Our Holocaust

Amir Gutfreund

OUR
HOLOCAUST

TRANSLATED BY

Jessica Cohen

The Toby Press

First English Language Edition 2006
The Toby Press LLC

POB 8531, New Milford, CT 06776-8531, USA
& POB 2455, London WIA 5WY, England
www.tobypress.com

First published in Hebrew as *Shoah Shelanu*
Copyright © Amir Gutfreund and Kinneret, Zmora-
Bitan, Dvir – Publishing House Ltd, Tel Aviv, 2001

ISBN 1 59264 139 3, *hardcover*

A CIP catalogue record for this title is
available from the British Library

Typeset in Garamond by Jerusalem Typesetting

Printed and bound in the United States
by Thomson-Shore Inc., Michigan

1993: Our Laws

G

randpa used to say, "People have to die of something," and refused to donate to the war against cancer, the war against traffic accidents, or any other war. To avoid being considered stingy, he would occasionally burst into exemplary displays of tremendous generosity. He put on these shows with such proficiency that if not for us, his relatives, no one would have known the simple truth: he was a miser.

In his home, parsimony was the law of the land. He zealously collected empty bottles for their deposits, and when one of them broke he glued it back together with great artistry. Like a cuckoo, he tossed his shirts into other people's laundry hampers, staging stains when necessary. A wonderful ability to catch colds in tandem with us enabled him to use our cough syrup and conserve his own. He would declare the colds over prematurely, proclaiming, "We're better now!" and stockpile the remaining antibiotics. A bottle of liquid soap stood in his bathroom, and whenever the soap level dropped below a finger's width he watered it down in an endless process that ultimately produced a bottle of water convinced it was soap. But his most wonderful ruse involved a magical power over tea bags. Each bag, even upon its tenth descent into boiling water, yielded something of itself—the merest vapor of tea, just verging on physically tangible material. The hoisting of the bag out of the water was accompanied by an expertly suspicious look at the bag hanging off the teaspoon by its string. Based on signs perceptible only to himself, he would estimate the bag's vitality and decree its fate. *Selektion*, he called this ceremony when he wanted to be cruel to Grandpa Yosef. We suspected that even when the bags were exhausted he did not throw them away, but rather hoarded them in a secret location so that he could one day make them into a new mattress. We spent our childhood hunting for them, but even in our nosiest searches, when we exposed his letters to Joyce the dancer and his debt to the late Jew Finkelstein, we never found a single tea bag.

We were happy, at times, to remind ourselves that he wasn't even our real grandfather.

We called him Grandpa—Grandpa Lolek—due to our family's Law of Compression, a wonderful invention of our parents, the first generation of the Holocaust. Lacking brothers, uncles, fathers and mothers, they had done away with the requirement for precision. Anyone belonging to our parents' generation was simply called "Uncle." Their offspring were our cousins. Not that everyone was up for grabs. There were certainly rules. There had to be a corresponding sense of closeness among all the generations, so that the stitches holding us all together could heal and all individuals could find their relatives. A fond relationship among the parents' generation meant that we could acquire their offspring as our cousins. Introvert "uncles" who tended not to take an interest in family affairs denied us entire clusters of willing cousins. Denied. End of story. The Law of Compression left no room for compromise.

Our greatest need was for grandparents, and so we ploughed our way through the restrictions and gathered as many of them as we could. I never knew my father's father, Zev-Wolf. (In Dad's photo album, I was drawn to a small picture of his grave.) We chose his cousins, Grandpa Lolek and Grandpa Hainek, to be our grandfathers. On Mom's side we devised a similar ploy. Her father, sick Grandpa Shalom—who had yet to emerge from the Holocaust—was locked in the depths of a terminal illness brought on by Gestapo tortures, and so we annexed a distant relative of his as an official grandfather, Grandpa Menashe. At other opportunities we acquired Grandpa Ernst, Grandma Eva and Grandpa Weil.

How pitifully small was my real family, the one we covered up with camouflage relatives:

Grandpa Shalom, 1912–1980.

One aunt.

Her son, one real cousin.

And yes, there was actually another uncle, my mother's half-brother.

"You don't need a psychologist to understand that," Effi responded when I told her once how I yearn to sleep with Anat every time we come home from one of her family weddings. Still in the car, both tired, I reach out to unbutton her dress and she barely has time to take her shoes off. From the back seat come the grumblings of Yariv, our five-year-old prince.

Grandpa Lolek, the tea artiste, was not the first of the grandpas. We got hold of him fairly late in the day. But he was a powerful axis in our lives, a figure who showered sparks onto our daily routines. He usually burst into our world in his 1970 Vauxhall, a moribund chassis of protestations upon which only he could impose life. Always wearing a tie, always smoking and dressed in colorful grandeur, he would emerge from the Vauxhall as if he were Kaiser Franz Josef out to wave at the masses from his balcony. Within minutes he would be sitting at the table drinking tea, eating whatever cake he was served, and smoking a cigarette.

Grandpa Lolek, the clear anomaly in our environment, was not a Holocaust survivor at all. World War II had caught him serving in the Polish cavalry, one of those wretched madmen who stormed German tanks yelling "Hurrah!" and waving swords. When his unit fell apart, Grandpa Lolek fled to Russia, where he joined the volunteer army of the Polish General Anders. With Anders, he set off on a voyage through Persia and Palestine to England, to reenter the war. Anders' soldiers, with Grandpa Lolek among them, were thrown into some of the toughest battles and suffered the most terrible losses.

These dime-a-dozen soldiers who were sent into battle every time a general in some war-room mumbled "let's give them a try," sustained heavy losses that filtered and distilled them until all that remained were Grandpa-Lolek-types, people coated with a layer of pure luck, fearless in the face of their old friend Death. They faced it every day, watched it go about its business, and grew accustomed to acknowledging it with a polite nod or a tip of the hat. They did not meddle in Death's business, nor Death in theirs.

When World War II was over, the members of Anders' Army, the remnants of the remnants, were rewarded for their service with British citizenship. But Grandpa Lolek was in love with an American dancer from Kentucky by the name of Joyce, and besides which, he needed to return to Poland to find out what remained of his family. Joyce was lost on the way, abdicating her chance to become Grandma Joyce (to be precise, she replaced Grandpa Lolek with a Viennese pianist). Lolek's family had perished in the gas chambers. Only his younger brother Hainek remained, and together they immigrated to Palestine, where Lolek renewed his war against all the wretches who lamented their fates, whispering tales of Auschwitz and Buchenwald.

Grandpa Lolek would rebuke the survivors. "You had terrible *Selektion*? One out of three, they took from you? Ten hours, naked in snow in *Appellplatz*? Well, what coddling! With us, against the Germans at Monte Cassino, if only it was being one out of three! Two nights and two days, person that rests a little, they die. Come on, let's move, no rest. Well, such trouble for you…"

His Hebrew was a tale of one-thousand Hebraic mistakes, an octagon of errors rolling through almost every sentence. He used to raise his glass and proclaim, "Life is good, Jews!" A bit of an anti-Semite. Drank a lot. Smoked. Always upright with a straight spine, despite his backache.

He owned a piece of land near Gedera, which he had been led to understand by certain-officials-in-the-right-places would soon be rezoned for construction. From time to time, over the course of thirty years, he went off to examine his treasure, which was agricultural for the time being, covered with heads of lettuce and strawberries like baby teeth, soon to be shed to make way for the main event. The officials, over the course of thirty years, were replaced, but Grandpa Lolek did not lose faith. He had complete confidence in the reliability of corruption and refused to sell his land to some bothersome farmer from Moshav Kidron. The farmer made repeated offers, all rejected by Grandpa Lolek.

"On my land no vegetable will to be grown!" he declared with ideological fervor. He would not stand for land being humiliated by such ridiculous things as kohlrabi. His land would be a piece of pure real estate.

Every time Grandpa Lolek came back from Gedera, he drove directly to Green the Mechanic, because the Vauxhall could not travel all those miles without a resuscitation service. There, sitting among the Arab laborers while the car was serviced, he was immediately provided with a chair and a glass of bitter coffee, for which he paid with war stories. The laborers loved him: a Jew who could tell of victories, but not over Arabs. They could relax around him, listen without pangs of guilt to stories of battles and ruses. For a wax-and-polish they were even treated to a good word about Salah a-Din.

The 1970 Vauxhall was a rare hothouse of now-extinct spare parts. The car, which had long ago driven off the standard path of licenses-insurance-tests, was patched up with any spare part that came cheaply. "The cheapest are chosen and the fittest survive," was the modus operandi in the Vauxhall, to the point where all other garage owners had washed their hands of it. Only Green the Mechanic, a pure soul, agreed to touch the Vauxhall. He offered no warranties, no reports, no nothing. There was a mutual understanding between the two men, and Green the Mechanic had Grandpa Lolek's blessing to explore every solution. He gave the Vauxhall a radiator from an old Volvo and a pump from a Saab. Screws that were no longer manufactured anywhere in the world found their way into the Vauxhall, as well as Fiat, Renault and DAF windows. The awe-inspiring jewel in the crown was concealed within the Vauxhall's maze of pipes: a Chevrolet carburetor, the last of its kind.

Green the Mechanic did these favors for no one but Grandpa Lolek. He looked surprised when I took him my Subaru for repairs one day, and reminded me that his was a Volkswagen garage—How, in my opinion, was he supposed to repair my Subaru? He wanted to know when I would start driving a Volkswagen, at which point I explained that I was opposed to German cars on principle.

"Because of the price?"

"Because of the Holocaust."

Green the Mechanic was very understanding. There are people who don't buy Japanese because of their metal, on principle. The Holocaust was a principle too, but in that case, he said, I had to go to a Subaru garage. Grandpa Lolek and his Vauxhall were a special case.

Grandpa Lolek loved the Vauxhall dearly, and he always paid Green the Mechanic on time. Elsewhere he was stingy, refusing to follow through with the activity known as payment. He continually enhanced his debtism until the accumulation of debt became an art form. His debts were his fountain of youth. They gave him strength and energized his spirit. We could imagine no finer event than Grandpa Lolek setting off to discuss a debt. He met his creditors proudly, presented his demands, occasionally listened. The tougher and more well-to-do creditors who could back their demands more concretely only increased Grandpa Lolek's grandeur. Sometimes he would orchestrate our attendance at the discussions, sitting us down in a corner of the room. The sweet presence of a child takes the sting out of many hostilities, he reasoned. We sat silently, somewhat aware of our function, watching as Grandpa Lolek pulled out thick binders full of papers and bills. He would leaf through them, examining them, and suddenly his eyes would light up. Looking up at the creditor, he would exclaim, "Here! We've found you!" He would display the papers, glowing with satisfaction, as if half the problem had already been solved. With quick fingers that were speckled with a few brown old-age stains, he would draw some papers from the thick pile and spread them on the table. "Here!" He would slap his hand on them. And the interlocutor was expected to ease up his demands a little. Not all the creditors were gullible. Some tended to be violent. But the hero of Anders' Army would pierce them with his icy blue eyes and plunge them into a river of agreements, words, choices, debts, arrangements, restrictions and guarantees. Grandpa Lolek was a juggler. Dates were set, systems drafted, on occasion a payment date was even considered. Sometimes another loan would spontaneously materialize from the very force of the new agreement. Some of the creditors took Grandpa Lolek to court, where justice entered a dizzying series of wonders. Grandpa Lolek's cases dragged on through delays and mistakes. The court reversed its opinions again and again. It set dates and then canceled them, summoned meetings and withdrew from them. The court's transformation was incomprehensible, as if Doubt had sat down in the central office to translate pangs of conscience into cancelled hearings. Or else it was because Grandpa Lolek had found an old court clerk who admired his past in Anders' Army. Not because of Grandpa Lolek's own service, but out of reverence for another of General Anders' soldiers, the late Prime Minister Menachem Begin. Admittedly, Begin, like many other Jews, had defected even before the battles began, when Anders' Army passed through Palestine en route from Russia to England, and had joined the Zionist fight here. Nonetheless, Begin had been affected by his days in Anders' Army, and in return for Grandpa Lolek's recollections of him, the clerk would do his best with the court dates, arranging delays and postponements. Grandpa Lolek, regretfully, had not known Menachem Begin at all in those days, but as far as he was concerned a soldier was a soldier. And so he told stories upon stories, sometimes carelessly sweeping Begin along with Anders' Army to Europe instead of leaving him here to lead the Etzel underground movement. He took him to the battles of Monte Cassino, Loretto, Ancona, to the river fordings in Italy. His interlocutor, rather than protesting, enthused, "And all this, while the Zionist struggle was raging here!"

Alongside his debtism, Grandpa Lolek perfected the art of opportunity. Whenever time, usually a galloper, made the mistake of slowing down to a trot, Grandpa Lolek immediately swatted it. His newspapers were always spread out, open to the classifieds and the obituary pages. He rapidly connected this notice with that announcement, put on his most appropriate tie, and set off in the Vauxhall to hunt down an opportunity. Grandpa Lolek, a foot soldier, did not discount minor gains. He nurtured small accounts, sometimes tiny, in every bank. He transferred pennies from one account to the other, bearing the pain of commissions, and waited for a surprising event on a cosmic scale that would hit the pennies en route and turn them into billions. His life was guided by special offers. He would purchase sixty packets of spaghetti on sale without a qualm and lie patiently in wait for ketchup prices to go down. He smoked remorselessly, with the enjoyment of those who know that cancer will not kill them. This was one area in which he was never thrifty. He bought fine imported cigarettes even in the hardest economic times, and smoked them lovingly without fear. He would not take a cigarette from anyone and he gave them freely to others. One cigarette, two. And once, right in front of my eyes, he gave a whole pack to a panhandler on the street.

His debtism, miserliness and frugality, coupled with his lust for business, gave rise to a large amount of property. We reminded him of the possibility that someone might someday inherit all of this. Grandpa Lolek avoided heirs like the plague. He thwarted any attempts at producing offspring, who were nothing but temporarily disguised successors. He was not of the opinion that "after his passing" would be an appropriate time to allow someone to enjoy his money. When the subject came up he became aggravated, waving his fist at non-existent sons to ward them off. He went to bed every night alive, and in the morning inherited his own property.

This was a flawless arrangement. Ostensibly. For alongside the strait of his life another channel rolled along, an ever-multiplying serpent of offspring in the form of a gang of boys entitled to address him as "Uncle." They had been produced in quick succession by Grandpa Lolek's only brother, Grandpa Hainek.

Our anointing of Grandpa Hainek as a grandfather was solely due to Grandpa Lolek. He himself was not of much use, but when we adopted Grandpa Lolek we simply reached out and added Grandpa Hainek, just in case. He was distinguished by his blue eyes and blond hair, which had turned white over the long and torpid snowy years. His body was heavy and solid, almost dwarfish, and his face was handsome. At the beginning of the war, aged eleven, he had been given to a Polish family. His Aryan looks and his youth enabled him to fit in easily with the farmer's children. For five years he ran barefoot with the peasant children, earned his keep, learned about life. When Grandpa Lolek came for him at the end of the war, Grandpa Hainek did not recognize this man who was trying to separate him from his parents. The Polish family wanted to adopt him: He didn't look like a Yid anyway, and soon they would need more hands for the harvest. But Grandpa Lolek, hero of Anders' Army, persisted in his mission, and led Grandpa Hainek all the way to a cot in the youth hut of a kibbutz in the Naftali Mountains.

On the kibbutz, they took one look at Grandpa Hainek, wearing a black coachman's cap and boots in the middle of August, and sent him to work in the hay. He slowly grew accustomed to the Yids surrounding him, but was barely able to pick up their language and their ideas remained incomprehensible. Why was it bad to accumulate property on the kibbutz? He stole eggs, bread and knives from the kitchen, which he buried who-knew-where, the-devil-knows-why. He did find a common language with the local Arabs, those who hung around the edges of the fields, keenly interested in wagon shafts, tractor parts, anything Grandpa Hainek brought them in return for sheep skins and good pitchforks.

It was with the Arabs that he arrived in Tiberias. He found himself a pair of strong horses and started working as a porter and hauler of goods. Wearing heavy boots and a redolent sheep skin slung over his shoulders year-round, with what little broken Hebrew he spoke, Grandpa Hainek continued his life in the land of the Yids. He ate a lot of beets and a lot of cabbage. He distilled his own vodka from potatoes, and from the Christians in the Galilee he bought huge cuts of pork which he hung in his room alongside his coachman's overcoat, whip and sheep skin.

In one of the Yids' villages he found a wife, Tamar, and they had three sons together before she died of a nameless disease, most likely typhoid fever. Apart from his sons, she also left him her Shabbat candlesticks, an assortment of feminine items bundled together in a purse, and a book of Psalms that she was extremely fond of, and which Grandpa Hainek nailed to the wall above his bed as a talisman against witches. When he returned to the kibbutz for a short while to deposit his sons and make sure his treasures were still well hidden, he met Naomi. She was the educational coordinator on the kibbutz, and he was referred to her to take in his sons. After she had performed her job impeccably, she followed him, to live with him wherever he should choose. They bought a plot of land on an old moshav and lived off the fruits of their labors. They had no real connection with the State of Israel and were cut off from its institutions. Naomi would chat a little with the neighbors, Grandpa Hainek would not. He had heard of the Israel Defense Forces (he found the concept of a Yid army impressive) but not of the Sick Fund. He traded in straw, sowed oats, beets and potatoes. He fattened calves and pigs. He wanted to have children with Naomi but could not. He took her to Arab witch-doctors, to a rabbi in Tiberias, to anyone who offered a cure, but none was found.

He did not maintain contact with our family. Yids. Grandpa Lolek always knew where he was and how many children he had—that was enough. As long as there were no monetary demands he took no interest in Grandpa Hainek's affairs, not even when he left the moshav and settled on the outskirts of the abandoned Arab villages, Ikrit and Biram. Grandpa Hainek, roaming the Galilee, had found the villages deserted and free for the taking. He was immediately drawn to a church with a ruined bell tower at its peak, and to the expansive wilderness enveloped in low-growing weeds, where the only sound was the screeching of crows. He spent long days on the barren hilltops and in the *wadi* beds, where gray rivers groaned in wintertime. On snowy nights, when black rain threatened to wash everything into the rivers, Grandpa Hainek liked to roam about, battling the winds, in fear that the darkness descending from the woods of Mount Meron would settle on him. He scanned each and every ruin in the villages, examining the opportunities afforded by this Eden.

One day he took Naomi and housed her in one of the ruins. He gathered new bricks and built walls, a fireplace and chimneys. With his own two hands he installed a kitchen and cabinets, a wash-basin and house wares. He brought her feathers to make down comforters. He brought her windows that he stole from the Arab villages, and even sewed curtains for the windows. Adjacent to the house he turned a few ruins into covered barns. He fenced in some yards and raised goats. With the displaced villagers of Ikrit and Biram, who returned from time to time to examine their villages, he did not have many dealings. He respected them, and forced them to respect him. He usually made them leave. Sometimes he bought jewelry for Naomi from them, and in return sold them aspirins stolen from kibbutzim.

By a circuitous route, Naomi found religion. She suddenly began to observe the mitzvahs, pray, light Shabbat candles. Grandpa Hainek had to go with her to Tzfat to buy kosher meat, wait for her to bathe in the ritual *mikvah*, sit with her with rabbis, in congregants' houses, in synagogues.

He bore her barrenness silently. He was not angry at having to hire laborers to gather the potatoes instead of using his own sons. He built her a life of royalty and did not resent her tendency to visit with her family members, the Yids, to escape once in a while who knows where.

Naomi and Grandpa Hainek lived on the edge of the abandoned villages, childless, far from the family. Even when she persuaded him to take in the late Tamar's three children so she could bring them up properly at their father's side, and even when she dragged him to meet a few people—her family, Jewish friends from Tzfat, friends from the kibbutz—it never occurred to Grandpa Hainek to establish contact with us.

It is said that his first appearance in our family was at my *briss*, which happened to be held on the *Tisha B'Av* fast of 1963. He turned up for some reason, dressed festively in a white shirt. His yellowish hair was neatly combed and he had wiped the grease stains off his cap. No one looked at him much, and they ignored him when he ungrammatically and unabashedly wondered, "And the food, where is? And drinks, where are?" even though it was a fast day. Dumbstruck, they all gaped at Naomi with her light blue eyes and grey hair, her aquiline nose and high cheekbones. An angelic vine, a beautiful, noble icon with a white peasant's dress and a shy look. We immediately wanted her to give us children. To breathe life into our family. That tall, serene body was made for our offspring. We wanted to drink from this well of life, even at the cost of mingling with Grandpa Hainek.

The family members greeted her warmly, connected with her.

They asked—where had she left the children? Whispers traveled through the room: she was barren. Acting on a vague instinct, they brought her to my cradle, a fertility charm concocted on the spot.

Many more prayers were whispered for her, countless blessings were showered upon her, and finally they also thought to ask—it turned out that she had no Sick Fund membership and had not tried any doctors. Only witches and a soothsayer and one medic. Naomi was sent to the doctors and a year later she began to have children. Despite having been the source of the charm, I myself was somewhat forgotten, and her children—whom she bore at the ages of thirty-five, thirty-six and thirty-seven, until the midwife was unable to stop the bleeding when she gave birth to Oz, her fourth son—are not attributed to me.

Naomi had been loved and was deeply mourned. The family could not accept her death—we had touched the well of life itself. How could it be that instead of Aunt Ecka or Aunt Frieda, Naomi had suddenly been taken? Nor did Grandpa Hainek come to terms with her death. Perhaps he blamed himself. On the night when she gave birth to Oz, prematurely, he had run twelve miles in the snow after his horses had veered off the path, frightened by bright lights. But by the time he came back with the midwife, an old woman from one of the villages, it was too late to save Naomi. He went back to the kibbutz with his sons.

At the end of that year, the Yom Kippur War broke out. After the war, Grandpa Hainek's oldest son with Tamar, Ze'ev (1953–1975), left the kibbutz. He went to Canada to work in the oil fields, where he was killed in a glacier accident. Grandpa Hainek mourned the loss of his eldest son heavily, but there were those who subtly claimed that his expression gave off a hint of satisfaction—after all, this was death by drowning in a freezing lake, just like in the old days, in the Wisła near Krakow.

A year later, Dov (1954–1976) was killed. Dov was the second son. Some say he was a Mossad agent, some say something even more secretive. In Europe, on a mission, two bullets. Three people, one dressed as a priest.

In 1978, a hay wagon ran over Sagi, Naomi's second son.

Grandpa Hainek took his remaining sons and began an endless journey through the little Land of Israel, to get away from his Polish legacy and from the fate of the peasant coachman. He went from town to town, from vocation to vocation. He was an agricultural laborer in the Sharon region, a porter in Petach Tikva, a print worker in Haifa. He got as far south as Beersheba, far from the snow, and found work as a taxi driver. He changed his clothes, learned Hebrew, even voted in the elections. (Once. He stole an identity card and voted as Ernst Rabinowitz.) But all the roles he played, all the vocations, the attempts, the distance from the snow, none of these could rescue him from the claws of his true identity, the only possible one: a Polish coachman in the town of Kielce, wearing coachman's boots and a black cap.

Still, despite long snowy years under scorching *khamsin* heat waves, despite sauerkraut and vodka that destroyed his teeth, despite his dead wives and tragically killed sons, at the age of fifty-two, thanks to an argument over change at the grocery store, Grandpa Hainek met his third wife, Atalia. She quickly gave him three children from her young body. To protect her and her children, he took them even further south, to Machtesh Ramon. He went north only when snow capped the high mountains, after which he would return to Beersheba, startled, to a heat that had no snow and no woods and no slowly descending darkness. He went back to making a living driving a taxi, with the windows rolled up even in the heaviest *khamsin*, ignoring his passengers' pleas, sweating, his skin turning red. In Beersheba he had another child with Atalia.

Grandpa Hainek was the fertile opposite of our family: a Polish peasant, ignorant and uncomplicated. We never found any interest or use in him apart from his butterfly collection, which included an impossibly purple cabbage butterfly, and apart from his third son, Eitan, who was the first to show me pictures of naked ladies who were more developed than Effi was on the day she showed me her body.

Atalia was a different matter.

Aristocratic, tender and radiant, as were all of Grandpa Hainek's known women, she was a tall, slender Yemenite. She was always barefoot and her fingers were adorned with rings of white copper. She was twenty-three when she married Grandpa Hainek, only a few years older than us, and boundlessly in love with her white-haired partner. Atalia's sons ("the Lubliner Yemenites," Effi called them), shared the appearance Grandpa Hainek gave all his sons regardless of the ethnicity of his partner. Each of his eleven sons had an identical hardened look. They could never be seen in one full group (Grandpa Hainek's eldest were killed before Atalia's children were born), but partial gatherings were sometimes convened for Grandpa Lolek's ceremonious camera. These grandchildren of the headmaster of Kielce's Hebrew Gymnasium, the pedagogue and man of letters Dr. Feuer, appear in pictures surrounding their father. Their calves wrapped in leg-warmers, they wear clothes that look heavy and sour. Spanning all ages, their countenances are identical. A dark, boorish crew of mute masculinity, a gang fifty years too late to join the ranks of Alexander Zaid's nascent Shomer movement.

From a very young age, they paved their ways to living on moshavim or military academies. They were bulky and lonely. Their hair turned grey before they reached eighteen. In the army, they served in tight-lipped units. They had girlfriends, always moshav girls, always fair-haired. In time they each found an exciting line of work, but even their intriguing professions—hunters, spies, commandos, coal-miners—never gave them an aura of interest. They were ascetic, hardened types, who connected with the world only infrequently, to sleep with its girls or buy its spare tractor parts. Grandpa Lolek photographed them often. He enjoyed gathering them in front of his camera to immortalize his younger brother and nephews.

In the family, it was usually Grandpa Lolek who took pictures. He generously erected his Leica camera, a black metal monster with personality disorders, everywhere he went. It was no simple matter to produce a good picture with the Leica. Its internal mechanisms were controlled with one seemingly simple button that required no more than a click. But inside, the camera teemed with a religion of restrictions and mishaps. While the Leica produced attempts, failures and repeated adjustments, the audience opposite it grew increasingly impatient. Finally, the button. Pressing it produced an impressive sound and sometimes a picture.

(Effi: "If you press twice, you get an X-ray.")

Grandpa Hainek and his sons usually agreed to pose. The pictures always captured them eyeing the lens suspiciously with a cautionary look, as if to say, "No tricks, I'm warning you." They never asked for the pictures afterwards, uninterested in what had happened to the moment frozen by the Leica. Grandpa Lolek enjoyed photographing them and uncharacteristically overcame his sorrow at the lack of payment. He amassed the photos of his nephews, who had been imposed upon him as a calamity of potential heirs, and collected payment indirectly from other photography subjects.

The family members usually liked to be photographed, eternalized. The relatives, the friends, the acquaintances—all the survivors from *there*. After the Holocaust, eternity was as vital to them as oxygen, food, and good health. Even before they arrived in Israel, they photographed themselves with heavy black cameras at all sorts of events, proving that they existed, that they were real, a mathematical truth, a concept supported by science. They existed. They were photographed at resorts, on holidays, on afternoons of idle laziness, forgotten moments that they wished to immortalize so that future generations could not claim these people were never idle. The pictures were rarely gathered into albums. They generally bustled by the dozen, disorganized, in a chaos we spent evenings poring over, makings sudden discoveries of Mrs. Tsanz in a bathing suit, Uncle Antek embracing two young women. Smiling. Mrs. Tsanz too. There she was at the center of a merry group on a waterfront bench, a snowy background and a road-sign suggesting a season, a place. An unnamed park, perhaps in Krakow, chestnut trees overhead, and the people in the photograph are smiling. The awkward smile of a young girl, our Grandpa Yosef with his arm around her waist as if there were no prohibitions and no sins in this world. A snowman with a carrot nose, three anonymous people and Uncle Mendel kneeling at its feet, smiling. Springtime in a field divided by a walking path, a gang of people lingering briefly for the camera, smiling. Their clothes are heavy in summer too, their faces grave—here we are, living the good life. Recovering. Sated. Satisfied. Grumbling about this and that. And the park benches and the sidewalks and the doorways are full of them, gathered, smiling, the camera casting their images onto the negative. One click, and eternity.

Grandpa Lolek enjoyed taking photographs, but developing them for free was too much. He demanded money and made no superfluous niceties about it. He set a regular price for "regular" photos and a special price for "special" photos. What constituted "special"? Unclear. But Grandpa Lolek determined, "This one is special," and demanded a special price. Quarrels erupted. The relatives were furious. The Leica contained a precious moment of their new lives and in order to bring it out into the light they were being robbed. The impertinence of it. They would pay, of course they would, but so much? Goldberg on HaChalutz Street, the finest in Haifa, charges less. Why so much? The disputes thickened. Grandpa Lolek was not one to allow battles to simply die down. From the summits of Monte Cassino he taunted his adversaries.

The only person capable of moderating and untying these knots, sometimes by force of personality, sometimes with a little something from his wallet, was Grandpa Yosef. There should be no fighting among Jews, he believed.

Our kaleidoscope of memories, which turned everything upside-down, always contained a thousand colorful, crumbling versions of Grandpa Lolek arguing. Complaints from the audience, harsh words from Grandpa Lolek, back and forth. And everyone waited: When would Grandpa Yosef finally intervene? The kaleidoscope holds endless versions of one single dispute, until Grandpa Yosef arrives. He had been busy, someone needed his assistance, but now he was here. Why were they fighting?

Grandpa Yosef. The polar opposite of Grandpa Lolek. Our parents' generation found him and declared without hesitation: a grandfather. A short man with a yarmulke, his face was always locked with sorrow, his strides always small. A champion of the needy, always helping, rescuing, supporting. From morning to evening he was busy doing mitzvahs. He rode his bicycle everywhere. Always modest, always in the shadows. The needy knew how to find him. Not only the truly needy, but the family too. Every time we had to temporarily pass through the straits of religion, Grandpa Yosef the kindly ferry man was summoned. At funerals, memorials, sitting *shiva*, marriage ceremonies, bar-mitzvah lessons. In each of these, Grandpa Yosef played the role so needed by the secular heart: a man intimately familiar with the ceremonial, a purveyor of benevolent versions to those who could not make head or tail of it all. Beneath his tender face burned a blaze of faith that could have scorched the entire world if Grandpa Yosef had not trimmed it down to the measurements of a quiet, retiring man.

Grandpa Yosef knew hundreds of Jewish precepts by heart, as well as the length of the Orinoco River. We could find out from him how the price of milk had increased, month by month, starting at any year we requested. He could recite the Book of Esther, the names of the Shetland Islands, and the birthplaces of Galician rabbis lost in the Holocaust. He was a stormy genius, very quiet, always soft-spoken, with a tired gaze, his face lined with furrows of wisdom and tiny white specks of unshaveable stubble on his yellowish cheeks. He had a soft French accent; no one knew why. But his compassionate voice sounded wonderful with its French enunciation. Because of his accent, people believed he had a refined approach to food and that he was knowledgeable about wine. In truth, he rarely encountered wine, and only then by force of mitzvahs. At family meals he gargled peach-flavored sparkling wine and mumbled something about its "delicate savor," believing he was giving his audience what it wanted. In matters of food he was even less fussy. When he ate, his throat grew a pelican's crop, into which he rolled any kind of food without needless enquiries. He ate to his fill at every meal and accepted offers of coffee and dessert. He had no potbelly, thanks to the bicycle and the mitzvahs and due to a metabolic problem which allowed food to pass through his body like a roller-coaster. Precious little of his meals remained for him to grow strong on.

He lived in a small neighborhood where almost all the residents were Holocaust survivors, at the edge of the Haifa suburb of Kiryat Haim. Little houses, little yards. We went to visit him almost every Saturday, desecrating the Sabbath by driving, but not to worry. We spent whole weeks with him during summers. We attached ourselves to him like tropical ferns to the juicy core of an enormous trunk.

At his home, in the little room *they* called the "hall," which increased the value of the apartment, Grandpa Yosef had an old heavy desk made of brown wood, the only notable piece of furniture in his entire modest home. Behind it, on the wall, were book-lined shelves. First, gold-embossed volumes of the Scriptures, the six sections of the Mishna, the Babylonian Talmud, Rashi and Rambam. Then there were "liberal" books, which Grandpa Yosef knew by heart—Sholem Aleichem and Berdyczewski, Burla and Frischmann, Haim Nachman Bialik and Tchernichowsky. There was also an *Encyclopedia Hebraica*, which Grandpa Yosef did not know entirely by heart (he half apologized, explaining that it was wrong to know everything by heart as it only took up space in one's mind), and Eben-Shoshan's Hebrew dictionary (on occasion, he could be caught not knowing the definition of a word like 'batten' or 'burette'). The desk itself was usually scattered with volumes of the Scriptures, textbooks and fine literature. Also a glimpse of a little dish of pickled herring, which Grandpa Yosef preserved himself, and the pit of a fruit. Grandpa Yosef would be sitting hunched over, studying. A small lamp illuminated his face.

Despite the yellowing cheeks, the stubble and the folds of skin, the image of Grandpa Yosef the righteous scholar was forever a cornerstone in our lives. In the Garden of Eden that was our childhood, he was the Tree of Knowledge, just as Grandpa Lolek was the Tree of Life. To this very day, although we have grown up, Grandpa Yosef is still the Tree of Knowledge. He always wore loose slacks and white dress shirts tucked in tightly, with large cumbersome jackets that conquered his body and covered up the fine shirts. Grandpa Yosef tried to dress carefully, but the flap of something always peeked out from something else.

He came from the same little town as Dad, Bochnia, and although he was not related to my father's family, he knew them well. He would say things like, "He was a little rascal, your father, but a good boy. Got hold of lots of stamps for me," (a slightly enigmatic compliment, which I sanctified without further contemplation). In his distant way he was a disciple of the Admor of Belz, and he feebly fumed when Effi referred to him under her breath as "the Admor of Belzec." In our family's underground cell of Bochnia ghetto graduates, it was a known fact that before the Admor of Belz boarded the train from Hungary to Switzerland, leaving his disciples behind to perish in Auschwitz, he had spent time in the Bochnia ghetto until the collaborator Landau was able to transfer him to Hungary, then a safe-haven, leaving his believers to contend with the nuisance of the gas chambers at Belzec. Grandpa Yosef did not reach Belzec or Auschwitz, but his Holocaust trail was the longest and most intricate of all the survivors we knew. Over the course of the war he passed through no less than twelve concentration camps, ghettos and extermination camps. He never explained why. He did not dwell much on depictions of those days, but often tied the present to the past.

"It was in the Bochnia ghetto that I met Attorney Perl, and then we met again in Haifa."

"Mr. Hirsch was very helpful to me in the Lodz ghetto. If not for him, who knows…"

"I was at the men's camp in Ravensbrück and then I was transferred to Stutthof, but in any case Ravensbrück was officially affiliated with Stutthof. Officially, I stayed in the same place. In the train car, it took three days."

"The Death March? No, I wasn't there. Fortunately, I was transferred from Gross-Rosen to Waldenburg, so I was saved."

"Buchenwald uprising? Haven't heard of it. Perhaps it was after I was transferred from Buchenwald to Gross-Rosen."

The Shoah raged through the world, and Grandpa Yosef traveled to and fro on trains. We sometimes wondered why.

"He wasn't a good social fit at Buchenwald, so they transferred him to Gross-Rosen," Effi suggested.

Fifty years later, Grandpa Yosef himself explained. "It was not the Nazis who moved me from one place to the other, it was my heart that moved worlds until I found her, Feiga."

Feiga was his wife, the princess of his youth, his queen, who lay eternally ill in her room. When he stepped off the last train into a world turned upside-down at the end of the World War, he found his fiancée from before the war, Feiga, and married her, as their parents had agreed six years earlier in the spring of 1939. They were engaged at nineteen, married at twenty-five, and gave birth to Moshe.

Moshe was Grandpa Yosef and Feiga's only child, and from the moment he was born, it seemed, the angels had showered him with a host of disasters. He was mentally retarded, but not profoundly enough so that he could exist in a dulled serenity. He had slight brain damage, which tormented his movements, pulled his limbs as taught as springs and did not let go, only twisted them in pain. And adenopathy, a disease of the lymph nodes which caused internal sorrow to hide beneath his sealed face. "He has pain, sometimes. Try not to let him eat food that's too spicy or too sweet," said Doctor Gnessin. And there was something else. Not exactly autism, but a nameless disjointedness that thwarted all known methods for treating autism, prevented him from being taken in at autistic homes, and finally left him in his place under the sun on the low fence opposite his house, where he sat upright all day long.

Between sick Feiga and Moshe, Grandpa Yosef was in constant motion: Gemara, mitzvahs, preparing food, washing dishes, biking here and there. Medication for Feiga. Medication for Moshe. Even so, we were not amazed when Grandpa Yosef announced one day that he had decided to take some courses at the Open University. Why not? After all, Grandpa Yosef was a prodigy whose rabbinical dreams had been cut short by the Holocaust, and in any case he always had fifteen minutes to spare here and there. He would get his bachelor's degree and then see.

He signed up. Disappointed by the slow pace and the meager load of material, he decided to register at a regular university. He took the entrance exams and was accepted. He was even interviewed by the student newspaper; the university was happy to publicize their elderly student. But their delight was somewhat marred when, six months later, Grandpa Yosef applied for permission to take all the required exams for the bachelor's degree. His request was rejected, of course, and Grandpa Yosef dared not appeal ("Do not presume to defy the rulership," he had learned). The one thing Grandpa Yosef did accomplish with his request was to be taken under the wing of Professor Shiloni, a kindly renaissance man who was impressed by this elderly beacon of knowledge and arranged a customized course of study for him. And so on Chanukah of 1985, Grandpa Yosef was awarded an MA in Jewish History.

The Masters degree did not quench the predator's thirst. Grandpa Yosef decided he wanted a doctorate, claiming this had been his goal from the first. It was his life's duty to earn a doctorate on the topic of Jewish heroism in the Middle Ages—this and no other. We were surprised by his narrow focus: Why would Grandpa Yosef be interested in Jewish heroism in the Middle Ages? But under the guidance of Professor Shiloni, during Grandpa Yosef's plentiful quarter-hour openings, a foundation for the dissertation was laid. To this very day, the end of 1993, Grandpa Yosef can still be found scratching away at drafts he is never pleased with.

The years of our childhood solidified our belief that Grandpa Yosef knew everything, and this estimation was not diminished when we grew older. The main tenets of his knowledge—Talmud and Jewish history—were barely tested by us. Astronomy, meteorology, zoology—absolutely. When Brandy the dog gave birth to six piebald puppies underneath his brown desk, Grandpa Yosef was forced to elucidate for us the riddle of procreation. Even in the strangest corners of human knowledge, Grandpa Yosef was never without a response.

"Grandpa Yosef, when was the kite invented?"

"Grandpa Yosef, are giraffes kosher?"

He was our resource for settling any argument. The matter would be brought before him and the loser would reap consolation thanks to Grandpa Yosef's slight bending of the facts, allowing him or her to squeeze in next to the winner at the last minute.

"The longest river in the world? The Amazon."

Effi loses.

"But the Mississippi is the longest of the North American rivers."

Effi takes her place alongside the winner.

We would lie on our backs in the garden at our place, beneath the trees, and let our thoughts fly, contemplating the farthest or the strangest, to the very edge of our wits. Even before the era of Brandy the dog, we learned to love a good game of fetch. We would toss our questions as far as we possibly could, and wait for Grandpa Yosef to return with a proud answer in his mouth.

"Grandpa Yosef, what else can you grit, other than teeth?"

"Grandpa Yosef, why doesn't a spider float in grape juice?" (A failed experiment.)

Our memories were crumbled into the flakes of a kaleidoscope, and the answers are difficult to see. Things get forgotten, scattered, but Grandpa Yosef's gravity is remembered well. He would never belittle our questions.

"Grandpa Yosef, who would win: a thousand scorpions or a bear?"

"Grandpa Yosef, which prison is the hardest to escape from in the world?"

Grandpa Yosef considered. Were we counting the camps in Siberia as prisons? Would we count prisons that have been closed down? Like Alcatraz? Instead of a simple answer, Grandpa Yosef told us about the most terrifying prisons, lying with us on a blanket with blades of grass crumpled beneath our backs, roots crushed. We listened with eyes closed, pondered prisons, and enjoyed the strength infused in us by their force.

Wherever religious ceremonies were concerned, Grandpa Yosef's advantages were enjoyed by all. He was handed the field marshal's baton and asked to lead the way. He always positioned himself on the front, at the edge of the rabbi's beard, where he could hum with him, emphasize and echo certain syllables of his prayers, and cover for our awkward silences. And when necessary, with a reassuring look, he would urge orphans to recite *kaddish*, fathers to sign documents for their children's nuptials, bar-mitzvah boys to squeak out the readings he himself had taught them with the utmost patience and grace. Salvation and redemption were for him simple tokens to be distributed for the asking. He was summoned to every ceremony to stand as advocate between us and God, or at least between us and Uncle Mendel.

Uncle Mendel, a member of Grandpa Yosef's generation, was never even honored with candidacy for grandfatherhood. We had no choice but to tolerate his presence at funerals and *brisses*, where he would rapidly ignite with holy furor and terrible wrath against us idol worshippers. His eyes dispersed threats against the family and the officiating rabbi. His hints were clear: the slightest deviation from tradition, and heads would roll. The presence of Grandpa Yosef was able to slightly dilute the anxiety. "Shhh...Shhh...," he would calm Uncle Mendel with an enchanting whisper, unburdening the holy man of his anger and extracting from him a momentarily turned blind eye.

Uncle Mendel was invited to the celebratory events because it would have been unbefitting not to. And anyway, it was difficult to get around Uncle Mendel. He had managed to position himself both as a relative of some sort and as Grandpa Yosef's neighbor, and he lay in wait for any family gathering, so that circumventing him was both unpleasant and impossible. At family meals he took his place at the edge of the room in an observation armchair, vigilantly watching for any transgression. People examined their words carefully, omitted details that might set off Uncle Mendel, and gingerly approached the buffet table to take their fill. Sin could be lurking anywhere, you never knew. When Uncle Mendel himself finally drew near the buffet, he acted like a man preparing to dismantle an explosive device. He walked from his holy throne of an armchair to the table, rolling his sleeves up to his elbows. Mumbled assurances of "It's all kosher, it's all kosher," would be uttered righteously all around him when the crowd saw the patron of Godliness going to sample the food. Uncle Mendel, sternly dismissing these heretics' oral oaths, stood breathlessly surveying the bounty. This Buchenwald survivor, in whose hut people driven mad by starvation had gnawed on the dead as they lay on their bunks, stood within arm's reach of sin: golden-brown chicken thighs, cuts of beef, dumplings. Pink radishes, mounds of peas and bowls of sautéed cabbage winked at him from the side. Potatoes up to their chins in sauce, squares of quiche notched with a knife. Uncle Mendel stood there, temptation enveloping him like a prayer shawl.

The bridge of mercy, more often than not, was Grandpa Yosef. Somewhat embarrassed, his fork busy with a full plate, he would remark in Uncle Mendel's direction, "The cholent is excellent." Beneath this culinary judgment ran a subterranean confirmation of *kashrut,* and Uncle Mendel would begin to forgive the world. First a mound of cholent. Then a second helping. He shovels the piles into his mouth and helps himself to more. Walking this way and that in front of the table, heaped dishes set out before him, rich and dark as a Dutch still-life, he perspires. His jaws move too quickly. He coughs. Holds a pickle and clears his throat. Other people approach the buffet to demand their rights. Uncle Mendel bumps, clashes. His plate wobbles. People pass him left and right, rushing, the signs of his authority blurring. A mass of camp prisoners carries quivering plates piled with knolls of food, exhaling hot ashes and smoke through their nostrils. Grandpa Lolek uproots mountains of dumplings with his fork. Grandma Eva's strength is restored, her face glimmers with a copper tone as she clenches her jaw to defeat a stubborn bone. And Uncle Mendel, still there, waves a red napkin like a matador and burdens his plate further. Elbows jostle around the table, retiringly, politely. They will not let anyone beat them to it—not today, not here too. Conversations. Public opinion on the kreplach. One man talks, the crowd listens with joyful apprehension and a hesitant heart. They listen and pile on food. The brisket elicits cries for help. The plates are already dizzy. They rub against each other, shoving. No thoughts except seconds, the next course, and dessert.

Dessert was always compote, and it brought with it a quiet time when all was comfortable, shallow, at the end of the ends—the river's estuary. The compote had a ritual structure that permitted no deviations. Swollen cheeks of sugared apples drowning in compote syrup. Purple plums with stems removed, looking as if their flesh has been shredded by a Doberman. Grapes floating palely like skulls at the bottom of the bowl. That was the compote and there was no other. Afterwards, there was coffee for those who were allowed. The guests were exhausted by this time, their faces expressionless. A slight sense of suffering. And inside they would embark on glorious journeys, Mongolian horsemen whipping time away in their memories.

Eventually we would detect the softened look and slight quickness of breath that signaled the awakening of their nostalgic yearning for jam. They would open the cabinet, lips puckered, and take out sickening plum or blueberry preserves, holding them out for us to taste. We would flee in horror.

The family meals wandered from one house to the other by order of a secret code of generosity. But usually we met at Grandpa Yosef's. He was the uncontested focus, a patient host who served tea and home-made cakes—huge rounds of dough from which we pulled out raisins in disgust. At his home the Sabbath was desecrated almost every Saturday. Four generations happily watched soccer on TV, but Grandpa Yosef did not protest. He disappeared once in a while to take care of Feiga, Moshe, or a neighbor. At noon he went to synagogue. But in between business and caretaking he was an exemplary host. He bought the television himself, so the Sabbath desecrators would not be bored while he was busy. Television was permitted, he explained. They show educational programs and documentaries. But we caught him watching current affairs and the evening news. "Well, news is important," he responded.

When the anarchy increased, the television found its way to Feiga's bedroom. She tolerated only afternoon soaps and children's programs, which were important. And once we caught her cheering on Maccabi Tel Aviv, blessing the star player Miki Berkowitz and his family for generations to come. Grandpa Yosef bought another television to put in the living room for the Sabbath desecrators.

Grandpa Yosef was no saint. As proof, there was his support of the Maccabi Haifa soccer team. The family tradition was one of illogical support for HaPoel Haifa, a support that nurtured in us all the appropriate character traits. We learned how to lose honorably—it became our specialization. We learned to bear disappointment, to settle for less. We acquired modesty. And against these virtues, earned through our unwavering support of HaPoel Haifa, Grandpa Yosef infuriatingly fell under the spell of Maccabi Haifa. It was all those Saturdays when he let us turn on the TV at his home, desecrating the Sabbath with live soccer broadcasts, that gave rise to the calamity. He himself, of course, never participated openly in this public sin. But here and there his gaze lingered on the screen for just a moment. Unable to reveal that we had noticed his interest, we left him without guidance, without instruction. And so Grandpa Yosef, as a soccer fan, grew into a savage. The one man who might have been able to turn God's favor toward HaPoel accidentally became a fan of Maccabi. He won the championship with them, and the state cup final. He cheered and glowed, disinherited from all the characteristics we had attained through our love of the underdog.

Over the years, the rift grew. In Grandpa Yosef's heart, the halfback king Reuven Atar battled the Shabbat Queen. When we watched the Saturday match on TV, he lurked between the couches. When Maccabi Haifa worked its magic against helpless opponents, he could no longer pretend. The King had outdone the Queen. We were good to him. In the early summer days of soccer, when Grandpa Yosef was buried in prayer in the synagogue or on his veranda, we would pass by with a transistor radio playing the weekly soccer broadcast and yell out to an anonymous listener, "Maccabi Haifa still leading, three minutes to match time!" A holy rustle would sweep through the congregation. Grandpa Yosef was not the only one who secretly furrowed his brow. Three minutes! They have to make it! May the Lord be with them.

Grandpa Lolek would sit with us at Grandpa Yosef's on Saturdays, smoking, perplexed by this interest in soccer. He found it inconceivable that anyone could be excited over a profit divided among eleven men. And he had other criticisms of Grandpa Yosef's preferences: "How is it that with all those brains in his noggin, he married that woman?" ·

That woman. Feiga.

Feiga was, simply stated, a princess. The world had mixed things up and sent her to Kiryat Haim by mistake. World War II had shuffled the deck of history cards and Feiga had been uprooted from the life she was supposed to lead, but she let it slide. True, she had been destined to inherit kingdoms—the Sheba Kingdom, the ancient city of Cadiz, the Inca Palaces—but, exiled in Kiryat Haim, she established a little court and spread her monarchy over one subject, Grandpa Yosef. He was her foremost knight, her royal counselor and her stable boy. He slaved away without a grumble, tending to her and to the affairs of the kingdom—Moshe, the kitchen sink, the bills, the medications.

Ever since we could remember, Feiga had lain ill in her room. She was always cold, a stable condition unchanged by *khamsin* days or by the bundles of clothes in which she wrapped herself. A mixture of dresses, robes and sweaters arranged itself on her body in lumps and bulges, layer upon layer, until she looked like a bunch of grapes covered up beneath the blankets. Caretakers and cleaners were forbidden to enter Feiga's palace and any attempts they made, for Grandpa Yosef's sake, she torpedoed. She set extremely rigid terms. Feiga demanded perfection—an utter absence of errors. When this was achieved she had no complaints, but she rarely permitted Grandpa Yosef to attain this state for long. His failures were many and they begat one another, branching and mingling into a suffocating network of omissions. Had Feiga not been a princess, she surely would not have tolerated it all. She would have taken harsh steps. But as it was, she made do with complaining. Her complaints were a constant echo in the house, lacking any logic comprehensible to an outsider. Like the call of a mating bird in a forest that would mean nothing to a weekend hiker, Feiga's cuckoo call set the pace of time, changed the clocks.

Between her engagement to Grandpa Yosef and the end of the war, Feiga had found herself embroiled in a mysterious marriage to a young rabbi. It was not through any passion that suddenly overcame the man in the shadow of the *Aktionen* and the annihilation, but a desperate magical attempt to put creation right, or something of the sort. A few weeks after the mystical ceremony, the rabbi was shot on the street in down-to-earth simplicity, his attempt to change the world ending in nothing but Feiga's widowhood.

As soon as we found out about this, we confronted Grandpa Yosef with his embarrassing deputyship.

"So you were her second," Effi determined.

The silver medal winner graciously granted an interview. "Well, yes, the second," he said consolingly.

Grandpa Yosef worshipped Feiga.

We, conversely, found it difficult to take an interest in her.

In the face of her first husband, a spiritual giant, her intellectual prowess had been cowed. The few weeks spent between the holy rabbi's sheets had absolved her from the need to prove anything at all. Grandpa Yosef could make his own efforts, study Talmud, do righteous deeds—she had done her bit.

She did marry Grandpa Yosef when the opportunity arose, but her first marriage was the pillar of fire in her life. After being within a hair's breadth from the Lord of Creation, she was less than eager to relocate to suburban Haifa. And since she had been fortunate enough to serve as a holy vessel, Feiga had no choice but to continue her stormy life beneath the covers. In her own eyes, she was akin to the lantern of the temple, plundered by the evil Titus, cast upon her bed beside a window that, curiously, looked out onto the Acre-Haifa train tracks.

She generally spoke with the grammar of diseases, a language in which the subject and predicate of the sentence were diminished in the face of its object, where the true essence of the sentence occurred. Sometimes the subject and predicate were completely dropped in favor of a daring voyage into tempestuous auxiliary clauses:

"Pain in my forehead because the crows did not rest the tree will fall."

"When no blood in the feet, like a wild animal from the stomach down."

"Rain, *tsk, tsk,* no energy to the bones, all day, amen, Doctor Brattlebaum."

The Oracle of Kiryat Haim also gave blessings to the needy. People came to her and, by virtue of the late rabbi's holy sheets, she blessed them. Her days in the presence of the deceased had imbued her with a vast reserve of holiness. On her finger, she wore two wedding bands. This was not sanctioned by Jewish law, but it was by Feiga.

What Grandpa Yosef saw in her was unclear. How he withstood it—unknown. We could not understand how he was able to perform all his jobs and study a page of Gemara every day, and keep up his prayers and run around doing good deeds—his *tzedakah*—and study at the university. Genius could not explain everything, and so we had to add the factor of love to the equation. Grandpa Yosef broke the record of Jacob our Father, who worked for seven whole years to win Rachel, and then another seven. Grandpa Yosef worked for Feiga for forty-five years, well on his way to the perfectly biblical sum of seven times seven years. Inside his home, Grandpa Yosef was tantamount to a slave, while outside, in the neighborhood, he was the king of kings, the beacon of salvation. He was a patron for the needy, a solver of problems. As he walked or rode his bike, people stopped him to present a new problem, report on an old one, or remind him of problems long solved but still bothersome. Those who were unable to get out of bed to present their claims to Grandpa Yosef were treated to personal visits.

In that neighborhood, the Holocaust—the Shoah—had never ended. People had settled there after the war with their memories, their stories, their grudges. Like a huge flock of storks, they came all at once and landed near the woods on the edge of Kiryat Haim, and there they remained. Sick people, confined by their memories. After the war they had families, they existed, they made a living. They took cautious little steps. Every day they dragged themselves around anew, tied to the rotating minute hand of a clock. Distorted, bound, hauled. Date after date fell away on the calendar. The windows of their homes were closed, a slit in the blinds sufficed to see everything. Most stayed at home, where they sat by large radios that broadcast news in *their* languages. They sat quietly. Illegal-immigrants-for-ever-and-ever. If the day came to a close and nothing had happened—so much the better. Sometimes their heavyset bespectacled sons came to visit. Not often.

Everyone in the neighborhood had two types of past: there was "what you did during the war" and "where you came from before the war." The present and the future languished insignificantly in the distance. Everyone knew everyone else's stories, and bit by bit they were elucidated until thoroughly comprehended. The tales accompanied people's lives, never lost, never growing old. When the owner of a story died, the story went on without him, leaning on other stories on either side, plodding along in a row. Like in the camps, in rows of five, the weak leaning on the strong, the rows proceeded.

The place had a complex arc of supervisors and supervised, patients and caregivers, with no clear partition between the two. Helpless bedridden dependents would suddenly rise in afternoon miracles and go to care for a needy friend. Each of them jealously guarded *their* story, *their* troubles, *their* business, a possessiveness that led to a lot of sighs. They were always sighing. They gathered together to sigh, as if something too large was sitting inside of them and could not be released all at once for fear of explosion. And so they had meetings where they sat and sighed, let it all out in little pieces, looking for opportunities to sigh. And they cheated the rules by speaking in Yiddish, which allows for the release of larger portions.

We liked to listen to them, although in our presence (by Grandpa Yosef's orders) they did not delve too deeply into the Shoah itself. We sat at their feet, an inner ring inside the circle of tea-drinkers, enjoying a wonderful childhood in the shadow of their terrors. When Grandpa Lolek was not around they could compare stories, rate their suffering, measure their sorrow. And they could quarrel, declaring things like, "*Nu*, you, let's see you in Stutthof! Let's see you survive just two days there..." As if the possibility existed—a simple matter of addressing the package correctly, and the man would be sent off to Stutthof for two days.

Behind them, on invisible benches, sat their actions. Thanks to those actions they were here. They had survived.

Sometimes Dad would come to the neighborhood after work, at Grandpa Yosef's behest, to fix a closet for one poor man, do some electrical work for another. Dad's magic hands enabled Grandpa Yosef to implement righteous intentions, since he himself did not get along with things like soldering irons and screws. He paid Dad with his own pickled herring, a good cup of tea and a vague assurance of a place in heaven, to which he sometimes alluded as if he himself went up there once in a while to oversee construction.

There were a few rays of light in the neighborhood too. For example, Yehoshua's barbershop, where Dad stopped in when he visited the neighborhood to get haircuts for himself and for me. The barbershop was not exactly in the neighborhood, but across the way. Still, the whole neighborhood went to cut their hair at Yehoshua's. His name was known far and wide because he had once cut the hair of the Queen of Belgium (so they said), and also because he gave haircuts to the elderly in their homes. That was the greatness of Yehoshua:

anyone who could no longer leave their home and was lying ill in bed, earned a visit from him. He gave haircuts to the needy for free until their final days, never shirking, working diligently to fulfill his clients' requests. The caveat in this act of righteousness was his rule that the elderly person had to be a loyal client, to keep getting his hair cut at Yehoshua's as long as he could make it there. Under no circumstances could he get his hair cut at any other barber. And the temptation was there. On trips to Haifa, after errands and the market, after the plumber and the bank. On Herzl Street, for example, there were little shop windows that revealed barbers with white cloaks chatting inside. Behind them, on chairs, rows of people waited. You could go in and have a chat while you waited. *And where are you from? Ohanov? Nu, myself too, not far. Rawa-Ruska. Kapler was our name.* And the talk would go on.

But all that was forbidden. With Yehoshua the barber there were no compromises. Having no choice, in return for service during their old age, they enslaved themselves to him and took pains not to be absent, not to wait too long between cuts, certainly never to try a competitor. The touch of a foreign hand, even covered by months of growth, was immediately exposed, including the barber's name.

"So, you went to Pollack in town, eh?"

And the traitor was out of the charity program.

"Just thought we'd give Antek a try, eh? On HaNevi'im Street, yes? Thought Yehoshua wouldn't notice his livelihood was being robbed?"

And gone was the chance for free haircuts by Yehoshua during old age.

There was no forgiveness from Yehoshua-who-cut-the-queen-of-Belgium's-hair. Except for Gershon Klima, who did as he wished and Yehoshua did not protest. No one messed with Gershon Klima.

The main feature in Yehoshua's barbershop was a wall of mirrors across from the barber chairs. The entire barbershop was reflected in these mirrors, all the way to the opposite wall, where people sat waiting. You could see their closed eyes, their tired thoughts, and the magazines they glanced at once in a while, just scanning the letters. Nothing could be hidden from the mirrors, but even so, I sometimes found magazines with pages secretly cut out, only a woman's foot remaining on the page, or a crown of hair and the edge of an opulent bed. The mirrors were large; from my height they reflected the white ventilator, spider webs, the lamp. Old photographs were taped on the corners: two soccer players in black and white, shaking hands and exchanging little flags, and a scene in front of a goal with a soccer player jumping up for a never-to-be-materialized head-butt. I never asked who the player was. It seemed wrong.

Beneath the pictures on the counter were dozens of knives and other weapons of destruction, little bottles and containers with tubes protruding at odd angles. Yehoshua cut my hair using only scissors and a little tap water. Before the cut he rubbed the water into my scalp mercilessly with his thick fingers. (The Queen of Belgium?) I was even dispossessed of the little mirror that displayed the backs of the customers' heads for them afterwards. Deprived, I looked on as the adult customers were treated to shears and files, clippers and tweezers. At the end of his work, and sometimes during, he even squirted them with a toxic cloud of eau de cologne. Not sufficing with heads alone, the shrapnel of scent moved through the air like a little fish, floated across the mirror and made its way to the storefront window, where it sat down in little beads on top of the words, "Barber Yehoshua Elegant—Appointments Needed," (you came in and sat down—that was how you made an appointment), its glistening turning Yehoshua's barbershop into a feast of light. On the high wall above the lamps were pictures of all the Chiefs of Staff, apart from Moshe Dayan, who, in the Yom Kippur War, had killed Yehoshua's son. I memorized their faces, their names, the years they served in office.

Once, after much whispering in Dad's ear, on the special occasion of my birthday, Yehoshua consented to give me one squirt of eau de cologne. The burning sensation, the fire in my nostrils, the oddness of the occasion, all paled in comparison with the peaks on which my soul rested for a brief moment, a shepherd in the Garden of Eden. I felt as though I might burst. Through the tears, the excitement, and the mirrors, I could see the ancient picture of the soccer player rising up to butt the ball.

"Who is that?" I finally dared to ask, pointing. (After all, today I had entered the secret world of grownups.)

Dad and Yehoshua adopted solemn expressions and grew sad. Many years of stone bleachers and *Totto* betting forms, listening to little radios on Saturday nights, and memories of stadiums in Poland, all solidified in Dad's response: "That's Duncan Edwards from Manchester United."

"May God avenge his blood," Yehoshua added, but he looked at the row of Chiefs of Staff.

It turns out that Duncan Edwards had not been murdered at all, but had perished in February 1958, in a plane crash in which the entire Manchester United team was killed. And so I learned of new ways to love, to set one's heart on a single thing, to defeat logic in the face of the soul's devotion. Manchester United was engraved on my father's heart and on Yehoshua's heart, and on the hearts of those waiting their turn at Yehoshua's. And now it was engraved on mine too. The Mancunian induction was a gateway into the world of true love.

Anat.

We married a year after we met. The first time I heard her speak, she was uttering a lament: "But sir, eighteen thousand cases just this year. Doesn't that seem important to you?"

Desperately enveloped in the thread of an argument, trapped in Grandpa Lolek's net, she was not able to concede. He faced her as she stood in his doorway, stubbornly refusing to donate money, but more than willing to donate an opinion or two.

People soliciting for donations knocked on his door all the time. Pairs of children, slippery professionals, innocent young women like Anat. They were all treated alike. When knuckles rapped on the door, it was not enough for him to wait in tense silence for the nuisance to go away. Nor did he use any of the wonderfully odd phrases that thrive in the world of supplicants and their resisters: "No one's home," "We gave yesterday," "Mom's sleeping" (in a masculine, childish low voice). Grandpa Lolek's door was open to all—he was an equal-opportunity resister. Usually the supplicant would leave and turn to nearby doors, waiting for some reason for the resister's door to close. Sometimes things developed into a casual conversation or a lively debate. Bitterness fueled by tired feet often inflamed hostility and led to implied ill-wishes. Grandpa Lolek enjoyed the conversations. "Is important to stay in touch with young generation," he said.

When I met Anat, they were already in the depths of an argument. Anat, justice at her feet as always, like a faithful puppy, was pleading with Grandpa Lolek. She wanted to show him diagrams and reports. Perhaps he would like to visit their headquarters one day? A lovely, red-faced Andromeda, with no way out. Grandpa Lolek was unperturbed. When he saw me coming, he asked if I had had any luck with the blender.

Anat turned to me. She, a righteous soul, and me with the blender.

"Your grandfather is against donations on principle!" She exposed Grandpa Lolek's terrible secret.

"My grandfather is against lots of things," I said, slightly taken aback. Why had she assumed we were grandfather and grandson? I could have been a technician. We could have been, as indeed we were, extremely distant relatives, were it not for the Law of Compression.

"Are you in favor of donations?"

We looked at each other. Anat was the first to recover.

"You can donate five, ten or twenty shekels," she said.

I bought two vouchers for ten and one for twenty. Grandpa Lolek grunted contemptuously. "How's the blender?" he asked.

Electrical appliances went to die in his home. Pushing a button was, for him, only one of a dozen options, an unimaginative way to give life to an appliance. Knocking, shaking, rattling and all their various permutations were more correct methods, expressive of the relationship between man and his property. And when an appliance broke, he would find an opportunity to give it to me so I could get it fixed for cheap by my friend. There was no friend—just a repairman. Nor was he cheap, his prices were the same as everyone else's. But Grandpa Lolek insisted that I had a friend who fixed things practically for free. So he allowed himself to saddle me with the bills.

Long afterwards, Grandpa Lolek reconstructs the course of that fateful day. "For you, I did it all. To keep Anati at mine house. I knew you were to be coming, and she, what sweetheart." Happily hugging Yariv, he perceives his own role in my son's existence. He worries a little—Yariv is five now, already going to kindergarten, where they teach him all sorts of nonsense about Chanukah *gelt* and such.

Yariv is also worried. Grandpa Lolek has started teaching him to clean out the ashtrays in the Vauxhall, buy cigarettes, polish shoes. Grandpa Yosef is easier for Yariv to handle. Theirs is a boundless love. Grandpa Yosef was Yariv's godfather at his *briss*, where the flames of his pride threatened to burn down the hall. Every encounter between them involves trade in chewing gum and kisses. Grandpa Yosef rocks Yariv on his slightly rheumatic knee, switches him to his arthritic knee, and back again. "Grandpa, horsey!" Yariv commands. And to hear the word "Grandpa," Grandpa Yosef is willing to work hard.

Effi looks at righteous Grandpa Yosef playing with Yariv and says, "God aims and misses…" And our thoughts go to Moshe.

We wanted Grandpa Yosef to have a consolation son, something to give meaning to his difficult life. We wanted Moshe to get up one day, take the mask off his face, and explain that the whole thing had been a test—some sort of Jobian trial. We looked at Moshe, wondering if the moment was approaching. We glanced at Grandpa Yosef looking at his son. But we never saw complaint in his eyes. Only once in a while, it seemed, there was a glimpse. A thought exposed: "It's because of our seed, we who came from *there*." But the words never left his lips.

Moshe lived most of his life sitting on the low fence across from the apartment building. That was where a long life spent in institutions in which he did not fit and in futile attempts to improve his condition culminated. In his thirtieth year, he sat down on the fence and got on with his life. Year after year after year. Morning to evening, the hours anchored Moshe's life. Like moored ferries, swaying slightly, they lapped at each other with a gentle sound. A ritual strand of saliva hung from his lips. Expressions appeared on his face and dropped away, not belonging to him, just passing as if he were a bustling train station. His limbs lacked coordination. Enormous, doleful powers stood him tensely in one spot, his back and hands seeking respite but not finding it, just freezing for a few moments in a rigid position like a Shakespearean actor before a monologue.

In the morning, on his way back from synagogue, Grandpa Yosef would pick up a roll. He would sit Moshe on the low fence next to the red mailbox and put the roll in his hand. He would wrap Moshe's fingers around it and squeeze lightly until Moshe's hand stirred. Then he would put down a plastic water canteen and a little hat with a picture of an anchor. When everything was ready, Brandy would take up her position and the shift would begin. Moshe, from early morning until sundown, alone on the fence. The birds, the lawns, the paved path, the old almond tree—their groans, their rustles, their bows. Moshe was at one with them.

As the long days sailed across his face, Moshe did not withdraw in the face of crises, fearless of danger. Around him, in the neighborhood, nature took its toll, disasters befell the shores of the gardens and the palely whitewashed houses. But Captain Moshe remained silent and erect, his face watchful. He stood on deck when life beat down Regina from the second floor and Adella Greuner from next-door. By all appearances, he concerned himself only with his bread roll. Took bites out of it, chewed, massaged its body with rhythmic, sleepy prods. Only the sun frightened him, and he moved his cap and tilted it according to some internal mechanism, defensive and respectful of the one who was always above. And sometimes, making a Captain's decision, Moshe would get up and set off on a voyage. He was blessed with two strong and sturdy legs, which he exploited for long journeys. From his still position on the low fence he would suddenly erupt into purposeful walking, as if called to duty. But the journeys' endings—at a garage in the industrial zone, a butcher in the next *Kirya*, in the middle of an intersection—put to question the existence of any organized plan. Before Brandy came along, Grandpa Yosef was the one who took him back to the fence, where he rubbed his feet and back. Once Brandy entered Moshe's life, she handled everything.

But Moshe's outward journeys were rare. He usually remained on the fence, internally a Marco Polo. In wonderful China he discovered silk, drooling a thread of saliva for us, hinting, hinting as hard as he could, if only we could concentrate and understand. He discovered gunpowder. His eyes black, pain traveling from his extremities to every part of his body. Rapid, bustling commerce across all borders, over all waterways and land. Undeterred by the Mongolian wilderness, the Yellow Sea of China, or the overflowing Yang-Tse River, Moshe closed his eyes for a moment while blocks of pain changed hands. Goods in return for goods. A bustling city, and Marco Polo stares inside, wide-eyed.

Sometimes children kidnapped him from the fence and led him afar in merry processions. He would be returned hours later. They were always careful to put him back where they had found him, on the fence next to the red mailbox. And they carefully removed any hint of the last few hours—something stuck to his shirt or hanging from his neck or glistening in his hair. But when Brandy arrived, all trade in Moshe ceased. The children didn't dare. Captain Moshe was left master of his own time. He sat on the fence when he wanted to and set off on voyages when he wanted to. Got up suddenly with no hesitation and started walking on his strong feet. Quickly, quickly. A lot to get done. Other plans null and void. Only an army of ants could steer him off his chosen path. Moshe, in his enigmatic way, was in awe of ants. Something about their motion, the unspoken command that drove these little creatures one after the other, imposed the same law of procession on him. With heavy, hypnotic steps, he veered from his original path to join the convoy. Sometimes the line circled around a yard, or traveled far away to the fields beyond the neighborhood, in front of the row of eucalyptus trees that hid the train from the residents (but not its whistle—oh, the whistle). Moshe marched, his soul gradually changing, filling with antness. He was accompanied by Brandy, who trotted along at a safe distance from the black line, the blind procession that gathered up anything in its way. Sometimes she would hurry over to Moshe to make sure all was well, lick a few of his new bruises, sneeze, and run back to follow alongside the procession. By that time, in the center of the line, Moshe had already become an ant. A giant, anonymous creature in a long row, and his roll was a crumb for the queen. Only when they reached the nest, at the point where the ants disappeared one by one into a little hole, did Moshe encounter the inadequacy of his human form. He stood bewildered on the edge of the nest while harried ants angrily passed him by. The body of a human, the soul of an ant. One could imagine that deep animal desperation would erupt from his sealed core in a chilling wail, a howl of anguish. But no. After a few moments, Moshe would set down the roll—a delight for the astonished ants—and, having done his part, go home. Brandy led the way.

Every other Tuesday afternoon, Grandpa Yosef would put on a nice shirt, dress Moshe up elegantly, and together they would go to see a movie, preferably something by Walt Disney. Sometimes Moshe protested, presenting Grandpa Yosef with an impenetrable line of thought until the expedition was cancelled. Then Grandpa Yosef, disappointed, would go and study a page of Gemara and Moshe would go out to the fence to sit in his rightful place.

We usually found him there. When we came to visit Grandpa Yosef, Moshe would be sitting motionless, sparrows perched on his roll, holding it with their tiny feet and pecking. They were not afraid of the holder of the roll, apparently attributing a lesser consciousness to him than to the scarecrow in the yard across the way. The scarecrow belonged to Adella Greuner and for a long time we believed that this was the creature to whom she shouted through the window, "Kalman, *vi geystu? Vi geystu?*" The phrase was once clumsily translated for us as, "Kalman, where did you go?"—a fairly common shout among the bereaved neighbors. But Grandpa Lolek obligingly provided us with the more accurate translation of, "Kalman, where are you going?" This rendition testified to an ongoing dramatic state, a fixed presence in Adella's world, an event unable to become past tense, simply stuck. We thought we would have to set up a rescue team to get Adella Greuner out of her unfortunate situation, but Grandpa Lolek beat us to it. He started going up to her apartment for tea between two and four every Thursday, and ever since then the shouting stopped. Kalman, apparently, had gone.

We also practiced rescuing Moshe. Using methods that had proven successful in the books we borrowed from Mrs. Gottmartz's library, we furtively tried to cure him. We hoped to be able one day to present Grandpa Yosef with his new son: a cheerfully chattering, multilingual, musically talented Chief Mechanical Officer in the Navy.

"Here, this is your son, Moshe," Effi practiced the great moment when our Pinocchio, the wondrous wooden child, would be presented to Grandpa Gepetto-Yosef. In the meantime, we read him books and whispered secrets in his ear. We drew him cards with letters and tried to hypnotize him and find hidden reflexes in his body. But we had gravely underestimated the distance between Moshe and the light.

One day, for some unknown reason, Grandpa Yosef decided to build us an igloo. Excited by something he had recently read, he hurriedly set about his construction project. In the yard, he spread out a layer of white plastic sheeting on a truss of cardboard. He worked hard, laboring with the helplessness of a man not designed to perform handicrafts. But finally he declared: an igloo. We squeezed into the igloo with Moshe and were left to enjoy ourselves. We sat there, slightly cramped, and Grandpa Yosef abandoned us. Our condition was one of being in an igloo. It was a state of consciousness.

The state continued.

We did not know what came next. What does one do in an igloo?

We tried to think back to the seals from our *Tarbut* encyclopedia, and Neeluk the brave Eskimo boy. We sat across from Moshe with our limbs cramped, dripping with sweat, sweltering in the heat, playing at igloo. Suddenly Moshe began neighing in a strange, animal voice. Then he switched to soft bleating. After that, following a brief pause, he yelled at the top of his lungs. Traversing great chasms of damaged consciousness, the yell cut across like a wilderness train. Someone pulled the stop bell. Someone shouted to pull down the crank wheels. Moshe yelled with all his might and tried to get up, flailing his arms in all directions. Frightened, we rolled away from him. For a moment we got caught up in his reality, growing as distant as he was. We were lost inside the white sheets of plastic.

Grandpa Yosef came to the rescue. We were saved, but from that day on we understood how great the distance was. Moshe was farther than the expanses of wilderness illustrated in our Brawer

Atlas, beyond the Kazak plains, beyond Novaya Zemlya, beyond Franz Josef Land. Moshe could not be reached. Grandpa Yosef had been trying all of Moshe's life, and had not succeeded. Professionals had tried. We had tried. Good people had tried. The Moshe Pole was beyond reach.

Once we saw Grandpa Yosef helping Moshe get dressed in his room. He caressed Moshe's hair for a brief moment, and said, "My child, how shall I reach your inner sanctum?" in a desperate voice we did not know.

How strange, then, that the one and only person who not only could reach the darkness of Moshe's inner sanctum, but could come and go there as he wished, was Grandpa Lolek. As soon as his car appeared in the neighborhood, Moshe would change. The slow-witted figure became an energetic creature with volition, to the great satisfaction of Grandpa Lolek, as Moshe's primary desire was to wash the Vauxhall. Washing the car was his great love, one of his few privileges, and he kept a bucket and rag under his bed for the occasion. Moshe was so quick to sense Grandpa Lolek's presence that the scene would sometimes blur and it would be hard to tell which came first—Moshe running sprightly with the bucket, or Grandpa Lolek driving up in the Vauxhall, struggling to park. With rebellion bubbling in his body, Moshe also tended to add a certain majesty to his persona as he fished a wet rag out of the bucket and waved it, dripping with soap, to demonstrate his serious intentions. Perhaps he wished to banish potential competitors, guys who might emerge from nearby yards, buckets in hand, and Grandpa Lolek's car was willing to indulge them too. He would swing his bucket and run to the car like a crazed puppy. Then he would jump around the Vauxhall uncontrollably, interfering with Grandpa Lolek's parking maneuvers. He would begin scrubbing the windows with a sponge while Grandpa Lolek, a cigarette between his fingers, exhaled angrily into the windshield as he struggled to subdue the car into a parking space. Moshe would open the door to greet the newcomer and try to empty the ashtray, and would be left almost with the door in his hand when the car spluttered backwards.

The more profound layers of this relationship were evident

in the serenity of Moshe's movements when he was with Grandpa Lolek. Only Brandy reached deeper levels of influence. But Grandpa Lolek came first.

When we enthused over Brandy's accomplishments, Grandpa Lolek would repeatedly remind us, "I was the first."

It was true, but we betrayed him unflinchingly, increasing our excitement over Brandy. Grandpa Lolek did not give in. Hero of the battle at Monte Cassino, the man for whom Joyce-the-American-dancer had danced with two umbrellas on the rainy dock at Portsmouth kept up his fight.

"With me he really talks," he stressed.

"With her too, sometimes," we replied, defending Brandy.

"With me he explains what hurts!" he boasted.

"With Brandy nothing hurts!" we struck back.

Grandpa Lolek and Brandy were in a race to reach the Moshe Pole. It was a dead heat. The opponents had a lot in common—stubbornness, depth of thought, a shirking of kitchen duties. But there were differences, and most of them favored Brandy. In the race to the Moshe Pole, Grandpa Lolek felt like Sir Robert Scott left behind in the snow while everyone admired the winner, Roald Amundsen—licking Moshe as he stomped his paws and rubbed up against him. But we had to concede that it was only with Grandpa Lolek that Moshe spoke in charmingly complete, if somewhat clumsy, sentences and desires. As if the painful disarray inside Moshe managed to find its shattered hands and feet, and from the newly assembled fractures even table manners flowered.

Grandpa Lolek's approach to Moshe lacked the restraint we all embodied. The hesitation and the caution which, even when barely perceptible in the kindliest of people, was still real enough to shut Moshe behind a screen. Grandpa Lolek crossed the wilderness of Moshe alone, hugging him with ease, asking as he would ask anyone, "How are you doing?"

A blushing reply, struggling somewhat through his lips, crossed Moshe's dark throat: "Better today."

This was not his own phrase, but a plagiarized version of his mother Feiga's routine response. She always started with, "Better

43

today," carefully maintaining the literary structure of the idyll, which first provides the reader with reassuring content, only to surprise him with imminent tragedy. "Better today" was directed at the past and hinted heavily at yesterday's sorrows. "Better today" also addressed the future. The persistence in this reply forced us to estimate a consistent improvement in Feiga's condition from day to day, going forth to some imaginary day in the future when she would reach Venus-like perfection, approaching the likes of Diana, goddess of hunters, whereupon she would kiss Rhea, Mother of the Gods. And then on to great Zeus.

Moshe's human voice filled anyone who witnessed it with admiration for Grandpa Lolek. They stared at him with glistening eyes. Grandpa Lolek sanctimoniously brushed off the respect, mumbling modestly. He hoped to plant the impression that if Moshe had been in his care from a young age, today he would have been, at the very least, a goalkeeper for the Israeli soccer team.

"Don't forget that Moshe is the only one who never asks him for pocket money," Effi noted, attempting to explain the wonderful relationship between the two.

Vested with this responsibility, Grandpa Lolek altered his manners and behaved carefully around Grandpa Yosef, even abandoning his tea bag *Selektion* ritual out of consideration. When pushed, he would go so far as to buy candy for Moshe, or preferably something they could share, like a poppy-seed cake. After recovering from the novelty of it all, Grandpa Lolek began to ponder out loud if perhaps there was a profit to be made from this relationship, some sort of respectable circus act. Of course, he unfettered his tongue only at a safe distance from Grandpa Yosef or from anyone who might inform on him to Grandpa Yosef—namely, us.

Until he dared propose his commercial ideas out in the open, the relationship between Grandpa Lolek and Moshe was exploited purely for medical purposes. Moshe suffered greatly from his adenopathy, and the doctors informed Grandpa Yosef that the disease had damaged his internal organs. His body was bound up in pain. Even if it was only slightly visible on the outside, his suffering was great. They prescribed pills to dull the pain, but they could not give

Moshe sedatives every time his face contorted with pain. The spasms might be simply the outcome of some internal rustle in the nervous system, or they might be due to intense pain. Grandpa Lolek would be called in to interpret. He would sit at Moshe's side and slowly decipher the complex language of his brow. "It hurts? Everything okay?" Based on the diagnosis, the pills were either administered or saved for the next onslaught. He drove without a grumble from his house in Haifa's Achuza neighborhood all the way to Kiryat Haim, sometimes at three o'clock in the morning, to ask Moshe, "It hurts? Everything okay?"

Grandpa Yosef used him sparingly. Fearfully.

But despite the language barrier, despite the four legs and the tail, the deepest reach of all was made by Brandy. Sometimes all that was needed was the presence of her clinging canine body to banish the pain and spasms. Not the pills, not Grandpa Lolek, but the maternal bodily warmth, the courage contained in those jaws.

Brandy.

One day when Grandpa Yosef walked home from synagogue, he had been joined by an unsightly little dog, panting and stubbornly trotting in the steps of her newfound master. Grandpa Yosef and Brandy walked on together, moderately aware of one another, he contemplating a Talmudic conundrum, she the hibiscus beds. After concluding their respective digressions, they returned breathlessly to the narrow path. Grandpa Yosef clucked his tongue. Finally, they arrived home, where Moshe was sitting by the fence. Grandpa Yosef wiped away a strand of saliva hanging from Moshe's mouth. Brandy joined in. She licked Moshe's face lovingly with her gentle puppy tongue. Grandpa Yosef did not object, amazed at her lack of aversion, at the simple way her paws rested on Moshe's knees and, moreover, at the ease with which Moshe's hand reached out to her, surprising, gentle, not recoiling, running five fingers over her furry head. Adoption was declared.

Brandy had been reared with no clear plan for her future. Her body had prepared itself for an ownerless life amidst the trash, a slow implementation of her original blueprints. The newfound bounty of food and rest necessitated constant repairs and improvements. Faulty supervision over this accelerated and architecturally unsound project impelled her tail to grow twice as long as her trunk and then, when it stopped, to give her legs exaggerated prominence over her tiny body. Her ears, never flattering, sailed like leaves in the wind. Her hips, destined to broaden due to the tendencies toward harlotry she was secretly harboring, first accumulated some meager flesh, small in comparison to her bulky chest, and then leapt forward like a canon muzzle, even gaining a pair of fleshy cheeks that protruded from her bottom like an extra face. No architect, no contractor, no accountant would have authorized these plans. But Brandy managed herself, willfully ignoring supervision and criticism, growing limbs that fought for precedence over one another, unregulated, working on requests from relatives, winks from patrons, kickbacks from thugs. This entire corrupt mess, a scandal that occurred against the public good and without any accountability (where were all the sausages, the chicken, the cheese, the *kishke*, the *gorgele*, the wings, the vitamins, and Feiga's pills—the latter were our own initiative—being invested?) eventually worked out for the best. Quicker than one could have guessed, a new persona emerged from the orphaned puppy. Brandy became a large, comfortable dog with only one thought in her mind: Moshe. Even for mating purposes, she refused to stray far from him, and the male dogs accepted her rules without argument. Many dogs sought the favors of the bitch owned by Grandpa Yosef the *Tzaddik*, whose reputation traveled far and wide. They came to her from the northern neighborhoods of Kiryat Bialik and the industrial zones near Kiryat Ata. Brandy, a modest soul, deprived no seeker of her body. Miraculously, this vast celebration of semen produced no puppies, most of the time. Brandy had trouble conceiving. Sometimes, a few months after being in heat, a passing dog would give her a questioning look, as if to ask, how much? But still, these creditors did not despair. Again and again, when the season arrived, they returned to her.

Brandy's relationship with Feiga was civil. Faced with Feiga's complaints—the dirt, the barking, the fleas, the ticks—she was considerate to a fault, making herself available for bathing whenever asked, and doing her business far away. Her barks served only Moshe's welfare. Our treatment of her was more fitting. Anyone who came

46

to visit Grandpa Yosef remembered to bring something for Brandy; a little token of appreciation, usually made of salami. Although she was well fed by Grandpa Yosef, she never insulted the pilgrims, sticking her snout into anything they offered and even tasting a morsel. Once in a while, Feiga interfered with Brandy's feeding, furious at the waste. Weren't bones good enough? Grandpa Yosef, in trembling silence, repeatedly transgressed Feiga's laws, filling Brandy's bowl with the finest fare. He stroked her head, her ears, her shoulders. Whispered lovingly to her as her snout inhaled the aroma of chicken and the scent of pink sausages. With her tail, she would signal, "Your love has been duly noted."

1985 was a year of great consequence for Brandy. Due to some business in a distant neighborhood, Grandpa Yosef found himself doing the grocery shopping in a modern supermarket, where he discovered the dog kibble named Bonzo. That same day, his newly powerful shoulders hauled a forty-pound bag of Bonzo home, from which a few pellets were poured into Brandy's bowl as an introductory portion. Brandy sniffed and grimaced in surprise. She must have let something slip because Grandpa Yosef grew angry:

"What? No good? What now? *Nu*, enough. Every day, day in day out, twenty years, and never a word of thanks. I break my back and there's no regard, not one word. *Nu*, enough. How many years? How long can this go on? Just one kind word. Let me hear something. But *nu, nu*, we mustn't think badly…"

Grandpa Yosef pulled himself together and his anger was all but gone. He quickly restored his calm and put the world back in order. Brandy's bowl resumed carrying its normal contents: chicken necks and fatty bones. Only a few pellets of Bonzo, at Grandpa Yosef's insistence, were added to the menu to commemorate their fight. He asked us expressly not to bring her food—there was no need to spoil her. Only if there were leftovers, that was all right. The family ignored his request and brought Brandy the finest. Leftovers were for other animals.

In our homes, food was not thrown out. This was another basic axiom, almost as vital as the Law of Compression: Food is Not Thrown Out.

Why?

Because.

Why because?

Because Food is Not Thrown Out.

The true reasons:

Because people died for a single potato.

Because people turned their parents in for a morsel of cabbage.

Because people were so starved that they ate wooden planks in their huts in Buchenwald.

Because people stole soup. Because they had their heads whipped and they kept on eating. Because their bodies had already died from the beatings, and yet their mouths kept on chewing.

But we were not told these reasons, not given explanations. The third rule was that we had to be Old Enough to hear things. Becoming Old Enough was a purpose, a mission. Every year they told us stories about the war. Every year, the appropriate dose of horror. In order to climb up the rungs of horror we had to wait, restrained, until we were Old Enough. In the meantime, don't ask why. Food is Not Thrown Out.

My mother had a rigid set of rules. Hard bones were collected for the dog downstairs. Leftover tender meat and expired cheese for the stray cats in the yard. Dried bread that couldn't be toasted—add a little water and put it out for the birds. The fundamental law, the underlying notion governing her rules, was that any food could satisfy someone's hunger. Never throw out anything that contains protein, fat, or carbohydrates. Someone needs it. It can't simply be tossed into the trash to rot or rust. It must be given to someone, and not just given—arranged and presented so it becomes edible. Crack the eggs and remove the shells. Take the lids off the containers of cheese. Pour the milk into a bowl. Even orphaned leftovers (a moldy pickle, puff pastry forgotten in the freezer) were gathered into a little pile. Someone would eat them. Hunger leads to compromise.

In this kingdom of the living, surviving on my mother's generosity, there was only one exception: ants. In this Garden of Eden, ants had replaced the snake, persecuted to the point of total eradication. Terms of negotiation never existed between my mother and the ants.

Mom, why do you hate ants?

A question I never asked.

Why not?

Because you didn't ask. Because there were questions without answers, and questions you didn't ask.

At home, we led ordinary lives. Mom was two years old when the war started and Dad was nine, both young enough to recover from the Holocaust and eventually start a normal family. We children were not the "second generation" of the Holocaust—we were the second *and-a-half* generation. That slight shift, just half a rung on the generational ladder, gave us a simpler, healthier life, with parents who smiled, who found it easy to love, to hug, to talk with us. But beneath the surface was an enchanted tapestry of musts and mustnots. Questions you didn't ask Mom, questions you didn't ask Dad. And questions you did ask, but which had no answers. Hints picked up in a hesitant breath, answers that seemed disoriented—at first they were simple, benevolent, but then rather than thrust themselves into the light, they squirmed around in circles, lost in the darkness.

Where were you, Mom, in the war? Were you in the ghetto, like Dad? How did you walk barefoot in the snow for a whole winter?

Mom, why do you hate ants?

Don't ask.

We knew there was something in common, a shared basis that could provide all the answers, and it was called "the Shoah," although they usually referred to it simply as "the War." The Shoah could explain things, expose the truth—the real truth, not the answers passed off to us as the truth. It was a deep and hidden Shoah, unrelated to the one declared each year with a siren. That was the Shoah that made everyone angry at Effi year after year because she couldn't help bursting out in peals of laughter during the moment of silence.

The Shoah was a dual entity: there was the one declaimed at school ceremonies with torches and handmade black placards and the six million, and there was its twin, the familial one, the one that had not enlisted six million into its ranks but contained instead a vivid cast of characters—not only Grandpa Yosef and Mom and Dad, but also the banal personas on the margins of life. There was Aunt Frieda, whose life was no life at all, and Aunt Zusa, who had nothing but trouble. Aunt Riesel, whom God did not take because he knew what a mouthful he'd get when he did. And Uncle Lunkish, who had an unusual name but nothing else unusual—we couldn't find out anything about him: when we asked, we were shushed. There was Uncle Antek, the Auschwitzian prophet who could predict what happened there, and Aunt Ecka, who didn't seem to fit into any of our categories (was she animal, vegetable, or mineral?) as she sat clammy and wrinkled at the edge of every family affair. Always by her side was Mrs. Kopel, who had no children—she wanted them, but "her womb had dried up." And there was Uncle Menashe, the bachelor, who owned a little butcher shop in Netanya. When he showed up at weddings, unannounced, Aunt Frieda would faint because his hands always smelled of poultry, even after he had showered and put on aftershave. It made no difference to Aunt Frieda who was being slaughtered—she counted any death as a strike against her. In order for them to be able to sit together, because otherwise it would be embarrassing (and Uncle Menashe was actually a very nice man), he had to learn how to come up close to her instead of disappearing into a far corner, because with Aunt Frieda death was unaffected by distance—quite the opposite: you had to come right up to her, cautiously, taking apologetic and slightly peculiar steps that Uncle Menashe had invented and which could generally only be seen in nature films that showed male birds courting a female.

Our immediate surroundings were occupied by Mom and Dad and Effi's mom and dad. They were younger characters, who would hand down their stories to us every year when we were Old Enough.

Except for my Mom, who kept quiet.

What did we know of my Mom's past?

In a village among Christians, a five-year-old Jewish girl fearfully recites Hail Marys, a prayer differentiating life from death. Later, with her mother and father, in the woods with the partisans. And years later, when we were Old Enough: an ambush in the forest, shots fired, everyone escapes, leaving her behind. Her mother, alone, comes back for her. More shots. Mom wakes up hours later in the arms of her dead mother, hidden beneath her body. Her mother is covered with blood. And ants.

How could she not hate ants?

And what else happened to you, Mom?

You mustn't know.

By the time she passed away, only a few tiny episodes of her story had come to light. A detail here, a detail there, in between the gaps. But Mom's story was like Braille—it was the gaps that produced the content.

After Mom died, we went to Poland with Dad. I asked him, "Dad, is there anything about Mom that you know and we don't?"

No.

Mom and Dad were surrounded by uncles and aunts, grandfathers and grandmothers, people related to us by the Law of Compression. They all had their own stories, which we tried to understand, but mainly they spoke about each other. Although our families were small, they still tended to disconnect, to distance themselves. Calls were made on Rosh Hashanah and Passover. "We must get together," they would say, then dig themselves in—stations broadcasting not distress signals, but boxes of bonbons.

We were seldom bought candy, since there would be plenty of bonbons every holiday. We never ate the bonbons because they could be given as gifts. And so each holiday, bonbons were hurled from one family to the next. Happy holidays. And between the holidays, the boxes were stored on the top shelf next to Uncle Tulek's African figurine, which simply could not be displayed because of its huge black penis. Poor Uncle Tulek had lost his mind in the African heat. And you couldn't throw the figurine away because there might come a day when he would visit and want to see it.

We wanted to know what had happened to them *there*.

Why wouldn't they say?

Why did they keep their distance, not spend time together?

We knew their war had begun in 1939. Way back at the beginning of time, in 1939, the Big Bang had occurred, and the meaning of its visible crumbs would become apparent only if we could comprehend the instant of that explosion.

*

The residue left by the Big bang was evident in Grandpa Yosef's neighborhood. The crumbs, the people closed off behind blinds. The ill people, the strange ones. Gershon Klima, labeled a madman with the endorsement of district psychiatrists, but to us the greatest of friends. And Crazy Hirsch, undiagnosed, who lived in a scary hut in the woods and who must have possessed parts of the truth. And Rachela Kempler. And Eva Lanczer. And Adella Greuner. And Asher Schwimmer.

We got to know the neighborhood residents on summer vacations spent with Grandpa Yosef. Almost every summer, for half the vacation—after the unavoidable fate of going to camp, where there was horse-riding and pottery and swimming and soccer and team games—we came to the neighborhood, thirsty for the truth, to meet the people and their miracles. It was a marginal neighborhood, mostly paths and yards, with only one real street, Katznelson Street, and the rows of houses that branched off the main street made do with the proximity of its name. Grandpa Yosef, for example, lived at 8-B Katznelson, even though his house was some distance from the real Katznelson, the main one, which was a paved road. Katznelson Street ran down the length of the neighborhood, affixing its name even to the distant houses, but the name was shrouded in mystery. Which Katznelson?

The main hypothesis was Berl Katznelson, the leader of the Zionist labor movement, just like the streets in every other town in Israel. But some of the neighbors supported their own Katznelson, the poet and author, whose first name was Yitzhak. They remembered him from Lodz before the war, and from the days in the Warsaw ghetto. And Mr. Orgenstern recalled yet another Katznelson, a furniture merchant in Jezupol. It seemed as though the residents had enough problems—why did they care which Katznelson this was? But there was unrest in their hearts. They had to know—was it Berl or Yitzhak? They very much hoped it was Yitzhak. At least in their neighborhood.

52

He had perished in Auschwitz, poor man, after managing to escape to France. From there they took him, from Paris to Auschwitz.

Year after year, the doubt would suddenly be hurled into the most innocent conversations: Berl or Yitzhak? So one day I went to find out. I was fourteen, and wanted to put an end to doubt in the world. I went to the Municipality of Haifa, which had jurisdiction over Kiryat Haim, and found a clerk to interrogate. "Which Katznelson is the street named after? The famous Katznelson, or their Katznelson?" I demanded. The clerk made his enquiries with a grave expression and replied, "Berl Katznelson, of course." I told him that the neighborhood residents would prefer their own Katznelson, and would it be possible to change it? I explained that their Katznelson had been a great poet in Poland, and since he had perished in the Holocaust it made a lot of sense for his street to be in their neighborhood. The clerk nodded silently, then asked, "Kid, are you doing a school project or something?" To call me a kid that year was a very serious transgression. I left, hunching my shoulders in the leather jacket I wished I had.

Effi put an end to the problem.

She walked up to the sign, wrote "Yitzhak" in front of "Katznelson," and told everyone it was Yitzhak, not Berl. And ever since then everything has been fine. The residents are happy and the postmen don't get confused. Only Orgenstern, even though he's been dead for two years, still has a sour face. There really was a furniture merchant in Jezupol called Katznelson. You could order all sorts of bureaus from him and once a year, before Passover, he would bring all the orders in from town. He had two daughters, this Katznelson did, and the eldest one had married a *goy*.

It was a neighborhood of slow troubles. Every moment lingered long enough to have a bite taken right out of it. Even the sun was sober there. Every morning it carefully infiltrated the neighborhood and its rays climbed up the walls. As soon as they reached the windowsills, they encountered pillows, comforter covers and blankets waiting to be aired out. Heavy clothing hung on laundry lines. Waving excitedly, motivated partly by wind and partly by urgency, the damp clothes prodded the sun: Please start drying! That white shirt over there, for example, we'll be needing that tonight. And onwards the sun climbed. Blinds drawn. Why stop here? Why lash white-hot blinds with sparks of fire? Just get to work. Go up top, to the solar panels. Save these people some money. Theirs was a blue-collar sun, a day laborer, without benefits. They had no need for light flickering among the leaves, for emeralds of dew, mulberry rubies, shadows in the pitanga tree. What use was that? They simply needed it to dry, to warm, to flood with light. Before noon, a thorough job. Towards evening, indifferent brush-strokes among the shadows, another afternoon load of laundry spat out from the windows onto the lines, a few more tomatoes set out in Pyrex bowls: Please ripen these as quickly as you can.

If anyone thanked the sun, it was the garden plants. A stunning profusion spilling from one garden to the next, a large wave of lawns and bushes and flowers and fruit. Trees stood in every lot, their shadows falling on the lawns and bursting onto Katznelson, where they skipped over hedgerows of hibiscus and Turk's cap, oleander and wild roses. Crazed bees and flies flew around dizzily, not only in the springtime. Jostling one another, the bushes concealed an anonymous array of creepy crawly life. Ants crossed the paths, foppishly bearing colorful petals and pitanga berry carcasses. The treetops were abuzz with wind and birds, among the roots emerged toxic fungi, shoots and mole whiskers.

Even Mr. Bergner, who was highly educated, and only in Israel had become what he'd become, God help him, had a soft spot for the sun. When given a cup of tea, he would recount to whomever wished to hear that it was at Jagiellońska, the ancient university of Krakow, that Copernicus had first conceived the notion that the earth revolves around the sun. And since it had been back there in Galicia that human thought had first restored the sun to its rightful status at the center of the planets, and since many of the Galicians in the neighborhood remembered that in school they had dwelled at length on this affair, which illuminated Galicia with a scientific glow—somewhat surprising in a land of shopkeepers and small-time farmers—many of them turned to the sun with arrogance in their eyes. Just a little patronizing. Here you go, they seemed to be saying. Now it's your turn to repay the favor. They shot it secretive, Copernican sideways glances, as if they were partners in a galactic voyage.

And there was Asher Schwimmer, a man of the sun, who had been a Hebrew poet in Poland before the war and had taught beautiful Hebrew, and his poems had even been published in *HaSolel* newspaper. But after the war his Hebrew had simply disappeared and to this day he has no grasp of it, not even a word. This man who had once written, in intricately fluent Hebrew, lines like "Fleeces of raindrops unearth life from the inanimate," now has trouble understanding the bus driver. He no longer lives in the neighborhood, they say he's in Acre, or perhaps on a kibbutz with his brother. Sometimes he turns up and sits with the neighbors on hot *khamsin* days. Chatters in startled Polish, uses his hands a lot, doesn't laugh, sometimes in the middle of a cup of tea he gets a nosebleed.

The seasons bubbled in the neighborhood as if they were bottled up. The winter rain was cruel, cutting out paths for itself between the houses, appearing in windows like a frightened face. Summer entered the closed apartments, where it went mad, multiplied its heat, and danced and danced, sweat pouring down the blinds, the air turning practically white. Spring was lovely. The bauhinia flowers fell to the ground. The huge bombax tree blossomed. The bottlebrushes waved their spiky red wands. Tiny flowers rose up from the wild shrubs, frantic beetles flipped onto their backs. Spring was lovely, but people were unhappy. Gershon Klima, his own brother, tried to hospitalize himself almost once a week instead of every two months. Feiga would complain and suffer in her room. Mr. Bergner would do-what-he-would-do, only more so, and Mrs. Tsanz couldn't bear it any more.

There were not many possibilities in this neighborhood, only cracks of possibilities. Every day the same people walked to the same places with the same problems. Every day before sunrise, Rachela Kempler stood at the window of her house, 4 Katznelson, and stared into the expanses that ended at 3 Katznelson. Opposite her, with closed blinds and aching joints, crazy Itcha Dinitz, in love with himself, winked and blinked, some say giving his body to young men. This was no neighborhood for mortals. The great catastrophes had already happened to them long ago, in the war. Now was the time for the little catastrophes. Aging. Bad backs. Weak hearts. Brothers from Ness Ziona dying suddenly. So young—what happened?

Tragedy was commonplace, a daily occurrence, like drinking. They passed it by in much the same way that their looks skipped over the uninteresting hibiscus shrubs in the yards. Those who had not lost their entire families in the camps got no respect. Loss of a spouse didn't even register. Loss of children was a little more touching, but one child was usually not enough. Simple dramas were dwarfed when compared to the lot of Rachela Kempler, who had lost her three children and a baby she had carried in her womb for nine months in Plaszow and had managed to deliver thanks to unspoken sins—a silence fee. Her mantle of grief cloaked the entire neighborhood, casting a dampening shadow on such petty losses as that of one child, a husband, brothers, parents. Nickels and dimes against the gleaming piece of gold she had paid to the author of history, a glistening coin that rose into the neighborhood's sky every day disguised as the sun (not fooling anyone), a reminder of the cursed silence fee, a simple, daily act in the reality of those days, because what else did a woman have to sell, after all, and yet it would not let up, that reminder, perhaps because of the failure, perhaps because the baby she had paid for was also lost.

The loss of Feiga's young rabbi was, for some reason, emotionally captivating, acknowledged with profound grief despite the relative shallowness of the case. No one felt sorry for Adella Greuner because "she did it with Germans of her own free will." No one apart from us, that is, even when we were older and understood exactly what she had done with Germans. Her home, 7 Katznelson, first floor, remained for us a pleasant sanctuary of aromatic smells. Against the cooking odors that permeated the neighborhood—the *cholent*, the *gefilte* fish, the chicken soup turning the sky a pale shade of yellow—Adella Greuner's window insisted on infusing the air with French perfume, floral bouquets, dried retama flowers, and the eau de toilette that every proper woman should wear. Adella Greuner had rows of neatly arranged colorful little parasols, white gloves and very light purses. She stored lipstick, bottles of cosmetics and photographs on immaculate shelves. Her closets held corsets and pantyhose and hairpins, all burning with the heat of her body. It wasn't only the scents tickling the air outside her house, but also the radio, which was always playing dancing music. Birds gathered to chat there, hopping along the branches of the dying bauhinia. And Adella herself, in the evening hours, behind closed curtains, sometimes leaned out the window and called out, "Kalman, *vi geystu? Vi geystu?*" and on rare occasions poked her head out the door, distraught. Adella Greuner took the quick route to the streets beyond Katznelson, to the bus stop, to freedom, wearing a handsome hat, a delicate dress, gloves and impeccable makeup. "She goes with men." "Wanton." Words said with ease. Who could be bothered to deal with other people? The Angel of Death would see to her. "He'll put gloves on his hands when he takes her," another venomous spark erupts. And more than that, no one could really be bothered.

It was a neighborhood of walking in pairs, in little groups. As if by chance the individuals met up to walk together to the bus stop, the greengrocer, Littman's corner store. Woe to anyone caught alone. Only Grandpa Yosef, protected by his God, and Gershon Klima, a radical loner, an Essene, did not fear solitary walking. And Genia Mintz. Crazy Hirsch didn't count.

There were those who did not fear the outside world. They worked, they functioned, everything was fine. Uncle Antek, 10-B Katznelson, served every day as an efficient clerk at the water commissioner's office, and only when evening came did he sit down in front of his huge radio and turn into a prophet. Even though Auschwitz was over and done with and the huts had become a museum, possibilities still stirred in the past. Uncle Antek roamed through the depths of what-was, writing his prophecies in a thick notebook, and every evening he went to sleep only to get up in the morning for work and make a living like an ordinary man. Not far from him, at 11-B Katznelson, lived Haim Mintzer, who managed a warehouse. In the war he had had an identical twin and no one could tell them apart. But the electric fence had known the difference; the length of fence over which Haim climbed was not connected to the current. He alone managed to jump over the fence and run to the woods. Today he walks with a limp and a hunched body, and the doctors can't figure out what's wrong. At 6-A Katznelson lived Genia Mintz, a survivor of the Ravensbrück Death March, who was a schoolteacher. A short, straight, single-mast sailboat with her black hair tied in a tight bun. She walked slowly. Alone. The neighborhood shook its head behind her back as if this solitary, peaceful walking was madder than any other behavior. Genia Mintz kept walking without fear and her demonic, tranquil isolation cast doubts about her true nature. Rumors flourished. People looked right and left, spoke cautiously. And when she died, collapsing at the tail-end of the Ravensbrück march, not everyone believed that Genia Mintz was really gone. They kept raising hypotheses, looking now not only to the sides but up above.

In contrast to Adella Greuner and the rumors, in contrast to Genia Mintz and the suspicions, in the window of 12 Katznelson there usually stood the angelic character of Eva Lanczer. She was young and beautiful and had come to the neighborhood with her mother, who died shortly thereafter and whose name they could barely remember. It was quickly discovered that Lanczer was searching for her fiancé. They sat her down by the radio to listen to the Bureau for Missing Relatives broadcast and went to great efforts, searching everywhere. Anyone able was enlisted for the benefit of Eva Lanczer, because she was young and beautiful and never smiled or wore makeup or met nice young boys—she had a fiancé. Grandpa Yosef spearheaded the campaign and made every effort to locate the fiancé.

The fiancé was named Meirke Geltzner, from Dynow, and the entire neighborhood searched for him. One day, they found him. In Dimona. They dressed up Eva Lanczer like a bride, persuaded her to put makeup on, and Yehoshua gave her a free haircut, modeled on the style of the Queen of Belgium. When everything was ready, one last thing was required: Eva Lanczer put on a smile and became a princess.

That evening, she came back home. It wasn't him. There were those who claimed that it was him, and others who simply said, Why not? According to the testimonies, this Meirke Geltzner wanted her to stay with him. But Eva Lanczer came home, turned off the Missing

Relatives program, gave back the clothes and removed her makeup. Only the smile remained.

The encounter with Meirke Geltzner from Dimona, who some say even came to the neighborhood once to try another proposal, happened before we were born. We had always known Eva Lanczer like a picture, standing in the window at 12 Katznelson with a frozen smile on her lily-white face. She stood in her window like Rachela Kempler, but without Rachela Kempler's strength. She dressed palely, in clothes that aged quickly, emphasizing how much she herself did not change. She lived a small life. No complaints, no sounds. Not even a murmur. She stood with pursed lips, arms hanging at the sides of her body, a white sentry. A man named Eliyahu brought her cotton threads and she made strange and colorful embroidery which he sold in stores. They used to find her sometimes in all sorts of places where she walked to without realizing she was walking, like Moshe but without Moshe's thwarted sense of purpose. She went out sailing, not walking. Drifting away. Floating like a fairy among the falling leaves, only to be discovered near the train station, in a kiosk, or at an intersection. Once, the doctors found that she had been taken advantage of. The virginal Eva Lanczer was no longer a virgin. Several times they talked to Grandpa Yosef, who acted as neighborhood consul for the insane. They explained the situation and sought his advice. But Eva Lanczer kept standing at the window, weakening, imperceptibly detaching, disappearing on little journeys with her white smile, her slender hands and her clean dress. It always ended with a voyage.

We always heard that Eva Lanczer was only doing "what she had to." That was it. Adella Greuner, they did not forgive. Eva Lanczer they did. Because they loved Eva Lanczer and she was only doing what she had to. Here lay the key to the delicate balance, the watershed line between hatred and compassion.

Her life trickled down into points of silence. You could not hear her living—eating, bathing, cleaning. A transparent silence lay on her house. Movement in the two little rooms winnowed down to the flickers of her mouth, bodily flutters barely detectible through the cracks. We did not bother Eva Lanczer. Her window image begged us to let her be, and we did.

With others, we were less kind. Not much further, at 10-A Katznelson, lived Linow Community. Her real name was Hinda Goldberg, but since it was said that she alone remained out of all the Jews in her town of Linow, Effi came up with her nickname, Linow Community. Right below her lived Sarkow Community, a similar case. They had lost husbands, parents, families. And every morning at precisely nine o clock, their two green front doors opened. Linow Community and Sarkow Community went down to buy vegetables at Sammy's. One tomato, one onion, a cucumber or a carrot. They peeked at the watermelons, prodded the apricots, bought another onion. They walked down the path, diminutive and unsteady. A green basket for Linow Community, a yellow one for Sarkow Community. They walked. Deadly afraid of Sammy the greengrocer. His voice. His huge belly. His chest-hair.

The mechanism kicked in every day at nine and there was no stopping it. Once every seven days: Shabbat. Malfunction. Linow Community and Sarkow Community walk down the path with baskets in hand. They get to the bars in front of the store and put their thin cold hands on the fence. Their knuckles turn white. Linow Community wears wine-red nail polish, reflected as dark brown in the store window. Who knows what is reflected on the vegetables beyond, lying in wooden crates, no reaching them through the fence. Sarkow Community gives in first and turns around. Linow Community follows. A dim recollection of yesterday, when Sammy put another cucumber in their baskets, another carrot, another onion. "All the best, Ma'am." They walk, swerving. Disappear until the next day at nine.

We used to follow the Communities. We suspected there were still a few remaining Jews from Linow and Sarkow and that they were hiding them; they had reason to. Linow Community had a kind face and we hoped to find her a little Linowik man one day. Sarkow Community, with a mole on her cheek, we did not like. We carefully checked every piece of mail she got to see if there wasn't someone from Sarkow corresponding with her. We read the addresses, in Polish letters that looked almost like English, and compared them with the stamps to make sure they matched. She wasn't the only one we checked up on. Whenever we heard talk about someone the others couldn't be bothered to deal with, we took the responsibility upon ourselves. We tailed the seven-thirty AM postman like crows behind a plough, removing everything he dropped in the boxes, just to check.

There were a few address-less people in the neighborhood. Crazy Hirsch, for example. A pasty old man, not much more than a yellowing beard with red lips that stood out against the pale whiteness of his face. Sometimes he roved the neighborhood in daylight, emerging from a distance and disappearing back into it. Roaming evil-faced on Katznelson, he reeked and jabbered, sometimes even sitting himself down on a bench. He had a long black coat like Orthodox men wore, and a book of Psalms in his hand. You never knew when he would start ripping out pages, tossing them into the bushes or up into the air or into houses through low windows. But you knew he would always find just the right minute to stop, stand in front of the neighbors or simply in front of thin air and scream, "Only saints were gassed?!" Rebuking. Spraying his question. His one and only question. Then he would disappear. We brushed his question off. Even when left without answers to our many questions, we never touched Crazy Hirsch's. First we needed the energy to gather answers to the straightforward questions. Crazy Hirsch could come later.

You could ask lots of questions in the neighborhood—it was populated by people with answers. But Grandpa Yosef forbade them from talking. "Don't get worked up about things that don't matter anymore," he said. He believed the Holocaust was not for children, and he imposed this opinion tyrannically.

We tried. We harassed old people. Interrogated them, told them what others had said, snitched and invented. It wasn't bad enough the fights they already had, the old accounts to settle, we had to add new reasons. "What do you mean by saying that—?" "I was in—?" We had no choice. We had to understand. Had to know. Effi had to understand why her mother cried at nights. Why Uncle Antek, who was a real relative of hers and also lived in the neighborhood, had numbers on his arm that never came off. We searched for hidden gaps.

Like Mr. Pepperman, whom we visited just to tell him that Grandpa Yosef had been to the Municipality for him and everything would be fine, but he offered us grape juice and told us he had had two children our age, and his daughter had eyes like Effi's. He told us, without being forced, how they took her in the *Aktion* at Kovno. Ruchaleh, ten years old. Then he said it was no story for children and that we shouldn't tell Grandpa Yosef he'd told us.

The fonts of knowledge were well-hidden. Sometimes we passed by blocked-up walls without sensing that behind the wall was a spring yearning to burst. Still, we developed subtle senses, able to know who was worth hanging around, and we learned to listen. The stories were not straightforward. The old people mixed up their time-lines. They jumped years ahead to the final moments before Libera-tion, then suddenly remembered the ghetto, their children, the camp commandant's dog, the Passover Seder before the war even started. Suddenly, a train journey, scared to death, no ticket. How could they have a ticket? It was only 1940, before the exterminations, before they closed them off in a ghetto, and Jews were no longer allowed to ride the trains. They talked about the Death Marches, a moment before Liberation, snow and summer got mixed up and they mentioned a man and the store he owned before the war, so they could tell about how he was shot in front of their eyes during the Death March two hours before Liberation. He didn't make it.

The stories were complicated, non-linear. But we were experts by then, knowing that time marched in a straight line only for those who slept at night. We listened quietly and later unraveled the stories and re-stitched them in the right order. We were not picky; it was hard to find people who would talk. The kaleidoscope of memories accumulated both successes and failures. Ella Pruchter, who wouldn't talk, went to Grandpa Yosef to complain—not only about that but also about what we did to her plants. Beady-eyed Uncle Antek, wear-ing a white undershirt, smiled when we asked what happened in Auschwitz. He spread his hands out. He couldn't help us. Auschwitz? Who could tell? He gave us toffee candies and went to snitch on us to Grandpa Yosef. And in contrast to them, at the last minute there was Zvi Alpert, who had already left the neighborhood with a new wife. He didn't mind talking. His father threw him out of the train on the way to Belzec. A Polish farmer took him in, a six-year-old boy with broken legs.

Sometimes there was no choice. We came to Grandpa Yosef embroiled in the tangle of a story, a congestion of details whose every partial component put fear in our hearts.

"Grandpa Yosef, we need to know about Kurt Franz from Treblinka for a school project."

But Holocaust Remembrance Day was still a long way away— we had barely scraped the mud off our boots from planting trees on Tu B'Shvat. Grandpa Yosef interrogated us. Where had we come up with that question? He didn't believe the school project story. His expression was stern. Who had told us about "Doll"? He tracked down the source of the leak and Mr. Levertov was caught. Grandpa Yosef picked him up by the scruff of his neck like a bunny and extracted an oath that he would never talk to us about the war again. Children shouldn't hear about Untersturmführer Kurt Franz, known as Doll.

But Kurt Franz had sunk in. Levertov's transgression had been brief and incidental, barely two sentences as he stood outside the grocery with a bag of milk in his hand. But Kurt Franz, Doll, had been sown within us. Slowly but surely he would sprout. Slowly but surely he would grow. We would yet suffer because of him. Doll joined the heap of fragments—Majdanek, Belzec, Birkenau—and the names that kept reappearing—Warsaw, Lodz, Vilnius—among the terrible screeches of glass—Herman Goering, Ilse Koch, Dr. Mengele. From the center of the kaleidoscope an inviting hand was outstretched by Untersturmführer Kurt Franz, Doll. He drew us in.

We never stopped trying to outsmart them. We counted the days until Holocaust Remembrance Day and then came to Grandpa Yosef, a pair of scoundrels. Effi spoke for us both.

"Grandpa Yosef, everyone in class has to have someone tell them about the Shoah, so we can write essays about it. Everyone else has already done theirs."

"Everyone?"

"Everyone."

"Even Yossi, Avraham Buskila's son?"

Grandpa Yosef knew the names of all the children in the classes and the names of their parents, because he had once glanced at the registers.

An awkward moment.

And then, without batting an eyelid: "The teacher said we could do it in pairs, and Yossi Buskila did it with fat Dorit whose dad was in the Shoah."

"But the two of you aren't even in the same class!" Grandpa Yosef pointed out, embarrassing us again.

We went for double or nothing.

"That's why we need two stories!"

And we won.

But Grandpa Yosef merely scratched off some stories from the outer peel for us, not even a hint of the burning core. Disappointment. He tried to interest us in the structure of the microscope, the life and times of Rashi, American Indians, and the 1920 riots in Palestine. But we demanded Shoah stories. The misshapen Shoah, the one on the other side of the fence, the one we were not yet Old Enough for. We weren't happy with what we were allowed and our senses picked up on what was beyond, the bigger Shoah, where the pale neighborhood characters turned into protagonists in a plot.

We were twelve years old when we began to rebel. Up to then we had settled for the random stories, the hidden fountains, what little our family consented to give—what they thought was appropriate for our age. At twelve, our sense of internal order began to make its own demands. We tossed out childhood materials to make way for consciousness. We wanted to know what our parents had been through, to know about the people who had been lost, the people that looked out at us from black-and-white photographs with handsome moustaches and serious eyes. We wanted Grandpa Yosef's story. What had he been through? Why had he gone through so many ghettos and camps? How was he saved? Everything we knew was punctured, perforated, full of pauses. Stories lacking continuity, with torn out pages, one episode after another after another, but between the events lay chasms. There was no integral whole, only a kind of Morse code, dot-dash-dot dash-dash-dot. Our rebellion declared: If we can't know about your Shoah, we'll find out about everybody else's.

We began to study, to acquire knowledge. We went to public libraries every day after school, just the two of us. Our day truly began after English and Grammar were over. We read, we studied. We made good use of our reading glasses. Auschwitz and Buchenwald, Treblinka and Majdanek flew across the pages of our books. Eternal, perpetual, in a solar system whose maps were becoming clearer. Now the questions burned in us from two directions. Not only, "Dad, what happened to you in the *Aktion* in Bochnia?" but also, "What did the Commandant at Magdeburg do to the prisoners with his dog?" Not just, "Why did Adella Greuner's husband complain to a Nazi general about the handsome ghetto commander?" but also, "What was the difference between the regular Bergen-Belsen camp and the exchange camp?" We cultivated questions at an age that did not yet enable us to completely understand them. We collected stars and comets, and later we would figure out the laws, the paths.

We wanted to bring what was written in the books to our family, to the neighborhood, to find out what we might read if they wrote books. We couldn't, we weren't yet Old Enough. Grandpa Yosef sealed off the shores better than the British had—illegal immigrants hardly dared approach. People knew how to close themselves off uninstructed, intuitively, a perk for anyone who had been through a life like theirs. We didn't have many chances, we were up against too many enemies, like the heroic Paladins in our *Tarbut* encyclopedia. But we declared an emergency mobilization. We mustered all our resources. Courage and schemes and flattery and lies and blackmail and planning. All orchestrated from the rear by a level-headed mechanism, relying on a childish confidence that our punishment would not be too severe. We collected what we could, picked everything that could be picked. We created a shape. Established a shuffled world of Shoah, a valid world in which the Holocaust was a geographical area, a district with a postal authority and a written history. Whatever we knew about the family, about the elderly neighborhood residents, found a place and was given citizenship and land. It was not organized research, it was begging. No—it was a hunt.

With slanted rifles and hunting caps, we marched through the forest on the lookout for prey. On the paths, in the branches, in the bare patches, we hunted. We hunted Mr. Orgenstern (1914–1991), Jezupol *Aktion*, and we hunted Mr. Cogen through the Vilnius woods, Majdanek, Sobibor. We hunted Littman, Buchenwald, and Mrs. Rudin. We hunted Genia Mintz (1920–1976), Krakow ghetto and Ravensbrück, and we hunted Olinowsky (1921–1980), Kovno. We walked up proudly to the fruits of our hunt and held out our hat for a penny.

"Mrs. Rudin, is it true you were in Stutthof? Tell us about Stutthof camp."

"Mr. Cogen, is it true that Ilse Koch used to mark up the Jews before the gas chambers, to make lampshades out of their skin?"

"Mr. Orgenstern, Dad says thanks for the pruning shears, and we wanted to ask, what happened at Magdeburg? In the book it says there was a dog that ate prisoners."

Once in a while, as we entered the thicket, we came across Crazy Hirsch, but we were loath to conquer that lying beast. We wanted none of Hirsch. We were after the nimble deer like Gershon Klima. We wanted our arrows to strike Adella Greuner, Mr. Bergman, Itcha Dinitz, one of the burrow-dwellers who might—if we could only penetrate their habitat—provide the magic key.

Disobeying the librarian, we furtively read Ka-Tzetnik's novel, *Piepel*, and we knew then what Itcha Dinitz was and what the kapos did with young boys. We read testimonies from the Vilnius ghetto. Now Mr. Cogen's mumblings began to make sense. Needy people from the testimonies had come to his father's pharmacy. The testimonies confirmed that the pharmacist Cogen had taken a hundred final pills with his wife and son. Mr. Cogen explained to us that he spat them all out when his father wasn't watching, went to sleep and woke up an orphan.

And once a year, there was a big surprise. Grandpa Yosef's font of knowledge opened up.

On the same day every year he would go to Tel Aviv. He wore a white shirt that was smarter than the usual ones, and insisted on taking the train. Despite three-days-closed-up-standing-upright-in-a-traincar-between-Ravensbrück-and-Sachsenhausen, despite the deaths on the way between Dora-Mittelbau and Buchenwald, between Buchenwald and Gross-Rosen, he rode the train. Against his better judgment, he took us with him. Once we arrived, he left us with a man by the name of Yehezkel, nicknamed Hezi, and disappeared for a few hours while we ran around the amusement park with its Ferris wheel and motorbike show and cotton candy. Meanwhile, Grandpa Yosef took part in the annual memorial service for the Jews of Bochnia. On the way home, with us still flushed from the haunted house and the rollercoaster and the bumper cars, he became a gushing fountain. Later there were regrets, but on the train, instead of telling us about magnetic fields or King Solomon, he spoke of *kiddush Hashem* and Buchenwald and the Warsaw ghetto uprising. He suddenly took an interest in what we were learning at school and what we knew (somewhat surprised). Unable to dam up his flow of stories, *his* Shoah erupted: the Lodz ghetto, children starving to death, the child he saw ripped to shreds by dogs, little bodies covered with lime so they wouldn't spread diseases.

Small stations pass by outside, faces on platforms, and the landscape sticks it tongue out at us. Large buildings with cranes above them, railway sleepers in heaps, trees as yellow as a lemon-ice ("Not now, we're listening"), and the stories somehow involve a real puppet show in a concentration camp and a lion trainer whom Grandpa Yosef knew and a merry-go-round on which Grandpa Weil rode in the middle of his escape from a death march, and there's snow in different colors and someone who ate twenty candied apples ("Not now, we're listening to Grandpa Yosef's Shoah"), and we wait for the story to come back to him—his story. The train charges on. Grandpa Yosef talks. Down below the pistons chug doubtfully, the *get your lemon-ice strawberry-ice here* man comes and goes, ticket collectors flow through the cars, passengers search for their tickets. Grandpa Yosef gushes. Outside, platform signs smear by—"Netanya North," "Hadera West"—many towns in all directions, all with train stations we must pass, and trains rush by in the opposite direction, their rows of windows as long as Katznelson, the air trapped between the two trains transparent, tremulous. Again the Lodz ghetto, again children starved to death. Again the boy devoured by dogs, again the bodies covered in lime.

By the time we get to Haifa it all falls apart. Grandpa Yosef dozes off. We go to the snack bar and use the coins he gave us. Kibbutz Ma'agan Michael has passed us by, Atlit floats behind the dusty window. Southern Haifa welcomes the train, finding a spot for it between the ocean and the neighborhood houses. The train whistles as it enters the station, waking Grandpa Yosef. A little confused, a little alarmed, he looks at our faces that are dotted with powdered sugar from cold donuts. The board says the train goes on to Kiryat Haim and Kiryat Motzkin, but Grandpa Yosef ignores these facts. As far as he is concerned there is no train to Kiryat Haim. As far as he is concerned we'd be better off without any trains. He waits for the train to stop so he can get off first, his body still a little slow, his face sleepy. On the platform, we flank him on either side, in charge of the bags, the packages, the bonbons from Tel Aviv. Our hands, sticky from juice, grasp his sleeves. Grandpa Yosef slowly restores himself, awakens, next to the eternally inaccurate clock, recovering just in time to explain why in our country we should have done without trains.

Grandpa Yosef was impassioned about this idea. Even though you had to take two buses to get from the Haifa train station to his house—a journey that twice defeated you—and even though he insisted on taking the train to Tel Aviv, he obstinately claimed that in our country we should have done away with trains. Trains could be used to transport anything you wanted, far away from people. Things should not be allowed to be transported far away from people. Everything should be on the main routes, on the roads, among cars, so that everyone knows what's going on. Year after year, Grandpa Yosef's explanation glimmered in the kaleidoscope of memories, recording itself as something-we-must-remember. Year after year, with slight variations, it asserted itself at the schedule board or on the way out as we passed by the kiosk without buying anything. Once Effi lost a ball while we were still on the train—we were the last ones in the car, hoping to find the ball before the train set off for Kiryat Haim. Even when we stood in crowded buses, dripping with uncomfortable sweat and holding too many packages and gooey boxes of bonbons, Grandpa Yosef insisted.

We would barely listen to him, still breathless from our Tel Aviv adventure at the amusement park and from the gushing well of Grandpa Yosef now sealed off, now regretting his words. But it was too late, the stories were already inside us, being marched down the road like hostages to a large camp, and new hostages were added every year. There was no choice, this was the only way to gather information. But the hoarded material still did not form a clear picture. The events, the people, the acts, were all fragments and crumbs, meaningless on their own, but an abstract picture emerged from their collective. Not a picture we could explain or describe, but a rich image whose details had no significance. Everything we learned, each additional story, formed a new sliver for the kaleidoscope, where the pictures spun around, erased themselves, and a new model was created.

We spent the nights after the trips to Tel Aviv at Grandpa Yosef's, lying wide-eyed in the dark, listening. Every so often we heard trains faraway. And in later years, when I was a soldier taking ordinary train rides, catching a nap on the way, suddenly there would be a click and the trains would change with the light whisper of a well-oiled machine. Something full of innocent passengers was taken away, lunch-boxes-scattered-newspapers-do-you-have-the-sportspage-and-children-running-around-yelling-and-even-an-impudent-spit-ball-flying-out-the-window-hitting-a-stunned-face. All this was replaced with narrow-high-windows-no-air-down-there-bodies-squirming-devilish-siren-who-knows-what-village-passing-by-long-stops-hours-and-days-without-moving-tiny-sobbing-stops.

Our trains would travel beyond the woods. We let them run over the tracks near our sleep, their chilling sounds setting music to our dreams. In our sleep we listened to the footsteps on the paths (someone walking), to the wanderers wandering (someone unable to find peace), to the quiet conversations, the calls into rooms, "Everything all right?" (someone worried about someone).

One person we could ask, even though he was officially insane, was Gershon Klima, his own brother. Three generations of psychiatrists had confirmed his madness and if anyone questioned him, Gershon Klima had the documents to prove it. He was one of the younger people in the neighborhood, born in fact in 1939, the year of the Big Bang. He came to Israel after the war with an older uncle and aunt and strayed through many places, living a virtually normal life, until he found the neighborhood. Gershon Klima was an expert plumber who worked for Kiryat Haim's department of sewage. He spoke Hebrew like ours and worked for a living. He gave out toffee candies, and there was always the hope that he would take us on a trip through the sewage system. We worshipped Gershon Klima. His privilege of going down into the sewer, trivial as it may have seemed to other people, was inestimable in our world, in which every dark opening was a gateway to our hearts. We were drawn to the secrecy inherent in hollow spaces. We liked caves, burrows, tunnels and hovels. Nor were we indifferent to always-closed-doors, basements or attics. But in our heaven, had we been asked to come up with one, we would have given first priority to the sewer.

We went to see Gershon Klima often. Not in his house—no one went there. But to the open manhole that marked his whereabouts. We would sit with our legs dangling into the hole—a test of courage—and direct our questions downwards.

"Gershon, can we come down?"

"Why not?"

"Gershon, when will you take us on a tour of the tunnels?"

Gershon Klima did not answer. Busy. He poked his head out only when he felt comfortable, like a turtle whose shell is all the sidewalks and yards and gardens around the manhole. He smiled at us. Asked how we were. Asked us to move a little so he could climb out, and told us what kind of problem he was fixing down there and why he was officially barred from letting anyone in. It later turned out that, officially, Gershon Klima himself was barred from going in because the neighborhood wasn't even his work area. But the Kiryat Haim sewage authorities turned a blind eye: Gershon Klima solved all their problems, and besides—you didn't mess with Gershon Klima.

Gershon Klima was a quiet, wise man. But he did peculiar

things and lived a peculiar life, so he had a bad reputation. No one in the neighborhood wanted to talk about Gershon Klima and no one wanted to talk with him, apart from Grandpa Yosef, who was above the normal rules. People thought Gershon Klima was scary just because he lived such an utterly different life. But Gershon Klima was a wonderful friend and a very useful one. Before Brandy, whenever someone had to find Captain Moshe, it was usually Gershon who came through. He had a sense.

His craziness came in an orderly fashion. Usually Gershon Klima beat the craziness to it, arranging his own hospitalization with one calm telephone call. Neatly following an internal debate that led to a clear-cut decision, he would leave his house after dawn and sit on the little bench beneath the huge Indian bombax tree. A little bag lay beside him. In the bag, Gershon Klima had packed a few clothes, some medications and a large, heavy pipe wrench. His skilled hands were exploited even at the mental institution in Tirat HaCarmel, where there was always a repair or two for him to do. Of all things, it would be the arrival of the four male nurses which enraged him. He would leap up like a demon at them, thrashing against their grip. The struggle was quickly decided. Gershon Klima calmed down. Mumbling, his arms slowly waved in the air. "Never mind, never mind…" he would reassure himself, the commotion with the nurses suddenly seeming needless and inappropriate. He would drape his arms over their shoulders, then smile and mutter, "It was…that was it," as if having explained something fundamental, something that had always darkened his sunlight. Now he could rest. But then he would squirm in their arms again, almost wrenching one arm free, his eyes glistening with the possibilities should he be able to free one arm. The nurses would overcome him and Gershon Klima was swallowed up inside the ambulance.

Once or twice we went out at night and were able to see Gershon Klima being institutionalized. When he caught our eyes, he stopped fighting his captors. He smiled at us like a rabbit slung over a hunter's shoulder. "Everything…it was…it's all right…" And he was taken away.

We wanted to know why he was known as 'his own brother.'

But no one would tell us. You could peek into his home from 17-B Katznelson, or boldly climb the huge bombax that rose from his modest yard halfway up the sky. He had an empty apartment. Utterly empty. No furniture, no tables, no boxes. Nothing. Walls and white-wash.

"I've always lived this way, this is how I like it," he explained. He didn't ask how we knew what the inside of his apartment looked like, just smiled sheepishly and promised to take us down the sewage tunnels one day.

"How far?" we wanted to know.

"Caesarea. Or Tiberias."

He debated pros and cons to which we were not privy, then secretly settled them in his mind. "I lived like this on the kibbutz too." A late-blooming thought to explain his empty apartment.

A few years after immigrating to Israel and bouncing around various places until the age of twenty-five, Gershon Klima had joined one of the most severe of the Shomer HaTzair movement's kibbutzim. There, his request to live in a room without objects was reviewed and they allowed him to live between bare walls in a drafty room. They were impressed. His name was even mentioned at one of the national conferences as a model of ascetic extremism. Gains were reaped. Gershon Klima was briefly upheld as a paragon but was soon forgotten, to the relief of the kibbutz representatives. Better to suffice with brief symbolism and not expose the embarrassing flaw in his character, his insistent tendency to collect expensive fabrics as bedding. In the center of his room, on the bare floor, he scattered lengths of utterly non-socialist fabrics: satin, velvet, brocade and silk. A princely bed was formed from these broad sheets of fabric with cascading folds which, if not for the sour odor of perspiration and hay that clung to it, might have engendered thoughts of a harem. When he was kicked off the kibbutz because of something that happened, he gathered up his fabrics and came to the neighborhood. Peering through his window from the bombax branches, one could just make out his luxurious bedding in the corner of the room. We once stole a few silk shirts from Grandpa Lolek and gave them to Gershon Klima for his pile. He was touched.

"It's a gift," he explained our deed to us. He promised to get a permit and take us on a tour of the sewage tunnels.

"How far?" we pressed.

"Caesarea." This time he was determined. "Too hot in Tiberias."

His voice heralded a prediction about to come true. Caesarea! We could not immediately digest all the fun of anticipating this walk. For weeks and months we sat daydreaming, breaking the walk down into smaller units. We imagined a dark passage, numerous dangers and enemies, a treasure trunk. Arguments broke out—would there be bats? Would they bite? How many candles should we take? Were flashlights allowed? Would we ever return to our worried families? A sewage-full Caesarea was about to cleave our souls before we could even see it. Every few days we had to unload a dose of excitement upon Gershon Klima:

"Will you really take us to Caesarea?"

"All the way to Caesarea, not just half-way?"

The promise was ratified and a bag of toffee candies placed in our hands, to fortify mind with matter.

Sometimes, usually at summer's end, Gershon Klima surprised the neighborhood residents by appearing in an IDF uniform, thanks to the reserve duty for which he continued to volunteer even at the age of fifty-three. As soon as Gershon Klima turned up at his army base somewhere in the south of Israel, his fellow unit members showered him with respect and praise. They walked him inside and danced around him. Senior officers came up to shake his hand, quickly asking, "Gershon, where are the mains?" Because, as it turned out, Gershon Klima was the only person who knew how to find the water mains that united the water and sewage systems of the entire base, and he had been jealously guarding the secret since 1963. The visible mains, the straightforward ones, which any hand could touch, were nothing but an empty vessel—a superfluous component that had been maliciously circumvented and left completely without function. The real mains were hidden somewhere, probably in the thick of the earth, lording over the supply of water to the base with demonic whims. Only Gershon Klima could work his magic on them to make them keep working. A certain deviousness snuck into Gershon Klima when he put his IDF uniform on, a-completely-different-Gershon-Klima, and in order to keep the scandal to a minimum he was willing at any moment to turn up at the base and repair the mains, even if it meant leaving in mid-hospitalization. He had already been summoned by two base commanders to offices with brigade maps hanging on their walls, where, with grave expressions, they pressed, "Gershon, where are the mains?" The maintenance commanders, who were replaced every few years, hated him. One of them once spent thirteen thousand shekels on sophisticated equipment to locate the real mains. He reasoned, how difficult could it be? It was simply a matter of following the pipes. But the operation failed and the pipes lay still, never betraying Gershon Klima. As Grandpa Yosef served him a slice of watermelon, Gershon Klima recounted gleefully, "They almost struck oil with their thirteen grand, but they didn't find the mains." He chuckled, treating the thirteen thousand shekels as if he had donated them to an important cause.

Gershon Klima was unaware of the role his apartment played during his reserve duty days. In his absence, we reconstructed the terrorist takeover of the Savoy Hotel in Tel Aviv (we were both the late Colonel Uzi Yairi, the first of the forces to be killed), and we freed the Sabena airliner hostages at Ben-Gurion Airport (united against the terrorists but resentful of one another, since we were both the commanding officer of the Sayeret Matkal special forces unit, neither of us wanting to be a hostage). In '76 we would have freed the Entebbe hostages seven days before a government meeting authorized a similar operation, were it not for Gershon Klima's early return.

We needed Gershon Klima. His hands alone could uncover manholes to reveal the thrilling, multifaceted belly of the underworld. Ever since we had been given a *Tarbut* encyclopedia set, we had become acquainted with the properties of Planet Earth, and knew that it was made up of layer inside layer inside layer. We envisioned us humans as tiny people who stood on the outer layer, not knowing that down below it was burning—not even knowing that there *was* a below, that below was the source of everything that occasionally burst forth up here, volcanic eruptions and streams of lava, and steaming geysers and earthquakes, and a horrible smell of sulfur in ordinary-looking places. Our minds wrestled with the structure of the Earth's layers, the thin layer we lived on, only its outer skin viable. Underneath was the cloak layer, in moderate burning colors, and finally the core, storing iron in a fluid state. Effi claimed Gershon Klima had never gone down deeper than the Earth's layer. I believed the core of the Earth was within his reach, as evidenced by the fact that his clothes were covered with grey and brown stains, which must have come from the iron and manganese so plentiful in the Earth's core. In any event, Gershon Klima had the key to the heart of Planet Earth.

He also held another key: if he was born in 1939, the time of the Big Bang, well then he must have known what had happened, and he was obliged to tell us.

We never walked up to him and asked questions just like that. We were conscious of the magnitude of caution required, of the once-in-a-lifetime opportunity we would be given one day in the future to ask the true questions, and of our obligation to wait, to ambush, to sense the right moment. We circled Gershon Klima, giving each other meaningful looks before each question and conducting silent consultations to avoid asking the wrong question, the kind that might destroy our chance to one day be able to ask: What happened to you in the war? How were you saved as a baby? How far down into the earth have you reached? Why do the people who come to take you away to the hospital call you 'your own brother'? And above all, when will you finally take us on a tour inside Earth? We proceeded with caution. Edged around the nerve centers with a subtlety beyond our age, a concentration beyond our abilities.

"Gershon, how do you know when you need to go to the hospital? Do you feel it? Can anyone feel it when they need to?"

"Gershon, is Adella Greuner really a whore, or did she just do it once of her own free will?"

And the questions branched off:

"Gershon, what's it like to be a whore?" (Effi.)

"Gershon, what exactly *is* a whore?" (Me. Whispered into his ear at an opportune moment when Effi wasn't around.)

"Whore" wasn't an entry in the *Tarbut* encyclopedia, despite illustrations of Cleopatra and pictures of amazingly curvaceous Romans, and an exciting picture of the French revolutionary Charlotte Corday murdering Jean-Paul Marat in his bathtub. Her stretched out hand, as it brandished the knife, revealed the curves of her breast beneath her blouse.

We investigated the Holocaust. Twelve years old, we charged into the barren wilderness, the murderous expanses in which Gershon Klima stood as a lone tree, and only rarely at that. We did not know how terrible and hostile the expanses were—we could not have imagined. We watched Grandpa Lolek play rummy with Holocaust survivors, winning money out of their compensation payments, and assumed the expanses were not all that hostile. We could step into their depths.

The case of Eva Lanczer exposed their true nature.

It was springtime, during Passover vacation. We were sleeping over at Grandpa Yosef's on the night Eva Lanczer couldn't bear it anymore. We were in bed by then, playing a game of "ten strokes for ten strokes," when a massive scream pierced the darkness. The lights did not come on—one scream was not enough for that in this neighborhood—but a second scream, right on Katznelson, alerted Grandpa Yosef. We followed him.

Before they made us leave we had time to see, or so we imagined, Eva Lanczer on fire—almost on fire—in a dress turned orange by the light, her bare feet glistening on the lawn and her two arms, in sleeves of flames, clutching her shoulders as her painted fingernails dug into her flesh. Her lips were painted too and there was a smudge of lipstick on her cheek. Small white earrings hung from her lobes, their dangling more kinetic than anything that moved and bustled on the lawn—the people, the lights from the windows, and the shouting. Neighbors came out in their white night-shirts and hovered like moths by the lamp in crazed circles. Exclamations of *"Oy vey, oy vey"* punctuated their sentences. A confused Gershon Klima came down with his bag and sat on the bench. Grandpa Yosef tried to impose order and calm, almost succeeding, until an ambulance arrived and drove over the lawn and Eva Lanczer screamed again. We wouldn't leave. We didn't want to move and didn't want to be in the world while this was happening. With our reasonably good grades and our teachers' notes about good behavior and the Passover vacation, everything should have been fine in the world. But nothing was.

The orderlies stepped out of the ambulance, skipped over Gershon Klima, and Eva Lanczer's mouth took control of her and screamed and scratched and bit. The orderlies grabbed her with stubborn hands, grasping her bubbling flesh. It was hard to discern a face and a body within the whirlwind—only her usual fey flickering and her mouth that seemed to grow and expand. Her screams rang back from the woods, pleas emerged from the puddles. Eva Lanczer's flesh was taken into the ambulance and her blood boiled on the path and on the orderlies' white coats and in her fingernails. When the doors were slammed closed, one last scream escaped and the whole world clapped its hands for a moment—the mouths of its lakes cried out, its birds turned to owls and its bats took to the sky.

And then, silence. They took Eva Lanczer away. Forever.

We tried to sleep that night, shutting our eyes tightly. Beneath my closed eyelids I glimpsed shapes of darkness, hovering stains. Letters, instructions, laws. That night, I think, my hatred of Germany was quadrupled. I hated Germans, hated Germany, would never go there. Effi, in bed next to me, shut her eyes tight as well. She wet the bed too, a thin trickle that spread through the mattress and over the sheets all the way to me. In the morning, Grandpa Yosef would have trouble deciding who was to blame. We should have woken up identical, both hating Germany. One night, one conclusion. When morning came we brushed our teeth without protest and ate what Grandpa Yosef served us without complaint. A silence had befallen the whole neighborhood. It was a day no one felt like starting. But Effi, who was quiet like I was and looked like I did, as if she too had spent all night studying by the light of Eva Lanczer, awoke carefree and forgiving. I learned years later that she had not thought about Germany that night, nor about Germans. She had not seen stains of darkness in the form of Eva Lanczer, had not read letters and laws, instructing: Do not forgive the Germans.

In the morning we roamed the neighborhood aimlessly, almost

without touching the ground. Two little hovercrafts with reasonably good grades—what was it all for? We wandered this way and that, not knowing what to do about Eva Lanczer. We wanted the story to go on. We couldn't accept the first ending, could not conceive that it would be the final ending, with no sequels. We waited many days for Eva Lanczer to come back, watched her window often, trying to persuade it to produce her. We came at daytime, on Saturdays, and sometimes when it was dark. We wanted to surprise her apartment and find it with Eva Lanczer outside, half-smiling, pale.

On one of our night-time excursions we discovered that we were not alone outside the dark houses. In the middle of the path we found a hunched character dressed in black.

"It's the Angel of Death, come for Eva Lanczer's soul," Effi said.

And indeed, the burglar turned to Eva Lanczer's house, although it turned out he was after more material assets than Eva's soul. Opposite, Adella Greuner opened her blinds and like a large cuckoo clock in a huge white night-dress, yelled out, "Kalman, *vi geystu? Vi geystu?*" just as usual. The burglar fled, half-cat half-bird, rolled over the flowerbed at the foot of the scarecrow and broke into a mad dash. He took all of Katznelson—which I could do in fourteen seconds wearing shorts and cheating the start gun just a little—in less than six seconds. Just before the end of Katznelson, he turned off into a side alley and was gone.

Autumn came. The days grew shorter. More tea was sipped behind the blinds, more memories. The sky waited for the rain to finish off autumn. "The splendor of Carmel falls / Bows / To the ends of autumns whose first rains are severed," wrote Asher Schwimmer back in Poland. In November a thuggish guava tree awoke from its slumber and flooded the neighborhood with its scent. The elderly neighbors seemed pleased. Guavas smelled of health, they claimed. And no less important, the aroma aroused their senses, emboldening their belief that not everything had weakened in them. All they needed was for someone to make a proper effort and everything would work fine. They tended to take their glasses off during guava days, dared to leave their walking sticks at home, reconsidered medication dosages. The guava flowed and flowed in a great stream. Hearing aids were cautiously removed, jaws moved in unabashed appetite. Once in a while, in random conversations, they expressed opinions and demonstrated knowledge.

"Lots of vitamin c in guavas," they would say. To show that modernity had not passed them by. That they too were in the twentieth century.

We would come on rainy Saturdays to visit Grandpa Yosef, careful not to track mud into the house—he had enough trouble as it was. We sat with the family and the neighbors, watching the rain, talking. Winter, the mire and the rain, for some reason did not bring back memories from the camps. On the contrary, winter was good. Their heavy faces were flushed from the heaters. The couches bore their weight. They flew. Childhood memories hovered. They themselves, their childhoods in snow and mud—they did not need us there. In their pictures they were fair-eyed toddlers sledding down the snow with a screech and walking with Father, holding his big hand. Always with them it was prayer shawls and Shabbat, narrow alleyways and, in the distance, the forest. The forests had long names. Niepolomice, Naliboki, Zielona. Sometimes there were weekdays too—haberdasheries, markets and synagogues. Tall *goyim*. Tomorrow it will snow.

And we were outside.

Sometimes other life forms tried to infiltrate the neighborhood. Young couples grew excited by the cheap real estate, and suddenly there were baby clothes hanging from the laundry lines. Crying at night, a soft, continuous sound. For some reason the young people did not last long. They moved away, leaving only the regular crying, lights on all night, the smell of old fabric on the lines. And sometimes kids were sent to the neighborhood to do fundraising.

On one side the children wait, sometimes giggling at the funny names on the doorbells. On the other side, life comes to a standstill. Quiet! Someone's at the door! The children of Israel wait with their vouchers in denominations of five, ten and twenty. Beyond the door the Gestapo is knocking—someone has turned us in.

Black clouds of starlings also invaded in season, finding the neighborhood a wonderful place for their needs, chattering on the trees, increasing the value of every branch. Footballs suddenly appeared in the air, kicked over from a nearby practice field. A young boy soon emerges and looks around for the ball, somewhat surprised at this neighborhood, this quiet. Sometimes he spots a resident in a window. Impudently, the boy asks Uncle Antek if perhaps he's seen the ball, not knowing that sundown is approaching and in Auschwitz the prisoners are being counted. The inmates stand for roll-call, the shadows of their tortured bodies hidden in the earth, and when the roll-call drags on and on it seems as if only a small step separates the natural state from its opposite: the shadow straightening up while the body falls to the ground to rest.

We invade too. Our neighborhood vacation. Halfway through summer, before we arrive, a sudden blossoming in the yards. Gloomy trees light up with color. Pink, red and purple glimmer trivially in the yards. Then we show up, Effi and I. Tanned, unkempt, full of ideas. After a whole session at camp, bursting with our little disputes, bitter grudges erupting every hour. How could Effi have made us lose the indoor-soccer match? How could I have forgotten the right answer in the group quiz? Effi still resentful over the gray horse I got to ride on horse-riding day. Carried on its back, I felt afraid, with a foolish smile on my lips, hesitant but victorious. Effi got a skinny horse without a mane.

Effi was older than me. She was always a year ahead of me and always beat me at everything. A poem she wrote was published in *Ha'aretz Shelanu*; mine wasn't. She got work as a photographer for *Maariv LaNoar* magazine; I didn't even get a response to my application. She managed to get herself a cast on her arm at least once every two years; I never even had one. She had braces and she was sent to have her eyes tested. Every other summer when she got her cast, everyone wrote lines and poems and signed their names with colorful markers. Every year I plucked up the courage to rebel, to reverse the order of things and try to lead. Effi would rise to the challenge. For that reason we set up a summer camp, an arena in which everything would be decided. Moshe attended our camp, and very quickly he also became the janitor and the judge. When Moshe wasn't quick enough and the fights were too great, Effi would declare—to the woods! That was where I lost.

Above us the Carmel mountains towered, and behind them the woods of Minsk. We were partisans and we were American-Indians and we were ghetto-fighters, day in day out. Time was thrown into disarray. German trucks were attacked and taken down whenever a path met a road. The rivers flowed with opportunities to wade through the water and join the partisans. Uprisings broke out in the ghettos every day. We escaped to the woods and hid. We poked around all the houses of Katznelson, climbing through windows, invading closets. We opened sealed boxes and read impenetrable certificates in foreign Polish on paper that smelled like dead countries. We picked up the rules from the grownups' conversations: if you get caught, better to be caught by the Germans. Worse to be caught by the Poles. Worst of all—Ukrainians or Lithuanians. We were afraid of Mrs. Dopochek, who was Lithuanian. We tried to find evidence to ascertain who was Ukrainian. We carved oaths of silence-if-taken-hostage on all the trees except Gershon Klima's Indian bombax, which we regarded as slightly holy. And we celebrated our childhood, our wildness. Apart from Menachem, the only child in the neighborhood, we had no competitors there, and we sucked everything we could out of it. Every year, the same things. Momentous events tried, unsuccessfully, to distinguish the years from one another, but one year skipped into the next and they all turned into one huge, borderless year. A year in which everything happened, then, now, forever. A tremendous year, its details bursting forth, every memory picking out arbitrary details from many places; contradictions and amazements jostle, huddle, one thuggish version wins for a moment then disappears into the pile, kicking and screaming. The Great Year plays innocent: I am not one year, I am all of childhood. But we think only of the summers with Grandpa Yosef and the Great Year quickly stands at attention, buttons itself up into the measurements of a single year, barely standing, rocking on its heels.

Genia Mintz, the teacher, who kept a little parrot on her windowsill, comes to complain that we threw chewing gum and toffees into the bird-cage. (She dies on a Saturday; they wheel her out of the house and take her away in a black car.) In the middle of summer, she pets Effi's head and asks math questions, questions for tanned skin and sandals. "Tell us about Ravensbrück, Mrs. Mintz." Little Genia Mintz walks down Katznelson, alone.

Mr. Bergman is hospitalized for a whole year, allowing us to investigate the contents of his home. Grandpa Yosef goes over to return a book in Polish about Herod and we agree to just stand at the window. Mr. Bergman's plants need to be watered, he's been in "convalescence" near Jerusalem for two weeks, and Grandpa Yosef goes inside with us and a watering can.

During that Great Year we were American Indians and soldiers and illegal immigrants and astronauts. But mostly we were partisans, of the vengeful type. We sought out victims. Once, on the side of the road that ran between the two forests, we found an abandoned car whose driver had gone into the woods for a pit-stop. Bleary-eyed, we crawled into the car. We stole candy from the glove compartment, let the air out of one tire and spat on the seats.

The road at the edge of the first forest was, for me, the final frontier, never to be crossed. Something about the way it popped up after a long run among the trees was inexplicably frightening. Nature, nature, nature, then suddenly a break, a road—human presence. Effi used to mock me. Complacently crossing the road, she would disappear into the other forest, then come back and tell me how she'd gone "to the edge." I didn't know that just beyond "the edge," behind another forest, was the Kiryat Haim soccer stadium where I went on Saturdays with Dad and yelled cheers that reached the heights of the treetops in the woods.

One day, when we accidentally discovered that the woods were where Crazy Hirsch lived, our blood curdled. We were too afraid to go back for a whole year. We made enquiries. Learned the facts. Pictured the hut he had built himself, with its wooden fences and the light coming from a little window. The next year there was a suffocating journey to the edge of the woods. Trembling steps. A darkening world, the scent of panic. More and more steps, until our surrender. We could not find the hut. In subsequent journeys we went deeper, further. Finally we found the hut. We fled with beating hearts and wild breath and footprints—that was what we thought about: the footprints, which would lead Crazy Hirsch all the way to Grandpa Yosef's if he chose to follow us. We went back, our breath ragged, our courage compelled. We erased the footprints and made others, leading the soles of our shoes to Brachaleh's empty house, to Gershon Klima's house—no one would dare harm him. And the year after that we went back to the woods and took up our games again, steeped in the knowledge that Crazy Hirsch's hut was right there, a gentle pattering of absolute terror, a suffocating veil descending upon our recreational pleasure.

When Crazy Hirsch suddenly appeared in the middle of the neighborhood, we would freeze as we waited, lifeless, for him to find an appropriate place to scream his question:

"Only saints were gassed?"

Then he would leave and we would breathe again. Children again, as usual, but those skeletal seconds before he left, long as the bones of a whale, exposed us to the true nature of the neighborhood. The character of the people. The family. The real truth. Stripped of the houses, the gardens, the paths, the trees, the sun, we clearly saw the people among whom we were playing. The dim message that could not be deciphered with words or with entries from the encyclopedia, like "tropical forest," "first aid," "the Stone Age." For a moment we comprehended the real figure, the one morbidly pushed into a corner. The dwellers of these little houses, tied to one another in a wondrous braid. Elderly gods, sitting on the Olympus of a senior citizen neighborhood, spinning plots of flesh and blood, determining the fates of us mortals. They were free of weak spots. Afraid only of the mailman, oddly affected by his shiny cap. Dining on ambrosia out of faded crockery. Orbiting through zodiacal constellations. From the early sunrise of Mrs. Kempler in her window, through Grandpa Yosef's route to synagogue, to the sunset of Adella Greuner's face as she waited in the evening breeze behind angry drapes, rolling in the image of a burning comet, yelling, "Kalman, *vi geystu? Vi geystu?*" Anonymous shouts discharged from dreams, shooting stars ineligible for wish-making. Grandpa Lolek like furious Apollo in his Vauxhall chariot, untouched by the suffering, a mischievous Pan in the forest of the miserable. And Neptune, Gershon Klima, his own brother, ascending from the water, a miracle being torn from its axis. The marching fire, Uncle Mendel, judging every being. And young Narcissus, crazy Itcha Dinitz. Saintly and amiable, walking to the grocery to the beat of an African drum, discovering new lands every day. Nobel laureates behind closed doors, sealed off geniuses living on pills. Their illnesses were picturesque, sprouting out of nothing. They went to the Sick Fund, that barn of pills, to ask the Pharaonic clerks to fill their prescriptions from the huge dark bottles on the upper floors. (We never got anything from the interesting bottles. No matter what disease we managed to catch we were always given syrup taken down nonchalantly from the lower shelf. The pitchers of pills, the wonders of the high shelves, were only for the patched up old people in slippers and layers of robes. And for Feiga, sometimes, there was even a trip behind the cabinet for a secretive pharmacists' huddle, and a little bag that emerged from the darkness full of yellow pills that we once tasted and which Effi promptly threw up; I did not.)

These prematurely old people waiting mutely on benches at the Sick Fund, spinning their memories around and around, were aqueducts that carried life and memories. Afterwards, at home, they philosophized quietly in their rooms, men and women of ideas (some were modest, having only one idea). Dam-builders, forest-choppers, mountain-climbers, gold-miners, land-birthers. A multitude of gold and wine-like light in impenetrable eyes—only memories could light sparks in those eyes. Crinoline dresses danced tenderly to the sounds of the radio at Adella Greuner's. The margosa trees dripped with barren fruit that turned yellow as it fell. Only the yard of Gershon Klima, his own brother, was blessed with a massive Indian bombax. Feiga also had a tree by her window, a mad poinciana whose branches groaned in the wind. As if her real demons were not bad enough, in the rain she imagined devils hanging from the stems of the leaves.

*

The Holocaust extended its reach beyond the neighborhood. Traces of Shoah lurked in the most surprising places, like the little shops where

Dad went to order wallpaper or buy light bulbs. He often took me with him to Attorney Perl's hardware store on Yonah HaNavi Street. Apart from buying plaster or little boxes of screws, it was a place where you could talk, ask questions and watch Attorney Perl at work. People used to stand with their elbows on the counter and gaze at the wall behind Attorney Perl, which was a patchwork of small metal drawers, each containing its own peculiar occupants: nails, screws, nuts, bolts, hooks, latches, washers, rubber bands. Attorney Perl would be up on the ladder in his blue smock, scaling the length and height of the wall like Spiderman, filling the customers' orders. Words cannot adequately convey the splendor of his motion. The slowness. The precision. His serene voice enquiring from above, "I've only got half-inch ones. Will they do?" Clinging to the wall as he moved up and down, right and left, Attorney Perl would descend for a brief moment to hand over the goods and take the customer's money. Then up the ladder again to retrieve something from another metal drawer. Measure out the contents. Wrap the correct amount in a small paper bag. Climb down. Deliver the goods.

Attorney Perl was born in 1900. Before the war he was a practicing attorney. In his town of Stanislaw, near Lvov, he was known even among the *goyim* as an expert in business, commerce, and property law. His voice echoed beautifully through the courtroom, as if the dimensions of the space had been designed precisely for his vocal chords. Had he not been Jewish, he might have been appointed a judge in Lvov. At the beginning of the war he lived in the Bochnia ghetto, in the same house as Dad's family, 7 Leonarda Street. Then he was sent to Auschwitz, and later to work in Dora-Mittelbau. This camp, with its tender, womanly name, is hardly mentioned in Holocaust stories because very few of its inhabitants survived. Attorney Perl would have been lost too, if he hadn't found his way to one of the Dora-Mittelbau satellite camps, where he operated Obersturmführer Jürgen Licht's puppet theater. After the war, he came to Israel. His days in the camps had not only left the attorney barely more than skin and bones, but had also rendered him skeptical of the validity of the law. So he opened a little hardware store. But even after all those years, even to people who knew nothing of his aborted career as a lawyer in the courtrooms of Lvov, when he called out from up top, "Coated or uncoated, the nuts?" he still exuded a stifling sense of eminence. People answered cautiously. Put their hands to their chins. Pondered.

Sometimes he would take Dad and me into the little chamber behind the wall of drawers. He would tell his assistant, "Yakov, mind the store for a while" (his assistants were always called Yakov), and take us to the back room. There, to my surprise, was a mirror image of the store. On the reverse side of the wall was another wall of drawers, containing the store inventory. The space below the counter looked just like its front-end counterpart. But the width of the chamber was different, and I soon noticed other dissimilarities, including a black-and-white photograph of a woman, a tea kettle, two fountain pens, and a book in Latin.

Sometimes Attorney Perl would point to the picture of the woman and ask Dad if he remembered her, forgetting that he had asked the same question many times. Dad would answer politely, "No, I don't remember her," and Attorney Perl, astonished, would wonder how this was possible. After all, they had lived together in the same house in the Bochnia ghetto until she was taken away. During those brief moments, Attorney Perl found the world to be a strange place. His fingers caressed the kettle as he contemplated how it could have happened. In Stanislaw, before they were married, half the town had courted her. Everyone knew her. And here, now—no one. Not even the people from the ghetto. Gradually, he would regain his composure. We would wait patiently as he went about making us tea in his calm manner. He talked with Dad, and a little with me. I liked to listen to the majesty in his voice, especially when he argued. He could quote from books in all sorts of languages and knew every minute detail of Polish history, as if it had been tailor-made for him. The only match for him was a wizard like Grandpa Yosef. Occasionally, one of Dad's responses to his questions would leave Attorney Perl hesitant, momentarily disarmed, but he would soon perk up and produce a witty retort, replete with dates and quotations. Still, there was respect in his eyes when he looked at Dad (*Nu*, and this is the boy who was so mischievous in the ghetto!).

I sat between them, coveting the appreciative looks. The kaleidoscope of memories came by like a large fish, swallowing up the flakes: *Attorney Perl argues with Dad. Dad wins. Attorney Perl slurps his tea and says nothing.* Colorful flakes. Soon they would be gone and I would no longer remember them. But the scenes still echo, chipped and crushed, inside the kaleidoscope.

Sometimes the arguments led to the topic of Attorney Perl's great plan—his despoiled, lost plan. He wondered out loud, now did they understand how far-reaching his predictions had been? At the end of the war, when Jews were thinking only of themselves, of food and of family members who may or may not have survived, Attorney Perl was busy scurrying back and forth among offices and embassies. His feverish momentum thwarted any notion of throwing him out onto the street. He was surrounded by desperate people trying to slip into offices and present their documents with trembling hands, petitioning bureaucrats on their own behalf or for a family member. Negotiations were attempted in reception rooms between a certain Yakov Zweig, tailor, and the government of the United States of America. People retreated in despair, sighed and went to try their luck elsewhere. They took no notice of retired Attorney Perl—his skin covered with eczema and his body little more than a skeleton—as he proclaimed his sacred mission at every embassy and bureau: Clemency must be granted to all the Nazi leaders. Under no circumstances should they be hanged.

This was the essence of Attorney Perl's position and the impetus for his bureaucratic endeavors. Fifty years from now, he explained, we will regret not having kept them alive, not having bothered to collect their versions. Not the rushed testimonies obtained from shattered officers during two weeks of interrogation. Not the court rendering, but rather a version for the history books. So that we might comprehend what exactly they were thinking, which orders were spoken, who said what. We must not be satisfied with the statements they give in court before they are hanged, their mouths contorted in contempt or terror. We must leave them to patiently document every tiny detail. Because if we hang the wretches, we shall never know both sides of the truth. We will keep digging our heels into our own versions.

Historians born after the war will try to understand the other side based on the inconsequential utterances of junior officers. We will all stand in front of the mirror that reflects us, our side, and we will deny the other side, the dark one. Regrets will be of no use. It is the heart's duty—humanity's duty, to keep these criminals alive, and it will be far more useful for us than any revenge could ever be. Many years after it had failed, after the Nuremberg hangings had disastrously killed all those who could testify, Attorney Perl never tired of his plan. What exactly were they thinking? What orders were they given?

Dad was practical. "*Nu*, but where would we have kept them? In the end they would have escaped, and then where would we be?"

But Attorney Perl had thought of everything. "Where? In the camps, of course. The barracks and fences were still standing. We could have housed the criminals there. Under guard. Why not? Every day we would have made them walk five miles to the testimony stand. In the freezing cold, yes. And we would have made them wear our clothes and eat our food, and walk in those 'fine' shoes, and they would have received medical treatment right there in their precious *revier*. And we would have whipped them. Yes! Whipped! Even unto death! Death to anyone who is careless with his testimony!"

He falls silent. His back hunches over, he shuts his eyes. A small vein throbs in his forehead.

We drink another cup of tea in silence. Birds of memory flutter overhead. Finally, my moment comes: Attorney Perl lets me choose whatever I want from the drawers of bolts, rubber bands and screws.

I don't know where Effi was during those hours when I settled down on the little chair at Attorney Perl's. Did her father also have a wise old friend who knew the names of all the Nazi criminals, the dates of their court cases, their sentences, and the extent to which those sentences were enforced? Did she sit in a little back room where the dense air was sweetened with tea, hearing about appeals, sentence mitigations, re-trials? Did she also hear a list of names—a long, long list naming criminals who had evaded trial and were living somewhere comfortably, hiding behind borrowed identities, ordinary members of communities—*forgiven*? Attorney Perl was mine, all mine, and when he was invited to family affairs, I didn't tell Effi quite how distinguished he was. It didn't matter. Her side also had anonymous guests who would show up unknown, ever-changing, recurring, replaceable, eternal. We maintained a certain distance from one another, fearing our similarities might one day make us virtually interchangeable. Attorney Perl, with his sublime hatred and his neat lists of Nazis carved out like steps, was mine alone.

When I was about nine, Attorney Perl gave my brother Ronnie the *Tarbut* encyclopedia set for his bar mitzvah. In my world this was an incredible gift, more precious than anything I could conceive of. A great deal of the affection which *they* did not know how to express in the usual ways was embodied in this gift. The Holocaust was concealed within the pages of the *Tarbut* encyclopedia, overshadowed by other entries. "The Massacres of 1648–49" and "The Pogrom Horrors" were more impressive, more direct. But even more powerful than the pogroms was the colorful, illustrated world waiting to be deciphered. The entries were arranged according to an unfathomable order, each entry following a set outline. First, an introductory narrative composed by the author, recreating the private meditations of Alexander the Great, behind-the-scenes secrets from the French Revolution, an encounter with a gorilla. After the introduction, printed in a different typeface and composed in formal language, came the encyclopedic data, a refreshing assortment of information, explications and subplots. Each page was embellished with an illustration, whatever the entry. That was where we learned how dinosaurs fought and what the Vilna Gaon looked like, how the Battles of Hannibal were won and how Thomas Edison gazed at the first electric bulb as it shone on his desk. The *Tarbut* encyclopedia paved roads, expanded the world, colored it and outlined its rules. It also clipped the wings of the Holocaust's voracity and defined its boundaries, demanding equal measures of attention for both *tarbut*—culture—and Shoah.

Grandpa Yosef wrinkled his nose when he saw Attorney Perl giving Ronnie the entire encyclopedia set, because he was the tree of knowledge in our family and encyclopedias were supposed to be his domain. When Grandpa Yosef himself bought me a very fancy book, *Sayings of Wisdom*, he suffered yet another setback, because that was exactly what Sammy the greengrocer had given me. When it turned out that Uncle Menashe had bought me yet another *Sayings of Wisdom*, an inquiry was conducted and all the *Sayings of Wisdom* givers issued a joint statement: It was on sale at Goldberg's on Shapira Street. An appendix to the statement clarified that the book was still expensive even after the discount.

We forgave them quite easily:

Grandpa Yosef, because of the money, of which he had none. Whenever he had a penny, he would find someone who didn't and give it to them.

Uncle Menashe, because he lived far away and there was an unwritten, dimly comprehended rule that defined a correlation between mileage and gift-size. Various distances and degrees of familial relationship were plugged into this formula, resulting in the appropriate expenditure for a gift.

Sammy, because when his son, Tzachi, had his bar-mitzvah, Dad had given him a very fancy *Interpretations of the Torah and Prophets* that was on sale at Goldberg's on Shapira Street.

Besides, Dad could never be angry at Sammy, because of all the people with whom he bought lottery tickets (they faced God in pairs, hoping He would hand out a measure of good fortune in proportion to their joint rights), Sammy was the only one who didn't cheat Dad when they won, or rely on his indulgence in financial matters. Hillel, the barber from Herzl Street, cheated him. And a guy from the army reserves cheated him. But Sammy would always run to find Dad and announce the winnings.

Sammy had a little fruit and vegetable store at the edge of Grandpa Yosef's neighborhood. He wore a gold chain around his neck and had a thundering voice, and his potbelly always stuck out of the bottom of a shirt that proclaimed, in English, "Harvard University." With his mustache and bald head, Sammy looked like a hardened thug, but he had small, green eyes that took on the color of tea in the sun. Inside the store, his eyes had a strained tone of green, sometimes Ganges-green, reminding everyone that Sammy was half-Indian. He kept two different kinds of tabs for his customers in the neighborhood: one for those who had to pay, and another for those who didn't have to pay because they had suffered enough in the Holocaust. Sammy spoke of the Holocaust like normal greengrocers talked about soccer. The Holocaust, for him, was a physical entity, a body with character traits. A transparent globe which you could hold in your hands and gaze into to see figures and snowflakes and all sorts of colorful things. "The Shoah..." he used to say, and coming from his lips the word sounded different. Finally, here was the perspective of a man with both feet on the outside, with true compassion and unexaggerated kindness. "They suffered over there, the poor souls," he explained, and nothing was hiding behind his words. "Suffered" did not conceal two-days-under-a-mountain-of-bodies-with-his-mother-and-father-dead-on-top-of-him-until-he-got-out-and-ran-to-the-forest. "Poor souls" was not their-children-died-in-the-ghetto-and-after-the-war-they-tried-to-have-children-and-could-not-something-in-her-body-or-her-mind-the-doctors-gave-up.

Sammy employed three assistants, and they were told to be nice to the customers. When he said "customers," it was clear that he did not mean the ones in sunglasses who stopped their cars outside for a minute to run in and get something for Shabbat, but rather the ones like Gershon Klima, for example, who would sometimes stand among the crates of produce without any idea of what he wanted. They had to let him stand there like a waxwork, with his own rhythm of confusion, no urgency, until a healthy thought about plumbing drew him out of the confusion and instantly cured him, and as if on the wings of Superman's cloak he would take hold of his six-inch pipe and emerge a regular customer, grumbling, "How much are the tomatoes today?"

Sammy worshipped Grandpa Yosef, and personally delivered his groceries for free. In the middle of the workday he would sit down with Grandpa Yosef and discuss the affairs of the day, the political situation. They explored various possibilities, like a truce between Sammy and Littman from the corner store. (Sammy's fight with Littman, who owned the corner store next-door to the vegetable store, had been going on for thirty years, ever since the business with the pickles. Sammy had attempted to market pickles made by his sister-in-law, thereby diverging from his legitimate domain of fresh vegetables.)

Littman was also a saint. Prices, with Littman, were a flexible matter. Bills were totaled in pencil on a little roll of paper, quick computations in Yiddish, impossible to follow. The neighborhood residents came, looked at a product, and whatever was reflected in their pupils—their past in the camps, the sum of their compensation payments, their pensions—formed an image that was turned into a price. They ran tabs that sometimes lasted a lifetime. Debts were dropped, erased. At Littman's, they could come and chat, and he would always ask how they were doing; this was as important as the shopping. His corner store was a valley of sorts, where shepherds came to rest with their herds in a place virtually untouched by the winds. Even Crazy Hirsch found refuge at Littman's, where he would idle with his elbow leaning on a barrel of pickles. Sometimes Linow Community and Sarkow Community came too. Littman encouraged them, reminding them that he had seen the greengrocer in the Turkish market buying spoiled pickles and then putting them in hot water to make them look fresh.

In the conflict between Littman and Sammy, the neighborhood's heart leaned towards Littman, who, after all, had a number on his arm from Auschwitz, and had also been in Buchenwald. But I preferred Sammy because he looked normal, like Dad, and a couple of times he took me to play soccer on the beach with his team, "Maccabi Sammy Vegetables and Son." Sometimes, when the store was empty, Sammy would ask me to toss him a mandarin orange, and he would cheerfully head-butt it back to its place. Sometimes he missed. Then we would look sheepishly at the mandarin as it rolled across the floor.

"You shouldn't throw away food," I said.

"You shouldn't say 'yuck' about food," Sammy retorted.

"People died for a bit of cabbage," I escalated.

"Bread is sacred," Sammy giggled.

We shouted out all the battle-cries, only after making absolutely sure we were alone.

A little of Sammy's hegemony was disrupted in favor of Littman during one of our trips to Tel Aviv with Grandpa Yosef, when we were delivered into the caring hands of Hezi for our day at the amusement park. We found Hezi in a garrulous mood. Until that day, we had believed that Hezi was created only once a year to welcome us in Tel Aviv and take us to the amusement park, then disappear into thin air until the next year. But there he was, not only talking and taking on the form of flesh and blood, but very quickly also revealing a solid connection to our life: he announced that he was the son of Littman from the corner store, didn't we know? He told us off-handedly about Buchenwald and the mad hunger. The people who ate corpses. Ate clothes. Ate wood from the hut walls. Their teeth crumbled as they gnawed on the wood but they could not stop. Only those who gained the protection of criminals or Russian POWs, the kings of the camps, could survive.

Hezi was an utterly unexpected fountain of information, and an incautious one. He was apparently reprimanded by Grandpa Yosef because the next year he was completely silent, as if the Hezi who had snuck into the previous year's amusement park day had been an impostor. We failed to see how he could be Littman's son, and how he could suddenly have talked. The year after that, Hezi was abolished altogether.

Hezi was abolished, but not the impressions of Buchenwald. We had finally found a magic key to the Shoah: hunger was something we too could experience. Hunger. That, we could do ourselves.

But it was hard to stop eating just like that. Mom's radar eyes would have picked up on it immediately, and things were no different in Effi's household. We waited for our chance, knowing that we had to taste Buchenwald. The opportunity did not come quickly, but it came. We were sent to the kibbutz.

The original plan was to spend summer with Grandpa Yosef as usual, but a severe deterioration in Feiga's health necessitated a change of plans. We oscillated between the threat of a session at camp (after already having announced that we were through with camp—thirteen years old, enough is enough), lounging around at my place, lounging around at Effi's place, or going to the kibbutz. We wanted to stay with Grandpa Yosef, even prayed for Feiga's health, but this time her decline was so severe that all the pale bones at the foundation of her illnesses were exposed, revealing a ruined network of body-soul connections. The die was cast: kibbutz.

The kibbutz was where Grandpa Hainek's eldest sons lived. Ze'ev had already been killed. It was the year in which Dov was to be killed, in November, but that summer he still welcomed us warmly. His task was to host us for a month, and he did just that, with the help of Eitan, Grandpa Hainek's third son, who was well-suited to the mission. He had just finished his army service and he liked to talk once in a while, which, by family standards, made him garrulous.

Most of the time we were left to our own devices, and we made the most of it: this was what we had been waiting for. Buchenwald. The rules of the game were simple: no eating. Then we replaced the absolute rule with less severe derivatives: eating was allowed, but only scraps from the kibbutz trash-cans, fruit peel, waste, bones. We were willing to be disgusted, to get ill. We toughened our spirits. It was not a game played for immediate victory, but in the service of the senses, to acquire skill, depth, and the possibility of touching the truth. Then we added another rule: we could eat whatever we stole.

It was not an easy time between Effi and me. She was fourteen, I was at bar mitzvah age ("Comfort, comfort my people," began the *haftorah* I was learning to recite), and all sorts of things were erupting in my body. Strange discoveries emerged constantly, everything seemed peculiar, in constant flux. Effi had begun to hide things from me and was often busy. She had recruited a staff of girlfriends. When I wanted to go to the library, she would say she was busy, and eventually she confessed: "I'm kind of sick of the Shoah." I felt betrayed. With great anger, I would go alone to read in the library, more diligent than ever, now representing the righteous, the neglected, the abandoned. I traded horrible thoughts and self-pity for studious reading. What I found out, I kept to myself, a little treasure for the treasureless.

On the kibbutz, the rift was somewhat healed. We knew it was Buchenwald time. Effi put her new interests (which, to my horror, had begun to take on the corporeal form of Yaron from the ninth grade) on hold. We played Buchenwald. We fasted and did not drink. We licked water from leaking taps, slipped behind the dining hall, stole old hunks of cheese and ate with trembling hands. We even sucked on straw, like Littman had done when he had escaped. We shared a sour, blackened banana peel in a tender moment of mutual destiny. Then, one day, there was an event of a different kind.

At the burning hour of midday we went to the distant fields near the entrance to the cowshed and the dairy. The heat was relentless. Our breath was lethargic from the Buchenwald hunger and the oppressive heat, colorful circles of sunlight hovered in front of our eyes. No one dared go outside in the heat wave. Only a few stunned pigeons wandered on the lawns and in the shade of the oleander shrubs, and the cows mooed plaintively in the distance. We walked slowly. I felt as if my legs were acting of their own accord. A strange sensation. Hunger had weakened my thoughts. For four days it had been nothing but sour banana peels, straw, cheese from a discarded container, and some apple rinds Effi had got hold of—the most nutritious thing I had consumed.

Effi dragged me into the oleander shade. She did not speak. She was breathing heavily and I saw a strange look in her eyes, beneath fluttering eyelids. Without warning, she lay down on her back on the slightly putrid bed of leaves, and slowly took off her blouse, crushing the leaves as she squirmed. Her nipples were presented to me with the hem of her blouse still draped over her forearms. Curiously, I surveyed the revelation, the fair mounds which bore her nipples on their peaks, and my heart did not demand a thing. Effi ordered me to come closer, laid down the law. She let me touch her with my tongue, but only on her belly-button, her earlobes, and the tip of her nose. She warned me against deviating from this crucifix of flesh. I knelt, examining my options, looking for interest in them. Effi breathed heavily. Nerve endings bustled just beneath the surface of her skin, invisible channels of sweetness perceptible only in her rosy blush. I kissed her earlobes undesiringly, cautiously touched the edge of her nose, then licked her navel. I sat up straight.

Effi sighed with her eyes closed. "Again."

I was scared. "Again?"

Effi felt for my hand. She dragged it over her skin, letting me find the tracks on my own. "Use your tongue too," she ordered.

I chose the safest looking path, the four points that had already proven themselves. I flitted over her navel, her ears, her nose. I sniffed. Effi exuded a new scent of budding perspiration. I gained courage and touched a nipple. I put my lips to it and tried to drink. I placed my hand on her abdomen and attempted to draw out a single drop, the way we had once both sucked on the udders of Lassie, the barn dog. She had not put up much resistance as we removed her puppies and tasted her udders, only a look that said, "Kids, it's not pasteurized," and slight amazement, perhaps also resentment at the temporary suspension of her puppies. (We didn't drink much. It was a little bitter and unpleasantly warm. Unlike Romulus and Remus, we preferred grape juice.) I could not find a drop in Effi's nipples. And she too, fairly soon, grew bored. But a new idea glistened.

At my cousin Zevik's wedding, Grandpa Hainek's son Eitan had been kind enough to explain to me about the schlong. He pulled me aside at one of the tables and went into great detail regarding whom he had given his schlong to, whom he was planning to give his schlong to, and how one gives one's schlong. Later, in the restroom, he pulled down his pants and showed me this mysterious creature, the schlong, which had-been and was-being and would-be given according to a carefully implemented plan. I discovered with Columbus-like excitement that I too had a fragile schlong in my pants, and that its thus-far monotonous functions (sometimes, to my chagrin, at night in bed) were merely a spiritual weakening whose time was up. Now I looked at Effi and was guided by an unspoken sensation—her fluttering eyelids, her trembling lips, her expectant look. I put my worlds together and enquired, "Do you want to get my schlong?"

The days were days of Buchenwald, and I was dizzy from barely eating, and Effi's slap sent me reeling into deep darkness. I could not believe how much Jewish strength still remained in the hand of this girl who had been testing her limits by starving herself for a week. Years later, she told me I was the only one who had been in the throes of Buchenwald starvation. She was secretly gobbling down double meals, fattening herself up in the dining room and at Dov's. "I thought about it," she generously explained, "about whether both of us really needed to do it, to understand." And she had a complaint too. "Do you have any idea how many apples I had to eat, to make you those scraps?"

I woke up alone. Effi had left and gone to Dov's room, where she sat comfortably eating jam and loquats, preparing me some apple rinds as she munched her way through a bag of toffee candies. The sun stole in between the oleanders, striking my face. I opened my mouth wide, feeling singed. Voices came from afar, people walking. My eyes could not see, shadows were distorted, glimpses of color danced around. I vomited, still lying on my back, almost choking. I could not open my eyes. How would I get up? I lay helpless, wanting to drink just one drop. I tried to move again, in vain. Nausea. I wanted to pass out, not to suffer the dizziness, the thirst. At the last minute, before giving in, I made one more effort. I rolled onto my side and sat up on my knees. Things were dripping inside my head. Circles running in my eyes. I vomited again. I got up very slowly and opened my eyes. I walked, lightly touching the branches, anchoring myself in the spinning world. I followed the shrubs all the way to where the path began and made my way to Dov's room. Got to survive.

I ate three dinners that evening, and for the next two days I kept drinking from every tap I came across, just in case. But at the moment when I touched the door to Dov's room, on the border between an Israeli kibbutz and Cell Block 55 in Buchenwald, I touched a speck of Shoah. Only a hint, just for a moment, but I will never again be as close. The Buchenwaldian moment was over as soon as I washed my face, but a glowing spot remained inside of me. And there remained Effi's look when I turned up at the door, my face and shirt stained with vomit and blood, my eyes vacant, unresponsive, as I walked to the sink with a strange quaver. A speck also remained deep inside her. I had been to Buchenwald, she had not. A solid stain of failure that no future victories could melt away. An Archimedean point that marked new directions in our relationship.

To console herself, she stood on the peaks of Monte Cassino with Grandpa Lolek the hero. When we went back to school, she brought him in to tell his story to her class. Despite his broken Hebrew and the hollow ring of his tales, when he faced an audience of thirteen-year-olds, Grandpa Lolek might as well have been a recruiter for the Israel Defense Forces: six armor officers, five paratroopers, two pilots and one Mossad agent were ready to sign up. At the end of the class, Effi stood beside him on that glorious mountaintop with her eyes lowered modestly, basking in admiration. He wouldn't come to my class. Even one free appearance was beyond his emotional strength. For Effi, he agreed. She was always his favorite. He had plans to marry her off for a good price one day. "What a beauty! My woman! Men will be around her like flies!" The object of these compliments, barely fourteen years old, was less excited. Men were always like flies. Sometimes the compliments were dual. He would gather us both in his arms and gush, "You are *mamelach*, like my children." He shoved the word *like* to the front, its prominence thwarting any ideas of offspring-hood we might have.

Later that summer the anarchy continued. Due to a coordination mishap, we were sent to spend two whole days with Grandpa Lolek. There was no telling what he was promised, and he usually collected his debts promptly and firmly. In any event, he managed the first day nobly, took us to the Carmel Center and with a flourish of generosity bought us each two swimsuits. He even took us out, like grownups, to a café, where he let us order chocolate cake and hot cocoa while he smoked his cigarettes and sipped a cup of tea. The cakes and cocoa were our reward for listening to him once again recount the story of Joyce the American dancer, the one who came with a troupe from Kentucky to entertain the soldiers, but one of the generals took a liking to her and she was ordered to stay behind when the troupe left and entertain him alone. Once he was sufficiently entertained, he wanted to send her to entertain another general, but our Queen Esther responded with a stinging slap on his cheek. Lonely and tearful, she walked the streets until she met her savior, Grandpa Lolek, a soldier in Anders' Army waiting to be deployed to the front. On the rainy dock, she danced for him with two umbrellas in her hands, etc., etc., etc.

We tried to ask him about the war.

"Grandpa Lolek, why won't Grandpa Yosef tell us about what happened to him in Buchenwald?"

"Grandpa Lolek, what do you know about Adella Greuner?"

"Grandpa Lolek, what happened to my mom in the village when she hid with Christians?"

But we gave up in despair. Grandpa Lolek knew only one war, his, and it sounded very similar to the wars we had here. The Six Day War, for example. His description of the battle at Monte Cassino, May '44, week after week after week, melted away the delight of chocolate cake and cocoa. Grandpa Lolek tried to impress us with descriptions of the final hilltop battle. "Seven days, we skip on foot, from rock to rock."

"It was probably cheapest to travel by foot," Effi whispered, her face a study of chocolate.

But I noticed the unusual words Grandpa Lolek used—'skip', 'from rock to rock'—and it occurred to me that he might have read about Monte Cassino in books, impressed at his own feats.

Grandpa Lolek grew animated as he continued to broaden our education. "Monte Cassino, what do you know? Germans were positioned there, not to move. You move, you lose all of Italy, all the war. Fighting there, the Germans. Everybody against them, no good. No passing. They bomb from the sky, day and night. From the land we try to get up. Germans slaughter everyone. Through the rocks, not possible. Uphill. Difficult. Anywhere a soldier walks, a German is hiding, and bang-bang. They tried everything, the generals. No more soldiers of theirs left, and the Australians tried and the New Zealanders tried. Fighting, fighting, and no doing. All day, all night, they bring bodies down. No getting by the Germans. Strong, those Germans. Animals. They decided: Send the Poles in. Anders' soldiers. Why not? Soldiers for free. In May, we start to conquer. Fifteen of May, the beginning of the end. Last battle, they said. Well, ask your father. That was the day when his mother, Rachela, went in Auschwitz. Exactly that same day. Fifteen of May. Ask him, ask him. And me on the hilltop, Monte Cassino, fighting the Nazis. There were casualties, you should know. For two weeks now, we, the Poles, on the mountain. The Germans were men, lions. Us Poles, we had more hate. Up we went, and took the Germans, one at a time, with bayonets. Until no more. We slaughtered the last German. Anders' Army on the mountain. Me, the Jew, on the mountain. Your father's mother, Rachela, a righteous woman, Auschwitz. Your father and his father in train car, to a new concentration camp, they have luck, not

Auschwitz. Strong. Your father is good boy, his father sick already. But me, a Jew, on Monte Cassino, up top, and no one has bad word for me. Germans, only with bullet in the head, and if all Jews were like that, no Hitler. There would not have been…"

He calmly ordered another cup of tea, leaving us wide-eyed, with many new questions racing through our minds. For me, my mother's birthday, May 15th, now connected with the new date, the day of Grandma Rachel's death in Auschwitz. I would have to ask Dad about it. But I soon forgot. The loyal mechanism worked every time: whatever we weren't allowed to ask, we forgot to ask. Dad would continue to hide the date, celebrate Mom's birthday with her and quietly think about his mother. Mom mustn't know, not to ruin her celebration. Only after Mom died, did he tell us how all those years…

The cup of tea came. Grandpa Lolek stirred in three teaspoons of sugar (courtesy of the café) and jolted the teabag around in the boiling water to get everything out. After fishing out the bag, forgoing his usual *Selektion* process, he put it with its predecessors in the saucer and sighed. "Such a pity you cannot smoke what's left of tea." He stared at us with his crystal blue eyes and sighed again, from the depths of his chest.

Fake.

If not for our keen senses, he might have been able to trick us. But something about the sentence rang false, something in the sigh he had amateurishly copied from Grandpa Yosef. Since when did Grandpa Lolek sigh? As we left, we were not surprised to see him stealthily collecting the used tea bags in a little plastic bag, intending to produce another eight cups out of every bag, and then on to his great mattress plan.

We had fun at his house. We learned new shades of miserliness, ones that were not evident to us during regular encounters. In his kitchen window boxes we found herbs he had planted following the guidance of a television program, with plenty of sun and a little water. In his lamps he used only monastic low-wattage bulbs, which produced a brownish-golden light. In the kitchen, he required every match to last for three uses. When he tried to make us soft-boiled eggs, the first match completely failed and Grandpa Lolek looked at us accusingly. Before bed-time we took showers. We wanted baths with water up to our chins, but Grandpa Lolek recommended showers. "After beach, it washes better the sand." We reminded him that we hadn't been to the beach, but our protests were drowned out in a stream of water. He kept us apart ("No romances should be here") and sent Effi in first. To pass the time until it was my turn, and since I was going to wash soon anyway, I helped him polish shoes, wash the dishes in the sink, throw out the trash.

After my shower, Effi and I shared our astonishment at the soap. We discovered that not only did he dilute the liquid soap by the sink down to nothing, but that the bar of soap for use in the shower had also been subjected to his artistry. In a painstaking process, he had hoarded and united the tail-ends of countless bars of soap, and with the skillfulness of a goldsmith had fused them into one multicolored lump, a bumpy hedgehog ready for use. This hedgehog, when it reached the end of its days, was also reduced to a soap tail-end and used, in turn, in a further welding. Through this process of reduction and fusing, Grandpa Lolek created a new entity, a bar of soap in which every particle had its own age and its own parent-soap. This alchemical creature, "a wise man's soap" that resulted from the filtering down of hundreds of initial bars, astounded us with its multitude of colors. At home, our soap had only one color, usually a faded shade of brown.

And we discovered more rules. When he had a headache, he left his house to have a cup of tea with a neighbor. Then he would suddenly murmur, "Happen to have a pill for my headache?" That way, he also gained a glass of water to swallow the pill with. He was distressed by the red light on the hot water heater, which lit up every time it was turned on. Grandpa Lolek wanted hot water, not light. They explained to him that the light was in fact intended to conserve power, to remind him to turn the boiler off. Grandpa Lolek could not comprehend this. How could anyone leave the boiler on? Who would do that? He blamed the boiler for the waste, as if the hot water was designed to pamper the heating elements.

We came to believe that Grandpa Lolek existed on a level of miserliness that few could achieve. We could not have known that he was still only half-way up the peaks he was yet to scale. But even then, we sensed how to wind him up. "Starting next month, it will cost money to call an ambulance," we told him. Or, "They said on the news there's going to be a tax on bus fare." (He rode the bus to preserve the Vauxhall.)

By the second day of our visit, Grandpa Lolek was shirking his duties. He handed a thimble-full of cleaning fluid to the maid who came in the morning, instructed her to wash everything twice, then hid the container. He took us for a measly trip to the Carmel Center, where he walked around with us impatiently. Too many hours had already been robbed from his life. When lunchtime arrived, he did not hesitate to set off to his regular restaurant. He left us at home without much remorse. The maid had left us a pot of mashed potatoes to heat up with beans, two rolls wrapped in plastic, and compote for dessert. In disgust, we ate nothing but the rolls, saving time for the main event: a thorough rummage through Grandpa Lolek's house of wonders. We cautiously opened closets, bureaus, draws, cabinets. We found account ledgers and binders and lots of pictures of smiling people, including some of ourselves at Nathan's bar mitzvah. We found a crystal swan with a broken neck—more precisely, we found only the hook of its neck and head, with no body. We found two envelopes stuffed with stamps, all in the same color, red. When I stood on a chair and Effi risked her life by climbing up on my shoulders, we discovered a treasure. From that height, Effi saw something in the rug on the floor. The rug was nicely spread beneath the table, with its edges under the armchairs and couch, but from up above she saw an indentation down the length of the rug. A bunker! We quickly uprooted the table, the couch, the armchairs and the rug, revealing a trapdoor that led to a cellar. And there it was. Our dreams had come true.

Grandpa Lolek's house stood on a small hill, a position which created interesting geometrical possibilities. It had been built by a founding member of the underground Haganah movement in the thirties, and he had exploited every single possibility. When the Haganah man was killed, the house was left to its tenant, Grandpa Lolek, who managed to defend it against claims by the legal heirs.

After a generation of fighting, the heirs were exhausted, but to this day, every few years, a feeble legal bleating comes from the direction of Ness Ziona.

Now we stood over the opening of a hidden cellar, a weary cloud of dust rising up from below. We looked inside. All we could see was a dark staircase winding its way down. We were drawn to this Pharaonic tomb, and despite our familiarity with the curse (*Death shall come on swift wings to him who disturbs the peace of the king*), we had to go down. Guided by some force of maturity, we descended, older than our years, and crossed an invisible line between childhood and what comes after.

We advanced slowly. Effi went first. We stood blinded on the cellar floor, inhaling a stench of dead lizards and bricks touched only by dampness. Dust, dust, wormy and horrible. The moment was too sacred for words. We tried to accustom our eyes to the darkness. No light deigned to enter. Above us, through the cellar opening that faced the living room, daylight loomed, but in the heart of dustiness darkness reigned. We could vaguely see that the cellar continued far on into the darkness. We walked slowly, hoping for the best, until we touched a damp wall. There were two windows of a sort there, which gave way to the yard above, but no light shone in through them. Mosquito screens had been hung long ago and they were thick with spider webs, allowing only a slim line of light to barely penetrate and drag its shadow behind with a limp. Effi decreed that someone had to go up for matches.

It was me, of course. Out I went, passing through the rooms like a short apparition, pausing in astonishment opposite the hallway mirror to scan the mass of cobwebs on my body. I found two flashlights in the kitchen cabinet (the battery was kept separately, of course, in the refrigerator) and I also took candles, matches and a lighter. I looked around at the house. The furniture and rugs were coated with dust. Punishment hovered over our heads. I went back to the cellar, concealing the dusty horrors from Effi. We turned the flashlights on and dark objects sparkled and crackled in surprise from every corner. Light! Light!

Together we scanned a cellar crowded with items, furniture

parts, pictures, and an inexplicable blonde wig that took our breath away. We went a little further inside. The dust glimmered in the beams of our flashlights, exposing cobwebs of withered geometry. Effi led us further inside. At the edge of the cellar was a hidden opening, concealed behind two kerosene heaters that stood like eternal guards—reeking sphinxes.

"This is probably going to lead to some secret army headquarters," Effi decided, in a voice grown weary of secret tunnels. But when we opened the cover we found only a recess, and inside, oddly, two more kerosene heaters. The heaters were guarding heaters. The dust kept billowing out. We cast our flashlight's glow on a small metal box and opened it, revealing envelopes and pages written in crowded Polish characters. We trembled. These were not our first stolen documents. In the houses in Grandpa Yosef's neighborhood we got our paws on any available box. But this time we knew—these were secrets. This was a clue to something.

We made our way out and collapsed on the dusty rug, our faces colored with war-paint of soot and dust. We looked at the distant ceiling and did not talk. We saw the room around us enveloped in a frock of dust, but that was not what we were thinking of. In our hands shone the box that contained letters, possibilities. We each pondered separately but our breaths were intertwined, our souls melded. There would be no more Effi-without-a-little-Amir, no more Amir-without-a-little-Effi.

Later, we spent three hours cleaning the house meticulously to eradicate all traces of dust. We unrolled the rug, and restored the overturned furniture. And we stole the box.

The letters were in Polish, in Grandpa Lolek's handwriting, except for one page. The page at the bottom of the box was written in a different ink in an unidentified, square handwriting, and it had no illustrations of blood-red hearts. We needed someone to translate them for us. We had an entire family of Polish speakers at our disposal but we could not give them the papers just like that and say, Please, translate these letters we stole from Grandpa Lolek's secret cellar. We hatched a plan to translate the sentences word by word, separately, each word from a different source. We copied the words onto separate pieces of paper (we knew the English alphabet, so the Polish characters did not pose much of a problem). Next to each word we wrote down the name of the person we intended to ask. We were careful not to give any one person a sequence of words or too many words from one letter. We set off on every mission with one word and, in a roundabout way, deciphered its meaning. Each deciphered word was written on a new page. Using this mosaic approach, we slaved with a dedication usually associated with pyramid builders, and slowly created the Hebrew translation of the letters.

There were a few hitches. For example, the stubbornly puzzling sentence, "Life is a roll." Cross-referencing, enquiries, parsing and assembling, led to the decipherment: "Life is a *partnership*." Instead of *spółka*, partnership, we had copied down *bułka*, roll.

Some people were dismissed after being found unsuitable—suspicious, questioning. But we did discover a few great talents. Uncle Pessl, for example, whom everyone in the family had always considered—to put it mildly—an idiot, asked no questions, made no enquiries, and was utterly unsuspecting as he sat gobbling down a dish of chicken and providing us with translations of entire sentences.

And then there was Uncle Menashe from Netanya. We came to him and asked about the word *brzoza*. But Uncle Menashe looked us in the eye and said calmly, "You've found a letter in Polish and you're trying to figure it out. Why work so hard? Bring me the letter, I'll translate it."

We held a brief and silent consultation with our eyes. And two days later, with the box on our knees, instead of going to school we were on our way to his butcher shop in Netanya. We sat in Menashe's shop for a few hours, surrounded by freezers full of meat and slaughtered chickens hanging on the walls like *sukkah* decorations. He read out loud and translated, no wise-cracks.

What we had found were Grandpa Lolek's letters to his dancer, Joyce. (He must have written them in Polish and had someone translate them into English for him, keeping the Polish copies himself). The content of the letters was not rewarding—silly love lines, promises, pleas, plans for a life together. For a while we were partners to this mythological episode in Grandpa Lolek's life. With him, we were left for the Viennese pianist. We sent her pleas. We hoped. We knew in the bottom of our hearts that now, after the war was over, the future belonged to the pianists of the world. But still we tried, even writing poetically, "…you know, battles on the plains are still sadder," but we did not win back her heart. We lost Joyce. We also lost interest in the letters. We asked Uncle Menashe to skim them, thinking perhaps he might come up with something of interest after all. Then we showed him the last page, written in a different ink, the one without hearts. This page piqued Uncle Menashe's interest.

"This, you must not talk about!" he ordered. "And put the box back straight away, so no one will know you took it."

"What is it?" we demanded.

It was a letter from Moishe Finkelstein, a Jew from Bielsko-Biala, dated September 1st, 1939. That was the day the war broke out—the occupation of Poland, the Big Bang. We had found a dark moon orbiting the glowing planet of Grandpa Lolek.

Uncle Menashe made light of the matter: all that had happened was that Grandpa Lolek had received a lot of gold from Finkelstein, which he was supposed to deliver after the war to Finkelstein's son in America. Half was to go to the son, half to stay with Grandpa Lolek. "And if I know Lolek," he added, "gold, he didn't see, Finkelstein's son. Oh well, not to worry. It's only money. Believe me, Jews over there did worse things than that."

"Worse?"

"*Nu*, it's not for children."

We were not Old Enough. But we were reminded of Crazy Hirsch's yell. Until that day we had not devoted sufficient attention to his recurrent question, "Only saints were gassed?"

We were not Old Enough.

Before childhood could end, we had to fit it all in:

Find out what happened to Finkelstein's gold.

Understand the important things.

Discover all sorts of things.

Invent something important.

Find a profession for Effi, something that would combine her desire to always be tanned with her hatred of hard cheese.

Descend, finally, into Gershon Klima's sewer.

Stand facing Hirsch. Without fear.

And for that we had to remain kids. We had to investigate. The tea bags, the mattress, the hidden gold, it all joined into one enigmatic picture of a land begging to be explored. Finkelstein's moon hovered above us, dimming, shining, dimming, shining, trembling in its orbit. In order to understand the Kepler Laws of this astronomy, we would have to go back into the cellar.

Having no alternative, we landed—two small space-ships with reasonable grades—on Grandpa Lolek's planet. A search party. Into the cellar. We forced ourselves. Sensing the uncompromising smell of hidden gold within the odor of a-punishment-we-could-not-even-imagine, we positioned ourselves on Planet Lolek. We replaced our deadly fear with a dry sense of purpose. We sorted items, catalogued. Over and over we went down to the cellar, creating opportunities out of thin air, plots hatched behind Grandpa Lolek's back. One slip and we'd all be exposed. Once in a while, we delved deeper. The forest of dust revealed itself to us, vaults, treasures and all. We found camera parts arranged in towers, the smaller ones on top. Hundreds of neatly rolled mosquito nets. Metal objects that gave light in return for light. Aluminum strips robbed from windows, blinds, closet hinges. A washing machine engine leaning on its side like a sunken ship in the sandy floor. A fan with all its blades broken, like the prop for a bad joke. We found an accordioned roll of barbed wire that we tried, unsuccessfully, to unroll, and had to grow accustomed to it jumping up suddenly every so often, like Archimedes submerged in his bathtub, shouting, "Eureka! Eureka!" but without revealing a thing. Rapidly adapting, we learned to use the barbed wire to rake the cobwebs, forming dusty clumps. We exposed more and more. Empty bottles that always glistened, like a chorus hungry for the light of a flashlight. Empty packing crates. Matted bundles of rubber bands, sticky and crushed. And finally, a mouse on its back with its feet sticking straight up. Its eyes turned golden in the flashlight beam.

The mouse opened the door to desperation. Finkelstein's moon was disappointed in us; we had not found wonders or secrets. Not even a note. Only worthless material treasures coated in dust. We hoped for a miracle, hoped to stumble upon a box containing Grandpa Lolek's confessions, explaining what he had done with the gold, or an incensed communication from Finkelstein's son demanding to know where the gold was. We looked for envelopes with American stamps, papers written in foreign languages, Polish letters.

In between one descent and the next, we continued to orbit within the gravity of Planet Lolek. We tried to approach the core issue—the gold—with words. Out of the blue, we would ask him about the price of gold. Where did they sell gold? How did you get gold? We talked to him about El Dorado, the mythical land of gold. We talked about golden retrievers and asked him to buy us a golden hamster. We showed him the picture in the *Tarbut* encyclopedia of the Indian chief whose wife and son fled his cruelty and drowned themselves in a river, and every year he threw gifts of gold into the river to plead for their return. To our surprise, Grandpa Lolek showed no interest in where the river was, how one got there, or how much gold exactly this Indian had thrown in there. He only wanted to know if the gifts had helped, if the wife and son came back.

Again and again we went down to the cellar. And once, as expected, it happened. Just as we were starting to roll up the rug, Grandpa Lolek, who-was-only-supposed-to-be-back-in-an-hour, caught us. In his hand was a glistening new camera and on his face a furious suspicion. "What goes on here?"

I was the first to respond, before Effi. "Grandpa Lolek, my pen got lost under the rug."

That was practical-Amir, a distant relative of regular-Amir. He was hardly ever seen. Sometimes, at weddings, he would choose the furthest slice of cake from the one Aunt Ecka had touched.

Effi did not cooperate. She should have said, "Yes, the pen," but instead she stood facing Grandpa Lolek with her hands on her hips and demanded, "We want to know, what did you do with Finkelstein's gold?"

Eyes met eyes. One look said: more locks, more bolts, fewer guests. Two looks said: have mercy, Sir, take pity on these small children.

Flashes, looks, thoughts, prayers. A breeze passed through us as we stood sturdy as cypress trees.

Finally, "Finkelstein got the gold." Simply put.

Meaning, no punishment (for now). Meaning, Grandpa Lolek was unaware of his entitlement to punish children when there was no other way out. When asked a question, he answered it.

"Got more than was he deserved," he added.

"He deserved half," Effi said, representing the parties in absentia.

"Half?!" Grandpa Lolek came closer, furious.

Effi continued cautiously, "According to the letter…"

Grandpa Lolek sat down slowly on the couch. A mistake. We immediately flanked him on either side.

"Tell us about Finkelstein. How much gold was there? How did you give him half? Was it hard? What happened to Finkelstein?"

Grandpa Lolek put his new camera in his lap and drummed on it with two fingers. Perhaps he was waiting for us to ask about it and forget about unnecessary questions. But he had no choice and so he spoke. He told us the entire story, omitting no detail, as if what we had found in the letter was needless, as if he had always been willing to tell us everything, but hadn't thought anyone cared to know. He talked at length and also stole in a little bit of Joyce, her umbrellas, the dock, the rain, the damp rose in her hair.

"What do you understood about half? After war, no getting money out of Poland. No doing. Not allowed. And where I buried the gold, to send to America, to the son over there, a lot of money I gave people, so gold will arrive to America good. My head was having shiny with sweat, not with money, until there came for me a telegram that okay, that says to me thank you from Finkelstein the son, that his wife she says thank you also. Half mine, what was left, not so big this half, after the people took for them."

"And what did you do with your half?"

We hoped to hear that he had kept the gold without touching it. We hoped he would open a secret door and reveal a room full of cobwebs with a stack of pale bars of gold on the floor.

"What I used, when was needed," Grandpa Lolek said disappointingly.

But we were relieved. "So you weren't a bad Jew?"

"Bad Jew?"

"Who did bad things in the war...?"

"Who do you think you are, Haim Nachman Bialik?! There is no bad Jew, good Jew. There is alive and there is dead. That's it."

Grandpa Lolek's philosophy. A dogma handed down from on high. Dead Germans, bodies of Anders' soldiers. All our lives, Grandpa Lolek showered us with sayings coined on that mountain:

"What you take, you have not give back."

"Hold in your teeth, and not yet is yours."

"If hit, hit back. No hit, very good. That means, you hit."

We disagreed. "No bad Jew, good Jew" was too simple. We had stored up enough thoughts of Adella Greuner, Mr. Bergman, Itcha Dinitz. For too long we had become acquainted with Finkelstein, with Crazy Hirsch's words. Something strong, an evil Jew, had to exist—the opposite of Grandpa Yosef. The war could not have sufficed with bad Germans. We rejected Grandpa Lolek's philosophy but felt that he himself was becoming purer, not a bad Jew or a good Jew, but rather, our grandfather. We breathed a sigh of relief that flung open floodgates, an eternal, lucid horizon, over which anything could gallop, anything could fly. Spotless light flowed easily. Two little spaceships with reasonable grades could finally let go and Finkelstein's moon lifted off like a balloon and disappeared. We felt like going out with Grandpa Lolek so he could buy us popsicles, or so we could buy them, whichever—as long as we could sit and lick them and no one would be to blame.

Only a single letter in Polish stayed on its course through space. What had the textile merchant Finkelstein written to his son in America? For many years in the dark, Polish characters concocted a frightening truth. The letter opened with the hackneyed lines, "When you read these words, son, your mother and I will not be among the living…" Then more words, Finkelstein the textile merchant's explanations of what was about to happen in the world, why he did what he did, and what the son should do.

Today, now that I am Old Enough, I know. Finkelstein realized, days before the war broke out, what the Holocaust would be. His thoughts were lucid, with none of the enveloping mist of illusion. Crystal clear. Even before the Nazis imagined how far they would go, before Adolf Eichmann hatched his ingenious plans, before Hitler conceived the only solution to the world's troubles, the textile merchant from Bielsko-Biala knew—*knew*, not guessed—the future in great detail. He sold his business. He instructed his only son to stay in America despite the hardships. He had all his gold fillings removed and forced his wife to do the same. Even before Auschwitz was built, before the incinerators, before the Sonderkommando and the "Kanada" commando that collected belongings from the dead, he had deprived himself of the immediate reasons to send him to his death. He melted down the gold from their teeth, from his wife's jewelry, from the sale of his shop. Then he waited for an opportunity, for a man to whom he could give the money, someone he could trust who wouldn't ask questions and would survive the imminent war. On the street in town he met a hardened corporal from the Polish army, a Jew by the name of Feuer, son of the headmaster of the Hebrew Gymnasium in Kielce. Finkelstein the merchant looked the Jewish corporal up and down and knew he had found his man. They settled on the terms. Shook hands. Corporal Lolek Feuer went back to his unit. The next morning, the war broke out, inflicting six years of suffering upon the world. Finkelstein the textile merchant and his wife perished. At a certain point during those years they joined the six million Jews, perhaps in a ghetto, perhaps in a concentration camp, perhaps in a death camp. They may not have been killed as Jews but simply, without ideology, like the ten million other citizens who died in the war. One moment they were human beings, parents of a son in America, and the next—dead.

One Jew, before the war, knew everything. And even in 1942, with the extermination at its height, Jews would disbelieve living witnesses and refuse to accept the impossible. A man by the name of

Rosenthal would manage to send a postcard to the Bochnia ghetto from Belzec, reporting explicitly what befell those who went to Belzec and exposing the true purpose of the transports to "resettle the Jews in the East." People would doubt him. Suspicions would flicker, fear too. But they would refuse to believe. A letter from the Rabbi of Grabow would be smuggled into the Lodz ghetto, explaining precisely what the Chelmno camp on the Ner River was. People would not believe. At the height of the war, the *Aktionen*, babies' heads smashed against walls, still they would not believe that there could be such a thing as death camps, such a thing as gas chambers, such a thing as industrial use of hair, skin and fat. War, people perpetrating horrors on other people, yes. But gas chambers? Incinerators? Not possible.

Zagazowani.

That was what Rosenthal would write from Belzec to the residents of the Bochnia ghetto. The first word that would explain that people were being put to death with gas. (Dad tried to explain the Polish grammar to me, the way the noun *gas* is inflected as a verb that kills people. *Zagazowani.*) A word that would be a gateway to the coming years. Secretly, the congregation leaders in the ghetto would pass the postcard from hand to hand. My father, a curious child, playing down among the chair legs, would listen. Above him there would be doubts, suspicions—why would the Germans let someone send a postcard out?

Only one Jew, in 1939, the textile merchant Finkelstein, knew everything, and he wrote a letter to his son. Not a historical or scholarly record, but a practical abstract of thoughts. The textile merchant had no spare time to sit and write at length. What good would writing do? Leave the writing for the intellectuals. All he needed was to explain to his son what would happen, what to watch out for, how much gold to demand from the soldier and where to invest it.

Once I became Old Enough and was allowed to know more, I asked Dad about 1939. That year, just before it all began, when only Finkelstein knew, is more frightening than anything Dad could tell me about "afterwards." Because 1939 is similar to the years I live in. In 1939, level-headed Jews had moderate opinions. They had worries that could be dismissed by reason. Sensible people made assumptions, felt apprehensive, found solutions. The Jewish newspapers were full of keen, thorough editorials. Everything was so reasonable, so progressive, so modern. In the cemeteries, deceased Jews were led to their eternal rest. Kaddish prayers were whispered. A little before September 1939 they still recited, *Let He who makes peace in the heavens grant peace to all of us and to all Israel,* and the congregants responded, *Amen.* The year 1939 is the year I could be living in. Every year could be 1939. Everything around me is so democratic, so reasonable. A world of public statements, petitions, strong protests. Everything could be reversed in the blink of an eye. Sometimes I know that if a totalitarian regime were to be established here, decimating minorities, only time and a few moral convulsions would delay a Jewish incarnation of the Reich. Here too, it could rise. There would be opponents, yes, even in the mainstream. But they too would disappear. Not straight away, but all of them. I recognize around me the types who would construct the new regime. They are all here already: the king of the black market, the collaborator, the informer with eyes torn wide in terror. The chief of police, the loyal soldiers, the implementers of orders. They are here, they are living and multiplying. They are decent citizens concealed by comfortable circumstances. Never (one assumes) will their dark natures be exposed. Throughout their lives, perhaps only a moment or two will touch the core of their souls. Commonplace life produces moderate versions of these people, the outcome of routine and of the flourishing State of Israel. The king of the black market will be no more than a crooked insurance agent. The collaborators will be tailors, policemen, physicians. The chief of police will be an unlikable man, perhaps the manager of a supermarket, that's all. If the day comes and reality is overturned, Grandpa Yosef will be an intellectual opposing the regime. His skull will be cracked in the public square, crowds will cheer. Or in secret, three thugs will knock on his door in the middle of the night. The car will drive away. Neighbors will murmur sorrowfully. Someone will make a derisive comment about him and a few will nod in agreement. The regime will provide them with material and they will recite it. They will forget.

Yes, it is here, but it will not come to fruition. There is too much good sun, blue skies. But what is important is that it is here, that it threatens my Yariv, that it will want to take my father away again to Plaszow camp, but I won't let it. That I do not know how I will not let it. I pick Yariv up from kindergarten. We walk down the street and pass by the collaborators, the volunteers, the informants, the black market merchants. People with simple faces. At any moment it is possible. The wind will change, the makeup will scatter, and Yariv and I will stand facing them. It would take even less than a change in the way the wind blows. They could be exposed just like that, simply because they want to be. And my skull too will be smashed on some night-time street in some immaterialized reality in some world which I am mocked for even positing the existence of. Anat too. Why, for God's sake, don't they see it?

I raise my Yariv to be strong, to know how to suffer, to survive. Anat takes the seeds out of tomatoes before he eats them. I get annoyed. She does, too. "Yariv belongs to both of us. You can raise your half in Buchenwald, but I'm sending mine to Mira's Daycare!"

Anything he has not been fully prepared for deters him, afraid, confused. I want him to peel his hard-boiled egg. He refuses. The shell is hot, it scares him. Anat takes it and peels it for him. My father was in the camps. He knows what can happen. But Yariv's babyish fears don't bother him. He plays with him, sees how afraid he is of the ball, how he starts crying. He runs to reassure him.

I cannot understand them. *Zagazowani.*

How good it was then, two little spaceships resting beside Grandpa Lolek, our voyage over, and Grandpa Lolek between us with a camera in his lap. I did not know everything I know today: that you don't need a Holocaust to have bad Jews. That people like Grandpa Lolek, even if they do steal gold, are not the bad ones. We only knew that that was it, we could breathe easy, Grandpa Lolek was not a bad Jew. The camera on his lap started to glimmer, capturing half and more of our attention, pushing aside letters and dust and bad Jews. We started to take an interest. The price-tag was intriguing; it was a very expensive camera. We looked at Grandpa Lolek full of hope.

He who was absolved of all guilt erased his anger. "Here, Nikon make this, is very expensive, I brought for Effi as present."

We passed the enchanted object between us, a gift for Effi, not for me. His preference for Effi was immortalized.

Grandpa Lolek hadn't meant it. He did prefer Effi, but hadn't intended to insult one of his "like grandchildren" on the couch in his home, after a dark moon had melted away. There was no reason for tears, even though they almost burst from my eyes. (It was at that moment that I made up my mind: I would go to the Municipality on my own and find out who Katznelson Street was named after.) In any case, the bestowal of the Nikon upon Effi was unplanned, and it was not the product of generosity. An hour earlier the camera had still sat in a display window at Carmel Center, scanning with a shuttered eye the passersby who did not buy it because it was too expensive, who only lingered briefly, eye to eye, to exercise their longing, to covet, to finally glance askance at a cheaper model displayed two shelves below. The look in their eyes changed—this was something they could afford—and they gazed at the plain model with the loathing of compromise, as if to say, "We're doing you a favor." Eyes yearned, calculated, went into the store to buy the simpler models. Two gentleman stood opposite the camera, ignoring the display window, busy doing business. The one wondered quietly whether the other was capable of meeting his financial obligations—he'd been warned against doing business with him. The other, dressed in finery, a hero of Monte Cassino with blue metallic eyes, sensed the man's doubts and feared the transaction would fall through. He had to make a quick impression. His look fell on the camera in the display window. He scanned the price. Panic. Contemplation. Vacillation. Decision. The hero of Monte Cassino walked into the store and came out with the Nikon in hand, explaining to his interlocutor, "This I bought for Effi, so it will make her happy. She is like my granddaughter, Effi." This time the *like* was intended to clarify that he gave his *like* relatives expensive gifts without a moment's hesitation. Imagine, then, what gifts he must give his real relatives. Imagine how financially secure he must be.

"Thanks, but what am I supposed to do with a camera?" Effi asked. And a minute later, "Oh well, stand up and pose, we'll give it a try." And we stood up.

At first she photographed everything she came across, then landscapes on Saturday hikes, and finally family affairs. This blatant invasion of Grandpa Lolek's domain came after he had been defeated by Brandy in the fight to reach the Moshe Pole, and after the family members had begun, one by one, to buy small, modest cars, doing away with hegemony of the Vauxhall once and for all. The battle was fought through two weddings and one *briss*. Finally, a moderate victory was achieved because:

Effi took nice pictures.

She didn't ask for payment.

Grandpa Lolek was in her pictures.

The latter was an advantage praised even by the loser. In almost all of Effi's pictures stood a tall, serious man, a hero of Monte Cassino, and his look at the lens took into account generations to come, who would ask, who is that? The masculine one, standing in his finest suit?

Effi did not like spontaneous photographs. She preferred the formal kind, arranging people like bowling pins. One click and they were dismissed. Then, "No, actually, stand that way again, it may not have come out well." Smiles were arranged in rows, lips frozen. At weddings, parties, everywhere. Rows, lines. Little trapeze shapes with the adults in the back row, gathering with-gentle-hands-on-shoulders the children in the front row. It was the beginning of the photography era. Effi with a camera around her neck, always arranging people. As soon as people saw her, they would arrange themselves in rows. Women would reach up to their hair, men—down to their flies. They smiled when they saw her; you never knew. Always flashes, always instructions. In winter she blended with the lightening. In summer—the heat, the flies. "Stand, I'll take a picture." "Smile now." They built her a fully equipped dark-room with chemicals that only two or three years earlier we would have tried to drink. Now she was careful, gave warnings, behaved responsibly, sealed the bottles, made labels with thick markers, separated containers.

Grandpa Lolek's passing on of the photography obsession and the natural effects of age began to come between us. Effi signed up for a photography course, and I for an amateur radio course (which was a little too amateur for my taste). She graduated to a photography course for gifted children. I responded by winning an essay competition on Jerusalem. The distancing continued, became more sophisticated, swept along deposits of grudges and hostility. Substances long ago fixed into the river banks were swept along, renewing forgotten arguments. At the apex of the route—the apogee—Effi's photographs were accepted by *Maariv Lanoar* magazine. My turn. I was appointed head of a ship in my seafaring course (salt water when falling overboard at the port, filthy water when falling in at the mouth of the Kishon River). That wasn't enough. In a desperate step I defected from *Tarbut* encyclopedia and switched to the *Hebrew Encyclopedia*. I began at "*a cappella*" and started reading.

Then we started to divide our assets. Effi demanded the four-part poster of Yehoram Gaon, which we had both labored to compile. I demanded that she apologize for her comments about Mike Brandt.

No.

Me neither then.

The poster stayed with me, a hostage for an apology never given.

It had started two years previously, when news came that Mike Brandt had committed suicide in Paris. I was overcome with grief. He was from Haifa, one of ours, and had become a famous singer in France and in the world. Then suddenly they said he had jumped out of a window, and despite all his success in Paris it was decided that he would be buried here in Haifa, in the same cemetery where Aunt Zusa owned a plot. Effi said, "So what?" and showed no understanding. I was used to national grief, when everyone was sad for a lot of people, but this time I felt a new sadness, only for Mike Brandt, the way I felt when I read in the encyclopedia about Katznelson the poet, the Katznelson for whom we had named the neighborhood street. It said that he had managed to escape the Warsaw ghetto and get to Paris, and there he sat, a brand snatched from the burning fire, lamenting his perished wife and children. He wrote poems, expressed hope—if only he had died with them. And it was this prayer that was heard, of all the prayers uttered in all those years all over the world. A train came especially to take him from Paris to Auschwitz, to the gas chambers. A whole train for one weeping Jew, while war was raging and trains were an expensive commodity.

I thought about Katznelson when they brought Mike Brandt back here. It was a sorrow that Effi could not comprehend. We fought, with hatred. We found more and more things to divvy up. We halved joint collections and erased each other from important lists. We left no detail in our lives that did not bear the stamp, "Inspected. Proper procedures followed." We even divided the grandparents, all of whom had been tirelessly collected under the Law of Compression. Borders were demarcated. Partitions that had previously symbolized mere preferences were lined with barbed wire fences: No Entry. Grandpa Lolek and Grandpa Weil went to Effi. Grandpa Menashe to me. Grandma Eva was divvied up as an afterthought. Grandpa Yosef was undecided. It seemed that if there had to be a decision, Grandpa Yosef would prefer me, because of the scholarliness. But we found Grandpa Yosef high above territorial borders, even during this nationalistic frenzy of the separation of grandparents. Grandpa Yosef remained the only thing that would still connect us.

Agreed.

And what about Grandpa Shalom? After all, he was my real grandfather, only mine, my mother's father. The only actual grandfather. Ostensibly there was no question that Grandpa Shalom was mine. At my *briss* on the ninth of Av he had held me in his arms. He had looked at me, his second grandchild, and seen yet another root struck in the new land. He had watched me grow up, not knowing that inside of him someone had already rapped three times on the door, that in the dressing room his disease was already preparing for its performance. One final moment before it came out. A glance in the mirror. A long breath. And the curtain began to rise. Grandpa Shalom got Parkinson's disease and sunk into his trembling body. The Gestapo tortures, the room in which he awoke on the floor after being interrogated, bathed in his own blood, would be portrayed in a symbolic illness—his body was now his prison. Grandpa Shalom the strong man, championed by all, helper of the needy, a poor man in aid of the poor, would become Grandpa Shalom who smelled of medicine, his tortured body emitting vapors of rotten fruit. Barely walking, barely talking, only Grandma Chava could understand what the thin purple lips were saying. And the cold mouth that tried to kiss us, which we dreaded even before leaving home and on the way there. Grandpa Shalom, who loved through all obstacles, but whom we could not love. We simply could not.

Effi could. When we came to visit (preferably during Chanukah; on Passover Seder and Rosh Hashanah we had no choice), only she hugged and kissed him without hesitation. It was not courage or purity of soul—she simply had no problem doing it. Effi with a camera round her neck and complaints about everything. How could we not have seen how obvious it was that she would grow up to be a doctor? A merciful mother to the Sick Fund patients. She did not photograph Grandpa Shalom in rows of people, but always alone, looking straight at the camera.

How would we divide Grandpa Shalom? It seems we did not. We left a grey area, a demilitarized zone in the interest of both parties. After a while there was a truce of sorts. We emptied out our pockets into one joint pile of grandparents for us both. What did we need the silly division for? We reconstructed from memory what we had been before the fights. We gathered the strength needed for what was about to occur in just a few weeks, the affair of Levertov and the Formacil pills.

In Grandpa Yosef's neighborhood, medicine healed the body and uplifted the spirit. Prescriptions were status symbols, property, business cards, legal tender. Your medications were who you were. Everyone in the neighborhood knew their neighbors' prescriptions. A few who had unique prescriptions were modest in their pride, walking along their Mount Everests, shrugging their shoulders—they really didn't know what they'd done to be so fortunate. But it was a dynamic world. Prescriptions were renewed and terminated at doctors' whims, based on pharmaceutical trends. Everyone in the neighborhood knew the rules well and they knew they needed to stay vigilant. You had only to look away for a second and a prescription could be lost. And then no amount of pleading ("it was so good with the old pill," "the new one's no good") would help. Dishonest complaints during medical exams wouldn't help. Does it hurt here? Yes. Here? Yes. And here? Yes. Everything hurts? Yes, but with the pill from before it didn't hurt at all! Narrow-mindedness grew naturally, like weeds on the edge of a puddle. If you were taken off a pill but your neighbor was not, the insult was threefold—where was justice?

Feiga's prescriptions were a relatively constant anchor. Her diseases complicated one another and no physician dared touch this house of cards—one false move could bring it tumbling down. This stability was a thorn in the side of some of the neighbors. People were jealous. Sometimes we heard remarks. We stored them up as if sensing that one day we would make use of them.

It happened with Mr. Levertov.

It happened with the Formacil.

It happened during a ceasefire. And during the days when we had stopped wondering about the Shoah: There was a war, and the Germans wanted to murder all the Jews, and they managed to murder six million, and the ones who survived lost so much that even they did not emerge completely alive. That was it. That explained it. The questions had settled down to a lower level. We were able to connect the Shoah we found at home with the one we learned at school, the black placards, the recitations, the minute of silence. For a moment we believed everything was clear. And it was then, of all times, just when we didn't want to ask anything more and everything had become simple, that Untersturmführer Kurt Franz from Treblinka, known as "Doll," emerged like a sandbank for us to run aground on. Something made us think of him again. Levertov had once tried to tell us something about him but Grandpa Yosef had put an end to it. And now, despite what we'd thought we wanted, we simply had to know everything about him.

The idea percolated for a long time. Two river banks faced each other. On the one was Levertov, yearning for the Formacil they had taken away from him—Why did Feiga still have hers? On the other bank was Treblinka, where Levertov had been with Untersturmführer Kurt Franz, Doll. The two banks glistened, the water turned silver at night, churning and rising in daylight. One ferry ride with the Formacil in our possession, and Levertov would agree to tell us about Untersturmführer Kurt Franz, Doll, the Commandant of Treblinka, despite Grandpa Yosef's prohibition. Levertov was afraid. He had already turned us down twice. But he was the only one in the neighborhood who had been in Treblinka—one of the few who had been with Doll and survived. We had to know.

From the heart of the kaleidoscope, Kurt Franz, Doll, looked out at us. *I am the Shoah of Shoahs,* he seemed to be saying. I am what you will not understand even if you understand everything. I am the only one who, even twenty or thirty years from now, when you're grown up, when you're old, when you understand—you will not understand. I am Kurt Franz, Doll, and I had Levertov in Treblinka. He escaped during the little uprising here, but that's not important. My commander, Stangl, was dismissed and I remained, no longer Deputy Commandant but Commandant. Me, Untersturmführer Kurt Franz, Doll, Commandant of Treblinka. Finally. Levertov did not see me when I was Commandant, he had already escaped. But he can guess, he can tell you. He saw me when I was Deputy Commandant, subject to orders, restrictions, rules. He can guess who I became afterwards, alone, here in Treblinka. Ask Levertov.

We did.

Levertov was afraid. "He was a terrible man. It's not for kids. And anyway, your grandfather asked me not to talk to you about it and he's right. Why don't you tell me what you learned in math today?"

But Feiga had the Formacil on the other river bank. The two sides of Katznelson glimmered: Levertov at 7-A, Grandpa Yosef at 8-B. The Formacil here, Levertov there. What if we brought him some Formacil?

After many days we said it out loud. "And if we bring you Formacil?"

It was a sentence we had practiced saying, recited, encouraged each other. A sentence Levertov had hoped to draw out of us. A sentence both sides were expecting.

Now the waiting. We got down on our knees to offer our gift. Now Levertov had to say yes. Let him say yes. How long could we wait?

It was the height of summer. Scorching heat. Katznelson was

a river, a dreamy Nile. At midday we passed by its banks to check the other side. Was Levertov there? Would he call us? Say yes? No? We walked back and forth. We passed by Mr. and Mrs. Tsanz, Uncle Mendel. From the mud Gershon Klima appeared like a frog. On the fence was Moshe, sitting alone, a captain. By his side an empty space waited for a dog named Brandy to be born, to be adopted, to sit down and keep watch. Menachem, the neighborhood kid, called to us to play with him. He said we could build a tree house in the eucalyptus. He looked at Effi, his thick thighs a pale pink color. Girls were allowed too, he stressed. We got rid of him. On the banks of Katznelson we sat among the reeds of hibiscus, Turk's cap, and orange honeysuckle, waiting for a signal from the other bank.

Finally it came. "Yes. But I will decide what to tell you."

Our hearts trembled: Levertov said yes. The kaleidoscope overturned. But one spot still remained inside, calling us. We had to. We would give him Feiga's Formacil. We would steal it and give it to him. Within the kaleidoscope was one dot of fear named Kurt Franz, Doll. We could hear him calling: I will not leave you, children, I am the Shoah, I am the elucidation, I am the explanation that will not help you comprehend, but without me you have no chance of understanding your family. Your mother, Effi. Your mother, Amir. Grandpa Shalom. And Grandpa Yosef. Do you think he doesn't have a story of his own? You steal the Formacil from Feiga and give it to Levertov. If he tells you what he saw, you'll know who I was. Untersturmführer Kurt Franz, Doll, Commandant of Treblinka. In the library you read that I was a very cruel Nazi and that my nickname was Doll because I was handsome and my face was like a young boy's. Did they mention that I was tall? That I loved to be seen riding horses? But Levertov will tell you, he'll tell everything. Ask Levertov. Steal the Formacil.

Levertov gave us a precise description. We wrote down Hebrew characters, Latin characters, color, size and shape. We memorized F-O-R-M-A-C-I-L from one pill, a refugee from an old packet that Levertov found in his cabinet. We had to remove the Formacil without Grandpa Yosef noticing. He was used to whole packets of pills disappearing occasionally, because Feiga would sometimes secretly throw things out the window, acting on some logic known only to her. She would throw things out and then complain, where is the napkin? Where is the pill? Where is the soup spoon? When we were guests of Grandpa Yosef, we took over his chore of collecting the objects (until Brandy came into our lives and spent her morning walks gently picking up what she found with her teeth and bringing it to Grandpa Yosef). In order to barter with Levertov, we had to make the pills completely disappear, something that would explain why we could not find anything under the poinciana tree. We considered a few methods of deceit and finally adopted Effi's idea. To add to Grandpa Yosef's perplexity, we hid a slingshot among Feiga's things. He would find it and wonder in astonishment, could it be? And would vainly expand his search all the way to the edge of the hibiscus at 6-B Katznelson.

When we finally got hold of the Formacil, we went to see Levertov. He panicked. "No! Not here! All I need is for…" He rolled his eyes as he scanned the paths along Katznelson to see if anyone was giving us unwanted looks. He greedily snatched the Formacil and forbade us to come to his home. He gave us a meeting place, a real one like in the movies, in the neighborhood across the way, next to the drapery store, a bench, a tree, next to a payphone, where we could talk.

Effi snatched the Formacil back from Levertov. "You'll get it there," she announced, staring at him with Grandpa-Lolek-eyes.

And that was how we found him, waiting on the bench with restless eyes. We sat down full of questions and excitement, our souls practically bursting out of our shirts. Levertov demanded the Formacil. Effi handed it over. He gave it a long look to make sure everything was in order. He checked the expiration date and made sure the pack was sealed. He mumbled something nervously and shoved the bag into the pocket furthest from us. Then he breathed heavily. "I'll tell you, but I'm deciding what to tell and how far to go."

We nodded, prepared for anything. Our questions were clambering over one another to get out. But we remained silent, a spot in the kaleidoscope spreading large as an ink-stain.

"I was in Treblinka only two weeks before we escaped. They bought weapons from the Ukrainian guards and we killed the

Ukrainians. Fools! Then like heroes we hid in the woods. Until the war was over, in the woods. But first, before Treblinka, I was a Jew from Radom. Then I got married and moved to Siedlce. I have many stories to tell about how they slaughtered the people in the ghetto, how I escaped alone to the partisans, and how they tried to kill me too, the *goyim*, anti-semites. I hid in a village with good people but in the end they informed on me and they took me to a camp. Then Treblinka. I arrived in a train car. When they opened the doors I was almost dead. I don't want to talk about what went on next to me. It shouldn't be told. Outside was a little station with a clock and a schedule for other stations. Everything neat and orderly, even a small shop. So we'd think the suffering was over, that now was no time for problems. If we had known where we were, we wouldn't have done everything they told us so well. I was strong, not like today how you see me now, an old man without strength. I was well-built, with good muscles, and they chose me for the work group. Everyone who came with me, one-two to the gas, but me, they took me aside to work. God help us, what hard work. Right after the gas with what was left, we had to do what the SS told us. All sorts of things. Whatever they said. And anyone who couldn't, who didn't work well—gone. One-two."

"What about Doll? He killed children, right?"

"I didn't see everything. That man, *Lalka*, whom you call Doll, there were things he liked. There were things that made him angry. Children who slowed things down, yes. And naked women, it angered him if they didn't go in quickly. If in the middle of the gassing the engine broke with people stuck inside, and outside another load was waiting, then he would go wild. Then the whole Lager would be afraid. That he liked, to punish. To beat with fists and with a whip. But he had a huge dog. I remember he was beautiful, his name was Barry, and together with the dog, or sometimes just the dog, they punished prisoners. God help me for telling this, but the dog would finish people off. Eat them. Yes, I mean he ate them. And especially he was trained to bite there, *nu*, you know, in the pants, where the thingamajig is, to tear it. And it was better if the dog finished off the prisoner completely, otherwise he would suffer. And all this we had to see in front of our eyes at the roll-calls, everything there happened during roll-call so that everyone would see, and we thought how we would be next, always we thought about the dog, that it would be us if we made a mistake. One day a Jew went berserk by the gas and attacked an SS man. Commandant Stangl ordered Doll to have a roll-call and kill one out of ten. But he killed one out of ten and then kept killing, slowly but surely. Time, he had plenty. We stood there wetting our pants, really and truly, and he kept pulling people out, sometimes to kill, sometimes to whip them and leave them alive. When it would end we did not know. We were happy every time it wasn't us. That they took someone else out, for the dog, or for a bullet in the head, or just lashings, as usual. That was every evening, the lashings. All day he walked around, and for little things he would say how many lashings he would give that evening. He would have a roll-call, and everyone who was getting a punishment had to come, say he needed to be lashed, and say exactly how many lashings. No one lied, it wasn't worth it. And the men had to count the lashes themselves. Even if they were almost dying from the beatings, they had to count out loud. And if they lost count, they would start from scratch. Some did not get up from those lashings, better to get a bullet in the head…"

Levertov fell quiet. Thought quiet thoughts. We sat silently.

Suddenly he said, "That's it for today. Enough now."

We were amazed—so little? We wanted to rebel but something within us did not. Something inside completely agreed and told us to go, there would be time to hear it all. Effi got up first. I stood up too. Levertov stayed behind. We didn't look back until we'd rounded the corner, and then we ran down the main road back to Katznelson, to Grandpa Yosef's neighborhood.

The next day we wanted to hear more, but we discovered that Levertov was not in such a hurry. He had enough Formacil for a few days. He would tell us when to meet by the bench again. We were annoyed, but it was no use. It was during the school year and it was hard to get to Grandpa Yosef's just like that. Still, we tried twice, until Levertov found us, and we didn't even need to say anything. "In an hour," he told us, and we synchronized our watches.

We got to the bench half an hour early and Levertov was already there. Effi gave him six Formacil and kept the rest in her pocket. Levertov got angry.

"I need it all!" he shouted.

Effi kept her cool. "It goes by how much you tell!"

Levertov looked at her and at me, wondering what he could say to prevail. His look was hateful, but he simply said quietly, "Two more."

And Effi agreed.

He grabbed the pills from her and looked around, waiting for the street to empty out.

"Today I will tell you about how he was, Doll, from a work point of view I mean. He was the Deputy Commandant in Treblinka and he wanted to do well, so they would make him Commandant. He was always making plans to improve, to fit in more of the transports that arrived all the time, day and night. Long before I came he already had an idea that went very well for him. He realized that he wasn't getting as much done as he wanted, because elderly people and cripples did everything slowly. So he had an idea. Near the beginning of the route he closed off a piece of land as if there was a hospital there, put up a sign and a red cross. Anyone who was elderly or handicapped was sent there straight way. Inside there was nothing, just a pit, where they did away with people on the spot. Doll was pleased with his idea. With my own eyes I saw how he went up to an old man and asked him politely why he wasn't keeping up with the group. The old man answered something and Doll graciously pointed to the hospital. He even got a thank you from the old man, you see. That, he liked. One-two, no more old man. And he always made sure to receive the transports himself, for this pleasure. Where people were stripping down he interfered too, and did things. If he found that women were trying to keep their babies and children with them, he got angry because that was against his rules. He got rid of the children himself. And listen to this: Once I saw how his assistant, Hirtreiter, took hold of a baby by both feet and, hear this, he slammed the baby against the wall until it was over. And Doll got angry and yelled at Hirtreiter that that wasn't the way to do it, and he stopped everything, even though that was a waste of time, so that he could teach him. He grabbed a different baby by its feet and with one blow, that's it. Then he told Hirtreiter that was how it was done, with one blow, and he left. God help me, the things I saw. He had strange behaviors, this man. One minute he would go through the camp on his horse, tall you know, and clean. The face of an angel, he had, the Angel of Death, and on the horse he was distant from it all, thinking to himself, clean sort of. And another time he would sneak into the latrines where the Jews went to get a breather, and shoot people doing their business. He found that very funny. There was a man, Itzik Konchinski, whom he hit right as he was using the latrine, and he fell inside and Doll was very happy, as if he had succeeded at something he had wanted to do for a long time. Sometimes he did things where you couldn't tell what was going on in his mind. Once, so I heard, there was a Jew who came to Treblinka and he was injured when they took him out of the train car. He begged for water and Doll gave an order to bring him a bucket. And they said that the Jew tried to drink and then Doll attacked him and shoved his head in the bucket and kept hitting him with the butt of his rifle until it was over. They always told stories about him quietly, and I can't explain how frightened we were to think that it would be our turn soon. First the man to your left, then the man to your right, and all the time you had the feeling that that was it. I was there for only two weeks, thank God, until the uprising. Afterwards, this was only what I heard, because of our uprising they got rid of the Commandant of Treblinka and made Doll the Commandant, and that was his dream. That, thank God, I did not see. I was in the woods until the end of the war."

That was the end of the conversation, for eight Formacils. Effi tried to offer him more, to make him go on, but Levertov refused. He had decided to teach us a lesson. "Same time tomorrow. And bring me a whole packet, otherwise nothing," he threatened.

We left. We had to find a way to steal more medicine. We thought about substituting similar looking pills and searched our medicine cabinets at home, but we found only one little packet that looked almost the same. We exchanged it for the Formacil. We volunteered to help Grandpa Yosef prepare Feiga's pills and lukewarm tea and arranged everything nicely on a tray, not forgetting a saucer for the teacup.

Those were trying times. We would come up with all sorts of excuses to come to the neighborhood. After school, even on Saturdays. We met Levertov to hear more of his stories. We stole Formacil and gave Feiga replacement pills. Feiga did not complain but we detected something menacing lurking under the surface of her silence. We imagined Feiga turning blue or yellow. We imagined a multicolored Feiga. We imagined worms erupting out of her body and Feiga erupting out of the house like Godzilla, people scattering. Our imagination spun around the true fear, the one we could not imagine—what would we tell Grandpa Yosef if we were caught?

The neighborhood lived its life in ignorance; Katznelson flowed slowly while we secretly passed Formacil pills from one bank to the other. We felt empowered by the pills Levertov grabbed from us, his eyes glimmering with redness and guilt, and by the secret that went everywhere with us. We were filled with the power of the traitor and the smuggler. It showed in our eyes, in our gait, in the way we held our heads up high. Menachem, the only kid in the neighborhood, dragged around behind us. He was older than us, our undisputed leader, but he surrendered to a force he could not comprehend. He built us tree houses but we refused to enter them, and found all sorts of petty faults in everything he did. He brought Effi new pedals for her bike and gave me books he'd been given for his birthday.

We went to Gershon Klima and asked menacingly why he wouldn't take us to the sewer. We faced Grandpa Yosef, supported by the force of fear and betrayal, and instead of being ashamed of ourselves, we made demands:

"Why did they move you around in the Holocaust through so many places?"

"Why weren't you in Auschwitz?"

"Tell us about Hirsch, when did you meet him?"

"Why do you apologize so much when Mrs. Tsanz gets angry?"

Mrs. Tsanz came from Lodz, and for some reason Grandpa

Yosef was self-deprecating in front of Lodzniks. A constant tone of self-justification and apology, even when it wasn't us who had kicked the ball into Mrs. Tsanz's window.

Our latent power affected the neighborhood. Unlikely events occurred offhandedly. The Frequent gave way to the Rare. A red-capped parrot took up residence in the treetops and for two days squawked from up high, "I'm lost, come and get me!" Or "I ran away, I promised I would!" Then it disappeared. Over at Sammy the greengrocer, a crate of plums was found covered with strange little bite-marks. A great mystery, until they found a small bat and a hole in the wall that had operated in tandem. In the middle of the day, a eucalyptus tree crashed down from the woods into the garden at 12-C Katznelson. We took a book out of the library and from the pages fell a postcard sent from Cypress to a woman named Hedva. Someone had written her a love letter and signed it "Everyman." Even Adella Greuner sensed something. In the throes of the Era of Things That Should Not Happen, she came to visit Grandpa Yosef. In her hand was a letter from the Municipality. Her dress was light blue and clean. She asked Grandpa Yosef for advice.

"Please come in," he said.

Adella Greuner and Grandpa Yosef sat at his desk for a long while, but the world could not tolerate such behavior. Feiga fluttered in her bed. The fridge rattled in the kitchen, emitting a series of complaints. Planes overhead shocked the neighborhood with distant sonic booms, the windows shook and rattled, even the walls could barely stand up around the two of them. The Frequent knocked and asked to come back—enough already with the Rare. But Grandpa Yosef sat with Adella and explained what the City wanted, who she must see, what to say.

It was difficult. It was up to us. We had to hear as much as we could about Doll, to fill in the empty gaps, to get it done before everything blew up and we would have to explain ourselves, standing in a shower of shrapnel, facing Grandpa Yosef and hoping everything would scatter and there would be an end to it. We had to get through.

Levertov kept talking.

"He planned 'portions' for the gas chambers. He knew exactly how many went in with each portion, the children and everything. They kept the children for last and when it was already crowded they threw the children in between the heads and the ceiling, and finally the babies too. If he couldn't push them all in, he got angry. That was when you wanted to escape his look. Us, and the Ukrainians, and his SS."

Six Formacil.

"One day I'm walking through the camp. On duty, not just like that. You didn't walk through the camp just like that. There was a man from my hut, Yankel Klein, standing there petting the dog Barry. Petting him! And Yankel says to me, completely calm, that when Doll isn't around there is no sweeter dog than Barry. He was one of those big Saint Bernards that never really do anything, just drool a lot and have a stupid look on their face. And Yankel said I should pet him, he was a good dog. God help me, I didn't pet that dog. That, I would not do. But exactly one week later, just before the uprising when we escaped, I watched that dog finish off Yankel Klein. He bit Yankel until he stopped yelling, and Doll stood on the side, lashing him with a whip. That, I saw."

He got a whole packet of Formacil, even though we had agreed on only six pills. He looked thankful. The next day, a horse with a shiny chestnut-colored coat passed through the neighborhood, stopped briefly on Katznelson opposite Gershon Klima's house, stood up on his hind legs, his coat glimmering in the sun, neighed and ran away.

From Adella Greuner's garden, the scarecrow disappeared. The one we thought she was yelling at, "Kalman, *vi geystu*? Kalman, *vi geystu*?" Peculiar hypotheses were suggested. There was even an explicit accusation against Grandpa Lolek, who snorted disdainfully, "I am to be lucky if I can get ten shekels for the wool hat, and nothing at all for those clothes, which the rain eats, and his plank also worth nothing. Who would buy from me such plank?"

From which we surmised that he had given the scarecrow an economical appraisal but had rejected it. We tried to picture Grandpa Lolek in his suit, haggling over the price of a scarecrow with a rag merchant. We couldn't. Proof. We acquitted him beyond a doubt.

"Once he went up to an old man to offer him his 'hospital,' but suddenly he couldn't hold back and he started to strangle the old man. He didn't shoot him, nothing, just strangled him, like a madman. Suddenly he stopped, as if everything was fine, and after a moment not fine again; he strangled him and strangled him until that was it…"

Two Formacil, even though we had promised more. There was no more. Levertov was angry, but to no avail. And the next day it rained hard, out of season. (Asher Schwimmer, having learned from the pioneers' letters about the strangeness of the Israeli skies between the dry season and the transition season, wrote in Poland, "A land of trespassing clouds / Their constitution of wilderness.") The laundry had not yet recovered from the miracle of rain when Grandpa Lolek's Vauxhall suddenly showed up. He brought Grandpa Yosef a wonderful edition of the Babylonian Talmud, with all volumes intact. He'd found a good deal—seventy-five percent off on the whole thing—and he gave it to an excited Grandpa Yosef for free, why not?

"Doll, he fancied himself a boxer, and he trained in the camp. He would get hold of a prisoner and that was it. The prisoner had to hold his head straight so Doll could hit it, and Lord have mercy on anyone who couldn't hold his head up straight after a round of boxing. But it didn't matter anyway because after Doll was finished they didn't stand much of a chance. SS Miete, damn him and all the rest of them, who was in charge of the 'hospital' that Doll invented, he would always walk around wherever Doll had been because he knew he'd find clients for his hospital. A bullet in the back of their neck, straight into the pit and that was that. And anyone Doll left after the boxing, this Miete would come quickly to take him to the hospital, one-two. Once, so they said, this was before I came, back in '42, Doll heard that a real boxer from Krakow had come on a transport. He made a big deal, organized a fight with gloves and everything, on a Sunday, their day of rest. But Doll was well-prepared. Inside his glove he put a little pistol, just in case. As soon as the fight started, while they were still facing each other with their gloves, he couldn't resist. Through his glove he shot the young man from Krakow. On the spot, that's that."

Four more Formacil and some other pills we had gathered up to offer Levertov because we couldn't get any more Formacil.

One Saturday, we came to visit Grandpa Yosef with our parents. We were strong, fortified by our betrayal. We glanced at Feiga, everything seemed fine. When it was time for tea and the conversation began to slow down to make way for the silence, the dreams, we went outside to play. We walked slowly down Katznelson. In the midday heat only Moshe survived outside, rubbing his hands together, something passing across his face, a kind of smile, as if inside he had completed a quick transaction. The shade from Gershon Klima's bombax attracted us. We went to see if the trunk had grown any new thorns (someone, perhaps one of the night wanderers, liked to abuse the tree, cutting off its thorns every night). We found a few that had slipped by. We touched them carefully, pricking ourselves painlessly. Our eyes traveled upwards, to Gershon Klima's forbidden window. We didn't have to look at each other. The Formacil, the power, the boldness. We decided that today was the day Gershon Klima would take us to the sewer.

We started climbing without a second thought. We skipped easily among the branches all the way to the open window. From there a small jump, and we'd be in the bathroom. We poked our heads in. Before us, inside the bathtub, lay the scarecrow from Adella Greuner's garden. We wondered, frightened, what was it doing there? We pushed our questions aside to make way for more important matters, but our astonishment kept showering us with its sparks. We found Gershon Klima standing in his room (Not sitting? Always standing or lying?), and before we could formulate our request, he said, "I'll tell you whatever you want."

We wanted him to take us to the depths of the earth, to the core, but the power of the Formacil had gone too far and had mistakenly melted away an ancient emotional strength, a cloak of silence forged over many years. All of a sudden Gershon Klima agreed to tell his story, to explain why he was "his own brother." We had subdued him by way of error, or perhaps (so we contemplated), Gershon Klima had captured us in his lair and we were finally caught, so he could tell his story.

Effi struck a hard bargain. "Do you have any juice?" she enquired.

I was anxious that we were about to lose Gershon Klima. Here he was, willing to tell us his story and make us the first to land on that moon, when suddenly—juice. But still Effi guided the ritual, in control of all aspects.

"I have no juice. I have no refrigerator at home," said Gershon Klima, and the simple politeness of his response became, in the air of the room, something greater. Gates were opened, the room filled with the sense of his clear declaration: This is Gershon Klima and this is his empty home, and his life, and we would hear his story here in the heart of the being that created it. "His own brother" was about to be deciphered. His own brother. So simple.

When Gershon Klima was born, he had an identical twin brother. Only their mother could tell her two drops of bliss apart. In a bunker during the Görlitz *Aktion*, sixteen adults and two children spent two days underground. Gershon and Hezkel Klima, aged one-and-a-half, were given sleeping pills so they wouldn't cry and give everyone away. But the Germans didn't need cries. Someone informed. In return for his life or the lives of his family members, or in return for one of the things that functioned as currency during the *Aktionen*, someone gave up the bunker. One by one, the people came out. The first were shot even before the last emerged. A moment before the mother went out into the light to be shot, she threw her twins into an empty water barrel.

They lay there, still, for an unknown length of time. First drugged, then dazed by the darkness and the shock. When one of them began to cry, someone heard him and crawled into the hiding place. He found one living twin, crying, and one dead twin. No one knew which of the two had survived—Gershon or Hezkel? But not only the external name had been lost. The sleeping pills had also taken the inner name. A warm child had woken up beside his cold brother, everything was dark, no one around. For several long hours a one-year-old soul had stirred, lost in the dark, crying, in a slumber that came and went, lowering blinds and partitions. Years would pass and only prescription pills could raise those blinds even a crack.

He spent the entire war hiding in the woods and in the homes of kind *goyim*. When the war was over, relatives came to collect him and they raised him devotedly, giving him generously from what little they had. Their looks enquired—Gershon or Hezkel? Not once did they call him by name, so as not to make the decision. He silently bore the appellations, "good boy," "our beloved," aliases that evaded the need to use an explicit name. Years went by and no decision was made. When they arrived at the port of Haifa in Israel, the immigration officer leaned down to the boy and pinched his chin affectionately. For some reason, after hundreds of children, all wide-eyed and imploring, the officer was moved by this boy grasping his uncle's hand.

"What should we call you, boy?" he asked in crude rustic Polish.

Gershon Klima, frightened and suddenly obligated, found himself committing. "I'm Gershon."

End of story.

We listened to Gershon, who now was quite possibly Hezkel, and understood everything.

"Is it because of Hezkel that you go to the nuthouse?"

Gershon Klima smiled. Yes, all was understood. Hezkel wanted a life too. Sometimes he demanded everything, sometimes only a little—just a walk outside.

We were not happy. "His own brother" had been deciphered but we felt empty and worn out. Something we should have left with its owner had been given to us. We should not have taken it. We left Gershon Klima's home in the usual way, through the front door, remembering to observe how the world looked from inside the house, through its windows, from its doorway, from its porch. We walked very slowly, already thinking about our meeting with Levertov later that evening, and even before that, our task of stealing more Formacil from Feiga.

We were not prepared for the next surprise. Trapped in broad daylight in the middle of Katznelson, we ran into Hirsch. His feet were planted solidly in the middle of a row of hibiscus flowers, his coat raised in his right hand above his knees. He was peeing on the flowers. In his left hand he held a book of Psalms, lifting it as high as he could, far away from the urgent downward stream. We stood frozen opposite this statue of liberty—we were immigrants in America, standing dazed at the port with a suitcase at our feet and our brother's address in our pocket. We thought about Mr. Bergman, who had a brother in America. About Finkelstein the son, of whom we knew nothing except what had been addressed to him. We recalled Adella Greuner's brother, who once came to visit from America, rolling into the neighborhood in a taxi. After less than half an hour at Adella's, the whole neighborhood watched through their blinds as he slapped her on the cheek, got back into the waiting taxi and left. Astonishing. Everyone stood limply behind their blinds—imagine coming all the way from America to slap Adella Greuner and go back home! That evening, the sky had seemed higher over the neighborhood, although the swallows had come down at twilight as usual, following the insects that stuck to the lamps. By morning, the neighborhood had not yet wiped off its look of astonishment. People pondered the broadness of life, sensed a Mississippi River that had burst onto Katznelson for one single day and submerged it. All the way from America for one slap and back home!

Hirsch concluded his business and walked onto the paved portion of Katznelson. His right hand still lifted his coat, his left shook the Psalms up and down. Up and down, as if he were clutching a J N F donation box, listening to the letters jingle inside. We saw him turn to us and approach. We thought he would choose us, stand facing us and open his terrible mouth:

"Only saints were gassed?"

We stood. Eyes closed. We felt Hirsch's breath on our face. Then he was gone, leaving his leaden dramas at an insignificant point near the plumbago shrubs far behind us.

We went home and we were almost unsurprised to see Levertov coming out of Grandpa Yosef's apartment. He looked at us for a moment like a captured jackal, exposing his teeth in an evasive sort of smile. We didn't have to ask. We hurried to Feiga's room. The Formacil had already been swapped. Grandpa Yosef scurried after us, explaining, "Mr. Levertov came to see how Feiga was. It's so nice that there is someone willing to sit with her a little when I'm busy. And Levertov, he has enough problems of his own."

We left. Our hearts yearned for the woods but our feet took us only as far as the upper border demarcated by long yellow skeletons of leaves and little pieces of junk tossed, over the years, into the point that connected the place of human residence with the beginning of savagery. At the point where the neighborhood disconnects from the rest of the woods, we returned to Katznelson. That was the precise moment when childhood ended.

We walked quietly back and forth along Katznelson. We wanted to vandalize something at Levertov's, to go to Grandpa Yosef and blurt out a confession: Feiga has been poisoned, someone faked the Formacil! Or perhaps do a good deed and carry Linow Community's shopping for her or rake some leaves from the path next to Moshe.

We had wasted our power and we sensed it ebbing away, beaten down, weakening. So many things had been missed. We had not gone to Hirsch's hut to knock on his door and see what he did when he wasn't shouting on Katznelson. We had not gone down into the sewer to walk all the way to Caesarea. So much truth we could have acquired, enough to fill our pockets with. But we had wasted it, wasted it all. Childhood was over. We were thrown out and barred from taking anything with.

The following Saturday, when Mom suggested a visit to Grandpa Yosef, I asked instead to go hiking in the Jezreel Valley. (In class we had learned about Hankin, the Zionist who had redeemed lands in the valley). Effi, at home, used the flu.

We began to withdraw from the neighborhood, from Grandpa Yosef. We abandoned the Shoah. We were repelled by something. Levertov's betrayal was the seed of something greater, and it only grew larger and darker, with onion-like layers. We gave ourselves up to maturity.

We were fourteen when Levertov betrayed us. After that, we were seduced by a new world. With Tal Brody, we led Maccabi Tel Aviv to victory in the European Cup Championship. With Yizhar Cohen, we won the Eurovision Song Contest. The world glowed with lights of victory and we lapped them up. It was the start of our years of Imaginary Purposefulness. Growing up. Aspiring to things that were bigger, less alive. We allowed ourselves to be painted with the right colors, to assimilate, to blend in. The instructions were precise and we followed them, no questions asked. And whatever we didn't do, our bodies rushed to achieve on their own, treacherously, with an apologetic grin but pleased with the changes.

We were dropped off on an unfamiliar platform. Adolescence. Things happened.

Occurrences.

But only to us.

Around us, stagnation. The years passed by. In the family, everything stayed as it was. Grandpa Yosef's neighborhood remained unchanged. The people we knew added twenty years on to their ages, years swallowed up like pills taken and forgotten. For them the years were pushed into drawers, closets, lives with secret bottoms. Things stopped changing. A spell brought it all to a standstill and let us run ahead and grow up. Blindly, we ran.

There was Rachela Kempler, every day before dawn in her window. Opposite her, with drawn blinds, was mad Itcha Dinitz. Linow Community, Sarkow Community, swayed slightly more as they walked with their baskets of vegetables. In season, the bombax bloomed. The bauhinia. The poinciana. Katznelson, calm as always, flowed in numbers and letters. A frozen world where nothing changed. Not even Eva Lanczer. Twenty years have passed since they took her away and she still lies in a hospital bed all in white. Eliyahu goes to visit her. Wondrously, she still embroiders strange and beautiful things for him to sell. All those years she spent resting, we devoted to growing up. The people around us grew older, sicker, much the same as always, determined to go on without aging, as if the secret of longevity was unhappiness. Avoid happiness and you have as good as avoided dampness, wetness, any danger to your health.

The family stuck to itself and clenched its teeth against change. Nothing could happen. When someone died, everyone rushed to the funeral and huddled around the muddy grave with wintry umbrellas, or sweltered in midday in a desert of white gravestones—just as long as we huddled around the plot, piled up the dirt to stop a hole in the ship.

Grandpa Shalom died in 1980. Effi's camera captured Aunt Ecka for the final time. We had her face as a souvenir, next to a table spread with whipped cream and desserts. Uncle Tulek also died (finally, the African statuette could be removed from the living room). In the unknown distances at the edges of the family with-whom-we-never-met, people died. But the bonbons still arrived at the holidays. People died, but the bonbons could not be stopped, they were like a herd of buffalo galloping by on the holidays, kicking up dust. Every year a Passover Seder managed to somehow be arranged. We managed to meet at the dinner table. If we had photographed ourselves and sent the picture to a lab, the report would have come back and certified: this is a family.

The family friends did not abandon us either. Attorney Perl was still in his store. Now he had two assistants, both named Yakov, but only he went up the ladder. A ninety-year-old Spiderman in 1990. And it wasn't only Dad sitting with him in the backroom—I started to sit there too. The years brought Attorney Perl and myself together in an unexpected way. At the age of fifteen I tried my hand at a woodworking course held near his store. I wanted to drop the course almost immediately, but the teacher was a friend of Dad's from the army reserves and lots of warm regards were exchanged between them. I stuck it out for more than a year, fulfilling my messenger duties, and built a wooden *menorah*, a bookshelf, a wine rack, and a model airplane. My consolation was that I could go into Attorney Perl's store on my own, without Dad, as a grownup. Attorney Perl welcomed me into the little back room, the mirror room, where he made me tea, told me about his late spouse, about the Nuremberg Trials that had put an end to all hope, and about Eichmann, who was put to death just like that, without us knowing his thoughts.

I kept going to see him even after squirming my way out of the woodworking course, sometimes before seeing a movie in town, sometimes for no reason. During my army service, too. I was welcomed respectfully, pleasantly, with a cup of tea that suspended all commerce. He ordered his assistant, "Yakov, mind the store for a while," and took me to the back room, the mirror reflection of his store. Every visit opened with a short discussion of my military service. A meeting of the special staff. "How's it going at your Lager?" Attorney Perl would enquire. They have their own words. *Camp*, with them, is *Lager*. A *pass* is a *Certifikat*. Even here in Israel, after years of independence. But they do have Hebrew words. Even those who speak only broken Hebrew acquire essential words. *A draft*, for example. They must have stepped off the boat and enquired, "How do you say in Hebrew when the windows are not sealed properly? A draft?" And that was it. Absorption in Israel.

Attorney Perl did not allow the Holocaust to disappear. He regretted the Nazi criminals who had been hanged before we could understand their thoughts, and he regretted those who were not hanged at all and whom the world had found swift ways to forgive. His memory catalogued hundreds of names of war criminals, their deeds, their verdicts. His map of the world included every country that had taken in Nazis after the war, every country that had served as a means of transit, every country whose agents had assisted the criminals in their escapes. In the air of the little room among the shadows of tea, he made long lists, calmly, meticulously.

—Martin Sandberger. Sentenced to death during the Einsatzgruppen Case for having engaged in mass extermination of Jews in occupied territories. Set free as early as 1953.

—Dr. Carl Clauberg, "the sterilizing doctor." Conducted horrific experiments on Jewish and Gypsy women in order to improve methods for quick sterilization. His lethal experiments were carried out in a special hut at Auschwitz. Released in 1955 from a Russian prison and transferred to Germany. No legal proceedings were initiated against him there, and only under pressure from the Jewish communities did an investigation begin. Preparations for his trial were cut short due to his death.

—Dr. Wilhelm Beiglböck. Conducted human experiments designed to ascertain whether man could subsist on seawater, and concluded that he could not. Sentenced to fifteen years in prison in 1947 but set free in 1951.

—Dr. Karl Genzken, physician. A typhus 'researcher' who

killed hundreds of prisoners in his experiments at Buchenwald camp. Sentenced to life in prison, but his sentence was reduced to twenty years and he was released to live in freedom in 1954.

—Wilhelm Speidel. Convicted of participating in the extermination of Serbian Jews and in war crimes related to the expulsion of Greek Jews to extermination camps. Sentenced in 1948 to twenty years in prison but released in 1951.

He listed some familiar names too:

—Untersturmführer Kurt Franz, referred to by the prisoners as *Lalka*, meaning "Doll." Arrested only in 1959 and brought to trial. For almost fifteen years, he lived a normal life in his community. Despite the harsh testimonies, his punishment was only imprisonment. As an exceptional case, the court also addressed the culpability of Barry, the St. Bernard dog who took an active part in killing prisoners. The dog was adopted after the war by a German physician, Dr. Strobe, and harmed no one. He reached old age and was euthanised in 1947.

—Erich Lachmann. The original owner of Barry, and the man who instilled his murderous tendencies in him. Also charged with murdering inmates in the Sobibor camp, but acquitted of all charges.

—Heinrich Lohse, Reichskommissar of the Baltic areas. A brutal implementer of the Final Solution, who ordered that Jews in areas under his control be rationed no more than the minimal essentials to sustain life. Sentenced to ten years of penal servitude, but released after three years for medical reasons. Lived in freedom until his death thirteen years later.

—Wilhelm Koppe. A leading figure in the establishment of the Chelmno extermination camp, a ghetto "liquidator" in the Wartheland and a senior SS commander of occupied Poland. Lived under an assumed name after the war and was only captured in 1961. His trial was discontinued due to medical problems. Lived in freedom until 1975.

Endless lists.

Again and again, I am struck by one mounting impression: how quick the world was to forgive, to mitigate death sentences, to release life-term prisoners. Something larger than the Nazis' crimes was at work here. Something global. It was not only the Nazis whom Attorney Perl was condemning. His explanations encompassed all human beings—otherwise, the Nazis would not be understood. He spread before me the treasures of the Holocaust, rolling them out like a fabric merchant. Together we tore up everything I had learned at school; the Shoah recited in ceremonies, the placards displaying numbers of casualties. It was a competition of sorts, a hope to impress, to shock, to emphasize the magnitude of the catastrophe.

Attorney Perl led the conversations. I, in turn, modestly provided material from encyclopedias, from school, from the books on the shelves in Mrs. Gottmartz's public library. I also brought to our conversations what little I knew of my family history. Minute details in punctured containers. But Attorney Perl removed our families from his words, so as not to divert the line of logic. His own private Shoah grief rarely emerged, and was quickly covered over when it did. He was authoritative in his speech. Precise, impartial.

"In order to judge the Nazis' deeds," he explained, "we need something moral and axiomatic that includes the obligations of both the judged and the judges. Feelings must not be an active factor, but only an additional examination method."

And when the explanations got complicated, we always went back to the endless lists.

—Heinz Schubert. Sentenced to death at the Einsatzgruppen Case. Released in 1951.

—Erhard Milch, head of the Nazi regime's Central Planning Board. Charged with exploiting the slave labor economy throughout the Reich and overseeing morbid medical experiments conducted by physicians on camp inmates. Sentenced to life in prison in 1947 but his sentence was commuted to fifteen years and he was in fact released in 1954.

—Walter Kuntze, a general in the German army. Responsible for the murder of thousands of Serbian Jews with the SS. Sentenced to life in prison in 1948 but released in 1953 due to reasons described as "health considerations."

Outside Attorney Perl's store, life went on as usual. Yehoshua the barber had to make good on more and more promises to cut the hair of loyal customers at their homes until their dying days. He arrived punctually, not reneging even on the vaguest of vows, but boosting himself by mumbling around his customers' heads, "Believe me, I'm certain it was you in '64 over at Golchik the barber on HaNevi'im Street. Not anyone else. So help me God, I shouldn't have come to you."

In the neighborhood, the fight between Littman and Sammy raged on—proof that the world did not change. But it did change: Littman installed air conditioning in his corner store ("enough suffering," he said), paving the way for two frenetic months during which the entire neighborhood fattened up their walls with little air conditioners. A victory for progress.

Littman did not grow old. Neither did Grandpa Lolek. Why would he? He had already been eligible for discounted bus fares for a while now, and besides, there was not much to be gained by old age. His Vauxhall was not what it used to be; every time the engine was turned off, its cooling body trickled out grumbles and complaints. But Grandpa Lolek remained loyal. Thanks to Green the Mechanic, the Vauxhall could still make it to Gedera and back. When Anat was pregnant with Yariv, Grandpa Lolek bought her a car. One day he simply placed the keys to a Fiat Uno in the palm of her hand, as if to say, "I always buy cars for pregnant women." We tried to graciously refuse, and finally, perplexed, we consented. There were no words. Only the *Tarbut* encyclopedia could express the sentiment (Everyman, Plate Tectonics, Seventh Wonder).

Grandpa Yosef did not grow old either. His justification was the bike. His wrinkles deepened, his wisdom grew heavier. The university studies breathed new life into him, dragon wings that he politely dragged through the shrubs along Katznelson. His decision to continue his academic adventures even after obtaining his Masters' impressed us. The topic of his doctoral thesis, Jewish heroism in the Middle Ages, aroused a certain curiosity. By the time he reached the graduation ceremony in 1985, Effi was a medical student and I was an officer—two perfect icons of *naches* for Grandpa Yosef. Except in our case it was the grandfather who brought *naches* to his grandchildren. Each of us secretly vowed to fill our lives with rich content, to somehow aspire to be the equal of Grandpa Yosef, who struggled against a lack of time, a multitude of worries and old age. Many other family members seemed to be in a constant flux of hidden motion—a change perceptible only to those proficient in this morphology.

We would come to Grandpa Yosef whenever we could, to eat the ever-changing contents of the fruit bowl, to talk, to fortify ourselves. Around us strange years flew by. We sat with Grandpa Yosef. Things occurred outside. Grandpa Yosef came and went, brought cold fruit, juice. We saw the books on his desk change. Less of Rambam and Radak's scriptural commentaries, more *Traditional Anti-Semitism in Western Europe* and *The Jewish Leadership's Interpretation of the Crusades*. We went to make coffee in the kitchen and came back. Effi began her studies. Still taking pictures in bursts, but the periodic excess now concealed an impaired desire to photograph. I became an officer and completed a short term of service in the standing army. Grandpa Yosef reveled in the anti-aircraft weaponry I was put in charge of, slightly miffed that I wasn't allowed to try my hand against real aircraft. Effi's books, *Introduction to Surgery* and *Biology for Physicians*, were respectfully leafed through.

Grandpa Yosef did not have a porch-and-a-loquat-tree-to-sit-beneath. When we came, sometimes both of us, but usually only one, we made do with the big wooden table. There we sat, all grown up, comprehending the amazing power with which its location had been selected: the precise center of an equilateral triangle between Brandy's calls (Moshe's needs), Feiga's calls (Feiga's needs), and the window (public needs). Grandpa Yosef, the loyal emissary, left his post once in a while to head this way or that to answer a call. Sometimes he went far, if the summons required it. Moshe, Feiga, someone else, Moshe again, Feiga once more, someone else again. Grandpa Yosef on his orbits, never resting, never finished. And he always came back to us, looking straight ahead with severity, even threatening: No pity. God forbid, do not dare pity me.

Sometimes serendipity brought Effi and me together at Grandpa Yosef's. Like a pair of lemmings, we dropping everything—university, marriage—to answer the call of our species and come to Grandpa Yosef. We convened with him to debate the problems of

life, offer advice, comments, slight derisions and sometimes encouragement. We never left Grandpa Yosef without playing a game of
"Categories." It was good to lose, as we had done in our childhood.
Grandpa Yosef showed no mercy when it came to Categories. He
became a vengeful warrior. His arms thickened. His voice turned
crude. In the interest of fairness, we made him come up with two
terms instead of one to gain any points. Grandpa Yosef obeyed, but
in return, we agreed that he could play his beloved double turns—
once as Grandpa Yosef, once as Feiga. He placed two pieces of paper
in front of him, one with his own name, and on the other he wrote
tenderly, "Feiga."

Feiga was the winner. Always. Grandpa Yosef left himself the
common terms and decorated Feiga's page with the best of exotica.
An animal with "Z" was "zebra" for himself and "zebu" for Feiga. A
vegetable with "T" was "tomato," destined to battle our own identical
choices, leaving Feiga as the lead with "turnip." If the letter H was
called out, Grandpa Yosef would blink, his Adam's apple bobbing,
bits of thought dripping down his temples. He would write down
"Honduras" or "Holland" for himself, and for Feiga, "Hungary." A
very mediocre stroke of genius, connected to the as-of-yet-unexplained
escape by Feiga and her family from Bochnia to Hungary one fine day
before the *Aktionen* and the Holocaust horrors. The insult was not
yet digested, Grandpa Yosef still did not dare take a first bite out of
the affair: one moment the two of them were in the ghetto, engaged,
and the next—Feiga was gone.

After the games he would make sure to pad into Feiga's room
and announce, "You won!" Pleased with his achievement, he would
pamper himself with a piece of pickled herring or some lox or a pickle
spear. Happiness radiated from his stubble, from the wrinkles on his
face. He happily sipped a cup of weak tea right in front of our eyes,
restoring in himself the powers dissipated by victory.

Every time we visited, we asked about the doctorate. Grandpa
Yosef was secretive. "Grandpa Yosef, let us read it," we would beg, but
our attempts were met with raised eyebrows and waves of the hand.
He would grumpily complain: there was progress, but not the progress he wanted. Something…something was missing. Something to

give life…validity. He was waiting for an omen, a sign from above. As if engaged not in scientific research but in a kind of religious purification.

"Maybe if you wrote about Jewish cowardice in the Middle Ages you'd have more ideas," Effi says, annoying Grandpa Yosef. Jewish cowardice. Not funny at all.

Angrily, he responds, "I knew a man in the camps…Adler… *nu.*" And falls silent. As if he has touched a thought not yet fully molded. He suspends our fruit bowl rights by taking the bowl into the kitchen to preoccupy himself, to hide his anger, leaving us with a hankering for grapes. The hasty reference to "Adler" gives rise to a common thought: Grandpa Yosef had managed to successfully ford our childhood without telling us much about his Shoah. A series of Morse code was all we ever had, event-event-occurrence, that's it.

There are moments when Grandpa Yosef lobs a confession attempt in our direction. "The things I saw…the people I recall…in the Lord's name! Sometimes I sit here in my chair and think: I am alive. And I think about them, so many years have passed since they too hoped to live, to survive the camps. I sit here and tremble, children, I sit and tremble…"

As if he wants us to sit and listen as he talks, but there is no one to talk to. We look back at the years during which we chased down the questions of the Holocaust. Caged years that began with ordinary days, when we were ten, and ended with Levertov's betrayal and our banishment from childhood. We did not find answers to our questions, and it seems we stopped seeking them.

Grandpa Yosef's dissertation was to continue at a painfully slow rate, and in fact is still not complete today. But during the lucid days of 1985 we imagined it was just within his reach. Every meeting with him opened with the question, "How's it going?" and with the answer, "Still not…still not," with a grumbling sigh. If we had focused our attention correctly, the delay would have revealed to us the secret of the stagnation that had befallen the world around us. We should have taken the hint. The neighborhood had come to a standstill. Everything had frozen. The world does *not* change.

We would run into the neighborhood residents and find them

identical to the characters of our childhood, unchanged, not a comma or a wrinkle different. Continuing to survive. Magical people. Day after day, experts at survival. Forces of nature pushed them into the neighborhood (volcanoes disguised as historical dates; raging fires known as Auschwitz, Belzec, Bergen-Belsen; thunder storms on train tracks; the thick fog of transports; sub-zero temperatures—the locals' indifference) and now they sit in the depths of their compensation payments—the only support they have, a flow of coins from Germany. Only the Germans are left to atone, to compensate them every month for their suffering, for families lost and lives unblossomed. There are no professors among them, no big-time merchants, statesmen, legislators. Their lives have been diverted to this neighborhood, to this wasteland. Their lives are unlived. They came here as a torrent of refugees after the war, to the heat waves and the rationing, to a place with no trees and no snow. They were forced to live other people's lives, chosen from a pile like clothes in the camps without trying them on, no exchanges allowed—pause too long and the whip will crack. They took tattered lives, lives that fit no one, and lived them complacently. They married. Had children. Listened to the radio. There were holidays—Rosh Hashanah, Passover. But what could compare to the Passover Seder at home in Sosnowitz, where Father blessed the *matzo* with Elijah's trembling cup of wine on the table? Where were their lives? The continuity? Things begun during the first year of studies at the Polytechnikum or a renowned *yeshiva*? In a successful business inherited from Father, full of ideas to double and triple the profits? Where were those lives?

They sit. They sigh. Sometimes a thought creeps in, a certain sacred relief: We are not to blame. Our lives have been nothing, but it is not our fault. The Shoah. The war. We were saved, and more than that we could not do. We were absolved from a life that demands successes, accomplishments, proof. Not like our children, who grew up here and were given everything—and what do they have? Nothing. We are here, surviving.

We looked at them with wonderment, amazed and alarmed—they did not change. The years passed us by like a cat's scratches. We could feel each one of them. Those later years were not as easy as our childhood had been. Life surged around us and we clung to our seats trying not to drift away. We were abandoned, weak, in need of Grandpa Yosef. We came to him: Go on, Grandpa Yosef, pull us along, you are the strongest sleigh dog. We sat with him to catch our breath. To rest. To check in—was the world changing? Not changing? And us? What about us?

The neighborhood does not change. Every evening, Uncle Antek turns on the huge radio and the inmates are counted in Auschwitz. Gershon Klima is down in the sewer. The occasional hospitalization, slightly less frequent. Twice a month is just too much at his age. Adella Greuner is still despised behind curtains. Haim Mintzer limps along Katznelson.

Sometimes outside, for a moment, the yell comes:

"Only saints were gassed?"

The world does not change, just grows old and more complicated. A scruffy beard and cracked lips. Doesn't it ever get sick? Doesn't it ever need help?

And Moshe? What will happen with Moshe? There he sits on the low fence.

Everything remains as it was.

Without even noticing it, we grew Old Enough. Dad started to talk with me. Cautiously laconic, only the bare facts. He told many stories—at-age-twelve-condemmed-up-against-a-wall-in-the-ghetto-a-German-SS-officer-puts-a-bullet-in-raises-his-rifle-suddenly-a-messenger-comes-with-an-order-to-stop-shooting-the-German-lowers-his-rifle-what-did-you-think-about-Dad-a-moment-before-the-shooting?-I-don't-know-I-just-thought-let-it-not-hurt. Then-in-the-camp-during-*Selektion*-they-sent-him-to-die-put-his-name-down-on-the-list-of-condemned-then-they-couldn't-find-him-on-the-list-he-didn't-wait-around-just-ran-to-the-ranks-of-those-chosen-to-stay-alive-and-of all these stories, the most moving was a particular moment after the war. Dad tried to finish his primary school education. In the entrance exam he was required to submit an essay in Polish. The school headmaster asked him to write on "My Life Story." And so Dad wrote his life story. When he came to get his grade, the headmaster asked him, "All this, everything you wrote in your essay…Did this really happen to you?"

Dad said, "Yes."

The headmaster said, "Poor boy." And caressed his head.

A simple gesture—an educator pats the head of a boy whose life has been difficult. But Dad was not a boy. He was already sixteen. The hand was caressing the head of the boy from the essay, who had already lived, who was no longer, whom no one had caressed when he was selected for death in Plaszow camp, on whom no one took pity when he was ill, when it was clearly just a matter of time before they put a bullet in him. The boy who stole food to keep his parents alive. Who was unable to keep them alive. Whose friends—all his friends from school, from the playground, from the screaming and shouting during recess—were dead. Gone. The hand caressed a subterranean boy, a non-boy. The caress was too late.

That caress had to traverse many light years and cross many firmaments to land, to settle, to show a natural motion, an educator-patting-the-head-of-a-boy-whose-life-had-been-so-difficult. Six years earlier, German educators had joined the ranks of the SS and the Gestapo. Polish educators had cooperated willingly, even when the victims were little children. Six years earlier, Dad had come to school for the first day of the third grade, and the homeroom teacher, Professor Wronewitz, had called the five Yids up to the front of the classroom to inform them that from that day onward they were no longer students at the school. He was following the orders of the Germans, who had recently occupied Poland. Just following orders. But the Germans had not ordered him to refer to the children he had been educating since the first grade as *Kikes*. The Germans had not ordered him to sweetly add, "Goodbye but not farewell." Dad still remembers his smile.

A country beginning with P? The Philippines, Peru, Portugal, Pakistan. We silently agreed never to choose "Poland." Revenge.

And Attorney Perl in the back room:

"Let us closely examine words from a command issued by Walter Von Reichenau, Commander of the Army Group South, as a spiritual guideline for the operating forces of the liquidation: 'The soldier must fully understand the necessity of meting out severe yet fair retribution to the Jewish sub-humans.' These words were intended to strengthen the spirits of soldiers engaged in the liquidation, and they represent an extremely prevalent frame of mind, which informed the way Jews were treated even by those who had nothing to do with the SS, such as anti-semites among the Polish civilian population, the collaborators."

Circuitously, Attorney Perl found his way to Grandpa Yosef. A respectful friendship grew. The presence of the elderly man enriched our games of Categories. Attorney Perl observed the game, respecting its rules, amazed at the treasures of knowledge to which he was not privy.

A city beginning with M? Minatitlan. (The points go to Feiga.)

A country beginning with T? Tuvalu, the capital of which is, of course, Fongafale.

But in the back room of Attorney Perl's store, the directions of amazement and knowledge were reversed:

—Emil Johann Puhl. Actively engaged in handling gold teeth collected in the death camps and storing them in the Reichsbank coffers. Sentenced to only five years in prison.

—Franz Rademacher. One of the greatest 'desk-bound' murderers, in his capacity as head of the German Foreign Office's "Jewish Desk." Escaped after the war to Syria, returned to Germany in 1966 and died before legal proceedings against him were concluded.

—Hauptsturmführer Hans Krüger. One of the most efficient and energetic murderers in the SS. Served as commander of a small border station in the Stanislawow district of Eastern Galicia. Although he commanded a tiny force of about twenty-five men, he managed to organize and implement the executions of some 70,000 Jews, possibly more. After the war he was not arrested at all, and was even bold enough to assimilate into public life and run for local parliament. Only in 1959 was he placed under investigation, and in 1968 sentenced to life in prison. He was released in 1986 and died two years later.

—Erich Koch, a founding member of the Nazi party. Reichskommissar of the Ukraine. Sentenced to death in 1959 for his actions, but his sentence was not implemented due to poor health. He lived on in prison until 1986.

—Alfried Krupp. Chairman of the Krupp family industrial conglomerate, which employed close to one hundred thousand forced laborers under conditions of slavery and terror. Sentenced in 1947 to twelve years in prison, but released in 1951. In 1953 he was restored to his previous position as head of Krupp industries.

—Richard Korherr, statistician. Author of the "Korherr Report," a publication containing updated data on the number of killings and the number of Jews still populating each area throughout Europe. His work was used by Adolf Eichmann to enable the planning stages of the extermination. After the war he was investigated but never brought to trial.

Endless lists of bad Germans swarm through my memory like frenzied flies.

I asked Attorney Perl an ancient question. "Mr. Perl, were there bad Jews?"

Attorney Perl prepared for his reply. Rapped his knuckles on the empty kettle. Twirled a finger behind his ear as if pulling an imaginary side-lock. "Bad Jews…you have to understand that the Germans…they had methods. Jews…they wanted to live."

He fell silent. A preparatory silence.

"First we must understand how far it is possible to go with the law. Where is the line from which we draw conclusions about who was good and who was bad? Up to a certain point, a person's morality struggles and he must choose between options. After that, there is no control, you cannot judge or accuse. A person commits an act—turns in his mother, his father, his brother. And it is not his thoughts that issue the command, and not his faith that interferes. It is not the person who acts, but the molecules of his body. The molecules wish to exist, they tell the Germans, 'There is the door, behind the oven, the bunker.' They desire only to live, to stay together in some human form. Families turned in, friends turned in. It was not the person who betrayed, but the molecules, the corporeal level, and that cannot be judged. There was in our ghetto, in Bochnia, a family by the name of Zomer. One day the Germans caught them—an informant had told them that the Zomers, father and son, knew where other people were hiding in bunkers. I believe they were bakers and they secretly delivered bread to hiding places, so they knew everything. They were told to inform, otherwise they would be shot immediately. The son, a young man roughly your age, wanted to live and so he started to talk. The father ordered him, 'Shut up and start undressing,' because the Germans would not shoot people in their clothes, that would be a waste. The son obeyed. They took their clothes off. They were shot. They did not give up the bunker. And the son? Like you. He wanted to live. So where are good Jews and bad Jews? Where?"

He told me about good Germans, bad Germans. Good Poles, bad Poles. Good Jews, bad Jews. He told me about Landau, a Jewish collaborator whom the Gestapo used to drive proudly through the streets of the Bochnia ghetto. And Count Simon, who was a fool, not a bad person, a persistent collaborator. These were not the worst, he cautioned. And he told me about the Jewish Kapo Yehezkel Ingster, and the Jewish Kapo Yakov Honigman. I was Old Enough.

Effi was also Old Enough. "Mom, why do you cry?"

Some things were told. Some were not. Even though we were Old Enough, questions still remained.

Why don't they spend time together?

Why is Mrs. Kopel infertile?

Why is Uncle Menashe from Netanya still a bachelor?

What about Mr. Bergman?

Suddenly, like a redemptive wave of nausea, we remembered: What did Grandpa Lolek do with Finkelstein's gold?

The wave of nausea went off to ask Grandpa Lolek. We were Old Enough.

"I give it to people without food after war, I give so they make graves for families, make new graves that the *goyim* destroyed. Also my family I made graves. Everything I gave, I thought after war there will be world without money, that is what I thought."

Grandpa Lolek's ideological era.

"On that, I was much mistaken," he admitted.

"You gave it all? All of it?"

"All of it."

To believe, not to believe, to believe, not to believe, to believe, not to believe—an entire field of marigolds was picked, petals plucked off. Believe, not believe, believe, not believe.

A hurt look from blue eyes interfered.

We believed.

The years passed by, Moshe celebrated his fortieth birthday, still sailing away as he sat on the low fence. There were no more attempts to find him a framework. He had found his framework. Maturation had given his face a stamp of contemplation, a gravity which brought to mind an internal change, perhaps a thought about to burst through, finally erupt, a thought that had been stymied all his life by a mind too bureaucratic, too clerk-like, and now the dull era would be over and the sweeping thought would burst forth to make amends, to express with simplicity everything that had not been understood his whole life, had been hidden in a distorting mirror. Brandy at his feet, an old dog now, tired of lovers, knowing her duty, loving the essence of her existence. A heavy slumber had spread over her limbs. Over the years some of Grandpa Yosef's qualities had poured into her. The altruism, mainly. When Moshe was resting in his room, if there was no urgent canine season, she could be seen hurrying to the pedestrian crossing nearby. She excelled at helping the elderly and children, granting confidence to those who lacked it. Every visit to Grandpa Yosef's began with a thorough indulgence of Brandy. We scratched the soft spots behind her ears and the hard box of her forehead. Looked straight into her eyes, trying to find the nobility that lay behind that canine face. Whiskers straight as a wand. Open mouth. Dots of foam always on her tongue. Not a face to break hearts. But still, Brandy.

Over the years we could sense how even Brandy went through changes. Death, in particular, was reflected through her—it tried her on like a suit of clothes. When someone came close to her she perked her head up, wagged her tail and yawned, as dogs do. But if you concentrated you could pick up certain notes. Death was apparent in her. Something not yet issued, a license held up by a clerk dazed from the heat, subject to continuous delays and the capriciousness of a bureaucrat. She strode down the paths with exemplary steps, careful not to skip too far into the next world—bad enough the trees she sometimes forgot to circle and the walls she crossed distractedly. Fifteen years old in 1991, Brandy was a demonic and yet tranquil dog. A sober island of wisdom, only the scruffy face preventing her from taking on a saintly halo.

Sometimes, on Katznelson, we would run into Menachem the neighborhood kid. We would stop and smile. "How's it going?" And in his eyes was wonder and astonishment. You left me here, he seemed to be accusing. You went off and I'm still here. I went to military school, got a job in Haifa, and I can barely make ends meet, and when we were kids we went to the woods together and climbed trees, even Gershon Klima's bombax, and you left me here. We say goodbye, somewhat awkwardly. I head to Grandpa Yosef, Menachem makes his way to the parents who gave birth to him many years ago, in the neighborhood, with wonderment, with embarrassment, as if they were being accused—where did this child come from? After all, we barely have the strength to live, so how did you find enough joy to give birth?

I too am amazed. When we were kids—I am certain of this—he was called Nimrod. I remember everything, and he was called Nimrod. When we were kids, Nimrod. There were no other kids in the neighborhood, so it was easy to remember. Grandpa Yosef remembers Menachem, everyone remembers Menachem, and yet I am certain: Nimrod. After the birth, for a short while, the parents had been filled with a placental life force, they grew impudent and named their son Nimrod after the biblical hunting hero. But now suddenly it was Menachem. According to him it had always been Menachem. To his mother he was Nahche, with teary eyes, after her brother, Nahche Osterman, may God avenge his blood. Fourteen years old, sent to Belzec. The eyes are the same, but her Nahche is heavier set.

If Grandpa Yosef wrote down 'Leibeleh' for a boy's name with L, we did not point out that for us 'Leibeleh' was not considered a boy's name. We trusted him. Our game of Categories was played in a spirit of generosity, which came easily. Sometimes, though, disputes arose. Effi, a charming ignoramus, fanatical over every point, once insisted that marshmallow was a vegetable. A radical player, she spread her hands out to the heavens for proof that might spring from the evening night. "Isn't marshmallow a vegetable?" Then she demanded points for Sodom. Sodom, she claimed, was a city!

Tasked with finding a country beginning with "B," Effi got points for Britain, I for Bahrain, Grandpa Yosef for Bermuda, Feiga for Barbados. Grandpa Yosef commented, "Interesting, we all chose islands…"

Effi was astonished. "Britain is an island?" She looked around at us. Was she being mocked? "But Germany isn't, right?" Just checking.

I consulted Grandpa Yosef's eyes. Geographically, the answer was clear. But Effi's question had raised a thought-provoking cultural image that could not be dismissed at hand. Could Germany be an island?

Grandpa Lolek interrupted our thoughts, manifested in his role as geographer. "What island?! Germany is connects nicely with Poland, and is connects nicely with Austria, where I have been when my Joyce got mixed up with the player on the piano in a café."

He was sitting with us because his neighborhood game of rummy had been cancelled. And as long as he had dragged the Vauxhall all the way here (and now it needed to rest), why not sit with some company, smoke a cigarette, drink some tea? He could also dangle a tea bag in front of Grandpa Yosef and do his *Selektion*, deciding to let the bag live but regretful that it would live on at Grandpa Yosef's. But not to worry, dinnertime was nearing, which might offer some prospects. He could browse Grandpa Yosef's papers and circle some notices. Then we'd see. He often turned up at our meetings, where he existed alongside us without wasting his time on our games and conversations. We would find him sitting quietly, diluting his cigarettes with tea, thinking. He never allowed his thoughts to be revealed, only their shadow exposed, disguised as tea vapors or wisps of smoke.

A more frequent guest than him, steady and respectful, was Gershon Klima. His tiger-like nostrils, unscathed by the sewage, always detected our arrival. Then he would hurry to Grandpa Yosef's and sit down to watch us play Categories. He never dared play, confounded by the supra-terranean concepts. He sat stiffly on his chair without even reaching for the fruit in the center of the table, which was meant for him, too. We respected his presence and looked forward to the letter S coming around so we could demonstrate our fondness. We silently conspired to all write 'sewage' under 'inanimate' (except for Feiga, who put down 'skippet' and took all the points again). Gershon Klima thanked us with a nod of the head, but seemed to disagree with those who did not know that sewage was in fact 'animate' and sometimes even 'vegetable,' and perhaps also 'personality' or even 'boy/girl'—two of them, begging to be taken down into the mystery smelling of mildew and zucchini.

Gershon-please-take-us-on-a-tour-of-the-sewer had been a failure, when childhood was said and done. During our games of Categories we began to comprehend Gershon Klima's strategy of promises. He employed a miraculous mechanism of rejection, one thousand and one nights, and in each promise the next rejection was ingrained. We looked for guile in the eyes of our childhood friend, but all we found was a desire to keep himself a little piece of the world, one freedom, a place that could act as a sort of balance to the empty, unfurnished house that contained only a bed made of satin, silk, brocade and velvet. This was Gershon Klima: three generations of psychiatrists had certified him as insane, hospitalized him when he asked, diluted his gentle personality with pills and taken slight advantage of his strong hands to do a few repairs here and there on the hospital pipes. We sat across from him, grown up. 'His own brother' deciphered, cracked. We had imagined this deciphering for many long years of toffee candies, believing that the moment of discovery would shatter planets in our face, alloy saliva and breath in our throats. But no. Gershon Klima talked, we listened, and nothing. Was this the moment of maturation? Compassion exceeding curiosity? Even before the betrayal of Levertov, which had dispossessed us, banishing innocence into exile?

We kept growing up. We changed. Sent forth versions of ourselves to live, to try things outside. Every version that succeeded we wore as an overcoat, layer upon layer. But inside, a wholesome core still enquired once in a while:

Why don't they spend time together?

Why is Mrs. Kopel infertile? (The long years sent forth the tail-end of an answer. Dr. Mengele.)

Why is Uncle Menashe from Netanya still a bachelor?

What about Mr. Bergman?

Versions of us asked questions. We did not abandon the Shoah but we bundled it up into one single day like everyone else did. Holocaust Remembrance Day. Like a pile of leaves neatly raked. We stood for the moments of silence. Watched the national ceremony. Communed. But daily life overcame us. The passing years. Only one connection remained to the lands of Shoah, one single flimsy ladder in the form of Attorney Perl. In his store there were debates over the culpability of the German nation, of the Nazis, of the SS. Everything I quickly convicted, Attorney Perl delayed, sentencing to caution and investigation. He walked his conclusions in a cold row of facts, enslaved by data and evidence.

"Every factor must be considered independently, and every pair of factors together, in terms of their influence on one another, and every group of factors, and so forth, in a neat order, with a settling of the conclusions at every stage, integrating them with what has already been concluded and what we aspire to.

"Let us read as testimony the words of Hans Karl Moeser, given during his trial in August in the year nineteen-hundred and forty-seven. Listen: 'The same way, with the same pleasure as you shoot deer, I shoot a human being. When I came to the SS and had to shoot the first three people, my food didn't taste good for three days, but today it is a pleasure. It is a joy for me.'"

Attorney Perl constructs ineradicable sentences within me. The bottom of my soul is paved with words. "With the same pleasure as you shoot deer, I shoot a human being."

And always, always, it ended with the recitation of lists.

—Erich von dem Bach-Zelewski, Obergruppenführer. A general in the Einsatzgruppen. Sentenced to only ten years in prison, released after five years. In 1961 he was sentenced again to a period of four more years.

—Erich Fuchs. A mechanical expert who installed gas chambers in the Eastern death camps. Arrested only in 1963. Sentenced to four years in prison and revocation of citizenship.

—Dr. Karl Blaurock, chemist. An expert on asphyxiating gases, a consultant for the gas chamber program. Not found to this day.

—Hermann Michel. SS member, nicknamed "the Preacher of Sobibor." Not found to this day.

—Adolf (Karl) Müller. One of the more brutal of the Sobibor staff members, whose name came up repeatedly in survivor testimonies. Not found to this day.

"What do you mean, 'not found to this day'?" I asked. How do people disappear in such a precise nation? It was unacceptable. Unpaid sins. Names and more names. The list was merciless. Its length, its breadth. One after the other in an orderly march. The hatred was fanned. The helplessness. How could so many have got away? Who forgave them? Who let them live, and bear children?

The hours I spent with Attorney Perl passed through underground burrows. These were hours unaware of the questions that arose: Does the world change? Does it not change? Outside the store, in the silence that prevailed when my footsteps returned to the world, the underground hours reunited with real time. Maturation. Grown up life. Continuity. Within the store there was still the reign of logic and precision, the Holocaust up for study. Inside his little back room we spun a world and attempted to comprehend it. I suggested it might have been a different world back then, with different rules, incomprehensible to us.

Attorney Perl dismissed my claims. "People were as they are today. Everything worked according to the regular rules, it was not a different world. It was our world, familiar and examined. My Laura came to Belzec on a train whose travel time was precisely the distance of the route divided by its average speed of travel. The gas in the chambers behaved according to the laws of gas formulated by the chemist Avogadro. The engine output determined the speed at which the gas diffused through the given volume of the chambers. And from there, physiology. The duration of time until death was determined by certain parameters: the ratio of gas to air, lung supply, the rate of metabolism in the body. Even Laura's final seconds, inside, can be described. Everything she went through during her final breaths. Doctors and experts have helped me to understand. And I talked with a survivor from the Sonderkommando who was somehow saved from death. His job was to clean the excrement and blood from the gas chambers. He described, at my request, everything he saw inside the chambers themselves. So you see, I know everything. I can go on with her until the last moment. And my Laura was so concerned with cleanliness and aesthetics. Even in the ghetto, despite the difficulties, she was so good about maintaining hygiene. Never let the crowdedness and the hunger sabotage her upbringing. And to die like that. Damn them…"

He breathed heavily.

"Damn them…"

A vein throbbed in his forehead.

"Damn them. Damn them."

Outside his store, time passed by. The hours piled up, massed at the door like uncleared snow. When I went out the spell was lifted, the crawling time in Attorney Perl's store disappeared in the flow of reality. A bus home. Falafel on HaChalutz Street. Car horns and stoplights. Only inside me the accumulating hours still lingered, constructing the only thing they were meant to construct: hatred for everything that went unpunished and still lives in our world, gazing fondly at its grandchildren. All the "not found to this day" who water their little suburban gardens, pay their taxes, wait for the weekend when their oldest son will come to visit with little Hans.

But the burrowing hours at Attorney Perl's did not dam time completely. I met Anat in 1986. I got married in 1987. Alongside my life, Effi grew up. She had loves. She studied. In the army, they sent her to take photographs too. After the army she chose medical school, seemingly for all the right reasons: they told her it was hard to get in but then it was easy, you just needed a good memory. She wouldn't have to stop taking photographs. But inside her, a hidden well of natural healing talent was crawling, waiting to spring. After seven years of school, she forgot about the camera.

1989. She earned her M.D. An impressive ceremony. She stood in the heart of a proud family while one man, a hero of Monte Cassino, clicked the button on a black Leica as if finally shutting a stubborn lid. Then two years at Ichilov Hospital in Tel Aviv. A shabby job, her hands longing for patients but touching only sterile bottles. Later, a partial transition to Carmel Hospital in Haifa. In the meantime, a position at the General Sick Fund in one of the Haifa suburbs, until a full-time position opened up at Carmel Hospital. But the temporary job won her over. Like a scientific researcher who does not find his place in human society, but in the heart of Africa, with a tribe he discovers (and perhaps names after himself—a simple matter of finessing the reports), he suddenly finds tranquility and love. The simplicity of the people wins him over, their love is the emotion he never found at home.

The Sick Fund patients loved her, and affection breeds affection. Sometimes I went to visit, surprised to see Effi's tribe at the entrance to her room, huddled in their troubles, talking about the doctor inside with a few complaints and a lot of love. They came bundled up in heavy clothing or flaccid robes, to gain her listening ear for their suffering, to present documents and test results. Among them were the shamefaced, the secretive. Apologizing for their illnesses, they kept their suffering folded up in little plastic bags. Their eyes were watery, frozen on a particular point on the floor (no doubt a puddle of memory had gathered there). Others were more demanding, masters of their illnesses. Standing in line, they regaled their fellow patients with the wondrous thicket of their aches and pains, and when their turn came they could barely bring themselves to leave the crowd—they had not yet given their opinion on the latest blood test. Determined, on the arc of a storm, they would sit down with Effi, charged with strength and courage, their illness practically escaping. Their debates were lengthy, involving pills, prescriptions, tests, forms—a hybrid treasure clutched in the palm of their hand, which they waved victoriously at the waiting congregation as they left.

The patients came to her one after the other, with more than simple illnesses to be treated. They did not always remember the true nature of their needs. Sometimes, like a watch forgotten at home, they left their complaints behind and came only with memories. They brought a mixture of backaches and service in the Russian military and new desires and the constraints of reality. Effi sat the mixtures down in a chair and talked to their memories. She had the depth to sense, to treat what needed to be treated. They acquiesced to her genuine compassion, to her concern for their welfare. Her fingers touched them and the touch said, "this body is important, someone cares that health should prevail here, too." She asked questions, remembered minute grievances, the fingerprint of each of her patients.

There was one disadvantage to the relationship between Effi and her patients: Effi was the first to get any round of flu. She could easily have served as a public alarm system, like canaries in a coalmine. She always fell to bed and turned red, then pale, her breathing labored. Then her patients would come up against a note that said, "Out sick," and would be referred to someone else, Dr. Reut or Dr. Mitelbien or Dr. Sachs, who were never sick. Whenever a flu outbreak began, the patients ran quickly to storm the clinic, hoping to beat Effi to it. But no. Already sick. Dr. Sachs instead. Her absences were no great crises. Most of her patients had flexible illnesses that happily accommodated delays. Only a small minority, a demanding handful, packed up their grudges in little boxes and came as soon as Effi was well to demand compensation. More pills, perhaps. Another test. Maybe the medication they were taken off that the doctor wouldn't give them, now she had to! Effi did not give in. The hagglers left her office, roaring their complaints and sometimes cursing Effi. Horrible words were uttered. Neither hisses nor utterances of "you should be ashamed of yourself" from the crowd could calm them. And Effi forgave, always. The curses were never mentioned at the next meeting. How did she forgive?

The old people from Grandpa Yosef's neighborhood could not come to see Effi. Sadly, the neighborhood had its own separate branch of the clinic. Only just over a mile away as the crow flies, but the distance of infinite Sick Fund bureaucracy. So they had to make do with *naches*, proud of Effi, whom they had known as a child, now with the most precious of gemstones in her hands: a prescription pad. Only one person in the neighborhood, Levertov of all people, somehow slipped through the fences of bureaucracy and got himself registered as a patient of Effi's. He came and sat down in her office. The world *does not change*. Effi prescribed Formacil, knowing he needed it. Levertov said "thank you" and sometimes wanted to tell her about Treblinka. He wished her well. "May you marry soon." He thanked her again and left.

I got married. Effi did not. From the beginning she took the path of multiple lovers, trying out men of all kinds. Almost every time we met she talked of someone new, predicting eternity for the new love, but completely aware that there was no eternity and that there was still a long list of men ahead. She was like a competitive eating candidate, preparing to eat a hundred and four crabs, two more than the current record (set by a Korean student). The rules were clear: every crab must weigh at least one pound after cooking. One ten-minute rest every hour, on the hour. Three hours at most. Water is allowed, with lemon. No alcohol. Someone set the rules and Effi obeyed. A long, observant attempt, whose chapters were conveyed to me in dry, embarrassed reports.

To transfer our relationship from childhood to adulthood, we sawed the connection between us in half so it could squeeze through. We assumed we could put it back together again on the other side. And indeed, here and there the halves came together. We remained wondrous, suspicious. The halves were in our hands, everything was intact, but the relationship did not connect. Something had gone wrong.

Time passed. Thunder slammed against the ground. The sounds of a drumbeat. My Yariv was born, fanning flames of *naches* in the family. An echo came from Netanya: Aunt Frieda's Rina gave birth to her first son. Then Miri, then Ronnie. Roots erupted into the air. Grandchildren, great-grandchildren. You could take pictures, put them in your wallet, pull them out when necessary and proudly present roots. Fertility came easily. Not sadly, not sorrowfully. Children and more children. How many more would you like?

The family was stirred up with births and deaths. We could no longer take the stagnation. Something was about to change. We had to choose a moment of flux, a worldwide event that would give us momentum and cancel out the years-without-occurrences.

We chose the Gulf War.

In August 1990 the Iraqi army invaded Kuwait, shocking the world and surprising both experts and laymen. The cracks continued to emerge until 1991, alliances formed, tempers raged. In January the war broke out, but by then we were completely different than we had been in August 1990.

*

We were the first to understand Iraq's intentions, to absorb their significance through the short moments of history.

In a game of Categories, the letter "K" was declared. Panic! We knew there were not enough countries beginning with K to go around! Years after we had disallowed Kurdistan because Iraq had stubbornly prevented the independence of the Kurdish region, forcing us to rely on the same old Kenya, Korea and Kuwait over and over again, often resulting in a draw, suddenly "Kuwait" was gone too. The plot of the dictator from Baghdad, a malicious step impenetrable by all strategic experts, was revealed as clear as crystal on our Categories score sheets. Alongside his plot, the events also exposed an ancient scheme of Grandpa Yosef's. As if he had been waiting for the Iraqi tyrant to make his move so that he could comfortably complete a maneuver of his own, he stunned us by writing down "Kiribati" on Feiga's sheet. It was a tiny republic in the Pacific Ocean. Disputes arose, the old Brawer atlas was summoned, and evidence presented itself on page sixty-five. How had it gotten away all these years? Grandpa Yosef hurried to Feiga's room to report to the island princess how polished her game was this evening, how sweet her victory.

After a few months the war itself broke out. Rockets fell. Perhaps Saddam Hussein was after more than annihilating the letter K. But even before the rockets, the main events had already occurred in the family. An era of traveling had begun. Effi decided to take advantage of a school vacation to go to Japan. In her room she piled up guidebooks, descriptions, recommendations. She was too lazy to read them, demanding instead that I give a brief, efficient summary—after all, I had read all the encyclopedias. I started my attempt, but after a moment she cut me off in astonishment. "Wait a minute, Japan is an island?" Fearful, perhaps she wouldn't go after all. "An island? Tokyo is in the ocean?"

We took a trip with Dad to trace our roots in Poland, to see it all. Ronnie came back and then squeezed in a trip to the US. Effi finally set off for Japan. A frenetic pace took hold of the family. Something had decided to iron out the creases and reorganize things. We were all troubled. Business. Pleasure. Roots. Constant travel. Ostensibly independent trips—what did Japan have to do with Poland? But from above, something larger was waiting to rip out everything and dismantle it. Even the backdrops would be torn apart, destroyed (just in case we thought we might come back one day, everything was demolished).

First, Feiga died. Just like that. The impossible occurred without a second thought. One morning a trembling phone call came from Grandpa Yosef. Then a momentary dizziness. With him. At the graveside. With neighbors. At home at the *shiva*. We allowed him to mourn. Even Moshe improvised a quiet *shiva*. People went into Feiga's room to believe. Her death, which had occurred opposite the surprised branches of the poinciana, was not yet apparent. The blankets did not look as if they had given up their place. There was still an odor of medication in the air. On the windowsill, the same delicately peeling old paint. The same thin branch staring inside. The impression of death was delayed.

Effi was in Japan. I had to locate her. She cried a lot. I had not realized how attached she was to Feiga. She was incomprehensible. She wanted to come home right away, but something went wrong, constraints beyond her control. When the *shiva* was over, I received postcards she had slipped one by one into a Japanese mailbox. She wrote how much she loved Grandpa Yosef, how everything was different now, how impossible it was. How could she have missed the funeral? I tried to locate her so I could cheer her up with the existence of Grandpa Yosef and replace him with Feiga, but in the meantime she had traveled home, just in time for Moshe's death.

Moshe died.

It happened suddenly, not even as a result of one of his diseases.

Heart failure. Another infliction he had been cursed with and which had hidden among his disasters, taking a backseat to the dramatic lead roles of retardation, brain damage, autism, adenopathy. A modest ghostly infliction, an unassuming stagehand to the great dramaturgy of Moshe's life, turning up all at once to lower the curtain.

We could not ignore the proximity of the events. Moshe's death followed Feiga's as if a lifeline that had been obscured in the shadow of Grandpa Yosef's grace had suddenly erupted, proving its vital existence only in its absence. Moshe had survived, ostensibly, with the support of Grandpa Lolek and Brandy and ourselves. But Feiga's death had pierced the gentle artery of his will to live.

A slow, merciful wave enveloped the house. Mourners gathered from the edges of the neighborhood, from the city, taking routes usually traversed by Grandpa Yosef in the opposite direction. Even those who had not come to the house for Feiga's death uprooted themselves and came this time. Adella Greuner, fragrant and despondent. Itcha Dinitz, unsure if it was the right thing to do. Mr. Bergman, restrained and heavy, sat and spoke in Polish about the sun rays.

We never noticed the disappearance of Brandy. On the day Moshe died she wailed like a wolf, and at some point during the *shiva* Grandpa Yosef asked if we had fed her.

Feiga was gone. Moshe was gone. Brandy was gone. *The world does change.*

During that *shiva* Grandpa Yosef conducted himself silently, with internal precision. He sat small and covered in his corner, addressing us only seldomly, to clarify confusing customs. "Now we need a *minyan* for the evening prayer." "Tomorrow is Shabbat, no *shiva* tomorrow." A lone sailor, leading himself on without us, we could not even pick up an oar to help him. At the end of the *shiva* he rose, his skin yellowing, his eyes bloodshot, and with a decisiveness that could have only emerged from focused contemplation, he announced that he intended to sail to the Caribbean islands.

The family was taken aback. The Caribbean? Haiti, Guadeloupe, Tobago, Martinique?

The Caribbean.

Why?

That question was not asked. And there was no answer.

We waited for the peculiar idea to pass, along with the sorrow and the layers of shock. This unwise plan would surely fade away as a mere fragment of thought that had offered him some consolation. It was an incomprehensible notion and would soon be gone. But the days went on and Grandpa Yosef went about his business, keeping secrets, making preparations.

The Caribbean?

Events proceeded at a surprising pace, and at the end of 1990 Grandpa Yosef took off in the estimated direction of Bermuda. He was a tourist with maps and a suitcase.

1991: Grandpa Yosef's Travels

T hey eat lots of coconut and pork here," his first postcard announced. He sounded disappointed, as if he had expected to find an observant congregation on the Caribbean islands. But his second postcard focused on the "amazing dark-skinned ladies," whose supple gait made a great impression on the wise scholar. On the front of the postcard, to our regret, were only a modestly-topped palm tree and a stretch of blue ocean. A disgruntled Grandpa Lolek suggested sending a quick telegram demanding to see the glistening dark buttocks with our very own eyes. We ignored him and continued to peruse the postcard, on which Grandpa Yosef detailed his impressions of a cave he had toured and his pending voyage to an abandoned island (a pirate stronghold from the good old days), but Grandpa Lolek would not let go. Finally, he confessed: his dancer, Joyce, was black. We were amazed. We quickly had to repaint a reel of memories in Joyce's new color and add the necessary features, somewhat awkwardly, to each imaginary scene. Even the color of the umbrellas with which she had danced for Grandpa Lolek on the rainy dock at Portsmouth had to be revised.

"Did you leave out any other details?" we asked firmly. We

meant to straighten out the memories once and for all. These recollections were the fruit of so many stories, and suddenly, in the midst of a postcard from Grandpa Yosef—the first to lose his mind—now this grandpa was going mad too. We waited.

"She had a little yellow parasol. She carried it rain or shine."

We were a little thrown off by the combination of rainy England and yellow parasols. How did the dance fit in? And what was the difference between an umbrella and a parasol? Like weary painters, we were forced to refinish our imaginations with the right colors. Joyce the dancer grew darker and more beautiful. The trivial objects that surrounded her also took on the appropriate characteristics (we threw in scarves, high-heels, purses). The exhausting engagement in color and details almost caused us to overlook the true hero of the evening, the supposedly unruly Grandpa Yosef. We still did not understand his fascination with the Caribbean, nor how these islands of palm trees had found themselves caught up in a life of prayer shawls, chopped liver and pickled herring with onion. At the edge of his postcard we identified a grease stain that demanded rigorous investigation. Was it possible that Grandpa Yosef was secretly committing transgressions over there? Ultimately, the source of the stain was officially determined to be okra, or possibly coconut. Case closed.

In his third postcard he claimed to have discovered fruits whose existence he had not previously imagined. For the first time in his life he was eating without knowing the names of the foods. He also expressed his astonishment at the color of the ocean, the peoples' eyes, the way night-time appeared. He wrote that as far as the purpose of his travels was concerned, he was not getting much closer, but the bottom line was that he did not find himself sensing any regret. We remained puzzled by all the mysteriousness—what was he up to there?

It was a good thing the Gulf War broke out, replete with Scud missiles, plastic sheeting, and gas masks. Grandpa Yosef's postcards tumbled into our post boxes as if from a faraway world, filled with coconuts and treasure chests and his increasingly worried enquiries as to what was happening over here. On a series of grease-stained postcards, he attempted to commiserate with our missile anxieties. Even years later, when the synagogue congregation reminisced about the Gulf War days, Grandpa Yosef would whisper apologetically, "And there I was in the Caribbean…" He was never sure how to utter this truth, especially in front of guests who had come to spend the Shabbat with relatives. They looked at him in astonishment—the Caribbean?

And indeed, he tried to come home early due to the Gulf War, so he could worry with us. He informed us of his intentions and was rebuked—he should stay there and complete his trip. We told him to stay where he was and agreed to follow his instructions regarding what to do with his needy neighbors during these stressful days, for as long as he was gone. The instructions were precise, like those for tending to plants. The postcards specified what to watch for with Mr. Bergman and what to do if Mr. Pepperman turned up again with old papers from the Municipality. The names of Mr. Cogen, Ella Pruchter and Itcha Dinitz reached us like the coconuts in the *Tarbut* encyclopedia, traveling the seas in their tough shells, finding islands to wash up on and take seed. Each postcard was signed by the palm tree himself, Grandpa Yosef, always adding a tail-end of questioning—Perhaps he should come home early after all? He did not imagine the extent to which his early return would have gotten us into trouble. Because in his empty apartment, in the meantime, a tenant had been installed. A tourist.

A short while after Grandpa Yosef's departure for the Caribbean, I received a phone call from Professor Shiloni, his academic advisor. He informed me that Dr. Hans Oderman, a research colleague from Frankfurt University, was arriving on the next El Al flight to make his way to the University of Haifa, where he would spend time on a research grant.

And the problem?

"Well, we agreed that he would be a guest in my home, but all of a sudden my in-laws from New York have turned up. They heard about Saddam Hussein's threats and came to show solidarity, the nuts, instead of inviting me to their place. And now this young man, Dr. Oderman, tells us he's decided not to cancel. He too believes that now is the time to support the people of Israel. So I thought that if Yosef's apartment was empty, perhaps, just until I find something better, we could put him there. Only temporarily, until we come up with something. Just until the first missile lands here, and then all the friends of Israel will be gone in a flash."

"He's German?"

Embarrassment in Professor Shiloni's voice. "Yes…. Is that a problem?"

"No, no, of course not."

The elderly residents in Grandpa Yosef's neighborhood were trying on gas masks, and I would be housing a German in 8-B Katznelson.

I didn't have to pick him up at the airport. Someone else brought Dr. Hans Oderman of Frankfurt to the faculty lounge at the University of Haifa, where we were introduced. Six-foot-three-sapphire-blue-eyes-golden-locks shook my hand.

"Nice to meet you."

A limp handshake.

I politely carried his luggage and led him to my car. A simple drive. No conversation. We drove down the Carmel hillside through Neveh Sha'anan and round the bends that hug the mountain. I looked at him as he sat erect and glanced at the cascading landscape. He stared at the lights, the intersections, the industrial zone in the valley below us. Our eyes met briefly. His were islands of steel. I looked at his hands resting firmly in his lap over the safety belt. Six-foot-three-inches of neatly divided parts. We passed by traffic lights, junctions, and the colorful commercial area. Heavy industry sprawled on both sides. Fences, chimneys, guard towers. The objects stood out against the landscape, distant deviations that looked as if they were running toward the road, waving, urgently introducing themselves. I drove among barbed wire and guard huts with a Nazi poster child sitting beside me.

The industrial stench provoked a look of discomfort on Hans Oderman's face. He wondered where he was being taken to. Breaking out of his polite silence, he tried a few lines. But the conversation did not progress much. Hans Oderman sensed the reservation in my voice and wondered whether everything was all right. He began to apologize even before I could reply. He was afraid something had been imposed upon me and asked again if everything was all right. He could always find a hotel room, he said.

"Everything is all right."

But then I took advantage of an uneventful stop light near Volkan Intersection:

"I just want you to know that, personally, I have a bit of a problem with Germans. That my parents' families were obliterated in the Holocaust. That I won't buy German appliances. That I fought with my wife because she bought a German washing machine. That I won't drive a Volkswagen because I haven't forgotten that in the war they employed Jews as slave laborers at vw factories. That all the cars you see on our roads, including lots of vws, are to my mind a desecration of the honor of those who died in slavery. That even so, I have nothing against you personally."

Silence. The light turned to green. We were saved.

As we approached Kiryat Haim, trees and residential buildings began to appear around the intersections. I said, "It will be a bit of a schlep for you to get to campus every day."

Hans Oderman nodded.

We turned onto the road leading to Grandpa Yosef's neighborhood. We passed by parks full of mothers and children, and I said, "If you need something, anything, just call us."

He nodded. He looked at a group of golden-haired children trying to take over a see-saw from a stubborn little girl, and possibly remembered his home. In Frankfurt.

I told him that if he called because he needed something and there was no one home, he could always call my parents or leave a message.

He nodded.

We reached the edge of the neighborhood, marked with a cypress tree at the beginning of Katznelson Street. I stopped there. When we got out of the car I had an idea. I took the suitcases out of the car and walked away, to make it clear that this time he was carrying them all by himself. I hoped the three suitcases would make him look slightly hunched, just a little ridiculous. So he wouldn't appear before the elderly neighbors in his full glory. Why shouldn't *they* carry things for once? I saw no curtains pulled back but I knew they were watching. Eyes at every window. They were experts at it.

Hans Oderman carried his suitcases with a straight back. He walked slowly, erect, elegant. Too elegant, to my mind. He walked down Katznelson just ahead of me, without slowing down, without even glancing at me to enquire which house to go to. I looked at his steps as he strolled down Katznelson as if it were his own street, and from beyond the windows, from behind the blinds—they saw.

They saw Hauptsturmführer Amon Goeth, commandant of Plaszow camp.

They saw Gruppenführer Jürgen Stroop, liquidator of the Warsaw ghetto.

They saw Hauptsturmführer Fritz Suhren, commandant of Ravensbrück camp.

They saw Hauptsturmführer Josef Kramer, commandant of Bergen-Belsen camp.

They saw Obersturmbannführer Rudolf Höss, commandant of Auschwitz.

They saw Hauptsturmführer Hans Bothmann, commandant of the Chelmno death camp, liquidator of the Lodz ghetto.

Marching in front of me. Come to stay. Soon he would put his suitcases down in Grandpa Yosef's home, place his ironed clothes on the shelves in the closet, hang his suits. Make himself a first cup of tea. Him. Here.

But when we reached Grandpa Yosef's apartment we found Effi standing in the doorway, eating a carrot. It turned out she had been settled in at Grandpa Yosef's for two days now, and was painting the apartment. She looked at Hans.

"Oy, the Nazi creature!" she said. She wore a long tank-top and nothing else.

"Effi, what are you doing here?"

"Look at you! You've really brought a Nazi," she continued, examining Hans, offering him a carrot and pulling him into the apartment as if introductions had been made and all that was left was to divvy up Grandpa Yosef's apartment.

174

"Effi, what are you doing here?" I chased after her, stepping over the plastic tarps she had spread throughout the apartment. "Effi, what are you doing here?"

She turned to me and promised, "Adolf and I will get along just fine."

And that's when I began to feel bad—he had suffered enough cruelty.

"His name is Hans," I said to Effi, but you could tell he had picked up on the 'Adolf.' With one awkward wave of the hand he played out the entire requisite sequence—expressed shock, indicated that he understood the humor and knew that it was imposed by his persona, voiced his objection nonetheless, then downplayed it—he would give in if he had to.

"He can stay here," Effi said generously, "we'll be two doctors in one apartment."

It seemed to me that she already had her eye on him. Him, Dr. Hans Oderman, six-foot-three-sapphire-blue-eyes-golden-locks. She led him to Feiga's room and opened the windows to banish death, if there was any still remaining. She helped him lay his clothes out on the empty shelves (in the midst of the *shiva* Feiga's clothes had been donated to an old age home; Grandpa Yosef's charity campaigns never rested for a moment). As her hands took control of Hans's property, with her face buried in the closet, she explained that her apartment lease was almost up, it was close to her work here, and the apartment needed to be fixed up a little before Grandpa Yosef got back.

A short while later we sat drinking tea at Grandpa Yosef's wooden table. We talked. We asked Dr. Hans Oderman about his plans, his intentions, his family, the city of Frankfurt. We generously bypassed questions about things that should not be discussed, but tried to extract an admission of guilt—a happy childhood, grandmas and grandpas, the whole thing. Hans Oderman pleaded not guilty: he never knew his grandparents on either side. Things were not that easy for him either. His father had been orphaned as a child.

And what did he think about Israel?

We demanded love. Not just for us but for the elderly people who lived here, who would see him as he left the apartment every day, walked through the yard and down Katznelson. We could not imagine how easy it would be for Hans to integrate into the life of the neighborhood. Within a few days we would find that he had already been enlisted to perform the requisite tasks, helping the old people choose a room to seal off, measuring sheets of plastic as they buttressed themselves inside in preparation for another battle. (They grit their teeth, their elderly fingers caught up in masking tape, their faces wearing determined expressions—they would survive.)

During the first days of his stay we plodded around behind him responsibly, checking up—Effi in her capacity as roommate, and myself as liaison with Professor Shiloni. I felt obliged to report to him should anything occur, some fatal mistake or a case for the authorities to handle. We did not need to report his lingering visits at Sammy's vegetable shop. Nor the cups of tea at Mrs. Rudin's. We gradually eased up our supervision. We came to check up, to see how the neighborhood was getting along with Dr. Hans Oderman, and found him nicely assimilated. Sipping tea with Mrs. Rudin. Eating Mrs. Tsanz's *kugel*. Chatting with Sammy about the crisis in German soccer, complaining about the price of tomatoes. He was doing well. He even had an encounter with Hirsch. Later, he asked for explanations. What was he yelling? Why did he yell? And finally we had an opportunity to explain this neighborhood, these people, the hidden significance of what occurred here.

We carefully monitored his opinions and actions. On his free days, we learned, he liked to go to Jerusalem, to Lake Kinneret, or to the Galilee. He also went to Masada, the Yad Vashem Holocaust museum, and the Ghetto Fighters' Kibbutz. Our courteous offers were met with dismissal: Hans Oderman preferred to take the bus, so he could meet people. He came back from his travels full of impressions. He connected easily with people and learned to understand the different pieces of Israeli existence. He sat with us trying to fill in the gaps in his knowledge. Were Jews of Bulgarian origin considered Sephardic? What was the difference between a cooperative moshav and a regular moshav? Where exactly had the Cochin Jews come from?

He also found the beach, and he took slow walks there with

his lustrous Atlas-like body, regally scanning the seashell-clutching women who stared at him and engaged him in conversation. He made no effort to avoid the streets of Haifa, especially the Carmel, amazed at the mottled mass of Eastern, Western, Southern and Northern notes. Women and young girls strolled up and down the streets of the Carmel—a miracle ignoring its own importance, coming and going from the houses, the stores, the cafés.

It sometimes seemed that an impenetrable contemplation flickered in his mind, something that might have taken on the shape of a thought—You mean these were the kinds of people they wanted to annihilate in the gas chambers? But the thought did not ripen. It remained in its crude form, hovering, bothering every other thought like a troublesome grain.

People asked us what he was doing at the university.

"Hans is completing a historical study on the subject of orphanhood," I replied.

Meaning?

"Meaning, how they treated orphans in different cultures and through the prism of history."

("Very useful," Effi pointed out.)

They wanted to know if he himself was an orphan.

I answered, "No."

Anat said, "He looks a bit like an orphan." (Finding even in Dr. Hans Oderman, six-foot-three-sapphire-blue-eyes-golden-locks, the orphan in need of help. Anat.)

We slowly came to understand his personality. Hans Oderman from Germany was an expert at awkwardness. Like a mouse trained to find cheese, praised every time he makes it through a maze, so was Hans, finding in every situation the way to be embarrassed, to hesitate, to grope his way out with cautious words. Six-foot-three-sapphire-blue-eyes-golden-locks was only a camouflage.

Towards the end of January the war came true. Missiles started falling. Worried, we scurried around on Hans's behalf, trying to get him a gas mask. He didn't want one. It wasn't necessary, he believed. And in general, he had a tough time with masks and found it difficult to breathe with them because of respiratory problems. In between the air-raid sirens he cared for the sealed rooms, replacing plastic tarps and fixing strips of tape that had fallen away here and there.

Effi's liked to look me over and say, "You see, there are good Germans."

I never said there weren't. There were back then too. Dad told me about German soldiers who cried when they saw a pile of dead children in the Bochnia ghetto. Who said there weren't any good Germans? But within the current admixture of euphemisms—New Germany, the New Germans, Democratic Germany—hides the thing that allowed the criminals to keep on living, the thing that granted sweeping clemencies, gave them back their status, let them raise sweet grandchildren—Hans and Peter and Jorgen, who sometimes came to plant trees here in the Land of Israel. I despise those unwilling to confess to their crimes, the banks that traded in gold teeth, the factories that killed prisoners through slave labor, anyone who allowed these institutions to continue being part of the nation, to function under the patronage of national denial. I despise the hands raised in the Bundestag on May 8th 1960—only fifteen years after the war had ended—and voted to allow the expiration of the statute of limitation for minor crimes such as manslaughter, wrongful injury resulting in death, and denial of freedom resulting in death. I despise those hands, a democratic majority. But who ever said there weren't any good Germans?

We invited Hans over to our place on weekends. As we sat around waiting for air-raid sirens, we grew more friendly. We slowly roamed through different conversation topics. First, orphanhood. What exactly was he researching? Then, the war. Germany. The Holocaust.

Hans Oderman took part in the conversations reluctantly. His scripted role was that of the culprit, and he took it upon himself without protest. We set him free in the swampy reeds of our intentions, a jet-black wolf for us to target and hit. But Hans Oderman sat frozen like a frightened duck. His function was to stand before us, accused. But we could not draw the lines that would differentiate us from him.

"What did your father do during the war?"

"My father? He was only born during the war."

"And his father?"

"He was a soldier, killed on the Russian front near Leningrad."

"And your mother's family?"

"They were soldiers. One was a pilot. And there were two dissidents, one was imprisoned in Dachau for five years."

But there was an uncle who belonged to the SS, he remembered, sheathing himself with the blanket of culpability after all.

Even without words (after all, many of the worst Nazis found these sorts of biographical responses for themselves), there was in him a sort of innocence. Guilt did not stick to him. A hidden line of defense came together from his looks, his embarrassment, his explanations. He was exonerated by the words we sensed hiding within his thoughts. He did not say everything, and what he left out was not damning—on the contrary, it might even have connected us to him. A riddle.

We introduced Hans to the family so he could wriggle under the light of their looks for a while. If he survived that, we would know he was innocent.

The family was enchanted by Hans's politeness. Grandpa Lolek interrogated him and observed, "I killed a lot like him."

The days went by and the Gulf War began to die out. Everyone was used to Dr. Hans Oderman, no longer excited by the appearance of this man who seemed to have been drawn from a Nazi leader's dream. And then suddenly, in the midst of the routine days, without warning, Grandpa Yosef was back. He had been struck by a mysterious virus, courtesy of the Caribbean humidity, which had graced his pale yellow cheeks with a healthy flush and quickened his breath. He returned with a newly ardent and life-loving temperament and seemed agitated by the slow pace of routine events. He did not object to Hans Oderman's presence in the empty apartment, which was now full of dead people with whom Grandpa Yosef had a thing or two to sort out privately. He warmly hosted him in his home. In fact, he deepened the intensity of the German doctor's residence, cooking him food and washing his clothes, willfully and affectionately melting away Hans Oderman's intentions to move a little closer to campus—there wasn't even a bus route in this sleepy neighborhood.

In a sort of destruction of the sanctity of grief, in this house without Feiga and without Moshe, Grandpa Yosef and Hans organized a cooperative life for themselves. They cooked, cleaned and studied. They seemed thankful for each other's company. Grandpa Yosef enjoyed the refreshing proximity of scholarliness. After the heat of the Caribbean days, he happily breathed in the cool air of science. Hans was charmed by his host, easily won over by Grandpa Yosef's personality. He was especially happy to speak fluent German in the Holy Land. And he made the mistake of asking where Grandpa Yosef had acquired such fine German.

"I was in your land," Grandpa Yosef clarified. As if he had spent time in Germany to inspect some furniture.

They sat often at Grandpa Yosef's wooden table, talking about the problem Hans was working on at the university. Grandpa Yosef understood little, and was sorry that no miracle occurred, such as a brilliant idea that would come to him in a flash after one hearing. The Caribbean force still pulsed in him, and slow business irritated him.

Every evening, Hans Oderman came home from his studies and Grandpa Yosef from his do-gooding. They unloaded their daily baggage, two hunters laying their loot on the table. They talked, debated, argued. Our visits were not rejected, but were received somewhat indifferently. As if for our sake Grandpa Yosef was keeping up a demeanor appropriate for a man in mourning. We would come and find them walking around Katznelson together, in the parks, even the woods. They talked. Like two intellectual giants projecting their charms upon each other. They would stop for a moment to exchange an opinion and glance at one another. Two magicians, mutually awed, but each suspicious of the other's tricks, wondering what was the secret of the other's magic.

When Hans Oderman went back to Germany, the vivid impression he had made continued to accompany us in conversations, in thoughts, in meetings, until it became doubtful whether his physical presence could have added anything more. We felt as if he were with us. Phone calls also fostered the relationship. After one such conversation, we thought he had said his research was not done and that he would have to come back soon. We nibbled out of the air a feeling that such a promise had been made, and we nurtured it. (Effi tried to tempt him: "Come, come back. We have lots of wars here. Every decade or so there's a good orphan season.") We perceived Hans Oderman's appearance in our lives as having a greater function than what had been revealed thus far, and could not accept that his return to Germany had put an end to it all. With uncommon generosity, we agreed to wait for months, even years, until the true role of Hans Oderman would be revealed. Only Grandpa Yosef turned out to be a realist. He viewed the separation straightforwardly: Hans had left. But a sadness befell him. He cut down on his bike rides and even considered a moped or a car. With an increased sense of charity he fell on the patients he had neglected for weeks in favor of the Caribbean, and still we did not understand—what had he found in the islands?

But we did not ask. The Caribbean adventure was over. That was it, and it was best forgotten. Why would we go searching for something that would supposedly explain a connection between the mourning in Kiryat Haim and the coconut trees of Tobago? We offered him a trip to Jerusalem, he hadn't been to the holy city for years. We even suggested, somewhat anxiously, the reckless city of Eilat. Maybe there, in the Caribbean sphere, he would shake off the burning in his blood. But Grandpa Yosef rejected our offers and quickly accustomed himself to a life with new troubles. There were many needy people and no time to rest. He forged relationships with elderly people outside the neighborhood, and reconnected with an old love, the community of Belz Chassidim, where he found some good to do. He volunteered in the northern neighborhoods, where new immigrants began to look forward to his frequent visits. He was quick to commit to any affair, rushing to lend a shoulder.

It was clear that new powers had taken control of Grandpa Yosef. This was evidenced by the fact that one day, while he was being driven by a colleague to visit a mutual acquaintance who was sick, a policeman popped up and accused the driver of disobeying a stop sign. Grandpa Yosef was overtaken by a rebellious spirit.

Disobeying?

Failure to come to a complete stop with all four wheels behind the line?

The wheels, after all, are all on one axis. If one stops, they all stop. And Grandpa Yosef was prepared to testify that the front wheel had stopped. And if *it* had stopped, it stood to reason that its siblings had too.

The policemen, at first, was extremely patient, responding calmly to his elderly interlocutor. But Grandpa Yosef entered into Talmudic debates and arguments, later telling us how he struck down the policeman's claims one after the other until victory. The policeman grew angry and began to make threats. Grandpa Yosef fumed as well. Things were fast approaching the most dreaded outcome. Grandpa Yosef was not hauled off to jail, but he came close. He gave the policeman quite an argument, and earned a ticket to show for it.

He dug through his pockets and pulled out the official confirmation for us, then looked at the report covered in Hebrew letters. "*Nu*, at least it's one of our own policemen." And he breathed a breath of calmness, inhaling the flavor of a Hebrew ticket, in Hebrew characters, from "one of our own" policemen. Even the argument seemed to take on a renewed form in his thoughts—softer, entirely conducted in the language of Eliezer Ben-Yehuda, inventor of the modern Hebrew language.

We hoped the pale light and the tart aromas of cooking from the neighborhood windows would quiet his blood. But in the Turkish market Grandpa Yosef found curry powder, and from Sammy of the vegetables he demanded mango, fresh coconut and ginger. He replaced his tea with strong coffee. Then he began researching names—Arabica, Robusta, Segafredo, Jamaican Blue Mountain.

At times it seemed as if the new, temporary persona would soon settle down and put forth roots. Grandpa Yosef scurried around even when he had no reason to. He could not find tranquility in his armchair, and changed outfits a few times a day. At some point, a great secret almost escaped him: since his return, the Gemara had struck him as too slow, too lingering. How long could one debate a *seah* of carobs? And so instead of studying Gemara pages, he sometimes took off to the beach—the actual beach. Red sunsets. Beautiful young women, excuse-me-sir-what-time-is-it? And an oceanfront café where you could buy cocoa and fruit juices. The Caribbeanism within him radiated to the outside, pulling out his personality like a rabbit from a hat. But we gradually sensed that a great weight had sat itself down in Grandpa Yosef's garden, clarifying: things will be tough. There was no Feiga, no Moshe, no one to make an effort for.

Grandpa Lolek continued to visit. When the Vauxhall showed up the yard looked briefly as it had in days past. Hope glistened; perhaps Moshe's quick figure would emerge from the distance to wash off the nettlesome dust. Grandpa Lolek sat down for a cup of tea, his face respectable, and inspected the new reality. He missed Moshe and, more than Moshe, he missed the wondrous miracle that could flourish thanks to him. (There was something disrespectful about the way he missed him, like a magician who had lost his rabbit.) We were amazed to learn that it was he who had bought a triple burial plot for Grandpa Yosef and his two loves. He had gritted his teeth and financed the erection of two marble tombstones. For now, Grandpa Yosef had saved him a third. No need. Grandpa Lolek had no qualms about taking pride in this act of charitableness, recounting in great detail how he had acquired the triple plot against all odds, outdoing competitors. As if he had completed a winning row of three in a game of tic-tac-toe.

"They said, take two, this here and this another separate, they said is expensive here, no possible three because of wall. They said here is good plot, no possible three, one in middle is already taken. Not possible to cancel. Very expensive. Here in middle is already taken, there is others who want three together. That's it. Must give up. Then suddenly, yes! On the side, in shade. A good plot! They already jumped on it, to take it. From between teeth I took it away, bam! There is nothing which that money cannot do."

And yet it was with him, of all people, one fine day, that the incident occurred.

We were drinking tea (strong "Eva" coffee for Grandpa Yosef), and as on every day, Grandpa Lolek waved his tea bag, hanging it from the edge of a cake-fork by its string. *Selektion*. When he held the bag up close to Grandpa Yosef's face, teasing him in his customary way, Grandpa Yosef suddenly snatched the bag away. He held it in his hand and contemplated whether to throw it in Grandpa Lolek's face or do something else. But in the end he just crushed it in his fist. Dark brown rivets of tea trickled from his hand to the table as Grandpa Yosef squeezed and squeezed.

All his life Grandpa Yosef had held back, exercising restraint for the sake of the little miracle that was Moshe. We could actually sense the word, RESTRAINT, appearing on his face, and further inside. But now it all fell apart. There was no Moshe. No Feiga. No one to make an effort for. With the tea bag in his hand, Grandpa Yosef hurried to the kitchen, where he traded his anger for some trivial business and then returned to us slightly calmer.

Grandpa Lolek, in a rare outburst of sensitivity to what was occurring, quickly found a reason to leave.

Grandpa Yosef was left alone, not only on that day. There began a period of isolationism. He had finally found the strength to declare himself a mourner with rights. He fenced himself off and avoided the family. He made us feel punished, unworthy. We tried. We came up to the foot of the cliff of righteousness, and there we broke down, wretched, spilling over with shortcomings.

Grandpa Yosef taught us a chapter in remorse. He did not have to use many looks or words, he trusted that we would sense the nuanced emotions, the hidden meanings of his gestures of withdrawal. But with Grandpa Lolek it was simple and determined. As if to pay him back for many seconds, many hours, for the six million whom Grandpa Lolek had continuously humiliated without anyone doing anything about it. Instead of the whole six million, *they* usually focused their grief on one or two people, becoming their voice.

Grandpa Lolek's response was surprising. It would seem that he could have avoided Grandpa Yosef's presence—what was bringing them together? But instead he repeatedly asked for Grandpa Yosef's forgiveness, insistently, innocently, without complaint. He admitted that he had behaved badly. And he was prepared to apologize, to atone. We could see that he cared. Delegations were sent. Grandpa Yosef welcomed the guests with his usual humbleness, taking his doughy cakes out of the oven, serving herring and home-made pickles. But despite the normal hospitality, in the matter of Grandpa Lolek he would not budge. His face hardening, his temples sprouted veins as he announced that he was unwilling to make up. "May he go to hell and go in peace," he blessed the banished relative.

We kept trying. Our self-declared role as mediators allowed us to feel objective, outside the fan of Grandpa Yosef's anger. We were merely the organizers of a transaction, not a party to the affair. A number of times the reconciliation was about to come to fruition. The two were already positioned on either side of the bridge, the exchange ceremony about to begin, when suddenly Grandpa Yosef would brush off the agreement—he would never forgive, never! We tried to persuade him. Tried to demand explanations. Grandpa Yosef extricated himself from us. Trembling. He wagged his finger, mumbled, grumbled, rubbed one fist against the other. His temples lit up in rage. Words tried to escape. Commotions. Little crackles in the pipe works. Sweat glistening on his forehead.

We were amazed. This was not the Grandpa Yosef we knew. This was not the Grandpa Yosef he himself knew from looking in the mirror. And so we summoned time to come and heal. We invited the months to pass by, to place cold compresses on his face. We sensed that Grandpa Yosef did not wish to alienate the Caribbean-ism in which he was slowly coming to know himself, his condition, his widowerhood. He fumbled alongside a dark wall, finding only a grieving father and no one to make the effort for. No one at all. He was preparing for a great battle, a desert front: life ahead without Feiga, without Moshe. With a burning silence he shed colorful layers, rainbow-colored feathers, war paint. He shrunk down to the right size, a life of austerity around the darkness of routine and family events. Only towards Grandpa Lolek did his resentment maintain its tropical nature, devouring our attempts to alleviate, to lighten, to conciliate.

Grandpa Lolek stopped relying on us and tried a few of his own reconciliation methods. He failed. He tried again, and failed again. Then he made up his mind that he had no choice. As an emergency ploy, like a pilot abandoning his plane, he produced his final attempt:

a cancerous tumor in his head. He may have six months left to live. In the meantime, tests were to be run.

After Grandpa Lolek lost consciousness on the steps outside his house and was rushed to the hospital, the harsh prognosis was pronounced: the growth was cancerous, his chances slim. Later, a more moderate possibility emerged. There might even be full recovery. We sat there, Grandpa Yosef and I, on a little bench in Rambam Hospital, waiting for a doctor, for solid information. Anxiety took hold of Grandpa Yosef's face, somehow looking more natural than the Caribbean vigor.

Effi arrived, alarmed. "What happened? He lost consciousness? On the front steps?'

She pushed open closed doors and talked with doctors. Grandpa Lolek suddenly became the most urgent case there, although he himself was by then lying calmly on a clean bed, his blue eyes shut, tranquility in his bones. After an hour Effi calmed down too. She sat down tiredly on the bench with us and became a worried relative once again. No more being a doctor.

Grandpa Yosef was curious, still clinging to her in her role as a doctor. "What does it mean that he passed out like that?"

"Lots of things. It could be lots of things."

"But to pass out? All of a sudden, in the middle of the day?"

"That was so he wouldn't have to make the call to the hospital, so someone else would pay for the call, that's why," Effi said, completely restored.

"My Feiga never passed out. It was hard for her, but she always kept her eyes open." Already making comparisons between the new patient and his patient. (Feiga won. Her refreshing morbidity was inimitable.)

We organized shifts when Grandpa Lolek woke up and wanted to know what the fuss was about, when he could leave, and whether the Sick Fund would cover his expenses. The doctors told him he had suffered "a kind of stroke." There seemed to be something pressing on his brain, a tumor—no, not cancerous, it could be lots of things. They reassured him that the Sick Fund would likely cover all the treatments. For now they would leave him under observation. They needed to do some X-rays. And a CT. They left me with him while the family went to get some sleep and organize things.

We waited for the CT. Grandpa Lolek, from one moment to the next, grew stronger. He demanded food, cigarettes. He tried to get out of bed, embarrassed—how could a hero of Anders' Army be lying on a stretcher bed in a hospital? By the time they were ready for the CT, he had worn me out with his plethora of demands, opinions, schemes (three escape attempts in four hours, one grab for a meal in the closed kitchen). Grandpa Lolek flew into a rage when they would not let me in the CT room. I whispered to the nurse, "I'll just go in with him and come straight out." We went in. Grandpa Lolek was very alert, waving a stick he had gotten hold of the devil knows where. He held it close to him, giving the impression that the stick was an old friend and no one could possibly take away this old man's support. He also used the stick to rap on the side of the CT machine and wink at me inexplicably, a wink I suspected was related to the tumor in his brain. He rapped impatiently on the machine, again and again, as the nurses grew angry. Finally I saw it. A little label on the side of the machine read, "Donated by the Society for the War on Cancer." Grandpa Lolek was clarifying that for this machine, he had not given a penny. I went out and sat on the bench while inside the CT machine scanned Grandpa Lolek for free.

After half an hour a commotion broke out in the room. The closed space into which Grandpa Lolek had been slid like a cake in an oven had a negative affect on the old warrior. He lost consciousness. The doctors, alarmed, rushed him to the treatment room. For long hours, it turned out, Grandpa Lolek fought for his life. A kind of sudden collapse. Not something the CT was supposed to cause, it was a completely routine test. But still, tubes were inserted into his nose and body while the doctors tried to save him. In the morning his condition was stable but he lay in bed unconscious. The family came. Even Atalia and Grandpa Hainek. They were amazed to hear about the overnight crisis. Why hadn't I called anyone? How could there be such a sudden deterioration?

Everyone thought of Uncle Pessl. Uncle Pessl had been a robust man whose eighty-five years were apparent only in his Austro-

Hungarian opinions. We had always admired him, despite his dim-wittedness, because he was a partisan and had strangled five Nazis to death with his bare hands, and even when anti-Semitic peasants had turned him in he had gone on to survive the camps and even the death march from Gross-Rosen. Since then, he always walked upright, elegantly. Always with few words and a bow tie. Last Sukkot he was walking through the shopping center and fell down. People quickly helped him up; he only had a slight bruise on his knee. But since then, Uncle Pessl had not recovered. Now he was in a nursing home and wanted to die.

One after the other we went into Grandpa Lolek's room and examined the silent figure lying quietly in bed. We were filled with thoughts and worries. Anat came and sent me home. In the evening we changed shifts. When my shift began, I was amazed to find Grandpa Yosef sitting at the bedside of excommunicated Grandpa Lolek as if there was no more natural a feature than him in the hospital landscape.

We sat on either side of the bed in a small room of which Grandpa Lolek was the sole inhabitant. To the west was a pleasant window, where Grandpa Yosef stood and attempted the afternoon *mincha* prayer. His short figure covered half the window. A Caribbean sun set over the ocean, winking with its final strength, trying to stir up Grandpa Yosef's new personality. Its efforts were in vain. He was here, a praying Jew, come to care for a needy patient, to do good, to give support in times of trouble.

When he finished praying we talked about this and that. Our eyes avoided Grandpa Lolek's figure, as it was still unclear whether the ban had been lifted, the excommunication called off. We talked about Yariv, about Anat, about the weather. We shared our astonishment at winter's failure to arrive. It was almost November, the days were getting cool, the nights still cooler, but it had yet to rain. Everyone knew the rain would come, but for now there was a drought. Between our sentences lay Grandpa Lolek. My presence seemed natural. And Grandpa Yosef also blended into the landscape of unsurprising elements—the curtain, the water pitcher, the little sink. Between us, slightly more out of place, lay Grandpa Lolek.

His eyes were closed, but his right one was open a slit, just to make sure the world remembered that he always said, "People have to die of something." He would not close his eyes until the world admitted that he did, indeed, say that. He had lived with that one opinion and would die with it. In fact, we should bury him with that victorious belief, like a Pharaoh entombed with his jewels so they can serve him on his eternal journey. We could leave his suits outside the grave, as well as his decorations, his certificates, the promissory notes and the papers for the land near Gedera—a good piece of land, one day its value will increase—but his opinions would be placed beside his body.

Grandpa Yosef broke down first and acknowledged Grandpa Lolek's presence. He pointed to the silent man and tried to rationalize him. "*Nu*, after all, one cannot forget. Jews in the war went like lambs to the slaughter, exterminated in the gas chambers, and this man here fought heroically. I heard stories about him from people who were there. A true lionheart. And me, with all my wanderings, all the pain and suffering, perhaps it would have been better if I had been like him."

Fresh envy in Grandpa Yosef's eyes. His look roamed worriedly over the still body, which somehow did not appear helpless. Grandpa Lolek was silent on his bed, stiff and still, like a Viking set adrift by his friends for one last voyage. The glory still enveloped him. It was hard to pity a body so taut—it seemed at any moment this Viking might sit up and smoke a cigarette. But for now he was afloat on the current, summing up his life with satisfaction, eyes shut. If not for the tiny slit in his right eye, which turned to a tremor like a wink, his image would have been perfect. The slight wink tarnished the glory. Grandpa Lolek was alive and planned to return.

Grandpa Yosef prepared for his defense. "Believe me, in the camps and the ghettos I also saw heroism." His voice strengthened. "Individuals sacrificed themselves. Lone soldiers, without uniforms or orders. At the moment of truth they flung themselves into death. And who will tell their stories?"

His question lingers in the air.

Who will tell their stories?

Grandpa Yosef stands up. He thinks he saw some "Swiss coffee" in the vending machine at the end of the hallway. That was what the label said. He has no idea what it means. Would I like a cup too?

No.

Grandpa Yosef goes off to examine the mystery of the vending machine label. By my side Grandpa Lolek lies tall and still, ready for inspection.

Who will tell their stories?

Grandpa Yosef managed to traverse our entire childhood without giving away too much. His attempts at concealment were successful. On the train, on the trips to Tel Aviv, the spring poured forth once a year. No more. Strategically, Grandpa Yosef had won. And now he cautions—who will tell their stories? As if now of all times, from within his victory, he is considering the possibility of taking a loss. Perhaps he wishes to offer himself up: He will tell, I will listen. We will sit on either side of Grandpa Lolek and whatever manages to cross over his bed will be mine. But I have my own reservations. It has been fifty years. Whatever has been told, has been told. I once pursued these stories. I poisoned Feiga with fake pills for them, and knelt before any old man willing to talk. Now we have grown up. We are the second-and-a-half generation to the Shoah, living our lives, and we have no need to adhere to the past anymore. Life flows vigorously enough. I still visit Attorney Perl and talk with him. With him the Shoah lives on, a climbing plant that never ceases to sprout new branches. But the conversations with him are the *malkosh*—the last rain of the season. The final rains of a great winter that has come and gone.

When we went to Poland with Dad to see his stories made real (the imaginary pictures solidified, we could even take photographs), we discovered that we did not need the Holocaust stories as much as we wanted the stories of his childhood—the happy one, the forgotten one, in Bochnia before the war. Dad showed us places, houses, abandoned gaps of time. He gestured with his hands—this happened here, that happened there.

The house he was born in.

The soccer field across the street.

The rooftop where he chased pigeons and almost fell off.

The chestnut trees whose fruit he used to gather with his friend Penek Lamensdorf (1930–1942), intending—based on a personal scientific hypothesis—to manufacture sophisticated glue.

There was a certain discord between our childhood stories and the reality we found. Things turned out to be the opposite of what they had seemed. Our memories stood gravely in attendance, prepared to defend the childhood stories in this complicated suit—after all, this conspiratorial reality was scandalous. But as we walked behind Dad through the ghetto, reality went through the stories with a fine-tooth comb, dismantling everything. Dad left nothing whole.

"Here, look," he pointed to a little path between pretty houses, trees and greenery. There, in front of our eyes, was the-lane-Dad-zig-zagged-through.

Since we were little kids, every year, Dad had told us about the day he and a friend had tried to hide their stamp collection. The Germans called out to them to stop. They ran away down the alley. Dad's father had instructed him to always run in zigzags when shots were being fired. (I think of Yariv. What will I teach him?) His friend ran in a straight line and was killed. It was a simple story for Dad. We became Old Enough for this story fairly early. Perhaps from his point of view it was a trivial tale—only one child was killed. But it was imprinted in our memories, and its visual traits gave us many versions of Dad running, dodging the bullets, the zigzag overcoming everything. We did not hesitate to dramatize the different versions in dusty lanes on dry, colorless, pitiful gravel. When we were older we learned to add shades of color we came to know in the alleys of Gaza, in Khan-Younis.

We gazed in wonder. Here, in front of us, was the zigzag lane. It was raining, everything was glimmering, giving off a fresh smell. And the ghetto. The ghetto where people had to line up on the sidewalks to die. A violent and pale ghetto, surrounded by walls, crowded, morbid. But we walked down narrow streets and stood in front of the house at 7 Leonarda Street, the mythological house from the stories. We looked at a little yard where a swing hung from a tree, and there were bushes, and flowers. At this moment it became clear that of everything in this journey to Poland, we would remain with only one accurate link between the childhood stories and the Polish reality: The famous window from which a cat willingly leapt sixty years ago after Dad gave it a bottle of ammonia to sniff. A thousand forms of this window had been imagined since Dad told the story, a thousand cats leaping, a thousand versions of its hesitant return home a few days later.

Dad pointed to the window. The thousand windows of our imagination murmured satisfactorily, pleased with the father who begat them.

In the meantime a small door had opened at 7 Leonarda. Mr. Petrovich, the resident, came out to see us. He was the son of the man who had owned the house at the time when its owners were thrown out so that Jews could be housed in it. The father, an educated Polish Christian, was sent to Auschwitz, one of the first from Bochnia. The son was friendly. He recalled how his father used to send him to the confiscated house to see how it was getting along. He even found an old document listing the Jewish tenants during the ghetto period. Someone had written everything down in neat handwriting, every single detail, seemingly assigning the utmost importance to the lives of these people, most of whom would soon be murdered in the gas chambers at Belzec.

Dad read the list and filled up with new memories. The Marsend family. Father, mother, little Etinka.

Who was little Etinka? Why didn't you ever tell us about her? Where is Attorney Perl on the list? Didn't he live with you at 7 Leonarda?

Dad struggled to explain, to bring order. The Perls were taken in the first *Aktion*. This was a list from the time between the first and second *Aktionen*. The Marsends came after the first *Aktion*. They were taken in the third *Aktion*.

And who is little Etinka?

Before I can finish the thought, Grandpa Yosef comes back carrying two cups of "Swiss coffee." One for me. Didn't I ask for one? He thought I did. Really? Won't I drink it? It's a pity to waste it.

Grandpa Lolek's eye gives its quick wink. The scent of wasted money disturbs his rest.

I take the coffee and sip unwillingly. It has no sugar—a double punishment.

Grandpa Yosef makes himself comfortable, surrendering to the flavor of the coffee. He looks up at me and says, "When it comes down to it, the ghetto was not completely bad." As if finishing up a story, or starting one, or interfering in Dad's. Unclear.

He sips from his cup. One hand rests on the edge of Grandpa Lolek's bed.

"Up until they closed us off in the ghetto, the lives of Jewish people were not too bad. Everyone suffered, *goyim* and Jews. The beginnings of the ghetto did not foreshadow what was about to happen to the Jewry of Bochnia, to all Jewry. The ghetto commandant, Müller, was not an evil villain. Perhaps if he had been as abusive as some other SS officers, we might have been more on our guard, might have dared to find any way possible to escape. Even the Gestapo chief, an older German by the name of Schomburg, did not help us divine the true circumstances faced by Bochnia Jewry. He did not treat us harshly, and in return for bribes he was willing to issue authorizations, certificates, whatever was needed. We were closed off in the ghetto, waiting for the gloom to lift, not imagining what lay ahead. It was crowded, there was little food, there were worries. But Bochnia was known throughout the region as a good place to live. Jews flocked there to become a part of the imprisoned community. The Germans did not stop them. They sat in their offices and rubbed their hands together gleefully. This was their plan, after all. First, to gather the Jews from the small villages and farms into the towns. Then, to concentrate the town Jews in the district centers, and finally, to lead them all into the large cities. A diligent and thorough cleansing plan. They implemented it with force, with decrees, with train cars. And at the same time, Jews flowed in of their own free will. Bochnia was filled with them. And what can I say? Until the first *Aktion*, life was bustling. Within the crowdedness and the density, people grew closer—some through love, some through strife, some through communal study, some through screaming to high heavens. It was hard, but life burst through. There was a little field on the outskirts of the ghetto in a deforested piece of land, where I would meet Feiga every day. We would sit and talk of important matters like spring, the prophets, silly Marushka. But the ghetto children also liked the field, those rascals, your father too, and when we wanted to be alone we had to go up to an isolated wooden hut on a hilltop on Leonarda Street. In the middle of the little ghetto was this magnificent hilltop. Around it were crowded houses and noisy masses, but on the hilltop—not a thing. Our own Noah's Ark. You could sense the gathering, more and more Jews streaming into the ghetto from the villages of the Bochnia district. Tiny ghettos were shut down and their Jews were sent to us. Slowly and diligently the Germans labored to convene all the rural Jews in our ghetto. The crowdedness became worse and worse, you wouldn't believe how the skirmishes and the screaming outweighed the love and friendship. How people became less happy with the imposed communality, and the Jewish heart with its righteousness and patience could no longer suffice. Something had to break—even Noah's Ark had room only for couples.

"But I had Feiga, and what else did I need in the world?

"One day, all of a sudden, no Feiga. Thunder on a bright day. Her family disappeared, and the rumor was that they had secretly escaped. They were heading to Hungary, which was often the destination at that time for those who had the means or the connections."

"Your rabbi did that too, the Admor of Belz," I charge. "But his disciples stayed behind for the *Aktionen*."

"*Nu, nu*," Grandpa Yosef protests.

Grandpa Lolek's winking eye stirs a little; it seems his opinion of the religious in general has been voiced.

"What will be the end of this?" Grandpa Yosef sighs, straightening the blanket on Grandpa Lolek, short, elderly fingers expertly tucking the blanket beneath his body.

I begin to be frightened that he might stop talking. I suddenly realize that Grandpa Yosef is sitting here about to tell me his story. The entire story. Childhood bustles within me excitedly, gratefully. I must not disturb him, he must not stop talking. Grandpa Yosef comes through.

"I could not understand how Feiga had left without saying a word," he says, returning to the point at which he left off. And he quickly rejects my unvoiced question. "No, I was not hurt. At first perhaps, there was a grain of anger, but even before the grain sprouted, my heart was flooded with joy: my love was in a safe place, a great worry had been lifted.

"But after a few days the rumors began. They said her family had been betrayed by its guides, they had been captured. They said some were dead, some taken away. Feiga had been taken north, for some reason. The Germans were lacking a beautiful Jewish woman in northern Poland, so instead of killing Feiga they fished her out of the south and handed her over to the north, to balance out their world. *Nu.*"

"How did the rumors start?"

"They just did. In the ghetto, rumors had the healthiest of legs. All day long they hurried around from here to there, never tiring. They ran around and built up strength, not like us humans. *Nu.* And there were people who still traveled around in all sorts of ways among the ghettoes, bearing news and rumors. They knew what was going on. Everyone knew. The only thing they didn't know was that only thirty days away, death was waiting for us all. Feiga disappeared in July, and in August they suddenly declared a roll-call. They ordered us to line up in the military camp courtyard adjacent to the ghetto.

"It was the *Aktion*, which meant a transport of Jews to the death camps. We knew nothing of the liquidation. We were told of a campaign for resettlement in the East, where they would turn Jewish people into productive citizens. We were even ordered to pack bags for the journey. The deceit worked beautifully. We gathered obediently in the empty camp, where they would separate people intended for the transport from those permitted to stay. Anyone who had a permit to stay in the ghetto felt safe, and the others, without knowing a thing, sensed death. People hid out, dug themselves into attics, hollows, anywhere they could. The Germans went from door to door, aided by Polish policemen and local assistants. Whoever was caught was shot on the spot. Women, elderly people, children. The whole ghetto filled with the sounds of screaming and shooting. Bodies rolled down the streets.

The *Aktion* continued for three days. To the credit of this *Aktion* one could say that it was easy compared to the two *Aktionen* that would come later in ghetto Bochnia, until the liquidation. I myself saw no more than the first *Aktion*. I was destined for a transport.

"I stood there indifferently, facing death in the gas chambers but pondering the East, to which we had been promised we were being taken. The rumors about Feiga had spoken of a northern camp, but how could the rumor-mongers know where she had been taken? Why not to the East? Had the Germans who had captured her bothered to show them their orders? People gossip, they want to be considered knowledgeable, and so they embellish. I stood in the large courtyard, around me much grief and chaos, commotions erupting once in a while when people were separated from their families or holders of legal permits were suddenly placed in the transport group, their protests to no avail. In my family too there were many tears and much confusion. My mother fainted and I ran to ask for some water for her, but nothing. Two Jewish policemen returned me by force to the row, humiliated me. Nearby a commotion broke out and someone was shot. I was overtaken by a sense of apathy. I thought about Feiga. Will we meet in the East? Might we have a marriage ceremony there? Set up a home for ourselves?

"Suddenly, my name was called out. I was told to go with a small group being sent to the labor camp at Rakowice airfield. I was simply pulled out of the transport waiting to die in the gas chambers of Belzec, and sent off to live a good long life. Why me? Who was the angel who had put my name on that list? I do not know. Perhaps it was Yanek, your father's uncle, who was in the Judenrat and had very helpful connections. They were not much help for him, though. In that very same transport he himself was sent away with his family. To the gas chambers. And the same for my mother and father and sister and two brothers. Also my uncles, friends. Everyone. Only me, to Rakowice…"

Grandpa Yosef stops talking. Rakowice pads through the room. An unfamiliar name, its letters tread firmly. Ra-ko-wi-ce.

Grandpa Yosef's thoughts wander. I assume he is thinking of

his family, their last moments together. But he is dwelling on the wonder of his being sent to Rakowice.

"Strange. Craftsmen were sent to Rakowice. A small group of skilled laborers. And me. Why me? Rakowice was not just another camp. Airplanes! An airfield! Engineers worked there."

He sounds almost boastful. He is short of breath. For a moment he scans his surroundings—me, Grandpa Lolek, the bed, the room. As if only at this moment has it become apparent to him that he has begun to tell his story. He needs to devote his attention to the place, to observe before he opens his mouth, as all good orators do. Here, in a wondrous way, is a coming together of opportunity and the need he has harbored for a long time. In this silence, which only Grandpa Lolek can disturb, we will spread out the story. There is plenty of time, every detail is important. Outside, night has fallen. Silence in the ward, silence in the room. Grandpa Yosef sets the time for his story: evening.

"We arrived in Rakowice in the evening hours. They rushed us into a group of huts. They started yelling. Beating us. What they wanted from our shattered souls, we could not tell. And in the distance was the airfield with the runway lit up. We squinted at the lights, fearful. Everything was too overwhelming, happening too quickly. We wanted just a moment of reprieve.

"Our gazes were drawn to beyond the fence. There, near the ugly barracks that formed the staff housing, was a fancy black car. In the chill of the night, against the backdrop of the runway lights, the body of the car shone like marble. So shiny and black, standing still and demanding our attention. But we were not permitted to look at the car for long. We were soon thrown from the gate area onwards, into the camp. Then there were beatings, searches, shouts. They acted as though they did not understand why we had come, and the whole business of our arrival was an unnecessary nuisance. From their point of view, we could have left. But I say this only jokingly. Leaving, even attempting to leave for just a second, was a death sentence. They hit and yelled just indiscriminately, for no reason. Shouts and lashings that made your mind dizzy with fear. We could not contemplate anything, not even the town we had left, or our families. All we could do was bow our heads and obey orders, ignore what was going on.

"But still, I must admit, once in a while my thoughts strayed to that black car. For some reason I sensed that I would be brought together with that fabulous machine in a few hours. There were beatings, punishments, crazed thoughts, and yet the car took hold of my mind. What was such a car doing in this ugly camp, among the crude trucks and a few simple vehicles parked in the mud? Was a high-ranking official about to take off from the airfield? Was the car waiting to pick up an official about to land here? The soldiers and personnel moving around in the distant airfield seemed unconcerned with the car. Why here, then? All that was happening here was our absorption into this pathetic, wearisome camp, implemented by low-ranking cruel beasts. Yes, this was what I would contemplate as the blows were being delivered, punishments and yelling around me. Still, I was drawn by the idea that the car was there for us. As if the absorption in Rakowice was an exemplary act, an operation to which senior officials were invited to watch and be impressed.

"As I contemplated these nonsensical thoughts, a sergeant suddenly grabbed hold of me, a Scharführer in uniform, and asked me to my face, 'Speak German, kike?'

"I replied, 'Yes,' with terror in my soul. My father, may God avenge his blood, Reb Mordechai Halevi Ingberg, had always admired the Germans. He learned their language and read their books. In the First World War he even served in one of the Austrian army's regiments. He taught me the language too, and I was fluent. But why did they need my German?

"I was not given much time to think. I was pulled away from the group to an isolated courtyard near a black wall. Did they shoot German-speaking Jews immediately? And for that they had dragged me all the way from Bochnia?

"I was left alone for a moment or two, and then came two prisoners, Jews, servants of the camp. They silently instructed me to strip, so they could wash and disinfect me. I obeyed, saying nothing, but my heart wished to know—what would be my fate?

"At first the two men did not speak much. They left me to my thoughts, which were few: *Shema Yisrael*, Feiga, Mother. Why disinfect me if I was condemned? Would I dirty their bullets? Or did this mean that I was not going to die? It seemed unreasonable, after all, to wash and disinfect someone about to die. Then again, the Germans had already shown us quite clearly in the ghetto that they had their own logic, a very cunning kind, which became apparent only in retrospect—usually too late.

"The Jews gradually began to loosen their tongues. They whispered to me that they didn't know much, but a Nazi general was waiting with the camp commandant. He had demanded to be given a German speaking inmate. They had heard him ask for 'a short Jew,' and they had no idea why. The car, over there, had I seen it? It was his. More than that they did not know.

"I was terrified. What did he need a 'short Jew' for? What was he going to do with me? My throat closed up, images darting between the walls of my imagination. What would the Nazi do with me?

"The Jews finished washing my body. I was freezing, naked in the night air. They rubbed me dry, then sprayed me with a foul-smelling disinfectant. Then they rubbed me again with a different rag, doing their work carefully like loyal servants. All that was left was to dress me. Not in a prisoner's uniform, but in civilian clothes. They were instructed to dress me well, neatly and cleanly. As if I were a bride being lead to her *chuppah*. And my heart sank—what misdeeds would they inflict upon me? Why did they need someone short?

"First they put an awful pale pink shirt on me, as if I were a man of leisure in Krakow, one of those debauched people I had heard so much about, and had even seen in Brzesko once. And they gave me shoes that were almost the right size, a small consolation, and plain brown trousers. Then an overcoat to cover the pink shirt.

"I asked my fellow Jews where they were from, what their names were. But they were silent. Their eyes showed fear. They were forbidden to talk. A single word could result in lashings. But one of them, who must have been naturally garrulous, was eager to convey something, and he began to whisper. The general was very senior. He had earned commendations on the Eastern front. He was high-ranking. 'And they say he has a lover,' he whispered secretively. A little SS sweetheart somewhere in the north, and he was traveling to her. She had fled him, the lover, and he was pursuing her. A whole affair.

"'A lover?' I asked. The man said he had overheard the German policemen gossiping. More than that he did not know.

"More than that I did not need. Horrific images sprung up in my mind. My heart trembled. What would they do with me? Would he present me to his SS woman? A lover's gift? And why did he need 'a short Jew'? I had known great fear in the ghetto, but now I could no longer abide it. From the *Kadosh Baruch Hu*, from Him I asked for strength. Perhaps I will kill myself here and now, in the name of the Lord, I thought, before they do to me what they wish to do. But then I thought of Feiga. And like a white feather descending from a dark sky, I suddenly found determination in a new thought: I was going to Feiga. To rescue her. This whole journey, the plan of this Nazi general, damn him, was nothing but a trick being played upon me by the *Kadosh Baruch Hu*. He was making the villain lead me to Feiga. And so it was. I had asked my Lord many times: Take me, lead me to Feiga. And how had I thought my Lord would answer my prayers? Would he provide me with a private jet? An automobile? No. Instead, he had given me a Nazi general in pursuit of a fleeing lover. For some reason the bastard had concocted a need for a Jew, and he had to be short, and had to speak German fluently. Of the whole shipment he had chosen me. And now I was going to rescue Feiga!

"The newfound joy in my heart must have transferred a spark to my eyes and face, because the two Jews looked at me in amazement. My fortitude had sent a shudder through them.

"'Are you not afraid, Reb?' the talkative one wanted to know.

"'With God's help, *chazak chazak venitchazek*, be strong, be strong, and we shall be strengthened,' I whispered, and they stood up straight in the darkness upon hearing the holy prayer. My strength imbued their limbs with power too. And that force that I showered upon these two poor Jews, servants of the Nazi camp, strengthened me even more. I had become a leader of sorts, a small-time leader, who saw the trouble of his people and gave them strength. Like Moses our Teacher, who smote the Egyptian, I whispered words of encouragement to them, now completely separate from the torture, the nightmare, the terrible fate of Jewish souls from all corners of the Nazi land. And me—I was going to Feiga. I could barely contain my impatience. Let the Nazi come, that evil Haman, and lead me like Mordechai on his horse.

"I was eager and excited, but they left me alone for two days in a frozen room with no windows, with only a waste-water container to keep me company. My heart was burning, my body freezing. The cement dug into my bones. The cold tortured me, but worse was the loneliness, the uncertainty, the harsh anticipation. I wanted a journey! Right then and there! Every twelve hours a door opened and a 'black,' which was what we called the Ukrainian guards, placed a dish of rotting food out for me. Two days later, in the evening, I was sent out to the yard again. They undressed me. Washed me in freezing cold water. Dried and disinfected me again. Gave me back my clothes, including the pink shirt. They added a hat. Even gloves. Yes, yes. Yosef Ingberg in kid gloves!

"After all these arrangements, one of the 'blacks' led me to the huts and then my eye caught sight of the black marble car, washed and shining, waiting. Oh horror and fear, an SS general was already sitting in the driver's seat, his black uniform stifling my courage—perhaps I was wrong about Feiga. But a moment later I found encouragement. How could I be wrong about the Lord's salvation?

"I was put in the passenger's seat next to the general, a large upright Amalek, and when I shot him a trembling look the Ukrainian guard hit me. Kikes mustn't look! The SS general had been still, but now he moved his hand slightly, as if brushing something off, and the guard who had struck me pulled away. I realized he had been ordered to leave me alone. There I was between two Amalekites, and one cancelled out the wickedness of the other. I was certain of the Lord's salvation, but in such proximity to a Nazi's body, the soul takes fright. His cap especially, shiny black on his head, put fear in me.

"The general reached out and turned the engine on. Policemen, Gestapo and Ukrainian guards bustled outside. And camp staff. They all came to see the general off on his journey. They did not realize it was my journey. My journey to Feiga. And off we went. An SS general holding the wheel, and me, Yosef Ingberg of Bochnia, beside him. Really and truly on the seat beside him. The seat was soft, made of fine leather. My fingers found pleasure touching it, feeling it. God forgive me for saying so, but it was as fine as the *paroches* that covers the holy ark. Through the windshield in front of me I could see everything clearly. Beneath the windshield, on his side, was the instrument panel with its dials and gauges. And the wheel—a butting ram, driving the engine that roared in its innards."

Grandpa Yosef blushes slightly at his own excitement. After all, this is a car he is describing. The air is charged with a sense of confession.

"*Nu*, you see, back then I had never driven in a car before. It just hadn't happened. And here was this wonderful carriage, all in black, and the whole world hurriedly making way for us. Trees, houses, even the clouds. Every time we passed a security point or a group of soldiers, they saluted us in fearful reverence. I had no idea where we were going. My heart was frozen. Was I bound for her? Terror struck me from my knees to my chest, but one sliver of thought did not abandon me: Have no fear, we are going to Feiga. But elsewhere was gloom and darkness. What would they do to me?

"We drove without stopping until midday. He was untiring, the general. His face was frozen, fixed on the wheel, and on he sailed. At noon we went into a military camp for lunch. I was left in the car and a guard was posted to watch me. I realized that I had eaten nothing for twenty-four hours. I did not yet know what days of hunger were ahead of me in my miserable future. But when we got back on the road, after some way, Amalek reached into his coat pocket and took out a wrapped parcel of food. Meat and salami and beets and cabbage. I gobbled it all down without saying a blessing, without a thought. The food was like pebbles in my throat, but I overcame that.

"So we kept driving in silence. In the evening he stopped again and had another meal. Again he secretly put aside a portion of food for me. Even poured me a hot drink. Such a merciful caretaker! And it was all done in silence, without so much as a glance in my direction. As if I were nothing but an object. Still I did not know, what did he want? What would he do with me? My mouth gobbled, my heart quavered. My knees trembled, my gut rejoiced. In between meals this

Pharaoh needed no rest. He kept driving the whole night through. I, in great terror, fell asleep. I woke up with an empty stomach. My body ached from the endless sitting. And he, the devil, acted as if he had not been robbed of any sleep. Around us, although it was summer, the pine trees were sparse and it was very cold, mud piled up alongside the roads. Forests came into view to the east. To the west as well. I wondered about Feiga. Was my little bird near or far?"

Grandpa Yosef comes to a stop with screeching brakes. "Do you know what *Feiga* means? *Feigaleh*? It's a bird. A female bird. A little female bird."

He continues his story.

"This Amalek did not let go of the wheel until the roads led to another camp. I felt them immediately; the fences, the huts, the terror. My general was tensely welcomed by an SS man, the camp commandant, who gave him their *heil* salute. It seemed my general had taken him by surprise. They both disappeared into a building, where they sat down to eat and talk. They spent six hours there while I was trapped in the car, watching the camp routine through the windows. The daylight was dark through the heavy glass and the scenes were dim. No sounds penetrated the car. Beyond the fences were inmates, exhausted and skeletal. No one came close. They did not dare. I sat watching, not knowing at all that I was in the height of the days that would come to be called the Shoah, believing that my suffering was due to loneliness, with Feiga somewhere out there, unrevealed. I believed my family was in the East, perhaps in the Ukraine, working hard, if they had not met with some disaster on their difficult journey. I myself was at the mercy of a Nazi general and I did not know what would be done with me. There was terror in my heart but there was a certain sweetness too—I was going to Feiga, I was destined for a great adventure. A black car was driving me through places I had only dreamed of as a boy, when I used to sit at the edge of Bochnia looking at the faraway landscape, my heart hollow with vague longings, weeping with love—Feiga, Feiga.

"A faint smell wafted into the car. My senses immediately conjured up a thought—potatoes! But that smell belied something else, and to the left of the car I could see a billow of smoke. A hut obscured my view of the source of the smoke. I stretched my neck out, my body leaning as far sideways as possible, but I could not see around the hut. The smoke billowed upwards from the earth as if someone were stoking that fire well, and the smell became more and more pronounced as the smoke thickened. For a moment I contemplated moving to the general's seat, where I would be able to see, but the mere thought was enough to cover my heart with ice. I must not! I remained in my seat, turned away from the billow of smoke, and a moment later I thanked my lucky stars because the general came out, surrounded by officers. They looked excited, as if they had been vigorously commended, their fear of criticism gone. They saluted him and walked him to our car with ingratiating looks. They did not move from the road until the car drove through the gates.

"We drove north. All the car's movements, the official stops at SS camps, all were directed northward. An iron plan was in his heart, to reach his escaped lover, and he did not sleep, and did not cease, and only for the sake of good order, damn them, did he visit his officers on the way.

"By that time I had already found a name for him, for the Nazi general. From the first I felt the need to give him a name. A nickname. If I were to die at his hands, he might as well have a name. I had already named the woman he was traveling to, Little Lover. And him, I had already silently called him Amalek, murderer, cruel soldier, Pharaoh, Haman, murderer. And possibly because of Haman, I suddenly determined to name him after Ahasuerus, the King of Persia who was incited by Haman to kill all the Jews. Perhaps this was not emblematic of his character, not an appropriate name for such an evil man, but it was what my heart decided.

"Evening came. We visited our fourth camp in a single day. My heart was dimly terrified, sensing we were getting closer to the end of our voyage. Ahasuerus would deliver me to the Little Lover. Sacrifice me on her altar. May God have mercy. But when we left the camp gates, Ahasuerus's face had changed. I dared not look at him directly, knowing it was better not to, but out of the corner of my eye I could see a glimpse of his face. It was gray and drawn and deadened. As if he had learned of a great disaster that had befallen his family. His hands, seemingly uninformed of the bad news, grasped the wheel strongly as they drove the car. These people seemed to have no connection between their hearts and their hands. But then finally the broken heart reached the hands, and Ahasuerus slowed down and drove his car onto the shoulder of the road, where he stopped beside a small puddle of mud. He did not explain the stop to me, as if I were nothing to him. He sat clutching the wheel, his back straight. He sat that way for a long time. Ahasuerus was silenced. The whole world was still. Ahasuerus's breath counted time—the seconds, the minutes. In and out it went, heavy and slow. Ahasuerus was tormented.

"I stared straight ahead, careful not to look at him, God forbid. Suddenly, there was a sound. The door opened and Ahasuerus got out. He walked alongside the car. He dug into the hollows of his eyes with his thumb and finger to rub the tiredness and trouble away from them, as I used to do when I was studying. Then he put his hand over his eyes as if he were crying. Suddenly he moved his hand to reveal his eyes and there was nothing to separate him from me. He looked at me, the Angel of Death.

"Ahasuerus got back into the car. The end is near, I thought, and suddenly it seemed that a bundle of pictures I had stored away in my memory was erupting. The Nazis shoot Metzger the baker in the hiding place he made for himself behind the oven, and while being led to Rakowice, I pass his body, bullet-ridden and white as ice. The body of young Yehezkel, my classmate, on his back, his eyes facing me. Mrs. Otkova yelling, running through the courtyard, no one knows what she wants. And Rabbi Halberstam, what of Rabbi Halberstam? With his wife, both shot against the wall.

"Nothing in my heart was apparent to Ahasuerus. He wanted to get back on the road, to keep going north. But the car would not cooperate. He could not start it. He got out, checked the engine, got back in. In and out again, he hurried around, regal and slow, but his concern was apparent. Around us night was falling, the woods, wild beasts. *Nu*, may God protect. For some reason, I was confident that he would manage. In my mind I could not envision a Nazi general failing, damn them. We believed in them so, those sons of death. But the car did not fear him. It remained silent and still, as if this marble angel was insulted at having been made to stop on a muddy road.

"Ahasuerus got back into the car. Silence prevailed. The cold began to seep in. Night was falling. Not a soul was on the road. Forests on both sides. Trees. A few birds fluttered through the treetops, screeching, groaning, demanding to know why the Creator had brought them to this remote land. And suddenly I sensed sleep fossilizing on the general's face. But then something moved in the stoniness of his strong chin and he left me in the car again, going out to explore the wilderness. His boots creaked in the freezing cold. Birds screeched and an echo passed from one end of the world to the other. We were alone. Around us an endless forest. No salvation.

"I looked through the window of the car. Ahasuerus's fingers rested on his eyes. His figure was hunched over for a moment. Tired and irritated and helpless. Lightening struck in my heart: He will kill me here with his gun. I tried to diminish my presence, shrinking into my pink shirt like a miserable reptile—perhaps he would take pity. Indeed. An evil Gestapo man, a general, and from him I expected mercy. Still fresh in my mind were pictures of shattered babies, Rabbi Halberstam shot with his wife. And there I was, expecting compassion. Still, my body was taut, hoping for mercy, mercy.

"Ahasuerus returned and sat down beside me in his place. I dared to steal a quick look. His face was still hard and his sorrow evident. What was going on in his soul? Had he heard bad news of his escaped lover? Had he seen her? Was she not impressed by his efforts, had she simply told him that everything they had told each other previously was revoked?

"Silence.

"Suddenly a small, sharp sound. Forgetting my vigilance, I looked straight at him. Ahasuerus was cracking a nut. With the fingers of one hand, with Herculean strength, he broke the shell and removed the debris. Carefully, unrushed, he took out the fragments. The nuts cracked like skulls between his hands. I looked away from him, frightened. I remembered that he had forgotten to give me part of his dinner. He had been lost in thought when we left the last camp and forgot about me. But it was not hunger that rose in me—rather, it was fear. The smell of the nuts terrified me. Ahasuerus pressed on. Breathing slowly. Cracking nuts. Every nut got its turn.

"Thoughts rushed through my mind. Metzger the baker came back again, as if his body wanted to tell me something. Lying, shot dead, in front of the bakery where every Friday we used to feast our eyes on the window display, the soft *challahs* and the raisin bread. In our home, Mother baked the bread, the *challahs* too, but to this day I can smell the aromas from Metzger's. Feiga used to go there to buy bread for her family and Metzger would give her a little crown of *challah* for good luck. I thought about Mother. The last time I had seen her she had fainted in the military lot. Who knew where she was. My heart filled with self-pity. My loneliness enveloped me. I took consolation in the distant memory of a walk I had taken with Feiga before the war. Against that backdrop I saw a scene from the last camp Ahasuerus had taken me to: a prisoner stands looking at me with wild eyes. His whole face is black. A skeleton of a man. He stands and stares as if it's worth looking at the car despite the risks. He tilts his head for a moment, hearing a sound. Then he leaves. I, for some reason, wonder what his name is. As if there is any importance to the name of this suffering man behind the fences, who looked at me for two minutes and in a few days will be among the dead. And still I ask myself, Yanek? Hetzkel? Shmuel? Perhaps Yosef, like myself? Suffering and tortured and about to die, and his name is my name?

"Ahasuerus moved briefly beside me. He had collected his nuts and hid them somewhere. He sat erect but his weariness was now obvious. He had not shut his eyes for two days, maybe more. For his lover's sake he overcame tiredness, hardened himself, but the car's breakdown had collapsed everything. Now his eyes demanded sleep. Ahasuerus struggled, there was no salvation. I was tired too, but fear would not allow me to close my eyes. First the villain had to sleep, then we'd see.

"Ahasuerus gave in first. He prepared himself for sleep, wrapping his body in his officer's coat and digging his hands in his pockets. He turned to look at me for a moment, as if remembering that this human package sitting beside him still existed. He seemed to be considering something. Suddenly he turned to me. Truly turned his head to me and spoke:

"'I've always hated Jews, but not like this.'

"When he said 'but not like this,' his hand made a gesture in the air as if to envelop the entire world, the *Aktionen* and the torture and the blood of Rabbi Halberstam on the street in the ghetto. He turned his side to me, mumbled something and fell asleep.

"Those were his first words to me and, in my innocence, I thought that from then on we would talk. But I was mistaken. He never addressed me again as long as we were together, except one more time to say one sentence. But that day is still far off. Perhaps you'd like some more of the Swiss coffee? Tasty, isn't it?"

I decline. Grandpa Yosef patters down to the end of the hallway. It's night time here in the hospital ward. Absolute night. Ahasuerus is asleep with his hands folded beneath his black coat, and Grandpa Yosef has positioned himself as a guard. The night is dark and there are sounds of menacing creatures. Trees sway in the wind. Grandpa Yosef's eyes will not shut. He sits and stretches, and thoughts pass through him unfettered.

Grandpa Yosef comes back from the vending machine, looking bitter. The machine is broken. Someone poked their fingers into the mechanism and stuck something in there and now nobody can get any coffee.

Grandpa Lolek sighs as something inside him stirs—perhaps the stroke, trying to heal—and his body emits a kind of whimper. Grandpa Yosef sits silently, his flow of talk ceased, wondering if there might be an awakening, a feeble word uttered. We watch Grandpa Lolek, lurking for a disturbance in his deep rest. Only the strange wink moves slowly. The eye opens to a narrow slit, then closes, as if satisfied by one open instant. His still body convinces us that there will be no more motion. Grandpa Yosef hurries on, reminded by the soft sigh that his time to tell the tale is not unlimited. If Grandpa Lolek wakes up, if he recovers, it will put an end to the time allotted for listening, for telling, for continuing his journey.

"The general slept the whole night through. His sleep was not peaceful. His head moved, sighs and whimpers erupted from his chest.

I wondered if he was plagued by scenes of babies smashed, children with heads cracked open on the walls of houses. Or perhaps his Little Lover, the SS woman, who had fled him. And myself—if I closed my eyes, would I be in the arms of Feiga? Or would I too reach the walls of the ghetto, our elderly neighbors, like Bergman, shot in the back of their heads? My eyes would not shut. Forbidden. My eyelids kept drooping, but then I would see Kowalska Street, covered with people lying dead as I walk among them. And the eyes would shoot open. No sleep. By my side Ahasuerus moved his head restlessly. Two people suffering; around them, wilderness.

"Just before dawn, the birds began to chirp and a car approached. I looked at Ahasuerus. He did not wake up. He lay restfully, curled up in a dream, perhaps having found peace in the arms of his Little Lover. He had no idea that a car was about to pass us, that he would sleep away an opportunity. I asked myself if I should let the car pass and leave us there, the two of us, hungry and cold, perhaps unto death. That would be my revenge for Metzger the baker, for Yehez-kel, for Rabbi Halberstam.

"The car was audible now, its sounds clear. My hand reached out and one finger impudently tapped his neck. Ahasuerus woke without even giving me a glance. He got out and stopped the car. The soldiers in the car were eager to help. They rescued us. A short soldier reached under the engine hood and did something in there that fixed the problem. In the meantime, they danced around the general, star-struck, offering him their food. They saluted him and asked if they could do anything. Confused, they saluted again. They shot glances at me but did not dare ask what the general was doing with a Jew in a pink shirt. But their looks were curious. Ahasuerus dismissed them and I thought we would set off on our voyage again, determined. The breakdown had cost us precious time. My body was slowly thawing, its heat eager to get to work, to find Feiga's camp. But Ahasuerus was in no hurry. The moment the car was fixed, he began to plan the day ahead. From his coat pocket he gave me a hunk of bread. He had put it aside from what they had given him. Then, to my surprise, he went off to do his business.

"Even crouching behind a shrub, he still looked regal. Straight as an eagle. I allowed him some privacy, turning my face. But the odor of his bowel movement spread through the fresh air. The smell was unpleasant but I persisted in inhaling it, sensing his health—for months, begging your pardon, everything with me had been sick and watery. After a while he reemerged and walked toward me in his neat uniform. He rubbed his hands on the leaves of a bush and was spotlessly clean. He proceeded, not to his side of the vehicle, but straight to me, motioning with his head at the bush. I grew frightened. Was I to die there? But my fear was unfounded as I soon understood. There was a long way ahead of us, most likely, and I too, begging your pardon, had to relieve myself. My heart wished to lead me to a different bush, far from the one he had used. But my legs positioned me behind the very same bush. *Nu.* I pulled my pants down and looked aside. There were two of them, laying like babes in a cradle on the leafy grass, solid and identically sized. I hoped I would not emit the soft stream again, not the usual output, not in front of those two. But my bowels quickly erupted in a dirty, unpleasant flow. Flies had already appeared. I could barely stand up and tuck my pink shirt into my pants. Disgusted and miserable, I sat down beside him in the car. I recalled the sentence he had said to me and, for some reason in that moment my heart believed that the journey had somehow brought us closer, that perhaps we would talk. But the general's concern was only for his car. He drove the marble angel back onto the road to his lover, to my Feiga.

"At midday we visited a camp. Again I sat imprisoned in the car while Ahasuerus met with the camp personnel. This time I saw women. Female prisoners and policewomen. Was the journey to Feiga over? Suddenly there was a knock on the window. A prisoner, an actual prisoner, was knocking urgently. His face looked like the skeleton I had seen the day before. That one had just stood and looked at me, a nameless figure with crazed eyes, but this one was more daring. I opened the window a crack and asked hurriedly, 'Feiga, née Blau, is she here?'

"'Bread?' the prisoner asked. 'Anything?'

"His skeletal face was crazed with fear. My reaction was too slow for him and he skipped away and disappeared among the huts without waiting for my answer. A moment later two SS men passed by and stared lengthily at the car. In my heart I knew that Feiga was not there. When I reached her camp I would know, I would not need conversations.

"I waited for Ahasuerus and did not trouble my mind with thoughts of the prisoner, that skeletal face of his, the likes of which I had never seen in the ghetto. I did not bother with thoughts of the type of life that engenders such terror. My heart was directed elsewhere, to an uncomfortable flutter, a dense sort of desperation. As if my heart was a true prophet, when Ahasuerus came out his steps seemed weak, his expression strange. I looked at him and suddenly all was clear: the voyage was over, no more. Ahasuerus had given up on his journey. Why the confidence? Why the certainty? It was his face. I could tell without a doubt that he was no longer determined, that he had lost his purpose. He got into the car without even glancing at me, and started to drive. The previous night had broken something in him, something greater than mere time lost. I could see this with certainty. Though in fact he appeared more at ease, as if something in him had found calmness, or had been lost, disappeared. But my heart was not available to study the inner workings of a Nazi general. It was Feiga that I was thinking of. Was my voyage still going ahead as planned? Ahasuerus, after all, knew nothing of the journey's purpose. Only the Little Lover was in his head, and now, no Little Lover, and no more need for the 'short Jew' he had wanted to bring her as a gift. What would he do with me?

"The roadsides began to be dotted with villages. The villages grew denser and denser. We were driving through the outskirts of a town. German army guard posts, roadblocks, inspections, examinations. Everyone let Ahasuerus go on his way, retreating with a salute. We sailed deeper in. I slowly began to read names on the road-signs, and realized we had reached the city of Lodz. Why Lodz, I did not know. Had Feiga been taken there? Why was Ahasuerus bringing me to Lodz? What was he scheming? Was he planning to get rid of me now that I was unnecessary? And why not simply put a bullet through my head right there?

"From the fear, not only my heart shrunk. Begging your pardon, my bladder did too. To this day I remember the endless, painful pressure. My life was on the line, but it was my bladder that preoccupied me. If only Ahasuerus would stop for a moment, I could jump out and urinate. He might think I was escaping. He might shoot me. But my thoughts could not tolerate the caution that might delay urination. Still suffering, my bladder so full that it was almost erupting, we reached the gates of a low wall, and beyond it, I knew immediately, was a ghetto. Far larger than the Bochnia ghetto, unfamiliar and crowded, but there was no mistaking it. A ghetto is immediately recognizable. An entire town of hungry, ill Jews. The Lodz ghetto.

"To this day I wonder why Ahasuerus brought me to the Lodz ghetto. Was it so I would be killed in the *Aktion* that was planned for the next few days? He must have known about it (perhaps even ordered it). Or maybe it was just the opposite—it was life that he ordered for me. He knew what everyone knows today, that after the next *Aktion* this ghetto would be allowed to survive, the last of the ghettos. So his was an act of grace. Or maybe it was neither. Here was simply a place where he could leave me among the hundreds of thousands of people crowded into the ghetto, who walked its streets daily, characters coming and going with the wind. Here no questions would be asked. But why would a Gestapo general need to be so cautious? In the Bochnia ghetto they shot hundreds like me, lined up against the walls, so why would a general inconvenience himself for one miserable Jew? He could have shot me, no questions asked, on the side of the road.

"Back then, much like today, I was full of questions. But Ahasuerus was indifferent. We were destined to meet again several days later, and as I have said, Ahasuerus would address me one more time. But on that day he left me by the entrance to a building. He gave me some sort of *Certifikat* and a little bag which contained, I discovered, Polish and German currency. Dispensing with niceties, he left me and disappeared. As if the neglected regions of the world had never been traversed together by these two: a Nazi general and a short Jew. At that moment I still did not know how much future we were yet to have together.

"I soon realized that I had been left outside the German police headquarters. I was promptly led to the office of the Jewish police by two German officers who treated me with inexplicable respect. The Jewish clerks I was delivered to also treated me with caution, even deference. They interviewed me, asked questions. They explained to me about the difficulties, the rationing. They promised to help with housing, although the situation was practically hopeless, and in any case it was warm on these summer nights and the street was a good option for now. Better the street than the houses, where typhus and boils were raging. The streets were cleaner. They dared to ask, in hushed voices, if I had any particular desires, if I required assistance in my mission, any requests?

"No, they said, they hadn't heard of Feiga, née Blau, but they would find out. Two-hundred thousand Jews in the ghetto, but not to worry, everything was in the records. Order, there was. Law, there was. The clerks would do their jobs and Feiga would be located. Did I wish to make any further inquiries of another kind? Any orders, for example?

"I was naïve. I did not realise that to them, a man dropped off in the middle of the Lodz ghetto in the black car of a Gestapo general, dressed in fine clothes and a pink shirt, had to be an agent. They were in awe of my unabashed scheming; I had not slipped into the ghetto dressed in plain clothes, but had arrived demonstratively in a black car that had stopped right outside the police headquarters. And they must have pondered the pink shirt. What kind of an agent dressed like that? In my innocence, I did not divine the thoughts surrounding me. I did not yet conceive of the size of the Lodz ghetto, the two hundred thousand Jews crowded into it, the hundred Jews who died there routinely every day, in hunger and in sickness, in suicide and over-crowdedness. I did not imagine the thieves, the agents, the informers, the policemen, the underground activists, a great tapestry of people in conflict with one another, fighting over a hunk of bread, over a sliver of authority. An entire city full of passions and torments. In this city there were people who jumped out of windows, and there were those who were selflessly charitable. There was a woman in this city, a simple daughter of Israel, who was accused of having eaten from the flesh of her own son's body. And there were martyrs who died for *kiddush hashem*. A city that even had strikes and labor riots, instructions from foremen, and weddings and prayers and distinguished gentlemen. And into this cauldron, the vast Lodz ghetto, tenfold larger than our ghetto in Bochnia, I descended in a pink shirt.

"The clerks asked if I had any further desires. Amazingly, I expressed my urgent desire—begging your pardon—for a place to relieve myself. My bladder could take no more. And thus began my time in the Lodz ghetto.

"The first days were terrible. All the ghetto streets were so clean as to be practically spotless. Countless people made it their business to clean them, countless others supervised their work. With untiring efforts, they scrubbed the streets to stop the spread of disease as much as was possible. But on top of this bed of cleanliness teemed terror and fear. Everything was crowded and morbid. People were hungry. The money on my person was of practically no use. I was afraid to take out a coin. I was among Jewish brethren, but there was hunger in their eyes, and thieving looks. And my own fear was dwarfed by everyone else's fear of me. The rumor had already spread: the high priest of agents had come to the ghetto.

"At first I walked alone. Without a friend, without a living soul. Around me the streets bustled with the furor of life, thousands of people going about their business. Troubles and pleas and lobbying and attempts to deceive bitter fate. There was no going outside the ghetto. Closed off. But inside people flowed, together or alone, including a few strange creatures like myself. Who could imagine the travels that had led a driven leaf like myself from our little Bochnia to 32 Dolna Street in the Lodz ghetto? One way or another, all these scattered leaves seemed to gather together in their wanderings, and I quickly found myself some company. Not wise men. Good people, also lonely. We wandered the streets like ragamuffins, and it was good. We spoke of our loved ones, our homes. Each man extolled the place he had come from, his family, his loves. There were lies, and foolishness, and it was all in good spirits, to warm the heart. I alone did not have to lie: I described Feiga just as she was, unembellished.

"I found consolation in this gang. By all appearances, they were lonesome unworthies. But the closer our ties grew, the more confessions we made, and each man shone through with the miracles of his life. You would look at one of us, a lifeless man dressed in rags, the dregs of the dregs, and an unparalleled story of life would emerge, a unique, wonderful soul that could not be imagined.

"We walked and we talked. All like me, driven leaves. Brought from distant places, each with his own story, longing to tell it thoroughly, to amaze, to share, to sigh a little together. It seemed, at times, that life was not yet that bad. We were hungry, but a sweet sorrow lingered in the air. The two trees on Balut Street, where our 'parliament' met, were like an orchard to us. We did not imagine that on September fifth, 1942, the terrible Lodz ghetto *Aktion* would begin—the one infamously known as *Sperre*. Afterwards, the ghetto was untouched until 1944, the last of the ghettos allowed to live out its life. Outside the ghetto, Jews everywhere were taken to concentration and extermination camps, murdered and tortured, while the Lodz ghetto was left in peace. But the ghetto paid a price for this respite in the form of the *Sperre*.

"I have already said that I was naïve. I did not imagine that even as I was wandering around among the unknowns, I was not anonymous at all. Many in the ghetto took an interest in me, for various reasons. People often turned up in the ghetto like I had, sent by the Germans as agents. And just as suddenly, they disappeared. No one could keep track of all the movements and transports. But I had come straight from a general's car to the police headquarters, and such a thing had never been witnessed before. People privately commented that this was no way to plant an agent—so publicly, wearing a pink shirt like some sort of peacock. And rumor soon spread that I had no shortage of money. There were many thieves in the ghetto, as well as real murderers. But apparently they were afraid of me. I am ashamed to say that I had gained a reputation as a high-ranking secret agent of the Germans who should not be messed with. All my efforts to refute the rumors were to no avail, and within a few days I began to comprehend that in fact I might be better off protected by them.

"I would walk through the masses, sad and hungry. All sorts of people attached themselves to me, mostly intrigued by my alleged role as chief agent, and undoubtedly also drawn by the rumors of my money. Fearful characters stole up to me, pressed my arm and offered me a piece of wax, or cabbage, or a lock. They tried to complete the transactions quickly, retreating in haste when I hesitated. In the morning I would hear that a supply of boots had been stolen from the warehouse, and in the evening a Jew would come up to offer me a pair for cheap. Others behaved like royalty. *Malchus.* Turning to me, they beckoned secretively, hinting at a proposal, expecting that we would gradually reveal our business to one another. The one would expose his money. The other would name a price for a fake authorization, for getting a letter to any address in Poland, for a special favor at the ghetto organization offices. They were surprised I did not want these services, which were offered only to the distinguished—to those who could pay gold for small favors.

"Not only merchants hassled me. Some came to me with complaints about this or that official, expecting the grievance to make its way to the powers that be. Some came with bubbling anger, regaling me with stories of wrongdoing. Demanding compensation, threatening, saying, 'The day is not far…The day is not far.' And some did not speak. They followed me around with hawk-eyes for a day or two. My money put them on my heels, the title of agent melted their hearts. For one or two days they did not dare approach, but did not give up. And every such attempt increased my resolution: I would cloak myself in the rumor and the thieves would stay away. Better that way. I had no idea of the danger lurking beneath the surface.

"There was in our gang a narrow-eyed Jew from Koźminek. His wife had died of typhus in the ghetto and he had lost his children to pneumonia. He hung around with us, not entirely belonging, sometimes talking of his wife, sometimes of his children, but his main concern was potatoes. His mind was completely obsessed with the topic, and he would stand among us discussing a shipment of potatoes he had seen being unloaded on Limanowa Street, which would probably go to the sycophants of the Authority. He discussed potatoes distributed in the public kitchens, which were damaged from faulty storage over winter. This was his entire preoccupation: potatoes that were, that would be, that he intended to get hold of. Potatoes. And between them, like drops of rain, a word or two about his children. Antek, three years old, had died in the hospital. His Rozka had not even seen the inside of a hospital. For two days she lay coughing at home, and suddenly one night she got a high fever. He wrapped her in a blanket and took her in the middle of the night, hoping they would treat her. They told him the hospital was over-flowing with typhus and boils patients. She should have hot drinks and she would get better. He offered all his food stamps and a small treasure of hoarded potatoes as bribery. But the sacrifice did not help. She died in his arms, six-year-old Rozka. He would have given his entire stock of potatoes, but they did not want it. Why would they? Bursting with fatty foods, hiding huge storehouses from the masses, full of potatoes, only for them. And here the potatoes erupted again. The unfair allocations. The shipment rotting in a warehouse because a few clerks in the office were lazy. A certain type of potato that was a curse, causing the stomach to bloat, God save us, we had to watch out. And so on and so forth.

"One day, when there was great hunger, this Jew from Koźminek decided to attach himself to me. He stood close to my body and for a moment I thought that was it—a knife and I would be done for. He had a thieving look in his eyes, which led me to believe that it would be him, of all the men in our gang, who would overcome the force of the rumors and rob me for my potatoes. But the Jew from Koźminek, it turned out, was seeking my wellbeing. Standing close to me, his words crazed, frightened, he was actually trying to warn me:

"'In our circle…*hmm*…they think about you, *nu*…Where did you come from? And some believe we should…*nu*, in the neck…there are youths here…'

"He was trying to tell me that my life was in danger, and at the hands of whom?! The rumors protected me from regular thieves, but the underground, the people who acted in the name of ideology, considered me a target. Oh dear! Why did Ahasuerus bring these troubles on me? He could have left me at some distance from the town, where I would have ended up wherever I ended up. What did he care? I knew my condition was grave. I did not know how grave it was yet to become.

"In the meantime, something of note occurred. The chairman

of the Lodz ghetto Judenrat, Rumkowski, the "Elder of the Jews," who lorded over the small kingdom of two hundred thousand ghetto subjects, summoned me to see him. He wanted to talk. The most important of the ghetto Jews, the 'president,' as we were required to call him, invited a lonesome Jew of the Wesoła Street wanderers to his room.

"He talked to me for a long time, trying to figure me out. If I were an agent, how did he not know? There were agents about whom the Gestapo notified Rumkowski, and others, if the Gestapo hid them from him, Rumkowski the fox uncovered on his own. And me? Who was I? He stared at me. An elderly man with a strong face. He asked where I had come from, what I did. He chatted about himself and the troubles of his kingdom. And all this time his eyes were watching me, wondering who I was. A cunning and wise man, this Rumkowski was. Some say he was bad for the Jews, some say he did great things for them, finding himself between a rock and a hard place. Who can judge? He met his end in Auschwitz too, may God avenge his blood. With me he was relaxed. He asked if my life in the ghetto was adequate, if I was finding nourishment, if I was treated well by his subordinates. He asked how he could help. I gave him a detailed description of Feiga, which he wrote down, and he said his people could make enquires in nearby ghettos.

"All this time I wondered—should I confess? Open my heart to this grandfatherly Jew and tell him that I was no agent and no nothing? Should I restore myself to the people of Israel, or cloak myself in secrecy and preserve the confusion? After all, it was only my secret that protected me from the robbers, like a coat of armor. Perhaps I could give him my money to keep? German and Polish bills were forbidden in the ghetto and were of no use in any case. But I did not reveal it to him. Not a thing. I went back to the street, and he, in his office, was left wondering who I was.

"I kept roaming here and there through the streets. A lonesome Jew, longing for life. Thieves in pursuit, murderers lurking for the money hidden deep in my coat pocket. I could not spend a penny of Ahasuerus's treasure. And whom did I fear? The underground youths. I did not want to die like an agent, a traitor. Better to be killed by a robber, better tuberculosis, typhus. Every young man who came in my direction looked like an assassin to me. I tried to find ways to contact the underground—perhaps I would knock on their door and settle the misunderstanding. Take the entire treasure out of my coat pocket and say, Here, all my money can go to your cause. But what door could I knock on? How could I, the chief of agents, find out on the streets where the underground met? *Nu*, what an affair!

"One day there was a chance of sorts. On Dolna Street, I happened to meet a man by the name of Yanek Leib, a Jew of short stature who used to be in our gang of misfits and then disappeared. A peculiar sort of Jew. His eyes were extremely large, made even more pronounced by a pair of bushy eyebrows. From the first I had sensed something odd about him, as if despite spending time with us, he did not wish for human company, only needed it so he would not stray too far. He was silent when he was with us, his head bowed, and he never made any efforts to introduce himself. If he was forced to talk, he would immediately grow anxious, emitting sort of 'humpf humpf' noises between his words, waving his hands, wishing to finish his piece in any way possible. He behaved as if a secret were burdening him and he was afraid it would escape—he could not find anyone to share his secret with. Then he found me.

"When I met him he was in a fever, walking towards me as energetically as a defense attorney hurrying to defend the town dignitaries in court. When I enquired as to his destination, he at first tried to conceal his excitement, as if our meetings were a daily occurrence—why would today be anything special? But within a moment or two his appearance changed. He wanted to tell me something right away. I have already told you that, sadly, ordinary Jews, regular people, kept their distance from me, while certain characters stuck to me. And Yanek Leib, he was the greatest of characters. He sat me on an odd-looking staircase that was not connected to any building, serving only the backsides of two conversationalists. He began to talk. Then he stopped. He inhaled, as if trying out his words. He whispered, 'humpf humpf,' preparing his vocal chords. Finally he looked at me.

"'I am a simple Galician, as you know. Yanek Leib, from the

township of Okhanow. From a young age I aspired to reach great distances, humpf, and great distances I have reached…'

"He briefly scanned my face. Was his story making an impression? Then he hurried on, likely short of time.

"'I was a merchant's apprentice and an aid to a *tzaddik*, and also, forgive me, I was a thief. Humpf. I tumbled from land to land, I crossed Silesia, and I crossed the land of Czechia. A merchant and a tramp and a juggler. Yes. Hungry all the time. And the police in pursuit…humpf. Locked me up in winter, let me go in summer. Until I crossed the Alps, yes, the great mountains! Humpf. And in the land of Italy, where it was warm, I found the world famous Enrico circus. Having no choice, for my stomach, I became an acrobat, performing magnificent feats for the audience. But then I twisted my foot, to this day it is crooked and makes me short, shorter than the day I was born. For seven days and seven nights I lay in pain, bedridden, and Mrs. Gazella, the wife of Enrico, cared for me like a mother, humpf, and on the seventh night something went wrong with the lion tamer, his head was bitten off. He put it into the mouth of a lion but never took it out. Humpf. They gave me a choice: they needed a lion-tamer, and acrobatic jumps I could do no longer. I could either tame lions or go back to the dumps, humpf. Of course, I preferred the dumps. There, I would have my head intact, humpf. But the circus master, Enrico himself, hovered over me for seven days and seven nights, entreating and persuading. After all that time I didn't know if I was coming or going, and then he added a final temptation, humpf. He would teach me a magic whisper to subdue the lions. I said no, of course. What good would the magic whisper be when I was in the lion's gut? But Enrico put his lips to my ear and whispered the magic whisper, which had been passed down through many generations in his family, and which included one Hebrew word. Yes, one word in *lashon hakodesh*, the Holy Tongue. For some reason, humpf, far from my people, from Okhanow, one word was more enchanting than the wholeness of my head. Yes, a Hebrew word. I did not even speak Hebrew, except for a few prayers. And so I became the lion tamer in the famous Enrico circus, traveling through the towns of all the world! I had seven lions and seven lionesses, all at my command. No thanks to my stature, which was not tall, humpf, but due to the whisper. After I whispered the charm, looking into their eyes, I fearlessly put my head between their jaws and sometimes placed my neck beneath their paws. Humpf. Humpf.'"

Grandpa Yosef looks serious. "I was beginning to believe that his 'humpf' was the magic whisper, but it turned out not to be. And the whole story turned out to be a long introduction to one more secret.

"Yanek Leib purses his lips and his eyes sparkle. 'Here in Lodz,' he says, 'I discovered that the lion whisper also works against the Nazis, damn them! Yes, humpf, it calms them like little lambs, it calms them. Indeed, only yesterday one such man stood opposite me and I faced him coolly. I began to whisper the magic words and looked deep into his eyes, damn him. He opened his eyes wide—how dare this Jew stand right across from him? Humpf. He was already thinking of his whip, perhaps his pistol. But after a moment his heart became as tender as a lamb. An innocent kid stood before me with no thoughts in his head. Had I wished to, I could have taken his handkerchief from his pocket, blown my nose and put it back. But no! The authorities must not be provoked. You should not be too smart for your own good. A lion is a lion, and a Nazi is a Nazi, damn them, humpf. So I simply walked away and left him to his perplexity. In a moment or two he would awake and have no idea where he was, what he had done, or indeed the name of the cursed mother who had borne him. Humpf!'

"Yanek's face was flushed and excited, he was agitated. His 'humpfs' became more frequent, sticking in his throat.

"'I have already offered myself to the underground. I could play my trick on the authorities, transfer information. Humpf. But they are disbelieving, humpf, they almost threw me out. Humpf, they demand a demonstration, humpf. They'll get one, humpf, tomorrow. In front of the congregation's eyes, I, Yanek Leib, will subdue a *goy*, humpf.'

"He subsided for a moment. His breath grew quiet. But suddenly his face filled with fear. 'I will not reveal the words, I will not!' he screamed, and started digging through his coat pockets, and bleating and mumbling.

"It had never occurred to me to steal his whisper—this whisper was his only asset, worth a multitude of food stamps and more. And in any case it was the underground I was thinking of. Was he connected to the underground? Perhaps he could help me with my affair. There was a sword hanging over my neck, after all. I laid out my plea before him. Yanek Leib arched his eyebrows and gravely considered the request. He could not promise anything. But I was already excited and I urged him, 'Please, for me.' Yanek Leib stood up as if in a hurry again. I chased after him, one block, two, urging him, my heart pounding, 'The underground, the underground, please help.'

"Finally he consented. He knotted his eyebrows together, sighed, and agreed to present my case before the underground the next day. But from that day onwards, until the end of time, I never saw Yanek again. What happened to him, I do not know. I wanted to ask, but people kept their distance. As far as they were concerned, the chief agent had conversed with a man, and the next day the man was gone. And a few days later came the *Sperre*.

"Have you heard the word? *Sperre*? That was what they called the Lodz ghetto *Aktion*. What can I say about the *Aktion*? Every horror you can imagine occurred. A baby taken from its mother's arms, speared on the gun's bayonet, and put back in her arms with wild laughter—she wanted her baby back, didn't she? People were thrown out of windows...children too. Lying broken-boned on the sidewalks, no one coming to their aid. Your heart could not contain all that the Nazis inflicted, in the streets, in houses, lines of people going to Chelmno, the death camp. To this day, sometimes, still, my eyelids close in the middle of the day, my head droops, and from that cursed place those scenes pour forth in front of my eyes.

"First the announcement went through the ghetto: the Gestapo authorities had given an order to evacuate some of the residents. 'Evacuate' was the term they used. At first it was the sick and the weary, then the elderly. Then—the children. The ghetto community leaders had to hand over a list of twenty-thousand people. And to where would they be evacuated? God help them, now we know it was to Chelmno. Back then? We knew and we did not know; we understood and we did not understand. And what can I say…the entire ghetto was panic-stricken, and an uprising was organized. In our hearts we knew where the evacuees would be taken, and it shook people up. The demand passed by word of mouth: Do not give anyone up. Let the *goyim* come and take them themselves. Even the Rambam decreed it is forbidden to give a person up for death, even if it is to the advantage of the entire congregation. Forbidden.

"President Rumkowski gave a speech. He entreated us to hand the people over, otherwise it would get worse. Committees began to meet and divide people up. There were lists. People looked out for their loved ones, pushed people off the lists, wrote others in. Anyone with power, anyone capable of accessing the lists. And there was wailing all the time. I myself was not on the lists of those going to death. No one dared write down the name of the chief agent, for fear their own name might replace it at the last minute, reversing their fortunes.

"On September fifth a curfew was declared. The *Aktion* had begun. Eight days and eight nights of terror. I have said already that in our hearts we knew where they were going. And testimonies had crept into the ghetto. The Rabbi of Grabow sent a letter, a voice of truth to his brethren in the ghetto. True, there were also denials, letters signed by people in the deportations, even rabbis, asking how we were and reporting how fortunate they had been. A moment or two before the gas chambers they were forced to write comforting letters, planting doubt against the cautioning testimonies. But in our hearts we knew the truth. We believed there was annihilation. Everyone thought about their relatives and stopped imagining their lives in the East, trying instead to come to terms with their deaths. I too, from the little window in the room I called home, peeked out at the goings-on in the streets and my memory called up the *Aktion* in Bochnia, the military courtyard, Mother, Father, my sister, my brother. I thought about the large group from which I had been removed to be sent to Rakowice. In the streets below mothers begged, children were dragged kicking into carts, and I recalled four-year-old Irenka standing next to me in line, waiting quietly. A little angel with golden hair. I remembered how she used to sing for us in the ghetto when they organized concerts. Her mother, Bronia, who was a musician at the Krakow Conservatory, would write songs, and Irenka would stand with a violin, playing and singing."

Grandpa Yosef begins to sing a Polish song:

Bo ja jadę dzisiaj do Palestyny
Po radośniejszego życia los
Tam przy cichem gaju pomarańczowym
Będę snuć życia radosnego nić

Grandpa Lolek's eyelid flutters a little. How far are the Polish words reaching?

I ask for a translation.

Grandpa Yosef thinks for a while. It will be hard in Hebrew, he thinks; the words embrace one another less. His lips test the words, gain confidence. Then he hums Irenka's song in Hebrew:

Today I travel to Palestine
To the fate of a more joyful life
There in a tranquil orange grove
I will spin the thread of life's joy

"It sounds better in Polish," Grandpa Yosef emphasizes. "And the song was so beautiful when Irenka sang it. She sang many songs, but unfortunately only this one remains in my memory. They took Irenka, with Bronia, and with her father Leon, to Belzec. *Nu*, four years old, with such angel eyes and golden hair. *Nu*, that was how Irenka went. For many years Leon waited to be blessed with that daughter. In the First World War he fought in the Austrian army. He was taken hostage and held for a long time. When he came home he worked with his father as a barber, he had to make a living, but he never gave up his dream of studying music, and every spare moment he played his violin in the barbershop. 'Chasing away the customers,' his father used to grumble. That was your father's grandfather, Sigmund Shlomo. At a late age, Leon was able to see his dream come true, and at the Conservatory he met the woman of his dreams, Bronia, whom everyone called Ronia. They fell in love and got married. How beautiful the world seemed when Irenka was born, such an angel. All their dreams were coming true, and then Belzec. But our Irenka was just one little angel, and there in the *Sperre*, through my window, we saw dozens of angels crowded onto a wagon and taken away. People followed the wagon, screaming. Shots were fired. People lay in their coats on the street, blood spurting, as the wagon went off into the distance. Screaming, wailing.

"*Nu*, imagine all this, and when the *Sperre* was over, I found out that word on the street was that it had been my mission. I, the chief agent, had brought about the *Sperre*. So went the rumor. *Nu*, me. Nothing could have been further from the truth. But the rumor persisted. People talked. I could not go around to everyone and convince them. Rumors had the strength to walk, while we no longer did. And who would talk with me? To this day, I hate to think of it. I was taken forever from the Lodz ghetto a few months later, and perhaps there are still survivors who remember Reb Yosef Ingberg as an agent of the Germans, their error never corrected. Who knows? Perhaps in the gas chambers at Chelmno, in the minutes during which they convulsed before death, not only the faces of their loved ones passed before their eyes, but also those they hated, and they whispered horrible curses unto death. Was there a Jew who whispered my name? Did I rise up in front of the eyes of so-and-so, in my pink shirt, as his lips entreated?"

Grandpa Yosef stands up and faces the window. In the west, over the ocean, the light from the east is reflected. The day has begun. Grandpa Yosef cracks his knuckles, moves this way and that. Time for prayers, a cup of coffee perhaps. He must go and see when the doctor is coming, we can't just leave Lolek this way. The door opens. A nurse comes in and announces that a doctor will be coming soon. Grandpa Yosef nods, calmly bobbing his head, as if having measured the time between his wish and its realization, he is pleased with the speed. The nurse leans over Grandpa Lolek's bed to check on him, straightens his head on the pillow, smoothes his sheets. Grandpa Yosef watches her movements—perhaps he can learn something new. Then he disappears from the room. Praying, no doubt. But he comes back with a cup of "Swiss coffee" (someone fixed the machine) and the physician follows him in with Effi at his side.

We are asked to leave the room. Effi stays—she is a doctor. Grandpa Yosef stays—he is not moving. I go out and call Anat. Yariv picks up the phone. He tries to figure out where I am and when I'll be back, reducing the complicated topic to his true interest: Will I bring him a present? We agree on a ball. Red. The kind that squeaks when you press it. I think about Irenka. The thread of life's happiness. I want to hold my son. What, I wonder, do you tell a boy in a train car on the way to Belzec? What do you explain to him when the doors open, orders are barked, and everyone must get off? The kid would be screaming, wouldn't he? But he mustn't scream. And if he is quiet, if he asks questions, what do you answer? Anat takes the phone and listens to the night's events, also wanting to take part in the shifts. She's giving a benefit evening for foster children, but she can find the time, perhaps not tonight, but tomorrow. She will look after Grandpa Lolek too, it's her prerogative. Strange, I think. Anat is half Iraqi, on her father's side, and in her huge family there are at least two celebrations almost every week. How is it that there are hardly any troubles? There should be a proportional relationship, shouldn't there? Her family is large. But with them we go to weddings, *brisses*, bar mitzvahs. With us—visiting the sick, funerals. How is that? Once we went to the funeral of Uncle Shmuel, her mother's brother. That was the Polish side. Strange indeed. I can hear Yariv in the background, wanting to be part of the conversation. He grabs the phone again and clarifies: The ball must squeak. A strict engineer, my child, formulating his desires in precise detail.

The doctor comes out. Not much news. They have to run tests and keep him under observation. His current condition may continue for some time, the bodily systems need to recover. We look at Grandpa Lolek. The change in him cannot be ignored. His face has taken on a tenderness, a strange glow. As if his soul has found an unfamiliar tranquility that he has no intention of giving up so quickly. Perhaps what is so striking is his silence. Finally, the ever-present handicap of his defective, limbless Hebrew has disappeared within the silence of his body, removed from Grandpa Lolek's face like a mask that has held him back all these years, a barrier between him and us. We look at him as we stand there, and it's like looking into a small pool of water. We perceive with clarity, finally seeing him as he was seen one day in the fifties by an anonymous photographer who needed to produce a suitable picture—perhaps for a poster, perhaps for a new Israeli stamp—and had found Grandpa Lolek a good model for his needs. He had tried to photograph him as a Zionist leader observing his vision, his gaze turned slightly upwards and forward, somewhat diagonal. But in the wonderful picture in his album, Grandpa Lolek wears an expression reserved for golfers, a second after the swing, his eyes searching for the ball in flight. Now we understand the photographer. On Grandpa Lolek's tranquil face lies the quiet radiance befitting leaders of nations.

Effi goes over to the window and draws the curtains. Grandpa Lolek's face fills with a dark sleepiness. "Go home, I'll sit here for a while," she says.

I agree. She comments to Grandpa Yosef, "You can take a break too. I'll be fine here."

Grandpa Yosef refuses. "No, no," he replies, somewhat hurt, "maybe later." Alex had said he would come, and Atalia too. She would come alone. Hainek had to go back to Beersheba for some urgent business.

We sit there and try to imagine Grandpa Hainek having urgent business.

*

Grandpa Lolek was in no hurry. The critical condition of the first few hours had been exchanged for the comforts of a sleepy empire where the king held court in bed. The doctors concluded that a benign tumor had developed in his head, which could be removed with one or two operations as soon as his body gained some strength. This diagnosis gave rise to a general sigh of relief, but the object of the diagnosis remained indifferent to the turn of events. Resting on his bed, he was quiet and free of worries. Only his fluttering wink reminded us of the life currently trapped inside a stroke.

Word of Grandpa Lolek's hospitalization spread through the

family by the usual means—phone calls and the fluctuation of the stars—and they came, teeming with urgency, soaked in sweat, three-busses-from-Netanya, local trains, aging cars, all come to peruse Grandpa Lolek and let out a murmur. A massive force collected them piecemeal from the troubles of life. The secret wings of the family that were scattered around the country, their connections normally hidden and disguised, were suddenly exposed and there they all were, summoned by the urgent alarm call of true trouble. The white room groaned, chairs were dragged in from the hallway, from the waiting room, and surreptitiously from the room next-door. The IV stand was wheeled against the wall. The empty bed next to Grandpa Lolek's became populated with visitors who settled themselves down close to one another, four or five in a row like heavy parrots.

And there were guests too. Unlike the family, they were notable for the temporary sense of their visits—they came for just a short while, didn't want to tire anyone out. What distinguished them from the family was also the absence of calculating looks at the other inhabitants of the room. Neighbors came. Friends came. Old creditors came. As they looked at Grandpa Lolek, they saw the silent debts within him, pondered their money and sighed. The elderly court clerk came, the one who delayed cases in return for stories of Anders' Army. He looked at his sleeping hero and sighed. There were visitors whose business with Grandpa Lolek was not apparent even by the end of their visits. They sighed and left. Green the Mechanic came. Why hadn't he been told anything, he asked angrily. He had begun to grow suspicious when the Vauxhall hadn't shown up, so he had made enquires and here he was. He stood with his hands spread wide and announced to the room: the Vauxhall, he would handle.

From the moment Grandpa Lolek began to command all horizontal attention as he lay in bed, Grandpa Yosef took the vertical attention, dashing this way and that, welcoming visitors and doctors, handling all the necessities. A great deal of motion circulated through Grandpa Lolek's room, and in the center of it all was Grandpa Yosef. He hardly left the hospital, devoting himself completely to care-giving. His shirts were clean but a faint odor wafted up from them, and from his body too. His eyes were bloodshot, his cheeks damp with glistening perspiration. He chopped up the endless time into shifts and handed them out to anyone who asked. Uncle Lunkish turned up with two umbrellas—so what if it wasn't raining—and got one shift, just one. Aunt Frieda came from Netanya, declaring, "*Nu*, you know I never got along with Lolek, but family is family," and demanded a shift. Uncle Menashe left the butcher shop and demanded a shift. Uncle Mendel came, inspected the *mezuzah* with his fingernail and sat down. Another shift.

Even at the end of the distribution, plenty of shifts were left over. Most of them were taken by us, Grandpa Lolek's *like*-grandchildren. We were recruited in different permutations, usually linking up with Grandpa Yosef, the lead caregiver. The *real* family—Grandpa Hainek—was represented by Atalia. She demanded and received one shift every day. In the hospital Grandpa Hainek wandered restlessly. Haifa. The north of the country. It might snow. And he rushed back to his southern city of Beersheba before his Polish destiny could awaken and strike, taking Atalia away from him. Every day he brought Atalia at the beginning of her shift, drove back to Beersheba in a taxi with the windows rolled up, and showed up again when her shift was over. He was consistent in the way he gave the obligatory ten minutes which Atalia forced him to allot to his oldest brother. He sat there polished, heavy, boots sticking out, sternly scanning the place.

In light of the grueling job he had taken upon himself (twice-a-day-Beersheba-Haifa-and-back) for Atalia's sake, and to ward off his fears, we hoped to discover something new in Grandpa Hainek. We looked at him and tried to comprehend. It was a good season for a little compassion. We thought about the beginning of the war. We tried to envision an eleven-year-old boy taken to a village he had never seen before, his father telling him this would be his new family, that he could not see his mother and father for a while. *You mustn't ever say you are a Jew.* He had to memorize prayers. *Here, this is your father, only him. Here, this is your mother, you cannot say she is not. Here are your brothers.* An eleven-year-old boy, left alone despite his tears. The farmer takes him to the barn and silently shows him how to work. From that boy our thoughts returned to the man sitting here in heavy boots, and we tried to envelope him with understanding, with tenderness. The thoughts lasted a second or two but then fell apart with a clatter and we had to think again about the eleven-year-old boy—if we wanted to.

The obligatory ten minutes passed and Grandpa Hainek escaped to his taxi. He spent a few minutes looking for passengers to take to Beersheba, but either way he was soon headed south, before the flakes could begin to whiten Haifa and clog everything up with mud and snow.

In the world, meanwhile, it was a dry winter. No rain. Freezing at night time, sometimes warm during the days. People said, "It's already November and no sign of winter." They gazed at the sky with astonishment, even some pride, practically hinting at a secret partnership in this decision of nature to flood the days with what had not ended in summer—light, heat, and strange winds. A violent and sterile winter, trying with all its might, but forgetting the main point. It glanced at the deeds of the previous winter and reproduced the freezing winds, doing its best, but there was no rain. Every night leaves fluttered through the darkness. The sea opposite Grandpa Lolek's room was full of great waves. Grandpa Yosef liked to stand at the window. At night you could hear the waves, and the wind sweeping paper from notice boards along the street.

In between visits, shifts, doctor's examinations and nuisances, Grandpa Yosef's journey continues. I try to time my shifts so I can continue on the voyage with him. My shifts are punctuated with essentially normal life. I come and go while the voyage waits. But gravity pulls the chapters together and the times between shifts are forgotten, dismissed from memory, leaving a continuity, an energetic and impatient journey.

Every time I come, Grandpa Yosef is in the midst of some burning matter, rushing past me, does-he-look-like-someone-who-has-time-to-sit-and-talk-about-what-happened-fifty-years-ago? Yet he is eager to talk of the voyage raging inside him, and very soon he sits me down, rids himself of all sorts of nuisances, including the ones I bother him with, and tells me offhandedly about Grandpa Lolek's status. He looks at me sternly: What do I mean by coming here and demanding miraculous improvements in the health of someone lying in bed like a sphinx? What could be new? Then he reaches out with impatient fingers to the bag I've brought, pulls out the clothes Anat prepared for him, the neatly cut sandwiches with little stickers noting the content of each one and whether they should be refrigerated. He nods, mumbles, "Thank you very much," and can't resist biting into the first sandwich, supplementing it with some coffee from a thermos. He sips and munches.

It seems to me that we both try to time our shifts so that we are together. But in fact Grandpa Yosef does most of the shifts, sharing days and nights with Effi too. One morning, between shifts, she asks me, "How many *Aktionen* were there in Bochnia anyway?" Atalia, at the end of a shift, asks me something about the ghettos. And I slowly begin to comprehend that the voyage is taking place during their shifts too. Or perhaps there is a completely different voyage going on there. The same places, the same events, and yet a different voyage. Grandpa Yosef does not divulge—he divides and conquers.

I come to take over from Dad on one of my shifts and find him and Grandpa Yosef laughing. They were recalling a day in Dad's childhood in Bochnia, when his mother sent him with his sister to the *dayan-posek*, the arbitrator, to check if the chicken for Shabbat was kosher even though she had found a tiny imperfection in it. Dad and his sister spoke only Polish, the *dayan* only Yiddish. With great effort they memorized their mother's question, learning the words by heart: *di mame hot geheysn fregn a shayle oyb dos hindl iz treyf oder kosher.* But on their way to the store, the syllables scattered in disarray. The two walked on worriedly, rapidly losing their arsenal of words as they neared the *dayan*. By the time they arrived, only a few confused letters and one simple phrase remained, a few sounds at the end of the sentence.

Dad and Grandpa Yosef laugh as they reminisce, and I realize there is no happenstance here: Grandpa Yosef is in the same era with everyone, the era of the voyage. I am not enough for him. During Dad's shifts the voyage slips through. It is planted in Atalia's shifts too. In Effi's shifts a twin voyage sneaks in. Grandpa Yosef is producing enough baby voyages to conquer the expanses of the family.

*

"Life went on after the *Sperre*. Those who had gone, were gone. Those who remained were overcome by hunger, thirst, and a will to live. It is hard to believe how quickly people went back to discussing the affairs of the day—potatoes, soup, the prospect of a cabbage shipment. Gradually the streets healed from the *Sperre* and, wondrously, new Jews flowed into the ghetto. As if the Germans had forgotten that they had evacuated Jews because of over-crowdedness, they continued to bring in more and more. Although I had not been taken away, I myself became a ghost after the *Sperre*. No one came close to me; they wouldn't dare. But I needed friends. My town of Bochnia was far beyond the mountains and the darkness, and the Jews here did not want me. Feiga was gone. I was not going to find her. It seemed the hunger and loss had weakened me so much that I no longer had the strength to get up and continue searching for my little bird. My legs longed to take me to Feiga, to awaken my heart. But my heart, what could it do? I could not just pick up my hat and go. All I could do was tire out my legs. There was not a day when I did not roam the ghetto in circles. I needed people, needed to talk, to socialize. I wanted to pray, to share a prayer with other Jews. I wanted to join a prayer *minyan*, to contribute my voice. But after the *Sperre* all religious life was forbidden, holy studies punishable by death. Even marriage ceremonies, when permitted, were conducted by Rumkowski. He was given sort of captain's duties. People gathered secretly to study and went on praying in underground groups. Me, they fled like the devil, exercising extreme caution.

"About a week after the end of the *Sperre*, Yom Kippur came, on September twenty-first. The ghetto was preoccupied with work, food and sickness. I walked far, as far as my legs could carry me, as if that were my way to somehow mark the torments of the holy day. And behold, from one of the houses emerged a distinguished Jew. He looked at me with penetrating eyes and asked, 'Would you like to pray on this holiest of days?' And wonder of wonders, he took me into an alcove in the house, where a secret prayer group was squeezed into the cellar. Jews wrapped in prayer shawls looked up at me and nodded their welcomes. I was handed my own *tallis*. A moment later, I, Yosef Ingberg of Bochnia, was praying in a *minyan*.

Guess who this miraculous man was, who dared to come out to me, to look into my eyes, to see that I was merely a Jew seeking prayers, not an agent or a chief agent?"

Grandpa Yosef wants me to guess. I give up. "Well, who was it?"

"It was Mr. Hirsch. Yes, Mr. Hirsch, the man who sometimes wanders through the neighborhood." He looks at me, detecting trains of amazement running over my face.

"Hirsch?"

"Yes, Mr. Hirsch. Now you have to make an effort and replace the person you know with his image from the ghetto days, when he was still an honorable rabbi, one of the senior beadles of the Admor of Tipow. Soon after I arrived in the ghetto I had noticed him on the streets; he stood out because of his great height, which did not result from the length of his body but from his gait—upright, arrogant even. He walked proudly through the ghetto, fraternizing only with similarly Orthodox men. They lived as a collective, a cohesive group from Tipow, obeying the rulership of their rabbi, the Admor, daring even to defy Rumkowski and his gang. In every matter they held Rumkowski accountable. They negotiated with him fearlessly over food rations and work quotas and housing. Everything. The Admor of Tipow gave the word, and his disciples went to battle.

"After the prayers, where I had been the tenth man to complete their *minyan*, Hirsch did not dismiss me. For some reason he attached me—not to his group, God forbid, but to himself, solely to himself. I found myself strolling the streets with him, just the two of us. We spoke a little, but mostly we were silent. Most of the words were spoken by Hirsch. He thought out loud, gave me his homiletics, and the things I heard from him I never imagined I would hear. Until the war I had been a man of Torah, I had studied diligently, but what I had learned was unlike anything I heard from Hirsch. He spoke pearls of wisdom and his persona was lofty and exalted, splendor in his appearance and splendor in his heart. To him, only to him, I poured out the entire truth, that I was not an agent nor anything of the kind. Only with him was I bold enough to let down my guard. I also gave him Ahasuerus's money. I told him to take it and give it to charity. But Hirsch only shook his head and laughed bitterly. 'Why would we want your money?' he asked mockingly, as if I had offered something forbidden.

"Sometimes he would erupt in fits of anger, accusing the whole world, accusing assimilated Jews, modernism, even myself. Sometimes there were long silences and I walked beside him quietly, waiting for his foul mood to pass. But usually he was in good spirits, and his Torah was as sweet as honey. During the hours I spent with him, life seemed to grow larger. It was so easy to believe that there was a world beyond the ghetto walls, and it was as if my soul had already been set free, comforted. I felt myself a man of freedom, walking wherever I pleased.

"We met almost every day. Each morning I hurried from my home on Dolna Street to meet him, and if he did not arrive, the whole day went badly. But when he did, we soon began to walk around the ghetto in conversation. He gradually began to unfetter his tongue. He asked me, 'Wherefore the destruction?' Standing at a crossroads, he grasped my shoulders and repeated the question: 'Wherefore the destruction?' It was a custom of his, to ask questions, when he was the one who had the answers. He came up with a question and repeated it over and over again, but it was not from me that he sought an answer—rather, from himself. Again and again, 'Wherefore the destruction?' And his reply: 'Due to the diminution of life.' What did this mean?

"Rabbi Hirsch explained. 'Even before the war, long before we could have imagined this state of affairs, I used to look around at life in our rabbi's court. Everything was so simple, the usual worries. In the *cheders* the little boys studied, and in the yeshivas the young men, and rabbis expounded upon the Torah, and Admors guided the simple people, and our minds did not engage in the greater questions of life. These wise men wished to delve deeper into rabbinic writings, to amend and revalue the laws, to interpret the sages' opinions. And the questions grew smaller and smaller, down to the scale of a feather, a bone, an egg. Oh, how small the questions grew. I gave notes to the rabbi on trivial matters—an onion fallen on an impure stovetop, or a crumb hidden among the straw. Tiny questions—shadows of questions. Where was the richness of life, the mystery?!

"'And when the questions grow small, so too does the soul and the faith. Our eyes suffice with small sins, and our hearts follow our eyes. Exploitation does not gnaw at one's conscience, lies do not sour one's breath. And life is pleasant, and worshipping *Hashem* is done offhand. Jews needed their lives to grow large again, after having diminished so. This is why everything now descends upon us. Because we stopped asking questions. Effortless existence weakened our questions. And here, now, everyone is asking questions...'

"Rabbi Hirsch's look turned cruel for a moment, vengeful. I had yet to learn of his tragedy, the tears he wept inside while he spoke so finely. Nothing I had learned had prepared me for such opinions. It was a desecration that was, somehow, not desecrating. As I lay in bed at night, I turned his words over and over in my mind. Life that had diminished...and what had befallen us because of it. I revisited scenes from the *Sperre*, the children, Rabbi Halberstam from Bochnia on the street, just like that, lying on the street, and for a moment I thought of Feiga, the comfort in her arms, and back came pictures from the *Sperre*, and up floated Hirsch's words.

"The diminution of life.

"In the morning my feet were drawn to Hirsch, and I spent entire days with him, with his relentless, unforgiving theories, and his words, which were unbefitting, and the likes of which I had never before heard. They were so sharp, and they compelled my heart to listen, to examine, to self-examine—was my own life so small? Were my questions small?

"I noticed that as the days passed, the fire of hatred grew stronger in him. His claims were harsh, bitter. 'How can we remonstrate?' he asked. 'After all, we ourselves are commanded in the holy Bible to destroy a people, Amalek. What is the difference between a command from our Lord, *Ribono shel olam*, and a command from their mustached god? What is the difference between annihilating Amalek and annihilating the Jews? We are commanded in the holy Torah, *Thou shalt blot out the remembrance of Amalek from under heaven;*

thou shalt not forget. Why, therefore, should we complain that the *goyim* too have been given their own Torah, in which they are commanded to kill us?'

"'And the children?' I asked. The children. Scenes of the *Sperre* flickered through my mind, and scenes of Bochnia, and beautiful Irenka, but Hirsch stood and faced me and his voice thundered, 'It is said in our Torah, *Now go and smite Amalek and spare them not...but slay both man and woman, infant and suckling...*do you understand, sir? *Infant and suckling*!!'

"He spoke the holy language, and it was so beautiful to hear it in the tortured ghetto, but his words were intolerable and I did not know how to respond, and at night the words mingled and Feiga appeared in a dream, and the infants of Amalek, and in the morning I ran to him to hear more.

"And so it went every day. I did not know the tragedy Hirsch bore in his heart, and I did not know that already then his soul was dismantled, that he was then the persona you know today, but under the authority of the Rabbi of Tipow, his Admor, all his parts were held together as one. To the outside he was still an elegant rabbi, the beadle of the Admor, and on the inside he was falling apart, betrayed, seeking revenge. Today, all that I did not know at the time is known and can be told. Today I know that during the *Sperre*, the Tipow group was required to hand over some of its members. The Admor of Tipow pronounced the names—these shall live, those shall die. And right in the midst of the *Sperre* days, he discovered that a relative of his wife's had recently arrived in the ghetto but had not yet joined the cohesive community, and all of his children were listed for deportation. The Admor ordered that the names be changed. Two of Hirsch's six children were put on the list. The searchers burst into Hirsch's house and pulled out all six of his children, although he had been promised that only two would be taken. By the time Hirsch learned of this awful affair and rushed to save his children, they had already been given to the Germans, from whose claws even the Admor of Tipow could not rescue them.

"And so his six children were lost, and his wife was lost—she jumped onto the wagon that took her children away. After the *Sperre*,

Hirsch was left on his own, and the Rabbi commanded him, 'Jew, take strength in the test that our Father in Heaven is giving you.' The Admor's authority was enough to strengthen the outer shell. But inside, Hirsch's soul was weeping, it did not want to live, and it was ashamed of its cowardice—his wife had thrown herself to death, and he? But Hirsch had no choice. Life had to go on. Even in the ghetto, the Admor's court carried on, and no words of mourning could be voiced because everyone had lost loved ones. Thoughts of revenge and heresy were forbidden. Then Rabbi Hirsch found me, Reb Yosef Ingberg of Bochnia, a Jew from the outside, and to me he released his thoughts—the question of destruction, the question of justice. Thanks to me, that which was confined within him could survive, and I served as a vessel for his anguish.

"I had no idea whatsoever of what was going on in Hirsch's soul, and was utterly unaware of my role, that by talking to me, a stranger, he was draining his embitterment just a little. I only knew that I heard wonders of wonders from him, terrible things. He would put his face close to mine and quote to me from the sages: 'Even if an Amalekite converts, we are commanded to smite him.' He would wag his finger in my face and ask, 'Where are these laws from?' And continue walking as if having spoken calmly, as if his words had not beaten my Jewish heart like a mallet, and I stayed behind him in the heart of the bustling ghetto. And the next day, the same thing.

"One morning something happened. It became known in the ghetto that the Admor of Tipow had escaped. To where, or how he did it, was not clear. But that morning his disciples awoke orphaned. Imagine to yourself what a betrayal that was, without warning, without a hint. The Admor had simply fled with his family. The disciples were not given much time to mourn. Rumkowski's people immediately saw their chance to nullify agreements, break up power, send the poor men off to work groups and deportation lists. They took the Admor's cronies out of the best places in the hospitals, out of the comfortable factories. All at once their privileges were revoked and given to those who found favor with the Judenrat. But worst of all was Hirsch. The Admor of Tipow had disappeared, and Hirsch's dismantled soul, which had been held together by the power of his authority, shattered into smithereens. Why go into detail? In short, *nu*, he completely lost his mind. From the moment the Admor abandoned them, not only did Hirsch's mind weaken, and not only did the Tipowik group's power fall apart, but all its secrets blossomed and spread through the ghetto, including the story of Hirsch. Only then did I learn of the fire that had been eating away at his heart. I was regretful—perhaps I could have offered him some consolation.

"One week later, Hirsch was taken away. I thought he was killed, but as you know, he was not lost in the camps; he is here with us in Eretz Yisrael. And it was the Admor of Tipow, may the memory of this *tzaddik* be a blessing, who did not survive. He was caught and taken with all his loved ones, may God avenge their blood, to Treblinka. He was captured near the town of Shedlitz, and instead of Chelmno, where the Lodz ghetto inhabitants were sent, he went to the gas chambers in Treblinka."

(Treblinka. Untersturmführer Kurt Franz, Doll.)

Grandpa Yosef seems to read my mind. "Yes, that was where that 'Doll' was, *Lalka*, but what difference does it make, one way or the other. Hirsch went, as did many others. And I too, just as I was getting used to life in the Lodz ghetto, I was grouped with some Jews sent to slave labor in a camp near Poznan. Someone dared put my name on the list and kick the chief agent out of the ghetto. And I, Yosef Ingberg, not an agent and not a chief, found myself leaving the Lodz ghetto forever. I cannot recall the name of the camp. How could I? As soon as we arrived, battered from our ride in a truck, after they whipped me and pulled out two teeth, and after two men were shot in front of my eyes (Why? No way to know), my gaze fell briefly on the camp personnel standing in the distance, and I saw the figure of Ahasuerus.

"There he stood, next to the camp commandant, and he seemed to be tutoring him, teaching the inexperienced commandant. I stared. I must have stood out from the distance—a Jew looking straight at death. Suddenly his eyes met mine. I saw him give the commandant an instruction and then all the personnel came up to us. Terror fell upon our group. All around me people sensed the shadow of death approaching. Only rarely did the senior officers interfere with the

Jews' lives. They left that job for junior officers, sergeants, the Ukrainians and the volunteers, damn them.

"I whispered to the Jews, 'Do not worry, he is a decent man.' They looked at me as if I had lost my mind. They could not have imagined the storm raging in my heart as a thought that was all but forgotten began to reappear: Feiga. We must set off on the road again. Here, the *Kadosh Baruch Hu* was renewing my voyage! I had no doubt of Ahasuerus's intentions. He might not have remembered me at all, but simply been astonished at this Jew staring at him. And yet he might have recognized me, only to wonder how I had not been killed in the *Sperre* as planned. Still, I was certain he would not kill me.

"Ahasuerus came closer. He stopped some six steps away from us. The personnel stood behind him. In front of him the Ukrainians and the sergeants, they too were frozen. They had ceased kicking us, cowed by the presence of authority. What did the general want? They did not know of my Feiga. Perhaps they did not conceive of his Little Lover either. We stood there, everyone around us completely unaware of the true significance of the situation, only Ahasuerus and myself in the center as he stared at me with steely eyes. A brief moment of human expression flitted over his face, a wrinkle that perhaps came from the heart, and an instant later there was nothing but frozen wilderness. He turned back and disappeared into the distance, and with him, like the wings of a crow, went the personnel. Silence lingered in the air for a moment, then all erupted. The whips began again. The shouts picked up. We were pushed, whipped. We were rushed into flimsy wooden huts without windows. We knew neither the name of the camp, nor what they would do with us.

"A whole day and night passed. We were not sent to work. Twice we were brought some disgusting soup, and once we were allowed to use the latrine. Then, from the edge of the window, I saw the car. It had a new hood ornament, a statue of an eagle with its talons digging into the flesh of the car, its bird-legs lifting up behind. And as my heart had foreseen, we were quickly forced out of the hut for a roll-call. The reason for the roll-call was me. A sergeant took hold of me and removed me from the group. They washed me again. And again the bridegroom's clothes. They put me in a closed room.

"Ahasuerus had tormented himself for a whole day and night. All those months, while I was in the Lodz ghetto, he had managed with great effort to banish the Little Lover from his heart, to devote himself to his duties, damn him, and now here I was. He agonized for a whole day and night but was unable to put out the fire kindled by the sight of me, and early the next morning we set off again. This time it was winter. Cold. Ahasuerus's face was strained. Who knew what obligations he had abandoned hastily, and what his punishment would be, how determined he was to be swallowed up in the black abyss of this unrequited love? For four months, more than a third of a year, we had not seen each other. I wondered, should I report anything? He had deposited me in the ghetto and the deposit had been returned. I should say something, should I not? But reality quickly reminded me who I was, and who he was. The months of hunger in the ghetto had mistreated my body and he, the king of evil, now had a higher rank, and it seemed he had also grown taller. He did not talk to me, my existence did not bother him at all. I was an object, like a comb found at the bottom of the sheets, bringing up forgotten emotions. We were driving to his Little Lover, or so he believed. Storing up energy for a decisive conversation with her. Perhaps he would beg. The devil would kneel before the she-devil and weep. He did not know who Feiga was, for whom he was urging his heart, straining his eyes, squeezing out the power from his car. I permitted myself a pause for thought. Leaning back in my seat, I asked myself like a merchant, should I give him back his money? I had spent almost none of it. But that nonsensical thought soon disappeared.

"What more can I say? For two days we drove. The routine of the journey was much like the previous one, but there were no break-downs, no chance for a word to be uttered. Two people driving. Thus far we had accumulated only one spoken sentence, uttered by Ahasuerus before he closed his eyes to sleep. The landscape changed. Flat lakes, black trees. The sky drizzled constantly. We crossed huge rivers and one massive Tigris, which in retrospect I believe was the Wisla, that same Wisla that crossed through Krakow, on to Warsaw, and all the way to Danzig on the North Sea. I was afraid—was Feiga here? In this terrible cold? Here, in such a barren landscape? The car drove on and on as if Ahasuerus could not interfere with its maneuvers. She knew her way, the car. Bilaam's donkey.

"We stopped at a camp. It was entirely black. Black trees and black fences, and all the huts were black, dipped in freezing cold and puddles. The gates opened for us, the camp guards practically danced around in fear. We made a strong impression on them. The camp personnel hurried to welcome Ahasuerus, and I, knowing my role, stayed in the car. I was left in a large square beside the command house. My eyes were glued to the hunched, black images walking to and fro. Jews rotting away from cold and torture, while I sat in a royal car and fine clothing, looking for lovers. I dared not get out and ask the Jews about Feiga. I reprimanded myself—after all, that was what I had come for—but caution held me back. Slowly my silhouette became apparent to the inmates, and Jewish faces began to stare at me. From afar I saw them, but sensed them coming closer. I did not dare get out, and they dared not approach. There was terror in the air, I could sense it. Their caution taught me caution. Ukrainian guards in black uniforms, similar to the SS uniform, walked around the camp arrogantly. They passed by the car, pretending not to notice me. Darkness fell. Calls were heard in the distance. Many footsteps. My body had been freezing for two hours in the car. Inside, Ahasuerus was still meeting with the officers. They were probably presenting their fine achievements to him, boasting of impressive killing quotas, damn them. And then a Jew tapped on the car window. I could tell immediately that it was a Jew. I was horrified by his skeletal face, his body wrapped in rags, but I knew it was a Jew. Afraid, I opened the window a crack.

"'Give me!'

"His Yiddish was crude. His eyes darted around. Black knobs on his face, bruises and cuts. His flesh was covered with wounds. I reached into my clothes. I had no food and was hungry myself, but I still had Ahasuerus's money. I asked about Feiga.

"'No woman here. Give!'

"And then, disaster. From the darkness a figure emerged. A Ukrainian guard. Before I knew what was happening, the whip had landed. The Jew fell. Right beneath my window, he disappeared from my eyes. The Ukrainian went up to him and raised his whip. He thrashed and then turned the whip around and beat the Jew's body with the handle. Another figure came out of the command house. The noise had disturbed the convening gentlemen. The Ukrainian took one step back as an SS officer approached. He looked at me first and my blood curdled. I thought about Yanek's lion whisper from the ghetto. The officer looked away from me—I was nothing to him. In the dark he aimed his pistol downwards. The pistol was hidden from me, but not the flash of lightening followed by a bang. All beneath my window, a step away from me, on the other side of the door, and I could not see a thing. The SS officer straightened up and examined his handiwork. He turned to the headquarters, where Balshazar's feast was going on. The Ukrainian went up to finish the job. He dragged the body away, which was then revealed to me. My heart sunk.

"In the dark, in the silence, I stayed shut in the car. I barely noticed Ahasuerus coming out, throwing himself onto the seat next to me, starting the engine, far from my world. He drove the car, cold, quiet, and I thought of Feiga. For a moment I felt angry at her. What was this journey for? The torture. Jews were dying, for God's sake, and she was holding back. Where was she? Why did she not make an effort, as I was doing, to traverse the distance? A gloom took hold of me, not only anger. I remembered that in the distant days before the war, too, I had sensed a speck of something amiss. My time with her was enjoyable, and she had agreed to marry me, but the balance, how shall I put it…for her I would have run through half of Bochnia, but she? No telling. She had a rich world inside of her, she was quiet, noble. She had many suitors. And yet she had chosen me. That was her way, her world was shut off under lock and bolt, no emotions escaped, no closeness."

Grandpa Yosef tries to explain Feiga. Ahasuerus can wait. The journey can wait. The Shoah can wait. Now, Feiga.

"You know, long before I was bold enough to speak to her, my entire life was devoted to Feiga. In Bochnia, before she even knew of my existence, I would keep track of her daily routine. She walked down Zandetzka Street every day to visit her friend Gittel. And there, on Zandetzka, lived Jozi, a classmate of mine. Not a smart fellow, not a likeable man, in fact. But every day at three forty-five I would turn up at his house and try to tempt him with stamps to trade. That was his only hobby, and for Feiga's sake I began to collect stamps too. There was no better place in the whole street than Jozi's window, where I would sit and wait for her while Jozi crumpled the stamps I had brought, displeased. He would haggle and try to bring my prices down, negotiating back and forth with me, without knowing that it was time that I was buying. Only time. It was not easy to find stamps for Mr. Jozi. Your father used to get hold of some for me, I did not ask how. And I stole from Uncle Marek's collection. I did business with the Polish mailman, helping him out with our maid, Marushka, with whom he was head over heels in love. It was hard to believe how such a great love was possible for that Marushka of ours. Spoiled and sickly, all she ever did was complain.

"At exactly four o'clock, Feiga would appear from down the street. She walked alone, with a straight back. In her heart she did not address the world, but the whole world turned to her. It was impossible not to join the breeze in the trees, the birds in the branches, the fallen leaves scattering at her feet. I practically flew out the window like one of the birds. If only I could be allowed to roll at her feet. But I did not fly, I was no bird. I leaned out of the window towards her like a deer yearning for rivers of water, and she, innocent and pure, walked along. She was modest and knowing, fully aware of the man swinging between life and death at Jozi's window.

"Behind me, Jozi annoyingly complained that the stamps were too ordinary. His complaints increased from day to day, and the time came when he declared that he was sick of stamps. Stamps were for kids.

"And in what would the honorable Jozi take an interest now, if not in stamps?

"Jozi giggled. His eyes sparkled like two balls of grease. '*Nu*, you know…' He rubbed his palms together and the blood pulsed through his face as he pursed his lips. Then he confided the worst. Of all the women in the world, it was Feiga's name that he uttered. He told me how every day at seven in the evening she hurried down the street outside his window on her way home, and that the little lass looked straight at his window.

"Alarms rang through my head. It turned out I was missing an entire show of Feiga at seven in the evening. I would have to stay longer at Jozi's, missing one prayer service. *Hashem* would forgive me. And Feiga was apparently interested in Jozi. If that was true, what good were prayers?

"Imagine, before I knew how many obstacles there were and how difficult it would be. *Nu,* her family, and mine too, they thought we should wait. And imagine the joy in my heart, imagine how I thanked the Lord, when finally everything fell into place. Feiga agreed to marry me. 'I will love you,' she said. What happiness my Feiga gave me. And after the war, as you know, we were married. Almost fifty years of marriage I had with her, and every day was good. And then her strength failed her and my Feiga passed away. I would have liked twenty more years of marriage. I did not have my fill, my thirst was not quenched."

Grandpa Yosef walks to the end of the hallway. Coffee. Ahasuerus's car drives on north through low fields and creeks. Little villages. A flat landscape.

Grandpa Yosef has left a few words behind:

"For one moment there, while the Jew's body was being dragged away and I waited in the car for Ahasuerus, I felt some anger at Feiga, as if the prolonging of this journey was her fault, and the sacrifice of the Jews was unacceptable."

While he is gone at the coffee machine, the story continues without him. Grandpa Yosef and Ahasuerus pass through Mielejewo camp. Ahasuerus gets out to surprise the personnel with an inspection. His appearance is harsh, but his steps slacken, this whole adventure is a loss. If only he could turn back the wheel of time. He cannot. The obligations. The damned Jews. At home he has a wife and child, but without his beloved, life is intolerable. The officers salute, the car is welcomed with respect and amazement. The general's presence is unwanted—in this damned place there is no good time for an inspection. Fortunately, he only goes through the list of staff, enquiring, where is this one? Where is that one? Transferred where? And where was this woman transferred to? Ravensbrück? The answer satisfies him. He gets up and leaves without even finishing his meal. Did they pass the inspection? Would he give a good report? Ahasuerus leaves. The gates shut. And the journey continues. Pruchnik camp, Nadbrzeże camp. Tiny satellites of Stutthof camp on the shores of the Baltic Sea. The journey has only just begun, it transpires. They are traveling to Ravensbrück. Ravensbrück. In Germany, not in Poland. A long journey west, to the heart of the Reich, less than seventy miles from Berlin. Ahasuerus oscillates between relaxation and anger.

Grandpa Yosef comes back with a cup of coffee.

"I feared for my life. This Ahasuerus, there was no telling what he would do when he was angry. Again I found myself afraid to look up, trying to diminish myself. During my hours of rest, I thought up a job for myself: I would sweep the floor of the car and polish the windows and mirrors with my sleeve. That was my instinct—to be necessary. Learn it once, and it will never leave you. I tried out different ideas. I very much wanted to open the hood and glance at the engine, at the bird's hidden organs. I was innocent, I had hardly ever seen cars, and to see one exposed beneath its robes, I had not even imagined possible. I was so close, longing to get to know the mechanism, the technique, to reach out and touch it, to see where the power flowed.

"And so we drove on, swallowing up countries. And then finally we were close to Ravensbrück, where the Little Lover was—where, my heart fluttered, my Feiga might be. But just before the camp, Ahasuerus stopped, as if to gather his strength, to remind himself who he was, an omnipotent general—why should he fear one woman, a minor staff member? He got out of the car with great momentum and walked out into the cold air. He strode confidently, his SS boots creaking in the mud. He stood beside a bush, his hand hovering over the leaves, as if examining his fingers to see whether he was still capable of touching a delicate body. His hand flitted over the bush and I could see he liked the touch. His chin was turned down, his eyes shut tight. And suddenly I saw that Ahasuerus was crying. His hand made a fist around the tendrils of that poor bush. His entire body was trembling.

"Thoughts spun through my mind. *Nu*, such a general, a creature in love, and he was a murderer. How could these two things flow together in his blood? Hot and cold, poison and tenderness. How did his strength not run out? Every hour without her was worse than death and harder than hell.

"Ahasuerus walked away from the bush and came back. Upright, he opened the door and sat down regally. Only his face disclosed the shock, the annihilation to which he was leading himself, betraying his duties. This whole journey was just false hope, and there was no telling how it would end. A moment passed. Another moment. Ahasuerus sat without making a sound. I felt that time was running out, convinced that in Ravensbrück camp I would find Feiga. Ahasuerus would soon start the car and our hearts would be reunited. But Ahasuerus was lost in thought. His breathing was quiet, slow. I turned to look at him, thinking perhaps I could divine his intentions. Would he have the strength to start the car, to go as far as the camp gates? And then another thought ignited—what did he need me for? Once he found his Little Lover, what would he need me for? My fright increased. He will kill me. Why not here? What need is there for me? Two trees along, the side of the road grew large in my eyes. Perhaps he would shoot me beneath one of them, without the traditional escort, without a *kaddish* prayer, without a Jewish burial. *Nu*, Jews were dying in the thousands, and I wanted a Jewish burial. And where were my parents? I no longer believed, of course, that they had been taken East. The truths that had penetrated my ears in the Lodz ghetto, the killings, Chelmno, had slowly connected with my parents who had been sent away. What Chelmno had been for the Jews of Lodz, Belzec had been for my family. Lost, all my loved ones were lost, and there I was, dressed in fine clothing.

"I sighed. And my sigh drew a look from Ahasuerus. He quickly turned back to look at the road, removing me from his field of vision. I froze. I had reminded him of my existence, my unnecessary existence. A mistake.

"He turned and looked at me. 'It's hard...It's hard for everyone...'

"And silence. Emptiness around us. He had not spoken only to me. Around us were woods, and behind them camps, and somewhere in the distance the Lodz ghetto, and more camps, and the whole world was at war. It was hard, it was hard for everyone."

Grandpa Yosef stops talking. He gets up and goes to the window. He looks at the clouds. No rain, no rain. What will be the end? Clouds gather, the sky presses down to the earth, the cold deepens and still the rain does not come. Grandpa Yosef stays by the window but his story does not wait. Behind his back, details slip through, little pieces of morse code that he has already told me an era ago, and they take me through the rest of the story without him.

Ahasuerus starts the car and drives it up to the camp gates. In the women's camp of Ravensbrück there is hunger and disease. The inmates are exhausted. Those who do not join a group, die. Any woman who makes the mistake of standing out in front of the murderous female SS officers is killed. Death is a method, a solution. In the heart of the camp, the "bunker" provides a solution for those whose death the SS murderesses want to slow. But the main point for us—for Grandpa Yosef, for me, for Ahasuerus—is that the Little Lover is there, serving at Ravensbrück.

The car crosses through the gates. There is not even a moment's delay before the meeting. Ahasuerus walks into the staff building. Then he goes to one of the huts. A conversation takes place there for a moment or two. A fair young woman emerges and walks away with heavy, angry steps. He follows her, pleading. She pushes his hands away, speeding up. She is not tall. Pretty, let us say. Her face is flushed with anger. She disappears behind a hut.

"There, in the savagery, they were not bound by their rules of etiquette," Grandpa Yosef mumbles. "I had not imagined such a thin little thing. She wasn't huge or red-faced, like so many of the cruel SS female officers. And it was clear that she was unhappy with Ahasuerus's advances. Unaccustomed to such crudeness. She had been taught that a woman should be treated politely. Gently. And he, the villain, would not let her alone.

"In the car I could see little and hear nothing. The minutes passed and I felt a strong desire to get out and look for my Feiga. But it was good that I didn't, because here was Ahasuerus marching towards me, getting into the car, slamming its door. He started the engine in a fury, in a storm. His face was red, evil, as if nothing else mattered in the world. The car's tires screeched on the road, burst through the gates, the sentries barely had time to fling them open. Ahasuerus made the car gallop. Imposing the roar of his heart upon it, he strained the engine to its limits. His face was determined, as if there were great intent in his driving, but I sensed that our journey was over. He looked right and left, his driving seemed very purposeful, but I could sense the truth in the regal car. She acquiesced to having her pedals pressed, her wheel turned, but her senses had been weakened, and she was no longer searching for a route but rather she was fleeing. It was over and done with—the search for Feiga had failed.

"Again I believed he would kill me. But he did not. And what did he do with me? I will tell you the truth. All the horrors of the Shoah that I saw, everything that is best forgotten, lives on lucidly in my memory. The memories are clear and transparent, like a beautiful landscape. But the end of Ahasuerus is dim. When did we part ways? I vaguely remember someone walking me down a path of wet gravel. That was probably no longer Ahasuerus, but an officer, I think. And then the memory is swallowed up. Rain drenches the world and I am in a suffocating space. Figures around me, prisoners. I too am a prisoner. I awake in the men's camp of Ravensbrück. A merciful figure comes up to me, shoves at me some sort of thing which I shall call a blanket, although that is not what it was. A hard, cold sheet. It was barely flexible enough to be placed on one's body, it was useless for heat. The memories return. I am completely frozen, a cut on my head and a deep gash from ankle to knee. The merciful man, the head of the hut, whose name is Adler, whispers in my ear that I will feel better by morning. Although I had not yet been a prisoner in any camp, only ghettos and strange journeys, my voyage with Ahasuerus had taught me plenty about camp life. I would not feel better in the morning. In the morning there would be slave labor. I would starve. They would beat me ceaselessly. They would rob me of my bread, the other inmates too. It would not be better in the morning.

"Do you know what they called the camp system there, in the north? *Vernichtung durch Arbeit.* Extermination through work."

(He finds strange pleasure in rolling the German words off his tongue, tasting them on his lips. *Vernichtung durch Arbeit.*)

"But this man, Adler, tries to lift my sprits. From somewhere they bring hot soup, as if a restaurant is open not far away. The soup is a bland concoction, but I sip it, inhale the broth, and sense that without this Adler I will have no life.

"And indeed, I was right. Adler was one of the saints. My days of Ravensbrück had begun. *Vernichtung durch Arbeit.* Extermination through work. In the morning, still dark, roll-calls that last for hours. Shouting, beating, physical punishments. People murdered right beside you. The living go off to work. A moribund mass of prisoners sets off shoulder to shoulder. The work is exhausting, our brains dizzied from fear. The German supervisors do not spare the rod. One of them had fit a silver knob on the end of his whip. Everyone knew that all that whip needed was one thrash. Prisoners were murdered over mistakes, over nothing, over boredom that took hold of a German. The Ukrainian guards were not allowed to kill. Only the Germans had that right, and there was much jealousy. We, the prisoners, worked. All we did was work. At lunch there was a hard hunk of bread and soup. A stench rose from it, but the prisoners fought over one more spoonful and stole each other's slices of bread. Simple people, everyday Jews, became murderous and loathsome. They would rip a piece of bread away from you and laugh in your face, crazed. There are no depths of hell lower than that. And in the midst of it all was Adler.

"This man, Adler, revealed himself from the first as a sort of Judah the Maccabi. A courageous Jew, he did not fear the prisoners, and even found courage in front of the SS. He knew his limitations and exercised caution, but he guarded the prisoners like a Hasmonean. His work was exhausting. There was no shortage of villains among the prisoners, and even those who were not villainous had been driven mad by hunger and were capable of anything. Even in the heart of suffering, on the brink of death, the power-hungry still lust for power, the traitorous still hand over their brethren, and the informants still collaborate.

"Among all these, with infinite dedication, stood Adler. He

pronounced verdicts like King Solomon, separated the Jewish hawks from one another like Moses, and brandished a sword like David. He was as kind as—to whom can I compare his kindness? It was infinite. Incredibly, before the war he was a Doctor of Humanities at the university of Lvov. A scholar, a researcher of history, an author of books on theories of the soul. A Jew who had forgotten his Judaism, wrapped up in the world of the *goyim*, and that was how he liked it. He researched Jewish history too, but in the way that a geologist studies rocks or a geographer the patterns of streams. It was in the camp that his Jewish soul was revealed. By the time I, Yosef Ingberg, arrived at Ravensbrück men's camp, which was attached to the infamous women's camp, Adler was already positioned as a leader of the people, one to guide them through the desert for forty years. *Nu*, I am exaggerating a little..."

Grandpa Yosef stops. He breathes heavily, clearly searching for the right words. He wants to paint me an accurate picture of Adler, as great as the man himself, but not ordinarily great like memorial statues.

"The head of the prisoners in the camp was called Farkelstein. Adler, on his part, stayed away from him. He could easily have become head of the prisoners, but he avoided that role. The SS themselves, damn them, although they did not appoint Adler to Farkelstein's position, used to come to him, recognizing his authority over the prisoners. They let Farkelstein bear the official title, a sort of badge of respect invented in the camps, but much to Farkelstein's chagrin, they ignored him and his title. Farkelstein could have designated Adler for the hard jobs, the more injurious ones, or handed him over to the Germans with a wink, but more than he hated Adler, he feared him, and more than he feared him, he was trapped in a superstitious conviction that without Adler there would be no Farkelstein. Where did this belief come from? What was the logic? But then, where did places like Ravensbrück come from; what logic was behind them? There was none. Farkelstein dealt every day with his hatred and his envy and his fears. And it was into this river of flames that I slid. Because for some reason, Farkelstein immediately began to hate me and harass me. And harassment by the head of the prisoners was tantamount to a death sentence.

"A few days had passed since I arrived in the camps, and already I was half-dead. The work was grueling. My body, sensing death, suffered from dysentery. Inside the rags of my trousers the excrement dribbled over my body. The end was nearing. I no longer had the strength to work. There were moments, my mind dizzied, when I was drawn to the whip, especially the one with the silver knob. To offer my head, to kiss the whip. Shut off the whole world, no strength, no desires, only the whip, that whip, sharp and clear. That silver knob was like a *rimon*—like the finial that decorates a Torah scroll.

"How did I not die?

"Adler.

"Was there any other way?

"During work he protected me. When food was distributed he looked out for me. He got hold of clean clothing for me. At night, in the hut, he fed me the secret soup which a few prisoners cooked up somewhere in the distance every night. Only a few were lucky enough to get a few drops of it.

"Strange. So many were dying. *Vernichtung durch Arbeit.* Extermination through work. On every bed, every night, a Jew fought for his life. No justice and no mercy. Here died the son of a rabbi, there a tailor, a father of ten. Here was a boy dying, no one knew his name, there an elderly man—who knew how he had survived that long? Jews were dying everywhere and yet Adler took pity on me, visiting my bedside as if I alone were a patient among vacationers. A spoiled tourist with a bad stomach on a pleasure cruise, and the captain making himself personally responsible for his health, embarrassed by the regretful mishap. Because of such a trivial problem, the traveler might miss the best of the itinerary.

"Every night Adler sat on the edge of my bed, untouched by tiredness, by hunger. And do you know what Adler did before the dying body of Yosef Ingberg? He recited his studies. He told me about the theories he investigated, the matters on which he had almost completed a conclusion or two that were important for humanity, before the world had lost its mind. I lay at his feet, deathly ill, with only a spark remaining in my soul, a small candle's light not yet extinguished. And to that flame, it seems, Adler talked, night after night. What little remained of me was there in the core of the flame, and each night I had to regain strength for the next day, another day of *Vernichtung durch Arbeit*. During work too, between the trenches of dirt we dug only to fill up again—the purpose, after all, was extermination—Adler recited his studies softly, as if leafing through pages he had left only a moment ago on his desk at Lvov University. He was respectful of his only student, the dying Yosef Ingberg, as I lay on the side of the trench while he himself worked a double quota. The supervisor turned a blind eye, and against the background noise of the picks softly tapping, only Adler's voice could be heard. Every day he took a book off the shelf and taught me its content. The great Khans of Mongolia and the travels of Attila the Hun. The history of the Ancients and the mystery of the Danube. The ascendance of Jewish agriculture and the travels of Alexander the Great. He spread before me everything he had studied of the past and the present, until the war had snatched him away from his desk. And he revealed a new topic to me, which he had only just begun to explore, a study on the true nature of pirates. Every night when we returned from work, after he had fed me the extra soup, Adler told me of his preliminary conclusions, and in those moments it seemed that for him the Holocaust was merely a slight nuisance, as if he had been called away from his office to discuss a tedious memorandum with the faculty treasurer. He was not pained by the whip that cut through his flesh, nor by the hangings in the center of the camp, nor the bad food. His spirit fell because of the pirate Subatol Deul, who was waiting for him, unexplored, on the deck of the *Costa Negra*. There he stood, the skull-and-bones flag above him, while Adler carried baskets of dirt from the trenches to the mounds.

"What can I say? My soul was tiny, practically devoid of life, but Adler's words penetrated it and brought health. Slowly but surely, thanks to his lectures, I recovered. And Adler? From the moment it became clear that I would live, it was as if I had graduated to the next class, and he added advanced topics to the curriculum. Adler taught me—to survive. He taught me the ruses of existence and the customs of the camp and what was required if one wished to live. Every day one had to wage a careful war against the SS, against the Ukrainians, against the Jewish police—God help us—and do not forget Farkelstein and his gang. Among all these troubles and hardships, Adler roamed like a king, a lion, directing justice, obtaining here and giving there, and all in aid of the weak, the sick, to save one more soul from death. Not that Adler was able to help much. Prisoners died every day, and every day new ones came, and there was no clear law dictating what saved a man from death, what brought him to death. But Adler did not give up. His dealings were many and dangerous, always engaged in quick transactions intended to maintain human dignity.

"It is very difficult to describe the greatness of a man like Adler in such a place. Many prisoners ended up in the Ravensbrück men's camp, rabbis and intellectuals, community leaders and public figures. You cannot imagine how quickly one's soul declines in a place like that, and if it does not decline, the body withers. It is hard, hard to survive, to remain human. Many struggled to save their lives, to save a human soul, and some managed, but someone like Adler...*nu*, how can I describe him?

"One day I told him I would like to be like him. Adler smiled, waved his pick, and kept on digging the trench.

"He dug twice as many trenches as he needed to, completing quotas for the sick and the weary, in return for the supervisors' silence. His Jewish soul burst through like a young lion. Sometimes he said nothing, and I was enveloped by a silence of awe. I examined this marvelous man closely, wondering if bad memories tormented him, as they did me, or if perhaps he was plowing ahead, making inroads in his research. My eyes examined, my ears mined. And slowly I noticed a series of grumbles escaping silently from his lips, kind of furious mumbles, as if he were conducting a bitter negotiation with someone. The anger and mumbling did not go on for long. A short time later he taught me about the Pharaonic kings, the education of children in Sparta, the customs of the Greek Olympics. But I was intensely curious—what went on during those silences? What was the cause of Adler's bitterness? I had already learned that it was best to stay away from the truth, better not to know of peoples' wounds. Had he lost six children like Hirsch had? Had some other disaster befallen him? Curiosity has a way of triumphing, so one day I dared to ask about the meaning of his mumblings and anger.

"Adler, embarrassed, admitted that these murmurs of his were a theory he was trying out, a survival method, and he did not know if the theory was ripe for instruction yet. I demanded—teach me! And Adler began to teach me a simple theory. He explained that I had to contemplate the future that had been robbed from me and cry out in bitter resentment—how had they dared take the future that had been planned for me?! 'Grow bitter! Be furious!' he urged me. 'Imagine the future that was ready for you, and cry out against the reality trying to cancel it out!' And that was not all. I also had to outline before him the precise details of my robbed future, and complain, and rage, and wave my fists at reality.

"And so, every day, we both bitterly protested the theft of our futures, and threatened like lions—who would dare take this future from us? Adler was extremely fanatical about this future theory. The past was completely forbidden. He demanded that I rid myself of memories, throw them all out, shake out my pockets. When one day I began to tell him about Feiga and our good days in Bochnia, he grew enraged. 'The future! The future! If you wish to live, think about her and you in the future, only in the future!' He waved his pick in the air and the Ukrainian supervisor looked up in surprise and curiosity, thinking he might be lucky enough to witness one Jewish prisoner murdering another.

"There was no choice. From morning to evening the future preoccupied us. We were full of anger at all that had been stolen from us. Adler commanded the future to appear in all its details. At roll-calls, at food distribution, always we lived in the future. Day after day I left the splendid house I had built for my Feiga and myself in Bochnia, to study at a fine *yeshiva*. In the evenings we sat and dined and talked about life. And Adler, who held a chair at a university, labored over his book about pirates. He went to the Caribbean once or twice to expand his studies. He tasted pineapple, palm fruit, papaya. Studied the world of the pirates. And life in the future was simple and good.

"When we grew slightly tired of the future, we dwelled on Adler's research. I began to gain courage and ask questions, make comments, even construct a few hypotheses and semi-proposals of my own. Every single moment, from before sunrise until after sundown, waving our picks up and down, it was inexplicable how death had not yet taken us, but with Adler the hours passed pleasantly. Pleasantly, *nu*, perhaps that is an exaggeration. But it was tolerable. There was a hint of a reason to go on living in the trenches, in the stench of the hut, with the horrible punishments and the dead we no longer counted or thought of. Every morning I longed for the moment when we would be positioned alongside the pits after roll-call, after the interminable march, after the morning punishments, and there, in the pits, a few cigarettes for the supervisor, and then I could regale Adler with ideas built up overnight. My lust for knowledge impressed and amused Adler. He straightened up over his pick for a moment, giggling, 'As soon as you were brought here, I knew I could not lose my best student.'

"His compliment embarrassed me but filled me with pride. I wished I could be his student at the real university in Lvov. In Bochnia they had said I had the character of a scholar. One day I asked Adler, 'Why, why this extermination? Why is all this occurring?'

"Adler stopped working and stood bewildered, holding his pick up in mid-air. Then he slowly lowered it. 'Why the extermination?' He repeated my question, mulling it over. He went back to work. He hummed the sentence to himself one more time, 'Why the extermination?' Then he demanded, 'The future, we must think only of the future.'

"And so I told him of the future, of Feiga and me holding a son, the baby's lavish *briss* ceremony, rabbis gathering from all corners of the land to see the newborn, and blessing him, not explaining why they have convened, but with hints in their eyes. They huddle secretively every once in a while and sip the good wine, *khamra taba*, and they closely examine the baby's face in silence. I listed for Adler the names of the rabbis, gather them from all the dynasties of Poland and Lithuania, as if my eyes are passing over a wall of radiance.

"Adler listens, encouraging, and asks, 'What will you name your firstborn?'

"And my heart cries out, 'I will name him after you!'

"One day there was an outbreak of typhus in the camp and Adler fell ill. He was simply one among many. At first he kept his strength and tried to join the work group, but he quickly weakened. From then on our roles were reversed. I, the healthy one, took it upon myself to save Adler from the disease, from being finished off with a shot, from some connivance of damned Farkelstein. I called out to him, 'Be angry! Be bitter!' and begged our Creator to take pity on this man. I gave him food from my meager allowance, and he ate from my palm like a baby. His kind eyes thanked me, and that was the greatest gift I could have sought from *Hashem*, blessed be He. But Adler was dying. There was no choice but to take him to the *rivier*, the infirmary, a place that offered no great cures, only sadistic doctors and reduced food rations; at the end of every week, those who had not recovered were killed.

"For a day or two I was left on my own, and then a sudden boldness took hold of me. I stole an extra portion of bread for Adler and rushed to the *rivier* with some excuse to visit him. I handed him the bread, proud and embarrassed—but Adler needed food no longer. Instead of the bread he grasped my hand and pulled me to him. He began to mumble in my ears, words that I believed at first came from the shock of his waning mind, but slowly they began to make sense. Adler was trying to tell me about a portion of research he had not sufficiently delved into, a section he had found but had not been able to investigate. One day, he suggested, I might want to look into this line of research. From the force of his excitement he rose feverishly from his bed, attempting to sit up. I tried to hold him down with both hands, afraid he would make a commotion in that *rivier* of those cursed people, where both the healthy and the sick could find themselves dead. But Adler's strength was greater than mine, like Jacob our father battling the angel.

"'You know,' he said, 'Jews did not always allow themselves to be killed without taking revenge.' His voice grew bitter, as if he were practicing the future, not discussing the past. 'Jews fought. They formed groups to plot against the plunderers. They preferred death by the sword to a pathetic death like ours. And more than anyone, you must know about the Jewish pirates. Subatol Deul was Jewish, he wrote his secrets in Hebrew. And more wondrous than him were the rabbis that went out to sea to take revenge on the Spaniards who expelled the Jews from Spain. Pirate rabbis sailed the seven seas, kept the Sabbath, observed the mitzvahs, and on weekdays they rampaged against their enemies!' Then he told me, 'After you are freed, study them.' His body radiated with a strong force and he was actually shaking me. I could not listen to his words, horrified by his strength and his awful vacant face, which contained both the most beautiful of professorial looks, and the terror of a man about to die.

"The *rivier* physician, Doctor Gosen, damn him, had begun his evening rounds, God help us, and I grew frightened. I extricated myself from Adler and promised to visit him the next day, but both he and I knew it was a lie. The next day I was told to work in a new group, with the corpse burners, God help us. Adler's body was at the top of the heap, ready for us to burn in the pits. The Nazis, damn them, had not been able to kill him. Adler had returned his soul to the Creator and I said a *kaddish* prayer over him, so the Lord of the Universe would know that a Jew still mourned for a Jew. That even here, someone was still dear to someone else's heart.

"From that day forward I decided to take up my prayers again. Since being deported from Bochnia I had evaded all the duties of a Jew. I ate *treif*, I did not say the blessings, did not pray. But I made up my mind to pray every day for Adler's soul, and to go back to saying the three daily prayers: *shacharit*, *mincha* and *ma'ariv*."

Grandpa Yosef remembers it is time to pray now. He pauses the tale of his journey and is about to go to the end of the hallway, where he has found a corner for his prayers by the vending machine.

"What happened to Farkelstein?" I ask.

Grandpa Yosef stops in his tracks, annoyed. "What happened to

Farkelstein? How would I know what happened to Farkelstein? And what happened to every single Jew I met? There were thousands and thousands there—how should I know what happened to them?"

He walks out briskly and prays. Then he uses the coins Anat sent for him (sometimes the thermos isn't enough) for a cup of "Swiss coffee" from the machine. He comes back with a hesitant look on his face, slightly ashamed of his outburst, and says, "I don't know about Farkelstein. There's no way to know. But today I am Shoah-smart, you could say, and I know that people like Adler were marked men from the beginning. Who would live? Who would die? Was there any way to predict? That's not what I'm saying. But there were those whose fate was marked on them from the beginning. The brazen would live, the pure would die. Adler, there were no two ways about it, was fated to die, as if the Angel of Death himself had seen to it.

"I did not have much time to mourn for Adler. The typhus plague did not subside, the SS themselves began to fear infection, and they started with the transports. At the beginning of March I packed up my belongings again, as they say (*nu*, it's a joke, I had no belongings at all), and I was sent with a large group to Sachsenhausen camp. Documents have shown that the men's camp of Ravensbrück belonged to Sachsenhausen from the beginning. So once again we were transferred, probably to satisfy the cursed Nazis' quotas and regulations. Sachsenhausen is less than twenty miles northeast of Berlin.

"In Sachsenhausen I learned a profession for the first time in my life. I softened leather boots for German soldiers. How? By walking. Instead of a German soldier getting a pair of painful new leather boots, they used our infinite supply of spare feet. Under the supervision of orthopedic specialists, we marched back and forth through the camp in new army boots, without socks, without rest. We walked and walked. When a boot was worn in and the experts decreed it suitable for the noble foot of a soldier, we were rewarded with a new boot to teach us new pain.

"Is it possible to describe such a deathly nightmare? Worse than working in the trenches of Ravensbrück. Endless. The routine was disturbed only by the occasional shot—another stumbler giving in to his body. Usually there were no shots. The stumblers did their best not to stumble. The guards did their best to kick, whip, and arouse in the prisoner, if not energy, at least the fear of death. They whipped and whipped until he would start walking again. Only seldom did they shoot. And for us, how can I put this aptly, the shots were a slight reprieve from routine. One's mind, unwillingly, created a sort of anticipation of the shots. One side of your soul urges you to feel nothing, hear nothing, see nothing, think nothing—only march. The other side, secretly, with an inexplicable perversion, waits for the sound of the shot. Your head is stupefied and your body marches on, waiting. The shot rings out.

"We walked back and forth in straight lines. Every day we passed a wretched group of young Russian POWs, who for some reason had the letter 'T' imprinted on their foreheads. They were forced to march in a circle, handcuffed to one another in pairs, from morning to night. They did not march to wear in boots—only to die. They marched in an endless circle from which only one fate could remove them. Why did the Germans torture them so? Why not shoot them and be done with it? No way to know. German logic. But those poor wretches, they all met the same fate, and it was slow and hopeless. We never saw the same prisoner twice. And why only the Russians? Why did we walk in straight lines with army boots, people of many nations, Jews and non-Jews? German logic.

"Day after day I marched, and in Sachsenhausen too there were beatings, abuse, hunger, death. As we marched, at first our brains were in a daze. One could not think, could not do anything. We were forbidden to talk. Punishable by death. Later, just a little, I found myself thinking of Adler and his orphaned research. And wondrously, I found myself gaining strength from these thoughts, from the Jewish pirates on their glorious ships. I practiced my future, coming up with adventures for the pirates, inventing things from my soul, and also contemplating the halakhic problems posed by their profession. After all, this was no simple matter, the pirates and the 613 commandments! Every day I found myself embroiled in complex thoughts that reached dead-ends. It was beyond my Talmudic knowledge to solve such intricate issues. Not giving in, I scanned every aspect of a pirate's life, identified the problems, debated them with myself until all possibilities were exhausted, and then made notes of what I would ask the rabbis once I was free. At night in bed, exhausted and hungry, I forced myself to stick with the pirates, divvying up their loot according to the laws of Gemara, muddling through the thicket of laws concerning hostages and the allowance of trade in the fruits of plunder. I was excited to realize that I was asking questions, and they were not small. These were large questions!

"My questions were large, but life, diminished life, did not arise in their wake. Adler's theory was all well and good, but without food, without rest for one's body, life had no chance. And Adler had not only empowered the spirit, he had also added the nightly portion of soup. Without the soup, what good were thoughts? The soul, you should know, needs a body. Wise men philosophize, they separate the spirit from the body, aspire to do away with the corporeal for the sake of the spiritual. But those who know hunger have no questions. A person needs a body.

"In the meantime, in Sachsenhausen, I sensed death approaching in my bones. The dysentery was back. There were days when I ate no more than a turnip leaf from morning to night. And my feet began to refuse to move. They swelled and cracked. I was growing weak. Day after day, Asmodeus came to claim what was his. I knew I would not last long. At night, I exchanged not a single word with my neighbors to the left or the right, and did not know who they were. Our bodies were so shattered, our souls so crushed. Every so often, a neighbor disappeared. Died, shot, replaced. A new one was thrown onto the cot and I remained indifferent, not knowing who he was, not wanting to know, even though he was my brother in this trouble and his suffering was a brother to my own suffering. But there was emptiness. The soul was empty, everything was empty. Death was so close. In the twilight of life, memories invaded, overcoming Adler's prohibition, and my thoughts turned to the past. Even memories were too weak to go very far—the Lodz ghetto seemed as if it had happened many years ago. I could barely remember Bochnia. Only occasionally did childhood memories emerge, with the cheder, the tutor, and the stones we threw in the afternoon into the little Babica brook that flowed beneath the bridge.

"And where, you might ask, was Feiga in all of this? I did not have in me enough Yosef to contain Feiga. At the edge of the very edge, Yosef Ingberg ended. My soul made a decision: Tomorrow I will not get up from this cot. They may whip me to death, but I will not rise.

"That night, two of my neighbors died suddenly, one from beatings, taken from bed to be punished and never returned, and the other from exhaustion. The one who died of exhaustion would be removed in the morning with all the dead, but in place of the one who was beaten to death they tossed in a new neighbor, a diminutive Jew. And this Jew, as if he did not see how miserable my condition was, as if neither bothered by the body that separated us, nor deterred by the death sentence awarded to those who whispered in their cots, immediately began trying to get acquainted, asking questions, telling me about himself. I, in the twilight of death, was somewhat taken aback. It seemed strange that this little Jew was unafraid of Adler's command, talking freely about his past, his history. When morning came, I got up from the cot despite myself, rising to a new day of death, and I knew my Jewish neighbor's entire story by heart.

"Until the war started my new neighbor had been a tramp and a beggar. He ate in soup kitchens and at rich people's houses. In summers he played the violin at weddings, and in winters he was hungry for bread. He stole. A dangerous sort of Jew, he was. And indeed, I feared him, but I was also drawn to his companionship. How can I put it? I sensed that with him I might survive. When he told me his name, Rothschild, I did not know if he was joking or truthful. I dared not ask. I soon discovered that my intuition about Rothschild was correct. He always knew where they were secretly giving out another portion, where they were selling something, which work group was better off. I tell you this without shame: I put my trust in Rothschild. Incredibly, he put his in me. One day he caught me in the latrine, or, forgive me, the crapper, which served as a general market in the camps, and he stood up close to me. Whispering, he proposed a deal. He would keep me going, look out for me, and I would pray for him. He had seen me praying for Adler and he wanted me to pray for him too, so his sins would not be counted against him. I was taken aback.

Such a deal, *nu*. But he shoved a piece of cooked potato into my hand and I quickly stuffed it in my mouth. We had a deal.

"From that day on, Rothschild really did take care of me. He was cunning and seemed to be without conscience. He stole and tricked and cheated and lied. And he brought me half of his earnings, or so he assured me. Everything gained through his wheeling and dealing, I swallowed up; my body wanted it. Every evening he came to me and asked pragmatically, 'Have you prayed for me yet today, Rabbi?' As if we had not a general agreement, but a detailed contract.

"He insisted on calling me 'Rabbi.' No matter how many times I told him I was not a rabbi, Rothschild explained that for him I was. In any case, he said, he had seen the rabbi of his town being dragged through the snow by his beard. His entire congregation had already died in the crematoria. Only he was left. So he was a congregation, and I—a rabbi.

"So we remained, the pair of us. Every day I prayed for myself, for him, and for Israel. I dared to bring Feiga's name to my lips, pleading. He brought to me from his takings, and saved me twice from prisoners who wanted to slaughter me for my portion of soup. So small, he was, and so bold. A savage. At the end of every day he checked, making sure I hadn't forgotten to pray for him. I did not know what sort of a trap I had fallen into, and did not give it much thought because my body was surviving thanks to another radish, another bit of soup, another potato. Many times, when the food was in my stomach, I grew terrified of this partner, a thief and a robber—how had I joined up with this burglar? But hunger came and pierced through my thoughts, and when Rothschild passed me a potato I did not ask where it came from, whether from the prisoners' kitchen or the jailors' kitchen or the hoard of another miserable prisoner. I grabbed it and ate.

"One day there was a special roll-call. There were shouts, and a group of us was sent to work in the woods. There, we knew, death was waiting. You did not come back from working in the woods with those villains. I was to be annexed to the group, separated from fortunate Rothschild. I had already began marching with the rows of people, extremely frightened, when suddenly Rothschild slid into our group and squeezed in next to me. 'Right behind you, Rabbi!' I no longer knew who this Rothschild was—a villain or a righteous man. For he had sentenced himself to death.

"After many hours of walking, we were hurried into a wooded area and ordered to chop down the trees. Our hands grasped dull axes and broken saws, and the supervisors made sure the work was done according to certain rules and with the requisite energy. Every so often, one of the supervisors lost his patience, burst into the group, chose himself a victim, and that victim had no recourse. Why did they not shoot us and be done with it? Who can tell. For days, they worked us from morning to night. They themselves were bored. The woods made them irritable and we paid the price. We bowed our heads and continued to work. There was no Adler to come to my help here. Rothschild, in the woods, was also waning. We were both losing our strength. Around us people collapsed, unresponsive to thrashes, beatings. Anything was better than another hour of work. Each one who gave up his life, we regretted, because we would have to carry his body back to the camp. The Germans could not tolerate inaccurate numbers or a discrepancy between the number that set off and the number that returned.

"Rothschild, it turns out, was not idling. Every night when we were brought back to the camp, shattered, he did not lie down on his bed as I did, one foot in the grave. He ran around stirring things up, investigating, lobbying. A few days later he found himself a job in the kitchen and was also able to get me out of the woods group and back to the boot-marchers. One night he woke me up and dragged me out of the hut, unafraid of the supervisor and the SS outside. He stealthily gave me a piece of meat, a real piece of meat, which if not for the freezing cold would have probably sent a stench throughout the entire camp. I swallowed it. My stomach ached for two days, having forgotten the taste of meat. And the pain, well. *Nu*, like a new baby that keeps you from sleeping. Like Yariv, your Yariv, when he was born. He wouldn't let you sleep, but the joy, the joy!"

(Suddenly, my Yariv, in the middle of the camps.)

"And of course, he said, 'Don't forget to pray for me, Rabbi.'

He took me back to the hut but did not go in. For Rothschild, night was the time for doing business. He was always busy with intrigues and commerce. As if he meant to get rich in this place. For one whole month he tormented himself with a major secret transaction. He twitched on his cot at night, hitting and kicking the planks. He hit me too, thrashing this way and that. He was seeking reprieve from the calculations he labored over all day, skipping among his confidants, hiding, helping, bribing, slipping away. I was not let in on the secret and had no idea what kind of transaction could be so worthy of these torments. Apart from life, what asset could he gain here? Perhaps that was his business. Life. Saving his own life in some way. Escaping was not his intention. Not a simple escape. He was derisive of escape plans, and often mocked some poor garrulous rookie boasting of his idea. He would tell him dismissively, '*Nu*, so you escape. What then? What afterwards?' Perhaps Rothschild was plotting a large-scale plan. What he was scheming, I do not know. But one day it was all over. His strength suddenly ran out. He went back to the little transactions, a stub of salami here, a potato there, cigarettes. At night his sleep was restful again.

"More than anything, Rothschild looked to Cell Block 18, where the Germans had built a sophisticated printing house to print counterfeit bills in other currencies. The printing house ignited a flame in Rothschild's eyes. All his instincts fired up for the chance to get himself a job there. He talked with this one, debated with the other. Walked alongside the fence at night, returned excitedly from hasty meetings. He waited expectantly for a conversation, just a few words, a partner to arrive. Truly like a suitor and a lover. Yes, even in a creature such as Rothschild there was a manifestation of love.

"But before he managed to establish a role for himself in Cell Block 18, he had already jumped on another opportunity. A rumor was going around that soon a group of prisoners would be evacuated from Sachsenhausen. Where to? That was unclear. Perhaps, like other times, to the nearby woods to be shot in the head. But perhaps elsewhere. Rothschild considered the opportunity from all points of view, and decided to get himself into the transport. He informed me that he had put my name down for this corrupt business too. As if he could not imagine leaving for a new place without the man who prayed for him.

"I was terrified. What was I doing with a murderous character like this? How had I gotten mixed up with him? But when the rumor turned into an actual transport, and the list was real, and both of our names were on it, I joined him without a word—what life did I have without Rothschild? And that was how we arrived at Dora-Mittelbau camp.

"We were in that hell for only a few weeks. Rothschild soon realized he had struck a foul bargain. After our welcome, which included roll-call, lashings and punishments, we were thrown into rock caves. That was the camp. Entirely made of dark, stifling tunnels. There we had to dig tunnels for the Germans to store their secret missiles. Not that we knew that. We only knew that we were digging from morning till evening, no food, horrendous conditions, without any light. They did not let us see the light of day. We worked and slept and ate in the tunnels. For our intestinal needs, the Germans built for us, in their mercy, a wonderful kind of facility. Fuel barrels cut in half, which we were invited to fill up to our hearts' content. Apparently there was no shortage of empty barrels throughout the German Reich, but we were given only a few, so as not to spoil us. As if they were saying, you're not getting fed anyway—how could you have any excrement? There were very few barrels and they were always overflowing. We stepped in human waste. People gave up all remnants of human dignity and left their waste wherever they happened to crouch. The aqueducts filled with the smell of excrement and a strong odor of grease and dust.

"You know, there are almost no accounts of Dora-Mittelbau camp. Why is that? Because there are so few survivors fortunate enough to be able to tell what happened there. Every day people dropped dead by the dozens and the hundreds. You cannot imagine how murderous and terrible that place was. Rothschild realized immediately that he had made a bad move, and, incredibly, he discovered that in a nearby camp they needed metal workers. Right there and then he became a metal artisan, pushing himself under the kapo's nose just in time so some other prisoner wouldn't be taken instead.

They took ten prisoners, including the metal artisan Yosef Ingberg of Bochnia. There is no way of knowing what Rothschild did to get me onto that list, but he did not forget me, he did not leave me in that awful cemetery Dora-Mittelbau. Cursed is the world in which camps such as Dora-Mittelbau are created to kill human beings.

"In the nameless new camp we were welcomed by a huge German prisoner, a criminal, who tested our knowledge of frames and metal. In the dark, Rothschild asked me, 'What do you know about metal work?' I answered in a panic, 'Tubal-cain, the forger of every cutting instrument of brass and iron...' Rothschild did not comprehend my scriptural quote, and I whispered, 'Genesis, chapter four, verse twenty-two. The first metal cutter, Tubal-cain.' Rothschild sighed and said, 'In that case, you know slightly more than I do.'

"I was seized by fear—what would we answer to the German? But Rothschild remained calm, his eyes already investigating in the dark, finding out where there might be a chance to do good business. As if he himself were orchestrating things, just as we stood before the German, a siren pierced the camp, the lights went off and we were thrown into a dark hut without any orders and with no questions asked. It turned out the Allied planes were attacking. It was already September of 1943, and the Germans were no longer so sure of themselves. Every siren sent them into a panic. When calm was restored, we were miraculously led to a large cauldron, which held our dinner, and were given pieces of soft, grey bread. At the end of the meal Rothschild was already part of the kitchen crew—don't ask how—and I was his assistant. It turned out they needed no more than two or three metal workers in the camp, and apart from the ones the huge German chose, and apart from Rothschild and me, the others were nonchalantly taken to a nearby clearing in the woods and shot in the back of their heads.

"We were saved from Dora-Mittelbau, saved too from the fate of the metal cutters, and a few days later the camp was shut down. Again we were rolled along, this time south, to Buchenwald."

Grandpa Yosef says the word 'Buchenwald' and into the room comes the nurse. Behind her, the doctor. He examines Grandpa Lolek, gives the nurse some instructions, and tells us Grandpa Lolek is out of danger and has in fact begun to recover. He can be discharged, he should be in a nursing home of some sort, like Flieman Hospital, where he can complete his little journey until he goes home. Grandpa Yosef objects with a stony face—supervision is essential. But he lets it slide. He will wait for Effi's shift. She's a doctor, he can recruit her to his battle and do away with their plan. In the meantime he lets it slide, protesting with an angry mumble. The doctor answers, trying to explain that the treatment in a convalescence home will be better than what he'll get here, and in any case, he doesn't belong in this ward. All he needs is rest. Rest and observation. Grandpa Yosef decides to ignore him, as if the argument is over. He sits down carelessly in his chair, gives the doctor a defiant look, ready for battle. He has in him a courage he did not have on the train going to Buchenwald, rattling in the dark, burnt with thirst, singed from the nights of waiting, frozen on the tracks without moving, waiting for the devil knows what, perhaps for a torture that will grow, burst forth, assail these people who are desperate anyway and starving anyway in the darkness of the train car. The doctor thinks the better of any further argument. He leaves the room and the nurse follows him. The train ride goes on for days, in the depths of darkness, Grandpa Yosef and Rothschild cast into a darkness deeper than the one Grandpa Lolek is now resting in. Outside sirens rip through villages. They cross bridges, the rain slams down, and inside the arid darkness the water bucket is empty, the windows are closed, there is no air. Finally, the screeching of tracks announces the end. The train doors are flung open. Light. Buchenwald.

Buchenwald is a vast camp. First thing in the morning, the kapo is already harassing Grandpa Yosef, two shots of the whip on his face, and screams. Grandpa Yosef does not understand what he wants, the kapo kicks him in the ribs. But then Rothschild, risking his life, jumps boldly in front of the kapo and the incident is over. In some way that is beyond normal comprehension, the kapo immediately realizes that people like Rothschild should be avoided. He screams for another moment or two, kicks and fumes, but then leaves. Rothschild drags Grandpa Yosef to his cot. Grandpa Yosef is stunned, still not understanding why the kapo fell on him, but knowing that

Rothschild had saved his life. Over the next few days he learns what kind of lowly murderer the kapo is, how he amuses himself with the prisoners, but Grandpa Yosef has Rothschild's protection.

Grandpa Yosef regulates his breath a little.

"In Buchenwald, finally, I had a little rest from my travels. I spent a whole year there, from November '43 to November '44. First we were sent to work in the quarry. Every morning we marched in rows, pounded rocks for sixteen hours, then marched back to the camp, where we had roll-calls and more marches. I no longer had any strength anyway, I was no more than a skeleton, and if not for Rothschild...*nu*. He soon joined up with the Russian POWs and the criminals, hardened people who would murder over nothing. Thanks to them he found easy work for both of us in a nearby town. Every day we were actually taken out of the camp into a German town where citizens lived their lives. Children peered at us through windows, and on the streets we passed women with baskets and gentlemen going off to work. A town, simply a town. We repaired the water reservoirs. Hard work, but only as hard as any manual laborer's work.

"Rothschild cast his net here too, doing business, various corrupt transactions. Such a devil. He started to place his confidence in me, asked me questions, sought advice. He told me of his plans and deeds and secrets. His heart was completely unhesitant. He would do anything. He struck terror and fear in me—he could betray me at any moment, sell me for a potato.

"Only one thing did Rothschild ask of me, as ever. 'Pray for me, Rabbi.' His face would strain as he forced a smile, but he was entirely serious, and he took the trouble to make sure the prayer was being said.

"He grew tired of working at the water reservoirs very quickly. His business was not booming and the danger was too great, so he found himself a job in the kitchen. There, for those who dared, business was good. Rothschild traded, bribed, cheated, orchestrated transactions. In January there was snow and the ground was frozen, so they did not need us in the town. Rothschild tried to sneak me into kitchen duty, but was unable. Having no choice, we found ourselves the job of pushing the wagons that carried the dead. Throughout the camps, this job was done by the Ukrainian POWs, a hardened and frightening group. How Rothschild penetrated this evil band...*nu*, Rothschild. He was pleased with his accomplishment and could not understand the way my face fell when he told me. 'The work is easy, no? We'll survive. Gain some weight.'

"And so we took the dead out of the huts every morning. People I knew, the dying who had completed their process. One day I would look into the eyes of a dead man, *nu*, and the next day I piled his corpse onto the wagon. Worst of all was the inspection we had to do. Sometimes the man was not dead, but did not get up; he lay still, awaiting his fate—the hand that would put him to death. I was the wagon man. And then I had to deal with the corpses. I don't want to talk about that.

"The months in Buchenwald went by. I survived. Rothschild was with me. I prayed, he took care of the rest. Thoughts of Feiga returned. Thoughts of Adler. I worked with the dead wagon and imagined the future in all its details. We did not gain any weight, none at all. A great hunger fell on Buchenwald. Rations were cut. The black water known as 'soup' was taken from us, the gray mess known as 'bread' all but disappeared. The hunger brought death to the huts and we were always busy. Those who did not die sometimes lit up with a fever like torches and became crazed. They drank mud and ate their own clothing. God help us, we even found gnawed bodies on the cots. Yes, gnawed bodies. And the eyes, everyone's eyes, even those whose minds were still sound, were crazed and glimmering, their hearts wanted only a chance to nibble at some food, their souls ignited—when would the chance come? When would it come?

"One evening there was a commotion. We were crowded into the *Appellplatz* for a special roll-call. The officers surrounded us, there was shouting, dogs barking, something bad had happened. For a long time all we heard were paralyzing shouts. We were counted, then counted again, and the roll-call went on into the night and it was not clear what had happened, but we knew in our hearts that it would not end well. We slowly began to understand that we were being accused of stealing twenty candied apples. Twenty candied apples! They had been prepared in the kitchen for the birthday celebration of one of the senior SS men, and lo and behold, the apples were gone.

"We were left to freeze in the snow, tormented, and the SS did nothing, only walked among us shouting and threatening. It became evident that they would not be satisfied with killing someone. They needed the apples. They were frightened themselves—what would they do without the apples? They waited for someone to open his mouth and confess, or to turn in someone else. And we stood there, stupefied from cold and fear. But there was joy hiding in our hearts. Twenty candied apples! If it had been one apple, or one rotting potato, we would have been jealous, our empty stomachs would have demanded the *kartoshka*. We would have suspected one another, even hoped that a few would be shot, including the one who had stolen the apple, because then maybe later we would find the apple in his cot. But twenty candied apples! We had to whisper explanations to the villagers among us, stressing that this was not just an apple with sugar, but an apple dipped in boiling syrup bubbling in a cauldron, and the syrup is sweet like honey and it coats the apple and hardens like red glass. First the excess syrup drips down the apple, then the drops freeze as if ordered to stop and decorate the head of the apple like snow on a hilltop. Twenty such apples!

"Late at night the SS men gave up. This truly was a mystery, the thief was never discovered, even the informants couldn't say. The roll-call commander ordered his officers to take out every fifth man and shoot him. A rustle of terror stirred among us. Our bodies began to awaken from the cold, the nausea of fear crept inside us. An SS officer walked among the rows, pushing aside certain men with his whip, instructing them to join the condemned. He walked in front of me and his whip touched me. Yes, the whip touched me. And the sergeant marching behind him motioned at me with his head to leave the row. But to my right Rothschild jumped out. The sergeant glanced at this exchange for an instant. He didn't care, as long as the number added up nicely. I froze in my place without moving, and Rothschild was already standing at the edge of the condemned group. From the end of the line he gestured at me with his hands, mimicking a prayer stance, to remind me that I should continue to pray for him.

"They walked them to a clearing in the woods where the SS liked to execute people. As he passed me, with a real grin on his murderous face, Rothschild dared to call out loud to me, 'I am Leibel Rothschild. If you have a son, call him Leibel!'

"And the group was swallowed up in the darkness. I remained among the living, owing my life to another man. How did my legs plant me down at that moment of the switch? How did I allow it to happen? Why did I allow...*nu*...

"They shot Rothschild. Gone. That's all I can tell you. I don't remember much of the days that followed. A long period, months, and the memories are gone. I probably continued to work with the dead wagons, since I was not dead myself. I was not taken to work at the quarry. And what else did I do? I believe I was entirely submerged in the future. I imagined it beautifully, and my aim was not bad. The present was not all that agreeable to me, so I turned my thoughts to the future, where things were good. I made *aliya* with Feiga to Palestine, to build a new life. And even if I never imagined my home in Kiryat Haim, and Ben Gurion, still, I did picture Palestine. Feiga and I were most certainly alive. We sat on the beach at Jaffa, gobbling down oranges in the sunshine, our feet reaching out to touch the convoys of camels, the local Arabs admiring our culture, our religion. I did not envision wars and conflicts, not like this. But in dark Buchenwald we definitely gobbled down oranges and tangerines.

"I recall only one moment of the present. I leaned against a rod or a wagon shaft for a brief moment of contemplation. I suddenly thought about my journey with Ahasuerus. It was, after all, a journey to rescue Feiga, and I believed that the *Kadosh Baruch Hu* had given me this journey and the black car. I suddenly realized that I had not achieved a thing. Not Feiga, not anything. And in that moment, which memory is kind enough to illuminate to this day, I was filled with great desperation and confusion. I leaned hard against the wagon shaft. I remember the shaft well.

"At the end of 1944 the Germans decided it was time for me

to move on again, to Gross-Rosen camp. At that time, all the camp Jews were being sent west, mass transports going with the Germans as they retreated from the Russians. But for some reason, I was sent east. To Gross-Rosen.

"At Gross-Rosen I received the usual welcome. A shower in the nude, pushing, shouting, a long roll-call in the snow. The Germans wore fur coats, protecting their bodies from the wind, while we stood naked. Night came, the cold took its victims, and the Germans too were tired of the roll-calls. It was cold. We were taken into huts, a hundred people shoved into a space big enough for ten.

"At Gross-Rosen there was no work. They kept us in huts and took us out to be counted or punished. Then back to the hut. I do not remember many people dying in the daily routine of Gross-Rosen; not like at Sachsenhausen, not like at Buchenwald. But those who did die stand out in my memory. After Rothschild's death, I was lucidly aware of each and every subsequent man shot dead. To this day I think not only about Rothschild, who was not successful in all of his schemes and who ultimately died. I think about everyone who was executed in front of my eyes. In Ravensbrück, in Sachsenhausen, in Buchenwald, in Gross-Rosen. All those anonymous people drawn out from the end of their rows so a dog could tear through their flesh or they could be whipped to death. In their own eyes, these people were the whole wide world. They alone perceived the miracle of their salvation up until that moment, and at the instant before their death they surely thought in terror, 'I have been marked, God help me,' and they hoped for life, for one more miracle. They looked at our impenetrable faces, hoping salvation might come from us. Until the very last second they hoped, in their dying convulsions, in their memories, between the teeth of a dog, and could not imagine a world without themselves. Do you understand? They could not imagine a world without themselves in it. Every such person who knelt down to get a bullet in the back of his neck was a whole wide world. And not only because that is what the Scriptures say. Simply a whole wide world. Each man with his memories, his loves, his history. Just like me. And I am living, here, and they…

"In Gross-Rosen I came to see Rothschild and Adler and Rabbi

Hirsch as chaperones who knew that liberation was close, that it would take just one more little effort, a stroke of luck. And indeed, near the end of the war I was transferred from Gross-Rosen to an auxiliary camp. Then to another camp. And another. Towards their end, damn them, as if the Germans did not know what to do with me, they transferred me again and again. Finally they put me in a little camp near the Polish town of Walbrzych, which was not far from Waldenburg camp, where your father was with his father. In that camp, things were relatively comfortable. I worked at a sort of carpentry shop. It was work for work's sake, not for death's sake, and the foreman was an elderly German man. There was little food and I was ill, but survival was possible. I spent a month there, no more. The Russians came, the Germans fled, and I was set free. With me, everything happened simply. No last minute torture, no death march, no burning huts with inhabitants still inside, no being buried alive in a pit. I was simply set free.

"Then there was a difficult period of freedom. The world was in shambles, and I was all sickness and hunger. But we overcame. *Nu*, there was life, the *Kadosh Baruch Hu* gave life and commanded that we live, and you cannot imagine my joy when, in Bochnia, I met Feiga. But before that, in the last camp, I had another encounter, a unique one. Of all the people I met in my days, none was as important as this brief meeting.

"In our camp I found a prisoner who drew my attention for some reason. He was a sick man, lying silently on a cot, barely able to get up. He walked softly to the latrine, conversing with no one. He was fairly young, around thirty, but his face was drawn and old. For some reason I felt pity for him, as if I somehow still contained pity, and one day I went to him and gave him a piece of bread. I was deathly ill, my condition no better than his, and yet I offered him my bread. He thanked me with a limp wave of the hand and rejected my offer. He motioned with his fingers—perhaps I had a cigarette? For some reason I rushed around as if commanded by a great Admor. I searched the camp for someone who would trade food for a cigarette, and went back to the patient to give him the gift. Two real Eckstein cigarettes.

"He smoked one cigarette. Then the next one. I sat waiting at his feet for the devil knows what. But from that day we became connected. I would sit at his side, looking into his pale face as he smoked cigarettes. I noticed that he did not eat, and I tried to entreat him. But he dismissed my pleas completely. Strange, I had yet to hear his voice or learn his name, and yet I felt that I had found a friend. He too bowed his tired head, welcoming my arrival. I found myself sensing an increased desire to help, to encourage the man, to tell him about Rothschild, about Adler, about Hirsch. And indeed I began to tell him my stories, the entire past. From day to day I could see the man weakening, as if he did not want his life and was actually beckoning death to approach. I implored him to gain strength. 'Life is holy!' I told him.

"One day I heard from some people that the man came from the village of Kalow. I tried to engage him in conversation. 'His honor is from Kalow, so I hear? A long way his honor has traveled. *Nu*, these times… In Kalow, did you happen to know the 'Fledgling Tree,' the Rabbi of Kalow?'

"His lips whispered, 'I am the Rabbi of Kalow.'

"I was stunned into silence. Not just for a brief moment, but for whole days. I continued to tend to him, kneeling at his feet. What were my stories, all my worthless tales of Hirsch and Adler? Who knew what this man was engaged in during his moments of silence, in what secret and wonderful worlds the Rabbi of Kalow, the Fledgling Tree, roamed, he and none other, while I intruded on his visions with my Feiga here, and Ahasuerus there. With my idle talk I was putting spokes in the wheels of a true holy man, the Rabbi of Kalow! The author of important new interpretations of Torah that had sent shockwaves from the farthest corner of Galicia all the way to the land of Lithuania. I looked into his pale face, which now appeared clean and pure, and I was overcome. The Rabbi of Kalow!

"The next day I moved to the cot next to his. I would be quiet and would be an aid. I would save the Rabbi of Kalow from the claws of death. I would feed him, give him water, guard him. But my longing to talk, to regale him with what was in my heart, would not let go. I was quiet but full of questions—about pirates, about their mitzvahs, about the diminished questions. I wanted to ask the Rabbi of Kalow, 'Why, why the annihilation?'

"But the Rabbi was not there to be questioned. He silently smoked the cigarettes I brought him. Once in a while he posed a question and I responded as concisely as possible, so he would understand my answer correctly without a single superfluous word. He asked about Bochnia, about my family, my engagement. Then he surprised me by saying, 'My wife Rachel and I were not blessed with children. It was not His wish, *Hashem*, blessed be He.'

"I already knew this, having heard that the Rabbi of Kalow was not blessed by *Hashem* with offspring, and that hundreds of Jews used to come to him for fertility blessings. He was known as a curer of barrenness.

"And so we counted the days until liberation. Rumors abounded, and we could hear the Americans bombing. Echoes of cannons, rumors of Russian artillery. The prisoners were excited, the Germans anxious and tense. Only the Rabbi of Kalow was in his own world. He lay on his bed communing with other spheres. I introduced him to the other prisoners and promised he would be our savior. Here, this is the Fledgling Tree, the Rabbi of Kalow, our hope. People dismissed him with a mumble of indifference, perhaps contempt. What did they care about one more rabbi? In any case, they hinted, the pure rabbis had all been killed in the crematoria. Whoever was loyal to his people was gone now. These weary people did not understand, they missed the hidden intentions of the Rabbi of Kalow, and even if I myself did not entirely understand them, I did see their beauty, like the face of a bride through a veil.

"The Rabbi of Kalow was unaffected by the prisoners' opinions. Like us, he was imprisoned behind fences, but his soul danced freely wherever the good Lord took him. I was his servant, I fed him soup, found him cigarettes, while he tended the plains, measured the heavens.

"One day he put his hand to his tired face as if returning from an exhausting thought, and told me, 'When you have a son, name him Moshe.'

"'Moshe?'

"'Name him Moshe, and he will be the savior of Israel!'

"He turned away from me and sunk into his contemplations.

"I let him be and went to wander through the huts and latrines. I examined the fences and the buildings and the entire world. The future suddenly seemed solid and tangible. I saw Feiga and myself embracing a child. The hope for liberation that had remained in my heart through all the camp years in a shapeless, faceless form, suddenly took on a simple outline. Here was the future—not the future I had barely known how to sketch back in Ravensbrück, but a corporeal future, a future that would not be stolen from me! I was ill, hungry, and weak, but I had ceased doubting. I knew that I would live, that I would be free.

"Soon, time itself joined the flight of my soul: liberation day was approaching. The whole camp could hear the beat of freedom, the prisoners were growing anxious, trying to fortify themselves for one more day, one more hour. Only the Rabbi of Kalow remained outside the flow of time, still in his own world. He was no longer accepting the soup I brought him, he rejected bread, even cigarettes. He did not rise from his bed. He lay with his eyes open as if standing on guard, not here, but in some loftier world, and his hand weakly dismissed my words, my pleas, my attentions.

"Right on the verge of the great day, when we were counting the hours and the minutes, he called to me. I came and stood by him. The Rabbi of Kalow's face, although no more than skin and bones, filled with light, as if while still in this world he had been delivered to the angels. He asked to deposit his story with me. That was how he put it. Not 'I want to tell you,' but 'I wish to deposit.' In his angelic language, each word was carefully chosen. I sat alert, entirely prepared to hear his tale. And the Rabbi of Kalow deposited it:

"'In the Kalow ghetto, there, my wife Rachel died in the typhus plague. She was taken away, *baruch dayan ha'emet*—Blessed be the true judge. One day three young men came to my room. They announced: Tomorrow we must escape. The ghetto has been condemned. No one will live. They demanded that I keep the news a secret. I would leave alone, at dawn. Everyone else, may God protect them.

"'They took me to the forest. There, in advance, a hiding place had been prepared. From childhood until manhood, I had never been in the woods. Always among streets and houses, roads paved through fields on either side. Only from a distance would I gaze at the woods, contemplating their secrets, and here I was, called to a life in the forest, in a crowded hiding place with twenty men and their troubles. Bread was scarce, we never saw the light of day.

"'One day, someone must have informed. Germans and Poles surrounded the place, shots were fired, I heard shouts. I escaped. Bullets whistled around me, and they ordered: Stop! I ran. I did not know where my legs were taking me, whether towards or away from any town. In the heart of the woods there was no sunlight, no moonlight, and I had no strength left. But my body kept walking so the wolves would not eat me alive. I prayed, I called out from the depths, where shall I go? Anyone I meet will turn me in. The Germans promise two pounds of bread and half a salami for every Jew. And why should they not turn me in? For half a salami, I would give myself up.

"'Like a blind man I walked on. Stumbling, defeated. Suddenly the darkness was cleaved with a great light. Opposite me stood a house with the front door ajar, and a light shining from it. In the doorway, under the light, stood a huge peasant woman with white hair—she was *erva*, unchaste—and she called out to me, "Come, Jew, come…I will help…"

"'And so I found myself sitting in a crude room inside the crowded, warm peasants' house, and the *goya* served me. She gave me hot soup. Fed me potatoes and butter. All *treif*, all forbidden. But my mouth ate. The *goya* gave me a chicken wing and heaped a bounty of food onto my plate. She told me, "My husband is working…shhh! He must not know…I will hide you in the cellar. It will be fine." Then she caressed my hair with her thick fingers.'"

Grandpa Yosef stops his story for a moment. It is hard for him. He softens his words. He puts his mouth up close to my face so that only my ears will hear the story of the Rabbi of Kalow.

"Starting the next day, he told me, she forced him to do with her as a man does with a woman. Yes, his life was on the line and she made her demands, set her terms. What could he do? Day and night he hid in the cellar, and in the morning when the farmer went to work, she came down to him. Gave him food. Drink. Took care of his sanitation. And then he had to…with the peasant woman."

Grandpa Yosef is practically whispering. His modest voice seems unworthy of the Rabbi of Kalow. To heal this wound it will take a great roar.

"'I prayed to the heavens, I begged, Take away from me this Lilith of the woods! Leave me! From the depths I called out. Asmodeus! Demon woman! Lilith! Inhabitor of the corners of the world! But no redemption came.

"'In the cellar I was encased like a bird in the belly of a great fish, ensnared in a crevasse, embittered as wormwood. She came down every day to give me food and drink, and by the grace of the shadows she took her dues from me. There was no escape. Only prayer remained. So I offered prayers and did not give up. And indeed, on one of the days, the cellar door suddenly opened at noon and the farmer led a young Jewess down to the hiding place. He prepared a bed for her and assuaged her fears. He did not scheme like the peasant woman, not at all. Indeed he let his spouse in on the secret of the Jewess's existence. He entreated her with words that my ears could hear. A drunken Polish *goy*, persuading his spouse to show a measure of mercy towards all creatures of the world. He reassured her, the war will be over, no one will know, it is our duty. She consented to his demand and agreed to hide the survivor woman in the cellar. She did not divulge to him the secret of my existence.

"'Downstairs, in the dark, I revealed myself to the survivor. I calmed her spirits and told her my tale, omitting my deeds with the peasant woman. When I told her I was a rabbi in Kalow, she fell to her knees. Only three years ago she had come to ask for my blessing: she had asked for a son and been granted one. The son had died in the forest with her husband and mother. *Baruch dayan ha'emet.* She hid her face in her hands, thankful that fate had brought about our encounter, as if she was already saved. But we were both in the dark, residents of the cellar, like clods of clay, like valley denizens, and above us was life.

"'All the while the young woman was in the hiding place, the peasant woman stopped coming to me. She helped to care for the woman, bringing down double portions of food, but she did not give away a thing. The *Kadosh Baruch Hu* had granted me some respite from her. One day the farmer came down and sadly told the woman that the Germans would be searching all the village houses. Someone had informed. He had to try and take her elsewhere, perhaps he would find a friend who would agree to hide her. Having no choice, she left with him, and I never found out what happened to her. I stayed in the cellar. If the Germans came down, the farmer would be surprised to find me and would be killed with his wife and myself.

"'Indeed, over the next few days the village was visited by Germans. They came into the house and looked down into the cellar. The *Kadosh Baruch Hu* saved me from them and took mercy on the household. But then the peasant woman began to come down to the cellar every day once again, to feed me of her bounty. She did not impose upon me the terror of her urges. She was good natured, serving me with respect. My heart filled with fear, as if disaster was imminent. How long would I sit through dark days, meager of deeds and poor of feats, a captive in the dwellings of Midian? My soul cried out: Escape!

"'One day the peasant woman brought down a hearty meal for me. Eggs, fat, groats, cream and potatoes. Suddenly the *goya* said, "I will bear you a child." The taste of cream was still on my lips, and she explained, "It won't be long now. At winter's end we shall have a child."

"'A number of months, then, had passed since she had become pregnant. In six months she would have a son.'"

Grandpa Yosef weighs in. "Imagine to yourself. The Fledgling Tree, and his firstborn was conceived by a *goya*!"

"'Harlot!' The rabbi screamed, his limbs frozen in terror. The peasant woman's face turned red."

Grandpa Yosef gets up and walks quickly to the window. He points to the distance, his fingers trembling. The Rabbi of Kalow's deposit still unsettles him, a fifty year old pregnancy demanding to be solved. It is unclear what might placate Grandpa Yosef. Perhaps a little rain in the window coming in from the ocean—finally a November rain, offering surrender.

"The Rabbi of Kalow thinks. He must escape and save his soul from this Lilith. He will be better off if the Nazis catch him and he can join his Rachela. But how can he leave his firstborn? He is consumed with fright and distress. How can he leave? Trapped inside her body, his only son is growing."

Grandpa Yosef comes back from the window, hunched over as if bearing a heavy weight. He has been recounting the torments of the Rabbi of Kalow during Effi's shifts too, and during mine, and Dad's. As he retells the journey, from within his raging spirit comes the stormy soul of the rabbi, counting the passing days, shut in the cellar, agonizing. Grandpa Yosef spreads his hands out, explaining, "His firstborn was…with the *goya*!"

I nod understandingly. The months go by, and time is more powerful than the rabbi's supplications, than Grandpa Yosef's explanations, than my quiet nod.

"The peasant woman continues to bring the rabbi food and water, trim his beard, clip his nails. She cares for him generously and her stomach grows larger, a monstrous swelling in front of his eyes. Having no choice, he survives. In the hours between dawn and day, when the farmer is out, he goes up into the house to pray and soak up some light and air. The peasant woman watches him pray, sighing, and she too moves her great body about. 'I will call him Moises,' she says."

Grandpa Yosef grows agitated. "To use the name of Moshe our Teacher, she wants!"

"The Rabbi of Kalow says nothing. He finishes his prayers and goes down to the cellar. Most days he huddles there, sometimes hearing the farmer and his wife speaking above the floorboards of his prison. The farmer happily awaits the arrival of his child. He makes promises to his wife. He will work hard, make money, the newborn shall want for nothing."

I press him. "How does everyone know it's a boy? Are you telling me they did an ultrasound?"

Grandpa Yosef dismisses my question with a wave of his hand.

He hints at the world of holy rabbis, *goya* witches, and life at the edge of the woods on the margins of darkness. It would be a son.

"And indeed, it was a son. Her time to give birth had come. Over the head of the rabbi, on the floorboards, many pairs of boots and shoes creak. Farmers walk around the house, young neighbor women come and go. The peasant woman falls ill, grows weak, and is ordered not to leave her bed. The neighbor women care for her. Smells of cooking fill the house. And downstairs, the rabbi starves. He nibbles on onions and raw potatoes from a sack. And he prays. He offers up many prayers."

"What did he pray for?"

"Just prayers. The duties of a Jew." Grandpa Yosef stares at me, trying to comprehend what I am really asking. What do I mean? "Just prayers," he says.

"And then, one night, a great commotion. Elderly women in the house, *babas* dressed in cloaks, satanic midwives, they deliver a male child. A large, healthy boy, the farmer immediately falls in love with him. He repeats his promises to his ailing wife, tenderly caresses her head, promises support, good health, everything."

The rabbi can no longer contain himself. The conduit of Grandpa Yosef is not sufficient, and so he speaks up himself:

"No sooner had the farmer set off to work than the cellar door opened. The peasant woman, weakened, padded over to me, wrapped in many clothes. Alone she came, without my son. She brought me food. She asked my forgiveness in a soft, pained voice. She could barely leave her bed, the labor had weakened her greatly. Her face looked old and wrinkled, her body had barely any strength left. And so, how can I say this…I caressed her hair. One caress. After all, she too was created in His image."

"Caressing is permitted," Grandpa Yosef interjects.

"The peasant woman said, 'His name will be Mieczslaw, that is my husband's wish. But we will call him Moises.'

"And the boy was flesh and blood, and he had a name, he was a living creature, the deed could not be undone."

"Such an affair," Grandpa Yosef mumbles.

"I remained in the cellar while above me, day and night, I

could hear my son crying. I too wept. Seven days and seven nights. The next day the peasant woman came down. She waited for me to finish my meal and said, 'I have circumcised our son.'

"That night there was madness. The baby cried out in pain. The farmer was beside himself. He did not know what had happened, but his instincts were unsettled. Something was wrong and he did not know what. The peasant woman cared for the baby, secretly changing his bandages. The madness descended as far as the cellar. I had pain in my feet and burning in my heart. In the chambers of my soul the rebellion stirred—I would run away, take the boy and flee. And where would I bring the child? Where would I go? The urge, barely roused, was lost. It rose and fell. Born, then dead."

Grandpa Yosef sighs. "You must recall that he told me this story, he gave me the deposit, in the camp, by which I surmised that one day he had made a decision and committed an act. What did he do? There is no knowing. Where is the child? No telling. He ended up in our camp, and more than that he did not wish to tell. 'Here I am,' he said with a gray face, and looked away from me. He leaned back into the world of his ponderings, having completed his part in this world. He motioned to me to leave him alone. I was helpless. Soon the gates of liberation would open for the Jews, but the life of the Rabbi of Kalow was draining into the Next World like a leaking well.

"The next morning the gates of the camp opened. Liberation! Everyone ran to the gates and I rushed to check on the Rabbi of Kalow. He was still alive. I gave him the good news. The *Kadosh Baruch Hu* had provided for us. 'Liberation!' I told him. 'Liberation!'

"'Liberation,' he whispered. He was free to go. He breathed into the depths of his lungs, as if taking a final taste of this world, and his soul departed. The Rabbi of Kalow was dead. *Baruch dayan ha'emet.* I was not able to ask, 'Why, why the annihilation?' And he was the last to be annihilated. He brought the people to freedom but did not see it. He came to the brink of Israel, but remained on Mount Nebo.

"From outside I heard the prisoners celebrating, shouting, cheering. Feet pattered this way and that, storehouses were raided, people roamed outside the fences. I sat in the shadows of the hut at the feet of the dead rabbi. I could not share in the happiness. I whispered my vow: 'When I have a son, I will name him Moshe.' The rabbi's tortured face, now pure and bathed in the brilliance of the afterworld, seems to repeat his promise: 'And he will be the savior of Israel!'"

*

During Atalia and Effi's shift, Grandpa Lolek opened his eyes and lay facing the white ceiling, looking slightly bewildered, as if his deep blue eyes had left something behind. It soon became clear that it was his vision. Grandpa Lolek's sight had not yet come back, but his eyes had taught themselves how to open again. He remained a still, helpless figure. His eyes opened with great desire, but his body would not yet cooperate.

The doctors told us that Grandpa Lolek's body had made up its mind to get better, but there was a slight delay in the process. They still needed to remove the benign tumor pressing on his brain, although it was unclear if they should risk removing the entire tumor. In Switzerland there were experts on this kind of tumor. They may decide to remove only part of it. There were modern treatments that did not require surgery. They had to consider the risks, the dangers, the experts' recommendations. In any case, Grandpa Lolek no longer needed the ward.

Somehow a decision turned out to have been made: Grandpa Lolek would move in with Grandpa Yosef for now, so he could take care of him. He needed this supervisory transition period before anyone took a risk and rushed into wasting money on some Swiss treatment that might not be the best solution. When the decision had been made, or when there had been discussions and deliberations, was unclear. That was how it worked with them. The decision materialized out of thin air without requiring any sort of debate or concrete words. The situation set its own course, and from the hospital Grandpa Lolek went straight to Grandpa Yosef's house, for-a-supervisory-transition-period.

Grandpa Yosef put Grandpa Lolek in Feiga's room. He laid his clothes and suits on the closet shelves (where he found a forgotten tie belonging to Hans Oderman). He scattered towels and toiletries in the bathroom. Cleared space on the kitchen shelves. Then he began sending us to Grandpa Lolek's house on the Carmel to bring whatever he thought necessary for the recovering patient. He made us bring fine bed linen and fancy teacups, and the Leica camera. Each item we brought found its place, but did not satisfy Grandpa Yosef. He scanned the newly arranged room and found fault. Off he sent us for another item.

There seemed to be something overwrought about Grandpa Yosef's conduct, but we did not bother to question him. We assumed he was simply being accommodating, trying to introduce a certain amount of grandeur to his modest home. We thought he was trying to fill the house up for his patient's sake. We smiled and obeyed—it was unwise to refuse Grandpa Yosef's requests at a time when the Caribbeanism seemed to be rearing its head again.

Out in the world, the rain finally began to fall. December took its revenge in the form of storms, and we drove back and forth between Kiryat Haim and the Carmel, on the seat beside us a transistor radio, sometimes a scarf, sometimes a vase.

"He's emptying out my home!" Effi complained, already well entrenched in Grandpa Lolek's empty house. ("Just for a while," she explained, insinuating herself like a cuckoo.)

Grandpa Yosef would not rest. He declared his intent to vacate another shelf, the top one, which housed various useless antiques (an ivory elephant from Uncle Tulek, a backup menorah in case the regular one broke, a bag of Bonzo he hadn't had the fortitude to throw out). He climbed up a ladder and passed the little treasures down to us. He grinned awkwardly when he found a bottle of rum he had brought back on a Caribbean whim. "Well, now you know..." he mumbled. "The doctorate. I went there because of Adler, to research the Jewish pirates."

He seemed to feel the need to tie up loose ends and lift the veil off whatever still remained mysterious. We were struck by an odd sensation—a slight aversion to Grandpa Yosef. His life was suddenly deciphered, suddenly clear, all the way down to his most recent secret, the journey to the Caribbean, a dream dreamt by another. That, and Moshe's name, and the doctorate, were all spread out before us. It was hard to look at Grandpa Yosef without feeling uncomfortable. This Grandpa Yosef was too open, too broken down into factors. The bare facts of his life story had become just that—bare. Something had been exposed which should have remained hidden. A bright light had come and flooded with clarity what had thus far squirmed inside towers of clues, fractures of truth that had come together into the form we loved: mysterious Grandpa Yosef, who goes to university despite his age, who writes a doctoral thesis, who rises from sitting *shiva* and sets off for the Caribbean. Everything was exposed—everything. Even the fog tormenting his soul, his son Moshe and the names he was not given—demons which, according to his belief, had taken their revenge.

We had to fight to reconstruct a Grandpa Yosef free of this aversion. There commenced an era of clearing away shards. We fought. But the feelings grew more complicated, emerging in an opposite form to the one we had envisioned. We were unable to look lucidly at this man into whose house once again flowed the needy and the troubled, demanding that Grandpa Yosef give them solutions, assistance, shelter. His good deeds were depicted in a new light. Against our will we saw Grandpa Yosef having to persist, to do only good, without ceasing. If he stopped even for a moment, his old deeds would catch up with him and crush him under their wheels.

The world filled with rain and we fought inside it, against the mist, the dragons, the aversion. One day Grandpa Yosef sent me for Grandpa Lolek's files that contained his bills and the certificates for the land in Gedera and his other property. He thought the recovering patient needed the files to be present beside him on the bedside table. When I returned I found Green the Mechanic in the little parking lot, bringing the Vauxhall at Grandpa Yosef's demand. Then suddenly Hirsch emerged, the almost-deciphered Hirsch, but a chasm still stretched between the end of his story in Grandpa Yosef's voyage and the filthy old man now standing on Katznelson and enquiring theologically,

"Only saints were gassed?"

The root of evil had been revealed: Grandpa Yosef's unfinished voyage. From within the voyage, from one end to the other, questions erupted, movements stirred. What had happened to Hirsch after he left the Lodz ghetto? What happened to Farkelstein? What happened to Ahasuerus? Fragments had been born so that we could contemplate them and think of everything we had not had time to ponder during his hurtling voyage. And Grandpa Yosef's voyage began to roam inside me. All the days he had casually mentioned ("Sometimes I ate nothing but a turnip leaf for a whole day") sprawled out before me. Whole days depicting the events and suffering that had surrounded Grandpa Yosef. A tiny dot with a world around it. I had to fight. If not the dragon, at least its wings.

I came to Grandpa Yosef. "I want you to tell me your whole story again."

"What for?"

"So I can document it."

"What do you want to do that for?" Anat asked.

"What's the point of that?" Effi asked. She was sitting in Grandpa Lolek's house on a new couch she had bought "to make him happy when he comes home." She had placed it exactly above the opening of his secret cellar, opposite her newly purchased television; she had even paid for cable TV ("it's instead of men"). She would leave everything for Grandpa Lolek, to make him happy when he came home.

"We have to document, to understand," I reply.

Grandpa Yosef's voyage kept rambling, great bright landscapes around every small section of his story.

Grandpa Yosef acquiesced. "All right, if you think it's important."

We sat together night after night, him talking and me writing. Every so often he got up, leafed through what I had written, reviewed his own story on the pages, pleased with what he saw. As if every letter wore a little tie, and his duty was to walk among the rows and inspect them, correcting little imperfections in their appearance.

Night after night, I acquired Grandpa Yosef's memories.

Dad was also willing to talk. I was Old Enough.

This time, I was the emotional one. His style was short and simple, with no inexpedient words. His life, his memories. The lost world in which he had been left to wander among ruins, people-who-would-no-longer-be, places-that-were-gone, a culture that had left only pointy headstones in little cemeteries and monuments at the edges of train tracks, and now the whole world that had once convened at the edge of the tracks was gathering its memories into the monuments, enlarging them, and so my father turned the years back, slowly retelling.

His words were clear. Simple. He had the talent to remember, a talent I inherited. Sometimes he struggled, *"Nu...what was the name of Einhorn's son from the furniture store?"* But he did not give in to the fifty years. I tried to comprehend how deeply he was casting these moments of concentration as I sat beside him, unable to help. In the evenings I transcribed his story, documenting, without changing a single word. I left it just as Dad said.

> I was born in Bochnia, Poland, in 1930. My father was a barber, my mother a housewife. Before the war I completed the third grade in a regular Polish school, the Jachowicza School. My family was middle class. My father was a Zionist. My mother had a Jewish National Fund collection box like all good Jewish women did. Father was very active in the Jewish community. He was involved in building a large synagogue in Bochnia. Until then there were many small synagogues, known as *stiebelech*. The Jews in Bochnia were divided. Some were very Orthodox, some traditional, and some were not religious. My grandfather on my father's side was traditional. On Mother's side I only knew Grandmother, and she was very religious. My mother was also very religious.
>
> Our lives were ordinary. That was, until the war. I played with Polish kids and felt like a Polish patriot. I knew I was Jewish, and after school I went to the *cheder,* which I was a little bitter about, but I had no choice...[Dad tells me, "In the Cheder we studied the *Chumash* and translated from *loshen koidesh* (Hebrew) into Yiddish. I did not know Hebrew or Yiddish, so for me it was like translating Chinese into French. I didn't understand a word. One day I came home and told

my father proudly, *'doszedłem do shlishi!*—I reached the third!'
I had no idea what *'shlishi'* was, but I usually reached only
sheini—the second."] I was not in a youth movement myself,
I was too young, but Father used to take me sometimes to a
Zionist youth movement. I can't remember which one, but
since Father was a socialist and a Zionist, it must have been
a Zionist socialist youth movement.

In 1939 the war broke out. About a week later the Germans entered Bochnia. We saw the German might and had not
believed that such a thing existed. We lived on the main street,
and we saw the Germans coming in with tanks and artillery
and infantry riding on armored vehicles. Before the Germans
came, there was a battle with a small Polish force, which was
destroyed by air strikes in the morning. The Germans had no
difficulty getting in. The bombardments were not in the center of town, so we did not suffer from them.

When the Germans arrived, at first they paid no attention to the Jews. After a while, the first prohibition was that
Jews were not allowed to walk down the main street. When
they did anyway, they were beaten. Then they set up a sort of
Jewish police, the *Ordnungsdienst*, or OD. They posted guards
at the entries and exits of the street so Jews would not pass
through. After a while, we were instructed to put a sort of
band on our sleeves. Not a yellow patch, but white with light
blue. It was obligatory from age thirteen, but I also started to
wear one at some point. The summer break came to an end
and we went back to school. After about a week the teacher
called us to the front. There were five of us Jewish children in
the class, and he said to us, "Goodbye and not farewell." He
simply kicked us out. We left.

The Judenrat had already been established by then, and
they set up a Jewish school. There were no advanced studies,
it was mainly to keep the children busy. My father's shop was
not confiscated—on the contrary, he was instructed to open
the shop and make it available to the German army. At first
they paid well. The soldiers knew he was Jewish, and that

was fine. Father kept running the shop, but after a while the Germans went elsewhere. That was until '41. Of course, during that period there were all sorts of *Kontributionen*—levies. You had to give so many pounds of copper, lead, all sorts of materials. You would buy the material and hand it over. They would publish a notice that everyone had to bring a certain amount, and no one dared not to.

We kept on living in our apartment. In the same building, they set up a residence for German soldiers. I don't know if they knew we were Jews, but in any case they treated us fine. Some of them were anti-semites who spoke about Jews, and others took no notice. In fact our landlord, who was a Polish anti-Semite and wanted to inform on us, was treated badly by them because they had been taught that wealthy landlords were Jews. We actually developed good relationships with some of the soldiers. They would hang around when they were on duty, and once in a while they came to visit. Father spoke excellent German, and it was nice for them to have someone to talk to far from home. Once, I remember, it was a Jewish holiday, and we had a festive meal at home. Suddenly we heard their vehicle stop outside. They had come to visit. Father quickly gathered everything up from the table, with the table-cloth, and threw it all into the next room. The soldiers came in and saw us sitting at an empty table. They asked why. Father said times were hard, and we just couldn't afford anything. They were moved and wanted to help, so they drove off and brought us back lots of food and other things.

That was how it was with those soldiers. They were just people. During that time there was some activity going on, they say there were Polish Partisans or some sort of underground. There was shooting at night, and they killed two or three Germans. The Germans hanged the two men who had done it. Then they took everyone who was in prison, and "just to be sure," they added in a few Jews. They led them all the way through town, we watched it, and executed them in a spot near the woods, and that was in fact the first execution in Bochnia.

In 1941 we received an order to move to the ghetto. We left our home and found an apartment in the ghetto. Father was given a permit to transfer his business to the ghetto. Poles were taken out of the ghetto area. There was still a school then, to keep the children occupied. At that time we didn't think much about escaping. There were no thoughts of extermination. There was no talk about extermination. People knew there would be trouble, they knew the Germans did not like Jews, but they thought it would be like in Germany, where Jews were restricted and their freedom of movement was curtailed, but there was no talk of extermination. Even when they talked about transports to the East, they knew the Jews were being sent to work. No one knew it was to be killed. Everyone thought they would somehow get through. Jews were always optimistic. Germans reached as far as Moscow and still people said, "These are extraordinary circumstances." Perhaps that was what kept them going, because otherwise people might not have survived.

My father had a barbershop, and at some point there came orders that everyone had to work. The luxury of school came to an end and I was allowed to work with Father in the barbershop. I studied hairdressing, learned how to shave, lather, that sort of thing. I worked there for quite a long time. It was a kind of village life, where people traded with each other. There were some people who did business, made money, and there were still some connections outside the ghetto, but the economic situation really began to deteriorate. That was until the first *Aktion* in the summer of '42.

In the summer of 1942 all the Jews of Bochnia were ordered to appear at the military base, except those who were given stamps in their work cards permitting them to stay. Anyone who wanted to stay tried to find a respectable workplace, because they thought if they sent people away, it would be those who did not have work. In that *Aktion,* virtually all the Jews who were originally from Bochnia went to Belzec. Well, we didn't know that Belzec was a death camp. We thought they were being sent to work in the East. My sister did not get a stamp, and she was already prepared with a bag and everything to go east. But at the last minute she was able to get a stamp. I remember we were standing next to our home in the ghetto when the Gestapo head, Schomburg, walked by with my Uncle Yanek, who was in the Judenrat. Yanek pointed out my sister to Schomburg, and that was all she needed. After that she got a stamp. Yanek himself was not helped by his 'status'; he was sent with his wife and his son Sigmund, three years old, to Belzec, stamps and all.

There was a hospital in the ghetto, and the head of the hospital was my uncle, Anatol Gutfreund. Since they said patients would not be sent east but would stay in Bochnia, my uncle hospitalized his mother. People found ways. But the Germans, as usual, did not keep their word, and they took all the hospital patients to the Baczkow forest and shot them, all of them, including my grandmother. That was apparently not enough for the Germans, because afterwards all the people who had been given permits to stay in Bochnia were ordered to come to the Judenrat courtyard, and they took us to the military base and had another *Selektion*. They asked each person what he or she did. My father said he was a barber. They said, "Good, we need a barber." They let him go. Then my sister came up. She had two jobs, at the bakery and in the street sanitation department. Then my mother said she worked with Father, so somehow they let her go. My mother took me by the hand so we could pass through together, but the man stopped me with his *Peitsche*, his horsewhip, putting it between my hand and Mother's. I was a twelve-year-old boy. At that moment a commotion broke out over by the main transport, I don't know what it was about. He looked over to see what was going on, and Mother quickly pulled me away and I went over to the other side and joined the group of people permitted to stay. That was my first *Selektion* and, as in dozens of cases, it was a matter of a split second this way or that.

After the *Aktion* was over they took us to collect the

dead from the streets. I saw murdered rabbis lying there, and I asked Father, "Father, tell me, what is this? Rabbis...why? Where are they and where are we...?" So my father said something like, "Because of sins, for what has happened...penance for the People of Israel," and so forth. I said to him, "Yes, but there are children here too. What about these children?" Then Father started crying. What could he say?

In that *Aktion*, the main core of the Bochnia Jews disappeared. We went back to the ghetto. Then they started bringing Jews in from all sorts of towns and villages in the area, and concentrated them all in the ghetto. What happened was that all the people who had hidden during the *Aktion* and had been found, they shot them right on the spot. Those they didn't find stayed hidden in the ghetto, then they let them out. There was no problem, they came out, they got a stamp, and they stayed. Then they divided the ghetto into Ghetto A and Ghetto B. In Ghetto A were people who worked, in Ghetto B people who didn't work. The Germans had a long-term plan to liquidate Ghetto B.

The second *Aktion* was in the winter of 1942, in November. The Jews were fairly confused and did not know what to do. We got permits to stay again, but we were afraid by then, because we had seen that there were *Selektionen*. And we saw that all the people who had hidden the first time were still there. So my father decided we would hide. He set up a bunker in the attic of a storehouse in our back yard. There was another family there, the Marsends. They had a little girl of about four, Etinka. That little girl was not just educated, but really trained. They trained her to stay quiet, not to open her mouth, and she could sit for hours without making a sound. They taught her that if she was put into a backpack and someone hit the backpack, she mustn't open her mouth. She was well trained. She was also a very fearful girl, very frightened. I admit that I tormented her quite a bit. I was bigger than her, and I used to tease her. I would tell her scary stories and she would stare at me without saying a word for a long time, then suddenly burst into tears. Whatever you did to her she would stay very quiet, until she suddenly started crying. That poor little girl.

We hid with the Marsends, and Grandma was also with us, my mother's mother. We hid and the searches began. We heard that every time they found people in a house, they shot them. They went from house to house and we heard yelling and shots. They shot and shot and shot. The house next-door to us too, they found a family there who we knew, and they killed them. We heard all the shouts. Then they reached our house. I remember that on the front door it said *'Ordnungsdienst Hollander.'* He was our neighbor. I remember that it was in the evening and they called his name out. They searched, turned things upside down, but they didn't find the storehouse where we were hiding. It must have been too dark for them to see. We were in a sort of attic, the entrance was through the storehouse. My father had put some heavy objects against the door, so it couldn't be opened from downstairs. At least we thought it couldn't. The next day we heard them starting the search all over again. They went through again and we heard shots fired. They were getting closer to us. They came right up to our storehouse. They looked at it and said, "There must be an attic here." They started searching. They pushed against the door with a pole and the things Father had put there started to shift. The German said, "There must be people here." They brought a ladder and sent people in through the roof. A Jewish man came in, a locksmith they had brought to open doors, and a Polish policeman.

Before the war we had lived in a building that belonged to the police, and all the policemen knew us. The policeman saw Father, and yelled, "Dear God, Mr. Gutfreund, what are you doing here?"

What are you doing here...

In any event, the policeman started trying to cover Father up, and the locksmith, who knew the Marsends, tried to cover them up. Then they opened the door. I was standing closest to the door, so they took me and threw me down. Mother screamed because she was afraid I would be hurt in the fall. She didn't consider that we were about to be shot. I came out of the warehouse and stood in the yard. The German called me over. There was one German there, and all the rest were Polish police. He told me to stand by the fence. He asked how many people were up there, but I didn't tell him. I knew they had covered up Father and the other family, so I said, "There's my mother, my sister, and my grandmother." I knew they had already been found, because they had been in the same place with me. Then he stood me up against the wall, took his rifle off his shoulder and put a bullet in it. And all I could think of was that I hoped it wouldn't hurt, because I knew it was the end. At that moment a messenger arrived on a motorcycle and shouted something at him in German. The German took the bullet out, put it back into the magazine, slung his rifle over his shoulder and went over to the messenger. They spoke in German, I couldn't hear what they were saying, and he signed an order for the messenger. In the meantime they had brought down Grandmother and Mother. And the German said, "Search, there are more people there. Search, there are more people up there." They searched and found the Marsends and Father.

What happened, we learned later, was that they didn't shoot me because an order came to stop all the shooting. In the military base that I mentioned before, there were German soldiers who had started asking questions about the shootings. The SS didn't want the soldiers to know what was going on, so they gave an order to stop shooting. So it was a stroke of luck that we weren't shot. It was my own private stroke of luck.

Father told the Polish officers, "Don't take us to the transport, we have a permit to stay in the ghetto. We hid here because we were late and we were afraid to go out during curfew. Take us to the Judenrat, they'll authorize it there."

They didn't care, the Polish officers. Terrible anti-semites.

Mother said, "Look, Grandmother isn't feeling well. Where is your conscience?"

One of the officers said, "My mother is already in her grave, why shouldn't yours be?"

Fortunately, a German citizen passed by, a Gestapo member. Father, who spoke excellent German because he had been in the Austrian Army in World War I, told him we had a permit to stay and that they should take us to the Judenrat. He took off a ring with gemstones. The German took the ring and said, "All right, take them to the Judenrat."

There at the Judenrat, they said, "Yes, they are on the list." But despite that, there was an instruction to put us in the transport, where everyone was gathered. After that, an order came from the Judenrat and we were taken back there. They left only my grandmother in the transport.

We sat in the Judenrat offices. I remember there was a baby boy there, a few months old, and they had given him sleeping pills so he wouldn't cry and give away the people hiding in his bunker. They must have given him too much, and he was dying. My uncle the doctor said, "Give him something, milk, I'll flush his stomach," but there was no milk. I think that boy died eventually, I don't know. In any case, we sat there until the afternoon, and saw how they moved all these people onto the train, all the ones who had to go, and those who couldn't walk were shot. Then we saw that they were taking the elderly people on wagons, and we saw my grandmother on one of the wagons. Where they took them to this day I do not know. Because all the ones on the train they took to Szebnie, a work camp. The elderly ones, I don't know. I have no idea. Either they took them somewhere and shot them, or to Belzec. We don't know.

By that time we already knew about the annihilation. Because in the same hospital where my uncle was a director, there was a nurse there, a medic, who had been taken in the first *Aktion*. After two or three weeks my uncle had received a letter from Belzec, with a stamp that said, 'Belzec.' In his letter, the man wrote, "Everyone is dead. I am the only one left alive. Everyone was gassed. [*zagazowani.*] I met an old school friend." (The man was from Bielsko-Biala, on the Czech border. The German he met was from Czechia, near the border, and he knew him and kept him alive.) But this Jew asked my uncle to send him poison because he didn't want to live. There was a problem of what to do with this postcard. They sensed panic, and were unsure whether or not to reveal it. Uncle and Father decided to give it to the Judenrat. They handed it over but the Judenrat also didn't know what to do with it. Then another postcard came, saying, "I am begging you, send me poison, I don't want to live." Then another postcard came, and that was it. Nothing more. So by then we already knew there was annihilation. That was the first time it was clear to us.

Now, after the second *Aktion*, they let us go back home. But first we had to collect all the dead bodies from bunkers and all that. They brought us to a kind of hilltop. First we put the dead into a wooden house, and they were going to set fire to the house and burn everything. That was the order. But there were too many, and they wouldn't fit in. So we were ordered to tear down the house and make a pile, a layer of wood and a layer of corpses, like that in layers. Just then three German soldiers came from the army base. They had heard the shots and wanted to know what was happening. They saw the pile of bodies and asked what was going on. My father, as I mentioned, spoke good German, and he said, "*Verbrecher.*" Criminals.

Criminals. All right.

But then they saw a heap of children over on the side, and asked, "Are those criminals too?"

Dad said, "Yes."

"What did they do?"

"Jews."

Then the soldiers realized what was happening. They said, "Those dogs, the SS, what they do in our name! And we will pay the price."

They went to the base and brought the whole division

back, and they were planning to fight the SS and kick up a storm about what was going on. We begged them not to do that because it would only hurt us and make things worse. And it wouldn't bring back the dead. We could see that the soldiers were really... They didn't know what was going on back then. They were horrified. They simply did not know what was going on. There may have been Wehrmacht units doing all sorts of things, but these soldiers did not know what was going on, clearly. [I ask Dad, "Your father was a little impudent, no? Saying things like that. They could have done something to him for talking back to them like that." Dad says, "Yes, but he was...at that moment I think he just didn't care. He also... there was another time, before the ghetto, when a German *Volksdeutsch* harassed him on the street, and Father wouldn't let it slide and he punched him. He didn't leave the house for three days after that, because they were looking for him, and his hand was injured. Sometimes he wouldn't give in, he did or said what he thought should be done or said. Maybe that's why he answered the soldiers like that, I think."]

We went back to our houses, and again they started bringing in Jews from the region. At some point they separated the men from the women and the place turned into a forced labor camp. Everyone worked. They set up a mess hall because there was no cooking at home. I remember once we were eating in the mess hall, and there was an execution across the way. Two brothers, Schentzer, they had a soap factory before the war. They tried to escape the ghetto and some Polish policemen caught them and beat them bloody. They threw them into the Babica, the brook. The next night, they tried again. They were, you know, macho, the two of them. The Germans caught them. I remember they shut them up in a cellar right across from the mess hall. They took out one of them and were about to shoot him, and he tried to resist. But the executioner, an older German, was quick as a fox. He grabbed the man quickly by the back of his neck, put the gun to his head, and shot. Then they took the second brother out.

He saw his brother on the ground and started struggling. Again the German grabbed him and shot him. Not that he had a chance—they were surrounded by SS men with guns. And the whole time this was happening, about twenty yards from us, we kept on eating.

Then they canceled the separation between men and women. That was probably because they wanted to concentrate as many Jews as possible into one place. They had their plans. We moved into a house again, all of us together, with my uncle the doctor, who was the hospital director. We lived on Solna Gora Street. That was when they divided the ghetto into Ghetto A and Ghetto B. There was a case where the ghetto commandant, the Lagerführer, found a woman from Ghetto A in Ghetto B. He warned her once. The second time he shot her dead.

The third *Aktion* was in the summer of 1943. One morning they started announcing, "Everybody out, everybody out, everybody to the *Appellplatz*," which was the roll-call square. "Everybody leave now, take small belongings with you." I had a stamp collection, and I went with my friend to hide it because we thought we would somehow get through it again. I went to the cellar with my friend and we hid the collection. We wrapped it up in some rags. When we came out, no one was there, they had taken everyone. We lived not far from the Judenrat, just a couple of hundred yards across the way. And next to the Judenrat a bunch of Germans were standing around. They saw us coming out and yelled, "*Stehen bleiben!*"— Stop! But I didn't really trust them and so we started running. My father had once taught me that if I was being shot at, I should run away in a zigzag. And so I did. My friend overtook me, he was about ten yards ahead of me. They opened fire on us and I suddenly saw a red spot spreading on his back. He fell down. I kept on running into an alleyway, then I ran to the *Appellplatz*, where everyone was gathered, and I found my family. The Germans chased me but they couldn't find me, there were a lot of people there. [I ask Dad, "Do you remember your friend's name?" (I wanted something of him to live on.) Dad says, "No. He was one of the kids who came to the ghetto from the outside, from somewhere else. I can't remember his name anymore." But a few days later he remembers. "I think his name was Salek. Salek was a nickname for Shlomo. I'm not certain. But I think so, Salek."]

Again we were left behind, among those who were supposed to stay for the ghetto liquidation. At the time we didn't know it would be liquidated. Father got a permit to stay. We all got permits to stay. They took us aside. All the others, they started putting in the transport. Then we saw the family that had lived with us, and the father was wearing a large backpack, and we knew that inside that backpack was little Etinka. We saw how the Germans hit the backpack with a stick. They hit everyone. We saw them hitting and poking, and that little girl kept quiet, didn't say a word. He managed to get her through and they went to Szebnie.

I learned later that when they were in Szebnie, the work camp, they found the girl and killed her. Etinka's father found out who the German was who had killed her, and during one of the roll-calls he broke out of line, attacked the German and strangled him. They shot him on the spot, but I was told that he managed to strangle the German who had killed his little girl. [From the list we got when we visited the ghetto with Dad on our trip to Poland, I copy his full name down: Noah (Noe) Marsend. Even though he was murdered long ago, and the details of his life have become insignificant, I document everything I know. His date of birth, 8/31/1904. The name of his wife, Manya. Her date of birth, 7/26/1904. And the name of his only daughter, Beata, known as little Etinka, who was born on 6/2/1938 and murdered in 1942 at Szebnie camp. She was four, exactly the age of my Yariv, who was born in 1988, and who now comes out of his room and sleepily asks me to check his buttons. "My pj's are all twisted." He can't sleep.]

That was a bit of a digression. In any case, a whole group of us sat and watched as they sent the other people to Szebnie.

Then we saw a Jew running away from the transport. We were sitting next to a Jewish slaughterhouse, a kosher one. The Jew broke in there and the Germans chased him. We heard shots, then we heard him shout, "*Shema Yisrael!*" And then everything went silent. After about ten minutes we heard him shout, "Water...water..." He was still alive. But no one could go to him. Then there was silence.

After that they took us to the house where the *Ord-nungsdienst* lived. It was a house on Kraszewska Street. There were supposed to be a hundred and sixty Jews left out of all the ghetto, and what happened was that there were two hundred and sixty left. So they took everyone. They called it the 'bloody roll-call.' They decided they had to kill a hundred people. They told the Judenrat head, Simcha Weiss, to give them the list of everyone who was left. So he said, "I have no list." He was hoping, you see, that without a list they would be able to save more people. For some reason, the camp comman-dant, Müller, also said he didn't have the list. In that respect he was pretty decent. The *Aktion* commander, a colonel, said, "You don't have a list? All right. Shoot the whole pile of them!" He got into his car and started driving away. Then Weiss ran after the car like a puppy and started begging, "Listen...we'll do something." The colonel stopped and said, "You choose who goes." So Simcha Weiss said, "I cannot choose, but I will go first." I remember that.

The Germans had a discussion and they started taking out all sorts of people from the group. At first we were con-vinced they were choosing the ones who would stay, because they took out all sorts of people who had connections with the Germans. But it turned out that every German who had an account to settle with a Jew took him out to kill him.

Then they said, "All the children stand in the front row." So I ran out, but Father grabbed me and wouldn't let go. He lifted me up behind his back and stood in front of me, hold-ing me, and someone from the row behind held me up by my pants so I would look taller. ["How long did he hold you

like that?" "Oh, it was a roll-call that lasted several hours..."
"And all that time he held you like that?" "Yes, with his hands
behind his back, holding me by my belt."] They went back
and forth, searching. They didn't notice that I was a kid. They
picked out a hundred people, took them aside and shot them
on the spot.

Then they took us to the *Appellplatz*, where they put us
into these kinds of shacks. We were ordered to start liquidat-
ing the ghetto. But first they took us to cover all the...to get
rid of all the dead people...and there were lots of them. Lots
of dead people. I can't give a number, but there were hundreds. We were left to liquidate the ghetto. A lot of Jews had
been hiding, and the way it went that time was, whenever
they found anyone, they killed them. Before that, whenever
they found people after an *Aktion* they had let them live. But
not this time. Whoever they found, they killed. There were
some that they threw into the Judenrat cellars, but mostly
they killed them.

I remember once I was with Father and they found two
children. The girl was maybe thirteen, and a boy of seven or
eight, something like that. Father called me and showed me a
tiny suitcase, and inside were a few carrots and radishes and
potatoes, because there was nothing to eat. They must have
been hiding for a long time. Father started crying when he
saw that. Of course, they shot those children. They took us to
light a fire. They put the children in a straw basket. In Poland
they had these big straw baskets. They burned them in the
basket, but the basket fell apart and I saw how their bodies
spilled out onto the pile with their arms and legs to the sides.
Then they scattered the ashes. ["Dad, how did you turn out
so normal, Dad?"] My father was the head of a work group,
and there was a woman who came out of her hiding place and
joined his work group. She wasn't legal, but Father covered
for her and helped her get in touch with the other side, the
Aryan side, and she was able to escape.

At a certain point, they had another *Selektion* during

the ghetto liquidation. There were a hundred and sixty of us and there were only supposed to be a hundred left. The truth is we were in a bind, because at that stage Father was 'in a spat' with the Lagerführer, Müller. One day some Gestapo men had come from Krakow, and without asking any questions they burst into the ghetto hospital and seized a whole treasure of gold and silver from under the bed of a Jew who was lying there. There must have been an informant, because they went straight to his bed. Müller was very angry that the whole treasure went to someone else, and he blamed my uncle and my father, insisting they had known about the treasure and helped hide it. He didn't exactly accuse them—I shouldn't even use the word 'accuse' because it's not like he had to say anything. He simply gave an order that Father should stop coming to shave him every day, as he had done up to then. He was the ghetto barber, and that was his great 'privilege.' ["What sort of a character was he, this Müller?" "You know. Nothing special." "You once told me he used to shoot out of his office window." "At bottles, not at people. He had one obsession, about women with makeup. He would personally supervise, and if he caught a woman with makeup on he would force her to remove it. That was at the beginning of the ghetto. Later, he didn't have to do that anymore—who walked around with makeup? He collected stamps, and he kept a Jewish expert to get hold of whatever he could find for him in the ghetto. Apart from that, nothing special. He wasn't even an officer, he was a sergeant or a sergeant major, a Scharführer. I don't know what their ranks were."]

Anyway, the Lagerführer was in a 'spat' with our family, and then came the *Selektion* announcement. We were worried, of course. But something that had happened two or three days before saved our lives. My father was the head of a work group, and he was a hard-working man. It was in his character to get the job done, and for some reason Müller, who used to ride around on a horse, saw that he was working hard and he must have liked that a lot. He called Father over, took out a cigar and gave it to him. It was a Saturday, and my father didn't smoke on the Sabbath. Go tell a German that you don't smoke on the Sabbath. So Father said, "I don't smoke while I'm working. I'll smoke it after work." And he liked that even more. So when the *Selektion* came, two or three days later, he let us go again. Gave us a permit. Our whole family was part of the remaining hundred. My mother and sister too.

At the end of 1943 the Bochnia ghetto was basically done with, liquidated. They took everything that was still there to the trains. Everything went to Germany, all neatly packed up. During the ghetto liquidation there was a case where a Jewish policeman escaped from the ghetto. His mother lived there, Mrs. Rothkopf, a very elderly lady. And so the camp commandant, Müller, took her out and killed her. Oberstrumführer Müller. Those were the two incidents when he personally shot someone. That time, and the case of the woman who wasn't supposed to be in Ghetto A. ["That's not true, Dad." Müller, although he was a nothing, is well known to Attorney Perl. People testified that he shot lots of people. True, he wasn't as murderous as some others, he was just a minor and obedient SS man who did not take his own initiative or commit extraordinary acts, but he did his job. When necessary, he shot people.] It's fate, the way one person is saved just because someone else isn't. Since the son had run away and Müller had killed the mother, he was missing two people to make the numbers work, and numbers were important to the Germans. Just then they caught a woman I knew, Mrs. Schwimmer, and her daughter, who were hiding. They wanted to shoot them right then and there, but Müller added them to the group to replace the missing two, so it worked out all right for him. And that was how Mrs. Schwimmer was saved, and she lived in Israel with her daughter until she was a hundred and three. Fate, that's what it is. But another son of hers was killed back in the first *Aktion*. He was an ordained rabbi, and during the *Aktion* he ran to the Judenrat as if it were an embassy that could save him. They shot him on the steps, and his glasses broke and pierced his eyes. He lay there like that. On the steps, face up.

In any case, they liquidated the ghetto. They put us all into one big house. One fine day they said, "Everybody out." They put us into train cars and took us to the Plaszow concentration camp. That was at the beginning of 1944, the winter of '43–'44. When we arrived in Plaszow, they put me and my father to work in the paper mill, and my mother and sister worked as seamstresses. They separated the men from the women, and only occasionally would we see my mother and sister behind the fence. At some point they needed lots of tools on the front, like pickaxes and spades. So they transferred all the men from the paper mill to the carpentry shop. The food was indescribable. There was hardly any of it. There was constant turnover of people. Some they sent away, some they killed.

The camp commandant was Goeth, Amon Goeth, who had an 'illustrious' career. He was huge, almost six-five, a sadist and a murderer. They said he was even crazier before we arrived. By the time we got there at the end of '43, he had already calmed down. Not that it helped us—he put the fear of death in us. I was a boy and I couldn't look at him...I just couldn't. He was truly the Angel of Death. The minute we saw him walk outside, we knew it would end badly. He was... simple...and he had assistants who were no less cruel than him. Sometimes all sorts of senior officials would come to the camp, but they didn't pay any attention to us. They came and went. [Sometimes I think it is because he went through the Shoah that Dad finds it difficult to understand. He survived on instinct, not thought. Germans who shot were bad; Germans who didn't—didn't count. But he gave no thought to a German who passed by in his car for a moment, looked around and drove on without a word. Dad couldn't pay any attention to whoever wasn't shooting or abusing him. That

German in the car scanned the square and thought to himself something like, "There are two hundred more than the estimate here. The train cars won't be big enough. If Spauser had worked faster with the transport from Jeklowicze we could have added another car, but now it's too late. We'll have to knock off a hundred here and squeeze in the rest. We'll send another telegram to Spauser and a reminder to HQ. We can't have things held up here." My father was too close, too persecuted, and the evil that concerned him was the simple kind, the obvious kind. But my thoughts go to that other evil, the one sitting in the car wearing wire-rimmed glasses.]

We worked in the carpentry shop. The foreman, I don't know his name, but he was known as 'Mongol.' He was a character. When we worked the night shifts it was good because there were air-raid sirens. The Allies were already bombing, and we hardly worked at night because when they bombed the lights were turned off and we couldn't work. But the work was very hard and very high-pressure. Next to the carpentry shop there was an execution area. They used a very nasty word to refer to it, *'Chujowa Gorka,'* which means "Dick Hill." And that's where they held executions. We saw a lot of them. At some point they started burning the corpses there. At first they buried them, but when the front got closer they started burning them because they wanted to hide that anything had happened there. They started taking the bodies out and there was an awful stench from the rotting corpses and the fire. We worked very nearby, about fifty yards away. Then they moved the execution place to a different area, on the other side of the carpentry shop.

One day I wanted to take a little rest and I hid in a pile of chopped wood. They used to put the logs out to dry and there was a gap inside the heap, where I sat. And then I saw that they were bringing...it must have been Germans. First, a German company in brown uniforms brought someone and shot him. A German in a brown uniform. Then came a company in black uniforms and shot someone in a black uniform. It was some sort of internal execution, but I almost died of fear, because if they had seen that I was watching it could have ended badly.

On May seventh, 1944, there was a big *Selektion*. We stood naked all day, and a doctor came, whose name I can't remember. [Attorney Perl remembers his name. He was Doctor Blancke, Hauptsturmführer Blancke.] He stood there in a huge fur coat and we stood naked all day, and it was raining, and he pointed with a little pencil and said, *"Links, Rechts, Links, Rechts"*—left, right, left, right. I, of course, went to the *Links* because I was a runt. The ones who went to the left were put on the list, and that was it, they were listed for the transport. The transport was a week later, and whoever was listed had to go. Somehow on that day they also wrote my mother down in the *Selektion* in the women's camp. And I got a cold that day. The Germans didn't mess around—if you had a cold, you went to the hospital. They were afraid of epidemics. After two or three days in the hospital, I felt better. I was just a kid, and one of the Germans, Doctor Kalfus, was building himself a fish pond next to his office. I came out and started bringing him cement and rocks. I later found out that he was the number one murderer in the hospital. He would inject kerosene into patients' veins to kill them. Yes, a real criminal.

The fifteenth of May arrived, a week after the *Selektion*, and everyone who had been listed was called to come to the transport. Of course my name was called out too, because I was on the list. They called and called and called but I was saved because I was in the hospital. Then they came and took the whole hospital away. When they came to get me, there was a Jewish doctor there who really liked me. Well, I was a kid, and he said something to Kalfus. Kalfus remembered that I had helped him, so he said, "He's still young, he can work," and they let me stay. Now, you see, if I had been healthy they would have taken me to begin with. If I had been sick they would have taken me from the hospital. There were about nine hundred people there, and out of all those people I was the only one who remained.

That was the day they took my mother away. It later turned out that the whole transport went to Auschwitz, straight to the crematoria, because they were sick and emaciated people who couldn't work. My mother had lost weight for a reason. She was very religious and she wouldn't eat *treif*. So she would exchange soup for bread and things like that. When Passover came, she wouldn't eat bread either. She lost a lot of weight and they took her...that was the end.

There were a few more *Selektionen*. Once they sent me to the left in the *Selektion* and they wrote me down for the transport, but something...they couldn't find me on the general list. There was a member of the Jewish police named Finkelstein. He was a criminal. Jewish. He looked through the lists and then he said in Yiddish, I don't know...something...his heart softened, and he said, "I hope I don't find you on this list." And suddenly I saw that all the people from my hut were going back to the hut, and I saw my father, and I didn't ask a lot of questions. I ran and joined that group of people and no one said anything. I got into the hut and was saved that time. [I've been counting, and that's the seventh time you've been saved, and me saved with you, thanks to resourcefulness, thanks to luck, thanks to your father, thanks to your mother. Every time you are saved, you save me. I was born easily, a normal child, without understanding what I understand now—the miracle of my existence. I am here thanks to the things that happened to you and did not happen to others, those whose children were not born, who do not exist. Sometimes, though, I think you can sense them in the air, maybe on holidays and large gatherings, you can sense the offspring of the man standing behind you, next to you, whose father did not hold him behind his back for three hours, for whom there was no order to stop shooting just in the nick of time, for whom no well-timed commotion arose just when the horse whip, the *Peitsche*, separated him from his mother.]

Life in Plaszow camp was very difficult because often, after work, they would make us do all sorts of things just to humiliate us and make our lives difficult. After a night shift, they would often take four people and load a wooden plank on their backs. There were these dismantled shacks that were made up of all sorts of pieces of wood and they would load a plank onto four people. The plank itself was heavy, and then they would load it up with anything we came across on the way. Rolls of barbed wire, stones, dirt. Until the people collapsed. He was simply a sadist, the officer who devised this game. I don't remember his name, some SS officer, this was his hobby. The four would collapse and he'd take another four. It was...almost every morning after the night shift. Living conditions were very harsh. We lived in shacks with beds...not exactly beds, triple bunks, and each section held three people, and there were lots of fleas. We called them 'paratroopers' because they were red and they would fall on us from above. It was impossible to sleep. We used to sleep outside, because inside it was impossible. Outside there was rain and cold and snow. But it was better to sleep outside in the rain and snow than inside, where it was impossible. We had a lot of lice. After work, people would sit and kill the lice. You couldn't wash or boil the linen.

Economically it was very difficult. There wasn't enough food. My father had left some money with a Polish man in Bochnia who used to work for him, Mieczslaw Kozek. This Pole, from time to time, would send sums of money to the concentration camp. It was possible to get it to Plaszow. How he did it, I do not know. There were Germans who helped him. They must have gotten ninety percent of the sums that went through, but the ten percent were enough for us to buy bread or something. After the war, the Polish assistant told us that one day he saw an SS officer coming up to his barbershop, and he thought they'd found out about him and so he ran. He spent a week away from Bochnia, afraid to go back. It turned out the officer he ran away from was actually the man who had come to transfer the money. But it was no laughing matter, they really could have killed him for that. It was a great help to us.

In any case, it was possible to get along for a while, but then it stopped. The economic situation was very difficult.

Then there was a time when Father was ill and had to be hospitalized. I also got ill. My joints were so inflamed I couldn't even walk. We used to pass twice a day through the gates, and they would count us. We walked in rows of five. So when we had to go through to be counted, they would pick me up and walk me through the gates so I would be counted. Then they would sit me on the side. I couldn't move. [Who would have cared if they had put a bullet through you? You lay there, unable to move, and for hundreds of miles around you there was no one who could help, no one to halt reality if a bullet shot out of the barrel. What did you think about? You say you didn't think about anything in particular. I understand why you are such a Zionist. That was when you realized something that is difficult for me to understand—what it is to be without your own country. Without independence. Without having someone with a gun on your side too. So many days, lying there without moving, people around you being murdered over nothing. It must be harder than standing against a wall in the Bochnia ghetto, harder than being sent to the left, to die, and waiting a week for the transport.] In the camp afterwards I just couldn't make it to the clinic. I couldn't. But somehow I made it, I don't remember how. They gave me some medicine. It helped me a little and I got better, but it was a very difficult time.

For a while they took us to work outside the camp and we built railroad tracks for Prokocim, a village near Krakow. Terrible conditions. The foremen were real murderers. They would beat us to death over any mistake, or not a mistake, just any little thing. And the walk was long, walking from Plaszow all the way to Prokocim and back. People collapsed, they couldn't do it. The one good thing was that we could buy things from the Poles and smuggle them back into the camp. At first there was no money, but then Father somehow organized some money to buy stuff and smuggle it in. But the Germans knew this, and every so often they conducted searches. One evening they started a search. Everyone who had anything would be beaten bloody. There were some cooking pots laid out on kind of wooden planks. I told someone, "Come on, let's take this plank and go." We took a plank and started walking away. A German saw us leaving so he chased us. He was certain we were hiding something in the pots. When he saw there was nothing, he hit me and we left. But I had lots of things on me, and then we were able to get money.

In Plaszow there were a few Jews who were no better than the Germans—and some that were worse. There was the Chilewicz, the 'head Jew.' This man was a criminal. There was also Finkelstein, the one I mentioned before, and the two of them were no less cruel than the Germans. Sometimes even worse. [I read in the testimonies about their fates. Just before the liquidation of the camp, the Germans took Finkelstein and Chilewicz and Chilewicz's wife, who was even worse than he was, to a hilltop and killed them. *Speak kindly of the dead.*] In that period there was nothing to eat. I always tried to find a way to sneak into the kitchen. I was a small, thin boy. I would burrow under the fences and steal soup and run with it to Father. On my shirt you could see the menu every week. There was no other way to survive. I also managed to get something through to my sister, in the women's camp. Mother, I already said, would not eat soup because it was *treif*. At the end of '44 they sent us in a transport to Gross-Rosen in Germany. At the same time they sent my sister to Auschwitz, and then to Ravensbrück. My father was already quite sick. We didn't know he was suffering from kidney problems. His legs swelled up horribly.

We came to Gross-Rosen. I remember at the station, we were met by Jewish prisoners in striped uniforms. They told us, "If you have anything, give it over quick, because you won't be needing it..." We thought they meant we were going to be gassed, but they must have meant that the Germans would take everything we had, and if we gave these people our things, at least the Germans couldn't take them. But we thought that was it, we were going to the gas chambers. We were ordered to strip. They put us in a little hall and we sat naked for three days and three nights, because Germans believed that people smuggled in gold and dollars in their bodies. Maybe there were people who did, I don't know. When someone needed to use the toilet they took him outside in the snow, naked, and he would have to do his business somewhere where they could search. There was a kind of container, and there were Jews who used sieves to find out if there was anything inside. We sat for three days and three nights without food or drink. Cold.

After three days they concluded that everyone had vacated themselves. They put us in cold showers and made us run in the snow for about a mile. We stood in a hut and they threw each of us a pair of pants, a shirt, a strange sort of wool hat, and shoes. Clothes with stripes. In the middle of winter, freezing cold, but those were the clothes they gave us. We slept in a little hall, if you can call it sleep. One man sat up against the wall and the next on his legs and the third on that one's legs, in rows and rows. If someone needed to go out to relieve himself, in the cold, he had to step on the other people's feet, because there was nowhere to walk. He had very little chance of reaching the door. On the way people held it in, they didn't want to go...but by the time they got to the door they didn't need to go out anymore. Whenever someone made a noise, a kapo would come in and make us exercise—up, down, up down, with murderous beatings. That's how the nights would go by. We worked in construction. The Germans were still building. Retreating on one end, building on the other. We were there for only two weeks. After that they sent us to Waldenburg.

In Waldenburg we lived in buildings. It wasn't a large camp. Most of the people worked. There was a chemical plant there, and some people worked in construction at all sorts of places where they walked on foot, over five miles, every day there and back. In Waldenburg we worked at peeling potatoes.

Next to the camp there was a bachelors' residence house. There were Italians and Frenchmen working at the plant because the Germans were all on the front. They were salaried civilians, and so they had this sort of bachelors' house where they lived, and whoever was able to get in there to work saw it as a boon, because the house matron was a Volksdeutsch, a Polish woman of German origin. Frau Paullina. She was very fair. Really, thanks to her my father was saved because his legs were very swollen, he was barely alive. She wasn't so strict about work. She was really all right. Once in a while people were beaten, but compared to other camps it was okay. The thing is, they were always preparing for an evacuation. They thought we would have to leave at any moment. [Dad was lucky. All the auxiliary camps of Gross-Rosen were ordered to go on Death Marches. Waldenburg was an auxiliary camp of Gross-Rosen, but there was no Death March, probably by personal order of the camp commandant. People went out on the marches from all the camps in the area, even from relatively comfortable camps like Waldenburg. People who believed they had gotten through it all, that they had been saved, went on the marches days and hours before the war was over. Cut off from the world. Around them was utter German defeat, the Russians were in Berlin, no more orders were coming through, but the lines marched on, a small disconnected world where there were still orders and shooting and an ostensible direction. On an endless course—a line of ants with no nest. Marching. No food, no water, no rest. The lines marched on and on. One step after the other. No questions asked. March on. Nazi Germany had surrendered, orders had stopped coming, and prisoners were being shot on the side of the road. The cruelty did not melt away—on the contrary, it grew harsher, more extreme. In the row of ants, the people with the guns clung to the familiar. Only if they kept on marching would the safe world, the good world, remain. If they stopped even for a moment it would all disappear. A row of ants with no nest, and I see those who falter shot immediately, and the shooters wipe the blood off a rifle butt held too close. I can actually see it. A row of ants with no nest, and Dad, because of an anonymous camp commandant, back on his cot in Waldenburg, while around him prisoners set off to march.] The camp commandant told us there were SS units going from camp to camp and killing whoever remained. I didn't hear it, but people told me that he said, "If they come here, everyone should run wherever they can." He was simply...well...he was all right.

The end of the war was getting closer. We saw German civilians gathering around our camp in increasing numbers because they were terribly frightened. They were already throwing food into the camp and trying to tell stories about how they weren't to blame, they didn't know and hadn't known. And then the eighth of May arrived. At two-thirty in the afternoon, the camp commandant closed the gates with a lock, threw the keys in and said, *"Jetzt seid Ihr frei"*—you're free now. And he fled. And that was that.

We didn't know what to do. People were frightened. We knew it was the end, but we didn't know what to do with our freedom. People didn't know what to do, they simply didn't know. They were afraid to go out in case the SS arrived after all. We didn't know what to do. So for a while we waited inside. After a couple of hours we broke open the gates and started running towards the main road. We got there at about four-thirty in the afternoon. That was when we saw the first Russian units. Russian troops rolled in on tanks. They had no food. They also had apparently not had much to eat. But people went into factories and houses and started eating. That was a disaster, because they got dysentery and food poisoning and had to be hospitalized. A lot of people died after that. Maybe it was my luck again that the Russians broke into a liquor factory—that's what they were after. I went in there and filled some bottles with all sorts of drinks. And for some reason I didn't think about food...I don't know why. I took it all back and brought it to Father. Father drank a little and I drank some, and we didn't have much strength left. We fell asleep. The next day we woke up and saw people vomiting, they were horribly sick. We realized that the little bit of drink had saved us.

Then we went to the German women. The German men were on the front, and the women wanted the people from the camps to come and protect them. We lived there for about two months. There were no trains, no means of transportation, so we couldn't get back. And we didn't know where to go back to. We lived there for about two months without doing anything. After two months we started to walk. We took a little wagon and loaded up a few things we had. At that time personal belongings had no value; when I needed a shirt I took one and threw away the old one. Who needed two shirts? In those circumstances, property had no value. So we took a wagon and loaded it with...I can't even remember what, and we started to walk. There were some stretches where there were trains and some where there weren't. When there were trains they were full. It wasn't well organized like it is today. Everywhere we went, we saw Poles standing around saying, "More Jews have come back."

I knew that my mother was not alive, because people who had been with me in Waldenburg, who had also been in Auschwitz, had told me. They said the transport that arrived on May 15th and 16th went straight to the gas chambers. I didn't tell my father anything. My sister went through very difficult things. She barely made it through alive. She was in Auschwitz, in Ravensbrück. In terrible conditions.

At Katowice there was a train to Krakow. In Krakow we caught a coal train to Bochnia, hoping someone would still be alive. We didn't know, but we hoped. We got to Bochnia. There was a horse and cart there, and the driver knew Father. He asked him in complete surprise, "You mean you're still alive? They said everyone was dead." He wasn't too happy, but he took us to the center of town, where we met a young man who had been in the concentration camp with us, and he said that my sister was in town. There were only a few Jews there, and my sister was among them. And so for a while we lived in Bochnia, but there was nothing to do there.

My father tried to rebuild the gravestones. The Germans had destroyed them all to pave roads. Mrs. Schwimmer was there. She was the elderly Jew who had been saved with her daughter because they shot the mother of the Jewish police-man who escaped. She was a serious woman. Together with my father they set up a lot of the gravestones they found. During the war, a Polish man had found my grandfather's gravestone in the road, and at night he came with his sons and took it and hid it in his barn. When we came back, he told Father that he couldn't allow himself to see the gravestone of Mr. Gutfreund on the road. He gave it back to Father and it still exists today.

I was basically illiterate. I had hardly had any schooling. Father sat me down and hired a private tutor who taught in the local high school, and within six months I finished elemen-tary school. I went through all the material. Then I took an exam at Jachowicza school, where I had gone before the war. The headmaster was the examiner. Amongst other things, he had me write about what I had been through during the war, in Polish. It was really the first time I sat down and thought about what had happened. He came into the class a few times, where I sat alone, and asked, "Haven't you finished yet?"

I wrote and wrote and wrote and wrote.

A few days later, I came to get my grade. He looked at me and said, "You wrote this?"

"Yes, I did."

"Are you sure?"

"No one was in the classroom, I was alone."

"And you went through all these things?"

"Yes," I said.

And then he said, *"biedny dziecko"*—poor boy. He patted my head and asked if I would be willing to leave the notebook with him. Stupidly, I left it. [I found out that the name of the headmaster was Witold Raganowitz.]

That's it. That was the end of the story in Bochnia. [After the war, Dad raised doves on the rooftops in Bochnia. Raising doves—that was good. A symbol of freedom. Something I will be proud to tell Yariv one day. He also sold contraband cigarettes. That's less good, but true. That's what happened. He used to go to Krakow to buy packs of cigarettes, then back to Bochnia to sell them in the market square. Competitors harassed him, policemen chased him down, but after the war they were no match for Dad. A man who had been blessed with so much cunningness and luck and survival skills—it took more than a Polish policeman to trip him up.] We moved to Krakow. In Krakow I went to high school, a Jewish school. And there we studied two classes every year to catch up. Then they demolished the Jewish school and I moved to a Polish school. At that time I was already active in the Shomer HaTzair movement, and my head was more in the movement and in making *aliya* to Israel than in my studies. But I studied because Father pressured me. He opened a barbershop in Krakow. He was always sick. He had uremia, a kidney disease, and he died in 1950. My sister left for Israel, leaving me on my own. I had an aunt and an uncle, but really I was alone. That was during the period when they didn't let people leave, it was a big problem. I went to Warsaw a few times, because the main *Shomer HaTzair* cell was there. Then they broke up the cell. Zionist movements were outlawed. My uncle was a captain in the Polish army, a dentist, and he was a first lieutenant in a military hospital. I lived in his apartment and I used to hold Shomer HaTzair cell meetings there. If he had known, he would have killed me. But it was a safe place, because a captain in the Polish army and all that...

The Israeli ambassador to Poland at that time was Barzilai, a member of Kibbutz Negba. He was very supportive, as much as he could be, of the Zionist issue, but we couldn't get exit visas. One day I decided to try. I went to the Ministry of the Interior in Warsaw. It was an office of the KGB and that sort of thing. Very secured. Guards everywhere. I searched for a way in, and managed somehow. There was a guard on every floor. When the guard was distracted by talking with someone I would sneak past. I got to the fourth or fifth floor, I can't remember, to the office of the Director General of the ministry. Getting there was...I myself don't know how I did it. Back then I could do those things.

When I walked into the office, the secretary started shouting, "Goodness gracious, how did you get in here?"

I said to her, "Listen, I'm Jewish, I have no one here, I want to go to Israel."

From all her yelling, because she was so afraid, the Director General came out. He asked, "What's going on here?"

So she said, "He snuck in."

He asked, "What are you doing here?"

I told him, "I'm Jewish, my father has died, my sister left, there's nothing for me here. I went through the whole war in the camps, I have nothing here."

He looked at me like this, put his arm around my shoulder, and said, "Go home, you'll get a travel permit."

So I said, "But you don't know my name."

"Give your name to the secretary."

I gave her my name and left the building legally. Two weeks later I received my passport. I believe to this day that he was Jewish. That's what I think. Because he...I could see that he...he was considerate. And the fact is, I got a passport.

So I made *aliya* to Israel. I went straight to Kibbutz Gan Shmuel. I came with a Shomer HaTzair group, part of a larger group. The Poles gave out exit permits, but only very few. We took trains through Czechia, Koshitza, Austria, Italy. In Venice we boarded the "Galila" ship, and that was how we arrived in Israel. Of course, they welcomed us by dousing us with DDT, but for some reason we did not complain. We understood. After Kibbutz Gan Shmuel, I went to Kibbutz Harel. Then I decided to join the army. I served for two and a half years, in the artillery. I finished my service. I was alone. My sister was in Israel, and there was an aunt, but...

Somehow I got a job at Ata. It was a big textile factory, one of the most famous in Israel. Getting a job there was a big deal, it was considered a good job. I worked there doing 'dirty work.' Before that I worked in construction and all sorts of other things. Slowly but surely, I made progress. I went through training, took courses, I was an instructor, a foreman, then a human resources manager. It took time. Thirty years. The factory closed down in 1985 and I got a job in the collections department at the municipality of Kiryat Bialik. Then I retired, and that was it.

1992: Yariv

L unch. Saturday. Yariv sits across from his grandfather—my father—contending with the revelation that Grandpa was once a little boy. A lovely crease ploughs its way across his forehead as he gazes at Dad suspiciously. Considering. Examining. Straining to find a place for this new truth. I watch as his mind processes the geology of knowledge. Effi watches too, still with an angry look on her face. Before lunch she had discovered that Yariv was unfamiliar with Little Red Riding Hood. She took him to his room to tell him the story, and emerged after a short while, announcing, "Your kid's a retard. He had no problems with the wolf, but he was afraid of Little Red Riding Hood!"

We eat in silence. What can we say? Our current life stories pale in comparison to the history evolving over at Grandpa Yosef's, where Grandpa Lolek's recuperation is rapidly progressing. Only two months have passed since Grandpa Yosef took him in, and Grandpa Lolek is already taking slow, probing steps around the neighborhood. He roams Katznelson Street, looks at his Vauxhall, even sits down in it for a furtive cigarette once in a while.

Except that doubt has seeped in. Something hasn't been sitting right. Grandpa Lolek's rehabilitation process has begun to seem suspiciously marginal, as if its true tenor is in fact the advancement of the capricious protagonist, Grandpa Yosef. Something about him strikes us as odd. At first, when he insisted that Grandpa Lolek come to his home to recuperate, we thought he was simply trying to buy some more time before the inevitable loneliness set in (no-one-to-make-an-effort-for-no-one-to-make-an-effort-for.) He had escaped to the Caribbean, had then seized the opportunity to fill his home with the presence of Hans Oderman, and finally spent a heroic era at Grandpa Lolek's side in the hospital. We thought he was now attempting to acquire yet another stretch of time. But that was merely the outer layer of a disorganized thought.

We monitored the recuperating Grandpa Lolek as he slowly returned to us. We applauded the internal powers that redrew him without losing an iota of his former character. We were optimistic, despite the slight and perhaps typical oddness of the way his health was restored. His limbs and senses convened in separate units to regain their strength, each disconnected from the other. The first to recover were his legs, along with his vision and appetite. His hands remained rigid, almost paralyzed, and not a word left his lips. When his left hand recovered enough so that he could leaf through the obituary pages in *Yediot Aharonot,* an anonymous notice representing an opportunity to make a quick profit sufficed to extract a cry of excitement from his lips; thus his vocal capabilities were rebirthed. His right hand recovered along with his hearing. He slowly relocated his back pain and the urge to smoke. The lust for opportunity, the debtism—it all came back. He regained strength daily, limb by limb, sense by sense, character trait by character trait, as if he were healing himself according to an old blueprint he had kept hidden away somewhere. Eventually he came back to us completely, the old Grandpa Lolek we knew. He took an interest in the world, in what was different and new, in the dollar exchange rate and the family's well-being. He was somewhat alarmed by the rainfall, unaware of the drought that had raged while he was gone. He did not entirely comprehend his medical condition, utterly surprised to discover that he had been considered 'ailing' for some time now. He was very curious about the treatment options, the physician referrals, the types of surgery to choose from. He converted the proposals into a line of prices, options and costs, which clarified his situation with surgical precision.

We were impressed. We monitored him. With Grandpa Lolek—everything was fine. Coming along nicely. But with Grandpa Yosef there was a wild and indeterminate motion. From the moment Grandpa Lolek awoke and regained his senses, our suspicion increased. At all hours of the day and night, Grandpa Yosef hastened to pick up on Grandpa Lolek's every wish, fulfilling each and every desire as though it were a holy mission. Even when we considered his usual personality, together with the uniqueness of the situation, we were still far from understanding the power of his enthusiasm.

The devoted care-giving affected Grandpa Lolek in many ways. We found him usually vibrant and cheerful, well cared for, his face joyous. Even when the discussion revolved around surgery and the correlated risks, his face was full of surging optimism. Talk of the costs still did not diminish the lightness of his wrinkles. It seemed that Grandpa Lolek was not in complete control of a burning desire to smile, to rejoice, to enthuse. We could not understand the source of this happiness. We suspected it might be the delicacy that Grandpa Yosef cooked up for him every day, the inactive ingredients of which were pickled herring and onion, but which was in fact a potion concealing powers that sometimes took the form of dillweed. Grandpa Lolek ate it eagerly, asking for more every day, longing for the next helping to the point of total dependency. A light glow enveloped him, a constant light into which the dish was poured onwards and inwards.

Grandpa Yosef had become a complete savage in the kitchen. He turned his soups golden with turmeric and scattered cardamom pods in his fritters. Ginger and cilantro enhanced his meatballs, while the flavor of cinnamon took hold of rice pudding like a tyrant. Whenever we came, at any time of day, we would find the table covered with leftovers from their banquets, and over in the kitchen a new feast being concocted in the oven. Whenever we tasted anything, we recoiled. Grandpa Yosef was exploiting the temporary malfunction of his recuperating guest's taste buds by embedding fiery spices in all his dishes, turning Grandpa Lolek's body into a refinery, a test-tube. Grandpa Lolek happily dined on the meatballs, the fritters and the dumplings, while mysterious reactions burned within his body. And Grandpa Yosef stood watching, concentrating, his eyes ablaze with purpose. "Stand back, stand back," he would urge, pushing us away.

Nutrition and digestion could not contain all of Grandpa Yosef's intentions. A fire was burning there, a great mystery. Perplexed, we watched as Grandpa Yosef rushed around and drained his energies. We asked ourselves what was going on. Effi was the first to understand: "Well, he's trying to turn back time."

We were amazed. No, not amazed, for this was an idea we had already considered—it had amazed us once and been rejected, but now it was clear. From the moment the idea was voiced, it seemed so obvious. How could it be otherwise? Grandpa Yosef was trying to turn back time. We looked at Grandpa Lolek, who had touched the brink of death and returned, rowing back into a life already lived. We looked at Grandpa Yosef staring longingly at him—if only Grandpa Lolek could recover and go back to the moment of the stroke. If only he could push and heal him a little more. Even the doctor had said, "Just give it time, take good care of him, and he'll be younger than he was before."

Grandpa Yosef was a realist, but he suffered from a mystical unconscious. His soul was preparing to create a miracle: to cure Grandpa Lolek with dizzying speed, to hasten the arrow of retreating time, and to use the momentum of his recuperation so that time would gallop backwards and restore Grandpa Lolek to his previous life, thereby also restoring Moshe. And by truly pushing reality to it limits, Feiga too would be restored. Grandpa Yosef's unconscious barely let him in on these plans. It only ran him around like a messenger boy, working towards the great purpose—to turn back time and demand that it give back Moshe and Feiga. To restore everything to the way it was.

Grandpa Yosef took in Grandpa Lolek like a beloved burden, a yoke worth its weight in gold. From his illness, from the regions of death he had touched, Grandpa Lolek was launched towards health, a load pulled back and released. Together with him, according to the laws of physics, and without disrupting the principle of inertia or the law of conservation, without transgressing the laws of this world, time was also supposed to be swept away, or at least to flutter and leave behind a twist, a fold, a dimple—that was enough.

We were concerned for his health. Grandpa-Yosef-against-time seemed like an unfair battle. We observed his desperation and endurance, and we fell in love anew. Matters were helped by the documentation of "Grandpa Yosef's Voyage." The pages, slowly accumulated, described a simple voyage that explained everything. I showed it to Effi and Dad. We fought off our aversion.

Grandpa Yosef's story was written down, as was Dad's. And then, in the spirit of the era, attention was turned to a more momentous task. I began to think about the other people in the family and in the neighborhood. Their stories. The Big Bang. I wanted to document it, to write everything down. Everything-that-had-happened-to-everyone-who-came-from-there. Everyone-I-knew. Everything-I-once-did-not-know. Everything-that-must-be-revealed-so-that-I-could-now-understand. Everything-that-must-be-written-so-it-was-not-lost.

Anat could not understand. "What do you need to deal with all this stuff for? It won't do them any good either."

During Grandpa Lolek's illness, she had joined forces with Grandpa Yosef. She could not contain herself for long while such an impressive nursing operation was taking place right in front of her eyes. She took over the domain of laundry and ironing, and contributed to the baking. We often met at the hospital, I with pages of documentation, she with piles of clothes on the Fiat seats.

"I don't want you to spend too much time with all that," she said.

"You're not letting it go, eh?" Effi said.

"It should be documented," Attorney Perl assured me.

I brought Yariv to see him in the store for the first time. He sat in the back room, in the corner at first, slightly frightened beneath the angular wall above him. He nervously kneaded the soles of his rain boots, a new acquisition, and examined the screws he had been given. He plucked up the courage to ask for a nut for each bolt, "So they won't be lonely."

Attorney Perl laughed and called out to his assistant in the front of the store, "Yakov, bring in a box with nuts for quarter-inches!"

He showed Yariv the photograph of his wife, Laura, and explained, "That was my wife."

"Whose mommy was she?" Yariv asked.

Attorney Perl rolled his eyes and sipped a cup of tea. Then he yelled, "Yakov?!"

Yakov came in with a box. It was a new Yakov, one we did not know. He scattered some nuts in front of Yariv and silently retreated to the front of the store.

The nuts bored Yariv. He started inspecting the little drawers along the back wall. He carefully pulled out one drawer, wondering if he would be rebuked, and revealed that the drawers did not contain the store inventory, as I had believed all those years, but rather notes of paper. The little drawers that filled the back room contained index cards bearing crowded notations.

"*Nu*, I've been collecting all these years." Attorney Perl took out a few cards and showed me his treasure trove of endless notations.

Franz Six. Head of the "ideological" branch at the Reich Security Main Office, responsible for disseminating material on the "Jewish question." Sentenced in 1948 to twenty years in prison, released four years later, in 1952.

Eduard Houdremont. A partner in the slave labor crimes at Krupp industries. Sentenced to ten years in prison in 1948, released in 1951.

Hermann Reinecke. Sentenced in the High Command trial to life imprisonment in 1948. Released in September 1954.

Walter Warlimont. Sentenced at the same trial to life imprisonment. His sentence was later commuted to eighteen years and he was released in 1957.

Endless lists. Crowded index cards with names and details, the stories of their lives after release from prison—the quiet lives, the little houses, the grandchildren, the longing for the good old days. Here, I realized, was where the treasure trove had always resided. Not in the memory of Attorney Perl, but in the little drawers.

"Could I read these?" I asked.

Attorney Perl gestured with his hand, putting all the drawers along the wall at my disposal. "Yes, yes. It would be interesting if someone finally did something with all this. You could write out all these notes nicely, with all the details. So if anyone in the world thinks the Nazi criminals were punished enough, they'll know."

Between my eyes and his there emerged a world in which I sat down immediately and began to toil. But Yariv pulled my hand, whispering, "I have a secret." He put his hand to my ear and explained gravely, "I have to go pee-pee." Then he announced, "Not here."

"Why not here?"

"Not here."

We went out to the street. Rain, as usual. A good time to try out his new boots. We found an old yard full of puddles glimmering under the street lamps.

"Here," Yariv chose.

And very quietly, like two bank robbers, we slipped into the yard "for a quick pee-pee." Later, at Yariv's demand, we went to "our" falafel stand, the one on Nevi'im Street. There, of course, came the memories. Dad used to take me to this stand, and I too had to be lifted up high so I could see over the counter laden with bowls of condiments. "Half a portion and juice," I used to say. The same place, so many years ago. Only the falafel guy is different—probably the son. "A ton of rain," he comments. "Yeah," I reply. I have no idea what his name is. So many years. This place has never been closed except for one week, when death notices covered the iron shutters, citing a name I have now forgotten. Then it opened up again. Same falafel, same flavor, only a different guy, but with the same features. He asks Yariv what he wants. Yariv does not speak, only points, cautious around strangers. But he stomps his feet in a puddle so everyone will see his new boots.

Lightning bolts through the sky, followed by thunder. Yariv is not scared, he likes it. He says, "rain," and his fingers mimic drops falling. "Lightning," he says, and one finger cuts through the air. He says, "thunder," and makes a tight fist, then opens it up as befitting thunder. Little Red Riding Hood scares him. Not thunder. At nights he gets out of bed and sings songs with the rain. They spent the whole fall at kindergarten looking forward to the rain, and when it was delayed, they sang the songs anyway and applauded. Now they're onto Chanukah songs, but Yariv happily wakes up at night, puts his nose against the window and sings for the rain. He thinks this is how it will be all year round. Rain and rain and rain and rain. He has no idea that something has happened this year, because of Grandpa Yosef and his war against time, and that the rain has already taken on the qualities of a deluge.

After the falafel, it's too late to go back to Attorney Perl's store. But over the next few days I go every day and stand in front of the great wall of drawers. (When Anat has to go out, I leave Yariv with the upstairs neighbor, the one who's always-happy-to-look-after-him-for-a-few-hours.) Attorney Perl lets me poke around and read, while on the other side of the wall he slowly climbs the ladder to take down bolts and nails for his customers.

Attorney Perl starts to bring me books from his home, endless volumes and pamphlets on the Holocaust. The Nazi trials are documented in thick brown volumes, testimonies bound in thin notebooks, anthologies of articles, the literature of Nazi laws, the speeches and verdicts of German leaders. "*Nu*, I've been collecting and buying for many years." Little notes and pencil markings indicate sections he finds particularly noteworthy. I read everything he has marked, and everything in-between.

He also starts sending me to Jerusalem, to the Yad Vashem library and archives. He gives me precise lists, citations in books, reports I have to read. He names documents, testimonies, protocols. The order and clarity in his ninety-two year old memory conflicts starkly with the labyrinthine archives. Energetic librarians do their best to search for my requests. Am I sure that's the name of the report? Being a well-briefed emissary, I insist. Sometimes Attorney Perl is vindicated, the report located. Other times—nothing, the report is missing. I go back to his store to peruse the documents with him, to hear explanations, opinions, further instructions.

"And don't forget," he says, supervising my work, "that you wanted to document testimonies from your family too."

I set up meetings with family members and come to demand

their recollections. I bring Yariv, the representative of sweetness and charm. We work as a team. His role—to extort wonder, excitement, attention. To soften them up. As soon as we arrive he makes himself comfortable on the rug, takes out two balls, a motorized car, an old plastic car, a water pistol. He never turns down a cup of juice, cookies, more juice. He rejects biographical questions, like "How are you doing?" "Do you like your teacher?" "What's your girlfriend's name at kindergarten?" In the meantime, his accomplice begins asking questions, listening, encouraging. The people acquiesce and their memories begin to pour out. First, happy memories. Always childhood. Always a town or a village, always with a market square (*rynek*, in their language). Mother. Father. Family. Sometimes the memories skip around, suddenly it is the post-war years. Pieces of family and fragments of encounters and life forces. At some undecipherable cue, the photo albums come out and great wings are spread. As the pages are turned, the storytellers are inspired to voice near-prophetic visions, although they are unable to belie the triviality of the photograph subjects—family displays and smiles in a row on chairs.

I let them talk. They roam through their memories, not always masters of their domain. Sometimes the storyline crosses the 1948 line, reaching the years of *aliya* to Israel and even as far as the Six Day War, in IDF uniforms with stories-you-wouldn't-believe, and yet it always reverts in the end, retreating back to 1939, the year of truth, the Big Bang.

On the rug, Yariv concocts battle and chase scenes, staging accomplishments for an imaginary enemy soon to be cowed by his own great victory. In the meantime, they reminisce. Sometimes in a flow, a series, an effortful sprint. Sometimes there are breaks and jumps and refusals and darkness. They cry too. Real tears. Yariv cranes his neck to see, one hand clutching a plastic car, the other on the table top as he stares.

Sometimes they say, "You know what, why do you need all these stories?"

"Documentation," I reply.

They ponder the word. It appeases them. Documentation. And they continue talking. Immortalized. Existing. Validated. Uncle

Lunkish and Aunt Frieda and Aunt Riesel and Aunt Zusa and Uncle Antek and Mrs. Kopel and Uncle Menashe. Darkness and ignorance and physical adjustments and escape and terror and trees and huts and people who once were and prayers and children and market squares and shooters and fear and quiet and silence.

In the evening I sit down to put it all into some sort of order. To document. I also copy down details from Attorney Perl's little cards. How do you form a coherent shape out of all this chaos?

Anat hovers around me, dissatisfied. "I'm telling you, you shouldn't be spending too much time with this."

Glowing embers.

"There's no such thing as too much!"

Because Walter Haensch, an Einsatzgruppe leader, was sentenced to death, but his sentence was commuted to fifteen years and in the end he was released after serving seven years in prison.

Because Heinz Schubert, another Einsatzgruppen leader, was sentenced to death, but his sentence was commuted to ten years and he was eventually released after three years in prison.

Because of their beautiful little houses in the newly formed Germany. Because of the gardens, the red roofs, the lawns to mow. The children, the grandchildren. The long weekends in the cold winters of Saxony, the autumns bursting through in the Erz mountains and painting the forests of Bavaria. And I am welcomed with open arms into a closed world of hands reaching out from the tiny windows of train cars, and Yariv's toothache, or maybe it was Anat's, fade away in my mind. I have to go down, down into that world, to repair it— that will repair the world above. Uncle Lunkish, in the world down there, promises to talk on condition I don't write it down, but in the end he doesn't tell me anything. "With my family in Tarnow…" he begins, and can't go any further. Mrs. Kopel went before Dr. Mengele's with her sister. Her sister died, Mrs. Kopel survived. Strange, he only tested her eyes, and she had no trouble with her vision, she could see perfectly—it was her womb that didn't work. Twice she got married, and twice went back to using Kopel, her maiden name, the name of her father, who died in the ghetto of a heart attack. Uncle Antek is surprised by my visit. Why don't we come more often? He asks about

Yariv, about Anat. And will there be another child? And how is Dad doing? He talks breezily about recent weddings, and remembers my *briss*, and Grandma Eva dancing. About Auschwitz he speaks slowly, not so lucid. "The winter in Auschwitz is hard, people don't know, in summer harder, diseases, people will die." I try to ask questions, to carefully turn back Uncle Antek's arrow of time, to get him to say one sentence about Auschwitz in the past tense. I touch ancient shards as I speak. All he can do is scatter his sentences around. "The head of our block, Prucher, thinks he'll survive because of his cruelty, but he'll go too. In Auschwitz you go, no matter how you behave. I'll end up going too, in the smoke. How long can you survive?" He warns me, "In the camps, even if you survive whole on the outside, thin as a skeleton, on the inside everything is finished. No dignity, no heart, no nothing."

Uncle Menashe doesn't want to talk in the evenings, before bed. He'll talk in the morning. He closes up the butcher shop for me again. "I was a five-year-old kid, what did you think, how could a five-year-old kid live?" He tells me about days spent hidden among kindly farmers—hidden not only from the Nazis, but from his current self. To this day he can't remember them, but he emphasizes, "The farmers were kind." He talks about his father, who paid a farmer he knew, and later, he remembers, he was moved to a different farm, a quiet place. As Uncle Menashe talks, Mom's story sneaks in. Her father also hid her with farmers, giving them all his money, and Uncle Menashe tells his story and I think about my mother, the prayers they made her learn in case the Germans interrogated her, the Hail Marys she kept on saying even when the war was over, even though they told her there was no need, and Uncle Menashe talks about the searches and the shootings in the village houses, he can't remember anything else, just that the farmers were kind, they gave him tasty bread with fat, and Mom walked barefoot for a whole winter, she remembered that, and that she was afraid of something, Dad told us that. She used to flee to the fields because something scared her, and Uncle Menashe says, "The farmers were kind. Once the farmer said, 'There's going to be trouble,' and he took me to another village for a few days, and there I saw a day-old lamb in a pen." That, he remembers; most everything else is gone. There was a light on in the pen. The lamb was almost white. That's all he can remember, and he apologizes for making me come all the way from Haifa to hear nothing. He says, "The main thing is that I turned out normal, right?" I smile. In our family, Uncle Menashe is one of the most normal people. He laughs, "Now, for thirty years, I'm the one who slaughters animals..."

Their stories collect and grow sharper. They tie into one another. I write and go back to ask questions, and write some more. Not infrequently, their memory betrays me. Something is related, but when I ask a question about it the next day, it's no longer clear—did it happen or didn't it? And when? With every passing day something is lost. Memory is like plaster—when you touch it, it crumbles. I struggle to leave as much as possible intact. Every evening at home the documentation continues like a stubborn battle. Grandpa Yosef's rains knock on the windows to remind me that somewhere out there another battle is raging. Grandpa Yosef fights against time. I pore over the testimonies, sometimes only understanding what I've written when I reread it at night. Then, sometimes, I understand their happiness—yes, it is happiness that I see erupting from them. They sit with me, unburdening themselves of massive gourds of memory, the gourds lying at an angle on the earth (thin stalks, unbelievably thin, nourish the huge resting bodies through connections forged among the leaves, into the earth, all the way far down and deep). They tell their stories, transferring their words to my notes, and stand back, leaving me to fight alone, to find order, to find the way, to document. (I combat memory while Grandpa Yosef battles time. We are both about to lose, but both as happy as victors.)

In Grandpa Yosef's house, meanwhile, the battle has intensified and reached a critical stage. Time will either turn back or not—the next few days will tell.

Pots simmer on the stove, the aromas of spices are absorbed into the walls. Grandpa Lolek has been cured despite himself; with food, with rest, with soft walks to the end of Katznelson, with the renewal of debtism, with slow appearances at court, with futile debates consisting mostly of the clerks' affection for him, pats on his shoulder and good wishes. Grandpa Yosef, constantly at Grandpa Lolek's side, manages the patient, guards him, and keeps a curious watch on events at the courthouse, consoling the neglected plaintiff. Sometimes, for Grandpa Lolek's and the car's sake, I take them for a spin in the 1970 Vauxhall. We circle the neighborhood, driving in rings of streets that grow longer and wider, the Vauxhall like a great centrifuge, accelerating more and more, producing power, until Grandpa Yosef is finally satisfied and announces, "Home, now."

On the surface, there is tranquility and responsibility in all his deeds. But the battle is raging. Every day he phones, and phones again, and forgets he has already phoned. He talks with me about Grandpa Lolek, boasting about the pounds he's gained. He invites Effi to give Grandpa Lolek a medical examination, demanding— "Come, weigh him." He talks with relatives, with friends, with all sorts of people he summons in no particular order, again and again, and it's no wonder that when the phone bill arrives, he is astounded and angry. Anger also erupts over the electricity and water bills (the flames fanned by Grandpa Lolek's objective estimation, "You're being robbed") and Grandpa Yosef, in a Caribbean mood, goes to enquire. The clerks welcome him warmly, who has he come for this time? But instead they are assailed by his wrath, lasting bitterness and furious demands, at the end of which Grandpa Yosef leaves with a slight look of shame on his face.

We believed he was losing. There were still only twenty-four hours in a day, and the hours were still only sixty minutes long. January proceeded at its dreary rate. Most of the time, the weather was still, but sometimes, especially at night, there would be a quick flash of lightning and a bolt of thunder that made the windows shudder and woke us, and we would wonder for a moment if perhaps Time was trying to overcompensate for its disgrace. November seemed to have returned, and even October. This downpour wasn't only January rain—everything that had been held back in November was now finally being added to the quota. In the mornings we would smile sheepishly. And then one day at the market, there was a sudden whiff of guavas. Sammy shrugged his shoulders. "I don't know how this is possible. Guavas in January? I heard they already have melons in the West Bank, and that shouldn't even happen in March."

Time's prophesying began to bother us. We noticed that lightning would strike, and only the next day would any thunder roll through the sky, born simply from itself.

The battle had reached its height. We were afraid for the loser's health—be it Grandpa Yosef's or Time's. We expressed our concern. Wasn't the care-giving exhausting him? Grandpa Yosef brushed off our worries. Artless and calm, entirely devoted to expediting the recovery, he found our questions mystifying. He used Anat as an alibi—she was doing half the work, after all, and besides, Grandpa Lolek was getting easier every day. He was already independent, self-sufficient. Why would it be difficult?

Inside, his subconscious forced him to keep working. Don't stop. There are things to do, plans to make, food to cook. Later—it will be heaven, with Feiga and Moshe. Grandpa Yosef toiled from morning to night (as if there were no Grandpa Lolek at the tail-end of his recovery, silently gaining weight; as if he was in fact fighting for his life), and from time to time, with triple and quadruple measures of cunning, he would remember his brief tourist days and start talking. Completely relaxed, chatting agreeably, lost in the sweet forests of his memory.

"They have, in the Caribbean, houses with pink shutters and lovely red roof-tops, and everything there is modest, and there are luscious plants. The children run around the streets with no worries, and the ocean is so clear. At sundown, red painted boats cast blue nets and the fishermen tug this way and that, pulling out stingrays and crabs from the sea, and shrimp and moonfish. The wooden doors are left ajar, and fine artisans engage in their labors for all to see. Women in pure white dresses patiently embroider, and their stores are so bright that it's blinding. In the market, everything is bustling, all the wares are out on display. Spotted fish and quivering seafood. Lemon-yellow bananas and other, nameless fruits. Strike them with your knife and their juice drips out, the aroma hitting your nostrils."

Grandpa Yosef furtively crawled towards his destination, outflanking time, ablaze, and out in the open he fried and cooked and rolled and whipped. Excited by the exotically named "Princess of the Nile"—which was in fact a simple Nile perch—he served it on fancy platters and fine dishes, garnished with chopped cilantro and nuts. Scattering slivered almonds as Grandpa Lolek looked on, he would comment, "Of course, I would prefer to fry it in palm oil."

He offered us a taste of the fish, dreamily reminiscing about the Caribbean as he handed out dishes. "There are restaurants scattered everywhere there, and cheerfully blazing fires. Fires in pits and fires under pots, and food wrapped in leaves and baked on coals. And I have not yet spoken of the little forests, and the lakes, and the light blue bays, and the coral reefs. The whole place is a Garden of Eden. As if there is not and never has been any suffering there."

We reminded him that much of the Caribbean population was descended from slaves led shackled onto ships, and that the islands' indigenous peoples had been completely eradicated. There was suffering there too. Grandpa Yosef mumbled, "Still…The quiet, the fruit," and continued his secret struggle. He and his adversary squeezed into a little arena, grasped each other's arms and pushed.

The decisive moment came unexpectedly on a simple February evening. Grandpa Lolek was sitting in the living room after dinner. He wiped his lips with the napkin Grandpa Yosef handed him, sighed a satisfied sigh and declared, "I think, time is for me to go home."

And for one tiny moment that was multiplied to the power of eternity, composed entirely of fragments of the present and fragments of the past and fragments of the future, standing ever-so-briefly on the scales of time to become present tense, the world froze. The second passed and it was followed by a new one. Everything continued as usual. Time went on its way. Grandpa Yosef had lost. He carefully packed up Grandpa Lolek's belongings. He emptied the closets, the drawers, the shelves. He left his home suitable for a single inhabitant.

Two days passed from the moment Grandpa Lolek made his pronouncement until we drove him in my car to his house. The hours of those two days lined up on either side of Grandpa Yosef and he walked between them, hour after hour, not so that they could whip him, but so that he could scan the hours as if they were a parade of honor. He walked towards the end of days, seeing us all the way to Katznelson. He respectfully bade farewell to Grandpa Lolek and turned back, erect, towards time, which was waiting for him at home. His look pierced us wildly, combatively. *Do you think I've forgotten Adler's philosophy? The future, that is what I am thinking of. The future. And I shall win.*

We left him there dolefully. Grandpa Yosef, without Moshe, without Feiga. How would he manage?

It soon turned out that the magical era had not come to an end without incident. From all the commotion, the fluttering of days, the prophetic time, the oscillating eras, the minutes pushed back like the poles of a magnet, a single distortion of time blossomed into a deed: Brandy came back. But not in her familiar canine form. Grandpa Yosef's neighborhood became filled with a plethora of dogs, passing transients of different breeds and different sizes. Each of them looked clearly like a particular aspect of Brandy—a rib of hers, something extracted from her wholeness and presented independently, developed into a whole dog, a barking puppy or a bitch pulled along on a leash.

We would see them and remember Brandy—because of a leg, because of an ear, because of a bark. It did not occur to us that the dogs were somehow related. Who was thinking of mysticism? We were thinking of what we missed. Even before Grandpa Yosef started battling the direction of time, if our thoughts went to Moshe, Brandy also waddled along and sat down to keep watch at his feet. Even in our thoughts, even after death, if Moshe was here, Brandy would come too, to make sure no harm came to him. Sometimes she turned up in our thoughts just like that, and we quickly conjured up a big lawn, butterflies, moles tunneling, even rabbits. Anything to make her happy. To excite her. To make her reach out with her ugly paws as she lunged, to make her run and jump, gaining full compensation for a life bound at Moshe's feet.

But now her appearance was clearly real. We could not ignore the dogs surrounding the house as if by chance. Effi was the first to say, "That dog has a nose exactly like Brandy's," and from that moment the silence was broken. Brandy's appearances were publicly discussed. It was Brandy—that much was clear. She was back. We simply had to explain how it could be that one dog could make such an exaggerated reappearance. We didn't have to try very hard: in that period, thanks to Grandpa Yosef, the reason for anything odd was easily hovering within arm's reach. The air disgorged explanations for any wonderment, logic defended even that which diverged from reason. For Brandy too, explanations gathered, and we could choose among them. We were persuaded by a particularly sobering explanation—Brandy was never a dog, but rather something intended to protect Moshe, which had taken on the form of a dog (probably so as not to raise any eyebrows). Now that Moshe was dead, the substance, which had planned on lasting for many more years of Moshe, was left uselessly out there somewhere, and had been summoned by the call of Grandpa Yosef. It had not found peace in the past, in the place where we had said goodbye to Brandy. All it needed was the moderate rocking which Grandpa Yosef gave time, to extract it from its unsuitable surroundings and fling it into our present-day, where it could re-embody Brandy. The new Brandy was only a drop of time splashed in our way, dismantled and multiplied into a host of dogs. And yet—it was Brandy.

We made do with Brandy in her reincarnated form, mystical and implausible, so long as she eased Grandpa Yosef's loneliness. From our point of view, all was clear. But explanations kept following us, waiting for us to adopt them despite their dwarfish appearance and unfounded claims. In their unfortunate ownerless state, the explanations united into a theory that charged our thoughts with wild speculations: the dramatic loss of Brandy during Moshe's *shiva* had been interpreted as death, but we had been mistaken. Brandy had disbanded into separate states. Her disappearance was not the result of death, but an act from the political sphere. Everything that had been held together, despite a genetic aversion, in order to serve the superpower that was Moshe, had been completely dismantled, eradicated, lost. The silent sitting at Moshe's feet turned out to have been quite the opposite of restful. Rather, it had been a concerted and desperate effort to keep herself united against internal factionalism, against the divisions made greater by micro-politicians. (Only after her death did we comprehend the concept of being *at Moshe's feet* to its full, cruel extent, a bound state of being, so difficult, so impossible.)

Brandy's dismantled existence, which surrounded the house with a cloud of damp tongues, wagging tails and loud barks, made it easier for Grandpa Yosef to accept the total failure of his plan to reverse time. Grandpa Lolek went back home, the grandiose attempt was concluded, without Feiga and without Moshe. But Grandpa Yosef began to come to terms with his new life—the desert in which only Brandy accompanied him, there to protect strips of existence from the past. Trickles of hidden possibilities nourished Grandpa Yosef's vacant hours and settled in as reality, as a restrained rendition of Feiga and Moshe. This was the garden in which Grandpa Yosef agreed to live.

There was no more tragedy.

*

From a speech given by Himmler, the Reichsführer, in October of 1943, to a group of senior officers:

"Most of you here know what it means when a hundred corpses lie next to each other, when five-hundred lie there or when a thousand are lined up. To have endured this and at the same time to have remained a decent person—with exceptions due to human weaknesses—has made us tough."

I wrote down Himmler's words on a white sheet of paper. I looked at them. The words were nothing new—I had copied them from one of Attorney Perl's little index cards, and they have been recorded in books. But I wanted to write them down. To write them myself. As I read the words, they approached one by one like customers going up to a counter with tense and hesitant steps, each preparing to present itself.

"Yes," said Attorney Perl, "the Nazi ideal was to create a human being who does his job without moral defects, without cruelty or harassment of his victims. In terms of the ideal, people like Kurt Franz, 'Doll,' or Amon Goeth, were utter failures, examples of the weakness of human beings engaged in an endeavor that is beyond their strength."

Himmler's speech continues:

"We have taken away the riches that they had…we have taken nothing from them for ourselves. A few, who have offended against this, will be judged in accordance with an order that I gave at the beginning: He who takes even one mark of this is a dead man...we have the moral right, we had the duty to our people to do it, to kill this people who wanted to kill us. But we do not have the right to enrich ourselves with even one fur, with one mark, with one cigarette, with one watch, with anything. That we do not have. Because at the end of this, we don't want, because we exterminated the bacillus, to become sick and die from the same bacillus."

Yes, Heinrich Himmler belonged to the genus of SS officers who fell in love with the persona of the clean, superior, moral man. His fellow senior leaders, particularly Goering, did not hesitate to plunder whatever property they could get their hands on. They did not care for Himmler's theories. But countless SS officers viewed his ideas as a gold standard.

Attorney Perl's cards contained quotes, speeches, orders, decisions made by the Nazi party. I dedicated a white sheet of paper to each sentence that caught my eye.

From an order issued by Generalfeldmarschall Erich von Manstein, dated November 20, 1941:

"Jewry constitutes the middleman between the enemy in the rear and the remainder of the Red Army Forces which is still fighting, and the Red leadership.... The Jewish-Bolshevik system must be exterminated once and for all.... The soldier must appreciate the necessity for the harsh punishment of Jewry." Von Manstein oversaw the operations of the Einsatzgruppe D task force, commanded by Otto Ohlendorf. After the war, he claimed to have had no knowledge of the exterminations.

In his speech at the Wannsee Conference, Reinhard Heydrich stated that "the evacuation of the Jews to the east has now emerged, after the appropriate prior approval of the Führer, as a further possible solution." The Jews would be utilized for labor in the east, Heydrich explained, and continued: "...a large part will doubtless fall away through natural diminution. The remnant that finally survives all this, because here it is undoubtedly a question of the part with the greatest resistance, will have to be treated accordingly, because this remnant, representing a natural selection, can be regarded as the germ cell of a new Jewish reconstruction if released."

"It was only thanks to the awareness of the personal responsibility of each one of the officers and the men that it was possible to get this plague under control in the shortest possible time," read the concluding remarks of the "Katzmann Report," authored by SS Gruppenführer Fritz Katzmann, a unit commander in the Galicia region. The report concerned the extermination of half a million Galician Jews. After the war, Katzmann lived under an assumed name. Only in 1960, three years after his death, was his true identity revealed.

At the bottom of the card devoted to Fritz Katzmann, Attorney Perl had noted, "Died in great agony from stomach cancer."

On the other side of the wall, in the front of the store, he calls out from the top of the ladder, "I've only got three-quarter inch nails with the plastic head, is that okay?"

An incredible man. Ninety-two years old in ninety-two. Ninety-three years old in ninety-three. An easily calculable miracle. He'll be ninety-four in ninety-four. Ninety-five in ninety-five. As his life progresses, another man also grows old: Edmund Veesenmeyer, born in 1904. Attorney Perl writes on his index cards every year:

"1981. Still alive."

"1982. Still alive."

"1983. Still alive."

He sounds almost apologetic when he tells me, "He's still alive, but I'm sick of checking, tired of the disappointment. I've checked every year since 1951. Here, it's all written down, his family and everything. Instead of shrinking, it's growing. What can you do? It's a shame."

The miracle of Attorney Perl's continuing life contends with the unending life of Edmund Veesenmeyer, a diplomat, Adolf Eichmann's partner in the implementation of the Final Solution in Hungary. In 1949 he was sentenced to twenty years in prison, but he was pardoned and released two years later. After that, he led a small, good life. Family, work.

On his little index cards, Attorney Perl tracks the war criminals. "My debtors," he calls them. He keeps track of what happens instead of hangings. Their punishments—the big ones, the little ones. The pardons. The commutations. The appeals, the retrials. The waiting.

The years that pass without any notes on the cards. Waiting, waiting. Sometimes the debtor moves to a different city, buys an apartment, starts up a business. And there are families, little European families that emerge as if from mazes, sending out offshoots that get further and further away from the center. The debtor integrates into society, gets appointed to positions where his talents are appreciated.

Siegfried Ruff, a superior of Dr. Rascher, who conducted gruesome medical experiments. Acquitted. Appointed head of the Institute for Aeronautical Medicine at the German Air Navigational Experiment Center, and later a professor at the University of Bonn.

Hermann Schmitz, senior member of I.G. Farben, the manufacturer of Zyklon B gas. Sentenced to four years, appointed honorary chairman of Rhein steel plants.

Friedrich Jaehne, senior member of I.G. Farben, manufacturer of Zyklon B gas. Sentenced to eighteen months detention. Awarded the Distinguished Service Cross of the Federal Republic of Germany.

Attorney Perl is not satisfied with general outlines. He carefully sketches the lack of revenge, assiduously noting every detail: First grandson; second marriage; promotion; date of death. Everything. He explains, "I thought, well, if I'm going to go mad, then I may as well do it like this, in this chair. Writing everything down." Then he goes back to the storefront to sell plaster and nails.

In the evening I go home. Anat is out, busy donating her time for the greater good. The neighbor from upstairs is watching Yariv. I think she just likes sleeping on our couch. Yariv comes out of his room and recites a well-rehearsed line: "Mom said there's rice in the pot and soup in the fridge." He stands watchfully opposite me and examines my face, wondering if he has conveyed the message successfully. It's important for him to do well.

I ask, "Have you eaten?"

"Yes."

"Where's Mom?"

"She went to help children who don't have a mommy and daddy."

Small, almost orphaned, he locates my wife in a place she will come home from late and tired. On the way to bed she'll pass by Yariv's room, the shower, the pots and pans, the things she needs to get ready for tomorrow, me. She'll look at the pages, at the memories I am acquiring. I show her the criminals, the families, the offspring carrying on their names. They love their grandpas. Nice children, well-bred. They support democracy, reject discrimination against foreigners. Sometimes they come to Israel and plant trees. They send postcards to Granddad and to Grandma Wilma, who waited five years for Granddad to get back from his missions in the East. She didn't give up on him, even though officers fell in love with her and offered her heaven and earth.

Anat goes to sleep, saying, "Yes, it's important, if you want to delve into it. But tomorrow don't forget to pick up Yariv from kindergarten early. He's not used to being the last one picked up. It makes him anxious."

We hardly see each other. She has her business, I have my index cards and the family testimonies. Yariv stands between us like a well to which we come at the end of the day.

From kindergarten I take him to Attorney Perl's. Instead of going home for lunch, we have "our" falafel. This makes Yariv happy; he thinks we're big-time criminals, although he is very worried about the pots of rice, *schnitzel* and fries that we're supposed to be heating up for lunch. He is buoyed by the thought of not having to eat the peas, but every so often, on the floor in the shop, among his soldier-screws, he is troubled by the uneaten rice. "What will we tell Mom?" he asks, his teeth glistening as he smiles. He knows we're committing a sin. Anat went to all that trouble to make us lunch, and besides, falafel-is-no-sort-of-food-for-a-growing-boy. Together, we come up with a solution—a different excuse each time, always successful. (In any case, I'm the one who spinelessly wolfs down two portions at home so Anat won't notice.)

He's already grown accustomed to Attorney Perl's store, and finds the front part more enchanting. He stands on a stool behind the counter like an extra salesman, in between Yakov the assistant and Attorney Perl, and watches the commerce in action. At the back, I sit among the cards. Everything is scattered around me, unprocessed, infinite. From day to day I gain insight—how quickly they forgave. If they weren't hanged immediately, their sentences simply melted away. Even the ones sentenced to long prison terms for crimes against humanity were released sooner than petty larcenists. We have already agreed, Attorney Perl and I, that the Nazis and their aids were not punished enough. Our disagreement concerns the appropriate punishment, if it had been up to us.

Attorney Perl clings to his fifty-year-old idea. "We should have kept them all alive, but in prison. Should have heard them. Even Eichmann. Should have marched him every morning from Ramleh prison to Latrun outside Jerusalem. There, we should have heard his story. Given him some water, not much. And in the evening, but only if he got there on time, a little 'soup,' like the kind they gave us."

I say, "No, they should have executed them. At least all the ones who were in SS units, not just the commanders. They should have executed everyone who took part in operations by army units and police. The Jewish collaborators too. No mercy. And all the clerks, the diplomats, the mayors, the volunteers. Everyone who knew that genocide was occurring and took an active part, even a small one. If they had executed all of them, we wouldn't need to 'understand' now."

Attorney Perl objects and grows slightly angry. He eagerly outlines a plan that will never come to fruition, things he tried to explain at the end of the war to ambassadors into whose offices he was able to sneak, to consuls who listened as they looked fearfully at this ghost of a man orating before them. When he talks about his plan, the thundering, lucid voice of Attorney Perl from before the war reawakens, recalling the way he sounded in the courts of Lvov and in his city of Stanislaw. Some time before 1939 he was sent to Bochnia for work and was trapped there when the war broke out. He was sent with his wife to the ghetto, to our house at 7 Leonarda. In the third *Aktion* he was sent to Szebnie camp, then transferred to Dora-Mittelbau. Between the lines, his own story emerges too. Sometimes he just starts talking about himself unprompted, then changes the subject. He mentions "Dora-Mittelbau" or "trains" and sighs, swept up in his own story again. He deposits his words at stops along the route, leaving me a sliver here and a morsel there, and they multiply and meld, as if Attorney Perl is challenging me to put the pieces of his story together.

At home, later, I edit the family stories and attempt to assemble his tale too. But in the shop, the story is the criminals, their restored lives after the war, the false identities, the borrowed personas. The lives dispersed among refuge countries—Argentina, Chile, Brazil, Canada, Syria. The irony of the diasporic dispersion of those who tried to destroy the diasporic nation. Their own Diaspora in Mexico, South Africa, Spain, Portugal, Bolivia. *The germ cell of a new reconstruction.* In the jungles of Brazil and in fenced suburbs of Buenos Aires, in wealthy South African homes and quiet villages in the heart of Germany. They were not killed and they continue to exist. *The germ cell of a new reconstruction.* We could have given them the great poet Yehuda Halevi's poems of yearning, the lamentations, the nostalgic liturgies. They had sent themselves to the Second World War, after all, to achieve *Lebensraum*—living space—for the German people, and now there they were, scattered around the world, absorbed in faraway diasporas. Two thousand years from now the Germans will look proudly at their accomplishment—a small German community in every remote spot, conducting its German life, maintaining a little German culture in foreign surroundings, its children longing for the homeland from which their parents were exiled. How did they get there? Ah, such a wonderful story. And some day, one of the curious young people will set off on a journey to trace his roots, and will expose the amazing adventure that led his founding fathers to Brazil, to South Africa, to the remote regions of Australia.

Is that their punishment? Living under false identities in humid jungles and faraway villages—is that the punishment? No. Too many of them were not exiled and did not escape, but continued to live under their real names in Germany. Sometimes they were pestered by the courts, more often left alone. Sometimes they were imprisoned and then released, assimilating nicely into their reconstructed lives. The worst criminals, the architects of the extermination, were sometimes not even investigated—these were the smart ones, the farsighted ones, those whose fingerprints disappeared from all incriminating documents and deeds.

"Especially the legalists," Attorney Perl said.

The talks with Attorney Perl do not finish when I leave his shop. I recreate them with Effi, with Dad, with Anat. Sometimes I come up against opposing opinions, reservations. Waving my papers and reading out lines, I explain what the people did, what they said, what they declared. I contend that they only tried the ones they could prove had committed murder or torture, or had been guards. But what about the ones who drafted laws? Recruited for the SS? Directed movies propagandizing the extermination of handicapped people? Testified to a trace of Jewish origin in a neighbor's blood? They did not murder, torture, or lock anyone up in gas chambers, but without them? Who will judge the faceless masses, the ones who will never be convicted because between them and what they deserve there will always be the graceful giants of the law: "lack of evidence," "reasonable doubt," "lack of public interest."

"Not everyone who spoke against the Jews is a Nazi who should be hanged," Effi said.

"Don't forget, there were and still are good Germans," said Grandpa Yosef. And of course, the example soon follows. "Take Hans Oderman, for example."

Faced with the kindheartedness of the orphan researcher Hans Oderman, accusations must bow. We cannot embrace opinions that do not consider the existence of the good German. Yes, I know, Hans Oderman is coming to Israel. The good German is coming back to serve as an example. Grandpa Yosef has already phoned me twice. "Hans said he's coming!" And Effi called too, "Hans is coming!" I count the days until the volcanic eruption.

The existence of the Hans Odermans of the world seems to be attempting to erase the non-erasable—Attorney Perl's index cards, every single one of them, and the declaration of Obersturmführer Moeser, Dora-Mittelbau's commandant, while on trial for his acts: *With the same pleasure as you shoot deer, I shoot a human being.* Attorney Perl recalls, "There, in Dora-Mittelbau, in the tunnels, people dropped like flies. Bad food and beatings, and everything covered with dust and the smell of excrement. We weren't allowed to use water. We had to pee on our hands and rub our faces just to get the dust off. That was forbidden too, but we did it anyway. If I had stayed there any longer, I wouldn't have made it. No chance. Fortunately, I was moved. They took me to a camp not far from Dora-Mittelbau. There we dug pits, God knows why, and we sawed wood, maybe for heat.

"The commandant at that camp was Obersturmführer Sahl, but one day he was removed from the camp, literally taken away by the SS military police, and in front of us stood our Angel of Death, the new camp Commandant, Obersturmführer Jürgen Licht."

I ask, "Did he kill lots of prisoners, this Licht?"

Attorney Perl is taken aback. "Obersturmführer Jürgen Licht," he corrects me. Even from a distance of fifty years he stands on ceremony, noting the rank and name. But he replies, "Indeed he did. But he was always very quiet, as if the whole business of war had nothing to do with him. As if managing the camp was a necessary duty, beneath his true aspirations. He would shoot prisoners without losing his temper, and never gave punishments that took up time, like roll-calls in the snow all night. The Ukrainian and German staff members were afraid of him, but us prisoners…we trembled at the thought of him showing up. It would mean death. His eyes, oh the eyes! Quiet, almost bored. If you had been allowed to look into them, you would have seen grayness, but we couldn't look. The Angel of Death!"

Attorney Perl is animated, his voice changes as he talks about SS-Obersturmführer Jürgen Licht, who killed people with his pistols, of which he was extremely fond, without a second thought. But more than his pistols, he was enamored with puppet theater, and every time he was transferred to a new camp he would bring a little truck lined with shelves of marionettes. Puppet theaters were officially banned by the Nazi party, and Obersturmführer Licht never considered disobeying the law, but a lengthy correspondence with indifferent supervisors finally resulted in a personal authorization to engage in his beloved hobby, and so at every camp he set up a small but active puppet theater. He never took harsh measures upon arriving at a new camp before enquiring whether any of the prisoners might be of use. Carpenters, engravers, arts and craftsmen, tailors, painters, and perhaps even a rare gem—a puppet maker. Attorney Perl was none of these, which meant that by rights he should have

joined the grey herd destined to die, the herd at which Obersturmführer Licht shot on its way to work, often out of mere curiosity, to
see who would fall. Would it be the tall man he was aiming at, or the
yellowing one hunched next to him? Or someone else? Pistol bullets
were so unpredictable at times. Attorney Perl should have waited his
turn to be hanged from the gallows in the center of the camp; they
were painted red, and the rope that hung from them swayed constantly like a live snake. Or else he should have crouched down and
knelt on the muddy ground. Or perhaps he should have survived by
simply working day after day in the trenches, with a pick, without
dying, without making any noise, without meeting the fate of being
shot and having his body dumped into cold water. Except that during the first inspection, he lifted a trembling hand—a hand stronger
than he himself—and whispered right in Obersturmführer Licht's face
that yes, he too could be of use. Of use? Yes. He offered his singular
contribution, which was his voice. The clear, sometimes thunderous
tone that he had used to great advantage when representing his clients
in court. Even if in his private life his voice was soft, withdrawn, in
the courthouse he was taken over by some sort of spirit, a devil that
gave him tremendous oration skills. As his words were barely whispered to Obersturmführer Licht through the lips of a skeleton, in
fluent German, the devil grabbed hold of him and awoke his voice,
which grew clear and loud. He boldly proposed to be the voice of
the marionettes in the puppet theater.

From the front of the shop, Yariv's voice reaches me in a wail.
One of the customers was joking around and told Yariv he would buy
him along with his bag of nails. Yakov the assistant played along and
together they staged a complex negotiation. *How-much-for-the-sweet-
little-mama's-boy?* At first Yariv sat quietly, following the negotiations
in awe. But suddenly his sorrow broke through and he was washed
over with great self-pity. He cried, "Where's my daddy?" and shouted,
and the customer apologized, red-faced, looking left and right to enlist
other customers to attest to his innocence; he hadn't meant any harm.
There was no one on the right, and the two on the left nodded, trying to reassure Yariv, not knowing how difficult a task that would
be. I arrive on the scene to find my son standing frozen on a bench,

waiting for me helplessly. We have no choice but to leave the store. Off we go. Where to? Where do you want to go? To the lawn. We go to the big lawn at Memorial Park, with the white pillars. Yariv finds a line of ants and kneels down, enchanted. With a little twig he tries to pose dilemmas to the ants. I sit facing the sea. The bay of Haifa is spread out before us. I think about the beach, where *they* never go. Just over half a mile as the crow flies and yet never, never do they take their cheery flip-flops and varicose-veined legs onto the sandy shores. Only Grandpa Yosef, thanks to his righteousness and with the help of his bicycle (especially since returning from the Caribbean), dares to go that far. Later, he comes home from an idle hour at the beach with shells in his pockets.

One ant climbs onto Yariv's twig. He shakes it, but the ant clings. Yariv lets go in a fright. He comes over to me, ready to go home. Already? Yes. Don't you want to sit a little longer? No. We leave. People pass us by. They are happy here. The park assuages troubles, slows down the pace of life. People can come from downtown, from doing errands at City Hall across the way, from the army induction center, from the courthouse. Such a Haifa park, close to errands and shopping. You can walk around without feeling as if you're wasting time, opposite Haifa's round bay. You can sit on the benches, looking at the dirty pool and the swings that someone insists on constantly re-painting to make them look nice. (There's always a patch of wet paint or a glossy new layer, and people know to check carefully before they put a kid down). Dad used to bring us here on Saturday afternoons in our good shoes, in the sixties. Thirty years apparently had to go by for me to notice the park's name, "Memorial Park." A strange name. I never paid attention to it before. We used to come here without thinking about names, to play and walk around. Once a year the park justified its name when the official memorial services were held here. First for Holocaust Remembrance Day, then for the IDF soldiers on Memorial Day. Then there would be fireworks set off for Independence Day. I remember people dancing in circles, and lots of people coming up to Dad, excited, shaking his hand as if they had won the Nobel prize together.

On Attorney Perl's little cards there is mention of the *Aktion* in the small town of Koretz, on the holiday of Shavuot. When the *Aktion* was over, the Gestapo officer addressed the Jews whose family members had just been sent away in transports, saying, "The *Aktion* is over. Tomorrow morning all remaining Jews must arrive at their workplaces." I think about the unbelievable passivity. To be a human being whose family has been sent to extermination and to be asked to show up to work on time the next day. Here, in Memorial Park, I think about the *Aktion* in Koretz and realize what it was that Dad was celebrating with us. The fireworks, the dances, the Nobel winners. The Independence Day I take Yariv to is not the Independence Day I went to with Dad. With us there is happiness, and wheeling and dealing among the various stalls—Yariv is only allowed to pick two things. But with Dad we would walk among the Nobel winners, everyone strolling happily, and a wild cry of joy—I-N-D-E-P-E-N-D-E-N-C-E—rose up from peoples' bones to the stars, just like the fireworks. Green, red and yellow trails bursting like little thoughts that run out on their way down, making way for a new idea that erupts and is soon forgotten. Six million prosecutors in our Memorial Park, and young people dancing in circles, and Dad watching with us, buying falafel and little flags, and a Bedouin man from the Negev selling rides on his camel, and eating pita with spicy humus. I-N-D-E-P-E-N-D-E-N-C-E, I-N-D-E-P-E-N-D-E-N-C-E. Nobel prizes bursting through the holes in flimsy pitas, pickles dying like heroes, pale-pale green, I take them out and very quietly drop them to the ground. Food is Not Thrown Out.

Even in Grandpa Yosef's neighborhood they celebrated Independence Day. It was quiet, with only the state flags sneaking out of the windows. But Grandpa Yosef assured us, "Oh, believe me, it's very joyous here." To prove that something exciting was hiding beneath the surface, on the morning of Independence Day he would walk to synagogue and pray loudly for Israel. He would come back from prayers sparkling and festive, and tell us how he had gone to see the celebrations in the center of Kiryat Haim the night before. He had watched the fireworks that were set off from where we live, from Memorial Park.

*

I finish writing, editing and typing the testimonies. I send each member of the family their testimony so they can make comments and corrections.

Uncle Lunkish phones. "Will you be sending me what you wrote about me too?"

"But you didn't really say much…"

"But what I did say, will you send it?" And on second thought he adds, "Could you perhaps come again? I think I can talk now." He voice grows stronger. "What's the worst that could happen?"

The next day, with Yariv, we sit in his little home. Uncle Lunkish talks. First the childhood, the village, the square. Then the war. The hardships, the ghetto, the concentration camp. And finally, Hermann Dunevitz.

"That was the worst. He made me his helper, that bastard. He forced me. I had to write down on lists the people he named. He was Jewish, but he did not have the heart of a Jew. The Nazis liked him, and as soon as he got to the camp they made him half-prisoner half-officer. They didn't give him a uniform but they let him walk around the camp wherever he wanted and be their detective. He wrote down punishments, gave out punishments himself, and issued all sorts of orders. I wore glasses before the war, but he took them away from me and I couldn't see a thing. Everything I did with him afterwards, I didn't see. I could still write. He made sure of that before he took them. He showed me a pile of glasses and laughed, and explained where the glasses came from, and then he threw mine onto the pile and said it was a great privilege for me that my glasses were on that pile but I was still standing. From that day on I was his assistant. He got me off work duty, and that's why I'm still alive today, because my strength had already run out and I knew I would not make it through the next *Selektion*, that they would send me where they had sent the people with the glasses. I don't know why he needed me. Maybe because they wouldn't let him be a real officer with rank, because he was Jewish, so he wanted to at least have an assistant. I would walk around with him, seeing everything blurred, and when he stopped in front of someone to decide whether or not to punish them, I had to write down his decision. People would stand across from me, I could barely see them, and they would tell me their number and block number and the name of their block leader, who was the only one who had a name. I would hold the notebook up to my eyes and write everything down, afraid he would kill me if I made a mistake or changed their punishments, because for him, killing was nothing. I may have written down people I knew, who I used to know before they took my glasses. Once someone whispered to me, 'Naftali, it's me, Gotleib, get him to let me off.' I wasn't entirely sure who Gotleib was, as if for a brief moment the glasses of my memory had also been removed. I wrote down his number and the other stuff, and I wrote down thirty lashings, and in the evening he must have got them.

"That was how it went, from the moment he made up his mind to make me his assistant. I ate well and rested and didn't see a thing. He used to hold roll-calls too, after the regular roll-calls were over and people were about ready to die of exhaustion. But the Germans allowed him to have them, and I remember, before he took me as his assistant, I would also stand in the cold without food, tired. Now his roll-calls were after the regular ones, and people used to collapse. I would stand opposite the group without seeing anything, and he would walk among them and tell me what to write. He was always looking for Jews from his hometown, to write them down for deportations or kill them himself. During work, if he caught a Jew who wasn't working properly and discovered he was from his town, he would beat him to death just like that, right in front of me. I couldn't see anything, but if they were from his town, that was the end. It was as if he had decided to be like the Nazis, but instead of going after all the Jews, he wanted only the Jews from his town. I don't know why he wanted revenge, it was his obsession. And anytime he issued a punishment for some Jew, he would offer him the option of turning in Jews from his town, if he knew any, and then the punishment would be eased. People snitched on each other, and Dunevitz would interrogate them and get the truth out.

"Finally, the camps came to an end, and the Germans took out everyone who was left and sent them on the Death March. Hermann Dunevitz was convinced he would be allowed to go with the Germans, but they laughed and whipped him, and threw him out to walk with all the other prisoners. I walked too, and I was glad that the nightmare of being with Dunevitz and his notebook was finally over. We walked for a few days, and anyone who no longer had the strength to walk was shot immediately. We didn't get any food or drink. The Nazis took turns riding a wagon, they ate and drank, and they wouldn't let us stop walking. I still had some flesh left on my bones, so I had more energy, but even I almost collapsed. You cannot believe what torture it is to keep walking without any rest, for no reason, just so we would die. We were saved by the airplanes that bombed us. From the sky they thought we were soldiers, and they shot at us. All the Germans ran away, it was a day or two before the war was over. Dunevitz also ran, because he knew the Jews would kill him even if it was the last thing they did. I stayed with the Jews and at first they didn't touch me. People simply lay down on the ground with no strength left. There were some who died that way, and others who started walking and looking for food in the wagon the Germans left. After two days some soldiers found us and took us to a camp, where they took care of us. And it was there that people started harassing me, saying, 'That's the partner of Dunevitz, the animal.' They wanted to kill me. I wouldn't have resisted, I no longer had the strength to live, even though I couldn't see anything. But one guy said, 'Leave him alone,' and they did. They didn't have the strength in them either. After a few days I got hold of a pair of glasses, and I met a friend from my hometown who had heard stories about me, but he believed me when I told him I hadn't been able to see, and together we made our way back to our town. That's it. I didn't hear anything more about Dunevitz. Some said he was killed, some said he escaped to America, but I don't know, goddamn him. Because of him, people have been saying I did bad things my whole life. But I couldn't see anything."

Dunevitz. Hermann Dunevitz. Something in the name rings a bell in my memory, trying to come through. Hermann Dunevitz. I ask Attorney Perl.

"Dunevitz? No, I don't know him. But there were quite a few of those characters; the war gave them an opportunity. You can read in my cards about Yakov Honigman, the kapo from the Gräditz and Faulbruck camps. I also have Hanoch Bayski, who was a Jewish policeman. When the Nazis hanged a Jew he would run after them to report if the hanged man was not dead and should be hanged again. And there was Moshe Puczich from the Ostrowiec ghetto, who was charged with many acts of cruelty, including burying a Jew alive, but he was acquitted in an Israeli court. He probably did the things attributed to him, but the testimonies got complicated because of unreliable witnesses. People testified against him, and it turned out that after the war they had sent him friendly letters, asking him to help them buy a pair of shoes. You see, not all the victims stopped being victims when the war was over. That complicated the testimonies. There were other issues too. People informed on each other because of petty grievances. They took advantage of the circumstances to get back at each other over little quarrels, even conflicts from before the war. But there were some whom they didn't need to do much investigating to convict. Yehezkel Ingster was also a kapo at Gräditz and Faulbruck, the only person in Israel ever sentenced to death at the time he was tried. A Jew, and he was sentenced to death, even before Eichmann. They didn't implement the sentence because at the time of the trial he was already very ill, a broken man. They incarcerated him for a short while and he died later."

"And Dunevitz? Don't you have anything on Dunevitz?" I can't get rid of the impression, a plea served up from the depths, something in me knows the name—Hermann Dunevitz.

"No, I told you I don't. But we had one in our camp too. Oh, if I could get my hands on him...but in our camp we were mainly afraid of Obersturmführer Jürgen Licht himself. He was our Angel of Death. I had to be close to him most of the time because I was the voice of the puppet theater. Every evening we put on a show for him. He built himself the theater on a little hill overlooking the *Appellplatz*, and the entire hill was covered with lovely rugs like a Persian palace; he put an armchair in the middle of all the rugs. We put on classical plays, adapted to fit the times, and plays that a German political prisoner wrote for Licht on topics he commissioned. I remember we put on a dramatization of *Wenn ich der Kaiser Wär*—If I Were the Emperor—which I knew from before the war. We did other plays too, it doesn't matter now. It was all for Obersturmführer Licht. Sometimes he would invent a protagonist and we had to make the puppet and give it a part in the play. It didn't matter, because he was the only spectator anyway, and if he was happy the evening finished without trouble. He especially liked a knight character he had invented, called Zibrus the Knight. We had to build ugly puppets with defects, in our own images, so that Zibrus the Knight could heroically save young German girls from us.

"One evening there was a disaster. Obersturmführer Licht invited the regional commander, Sturmbanführer Hes, to the play. Hes did not like puppet theater, and all throughout the play I could see him glaring at the carpeted ground. At the end of the play he politely refused to accept the Zibrus puppet and gave Obersturmführer Licht an odd look. I was at the front and I saw everything. I knew there would be trouble, I just didn't know what kind. The next day all the puppets were ordered burned, the stage too, and the wooden frame; everything. All the theater workers were called for roll-call, and Obersturmführer Licht walked among us. I was first in line, and he walked past without looking at me, and for a moment we thought nothing would happen. But the man next to me was a puppet maker and he shot a bullet into his head without even hesitating. Then he kept walking and stood by different people. Sometimes he lingered, standing pensively. When he finally made up his mind he either shot the man or kept going. And it went on that way. He shot the expendable ones. That was it. In the morning, the kapos came and took all the remaining theater workers to regular jobs with the rest of the prisoners, and for almost a week we didn't hear from Obersturmführer Licht. There were no plays and we didn't see him. The hunger came back, the beatings, the desperation, and once again I thought I would not survive. Every evening we would go back to the camp and see his empty armchair up on the hill. We hoped something would happen, that the theater would be revived. After all, there must have been a reason why he had left some of us alive—we had a use.

"Day after day went by and not much hope was left. But late one night after a week, the head of my hut told me to go to Obersturmführer Licht's office. My heart sensed disaster. He had already summoned someone to his office once, a typist, and had dictated an entire letter to him and then shot him in the head. What did Obersturmführer Licht want of me? They took me into his room. It was warm in there. A nice fire was burning, and there were dogs lying on a rug. My body was stiff as a rock. In front of the desk where Obersturmführer Licht sat was an empty chair. Was I supposed to sit down? Greet him? Salute? His adjutant handed me some papers. Obersturmführer Licht had written a play about his childhood, and my job was to read the pages out loud for him.

"His play was called *Verbrecher*—Criminals—and it recounted the story of an affair from his school days—some incident where he was assigned the duty of carrying the flag on a holiday parade, but something happened and the teacher let another boy carry it. Obersturmführer Licht gave precise instructions for making the puppet that would represent the teacher. It had to have small, Communist, Jewish eyes. He spent half a page on how to make the puppet of the other boy. And the kids who laughed at little Obersturmführer Licht. And the Jewish headmaster. And the priest. All of them. Lots of instructions in German. How the puppet makers managed to finally build the marionettes the way he instructed, God only knows. Perhaps they were helped by the fear of death. After the teacher and the headmaster and the priest, on a fresh new page, there were instructions on how to portray his beloved mother's voice; there was to be no puppet representing her body. Then there was Zibrus the Knight, who in Obersturmführer Licht's play had to appear and put a stop to the parade, take the flag away from the other boy and give it to Obersturmführer Licht.

"Obersturmführer Licht had poured many words onto paper, and I was required to read the lines aloud, to pleasure his ears with his own composition. I did the best I could, acting the parts out as I read. I cackled evilly when the teacher—who was a traitor, a Jew and a Communist—tripped up Obersturmführer Licht in class. I was emotional when the flag was given to the other child. And then Obersturmführer Licht the boy got up from his seat in class to make a speech. That was how it went in the play. He had written himself a long speech and as I tried to deliver it expertly, Obersturmführer Licht the commandant sat at his desk and, with his eyes shut and his hands beneath his chin holding a little pencil like a baton, instructed me to repeat my lines, make corrections, slow down the pace."

"How did you understand what he wanted?"

"I understood. Believe me, I understood. I was so scared, I almost went in my pants. I followed the pencil beneath his chin and understood everything Obersturmführer Licht wanted."

"And what happened in the end?"

"I got to the point where the voice of little Obersturmführer Licht's mother was supposed to come from behind a screen. She was to try and persuade the Jewish headmaster to reverse his terrible decision. I recited her noble pleas, some of which he had found, I believe, in party propaganda, and some of which were the sorts of things mothers really would say. The headmaster refused to listen to the mother's reasoning because little Obersturmführer Licht had a mark for misbehavior on the class roll, because he had thrown a spitball. I remember the headmaster's response to her: 'In our regime, as it is designed at present, in the year 1922, I am the one who decides which pupil shall march with the flag in the parade, and I am the one who decides that your son is not worthy of this great honor because he threw a spitball!'"

Attorney Perl does not need to recite the play for me. The tearful voice of a wronged child comes through amply in the space of the room: "But it was Heinrich who threw the spitball!" The mother's response is also superfluous. It is obvious that the headmaster, for whose puppet the prisoners will have to find a thick log of wood, will throw her out of his office. Obersturmführer Licht's lines need not continue either.

"He held up his hand: 'Stop!' and the play recitation ceased. The dogs perked up their ears and looked at me. The adjutant gave a brisk order and two guards came to take me away and deliver me back to the head of the hut. From the next day onwards, the whole camp was busy setting up the new theater and producing Obersturmführer Licht's play, *Verbrecher*."

Attorney Perl gets up to make us some more tea. With his

back turned to me he looks small and hunched. His feet still give him the strength to work. His hands tremble slightly, but he carries the tea confidently, cautiously, without spilling a drop. He sits down opposite me with a lucid mind—mercilessly lucid. I thank him, and from some troubled region of my memory I insist on murmuring, "I would still like to find out about Hermann Dunevitz."

Attorney Perl sighs. "You know, I think that maybe, somehow, with all my cards, you've gotten yourself headed in a bad direction. For every *dreck* like that Hermann Dunevitz or Yehezkel Ingster, there was a wonderful man who did more than you could imagine. Think about Mordecai Anielewicz, the leader of the Warsaw ghetto uprising—what a leader this country could have had if only he hadn't stayed in a bunker with the last of the insurgents. And think about Adam Czerniaków, head of the Warsaw Judenrat. Read about him. Such a wonderful man. And Robert Stricker, who could have used his connections to stay out of Auschwitz, but he insisted on going with his congregation precisely because 'that was where he was needed.' You have surely heard of Janusz Korczak. And just think of all the people whose names we don't even know but who gave morsels of bread to people who had no strength to get to the food because they were pushed away by the strong ones. Think of all the rabbis who did not flee but went with their people to death. Some of them carried Torah books in their hands, to give people courage in the train cars. And the people who sung *Hatikvah*, the national anthem, on the way to the crematoria. So many were killed in this Shoah—if only I had the courage and the strength to behave as they did. What happened there, in the Shoah, is more complex than what you can derive from my cards. All the educated people who committed acts of betrayal, and the simple Polish peasants who saved lives and were sometimes killed with their whole families because they hid a Jewish child. All the monks who were exterminated because they were caught hiding Jewish children. The people who informed on Jews, the people, even within the SS, who turned a blind eye and gave a prisoner one more chance to live. I told you, there were SS camp commandants who did their jobs without hating Jews. It didn't stop them from carrying out all their orders, and they killed prisoners to maintain discipline, but they tried to provide the Jews with the calorie quota dictated by their regulations, even during shortages. Then there were the Hanoch Bayskis, the Jews who hurried after hangmen to let them know a victim needed to be hanged again. Complicated, very complicated. Think of the Polish monk, Maximilian Kolbe, who volunteered at Auschwitz to go to his death in place of another prisoner. He knew his punishment would be death by starvation in a locked cellar beneath Cell Block 10, the hut of death. He knew he would lie in a dark hut until he died, but still he volunteered. It turns out that he was an anti-Semite and had published articles against Jews before the war. So what was he, this man? And what do we understand?"

We drink our tea.

But on the way home, Hermann Dunevitz floats to the surface like a strange dream trying to get out. Black markers are scattered through Memorial park. The kaleidoscope of memories is overturned, trying to record something. Upside down, it cannot find rest. On the pillow at night, troubled sleep, the kaleidoscope tries to emit a voice. There is something down there. Something down there.

The next day I ask Grandpa Yosef if he happens to know a Hermann Dunevitz. Grandpa Yosef struggles. His memory digs deep and enquires. Nothing. "Hermann Dunevitz, who is that?" He takes me into his house, although I have only come to pick up Grandpa Lolek's Vauxhall. It's Friday, Shabbat is almost here, and everyone has lots to get done. Grandpa Yosef pleads, "Come in, eat something, help me out. My pots and pans are bursting with food already. I don't know how it happened, the whole house is full of food." He takes my hand; the Vauxhall can wait, as well as my other errands. He sits me down in the kitchen and serves me plates of food. He chops, slices and waits for my reaction. Last night he insisted the Vauxhall had to go back to Grandpa Lolek's so it wouldn't be in the way here in his parking lot. Now the urgency is drowned out in steaming soup on the stovetop, in hot fritters he serves with grated fresh horseradish and ginger on top. "Taste these please." From the window I can see the edge of the parking lot. How is the Vauxhall in anyone's way? (Perhaps he wishes to erase all traces of the former tenant before he can host Hans Oderman wholeheartedly.)

Grandpa Yosef rushes off to his pots and in the window between the bushes, crazy Hirsch pops up. Motionless, he watches, looking straight at me. The man from the Lodz ghetto, the beadle of the Admor of Tipow, still dwelling on his question, "Only saints were gassed?" Perhaps he will come right up to the windowsill and scream his impenetrable question, shattering the days of my childhood. Yet the question is becoming clearer and clearer to me—I even have an answer. If he comes up to the window I will simply reply: Regular people were gassed. Righteous and evil people too, but mainly regular people, just like the ones who walk past me on the streets. If they were tossed into a reality of concentration camps, they would quickly settle into their roles—the attempts, the failures, the loss of sanity, the revelation of greatness. Hirsch knew this all along, and he questioned it. Ever since he began to ask in the Lodz ghetto, "Why, why the annihilation?" and to reply, "Because of the diminishment of life," all the way through the day he began asking his new question in the neighborhood, many thoughts must have passed through his mind, a theological debate beneath a cloak of filth and madness. Perhaps the debate continues still in secret, under cover of insanity. Perhaps he has found his role, to wander an entire lifetime on the path to one single conclusion—*the* conclusion, the essence of all contemplation.

I look at Hirsch in a new light. Perhaps he truly is the servant of a theological journey. But Hirsch simply disappears, going off to his daily routine in the bushes, and Grandpa Yosef comes back with a dish of sausage and cooked sauerkraut.

"Did you see Mr. Hirsch?" I ask.

Grandpa Yosef is daydreaming, not listening to my question, answering instead a question that was not asked at all. "Hans Oderman will stay with me, of course. He'll sit here and finish his research." He waits to see what I think about the dish. "Delicious, isn't it?"

Delicious.

"The Germans call it '*Bratwurst mit sauerkraut.*' Except of course, my sausage is kosher!"

I have trouble starting the Vauxhall. It would be better if Green the Mechanic took it to Grandpa Lolek's, but Grandpa Yosef called me last night urgently, as if the Vauxhall had to disappear at once.

"What's so urgent?" I angrily ask out loud. It's not as if Hans is arriving tomorrow. But the Vauxhall comes to Grandpa Yosef's assistance and wakes up. We can go, no answers needed.

On the way up to the Carmel neighborhood I pass by lights, intersections, a busy Friday coming to life. In the cars I see glum faces calculating lost time, trying to imagine a burst of salvation, a long wave of green lights rushing like a river all the way along their route. I have time. I only have to pick Yariv up from kindergarten at twelve. I need to talk to Grandpa Lolek and find out when he's planning to have the surgery—the tumor is still there and the doctors have urged him to get it treated.

"He's waiting for brain surgery to go on sale," Effi said.

She doesn't know why the name 'Hermann Dunevitz' sounds familiar to me either. I ask her when she comes over to talk with Anat. Anat is trying to recruit her to her army of volunteer women, to help them give out gift baskets to the poor on Purim. They sit talking in the kitchen, and before Effi leaves she comes by my desk.

"What's the deal with all the stuff you're documenting? Everyone's talking in the family. When will you show me?"

"Most of it's already finished, but not everything. There's so much material, you have no idea."

"Then show me what's ready, come on, the Shoah isn't a secret."

"You have no idea how much material there is." (My desperation grows right in front of her eyes.)

"Another reason why it's good the Shoah ended in '45. And oh yes, talking of Germans, I told you, didn't I? Hans Oderman is coming!"

"Yes, you told me already."

"Show me what you've finished."

She examines the pages, amazed at the length of the testimonies. She didn't know that Uncle Antek and Aunt Frieda and Aunt Zusa could remember so much, that there was so much unknown inside them.

"You know, I saw Hirsch today."

"So?"

"Hirsch…who we used to see around the neighborhood."

"Yeah, I know. So what happened?"

"Oh, nothing. But I was thinking about him. And you know, I dreamt about him a few days ago."

"About Hirsch? Nice choice."

"Well, never mind…"

She looks at me sitting among the pages, the drafts, the index cards. "You're going a little crazy," she opines.

"A little," I agree.

"It's only out of politeness that I still love you."

"Thanks."

"I really love you."

"Thanks again."

She leaves.

I really did have a dream about Hirsch, and my encounter with him has summoned up a fragmented memory of the extremely vivid dream. Hirsch was sitting in his hut in the woods. I came to him to ask for something. Something I'd been wanting for a long time, that everyone used to want, and now only the two of us had, except I didn't know where mine was. Hirsch's hut was surrounded by stray dogs, limping, exhausted. Tortured dogs with runny eyes, bald dogs. Old dogs thrown out of moving cars, resting with broken legs among bowls of bread and meat. Hirsch came out to me in his incarnation as the upright beadle of the Admor of Tipow, and said, "This is my penance. To right in dogs what I could not right in humans."

Crazy or not, that's what I dreamed. Crazy or not, I continue to document. It must be documented, the criminals and the victims. I must try and understand what is understandable. Crazy Hirsch struggles in his own way, Attorney Perl in his, and I in mine. Effi doesn't understand that something greater than the individual stories is emerging. Out of the chaos, a logic is transpiring. Everything can finally be combined, the framework comprehended. We can understand the clear process of the Nazi plan. Combine my father's story, random from his point of view, with the despotic framework of the plan around him, the simple cold calculation that declared *Aktionen* on certain dates in Bochnia, declared Bochnia "clean of Jews" on

October 1, 1943, performed a liquidation *Selektion* in Plaszow camp towards the middle of May, 1944, and sent his mother—Dad was saved—to a transport where no *Selektion* was held at all; they went straight from the train cars to the ovens, because in the organized formal procedure, the massive shipments from Hungary were supposed to have arrived at Auschwitz, according to the destruction plan drafted by Adolf Eichmann and Franz Novak. Orders, reports and commands were issued, postal trains passed by trains transporting Jews, Dad included, and documents containing action plans, dates, quotas—all of these together could explain each day in Dad's Shoah. They could also explain the transfer of Grandpa Yosef from one camp to the next and clarify why Attorney Perl was transferred to Dora-Mittelbau and why he was transferred again. Everything was in the documents, even answers to questions the family members asked themselves, sometimes out loud, sometimes silently, over and over and over again.

"I escaped in the middle of the Death March from Stutthof. Where did they end up taking the ones who didn't escape? How far did they get?" (Mrs. Kopel.)

"Why didn't they make allowances for our work permits in the Vilna ghetto? Why did they take my family away even though they had permits?" (Uncle Antek.)

"What was the end of SS Landau, Goddamn him, who was with us in Drohobicz?" (Aunt Frieda.)

"Perhaps you know what happened to the Greenspans from Koretz? Adella, Adella Greenspan, she was a friend of mine." (Aunt Zusa.)

And Dad, always practical. "Why did they want to send us to be gassed anyway?"

I should have shown Effi the Nazis' words too, the speeches, the declarations. So she would read and understand, so she would know that we mustn't stop thinking about the people who didn't hate Jews. The people who were just doing their jobs. The ones who did not derive pleasure from torture, from murder. The camp commandants who tried to give Jews the regulated calorie quotas even during shortages. The commandants who punished officers who cheated and withheld

the prisoners' codified rights. The original SS people who enlisted in
the purest of armies and swore not to lie or cheat or drink or curse.
The people who saw themselves as exemplary human beings, whose
enlistment in the SS was supposed to personify the oath they had taken
towards all that was noble in the human soul. Even when they ruled
over the lives of thousands and tens of thousands of people willing to
do anything for a chance to live, they did not harm a single prisoner
unless it was required for proper order in the camp. Pedantically and
gravely, they continued to do their jobs. Effective, fair, non-murderous
murderers. In the heart of a world gone mad they were not tempted
to sin by enjoying the suffering of others. They squeezed, yes, they
squeezed the gold out of Jews, out of their vessels, their teeth, out of
what they tried to hide in their bodies. But for themselves they took
not a crumb of loot. They produced raw materials—hair, teeth—for
a Germany at war. They managed the annihilation efficiently. They
shot anyone who hindered the process—the elderly, children—without
enjoyment, without evil. Non-murderous murderers. Around them
raged sadists, some in SS uniforms, uncurbed plunderers of property,
rapists, demented minds, psychopaths—the war gave them a boundless cushion for their actions. Around them raged SS people who, at
the beginning, did not demonstrate sadism or greed, but who slowly
discovered in the camps a simple, supreme fact—that everything was
allowed. The righteous purity of these paragons was vanquished by the
intoxicating feeling that everything was allowed. Torture and murder
and beatings and pranks—everything was allowed. Rape and plunder-
ing and a good laugh or two—everything was allowed. Simple souls
who gradually comprehended that there was no one to punish them,
no one to reprimand them. Sadism opened up like a fan and the
temptation drew them on—how much further could they go? Without
balance, without boundaries, these simple souls were dragged along
in amazement—they still hadn't reached the limit, everything was
still allowed. We-are-doing-the-unthinkable-and-still-it-is-allowed.
We-are-doing-everything-we-want-to-and-no-one-is-punishing-
us. Allowed! Like creatures erupting into a vacuum with nothing to
hold them back and prevent them from bursting forth, out came the
unstoppable urges. Everything was allowed, everything allowed. After

the war it would all go back inside neat boxes. Twenty years later, judges and prosecutors would ask in astonishment—is this the man accused of the charges?

Those sadists, I understand. It is not them that I fear. People like them are hiding everywhere around me today. I can guess who they will be and where they will come from if-what-happened-there-happens-here-too. What frightens me is the ones who maintained their integrity. The-people-who-did-not-hate-Jews. The-people-who-were-only-doing-their-job. Those people, I cannot understand, and I have no idea where they will come from.

I pick Yariv up from kindergarten and we walk through his world together. No one will be shot here. Pregnant women need not worry—no one will stab them in the stomach. Women pushing strollers can keep peeking at their babies to make sure they're not too warm, not too cold. No one will throw a baby in the air, wish the first shot had hit it in flight, and try again. But I know. The monsters are here. The only thing missing is the circumstances, and when the circumstances arise it will all happen here, and it will be directed against me because I will not collaborate. They will emerge, all of them, even the people-who-did-not-hate—although where they will come from I do not know—and the camp-commandants-who-tried-to-supply-the-regulated-calorie-quotas-even-during-shortages. In the midst of it all, like a sailboat stuck in the mud of Lake Tiberias, waiting for the tide to go out, waiting for a drought to spread its smooth mantle, Hermann Dunevitz's name rises up, more than half of him now exposed. I must remember.

In the evening, Grandpa Yosef calls to report cheerfully, "I kept thinking about Hermann Dunevitz all day, and I remembered. Anat's mother's maiden name was Dunevitz. Maybe that's why the name stuck in your mind?"

Anat is making our dinner, Yariv is already asleep in bed. (Anat thinks he's getting an ear infection again.) I go up and ask her.

"Yes, before she was married my mother's name was Dunevitz. Why?"

My memory already knows, but still it questions—perhaps it is wrong, perhaps the certainty is a mistake.

"What was your grandfather's name?"

"My grandfather? Hermann. What are all these questions for?"

Hermann Dunevitz.

First there is a trickle of blood, not a rushing feeling. At first it goes, "So what? So what if it's her grandfather?" But the "so what" loses out, trampled, and newly disorganized thoughts take its place. She says, "My grandfather? Hermann." And this is Anat, and I gave him a great-grandson, and it is with me, and what am I going to do? I gave him a great-grandson who is sleeping now and he might have an ear infection and I'm married to his granddaughter. His granddaughter. Who is his granddaughter? Why, it's Anat! It's Anat and it's Yariv, and what difference does it make?

But like a necessary torture, it does make a difference, and I am a breathless, silent volcano. I wait silently for the next emotion, the next thought, an uncontrollable internal torrent. In the accompanying transparent light everything comes out, bursts through from within fantastical treasure boxes and locked dowry chests. Gustav Richter, one of Eichmann's senior aids, a primary implementer of deportation plans and the organizer of a failed attempt to transfer Rumanian Jewry to the concentration camps, was tried only in 1981 and sentenced to four years. Franz Novak, Eichmann's assistant, particularly active in the deportation of Hungary's Jews, hid after the war under an assumed name. In 1957 he began using his real name again, but was not tried. He continued to live his life. Only in 1961, after his name came up repeatedly during the Eichmann trial, was he incarcerated and tried; he was sentenced to eight years. He was retried after an appeal and released in 1966. Anton Streitwieser, commandant of Melk camp, was captured at the end of the war but escaped and lived under an assumed identity. He was caught in 1956. He was free until his trial, which began only in 1967. He was given a life sentence and died in prison in 1972. Alfred Nossig, a Jewish collaborator in the Warsaw ghetto, was assassinated by ZOB, the Jewish Fighting Organization (*Zydowska Organizacja Bojowa*). Herta Bothe, a female camp guard at Bergen-Belsen, was sentenced for her acts in the camp to ten years in prison in 1945, but released in 1951. George Eliot said, "Cruelty, like every other vice, requires no motive outside of itself; it only requires opportunity." On one of the transports to Sobibor, some clown decided to spill chlorine into the moving train cars. The chlorine coated the people in the trains. By the time it arrived at Sobibor, the car was filled with pale green bodies whose skin peeled away when touched. Anat calls me for dinner. How can I eat dinner when Gottlieb Muzikant, SS-Sanitätsdienstgrad at the hospital in Melk camp, admitted at his trial, held only in 1960, that he had killed over ninety prisoners by injecting phenol into their hearts and had strangled at least one hundred patients to death? He was sentenced to life in prison, not death. Anat asks where I am and my thoughts need to stop, they must stop, they do stop. I can exist for now in the form of a breathing volcano. I can get up, eat dinner, keep going through the dark memory. I'll sit next to her, we'll eat, we'll think. "So what? So what? So what? Why did I even get mixed up in all this?"

Dinner. The volcano breathes heavily, absorbing little relief from the air, the omelet, the salad.

"Is everything all right?" Anat asks. She wants to talk. It's Purim soon and she'll be busy preparing the gift baskets.

The volcano asks, "What do you know about your grandfather, Hermann Dunevitz?"

"Grandpa Hermann?"

"Yes."

"Not much. He died in Canada, a long time ago. My mother was five."

"He came from the Lvov region, didn't he?"

"Maybe, yes, one of those towns. I don't know. Why? What have you found out?"

"What have I found out? I'll tell you what I've found out. Your grandfather was a murderer. He murdered Jews in the camps."

Her expression turns grave. "Really?"

I look at her face. Where will this go?

Anat wonders, "But he was Jewish, wasn't he?"

I tell her almost gleefully, "Yes, but he was a sadist, he was crazy. He hung around the camps and murdered Jews like the worst of the Nazis."

Silence. She spreads margarine on a slice of bread. The knife moves over the bread. Salt. Pepper. That's how she eats. "All right, well what do you want now?"

"Nothing."

I'm not accusing her, it's not her fault, is it? There's nothing to accuse her of. And if what came of Hermann Dunevitz is Anat, then everything must be all right, and the theories don't hold up. Except that now we have to forgive them too, the grandchildren of Nazis, who come here to plant forests.

Anat won't let it go. "It doesn't seem like nothing by the look on your face. Come on, tell me, what do you want?"

"Nothing, really nothing. It's not your fault."

We eat in silence. Pass the salt. I spread margarine on a slice of bread. I add salt, pepper. The flammable air above us—will it ignite or not?

"Just don't say anything to my mother! Even if it's true!"

"Okay."

We sit quietly. Drink coffee. Read the paper. We hear a noise and sigh. It's just Yariv stirring in his bed. We toss and turn on our bed until morning comes. Hermann Dunevitz is Anat's grandfather.

Grandpa Lolek's surgery became an urgent matter, something to busy ourselves with, because Grandpa Lolek was beginning to behave oddly. Whether it was old age or the tumor was unclear, but it became apparent that he had to have the surgery, and soon. Little defects flowed through his memory and thoughts. He announced that he was leaving the lands in Gedera to me—me and Joyce the dancer, jointly, as long as we didn't fight. He asked us all to give her the news when she arrived for her usual evening visit, and hoped she wouldn't be late this time. He was clearly going senile.

We gathered around him with suggestions and data. We took him to the doctor, and together consulted and recommended having the surgery here in Israel, at Hadassah Hospital—the best department. Grandpa Lolek looked frightened as he sat on his chair trying to understand our franticness and the urgent need to undergo surgery. He closed his light blue eyes for a moment, weighing the important decision. Then he opened them and said, "All right. You can have operation." And so we had to explain everything again, reintroduce the doctor, the room, the Sick Fund, and that the surgery was for *his* head, not anyone else's, and that it would be cheap and successful. The doctor would explain everything, here he was. Anat was among us, urging Grandpa Lolek, reassuring him, introducing him to the doctor. We all encouraged him and the doctor encouraged us, saying we should leave Grandpa Lolek in the room with him and let him explain. And Anat was among us, and we were living a quiet married life, kind to each other (shoving reasons to fight into the abyss). The panic over Grandpa Lolek's confusion was good for us, it softened our dormant troubles. Besides, I had convinced myself that everything was fine. At first I was angry, unable to tolerate the thought that she was the granddaughter of Hermann Dunevitz. But it all passed and I managed to say, "So what?" and to really feel, "So what?" So what if she's his granddaughter? We've been married for six years and I know everything about her, her love, her capacity to truly love people, to help them. She has a love of humankind. ("She has an ego that lives on the back porch," Effi said). I said, "So what?" and I felt, "So what?" I had simply been alarmed for a moment by the sound of shattering glass. I wasn't prepared for it. But nothing was broken, nothing had shattered.

Life got back on track. Documenting, talking with Attorney Perl, reading his books. Everything attested to routine. Grandpa Lolek broke an appliance and asked that my friend "who fixes things cheap" repair it. Effi found a new boyfriend. Anat said she'd be busy on Purim. Grandpa Yosef asked if I could bring back the Vauxhall, which Grandpa Lolek couldn't use anyway, because Hans might want to use it (for some time, his entire life had been dedicated to paving roads for Hans). I told him I had finished documenting most of the family stories, everything was ready, and he asked me to come over. He served me a dish of okra and banana. (Did I think Hans would like these sorts of exotic flavors?) I put down a neatly bound copy of everything I had documented. My documentary, on Grandpa Yosef's brown wooden table.

Grandpa Yosef left the bound pages where they were and did not even reach out a curious hand. He talked about how things were going in the neighborhood. Everything was the same as usual. Gershon Klima had decided he needed a rest and had found himself a suitable place near Tel Aviv. They were thinking of renting out his house here, but weren't sure they'd be able to. Not long ago, the Meretz party had rented the late Orgenstern's house and set up a local branch, but they had to leave after visiting dignitaries were bitten by dogs on two separate occasions, for no apparent reason. (Grandpa Yosef and I knew it was Brandy, who had become an extreme right-winger after her death.) Mr. Pepperman had stopped getting his mail, which alarmed him. They had to have a search. At the post office they said everything was in order. In the end they found all his mail lying in a puddle and no one knew who had done it. There was also a strange affair with the poet, Asher Schwimmer. He no longer lived with his brother; the brother had passed away. They took him to a place near Nazareth, a quiet place, so he'd be happy. But he suddenly started slapping people for no reason—the staff, the doctors, the caregivers. He yelled and made accusations and hit. Here in the neighborhood, Uncle Antek was losing his hearing, he couldn't hear at all in his right ear. The doctors were looking into it, and so was Effi. In the meantime she suggested he turn up the volume on his radio. Uncle Mendel was also losing his hearing, but he never listened to anyone anyway so it didn't matter.

"And how's Mr. Levertov?"

Mr. Levertov was absolutely fine. Ever since Effi had become his primary physician, he'd been truly exceptional. Like a young boy. People were envious; they wanted Effi to be their doctor too. Even Mrs. Tsanz. (And we both knew, because Effi had told us confidentially, that she was probably going to leave the clinic soon. A position had opened up for her at Hadassah Hospital in Jerusalem.)

The conversation naturally shifted to Grandpa Lolek. We agreed that he had to have the surgery—what was he waiting for? Grandpa Yosef asked about Yariv and how Anat was. We didn't talk about Hermann Dunevitz. As long as we didn't talk and didn't ask, everything would be fine. If-we-shut-our-eyes-the-monster-would-leave. Everything was fine. Simply fine. And really, I thought, it's no fault of hers. Everything is fine, I thought. Simply fine.

But at nights, our glaciers floated on as we slept.

Around the time Grandpa Lolek decided to leave me the lands in Gedera, I started feeling that I couldn't, I just couldn't. Not because of Anat, but because of Hermann Dunevitz. He had cunningly found a way to live on through me. To give himself a great-grandson, an eighth of himself, through me. Not only Hermann Dunevitz, but all the traitors, the murderers, the sadists. The people who made Hirsch wander the streets and gave Rachela Kempler that *look*. And Gershon Klima and Mr. Pepperman and Itcha Dinitz and Mr. Bergman and Linow Community and everyone.

In Effi's kangaroo court, I declared, "It won't leave me alone. You see, he's her grandfather, and Yariv is one eighth of him. One eighth. His blood is living on through her, through Yariv, through everyone who will come in the future. Precisely what shouldn't happen. Do you see?"

Effi bristled. "Are you listening to yourself? That's exactly what the Nazis said. They also looked for people with one eighth Jewish blood in them. They also said it coursed through one's blood and could not be helped. You've really lost your mind."

Attorney Perl said, "You have a wife, you mustn't do anything. Give it time. Trust me, don't do anything." He caressed the cover of a book, *The Protocols of the Nazi Trials, Volume IV*, printed in 1950. These were the protocols that should have explained, should have told us what the grandfathers did in Germany. They all kept telling me, "So what?" They told me to forget. But something stronger than "so what" had to come, it had to. I would give anything to be told how to go on, what to do. They told me, "So what?" and "Forget it," as if they were selling shiny objects to savages. As if I were incapable of understanding on my own that Anat was not to blame and neither were the German grandchildren who come here every summer to plant forests. Every summer, so I heard, they came to plant trees. Where were all these forests? Maybe you couldn't see them from the roads, but after a few more years of apologies, their trees would suddenly shoot up over the bald, white shoulders of the highways, and the roads would have to be paved through wooded fields. It wasn't her fault. I wished it was, so I could grasp at something. There wasn't even the edge of a thread, nothing to point to, to imagine, to locate the pain, to know what to heal. There was nothing to do, no way to go on. Still they disembarked on my island to sell me shiny objects. (My suffering could not be traded for simple glass beads.)

"You have a major problem," Effi said. "Everywhere you go, you take your hatred with you, like a dung beetle rolling a ball along. You need to stop. Get it in your head that there isn't as much black and white in the world as we would like. Just stop it."

"I don't want to stop it."

"I understand why it's bothering you, but enough, stop it. You're a grown man, you need to resolve this."

"How?"

"Well, think of a bridge, for example."

"A bridge?"

"Yes. When there's a river you can't cross, you build a bridge over it. It doesn't mean the river is gone, it just means now you can cross it. See?"

"Yes." I get the analogy. I get what she means. But Effi is enthusiastic about the idea and wants to keep explaining it. So what if I get it.

"That's what people do. They need bridges. See, no one is telling you to stop feeling what you're feeling. Just build a bridge. So you can cross over. You can even stand on the bridge and look down at the river, just without being inside it. Do you know how many bridges I've built?"

A bridge. I'm already taking measurements for the first supports, and Effi says, "Or maybe you could punish her."

"Punish?"

"Punish Anat, you know, maybe that's what you need."

"What do you mean, punish?"

"It has to be something you choose. Like you do with kids."

Punish Anat. Why should I punish Anat?

Effi comes to life. "For instance, another woman. Yes, something like that, so it won't be easy. Another woman, at least once, yes." (She is falling in love with the idea. She talks quickly, thinking, another woman, that's what will help.)

"What are you talking about?"

"Then think of something else."

"But why would I be with another woman?"

She gets annoyed. "Okay, you find something then. You're the child. Figure out what will make you feel that it's over and done with."

Another woman? Where did she get that peculiar idea? Anat is the only one, I'm not attracted to other women. Why would I be with another woman?

(There is one, oddly. We met not long ago at Yariv's kindergarten. I went to pick him up and it started raining. We stood beneath a small cornice that leaked; we were the last people in the kindergarten except for one of the teaching assistants, who jingled a large bunch of keys, put it in her bag, and stood next to us. She asked if I was Yariv's dad. I said, no, I was the infamous child-kidnapper, Heinrik Chapinski. She laughed and said, "Why didn't you say so? We give top honors to child-kidnappers around here!" I looked at her and wondered when kindergarten assistants got so pretty. Mine, Chana, was a half-mad dwarf who only liked quiet children, but she didn't like me even though I was quiet. I plucked up the courage to ask if she really was the teaching assistant. She laughed again and said actually she wasn't the assistant, she was also a child-kidnapper. In fact, Yariv was in her sights too because he was the cutest kid, but I, Heinrik Chapinski, had got to him first. I was surprised at how she had picked up the name and repeated it correctly. She didn't even know that Heinrik Chapinski was tried after the war for the sadistic extermination of Jews in the Bochnia ghetto. She smiled and said that if we were both child-kidnappers then we should get together some time to discuss professional hazards. I told her I was married. Happily, I stressed. I pointed to Yariv: "That's the result." She looked hurt and said she hadn't meant anything, she was just being nice. I wanted to say something friendly, to take it back, but Yariv started crying and tugged my hand. He wailed as only he knows how, without sentences, only words, leaving me responsible for the syntax. Half the words he was saying were "Itzik." Itzik was a daunting entity in Yariv's world, a kid who hit other kids and lorded over the sandbox and told all the other kids what to do. A kapo. Ever since that day, every time I come to pick Yariv up, I'm the embarrassed one. She seems quite cheerful. ("Hello, Heinrik!" She smiles prettily.)

Nothing will happen. There is love between Anat and me, six years of ever-growing love. I have no friends. Only Anat. I can't understand how other people keep up with their friends from the army. Effi is family. There are no other friends. Why would I punish her?

Just before Purim I come home to find Anat sitting with gift baskets for the poor scattered all over the living room. She conducts her campaigns from our little headquarters, all the rooms filled with cardboard boxes, items and notes. Everything has to fit in the packages and be sent off. Not everything is straightforward. There are different types of recipients, three sizes of boxes (the size of the package corresponds to the extent of the recipient's misfortune). She sits exhausted among the items. Yariv sits with her, curled up, obedient. He is as big as one of the packages. He doesn't try to reach into the gifts and sabotage them. A well bred and polite child.

I stand in the doorway and say, "Over there, just so you don't get mixed up, is our son. Should I mark him for you?"

She laughs, exhausted.

(Deep inside us our married life continues. Caution and apology and fragile affection. "Forget it" and "So what?" and "Go on.")

She smiles at me so that I will smile back at her. (How angry I was when she bought a German washing machine. For months I lay in wait, hoping for it to break, hoping for one non-German instant to penetrate the mechanism, the wrong kind of soap to tear up its innards—even if it meant our clothes would be ruined. I was angry at the machine, not at Anat, and I waited for a short, a blockage, knitwear washed too hot, even an electrical fire right here in my home. But that died down too, and the machine kept working quietly, became something that simply washed our clothes.) I have to smile, this needs to be over, this thing between us that slowly slinks and does not rest. Someone has to bridge the banks and I am the only one who can, I am the one who has to stop thinking it's important. But I was the one who saw Eva Lanczer on the lawn outside 12 Katznelson, and I saw Mr. Pepperman coming to Grandpa Yosef with his old bills to make sure his name was listed only to make sure he paid his bills. And I remember Finkelstein's gold, Finkelstein who knew everything back in 1939 and whose letter is still hidden in Grandpa Lolek's basement. I am the one who asks, why did Asher Schwimmer start slapping people? What did they do to him *there*, that made him forget all his Hebrew? Attorney Perl tries to calm me, to cancel out the affair, saying, "You have a good wife." Yet at the same time he stokes the engine with hot coals, saying, "Here, read this."

Orders issued by Reichsführer Heinrich Himmler concerning retaliation for the murder of six SS officers by Partisans near Kiev:

"I order that in the district of Kiev, ten thousand Jews shall die without regard to sex and age, for each of the six officers. Even a babe in the cradle must be trampled down like a poisonous toad.... We are living in an iron age, and there is no escape from using an iron broom."

Karl Jäger, commanding officer of Einsatzkommando 3, from a report summarizing his activities in Lithuania, dated December 1, 1941:

"I can confirm today that Einsatzkommando 3 has achieved the goal of solving the Jewish problem in Lithuania. There are no more Jews in Lithuania, apart from working Jews and their families.... I am of the opinion that the male working Jews should be sterilized immediately to prevent reproduction. Should any Jewess nevertheless become pregnant, she is to be liquidated."

I take the Karl Jäger index cards out of the drawers. What was his fate? The cards say nothing.

"Don't worry about him. I don't know how I could have forgotten to put it on the cards. After the war he hid, posing as a farmer. He was only exposed in 1959 and he committed suicide before his trial."

Don't worry about him. But there are others, and they cover the earth like weeds.

*

We finally took Grandpa Lolek to Hadassah Hospital. They promised he would only remain for a short while after the surgery, and then he could go home and be watched by Effi. The Lion of Life recited the terms to us and reminded me about the broken blender—what about my friend who fixed things for cheap? His blue eyes hinted at how lovely it would be if the repaired blender was waiting for him when he got back from his dangerous surgery.

Dangerous?

No.

They explained that the location of the tumor made Grandpa Lolek's surgery a fairly easy case. Very easy. They had to operate so there wouldn't be any more unpleasant surprises. Still, during evening phone calls, little drops of concern were voiced, fears for his well-being. We spoke our fears out loud so our hearts could make it through them. Here and there an explicit question was posed: Was there a chance he wouldn't make it?

Effi did not allow anyone to go too far. "Don't worry, he won't die. Before he goes under, we'll tell him the price of gravestones has gone up, and that will be that. No danger."

She greeted us in a white coat when we got to Hadassah, not yet a staff member, and in any case brain surgery was not her field. But for Grandpa Lolek, Effi in a white cloak was a good sign, evidence that someone was looking out for him. He agreed to be hospitalized without protest, saving us several hours we had planned to waste on a sudden refusal in the parking lot. Grandpa Lolek dismissed us, asked Dad to stay, and agreed to send me back to Haifa. (Behind the glass window in the door, far away, he turned back to me and twirled his finger around fast, to remind me about the blender. I nodded.)

Two days later, with his head bandaged, everything was behind him. As promised, it had been very simple. Grandpa Lolek was convinced we had come to release him from the doctors, he was sick-of-doctors, there-is-life-outside, there-is-business-outside, and he believed we would devise an impressive rescue operation, a kidnapping, something that would conclude at his home with a cup of tea and news from the neighbor's radio. His question for me was, "What about the blender?" He had been anesthetized for brain surgery, knives had sliced open his skull, blood infusions had been pumped into his veins, a tumor that had been pressing on a primary blood vessel had been cut out of him, and yet when he awoke, his desire to fix the blender on the cheap was still intact, having survived the procedure like a tightrope walker who tiptoes from one end to the other without losing his balance.

I looked at him and knew he would never die. He was the strength, the power. He had never come down from the peaks of Monte Cassino, and so he had no need for memories. He was the tree of life, and not only did he have no memories, he also had no hatred. No ball of loathing to roll around, only a large world full of profits and cups of tea, cigarettes to be smoked, and debts to accumulate. From him, from him I should be learning. Not bridges and not punishments. All I needed to do was ask, how do you get rid of the thoughts?

I did not forget his wish, and the next morning I turned up at his apartment to pick up the blender. (I was also there to move the Vauxhall back to Grandpa Yosef's parking lot. Twice he had called. "Hans is coming. Where's the Vauxhall?") I opened the darkened house and instead of going to the kitchen, where the blender was, I walked into the living room. Just to sit for a while on the couch, above the rug that covered the opening to the cellar and the box of letters to Joyce the dancer, and the letter from Finkelstein who knew everything back in 1939. The house of wonders was at my disposal. I could have opened the cellar door and found, with adult eyes, what we had not found as children, when Grandpa Lolek had walked in with the Leica camera. But the magic of the cellar had been dampened. We had grown up. On the couch at Grandpa Lolek's I could only rest and think, Yariv is an eighth of *him*. Who knew how many eighths like Yariv were running around in some kindergarten? Those eighths also had parents who, like me, had sat through Holocaust Remembrance Day ceremonies at school and recited words from black placards, and had learned to understand that we were the victims and that was it. Easy. We were the victims. We were. And that was that. Now life. Once a year our hearts would be sad, once a year we would remember what happened, and we would never look around us and realize that everything existed now too, here too. They did not see Mr. Pepperman checking his bills, they did not see Rachela Kempler. Itcha Dinitz, between the blinds, in the dark, living there; they did not see him either. They say I should build bridges, forget. But before the bridge-erectors came the abyss-builders. I am not willing to forget the abyss-builders. On Holocaust Day everyone stands for a moment of silence when the siren goes off, and everyone feels moved, and they all raise their children and do not know, and are sure of themselves, and do not understand. 1939, every year anew. 1939, and they do not know.

I went to check the blender. The only thing wrong with it was that it was unplugged. The power chord was lying cunningly on the counter, disconnected from the socket. When I plugged it in the blender started whirring loudly, ready to blend and mix. I took it with me anyway, for some reason, and placed it on the back seat of the Vauxhall. (There was a reddish-brown stain on the upholstery, as if right there was where the battle of Monte Cassino had ended, when Grandpa Lolek had spun around and stabbed a German on the back seat with his bayonet).

At Grandpa Yosef's house I opened the door to find him wearing an apron, holding a steaming pie fresh from the oven.

"I brought the Vauxhall."

"*Nu*, welcome, welcome. Come in please." He put the pie down and wiped his hands on the apron. On the brown wooden table was my documentation, bound and neat. Grandpa Yosef hadn't touched it.

"Haven't you read what I wrote?" I ask. Eighty well-written pages.

Grandpa Yosef squirmed. "*Nu*, no time. I didn't get to it. Hans is coming tomorrow morning, and the house...no time...." He sliced a piece of pie and served it to me, then continued to cut more slices for an invisible guest.

"All right. When you have time, read it."

"*Nu*, taste it, taste it. I'm a little...I'll read it, I'll read it all. I just haven't had time." He wouldn't leave the pie alone. He sliced and sliced, sinking the knife into the dough, attacking it nervously. He got up and asked, "Would you like some sugar for the pie?" Without waiting for an answer, he reached out and leafed through the pages. Then suddenly he said, "*Nu*, documentation. Naked in the snow for ten hours, can you know what that is? Hunger like there was in Buchenwald, can you know what that is? No, no. You cannot know what that is…" He darted into the kitchen.

I cautiously tasted the pie, another of Grandpa Yosef's strange concoctions. The sparks of his soul. He came back with sugar and scattered some on my pie without asking. I tasted it—cardamom and sugar.

"So, how are things?" I asked.

"Good, good. Just that there's no time for anything. Hans is coming and look, look at the state of the house."

"The house looks fine."

"Effi volunteered to pick him up at the airport. It's a good thing it worked out for her, and she's coming from Jerusalem. You're busy, I know, with Grandpa Lolek's operation. You can't do it, *nu*. It's a good thing Effi volunteered."

("Wherever Hans Oderman is concerned, I'm the first to volunteer," Effi said.)

I looked at Grandpa Yosef. In a white undershirt, his shoulders looked soft. His tiredness suddenly seemed very pronounced. A whole life of charity, of nerve-wracking righteousness, and one visit from Hans Oderman of Germany, of all things, was wearing him out to the point of exhaustion. (I suddenly understood and was seized by panic: He was not like Grandpa Lolek; he would die one day. There was a day waiting for us, a funeral, rain, umbrellas, a rabbi praying.)

"Aren't you a little tired?"

"Tired? Gracious no. I enjoy the work."

"Isn't it difficult for you like this here? Alone?"

"Difficult? No, not difficult. I get along fine, thank God."

Something strange in our conversation. Like forcing a puzzle piece that doesn't fit. Something wrong, but you ignore it.

Grandpa Yosef went into the kitchen again and reemerged with his pride and joy, a cake that looked like a hat with a battered rim. He declared, "Finally the *lekach* cake came out right! All those years my Feiga tried to teach me the recipe, and finally..." He placed the cake on the table to slice it. His pride was real, glowing. (Success, after years of failure, and there was no one to give him a prize.)

We both sat and ate. Grandpa Yosef wandered through his desert of life without Feiga, without Moshe. I pushed along a ball of hatred and they asked me to build bridges. To forget, to forgive. Hans Oderman was arriving soon, the orphan researcher.

"*Nu*, how's the cake?"

"Delicious."

"When my Feiga was still alive, she always knew how long to mix the batter, when to take it out of the oven. She would always remind me. Without her, sometimes strange things come out of the oven."

"It's still a little hard for you without Feiga, isn't it?"

"Oh...*nu*. When my Feiga was still alive, there was always someone to talk with, someone I could discuss an interesting Gemara page I had read with, or things they were saying in the neighborhood. Now there's no one to talk to, and my thoughts roll around inside and keep going. *Nu*, not to worry."

"It will be all right. Time heals, they say."

Grandpa Yosef looked up. "Time heals?" His face relaxed for a moment, gathering up a thought like a river collecting rivulets. Suddenly he shouted, "Time heals?! I still haven't healed from the people I lost long ago, and time heals? A little hard without Feiga? How about it's still a little hard without my brothers and my mother and father, who went in Belzec, and I still can't accept that? Maybe that's still a little hard?" He carved thick, moist slices of cake that fell on their sides, one on top of the other, on the dish.

I looked at him quietly. I had never heard Grandpa Yosef shout before.

He hummed and huffed as if to still himself. He moved his head from side to side, trying to understand. "*Nu*, I.... Well. You know...."

"It's all right."

"I'm actually a little...after I told you everything...things haven't been sitting well inside. *Nu*, the memories...."

He went to the kitchen and dragged some pots around. Opened and closed the oven door. Did what he knew best, putting himself into order. He pulled something off a shelf. Opened the fridge. Closed it. Came back and apologized again. I did too.

"Anat said it wasn't good of me to remind people of what happened."

"*Nu*, well, Anat. She knows how to feel things. Is everything okay with you two? With the issue?"

A ball of hatred rolled along. The dung beetle lost its ball.

"Everything's fine," I said.

"Yes...."

"There's nothing to be done."

"*Nu*, everybody has problems."

We spoke quietly, breaking down the previous exchange into small words, letters, tiny signs that meant nothing. Grandpa Yosef tried to find something to do with his hands. He started slicing the cake again. "You know, I still have trouble with Rothschild too. Since we spoke, it's been harder. I can't get rid of the thought that he somehow stayed there, for evermore in Buchenwald. That's where my last memory of him is, and apart from what is in my memory, what other existence does Rothschild have? Sometimes I think, if only I could get him out of there and have one memory of life after Buchenwald. For example, Rothschild managing a store here on Herzl Street, doing business. But how? That's where he stayed." He paused for a thought. "And Mr. Hirsch walking around the neighborhood, that's not easy for me, it reminds me of things. But you accept it. You live your life. With all sorts of things, you live."

Grandpa Yosef, our sleigh-dog, still pulling the corpse wagons.

We ate the cake silently. Grandpa Yosef pulled the pie towards himself and cut a slice. He tasted it. "I might have put too much cardamom in this," he mumbled. "Maybe it doesn't need any cardamom at all." He fell silent.

(He cannot be helped. Grandpa Yosef pulls the corpse wagons. Everyone here in the neighborhood, that's what they do. Pull wagons. White figures looking for things at night, sitting like tubers in warm homes, saying, "How are things?" and answering, "Life goes on," like a frightened lie, like something that redeems. Grandpa Yosef at least has the strength to live. Most of the people here have never lived after the camps. Even though they were liberated and sent to Israel on boats and given houses to live in, nothing truly alive came out from behind those fences. A massive fraud. Eating and drinking and sleeping for fifty years, with remarriages and new children—all a fraud. All that survived are shells with memories. Empty shells listening to the radio, walking to the grocery store, going to visit relatives. Fifty years, and in Germany the war is long over. The guard soldiers and the train conductors and the propaganda clerks have already forgotten. The foremen, the gas manufacturers, and the transport supervisors have already forgotten. The engine operators and the experimenters and the order-givers have already forgotten. Those who were not hanged have already forgotten. Those who were not shot by avengers—forgotten. Only here, in the neighborhood, shells with memories.)

I cut myself another slice of cake. To cheer him up. A cake he made from Feiga's recipe. Where did Feiga have recipes from? From her home, most likely, there, in Bochnia. We eat cake made from a recipe from a world destroyed. Grandpa Yosef, lost in thought, digs his fork into the crumbs. We don't know what to talk about. We try. There is always a way.

"*Nu*, what's new in the neighborhood?"

Littman from the grocery store may be closing down. His son might take over, or he might sell it to someone else. Adella Greuner has started singing. She's really disturbing the neighbors. They went to talk to her, and she promised, but nothing. (We both remember her brother who came from America in a taxi to slap her and go back home). Gershon Klima's bombax has started creaking in the wind, the branches must be old. Someone said it should be chopped down, but they won't let that happen.

"And Asher Schwimmer?"

"Asher Schwimmer. I really should go see him one of these days, poor man. I heard he's still slapping people. They don't know what to do with him."

"And Gershon?"

"Klima is all right. He asks about you and Effi. He's at home for now. *Nu*, things move slowly with him."

Before we say goodbye, Grandpa Yosef presents me with a twin brother of the *lekach* cake and a pie wrapped in foil ("In this one, thank God, I forgot to put cardamom"). He offers some home-made jam ("a little sour, but it's energizing"). He is back to his old self, our Grandpa Yosef. What happened to him before must have just been nerves. The preparations for Hans Oderman's arrival are exhausting him, and we all have bad days. He sends regards to Anat. "You have a wonderful wife," he says as he walks me down Katznel-son. I mustn't forget that I have a wonderful wife. He stops when a bark comes from the direction of his house. "Well, I have to go back to put out food. I'm sorry."

Of everything that happened at Grandpa Yosef's, his yelling, and our conversation, and the documentation that didn't affect him, and the corpse wagons, I suddenly think of Asher Schwimmer. I have to go and see him. He is the final riddle, the place where the marvel might be hiding, a true splinter from the Big Bang. I must go to his new place near Nazareth and talk to him, no matter in which language, whatever enables us to talk, to find some gem of King Solomon's wis-dom that will bring us together. Why did he forget his Hebrew? Why did he start slapping people? Grandpa Yosef spoke of him with worry, but I know that the slaps are in fact a sign that something has awoken. A blossoming of sorts. For fifty years he was quiet, his Hebrew lost (*The Carmel peaks shall I ascend / in His forest shall I prophesize. / The rivers of Levy shall be mine / a nest for the crow and a bed for the brambles*), but now he is returning, his powers are being restored and he has the courage to accuse. Something inside him is sprouting those slaps like brave flowers in a desert. I must see Asher Schwimmer. Whatever he says, I will use—kindling for everything I need.

I run after Grandpa Yosef, shouting, "Grandpa Yosef! Grandpa Yosef!" I explain to him, almost begging, and yet also commanding: "I'm taking the Vauxhall, I'll bring it back in a few hours." I run with the cake, the pie and the jam. I put them on the back seat next to the blender (I almost forgot about it, almost left it as prey for Hans Oderman). Forget about bridges and punishments. I'm going to Asher

Schwimmer, a dung beetle rolling a ball of hatred, but I already know: everything's all right with Anat, and with Yariv. An eighth of him—so what? That, I can forget. But I cannot rest inside. I have to keep going, to understand. To read everything I can about the Nazi criminals, the ideas, the acts committed by people who realized that everything-was-allowed-everything-was-allowed-no-one-would-punish-them. I have time. On the inside, I have time. But I must go on. Get help from Attorney Perl and investigate until I reach all the dead-ends. That is the goal, to reach every dead-end, to stop and realize that from there onwards only people like Hirsch can continue. Attorney Perl and I will stop at the dead-ends, we have no half-century-long theological journey, we do not have the strength not to die, to walk around Katznelson ill and injured, to be Mr. Hirsch-Who-Yells.

I drive the grumbling Vauxhall, lagging behind passing cars. I feel out of place—not spectacular enough, not as wonderful as Grandpa Lolek. Like an unwanted guest at the wheel. The Vauxhall carries me on and I try to imagine how it looks. (When Grandpa Lolek drove the Vauxhall it was always enveloped in velvety clouds and rings of cigarette smoke. The Vauxhall was a stormy tropical island. Something you could see only in the *Tarbut* encyclopedia and in Grandpa Yosef's parking lot. When Grandpa Lolek drove the Vauxhall, cigarette butts rolled around on the floor, sometimes still lit, under the seats too, embers scheming with red eyes. Every time he took a sharp turn, sparks flew, a substitute for the bulbs of the turn signal lights which had burned out in 1976 and could not be repaired because Green the Mechanic could not figure out what the matter was with the electrical wires.) The Vauxhall greets me with a restrained grumble and drives on. I am a grayish figure, propelled towards the convalescence home.

It was afternoon when I arrived. A pleasant corridor of large windows stretched from the entryway to the wards, displaying lawns and shrubs on either side. A bright, clear, beautiful light shone in. You could see almost the entire valley, but it was doubtful that anyone here looked at it. I passed elderly people wearing morbid looking robes, strolling along to somewhere. Elderly people sat on armchairs. They looked at me.

I did not have to search for long. I saw him in the hallway, standing opposite a doctor. He was waving his hands and shouting something and a frail group of old people surrounded him, talking excitedly. Only when I got closer did I realize they were translating. Asher Schwimmer was making accusations in Polish, and they were doing their best to interpret into old-fashioned Hebrew while the doctor listened. The slap came, not hard, but the doctor did not lose his attentive look, as if both the translated words and the slap itself contained a hint. Asher Schwimmer turned around, walked feebly to a bench and sat down. A friend wearing a faded suit hurried to his side, supporting Asher Schwimmer and sitting down beside him. I went up to him, wondering if he would recognize me. I scanned him as he sat with his eyes closed.

"Oh, oh! He once had a head of hair! Wild hair!" said his friend, as if, having noticed my look, he had assumed I was not doing justice to Asher Schwimmer in my thoughts. He held out his hand. "Nice to meet you. Dov Ber."

"Nice to meet you, Mr. Ber. I'm Amir. How is Mr. Schwimmer?" I addressed Mr. Ber as if he were Asher Schwimmer's spokesman, a position that he clearly aspired to. He accepted my greeting for both of them, and his look seemed to indicate that he would, at the very first opportunity, convey my good wishes to Asher Schwimmer himself (and for a moment it seemed that the transmission of the greeting would be delayed due to the infinite distance of Asher Schwimmer, rather than his sealed, extinguished face here on the bench beside us). "Not many people come here. One could say we've been forgotten. And your honor is…?"

I told him about Grandpa Yosef, about the little poetry book in his library, Asher Schwimmer's poems from the days when he knew Hebrew. I also sent warm regards from Grandpa Yosef to Asher Schwimmer. Asher Schwimmer opened his eyes. "Hello, Mr. Schwimmer. I said that Yosef Ingberg sends his warm regards!"

Asher Schwimmer replied, "*Todah.*" Thank you. In Hebrew. In Hebrew! I must have looked astonished.

Mr. Ber beamed. "I'm teaching him Hebrew." Teaching him Hebrew! Asher Schwimmer closed his eyes again, but Mr. Ber would not let his prodigy disappear from our conversation. "Just like he taught me Hebrew! From him I learned! Everything!"

"Did you know him *there?*" I emphasized the last word and Mr. Ber nodded, confirming, but he did not understand what I meant. As far as he was concerned, *there* was Warsaw, before the war, where Asher Schwimmer had ruled the eager poetry circles, the lovers of the Hebrew language.

Mr. Ber called out, "He was born for great things! Tremendous! At nineteen, we all surrounded him! Worshipped him!" He pointed to Asher Schwimmer, whose eyes were shut tightly as if the memories that gripped him were too strong, as if the Hebrew he was learning was illuminating difficult things. Mr. Ber continued excitedly. "The Romantic style, that was his style. A Byronist! Roses! Pallor! Affairs of the heart! Then he began to take an interest in *Eretz Yisrael* and all his poetry became filled with carobs and sunshine! We loved the carobs and the sunshine too! He was not like us. We ran around trying to find someone who would agree to publish our verses. But him, they chased after him. And he? He only allowed the very best to publish him. If only you had been fortunate enough, such verses!"

"Yes, I know. My grandfather has a copy of his book at home."

Mr. Ber ignored me. "A Zionist, he became! A Zionist! I was a Zionist too, but to go to Palestine? Being a Zionist was talking! Arguing! Proving a point! Big meetings! Good for the soul! But Asher Schwimmer? He was really bitten! He decided to go to *Eretz Yisrael*, to Palestine. To see with his own eyes the Carmel, and Jerusalem. *Nu*, such a young man! And where did he end up? The war broke out, and who knows? Neither in Polish nor in Hebrew, about that matter, he will not talk. But they said he was in Gräditz. Suffering! That's what they said!"

(I pulled out the information easily. Gräditz. Yehezkel Ingster was there. The Jewish kapo who was tried in Israel and sentenced to death. Was it possible that Asher Schwimmer had lost his Hebrew in Gräditz? Did he know Yehezkel Ingster? Could I find out about Yehezkel Ingster from him? But no, I did not want to ask. I had to stop. Enough. Stop right now.)

But I asked Mr. Ber, "You weren't with him?"

"Me? No! No! In Israel too, I didn't see him for fifty years. Here, I found him. Right here, suddenly standing in front of me, Asher Schwimmer! Hebrew I teach him! And take care of him! I serve him gladly! If only you had seen him in Warsaw!"

Asher Schwimmer opened his eyes. I smiled at him.

(Leave. Leave now. There is nothing for me here. It doesn't matter if he slaps people. It doesn't matter what happened in Gräditz. Leave. The bridge is starting to crumble.)

I gently shook Asher Schwimmer's hand. "I'll come and visit again. Grandpa Yosef will come too."

"Pass the salt, please," said Asher Schwimmer, his mouth slowly plucking out the letters.

And his teacher, Mr. Ber, beamed. "See? He's learning! We'll bring back all the Hebrew! All the Hebrew!" He pats Asher Schwimmer's shoulder. "God willing, before we die we'll be reading new verses! Poems by Asher Schwimmer! Here! In Zion! Begone with your feeble poets—long live Asher Schwimmer! Rage on!" He grabbed my hand as it held Asher Schwimmer's. I gently disengaged my hand and turned to leave. As I said goodbye to them both, Mr. Ber helped Asher Schwimmer stand up. "We'll go and sit in the sun. He likes the sun very much!"

(*Roaming opposite your fields / fading / opposite the houses of wine and bread, from evil departing. / She alone yields crops—my soul implored / stalks of grain for her alone / Make golden my maternal sky—wheat of radiance*).

In the Vauxhall, the blender still sat on the back seat. I took it out and ran back. I found Mr. Ber and Asher Schwimmer on their way to the sun. "Here, a little gift. I almost forgot," I said, out of breath.

Mr. Ber was moved. "A blender! A food processor!" He grasped Grandpa Lolek's gift (I would have to come up with an excuse and buy something else for him), waving it at Asher Schwimmer. "A food processor! A food processor!"

We both waited silently to see if the drooping mouth would form the necessary words. But no. Mr. Ber covered for his silence, instantly trampling the failure with his words. "He's tired today. He's just tired!"

Asher Schwimmer stood up—perhaps about to slap me. But no. He ambled over to the shade, fleeing the sun, and Mr. Ber hurried after him to correct his error. I walked back to the Vauxhall. I had to tell Grandpa Yosef to visit.

When I got home, Anat said, "Yakov the assistant called. Attorney Perl passed away."

The next day they carried him on a black stretcher, wrapped in burial shrouds.

1900–1993.

They put his body down in front of us, beneath a sheet. As if this were the proper way to explain, to make us understand. I thought, with us, the ones we need don't die (like Brandy, like Linow Community, who some say has already died, it's just Sarkow Community who makes her keep walking to the grocery every day.) With us people last. But Attorney Perl died.

His body was covered with earth, and I realized that despite the gathered crowds, he was a solitary man. I never asked him about children. Why weren't there any? His life with Laura was not talked of much. Everything that, in his memory, had contained the beautiful days of their married life, shrunk in my memory to a wife led away to Belzec, living ever after in the house at 7 Leonarda Street. Now there was only me, and the remainder of her life would be shut up in train cars, on a slow voyage that would continue on with me. And children? Why weren't there any children? Hadn't he talked once about the eternity of procreation? He had glorified fertility. Like an elaborate agricultural plan in which he was not to participate, only to admire. Why didn't he have any children? I considered infertility, random happenstance, or perhaps a joint decision, or simply the fruits of bad luck. Reasons. Then I thought, And if he had had children? If they had grown up to be Dad's age during the Shoah, would they have survived? They would have been around ten in 1939, and would have fallen into the hands of Hermine Braunsteiner, "the Stomping Mare," or Kurt Franz, "Doll," or all the hands that had waited unknowingly from the moment the children of the thirties were conceived. Anat and I had Yariv. Eternity was ours. And Attorney Perl? His eternity was broken down on little index cards, and I could already envision them as crumbling shreds in a crate stored in a faraway basement. Seventy years on, someone nosy would find the swollen box and investigate the round handwriting. Hermine Braunsteiner, "the Stomping Mare," was charged with the sadistic murder of children and infants at Majdanek. She shot children at close range and whipped their eyes. She managed to immigrate to the United States, was exposed in the early seventies, extradited to Germany and sentenced to life imprisonment. Attorney Perl's eternity was assigned by topic, separated in drawers, hopeless. Why did he not have children?

Anat and I had already discussed having more children, and we probably would (the castles they convince us to build). I thought about the madness of procreation. The families who at the beginning of the century raised children who would become inmates of concentration camps. The families who raised children who would become SS officers. Pitted against one another. At the beginning of the century, on both sides, families feared for the fates of their loved ones on the front of the First World War. My family sent four sons to the war. Four sons who fought for Germany, shoulder to shoulder with people who would one day join the SS and participate in the extermination. Dad's father, Ze'ev, marched all the way to the Italian front. His brother, Dr. Anatol, served in a military hospital. Moshe Gutfreund, aged nineteen, was killed on the Carpathian front, and Leon Gutfreund was taken hostage by the Russians and came home after many years; in World War II he was taken to Belzec. Among those who guarded them, among the jailors, the commanders, the shooters, were the war veterans who-could-be-trusted, the people who didn't flinch at a few heaps of women and children.

When I documented *them*, I recalled, sometimes they looked at me as if to say, "We are documented. Now we are eternalized. And you? Your child, is that your eternity? We had children too, but it was not enough." I thought and thought. Behind the thoughts lurked a fear of sorts; it did not move, but it threatened to cave in, held together only by the thoughts.

The rabbi prayed. A lot of people came to Attorney Perl's

funeral. The many assistants he had employed over the years came, including predecessors of the predecessors. A trail of Yakovs scattered throughout the crowd, prominent in name, visible to strangers. The rabbi had apparently been expecting a quick funeral for a solitary man, and was surprised by the crowds. He prolonged and drew out and glorified the ceremony, trying to catch the relatives' eyes, surprised again, and somewhat vexed, when he invited an orphan to recite the *kaddish* and there was none. Nor was there a brother, or any relatives at all. He looked around sharply to show he wasn't joking around, and Grandpa Yosef came to his rescue. The outcome of their quiet convening was an appropriate *kaddish* prayer.

For a moment it seemed that a true lamentation erupted from the rabbi. The deceased man described in his notes as "a solitary man with no relatives," who had surprised him with a large, grieving crowd, wrung sorrow from his heart. Something stole into his prayers and nested in the routine words and took hold. His voice changed. He recited the letters of the deceased's name, adding a small prayer for each letter, and his anxiety was perceptible (he looked into my eyes—if there was no orphan, he would make do with me). At the end of the ceremony, the mourners filed past me is if I were a relative. They sweltered on the April asphalt (talking about Attorney Perl, about Bochnia, about the city of Stanislaw, about yesterday's news, about the new couch, which had cost a fortune, about a new immigrant technician who repairs televisions, good and cheap, about the uncomfortable shoes, they said it would take a week to wear them in but it's been two weeks and they still hurt). The rabbi shook my hand and bid me farewell. The Yakovs passed me by, their faces familiar. Memories, like a breeze, blew all the way to the deep days of the past. At the end of the row, like a uniter of them all, Yakov the current assistant came up to me. He said he would take care of "all the necessary payments," but he needed to talk to me about something. He asked me to come to the store. Then a figure appeared on the edge of the landscape like a ghostly apparition, six-foot-three-sapphire-blue-eyes-golden-locks. Effi and Hans Oderman had come straight from the airport to meet Grandpa Yosef. What could they do, who could plan on a funeral? Hans Oderman, the artiste of awkwardness, marched behind Effi, passing cautiously among the tombstones. He came up and shook my hand heartily. He pressed Dad's hand too, and Grandpa Yosef's, but our handshake was resonant—the other shakes could not push away a truly gloomy impression. Hans Oderman came back to me and shook my hand again, as if to close the circle of all his impressions of the moment. He stood tensely above the mounds of earth, looking down. The irony could not be ignored: Six-foot-three-sapphire-blue-eyes-golden-locks standing above the lonesome grave of Attorney Perl.

*

We came to the store, Anat and I. (She was the one who asked to come. We're building bridges.) Yakov the assistant welcomed us.

"Mr. Perl, of blessed memory, left the store to me and to Yakov Zimra, who used to work here, on condition that we help the people he always helped. He left a list. He asked that everything behind the wall be given to you. That means the kettle, the towel, the picture of his wife, of blessed memory, and everything in the drawers."

He listed all the things lacking from his inheritance with a cautious look of authority on his face, not yet knowing how far he would take it, what was permitted and what was not. He sized me up, somehow believing I had the power to revoke everything, his share too, and waited for me to say something.

"All right," I said.

I took Anat to the back room. The kettle. The cups. The photograph.

She opened a drawer and took out a little index card. She read it and took out another. "Why was this Hermann Michel called 'the Preacher of Sobibor'?"

"He was responsible for receiving the new transports of Jews. His job was to gather all the Jews as they stepped off the trains and give them a speech about the rosy future waiting for them in the East, and about the importance of work and all sorts of values. It reassured the Jews, and from the Germans' point of view it made the process more efficient. It was easier to lead them to the gas chambers.

Hermann Michel gave speeches to shipment after shipment, twenty minutes before they started shoving them into the gas chambers."

"It says here that he disappeared."

"Yes, they couldn't find him after the war, in the big land of the Germans."

She looked at some more cards, taking an interest.

"You know," I tell her, "they tried out different methods in Sobibor. They suspected the Jews were managing to code warnings into the letters they were forced to write just before being gassed. So in Sobibor they changed the system. When the Jews arrived, they were welcomed at the train platform with light refreshments, cigarettes, hot drinks. They apologized for the difficult transport conditions, explained that the state of war prevented them from using more humane means. They chatted with the Jews, took an interest in their problems and requests. Then they casually encouraged them to go and write postcards to their relatives, for free, before continuing their journey to the East. After the postcards were written, the extermination began."

Anat sighed. "There's no limit to what people can come up with."

"Yes, think of how they looked at the Jews while they wrote their postcards. How they waited for them to finish. Impatiently, but with a gracious expression. They knew they had to restrain themselves just a little longer, just another few moments."

I'm on fire now—she thinks she has an inkling of what the limit is. *There's no limit*, she says, still imagining she knows, more or less, what the limit in fact was.

"You asked about Hermann Michel from Sobibor. Well, I'll tell you about Sobibor. One day the gas chamber engines broke down in Majdanek. There were dying prisoners there, who were supposed to be gassed that day, but because of the break-down they couldn't do it. They found a solution. They transferred them on a special shipment to Sobibor. It was already getting dark when they arrived and the camp staff were resting in their rooms. So they just threw them in a heap in the rain and mud, and left them there until the next morning. You know, survivors of Sobibor testified about that night. They thought they'd seen everything in Sobibor. That's what they thought, but they were wrong. The dying people wailed and sobbed. They were skeletal, ill, without much life left in them, but the rain and cold brought even more suffering. At some point the SS people lost their patience. They went out to the dying people and whipped and whipped and whipped them, until the last whimper died down. Do you still think you have any idea what the limit is?"

"Okay, enough," Anat says.

But I persist, cruelly struggling on—I want her to understand the drawers. Bridges are built from two sides.

"You know, there were Jews who cleaned out the transport trains, to get rid of everything left by those who died or were dying on the way. They were also used to everything by that time. But one day they were forced to open the doors to some train cars and they found them full of greenish corpses. Piles of bodies whose skin peeled away as soon they touched it. Someone had poured chlorine into the cars while the train was in motion. Try to imagine now, the people who had chlorine poured on them, inside moving train cars..."

"Okay, stop, enough."

I have to go on, so she understands. (This is our lust for the abyss). So she realizes that she thinks she knows what went on in the concentration camps, but she doesn't. That only these drawers can bring the truth out. That only through these drawers will she know that Dr. Gohrbandt, in Dachau, investigated how inmates would behave when forced to stand naked for fourteen hours in sub-zero temperatures. She needs to know that because of their screams they could not continue the experiment in Dachau; it was too close to civilian residential areas. And she needs to know that inmates were infected with epidemics and pus was injected under their skin, to see how they would handle the infection. She needs to know that Dr. Mengele pierced the eyes out of little children and he was never caught. She needs to know.

I keep quiet and Anat shuts the drawers, looking pale. "What are you planning to do with all this?"

(Meaning, how far are you intending to go—where are you thinking of arriving?)

"I'm planning to leave it, to quit. I'll put it all in a sealed box in Grandpa Lolek's basement."

(Seventy years from now, someone nosy will find the bloated box and investigate the round handwriting. Hermine Braunsteiner, "the Stomping Mare" of Majdanek.)

She understands—I am quitting for her. Building a bridge. She hugs me.

"Okay…All right, well…" I say. Not only my words are mumbled, but my thoughts too. (We embrace, everything seemingly back to the elemental materials. We will have to refurnish our emotions. Refurnish what is now empty and hard. And the documentation? Should I betray it? Betray Attorney Perl? Should I really quit?)

Anat picks up the photograph of Laura Perl, who was killed in the gas chambers at Belzec, and whose husband taught himself what she had been through in her final moments, and was sad because she had always been so conscientious about cleanliness, even in the harsh ghetto conditions. From the day they took his wife from the house at 7 Leonarda Street, he had launched himself on a route of investigation, pierced a pinhole in the atmosphere and shot off into the distance to watch the ongoing world from high above.

Anat asks, "And the things Attorney Perl went through in the war, did you document them?"

No.

I didn't have time.

*

Obersturmführer Licht mobilized the whole camp to work on *Verbrecher*. But then what? I had no idea. But I had read so much, so many survivor testimonies, that from that endless mass I learned that in fact there were not that many stories, only a multitude of versions of one story, versions that duplicated themselves and were distinguishable only by minute details. I realized I could tell Anat the rest of the story without making too many mistakes. Only trivial details would differentiate what I told her from the truth. The main thing was not to say "Licht," but "Obersturmführer Licht." It could have been another part of the bridge, and the bridge itself was more important than the little details. I would tell her about Obersturmführer Jürgen Licht, about his deadly gray eyes and his love of guns and puppet theater. After all, here in the store I was taking revenge on her for Attorney Perl's death, and again—what fault was it of hers? Instead of taking revenge, better to tell her about Obersturmführer Licht's play, *Verbercher*, and convince her that a grown man had actually written these things. Explain to her how in the camp that was at his disposal, where everything was allowed, where nothing-can-stopus-when-we-want-something, a seed of insult planted in his childhood sprouted, and he used his prisoners to produce the play. Yes, that madness too was allowed in the world of the camps, something as innocent and colorful as a puppet theater, among guard towers and fences. Yes, a world in which they could say, "The *Aktion* is over, be at work on time tomorrow," was a world of fairytales, and from what Attorney Perl had started to tell me about the true existence of the puppet theater, anything could have happened.

In order to tell her, one would have to imagine that the puppet theater had become the main facet of life in the camp, and to guess that even so, routine was not abandoned. Every morning rows of prisoners were taken out to dig pits and chop wood. Only those involved in the theater in some way were treated well. It is easy to imagine how work on the theater progressed, and how Obersturmführer Licht treated Attorney Perl like a personal assistant in a striped uniform. The adjutant was cast aside—his reports and documents were uninteresting. Obersturmführer Jürgen Licht avoided almost any interference in the camp life—that work had always bored him. He devoted all his attention to the play, ignoring orders that came from the outside, until one of his officers, the adjutant for example, complained to senior officers. Then Sturmbanführer Hes came to conduct an inspection visit and Obersturmführer Licht gave him an SS officer's word of honor that everything was as it should be in the camp. In the meantime, the inmates on their way to work began to see refugees on the streets. German civilians. They traveled in long lines with wagons, and the looks on their faces told the inmates that the war was coming to an end. Then the rumors sprung up: all the inmates would be marched on long walks whose purpose was death.

In the camp things were no longer in order. Roll-call was held later and later in the day. Work was stopped before dark and the SS officers hurried back behind the fences. The skies were now the domain of the Americans, and almost every day there were planes dropping bombs, engines always roaring in the distance. Obersturm-führer Licht's camp did not constitute a target, but stray bombs found their way inside every so often. The officers were nervous, looking up at the sky even when it was empty. Some of them simply left, and Obersturmführer Licht did not object. Some inmates escaped too. I can already picture the final scene, in which Obersturmführer Licht and Attorney Perl remain on their own on the theater hilltop. Yes, that will be the scene. I will use all the adventure stories I used to read in Mrs. Gottmartz's library, all the Karl May books about the Wild West, to imagine the finale. Anat will believe it, she has to. Anyone who says "there is no limit" and thinks they are capable of imagining the limit, must believe. Because if Sobibor happened and Majdanek happened, anything could happen between Obersturmführer Licht and Attorney Perl, even a duel. No one could protest even if that was the final scene, even if I decide right now that Obersturmführer Licht's black pistol has a twin, a silver pistol on his right hip.

Up until the final duel, everything was devoted to the play. That was the new order of the camp. The production of *Verbercher* had to go on. Some of the Ukrainian policemen, perhaps because they liked working with wood, were assigned to work on the puppets. Whips and guns were laid down, and guards and inmates began convers-ing with one another. Everything revolved around the theater, while planes flew through the skies and a stream of refugees filed past the camp. Obersturmführer Licht's officers had already decided to wrest the reins of power from him, but he outsmarted them by quickly ordering a rapid organization of death marches. Three rows left the camp, all of his officers and soldiers leading lines of those inmates who were not essential to the theater. Most of the puppet makers were sent off too, and the carvers and tailors—anyone who's work was already done. Obersturmführer Licht instructed that the camp gates be locked and guard posts reinforced. He summoned his adjutant and shot him. The Ukrainian guards were ordered not to allow anyone in, not even SS. The camp became Obersturmführer Licht's fortress. There would be a puppet theater.

American planes kept bombing, and their shattering trail of bombardments fell inside the camp too. The Ukrainian guards began to flee. Obersturmführer Licht did not stop them. He remained alone with his two pistols among the inmates still at work on his play, at his side only two Ukrainians who chose to continue their puppet-building work.

On April 6th everything was ready. Obersturmführer Licht set curtain time for six in the evening. Planes had been attacking in the distance as early as noon, sounds of artillery reverberating through the air. The distant noise grew closer and closer, as if the planes were about to blindly assail the camp. Two Ukrainians tried to escape. From over forty yards away, with only two bullets, Obersturmführer Licht shot them. There were whispers among the inmates, some conjectured that he had no bullets left, but no one dared attack him. Alone among twenty-one inmates and three Ukrainians, Obersturmführer Licht annihilated any intentions of rebellion, any hopes of liberation, any lust for revenge; the play would go on at six.

At six in the evening he sat down in his armchair on the rugs. The rectangular stage was lit up and the play began. Attorney Perl stood on the little wooden stage and began the opening speech in his lucidly thundering voice, just as a pulverizing barrage of artillery landed between the fences. Obersturmführer Licht drew his pistol and placed it on his lap. "Continue!"

The artillery was merciless. A battle was raging in the distance. When the puppet of the Communist teacher appeared in the window, about to confiscate little Obersturmführer Licht's flag, a shell exploded at the foot of the hill and shrapnel sparked through the night sky. The puppeteers ran away. Behind the curtain they fled on their hands and knees and ran down the hill as Obersturmführer Licht's bullets whistled around them. The remaining inmates burst out of the camp and disappeared into the dark. The dim thundering of plane engines could be heard, and after a few moments there were bombardments that set a nearby hill ablaze. The only figures remaining on the theater hilltop were Obersturmführer Licht and Attorney Perl.

Anyone who says, *There is no limit*, and thinks they can imagine the limit, must believe.

Obersturmführer Licht looked at Attorney Perl as he stood thundering on the wooden stage. The Commandant approached his prisoner. He thrust his silver pistol into Attorney Perl's hand and set the terms. "Ten steps, then turn and shoot!" He turned and began walking.

And I have no idea if the Jew Attorney Perl will fight the Nazi officer, like the Jew Grandpa Lolek did, or if he will wisely escape, like the Jew Grandpa Yosef did. Or whether he might do something unexpected, like the Jew Hirsch, something that will transcend logic and imagination.

Anat will ask me, "So, what happened?"

And I will smile at her and say something like, "He ran away." I have to say something. After all, we know he survived. "Attorney Perl lived, as you know."

*

All the wonders, all the treasures, all the miracles. All the secrets, all the riddles, all the questions. It all spun into a gleaming cloud whose center hung over the brown wooden table in Grandpa Yosef's house.

For three days he asked, and finally I came to meet Hans Oderman at his house. Effi said, "Come this evening, I'll be there too." So I did.

We sit within circles of pleasant conversation, bringing each other up to date on what's new, telling stories, reporting how we're doing. But over the circles looms a pulsating cloud, its vapors dripping down and baptizing us—the end is near. The childhood riddles, Gershon Klima's sewage, the letter from Finkelstein, the battle at Monte Cassino, Grandpa Hainek's sons, the questions I asked Attorney Perl, Grandpa Yosef's journey, Adler's philosophy, Hirsch's theological inquiries, a ray of light from the Rabbi of Kalow, and the memory of Rothschild—all come together like clouds at the edge of a landscape. We sit at the table and talk comfortably, and I am certain: There will be closure here.

Grandpa Yosef serves us dinner. He brings out more and more dishes of increasingly peculiar concoctions. Effi helps him, leaving me and Hans to face one another. Six-foot-three-sapphire-blue-eyes-golden-locks and I converse. Every so often she comes in to interfere:

"I told Hans about your documentation. Talk to him, he's very interested."

She has an agenda; she's promoting a scheme.

Hans smiles awkwardly, having partially understood what Effi said in Hebrew.

"They told me that you have documented what happened to your family in the war. I'm very interested in this."

"Interested?"

"Yes, Mr. Ingberg said he would translate what you wrote into German for me, if you would agree." Hans looks at me with a certain discomfort on his face. As if things are about to float to the surface and he can already sense them erupting. "Effi said you found out some unpleasant things about your wife's grandfather."

(What else did she tell him? She looks like she's plotting something. She seems too directed, too arrow-like. As if she is assassinating the life I have now. But she walks past us innocently and asks, "Coffee, anyone?")

"Umm…yes. He was a sort of Jewish collaborator," I tell Hans. That's enough.

"You know, something similar happened to me."

Similar?

Tribal stories unfold around the campfire, and Grandpa Yosef arrives from somewhere and sits down, and Effi comes, with the coffee miraculously already brewed. We linger over our mugs for a while. Add sugar cubes. Stir politely. More milk?

"When I was here last year and you asked me what my family did during the war, you could say that I lied. Actually, I did not lie. Everything I said was the truth, but it was the truth that I am comfortable with. My father really was an orphan, and he was adopted by a family when he was ten. Everything I told you was about that family. I did not tell you about the real family, not because of lies, but because I have no idea who my family is."

(All of us are sitting at the table, yet Hans Oderman is talking to me.)

"My father grew up an orphan. As a child, he was moved around from one orphanage to another. He told me very little about that period. It was an unspoken matter in our home. I'm sure you understand…"

(All the secrets, all the riddles, all the questions.)

"It was as though his orphanhood concealed a great secret. Perhaps because of how little he told and how much I tried to fill in with my imagination, I began to take an interest in orphanages. That was how I got to my academic research. And when I was writing my dissertation, I read one day something about the "Fountain of Life" project, *Lebensborn* in German. This is not something that is talked about very much. There I was, an academic researcher in the field, and I had never even heard of *Lebensborn*. Much less a layman. The *Lebensborn* was part of a plan devised by Himmler to encourage the procreation of the Aryan race. That word, *Lebensborn*, would not leave my thoughts. I felt that it had some connection to my father. I had a clear intuition. Something you cannot understand, but still you sense. I'm sure you understand…

"I began to make calculations, you see. My father never mentioned any details, and in Germany it was not so customary to investigate what had happened during the war years. But I began asking Father about his early years and, as if he had been waiting all that time for me to uncover his secret on my own, he said, 'Yes, I am a *Lebensborn* child, and I have no idea where I come from.'"

"What do you mean, 'no idea where he comes from'?" I ask.

But Hans Oderman heatedly continues a flow of talk that has long been welling inside of him. Questions can be answered later. He tells me about Heinrich Himmler—Reichsführer Himmler—who, more than all the other Nazi leaders, had the appearance of a modest clerk, shy and withdrawn. Behind his small glasses hid a disturbed personality bound by hallucinations, aspiring to fame, unfeeling. He constructed ideals of an eternal Reich and tried to make them come true; he failed, but the remnants of his ideas were left in the world to suffer. He had his scientists calculate the rate of exterminating unwanted peoples and the rate of building the German Aryan race, and they indicated a discrepancy between the required number and the expected outcome. Riechsführer Himmler hatched a scheme. He promised his Führer a hundred and twenty million Aryan Germans by 1980. He came up with a plan that would, in the future, produce half a billion Aryan Germans if everything went according to his calculations. First he began a campaign to encourage higher birthrates, supporting every German child-bearing woman through any possible circumstances of childbirth—every child was adopted by the Reich. Even children born from relations between German soldiers and suitable women in the occupied lands were adopted by the Reich. Heinrich Himmler instructed that not even a drop of German seed should be lost. Still, that was not enough. The population growth was too small and too slow. Himmler ordered that children and babies in occupied countries with potentially Aryan qualities be either kidnapped or purchased. Children were taken from their parents by bribery or by force. In problematic cases, the parents were liquidated, labeled as partisans or outlaws or enemy agents. The children, from all over Europe, were educated in special boarding schools. Those who grew up to be disappointments, lacking in Aryan traits, were exterminated. Those who met expectations joined the Reich. The little girls were treated with hormones to expedite their sexual maturation—without the ability to quickly produce offspring, their annexation to the Reich would be fruitless.

Despite the kidnapping and adoption programs, the birthrate was not promising. And so Himmler declared a new program: *Lebensborn*, the Fountain of Life. Pure Aryan women were housed in convalescence homes in order to bear children for the Reich. The fathers were all SS men, the purest of the race. Each woman and her offspring were awarded the finest of conditions, in a world completely cut off from the hardships and hunger that were slowly descending upon the people of Germany. All that was required of these women was to give birth, to produce more and more babies for the Reich.

The essence of the *Lebensborn* scheme was to fill the wombs of German women with fetuses, to quickly manufacture rushed progeny and deliver them so the wombs would be available for the next batch of offspring.

Hans Oderman keeps talking without a pause, and I realize that the two polarities of the German Reich are coming to light simultaneously: On the one hand, a twisted enterprise of death is taking place, a burning urgency to shove more and more transports into the gas chambers, each transport making way for the next. On the other, an equally twisted enterprise of life, the chambers of female wombs being stuffed to capacity, one fetus making way for the next. This animalistic machine does not rest for a moment, so urgent are the needs of the Reich.

Within this wild, confused enterprise, born of the yearnings of Reichsführer Himmler, Hans Oderman's father is created. Born, perhaps, or possibly kidnapped and reeducated. Hans Oderman has no idea. Hans's father did not remember the *Lebensborn* years. The four-year-old's memories go back only to the post-war years, after German defeat. He told Hans very little about those blurred years of hunger. Huge orphanages, endless hours of enforced sleep. Facing the broken window of an abandoned house. A large hole behind a tree. For some reason, the hole becomes his friend, he likes to look at it, in the dark too, when he must sleep, sleep, sleep.

The war left thousands of infants, a master race that no one wanted, and there was no one to keep the promises that had created them.

"I began a tireless investigation. Most of the *Lebensborn* files were destroyed by the officials before the *Lebensborn* houses were occupied. A few papers were left, some memos, but there was no way to find my father. He was born a *Lebensborn*, that much he knew. An elderly childless couple had taken him in after the war, but they died and my father went back to the orphanages. He still had an aunt from his adoptive parents, and she told him everything she knew, which was very little. I searched through all the remaining files and documents. My father's father might have been an SS man, my father might have been a kidnapped child, perhaps Polish.

Hundreds of thousands of children were kidnapped in the war years, and who knows? I asked my dad what he thought, and he told me that sometimes he felt as if the Polish language sounded familiar. I would like to think that my father was kidnapped, rather than the planned child of an SS man, but look at me..."

Six-foot-three-sapphire-blue-eyes-golden-locks looks at me and I find myself convicting him against my own will. Then I think, "So what? So what if his father's father was in the SS?"

(All the wonders, all the treasures, all the miracles.)

"I would like to believe that my father was kidnapped. The children they kidnapped were usually a little older, but still. Or maybe my father was the offspring of a simple German army man. They usually only allowed party members to impregnate women in the *Lebensborn* houses, but sometimes, towards the end, regular soldiers were given the chance too."

We sit quietly. Grandpa Yosef remembers that we haven't eaten dessert yet. Something hovers over Hans and myself, the story of my documentation and the story of his research, the truth I did not want to reach and the truth Hans wished not to find. From that clashing of wings comes a deceitful sort of lesson that says loudly: Never enquire.

"When you asked me what my family did during the war, I told you what was convenient, I didn't exactly lie."

(Still making excuses, Hans Oderman the artiste of awkwardness.)

"My father built his life without complaints. He built a house. He built a family. He started from nothing and achieved everything. I respect him very much, admire him even. It's a shame I never had a grandfather like everyone else did. There was the aunt, and I called her Grandma, but it wasn't really...."

(All the wonders, all the treasures, all the miracles.)

As I look at Hans Oderman, I realize what his role is, what it has been from the first day I saw him. He is my reflection. That's it. I can no longer say *us* and *them*. Every move I make, every line I draw, there will be a line on my reflection too. Every thought of

mine will produce a thought on the other side too. There is no more
us and *them*.

"I want to write a book about the *Lebensborn*, about the kidnapping operation and the breeding farms. Today in Germany there
are hundreds of thousands of people who are assumed to be *Lebensborn* children. There were more. Some were returned to their parents,
if there were any. But there are many left without fathers, without
mothers, without memories. You know, no one ever punished the
Lebensborn directors, Dr. Gregor Ebner and Dr. Max Sollmann. And
they were the people who signed documents ordering that a disap-
pointing baby be liquidated. They allowed transports of kidnapped
children with unsatisfactory data to be left to die. No one even bothered to investigate them. Strange, isn't it?"

A reflection. A transparency. An unwanted world of mirrors, all
the lines between me and him are reflected, joined together, insepa-
rable. Since the day I let him carry his own suitcases, it was clear—he
was destined to finish my search. To show me that everything was
more complicated than I could even conceive.

A gleaming cloud whose center hung over the brown wooden
table in Grandpa Yosef's house opens up. All the wonders shower
down, all the treasures, all the miracles. All the secrets, all the riddles,
all the questions.

I did not go straight home that evening. After what Hans had
told me, after the *Lebensborn*, after what I had come to understand,
the reflection that trapped me and the realization that there was no
simple explanation, I just stayed there. I could not leave. In order
to be capable of being at home with Anat and Yariv, in order to be
capable of living my life, the world had to operate differently. Like
turning a sock inside out, the world simply spun around us, leaving us
in our place, in our time, but it came in closer, upside-down, joining
in. Time would have to figure out how to make things settle down—
with us everything continued as usual. Hans stayed at Grandpa Yosef's,
washing dishes I suppose, speaking German. Effi disappeared somewhere—probably home, or perhaps to another place in her life (she
too had bridges), and I found myself walking down Katznelson in

the direction of home. At the end of all days, I believe, I will be sitting on a couch opposite Hans Oderman in Grandpa Yosef's house. That will be the revenge of time. But that night, I walked down Katznelson without a thought in my head, and looked up at one of the tall poplar trees. Some of its bark was starting to shed, hanging limply as if I had caught it in the middle of an escape attempt. I stood and thought of those neighborhood trees for a long time. Who had planted them? Who had chosen poplars and poincianas and pepper trees and pink bauhinias and purple jacarandas and divided them up among the yards by some secret code? Who had taken the time? The people who lived here had never planted a tree, and I could not imagine a single one of them dropping everything to dig a hole for a sapling. Someone, perhaps a municipal clerk, must have picked out the trees when this neighborhood was designed. It was designed, after all, wasn't it? And the trees, to which I had never given much thought before, suddenly appeared before me: the poplar, the poinciana, Gershon Klima's Indian bombax. Hirsch emerged from the hibiscus shrubs, as if summoned for a purpose. Hirsch.

He looked at me with his lost gaze, seeming unsure of how he had come to be standing in front of me. The usual madness was gone from his face. He looked at me as if he knew me, as if I were doomed to be his audience, the first to hear the conclusion of a lifetime of enquiry, a theological exploration that, to the outside, had always appeared to be a frightening madness, but inside was profound erudition.

Hirsch stood facing me and found himself with no choice but to expose, precisely and terrifyingly, the final, definitive sentence, the conclusion of an irrevocably sealed life: Everything, the Shoah, had been an ordinary occurrence. Ordinary people made it happen and ordinary people were its victims.

I looked at him and answered silently, yes.

Afterword

Lolek and Hainek were my father's cousins, the sons of Gustava Gutfreund, who died of cancer at the age of thirty-one, before Dad was born. They lived in Kielce with their father, the educator Doctor Feuer, headmaster of the Hebrew Gymnasium in Kielce, and with his second wife. Dad never saw Hainek and Lolek. Only his sister, Aunt Anola, once saw Hainek, the younger brother. She was around twelve, he was thirteen or so, and to this day she carries the impression of their encounter. From their one conversation, as they walked down the streets of Bochnia, she remembers that he was handsome and had the aura of being a "man of the world." Fifty years later, she remembers exactly what he told her.

His older brother, Lolek, who was several years older than Hainek, was never seen. They know he had planned to go to *Eretz Yisrael* to study, but did not make it. The war broke out. As far as is known, Dr. Feuer and his sons, Hainek and Lolek, were killed in the region of Lvov, or perhaps somewhere else. The Kielce memorial book mentions Dr. Feuer and his second wife. Hainek and Lolek are not mentioned. We looked for the grave of their mother, Gustava, in the Bochnia cemetery, but it is gone too.

I continued the lives of Lolek and Hainek in their new, surviving, personas, two brothers from the generation of our grandfathers. Grandpa Lolek's service in the volunteer army of the Polish General Anders is based on the service of Avraham (Romek) Gutfreund, my father's uncle, in that same army.

Grandpa Yosef is a purely invented character. He is probably inspired by my true grandfather, Grandpa Shalom, who was tortured by the Gestapo. The tortures caused the onset of his disease, and I only knew him through the barriers of illness. When I grew up I heard stories of the man he had been before he became ill, and I recreated his character with a different name, far from the one and only persona of Grandpa Shalom I can imagine.

Attorney Perl from Stanislaw lived in the house at 7 Leonarda Street in the Bochnia ghetto, with my father's family. He and his wife, whose name I do not know, were killed in Belzec together. Dad remembers him as an educated and dignified attorney, an imposing persona. He was born in 1872 and his full name was Solomon (Shlomo) Perl. During the course of writing this book I discovered that the couple had a daughter, Genya, and a granddaughter, Danusha, of whom the Perls spoke incessantly. I have no information about their fates. I recreated him so that he could expose a little of the truth about that period. The names, quotes and other details from Attorney Perl's index card are true, to the extent I was able to verify through publicly available sources.

Only a fraction of the Nazi criminals were tried or served any significant sentences. Contrary to popular belief, the vast majority of those who committed or collaborated in atrocities accepted no responsibility for their actions. Formal pardons, shady deals, and a conspiracy of forgiveness and silence enabled the committers of atrocities to live out their lives in freedom.

Characters who are part of the plot, such as Ahasuerus and Obersturmführer Licht, never existed, but were forged out of a mosaic of the extreme figures who most certainly did exist in the mad world of the Nazi regime.

Persons mentioned in the plot such as Kurt Franz, 'Doll,' of Treblinka, or the Jewish kapo Yehezkel Ingster, absolutely existed. One can read of their misdeeds and those of hundreds and thousands like them, in the Yad Vashem library and archives.

The mad enterprise of the *Lebensborn*, the "Fountain of Life," is chronicled in *Of Pure Blood*, by Mark Hillel and Clarissa Henry.

About the Author

Amir Gutfreund

Amir Gutfreund was born in Haifa in 1963. After studying applied mathematics at the Technion, he joined the Israeli Air Force and became a Lieutenant Colonel. *Our Holocaust* was his first novel. It was awarded the Buchman Prize by the Yad Vashem Holocaust Remembrance Institute. His second novel, *Shoreline Mansions*, won the prestigious Sapir Prize in 2003, and is forthcoming from *the* Toby Press. His third novel, *The World, a Little Later*, was recently published in Israel. Gutfreund lives in the Galilee with his wife, Netta, a clinical psychologist, and their two children, Romi and Nimrod.

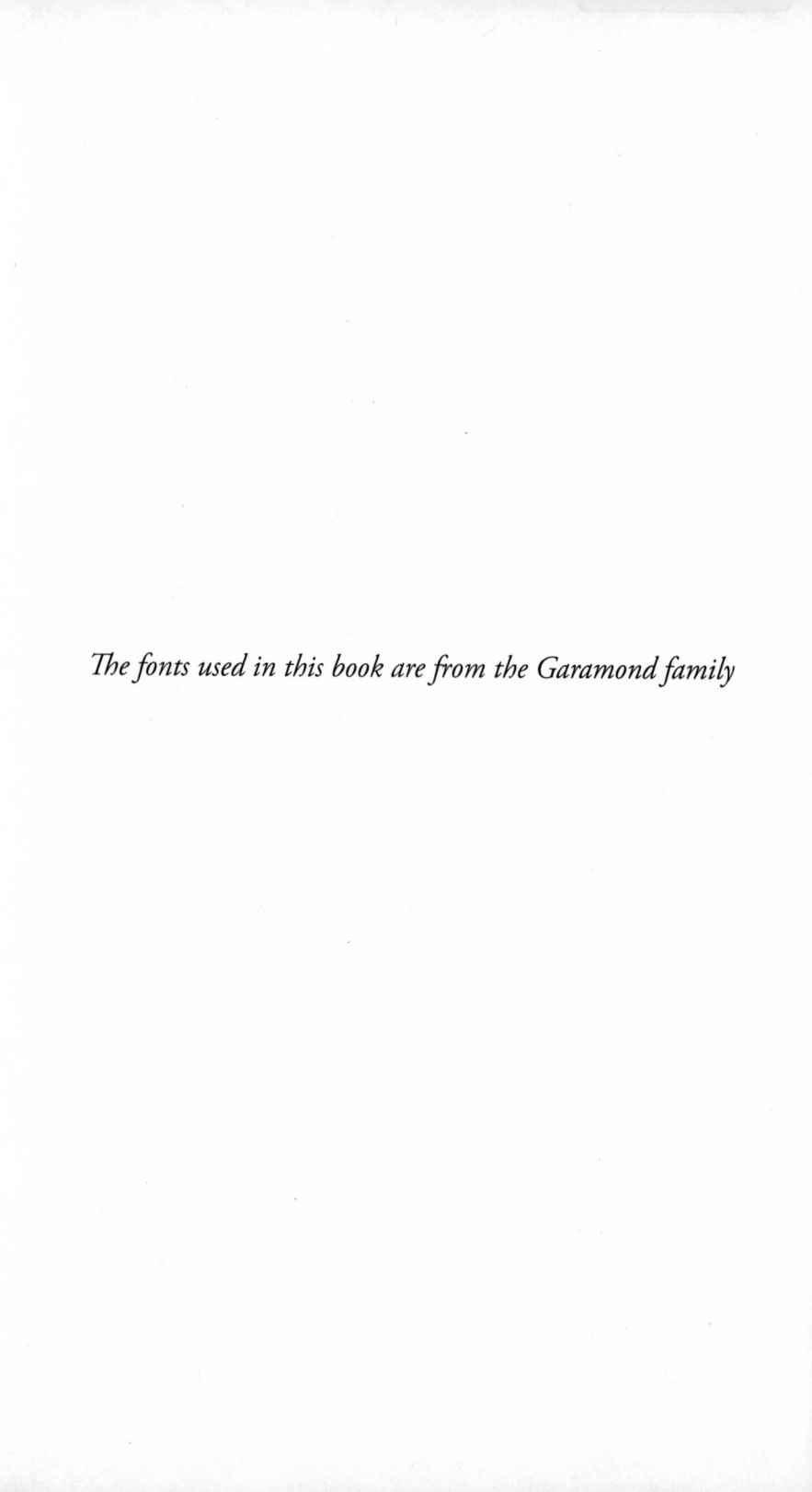

The fonts used in this book are from the Garamond family

PRINCIPLES OF
ECONOMICS
THIRD EDITION

PRINCIPLES OF ECONOMICS

THIRD EDITION

Dirk Mateer

University of Arizona

Lee Coppock

University of Virginia

W. W. NORTON & COMPANY
Independent Publishers Since 1923

W. W. Norton & Company has been independent since its founding in 1923, when William Warder Norton and Mary D. Herter Norton first published lectures delivered at the People's Institute, the adult education division of New York City's Cooper Union. The firm soon expanded its program beyond the Institute, publishing books by celebrated academics from America and abroad. By midcentury, the two major pillars of Norton's publishing program—trade books and college texts—were firmly established. In the 1950s, the Norton family transferred control of the company to its employees, and today—with a staff of five hundred and hundreds of trade, college, and professional titles published each year—W. W. Norton & Company stands as the largest and oldest publishing house owned wholly by its employees.

Editor: Eric Svendsen

Developmental Editor: Kurt Norlin

Manuscript Editor: Carla Barnwell

Project Editor: Laura Dragonette

Media Editor: Miryam Chandler

Associate Media Editor: Victoria Reuter

Assistant Editor: Jeannine Hennawi

Media Editorial Assistant: Christina Fuery

Marketing Manager, Economics: Janise Turso

Production Manager: Eric Pier-Hocking

Photo Editor: Ted Szczepanski

Photo Researcher: Dena Digilio Betz

College Permissions Specialist: Elizabeth Trammell

Text Design: Jen Montgomery

Art Director: Rubina Yeh

Cover Design and "Snapshot" Infographics: Kiss Me I'm Polish

Composition: Graphic World

Manufacturing: Transcontinental Printing

Library of Congress Cataloging-in-Publication Data

Names: Mateer, G. Dirk, author. | Coppock, Lee, author.
Title: Principles of economics / Dirk Mateer, Lee Coppock.
Description: Third Edition. | New York : W. W. Norton & Company, 2020. |
   Revised edition of the authors' Principles of economics, [2018] |
   Includes bibliographical references and index.
Identifiers: LCCN 2019045451 | ISBN **9780393679175** (hardcover)
Subjects: LCSH: Economics.
Classification: LCC HB171.5 .M435 2020 | DDC 330—dc23
LC record available at https://lccn.loc.gov/2019045451

W. W. Norton & Company, Inc., 500 Fifth Avenue, New York, NY 10110-0017
wwnorton.com

W. W. Norton & Company Ltd., 15 Carlisle Street, London W1D 3BS
1 2 3 4 5 6 7 8 9 0

BRIEF CONTENTS

CONTENTS

PART I Introduction

1 Five Foundations of Economics 4

2 Model Building and Gains from Trade 26

PART II The Role of Markets

3 The Market at Work: Supply and Demand   72

4 Elasticity   114

7 Market Inefficiencies: Externalities and Public Goods   218

PART III The Theory of the Firm

PART IV Labor Markets and Earnings

14 The Demand and Supply of Resources   434

PART V Special Topics in Microeconomics

16 Consumer Choice   510

PART VI Macroeconomic Basics

19 Introduction to Macroeconomics and Gross Domestic Product   600

PART VII The Long and Short of Macroeconomics

24 Economic Growth and the Wealth of Nations   760

27 Recessions, Expansions, and the Debate over How to Manage Them   864

PART VIII Fiscal Policy

28 Federal Budgets: The Tools of Fiscal Policy 908

29 Fiscal Policy 936

PART IX Monetary Policy

30 Money and the Federal Reserve   968

31 Monetary Policy   1000

PART X International Economics

32 International Trade 1036

PREFACE

We are teachers of principles of economics. That is what we do. We each teach principles of microeconomics and macroeconomics to over a thousand students a semester, every single semester, at the University of Arizona and the University of Virginia. To date, we have taught over 50,000 students.

We decided to write our own text for one big reason. We simply were not satisfied with the available texts and felt strongly that we could write an innovative book to which dedicated instructors like us would respond. It's not that the already available texts were bad or inaccurate; it's that they lacked an understanding of what we, as teachers, have learned through fielding the thousands of questions that our students have asked us over the years. We do not advise policymakers, but we do advise students, and we know how their minds work.

For instance, there really was no text that showed an understanding for where students consistently trip up (for example, cost curves) and therefore provided an additional example or, better yet, a worked exercise. There really was no text that was careful to reinforce new terminology and difficult sticking points with explanations in everyday language. There really was no text that leveraged the fact that today's students are key participants in the twenty-first-century economy and that used examples and cases from markets in which they interact all the time (such as the markets for cell phones, social networking sites, computing devices, and online booksellers).

What our years in the classroom have brought home to us is the importance of meeting students where they are. This means knowing their cultural touchstones and trying to tell the story of economics with those touchstones in mind. In our text, we meet students where they are through resonance and reinforcement. In fact, these two words are our mantra—we strive to make each topic resonate and then make it stick through reinforcement.

Whenever possible, we use student-centered examples that resonate with students. For instance, many of our examples refer to jobs that students often hold and businesses that often employ them. If the examples resonate, students are much more likely to dig in to the material wholeheartedly and internalize key concepts. This revision process is not new to us; every time a new term begins, we update our course materials. What you see in the Third Edition of this book is a reflection of current economic theory, the contributions of students (past and present), and the changes in society around us. As professional instructors, we have an unfailing commitment to reach every student who crosses our paths and equip them for success. This book, like our classrooms, reflects this goal.

When we teach, we try to create a rhythm of reinforcement in our lectures that begins with the presentation of new material, is followed by a concrete example and then a reinforcing device, and then closes with a "make it stick" moment. We do this over and over again. We have tried to bring that rhythm to the book. We believe strongly that this commitment to reinforcement works. To give an example, in our chapter "Oligopoly and Strategic Behavior," while presenting the crucial yet difficult subject of game theory, we work through the concept of the prisoner's dilemma at least six different ways.

No educator is happy with the challenge we all face to motivate our students to read the assigned text. No matter how effective our lectures are, if our students are not reinforcing those lectures by reading the assigned text chapters, they are only partially absorbing the key takeaways that properly trained citizens need in order to thrive in today's world. A second key motivation for us to undertake this ambitious project was the desire to create a text that students would read, week in and week out, for the entire course. By following our commitment to resonance and reinforcement, we are confident that we have written a text that's a good read for today's students. So good, in fact, that we believe students will read entire chapters and actually enjoy them. Many users of the first two editions have indicated that this is the case.

What do we all want? We want our students to leave our courses having internalized fundamentals that they will remember for life. The fundamentals (such as understanding incentives, opportunity cost, and thinking at the margin) will help them to make better choices in the workplace, in their personal investments, in their long-term planning, in their voting, and in all their critical choices. The bottom line is that they will live more fulfilled and satisfying lives if we succeed. The purpose of this text is to help all of us succeed in this quest.

What does this classroom-inspired, student-centered text look like?

A Simple Narrative

First and foremost, we keep the narrative simple. We always bear in mind all those office-hour conversations with students where we searched for some way to make sense of this foreign language—for them—that is economics. It is incredibly satisfying when you find the right expression, explanation, or example that creates the "Oh, now I get it . . ." moment with your student. We have filled the narrative with those successful "now I get it" passages.

Real-World, Relatable Examples and Cases that Resonate

Nothing makes this material stick for students like good examples and cases that they relate to, and we have peppered our book with them. They are part of the narrative, set off with an Economics in the Real World heading. We further feature Economics in the Media boxed examples that use scenes from sources like movies and TV shows that illustrate economic concepts. One of us has written the book (literally!) on economics in the movies, and we have used these clips year after year to make economics stick with students.

In addition, we have continued to work hard to create a text that represents the student population. Economics as a discipline is less diverse than many other fields of study, and that's something we've been trying to change, at the ground level, for decades. How do we do this? We listen to our students in our office hours, through email and informal conversations, and by observing the level of engagement in our classrooms. We also go out of our way to reach out and help those in need to learn and feel welcome. We hope you get this same feeling when you read this book! The style of writing is clear but intentionally conversational—the photos and captions are designed to draw you in, just as a lecture would. Take a quick read or flip through the pages, and you will see what we mean.

ECONOMICS IN THE REAL WORLD

CRYPTOCURRENCY IS MONEY, TOO

Bitcoin, Ethereum, and other cryptocurrencies have captured the imagination of many investors around the globe. Although cryptocurrencies are different from traditional money, in that they are not issued by national governments, cryptocurrencies can serve as a medium of exchange and this feature makes them a form of money: they are accepted as payment for goods and services. You can, for example, buy a pizza from Domino's or Pizza Hut using Bitcoin, or you can buy airline tickets via Expedia.com.

A main rationale for manipulated by the go cryptocurrency's valu is regulated not by a c called blockchain. By fashion, the blockchai rency. In nations whe can provide an alterna Venezuela, for examp

Owning cryptocu side can be unpredict currencies, but the va investment. In 2017, t By year's end, the pri wishing they'd gotten spike attracted new sp Some observers see cr believe that it will per

Dogecoin is a popular crypto-currency. In 2018, the total market value of all Dogecoins was around $300 million.

· ECONOMICS in the MEDIA ·

Costs in the Short Run

OCEAN'S 8

In *Ocean's 8* (2018), Sandra Bullock and Cate Blanchett recruit six partners in crime to help them steal a diamond necklace worth $150 million. Part of the joy in watching any of the *Ocean's* films is seeing a star-studded cast of A-list actors pull off the perfect heist. Each partner has a specific skill: one is a jewelry maker, another a computer hacker, a third a pickpocket, and so on.

Beyond a certain point, however, adding more specialists mostly just means an extra person to split the take with. The Bullock and Blanchett characters know exactly how big a core team they want. That's

Applying Economic Decision-Making Through Problem-Solving

Most instructors in this course want students to learn to think like economists and to apply economic principles to their decision-making. This text shares this goal. To get students thinking about economics, we open each chapter with a scenario to illustrate a popular concept or to point out a misconception. Students come to our classes with a number of strongly held beliefs about economics and the economy, so we begin each chapter recognizing that fact and then establishing what we will do to illuminate and clarify that subject area. Then, in each chapter, several Practice What You Know features allow students to self-check their comprehension while also laying the foundation for the step-by-step problem solving required for the end-of-chapter Study Problems. And throughout the text, key equations are used, and the five core foundations of economics (incentives, trade-offs, opportunity cost, marginal thinking, and trade creates value) are reinforced with a special icon to ensure that students are constantly connecting the dots.

Incentives
Trade-offs
Opportunity cost
Marginal thinking
Trade creates value

PRACTICE WHAT YOU KNOW

Price Elasticity of Demand

Take a look at this IKEA advertisement and think about the determinants of the price elasticity of demand.

QUESTION: Do you think IKEA's "Rainy day special" price makes sense?

ANSWER: Let's start by figuring out whether the demand for umbrellas is elastic or inelastic when it is raining. The GRÖSSBY umbrella is quite inexpensive even at full price, so the purchase would represent only a small share of a consumer's budget. That would tend to make the demand inelastic. Also, when do you need an umbrella? When it's raining, of course! Consumers without umbrellas need them immediately, and that [...]d inelastic. Finally, how many good substitutes are there for [...] or poncho, maybe, but it's a lot harder for two people to share [...]lla. The lack of good substitutes is another factor that tends to [...]n rainy days, then, demand is even more inelastic than usual. [...] more and raised the price of the GRÖSSBY on rainy days, [...] store would have increased revenues.

Umbrella
GRÖSSBY
blue/yellow

$4⁹⁹

$2⁵⁰

Offer valid on GRÖSSBY umbrella only.

IKEA

PRACTICE WHAT YOU KNOW

Changes in Resources: Natural Disasters

In September 2017, Hurricane Maria slammed into Puerto Rico, killing many people and destroying significant capital, including roads, homes, factories, and bridges.

QUESTION: How would you use an aggregate production function to illustrate the way a major destruction of capital affects a macroeconomy in the short run?

ANSWER:

Hurricane Maria caused an estimated $90 billion in damage to Puerto Rico and the U.S. Virgin Islands.

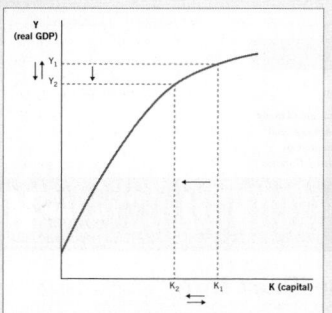

This is an unusual situation, in which the level of capital actually falls. Because capital (K) is on the horizontal axis of the production function, the decline in capital moves Puerto Rico back along its production function. Assuming the original level of capital is indicated as K_1, we can illustrate the effect of Maria as a change to a lower level, say K_2. This means less GDP for Puerto Rico (Y falls from Y_1 to Y_2) until the capital is rebuilt.

QUESTION: With no further changes, what happens to real GDP in the long run?

ANSWER: With no further changes, real GDP returns to the steady-state output level (K_1) in the long run. At the new level of capital after the storm (K_2), the marginal product of additional capital is relatively high, so there is a greater return to building new capital. But in the long run, because there was no shift in the production function, the level of capital returns to the steady-state level (K_1), which means output also returns to its steady-state level (Y_1).

[...]venue that tax will generate. These are questions about [...]valuate by using a mathematical formula.

[...]ICITY OF DEMAND FORMULA Let's begin with [...] shop. Consider an owner who is trying to attract more [...]nth, he lowers the price of a pizza by 10% and is pleased [...] by 30%.

[...]la for the price elasticity of demand (E_D):

$$\text{[...]nd} = E_D = \frac{\text{percentage change in the quantity demanded}}{\text{percentage change in price}}$$ (EQUATION 4.1)

[...]rom the example, we calculate the price elasticity of

$$\text{[...]asticity of demand} = E_D = \frac{30\%}{-10\%} = -3$$

[...]y of demand, −3 in this case, is expressed as a coefficient [...] (it has a minus sign in front of it). The coefficient tells us [...] demanded has changed (30%) compared with the price [...] case, the percentage change in the quantity demanded [...]centage change in the price. Whenever the percentage

Big-Picture Pedagogy

For beginning students, economics can be a subject with many new concepts and seemingly many details to memorize. To help students stay focused on the big ideas of each chapter while continuing to emphasize critical thinking, we use several unique features. First we introduce students to the objectives in each chapter in the form of Big Questions that students will explore rather than memorize. Then we come back to the Big Questions in the conclusion to the chapter with Answering the Big Questions.

· BIG QUESTIONS ·

- What are the factors of production?
- Where does the demand for labor come from?
- Where does the supply of labor come from?
- What are the determinants of demand and supply in the labor market?
- What role do land and capital play in production?

· ANSWERING the BIG QUESTIONS ·

What are the factors of production?

- Labor, land, and capital are the factors of production, or the inputs used in producing goods and services.

Where does the demand for labor come from?

- The demand for each factor of production is a derived demand that stems from a firm's desire to supply a good in another market. Labor demand is contingent on the value of the marginal product that is produced, and the value of the marginal product is equivalent to the firm's labor demand curve.

Where does the supply of labor come from?

- The supply of labor comes from the wage rate that is offered. Each worker faces the labor-leisure trade-off. At high wage levels, the income effect may become larger than the substitution effect and cause the labor supply curve to bend backward. Changes in the supply of labor can result from other employment opportunities, the changing composition of the workforce, immigration, and migration.

What are the determinants of demand and supply in the labor market?

- Labor markets bring the forces of demand and supply together in a wage signal that conveys information to both sides of the market. At wages above the equilibrium, the supply of workers exceeds the demand for labor. The result is a surplus of available workers that places downward pressure on wages until they reach the equilibrium wage, at which point the surplus is eliminated. At wages below the equilibrium, the demand for labor exceeds the available supply of workers, and a shortage develops. The shortage forces firms to offer higher wages to attract workers. Wages rise until they reach the equilibrium wage, at which point the shortage is eliminated.
- There is no definitive result for outsourcing of labor in the short run. In the long run, outsourcing moves jobs to workers who are more productive and enhances overall social welfare.

What role do land and capital play in production?

- Land and capital (as well as labor) are the factors of production across which firms compare the value of the marginal product per dollar spent. Firms seek to equalize the revenue per dollar spent on each input, thereby maximizing their efficiency.

Another notable reinforcement device is the Snapshot that appears in most chapters. We have used the innovation of modern infographics to create a memorable story that reinforces a particularly important topic. By combining pictures, text, and data in these unique features, we encourage students to think about and understand different components of a concept working together.

Solved-Problems Pedagogy

Last but certainly not least, we conclude each chapter with a selection of fully solved problems. These problems show students how to approach material they will see in homework, quizzes, and tests.

Solved Problems

5a. The equilibrium price is $4, and the equilibrium quantity is 60 quarts. The next step is to graph the curves, as shown here.

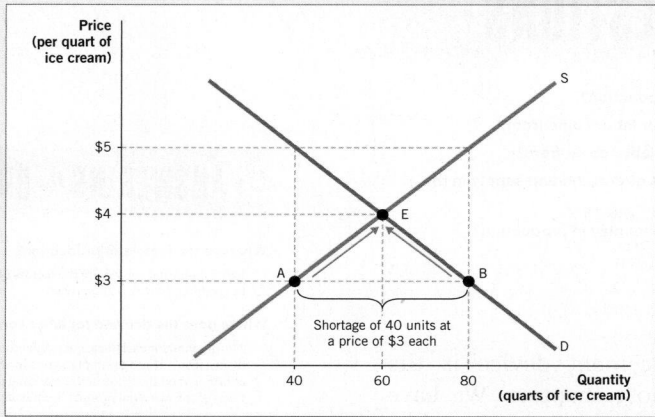

b. A shortage of 40 quarts of ice cream exists at $3 (quantity demanded is 80 and the quantity supplied is 40); therefore, there is excess demand. Ice cream sellers will raise their price as long as excess demand exists—that is, as long as the price is below $4. It is not until $4 that the equilibrium point is reached and the shortage is resolved.

8.a. The first step is to set $Q_D = Q_S$. Doing so gives us $90 - 2P = P$. Solving for price, we find that $90 = 3P$, or $P = 30$. Once we know that $P = 30$, we can plug this value back into either of the original equations, $Q_D = 90 - 2P$ or $Q_S = P$. Beginning with Q_D, we get $90 - 2(30) = 90 - 60 = 30$, or we can plug it into $Q_S = P$, so $Q_S = 30$. Because we get a quantity of 30 for both Q_D and Q_S, we know that the price of $30 is correct.

b. In this part, we plug $20 into Q_D. Doing so yields $90 - 2(20) = 50$. Now we plug $20 into Q_S. Doing so yields 20.

c. Because $Q_D = 50$ and $Q_S = 20$, there is a shortage of 30 quarts.

d. Whenever there is a shortage of a good, the price will rise in order to find the equilibrium point.

9a. The reduction in consumer income led to a negative, or leftward, shift in the demand curve for gasoline. Because this is the only change, the equilibrium price of gasoline fell. In fact, by the

end of 2008, the price of gasoline had fallen to under $2 per gallon in the United States.

b. The significant drop in the cost of production led to a large increase, or rightward, shift in the supply of gasoline. This increase in supply led to a decrease in price. In fact, by early 2015, the average price of a gallon of regular gasoline in the United States fell to under $2 per gallon.

Looking at parts (a) and (b) together, you can see that very different causes led to steep drops in the price of gasoline. In 2008 the cause was a decline in demand; in 2014 it was an increase in supply.

10. Because alcohol and Solo cups are complements, the key here is to recall that a change in the price of a complementary good shifts the demand curve for the related good. Lower alcohol prices will cause consumers to purchase more alcohol and therefore demand more Solo cups. In other words, the entire demand curve for Solo cups shifts to the right.

12a. The price of related goods is a demand shifter so, it is incorrect.

b. Income is a demand shifter so, it is incorrect.

c. The cost of inputs is a supply shifter so, it is correct.

d. The price causes a movement along the supply curve so, it is incorrect.

Principles of Microeconomics— Hallmarks and Updates to the Third Edition

When we wrote the First Edition of *Principles of Microeconomics,* we decided to follow the traditional structure found in most texts. Though every chapter is critical, we believe that those covering supply and demand, elasticity, and production costs are the *most* fundamental, since so many other insights and takeaways build on them. We tried triply hard to reinforce these chapters with extra examples and opportunities for self-assessment.

Enthusiastic feedback from the Second Edition told us that our readers were happy with the organization of the book, so in this edition we were able to drill down and focus our updates on elements that we believe add tremendous value. We did a big rethink on every example in the textbook, updating and changing examples so that they are relatable, inclusive, culturally relevant, and interesting, and so the reader is engaged. This involved updating text content, features boxes, images, and illustrations. We took a hard look at many chapters, considering where we might introduce the work of different economists, especially women, who are often not well represented in principles texts. In trying to be relatable to a varied student body, we always looked for places where we could make sure every reader finds themselves represented repeatedly throughout the book.

Several other important changes were made to the chapter pedagogy. Each chapter now starts with a large and engaging photo that works with the chapter opener and the caption. Images and stories engage students, and we wanted to improve on our treatment in previous editions. Each chapter now includes a challenge question in our practice boxes. These challenge questions give curious students the opportuntiy to analyze problems in-depth so that deeper learning occurs. Further, Economics for Life boxes have both revised content and bullets that summarize the key takeaways at a glance. Based on reviewer feedback, we have updated and simplified Snapshots, and we eliminated those that were found to be repetitive with the text material. We also have built a closer connection to the book and the media package, especially elements of Smartwork5 and Inquizitive. This is described in more detail below.

A sampling of specific updates to the text includes new material featuring the research of economists like Joan Robinson, Elinor Ostrom, and Ulrike Malmendier, among others. New media examples feature *Shark Tank, Ocean's 8, Breaking Bad, Superior Donuts, Mad Men, Superstore, Captain America: Civil War, Last Week Tonight with John Oliver, Worth It, Inside Out, The Onion,* and *Planet Money.* Updated examples include new data on the relationship between educational attainment and pay; a full explanation of the gender wage gap along with a study on why the gender gap exists at Uber; and a figure showing gender differences among the most common jobs. We dug deeper to give our students the best data so that they can become more informed.

One hallmark of this textbook that is not found anywhere else in the principles markets remains. This text includes a separate chapter on price discrimination. We have done this because the digital economy has made price discrimination much more common than it ever was before, so what was once a fun but somewhat marginal topic is no longer marginal. What's more, students really relate to it because they experience it in many of the markets in which they participate—for example, college sporting events.

We also place a stand-alone consumer theory chapter toward the end of the volume, but that does not mean that we consider it an optional chapter. We have learned that there is tremendous variation among instructors for when to present this material in the course, and we wanted to allow for maximum flexibility.

Principles of Macroeconomics— Hallmarks and Updates to the Third Edition

Principles of Macroeconomics follows the traditional structure found in most texts, but it contains several chapters on new topics that reflect the latest thinking and priorities in macroeconomics. First, at the end of the unit on macroeconomic basics, we have an entire chapter on financial markets, including coverage of securitization and mortgage-backed securities. The economic crisis of 2008–2009 made everyone aware of the importance of financial markets for the worldwide economy, and students want to know more about this fascinating topic.

Economic growth is presented before coverage of the short run, and we have two chapters devoted to the topic. The first focuses on the facts of economic growth. It discusses in largely qualitative terms how nations like South Korea and Singapore can be so wealthy while nations like North Korea and Liberia are so impoverished. The second chapter on growth presents the Solow model in very simple terms. We've included this chapter to highlight the importance of growth and modeling. That said, it is optional and can be skipped by those instructors who have time for only one chapter on growth.

Coverage of the short run includes a fully developed chapter on the aggregate demand–aggregate supply model, and a second chapter that uses this key model to analyze—essentially side by side—the Great Depression and the Great Recession. We feel this is a very effective way of presenting several of the key debates within economics.

Finally, we have written a unique chapter on the federal budget, which has allowed us to discuss at length the controversial topic of entitlements and the foreign ownership of U.S. national debt.

Feedback from the Second Edition has driven important revisions. Reviewers have noted how important it is to frame chapters at the start, to introduce students to economic concepts. For this edition, almost every opener has been rewritten and updated, and uses an extra-large photograph to draw students in. Also, addressing a concern in the discipline, we have tried to add the voices of a more diverse group of economists, including people like Joan Robinson, Carol Graham, Dambisa Moyo, Valerie Ramey, Esther Duflo, and Caren Gaffney. We have added important new material on topics like the Tax Cuts and Jobs Act, why recessions occur, the savings rate in America, and understanding cryptocurrencies. Further, we continue to fine-tune our aggregate demand–aggregate supply chapter after a large revision in the Second Edition, and also our appendix on the aggregate expenditures model. Of course, we have updated the examples in the book, including new features from *The Onion, Planet Money, Breaking Bad*, and the work of Hans Rosling. We have also evaluated the purpose of every Snapshot feature in the text and have simplified many of them, as well as eliminating some that overlapped with material already in the text.

Supplements and Media

This text comes with robust support. Most can be accessed electronically either at digital.wwnorton.com/prineco3 or by locating this title's catalog page at wwnorton.com.

SMARTWORK5

Smartwork5 (SW5) for *Principles of Economics* is an online learning environment that helps instructors meet the teaching goal of connecting concepts and showing applications. Richly varied questions and intuitive functionality give users the flexibility to create the type of learning that works best for their students. Try a demo of the following features at digital.wwnorton.com/prineco3.

Easy to launch, easy to use

Simple course setup and intuitive student registration minimize administrative headaches at the beginning of the semester. Instructors can use prebuilt activities or customize their own assignments and questions to suit their needs.

Integration with campus LMS platforms

Smartwork5 integrates with campus learning management systems. Student grades flow automatically to the instructor's LMS course. A single sign-on between the LMS and Norton digital products simplifies student access—and this means fewer password/log-in woes.

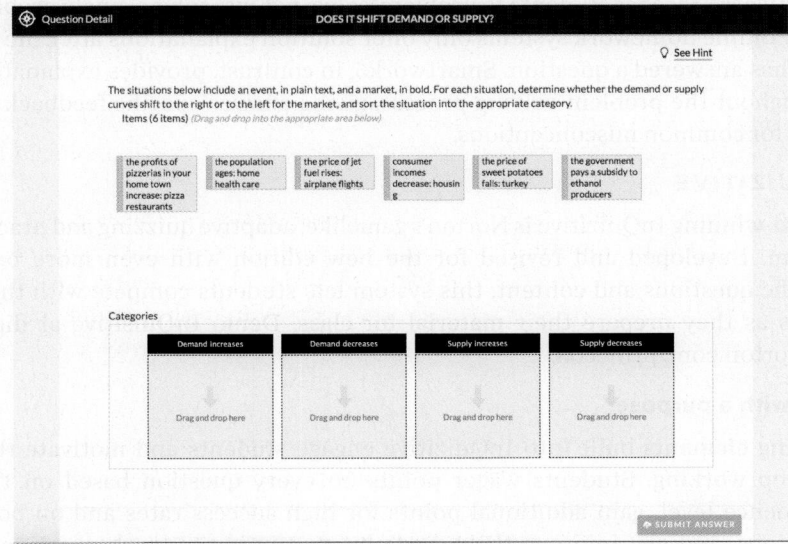

Smartwork5 Norton's easy-to-use homework system designed to integrate with your LMS.

Trusted economics tools and content

Smartwork5 teaches students not just how to solve problems but how to problem-solve, connecting concepts to learned skills through varied applications. Smartwork5 includes assignments based on real-world economic scenarios, "Office Hours" video tutorials presented in the learning moment, analytical and interactive graphing questions, and application problems. Rich answer-specific feedback builds students' confidence and economic skills. Questions are book specific, matching the terminology and conventions that students see in their textbook. They were developed in collaboration with instructors actively teaching with the Mateer and Coppock textbook.

NEW for this edition are several reviewer-tested improvements and content types. Smartwork5 now also includes questions keyed in to Practice What You Know examples in each chapter, building a strong support system between Smartwork5 and the text. Further, up-to-date news feature questions have been added to each chapter. In total, there are close to 500 new questions in the latest release of Smartwork5.

Rich performance reports

Intuitive performance reports for both individual students and entire classes help instructors gauge student comprehension and adjust their teaching accordingly.

An intuitive, easy-to-use graphing tool

The Smartwork5 graphing interface consistently uses the same colors and notation as the in-text art to enhance continuity and reduce confusion. The interface is easy to understand and was designed for both computers and tablet devices. Students are invited to manipulate existing graphs or to draw their own graphs from scratch.

Answer-specific feedback and hints

Smartwork5 teaches students to problem-solve, not just solve a single problem. Many online homework systems only offer solution explanations after the student has answered a question. Smartwork5, in contrast, provides explanations throughout the problem-solving process, giving answer-specific feedback and hints for common misconceptions.

INQUIZITIVE

Award-winning InQuizitive is Norton's gamelike, adaptive quizzing and practice system. Developed and revised for the new edition with even more book-specific questions and content, this system lets students compete with themselves as they prepare their material for class. Demo InQuizitive at digital .wwnorton.com/prineco3.

Play with a purpose

Gaming elements built into InQuizitive engage students and motivate them to keep working. Students wager points on every question based on their confidence level, gain additional points for high success rates and on bonus questions, and can improve their grade by continuing to work questions in InQuizitive.

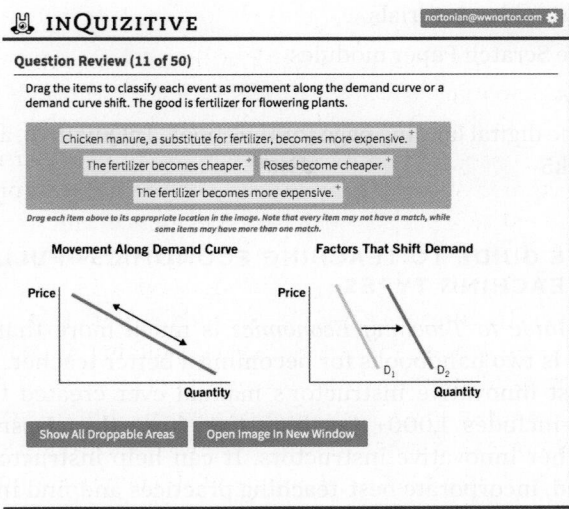

Inquizitive offers adaptive quizzing with gamelike features.

Active learning, helpful feedback

InQuizitive includes a variety of question types beyond basic multiple choice. Image-click, numeric entry, and various graph interpretation questions build economic skills and better prepare students for lecture, quizzes, and exams. Rich answer-specific feedback helps students understand their mistakes.

Easy to use, and integrates with your campus LMS

Instructors can set up InQuizitive for their students in less than 5 minutes. Students can access InQuizitive on tablet devices as well as on computers, making it easy to study on the go. InQuizitive integrates with campus learning management systems; when integration is enabled, grades flow automatically to campus LMS gradebooks. A single sign-on between the LMS and Norton digital products simplifies student access.

Formative assessment works

The efficacy of formative assessment is backed by education and psychology research (see inquizitive.wwnorton.com). Furthermore, performance-specific feedback, varied question types, and gaming elements built into InQuizitive have been shown to increase student engagement and retention of material.

NORTON COURSEPACK

Bring tutorial videos, assessment, and other online teaching resources directly into your new or existing online course with the Norton Coursepack. It's easily customizable and available for all major learning management systems, including Blackboard, Desire2Learn, Moodle, and Canvas.

The Norton Coursepack for *Principles of Economics* includes:

- Concept Check quizzes
- Homework quizzes

- Office Hours video tutorials
- Interactive Scratch Paper modules
- Flashcards
- Links to the digital landing page for the ebook, InQuizitive, and Smartwork5
- Test bank

THE ULTIMATE GUIDE TO TEACHING ECONOMICS—FULLY UPDATED WITH NEW TEACHING TYPES

The Ultimate Guide to Teaching Economics is much more than an instructor's manual; it is two handbooks for becoming a better teacher. *The Ultimate Guide*—the most innovative instructor's manual ever created for principles of economics—includes 1,000+ teaching tips from the classrooms of the authors and other innovative instructors. It can help instructors, both new and experienced, incorporate best-teaching practices and find inspiring ideas for enlivening their lectures.

The tips in *The Ultimate Guide to Teaching Microeconomics* and *The Ultimate Guide to Teaching Macroeconomics* include:

- Think-pair-share activities to promote small-group discussion and active learning
- "Recipes" for in-class activities and demonstrations that include descriptions of the activity, required materials, estimated length of time, estimated difficulty, recommended class size, and instructions. Improved and ready-to-use worksheets are also available for select activities, now with additional instructions to make them easier to use in class.
- Descriptions of movie clips, TV shows, commercials, and other videos that can be used in class to illustrate economic concepts
- Clicker questions and questions designed for other classroom signaling systems
- Ideas for music examples that can be used as lecture starters
- Suggestions for additional real-world examples to engage students
- A Taking It Online appendix in each chapter that shows how *The Ultimate Guide*'s class-tested teaching ideas can be adapted to online teaching environments
- Writing to Learn tips that give instructors short (one-page or less) paper prompts with ideas for potential student responses
- Worksheets and exercises to help you introduce and utilize the Federal Reserve's FRED economic data site in class.

Each chapter ends with solutions to the unsolved end-of-chapter problems in the textbook.

INTERACTIVE INSTRUCTOR'S GUIDE

The Interactive Instructor's Guide (IIG) brings all the great content from *The Ultimate Guide to Teaching Economics* into an online database that can be searched and filtered by a number of criteria, such as topic, chapter, key word, media format, and resource type. Instructors can even save their favorite assets to a list so they don't need to hunt for them each time they revisit the IIG.

To make it quick and easy for instructors to incorporate the tips from *The Ultimate Guide to Teaching Economics,* the IIG also includes:

- Downloadable versions of student worksheets for activities and demonstrations
- Downloadable PowerPoint slides for clicker questions
- Additional teaching resources not found in *The Ultimate Guide*

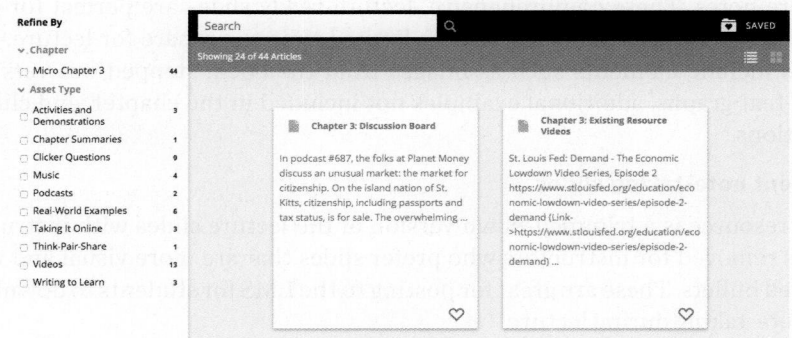

Interactive Instructor's Guide This searchable database of premium resources makes lecture development easy.

OFFICE HOURS VIDEO TUTORIALS

This collection of now more than 85 videos brings the office-hours experience online. Each video explains a fundamental concept. Videos were developed and filmed working with the authors, as well as a new team of presenters.

Perfect for online courses, each Office Hours video tutorial is succinct (90 seconds to 2 minutes in length) and mimics the office-hours experience. The videos focus on topics that are typically difficult to explain just in writing (or over email), such as shifting supply and demand curves.

The Office Hours videos have been incorporated throughout the Smartwork5 online homework system as video feedback for questions, integrated into the ebook, and included in the Norton Coursepack.

TEST BANK

NEW Two versions of the test bank are now available to better serve very large courses and offer you more question options for quizzes and tests each semester you teach. Each version has over 6,000 questions, with over 3,000 of those questions either new or substantively revised. Both test banks have been fully updated and expanded based on reviewer feedback. Each chapter includes between 100 and 150 questions and incorporates graphs and images where appropriate. The test bank has been developed using the Norton Assessment Guidelines. Each question in the test bank is classified according to Bloom's taxonomy of knowledge types (remembering, understanding and applying, analyzing and evaluating, and creating). Questions are further classified by section and difficulty, making it easy to construct tests and quizzes that are meaningful and diagnostic.

PRESENTATION TOOLS

Norton offers a variety of presentation tools so that new instructors and veteran instructors alike can find the resources that are best suited for their teaching style.

Enhanced lecture PowerPoint slides

NEW Revised lecture PowerPoints now also use key images from the text to convey complex economic concepts. All slides are supported with complete lecture notes. These comprehensive, lecture-ready slides are perfect for new instructors and instructors who have limited time to prepare for lecture. The slides include elements such as images from the book, stepped-out versions of in-text graphs, additional examples not included in the chapter, and clicker questions.

Student note-taking slides

This resource is a trimmed-down version of the lecture slides with instructor notes removed for instructors who prefer slides that are more visual and with limited bullets. These are great for posting to the LMS for students to download for note-taking during lecture.

Art slides and art JPEGs

For instructors who simply want to incorporate in-text art into their existing slides, all art from the book (tables, graphs, photos, and Snapshot infographics) is available in both PowerPoint and .jpeg formats. Stepped-out versions of in-text graphs and Snapshot infographics are also provided and optimized for screen projection.

DIRKMATEER.COM

Visit dirkmateer.com to find a library of hundreds of recommended movie and TV clips and links to online video sources to use in class.

LEECOPPOCK.COM

This blog serves as a one-stop-shop for all the "econ news you can use." Here you will find timely economic data, graphics, and teaching materials you will need to keep your course fresh and topical.

ACKNOWLEDGMENTS

We would like to thank the literally hundreds of fellow instructors who have helped us refine both our vision and the actual words on the page for three editions of this text. Without your help, we would never have gotten to the finish line. We hope that the result is the economics teacher's text that we set out to write.

Our class testers:

Jennifer Bailly, California State University, Long Beach
Mihajlo Balic, Harrisburg Community College
Erol Balkan, Hamilton College
Susan Bell, Seminole State College
Scott Benson, Idaho State University
Joe DaBoll-Lavoie, Nazareth College
Michael Dowell, California State University, Sacramento
Abdelaziz Farah, State University of New York, Orange
Shelby Frost, Georgia State University
Karl Geisler, University of Nevada, Reno
Nancy Griffin, Tyler Junior College
Lauren Heller, Berry College
John Hilston, Brevard Community College
Kim Holder, University of West Georgia
Todd Knoop, Cornell College
Katharine W. Kontak, Bowling Green State University
Daniel Kuester, Kansas State University

Herman Li, University of Nevada, Las Vegas
Gary Lyn, University of Massachusetts, Lowell
Kyle Mangum, Georgia State University
Shah Mehrabi, Montgomery College
Sean Mulholland, Stonehill College
Vincent Odock, State University of New York, Orange
J. Brian O'Roark, Robert Morris University
Michael Price, Georgia State University
Matthew Rousu, Susquehanna University
Tom Scales, Southside Virginia Community College
Tom Scheiding, University of Wisconsin, Stout
Clair Smith, St. John Fisher College
Tesa Stegner, Idaho State University
James Tierney, State University of New York, Plattsburgh
Nora Underwood, University of Central Florida
Michael Urbancic, University of Oregon
Marlon Williams, Lock Haven University

Our reviewers and advisors from focus groups:

Mark Abajian, California State University, San Marcos
Teshome Abebe, Eastern Illinois University
Casey R. Abington, Northwest Missouri State University
Charity-Joy Acchiardo, University of Arizona
Rebecca Achee Thornton, University of Houston
Mehdi Afiat, College of Southern Nevada
Carlos Aguilar, El Paso Community College
Clelia Aguirre, Miami Dade College
Seemi Ahmad, State University of New York, Dutchess
Abdullah Al-Bahrani, Northern Kentucky University
Frank Albritton, Seminole State College
Rashid Al-Hmoud, Texas Tech University
Farhad Ameen, Westchester Community College
Giuliana Andreopoulos, William Paterson University
Tom Andrews, West Chester University
Becca Arnold, San Diego Mesa College
Giant Aryani, Collin College
Lisa Augustyniak, Lake Michigan College
Dennis Avola, Bentley University

Roberto Ayala, California State University, Fullerton
Nahata Babu, University of Louisville
Philip Baca, New Mexico Military Institute
Sahar Bahmani, University of Wisconsin, Parkside
Diana Bajrami, Diablo Valley College
Ron Baker, Millersville University
Saad Bakir, Alabama State University
Mihajlo Balic, Harrisburg Area Community College
Kuntal Banerjee, Florida Atlantic University
Gyanendra Baral, Oklahoma City Community College
Ryan Baranowski, Coe College
Ruth Barney, Edison Community College
David Barrus, Brigham Young University, Idaho
Clare Battista, California Polytechnic State University
Jude Bayham, Washington State University
Mary Beal-Hodges, University of North Florida
Michael Bech, University of Southern Denmark
Stacie Beck, University of Delaware
Q Beckman, Delta College
Christian Beer, University of North Carolina, Wilmington

Jodi Beggs, Northeastern University
Richard Beil, Auburn University
Ari Belasen, Southern Illinois University
Doris Bennett, Jacksonville State University
Karen Bernhardt-Walther, The Ohio State University
Joel Beutel, Delta College
Prasun Bhattacharjee, East Tennessee State University
Richard Bilas, College of Charleston
Kelly Blanchard, Purdue University
Wesley Blundell, California State University, East Bay
Inácio Bo, Boston College
Michael Bognanno, Temple University
Antonio Bojanic, California State University, Sacramento
David Boldt, University of West Georgia
Michael Bonnal, University of Tennesse, Chattanooga
Heather Bono, University of West Georgia
Andrea Borchard, Hillsborough Community College
Feler Bose, Alma College
Inoussa Boubacar, University of Wisconsin, Stout
Donald Boudreaux, George Mason University
Austin Boyle, Penn State
Jared Boyd, Henry Ford Community College
Elissa Braunstein, Colorado State University
Elizabeth Breitbach, University of Southern California
Kristie Briggs, Creighton University
Stacey Brook, University of Iowa
Bruce Brown, California State Polytechnic University, Pomona
John Brown, Clark University
Vera Brusentsev, Swarthmore College
Laura Maria Bucila, Texas Christian University
Bryan Buckley, Northeastern State University
Benjamin Burden, Temple College
Richard Burkhauser, Cornell University
Whitney Buser, Young Harris College
W. Jennings Byrd, Troy University
Joseph Calhoun, Florida State University
Charles Callahan, State University of New York, Brockport
Douglas Campbell, University of Memphis
Giorgio Canarella, University of Nevada, Las Vegas
Laura Carolevschi, Winona State University
Nancy Carter, Kilgore College
Mike Casey, University of Central Arkansas
Amber Casolari, Riverside Community College
Nevin Cavusoglu, James Madison University
Valbona Cela, TriCounty Technical College
Semih Cekin, Texas Tech University
Rebecca Chambers, University of Delaware
Jason Chang, California Polytechnic State University, Pomona
Myong-Hun Chang, Cleveland State University
June Charles, North Lake College
Sanjukta Chaudhuri, University of Wisconsin, Eau Claire
Parama Chaudhury, University College of London
Chuiping Chen, American River College
Shuo Chen, State University of New York, Geneseo

Monica Cherry, State University of New York, Buffalo
Larry Chisesi, University of San Diego
David L. Cleeton, Illinois State University
Marcelo Clerici-Arias, Stanford University
Steve Cobb, University of North Texas
John Colletti, North Central College
Kristen Collett-Schmitt, University of Notre Dame
Rhonda Collier, Portland Community College
Simon Condliffe, West Chester University
Christopher K. Coombs, Louisiana State University
Michael Coon, Hood College
Gary Cooper, University of Minnesota
William Cooper, University of Kentucky
Doug Copeland, Johnson County Community College
Joab Corey, University of California, Riverside
Carlos Cortinhas, University of Exeter
Allen Coson, East Los Angeles College
Chad D. Cotti, University of Wisconsin, Oshkosh
Richard Cox, Arizona State University
Erik Craft, University of Richmond
Antoinette Criss, University of South Florida
Zachary Cronin, Hillsborough Community College
Glynice Crow, Wallace State Community College
Patrick Crowley, Texas A&M University, Corpus Christi
Sarah E. Culver, University of Alabama at Birmingham
Damian Damianov, University of Texas, Pan American
Morassa Danai, California State University, Fullerton
Alexander Danel, University of Virginia
Ribhi Daoud, Sinclair Community College
Patrick Dolenc, University of Massachusetts, Amherst
John Donahue, Estrella Mountain Community College
Oswaldo Donoso, Lone Star College, North Harris
Kacey Douglas, Mississippi State University
Whitney Douglas-Buser, Young Harris College
Chelsea Dowell, Upper Iowa University
Alissa Dubnicki
William Dupor, The Ohio State University
Renee Edwards, Houston Community College
Harold W. Elder, University of Alabama
Diantha Ellis, Abraham Baldwin Agricultural College
Harry Ellis, University of North Texas
Amani Elobeid, Iowa State University
Tisha Emerson, Baylor University
Lucas Englehardt, Kent State University
Michael Enz, Framingham State University
Erwin Erhardt, University of Cincinnati
Jonathan Ernest, Clemson University
Mary Ervin, El Paso Community College
Molly Espey, Clemson University
Jose Esteban, Palomar Community College
Sarah Estelle, Hope College
Patricia Euzent, University of Central Florida
Brent Evans, Mississippi State University
Carolyn Fabian Stumph, Indiana University–Purdue University, Fort Wayne
Leila Farivar, The Ohio State University

Ben Fitch-Fleischmann, University of Oregon
Va Nee Van Fleck, California State University, Fresno
Oscar Flores, Minnesota State University, Moorhead
Michael Forney, Austin Community College
Irene Foster, George Washington University
Roger Frantz, San Diego State University
Shelby Frost, Georgia State University
Gnel Gabrielyan, Washington State University
Craig Gallet, California State University, Sacramento
Susan Garrigan-Piela, Hudson Valley Community College
Wayne Geerling, Pennsylvania State University
Karl Geisler, Idaho State University
Elisabetta Gentile, University of Houston
Erin George, Hood College
Menelik Geremew, Texas Tech University
Linda Ghent, Eastern Illinois University
Dipak Ghosh, Emporia State University
Edgar Ghossoub, University of Texas at San Antonio
J. Robert Gillette, University of Kentucky
Gregory Gilpin, Montana State University
Joana Girante, Arizona State University
Lisa Gloege, Grand Rapids Community College
Robert Godby, University of Wyoming
John Goddeeris, Michigan State University
Rajeev Goel, Illinois State University
Bill Goffe, State University of New York, Oswego
Michael Gootzeit, University of Memphis
Aspen Gorry, Clemson University
Paul Graf, Indiana University, Bloomington
Alan Green, Stetson University
Barbara Grey, Brown Foundation
Natalia Grey, Southeastern Missouri State University
Daniel Grossman, West Virginia University
Jeremy Groves, Northern Illinois University
Sheryl Hadley, Johnson County Community College
Gail Hayne Hafer, St. Louis Community College
Dan Hamermesh, University of Texas at Austin
Gabriela Q. Hamilton, Hillsborough Community College-
Dale Mabry Campus
Mehdi Haririan, Bloomsburg University
Oskar Harmon, University of Connecticut
David Harrington, The Ohio State University
David Harris, Benedictine College
Darcy Hartman, The Ohio State University
Jenny Hawkins, Case Western Reserve University
John Hayfron, Western Washington University
Beth Haynes, East Tennessee State University
Jill Hayter, East Tennessee State University
Densie Hazlett, Whitman College
Phil Heap, James Madison University
Douglas Heiwig, Ivy Tech Community College
Marc Hellman, Oregon State University
Amy Henderson, St. Mary's College Maryland
Jessica Hennessey, Furman State
Wayne Hickenbottom, University of Texas at Austin
Mike Hilmer, San Diego State University

John Hilston, Eastern Florida State College
Ashley Hodgson, St. Olaf College
Adam Hoffer, University of Wisconsin, La Crosse
Jan Höffler, University of Göttingen
Lora Holcombe, Florida State University
Suneye Holmes, Spelman College
Charles Holt, University of Virginia
James Hornsten, Northwestern University
Nancy Howe, Hudson Valley Community College
Gail M. Hoyt, University of Kentucky
Yu-Mong Hsiao, Campbell University
Alice Hsiaw, College of the Holy Cross
Yu Hsing, Southeastern Louisiana University
Amanda Hughey, University of Delaware
Brad R. Humphreys, West Virginia University
Greg W. Hunter, California State Polytechnic University,
Pomona
Rebecca Innerarity, Angelina College
Miren Ivankovic, Anderson University
Oleg Ivashchenko, University of Albany
Meredith Jackson, Snead State Community College
Sarah Jenyk, Youngstown State University
Michal M. Jerzmanowski, Clemson University
Kristen Johnson, Metropolitan State University of Denver
Paul Johnson, University of Alaska, Anchorage
David Kalist, Shippensburg University of Pennsylvania
Mustafa Karakaplan, Oregon State University
Nicholas Karatjas, Indian University of Pennsylvania
Reza Karim, Des Moines Area Community College
Hossein Kazemi, Stonehill College
Janis Kea, West Valley College
Michael Kelley, Oakwood University
Sukanya Kemp, University of Akron
Carrie B. Kerekes, Florida Gulf Coast University
Frank Kim, University of San Diego
Sandra Kinel, Monroe Community College
Linda Kinney, Shepherd University
Vivian Kirby, Kennesaw State University
Ara Khanjian, Ventura College
Colin Knapp, University of Florida
Mary Knudson, University of Iowa
Brian Koralewski, Suffolk County Community College,
Ammerman
Dmitri Krichevskiy, Elizabethtown College
Lone Grønbæk Kronbak, University of Southern Denmark
Daniel Kuester, Kentucky State University
Jean Kujawa, Lourdes University
Sylvia Kuo, Brown University
MAJ James Lacovara, United States Military Academy at
West Point
Becky Lafrancois, Colorado School of Mines
Ermelinda Laho, LaGuardia Community College
Bree Lang, University of California, Riverside
David Lang, California State University, Sacramento
Ghislaine Lang, San Jose State University
Nancy Lang, Northern Kentucky University

Carsten Lange, California State Polytechnic University, Pomona
Tony Laramie, Merrimack College
Paul Larson, University of Delaware
Teresa Laughlin, Palomar College
Jason Lee, University of California, Merced
Logan Lee, University of Oregon
Jenny Lehman, Wharton County Junior College
Mike Leonard, Kwantlen Polytechnic
Tesa Leonce, Columbus State University
Amy Leung, Cosumnes River College
Eric Levy, Florida Atlantic University
Herman Li, University of Nevada, Las Vegas
Ishuan Li, Minnesota State University, Mankato
Daniel Lin, American University
Jaclyn Lindo, University of Hawaii, Manoa
Charles Link, University of Delaware
Delores Linton, Tarrant County College
Arthur Liu, East Carolina University
Bo Liu, Southern New Hampshire University
Weiwei Liu, Saginaw Valley State University
Xuepeng Liu, Kennesaw State University
Monika Lopez-Anuarbe, Connecticut College
Heriberto Lozano, Mississippi State University
Josephine Lugovskyy, University of Kansas
Ed Lukco, Ohio State University at Marion and Ohio Dominican University
Brian Lynch, Lake Land College
Martin Ma, Brigham Young University-Idaho
Lynn MacDonald, St. Cloud State University
Zachary Machunda, Minnesota State University, Moorhead
Bruce Madariaga, Montgomery College
Brinda Mahalingam, University of California, Riverside
Chowdhury Mahmoud, Concordia University
David Mahon, University of Delaware
Mark Maier, Glendale Community College
Lucy Malakar, Lorain County Community College
Len Malczynski, University of New Mexico
Ninos Malek, San Jose State University
Margaret Malixi, California State University, Bakersfield
Khawaja Mamun, Sacred Heart University
Nimantha Manamperi, St. Cloud University
Amber Mann, Corretta Scott King High School
Sonia Mansoor, Westminster College
Fady Mansour, Columbus State University
Daniel Marburger, Arkansas State University
Emily Marshall, Dickinson College
Kerry Martin, Wright State University
Erika Martinez, University of South Florida
Jim McAndrew, Luzerne County Community College
Michael McAvoy, State University of New York, Oneonta
Kate McClain, University of Georgia
Myra McCrickard, Bellarmine University
Cara McDaniel, Arizona State University
Scott McGann, Grossmont College
Christopher McIntosh, University of Minnesota, Duluth

Craig McLaren, University of California, Riverside
Kris McWhite, University of Georgia
Shah Mehrabi, Montgomery College
Mark Melichar, Tennessee Technical University
Diego Mendez-Carbajo, Illinois Wesleyan University
Evelina Mengova, California State University, Fullerton
William G. Mertens, University of Colorado, Boulder
Charles Meyrick, Housatonic Community College
Frannie Miller, Texas A&M University
Laurie Miller, University of Nebraska, Lincoln
Edward L. Millner, Virginia Commonwealth University
Ida Mirzaie, The Ohio State University
Kaustav Misra, Saginaw Valley State University
Kara Mitchell, Belmont University
Michael A. Mogavero, University of Notre Dame
Mehdi Mohaghegh, Norwich University
Conor Molloy, Suffolk County Community College
Moon Moon Haque, University of Memphis
Francis Mummery, Fullerton College
Sheena Murray, University of Colorado, Boulder
Yolunda Nabors, Tennessee Technical University
Max Nagiel, Daytona State University
Mijid Naranchimeg, Central Connecticut State University
Mike Nelson, Oregon State University
Gibson Nene, University of Minnesota, Duluth
Boris Nikolaev, University of South Florida
Jasminka, Ninkovic, Emory University
Caroline Noblet, University of Maine
Daniel Norgard, Normandale Community College
Stephen Norman, University of Washington, Tacoma
Farrokh Nourzad, Marquette University
Grace O, Georgia State University
Ichiro Obara, University of California, Los Angeles
Fola Odebunmi, Cypress College
Vincent Odock, State University of New York, Orange
Constantin Ogloblin, Georgia Southern University
Lee Ohanian, University of California, Los Angeles
Paul Okello, Tarrant County College
Gregory Okoro, Georgia Perimeter College, Clarkston Campus
Ifeakandu Okoye, Florida A&M University
Neal Olitsky, University of Massachusetts, Dartmouth
Martha Olney, University of California, Berkeley
EeCheng Ong, National University of Singapore
Stephen Onyeiwu, Allegheny College
Sandra Orozco-Aleman, Mississippi State University
Lynda Marie Ortega, Saint Phillip's College
Christopher Otrok, University of Missouri
Stephanie Owings, Fort Lewis College
Caroline Padgett, Francis Marion University
Jennifer Pakula, Saddleback College
Kerry Pannell, DePauw University
Pete Parcells, Whitman College
Darshak Patel, University of Kentucky
R. Scott Pearson, Charleston Southern University
Jodi Pelkowski, Wichita State University
Faye Peng, University of Wisconsin, Richland

Erica Perdue, Virginia Polytechnic Institute and State University
Andrew Perumal, University of Massachusetts, Boston
Brian Peterson, Central College
Dorothy Peterson, Washington University
Michael Petrowsky, Austin Community College
Van T.H. Pham, Salem State University
Rinaldo Pietrantonio, West Virginia University
Inna Pomorina, Bath Spa University
Steve Price, Butte College
Irina Pritchett, North Carolina State University
Guangjun Qu, Birmingham—Southern College
Jason Query, Western Washington University
Gabriela Quevado, Hillsborough Community College
Sarah Quintanar, University of Arkansas at Little Rock
Aleksander Radisich, Glendale Community College
Tobi Ragan, San Jose State University
Robi Ragan, Mercer University
Nahreen Rahman, University of Cincinnati
Mona Ray, Morehouse College
Ranajoy Ray-Chaudhuri, The Ohio State University
Mitchell Redlo, Monroe Community College
Dawn Renninger, Penn State Altoona
Ann Rhoads, Delaware State University
Jennifer Rhoads, St. Catharine University
Samual Riewe, Sonoma State University
Matthew Rolnick, City College of New York
Leanne Roncolato, American University
Debasis Rooj, Northern Illinois University
Brian Rosario, American River College
Ildiko Roth, North Idaho College
Matthew Rousu, Susquehanna University
Jason Rudbeck, University of Georgia
Nicholas G. Rupp, East Carolina University
Anne-Marie Ryan-Guest, Normandale Community College
Martin Sabo, Community College of Denver
Hilary Sackett, Westfield State University
Shrawantee Saha, College of St. Benedict
Ravi Samitamana, Daytona State College
Rolando Sanchez, Northwest Vista College
Jeff Sarbaum, University of North Carolina, Greensboro
Naveen Sarna, Northern Virginia Community College
Supriya Sarnikar, Westfield State University
Noriaki Sasaki, McHenry County College
Thomas Scheiding, University of Hawaii-West Oahu
Douglas Schneiderheinze, Lewis & Clark Community College
Jessica Schuring, Central College
Robert Schwab, University of Maryland
James Self, Indiana University, Bloomington
Sean Severe, Drake University
Sheikh Shahnawaz, California State University, Chico
Gina Shamshak, Goucher College
Neil Sheflin, Rutgers University
Brandon Sheridan, North Central College
Dorothy R. Siden, Salem State College
Cheri Sides, Lane College
Joe Silverman, Mira Costa College

Scott Simkins, North Carolina A&T State University
Robert Simonson, Minnesota State University, Mankato
Michael C. Slagel, College of Southern Idaho
Brian Sloboda, University of Phoenix
Gordon Smith, Anderson University
Kara Smith, Belmont University
John Solow, University of Iowa
Robert Sonora, Fort Lewis Collge
Todd Sorensen, University of California, Riverside
Maria Sorokina, West Virginia University
Christian Spielman, University College London
Denise Stanley, California State University, Fullerton
Leticia Starkov, Elgin Community College
Kalina Staub, University of North Carolina, Chapel Hill
Tesa Stegner, Idaho State University
Rebecca Stein, University of Pennsylvania
Joe Stenard, Hudson Valley Community College
Heather Stephens, California State University, Long Beach
Liliana Stern, Auburn University
Joshua Stillwagon, University of New Hampshire
Burak Sungu, Miami University
Paul Suozzo, Centralia College
Dan Sutter, Troy University
David Switzer, St. Cloud Sate University
Vera Tabakova, East Carolina University
Ariuna Taivan, University of Minnesota, Duluth
Yuan Emily Tang, University of California, San Diego
Anna Terzyan, Loyola Marymount University
David Thomas, Ball State University
Henry Thompson, Auburn University
James Tierney, Pennsylvania State University
Aleksander Tomic, Macon State College
Suzanne Toney, Savannah State University
Mehmet Tosun, University of Nevada, Reno
Steve Trost, Virginia Polytechnic Institute and State University
Mark Trueman, Macomb College
Melissa Trussell, College of Coastal Georgia
Phillip Tussing, Houston Community College
Nora Underwood, University of Central Florida
Gergory B. Upton, Jr., Louisiana State University
Mike Urbancic, University of Oregon
Jesus Valencia, Slippery Rock University
Robert Van Horn, University of Rhode Island
Adel Varghese, Texas A&M University
Marieta Velikova, Belmont University
Tatsuma Wada, Wayne State University
Jaime Wagner, University of Nebraska, Lincoln
Annie Walker, Boise State University
Will Walsh, Samford University
Yongqing Wang, University of Wisconsin, Waukesha
Mark V. Wheeler, Western Michigan University
Thomas White, Assumption College
Katie Wick, Abilene Christian University
Johnathan Wight, University of Richmond
Eric Wilbrandt, Auburn University

Nick Williams, University of Cincinnati
Douglas Wills, University of Washington, Tacoma
Ann Wimmer, Iowa Lakes Community College
Kafu Wong, University of Hong Kong
Kelvin Wong, University of Minnesota
Ken Woodward, Saddleback College
Jadrian Wooten, Washington State University
Ranita Wyatt, Paso-Hernando State College
Kuzey Yilmaz, Cleveland State University
Young-Ro Yoon, Wayne State University

Anne York, Meredith College
Han Yu, Southern Connecticut State University
Kristen Zaborski, State College of Florida
Arindra Zainal, Oregon State University
Erik Zemljic, Kent State University
Tianwei Zhang, University of Georgia
Ying Zhen, Wesleyan College
Dmytro Zhosan, Glendale Community College
Alex Zhylyevskyy, Iowa State University
Kent Zirlott, University of Alabama

All of the individuals listed above helped us to improve the text and ancillaries for the first three editions, but a smaller group of them offered us extraordinary insight and support. They went above and beyond, and we would like them to know just how much we appreciate it. In particular, we want to recognize Alicia Baik (University of Virginia), Jodi Beggs (Northeastern University), Dave Brown (Penn State University), Jennings Byrd (Troy University), Douglas Campbell (University of Memphis), Shelby Frost (Georgia State University), Wayne Geerling (Penn State University), Karl Geisler (Idaho State University), Paul Graf (Indiana University), Oskar Harmon (University of Connecticut), Jill Hayter (East Tennessee State University), Phil Heap (James Madison University), John Hilston (Brevard Community College), Kim Holder (University of West Georgia), Todd Knoop (Cornell College), Katie Kontak (Bowling Green State University), Brendan LaCerda (University of Virginia), Paul Larson (University of Delaware), David Mahon (University of Delaware), Lucy Malakar (Lorain County Community College), Kerry Martin (Wright State University), Kris McWhite (University of Georgia), Ida Mirzaie (The Ohio State University), Yolunda Nabors (Tennessee Technical University), Charles Newton (Houston Community College), Boris Nikolaev (University of South Florida), J. Brian O'Roark (Robert Morris University), Andrew Perumal (University of Massachusetts, Boston), Irina Pritchett (North Carolina State University), Robi Ragan (Mercer University), Matt Rousu (Susquehanna College), Tom Scheiding (University of Hawaii-West Oahu), Brandon Sheridan (North Central College), Clair Smith (Saint John Fisher College), James Tierney (Penn State University), Phillip Tussing (Houston Community College), Nora Underwood (University of Central Florida), Joseph Whitman (University of Florida), Erin Yetter (University of Arizona), Erik Zemljic (Kent State University), and Zhou Zhang (University of Virginia).

We would also like to thank our partners at W. W. Norton & Company, on all three editions, who have been as committed to this text as we've been. They have been a pleasure to work with and we hope that we get to work together for many years. We like to call them Team Econ: Melissa Atkin, Hannah Bachman, Jack Borrebach, Miryam Chandler, Cassie del Pilar, Laura Dragonette, Christina Fuery, Sam Glass, Jeannine Hennawi, John Kresse, Pete Lesser, Sasha Levitt, Lindsey Osteen, Eric Pier-Hocking, Jack Repcheck, Victoria Reuter, Spencer Richardson-Jones, Carson Russell, Nicole Sawa, Megan Schindel, Eric Svendsen, Elizabeth Trammel, Janise Turso, and Stefani Wallace. Our development editors, Becky Kohn, Steve Riglosi, and Kurt Norlin were a big help, as were our copy editors, Alice Vigliani, Janet Greenblatt, and Carla Barnwell. The visual appeal of the book is the result of our photo researchers, Dena Digilio Betz, Nelson Colón, and Ted Szczepanski, and the design teams at W. W. Norton and Kiss Me I'm Polish: Jen Montgomery, Debra Morton-Hoyt, Tiani Kennedy, Rubina Yeh, Agnieszka Gasparska, Andrew Janik, and Annie Song.

Finally, we would like to thank Kaitlyn Amos for the help she provided generating photo ideas, and Courtney Fox for helping to supply the idea for Figure 24.1. Thanks to all.

ABOUT THE AUTHORS

Dirk Mateer is the Gerald J. Swanson Chair in Economic Education at the University of Arizona. His research has appeared in the *Journal of Economic Education* as well as other journals and focuses on media-enriched learning. He is the author of *Economics in the Movies* (2005) and is an award-winning instructor. He has been featured in the "Great Teachers in Economics" series and he was also the inaugural winner of the Economic Communicator Contest sponsored by the Association of Private Enterprise Education. While he was at Penn State, he received the George W. Atherton Award, the university's highest teaching award, and was voted the best overall teacher in the Smeal College of Business by the readers of *Critique Magazine*. Now at Arizona, he received the best large class lecture award in the Eller College of Management.

Lee Coppock is professor of economics and director of undergraduate studies in the Department of Economics at the University of Virginia, where he has taught more than 15,000 students in principles of macroeconomics. He has received several teaching awards, including the 2017 Kenneth G. Elzinga Distinguished Teaching Award from the Southern Economics Association and the 2018 UVA Alumni Distinguished Professor Award. Along with Krista, his wife of 30 years, he has four children: Bethany, Lee III, Kara, and Jackson.

PRINCIPLES OF ECONOMICS

THIRD EDITION

PART

I

Introduction

Five Foundations
of Economics

Economics Is About More Than Money.

Have you ever thought about what it would be like to have a money tree in your backyard? Imagine walking outside, picking cash off the branches, and using it to buy whatever you desired. If that sounds too good to be true, it is—and not just because money doesn't grow on trees. The problem is, if money did grow on trees, it wouldn't be scarce. Everyone would have their own money tree, and therefore they wouldn't have any reason to give you something in return for the greenbacks you waved in front of them. You'd have all the money you could possibly want, and yet in practical terms you'd be as poor as if you had none at all.

The money-tree story teaches a lesson about the value-destroying nature of inflation; we'll get to that in a later chapter. But there's another, even more basic moral, namely that money itself is not really what we care about. What we care about is what we use money to acquire: the actual goods and services that make our lives more enjoyable.

Economist Carol Graham, who studies "the economics of happiness," argues that human happiness provides an alternative measure of well-being, one that covers more than a snapshot of people's finances at a single point in time. For many people, income is variable, with periods of unemployment causing them to move in and out of poverty. Even when these folks are working, uncertainty about the future subtracts from their happiness. Other people's variations in

A personal money tree would be awesome, especially if no one else had one!

income follow a more predictable course: these folks are relatively poor when young, earn more and build up savings during middle age, and then draw down those savings once they retire. These people, for the most part, avoid the happiness-undermining effects of financial uncertainty.

Money also can't tell us about neighborhood effects, like the fact that New York City is a way more expensive place to live than Charlottesville, Virginia, or Tubac, Arizona (where your authors live). These are some reasons why economists are concerned about human happiness just as much, if not more, than simply how much money you make.

This textbook provides the tools you need to fill in more of the picture and make your own assessments about the economy. What other discipline helps you discover how the world works, how to be an informed citizen, and how to live your life to the fullest? Economics can improve your understanding of the stock market and help you make better decisions. If you are concerned about Social Security, this textbook explains how it

Even in New York's pricey Greenwich Village, money doesn't grow on trees. The people living here do make a lot more money than most people, though. So do the residents of Miami Beach and Beverly Hills. Does that make them happier? Not necessarily.

works. If you are interested in learning more about the economics of health care and some of the challenges it faces, the answers are here.

In this chapter, you will learn about five foundations of economics—incentives, trade-offs, opportunity cost, marginal thinking, and the principle that trade creates value. You will find that many of the more complex problems presented later in the text are based on these foundations, either singly or in combination. Think of this chapter as a road map that provides a broad overview of your first journey into economics. Let's get started!

· BIG QUESTIONS ·

- What is economics?
- What are five foundations of economics?

What Is Economics?

Economists study how decisions are made. Examples of economic decisions include whether you should buy or lease a car, sublet your apartment, or buy that Gibson guitar you've been eyeing. And just as individuals must choose what to buy within the limits of their income, society as a whole must determine what to produce from its limited set of resources.

Of course, life would be a lot easier if we could have whatever we wanted whenever we wanted it. Unfortunately, life does not work that way. Our wants and needs are practically unlimited, but the resources available to satisfy these wants and needs are always limited. The term used to describe the limited nature of society's resources is **scarcity**. Even the most abundant resources, like the water we drink and the air we breathe, are not always abundant enough everywhere to meet the wants and needs of every person. So how do individuals and societies make decisions about scarce resources? This is the basic question economists seek to answer. **Economics** is the study of how individuals and societies allocate their limited resources to satisfy their practically unlimited wants.

Scarcity
refers to the inherently limited nature of society's resources, given society's unlimited wants and needs.

Economics
is the study of how individuals and societies allocate their limited resources to satisfy their practically unlimited wants.

Water is scarce...

...and so are diamonds!

Microeconomics and Macroeconomics

Microeconomics
is the study of the individual units that make up the economy.

Macroeconomics
is the study of the overall aspects and workings of an economy.

The study of economics is divided into two subfields: microeconomics and macroeconomics. **Microeconomics** (micro) is the study of the individual units that make up the economy, such as households and businesses. **Macroeconomics** (macro) is the study of the overall aspects and workings of an economy, such as inflation (an overall increase in prices), growth, employment, interest rates, and the productivity of the economy as a whole. To understand the difference, consider a worker who gets laid off and becomes unemployed. Is this an issue that would be addressed in microeconomics or macroeconomics? The question seems to fit parts of both definitions. The worker is an individual, which is micro, but employment is one of the broad areas of concern for the economy as a whole, which is macro. However, because only one worker is laid off, this is a micro issue. If many workers were laid off and the result was a higher unemployment rate across the entire economy, the issue would be broad enough to be studied by macroeconomists. However, macroeconomics is more than just an aggregation of microeconomics. Macroeconomists examine, among other things, government policies regarding the federal budget and money supply, the reasons for inflation and unemployment, economic growth, international trade, and government borrowing—topics that are too complex to be understood using only microeconomic analysis.

What Are Five Foundations of Economics?

The study of economics can be complicated, but we can make it very accessible by breaking it down into a set of component parts. The five foundations presented here are key components of economics. They are a bit like the natural laws of physics or chemistry. Almost every economic subject can be analyzed through the prism of one of these foundations. By mastering the five

Scarcity

NATION JUST WANTS TO BE SAFE, HAPPY, RICH, COMFORTABLE, ENTERTAINED AT ALL TIMES

A short video from the satirical website *The Onion* describes a fictitious report from the Pew Research Center, about what Americans want and expect from life. After a graphic details how practically all Americans would like to be everything from "safe" to "romantically fulfilled," the video segues to interviews with individuals whose "all I want" lists range from the endearing (a big happy dog) to the quirky (a new Wes Anderson movie), the unrealistic (quick and easy weight loss), and the impossible ("I don't want to die").

We live in a world of scarcity. But that alone doesn't explain why we're unable to meet everyone's wants. Couldn't we just redistribute goods and services more evenly, to satisfy everyone? No chance, because our wants exceed our needs, and when all our wants are met, we come up with new ones. Many people spend their lives trying to "keep up with the Joneses." This isn't all bad, because competitive drive causes people to work longer and harder, which makes the economy more productive. At the same time, when we purchase

Safe	97%
Happy	100%
Rich	98%
Comfortable	99%
Entertained	100%
Thin	96%

Based on a fictitious report on the satirical website *The Onion,* this graphic shows what Americans want. Of course, part of the joke is that this is not far from the truth for most of us, right?

one good, we have less to spend on other goods we also desire, and therefore we face trade-offs and opportunity costs.

foundations, you will be on your way to succeeding in this course and thinking like an economist. The five foundations of economics are:

- Incentives
- Trade-offs
- Opportunity cost
- Marginal thinking
- Trade creates value

Each of these five foundations reappears throughout the book and enables you to solve complex problems. Every time you encounter one of the five concepts, you will see an icon of a house in the margin. As you become more adept at economic analysis, you will often use two or more of these foundational ideas to understand the economic world around you.

Incentives
Trade-offs
Opportunity cost
Marginal thinking
Trade creates value

Incentives

Incentives
are factors that motivate a
person to act or exert effort.

When you are faced with making a decision, you usually make the choice that you think will most improve your situation. In making your decision, you respond to **incentives**—factors that motivate you to act or exert effort. For example, your choice to study for an exam you have tomorrow, instead of spending the evening with your friends, is based on your belief that doing well on the exam will provide a greater benefit. You have an incentive to study because you know that an A in the course will raise your grade-point average and make you a more attractive candidate on the job market when you are finished with school. We can further divide incentives into two paired categories: positive and negative; and direct and indirect.

PRACTICE WHAT YOU KNOW

Microeconomics and Macroeconomics: The Big Picture

Decide whether each of the following statements identifies a microeconomic issue or a macroeconomic issue.

STATEMENT: The national savings rate is less than 2% of income.

ANSWER: The national savings rate is a statistic based on the average amount each household saves as a percentage of income. As such, it is a broad measure of savings that describes a macroeconomic issue.

STATEMENT: Maya was laid off from her job and is currently unemployed.

This mosaic of the flag illustrates the difference between micro and macro. The tiny pictures represent microeconomics and the roles that individual decisions play in the overall health of the economy, which is the composite we see when we look at the entire picture.

ANSWER: Maya's personal financial circumstances constitute a microeconomic issue, because she is an individual worker.

STATEMENT: Apple decides to open 100 new stores.

ANSWER: Even though Apple is a very large corporation and 100 new stores will create many new jobs, Apple's decision is a microeconomic issue because it is best understood as part of an individual firm's competitive strategy.

STATEMENT: The government passes a jobs bill designed to stabilize the economy during a recession (an economic downturn).

ANSWER: You might be tempted to ask how many jobs are created, but that information is not relevant to answering this question. The key part of the statement refers to "stabilize the economy during a recession," which is an example of the government taking an active role in managing the overall workings of the economy. Therefore, it is a macroeconomic issue.

POSITIVE AND NEGATIVE INCENTIVES *Positive incentives* encourage action by offering rewards or payments. For example, end-of-year bonuses motivate employees to work hard throughout the year, higher oil prices cause suppliers to extract more oil, and tax rebates encourage citizens to spend more money. *Negative incentives* discourage action by providing undesirable consequences or punishments. For instance, the fear of receiving a speeding ticket keeps motorists from driving too fast, higher oil prices might spur some consumers to use less oil, and the dread of a trip to the dentist motivates people to brush their teeth regularly. In each case, we see that incentives spur individuals to action.

Conventional wisdom tells us that "learning is its own reward," but try telling that to most students. Teachers are aware that incentives, both positive and negative, create additional interest among their students to learn the course material. Positive incentives include bonus points, gold stars, public praise, and extra credit. Many students respond to these encouragements by studying more. However, positive incentives are not enough. Suppose your instructor never gave any grade lower than an A. Your incentive to participate actively in the course, do assignments, or earn bonus points would be small. For positive incentives to work, they generally need to be coupled with negative incentives. This is why instructors require students to complete assignments, take exams, and write papers. Students know that if they do not complete these requirements, they will get a lower grade, or perhaps even fail the class.

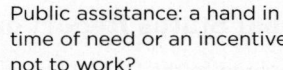

Incentives

DIRECT AND INDIRECT INCENTIVES Incentives can also be direct or indirect. For instance, if one gas station lowers its prices, it most likely will get business from customers who would not usually stop there. This is a *direct incentive*. Lower gasoline prices also work as an *indirect incentive*, because lower prices might encourage consumers to use more gas.

Direct incentives are easy to recognize. "Cut my grass and I'll pay you $30" is an example of a direct incentive. Indirect incentives are more difficult to recognize. But learning to recognize them is one of the keys to mastering economics. For instance, consider the indirect incentives at work in welfare programs. Almost everyone agrees that societies should provide a safety net for those without employment or whose income isn't enough to meet their basic needs. In other words, a society has a direct incentive to alleviate suffering caused by poverty. But how does a society provide this safety net without taking away the incentive to work? If the amount of welfare a person receives is higher than the amount that person can hope to make from a job, the welfare recipient might decide to stay on welfare rather than go to work. The indirect incentive to stay on welfare creates an *unintended consequence*: people who were supposed to use government assistance as a safety net until they can find a job use it instead as a permanent source of income.

Policymakers have the tough task of deciding how to balance such conflicting incentives. To decrease the likelihood that a person will stay on welfare, policymakers could cut benefits. But this decision might leave some people without enough to live on. For this reason, many

Public assistance: a hand in time of need or an incentive not to work?

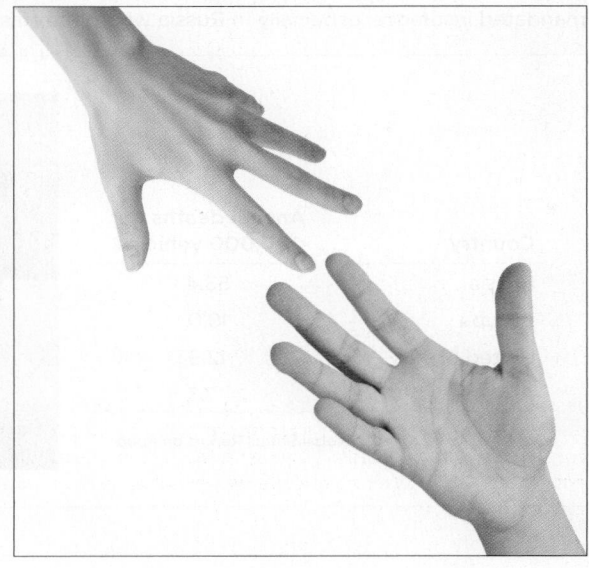

government programs specify limits on the amount of time people can receive benefits. Ideally, this limit allows the welfare programs to continue meeting people's basic needs while creating incentives that encourage recipients to search for a job and acquire skills that will help them get a job. We'll learn more about welfare issues in Chapter 15.

ECONOMICS IN THE REAL WORLD

WHY ARE THERE SO MANY DASHBOARD CAMERAS IN RUSSIA?

Let's look at an example of how incentives operate in the real world and how they can produce surprising consequences. Compared to the United States, Russia is quite a dangerous place to drive (see Figure 1.1). On top of the collisions that occur due to chaotic traffic conditions, insurance scammers regularly stage accidents. To protect themselves against scammers, most Russian motorists have "dash cams," which provide video evidence of a driver's innocence in court. The fact that so many Russian drivers are willing to invest in dash cams strongly suggests that the benefits of having a cam exceed the cost.

In the United States, and in most other countries where there are fewer annual deaths (and accidents) per vehicle, staged accidents are much less common, and consequently dash cams are much less prevalent.

FIGURE 1.1

Global Status Report on Safety

Compared to the United States, Russia is quite a dangerous place to drive. Widespread insurance scamming in Russia has led most motorists to install dash cams. The fact that insurance scammers exist is an unintended consequence of mandated insurance, especially in Russia where the rules of the road and safe driving are often ignored.

Country	Annual deaths per 100,000 vehicles
Russia	53.4
Europe	19.0
United States	12.9
Australia	7.3

Source: See, WHO, ed., "Global Status Report on Road Safety 2015" (2015).

INCENTIVES AND INNOVATION Incentives also play a vital role in innovation, the engine of economic growth. An excellent example is Steve Jobs. He and the company he founded, Apple, held over 300 patents at the time of his death in 2011.

In the United States, the patent system and copyright laws guarantee inventors a specific period of time in which they have the exclusive right to sell their work. This system encourages innovation by creating a powerful financial reward for creativity. Without patents and copyright laws, inventors would bear all the costs, and almost none of the rewards, for their efforts. Why would firms invest in research and development or artists create new music if others could immediately copy and sell their work? To reward the perspiration and inspiration required for innovation, society allows patents and copyrights to create the right incentives for economic growth.

In recent years, new forms of technology have made the illegal sharing of copyrighted material quite easy. As a result, illegal downloads of books, music, and movies are widespread. When writers, musicians, actors, and studios cannot effectively protect what they have created, they earn less. So illegal downloads reduce the incentive to produce new content. Will the next John Lennon or Jay-Z work so hard? Will the next Suzanne Collins (author of *The Hunger Games*) or J. K. Rowling (author of the Harry Potter books) hone their writing craft so diligently if there is so much less financial reward for success? Is the "I want it for free" culture causing the truly gifted to be less committed to their craft, thus depriving society of excellence? Maintaining the right rewards, or incentives, for hard work and innovation is essential for making sure that inventors and other creative people are compensated for their creativity and vision. Some see services like Spotify, Tidal, and Soundcloud as the answer. While streaming services are now very successful, the amount artists receive is still far lower than is used to be.

Incentives

INCENTIVES ARE EVERYWHERE One very powerful incentive is saving time. You can test out your time-savings skills when you walk across campus to a class. An app will give you a detailed route and an estimated time of arrival, but your app won't know the local shortcuts. Sometimes the shortcuts everyone takes are through buildings or along dirt paths. Sometimes all you have to do is crowdsource the best route by following others. The paths worn into greens by students' feet will show you how to get across campus as quickly as possible.

Understanding incentives, from positive to negative and direct to indirect, is the key to understanding economics. If you remember only one concept from this course, it should be that incentives matter.

Trade-Offs

In a world of scarcity, each and every decision incurs a cost. Even time is a scarce resource; after all, there are only 24 hours in a day. So deciding to play Fortnite now means you won't be able to read one of the

Taking a shortcut saves time.

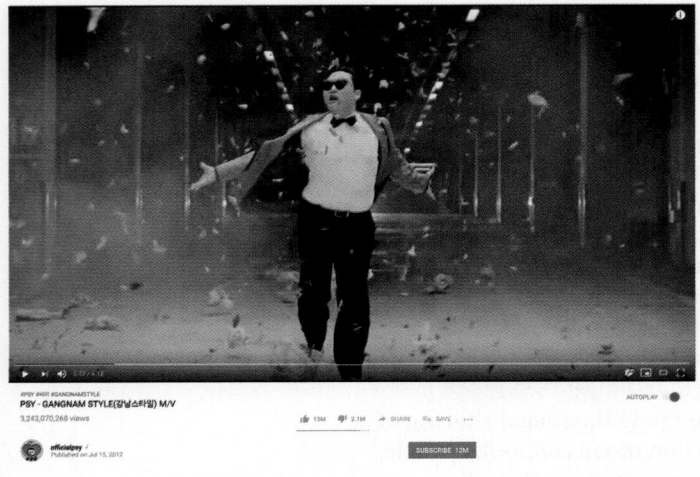

PSY - GANGNAM STYLE(강남스타일) M/V

3,243,070,268 views

officialpsy
Published on Jul 15, 2012

SUBSCRIBE 12M

What might have been achieved in the time it has taken to watch this video over 3 billion times?

Trade-offs

Harry Potter books until later. More generally, doing one thing often means you will not have the time, resources, or energy to do something else. Similarly, paying for a college education can require spending tens of thousands of dollars that might be used elsewhere instead.

Understanding the trade-offs that exist in life can completely change how you view the world. Let's look at Psy's song "Gangnam Style." The video for this song has been viewed over 3 billion times on YouTube, making it one of the most watched videos of all time. Imagine what could have been accomplished if people had used that time differently. *The Economist* magazine considered this question and came up with a list of the trade-offs. "Gangnam Style" is 4 minutes and 12 seconds long, which means that more than 200 million hours have been spent watching the video. In the same amount of time, eight Burj Khalifas (one of the world's tallest buildings, located in Dubai, United Arab Emirates) or five Great Egyptian Pyramids could have been built or the entire contents of Wikipedia entered—twice!

People who don't understand economics sometimes ignore the trade-offs that are natural in a world of scarcity. They unconsciously assume that we can (as individuals or a group) have more of everything we want. But in fact, decision-making generally involves trade-offs. For example, if you decide to increase your time allotment for studying economics, you need to give up something else: you might study less for other courses, work fewer hours at your job, or socialize less. That is, there is a trade-off between higher economics grades and other things you desire. As a nation, we may wish to increase subsidies to college education, or to increase international aid, or to strengthen our national defense. Economists are the ones who then ask: What about the trade-offs? That is, what must we give up to increase spending on education or international aid, or on a stronger military?

Here's how President Dwight Eisenhower put the point in a 1953 speech:

> The cost of one modern heavy bomber is this: a modern brick school in more than 30 cities. It is two electric power plants, each serving a town of 60,000 population. It is two fine, fully equipped hospitals. It is some 50 miles of concrete highway. We pay for a single fighter plane with a half million bushels of wheat. We pay for a single destroyer with new homes that could have housed more than 8,000 people.

Ultimately, thinking about trade-offs means that we will make more informed decisions about how to utilize our scarce resources.

Opportunity Cost

Opportunity cost

The existence of trade-offs requires making hard decisions. Trade-offs are about having to give something up, and opportunity cost quantifies "what" or "how much" is being given up. Choosing one thing means giving up something else. Suppose you receive two invitations—the first to spend the day hiking and the second to go to a concert—and both events occur at the same time. No matter which event you choose, you have to sacrifice the other option. In this example, you can think of the cost of going to the concert as the lost opportunity to go on the hike. Likewise, the cost of going hiking is the lost opportunity to go to the concert. No matter what choice you make, there is an opportunity cost, or next-best alternative, that must be sacrificed. **Opportunity cost** is the highest-valued alternative that must be sacrificed to get something else.

Every time we make a choice, we experience an opportunity cost. The key to making the best possible decision is to minimize your opportunity cost by selecting the option that gives you the largest benefit. If you prefer going to a concert, you should go to the concert. What you give up (the hike) has less value to you than the concert, so it represents an opportunity cost.

The hiking/concert choice is a simple and clear example of opportunity cost. Usually, it takes deliberate effort to see the world through the opportunity cost prism. But it is a worthwhile practice because it will help you make better decisions. For example, imagine you are a small business owner. Your financial officer informs you that you have had a successful year and made a sizable profit. So everything is good, right? Not so fast. An economist will tell you to ask yourself, "Could I have made *more* profit doing something else?" Good economic thinkers ask this question all the time. "Could I be using my time, talents, or energy on another activity that would be even more profitable for me?"

Profits on an official income statement are only part of the story, because they only measure how well a business does relative to the bottom line. Accountants cannot measure what *might* have been better. For example, suppose you had decided not to open a new store. A few months later, a rival opened a very successful store in the same location you had considered. Your profits were good for the year, but if you had opened the new store, your profits could have been even better. So when economists talk about opportunity cost, they are assessing whether the alternatives are better than what you are currently doing, which considers a larger set of possible outcomes.

Before Ellen DeGeneres achieved stardom, she spent one semester studying communication at the University of New Orleans. Ellen defied the usual wisdom about staying in school and completing her degree, because she understood opportunity cost. Given her show's success and her entrepreneurial acumen starting a number of successful derivative companies, it is hard to fault her decision. If Ellen had finished her degree, she most likely never would have become the likeable star we know today.

Can you come up with a witty one-liner as fast as Ellen can?

Opportunity cost

The Opportunity Cost of Attending College

QUESTION: What is the opportunity cost of attending college?

ANSWER: When people think about the cost of attending college, they usually think of tuition, room and board, course materials, and travel-related expenses. While those

Spending thousands on college expenses? You could be working instead!

expenses are indeed a part of going to college, they are not its full cost. The opportunity cost is the next-best alternative that is sacrificed. This opportunity cost—or what you potentially could have done if you were not in college—includes the lost income you could have earned working a full-time job. If you consider the cost of attending college plus the forgone income lost while in college, you can see that college is a very expensive proposition. Setting aside the question of how much more you might have to pay for room and board at college rather than elsewhere, consider the cost of tuition, which can be $40,000 or more at many of the nation's most expensive colleges. Add that out-of-pocket expense to the forgone income from a full-time job that might pay $40,000 a year, and your four years in college can easily cost over a quarter of a million dollars.

CHALLENGE QUESTION: Ellen DeGeneres honed her trademark comedy routines in small venues until she became famous. But for every Ellen, there are thousands of other comedians who never made it big. What advice would you give to someone wrestling with the decision to leave college?

ANSWER: The question is tricky. We can't know the future, and staying in college and leaving college both have opportunity costs. By staying, you forgo the opportunity to try new things and, perhaps, discover in the process something else you excel at. However, leaving means a college degree will not be part of your resume. Making decisions when there is uncertainty about how the future will unfold is what makes choices difficult, because there are opportunity costs in both directions.

ECONOMICS IN THE REAL WORLD

HOW LONG WOULD YOU WAIT IN LINE ON BLACK FRIDAY TO SAVE $300?

How long would you wait in line to save $300?

A few years ago in Beaumont, California, Vicky Torres and Juanita Alva were first in line to secure a large-screen television at Best Buy during the Black Friday Sale. The TV they wanted was advertised at $199. Let's say that was a markdown from $499. How many hours would you wait in line to save $300? Two hours? Five? Ten? How about 500 hours? That's how long the two women waited, because they arrived *three weeks* early. By all accounts they enjoyed their time waiting, spending their days talking to strangers and taking turns saving each other's spots in line over night. However, there's an opportunity cost here that makes Vicky and Juanita's decision puzzling. Think of the many trade-offs they faced: missed sleep, time they could have spent with friends and family, and the time they could be working instead of waiting in line, to name just a few. It is hard to justify the women's choices using marginal analysis. Saving $300 by spending 500 hours makes their time worth 60 cents an hour. They could have spent 30 hours working an extra job at $10 an hour and each earned enough money to purchase the TV at full price—and still had 470 hours to do other things. In short, they don't seem to have been aware of the opportunity cost of waiting in line.

Marginal Thinking

The process of systematically evaluating a course of action is called economic thinking. **Economic thinking** involves a purposeful evaluation of the available opportunities to make the best decision possible. In this context, economic thinkers use a process called *marginal analysis* to break down decisions into smaller parts. Often, the choice is not between doing and not doing something, but between doing more or less of something. For instance, if you take on a part-time job while in school, you probably wrestle with the question of how many hours to work. If you work a little more, you can earn additional income. If you work a little less, you have more time to study. Working more has a tangible benefit (more money) and a tangible cost (lower grades). All of this should sound familiar from our earlier discussion about trade-offs. The work-study trade-off affects how much money you have and what kind of grades you earn.

An economist would say that your decision—weighing how much money you want against the grades you want—is a decision at the *margin*. What exactly does the word "margin" mean as used in economics? In economics, **marginal thinking** requires decision-makers to evaluate whether the benefit of one more unit of something is greater than its cost. Understanding how to analyze decisions at the margin is essential to thinking like a good economist.

For example, have you ever wondered why people vacuum, dust, scrub the bathrooms, clean out their garages, and wash their windows, but leave the dust bunnies under the refrigerator? The answer lies in thinking at the margin. Moving the refrigerator out from the wall to clean requires a significant effort for a small benefit. Guests who enter the kitchen can't see under the refrigerator. So most of us ignore the dust bunnies and just clean the visible areas of our homes. In other words, when economists say you should think at the margin, what they really mean is that you should weigh the costs and benefits of your actions and choose to do the things with the greatest payoff. For most of us, that means being willing to live with dust bunnies. The *marginal cost* of cleaning under the refrigerator (or on top of the cabinets or even behind the sofa cushions) is too high, and the added value of making the effort, or the *marginal benefit*, is too low to justify the additional cleaning.

Trade

Imagine trying to find food in a world without grocery stores. The task of getting what you need to eat each day would require visiting many separate locations. Many centuries ago, this need to bring buyers and sellers together was met by weekly markets, or bazaars, in central locations like town squares. **Markets** bring buyers and sellers together to exchange goods and services. As commerce spread throughout the ancient world, trade routes developed. Markets grew from infrequent gatherings, where exchange involved trading goods and services for other goods and services, into more sophisticated systems that use cash, credit, and other financial instruments. Today, when we think of markets, we often think of eBay or Craigslist. For instance, if you want to find a rare Hot Wheels Black Panther Movie Die-Cast Vehicle, an excellent place to look is eBay, which allows users to search for just about any product, bid on it, and then have it sent directly to their home.

Economic thinking
requires a purposeful evaluation of the available opportunities to make the best decision possible.

Marginal thinking
requires decision-makers to evaluate whether the benefit of one more unit of something is greater than its cost.

Marginal thinking

Markets
bring buyers and sellers together to exchange goods and services.

Trade creates value

THE CIRCULAR FLOW When we consider all the trade that occurs in an economy, it is helpful to use a **circular flow diagram**. This shows how goods, services, and resources flow through the economy via commerce between households and firms. Households are made up of consumers, as we usually picture them. Firms are businesses. Households desire the goods and services produced by firms, but to produce those goods and services, firms require the resources owned by households. The circular flow diagram illustrates the movement of goods, services, and resources that results when firms and households do business with each other.

In the circular flow in Figure 1.2, households are on the left and firms on the right. Households buy goods and services from firms in product markets, at the top of the diagram. This is the kind of transaction you undertake all the time: when you buy groceries or school supplies, you purchase these in product markets, from firms. But households are also sellers, in that they provide the inputs or resources that firms use to produce their output. These transactions take place in resource markets, at the bottom of the diagram. When you put in time at your job and get a paycheck in return, that is a resource market transaction.

The green arrows that form the counterclockwise outer loop show goods and services flowing from firms to households across the top of the circle and resources flowing from households to firms across the bottom. Goods, services, and resources are paid for with *funds*. The red arrows forming the inner loop show how funds flow in the opposite direction of whatever they are paying for. Each loop is closed. On the outside, resources go into the production of goods and services, which in turn go into sustaining households so they can continue to provide firms with resources. On the inside, funds are transferred from households' bank accounts to firms' accounts as

---

FIGURE 1.2

The Circular Flow

Goods and services move counterclockwise from one part of the economy to another. Firms produce goods and services and trade them for funds from households in the product market. Households sell resources to produce goods and services in the resource market. The circular flow of goods and services appears as the green outer loop, and the circular flow of funds to purchase goods and services appears as the red inner loop.

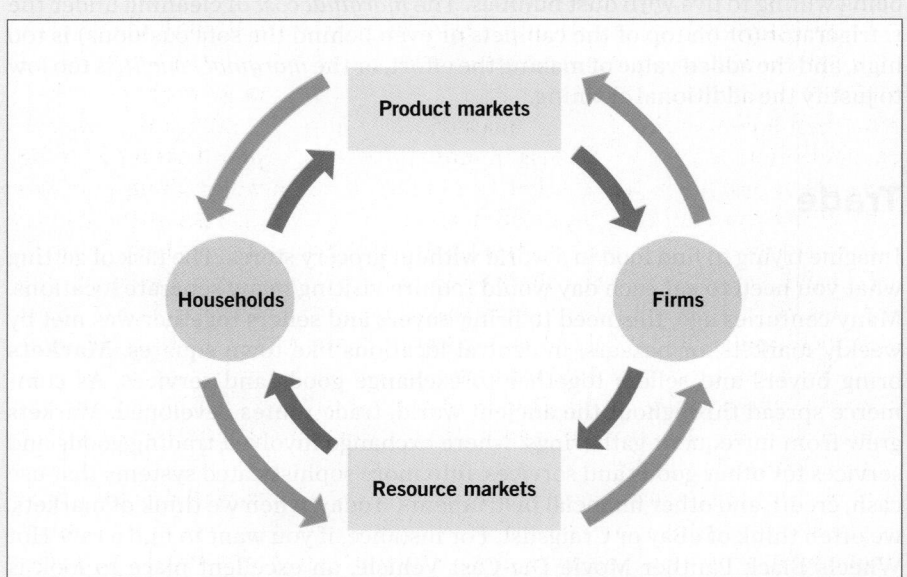

payment for goods and services, and then return to households as payment for resources.

Consider a simple example. Let's say you spend $1,000 on a new Dell computer. You trade for your computer in a product market, and Dell gets the $1,000: this takes place in the top half of the circular flow diagram. Then Dell uses the $1,000 to pay its workers' wages and other suppliers for the use of resources. This happens in the bottom half of the diagram. In the end, the funds make the complete circuit back to households.

This simple circular flow diagram leaves out some details. For one thing, government is an important player in any economy. Funds flow into and out of governments, which participate in both the product and resource markets. In addition, households and firms also interact with foreign firms and households. We consider the roles of government and foreign firms and households later in the text, but for now, this simple circular flow diagram serves as a schematic summary of how households and firms interact through trade in an economy.

TRADE CREATES VALUE **Trade** is the voluntary exchange of goods and services between two or more parties. Voluntary trade among rational individuals creates value for everyone involved. Imagine you are on your way home from class and you want to pick up a gallon of milk. You know that milk will be more expensive at a convenience store than at the grocery store 5 miles away, but you are in a hurry to study for your economics exam and are willing to pay up to $5 for the convenience of getting the milk quickly. At the store, you find that the price is $4 and you happily purchase the milk. This ability to buy for less than the price you are willing to pay provides a positive incentive to make the purchase. But what about the seller? If the store owner paid $3 to buy the milk from a supplier, and you are willing to pay the $4 price she has set in order to make a profit, the store owner has an incentive to sell. This simple voluntary transaction has made both of you better off.

By fostering the exchange of goods, trade helps to create additional growth through specialization. **Comparative advantage** refers to the situation in which an individual, business, or country can produce at a lower opportunity cost than a competitor can. Comparative advantage harnesses the power of specialization, a topic we discuss in more detail in Chapter 2. As a result, it is possible to be a physician, teacher, or plumber and not worry about how to do everything yourself. The physician becomes proficient at dispensing medical advice, the teacher at helping students, and the plumber at fixing leaks. The physician and the teacher call the plumber when they need work on their plumbing. The teacher and the plumber see the doctor when they are sick. The physician and the plumber send their children to school to learn from the teacher.

The same process is at work among businesses. For instance, Starbucks specializes in making coffee, Honda in making automobiles. You would not want to get your morning cup of joe at Honda any more than you would want to buy a car from Starbucks!

On a broader scale, specialization and trading of services exist at the international level as well. Some countries have highly developed workforces capable of managing and solving complex processes. Other countries have large pools of relatively unskilled labor. As a result, businesses that need skilled labor gravitate to countries where they can easily find the workers they need. Likewise,

Trade
is the voluntary exchange of goods and services between two or more parties.

Incentives
Trade creates value

Comparative advantage
refers to the situation where an individual, business, or country can produce at a lower opportunity cost than a competitor can.

Our economy depends on specialization.

firms with production processes that rely on unskilled labor look for employees in less developed countries, where workers are paid less. By harnessing the power of increased specialization, global companies and economies create value through increased production and growth.

However, globalized trade is not without controversy. When goods and jobs are free to move across borders, not everyone benefits equally, nor should we expect this outcome. Consider the case of a U.S. worker who loses her job when her position is outsourced to a call center in India. The jobless worker now has to find new employment—a process that requires significant time and energy. In contrast, the new position in the call center in India provides a job and an income that improve the life of another worker. Also, the U.S. firm enjoys the advantage of being able to hire lower-cost labor elsewhere. The firm's lower costs often translate into lower prices for domestic consumers. None of those advantages make the outsourcing of jobs any less painful for affected workers, but outsourcing is an important component of economic growth in the long run.

Conclusion

Economists ask, and answer, big questions about life. This is what makes the study of economics so fascinating. Understanding how an entire economy functions may seem like a daunting task, but it is not nearly as difficult as it sounds. Remember when you learned to drive? At first, everything was difficult and unfamiliar. But as you probably found, becoming a good driver is just a matter of mastering a few key principles, and then, with a little experience under your belt, you can drive any car on the road. In the same way, once you have learned the fundamentals of economics, you can use them to analyze almost any problem. In the next chapter, we use the ideas developed in this chapter to explore trade in greater depth. ✳

Five Foundations of Economics

In this book, we study five foundations of economics—incentives, trade-offs, opportunity cost, marginal thinking, and the principle that trade creates value. Once you have mastered these five concepts, even complex economic processes can be reduced to smaller, more easily understood parts. If you keep these foundations in mind, you'll find that understanding economics is rewarding and fun.

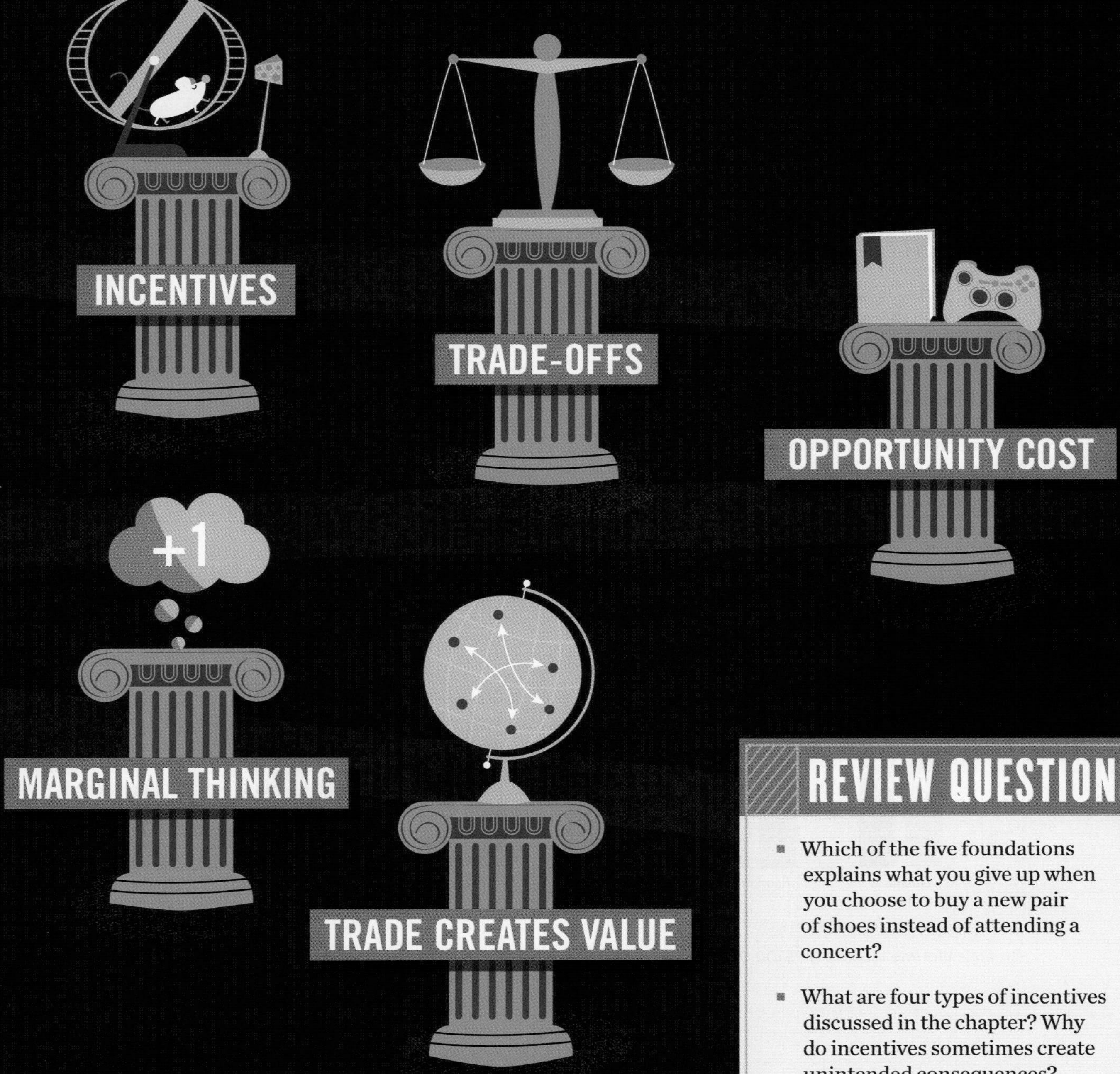

INCENTIVES

TRADE-OFFS

OPPORTUNITY COST

MARGINAL THINKING

TRADE CREATES VALUE

REVIEW QUESTIONS

- Which of the five foundations explains what you give up when you choose to buy a new pair of shoes instead of attending a concert?

- What are four types of incentives discussed in the chapter? Why do incentives sometimes create unintended consequences?

So You Wanna Be a Billionaire? Study Economics

- Economics majors are more likely to become billionaires than majors in any other subject.
- Economics majors, on average, make 3.4 million dollars in career earnings.
- Economics majors are also top performers on the Law School Admission Test.

Travie McCoy and Bruno Mars collaborated on the mega-hit "Billionaire" in 2010. Little did they know that majors in economics are most likely to make the Forbes 400, a list of the richest people in the United States. In this graphic, we report the six majors that produce the highest number of billionaires and cross-reference those findings with projected lifetime earnings to give you a sense of how much the average college graduate with one of these degrees is likely to earn. We've intentionally used lifetime earnings, since they are a better indicator of financial well-being than the typical starting salary ranges you might be more familiar with. It is how much money you make over your entire career that matters!

Majoring in economics gives you the best chance of becoming a billionaire.

The financial rewards are nice, but that's not the only reason to choose economics. Economics majors are also versatile in other ways: they are top performers on the LSAT (Law School Admission Test) and are in demand as policy experts, consultants, and forecasters.

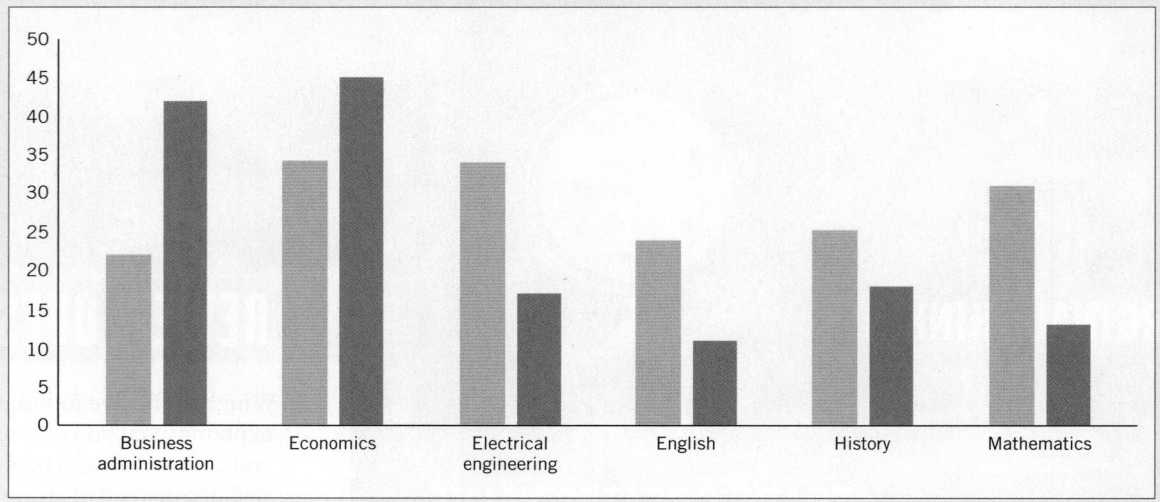

Green is lifetime income (in $100,000s) and red is the number of billionaires in the Forbes 400.

· ANSWERING *the* BIG QUESTIONS ·

What is economics?

- Economics is the study of how people allocate their limited resources to satisfy their practically unlimited wants. Because of the limited nature of society's resources, even the most abundant resources are not always plentiful enough everywhere to meet the wants and needs of every person. So how do individuals and societies make decisions about how to use the scarce resources at their disposal? This is the basic question economists seek to answer.

What are five foundations of economics?

Five foundations of economics are incentives, trade-offs, opportunity cost, marginal thinking, and the principle that trade creates value.

- Incentives are important because they help explain how rational decisions are made.
- Trade-offs exist when a decision-maker has to choose a course of action.
- Each time we make a choice, we experience an opportunity cost, or a lost chance to do something else.
- Marginal thinking requires a decision-maker to weigh the extra benefits against the extra costs.
- Trade creates value because participants in markets are able to specialize in the production of goods and services they have a comparative advantage in making.

· CHAPTER PROBLEMS ·

Concepts You Should Know

circular flow diagram (p. 18)
comparative advantage (p. 19)
economics (p. 7)
economic thinking (p. 17)

incentives (p. 10)
macroeconomics (p. 8)
marginal thinking (p. 17)
markets (p. 17)

microeconomics (p. 8)
opportunity cost (p. 15)
scarcity (p. 7)
trade (p. 19)

Questions for Review

1. How would you respond if your instructor gave daily quizzes on the course readings? Are these quizzes a positive incentive or a negative incentive?

2. Explain why many seniors often earn lower grades in their last semester before graduation. (**Hint:** This is an incentive problem.)

3. What is the opportunity cost of reading this textbook?

4. Evaluate the following statement: "Trade is like football: one team wins and the other loses."

Study Problems (*solved at the end of the section)

* 1. What role do incentives play in each of the following situations? Are there any unintended consequences?
    a. You learn you can resell a ticket to next week's homecoming game for twice what you paid.
    b. A state government announces a "sales tax holiday" for back-to-school shopping during one week each August.

2. Compare your standard of living with that of your parents when they were the age you are now. Ask them or somebody you know around their age to recall where they were living and what they owned. How has the well-being of the typical person changed over the last 25 years? Explain your answer.

3. By referencing events in the news or something from your personal experiences, describe one example of each of the five foundations of economics discussed in this chapter.

* 4. Suppose that Colombia is good at growing coffee but not very good at making computer software and that Canada is good at making computer software but not very good at growing coffee. If Colombia decided only to grow coffee and Canada only to make computer software, would both countries be better off or worse off? Explain. Can you think of a similar example from your life?

5. After some consideration, you decide to hire someone to help you move from one apartment to another. Wouldn't it be cheaper to move yourself? Do you think the choice to hire someone is a rational choice? Explain your response.

* 6. When a town gets snowed in for a couple of days— the urban legend goes—the local hospital is likely to see a boost in births nine months later. In other words: blizzards might be prime baby-making time. Explain, using *economic* reasoning, why snowstorms may indeed cause an uptick in births nine months down the road.

7. *Whiplash* (2014) is about an aspiring college-age drummer who wants to become the best drummer in the world. He is willing to sacrifice personal relationships, practices tens of thousands of hours, and suffers mental and physical abuse from his teacher in order to achieve his goal and earn the recognition he craves. Watch the full movie trailer on IMDB.com or go to www.youtube.com/watch?v=MsWlktW0kj4 and watch the break-up scene with his girlfriend. What trade-offs are you making in your life right now to achieve your goals?

✴ **8.** We have talked about how trade creates value. Use the information in each example below to compute the total value created in each exchange:

  a. Patrick bought an orange pen from Jill for $2.00. Patrick would have been willing to pay $2.50 for the pen, and Jill would have been willing to sell the pen for $1.25.

  b. Hillary found a car on Craigslist for which she would have been willing to pay up to $10,000. The car's owner, Jason, needed to sell the car right away and would have accepted $6,000. The price they agreed on was $7,500.

9. What concept best explains why you wouldn't want to make your own clothes completely from scratch and instead will normally prefer to buy them from a retailer?

Solved Problems

1.a. Because your tickets are worth more than you paid for them, you have a direct positive incentive to resell them.

  b. The "sales tax holiday" is a direct positive incentive to buy more clothes during the back-to-school period. An unintended consequence of this policy is that fewer purchases are likely to be made both before and after the tax holiday.

4. If Colombia decided to specialize in the production of coffee, it could trade coffee to Canada in exchange for computer software. This process illustrates gains from specialization and trade. Both countries have a comparative advantage in producing one particular good. Colombia has ideal coffee-growing conditions, and Canada has a workforce that is more adept at writing software. Since both countries specialize in what they do best, they are able to produce more value than they could produce by trying to make both products on their own.

6. The situation has changed the incentives people face. In other words, the perceived costs and benefits of their choices have changed. Inclement weather makes it more costly to go outside; thus, more people will choose to stay home and engage in at-home activities.

8.a. In this example, Patrick is better off by $0.50, because he was willing to pay $2.50 but paid just $2.00. And Jill is better off by $0.75, because she would have accepted $1.25 but received $2.00. So the total value created is the additional value to Patrick ($0.50) plus the additional value to Jill ($0.75), which sums to $1.25.

  b. The value added for Jason is $1,500, which is the difference between the minimum price he would have accepted ($6,000) and the price he received ($7,500). The value added for Hillary is $2,500, which is the difference between the maximum price she would have paid ($10,000) and the price she actually paid ($7,500). In total, $1,500 + $2,500 = $4,000 in new value was created through the exchange.

Model Building and
Gains from Trade

When People Trade, Both Sides Normally Win.

It's only common sense that trade benefits both parties. After all, if it's voluntary, both sides must be getting something out of it. But there's more to the story: we can quantify the extent to which trade makes each side better off. We do this by establishing how much more productive a person can become through trade, given that trade allows people to specialize in what they're good at. That's what we're going to learn about in this chapter.

Consider the interaction between a contractor and an architect. They each have a vital role to play in the building process. The architect designs the plans to the buyer's specifications. The contractor is an expert at bringing the architect's design to fruition by organizing the equipment, supplies, and labor to complete the project on time. The architect is the creative genius and the contractor is a genius at managing the construction workflow. The architect understands how to design plans that pass engineering tests and meet building codes. The contractor understands the supply chain. By specializing, each becomes more productive and gets their part of the project done faster, trading their expertise and time for monetary payment.

In 2004, world-renowned architect Zaha Hadid became the first woman to win the Pritzker Architecture Prize. She was well aware that building her designs, like this Riverside Museum in Glasgow, Scotland, required the work of many specialized builders, all managed by a highly skilled contractor. She also looked to other specialists for creative inspiration. "Our designs become more ambitious," she says, "as we see the new possibilities created by the technology of other industries."

To help understand how trade works, we will develop our first economic model, the production possibilities frontier, so we can explore the more nuanced reasons why trade creates value.

· BIG QUESTIONS ·

- How do economists study the economy?
- What is a production possibilities frontier?
- What are the benefits of specialization and trade?
- What is the trade-off between having more now and having more later?

How Do Economists Study the Economy?

Economics is a social science that uses the scientific method to develop *economic models*. To create these models, economists make many assumptions to simplify reality. These models help economists understand the key relationships that drive economic decisions.

The Scientific Method in Economics

The television show *MythBusters* puts popular myths to the test by replicating the circumstances and then showing the results. The entire show is dedicated to scientific testing of the myths. At the end of each episode, the myth is confirmed, deemed plausible, or busted. For instance, in a memorable episode, the show explored the reasons behind the *Hindenburg* disaster. The *Hindenburg* was a German passenger airship, or zeppelin, that caught fire and became engulfed in flames as it attempted to dock in New Jersey on May 6, 1937. Thirty-six people died.

Some people have claimed that the fire was sparked by the painted fabric in which the zeppelin was wrapped. Others have suggested that the hydrogen used to give the airship lift was the primary cause of the disaster. To test the hypothesis (proposed explanation) that the paint used on the fabric was to blame, the MythBusters built two small-scale models. The first model was filled with hydrogen and had a nonflammable skin. The second model used a replica of the original fabric for the skin but did not contain any hydrogen. Hyneman and Savage then compared their models' burn times with original footage of the disaster.

After examining the results, they "busted" the myth that the paint was to blame. Why? The model containing the hydrogen burned twice as fast as the one with just the painted fabric skin. It seems reasonable to conclude that hydrogen caused the disaster, not paint.

Economists work in much the same way as the Myth-Busters: they use the scientific method to answer questions about observable phenomena and to explain how the world works. The scientific method consists of four steps:

- First, researchers observe a phenomenon that interests them.
- Next, based on these observations, researchers develop a *hypothesis*, which is a proposed explanation for the phenomenon.
- Then they construct a model to test the hypothesis.
- Finally, they look for opportunities to test how well the model (which is based on the hypothesis) works. After collecting data, they use statistical methods to verify, revise, or refute the hypothesis.

The scientific method was used to discover why the *Hindenburg* caught fire.

The economist's laboratory is the world around us, and it ranges from the economy as a whole to the decisions made by firms and individuals. As a result, economists cannot always design experiments to test their hypotheses. Often, they must gather historical data or wait for real-world events to take place—for example, the Great Recession (economic downturn) of 2007–2009—to better understand the economy. When real-world events meet the criteria of an experiment designed to test a hypothesis, we have what's called a *natural* experiment.

Positive and Normative Analysis

As scientists, economists strive to approach their subject with objectivity. This means they rigorously avoid letting personal beliefs and values influence the outcome of their analysis. To be as objective as possible, economists deploy positive analysis. A **positive statement** can be tested and validated. Each positive statement can be thought of as a description of "what is." For instance, the statement "The unemployment rate is declining" is a positive statement, because it can be tested by gathering data. If the unemployment rate is indeed going down, then the statement is true, whereas if instead unemployment is rising, the statement is false.

A **positive statement** can be tested and validated; it describes "what is."

In contrast, a **normative statement** cannot be tested or validated; it is about "what ought to be." For instance, the statement "An unemployed worker should receive financial assistance to help make ends meet" is a matter of opinion. One can reasonably argue that financial assistance to the unemployed is beneficial for society as a whole because it helps eliminate poverty. However, many argue that financial assistance to the unemployed provides the wrong incentives. If the financial assistance provides enough to meet basic needs, workers may end up spending more time unemployed than they otherwise would. Neither opinion is right or wrong; they are differing viewpoints based on values, beliefs, and opinions.

A **normative statement** is an opinion that cannot be tested or validated; it describes "what ought to be."

Incentives

The Wright brothers' wind tunnel.

Economists are concerned with positive analysis. In contrast, normative statements are the realm of policymakers, voters, and philosophers. For example, if the unemployment rate rises, economists try to understand the conditions that created the situation. Economics does not attempt to determine who should receive unemployment assistance, which involves normative analysis. Maintaining a positive framework is crucial for economic analysis because it allows decision-makers to observe the facts objectively.

Economic Models

Thinking like an economist means learning how to analyze complex issues and problems. Many economic topics, such as international trade, Social Security, job loss, and inflation, are complicated. To analyze these phenomena and to determine the effect of various government policy options related to them, economists use economic models, which are simplified versions of reality. Models help us analyze the components of the economy.

A good model should be simple, flexible, and useful for making accurate predictions. Let's consider one of the most famous models in history, designed by Wilbur and Orville Wright. Before the Wright brothers made their famous first flight in 1903, they built a small wind tunnel out of a 6-foot-long wooden box. Inside the box they placed a device to measure aerodynamics, and at one end they attached a small fan to supply the wind. The brothers then tested over 200 different wing configurations to determine the lifting properties of each design. Using the data they collected, the Wright brothers were able to determine the best type of wing to use on their aircraft.

Similarly, economic models provide frameworks that help us to predict the effects of changes in prices, production processes, and government policies on real-life behavior.

Ceteris paribus
[pronounced KETeris PAReebus] means "other things being equal" or "all else equal" and is used to build economic models. It allows economists to examine a change in one variable while holding everything else constant.

CETERIS PARIBUS Using a controlled setting that held many other variables constant enabled the Wright brothers to experiment with different wing designs. By altering only a single element—for example, the angle of the wing—they could test whether the change in design was advantageous. The process of examining a change in one variable while holding everything else constant involves a concept known as **ceteris paribus**, from the Latin meaning "other things being equal" or "all else equal."

The *ceteris paribus* assumption is central to model building. If the Wright brothers had changed many design elements simultaneously and found that a new version of the wing worked better, they would have had no way of knowing which change was responsible for the improved performance. For this reason, engineers generally modify only one design element at a time and test only that one element before testing additional elements.

Like the Wright brothers, economists start with a simplified version of reality. Economists build models, change one variable at a time, and ask whether the change in the variable had a positive or negative impact on performance. Perhaps the best-known economic model is supply and demand, which we study in Chapter 3.

ENDOGENOUS VERSUS EXOGENOUS FACTORS Models must account for factors we can control (*endogenous*) and factors we can't (*exogenous*). Factors that are accounted for inside the model are **endogenous factors**. The Wright brothers' wind tunnel was critical to their success because it allowed them to control for as many endogenous factors as possible. For example, the wind tunnel enabled the Wright brothers to see how well each wing design—an important part of the model—performed under controlled conditions.

Factors beyond our control—outside the model—are **exogenous factors**. Once the Wright brothers had determined the best wing design, they built the full-scale airplane that took flight at Kitty Hawk, North Carolina. At that point the plane, known as the "Flyer," was no longer in a controlled environment. It was subject to the gusting wind and other exogenous factors that made the first flight so challenging.

Building an economic model is very similar to the process Wilbur and Orville used. We need to be mindful of three factors: (1) what we include in the model, (2) the assumptions we make when choosing what to include in the model, and (3) the outside conditions that can affect the model's performance. In the case of the first airplane, the design was an endogenous factor because it was within the Wright brothers' control. In contrast, the weather (wind, air pressure, and other atmospheric conditions) was an exogenous factor because the Wright brothers could not control it. Because the world is a complex place, an airplane model that flies perfectly in a wind tunnel may not fly reliably when it is exposed to the elements. Therefore, if we add more exogenous variables, or factors we cannot control—for example, wind and rain—to test our model's performance, the test becomes more realistic.

> **Endogenous factors** are the variables that are inside a model.

> **Exogenous factors** are the variables that are outside a model.

THE IMPORTANCE OF ASSUMPTIONS When we build a model, we need to make choices about which variables to include. Ideally, we would like to include all the important variables inside the model and exclude all the variables that can safely be ignored. Then we have made reasonable simplifying assumptions. Excluding the wrong variables, on the other hand, can lead to spectacular failures. So can making *false* assumptions. An excellent example is the financial crisis and Great Recession that began in December 2007.

In the years leading up to the crisis, banks sold and repackaged mortgage-backed investments under the faulty assumption that real estate prices will always rise. This assumption seemed perfectly reasonable in a world where real estate prices were rising annually. Unfortunately, the assumption turned out to be false. From 2007 to 2008, real estate prices fell dramatically. Because of one faulty assumption, the entire financial market teetered on the edge of collapse.

Throughout this textbook we will assume that firms and households are rational benefit-maximizers who both respond to incentives predictably and thoughtfully consider the costs and benefits of their actions. Rationality is a cornerstone of most economic theory. It's a simplifying assumption, and in Chapter 17 we will see how it sometimes fails in real life, but for the most part we treat it as 'true enough.'

> In the early 2000s, some investors believed that real estate prices could only rise.

Positive versus Normative Statements

QUESTION: Which of the following statements are positive and which ones are normative?

1. Winters in Arkansas are too cold.

2. Everyone should work at a bank to learn the true value of money.

3. The current exchange rate is 0.7 British pound per U.S. dollar.

4. On average, people save 15% on insurance when they switch to Geico.

5. Everyone ought to have a life insurance policy.

6. University of Virginia graduates earn more than Duke University graduates.

7. Harvard University is the top educational institution in the country.

8. The average January temperature in Fargo, North Dakota, is 56°F.

ANSWERS

1. The phrase "too cold" is a matter of opinion. This is a normative statement.

2. While working at a bank might give someone an appreciation for the value of money, the word "should" indicates an opinion. This is a normative statement.

3. This is a positive statement. You can look up the current exchange rate and verify if this statement is true or false.

4. Geico made this claim in one of its commercials. It is a positive statement because it is a testable claim. If you had the data from Geico, you could determine if the statement were correct or not.

5. This sounds like a true statement, or at least a very sensible one. However, the word "ought" makes it an opinion. This is a normative statement.

6. You can look up the data and see which university's graduates earn more. This is a positive statement.

7. Some national rankings indicate that this statement is true, but others do not. Because different rankings are based on different assumptions, it is not possible to identify a definitive "top" school. This is a normative statement.

8. This is a positive statement, but the statement is wrong. North Dakota is much colder than that in January. The statement can be verified (in this case, proved wrong) by climate data.

CHALLENGE QUESTION: Some statements aren't simple declarative sentences but instead take the form of hypotheticals. Are the following hypotheticals positive or normative?

9. If Steph Curry makes 50% of his two-point shots and 40% of his three-point shots, his "effective field goal percentage" calculates higher than 50% since this statistic weighs three-point shots more than two-point shots.

10. If Steph Curry makes 40% of his three-point shots, he should shoot only three-pointers.

11. If you earn a college degree, you may earn less income than someone who only completes high school.

12. If you earn a college degree, you should share what you learned with the less fortunate.

NBA star Steph Curry has made three-pointers his trademark.

ANSWERS

9. This hypothetical statement is mathematically verifiable, so the statement is positive.

10. This is a hypothetical statement where the second part is an opinion, so the statement is normative.

11. This statement is factually verifiable, so the statement is positive.

12. The second part of this statement is an opinion, so the statement is normative.

What Is a Production Possibilities Frontier?

Now it's time to learn our first economic model. However, before you go on, you might want to review the appendix on graphing at the end of this chapter. Graphs are a key tool in economics because they display the relationship between two variables. Your ability to read a graph and understand the model it represents is crucial to learning economics.

In Chapter 1, we learned that economics is about the trade-offs individuals and societies face every day. For instance, you may frequently have to decide between spending more time studying or hanging out with your friends. The more time you study, the less time you have for your friends. Similarly, a society has to determine how to allocate its resources. The decision to build new roads will mean that there is less money available for new schools, and vice versa.

A **production possibilities frontier (PPF)** is a model that illustrates the combinations of outputs a society can produce if all of its resources are being used efficiently. An outcome is considered *efficient* when resources are fully utilized and potential output is maximized. To preserve *ceteris paribus,* we assume that the technology available for production and the quantity of resources remain fixed, or constant. These assumptions allow us to model trade-offs more clearly.

Let's begin by imagining a society that produces only two goods—pizza and chicken wings. This may not seem like a very realistic assumption, since a real economy produces millions of different goods and services, but this approach helps us understand trade-offs by keeping the analysis simple.

Figure 2.1 shows the production possibilities frontier for our simplified two-product society. Remember that the number of people and the total resources in this two-product society are fixed. If the economy uses all of its resources to produce pizza, it can produce 100 pizzas and 0 wings. If it uses all of its resources to produce wings, it can make 300 wings and 0 pizzas. These outcomes are represented by points A and B, respectively, on the production possibilities frontier. It is unlikely the society will choose either of these extreme outcomes, because it is human nature to enjoy variety.

If our theoretical society decides to spend some of its resources producing pizzas and some of its resources making wings, its economy will end up with a combination of pizza and wings somewhere along the PPF between points A and B. At point C, for example, the society would deploy its resources to produce

Trade-offs

A **production possibilities frontier (PPF)** is a model that illustrates the combinations of outputs a society can produce if all of its resources are being used efficiently.

FIGURE 2.1

The Production Possibilities Frontier for Pizza and Chicken Wings

The production possibilities frontier (PPF) shows the trade-off between producing pizza and producing wings. Any combination of pizza and wings is possible along, or inside, the line. Combinations of pizza and wings beyond the production possibilities frontier—for example, at point E—are not possible with the current set of resources. Point F and any other points located in the shaded region are inefficient.

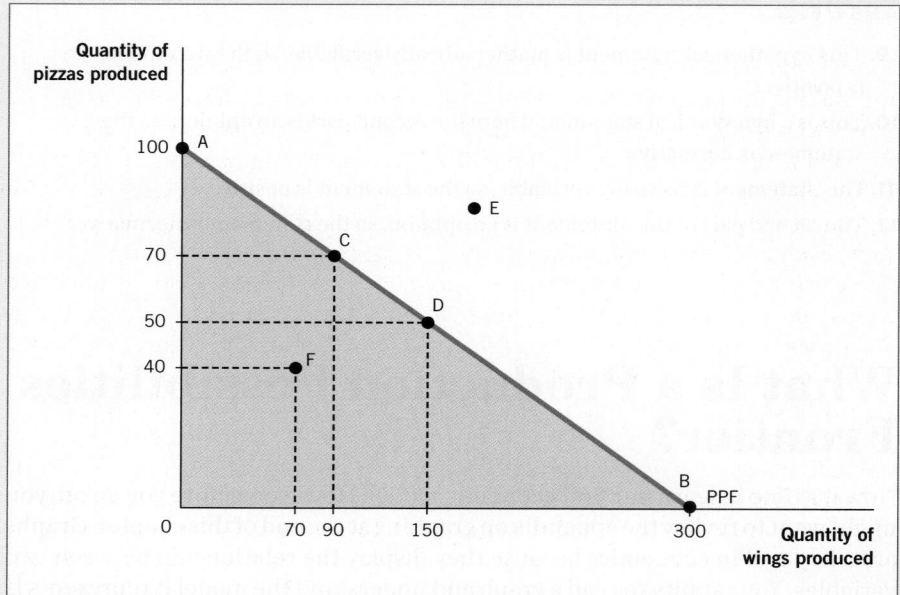

70 pizzas and 90 wings. At point D, the combination would be 50 pizzas and 150 wings. Each point along the production possibilities frontier represents a possible set of outcomes the society can choose if it uses all of its resources efficiently.

Notice that some combinations of pizza and wings cannot be produced because not enough resources are available. Our theoretical society would enjoy point E, but given the available resources, it cannot produce that output level. Points beyond the production possibilities frontier are desirable but not feasible with the available resources and technology.

At any combination of wings and pizzas along the production possibilities frontier, the society is using all of its resources in the most efficient way possible. But what about point F and any other points located in the shaded region? These points represent outcomes inside the production possibilities frontier, and they indicate an inefficient use of the society's resources. Consider, for example, the labor resource. If employees spend many hours at work surfing the Web instead of doing their jobs, the output of pizza and wings will drop and the outcome will no longer be efficient. As long as workers use all of their time efficiently, they will produce an efficient amount of pizza and wings, and output will lie somewhere on the PPF.

Whenever society is producing on the production possibilities frontier, the only way to get more of one good is to accept less of another. Because an economy operating at a point on the frontier will be efficient, every point on the frontier represents full-capacity output. But a society may favor one point over another because it prefers that combination of goods. For example, in our theoretical two-good society, if wings suddenly become more popular, the movement from point C to point D will represent a desirable trade-off. The society will produce 20 fewer pizzas (decreasing from 70 to 50) but 60 additional wings (increasing from 90 to 150).

Trade-offs

The Production Possibilities Frontier and Opportunity Cost

Because our two-good society produces only pizza and wings, the trade-offs that occur along the production possibilities frontier represent the opportunity cost of producing one good instead of the other. As we saw in Chapter 1, an opportunity cost is the highest-valued alternative given up to pursue another course of action. As Figure 2.1 shows, when society moves from point C to point D, it gives up 20 pizzas; this is the opportunity cost of producing more wings. The movement from point D to point C has an opportunity cost of 60 wings.

Until now, we have assumed a constant trade-off between the number of pizzas and the number of wings produced. However, not all resources in our theoretical society are perfectly adaptable for use in making pizza and wings. Some workers are good at making pizza, and others are not so good. When the society tries to make as many pizzas as possible, it will be using both types of workers. That is, to get more pizzas, the society will have to use workers who are increasingly less skilled at making them. For this reason, pizza production will not expand at a constant rate. You can see this effect in the new production possibilities frontier in Figure 2.2; it is bowed outward rather than a straight line.

Opportunity cost

FIGURE 2.2

The Law of Increasing Opportunity Cost

To make more pizzas, the society will have to use workers who are increasingly less skilled at making them. As a result, as we move up along the PPF, the opportunity cost of producing an extra 20 pizzas rises from 30 wings between points D and C to 80 wings between points B and A.

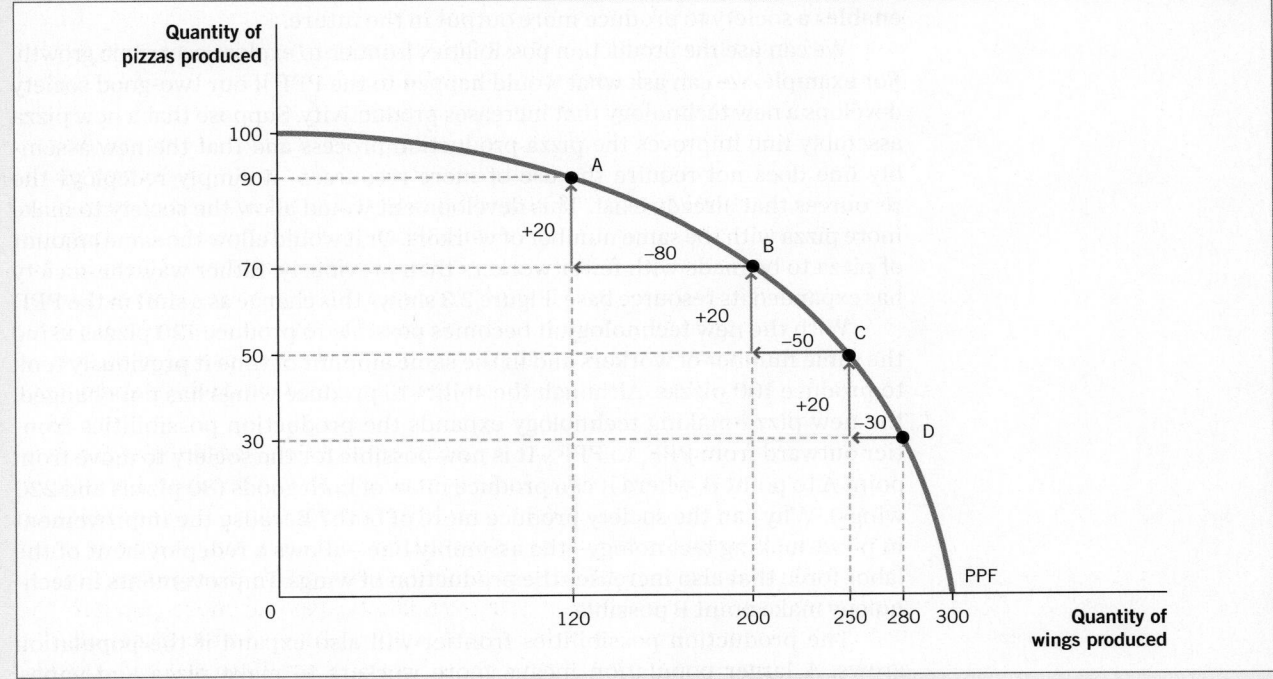

Opportunity cost

Because resources are not perfectly adaptable, production does not expand at a constant rate. For example, to produce 20 extra pizzas, the society can move from point D (30 pizzas) to point C (50 pizzas). But moving from point D (280 wings) to point C (250 wings) means giving up 30 wings. So moving from point D to point C has an opportunity cost of 30 wings.

Now suppose that the society decides it wants even more pizzas and moves from point C (50 pizzas) to point B (70 pizzas). Now the opportunity cost of 20 more pizzas is 50 wings, because wing production declines from 250 to 200. If the society decides that 70 pizzas are not enough, it can expand pizza production from point B (70 pizzas) to point A (90 pizzas). Now the society gives up 80 wings. Notice that as we move up along the PPF from point D to point A, the opportunity cost of producing an extra 20 pizzas rises from 30 wings to 80 wings. This higher opportunity cost reflects the increased trade-off necessary to produce more pizzas.

The **law of increasing opportunity cost** states that the opportunity cost of producing a good rises as a society produces more of it.

A bowed-out production possibilities frontier reflects the increasing opportunity cost of production. Figure 2.2 illustrates the **law of increasing opportunity cost**, which states that the opportunity cost of producing a good rises as a society produces more of it. Changes in relative cost mean that a society faces a significant trade-off if it tries to produce an extremely large amount of a single good.

The Production Possibilities Frontier and Economic Growth

So far, we have modeled the production possibilities frontier based on the resources available to society at a particular moment in time. However, most societies hope to create economic growth. *Economic growth* is the process that enables a society to produce more output in the future.

We can use the production possibilities frontier to explore economic growth. For example, we can ask what would happen to the PPF if our two-good society develops a new technology that increases productivity. Suppose that a new pizza assembly line improves the pizza production process and that the new assembly line does not require the use of more resources—it simply redeploys the resources that already exist. This development would allow the society to make more pizza with the same number of workers. Or it would allow the same amount of pizza to be made with fewer workers than previously. Either way, the society has expanded its resource base. Figure 2.3 shows this change as a shift in the PPF.

With the new technology, it becomes possible to produce 120 pizzas using the same number of workers and in the same amount of time it previously took to produce 100 pizzas. Although the ability to produce wings has not changed, the new pizza-making technology expands the production possibilities frontier outward from PPF$_1$ to PPF$_2$. It is now possible for the society to move from point A to point B, where it can produce more of both goods (80 pizzas and 220 wings). Why can the society produce more of both? Because the improvement in pizza-making technology—the assembly line—allows a redeployment of the labor force that also increases the production of wings. Improvements in technology make point B possible.

The production possibilities frontier will also expand if the population grows. A larger population means more workers to make pizza and wings. Figure 2.4 illustrates what happens when the society adds workers to help

FIGURE 2.3

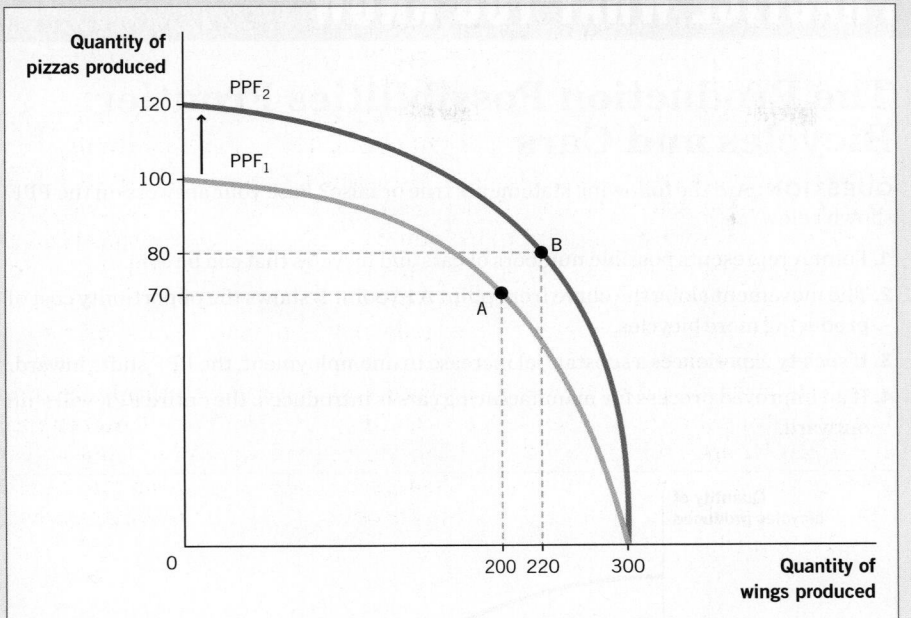

FIGURE 2.3

A Shift in the Production Possibilities Frontier

A new pizza assembly line that improves the productive capacity of pizza makers shifts the PPF upward from PPF$_1$ to PPF$_2$. More pizzas can be produced. Comparing points A and B, you can see that the enhanced pizza-making capacity also makes it possible to produce more wings at the same time.

FIGURE 2.4

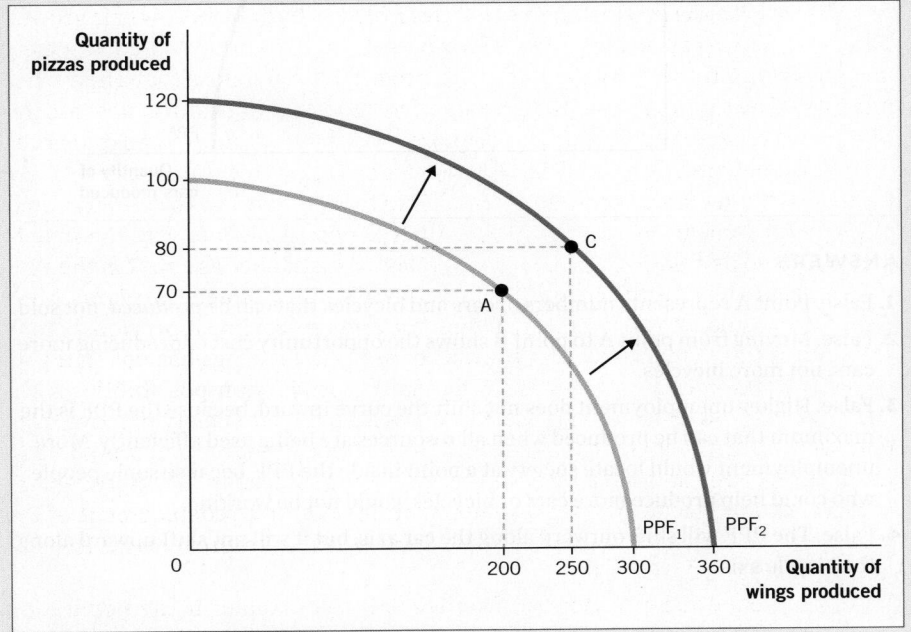

More Resources and the Production Possibilities Frontier

When more resources (such as additional workers) are available for the production of either pizza or wings, the entire PPF shifts upward and outward. This shift makes point C, along PPF$_2$, possible.

The Production Possibilities Frontier: Bicycles and Cars

QUESTION: Are the following statements true or false? Base your answers on the PPF shown below.

1. Point A represents possible numbers of cars and bicycles that can be sold.

2. The movement along the curve from point A to point B shows the opportunity cost of producing more bicycles.

3. If society experiences a substantial increase in unemployment, the PPF shifts inward.

4. If an improved process for manufacturing cars is introduced, the entire PPF will shift outward.

There is a trade-off between making bicycles and making cars.

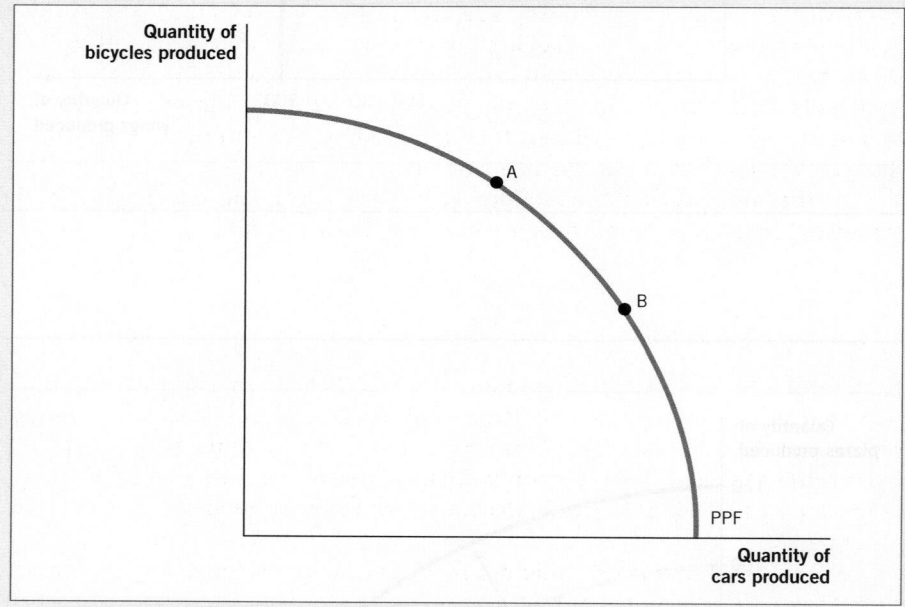

ANSWERS

1. False. Point A represents numbers of cars and bicycles that can be *produced*, not sold.

2. False. Moving from point A to point B shows the opportunity cost of producing more cars, not more bicycles.

3. False. Higher unemployment does not shift the curve inward, because the PPF is the maximum that can be produced when all resources are being used efficiently. More unemployment would locate society at a point inside the PPF, because some people who could help produce more cars or bicycles would not be working.

4. False. The PPF will shift outward along the car axis, but it will not shift upward along the bicycle axis.

produce pizza and wings. With more workers, the society can produce more pizzas and wings than before. The PPF curve shifts from PPF$_1$ to PPF$_2$, expanding up along the *y* axis and out along the *x* axis. Like improvements in technology, additional resources expand the frontier and allow the society to reach a point—in this case, point C—that was not possible before. The extra workers have pushed the entire frontier out—not just one end of it, as the pizza assembly line did.

What Are the Benefits of Specialization and Trade?

We have seen that improving technology and adding resources make an economy more productive. A third way to create gains for society is through specialization and trade. **Specialization** is the limiting of one's work to a particular area. Determining what to specialize in is an important part of the process. Every worker, business, or country is relatively good at producing certain products or services. Suppose you decide to learn about information technology. You earn a certificate or degree and find an employer who hires you for your specialized skills. Your information technology skills determine your salary. You can then use your salary to purchase other goods and services that you desire and that you are not so skilled at making yourself.

In the next section, we explore why specializing and exchanging your skilled expertise with others makes gains from trade possible.

Specialization is the limiting of one's work to a particular area.

Gains from Trade

Let's return to our two-good economy. Now we'll make the further assumption that this economy has only two people. One person is better at making pizzas, and the other is better at making wings. In this case, the potential gains from trade are clear. Each person will specialize in what he or she is better at producing and then will trade to acquire some of the good produced by the other person.

Figure 2.5 shows the production potential of the two people in our economy, Gwen and Blake. From the table at the top of the figure, we see that if Gwen devotes all of her work time to making pizzas, she can produce 60 pizzas. If she does not spend any time on pizzas, she can make 120 wings. In contrast, Blake can spend all his time on pizzas and produce 24 pizzas or all his time on wings and produce 72 wings.

The graphs illustrate the amount of pizza and wings each person produces daily. Wing production is plotted on the *x* axis, pizza production on the *y* axis. Each production possibilities frontier is drawn from the data in the table at the top of the figure.

Because the production possibilities frontiers here are straight, not bowed, Gwen and Blake each face a *constant* trade-off between producing pizza and producing wings. Gwen produces 60 pizzas for every 120 wings; this means her trade-off between producing pizza and producing wings is fixed at 60:120, or 1:2. Blake produces 24 pizzas for every 72 wings. His trade-off between producing pizza and producing wings is fixed at 24:72, or 1:3. Because Gwen and

Trade creates value

Trade-offs

FIGURE 2.5

The Production Possibilities Frontier with No Trade

(a) If Gwen cannot trade with Blake, she chooses to produce 40 pizzas and 40 wings, because she likes both foods equally.
(b) If Blake cannot trade with Gwen, he chooses to produce 18 pizzas and 18 wings, because he likes both foods equally.

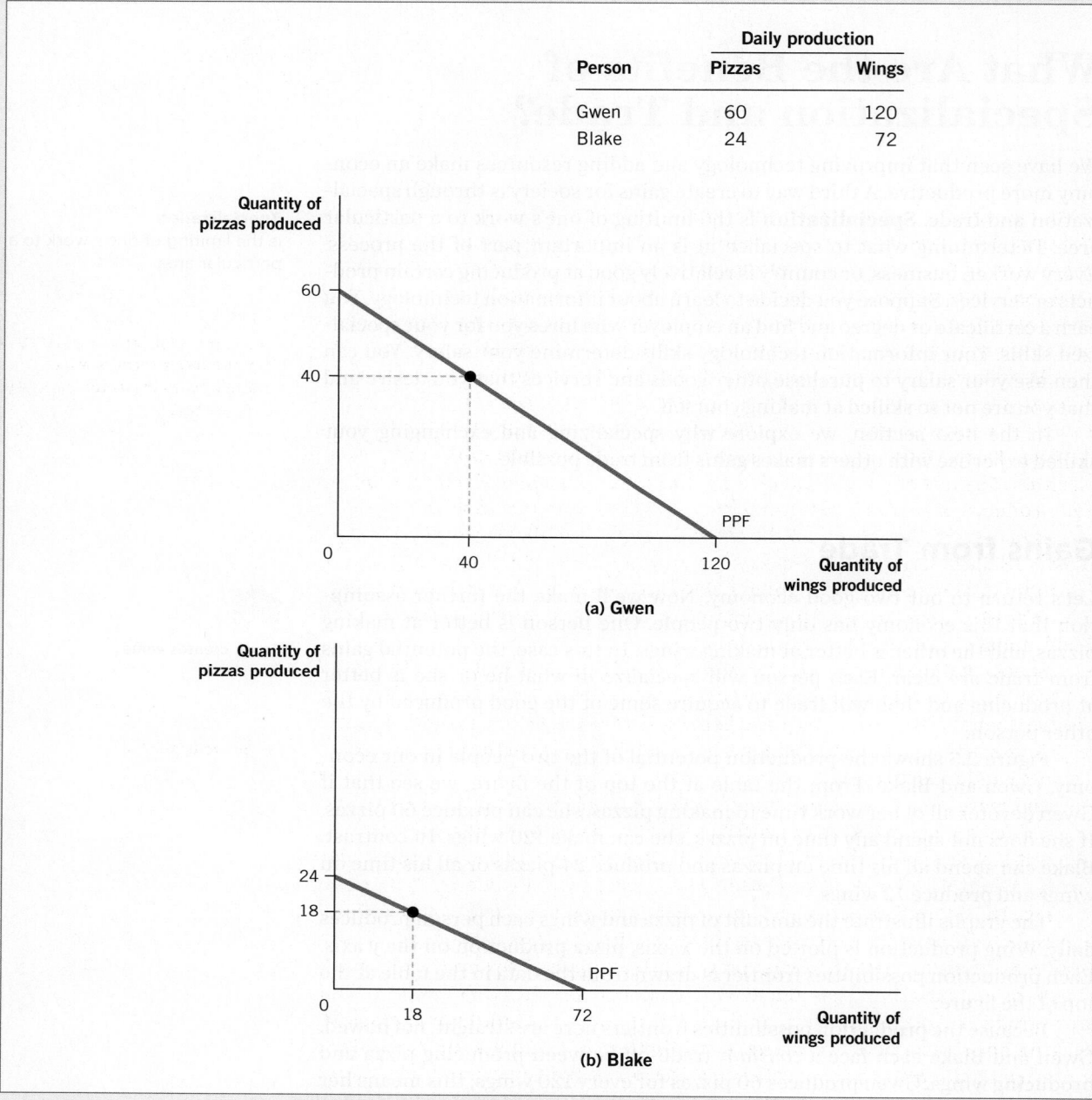

	Daily production	
Person	Pizzas	Wings
Gwen	60	120
Blake	24	72

TABLE 2.1

		Without trade		With specialization and trade		
Person	**Good**	**Production**	**Consumption**	**Production**	**Consumption**	**Gains from trade**
Gwen	Pizza	40	40	60	41 (keeps)	+1
	Wings	40	40	0	47 (from Blake)	+7
Blake	Pizza	18	18	0	19 (from Gwen)	+1
	Wings	18	18	72	25 (keeps)	+7

The Gains from Trade

Blake can choose to produce at any point along their production possibilities frontiers, let's assume they each want to produce an equal number of pizzas and wings. In this case, Gwen produces 40 pizzas and 40 wings, while Blake produces 18 pizzas and 18 wings. Since Gwen is more productive in general, she produces more of each food. Gwen has an **absolute advantage**, meaning she can produce more than Blake can produce with the same quantity of resources.

At first glance, it would appear that Gwen should continue to work alone. But consider what happens if Gwen and Blake each specialize and then trade. Table 2.1 compares production with and without specialization and trade. Without trade, Gwen and Blake have a combined production of 58 units of pizza and 58 units of wings (Gwen's 40 + Blake's 18). But when Gwen specializes and produces only pizza, her production is 60 units. In this case, her individual pizza output is greater than the combined output of 58 pizzas (Gwen's 40 + Blake's 18). Similarly, if Blake specializes in wings, he is able to make 72 units. His individual wing output is greater than their combined output of 58 wings (Gwen's 40 + Blake's 18). Specialization has resulted in the production of 2 additional pizzas and 14 additional wings.

Specialization leads to greater output. But Gwen and Blake would like to eat both pizza and wings. So if they specialize and then trade with each other, they will benefit. If Gwen gives Blake 19 pizzas in exchange for 47 wings, they are each better off by 1 pizza and 7 wings. This result is evident in the final column of Table 2.1 and in Figure 2.6.

In Figure 2.6a, we see that at point A, Gwen produces 60 pizzas and 0 wings. If she does not specialize, she produces 40 pizzas and 40 wings, represented at point B. If she specializes and then trades with Blake, she can have 41 pizzas and 47 wings, shown at point C. Her value gained from trade is 1 pizza and 7 wings. In Figure 2.6b, we see a similar benefit for Blake. If he produces only wings, he will have 72 wings, shown at point A. If he does not specialize, he produces 18 pizzas and 18 wings (point B). If he specializes and trades with Gwen, he can have 19 pizzas and 25 wings, shown at point C. His value gained from trade is 1 pizza and 7 wings. In spite of Gwen's absolute advantage in making both pizza and wings, she is still better off trading with Blake. This amazing result occurs because of specialization. When Gwen and Blake spend their time on what they do best, they are able to produce more collectively and then divide the gain.

Absolute advantage refers to one producer's ability to make more than another producer with the same quantity of resources.

Trade creates value

FIGURE 2.6

The Production Possibilities Frontier with Trade

(a) If Gwen produces only pizza, she will have 60 pizzas, shown at point A. If she does not specialize, she will produce 40 pizzas and 40 wings (point B). If she specializes and trades with Blake, she will have 41 pizzas and 47 wings (point C). (b) If Blake produces only wings, he will have 72 wings (point A). If he does not specialize, he will produce 18 pizzas and 18 wings (point B). If he specializes and trades with Gwen, he can have 19 pizzas and 25 wings (point C).

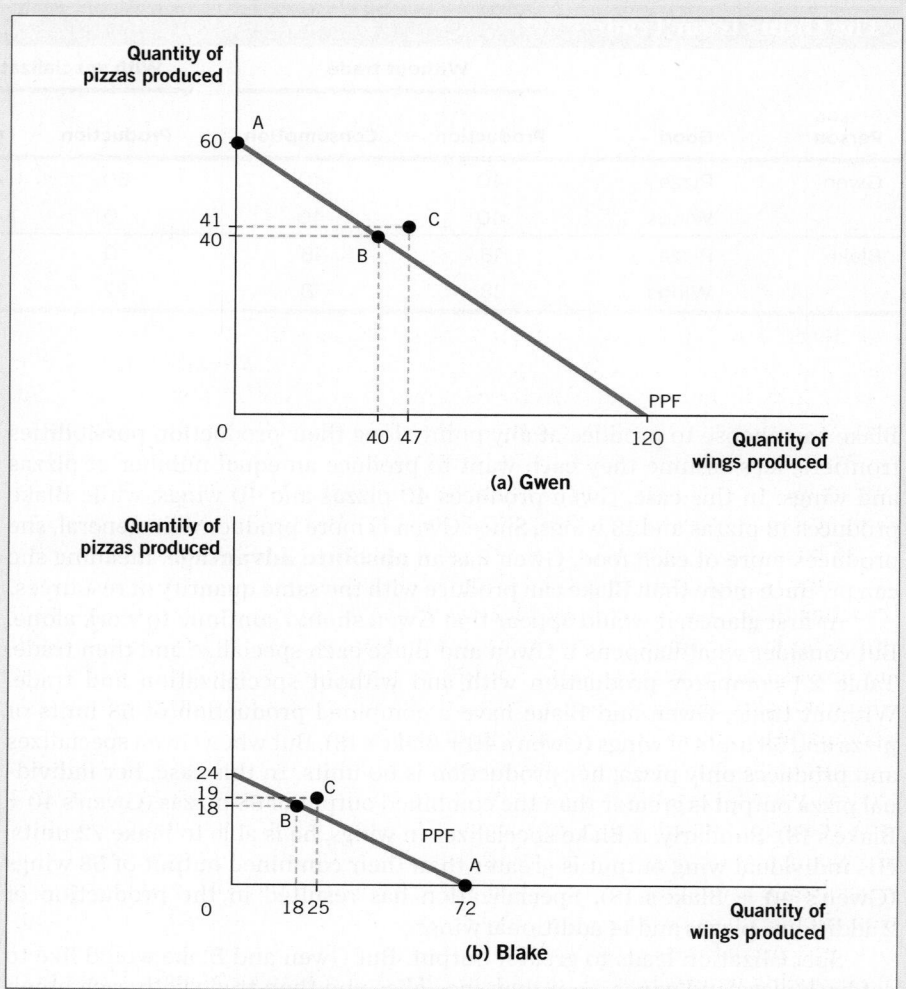

(a) Gwen

(b) Blake

Comparative Advantage

Opportunity cost

We have seen that specialization enables workers to enjoy gains from trade. The concept of opportunity cost provides us with a second way of validating the principle that trade creates value. Recall that opportunity cost is the highest-valued alternative that is sacrificed to pursue something else. Looking at Table 2.2, you can see that in order to produce 1 more pizza, Gwen must give up producing 2 wings. We can say that the opportunity cost of 1 pizza is 2 wings. We can also reverse the observation and say that the opportunity cost of one wing is $\frac{1}{2}$ pizza. In Blake's case, each pizza he produces means giving up the production of 3 wings. In other words, the opportunity cost for him to produce 1 pizza is 3 wings. In reverse, we can say that when he produces 1 wing, he gives up $\frac{1}{3}$ pizza.

TABLE 2.2

The Opportunity Cost of Pizza and Wings

| Person | Opportunity cost | |
	1 Pizza	1 Wing
Gwen	2 wings	$\frac{1}{2}$ pizza
Blake	3 wings	$\frac{1}{3}$ pizza

Recall from Chapter 1 that comparative advantage is the ability to make a good at a lower opportunity cost than another producer. Looking at Table 2.2, you can see that Gwen has a lower opportunity cost of producing pizza than Blake does—she gives up 2 wings for each pizza she produces, while he gives up 3 wings for each pizza he produces. In other words, Gwen has a comparative advantage in producing pizzas. However, Gwen does not have a comparative advantage in producing wings. For Gwen to produce 1 wing, she would have to give up production of $\frac{1}{2}$ pizza. Blake, in contrast, gives up $\frac{1}{3}$ pizza each time he produces 1 wing. So Gwen's opportunity cost of producing wings is higher than Blake's. Because Blake is the low-opportunity-cost producer of wings, he has a comparative advantage in producing them. Recall that Gwen has an absolute advantage in the production of both pizzas and wings; she is better at making both. However, from this example we see that she cannot have a comparative advantage in making both goods.

Applying the concept of opportunity cost helps us see why specialization enables people to produce more. Gwen's opportunity cost of producing pizzas (she gives up 2 wings for every pizza) is less than Blake's opportunity cost of producing pizzas (he gives up 3 wings for every pizza). Therefore, Gwen should specialize in producing pizzas. If you want to double-check this result, consider who should produce wings. Gwen's opportunity cost of producing wings (she gives up $\frac{1}{2}$ pizza for every wing she makes) is more than Blake's opportunity cost of producing wings (he gives up $\frac{1}{3}$ pizza for every wing he makes). Therefore, Blake should specialize in producing wings. When Gwen produces only pizzas and Blake produces only wings, their combined output is 60 pizzas and 72 wings.

Finding the Right Price to Facilitate Trade

We have seen that Gwen and Blake will do better if they specialize and then trade. But how many wings should it cost to buy a pizza? How many pizzas for a wing? In other words, what trading price will benefit both parties? To answer this question, we need to return to opportunity cost. For context, think of the process you likely went through when trading lunch food with friends in grade school. Perhaps you wanted a friend's apple and he wanted a few of your Oreos. If you agreed to trade three Oreos for the apple, the exchange benefited both parties, because you valued your three cookies less than your friend's apple, and your friend valued your three cookies more than his apple.

In our example, Gwen and Blake will benefit from exchanging a good at a price that is lower than the opportunity cost of producing it. Recall that Gwen's opportunity cost is 1 pizza per 2 wings, or half a pizza per wing. This means that

Opportunity cost

Specialization

HOW TO MAKE A $1,500 SANDWICH IN ONLY SIX MONTHS

This video on the YouTube channel "How to Make Everything" features a YouTuber who takes building a sandwich from scratch to new lengths. We're not talking about going the store and getting the needed ingredients. We're talking 100% do-it-yourself: growing the vegetables, evaporating seawater for salt, milking a cow and using the milk to make cheese, slaughtering a chicken for the protein, and grinding wheat to make bread flour. It is all quite fascinating to watch. At the end he taste tests the sandwich. "Not bad" he says, "not bad for six months of my time"—and then he puts his head down on the table.

When you decide to forgo specialization and comparative advantage, you're effectively turning back the clock on economic progress and living like our ancestors did. Without any help, we end up doing everything ourselves. When that happens, we are not getting the benefits of comparative advantage. So the next time you think to yourself, "I can do this on my own," think again.

How long would it take you to make a sandwich from scratch?

Sandwiches only take a few minutes to make, precisely because in a modern economy we rely on others to make the component parts we want. You can even get your sandwich made to order for you at any number of shops, and that's a wonderful thing!

---

any exchange where she can get a wing for less than half a pizza will be beneficial to her, because she ends up with more pizza and wings than she had without trade. Blake's opportunity cost is 1 pizza per 3 wings, so any trade where he can get a pizza for less than three wings will be beneficial to him. For trade to be mutually beneficial, the exchange ratio must fall between Gwen's opportunity cost ratio of 1:2 (0.50) and Blake's opportunity cost ratio of 1:3 (0.33). Outside of that range, either Gwen or Blake will be better off without trade, because the trade will not be attractive to both parties. In the example shown in Table 2.3, Gwen trades 19 pizzas for 47 wings. The ratio of 19:47 (0.40) falls between Gwen's and Blake's opportunity cost ratios and is therefore advantageous to both of them.

As long as the terms of trade fall between the trading partners' opportunity costs, the trade benefits both sides. But if Blake insists on a trading ratio of 1 wing for 1 pizza, which would be a good deal for him, Gwen will refuse to trade because she will be better off producing both goods on her own. Likewise, if Gwen insists on receiving 4 wings for every pizza she gives to Blake, he will refuse to trade with her because he will be better off producing both goods on his own.

Trade creates value

TABLE 2.3

Gaining from Trade

Person	Opportunity cost	Ratio
Gwen	1 pizza equals 2 wings	1:2 = 0.50
Terms of trade	19 pizzas for 47 wings	19:47 = 0.40
Blake	1 pizza equals 3 wings	1:3 = 0.33

PRACTICE WHAT YOU KNOW

Opportunity Cost

QUESTION: Imagine that you are planning to visit your family in Chicago. You can take a train or a plane. The plane ticket costs $300, and traveling by air takes 2 hours each way. The train ticket costs $200, and traveling by rail takes 12 hours each way. Which form of transportation should you choose?

Opportunity cost

ANSWER: The key to answering the question is learning to value time. The simplest way to do this is to calculate the cost savings of taking the train and compare that with the value of the time you would save if you took the plane.

Cost savings with train	Round-trip time saved with plane
$300 − $200 = $100	24 hours − 4 hours = 20 hours
(plane) − (train)	(train) − (plane)

Will you travel by plane or by train?

A person who takes the train can save $100, but it will cost 20 hours to do so. At an hourly rate, the savings would be $100/20 hours = $5 per hour. If you value your time at exactly $5 an hour, you will be indifferent between plane and train travel (that is, you will be equally satisfied with both options). If your time is worth more than $5 an hour, you should take the plane. If your time is worth less than $5 an hour, you should take the train.

It is important to note that this approach to calculating opportunity cost gives us a more realistic answer than simply observing ticket prices. The train has a lower ticket price, but very few people ride the train instead of flying, because the opportunity cost of their time is worth more to them than the difference in the ticket prices. Opportunity cost explains why most business travelers fly—it saves valuable time. Good economists learn to examine the full opportunity cost of their decisions, which must include both the financials and the cost of time.

We have examined this question by holding everything else constant (that is, applying the principle of *ceteris paribus*). In other words, at no point did we discuss possible side issues such as the fear of flying, sleeping arrangements on the train, or anything else that might be relevant to someone making the decision.

WHY LEBRON JAMES HAS SOMEONE ELSE HELP HIM MOVE

LeBron James is a giant of a man—6'8" and 260 pounds. He is a professional basketball player in the NBA, and he has moved from one team to another multiple times, requiring him to relocate to another city. Given his size and strength, you might think that LeBron would move his household himself. But despite the fact that he could likely do the work of two ordinary movers, he kept playing basketball and hired movers. Let's examine the situation to see if this was a wise decision.

LeBron has an absolute advantage in both playing basketball and moving furniture. But as we have seen, an absolute advantage doesn't mean that LeBron should do both tasks himself. When he signed with a new team, he could have asked for a few days to pack up and move, but each day spent moving would have been a day he was unable to work with his new team. When you are paid millions of dollars to play a game, the time spent moving is time lost practicing or playing basketball, which incurs a substantial opportunity cost. The movers, with a much lower opportunity cost of their time, have a comparative advantage in moving—so LeBron made a smart decision to hire them!

Opportunity cost

What Is the Trade-Off between Having More Now and Having More Later?

So far, we have examined short-run trade-offs. In looking at our wings–pizza trade-off, we were essentially living in the moment. But both individuals and society as a whole must weigh the benefits available today (the short run) with those available tomorrow (the long run). In the **short run**, we make decisions that reflect our immediate or short-term wants, needs, or limitations. In the short run, consumers can partially adjust their behavior. In the **long run**, we make decisions that reflect our wants, needs, and limitations over a much longer time horizon. In the long run, consumers have time to fully adjust to market conditions.

The **short run** is the period in which we make decisions that reflect our immediate or short-term wants, needs, or limitations. In the short run, consumers can partially adjust their behavior.

The **long run** is the period in which we make decisions that reflect our needs, wants, and limitations over a long time horizon. In the long run, consumers have time to fully adjust to market conditions.

Many of life's important decisions are about the long run. We must decide where to live, whether and whom to marry, whether and where to go to college, and what type of career to pursue. Getting these decisions right is far more important than simply deciding how many wings and pizzas to produce. For instance, the decision to save money requires giving up something you want to buy today for the benefit of having more money available in the future. Similarly, if you decide to go to a party tonight, you benefit today, while staying home to study creates a larger benefit at exam time. We are constantly making decisions that reflect this tension between today and tomorrow—eating a large piece of cake or a healthy snack, taking a nap or exercising at the gym, buying a jet ski or purchasing stocks in the stock market. Each of these decisions is a trade-off between the present and the future.

Trade-offs

Opportunity Cost

XBOX OR PLAYSTATION?

In *The Big Bang Theory*, Sheldon wants to buy either a new Xbox or a new PlayStation. He explains to his girlfriend, Amy, over dinner that because each system has many advantages, it is hard to choose. Eventually, he settles on an Xbox, but after picking one up at the store, he begins to have second thoughts. He starts by recalling decisions from his past that in hindsight were poor choices: he bought a Betamax instead of a VHS player, an HD-DVD player instead of a Blu-ray player, and a Zune instead of an iPod. Sheldon puts the Xbox back, because he doesn't want to experience regret.

Seeing that Sheldon is unable to choose, Amy intervenes and offers to buy him both systems! Problem solved, right? Not quite, because Sheldon only has one slot open on his entertainment system. Amy counters that she'll buy him a new entertainment center, only to have Sheldon respond, "Which one?" because he knows he won't be able to make that choice easily, either! Hours later, we see Sheldon and Amy lying on the floor while Sheldon is still deciding. Eventually the store closes and they are forced to come back another day.

We may not be as indecisive as Sheldon, but we face the same basic problem all the time. When you buy a new phone, rent a new apartment, buy a new outfit,

Which would you choose, an Xbox or a PlayStation?

go out to eat, or decide where to go to college, you give up your next-best option. The more important the decision and the better the alternatives, the harder the choice becomes. In those situations, the choice involves a high opportunity cost. If the choice is trivial or the second-best option isn't appealing, the choices we make involve low opportunity costs.

Consumer Goods, Capital Goods, and Investment

We have seen that the trade-off between the present and the future is evident in the tension between what we consume now and what we plan to consume later. Any good that is produced for present consumption is a **consumer good**. These goods help to satisfy our needs or wants now. Food, entertainment, and clothing are all examples of consumer goods. **Capital goods** help in the production of

Consumer goods are produced for present consumption.

Capital goods help produce other valuable goods and services in the future.

other valuable goods and services in the future. Capital goods are everywhere. Roads, factories, trucks, and computers are all capital goods.

Education is a form of capital. The time you spend earning a college degree makes you more attractive to future employers. When you decide to go to college instead of working, you are investing in your *human capital*. **Investment** is the process of using resources to create or buy new capital.

Because we live in a world with scarce resources, every investment in capital goods has an opportunity cost of forgone consumer goods. For example, if you decide to buy a new laptop, you cannot use the money to travel over spring break. Similarly, a firm that decides to invest in a new factory to expand future production is unable to use that money to hire more workers now.

The decision between whether to consume or to invest has a significant impact on economic growth in the future, or long run. What happens when society chooses to produce many more consumer goods than capital goods? Figure 2.7a shows the result. When relatively few resources are invested in producing capital goods in the short run, very little new capital is created. Because new capital is a necessary ingredient for economic growth in the future, the long-run production possibilities curve expands only a small amount.

What happens when society chooses to plan for the future by producing more capital goods than consumer goods in the short run? Figure 2.7b shows the result. With investment in new capital, the long-run production possibilities curve expands outward much more.

All societies face the trade-off between spending today and investing for tomorrow. Mexico and Turkey are good examples of emerging global economies investing in the future. Over the last 20 years, the citizens of these countries have invested significantly more in capital goods than have the citizens of wealthier nations in North America and Europe. Not surprisingly, economic growth rates in Mexico and Turkey are much higher than they are in more developed countries. Part of the difference in these investment rates can be explained by the fact that the United States and Europe already have large capital stocks per capita (per person) and therefore have less to gain from operating at point B in

Investment
is the process of using resources to create or buy new capital.

Trade-offs

Study Now…

…play later.

The Trade-Off between the Short Run and the Long Run

A KNIGHT'S TALE

In this movie, three peasants unexpectedly win a jousting tournament and earn 15 silver coins. Then they face a choice about what to do next. Two of the three want to return to England and live the high life for a while, but the third, played by Heath Ledger, suggests they take 13 of the coins and reinvest them in training for the next tournament. He offers to put in all 5 of his coins and asks the other two peasants for 4 coins each. His partners are skeptical about the plan because Ledger's character is good with the sword but not very good with the lance. For them to win additional tournaments, they will have to invest considerable resources in training and preparation.

The movie illustrates the trade-off between enjoying consumer goods in the short run and investing in capital goods in the long run. The peasants' choice to forgo spending their winnings to enjoy themselves now in order to prepare for the next tournament is not easy. None of the three has ever had any money. Five silver coins represent an opportunity, at least for a few days, to live the good life. However, the plan will elevate the three out of poverty in the long term if they

Learning to joust is a lifetime skill.

can learn to compete at the highest level. Therefore, investing the 13 coins is like choosing point B in Figure 2.7b. Investing now will allow their production possibilities frontier to grow over time, affording each of them a better life in the long run.

Figure 2.7b than developing countries do. Mexico clearly prefers point B at this stage of its economic development, but point B is not necessarily better than point A. Developing nations, such as Mexico, are sacrificing the present for a better future, while many developed countries, such as the United States, take a more balanced approach to weighing current needs against future growth. For Mexican workers, this trade-off typically means longer work hours and higher savings rates than their U.S. counterparts can claim, despite far lower average salaries for the Mexican workers. In contrast, U.S. workers have much more leisure time and more disposable (spendable) income, a combination that leads to much higher rates of consumption in the United States.

FIGURE 2.7

Investing in Capital Goods and Promoting Growth

(a) When a society chooses point A in the short run, very few capital goods are created. Because capital goods are needed to enhance future growth, the long-run PPF$_2$ expands, but only slightly.
(b) When a society chooses point B in the short run, many capital goods are created, and the long-run PPF$_2$ expands significantly.

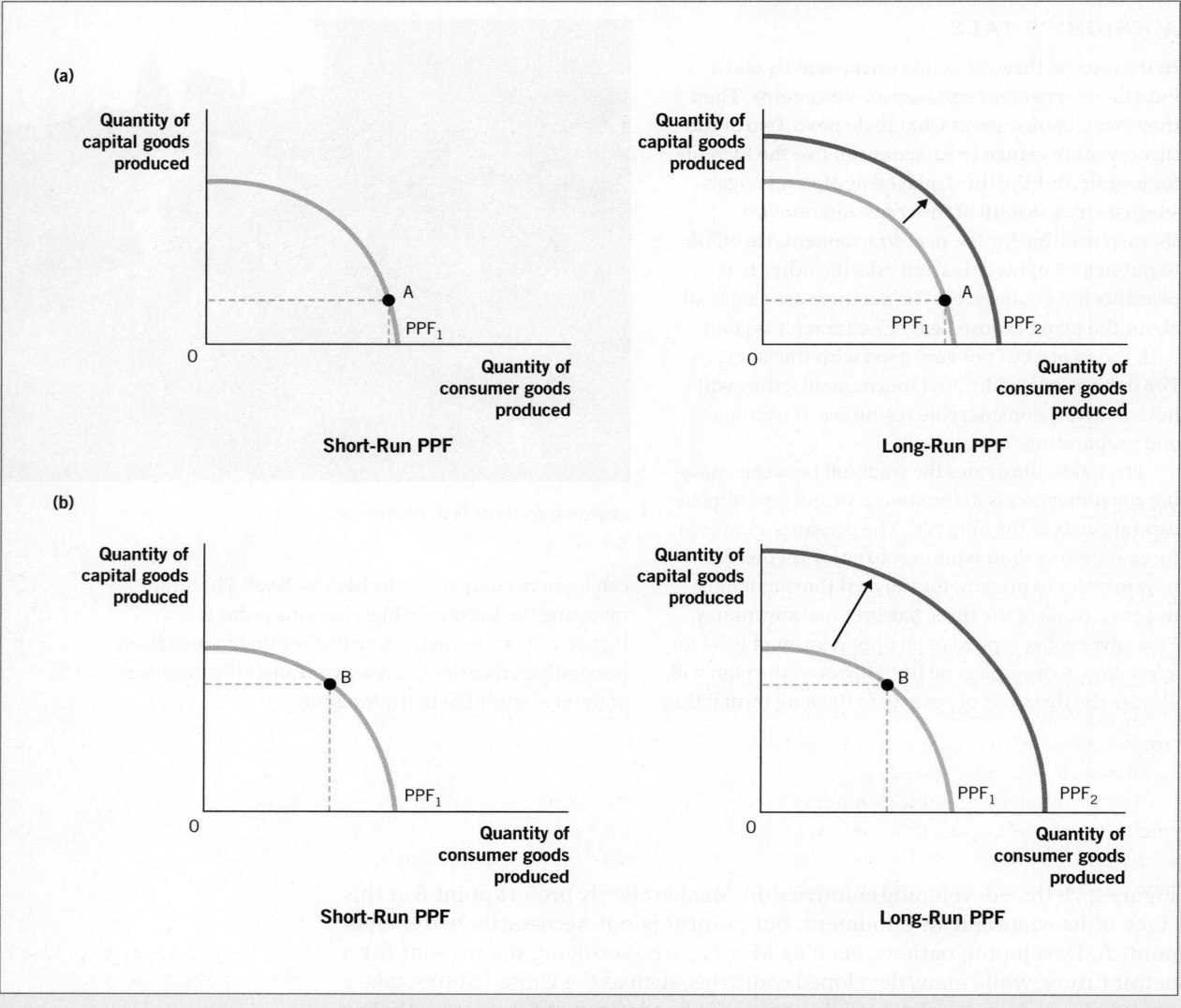

(a)

Quantity of capital goods produced

A

PPF$_1$

0

Quantity of consumer goods produced

Short-Run PPF

Quantity of capital goods produced

A

PPF$_1$ PPF$_2$

0

Quantity of consumer goods produced

Long-Run PPF

(b)

Quantity of capital goods produced

B

PPF$_1$

0

Quantity of consumer goods produced

Short-Run PPF

Quantity of capital goods produced

B

PPF$_1$ PPF$_2$

0

Quantity of consumer goods produced

Long-Run PPF

Trade-Offs

QUESTION: Your friend is fond of saying he will study later. He eventually does study, but he often doesn't get quite the grades he had hoped for because he doesn't study enough. Every time this happens, he says, "It's only one exam." What advice would you give him about trade-offs?

ANSWER: Your friend doesn't understand long-run trade-offs. You could start by reminding him that each decision has a consequence at the margin and also later in life. The marginal cost of not studying enough is a lower exam grade. To some extent, your friend's reasoning is correct. How well he does on one exam over four years of college is almost irrelevant. The problem is that many poor exam scores have a cumulative effect over the semesters. If your friend graduates with a 2.5 GPA instead of a 3.5 GPA because he did not study enough, his employment prospects will be significantly diminished.

No pain, no gain.

Marginal thinking

Incentives

ECONOMICS IN THE REAL WORLD

ZIFERBLAT CAFÉ UNDERSTANDS INCENTIVES

Ziferblat is a small but growing café chain with locations in the UK and Eastern Europe. Their slogan is "Everything is free inside; except the time you spend." Unlike most cafés, which charge for the items you order, Ziferblat charges 8 pence a minute (about $7.00/hour), and everything (Wi-Fi, dozens of brands of tea and coffee, biscuits, and cakes) is included.

In most cafés the scarcest resource is table space. The reason is that once a customer purchases something, they are allowed to sit as long as they want. Ziferblat has solved the "squatting" problem that plagues other cafés by giving each customer a clock that charges them based on how long they stay. This nontraditional pricing structure creates an incentive to take time into account, by raising the cost of staying after you have finished your refreshment.

Ziferblat is a good example of voluntary trade. Customers can use Ziferblat for a quick bite or beverage and also use it as a shared office or meeting space. Ziferblat sets a price per minute that allows it to make a profit, and customers are willing to pay for the comforts provided. That's a win-win exchange.

How long would you stay, if each minute costs you 12 cents?

Trade creates value

Conclusion

The simple, yet powerful idea that trade creates value has far-reaching consequences for how we should organize our society. Since we all win when voluntary trade takes place, creating opportunities for more trades to take place between consumers and producers and across countries enriches all of our lives.

We have developed our first model, the production possibilities frontier. This model illustrates the benefits of trade and also enables us to describe ways to grow the economy. Trade and growth rest on a more fundamental idea—specialization.

Why Men Should Do More Housework

- Men spend, on average, 50 minutes less than women on household chores.
- If labor in the household is allocated in a gender-neutral way, output-per-hour increases by 5.4%.
- Reducing the amount of time talented women spend doing household chores helps them earn pay equal to their male counterparts.

According to the U.S. Census Bureau's American Time Use Survey, the division of household chores falls disproportionately on females. It turns out that this imbalance is a contributor to the wage gap that exists between men and women (more on that in Chapter 15). Researchers at the National Bureau of Economic Research, a private nonprofit organization, found that women earn less than men do because they are less willing to work jobs that require long hours.

When men share chores equally, it's good for all of us.

The researchers determined that if labor in the household is allocated in a gender-neutral way, this increases output-per-hour by 5.4%, as people make better use of their time, given their respective skills. Freeing up talented women from household chores also helps them earn pay equal to that of their male counterparts.

The life lesson is clear here. When partners both work outside the home, they should each pull their weight by spending equal amounts of time completing chores at home. Each partner should specialize in the chores they are comparatively good at, enabling the other partner to do likewise.

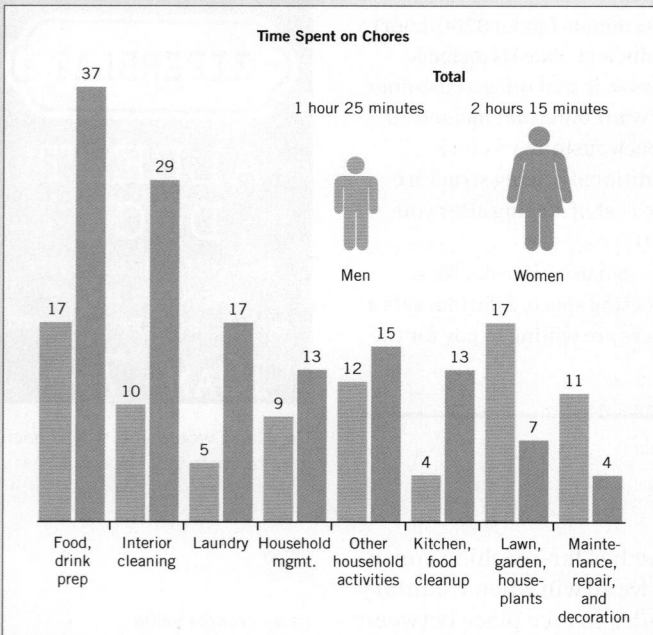

Women on the average spend more of their time than men do on household activities. Households that break up tasks more based on skill increase household labor per hour by 5.4%. This earns the family more money. If women participated in the economy identically to men, one report estimates it would add $28 trillion or 26% to the annual global economy.

Sources: NBER Study, 2017; McKinsey & Company, www.mckinsey.com/featured-insights/employment-and-growth/how-advancing-womens-equality-can-add-12-trillion-to-global-growth.

When producers specialize, they focus their efforts on those goods and services for which they have the lowest opportunity cost and they trade with others who are good at making something else. To have something valuable to trade, each producer, in effect, must find its comparative advantage. As a result, trade creates value and contributes to an improved standard of living in society.

In the next chapter, we examine the supply and demand model to illustrate how markets work. While the model is different, the fundamental result we learned here—that trade creates value—still holds. ✳

Opportunity cost
Trade creates value

· ANSWERING *the* BIG QUESTIONS ·

How do economists study the economy?

- Economists design hypotheses (proposed explanations) and then test them by collecting real data. The economist's laboratory is the world around us.

- A good model should be simple, flexible, and useful for making accurate predictions. A model is both more realistic and harder to understand when it involves many variables. To keep models simple, economists often use the concept of *ceteris paribus*, or "all else equal." Maintaining a positive (as opposed to normative) framework is crucial for economic analysis because it allows decision-makers to observe the facts objectively.

What is a production possibilities frontier?

- A production possibilities frontier (PPF) is a model that illustrates the combinations of outputs a society can produce if all of its resources are being used efficiently. An outcome is considered efficient when resources are fully utilized and potential output is maximized. Economists use the PPF to illustrate trade-offs and to explain opportunity costs and the role of additional resources and technology in creating economic growth.

What are the benefits of specialization and trade?

- Society is better off if individuals and firms specialize and trade on the basis of the principle of comparative advantage.

- Parties that are better at producing goods and services than all their potential trading partners (and thus hold an absolute advantage) still benefit from trade. Trade allows them to specialize and trade what they produce for other goods and services they are relatively less skilled at making.

- As long as the terms of trade fall between the opportunity costs of both trading partners, the trade benefits both sides.

What is the trade-off between having more now and having more later?

- All societies face a crucial trade-off between consumption in the short run and economic growth in the long run. Investments in capital goods today help to spur economic growth in the future. However, because capital goods are not consumed in the short run, society must be willing to sacrifice how well it lives today in order to have more later.

Concepts You Should Know

absolute advantage (p. 41)
capital goods (p. 47)
ceteris paribus (p. 30)
consumer goods (p. 47)
endogenous factors (p. 31)
exogenous factors (p. 31)

investment (p. 48)
law of increasing opportunity
   cost (p. 36)
long run (p. 46)
normative statement (p. 29)
positive statement (p. 29)

production possibilities frontier
   (PPF) (p. 33)
short run (p. 46)
specialization (p. 39)

Questions for Review

1. What is a positive economic statement? What is a normative economic statement? Provide an example of each (other than those given in the chapter).

2. Is it important to build completely realistic economic models? Explain your response.

3. Draw a production possibilities frontier curve. Illustrate the set of points that is feasible, the set of points that is efficient, the set of points that is inefficient, and the set of points that is not feasible.

4. Why does the production possibilities frontier bow out?

5. Does having an absolute advantage mean that you should undertake to produce everything on your own? Why or why not?

6. What criteria would you use to determine which of two workers has a comparative advantage in performing a task?

7. Why does comparative advantage matter more than absolute advantage for trade?

8. What factors are most important for economic growth?

Study Problems (✳ *solved at the end of the section*)

✳ **1.** Michael and Angelo live in a small town in Italy. They work as artists. Michael is the more productive artist. He can produce 10 small sculptures each day but only 5 paintings. Angelo can produce 6 sculptures each day but only 2 paintings.

	Output per day	
	Sculptures	**Paintings**
Michael	10	5
Angelo	6	2

a. What is the opportunity cost of a painting for each artist?

b. Based on your answer in part (a), who has a comparative advantage in producing paintings?

c. If the two men decide to specialize, who should produce the sculptures and who should produce the paintings?

✳ **2.** The following table shows scores a student can earn on two upcoming exams according to the amount of time devoted to study:

Hours spent studying for economics	Economics score	Hours spent studying for history	History score
10	100	0	40
8	96	2	60
6	88	4	76
4	76	6	88
2	60	8	96
0	40	10	100

a. Plot the production possibilities frontier.

b. Does the production possibilities frontier exhibit the law of increasing relative cost?

c. If the student wishes to move from a grade of 60 to a grade of 88 in economics, what is the opportunity cost?

3. Think about comparative advantage when answering this question: Should your professor, who has highly specialized training in economics, take time out of his or her teaching schedule to mow the lawn? Defend your answer.

✱ **4.** Are the following statements positive or normative?

    a. My dog weighs 75 pounds.

    b. Dogs are required by law to have rabies shots.

    c. You should take your dog to the veterinarian once a year for a checkup.

    d. Chihuahuas are cuter than bulldogs.

    e. Leash laws for dogs are a good idea because they reduce injuries.

5. How does your decision to invest in a college degree add to your human capital? Use a projected production possibilities frontier for 10 years from now to compare your life with and without the college degree.

✱ **6.** Suppose that an amazing new fertilizer doubles the production of potatoes. How would this invention affect the production possibilities frontier for an economy that produces only potatoes and carrots? Would it now be possible to produce more potatoes *and* more carrots or only more potatoes?

7. Suppose that a politician tells you about a plan to create two expensive but necessary programs to build more production facilities for solar power and wind power. At the same time, the politician is unwilling to cut any other programs. Use the production possibilities frontier graph below to explain if the politician's proposal is possible.

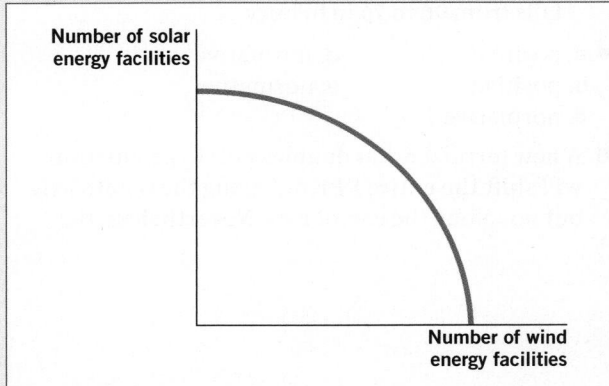

✱ **8.** Two friends, Rachel and Joey, enjoy baking bread and making apple pie. Rachel takes 2 hours to bake a loaf of bread and 1 hour to make a pie. Joey takes 4 hours to bake a loaf of bread and 4 hours to make a pie.

    a. What are Joey's and Rachel's opportunity costs of baking bread?

    b. Who has the absolute advantage in making bread?

    c. Who has a comparative advantage in making bread?

    d. If Joey and Rachel both decide to specialize to increase their joint production, what should Joey produce? What should Rachel produce?

    e. The price of a loaf of bread can be expressed in terms of an apple pie. If Joey and Rachel are specializing in production and decide to trade with each other, what range of ratios of bread and apple pie would allow both parties to benefit from trade?

9. Where would you plot unemployment on a production possibilities frontier? Where would you plot full employment on a production possibilities frontier? Now suppose that in a time of crisis everyone pitches in and works much harder than usual. What happens to the production possibilities frontier?

10. Read the poem "The Road Not Taken," by Robert Frost. What line(s) in the poem capture the opportunity cost of decision-making?

✱ **11.** Suppose that you must decide between attending a Taylor Swift concert or a Maroon 5 concert. The concerts are at the same time on the same evening, so you cannot see both. You love Taylor Swift and would pay as much as $200 to see her perform. Tickets to her concert are $135. You are not as big a Maroon 5 fan, but a friend has just offered you a free ticket to the concert. If you decide to take the free ticket to see Maroon 5, what is your opportunity cost?

✱ **12.** In this chapter we have seen that the PPF could be bowed-out or a straight line.

    a. Provide an example of two goods where the PPF would be bowed-out.

    b. Provide an example of two goods where the PPF would be a straight line.

c. It also turns out that the PPF can bow in. This occurs when the production process produces economies of scale, which means that it is possible to make *more* of each good as production expands. Can you think of two goods where the PPF would be bowed-in?

13. Barrville is a country that produces either all dumbbells, or all sandals, or a combination of the two.

    a. Draw a production possibilities frontier and label the *x* and *y* axes appropriately.

b. Place a point that shows where the country would be operating if a recession hits and companies are laying off workers. Label this point B.

c. Place a point that shows an unattainable point under the current situation. Label this point C.

d. If a point is unattainable now, will it always be unattainable? If you write that it can be attainable, what would cause it to become attainable?

Solved Problems

1.a. Michael's opportunity cost is 2 sculptures for each painting he produces. How do we know this? If he devotes all of his time to sculptures, he can produce 10. If he devotes all of his time to paintings, he can produce 5. The ratio 10:5 is the same as 2:1. Michael is therefore twice as fast at producing sculptures as he is at producing paintings. Angelo's opportunity cost is 3 sculptures for each painting he produces. If he devotes all of his time to sculptures, he can produce 6. If he devotes all of his time to paintings, he can produce 2. The ratio 6:2 is the same as 3:1.

b. For this question, we need to compare Michael's and Angelo's relative strengths. Michael produces 2 sculptures for every painting, and Angelo produces 3 sculptures for every painting. Because Michael is only twice as good at producing sculptures, his opportunity cost of producing each painting is 2 sculptures instead of 3. Therefore, Michael is the low-opportunity-cost producer of paintings.

c. If they specialize, Michael should paint and Angelo should sculpt. You might be tempted to argue that Michael should just work alone, but if Angelo does the sculptures, Michael can concentrate on the paintings. This is what comparative advantage is all about.

2.a.

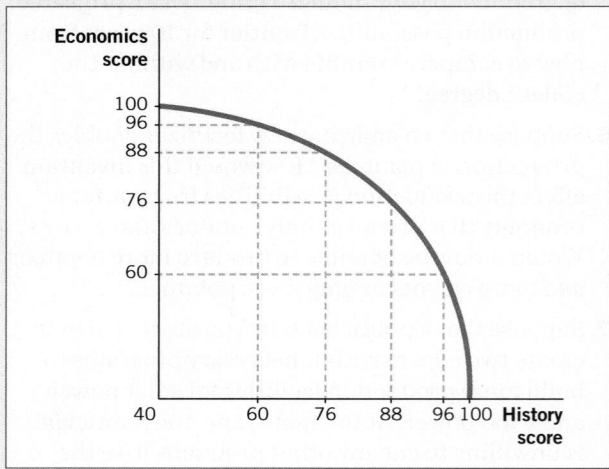

b. Yes, because it is not a straight line.

c. The opportunity cost is that the student's grade falls from 96 to 76 in history.

4.a. positive   **d.** normative
    b. positive   **e.** normative
    c. normative

6. A new fertilizer that doubles potato production will shift the entire PPF out along the potato axis but not along the carrot axis. Nevertheless, the added ability to produce more potatoes means that less acreage will have to be planted in potatoes and more land can be used to produce carrots. This makes it possible to produce more potatoes and carrots at many points along the production possibilities frontier. Figure 2.3 has a nice illustration if you are unsure how this process works.

8.a. Rachel gives up 2 pies for every loaf she makes. Joey gives up 1 pie for every loaf he makes.

   b. Rachel

   c. Joey

   d. Joey should make the bread and Rachel the pies.

   e. Rachel makes 2 pies per loaf and Joey makes 1 pie per loaf. So any trade between 2:1 and 1:1 would benefit them both.

11. Despite what you might think, the opportunity cost is *not* $200. You would be giving up $200 in enjoyment if you go to the Maroon 5 concert, but you would also have to pay $135 to see Taylor Swift, whereas the Maroon 5 ticket is free. The difference between the satisfaction you would have experienced at the Taylor Swift concert ($200) and the amount you must pay for the ticket ($135) is the marginal benefit you would receive from her concert. That amount is $200 − $135 = $65. You are not as big a Maroon 5 fan, but the ticket is free. As long as you think the Maroon 5 concert is worth more than $65, you will get a larger marginal benefit from seeing Maroon 5 perform than from seeing Taylor Swift perform. Therefore, the opportunity cost of using the free ticket is $65.

12.a. tattoos and (in-ground) swimming pools

   b. left shoes and right shoes

   c. The cost of producing some goods goes down as production increases. Computers, automobiles, and fast food are good examples. For such goods, the PPF would bow in.

02A

Graphs in Economics

Many students try to understand economics without taking the time to learn how to read and interpret graphs. This approach is shortsighted. You can "think" your way to the correct answer in a few cases, but the models we build and illustrate with graphs are designed to help analyze the tough questions, where your intuition can lead you astray.

Economics is fundamentally a quantitative science. That is, economists often solve problems by finding a numerical answer. For instance, economists determine the unemployment rate, the inflation rate, the growth rate of the economy, prices, costs, and much more. Economists also like to compare present-day numbers with numbers from the immediate past and historical data. Throughout your study of economics, you will find that many data-driven topics—for example, financial trends, transactions, the stock market, and other business-related variables—naturally lend themselves to graphic display. You will also find that many theoretical concepts are easier to understand when depicted visually in graphs and charts.

Economists also find that graphing can be a powerful tool when attempting to find relationships between different sets of variables. For example, the production possibilities frontier model presented in this chapter involves the relationship between the production of pizza and the production of chicken wings. The graphical presentations make this relationship, the trade-off between pizza and wings, much more vivid.

In this appendix, we begin with simple graphs involving a single variable. We then move to graphs that consist of two variables.

Graphs That Consist of One Variable

A **variable** is a quantity that can take on more than one value.

There are two common ways to display data with one variable: bar graphs and pie charts. A **variable** is a quantity that can take on more than one value. Let's look at the market share of the largest carbonated-beverage companies. Figure 2A.1 shows the data in a bar graph. On the vertical (y) axis is the market share held by each firm. On the horizontal (x) axis are the three largest firms (Coca-Cola Co., PepsiCo Inc., and Keurig Dr Pepper) and a separate category for the remaining firms, called "Others." Coca-Cola Co. has the largest market

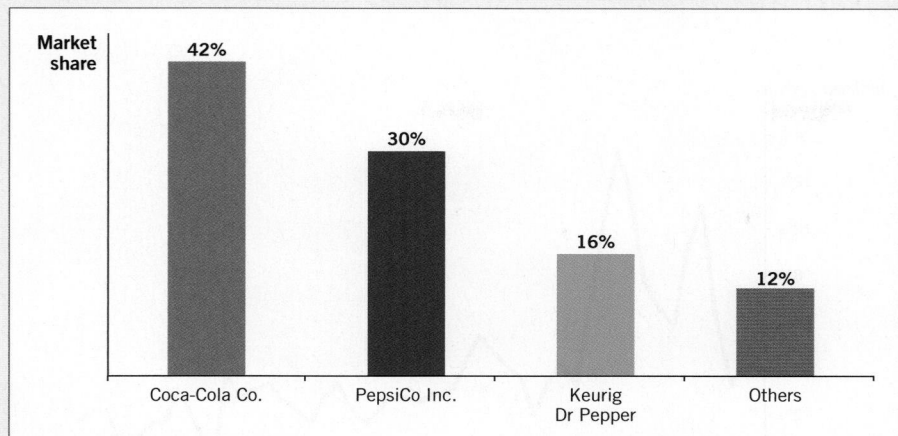

Bar Graphs

Each firm's market share in the beverage industry is represented by the height of the bar.

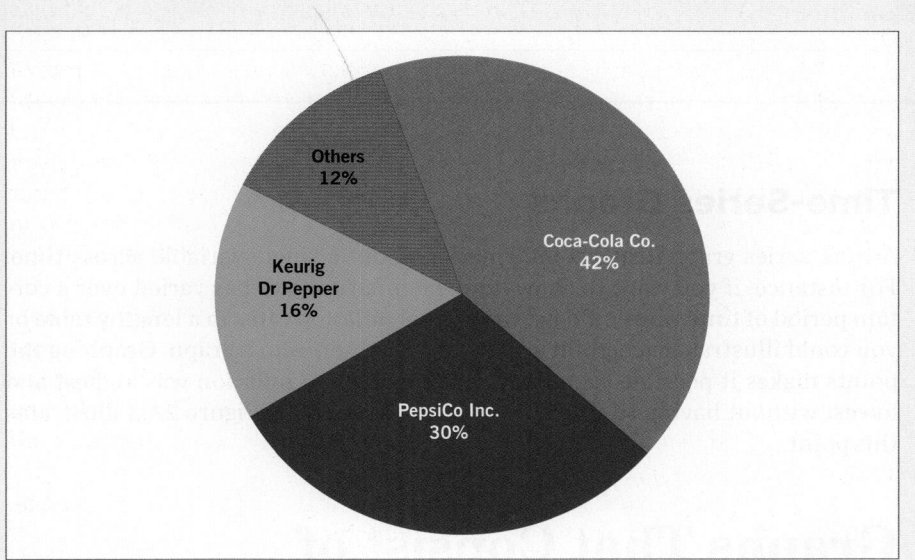

Pie Chart

Each firm's market share in the beverage industry is represented by the size of the pie slice.

share of the U.S. market at 42%, followed by PepsiCo Inc. at 30% and Keurig Dr Pepper at 16%. The height of each firm's bar represents its market-share percentage. The combined market share of the other firms in the market is 12%.

Figure 2A.2 illustrates the same data from the beverage industry on a pie chart. Now the market share is expressed as the size of the pie slice for each firm.

The information in a bar graph and a pie chart is the same, so does it matter which visualization you use? Bar graphs are particularly good for comparing sizes or quantities, while pie charts are generally better for illustrating proportions (parts of a whole).

Time-Series Graph

In a time-series graph, you immediately get a sense of when the inflation rate was highest and lowest, the trend through time, and the amount of volatility in the data.

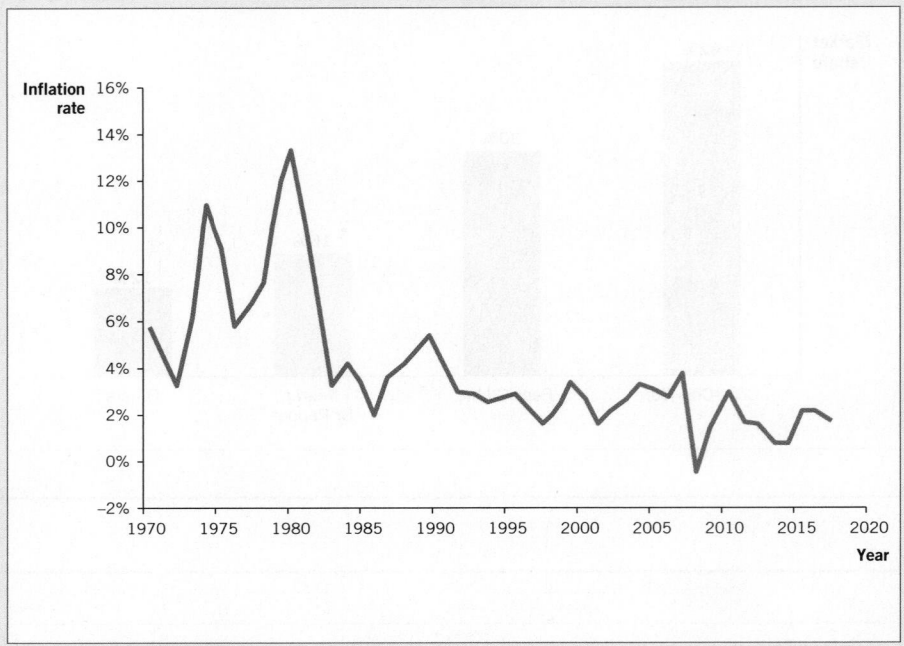

Time-Series Graphs

A time-series graph displays information about a single variable across time. For instance, if you want to show how the inflation rate has varied over a certain period of time, you could list the annual inflation rates in a lengthy table or you could illustrate each point as part of a time series in a graph. Graphing the points makes it possible to quickly determine when inflation was highest and lowest without having to scan through the entire table. Figure 2A.3 illustrates this point.

Graphs That Consist of Two Variables

Sometimes, understanding graphs requires you to visualize relationships between two economic variables. Each variable is plotted on a coordinate system, or two-dimensional grid. The coordinate system allows us to map a series of ordered pairs that show how the two variables relate to each other. For instance, suppose we examine the relationship between the amount of lemonade sold and the air temperature, as shown in Figure 2A.4.

The air temperature is graphed on the x axis (horizontal) and cups of lemonade sold on the y axis (vertical). Within each ordered pair (x, y), the first value, x, represents the value along the x axis and the second value, y, represents the value along the y axis. For example, at point A, the value of x, or the

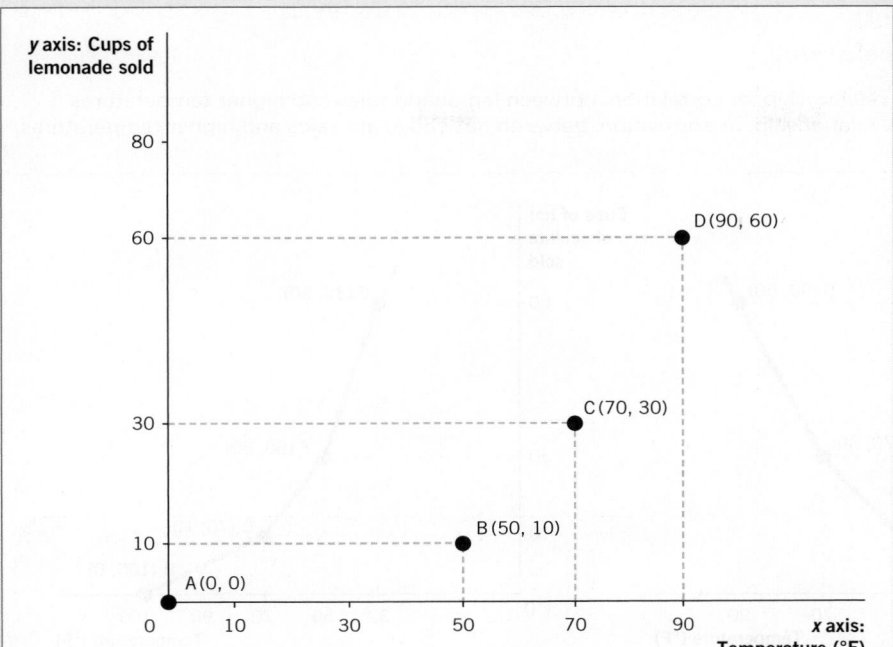

Plotting Points in a
Coordinate System

Within each ordered pair
(*x*, *y*), the first value, *x*, represents the value along the
x axis, and the second value,
y, represents the value along
the *y* axis. The combination of
all the (*x*, *y*) pairs is known as
a scatterplot.

temperature, is 0 and the value of *y*, or the amount of lemonade sold, is also 0.
No one would want to buy lemonade when the temperature is that low. At point
B, the value of *x*, the air temperature, is 50°F, and the value of *y*, the number
of cups of lemonade sold, is 10. By the time we reach point C, the temperature
is 70°F and the amount of lemonade sold is 30 cups. Finally, at point D, the
temperature has reached 90°F, and 60 cups of lemonade are sold.

The graph you see in Figure 2A.4 is known as a **scatterplot**; it shows
the individual (*x*, *y*) points in a coordinate system. Note that in this example,
the amount of lemonade sold rises as the temperature increases. When the
two variables move together in the same direction, we say there is a **positive
correlation** between them (see Figure 2A.5a). Conversely, if we graph the relationship between hot chocolate sales and temperature, we find they move in
opposite directions; as the temperature rises, hot chocolate consumption goes
down (see Figure 2A.5b). This data set reveals a **negative correlation**, which
occurs when two variables, such as cups of hot chocolate sold and temperature,
move in opposite directions. Economists are ultimately interested in using
models and graphs to make predictions and test theories, and the coordinate
system makes both positive and negative correlations easy to observe.

Figure 2A.5 illustrates the difference between a positive correlation and a
negative correlation. Figure 2A.5a shows the same information as Figure 2A.4.
When the temperature increases, the quantity of lemonade sold increases as
well. However, in Figure 2A.5b we have a very different set of ordered pairs. As
the temperature increases, the quantity of hot chocolate sold falls. We can see
this relationship by starting with point E, where the temperature is 32°F and

A **scatterplot** is a graph that
shows individual (*x*, *y*) points.

Positive correlation
occurs when two variables
move in the same direction.

Negative correlation
occurs when two variables
move in opposite directions.

Positive and Negative Correlations

(a) This graph displays the positive relationship, or correlation, between lemonade sales and higher temperatures.
(b) This graph displays the negative relationship, or correlation, between hot chocolate sales and higher temperatures.

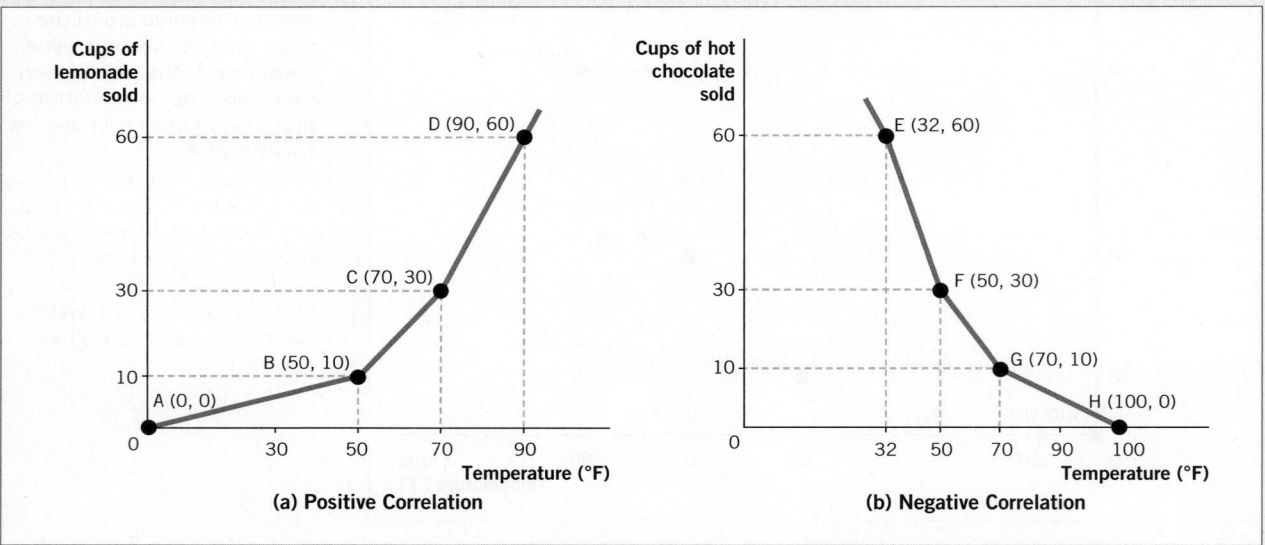

(a) Positive Correlation

(b) Negative Correlation

hot chocolate sales are 60 cups. At point F, the temperature rises to 50°F, but hot chocolate sales fall to 30 cups. At point G, the temperature is 70°F and hot chocolate sales are down to 10 cups. The purple line connecting points E–H illustrates the negative correlation between hot chocolate sales and temperature, because the line is downward sloping. This relationship contrasts with the positive correlation in Figure 2A.5a, where lemonade sales rise from point A to point D and the line is upward sloping. But what exactly is slope?

The Slope of a Curve

Slope
refers to the change in the rise along the *y* axis (vertical) divided by the change in the run along the *x* axis (horizontal).

A key element in any graph is the **slope**, or the rise along the *y* axis (vertical) divided by the run along the *x* axis (horizontal). The *rise* is the amount the vertical distance changes. The *run* is the amount the horizontal distance changes.

$$\text{Slope} = \frac{\text{change in } y}{\text{change in } x}$$

A slope can have a positive, negative, or zero value. A slope of zero—a straight horizontal line—indicates that there is no change in *y* for a given change in *x*. The slope can also be positive, as it is in Figure 2A.5a, or negative, as it is in Figure 2A.5b. Figure 2A.6 highlights the changes in *x* and *y* between the points

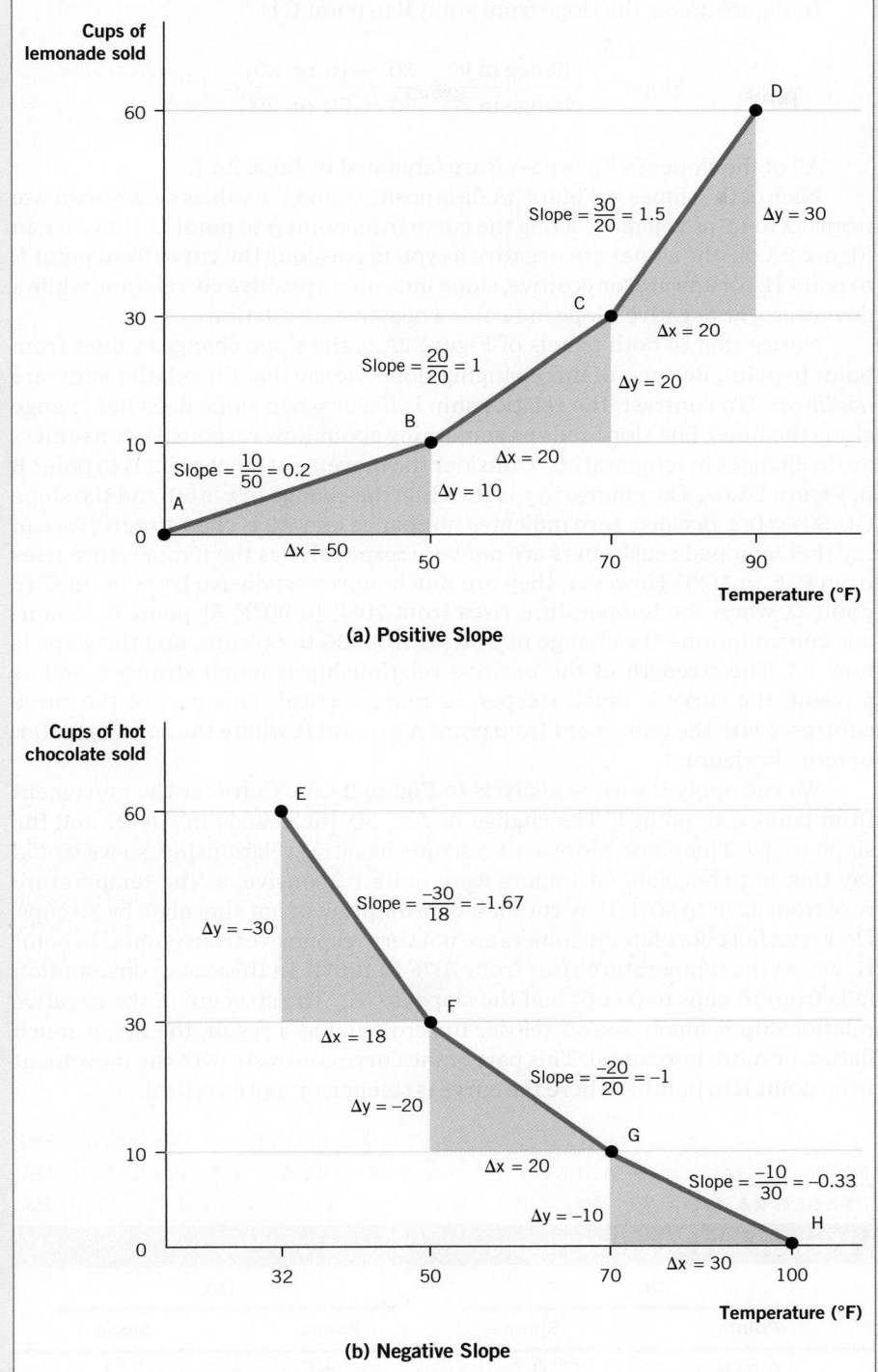

(a) Positive Slope

(b) Negative Slope

Positive and Negative Slopes

Notice that in both panels the slope changes value from point to point. Because of this changing slope value, we say that the relationships are nonlinear. In (a), the slopes are positive as you move along the curve from point A to point D. In (b), the slopes are negative as you move along the curve from point E to point H. An upward, or positive, slope indicates a positive correlation, while a negative, or downward, slope indicates a negative correlation.

on Figure 2A.5. (The change in a variable is often notated with a Greek delta symbol, Δ, which is read "change in.")

In Figure 2A.6a, the slope from point B to point C is

$$\text{Slope} = \frac{\text{change in } y}{\text{change in } x} = \frac{30 - 10 \text{ or } 20}{70 - 50 \text{ or } 20} = 1$$

All of the slopes in Figure 2A.6 are tabulated in Table 2A.1.

Each of the slopes in Figure 2A.6a is positive, and the values slowly increase from 0.2 to 1.5 as you move along the curve from point A to point D. However, in Figure 2A.6b, the slopes are negative as you move along the curve from point E to point H. An upward, or positive, slope indicates a positive correlation, while a downward, or negative, slope indicates a negative correlation.

Notice that in both panels of Figure 2A.6, the slope changes values from point to point. Because of this changing slope, we say that the relationships are *nonlinear*. (In contrast, the relationship is *linear* when slope does not change along the line.) The slope tells us something about how responsive consumers are to changes in temperature. Consider the movement from point A to point B in Figure 2A.6a. The change in y is 10, while the change in x is 50, and the slope (10/50) is 0.2. Because zero indicates no change and 0.2 is close to zero, we can say that lemonade customers are not very responsive as the temperature rises from 0°F to 50°F. However, they are much more responsive from point C to point D, when the temperature rises from 70°F to 90°F. At point D, lemonade consumption—the change in y—rises from 30 to 60 cups, and the slope is now 1.5. The strength of the positive relationship is much stronger, and as a result, the curve is much steeper, or more vertical. This part of the curve contrasts with the movement from point A to point B, where the curve is flatter, or more horizontal.

We can apply the same analysis to Figure 2A.6b. Consider the movement from point E to point F. The change in y is –30, the change in x is 18, and the slope is –1.7. This value represents a strong negative relationship, so we would say that hot chocolate customers were quite responsive; as the temperature rose from 32°F to 50°F, they cut their consumption of hot chocolate by 30 cups. However, hot chocolate customers are not very responsive from point G to point H, where the temperature rises from 70°F to 100°F. In this case, consumption falls from 10 cups to 0 cups and the slope is –0.3. The strength of the negative relationship is much weaker (closer to zero), and as a result, the line is much flatter, or more horizontal. This part of the curve contrasts with the movement from point E to point F, where the curve is steeper, or more vertical.

TABLE 2A.1			
Positive and Negative Slopes			
(a)		(b)	
Points	Slope	Points	Slope
A to B	0.2	E to F	−1.7
B to C	1.0	F to G	−1.0
C to D	1.5	G to H	−0.3

Formulas for the Area of a Rectangle and a Triangle

Sometimes, economists interpret graphs by examining the area of different sections below a curve. Consider the demand for Bruegger's Bagels shown in Figure 2A.7. The demand curve (labeled D) has a downward slope, which tells us that when the price of bagels falls, consumers will buy more bagels. (We will learn more about demand curves in Chapter 3.) But this curve also can tell us about the revenue the seller receives—one of the most important considerations for the firm. In this case, let's assume that the price of each bagel is $0.60 and Bruegger's sells 4,000 bagels each week. We can illustrate the total amount of Bruegger's revenue by shading the area bounded by the number of sales and the price—the green rectangle in the figure. In addition, we can identify the surplus benefit consumers receive from purchasing bagels; the blue triangle shows this amount. Because many buyers are willing to pay more than $0.60 per bagel, we can visualize the "surplus" consumers get from Bruegger's Bagels by highlighting the blue triangular area under the demand curve and above the price of $0.60.

To calculate the area of a rectangle, we use the formula

$$\text{Area of a rectangle} = \text{height} \times \text{base}$$

In Figure 2A.7, the green rectangle is the amount of revenue that Bruegger's Bagels receives when it charges $0.60 per bagel. The total revenue is $0.60 × 4,000, or $2,400.

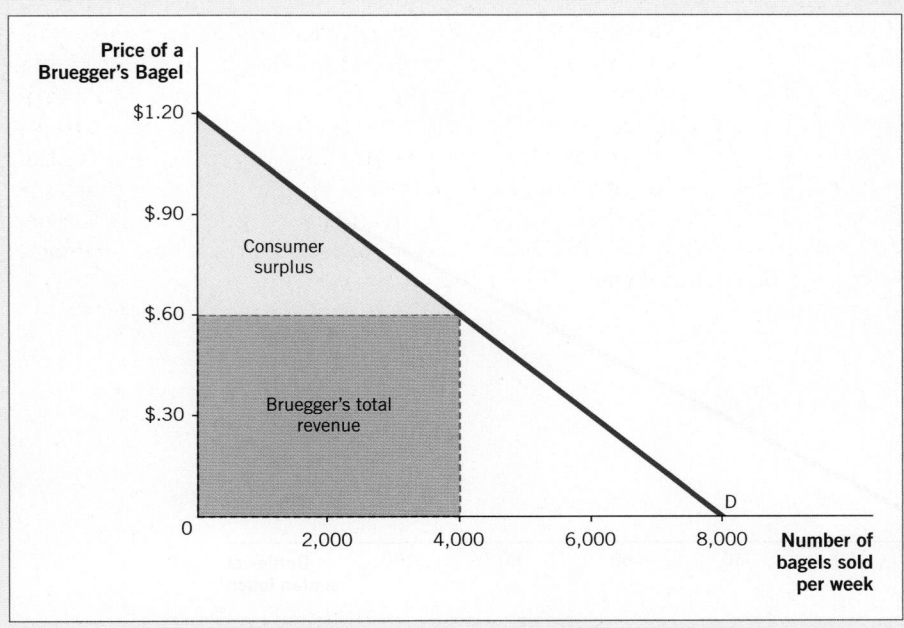

Working with Rectangles and Triangles

We can determine the area of the green rectangle by multiplying the height by the base. This gives us $0.60 × 4,000, or $2,400 for the total revenue earned by Bruegger's Bagels. We can determine the area of a triangle by using the formula $\frac{1}{2} \times$ height $\times$ base. This gives us $\frac{1}{2} \times$ $0.60 × 4,000, or $1,200 for the area of consumer surplus.

To calculate the area of a triangle, we use the formula

$$\text{Area of a triangle} = \tfrac{1}{2} \times \text{height} \times \text{base}$$

In Figure 2A.7, the blue triangle represents the amount of surplus consumers get from buying bagels. The amount of consumer surplus is $\tfrac{1}{2} \times \$0.60 \times 4{,}000 = \$1{,}200$. Note that the value of the height, $0.60, comes from reading the y axis: $1.20 at the top of the triangle $-$ $0.60 at the bottom of the triangle $=$ $0.60.

Cautions in Interpreting Numerical Graphs

In Chapter 2, we utilized *ceteris paribus*, which entails holding everything else around us constant (unchanged) while analyzing a specific relationship. Suppose that you omitted an important part of the relationship. What effect would this omission have on your ability to use graphs as an illustrative tool? Consider the relationship between sales of lemonade and sales of bottles of suntan lotion. The graph of the two variables would look something like Figure 2A.8.

FIGURE 2A.8

Graph with an Omitted Variable

What looks like a strongly positive correlation is misleading. What underlying variable is causing lemonade and suntan lotion sales to rise? The demand for both lemonade and suntan lotion rises because the temperature rises.

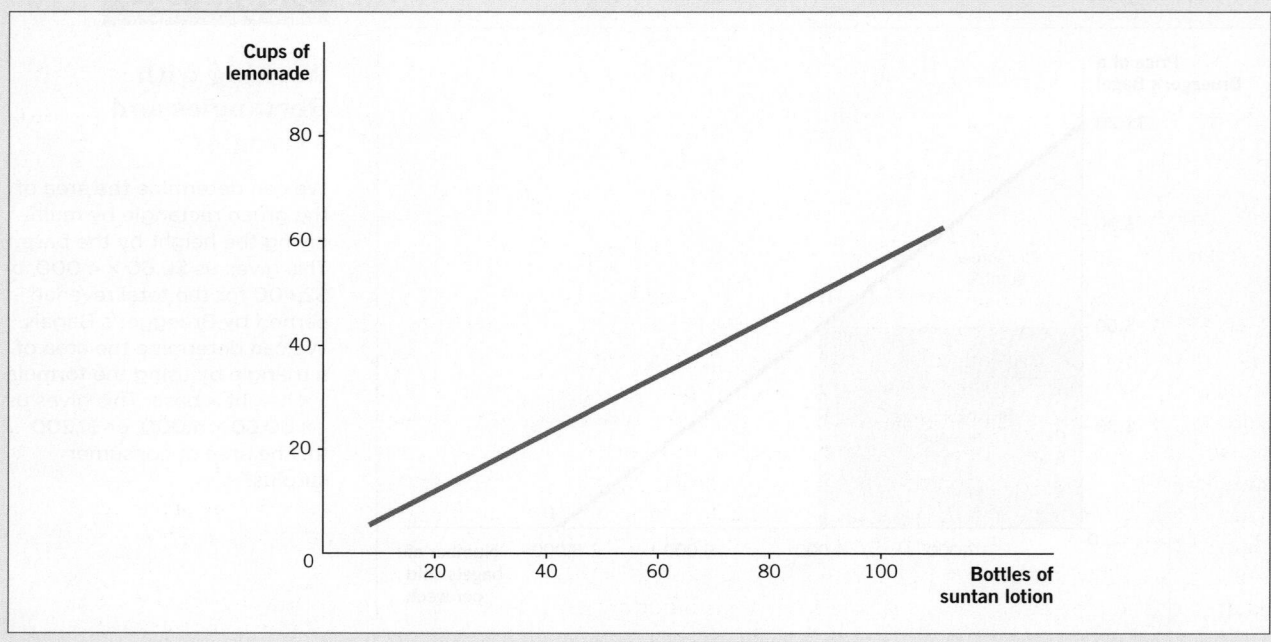

Reverse Causation

AIDS deaths are associated with having more doctors in the area. But the doctors are there to help and treat people, not harm them. Suggesting that more doctors in an area causes more deaths from AIDS would be a mistake—an example of reverse causation.

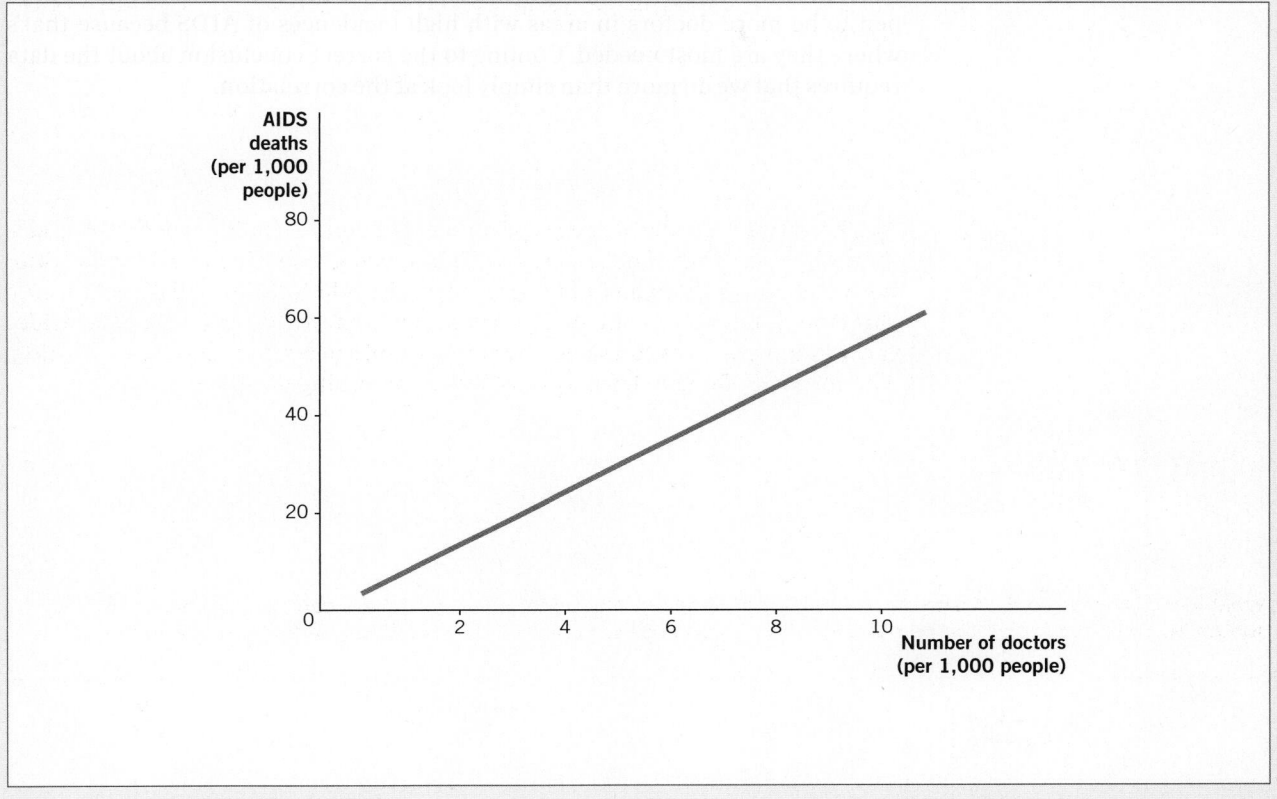

Looking at Figure 2A.8, you would not necessarily know that it is misleading. However, when you stop to think about the relationship, you quickly recognize that the graph is deceptive. Because the slope is positive, the graph indicates a positive correlation between the number of bottles of suntan lotion sold and the amount of lemonade sold. At first glance this relationship seems reasonable, because we associate suntan lotion and lemonade with summer activities. But the association does not imply **causality**, which occurs when one variable influences the other. Using more suntan lotion does not cause people to drink more lemonade. The **common cause** is that when it is hot outside, more suntan lotion is used and more lemonade is consumed. In this case, the causal factor is heat! The graph makes it look like the number of people using suntan lotion affects the amount of lemonade being consumed, when in fact the two variables are not directly related.

Causality
occurs when one variable influences another.

A **common cause** is a single cause responsible for two phenomena observed to correlate with each other.

Another possible mistake is **reverse causation**, which occurs when causation is incorrectly assigned among associated events. Suppose that in an effort to fight the AIDS epidemic in Africa, a research organization notes the correlation shown in Figure 2A.9.

After looking at the data, it is clear that as the number of doctors per 1,000 people goes up, so do death rates from AIDS. The research organization puts out a press release claiming that doctors are responsible for increasing AIDS deaths, and the media hypes the discovery. But hold on! Maybe there happen to be more doctors in areas with high incidences of AIDS because that's where they are most needed. Coming to the correct conclusion about the data requires that we do more than simply look at the correlation.

·APPENDIX PROBLEMS·

Concepts You Should Know

causality (p. 67)
common cause (p. 67)
negative correlation (p. 61)

positive correlation (p. 61)
reverse causation (p. 68)
scatterplot (p. 61)

slope (p. 62)
variable (p. 58)

Study Problems *(✳ solved at the end of the section)*

1. The following table shows the price and the quantity demanded of apples (per week).

Price per apple	Quantity demanded
$0.25	10
$0.50	7
$0.75	4
$1.00	2
$1.25	1
$1.50	0

a. Plot the data provided in the table into a graph.
b. Is the relationship between the price of apples and the quantity demanded negative or positive?

✳ **2.** In the following graph, calculate the value of the slope if the price rises from $20 to $40.

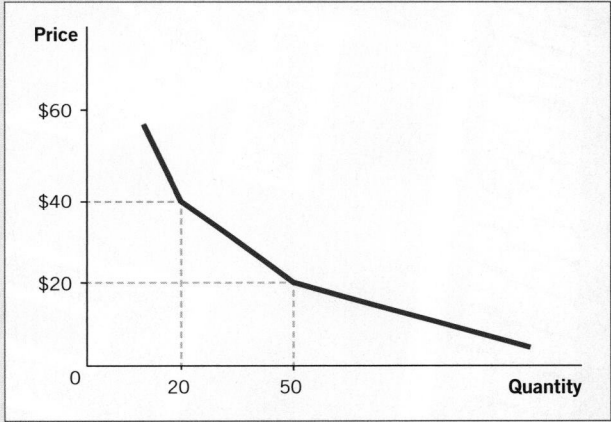

3. Explain the logical error in the following sentence: "As ice cream sales increase, the number of people who drown increases sharply. Therefore, ice cream causes drowning."

4. Of the following relationships, which are the result of a common cause or reverse causation?

a. Increased dash cam use causes more accidents to happen.
b. Increased sales of life jackets lead to more shark attacks.
c. When people wear sandals more often, it's because they're wearing shorts more often.

Solved Problem

2. The slope is calculated by using the formula:

$$\text{Slope} = \frac{\text{change in } y}{\text{change in } x} = \frac{\$40 - \$20}{20 - 50} = \frac{\$20}{-30} = -0.6667$$

PART II

The Role of
MARKETS

■ CHAPTER ■

03

The Market at Work:
Supply and Demand

Buyers and Sellers Together Determine the Price of the Good.

What do Starbucks, Nordstrom, and Amazon have in common? If you guessed that they all have headquarters in Seattle, that's true. But even more interesting is that each company supplies a product much in demand by consumers. Starbucks supplies coffee from coast to coast and seems to be everywhere someone wants a cup of coffee. Nordstrom, a giant retailer with hundreds of department stores, supplies fashion apparel to meet a broad spectrum of individual demand, from the basics to designer collections. Amazon delivers online products to customers all over the world. Demand for Amazon's products has made Jeff Bezos the richest person in the world.

Notice the two recurring words in the previous paragraph: "supply" and "demand." Sometimes buyers set the price— through live auctions, on eBay, or at shopgoodwill.com. Other times, sellers set the price and then adjust it based on how well an item sells and how much inventory remains. Buyers and sellers each influence both prices and quantities traded, so that these end up being determined by how buyers' and sellers' price-versus-quantity calculations interact.

This chapter describes how markets work and discusses the nature of competition. To shed light on the process, we introduce the formal model of demand and supply. We begin

Black Friday rush at Macy's means more demand. Customers storm the door while taking selfies to share the moment with their friends. Macy's and other Black Friday retailers offer a limited supply of dramatically reduced merchandise to get customers into their stores.

by looking at demand and supply separately. Then we combine them to see how they interact to establish the market price and determine how much is produced and sold.

· BIG QUESTIONS ·

- What are the fundamentals of markets?
- What determines demand?
- What determines supply?
- How do supply and demand interact to create equilibrium?

What Are the Fundamentals of Markets?

In a **market economy**, resources are allocated among households and firms with little or no government interference.

The **invisible hand** is a phrase coined by Adam Smith to refer to the unobservable market forces that guide resources to their highest-valued use.

Peak season is expensive…

Markets bring trading partners together to create order out of chaos. Companies supply goods and services, and customers want to obtain the goods and services that companies supply. In a **market economy**, resources are allocated among households and firms with little or no government interference. Adam Smith, the founder of modern economics, described the dynamic best: "It is not from the benevolence of the butcher, the brewer, or the baker, that we expect our dinner, but from their regard to their own interest." In other words, producers earn a living by selling the products consumers want. Consumers are also motivated by self-interest; they must decide how to use their money to select the goods they need or want the most. This process, which Adam Smith called the **invisible hand**, guides resources to their highest-valued use.

The exchange of goods and services in a market economy happens through prices that are established in markets. Those prices change according to the level of demand for a product and how much is supplied. For instance, hotel rates near Disney World are reduced in the fall when demand is low, and they peak in March when spring break occurs. If spring break takes you to a ski resort instead, you will find lots of company and high prices. But if you are looking for an outdoor adventure during the summer, ski resorts have plenty of lodging available at great rates.

Similarly, many parents know how hard it is to find a reasonably priced hotel room in a college town on graduation weekend. Likewise, a pipeline break or unsettled political conditions in the Middle East can disrupt the supply of oil and cause the price of gasoline to spike overnight. When higher gas prices continue over a period of time, consumers respond by changing their driving habits or buying more fuel-efficient cars.

Why does all of this happen? Supply and demand tell the story. We begin our exploration of supply and demand by looking at where they interact—in markets. A firm's degree of control over the market price is the distinguishing feature between *competitive markets* and *imperfect markets*.

... but off-season is a bargain.

Competitive Markets

Buyers and sellers of a specific good or service come together to form a market. Formally, a *market* is a collection of buyers and sellers of a particular product or service. The buyers create the demand for the product, while the sellers produce the supply. The interaction of the buyers and sellers in a market establishes the price and the quantity produced of a particular good or the amount of a service offered.

Trade creates value

Markets exist whenever goods and services are exchanged. Some markets are online, and others operate in traditional "brick and mortar" stores. Pike Place Market in Seattle is a collection of markets spread across 9 acres. For over a hundred years, it has brought together buyers and sellers of fresh, organic, and specialty foods. Because there is a large number of buyers and sellers for each type of product, we say that the markets at Pike Place are competitive. A **competitive market** is one in which there are so many buyers and sellers that each has only a small impact on the market price and output. In fact, the impact is so small that it is negligible.

A **competitive market** exists when there are so many buyers and sellers that each has only a small (negligible) impact on the market price and output.

At Pike Place Market, like other local markets, the goods sold by each vendor are similar. Because each buyer and seller is just one small part of the whole market, no single buyer or seller has any influence over the market price. These two characteristics—similar goods and many participants—create a highly competitive market in which the price and quantity sold of a good are determined by the market rather than by any one person or business.

One of many vendors at Pike Place Market.

To understand how competition works, let's look at sales of salmon at Pike Place Market. On any given day, dozens of vendors sell salmon at this market. If a single vendor is absent or runs out of salmon, the quantity supplied that day will not change significantly—the remaining sellers will have no trouble filling the void. The same is true for those buying salmon. Customers will have no trouble finding salmon at the remaining vendors. Whether a particular salmon buyer decides to show up on a given day makes little difference when hundreds of buyers visit the market each day. No single buyer or seller has any

The Empire State Building has one of the best views in New York City.

An **imperfect market** is one in which either the buyer or the seller can influence the market price.

Market power is a firm's ability to influence the price of a good or service by exercising control over its demand, supply, or both.

A **monopoly** exists when a single company supplies the entire market for a particular good or service.

appreciable influence on the price of salmon. As a result, the market for salmon at Pike Place Market is a competitive one.

Imperfect Markets

Markets are not always fully competitive. British economist Joan Robinson wrote that in imperfect competition, "a certain difficulty arises [because] the individual demand curve for the product of each of the firms . . . will depend to some extent upon the price policy of the others."[*] Accordingly, we define these **imperfect markets** as markets in which either the buyer or the seller can influence the market price. For example, the Empire State Building affords an iconic view of Manhattan. Not surprisingly, the cost of taking the elevator to the top of the building is not cheap. But many customers buy the tickets anyway because they have decided that the view is worth the price. The managers of the Empire State Building can set a high price for tickets because there is no other place in New York City with such a great view. From this example, we see that when sellers produce goods and services that are different from their competitors', they gain some control, or leverage, over the price they charge. The more unusual the product being sold, the more control the seller has over the price. When a seller has some control over the price, we say that the market is imperfect. Specialized products, such as popular video games, front-row concert tickets, or dinner reservations at a trendy restaurant, give the seller substantial pricing power. **Market power** is a firm's ability to influence the price of a good or service by exercising control over its demand, supply, or both.

In between the highly competitive environment at the Pike Place Market and markets characterized by a lack of competition, such as the Empire State Building with its iconic view, there are many other types of markets. Some, like the market for fast-food restaurants, are highly competitive but sell products that are not identical. Other businesses—for example, Comcast Cable—function like monopolies because they are the only provider of a service in a geographic area. A **monopoly** exists when a single company supplies the entire market for a particular good or service. We'll talk a lot more about different market structures, such as monopoly, in later chapters. But even in imperfect markets, the forces of supply and demand significantly influence producer and consumer behavior. For the time being, we'll keep our analysis focused on supply and demand in competitive markets.

What Determines Demand?

Demand exists when an individual or group wants something badly enough to pay or trade for it. How much an individual or group actually buys depends on the price of the good or service. In economics, the amount of a good or service that buyers are willing and able to purchase at the current price is known as the **quantity demanded**.

When the price of a good increases, consumers often respond by purchasing less of the good or buying something else. For instance, many consumers

The **quantity demanded** is the amount of a good or service that buyers are willing and able to purchase at the current price.

---

[*]Source: Joan Robinson, *The Economics of Imperfect Competition* (London: Macmillan, 1933).

Markets and the Nature of Competition

QUESTION: Which of the following are competitive markets? How will each firm price its products, and how much market power does each firm have?

1. gas stations at a busy interstate exit

2. a furniture store in an isolated small town

3. a fresh produce stand at a farmers' market

ANSWERS

1. Because each gas station sells the same product and competes for the same customers, they often charge the same price. This is a competitive market. However, gas stations also differentiate themselves by offering conveniences such as fast food, clean restrooms, ATM machines, and so forth. The result is that individual stations have some market power.

2. Residents would have to travel a significant distance to find another furniture store. This situation allows the small-town store to charge more than other furniture stores. The furniture store has some monopoly power. This is not a competitive market.

3. Because consumers can buy fresh produce in season from many stands at a farmers' market, individual vendors have very little market pricing power. They must charge the same price as other vendors in order to attract customers. This is a competitive market.

Is this a competitive market?

who would buy salmon at $5 per pound would likely buy something else if the price of salmon rose to $20 per pound. Therefore, as price goes up, quantity demanded goes down. Similarly, as price goes down, quantity demanded goes up. This negative (opposite) relationship between the price and the quantity demanded is the law of demand. The **law of demand** states that, all other things being equal, the quantity demanded falls when the price rises, and the quantity demanded rises when the price falls. The law of demand holds true over a wide range of goods and settings.

The Demand Curve

A table that shows the relationship between the price of a good and the quantity demanded is known as a **demand schedule**. To discuss this idea (and to take a break from fish markets), let's introduce a new hypothetical involving action hero and former athlete Dwayne "The Rock" Johnson. The Rock gets a lot of bumps and bruises in his active career, and Table 3.1 shows The Rock's hypothetical demand schedule for healing crystals. When the price is $20.00 or more per crystal, The Rock will not purchase any crystals. However, below $20.00, the amount The Rock purchases is negatively related to the price. For instance, at a price of $10.00, The Rock demands 4 crystals. If the price rises to $12.50, he demands 3 crystals. Every time the price increases, The Rock buys fewer crystals. In contrast, every time the price falls, he buys more. If the price falls to zero, The Rock would demand 8 crystals. That is, even if the crystals are free, there is a limit to his demand because he would grow tired of using the crystals.

Trade creates value

The **law of demand** states that, all other things being equal, quantity demanded falls when the price rises, and rises when the price falls.

A **demand schedule** is a table that shows the relationship between the price of a good and the quantity demanded.

Incentives

TABLE 3.1

The Rock's Demand for Healing Crystals

Price of healing crystals	Number demanded
$20.00	0
17.50	1
15.00	2
12.50	3
10.00	4
7.50	5
5.00	6
2.50	7
0.00	8

A **demand curve** is a graph of the relationship between the prices in the demand schedule and the quantity demanded at those prices.

The numbers in The Rock's demand schedule from Table 3.1 are plotted on a graph in Figure 3.1, known as a demand curve. A **demand curve** is a graph of the relationship between the prices in the demand schedule and the quantity demanded at those prices. For simplicity, the demand "curve" is often drawn as a straight line. Economists always place the independent variable, which is the price, on the *y* (vertical) axis and the dependent

FIGURE 3.1

The Rock's Demand Curve for Healing Crystals

The Rock's demand curve for healing crystals plots the data from Table 3.1. When the price of a crystal is $10.00, he buys 4. If the price rises to $12.50, The Rock reduces the quantity he buys to 3. The figure illustrates the law of demand by showing a negative relationship between price and the quantity demanded.

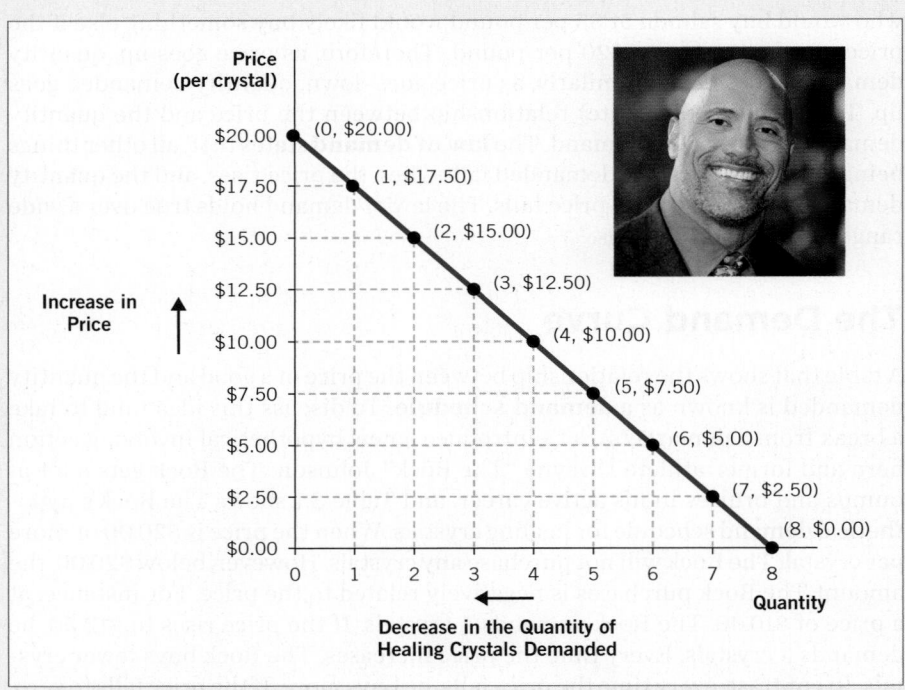

variable, which is the quantity demanded, on the *x* (horizontal) axis. The relationship between the price and the quantity demanded produces a downward-sloping curve. In Figure 3.1, we see that as the price rises from $0.00 to $20.00 along the *y* axis, the quantity demanded decreases from 8 to 0 along the *x* axis.

Market Demand

So far, we have studied individual demand, but a market is composed of many different buyers. In this section, we examine the collective demand of all of the buyers in a given market.

The **market demand** is the sum of all the individual quantities demanded by each buyer in a market at each price. During a typical day, thousands of individuals buy healing crystals. However, to make our analysis simpler, let's assume that our market consists of only two buyers, The Rock and Emma Stone, each of whom enjoys using healing crystals. Figure 3.2 shows individual demand schedules for the two people in this market, a combined market demand schedule, and the corresponding graphs. At a price of $10, Emma buys 2 crystals, while The Rock buys 4. To determine the market demand curve, we add Emma's 2 to The Rock's 4 for a total of 6 crystals. As you can see in the table within Figure 3.2, by adding Emma's demand and The Rock's demand, we arrive at the total (that is, combined) market demand. Any demand curve shows the law of demand with movements along (up or down) the curve that reflect the effect of a price change on the quantity demanded of the good or service. Only a change in price can cause a movement along a demand curve.

Market demand
is the sum of all the individual quantities demanded by each buyer in the market at each price.

Shifts of the Demand Curve

We have examined the relationship between price and quantity demanded. This relationship, described by the law of demand, shows us that when price changes, consumers respond by altering the amount they purchase. But in addition to price, many other variables influence how much of a good or service is purchased. For instance, news about the possible risks or benefits associated with the consumption of a good or service can change overall demand.

Suppose the government issues a nationwide safety warning that cautions against eating cantaloupe because of a recent discovery of *Listeria* bacteria in some melons. The government warning would cause consumers to buy fewer cantaloupes at any given price, and overall demand would decline. Looking at Figure 3.3, we see that an overall decline in demand will cause the entire demand curve to shift to the left of the original curve, from D_1 to D_2. Note that though the price remains at $5 per cantaloupe, demand has moved from 6 melons to 3. Figure 3.3 also shows what does *not* cause a shift of the demand curve: the price. The orange arrow alongside D_1 indicates that the quantity demanded will rise or fall in response to a price change. *A price change causes a movement along a given demand curve, but it cannot cause a shift of the demand curve.*

FIGURE 3.2

Calculating Market Demand

To calculate the market demand for healing crystals, we add Emma Stone's quantity demanded and The Rock's quantity demanded.

Price of healing crystals	Emma's demand	The Rock's demand	Combined market demand
$20.00	0	0	0
17.50	0	1	1
15.00	1	2	3
12.50	1	3	4
10.00	2	4	6
7.50	2	5	7
5.00	3	6	9
2.50	3	7	10
0.00	4	8	12

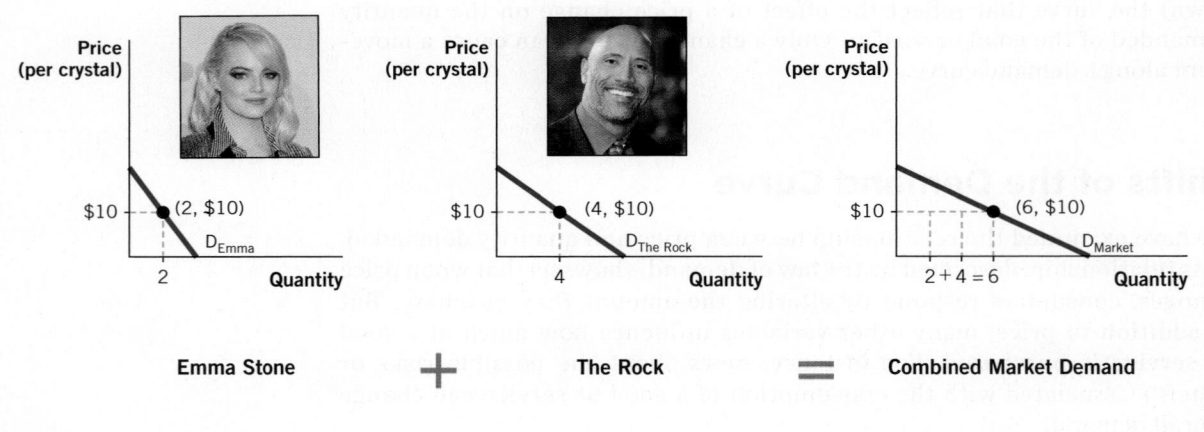

Emma Stone   +   The Rock   =   Combined Market Demand

A decrease in overall demand shifts the demand curve to the left. What happens when a variable causes overall demand to increase? Suppose that the news media have just announced the results of a medical study indicating that cantaloupe contains a natural substance that lowers cholesterol. Because of the newly discovered health benefits of cantaloupe, overall demand for it will increase. This increase in demand shifts the demand curve to the right, from D_1 to D_3, as Figure 3.3 shows.

Incentives

FIGURE 3.3

A Shift of the Demand Curve

When the price changes, the quantity demanded changes along the existing demand curve, as indicated by the orange arrow. A shift of the demand curve, indicated by the black arrows, occurs when something other than price changes.

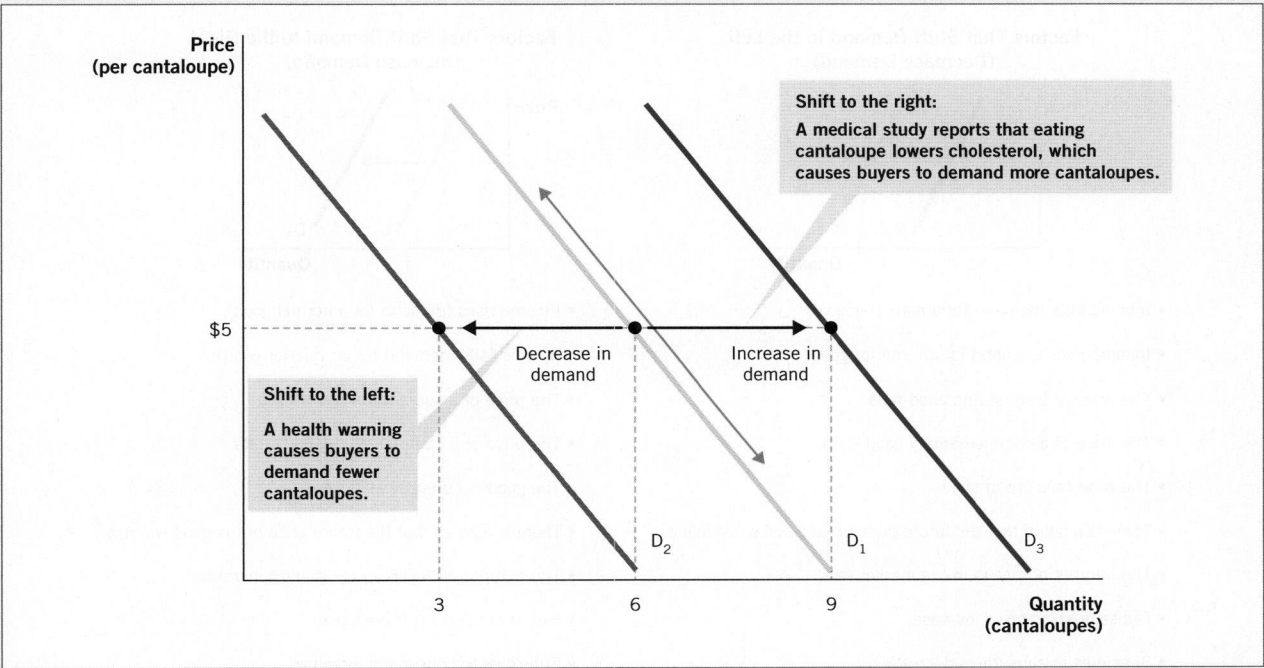

In our cantaloupe example, we saw that demand shifted because of changes in consumers' tastes and preferences. However, many different variables can shift demand. These include changes in buyers' income, the price of related goods, changes in buyers' tastes and preferences, price expectations, the number of buyers, and taxes.

Figure 3.4 provides an overview of the variables, or factors, that can shift demand. The easiest way to keep all of these elements straight is to ask yourself a simple question: Would this change cause me to buy more or less of the good? If the change reduces how much you would buy at any given price, you shift the demand curve to the left. If the change increases how much you would buy at any given price, you shift the curve to the right.

CHANGES IN BUYERS' INCOME When your income goes up, you have more to spend. Assuming that prices don't change, individuals with higher incomes are able to buy more of what they want. Similarly, when your income

If a new medical study indicates that eating more cantaloupe lowers cholesterol, would this finding cause a shift in demand, or a movement along the demand curve?

FIGURE 3.4

Factors That Shift the Demand Curve

The demand curve shifts to the left when a factor decreases demand. The demand curve shifts to the right when a factor increases demand. (*Note*: A change in price does not cause a shift. Price changes cause movements along the demand curve.)

Factors That Shift Demand to the Left
(Decrease Demand)

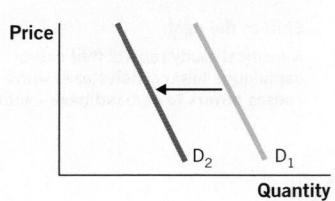

Factors That Shift Demand to the Right
(Increase Demand)

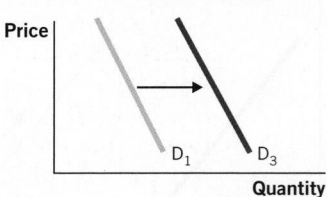

• Income falls (demand for a normal good).
• Income rises (demand for an inferior good).
• The price of a substitute good falls.
• The price of a complementary good rises.
• The good falls out of style.
• There is a belief that the future price of the good will decline.
• The number of buyers in the market falls.
• Excise or sales taxes increase.
• Subsidies to consumers decrease.

• Income rises (demand for a normal good).
• Income falls (demand for an inferior good).
• The price of a substitute good rises.
• The price of a complementary good falls.
• The good is currently in style.
• There is a belief that the future price of the good will rise.
• The number of buyers in the market increases.
• Excise or sales taxes decrease.
• Subsidies to consumers increase.

Purchasing power is the value of your income expressed in terms of how much you can afford.

Consumers buy more of a **normal good** as income rises, holding all other factors constant.

An **inferior good** is one where demand declines as income rises.

declines, your **purchasing power**, or how much you can afford, falls. In either case, your income affects your overall demand.

When economists look at how consumers spend, they often differentiate between two types of goods: normal and inferior. Consumers will buy more of a **normal good** as their income goes up (assuming all other factors remain constant). An example of a normal good is a meal at a restaurant. When income goes up, the demand for restaurant meals increases and the demand curve shifts to the right. Similarly, if income falls, the demand for restaurant meals goes down and the demand curve shifts to the left.

While consumers with an increased income may purchase more of some things, the additional purchasing power will mean they purchase fewer inferior goods. An **inferior good** is one where demand declines as income rises. Examples include rooms in boarding houses, as opposed to one's own apartment or house, and hamburgers and ramen noodles, as opposed to filet mignon. As income goes up, consumers buy less of an inferior good because they can afford something better. Within a specific product market, you can often find examples of inferior and normal goods in the form of different brands.

THE PRICE OF RELATED GOODS Another factor that can shift the demand curve is the price of related goods. Certain goods directly influence the demand for other goods. **Complements** are two goods that are used together. **Substitutes** are two goods that are used in place of each other.

Consider this pair of complements: smartphones and phone cases. What happens when the price of one of the complements—say, the smartphone—rises? As you would expect, the quantity demanded of the smartphone goes down. The demand for its complement, the phone case, also goes down because people are not likely to use one without the other.

Substitute goods work the opposite way. When the price of a substitute good increases, the quantity demanded declines, and the demand for the alternative good increases. For example, if the price of the PlayStation 4 goes up and the price of Microsoft's Xbox remains unchanged, the demand for Xbox will increase while the quantity demanded of the PS4 will decline.

CHANGES IN TASTES AND PREFERENCES Fashion goes in and out of style quickly. Walk into Nordstrom or another clothing retailer, and you will see that fashion changes from season to season and year to year. For instance, what do you think of heavily distressed jeans? They became popular a few years ago and are still a common sight today, but it is safe to assume that in a few years they will once again go out of style. While something is popular, demand increases. As soon as it falls out of favor, you can expect demand for it to decrease. Tastes and preferences can change quickly, and this fluctuation alters the demand for a particular good.

Though changes in fashion trends are usually purely subjective, other changes in preferences are the result of new information about the goods and services we buy. Recall our example of shifting demand for cantaloupe as the result of either the *Listeria* infection or new positive medical findings. This is one example of how information can influence consumers' preferences. Contamination would cause a decrease in demand because people would no longer want to eat cantaloupe. In contrast, if people learn that eating cantaloupe lowers cholesterol, their demand for the melon will go up.

PRICE EXPECTATIONS Have you ever waited to purchase a sweater because warm weather was right around the corner and you expected the price to come down? Conversely, have you ever purchased an airline ticket well in advance because you figured that the price would rise as the flight filled up? In both cases, expectations about the future influenced your current demand. If we expect a price to be higher tomorrow, we are likely to buy more today to beat the price increase. The result is an increase in current demand. Likewise, if you expect a price to decline soon, you might delay your purchases to try to get a lower price in the future. An expectation of a lower price in the future will therefore decrease current demand.

Complements
When the price of a complementary good rises, the quantity demanded of that good falls and the demand for the related good goes down.

Substitutes
are two goods that are used in place of each other. When the price of a substitute good rises, the quantity demanded of that good falls and the demand for the related good goes up.

Are these jeans stylish or fit for the dumpster? It depends on consumers' tastes in fashion at the time.

Shifting the Demand Curve

THE HUDSUCKER PROXY

This 1994 film by the Coen brothers, who would go on to bring us *Fargo* (1996) and the TV series based on it, chronicles the introduction of the hula hoop, a toy that set off one of the greatest fads in U.S. history. According to Wham-O, the manufacturer of the hoop, when the toy was first introduced in the late 1950s over 25 million were sold in four months.

One scene from the movie clearly illustrates the difference between movements along the demand curve and a shift of the entire demand curve.

The Hudsucker Corporation has decided to sell the hula hoop for $1.79. We see a toy store owner leaning next to the front door waiting for customers to enter. But business is slow. The movie cuts to the president of the company, played by Tim Robbins, sitting behind a big desk waiting to hear about sales of the new toy. It is not doing well. So the store lowers the price, first to $1.59, then to $1.49, and so on, until finally the hula hoop is "free with any purchase." But even this generous offer is not enough to attract consumers, so the toy store owner throws the unwanted hula hoops into the alley behind the store.

One of the unwanted toys rolls across the street and around the block before landing at the foot of a boy who is skipping school. He picks up the hula hoop and tries it out. He is a natural. When school lets out, a throng of students round the corner and see him

How did the hula hoop craze start?

playing with the hula hoop. Suddenly, everyone wants a hula hoop and there is a run on the toy store. Now preferences have changed, and the overall demand has increased. The hula hoop craze is born. In economic terms, we say that the increased demand has shifted the entire demand curve to the right. The toy store responds by ordering new hula hoops and raising the price to $3.99—the new market price after the increase, or shift, in demand.

This example reminds us that changes in price cannot shift the demand curve. Shifts in demand can happen only when an outside event influences human behavior.

THE NUMBER OF BUYERS Recall that the market demand curve is the sum of all individual demand curves. Therefore, another way for market demand to increase is for more individual buyers to enter the market. The United States adds 3 million people each year to its population through immigration and births. All those new people have needs and wants, just as the existing population of 325 million does. Collectively, the new people add about 1% to the overall size of many existing markets on an annual basis.

The number of buyers also varies by age. Consider two markets—one for baby products (such as diapers, high chairs, and strollers) and the other for health care (including medicine, cancer treatments, hip replacement surgery,

Shift of the Curve or Movement along the Curve?

Cheap pizza or...

...cheap drinks?

QUESTION: Suppose that a local pizza place likes to run a late-night special. The owners have contacted you for some advice. One of the owners tells you, "We want to increase the demand for our pizza." He proposes two marketing ideas to accomplish this goal:

1. Reduce the price of large pizzas.

2. Reduce the price of a complementary good—for example, offer two half-priced bottles or cans of soda with every large pizza ordered.

Which strategy will you recommend?

ANSWER: First, consider why late-night specials exist in the first place. Because most people prefer to eat dinner early in the evening, the pizzeria has to encourage late-night patrons to buy pizzas by stimulating demand. "Specials" are used during periods of low demand, when regular prices would leave the establishment largely empty.

Incentives

Next, look at what the question asks. The owners want to know which option would "increase demand" more. The question is very specific; the owners are looking for something that will increase (or shift) demand.

Consider the first option, a reduction in the price of pizzas. Let's look at this option graphically (see next graph). A reduction in the price of a large pizza causes a movement along the demand curve, or a change in the quantity demanded.

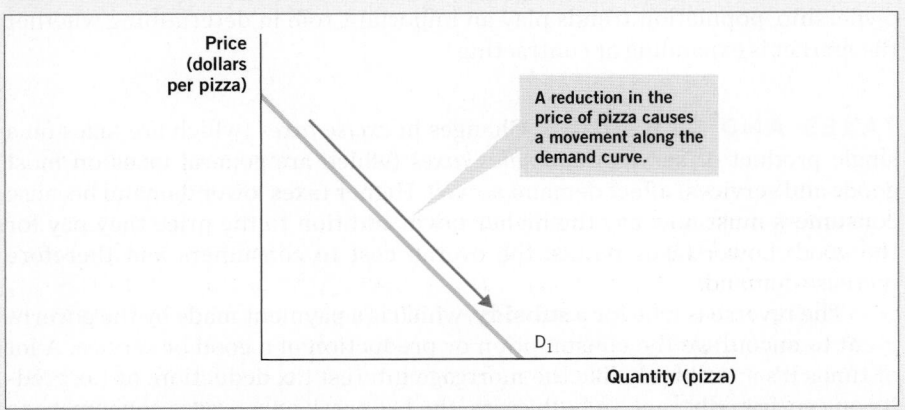

Price (dollars per pizza)

A reduction in the price of pizza causes a movement along the demand curve.

D₁

Quantity (pizza)

Now consider the second option, a reduction in the price of a complementary good. Let's look at this option graphically (next graph). A reduction in the price of a complementary good (for example, soda) causes the entire demand curve to shift. This is the correct answer, because the question asks which marketing idea would increase (or shift) demand more.

Recall that a reduction in the price of a complementary good shifts the demand curve to the right. The other answer, cutting the price of pizzas, causes a movement along the existing demand curve, which does not increase demand.

If you move along a curve instead of shifting it, you will analyze the problem incorrectly.

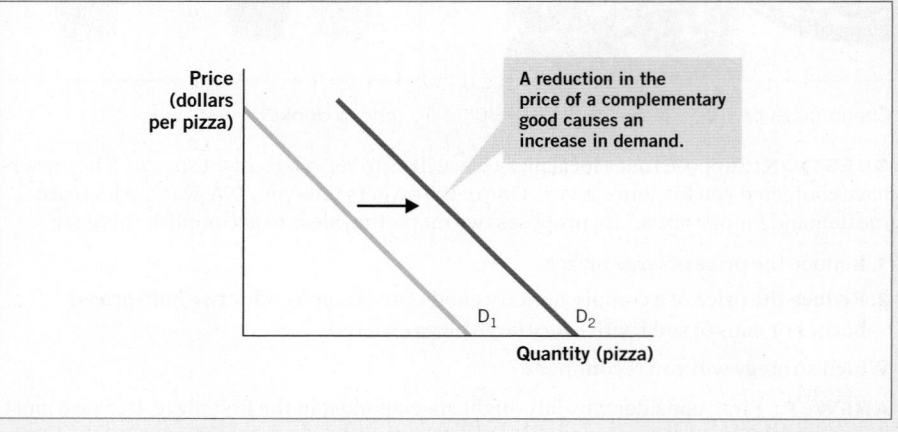

and nursing facilities). In countries with aging populations—for example, in Italy, where the birthrate has plummeted over several generations—the demand for baby products will decline and the demand for health care will expand. In other words, demographic changes in society are another source of shifts in demand. In many markets, ranging from movie theater attendance to home ownership, population trends play an important role in determining whether the market is expanding or contracting.

Incentives

A **subsidy** is a payment made by the government to encourage the consumption or production of a good or service.

TAXES AND SUBSIDIES Changes in *excise taxes* (which are taxes on a single product or service) and *sales taxes* (which are general taxes on most goods and services) affect demand as well. Higher taxes lower demand because consumers must now pay the higher tax in addition to the price they pay for the good. Lower taxes reduce the overall cost to consumers and therefore increase demand.

The reverse is true for a **subsidy**, which is a payment made by the government to encourage the consumption or production of a good or service. A lot of times it's a tax break, like the mortgage interest tax deduction, or tax credits on eco-friendly cars. In both cases, the tax break encourages consumers to purchase more of the subsidized good.

What Determines Supply?

Even though we have learned a great deal about demand, our understanding of markets is incomplete without also analyzing supply. Let's go back to Seattle's Pike Place Market and focus on the behavior of producers selling goods there.

We have seen that with demand, price and output are *negatively related*. That is, they move in opposite directions. With supply, however, the price level and quantity supplied are *positively related*. That is, they move in the same direction. For instance, few producers would sell salmon if the market price were $2.50 per pound, but many would sell it at a price of $20.00 per pound. (At $20.00, producers earn more profit than they do at a price of $2.50.) The **quantity supplied** is the amount of a good or service that producers are willing and able to sell at the current price. Higher prices cause the quantity supplied to increase. Conversely, lower prices cause the quantity supplied to decrease.

When price increases, producers often respond by offering more for sale. As price goes down, quantity supplied also goes down. This direct positive relationship between price and quantity supplied is the law of supply. The **law of supply** states that, all other things being equal, the quantity supplied increases when the price rises, and the quantity supplied falls when the price falls. This law holds true over a wide range of goods and settings.

The **quantity supplied** is the amount of a good or service producers are willing and able to sell at the current price.

The **law of supply** states that, all other things being equal, the quantity supplied of a good rises when the price of the good rises, and falls when the price of the good falls.

The Supply Curve

A **supply schedule** is a table that shows the relationship between the price of a good and the quantity supplied. The supply schedule for salmon in Table 3.2 shows how many pounds of salmon Sol Amon, owner of Pure Food Fish, would sell each month at different prices. (Pure Food Fish is a fish stand that sells all kinds of freshly caught seafood.) When the market price is $20.00 per pound, Sol is willing to sell 800 pounds. At $12.50, Sol's quantity offered is 500 pounds. If the price falls to $10.00, he offers 400 pounds. Every time the price falls, Sol offers less salmon. This means he is constantly adjusting the amount he offers.

A **supply schedule** is a table that shows the relationship between the price of a good and the quantity supplied.

TABLE 3.2

Pure Food Fish's Supply Schedule for Salmon

Price of salmon (per pound)	Pounds of salmon supplied (per month)
$20.00	800
17.50	700
15.00	600
12.50	500
10.00	400
7.50	300
5.00	200
2.50	100
0.00	0

FIGURE 3.5

Pure Food Fish's Supply Curve for Salmon

Pure Food Fish's supply curve for salmon plots the data from Table 3.2. When the price of salmon is $10.00 per pound, Pure Food Fish supplies 400 pounds. If the price rises to $12.50 per pound, Pure Food Fish increases its quantity supplied to 500 pounds. The figure illustrates the law of supply by showing a positive relationship between price and the quantity supplied.

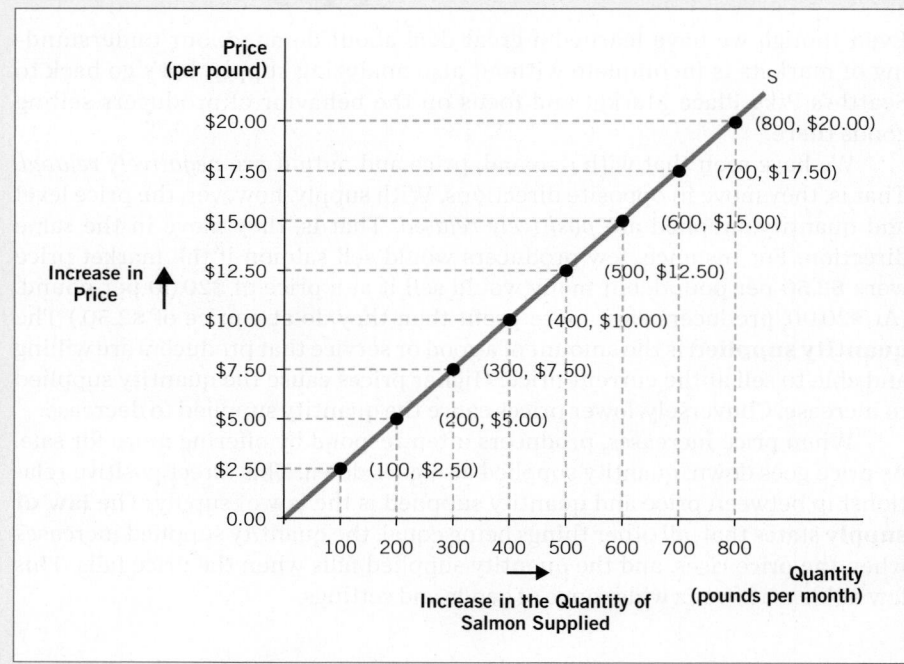

A **supply curve** is a graph of the relationship between the prices in the supply schedule and the quantity supplied at those prices.

As the price of salmon falls, so does Sol's profit from selling it. Because Sol's livelihood depends on selling seafood, he has to find a way to compensate for the lost income. So he might offer more cod instead.

Sol and the other seafood vendors must respond to price changes by adjusting what they offer for sale in the market. This is why Sol offers more salmon when the price rises and less salmon when the price declines.

When we plot the supply schedule in Table 3.2, we get the supply curve shown in Figure 3.5. A **supply curve** is a graph of the relationship between the prices in the supply schedule and the quantity supplied at those prices. As you can see in Figure 3.5, this relationship produces an upward-sloping curve. Sellers are more willing to supply the market when prices are high, because this higher price generates more profits for the business. The upward-sloping curve means that the slope of the supply curve is positive, which illustrates a direct (positive) relationship between the price and the quantity offered for sale. For instance, when the price of salmon increases from $10.00 per pound to $12.50 per pound, Pure Food Fish will increase the quantity it supplies to the market from 400 pounds to 500 pounds.

Incentives

Market Supply

Market supply is the sum of the quantities supplied by each seller in the market at each price.

Sol Amon is not the only vendor selling fish at the Pike Place Market. The **market supply** is the sum of the quantities supplied by each seller in the market at each price. However, to make our analysis simpler, let's assume that

FIGURE 3.6

Calculating Market Supply

Market supply is calculated by adding together the quantity supplied by individual vendors. The total quantity supplied, shown in the last column of the table, is illustrated in the market supply graph below.

Price of salmon (per pound)	City Fish's supply (per month)	Pure Food Fish's supply (per month)	Combined market supply (pounds of salmon)
$20.00	200	800	1000
17.50	175	700	875
15.00	150	600	750
12.50	125	500	625
10.00	100	400	500
7.50	75	300	375
5.00	50	200	250
2.50	25	100	125
0.00	0	0	0

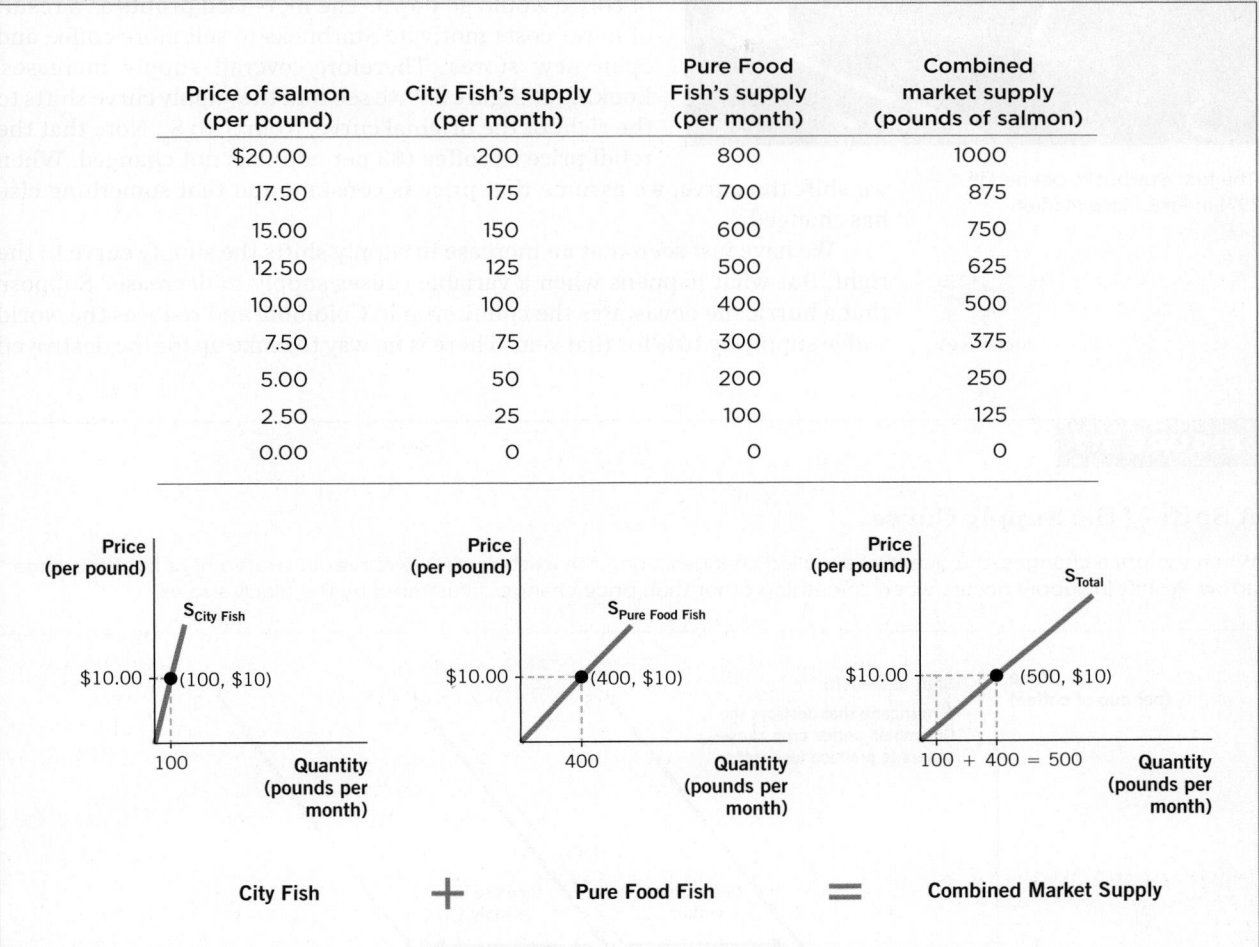

our market consists of just two sellers, City Fish and Pure Food Fish, each of which sells salmon. Figure 3.6 shows supply schedules for those two fish sellers and the combined, total-market supply schedule and the corresponding graphs.

Looking at the supply schedule (the table within the figure), you can see that at a price of $10.00 per pound, City Fish supplies 100 pounds of salmon, while Pure Food Fish supplies 400 pounds. To determine the total market supply, we add City Fish's 100 pounds to Pure Food Fish's 400 pounds for a total market supply of 500 pounds.

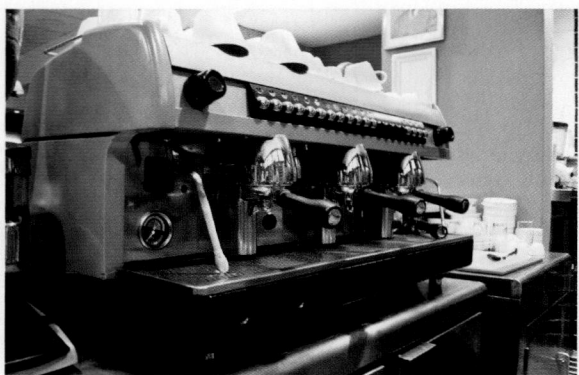

The first Starbucks opened in 1971 in Pike Place Market.

Incentives

Shifts of the Supply Curve

When a variable other than the price changes, the entire supply curve shifts. For instance, suppose that beverage scientists at Starbucks discover a new way to brew a richer coffee at half the cost. The new process would increase the company's profits because its costs of supplying a cup of coffee would go down. The increased profits as a result of lower costs motivate Starbucks to sell more coffee and open new stores. Therefore, overall supply increases. Looking at Figure 3.7, we see that the supply curve shifts to the right of the original curve, from S_1 to S_2. Note that the retail price of coffee ($3 per cup) has not changed. When we shift the curve, we assume that price is constant and that something else has changed.

We have just seen that an increase in supply shifts the supply curve to the right. But what happens when a variable causes supply to decrease? Suppose that a hurricane devastates the coffee crop in Colombia and reduces the world coffee supply by 10% for that year. There is no way to make up for the destroyed

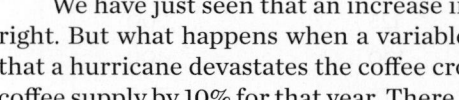

FIGURE 3.7

A Shift of the Supply Curve

When the price changes, the quantity supplied changes along the existing supply curve, illustrated here by the orange arrow. A shift in supply occurs when something other than price changes, illustrated by the black arrows.

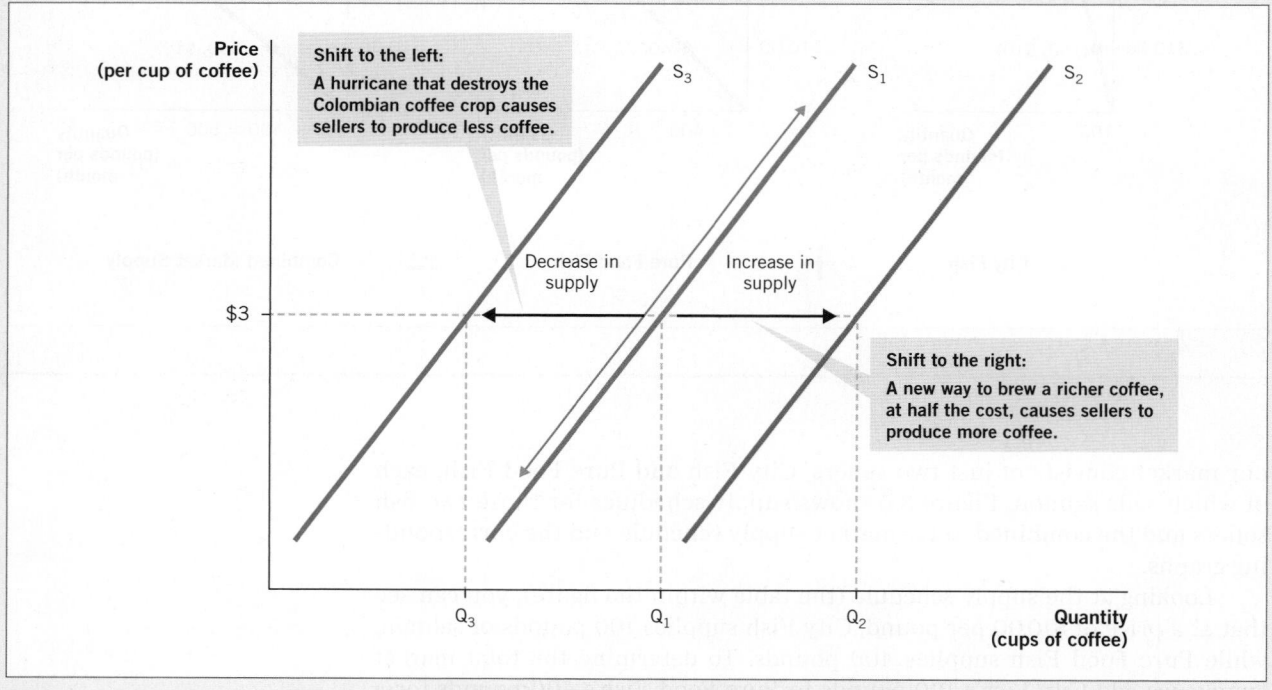

coffee crop, and for the rest of the year at least, the quantity of coffee supplied will be less than the previous year. This decrease in supply shifts the supply curve in Figure 3.7 to the left, from S_1 to S_3.

Many variables can shift supply, but Figure 3.7 also reminds us of what does *not* cause a shift in supply: the price. Recall that price is the variable that causes the supply curve to slope upward. The orange arrow alongside S_1 indicates that the quantity supplied will rise or fall in response to a price change. *A price change causes a movement along the supply curve, not a shift in the curve.*

Factors that shift the supply curve include the cost of inputs, changes in technology or the production process, taxes and subsidies, the number of firms in the industry, and price expectations. Figure 3.8 provides an overview of these variables that shift the supply curve. The easiest way to keep them straight is to ask yourself a simple question: Would the change cause a business to produce more of the good or less of the good? If the change would reduce the amount of a good or service a business is willing and able to supply at every given price, the supply curve shifts to the left. If the change would increase the amount of a good or service a business is willing and able to supply at every given price, the supply curve shifts to the right.

THE COST OF INPUTS **Inputs** are resources used in the production process. Inputs may include workers, equipment, raw materials, buildings, and capital goods. Each of these resources is critical to the production process.

Inputs
are resources used in the production process.

FIGURE 3.8

Factors That Shift the Supply Curve

The supply curve shifts to the left when a factor decreases supply. The supply curve shifts to the right when a factor increases supply. (*Note*: A change in price does not cause a shift. Price changes cause movements along the supply curve.)

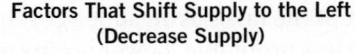

Factors That Shift Supply to the Left (Decrease Supply)

Factors That Shift Supply to the Right (Increase Supply)

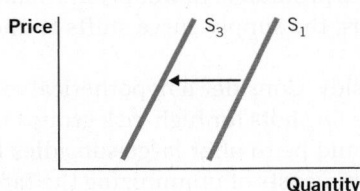

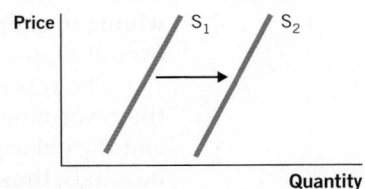

- The cost of an input rises.

- Business taxes increase or subsidies decrease.

- The number of sellers decreases.

- The price of the product is anticipated to rise in the future.

- Capital or resource destruction (e.g. damage caused by a hurricane).

- The cost of an input falls.

- Business taxes decrease or subsidies increase.

- The number of sellers increases.

- The price of the product is expected to fall in the future.

- The business deploys more efficient technology.

Baristas' wages make up a large share of the cost of selling coffee.

When the cost of inputs change, so does the seller's profit. If the cost of inputs declines, profits improve. Improved profits make the firm more willing to supply the good. So, for example, if Starbucks is able to purchase coffee beans at a significantly reduced price, it will want to supply more coffee. Conversely, higher input costs reduce profits. For instance, at Starbucks, the salaries of Starbucks store employees (or baristas, as they are commonly called) are a large part of the production cost. An increase in the minimum wage would require Starbucks to pay its workers more. This higher minimum wage would raise the cost of making coffee and make Starbucks less willing to supply the same amount of coffee at the same price.

CHANGES IN TECHNOLOGY OR THE PRODUCTION PROCESS *Technology* encompasses knowledge that producers use to make their products. An improvement in technology enables a producer to increase output with the same resources or to produce a given level of output with fewer resources. For example, if a new espresso machine works twice as fast as the old machine, Starbucks could serve its customers more quickly, reduce long lines, and increase its sales. As a result, Starbucks would be willing to produce and sell more espressos at each price in its established menu. In other words, if the producers of a good discover a new and improved technology or a better production process, there will be an increase in supply. That is, the supply curve for the good will shift to the right.

TAXES AND SUBSIDIES Taxes placed on suppliers are an added cost of doing business. For example, if property taxes are increased, the cost of doing business goes up. A firm may attempt to pass along the tax to consumers through higher prices, but higher prices will discourage sales. So, in some cases, the firm will simply have to accept the taxes as an added cost of doing business. Either way, a tax makes the firm less profitable. Lower profits make the firm less willing to supply the product; thus, the supply curve shifts to the left and the overall supply declines.

The reverse is true for a subsidy. Consider a hypothetical example where the government wants to promote flu shots for high-risk groups like the young and the elderly. One approach would be to offer large subsidies to clinics and hospitals, thus offsetting those firms' costs of immunizing the targeted groups. The supply curve of immunizations greatly shifts to the right under the subsidy, so the price falls. As a result, vaccination rates increase over what they would be in a market without the subsidy.

THE NUMBER OF FIRMS IN THE INDUSTRY We saw that an increase in total buyers (population) shifts the demand curve to the right. A similar dynamic happens with an increase in the number of sellers in an industry. Each additional firm that enters the market increases the available supply of a good. In graphic form, the supply curve shifts to the right to reflect

WHY DO THE PRICES OF NEW ELECTRONICS ALWAYS DROP?

The first personal computers (PCs) released in the 1980s cost as much as $10,000. Today, you can purchase a laptop computer for less than $500. When a new technology emerges, prices are initially very high and then tend to fall rapidly. The first PCs profoundly changed the way people could work with information. Before the PC, complex programming could be done only on large mainframe computers that often took up an entire room. But at first only a few people could afford a PC. What makes emerging technology so expensive when it is first introduced and so inexpensive later in its life cycle? Supply tells the story. Advances in manufacturing methods lead to an increased willingness to supply, and therefore the supply curve shifts out. When the supply expands, there is both an increase in the quantity sold and a lower price.

Technological progress is also driving newer markets, like the market for custom shoes. 3D printing makes it possible for anyone go online, or enter information at a kiosk in a store, and order shoes that are 100% customized. You can design the uppers, insoles, and tread however you like, and in about an hour, your shoes will be printed for you. If your two feet are slightly different sizes, you will get two different-size insoles, to match your feet perfectly! Fully customized 3D printed shoes are still pretty pricey (about $300), but the price is dropping rapidly as the process becomes more efficient and designers build templates that make it easier for customers to get exactly what they want. As the technology continues to improve, the supply curve will continue to shift out. With time, customized shoes may eventually become so cheap that almost everyone will be able to afford them easily—just like computers today!

Why did consumers pay $5,000 for this?

the increased production. By the same reasoning, if the number of firms in the industry decreases, the supply curve shifts to the left.

Changes in the number of firms in a market are a regular part of business. For example, if a new pizza joint opens up nearby, more pizzas can be produced and supply expands. Conversely, if a pizzeria closes, the number of pizzas produced falls and supply contracts.

PRICE EXPECTATIONS A seller who expects a higher price for a product in the future may wish to delay sales until a time when the product will bring a higher price. For instance, florists know that the demand for roses spikes on Valentine's Day and Mother's Day. Because of higher demand, they can charge higher prices. To be able to sell more flowers during the times of peak demand, many florists work longer hours and hire temporary employees. These actions allow them to make more deliveries, so supply increases.

Likewise, the expectation of lower prices in the future will cause sellers to offer more while prices are still relatively high. This effect is particularly noticeable in the electronics sector, where newer—and much better—products are constantly being developed and released. Sellers know that their current offerings will soon be replaced by something better and that consumer demand for the existing technology will then plummet. This means that prices typically fall when a product has been on the market for a time. Because producers know that the price will fall, they supply as many of the current models as possible before the next wave of innovation cuts the price they can charge.

PRACTICE WHAT YOU KNOW

Ice Cream: Supply and Demand

I scream, you scream, we all scream for ice cream.

QUESTION: Which one of the following will increase the demand for ice cream?

a. a decrease in the price of the butterfat used to make ice cream

b. a decrease in the price of ice cream

c. an increase in the price of the milk used to make ice cream

d. an increase in the price of frozen yogurt, a substitute for ice cream

ANSWER: If you answered b, you made a common mistake. A change in the price of a good cannot change overall market demand; it can only cause a movement along an existing curve. So, as important as price changes are, they are not the right answer. Instead, you need to look for an event that shifts the entire curve.

Choices a and c refer to the prices of butterfat and milk. Because these are the inputs of production for ice cream, a change in their prices will shift the supply curve, not the demand curve. That leaves choice d as the only possibility. Choice d is correct because the increase in the price of frozen yogurt will cause consumers to substitute away from frozen yogurt and toward ice cream. This shift in consumer behavior will result in an increase in the demand for ice cream even though its price remains the same.

QUESTION: Which one of the following will decrease the supply of chocolate ice cream?

a. a medical report finding that consuming chocolate prevents cancer

b. a decrease in the price of chocolate ice cream

c. an increase in the price of chocolate, an ingredient used to make chocolate ice cream

d. an increase in the price of whipped cream, a complementary good

ANSWER: We know that b cannot be the correct answer because a change in the price of the good cannot change supply; it can only cause a movement along an existing curve. Choices a and d would both cause a change in demand without affecting the supply curve. That leaves choice c as the only possibility. Chocolate is a necessary ingredient in the production process. Whenever the price of an input rises, profits are squeezed. The result is a decrease in supply at the existing price.

How Do Supply and Demand Interact to Create Equilibrium?

We have examined supply and demand separately. Now it is time to see how the two interact. The real power of supply and demand analysis is in how well it predicts prices and output in the entire market.

Supply, Demand, and Equilibrium

Let's consider the market for salmon again. This example meets the conditions for a competitive market because the salmon sold by one vendor is essentially the same as the salmon sold by another, and there are many individual buyers.

In Figure 3.9, we see that when the price of salmon fillets is $10 per pound, consumers demand 500 pounds and producers supply 500 pounds. This situation is represented graphically at point E, known as the point of **equilibrium**, where the demand curve and the supply curve intersect. At this point, the two opposing forces of supply and demand are perfectly balanced.

Notice that at $10 per pound, the quantity demanded equals the quantity supplied. At this price, and only this price, the entire supply of salmon in the market is sold. Moreover, every buyer who wants salmon is able to find some and every producer is able to sell his or her entire stock. We say that $10 is the **equilibrium price** because the quantity supplied equals the quantity demanded. The equilibrium price is also called the *market-clearing price*, because this is the only price at which no surplus or shortage of the good exists. Similarly, there is also an **equilibrium quantity** at which the quantity supplied equals the quantity demanded (in this example, 500 pounds). When the market is in equilibrium, we sometimes say that *the market clears* or that *the price clears the market*.

The equilibrium point has a special place in economics because movements away from that point throw the market out of balance. The equilibrium process is so powerful that it is often referred to as the **law of supply and demand**, the idea that market prices adjust to bring the quantity supplied and the quantity demanded into balance.

Equilibrium occurs at the point where the demand curve and the supply curve intersect.

The **equilibrium price** is the price at which the quantity supplied is equal to the quantity demanded. It is also known as the *market-clearing price*.

The **equilibrium quantity** is the amount at which the quantity supplied is equal to the quantity demanded.

The **law of supply and demand** states that the market price of any good will adjust to bring the quantity supplied and the quantity demanded into balance.

FIGURE 3.9

The Salmon Market

At the equilibrium point, E, quantity supplied and quantity demanded are perfectly balanced. At prices above the equilibrium price, a surplus exists. At prices below the equilibrium price, a shortage exists.

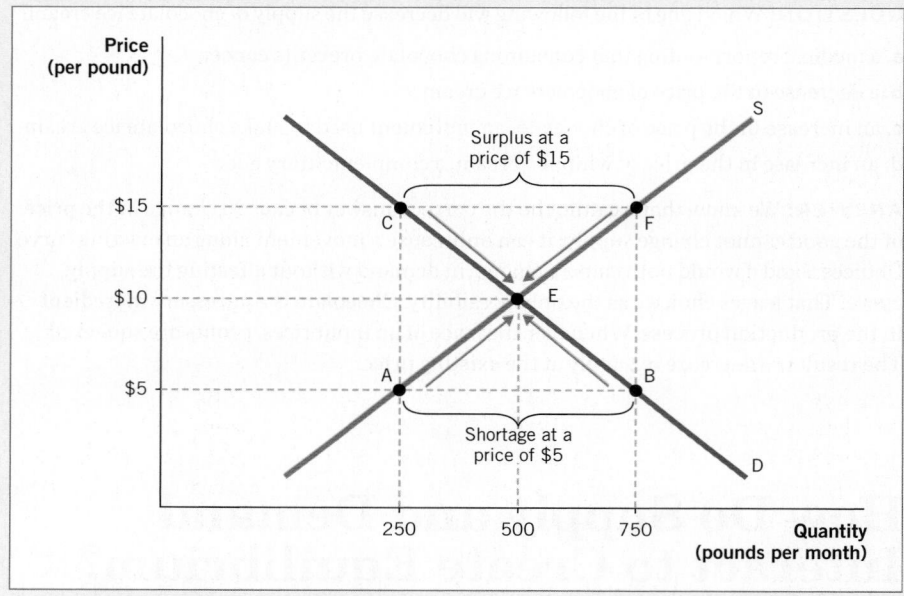

SHORTAGES AND SURPLUSES How does the market respond when it is not in equilibrium? Let's look at two other prices for salmon shown on the y axis in Figure 3.9: $5 per pound and $15 per pound.

At a price of $5 per pound, salmon is quite attractive to buyers but not very profitable to sellers. The quantity demanded is 750 pounds, represented by point B on the demand curve (D). However, the quantity supplied, which is represented by point A on the supply curve (S), is only 250 pounds. So at $5 per pound there is an excess quantity of 750 − 250 = 500 pounds demanded. This excess demand creates disequilibrium in the market.

When there is more demand for a product than sellers are willing or able to supply, we say there is a shortage. A **shortage**, or *excess demand*, occurs whenever the quantity supplied is less than the quantity demanded. In our case, at a price of $5 per pound of salmon, there are three buyers for each pound. New shipments of salmon fly out the door, providing a strong signal for sellers to raise the price. As the market price increases in response to the shortage, sellers continue to increase the quantity they offer. You can see the increase in quantity supplied on the graph in Figure 3.9 by following the upward-sloping arrow from point A to point E. At the same time, as the price rises, buyers demand an increasingly smaller quantity, represented by the arrow from point B to point E along the demand curve. Eventually, when the price reaches $10 per pound, the quantity supplied and the quantity demanded are equal. The market is in equilibrium.

What happens when the price is set above the equilibrium point—say, at $15 per pound? At this price, salmon is quite profitable for sellers but not very attractive to buyers. The quantity demanded, represented by point C on the demand curve, is 250 pounds. However, the quantity supplied, represented by point F on the supply curve, is 750 pounds. In other words, sellers provide 500 pounds more than buyers wish to purchase. This excess supply creates disequilibrium in the

A **shortage** occurs whenever the quantity supplied is less than the quantity demanded. A shortage is also called *excess demand*.

market. Any buyer who is willing to pay $15 for a pound of salmon can find some because there are 3 pounds available for every customer. A **surplus**, or *excess supply*, occurs whenever the quantity supplied is greater than the quantity demanded.

When there is a surplus, sellers realize that salmon has been oversupplied, giving them a strong signal to lower the price. As the market price decreases in response to the surplus, more buyers enter the market and purchase salmon. Figure 3.9 represents this situation on the demand side by the downward-sloping arrow moving from point C to point E along the demand curve. At the same time, sellers reduce output, represented by the arrow moving from point F to point E on the supply curve. As long as the surplus persists, the price will continue to fall. Eventually, the price reaches $10 per pound. At this point, the quantity supplied and the quantity demanded are equal and the market is in equilibrium again.

In competitive markets, surpluses and shortages are resolved through the process of price adjustment. Buyers who are unable to find enough salmon at $5 per pound compete to find the available stocks; this competition drives the price up. Likewise, businesses that cannot sell their product at $15 per pound must lower their prices to reduce inventories; this desire to sell all inventory drives the price down.

Every seller and buyer has a vital role to play in the market. Venues like the Pike Place Market bring buyers and sellers together. Amazingly, market equilibrium occurs without the need for government planning to ensure an adequate supply of the goods consumers want or need. You might think that a decentralized system would create chaos, but nothing could be further from the truth. Markets work because buyers and sellers can rapidly adjust to changes in prices. These adjustments bring balance. When markets were suppressed in communist countries during the twentieth century, shortages were commonplace, in part because there was no market price system to signal that additional production was needed.

In summary, Figure 3.10 provides four examples of what happens when either the supply curve or the demand curve shifts. As you study these examples, you should develop a sense for how price and quantity are affected by changes in supply and demand. When one curve shifts, we can make a definitive statement about how price and quantity will change.

In Appendix 3A, we consider what happens when supply and demand change at the same time. There you will discover the challenges in simultaneously determining price and quantity when more than one variable changes.

PRACTICE WHAT YOU KNOW

Bacon: Supply and Demand

QUESTION: Suppose that the government decides to subsidize bacon producers. What is the impact on the equilibrium market price and output?

ANSWER: In order to answer this question, you first need to determine whether the supply curve or the demand curve shifts in response to the subsidy. Since the subsidy is given to the bacon producers, the supply curve shifts out. The end result is that the market price falls to P_2 and the market output increases to Q_2.

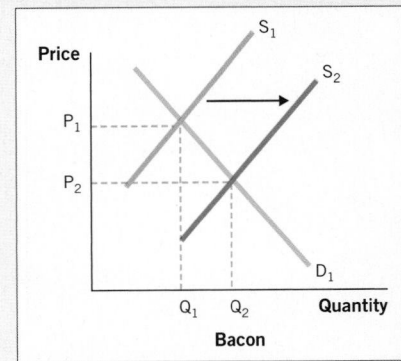

CHALLENGE QUESTION: Is the statement in the meme true or false?

They were made for each other

Let's lower our price and raise our demand

ANSWER: By now you should know that a price decrease causes a change in the quantity demanded, not a change in demand. Therefore, you might be tempted to judge the meme false. But if you did, you would be wrong! Let's see why. The first step is recognizing that bacon and eggs are complements. Therefore, a reduction in the price of the one increases the demand for the other. Recall that a reduction in the price of a complementary good shifts the demand curve to the right. The second step is to look at this graphically (see the graphs below). Using the color-coded letters, we see that (B_1) the price drop on bacon causes an increase in the quantity demanded of bacon (a slide along the existing demand curve) and (E_2) since consumers buy more bacon than before, this increases the demand for eggs (demand shifts to the right) in the egg market. At the same time, (E_1) the price drop on eggs causes an increase in the quantity demanded of eggs (a slide along the existing demand curve) and (B_2) since consumers buy more eggs than before, this increases the demand for bacon (demand shifts to the right) in the bacon market. We model this by showing the two related markets, bacon and eggs, side by side so you can see how a price reduction of the related goods increases the "demand for each other." Since both curves shift out, the meme is true!

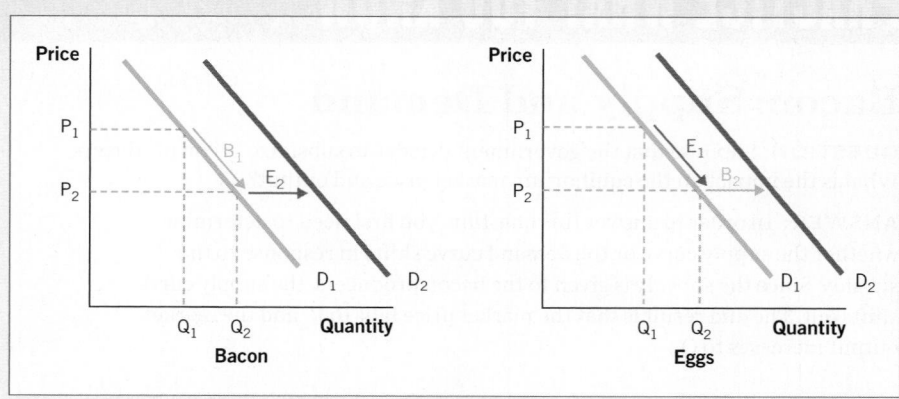

FIGURE 3.10

Price and Quantity When Either Supply or Demand Changes

Change	Illustration	Impact on price and quantity
1. Demand increases; supply does not change.		The demand curve shifts to the right. As a result, the equilibrium price and the equilibrium quantity increase.
2. Supply increases; demand does not change.		The supply curve shifts to the right. As a result, the equilibrium price decreases and the equilibrium quantity increases.
3. Demand decreases; supply does not change.		The demand curve shifts to the left. As a result, the equilibrium price and the equilibrium quantity decrease.
4. Supply decreases; demand does not change.		The supply curve shifts to the left. As a result, the equilibrium price increases and the equilibrium quantity decreases.

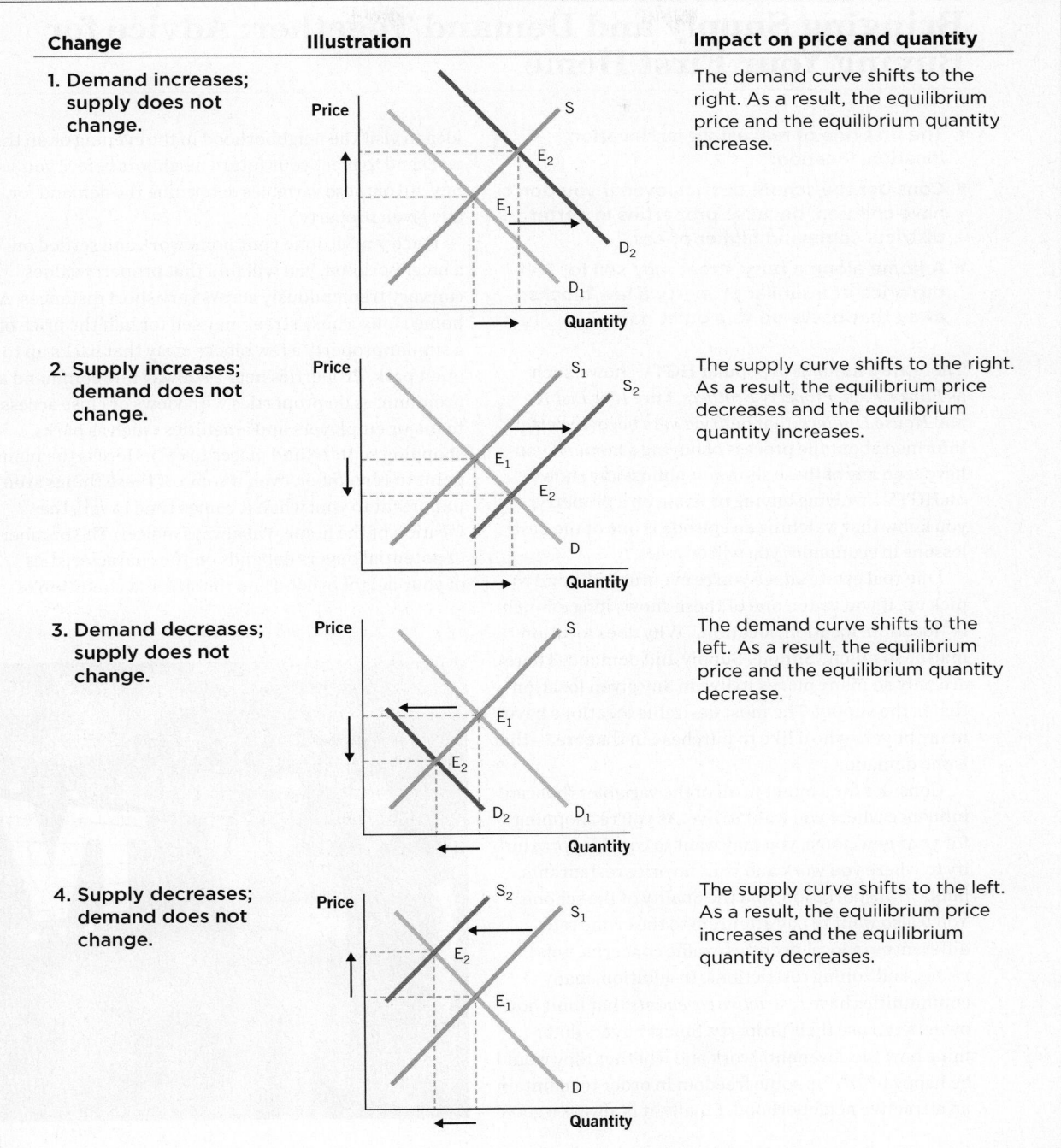

Bringing Supply and Demand Together: Advice for Buying Your First Home

- The first rule of real estate is, "location, location, location."
- Consider the school district, even if you don't have children, because properties in better districts command higher prices.
- A home along a busy street may sell for half the price of a similar property a few blocks away that backs up to a quiet park.

There are a number of popular HGTV shows, such as *Flip or Flop, Property Brothers, Love It or List It,* and *House Hunters,* that help viewers become better informed about the process of buying a home. If you have seen any of these shows, or almost any show on HGTV involving buying or fixing up a property, you know that watching an episode is one of the best lessons in economics you will ever get.

One real estate adage you're eventually bound to pick up, if you watch one of these shows long enough, is "location, location, location." Why does location matter so much? Simple. Supply and demand. There are only so many places to live in any given location—that is the supply. The most desirable locations have many buyers who'd like to purchase in that area—that is the demand.

Consider for a moment all of the variables that can influence where you want to live. As you're shopping for your new home, you may want to consider proximity to where you work and your favorite restaurants, public transportation, and the quality of the schools. You'll also want to pay attention to the crime rate, differences in local tax rates, traffic concerns, noise issues, and zoning restrictions. In addition, many communities have *restrictive covenants* that limit how owners can use their property. Smart buyers determine how the covenants work and whether they would be happy to give up some freedom in order to maintain an attractive neighborhood. Finally, it is always a good

idea to visit the neighborhood in the evening or on the weekend to meet your future neighbors before you buy. All of these variables determine the demand for any given property.

Once you've done your homework and settled on a neighborhood, you will find that property values can vary tremendously across very short distances. A home along a busy street may sell for half the price of a similar property a few blocks away that backs up to a quiet park. Properties near a subway line command a premium, as do properties with views or close access to major employers and amenities (such as parks, shopping centers, and places to eat). Here is the main point to remember, even if some of these things aren't important to you: when it comes time to sell, the location of the home will always matter. The number of potential buyers depends on the characteristics of your neighborhood and the size and condition of

your property. If you want to be able to sell your home easily, you'll have to consider not only where you want to live now but who might want to live there in the future.

All of this discussion brings us back to supply and demand. The best locations are in short supply and high demand. The combination of low supply and high demand causes property values in those areas to rise. Likewise, less desirable locations have lower property values because demand is relatively low and the supply is relatively high. Because first-time buyers often have wish lists that far exceed their budgets, considering the costs and benefits will help you find the best available property.

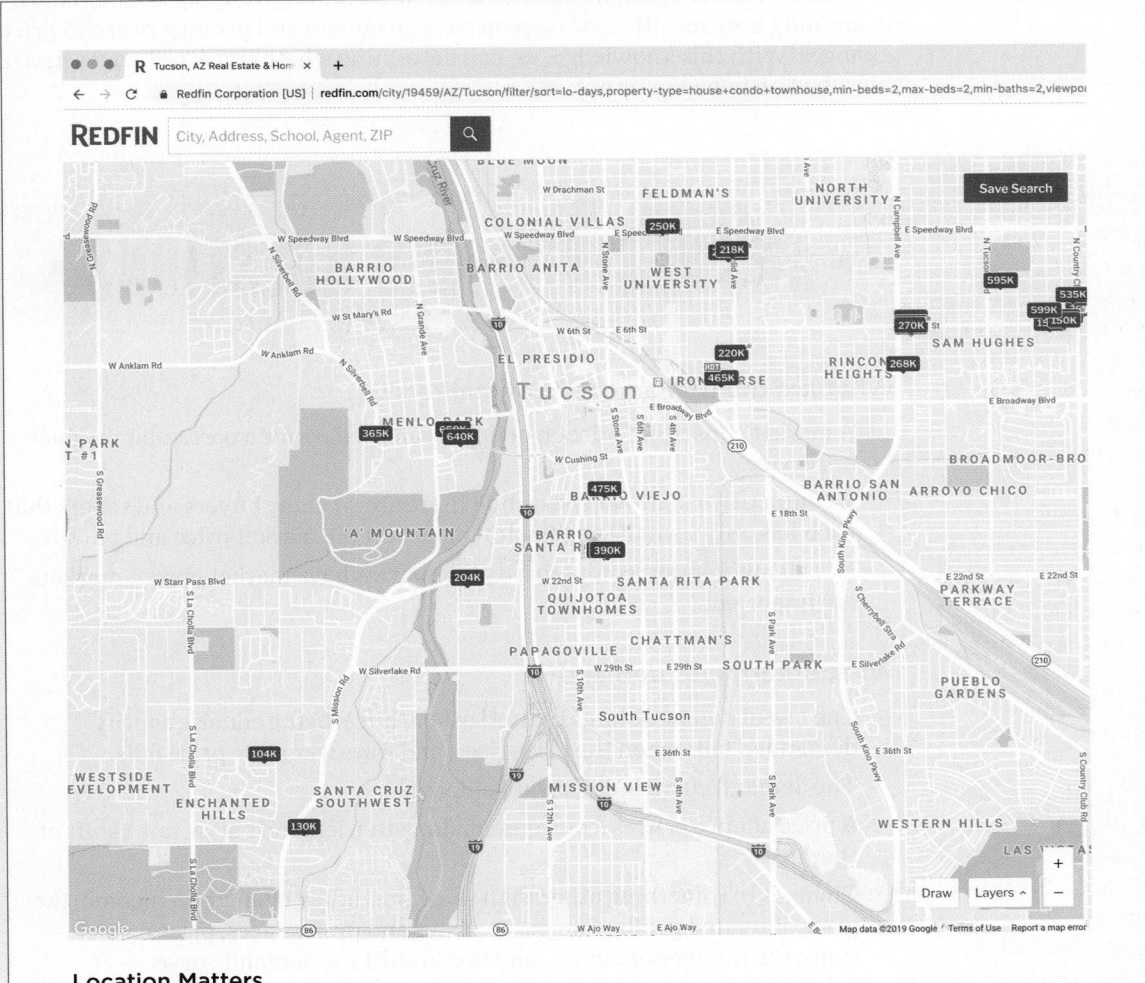

Location Matters
This graphic shows listings for prices of 2-bedroom, 2-bath houses on the market in Tucson, AZ. Prices range from $104–640K. What are some rules of thumb to remember?

Conclusion

Five years from now, if someone asks you what you remember about your first course in economics, you will probably respond with two words: "supply" and "demand." These two forces allow us to model market behavior through prices. Supply and demand help establish the market equilibrium, or the price at which quantity supplied and quantity demanded are in balance. At the equilibrium point, every good and service produced has a corresponding buyer who wants to purchase it. When the market is out of equilibrium, either a shortage or surplus exists. This condition persists until buyers and sellers have a chance to adjust the quantity they demand and the quantity they supply, respectively.

In the next chapter, we extend our understanding of supply and demand by examining how sensitive, or responsive, consumers and producers are to price changes. With this knowledge, we can determine whether price changes have a big effect on behavior or not. ✳

· ANSWERING *the* BIG QUESTIONS ·

What are the fundamentals of markets?

- A market consists of a group of buyers and sellers for a particular product or service.
- A competitive market exists when there are so many buyers and sellers that each has only a small (negligible) impact on the market price and output.
- Not all markets are competitive. When firms have market power, markets are imperfect.

What determines demand?

- The law of demand states that, all other things being equal, quantity demanded falls when the price rises, and rises when the price falls.
- The demand curve is downward sloping.
- A price change causes a movement along the demand curve, not a shift of the curve.
- Changes in something other than price (including changes in income, the price of related goods, changes in tastes and preferences, price expectations, the number of buyers, and taxes) shift the demand curve.

What determines supply?

- The law of supply states that, all other things being equal, the quantity supplied of a good rises when the price of the good rises, and falls when the price of the good falls.

- The supply curve is upward sloping.
- A price change causes a movement along the supply curve, not a shift of the curve.
- Changes in something other than price (the cost of inputs, changes in technology or the production process, taxes and subsidies, the number of firms in the industry, and price expectations) shift the original supply curve.

How do supply and demand interact to create equilibrium?

- Supply and demand work together in a market-clearing process that leads to equilibrium, the balancing point between the two forces. The market-clearing price and output are determined at the equilibrium point.
- When the price is above the equilibrium point, a surplus exists and inventories build up. Suppliers lower their price in an effort to sell the unwanted goods. The process continues until the equilibrium price is reached.
- When the price is below the equilibrium point, a shortage exists and inventories are depleted. Suppliers raise the price until the equilibrium point is reached.

·CHAPTER PROBLEMS·

Concepts You Should Know

competitive market (p. 75)
complements (p. 83)
demand curve (p. 78)
demand schedule (p. 77)
equilibrium (p. 95)
equilibrium price (p. 95)
equilibrium quantity (p. 95)
imperfect market (p. 76)
inferior good (p. 82)
inputs (p. 91)

invisible hand (p. 74)
law of demand (p. 77)
law of supply (p. 87)
law of supply and
   demand (p. 95)
market demand (p. 79)
market economy (p. 74)
market power (p. 76)
market supply (p. 88)
monopoly (p. 76)

normal good (p. 82)
purchasing power (p. 82)
quantity demanded (p. 76)
quantity supplied (p. 87)
shortage (p. 96)
subsidy (p. 86)
substitutes (p. 83)
supply curve (p. 88)
supply schedule (p. 87)
surplus (p. 97)

Questions for Review

1. What is a competitive market, and why does it depend on the existence of many buyers and sellers?

2. Why does the demand curve slope downward?

3. Does a price change cause a movement along a demand curve or a shift of the entire curve? What factors cause the entire demand curve to shift?

4. Describe the difference between inferior goods and normal goods. Give an example of each type of good.

5. Why does the supply curve slope upward?

6. Does a price change cause a movement along a supply curve or a shift of the entire curve? What factors cause the entire supply curve to shift?

7. Describe the process that leads a market toward equilibrium.

8. What happens in a competitive market when the price is above the equilibrium price? Below the equilibrium price?

9. What roles do shortages and surpluses play in the market?

Study Problems (* solved at the end of the section)

1. In the song "Money, Money, Money" by ABBA, one of the lead singers, Anni-Frid Lyngstad, is tired of the hard work that life requires and plans to marry a wealthy man. If she is successful, how will this marriage change her demand for goods? How will it change her supply of labor? Illustrate both changes with supply and demand curves. Be sure to explain what is happening in the diagrams. (*Note*: The full lyrics for the song can be found by Googling the song title and ABBA. For inspiration, try listening to the song while you solve the problem.)

2. For each of the following scenarios, determine if there is an increase or a decrease in demand for the good in *italics*.

   a. The price of *oranges* increases.
   b. The cost of producing *tires* increases.

   c. Samantha Brown, who is crazy about *air travel*, gets fired from her job.
   d. A local community has an unusually wet spring and a subsequent problem with mosquitoes, which can be deterred with *citronella*.
   e. Many motorcycle enthusiasts enjoy riding without *helmets* (in states where this is not prohibited by law). The price of new motorcycles rises.

3. For each of the following scenarios, determine if there is an increase or a decrease in supply for the good in *italics*.

   a. The price of *silver* increases.
   b. Growers of *tomatoes* experience an unusually good growing season.

c. New medical evidence reports that consumption of *organic products* reduces the incidence of cancer.

d. The wages of low-skilled workers, a resource used to help produce *clothing*, increase.

e. The price of movie tickets, a substitute for *Netflix video rentals*, goes up.

4. Are laser pointers and cats complements or substitutes? (Not sure? Search for videos of cats and laser pointers online.) Discuss.

✳ **5.** The market for ice cream has the following demand and supply schedules:

Price (per quart)	Quantity demanded (quarts)	Quantity supplied (quarts)
$2	100	20
3	80	40
4	60	60
5	40	80
6	20	100

a. What are the equilibrium price and equilibrium quantity in the ice cream market? Confirm your answer by graphing the demand and supply curves.

b. If the actual price is $3 per quart, what would drive the market toward equilibrium?

6. Starbucks Entertainment announced in a 2007 news release that Dave Matthews Band's *Live Trax* CD was available only at the company's coffee shops in the United States and Canada. The compilation features recordings of the band's performances dating back to 1995. Why would Starbucks and Dave Matthews have agreed to partner in this way? To come up with an answer, think about the nature of complementary goods and how both sides can benefit from this arrangement.

7. The Seattle Mariners baseball team wishes to determine the equilibrium price for seats for each of the next two seasons. The supply of seats at the ballpark is fixed at 45,000.

Price (per seat)	Quantity demanded in year 1	Quantity demanded in year 2	Quantity supplied
$25	75,000	60,000	45,000
30	60,000	55,000	45,000
35	45,000	50,000	45,000
40	30,000	45,000	45,000
45	15,000	40,000	45,000

Draw the supply curve and each of the demand curves for years 1 and 2.

✳ **8.** Demand and supply curves can also be represented with equations. Suppose that the quantity demanded, Q_D, is represented by the following equation:

$$Q_D = 90 - 2P$$

The quantity supplied, Q_S, is represented by the equation

$$Q_S = P$$

a. Find the equilibrium price and quantity. (**Hint:** Set $Q_D = Q_S$ and solve for the price, P, and then plug your result back into either of the original equations to find Q.)

b. Suppose that the price is $20. Determine Q_D and Q_S.

c. At a price of $20, is there a surplus or a shortage in the market?

d. Given your answer in part (c), will the price rise or fall in order to find the equilibrium point?

✳ **9.** Let's take a look at two real-world episodes in the market for gasoline and try to figure out why the price fluctuates so much.

a. In the summer of 2008, the price of regular gasoline in the United States soared to over $4 per gallon. Then, in the fall of that year, the U.S. economy fell into a deep recession that significantly reduced consumers' income. Use the supply and demand model to determine which curve shifted and what happened to the equilibrium price of gasoline. For this part of the question, assume no other changes in the market for gasoline.

b. By the summer of 2014, the price of regular gasoline in the United States was hovering around $3.50 per gallon. But innovations in oil extraction technology, such as hydraulic fracking, reduced the price of crude oil significantly. Crude oil is the primary input for gasoline production. Use the supply and demand model to determine which curve shifted and then what happened to the equilibrium price of gasoline. For this part of the question, assume no other changes in the market for gasoline.

✳ **10.** If the price of alcohol decreases, what happens to the demand for red Solo (plastic) cups?

11. Consider the market for the Samsung Galaxy S9.

   a. Scenario 1: Using a supply and demand graph, show what will happen to the current equilibrium price and quantity of Galaxy S9s

if people expect the price of S9s to fall in the future.

   b. Scenario 2: Now, using a second supply and demand graph, show instead what will happen to the equilibrium price and quantity of S9s if the price of the iPhone X falls. In answering your question, assume that the S9 and iPhone X are substitutes in consumption.

   c. Scenario 3: You observe that the price of S9s increases. Can you definitively conclude that there has been an increase in demand? If not, what besides an increase in demand could explain the price increase?

✳ **12.** One of the responses completes this list of things that shift the supply curve: technology, expectations, the number of sellers, and _____. Identify the correct answer and also explain why the other three responses are incorrect.

   a. the price of related goods
   b. income
   c. the cost of inputs
   d. the price

Solved Problems

5a. The equilibrium price is $4, and the equilibrium quantity is 60 quarts. The next step is to graph the curves, as shown here.

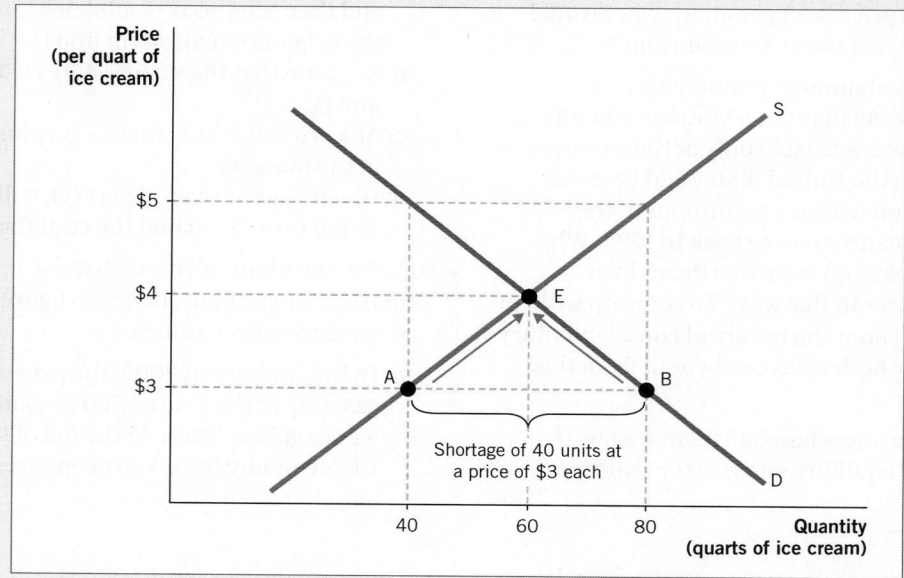

b. A shortage of 40 quarts of ice cream exists at $3 (quantity demanded is 80 and the quantity supplied is 40); therefore, there is excess demand. Ice cream sellers will raise their price as long as excess demand exists—that is, as long as the price is below $4. It is not until $4 that the equilibrium point is reached and the shortage is resolved.

8.a. The first step is to set $Q_D = Q_S$. Doing so gives us $90 - 2P = P$. Solving for price, we find that $90 = 3P$, or $P = 30$. Once we know that $P = 30$, we can plug this value back into either of the original equations, $Q_D = 90 - 2P$ or $Q_S = P$. Beginning with Q_D, we get $90 - 2(30) = 90 - 60 = 30$, or we can plug it into $Q_S = P$, so $Q_S = 30$. Because we get a quantity of 30 for both Q_D and Q_S, we know that the price of $30 is correct.

b. In this part, we plug $20 into Q_D. Doing so yields $90 - 2(20) = 50$. Now we plug $20 into Q_S. Doing so yields 20.

c. Because $Q_D = 50$ and $Q_S = 20$, there is a shortage of 30 quarts.

d. Whenever there is a shortage of a good, the price will rise in order to find the equilibrium point.

9a. The reduction in consumer income led to a negative, or leftward, shift in the demand curve for gasoline. Because this is the only change, the equilibrium price of gasoline fell. In fact, by the end of 2008, the price of gasoline had fallen to under $2 per gallon in the United States.

b. The significant drop in the cost of production led to a large increase, or rightward, shift in the supply of gasoline. This increase in supply led to a decrease in price. In fact, by early 2015, the average price of a gallon of regular gasoline in the United States fell to under $2 per gallon.

Looking at parts (a) and (b) together, you can see that very different causes led to steep drops in the price of gasoline. In 2008 the cause was a decline in demand; in 2014 it was an increase in supply.

10. Because alcohol and Solo cups are complements, the key here is to recall that a change in the price of a complementary good shifts the demand curve for the related good. Lower alcohol prices will cause consumers to purchase more alcohol and therefore demand more Solo cups. In other words, the entire demand curve for Solo cups shifts to the right.

12a. The price of related goods is a demand shifter so, it is incorrect.

b. Income is a demand shifter so, it is incorrect.

c. The cost of inputs is a supply shifter so, it is correct.

d. The price causes a movement along the supply curve so, it is incorrect.

03A

Changes in Both Demand and Supply

We have considered what would happen if supply *or* demand changes. But life is often more complex than that. To provide a more realistic analysis, we need to examine what happens when supply and demand both shift at the same time.

Suppose that a major drought hits the northwestern United States. The water shortage reduces both the amount of farmed salmon and the ability of wild salmon to spawn in streams and rivers. Figure 3A.1a shows the ensuing decline in the salmon supply, from S_1 progressively leftward, represented by the dotted supply curves. At the same time, a medical journal reports that people who consume at least 4 pounds of salmon a month live five years longer than those who consume an equal amount of cod. Figure 3A.1b shows the ensuing rise in the demand for salmon, from D_1 progressively rightward, represented by the dotted demand curves. This scenario leads to a twofold change. Because of the water shortage, the supply of salmon shrinks. At the same time, new information about the health benefits of eating salmon causes demand for salmon to increase.

It is impossible to predict exactly what happens to the equilibrium point when both supply and demand are shifting. We can, however, determine a region where the resulting equilibrium point must reside.

In this situation, we have a simultaneous decrease in supply and increase in demand. Since we do not know the magnitude of the supply reduction or demand increase, the overall effect on the equilibrium quantity cannot be determined. This result is evident in Figure 3A.1c, as illustrated by the purple region. The points where supply and demand cross within this area represent the set of possible new market equilibria. Because each of the possible points of intersection in the purple region occurs at a price greater than $10 per pound, we know that the price must rise. However, the left half of the purple region produces equilibrium quantities that are lower than 500 pounds of salmon, while the right half of the purple region results in equilibrium quantities that are greater than 500. Therefore, the equilibrium quantity may rise, fall, or stay the same if both shifts are of equal magnitudes.

The world we live in is complex, and often more than one variable will change simultaneously. In such cases, it is not possible to be as definitive as when only one variable—supply or demand—changes. You should think of the new equilibrium not as a single point but as a range of outcomes represented by the purple area in Figure 3A.1c. Therefore, we cannot be exactly sure at what point the new price *and* new quantity will settle. For a closer look at four possibilities, see Figure 3A.2, where E_1 equals the original equilibrium point and the new equilibrium (E_2) lies somewhere in the purple region.

A Shift in Supply and Demand

When supply and demand both shift, the resulting equilibrium can no longer be identified as an exact point. We can see this effect in (c), which combines the supply shift in (a) with the demand shift in (b). When supply decreases and demand increases, the result is that the price must rise, but the equilibrium quantity can either rise or fall, or stay the same if both shifts are of equal magnitudes.

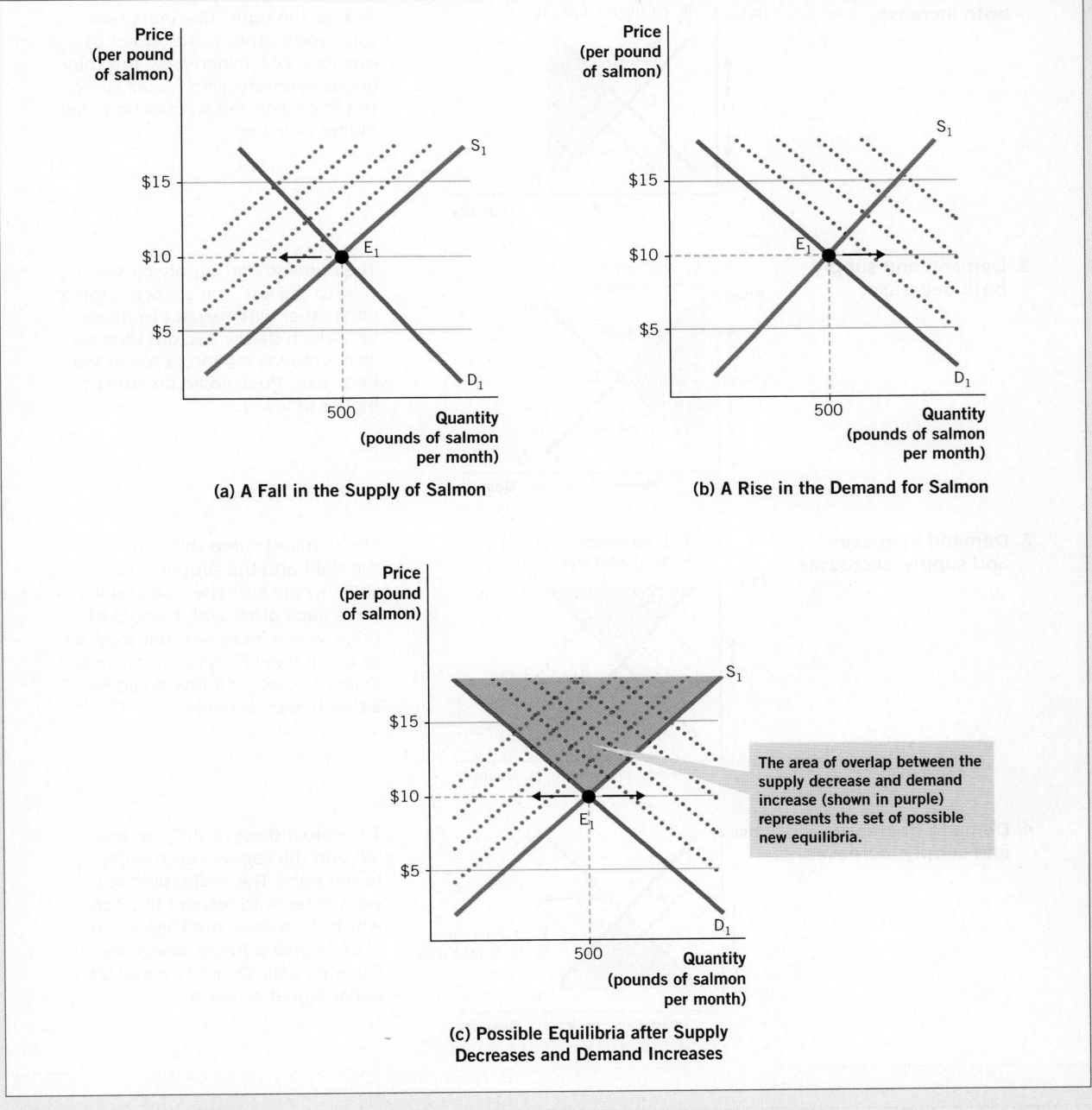

(a) A Fall in the Supply of Salmon

(b) A Rise in the Demand for Salmon

The area of overlap between the supply decrease and demand increase (shown in purple) represents the set of possible new equilibria.

(c) Possible Equilibria after Supply Decreases and Demand Increases

Price and Quantity When Demand and Supply Both Change

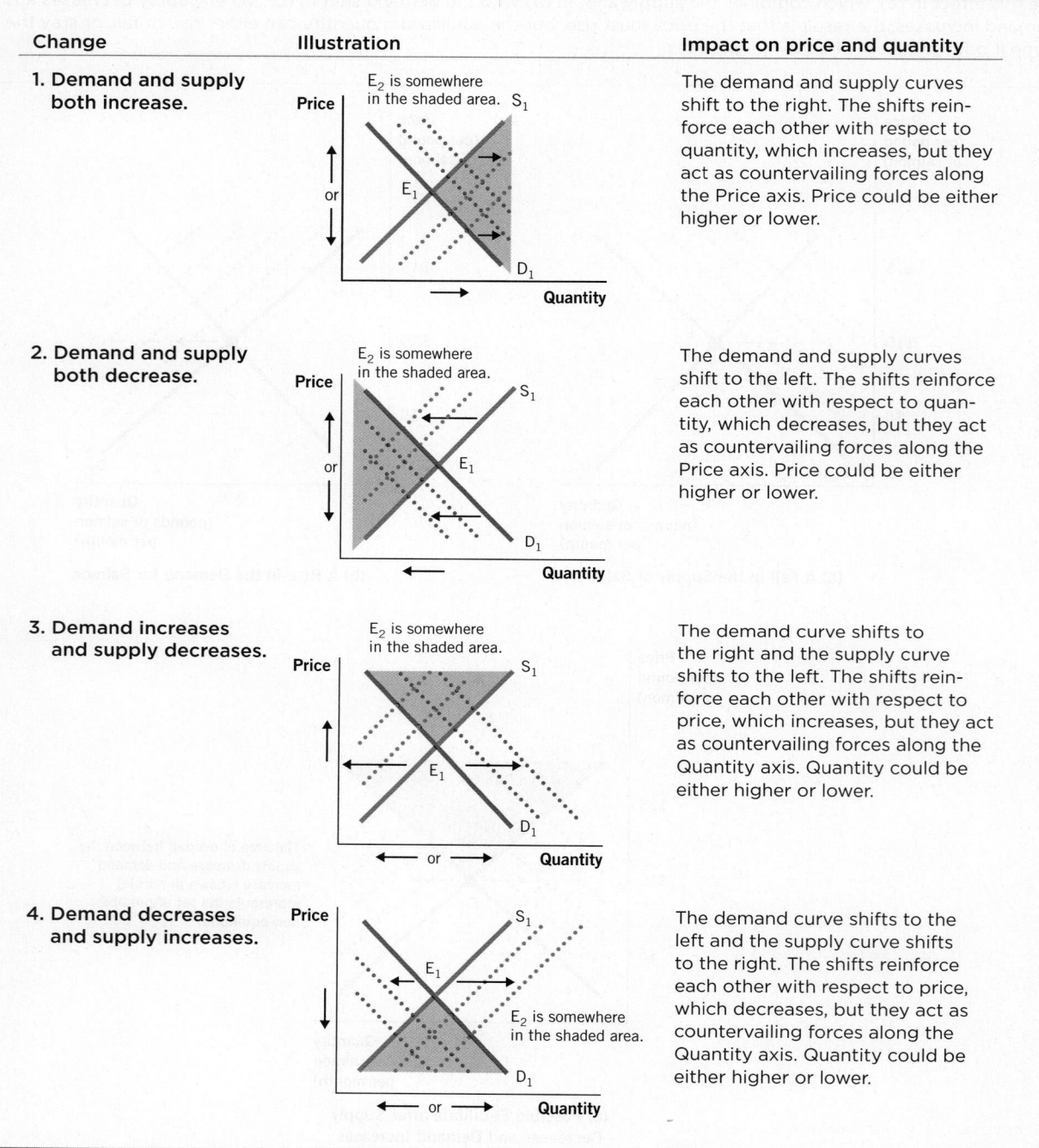

Change	Illustration	Impact on price and quantity
1. Demand and supply both increase.	E_2 is somewhere in the shaded area.	The demand and supply curves shift to the right. The shifts reinforce each other with respect to quantity, which increases, but they act as countervailing forces along the Price axis. Price could be either higher or lower.
2. Demand and supply both decrease.	E_2 is somewhere in the shaded area.	The demand and supply curves shift to the left. The shifts reinforce each other with respect to quantity, which decreases, but they act as countervailing forces along the Price axis. Price could be either higher or lower.
3. Demand increases and supply decreases.	E_2 is somewhere in the shaded area.	The demand curve shifts to the right and the supply curve shifts to the left. The shifts reinforce each other with respect to price, which increases, but they act as countervailing forces along the Quantity axis. Quantity could be either higher or lower.
4. Demand decreases and supply increases.	E_2 is somewhere in the shaded area.	The demand curve shifts to the left and the supply curve shifts to the right. The shifts reinforce each other with respect to price, which decreases, but they act as countervailing forces along the Quantity axis. Quantity could be either higher or lower.

When Supply and Demand Both Change: Hybrid Cars

QUESTION: At lunch, two friends are engaged in a heated argument. Their exchange goes like this:

The first friend begins, "The supply of hybrid cars and the demand for hybrid cars will both increase. I'm sure of it. I'm also sure the price of hybrids will go down."

The second friend replies, "I agree with the first part of your statement, but I'm not sure about the price. In fact, I'm pretty sure that hybrid prices will rise."

They go back and forth endlessly, each unable to convince the other, so they turn to you for advice. What do you say to them?

ANSWER: Either of your friends could be correct. In this case, supply and demand both shift out to the right, so we know that the quantity bought and sold will increase. However, an increase in supply would normally lower the price, and an increase in demand would typically raise the price. Without knowing which of these two effects on price is stronger, you can't predict how price will change. The overall price will rise if the increase in demand is larger than the increase in supply. However, if the increase in supply is larger than the increase in demand, prices will fall. But your two friends don't know which condition will be true—so they're locked in an argument that neither can win! As an aside, Tesla came out with their priciest model first, then their midrange model, and they're now trying to roll out the model for the masses, which suggests that they are betting on hybrid prices going down over time.

Hybrid cars are becoming increasingly common.

POLAR VORTEX ECONOMICS

Every few years, the jet stream buckles and the polar vortex drops into the eastern United States. When the vortex descends, temperatures plummet, the demand for propane skyrockets, and supplies of propane are tight. The economic effects of the polar vortex provide a textbook example of a positive demand shock and negative supply shock (a "shock" is an unexpected event) hitting at the same time. Let's consider the effects of the polar vortex that hit the United States in the winter of 2013–2014.

Incentives

First, the positive demand shock. It is easy to understand. Bitter cold dramatically increases (that's why we say "positive") the demand for propane, because much more propane than usual is needed to heat homes.

Second, the negative supply shock. There are actually two negative shocks. It turns out that farmers used more propane than usual in the fall of 2013 to dry out their grain crops, thus lowering (that's why we say "negative") supplies of propane for heating homes. Then, during the first cold snap, pipelines across the Midwest froze, disrupting the delivery of propane to holding tanks and then to homes. The frozen pipes were the second negative supply shock.

Third, the complication. Because of the booming supply of natural gas (propane is made from natural gas) in the United States, the price had dropped so low (again, basic supply and demand at work) that very large quantities of propane were exported to markets where suppliers could get a higher price. The supplies that were exported out of the country could have been used in the United States in the winter of 2013–2014, but because they were not here, the shortage was exacerbated.

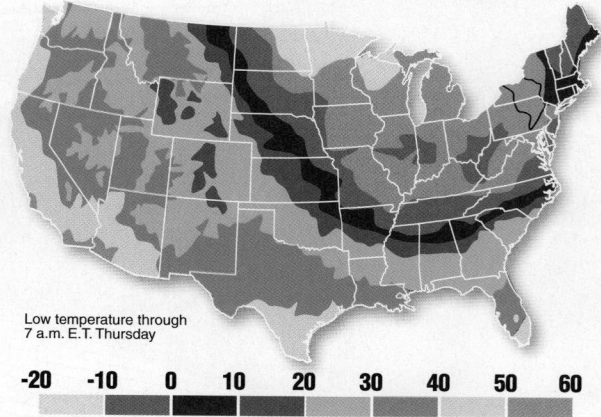

Bitter cold to continue all week

The unusually cold weather is forecast to continue through much of the week for the eastern U.S. Some places from the Carolinas to the Mid-Atlantic may see some of the coldest weather since the mid-1990s. Numerous record low temperatures are expected.

Low temperature through
7 a.m. E.T. Thursday

-20 -10 0 10 20 30 40 50 60

Source: NOAA
Graphic: Tribune News Service

The polar vortex is coming. Do you have enough propane?

· APPENDIX PROBLEMS ·

Questions for Review

1. What happens to price and quantity when supply and demand change at the same time?

2. Is there more than one potential equilibrium point when supply and demand change at the same time? Explain.

Study Problems *(✳ solved at the end of the section)*

✳ **1.** Assume that, over time, consumer incomes generally increase but also that technological advancements in oil extraction lead to lower prices of crude oil (the primary input for gasoline).

   a. If consumer incomes increase by significantly more than input prices fall, what happens to both the price and quantity of gasoline?

   b. If, instead, consumer incomes increase relatively less than input prices fall, what happens to the price and quantity of gasoline?

2. Every Valentine's Day, the price of roses spikes. Using your understanding of the factors that shift both demand and supply, draw the equilibrium in the rose market on January 31 and then draw the new equilibrium that occurs on February 14.

Solved Problem

1a. The increase in consumer income increases demand and shifts the demand curve to the right. The decrease in input prices increases supply and shifts the supply curve to the right. Equilibrium quantity unequivocally increases. The demand shift is relatively larger, so price also increases.

   b. Again, we see that the increase in consumer income increases demand and shifts the demand

curve to the right; and the decrease in input prices increases supply and shifts the supply curve to the right. Equilibrium quantity increases. But in this question, the demand shift is relatively smaller, so price falls. This example provides a good description of events in the gasoline market at the end of 2014, when price was falling even though consumer incomes were rising.

Elasticity

Should Sellers Charge the Highest Price Possible?

Many people believe that sellers charge the highest price possible for their product or service—that if sellers can get one more penny from a customer, they will, even if it makes the customer angry. It turns out that this belief is wrong. What *is* accurate is that producers charge the highest price they can while maintaining the goodwill of most of their customers.

Suppose that your gas tank is nearly empty. How much of a price difference would it take for you to switch from one station to another? Charging a high price might seem like a good strategy, because the station would make a sizable profit on each gallon sold, but this only works if most customers are not price sensitive. If customers are price sensitive, the station with the lower price might get two or three times more customers than the more expensive station does, and they could end up making more profits because they had more sales.

In the previous chapter, we learned that demand and supply regulate economic activity by balancing the interests of buyers and sellers. We also observed how that balance is achieved through prices. A higher price causes the quantity supplied to rise and the quantity demanded to fall. In contrast, a lower price causes the quantity supplied to fall

Where would you fill up? A ten-cent price difference may not seem like a lot but when you multiply that price difference by the number of gallons in your tank, you can easily save a couple of dollars by driving a few feet more.

and the quantity demanded to rise. In this chapter, we examine how decision-makers respond to differences in price and also to changes in income.

The concept of *elasticity*, or responsiveness to a change in market conditions, is a concept that we need to grasp if we are to fully understand supply and demand. Understanding elasticity helps us to determine the impact of government policy on the economy, to vote more intelligently, and even to make wiser day-to-day decisions.

· BIG QUESTIONS ·

- What is the price elasticity of demand, and what are its determinants?
- How do changes in income and the prices of other goods affect elasticity?
- What is the price elasticity of supply?
- How do the price elasticities of demand and supply relate to each other?

What Is the Price Elasticity of Demand, and What Are Its Determinants?

Trade-offs

Many things in life are replaceable, or have substitutes: boyfriends come and go, people stream videos instead of going out to a movie, and students ride their bikes to class instead of taking the bus. Pasta fans may prefer linguini to spaghetti or angel hair, but all three taste about the same and can be substituted for one another in a pinch. With goods like pasta, where consumers can easily purchase a substitute, we think of demand as being *responsive*. That is, a small change in price will likely cause many people to switch from one good to another.

In contrast, many things in life are irreplaceable or have few good substitutes. Examples include electricity and a hospital emergency room visit. A significant rise in price for either of these items would probably not cause you to consume a smaller quantity. If the price of electricity goes up, you might try to cut your usage somewhat, but you would probably not start generating your own power. Likewise, you could try to treat a serious medical crisis without a visit to the ER—but the consequences of making a mistake would be enormous. In these cases, we say that consumers are *unresponsive*, or unwilling to change their behavior, even when the price of the good or service changes.

Elasticity is a measure of the responsiveness of buyers and sellers to changes in price or income. Elasticity is a useful concept because it allows us to measure *how much* consumers and producers change their behavior when either price or income changes. In the next section, we look at the factors that determine the price elasticity of demand.

Elasticity
is a measure of the responsiveness of buyers and sellers to changes in price or income.

Determinants of the Price Elasticity of Demand

The law of demand tells us that as price goes up, quantity demanded goes down, and as price goes down, quantity demanded goes up. In other words, there is a negative relationship between the price of a good and the quantity demanded. Elasticity allows us to measure how much the quantity demanded changes in response to a change in price. If the quantity demanded changes significantly as a result of a price change, then demand is *elastic*. If the quantity demanded changes a small amount as a result of a price change, then demand is *inelastic*.

The **price elasticity of demand** measures the responsiveness of quantity demanded to a change in price. For instance, if the price of a sweatshirt with a college logo rises by $10 and the quantity demanded falls by a large amount (say, half), we'd say that the demand for those sweatshirts is elastic. But if the $10 rise in price results in very little or no change in the quantity demanded, the demand for the sweatshirts is inelastic.

The **price elasticity of demand** measures the responsiveness of quantity demanded to a change in price.

Five determinants play a crucial role in influencing whether demand will be elastic or inelastic: the existence of substitutes, the share of the budget spent on a good, whether the good is a necessity or a luxury good, how broadly defined the market is, and time.

THE EXISTENCE OF SUBSTITUTES The most important determinant of price elasticity is the number of substitutes available. When substitutes are plentiful, market forces tilt in favor of the consumer. For example, imagine that an unexpected freeze in Florida reduces the supply of oranges. As a result, the supply of orange juice shifts to the left (picture the supply curves we discussed in Chapter 3). Because demand remains unchanged, the price of orange juice rises. However, the consumer of orange juice can find many good substitutes. Because cranberries, grapes, and apple crops are unaffected by the Florida freeze, prices for juices made from those fruits remain constant. This situation leads to a choice: a consumer can continue to buy orange juice at a higher price or choose to pay a lower price for a fruit juice that may not be his first choice but is nonetheless acceptable. Faced with higher orange juice prices, some consumers will switch. How quickly this switch takes place, and to

Your "average"-looking boyfriend is replaceable.

Beyoncé is irreplaceable.

what extent consumers are willing to replace one product with another, determines whether demand is elastic or inelastic. Because many substitutes for orange juice exist, the demand for orange juice is elastic, or responsive to price changes.

What if there are no good substitutes? There is no amusement park quite like Disney. Where else can you see all your favorite Disney characters? Nowhere! Because the experience is unique, the number of close substitutes is small. Therefore, demand is more inelastic, or less responsive to price changes.

To some degree, the price elasticity of demand depends on consumer preferences. For instance, sports fans are often willing to shell out big bucks to follow their passions. Amateur golfers can play the same courses that professional golfers do. But the opportunity to golf where the professionals play does not come cheaply. A round of golf at the Tournament Players Club at Sawgrass, a famous course in Florida, costs close to $300. Why are some golfers willing to pay that much? For an avid golfer with the financial means, the experience of living out the same shots seen on television tournaments is worth $300. In this case, demand is inelastic—the avid golfer does not view other golf courses as good substitutes. However, a less enthusiastic golfer, or one without the financial resources, is happy to golf on a less expensive course even if the pros don't play it on TV. When less expensive golf courses serve as good substitutes, the price tag makes demand elastic. Ultimately, whether demand is inelastic or elastic depends on the buyer's preferences and resources.

THE SHARE OF THE BUDGET SPENT ON THE GOOD Despite our example of an avid and affluent golfer willing to pay a premium fee to play at a famous golf course, in most cases price is a critical element in determining what we can afford and what we choose to buy. If you plan to purchase an 80-inch-screen TV, which can cost as much as $2,000, you will probably be willing to take the time to find the best deal. Because of the high price, even a small percentage discount can cause a relatively large change in consumer demand. A 10% off sale may not sound like much, but when purchasing a big-ticket item like a TV, it can mean hundreds of dollars in savings. In this case, the willingness to shop for the best deal indicates that the price matters, so demand is elastic.

Incentives

Saving 10% on this purchase amounts to a few pennies.

Demand is much more inelastic for inexpensive items on sale. For example, if a candy bar is discounted 10%, the price falls by pennies. The savings from switching candy bars is not enough to make a difference in what you can afford elsewhere. Therefore, the incentive to switch is small. Most consumers still buy their favorite candy because the price difference is so insignificant. In this case, demand is inelastic because the savings gained by purchasing a less desirable candy bar are small in comparison to the consumer's budget.

NECESSITIES VERSUS LUXURY GOODS A big-screen TV and a candy bar are both luxury goods. You don't need to have either one. But some goods are necessities. For example, you have to pay your rent and water bill, purchase gasoline for your car, and eat. When consumers purchase a necessity, they are generally thinking about the need, not the price. When the need trumps the price, we expect demand to be relatively inelastic. Therefore, the demand for things like cars, textbooks, and heating oil all tend to have inelastic demand.

Saving 10% on this purchase adds up quickly.

WHETHER THE MARKET IS BROADLY OR NARROWLY DEFINED The more broadly we define a market for a good, the harder it is to live without. For instance, demand for housing in general is quite inelastic because without some form of housing you'd be living on the street. However, the demand for a particular apartment or house is much more price sensitive because you don't need to live in *that* exact place. Therefore, a good falling into a narrowly defined category, such as Crest toothpaste, will have more elastic demand than a broadly defined category, such as toothpaste, which has more inelastic demand.

TIME AND THE ADJUSTMENT PROCESS When the market price changes, consumers and sellers respond. But that response does not remain the same over time. As time passes, both consumers and sellers are able to find substitutes. To understand these different market responses, when considering elasticity economists consider time in three distinct periods: the *immediate run*, the *short run*, and the *long run*.

In the **immediate run**, there is no time for consumers to adjust their behavior. Consider the demand for gasoline. When the gas tank is empty, you have to stop at the nearest gas station and pay the posted price. Filling up as soon as possible is more important than driving around searching for the lowest price. Inelastic demand exists whenever price is secondary to the desire to attain a certain amount of the good. So in the case of an empty tank, the demand for gasoline is inelastic.

But what if your tank is not empty? The **short run** is a period of time when consumers can partially adjust their behavior (in this case, can search for a good deal on gas). In the short run, we make decisions that reflect our immediate or short-term wants, needs, or limitations. When consumers have some time to make a purchase, they gain flexibility. They can shop for lower prices at the pump, carpool to save gas, or even change how often they drive. In the short run, flexibility reduces the demand for expensive gasoline and makes consumer demand more elastic.

Finally, if we relax the time constraint completely, it is possible to use even less gasoline. The **long run** is a period of time when consumers have time to fully adjust to market conditions. In the long run, we make decisions that reflect our wants, needs, and limitations over a long time horizon. If gasoline prices are high in the long run, consumers can relocate closer to work and purchase fuel-efficient cars. These changes further reduce the demand for gasoline. As a result of the flexibility that additional time gives the consumer, the demand for gasoline becomes more elastic.

This is *not* the time to try and find cheap gas.

In the **immediate run**, there is no time for consumers to adjust their behavior.

The **short run** is a period of time when consumers can partially adjust their behavior. In the short run, we make decisions that reflect our immediate or short-term wants, needs, or limitations.

The **long run** is a period of time when consumers have time to fully adjust to market conditions. In the long run, we make decisions that reflect our wants, needs, and limitations over a long time horizon.

TABLE 4.1

Developing Intuition for the Price Elasticity of Demand

Example	Discussion	Overall elasticity
Football tickets for a true fan	Being able to watch a game in person and go to pregame and postgame tailgates is a unique experience. For many fans, the experience of going to the game has few close substitutes. In addition, this is a narrowly defined experience. Therefore, the demand is relatively inelastic.	Tends to be relatively inelastic
Assigned textbooks for a course in your major	The information inside a textbook is valuable. Substitutes such as older editions and free online resources are not exactly the same. As a result, most students buy the required course materials. Acquiring the textbook is more important than the price paid; therefore, the demand is inelastic. The fact that a textbook is needed in the short run (for a few months while taking a class) also tends to make the demand inelastic.	Tends to be inelastic
A slice of pizza from Domino's	In most locations, many pizza competitors exist, so there are many close substitutes. The presence of so much competition tends to make the demand for a narrowly defined brand of pizza elastic.	Tends to be elastic
A Yellow Kia Soul	There are many styles, makes, and colors of cars to choose from. With large purchases, consumers are sensitive to smaller percentages of savings. Moreover, people typically plan their car purchases many months or years in advance. The combination of all these factors makes the demand for any narrowly defined model relatively elastic.	Tends to be relatively elastic

We have looked at five determinants of elasticity—substitutes, the share of the budget spent on the good, necessities versus luxury goods, whether the market is broadly or narrowly defined, and time. Each is significant, but the number of substitutes tends to be the most influential factor and dominates the others. Table 4.1 will help you develop your intuition about how different market situations influence the overall elasticity of demand.

Computing the Price Elasticity of Demand

Until this point, our discussion of elasticity has been descriptive. However, to apply the concept of elasticity in decision-making, we need to view it more quantitatively. For example, if the owner of a business is trying to decide whether to put a good on sale, he or she needs to estimate how many new customers would purchase it at the sale price. If a government is considering a new tax, it needs

Price Elasticity of Demand

Take a look at this IKEA advertisement and think about the determinants of the price elasticity of demand.

QUESTION: Do you think IKEA's "Rainy day special" price makes sense?

ANSWER: Let's start by figuring out whether the demand for umbrellas is elastic or inelastic when it is raining. The GRÖSSBY umbrella is quite inexpensive even at full price, so the purchase would represent only a small share of a consumer's budget. That would tend to make the demand inelastic. Also, when do you need an umbrella? When it's raining, of course! Consumers without umbrellas need them immediately, and that also tends to make demand inelastic. Finally, how many good substitutes are there for an umbrella? A raincoat or poncho, maybe, but it's a lot harder for two people to share a raincoat than an umbrella. The lack of good substitutes is another factor that tends to make demand inelastic. On rainy days, then, demand is even more inelastic than usual. If IKEA decided to charge more and raised the price of the GRÖSSBY on rainy days, instead of lowering it, the store would have increased revenues.

to know how much revenue that tax will generate. These are questions about elasticity that we can evaluate by using a mathematical formula.

THE PRICE ELASTICITY OF DEMAND FORMULA Let's begin with an example of a pizza shop. Consider an owner who is trying to attract more customers. For one month, he lowers the price of a pizza by 10% and is pleased to find that sales jump by 30%.

Here is the formula for the price elasticity of demand (E_D):

$$\text{price elasticity of demand} = E_D = \frac{\text{percentage change in the quantity demanded}}{\text{percentage change in price}} \qquad \textbf{(EQUATION 4.1)}$$

Using the data from the example, we calculate the price elasticity of demand as follows:

$$\text{price elasticity of demand} = E_D = \frac{30\%}{-10\%} = -3$$

The price elasticity of demand, −3 in this case, is expressed as a coefficient (3) with a specific sign (it has a minus sign in front of it). The coefficient tells us how much the quantity demanded has changed (30%) compared with the price change (−10%). In this case, the percentage change in the quantity demanded is three times the percentage change in the price. Whenever the percentage change in the quantity demanded is larger than the percentage change in price, the demand is elastic. In other words, the price drop made a big difference in how much pizza consumers purchased from the pizza shop. If the opposite occurs and a price drop makes a small difference in the quantity that consumers purchase, demand is inelastic (see Table 4.2).

Price Elasticity of Demand

THE BIG BANG THEORY

The Mystic Warlords of Ka'a (an obvious spoof of Magic: The Gathering) is a fictional trading card game that Sheldon, Leonard, Raj, and Howard all enjoy playing. Howard complains about the release of a new expansion pack called Wild West Witches:

RAJ: Hey, look, the new Warlords of Ka'a expansion pack is out.

HOWARD: A new one? Unbelievable. They just keep making up more cheesy monsters, slapping them on cards, and selling them at 25 bucks a pop.

RAJ: Stuart, settle an argument for us. Who would win, Billy the Kid or the White Wizard?

STUART: If I tell you that, I'm robbing you of the hours of fun you could have for the magical, rootin' tootin' low price of $24.95.

RAJ: I'll take one.

HOWARD: Mmm, make it two.

LEONARD: I hate all of you and myself. Three.

STUART: I'll ring it up. Like shooting nerds in a barrel.

Analysis: Expansion packs allow players of Mystic (and other role-playing games) the opportunity to

Howard considers buying an expansion pack.

improve the deck of cards with which they play the game. Because all of the guys are smart and competitive, new expansion packs make Mystic more challenging to play and also increases the chance of winning when you play against others who do not have the latest cards. The demand for new expansion packs is quite inelastic because the purchase is made in the short run, the share of the budget that each guy spends on the item ($25) is relatively small, and the number of available substitutes for cards with new powers is effectively zero.

The negative (minus) sign in front of the coefficient is equally important. Recall that the law of demand describes a negative relationship between the price of a good and the quantity demanded; when price rises, the quantity demanded falls. The E_D coefficient reflects this negative relationship with a negative sign. In other words, the pizza shop drops its price and consumers buy more pizza. Because the price of pizza and consumer purchases of pizza generally move in opposite directions, the sign of the price elasticity of demand is almost always negative.

THE MIDPOINT METHOD Our earlier calculation was simple because we looked at the change in price and the change in the quantity demanded from only one direction—that is, from a high price to a lower price and from the corresponding lower quantity demanded to the higher quantity demanded. However, the complete—and proper—way to calculate elasticity is from both directions. Consider the following demand schedule for pizza:

Price	Quantity demanded
$12	20
6	30

Let's calculate the elasticity of demand. If the price drops from $12 to $6—a drop of 50%—the quantity demanded increases from 20 to 30—a rise of 50%. Plugging the percentage changes into the E_D formula yields

$$\text{price elasticity of demand} = E_D = \frac{50\%}{-50\%} = -1.0$$

But if the price rises from $6 to $12—an increase of 100%—the quantity demanded falls from 30 to 20, or decreases by 33%. Plugging the percentage changes into the E_D formula yields

$$\text{price elasticity of demand} = E_D = \frac{-33\%}{100\%} = -0.33$$

This result occurs because percentage changes are usually calculated by using the initial value as the base, or reference point. In this example, we worked the problem two ways: by using $12 as the starting point and dropping the price to $6, and then by using $6 as the starting point and increasing the price to $12. Even though we are measuring elasticity over the same range of values, the percentage changes are different.

To avoid this problem, economists use the *midpoint method*, which gives the same answer for the elasticity no matter what point you begin with. Equation 4.2 uses the midpoint method to express the price elasticity of demand. While this equation looks more complicated than Equation 4.1, it is not. The midpoint method merely specifies how to plug in the initial and ending values for price and quantity to determine the percentage changes. Q_1 and P_1 are the initial values, and Q_2 and P_2 are the ending values.

$$E_D = \frac{\text{change in Q} \div \text{average value of Q}}{\text{change in P} \div \text{average value of P}}$$

$$= \frac{(Q_2 - Q_1) \div [(Q_1 + Q_2) \div 2]}{(P_2 - P_1) \div [(P_1 + P_2) \div 2]}$$

(EQUATION 4.2)

The change in the quantity demanded, $(Q_2 - Q_1)$, and the change in price, $(P_2 - P_1)$, are each divided by the average of the initial and ending values, or $[(Q_1 + Q_2) \div 2]$ and $[(P_1 + P_2) \div 2]$.

The midpoint method is the preferred method for solving elasticity problems. To see why, let's return to our pizza demand example.

If the price rises from \$6 to \$12, the quantity demanded falls from 30 to 20. Here the initial values are $P_1 = \$6$ and $Q_1 = 30$. The ending values are $P_2 = \$12$ and $Q_2 = 20$. Using the midpoint method,

$$E_D = \frac{(20 - 30) \div [(30 + 20) \div 2]}{(\$12 - \$6) \div [(\$6 + \$12) \div 2]} = \frac{-10 \div 25}{\$6 \div \$9} = -0.60$$

If the price falls from \$12 to \$6, quantity demanded rises from 20 to 30. This time, the initial values are $P_1 = \$12$ and $Q_1 = 20$. The ending values are $P_2 = \$6$ and $Q_2 = 30$. Using the midpoint method,

$$E_D = \frac{(30 - 20) \div [(20 + 30) \div 2]}{(\$6 - \$12) \div [(\$12 + \$6) \div 2]} = \frac{10 \div 25}{-\$6 \div \$9} = -0.60$$

When we calculated the price elasticity of demand from \$6 to \$12 using \$6 as the initial point, $E_D = -0.33$. Moving in the opposite direction, from \$12 to \$6, made \$12 the initial reference point and $E_D = -1.0$. The midpoint method splits the difference and uses \$9 and 25 pizzas as the midpoints. This approach makes the calculation of the elasticity coefficient the same, -0.60, no matter what direction the price moves. Therefore, economists use the midpoint method to standardize the results.

So, using the midpoint method, we arrive at an elasticity coefficient of -0.60, which is between 0 and -1. What does that number mean? In this case, the percentage change in the quantity demanded is less than the percentage change in the price. Whenever the percentage change in the quantity demanded is smaller than the percentage change in price, we say that demand is inelastic. In other words, the price drop does not make a big difference in how much pizza consumers purchase from the pizza shop. When the elasticity coefficient is less than -1, the opposite is true, and demand is elastic.

Graphing the Price Elasticity of Demand

Visualizing elasticity graphically helps us understand the relationship between elastic and inelastic demand. Figure 4.1 shows elasticity graphically. As demand becomes increasingly elastic, or responsive to price changes, the demand curve flattens. The range of elasticity runs from perfectly inelastic through perfectly elastic.

PERFECTLY INELASTIC DEMAND Figure 4.1, panel (a), depicts the price elasticity for pet care. Many pet owners report that they would pay any amount of money to help their sick or injured pet get better. For these pet owners, the demand curve is a vertical line. If you look along the quantity axis in panel (a), you will see that the quantity of pet care demanded (Q_D) remains constant no matter what it costs. At the same time, the price increases from P_0 to P_1. We can calculate the price elasticity coefficient as follows:

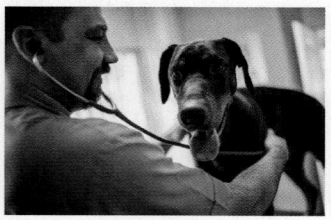

For many pet owners, the demand for veterinary care is perfectly inelastic.

$$E_{\text{pet care}} = \frac{\text{percentage change in } Q_D}{\text{percentage change in P}} = \frac{0}{\text{percentage change in P}} = 0$$

When zero is in the numerator, we know that the answer will be zero no matter what we find in the denominator. This conclusion makes sense. Many pet owners will try to help their pet feel better no matter what the cost, so we can say that their demand is *perfectly inelastic*. This means that the value of E_D will always be zero. (Of course, pet care is not perfectly inelastic, because there is certainly a price beyond which some pet owners would not or could not pay; but for illustrative purposes, let's say that pet care *is* perfectly elastic.) As you continue reading this section, refer to Table 4.2 on page 128 to help you keep track of the different types of elasticity.

The demand for electricity is relatively inelastic.

RELATIVELY INELASTIC DEMAND Moving on to panel (b) of Figure 4.1, we consider the demand for electricity. Whereas many pet owners will not change their consumption of health care for their pet no matter what the cost, consumers of electricity will modify their use of electricity in response to price changes. When the price of electricity goes up, they will use less, and when the price goes down, they will use more. Because living without electricity is not practical, using less is a matter of making relatively small lifestyle adjustments—buying energy-efficient light bulbs or adjusting the thermostat a few degrees. As a result, the demand curve in panel (b) is relatively steep, but not completely vertical as in panel (a).

When the change on the quantity axis is small compared with the change on the price axis, the price elasticity is *relatively inelastic*. Plugging these changes into the elasticity formula, we get

$$E_{electricity} = \frac{\text{percentage change in } Q_D}{\text{percentage change in P}} = \frac{\text{small change}}{\text{large change}}$$

The demand for apples is relatively elastic.

Recall that the law of demand describes a negative relationship between price and quantity demanded. Therefore, the changes along the price and quantity axes will always be in opposite directions. A price elasticity of zero tells us there is no change in the quantity demanded when price changes. So when demand is relatively inelastic, the price elasticity of demand must be relatively close to zero. The easiest way to think about this scenario is to consider how a 10% increase in electric rates affects most households. How much less electricity would you use? The answer for most people would be a little less, but not 10% less. You can adjust your thermostat, but you still need electricity to run your appliances and lights. When the price changes more than quantity changes, there is a larger change in the denominator. Therefore, the price elasticity of demand is between 0 and –1 when demand is relatively inelastic.

RELATIVELY ELASTIC DEMAND In Figure 4.1, panel (c), we consider apples. Because there are many good substitutes for apples, the demand for apples is *relatively elastic*. The flexibility of consumer demand for apples is illustrated by the degree of responsiveness we see along the quantity axis relative to the change exhibited along the price axis. We can observe this responsiveness by noting that a relatively elastic demand curve

The demand for a $10 bill is perfectly elastic.

is flatter than an inelastic demand curve. So, whereas perfectly inelastic demand shows no change in demand with an increase in price, and relatively inelastic demand shows a small change in quantity demanded with an increase in price, relatively elastic demand shows a relatively large change in quantity demanded with an increase in price. Placing this information into the elasticity formula gives us

$$E_{apples} = \frac{\text{percentage change in Q}_D}{\text{percentage change in P}} = \frac{\text{\large large} \text{ change}}{\text{\small small} \text{ change}}$$

Now the numerator—the percentage change in Q_D—is large, and the denominator—the percentage change in P—is small. E_D is less than −1. Recall that the sign must be negative, because there is a negative relationship between price and the quantity demanded. As the price elasticity of demand moves farther away from zero, the consumer becomes more responsive to a price change. Because many other fruits are good substitutes for apples, a small change in the price of apples will have a large effect on the quantity demanded.

PERFECTLY ELASTIC DEMAND Figure 4.1, panel (d), provides an interesting example: the demand for a $10 bill. Would you pay $11.00 to get a $10 bill? No. Would you pay $10.01 for a $10 bill? Still no. However, when the price drops to $10.00, you will probably become indifferent (that is, you will be equally satisfied with paying $10.00 for the $10 bill or not making the trade). The real magic here occurs when the price drops to $9.99. How many $10 bills would you buy if you could buy them for $9.99 or less? The answer: as many as possible! This is exactly what happens in currency markets, where small differences among currency prices around the globe motivate traders to buy and sell large quantities of currency and clear a small profit on the difference in exchange rates. This extreme form of price sensitivity is illustrated by a perfectly horizontal demand curve, which means that demand is *perfectly elastic*. Solving for the elasticity yields

$$E_{\$10\,bill} = \frac{\text{percentage change in Q}_D}{\text{percentage change in P}} = \frac{\text{nearly infinite change}}{\text{\small very small}\ (\$0.01)\ \text{change}}$$

We can think of this very small price change, from $10.00 to $9.99, as having essentially an unlimited effect on the quantity of $10 bills demanded. Traders go from being uninterested in trading at $10.00 to seeking to buy as many $10 bills as possible when the price drops to $9.99. As a result, the price elasticity of demand approaches negative infinity (−∞).

UNITARY ELASTICITY There is a fifth type of elasticity, not depicted in Figure 4.1. *Unitary elasticity* describes the situation in which elasticity is neither elastic nor inelastic. This situation occurs when E_D is exactly −1, and it happens when the percentage change in price is exactly equal to the percentage change in quantity demanded. This characteristic of unitary elasticity will be important when we discuss the connection between elasticity and total revenue later in this chapter. You're probably wondering what an example of a unitary good would be. Relax. It is impossible to find a good that has a price elasticity

FIGURE 4.1

Elasticity and the Demand Curve

For any given price change across two demand curves, demand will be more elastic on the flatter demand curve than on the steeper demand curve. In (a), the demand is perfectly inelastic, so the price does not matter. In (b), the demand is relatively inelastic, so the price is less important than the quantity purchased. In (c), the demand is relatively elastic, so the price matters more than quantity. In (d), the demand is perfectly elastic, so price is all that matters.

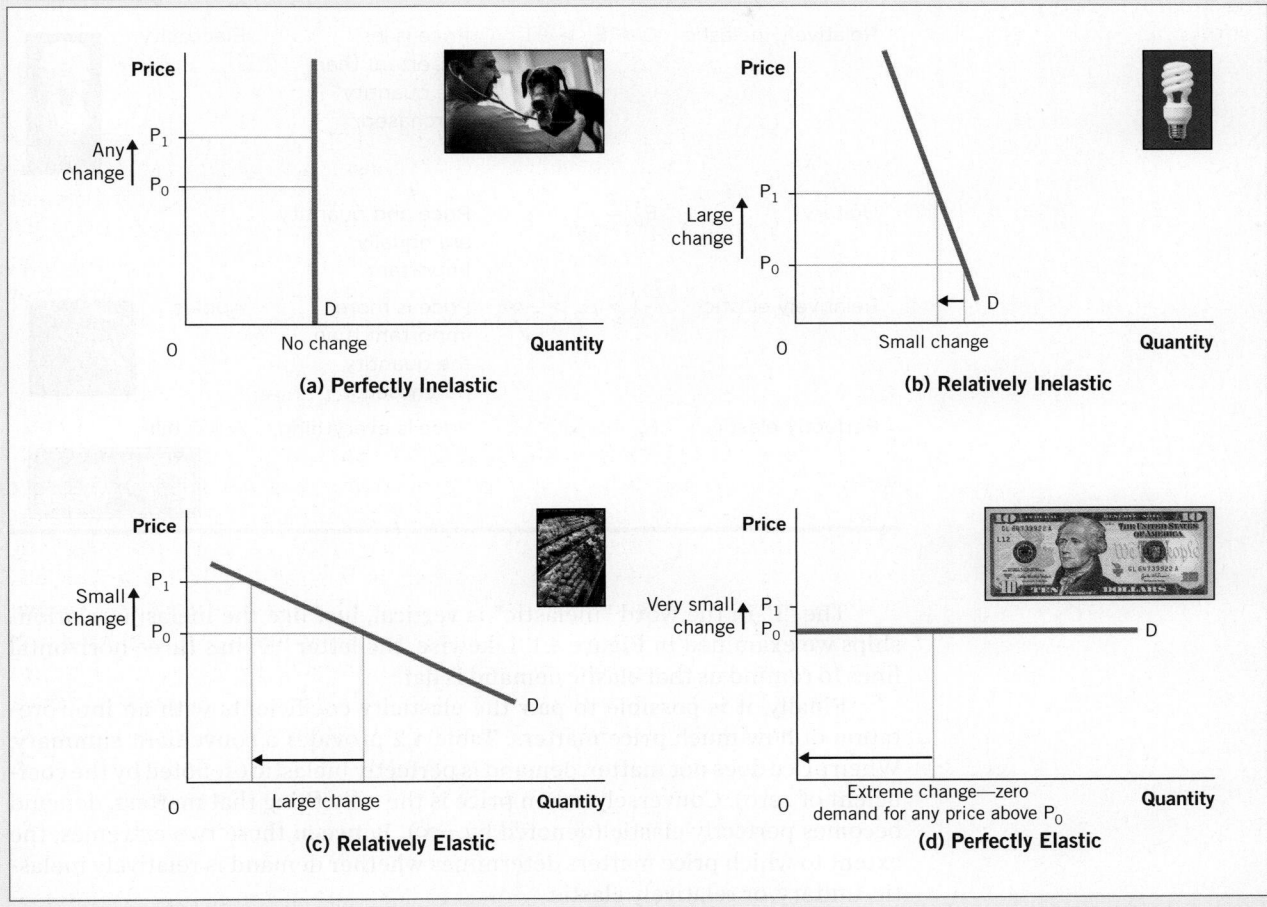

of exactly −1 at all price points. It is enough to know that unitary demand represents the crossover from elastic to inelastic demand.

PRICE ELASTICITY OF DEMAND: A SUMMARY Now that you have had a chance to look at all four panels in Figure 4.1, here is a handy trick you can use to keep the difference between inelastic and elastic demand straight.

$$\textbf{I} = \text{inelastic and} \quad \textbf{E} = \text{elastic}$$

TABLE 4.2

The Relationship between Price Elasticity of Demand and Price

Elasticity	E_D coefficient	Interpretation	Example in Figure 4.1
Perfectly inelastic	$E_D = 0$	Price does not matter.	Saving your pet
Relatively inelastic	$0 > E_D > -1$	Price is less important than the quantity purchased.	Electricity
Unitary	$E_D = -1$	Price and quantity are equally important.	
Relatively elastic	$-1 > E_D > -\infty$	Price is more important than the quantity purchased.	Apples
Perfectly elastic	$E_D \rightarrow -\infty$	Price is everything.	A $10 bill

The "I" in the word "inelastic" is vertical, just like the inelastic relationships we examined in Figure 4.1. Likewise, the letter "E" has three horizontal lines to remind us that elastic demand is flat.

Finally, it is possible to pair the elasticity coefficients with an interpretation of how much price matters. Table 4.2 provides a convenient summary. When price does not matter, demand is perfectly inelastic (denoted by the coefficient of zero). Conversely, when price is the only thing that matters, demand becomes perfectly elastic (denoted by $-\infty$). Between these two extremes, the extent to which price matters determines whether demand is relatively inelastic, unitary, or relatively elastic.

TIME, ELASTICITY, AND THE DEMAND CURVE We have already seen that increased time makes demand more elastic. Figure 4.2 shows this result graphically. When the price rises from P_1 to P_2, consumers cannot avoid the price increase in the immediate run, and demand is represented by the perfectly inelastic demand curve, D_1. For example, if your gas tank is almost empty, you must purchase gas at the new, higher price. Over a slightly longer time horizon—the short run—consumers are more flexible and drive less in order to buy less gasoline. Demand rotates to D_2, and in the short run consumption declines to Q_2. In the long run, when consumers have time to purchase a more fuel-efficient vehicle or move closer to work, demand rotates to D_3 and gas purchases fall even further. As the demand curve continues to flatten, the quantity demanded falls to Q_3.

FIGURE 4.2

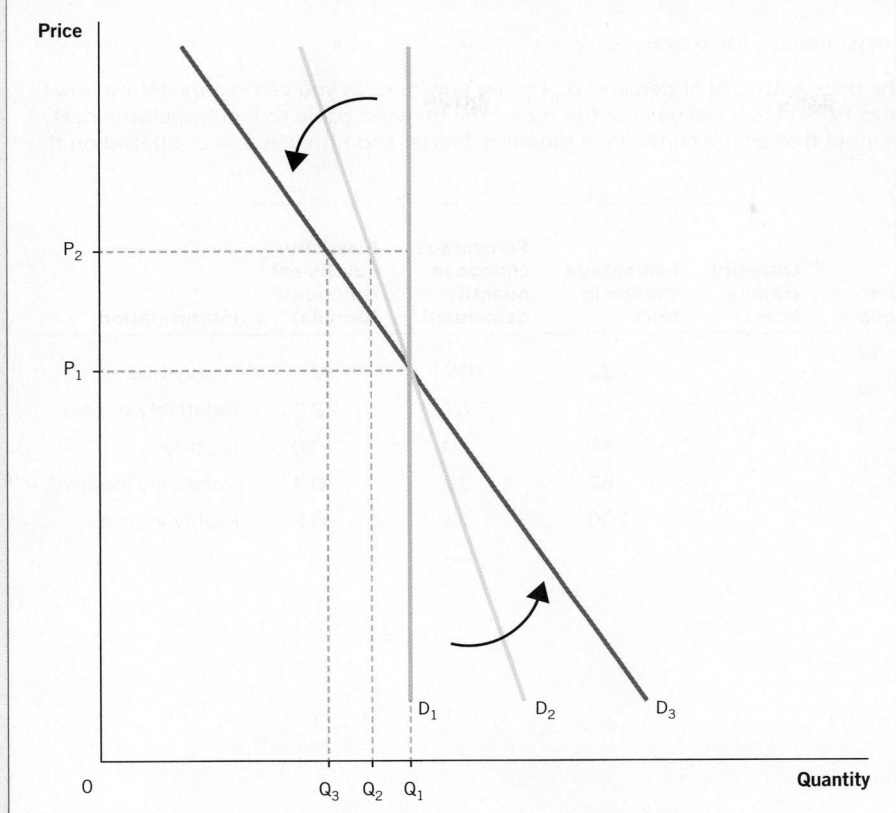

Elasticity and the Demand Curve over Time

Demand becomes more elastic over time. When the price rises from P_1 to P_2, consumers are unable to avoid the price increase in the immediate run (D_1). In the short run (D_2), consumers become more flexible and consumption declines to Q_2. Eventually, in the long run (D_3), there is time to make lifestyle changes that further reduce consumption. As a result, the demand curve continues to flatten and the quantity demanded falls to Q_3 in response to the higher price.

SLOPE AND ELASTICITY In this section, we pause to make sure that you understand what you are observing in the figures. The demand curves shown in Figures 4.1 and 4.2 are straight lines, and therefore they have a constant slope, or steepness. (A refresher on slope is found in the appendix to Chapter 2.) So, looking at Figures 4.1 and 4.2, you might think that slope is the same as the price elasticity. But slope does not equal elasticity.

Consider, for example, a trip to Starbucks. Would you buy a tall skinny latte if it costs $10? How about $7? What about $5? Say you decide to buy the skinny latte because the price drops from $5 to $4. In this case, a small price change, a drop from $5 to $4, causes you to make the purchase. You can say that the demand for skinny lattes is relatively elastic. Now look at Figure 4.3, which shows a demand curve for skinny lattes. At $5 the consumer purchases zero lattes, at $4 she purchases one latte, at $3 she purchases two, and she continues to buy one additional latte with each $1 drop in price. As you progress downward along the demand curve, price becomes less of an inhibiting factor, and as a result, the price elasticity of demand slowly becomes more inelastic. Notice that the slope of a linear demand curve is constant. However, when we calculate the price elasticity of demand between the various points in Figure 4.3, it becomes clear that demand is increasingly inelastic as we move

FIGURE 4.3

The Difference between Slope and Elasticity

Along any straight demand curve, the price elasticity of demand (E_D) is not constant, as you can see by noting how the price elasticity of demand changes from highly elastic near the top of the demand curve to highly inelastic near the bottom of the curve. In the table, note that all the numbers in the third, fourth, and fifth columns are based on the midpoint formula.

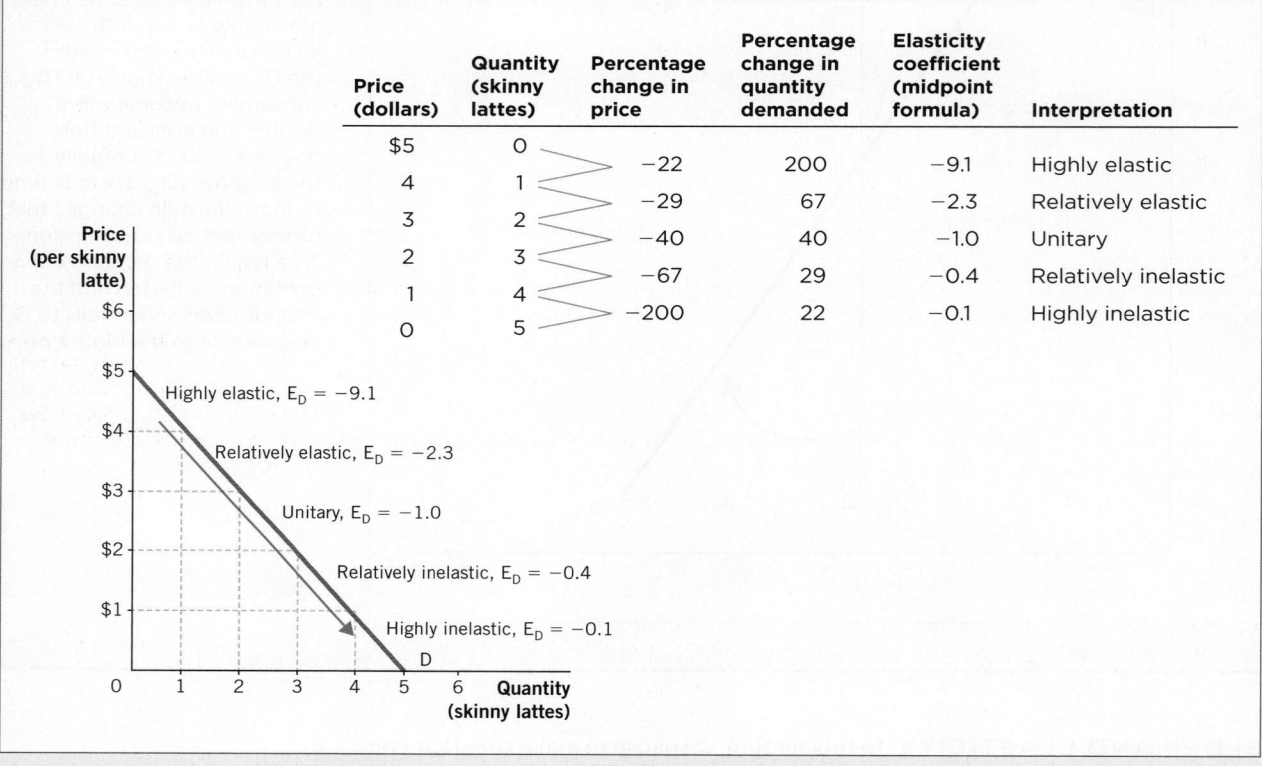

Price (dollars)	Quantity (skinny lattes)	Percentage change in price	Percentage change in quantity demanded	Elasticity coefficient (midpoint formula)	Interpretation
$5	0				
4	1	−22	200	−9.1	Highly elastic
3	2	−29	67	−2.3	Relatively elastic
2	3	−40	40	−1.0	Unitary
1	4	−67	29	−0.4	Relatively inelastic
0	5	−200	22	−0.1	Highly inelastic

down the demand curve. You can see this in the change in E_D; it steadily increases from −9.1 to −0.1.

Perfectly inelastic demand would exist if the elasticity coefficient reached zero. Recall that a value of zero means that there is no change in the quantity demanded as a result of a price change. Therefore, values close to zero reflect inelastic demand, while those farther away from zero reflect more elastic demand.

Price Elasticity of Demand and Total Revenue

Understanding the price elasticity of demand for the product you sell is important when running a business. Consumer responsiveness to price changes determines whether a firm would be better off raising or lowering its price for

TABLE 4.3

The Price Elasticity of Demand and Total Revenue

Price (P) (per skinny latte)	Quantity (Q) (skinny lattes)	Total revenue P × Q	Percentage change in price	Percentage change in quantity	Elasticity coefficient	Interpretation
$5	0	$0				
			−22	200	−9.1	Highly elastic
4	1	4				
			−29	67	−2.3	Relatively elastic
3	2	6				
			−40	40	−1.0	Unitary
2	3	6				
			−67	29	−0.4	Relatively inelastic
1	4	4				
			−200	22	−0.1	Highly inelastic
0	5	0				

a given product. In this section, we explore the relationship between the price elasticity of demand and a firm's total revenue.

But first we need to understand the concept of total revenue. **Total revenue** is the amount that a firm receives from the sale of goods and services. Total revenue for a particular good is calculated by multiplying the price of the good by the quantity of the good that is sold. Table 4.3 reproduces the table from Figure 4.3 (with numbers based on the midpoint formula) and adds a column for the total revenue. We find the total revenue by multiplying the price of a tall skinny latte by the quantity purchased.

After calculating total revenue at each price, we can look at the column of elasticity coefficients to determine the relationship. When we link revenues with the price elasticity of demand, a trade-off emerges. (This trade-off occurs because total revenue and elasticity relate to price differently. Total revenue involves multiplying the price by the quantity, while elasticity involves dividing the percentage change in quantity demanded by the percentage change in price.) Total revenue is zero when the price is too high ($5 or more) and when the price is too low ($0). Between these two extremes, prices from $1 to $4 generate positive total revenue.

Consider what happens when the price drops from $5 to $4. At $4, the first latte is purchased. Total revenue is $4 × 1 = $4. This is also the range at which the price elasticity of demand is highly elastic. As a result, lowering the price increases revenue. Revenue continues to increase when the price drops from $4 to $3. Now two lattes are sold, so the total revenue rises to $3 × 2 = $6. At the same time, demand remains elastic. We thus conclude that when demand is elastic, lowering the price will increase total revenue. This relationship is shown in panel (a) of Figure 4.4. By lowering the price from $4 to $3, the business has generated $2 more in revenue. But to generate this extra revenue, the business has lowered the price from $4 to $3 and therefore has given up $1 for each unit it sells. This lost revenue is represented by the red area under the demand curve in panel (a).

When the price drops from $3 to $2, the total revenue stays at $6. This result occurs because demand is unitary, as shown in panel (b). This special condition exists when the percentage price change is exactly offset by an equal percentage change in the quantity demanded. In this situation, revenue remains constant. At $2, three lattes are purchased, so the total revenue is $2 × 3, which is the same as it was when the price was $3. As a result, we can

Total revenue is the amount that a firm receives from the sale of goods and services. Total revenue for a particular good is calculated by multiplying the price of the good by the quantity of the good that is sold.

Trade-offs

FIGURE 4.4

(a) The Total Revenue Trade-Off When Demand Is Elastic

In the elastic region of the demand curve, lowering the price will increase total revenue. The gains from increased purchases, shown in the light green area, are greater than the losses from a lower purchase price, shown in the red area. The dark green area is part of the total revenue that exists at both prices.

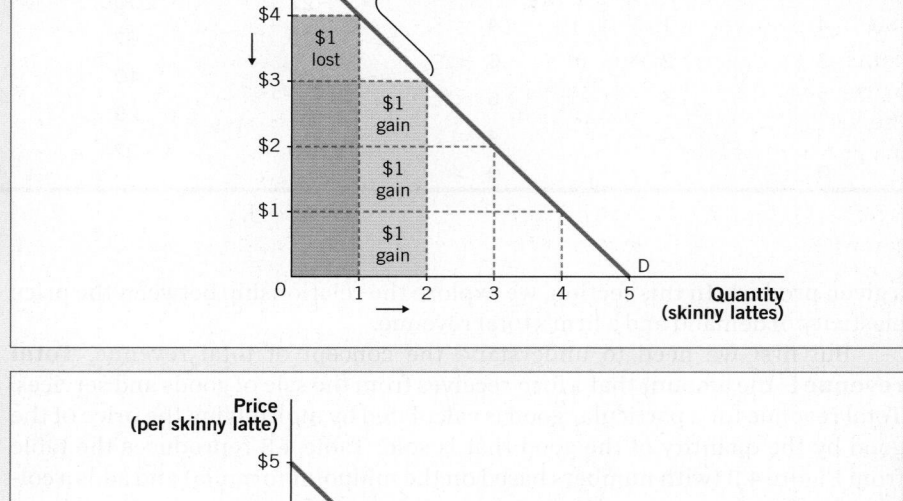

(b) ...When Demand Is Unitary

When demand is unitary, lowering the price will no longer increase total revenue. The gains from increased purchases, shown in the light green area, are equal to the losses from a lower purchase price, shown in the red area.

(c) ...When Demand Is Inelastic

In the inelastic region of the demand curve, lowering the price will decrease total revenue. The gains from increased purchases, shown in the light green area, are smaller than the losses from a lower purchase price, shown in the red area.

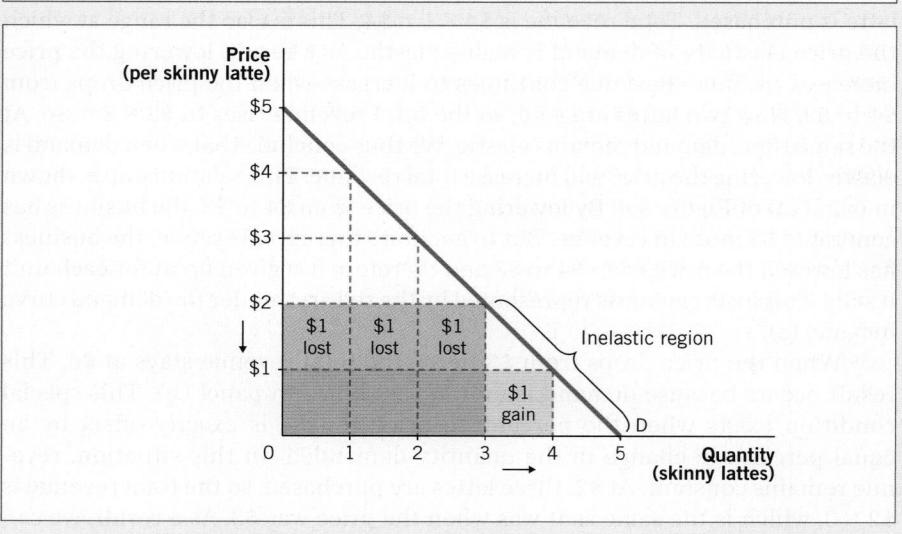

see that total revenue has reached a maximum. Between \$3 and \$2, the price elasticity of demand is unitary. This finding does not necessarily mean that the firm will operate at the unitary point. Maximizing profit, not revenue, is the ultimate goal of a business, and we have not yet accounted for costs in our calculation of profits.

Once we reach a price below unitary demand, we move into the realm of inelastic demand, shown in panel (c). When the price falls to \$1, total revenue declines to \$4. This result occurs because the price elasticity of demand is now relatively inelastic, or price insensitive. Even though the price is declining by \$1, price is increasingly unimportant; as you can see by the light green square, lowering the price to \$1 does not spur a large increase in consumption.

As we see in panel (c), at a price of \$2, three units are sold and total revenue is \$2 × 3 = \$6. When the price falls to \$1, four units are sold, so the total revenue is now \$4 × 1 = \$4. By lowering the price from \$2 to \$1, the business has lost \$2 in extra revenue because it does not generate enough extra revenue from the lower price. Lowering the price from \$2 to \$1 causes a loss of \$3 in existing sales revenue (the red boxes). At the same time, it generates only \$1 in new sales (the light green box), so the net change is a loss of \$2.

In this analysis, we see that once the demand curve enters the inelastic area, lowering the price decreases total revenue. This outcome is unambiguously bad for a business. The lower price brings in less revenue and requires the business to produce more goods. Because making goods is costly, it does not make sense to lower prices into the region where revenues decline. We can be sure that no business will intentionally operate in the inelastic region of the demand curve because it will earn less profit.

ECONOMICS IN THE REAL WORLD

PRICE ELASTICITY OF DEMAND: THE NUTELLA RIOTS OF 2018

Nutella is a chocolate hazelnut spread with a distinctive flavor and legions of loyal fans (32 million Facebook followers). There's even a medical condition known as "Nutella Addiction." When Intermarché supermarkets in France slashed their Nutella prices by 70% from €4.50 to €1.40 (\$5.00 to \$1.50), people went crazy. Want to see the reaction for yourself? Check out this link: www.youtube.com/watch?v=UyjM62yLGFQ.

What makes this story so interesting is the overwhelming reaction the price drop created. Nutella is a brisk seller in many European countries at its retail price. But when Intermarché lowered the price, sales exploded and Nutella sold out in every store. The overwhelming reaction is strong evidence that the demand for Nutella is quite elastic, since the price reduction caused a massive increase in the quantity demanded.

What would you do if the price of Nutella suddenly dropped 70%?

Incentives

Price Elasticity of Demand

The following two questions ask you to compute price elasticity of demand. Before we do the math, ask yourself whether the price elasticity of demand for sandwiches or the antibiotic amoxicillin is elastic.

QUESTION: A deli manager decides to lower the price of a featured sandwich from $3 to $2, and she finds that sales during the week increase from 240 to 480 sandwiches. Is demand elastic?

ANSWER: Consumers were flexible and bought significantly more sandwiches in response to the price drop. Let's calculate the price elasticity of demand (E_D) using Equation 4.2. Recall that

$$E_D = \frac{(Q_2 - Q_1) \div [(Q_1 + Q_2) \div 2]}{(P_2 - P_1) \div [(P_1 + P_2) \div 2]}$$

Plugging in the values from the question yields

$$E_D = \frac{(480 - 240) \div [(240 + 480) \div 2]}{(\$2 - \$3) \div [(\$3 + \$2) \div 2]} = \frac{240 \div 360}{-\$1 \div \$2.50}$$

Therefore, $E_D = -1.67$.

Whenever the price elasticity of demand is less than −1, demand is elastic: the percentage change in the quantity demanded is greater than the percentage change in price. This outcome is exactly what the store manager expected. But sandwiches are just one option for a meal; there are many other choices, such as salads, burgers, and chicken—all of which cost more than the now-cheaper sandwich. Therefore, we should not be surprised that there is a relatively large percentage increase in sandwich purchases by price-conscious customers.

QUESTION: A local pharmacy manager decides to raise the price of a 50-pill pre-scription of amoxicillin (an antibiotic) from $8 to $10. The pharmacy tracks the sales of amoxicillin over the next month and finds that sales decline from 1,500 boxes to 1,480. Is demand elastic?

ANSWER: First, let's consider the potential substitutes for amoxicillin. To be sure, it's possible to substitute other drugs, but they might not be as effective. Therefore, most patients prefer to use the drug prescribed by their doctor. Also, in this case the cost of the drug is relatively small. Finally, patients' need for amoxicillin is a short-run consideration. They want the medicine now so they will get better! All three factors would lead us to believe that the demand for amoxicillin is relatively inelastic. Let's find out if the data confirm that intuition.

The price elasticity of demand using the midpoint method is

$$E_D = \frac{(Q_2 - Q_1) \div [(Q_1 + Q_2) \div 2]}{(P_2 - P_1) \div [(P_1 + P_2) \div 2]}$$

Is the demand for a sandwich elastic or inelastic?

AMOX   500

Is the demand for amoxicillin elastic or inelastic?

Plugging in the values from the question yields

$$E_D = \frac{(1480 - 1500) \div [(1500 + 1480) \div 2]}{(\$10 - \$8) \div [(\$8 + \$10) \div 2]}$$

Simplifying produces this equation:

$$E_D = \frac{-20 \div 1490}{\$2 \div \$9}$$

Therefore, $E_D = -0.06$.

Recall that an E_D near zero indicates that the price elasticity of demand is highly inelastic, which is what we suspected. The price increase does not cause consumption to fall very much. If the store manager was hoping to bring in a little extra revenue from the sales of amoxicillin, his plan is successful. Before the price increase, the business sold 1,500 units at $8, so total revenue was $12,000. After the price increase, sales decrease to 1,480 units, but the new price is $10, so total revenue is now $14,800. Raising the price of amoxicillin has helped the pharmacy make an additional $2,800 in total revenue.

CHALLENGE QUESTION: Now suppose that the local pharmacy manager decides to raise the price of a 50-pill prescription of amoxicillin from $8 to $40, instead of just to $10. Again the pharmacy tracks the sales, and this time it finds that sales decline from 1,500 boxes all the way down to 50 boxes. Is demand still elastic?

ANSWER:

Plugging in the values from the question using the midpoint method yields

$$E_D = \frac{(50 - 1500) \div [(1500 + 50) \div 2]}{(\$40 - \$8) \div [(\$8 + \$40) \div 2]}$$

Simplifying produces

$$E_D = \frac{-1450 \div 775}{\$32 \div \$24}$$

Therefore $E_D = -1.41$

An E_D value below -1 represents relatively elastic demand. At this point, the price increase has clearly backfired. Total revenue has gone from $12,000 (1,500 boxes at $8 each) down to 50 boxes $\times$ $40 per box = $2,000. Raising the price of amoxicillin to a point where demand is elastic has cost the pharmacy $10,000 in total revenue. This is a vivid reminder that the elasticity of demand steadily becomes more elastic as the price rises.

Price Elasticity of Demand

Determining the price elasticity of demand for a product or service involves calculating the responsiveness of quantity demanded to a change in the price. The chart below gives the actual price elasticity of demand for ten common products and services. Remember, the number is always negative because of the negative relationship between price and the quantity demanded. Why is price elasticity of demand important? It reveals consumer behavior and allows for better pricing strategies by businesses.

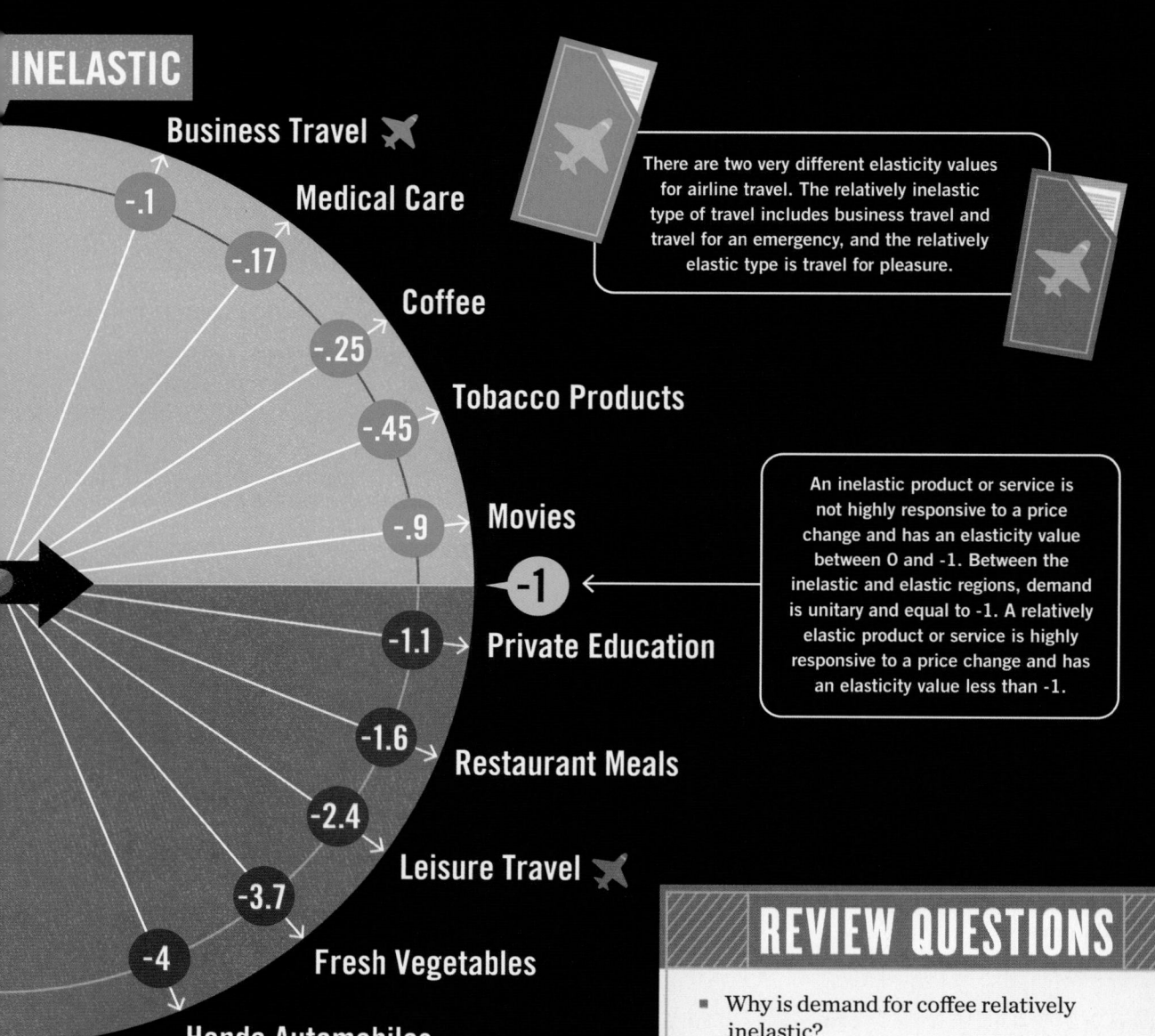

INELASTIC

Business Travel ✈ −.1

Medical Care −.17

Coffee −.25

Tobacco Products −.45

Movies −.9

−1

Private Education −1.1

Restaurant Meals −1.6

−2.4

Leisure Travel ✈ −3.7

Fresh Vegetables −4

Honda Automobiles

ELASTIC

There are two very different elasticity values for airline travel. The relatively inelastic type of travel includes business travel and travel for an emergency, and the relatively elastic type is travel for pleasure.

An inelastic product or service is not highly responsive to a price change and has an elasticity value between 0 and -1. Between the inelastic and elastic regions, demand is unitary and equal to -1. A relatively elastic product or service is highly responsive to a price change and has an elasticity value less than -1.

REVIEW QUESTIONS

- Why is demand for coffee relatively inelastic?

- For business owners, why is it important to understand whether demand for their products is elastic or inelastic?

Price Elasticity of Demand and Total Revenues

SHARK TANK: VURTEGO POGO

Do you increase revenue by lowering or raising prices?

The answer, according to economist Charity-Joy Acchiardo, is that "it all depends on the price elasticity of demand for your product or service." Acchiardo is one of the creators of econshark.com, a website dedicated to dissecting the economic principles on display in the popular TV show *Shark Tank*. In one episode, Brian Spencer is looking for an investment from the Sharks so he can mass-market his amazingly cool, extreme-sport pogo stick, the "Vurtego Pogo." However, Shark Robert Herjavec questions whether high-end pogo sticks are a good fit for the mass market. Spencer's current price of $330, Robert feels, is too low for a specialty product like a high-performance pogo stick, but too high for the mass market. The other Sharks agree. They urge Spencer to raise his price and concentrate on dominating the niche he's carved out for himself. Spencer leaves the Shark Tank empty-handed but realizing that he's been given good advice. When something is cool and there is nothing else exactly like it on the

How much would you pay to be able to do flips on a pogo stick?

market, people are willing to pay more to buy one. Translation: when demand is inelastic, don't price your product too low.

How Do Changes in Income and the Prices of Other Goods Affect Elasticity?

We have seen how consumer demand responds to changes in the price of a single good. In this section, we examine how responsive demand is to changes in income and to price changes in other goods.

Income Elasticity

Changes in personal income can have a large effect on consumer spending. After all, the money in your pocket influences not only how much you buy, but also the types of purchases you make. A consumer who is low on money may opt to buy a cheap generic product, while someone with a little extra cash can afford to upgrade. The grocery store aisle reflects different shoppers' budgets. Store brands and name products compete for shelf space. Lower-income shoppers can choose the store brand to save money, while more affluent shoppers can choose their favorite brand-name product without worrying about the purchase price. The **income elasticity of demand** (E_I) measures how a change in income affects spending. It is calculated by dividing the percentage change in the quantity demanded by the percentage change in personal income:

(EQUATION 4.3)

$$E_I = \frac{\text{percentage change in the quantity demanded}}{\text{percentage change in income}}$$

Unlike the price elasticity of demand, which is negative, the income elasticity of demand can be positive or negative. When a higher level of income enables the consumer to purchase more, the goods that are purchased are *normal goods*, a term we learned in Chapter 3. Because the demand for normal goods goes up with income, they have a positive income elasticity; a rise in income causes a rise in the quantity demanded. For instance, if you receive a 20% pay raise and you decide to pay an extra 10% on your cable TV bill to add HBO, the resulting income elasticity is positive, because 10% divided by 20% is 0.5. Whenever a good is normal, the result is a positive income elasticity of demand, and purchases of the good rise as income expands and purchases of the good fall as income falls.

Normal goods fall into two categories: *necessities* and *luxuries*. Goods that people consider necessities generally have income elasticities between 0 and 1. For example, expenditures on items such as clothing, electricity, and gasoline are unavoidable, and consumers at any income level must buy them no matter what. Although purchases of necessities will increase as income rises, they do not rise as fast as the increase in income does. Therefore, as income increases, spending on necessities will expand at a slower rate than the increase in income.

Rising income enables consumers to enjoy significantly more luxuries, producing an income elasticity of demand greater than 1 for luxuries. For instance, a family of modest means may travel almost exclusively by car. However, as the family's income rises, they can afford air travel. A relatively small jump in income can cause the family to fly instead of drive.

In Chapter 3, we saw that *inferior goods* are those that people will choose not to purchase when their income goes up. Inferior goods have a negative income elasticity, because as income expands, the demand for these goods declines. We see this effect in Table 4.4 with the example of macaroni and cheese, an inexpensive meal. As a household's income rises, it is able to afford healthier food and more variety in its meals. Consequently, the number of times that mac and cheese is purchased declines. The decline in consumption indicates that mac and cheese is an inferior good, as reflected in the negative sign of the income elasticity.

Clothing purchases expand with income.

Cross-Price Elasticity

Now we will look at how a price change in one good can affect the demand for a related good. For instance, if you enjoy pizza, the choice between ordering from Domino's or Pizza Hut is influenced by the price of both goods. The **cross-price elasticity of demand** (E_C) measures the percentage change in the quantity demanded of one good to the percentage change in the price of a related good:

Air travel is a luxury good.

$$E_C = \frac{\text{percentage change in the quantity demanded of one good}}{\text{percentage change in the price of a related good}}$$

(EQUATION 4.4)

The **cross-price elasticity of demand** (E_C) measures the percentage change in the quantity demanded of one good to the percentage change in the price of a related good.

Consider how two goods are related. If the goods are substitutes, a price rise in one good will cause the quantity demanded of that good to decline. At the same time, because consumers can purchase the substitute good for the same price as before, demand for the substitute good will increase. When the price of Domino's pizza rises, consumers will buy more pizza from Pizza Hut. This means that the cross-price elasticity of demand is positive.

The opposite is true if the goods are complements. In that case, a price increase in one good will make the joint consumption of both goods more expensive. Therefore, the consumption of both goods will decline. For example, a price increase for turkeys will cause the quantity demanded of both turkey and gravy to decline, and a price decrease for turkeys will cause the quantity demanded of both turkey and gravy to increase. This means that the cross-price elasticity of demand is negative.

What if there is no relationship between two goods? For example, if the price of basketballs goes up, that price increase probably will not affect the quantity demanded of bedroom slippers. In this case, the cross-price elasticity is neither positive nor negative; it is zero. Table 4.5 lists cross-price elasticity values according to type of good.

Trade-offs

TABLE 4.4			
Income Elasticity			
Type of good	**Subcategory**	**E_I coefficient**	**Example**
Inferior		$E_I < 0$	Macaroni and cheese
Normal	Necessity	$0 < E_I < 1$	Milk
Normal	Luxury	$E_I > 1$	Diamond ring

TABLE 4.5

Cross-Price Elasticity

Type of good	E_C coefficient	Example	
Substitutes	$E_C > 0$	Pizza Hut and Domino's	
No relationship	$E_C = 0$	A basketball and bedroom slippers	
Complements	$E_C < 0$	Turkey and gravy	

PRACTICE WHAT YOU KNOW

Cross-Price Elasticity of Demand

To learn how to calculate cross-price elasticity, let's consider enjoying the soft drink Mr. Pibb with Red Vines candy. If you have never tried this combination, you should!

QUESTION: Suppose that the price of a 2-liter bottle of Mr. Pibb falls from $1.49 to $1.29. In the week immediately preceding the price drop, a local store sells 60 boxes of Red Vines. After the price drop, sales of Red Vines increase to 80 boxes. What is the cross-price elasticity of demand for Red Vines when the price of Mr. Pibb falls from $1.49 to $1.29?

ANSWER: The cross-price elasticity of demand using the midpoint method is

$$E_C = \frac{(Q_{RV2} - Q_{RV1}) \div [(Q_{RV1} + Q_{RV2}) \div 2]}{(P_{MP2} - P_{MP1}) \div [(P_{MP1} + P_{MP2}) \div 2]}$$

Notice that there are now additional subscripts to denote that we are measuring the percentage change in the quantity demanded of good RV (Red Vines) in response to the percentage change in the price of good MP (Mr. Pibb).

Plugging in the values from the example yields

$$E_C = \frac{(80 - 60) \div [(60 + 80) \div 2]}{(\$1.29 - \$1.49) \div [(\$1.49 + \$1.29) \div 2]}$$

Simplifying produces

$$E_C = \frac{20 \div 70}{-\$0.20 \div \$1.39}$$

Have you tried Mr. Pibb and Red Vines together?

Solving for E_C gives us a value of −1.99. The result's negative value confirms our intuition that two goods that go well together are complements, since the decrease in the price of Mr. Pibb causes consumers to buy more Red Vines.

TENNIS, ANYONE?

Are you a casual tennis player or passionate about your game? The answer to that question helps us understand a real-life elasticity experiment.

In 2011, the New York City Parks Department doubled the prices paid by tennis players between the ages of 18 and 61. Single-pay passes for an hour of court time jumped from $7 to $15, while season passes rose from $100 to $200.

Far fewer tennis permits were sold under the new prices, according to data from the Parks Department. Sales of season passes for most players slipped by 40%, with 7,400 sold in 2011 as compared to 12,400 in 2010. Sales of one-day passes took a big hit as well, dropping by nearly a third from more than 40,000 for the 2010 season to 27,000.

How much would you be willing to pay for court time?

Type of pass	Price in 2010	Price in 2011	Passes sold in 2010	Passes sold in 2011	Total revenue in 2010 (in millions)	Total revenue in 2011 (in millions)	E_D
One-day	$7	$15	40,000	27,000	$0.28	$0.41	−0.53
Annual	100	200	12,400	7,400	1.24	1.48	−0.75
Total					$1.52	$1.89	

We calculated the price elasticity of demand, E_D, using the midpoint formula. Because the coefficients for the one-day and annual passes are between 0 and −1, we know that demand is relatively inelastic at these prices. We also know that when demand is inelastic and prices increase, total revenue should increase, and that is exactly what happened. Tennis court revenues increased from $1.52 million in 2010 to $1.89 million in 2011.

As you might guess, many tennis players in New York City were quite upset with the sudden price increase. However, the data show that many tennis players decided to keep playing rather than quit. This result shouldn't surprise you too much. Tennis is good exercise, a social experience, and a hobby that many people enjoy. While the price increases were dramatic on a percentage basis (they doubled!), the increase in price is a relatively small part of most New Yorkers' budgets. Because there are not many good substitutes for tennis available in New York City, we'd expect many to continue playing, as the data confirmed.

Sources: Author's calculations. Data from Matt McCue, "Tennis Fees Ace Out Many," *Wall Street Journal*, August 5, 2012. http://www.wsj.com/articles/SB10000872396390443687504577564933033308176.

Income Elasticity

Yummy, or all you can afford?

QUESTION: A college student eats ramen noodles twice a week and earns $300 a week working part-time. After graduating, the student earns $1,000 a week and eats ramen noodles once every other week , or 0.5 time a week. What is the student's income elasticity?

ANSWER: The income elasticity of demand using the midpoint method is

$$E_I = \frac{(Q_2 - Q_1) \div [(Q_1 + Q_2) \div 2]}{(I_2 - I_1) \div [(I_1 + I_2) \div 2]}$$

Plugging in the values from the question yields

$$E_I = \frac{(0.5 - 2.0) \div [(2.0 + 0.5) \div 2]}{(\$1000 - \$300) \div [(\$300 + \$1000) \div 2]}$$

Simplifying yields

$$E_I = \frac{-1.5 \div 1.25}{\$700 \div \$650}$$

Therefore, $E_I = -1.1$.

The income elasticity of demand is positive for normal goods and negative for inferior goods. Therefore, the negative coefficient indicates that ramen noodles are an inferior good over this person's range of income—in this example, between $300 and $1,000 per week. This result should confirm your intuition. The higher postgraduation income enables the student to substitute away from ramen noodles and toward other meals that provide more nourishment and enjoyment.

What Is the Price Elasticity of Supply?

The **price elasticity of supply** is a measure of the responsiveness of the quantity supplied to a change in price.

Like consumers, sellers are sensitive to price changes. However, the determinants of the price elasticity of supply are substantially different from the determinants of the price elasticity of demand. The **price elasticity of supply** is a measure of the responsiveness of the quantity supplied to a change in price.

In this section, we examine how much sellers respond to price changes. For instance, if the market price of gasoline increases, how will oil companies respond? The answer depends on the elasticity of supply. Oil must be refined into gasoline. If it is difficult for oil companies to increase their output of gasoline significantly, the quantity of gasoline supplied will not increase much even if the price increases a lot. In this case, we say that supply is inelastic, or unresponsive. However, if the price increase is small and suppliers respond by offering significantly more gasoline for sale, then supply is elastic. We would expect to observe this outcome if it is easy to refine oil into gasoline.

When supply is not able to respond to a change in price, we say it is inelastic. Think of an oceanfront property in Southern California. The amount of land next to the ocean is fixed. If the price of oceanfront property rises, the supply of land cannot adjust to the price increase. In this case, the supply is perfectly inelastic and the price elasticity of supply is zero. Recall that a price elasticity coefficient of zero means that quantity supplied does not change as price changes.

When the supplier's ability to make quick adjustments is limited, the elasticity of supply is less than 1. For instance, when a cellular network becomes congested, it takes suppliers a long time to provide additional capacity. They have to build new cell towers, which requires the purchase of land and additional construction costs. In contrast, a local hot dog vendor can easily add another cart in relatively short order. As a result, for the hot dog vendor, supply is elastic, with an elasticity coefficient that is greater than 1.

Table 4.6 examines the price elasticity of supply (E_s). Recall the law of supply, which states that there is a direct relationship between the price of a good and the quantity that a firm supplies. As a result, the percentage change in the quantity supplied and the percentage change in price move in the same direction. The E_s coefficient reflects this direct relationship with a positive sign.

What would it take to own a slice of paradise?

Determinants of the Price Elasticity of Supply

When we examined the determinants of the price elasticity of demand, we saw that consumers have to consider the number of substitutes, how expensive the item is compared to their overall budget, whether the good is a necessity or

TABLE 4.6

A Closer Look at the Price Elasticity of Supply

Elasticity	E_s coefficient	Example	
Perfectly inelastic	$E_s = 0$	Oceanfront land	
Relatively inelastic	$0 < E_s < 1$	Cell phone tower	
Relatively elastic	$E_s > 1$	Hot dog vendor	

a luxury, and the amount of time they have to make a decision. Time and the adjustment process are also key elements in determining the price elasticity of supply. However, there is a critical difference: the degree of flexibility that producers have in bringing their product to the market quickly.

The Flexibility of Producers

When a producer can quickly ramp up output, supply tends to be elastic. One way to maintain flexibility is to have spare production capacity. Extra capacity enables producers to quickly meet changing price conditions, so supply is more responsive, or elastic. The ability to store the good is another way to stay flexible. Producers who have stockpiles of their products can respond more quickly to changes in market conditions. For example, De Beers, the international diamond conglomerate, stores millions of uncut diamonds. As the price of diamonds fluctuates, De Beers can quickly change the quantity of diamonds it offers to the market. Likewise, hot dog vendors can relocate quickly from one street corner to another or add carts if demand is strong. However, many businesses cannot adapt to changing market conditions quickly. For instance, a golf course cannot easily add nine new holes to meet additional demand. This constraint limits the golf course owner's ability to adjust quickly, preventing the owner from quickly increasing the supply of golfing opportunities as soon as the fee changes.

Time and the Adjustment Process

In the immediate run, businesses are stuck with what they have on hand. For example, a pastry shop that runs out of chocolate glazed doughnuts cannot bake more instantly. As we move from the immediate run to the short run and a price change persists through time, supply—just like demand—becomes more elastic. For instance, a golf resort may be able to squeeze extra production out of its current facility by staying open longer hours or moving tee times closer together, but those short-run efforts will not match the production potential of adding another golf course in the long run.

Figure 4.5 shows how the two determinants of supply elasticity are mapped onto the supply curve. In the immediate run, the supply curve is vertical (S_1). A vertical curve tells us that there is no responsiveness when the price changes. As producers gain additional time to make adjustments, the supply curve rotates from S_1 (the immediate run) to S_2 (the short run) to S_3 (the long run). Like the demand curve, the supply curve becomes flatter through time. The only difference is that the supply curve rotates clockwise; in contrast, as we saw in Figure 4.2, the demand curve rotates counterclockwise. With both supply and demand, the most important thing to remember is that more time allows for greater adjustment, so the long run is always more elastic.

CALCULATING THE PRICE ELASTICITY OF SUPPLY We can use a simple formula to calculate the price elasticity of supply. Doing so is useful when a business owner must decide how much to produce at various prices. The elasticity of supply measures how quickly the producer is able to change production in response to changes in price. When supply is elastic, producers

FIGURE 4.5

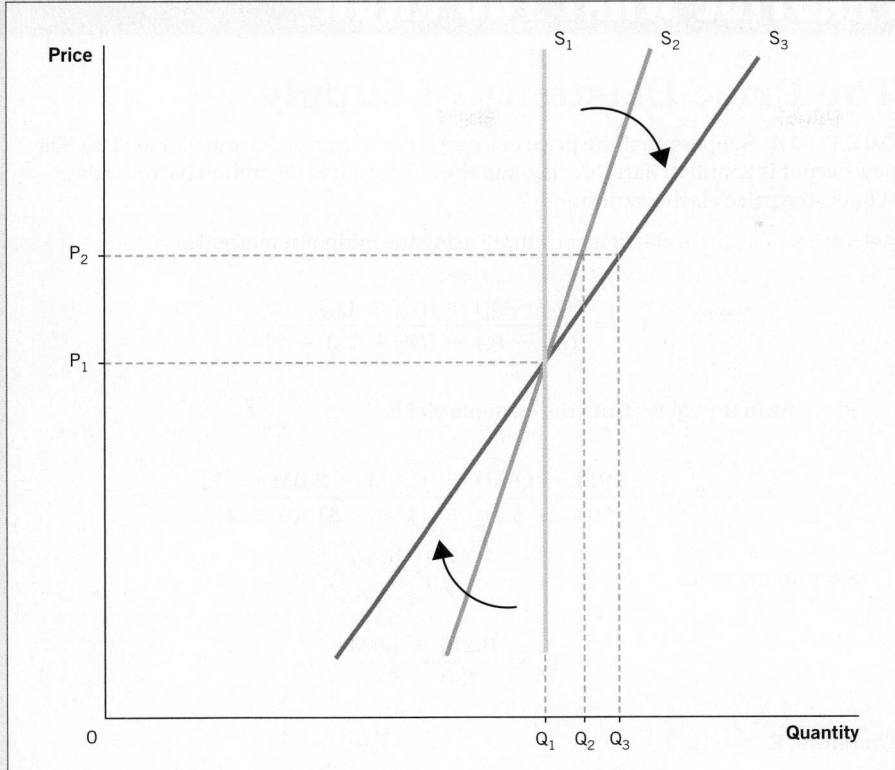

Price

S₁   S₂   S₃

P₂

P₁

0   Q₁ Q₂ Q₃   **Quantity**

Increased flexibility and more time make supply more elastic. When price rises from P_1 to P_2, producers are unable to expand output immediately and the supply curve remains at Q_1 in the immediate run. In the short run (S_2), the firm becomes more flexible and output expands to Q_2. Eventually, in the long run (S_3), the firm is able to produce even more, and it moves to Q_3 in response to higher prices.

are able to quickly adjust production. If supply is inelastic, production tends to remain roughly constant, despite large swings in price.

Here is the formula for the price elasticity of supply (E_S):

$$E_S = \frac{\text{percentage change in the quantity supplied}}{\text{percentage change in the price}}$$

(EQUATION 4.5)

Consider how the manufacturer of Solo cups might respond to an increase in demand that causes the cups' market price to rise. The company's ability to change the amount it produces depends on the flexibility of the manufacturing process and the length of time needed to ramp up production. Suppose that the price of the cups rises by 10%. The company can increase its production by 5% immediately, but it will take many months to expand production by 20%. What can we say about the price elasticity of supply in this case? Using Equation 4.5, we can take the percentage change in the quantity supplied immediately (5%) and divide that by the percentage change in price (10%). This calculation gives us $E_S = 0.5$, which signals that supply is relatively inelastic. However, with time the firm is able to increase the quantity supplied by 20%. If we divide 20% by the percentage change in the price (10%), we get $E_S = 2.0$, which indicates that supply is relatively elastic in the long run.

How would the manufacturer of Solo cups respond to a price increase in the short run and in the long run?

The Price Elasticity of Supply

Oil companies cannot quickly respond to rising prices.

QUESTION: Suppose that the price of a barrel of oil increases from $50 to $100. The new output is 2 million barrels a day, and the old output is 1.8 million barrels a day. What is the price elasticity of supply?

ANSWER: The price elasticity of supply using the midpoint method is

$$E_s = \frac{(Q_2 - Q_1) \div [(Q_1 + Q_2) \div 2]}{(P_2 - P_1) \div [(P_1 + P_2) \div 2]}$$

Plugging in the values from the example yields

$$E_s = \frac{(2.0M - 1.8M) \div [(1.8M + 2.0M) \div 2]}{(\$100 - \$50) \div [(\$50 + \$100) \div 2]}$$

Simplifying yields

$$E_s = \frac{0.2M \div 1.9M}{\$50 \div \$75}$$

Therefore, $E_s = 0.16$.

Recall that the law of supply specifies a direct relationship between the price and the quantity supplied. Because E_s in this case is positive, we see that output rises as price rises. However, the magnitude of the output increase is quite small, as reflected in the coefficient 0.16. Because oil companies cannot easily change their production process, they have a limited ability to respond quickly to rising prices. That inability is reflected in a coefficient that is relatively close to zero. A zero coefficient would mean that suppliers could not change their output at all. Here suppliers are able to respond, but only in a limited capacity.

How Do the Price Elasticities of Demand and Supply Relate to Each Other?

The interplay between the price elasticity of supply and the price elasticity of demand allows us to explain more fully how the economy operates. With an understanding of elasticity at our disposal, we can conduct a much richer and deeper analysis of the world around us.

For instance, suppose that we are concerned about what will happen to the price of oil as economic development spurs additional demand in China and India. An examination of the determinants of the price elasticity of supply quickly confirms that oil producers have a limited ability to adjust production in response to rising prices. Oil wells can be uncapped to meet rising demand, but it takes years to bring the new capacity online. Moreover, storing oil reserves, while possible, is expensive. Therefore, the short-run supply of oil is quite inelastic. Figure 4.6 shows the combination of inelastic supply-side production constraints in the short run and the inelastic short-run demand for oil (D_1).

An increase in global demand from D_1 to D_2 will create significantly higher prices (from $50 to $90 per barrel) in the short run. This result occurs because increasing oil production is difficult in the short run. Therefore, the short-run supply curve (S_{SR}) is relatively inelastic. In the long run, though, oil producers are able to bring more oil to the market when prices are higher, so the supply curve rotates clockwise (to S_{LR}), becoming more elastic, and the market price falls to $80 per barrel (point E_3). (Note that we are using an arbitrary price for a barrel of oil. The price of oil has swung widely over the last decade, making it difficult to predict.)

What does this example tell us? It reminds us that the interplay between the price elasticity of demand and the price elasticity of supply determines the magnitude of the resulting price change. We cannot observe demand in isolation without also considering how supply responds. Similarly, we cannot simply think about the short-run consequences of demand and supply shifts; we also must consider how prices and quantity will vary in the long run. Armed with this knowledge, you can begin to see the power of the supply and demand model to explain the world around us.

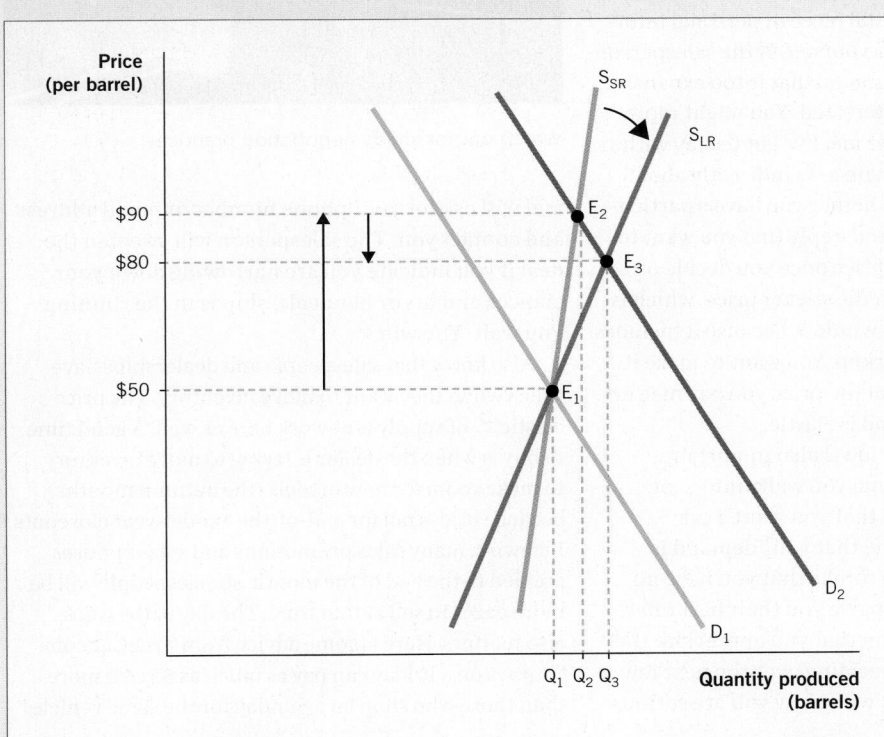

FIGURE 4.6

A Demand Shift and the Consequences for Short- and Long-Run Supply

When an increase in demand causes the price of oil to rise from $50 to $90 per barrel, initially producers are unable to expand output very much—production expands from Q_1 to Q_2. However, in the long run, as producers expand their production capacity, the price will fall to $80 per barrel.

Price Elasticity of Supply and Demand: Buying Your First Car

- Never buy a car on your first visit. Walking away shows that your demand is elastic and gives you a bargaining advantage.
- Don't give the salesperson information about your budget or allow them to run your credit.
- Shop when prices tend to be lower (end of the month, end of the model year, on a Sunday).

When you buy a car, your knowledge of price elasticity can help you negotiate the best possible deal.

Recall that three of the determinants of price elasticity of demand are (1) the share of the budget, (2) the number of available substitutes, and (3) the time you have to make a decision.

Let's start with your budget. You should have one in mind, but don't tell the salesperson what you are willing to spend; that is a vital piece of personal information you want to keep to yourself. If the salesperson suggests that you look at a model that is too expensive, just say that you are not interested. You might reply, "Buying a car is a stretch for me; I've got to stay within my budget." If the salesperson asks indirectly about your budget by inquiring whether you have a particular monthly payment in mind, reply that you want to negotiate over the invoice price once you decide on a vehicle. Never negotiate on the sticker price, which is the price you see in the car window, because it includes thousands of dollars in markup. You want to make it clear to the salesperson that the price you pay matters to you—that is, your demand is elastic.

Taking your time to decide is also important. Never buy a car the first time you walk onto a lot. If you convey the message that you want a car immediately, you are saying that your demand is inelastic. If the dealership thinks that you have no flexibility, the staff will not give you their best offer. Instead, tell the salesperson that you appreciate the help and that you will be deciding over the next few weeks. A good salesperson will know you are serious

Watch out for shady negotiation practices!

and will ask for your phone number or email address and contact you. The salesperson will sweeten the deal if you indicate you are narrowing down your choices and his or her dealership is in the running. You wait. You win.

Also know that salespeople and dealerships have times when they want to move inventory. The price elasticity of supply is at work here as well. A good time to buy is when the dealer is trying to move inventory to make room for new models (the autumn months), because prices fall for end-of-the-model-year closeouts. Likewise, many sales promotions and sales bonuses are tied to the end of the month, so salespeople will be more eager to sell at that time. The day of the week also matters. Here is some advice from TrueCar.com: "buyers on a Friday can pay as much as $2,000 more than those who shop on a Sunday for the same vehicle."

Elasticity: Trick or Treat Edition

How much would you spend on a Halloween pumpkin?

QUESTION: An unusually bad growing season leads to a small pumpkin crop. What will happen to the price of pumpkins as Halloween approaches? Use elasticity to explain your answer.

ANSWER: The demand for pumpkins peaks in October and rapidly falls after Halloween. Purchasing a pumpkin is a short-run decision to buy a unique product that takes up a relatively small share of the consumer's budget. As a result, the price elasticity of demand for pumpkins leading up to Halloween tends to be quite inelastic. At the same time, a small crop causes the entire supply curve to shift left. As a result, the market price of pumpkins rises. Because the demand is relatively inelastic in the short run and the supply of pumpkins is fixed, we expect the price to rise significantly. After Halloween, the price of any remaining pumpkins falls, because demand declines dramatically.

Conclusion

Do sellers charge the highest price possible? We can now address this misconception definitively: no. Sellers like higher prices in the same way consumers like lower prices, but that does not mean that sellers will charge the highest price possible. At very high prices, consumer demand is quite elastic. Therefore, a seller who charges too high a price will not sell much. As a result, firms learn that they must lower their price to attract more customers and maximize their total revenue.

Incentives

   The ability to determine whether demand and supply are elastic or inelastic enables economists to calculate the effects of personal, business, and policy decisions. When you combine the concept of elasticity with the supply and demand model from Chapter 3, you get a very powerful tool. In subsequent chapters, we use elasticity to refine our models of economic behavior and make our results more realistic. ✳

· ANSWERING *the* BIG QUESTIONS ·

What is the price elasticity of demand, and what are its determinants?

- The price elasticity of demand is a measure of the responsiveness of quantity demanded to a change in price.
- Demand will generally be more elastic if there are many substitutes available, if the item accounts for a large share of the consumer's budget, if the item is a luxury good, if the market is more narrowly defined, or if the consumer has plenty of time to make a decision.

- Economists categorize time in three distinct periods: (1) the immediate run, when there is no time for consumers to adjust their behavior; (2) the short run, when consumers can adjust, but only partially; and (3) the long run, when consumers have time to fully adjust to market conditions.

- The price elasticity of demand is calculated by dividing the percentage change in the quantity demanded by the percentage change in price. A value of zero indicates that the quantity demanded does not respond to a price change; if the price elasticity is zero, demand is said to be perfectly inelastic. When the price elasticity of demand is between 0 and −1, demand is inelastic. If the price elasticity of demand is less than −1, demand is elastic. When price elasticity is exactly −1, the item has unitary elasticity.

How do changes in income and the prices of other goods affect elasticity?

- The income elasticity of demand measures how a change in income affects spending. Normal goods have a positive income elasticity. Inferior goods have a negative income elasticity.

- The cross-price elasticity of demand measures the responsiveness of the quantity demanded of one good to a change in the price of a related good. Positive values for the cross-price elasticity mean that the two goods are substitutes, while negative values indicate that the two goods are complements. If the cross-price elasticity is zero, then the two goods are not related to each other.

What is the price elasticity of supply?

- The price elasticity of supply is a measure of the responsiveness of the quantity supplied to a change in price. Supply will generally be more elastic if producers have flexibility in the production process and ample time to adjust production.

- The price elasticity of supply is calculated by dividing the percentage change in the quantity supplied by the percentage change in price. A value of zero indicates that the quantity supplied does not respond to a price change; if the price elasticity of supply is zero, supply is said to be perfectly inelastic. When the price elasticity of supply is between 0 and 1, demand is relatively inelastic. If the price elasticity of supply is greater than 1, supply is elastic.

How do the price elasticities of demand and supply relate to each other?

- The interplay between the price elasticity of demand and the price elasticity of supply determines the magnitude of the resulting price change.

· CHAPTER PROBLEMS ·

Concepts You Should Know

cross-price elasticity of
demand (p. 139)
elasticity (p. 117)
immediate run (p. 119)

income elasticity of demand
(p. 138)
long run (p. 119)
price elasticity of demand (p. 117)

price elasticity of supply (p. 142)
short run (p. 119)
total revenue (p. 131)

Questions for Review

1. Define the price elasticity of demand.

2. What are the four determinants of the price elasticity of demand?

3. Give an example of a good that has elastic demand. What is the value of the price elasticity if demand is elastic? Give an example of a good that has inelastic demand. What is the value of the price elasticity if demand is inelastic?

4. What is the connection between total revenue and the price elasticity of demand? Illustrate this relationship along a demand curve.

5. Explain why slope is different from elasticity.

6. Define the price elasticity of supply.

7. What are the two determinants of the price elasticity of supply?

8. Give an example of a good that has elastic supply. What is the value of the price elasticity if supply is elastic? Give an example of a good that has an inelastic supply. What is the value of the price elasticity if supply is inelastic?

9. Give an example of a normal good. What is the income elasticity of a normal good? Give an example of a luxury good. What is the income elasticity of a luxury good? Give an example of a necessity. What is the income elasticity of a necessity? Give an example of an inferior good. What is the income elasticity of an inferior good?

10. Define the cross-price elasticity of demand. Give an example of a good with negative cross-price elasticity, another with zero cross-price elasticity, and a third with positive cross-price elasticity.

Study Problems (✳ solved at the end of the section)

✳ **1.** If the government decided to impose a 50% tax on gray T-shirts, would this policy generate a large increase in tax revenues or a small increase? Use elasticity to explain your answer.

✳ **2.** College logo T-shirts priced at $15 sell at a rate of 25 per week, but when the bookstore marks them down to $10, it finds that it can sell 50 T-shirts per week. What is the price elasticity of demand for the logo T-shirts?

3. Black Friday, the day after Thanksgiving, is the largest shopping day of the year. Do the early shoppers, who often wait in line for hours in the cold to get doorbuster sale items, have elastic or inelastic demand? Explain your response.

4. If a 20% increase in price causes a 10% drop in the quantity demanded, is the price elasticity of demand for this good elastic, unitary, or inelastic?

5. Characterize the demand for each of the following goods or services as perfectly elastic, relatively elastic, relatively inelastic, or perfectly inelastic.

a. a lifesaving medication
b. photocopies at a copy shop, when all competing shops charge 10 cents per copy
c. a fast-food restaurant located in the food court of a shopping mall
d. the water you buy from your local utility company

6. A local paintball business receives a total revenue of $8,000 a month when it charges $10 per person and $9,600 in total revenue when it charges $6 per person. Over that range of prices, does the business face elastic, unitary, or inelastic demand?

7. At a price of $200, a cell phone company manufactures 300,000 phones. At a price of $150, the company produces 200,000 phones. What is the price elasticity of supply?

8. Do customers who visit convenience stores at 3 a.m. have a price elasticity of demand that is more elastic or less elastic than those who visit at 3 p.m.?

✳ 9. A worker eats at a restaurant once a week. He then gets a 25% raise. As a result, he decides to eat out twice as much as before and cut back on the number of frozen lasagna dinners from one frozen dinner a week to one every other week. Determine the income elasticity of demand for eating at a restaurant and for having frozen lasagna dinners.

10. The cross-price elasticity of demand between American Eagle and Hollister is 2.0. What does that coefficient tell us about the relationship between these two stores?

11. A local golf course is considering lowering its fees in order to increase its total revenue. Under what conditions will the fee reduction achieve its goal?

12. A private university notices that in-state and out-of-state students seem to respond differently to tuition changes.

Tuition	Quantity demanded (in-state applicants)	Quantity demanded (out-of-state applicants)
$10,000	6,000	12,000
15,000	5,000	9,000
20,000	4,000	6,000
30,000	3,000	3,000

As the price of tuition rises from $15,000 to $20,000, what is the price elasticity of demand for in-state applicants and also for out-of-state applicants?

✳ 13. The TV show *Extreme Couponing* features coupon users who go to extraordinary measures to save money on their weekly purchases. The show follows these coupon users throughout the week as they assemble coupons and scout out stores to see which have the best deals, and then follows them to the store for the big buy. Do extreme "couponers" have extremely elastic demand or extremely inelastic demand? Explain. (*Note:* If you are unfamiliar with the show, you can Google it and watch a segment.)

14. Suppose a hotel raises the price of the bottled water in the minibar in each room from $3 to $5. The hotel tracks the number of customers who buy the bottled water and finds that consumption drops from 1,000 bottles a week to 900 bottles. Is demand elastic or inelastic? Explain.

15. Americans bought 143 billion gallons of gas in 2016 when the price was $2.25. Back in 2012, when the price was $3.64, they bought 133 billion gallons. Is the demand for gasoline elastic, unitary, or inelastic?

16. In 2018, the NFC football team the Atlanta Falcons moved to a new stadium. As part of this move, they dropped their stadium's food and beverage prices 50% versus prices at the old stadium. In order for this pricing strategy to work, the Falcons must believe that consumer demand is _____. Explain your answer.

Solved Problems

1. To answer this question, we need to consider the price elasticity of demand. The tax is only on gray T-shirts. This means that T-shirt customers who buy other colors can avoid the tax entirely—which means that the demand for gray T-shirts is relatively elastic. Not many gray T-shirts will be sold, so the government will generate only a small increase in revenues from the tax.

2. Plugging into the formula for E_D gives us

$$E_D = \frac{(50 - 25) \div [(25 + 50) \div 2]}{(10 - 15) \div [(15 + 10) \div 2]} = -1.67$$

9. In this question a worker gets a 25% (or 0.25) raise, so we can use this information in the denominator when determining the income elasticity of demand. We are not given the percentage change for the meals out, so we need to plug in how often the worker ate out before (once a week) and the amount he eats out after the raise (twice a week) into the numerator.

   Plugging into E_I gives us

$$E_I = \frac{(2 - 1) \div [(1 + 2) \div 2]}{0.25}$$

   Simplifying yields

$$E_I = \frac{1 \div 1.5}{0.25}$$

   Therefore, $E_I = 2.67$.

The income elasticity of demand for eating at a restaurant is positive for normal goods. Therefore, eating at a restaurant is a normal good. This result should confirm your intuition.

Let's see what happens with frozen lasagna once the worker gets the 25% raise. Now he cuts back on the number of lasagna dinners from once a week to once every other week. This information is plugged into the numerator, while the 25% change in income, or 0.25, is plugged into the denominator.

Plugging into E_I gives us

$$E_I = \frac{(0.5 - 1) \div [(1 + 0.5) \div 2]}{0.25}$$

Simplifying yields

$$E_I = \frac{-0.5 \div 0.75}{0.25}$$

Therefore, $E_I = -2.67$.

The income elasticity of demand for having frozen lasagna is negative. Therefore, frozen lasagna is an inferior good. This result should confirm your intuition.

13. The show is called *Extreme Couponing* for a reason. Ordinary people don't spend more than 20 hours a week trying to find the best deals on grocery items, scouting stores, comparing prices, and make purchases based solely on what's on sale. The persons featured in the show are obsessive about saving money. When the price you pay is the most important determinant of what you buy, demand is extremely elastic.

Market Outcomes and Tax Incidence

Taxes on Firms Affect Consumers.

Many people believe that when the government taxes businesses, consumers catch a break because firms pay the tax. If only life worked that way! As this chapter explains, who actually pays the tax often is quite different from the party that is legally responsible for making the tax payment.

Gasoline prices are a common and visible sign of the market at work. It is hard not to notice when gasoline prices rise or fall, because every gas station posts its prices prominently. But there are a few things you might not know. First, gasoline taxes vary significantly from state to state, and they vary wildly from country to country. Residents of Saudi Arabia pay some of the lowest gasoline prices in the world, while Israelis have to put up with the world's third-highest gas prices. This occurs because the governments of certain oil-rich countries, such as Saudi Arabia, subsidize gasoline so that their citizens pay less than the market price. In countries where gasoline is subsidized, consumers drive their cars everywhere, mass transportation is largely unavailable, and there is less concern for fuel efficiency. As you might imagine, the opposite is true in countries with high gasoline taxes, like Israel, where consumers drive less, use public transportation more often, and tend to purchase fuel-efficient vehicles.

In countries with high gasoline taxes, close to $50 for every fill-up can be for taxes. However, in Saudi Arabia, gasoline taxes are almost nonexistent and gasoline is less expensive than bottled water.

What do gasoline taxes and subsidies around the world have in common? They are all folded into the price you see at the pump, which might lead you to believe that the seller is paying all of the tax or receiving the entire subsidy. Nothing could be further from the truth. The firm will try to pass along the tax to consumers in the form of higher prices. Likewise, in countries with subsidies, the firm must pass along lower prices to consumers. After reading this chapter, you will understand how this process works.

We begin this chapter by discussing consumer and producer surplus, two concepts that illustrate gains from trade. These concepts help us measure the efficiency of markets and the effects of taxation. Then we examine how taxation creates distortions in economic behavior by altering the incentives people and firms face when consuming and producing goods that are taxed.

· BIG QUESTIONS ·

- What are consumer surplus and producer surplus?
- When is a market efficient?
- Why do taxes create deadweight loss in otherwise efficient markets?

Trade creates value

Welfare economics
is the branch of economics
that studies how the allocation
of resources affects economic
well-being.

What Are Consumer Surplus and Producer Surplus?

Markets create value by bringing together buyers and sellers so that consumers and producers can mutually benefit from trade. **Welfare economics** is the branch of economics that studies how the allocation of resources affects economic well-being. In this section, we develop two concepts that help us measure the value markets create: *consumer surplus* and *producer surplus*.

In competitive markets, the equilibrium price is simultaneously low enough to attract consumers and high enough to encourage producers. This balance between demand and supply enhances the *welfare* (well-being) of society. That is not to say that society's welfare depends solely on markets. People also find satisfaction in many nonmarket settings, including spending time with families and friends, doing hobbies, and helping with charity work. We incorporate aspects of personal satisfaction into our economic model in Chapter 16. For now, let's focus on how markets enhance human welfare.

Consumer Surplus

Consider three students: Ron, Leslie, and Donna, all city government employees in the small Midwestern town of Pawnee (you may recognize them from the TV series *Parks and Recreation*). They need to take a class in basic economics, to better understand Pawnee's business environment. Like students everywhere, each of them has a maximum price he or she is willing to pay for a new economics textbook. Ron has a keen interest in financial matters, and he is prepared to invest quite a bit of money in a new book. Leslie is extremely conscientious but on a tighter budget than Ron and also not quite so committed to that particular class. Donna is a departmental colleague who is a confident negotiator and is also successful in her outside life. Table 5.1 shows the value each student places on the textbook. This value, called the **willingness to pay**, is the maximum price a consumer will pay for a good or service. The willingness to pay is also known as the *reservation price*. In an auction or a negotiation, the willingness to pay, or reservation price, is the price beyond which the consumer decides to walk away from the transaction.

These Pawnee city employees want to earn a consumer surplus.

Willingness to pay
also known as the *reservation price,* is the maximum price a consumer will pay for a good or service.

Consider what happens when the price of the book is $151. If Ron purchases the book at $151, he pays $49 less than the $200 maximum he was willing to pay. He values the textbook at $49 more than the purchase price, so buying the book makes him better off.

Consumer surplus is the difference between the willingness to pay for a good (or service) and the price paid to get it. While Ron gains $49 in consumer surplus, a price of $151 is more than either Leslie or Donna is willing to pay. Because Leslie is willing to pay only $150, if she purchases the book she will experience a consumer loss of $1. Donna's willingness to pay is $100, so if she buys the book for $151 she will experience a consumer loss of $51. Whenever

Consumer surplus
is the difference between the willingness to pay for a good (or service) and the price paid to get it.

TABLE 5.1

Willingness to Pay for a New Economics Textbook

Buyer	Willingness to pay
Ron	$200
Leslie	150
Donna	100

FIGURE 5.1

Demand Curve for an Economics Textbook

The demand curve has a step for each additional textbook purchase. As the price goes down, more students buy the textbook.

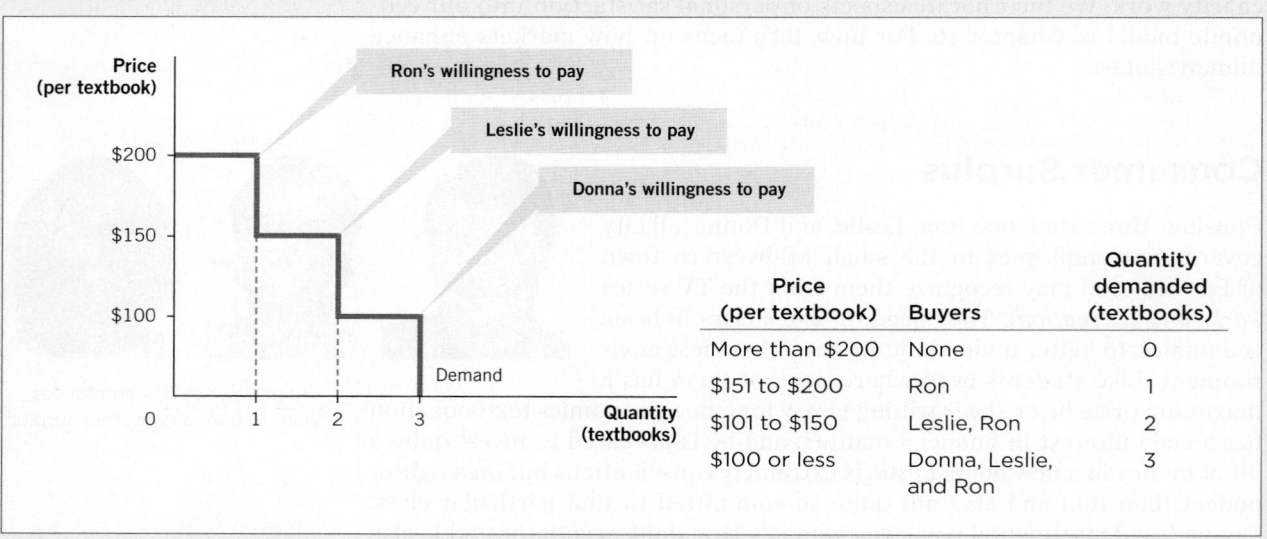

Price (per textbook)	Buyers	Quantity demanded (textbooks)
More than $200	None	0
$151 to $200	Ron	1
$101 to $150	Leslie, Ron	2
$100 or less	Donna, Leslie, and Ron	3

the price is greater than the willingness to pay, a rational consumer will decide not to buy.

Using Demand Curves to Illustrate Consumer Surplus

In the previous section, we discussed consumer surplus as a dollar amount. We can illustrate it graphically with a demand curve. Figure 5.1 shows the demand curve drawn from the data in Table 5.1. Notice that the curve looks like a staircase with three steps—one for each additional textbook purchase. Each point on a market demand curve corresponds to a specific number of units sold.

At any price above $200, none of the students wants to purchase a textbook. This relationship is evident on the x axis where the quantity demanded is 0 at a price of $200. At any price between $151 and $200, Ron is the only buyer, so the quantity demanded is 1. At prices between $101 and $150, Ron and Leslie are both willing to buy the textbook, so the quantity demanded is 2. Finally, if the price is $100 or less, all three students are willing to buy the textbook, so the quantity demanded is 3. As the price falls, the quantity demanded increases.

We can measure the total extent of consumer surplus by examining the area under the demand curve for each of our three consumers, as shown in Figure 5.2. In panel (a), the price is $175, and only Ron decides to buy. Because his willingness to pay is $200, he is better off by $25, which is his consumer

FIGURE 5.2

Determining Consumer Surplus from a Demand Curve

(a) At a price of $175, Ron is the only buyer, so the quantity demanded is 1. (b) At a price of $125, Ron and Leslie are both willing to buy the textbook, so the quantity demanded is 2.

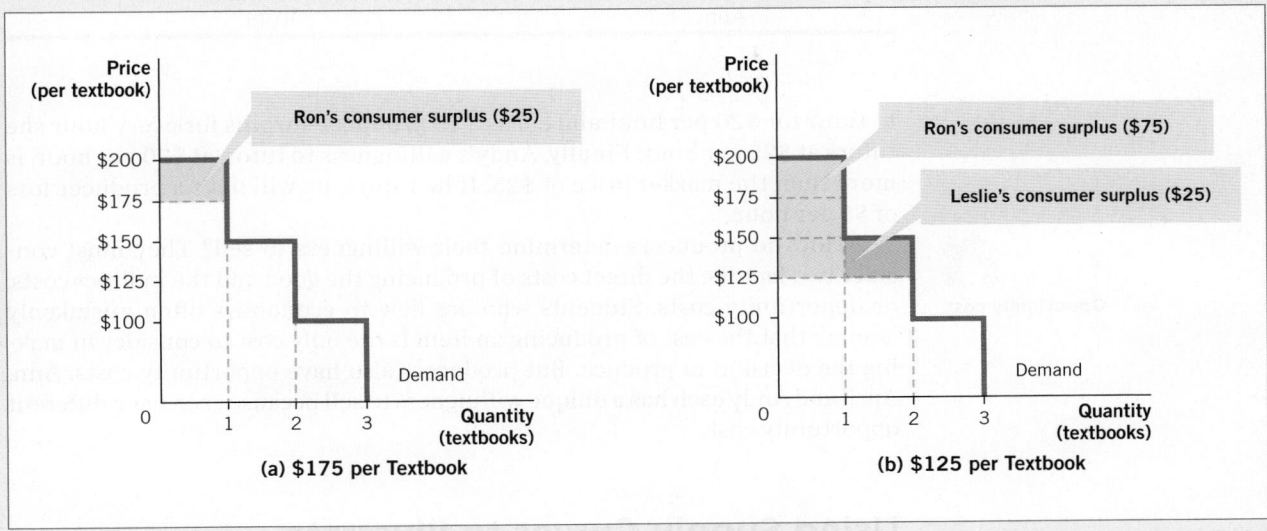

(a) $175 per Textbook

(b) $125 per Textbook

surplus. The light blue area under the demand curve and above the price represents the benefit Ron receives from purchasing a textbook at a price of $175. When the price drops to $125, as shown in panel (b), Leslie also decides to buy a textbook. Now the total quantity demanded is 2. Leslie's willingness to pay is $150, so her consumer surplus, represented by the darker blue area, is $25. However, since Ron's willingness to pay is $200, his consumer surplus rises from $25 to $75. So a textbook price of $125 raises the total consumer surplus from $25 at a price of $200 to $75 + $25 = $100. In other words, lower prices create more consumer surplus in this market—and in any other.

Producer Surplus

Sellers also benefit from market transactions. In this section, three other Pawnee city employees, Ann, April, and Andy, discover that they are good at economics and decide to go into the tutoring business. They do not want to provide this service for free, but each has a different minimum price. The **willingness to sell** is the minimum price a seller will accept to sell a good or service. Table 5.2 shows each tutor's willingness to sell their services.

Consider what happens at a tutoring price of $25 per hour. Because Ann is willing to tutor for $10 per hour, every hour she tutors at $25 per hour earns her $15 more than her willingness to sell. This extra $15 per hour is her producer surplus. **Producer surplus** is the difference between the willingness to sell a good or service and the price the seller receives. April is willing

Willingness to sell
is the minimum price a seller will accept to sell a good or service.

Producer surplus
is the difference between the willingness to sell a good (or service) and the price the seller receives.

TABLE 5.2	
Willingness to Sell Tutoring Services	
Seller	**Willingness to sell**
Andy	$30/hr
April	20/hr
Ann	10/hr

to tutor for $20 per hour and earns a $5 producer surplus for every hour she tutors at $25 per hour. Finally, Andy's willingness to tutor, at $30 per hour, is more than the market price of $25. If he tutors, he will have a producer loss of $5 per hour.

Opportunity cost

How do producers determine their willingness to sell? They must consider two factors: the direct costs of producing the good and the indirect costs, or opportunity costs. Students who are new to economics often mistakenly assume that the cost of producing an item is the only cost to consider in making the decision to produce. But producers also have opportunity costs. Ann, April and Andy each has a unique willingness to sell because each has a different opportunity cost.

Using Supply Curves to Illustrate Producer Surplus

Continuing our example, the supply curve in Figure 5.3 shows the relationship between the price for an hour of tutoring and the number of tutors who are willing to sell their services. As you can see on the supply schedule (the table within the figure), at any price less than $10 per hour, no one wants to tutor. At prices between $10 and $19 per hour, Ann is the only tutor, so the quantity supplied is 1. Between $20 and $29 per hour, Ann and April are willing to tutor, so the quantity supplied rises to 2. Finally, if the price is $30 or more, all three coworkers are willing to tutor, so the quantity supplied is 3. As the price they receive for tutoring rises, the number of tutors increases from 0 to 3.

What do these relationships between price and quantity supplied tell us about producer surplus? Let's turn to Figure 5.4. By examining the area above the supply curve, we can measure the extent of producer surplus. In panel (a), the price of an hour of tutoring is $15. At that price, only Ann decides to tutor. Since she would be willing to tutor even if the price were as low as $10 per hour, she is $5 per hour better off tutoring. Ann's producer surplus is represented by the light red area between the supply curve and the price of $15. Because April and Andy do not tutor when the price is $15 per hour, they do not receive any producer surplus. In panel (b), the price for tutoring is $25 per hour. At this price, April also decides to tutor. Her willingness to tutor is $20, so when the price is $25 per hour, her producer surplus is $5 per hour, represented by the darker red area. Since Ann's willingness to tutor is $10, at $25 per hour her producer surplus rises to $15 per hour. By looking at the shaded boxes in panel (b), we see that an increase in the rates for tutoring raises the combined producer surplus of Ann and April to $15 + $5 = $20 per hour.

FIGURE 5.3

Supply Curve for Economics Tutoring

The supply curve has three steps, one for each additional coworker who is willing to tutor. Progressively higher prices will induce more coworkers to become tutors.

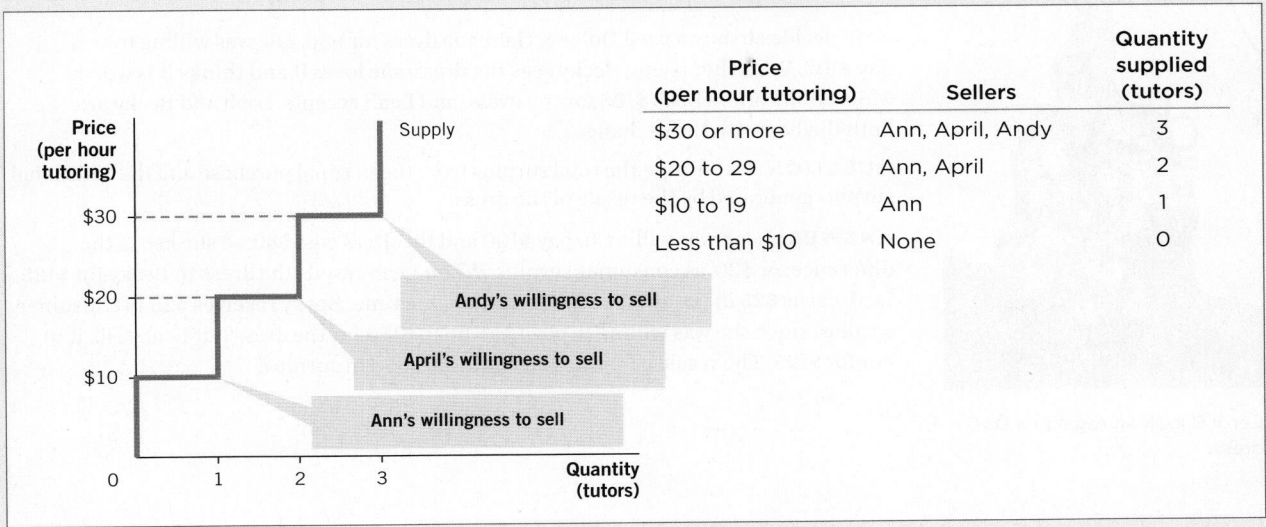

Price (per hour tutoring)	Sellers	Quantity supplied (tutors)
$30 or more	Ann, April, Andy	3
$20 to 29	Ann, April	2
$10 to 19	Ann	1
Less than $10	None	0

FIGURE 5.4

Determining Producer Surplus from a Supply Curve

(a) The price of an hour of tutoring is $15. At this price, only Ann decides to tutor. (b) The price for tutoring is $25 per hour. At this price, April also decides to tutor.

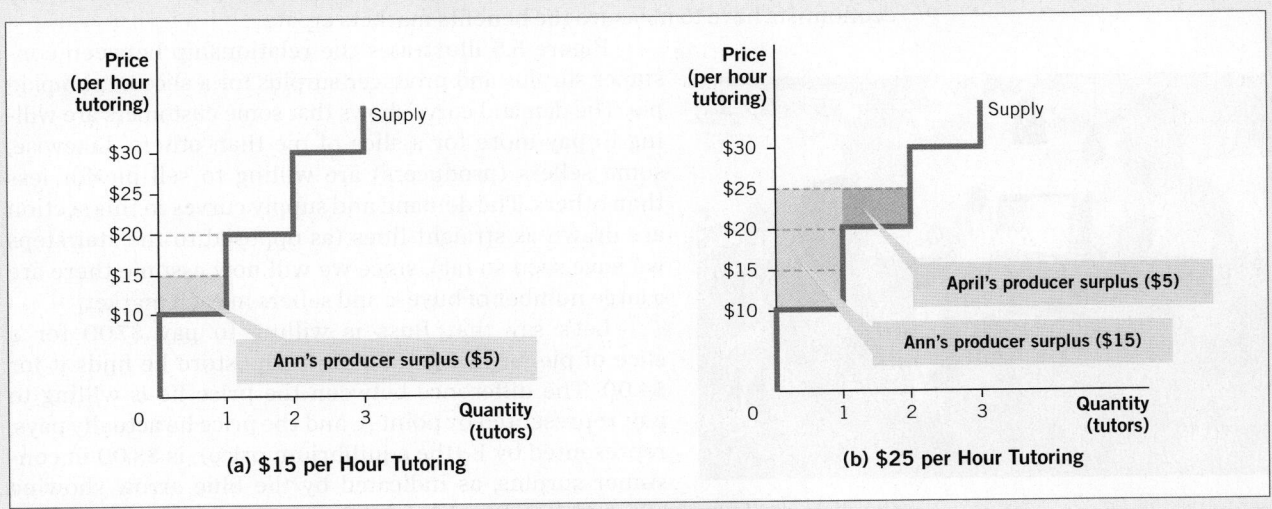

(a) $15 per Hour Tutoring

(b) $25 per Hour Tutoring

Consumer and Producer Surplus: Trendy Fashion

Cardi B looking regal in a D&G dress.

Leah decides to buy a used Dolce & Gabbana dress for $80. She was willing to pay $100. When her friend Becky sees the dress, she loves it and thinks it is worth $150. So she offers Leah $125 for the dress, and Leah accepts. Leah and Becky are both thrilled with the exchange.

QUESTION: Determine the total surplus from the original purchase and the additional surplus generated by the resale of the dress.

ANSWER: Leah was willing to pay $100 and the dress cost $80, so she keeps the difference, or $20, as consumer surplus. When Leah resells the dress to Becky for $125, Leah earns $25 in producer surplus. At the same time, Becky receives $25 in consumer surplus, since she was willing to pay Leah up to $150 for the dress but Leah sells it to her for $125. The resale generates an additional $50 in surplus.

When Is a Market Efficient?

Total surplus, also known as **social welfare**, is the sum of consumer surplus and producer surplus. It measures the well-being of all participants in a market, absent any government intervention.

We have seen how consumers benefit from lower prices and how producers benefit from higher prices. When we combine the concepts of consumer and producer surplus, we can build a complete picture of the welfare of buyers and sellers. Adding consumer and producer surplus gives us **total surplus**, also known as **social welfare**, because it measures the well-being of all participants in a market, absent any government intervention. Total surplus is the best way economists have to measure the benefits markets create.

Figure 5.5 illustrates the relationship between consumer surplus and producer surplus for a slice of pumpkin pie. The demand curve shows that some customers are willing to pay more for a slice of pie than others. Likewise, some sellers (producers) are willing to sell pie for less than others. The demand and supply curves in this section are drawn as straight lines (as opposed to the stairsteps we have seen so far), since we will now assume there are a large number of buyers and sellers in each market.

Let's say that Russ is willing to pay $7.00 for a slice of pie, but when he gets to the store he finds it for $4.00. The difference between the price he is willing to pay, represented by point A, and the price he actually pays, represented by E (the equilibrium price), is $3.00 in consumer surplus, as indicated by the blue arrow showing

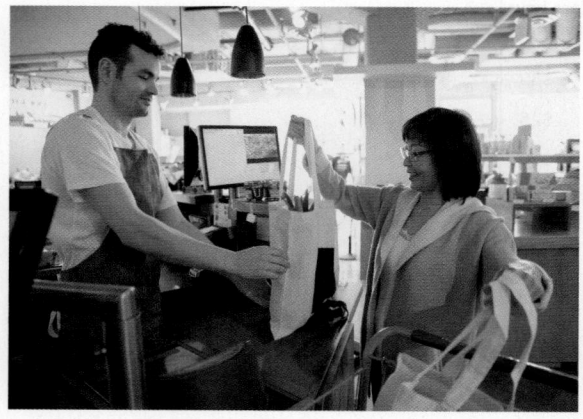

The buyer and seller each benefit from this exchange.

the distance from $4.00 to $7.00. Russ's friend Audrey is willing to pay $5.00 for a slice of pie, but, like Russ, she finds it for $4.00. Therefore, she receives

FIGURE 5.5

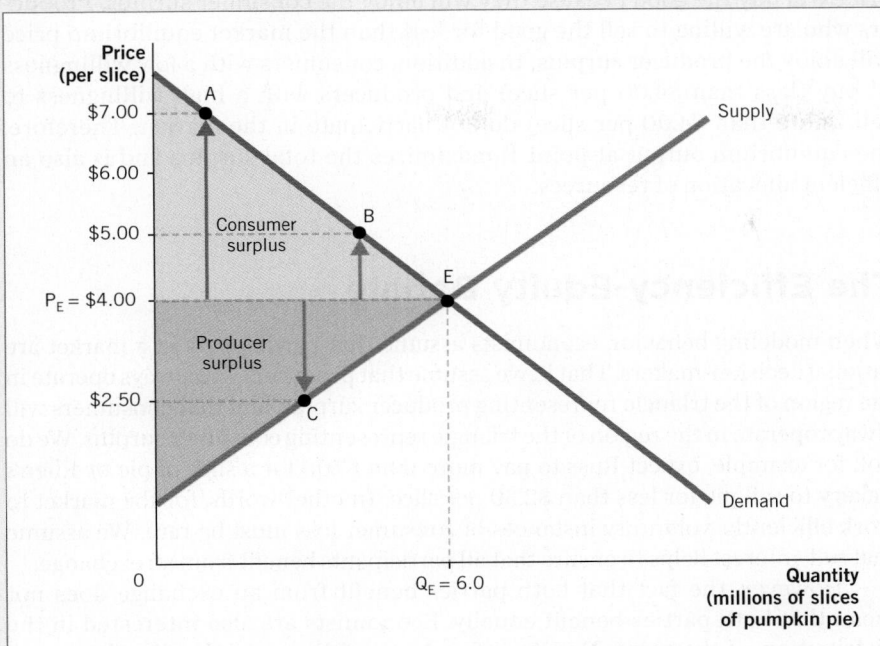

Consumer and Producer Surplus for Pumpkin Pie

Consumer surplus is the difference between the willingness to pay along the demand curve and the equilibrium price, P_E. It is illustrated by the blue triangle. Producer surplus is the difference between the willingness to produce along the supply curve and the equilibrium price. It is illustrated by the red triangle.

$1.00 in consumer surplus, as indicated by the green arrow at point B showing the distance from $4.00 to $5.00. In fact, all consumers who are willing to pay more than $4.00 are better off when they purchase the slice of pie at $4.00. We can show this total area of consumer surplus on the graph as the blue triangle bordered by the demand curve, the y axis, and the equilibrium price (P_E). At every point in this area, consumers who are willing to pay more than the equilibrium price for pie are better off.

Continuing with Figure 5.5, to identify producer surplus we follow a similar process. Suppose that Ellen's Bakery is willing to sell pumpkin pie for $2.50 per slice, represented by point C. Because the equilibrium price is $4.00, the business makes $1.50 per slice in producer surplus, as indicated by the red arrow at point C showing the distance from $4.00 to $2.50. If we think of the supply curve as representing the costs of many different sellers, we can calculate the total producer surplus as the red triangle bordered by the supply curve, the y axis, and the equilibrium price. The blue triangle (consumer surplus) and the red triangle (producer surplus) describe the increase in total surplus, or social welfare, created by the production and exchange of the good at the equilibrium price. At the equilibrium quantity of 6 million slices of pie, output and consumption reach the largest possible combination of producer and consumer surplus. In the region of the graph beyond 6 million units, buyers and sellers will experience a loss of surplus.

When an allocation of resources maximizes total surplus, the result is said to be **efficient**. In Figure 5.5, efficiency occurs at point E, where the market is in equilibrium. To think about why the market creates the largest possible total surplus, or social welfare, it is important to recall how the market allocates

Trade creates value

An outcome is **efficient** when an allocation of resources maximizes total surplus.

resources. Consumers who are willing to pay more than the market equilibrium price will buy the good because they will enjoy the consumer surplus. Producers who are willing to sell the good for less than the market equilibrium price will enjoy the producer surplus. In addition, consumers with a low willingness to buy (less than $4.00 per slice) and producers with a high willingness to sell (more than $4.00 per slice) do not participate in the market. Therefore, the equilibrium output at point E maximizes the total surplus and is also an efficient allocation of resources.

The Efficiency-Equity Debate

When modeling behavior, economists assume that participants in a market are rational decision-makers. That is, we assume that producers will always operate in the region of the triangle representing producer surplus, and that consumers will always operate in the region of the triangle representing consumer surplus. We do not, for example, expect Russ to pay more than $7.00 for a slice of pie or Ellen's Bakery to sell pie for less than $2.50 per slice. In other words, for the market to work efficiently, voluntary instances of consumer loss must be rare. We assume that self-interest helps to ensure that all participants benefit from an exchange.

However, the fact that both parties benefit from an exchange does not mean that both parties benefit equally. Economists are also interested in the distribution of the gains. **Equity** refers to the fairness of the distribution of benefits among the members of a society. In a world where no one cared about equity, only efficiency would matter and no particular division would be preferred. Another way of thinking about fairness versus efficiency is to consider a pie. If our only concern is efficiency, we will simply want to make sure that none of the pie goes to waste. But if we care about equity, we will also care about how the pie is divvied up, perhaps making sure that everyone gets a bite of the pie or at least has access to the pie.

In our first look at consumer and producer surplus, we have assumed that markets produce efficient outcomes. But in the real world, efficient outcomes are not guaranteed. Markets also fail; their efficiency can be compromised in a number of ways. We discuss market failure in much greater detail in subsequent chapters. For now, all you need to know is that failure can occur.

Trade creates value

Equity
refers to the fairness of the distribution of benefits among the members of a society.

Efficiency only requires that the pie get eaten. Equity is a question of how the pie gets divided.

Efficiency

ADAM RUINS EVERYTHING: WHY GIFT GIVING MAKES NO ECONOMIC SENSE

In this 2016 episode of the truTV series *Adam Ruins Everything*, Adam Conover pops into Emily and Murph's living room on the morning of their first Christmas together, just as they are opening gifts. Adam begins his lecture by defining economic value. He states that the value of an object is "how much it's worth to you," and immediately dollar amounts appear next to items throughout the room. Adam observes that a giant cardboard cutout of The Rock (a.k.a. Dwayne Johnson) standing in one corner is worth $100 to Emily. "But I only paid $50 for it," she happily replies. Adam then explains that in that case, "when you bought it, you literally created $50 in value. You're $50 richer." Emily is pleased. "Let's go to Vegas!" she exclaims.

While this lesson in basic economics is going on, a voice from the chimney signals the arrival of another visitor—not Santa, to Murph's disappointment, but economist Joel Waldfogel. He explains that while we are all really good at knowing what we like, we are not so good at knowing what others want. As Waldfogel talks, Emily unwraps a gift from Murph, a "Rock the Vote" T-shirt. Emily is less than impressed. She says she will probably wear it to bed but wouldn't have paid more than $15 for it. Murph, annoyed, declares that he paid $50 for it, to which Waldfogel responds, "Well, Murph, you just destroyed $35 worth of value." Adam piles on: "You might as well have set it on fire."

The cameo by Joel Waldfogel is a result of his research on "The Deadweight Loss of Christmas." He found that poor gift buying results in a loss of economic value of anywhere from 10 to 33% of the money spent during the holidays. That has led some economists to conclude that cash is the most efficient gift, since the recipient can simply spend the money as they see fit. Angus Deaton, however, pointed out that Waldfogel did not ask respondents to include any sentimental value they received from the gifts.

When we spend more on a gift than the recipient values it at, we destroy economic value.

Deaton states, "Money would be better than a gift if you define the problem narrowly enough. And that insight, like a lot of insights in economics, is valuable to have. But stopping there is the problem." Judy Chevalier thinks that Waldfogel and Deaton both make good points. She agreed with Waldfogel that giving gifts is often inefficient, but she also agrees with Deaton: "You can't stop there. If you ask people after Christmas how much they value this sweater, it's almost always less than what the giver spent on it. Does that mean I don't give Christmas gifts? No, I give Christmas gifts!" Most of us merrily exchange gifts each year, and we don't feel worse off for it. We value the sense of family that gift giving creates, and many gifts we receive convey a message that has immense intangible value: we know that someone loves us. It's hard to put a price on that.

Total Surplus: How Would Lower Consumer Income Affect Urban Outfitters?

Does less consumer income affect total surplus?

QUESTION: If a drop in consumer income occurs, what will happen to the consumer surplus that customers enjoy at Urban Outfitters? What will happen to the amount of producer surplus Urban Outfitters receives? Illustrate your answer by shifting the demand curve appropriately and labeling the new and old areas of consumer and producer surplus.

ANSWER: Because the items sold at Urban Outfitters are normal goods, a drop in income shifts the demand curve (D) to the left. The black arrow shows the leftward shift in the second graph below. When you compare the area of consumer surplus (in blue) before and after the drop in income—that is, graphs (a) and (b)—you can see that consumer surplus shrinks. Producer surplus (in red) also shrinks.

Your intuition might already confirm what the graphs tell us. Because consumers have less income, they buy fewer clothes at Urban Outfitters—so consumer surplus falls. Likewise, because fewer customers buy the store's clothes, Urban Outfitters sells less—so producer surplus falls. This result is also evident in graph (b), because $Q_2 < Q_1$.

CHALLENGE QUESTION: Now let's add an additional consideration. Suppose that Urban Outfitters also faces high manufacturing costs at the same time that consumer income drops. Will consumer and producer surplus continue to shrink in size or rebound?

ANSWER: Higher manufacturing costs will cause the supply curve to shift left. If you look at the second panel, you can visualize how a leftward shift in the supply curve will cause the new equilibrium to occur at a price above P_2 and the new equilibrium quantity to be less than Q_2. Since the overall quantity supplied shrinks, the areas of consumer and producer surplus will shrink as well.

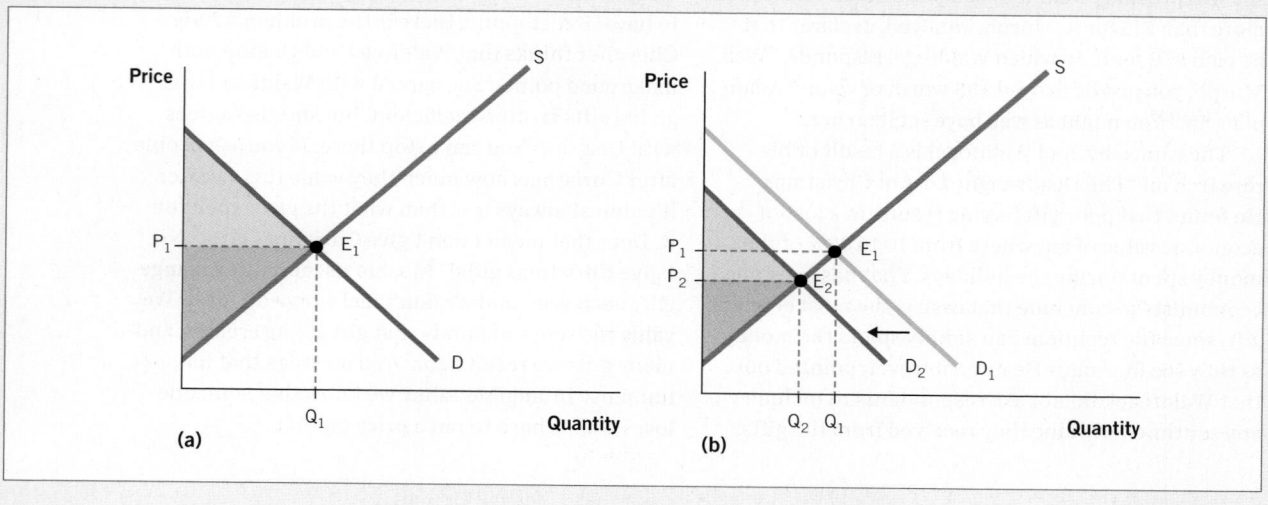

Why Do Taxes Create Deadweight Loss in Otherwise Efficient Markets?

Taxes provide many benefits. Taxes help to pay for many of society's needs—public transportation, schools, police, the court system, and the military, to name just a few. Most of us take these services for granted, but without taxes it would be impossible to pay for them. How much do all of these services cost? When you add all the federal, state, and local government budgets in the United States, you get over $6 trillion a year in taxes!

Spending tax dollars incurs opportunity costs, because the money could have been used in other ways. In this section, we use the concepts of consumer and producer surplus to explain the effect of taxation on social welfare and market efficiency. Taxes come in many sizes and shapes. There are taxes on personal income, payroll, property, corporate profits, sales, and inheritance, for example. Fortunately, we do not have to examine the entire tax code all at once. In the pages that follow, we explore the impact of taxes on social welfare by looking at one of the simplest taxes, the *excise tax*.

Opportunity cost

Tax Incidence

Economists want to know how taxes affect the choices that consumers and producers make. When a tax is imposed on an item, do buyers switch to alternative goods that are not taxed? How do producers respond when the products they sell are taxed? Because taxes cause prices to rise, they can affect how much of a good or service is bought and sold. This outcome is especially evident with **excise taxes**, which are taxes levied on a particular good or service. For example, all 50 states levy excise taxes on cigarettes, but the amount assessed varies tremendously. In New York, cigarette taxes are over $4.00 per pack, while in a handful of tobacco-producing states (including Virginia and North Carolina), the excise tax is less than $0.50 per pack. Overall, excise taxes, such as those on cigarettes, alcohol, and gasoline, account for less than 4% of all tax revenues. But because we can isolate changes in consumer behavior that result from taxes on one item, excise taxes help us understand the overall effect of a tax.

In looking at the effect of a tax, economists are also interested in the **incidence** of taxation, which refers to the burden of taxation on the party who pays the tax. To understand this idea, consider a $1.00 tax on milk purchases. We consider two cases: a tax placed directly on buyers and a tax placed directly on sellers.

Excise taxes
are taxes levied on a particular good or service.

Incidence
refers to the burden of taxation on the party who pays the tax through higher prices, regardless of whom the tax is actually levied on.

EXAMPLE 1: TAX ON BUYERS Each time a consumer buys a gallon of milk, the cash register adds $1.00 in tax. This means that to purchase the milk, the consumer must be willing to pay the price of the milk plus the $1.00 tax.

The result of the $1.00 tax on milk is shown in Figure 5.6. Because of the tax, consumers' willingness to pay for milk goes down, and the demand curve shifts down from D_1 to D_2. Why does the demand curve shift? The extra cost makes consumers less likely to buy milk at every price,

Why do we place excise taxes on cigarettes . . .

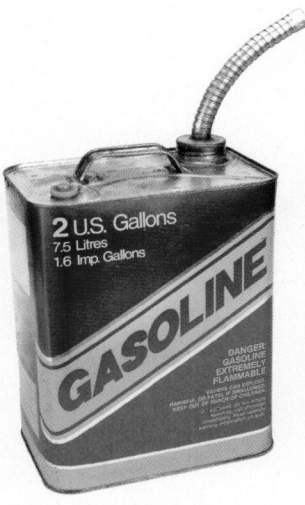

. . . and gasoline?

FIGURE 5.6

A Tax on Buyers

After the tax, the new equilibrium price (E$_2$) is $3.50, but the buyer must also pay $1.00 in tax. Therefore, despite the drop in equilibrium price, the buyer still pays more for a gallon of milk: $4.50 instead of the original equilibrium price of $4.00. A similar logic applies to the producer. Because the new equilibrium price after the tax is $0.50 lower, the producer shares the tax incidence equally with the buyer in this example. The consumer pays $0.50 more, and the seller nets $0.50 less.

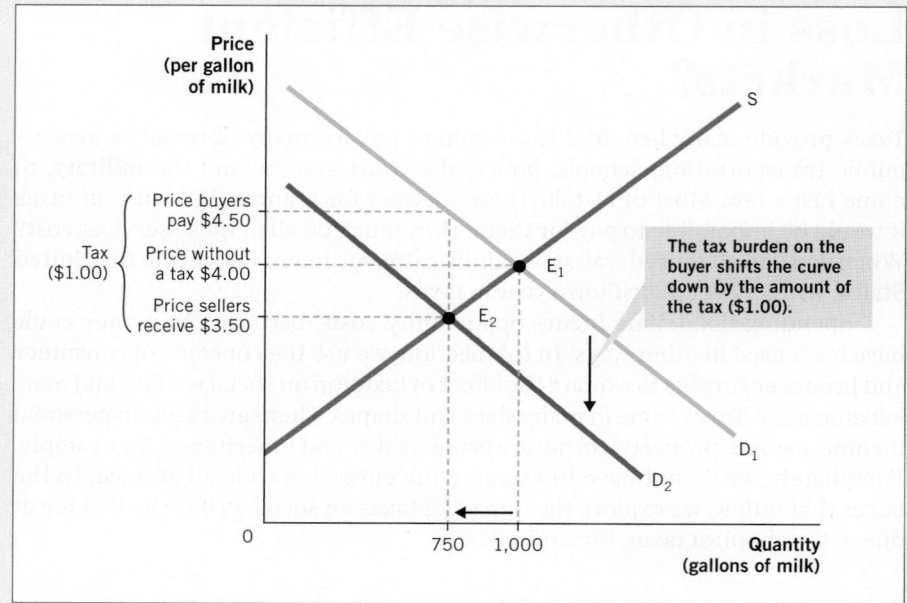

which causes the entire demand curve to shift down. The intersection of the new demand curve (D$_2$) with the existing supply curve (S) creates a new equilibrium price of $3.50 (E$_2$), which is $0.50 lower than the original price of $4.00 per gallon. But even though the base price is lower, consumers are still worse off. Because they must also pay part of the $1.00 tax, the total price to them rises to $4.50 per gallon. Many students mistakenly believe that the new equilibrium price will be $5.00, but that would only be the case if demand were perfectly inelastic. We will take a look at that scenario shortly.

At the same time, because the new equilibrium price after the tax is $0.50 lower than it was before the tax, the producer splits the tax incidence with the buyer. The producer receives $0.50 less, and the buyer pays $0.50 more.

The tax on milk purchases also affects the amount sold in the market, which we also see in Figure 5.6. Because the after-tax equilibrium price (E$_2$) is lower, producers of milk reduce the quantity they sell to 750 gallons. Therefore, the market for milk becomes smaller than it was before the good was taxed.

Excise taxes are rarely levied on consumers because these taxes are highly visible. If you were reminded that you have to pay a $1.00 tax every time you buy a gallon of milk, it would be hard for you to ignore the tax. As a result, politicians often prefer to place the tax on the seller.

EXAMPLE 2: TAX ON SELLERS Now let's look at what happens when the $1.00 tax on milk is placed on sellers. Figure 5.7 shows the result. First, look at the shift in the supply curve. Why does it shift? The $1.00-per-gallon tax on milk lowers willingness to sell, which causes producers to offer less milk at every price level. As a result, the entire supply curve shifts up in response to the tax that milk producers owe the government. The intersection of the new supply curve (S$_2$)

FIGURE 5.7

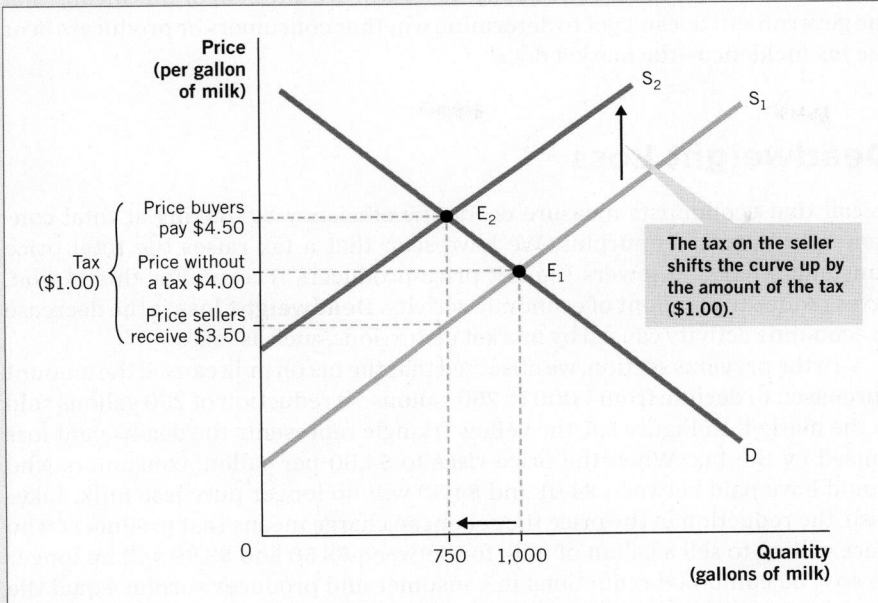

After the tax, the new equilibrium price (E_2) is $4.50, but $1.00 must be paid in tax to the government. Therefore, despite the rise in price, the seller nets only $3.50. Similar logic applies to the consumer. Because the new equilibrium price after the tax is $0.50 higher, the consumer shares the $1.00-per-gallon tax incidence equally with the seller. The consumer pays $0.50 more, and the seller nets $0.50 less.

with the existing demand curve creates a new equilibrium price (E_2) of $4.50 per gallon—which is $0.50 higher than the original equilibrium price of $4.00 ($E_1$). Many students mistakenly believe that the new equilibrium price will be $5.00, but again, that would only be the case if supply were perfectly inelastic. This higher equilibrium price occurs because the seller passes part of the tax increase along to the buyer in the form of a higher price. However, the seller is still worse off. After the tax, the new equilibrium price is $4.50 per gallon, but $1.00 goes as tax to the government. Therefore, despite the rise in price, the seller nets only $3.50 per gallon, which is $0.50 less than the original equilibrium price.

The tax also affects the amount of milk sold in the market. Because the new equilibrium price after the tax is higher, consumers reduce the quantity demanded from 1,000 gallons to 750 gallons.

SO WHO BEARS THE INCIDENCE OF THE TAX?

It's important to notice that the result in Figure 5.7 looks much like that in Figure 5.6 because it does not matter whether a tax is levied on the buyer or the seller. The tax places a wedge of $1.00 between the price buyers ultimately pay ($4.50) and the net price sellers ultimately receive ($3.50), regardless of who is actually responsible for paying the tax.

Continuing with our milk example, when the tax was levied on sellers, they were responsible for collecting the entire tax ($1.00 per gallon), but they transferred $0.50 of the tax to the consumer by raising the market price to $4.50. Similarly, when the tax was levied on consumers, they were responsible for paying the entire tax, but they essentially transferred $0.50 of it to producers, because the market price fell to $3.50. Therefore, we can say that the incidence of a tax is independent of whether it is levied on the buyer or the seller. However, depending on the price elasticity of supply and demand, the tax incidence need not be shared equally, as we will see later. All of this means that the government doesn't get to determine whether consumers or producers bear the tax incidence—the market does!

Deadweight Loss

Recall that economists measure economic efficiency by looking at total consumer and producer surplus. We have seen that a tax raises the total price consumers pay and lowers the net price producers receive. For this reason, taxes reduce the amount of economic activity. **Deadweight loss** is the decrease in economic activity caused by market distortions, such as taxes.

In the previous section, we observed that the tax on milk caused the amount purchased to decline from 1,000 to 750 gallons—a reduction of 250 gallons sold in the market. In Figure 5.8, the yellow triangle represents the deadweight loss caused by the tax. When the price rises to $4.50 per gallon, consumers who would have paid between $4.01 and $4.50 will no longer purchase milk. Likewise, the reduction in the price the seller can charge means that producers who were willing to sell a gallon of milk for between $3.50 and $3.99 will no longer do so. The combined reductions in consumer and producer surplus equal the deadweight loss produced by a $1.00 tax on milk.

In the next three sections, we examine how differences in the price elasticity of demand lead to varying amounts of deadweight loss. The tax is placed on the seller, and we evaluate what happens when the demand curve is perfectly inelastic, somewhat elastic, and perfectly elastic.

FIGURE 5.8

The Deadweight Loss from a Tax

The yellow triangle represents the deadweight loss caused by the tax. When the price rises, all consumers who would have paid between $4.01 and $4.50 no longer purchase milk. Likewise, the reduction in revenue the seller receives means that producers who were willing to sell a gallon of milk for between $3.50 and $3.99 will no longer do so.

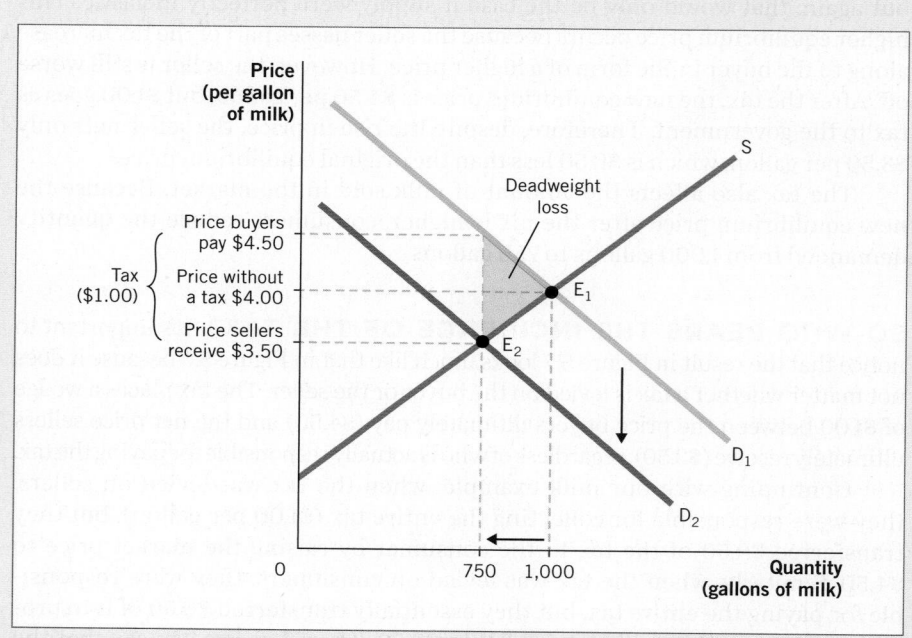

Is Soda Demand Elastic or Inelastic?

PARKS AND RECREATION: SODA TAX

Leslie Knope, now serving on the Pawnee city council, has to decide whether to vote for a citywide tax on sugary soda drinks. Leslie wants to understand both sides of the issue, so she meets with Pawnee Restaurant Association spokeswoman Kathryn Pinewood, to discuss the city's growing drink sizes. Leslie is concerned about the obesity problem in Pawnee, so she is horrified to learn that the sodas come in 64-, 128- and 512-ounce containers. She can't imagine why anyone would want so much soda. Kathryn won't allow Leslie to drag her into that discussion and instead touts the incredible value for consumers. Kathryn also argues that the tax would mean lost jobs in the local restaurant industry. Leslie and Kathryn, though on opposite sides, agree on this much: if passed, the tax will have a negative effect on the quantity demanded.

Since this episode first aired in 2012, soda taxes have been implemented throughout Mexico (2014) and in a number of major U.S. cities (San Francisco, Chicago, and Philadelphia). Researchers studied the impact of the sugary drink tax in Mexico and found that a 10% increase in the price of sweetened sugar beverages was associated with an 11.6% decrease

Mexico's sugary drink tax cut consumption by about 12%.

in quantity consumed.[*] That translates into a price elasticity of demand of –1.16 (slightly elastic). For proponents of soda taxes, this indicates that even a relatively small increase in price will meaningfully reduce consumption and lessen obesity.

---

*Source: M. A. Colchero, J. C. Salgado, M. Unar-Munguía, M. Hernández-Ávila, and J. A. Rivera-Dommarco. "Price elasticity of the demand for sugar sweetened beverages and soft drinks in Mexico," *Economics & Human Biology*, vol. 19 (December 2015): 129–137.

TAX REVENUE AND DEADWEIGHT LOSS WHEN DEMAND IS INELASTIC In Chapter 4, we saw that necessary goods and services—for example, water, electricity, and phone service—have highly inelastic demand. These goods and services are often taxed. For example, consider all the taxes associated with your cell phone bill: sales tax, city tax, county tax, federal excise tax, and annual regulatory fees. In addition, many companies add surcharges, including activation fees, local-number portability fees, telephone number pooling charges, emergency 911 service, directory assistance, telecommunications relay service surcharges, and cancellation fees. Of course, there is a way to avoid all these fees: don't use a cell phone! However, many people today feel that cell phones are a necessity. Cell phone providers and government agencies take advantage of consumers' strongly inelastic demand by tacking on these extra charges.

How do phone companies get away with all the added fees per month? Answer: inelastic demand.

FIGURE 5.9

A Tax on Products with Almost Perfectly Inelastic Demand

(a) Before the tax, the consumer enjoys the consumer surplus (C.S.) shaded in blue, and the producer enjoys the producer surplus (P.S.) shaded in red. (b) After the tax, the incidence, or the burden of taxation, is borne entirely by the consumer. A tax on a good with perfectly inelastic demand, such as phone service, represents a transfer of welfare from consumers to the government, as reflected by the reduced size of the blue rectangle in (b) and the creation of the green tax revenue rectangle between P_1 and P_2.

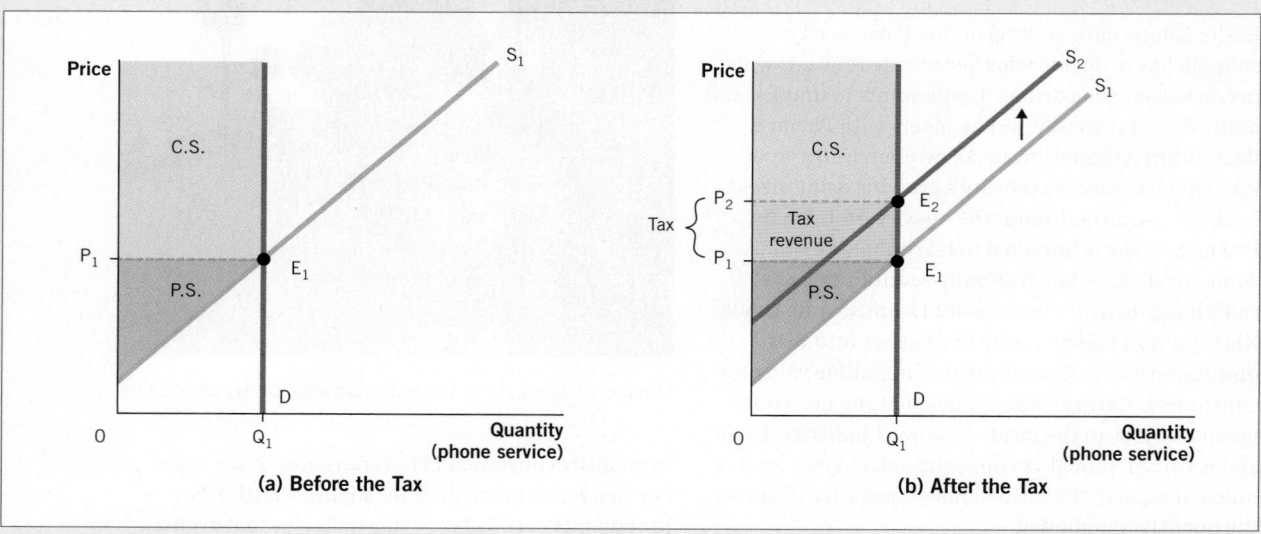

(a) Before the Tax

(b) After the Tax

Figure 5.9 shows the result of a tax on products with perfectly inelastic demand, such as phone service—something people feel they need to have no matter what the price. For our purposes, the demand for access to a phone (either a landline or a cell phone) can be considered perfectly inelastic. Recall that whenever demand is perfectly inelastic, the demand curve is vertical. Panel (a) shows the market for phone service before the tax. The blue rectangle represents consumer surplus (C.S.), and the red triangle represents producer surplus (P.S.). Now imagine that a tax is levied on the seller, as shown in panel (b). The supply curve shifts from S_1 to S_2. The shift in supply causes the equilibrium point to move from E_1 to E_2 and the price to rise from P_1 to P_2, but the quantity supplied, Q_1, remains the same. We know that when demand is perfectly inelastic, a price increase does not alter how much consumers purchase. So the quantity demanded remains constant at Q_1 even after the government collects tax revenue equal to the green rectangle.

There are two reasons why the government may favor excise taxes on goods with almost perfectly (or highly) inelastic demand. First, because these goods do not have substitutes, the tax will not cause consumers to buy less. Thus, the revenue from the tax will remain steady. Second, because the number of transactions, or quantity demanded (Q_1), remains constant, there will be no deadweight loss. As a result, the yellow triangle we observed in Figure 5.8 disappears in Figure 5.9 because the tax does not alter the efficiency of the market. Looking at Figure 5.9, you can see that the same number of transactions exist in panels

(a) and (b); the total surplus, or social welfare, is equal in both panels. You can also see this equality by comparing the full shaded areas in both panels. The sum of the blue area of consumer surplus and the red area of producer surplus in panel (a) is equal to the sum of the consumer surplus, producer surplus, and tax revenue in panel (b). The green area in panel (b) is subtracted entirely from the blue rectangle in panel (a), which indicates that the surplus is redistributed from consumers to the government. But society overall enjoys the same total surplus (even though some of this surplus is now in the form of a tax). Thus, we see that when demand is perfectly inelastic, the incidence, or the burden of taxation, is borne entirely by the consumer. A tax on a good with almost perfectly inelastic demand represents a transfer of welfare from consumers of the good to the government, reflected by the reduced size of the blue rectangle in panel (b).

TAX REVENUE AND DEADWEIGHT LOSS WHEN DEMAND IS MORE ELASTIC Now consider a tax on a product with more elastic demand, such as milk, the subject of our earlier discussion. The demand for milk is price sensitive, but not overly so. This elasticity is reflected in a demand curve with a typical slope as shown in Figure 5.10. Let's compare the after-tax price, P_2, in panel (b) of Figures 5.9 and 5.10. When demand is perfectly inelastic, as it is in panel (b) of Figure 5.9, the price increase from P_1 to P_2 is absorbed entirely by consumers. But in panel (b) of Figure 5.10, because demand is flatter and

FIGURE 5.10

A Tax on Products with More Elastic Demand

(a) Before the tax, the consumer enjoys the consumer surplus (C.S.) shaded in blue, and the producer enjoys the producer surplus (P.S.) shaded in red. (b) A tax on a good for which demand and supply are both somewhat elastic will cause a transfer of welfare from consumers and producers to the government, the revenue shown as the green rectangle. It will also create deadweight loss (D.W.L.), shaded in yellow, because the quantity bought and sold in the market declines (from Q_1 to Q_2).

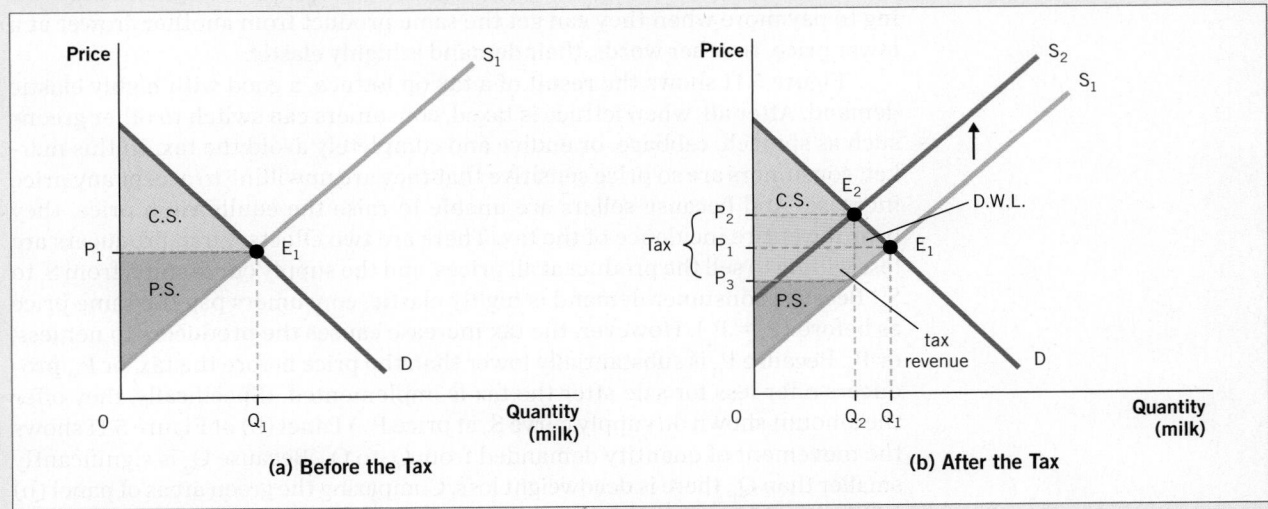

therefore more sensitive to price, suppliers must absorb part of the tax themselves (from P_1 to P_3). Thus, the net price they charge, P_3, is less than what they received when the good was not taxed. In addition, the total tax revenue generated (the green area) is not as large in panel (b) of Figure 5.10 as in panel (b) of Figure 5.9 because as the price of the good rises to P_2, some consumers no longer buy it and the quantity demanded falls from Q_1 to Q_2.

Notice that both consumer surplus (C.S., the blue triangle) and producer surplus (P.S., the red triangle) in Figure 5.10, panel (b), are smaller after the tax. Because the price rises after the tax increase (from P_1 to P_2), those consumers with a relatively low willingness to pay for the good are priced out of the market. Likewise, sellers with relatively high costs of production will stop producing the good, because the price they net after paying the tax drops to P_3. The total reduction in economic activity, the change from Q_1 to Q_2, is the deadweight loss (D.W.L.) indicated by the yellow triangle.

A tax on a good for which demand and supply are both somewhat elastic will cause a transfer of welfare from consumers and producers of the good to the government. At the same time, because the quantity bought and sold in the market declines, deadweight loss is created. Another way of seeing this result is to compare the red and blue areas in Figure 5.10, panel (a), with the red and blue areas in panel (b) of Figure 5.10. The sum of the consumer surplus and producer surplus in panel (a) is greater than the sum of the consumer surplus, tax revenue, and producer surplus in panel (b) because the deadweight loss in panel (b) is no longer a part of the surplus. Therefore, the total surplus is lower, which means that the efficiency of the market is smaller. The tax is no longer a pure transfer from consumers to the government, as was the case in Figure 5.9 with perfectly inelastic demand.

TAX REVENUE AND DEADWEIGHT LOSS WHEN DEMAND IS HIGHLY ELASTIC

We have seen the effect of taxation when demand is inelastic and somewhat elastic. What happens when demand is highly elastic? For example, a customer who wants to buy fresh lettuce at a produce market will find many local growers charging the same price and many varieties to choose from. If one of the vendors decides to charge $1 per pound above the market price, consumers will stop buying from that vendor. They will be unwilling to pay more when they can get the same product from another grower at a lower price. In other words, their demand is highly elastic.

Figure 5.11 shows the result of a tax on lettuce, a good with highly elastic demand. After all, when lettuce is taxed, consumers can switch to other greens such as spinach, cabbage, or endive and completely avoid the tax. In this market, consumers are so price sensitive that they are unwilling to accept any price increase. And because sellers are unable to raise the equilibrium price, they bear the entire incidence of the tax. There are two effects. First, producers are less willing to sell the product at all prices, and the supply curve shifts from S_1 to S_2. Because consumer demand is highly elastic, consumers pay the same price as before ($P_1 = P_2$). However, the tax increase causes the producers to net less, or P_3. Because P_3 is substantially lower than the price before the tax, or P_2, producers offer less for sale after the tax is implemented. (Specifically, they offer the amount shown on supply curve S_2 at price P_2.) Panel (b) of Figure 5.11 shows the movement of quantity demanded from Q_1 to Q_2. Because Q_2 is significantly smaller than Q_1, there is deadweight loss. Comparing the green areas of panel (b) in Figures 5.10 and 5.11, you see that the size of the tax revenue continues to shrink. There is an important lesson here for policymakers. They should tax

FIGURE 5.11

A Tax on Products with Highly Elastic Demand

(a) Before the tax, the producer enjoys the producer surplus (P.S.) shaded in red. (b) When consumer demand is highly elastic, consumers pay the same price after the tax as before. But they are worse off because less is produced and sold; the quantity produced moves from Q_1 to Q_2. The result is deadweight loss (D.W.L.), as shown by the yellow triangle. The total surplus, or efficiency of the market, is much smaller than before. The size of the tax revenue (shaded in green) is also noticeably smaller in the market with highly elastic demand compared to the market with highly inelastic demand.

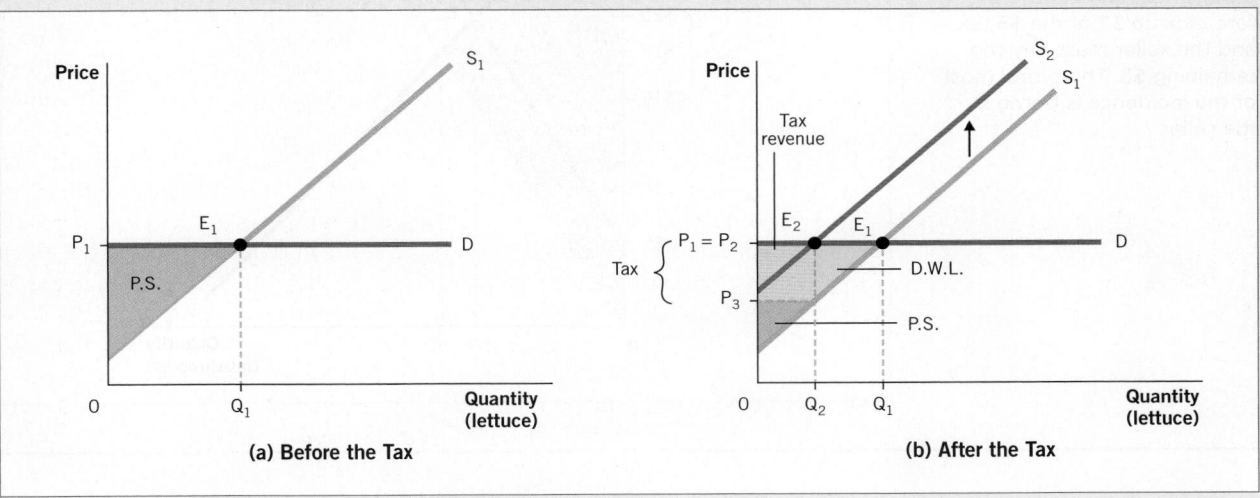

(a) Before the Tax

(b) After the Tax

goods with relatively inelastic demand (if the goal is to generate tax revenue or minimize efficiency losses). Doing so will not only lessen the deadweight loss of taxation, but also generate larger tax revenues for the government.

INTERACTION OF DEMAND ELASTICITY AND SUPPLY ELASTICITY

The incidence of a tax is determined by the relative steepness of the demand curve compared with the supply curve. When the demand curve is steeper (more inelastic) than the supply curve, consumers bear more of the incidence of the tax. When the supply curve is steeper (more inelastic) than the demand curve, suppliers bear more of the incidence of the tax. Also, whenever the supply and/or demand curves are relatively steep, deadweight loss is minimized.

Let's explore an example in which we consider how the elasticity of demand and elasticity of supply interact. Suppose that a $5-per-pound tax is placed on shiitake mushrooms. Given the information in Figure 5.12, we will compute the incidence, deadweight loss, and tax revenue from the tax.

Let's start with the incidence of the tax. After the tax is implemented, the market price rises from $18 per pound (at E_1) to $20 per pound (at E_2). But since sellers must pay $5 per pound to the government, they keep only $15.

How much would you pay per pound for these mushrooms?

FIGURE 5.12

A Realistic Example

A $5-per-pound tax is placed on mushroom suppliers, driving the equilibrium price up from E₁ ($18) to E₂ ($20). Notice that the price rises by only $2. Consumers therefore pick up $2 of the $5 tax and the seller must pay the remaining $3. Therefore, most of the incidence is borne by the seller.

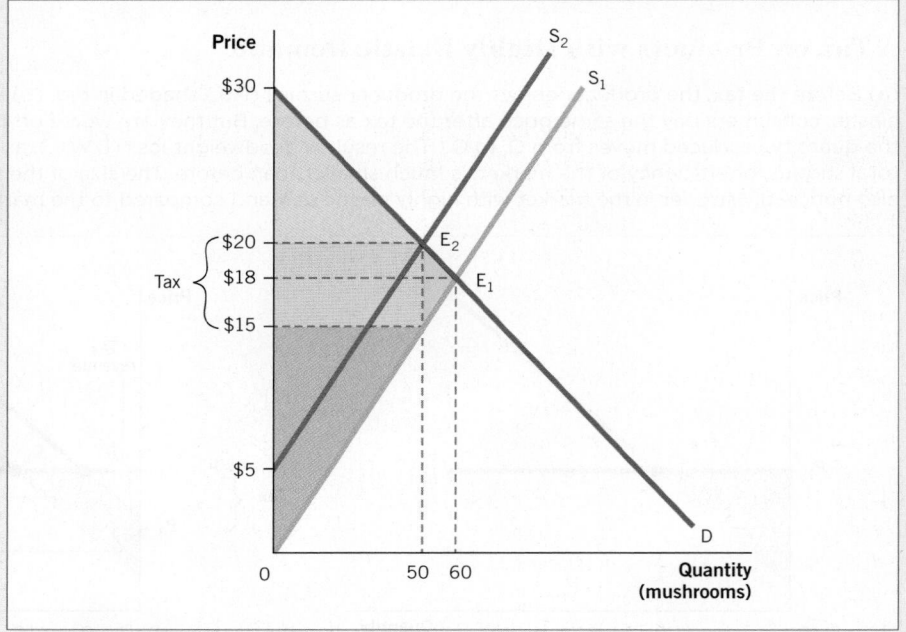

Tax incidence measures the share of the tax paid by buyers and sellers, so we need to compare the incidence of the tax paid by each party. Because the market price rises by $2 (from $18 to $20), buyers are paying $2 of the $5 tax, or $\frac{2}{5}$. Because the amount the seller keeps falls by $3 (from $18 to $15), sellers are paying $3 of the $5 tax, or $\frac{3}{5}$. Notice that the demand curve is slightly more elastic (flatter) than the supply curve; therefore, sellers have a limited ability to raise their price.

Now let's determine the deadweight loss caused by the tax—that is, the decrease in economic activity. Deadweight loss is represented by the decrease in the total surplus found in the yellow triangle in Figure 5.12. To compute the amount of the deadweight loss, we need to determine the area of the triangle:

(EQUATION 5.1)

$$\text{area of a triangle} = \frac{1}{2} \times \text{base} \times \text{height}$$

The triangle in Figure 5.12 is sitting on its side, so its height is $60 - 50 = 10$, and its base is $20 - 15 = 5$.

$$\text{deadweight loss} = \frac{1}{2} \times 10 \times \$5 = \$25$$

This means that $25 worth of mushroom sales will not take place because of the tax.

THE SHORT-LIVED LUXURY TAX

The Budget Reconciliation Act of 1990 established a special luxury tax on the sale of new aircraft, yachts, automobiles, furs, and
jewelry. The act established a 10% surcharge on new purchases as
follows: aircraft over $500,000; yachts over $100,000; automobiles over $25,000; and furs and jewelry over $10,000. The taxes
were expected to generate approximately $2 billion a year. How-
ever, revenue fell far below expectations, and thousands of jobs
were lost in each of the affected industries. Within three years,
the tax was repealed. Why was the luxury tax such a failure?

If you were rich, would this be
your luxury toy?

When passing the Budget Reconciliation Act, lawmakers
failed to consider basic demand elasticity. Because the purchase
of a new aircraft, yacht, car, fur, or jewelry is highly discretionary, many wealthy consumers decided that they would buy substitute products that fell
below the tax threshold or buy a used product and refurbish it. Therefore, the demand
for these luxury goods turned out to be highly elastic. We have seen that when goods
with elastic demand are taxed, the resulting tax revenues are small. Moreover, in this
example, the resulting decrease in purchases was significant. As a result, jobs were lost
in the middle of an economic downturn. The combination of low revenues and crippling
job losses was enough to convince Congress to repeal the tax in 1993.

The failed luxury tax is a reminder that the populist idea of taxing the rich is far more
difficult to implement than it appears. In simple terms, it is nearly impossible to tax the toys
that the rich enjoy because wealthy people can spend their money in so many different ways.
They have options about whether to buy or lease, as well as many good substitutes to choose
from. In other words, in many cases, they can avoid paying luxury taxes.

Finally, what is the tax revenue generated by the tax? In Figure 5.12, the tax
revenue is represented by the green-shaded area, which is a rectangle. We can
calculate the tax revenue by determining the area of the rectangle:

$$\text{area of a rectangle} = \text{base} \times \text{height}$$

(EQUATION 5.2)

The height of the tax revenue rectangle is the amount of the tax ($5), and
the number of units sold after the tax is 50 (the base).

$$\text{tax revenue} = \$5 \times 50 = \$250$$

Balancing Deadweight Loss and Tax Revenues

Up to this point, we have kept the size of the tax increase constant. Doing so enabled
us to examine the impact of the elasticity of demand and supply on deadweight
loss and tax revenues. But what happens when a tax is high enough to significantly
alter consumer or producer behavior? For instance, in 2002, the Republic of
Ireland instituted a tax of 15 euro cents on each plastic bag in order to curb litter

and encourage recycling. Since the cost of production of each plastic bag is just a few pennies, a 15-euro-cent tax is enormous by comparison. As a result, consumer use of plastic bags quickly fell by over 90%. Thus, the tax was a major success because the government achieved its goal of curbing litter. In this section, we consider how consumers respond to taxes of different sizes, and we determine the relationship between the size of a tax, the deadweight loss, and tax revenues.

Incentives

Figure 5.13 shows the market response to a variety of tax increases. The five panels in the figure begin with a reference point, panel (a), where no tax is levied, and progress toward panel (e), where the tax rate becomes so extreme that it curtails all economic activity.

Trade-offs

As taxes rise, so do prices. You can trace this price rise from panel (a), where there is no tax and the price is P_1, all the way to panel (e), where the extreme tax causes the price to rise to P_5. At the same time, deadweight loss (D.W.L.) also rises. You can see this increase by comparing the sizes of the yellow triangles. The trade-off is striking. Without any taxes, deadweight loss does not occur. But as soon as taxes are in place, the market equilibrium quantity demanded begins to decline, moving from Q_1 to Q_5. As the number of transactions (quantity demanded) declines, the area of deadweight loss rapidly expands.

When taxes are small, as in panel (b), the tax revenue (green rectangle) is large relative to the deadweight loss (yellow triangle). However, as we progress through the panels, this relationship slowly reverses. In panel (c), the size of the tax revenue remains larger than the deadweight loss. In panel (d), however, the

PRACTICE WHAT YOU KNOW

What is the optimal tax rate?

Deadweight Loss of Taxation: The Politics of Tax Rates

Imagine that you and two friends are discussing the politics of taxation. One friend, who is fiscally conservative, argues that tax rates are too high. The other friend, who is more progressive, argues that tax rates are too low.

QUESTION: Is it possible that both friends are right?

ANSWER: Surprisingly, the answer is yes. When tax rates become extraordinarily high, the amount of deadweight loss dwarfs the amount of tax revenue collected. We observed this result in our discussion of the short-lived luxury tax. Fiscal conservatives often note that taxes inhibit economic activity. They advocate lower tax rates and limited government involvement in the market, preferring to minimize the deadweight loss on economic activity—see panel (b) in Figure 5.13. However, progressives prefer somewhat higher tax rates than fiscal conservatives, because a moderate tax rate—see panel (c)—generates more tax revenue than a small tax does. The additional revenues that moderate tax rates generate can fund more government services.

Therefore, a clear trade-off exists between the size of the public (government) sector and market activity. Depending on how you view the value created by markets versus the value added through government provision, there is ample room for disagreement about the best tax policy.

Trade-offs

FIGURE 5.13

Examining Deadweight Loss and Tax Revenues

The panels show that increased taxes result in higher prices. Progressively higher taxes lead to more deadweight loss (D.W.L.), but higher taxes do not always generate more tax revenue, as evidenced by the reduction in tax revenue that occurs when tax rates become too large in panels (d) and (e).

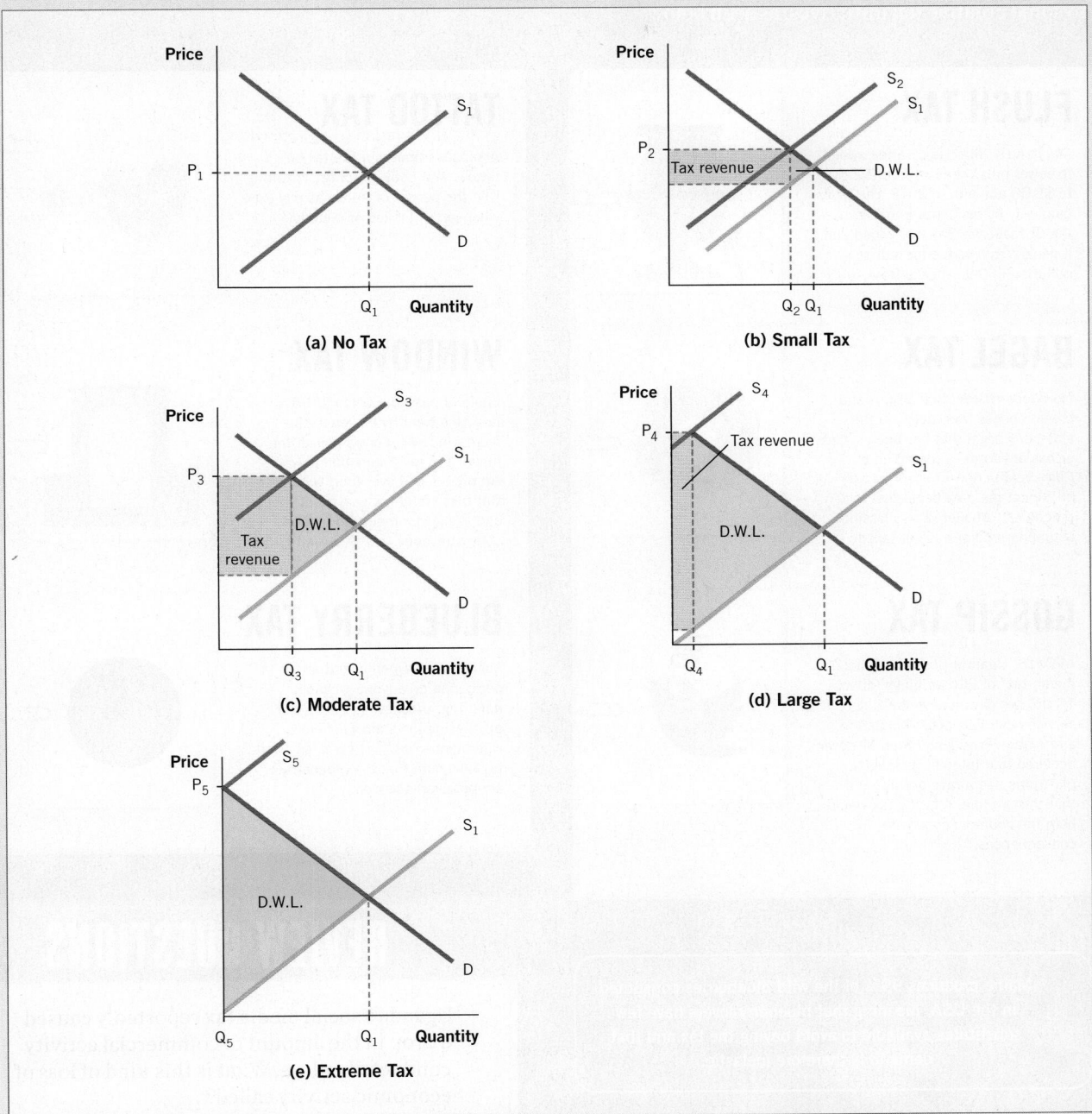

(a) No Tax

(b) Small Tax

(c) Moderate Tax

(d) Large Tax

(e) Extreme Tax

Unusual Taxes

Governments tax their citizens for a variety of reasons. Often it's to raise revenue. Sometimes, taxes are levied to influence citizens' behavior. Occasionally, both of these reasons are in play. These two motivations have led to some creative tax initiatives, as seen below.

FLUSH TAX

Maryland's "flush tax," a fee added to sewer bills, went up from $2.50 to $5.00 a month in 2012. The tax is paid only by residents who live in the Chesapeake Bay Watershed, and it generates revenue for reducing pollution in Chesapeake Bay.

BAGEL TAX

New Yorkers love their bagels and cream cheese from delis. In the state, any bagel that has been sliced or has any form of spread on it (like cream cheese) is subject to an 8-cent tax. Any bagel that is purchased "unaltered" is classified as unprepared and is not taxed.

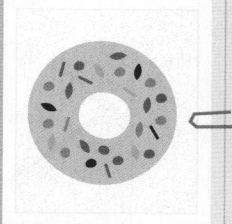

GOSSIP TAX

In 2018, Uganda passed a "social media tax" of 200 shillings (about $0.05) per day on anyone using online services like Facebook, WhatsApp, and Twitter. President Yoweri Museveni declared that Internet messaging platforms encourage gossip, and that the revenue from the tax would help the country "cope with the consequences."

TATTOO TAX

Arkansas imposes a 6% tax on tattoos and body piercings, meaning that the people of Arkansas pay extra when getting inked or pierced.

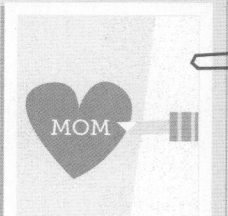

WINDOW TAX

England passed a tax in 1696 targeting wealthy citizens—the more windows in one's house, the higher the tax. Many homeowners simply bricked over their windows. But they could not seal all of them, and the government did indeed collect revenue.

BLUEBERRY TAX

Maine levies a penny-and-a-half tax per pound on anyone growing, handling, processing, selling, or purchasing the state's delicious wild blueberries. The tax is an effort to make sure that the blueberries are not overharvested.

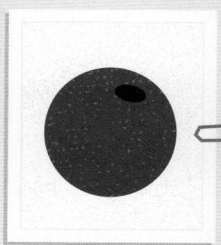

Maine produces 99% of the wild blueberries consumed in the USA, meaning that blueberry lovers have few substitutes available to avoid paying the tax and that demand is therefore inelastic.

Marylanders are being taxed on a negative externality, which we cover in Chapter 7.

REVIEW QUESTIONS

- Uganda's social media tax reportedly caused a drop in the amount of commercial activity conducted online. What is this kind of loss of economic activity called?

- Do you think the New York bagel tax is an effective tool to raise government revenue? Think about how the tax may or may not affect the purchasing behavior of New Yorkers.

magnitude of the deadweight loss is far greater than the tax revenue. The size of the tax in panel (d) is creating a significant cost in terms of economic efficiency. Finally, panel (e) shows an extreme case in which all market activity ceases as a result of the tax. Because nothing is produced and sold, there is no tax revenue.

Conclusion

The government largely taxes goods that have inelastic demand, which means that firms are able to transfer most of the tax incidence to consumers through higher prices.

In the first part of this chapter, we learned that society benefits from unregulated markets because they generate the largest possible total surplus. However, society also needs the government to provide an infrastructure for the economy. The taxation of specific goods and services gives rise to a form of market failure called deadweight loss, which reflects reduced economic activity. Thus, any intervention in the market requires a deep understanding of how society will respond to the incentives created by the legislation. In addition, unintended consequences can affect the most well-intentioned tax legislation and, if the process is not well thought through, can cause inefficiencies with far-reaching consequences. None of this means that taxes are undesirable. Rather, society must balance (1) the need for tax revenues and the programs those revenues help fund with (2) trade-offs in the market. ✳

Incentives

Trade-offs

Excise Taxes Are Almost Impossible to Avoid

- Excise taxes are placed on specific products.
- Excise taxes are typically levied on goods with inelastic demand.
- A typical household of four pays over $1,000 in excise taxes annually.

The federal government collected $83 billion in excise taxes in 2017. Excise taxes are placed on many different products, making them almost impossible to avoid. They also have the added advantages of being easy to collect, hard for consumers to detect since the producer is responsible for paying the tax, and easier to enact politically than other types of taxes. You'll find federal excise taxes on many everyday household expenses—what you drink, the gasoline you purchase, plane tickets, and much more. Let's add them up over the course of a typical year.

Excise taxes are everywhere.

1. **Gasoline (and Diesel).** 18.4 cents per gallon (and 24.4 cents per gallon), generating $41 billion to help finance the interstate highway system.
2. **Cigarettes.** $1.01 per pack, generating $10 billion for the general federal budget.
3. **Air travel.** 7.5% of the base price of the ticket plus $4 per flight segment, generating $14 billion for the Transportation Security Administration and the Federal Aviation Administration.
4. **Alcohol.** 5 cents per can of beer, 21 cents per bottle of wine, and $2.14 per bottle of spirits, generating $10 billion for the general federal budget.

These four categories account for $75 billion in excise taxes. You could still avoid the taxman with this simple prescription: don't drink, don't travel, and don't smoke. Where does that leave you? Way out in the country somewhere far from civilization. Since you won't be able to travel to a grocery store, you'll need to live off the land, grow your own crops, and hunt or fish.

But there is still one last federal excise tax to go.

5. **Hunting and fishing.** Taxes range from 3 cents for fishing tackle boxes to 11% for archery equipment, generating over $1 billion for fish and wildlife services.

Living off the land and avoiding taxes just got much harder, and that's the whole point. The government taxes products with relatively inelastic demand because most people will still purchase them after the tax is in place. As a result, avoiding excise taxes isn't practical.

▪ ANSWERING *the* BIG QUESTIONS ▪

What are consumer surplus and producer surplus?

- Consumer surplus is the difference between the willingness to pay for a good or service and the price is paid to get it. Producer surplus is the difference between the price the seller receives and the price at which the seller is willing to sell the good or service.

- Total surplus (social welfare) is the sum of consumer and producer surplus that exists in a market.

When is a market efficient?

- Markets maximize consumer and producer surplus, provide goods and services to buyers who value them most, and reward sellers who can produce goods and services at the lowest cost. As a result, markets create the largest amount of total surplus possible.

- Whenever an allocation of resources maximizes total surplus, the result is said to be efficient. However, economists are also interested in the distribution of the surplus. Equity refers to the fairness of the distribution of the benefits within the society.

Why do taxes create deadweight loss in otherwise efficient markets?

- Deadweight loss occurs because taxes increase the purchase price, which causes consumers to buy less and producers to supply less. Deadweight loss can be lessened by taxing goods or services that have inelastic demand or supply.

- Economists are also concerned about the incidence of taxation. Incidence refers to the burden of taxation on the party who pays the tax through higher prices, regardless of whom the tax is actually levied on. The incidence is determined by the balance between the elasticity of supply and the elasticity of demand.

Concepts You Should Know

consumer surplus (p. 157)
deadweight loss (p. 170)
efficient (p. 163)
equity (p. 164)

excise taxes (p. 167)
incidence (p. 167)
producer surplus (p. 159)
social welfare (p. 162)

total surplus (p. 162)
welfare economics (p. 156)
willingness to pay (p. 157)
willingness to sell (p. 159)

Questions for Review

1. Explain how consumer surplus is derived from the difference between the willingness to pay and the market equilibrium price.

2. Explain how producer surplus is derived from the difference between the willingness to sell and the market equilibrium price.

3. Why do economists focus on consumer and producer surplus and not on the possibility of consumer and producer loss? Illustrate your answer on a supply and demand graph.

4. How do economists define efficiency?

5. What type of goods should be taxed in order to minimize deadweight loss?

6. Suppose that the government taxes a good that has very elastic demand. Illustrate what will happen to consumer surplus, producer surplus, tax revenue, and deadweight loss on a supply and demand graph.

7. What happens to tax revenues as tax rates increase?

Study Problems *(✳ solved at the end of the section)*

1. A college student enjoys eating pizza. Her willingness to pay for each slice is shown in the following table:

Number of pizza slices	Willingness to pay (per slice)
1	$6
2	5
3	4
4	3
5	2
6	1
7	0

2. A cash-starved town decides to impose a $6 excise tax on T-shirts sold. The following table shows the quantity demanded and the quantity supplied at various prices.

Price per T-shirt	Quantity demanded	Quantity supplied
$19	0	60
16	10	50
13	20	40
10	30	30
7	40	20
4	50	10

a. If pizza slices cost $3 each, how many slices will she buy? How much consumer surplus will she enjoy?

b. If the price of slices falls to $2, how much consumer surplus will she enjoy?

a. What are the equilibrium quantity demanded and the quantity supplied before the tax is implemented? Determine the consumer and producer surplus before the tax.

b. What are the equilibrium quantity demanded and quantity supplied after the tax is implemented? Determine the consumer and producer surplus after the tax.

c. How much tax revenue does the town generate from the tax?

3. Andrew pays $30 to buy a potato cannon, a cylinder that shoots potatoes hundreds of feet. He was willing to pay $45. When Andrew's friend Nick learns that Andrew bought a potato cannon, he asks Andrew if he will sell it for $60, and Andrew agrees. Nick is thrilled, since he would have paid Andrew up to $80 for the cannon. Andrew is also delighted. Determine the consumer surplus from the original purchase and the additional surplus generated by the resale of the cannon.

4. If the government wants to raise tax revenue, which of the following items are good candidates for an excise tax? Why?

a. granola bars
b. cigarettes
c. toilet paper
d. automobile tires
e. bird feeders

✳ **5.** If the government wants to minimize the deadweight loss of taxation, which of the following items are good candidates for an excise tax? Why?

a. bottled water
b. prescription drugs
c. oranges
d. batteries
e. luxury cars

6. A new medical study indicates that eating blueberries helps prevent cancer. If the demand for blueberries increases, what will happen to the size of the consumer surplus and producer surplus? Illustrate your answer by shifting the demand curve appropriately and labeling the new and old areas of consumer and producer surplus.

7. Use the following graph to answer questions a–f.

a. What area represents consumer surplus before the tax?

b. What area represents producer surplus before the tax?

c. What area represents consumer surplus after the tax?

d. What area represents producer surplus after the tax?

e. What area represents the tax revenue after the tax?

f. What area represents the deadweight loss after the tax?

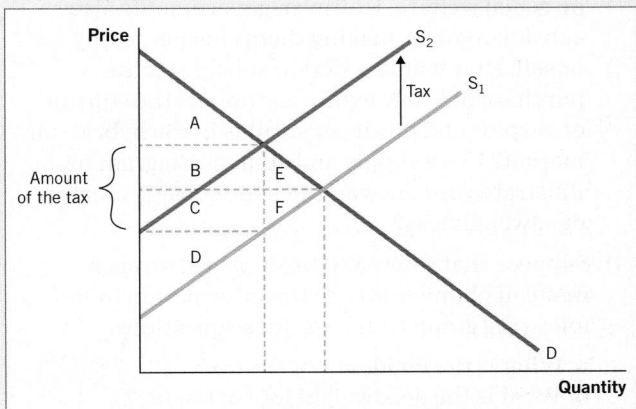

8. The cost of many electronic devices has fallen appreciably since they were first introduced. For instance, computers, cell phones, microwave ovens, and calculators not only provide more functions but also do so at a lower cost. Illustrate the impact of lower production costs on the supply curve. What happens to the size of the consumer surplus and producer surplus? If consumer demand for cell phones is relatively elastic, who is likely to benefit the most from the lower production costs?

9. Suppose that the demand for a concert, Q_D, is represented by the following equation, where P is the price of concert tickets and Q is the number of tickets sold:

$$Q_D = 2500 - 20P$$

The supply of tickets, Q_S, is represented by the equation

$$Q_S = -500 + 80P$$

a. Find the equilibrium price and quantity of tickets sold. (**Hint:** Set $Q_D = Q_S$ and solve for the price, P, and then plug the result back into either of the original equations to find Q_E.)

b. Carefully graph your result from part a.

c. Calculate the consumer surplus at the equilibrium price and quantity. (***Hint:*** Because the area of consumer surplus is a triangle, you will need to use the formula for the area of a triangle, $\frac{1}{2} \times$ base $\times$ height, to solve the problem.)

10. In this chapter, we focused on the effect of taxes on social welfare. However, governments also subsidize goods, making them cheaper to buy or sell. How would a $2,000 subsidy on the purchase of a new hybrid car impact the consumer surplus and producer surplus in the hybrid-car market? Use a supply and demand diagram to illustrate your answer. Does the subsidy create deadweight loss?

✳ **11.** Suppose that a new $50 tax is placed on each new cell phone sold. Use the information in the following graph to answer these questions.

   a. What is the incidence of the tax?
   b. What is the deadweight loss of the tax?
   c. What is the amount of tax revenue generated?

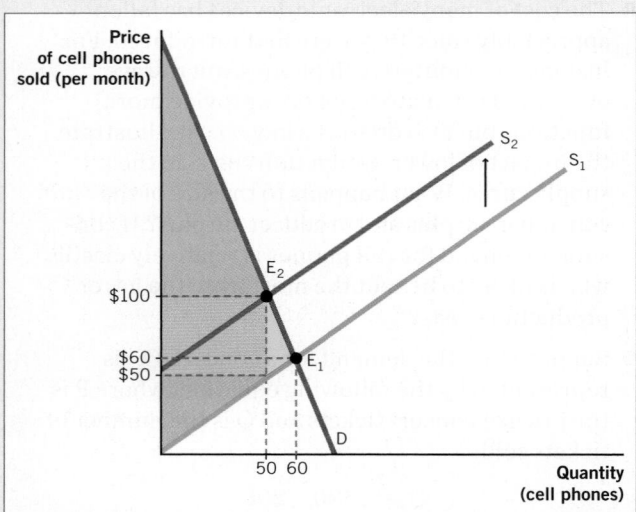

✳ **12.** A well-known saying goes, "Honesty is not only morally right, it is also highly efficient." Explain why firms that practice honesty generate more social welfare than firms that practice dishonesty.

13. We defined deadweight loss as the decrease in economic activity caused by market distortions. One place where we see deadweight loss is during Halloween's trick-or-treat. Children of all ages return home with bags of candy, some of which they love and some of which they don't care for. A lot of candy ends up uneaten. In this context, we can think of uneaten candy as not being distributed effectively by the market; therefore, deadweight loss occurs. What ways can you think of to improve how candy is given away during trick-or-treat so that children would receive more candies they enjoy? Provide three possible solutions.

✳ **14.** Assume that a $0.25/gallon tax on milk causes a loss of $300 million in consumer and producer surplus and creates a deadweight loss of $75 million. From this information, we know that the tax revenue from the tax is _____.

✳ **15.** For each of three potential buyers of avocados, the table displays the willingness to pay for the first three avocados of the day. Assume Carri, Carina, and Carlos are the only three buyers of avocados.

	First avocado	Second avocado	Third avocado
Carri	$2.00	$1.50	$0.75
Carina	1.50	1.00	0.80
Carlos	0.75	0.25	0.00

If the market price of avocados increases from $0.70 to $1.40, what is the change in total consumer surplus?

16. Suppose that the government imposes a $2 tax on consumers of donuts. What will happen to the market price?

Solved Problems

5.a. Many good substitutes are available: consumers can drink tap water, filtered water, or other healthy beverages instead of bottled water. Therefore, bottled water is not a good candidate for an excise tax.

b. Taxing prescription drugs will generate significant revenues without reducing sales much, if at all. There is almost no deadweight loss because consumers have few, if any, alternatives. Thus, prescription drugs are a good candidate for an excise tax.

c. Consumers can select many other fruits to replace oranges. The deadweight loss will be quite large. Therefore, oranges are not a good candidate for an excise tax.

d. Without batteries, many devices won't work. The lack of substitutes makes demand quite inelastic, so the deadweight loss will be small. Thus, batteries are an excellent candidate for an excise tax.

e. Wealthy consumers can spend their income in many ways. They do not have to buy luxury cars. As a result, the tax will create a large amount of deadweight loss. Therefore, luxury cars are a poor candidate for an excise tax.

11.a. After the tax is implemented, the market price rises from $60 to $100; but because sellers must pay $50 to the government, they net only $50. Tax incidence measures the share of the tax paid by buyers and sellers. Because the market price rises by $40 (from $60 to $100), buyers are paying $40 of the $50 tax, or $\frac{4}{5}$. Because the net price falls by $10 (from $60 to $50), sellers are paying $10 of the $50 tax, or $\frac{1}{5}$.

b. The deadweight loss is represented by the decrease in the total surplus found in the yellow triangle. To compute the amount of the deadweight loss, we need to determine the area inside the triangle. The area of a triangle is found by taking $\frac{1}{2} \times$ base $\times$ height. The triangle is sitting on its side, so the height of the triangle is 10 (60 – 50) and the base is $50 ($100 – $50). Hence the deadweight loss is $\frac{1}{2} \times 10 \times \$50 = \$250$.

c. The tax revenue is represented by the green area. You can calculate the tax revenue by multiplying the amount of the tax ($50) by the number of units sold after the tax (50), which equals $2,500.

12. For markets to benefit both the buyer and the seller, both parties must have accurate information about the good. We learned that an efficient allocation maximizes total surplus. Think about how dishonesty disrupts trade. Suppose a seller misrepresents the qualities of the good she is selling. A consumer buys the good and finds it to be defective or undesirable. As a result, the consumer does not get any consumer surplus from the transaction. In this case, total surplus is less than it otherwise would be. In addition, the consumer will no longer purchase from the dishonest seller, which means that potential gains from trade in the future will be lost as well.

14. The tax revenue is the lost consumer surplus plus the lost producer surplus minus the deadweight loss. Therefore the answer is $300M − $75M = $225M.

15. When avocados are $0.70, Carri buys three and receives ($2.00 + $1.50 + $0.75 − $0.70 × 3 =) $2.15 in consumer surplus, and Carina buys three and receives ($1.50 + $1.00 + $0.80 − $0.70 × 3 =) $1.20 in consumer surplus. Carlos buys one and receives ($0.75 − $0.70 =) $0.05 in consumer surplus. Totaling the combined consumer surplus gives us $2.15 + $1.20 + $0.05 = $3.40.

After the price rises to $1.40, Carri buys two and receives ($2.00 + $1.50 − $1.40 × 2 =) $0.70 in consumer surplus, and Carina buys one and receives ($1.50 − $1.40 =) $0.10 in consumer surplus. Carlos no longer buys avocados. Totaling the combined consumer surplus gives us $0.70 + $0.10 = $0.80.

Therefore the change in consumer surplus is $0.80 − $3.40 = −$2.60.

Price Controls

Price Controls Do More Harm Than Good.

Nineteen-year-old Monica Savaleta is just like a lot of us, but she lives in Caracas, Venezuela, where the prices charged for basic necessities are strictly regulated. On the surface this sounds like an intriguing idea. Lower prices for essential items, like rice and sugar, means that those items are more affordable for everyone, right? Unfortunately, nothing in life is free. Sure, Venezuelan supermarkets sell food staples at prices that are kept low not just by law but though government subsidies. But the reality is that to buy those products you have to wait in line for many hours, with no assurance that there will be any left when it's your turn to roam the aisles.

Meanwhile, black market profiteers called *bachaqueros* do sell commodities like rice and sugar—for more than $5 a pound, a tremendous expense for a typical Venezuelan earning the minimum wage, equivalent to about $50 month. Monica is faced with two bad choices: wait in line at the supermarkets, or pay the bachaqueros. "I've been waiting in line since 3 a.m. and have only managed to get two tubes of toothpaste," she says. "If I buy from the bachaqueros, my whole salary is blown on three kilos of rice."[*]

Price controls are not a new idea. The first recorded attempt to regulate prices was 4,000 years ago in ancient

---

[*]Source: Charner, Flora, Clarke, Rachel, Venezuale, "Where flour, pasta, and milk can cost a month's pay," CNN.com, August 2, 2016. http://edition.cnn.com/2016/08/02/americas/venezuela-food-prices/index.html.

Price controls in Venezuela have made it harder for stores to keep basic necessities in stock. Here, shoppers in the nation's capital, Caracas, wait their turn to enter a supermarket and hope to find at least a few of the items they came for.

Babylon, when King Hammurabi decreed how much corn a farmer could pay for a cow. Similar attempts to control prices occurred in ancient Egypt, Greece, and Rome. Each attempt ended badly. History has shown us that price controls generally do not work. Why? Because they disrupt the normal functioning of the market. By the end of this chapter, you will understand why price controls are rarely the win-win propositions that legislators often claim. To help you understand why price controls lead to disequilibrium in markets, this chapter focuses on the two most common types of price controls: *price ceilings* and *price floors*.

· BIG QUESTIONS ·

- When do price ceilings matter?
- What effects do price ceilings have on economic activity?
- When do price floors matter?
- What effects do price floors have on economic activity?

When Do Price Ceilings Matter?

Price controls attempt to set prices through government regulations in the market. In most cases, and certainly in the United States, price controls are enacted to ease perceived burdens on society. A **price ceiling** creates a legally established maximum price for a good or service. In the next section, we consider what happens when a price ceiling is in place. Price ceilings create many unintended effects that policymakers rarely acknowledge.

Understanding Price Ceilings

To understand how price ceilings work, let's try a simple thought experiment. Suppose that most prices are rising as a result of *inflation*, an overall increase in prices. The government is concerned that people with low incomes will not be able to afford to eat. To help the disadvantaged, legislators pass a law stating that no one can charge more than $0.50 for a loaf of bread. (Note that this price ceiling is about one-third the typical price of a loaf of generic white bread.) Does the new law accomplish its goal? What happens?

The law of demand tells us that if the price drops, the quantity that consumers demand will increase. At the same time, the law of supply tells us that the quantity supplied will fall because producers will be receiving lower profits for their efforts. This combination of increased quantity demanded and reduced quantity supplied will cause a shortage of bread.

On the demand side, consumers will want more bread than is available at the legal price. There will be long lines for bread, and many people will not be able to get the bread they want. On the supply side, producers will look for ways to maintain their profits. They can reduce the size of each loaf they produce. They can also use cheaper ingredients, thereby lowering the quality of their product, and they can stop making fancier varieties.

In addition, *black markets* will develop. For instance, in 2014 Venezuela instituted price controls on flour, which has led to severe shortages of bread. In this real-life example, many people who do not want to wait in line for bread or who do not obtain it despite waiting in line will resort to illegal means to obtain it. In other words, sellers will go "underground" and charge higher prices to customers who want bread. **Black markets** are illegal markets that arise when price controls are in place.

Table 6.1 summarizes the likely outcomes of price controls on bread.

Long lines for bread in Venezuela.

Incentives

Black markets
are illegal markets that arise when price controls are in place.

TABLE 6.1
A Price Ceiling on Bread

Question	Answer / Explanation	Result
Will there be more bread or less bread for sale?	Consumers will want to buy more because the price is lower (the law of demand), but producers will manufacture less (the law of supply). The net result will be a shortage of bread.	Empty shelves
Will the size of a typical loaf change?	Because the price is capped at $0.50 per loaf, manufacturers will try to maintain profits by reducing the size of each loaf.	No more giant loaves
Will the quality change?	Because the price is capped, producers will use cheaper ingredients, and many expensive brands and varieties will no longer be profitable to produce. Thus the quality of available bread will decline.	Focaccia bread will disappear
Will the opportunity cost of finding bread change?	The opportunity cost of finding bread will rise. Consumers will spend significant resources going from store to store to see if a bread shipment has arrived and waiting in line for a chance to get some.	Bread lines will become the norm
Will people have to break the law to buy bread?	Because bread will be hard to find and people will still need it, a black market will develop. Those selling and buying on the black market will be breaking the law.	Black-market bread dealers will help reduce the shortage

If you can touch the ceiling, you can't go any higher. A binding price ceiling stops prices from rising.

Incentives

The Effect of Price Ceilings

Now that we have some understanding of how a price ceiling works, we can transfer that knowledge into the supply and demand model for a deeper analysis of how price ceilings affect the market. To explain when price ceilings matter in the short run, we examine two types of price ceilings: nonbinding and binding. Both are set by law, but only one actually makes a difference to prices.

NONBINDING PRICE CEILINGS The effect of a price ceiling depends on the level at which it is set relative to the equilibrium price. When a price ceiling is above the equilibrium price, we say it is *nonbinding*. Figure 6.1 shows a price ceiling of $2.00 per loaf in a market where $2.00 is above the equilibrium price (P_E) of $1.00. All prices at or below $2.00 (the green area) are legal. Prices above the price ceiling (the red area) are illegal. But because the market equilibrium (E) occurs in the green area, the price ceiling does not influence the market; it is nonbinding. As long as the equilibrium price remains below the price ceiling, price will continue to be regulated by supply and demand.

BINDING PRICE CEILINGS When a price ceiling is below the market price, it creates a binding constraint that prevents supply and demand from clearing the market. In Figure 6.2, the price ceiling for bread is set at $0.50 per loaf. Because $0.50 is well below the equilibrium price of $1.00, the price ceiling is *binding*. Notice that at a price of $0.50, the quantity demanded (Q_D) is greater than the quantity supplied (Q_S); in other words, a shortage exists. Shortages typically cause prices to rise, but the imposed price ceiling prevents that from happening. A price ceiling of $0.50 allows only the prices in the green area. The market cannot reach the equilibrium point E at $1.00 per loaf because it is located above the price ceiling, in the red area.

The black-market price is also set by supply and demand. Because prices above $0.50 are illegal, sellers are unwilling to produce more than Q_S. Because a shortage exists, an illegal market will form in response to the shortage. In the black market, purchasers can illegally resell what they have just bought at $0.50 for far more than what they just paid. Because the supply of legally produced bread is Q_S, the intersection of the vertical dashed line that reflects Q_S with the demand curve D_{SR} at point $E_{black\ market}$ establishes a black-market price ($P_{black\ market}$) at $2.00 per loaf for illegally sold bread. The black-market price is substantially more than the market equilibrium price (P_E) of $1.00. As a result, the black-market price eliminates the shortage caused by the price ceiling. However, the price ceiling has created two unintended consequences: a smaller quantity of bread supplied (Q_S is less than Q_E), and a higher price for those who purchase it on the black market.

Price Ceilings in the Long Run

In the long run, supply and demand become more elastic, or flatter. Recall from Chapter 4 that when consumers have additional time to make choices, they find more ways to avoid high-priced goods and more ways to take advantage of low prices. Additional time also gives producers the opportunity to

FIGURE 6.1

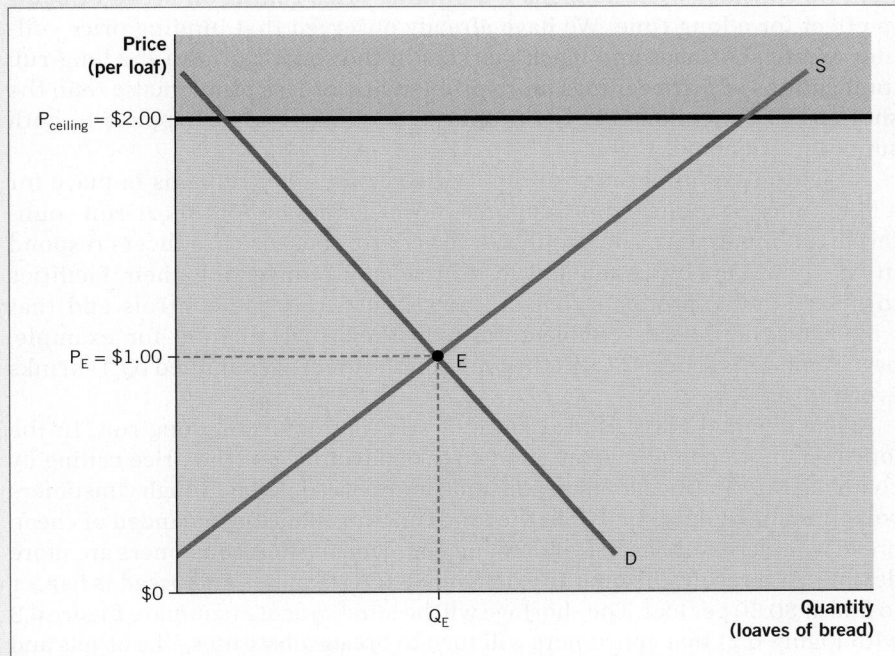

The price ceiling ($2.00) is set
above the equilibrium price
($1.00). Because market prices
are set by the intersection of
supply (S) and demand (D), as
long as the equilibrium price
is below the price ceiling, the
price ceiling is nonbinding and
has no effect.

FIGURE 6.2

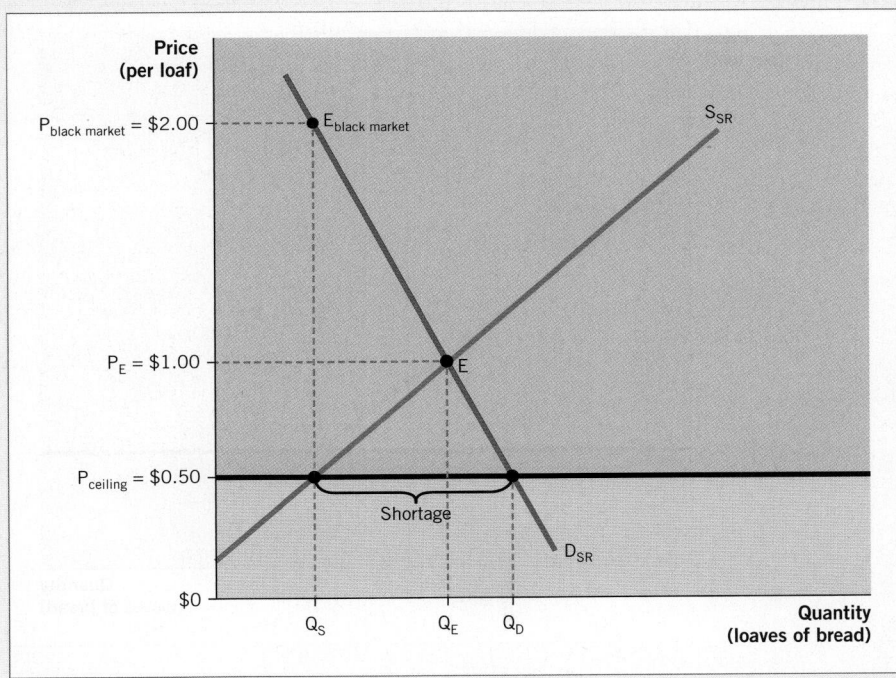

**The Effect of a
Binding Price Ceiling
in the Short Run**

A binding price ceiling
prevents sellers from
increasing the price and
causes them to reduce the
quantity they offer for sale.
As a consequence, prices no
longer signal relative scarcity.
Consumers desire to purchase
the product at the price ceiling
level, which creates a shortage
in the short run (SR); many will
be unable to obtain the good.
As a result, those who are shut
out of the market will turn to
other means to acquire the
good, establishing an illegal
market for the good at the
black-market price.

produce more when prices are high and less when prices are low. In this section, we consider what happens if a binding price ceiling on bread remains in effect for a long time. We have already observed that binding price ceilings create shortages and black markets in the short run. Are the long-run implications of price ceilings more problematic or less problematic than the short-run implications? Let's find out by looking at what happens to both supply and demand.

Figure 6.3 shows the result of a price ceiling that remains in place for a long time. Here the supply curve is more elastic than its short-run counterpart in Figure 6.2. The supply curve is flatter because producers respond in the long run by producing less bread and converting their facilities to make similar products that are not subject to price controls and that will bring them a reasonable return on their investments—for example, bagels and rolls. Therefore, in the long run the quantity supplied (Q_S) shrinks even more.

The demand curve is also more elastic (flatter) in the long run. In the long run, more people will attempt to take advantage of the price ceiling by changing their eating habits to consume more bread. Even though consumers will often find empty shelves in the long run, the quantity demanded of cheap bread will increase. The flatter demand curve means that consumers are more flexible. As a result, the quantity demanded (Q_D) expands and bread is harder to find at $0.50 per loaf. The shortage will become so acute (compare Figure 6.3 with Figure 6.2) that consumers will turn to bread substitutes, like bagels and rolls, that are more plentiful because they are not price controlled.

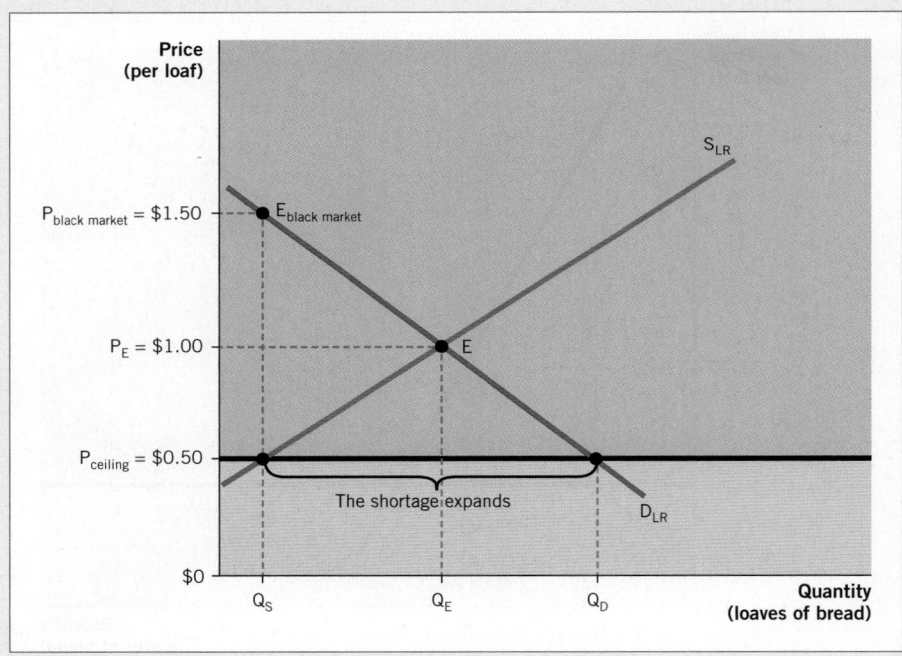

Price Ceilings

SLUMDOG MILLIONAIRE

The setting for the Academy Awards Best Picture of 2008 is Mumbai, India. Eighteen-year-old Jamal Malik is an Indian Muslim who is a contestant on the Indian version of *Who Wants to Be a Millionaire?* Dharavi, where the film is set, is a Mumbai slum about half the size of New York's Central Park. Over 1 million people call Dharavi home. Malik is one question away from the grand prize. However, he is detained by the authorities, who suspect him of cheating because they cannot comprehend how a "slumdog" could know all the answers. The movie beautifully chronicles the events in Jamal's life that provided him with the answers. Jamal, contrary to the stereotype of the people that live in the Dharavi slum, is intelligent, entrepreneurial, and fully capable of navigating life in the 21st century.

Rent controls have existed in Mumbai since 1947. Under the Rents, Hotel and Lodging House Rates Control Act, the government placed a cap on the amount of rent a tenant pays to a landlord. This limit has remained virtually frozen despite the consistent rise in market prices over time. As economists, we know that this policy will create excess demand. Renters are lined up for housing, and therefore, landlords can offer substandard accommodations and still have many takers. When this process continues for generations, as it has in Mumbai, the cumulative effect is that many buildings are unsafe to live in.

Price ceilings set the regulated price below the market equilibrium price determined by supply and demand. As a result, there is an increase in the quantity

The Dharavi slum in Mumbai is the setting for *Slumdog Millionaire*.

demanded. At the same time, since the price that landlords can charge is below the market equilibrium price, many landlords have left the apartment market to sell and invest elsewhere. As a consequence, the supply of rental units is reduced over time, which leads to long wait lists for apartments. Since demand exceeds supply, some landlords also impose additional requirements on potential tenants, leading to discrimination against certain groups of people.

Increased elasticity on the part of producers and consumers magnifies the unintended consequences we observed in the short run. Therefore, products subject to a price ceiling become progressively harder to find in the long run and the black market continues to operate. However, in the long run our bread consumers will choose substitutes for expensive black-market bread, leading to somewhat lower black-market prices in the long run.

Price Ceilings: Ridesharing

Need a Lyft in an emergency? Better hope there's one available!

QUESTION: Surge pricing is the practice of raising prices during periods of increased demand, sometimes for just a few hours at a stretch. Suppose that users of rideshare services, such as Lyft and Uber, persuade Congress to ban surge pricing when emergencies are declared. How will this policy affect the number of people who can use ridesharing in times of crisis?

ANSWER: The price that makes quantity supplied equal to quantity demanded is now illegal, because of the binding price ceiling. As a result, there will be a shortage of drivers willing to supply their service. Because rideshare drivers control when and where they choose to work, many will choose to stay home or work other areas not affected by the emergency. Consumers seeking a ride in the affected areas will turn to taxi cabs, buses and other forms of mass transit, but those services are also likely to be disrupted. In sum, the supply of available transportation options will dwindle. So the answer to the question is that fewer people will be able to get a rideshare, and this problem will be most acute in the worst-hit areas.

What Effects Do Price Ceilings Have on Economic Activity?

We have seen the logical repercussions of a hypothetical price ceiling on bread and the incentives it creates. Now let's use supply and demand analysis to examine two real-world price ceilings: *rent control* and *price gouging laws*.

Rent Control

Rent control
is a price ceiling that applies to the market for apartment rentals.

Under **rent control**, a local government caps the price of apartment rentals to keep housing affordable. While this goal may be laudable, rent control doesn't work. In fact, it doesn't help the poor residents of a city find affordable housing or gain access to housing at all. In addition, these policies contribute to dangerous living conditions.

Mumbai, India, provides a chilling example of what can happen when rent controls are applied over an extended period. In Mumbai, many rent-controlled buildings have become dilapidated. Every monsoon season, several of these buildings fall—often with tragic consequences. Because the rent that property owners are permitted to charge is so low, they have less income to use for maintenance on the buildings. They cannot make a reasonable profit and afford to maintain the buildings properly. As a result, rent control policies have led to the decay of many apartment buildings. Similar controls have caused the same problem in cities worldwide.

To understand how a policy can backfire so greatly, let's look at the history of rent control in New York City. In 1943, in the midst of World War II, the federal government established the Emergency Price Control Act. The act was designed to keep inflation in check during the war, when many essential commodities were scarce. After the war, the federal government ended price controls, but New York City continued rent control. Today, there are approximately 1 million rent-controlled units in New York City. Rent controls limit the price a landlord can charge a tenant for rent. They also require that the landlord provide certain basic services; but not surprisingly, landlords keep maintenance to a minimum.

Does the presence of so many rent-controlled apartments mean that less affluent households can easily find a cheap place to rent? Hardly. When a rent-controlled unit is vacated, the property is generally no longer subject to rent control. Laws allow the tenants of rent-controlled apartments to pass those apartments from generation to generation, which keeps the apartments in the rent control program. Because so many rent-controlled apartments are inherited, rent control no longer even remotely serves its original purpose of helping low-income households. Clearly, the law was never intended to subsidize fancy vacation homes, but that's what it does! This outcome has happened, in part, because some tenants who can afford to live elsewhere choose not to. Their subsidized rent enables them to afford a second or third home in places such as upstate New York, Florida, or Europe.

The attempt to make housing more affordable in New York City has, ironically, made housing harder to obtain. It has encouraged the building of upscale properties rather than low-income units, and it has created a set of behaviors among landlords that is inconsistent with the affordability that rent control was designed to address. Figure 6.4 shows why rent control fails.

Many apartment buildings in Mumbai, India, are dilapidated as a result of rent control laws.

Incentives

FIGURE 6.4

Rent Control in the Short Run and the Long Run

Because rent-controlled apartments are vacated slowly, the quantity supplied decreases in the short run and the supply curve becomes more elastic in the long run, causing the quantity supplied to fall. Demand also becomes more elastic in the long run, causing the quantity demanded to rise. The combination of fewer units available to rent and more consumers looking to find rent-controlled units leads to a larger shortage in the long run.

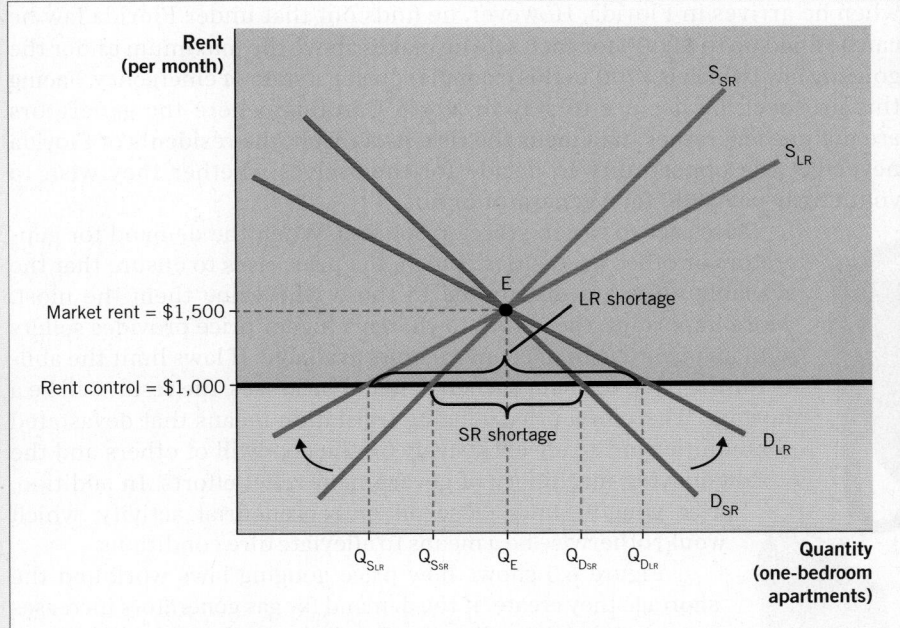

As with any binding price ceiling, rent control causes a shortage because the quantity demanded in the short run ($Q_{D_{SR}}$) is greater than the quantity supplied in the short run ($Q_{S_{SR}}$). The combination of fewer available units and more consumers looking for rent-controlled units leads to a larger shortage in the long run.

Price Gouging

Price gouging laws
place a temporary ceiling on the prices that sellers can charge during times of emergency.

Another kind of price control, **price gouging laws**, places a temporary ceiling on the prices that sellers can charge during times of emergency until markets function normally again. Over 30 U.S. states have laws against price gouging. Like all price controls, price gouging laws have unintended consequences. These consequences became very apparent after Hurricane Irma in 2017.

When Hurricane Irma hit Florida in September, a state of emergency activated the state's price gouging laws. The statute makes it illegal to charge an "excessive" price immediately following a natural disaster. The law is designed to prevent the victims of natural disasters from being exploited in a time of need. As Irma approached Florida, there were hundreds of complaints about suspected price gouging, including one retailer wanting $99.99 for cases of bottled water that normally retailed for $10.00—clear gouging under the statute. Airline prices, however, are not covered by gouging laws because they fluctuate quite a bit even in normal times. Prices on flights out of the affected areas skyrocketed to as much as $2,000 for last-minute bookings, as people tried to escape the storm.

Incentives

So what's better? Try to keep a lid on prices, or let them shoot up? Suppose that an entrepreneur from North Carolina is interested in delivering generators to parts of Florida about to be hit by Hurricane Irma. He can purchase generators for $530 where he lives, and he hopes to sell them for $900 when he arrives in Florida. However, he finds out that under Florida law he can be fined up to $1,000 for each sale he makes above the maximum under the gouging law (which is $700 in this example) during a state of emergency. Facing this prospect, he decides to stay in North Carolina, where the generators are not needed, rather than incur the risk. As a result, the residents of Florida never get the opportunity to decide for themselves whether they wish to voluntarily pay $900 for a generator or not.

Large generator: demand increased after Hurricane Irma hit.

Prices act to ration scarce resources. When the demand for generators or other necessities is high, the price rises to ensure that the available units are distributed to those who value them the most. More important, the ability to charge a higher price provides sellers with an incentive to make more units available. If laws limit the ability for the price to change when demand increases, the result will be a shortage. Therefore, price gouging legislation means that devastated communities must rely exclusively on the goodwill of others and the slow-moving machinery of government relief efforts. In addition, price gouging laws close off entrepreneurial activity, which would otherwise be a means to alleviate dire conditions.

Figure 6.5 shows how price gouging laws work and the shortage they create. If the demand for gas generators increases immediately after a disaster (D_{after}), the market price rises from $530 to $900. But because $900 is considered excessive, sales

FIGURE 6.5

Price Gouging

Price gouging laws serve as a nonbinding price ceiling during normal times. However, when a natural disaster strikes, price gouging laws go into effect. In our example, the demand curve for generators shifts to the right as a result of the natural disaster, causing the new equilibrium price (E_{after}) to rise above the legal limit. The result is a shortage. When the emergency is lifted, the market demand returns to normal, and the temporary shortage created by price gouging legislation is eliminated.

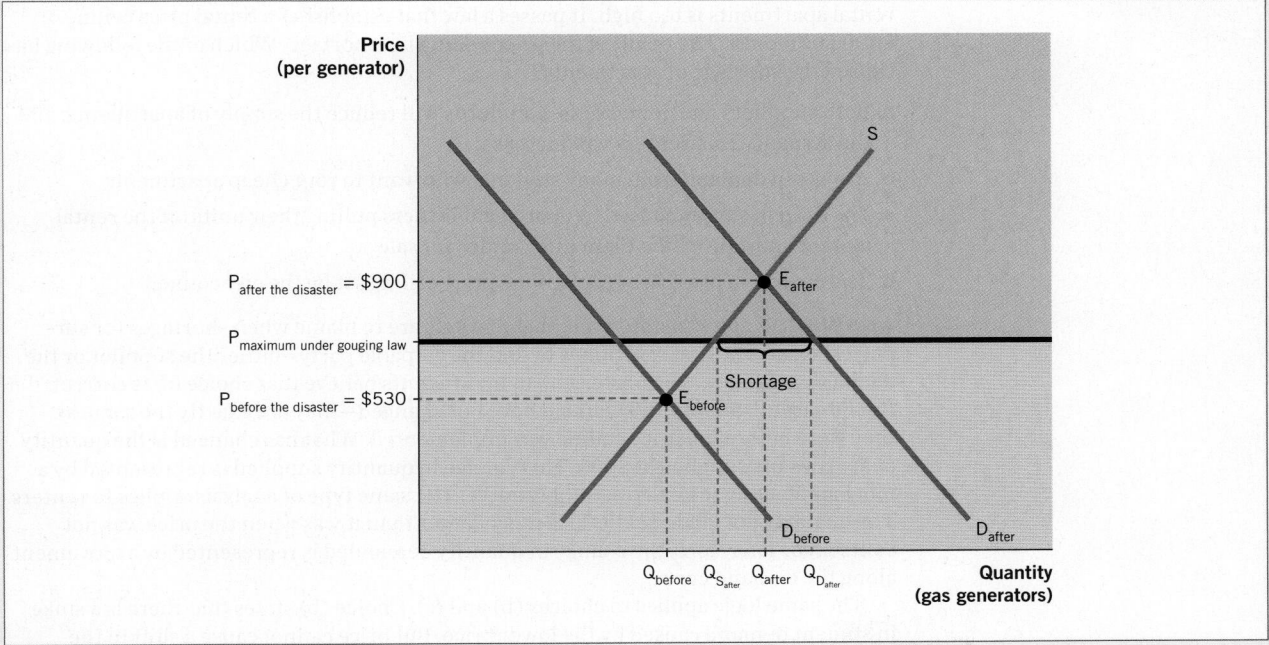

at that price are illegal. The result is a binding price ceiling for as long as a state of emergency is in effect. A binding price ceiling creates a shortage. You can see the shortage in Figure 6.5 in the difference between quantity demanded and quantity supplied at the price ceiling mandated by the law. In this case, the normal ability of supply and demand to ration the available generators is short-circuited. Because more people demand generators after the disaster than before it, those who do not get to the store soon enough are out of luck. When the emergency is lifted and the market returns to normal, the temporary shortage created by price gouging laws is eliminated.

When Do Price Floors Matter?

A **price floor** creates a legally established minimum price for a good or service. The minimum wage law is an example of a price floor in the market for labor. Like price ceilings, price floors create many unintended effects that policymakers rarely acknowledge. However, unlike price ceilings, price floors result

A **price floor** is a legally established minimum price for a good or service.

Price Ceilings: Student Rental Apartments

Here is a question that often confuses students.

QUESTION: Imagine that a city council decides that the market price for student rental apartments is too high. It passes a law that establishes a rental price ceiling of $600 per month. The result of the price ceiling is a shortage. Which of the following has caused the shortage of apartments?

a. Both suppliers and demanders. Landlords will reduce the supply of apartments, and the demand from renters will increase.

b. A spike in demand from many students who want to rent cheap apartments

c. The drop in supply caused by apartment owners pulling their units off the rental market and converting them into condos for sale

d. The change in price as a result of the price ceiling set by the city council

ANSWER: Many students think that markets are to blame when shortages (or surpluses) exist. The first reaction is to find the culpable party—either the supplier or the demander, or both. For this reason, many students believe that choice (a) is correct. But be careful. Supply and demand have not changed—they are exactly the same as they were before the price ceiling was implemented. What has changed is the quantity of apartments supplied at $600. This change in quantity supplied is represented by a movement along the existing supply curve. The same type of analysis applies to renters. The quantity demanded at $600 is much larger than it was when the price was not controlled. Therefore, the change in quantity demanded is represented by a movement along the demand curve.

The same logic applies to choices (b) and (c). Choice (b) states that there is a spike in student demand caused by the lower price. But price cannot cause a shift in the demand curve; it can only cause a movement along a curve. Likewise, choice (c) states that apartment owners supply fewer units for rent. The fact that fewer apartments are available at $600 per month would be represented by a movement along the apartment supply curve.

So we are left with choice (d), which is the correct answer. There is only one change in market conditions: the city council has passed a new price ceiling law. A binding price ceiling disrupts the market's ability to reach equilibrium. Therefore, we can say that the change in the price as a result of the price ceiling has caused the shortage.

from the political pressure of suppliers to keep prices high. Most consumers prefer lower prices when they shop, so the idea of a law that keeps prices high may sound like a bad one to you. However, if you are selling a product or service, you might think that legislation to keep prices high is a very good idea. For instance, many states establish minimum prices for milk. As a result, milk prices are higher than they would be if supply and demand set the price.

In this section, we follow the same progression that we did with price ceilings. We begin with a simple thought experiment. Once we understand how price floors work, we use supply and demand analysis to examine the short- and long-run implications for economic activity.

Understanding Price Floors

To understand how price floors affect the market, let's try a thought experiment. Suppose that a politician suggests we should encourage dairy farmers to produce more milk so that supplies will be plentiful and everyone will get enough calcium. To accomplish these goals, the government sets a price floor of $6 per gallon—about twice the price of a typical gallon of fat-free milk—to make production more attractive to milk producers. What repercussions should we expect?

First, more milk will be available for sale because the higher price will cause dairies to increase the quantity that they supply. At the same time, because consumers must pay more, the quantity demanded will fall. The result will be a surplus of milk. Because every gallon of milk that is produced but not sold hurts the dairies' bottom line, sellers will want to lower their prices enough to get as many sales as possible before the milk goes bad. But the price floor will not allow the market to respond, and sellers will be stuck with milk that goes to waste. They will be tempted to offer illegal discounts in order to recoup some of their costs.

What happens next? Because the surplus cannot be resolved through lower prices, the government will try to help equalize the quantity supplied and the quantity demanded through other means. It can do so in one of two ways: by restricting the supply of the good or by stimulating additional demand. Both solutions are problematic. If production is restricted, dairy farmers will not be able to generate a profitable amount of milk. Likewise, stimulating additional demand is not as simple as it sounds. Let's consider how these government programs work with other crops.

In many cases, the government purchases surplus agricultural production, most notably with corn, soybeans, cotton, and rice. Once the government buys the surplus production, it often sells the surplus below cost to developing countries to avoid wasting the crop. This strategy has the unintended consequence of making it cheaper for consumers in these developing nations to buy excess agricultural output from developed nations like the United States than to have local farmers grow the crop. International treaties ban the practice of dumping surplus production, but it continues under the guise of humanitarian aid. This practice makes little economic sense. Table 6.2 summarizes the result of our price floor thought experiment using milk.

If you're doing a handstand, you need the floor for support. A binding price floor keeps prices from falling.

The Effect of Price Floors

We have seen that price floors create unintended consequences. Now we will use the supply and demand model to analyze how price floors affect the market. We look at the short run first.

Got milk? Maybe not, if there's a price floor.

NONBINDING PRICE FLOORS Like price ceilings, price floors can be binding or nonbinding. Figure 6.6 illustrates a nonbinding price floor of $2 per gallon on milk. As you can see, at $2 the price floor is below the equilibrium price (P_E), so the price floor is nonbinding. Because the actual market price is above the legally established minimum price (P_{floor}), the price floor does not prevent the market from reaching equilibrium at point E. Consequently, the

TABLE 6.2

A Price Floor on Milk

Question	Answer / Explanation		Result
Will the quantity of milk for sale change?	Consumers will purchase less because the price is higher (the law of demand), but producers will manufacture more (the law of supply). The net result will be a surplus of milk.	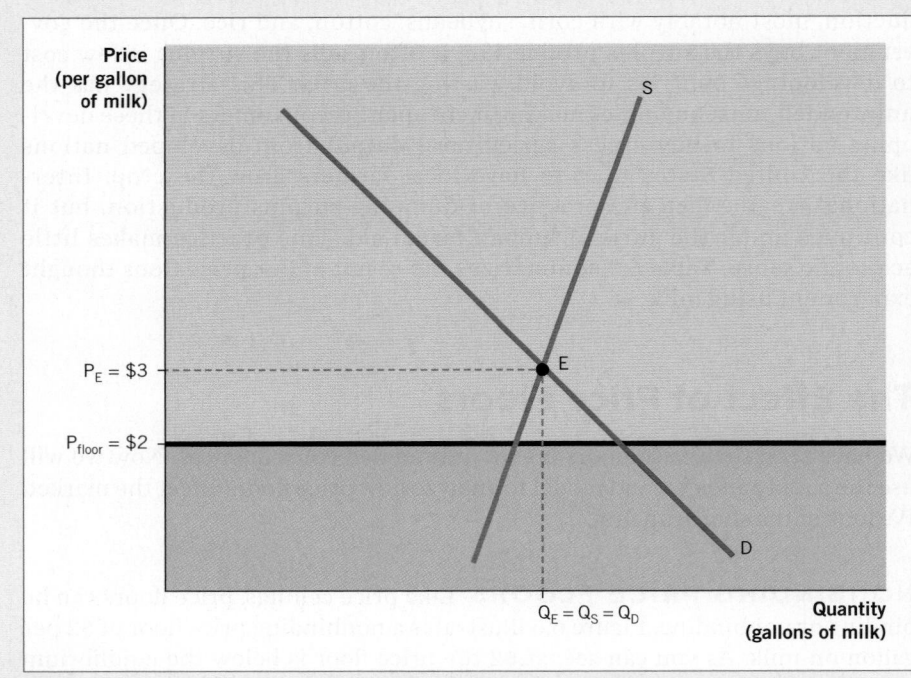	There will be a surplus of milk
Would producers sell below the price floor?	Yes. A surplus of milk would give sellers a strong incentive to undercut the price floor to avoid having to discard leftover milk.	**REDUCED MILK AHEAD**	Illegal discounts will help reduce the milk surplus
Will dairy farmers be better off?	Not if they have trouble selling what they produce.	not for Sale no good.	There might be a lot of spoiled milk

FIGURE 6.6

A Nonbinding Price Floor

Under a nonbinding price floor, price is regulated by supply and demand. Because the price floor ($2) is below the equilibrium price ($3), the market will voluntarily charge more than the legal minimum. Therefore, this nonbinding price floor will have no effect on sales and purchases of milk.

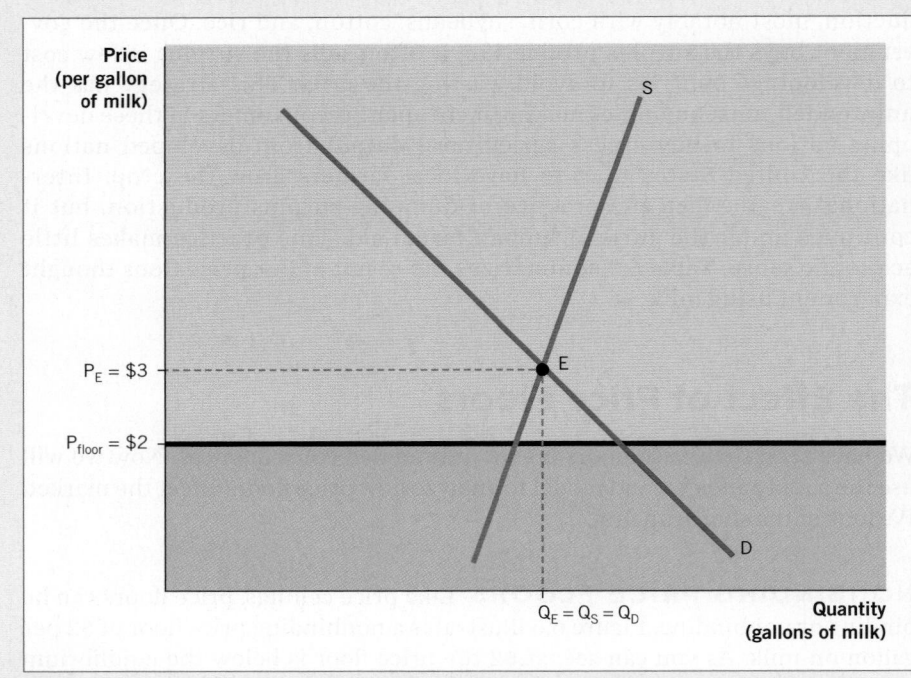

price floor has no impact on the market. As long as the equilibrium price remains above the price floor, price is determined by supply and demand.

BINDING PRICE FLOORS For a price floor to have an impact on the market, it must be set above the market equilibrium price. In that case, it is a binding price floor. With a binding price floor, the quantity supplied will exceed the quantity demanded. Figure 6.7 illustrates a binding price floor in the short run. Continuing our example of milk prices, at $6 per gallon the price floor is above the equilibrium price of $3. Market forces always attempt to restore the equilibrium between supply and demand at point E. So we know that there is downward pressure on the price. At a price floor of $6, we see that $Q_{S_{SR}} > Q_{D_{SR}}$. The difference between the quantity supplied and the quantity demanded is the surplus. Because the market's price adjustment mechanism is not permitted to work, sellers find themselves holding unwanted inventories of milk. To eliminate the surplus, which will spoil unless it is sold, a black market may develop with prices substantially below the legislated price. At a price ($P_{black market}$) of $2, the black market eliminates the surplus that the price floor caused. However, the price floor has created two unintended consequences: a smaller demand for milk ($Q_{D_{SR}} < Q_{E_{SR}}$) and a black market to eliminate the glut.

Full shelves signal a market at equilibrium.

Incentives

FIGURE 6.7

A Binding Price Floor in the Short Run

A binding price floor creates a surplus, which has two unintended consequences: (1) a smaller quantity demanded than the equilibrium quantity ($Q_{D_{SR}} < Q_{E_{SR}}$) and (2) a lower black-market price to eliminate the glut of the product.

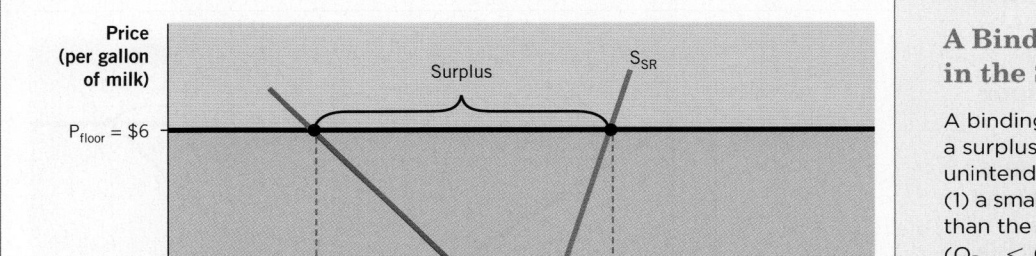

Price Floors in the Long Run

Once price floor legislation is passed, it can be politically difficult to repeal. What happens if a binding price floor on milk stays in effect for a long time? To answer that question, we need to consider elasticity. We have already observed that in the short run, binding price ceilings cause shortages and that black markets follow.

Figure 6.8 shows a price floor for milk that remains in place well past the short run. The long run gives consumers a chance to find milk substitutes—for example, products made from soy, rice, or almond that are not subject to the price floor—at lower prices. This added consumer flexibility makes the long-run demand for milk more elastic. As a result, the demand curve depicted in Figure 6.8 is more elastic than its short-run counterpart in Figure 6.7. The supply curve also becomes flatter (more elastic) because firms (dairy farms) are able to produce more milk by acquiring additional land and production facilities. Therefore, a price floor ($6) that remains in place over time causes the supply and demand curves to become more elastic, magnifying the surplus.

What happens to supply? In the long run, producers are more flexible and therefore supply is more elastic. The pool of potential milk producers rises as other closely related businesses retool their operations to supply more milk. The flatter supply curve in Figure 6.8 reflects this flexibility. As a result, $Q_{S_{LR}}$ expands and becomes much larger than it was in Figure 6.7. The increased elasticity on the part of both producers and consumers makes the surplus larger in the long run and magnifies the unintended consequences we observed in the short run.

FIGURE 6.8

The Effect of a Binding Price Floor in the Long Run

When a price floor is left in place over time, supply and demand both become more elastic. The result is a larger surplus ($Q_{S_{LR}} < Q_{D_{LR}}$) in the long run. Because sellers are unable to sell all that they produce at $6 per gallon, a black market develops to eliminate the glut of milk.

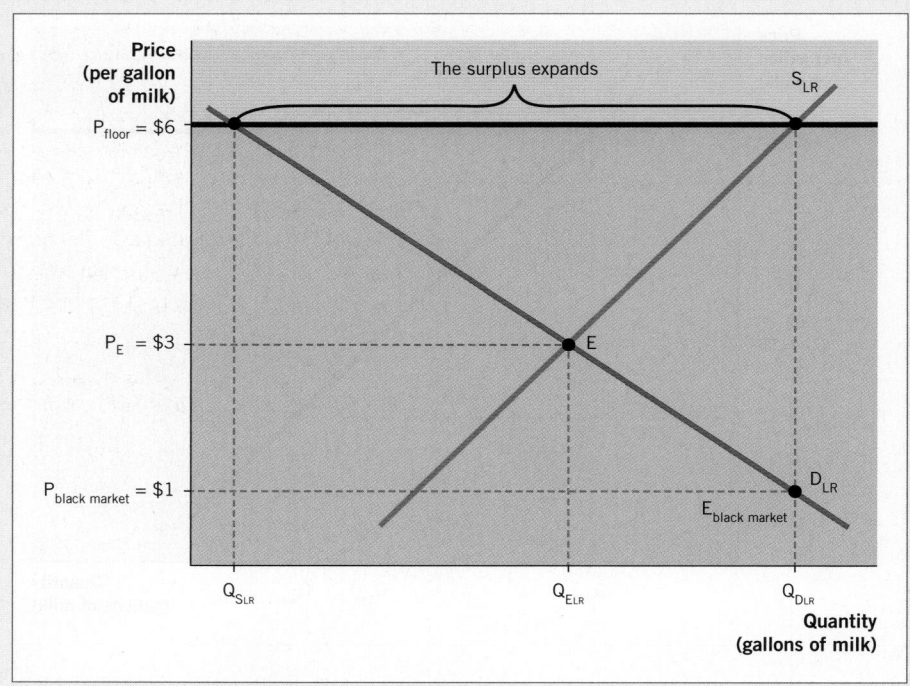

Price Floors: Fair-Trade Coffee

Fair-trade coffee is sold through organizations that purchase directly from growers. The coffee is usually sold for a higher price than standard coffee. The goal is to promote more humane working conditions for the coffee pickers and growers. Fair-trade coffee has become more popular but still accounts for a small portion of all coffee sales, in large part because it is substantially more expensive to produce.

Would fair-trade coffee producers benefit from a price floor?

Opportunity cost

QUESTION: Suppose that the price of a 1-pound bag of standard coffee is $8 and the price of a 1-pound bag of fair-trade coffee is $12. Congress decides to impose a price floor of $10 per pound on all 1-pound bags of coffee. What will most likely happen?

ANSWER: Fair-trade producers typically sell their product at a higher price than mass-produced coffee brands. Therefore, a $10 price floor is binding for inexpensive brands like Folgers but nonbinding for premium coffees, which include fair-trade sellers. The price floor will reduce the price disparity between fair-trade coffee and mass-produced coffee.

To see how the market will respond, consider a fair-trade coffee producer who charges $12 per pound and a mass-produced brand that sells for $8 per pound. A price floor of $10 reduces the difference between the price of fair-trade coffee and the inexpensive coffee brands, which now must sell for $10 instead of $8. The consumer's opportunity cost of choosing fair-trade coffee is now lower. Therefore, some consumers of the inexpensive brands will opt for fair-trade coffee instead. As a result, fair-trade producers will benefit indirectly from the price floor. Thus, the answer to the question is that more people will buy fair-trade coffee as a result of this price floor policy.

CHALLENGE QUESTION: Suppose the price floor is imposed and consumption of fair-trade coffee actually goes down. How might you explain this?

ANSWER: This could happen in a setting where the consumers are low-income, socially conscious coffee addicts. These consumers buy regular coffee when money is tight but fair-trade coffee when they feel they can afford it. When regular coffee gets more expensive, these consumers buy more of it and less of the fair-trade stuff. Since few locales have a large population of socially conscious coffee guzzlers on tight budgets, this scenario would require exceptionally strong consumer preferences.

Unintended Consequences

College Humor created a short YouTube video, "Buy Food Ethically, Unless It is Too Hard," that illustrates the trade-offs people face when they make purchases at a local farmer's market. The people interviewed in the video have the best of intentions: they want to save the environment, eat healthier, and support local growers. But their responses indicate that they don't always buy at the farmer's market despite their stated intentions. One of the primary reasons they don't go there as often as they would like to is the price. Each of the persons interviewed is young and socially conscious, but prices matter to them as well, and that, combined with the inconvenience of going to the farmer's market, means that they rarely go. The video illustrates a very important point: prices matter, whether those prices are naturally set in the market or artificially set through price controls.

Do you buy your produce at the farmer's market?

Trade-offs
Incentives

What Effects Do Price Floors Have on Economic Activity?

We have seen the logical repercussions of a hypothetical price floor on milk and the incentives it creates. Now let's use supply and demand analysis to examine two real-world price floors: *minimum wage laws* and *sugar subsidies*.

The Minimum Wage

The **minimum wage** is the lowest hourly wage rate that firms may legally pay their workers. Minimum wage workers can be skilled or unskilled and experienced or inexperienced. The common thread is that these workers, for a variety of reasons, lack better prospects.

A minimum wage functions as a price floor. Figure 6.9 shows the effect of a binding minimum wage. Note that the wage, or the cost of labor, on the y axis ($10 per hour) is the price that must be paid. However, the market equilibrium wage ($7), or W_E, is below the minimum wage. The minimum wage prevents the market from reaching W_E at E (the equilibrium point) because only the wages

The **minimum wage** is the lowest hourly wage rate that firms may legally pay their workers.

FIGURE 6.9

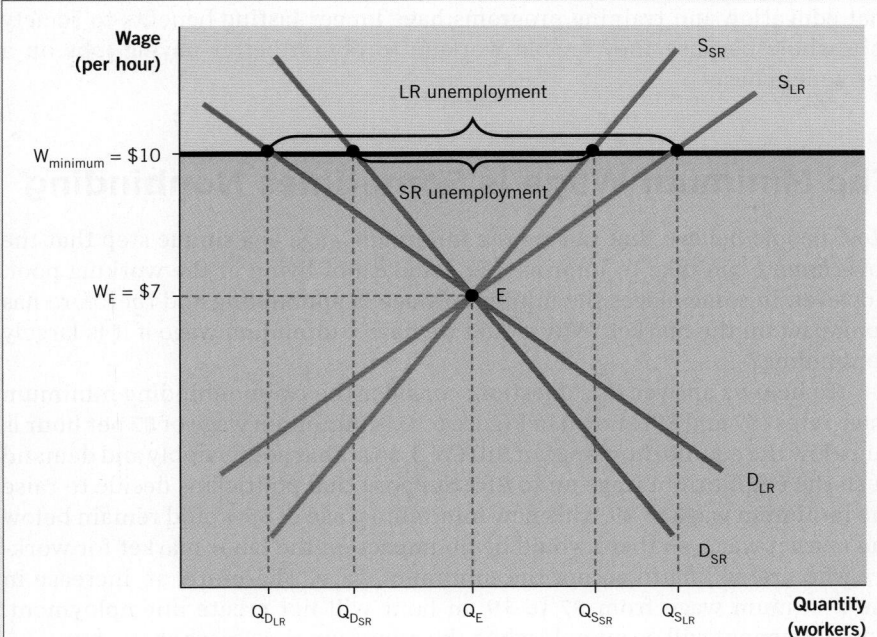

A binding minimum wage is a price floor above the current equilibrium wage, W_E. At $10 per hour, the number of workers willing to supply their labor ($Q_{S_{SR}}$) is greater than the quantity demanded of workers ($Q_{D_{SR}}$). The result is a surplus of workers (which we recognize as unemployment). Because the supply of workers and demand for workers both become more elastic in the long run, unemployment expands $(Q_{S_{LR}} - Q_{D_{LR}}) > (Q_{S_{SR}} - Q_{D_{SR}})$.

in the green area are legal. The minimum wage raises the cost of hiring workers. Therefore, a higher minimum wage will lower the quantity of labor demanded. At the same time, firms will look for ways to substitute capital for workers. As a result, a binding minimum wage results in unemployment in the short run because $Q_{S_{SR}} > Q_{D_{SR}}$.

Businesses generally want to keep costs down, so in the long run they will try to reduce the amount they spend on labor. They might replace workers with machinery, shorten work hours, offer reduced customer service, or even relocate to countries that do not have minimum wage laws. As we move past the short run, more people will attempt to take advantage of higher minimum wages. Like firms, workers will adjust to the higher minimum wage over time. Some workers who might have decided to go to school full-time or remain retired or who simply want some extra income will enter the labor market because the minimum wage is now higher. As a result, minimum wage jobs will become progressively harder to find and unemployment will increase. The irony is that in the long run, the minimum wage, just like any other price floor, has created two unintended consequences: a smaller demand for workers by employers ($Q_{D_{LR}}$ is significantly less than Q_E) and a larger supply of workers ($Q_{S_{LR}}$) looking for jobs.

Proponents of minimum wage legislation are aware that it often creates unemployment. To address this problem, they support investment in training, education, and the creation of government jobs programs to provide more work opportunities. While jobs programs increase the number of minimum wage

Incentives

jobs, training and additional education enable workers to acquire skills needed for jobs that pay more than the minimum wage. Economists generally believe that education and training programs have longer-lasting benefits to society as a whole because they enable workers to obtain better-paying jobs on a permanent basis.

The Minimum Wage Is Sometimes Nonbinding

Most people believe that raising the minimum wage is a simple step that the government can take to improve the standard of living of the working poor. However, in some places the minimum wage is nonbinding and therefore has no impact on the market. Why would we have a minimum wage if it is largely nonbinding?

To help us answer this question, consider the two nonbinding minimum wage rates ($7 and $9) shown in Figure 6.10. A minimum wage of $7 per hour is far below the equilibrium wage of $10 ($W_E$), so at that point supply and demand push the equilibrium wage up to $10. Suppose that politicians decide to raise the minimum wage to $9. This new minimum wage of $9 would remain below the market wage, so there would be no impact on the labor market for workers who are willing to accept the minimum wage. Therefore, an increase in the minimum wage from $7 to $9 an hour will not create unemployment. Unemployment will occur only when the minimum wage rises above $10.

FIGURE 6.10

A Nonbinding Minimum Wage

An increase in the minimum wage from $7 to $9 remains nonbinding. Therefore, it will not change the quantity demanded for labor or the unemployment rate. If the minimum wage rises above the market wage, unemployment will occur.

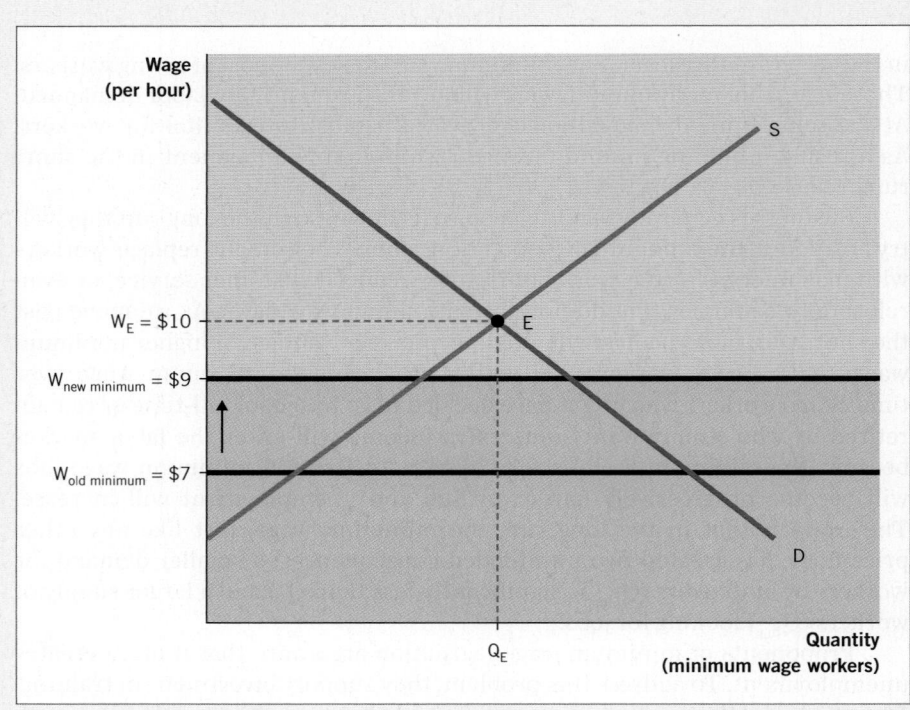

Minimum Wage: Always the Same?

A minimum wage is a price floor, a price control that doesn't allow prices—in this case the cost of labor—to fall below an assigned value. Although the media and politicians often discuss the minimum wage in the United States as if there is only one minimum wage, there are numerous minimum wages in the USA. In states where the state minimum wage is not the same as the federal minimum wage, the higher of the two wage rates takes effect.

■ **Minimum Wage Higher than Federal** ■ **Minimum Wage Equal to Federal** ■ **Minimum Wage Lower than Federal (Federal Rate Applies)** ■ **No Minimum Wage (Federal Rate Applies)**

WASHINGTON

Washington's minimum wage of $13.50/hour is significantly higher than the federal rate and takes precedence over the federal rate in that state.

$13.50

FEDERAL MINIMUM WAGE **$7.25**

Washington, DC

Georgia has a minimum wage of $5.15/hour on the books, but employers must pay their workers the higher federal rate.

GEORGIA **$5.15**

Puerto Rico

HIGHEST MINIMUM WAGES, 2020

District of Columbia	$14.00
Washington	$13.50
California	$13.00
Massachusetts	$12.75

Source: U.S. Department of Labor.

REVIEW QUESTIONS

- Suppose you live in Oklahoma and are looking for a job. The state minimum wage rate is $7.25/hour, the federal minimum wage rate is $7.25/hour, and the market equilibrium wage for the job is $8.00/hour. What wage will you be paid? Are the state and national minimum wages binding or non-binding price floors?

- Suppose Wisconsin increases its minimum wage from $7.25/hour, which is below the market wage for low-skill labor, to $11.00/hour, which is above the market wage. Using supply and demand curves, show how this might increase the number of unemployed workers.

In many locations there is a push to raise the minimum wage to $15 an hour. To consider the effectiveness of such a move, let's look at Seattle, Washington. Researchers who examined the Seattle Minimum Wage Ordinance have found conflicting results. What would explain the differences in their findings? For an answer we turn to a group of economists, including Ekaterina Jardim, who evaluated the wage, employment, and work hours of the first and second phase-in of the ordinance, which raised the minimum wage from $9.47 to $11 per hour in 2015 and to $13 per hour in 2016. For the first increase, from $9.47 to $11 an hour, the team found that the overall effect on low-wage workers' earnings was minimal. However, Jardim and the other researchers found that the second wage increase, to $13, reduced hours worked in low-wage jobs by around 9%, while hourly wages in such jobs increased by around 3%. Consequently, total payroll fell for such jobs, implying that the Minimum Wage Ordinance lowered low-wage employees' earnings by an average of $125 per month in 2016. Somewhere between $11 and $13 per hour, then, the minimum wage became binding.

That's not to say that efforts to raise the minimum wage in other places will have the same impact as Seattle. San Francisco became the first city with a $15 minimum wage in 2018. It is too early to tell whether that wage is binding or nonbinding. Moreover, just because a minimum wage is binding does not mean that low-wage workers can't benefit as a whole. If enough low-wage workers retain their jobs when the minimum wage is increased, the total payroll that workers receive can still increase even though some workers will have lost their jobs.

ECONOMICS IN THE REAL WORLD

WHY IS SUGAR CHEAPER IN CANADA, WHEN CANADA DOESN'T GROW SUGARCANE?

Sugar is one of life's small pleasures. It can be extracted and refined from sugarcane and sugar beets, two crops that can be grown in a variety of climates around the world. Sugar is both plentiful and cheap. As a result, Americans enjoy a lot of it—an average of over 100 pounds of refined sugar per person each year!

We would consume a lot more sugar if it were not subject to price controls. After the War of 1812, struggling sugarcane producers asked the government to pass a tariff (tax) that would protect domestic production. Over the years, price supports of all kinds have served to keep domestic sugar production high. The result is an industry that depends on a high price to survive. Under the current price-support system, the price of U.S.-produced sugar is roughly two to three times the world price. This situation has led to a bizarre set of incentives whereby U.S. farmers grow more sugar than they should and use land that is not well suited to the crop. For instance, sugarcane requires a subtropical climate, but most of the U.S. crop is grown in Louisiana, a region that is prone to hurricanes in the summer. As a result, many sugarcane crops there are completely lost. Have farmers turned to other, more locally suited crops? Not so much! What's happened is that frost-resistant strains have been developed that will grow farther inland, at colder locations.

Why do farmers persist in growing sugarcane in Louisiana? The answer lies in the political process: sugar growers have effectively lobbied to keep prices high

Incentives

through tariffs on foreign imports. Because lower prices would put many U.S. growers out of business and cause the loss of many jobs, politicians have given in to their demands.

Meanwhile, the typical sugar consumer is largely oblivious to the political process that sets the price floor. It has been estimated that the sugar subsidy program costs consumers over $1 billion a year. To make matters worse, thanks to corn subsidies, high-fructose corn syrup has become a cheap alternative to sugar and is often added to processed foods and soft drinks. In 1980, Coca-Cola replaced sugar with high-fructose corn syrup in its U.S. factories to reduce production costs. However, Coca-Cola continues to use sugarcane in many Latin American countries because it is cheaper there. Research shows that high-fructose corn syrup causes a metabolic reaction that makes people who ingest it more inclined to obesity. This is an example of an unintended consequence that few policymakers could have imagined. There is no reason why the United States must produce its own sugarcane. Ironically, sugar is cheaper in Canada than in the United States, primarily because Canada has no sugar growers—and thus no trade restrictions or government support programs. So here's another unintended consequence: Life Savers moved production of their quintessentially American candy treat to Canada, as a result of high U.S. production costs.

Which of these is the *real* thing? The Coke on the right, with high-fructose corn syrup, was made in the United States; the others, with sugar, were made in Mexico.

PRACTICE WHAT YOU KNOW

Price Ceilings and Price Floors: Would a Price Control on Internet Access Be Binding?

A recent study found the following demand and supply schedule for high-speed Internet access:

In today's Internet age, four degrees of separation are all that stand between you and the rest of the world.

Price of Internet	Connections demanded (millions of units)	Connections supplied (millions of units)
$60	10.0	62.5
50	20.0	55.0
40	30.0	47.5
30	40.0	40.0
20	50.0	32.5
10	60.0	25.0

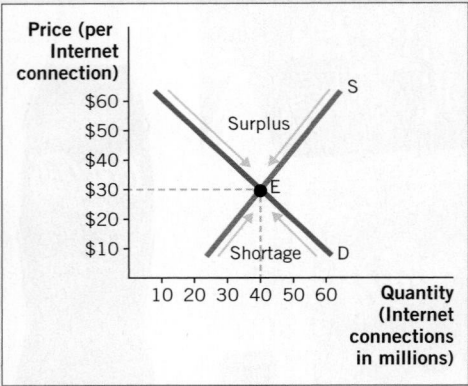

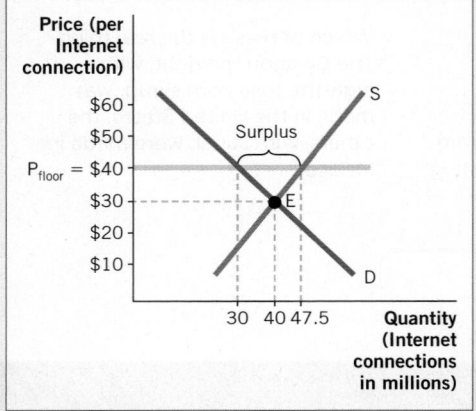

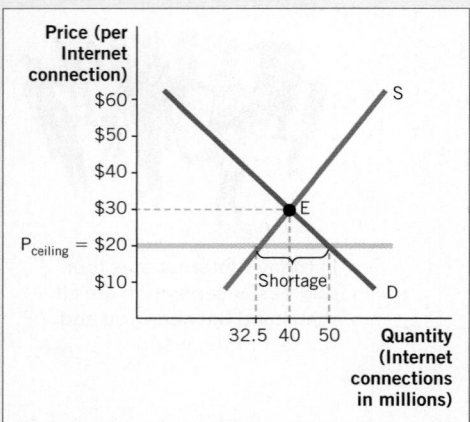

QUESTION: What are the equilibrium price and equilibrium quantity of Internet service?

ANSWER: First, look at the table on the previous page to see where quantity supplied and quantity demanded are equal. At a price of $30, consumers purchase 40 million units and producers supply 40 million units. Therefore, the equilibrium price is $30 and the equilibrium quantity is 40 million. At any price above $30, the quantity supplied exceeds the quantity demanded, so there is a surplus. The surplus gives sellers an incentive to cut the price until it reaches the equilibrium point, E. At any price below $30, the quantity demanded exceeds the quantity supplied, so there is a shortage. The shortage gives sellers an incentive to raise the price until it reaches the equilibrium point, E.

QUESTION: Suppose that providers convince the government that maintaining high-speed access to the Internet is an important element of technology infrastructure. As a result, Congress approves a price floor at $10 above the equilibrium price to help companies provide Internet service. How many people are able to connect to the Internet?

ANSWER: Adding $10 to the market price of $30 gives us a price floor of $40. At $40, consumers demand 30 million connections. Producers provide 47.5 million connections. The result is a surplus of 17.5 million units (shown in the graph). A price floor means that producers cannot cut the price below that point to increase the quantity that consumers demand. As a result, only 30 million units are sold. So only 30 million people connect to the Internet.

QUESTION: When consumers realize that fewer people are purchasing Internet access, they demand that the price floor be repealed and a price ceiling be put in its place. Congress acts immediately to remedy the problem, and a new price ceiling is set at $10 below the market price. Now how many people are able to connect to the Internet?

ANSWER: Subtracting $10 from the market price of $30 gives us a price ceiling of $20. At $20 per connection, consumers demand 50 million connections. However, producers provide only 32.5 million connections. The result is a shortage of 17.5 million units (shown in the graph). A price ceiling means that producers cannot raise the price, which will cause an increase in the quantity supplied. As a result, only 32.5 million units are sold, so only 32.5 million people connect to the Internet.

QUESTION: Which provides the greatest access to the Internet: free markets, price floors, or price ceilings?

ANSWER: With no government intervention, 40 million connections are sold. Once the price floor is established, 30 million people have an Internet connection. Under the price ceiling, 32.5 million people have an Internet connection. Despite legislative efforts to satisfy both producers and consumers of Internet service, the best solution is to allow free markets to allocate the good.

Price Gouging: Disaster Preparedness

- Set aside money in a long-term emergency fund.
- Keep a simple disaster supply kit.
- Safeguard your financial and legal records.

During a disaster, shortages of essential goods and services become widespread. In the more than 30 states where price gouging laws are on the books, merchants are prevented from charging unusually high prices. If you live in one of these states, cash alone can't save you. You will have to survive on your own for a time before help arrives and communication channels are restored.

"(It was) a little bit of a pandemonium," Orlando-area resident Diane Williams said, describing shoppers' efforts to stock up on supplies just before Hurricane Irma struck Florida in 2017. "It's just that everybody is panicked, so they are preparing, which is wise, but it's just, like, crazy."*

Taking measures to prepare for a disaster reduces the likelihood of injury, loss of life, and property damage far more than anything you can do after a disaster strikes. An essential part of disaster planning should include financial planning. Let's begin with the basics. Get adequate insurance to protect your family's health and property; plan for the possibility of job loss or disability by building a cash reserve; and safeguard your financial and legal records. It is also important to set aside extra money in a long-term emergency

Will you be ready if disaster strikes?

fund. Nearly all financial experts advise saving enough money to cover your expenses for six months. Most households never come close to reaching this goal, but don't let that stop you from trying.

Preparing a simple disaster supply kit is also a must. Price gouging laws make it important to stock a bunch of stuff, because you can't rely on just having cash on hand to buy what you need on short notice. Keep enough water, nonperishable food, sanitation supplies, batteries, medications, and cash on hand for three days. Often, the power is out after a disaster, so you cannot count on ATMs or banks to be open. These measures will help you to weather the immediate impact of a disaster.

---

*Source: "Irma Eyes the U.S.: 'Everybody Is Panicked'; Shelves Empty; Gas Pumps Run Dry," Offthegridnews.com, September 7, 2017. https://www.offthegridnews.com/current-events/irma-eyes-the-u-s-everybody-is-panicked-shelves-empty-gas-pumps-run-dry/.

Conclusion

The policies presented in this chapter—rent control, price gouging laws, the minimum wage, and agricultural price controls—create unintended consequences. Attempts to control prices should be viewed cautiously. When the price signal is suppressed through a binding price floor or a binding price ceiling, the market's ability to allocate goods and services is diminished, surpluses and shortages develop and expand through time, and obtaining goods and services becomes difficult.

The role of markets in society has many layers, and we've only just begun our analysis. In the next chapter, we consider two cases—externalities and public goods—in which the unregulated market produces an output that is not socially desirable. ✷

▪ ANSWERING *the* BIG QUESTIONS ▪

When do price ceilings matter?

▪ A price ceiling is a legally imposed maximum price. When the price is set below the equilibrium price, the quantity demanded will exceed the quantity supplied. The result is a shortage. Price ceilings matter when they are binding (below the equilibrium price).

What effects do price ceilings have on economic activity?

▪ Price ceilings create two unintended consequences: a smaller quantity supplied of the good (Q_s) and a higher price for consumers who turn to the black market.

When do price floors matter?

▪ A price floor is a legally imposed minimum price. The minimum wage is an example of a price floor. If the minimum wage is set above the equilibrium wage, a surplus of labor will develop. However, if the minimum wage is nonbinding, it will have no effect on the market wage. Thus, price floors matter when they are set above the equilibrium price.

What effects do price floors have on economic activity?

▪ Price floors lead to many unintended consequences, including surpluses, the creation of black markets, and artificial attempts to bring the market back into balance. For example, proponents of a higher minimum wage are concerned about finding ways to alleviate the resulting surplus of labor, or unemployment.

· CHAPTER PROBLEMS ·

Concepts You Should Know

black markets (p. 191)
minimum wage (p. 206)
price ceiling (p. 190)

price controls (p. 190)
price floor (p. 199)

price gouging laws (p. 198)
rent control (p. 196)

Questions for Review

1. Does a binding price ceiling cause a shortage or a surplus? Provide an example to support your answer.

2. Does a nonbinding price floor cause a shortage or a surplus? Provide an example to support your answer.

3. Will a surplus or a shortage caused by a price control become smaller or larger over time? Explain.

4. Are price gouging laws an example of a price floor or a price ceiling?

5. What will happen to the market price when a price control is nonbinding?

6. Why do most economists oppose attempts to control prices? Why does the government attempt to control prices anyway in a number of markets?

Study Problems *(*solved at the end of this section)*

1. In the song "Minimum Wage," the punk band Fenix TX comments on the inadequacy of the minimum wage for making ends meet. Using the poverty thresholds provided by the Census Bureau,* determine whether the federal minimum wage of $7.25 an hour provides enough income for a single full-time worker to escape poverty.

✱ **2.** Imagine that the community you live in decides to enact a rent control of $700 per month on every one-bedroom apartment. Using the following table, determine the market price and equilibrium quantity without rent control. How many one-bedroom apartments will be rented after the rent control law is passed?

Monthly rent	Quantity demanded	Quantity supplied
$600	700	240
700	550	320
800	400	400
900	250	480
1,000	100	560

*Source: https://www.census.gov/data/tables/2017/demo/supplemental-poverty-measure/poverty-thresholds.html.

3. Suppose that the federal government places a binding price floor on chocolate. To help support the price floor, the government purchases all of the leftover chocolate that consumers do not buy. If the price floor remains in place for a number of years, what do you expect to happen to each of the following?

a. quantity of chocolate demanded by consumers
b. quantity of chocolate supplied by producers
c. quantity of chocolate purchased by the government

4. Suppose that a group of die-hard sports fans are upset about the high price of tickets to many games. As a result of their lobbying efforts, a new law caps the maximum ticket price to any sporting event at $50. Will more people be able to attend the games? Explain your answer. Will certain teams and events be affected more than others? Provide examples.

5. Many local governments use parking meters on crowded downtown streets. However, the parking spaces along the street are typically hard to find because the metered price is often set below the market price. Explain what happens when local governments set the meter price too low. Why do you think the price is set below the market-clearing price?

6. Imagine that local suburban leaders decide to enact a minimum wage. Will the community lose more jobs if the nearby city votes to increase the minimum wage to the same rate? Discuss your answer.

✱ 7. Examine the following graph, showing the market for low-skilled laborers.

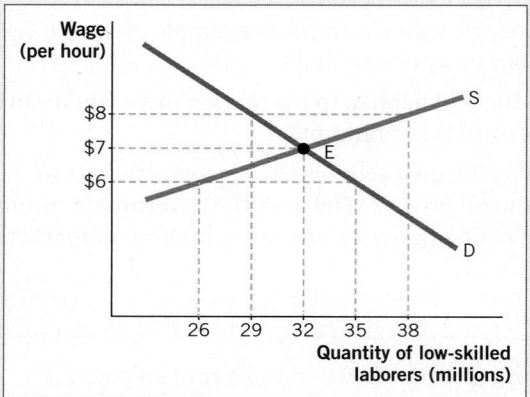

How many low-skilled laborers will be unemployed when the minimum wage is $8 an hour? How many low-skilled workers will be unemployed when the minimum wage is $6 an hour?

8. Demand and supply curves can be represented with equations. Suppose that the demand for low-skilled labor, Q_D, is represented by the following equation, where W is the wage rate:

$$Q_D = 53{,}000{,}000 - 3{,}000{,}000W$$

The supply of low-skilled labor, Q_S, is represented by the equation

$$Q_S = -10{,}000{,}000 + 6{,}000{,}000W$$

a. Find the equilibrium wage. (**Hint:** Set $Q_D = Q_S$ and solve for the wage, W.)

b. Find the equilibrium quantity of labor. (**Hint:** Now plug the value you got in part (a) back into Q_D or Q_S. You can double-check your answer by plugging the answer from part (a) into both Q_D and Q_S to see that you get the same result.)

c. What happens if the minimum wage is $8? (**Hint:** Plug W = 8 into both Q_D and Q_S.) Does this minimum wage cause a surplus or a shortage?

d. What happens if the minimum wage is $6? (**Hint:** Plug W = 6 into both Q_D and Q_S.) Does this minimum wage cause a surplus or a shortage?

9. Most of us would agree that movie theater popcorn is outrageously priced. Why don't price gouging laws result in arrests and prosecutions of theater operators and other firms that charge prices far beyond the actual cost of production?

✱ 10. More than 5,000 people in the United States die each year because they cannot find a suitable kidney donor. Under U.S. law, citizens cannot sell their spare kidney, which effectively means that there is a price ceiling on the sale of kidneys equal to $0. What do you think would happen to the number of deaths caused by kidney failure each year if the law prohibiting the sale of kidneys were repealed?

✱ 11. Scotland has introduced price floors on alcohol as a public health measure. Higher alcohol prices will lower sales, which would seem to hurt producers. If you were a producer in Scotland, would you necessarily be against this proposal?

12. Suppose the equilibrium rent for one-bedroom apartments in your neighborhood is $1,000 per month. If the government imposes a rent ceiling of $750 per month, what will happen to the number of one-bedroom apartments rented out each month?

a. It will increase, since more people will want to rent apartments when they are cheaper.

b. It will decrease, since fewer landlords will want to rent out their apartments when they can't charge as much.

c. It will not change, since the rent control is set below the equilibrium rent.

d. None of the above

✱ 13. Suppose the government imposes a minimum wage that is above the equilibrium wage. Will workers be better off or worse off?

Solved Problems

2. The equilibrium price occurs where the quantity demanded is equal to the quantity supplied. This equilibrium occurs when $Q_D = Q_S = 400$. When the quantity is 400, the monthly rent is $800. Next, the question asks how many one-bedroom apartments will be rented after a rent control law limits the rent to $700 a month. When the rent is $700, the quantity supplied is 320 apartments. It is also worth noting that the quantity demanded when the rent is $700 is 550 units, so there is a shortage of $550 - 320 = 230$ apartments once the rent control law goes into effect.

7. The first question asks how many low-skilled laborers will be unemployed when the minimum wage is $8 an hour. The quantity demanded is 29 million, and the quantity supplied is 38 million. The result is 38 million $-$ 29 million $=$ 9 million unemployed low-skilled workers.

The next question asks how many low-skilled workers will be unemployed when the minimum wage is $6 an hour. Because $6 an hour is below the market equilibrium wage of $7, it has no effect. In other words, a $6 minimum wage is nonbinding, and therefore no unemployment is caused.

10. Despite the repugnant nature of organ sales, there is no doubt that a price exists that would alleviate the kidney shortage and save lives. Under the current system, market prices are unable to identify people who would sell their spare kidney and match those sellers with the people who would be willing to buy a kidney. In the absence of a legal market, black markets have arisen to bring buyers and sellers together. The black-market price for a kidney ($250,000) is far higher than the market equilibrium price ($20,000) that economists estimate would exist if organ sales were legal.

11. If demand for alcohol is relatively inelastic, a price floor could increase revenues for most suppliers.

13. This is an empirical question. Low-wage workers may be better off, if enough of them keep their jobs and subsequently earn a higher wage, compared to the number of workers who lose their jobs and become unemployed.

Market Inefficiencies: Externalities and Public Goods

Should We Eliminate All Pollution?

We would all agree that it's important to protect the environment. So when we face pollution and other environmental degradation, should we eliminate it? If your first thought is "yes, always," you're not alone. After all, there's only one Earth, and we'd better get tough on environmental destruction wherever we find it, whatever it takes. Right?

It's tempting to think this way, but the prescription comes up short as a useful social policy. No one wants to go back to the way it was when businesses were free to dump their waste anywhere they chose, but it is also impractical to eliminate all pollution. Some amount of environmental damage is inevitable whenever we extract resources, manufacture goods, fertilize croplands, or power our electrical grid—all activities that are integral to modern society. But how do we figure out what the "right" level of pollution is, and how do we get there? The answer is to examine the tension between social costs and benefits and to ensure that participants in markets are fully accounting for both.

In the preceding chapters, we saw that markets provide many benefits and that they work because participants pursue their own self-interests. But sometimes markets need a

This outflow looks like lava flow from Mount Kilauea in Hawaii, but it's from a nickel refinery in Canada—what a catastrophe! No doubt we'd like to make it go away. But are we willing to do without the jobs the factory provides? What if we could keep the factory open and have just a *little* outflow? The scary red color is mostly iron oxides, a.k.a. rust. Are we willing to shut down any factory that puts even a little bit of rust into the groundwater? For an economist, deciding what to do about pollution isn't as easy as it may at first seem.

helping hand. For example, some market exchanges harm innocent bystanders, and some trades are not efficient because the
ownership of property is not clearly defined or actively enforced.
To help explain why markets do not always operate efficiently,
this chapter explores two important concepts: externalities and
the differences between private and public goods.

· BIG QUESTIONS ·

- What are externalities, and how do they affect markets?
- What are private goods and public goods?
- What are the challenges of providing nonexcludable goods?

What Are Externalities, and How Do They Affect Markets?

We have seen that buyers and sellers benefit from trade. But what about the
effects trade might have on bystanders? **Externalities**, or the costs and benefits of a market activity that affect a third party, often lead to undesirable
consequences. **Market failure** occurs when there is an inefficient allocation
of resources in a market. Externalities are a type of market failure. For example, in 2010, an offshore oil rig in the Gulf of Mexico operated by British Petroleum (BP) exploded, causing millions of barrels of oil to spill into the water and
resulting in over $40 billion in damage. Even though both BP and its customers
benefit from the production of oil, others along the Gulf Coast had their lives
severely disrupted. Industries dependent on high environmental quality, like
tourism and fishing, were hit particularly hard by the costs of the spill.

For a market to work as efficiently as possible, two things must happen. First, each participant must be able to evaluate the **internal costs** of
participation—the costs that only the individual participant pays. For example, when we choose to drive somewhere, we typically consider our internal
(also known as personal) costs—the time it takes to reach our destination, the
amount we pay for gasoline, and what we pay for routine vehicle maintenance.
Second, for a market to work efficiently, the external costs must also be paid.
External costs are the costs of a market activity imposed on people who
are not participants in that market. In the case of driving, the congestion and
pollution our cars create are external costs. Economists define **social costs** as
the sum of the internal costs and external costs of a market activity.

Externalities
are the costs or benefits of a
market activity that affect a
third party.

Market failure
occurs when there is an inefficient allocation of resources in
a market.

Internal costs
are the costs of a market
activity paid only by an
individual participant.

External costs
are the costs of a market activity imposed on people who are
not participants in that market.

Social costs
are the sum of the internal
costs and external costs of a
market activity.

In this section, we consider some of the mechanisms that encourage consumers and producers to account for the social costs of their actions.

The Third-Party Problem

An externality exists whenever an internal cost (or benefit) diverges from a social cost (or benefit). For example, manufacturers who make vehicles and consumers who purchase them benefit from the transaction, but making and using those vehicles lead to externalities—including air pollution and traffic congestion—that adversely affect others. A **third-party problem** occurs when those not directly involved in a market activity experience negative or positive externalities.

If a third party is adversely affected, the externality is negative. For example, a negative externality occurs when the number of vehicles on the roads causes air pollution. Negative externalities present a challenge to society because it is difficult to make consumers and producers take responsibility for the full costs of their actions. For example, drivers typically consider only the internal costs (their own costs) of reaching their destination. Likewise, manufacturers generally prefer to ignore the pollution they create, because addressing the problem would raise their costs without providing them with significant direct benefits.

In general, society would benefit if all consumers and producers considered both the internal and external costs of their actions. Because this expectation is not reasonable, governments design policies that create incentives for firms and people to limit the amount of pollution they emit.

An effort by the city government of Washington, D.C., shows the potential power of this approach. Like many communities throughout the United States, the city instituted a 5-cent tax on every plastic bag a consumer picks up at a store. While 5 cents may not sound like much of a disincentive, shoppers have responded by switching to cloth bags or reusing plastic ones. In Washington, D.C., the number of plastic bags used every month fell from 22.5 million in 2009 to 3 million in 2018, significantly reducing the amount of plastic waste entering landfills in the process.

Not all externalities are negative, however. Positive externalities also exist. For instance, education creates a large positive externality for society beyond the benefits to individual students, teachers, and support staff. A more knowledgeable workforce benefits employers looking for qualified employees and is more efficient and productive than an uneducated workforce. And because local businesses experience a positive externality from a well-educated local community, they have a stake in the educational process.

A good example of the synergy between local business and higher education is California's Silicon Valley, which is home to many high-tech companies and Stanford University. As early as the late nineteenth century, Stanford's leaders felt that the university's mission should include fostering the development of self-sufficient local

A **third-party problem** occurs when those not directly involved in a market activity experience negative or positive externalities.

Incentives

Many of the most successful businesses associated with Stanford have made large donations to the university.

When oil refineries are permitted to pollute the environment without any limitations, they are likely to overproduce.

The **social optimum** is the price and quantity combination that would exist if there were no externalities.

industry. After World War II, Stanford encouraged faculty and graduates to start their own companies, which led to the creation of Hewlett-Packard, Bell Labs, and Xerox. A generation later, this nexus of high-tech firms gave birth to leading software and Internet firms like 3Com, Adobe, Facebook, and Snapchat, and—more indirectly—Cisco, Apple, and Alphabet.

Recognizing the benefits they received, many of the most successful businesses associated with Stanford have donated large sums to the university. For instance, the Hewlett Foundation gave $400 million to Stanford's endowment for the humanities and sciences and for undergraduate education—an act of generosity that highlights the positive externality Stanford University had on Hewlett-Packard.

CORRECTING FOR NEGATIVE EXTERNALITIES In this section, we explore ways to correct for negative externalities. To do so, we use supply and demand analysis to understand how the externalities affect the market. Let's begin with supply and compare the difference between what market forces produce and what is best for society in the case of an oil refinery. A refinery converts crude oil to gasoline. This complex process generates many negative externalities, including the release of pollutants into the air and the dumping of waste by-products.

Figure 7.1 illustrates the contrast between the market equilibrium and the social optimum in the case of an oil refinery. The **social optimum** is the price

FIGURE 7.1

Negative Externalities and Social Optimum

When a firm is required to internalize the external costs of production, the supply curve shifts to the left, pollution is reduced, and output falls to the socially optimal level, Q_s. The deadweight loss that occurs from overproduction is eliminated.

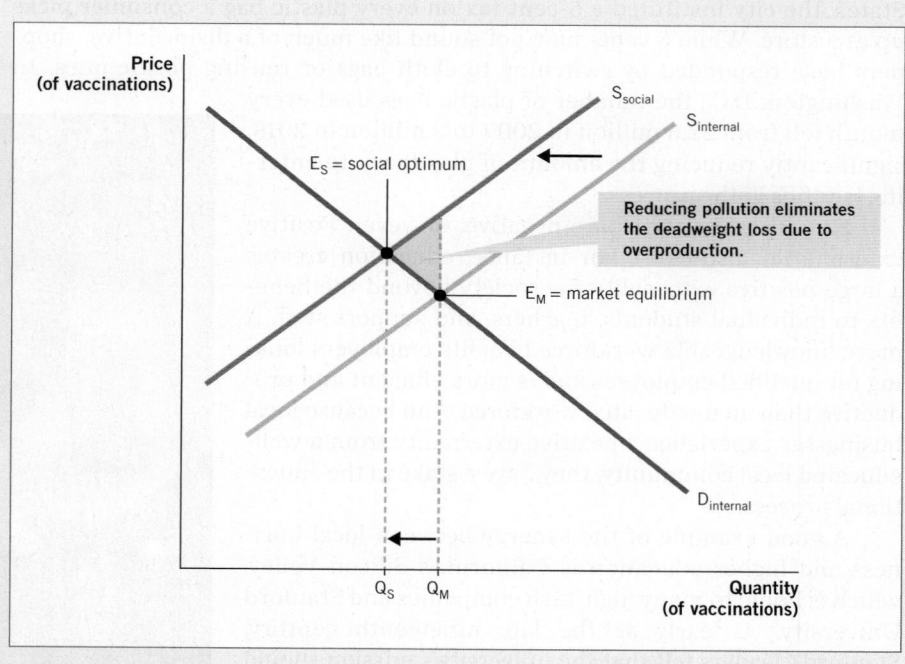

and quantity combination that would exist if there were no externalities. The supply curve $S_{internal}$ represents how much the oil refinery will produce if it does not have to pay for the negative consequences of its activity. In this situation, the market equilibrium, E_M, accounts only for the internal costs of production.

When a negative externality occurs, the government may be able to restore the social optimum by requiring externality-causing market participants to pay for the cost of their actions. In this case, there are three potential solutions. First, the refinery can be required to install pollution abatement equipment or change production techniques to reduce emissions and waste by-products. Second, the government can levy a tax on the refinery as a disincentive to produce. Finally, the government can require the firm to pay for any environmental damage it causes. Each solution forces the firm to **internalize** the externality, meaning that the firm must take into account the external costs (or benefits) to society that occur as a result of its actions.

Having to pay the costs of imposing pollution on others reduces the amount of the pollution-causing activity. This result is evident in the shift of the supply curve to S_{social}. The new supply curve reflects a combination of the internal and external costs of producing the good. Because each corrective measure requires the refinery to spend money to correct the externality and therefore increases overall costs, the willingness to sell the good declines, or shifts to the left. The result is a social optimum at a lower quantity, Q_S, than at the market equilibrium quantity demanded, Q_M. The trade-off is clear. We can reduce negative externalities by requiring producers to internalize the externality. However, doing so does not come without cost. Because the supply curve shifts to the left, the quantity produced is lower and the price rises. In the real world, there is always a cost.

In addition, when an externality occurs, the market equilibrium creates deadweight loss, as shown by the yellow triangle in Figure 7.1. In Chapter 5, we considered deadweight loss in the context of government regulation or taxation. These measures, when imposed on efficient markets, create deadweight loss, or an undesirable amount of economic activity. In the case of a negative externality, the market is not efficient because it is not fully capturing the cost of production. Once the government intervenes and requires the firm to internalize the external costs of its production, output falls to the socially optimal level, Q_S, and the deadweight loss from overproduction is eliminated.

Table 7.1 outlines the basic decision-making process that guides private and social decisions. Private decision-makers consider only their internal costs, but society as a whole experiences both internal and external costs. To align the incentives of private decision-makers with the interests of society, we must find mechanisms that encourage the internalization of externalities.

Incentives

Firms **internalize** an externality when they take into account the external costs (or benefits) to society that occur as a result of their actions.

Trade-offs

TABLE 7.1

Private and Social Decision-Making

Personal decision	Social optimum	The problem	The solution
Based on internal costs	Social costs = internal costs plus external costs	To get consumers and producers to take responsibility for the externalities they create	Encourage consumers and producers to *internalize* externalities

EXPRESS LANES USE DYNAMIC PRICING TO EASE CONGESTION

Metro Washington, D.C., is notorious for traffic, especially on the Capital Beltway (Interstate 495). New express lanes keep traffic moving by using dynamic pricing, which adjusts tolls based on real-time traffic conditions. Dynamic pricing helps manage the quantity demanded and keeps motorists moving at highway speeds. I-495 express-lane tolls can range from as low as $0.20 per mile during less busy times to approximately $1.25 per mile in some sections during rush hour. The higher rush-hour rates are designed to ensure that the express lanes do not become congested. Motorists thus have a choice: pay more to use the express lanes and arrive faster, or use the regular lanes and arrive later. The decision about whether to use the express lanes is all about opportunity cost. High-opportunity-cost motorists regularly drive the express lanes, while others with lower opportunity costs avoid the express lanes.

Because dynamic prices become part of a motorist's internal costs, they cause motorists to weigh the costs and benefits of driving into congested areas. In addition, the dynamic pricing of express lanes causes motorists to make marginal adjustments in terms of the time when they drive. High-demand times, such as the morning and evening rush, see higher tolls for using the express lanes and also longer waits in the regular lanes. Faced with either sitting in traffic (if they don't pay the toll) or being charged more to enter the express lanes at peak-demand times, many motorists attempt to use the Beltway at off-peak times. Since drivers internalize the external costs as a result of the dynamic toll prices even more precisely, the traffic flow spreads out over the course of the day so the existing road capacity is used more efficiently.

How much would you pay to avoid sitting in traffic?

Opportunity cost

Marginal thinking

CORRECTING FOR POSITIVE EXTERNALITIES Positive externalities, such as vaccines, are the result of economic activities that have benefits for third parties. As with negative externalities, economists use supply and demand analysis to compare the efficiency of the market with the social optimum. This time, we focus on the demand curve. Consider a person who gets a flu shot. When the vaccine is administered, the recipient is immunized, which creates an internal benefit. But there is also an external benefit. Because the recipient likely will not come down with the flu, fewer other people will catch the flu and become contagious, which helps to protect even those who do not get flu shots. Therefore, we can say that vaccines provide a positive externality to the rest of society.

Why do positive externalities exist in the market? Using our example of flu shots, there is an incentive for people in high-risk groups to get vaccinated for the sake of their own health. In Figure 7.2, we capture this internal benefit in the demand curve labeled $D_{internal}$. However, the market equilibrium, E_M, only accounts for the internal benefits of individuals deciding whether to get vaccinated. To maximize the health benefits for everyone, public health officials need to find a way to encourage people to consider the external benefit of their vaccination, too. For instance, making flu shots mandatory for hospital staff and other healthcare workers produces positive benefits for all members of society, by internalizing the externality, and helps nudge the market toward the socially optimal number of vaccinations.

Despite the benefits, however, vaccination rates in the United States have been steadily falling for years. The lower vaccination rate led to an outbreak of measles at Disneyland in California in late 2014, where it was believed a foreign visitor introduced the disease and unvaccinated children were exposed to it. The outbreak eventually spread to six U.S. states, Mexico, and Canada—demonstrating just how quickly measles can spread when the vaccination rate is not 100%. This disease continues to be a problem, worldwide, with major outbreaks in 2018 in places like Algeria, Greece, and Indonesia.

Vaccines offer both internal and external benefits.

Government can also promote the social optimum by encouraging economic activity that helps third parties. For example, it can offer a subsidy, or price break, to encourage more people to get vaccinated. The subsidy lowers the price to individuals but increases the demand for vaccines, which raises the overall market price.

Governments routinely provide free or reduced-cost vaccines to those most at risk from flu and to their caregivers. Because the subsidy enables

FIGURE 7.2

Positive Externalities and Social Optimum

The subsidy encourages consumers to internalize the externality. As a result, consumption moves from the market equilibrium (Q_M) to a social optimum at a higher quantity (Q_S), vaccinations increase, and the deadweight loss from insufficient market demand is eliminated.

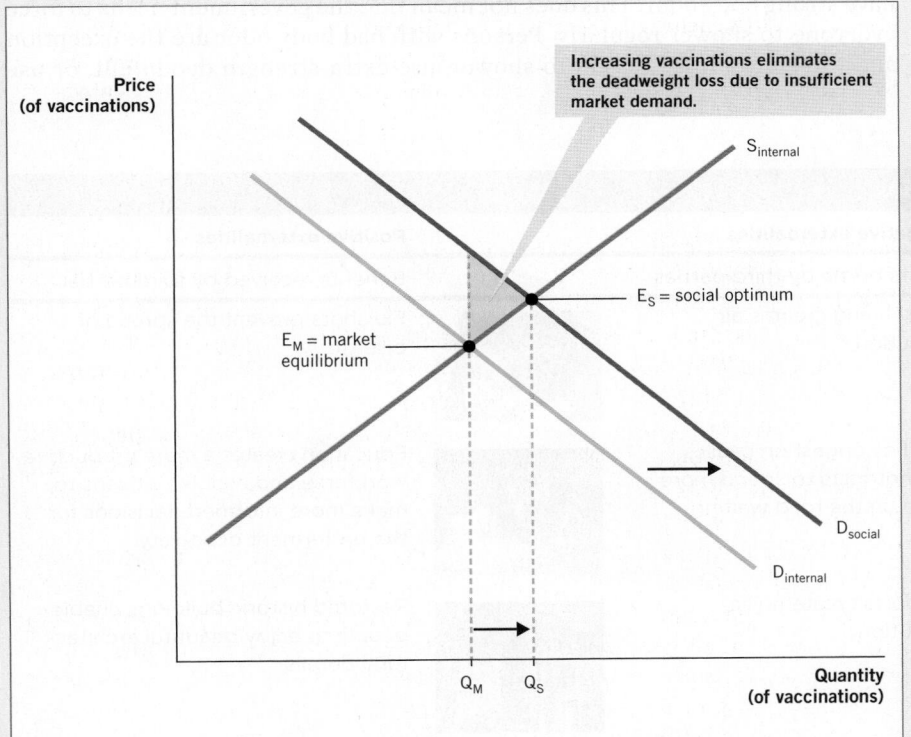

Increasing vaccinations eliminates the deadweight loss due to insufficient market demand.

Price (of vaccinations)

$S_{internal}$

E_S = social optimum

E_M = market equilibrium

D_{social}

$D_{internal}$

Q_M Q_S

Quantity (of vaccinations)

Incentives

consumers to spend less money, their willingness to get the vaccine increases, shifting the demand curve in Figure 7.2 from $D_{internal}$ to D_{social}. The social demand curve reflects the sum of the internal and external benefits of getting the vaccination. In other words, the subsidy encourages consumers to internalize the externality. As a result, the output moves from the market equilibrium quantity demanded, Q_M, to a social optimum at a higher quantity, Q_S.

Markets do not handle externalities well. With a negative externality, the market produces too much of a good. But in the case of a positive externality, the market produces too little. In both cases, the market equilibrium creates deadweight loss. When positive externalities are present, the private market is not efficient because it is not fully capturing the social benefits. In other words, the market equilibrium does not maximize the gains for society as a whole. When positive externalities are internalized, the demand curve shifts outward and output rises to the socially optimal level, Q_S. The deadweight loss that results from insufficient market demand, and therefore underproduction, is eliminated.

Table 7.2 summarizes the key characteristics of positive and negative externalities and presents additional examples of each type.

Before moving on, it is worth noting that not all externalities warrant corrective measures. There are times when the size of the externality is negligible and does not justify the cost of increased regulations, charges, taxes, or subsidies that might achieve the social optimum. Because corrective measures have costs, the presence of negligible externalities does not by itself imply that the government should intervene in the market. For instance, some people have strong body odor. This does not mean that the government needs to force everyone to shower regularly. Persons with bad body odor are the exception and they have every reason to shower, use extra-strength deodorant, or use

TABLE 7.2

A Summary of Externalities

	Negative externalities	Positive externalities
Definition	Costs borne by third parties	Benefits received by third parties
Examples	Oil refining creates air pollution.	Flu shots prevent the spread of disease.
	Traffic congestion causes all motorists to spend more time on the road waiting.	Education creates a more productive workforce and enables citizens to make more informed decisions for the betterment of society.
	Airports create noise pollution.	Restored historic buildings enable people to enjoy beautiful architectural details.
Corrective measures	Taxes or charges	Subsidies or government provision

Externalities: Fracking

In 2003, energy companies began using a process known as hydraulic fracturing, or fracking, to extract underground reserves of natural gas in certain states, including Pennsylvania, Texas, West Virginia, and Wyoming. Fracking involves injecting water, chemicals, and sand into rock formations more than a mile deep. The process releases the natural gas that is trapped in those rocks, allowing it to escape up the well. The gas comes to the surface along with much of the water and chemical mixture, which now must be disposed of. Unfortunately, the chemicals in the mix make the water toxic. Consequently, as fracking has expanded to more areas, controversy has grown about the potential environmental effects of the process.

What the frack?

QUESTION: What negative externalities might fracking generate?

ANSWER: People who live near wells worry about the pollutants in the water mixture and their potential to leach into drinking-water supplies. Additionally, the drilling of a well is a noisy process. Drilling occurs 24 hours a day for a period of a few weeks. This noise pollution affects anyone who lives close by. Another issue is that the natural gas has to be trucked away from the well. Additional truck traffic can potentially damage local roads and cause even more pollution.

QUESTION: What positive externalities might fracking generate?

ANSWER: Fracking has brought tremendous economic growth to the areas where it is occurring. The resulting jobs have employed many people, providing them with a good income. Local hotels and restaurants have seen an increase in business as temporary employees move from one area to another. As permanent employees take over the operation of a well, housing prices climb as a result of increasing demand, which benefits local homeowners.

cologne to mask the smell on their own. If they choose not to avail themselves of these options, they'll be ostracized in many social situations. Because the magnitude of the negative externality is small and government regulations to completely eliminate the externality would be quite onerous, it is best to leave well enough alone.

What Are Private Goods and Public Goods?

The presence of externalities reflects a divide between the way markets operate and the social optimum. What creates this divide? The answer is often related to property rights. **Property rights** give the owner the ability to exercise control over a resource. When property rights are not clearly defined, resources

Property rights
give the owner the ability to exercise control over a resource.

Incentives

can be mistreated. For instance, because no one owns the air, manufacturing firms often emit pollutants into it.

To understand why firms sometimes overlook their actions' effects on others, we need to examine the role of property rights in market efficiency. When property rights are poorly established or not enforced effectively, the wrong incentives come into play. The difference is apparent when we compare situations in which people do have property rights. Private owners have an incentive to keep their property in good repair because they bear the costs of fixing what they own when it breaks or no longer works properly. For instance, if you own a personal computer, you will probably protect your investment by treating it with care and dealing with any problems immediately. However, if you access a public computer terminal in a campus lab or library and find that it is not working properly, you will most likely ignore the problem and simply look for another computer that is working. The difference between solving the problem and ignoring it is crucial to understanding why property rights matter.

Private Property

Private property
provides an exclusive right of ownership that allows for the use, and especially the exchange, of property.

One way to minimize externalities is to establish well-defined private property rights. **Private property** provides an exclusive right of ownership that allows for the use, and especially the exchange, of property. This right creates incentives to maintain, protect, and conserve property and to trade with others. Let's consider these four incentives in the context of automobile ownership.

1. *The incentive to maintain property.* Car owners have an incentive to maintain their vehicles. Routine maintenance, replacement of worn parts, and repairs keep the vehicle safe and reliable. In addition, a well-maintained car can be sold for more than one in poor condition.

Incentives

2. *The incentive to protect property.* Owners have an incentive to protect their vehicles from theft or damage. They protect their property by using alarm systems, locking the doors, and parking in well-lit areas.

3. *The incentive to conserve property.* Car owners also have an incentive to extend the usable life of their automobiles by limiting the number of miles they put on their cars each year.

Opportunity cost

4. *The incentive to trade with others.* Car owners have an incentive to trade with others because they may profit from the transaction. Suppose someone offers to buy your car for $5,000 and you think it is worth only $3,000. Because you own the car, you can do whatever you want with it. If you decline to sell, you will incur an opportunity cost: you will be giving up $5,000 to keep something you value at $3,000. There is no law requiring you to sell your vehicle, so you *could* keep the car—but you probably won't. Why? Because private property gives you as the owner an incentive to trade for something better in the market.

The incentives to maintain, protect, and conserve property help to ensure that owners keep their private property in good shape. The fourth incentive, to trade with others, helps to ensure that private property is held by the person with the greatest willingness to pay for it.

THE COASE THEOREM In 1960, Nobel-prize winning economist Ronald Coase argued that establishing private property rights can close the gap between internal costs and social costs.

Consider an example involving two adjacent landowners, one who raises cattle and another who grows wheat. Because neither landowner has built a fence, the cattle wander onto the neighboring land to eat the wheat. Coase concluded that in this situation, both parties are responsible for the dilemma. He arrived at that conclusion by considering two possible scenarios.

The first scenario supposes that the wheat farmer has the legal right to expect cattle-free fields. In this scenario, the cattle rancher is liable for the damage caused to the wheat farmer. If the damage is costly and the rancher is liable, the rancher will build a fence to keep the cattle in rather than pay for the damage they cause. The fence internalizes the negative externality and forces the rancher to bear the full cost of the damage. If the cost of the damage to the crop is much smaller than the cost of building a fence, then the rancher is more likely to compensate the wheat farmer for his losses rather than build the fence.

What if the wheat farmer does not have the legal right to expect cattle-free fields? In this scenario, the cattle rancher is not liable for any damages his cattle cause to the wheat farmer. If the damage to the nearby wheat field is large and the rancher is *not* liable, the wheat farmer will build a fence to keep the cattle out. The fence internalizes the negative externality and forces the wheat farmer to bear the full cost of the damage. If the amount of damage is smaller than the cost of a fence, the farmer may accept occasional damage as the lower-cost option.

From comparing these two scenarios, Coase determined that whenever the externality is large enough to justify the expense, the externality gets internalized. As long as the property rights are fully specified (and there are no barriers to negotiations), either the cattle rancher or the wheat farmer will build a fence. The fence will keep the cattle away from the wheat, remove the externality, and prevent the destruction of property.

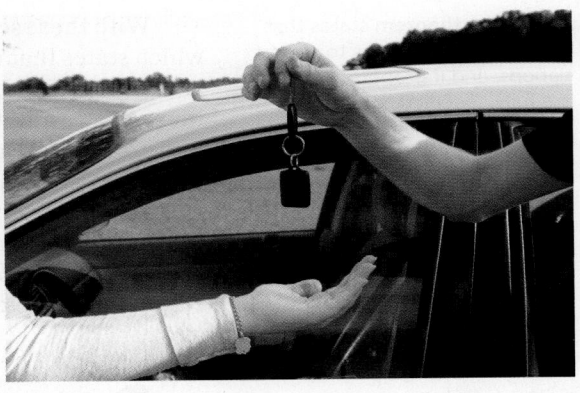

Selling a car, an exchange of private property, benefits both the owner and the buyer.

The cattle are near the wheat to the same extent . . .

. . . that the wheat is near the cattle.

With these scenarios in mind, we can now appreciate the **Coase theorem**, which states that if there are no barriers to negotiations, and if property rights are fully specified, interested parties will bargain privately to correct externalities. As a result, the assignment of property rights under the law gives each party an incentive to internalize any externalities. If it is difficult to bargain (because the costs of reaching an agreement are too high), private parties will be unable to internalize the externality between themselves. Therefore, the Coase theorem also suggests that private solutions to externality problems are not always possible, implying a role for government in solving complex externality issues.

To think about the case for a government role, consider the difference between the example of a rancher and a farmer with adjacent land and the example of a community-wide problem such as pollution. With two landowners, a private solution should be possible because the parties can bargain with each other at a low cost. With pollution, though, so many individuals are affected that the polluting company cannot afford to bargain with each one. Because bargaining costs are high in the case of pollution, an intermediary, like the government, may be necessary to ensure that externalities are internalized.

A fence internalizes the externality.

Private and Public Goods

When we think of private goods, most of us imagine something that we enjoy, like a slice of pizza or a favorite jacket. When we think of public goods, we think of goods provided by the government, like roads, the post office, and the military. The terms "private" and "public" typically imply ownership or production, but that is not the criterion economists use to categorize private and public goods. To understand the difference between private and public goods, you need to know whether a good is excludable, rival in consumption, or both. An **excludable good** is one for which access can be limited to paying customers. A **rival good** is one that cannot be enjoyed by more than one person at a time.

PRIVATE GOODS A **private good** is both excludable and rival in consumption. For instance, a slice of pizza is excludable because you must purchase it before you can eat it. Also, a slice of pizza is rival; only one person can eat it. These two characteristics, excludability and rivalry, allow the market to work efficiently in the absence of externalities. Consider a pizza business. The pizzeria bakes pizza pies because it knows it can sell them to consumers. Likewise, consumers are willing to buy pizza because it is a food they enjoy. Because the producer gets to charge a price and the consumer gets to acquire a rival good, the stage is set for mutual gains from trade.

Trade creates value

PUBLIC GOODS Markets have no difficulty producing purely private goods, like pizza, because in order to enjoy them you must first purchase them. But when was the last time you paid to see a fireworks display? Hundreds of thousands of people view many of the nation's best fireworks displays, but only a small percentage of them pay admission to get a preferred seat. Fireworks displays are a **public good** because (1) they are consumed by more than one person and (2) it is difficult to exclude nonpayers. Because consumers cannot be easily forced to pay to observe fireworks, they may desire more of the good than is typically supplied. As a result, a market economy underproduces fireworks displays and many other public goods.

Public goods are consumed by more than one person, and nonpayers are difficult to exclude.

Public goods are often underproduced because people can get them without paying for them. This means that public goods, like externalities, also result in market failure. Consider Joshua Bell, one of the most famous violinists in the world. The day after giving a concert in Boston for which patrons paid $100 a ticket, he decided to reprise the performance in a Washington, D.C., subway station and just ask for donations.* Any passerby could listen to the music—it did not need to be purchased to be enjoyed. In other words, it was nonexcludable and nonrival in consumption. But because it is impossible for a street musician to force bystanders to pay, it is difficult for the musician—even one as good as Joshua Bell—to make a living. Suppose he draws a large crowd and the music creates $500 worth of enjoyment among the audience. At the end of the performance, he receives a loud round of applause and then motions to the donation basket. A number of people come up and donate, but when he counts up the contributions, he finds only $30—the actual amount he earned while playing in the Metro.

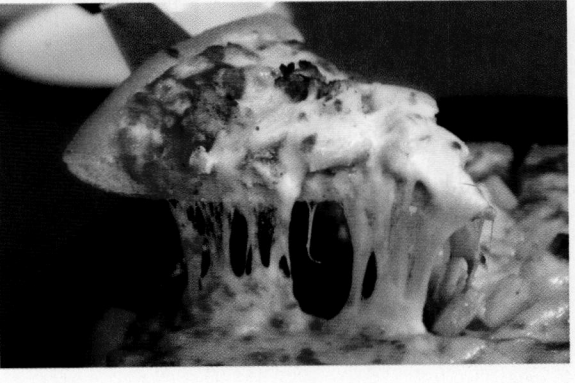

Pizza is a private good.

Why did Joshua Bell receive $30 when he created many times that amount in value? This phenomenon, known as a **free-rider problem**, occurs whenever people receive a benefit they do not pay for. A street musician provides a public good and must rely on the generosity of the audience to contribute. If very few people contribute, many potential musicians will not find it worthwhile to perform. We tend to see very few street performances because free-riding lowers the returns to performing, and the private equilibrium amount of street performances is undersupplied in comparison to the social optimum. When payment cannot be linked to production or consumption, the efficient quantity is not produced.

A **free-rider problem** occurs whenever someone receives a benefit without having to pay for it.

Street performances are just one example of a public good. National defense, lighthouses, streetlights, clean air, and open-source software such as Mozilla Firefox are other examples. Let's examine national defense because it is a particularly clear example of a public good that is subject to a free-rider problem. All citizens value security, but consider the difficulty of trying to organize and provide adequate national defense through private contributions alone. How could you get enough people to voluntarily coordinate a missile defense system or pay for an aircraft carrier and the personnel to operate it? Society would be underprotected because many people would not

*This really happened! The *Washington Post* and Bell conducted an experiment to test the public's reaction to performances of "genius" in unexpected settings. Our discussion here places the event in a hypothetical context. For the real-life result, see Gene Weingarten, "Pearls before Breakfast," *Washington Post,* April 8, 2007.

Concerned about security? Only the government is capable of providing adequate national defense.

voluntarily contribute their fair share of the expense. For this reason, defense expenditures are normally provided by the government and funded by tax revenues. Because most people pay taxes, the free-rider problem is almost eliminated in the context of national defense.

Most people agree that government should provide certain public goods for society, including national defense, the interstate highway system, and medical and science-related research to fight pandemics. In each case, public-sector provision helps to eliminate the free-rider problem and create the socially optimal level of activity.

ECONOMICS IN THE REAL WORLD

GROUP WORK

Perhaps you've taken a class where group work is required. These assignments are valuable opportunities to develop a skill businesses are looking for in potential employees: the ability to work as a team to accomplish a task. However, group work in class or in the workplace creates an environment for the free-rider problem. In many groups, one of the members doesn't put in the time or effort to complete the project. This person realizes he or she will get the benefit of the group grade without incurring the full cost. You may think that this behavior is lazy or inconsiderate, and it is, but it is nonetheless quite rational. The question for the free-rider is whether his or her actions will marginally affect the group's grade. Does the cost of completing part of the project justify what is likely to be only a small change in the grade earned by every member in the group? If the work raises the group's grade from a B− to a B, the free-rider may find that it is too costly to participate. To avoid the free-rider problem, teachers often ask the group to grade each group member's contribution to the group's overall output, and this determines the part of the project grade attributed to individual effort. The hope is that this system will give free-riders the incentive to pull their own weight.

Incentives

CLUB GOODS AND COMMON-RESOURCE GOODS There are two additional types of goods we have not yet introduced. Because club goods and common-resource goods have characteristics of both private and public goods, the line between private provision and public provision is often blurred.

A **club good** is nonrival in consumption and excludable. Satellite television is an example. It is excludable because you must pay to receive the signal, but it is nonrival in consumption because more than one customer can receive the signal at the same time. Because customers who wish to enjoy club goods can be excluded, markets typically provide these goods. However, once a satellite television network is in place, the cost of adding customers is low. Firms are motivated to maximize profits, not the number of people they serve, so the market price is higher and the output is lower than what society desires.

A **common-resource good** is rival in consumption but nonexcludable. King crab in the Bering Sea off Alaska is an example. Because any particular crab can be caught by only one boat crew, the crabs are a rival resource. At the same time, exclusion is not possible because any boat crew that wants to brave the elements can catch crab.

We have seen that the market generally works well for private goods. In the case of public goods, the market generally needs a hand. In between, club and common-resource goods illustrate the tension between the private and public provision of many goods and services. Table 7.3 summarizes the four types of goods we have discussed.

4-20
© 2006 Bil Keane, Inc.
Dist. by King Features Synd.
www.familycircus.com

"How much would it cost to see a sunset if God decided to charge for it?"

A **club good** has two characteristics: it is nonrival in consumption and excludable.

A **common-resource good** has two characteristics: it is rival in consumption and nonexcludable.

Satellite television is a club good.

Alaskan king crab is a common-resource good.

TABLE 7.3

The Four Types of Goods

		Consumption	
		Rival	**Nonrival**
Excludable?	**Yes**	*Private goods* are rival and excludable: pizza, watches, automobiles.	*Club goods* are nonrival and excludable: satellite television, education, country clubs.
	No	*Common-resource goods* are rival and nonexcludable: Alaskan king crab, a large shared popcorn at the movies, congested roads.	*Public goods* are nonrival and nonexcludable: street performers, national defense, tsunami warning systems.

PRACTICE WHAT YOU KNOW

Are Parks Public Goods?

Many goods have the characteristics of a public good, but few goods meet the exact definition.

QUESTION: Are parks public goods?

ANSWER: We tend to think of public parks as meeting the necessary requirements to be a public good. But not so fast. Have you been to any of America's top national parks on a peak summer weekend? Parks are subject to congestion, which makes them rival. In addition, most national and state parks require an admission fee—translation: they are excludable. Therefore, public parks do not meet the exact definition of a public good.

Not surprisingly, there are many good examples of private parks that maintain, protect, and conserve the environment alongside their public counterparts. For instance, Meteor Crater is a privately owned and operated park in Arizona that showcases an extremely well-preserved meteor strike. The United States is dotted with private parks that predate the establishment of the national park system. Like their public counterparts, private parks are also not public goods.

CHALLENGE QUESTION: Suppose you have pitched your tent at a campsite with a lovely view, when another party comes along and prepares to pitch their tent where it will block your view. They explain that the ground is conveniently level and soft in the spot they chose. What could be done about this, assuming that people have a right to pitch their tent wherever they want? What would the solution be if instead whoever arrived first had a right, by park rules, to an unobstructed view?

ANSWER: To answer this question we recall the Coase Theorem. In the first case you could offer them money to shift to an acceptable if less comfortable part of their campsite. In the second case they could offer you money as compensation for your loss of view so they can pitch their tent where they want.

Meteor Crater in Arizona.

What Are the Challenges of Providing Nonexcludable Goods?

Understanding the four types of goods provides a solid foundation for understanding the role of markets and the government in society. Next, we consider some of the special challenges that arise in providing nonexcludable goods.

Cost-Benefit Analysis

To help make decisions about providing public goods, economists turn to **cost-benefit analysis**, a process used to determine whether the benefits of providing a public good outweigh the costs. Costs are easier to quantify than benefits. For instance, if a community puts on a Fourth of July celebration, it will have to pay for the fireworks and labor involved in setting up the event. The costs are a known quantity. But benefits are difficult to quantify. Because people do not need to pay to see the fireworks, it is hard to determine how much benefit the community receives. If asked, people might misrepresent the social benefit in two ways. First, some residents who value the celebration highly might claim that the fireworks bring more benefit than they actually do, because they want the community fireworks to continue. Second, those residents who dislike the crowds and noise might understate the benefit of the fireworks, because they want the fireworks to cease. Since there is no way to know how truthful people are when responding to a questionnaire, the actual social benefit of a fireworks show is hard to measure.

Because people do not pay to enjoy public goods, and because the government provides them without charging a direct fee, determining the socially optimal amount typically takes place through the political system. Generally speaking, elected officials do not get reelected if the populace believes they have not done a good job with their cost-benefit analyses.

Cost-benefit analysis is a process that economists use to determine whether the benefits of providing a public good outweigh the costs.

Figuring out the social benefit of a fireworks display is quite difficult.

INTERNET PIRACY

The digitization of media, along with the speed with which it can be transferred across the Internet, has made the protection of *intellectual property rights* (that is, the protection of patents, copyrights, and trademarks) very difficult to enforce. Many countries either do not have strict copyright standards or fail to enforce them. The result is a black market filled with bootlegged copies of movies, music, and other media.

Because digital "file sharing" is so common these days, you might not fully understand the harm that occurs. Piracy is an illegal form of free-riding. Every song and every movie that is transferred takes away royalties that would have gone to the original artist or the studio. After all, producing content is expensive, and violations of copyright law prevent businesses from making a fair return on their investments. However, consumers of content don't often see it this way. Some believe that breaking the copyright encryption is fair game because they "own" the object in question or bought it legally or got it from a friend. The reality is different. One reason copyright law exists is to limit free-riding. When copyrights are fully specified and enforced across international boundaries, content creators receive compensation for their efforts. But if copyrights are routinely violated, revenues to private businesses will decline and the amount of music and movies produced will decrease. In the long run, artists will produce less and society will suffer. (For other benefits of copyright law, see Chapter 10.)

Think about the relationship between artists and the public as reciprocal: each side needs the other. In that sense, the music you buy or the movie you watch is not a true public good, but more of a club good. Copyright laws make the good excludable but nonrival. For this reason, some people will always have an incentive to violate copyright law, artists and studios will insist on ever more complicated encryption methods to protect their interests, and for the betterment of society as a whole, the government will have to enforce copyright law to prevent widespread free-riding.

Incentives

Common Resources and the Tragedy of the Commons

The tragedy of the commons occurs when a common-resource good becomes depleted.

Common resources often give rise to the **tragedy of the commons**, a situation that occurs when a common-resource good becomes depleted. The term "tragedy of the commons" refers to a phenomenon ecologist Garrett Hardin wrote about in the magazine *Science* in 1968. Hardin described the hypothetical use of a common pasture shared by local herders in a pastoral community. Herders know that intensively grazed land will be depleted and that this depletion is very likely to happen to common land. Knowing that the pasture will be depleted creates a strong incentive for individual herders to bring their animals to the pasture as much as possible while it is still green, because every other herder will be doing the same thing. Each herder has the same incentive to overgraze, which quickly makes the pasture unusable. The overgrazing is a negative externality brought about by poorly designed incentives and the absence of clearly defined private property rights.

Incentives

Even though the concept of common ownership sounds ideal, it can be a recipe for resource depletion and economic disaster. Common ownership, unlike private ownership, leads to overuse. With a system of private property rights, an owner can seek damages in the court system if his property is damaged or destroyed. But the same cannot be said for common property, because joint ownership allows any party to use the resource as he or she sees fit. This situation creates incentives to use the resource now rather than later and to neglect it. In short, common property leads to abuse and depletion of the resource.

Consider global warming. Scientific evidence clearly links increasing amounts of CO_2 (carbon dioxide) in the atmosphere and global warming. This negative externality is caused by some but borne jointly by everyone. Because large CO_2 emitters consider only the internal costs of their actions and ignore the social costs, the amount of CO_2 released, and the corresponding increase in global warming, is larger than optimal. The air, a common resource, is being "overused" and degraded.

Private property rights give owners an incentive to maintain, protect, and conserve their property and to transfer it if someone else values it more than they do. How are those incentives different under a system of common ownership? Let's examine a real-world example of the tragedy of the commons: the collapse of cod populations off Newfoundland, Canada, in the 1990s. Over the course of three years, cod hauls fell from over 200,000 tons annually to close to zero. Why did the fishing community allow this to happen? The answer: incentives. Let's consider the incentives associated with common property in the context of the cod industry.

Incentives

1. *The incentive to neglect.* No one owns the ocean. As a result, fishing grounds in international waters cannot be protected. Even fishing grounds within territorial waters are problematic because fish do not adhere to political borders. Moreover, the fishing grounds in the North Atlantic cannot be maintained in the same way one can, say, check the oil in an automobile. The grounds are too large, and the cod population depends on variations in seawater temperature, salinity, and availability of algae and smaller fish to eat. The idea that individuals or communities could "maintain" a population of cod in this wild environment is highly impractical.

2. *The incentive to overuse.* Each fishing boat crew would like to maintain a sustainable population of cod to ensure future harvests. However, conservation on the part of one boat is irrelevant because other boats would catch whatever the first boat leaves behind. Because cod are a rival and finite resource, boats have an incentive to harvest as much as they can before another vessel does. With common resources, no one has the authority to define how much of a resource can be used. Maintaining economic activity at a socially optimal level would require the coordination of thousands of vested interests, each of which could gain by free-riding. For instance, if a socially responsible boat crew (or country) limits its catch in order to protect the species from depletion, this action does not guarantee that rivals will follow suit. Instead, rivals who disregard the socially optimal behavior stand to benefit by overfishing what remains.

Because cod are a common resource, the incentives we discussed under a system of private ownership do not apply. With common property, resources are neglected and overused.

Common resources, such as cod, encourage overuse (in this case, overfishing).

Possible Solutions to the Tragedy of the Commons

Preventing the tragedy of the commons requires planning and coordination. Unfortunately, in our cod example, officials were slow to recognize that there was a problem with Atlantic cod until it was too late to prevent the collapse. Ironically, just as they placed a moratorium on catching northern cod, the collapse of the fish population became an unprecedented disaster for all of Atlantic Canada's fisheries. Cod populations dropped to 1% of their former sizes. The collapse of cod and many other species led to the loss of 40,000 jobs and over $300 million in income annually. Because communities in the affected region relied almost exclusively on fishing, this outcome crippled their economies.

The lesson of the northern cod is a powerful reminder that efforts to avoid the tragedy of the commons must begin before a problem develops. For example, king crab populations off the coast of Alaska have fared much better than cod, thanks to proactive management. To prevent the collapse of the king crab population, the state and federal governments enforce several regulations. First, the length of the fishing season is limited so that populations have time to recover. Second, there are limitations on how much fishing boats can catch. Third, to promote sustainable populations, only adult males are harvested. It is illegal to harvest females and young crabs, because these are necessary for repopulation. Government regulations like these help avoid a tragedy of the commons.

Trade-offs

Nobel-winning economist Elinor Ostrom examined how some commons are sustainably managed without government, despite the tragedy of the commons and free-rider problems. She understood many of the problems we face today. "[N]o one communicates, everyone acts independently, no attention is paid to the effects of one's actions, and the costs of trying to change the structure of the situation are high."* Her advice was for individuals to communicate often with one another, in order to develop shared norms from which intuitional arrangements would naturally arise to address common-resource dilemmas.

Can the misuse of a common resource be foreseen and prevented? If predictions of rapid global warming are correct, our analysis points to a number of solutions to minimize the tragedy of the commons. Businesses and individuals can be discouraged from producing emissions through carbon pricing, which charges firms by the ton for the CO_2 they put into the atmosphere. This policy encourages parties to internalize the negative externality, because carbon pricing acts as an internal cost that must be considered before creating carbon pollution.

Cap and trade
is an approach used to curb pollution by creating a system of emissions permits that are traded in an open market.

Another solution, known as **cap and trade**, is an approach to emissions reduction that has received much attention lately. The idea behind cap and trade policy is to encourage carbon producers to internalize the externality by establishing markets for tradable emissions permits. As a result, a profit motive is created for some firms to purchase, and others to sell, emissions permits. Under cap and trade, the government sets a *cap*, or limit, on the amount

*Source: Elinor Ostrom. *Governing the Commons: The Evolution of Institutions for Collective Action* (New York: Cambridge University Press, 1990).

of CO_2 that can be emitted. Businesses and individuals are then issued permits to emit a certain amount of carbon each year. Also, permit owners may *trade* permits. In other words, companies that produce fewer carbon emissions can sell the permits they do not use. By establishing property rights that control emissions permits, cap and trade causes firms to internalize externalities and to seek out methods that lower emissions. Global warming is an incredibly complex process, but cap and trade policy is one tangible step that minimizes free-riding, creates incentives for action, and promotes a socially efficient outcome.

Cap and trade is a good idea, but there are issues that must be overcome to make it work effectively. For example, cap and trade presumes that nations can agree on and enforce emissions limits, but international agreements have proved difficult to negotiate. Without binding international agreements, nations that adopt cap and trade policies will experience higher production costs, while nations that ignore them—and free-ride in the process—will benefit.

What is the best way to curb global warming?

Trade creates value

ECONOMICS IN THE REAL WORLD

THE GREAT PACIFIC GARBAGE PATCH

The Great Pacific Garbage Patch is an immense swirl of floating debris in the central North Pacific Ocean. It was first discovered in 1988 and is roughly twice the size of Texas! One would think that an environmental calamity of that scale would prompt significant intervention. That has not happened, because no one person or country "owns" the open Pacific. When trash makes its way out to sea from the shorelines of the Philippines, Vietnam, China, Japan, South and North Korea, Russia, Canada, the United States, and Mexico, it all eventually ends up in the Garbage Patch.

The Great Pacific Garbage Patch is an extreme example of the tragedy of the commons. Its tragedy is especially striking because many people care deeply about marine quality. The tragedy occurs because no one individual, group, or country has the means to solve the problem on its own. Even if you and I, and all our friends, consciously make sure we never let any trash enter the ocean, this won't stop debris from elsewhere. Likewise, if Japan unilaterally decided to filter the outflow from all its rivers before entering the ocean, debris from other countries would still litter the garbage patch. Complicating matters, once in the ocean the debris is hard to detect from satellites and even harder to collect and dispose of properly. The only real solution would be a cooperative agreement among all North Pacific Rim nations to filter ocean-bound debris. That's a very expensive proposition to a problem in a location so remote that it is out of sight, and therefore, out of mind.

Can anything be done to clean up the Great Pacific Garbage Patch?

Common Resources: Why Do Tailgaters Trash Parking Lots?

Tailgating can be one of the best parts of attending a big game or concert. You enjoy a great time with your friends and take in the action, leaving quickly afterward with little concern about the trash left behind. Consider this example: In 2014, country artist Luke Bryan played at Heinz Field in Pittsburgh. No doubt his fans care about the environment, but they absolutely trashed the parking lot. It was so bad, it made the local news. On the plus side, some city officials said the trash wasn't as bad as the Kenny Chesney concert the year before!

Why don't these tailgaters make a "concerted" effort to clean up?

QUESTION: What economic concept explains why so many people left so much trash behind?

ANSWER: Tailgaters brought snacks, drinks, cups, napkins, and all kinds of things to party before the concert, so a lot of trash was generated. Would you throw your trash on your driveway? Of course not. But otherwise conscientious individuals often don't demonstrate the same concern for public property. As a public space, the Heinz Field parking lot is subject to the tragedy of the commons. No one person can keep the lot clean, so overuse and littering occur. The effects of littering can be especially apparent when 50,000 people fill a stadium at one time.

Conclusion

Trade-offs

Although it's tempting to believe that the appropriate response to pollution is always to eliminate it, this belief is a misconception. As with all things, there are trade-offs. When pollution is taxed or regulated, business activity declines. It's possible to eliminate too much pollution, forcing businesses to shut down, creating undesirably high prices for anything from groceries to gasoline to electronics, and all in all creating an enormous deadweight loss to society. When you think about pollution like an environmental economist, you realize that eliminating pollution would create benefits and also costs. A truly "green" environment without any pollution would leave most people without enough "green" in their wallets. Therefore, the goal for pollution isn't zero, because the cost of attaining zero pollution outweighs the benefit.

In this chapter, we have considered two types of market failure: externalities and public goods. When externalities and public goods exist, the market does not provide the socially optimal amount of the good or service. One solution is to encourage businesses to internalize externalities. The government can aid the process through taxes and regulations that force producers to account for the negative externalities they create. Similarly, subsidies can spur the production of activities that generate positive externalities.

Tragedy of the Commons

SOUTH PARK AND WATER PARKS

If you have ever been to a water park or community pool, you know that the staff checks the pH of the water regularly to make sure it is clean. However, in an episode of *South Park*, everyone is peeing in Pi Pi's water park. The resulting pee concentration ends up being so high that it triggers a disaster-movie-style cataclysm, unleashing a flood of pee that destroys the place.

Why did this happen? Because each person looked at all the water and thought it wouldn't matter if *he* or *she* peed in it. But when *everyone* thought the same way, the water quality was affected. This led to the tragedy of the commons, in which the overall water quality became degraded. Pee-ew.

Thankfully, the real world is cleaner than South Park!

Likewise, public goods present a challenge for the market. Free-riding leads to the underproduction of goods that are nonrival and nonexcludable. Because not enough is produced privately, one solution is to eliminate free-riding by making involvement compulsory through taxation or regulation. A second problem occurs whenever goods are nonexcludable, as is the case with common-resource goods. This condition gives rise to the tragedy of the commons and can lead to the overuse of valuable resources. ✳

Buying Used Can Be Good for Your Wallet and for the Environment

- When you buy used you don't pay the "new" price markup.
- When you buy used you extend the usable life of a product, which is good for the environment.
- Some items are available for significant discounts soon after they are first sold.

Many people often spend their hard-earned money buying new, when choices to buying *almost* new instead are available. While some customers are willing to pay a premium for that "new" feeling, if you avoid that price markup for untouched goods, you'll usually save money *and* extend the usable life of a product. Here are a few ideas.

1. **Thrift-shop clothing**. Why would you buy something that immediately drops in value by 70%? When you buy new clothes at a retail store, you'll rarely get even a third of it back if you need to sell it at a consignment store or garage sale. Pick up bargains on lightly used clothing at your local thrift store instead.

2. **Sports equipment**. Let the enthusiasts buy the latest equipment. When they tire of it and switch to the newest golf clubs or buy a new kayak, you can swoop in and save big bucks. Play It Again Sports is a retailer that sells new and used equipment side-by-side so you can decide for yourself if new is worth the price difference.

3. **Video game consoles and games**. You can buy used and pay half price or less. The catch is you'll have to wait. But the good news is that you'll never find out that your expensive new system isn't as exciting as advertised. Waiting means better information *and* lower prices. That's how you find a good deal.

Listen to Macklemore's "Thrift Shop" advice: "It was 99 cents!"

4. **Automobiles**. The average new car can lose as much as 20% of its value during the first year after purchase. For a $30,000 car, that means $6,000 in lost value. Let someone else take that hit and buy a used vehicle instead.

5. **Tools and yard equipment**. Think twice before heading to the hardware store. Many tools like hammers and shovels are designed to last. Used tools might not look shiny-new, but they work just as well.

Every time you buy used, you extend the usable life of a product, which helps maximize the value society gets from its resources. These examples also illustrate the benefit of private property: recall that owners have incentives to (1) maintain, (2) protect, and (3) conserve the products they own so that they can (4) maximize the value when they sell them.

· ANSWERING *the* BIG QUESTIONS ·

What are externalities, and how do they affect markets?

- An externality exists whenever an internal cost (or benefit) diverges from a social cost (or benefit). Third parties can experience negative or positive externalities from market activity. Externalities are a type of market failure, which occurs when there is an inefficient allocation of resources in a market.

- Social costs are the sum of an activity's internal costs and external costs.

- When a negative externality exists, government can restore the social optimum by discouraging economic activity that harms third parties. When a positive externality exists, government can restore the social optimum by encouraging economic activity that benefits third parties.

- An externality is internalized when decision-makers must pay for the externality created by their participation in the market.

What are private goods and public goods?

- Private goods (or private property) ensures that owners have an incentive to maintain, protect, and conserve their property and also to trade it with others.

- A public good has two characteristics: it is nonexcludable and nonrival in consumption. Public goods give rise to the free-rider problem and result in the underproduction of the good in the market. Public goods give rise to market failure.

What are the challenges of providing nonexcludable goods?

- Economists use cost-benefit analysis to determine whether the benefits of providing a particular good outweigh the costs, but benefits can be hard to determine.

- Under a system of common property, the incentive structure encourages neglect and overuse.

Concepts You Should Know

cap and trade (p. 238)
club good (p. 233)
Coase theorem (p. 230)
common-resource good (p. 233)
cost-benefit analysis (p. 235)
excludable good (p. 230)
external costs (p. 220)

externalities (p. 220)
free-rider problem (p. 231)
internal costs (p. 220)
internalize (p. 223)
market failure (p. 220)
private good (p. 230)
private property (p. 228)

property rights (p. 227)
public good (p. 231)
rival good (p. 230)
social costs (p. 220)
social optimum (p. 222)
third-party problem (p. 221)
tragedy of the commons (p. 236)

Questions for Review

1. Does the market overproduce or underproduce when third parties enjoy positive externalities? Show your answer on a supply and demand graph.

2. Is it possible to use bargaining to solve externality problems involving many parties? Explain your reasoning.

3. Describe all of the ways in which externalities can be internalized.

4. Does cost-benefit analysis apply to public goods only? If yes, why? If not, name situations in which economists would use cost-benefit analysis.

5. What is the tragedy of the commons? Give an example that is not in the chapter.

6. What are the four incentives of private property? How do they differ from the incentives found in common property?

7. Give an example of a good that is nonrival in consumption and nonexcludable. What do economists call goods that share these characteristics?

Study Problems (✳ solved at the end of the section)

1. Many cities have noise ordinances that impose especially harsh fines and penalties for early-morning and late-evening disturbances. Explain why these ordinances exist.

2. Indicate whether the following activities create a positive or negative externality:

  a. Late-night road construction begins on a new bridge. As a consequence, traffic is rerouted past your house while the construction takes place.

  b. An excavating company pollutes a local stream with acid rock.

  c. A homeowner whose property backs up on a city park enjoys the sound of kids playing soccer.

  d. A student uses her cell phone discreetly during class.

  e. You and your friends volunteer to plant wildflowers along the local highway.

3. Indicate whether the following are private goods, club goods, common-resource goods, or public goods:

  a. a bacon double cheeseburger

  b. an NHL hockey game between the Detroit Red Wings and Boston Bruins

  c. a Fourth of July fireworks show

  d. a swimming pool

  e. a vaccination for the flu

  f. streetlights

4. Can you think of a reason why making cars safer would create negative externalities? Explain.

5. Which of the following activities give rise to the free-rider problem?

  a. recycling programs

  b. biking

  c. studying for an exam

  d. riding a bus

✳ 6. The students at a crowded university have trouble waking up before 10 a.m., and most work jobs after 3 p.m. As a result, there is a great deal of demand for classes between 10 a.m. and 3 p.m., and classes before and after those hours are rarely full. To make matters worse, the university has a limited amount of classroom space and faculty. As a result, not every student can take classes during the most desirable times. Building new classrooms and hiring more faculty are not options. The administration asks for your advice about the best way to solve the problem of demand during the peak class hours. What advice would you give?

7. Two roommates are opposites. One enjoys playing Modern Warfare with his friends all night. The other likes to get to bed early for a full 8 hours of sleep. If Coase is right, the roommates have an incentive to solve the noise externality issue themselves. Name at least two solutions that will internalize, or eliminate, the externality.

✳ 8. Two companies, Toxic Waste Management and Sludge Industries, both pollute a nearby lake. Each firm dumps 1,000 gallons of goo into the lake every day. As a consequence, the lake has lost its clarity and the fish are dying. Local residents want to see the lake restored. But Toxic Waste's production process depends heavily on being able to dump the goo into the lake. It would cost Toxic Waste $10 per gallon to clean up the goo it generates. Sludge can clean up its goo at a cost of $2 per gallon.

    a. If the local government cuts the legal goo emissions in half for each firm, what are the costs to each firm to comply with the law? What is the total cost to both firms in meeting the goo-emissions standard?

    b. Another way of cutting goo emissions in half is to assign each firm tradable pollution permits that allow 500 gallons of goo to be dumped into the lake every day. Under this approach, will each firm still dump 500 gallons of goo? Would the firms be willing to trade permits with one another?

9. A study finds that leaf blowers make too much noise, so the government imposes a $10 tax on the sale of every unit to correct for the social cost of

the noise pollution. The tax completely internalizes the externality. Before the corrective tax, Blown Away Manufacturing regularly sold blowers for $100. After the tax is in place, the consumer price for leaf blowers rises to $105.

    a. Describe the impact of the tax on the number of leaf blowers sold.

    b. What is the socially optimal price to the consumer?

    c. What is the private market price?

    d. What net price is Blown Away receiving after it pays the tax?

10. In most areas, developers are required to submit an environmental impact study before work can begin on a new construction project. Suppose that a commercial developer wants to build a new shopping center on an environmentally protected piece of property that is home to a rare three-eyed toad. The shopping complex, if approved by the local planning commission, will cover 10 acres. The planning commission wants the construction to go forward because the shopping complex means additional jobs for the local community, but it also wants to be environmentally responsible. One member of the commission suggests that the developer relocate the toads. She describes the relocation process as follows: "The developer builds the shopping mall and agrees to create 10 acres of artificial toad habitat elsewhere." Will this proposed solution make the builder internalize the externality? Explain.

✳ 11. Describe the difference between the way an environmental economist thinks about policy and the way an environmentalist thinks about policy. (***Hint:*** Recall the difference between positive economics and normative economics from Chapter 2.)

12. If a company pollutes the water and transactions costs are high, which of the following makes the most economic sense?

    a. All parties connected with the pollution should negotiate.

    b. The company should be allowed to pollute.

    c. The company should be liable for the damages it causes.

    d. The company should go out of business.

13. A homeowner is piling debris near his lot line. It would be $300 worth of trouble to put it elsewhere. The next-door neighbor is worried that the unsightly debris drops $5,000 from the market value of the home she's trying to sell.

  a. How might the two parties voluntarily resolve this conflict?
  b. If the local homeowners association prohibits debris piles, how is the dispute likely to get resolved? Is this a socially beneficial solution?

✳ 14. Does antibiotic use entail an external cost or an external benefit?

✳ 15. Suppose Heesun lives alone. She has two pet hamsters; she likes the hamsters because they are cute. But cleaning their cage every day is a hassle. In this case, Heesun's hamsters entail

  a. an external cost.
  b. an external benefit.
  c. neither an external cost nor an external benefit.

16. A cattle rancher and a wheat farmer own adjacent properties. The accompanying table identifies the annual profit received by each party in the event there is, or there is not, a fence. If there is no fence, one can be installed and maintained at an annual cost of $15,000.

	Fence	No fence
Cattle rancher	$40,000	$50,000
Wheat farmer	50,000	20,000

If legal rights are assigned to the wheat farmer so that the cattle rancher is liable for any damage caused by her cattle to the wheat crop, will the cattle rancher build a fence?

Solved Problems

6. A flat-fee congestion charge is a good start, because this charge would reduce the quantity demanded between 10 a.m. and 3 p.m., but such a fee is a blunt instrument. Making the congestion charge dynamic (or varying the price by the hour) will encourage students to move outside the window with the most popular class times in order to pay less. For instance, classes between 11 a.m. and 2 p.m. would have the highest fee. Classes between 10 and 11 a.m. and between 2 and 3 p.m. would be slightly discounted. Classes between 9 and 10 a.m. and between 3 and 4 p.m. would be cheaper still, and those earlier than 9 a.m. and after 4 p.m. would be the cheapest. By altering the price of different class times, the university would be able to offer classes at less popular times and fill them up regularly, thus efficiently using its existing resources.

8.a. If the local government cuts the legal goo emissions in half for each firm, Toxic Waste will cut its goo by 500 gallons at a cost of $10 per gallon, for a total cost of $5,000. Sludge Industries will also cut its goo by 500 gallons; at $2 per gallon, the cost is $1,000. The total cost to both firms in meeting the goo-emissions standard is $5,000 + $1,000 = $6,000.

  b. It costs Toxic Waste $10 per gallon to clean up its goo. It is therefore more efficient for Toxic to buy all 500 permits from Sludge—which enables Toxic to dump an additional 500 gallons in the lake and saves the company $5,000 minus the price it pays to Sludge for its permits. At the same time, Sludge could decide not to dump any goo in the lake. Because it costs Sludge $2 per gallon to clean up its goo, it will have to pay $1,000 unless it sells its permits to Toxic, in which case it might actually make a profit. Because Toxic is saving more than it costs Sludge to clean up the goo, the two sides have an incentive to trade the permits.

11. Thinking like an economist requires one to consider the marginal benefits and the marginal costs of every policy. This perspective allows environmental economists to assess whether a particular policy will create enough benefits to outweigh the costs. It is this positive (dispassionate) perspective that causes an environmental economist to argue that the optimal rate of pollution is above zero. In contrast, an environmentalist sees policy solutions through a normative lens. Environmentalists weigh the benefits of protecting the environment much more heavily than the costs and therefore advocate for policies that protect the environment even when the costs are quite high.

14. Antibiotics create both an external cost and an external benefit. There is external cost because overuse makes bacteria more resistant to future treatment, and an external benefit because the use of antibiotics helps to slow the spread of bacteria.

15. The correct answer is c. There is no third party, so there is no negative or positive externality.

PART

III

The Theory of THE FIRM

08 Business Costs and Production

Do Larger Firms Always Have a Cost Advantage Over Their Smaller Rivals?

Walmart, the nation's largest retailer, leverages its size to get price breaks on bulk purchases from its suppliers. People commonly believe that this kind of leverage enables larger firms to operate at lower costs than smaller firms do. It is true that large firms have broader distribution networks, and they benefit from more specialization and automation compared with their smaller competitors. However, not all industries enjoy lower costs with additional sales the way retailers do. Even Walmart, known for its very low prices, can be undercut by online outlets that have lower costs and therefore lower prices. In other words, larger firms do not always have the lowest costs.

More generally, in any industry where transportation and advertising costs are high, smaller localized firms are not always at a disadvantage in terms of pricing. In fact, they often have the edge. For instance, in most college towns you will find many pizza shops—the national brands (Pizza Hut, Domino's, Little Caesars) and the local shops. Often, the local shop is the one with the cheapest pizza special, while the name brands charge more. By the end of this chapter, you will appreciate the importance of cost and understand why smaller and more nimble firms are sometimes able to undercut the prices of larger companies.

The guy flipping pizza dough at this pizzeria is happy, because he knows there's nothing the big national chains can do that he can't. Making pizza is a craft, not a factory process, and what he's doing here took years of practice.

We begin the chapter with an examination of costs and how they relate to production. After we understand the basics, we consider how firms can keep their costs low in the long run by choosing a scale of operation that best suits their needs.

· BIG QUESTIONS ·

- How are profits and losses calculated?
- How much should a firm produce?
- What costs do firms consider in the short run and the long run?

How Are Profits and Losses Calculated?

To determine the potential profits of a business, the first step is to look at how much it will cost to run it. Consider a McDonald's restaurant. While you are probably familiar with the products McDonald's sells, you may not know how an individual franchise operates. For one thing, the manager at a McDonald's must decide how many workers to hire and how many to assign to each shift. Other managerial decisions involve the equipment needed and what supplies to have on hand each day—everything from hamburger patties to paper napkins. In fact, behind each purchase a consumer makes at McDonald's, there is a complicated symphony of delivery trucks, workers, and managers.

For a company to be profitable, it is not enough to provide products consumers want. It must simultaneously manage its costs. In this section, we discuss how profits and costs are calculated.

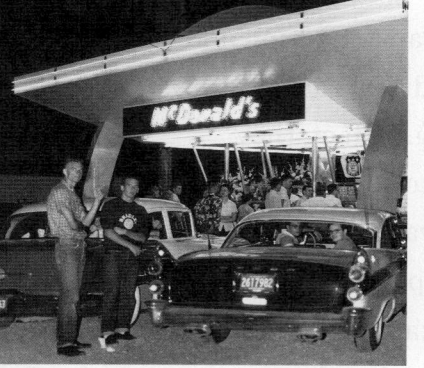

The first McDonald's—much like the one pictured here—opened in San Bernardino, California, in 1940.

Total revenue is the amount a firm receives from the sale of goods and services.

Total cost is the amount a firm spends to produce and/or sell goods and services.

A **profit** results when total revenue is higher than total cost.

Calculating Profit and Loss

The simplest way to determine profit or loss is to calculate the difference between revenue and expenses (costs). The **total revenue** of a business is the amount the firm receives from the sale of goods and services. In the case of McDonald's, the total revenue is determined by the number of items sold and their prices. **Total cost** is the amount a firm spends to produce and/or sell goods and services. To determine total cost, the firm adds the individual costs of the resources used in producing and/or selling the goods. A **profit** occurs whenever total revenue is higher than total cost. A **loss** occurs whenever total revenue is less than total cost. We can express this relationship as an equation:

A **loss** results when total revenue is less than total cost.

$$\text{profit (or loss)} = \text{total revenue} - \text{total cost}$$

(EQUATION 8.1)

To calculate total revenue, we look at the dollar amount the business takes in over a specific period. For instance, suppose that in a given day McDonald's sells 1,000 hamburgers for $1.00 each, 500 orders of large fries for $2.00 each, and 100 shakes for $2.50 each. The total revenue is the sum of all of these values, or $2,250. The profit is therefore $2,250 (total revenue) minus the total cost.

Calculating costs, however, is a little more complicated than calculating revenue; we don't simply tally the cost of making each hamburger, order of large fries, and shake. Total cost has two parts—one that is visible and one that is largely invisible. In the next section, we will see that determining total costs is part art and part science.

Explicit Costs and Implicit Costs

Economists break costs into two components: explicit costs and implicit costs. **Explicit costs** are tangible out-of-pocket expenses. To calculate explicit costs, we add every expense incurred to run the business. For example, in the case of a McDonald's franchise, the weekly supply of hamburger patties is one explicit cost; the owner receives a bill from the meat supplier and has to pay it. **Implicit costs** are the costs of resources already owned, for which no out-of-pocket payment is made. Implicit costs are also opportunity costs, because the use of owned resources means that the next-best alternative use is forgone.

Explicit costs are tangible out-of-pocket expenses.

Implicit costs are the costs of resources already owned, for which no out-of-pocket payment is made.

Let's consider an example. Purchasing a McDonald's franchise costs about $1 million; this is an explicit cost. However, there is also a high opportunity cost—the next-best possibility for investing $1 million. That money could have earned interest in a bank, been used to start a different business, or been invested in the stock market. Each alternative is an implicit cost.

Implicit costs are hard to calculate and easy to miss. For example, it is difficult to determine how much an investor could have earned from an

TABLE 8.1

Examples of a Firm's Explicit and Implicit Costs

Explicit costs	Implicit costs
The electricity bill	The labor of an owner who works for the company but does not draw a salary
Advertising in the local newspaper	The opportunity cost of the capital invested in the business
Employee wages	The use of the owner's car, computer, or other personal equipment to conduct company business

Opportunity cost

alternative activity. Is the opportunity cost the 3% interest he might have earned by placing the money in a bank, the 10% he might have hoped to earn in the stock market, or the 15% he might have gained by investing in a different business? We can be sure there is an opportunity cost for owner-provided capital, but we can never know exactly how much that might be.

In addition to the opportunity cost of capital, implicit costs include the opportunity cost of the owner's labor. Often, business owners do not pay themselves a direct salary. However, because they could have been working somewhere else, it is reasonable to consider the fair value of the owner's time—income the owner could have earned by working elsewhere—as part of the business's costs.

To fully account for all the costs of doing business, we must calculate the explicit costs, determine the implicit costs, and add them together:

(EQUATION 8.2)

$$\textbf{total cost} = \text{explicit costs} + \text{implicit costs}$$

A simple way of thinking about the distinction between explicit costs and implicit costs is to consider someone who wants to build a bookcase. Suppose that John purchases $30 in materials and takes half a day off from work, where he normally earns $12 an hour. After 4 hours, he completes the bookcase. His explicit cost is $30, but his total cost is much higher because he also gave up 4 hours of work at $12 an hour. His implicit cost is therefore $48. When we add the explicit cost ($30) and the implicit cost ($48), we get John's total cost ($78).

Table 8.1 shows examples of a firm's explicit and implicit costs.

Accounting Profit versus Economic Profit

Now that you know about explicit and implicit costs, we can refine our definition of profit. In fact, there are two types of profit—accounting profit and economic profit.

A firm's **accounting profit** is calculated by subtracting only the explicit costs from total revenue. Accounting figures permeate company reports, quarterly and annual statements, and the media.

Accounting profit is calculated by subtracting the explicit costs from total revenue.

(EQUATION 8.3)

$$\textbf{accounting profit} = \text{total revenues} - \text{explicit costs}$$

As you can see, accounting profit does not take into account the implicit costs of doing business. To calculate the full cost of doing business, we need to consider both implicit and explicit costs. Doing so yields a firm's economic profit. **Economic profit** is calculated by subtracting both the explicit and the implicit costs from total revenue. Economic profit gives a more complete assessment of how a firm is doing.

Economic profit
is calculated by subtracting both the explicit costs and the implicit costs from total revenue.

$$\text{economic profit} = \text{total revenues} - (\text{explicit costs} + \text{implicit costs})$$

(EQUATION 8.4)

Simplifying Equation 8.4 gives us

$$\text{economic profit} = \text{accounting profit} - \text{implicit costs}$$

(EQUATION 8.5)

Therefore, economic profit is always less than accounting profit.

The difference in accounting profits among various types of firms can be misleading. For instance, if a company with $1 billion in assets reports an annual profit of $10 million, we might think it is doing well. After all, wouldn't you be happy to make $10 million in a year? However, that $10 million is only 1% of the $1 billion the company holds in assets. As Table 8.2 shows, a 1% return is far less than the typical return available in a number of other places, including the stock market, bonds, or a savings account at a financial institution.

If the return on $1 billion in assets is low compared with what an investor can expect to make elsewhere, the firm with the $10 million accounting profit actually has a negative economic profit. For instance, if the firm had invested the $1 billion in a savings account, according to Table 8.2 it would have earned 2% on $1 billion—that is, $20 million. In that case,

$$\begin{aligned}
\text{economic profit} &= \text{accounting profit} - \text{implicit costs} \\
&= \$10 \text{ million} - \$20 \text{ million} \\
&= - \$10 \text{ million}
\end{aligned}$$

As you can see, economic profit can be negative, since the minus dollar amount is a loss. If a business has an economic profit, its revenues are larger than the combination of its explicit costs and implicit costs. Likewise, a business has an economic loss when its revenues are smaller than the combination of its explicit and implicit costs. The difficulty in determining economic profit lies in calculating the tangible value of implicit costs.

TABLE 8.2	
Historical Rates of Return in Stocks, Bonds, and Savings Accounts, 1928–2018	
Financial instrument	**Historical average rate of return since 1928 (adjusted for inflation)**
Stocks	8%
Bonds	3
Savings account at a financial institution	2

Source: Federal Reserve database in St. Louis (FRED) and author's adjustments. Data from 1928–2018.

Accounting Profit versus Economic Profit: Calculating Summer Job Profits

How much economic profit do you make from painting?

Kyle is a college student who works during the summer to pay for tuition. Last summer he worked at a fast-food restaurant and earned $2,500. This summer he is working as a painter and will earn $4,000. To do the painting job, Kyle had to spend $200 on supplies.

QUESTION: What is Kyle's accounting profit?

ANSWER: accounting profit = total revenues − explicit cost
= $4,000 − $200 = $3,800

QUESTION: If working at the fast-food restaurant was Kyle's next-best alternative, how much economic profit will Kyle earn from painting?

ANSWER: To calculate economic profit, we need to subtract the explicit and implicit costs from the total revenue. Kyle's total revenue from painting will be $4,000. His explicit costs are $200 for supplies, and his implicit cost is $2,500—the salary he would have earned in the fast-food restaurant. So Kyle's

economic profit = total revenue − explicit cost + implicit cost
= $4,000 − ($200 + $2,500) = $1,300

QUESTION: Suppose that Kyle can get an internship at an investment bank. The internship provides a stipend of $3,000 and tangible work experience that will help him get a job after graduation. Should Kyle take the painting job or the internship?

ANSWER: The implicit costs have changed because Kyle now has to consider the $3,000 stipend and the increased chance of securing a job after graduation versus what he can make painting houses. Calculation of economic profit from painting is now

economic profit = $4,000 − ($200 + $3,000) = $800

So at this point, Kyle's economic profit from painting would be only $800. But this number is incomplete. There is also the value of the internship experience. If Kyle wants to work in investment banking after graduation, then this decision is a no-brainer. He should take the internship—that is, unless some investment banks value painting houses more than work experience!

How Much Should a Firm Produce?

Every business must decide how much to produce. In this section, we describe the factors that determine output, and we explain how firms use inputs to maximize their production. Because it is possible for a firm to produce too little or too much, we must also consider when a firm should stop production.

Keeping Costs Down

INCREDIBLES 2

The 2018 sequel to *The Incredibles* opens where the original left off, with the Incredible family fighting to stop The Underminer. By now, all superheroes have been forced into hiding by public outrage over the collateral damage that the crime-fighting Supers habitually leave in their wake. Enter Winston Deavor, the head of a major telecommunications company. Not long after the Supers were banned, robbers broke into the Deavor mansion and shot his father. Winston always believed that if the Supers had been allowed to continue helping people, his father would still be alive. So when he and his sister inherited the company, they decided to create a campaign to bring back the superheroes.

To do this, Winston wants to change the public's perception by filming a superhero saving the day. He wants Elastigirl to lead the campaign, because a cost-benefit analysis by his sister determined that Elastigirl is able to solve crimes with far less damage than her husband, Mr. Incredible. That leaves the

Winston Deavor explains why he wants Elastigirl to fight the villains, while Mr. Incredible stays home with the kids.

big guy in the role of stay-at-home dad. Elastigirl changes public opinion about the Supers as she defeats the villains, because she is adept at minimizing property damage and loss of life. Good economists do likewise, by keeping costs as low as possible while getting the job done.

The Production Function

For a firm to earn an economic profit, it must produce a product that consumers want. This product is the firm's **output**. A firm should produce an output that is consistent with the largest possible economic profit.

The firm must also control its costs. To do so, the firm must use resources efficiently. There are three primary **factors of production**: labor, land, and capital. Each factor of production is an *input*, or a resource used in the production process to generate the firm's output. *Labor* consists of workers, *land* consists of the geographical location used in production, and *capital* consists of all the resources the workers use to create the final product. Consider McDonald's as an example. The labor input includes managers, cashiers, cooks, and janitorial staff. The land input includes the land on which the McDonald's building sits. The capital input includes the building itself, the equipment used, the parking lot, the signs, and all the hamburger patties, buns, fries, ketchup, and other foodstuffs.

Output
is the product the firm creates.

Factors of production
are the inputs (labor, land, and capital) used in producing goods and services.

The **production function** describes the relationship between the inputs a firm uses and the output it creates.

To keep costs down in the production process, a firm needs to find the right mix of these inputs. The **production function** describes the relationship between the inputs a firm uses and the output it creates. As we saw at the beginning of the chapter, the manager of a McDonald's must make many decisions about inputs. If she hires too little labor, some of the land and capital will be underutilized. Likewise, with too many workers and not enough land or capital, some workers will not have enough to do to stay busy. For example, suppose that only a single worker shows up at McDonald's one day. This employee will have to do all the cooking; bag up the meals; handle the register, the drive-through, and the drinks; and clean the tables. This single worker, no matter how productive, will not be able to keep up with demand. Hungry customers will grow tired of waiting and take their business elsewhere—maybe for good!

When a second worker shows up, the two employees can begin to specialize in what they do well. Recall that specialization and comparative advantage lead to higher levels of output (see Chapter 2). Therefore, individual workers will be assigned to tasks that match their skills. For example, one worker can take the orders, fill the bags, and get the drinks. The other can work the grill area and drive-through. When a third worker comes on, the specialization process can extend even further. Specialization and division of labor are key to the way McDonald's operates. Production per worker expands as long as additional workers become more specialized and there are enough capital resources to keep each worker occupied.

McDonald's needs the correct amount of labor to maximize its output.

When only a few workers share capital resources, the resources each worker needs are readily available. But what happens when the restaurant is very busy? The manager can hire more staff for the busiest shifts, but the amount of space for cooking and the number of cash registers, drink dispensers, and tables in the seating area are fixed. Because the added employees have less capital to work with, beyond a certain point the additional labor will not continue to increase the restaurant's output at the same rate as it did at first. You might recognize this situation if you have ever gone into a fast-food restaurant at lunchtime. Even though the space behind the counter bustles with busy employees, they can't keep up with the orders. Only so many meals can be produced in a short time and in a fixed space; some customers have to wait.

The restaurant must also maintain an adequate supply of materials. If a shipment is late and the restaurant runs out of hamburger patties, sales (and total revenue) will decrease. The manager must therefore (1) decide how many workers to hire for each shift and (2) manage the inventory of supplies.

Let's look more closely at the manager's decision about how many workers to hire. On the left side of Figure 8.1, we see what happens when workers are added, one by one. When the manager adds one worker, output goes from 0 meals to 5 meals. Going from one worker to two workers increases total output to 15 meals. The second worker has increased the number of meals produced from 5 to 15, an increase of 10 meals. This increase in output is the **marginal product**, which is the change in output associated with one additional unit of an input. In this case, the change in output (10 additional

Marginal thinking

Marginal product is the change in output associated with one additional unit of an input.

FIGURE 8.1

The Production Function and Marginal Product

(a) Total output rises rapidly in the green zone from zero to three workers, rises less rapidly in the yellow zone between three and eight workers, and falls in the red zone after eight workers. (b) The marginal product of labor rises in the green zone from zero to three workers, falls in the yellow zone from three to eight workers but remains positive, and becomes negative after eight workers. Notice that the marginal product becomes negative after total output reaches its maximum at eight workers. As long as marginal product is positive, total output rises. Once marginal product becomes negative, total output falls.

Marginal thinking

Number of workers	Total output (number of meals served per hour)	Marginal product of labor
0	0	
		5
1	5	
		10
2	15	
		15
3	30	
		12
4	42	
		10
5	52	
		8
6	60	
		5
7	65	
		2
8	67	
		−3
9	64	
		−8
10	56	

(Graphs (a) and (b) appear to the right of the table.)

(a)

(b)

meals) divided by the increase in input (1 worker) gives us a marginal product of 10 ÷ 1, or 10. Because the table in Figure 8.1 adds one worker at a time, the marginal product is just the increase in output shown in the third column. Conversely, for any given number of workers, the total output is the sum of the individual workers' marginal products.

Looking down the three columns, we see that the total output continues to expand, and it keeps growing through eight workers. But after the first three workers, the rate of increase in the marginal product slows down. Why? The gains from specialization are slowly declining. With the ninth worker (going from 8 to 9), we see a negative marginal product. Once the cash registers, drive-through, grill area, and other service stations are fully staffed, there is not much for an extra worker to do. Eventually, extra workers will get in the way or distract other workers from completing their tasks.

The graphs on the right side of Figure 8.1 show (a) total output and (b) marginal product of labor. The graph of total output in (a) uses data from the second column of the table. As the number of workers goes from 0 to 3 on the *x* axis, total output rises at an increasing rate from 0 to 30. The slope of the total output curve rises until it reaches three workers at the first dashed vertical line. Between three workers and the second dashed vertical line at eight workers, the total output curve continues to rise, though at a slower rate; the slope of the curve is still positive, but the curve becomes progressively flatter. Finally, once we reach the ninth worker, total output begins to fall and the slope becomes negative. At this point, it is not productive to have so many workers.

Diminishing Marginal Product

The marginal product curve in panel (b) of Figure 8.1 explains the shape of the total output curve in panel (a). Consider that each worker's marginal productivity either adds to or subtracts from the firm's overall output. Marginal product increases from 5 meals served per hour with the first worker to 15 meals per hour with the third worker. From the first worker to the third, each additional worker leads to increased specialization and teamwork, which explains the rapid rise—from 0 to 30 meals—in the total output curve. By the fourth worker, marginal product begins to decline. Looking back to the table, you can see that the fourth worker produces 12 extra meals—3 fewer than the third worker. The point at which successive increases in inputs are associated with a slower rise in output is known as the point of **diminishing marginal product**.

Why does the rate of output slow? In our example, the size of the McDonald's restaurant is fixed in the short run. Because the size of the building and the amount of equipment do not increase, at a certain point additional workers have less to do or can even interfere with the output of other workers. After all inputs are fully utilized, additional workers cause marginal product to decline, which we see in the marginal product curve in Figure 8.1, panel (b).

What does diminishing marginal product tell us about the firm's labor input decision? Turning again to the two graphs, we see that in the green area, as the number of workers increases from zero to three, the marginal product and total output also rise. But when we enter the yellow zone with the fourth worker, we reach the point of diminishing marginal product where the curve starts to decline. Total output continues to rise, though at a slower rate. Finally, in the red zone, which we enter with the ninth worker, marginal product becomes negative and total output declines. No rational manager would hire more than eight workers in this scenario, because doing so would cause total output to drop.

A common mistake when considering diminishing marginal product is to assume that a firm should stop production as soon as marginal product starts to fall. This is not necessarily true. "Diminishing" does not mean "negative." There are many times when marginal product is declining but still relatively high. In our example, diminishing marginal product begins with the

Diminishing marginal product occurs when successive increases in inputs are associated with a slower rise in output.

Marginal thinking

fourth worker. However, that fourth worker still produces 12 extra meals. If McDonald's can sell those 12 additional meals for more than it pays the fourth worker, the company's profits will rise.

What Costs Do Firms Consider in the Short Run and the Long Run?

Production is one part of a firm's decision-making process. If you have run even a simple business—for example, mowing lawns—you know that it requires decision-making. How many lawns do you want to be responsible for? Should you work on different lawns at the same time or specialize by task, with one person doing all the mowing and another taking care of the trimming? These are the kinds of production-related questions every firm must address. The other major component of production is cost. Should you invest in a big industrial-size mower? How much gasoline will you need to run your mowers? What does it cost to hire someone to help get the work done? These are some of the cost-related concerns firms face. Each one may seem like a small decision, but the discovery process that leads to the answers is crucial.

PRACTICE WHAT YOU KNOW

Diminishing Returns: Snow Cone Production

It's a hot day, and customers are lined up for snow cones at your small stand. The following table shows your firm's short-run production function for snow cones.

Number of workers	Total output of snow cones per hour
0	0
1	20
2	50
3	75
4	90
5	100
6	105
7	100
8	90

How many workers are too many? Use marginal product to decide.

(CONTINUED)

QUESTION: When does diminishing marginal product begin?

ANSWER: You have to be careful when calculating this answer. Total output is maximized when you have six workers, but diminishing marginal return begins before you hire that many workers. Look at the following table, which includes a third column showing marginal product.

Number of workers	Total output of snow cones per hour	Marginal product
0	0	
		20
1	20	
		30
2	50	
		25
3	75	
		15
4	90	
		10
5	100	
		5
6	105	
		−5
7	100	
		−10
8	90	

Marginal thinking

The marginal product is highest when you hire the second worker. After that, each subsequent worker you hire has a lower marginal product. Therefore, the answer to the question is that diminishing marginal product begins after the second worker.

Every firm, whether just starting out or already well established and profitable, can benefit by assessing how much to produce and how to produce it more efficiently. In addition, production and cost considerations are different in the short run and in the long run. We begin with the short run because the majority of firms are most concerned with making the best short-run decisions, and then we extend our analysis to the long run, where planning ahead plays a central role.

Costs in the Short Run

All firms experience some costs that are unavoidable in the short run. These unavoidable costs—for example, a lease on space or a contract with a supplier—are a large part of short-run costs. In the short run, costs can be variable or fixed.

Variable costs change with the rate of output. Let's see what this means for a McDonald's and further simplify our example by assuming that the McDonald's produces only Big Macs. In this case, the variable costs include the number of workers the firm hires; the electricity the firm uses; the all-beef patties, special sauce, lettuce, cheese, pickles, onions, and sesame seed buns needed to create the Big Macs; and the packaging. These items are variable costs because the restaurant doesn't need them unless it has customers. The amount of these resources varies with the amount of output the restaurant

Variable costs change with the rate of output.

produces. You might be thinking that a firm should decide to produce at an output where its average variable costs are lowest; but be careful—you don't have all the facts yet. In Chapter 9, we add demand to our analysis to determine how much the firm should produce. For now, we stay focused on the cost side.

Fixed costs are unavoidable; they do not vary with output in the short run. For instance, no matter how many Big Macs the McDonald's sells, most of the costs associated with the building remain the same and the business must pay for them. These fixed costs—also known as *overhead*—include rent, insurance, and property taxes.

Fixed costs
are unavoidable; they do not vary with output in the short run. Fixed costs are also known as overhead.

INTERPRETING TABULAR DATA Every business must be able to determine how much it costs to provide the products and services it sells. Table 8.3 lists many different ways to measure the costs associated with business decisions.

Let's begin with total variable cost (TVC) in column 2 and total fixed cost (TFC) in column 3. Notice that when output—the quantity (Q) of Big Macs produced per hour—is 0, total variable cost starts at $0 and rises with production at an uneven rate, depending on output and the cost of the ingredients that go into each Big Mac. We attribute this increase in TVC to the simple fact that additional workers and other inputs are needed to generate additional output. In contrast, total fixed cost starts at $100, even when output is 0, and remains constant as output rises. As already noted, fixed costs include overhead expenses such as rent, insurance, and property taxes.

TABLE 8.3
Measuring Costs

(1)	(2)	(3)	(4)	(5)	(6)	(7)	(8)
Quantity (Q = Big Macs produced per hour)	Total variable cost	Total fixed cost	Total cost	Average variable cost	Average fixed cost	Average total cost	Marginal cost
Abbreviation: TVC	TFC	TC	AVC	AFC	ATC	MC
Formula:			TVC + TFC	TVC ÷ Q	TFC ÷ Q	TC ÷ Q or AVC + AFC	ΔTVC ÷ ΔQ or ΔTC ÷ ΔQ
0	$0.00	$100.00	$100.00				
10	30.00	100.00	130.00	$3.00	$10.00	$13.00	$3.00
20	50.00	100.00	150.00	2.50	5.00	7.50	2.00
30	65.00	100.00	165.00	2.17	3.33	5.50	1.50
40	77.00	100.00	177.00	1.93	2.50	4.43	1.20
50	87.00	100.00	187.00	1.74	2.00	3.74	1.00
60	100.00	100.00	200.00	1.67	1.67	3.34	1.30
70	120.00	100.00	220.00	1.71	1.43	3.14	2.00
80	160.00	100.00	260.00	2.00	1.25	3.25	4.00
90	220.00	100.00	320.00	2.44	1.11	3.55	6.00
100	300.00	100.00	400.00	3.00	1.00	4.00	8.00

For simplicity, we assume that this amount is $100 a day. When we add fixed cost and variable cost together, we get total cost (TC), listed in column 4: TC = TVC + TFC.

Columns 5 and 6 enable us to determine the cost of producing a Big Mac by examining the average cost of production. **Average variable cost (AVC)**, in column 5, is the total variable cost divided by the output produced: AVC = TVC ÷ Q. Notice that the average variable cost declines until 60 Big Macs are produced at an average variable cost of $1.67, which is the lowest average variable cost. Why should we care about AVC? Because it can be a useful signal. In this case, total variable costs in column 2 always rise, but the average variable cost falls until 60 Big Macs are produced.

Average fixed cost (AFC), listed in column 6, is calculated by dividing total fixed cost by the output: AFC = TFC ÷ Q. Because total fixed cost is constant, dividing these costs by the output means that as the output rises, the average fixed cost declines. In other words, higher output levels spread out the total fixed cost across more units. As Table 8.3 shows, average fixed cost is lowest at an output of 100 Big Macs, where

$$AFC = TFC \div Q$$
$$AFC = \$100 \div 100$$
$$AFC = \$1$$

What does this example tell a business that wants to lower its costs? Because overhead costs such as rent cannot be changed, the best way to lower average fixed costs is to raise output.

Average total cost (ATC), shown in column 7, is calculated by adding the AVC and AFC. It can also be calculated by dividing total cost by quantity (TC ÷ Q). Let's look at the numbers to get a better understanding of what average total cost tells us. Even though the average variable cost rises from $1.67 to $1.71 after 60 Big Macs are produced, the average fixed cost is still falling, from $1.67 to $1.43. The decline in average fixed cost is enough to pull the average total cost down to $3.14. Eventually, increases in variable cost overwhelm the cost savings achieved by spreading fixed cost across more production. We can see this result if we compare the average total costs of making 70 Big Macs and 80 Big Macs.

For 70 Big Macs:

$$ATC = AVC + AFC$$
$$ATC = \$1.71 + \$1.43 = \$3.14$$

For 80 Big Macs:

$$ATC = AVC + AFC$$
$$ATC = \$2.00 + \$1.25 = \$3.25$$

At 80 Big Macs, the average variable cost rises from $1.71 to $2.00. And the average fixed cost falls from $1.43 to $1.25. Therefore, the rise in average variable cost—$0.29—is higher than the fall in average fixed cost—$0.18. ATC therefore rises, removing the benefit of higher output.

Average variable cost (AVC) is determined by dividing total variable cost by the output.

Average fixed cost (AFC) is determined by dividing total fixed cost by the output.

Average total cost (ATC) is the sum of average variable cost and average fixed cost.

INTERPRETING DATA GRAPHICALLY Now that we have walked through the numerical results in Table 8.3, it is time to visualize the cost relationships with graphs. Figure 8.2 shows a graph of total cost curves (a) and the relationship between the marginal cost curve and the average cost curves (b).

In panel (a) of Figure 8.2, we see that although the total cost curve continues to rise, the rate of increase in total cost is not constant. For the first 50 Big Macs, the total cost rises at a decreasing rate, reflecting the gains of specialization and comparative advantage that come from adding workers who concentrate on specific tasks. After 50 Big Macs, diminishing marginal product causes the total cost curve to rise at an increasing rate. Because a McDonald's restaurant has a fixed capacity, producing more than 50 Big Macs requires a significantly higher investment in labor, and those workers do not have any additional space to work in—a situation that makes the total cost curve rise more rapidly at high production levels. The total cost (TC) curve is equal to the sum of the total fixed cost and total variable cost curves, as shown in panel (a). Total fixed cost (TFC) is constant, so it is the total variable cost (TVC) that gives the TC curve its shape.

But that is not the most important part of the story. Any manager at McDonald's can examine total costs. Likewise, she can look at the average cost

Marginal thinking

FIGURE 8.2

The Cost Curves

(a) The total variable cost (TVC) dictates the shape of the total cost (TC) curve. After 50 Big Macs, diminishing marginal product causes the total cost curve to rise at an increasing rate. Notice that the total fixed cost curve (TFC) stays constant, or flat. (b) The marginal cost curve (MC) reaches its minimum before average variable cost (AVC) and average total cost (ATC). Marginals always lead the average variable and average total costs either up or down. Average fixed cost (AFC), which has no variable component, continues to fall with increased quantity, because total fixed costs are spread across more units.

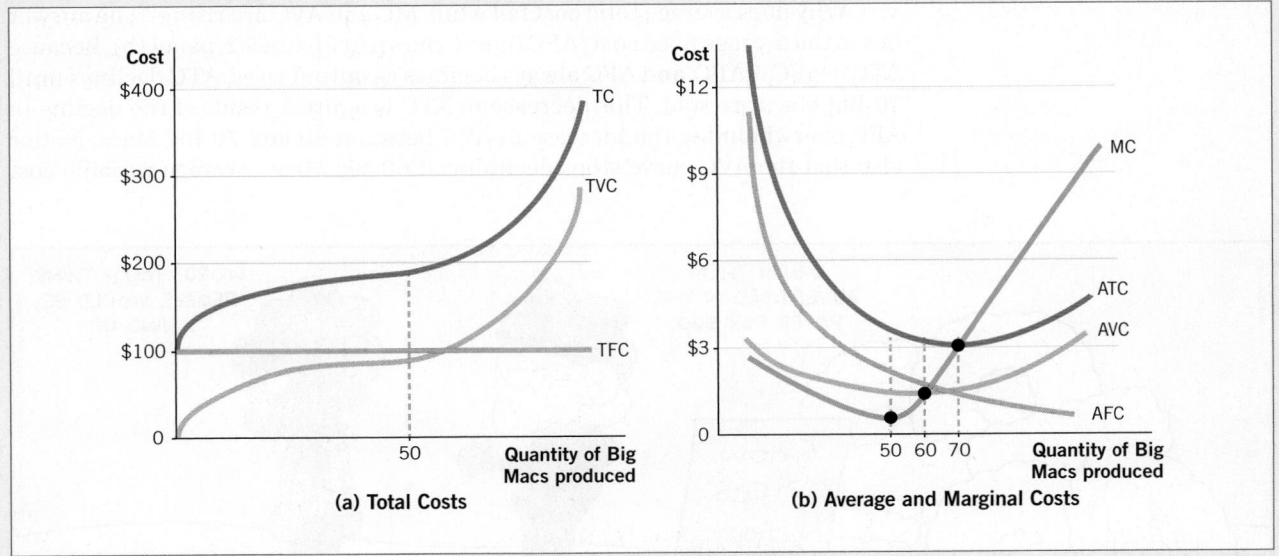

(a) Total Costs

(b) Average and Marginal Costs

and compare that information with the average cost at other local businesses. But neither the total cost of labor nor the average cost will tell her anything about the cost of making additional units—that is, Big Macs.

A manager can make even better decisions by looking at marginal cost. The **marginal cost** (**MC**) is the increase in cost that occurs from producing one additional unit of output. (In column 8 of Table 8.3, this relationship is shown as the change in TVC divided by the change in quantity produced, where "change" is indicated by Δ [the Greek letter delta]). For example, in planning the weekly work schedule, the manager has to consider how many workers to hire for each shift. She wants to hire additional workers when the cost of doing so is less than the expected boost in profits. In this situation, it is essential to know the marginal cost, or extra cost, of hiring one more worker.

In Table 8.3, marginal cost (MC) falls to a minimum of $1.00 when between 40 and 50 Big Macs are produced. Notice that the minimum MC occurs at a lower output level than average variable cost (AVC) and average total cost (ATC) in panel (b) of Figure 8.2. When output is less than 50 Big Macs, marginal cost is falling because over this range of production the marginal product of labor is increasing due to better teamwork and more specialization. After the fiftieth Big Mac, MC rises, acting as an early warning that average variable and total costs will soon follow suit. Why would a manager care about the marginal cost of the last few units being produced more than the average total cost of producing all the units? Because marginal cost helps the manager decide if making one more unit of output will increase profits or not!

The MC curve reaches its lowest point before the lowest point of the AVC and ATC curves. For this reason, a manager who is concerned about rising costs would look to the MC curve as a signal that average total cost will eventually increase as well. Once marginal cost begins to increase, it continues to pull down average variable cost until sales reach 60 Big Macs. After that point, MC is above AVC, and AVC begins to rise as well. However, ATC continues to fall until 70 Big Macs are sold. Note that the MC curve intersects the AVC and ATC curves at the minimum point along both curves.

Why does average total cost fall while MC and AVC are rising? The answer lies in the average fixed cost (AFC) curve shown in Figure 8.2, panel (b). Because ATC = AVC + AFC, and AFC always declines as output rises, ATC declines until 70 Big Macs are sold. This decrease in ATC is a direct result of the decline in AFC overwhelming the increase in AVC between 60 and 70 Big Macs. Notice also that the AVC curve stops declining at 60 Big Macs. Average variable cost

Marginal cost (MC) is the increase in cost that occurs from producing one additional unit of output.

Marginal thinking

Costs in the Short Run

OCEAN'S 8

In *Ocean's 8* (2018), Sandra Bullock and Cate Blanchett recruit six partners in crime to help them steal a diamond necklace worth $150 million. Part of the joy in watching any of the *Ocean's* films is seeing a star-studded cast of A-list actors pull off the perfect heist. Each partner has a specific skill: one is a jewelry maker, another a computer hacker, a third a pickpocket, and so on.

Beyond a certain point, however, adding more specialists mostly just means an extra person to split the take with. The Bullock and Blanchett characters know exactly how big a core team they want. That's why two people who play key but secondary roles— namely Yen, the acrobat from *Ocean's 11*, and Veronica, the younger sister of Nine Ball (Rihanna)—in effect function as contractors. They get a payoff, but they don't get a proportional share of the loot—because the marginal product of labor they contribute doesn't warrant a share.

How many accomplices does it take to pull off the perfect heist?

Marginal thinking

should initially decline as a result of increased specialization and teamwork. However, at some point the advantages of continued specialization are overtaken by diminishing marginal product, and average variable cost begins to rise. The transition from falling costs to rising costs is of particular interest because as long as average total cost is declining, the firm can lower its costs by increasing its output.

Once the marginal cost in Table 8.3 rises above the average total cost, the average total cost begins to rise as well. This result is evident if we compare the average total cost of making 70 Big Macs ($3.14) and 80 Big Macs ($3.25) with the marginal cost ($4.00) of making those extra 10 Big Macs. Since the marginal cost ($4.00) of making Big Macs 71 through 80 is higher than the average total cost at 70 ($3.14), the average total cost of making 80 Big Macs goes up (to $3.25).

Marginal cost always leads (or pulls) average variable cost and average total cost along. The MC eventually rises above the average total cost because of diminishing marginal product. Because the firm has to pay a fixed wage in our McDonald's example, the cost to produce each hamburger increases as each worker's output decreases.

Note that there is one "average" curve that the marginal cost does not affect: average fixed cost. Notice that the AFC curve in panel (b) of Figure 8.2 continues to fall even though marginal cost eventually rises. The AFC curve declines with increased output. Because McDonald's has $100.00 in fixed costs each day, we can determine the average fixed cost by dividing the total fixed cost ($100.00) by the number of Big Macs sold. When 10 Big Macs are sold, the average fixed cost is $10.00 per Big Mac, but this value falls to $1.00 per Big Mac if 100 burgers are sold. Because McDonald's is a high-volume business that relies on low costs to compete, being able to produce enough Big Macs to spread out the firm's fixed costs is essential.

Costs in the Long Run

We have seen that in the short run, businesses have fixed costs and fixed capacities. In the long run, all costs are variable and can be renegotiated. Thus, firms have more control over their costs in the long run, which enables them to reach their desired level of production. One way firms can adjust in the long run is by changing the **scale**, or size, of the production process. If the business is expected to grow, the firm can ramp up production. If the business is faltering, it can scale back its operations. This flexibility enables firms to avoid a situation of negative marginal product. Economists refer to the quantity of output that minimizes the average total cost in the long run as the **efficient scale**.

A long-run time horizon allows a business to choose a scale of operation that best suits its needs. For instance, if a local McDonald's is extremely popular, in the short run the manager can only hire more workers or expand the restaurant's hours to accommodate more customers. However, in the long run all costs are variable; the manager can add drive-through lanes, increase the number of registers, expand the grill area, and so on.

The absence of fixed factors in the long-run production process means that we cannot explain total costs in the long run in the same way we explained short-run costs. Short-run costs are a reflection of diminishing marginal product, whereas long-run costs are a reflection of scale and the cost of providing additional output. Because diminishing marginal product is no longer relevant in the long run, one might assume that costs would fall as output expands. However, this is not necessarily the case. Depending on the industry and the prevailing economic conditions, long-run costs can rise, fall, or stay approximately the same.

Scale refers to the size of the production process.

The **efficient scale** is the output level that minimizes average total cost in the long run.

Building more than one house at a time would represent economies of scale.

Economies of scale occur when long-run average total costs decline as output expands.

THREE TYPES OF SCALE In this section, we describe three different scenarios for a firm in the long run. A firm may experience *economies of scale*, *diseconomies of scale*, or *constant returns to scale*. Let's consider each of these in turn.

If output expands and long-run average total costs decline in the long run, a business experiences **economies of scale**. National homebuilders, such as Toll Brothers, provide a good example of economies of scale. All builders, whether they are local or national, do the same thing—they build houses. Each builder needs lumber, concrete, excavators, electricians, plumbers, roofers, and many more specialized workers or subcontractors. A big company, such as Toll, is able to hire many specialists and also buy the equipment it needs in bulk. As a result, Toll can manufacture the same home as a local builder but at a much lower cost.

But bigger isn't always better! Sometimes a company grows so large that coordination problems make costs rise. For example, as an enterprise expands its scale, it might require more managers, highly specialized workers, and a coordination process to pull everything together. As the layers of management expand, the coordination process can break down. For this reason, a larger firm can become less effective at holding down long-run average total costs and experience **diseconomies of scale**, or higher costs as output expands in the long run.

The problem of diseconomies of scale is especially relevant in the service sector of the economy. For example, large regional hospitals have many layers of bureaucracy. These added management costs and infrastructure expenses can make medical care more expensive beyond a certain point. If you are not convinced, ask yourself why large cities have many smaller competing hospitals rather than one centralized hospital. The answer becomes obvious: bigger doesn't always mean less expensive (or better)!

When long-run average total costs remain constant even as output expands in the long run, we say that the firm has **constant returns to scale**. For example, large national restaurant chains like Panda Express, which specializes in Chinese cuisine, compete with local Chinese restaurants. In each case, the local costs to hire workers and build the restaurant are the same. Panda Express does have a few advantages; for example, it can afford to advertise on national television and buy food in bulk. But Panda Express also has more overhead costs for its many layers of management. Constant returns to scale in the bigger chain mean that a small local Chinese restaurant will have approximately the same menu prices as its bigger rivals.

LONG-RUN COST CURVES Now it is time to illustrate the long-run nature of cost curves. We have seen that increased output may not always lead to economies of scale. Average total costs can decline, be constant, or rise with output. Figure 8.3 illustrates each of the three scale possibilities graphically. The long-run average total cost curve (LRATC) is actually a composite of many short-run average total cost curves (SRATC), which appear as the faint U-shaped dashed curves drawn in gray. By visualizing the short-run cost curves at any given output level, we can develop a composite of them to create the LRATC curve, which comprises all the short-run cost curves the firm may choose to deploy in the long run. In the long run, the firm is free to choose

Would you rather see the ER's doctor du jour or your own physician?

Diseconomies of scale occur when long-run average total costs rise as output expands.

Constant returns to scale occur when long-run average total costs remain constant as output expands.

Will you find lower prices at Panda Express or your local Chinese restaurant?

any of its short-run curves, so it always picks the output/cost combination that minimizes costs.

In the long run, there are three distinct possibilities: economies of scale, constant returns to scale, and diseconomies of scale. At first, each LRATC curve exhibits economies of scale as a result of increased specialization, the utilization of mass production, bulk purchasing power, and increased automation. The main question in the long run is whether the cost curve will continue to decline, level off, or rise. In an industry with economies of scale at high output levels—for example, homebuilding—the cost curve continues to decline, and the most efficient output level is always the largest output: the purple curve in Figure 8.3. In this situation, we would expect only one large firm to dominate the industry because large firms have significant cost advantages. However, in an industry with constant returns to scale—for example, restaurants—the cost curve flattens out: the red line. Once the curve becomes constant, firms of varying sizes can compete equally with one another because they have the same costs. Finally, in the case of diseconomies of scale—for example, big-city hospitals—bigger firms have higher costs: the orange curve.

FIGURE 8.3

Costs in the Long Run

In the long run, there are three distinct possibilities: the long-run average total cost curve (LRATC) can exhibit economies of scale (the purple curve), constant returns to scale (the red curve), or diseconomies of scale (the orange curve).

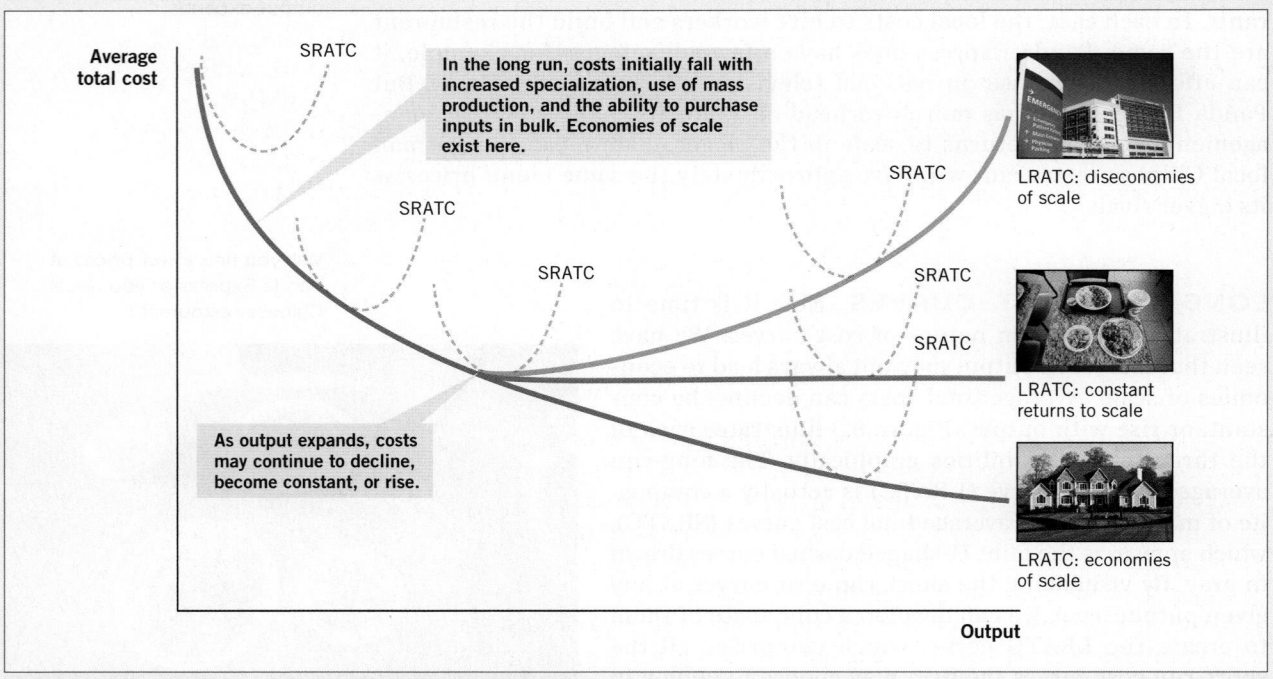

Economies of Scale

THE BIG BANG THEORY: THE WORK SONG NANOCLUSTER

In an episode of the long-running TV series *The Big Bang Theory*, Penny decides to make flower barrettes in her spare time to supplement her pay as a waitress. Because Penny is not very good at math, when Sheldon stops by she seeks his advice about how she can earn more money. What transpires can only be described as the best explanation of business costs you'll ever see.

As Sheldon explains to Penny: "If you took advantage of modern marketing techniques and optimized your manufacturing process, you might make this a viable business." They get to work and Sheldon starts timing how long it takes Penny to make a flower barrette. It takes her 12 minutes and 17 seconds, and Penny seems quite happy until Sheldon says, "That's 4.9 Penny Blossoms per hour. Based on your cost of materials and your wholesale selling price, you'll effectively be paying yourself $5.19 a day. There are children in a sneaker factory in Indonesia who outearn you." To increase Penny's productivity, he suggests they create an assembly line to lower the cost of manufacturing the barrettes, and they begin working together to make the Penny Blossoms, even singing a rhythmic work song to increase their productivity.

Creating flower barrettes by hand in your apartment misses out on economies of scale.

Together they can now make each Penny Blossom in under 3 minutes!

At this point, Leonard, Howard, and Raj enter Penny's apartment and start to ask questions about what is going on. Everyone quickly realizes they will have to expand the scale of the operation to fully optimize the production process to lower costs even further. The result is that you see the production process evolve from a small-scale operation in Penny's apartment in the short run to a sophisticated large-scale enterprise in the long run. All of this is done in one very funny 22-minute episode.

Costs are defined in a number of ways, but marginal cost plays the most crucial role in a firm's cost structure. By observing what happens to marginal cost, you can understand changes in average cost and total cost. This simple fact explains why economists place so much emphasis on marginal cost. Going forward, a solid grasp of marginal analysis will help you understand many of the most important concepts in microeconomics.

Marginal thinking

You now understand the cost, or supply side, of business decisions. However, to provide a complete picture of how firms operate, we still need to examine how markets work. Costs are only part of the story, and in the next chapter we take a closer look at profits.

ECONOMIES OF SCALE

Bike sharing is big business throughout China, with millions of bikes in use. It costs just pennies per hour to rent a bike, which means profit margins are thin, so firms have to be careful how quickly they expand into new markets. China's third-largest bike share company, Bluegogo, went out of business in 2017, when it expanded too rapidly and ran out of the cash needed to keep going. Bluegogo's chief executive said he had been "filled with arrogance" and believed that all they had to do was flood the market with bikes and people would use them.

Many firms mistakenly believe that expanding will make them more profitable. Bluegogo's two main rivals, Ofo and Mobike, followed the same strategy but survived because they generated more revenues. What does it look like when firms expand too rapidly? Check out this bicycle scrap pile, littered with broken shared bicycles that the companies would rather discard than fix.

Bike share graveyard in Xiamen, China, a testament to the perils of expanding too quickly.

Marginal Cost: The True Cost of Admission to Universal Studios

You and your family visit Orlando for a week. While there, you decide to go to Universal Studios. When you arrive, you notice that each family member can buy a day pass for $115 or a two-day pass for $150. Your parents are concerned about spending too much, so they decide to calculate the average cost of a two-day pass to see if it is a good value. The average cost is $150 \div 2$, or $75 per day. Their math is correct, but something you learned in economics tells you they are not thinking about this situation in the correct way.

QUESTION: What concept can you apply to make the decision clearer?

ANSWER: Tell your parents about *marginal cost*. The first day costs $115, but the marginal cost of going back to the park on the second day is only the extra cost per person, or $150 − $115, which equals $35. Your parents still might not want to spend the extra money, but spending only an extra $35 for a second day makes it an attractive value. Someone who does not appreciate economics might think the second day costs an extra $75 because that is the average cost, but the average cost is misleading. Looking at marginal cost is the best way to weigh these two options. By the way, if you want a three-day pass the price is $170, making the marginal cost of the third day just $170 − $150, which equals $20. That sounds ridiculously low, but the incremental increase in the price is low because no matter how much you like Harry Potter, a third straight day in the same theme park becomes repetitive quickly.

CHALLENGE QUESTION: Suppose you are considering a single-day three-park pass to Universal Studios, Islands of Adventure, and Volcano Bay. The price for the three-park pass is $170. If you value Universal Studios at $140, Islands of Adventure at $30, and Volcano Bay at $20, should you buy the three-park pass instead of the single-day pass to just Universal Studios?

ANSWER: The total value of the three-park pass to you is $140 + $30 + $20 = $190, which is more than enough to justify the expense of the park hopper ticket ($170), since you'd earn $20 in consumer surplus. However, you'd earn more consumer surplus if you purchased the day pass to just Universal Studios, since $140 − $115 = $25 in consumer surplus. That means you are better off sticking just with Universal Studios, since the price of the three-park pass doesn't save you enough money to justify the added expense.

Is one day enough to see Hogwarts?

Marginal thinking

Conclusion

Do larger firms have lower costs? Not always. When diseconomies of scale occur, average total costs will rise with output. This result contradicts the common misconception that bigger firms have lower costs than their smaller competitors. Simply put, sometimes a leaner firm with less overhead can beat its larger rivals on cost. ✳

How Much Does It Cost to Raise a Child?

- Raising a child costs approximately $250,000.
- Families that have three or more children spend an average of 22% less on each child.
- The cost of raising children also forces families to make trade-offs. In many households, both parents must work or work longer hours.

Raising a child is one of life's most rewarding experiences, but it can be very expensive. According to the U.S. Department of Agriculture, the cost for a middle-income, two-parent family to raise a child from birth to age 18 is about $250,000 (not including college). To determine this number, the government considers all the costs related to raising a child, such as food, clothing, medical care, and entertainment. In addition, the government apportions a share of the costs of the family home and vehicles to each child in the household. To put the cost of raising a child in perspective, the median home value in 2018 was **Opportunity cost** $239,000. Talk about opportunity cost!

What if a family has more than one child? You wouldn't necessarily multiply the cost by 2 or 3, because there are economies of scale in raising more children. For example, some things can be shared: the children might share a bedroom and wear hand-me-downs. Also, the family can purchase food in bulk. As a result, families that have three or more children can manage to spend an average of 22% less on each child.

Trade-offs The cost of raising children also forces families to make trade-offs. In many households, both parents must work or work longer hours. When one parent steps out of the workforce, the household loses a paycheck. While leaving the workforce may save in expenses associated with working, including certain clothes, transportation, and childcare, there are also hidden costs. For example, the lack of workplace continuity lowers the stay-at-home parent's future earning power.

Raising a child is an expensive proposition in both the short run and the long run. But don't let this discourage you; it is also one of the most rewarding personal investments you will ever make. More importantly, there are large benefits to society as well, as Nancy Folbre, author of *Valuing Children: Rethinking the Economics of the Family* notes. "When you raise children, they grow up to become workers and taxpayers and participants in an economic system that reproduces itself over time."[*] This has large implications for how the costs of raising children should be distributed among parents and society.

---

[*]Nancy Folbre, *Valuing Children: Rethinking the Economics of the Family* (Cambridge, M.A.: Harvard University Press, 2010).

Raising Hope, a TV show that ran from 2010 to 2014, is about Jimmy, a single father who wants to give his daughter a better childhood than the one he had.

· ANSWERING *the* BIG QUESTIONS ·

How are profits and losses calculated?

- Profits and losses are determined by calculating the difference between expenses (total cost) and total revenue.
- There are two types of profit: economic profit and accounting profit. If a business has an economic profit, its revenue is larger than the combination of its explicit and implicit costs.
- Economists break costs into two components: explicit costs, which are easy to calculate, and implicit costs, which are hard to calculate. Because economic profit accounts for implicit costs, the economic profit is always less than the accounting profit.

How much should a firm produce?

- A firm should produce an output that is consistent with the largest possible economic profit.
- To maximize profit, firms must effectively combine land, labor, and capital in the right quantities.
- In any short-run production process, a point of diminishing marginal product will occur at which additional units of a variable input no longer generate as much output as before. Diminishing marginal product is a result of fixed inputs (such as capital and land) in the short run.
- Marginal cost (MC) is the key variable in determining a firm's cost structure. The MC curve always leads the average total cost (ATC) and average variable cost (AVC) curves up or down.

What costs do firms consider in the short run and the long run?

- In the short run, firms consider variable and fixed costs, as well as marginal cost. Firms also consider average variable cost (AVC), average fixed cost (AFC), and average total cost (ATC).
- With the exception of the average fixed cost (AFC) curve, which always declines, short-run cost curves are U-shaped. All variable costs initially decline due to increased specialization. At a certain point, the advantages of continued specialization give way to diminishing marginal product, and the MC, AVC, and ATC curves begin to rise.
- Long-run costs are a reflection of scale. Firms can experience diseconomies of scale, economies of scale, or constant returns to scale, depending on the industry.

·CHAPTER PROBLEMS·

Concepts You Should Know

accounting profit (p. 254)
average fixed cost (AFC) (p. 264)
average total cost (ATC) (p. 264)
average variable cost (AVC) (p. 264)
constant returns to scale (p. 269)
diminishing marginal
    product (p. 260)
diseconomies of scale (p. 269)
economic profit (p. 255)

economies of scale (p. 268)
efficient scale (p. 268)
explicit costs (p. 253)
factors of production (p. 257)
fixed costs (p. 263)
implicit costs (p. 253)
loss (p. 253)
marginal cost (MC) (p. 266)

marginal product (p. 258)
output (p. 257)
production function (p. 258)
profit (p. 252)
scale (p. 268)
total cost (p. 252)
total revenue (p. 252)
variable costs (p. 262)

Questions for Review

1. What is the equation for the profit (or loss) of a firm?

2. Why is economic profit a better measure of profitability than accounting profit? Give an example.

3. What role does diminishing marginal product play in determining the ideal mix of labor and capital a firm should use?

4. Describe what happens to the total product of a firm when marginal product is increasing, decreasing, and negative.

5. Explain why marginal cost is the glue that connects average variable cost and average total cost.

6. Compare the short-run and long-run cost curves. In a few sentences, explain their differences.

7. Name examples of industries that illustrate each of the following: economies of scale, constant returns to scale, and diseconomies of scale. Think creatively; do not use the textbook examples.

Study Problems (＊solved at the end of this section)

1. Go to www.lemonadegame.com. This free online game places you in the role of a lemonade seller. Nothing could be simpler, right? Not so fast! You still need to control costs and ensure that you have the right ingredients on hand to be able to sell lemonade. You will need to manage your supply of lemons, sugar, ice, and cups. You will also have to set a price and decide how many lemons and how much sugar and ice to put in each glass of lemonade you produce. This is not a trivial process, so play the game. Your challenge is to make $20 in profit over the first five days. (Your business starts with $20, so you need to have $40 in your account by the end of day 5 to meet the challenge. Are you up to it?)

2. The following table shows a short-run production function for laptop computers. Use the

data to determine where diminishing product begins.

Number of workers	Total output of laptop computers
0	0
1	40
2	100
3	150
4	180
5	200
6	205
7	200
8	190

3. A pizza business has the cost structure described below. The firm's fixed costs are $25 per day. Calculate the firm's average fixed costs, average variable costs, average total costs, and marginal costs.

Output (pizzas per day)	Total cost of output
0	$25
10	75
20	115
30	150
40	175
50	190
60	205
70	225
80	250

✳ **4.** A firm is considering changing its plant size, so it calculates the average cost of production for various plant sizes, shown below. If the firm is currently using plant size C, is the firm experiencing economies of scale, diseconomies of scale, or constant returns to scale?

Plant size	Average total cost
A (smallest)	$10,000
B	9,500
C	9,000
D	8,800
E	8,800
F (largest)	8,900

5. True or false?

a. The AFC curve can never rise.

b. Diminishing marginal product is a long-run constraint that prevents lower costs.

c. The MC curve intersects the AVC and ATC curves at the minimum point along both curves.

d. Accounting profit is smaller than economic profit.

e. Total cost divided by output is equal to marginal cost.

6. Digital media distributed over the Internet often have marginal costs of zero. For instance, people can download music and movies instantly through many providers. Do these products exhibit economies, diseconomies, or constant returns to scale?

7. An airline has a marginal cost per passenger of $30 on a route from Boston to Detroit. At the same time, the typical fare charged is $300. The planes that fly the route are usually full, yet the airline claims that it loses money on the route. How is this possible?

8. Many amusement parks offer two-day passes at dramatically discounted prices. If a one-day pass costs $40 but the two-day pass costs $50, what is the average cost for the two-day pass? What is the marginal cost of the second day pass?

✳ **9.** Suppose that you own a yard care business. You have your own mower, flatbed truck, and other equipment. You are also the primary employee. Why might you have trouble calculating your profits? (**Hint:** Think about the difference between accounting profits and economic profits.)

10. Use the information provided in the following table to fill in the blanks.

Output	Total fixed cost	Total variable cost	Total cost	Average fixed cost	Average variable cost	Average total cost	Marginal cost
0	$500	$0	$500	___	___	___	
1	500	200	___	___	___	___	___
2	___	___	800	___	___	___	___
3	___	___	875	___	___	___	___
4	___	___	925	___	___	___	$25
5	___	___		$100	___	___	___
6	___	450	___	___	___	___	___

11. If you are a fan of cold dessert treats, you'll recognize that the production process at Cold Stone Creamery differs a great deal from frozen yogurt places. At Cold Stone you give the server your order and the mix-ins you want, and the server creates your treat for you. This process is labor intensive. At a frozen yogurt place, you pick up a cup, choose your flavor from the self-serve machine, serve it yourself, and add in your own mix-ins. You put your creation on a scale and the worker then rings you up. This process is capital intensive. Given this information, which type of frozen dessert business will have the lower marginal cost of production?

✱ **12.** Watch the Reebok commercial on "Terry Tate, Office Linebacker" (www.youtube.com/watch?v=tbSpAsJSZPc). Is the firm that hires Terry Tate experiencing economies, constant returns, or diseconomies of scale? Explain your answer.

13. Take a look at the table in Problem 10. What is happening to the marginal cost as more and more units are produced? Can you think of an industry where this might be expected?

✱ **14.** All else equal, when the marginal product of labor is falling, the marginal cost of producing output

  a. is falling.
  b. is rising.
  c. could be rising or falling.

Solved Problems

4. The key to solving this problem is recognizing the direction of change in the average total cost. If the firm were to switch to a smaller plant, like B, its average total cost would rise to $9,500. Because the smaller plant would cost more, plant C is currently enjoying economies of scale. When we compare the average total cost of C ($9,000) to D ($8,800), it continues to fall. Because the average total cost is falling from B to D, we again know that the firm is experiencing economies of scale.

9. When calculating your costs for the mower, truck, and other expenses, you are computing your explicit costs. Subtracting the explicit costs from your total revenue will yield the accounting profit you have earned. However, you still do not know your economic profit because you haven't determined your implicit costs. Because you are the primary employee, you also have to add in the opportunity cost of the time you invest in the business. You may not know exactly what you might have earned doing something else, but you can be sure it exists—this is your implicit cost. Implicit costs are the reason you may have trouble computing your profits. You might show an accounting profit only to discover that what you thought you made was less than you could have made by doing something else. If that is the case, your true economic profit is actually negative.

12. Terry Tate enforces company policies and helps to reduce the amount of slacking, making the workforce more productive. However, at the same time, the company needs to hire Terry Tate to reduce slacking, and this is costly, which means that the company is experiencing diseconomies of scale.

14. When the marginal product of labor is falling, the marginal cost of production is rising, since each worker is becoming less productive and therefore each unit requires more labor to produce.

Firms in a
Competitive Market

Why Do Firms Charge the Price They Do?

You want to send your mom flowers for Mother's Day, but when you check out the price of an arrangement from your favorite local florist, Diane's Flower Cottage, you have an attack of sticker shock. Why in the world are flowers so expensive?

Let's consider things from Diane's point of view, though. Growing flowers is labor intensive, since they must be carefully tended and then harvested by hand. Being highly perishable, they then have to be shipped rapidly, under refrigeration, to the point of sale. Diane has to charge enough to cover all the costs associated with getting the flowers to her shop. She then has to cover the expense of storing the flowers, again under refrigeration, and the spoilage loss of those that go unsold. Diane also has to pay the staff she relies on to market, design, and sell arrangements and deliver them on time. So while flower delivery might seem expensive to the consumer, Diane is just charging the market rate and can't go lower, due to her many behind-the-scenes costs. She might wish she could charge more, but since there are many florists, all of whom sell essentially the same services, competition drives prices down, which limits any one firm's ability to charge as much as it would like.

Such a lovely sight! But a lot of money probably went into this gorgeous display. These flowers may well have been grown in Colombia or Ecuador, the main foreign suppliers to the U.S. flower market. Getting them to the shop was not cheap.

In this chapter and the next four, we look in more detail at how markets work, the profits firms earn, and how market forces determine the price a firm can charge for its product or service. We begin our examination of *market structure,* or how individual firms are interconnected, by looking at the conditions necessary to create a competitive market. Although few real markets achieve the ideal market structure described in this chapter, this model provides a good starting point for understanding other market structures.

Our analysis of competitive markets shows that when competition is widespread, firms have little or no control over the price they can charge, and they make little or no economic profit. Thus, in competitive markets, firms are completely at the mercy of market forces that set the price. Let's find out why.

· BIG QUESTIONS ·

- How do competitive markets work?
- How do firms maximize profits?
- What does the supply curve look like in perfectly competitive markets?

How Do Competitive Markets Work?

Competitive markets exist when there are so many buyers and sellers that each one has only a small impact on the market price and output. Recall that in Chapter 3 we used the example of the Pike Place Market, where each fish vendor sells similar products. Because each fish vendor is small relative to the whole market, no single firm can influence the market price. It doesn't matter where you buy salmon because the price is the same or very similar at every fish stall. When buyers are willing to purchase a product anywhere, sellers have no control over the price they charge. These two characteristics—similar goods and many participants—create a highly competitive market where the price and quantity sold are determined by the market conditions rather than by any one firm.

In competitive markets, buyers can expect to find consistently low prices and a wide availability of the good they want. Firms that produce goods in competitive markets are known as price takers. A **price taker** has no control over the price set by the market. It "takes"—that is, accepts—the price determined by the overall supply and demand conditions that regulate the market. One of the reasons why firms are price takers is that each seller is small compared to the overall market. This means that any individual seller's decision (to either increase or decrease production) has no impact on the market price.

Competitive markets have another important feature: new competitors can easily enter the market. If you want to open a copy shop, all you have to do is rent store space and several copy machines. There are no licensing or regulatory obstacles in your way. Likewise, there is very little to stop competitors from leaving the market. If you decide to shut down your business, you can lock the doors, return the equipment you rented, and move on to do something else. When barriers to entry into a marketplace are low, new firms are free to compete with existing businesses, which ensures the existence of competitive markets and low prices. Table 9.1 summarizes the characteristics of competitive markets.

Real-life examples of competitive markets usually fall short of perfection. Markets that are almost perfectly competitive, shown in Table 9.2, include the stock market, farmers' markets, online ticket auctions, and currency trading. Of all the market structures, perfect competition is the most beneficial to society because it creates the maximum combined consumer surplus and producer surplus (as we saw in Chapter 5). The more imperfectly competitive a market is, the lower is the total of the two types of surplus and the less beneficial it is to society overall.

In the next section, we examine the profits competitive firms make. After all, profits motivate firms to produce a product, so knowing how a business can make the most profit is central to understanding how competitive markets work.

TABLE 9.1

Characteristics of Competitive Markets

- Many sellers
- Similar products
- Free entry and exit
- Price taking
- Every firm is small

TABLE 9.2

Almost Perfect Markets

Example	How it works	Reality check
Stock market 	Millions of shares of stocks are traded every day on various stock exchanges, and generally the buyers and sellers have access to real-time information about prices. Because most of the traders represent only a small share of the market, they have little ability to influence the market price.	Because of the volume of shares that they control, large institutional investors, like Pacific Investment Management Company (PIMCO), manage billions of dollars in funds. As a result, they are big enough to influence the market price.
Farmers' markets 	In farmers' markets, sellers are able to set up at little or no cost. Many buyers are also present. The gathering of numerous buyers and sellers of similar products causes the market price for similar products to converge toward a single price.	Many produce markets do not have enough sellers to achieve a perfectly competitive result. With fewer vendors, individual sellers can often set their prices higher.
Online ticket auctions 	The resale market for tickets to major sporting events and concerts involves many buyers and sellers. The prices for seats in identical sections end up converging quickly toward a narrow range.	Some ticket companies and fans get special privileges that enable them to buy and sell blocks of tickets before others can enter the market.
Currency trading 	Hundreds of thousands of traders around the globe engage in currency buying and selling on any given day. Because all traders have very good real-time information, currency trades in different parts of the world converge toward the same price.	Currency markets are subject to intervention on the part of governments that want to strategically alter the prevailing price of their currency.

ECONOMICS IN THE REAL WORLD

AALSMEER FLOWER AUCTION

The world's largest flower auction takes place in Aalsmeer, a small town in the Netherlands. Each week, producers sell over 100 million flowers there. In fact, over one-third of all the flowers sold in the world pass through Aalsmeer. Because the Aalsmeer market serves thousands of buyers and sellers, it is one of the best examples of a competitive market you will ever find. The supply comes from approximately 6,000 growers worldwide. More than 2,000 buyers attend the auction to purchase flowers.

Aalsmeer uses a method known as a Dutch auction to determine the price for each crate of flowers sold. Most people think of an auction as a situation in which two or more individuals try to outbid each other. However, in Aalsmeer that process is reversed. As each crate of flowers goes on sale, the price on a huge board starts at 100 euros and then goes down until the lot is sold. This special kind of auction was invented here, and it is a very efficient way of getting the highest price out of the buyer who wants the lot the most.

At Aalsmeer, individual buyers and sellers are small compared with the overall size of the market. In addition, the flowers offered by one seller are almost indistinguishable from those offered by the other sellers. As a result, individual buyers and sellers have no control over the price set by the market.

The Aalsmeer flower market is almost perfectly competitive.

How Do Firms Maximize Profits?

All firms, whether they are active in a competitive market or not, attempt to maximize profits. Making a profit requires that a firm have a thorough grasp of its costs and revenues. In the previous chapter, we learned about the firm's cost structure. In this section, we examine its revenues. Combining the firm's revenues with its costs enables us to determine how much profit the firm makes.

Profits are a key goal of almost every firm, but they don't always materialize. Sometimes, firms experience losses instead of profits, so we also explore whether a firm should shut down or continue to operate in order to minimize its losses. Once we fully understand the firm's decision-making process, we

PRACTICE WHAT YOU KNOW

Price Takers: Mall Food Courts

Your instructor asks you to find an example of a competitive market nearby. Your friend suggests that you visit the food court at a nearby mall.

QUESTION: Does each restaurant in a food court meet the definition of a price taker, thereby signaling a competitive market?

ANSWER: Most food courts contain many sellers. Customers can choose among burgers, sandwiches, salads, pizza, and much more. Everywhere you turn, there is another place to eat and the prices at each place are comparable. Is this enough to make each restaurant a price taker? Not quite. Each restaurant has some market power because it serves different food, enabling the more popular places to charge somewhat more.

Are the restaurants in a food court price takers?

While the restaurants in the court are not price takers, the drinks (both fountain drinks and bottled water) that they sell are essentially the same. Any customer who is only interested in getting something to drink has a highly competitive market to choose from.

Competitive Markets

THE SIMPSONS: MR. PLOW

In this episode, Homer buys a snowplow and goes into the snow removal business. After a few false starts, his business, Mr. Plow, becomes a huge success. Every snowy morning, he looks out the window and comments about "white gold."

The episode illustrates each of the factors that go into making a competitive market. Businesses providing snow removal all offer the same service. Because there are many buyers (homeowners) and many businesses (the "plow people"), the market is competitive.

However, Homer's joy, profits, and notoriety are short-lived. Soon his friend Barney buys a bigger plow and joins the ranks of the "plow people." Barney's entry into the business shows how easy it is for competitors to enter the market. Then Homer, who has begun to get lazy and rest on his success, wakes up late one snowy morning to find all the driveways in

Homer's great idea is about to melt away.

the neighborhood already plowed. A nasty battle over customers ensues.

When firms can easily enter the market, any positive economic profit a firm enjoys in the short run will dissipate in the long run, due to increased competition. As a result, we can say that this *Simpsons* episode shows a market that is not just competitive; it is perfectly competitive.

---

will better comprehend how the entire market functions. To make this process easier, throughout this section we refer to Mr. Plow (from the *Simpsons* episode mentioned in the Economics in the Media box above) to examine the choices every business must make. We look at the price Mr. Plow (Homer Simpson) charges and how many driveways he clears, and then we compare his revenues to his costs to determine whether he is maximizing his profit.

The Profit-Maximizing Rule

Let's imagine how much revenue Mr. Plow will make if the competitive price is $10 for each driveway he clears. Table 9.3 shows how much profit he might make if he clears up to 10 driveways. As we learned in Chapter 8, total profit (column 4) is determined by taking the total revenue (column 2) and subtracting the total cost (column 3). Mr. Plow's profits start out at −$25 because even if he does not clear any driveways, he incurs a fixed cost of $25 to rent a snow plow each day. To recover the fixed cost, he needs to generate revenue by clearing driveways. As Mr. Plow clears more driveways, the losses (the negative numbers) shown in column 4 gradually contract; he begins to earn a profit by the time he plows 6 driveways.

What does Table 9.3 tell us about Mr. Plow's business? Column 4 shows the company's profits (π) at various output (Q) levels. Profit reaches a maximum of $10 at 8 driveways. From looking at this table, you might suppose that the firm can make a production decision based on the data in the profit column. However, firms don't work this way. The total profit (or loss) is typically determined after the fact. For example, Homer may have to fill up with gas at the end of the day, buy new tires for his plow, or purchase liability insurance. His accountant will take his receipts and deduct each expense to determine his accounting profit. This process takes time. An accurate understanding of Homer's profits may have to wait until the end of the quarter, or even the year, in order to fully account for all the irregular expenses associated with running a business. This means that the information found in the profit column is not available until long after the business decisions have been made. So, in day-to-day operations, the firm needs another way to make production decisions.

The key to determining Mr. Plow's profits comes from understanding the relationship between marginal revenue (column 5) and marginal cost (column 6). The **marginal revenue** is the change (Δ) in total revenue when the firm produces one additional unit of output. So, looking down column 5, we see that for every driveway Mr. Plow clears, he makes $10 in extra revenue. The marginal cost (column 6) is the change (Δ) in total cost when the firm produces one additional unit. Column 7 calculates the difference between the marginal revenue (column 5) and marginal cost (column 6).

Marginal thinking

Marginal revenue
is the change in total revenue a firm receives when it produces one additional unit of output.

TABLE 9.3
Calculating Profits for Mr. Plow

(1) Quantity (Q = driveways cleared)	(2) Total revenue	(3) Total cost	(4) Total profit	(5) Marginal revenue	(6) Marginal cost	(7) Change (Δ) in profit
Abbreviation:	TR	TC	π	MR	MC	Δπ
Formula:	P × Q		TR − TC	ΔTR	ΔTC	MR − MC
0	$0	$25	−$25	$10	$9	$1
1	10	34	−24	10	7	3
2	20	41	−21	10	5	5
3	30	46	−16	10	3	7
4	40	49	−9	10	2	8
5	50	51	−1	10	3	7
6	60	54	6	10	7	3
7	70	61	9	10	9	1
8	80	70	10	10	25	−15
9	90	95	−5	10	50	−40
10	100	145	−45			

If you already own a truck and a plow, starting your own snow-plow business is inexpensive.

In Chapter 8, we saw that to understand cost structure, a firm focuses on marginal cost. The same is true on the revenue side. To make a good decision on the level of investment, Mr. Plow must use marginal analysis. Looking at column 7, we see that for output levels at or below 8, MR − MC is positive, as indicated by the numbers in green. Expanding output to 8 driveways adds to profits. But as Mr. Plow services more driveways, the marginal cost rises dramatically. For instance, Mr. Plow may have to seek driveways farther away and thus incur higher transportation costs for those additional customers. Whatever the cause, increased marginal cost (column 6) eventually overtakes the constant marginal revenue (column 5), causing MR − MC to go negative (shown in red in column 7).

Recall that we began our discussion by saying that a firm can't wait for the yearly, or even quarterly, profit statements to make production decisions. By examining the marginal impact, shown in column 7, a firm can make good day-to-day operational decisions. Each time it snows, Mr. Plow has to decide whether or not to clear more driveways. For instance, if he is plowing 4 driveways, he may decide to work a little harder the next time it snows and plow one more. At 5 driveways, his profits increase by $8. Since he enjoys making this extra money, he could expand again from 5 to 6 driveways. This time, he makes an extra $7 in profit. From 6 to 7 driveways, he earns $3 more in profit, and from 7 to 8 driveways he earns $1 in profit. However, when Mr. Plow expands beyond 8 driveways, he discovers that at 9 driveways he loses $15. This loss would cause him to scale back his efforts to a more profitable level of output.

Marginal thinking

The **profit-maximizing rule** states that profit maximization occurs when a firm chooses the quantity of output that equates marginal revenue and marginal cost, or MR = MC.

Marginal thinking helps Mr. Plow discover the production level at which his profits are maximized. The **profit-maximizing rule** states that profit maximization occurs when a firm expands output as long as marginal revenue is greater than marginal cost, stopping as close to MR = MC as practical. According to the MR = MC rule, production should stop at the point at which profit opportunities no longer exist. In the case of Mr. Plow, he should stop adding new driveways once he reaches 8.

Deciding How Much to Produce in a Competitive Market

We have observed that a firm in a highly competitive market is a price taker; it has no control over the price set by the market. Because all snow removal companies provide the same service, they must charge the price determined by the overall supply and demand conditions that regulate that particular market.

To better understand these relationships, we can look at them visually. In Figure 9.1, we use the MR and MC data from Table 9.3 to illustrate the profit calculation. For reference, we also include the average total cost curve. Recall from Chapter 8 that the marginal cost curve (MC, shown in orange) always crosses the average total cost curve (ATC) at the lowest point. Figure 9.1 illustrates the relationship between the marginal cost curve (MC) and the marginal revenue curve (MR). Because the price (P) Mr. Plow charges is constant at $10, marginal revenue is horizontal. Unlike MR, MC at first decreases and then rises due to diminishing marginal product. Therefore, the firm wants to expand production as long as MR is greater than MC, and it will stop production at the quantity where MR = MC = $10. When

FIGURE 9.1

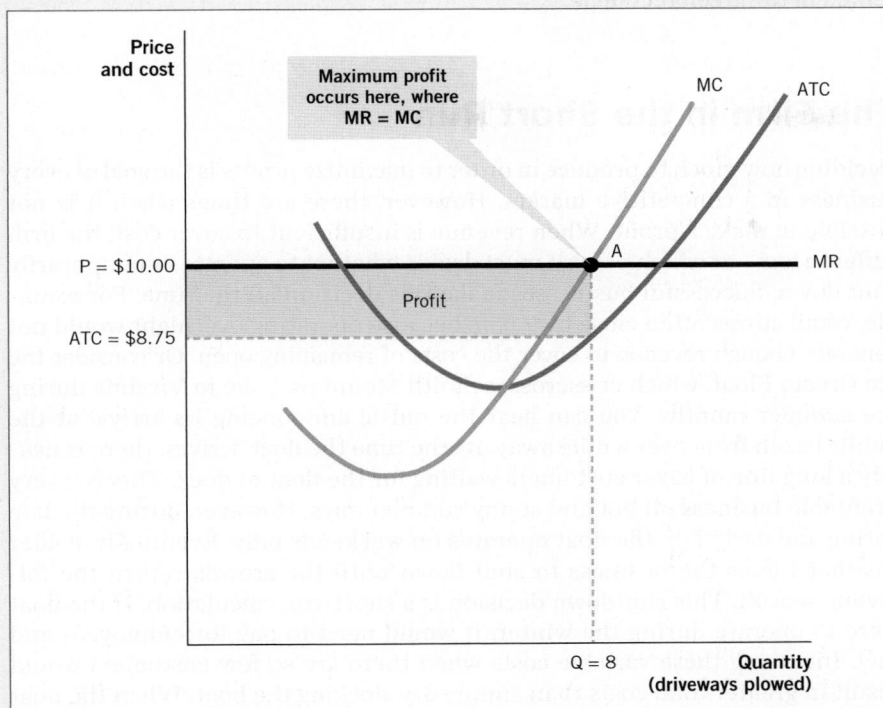

Profit Maximization

Mr. Plow uses the profit-maximizing rule to locate the point at which marginal revenue equals marginal cost, or MR = MC. This point determines the ideal output level, Q. The firm takes the price from the market; price is shown as the horizontal MR curve at P = $10.00. Because the price charged is higher than the average total cost curve along the dashed line at quantity Q, the firm makes the economic profit shown in the green rectangle.

Q = 8, MR = MC and profits are maximized. At quantities beyond 8, the MC curve is above the MR curve. Marginal cost is higher than marginal revenue, and the firm's profits fall.

Note that we can use the profit-maximizing rule, MR = MC, to identify the most profitable output in a two-step process:

1. Locate the point at which the firm will maximize its profits: MR = MC. This is the point labeled A in Figure 9.1.

2. Look for the profit-maximizing output: move down the vertical dashed line to the *x* axis at point Q. Any quantity greater than or less than Q would result in lower profits.

Once we know the profit-maximizing quantity, we can determine the average cost of producing Q units. From Q, we move up along the dashed line until it intersects with the ATC curve. From that point, we move horizontally until we come to the *y* axis. Doing so tells us the average cost of making 8 units. Because the total cost in Table 9.3 is $70 when 8 driveways are plowed, dividing 70 by 8 gives us $8.75 for the average total cost. We can calculate Mr. Plow's profit rectangle from Figure 9.1 as follows:

profit = (price − ATC [along the dashed line at quantity Q]) × Q

This equation gives us (10 − 8.75) × 8 = $10, which is the profit we see in Table 9.3, column 4, in red. Because the MR is the price, and because the price is higher than the average total cost, the firm makes the profit visually represented in the green rectangle.

The Firm in the Short Run

Deciding how much to produce in order to maximize profits is the goal of every business in a competitive market. However, there are times when it is not possible to make a profit. When revenue is insufficient to cover cost, the firm suffers a loss—at which point it must decide whether to operate or temporarily shut down. Successful businesses make this decision all the time. For example, retail stores often close by 9 p.m. because operating overnight would not generate enough revenue to cover the costs of remaining open. Or consider the Ice Cream Float, which crisscrosses Smith Mountain Lake in Virginia during the summer months. You can hear the music announcing its arrival at the public beach from over a mile away. By the time the float arrives, there is usually a long line of eager customers waiting for the float to dock. This is a very profitable business on hot and sunny summer days. However, during the late spring and early fall, the float operates on weekends only. Eventually, colder weather forces the business to shut down until the crowds return the following season. This shutdown decision is a short-run calculation. If the float were to operate during the winter, it would need to pay for employees and fuel. Incurring these variable costs when there are so few customers would result in greater total costs than simply dry-docking the boat. When the float is dry-docked over the winter, only the fixed cost of storing the boat remains.

Fortunately, a firm can use a simple, intuitive rule to decide whether to operate or shut down in the short run: if the firm would lose less by shutting down than by staying open, it should shut down. Recall that costs are broken into two parts—fixed and variable. Fixed costs must be paid whether the business is open or not. Because variable costs are incurred only when the business is open, if it can make enough to cover its variable costs—for example, employee wages and the cost of the electricity needed to run the lighting—it will choose to remain open. Once the variable costs are covered, any extra money goes toward paying the fixed costs.

A business should operate if it can cover its variable costs, and it should shut down if it cannot. Figure 9.2 illustrates the decision using cost curves. As long as the firm's marginal revenue curve (MR) is greater than the minimum point on the average variable cost curve (AVC)—the green and yellow areas—the firm will choose to operate. (Note that the MR curve is not shown in Figure 9.2. The shaded areas in the figure denote the range of potential MR curves that are profitable and those that cause a loss.) Recalling our example of the Ice Cream Float, you can think of the green area as the months during the summer when the business makes a profit and the yellow area as the times during spring and fall when the float operates even though it is incurring a loss (because the loss is less than if the float were to shut down entirely). Finally, if the MR curve falls below the AVC curve— the red area—the firm should shut down. Table 9.4 summarizes these decisions.

The Ice Cream Float, a cool idea on a hot day at the lake.

FIGURE 9.2

When to Operate and When to Shut Down

If the MR (marginal revenue) curve is above the minimum point on the ATC (average total cost) curve, the Ice Cream Float will make a profit (shown in green). If the MR curve is below the minimum point on the ATC curve ($2.50) but above the minimum point on the AVC (average variable cost) curve ($2.00), the float will operate at a loss (shown in yellow). If the MR curve is below the minimum point on the AVC curve ($2.00), the float will temporarily shut down (shown in red).

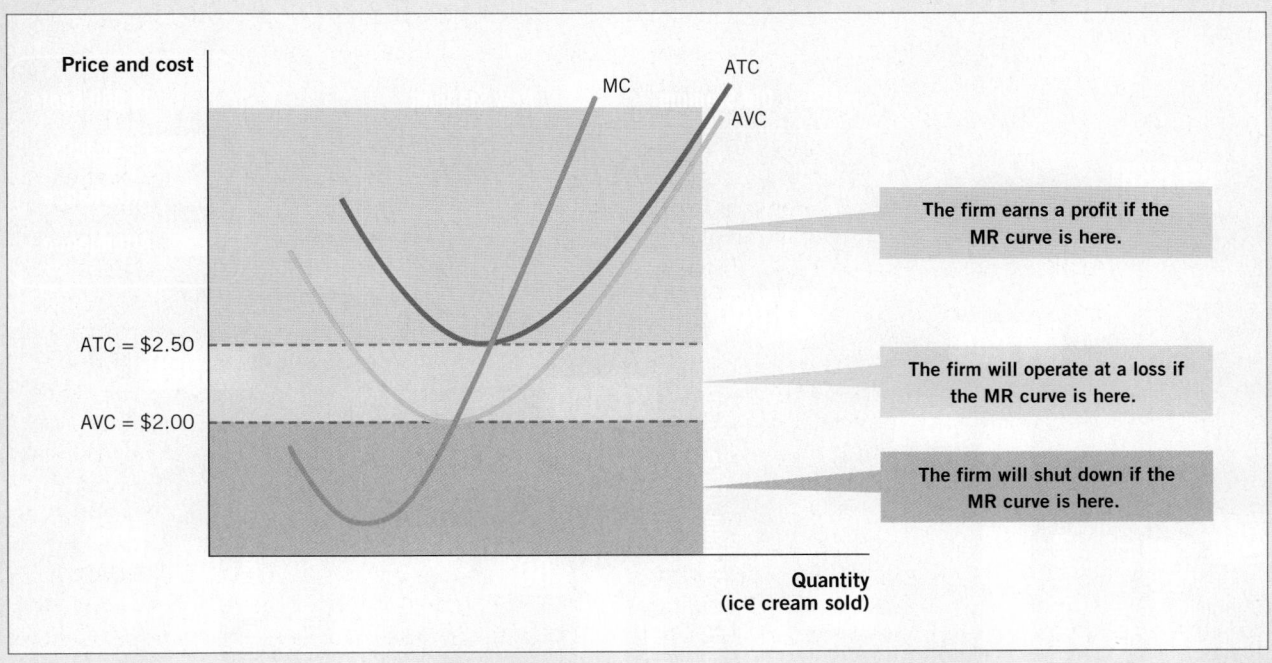

TABLE 9.4

Profit and Loss in the Short Run

Condition	In words	Outcome
P > ATC	The price is greater than the average total cost of production.	The firm makes a profit.
ATC > P > AVC	The average total cost of production is greater than the price the firm charges, but the price is greater than the average variable cost of production.	The firm will operate to minimize loss.
AVC > P	The price is less than the average variable cost of production.	The firm will temporarily shut down.

Sunk Costs: If You Build It, They Will Come

Replacing an old stadium with a new one is sometimes controversial. People often misunderstand sunk costs and argue for continuing with a stadium until it's completely worn down. But economics tells us not to focus on the sunk costs of the old stadium's construction. Instead, we should compare the marginal benefit of a new stadium to the marginal cost of demolition and new construction.

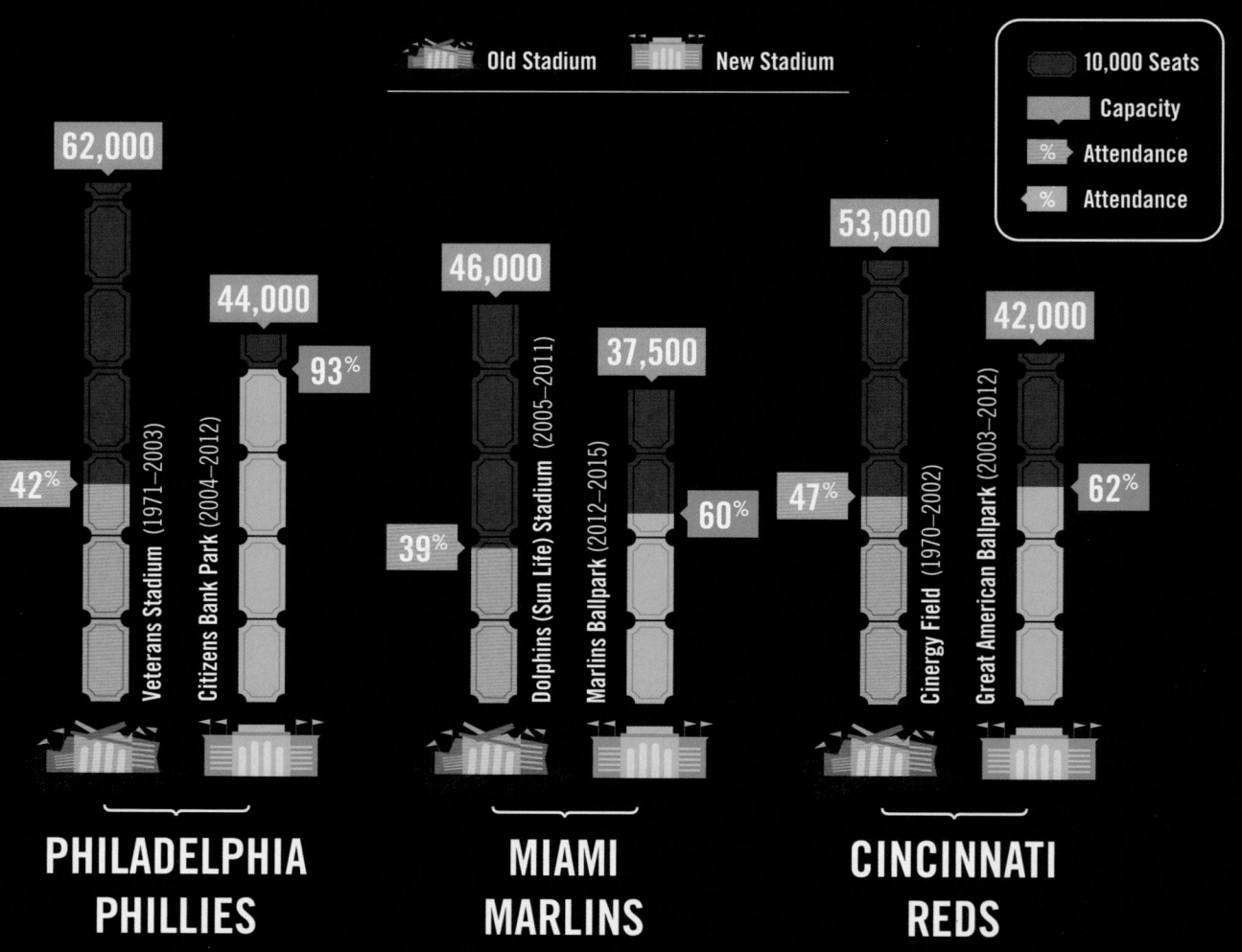

Old Stadium — **New Stadium**

10,000 Seats
Capacity
% Attendance
% Attendance

PHILADELPHIA PHILLIES

- 62,000 — Veterans Stadium (1971–2003) — 42%
- 44,000 — Citizens Bank Park (2004–2012) — 93%

MIAMI MARLINS

- 46,000 — Dolphins (Sun Life) Stadium (2005–2011) — 39%
- 37,500 — Marlins Ballpark (2012–2015) — 60%

CINCINNATI REDS

- 53,000 — Cinergy Field (1970–2002) — 47%
- 42,000 — Great American Ballpark (2003–2012) — 62%

The three new stadiums shown are considered successes. Higher attendance (especially in Philadelphia) and higher revenue per ticket—thanks to luxury boxes and better concessions—make the franchises happy.

An economist's analysis of the stadiums would go beyond attendance, however. The additional revenue generated by the new stadiums must be weighed against the costs of imploding the old stadiums and building new venues.

REVIEW QUESTIONS

- What effect do you think the reduced seating capacities of the new stadiums has on ticket prices, and why?

- Use the idea of sunk costs to analyze switching majors in college.

To make the shutdown decision more concrete, imagine that the Ice Cream Float's minimum ATC (average total cost) is $2.50 and its minimum AVC is $2.00. During the summer, when many customers line up on the dock waiting for it to arrive, it can charge more than $2.50 and earn a substantial profit. However, as the weather cools, fewer people want ice cream. The Ice Cream Float still has to crisscross the lake to make sales, burning expensive gasoline and paying employees to operate the vessel. If the Ice Cream Float is to keep its revenues high, it needs customers; but cooler weather suppresses demand. If the Ice Cream Float charges $2.25 in the fall, it can make enough to cover its average variable cost of $2.00, but not enough to cover its average total cost of $2.50. Nevertheless, it will continue to operate because it makes enough in the yellow region to pay part of its fixed cost. Finally, it reaches a point at which the price drops below $2.00. Now the business is no longer able to cover its average variable cost. At this point, it shuts down for the winter. It does this because operating when MR is very low causes the business to incur a larger loss.

The Firm's Short-Run Supply Curve

Cost curves provide a detailed picture of a firm's willingness to supply a good or service. We have seen that when the MR curve is below the minimum point on the AVC curve, the firm shuts down and production, or output, falls to zero. In other words, when revenues are too low, no supply is produced. For example, during the winter, the Ice Cream Float is dry-docked, so the supply curve does not exist. However, when the firm is operating, it bases its output decisions on the marginal cost. Recall that the firm uses the profit-maximizing rule, or MR = MC, to determine how much to produce. The marginal cost curve is therefore the firm's short-run supply curve as long as the firm is operating.

Marginal thinking

Figure 9.3 shows the Ice Cream Float's short-run supply curve. In the short run, diminishing marginal product causes the firm's costs to rise as the quantity produced increases. This is reflected in the shape of the firm's short-run supply curve, shown in orange. The supply curve is upward sloping above the minimum point on the AVC curve. Below the minimum point on the AVC curve, the short-run supply curve is vertical at a quantity of zero, indicating that a willingness to supply the good does not exist below a price of $2.00. At prices above $2.00, the firm will offer more for sale as the price increases.

Sunk Costs

Unrecoverable costs that have been incurred as a result of past decisions are known as **sunk costs**. For example, the decision to build a new sports stadium is a good application of the principle of sunk costs. Many professional stadiums have been built in the past few years, even though the arenas they replaced were built to last much longer. For example, Three Rivers Stadium in Pittsburgh and Veterans Stadium in Philadelphia were built in the early 1970s as multiuse facilities for both football and baseball, each with an expected life span of 60 or more years. However, in the 2000s, both were replaced. Each city built two new stadiums with features such as luxury boxes and better seats that generate more revenue than Veterans and Three Rivers did. The additional revenue makes the

Sunk costs are unrecoverable costs that have been incurred as a result of past decisions.

FIGURE 9.3

The Firm's Short-Run Supply Curve

The short-run supply curve (S_{SR}) and marginal cost curve (MC) are equivalent when the price is above the minimum point on the average variable cost curve (AVC). Below that point, the firm shuts down and no supply exists.

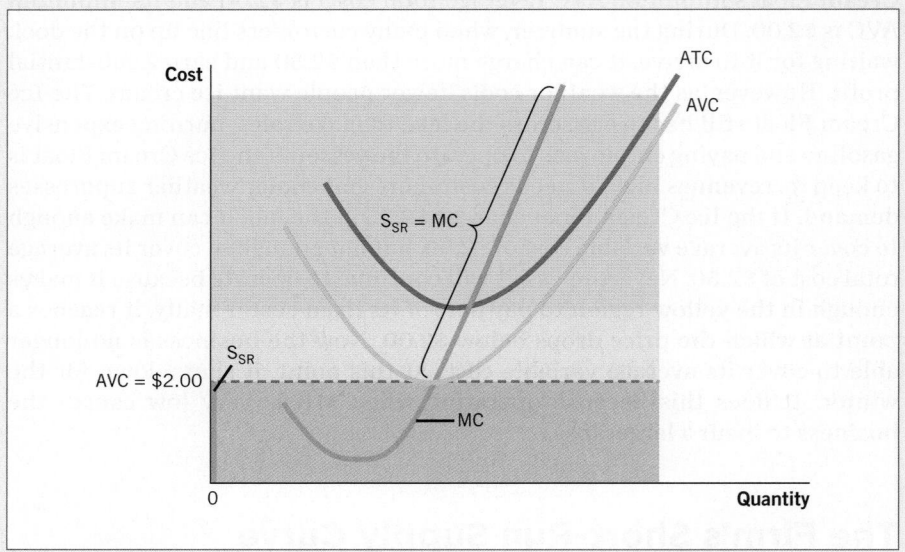

Opportunity costs can lead to stadium implosions.

Opportunity cost

new stadiums financially attractive even though the old stadiums were still structurally sound.

Demolishing a structure that is still in good working order may sound like a waste, but it can be good economics. When the extra benefit of a new stadium is large enough to pay for the cost of imploding the old stadium and constructing a new one, a city will do just that. In fact, because Pittsburgh and Philadelphia draw significantly more paying spectators with the new stadiums, the decision to replace the older stadiums has made the citizens in both cities better off. The new stadiums have created increased ticket sales, higher tax revenues, and a more enjoyable experience for fans.

Continuing to use an out-of-date facility has an opportunity cost. Those who do not understand sunk costs might point to the benefits of getting maximum use out of what already exists. But good economists learn to ignore sunk costs and focus on marginal value. They compare marginal benefits and marginal costs. If a new stadium and the revenue it brings in will create more value than the old stadium, the decision should be to tear the old one down.

The Firm's Long-Run Supply Curve

In the long run, a competitive firm's output decision is directly tied to profits. Because the firm is flexible in the long run, all costs are variable. As a result, the firm's long-run supply curve exists only when the firm expects to cover its total

The Profit-Maximizing Rule: Show Me the Money!

Here is a question that often confuses students.

QUESTION: At what point does a firm maximize profits: where the profit per additional unit is greatest, or where marginal revenue equals marginal cost?

ANSWER: Each answer sounds plausible, so the key is to think about each one in a concrete way. To help do that, we will refer back to the Mr. Plow data in Table 9.3. Making a large profit per unit sounds great. However, if the firm stops production when the profit per unit peaks—at $8 in column 7—it will fail to realize the additional profits, namely $7, then $3, and then $1 in column 7, that come from continuing to produce until MR = MC. The correct answer is where marginal revenue equals marginal cost. A firm maximizes profits where MR = MC, because at this point all profitable opportunities are exhausted. If Mr. Plow clears 8 driveways, his profit on the additional driveway is $1. If he clears 9 driveways, his profit on the additional driveway is −$15, because the marginal cost of clearing that ninth driveway, $25, is greater than the $10 he earns in marginal revenue.

What is the rule for making the most profit?

costs of production (because otherwise the firm would go out of business—that is, exit the market).

Returning to the Ice Cream Float example, recall that the boat shuts down over the winter instead of going out of business because demand is low but is expected to return. If for some reason the crowds do not come back, the float would go out of business. Turning to Figure 9.4, we see that at any point below the minimum point, $2.50, on the ATC curve, the float will experience a loss. Because firms are free to enter or exit the market in the long run, no firm will willingly produce in the market if the price is less than average total cost (P < ATC). As a result, no supply exists below $2.50. However, if price is greater than average total cost (P > ATC), the float expects to make a profit and thus will continue to produce.

The firm's long-run supply curve, shown in Figure 9.4 in orange, is upward sloping above the minimum point on the ATC curve, which is denoted by ATC on the *y* axis. The supply curve is vertical at a quantity of zero, indicating that a willingness to supply the good does not exist below a price of $2.50. In the long run, a firm that expects price to exceed ATC will continue to operate, because the conditions for making a profit seem favorable. In contrast, a firm that does not expect price to exceed ATC should cut its losses and exit the market. Table 9.5 outlines the long-run decision criteria.

So far, we have examined the firm's decision-making process in the short run in the context of revenue versus cost, which has enabled us to determine the profit each firm makes. However, a single firm represents only a small part of the overall supply in a competitive market. In the next section, we develop the short-run and long-run market supply curves.

FIGURE 9.4

The Firm's Long-Run Supply Curve

The long-run supply curve (S_{LR}) and marginal cost curve (MC) are equivalent when the price is above the minimum point on the average total cost curve (ATC). Below that point, the firm shuts down and no supply exists.

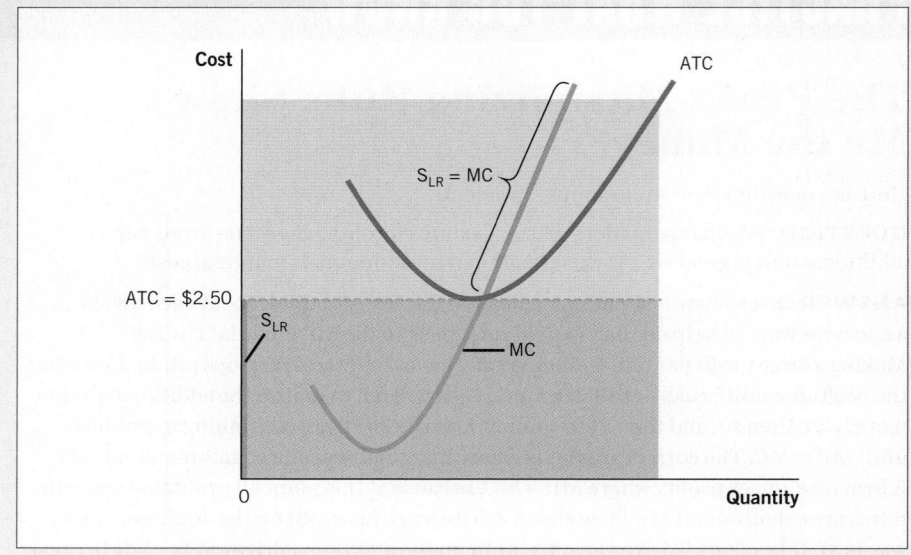

TABLE 9.5

The Long-Run Shutdown Criteria

Condition	In words	Outcome
P > ATC	The price is greater than the average total cost of production.	The firm makes a profit.
P < ATC	The price is less than the average total cost of production.	The firm should shut down.

ECONOMICS IN THE REAL WORLD

TOYS "R" US, CHANGES IN TECHNOLOGY, AND THE DYNAMIC NATURE OF CHANGE

What happens if your customers do not return? What if you simply had a bad idea to begin with, and the customers never arrived in the first place?

When the long-run profit outlook is bleak, the firm is better off shutting down. This is a normal part of the ebb and flow of business in a market economy. For example, once there were thousands of buggy whip companies. Today, as technology has improved and we no longer rely on horse-drawn carriages, few buggy whip makers remain. However, many companies now manufacture automobile parts.

Similarly, a succession of technological advances has transformed the music industry. Records were replaced by 8-track tapes, and then by cassettes and CDs. After that came iPods, MP3 players, and smartphones to help make music more portable. Websites and apps such as Pandora, Spotify, and the Apple music service allow streaming of almost any selection a listener wants to hear. However, there was a time when innovation meant playing music on the original Sony Walkman. What was cool in the early 1980s is antiquated today. Any business engaged in distributing music has had to adapt or shut down.

Similar changes are taking place in the toy industry. Toys "R" Us was founded in 1948 and experienced explosive growth. It was the nation's largest toy store seller until Walmart claimed that spot in 1998. By the early 2010s, Toys "R" Us faced stiff competition not only from large traditional retailers like Walmart but also from online vendors like Amazon. The last year Toys "R" Us made a profit was 2013. Eventually the firm filed for bankruptcy, and it closed its remaining stores in 2018.

In addition to changes in technology, other factors such as downturns in the economy, changes in tastes, demographic factors, and migration can all force businesses to close. These examples remind us that the long-run decision to go out of business has nothing to do with the short-term profit outlook.

Toys "R" Us once had over 1,600 stores worldwide.

What Does the Supply Curve Look Like in Perfectly Competitive Markets?

We have seen that a firm's willingness to supply a good or service depends on whether the firm is making a short-run or long-run decision. In the short run, a firm may choose to operate at a loss to recover a portion of its fixed costs. In the long run, there are no fixed costs, so a firm is willing to operate only if it expects the price it charges to cover total costs.

However, the supply curve for a single firm represents only a small part of the overall supply in a competitive market. We now turn to market supply and develop the short-run and long-run market supply curves.

The Short-Run Market Supply Curve

A competitive market consists of a large number of identical sellers. Because an individual firm's supply curve is equal to its marginal cost curve, if we add together all the individual supply curves in a market, we arrive at the short-run market supply curve. Figure 9.5 shows the short-run market supply curve in a two-firm model consisting of Mr. Plow and the Plow King. At a price of $10, Mr. Plow is willing to clear 8 driveways (Q_A) and the Plow King is willing to clear 20 driveways (Q_B). When we sum the output of the two firms, we get a total market supply of 28 driveways (Q_{market}), seen in the third graph.

The Long-Run Market Supply Curve

Recall that a competitive market is one in which a large number of buyers seek a product many sellers offer. Competitive markets are also characterized by easy entry and exit. Existing firms and entrepreneurs decide whether to enter and exit a market based on incentives. When existing firms are enjoying profits,

FIGURE 9.5

Short-Run Market Supply

The market supply is determined by summing the individual supplies of all the firms in the market. Although we have only shown this process for two firms, Mr. Plow and Plow King, the process extends to any number of firms in a market.

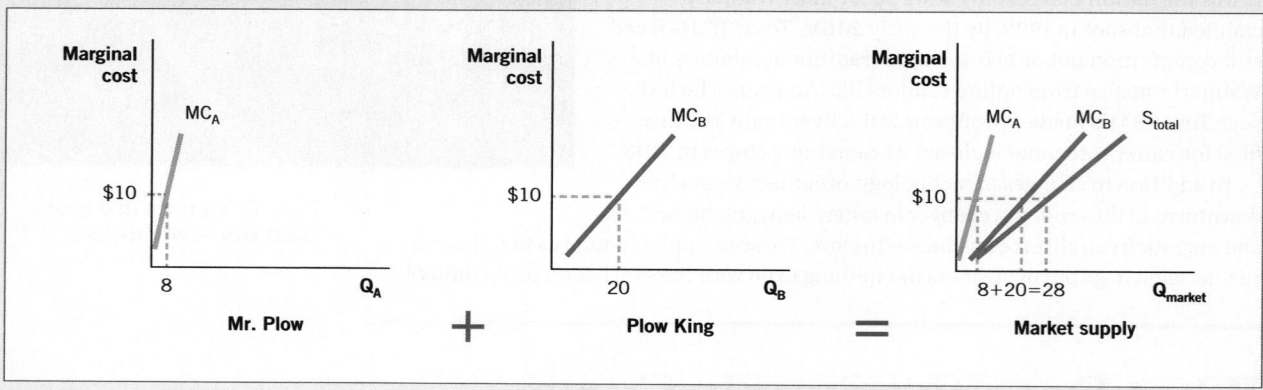

Incentives

The **signals** of profits and losses convey information about the profitability of various markets.

there is an incentive for them to produce more and also for entrepreneurs to enter the market. The result is an increase in the quantity of the good supplied. Likewise, when existing firms are experiencing losses, there is an incentive for them to exit the market; then the quantity supplied decreases.

Entry and exit have the combined effect of regulating the amount of profit a firm can hope to make in the long run. As long as profits exist, the quantity supplied will increase because existing firms expand production or other firms enter the market. When losses exist, the quantity supplied will decrease because existing firms reduce production or other firms exit the market. So both profits and losses signal a need for an adjustment in market supply. In other words, profits and losses act as signals for resources to enter or leave a market. **Signals** convey information about the profitability of various markets.

The only time an adjustment does not take place is when participants in the market make zero economic profit. In that case, the market is in long-run equilibrium. Existing firms and entrepreneurs are not inclined to enter or exit the market; the adjustment process that occurs through price changes ends.

The benefit of a competitive market is that profits guide existing firms and entrepreneurs to produce more goods and services that society values. Losses encourage firms to exit and move elsewhere. Without profits and losses acting as signals for firms to enter or exit the market, resources will be misallocated and surpluses and shortages will occur.

Figure 9.6 captures how entry and exit determine the market supply. The profit-maximizing point of the individual firm in panel (a), $MR = MC$, is located at the minimum point on the ATC curve. The price ($P = min. ATC$) that existing firms receive is just enough to cover costs, so profits are zero. As a result, new firms have no incentive to enter the market and existing firms have no reason to leave. At all prices above $P = min. ATC$, firms will earn a profit (the green

FIGURE 9.6

The Long-Run Market Supply Curve and Entry and Exit

Entry into the market and exit from it force the long-run price to be equal to the minimum point on the average total cost curve (ATC). At all prices above P = min. ATC, firms will earn a profit (the green area), and at all prices below P = min. ATC, firms will experience a loss (the red area). For this reason, the long-run supply curve (S_{LR}) must be horizontal at price P = min. ATC. If the price was any higher or lower, firms would enter or exit the market, and the market could not be in a long-run equilibrium.

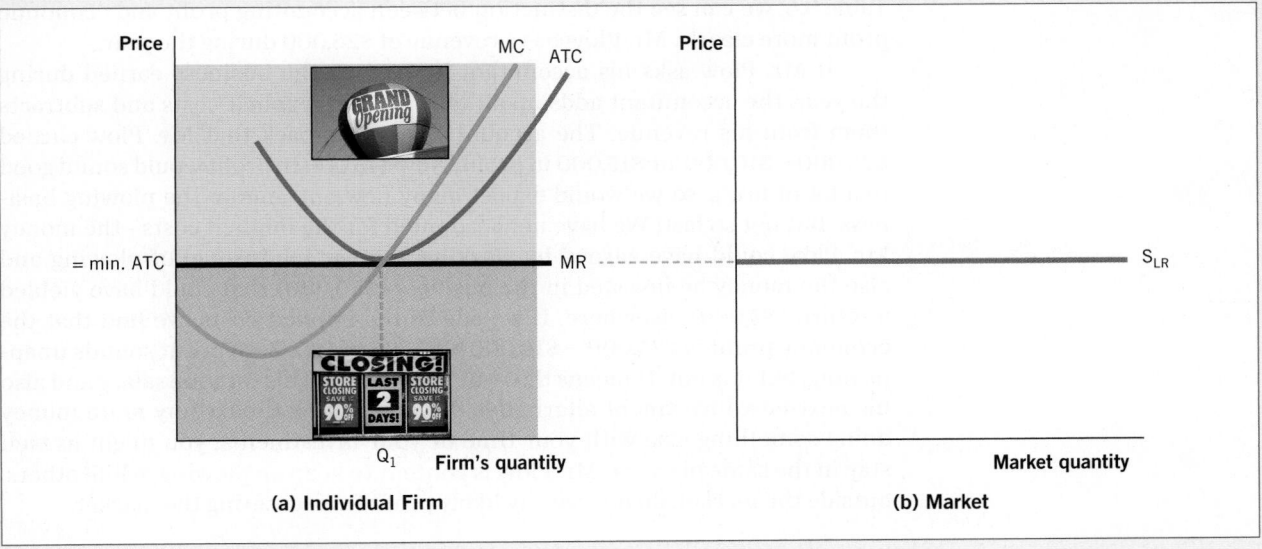

(a) Individual Firm

(b) Market

area), and at all prices below P = min. ATC, firms will experience a loss (the red area). This picture is consistent for all markets with free entry and exit; zero economic profit occurs at only one price, and that price is the lowest point of the ATC curve.

At this price, the supply curve in panel (b) must be a horizontal line at P = min. ATC. If the price were any higher, firms would enter, supply would increase, and price would be forced back down to P = min. ATC. If the price were any lower, firms would exit, supply would decrease, and price would be forced up to P = min. ATC. Because we know that these adjustments will have time to take place in the long run, the long-run supply curve must also be equal to P = min. ATC to satisfy the demand that exists at this price.

A REMINDER ABOUT ECONOMIC PROFIT Now that you have learned how perfect competition affects business profits in the long run, you may not think that a competitive market is a desirable environment for businesses seeking to earn profits. After all, if a firm cannot expect to make an economic profit in the long run, why bother? It's easy to forget the distinction between accounting profit and economic profit. Firms enter a market when they expect to be reasonably compensated for their investment. And they leave a market when the investment does not yield a satisfactory result. Economic profit is determined by deducting the explicit and implicit costs from total revenue. The remaining examples (graphs) in this chapter focus on our benchmark, economic profit. Therefore, firms are willing to stay in perfectly competitive markets in the long run when they are breaking even because they are being reasonably compensated for the explicit expenses they have incurred and also for the implicit expenses—like the opportunity costs of other business ventures—they would expect to incur elsewhere.

Opportunity cost

For example, if Mr. Plow has the explicit and implicit costs shown in Table 9.6, we can see the distinction between accounting profit and economic profit more clearly. Mr. Plow has a revenue of $25,000 during the year.

If Mr. Plow asks his accountant how much the business earned during the year, the accountant adds up all of Mr. Plow's explicit costs and subtracts them from his revenue. The accountant reports back that Mr. Plow earned $25,000 − $10,000, or $15,000 in profit. Now $15,000 in profit would sound good to a lot of firms, so we would expect many new entrants in the plowing business. But not so fast! We have not accounted for the implicit costs—the money Mr. Plow could have earned by working another job instead of plowing and also the money he invested in the business ($50,000) that could have yielded a return ($5,000) elsewhere. If we add in the implicit costs, we find that the economic profit is $25,000 − $10,000 − $15,000 = $0. Zero profit sounds unappealing, but it is not. It means that Mr. Plow covered his forgone salary and also his next-best investment alternative. If you could not make any more money doing something else with your time or your investments, you might as well stay in the same place. So Mr. Plow is content to keep on plowing, while others, outside the market, do not see any likely profit from entering the market.

How the Market Adjusts in the Long Run: An Example

We have seen that profits and losses may exist in the short run; in the long run, the best the competitive firm can do is earn zero economic profit. This section looks in more detail at the adjustment process that leads to long-run equilibrium.

TABLE 9.6	
Mr. Plow's Economic Profit and the Entry or Exit Decision	
Explicit costs per year	
Payment on the loan on his snowplow	$7,000
Gasoline	2,000
Miscellaneous equipment (shovels, salt)	1,000
Implicit costs	
Forgone salary	$10,000
The forgone income that the $50,000 invested in the business could have earned if invested elsewhere	5,000
Total cost	$25,000

FIGURE 9.7

A Competitive Market in Long-Run Equilibrium

When a market is in long-run equilibrium, the short-run supply curve (S_{SR}) and short-run demand curve (D_{SR}) intersect along the long-run supply curve (S_{LR}). At this point, the price the firm charges is equal to the minimum point along the average total cost curve (ATC). The existing firms in the market earn zero economic profit, and there is no incentive for firms to enter or exit the market.

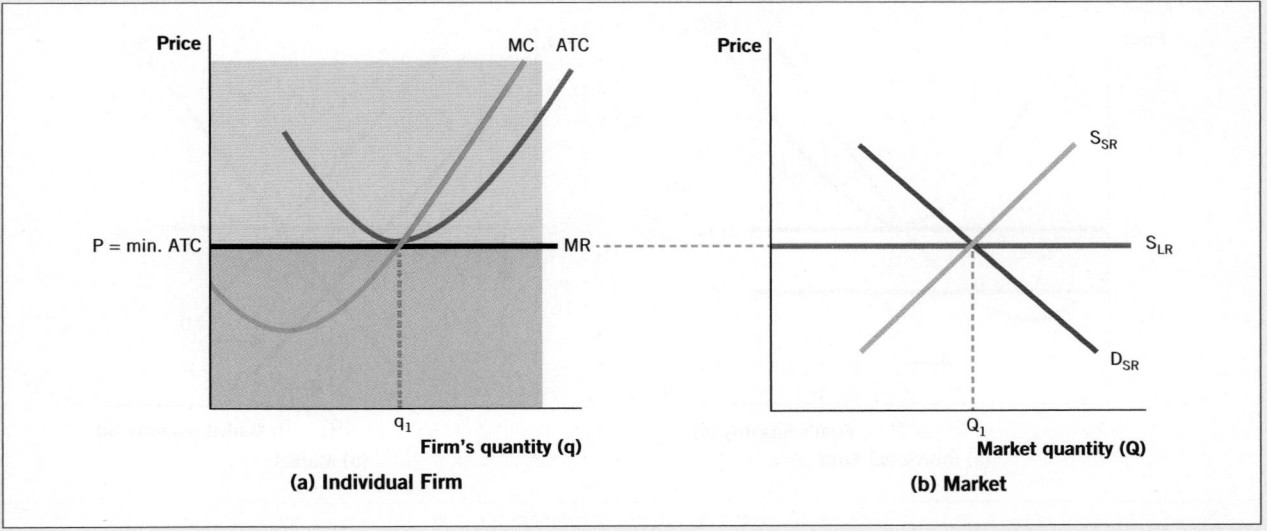

(a) Individual Firm   (b) Market

We begin with the market in long-run equilibrium, shown in Figure 9.7. Panel (a) represents an individual firm operating at the minimum point on its ATC curve. In long-run equilibrium, all firms are operating as efficiently as possible. Because the price is equal to the average cost of production, economic profit for the firm is zero. In panel (b), the short-run supply curve (S_{SR}) and the short-run demand curve (D_{SR}) intersect along the long-run supply curve (S_{LR}), so the market is also in equilibrium. But if the short-run supply curve and demand curve happened to intersect above the long-run supply curve, then the price would be higher than the minimum point on the ATC curve. The result would be short-run profits, indicating that the market is not in long-run equilibrium. And if the short-run supply curve and demand curve intersected below the long-run supply curve, then the price would be lower than the minimum point on the ATC curve. In that case, the result would be short-run losses.

Now suppose that demand declines, as shown in Figure 9.8. In panel (b), we see that the market demand curve shifts from D_1 to D_2. When demand falls, the equilibrium point moves from point A to point B. The price drops to P_2 and the market output drops to Q_2. The firms in this market take their price from the market, so the new marginal revenue curve shifts down from MR_1 to MR_2 at P_2 in panel (a). Because the firm maximizes profits where $MR = MC$, the firm will produce an output of q_2. When the output is q_2 the firm's costs, C_2, are higher than the price it charges, P_2, so it experiences a loss equal to the red area

FIGURE 9.8

The Short-Run Adjustment to a Decrease in Demand

A decrease in demand causes the price to fall in the market, as shown by the movement from D₁ to D₂ in panel (b). Because the firm is a price taker, the price it can charge falls to P₂. As we see in panel (a), the intersection of MR₂ and MC occurs at q₂. At this output level, the firm incurs the short-run loss shown by the red area in (a).

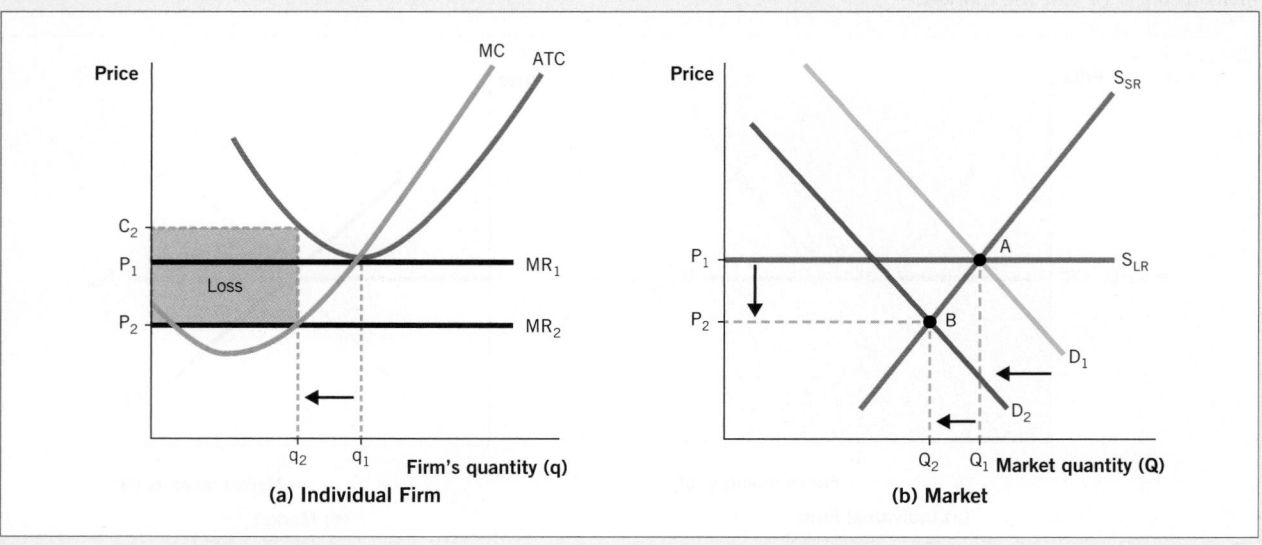

(a) Individual Firm

(b) Market

What does it take to produce more mangoes?

in panel (a). In addition, because the firm's output is lower, it is no longer producing at the minimum point on its ATC curve, so the firm is not as efficient as before.

Firms in a competitive market can exit the market easily. Some will do so to avoid further losses. Figure 9.9 continues the example from Figure 9.8. It shows that as firms exit, the market supply contracts from S_{SR1} to S_{SR2} and the market equilibrium moves from point B to point C. At point C, the price rises back to P₁ and the market output drops to Q_3. The firms that remain in the market no longer experience a short-run loss, because MR₂ returns to MR₁ and costs fall from C₂ to C₁. The end result is that the firm is once again efficient, and economic profit returns to zero.

For example, suppose there is a decline in demand for mangoes due to a false rumor that links the fruit to a salmonella outbreak. The decline in demand causes the price of mangoes to drop. As a consequence, mango producers experience negative economic profit—generating curves like the ones shown in Figure 9.8. In response to the negative profit, some mango growers will exit the market, the mango trees will be sold for firewood, and the land will be converted to other uses. With fewer mangoes being produced, the supply will contract. Eventually, the smaller supply will cause the price of mangoes to rise until a new long-run equilibrium is reached at a much lower level of output, as shown in Figure 9.9.

FIGURE 9.9

The Long-Run Adjustment to a Decrease in Demand

Short-run losses cause some firms to exit the market. Their exit shifts the market supply curve to the left in panel (b) until the price returns to long-run equilibrium at point C. Price is restored to P_1 and the MR_2 curve in panel (a) shifts up to MR_1. At P_1 the firm is once again earning zero economic profit.

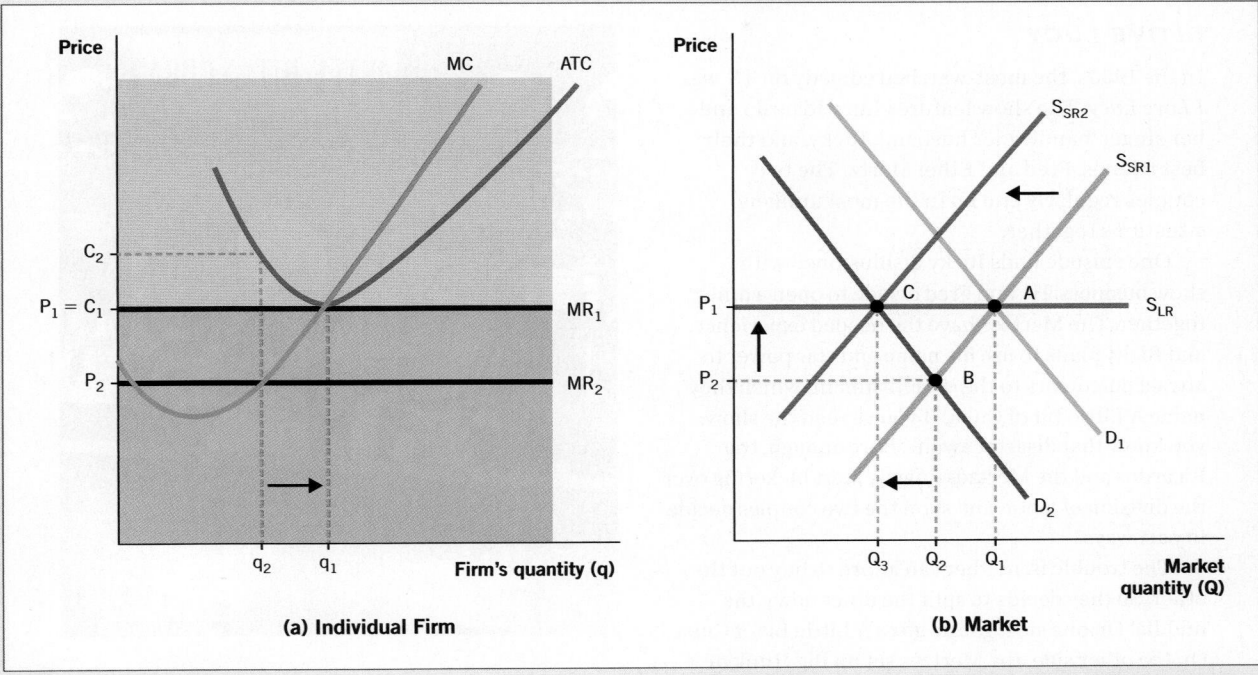

(a) Individual Firm

(b) Market

MORE ON THE LONG-RUN SUPPLY CURVE To keep the previous example as simple as possible, we assumed that the long-run supply curve was horizontal. However, this is not always the case. There are two reasons why the long-run supply curve may slope upward. First, some resources needed to produce the product may only be available in limited supplies. As firms try to expand production, they must bid to acquire those resources—a move that causes the average total cost curve to rise. For instance, a mango grower who wants to plant more trees must acquire more land. Because mangoes grow in tropical areas with warm, wet summers, not all land is perfectly suited to growing them. The limited supply of land will cause the price of producing more mangoes to rise, which will cause the supply curve to be positively sloped.

A second reason the long-run supply curve may be upward sloping is the opportunity cost of the labor used in producing the good. If you want to produce more mangoes, you will need more workers to pick the fruit. Hiring extra workers will mean finding people who are both willing and capable. Some workers are better than others at picking mangoes, and some workers have higher opportunity costs. As your firm attempts to expand production, it must increase

Opportunity cost

Entry and Exit

I LOVE LUCY

In the 1950s, the most-watched comedy on TV was *I Love Lucy*. The show features Lucy Ricardo and her singer-bandleader husband, Ricky, and their best friends, Fred and Ethel Mertz. The two couples regularly end up in the most unlikely situations together.

One episode finds Ricky disillusioned with show business. He and Fred decide to open a diner together. The Mertzes have the needed experience, and Ricky plans to use his name and star power to attract customers to the establishment, which they name A Little Bit of Cuba. If you've seen the show, you know that disaster awaits. Sure enough, the Ricardos and the Mertzes quickly start bickering over the division of labor, and soon the two couples decide to part ways.

The trouble is, neither can afford to buy out the other. So they decide to split the diner down the middle! On one side, guests go to A Little Bit of Cuba. On the other side, the Mertzes set up Big Hunk of America. Because the rival eateries sell the same food at the same facility, the only way they can differentiate themselves is through price. The result is a price war to attract customers.

When a new customer comes into the diner and starts to place an order for a 15-cent hamburger from Big Hunk of America, Lucy lowers the price at A Little Bit of Cuba to 10 cents. Ethel responds by lowering the price at Big Hunk of America to 5 cents. The two continue lowering the price until Ethel drops her price all the way down to 1 cent! (Even in the 1950s, a penny didn't cover the marginal cost of making a hamburger.) At this point, Lucy whispers in the customer's ear and gives him a dollar.

He then proceeds to Big Hunk of America and orders 100 hamburgers.

The scene illustrates how perfectly competitive markets work. Neither the Ricardos nor the Mertzes can stay in business selling one-cent burgers, so one of the couples will end up exiting the market. At that point, the remaining couple should be able to charge more. But if they end up making a profit, that profit will encourage entrepreneurs to enter the market. As the supply of hamburgers expands, the market price will be driven back down. Because we live in an economically dynamic world, prices are always moving toward long-run equilibrium.

Long-Run Profits: How Much Can a Firm Expect to Make?

QUESTION: True or false? "If firms in an industry are making economic profits, other firms will enter."

ANSWER: In the long run, a firm in a perfectly competitive market earns zero economic profit, so the opportunity in the short run to enjoy positive economic profits will cause existing firms to increase output and new firms to enter the market. The statement is true.

CHALLENGE QUESTION: The company you work for reported in its annual stockholder meeting that it made $1 million in profits last year. Should you invest?

ANSWER: The profit in the example is accounting profit. We don't know how large the firm is. If the firm had $5 million in assets, $1 million would represent a 20% return—which would be excellent. However, if the firm had $100 million in assets, the rate of return would only be 1%—which is poor. Economists are concerned with the rate of return adjusting for the implicit cost of the resources used. Recall that the stock market rises, on average, 8% a year. To account for this, when economists speak of profits they adjust the accounting profits downward for the implicit costs of doing business. For instance, let's take 8% off of the two hypothetical returns; 20% becomes a 12% return over the firm's next best alternative, that's why this outcome is "excellent." But when you subtract 8% from 1%, you get a return of −7%, which will drive firms out of the market. The firm could have used its assets more successfully by deploying them elsewhere.

So the answer to the question, "Should you invest?" is that it depends on the amount of economic profit—not the accounting profit—the firm expects to make going forward. Even then, you must be mindful about competition from other firms entering the market, since that will drive economic profits down to zero in the long run. Perhaps more pertinently, investing in a market characterized by no long-run economic profits should give you pause. In the next few chapters we will focus on imperfect competition. Firms with market power, barriers to entry, and differentiated products are able to consistently earn economic profits. That's where the smart investors look.

Calculating profits.

the wage it pays to attract additional help or accept new workers who are not quite as capable. Either way you slice it, the result is higher costs, which would be reflected in an upward-sloping long-run supply curve.

This discussion simply means that higher prices are necessary to induce suppliers to offer more for sale. None of it changes the basic ideas we have discussed throughout this section. The entry and exit of firms ensure that the market supply curve is much more elastic in the long run than in the short run.

Conclusion

In competitive markets, where firms are at the mercy of market forces that set the price, individual firms have no control over the price because they sell the same products as their competitors. In addition, profits and losses help regulate

Tips from the Sharks for Becoming a Millionaire

Before you go into business for yourself, you need to devise a plan. Over 80% of all small businesses fail within five years, because the businesses were ill-conceived or relied on unrealistic sales projections. Here is some advice from the stars of *Shark Tank*:

- **Barbara Corcoran:** "Every business is born out of an individual's intense passion and a real need to succeed, so you'll need enough passion to get started, but also enough to get through the intense 12-hour days when the chips are down and everything and everyone seems against you."

- **Mark Cuban:** "You've got to be good at something and not only be good at it, but you've got to love it, and then you're willing to work and do whatever it takes. Then, if you're fortunate, that turns into something that creates wealth for you."

- **Lori Greiner:** "Make sure you are hands-on and the one driving things because no one will care about your business like you do. Be involved in all details and be aggressive at attaining your goals, and know how to pivot when necessary."

- **Kevin O'Leary:** "If you can afford to take a risk and you're young enough, either start your own company or be involved with one where you're racking up equity."

- **Robert Herjavec:** "You've got to go back to the basics. Find a need, solve a problem and, most importantly, make sure you have a customer. If those things are in place, and you have the ability to scale, now we're talking. It's going to be incredibly hard work. Harder than you've ever

The Sharks may have a scary-sounding name, but they're rooting for you to succeed.

imagined, but it's the best time in America to start a business. The time is now!"

- **Daymond John:** "Go out there and do something that you really, really love, even if it's not something you went to school for. Find out what your passion is. I can't guarantee that you're ever going to make a dollar doing anything, but do something that you absolutely love and you're going to look back over the years and say that you enjoyed life."*

*Source: https://www.entrepreneur.com/slideshow/.

economic activity in competitive markets and promote economic efficiency. Profits reward producers for producing a good that is valued more highly than the resources used to produce it. Profits encourage entry into a market. Likewise, losses penalize producers who operate inefficiently or produce goods consumers do not want. Losses encourage exit from the market. The process of entry and exit ensures that resources flow into markets that are undersupplied and away from markets where too many firms exist.

In this chapter, we studied competitive markets to establish a benchmark that will help us understand how other market structures compare with this ideal. In the next few chapters, we explore imperfect markets, which provide a significant contrast with the results we have just seen. The closer a market is to meeting the criteria of perfect competition, the better the result for consumers and society in general. ✳

· ANSWERING *the* BIG QUESTIONS ·

How do competitive markets work?

- The firms in competitive markets sell similar products. Firms are also free to enter and exit the market whenever they wish.
- A price taker has no control over the price it receives in the market.
- In competitive markets, the price and quantity produced are determined by market forces instead of by the firm.

How do firms maximize profits?

- A firm maximizes profits by expanding output until marginal revenue is equal to marginal cost (MR = MC, or the profit-maximizing rule). The profit-maximizing rule is a condition for stopping production at the point where profit opportunities no longer exist.
- The firm should shut down in the short run if the price it receives does not cover its average variable costs. Because variable costs are incurred only when operating, if a firm can make enough to cover its variable costs in the short run, it will choose to continue to operate.
- In the long run, the firm should go out of business if it cannot cover its average total costs.

What does the supply curve look like in perfectly competitive markets?

- Profits and losses act as signals for firms to enter or leave a market. As a result, perfectly competitive markets drive economic profit to zero in the long run.
- The entry and exit of firms ensure that the market supply curve in a competitive market is much more elastic in the long run than in the short run.

Concepts You Should Know

marginal revenue (p. 287)
price taker (p. 283)

profit-maximizing rule (p. 288)
signals (p. 298)

sunk costs (p. 293)

Questions for Review

1. What are the necessary conditions for a perfectly competitive market to exist?

2. Describe the two-step process used to identify the profit-maximizing level of output.

3. Under what circumstances will a firm have to decide whether to operate or to shut down?

4. What is the difference between the decision to go out of business and the decision to shut down?

5. How do profits and losses act as signals that guide producers to use resources to make what society wants most?

6. What are sunk costs? Give an example from your own experience.

7. Why do competitive firms earn zero economic profit in the long run?

Study Problems (✱ solved at the end of this section)

1. Using the definition of a price taker as your guide, explain why each of the following industries does not meet the definition.

   a. the pizza delivery business
   b. the home improvement business
   c. cell phone companies
   d. cereal producers

2. A local snow cone business sells snow cones in one size for $3 each. It has the following cost and output structure per hour:

Output (cones per hour)	Total cost (per hour)
0	$60
10	90
20	110
30	120
40	125
50	135
60	150
70	175
80	225

   a. Calculate the total revenue for the business at each rate of output.
   b. Calculate the total profit for the business at each rate of output.
   c. Is the business operating in the short run or the long run?
   d. Calculate the profit-maximizing rate of output using the MR = MC rule. (*Hint:* First compute the marginal revenue and marginal cost from the table.)

3. Determine whether the following statements are true or false. Explain your answers.

   a. A firm will make a profit when the price it charges exceeds the average variable cost of the chosen output level.
   b. To maximize profits in the short run, a firm must minimize its costs.
   c. If economic profit is positive, firms will exit the market in the short run.
   d. A firm that receives a price greater than its average variable cost but less than its average total cost should shut down.

4. In the following table, fill in the blanks. After you have completed the entire table, determine the profit-maximizing output.

Output	Price	Total revenue	Marginal revenue	Total cost	Marginal cost	Total profit
1	$20	___	___	$40	___	−$20
2	___	___	___	50	___	___
3	___	___	___	60	___	___
4	___	___	___	65	$5	___
5	___	___	___	85	___	___
6	___	$120	___	120	___	___

5. Use the graph to answer the questions that follow.

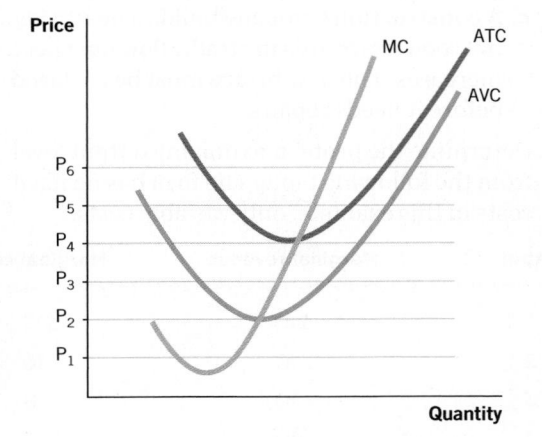

a. At what prices is the firm making an economic profit, breaking even, and experiencing an economic loss?

b. At what prices would the firm shut down?

c. At what prices does the firm's short-run supply curve exist? At what prices does the firm's long-run supply curve exist?

✱ 6. Identify as many errors as you can in the following graph.

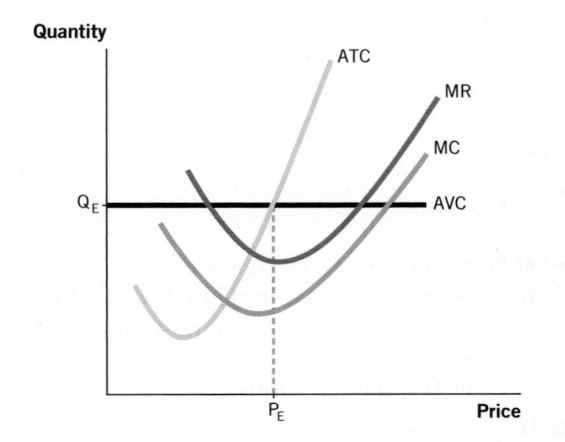

7. A firm is experiencing a loss of $5,000 per year. The firm has fixed costs of $8,000 per year.

a. Should the firm operate in the short run or shut down?

b. If the situation persists into the long run, should the firm stay in the market or go out of business?

c. Now suppose that the firm's fixed costs are $2,000. How would this level of fixed costs change the firm's short-run and long-run decisions?

8. Three students at the same school hear about the success of cookie delivery businesses on college campuses. Each student decides to open a local service. The individual supply schedules are shown below.

QUANTITY SUPPLIED

Delivery charge	Esra	Remzi	Camilo
$1	2	3	6
2	4	6	7
3	6	9	8
4	8	12	9
5	10	15	10
6	12	18	11

  a. Draw the individual supply curves.
  b. Sum the individual supply schedules to compute the short-run market supply schedule.
  c. Draw the market supply curve.

9. Do you agree or disagree with the following statement? "A profit-maximizing, perfectly competitive firm should select the output level at which the difference between the marginal revenue and marginal cost is the greatest." Explain your answer.

10. Barney's snow removal service is a profit-maximizing, competitive firm. Barney clears driveways for $10 each. His total cost each day is $250, and half of his total costs are fixed. If Barney clears 20 driveways a day, should he continue to operate or shut down? If this situation persists, will Barney stay in the market or exit?

✳ 11. Suppose you are the owner of a firm producing jelly beans. Your production costs are shown in the following table. Initially, you produce 100 boxes of jelly beans per time period. Then a new customer calls and places an order for an additional box of jelly beans, requiring you to increase your output to 101 boxes. She offers you $1.50 for the additional box. Should you produce it? Why or why not?

JELLY BEAN PRODUCTION

Number of boxes	Average cost per box
100	$1.00
101	1.01
102	1.02
103	1.03

12. In which of the following examples does the decision-maker avoid the sunk cost fallacy?

  a. You pay $10 to see *Furious 10* but realize 15 minutes into the film that the plot and acting are truly terrible, so you leave immediately.
  b. You sign up for a year-long membership at a local fitness center. You tire of the club visits quickly, but still go regularly to make sure you get the most out of your membership.
  c. A construction company builds a new bridge, but soon afterwards the traffic flow unexpectedly increases. The new bridge must be replaced before it needs repairs.

✳ 13. Determine the profit-maximizing output level from the following table. The firm has no fixed costs in this example, only variable costs.

Output	Marginal revenue	Marginal cost
1	$10	$13
2	10	10
3	10	8
4	10	7
5	10	9
6	10	11
7	10	14

14. Which of the following statements are true? Explain your reasoning.

  a. The marginal cost curve passes through the lowest points of the ATC, AVC, and AFC curves.
  b. The quantity for which MR = MC is the quantity for which the profit rectangle's area is maximized.
  c. The AVC curve can be derived from the MC curve.
  d. The AFC curve always slopes downward.

Solved Problems

6. Here is the corrected graph with the errors struck out and some explanation below.

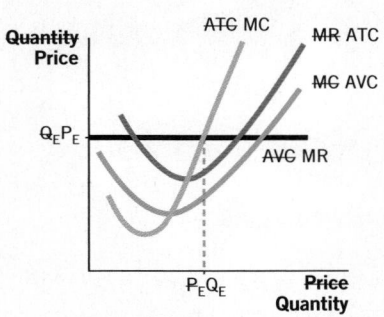

Also, the ATC and AVC curves did not intersect the MC curve at their minimum points. That is corrected here.

11. This problem requires marginal thinking. We know the profit-maximizing rule, MR = MC. Here all we need to do is compare the additional cost, or MC, against the additional revenue, or MR, to see if the deal is a good idea. We know that MR = $1.50, because that is what the customer is offering to pay for another box of jelly beans. Now we need to calculate the marginal cost of producing the additional box.

JELLY BEAN PRODUCTION

Number of boxes	Average cost per box	Total cost	Marginal cost
100	$1.00	$100.00	—
101	1.01	102.01	$2.01
102	1.02	104.04	2.03
103	1.03	106.09	2.05

First we compute the total cost. To do this, we multiply the number of boxes, listed in the first column, by the average cost, shown in the second column. The results are shown in the third column. Next we find the marginal cost. Recall that the marginal cost is the amount it costs to produce

one more unit. So we subtract the total cost of producing 101 boxes from the total cost of producing 100 boxes. For 101 boxes, MC = $102.01 − $100.00, or $2.01. Because MR − MC is $1.50 − $2.01, producing the 101st box would create a loss of $0.51. Therefore, at a price of $1.50, your firm should not produce the 101st box.

13. This problem confounds many students because if you've memorized only one thing from this chapter, it is the profit-maximizing rule, MR = MC, and it is clear that this condition is satisfied when the output is 2 (where MR and MC are both $10). But the answer 2 would be incorrect. A second part of the profit-maximizing rule is often overlooked: MR = MC, but MC must also be increasing. To see why 2 is not the profit-maximizing output, you should calculate the profit in a fourth column, as in the following table:

Output	Marginal revenue	Marginal cost	Profit (MR − MC)
1	$10	$13	− $3
2	10	10	0
3	10	8	2
4	10	7	3
5	10	9	1
6	10	11	−1
7	10	14	− 4

Profit is maximized at an output of 5, but why is this the case? Marginal cost is declining until output reaches 4, at which point the MR = $10 and MC = $7. So when the fourth unit is sold, it generates $3, and the firm is profitable for the first time. By the fifth unit, MC is rising but remains less than MR, so the profit rises. However, MC is higher than MR for the sixth unit, which causes profits to decline. The reason 2 is *not* the profit-maximizing output is that MC is falling, which means that the firm is at the point where additional output is just becoming profitable.

Understanding Monopoly

Monopolists Don't Always Make a Profit.

In this chapter, we explore another market structure: monopoly. Many people mistakenly believe that monopolists always make a profit. This is not true. Monopolists enjoy market power for their specific product, but they cannot force consumers to purchase what they are selling. The law of demand regulates how much a monopolist can charge. When a monopolist charges more, people buy less. If demand is low enough, a monopolist may even experience a loss instead of a profit.

While pure monopolies are unusual, it is important to study this market structure because many markets exhibit some form of monopolistic behavior. Google, the National Football League, the United States Postal Service (for first-class mail), and some small-town businesses are all examples of monopoly. The typical result of monopoly is higher prices and less output than we find in a competitive market.

Governments sometimes try to address the problems monopolies present. For example, governments split up the monopoly on phone service in the early eighties, which is generally seen as spurring the innovation that led to our modern systems. But governments can also be the cause of monopolies, sometimes in unexpected places. For example, in Winston-Salem, North Carolina, state law

Doctor Gajendra Singh wanted to make MRIs more affordable, but North Carolina wouldn't let him—so he took the state to court. Singh's lawyers are arguing that the certification requirement for MRI service providers interferes with his right, under the North Carolina constitution, to equal protection of the right to earn a living.

prevents doctors from becoming authorized providers of MRIs unless they first obtain a certificate of need, which can cost close to a half-million dollars. While this was originally done to regulate the quality of this service, the current result is that hospitals effectively have a monopoly on MRIs, keeping doctors or MRI centers from opening up and offering services at lower prices. So instead of Winston-Salem-area patients choosing the MRI provider they prefer, they are stuck going to a provider who charges $1,000 per MRI. Essentially, the state has made MRI services a monopoly market. In this chapter, we explore the conditions that give rise to monopolies and also the ways in which monopoly power can erode.

· BIG QUESTIONS ·

- How are monopolies created?
- How much do monopolies charge, and how much do they produce?
- What are the problems with, and solutions for, monopoly?

How Are Monopolies Created?

As we explained in Chapter 3, a monopoly exists when a single seller supplies the entire market for a particular good or service. Two conditions enable a single seller to become a monopolist. First, the firm must have something unique to sell—that is, something without close substitutes. Second, it must have a way to prevent potential competitors from entering the market.

Monopolies occur in many places and for several different reasons. For example, companies that provide natural gas, water, and electricity are all examples of monopolies that occur naturally because of economies of scale. But monopolies can also occur when the government regulates the amount of competition. For example, trash pickup, street vending, taxicab rides, and ferry service are often licensed by local governments. These licenses have the effect of limiting competition and creating **monopoly power**, which is a measure of a monopolist's ability to set the price of a good or service.

Monopoly power
is a measure of a monopolist's ability to set the price of a good or service.

A monopolist operates in a market with high **barriers to entry**, which are restrictions that make it difficult for new firms to enter a market. As a result, monopolists have no competition nor any immediate threat of competition. High barriers to entry insulate the monopolist from competition, which means that many monopolists enjoy long-run economic profits. There are two types of barriers to entry: natural barriers and government-created barriers. Let's look at each.

Natural Barriers

Some barriers exist naturally within the market. These include control of resources, problems in raising capital, and economies of scale.

CONTROL OF RESOURCES The best way to limit competition is to control a resource that is essential in the production process. This extremely effective barrier to entry is hard to accomplish. But if you control a scarce resource, other competitors will not be able to find enough of it to compete. For example, in the early twentieth century, the Aluminum Company of America (ALCOA) made a concerted effort to buy bauxite mines around the globe. Within a decade, the company owned 90% of the world's bauxite, an essential element in making aluminum. This strategy enabled ALCOA to eliminate potential competitors and achieve dominance in the aluminum market.

PROBLEMS IN RAISING CAPITAL Monopolists are usually very big companies that have grown over an extended period. Even if you had a wonderful business plan, it is unlikely that a bank or a venture-capital company would lend you enough money to start a business that could compete effectively with a well-established company. For example, if you wanted to design a new operating system to compete with Microsoft and Apple, you would need tens of millions of dollars to fund your start-up. Lenders provide capital for business projects when the chance of success is high, but the chance of a new company successfully competing against an entrenched monopolist is not high. Consequently, raising capital to compete effectively is difficult.

ECONOMIES OF SCALE In Chapter 8, we saw that economies of scale occur when long-run average costs fall as production expands. Low unit costs and the low prices that follow give some larger firms the ability to drive rivals out of business. For example, imagine a market for electric power where companies compete to generate electricity and deliver it through their own grids. In such a market, it would be technically possible to run competing sets of wire to every home and business in the community, but the cost of installation and the maintenance of separate lines to deliver electricity would be both prohibitive and impractical. Even if a handful of smaller electric companies could produce electricity at the same cost, each would have to pay to deliver power through its own grid. This system would be highly inefficient.

In an industry that enjoys large economies of scale, production costs per unit continue to fall as a firm expands. Smaller rivals then have much higher average costs that prevent them from competing with a larger company. As a result, firms in the industry tend to combine over time. These mergers lead to the creation of a **natural monopoly**, which occurs when a single large firm has lower costs than any potential smaller competitor.

Government-Created Barriers

The creation of a monopoly can be either intentional or an unintended consequence of a government policy. Government-enforced statutes and regulations, such as laws and regulations covering licenses and patents, limit the scope of competition by creating barriers to entry.

LICENSING In many instances, it makes sense to give a single firm the exclusive right to sell a good or service. To minimize negative externalities, governments occasionally establish monopolies, or near monopolies, through licensing requirements. For example, in some communities trash collection is licensed to a single company. The rationale usually involves economies of scale, but there are additional factors to consider. Because firms cannot collect trash without a government-issued operating license, opportunities to enter the business are limited, which leaves consumers with a one-size-fits-all level of service. This outcome is the opposite of what we'd expect to see in a competitive market, where there would be many varieties of service at different price points.

Licensing also creates an opportunity for corruption. In fact, in many parts of the world, bribery is so common that it often determines which companies receive licenses in the first place.

PATENTS AND COPYRIGHT LAW Another area in which the government fosters monopoly is that of patents and copyrights. For example, when musicians create a new song and copyright their work, they earn royalties over the life of the copyright. The copyright is the government's assurance that no one else can play or sell the work without the artist's permission. Similarly, when a pharmaceutical company develops a new drug, the company receives a patent under which it has the exclusive right to market and sell the drug for as long as the patent is in force.

Incentives

By granting patents and copyrights to developers and inventors, the government creates monopolies. Patents and copyrights create stronger incentives to develop new drugs and produce new music than would exist if market competitors could immediately copy inventions. As a result, pharmaceutical companies invest heavily in developing new drugs and musicians devote their time to writing new music. At least in theory, these activities make our society a healthier and culturally richer place. After the patent or copyright expires, rivals can mimic the invention. This new competition opens up the market and provides dual benefits: wider access to the innovation and more sellers—both of which are good for consumers in the long run.

Nonetheless, many economists wonder if patents and copyrights are necessary or have unintended consequences. Sometimes copyright holders benefit more from exposure than from exercising their right to charge consumers. For example, when a music video goes viral on YouTube, the exposure causes many people to buy the original artist's work. Consider Justin Bieber. He managed to leverage his YouTube fame into a successful album launch, concert tours,

TABLE 10.1

The Characteristics of Monopolies

- One seller
- A unique product without close substitutes
- High barriers to entry
- Price making

and appearance fees that might never have occurred if a music studio had tightly controlled his sound while he was an emerging artist. Conversely, Taylor Swift refused to allow her music on Spotify from 2014 to 2017, because she felt the service did not properly compensate her and all the other people involved in creating the music. The point to remember is that copyright protection gives artists the right to decide how to distribute their work and what price to charge. It also gives them the ability to litigate when their work is stolen, illegally downloaded, or improperly used.

Though market-created and government-created barriers occur for different reasons, they have the same effect—they create monopolies. Table 10.1 summarizes the key characteristics of monopolies. In the next section, we examine how the monopolist determines the price it charges and how much to produce, explaining the term "price making" listed in Table 10.1.

Taylor's fans wanted her to *stay, stay, stay* but there was a *blank space* on Spotify for three years.

ECONOMICS IN THE REAL WORLD

PFIZER'S LIPITOR

Lipitor is the best-selling drug of all time. Pfizer corporation spent millions of dollars developing the drug and bringing it to the market. Lipitor is highly effective in lowering blood cholesterol. It was also highly profitable for Pfizer, generating over $11 billion in annual revenues before the patent ran out in 2011. Lipitor is now available in an inexpensive generic formulation at a price that is 80% lower than the original patent-protected price. Even after the patent expired, many customers continued to ask for Lipitor—not the generic—so brand recognition and customer loyalty represent another entry barrier.

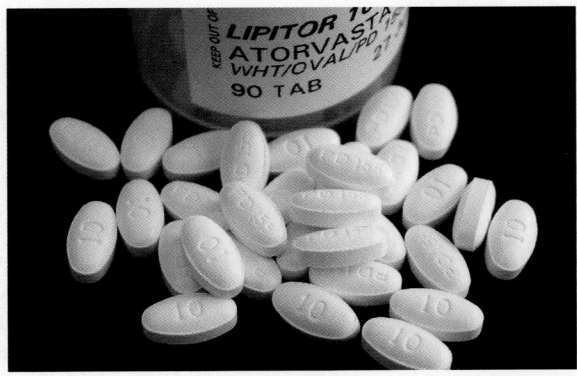

Do you want fries with that cholesterol medication?

Would Lipitor have been developed without patent protection? Probably not. Pfizer would have had little incentive to incur the cost of developing a cholesterol treatment if other companies could immediately copy the drug. In this case, society benefits because of the twofold nature of patents: they give firms the incentive to innovate, but they also limit the amount of time the patent is in place (20 years from the time of filing), thereby guaranteeing that competitive forces will govern long-run access to the product.

Incentives

Characteristics of Monopoly

THE OFFICE: PRINCESS UNICORN

Dwight Schrute buys up all of the Princess Unicorn dolls in local stores. As the Christmas holidays approach and parents become more desperate to find the dolls for their children, Dwight plans to sell his dolls marked way, way up—to $200! Toby wants to buy a doll for his daughter, Sasha, and is delighted to learn that Dwight has a stash he is selling, because now Toby has a chance to be a hero to his daughter. But he waits too long and learns that Dwight sold his last doll to Darryl. Distraught, Toby approaches Darryl, explains that he promised a doll to Sasha, and starts crying. Darryl decides to let Toby have the prized doll for $400, double what Darryl paid.

Dwight has a good understanding of the elements that create monopoly power. He is the sole seller in his area and he has a uniquely desirable product without close substitutes. That gives him monopoly power and the ability to raise the price he charges. Darryl also understands economics. He sees that Toby is desperate (has very inelastic demand) for the last doll and doubles Dwight's already high price.

FA-LA-LA-LA-LA, LA-LA, KA-CHING!

How Much Do Monopolies Charge, and How Much Do They Produce?

Both monopolists and firms in a competitive market seek to earn a profit. However, a monopolist is the sole provider of its product and holds market power. Thus, monopolists are price makers. A **price maker** has some control over the price it charges. As you learned in Chapter 9, a firm in a competitive market is a price taker.

A **price maker** has some control over the price it charges.

We can see the difference between price takers and price makers graphically in Figure 10.1. The demand curve for the product of a firm in a competitive market, shown in panel (a), is horizontal. When individual firms are price takers, they have no control over what they charge. In other words, demand is perfectly elastic—or horizontal—because every firm sells the same product. Demand for an individual firm's product exists only at the price determined by the market, and each firm is such a small part of the market that it can sell its entire output without lowering the price.

In contrast, because a monopolist is the only firm—the sole provider—in the industry, the demand curve for its product, shown in panel (b), constitutes the market demand curve. But the demand curve is downward sloping, which limits the monopolist's ability to make a profit. The monopolist would like to exploit its market power by charging a high price to many customers. However, the law of demand, which identifies a negative relationship between price and quantity demanded, dictates otherwise. Unlike the horizontal demand curve of a firm in a competitive market, the downward-sloping demand curve of the monopolist has many price-output combinations. If market demand is inelastic, a monopolist will choose a higher price. When market demand is more elastic, a monopolist will choose a lower price. As a result, monopolists must search for the profit-maximizing price and output.

PRACTICE WHAT YOU KNOW

Monopoly: Can You Spot the Monopolist?

Here are three questions to test your understanding of the conditions necessary for monopoly power to arise.

QUESTION: Is Amazon a monopolist?

ANSWER: Amazon is the nation's largest bookseller, with sales that dwarf those of its nearest retail rival, Barnes & Noble. Amazon is also by far the nation's leader in e-commerce with online sales that exceed the combined total of Walmart, Apple, Macy's, Home Depot, Best Buy, Costco, Nordstrom, Gap, and Target! Amazon's outsize market share, however, does not make it a monopolist. It still faces intense competition.

QUESTION: Is the only hairdresser in a small town a monopolist?

ANSWER: For all practical purposes, yes. He or she sells a unique service with inelastic demand. Because the nearest competitor is in the next town, the local hairdresser enjoys significant monopoly power. At the same time, the town's size limits potential competitors from entering the market, because the small community may not be able to support two hairdressers. Once one hairdresser is in place, a potential rival looks at the size of the market in the small town, calculates how many people he or she could expect to serve, and deduces that the potential revenue is too small to justify entrance into this market.

Monopoly profits!

CHALLENGE QUESTION: Which of these four firms do you think the government might, with good reason, allow to operate as a monopolist?

a. Tesla

b. Pacific Gas and Electric

c. Twitter

d. Walmart

ANSWER: The correct answer is B. Gas and electric companies are natural monopolies that have lower costs of production when they scale up. Dividing a natural monopolist into two or more smaller firms would drive costs significantly higher. Governments allow firms with significant economies of scale to remain monopolists and, as we shall learn, regulate the prices the firms can charge, to ensure that consumers are not gouged. Tesla, Walmart, and Twitter would, of course, like to be monopolists, too, but there is no compelling reason why society would be better off with just one large manufacturer of electric vehicles, or just one department store, or one social media outlet.

Barriers to Entry

FORREST GUMP

In this 1994 movie, Tom Hanks's character, Forrest Gump, keeps his promise to his deceased friend, Bubba, to go into the shrimping business after leaving the army. Forrest invests $25,000 in an old shrimp boat, but the going is tough—he catches only a handful of shrimp because of the competition for space in the shrimping waters. So Forrest tries naming his boat for good luck and brings on a first mate, Lieutenant Dan, who unfortunately is less knowledgeable and resourceful than Forrest. The fledgling enterprise continues to struggle, and eventually Forrest decides to pray for shrimp. Soon after, Forrest's boat, the *Jenny*, is caught out in the Gulf of Mexico during a hurricane. Miraculously, the *Jenny* makes it through the storm while the other shrimp boats, all anchored in the harbor, are destroyed. Boom! Forrest has a short-run monopoly.

The film suggests that Forrest's good luck—being in the right place at the right time—explains how he became a millionaire. But is Forrest's case realistic? Let's consider the situation in real-world economic terms.

Remember, Forrest was able to enter the business simply by purchasing a boat. To be sure, he will catch more shrimp in the short run, while the other boats are docked for repairs. However, once the competitors' boats return, they will resume catching shrimp, and Forrest's short-run profits will disappear. The reason we can be so confident of this result is that shrimping, with low barriers to entry and an undifferentiated product, is an industry that closely mirrors a perfectly competitive market. So when profits exist, new entrants will expand the supply produced and profits will return to the break-even level. Having Forrest become a "millionaire" makes for a good

If shrimping were easy, everyone would do it.

movie, but none of the elements are in place to suggest that he could attain a permanent monopoly. Forrest does not control an essential resource; the other shrimp captains will have little difficulty raising capital to repair their boats; and the economies of scale in this situation are small.

FIGURE 10.1

Comparing the Demand Curves of Perfectly Competitive Firms and Monopolists

(a) Firms in a competitive market face a horizontal demand curve. (b) Because the monopolist is the sole provider of the good or service, the demand for its product constitutes the industry—or market—demand curve, which is downward sloping. So while the perfectly competitive firm has no control over the price it charges, the monopolist gets to search for the profit-maximizing price and output.

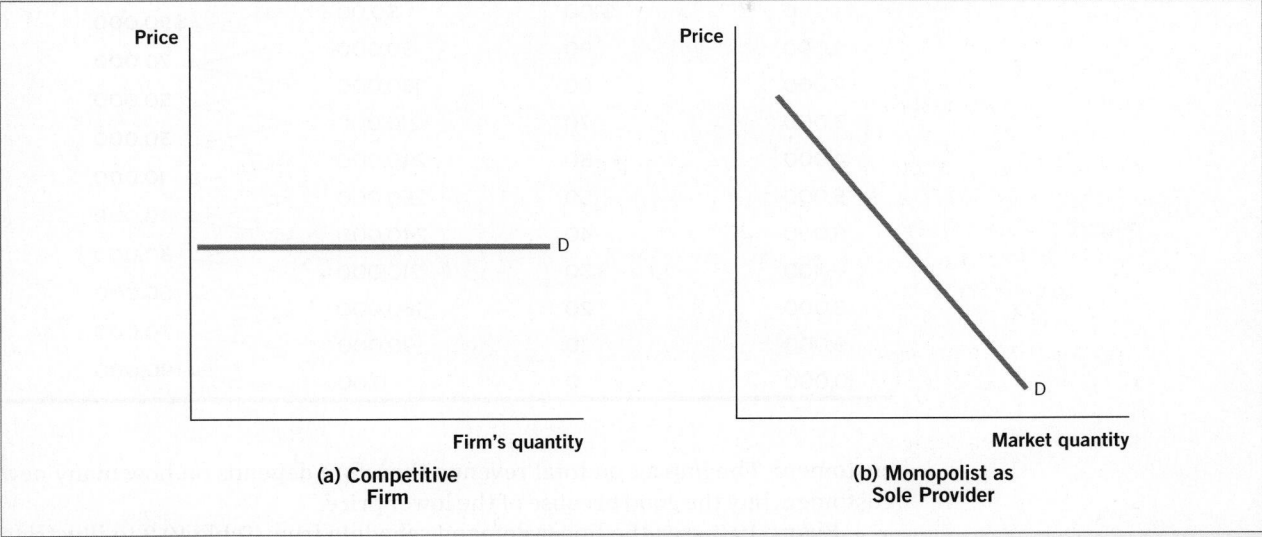

(a) Competitive Firm

(b) Monopolist as Sole Provider

The Profit-Maximizing Rule for the Monopolist

A competitive firm can sell all it produces at the existing market price. But a monopolist, because of the downward-sloping demand curve, must search for the most profitable price. To maximize profits, a monopolist can use the profit-maximizing rule we introduced in Chapter 9: MR = MC. For the price-taking firm, MR is just the market price, full stop. For the monopolist, however, there's a calculation involved.

Table 10.2 shows the marginal revenue for a cable company that serves a small community. Notice the negative relationship between output (quantity of customers) and price in columns 1 and 2: as the price goes down, the quantity of customers goes up. Total revenue is calculated by multiplying output by price ($TR = Q \times P$). At first, total revenue rises as the price falls. Once the price becomes too low ($40), total revenue begins to fall. As a result, the total revenue in column 3 initially rises to $250,000 before it begins to fall off. The final column, marginal revenue, shows the change (Δ) in total revenue. Here we see positive (though falling) marginal revenue associated with prices between $100 and $50 (see the green dollar amounts in column 4). Below $50, marginal revenue becomes negative (see the red dollar amounts in column 4).

The change in total revenue reflects the trade-off a monopolist encounters in trying to attract additional customers. To gain additional sales, the firm must lower its price. But the lower price is available to both new and existing

Marginal thinking

Trade-offs

TABLE 10.2

Calculating the Monopolist's Marginal Revenue

(1)	(2)	(3)	(4)
Quantity of customers	Price of service	Total revenue	Marginal revenue per 1,000 customers
(Q)	(P)	(TR)	(MR)
Formula:		Q × P	Δ TR
0	$100	$0.00	
			$90,000
1,000	90	90,000	
			70,000
2,000	80	160,000	
			50,000
3,000	70	210,000	
			30,000
4,000	60	240,000	
			10,000
5,000	50	250,000	
			−10,000
6,000	40	240,000	
			−30,000
7,000	30	210,000	
			−50,000
8,000	20	160,000	
			−70,000
9,000	10	90,000	
			−90,000
10,000	0	0.00	

customers. The impact on total revenue therefore depends on how many new customers buy the good because of the lower price.

Figure 10.2 uses the linear demand schedule from Table 10.2 to illustrate the two separate effects that determine marginal revenue. First, there is a *price effect*, which reflects how the lower price affects revenue. If the price of service drops from $70 to $60, each of the 3,000 existing customers saves $10, and the firm loses $10 × 3,000, or $30,000 in revenue, represented by the red area on the graph. But dropping the price also has an *output effect*, which reflects how the lower price affects the number of customers. Because 1,000 new customers buy the product (that is, cable service) when the price drops to $60, revenue increases by $60 × 1,000, or $60,000, represented by the green area. The output effect ($60,000) is greater than the price effect ($30,000). When we subtract the $30,000 in lost revenue (the red rectangle) from the $60,000 in revenue gained (the green rectangle), the result is $30,000 in marginal revenue at an output level between 3,000 and 4,000 customers.

Lost revenues associated with the price effect are always subtracted from the revenue gains created by the output effect. Now let's think of this data at the individual level. Because the firm adds 1,000 new customers, the marginal revenue per customer—$30,000 ÷ 1,000 new customers—is $30. Notice that this marginal revenue is less than the price, $60, that the firm charges. Because there is a price effect whenever the price drops, the marginal revenue curve lies below the demand curve. Therefore, in Figure 10.2, the *y* intercept is the same for the demand and marginal revenue curves and the *x* intercept of the MR curve is half of the demand curve's.

At high price levels—where demand is elastic—the price effect is small relative to the output effect. As the price drops, demand slowly becomes more inelastic. The output effect diminishes and the price effect increases. In other words, as the price falls, it becomes harder for the firm to acquire enough new

FIGURE 10.2

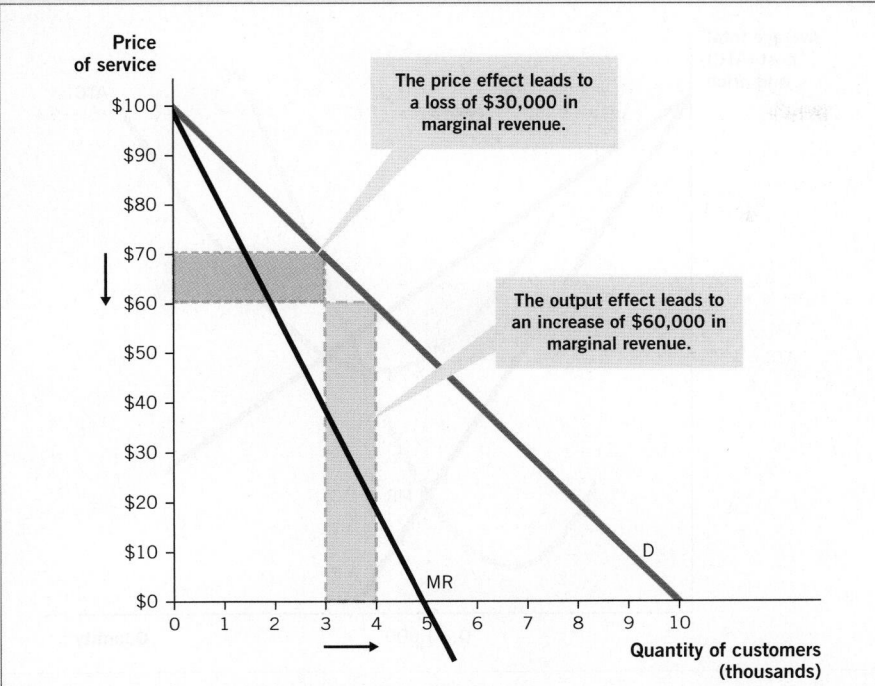

The Marginal Revenue Curve and the Demand Curve

A price drop has two effects. (1) Existing customers now pay less—this is the price effect. (2) New customers decide to purchase the good for the first time—this is the output effect. The relative size of the two effects, as shown by the red and green rectangles, determines whether the firm is able to increase its revenue by lowering its price. In this case, marginal revenue increases by $30,000.

customers to make up for the difference in lost revenue. Eventually, the price effect becomes larger than the output effect. This means that the marginal revenue curve will have the same *y* intercept as the demand curve and be twice as steep. As a result, marginal revenue becomes negative and dips below the *x* axis, as shown by the MR curve in Figure 10.2. When the marginal revenue is negative, the firm cannot maximize profit. This outcome puts an upper limit on the amount the firm will produce. This outcome is evident in Table 10.2: once the price becomes too low, the firm's marginal revenue is negative.

Marginal thinking

DECIDING HOW MUCH TO PRODUCE In Chapter 9, we explored the profit-maximizing rule for a firm in a competitive market. This rule also applies to a monopolist: marginal revenue should be equal to marginal cost. However, there is one big difference: a monopolist does not charge a price equal to marginal revenue.

Figure 10.3 illustrates the profit-maximizing decision-making process for a monopolist. We use a two-step process to determine the monopolist's profit:

1. Locate the point at which the firm will maximize its profits: MR = MC.
2. Set the price: from the point at which MR = MC, determine the profit-maximizing output, Q. From Q, move up along the dashed line until it intersects with the demand curve (D). From that point, move horizontally until you come to the *y* axis. This point on the *y* axis tells us the price (P)

FIGURE 10.3

The Monopolist's Profit Maximization

The firm uses the profit-maximizing rule to locate the point at which MR = MC. This condition determines the ideal output level, Q. Because the price (which is determined by the demand curve) is higher than the average total cost curve (ATC) along the dashed line at quantity Q, the firm makes the profit shown in the green area.

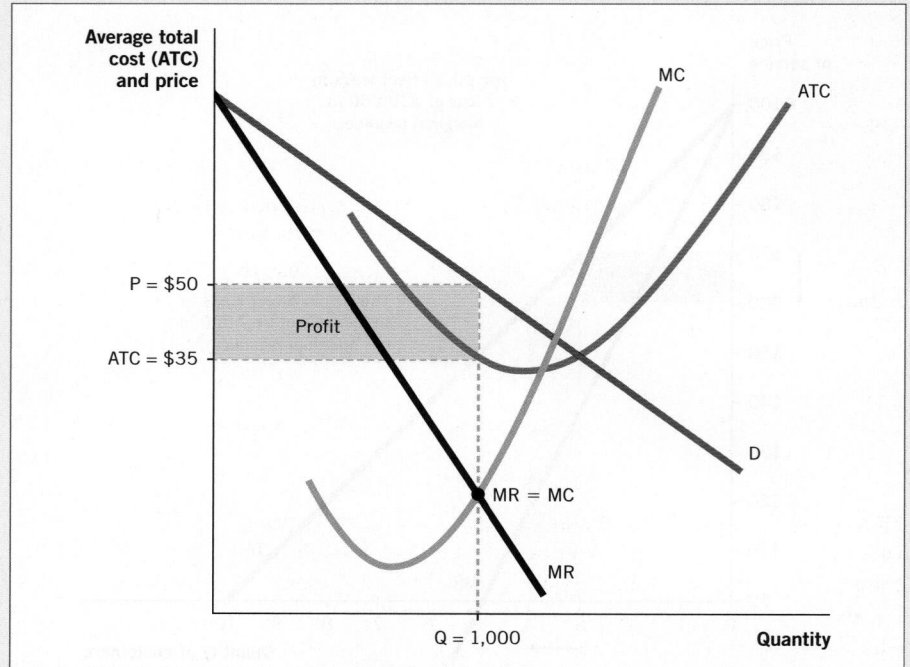

the monopolist should charge. Notice that the monopolist's price (P) is greater than MC (P > MC). This result differs from the competitive outcome, where P = MC.

Using this two-step process, we can determine the monopolist's profit. Locate the average total cost, ATC, of making Q units along the vertical dashed line. From that point, move horizontally until you come to the *y* axis. This point tells us the average total cost of making Q units. The difference between the price and the average total cost multiplied by Q tells us the profit (or loss) the firm makes. Any time the U-shaped ATC curve dips below the downward-sloping demand curve, D, there is a way to earn positive economic profits.

Because the price (P = $50) is higher than the average total cost (ATC = $35), the firm makes the profit shown in the green rectangle. For example, a profit-maximizing veterinarian will choose the point where MR = MC, and that means that the vet will serve 1,000 customers. Because the price at Q is $50 and the average total cost is $35, total profits are 1,000 × ($50 − $35) = $15,000.

Table 10.3 summarizes the differences between a competitive market and a monopoly. The competitive firm must take the price established in the market. If it does not operate efficiently, it cannot survive. Nor can it make an economic profit in the long run. The monopolist operates very differently. Because high barriers to entry limit competition, the monopolist may be able to earn long-run profits by restricting output. It operates inefficiently from society's perspective, and it has significant market power.

TABLE 10.3

The Major Differences between a Monopoly and a Competitive Market

Competitive market	Monopoly
Many firms	One firm
Cannot earn long-run economic profits	May earn long-run economic profits
Has no market power (is a price taker)	Has significant market power (is a price maker)
Produces an efficient level of output (because P = MC)	Produces less than the efficient level of output (because P > MC)

ECONOMICS IN THE REAL WORLD

THE BROADBAND MONOPOLY

Many markets in the United States have only a single high-speed Internet provider. The technology race strongly favors cable transmission over competing telephone lines. Internet access is provided by telephone companies using aging copper wiring, whereas cable companies use the latest fiber-optic technology. When it comes to truly high-speed Internet access, cable companies benefit from considerable barriers to entry. In many places, Comcast and Charter, the two largest cable companies in the United States by far, effectively own access to the Internet and can price their services accordingly.

Is there only one provider in your area?

The cable monopoly on high-speed Internet access affects both consumers and businesses. First, consumers increasingly need more bandwidth to stream movies, view YouTube, and load media-rich web sites. A slow connection can make surfing the Internet a chore. In other words, consumer demand is high and very inelastic. Second, businesses rely on bandwidth to maintain web sites and provide services to customers. Companies such as Netflix, Amazon Prime, and Hulu Plus, which deliver streaming content over the Internet, rely on access to a relatively affordable broadband Internet connection. Therefore, businesses also have high demand that is quite inelastic. For this reason, many people argue that relatively inexpensive access to the Internet is crucial if it is to continue as an engine of economic growth. Without competition, access will remain expensive.

Our dependence on the Internet invites a larger question. Where only one provider controls the bandwidth, should the government have a role in providing the infrastructure, or cables, in order to allow greater (or less-expensive) access? This is a concern in metropolitan areas served by only one Internet provider. Meanwhile, small rural communities may have no Internet access at all. For example, it is estimated that more than 25 million people in rural areas remain off the grid. Cable companies wouldn't make enough profit to connect these low-density areas, making it more difficult for their residents to participate in today's economy. The unfeasibility of having separate infrastructure for every would-be Internet provider makes this an example of a natural monopoly, a topic we'll take up toward the end of the chapter.

Is there a key profit takeaway?

Monopoly Profits: How Much Do Monopolists Make?

QUESTION: A monopolist always earns ____ economic profit.

a. a positive

b. zero

c. a negative

d. We cannot be sure about the profit a monopolist makes.

ANSWERS:

a. Incorrect. A monopolist is a price maker with considerable market power. This situation usually leads to a positive economic profit.

b. Incorrect. Zero economic profit exists in competitive markets in the long run. Because a monopolist, by definition, does not operate in competitive markets, it is protected from additional competition that would drive its profit to zero.

c. Incorrect. Whoa there! Negative profit? There is absolutely no reason to think that would happen. Monopolists sell a unique product without close substitutes in a market that is insulated from competitive pressures.

d. Correct. Because a monopolist benefits from barriers that limit the entry of competitors into the market, we would expect an economic profit. However, this outcome is not guaranteed. Monopolies do not control the demand for the product they sell. Consequently, in the short run the monopolist may experience a loss (if demand is low).

What Are the Problems with, and Solutions for, Monopoly?

Monopolies can adversely affect society by restricting output and charging higher prices than sellers in competitive markets do. This activity causes monopolies to operate inefficiently, provide less choice, promote an unhealthy form of competition known as *rent seeking* (addressed in a later section), and make economic profits that fail to guide resources to their highest-valued use. Recall that market failure occurs when there is an inefficient allocation of resources in a market. Once we have examined the problems with monopoly, we will turn to the potential solutions to the problems of monopoly.

The Problems with Monopoly

Monopolies result in an inefficient level of output, provide fewer choices to consumers, and encourage monopoly firms to lobby for government protection. Let's look at each of these concerns.

INEFFICIENT OUTPUT AND PRICE From an efficiency standpoint, the monopolist charges too much and produces too little. This result is evident in Figure 10.4, which shows what happens when a competitive market (denoted by the subscript C) ends up being controlled by a monopolist (denoted by the subscript M).

First, imagine a competitive fishing industry in which each boat catches a small portion of the fish, as shown in panel (a). Each firm is a price taker that must charge the market price. In contrast, panel (b) depicts pricing and output decisions for a monopoly fishing industry when it confronts the same cost structure as presented in panel (a). When a single firm controls the entire fishing ground, it is the sole supplier, so the supply curve becomes the monopolist's marginal cost curve. To set its price, it considers the downward-sloping demand and marginal revenue curves that serve the entire market. Therefore, it sets marginal revenue equal to marginal cost. The result is a smaller output than the competitive industry ($Q_M < Q_C$) and a higher price ($P_M > P_C$). The smaller output level is not efficient. In addition, the price the monopolist charges, P_M, is significantly above the marginal cost at the profit-maximizing level of output.

Figure 10.5 captures the deadweight loss (see Chapter 5) of the monopoly. The monopolist charges too high a price and produces too little of the product, so some consumers who would benefit from a competitive market lose out. Because the demand curve (the willingness to pay) is greater than the marginal

FIGURE 10.4

When a Competitive Industry Becomes a Monopoly

(a) In a competitive industry, the intersection of supply and demand determines the price (P_C) and quantity (Q_C).
(b) When a monopolist controls an entire industry, the supply curve becomes the monopolist's marginal cost curve. The monopolist uses MR = MC to determine its price (P_M) and quantity (Q_M). As a result, the monopolist charges a higher price and produces a smaller output than when an entire industry is populated with competitive firms.

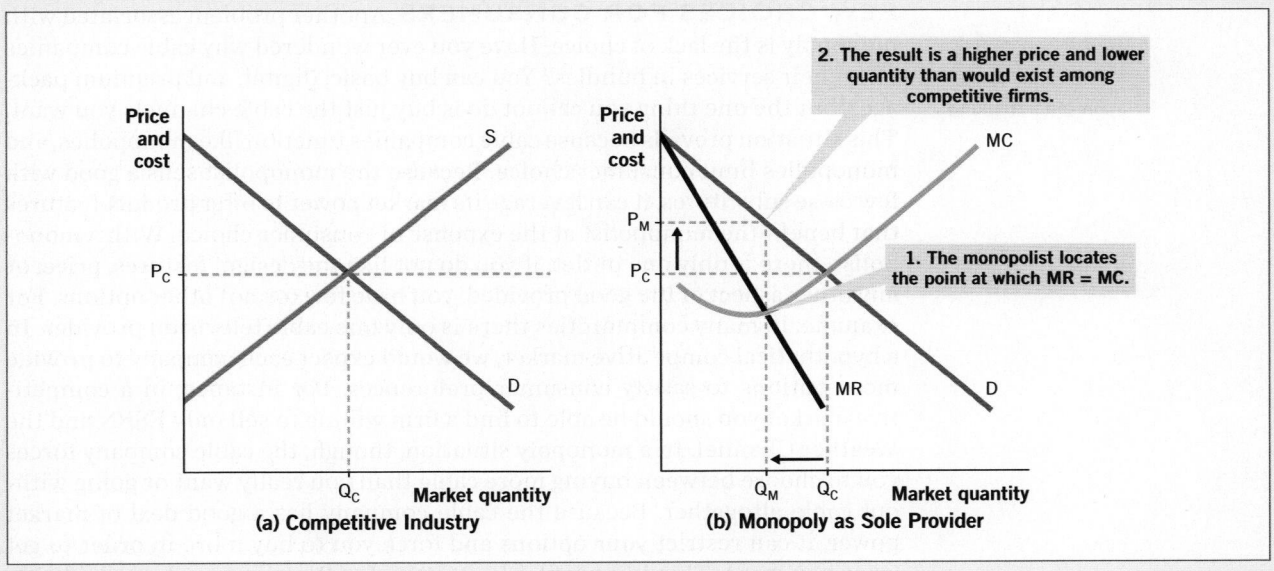

FIGURE 10.5

The Deadweight Loss of Monopoly

Because the profit-maximizing monopolist produces an output of Q_M, an amount that is less than Q_C, the result is the deadweight loss shown in the yellow triangle. The blue rectangle is the consumer surplus transferred to the monopolist.

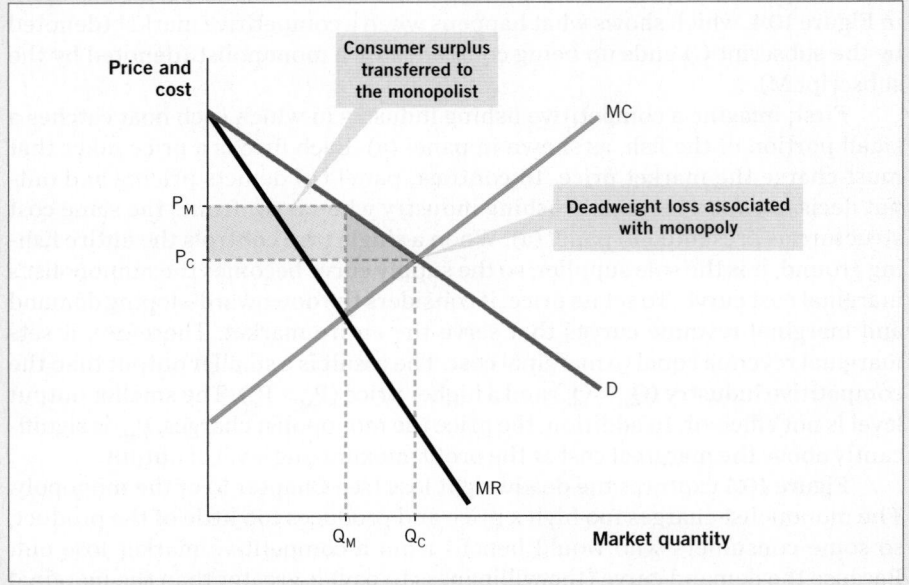

cost between output levels Q_M and Q_C, society would be better off if output expanded to Q_C. But a profit-maximizing monopolist will limit output to Q_M. The result, a deadweight loss equal to the area of the yellow triangle, is inefficient for society. Consumer surplus is also transferred to the monopolist, as shown in the blue rectangle.

Marginal thinking

FEW CHOICES FOR CONSUMERS Another problem associated with monopoly is the lack of choice. Have you ever wondered why cable companies offer their services in bundles? You can buy basic, digital, and premium packages, but the one thing you cannot do is buy just the cable channels you want. This situation prevails because cable companies function like monopolies, and monopolies limit consumer choice. Because the monopolist sells a good with few close substitutes, it can leverage its market power to offer product features that benefit the monopolist at the expense of consumer choice. With a monopolist, there is only one outlet: if you do not like the design, features, price, or any other aspect of the good provided, you have few (or no) other options. For example, in many communities there is only one cable television provider. In a hypothetical competitive market, we would expect each company to provide more options to satisfy consumer preferences. For instance, in a competitive market you should be able to find a firm willing to sell only ESPN and the Weather Channel. In a monopoly situation, though, the cable company forces you to choose between buying more cable than you really want or going without cable altogether. Because the cable company has a good deal of market power, it can restrict your options and force you to buy more in order to get what you want. This is a profitable strategy for the company but a bad outcome for consumers.

Would you rather watch the Weather Channel . . .   . . . or SportsCenter?

RENT SEEKING The term **rent seeking** was first coined by Anne Krueger in 1974. It refers to the attempt to gain monopoly power through the political process, by using lobbying and other means to secure legal monopoly rights. Throughout this text, we have seen the desirable effects of competition: lower prices, increased efficiency, and enhanced service and quality. However, rent seeking is a form of competition that produces an undesirable result. When firms compete to become monopolists, there is one winner without any of the benefits usually associated with competition. Consider the U.S. steel industry, which has been in decline for many years and has lost market share to steel firms in China, Japan, and Europe. If a U.S. steel company is losing money because of foreign competition, it can address the situation in one of two ways. It can modernize by building new facilities and using the latest equipment and techniques. (In other words, it can become competitive with the overseas competition.) Or it can lobby the government to limit imports. The domestic steel industry chose to lobby, and in 2002 the George W. Bush administration imposed tariffs of up to 30% on imported steel. Here is the danger: when lobbying is less expensive than building a new factory, the company will choose to lobby! If politicians give in and the lobbying succeeds, society is adversely affected because the gains from trade are smaller.

Supply and demand tell us that steel prices will rise in the absence of competition. This outcome is inefficient. Also, instead of pushing for legislation that grants market power, the lobbying resources could have gone into the production of useful products. As a result, the process of rent seeking potentially benefits the rent seeker but yields little direct benefit for society.

Rent seeking occurs when resources are used to secure monopoly rights through the political process.

Trade creates value

A former steel plant in Bethlehem, Pennsylvania.

Solutions to the Problems of Monopoly

We have learned that monopolies do not produce as much social welfare as competitive markets do. As a result, public policy approaches attempt to address this problem. The policy solutions include breaking up the monopoly, reducing trade barriers, and regulating markets.

Problems with Monopoly: Coffee Consolidation

A community has many competing coffee shops.

QUESTION: How can we use the market demand curve to illustrate the consumer surplus and producer surplus created by a competitive market?

When companies compete, consumers win.

ANSWER:

In a competitive market, supply and demand determine the price and quantity. In the figure, consumer surplus is represented by the blue area. Producer surplus is represented by the red area.

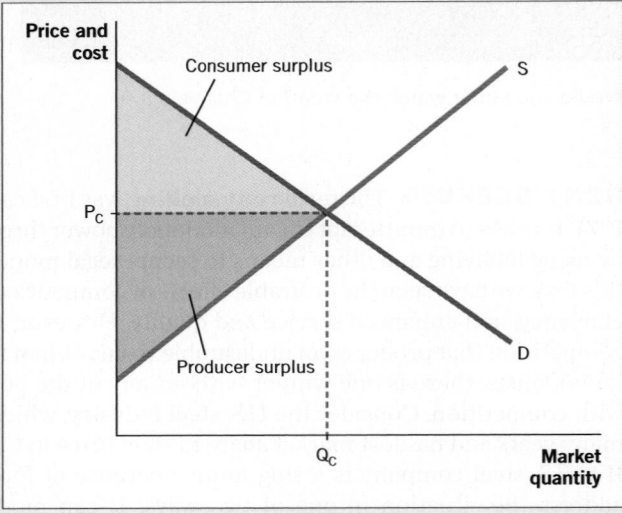

QUESTION: Now imagine that all the independent coffee shops combine under one fictional franchise, known as Harbucks. How can we create a new graph that illustrates the consumer surplus, producer surplus, and deadweight loss that occur when a monopolist takes over the market?

ANSWER:

In this figure, we see that the consumer surplus has shrunk, the producer surplus has increased, and the higher price charged by Harbucks creates deadweight loss. Allowing a monopolist to capture a market does not benefit consumers and is inefficient for society.

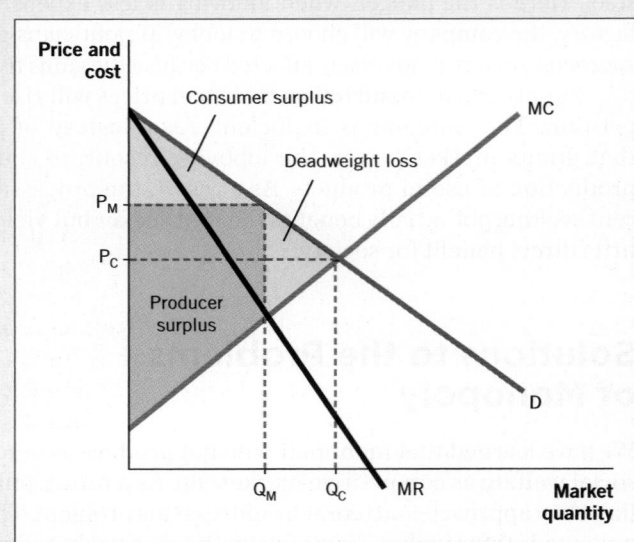

Monopoly Power

BREAKING BAD

Breaking Bad is widely regarded as one of the greatest television series of all time. It tells the story of Walter White, a depressed high school chemistry teacher diagnosed with lung cancer who turns to crime to secure his family's financial future before he dies. Together with a former student, Jesse Pinkman, the two produce and sell methamphetamine. Walt is the chemist who makes the best crystal meth in town. Jesse has the contacts Walt needs to sell it. Together, the two begin a long journey to take over the meth market in Albuquerque, NM.

In one scene Jesse is enthused about how well they are doing and says, "Gonna be some mad cheddar, yo. Cheddar, Mr. White. Fat stacks, dead presidents, cash money. Gonna own this city."

Walt immediately responds, "We're not charging enough."

JESSE: "What?"

WALT: "You corner the market, then raise the price. Simple economics."

Walt understands that you have to corner the market before you can raise your price.

BREAKING UP THE MONOPOLY Eliminating deadweight loss and restoring efficiency can be as simple as promoting competition. From 1913 until 1982, AT&T had a monopoly on the delivery of telephone services in the United States. As the years passed, however, it became progressively harder for AT&T to defend its position that having a single provider of phone services was good for consumers. By the early 1980s, AT&T was spending over $300 million to fend off antitrust lawsuits from the states, the federal government, and many private firms. The AT&T monopoly ended in 1982, when enormous pressure from the government led the company to split into eight smaller companies. Suddenly, AT&T had to compete to survive. The newly competitive phone market forced each of the phone companies to expand the services it offered—and sometimes even lower its prices—to avoid losing customers. For example, rates on long-distance calls, which were quite high before the break-up, plummeted.

Incentives

From this example, we see that the government can help to limit monopoly outcomes and restore a competitive balance. The government can accomplish this goal through antitrust legislation. Antitrust laws are designed to prevent monopoly practices and promote competition. The government has exercised control over monopoly practices since the passage of the Sherman Act in 1890, and the task currently falls to the Department of Justice. We discuss these regulations at greater length in Chapter 13.

REDUCING TRADE BARRIERS Countries use *tariffs*, which are taxes on imported goods, as a trade barrier to prevent competition and protect domestic business. However, any barrier—whether a tariff, a quota, or a prohibition—limits the possible gains from trade. For monopolists, trade barriers prevent rivals from entering their territory. For example, imagine that Florida could place a tariff on California oranges. For every California orange sold in Florida, the seller would have to pay a fee. Florida orange producers might like this tariff because it would limit competition from California. But California growers would cry foul and reciprocate with a tariff on Florida oranges. Growers in both states would be happy, but consumers would be harmed. For example, if a damaging freeze in Florida depleted the crop, Florida consumers would have to pay more than the demand-driven price for imported oranges from California. If, in contrast, Florida had a bumper crop, the tariff would keep prices artificially high, and much of the extra harvest would go to waste.

The United States has achieved tremendous growth by limiting the ability of individual states to place import and export restrictions on goods and services. The Constitution reads, "No State shall, without the consent of Congress, lay any imposts or duties on imports or exports." Rarely have so few words been more profound. With this simple law in place, states must compete on equal terms.

Reducing trade barriers creates more competition, lessens the influence of monopoly, and promotes the efficient use of resources. For example, prior to 1994, private air carriers accounted for less than 0.5% of the air traffic in India. In 1994, Indian airspace was opened to allow private airlines to operate scheduled service. This move forced the state-owned Air India to become more competitive. These changes in Indian aviation policies had the effect of raising the share of private airline operators in domestic passenger carriage to over 85% by 2018. Air India—which once controlled the market—has fallen to third place.

Since 1994, reduced barriers to competition have transformed India's airline industry.

REGULATING MARKETS In the case of a natural monopoly, it is not practical to harness the benefits of competition. Consider the economies of scale that utility companies experience. Breaking up a company that provides natural gas, water, or electricity would result in higher production costs. For instance, a second water company would have to build infrastructure to each residence or business in a community. Having redundant water lines with only a fraction of the customers would make the delivery of water extremely expensive, such that the final price to the consumer, even with competition, would be higher. Therefore, keeping the monopoly intact is the best option. In this situation, policymakers might attempt to create a more efficient outcome and maximize society's welfare by regulating the monopolist's prices. Theoretically, this process would be straightforward. However, the reality is that few regulators are experts in the fields of electricity, natural gas, water, and other regulated industries, so they often lack sufficient knowledge to make the regulations work as designed.

When a natural monopoly exists, the government may choose to use the marginal cost pricing rule, $P = MC$, to generate the greatest welfare for society. Because the price is determined along the demand curve, setting $P = MC$ guarantees that the good or service will be produced as long as the willingness to pay exceeds the additional cost of production. Figure 10.6 shows the difference in pricing and profits for a regulated monopoly and an unregulated natural monopoly. Recall that a natural monopoly is characterized by economies of scale, which we can idealize as a constant marginal cost that leads to a steadily dropping ATC curve, as in Figure 10.6.

To maximize profits, an unregulated monopolist sets $MR = MC$ and produces quantity Q_M at a price of P_M. Because P_M is greater than the average total cost of producing Q_M units, or C_M, the monopolist earns the profit shown in the

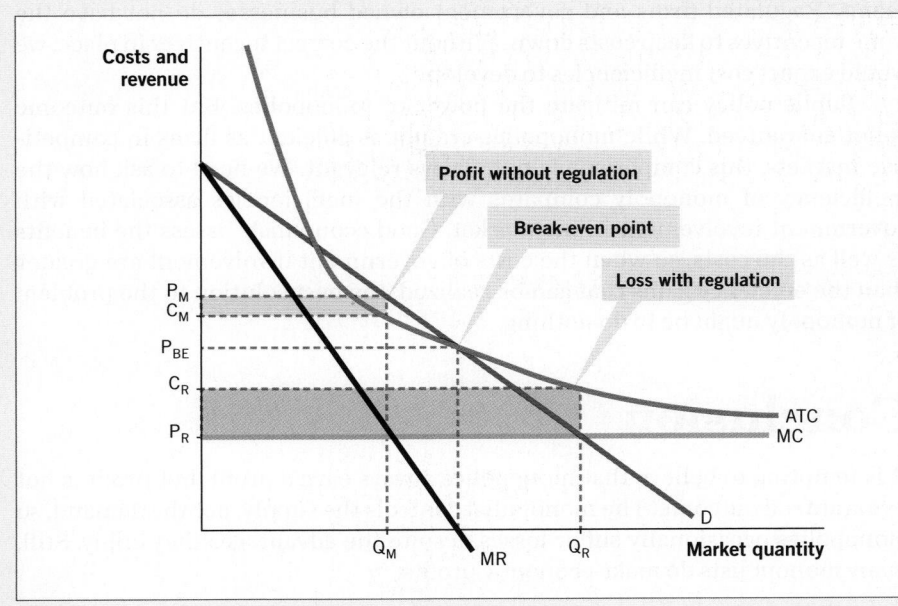

FIGURE 10.6

The Regulatory Solution for Natural Monopoly

An unregulated monopolist uses the profit-maximizing rule $MR = MC$ and earns a small profit, shown in the green rectangle. If the monopolist is regulated using the marginal cost pricing rule, $P = MC$, it will experience the loss shown in the red rectangle.

green rectangle. If the firm is regulated and the price is set at marginal cost, regulators can set P = MC, and the output expands to Q_R. (The subscript R denotes the regulated monopolist.) In this example, because the cost of production is subject to economies of scale, the cost falls from C_M to C_R and generates a large improvement in efficiency. The regulated price, P_R, is lower than the unregulated monopolist's price, P_M, and production increases. As a result, consumers are better off.

But what happens to the monopolist? It loses money in the amount of the red rectangle because the average total costs under the marginal cost pricing solution, C_R, are higher than the price allowed by regulators, P_R. This outcome is problematic because a firm that suffers losses will go out of business. That outcome is not desirable from society's standpoint, because the consumers of the product will be left without it. There are three possible solutions. First, to make up for the losses incurred at the higher output level, C_R, the government could subsidize the monopolist in order to achieve the socially efficient level of production. Second, the regulated price could be set at P_{BE}, where the ATC crosses the D curve, so that the firm breaks even; we can think of this as the second-best solution. Third, the government could own and operate the business in lieu of the private firm. This solution, however, has its own challenges, as we explore in the next section.

A CAVEAT ABOUT GOVERNMENT OVERSIGHT Firms with a profit motive have an incentive to minimize the costs of production, because lower costs translate directly into higher profits. If a firm's managers do a poor job reining in costs, they will be fired. The same cannot be said about government managers, or bureaucrats. Government employees are rarely let go, regardless of their performance. As a result, the government oversight and management of monopolies is problematic because there are fewer incentives to keep costs in check.

Consequently, the marginal cost pricing rule is not as effective as it first seems. Regulated firms and government-owned businesses do not have the same incentives to keep costs down. Without the correct incentives in place, we would expect cost inefficiencies to develop.

Public policy can mitigate the power of monopolies. But this outcome is not guaranteed. While monopolies are not as efficient as firms in competitive markets, this comparison is not always relevant. We need to ask how the inefficiency of monopoly compares with the inefficiencies associated with government involvement in the market. Good economists assess the benefits as well as the costs, so when the costs of government involvement are greater than the efficiency gains that can be realized, the best solution to the problem of monopoly might be to do nothing.

Conclusion

It is tempting to believe that monopolies always earn a profit, but profit is not a guaranteed outcome. The monopolist controls the supply, not the demand, so monopolies occasionally suffer losses despite the advantages they enjoy. Still, many monopolists do make economic profits.

Playing Monopoly like an Economist

■ Buy and trade properties with others. Recall that trade is one of our Five Foundations!

■ Some properties are landed on far more frequently than others. Buy or trade for them.

■ If you obtain a monopoly, develop it as quickly as possible.

In the game Monopoly, you profit only by taking from other players. The assets of its world are fixed in number. The best player drives others into bankruptcy and is declared the winner only after gaining control of the entire board.

Here is some advice on how to play the game like an economist.

Apply some basic economic principles, and you can win big.

- Remember that a monopoly is built on trade. You are unlikely to acquire a monopoly by landing on the color groups you need. Instead, you have to trade properties in order to acquire the ones you need. Because every player knows this, acquiring the last property to complete a color group is nearly impossible. Your competitors will never willingly hand you a monopoly unless they get something of great value in return.

- Don't wait to trade until it is obvious what you need. Instead, try to acquire as many properties as you can in order to gain trading leverage as the game unfolds. Always pick up available properties if no other player owns one of the same color group; purchase properties that will give you two or three of the same group; or purchase a property if it blocks someone else from completing a set.

- Think about probability. Mathematicians have determined that Illinois Avenue is the property most likely to be landed on and that B&O is the best railroad to own. Know the odds, and you can weigh the risks and rewards of trade better than your opponents. This is just like doing market research before you buy. Being informed matters in Monopoly and in business.

- When you get a monopoly, develop it quickly. Build three houses as quickly as you can, but don't build a fourth house or put a hotel on your property—the returns to those additional investments are not worth the price.

- Finally, if you gain the upper hand and have a chance to bankrupt a player from the game, do it. Luck plays a key role in Monopoly, as it does in life. Although it may sound harsh, eliminating a competitor moves you one step closer to winning the game.

Trade creates value

The decisions you make while playing Monopoly are all about cost-benefit analysis. You have limited resources and only so many opportunities to use them to your advantage. The skilled player understands how to weigh the values of tradable properties, considers the risk-return proposition of every decision, manages money effectively, and eliminates competitors when given a chance.

In this chapter, we examined the monopoly model and, along the way, compared the results under monopoly with the results of the competitive model that we developed in the previous chapter. While competitive markets generally yield welfare-enhancing outcomes for society, monopolies often do the opposite. Because monopolists do not produce an efficient outcome, government often seeks to limit monopoly outcomes and promote competitive markets.

Competitive markets and monopoly are market structures at opposite extremes. Indeed, we rarely encounter the conditions necessary for either a pure monopoly or a perfectly competitive market. Most economic activity takes place between these two alternatives. In the upcoming chapters, we examine monopolistic competition and oligopoly—two markets that constitute the bulk of the economy. Fortunately, if you understand the market structures at the extremes, understanding the middle ground is straightforward. As we move forward, we will deploy the same tools we used to examine monopoly in order to understand monopolistic competition (Chapter 12) and oligopoly (Chapter 13) ✳.

· ANSWERING *the* BIG QUESTIONS ·

How are monopolies created?

- Monopoly is a market structure characterized by a single seller that produces a well-defined product with no good substitutes.
- Monopolies operate in a market with high barriers to entry, the chief source of market power.
- Monopolies are created when a single seller supplies the entire market for a particular good or service.

How much do monopolies charge, and how much do they produce?

- Monopolists are price makers who may earn long-run economic profits.
- Like perfectly competitive firms, a monopolist tries to maximize its profits. To do so, it uses the profit-maximizing rule, $MR = MC$, to select the optimal price and quantity combination of a good or service.

What are the problems with, and solutions for, monopoly?

- From an efficiency standpoint, the monopolist charges too much and produces too little. Because the monopolist's output is smaller than the output that would exist in a competitive market, monopolies lead to deadweight loss.

- Government grants of monopoly power encourage rent seeking, or the use of resources to secure monopoly rights through the political process.

- There are three potential solutions to the problem of monopoly. First, the government may break up firms that gain too much market power in order to restore a competitive market. Second, the government can promote open markets by reducing trade barriers. Third, the government can regulate a monopolist's ability to charge excessive prices.

- When the costs of government involvement in regulating a monopoly are greater than the efficiency gains that can be realized, it is better to leave the monopolist alone.

Concepts You Should Know

barriers to entry (p. 315)   natural monopoly (p. 316)   rent seeking (p. 329)

monopoly power (p. 314)   price maker (p. 318)

Questions for Review

1. Describe the difference between a monopoly and a natural monopoly.

2. What are barriers to entry, and why are they crucial to the creation of potential long-run monopoly profits? Give an example of a barrier that can lead to monopoly.

3. Explain why a monopolist is a price maker but a perfectly competitive firm is a price taker.

4. Why is a monopolist's marginal revenue curve less than the price of the good it sells?

5. What is the monopolist's rule for determining the profit-maximizing output? What two steps does the monopolist follow to maximize profits?

6. Why does a monopolist operate inefficiently? Draw a demand curve, a marginal revenue curve, and a marginal cost curve to illustrate the deadweight loss from monopoly.

7. Why is it difficult to regulate a natural monopoly?

Study Problems (＊solved at the end of the section)

1. In the figure below, identify the price the monopolist will charge and the output the monopolist will produce. How do these two decisions on the part of the monopolist compare with the efficient price and output?

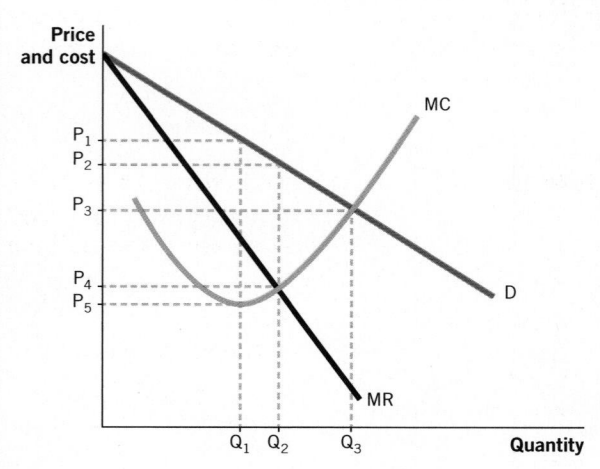

2. Which of the following could be considered a monopolist?

  a. your local water company

  b. Boeing, a manufacturer of airplanes

  c. Brad Pitt

  d. Walmart

  e. the only gas station along a 100-mile stretch of road

3. A monopolist has the following fixed and variable costs:

Price	Quantity	Fixed cost	Variable cost
$10	0	$8	$0
9	1	8	5
8	2	8	8
7	3	8	10
6	4	8	11
5	5	8	13
4	6	8	16
3	7	8	20
2	8	8	25

At what level of output will the monopolist maximize profits?

4. The year is 2278, and the starship *Enterprise* is running low on dilithium crystals, which are used to regulate the matter-antimatter reactions that propel the ship across the universe. Without the crystals, space-time travel is not possible. If there is only one known source of dilithium crystals, are the necessary conditions met to establish a monopoly? If the crystals are government owned or regulated, what price should the government set for them?

✳ 5. If demand falls, what is likely to happen to a monopolist's price, output, and economic profit?

✳ 6. A new musical group called The Incentives cuts a debut single. The record company determines a number of price points for the group's first single, "The Big Idea."

Price per download	Quantity of downloads
$2.99	25,000
1.99	50,000
1.49	75,000
0.99	100,000
0.49	150,000

The record company can produce the song with fixed costs of $10,000 and no variable cost.

a. Determine the total revenue at each price. What is the marginal revenue as the price drops from one level to the next?
b. What price would maximize the record company's profits? How much would the company make?
c. If you were the agent for The Incentives, what signing fee would you request from the record company? Explain your answer.

7. Recalling what you have learned about elasticity, what can you say about the connection between the price a monopolist chooses to charge and whether or not demand is elastic, unitary, or inelastic at that price? (**Hint:** Examine the marginal revenue curve of a monopolist. The fact that marginal revenue becomes negative at low prices implies that a portion of the demand curve cannot possibly be chosen.)

8. A small community is served by five independent gas stations. Gasoline is a highly competitive market. Use the market demand curve to illustrate the consumer surplus and producer surplus created by the market. Now imagine that the five independent gas stations are all combined under one franchise. Create a new graph that illustrates the consumer surplus, producer surplus, and deadweight loss after the monopolist enters the market.

9. A local community bus service charges $2.00 for a one-way fare. The city council is thinking of raising the fare to $2.50 to generate 25% more revenue. The council has asked for your advice as a student of economics. In your analysis, be sure to break down the impact of the price increase into the price effect and the output effect. Explain why the city council's estimate of the revenue increase is likely to be overstated. Use a graph to illustrate your answer.

10. Suppose that a monopolist's marginal cost curve shifts upward. What is likely to happen to the price the monopolist charges, the quantity it produces, and the profit it makes? Use a graph to illustrate your answer.

11. Suppose a firm collects $60 in revenues when it sells four units, $70 in revenues when it sells five units and $75 when it sells six units. You can infer that the firm is

a. perfectly competitive.
b. either a perfectly competitive firm or a monopolist.
c. a monopolist.

✻ **12.** Suppose Ambika, a graduate student in economics, tutors undergraduates to supplement her income as a teaching assistant. Ambika might tutor nine students each week. Their reservation prices for tutoring are given in the following table.

Each tutoring session lasts an hour. If the opportunity cost of Ambika's time is $20 per hour, and if she must charge each student the same price, how many students should she tutor each week? What price should she charge? What will be her economic profit?

Student	Reservation price
A	$50
B	46
C	42
D	38
E	34
F	30
G	26
H	22
I	18

Solved Problems

5. The following graph shows a monopolist making a profit:

Now we show what happens if demand falls:

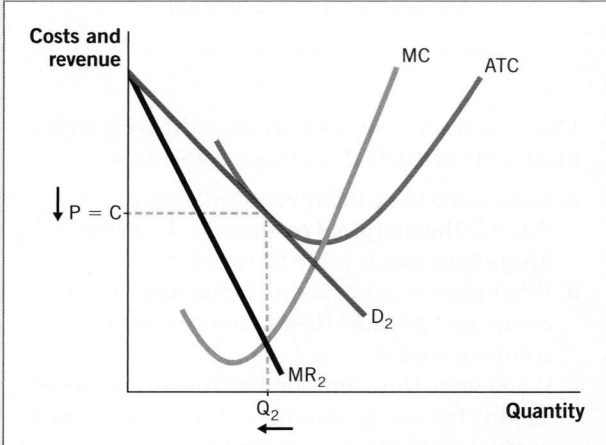

Lower demand causes the price to fall, the output to decline, and the profit to disappear.

6.a.

Price per download	Downloads	Total revenue	Marginal revenue
$2.99	25,000	$74,750	$74,750
1.99	50,000	99,500	24,750
1.49	75,000	111,750	12,250
0.99	100,000	99,000	−12,750
0.49	150,000	73,500	−25,500

b. Because marginal costs are $0, the firm would maximize its profits at $1.49. The company would make $111,750 − $10,000, or $101,750.

c. The company makes $101,750 from production, so as the agent you could request any signing fee up to that amount. Because determining a fee is a negotiation and both sides have to gain from trade, as the agent you should argue for a number close to $100,000, and you should expect the firm to argue for a much smaller fee.

12. She should tutor four students (students A–D). The marginal revenue of tutoring student D is $26, which is greater than Ambika's opportunity cost, but the marginal revenue of tutoring student E is only $18, which is less than Ambika's opportunity cost. So Ambika should stop at student D. She should charge $38, which is student D's reservation price. At this price, her economic profit will be 4($38) − 4($20) = $72.

Student	Reservation price	Total revenue	Marginal revenue
A	$50	$50	$50
B	46	92	42
C	42	126	34
D	38	152	26
E	34	170	18
F	30	180	10
G	26	182	2
H	22	176	−6
I	18	162	−14

Price Discrimination

Is Charging Different Prices to Different People Unfair and Harmful? Actually, No.

Have you ever wondered why private colleges have high sticker prices and then offer tuition discounts to some students but not others? And why theaters charge more for adults than for children, when everyone sees the same movie? In these examples, some customers pay more and others pay less. Is this practice unfair? Not really: everyone's paying what they're willing to pay. Anyway, two-tiered pricing usually works to the advantage of people who need a financial break, and in the big picture there are net social benefits, in the form of greater market efficiency.

Discounts for college students are a prime example. Here's a rundown of companies that will give you a price break if you can prove you're a student:

- clothing retailers like J. Crew, Eastern Mountain Sports, and TopShop
- tech companies such as Apple, Microsoft, Adobe, and MathWorks (makers of MATLAB)
- entertainment companies like Cinemark, Major League Baseball, museums, and most ski resorts and amusement parks
- travel and transportation companies such as Greyhound, Amtrak, many hotel brands, and some air carriers
- your favorite news publications, like *The New York Times* or *The Economist* (!)

College students win big with price discrimination—your student I.D. gets you hundreds of discounts!

- auto insurance (if you have good grades)
- all the major cell phone carriers
- last, but certainly not least: many national restaurant chains and almost all local restaurants

Price discrimination makes big winners out of college students! In this chapter, we examine many real-life pricing situations and how businesses can make additional profits if they charge different prices to different groups of customers. The study of *price discrimination* adds a layer of complexity to the simple models of perfect competition and monopoly. A thorough understanding of how price discrimination works is especially useful as we complete our study of market structure with monopolistic competition and oligopoly in the next two chapters.

· BIG QUESTIONS ·

- What is price discrimination?
- How is price discrimination practiced?

What Is Price Discrimination?

Price discrimination
occurs when a firm sells the same good or service at different prices to different groups of customers.

Price discrimination occurs when a firm sells the same good or service at different prices to different groups of customers. The difference in price is not related to differences in cost. Although "price discrimination" sounds like something illegal, in fact it is beneficial to both sellers and buyers. When a firm can charge more than one price, markets work more efficiently. Because price-discriminating firms typically charge a "high" and a "low" price, some consumers are able to buy the product at a low price. Of course, firms are not in business to provide goods at low prices; they want to make a profit. Price discrimination enables them to make more money by dividing their customers into at least two groups: those who get a discount and others who pay more.

We have seen that in competitive markets, firms are *price takers*. If a competitive firm attempts to charge a higher price, its customers will likely buy elsewhere. To practice price discrimination, a firm must be a *price maker*; it must have some market power before it can charge more than one price. Both monopolies and nonmonopolistic companies use price discrimination to earn higher profits. Common examples of price discrimination are movie theater tickets, restaurant menus, college tuition, airline reservations, discounts on academic software, and coupons.

Conditions for Price Discrimination

For price discrimination to take place, two conditions must be met. First, there must be at least two different types of buyers. Second, the firm must be able to prevent resale of the product or service. Let's look at each in turn.

DISTINGUISHING GROUPS OF BUYERS
To price-discriminate, a firm must be able to distinguish groups of buyers with different price elasticities of demand. Firms can generate additional revenues by charging more to customers with inelastic demand and less to customers with elastic demand. For instance, many restaurants offer lower prices, known as "early-bird specials," to people who eat dinner early. Who are these customers? Many, such as retirees and families with children, are on a limited budget. These early diners not only have lower demand but also represent demand that is more elastic; they eat out only if the price is low enough.

Trade-offs

Early-bird specials work for restaurants by separating customers into two groups: one that is price sensitive and another that is willing to pay full price. This strategy enables the restaurants to serve more customers and generate additional revenue.

PREVENTING RESALE
For price discrimination to be a viable strategy, a firm must also be able to prevent resale of the product or service. In some cases, preventing resale is easy. For example, airlines require that electronic tickets match the passenger's government-issued photo ID. This system prevents a passenger who received a discounted fare from reselling it to another passenger who would be willing to pay more. The process works well for airlines and enables them to charge more to groups of flyers with more inelastic demand, such as business travelers. It also works well for restaurants offering early-bird specials, because the restaurants can easily distinguish between customers who arrive in time for the specials and those who arrive later.

One Price versus Price Discrimination

A business that practices price discrimination would prefer to differentiate every customer by selling the same good or service at a price unique to that customer—a situation known as **perfect price discrimination**. To achieve this result, a business would have to know exactly what any particular customer would be willing to pay and charge him or her exactly that price. Many jewelry stores and automobile dealerships attempt to practice perfect price discrimination by posting high sticker prices and then bargaining with each customer to reach a deal. When you enter a jewelry store or a vehicle showroom, the

Perfect price discrimination occurs when a firm sells the same good or service at a unique price to every customer.

salesperson tries to determine the highest price you are willing to pay. Then he or she bargains with you until that price is reached.

In practice, perfect price discrimination is hard to implement, so most firms instead settle for charging two or three prices based on sorting customers into a few easily identified groups. To see how this works, let's look at a hypothetical example. Consider two small airlines, Flat Earth Air and Discriminating Fliers. Each airline has a monopoly on the route it flies, and each faces the same market demand curves and marginal costs. What happens if one of the airlines price-discriminates but the other does not?

In Figure 11.1, Flat Earth Air charges the same price to every passenger, while Discriminating Fliers uses two different price structures. To keep our example easy to work with, the marginal cost (MC) is set at $100, shown as a horizontal line.

Flat Earth Air sets its price by using the profit-maximizing rule, MR = MC. It charges $300 for every seat and serves 100 customers (that is, passengers).

One Price versus Price Discrimination

(a) A firm that charges a single price uses MR = MC to earn a profit. (b) When a firm price-discriminates, it takes in more profit than a firm that charges a single price. The discriminating firm increases its revenue by charging some customers more and other customers less, as shown in the dark green areas. The increase in profit is partly offset by the loss of revenue from existing customers who receive a lower price, as shown in the red area.

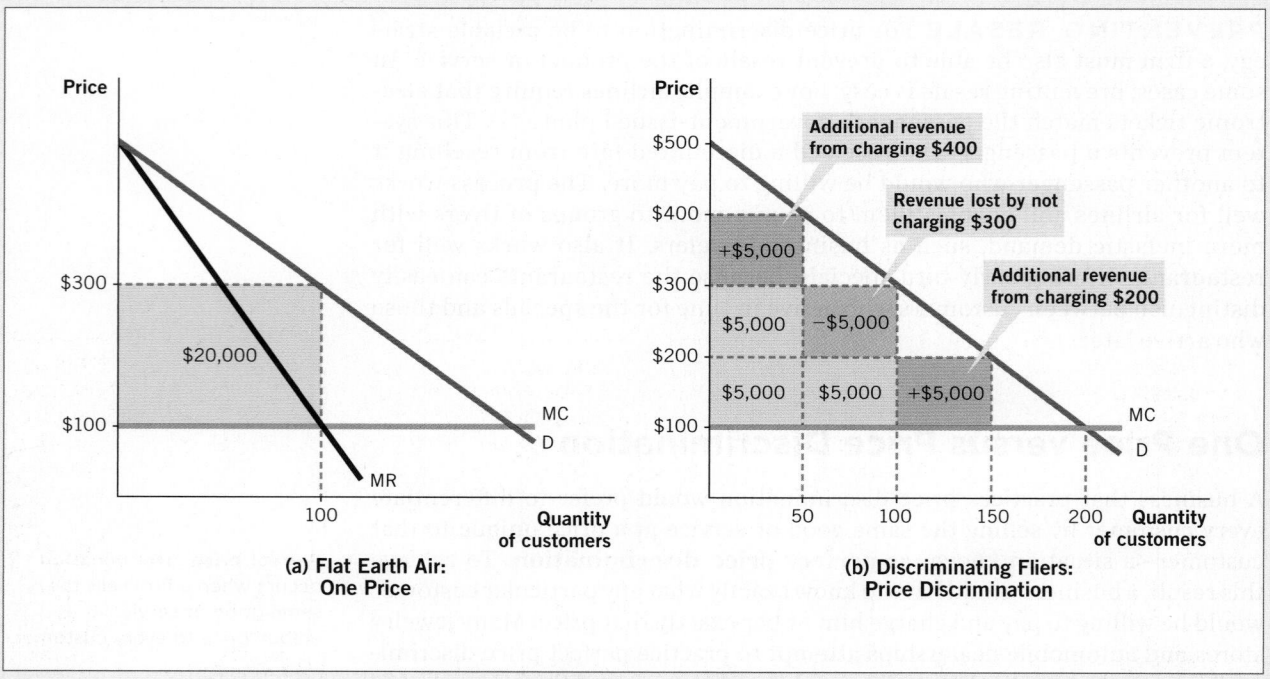

Because the marginal cost is $100, every passenger who gets on the plane generates $200 in producer surplus. The profit, represented by the green rectangle in panel (a), is $200 × 100, or $20,000. At 100 passengers, this airline has done everything it can to maximize profits at a single price. At the same time, there are plenty of unsold seats in the plane, which holds 200 passengers. Those unfilled seats represent a lost opportunity to earn additional revenue. As a result, airlines typically try to fill the plane by discounting the price of some seats. And this is precisely what Discriminating Fliers does.

Discriminating Fliers experiments with two prices, as shown in panel (b). Let's look at the reasoning behind these two prices. Because the firm faces a downward-sloping demand curve, the airline cannot sell every seat on the plane at the higher price. So it saves a number of seats, in this case 50, for last-minute bookings to capture customers with less flexibility who are willing to pay $400. These are travellers with inelastic demand, such as those who travel for business. The airline offers the rest of the seats at a low price, in this case $200, to capture customers with more elastic demand. The challenge for the airline is to make sure that the people who are willing to pay $400 do not purchase the $200 seats. So it makes the low fare available to customers who book far in advance, because these customers are typically more flexible and shop for the best deal. It is common for a business-person who needs to visit a client to make flight arrangements just days before the meeting, which precludes purchasing a $200 ticket weeks in advance. The customers who book early fill the seats that would otherwise be empty if the airline had charged only one price, as Flat Earth Air does. We can see this outcome by comparing the total number of passengers under the two strategies. Discriminating Fliers, with its two-price strategy, serves 50 passengers who pay $400 and 100 additional passengers who pay $200. Flat Earth Air's single price of $300 brings in only 100 passengers.

The net effect of price discrimination is apparent in the shaded areas of panel (b). By charging two prices, Discriminating Fliers generates more profit. The high price, $400, generates additional revenue equal to the upper dark green rectangle—$5,000—from passengers who must pay more than the $300 charged by Flat Earth Air. Discriminating Fliers also gains additional revenue with its low price of $200. The less-expensive tickets attract passengers with more elastic

Airlines offer lower fares if you are willing to take the red-eye.

Marginal thinking

SO WOULD YOU LIKE TO BUY A CUP OF COFFEE? THEY'RE $1 EACH.

A DOLLAR?!

JASON, THIS ISN'T FUNNY ANYMORE! I HAVE TO GET READY FOR WORK! AND I REALLY, REALLY, REALLY NEED MY MORNING COFFEE!

OH. WELL, THEN FOR YOU I WON'T CHARGE A DOLLAR.

THANK YOU.

FOR YOU IT'LL BE $5.

DON'T MAKE ME BEAN YOU, SON.

Perfect Price Discrimination

LEGALLY BLONDE

In this 2001 film, Reese Witherspoon stars as Elle Woods, who defies others' expectations by attending Harvard Law School. Believing that her boyfriend is about to propose to her, Elle and two friends go shopping to find the perfect dress for the occasion. They enter an exclusive boutique and start trying on dresses.

The saleswoman comments to another associate, "There's nothing I love more than a dumb blonde with daddy's plastic." She grabs a dress off the clearance sale rack and removes the "half price" tag. Approaching Elle, she says, "Did you see this one? We just got it in yesterday." Elle fingers the dress, then the price tag, and looks at the saleswoman with excitement.

ELLE: "Is this a low-viscosity rayon?"

SALESWOMAN: "Uh, yes—of course."

ELLE: "With half-loop topstitching on the hem?"

SALESWOMAN (smiling a lie): "Absolutely. It's one of a kind."

(Elle hands the dress back to her, no longer pretending to be excited.)

ELLE: "It's impossible to use a half-loop topstitch on low-viscosity rayon. It would snag the fabric. And you didn't just get this in, because I remember it from the June *Vogue* a year ago, so if you're trying to sell it to me at full price, you picked the wrong girl."

Do you know how to get the best price? Elle does!

The scene is a wonderful example of an attempt at price discrimination gone wrong. Unbeknownst to the saleswoman, Elle is majoring in fashion merchandising in college and knows more about fashion than the saleswoman does. Her effort to cheat Elle fails miserably.

What makes the scene powerful is the use of stereotypes. When merchants attempt to price-discriminate, they look for clues to help them decide whether the buyer is willing to pay full price or needs an incentive, or discount, to make a purchase. In this case, the saleswoman misjudges Elle, assuming she is an uninformed buyer with highly inelastic demand. Consequently, her strategy backfires.

demand, such as college students, vacationers, and retirees. The low-price tickets generate $5,000 in revenue, as shown by the lower dark green rectangle.

Some customers would have paid Discriminating Fliers more if the airline had charged a single price. Customers willing to pay $300 can acquire tickets on Discriminating Fliers for $200. The red rectangle represents the lost profit, equal to $5,000. The $10,000 in revenue represented by the dark green rectangles more than offsets the $5,000 in lost profit represented by the red rectangle. The airline that price-discriminates, depicted in panel (b), generates a profit of $25,000. The airline that charges a single price, depicted in panel (a), generates a profit of $20,000.

In reality, airlines often charge many prices. For example, you will find higher prices for travel on Friday and for midday flights. If your stay includes a Saturday night or if you choose a red-eye flight, prices are lower. Airlines charge more for last-minute bookings and less to customers who book in advance. Airlines also change prices from day to day and even from hour to hour. All of these price changes reflect efforts to price-discriminate.

Because passengers cannot resell their tickets or easily change their plans, airlines can effectively price-discriminate. In fact, if an airline could charge unique prices for every passenger booking a flight, it would transform the entire area under the demand curve and above the marginal cost curve into more profit.

The Welfare Effects of Price Discrimination

Price discrimination is profitable for the companies that practice it. But it also increases the welfare of society. How, you might ask, can companies make more profit and also benefit consumers? The answer: because a price discriminator charges a high price to some and a low price to others, more consumers are able to buy the good.

To illustrate this point, let's imagine an airline, Perfect Flights, that is able to perfectly price-discriminate. Perfect Flights charges each passenger a price exactly equal to what that passenger is willing to pay. As a result, some customers pay more and others pay less than they would under a single-price system. This outcome is evident in Figure 11.2, where a profit-maximizing firm charges $300. At this price, the firm captures the profit in the light green rectangle, B.

FIGURE 11.2

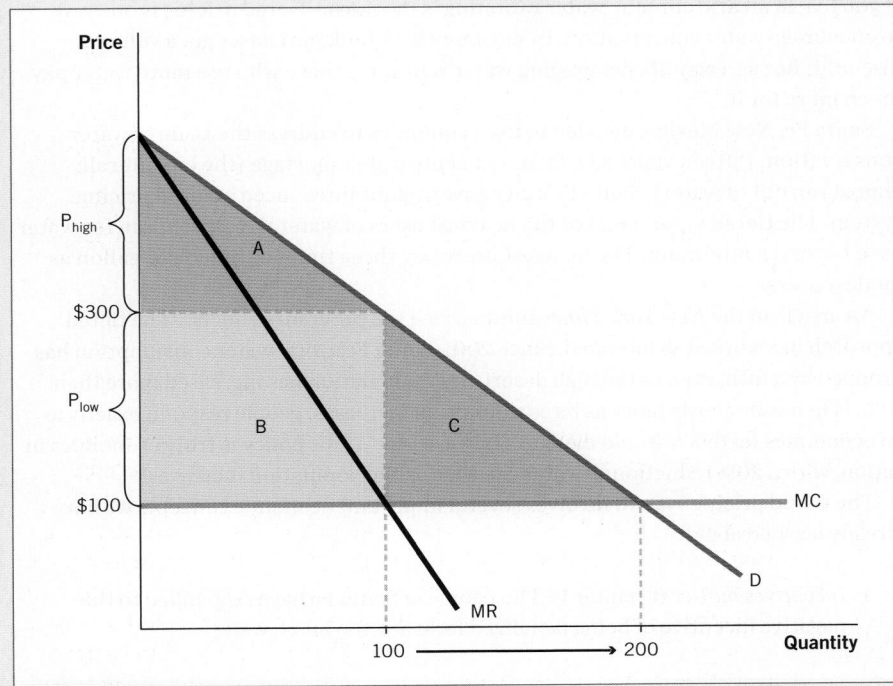

Perfect Price Discrimination

If the firm charges one price, the most it can earn is the profit in the light green rectangle. However, if a firm is able to perfectly price-discriminate, it can pick up the additional profit represented by the dark green triangles.

However, Perfect Flights charges each passenger a price based on his or her willingness to pay. Therefore, it earns significantly more profit. By charging higher prices (P_{high}) to those willing to pay more than $300, the firm is able to capture the additional profit in the upper dark green triangle, A. Likewise, by charging lower prices (P_{low}) to those not willing to pay $300, the firm is able to capture the additional profit in the lower dark green triangle, C. As a result, Perfect Flights is making more money and serving more customers.

Marginal thinking

By charging a different fare to every customer, Perfect Flights can also increase the quantity of tickets sold to 200. This strategy yields two results worth noting. First, in the long run, a perfectly competitive firm would charge a price just equal to marginal cost. In the case of Perfect Flights, the last customer who gets on the plane will pay an extraordinarily low price of $100—the price you might find in a competitive market. Second, this outcome mirrors the result of a government-regulated monopolist that uses the marginal cost pricing rule, $P = MC$, to enhance social welfare. Perfect Flights is therefore achieving the efficiency of a competitive market while also producing the output a regulated monopolist would choose. This strategy provides the firm with the opportunity to convert the area consisting of the two green triangles into more profit. In other words, the process maximizes the quantity sold. The efficiency of the market improves, and the firm generates more profit.

ECONOMICS IN THE REAL WORLD

SANTA FE, NEW MEXICO: USING NEGATIVE INCENTIVES AS PRICE DISCRIMINATION

Incentives

If you live in an arid climate, water rationing is the norm. Tiered pricing is one way to encourage water conservation. In most markets, bulk purchases get a volume discount. But as a way of encouraging water rationing, those who use more water pay much more for it.

Santa Fe, New Mexico, decided to use economics to address the issue of water conservation. Fifteen years ago, facing an acute water shortage (the city literally almost ran out of water), Santa Fe's city government introduced a tiered pricing system. The tiered system makes the heaviest users of water pay a premium for water used beyond a minimum. The heaviest users pay three times as much per gallon as modest users.

An article in the *New York Times* summarized the program's effects: "The tiered approach has worked as intended. Since 2001, Santa Fe's total water consumption has dropped by a fifth, even as the high desert city's population has increased more than 10%. When water costs more as its consumption increases, people respond exactly as an economics textbook would dictate: They use less."* This policy is truly economics in action, with a 20% reduction in water use even as the population increases!

The tiered pricing system involves several important economic concepts we have already learned about:

Tiered pricing encourages water conservation.

1. *Incentives matter* (Chapter 1). The people of Santa Fe have responded to the negative incentive of being penalized for using too much water.

---

*Nelson D. Schwartz, "Water Pricing in Two Thirsty Cities: In One, Guzzlers Pay More, and Use Less," *New York Times*, May 6, 2015.

2. *Internalizing the externality* (Chapter 7). Before 2001, heavy water users were affecting everyone in Santa Fe by creating periodic water shortages, but they did not have to pay extra for their actions. By paying much more for their water now, the heavy users are internalizing (paying for) the externality.

3. *Tragedy of the commons* (Chapter 7). Santa Fe has avoided a tragedy-of-the-commons scenario where all the water runs dry.

4. *The welfare effects of price discrimination* (this chapter). Dividing groups by their willingness to pay is beneficial to society, and that is what the Santa Fe water pricing system has achieved.

COMPARING PERFECT PRICE DISCRIMINATION WITH PERFECT COMPETITION AND MONOPOLY To understand the welfare effects of perfect price discrimination, we can compare the consumer and producer surplus in three scenarios: a competitive market, a market in which a monopolist charges a single price, and a market characterized by perfect price discrimination. The results, shown in Table 11.1, are derived by examining Figure 11.2.

In a perfectly competitive market, there are no barriers to entry and no firm has market power. In the long run, the price will be equal to the marginal cost. In our example of airline ticket prices, the price is driven down to $100. At this price, 200 tickets are sold. The entire area above the marginal cost curve (A + B + C) is consumer surplus, because the willingness to pay—as determined along the demand curve—is at least as great as the price. Because the ticket price is the same as the marginal cost, the producer surplus is zero. Because every customer who is willing to pay $100 or more can find a ticket, there is no deadweight loss. Under perfect competition, the market structure clearly favors consumers.

A monopoly holds substantial market power, so the firm in this scenario sets a price using the profit-maximizing rule, MR = MC, without having to worry about competition driving the price down to marginal cost. The monopolist's profit-maximizing price, or $300 in Figure 11.2, is higher than the $100 price under perfect competition. This higher price reduces the amount of consumer surplus to triangle A and creates a producer surplus equal to rectangle B. In addition, because the number of tickets sold falls to 100, there is now deadweight loss equal to triangle C. Economic activity associated with triangle C no longer exists, and the total welfare of society is now limited to A + B. From this analysis, we see that monopoly causes a partial transfer of consumer surplus to producers and a reduction in total welfare for society.

Marginal thinking

TABLE 11.1

The Welfare Effects of Perfect Price Discrimination

	Perfect competition	A monopolist that charges a single price	Perfect price discrimination
Consumer surplus	A + B + C	A	0
Producer surplus	0	B	A + B + C
Deadweight loss	0	C	0
Total welfare	A + B + C	A + B	A + B + C

In our third scenario, a firm that can practice perfect price discrimination is able to charge each customer a price exactly equal to the price that customer is willing to pay. This strategy enables the firm to convert the entire area of consumer surplus that existed under perfect competition into producer surplus (A + B + C). For the firm to capture the entire area of available consumer surplus, it must lower some prices all the way down to marginal cost. At that point, the number of tickets sold returns to 200, the market is once again efficient, and the deadweight loss disappears. Perfect price discrimination transfers the gains from trade from consumers to producers, but it also yields maximum efficiency.

Note that these examples give us a better understanding of what economists mean when they use the word "perfect" in connection with a market. It can mean that consumer surplus is maximized, as it is under perfect competition, or that producer surplus is maximized, as it is under perfect price discrimination. It does not specify an outcome from a particular perspective; instead, *perfect* describes any market process that produces no deadweight loss. If society's total welfare is maximized, economists do not distinguish whether the benefits accrue to consumers or producers. It is also important to note that while we compare the perfectly competitive result with the monopoly result and the result under perfect price discrimination as if those were the only three possible outcomes, those results are the extremes. Actual firms fall on a spectrum somewhere between these outcomes.

Marginal thinking

ECONOMICS IN THE REAL WORLD

OUTLET MALLS—IF YOU BUILD IT, THEY WILL COME

Incentives

Have you ever noticed that outlet malls along major roadways are often located a considerable distance from large population centers? Moreover, every item at an outlet mall can be found closer to home. The same clothes, shoes, and kitchenware are available nearby.

Logic tells us it would be more convenient to shop locally and forgo the time and hassle of getting to an outlet center. But that is not how many shoppers feel.

Discount shopping is a big deal. How big? Potomac Mills, 30 miles south of Washington, D.C., is Virginia's most popular attraction, with nearly 23 million visitors a year. (That figure rivals the number of annual visitors to Disney World's Magic Kingdom!)

Outlet shopping is an example of price discrimination at work. Traditional malls are usually situated in urban settings and offer a wide variety of choices, but not necessarily low prices. If you want convenience, the local shopping mall is right around the corner. But if you want a bargain, shopping at a traditional local mall is not the best way to go.

What makes outlets so attractive are the discounts. Bargain hunters have much more elastic demand than their traditional mall-shopping counterparts who desire convenience. Moreover, the difference in the price elasticity of demand between these two groups means that traditional malls can more easily charge full price, while outlets must discount their merchandise to attract customers. The difference between these two groups of customers gives merchants a chance to price-discriminate on the basis of location—which is another way of separating

How far would you drive to visit an outlet mall?

customers into two groups and preventing resale at the same time. Retailers can therefore earn additional profits through price discrimination, while price-sensitive consumers can find lower prices at the outlets.

It is noteworthy that the convenience of finding discounts online threatens not only the traditional malls but also the outlets. When savvy shoppers can simply click to find the best deal, will they continue to drive to the outlets? Online retailers that have built user-friendly web sites with fast shipping and a seemingly endless list of products—think Amazon—are building platforms that many shoppers prefer to in-person shopping. Internet shopping also facilitates price discrimination. Cookies that record your search history can be used to influence the price you are offered, in effect enabling firms to discover a price closer to your willingness to pay. Online retailers also track whether you arrive at their address on a Mac or PC and what operating system you use. Did you know that many web sites routinely place more expensive products higher up in the search results if you are a Mac user? That's another example of price discrimination, but this time groups are differentiated based on the gadgets they use.

Opportunity cost

PRACTICE WHAT YOU KNOW

Price Discrimination: Taking Economics to New Heights

Consider the table below, which shows seven potential customers who are interested in taking a 30-minute helicopter ride. The helicopter has room for eight people, including the pilot. The cost to the helicopter company of taking on each additional passenger is $5.

How much would you pay to fly in a helicopter?

Customer	Maximum willingness to pay	Age
Amelia	$80	66
Orville	70	34
Wilbur	40	17
Neil	50	16
Charles	60	9
Chuck	100	49
Buzz	20	9

QUESTION: If the company can charge only one price, what should it be?

ANSWER: First, create an ordered array of the customers, from those willing to pay the most to those willing to pay the least.

If the firm charges $100, only Chuck will take the flight. When the firm drops the price to $80, Chuck and Amelia both buy tickets, so the total revenue (TR) is 80×2, or $160. Successively lower prices result in higher total revenue from the first five

Customer	Maximum willingness to pay	Price	TR	MR
Chuck	$100	$100	$100	$100
Amelia	80	80	160	60
Orville	70	70	210	50
Charles	60	60	240	30
Neil	50	50	250	10
Wilbur	40	40	240	−10
Buzz	20	20	140	−100

customers. The firm will benefit from lowering its price as long as the marginal revenue is greater than the marginal cost, $5. When the price is $50, five customers get on the helicopter, for a total of $250 in revenue. Adding the fifth passenger brings in $10 in marginal revenue. The marginal revenue for the sixth passenger is negative, so $50 is the best possible price to charge. Because each of the five passengers has a marginal cost of $5, the company makes $250 − (5 × $5) or $225 in profit.

QUESTION: If the company could charge two prices, what should they be, and who would pay them?

ANSWER: First, arrange the customers in two distinct groups: adults and children.

Adult customers	Willingness to pay	Age	Price	TR	MR
Chuck	$100	49	$100	$100	$100
Amelia	80	66	80	160	60
Orville	70	34	70	210	50

Young customers	Willingness to pay	Age	Price	TR	MR
Charles	$60	9	$60	$60	$60
Neil	50	16	50	100	40
Wilbur	40	17	40	120	20
Buzz	20	9	20	80	−40

As you can see, two separate prices emerge. For adults, profits are maximized at a price of $70. For children, total profits are maximized at $40. The company should charge $70 to the adult customers, which brings in $70 × 3, or $210 in total revenue. The company should charge $40 for each child under the age of 18, which brings in $40 × 3, or $120.

Price discrimination earns the company $210 + $120 − (6 × $5), or $300 in profit. This is a $75 improvement over charging a single price. In addition, six passengers are now able to get on the helicopter, instead of only five under the single-price model. Of course, leaving nine-year-old Buzz on the ground by himself isn't a great idea! Let's hope there's an adult friend or relative who was planning to sit the ride out.

How Is Price Discrimination Practiced?

Price discrimination is one of the most interesting topics in economics because each example is slightly different from the others. In this section, we take a closer look at real-world examples of price discrimination at movie theaters and on college campuses. Movie theaters and college campuses would like to achieve perfect price discrimination, but it simply isn't possible to know each customer's exact willingness to pay. As you will see, price discrimination takes many forms—some that are easy to describe and others that are more nuanced.

Price Discrimination at the Movies

Have you ever gone to the movies early so you can pay less for tickets? Movie theaters price-discriminate based on the time of day, age, student status, and whether or not you buy snacks. Let's examine these pricing techniques to see if they are effective.

PRICING BASED ON THE TIME OF THE SHOW Why are matinees priced less than evening shows? To encourage customers to attend movies during the afternoon, theaters discount ticket prices for matinees. This strategy makes sense because customers who can attend matinees (retirees, people on vacation, and those who do not work during the day) either have less demand or are more flexible, or price elastic. Work and school limit the options for many other potential customers. As a result, theaters discount matinee prices to encourage moviegoers who have elastic demand and are willing to watch at a less-crowded time. Movie theaters also discount the price of matinee shows because they pay to rent films on a weekly basis, so it is in their interest to show a film as many times as possible during a given week. Because the variable cost of being open during the day is essentially limited to paying a few employees relatively low wages, the theater can make additional profits even with a relatively small audience. On weekends, matinees also offer a discount to families that want to see a movie together—adding yet another layer of price discrimination.

Theaters charge two different prices based on showtime because they can easily distinguish between inelastic-demand customers and price-sensitive customers who have the flexibility to watch a matinee. Those with inelastic demand have less-flexible schedules and must pay higher ticket prices to attend in the evening.

Even if you're at the matinee because your demand is highly elastic, be considerate of people who really want to watch the movie.

PRICING BASED ON AGE OR STUDENT STATUS Why are there different movie prices for children, seniors, students, and everyone else? This is a complex question. Income does not fully explain the discounts that the young, the old, and students receive. Movie attendance is highest among 13- to 24-year-olds and declines thereafter with age. Given the strong demand among teenagers, it is not surprising that "child" discounts are phased out at most theaters by age 12. But did you know that most "senior"

If you've ever smuggled food into a movie theater, it is because your demand for movie theater concessions is elastic.

discounts begin before age 65? In some places, senior discounts start at age 50. Now you might think that because people in their 50s tend to be at the peak of their earning power, discounting ticket prices for them would be a bad move. However, because interest in going to the movies declines with age, the "senior" discount actually provides an incentive for a population that might not otherwise go to a movie theater. However, as we have seen, age-based price discrimination does not always work perfectly. Theaters do not usually ask for proof of age, and it may be hard to tell the difference between a child who is just under 12 and one who is over 12. Nonetheless, price discrimination works well enough to make age or student status a useful revenue-generating tool. Empty seats represent lost revenue, so it makes sense to price-discriminate through a combination of high and low prices.

CONCESSION PRICING Have you ever wondered why it is so expensive to purchase snacks at the movie theater? The concession area is another arena in which movie theaters practice price discrimination. To understand why, we need to think of two groups of customers: those who want to eat while they watch movies and those who do not. By limiting outside food and drink, movie theaters push people with inelastic demand for snacks to buy from the concession area. Of course, that does not stop some customers with elastic demand from sneaking food into the theater. But as long as some moviegoers are willing to buy concession fare at exorbitant prices, the theater will generate more revenue. Movie theaters cannot prevent smuggling in of snacks, and they don't have to. All they really want to do is separate their customers into two groups: a price-inelastic group of concession-area snackers and a price-elastic group of nonsnackers and smugglers who fill up the remaining empty seats. This situation is very similar to the problem we examined with airlines.

Price Discrimination on Campus

Colleges and universities are experts at price discrimination. Think about tuition. Some students pay the full sticker price, while others enjoy a free ride. Some students receive the in-state rate, while out-of-state students pay substantially more. And once you get to campus, discounts for students are everywhere. In this section, we consider the many ways in which colleges and universities differentiate among their students.

TUITION Price discrimination begins before you ever set foot on campus, with the Free Application for Federal Student Aid (known as the FAFSA) that most families complete. The form determines eligibility for federal aid. Families that qualify are eligible for grants and low-interest loans, which effectively lower the tuition cost for low- and medium-income families. Therefore, the FAFSA enables colleges to separate applicants into two groups based on income. Because many colleges also use the FAFSA to determine eligibility for their own institutional grants of aid, the FAFSA makes it possible for colleges to precisely target grants and loans to the students who need the most financial help.

Many state institutions of higher education have a two-tiered pricing structure. In-state students get a discount on the tuition, while out-of-state students pay a much higher rate. Part of the difference is attributable to state subsidies that are intended to make in-state institutions more affordable for residents. In-state students pay less because their parents have been paying taxes to the state, often for many years, and the state then uses some of those tax dollars to support its system of higher education. However, in-state subsidies only partially explain the difference in pricing. Out-of-state tuition is higher than it would be if all students paid the same price because out-of-state students are generally less sensitive to price than in-state students.

Resort or college? Sky-high tuition and room and board are one way to help pay for a beautiful campus.

This two-tiered pricing structure creates two separate groups of customers with distinctly different elasticities of demand. Students choose an out-of-state college or university because they like what that institution has to offer more than the institutions in their home state. It might be that a particular major or program is more highly rated or simply that they prefer the location of the out-of-state school. Whatever the reason, they are willing to pay more for the out-of-state school. Therefore, out-of-state students have a much more inelastic demand. Colleges know this and price their tuition accordingly. Conversely, in-state students often view the opportunity to attend a nearby college as the most economical decision. Because price is a big factor in choosing an in-state institution, it is not surprising that in-state demand is more elastic.

Selective private colleges also play the price discrimination game by advertising annual tuition and room and board fees that exceed $60,000. With price discrimination, the "sticker" price is often discounted. Depending on how much the college wants to encourage a particular student to attend, it can discount the tuition all the way to zero. This strategy enables selective private colleges to price-discriminate by offering scholarships based on financial need, while also guaranteeing placements for the children of wealthy alumni and others willing to pay the full sticker price.

Colleges and universities also use "early decision" and campus visits to determine how eager you are to attend. That information is a measure of your price elasticity of demand. At the margin, students who commit to an early decision or visit campus have more inelastic demand than those who only apply for regular admission. This is yet another way colleges fine-tune student aid packages based on observed behavior.

STUDENT DISCOUNTS The edge of campus is a great place to look for price discrimination. Local bars, eateries, and shops all want college students to step off campus, so student discounts are the norm. Why do establishments offer student discounts? Think about the average college student. Price matters to that student. Knowing this, local merchants in search of college customers can provide student discounts without lowering their prices across the board. This means they can charge more to their regular clients while providing the necessary discounts to get college students to make the trek off campus.

Now Playing: Economics!

Have you ever gone to the movies early so you can pay less for tickets? Movie theaters price- discriminate based on the time of the movie and the age of the customer. In order to practice price discrimination, theaters must be able to identify different groups of moviegoers, where each group has a different price elasticity of demand.

MATINEE $9

Demand for matinees is typically low. These showings attract groups with relatively elastic demand, like families and those on a budget, who decide to attend matinees because of lower prices.

EVENING $13

Evening movie showings attract larger crowds that consist mainly of adults and couples on dates. This group has relatively inelastic demand, so price is not the determining factor of when and where they see a movie.

The concession counter also generates profit for the movie theater. The high prices mean that patrons who are price- conscious (having relatively elastic demand) skip the counter or smuggle in their own snacks, while those who are more concerned about convenience than price (having relatively inelastic demand) buy snacks at the counter.

REVIEW QUESTIONS

- Does price discrimination hurt all consumers? Think about the example of movie theaters as you craft your response.

- Your local movie theater is thinking about increasing ticket prices for just the opening day of a blockbuster movie. How would you explain the economics behind this price increase?

Price discrimination also occurs at entertainment venues near a college campus. For example, students typically receive discounts for campus activities like concerts and sporting events. Because students generally have elastic demand, price discrimination provides greater student access to events than charging a single price does.

PRACTICE WHAT YOU KNOW

Price Discrimination in Practice: Everyday Examples

Are Black Friday deals price discrimination or not?

QUESTION: Test your understanding by thinking about the examples below. Are they examples of price discrimination?

a. **Retail coupons.** Programs such as discount coupons, rebates, and frequent-buyer plans appeal to customers willing to spend time pursuing a deal.

b. **Using Priceline to make hotel reservations.** "Naming your price" on Priceline .com is a form of haggling that enables users to get hotel rooms at a discount. Hotels negotiate with Priceline to fill unused rooms while still advertising the full price on their web sites.

c. **The 1-2-3 Menu at McDonald's.** Customers who order off the 1-2-3 Menu get a variety of smaller menu items for $1, $2, or $3 each.

ANSWERS:

a. **Retail coupons.** Affluent customers generally do not bother with the hassle of clipping, sending in, and keeping track of coupons because they value their time more than the small savings. However, customers with lower incomes usually take the time to get the discount. This means that coupons, rebates, and frequent-buyer programs do a good job of price-discriminating.

b. **Using Priceline to make hotel reservations.** Priceline enables hotels to divide their customers into two groups: those who don't want to be bothered with haggling and those who value the savings enough to justify the time spent negotiating. This is a good example of price discrimination.

c. **The 1-2-3 Menu at McDonald's.** Anyone can buy off the 1-2-3 Menu at any time. Because McDonald's does not force customers to do anything special in order to get the deal, this is not price discrimination.

CHALLENGE QUESTION: Customers who line up in the early-morning hours after Thanksgiving get first dibs on a limited quantity of reduced-price items at many retailers. Are discounts for early shoppers on Black Friday a form of price discrimination?

ANSWER: The discounts are time sensitive. Shoppers who arrive before the deadline get a lower price; shoppers who arrive after the deadline do not. Any retailer can deploy this method and easily divide customers into two groups: those with elastic demand (willing to wait in line early in the morning to get a deal) and those with inelastic demand (they'd rather sleep and not hassle with waiting). Don't let the fact that anyone could wait in line distract you. Most people won't wait, and it is this fact that makes price discrimination possible.

Price Discrimination

JURASSIC PARK

Early on in the original *Jurassic Park* film, there's a discussion about the price of admission to the live-dinosaur theme park. "We can charge anything we want," muses the investors' lawyer, "two thousand a day, ten thousand a day, and people will pay it." Hammond, the park's visionary founder, objects, "This park was not meant to cater only for the super-rich. Everyone in the world has the right to enjoy these animals." The lawyer doesn't see a problem, "Sure. They will. We'll have a coupon day or something."

The ingenious thing about offering coupons, and about price discrimination in general, is that it would generate more total revenue for the firm while simultaneously increasing the number of visitors who are able to take in the park. The lawyer understands that some people's demand for dino-safaris is highly inelastic, but if that is the only market segment the park attracts, there may be times (off-season) when they can generate additional revenue by lowering the price to a separate group of tourists whose demand is more price-sensitive.

How much would you be willing to pay to see a real-life dinosaur in the wild?

Opportunity cost

Conclusion

The word "discrimination" has negative connotations, but not when combined with the word "price." Charging different prices to different groups of customers results in more economic activity and is more efficient than charging a single price across the board. Under price discrimination, many consumers pay less than they would if a firm had charged a single price, while other consumers will pay more because their demand is more inelastic. But overall, total social welfare increases, and the amount of deadweight loss in society is reduced.

Price discrimination also helps us understand how many markets actually function, because instances of perfectly competitive markets and monopoly are rare. ✳

Gender-Based Price Discrimination

On average, across the five industries surveyed, one report found that women paid:

- 7% more for toys and accessories.
- 4% more for children's clothing.
- 8% more for adult clothing.
- 13% more for personal care products.
- 8% more for senior/home health care products.

Throughout this chapter, we considered the shopping experience in the context of price discrimination. Here we focus on how firms separate men and women into different groups by making cosmetic changes to the products they sell.

In a report prepared for the New York City Department of Consumer Affairs, author Anna Bessendorf and her team compared nearly 800 products with clear male and female versions from more than 90 brands sold at two dozen New York City retailers, both online and in stores.

The report found that women frequently paid more than men for the same products. Specifically, the report found that women's products cost 7% more than similar products for men. To minimize differences between men's and women's items, Bessendorf's team selected products with male and female versions that were very similar in branding, appearance, materials, construction, and/or marketing. In all but five of the 35 product categories analyzed, products for female consumers were priced higher than those for male consumers. Across the entire sample, the report found that women's products cost more 42% of the time, while men's products cost more only 18% of the time.

Why do the same jeans cost $50 more for women?

Why would firms charge more for the female version of a product? The answer is price discrimination. When different groups (males and females) have different price elasticities of demand, price discrimination allows a firm to earn more revenue. In most of the products surveyed, females had more inelastic demand, which translates into higher prices for them in the marketplace compared to males.[*] If you are not happy about gender-based pricing there is a potential workaround: buy the comparable male product. Is a pink razor really something you have to have when a similar blue razor sells for less?

Source: https://www1.nyc.gov/assets/dca/downloads/pdf/partners/Study-of-Gender-Pricing-in-NYC.pdf.

What is price discrimination?

- Price discrimination occurs when firms can identify different groups of customers with varying price elasticities of demand and can prevent resale among their customers.

- A firm must have some market power before it can charge more than one price.

How is price discrimination practiced?

- Under price discrimination, some consumers pay a higher price and others receive a discount. Price discrimination is profitable for the firm, reduces deadweight loss, and leads to a higher output level.

· CHAPTER PROBLEMS ·

Concepts You Should Know

perfect price discrimination (p. 345)　　　　price discrimination (p. 344)

Questions for Review

1. What two challenges must a price maker overcome to effectively price-discriminate?

2. Why does price discrimination improve the efficiency of the market?

3. Why is preventing resale a key to successful price discrimination?

4. If perfect price discrimination reduces consumer surplus to zero, how can this situation lead to the most socially desirable level of output?

Study Problems (* solved at the end of the section)

1. Seven potential customers are interested in seeing a movie. Because the marginal cost of admitting additional customers is zero, the movie theater maximizes its profits by maximizing its revenue.

Customer	Maximum willingness to pay	Age
Allison	$8	66
Becky	11	34
Charlie	6	45
David	7	16
Erin	6	9
Franco	10	28
Grace	9	14

a. What price would the theater charge if it could charge only one price?

b. If the theater could charge two prices, what prices would it choose? Which customers would pay the higher price, and which would pay the lower price?

c. How much profit does the theater make when it charges only one price? How much profit does the theater make if it price-discriminates?

2. Which of the following are examples of price discrimination? Explain your answers.

a. A cell phone carrier offers unlimited calling on the weekends for all of its customers.

b. Tickets to the student section for all basketball games are $5.

c. A restaurant offers a 20% discount for customers who order dinner between 4 and 6 p.m.

d. A music store has a half-price sale on last year's guitars.

e. A well-respected golf instructor charges each customer a fee just under the customer's maximum willingness to pay for lessons.

3. At many amusement parks, customers who enter after 4 p.m. receive a steep discount on the price of admission. Explain how this practice is a form of price discrimination.

4. Name three products for which impatience on the part of the consumer enables a firm to price-discriminate.

* 5. Prescription drug prices in the United States are often substantially higher than in Canada, the United Kingdom, and India. Today, pharmacies in these countries fill millions of low-cost prescriptions through the mail to U.S. citizens. Given that the pharmaceutical industry cannot prevent the resale of these drugs, are the industry's efforts to price-discriminate useless? Explain your answer.

* 6. Metropolitan Opera tickets are the most expensive on Saturday night. There are often a very limited number of "student rush tickets," with which a lucky student can wind up paying $20 for a $250 seat. The student rush tickets are available first-come, first-served. Why does the opera

company offer these low-cost tickets? How does it benefit from this practice? Why are students, and not other groups of customers, offered the discounted tickets?

* **7.** Have you ever tipped a restaurant host in order to bypass a long wait and get a table more quickly? Would this be an example of price discrimination? Why or why not? Discuss.

8. Orbitz, the travel web site, routinely offers PC and Apple users different search results. Apple users typically have higher-priced hotels show up on the top page of the results, while PC users are presented with somewhat lower prices. Is Orbitz practicing price discrimination? Discuss.

* **9.** When Subway customers pay less per inch for footlong subs than they pay per inch for a six-inch sub, is this price discrimination or not?

10. When ride-sharing companies impose "surge pricing" during times of peak demand for rides and/or a low supply of drivers, is this price discrimination?

* **11.** If an app uses geolocation to understand where you are and offers different prices based on your location, is this price discrimination or not?

Solved Problems

5. Buying prescription drugs outside the United States is increasingly common. Because the pharmaceutical companies charge three to four times more for drugs sold domestically than they do in most other countries, it would seem that the drug industry's efforts to price-discriminate aren't working, but that is not true. Not everyone fills their prescriptions from foreign sources; only a small fraction of U.S. customers go to that much effort. Because most U.S. citizens still purchase the more expensive drugs here, the pharmaceutical companies are benefiting from price discrimination, even though some consumers manage to navigate around their efforts.

6. The Met hopes to sell all of its $250 tickets, but not every show sells out and some tickets become available at the last minute. The student rush tickets benefit both the opera company and the students: the company can fill last-minute seats, and the students, who have elastic demand and low income, get a steep discount. The Met is able to price discriminate, because the rush tickets require a student ID. Other groups of operagoers are therefore unable to buy the rush tickets. This practice effectively separates the customer base into two groups: students and nonstudents. Students make ideal rush customers because they are more willing to change their plans in hopes of obtaining last-minute tickets than other groups. Some opera companies also open up the rush tickets to seniors, another group that is easy to identify and generally has significant flexibility.

7. As a college student you probably don't have a lot of money to tip the restaurant host. But if you do have the money, it would make sense to tip the host. Here is why: First, your tip gets you seated sooner and avoids the wait time. Time is money, so you save right there. Second, the host has an incentive to let tippers in sooner, and that's not just good for the host. It is also good for the business because tippers have much more inelastic demand, which translates into customers who spend more while dining. So the host is actually separating customers into two groups: tippers with inelastic demand and nontippers with much more elastic demand. Third, the restaurant wins because when tippers with inelastic demand get tables faster, the restaurant makes more revenue.

9. Anyone could conceivably get the better deal, but only those with big appetites or a willingness to eat leftovers will choose a footlong. Those with smaller appetites are stuck paying more per inch for a six-inch sub. Since Subway can differentiate between those with big and smaller appetites by the size of sandwich they order, this is a form of price discrimination based on making a "bulk" purchase.

11. This is a form of price discrimination, and like all price discrimination efforts it will generate more revenue. Companies can use your location to raise or lower the price shown on the app. For instance, in 2018 Burger King offered its app users a free Whopper if they happened to be near a McDonald's!

12

Monopolistic Competition and Advertising

Advertising and Product Differentiation are Notable Features of Monopolistic Competition.

If you drive down a busy street, you will find many competing businesses, often right next to one another. These competing firms advertise heavily. The temptation is to see advertising as driving up the price of a product without any benefit to the consumer. However, in markets where competitors sell slightly differentiated products, advertising enables firms to inform their customers about new products and services. Yes, costs rise, but consumers also gain information to help make purchasing decisions.

Consumers also benefit from added variety, and we all get a product that's pretty close to our vision of a perfect good—no other market structure delivers that outcome. Consider California Pizza Kitchen (CPK). Since its inception in 1985, CPK has grown to over 200 restaurants throughout the United States and expanded to over a dozen countries. How did CPK break into an already crowded pizza market? By doing pizza differently. Instead of making traditional Italian-style pies, CPK is widely known for serving nontraditional pies with innovative ingredients. They popularized gourmet pizza, a style of pizza that combines an Italian thin crust with toppings from the California cuisine cooking style. In other words, CPK made pizza even better!

What do you like on your pizza? CPK probably has you covered. Do you want just sliced tomatoes and basil? If not, what about carrots and bean sprouts? Or eggplant? Or baby broccoli? Poblano chilies, anyone? Take your pick and make sure to share with a tablemate.

In this chapter, we look at *monopolistic competition*, a widespread market structure that has features of both competitive markets and monopoly. We also explore the benefits and disadvantages of advertising, which is prevalent in markets with monopolistic competition.

· BIG QUESTIONS ·

- What is monopolistic competition?
- What are the differences among monopolistic competition, competitive markets, and monopoly?
- Why is advertising prevalent in monopolistic competition?

What Is Monopolistic Competition?

Monopolistic competition
is a type of market structure characterized by low barriers to entry, many different firms, and product differentiation.

Product differentiation
is the process firms use to make a product more attractive to potential customers.

Some consumers prefer the fries at McDonald's, while others may crave a salad at Panera Bread or the chicken at KFC. Each fast-food establishment has a unique set of menu items. The different products in fast-food restaurants give each seller a small degree of market power. This combination of market power and competition is typical of the market structure known as monopolistic competition. Indeed, **monopolistic competition** is characterized by low barriers to entry, many different firms, and product differentiation. **Product differentiation** is the process firms use to make a product more attractive to potential customers. Firms use product differentiation to contrast their product's unique qualities with competing products. The differences, which we will examine in detail, can be minor and can involve subtle changes in packaging, quality, availability, and promotion. Or the differences can be very significant. For example, some soup companies specialize in organic soups, which the consumers they are targeting would find an extremely important characteristic.

How does monopolistic competition compare with other market structures we have studied? As Table 12.1 shows, monopolistic competition falls between competitive markets and monopoly in terms of the number of sellers, the types of products sold, and competing firms' ability to enter and exit the market.

We have seen that firms in competitive markets do not have any market power. As a result, buyers can expect to find consistently low prices and wide availability. And we have seen that monopolies charge more and restrict the availability of a good or service. In markets that are monopolistically competitive, firms sell differentiated products. This differentiation gives the

TABLE 12.1

Competitive Markets, Monopolistic Competition, and Monopoly

Competitive markets	Monopolistic competition	Monopoly
Many sellers	Many sellers	One seller
Similar products	Differentiated products	A unique product without close substitutes
Free entry and exit	Low barriers to entry and exit	Significant barriers to entry and exit

monopolistic competitor some market power, though not as much as a monopolist, which controls the entire market. Monopolistically competitive firms have a small amount of market power that enables them to search for the most profitable price.

To understand how monopolistic competition works, we begin with a closer look at product differentiation.

Product Differentiation

Monopolistically competitive firms create some market power through product differentiation. Differentiation can occur in a variety of ways, including style or type, location, and quality.

STYLE OR TYPE A trip to a mall is a great way to see product differentiation firsthand. For example, you will find many clothing stores, each offering a unique array of styles and types of clothing. Some stores, such as Abercrombie & Fitch, carry styles that attract younger customers. Others, such as Ann Taylor, appeal to older shoppers. Clothing stores can also vary by the type of clothing they sell, specializing in apparel such as business clothing, plus sizes, or sportswear. Each store hopes to attract a specific type of customer.

When you're ready for lunch at the mall, you can go to the food court, where many different places to eat offer a wide variety of choices. Where you decide to eat is a matter of your personal preferences and the price you are willing to pay. Like most consumers, you will select the place that gives you what you want while providing the best value for your money. Consumers' differing tastes make it possible for a wide range of food vendors to compete side by side with rivals who provide many good substitutes.

LOCATION Many businesses attract customers because of their convenient location. Gasoline stations, dry cleaners, barber shops, and car washes provide products and services that customers tend to choose on the basis of convenience of location rather than price. When consumers prefer to save time and to avoid the inconvenience of shopping for a better deal, a firm with a more convenient location will have some pricing power. As a result, producers who sell very similar products can generate some market power by locating their businesses along routes to and from work or in other areas where customers frequently travel.

Would you like your Mexican food cheaper . . .

. . . or fresher?

QUALITY Firms also compete on the basis of quality. For instance, if you want Mexican food, you can go to Taco Bell, which is inexpensive and offers food cooked in advance. In contrast, at Moe's Southwest Grill the food is freshly prepared and, as a result, more expensive. This form of product differentiation serves consumers quite well. Budget-conscious consumers can feast at Taco Bell, while those with a larger budget and a taste for higher-quality Mexican food can consider Moe's as another option.

PRACTICE WHAT YOU KNOW

Product Differentiation: Would You Recognize a Monopolistic Competitor?

Is Hollister a monopolistic competitor?

QUESTION: Which of the following is a monopolistic competitor?

a. a local apple farm that grows Red Delicious apples

b. Hollister, an apparel store

c. your local water company

ANSWERS:

a. Because Red Delicious apples are widely available at grocery stores, this local apple farm does not have a differentiated product to sell. In addition, it has many competitors that grow exactly the same variety of apples. This apple farm is part of a competitive market; it is not a monopolistic competitor.

b. Hollister has a slightly different mix of clothes than competitors Abercrombie & Fitch and American Eagle Outfitters. This differentiation gives the brand some pricing power. Hollister is a good example of a monopolistically competitive firm.

c. Because water is essential and people cannot easily do without it, the local water company has significant monopoly power. Moreover, purifying and distributing water are subject to economies of scale. Your local water company is definitely a monopolist, not a monopolistic competitor.

What Are the Differences among Monopolistic Competition, Competitive Markets, and Monopoly?

Monopolistic competition occupies a place between competitive markets, which produce an efficient output at low prices, and monopoly, which produces an inefficient output at high prices. To help explain whether monopolistic competition is desirable or not, we consider the outcomes that individual firms can achieve when facing monopolistic competition in the short run and in the long run. Once you understand how monopolistic competition works, we will be able to compare the long-run equilibrium result with that of competitive markets and then determine if monopolistic competition is efficient.

Monopolistic Competition in the Short Run and the Long Run

A monopolistically competitive firm sells a differentiated product and for this reason has some market power. Recall that in perfect competition, each firm sells the same product, so competitors' products are perfect substitutes, which means that demand is perfectly elastic (flat). In monopolistic competition, each competitor provides a differentiated product, so competitors' products are imperfect substitutes for one another, which means that demand is relatively elastic (less flat), but still flatter (more elastic) than monopoly. Like a monopolist, the monopolistic competitor uses the profit-maximizing rule, MR = MC, and locates the corresponding point on its demand curve to determine the best price to charge and the best quantity to produce. Whether the firm earns a profit, experiences a loss, or breaks even is a function of other firms entering and exiting the market. Recall that entry and exit do not take place in the short run. In the long run, however, firms are free to enter an industry when they see a potential for profits or leave if they are making losses. Therefore, entry and exit regulate how much profit a firm can make in the long run.

Marginal thinking

Suppose you own a Hardee's fast-food restaurant in Asheville, North Carolina. Your business is doing well and making a profit. Then one day a Five Guys opens up across the street. Some of your customers will try Five Guys and switch, while others will still prefer your fare. But your profit will take a hit. Whether or not you stay in business will depend on how much business you lose. To understand how a business owner makes the decision to keep operating or to shut down, we now turn to the short-run and long-run implications of monopolistic competition.

MONOPOLISTIC COMPETITION IN THE SHORT RUN Figure 12.1 depicts a firm, like Hardee's, in a monopolistically competitive environment. In panel (a), the firm makes a profit. Panel (b) shows the same firm incurring a loss after a new competitor, like Five Guys, opens nearby. In each case, the firm uses the profit-maximizing rule to determine the best price to charge by locating the point at which marginal revenue equals marginal cost. This calculation

FIGURE 12.1

The Monopolistically Competitive Firm in the Short Run

In this figure, we see how a single monopolistically competitive firm may make a profit or incur a loss depending on the demand conditions it faces. Notice that the marginal cost curve (MC) and average total cost curve (ATC) are identical in both panels because we are considering the same firm. The only functional difference is the location of the demand curve (D) and marginal revenue curve (MR). The demand in (a) is high enough for the firm to make a profit. In (b), however, there is not enough demand, so the firm experiences a loss.

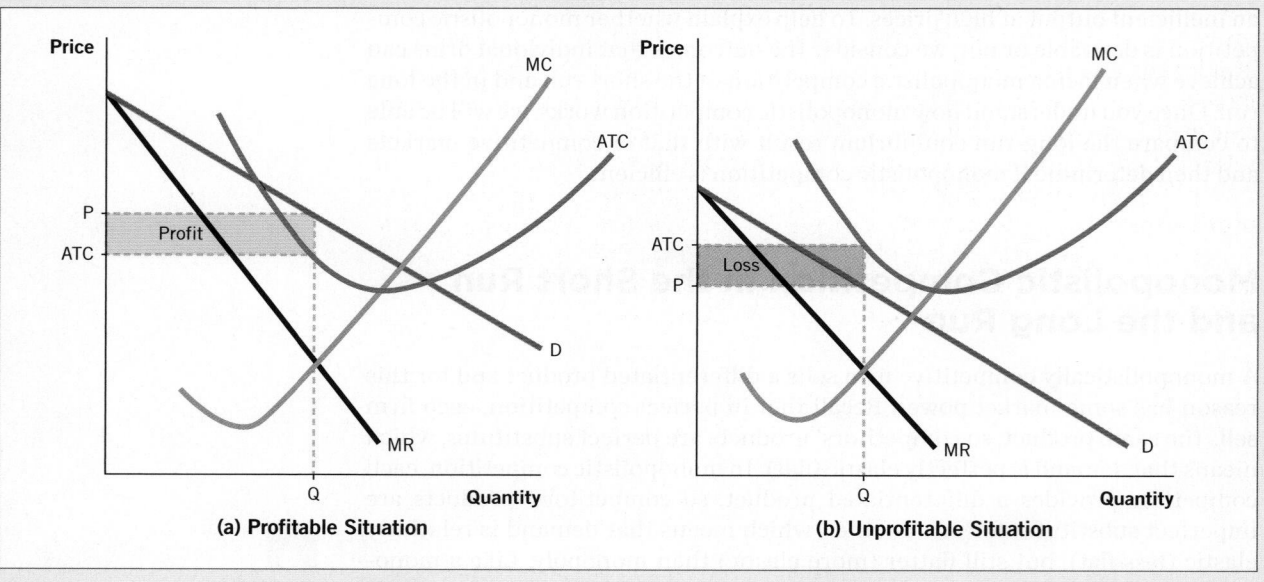

(a) Profitable Situation   (b) Unprofitable Situation

establishes the profit-maximizing output (Q) along the vertical dashed line. The firm determines the best price to charge (P) by following the dashed horizontal line from the demand curve to the vertical axis.

In panel (a), we see that because price is greater than average total cost (P > ATC), the firm makes a short-run economic profit. The situation in panel (b) is different. Because P < ATC, the firm experiences a short-run economic loss. What accounts for the difference? Because we are considering the same firm, the marginal cost (MC) and average total cost (ATC) curves are identical in both panels. The only functional difference is the location of the demand (D) and marginal revenue (MR) curves. The demand in panel (a) is high enough for the firm to make a profit. In panel (b), however, there is not enough demand; perhaps too many customers have switched to the new Five Guys. So even though the monopolistic competitor has some market power, if demand is too low, the firm may not be able to price its product high enough to make a profit.

MONOPOLISTIC COMPETITION IN THE LONG RUN In the long run, when firms can easily enter and exit a market, competition will drive economic profit to zero. This dynamic should be familiar to you from our previous discussions of competitive markets. If a firm is making an economic profit, that profit attracts new entrants to the business. Then the larger supply of competing firms will cause the demand for an individual firm's product to contract. Eventually, as more firms enter the market, it is no longer possible for existing firms to make an economic profit. A reverse process unfolds in the case of a market experiencing a loss. In this case, some firms exit the industry. Then consumers have fewer options to choose from, and the remaining firms experience an increase in demand. Eventually, demand increases to the point at which firms no longer experience a loss.

Figure 12.2 shows the market after the long-run adjustment process takes place. Price (P) is just equal to the average total cost of production (ATC) at the profit-maximizing rate of output (Q). At this point, firms are earning zero economic profit, as noted by P = ATC along the vertical axis; the market reaches a long-run equilibrium at the point where there is no reason for firms to enter or exit the industry. Note that the demand curve is drawn *tangent* to the average total cost curve (touching at one place). If demand were any larger, the result would look like panel (a) in Figure 12.1 and firms would experience an economic profit. Conversely, if demand were any lower, the result would look like panel (b) in Figure 12.1 and firms would experience an economic loss. Where entry and exit exist, profits and losses are not possible in the long run. In this way, monopolistic competition resembles a competitive market.

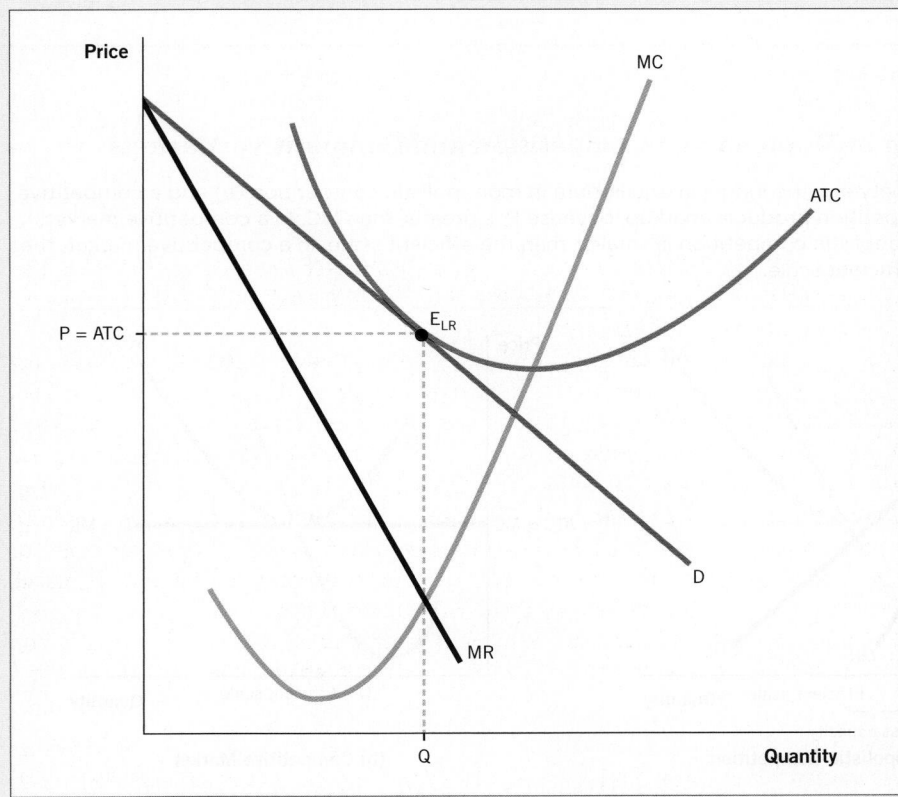

FIGURE 12.2

The Monopolistically Competitive Firm in the Long Run

Entry and exit cause short-run profits and losses to disappear in the long run, which means that the price charged (P) must be equal to the average total cost (ATC) of production. At this point, firms are earning zero economic profit, as noted by P = ATC along the vertical axis. The market reaches a long-run equilibrium (E_LR) at the point where there is no reason for firms to enter or exit the industry.

Incentives

Returning to our example of Hardee's, the firm's success will attract attention and encourage rivals, like Five Guys, to enter the market. As a result, the short-run profits that Hardee's enjoys will erode. As long as profits occur in the short run, other competitors will be encouraged to enter, while short-run losses will prompt some existing firms to close. The dynamic nature of competition guarantees that long-run profits and losses are not possible.

Monopolistic Competition and Competitive Markets

We have seen that monopolistic competition and competitive markets are similar; both market structures drive economic profit to zero in the long run. But monopolistic competitors enjoy some market power, which is a crucial difference. In this section, we compare pricing and output decisions in these two market structures. Then we look at issues of scale and output.

THE RELATIONSHIP BETWEEN PRICE, MARGINAL COST, AND LONG-RUN AVERAGE COST Monopolistically competitive firms have some market power, which enables them to charge slightly more than firms in competitive markets. Figure 12.3 compares the long-run equilibrium between monopolistic competition and a competitive market. Turning first to

---

FIGURE 12.3

The Long-Run Equilibrium in Monopolistic Competition and Competitive Markets

There are two primary differences between the long-run equilibrium in monopolistic competition (a) and a competitive market (b). First, monopolistic competition produces markup, because P is greater than MC. In a competitive market, P = MC. Second, the output in monopolistic competition is smaller than the efficient scale. In a competitive market, the firm's output is equal to the most efficient scale.

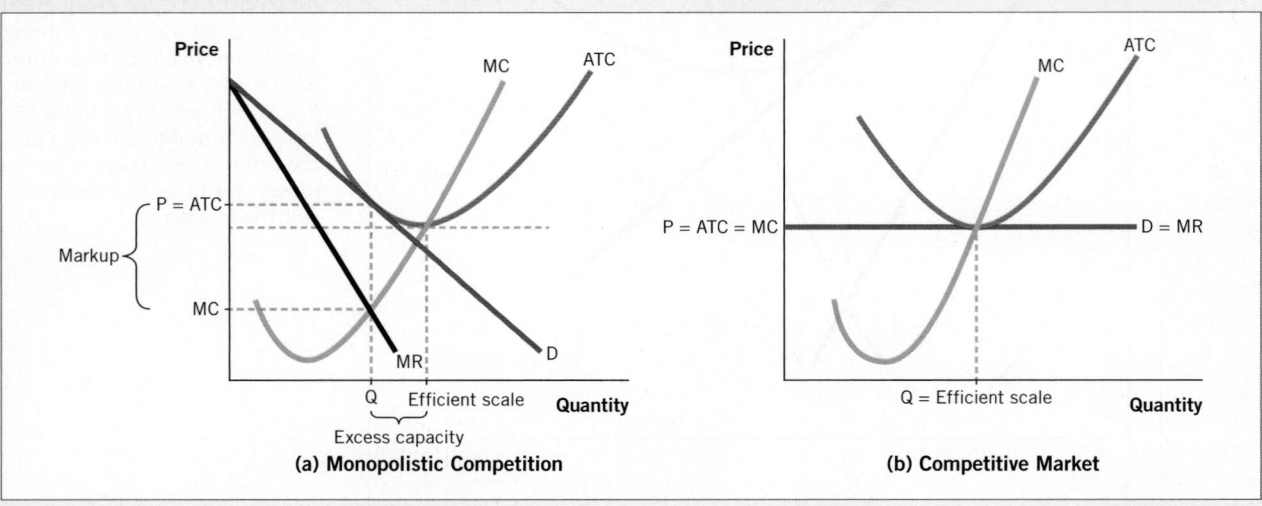

(a) Monopolistic Competition

(b) Competitive Market

---

the firm in a market characterized by monopolistic competition, shown in panel (a), notice that the price (P) is greater than the marginal cost (MC) of making one more unit. The difference between P and MC is known as the markup. **Markup** is the difference between the price the firm charges and the marginal cost of production.

Markup
is the difference between the price the firm charges and the marginal cost of production.

A markup is possible when a firm enjoys some market power. Products such as bottled water, cosmetics, prescription medicines, eyeglass frames, brand-name clothing, restaurant drinks, and greeting cards all have hefty markups. Let's focus on bottled water. In most cases, it costs just pennies to produce a bottle of water, but you're unlikely to find it for less than $1; there is a lot of markup on every bottle! Some firms differentiate their product by marketing their water as the "purest" or the "cleanest." Other companies use special packaging. While the marketing of bottled water is unquestionably a successful business strategy, the markup means that consumers pay more. You can observe this result in panel (a) of Figure 12.3, where the price under monopolistic competition is higher than the price in a competitive market, shown in panel (b).

Next, look at the ATC curves in both panels. Because a monopolistic competitor has a downward-sloping demand curve, the point of tangency between the demand curve and the ATC curve is different from the point of tangency in a competitive market. The point where P = ATC is higher under monopolistic competition. Panel (b) shows the demand curve just tangent to the ATC curve at ATC's lowest point in a competitive market. Consequently, we can say that monopolistic competition produces higher prices than a competitive market does. If this result seems odd to you, recall that entry and exit do not ensure the lowest possible price, only that the price is equal to the average total cost of production. In a competitive market, where the demand curve is horizontal, the price is always the lowest possible average total cost of production. This is not the case under monopolistic competition. However, the price in monopolistic competition often reflects quality; cheap food is cheap for a reason. Firms may charge more for higher-quality food, but there will still be zero economic profit.

SCALE AND OUTPUT When a firm produces at an output level smaller than the output level needed to minimize average total costs, we say it has **excess capacity**. Turning back to panel (a) of Figure 12.3, we see excess capacity in the difference between Q and the efficient scale.

Excess capacity
occurs when a firm produces at an output level smaller than the output level needed to minimize average total costs.

This result differs from what we see in panel (b) of Figure 12.3 for a competitive market. In a competitive market, the profit-maximizing output is equal to the most efficient scale of operation. This result is guaranteed because each firm sells an identical product and must therefore set its price equal to the minimum point on the average total cost curve. If, for instance, a corn farmer tried to sell a harvest for more than the prevailing market price, the farmer would not find any customers. In contrast, a monopolistic competitor in a food court enjoys market power because some customers prefer its product, which enables food court vendors to charge more than the lowest average total cost. Therefore, under monopolistic competition, the profit-maximizing output is less than the minimum efficient scale. Monopolistically competitive firms have the capacity to produce more output at a lower cost. But if they produced more, they would have to lower their price. Because a lower price decreases the firm's marginal revenue, it is more profitable for the monopolistic competitor to operate with excess capacity.

Monopolistic Competition, Inefficiency, and Social Welfare

Monopolistic competition produces a higher price and a lower level of output than a competitive market does. Recall that we looked at efficiency as a way to determine whether a firm's decisions are consistent with an output level beneficial to society. Does monopolistic competition display efficiency?

In Figure 12.3, panel (a), we observed that a monopolistic competitor has costs slightly above the lowest possible cost. So the average total costs of a monopolistically competitive firm are higher than those of a firm in a competitive market. This result is not efficient. To achieve efficiency, the monopolistically competitive firm could lower its price to what we would find in competitive markets. However, because a monopolistic competitor's goal is to make a profit, there is no incentive for the firm to lower its price. Every monopolistic competitor has a downward-sloping demand curve, so the demand curve cannot be tangent to the minimum point along the average total cost curve, as seen in panel (a).

Markup is a second source of inefficiency. We have seen that, for a monopolistically competitive firm at the profit-maximizing output level, P > MC by an amount equal to the markup. The price reflects the consumer's willingness to pay, and this amount exceeds the marginal cost of production. A reduced markup would benefit consumers by lowering the price and decreasing the spread between the price and the marginal cost. If the firm did away with the markup entirely and set P = MC, the output level would benefit the greatest number of consumers. However, this result would not be practical. At the point where the greatest efficiency occurs, the demand curve would be below the average total cost curve and the firm would lose money. It is unreasonable to expect a profit-seeking firm to pursue a pricing strategy that would benefit its customers at the expense of its own profit.

What if the government intervened on behalf of the consumer? Increased efficiency could be achieved through government regulation. After all, the government regulates monopolists to reduce market power and restore social welfare. Couldn't the government do the same in monopolistically competitive markets? Yes and no! It is certainly possible, but not desirable. Monopolistically competitive firms have a limited amount of market power, so they cannot make a long-run economic profit like monopolists do. In addition, regulating the prices that firms in a monopolistically competitive market can charge would put many of them out of business. Bear in mind we are talking about firms in markets like the fast-food industry. Doing away with a significant percentage of these firms would mean fewer places for consumers to grab a quick bite. The remaining restaurants would be more efficient, but with fewer restaurants the trade-off for consumers would be less convenience and fewer choices.

Regulating monopolistic competition through marginal cost pricing, or setting P = MC, would also create a host of problems like those we discussed for monopoly. A good proportion of the economy consists of monopolistically competitive firms, so the scale of the regulatory effort would be enormous. And because implementing marginal cost pricing would result in widespread losses, the government would need to find a way to subsidize the regulated firms to keep them in business. Because the only way to fund these subsidies would be higher taxes, the inefficiencies present in monopolistic competition do not warrant government action.

Perrier has a distinctive look—but how different is it from other mineral water?

Trade-offs

VARYING DEGREES OF PRODUCT DIFFERENTIATION We have seen that products sold under monopolistic competition are more differentiated than those sold in a competitive market and less differentiated than those sold under monopoly. At one end of these two extremes we have competitive markets where firms sell identical products, have no market power, and face a perfectly elastic demand curve. At the other end we have a monopolist that sells a unique product without good substitutes and faces a steep downward-sloping demand curve indicative of highly inelastic demand. What about the firm that operates under monopolistic competition?

Figure 12.4 illustrates two monopolistic competitors with varying degrees of product differentiation. Firm A enjoys significant differentiation. High levels of differentiation occur when the firm has an especially attractive location, style, type, or quality of product that is in high demand among consumers and that competitors cannot easily replicate. H&M, Urban Outfitters, and Abercrombie & Fitch are good examples. Consumers have strong brand loyalty for the clothes these firms sell, so the demand curve is quite inelastic. The relatively steep slope of the demand curve means that the point of tangency between the demand curve (D) and the average total cost curve (ATC) occurs at a high price, which produces a large amount of excess capacity. In contrast,

---

FIGURE 12.4

Product Differentiation, Excess Capacity, and Efficiency

The difference in product differentiation is represented by the steepness (elasticity) of the demand curve, since the demand curve for firm A enjoys more product differentiation. As a result, it has more excess capacity and is less efficient. Firm B sells a product that is only slightly different from its competitors'. In this case, consumers have only weak preferences about which firm to buy from, and consumer demand is elastic. The results are a small amount of excess capacity and a more efficient result.

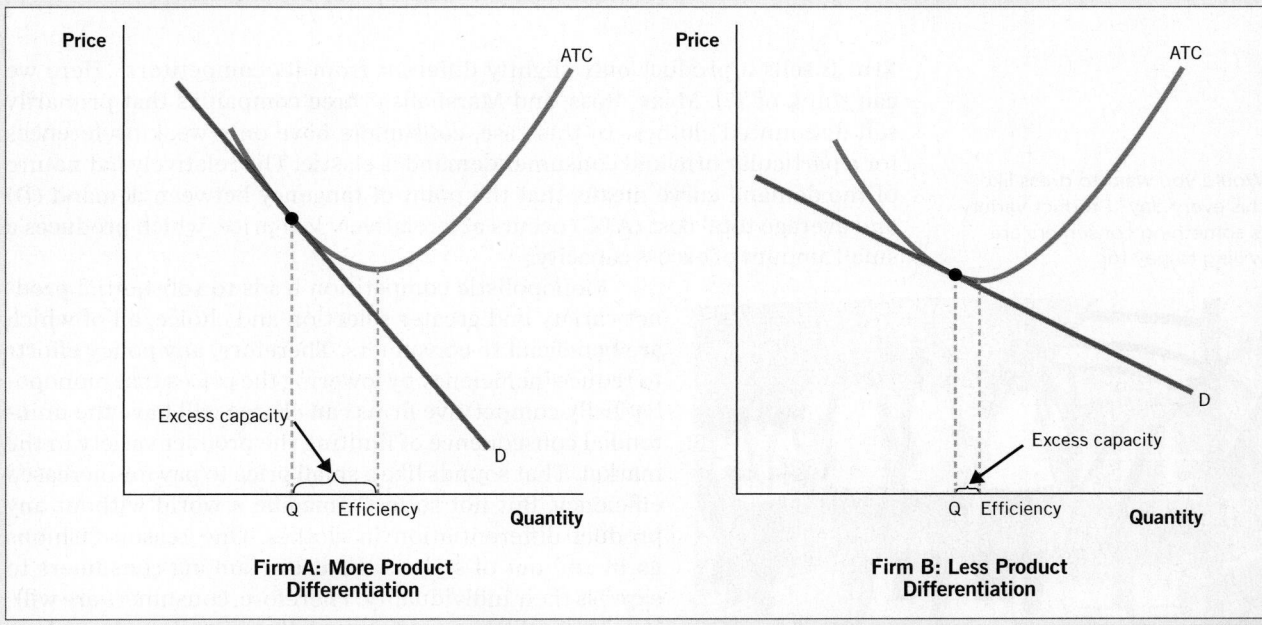

Firm A: More Product Differentiation

Firm B: Less Product Differentiation

Product Differentiation

SUPERIOR DONUTS

On the CBS sitcom *Superior Donuts*, Arthur is an old-school doughnut shop owner who runs the place with the help of a young employee, Franco. One day a new customer, Sofia, comes in and starts asking general questions about the neighborhood and how the shop operates. It turns out Sofia was doing recon, trying to gauge whether or not she should park her food truck out front! When she shows up a few minutes later, Arthur is incensed but Sofia doesn't care. She pops a few coins in a parking meter and opens her truck for business.

Sofia sells organic breakfast dishes at a much higher price point than Superior Donuts, so customers now have a second choice of where to eat. More importantly, since barriers to entering the market are low and the products served are differentiated, this is

Which do you prefer—an organic breakfast bowl or a donut?

a great example of how monopolistically competitive markets work to provide consumers with variety and reasonable prices.

firm B sells a product only slightly different from its competitors'. Here we can think of T.J. Maxx, Ross, and Marshalls—three companies that primarily sell discounted clothes. In this case, consumers have only weak preferences for a particular firm and consumer demand is elastic. The relatively flat nature of the demand curve means that the point of tangency between demand (D) and average total cost (ATC) occurs at a relatively low price, which produces a small amount of excess capacity.

Would you want to dress like this every day? Product variety is something consumers are willing to pay for.

Monopolistic competition leads to substantial product variety and greater selection and choice, all of which are beneficial to consumers. Therefore, any policy efforts to reduce inefficiency by lowering the prices that monopolistically competitive firms can charge will have the unintended consequence of limiting the product variety in the market. That sounds like a small price to pay for increased efficiency. But not so fast! Imagine a world without any product differentiation in clothes. One reason fashions go in and out of style is the desire among consumers to express their individuality. Therefore, consumers are willing to pay a little more for product variety in order to look different from everyone else.

Markup: Punch Pizza versus Pizza Hut

QUESTION: Punch Pizza is a small upscale chain in Minnesota that uses wood-fired ovens. In contrast, Pizza Hut is a large national chain. Which pizza chain would have a greater markup on each pizza?

ANSWER: If you ask people in the Twin Cities about their favorite pizza, you will find a cultlike following for Punch Pizza. That loyalty translates into inelastic demand. Punch Pizza claims to make the best Neapolitan pie. Fans of this style of pizza gravitate to Punch Pizza for the unique texture and flavor. In contrast, Pizza Hut competes in the middle of the pizza market and has crafted a taste that appeals to a broader set of customers. Pizza Hut's customers can find many other places that serve a similar product, so these customers are much more price sensitive.

Punch Pizza uses wood-fired ovens.

The marginal cost of making pizza at both places consists of the dough, the toppings, and wages for labor. At Pizza Hut, pizza assembly is streamlined for efficiency. Punch Pizza is more labor intensive, but its marginal cost is still relatively low. The prices at Punch Pizza are much higher than at Pizza Hut. As a result, the markup—or the difference between the price charged and the marginal cost of production—is greater at Punch Pizza than at Pizza Hut.

Marginal thinking

CHALLENGE QUESTION: If there's a higher markup for Punch Pizza, and therefore a higher economic profit, won't this attract new entrants?

ANSWER: Since barriers to entry into a monopolistically competitive market are relatively low, new firms will enter. As the supply expands, the market price drops and the demand for any particular pizza place becomes more elastic. This means that Punch Pizza's markup shrinks. So even though Punch Pizza is in an enviable position for now, competition will eventually reduce the price to a point where Punch Pizza earns zero economic profits—as is the case in every market where firms are free to enter.

Why Is Advertising Prevalent in Monopolistic Competition?

Advertising is a fact of daily life. It is also a means by which companies compete and therefore a cost of doing business in many industries. In the United States, advertising expenditures account for approximately 2% of all economic output annually. Worldwide, advertising expenses are a little less—about 1% of global economic activity. While the percentages are small in relative terms, in absolute terms worldwide advertising costs are over half a trillion dollars each year. Is this money well spent? Or is it a counterproductive contest that increases cost without adding value for the consumer? In this section, we will find that the answer is a little of both. Let's start by seeing who advertises.

Why Firms Advertise

No matter the company or slogan, the goal of advertising is to drive additional demand for the product being sold. Advertising campaigns use a variety of techniques to stimulate demand. In each instance, advertising is designed to highlight an important piece of information about the product (and remember the name of the company!). Table 12.2 shows how this process works. For instance, the FedEx slogan, "When it absolutely, positively has to be there overnight," conveys reliability and punctual service. Some customers who use FedEx are willing to pay a premium for overnight delivery because the company has differentiated itself from its competitors—UPS, DHL, and (especially) the United States Postal Service.

A successful advertising campaign will change the demand curve in two dimensions: it will shift the demand curve to the right and alter its shape. Turning to Figure 12.5, we see this change. First, the demand curve shifts to the right in response to the additional demand created by the advertising. Second, the demand curve becomes more inelastic, or slightly more vertical. This change in shape happens because advertising has highlighted features that make the product attractive to specific customers who are now more likely to want it. Because demand is more inelastic after advertising, the firm increases its market power and can raise its price.

In addition to increasing demand, advertising conveys information that consumers may find helpful in matching their preferences. Advertising tells us about the price of the goods offered, the location of products, and the introduction of new products. Firms also use advertising as a competitive mechanism to underprice one another. Finally, an advertising campaign signals quality. Firms that run expensive advertising campaigns are making a significant investment in their product. It is highly unlikely that a firm would spend a great deal on advertising if it did not think the process would yield a positive return. So a rational consumer can infer that firms spending a great deal on advertising are likely to have a higher-quality product than a competitor who does not advertise.

A wonderful example of this is Columbia Sportswear, a high-end maker and distributor of outerwear, sportswear, footwear, headgear, camping equipment, and ski apparel. Columbia ads feature the company CEO, Gert Boyle. She's better known as "Ma Boyle, One Tough Mother," thanks to a decades-long ad campaign for the company's outdoor apparel products. Columbia differentiated itself from its competitors, whose ads usually featured attractive young hikers and skiers, by chronicling the adventures of Boyle and her son, Tim, who gamely endured a variety of extreme conditions while bundled up in Columbia outerwear. The commercials reinforced the idea that Columbia products are worth a premium.

Advertising in Different Markets

Many firms engage in advertising, but advertising is not equally productive in all market structures. In our continuum from competitive markets to monopoly, markets that function under monopolistic competition invest the most in advertising.

ADVERTISING IN COMPETITIVE MARKETS As you know by now, competitive firms sell nearly identical products at an identical price. For this

TABLE 12.2

Advertising and Demand

Company / Product	Advertising slogan	How it increases demand
Convention and Visitors Authority / Las Vegas 	*What happens here stays here.*	The slogan attempts to convince travelers that they will have a better vacation than anywhere else.
John Deere / tractors 	*Nothing runs like a Deere.*	The emphasis on quality and performance appeals to buyers who desire a high-quality tractor.
Frito-Lay / potato chips 	*Betcha can't eat just one.*	The message that one potato chip is not enough to satisfy your craving appeals to chip buyers who choose better taste over lower-priced generics.
Energizer / batteries 	*He keeps going and going and going.*	The campaign focuses attention on longevity in order to justify the higher prices of top-quality batteries.
FedEx / delivery service 	*When it absolutely, positively has to be there overnight.*	Reliability and timeliness are crucial attributes of overnight delivery.
Visa / credit card 	*It's everywhere you want to be.*	Widespread acceptance and usability are two of the major reasons for carrying a credit card.
Skittles / candy 	*Taste the rainbow.*	The emphasis is on taste and a variety of flavors.

FIGURE 12.5

Advertising and the Demand Curve

A successful advertising campaign increases demand. Advertising also makes the demand curve more inelastic, or vertical, by informing consumers about differences they care about. After advertising, consumers desire the good more intensely, which makes the demand curve for the firm's product somewhat more vertical.

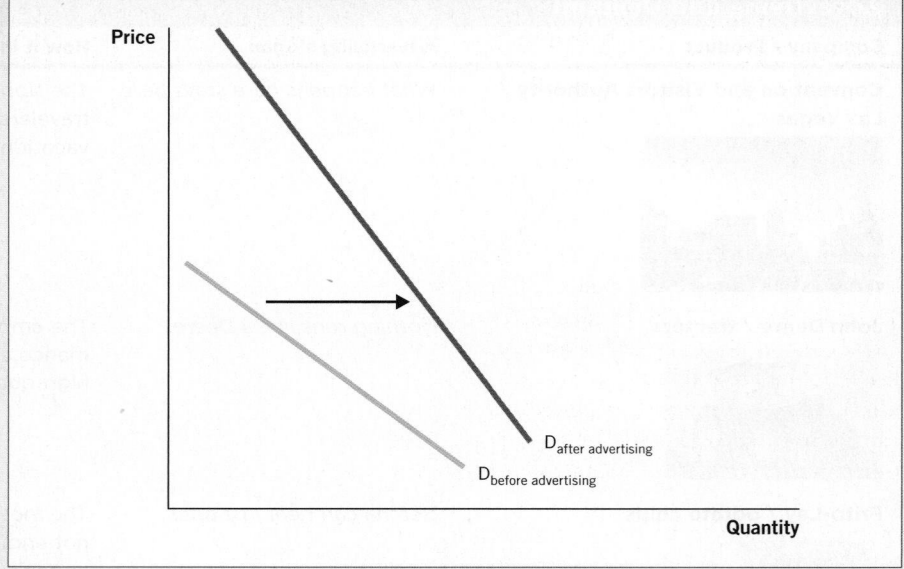

reason, advertising raises a firm's costs without directly influencing its sales. Advertising for an undifferentiated good functions like a public good for the industry as a whole: the benefits flow to every firm in the market through increased market demand for the product. Each firm sells essentially the same good, so consumers can find the product at many competing locations at the same price. An individual firm that advertises in this market is at a competitive disadvantage because it will have higher costs that it cannot pass on to the consumer.

This does not mean that we never see advertising in competitive markets. Although individual firms do not benefit from advertising, competitive industries as a whole can. For example, you have probably heard the slogan "Beef—it's what's for dinner." The campaign, which began in 1992, is recognized by over 80% of Americans and has been widely credited with increasing the demand for beef products. The campaign was funded by the National Cattlemen's Beef Association, an organization that puts millions of dollars a year into advertising. In fact, industrywide marketing campaigns such as "It's not just for breakfast anymore" by the Florida Orange Juice Growers Association or "Got milk?" by the National Milk Processor Board generally indicate that competitive firms have joined forces to advertise in an effort to increase demand. Other examples include "the incredible, edible egg" and "pork—the other white meat."

ADVERTISING UNDER MONOPOLISTIC COMPETITION Advertising is widespread under monopolistic competition because firms have differentiated products. Let's look at the advertising behavior of pizza companies.

Advertising

MAD MEN

Mad Men, which ran for seven seasons on AMC, is a show about the golden age of the advertising industry. The main character, Don Draper, is a marketing wiz. In season 6, he makes a pitch for a series of ads to sell ketchup. Gesturing at huge color photos of food that is just a condiment away from perfection, Draper explains the campaign's concept. "What's missing? One thing. Pass the Heinz." Draper understands that the goal of an ad campaign is to increase demand for a good or service and also to make the demand for whatever is being sold more inelastic. This gives the seller more pricing power and allows them charge a higher markup.

Draper's "Pass the Heinz" pitch is rejected, because the client can't wrap his head around the idea of ads that don't show the product. Fast forward fifty years, though, and in 2017, Heinz began running the ads, faithfully copied from Draper's presentation (with full credit given). The idea was brilliant—just ahead of its time.

This scene is missing just one thing.

Television commercials by national chains such as Domino's, Pizza Hut, Papa John's, and Little Caesars are widespread, as are flyers and advertisements for local pizza places. Because each pizza is slightly different, each firm's advertising increases the demand for its product and changes the slope of the demand curve. In short, the gains from advertising go directly to the firm spending the money. These benefits generate a strong incentive to advertise to gain new customers or to keep customers from switching to other products. Because each firm feels the same way, advertising becomes the norm among monopolistically competitive firms.

Incentives

Advertising and the Super Bowl

Super Bowl commercials are watched at least as closely as the football game itself. Fans love these usually creative and comedic ads. But economists pay close attention for different reasons. Who's advertising and what does it say about those industries? Are the ads money well spent, or do they increase business costs without making a noticeable difference in profits? Here we examine advertising from 1967 to 2019.

Inflation-adjusted Amount Spent   **# of Super Bowls Advertised in**   **Seconds of Super Bowl Ads**

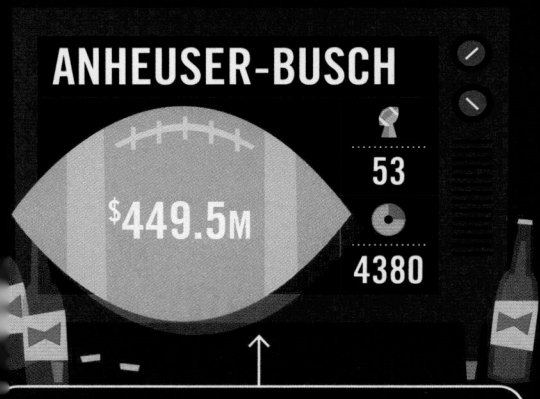

ANHEUSER-BUSCH

$449.5M   53   4380

Anheuser-Busch spends more than any other company on Super Bowl advertising to differentiate its product and create brand awareness.

PEPSI CO

$289.5M   34   3780

Coca-Cola has spent significantly less than PepsiCo on Super Bowl ads, yet it remains the market-leading soft drink brand. Coke has ramped up its Super Bowl efforts in the past few years to maintain this lead, however.

FORD

$109.8M   23   1800

COCA-COLA

$202M   29   2242

Some of these companies, especially Coca-Cola and Pepsi, are considered oligopolists rather than monopolistic competitors. We'll discuss oligopoly in the next chapter.

REVIEW QUESTIONS

- Draw what happens to a brand's demand curve when it successfully achieves product differentiation through advertising.

- Describe the risks and rewards of advertising from the perspective of both the brand and the consumer.

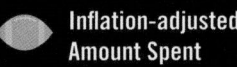
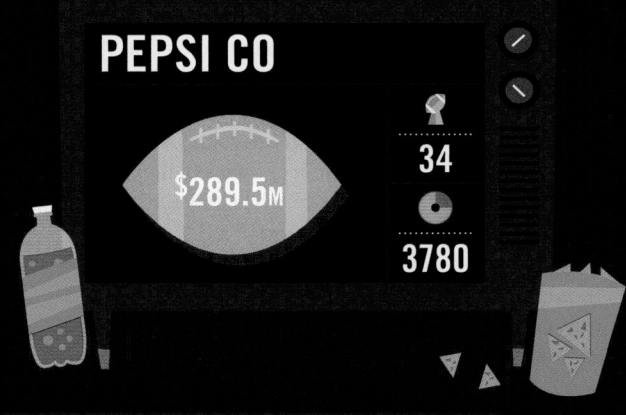

WHAT HAPPENED TO SEARS?

Sears, JCPenney, Kohl's, and The Gap are all famous brick-and-mortar retailers. Depending on how old you are, at some point in your life you probably spent a lot of time in one of these stores. Kohl's and The Gap struggled for a time but appear to be back on course for growth and viability. JCPenney and Sears, on the other hand, are all but done for. The last year Sears made a profit was 2010.

A few generations ago, a Sears credit card was as important as one from American Express. Sears is also historically important because it was the Sears catalog, first mailed in 1893, that allowed non-city dwellers access to products previously available only in cities.

So what has happened to Sears? Online giant Amazon and bad management have had major impacts since the mid-2000s. But Sears started losing business in the early 1990s. What happened then was the rapid rise of Walmart, which gave consumers significantly lower prices because of its sophisticated inventory control. By then, Sears had diversified into many areas, which caused it to lose focus on its main retail business. The rise of Walmart meant that Sears had to become more efficient (lower its markup) to survive, but because of the way Sears had expanded, its cost structure was higher than Walmart's.

What economics lesson can we extract from the Sears saga? A business must never take its success for granted, and you never know where your most fierce competitor will emerge from. Ever hear of Bentonville, Arkansas? That's where Walmart started (and is still headquartered).

Source: Hiroko Tabuchi and Rachel Abrams, "4 Different Turnaround Tales at Retailers Sears, Kohl's, Gap and J.C. Penney," *New York Times*, Feb. 26, 2015.

ADVERTISING AS A MONOPOLIST The monopolist sells a unique product without close substitutes. The fact that consumers have few, if any, good alternatives when deciding to buy the good makes the monopolist less likely to advertise than a monopolistic competitor. When consumer choice is limited, the firm does not have to advertise to get business. In addition, the competitive aspect is missing, so there is no need to advertise to prevent consumers from switching to rival products. However, that does not mean that the monopolist never advertises.

The monopolist may wish to advertise to inform the consumer about its product and stimulate demand. This strategy can be beneficial as long as the gains from advertising are enough to cover the cost of advertising. For example, De Beers, the giant diamond cartel, controls most of the world's supply of rough-cut diamonds. The company does not need to advertise to fend off competitors, but it advertises nevertheless because it is interested in creating more demand for diamonds. De Beers created the famous "A diamond is forever" campaign.

The Negative Effects of Advertising

We have seen the benefits of advertising, but there are also drawbacks. Two of the most significant drawbacks are that advertising raises costs and can be deceitful.

ADVERTISING AND COSTS Advertising costs are reflected in the firm's average total cost curve. Figure 12.6 shows the paradox of advertising for most firms. When a firm advertises, it hopes to increase demand for the product and sell more units—say, from point 1 at Q_1 to point 2 at the higher quantity Q_2. If the firm can sell enough additional units, it will enjoy economies of scale, and the average total cost will fall from ATC_1 to ATC_2. This return on the advertising investment looks like a good business decision.

However, the reality of advertising is much more complex. Under monopolistic competition, each firm is competing with many other firms selling somewhat different products. Rival firms will respond with advertising of their own. This dynamic makes advertising the norm in monopolistic competition. Each firm engages in competitive advertising to win new customers and keep the old ones. As a result, the impact on each individual firm's demand largely cancels out. This result is evident in the movement from point 1 to point 3 in Figure 12.6. Costs rise from ATC_1 to ATC_3 on the higher LRATC curve, but the quantity demanded may remain at Q_1. The net result is that advertising creates higher costs but no change in quantity produced and a decrease in profit. In this case, we can think of advertising as causing a negative *business-stealing externality* whereby no individual firm can easily gain market share but feels compelled to advertise to protect its customer base.

We have seen that advertising raises costs for the producer. It also raises prices for consumers. In fact, consumers who consistently favor a particular brand of a product have more inelastic demand than those who are willing to switch from one product to another. Therefore, brand loyalty often means higher prices. Let's look at an example.

FIGURE 12.6

Advertising Increases Cost

By advertising, the firm hopes to increase demand (or quantity) from point 1 to point 2. In this scenario, the increase in demand from Q_1 to Q_2 is large enough to create economies of scale even though advertising causes the long-run average total cost curve (LRATC) to rise. Because monopolistically competitive firms each advertise, the advertising efforts often cancel one another out. As a result, long-run average total costs rise without demand increasing much, so the firm may move from point 1 to point 3 instead.

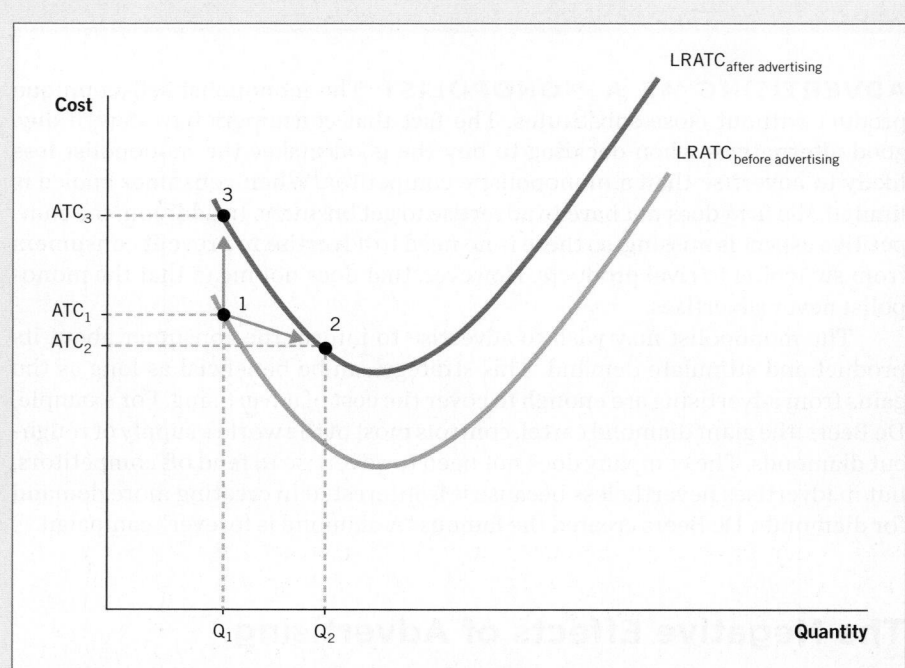

Pearl ear studs are a nice gift, but they are even better when they come in a . . .

. . . blue box.

Suppose you buy all your jewelry at Tiffany's. One day, you enter the store to pick up pearl ear studs. You can get a small pair of pearl studs at Tiffany's for $300. But it turns out you can get studs of the same size, quality, and origin (freshwater) at Pearl World for $43, and you can find them online at Amazon for $19. There are no identifying marks on the jewelry that would enable you, or a seasoned jeweler, to tell the ear studs apart! Why would you buy them at Tiffany's when you can purchase them for far less elsewhere? The answer, it turns out, is that buying ear studs is a lot like consuming many other goods: name recognition matters. So do perception and brand loyalty. Many jewelry buyers also take cues from the storefront, how the staff dress, and how the jewelry is packaged. Spending $300 total is a lot of money for the privilege of getting Tiffany's blue box. Consumers believe that Tiffany's jewelry is better, when all the store is doing is charging more markup.

TRUTH IN ADVERTISING Finally, many advertising campaigns are not just informative—they are designed to produce a psychological response. When an ad moves you to buy or act in a particular way, it becomes manipulative. Because advertising can be such a powerful way to reach customers, there is a temptation to lie about a product. To prevent firms from spreading misinformation about their products, the Federal Trade Commission (FTC) regulates

PRACTICE WHAT YOU KNOW

Advertising: Brands versus Generics

Why do some frozen pizzas cost more than others when brands that offer similar quality are only a few feet away in the frozen foods aisle? To answer that question, consider the following questions:

QUESTION: What would graphs showing price and output look like for DiGiorno and for a generic pizza? What is the markup for DiGiorno?

DiGiorno or generic?

ANSWER: Here is the graph for DiGiorno.

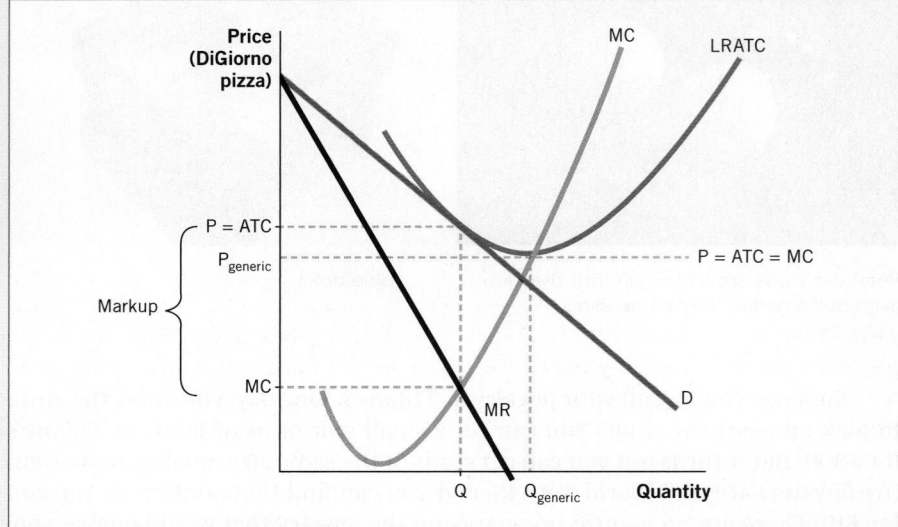

And here is the graph for the generic pizza.

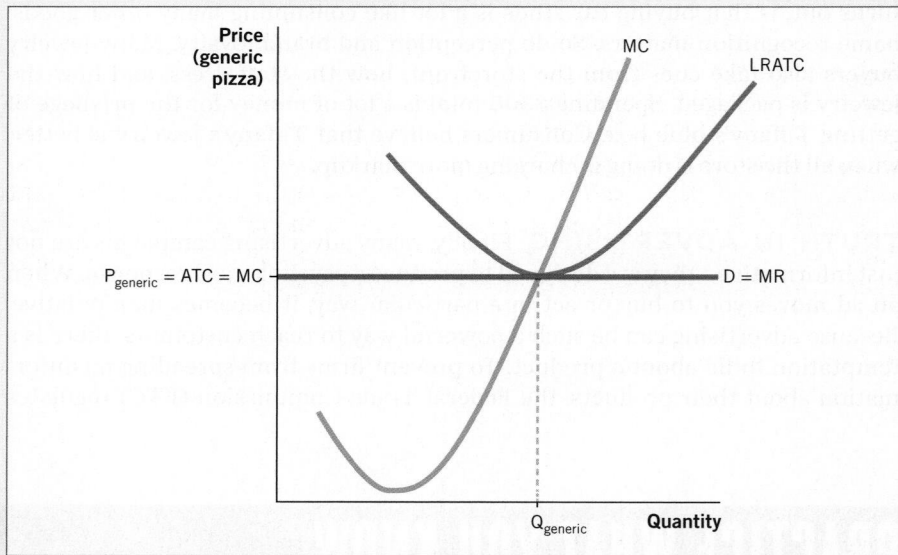

QUESTION: Which company has a stronger incentive to maintain strict quality control in the production process, DiGiorno or a generic brand? Why?

ANSWER: DiGiorno has a catchy slogan: "It's not delivery. It's DiGiorno!" This statement tries to position the product as being just as good as a freshly delivered pizza. Some customers who buy frozen pizzas will opt for DiGiorno over comparable generics because they are familiar with the company's advertising claim about its quality. Therefore, DiGiorno has a stronger incentive to make sure the product delivers as advertised. Because generic, or store-name, brands are purchased mostly on the basis of price, the customer generally does not have high expectations about the quality.

2xSnickers should really be called 1.5xSnickers. Shame on Mars for the deception.

advertising and promotes economic efficiency. At the FTC, the Division of Advertising Practices protects consumers by enforcing truth-in-advertising laws. While the commission does not have enough resources to track down every violation, it does pay particular attention to claims involving food, nonprescription drugs, dietary supplements, alcohol, and tobacco. Unsubstantiated claims are particularly prevalent on the Internet, and they tend to target vulnerable populations seeking quick fixes to a variety of medical conditions.

Of course, even with regulatory oversight, consumers must still be vigilant. At best, the FTC can remove products from the market and levy fines against companies that make unsubstantiated claims. However, the damage is often already done. The Latin phrase *caveat emptor*, or "buyer beware," sums up the dangers of false information.

Sometimes the way a product is advertised is not illegal but is still borderline unethical. Firms often engage in price deception, or tricks to make you think a price is lower than it really is. Gas stations deploy this technique by quoting prices ending in a 9/10 of a cent fraction, to slightly understate how much you are paying. But a more egregious example of price deception comes from Mars, which sells Snickers, far and away the most popular snack-sized candy bar sold in the United States. For a time, Mars sold Snickers and 2xSnickers. One would think that "two times" Snickers would be two Snickers in one longer package, right? That's the deception: the bars in 2xSnickers are smaller!

ECONOMICS IN THE REAL WORLD

THE FEDERAL TRADE COMMISSION VERSUS 1-800 CONTACTS

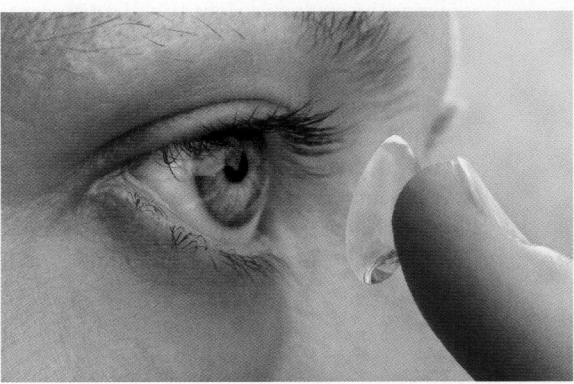

The FTC found 1-800 Contacts guilty of manipulative advertising.

When we search online, we trust that the most pertinent results are shown first. How would you feel—and how would it change your buying behavior—if you knew that the search results were being manipulated? That's what happened with 1-800 Contacts, America's largest online retailer of contact lenses. The firm was found guilty of unlawfully orchestrating a web of anticompetitive agreements with rival online contact lens sellers, to suppress competition in certain online search forums that advertise to consumers. So instead of buying contacts in a monopolistically competitive online space, consumers were shown search results with much higher prices.

Product Differentiation: Would You Buy a Franchise?

- Restaurant failures are very high and running a franchise can lower your risk.
- Franchises provide brand familiarity.
- However, rights to franchise can come with very high fees. The five restaurants with the highest combined franchise and start-up costs are:

  Golden Corral, $6.8M

  Buffalo Wild Wings, $3.2M

  Culver's, $2.8M

  KFC, $2.5M

  Denny's, $2.4M

Franchises are valuable in markets where product differentiation matters. McDonald's, Panera Bread, and KFC all have a different take on serving fast food. But what does it mean to own a franchise?

Franchises are sold to individual owners, who operate subject to the terms of their agreement with the parent company. For instance, purchasing a McDonald's franchise and opening a new store can cost over $2 million. McDonald's also requires the individual restaurant owner to charge certain prices and offer menu items selected by the parent corporation. As a result, customers who prefer a certain type and quality of food know that the dining experience at each McDonald's will be similar. Most franchises also come with noncompete clauses that guarantee that another franchise will not open nearby. This guarantee gives the franchise owner the exclusive right to sell a differentiated product in a given area.

Suppose you want to start a restaurant. Why would you, or anyone else, be willing to pay over $2 million just for the right to sell food? For that amount, you could open your own restaurant with a custom menu and interior, create your own marketing plan, and locate anywhere you like. For example, Golden Corral and Buffalo Wild Wings are two restaurants with high start-up costs exceeding $3 million. Golden Corral is the largest buffet-style restaurant in the country, and Buffalo Wild Wings is one of the top locations to watch sporting events. You might think it would make more sense to avoid the franchising costs by opening your own buffet or setting up a bank of big-screen TVs. However, failures in the restaurant industry are high. With a franchise, the customer knows what to expect. Translation: high franchise fees enable firms to charge a higher markup because consumer demand is more inelastic.

Franchise owners are assured of visibility and a ready supply of customers. Purchasing a franchise means more potential customers will notice your restaurant, and that drives up revenues. Is that worth $2 million or more? Yes, in some cases. Suppose you'll do $1 million in annual sales as part of a franchise, but only $0.5 million on your own. That half-million difference over 20 years means $10 million more in revenue, a healthy chunk of which will turn into profits. This is the magic of franchising.

How much would you pay for a KFC franchise?

Conclusion

Firms willingly spend on advertising because it can increase demand, build brand loyalty, and provide consumers with useful information about differences in products. Monopolistic competitors advertise and mark up their products like monopolists, but, like firms in a competitive market, they cannot earn long-run profits. While an economic profit is possible in the short run in all three types of market structure (perfect competition, monopolistic competition, and monopoly), only the monopolist, whose business has significant barriers to entry, can earn an economic profit in the long run. Entry and exit cause long-run profits to equal zero in competitive and monopolistically competitive firms.

Monopolistic competitors are price makers who fail to achieve the most efficient welfare-maximizing output for society. But this observation does not tell the entire story. Monopolistic competitors do not have as much market power or create as much excess capacity or markup as monopolists. Consequently, the monopolistic competitor lacks the ability to exploit consumers. The result is not perfect, but widespread monopolistic competition generally serves consumers and society well.

In the next chapter, we continue our exploration of market structure with *oligopoly*, which produces results that are much closer to monopoly than monopolistic competition. ✳

ᐧ ANSWERING *the* BIG QUESTIONS ᐧ

What is monopolistic competition?

- Monopolistic competition is a market structure characterized by low barriers to entry and many firms selling differentiated products.
- Differentiation of products takes three forms: differentiation by style or type, location, and quality.

What are the differences among monopolistic competition, competitive markets, and monopoly?

- Monopolistic competitors, like monopolists, are price makers with downward-sloping demand curves. Whenever the demand curve is downward sloping, the firm is able to mark up the price above marginal cost. The results are excess capacity and an inefficient level of output.
- In the long run, barriers to entry enable a monopoly to earn an economic profit. This is not the case for monopolistic competition or competitive markets.

Why is advertising prevalent in monopolistic competition?

■ Advertising performs useful functions under monopolistic competition: it conveys information about the price of the goods offered for sale, the location of products, and new products. It also signals differences in quality. However, advertising also encourages brand loyalty, which makes it harder for other businesses to successfully enter the market. Advertising can be manipulative and misleading.

Concepts You Should Know

excess capacity (p. 375)
markup (p. 375)

monopolistic competition (p. 368)
product differentiation (p. 368)

Questions for Review

1. Why is product differentiation necessary for monopolistic competition? What are three types of product differentiation?

2. How is monopolistic competition like competitive markets? How is monopolistic competition like monopoly?

3. Why do monopolistically competitive firms produce less than those operating at the most efficient scale of production?

4. Draw a graph that shows a monopolistic competitor making an economic profit in the short run and a graph that shows a monopolistic competitor making no economic profit in the long run.

5. Monopolistic competition produces a result that is inefficient. Does this outcome mean that monopolistically competitive markets should be regulated? Discuss.

6. Draw a typical demand curve for competitive markets, monopolistic competition, and monopoly. Which of these demand curves is the most inelastic? Why?

7. How does advertising benefit society? In what ways can advertising be harmful?

8. When you buy a generic product instead of its name-brand counterpart, is the good you purchase really inferior, or is it the same good, simply repackaged by the name-band manufacturer under another label?

Study Problems (✳ solved at the end of the section)

✳ **1.** At your high school reunion, a friend describes his plan to take a break from his florist shop and sail around the world. He says that if he continues to make the same economic profit for the next five years, he will be able to afford the trip. Do you think your friend will be able to achieve his dream in five years? What do you expect to happen to his firm's profits in the long run?

2. Which of the following could be considered a monopolistic competitor?

a. a local corn farmer
b. the Tennessee Valley Authority, a large electricity producer
c. a pizza delivery business
d. a grocery store
e. Stella McCartney, fashion designer

3. Which of the following are the same under monopolistic competition and in a competitive market in the long run?

a. the markup the firm charges
b. the price the firm charges to consumers

c. the firm's excess capacity
d. the average total cost of production
e. the amount of advertising
f. the firm's profit
g. the efficiency of the market structure

4. In competitive markets, price is equal to marginal cost in the long run. Explain why this statement is not true for monopolistic competition.

5. Econoburgers, a fast-food restaurant in a crowded local market, has reached a long-run equilibrium.

a. Draw a diagram showing demand, marginal revenue, average total cost, and marginal cost curves for Econoburgers.
b. How much profit is Econoburgers making?
c. Suppose that the government decides to regulate burger production to make it more efficient. Explain what would happen to the price of Econoburgers and the firm's output.

6. Consider two different companies. The first manufactures cardboard, and the second sells books. Which firm is more likely to advertise?

7. In the diagram that follows, identify the demand curve that is consistent with a monopolistic competitor making zero long-run economic profit. Explain why you have chosen that demand curve and why the other two demand curves are not consistent with monopolistic competition.

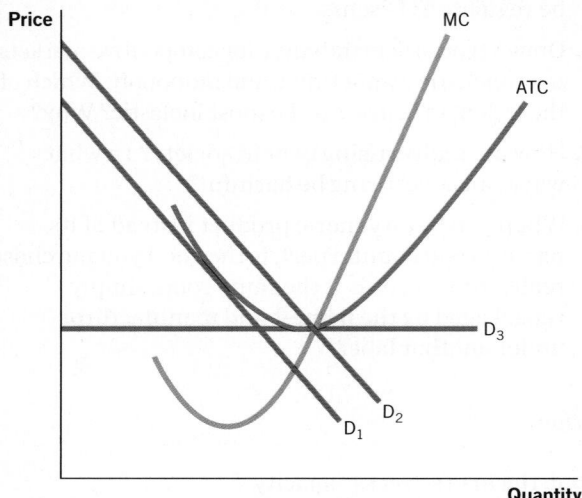

8. Titleist has an advertising slogan: "#1 ball in golf." Consumers can also buy generic golf balls. The manufacturers of generic golf balls do not engage in any advertising. Assume that the average total cost of producing Titleist and generic golf balls is the same.

   a. Create a graph showing the price and the markup for Titleist.

   b. In a separate graph, show the price and the output for the generic firms.

   c. Who has a stronger incentive to maintain strict quality control in the production process—Titleist or the generic firms? Why?

9. Taste of India is a small restaurant in a small town. The owner of Taste of India marks up his dishes by 300%. Indian Cuisine is a small restaurant in a large city. The owner of Indian Cuisine marks up her dishes by 200%. Explain why the markup is higher in the small town.

10. Read the following online article: http://20 somethingfinance.com/why-eyeglasses-are-so -expensive-how-you-can-pay-less. Using your understanding of monopolistic competition and markup, explain why retail customers pay so much more for eyeglasses than online customers do. You can also watch this video from *Adam Ruins Everything* for an interesting explanation: www.youtube.com/watch?v=CAeHuDcy_bY.

11. Consider a monopolistically competitive firm. From the point of view of the remaining firms, as firms leave the industry we can think of this as a shift to the

   a. left for each individual firm's supply curve.

   b. left in each individual firm's MC curve.

   c. right in each individual firm's ATC curve.

   d. right in each individual firm's demand curve.

Solved Problems

1. The florist business is monopolistically competitive. This means firms are free to enter and exit at any time. Firms will enter because your friend's shop is making an economic profit. As new florist shops open, the added competition will drive prices down, causing your friend's profits to fall. In the long run, this means he will not be able to make an economic profit. He will earn only enough to cover his opportunity costs, or what is known as a *fair return* on his investment. That is not to say he won't be able to save enough to sail around the world, but it won't happen as fast as he would like because other firms will enter the market and limit his profits going forward.

6. The cardboard firm manufactures a product that is a component used mostly by other firms that need to package final products for sale. As a result, any efforts at advertising will only raise costs without increasing the demand for cardboard. This situation contrasts with that of the bookseller, who advertises to attract consumers to the store. More traffic means more purchases of books and other items sold in the store. The bookstore has some market power and markup. In this case, it pays to advertise. A cardboard manufacturing firm sells exactly the same product as other cardboard producers, so it has no market power, and any advertising expenses will only make its cost higher than its rivals'.

10. There are many retailers (LensCrafters, Pearle, Sears, Target), but the brands they sell all come from Italian eyeglass manufacturer Luxottica. Luxottica prevents these major retailers from discounting the frames and will pull their brands if they do. However, if you don't care about the brand of eyeglasses you wear, you can find a pair online for well under $100. Online retailers aren't selling a brand, so they attract customers with much more elastic demand compared with customers who want their frames to be fashionable. This scenario fits perfectly with the idea of markup. Firms with brand-loyal customers have much higher markup than firms with customers who do not care about the brand they purchase.

11. The correct answer is d: each individual firm's demand curve shifts to the right. The reason is that as firms exit, each remaining firm picks up additional customers.

13

Oligopoly and Strategic Behavior

Cell Phone Companies are Competitive.

If you have a cell phone, chances are that you receive service from one of three major cell phone carriers in the United States: AT&T, Verizon, or T-Mobile. Together, these firms control 95% of all cellular service. In some respects, this market is very competitive. For example, cell phone companies advertise intensely, and they offer a variety of phones with voice and data plans. Also, there are differences in network coverage and in the number of applications users can access. But despite outward appearances, the cell phone companies do not do business in a competitive or even a monopolistically competitive market. One important reason for this is the expense of building and maintaining a cellular network. The largest cell phone companies have invested billions of dollars in infrastructure in order to attract customers based on cell phone network quality and speed and the plans and services the companies provide. Therefore, the cost of entry is very high. As we learned in Chapter 10, barriers to entry are a key feature of monopolies.

The cell phone industry has features of both competition and monopoly: competition is fierce, but smaller firms and potential entrants into the market find it difficult to enter and compete. This mixture of characteristics represents another form of market structure—*oligopoly*. In this chapter, we examine oligopoly by comparing it with other market

Gamers delight, 5G networks will make your cell phones even more powerful! Whatever this customer is seeing in her 3D display has apparently made quite an impression.

structures already familiar to you. We then look at some of the strategic behaviors firms in an oligopoly employ, an examination that leads us into the fascinating topic of game theory.

· BIG QUESTIONS ·

- What is oligopoly?
- How does game theory explain strategic behavior?
- How do government policies affect oligopoly behavior?
- What are network externalities?

What Is Oligopoly?

Oligopoly
is a form of market structure that exists when a small number of firms sell a differentiated product in a market with high barriers to entry.

Oligopoly is a form of market structure that exists when a small number of firms sell a product in a market with significant barriers to entry. An oligopolist is like a monopolistic competitor in that it often sells a differentiated product. But like pure monopolists, oligopolists enjoy significant barriers to entry. Table 13.1 compares the differences and similarities between the four market structures.

We have seen that firms in monopolistically competitive markets usually have a limited amount of market power. As a result, buyers often find low prices (but not as low as competitive markets) and wide availability. In contrast, an oligopolist sells in a market with significant barriers to entry and fewer rivals. Thus, the oligopolist has more market power than a firm operating under monopolistic competition. However, because an oligopolistic market has more than one seller, no single oligopolist has as much market power as a monopolist.

Our study of oligopoly begins with a look at how economists measure market power in an industry. We then work through a simplified model of oligopoly to explore the choices that oligopolists make.

TABLE 13.1

Comparing Oligopoly to Other Market Structures

Competitive market	Monopolistic competition	Oligopoly	Monopoly
Many sellers	Many sellers	A few sellers	One seller
Similar products	Differentiated product	Differentiated product (most of the time)	Unique product without close substitutes
Free entry and exit	Easy entry and exit	Barriers to entry	Significant barriers to entry

TABLE 13.2

Highly Concentrated Industries in the United States

Industry	Concentration ratio of the four largest firms (%)	Top firms
Search engines	98.5	Google, Yahoo, Microsoft
Wireless telecommunications	94.7	Verizon, AT&T, T-Mobile, Sprint
Satellite TV providers	94.5	DIRECTV, DISH Network
Soda production	93.7	Coca-Cola, PepsiCo, Dr Pepper Snapple
Sanitary paper products	92.7	Kimberly-Clark, Procter & Gamble, Georgia-Pacific
Lighting and bulb manufacturing	91.9	General Electric, Philips, Siemens
Tire manufacturing (domestic)	91.3	Goodyear, Michelin, Cooper, Bridgestone
Major household appliances	90.0	Whirlpool, Electrolux, General Electric, LG
Automobile manufacturing (domestic)	87.0	General Motors, Toyota, Ford, Fiat-Chrysler

Source: *Highly Concentrated: Companies That Dominate Their Industries*, www.ibisworld.com. Special Report, February 2012.

Measuring the Concentration of Industries

In markets with only a few sellers, industry output is highly concentrated among a few large firms. Economists use *concentration ratios* as a measure of the oligopoly power present in an industry. The most common measure, known as the four-firm concentration ratio, expresses the sales of the four largest firms in an industry as a percentage of that industry's total sales. Table 13.2 lists the four-firm concentration ratios for highly concentrated industries in the United States. This ratio is determined by taking the output of the four largest firms in an industry and dividing that output by the total production in the entire industry.

In highly concentrated industries like search engines, wireless telecommunications, and satellite TV providers, the market share held by the four largest firms approaches 100%. At the bottom of our list of most concentrated industries is domestic automobile manufacturing. General Motors, Fiat Chrysler, Ford, and Toyota (which has seven manufacturing plants in the United States) dominate the domestic automobile industry. These large firms have significant market power.

However, when evaluating market power in an industry, it is important to be aware of international activity. In several industries, including automobile and tire manufacturing, intense global competition keeps the market power of U.S. companies in check. For instance, domestic manufacturers that produce automobiles also must compete globally against cars produced elsewhere. This means that vehicles produced by Honda, Nissan, Volkswagen, Kia, and Volvo, to name just a few companies, limit the market power of domestic producers. As a result, the concentration ratio is a rough gauge of oligopoly power—not an absolute measure.

Competition from foreign car companies keeps the market power of the U.S.-based automobile companies in check.

Collusion and Cartels in a Simple Duopoly Example

In this section, we explore the two conflicting tendencies found in oligopoly: oligopolists would like to act like monopolists, but they often end up competing like monopolistic competitors. To help us understand oligopoly behavior, we start with a simplified example: an industry consisting of only two firms, known as a *duopoly*. Duopolies (such as Boeing and Airbus in the wide-body jet market) are rare in national and international markets, but not that uncommon in small, local markets. For example, in many small communities, the number of cell phone carriers is limited. Imagine a small town where only two providers have cell phone towers. In this case, the cell towers are a sunk cost (see Chapter 9); both towers were built to service all of the customers in the town, so each carrier has substantial excess capacity when the customers are divided between the two carriers. Also, because there is extra capacity on each network, the marginal cost of adding additional customers is zero.

Table 13.3 shows the community's demand for cell phones. Because the prices and quantities listed in the first two columns are negatively related, the data are consistent with a downward-sloping demand curve.

Column 3 calculates the total revenue from columns 1 and 2. With Table 13.3 as our guide, we will examine the output in this market under three scenarios: competition, monopoly, and duopoly.

Duopoly sits between the two extremes. Competition still exists, but it is not as extensive as you would see in competitive markets, which ruthlessly drive the price down to cost. Nor does the result always mirror that of monopoly, where competitive pressures are completely absent. In an oligopoly, a small number of firms feel competitive pressures and also enjoy some of the advantages of monopoly.

TABLE 13.3		
The Demand Schedule for Cell Phones		

Here we assume that 1 customer = 1 cell phone = 1 purchase of cell phone service.

(1) Price/month (P)	(2) Number of customers (Q)	(3) Total revenue (TR) (P) × (Q)
$180	0	$0
165	100	16,500
150	200	30,000
135	300	40,500
120	400	48,000
105	500	52,500
90	600	54,000
75	700	52,500
60	800	48,000
45	900	40,500
30	1,000	30,000
15	1,100	16,500
0	1,200	0

COMPETITIVE OUTCOME Recall that competitive markets drive prices down to the point at which marginal revenue is equal to the marginal cost. So if the market is highly competitive and the marginal cost is zero, we would expect the final price of cell phone service to be zero and the quantity supplied to be 1,200 customers—the number of people who live in the small town. At this point, anyone who desires cell phone service would be able to receive it without cost. Because efficiency exists when the output is maximized, and because everyone who lives in the community would have cell phone service, the result would be socially efficient. However, it is unrealistic to expect this outcome. Cell phone companies provide a good that is nonrival and also excludable; in other words, they sell a club good (see Chapter 7). Because these firms are in business to make money, they will not provide something for nothing.

Marginal thinking

MONOPOLY OUTCOME At the other extreme of the market structure continuum, a monopolist faces no competition, and price decisions do not depend on the activity of other firms. A monopolist can search for the price that brings it the most profit. Looking at Table 13.3, we see that total revenue peaks at $54,000. At this point, the price is $90 per month, and 600 customers sign up for cell phone service. Compared with a competitive market, the monopoly price is higher and the quantity sold is lower. The result is a loss of efficiency.

DUOPOLY OUTCOME In a duopoly, the two firms can decide to cooperate—even though this practice is illegal in the United States, as we will discuss shortly. If the duopolists cooperate, we say that they collude. **Collusion** is an agreement between rival firms that specifies the price each firm charges and the quantity it produces. The firms that collude can act like a single monopolist to maximize their profits. In this case, the monopolist would maximize its profit by charging $90 and serving 600 customers. If the duopolists divide the market equally, they will each have 300 customers who pay $90, for a total of $27,000 in revenue each.

Collusion
is an agreement among rival firms that specifies the price each firm charges and the quantity it produces.

When two or more firms act in unison, economists refer to them as a **cartel**. Many countries prohibit cartels. In the United States, **antitrust laws** prohibit collusion. However, even if collusion were legal, it would probably fail more often than not. Imagine that two theoretical cell phone companies, AT-Phone and Horizon, have formed a cartel and agreed that each will serve 300 customers at a price of $90 per month per customer. But AT-Phone and Horizon each have an incentive to earn more revenue by lowering their price while the rival company keeps the agreement. Suppose AT-Phone lowers its price to $75. Looking at Table 13.3, we see that at this price the total market demand rises to 700 customers—and AT-phone will capture the entire market, by selling at the lowest price. So AT-Phone will serve 700 customers, and its revenue will be 700 × $75, or $52,500. This is an improvement of $25,500 over what AT-Phone made when the market price was $90 and the customers were equally divided.

A **cartel** is a group of two or more firms that act in unison.

Antitrust laws
attempt to prevent oligopolies from behaving like monopolies.

Incentives

How would Horizon react? At the very least, unless it wants to earn $0, it had better match AT-Phone's lower price. Horizon would then attract 350 customers, half the market at a price of $75, and now AT-Phone and Horizon would each bring in revenue of 350 × $75, or $26,250, leaving each firm making $750 less than when they served only 600 customers total. From what we know about competitive markets, we might expect the competition

TABLE 13.4

Outcomes under Competition, Duopoly, and Monopoly

	Competitive markets	Duopoly	Monopoly
Price	$0	$0–90	$90
Output	1,200	600–1200	600
Socially efficient?	Yes	Only when the price is $0 and output is 1200	No
Explanation	Because the marginal cost of providing cell phone service is zero, the price is eventually driven to zero. Since firms are in business to make a profit, it is unrealistic to expect this result.	Because firms are mutually interdependent, each adopts a strategy based on the actions of its rival. The two firms may decide to collude and charge $90, or competitive pressures may lead them to charge a much lower price.	The monopolist is free to choose the profit-maximizing output. In the cell phone example, it maximizes its total revenue. As a result, the monopolist charges $90 and serves 600 customers.

between the two firms to cause a price war in which price eventually falls to zero. Duopolists are unlikely to participate in an all-out price war because both firms would no longer be making any profit, but we cannot know to what extent competitive pressures will determine each firm's decision.

Table 13.4 summarizes the different results under competition, duopoly, and monopoly using our cell phone example. From this example, we see that a market with a small number of sellers is characterized by **mutual interdependence**, which is a market situation in which the actions of one firm have an impact on the price and output of its competitors. As a result, a firm's market share is determined by the products it offers, the prices it charges, and the actions of its rivals.

Oligopolists want to emulate the monopoly outcome, but the push to compete with their rivals often makes it difficult to maintain a cartel. Yet the idea that cartels are unstable is not guaranteed. When a stable cartel is not achieved, firms in oligopoly fall short of fully maximizing profits. But they also do not compete to the same degree as firms in competitive markets. Therefore, when a market is an oligopoly, output is likely to be higher than under a monopoly and lower than within a competitive market. As you would expect, the amount of output affects the prices. The higher output (compared with monopoly) makes oligopoly prices generally lower than monopoly prices, and the lower output (compared with a competitive market) makes oligopoly prices higher than those found in competitive markets.

In many industries, smaller firms may take a cue from the decisions made by the price leader. **Price leadership** occurs when a single firm, known as the price leader, produces a large share of the total output in the industry. The price leader sets the price and output level that maximizes its own profits. Smaller firms then set their prices to match the price leader. Because the impact on price is small to begin with, it makes sense that smaller rivals tend to follow the price leader.

Price leadership is not illegal because it does not involve collusion. Rather, it relies on an understanding that an effort to resist changes implemented by the price leader will lead to both increased price competition and lower

Mutual interdependence is a market situation where the actions of one firm have an impact on the price and output of its competitors.

Price leadership occurs when a dominant firm in an industry sets the price that maximizes its profits and the smaller firms in the industry follow by setting their prices to match the price leader.

profits for every firm in the industry. Because the firms act in accordance with one another, this practice is commonly known as *tacit collusion*.

One well-known example of price leadership is pricing patterns in the airline industry. On almost any route with multiple carrier options, a price search for flights will reveal almost identical prices on basic economy-class flights. This similarity of prices happens even though the firms do not collude to set a profit-maximizing price. Rather, when one firm sets a fare, the other carriers feel compelled to match it. Price leadership works best when the largest firm in an industry raises or lowers its price and smaller rivals follow suit.

ECONOMICS IN THE REAL WORLD

OPEC: AN INTERNATIONAL CARTEL

The best-known cartel is the Organization of the Petroleum Exporting Countries, or OPEC, a group of oil-exporting countries that have a significant influence on the world price of crude oil and the output of petroleum. To maintain relatively high oil prices, the member nations collude to limit the overall supply of oil. While OPEC's activities are legal under international law, collusion is illegal under U.S. antitrust law.

OPEC controls almost 80% of the world's known oil reserves and accounts for almost one-third of the world's crude production, giving the cartel's 14 member nations significant control over the world price of oil. As is the case within any organization, conflict inevitably arises. In the 50 years OPEC

What would oil prices be like if OPEC didn't exist?

has existed, there have been embargoes (government prohibitions on the trade of oil), oil gluts, production disputes, and periods of falling prices. As a result, OPEC has been far from perfect in consistently maintaining high prices. In addition, OPEC has been careful to keep the price of oil below the cost of alternative energy options. Despite the limitations on OPEC's pricing power, OPEC has effectively acted as a cartel during the periods when it adopted output rationing to maintain price. However, the oil shale boom in the United States and Canada has significantly reduced OPEC's control over worldwide oil production, and as a result, the price is lower today than it was just a few years ago.

Oligopoly with More Than Two Firms

We have seen how firms behave in a duopoly. What happens when more firms enter the market? The addition of a third firm complicates efforts to maintain a cartel and increases the possibility of a more competitive result.

We can see this interaction in the cell phone market. The three major companies are not all equal. If AT&T and Verizon were the only two providers, the market might have very little competition. However, T-Mobile plays a crucial role in changing the market dynamic. Even though T-Mobile has significantly less market share than either of its bigger rivals, it still has developed an extensive cellular network in order to compete. Because T-Mobile has a smaller subscriber base and significant excess capacity, it aggressively competes on price. As a result, in many (but not all) respects, the entire cell phone industry functions competitively.

To see why, consider what the addition of a third firm will do to the market. When the third firm enters the market, there are two effects to consider—price and output. For example, if the third firm builds a cell tower, it will increase the overall capacity to provide cell phone service. As we observed in the duopoly example, if the total number of cell phone contracts (the supply) increases, all the firms must charge a lower price. This is the **price effect**, and it reflects how a change in price affects the firm's revenue. But because the marginal cost of providing cell phone service is essentially zero, the price each firm charges is substantially higher than the marginal cost of adding a new customer to the network. When the firm sells an additional unit, it generates additional revenues for the firm. This **output effect** occurs when a change in price affects the number of customers in a market.

The price effect and output effect make it difficult to maintain a cartel when there are more than two firms. Generally, as the number of firms grows, each individual firm becomes less concerned about its impact on the overall price, because any price above marginal cost creates a profit. Therefore, individual firms are more willing to lower prices because doing so creates a large output effect for the individual firm and only a small price effect in the market.

Of course, not all firms are the same size. Therefore, smaller and larger firms in an oligopolistic market react differently to the price and output effects. Increased output at smaller firms will have a negligible impact on overall prices because small firms represent only a tiny fraction of the market supply. But the same is not true for firms with a large market share. Decisions at these firms will have a substantial impact on price and output because the overall amount supplied in the market will change appreciably. In other words, in an oligopoly, the decisions of one firm directly affect other firms.

The **price effect** reflects how a change in price affects the firm's revenue.

The **output effect** occurs when a change in price affects the number of customers in a market.

PRACTICE WHAT YOU KNOW

Oligopoly: Can You Recognize the Oligopolist?

QUESTION: Which firm is the oligopolist?

a. Firm A is in retail. It is one of the largest and most popular clothing stores in the country. It also competes with many rivals and faces intense price competition.

b. Firm B is in the auto rental business. It is not the nation's largest rental company, but significant barriers to entry enable it to serve customers across the United States more conveniently and at a lower price than local rivals.

c. Firm C is a restaurant in a small, isolated community. It is the only local eatery. People drive from miles away to eat there.

ANSWER: Firm A sells clothing, a product with many competing brands and outlets. The competition is intense, which means that the firm has little market power. As a result, firm A is a player in a competitive market. It is not an oligopolist. Firm B faces competition from other large national car rental companies, but barriers to entry at many airports prevent smaller firms from securing space inside the terminal. This means that car rental companies are oligopolists. Firm C is a monopolist. It is the only place to eat out in the isolated community, and no other restaurant is nearby. It is not an oligopolist.

CHALLENGE QUESTION: Is the airline industry (a number of major airlines but many smaller rivals) a good example of oligopoly, or of monopolistic competition?

ANSWER: If you simply look at the number of airlines operating in the United States, you find dozens—more than enough, on a ground-level view—to make cartels and other monopoly-like behaviors seem unlikely. But if you look again, this time from 30,000 feet, you see that four major carriers (American, Delta, Southwest, and United) account for 80% of all domestic departures. In addition, many small airports are only served by one or two carriers, making price collusion relatively easy on many routes. Finally, significant start-up costs make the cost of entry into the market relatively high. That's not to say that airlines face no competition—one of the four largest U.S. carriers, Southwest, used to be a small regional airline but was so successful at building its brand and keeping cost low that it was able to expand across the country. Still, with the high barriers to entry (it is hard to secure gates at airports), consolidation among the largest carriers, and differentiated routes, each carrier enjoys pricing power. This makes the airline industry a better example of oligopoly than of monopolistic competition.

How Does Game Theory Explain Strategic Behavior?

Decision-making under oligopoly can be complex. **Game theory** is a branch of mathematics that economists use to analyze the strategic behavior of decision-makers who have to consider the behavior of others around them. In particular, game theory can help us determine what level of cooperation is most likely to occur. A game consists of a set of players, a set of strategies available to those players, and a specification of the payoffs for each combination of strategies. The game is usually represented by a payoff matrix that shows the players, strategies, and payoffs. It is presumed that each player acts simultaneously or without knowing the actions of the other.

In this section, we will learn about the prisoner's dilemma, an example from game theory that helps us understand how dominant strategies often frame short-run decisions. (In its simplest form, the prisoner's dilemma is a game played just once, not repeatedly over time.) We will use the idea of the dominant strategy to explain why oligopolists often choose to advertise. Finally, we will come full circle and argue that the dominant strategy in a game may be overcome in the long run, through repeated interactions.

Game theory
is a branch of mathematics that economists use to analyze the strategic behavior of decision-makers.

Strategic Behavior and the Dominant Strategy

We have seen that in oligopoly there is mutual interdependence: a rival's business choices affect the earnings the other rivals can expect to make. To learn more about the decisions firms make, we will explore a fundamental problem in game theory known as the *prisoner's dilemma*. The dilemma takes its name from a famous scenario devised by pioneer game theorist Al Tucker soon after World War II.

The scenario goes like this: Two prisoners are being interrogated separately about a crime they both participated in, and each is offered a plea bargain to cooperate with the authorities by testifying against the other. If both suspects refuse to cooperate with the authorities, neither can be convicted of a more serious crime, though they will both have to spend some time in jail. But the police have offered full immunity if one cooperates and the other does not. This means that each suspect has an incentive to betray the other. The rub is that if they both confess, they will spend more time in jail than if they had both stayed quiet. When decision-makers face incentives that make it difficult to achieve mutually beneficial outcomes, we say they are in a **prisoner's dilemma**. This situation makes the payoff for cooperating with the authorities more attractive than the result of keeping quiet.

We can understand the outcomes of the prisoner's dilemma by looking at the payoff matrix in Figure 13.1. Starting with the white box in the upper left corner, we see that if both suspects testify against each other, they each get 10 years in jail. If one suspect testifies while his partner remains quiet—the

The **prisoner's dilemma** occurs when decision-makers face incentives that make it difficult to achieve mutually beneficial outcomes.

FIGURE 13.1

The Prisoner's Dilemma

The two suspects know that if they both keep quiet, they will spend only 1 year in jail. The prisoner's dilemma occurs because the decision to testify results in no jail time for the one who testifies if the other does not testify. However, this outcome means that both are likely to testify and get 10 years.

		Tony Montana	
		Testify	**Keep quiet**
Manny Ribera	**Testify**	10 years in jail 10 years in jail	25 years in jail goes free
	Keep quiet	goes free 25 years in jail	1 year in jail 1 year in jail

---

upper right and lower left boxes—he goes free and his partner gets 25 years in jail. If both keep quiet—the result in the lower right corner—they each get off with 1 year in jail. This result is better than the outcome in which both prisoners testify.

Incentives

Because each suspect is interrogated separately, the decision about what to tell the police cannot be made cooperatively; thus, each prisoner faces a dilemma. The interrogation process makes the situation a noncooperative "game" and changes the incentives each party faces.

Under these circumstances, what will our suspects choose? Let's begin with the outcomes for Tony Montana. Suppose he testifies. If Manny Ribera also testifies, Tony will get 10 years in jail (the upper left box). If Manny keeps quiet, Tony will go free (the lower left box). Now suppose that Tony decides to keep quiet. If Manny testifies, Tony can expect 25 years in jail (the upper right box). If Manny keeps quiet, Tony will get 1 year in jail (the lower right box). No matter what choice Manny makes, Tony is always better off choosing to testify. If his partner testifies and he testifies, he gets 10 years in jail as opposed to 25 if he keeps quiet. If his partner keeps quiet and he testifies, Tony goes free as opposed to spending a year in jail if he also keeps quiet. The same analysis applies to the outcomes for Manny.

When a player always prefers one strategy, regardless of what his opponent chooses, we say it is a **dominant strategy**. We can see a dominant strategy at work in the case of our two suspects. They know that if they both keep quiet, they will spend one year in jail. The dilemma occurs because both suspects are more likely to testify and get 10 years in jail. The choice to testify is obvious for two reasons. First, neither suspect can monitor the actions of the other after they are separated. Second, once each suspect understands that his partner will save jail time if he testifies, he realizes that the incentives are not in favor of keeping quiet.

A **dominant strategy** exists when a player will always prefer one strategy, regardless of what his opponent chooses.

The dominant strategy in our example is also a Nash equilibrium, named for mathematician John Nash. A **Nash equilibrium** occurs when all economic decision-makers have no incentive to change their current decision. If each suspect reasons that the other will testify, the best response is also to testify. Each suspect may wish that he and his partner could coordinate their actions and agree to keep quiet. However, without the possibility of coordination, neither has an incentive to withhold testimony. So they both think strategically and decide to testify.

A **Nash equilibrium** occurs when all economic decision-makers opt to keep the status quo.

Incentives

Duopoly and the Prisoner's Dilemma

The prisoner's dilemma example suggests that cooperation can be difficult to achieve. What this means for oligopoly is that it is not natural or easy for firms to collude. To get a better sense of the incentives that oligopolists face, let's revisit the situation of AT-Phone and Horizon, each trying to decide whether to charge $90 or $75 for cell phone plans. Figure 13.2 puts some of the information from Table 13.3 into a payoff matrix and highlights the revenue AT-Phone and Horizon could earn, depending on the price each firm chooses.

We see that when AT-Phone sets a high price ($90), Horizon can earn either $27,000, by setting a high price, or $52,500, by setting a low price. When AT-Phone sets a low price ($75), Horizon can earn either $0 with a high price or $26,250 with a low price. Either way, Horizon is better off setting the low price. The same reasoning holds for AT-Phone: choosing the low price instead of the high one means getting either $52,500 instead of $27,000 or else $26,250 instead of $0, depending on what Horizon does. So the low price is the

Nash Equilibrium

A BRILLIANT MADNESS AND *A BEAUTIFUL MIND*

A Brilliant Madness (2002) is the story of a mathematical genius, John Nash, whose career was cut short by a descent into madness. At the age of 30, Nash began claiming that aliens were communicating with him. He spent the next three decades fighting paranoid schizophrenia. Before this time, while he was a graduate student at Princeton, Nash wrote a proof about noncooperative equilibrium. The proof established the Nash equilibrium and became a foundation of modern economic theory. In 1994, Nash was awarded a Nobel Prize in Economics. The documentary features interviews with John Nash, his wife, his friends and colleagues, and experts in both economics and mental illness. Nash died in 2015.

The 2001 film *A Beautiful Mind*, directed by Ron Howard, is based on the life of Nash but does not adhere strictly to the facts. If you watch *A Brilliant Madness* and then watch the famous bar scene in *A Beautiful Mind*, you'll see that Ron Howard attempts to depict a Nash equilibrium when we see the men and women dancing together. *A Beautiful Mind* won the Academy Award for Best Picture, but the film's most famous scene is infamous among economists because it does not depict a Nash equilibrium. If you are curious about why this is the case, read the spoiler in the conclusion of this chapter.

Russell Crowe plays John Nash, who revolutionized modern microeconomics.

Incentives

dominant strategy for both firms. This produces a Nash equilibrium, where both firms make $26,250. This is the prisoner's dilemma: each firm has an incentive to lower its price to generate more revenue than if they had colluded and kept prices high, but acting on this incentive causes them both to earn less revenue than if they had kept prices high.

Unfortunately for the two firms, it's not just a matter of settling for $26,250 instead of $27,000, because the Nash equilibrium is only for the given payoff matrix. Once the possibility of dropping the price to $60 floats into view, there's a new payoff matrix in which $75 is the high price and $60 is the low price. Lather, rinse, repeat with the price war "shampoo," and pretty soon both firms are practically giving cell phone service away for free. At that point they're

FIGURE 13.2

	AT-Phone	
	High price: $90	**Low price:** $75
Horizon **High price:** $90	$27,000 revenue $27,000 revenue	$52,500 revenue $0 revenue
Low price: $75	$0 revenue $52,500 revenue	$26,250 revenue $26,250 revenue

The Prisoner's Dilemma in Duopoly

Each company has a dominant strategy to serve more customers by lowering its price. But when both firms pursue that strategy, they end up in a Nash equilibrium where both firms are worse off than if they'd both chosen differently. They earn just $26,250, when $27,000 was seemingly within reach.

really, really wishing they'd figured out how to operate as a cartel and both earn $27,000, instead.

Advertising and Game Theory

We have seen that oligopolists function like monopolistic competitors in that they sell differentiated products. We know that advertising is commonplace in markets with a differentiated product. In the case of an oligopoly, mutual interdependence means that advertising can create a contest between firms trying to gain customers. The result may be skyrocketing advertising budgets and little, or no, net gain of customers. Therefore, oligopolists have an incentive to scale back their advertising, but only if their rivals also agree to scale back. Like all cooperative action among competitors, this is easier said than done.

Figure 13.3 highlights the advertising choices of Coca-Cola and PepsiCo, two fierce rivals in the soft-drink industry. Together, Coca-Cola and PepsiCo account for 72% of the soft-drink market, with Coca-Cola being the slightly larger of the two firms. Both companies are known for their advertising campaigns, which cost hundreds of millions of dollars. To determine if they gain anything by spending so much on advertising, let's look at the dominant strategy. In the absence of cooperation, each firm will choose to advertise, because the payoffs under advertising ($100 million or $150 million) exceed those of not advertising ($75 million or $125 million). When each firm chooses to advertise, it generates a profit of $100 million. This is a second-best outcome

Incentives

Prisoner's Dilemma

WHY DO SUPERHEROES FIGHT?

The movie *Captain America: Civil War* (2016) features a common comic trope: two groups of heroes end up fighting each other. After a superhero mishap results in the deaths of hundreds of people, the public demands that the government regulate the conduct of those with superpowers. Iron Man agrees with having the Avengers put under government control, while Captain America does not. The two heroes reach a stalemate, and they start to recruit members of the hero fraternity to their respective sides. Eventually Iron Man tries to bring Captain America in, and an epic battle ensues.

It's all very dramatic—but what is going on here? These are heroes, after all. Why would they fight each other, when there are so many villains to worry about? Many of the heroes are indeed concerned that fighting each other sends a bad message. And of course any battle where the fighters have superpowers is liable to result in a lot of civilian casualties. Nevertheless, the two sides lurch pell-mell into a messy (but of course highly watchable) confrontation.

While this seems like an outrageous outcome, fit only for the comics, there is a perfectly good economic explanation for this faceoff between two of Marvel's great protagonists: it's a prisoner's dilemma. In the payoff matrix, the dominant strategy is to fight. While we might like to see the two sides sit down and hash out their differences, each of them gets a bigger payoff for digging in their heels. The largest joint payoff (the combined benefit to both sides) occurs when both sides talk things out, but if one side decides to fight while the other side opts for peaceful talk, the "fight" side can get everything it wants, without compromising. These are the payoffs in the upper right and lower left boxes. Because

If you were a superhero, would you rather fight or talk it out?

the dominant strategy is to fight, the parties end up in the lower right box, even though the joint payoff is lowest there. Now it's time for civilians to head indoors and stay there, because things are about to get ugly.

		Captain America	
		Talk it out	Fight for what you believe
Iron Man	**Talk it out**	4 4	6 1
	Fight for what you believe	1 6	2 2

Why is there an Avengers Civil War? Or for that matter, why is it Batman versus Superman? The answer isn't that the comic characters are irrational, or are being blackmailed, or even that someone is controlling their minds. The answer is that they are in a prisoner's dilemma.

FIGURE 13.3

	Coca-Cola	
	Advertises	Does not advertise
PepsiCo Advertises	$100 million profit $100 million profit	$75 million profit $150 million profit
Does not advertise	$150 million profit $75 million profit	$125 million profit $125 million profit

The Prisoner's Dilemma and Advertising

The two companies each have a dominant strategy to advertise. We can see this strategy by observing that Coca-Cola and PepsiCo each make $25 million more profit by choosing to advertise. As a result, they both end up in the upper left box earning $100 million profit when they could have each made $125 million profit in the lower right box if they had agreed not to advertise.

compared with the $125 million profit each could earn if neither firm advertises. The dilemma is that each firm needs to advertise to market its product and retain its customer base, but most advertising expenditures end up canceling each other out and costing the companies millions of dollars.

ECONOMICS IN THE REAL WORLD

THE COLD WAR

The idea that companies benefit from spending less on advertising has an analogue in warfare. Countries benefit from a "peace dividend" whenever war ends. There is no better example than the Cold War between the Soviet Union and the United States that began in the 1950s. By the time the Cold War ended in the late 1980s, both countries had amassed thousands of nuclear warheads in an effort to deter aggression.

This buildup put enormous economic pressure on each country to keep up with the other. During the height of the Cold War, each country found itself in a prisoner's dilemma in which spending more in an arms race was the dominant strategy. When the Soviet Union ultimately dissolved, the United States was able to spend less money on deterrence. In the post–Cold War world of the 1990s, the U.S. military budget fell from 6.5% to 3.5% of gross domestic product (GDP) as the nation reaped a peace dividend. However, with China now aggressively upgrading its navy and the associated ability to project air power, and with Russia sinking money into advanced submarine technology, we may be sliding back into the same dynamic, this time with three players.

The Cold War created a prisoner's dilemma for the United States and the Soviet Union.

nes in the Prisoner's Dilemma

rlines and Delta Airlines once found themselves in a classic prisoner's dilemma. It all started when
to expand its share of the lucrative Dallas-to-Chicago route, where American was the dominant
a offered a substantial fare cut on that route to attract new travelers. American threatened a price
ng its own fare cut on the Delta-dominated Dallas-to-Atlanta route.

es had a dominant strategy to cut their
targeted route. Why? If one airline cut its
the other did not, the airline that did
a large profit ($100,000) while the other
large loss (-$200,000). This was each
irline's best possible outcome.

Even if the rival cut its fare too, lowering the
price was still the right move—the dominant
strategy—for each airline. Why? Because
if an airline failed to match the fare of its rival,
it would make less profit than before.

AMERICAN

	DISCOUNT	NO DISCOUNT
DISCOUNT	-$100,000 / -$100,000	-$200,000 / $100,000
NO DISCOUNT	$100,000 / -$200,000	$50,000 / $50,000

Chicago

Dallas

Atlanta

k of a prisoner's dilemma is when two
their dominant strategy and the result is
result for both. It would have been better
counts were ever considered.

ned? Fortunately for both airlines, they
planned fare cuts on a computer system
them to see what their rival was doing.
w the price war starting, backed down,
the prisoner's dilemma!

REVIEW QUESTIONS

- Which expected outcome in the matrix
  reflects the outcome of this American/Delta
  pricing war?

- Explain how the ability to communicate
  can allow two parties to escape a prisoner's
  dilemma.

Escaping the Prisoner's Dilemma in the Long Run

We have seen how game theory can be a useful tool for understanding strategic decision-making in noncooperative environments. However, the dominant strategy does not consider the possible long-run benefits of cooperation.

Game theorist Robert Axelrod decided to examine the choices participants make in a long-run setting. He ran a sophisticated computer simulation in which he invited scholars to submit strategies for securing points in a prisoner's dilemma tournament over many rounds. All the submissions were collected and paired, and the results were scored. After each simulation, Axelrod eliminated the weakest strategy and reran the tournament with the remaining strategies. This evolutionary approach continued until the best strategy remained. Among all strategies, including those that were solely cooperative or noncooperative, **tit-for-tat** dominated. **Tit-for-tat** is a long-run strategy that promotes cooperation among participants by mimicking the opponent's most recent decision with repayment in kind. As the name implies, a tit-for-tat strategy is one in which you do whatever your opponent does. If your opponent breaks the agreement, you break the agreement, too. If the opponent behaves properly, then you behave properly, too.

Because the joint payoffs for cooperation are high in a prisoner's dilemma, tit-for-tat begins with the players cooperating. In subsequent rounds, the tit-for-tat strategy mimics whatever the other player did in the previous round. The genius behind tit-for-tat is that it changes the incentives and encourages cooperation. Turning back to our example in Figure 13.3, suppose that Coca-Cola and PepsiCo want to save on advertising expenses. The companies expect to have repeated interactions, so they both know from past experience that any effort to start a new advertising campaign will be immediately countered by the other firm. Because the companies react to each other's moves in kind, any effort to exploit the dominant strategy of advertising will ultimately fail. This dynamic can alter the incentives the firms face in the long run and lead to mutually beneficial behavior.

Tit-for-tat
is a long-run strategy that promotes cooperation among participants by mimicking the opponent's most recent decision with repayment in kind.

Incentives

The Long-Run Benefits of Cooperation

THE EVOLUTION OF TRUST

Designer Nicky Case (a member of Forbes' "30 under 30" list for Games development) created an interactive simulation (https://ncase.me/trust/) based on Robert Axelrod's groundbreaking 1984 book, *The Evolution of Cooperation*. When you play the simulation, you encounter a variety of strategies that you might deploy in the repeated prisoner's dilemma.

In the repeated version of the game, it's important that neither player knows when the last round is. Why? If the players knew, then in the last round they would both definitely cheat, since there'd be no later rounds to worry about. But then by backward induction, each player should cheat in the second-last round, as well, since there will be no effect on the other player's choice in the last round. This logic continues until both players simply decide to cheat in the first round. That's a pretty depressing outcome, but it's not what Axelrod found in the long run with an unknown stopping point. Instead, he found that tit-for-tat did better than all other approaches. To observe Axelrod's

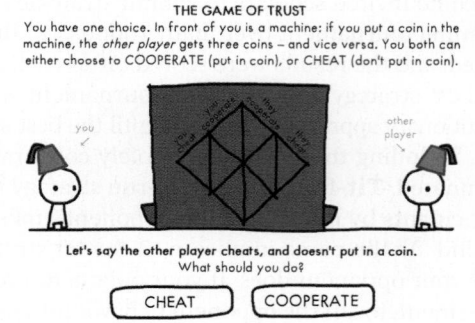

THE GAME OF TRUST
You have one choice. In front of you is a machine: if you put a coin in the machine, the *other player* gets three coins — and vice versa. You both can either choose to COOPERATE (put in coin), or CHEAT (don't put in coin).

Let's say the other player cheats, and doesn't put in a coin. What should you do?

[CHEAT] [COOPERATE]

Should your strategy be "copycat," "all cheat," "all cooperate," "grudger," or "detective"? Find out by trying the simulation!

result, Case has you play against five different strategies to show which are the most effective at creating cooperative outcomes. The entire simulation takes about thirty minutes to play—give it a try!

Tit-for-tat makes it less desirable to advertise by eliminating the long-run benefits. Advertising is still a dominant strategy in the short run because the payoffs with advertising ($100 million or $150 million) exceed those of not advertising ($75 million or $125 million). In the short run, the firm that advertises could earn $25 million extra, but in every subsequent round—if the rival responds in kind—the firm should expect profits of $100 million because its rival will also be advertising. As a result, there is a large long-run opportunity cost for not cooperating. If one firm stops advertising and the other follows suit, they will each find themselves making $125 million in the long run. Why hasn't this outcome happened in the real world? Because Coke and Pepsi don't trust each other enough to earn the dividend that comes from an advertising truce.

The prisoner's dilemma nicely captures why cooperation is so difficult in the short run. But most interactions in life occur over the long run. For example, scam artists and sketchy companies take advantage of short-run opportunities that cannot last because relationships in the long run—with businesses and with people—involve mutual trust. Cooperation is the default because you know that the other side is invested in the relationship. Under these circumstances, the tit-for-tat strategy works well.

Opportunity cost

Sequential Games

Not all games involve simultaneous decisions. Sometimes one player must move first and then the other player responds to the first move. In this case it is possible for the first player to utilize **backward induction** to get the best possible result. Backward induction in game theory is the process of deducing backward from the end of a scenario to infer a sequence of optimal actions.

To help visualize this situation, look at Figure 13.4. The payoff matrix summarizes the payoffs that Iggy and Azalea face in a noncooperative game. Neither Iggy nor Azalea has a dominant strategy, so it is impossible to predict what the final outcome will be.

However, if we let one player go first, the game has a predictable conclusion. To see this process at work, look at Figure 13.5. This type of diagram is known as a **decision tree**; it illustrates all of the possible outcomes in a sequential game. Let's imagine that Azalea goes first and Iggy chooses second.

In a sequential game, the first player can restrict the set of outcomes to one of the branches at the top of the decision tree. When Azalea chooses Agree, Iggy works off the lower left set of branches and must choose between making $20,000 if she agrees or $75,000 if she disagrees. Of course, Iggy chooses to disagree. In this case, the final outcome is $50,000 for Azalea and $75,000 for Iggy. If Azalea instead chose Disagree to start, Iggy would be faced with the payoffs on the lower right side of the decision tree. Here, Iggy would get $50,000 if she agrees and $25,000 if she disagrees,

Backward induction
in game theory is the process of deducing backward from the end of a scenario to infer a sequence of optimal actions.

A **decision tree** illustrates all of the possible outcomes in a sequential game.

FIGURE 13.4

To Cooperate or Not

Iggy and Azalea do not have dominant strategies, so the outcome of this game cannot be determined.

		Iggy		
		Agree		Disagree
	Agree		$20,000		$75,000
		$60,000		$50,000	
Azalea	Disagree		$50,000		$25,000
		$35,000		$75,000	

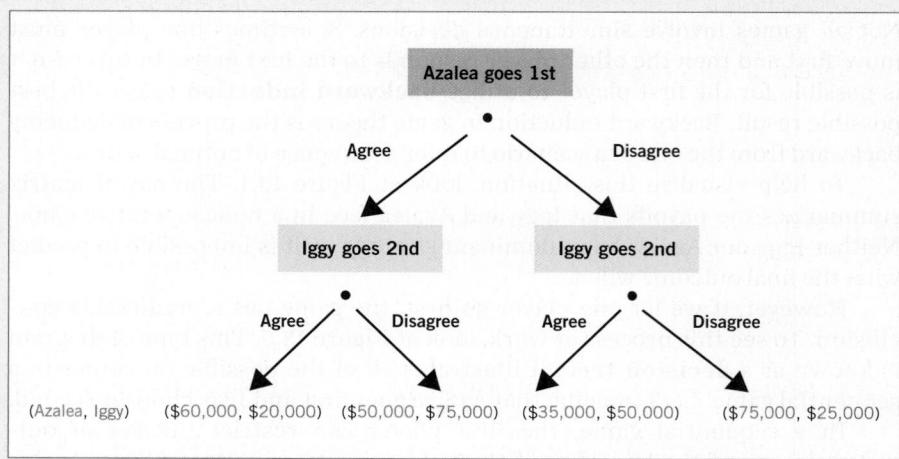

FIGURE 13.5

Decision Tree for a Sequential Game

Azalea will agree, knowing that Iggy will disagree. This game guarantees Azalea $50,000 and Iggy $75,000.

Azalea goes 1st

Agree — Disagree

Iggy goes 2nd   Iggy goes 2nd

Agree — Disagree   Agree — Disagree

(Azalea, Iggy)   ($60,000, $20,000)   ($50,000, $75,000)   ($35,000, $50,000)   ($75,000, $25,000)

so this time she agrees. Now the final outcome is $35,000 for Azalea and $50,000 for Iggy.

Because Azalea has full information about all of the payoffs in the matrix, she knows what Iggy will choose at the end of each set of branches. This knowledge allows her to use backward induction to earn $50,000 for herself by selecting Agree with the full knowledge that Iggy will choose Disagree.

There are many examples of sequential games in life. Chess and checkers are two popular board games that utilize backward induction. Likewise, many business decisions are also sequential in nature, and once a particular path is taken, it becomes easier to predict how future decisions will unfold. For instance, when a firm decides to launch a new advertising campaign, it is easier for the firm to predict how a rival will react by examining the remaining choices along a decision tree.

A Caution about Game Theory

Game theory is a decision-making tool, but not all games have dominant strategies that make player decisions easy to predict. Perhaps the best example is the game known as rock-paper-scissors. This simple game has no dominant strategy: paper beats rock (because the paper will cover the rock) and rock beats scissors (because the rock will break the scissors), but scissors beats paper (because the scissors will cut the paper). The preferred choice is strictly a function of what the other player selects. Many situations in life and business are more like rock-paper-scissors than the prisoner's dilemma. Winning at business in the long run often occurs because you are one step ahead of the competition, not because you deploy a strategy that attempts to take advantage of a short-run opportunity.

Consider two sisters who enjoy playing racquetball together. They are of equal ability, so each point comes down to whether a player guesses correctly about where the other player will hit the ball. Take a look at Figure 13.6. The

Rock-paper-scissors is a game without a dominant strategy.

Sequential Games

WHY DID RACHEL LET ELEANOR WIN A GAME OF MAHJONG?

In *Crazy Rich Asians* (2018), the lead character, Rachel, is an economics professor who teaches game theory at NYU, where her boyfriend, Nick, teaches history. After they've dated seriously for a year, Nick invites Rachel to Singapore to meet his crazy-rich family. Things do not go well. Nick's mother, Eleanor, wants to protect Nick from ending up with someone who, Eleanor thinks, is not right for Nick. The upshot is that Rachel and Eleanor end up in a prisoner's dilemma, making suboptimal decisions.

Rachel wants to keep Nick for herself because she earns either 2 or 5 "happiness points" playing that strategy, whereas giving Nick up brings her only 1 or 4 points. Eleanor's reasons for wanting to keep Nick for herself are exactly the same. As a result, there is a Nash equilibrium at (2, 2) in the upper left box.

The plot takes a remarkable turn when Rachel recognizes that she and Eleanor are stuck, and that if they remain at odds, neither of them will ever win. Ever the economist, Rachel decides to break the prisoner's dilemma by initiating a sequential game where she moves first, deliberately leaving herself vulnerable if Eleanor continues to play the dominant strategy.

An inspired scene where the two play mahjong sets the stage. As the game unfolds, Rachel lets Eleanor know that Nick has proposed to her earlier but Rachel did not accept. She goes on to explain that she knows Nick would never really be happy if he had to leave his family to be with her. Rachel then lays down a tile that Eleanor picks up in order to win the mahjong game. After Rachel finishes explaining her decision, she stands up and reveals all her tiles. The tile she gave Eleanor would have won Rachel the game. Rachel has communicated to Eleanor that she could have accepted Nick's proposal, but she respects Eleanor in her role as family matriarch enough to sacrifice for Nick's good. Rachel's strategic gesture, proving that she was willing to bend for the sake of family, breaks the cycle of mistrust and prompts Eleanor to bless the marriage.

We see the result of Rachel's actions in the following decision tree and payoff matrix.

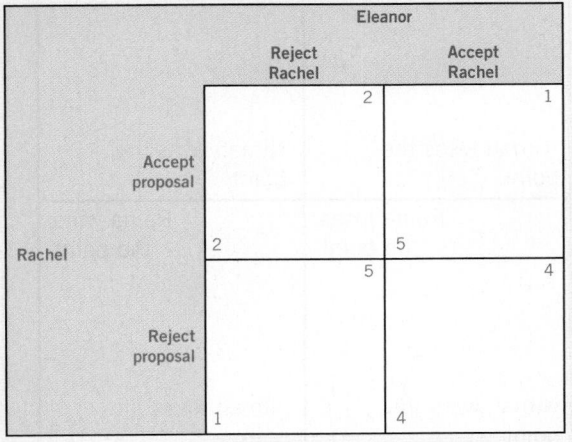

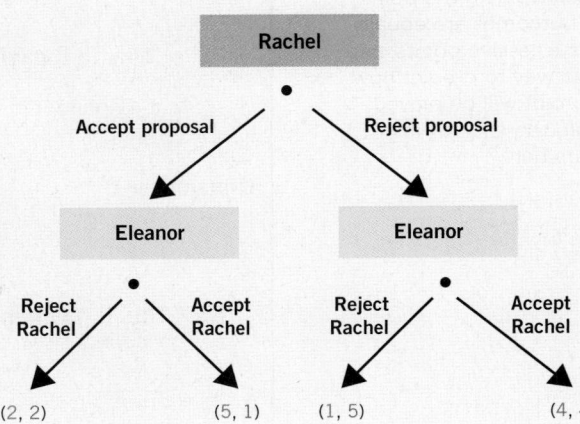

By saying no to Nick's proposal, Rachel has made Eleanor's choice simpler: she will gain either 5 or 4. She can still choose the 5 outcome, but Rachel has given her a very powerful reason to accept the (4, 4) outcome. Rachel makes one last statement before leaving: "So, I just wanted you to know that one day, when he marries another lucky girl who is enough for you . . . that it was because of me . . . a poor, raised-by-a-single-mother, low-class, immigrant nobody." Soon after, Eleanor understands that Rachel guaranteed her at least a 4, when Rachel could have chosen to say yes, and Eleanor would have earned no more than 2. This prompts Eleanor to reject the short-run dominant strategy and choose Rachel as her daughter-in-law. From that point forward, they are entering a long-run cooperative equilibrium, and (4, 4) maximizes their joint welfare by maximizing the sum of all payouts!

Good luck beating a game theorist at Mahjong!

FIGURE 13.6

No Dominant Strategy Exists

Neither Raina nor Nimah has a dominant strategy that guarantees winning the point. The four outcomes are equally likely on successive points, and there is no way to predict how the next point will be played. As a result, there is no Nash equilibrium here.

		Raina	
		Guesses to the left	**Guesses to the right**
Nimah	**Hits to the left**	Raina wins the point Nimah loses the point	Raina loses the point Nimah wins the point
	Hits to the right	Raina loses the point Nimah wins the point	Raina wins the point Nimah loses the point

success of Nimah and Raina depends on how well each one guesses where the other one will hit the ball.

In this competition, neither Raina nor Nimah has a dominant strategy that guarantees success. Sometimes Nimah wins when hitting to the right; at other times she loses the point. Sometimes Raina wins when she guesses to the left; at other times she loses. Each player guesses correctly only half the time. Because we cannot say what each player will do from one point to another, there is no Nash equilibrium. Any of the four outcomes are equally likely on successive points, and there is no way to predict how the next point will be played. In other words, we cannot expect every game to include a prisoner's dilemma and produce a Nash equilibrium. Game theory, like real life, has many different possible outcomes.

How Do Government Policies Affect Oligopoly Behavior?

When oligopolists in an industry form a cooperative alliance, they function like a monopoly. Competition disappears, which is not good for society. One way to improve the social welfare of society is to restore competition and limit monopoly practices through policy legislation.

Antitrust Policy

Efforts to curtail the adverse consequences of oligopolistic cooperation began with the **Sherman Antitrust Act** of 1890, the first federal law to place limits on cartels and monopolies. The Sherman Act was created in response to the increase in concentration ratios in many leading U.S. industries, including steel, railroads, mining, textiles, and oil. Prior to passage of the Sherman Act, firms were free to pursue contracts that created mutually beneficial outcomes. Once the act took effect, however, certain cooperative actions became criminal. Section 2 of the Sherman Act reads, "Every person who shall monopolize, or attempt to monopolize, or combine or conspire with any other person or persons, to monopolize any part of the trade or commerce among the several States, or with foreign nations, shall be deemed guilty of a felony."

The **Clayton Act** of 1914 targets corporate behaviors that reduce competition. Large corporations had been vilified during the presidential election of 1912, and the Sherman Act was seen as largely ineffective in curbing monopoly power. To strengthen antitrust policy, the Clayton Act added to the list of activities deemed socially detrimental, including:

1. *price discrimination* if it lessens competition or creates monopoly
2. *exclusive dealings* that restrict a buyer's ability to deal with competitors
3. *tying arrangements* that require the buyer to purchase an additional product in order to purchase the first
4. *mergers and acquisitions* that lessen competition, or situations in which a person serves as a director on more than one board in the same industry

As the Clayton Act makes clear, there are many ways to reduce competition.

The **Sherman Antitrust Act** (1890) was the first federal law limiting cartels and monopolies.

The **Clayton Act** (1914) targets corporate behaviors that reduce competition.

Dominant Strategy: To Advertise or Not—That Is the Question!

How much should a sandwich shop in a small college town charge for this sandwich?

QUESTION: University Subs and Savory Sandwiches are the only two sandwich shops in a small college town. If neither runs a special 2-for-1 promotion, both are able to keep their prices high and earn $10,000 a month. However, when both run promotions, their profits fall to $1,000. Finally, if one runs a promotion and the other does not, the shop that runs the promotion earns a profit of $15,000 and the other loses $5,000. What is the dominant strategy for University Subs? Is there a Nash equilibrium in this example?

ANSWER:

If University Subs runs the 2-for-1 promotion, it will make either $1,000 or $15,000, depending on its rival's actions. If University Subs keeps the price high, it will either lose $5,000 or make $10,000, depending on what Savory Sandwiches does. Suppose that Savory Sandwiches decides to run a 2-for-1 promotion. In this case, University Subs's best response is also to run a 2-for-1 promotion because $1,000 > −$5,000. Now imagine that Savory Subs uses the strategy of keeping the price high. University Subs's best response remains running the 2-for-1 promotion because $15,000 > $10,000. So regardless of what Savory Subs does, University Subs's best response—and therefore its dominant strategy—is to run a 2-for-1 promotion. Savory Sandwiches has the same dominant strategy and the same payoffs. Therefore, both companies will run the promotion and each will make $1,000. Neither firm has a reason to switch to the high-price strategy because one would lose $5,000 if the other company runs the 2-for-1 promotion. A Nash equilibrium occurs when both companies run the promotion.

	University Subs	
	Runs a 2-for-1 promotion	**Keeps price high**
Savory Sandwiches — Runs a 2-for-1 promotion	Makes $1,000 / Makes $1,000	Loses $5,000 / Makes $15,000
Keeps price high	Makes $15,000 / Loses $5,000	Makes $10,000 / Makes $10,000

Over the past hundred years, lawmakers have continued to refine antitrust policy. Additional legislation along with court interpretations of existing antitrust law have made it difficult to determine whether a company has violated the law. The U.S. Justice Department is charged with oversight, but it often lacks the resources to fully investigate every case. Antitrust law is complex, and cases are hard to prosecute, but these laws are essential to maintaining a competitive business environment. Without effective restraints on excessive market power, firms would organize into cartels more often or would find other ways to restrict competition. Table 13.5 briefly describes the most influential antitrust cases in history.

TABLE 13.5

Influential Antitrust Cases in History

Defendant	Year	Description
Standard Oil	1911	Standard Oil was founded in 1870. By 1897, the company had driven the price of oil down to 6 cents a gallon, which put many of its competitors out of business. Subsequently, Standard Oil became the largest company in the world. In 1906, the U.S. government filed suit against Standard Oil for violating the Sherman Antitrust Act. Three years later, the company was found guilty and forced to break up into 34 independent companies.
ALCOA	1944	The Aluminum Company of America (ALCOA), founded in 1907, maintained its position as the only producer of aluminum in the United States for many years. To keep that position, the company acquired exclusive rights to all U.S. sources of bauxite, the base material from which aluminum is refined. It then acquired land rights to build and own hydroelectric facilities in both the United States and Canada. By owning both the base materials and the only sites where refinement could take place, ALCOA effectively barred other firms from entering the U.S. aluminum market. In 1937, the Department of Justice filed suit against ALCOA. Seven years later, the Supreme Court ruled that ALCOA had taken measures to restrict trade and functioned as a monopoly. ALCOA was not broken apart because two rivals, Kaiser and Reynolds, emerged soon after.
AT&T	1982	In 1974, the U.S. Attorney General filed suit against AT&T for violating antitrust laws. It took seven years before a settlement was reached to split the company into seven new companies, each serving a different region of the United States. However, five of the seven have since merged to become AT&T Incorporated, which is now one of the largest companies in the world.
Microsoft	2001	When Internet Explorer was introduced in 1995, Microsoft insisted that it was a feature rather than a new Windows product. The U.S. Department of Justice did not agree and filed suit against Microsoft for illegally discouraging competition to protect its software monopoly. The government argued that Microsoft leveraged its monopoly power from the operating systems market into the browser market by strong-arming personal computer manufacturers like Dell into favoring Internet Explorer over Netscape. After a series of court decisions and appeals, a settlement ordered Microsoft to share application programming interfaces with third-party companies. Today, Internet Explorer has largely been replaced by Chrome and Firefox.
Google	2015	The European Union began investigating whether Google used its dominant market share as a search engine to gain an unfair advantage over competitors. After a lengthy investigation, the EU fined Google $2.8 billion in 2017 for diverting traffic away from search results that favored its rivals and toward results that favored Google's own products. As of 2019, Google remains the search engine of choice in 92% of all searches in Europe, and competitors continue to press for additional sanctions.

Predatory Pricing

Predatory pricing
occurs when firms deliberately set their prices below average variable costs with the intent of driving rivals out of the market.

While firms have a strong incentive to cooperate in order to keep prices high, they also want to keep potential rivals out of the market. **Predatory pricing** is the practice of setting prices deliberately below average variable costs with the intent of driving rivals out of the market. The firm suffers a short-run loss in order to prevent rivals from entering the market or to drive rival firms out of business in the long run. Once the rivals are gone, the firm should be able to act like a monopolist.

Predatory pricing is illegal, but it is difficult to prosecute. Neither the court system nor economists have a simple rule that helps to determine when a firm steps over the line. Predatory pricing can look and feel like spirited competition. Moreover, the concern is not the competitive aspect or lower prices, but the effect on the market when all rivals fail. To prove that predatory pricing has occurred, the courts need evidence that the firm's prices increased significantly after its rivals failed.

Walmart is often cited as a firm that engages in predatory pricing because its low prices effectively drive many smaller companies out of business. However, there is no evidence that Walmart has ever systematically raised prices after a rival failed. Therefore, its price strategy does not meet the legal standard for predatory pricing. Similarly, Microsoft came under intense scrutiny

Because Walmart keeps its prices low, there is no evidence that it engages in predatory pricing.

in the 1990s for giving away its browser, Internet Explorer, in order to undercut Netscape, which also ended up giving away its browser. Microsoft understood that the key to its long-term success was the dominance of the Windows platform. Bundling Internet Explorer with Microsoft Office enabled the company not only to gain over 80% of the browser market but also to keep its leadership with the Windows operating system. Eventually, Microsoft was prosecuted by the government—but not for predatory pricing, which could not be proved because Microsoft never significantly raised the price of Internet Explorer. Instead, the government prosecuted Microsoft for tying the purchase of

PRACTICE WHAT YOU KNOW

Predatory Pricing: Price Wars

Predatory pricing? Check out the competing signs in the photo!

You've undoubtedly encountered a price war at some point. It could be two gas stations, clothing outlets, or restaurants charging prices that seem unbelievably low.

QUESTION: Is a price war between two adjacent pizza restaurants evidence of predatory pricing?

ANSWER: One essential element for proving predatory pricing is evidence of the intent to raise prices after others are driven out of business. That is a problem in this example. Suppose one of the pizza places closes. The remaining firm could then raise its price substantially. But barriers to entry in the restaurant industry are low in most metropolitan areas, so any efforts to maintain high prices for long will fail. Customers will vote with their feet and wallets by choosing another pizza place a little farther away that offers a better value. Or a new competitor will sense that the victor is vulnerable because of the high prices and will open a new pizza parlor nearby. Either way, the market is monopolistically competitive, so any market power created by driving out one rival will be fleeting.

The aggressive price war is not evidence of predatory pricing. Instead, it is probably just promotional pricing to protect market share. Firms often price some items below their variable costs to attract customers. These firms hope to make up the difference and then some with high profit margins on other items, such as beverages and side dishes.

Internet Explorer to the Windows operating system in order to restrict competition. The Microsoft case lasted over four years, and it ended in a settlement that placed restrictions on the firm's business practices.

What Are Network Externalities?

We end this chapter by considering a special kind of externality that often occurs in oligopoly. A **network externality** occurs when the number of customers who purchase or use a good influences the demand. When a network externality exists, firms with many customers often find it easier to attract new customers and to keep their regular customers from switching to other rivals. In the early days of social networking, for example, MySpace had many more users than Facebook. How did Facebook gain over 2.2 billion users when it had to play catch-up? Facebook built a better social network, and MySpace was slow to respond to the threat. By the time MySpace did respond, it was too late: Facebook was on its way. Now the tables are turned, as Facebook is the dominant social networking platform. Moreover, among most demographics, the sheer size of Facebook makes it a better place to do social networking than Google+, Twitter, or LinkedIn. However, even though Facebook now enjoys significant network externalities, it must be mindful to keep innovating or else it might end up forgotten like MySpace.

Most network externalities involve the introduction of new technologies. For instance, some technologies need to reach a critical mass before consumers can effectively use them. Consider that today everyone seems to have a cell phone. However, when cell phones were introduced in the United States in 1983, coverage was quite limited. The first users could not surf the Internet, roam, text, or use many of the applications we enjoy today. Moreover, the phones were large and bulky. How did we get from that situation in 1983 to today? As additional people bought cell phones, networks expanded and manufacturers and telephone companies responded by building more cell towers and offering better phones. The expansion of networks brought more users, and the new adopters benefited from the steadily expanding customer base.

Other technologies have gone through similar transformations. The Internet, fax machines, and apps all depend on the number of users. If you were the only person on the Internet or the only person with the ability to send and receive a fax, your technical capacity would have little value. In a world with ever-changing technology, first adopters pave the way for the next generation of users.

In addition to the advantages of forming a larger network, customers may face significant switching costs if they leave. **Switching costs** are the

A **network externality** occurs when the number of customers who purchase or use a product influences the quantity demanded.

Switching costs are the costs incurred when a consumer changes from one supplier to another.

Users of the first-generation cell phone, the Motorola DynaTAC 8000X, created a positive network externality for future users.

costs incurred when a consumer changes from one supplier to another. For instance, the transition from listening to music on CDs to using digital music files involved a substantial switching cost for many users. Today, there are switching costs among the many digital music options. Once a consumer has established a library of MP3s or uses iTunes, the switching costs of transferring the music from one format to another create a significant barrier to change. When consumers face switching costs, the demand for the existing product becomes more inelastic. As a result, oligopolists not only leverage the number of customers they maintain in their network, but also try to make switching to another network more difficult. For instance, firms promote customer loyalty through frequent flier benefits, hotel reward points, and credit card reward programs to create higher switching costs.

An excellent example of the costs of switching are the costs associated with cell phone services. Contract termination fees apply to many cell phone agreements if the contract is broken. This tactic creates high switching costs for many cell phone customers. To reduce switching costs, the Federal Communications Commission in 2003 began requiring that phone companies allow customers to take their cell phone numbers with them when they change to a different provider. This change in the law has reduced the costs of switching from one provider to another and has made the cell phone market more competitive.

PRACTICE WHAT YOU KNOW

Examples of Network Externalities

Does Netflix benefit from network externalities?

QUESTION: In which two of these examples are network externalities important?

a. college alumni

b. Netflix

c. a local bakery that sells fresh bread

ANSWERS:

a. Colleges and universities with more alumni are able to raise funds more easily than smaller schools, so the size of the alumni network matters. The number of alumni also matters when graduates look for jobs, because alumni are often inclined to hire individuals who went to the same school. For example, Penn State University has the nation's largest alumni base. This means that each PSU graduate benefits from network externalities.

b. Netflix's size enables it to offer a vast array of DVDs, downloads, and streaming video. If it were smaller, Netflix would be unable to make as many obscure titles available. This means that Netflix customers benefit from network externalities by having more DVDs to choose from.

c. The local bakery is a small company. If it attracts more customers, each one will have to compete harder to get fresh bread. Because the bakery's supply of bread is limited, additional customers create congestion, and network externalities do not exist.

Oligopolists are keenly aware of the power of network externalities. As new markets develop, the first firm into an industry often gains a large customer base. When there are positive network externalities, the customer base enables the firm to grow quickly. In addition, consumers are often more comfortable purchasing from an established firm. These two factors favor the formation of large firms and make it difficult for smaller competitors to gain customers. As a result, the presence of significant positive network externalities causes small firms to be driven out of business or forces them to merge with larger competitors.

////// ECONOMICS IN THE REAL WORLD //////

NEW YORK CITY TAXIS

In 1932, during the depths of the Great Depression, New York City decided to license taxicabs. The goal was to standardize fares, operating procedures, and safety requirements. At that time, a taxicab license, or medallion, was available at no cost. Today, if you find one on the resale market, it costs around $200,000. That's a lot of money, but medallion prices peaked in 2013 at over $1,000,000! How did prices get so high, and why have they fallen so much? Let's find out.

The city did not intend to create an artificial oligopoly but that's what happened. From 1932 until the 1990s, the number of medallions, which represents the supply of taxis, was fixed at approximately 12,000. During the same 60-year period, population growth and an increase in tourism caused the demand for taxi services to rise steeply. The number of medallions would have had to quadruple to keep up with demand.

Medallion holders made huge profits and successfully lobbied the city to keep the supply of medallions low. Imagine what would happen if the city lifted restrictions on the number of available medallions and gave them out to any qualified applicant. Applications for licenses would increase, and profits for cab drivers and cab companies would fall until quantity supplied equalled quantity demanded. Conversely, if taxicab drivers experienced economic losses, the number of taxis operating would decline until the losses disappeared.

The medallion oligopoly worked effectively, until ridesharing came along. In 2012 it became possible to grab a ride without using a taxi. As ridesharing has caught on, the prices of the medallions have plummeted. Therefore, it is not surprising that medallion holders seek to keep the number of medallions as low as possible and to keep out Uber, Lyft, and other rivals. Because oligopolists make profits by charging higher prices than firms in competitive markets do, no one who already has a medallion wants the supply to expand.

Despite medallion owners' efforts to restrict the supply, ridesharing companies are having a big impact in the medallion market. The added competition has driven down medallion prices to $200,000 today.

Conclusion

Firms in oligopoly markets can compete or collude to create monopoly conditions. The result is often hard to predict. In many cases, the presence of a dominant short-run strategy causes firms to compete on price and advertising even though doing so yields a lower economic profit. In contrast, the potential success of a tit-for-tat strategy suggests that oligopolistic firms are capable of cooperating to jointly maximize their long-run profits. Whether oligopoly mirrors the result found in monopolistic competition or monopoly matters a

How Oligopolies Shape Our Lives as Consumers

- The rate at which new businesses are created has been steadily falling since the 1970s.
- Vertical integration allows a firm to exert enormous control over the prices consumers pay.
- Heavily consolidated industries can lose the incentive to innovate.

Who do you trust to tell you the truth? Jim Cramer or John Oliver?

Oligopolies are big business, and they shape our lives in many ways. HBO's John Oliver has a really informative and funny take on corporate consolidation on his show *Last Week Tonight* (stream this on YouTube). Oliver points out many of the features of oligopoly that are potentially problematic for consumers, but he also gives some screen time to Jim Cramer, a well-known pro-business personality. Watching this video will make you think about how consolidation plays a key role in a wide range of industries—everything from air travel to eyewear to beer.

Here are some ways corporate consolidation is shaping our lives:

- The rate at which new businesses are created has been steadily falling since the 1970s, and one reason for that is that big businesses are becoming more consolidated.
- Some brands you might think are indie, like Burt's Bees, Tom's deodorant, and Goose Island beer, are actually run by large corporations.

- Airline industry consolidation has allowed firms to raise $4.2 billion in ancillary fees for additional baggage, seat assignments, and priority check-in.
- In the eyewear industry, most of the name-brand frames (e.g., Prada, Dolce & Gabbana, Burberry, and Ralph Lauren) are manufactured by the same firm, Luxottica, which also owns most of the eyewear retailers (Pearle, Lens Crafters, Sunglass Hut, and Target Optical). This level of vertical integration allows Luxottica to exert enormous control over the prices consumers pay.
- Heavily consolidated industries can lose the incentive to innovate. (Think about your cable TV box and how antiquated the technology is!)

great deal because society's welfare is higher when more competition is present. Because oligopoly is not a market structure with a predictable outcome, each oligopolistic industry must be assessed on a case-by-case basis by examining data and utilizing game theory. For these reasons, the study of oligopoly is one of the most fascinating parts of the theory of the firm.

Revisiting *A Beautiful Mind*: Recall that a Nash equilibrium exists when all economic decision-makers opt to keep the status quo. In *A Beautiful Mind*, the famous bar scene is not a Nash equilibrium. If the most beautiful woman in the bar was without a dance partner, each of the gentlemen would have had an incentive to change his behavior and switch to her. ✴

Incentives

· ANSWERING *the* BIG QUESTIONS ·

What is oligopoly?

▪ Oligopoly is a type of market structure that exists when a small number of firms sell a differentiated product in a market with significant barriers to entry. An oligopolist is like a monopolistic competitor in that it sells differentiated products. It is like a monopolist in that it enjoys significant barriers to entry. The small number of sellers in oligopoly leads to mutual interdependence.

▪ Oligopolists have a tendency to collude and to form cartels in the hope of achieving monopoly-like profits.

▪ Oligopolistic markets are socially inefficient because price and marginal cost are not equal. The result under oligopoly falls somewhere between the competitive market and monopoly outcomes.

How does game theory explain strategic behavior?

▪ Game theory helps to determine when cooperation among oligopolists is most likely to occur. In many cases, cooperation fails to occur because decision-makers have dominant strategies that lead them to be uncooperative. As a result, firms compete with price or advertising when they could potentially earn more profit by curtailing these activities.

▪ Games become more complicated when they are played multiple times, so short-run dominant strategies often disappear. Whenever repeated interaction occurs, decision-makers fare better under tit-for-tat, an approach that maximizes the long-run profit.

How do government policies affect oligopoly behavior?

▪ Antitrust law is complex, and cases are hard to prosecute. Nevertheless, these laws are essential in providing oligopolistic firms an incentive to compete rather than collude.

▪ Antitrust policy limits price discrimination, exclusive dealings, tying arrangements, mergers and acquisitions that limit competition, and predatory pricing.

What are network externalities?

▪ A network externality occurs when the number of customers who purchase or use a good influences the quantity demanded. The presence of significant positive network externalities can cause small firms to go out of business.

· CHAPTER PROBLEMS ·

Concepts You Should Know

antitrust laws (p. 401)	game theory (p. 405)	price effect (p. 404)
backward induction (p. 415)	mutual interdependence (p. 402)	price leadership (p. 402)
cartel (p. 401)	Nash equilibrium (p. 407)	prisoner's dilemma (p. 406)
Clayton Act (p. 419)	network externality (p. 423)	Sherman Antitrust Act (p. 419)
collusion (p. 401)	oligopoly (p. 398)	switching costs (p. 423)
decision tree (p. 415)	output effect (p. 404)	tit-for-tat (p. 413)
dominant strategy (p. 407)	predatory pricing (p. 422)	

Questions for Review

1. Compare the price and output under oligopoly with that of monopoly and monopolistic competition.

2. How does the addition of another firm affect the ability of the firms in an oligopolistic industry to form an effective cartel?

3. What is predatory pricing?

4. How is game theory relevant to oligopoly? Does it help to explain monopoly? Give reasons for your response.

5. What does the prisoner's dilemma indicate about the longevity of collusive agreements?

6. What is a Nash equilibrium? How does it differ from a dominant strategy?

7. What practices do antitrust laws prohibit?

8. What are network externalities? Explain why network externalities matter to an oligopolist.

Study Problems (*solved at the end of this section)

1. Some places limit the number of hours that alcohol can be sold on Sunday. Is it possible that this sales restriction could help liquor stores? Use game theory to construct your answer. (**Hint:** Even without restrictions on the hours of operation, individual stores could still limit Sunday sales if they wanted to.)

2. Which of the following markets are oligopolistic?
   a. passenger airlines
   b. cereal
   c. fast food
   d. wheat
   e. golf equipment
   f. the college bookstore on your campus

✻ 3. Imagine that your roommate's alarm goes off at 4:30 every morning, and she hits snooze every 10 minutes until 6:00, when you both need to get up. She insists that this maddening procedure is the only way she is able to wake up. How would you respond? Is there a nonviolent way you can convince her to change her morning wake-up routine? (**Hint:** Think about a tit-for-tat strategy.)

4. After teaching a class on game theory, your instructor announces that if every student skips the last question on the next exam, everyone will receive full credit for that question. However, if one or more students answer the last question, all responses will be graded and those who skip the question will get a zero on that question. Will the entire class skip the last question? Explain your response.

5. For which of the following are network externalities important?
   a. gas stations
   b. American Association of Retired Persons (AARP)
   c. eHarmony, an Internet dating site

6. Your economics instructor is at it again (see question 4). This time, you have to do a two-student project. Assume that you and your partner

are both interested in maximizing your grade, but you are both very busy and would be happier if you could get a good grade with less work.

	Your partner	
	Work hard	**Work less hard**
You **Work hard**	Grade = A, but your partner had to work 10 hours. Happiness = 7/10.	Grade = A, and your partner only worked 5 hours. Happiness = 9/10.
	Grade = A, but you had to work 10 hours. Happiness = 7/10.	Grade = A, but you had to work 15 hours. Happiness = 4/10.
Work less hard	Grade = A, but your partner had to work 15 hours. Happiness = 4/10.	Grade = B, but your partner only worked 5 hours. Happiness = 6/10.
	Grade = A, and you only worked 5 hours. Happiness = 9/10.	Grade = B, but you only worked 5 hours. Happiness = 6/10.

a. What is your dominant strategy? Explain.
b. What is your partner's dominant strategy? Explain.
c. What is the Nash equilibrium in this situation? Explain.
d. If you and your partner are required to work together on a number of projects throughout the semester, how might this requirement change the outcome you predicted in parts (a), (b), and (c)?

7. Suppose that the marginal cost of mining gold is constant at $300 per ounce and the demand schedule is as follows:

Price (per oz.)	Quantity (oz.)
$1,000	1,000
900	2,000
800	3,000
700	4,000
600	5,000
500	6,000
400	7,000
300	8,000

a. If the number of suppliers is large, what would be the price and quantity?
b. If there is only one supplier, what would be the price and quantity?
c. If there are only two suppliers and they form a cartel, what would be the price and quantity?
d. Suppose that one of the two cartel members in part (c) decides to increase its production by 1,000 ounces while the other member keeps its production constant. What will happen to the revenues of both firms?

✷ 8. Trade agreements encourage countries to curtail tariffs (taxes on imports) so that goods may flow across international boundaries without restrictions. Using the following payoff matrix, determine the best policies for China and the United States.

		China	
		Low tariffs	**High tariffs**
United States **Low tariffs**		China gains $50 billion	China gains $100 billion
		U.S. gains $50 billion	U.S. gains $10 billion
High tariffs		China gains $10 billion	China gains $25 billion
		U.S. gains $100 billion	U.S. gains $25 billion

a. What is the dominant strategy for the United States?
b. What is the dominant strategy for China?
c. What is the Nash equilibrium for these two countries?
d. Suppose that the United States and China enter into a trade agreement that simultaneously lowers trade barriers in both countries. Is this agreement a good idea? Explain your response.

9. A small town has only one pizza place, The Pizza Factory. A small competitor, Perfect Pies, is thinking about entering the market. The profits of these two firms depend on whether Perfect Pies enters the market and whether The Pizza Factory—as a price leader—decides to set a high price or a low price. Use the payoff matrix below to answer the questions that follow.

		Perfect Pies	
		Enter	Stay out
The Pizza Factory	**High price**	Perfect Pies makes $10,000 The Pizza Factory makes $20,000	Perfect Pies makes $0 The Pizza Factory makes $50,000
	Low price	Perfect Pies loses $10,000 The Pizza Factory makes $10,000	Perfect Pies makes $0 The Pizza Factory makes $25,000

a. What is the dominant strategy of The Pizza Factory?

b. Does Perfect Pies have a dominant strategy?

c. What is the Nash equilibrium in this situation?

d. The combined profit for both firms is highest when The Pizza Factory sets a high price and Perfect Pies stays out of the market. If Perfect Pies enters the market, how will this entry affect the profits of The Pizza Factory? Would The Pizza Factory be willing to pay Perfect Pies not to enter the market? Explain.

10. Two brands of coffee makers, Keurig and Tassimo, are vying for the convenience market. Keurig is the market-share leader and has the largest variety of cups used to make coffees and teas. Tassimo makes a smaller machine that brews faster, but it lacks the variety of coffees and teas sold by Keurig. To complicate matters, Keurig and Tassimo users cannot easily switch from one manufacturer to the other, because the cups that each manufacturer uses are a different size. Which manufacturer is likely to dominate the market in the long run?

✴ 11. On the TV show *The Big Bang Theory*, the characters have an interesting way of resolving disputes. Watch the video at this link: www.youtube.com/watch?v=cSLeBKT7-sM. Is there a dominant strategy in rock-paper-scissors-lizard-Spock? Why do the guys always answer with Spock?

12. Most large banks charge the same or nearly the same interest rate. When market conditions require an adjustment, one of the major banks announces a change in its rate and other banks quickly follow suit. What model of oligopoly behavior explains why this happens?

✴ 13. Suppose that Muber is currently the only firm providing rideshares, but a second firm, Wyft, is considering entering the market. Prior to learning what Wyft will do, Muber must decide whether to make a costly investment to improve its own product. The decision tree for this game is diagrammed below, with the payoffs assumed to be the ones shown.

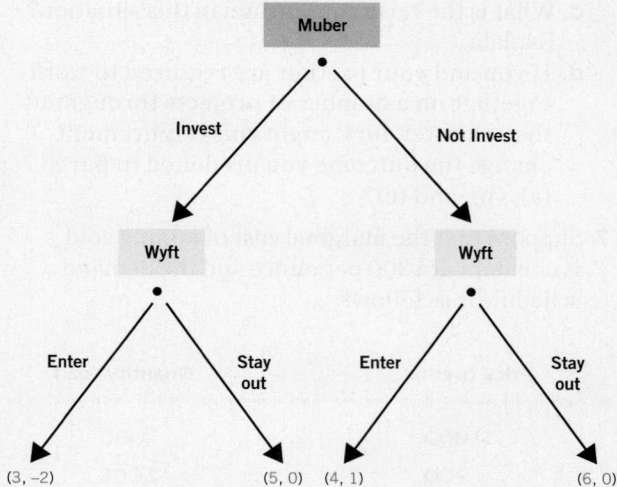

What is the equilibrium outcome of this game?

✴ 14. The owner of a small restaurant has one person who is responsible for keeping things clean throughout the day. Should the owner be more concerned that the restrooms are always clean, or the kitchen? Is there a dominant strategy?

Solved Problems

3. If your roommate does not wake up immediately, a tit-for-tat response would be for you to get up. Once up, you should turn on the lights, get dressed, and make enough noise that your roommate cannot easily sleep. If you use this approach, it won't take long for your roommate to realize that she should set the alarm for a more reasonable time and *not* hit the snooze button. When your roommate no longer relies on the snooze button to wake up, you can return to your normal sleeping pattern and stay in bed for as long as you wish.

8. a. The dominant strategy for the United States is to impose high tariffs, because it always earns more from that strategy than if it imposes low tariffs, no matter what policy China pursues.
  b. The dominant strategy for China is to impose high tariffs, because it always earns more from that strategy than if it imposes low tariffs, no matter what policy the United States pursues.
  c. The Nash equilibrium for both countries is to levy high tariffs. Each country will earn $25 billion.
  d. China and the United States would each benefit from cooperatively lowering trade barriers. In that case, each country would earn $50 billion.

11. There is not a dominant strategy in this variation of rock-paper-scissors, but the guys can't bring themselves to answer with paper, even though it disproves Spock, because they respect him so much.

13. Muber will invest, and Wyft will stay out. How do we know this? Muber will use backward induction to solve this sequential problem. If Muber decides to invest, it restricts Wyft's outcomes to either −2 (if it enters) or 0 (if it stays out). Wyft prefers 0 to −2, so it stays out. Now consider what happens if Muber does not invest. In this case, Wyft makes 1 (if it enters) or 0 (if it stays out). Wyft prefers 1 to 0, so it enters. Since Muber knows what Wyft will choose in both cases, Muber must examine how well it does based on Wyft's choices. When Muber invests, Wyft stays out and Muber earns 5. If Muber decides to not invest, Wyft enters and Muber earns 4. Muber prefers 5 to 4, so Muber will choose to invest.

14. Dirty restrooms cost businesses lost sales, customer referrals, and repeat business. This is especially important for restaurants. So the owner will direct the employee to clean the restrooms more often than the kitchen. Cleaning the restrooms is the dominant strategy, because customers routinely use the restrooms but rarely see the kitchen.

PART

IV

Labor Markets and EARNINGS

The Demand and Supply of Resources

Is Outsourcing Bad for the Economy?

When U.S. jobs are outsourced (sent to other countries), workers in the United States lose their jobs. People commonly think that outsourcing is bad for the U.S. economy, but the situation is not that simple. Outsourced jobs are relocated from high-labor-cost areas to low-labor-cost areas. Often, a U.S. job lost to outsourcing creates more than one job in another country. In addition, outsourcing lowers the cost of manufacturing goods and providing services. Those lower costs translate into lower prices for U.S. consumers and streamlined production processes for U.S. businesses. The improved efficiency helps U.S. firms compete in the global economy. In this chapter, we examine the demand and supply of resources throughout the economy. The outsourcing of jobs is a very visible result of these resource flows and an essential part of the market economy.

Consider Allen Edmonds, an American shoe company that has selectively shifted some of their production to the Dominican Republic. Quality footwear is stylish and hip, but consumers don't have unlimited budgets. To keep prices in the right range for the target market, Allen Edmonds decided to trim production costs by offshoring some of the early production stages. That enabled them to keep final assembly stateside. This move has made

These wingtips are assembled in the USA, but the uppers are probably stitched together overseas. If you want to buy American, how "American" must your shoes be?

their shoes a little more affordable for Americans who appreciate fine footwear, and it has helped keep the doors open at the main plant in Wisconsin. The point is that outsourcing is not a binary outcome. Products aren't made 100% in the United States or 100% elsewhere. The components are generally sourced from around the globe, and designed, manufactured, and assembled wherever these are most cost-effective.

In earlier chapters, we saw that profit-maximizing firms must decide how much to produce. For production to be successful, firms must combine the right amounts of labor and capital to maximize output while simultaneously holding down costs. Because labor often constitutes the largest share of the costs of production, we begin by looking at the labor market. We use supply and demand to illustrate the role of the labor market in the U.S. economy. We then extend the lessons learned about labor into the markets for land and capital. In Chapter 15, we expand our understanding of the labor market by examining income inequality, unemployment, discrimination, and poverty.

· BIG QUESTIONS ·

- What are the factors of production?
- Where does the demand for labor come from?
- Where does the supply of labor come from?
- What are the determinants of demand and supply in the labor market?
- What role do land and capital play in production?

What Are the Factors of Production?

Wages and salaries account for two-thirds of all the income generated by the U.S. economy. The remaining one-third of income goes to the owners of land and capital. Together, labor, land, and capital make up the *factors of production*, or the *inputs* used in producing goods and services. (For a review of these terms, see Chapter 8.)

For instance, let's imagine that Sophia wants to open a Mexican restaurant named Agaves. Sophia will need a dining room staff, cooks, dishwashers, and managers to coordinate everyone else; these are the labor inputs. She also will need a physical location; this is the land input. Finally, she will need a building in which to operate, along with ovens and other kitchen equipment, seating and tableware, and a cash register; these are the capital inputs.

Of course, Sophia's restaurant won't need any inputs if there is no demand for the food she plans to sell. The demand for each of the factors of production that go into her restaurant (land, labor, and capital) is said to be a *derived demand* because the factors are inputs the firm uses to supply a good in another market—in this case, the market for Mexican cuisine. Let's say Sophia secures the land, builds a building, and hires employees to produce the food she will serve. She is willing to spend a lot of money up front to build and staff the restaurant because she expects there to be demand for the food her restaurant will prepare and serve.

Derived demand—the demand for an input used in the production process—is not limited to the demand for a certain type of cuisine. For example,

A lack of customers is an ominous sign for restaurant workers.

Derived demand
is the demand for an input used in the production process.

PRACTICE WHAT YOU KNOW

Derived Demand: Tip Income

Your friend waits tables 60 hours a week at a small restaurant. He is discouraged because he works hard but can't seem to make enough money to cover his bills. He complains that the restaurant does not have enough business and that is why he has to work so many hours just to make ends meet.

QUESTION: As an economist, what advice would you give him?

ANSWER: Because labor is a derived demand, he should apply for a job at a more popular restaurant. Working at a place with more customers will help him earn more tip income.

Want more tip income? Follow the crowd.

Why do economists generally earn more than elementary school teachers?

consumer demand for iPads causes Apple to demand the resources needed to make them. The switches, glass, memory, battery, and other parts have little value alone, but when assembled into an iPad, they become a device that many people find very useful. Therefore, when economists speak of derived demand, they are differentiating between the demand for a product or service and the demand for the resources used to make or produce that product or service.

Where Does the Demand for Labor Come From?

As a student, you are probably hoping that one day your education will translate into tangible skills that employers will seek. As you choose a major, you might be thinking about potential earnings in different occupations. Have you ever wondered why there is so much variability in levels of salary and wages? For instance, economists generally earn more than elementary school teachers but less than engineers. Workers on night shifts earn more than those who do the same job during the day. And professional athletes and successful actors make much more for jobs that are not as essential as the work performed by janitors, construction workers, and nurses. In one respect, the explanation is surprisingly obvious: demand helps to regulate the labor market in much the same way that it helps to determine the prices of goods and services sold in the marketplace.

To understand why some people get paid more than others, we need to explore each worker's output at the margin, or the *marginal product of labor*. In fact, the value that each worker creates for a firm is highly correlated with the demand for labor. Then, to develop a more complete understanding of how the labor market works, we will examine the factors that influence labor demand.

The Marginal Product of Labor

To gain a concrete appreciation for how labor demand is determined, let's look at the restaurant business—a highly competitive market. In Chapter 8, we saw that a firm determines how many workers to hire by comparing the output of labor with the wages the firm must pay. We will apply this analysis of production to the labor market in the restaurant business. Table 14.1 should look familiar to you; it highlights the key determinants of the labor hiring process.

Let's work our way through the table. Column 1 lists the number of laborers, and column 2 reports the daily numbers of meals that can be produced with differing numbers of workers. Column 3 shows the **marginal product of labor**, or the change Δ (Greek delta) in output associated with adding one additional worker. For instance, when the firm moves from three employees to four, output expands from 120 meals to 140 meals. The increase of 20 meals is the marginal product of labor for the fourth worker. Note that the values in column 3 decline as additional workers are added. Recall from Chapter 8 that each successive worker adds less value, a phenomenon known as *diminishing marginal product*.

The **marginal product of labor** is the change in output associated with adding one additional worker.

TABLE 14.1

Deciding How Many Laborers to Hire

(1) Labor (number of workers)	(2) Output (daily meals produced)	(3) Marginal product of labor	(4) Value of the marginal product of labor	(5) Wage (daily)	(6) Marginal profit
		Δ Output	Price ($10) × marginal product of labor		Value of the marginal product of labor − wage
0	0				
		50	$500	$100	$400
1	50				
		40	400	100	300
2	90				
		30	300	100	200
3	120				
		20	200	100	100
4	140				
		10	100	100	0
5	150				
		0	0	100	−100
6	150				

It is useful to know the marginal product of labor, which tells us how much each additional worker adds to the firm's output. Combining the marginal product of labor with the price the firm charges gives us a tool we can use to explain how many workers the firm will hire. Suppose that Agaves charges $10 for each meal. When the firm multiplies the marginal product of labor in column 3 by the price it charges, $10 per meal, we see the value of the marginal product in column 4. The **value of the marginal product (VMP)** is the marginal product of an input multiplied by the price of the output it produces. The firm compares the gain in column 4 with the cost of achieving that gain—the wage that must be paid—in column 5. This process reduces the hiring decision to a simple cost-benefit analysis in which the wage (column 5) is subtracted from the value of the marginal product (column 4) to determine each worker's marginal profit (column 6).

The **value of the marginal product (VMP)** is the marginal product of an input multiplied by the price of the output it produces.

You can see from the green numbers that the marginal profit is positive for the first four workers. You might be tempted to argue that the firm should quit hiring once it has four workers because the marginal profit is zero for the fifth worker, shown in black. However, this argument is not valid because the firm can hire part-time workers. If the firm hires four full-time workers plus a fifth part-time worker, the fifth worker's VMP is greater than the wage the firm pays. Because the marginal profit is negative for the sixth worker, shown in red, the firm would not hire the sixth worker.

Marginal thinking

Figure 14.1 plots the value of the marginal product (VMP) from Table 14.1. Look at the curve: What do you see? Does it remind you of a demand curve? The VMP is the firm's willingness to pay for each laborer. In other words, it is the firm's labor demand curve.

The VMP curve slopes downward due to diminishing marginal product— which we see in column 3 of Table 14.1. As long as the value of the marginal product is higher than the market wage, shown in column 5 as $100 a day, the firm will hire more workers. For example, when the firm hires the first worker, the VMP is $500. This amount easily exceeds the market wage of hiring an

FIGURE 14.1

The Value of the Marginal Product

The value of the marginal product (VMP) is the firm's labor demand curve. When the value of the marginal product is higher than the market wage, the firm will hire more workers. However, because labor is subject to diminishing marginal product, eventually the value created by hiring additional labor falls below the market wage.

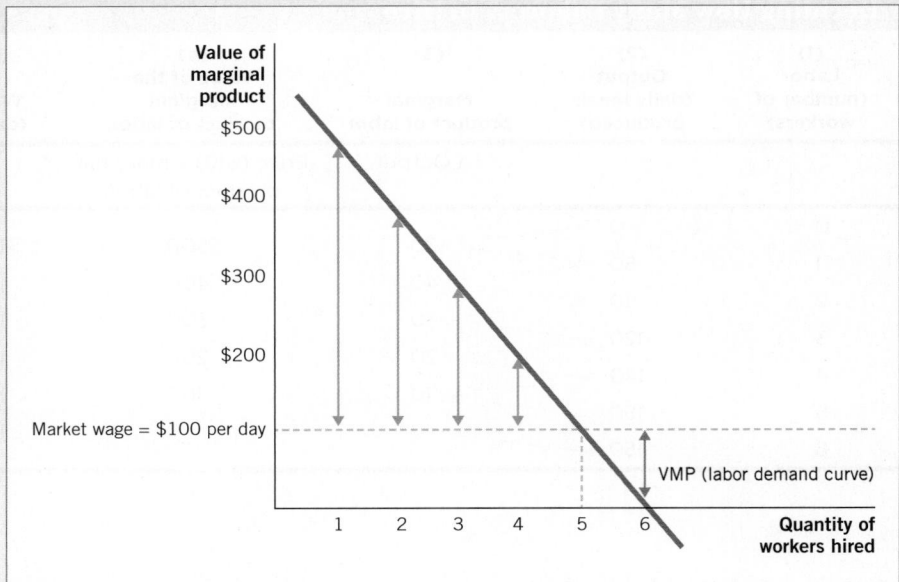

extra worker and creates a marginal profit of $400. Figure 14.1 illustrates the additional profit from the first worker with the longest green arrow under the labor demand curve and above the market wage. The second, third, and fourth workers generate additional profit of $300, $200, and $100, respectively, represented by the progressively shorter green arrows. As the value of the marginal product declines, there will be a point at which hiring additional workers will cause profits to fall. Because labor is subject to diminishing marginal product, the value created by hiring additional labor eventually falls below the market wage.

Changes in the Demand for Labor

We know that customers desire good food and that restaurants like Agaves hire workers to satisfy their customers. Figure 14.2 illustrates the relationship between the demand for restaurant meals and the demand for restaurant workers. Notice that the demand for labor is downward sloping; at high wages Agaves will use fewer workers; at lower wages it will hire more workers. We illustrate the law of demand with the blue arrow that moves along the original demand curve (D_1). Recall from Chapter 3 that a change in price results in a change in the quantity demanded. In addition, the demand for workers depends on, or is derived from, the number of customers who place orders. So changes in the restaurant business as a whole can shift the original demand curve and influence the number of workers the restaurant hires. For example, if the number of customers increases, the demand for workers will increase, or shift to the right to D_2. Likewise, if the number of customers decreases, the demand for workers will decrease, or shift to the left to D_3.

FIGURE 14.2

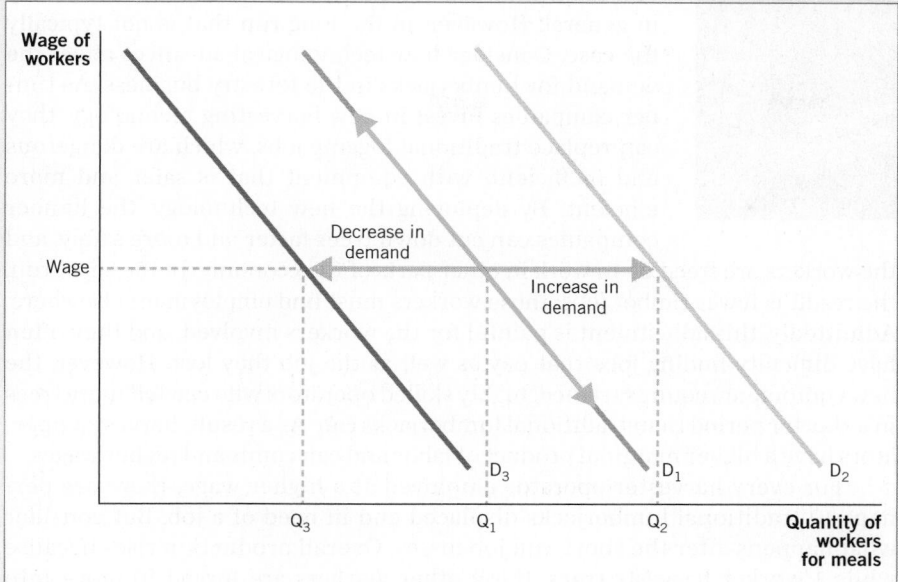

When the wages of workers change, the quantity of workers demanded, shown by the blue arrow moving along the demand curve D_1, also changes. Changes that shift the entire labor demand curve, shown by the gray horizontal arrows, include changes in demand for the product that the firm produces and changes in cost.

Two primary factors shift labor demand: (1) a change in demand for the product the firm produces and (2) a change in the cost of producing that product.

CHANGES IN DEMAND FOR THE PRODUCT THE FIRM PRODUCES

Because a firm is primarily interested in making a profit, it hires workers only when the value of the marginal product of labor is higher than the cost of hiring labor. Consider Agaves. If a rival Mexican restaurant closes down, many of its customers will likely switch to Agaves. Then Agaves will need to prepare more meals, which will cause the entire demand curve for cooks, table clearers, and waitstaff to shift outward to D_2 in Figure 14.2.

CHANGES IN COST
A change in the cost of production can sometimes be positive, such as when a new technology makes production less expensive. It can also be negative, such as when an increase in the cost of a needed raw material makes production more expensive.

In terms of a positive change for the firm, technology can act as a substitute for workers or can make existing workers more efficient. For example, microwave ovens enable restaurants to prepare the same number of meals with fewer workers compared to earlier technology. The same is true with the growing trend of using conveyor belts and automated systems to help prepare meals or even serve them. Therefore, changes in technology can lower a firm's demand for workers.

Marginal thinking

Touch screens at McDonald's automate order taking.

One John Deere 1270G harvester can replace 10 lumberjacks.

In the short run, substituting technology for workers may seem like a bad outcome for the workers and for society in general. However, in the long run that is not typically the case. Consider how technological advances affect the demand for lumberjacks in the forestry business. As timber companies invest in new harvesting technology, they can replace traditional logging jobs, which are dangerous and inefficient, with equipment that is safer and more efficient. By deploying the new technology, the lumber companies can cut down trees faster and more safely, and the workers are freed up to work in other parts of the economy. In the short run, the result is fewer timber jobs; those workers must find employment elsewhere. Admittedly, this adjustment is painful for the workers involved, and they often have difficulty finding jobs that pay as well as the job they lost. However, the new equipment requires trained, highly skilled operators who can fell more trees in a shorter period than traditional lumberjacks can. As a result, harvester operators have a higher marginal product of labor and can command higher wages.

For every harvester operator employed at a higher wage, there are perhaps 10 traditional lumberjacks displaced and in need of a job. But consider what happens after the short-run job losses. Overall production rises because while 1 worker harvests trees, the 9 other workers are forced to move into related fields or do something entirely different. It might take some of these displaced workers many years to find new work, but when they eventually do, society benefits in the long run. What once required 10 workers to produce now takes only 1, and the 9 other workers are able to work in other jobs and grow the economy in different ways.

PRACTICE WHAT YOU KNOW

Value of the Marginal Product of Labor: Flower Barrettes

In *The Big Bang Theory*, Penny starts a business making flower barrettes. Sheldon wonders if she can make a profit.

How many flower barrettes could you make in an hour?

QUESTION: Penny can make five flower barrettes each hour. She works 8 hours each day. Penny is paid $75.00 a day. The firm can sell the barrettes for $1.99 each. What is Penny's value of the marginal product of labor? What is the barrette firm's marginal profit from hiring her?

ANSWER: In 8 hours, Penny can make 40 barrettes. Because each barrette sells for $1.99, her value of the marginal product of labor, or VMP_{labor}, is $40 \times \$1.99$, or $79.60. Her VMP_{labor} is greater than the daily wage she receives, so the marginal profit from hiring her is $79.60 − $75.00, or $4.60.

CHALLENGE QUESTION: Suppose that the market price of barrettes begins to drop. At what price would Penny's job be in jeopardy?

ANSWER: Penny's VMP_{labor} is her output times the price the firm charges. Penny's wage is $75 a day, so with her making 40 barrettes per day, the VMP_{labor} pencils out to $75/40 = \$1.875$ per barrette. That's a scant 11.5 cents less than the current selling price. A small price drop will cause Penny to lose her job.

Changes in the Demand for Labor

WALL·E

In this classic animated sci-fi film from 2008, a future megacorporation called Buy N Large has caused so much overconsumption that Earth's resources are entirely used up. Humans escape their ruined home planet on spaceships where automation has rendered human labor superfluous. The humans become obese and ride around in hovering chairs while staring at computer screens all day long. The people in *Wall-E* drink "cupcakes-in-a-cup," they never exercise, and if they happen to fall off their hovering chairs, they can no longer walk and must wait for a robot to help them up.

This dystopian future occurs because automation and robots have left people with nothing to do, economically speaking. Yikes! But what will happen if, instead, automation and robotics *augment* our productivity? In that alternative future, we will have less work to do, but we will be able to devote our leisure time to travel and other hobbies and passions. There is

Getting replaced by automation and robots would be a drag, but the future doesn't have to look like *Wall-E*.

no doubt that the age of robots is nearing. You can be replaced, or you can find a way to work with, or alongside, robots to increase the value of the marginal product of your labor. The time to think about this is now, before you enter a field where automation is likely to replace you entirely.

To summarize, if labor becomes more productive, the VMP curve (demand for labor) shifts to the right, driving up both wages and employment, which is exactly what occurs with the demand for harvester operators. There is the potential for substitution as well, causing the demand for traditional labor to fall. This is what has happened to traditional lumberjack jobs, leading to a decrease in those workers' wages.

Where Does the Supply of Labor Come From?

In this section, we examine the connection between the wage rate and the number of workers who are willing to supply their services to employers. Because workers also value leisure, the supply curve is not always directly related to the wage rate. Indeed, at high wage levels, some workers may desire to cut back the number of hours they work. Other factors that influence the labor supply include other employment opportunities, the changing composition of the workforce, migration, and immigration; we explore these factors as well.

The Labor-Leisure Trade-Off

People work because they need to earn a living. While it is certainly true that many workers enjoy their jobs, this does not mean they would work for nothing. In other words, while many people experience satisfaction in their work, most of us have other interests, obligations, and goals. As a result, the supply of labor depends both on the wage that is offered and on how individuals want to use their time. We call this relationship the *labor-leisure trade-off*.

In our society today, most individuals must work to meet their basic needs. However, once those needs are met, a worker might be more inclined to use his or her time in leisure. Would higher wages induce an employee to give up leisure and work more hours? The answer is both yes and no!

At higher wage rates, workers may be willing to work more hours, or substitute labor for leisure. This effect is known as the **substitution effect**. One way to think about the substitution effect is to note that higher wages make leisure time more expensive, because the opportunity cost of enjoying more leisure means giving up more income. For instance, suppose Emeril is a short-order cook at Agaves. He works 40 hours at $10 per hour and can also work 4 hours overtime at the same wage. If Emeril decides to work the overtime, he ends up working 44 hours and earns $440. In that case, he substitutes more labor for less leisure.

But at higher wage rates, some workers may work fewer hours, or substitute leisure for labor. This effect is known as the **income effect**. Leisure is a normal good (see Chapter 3), so as income rises, some workers may use their additional income to demand more leisure. As a consequence, at high income levels the income effect may outweigh the substitution effect and cause the supply curve to bend backward. For example, suppose Rachael chooses to work overtime for $10 per hour. Her total pay (like Emeril's) will be $10 × 44, or $440. If her wage rises to $11, she may continue to work the overtime at a higher wage. However, if she does not work overtime, she will earn as much as she earned before the wage increase ($11 × 40 = $440), and she might choose to discontinue the overtime altogether or work fewer overtime hours. The income effect is at work when Rachael's wage goes up and she chooses to work fewer hours.

Figure 14.3 shows what can happen to the labor supply curve when the supply of labor responds directly to wage increases. When the wage rises progressively from W_1 to W_2 to W_3, the number of hours worked increases from Q_1 to Q_2 to Q_3, along the curve labeled S_{normal}. However, at high wage rates the number of hours worked is large. As a result, workers might experience diminishing marginal utility from the additional income and thus might value increased leisure time more than increased income. In this situation, workers might choose to work less, and the normal supply curve bends backward between W_2 and W_3 because as the wage goes up, the hours worked go down.

The **backward-bending labor supply curve** occurs when workers value additional leisure more than additional income. The labor supply curve bends backward when the income effect is large enough to offset the substitution effect that typically causes individuals to work more when the wage rate is higher. Because most workers in the real world do not reach wage level W_2 (that is, a wage at which they might begin to value leisure more than labor), we will draw the supply curve as upward sloping throughout the chapter. Nevertheless, it is important to recognize that the direct relationship we normally observe does not always hold.

Trade-offs

The **substitution effect** occurs when laborers work more hours at higher wages, substituting labor for leisure.

Opportunity cost

The **income effect** occurs when laborers work fewer hours at higher wages, using their additional income to demand more leisure.

A **backward-bending labor supply curve** occurs when workers value additional leisure more than additional income.

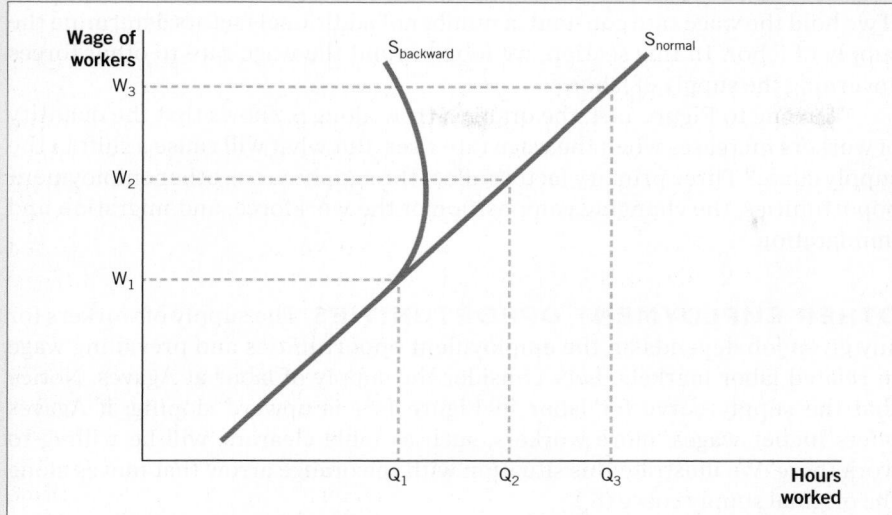

FIGURE 14.3

The Labor Supply Curve

At high wage levels (in this figure, above W_2), the income effect may become larger than the substitution effect and cause the labor supply curve to bend backward. The backward-bending supply curve occurs when additional leisure time becomes more valuable than additional income.

ECONOMICS IN THE REAL WORLD

THE LABOR-LEISURE TRADE-OFF

The statistician Nathan Yau created a simulation called "A Day in the Life of Americans," available at his site flowingdata.com, using data from the American Time Use Survey. As the clock on the upper left ticks along, you see 1,000 dots representing the ways Americans' days typically unfold. Watching the entire simulation will deepen your appreciation for what Americans typically do with their time, and all the trade-offs that take place during a work day.

Trade-offs

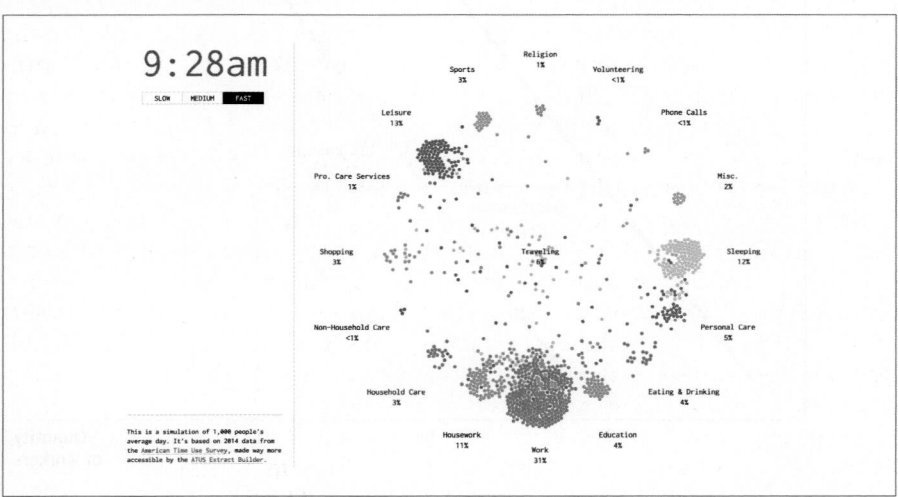

What do you do with your time when you are not working?

Changes in the Supply of Labor

If we hold the wage rate constant, a number of additional factors determine the supply of labor. In this section, we look beyond the wage rate to other forces governing the supply of labor.

Turning to Figure 14.4, the orange arrow along S_1 shows that the quantity of workers increases when the wage rate rises. But what will cause a shift in the supply curve? Three primary factors affect the supply curve: other employment opportunities, the changing composition of the workforce, and migration and immigration.

OTHER EMPLOYMENT OPPORTUNITIES The supply of workers for any given job depends on the employment opportunities and prevailing wage in related labor markets. Let's consider the supply of labor at Agaves. Notice that the supply curve for labor in Figure 14.4 is upward sloping; if Agaves offers higher wages, more workers, such as table clearers, will be willing to work there. We illustrate this situation with the orange arrow that moves along the original supply curve (S_1).

The supply of table clearers also depends on a number of nonwage factors. Because table clearers are generally young and largely unskilled, the number of laborers willing to work is influenced by the prevailing wages in similar jobs. For instance, if the wages of baggers at local grocery stores increase, some of the table clearers at Agaves will decide to bag at local grocery stores instead. The supply of table clearers will decrease and cause a leftward shift to S_3. If the wages of baggers were to fall below the wages of table clearers, the supply of

---

FIGURE 14.4

The Labor Supply Curve

A change in the quantity supplied of labor occurs when wages change, causing a movement along the supply curve S_1, shown by the orange arrow. Changes in the supply of labor (the quantity of workers), shown by the gray horizontal arrows, can occur due to other employment opportunities, the changing composition of the workforce, immigration, and migration.

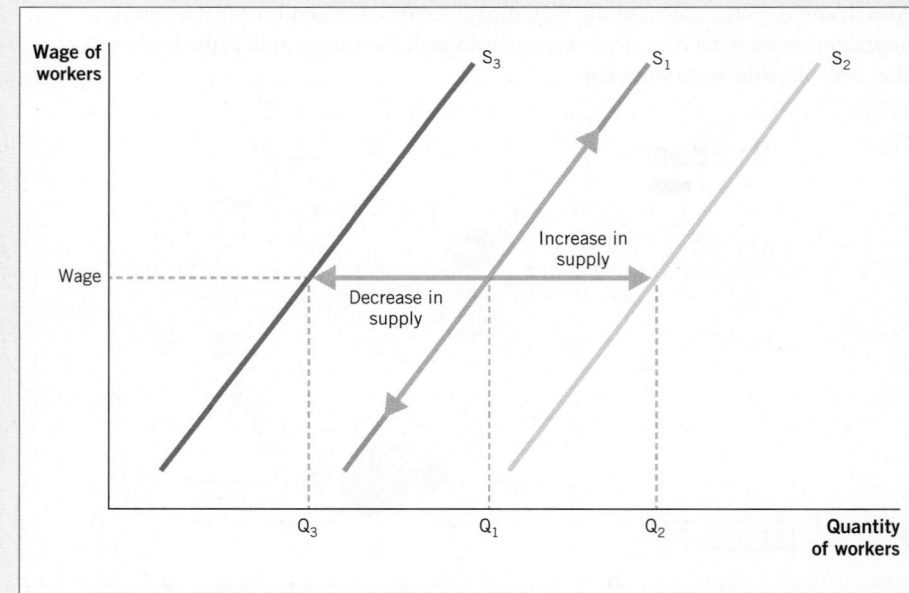

---

table clearers would increase, or shift to the right to S_2. These shifts reflect the fact that when jobs requiring comparable skills have different wage rates, the number of workers willing to supply labor for the lower-wage job will shrink and the number willing to supply labor for the better-paid job will grow.

THE CHANGING COMPOSITION OF THE WORKFORCE Over the last 30 years, the labor force participation rate (as measured by the female/male ratio) has increased significantly in most developed countries. A ratio of 100% indicates that females and males participated equally. According to the United Nations Development Programme, the United States saw its female/male ratio rise from 66% to 82%, Switzerland from 67% to 81%, and New Zealand from 65% to 84%. Overall, there are many more women employed in the workforce today than there were a generation ago, and the supply of workers in many occupations has expanded significantly as a result.

IMMIGRATION AND MIGRATION Demographic factors, including immigration and migration, also play a crucial role in the supply of labor. For example, immigration—both legal and illegal—increases the available supply of workers by a significant amount each year.

In 2015, over half a million people from foreign countries entered the United States through legal channels and gained permission to seek employment. There are over 40 million legal immigrants in the United States. In addition, illegal immigrants account for close to 10 million workers in the United States, many of whom enter the country to work as hotel maids, janitors, and fruit pickers. Often when states suggest or pass a tough immigration law, businesses in food and beverage, agriculture, and construction protest because they need inexpensive labor to remain competitive, and U.S. citizens are reluctant to work these jobs. Many states have wrestled with the issue, but policies that address illegal immigration remain controversial, and the solutions are difficult. The states need the cheap labor but don't want to pay additional costs, such as medical care and the cost of schooling the illegal immigrants' children.

For the purposes of this discussion, we consider migration to be the process of moving from one place to another within the United States. Although the U.S. population grows at an annual rate of approximately 1%, there are significant regional differences. Indeed, large population influxes lead to marked regional changes in the demand for labor and the supply of people looking for work. According to the U.S. Census Bureau, in 2010 the 10 fastest-growing states were in the South or West, with some states adding as much as 4% to their population in a single year. States in these areas provided 84% of the nation's population growth from 2000 to 2010, with Nevada, Utah, North Carolina, Idaho, and Texas all adding at least 20% to their populations.

It is worth noting that statewide data can hide significant localized changes. For example, census data from 2010 indicate that a number of counties experienced 50% or more population growth between 2000 and 2010. The biggest population gain was in Kendall County, Illinois, a far-flung suburb of Chicago that grew by nearly 100% between censuses. The county has been transitioning from an agricultural area to a bedroom community. Most of the fastest-growing counties are, like Kendall, relatively distant suburbs of major metropolitan areas. These are areas where new homes are available at comparatively reasonable prices.

SUPPLY OF LABOR

Where Have All the Teenagers Gone (and Who Is Going to Replace Them)?

In the mid-1990s there were 56 teenagers in the labor force for every fast-food restaurant. Today, there are half that many. Two factors are at work: teenagers are far less likely to participate in the workforce, and there has been explosive growth in the fast-food sector. Historically, fast-food restaurants relied on cheap labor to produce inexpensive food. Today, automation is being used to make up for the lack of workers. In 2018, Caliburger introduced Flippy, the first hamburger-flipping robot. Flippy costs $60,000, and there is also a $12,000 recurring annual fee for cleaning and maintenance, but Caliburger is confident that the investment is worth the high fixed cost. Caliburger is banking on decreased wait times, better consistency in food preparation, and less food waste. Plus, Flippy doesn't need health insurance. Also, he shows up for work on time and doesn't complain about the heat from the griddle.

Can't find reliable workers? No problem. Get a robot to do the job.

What Are the Determinants of Demand and Supply in the Labor Market?

In earlier chapters, we saw how markets reconcile the forces of demand and supply through pricing. Now that we have considered the forces governing demand and supply in the labor market, we are ready to see how the equilibrium

If you got a big raise, would you travel the world?

The Labor Supply Curve: What Would You Do with a Big Raise?

QUESTION: Your friend is concerned about his uncle, who just received a big raise. Your friend doesn't understand why his uncle wants to take time off from his job to travel. Can you help him understand why his uncle might want to cut back on his hours?

ANSWER: Ordinarily, we think of the labor supply curve as upward sloping, in which case higher wages translate into more hours worked and less leisure time. However, when the wage rate becomes high enough, some workers choose to substitute leisure for labor because they feel that enjoying free time is more valuable than earning more money. In this case, the labor supply curve bends backward, and the worker spends fewer hours working as his wage rises. Your friend's uncle is reflecting this tendency.

wage is established. We can then examine the labor market in greater detail and identify what causes shortages and surpluses of labor, why outsourcing occurs, and what happens when there is a single buyer of labor. The goal of this section is to provide a rich set of examples that help you become comfortable using demand and supply curves to understand how the labor market operates.

How Does the Market for Labor Reach Equilibrium?

We can think about wages as the price at which workers are willing to "rent" their time to employers. Turning to Figure 14.5, we see that at wages above equilibrium (W_E), the supply of workers willing to rent their time exceeds the demand for that time. The result is a surplus of available workers. The surplus, in turn, places downward pressure on wages. As wages drop, fewer workers are willing to rent their time to employers. When wages drop to the equilibrium wage, the surplus of workers is eliminated. At that point, the number of workers willing to work in that profession at that wage is exactly equal to the number of job openings that exist at that wage.

A similar process guides the labor market toward equilibrium from low wages. At wages below the equilibrium, the demand for labor exceeds

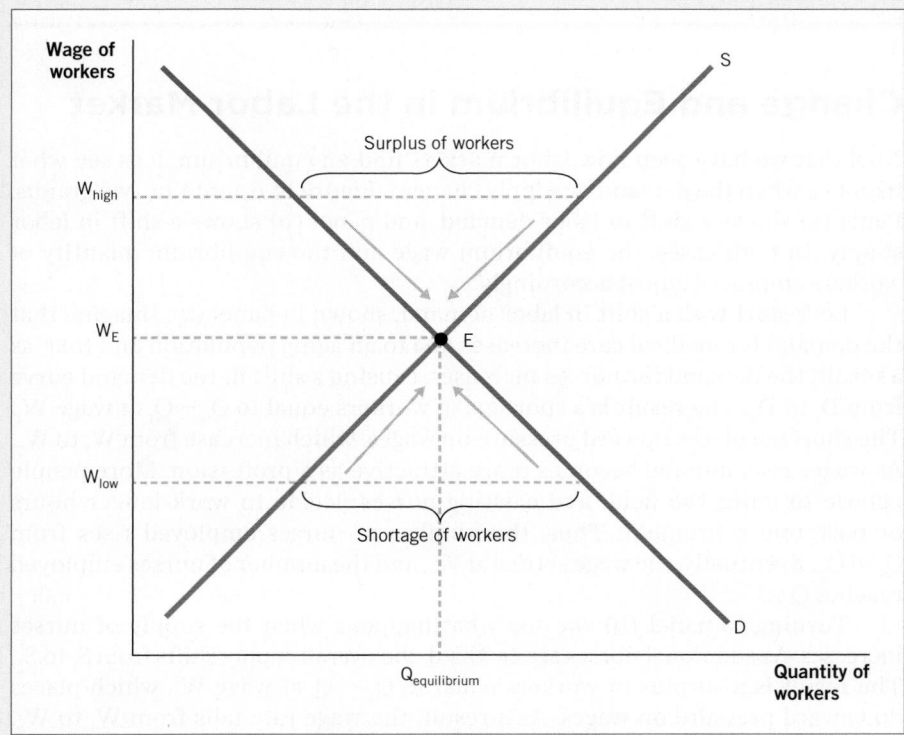

FIGURE 14.5

Equilibrium in the Labor Market

At high wages (W_{high}), a surplus of workers exists. The wage rate is driven down until the supply of workers and the demand for workers reach equilibrium. At low wages (W_{low}), a shortage occurs. The shortage forces the wage rate up until the equilibrium wage is reached and the shortage disappears.

the available supply. The shortage forces firms to offer higher wages to attract workers. As a result, wages rise until the shortage is eliminated at the equilibrium wage.

WHERE ARE THE NURSES?

The United States is experiencing a shortage of nurses. A stressful job with long hours, nursing requires years of training. As baby boomers age, demand for nursing care is expected to rise. At the same time, the existing pool of nurses is rapidly aging and nearing retirement. According to the Bureau of Labor Statistics, the shortage of nurses in America will approach 1 million by 2025, making nursing the number one job in the country in terms of growth prospects.

Because the training process takes two or more years to complete, the labor market for nurses won't return to equilibrium immediately. The nursing shortage will persist for a number of years, until the quantity of nurses supplied to the market increases. The median pay of nurses was $70,000 in 2017. Given the ongoing shortage, not only will you find immediate employment once trained, you'll also experience rising wages while the shortage lasts.

Economics tells us that the combination of more newly trained nurses entering the market and the transfer of certain nursing services to assistants and technicians will eventually cause the nursing shortage to disappear. Remember that when a market is out of balance, forces kick in to restore it to equilibrium.

Entering an occupation with a shortage of workers will result in higher pay.

Change and Equilibrium in the Labor Market

Now that we have seen how labor markets find an equilibrium, let's see what happens when the demand or supply changes. Figure 14.6 contains two graphs. Panel (a) shows a shift in labor demand, and panel (b) shows a shift in labor supply. In both cases, the equilibrium wage and the equilibrium quantity of workers employed adjust accordingly.

Let's start with a shift in labor demand, shown in panel (a). Imagine that the demand for medical care increases due to an aging population and that, as a result, the demand for nurses increases, causing a shift in the demand curve from D_1 to D_2. The result is a shortage of workers equal to $Q_3 - Q_1$ at wage W_1. The shortage places upward pressure on wages, which increase from W_1 to W_2. As wages rise, nursing becomes more attractive as a profession. More people choose to enter the field, and existing nurses decide to work longer hours or postpone retirement. Thus, the number of nurses employed rises from Q_1 to Q_2. Eventually, the wage settles at W_2, and the number of nurses employed reaches Q_2.

Turning to panel (b), we see what happens when the supply of nurses increases. As additional nurses are certified, the overall supply shifts from S_1 to S_2. The result is a surplus of workers equal to $Q_3 - Q_1$ at wage W_1, which places downward pressure on wages. As a result, the wage rate falls from W_1 to W_2. Eventually, the market wage settles at W_2, the new equilibrium point is E_2, and the number of nurses employed reaches Q_2.

FIGURE 14.6

Shifting the Labor Market Equilibrium

In panel (a), the demand for nurses increases, creating a shortage of workers equal to $Q_3 - Q_1$, which leads to a higher equilibrium wage (W_2) and a higher quantity of nurses employed (Q_2) than before. In panel (b), the supply of nurses increases. The result is a surplus of workers equal to $Q_3 - Q_1$, causing the equilibrium wage to fall (to W_2) and the number of nurses employed to rise (to Q_2).

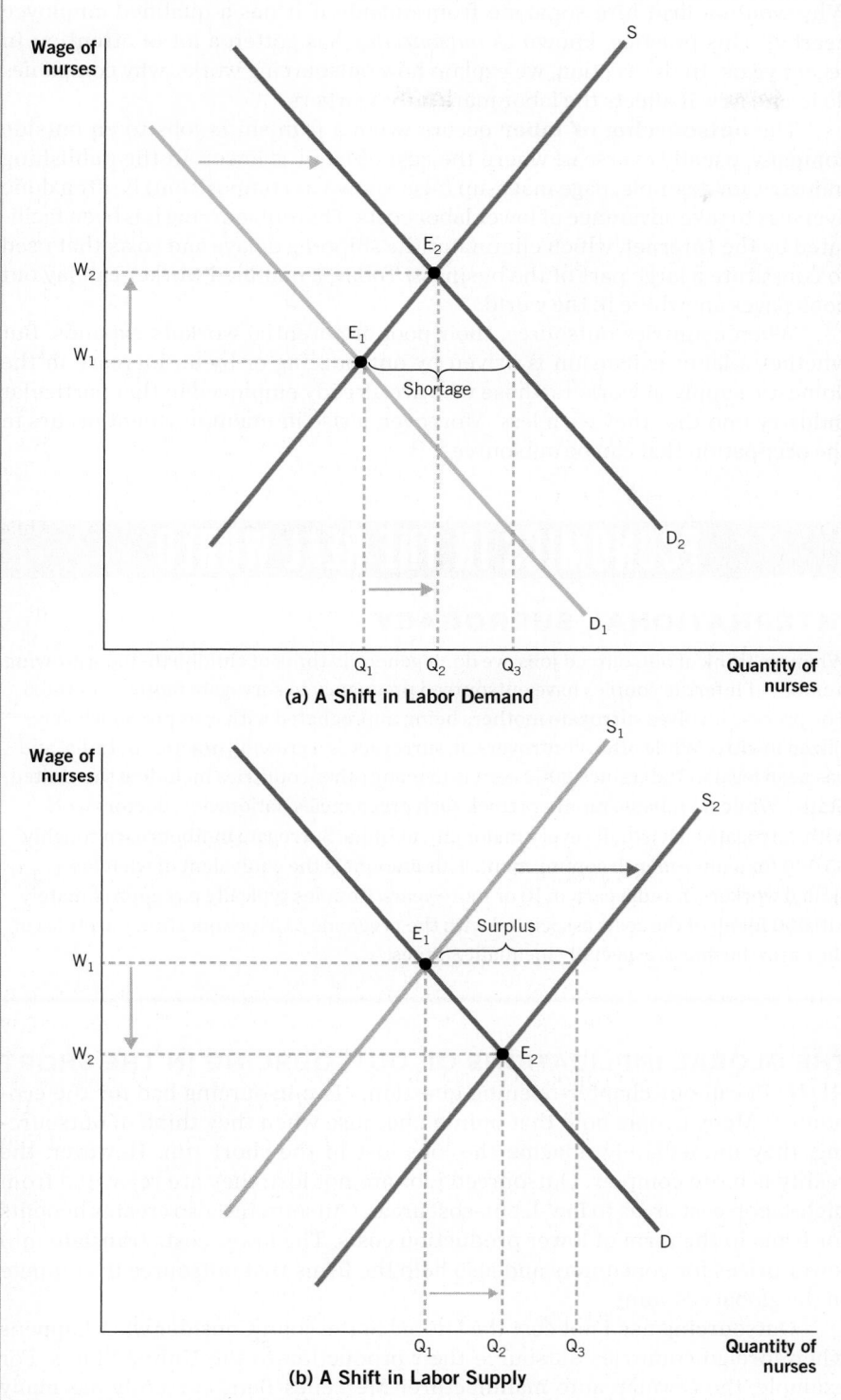

(a) A Shift in Labor Demand

(b) A Shift in Labor Supply

Outsourcing

Why would a firm hire someone from outside if it has a qualified employee nearby? This practice, known as *outsourcing*, has gotten a lot of attention in recent years. In this section, we explain how outsourcing works, why companies do it, and how it affects the labor market for workers.

The **outsourcing of labor** occurs when a firm shifts jobs to an outside company, usually overseas, where the cost of labor is lower. In the publishing industry, for example, page make-up (also known as composition) is often done overseas to take advantage of lower labor costs. This outsourcing has been facilitated by the Internet, which eliminates the shipping delays and costs that used to constitute a large part of the business. Today, a qualified worker can lay out book pages anywhere in the world.

When countries outsource, their pool of potential workers expands. But whether a labor expansion is driven by outsourcing or by an increase in the domestic supply of workers, those who are already employed in that particular industry find that they earn less. Moreover, a rise in unemployment occurs in the occupation that can be outsourced.

Outsourcing of labor
occurs when a firm shifts jobs to an outside company, usually overseas, where the cost of labor is lower.

ECONOMICS IN THE REAL WORLD

INTERNATIONAL SURROGACY

Kaival Hospital in Anand, India, matches infertile couples with local women, such as these surrogate mothers.

When we think of outsourced jobs, we don't generally think of childbirth. But a growing number of infertile couples have outsourced pregnancy to surrogate mothers in India. The process involves surrogate mothers being impregnated with eggs previously fertilized in vitro. While often controversial, surrogacy is a growing practice in India, and has been legal in India since 2002, as it is in many other countries including the United States. While no reliable numbers track such pregnancies nationwide, doctors work with surrogates in virtually every major city in India. Surrogate mothers earn roughly $5,000 for a nine-month commitment. This amount is the equivalent of what low-skilled workers in India earn in 10 or more years. Couples typically pay approximately $10,000 for all of the costs associated with the pregnancy. Critics question the ethics of the entire business, especially inequality issues.

THE GLOBAL IMPLICATIONS OF OUTSOURCING IN THE SHORT RUN Recall our chapter-opening question, "Is outsourcing bad for the economy?" Many people hold that opinion because when they think of outsourcing, they immediately imagine the jobs lost in the short run. However, the reality is more complex. Outsourced jobs are not lost; they are relocated from high-labor-cost areas to low-labor-cost areas. Outsourcing also creates benefits for firms in the form of lower production costs. The lower costs translate into lower prices for consumers and also help the firms that outsource to compete in the global economy.

Outsourcing need not cost the United States jobs. Consider what happens when foreign countries outsource their production to the United States. For example, the German auto manufacturer Mercedes-Benz currently has many of its cars built in Alabama. If you were an assembly-line worker in Germany

who had spent a lifetime making cars for Mercedes, you would likely be upset if your job was outsourced to North America. You would feel just like the American technician who loses a job to someone in India or the software writer who is replaced by a worker in China. Outsourcing always produces a job winner and a job loser. In the case of foreign outsourcing to the United States, employment in this country rises. In fact, the Mercedes-Benz plant in Alabama employs more than 3,000 workers. Those jobs were transferred to the United States because the company felt that it would be more profitable to hire American workers and make the vehicles in the United States rather than construct them in Germany and ship them across the Atlantic.

The Mercedes-Benz plant near Tuscaloosa, Alabama, illustrates that outsourcing is more than just a one-way street.

Figure 14.7 shows how outsourcing by foreign firms helps to increase U.S. labor demand. In panel (a), we see the job loss and lower wages that occur in Germany when jobs are outsourced to the United States. As the demand for labor in Germany falls from D_1 to D_2, wages drop to W_2 and employment declines to Q_2. Panel (b) illustrates the corresponding increase in demand for U.S. labor in Alabama. As demand shifts from D_1 to D_2, wages rise to W_2 and employment rises to Q_2.

Because each nation will experience outsourcing flows out of and into the country, it is impossible to say anything definitive about the overall impact of outsourcing on labor in the short run. However, it is highly unlikely that workers who lose high-paying jobs toward the end of their working lives will be able to find other jobs that pay equally well.

THE GLOBAL IMPLICATIONS OF OUTSOURCING IN THE LONG RUN Although we see mixed results for outsourcing in the short run, we can say that in the long run outsourcing benefits domestic consumers and producers. In fact, outsourcing is a key component in international trade. Throughout this book, we have seen that trade creates value. When companies and even countries specialize, they become more efficient. The efficiency gains, or cost savings, help producers to expand production. In the absence of trade barriers, lower costs benefit consumers in domestic and international markets through lower prices, and the outsourcing of jobs provides the income for foreign workers to purchase domestic imports. Therefore, the mutually interdependent nature of international trade enhances overall social welfare.

Trade creates value

FIGURE 14.7

Shifting the Labor Market Equilibrium

Outsourcing creates more demand in one market at the expense of the other. In panel (a), the demand for German labor declines from D_1 to D_2, leading to lower wages and less employment. Panel (b) shows the increase in the demand for labor from D_1 to D_2 in Alabama. The results are higher wages and more employment.

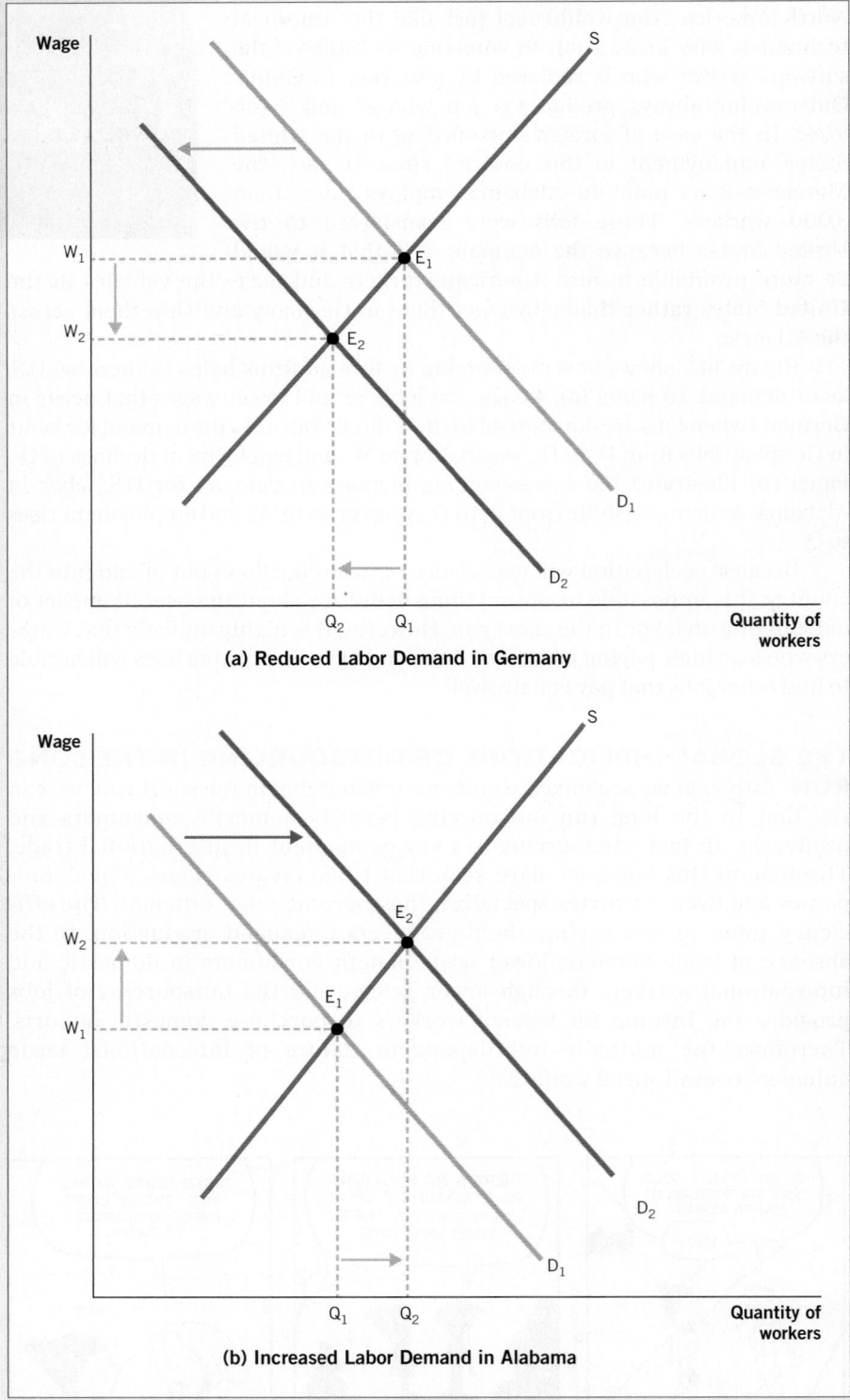

(a) Reduced Labor Demand in Germany

(b) Increased Labor Demand in Alabama

Monopsony

In looking at supply, demand, and equilibrium in the labor market, we have assumed that the market for labor is competitive. But that is not always the case. Sometimes the labor market has only a few buyers or sellers who are able to capture market power. One extreme form of market power is **monopsony**, which occurs when only a single buyer exists. Like a monopolist, a monopsonist has a great deal of market power. As a consequence, the output in the labor market will favor a monopsonist whenever one is present.

In Chapter 10, we examined how a monopolist behaves. Compared with a firm in a competitive market, the monopolist charges a higher price for the product it sells. Likewise, a monopsonist in the labor market can leverage its market power. Because it is the only firm hiring, it can pay its workers less. Isolated college towns are a good example. Workers who wish to live in such college towns often find that almost all the available jobs are through the college. Because it is the chief provider of jobs, the college has a monopsony in the labor market. It can use its market power to hire many local workers at low wages.

Monopsony is a situation in which there is only one buyer.

WHY DO SOME WORKERS MAKE MORE THAN OTHERS? While most workers generally spend 35 to 40 hours a week at work, the amount they earn varies dramatically. Table 14.2 presents a number of simple questions that answer the larger question, "Why do some workers make more than others?"

TABLE 14.2

Why Some Workers Make More than Others

Question	Answer
Why do economists generally earn more than elementary school teachers?	Supply is the key. There are fewer qualified economists than certified elementary school teachers. Therefore, the equilibrium wage in economics is higher than it is in elementary education. It's also important to note that demand factors may be part of the explanation. The value of the marginal product of labor of economists is generally higher than that of most elementary school teachers because many economists work in industry, which pays higher wages than the public sector.
Why do people who work the night shift earn more than those who do the same job during the day?	Again, supply is the key. Fewer people are willing to work at night, so the wage necessary to attract labor to perform the job must be higher. (That is, night shift workers earn what is called a *compensating differential*, which we discuss in Chapter 15.)
Why do professional athletes and successful actors make so much when what they do is not essential?	Demand and supply both play important roles here. The paying public is willing, even eager, to spend a large amount of income on entertainment. Thus, demand for entertainment is high. On the supply end of the equation, the number of individuals who capture the imagination of the paying public is small, and they are therefore paid handsomely. Since the value of the marginal product that they create is incredibly high, and the supply of workers with these skills is quite small, accomplished athletes and actors earn huge incomes.
Why do janitors, construction workers, and nurses—whose jobs are essential—have salaries that are a tiny fraction of celebrities' salaries?	Demand again. The value of the marginal product of labor created in these essential jobs is low, so their employers are unable to pay high wages.

Changes in Labor Demand

Labor is always subject to changes in demand.

QUESTION: A company builds a new facility that doubles its workspace and equipment. How is labor affected?

ANSWER: The company has probably experienced additional demand for the product it sells. Therefore, it needs additional employees to staff the facility, causing a positive shift in the demand curve. When the demand for labor rises, wages increase and so does the number of people employed.

QUESTION: A company decides to outsource 100 jobs from a facility in Indiana to Indonesia. How is labor affected in the short run?

ANSWER: This situation leads to two changes. First, a decrease in demand for labor in Indiana results in lower wages there and fewer workers hired. Second, an increase in demand for labor in Indonesia results in higher wages there and more workers hired.

The table shows how demand and supply determine wages in a variety of settings. Workers with a high-value marginal product of labor invariably earn more than those with a lower-value marginal product of labor. It is important to note that working an "essential" job does not guarantee a high income. Instead, the highest incomes are reserved for jobs with a high demand for workers and a low supply of them. In other words, our preconceived notions of fairness take a backseat to the underlying market forces that govern pay. In the next chapter, we consider many additional factors that determine wages, including wage discrimination.

What Role Do Land and Capital Play in Production?

In addition to labor, firms need land and capital to produce goods and services. In this section, we complete our analysis of the resource market by considering how land and capital enter into the production process. Returning to the restaurant Agaves, we know that the business hires labor to make meals. But to do their jobs, the workers need equipment, tables, chairs, cash registers, and a kitchen. Without a physical location and a host of capital resources, labor would be irrelevant.

The Market for Land

Like the demand for labor, the demand for land is determined by the value of the marginal product it generates. However, unlike the supply of labor, the supply of land is ordinarily fixed. We can think of it as nonresponsive to prices, or perfectly inelastic.

In Figure 14.8, the vertical supply curve reflects the inelastic supply. The price of land is determined by the intersection of supply and demand. Notice the label on the vertical axis, which reflects the price of land as the rental price necessary to use it, not the price necessary to purchase it. When evaluating a firm's economic situation, we do not count the entire purchase price of the land it needs. To do so would dramatically overstate the cost of land in the production process because the land is not used up, but only occupied for a certain period. For example, consider a car that you buy. You drive it for a year and put 15,000 miles on it. Counting the entire purchase price of the car would overstate the true operating cost for one year of service. The true cost of operating the vehicle includes wear and tear along with operating expenses, such as gasoline, maintenance, and service visits. A similar process is at work with land. Firms that own land consider the rent they could have earned if they had rented the land out for the year. This method nicely captures the opportunity cost of using the land.

Opportunity cost

Because the supply of land is usually fixed, changes in demand determine the rental price. When demand is low—say, at D_1—the rental price received, P_1, is also low. When demand is high—say, at D_2—the rental price of land is high, at P_2. Apartment rentals near college campuses provide a good example of the conditions under which the demand for land is high. Because students and faculty want to live near campus, the demand for land is often much higher there than even a few blocks away. Like labor, the demand for land is derived from

FIGURE 14.8

Supply and Demand in the Market for Land

Because the supply of land is fixed, the price it commands depends on demand. If demand increases from D_1 to D_2, the price will rise from P_1 to P_2. Note that "price" here reflects the rental price of the land, not the purchase price.

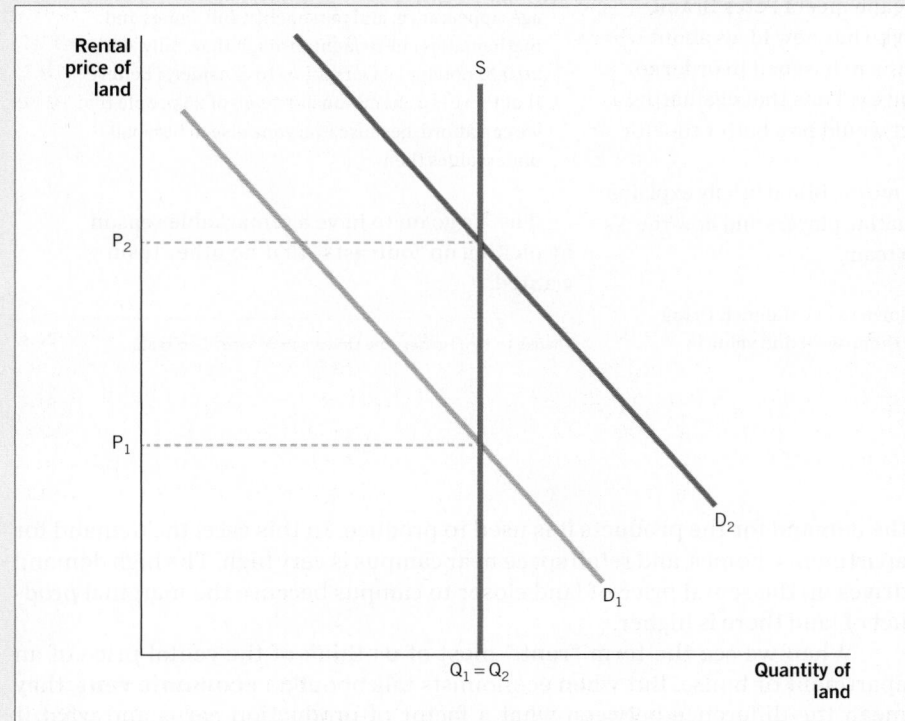

▪ ECONOMICS *in the* MEDIA ▪

Value of the Marginal Product of Labor

MONEYBALL

Moneyball (2011), a film based on Michael Lewis's 2003 book of the same name, details the struggles of the Oakland Athletics, a major-league baseball team. The franchise attempts to overcome some seemingly impossible obstacles with the help of its general manager, Billy Beane, by applying innovative statistical analysis, known as sabermetrics, pioneered by Bill James.

Traditional baseball scouts use experience, intuition, and subjective criteria to evaluate potential players. However, Beane, formerly a heavily recruited high school player who failed to have a successful professional career, knows firsthand that this method of scouting does not guarantee success. The Oakland A's lack the financial ability to pay as much as other teams. While trying to negotiate a trade with the Cleveland Indians, Beane meets Peter Brand, a young Yale economist who has new ideas about applying statistical analysis to baseball in order to build a better team. Brand explains that evaluating a player's marginal product would be a better tool for recruitment.

In the key scene in the movie, Brand briefly explains his methodology for evaluating players and how the A's can build a championship team:

It's about getting things down to one number. Using the stats the way we read them, we'll find value in

Can a young economist's algorithm save the Oakland A's?

players that no one else can see. People are overlooked for a variety of biased reasons and perceived flaws: age, appearance, and personality. Bill James and mathematics cut straight through that. Billy, of the 20,000 notable players for us to consider, I believe that there is a championship team of 25 people that we can afford, because everyone else in baseball undervalues them.

The A's go on to have a remarkable season by picking up "outcasts" that no other team wanted.

Thanks to Kim Holder (the University of West Georgia).

Marginal thinking

Economic rent
is the difference between what a factor of production earns and what it could earn in the next-best alternative.

the demand for the products it is used to produce. In this case, the demand for apartments, homes, and retail space near campus is very high. The high demand drives up the rental price of land closer to campus because the marginal product of land there is higher.

When we see the term "rent," most of us think of the rental price of an apartment or house. But when economists talk about an **economic rent**, they mean the difference between what a factor of production earns and what it could earn in the next-best alternative. Economic rent is different from *rent seeking*. Recall from Chapter 10 that rent seeking occurs when firms compete to

A satellite photo shows manufactured islands in Dubai, United Arab Emirates—an exception to our assumption that the amount of land is fixed.

seek a monopoly position. In contrast, economic rent refers to investors' ability to beat their opportunity cost. For instance, in the case of housing near college campuses, a small studio apartment generally commands a much higher rent than a similar apartment located 10 miles away. Why? The rent near campus must be high enough to compensate the property owners for using their land for an apartment instead of in other ways that might also be profitable in the area—for example, for a single residence, a business, or a parking lot. Once you move 10 miles farther out, the number of people interested in using the land for these purposes declines.

More generally, in areas where many people would like to live or work, rental prices are often very high. Take San Francisco, where the average rental unit costs a staggering $3,500 a month. That eye-popping amount makes most apartment rental prices in the United States seem downright inexpensive. Similarly, owners of property in Manhattan, Boston, and Washington, D.C., all receive more economic rent on properties than those who own similar rentals in Peoria, Idaho Falls, Scranton, or Chattanooga. The ability to earn a substantial economic rent comes back to opportunity costs: because there are so many other potential uses of property in densely populated areas, rents are correspondingly higher.

Opportunity cost

The Market for Capital

Capital, or the equipment and materials needed to produce goods, is a necessary factor of production. The demand for capital is determined by the value of the marginal product it creates. Like the demand for land and labor, the demand for capital is a derived demand: a firm requires capital only if the product it produces is in demand. The demand for capital is also downward sloping, reflecting the fact that the value of the marginal product associated with its use declines as the amount used rises.

When to Use More Labor, Land, or Capital

Firms must evaluate whether hiring additional labor, utilizing more land, or deploying more capital will constitute the best use of their resources. To do this, they compare the value of the marginal product per dollar spent across the three factors of production.

Let's consider an example. Suppose that a company pays its employees $15 per hour, the rental rate of land is $5,000 per acre per year, and the rental rate of capital is $1,000 per year. The company's manager determines that the value of the marginal product of labor is $450, the value of the marginal product of an acre of land is $125,000, and the value of the marginal product of capital is $40,000. Is the firm using the right mix of resources? Table 14.3 compares the ratios of the value of the marginal product (VMP) of each factor of production with the cost of attaining that value (this calculation gives us the "bang per buck" for each resource, or the relative benefit of using each resource).

Looking at these results, we see that the highest bang per buck (column 4) is the value $40 created by dividing the VMP of capital by the rental price of capital. When we compare this value with the bang per buck for labor and land, we see that the firm is getting more benefit per dollar spent on capital than from labor ($30) or land ($25). Therefore, the firm would benefit from using capital more intensively. As it does so, the VMP of capital in column 2 will fall due to diminishing returns, and the bang per buck for capital will drop from $40 in column 4 to a number that is more in line with bang per buck for labor and land. Conversely, the firm is using land ($25) too intensively, and it would benefit from using less. Doing so will raise the VMP it produces and increase its bang per buck for land. By using less land and more capital and by tweaking the use of labor as well, the firm will eventually bring the value created by all three factors to a point at which the bang per buck spent is equal for each of the factors. At that point, the firm will be utilizing its resources efficiently.

Why does all this matter? Because the world is always changing: wages rise and fall, as do property values and the cost of acquiring capital. A firm must constantly adjust the mix of land, labor, and capital it uses to get the largest return. Moreover, the markets for land, labor, and capital are connected. The amount of labor that a firm uses depends not only on the marginal product of labor, but also on the marginal product of land and capital. Therefore, a change in the supply of one factor will alter the returns of all factors. For instance, if wages fall, firms will be inclined to hire more labor. But if they hire more labor, they will use less capital. Capital itself is not any more, or less, productive. Rather, lower wages reduce the demand for capital. In this situation, the demand curve for capital would shift to the left, lowering the rental price of capital as well as the quantity of capital deployed.

Marginal thinking

TABLE 14.3

Determining the Bang per Buck for Each Resource

(1) Factor of production	(2) Value of the marginal product	(3) Wage or rental price	(4) Bang per buck
Labor	$450	$15	$450 ÷ 15 = $30
Land	125,000	5,000	125,000 ÷ 5,000 = 25
Capital	40,000	1,000	40,000 ÷ 1,000 = 40

Outsourcing

Outsourcing, though painful for those whose jobs are outsourced, is simply the application of a fundamental economic principle—keep costs as low as possible. Labor is usually the most expensive input for a business, so all managers must seek to pay the lowest wage that still ensures an effective workforce. Firms seek the right balance of costs and relevant skills when outsourcing jobs. Here is a look at three representative jobs in the United States, Mexico, China, and India, with salaries measured as a percentage of the typical U.S. salary.

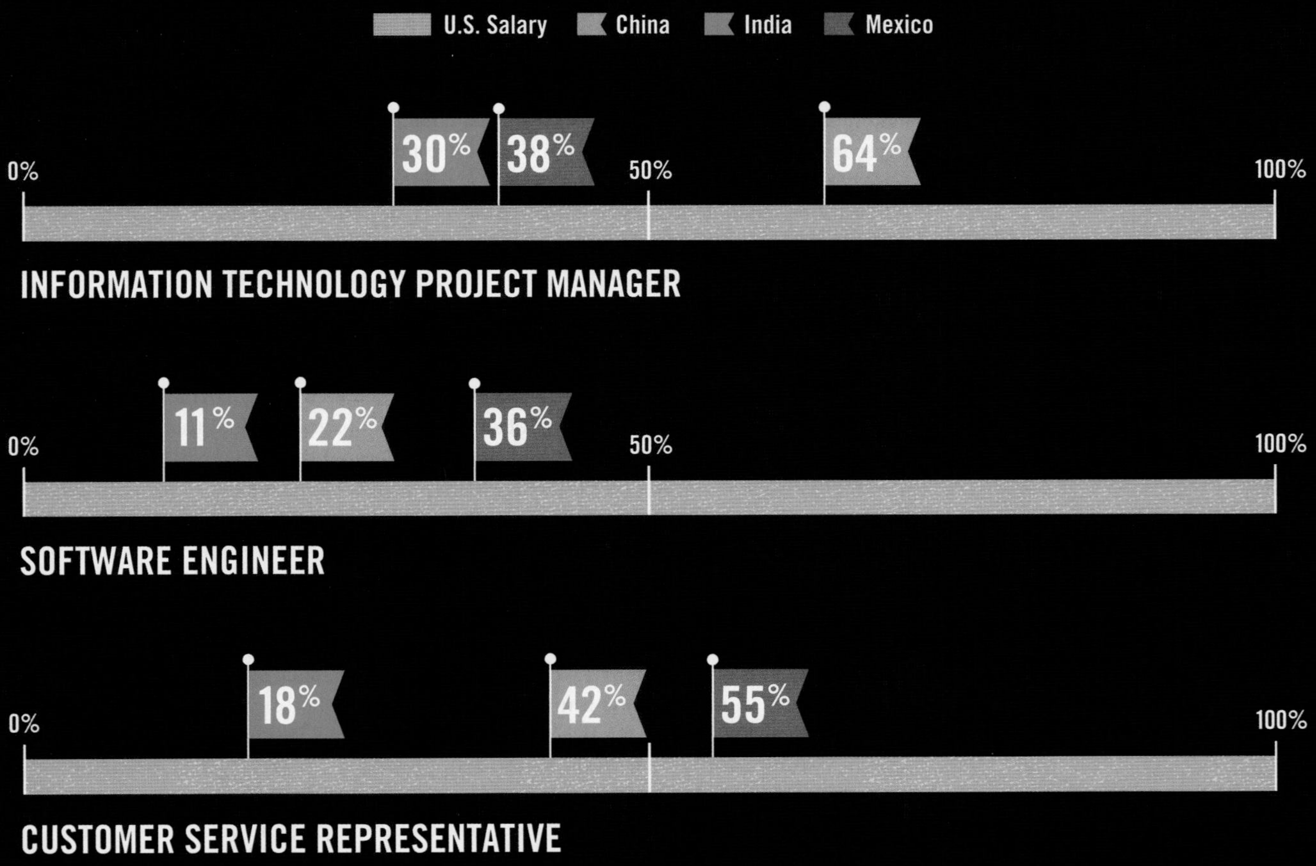

U.S. Salary   **China**   **India**   **Mexico**

0%   30%   38%   50%   64%   100%

INFORMATION TECHNOLOGY PROJECT MANAGER

0%   11%   22%   36%   50%   100%

SOFTWARE ENGINEER

0%   18%   42%   55%   100%

CUSTOMER SERVICE REPRESENTATIVE

The communications and transportation revolutions, along with the increasing skill level of foreign labor, have created conditions for the outsourcing of millions of U.S. jobs to China, India, and Latin America.

Outsourcing is about comparative advantage. Firms hire foreign workers who hold a comparative advantage and can produce a good or service more cheaply and at a lower opportunity cost than domestic workers.

REVIEW QUESTIONS

- Software engineering jobs are outsourced from the United States to India. Use supply and demand curves to sketch the effects on the U.S. and Indian labor forces.

- Outsourcing is controversial. Explain why by citing effects to the economy both in the short run and long run.

SKILLED WORK WITHOUT THE WORKER

Tesla factory in California. Where are the workers?

While the many robots in auto factories typically perform only one function, at the Tesla electric automobile factory in Fremont, California, a robot might perform up to four tasks. And it does it all without a coffee break—three shifts a day, 365 days a year. This is the future. A new wave of robots, far more adept than those now commonly used by automakers and other heavy manufacturers, are replacing workers around the world in both manufacturing and distribution. Factories like Tesla's are a striking counterpoint to those used by Apple and other consumer electronics giants, which employ hundreds of thousands of low-skilled workers.

The falling costs and growing sophistication of robots have touched off a renewed debate among economists and technologists over how quickly jobs will be lost. MIT economists Erik Brynjolfsson and Andrew McAfee argue that the transformation will be rapid: "The pace and scale of this encroachment into human skills is relatively recent and has profound economic implications." In their minds, the advent of low-cost automation foretells changes similar to those of the revolution in agricultural technology over the last century, which decreased farming employment in the United States from 40% of the workforce to about 2% today.

Robot manufacturers in the United States say that in many applications, robots are already more cost-effective than humans. In one example, a robotic manufacturing system initially cost $250,000 and replaced two machine operators, each earning $50,000 a year. Over the 15-year life of the system, the machines yielded $3.5 million in labor savings.

Some jobs are still outside the range of automation: construction jobs that require workers to move in unpredictable settings and perform different tasks that are not repetitive; assembly work that requires tactile feedback like placing fiberglass panels inside airplanes, boats, or cars; and assembly jobs where only a limited quantity of the product is made or where there are many versions of each product, which would require expensive reprogramming of robots. Moreover, Tesla may rely on automation in its Fremont plant, but it is still the area's biggest employer, with 10,000 workers compared to 3,200 for the local school district in the #2 spot—so there are still plenty of jobs that automation can't reach—yet.

But that list is growing shorter. Older robots cannot do such work because computer vision systems were costly and limited to carefully controlled environments where the lighting was just right. But thanks to an inexpensive stereo camera and software that lets the system see shapes with the same ease as humans, new types of robot can quickly discern the irregular dimensions of randomly placed objects.

"We're on the cusp of completely changing manufacturing and distribution," says Gary Bradski, a machine-vision scientist. "I think it's not as singular an event, but it will ultimately have as big an impact as the Internet."

Adapted from "Skilled Work, Without the Worker" by John Markoff, *New York Times*, August 18, 2012.

Conclusion

Throughout this chapter, we learned that the compensation for factor inputs depends on the interaction between demand and supply. Resource demand is derived from the demand for the final product a firm produces, and resource

Bang for the Buck: When to Use More Capital or More Labor

Suppose Agaves is considering the purchase of a new industrial dishwasher. The unit cleans faster and uses less labor and less water, but it costs $10,000. Should the restaurant make the capital expenditure, or would it be better off saving the money and incurring higher operating costs? To help decide what Agaves should do, consider this information: the dishwasher has a usable life of five years before it will need to be replaced. It will save the restaurant $300 a year in water and 10 hours of labor each week. Human dishwashers are currently paid $8 per hour.

How are all those dishes going to get clean?

QUESTION: Should Agaves purchase the new dishwasher?

ANSWER: This is the kind of question every business wrestles with on a regular basis. And the way to answer it is very straightforward. A firm should invest in new capital when the value of the marginal product it creates per dollar spent is greater than the value of the marginal product per dollar spent on the next-best alternative. In other words, a firm should invest in new capital when the bang per buck exceeds that of labor and other investments.

Let's compare the total cost of purchasing the dishwasher with the total savings. The total cost of the dishwasher is $10,000, but the savings are larger.

Item	Amount saved	Total for five years
Water	$300/year	$1,500
Labor	10 hours per week × $8/hour = $80/week × 52 weeks = $4,160/year	20,800
Total		22,300

The total savings over five years is $22,300. This makes the investment in the dishwasher the best choice!

---

supply depends on the other opportunities and compensation levels that exist in the market. As a result, the equilibrium prices and outputs in the markets for land, labor, and capital reflect, in large part, the forces of demand and supply.

In the next chapter, we examine income and poverty. As you will discover, there are many factors beyond the demand for and supply of workers that explain why some workers make more than others. For instance, wages also depend on the amount of human capital required for a job, as well as location, lifestyle choices, union membership, and the riskiness of the profession. Understanding these elements will deepen your understanding of why workers earn what they do.

It is true that outsourcing destroys some jobs in high-labor-cost areas, but it also creates jobs in low-labor-cost areas. As a result, it lowers the cost of manufacturing goods and providing services. This improved efficiency helps firms that outsource by enabling them to better compete in the global economy.

Will Your Future Job Be Automated?

- The best way to ensure that your future job is not automated is to be valuable to your organization.
- Developing new skills and knowledge is integral to maintaining and increasing the value of the marginal product of your labor.
- When you are highly valued, it will be difficult to replace you.
- Low-skill occupations tend to be the most at risk.

When you select an academic major and learn a set of skills, you hope they will enable you to find stable employment. Finding stable employment becomes more challenging in an environment where labor is easily automated. So as you seek employment, you need to consider the long-term likelihood that your job could be replaced. To help you think about your future career, let's consider jobs that are likely to be automated and jobs that are more likely to still be done by humans.

Researchers estimate that nearly half of all U.S. jobs may be at risk in the coming decades, with lower-paid occupations among the most vulnerable. In 2017 Bloomberg.com created a tool in an article to "Find Out If Your Job Will Be Automated." It projected which jobs are at increased risk of being replaced, which included nearly 50% of all U.S. jobs. Type your occupation into the search bar (as shown in the figure) to see where the researchers peg the probability of your job being automated.

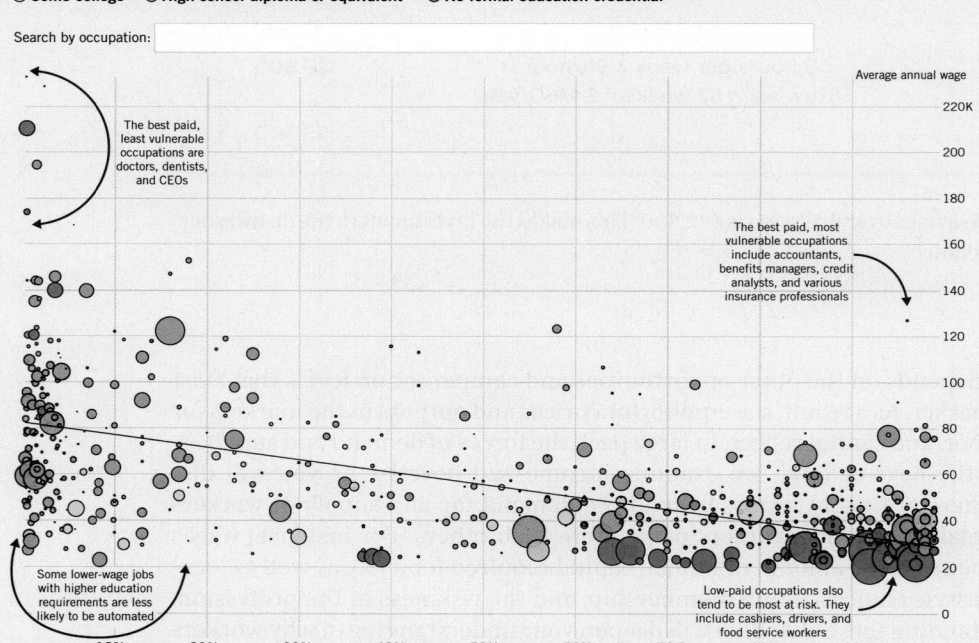

Might your job be automated? Bloomberg.com's search tool predicts it may be.

Outsourcing is one of the many ways firms adapt when labor costs rise. Firms also utilize more capital and deploy more technology when labor costs increase. And, workers must create a high value of the marginal product of labor to keep automation and robotics from making them superfluous as workers. ✳

· ANSWERING *the* BIG QUESTIONS ·

What are the factors of production?

- Labor, land, and capital are the factors of production, or the inputs used in producing goods and services.

Where does the demand for labor come from?

- The demand for each factor of production is a derived demand that stems from a firm's desire to supply a good in another market. Labor demand is contingent on the value of the marginal product that is produced, and the value of the marginal product is equivalent to the firm's labor demand curve.

Where does the supply of labor come from?

- The supply of labor comes from the wage rate that is offered. Each worker faces the labor-leisure trade-off. At high wage levels, the income effect may become larger than the substitution effect and cause the labor supply curve to bend backward. Changes in the supply of labor can result from other employment opportunities, the changing composition of the workforce, immigration, and migration.

What are the determinants of demand and supply in the labor market?

- Labor markets bring the forces of demand and supply together in a wage signal that conveys information to both sides of the market. At wages above the equilibrium, the supply of workers exceeds the demand for labor. The result is a surplus of available workers that places downward pressure on wages until they reach the equilibrium wage, at which point the surplus is eliminated. At wages below the equilibrium, the demand for labor exceeds the available supply of workers, and a shortage develops. The shortage forces firms to offer higher wages to attract workers. Wages rise until they reach the equilibrium wage, at which point the shortage is eliminated.

- There is no definitive result for outsourcing of labor in the short run. In the long run, outsourcing moves jobs to workers who are more productive and enhances overall social welfare.

What role do land and capital play in production?

- Land and capital (as well as labor) are the factors of production across which firms compare the value of the marginal product per dollar spent. Firms seek to equalize the revenue per dollar spent on each input, thereby maximizing their efficiency.

Concepts You Should Know

backward-bending labor supply
curve (p. 444)
derived demand (p. 437)
economic rent (p. 458)

income effect (p. 444)
marginal product of
labor (p. 438)
monopsony (p. 455)

outsourcing of labor (p. 452)
substitution effect (p. 444)
value of the marginal product
(VMP) (p. 439)

Questions for Review

1. Why is the demand for factor inputs a derived demand?

2. What rule does a firm use when deciding to hire an additional worker?

3. What are the two shifters of labor demand? What are the four shifters of labor supply?

4. What can cause the labor supply curve to bend backward?

5. If wages are below the equilibrium level, what would cause them to rise?

6. What would happen to movie stars' wages if all major film studios merged into a single firm, creating a monopsony for film actors?

7. If workers became more productive (that is, produced more output in the same amount of time), what would happen to the demand for labor, the wages of labor, and the number of workers employed?

8. How is economic rent different from rent seeking?

9. How does outsourcing affect wages and employment in the short run and in the long run?

Study Problems (✴ *solved at the end of this section*)

1. Maria is a hostess at a local restaurant. When she earned $8 per hour, she worked 35 hours per week. When her wage increased to $10 per hour, she decided to work 40 hours per week. However, when her wage increased again to $12 per hour, she decided to cut back to 37 hours per week. Draw Maria's supply curve. How would you explain her actions to someone who is unfamiliar with economics?

2. Would a burrito restaurant hire an additional worker for $10.00 an hour if that worker could produce an extra 30 burritos and each burrito made added $0.60 in revenues?

✴ 3. Pam's Pretzels has a production function shown in the following table. It costs Pam's Pretzels $80 per day per worker. Each pretzel sells for $3.

Quantity of labor	Quantity of pretzels
0	0
1	100
2	180
3	240
4	280
5	310
6	330
7	340
8	320

a. Compute the marginal product and the value of the marginal product that each worker creates.

b. How many workers should Pam's Pretzels hire?

4. Jimi owns a music school that specializes in teaching guitar. Jimi has a limited supply of rooms for his instructors to use for lessons. As a result, each successive instructor adds less to Jimi's output of lessons. The following table lists Jimi's production function. Guitar lessons cost $25 per hour.

Quantity of labor	Quantity of lessons (hours)
0	0
1	10
2	17
3	23
4	28
5	32
6	35
7	37
8	38

a. Construct Jimi's labor demand schedule at each of the following daily wage rates for instructors: $75, $100, $125, $150, $175, $200.
b. Suppose that the market price of guitar lessons increases to $35 per hour. What does Jimi's new labor demand schedule look like at the daily wage rates listed in part (a)?

5. In an effort to create a healthcare safety net, the government requires employers to provide healthcare coverage to all employees. What impact will this increased coverage have in the following labor markets in the short run?

a. the demand for doctors
b. the demand for medical equipment
c. the supply of hospital beds

6. A million-dollar lottery winner decides to quit working. How can you explain this behavior using economics?

7. Illustrate each of the following changes with a labor supply and demand diagram. (Use a separate diagram for each part.) Diagram the new equilibrium point, and note how the wage and quantity of workers employed changes.

a. There is a sudden migration out of an area.
b. Laborers are willing to work more hours.
c. Fewer workers are willing to work the night shift.
d. The demand for California wines suddenly increases.

✳ **8.** A football team is trying to decide which of two running backs (A or B) to sign to a one-year contract.

Predicted statistics	Player A	Player B
Touchdowns	7	10
Yards gained	1,200	1,000
Fumbles	4	5

The team has done a statistical analysis to determine the value of each touchdown, yard gained, and fumble to the team's revenue. Each touchdown is worth an extra $250,000, each yard gained is worth $1,500, and each fumble costs $75,000. Player A costs $3.0 million and player B costs $2.5 million. Based on their predicted statistics in the table above, which player should the team sign?

9. Farmers in Utopia experience perfect weather throughout the entire growing season, and as a result their crop is double its normal size. Draw a labor supply and demand diagram and use the diagram to explain how this bumper crop will affect each of the following.

a. the price of the crop
b. the marginal product of workers who harvest the crop
c. the demand for the workers who harvest the crop

10. What will happen to the equilibrium wage of crop harvesters in Dystopia if the price of the crop falls by 50% and the marginal product of the workers increases by 25%?

11. Suppose that the current wage rate is $20 per hour, the rental rate of land is $10,000 per acre, and the rental rate of capital is $2,500. The manager of a firm determines that the value of the marginal product of labor is $400, the value of the marginal product of an acre of land is $200,000, and the value of the marginal product of capital is $4,000. Is the firm maximizing profit? Explain your response.

✳ 12. What country made the shirt you are wearing? Go ahead and check the tag and write down your answer. Even though we can't predict the exact country your shirt is from, there is a surprising answer in the Solved Problems section, which you should check out.

13. Why are most iPhones manufactured and assembled in China and then shipped to the United States, even though Apple was founded in California and most of Apple's workforce still reside in this country?

✳ 14. We saw that a backward-bending supply curve of labor can cause individual workers to work less at high wage levels. But one doesn't generally see market supply curves bend backward. Can you explain why we don't generally see that but see it here?

15. Use labor supply and demand curves to illustrate what will happen to the wages of each of the following as the United States ages.

   a. teachers
   b. dog walkers

Solved Problems

3. a.

Quantity of labor	Quantity of pretzels	Marginal product	Value of the marginal product
0	0	0	$0
1	100	100	300
2	180	80	240
3	240	60	180
4	280	40	120
5	310	30	90
6	330	20	60
7	340	10	30
8	320	−20	−60

b. The VMP of the fifth worker is $90 and each worker costs $80, so Pam should hire five workers. Hiring the sixth worker would cause her to lose $20.

8.

Predicted statistics	Player A	VMP of Player A	Player B	VMP of Player B
Touchdowns	7	$1,750,000	10	$2,500,000
Yards gained	1,200	1,800,000	1,000	1,500,000
Fumbles	4	−300,000	5	−375,000
Total value		3,250,000		3,625,000

Player A has a predicted VMP of $3.25 million and a cost of $3.0 million. Player B has a predicted VMP of $3.625 million and a cost of $2.5 million. Since player B's predicted VMP exceeds his salary by $1.125 million and player A's predicted VMP exceeds his salary by only $0.25 million, the team should sign player B.

12. Forget the country of origin on your tag—that is just where the final product was assembled. Your shirt is actually a product of a global supply

chain that includes cotton seeds engineered in the United States, cotton grown in India, sewing machines manufactured in Germany, a collar lining from Brazil, and inexpensive labor from the place on your tag (where all the pieces were sewn together). The tag chronicles the end of your shirt's journey, so it gets the credit; but behind the scenes it takes a planet to make every shirt, and that is the surprising answer to the question.

14. In general, rising prices draw more suppliers. This is also true for wages in a particular market: as wages rise, more workers will choose that occupation, thereby ensuring that the market supply of labor increases. For the labor market as a whole, however, the supply of workers is more or less fixed (barring unrestricted immigration), and so there is a cap on the number of worker-hours per month that the market can supply. If wages continue to rise, the supply of labor becomes completely inelastic and the supply curve becomes vertical. This makes it possible for the income effect to begin to overtake the substitution effect if wages rise still further, as workers enjoy the same pay while working fewer hours.

15

Income, Inequality, and Poverty

Do You Think the Structure of Compensation in the Working World is Unfair?

If you wish to earn a sizable income, it is not enough to be good at something; that "something" needs to be an occupation that society values highly. What matters are your skills, what you produce, and the supply of workers in your chosen profession. How hard you work often has little to do with how much you get paid.

Just think about schoolteachers. They put in long hours, including evenings spent grading and prepping for the next day's classes. But the pay that teachers earn is low relative to the hours they put in and often teachers need to look for other income streams. One modern idea is to monetize their lesson plans. Second-grade teacher Nicki Dingraudo has an Instagram account, *The Sprinkle Topped Teacher*, with over thirty thousand followers. She lives in Arizona, where teachers are paid, on average, about $50,000 per year. That may sound like decent money, but it is not enough if you're a single parent who hopes to own a home and raise a family. Teachers like Nicki who have followers on Instagram or Pinterest in the tens or hundreds of thousands can earn more from social influence than they do from their salaries. How? On Instagram the same teacher helps thousands of other teachers by creating unique tools that make course preparation easier. Since

Social media puts one in touch with many thousands of adult followers. Teachers and many other "influencers" are using it to turn their work efforts into additional income.

time is the scarce resource many teachers wish they had more of, teachers often pay for lesson plans from trusted social influencers.

In this chapter, we continue our exploration of labor by examining income and inequality in labor markets, including the characteristics of successful wage earners and the impediments the poor face when they try to escape poverty. Examining those at the top and the bottom of the income ladder helps us explain the many forces that determine income. In addition, we explore the incidence of poverty, poverty trends, and measurement issues. Examining the poverty statistics, and understanding the causes of poverty, allows society to craft economic policies that more effectively help those in need.

· BIG QUESTIONS ·

- What are the determinants of wages?
- What causes income inequality?
- How do economists analyze poverty?

What Are the Determinants of Wages?

The reasons why some workers get paid more than others are complex. We learned in Chapter 14 that the forces of supply and demand explain a large part of wage inequality. However, numerous additional factors contribute to differences in earnings. Various nonmonetary factors cause some occupations to pay higher or lower wages than supply and demand would seem to dictate. In other contexts, discrimination on the basis of gender, race, or other characteristics is an unfortunate but very real factor in wages. And in some markets, a "winner-take-all" structure can lead to a small number of workers capturing a large majority of the total earnings.

The Nonmonetary Determinants of Wages

Some jobs have characteristics that make them more desirable or less desirable. Also, no two workers are exactly alike. Differences in jobs and worker ability affect the supply and demand of labor. In this section, we examine the nonmonetary determinants of wages, including compensating differentials, education and human capital, location and lifestyle, unions, and efficiency wages.

Are you being paid enough to risk a fall?

COMPENSATING DIFFERENTIALS Some jobs are more unpleasant, risky, stressful, inconvenient, or monotonous than others. If the characteristics of a job make it unattractive, firms must offer more to attract workers. For instance, roofing, logging, and deep-sea fishing are some of the most dangerous occupations in the world. Workers who do these jobs must be compensated with higher wages to offset the higher risk of injury. A **compensating differential** is the difference in wages offered to offset the desirability or undesirability of a job. If a job's characteristics make it unattractive, the compensating wage differential must be positive.

In contrast, some jobs are highly desirable. For example, restaurant critics sample a lot of great food, radio DJs spend the day playing their favorite music, and video game testers try beta versions before they are released. Some jobs are simply more fun, exciting, prestigious, or stimulating than others. In these cases, the compensating differential is negative and the firm offers lower wages. For example, newspaper reporters and radio DJs earn low pay. Video game testing is so desirable that most people who do it are not paid at all.

A **compensating differential** is the difference in wages offered to offset the desirability or undesirability of a job.

Incentives

EDUCATION AND HUMAN CAPITAL Many complex jobs require substantial education, training, and industry experience. Qualifying to receive the specialized education required for certain occupations—for example, getting into medical school—is often very difficult. Relatively few students are able to pursue these degrees. In addition, such specialized education is expensive, in terms of both tuition and forgone income.

The set of skills that workers acquire on the job and through education are collectively known as **human capital**. Unlike other forms of capital, investments in human capital accrue to the employee. As a result, workers who have high human capital can market their skills among competing firms. Engineers, doctors, and members of other professions that require extensive education and training can command high wages in part because the human capital needed to do those jobs is high. In contrast, low-skilled workers such as ushers, baggers, and sales associates earn less because the human capital required to do those jobs is quite low; it is easy to find replacements.

Table 15.1 shows the relationship between education and pay. Increased human capital (education) qualifies a worker for jobs paying higher wages. Workers who earn advanced degrees have a higher marginal product of labor because their extra schooling has presumably given them additional skills for the job. But they also have invested heavily in education. Higher wages are a compensating differential that rewards additional education.

Opportunity cost

Human capital is the set of skills workers acquire on the job and through education.

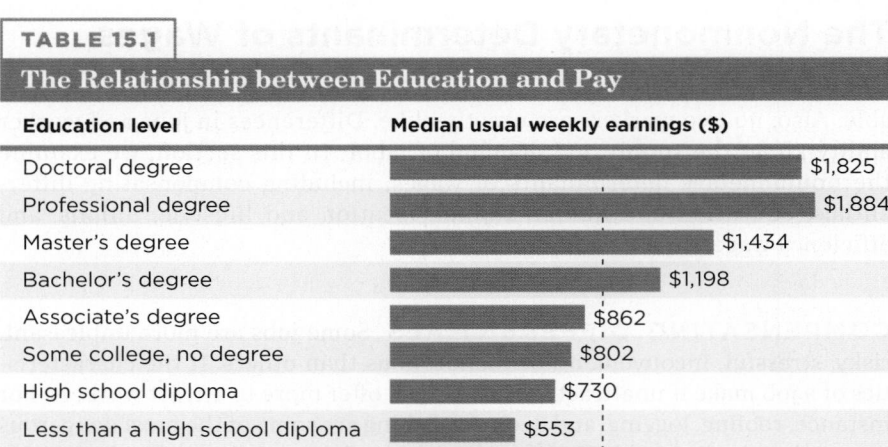

TABLE 15.1

The Relationship between Education and Pay

Education level	Median usual weekly earnings ($)
Doctoral degree	$1,825
Professional degree	$1,884
Master's degree	$1,434
Bachelor's degree	$1,198
Associate's degree	$862
Some college, no degree	$802
High school diploma	$730
Less than a high school diploma	$553
All workers	$932

Note: Data are for persons age 25 and over. Earnings are for full-time wage and salary workers.

Source: U.S. Bureau of Labor Statistics, Current Population Survey.

ECONOMICS IN THE REAL WORLD

DOES EDUCATION *REALLY* PAY?

An alternative perspective on the value of education argues that the returns to increased education are not the product of what a student learns, but rather a signal to prospective employers. In other words, the degree itself (specifically, the classes taken to earn that degree) is not evidence of a set of skills that makes a worker more productive. Rather, earning a degree and attending prominent institutions is a signal of a potential employee's quality. Prospective employers assume that a student who gets into college must be intelligent and willing to work hard. Students who have done well in college send another signal: they are able to learn quickly and perform well under stress.

It is possible to test the importance of signaling by looking at the returns to earning a college degree, controlling for institutional quality. At many elite institutions, the four-year price tag has reached extraordinary levels. For example, to attend Columbia University in New York City, the most expensive institution in the country, it cost $74,173 in 2018–2019. Over four years, that adds up to more than a quarter of a million dollars! What type of return do graduates of such highly selective (and expensive) institutions make on their sizable investments? And are those returns the result of a rigorous education or a result of the institution's reputation? It is difficult to answer this question because the students who attend more selective institutions are more likely to have higher earnings potential regardless of where they attend college. These students enter college as high achievers, a trait that carries forward into the workplace no matter where they attend school.

Is it the amount of education you obtain or other traits that determine your financial success?

Economists Stacy Dale and Alan Krueger examined the financial outcomes for over 6,000 students who were accepted or rejected by a comparable set of colleges. They found that 20 years after graduation, students who had been accepted at more selective colleges but decided to attend a less selective college earned the same amount as their counterparts from more selective colleges. This finding indicates that actually attending a prestigious school is less important for future career success than the qualities that enable students to get *accepted* at a prestigious school.

Although Table 15.1 shows that additional education pays, the reason is not simply an increase in human capital. There is also a signal that employers can interpret about other, less observable qualities. For instance, Harvard graduates presumably learn a great deal in their time at school, but they were also highly motivated and likely to be successful even before they went to college. Part of the increase in income attributable to completing college depends on a set of other traits that the student already possessed, independent of the school or the degree.

LOCATION AND LIFESTYLE For most people, sipping margaritas in Key West, Florida, sounds more appealing than living in Eureka, Nevada, along the most isolated stretch of road in the continental United States. Likewise, being able to see a show, visit a museum, or go to a Yankees game in New York City constitutes a different lifestyle from what you'd experience in Dodge City, Kansas. People find some places more desirable than others. So how does location affect wages? Where the climate is more pleasant, all other things being equal, people are willing to accept lower wages because the nonmonetary benefits of enjoying the weather act as a compensating differential. Similarly, jobs in metropolitan areas—where the cost of living is significantly higher than in most other places—pay higher wages as a cost-of-living adjustment. The higher wage helps employees afford a quality of life similar to what they would enjoy if they worked in less expensive areas.

How much more would you pay to live near here?

Choice of lifestyle is also a major factor in determining wage differences. Some workers are not particularly concerned with maximizing their income; instead, they care more about working for a cause. This is true for many employees of nonprofits or religious organizations or even for people who take care of loved ones. Others follow a dream of being a musician, writer, or actor. And still others are guided by a passion such as skiing or surfing. Indeed, many workers view their pay as less important than doing something they are passionate about. For these workers, lower pay functions as a compensating differential.

UNIONS A **union** is a group of workers who bargain collectively for better wages and benefits. Unions are able to secure increased wages by creating significant market power over the supply of labor available to a firm. A union's ability to achieve higher wages depends on a credible threat of a work stoppage, known as a **strike**. In effect, unions can raise wages because they represent labor, and labor is a key input in the production process. Because firms cannot do without labor, an effective union can use the threat of a strike to negotiate higher wages for its workers.

A **union** is a group of workers who bargain collectively for better wages and benefits.

A **strike** is a work stoppage designed to aid a union's bargaining position.

U.S. law prohibits some unions from going on strike, including those representing many transit workers, some public school teachers, law enforcement officers, and workers in other essential services. If workers in one of these industries reach an impasse in wage and benefit negotiations, the employee union is required to submit to the decision of an impartial third party, a process known as *binding arbitration*. The television show *Judge Judy* is an example of binding arbitration

Does going on strike result in higher wages?

in action: two parties with a small claims grievance agree in advance to accept the verdict of Judith Sheindlin, a noted family court judge.

The effect of unions in the United States has changed since the early days of unionization in the late 1800s. Early studies of the union wage premium found wages to be as much as 30% higher for unionized workers. At the height of unionization approximately 60 years ago, one in three jobs was a unionized position. Today, only about one in eight workers belongs to a union. Today, most empirical studies find the wage premium to be between 10% and 20%. The demise of many unions has coincided with the transition of the U.S. economy from a manufacturing base to one with a greater emphasis on the service sector, which is less centralized.

EFFICIENCY WAGES In terms of paying wages, one approach stands out as unique. Ordinarily, we think of wages being determined in the labor market at the intersection of supply and demand. When the labor market is in equilibrium, the wage guarantees that every qualified worker can find employment. However, some firms willingly pay more than the equilibrium wage. **Efficiency wages** exist when an employer pays its workers more than the equilibrium wage. Why would a business do that? Surprisingly, the answer is to make *more* profit. That outcome hardly seems possible when a firm using efficiency wages pays its workers more than its competitors do. But think again. Above-equilibrium wages (1) decrease turnover; (2) increase productivity by attracting a larger applicant pool, from which the most productive ones can be chosen; and (3) increase the cost of being fired, because other jobs in the same industry don't pay as well—giving every worker a greater incentive to work hard and not shirk. **Productivity** is the effectiveness of effort as measured in terms of the rate of output per unit of input. If the gains in overall labor productivity are higher than the increased cost, the result is greater profit for the firm.

Efficiency wages
are wages higher than equilibrium wages, offered to increase worker productivity.

Productivity
is the effectiveness of effort as measured in terms of the rate of output per unit of input.

Incentives

Henry Ford developed a visionary assembly process and also implemented efficiency wages at his plants.

Automaker Henry Ford used efficiency wages to generate more productivity on the Model T assembly line. In 1914, Ford decided to more than double the pay of assembly-line workers to $5 a day—an increase that his competitors did not match. He also decreased the workday from 9 hours to 8 hours. Ford's primary goal was to reduce worker turnover, which was frequent because of the monotonous nature of assembly-line work. By making the job so lucrative, he hoped that most workers would not quit so quickly. He was right. The turnover rate plummeted from over 10% per day to less than 1%. As word of Ford's high wages spread, workers flocked to Detroit. The day after the wage increase was announced, over 10,000 eager job seekers lined up outside Ford's Highland Park, Michigan, plant. From this crowd, Ford hired many temporary workers and gave each a 30-day trial. At the end of the trial period, he permanently hired the most productive workers and let the others go. The resulting productivity increase per worker was more than enough to offset the wage increase. In addition, reducing the length of each shift enabled Ford to add an extra shift, which increased productivity even more.

We have seen that wages are influenced by factors that include compensating differentials, human capital, location and

TABLE 15.2

The Key Nonmonetary Determinants of Wage Differences

Determinant	Impact on wages	In pictures
Compensating differentials	Some workers are eager to have jobs that are more fun, exciting, prestigious, or stimulating than others. As a result, they are willing to accept lower wages. Conversely, jobs that are unpleasant or risky require higher wages.	
Human capital	Many jobs require substantial education, training, and experience. As a result, workers who acquire additional amounts of human capital can command higher wages.	
Location and lifestyle	When the location is desirable, the compensating wage will be lower. Similarly, when employment is for a highly valued cause, wage is less important. In both situations, the compensating wage will be lower.	
Unions	Because firms cannot do without labor, unions can threaten a strike to negotiate higher wages.	
Efficiency wages	The firm pays above-equilibrium wages to help reduce slacking, decrease turnover, and increase productivity.	

lifestyle, union membership, and the presence of efficiency wages. Table 15.2 summarizes these nonmonetary determinants of income differences.

Wage Discrimination

When workers with the same ability as others are not paid the same because of their race, ethnic origin, sex, age, religion, or some other group characteristic, we say they are experiencing **wage discrimination**. Because of its importance for individuals and for policymakers, economists study the topic of wage discrimination by trying to understand its effects in the past and to help address wage discrimination today. In this section, we explore some of their observations. While most economists acknowledge that bias plays a role in wage discrimination, they believe that broader factors related to human capital play the major roles.

Wage discrimination occurs when workers with the same ability as others are not paid the same because of their race, ethnic origin, sex, age, religion, or some other group characteristic.

LOOKING AT THE DATA Table 15.3 presents median weekly earnings in the United States by sex, race or ethnic group, and age. Looking at the data, we see large earnings differences across many groups in U.S. society. In particular, female workers earn 19% less than their male counterparts. While most of us would like to believe that employers no longer pay men more than women for doing the same job, wage discrimination does still exist. In 2009, President Obama signed the Lilly Ledbetter Fair Pay Act, which

TABLE 15.3

Median Weekly Earnings by Group

Group	Median earnings in 2018	Percentage difference within each group
Males	$959	–
Females	780	–19%
White	907	–
Black	683	–25
Asian	1083	19
Hispanic	674	–26
Early-career workers (25–34)	794	–20
Mid-career workers (35–54)	978	–2
Late-career workers (55–64)	993	–

Source: U.S. Bureau of Labor Statistics, 2018. https://www.bls.gov/news.release/pdf/wkyeng.pdf.

gives victims of wage discrimination more time to file a complaint with the government. The act is named after a former Goodyear employee who sued the company in 2007. The courts determined that she was paid 15% to 40% less than her male counterparts. The fact that a major U.S. corporation was violating the Equal Pay Act of 1963 almost 50 years after its passage was a poignant reminder that wage discrimination still occurs in our society.

PRACTICE WHAT YOU KNOW

Efficiency Wages: Which Company Pays an Efficiency Wage?

Forbes magazine calls Facebook the best company to work for—and not just because you eat for free at work.

You are considering two job offers. Company A is well known and respected and offers a year-end bonus based on your productivity relative to other workers. This could substantially boost your income but the company's base wage is relatively low. Company B is not as well known, but its wages are higher than the norm in your field. This company does not offer a year-end bonus.

QUESTION: Which company, A or B, is the efficiency wage employer?

ANSWER: Efficiency wages are a mechanism that some companies use to reduce turnover, encourage teamwork, and create loyalty. Company A's bonus plan will reward the best producers, but the average and less-than-average workers will become frustrated and leave. Company A is not paying efficiency wages; it is simply using incentives tied to productivity. Company B is the efficiency wage employer because it pays every worker somewhat higher wages to reduce turnover.

CHALLENGE QUESTION: If firms in a given industry can become more profitable by paying efficiency wages rather than equilibrium wages, why don't all firms pay efficiency wages?

ANSWER: Efficiency wages work as an incentive to reduce turnover and boost productivity because they are higher than the equilibrium wage in the industry. If every firm paid higher wages, none of the firms would be at a competitive advantage in retaining workers or finding more productive workers from a larger-than-normal applicant pool. Therefore, if efficiency wages became the norm, they would lose their effectiveness.

Incentives

But economists try to study the topic of wage discrimination further by examining the data. For example, women and men often hold different types of jobs, and certain jobs pay more than others. Higher wages in jobs such as road work and construction reflect in part a compensating differential for exposure to extreme temperatures, bad weather, and other dangers, and men are more likely to work in these jobs. Additionally, more women than men take time off from work to raise a family, meaning that women ultimately have fewer years of work experience, put in fewer paid work hours per year, are less likely to work a full-time schedule, and leave the labor force for longer periods. In contrast, men normally take less, if any, time off to raise children. In the long term, these differences tend to lead to lower levels of human capital and overall lower wages for women.

Claudia Goldin's careful examination of the gender wage gap data suggests that the gap stems not from gender discrimination, but from work design. She found that people who work the longest and least flexible hours make the highest salaries per unit of time—and those people tend to be men, because women are more likely to be juggling caregiving responsibilities. Framed differently, one way to help close the gap is for employers to be more flexible about work hours and pay part-time workers a pro-rated share of what full-time workers earn. This is also more of a work-life balance issue. Added flexibility helps all workers juggle careers, family, and other interests. The work of Francine Blau and Lawrence Kahn explains some of the important causes of the gender pay gap. Their research finds that 62% of the pay gap is attributable to the first six causes listed in Figure 15.1. Unmeasured factors—including discrimination—account for the other 38% of the gap.

Similarly, differences in human capital can help explain wide gaps in earnings data by race or ethnic group. Asian Americans (56% of whom have a bachelor's degree or higher) have higher education levels than whites (44%), who in turn generally have much higher levels than blacks (24%) and Hispanics (20%). Economists expect the wage disparities between groups to decrease as these educational differences (and the resulting differences in human capital) become less pronounced. Socioeconomic factors also play a significant role in these disparities. For instance, the low quality of some inner-city schools can limit the educational attainment of students, many of whom are minorities.

For every $1 men make, women make, on average, 81 cents.

HUMAN CAPITAL AND THE LIFE-CYCLE WAGE PATTERN The earnings gap between mid-career workers and others also reflects differences in human capital. After all, workers who are just starting out have limited experience. As these workers age, they accumulate on-the-job training and experience that make them more productive

FIGURE 15.1

What Do We Know about What Causes the Gender Pay Gap?

Studies show that a large portion of the gender pay gap comes from factors that cannot be measured.

Source: Journal of Economic Literature, 2017.

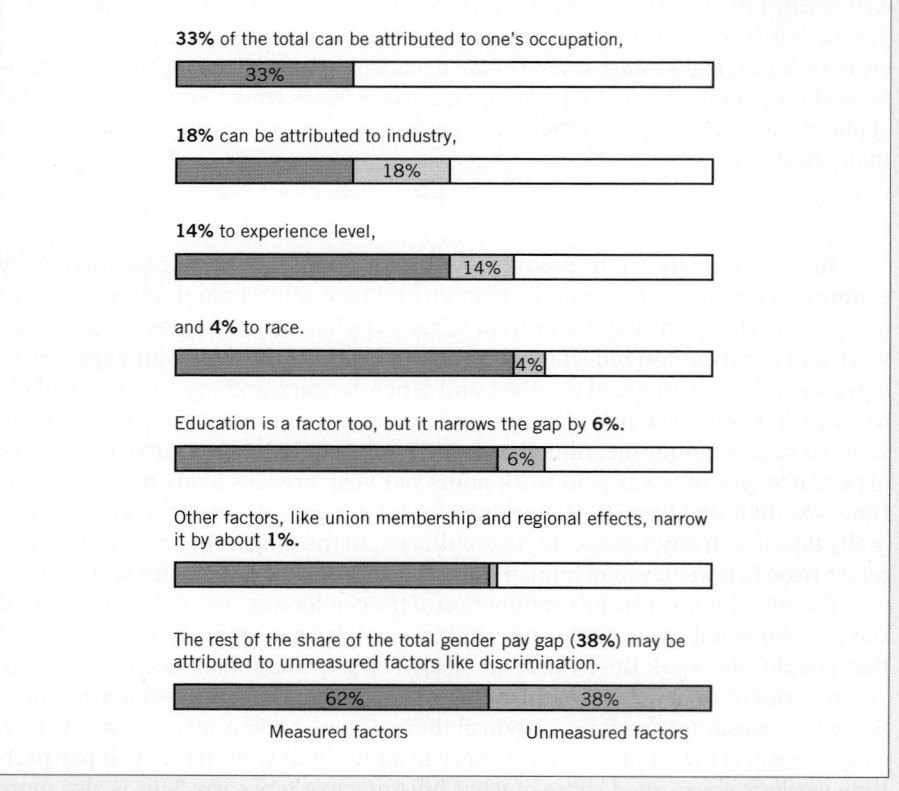

33% of the total can be attributed to one's occupation,

33%

18% can be attributed to industry,

18%

14% to experience level,

14%

and **4%** to race.

4%

Education is a factor too, but it narrows the gap by **6%**.

6%

Other factors, like union membership and regional effects, narrow it by about **1%**.

The rest of the share of the total gender pay gap (**38%**) may be attributed to unmeasured factors like discrimination.

| 62% | 38% |
| Measured factors | Unmeasured factors |

The **life-cycle wage pattern** refers to the predictable effect age has on earnings over the course of a person's working life. Wages peak for people in their early 60s and then slowly fall thereafter.

and enable them to obtain higher wages. However, for older workers the gains from increased experience are eventually offset by diminishing returns. Consequently, wages peak when these workers are in their early 60s and then slowly fall thereafter. This pattern, known as the **life-cycle wage pattern**, refers to the predictable effect age has on earnings over a person's working life.

ECONOMICS IN THE REAL WORLD

THE EFFECTS OF BEAUTY ON EARNINGS

According to research that spans the labor market from the law profession to college teaching and in countries as different as the United States and China, beauty matters. How much? You might be surprised. As related by economist Daniel S. Hamermesh in his book *Beauty Pays*, beautiful people make as much as 10% more than people with average looks, while those whose looks are considered significantly below average may make as much as 25% below normal.

The influence of beauty on wages can be viewed in two ways. First, beauty can be seen as a marketable trait that has value in many professions. Actors, fashion models, restaurant servers, and litigators all rely on their appearance to make a living, so it is not surprising that beauty is correlated with wages in those professions. If beautiful

Sandra Bullock, Lupita Nyong'o, Chris Hemsworth—three of the decade's most beautiful people.

people are more productive in certain jobs because of their beauty, then attractiveness is simply a measure of the value of the marginal product they generate. In other words, being beautiful is a form of human capital the worker possesses.

However, a second interpretation finds evidence of discrimination. If employers prefer "beautiful" people as employees, then part of the earnings increase associated with beauty might reflect that preference. In addition, the success of workers who are more beautiful could also reflect the preferences of customers who prefer to buy products and services from attractive people.

Because it is impossible to determine whether the beauty premium is a compensating differential or the result of overt discrimination, we have to acknowledge the possibility that the truth, in many situations, could be a little bit of both.

Also, height and earnings are correlated. A study found that for every inch taller you are, you make on average $800 more per year (the study controlled for gender, weight, and age).

OCCUPATIONAL CROWDING: HOW DISCRIMINATION AFFECTS WAGES Another factor deserving particular attention is **occupational crowding**—the phenomenon of relegating a group of workers to a narrow range of jobs in the economy. To understand how occupational crowding works, imagine a community named Utopia with only two types of jobs: a small number in engineering and a large number in secretarial services. Furthermore, men and women are equally proficient at both occupations, and everyone in the community is happy to work either job. Under these assumptions, we would expect the wages for engineers and secretaries to be the same.

Now imagine that not everyone in Utopia has the same opportunities. Suppose we roll back the clock to a time when women in Utopia are not allowed to work as engineers. Women who want to work can only find employment as secretaries. As a result of this occupational crowding, workers who have limited opportunities (women, in this example) find themselves competing with one another, as well as with the men who cannot get engineering jobs, for secretarial positions. As a result, wages fall in secretarial jobs and rise in engineering. Because only men can work in engineering, they are paid more than their similarly qualified female counterparts, who are crowded into secretarial positions and

Occupational crowding is the phenomenon of relegating a group of workers to a narrow range of jobs in the economy.

earn less. Furthermore, because women who want to work can only receive a low wage as a secretary, many effectively decide to stay at home and produce nonmarket services, such as child-rearing. These services have a higher value to the women who make this choice than the wages they could earn as secretaries.

Of course, women today are not restricted to secretarial jobs, but they still hold more of the lower-paying jobs in our society. The first column of Figure 15.2

FIGURE 15.2

Percentages of Male and Female Workers in the Most Common Occupations

In the United States, the most common jobs categories tend to be occupied by either women or men. Very few occupations have a roughly equal split of women and men. Women are also paid less than men across the board, though this is improving.

Source: US Census Bureau, 2017.

Common Occupations in USA, Gender and Pay Level

Occupation	Share of female workers in the occupation (percent)	Women's median weekly earnings	Men's median weekly earnings	Women's earnings as a percent of men's
Secretaries and admin assistants	94.5	735	852	86.3
Receptionists and information clerks	92.6	599	652	91.9
Registered nurses	88.8	1143	1260	90.7
Nursing, psychiatric, and home health aides	88.2	493	583	84.6
Bookkeeping, accounting, and auditing clerks	87.0	716	743	96.4
Office clerks, general	84.8	670	780	85.9
Maids and housekeeping	84.3	439	508	86.4
Elementary and middle school teachers	78.4	987	1139	86.7
Cashiers	72.2	422	493	85.6
Supervisors of office and admin support	67.7	819	987	83.0
Customer service representatives	65.6	637	712	89.5
Accountants and auditors	58.9	1065	1389	76.7
Retail supervisors	42.4	639	891	71.7
Retail salespersons	38.8	523	704	74.3
Managers, all other	38.7	1251	1629	76.8
Cooks	37.1	436	481	90.6
Stock clerks and order fillers	34.5	538	571	94.2
Janitors and building cleaners	28.8	481	574	83.8
Sales representatives, wholesale and manufacturing	27.9	956	1222	78.2
Software developers, applications and systems software	18.4	1543	1863	82.8
Laborers and freight, stock, and material movers, hand	17.5	500	595	84.0
Driver/sales workers and truck drivers	4.9	589	807	73.0
All full-time workers	**44.4**	**770**	**941**	**81.8**

shows the percentages of female workers in many of the most common jobs in the United States. Not surprisingly, given the low wages, neither men nor women rush into many of the lowest-paying jobs.

Why do occupational crowding and wage differentials continue? Rigidity in changing occupations, social customs (including discrimination), and personal preferences are all part of the explanation. However, many economists see a change coming. Because more women than men attend colleges and universities, women are now primarily responsible for expanding the supply of workers in most fields. As the supply of workers expands, the net effect will likely be lower wages in traditionally male-dominated jobs. At the same time, traditionally female-dominated jobs will see rising wages as women leave those jobs for better opportunities. The net result is that the wage gap will narrow over time.

Was your kindergarten teacher male or female?

A CAUTIOUSLY OPTIMISTIC OUTLOOK Because no employer will admit to discriminating, researchers can only infer the amount of bias driven discrimination after first correcting for observable differences from compensating differentials and differences in human capital. The unobservable differences that remain are presumed to reflect discrimination. While the number is hotly debated, most economists estimate that discrimination accounts for less than 5% of observed wage differences. They also see many signs of improvement.

Though it is still real, the gender gap is shrinking. In 1960 women in the workforce earned, on average, 60 cents for every dollar men earned. Today women earn 81 cents for every dollar men earn (see the second, third, and fourth columns of Figure 15.2), and the gap continues to close by about half a cent each year. In addition, women are no longer clustered in less rigorous academic programs than men, so women are more prepared to get jobs that pay better. In 2018, for example, more women than men in the United States received doctoral degrees. The number of women at every level of academia has been rising for decades. There are now three women for every two men enrolled in postsecondary education. Over time, this education advantage may offset some of the other compensating differentials that have kept men's wages higher than women's.

ECONOMICS IN THE REAL WORLD

WAGE INEQUALITY: WHAT UBER CAN TEACH US ABOUT THE GENDER PAY GAP

Uber pays drivers based on an algorithm that is gender-blind. Driver pay is determined by a pay structure tied to output (rides completed) and a surge multiplier (for peak demand times). Researchers studied data from over one million Uber drivers and found that men earned 6% more per hour than women. Perplexed, they dug deeper into the data to find the causes of the gender pay gap. What they found was that the entire gender gap could be explained by three factors: experience (men, on average, have worked for Uber longer), preferences over when and where to work (men tend to work later at night and more often in less-safe areas), and preferences for driving speed

Do male Uber drivers earn more than females? Read more to find out.

	All	Men	Women
Weekly earnings	$376.38	$397.68	$268.18
Hourly earnings	$21.07	$21.28	$20.04
Hours per week	17.06	17.98	12.82
Trips per week	29.83	31.52	21.83
Six-month attrition rate	68.1%	65.0%	76.5%
Number of drivers	1,873,474	1,361,289	512,185
Number driver/weeks	24,832,168	20,210,399	4,621,760
Number of Uber trips	740,627,707	646,965,269	93,662,438

(men drive faster, on average, than women). One of the researchers, Rebecca Diamond, sums up the findings nicely:

> Uber shows that even when you strip away all of this stuff, you definitely don't go to a gender gap of zero, and you still have this important experience component, where you work more and you learn about how to do the job better, and you get better at doing the job. So you can't say it's all going to be perfect in this new gig economy. [But it's] not because of discrimination, or problems in how we compensate workers. It really is about working more hours and gaining knowledge on the job, and differences in gender preferences.

Since Uber's algorithm does not discriminate, gender-based preferences are the cause of the pay gap.

Source: Cody Cook et al., "The Gender Earnings Gap in the Gig Economy: Evidence from over a Million Rideshare Drivers," (Stanford: Stanford Institute for Economic Policy Research [SIEPR], 2018).

Winner-Take-All

In 1930, baseball legend Babe Ruth demanded and received a salary of $80,000 from the New York Yankees. This would be approximately $1 million in today's dollars. Babe Ruth earned a lot more than the other baseball players of his era. When told that President Herbert Hoover earned less than he was asking for, Ruth famously said, "I had a better year than he did." In fact, the annual salary of the president of the United States is far less than that of top professional athletes, movie stars, college presidents, and many corporate CEOs.

Why does the most important job in the world pay less than jobs with far less value to society? Part of the answer involves compensating differentials. Being president of the United States means being the most powerful person in the world, so paid compensation is only a small part of the benefit of holding that office. The other part of the answer has to do with the way labor markets function. Pay at the top of most professions is subject to a form of competition known as **winner-take-all**, which occurs when extremely small differences in ability lead to sizable differences in compensation. This compensation structure has been common in professional sports and in the entertainment industry for many years, but it also exists in the legal profession, medicine, journalism, investment banking, fashion design, and corporate management.

Winner-take-all occurs when extremely small differences in ability lead to sizable differences in compensation.

In a winner-take-all market, being a little bit better than one's rivals can be worth a tremendous amount. For example, in 2019, baseball star Manny Machado earned $30 million with the San Diego Padres. As good as Machado is, he is not 7.5 times better than an average major-league baseball player, who makes $4 million. Nor is he a thousand times better than a typical minor-league player, who earns a few thousand dollars a month. In fact, it is hard to tell the difference between a baseball game played by major- and minor-leaguers. Minor-leaguers run almost as fast, and the fielding is almost as good. Yet major-league players make hundreds of times more.

Paying so much to a relatively small set of workers may seem unfair, but the prospect of much higher pay or bonuses motivates many ambitious employees to exert maximum effort. If we look beyond the amount of money that some people earn, we can see that winner-take-all creates incentives that encourage supremely talented workers to maximize their abilities.

Manny Machado has 30 million reasons a year to practice, but not all professional baseball players are as fortunate.

Incentives

What Causes Income Inequality?

Income inequality occurs when some workers earn more than others. Compensating differentials, discrimination, corruption, and differences in the marginal product of labor all lead to inequality of income. In this section, we first examine why income inequality exists. Once we understand the factors leading to income inequality, we examine how it is measured. Because income inequality is difficult to measure and easy to misinterpret, we explain how observed income inequality statistics are constructed and what they mean. We end by discussing income mobility, a characteristic in many developed nations that can lessen the impact of income inequality on the life-cycle wage pattern.

Factors That Lead to Income Inequality

To illustrate the nature of income inequality, we begin with a simple question: what would it take to equalize wages? For all workers to get the same wages, three conditions would have to be met. First, every worker would have to have the same skills, ability, and productivity. Second, every job would have to be equally attractive to potential employees. Third, all workers would have to be perfectly mobile. In other words, perfect equality of income would require that workers be clones who perform the same job. Needless to say, we do not live in such a world. In the real world, some people work harder than others and are more productive. Some people, such as humanitarian aid workers, missionaries, teachers, and even ski bums, choose occupations where they know they will earn less. In fact, our traits, our desires, and our differences all help to explain income inequality, which is the natural result of a market economy.

Next we look at five factors that can contribute to income inequality: ability, training and education, discrimination, wealth, and corruption.

ABILITY Workers who have more ability (for example, mental acuity, physical strength, fortitude) than less-able workers generally earn higher wages. Differences in ability can lead to large differences in wages because more-able workers have the potential to create much larger marginal products than their less-able counterparts.

TRAINING AND EDUCATION More ability is a necessary but not sufficient condition for high wages. Workers of all ability levels benefit from receiving additional training and education. The acquisition of specific skills through training and additional education enhances each worker's human capital. More human capital often makes workers more valuable in the marketplace, helping them earn higher wages.

DISCRIMINATION Discrimination harms the workers who are discriminated against, and it makes the overall distribution of income in a country more unequal. Workers who are passed over for promotions or job openings because of their gender, race, age, religion, or other traits earn lower wages that do not reflect their ability, training, or education. Discrimination in this context acts as a price ceiling that limits some workers' ability to earn more. Since discriminated workers are concentrated among women and minorities, the net effect is that discriminated groups end up concentrated among the lowest-paid groups—leading to more income inequality.

THE ROLE OF WEALTH How much does a privileged background matter? According to controlled studies, children born into wealthy households earn about 10% more than children born into low-income households. Wealth gives a child from an affluent home access to better education, private tutoring, a healthier diet, and many other intangible benefits that provide a head start in life. These early advantages often lead to higher levels of human capital that translate into higher wages.

THE ROLE OF CORRUPTION IN INCOME INEQUALITY All economic systems require trust in order to achieve gains from trade. However, some societies value the rule of law more than others. Many less developed countries suffer from widespread corruption. Consider Somalia, a country without a functional central government. This situation has led to lawlessness in which clans, warlords, and militia groups fight for control. The situation is so dire that international aid efforts often require the bribing of government officials to ensure that the aid reaches those in need.

Corruption can play a large role in income inequality. In societies where corruption is common, working hard or being innovative is not enough; getting ahead often requires bribing officials to obtain business permits or to ward off competitors. Moreover, when investors cannot be sure their assets are safe from government seizure or criminal activity, they are less likely to develop a business. Under political systems that are subject to bribery and other forms of corruption, dishonest people benefit at the expense of the poor. Corruption drives out legitimate business opportunities and magnifies income inequality.

Measuring Income Inequality

How do we measure income inequality in a country? To answer this question, we begin by looking at income inequality in the United States. Economists study the distribution of household income in the United States by quintiles, or five groups of equal size, ranging from the poorest fifth (20%) of households to the top fifth. Figure 15.3 shows the data from 2017.

According to the U.S. Bureau of the Census, the poorest 20% of households makes just 3.1% of all income earned in the United States. The next quintile, the second fifth, earns 8.2% of income. In other words, fully 40% of U.S. households (the bottom two quintiles) account for only 11.3% of earned income. The middle quintile earns 14.3%, the second-highest quintile 23.0%, and the top quintile 51.4%. Being a pie chart, Figure 15.3 vividly shows the wide disparity between the percentage of total U.S. income earned by the poorest households (3.1%) and by the richest households (51.4%). If we divide the percentage of income earned by households in the top fifth (51.4%) by the percentage of income earned by households in the bottom fifth (3.1%), we get an **income inequality ratio** of about 16.5. Looking at the numbers this way, we can say that households in the top fifth have approximately 16 to 17 times the income of those in the bottom fifth. Viewing that number in isolation makes the amount of income inequality in the United States seem large. However, we have not yet adjusted the data to reflect disposable income. When taxes and subsidies are included the U.S. income inequality ratio drops to 9.9.

To provide some perspective, Table 15.4 compares the income inequality in various other countries using disposable income. The countries above the line are more developed, and those below are less developed.

As you can see, the U.S. income inequality ratio of 9.9 after controlling for taxes and subsides is high compared with that of other highly developed nations but relatively low compared with that of less developed nations. In general, highly developed nations have lower degrees of income inequality.

The **income inequality ratio** is calculated by dividing the top quintile's income percentage by the bottom quintile's income percentage.

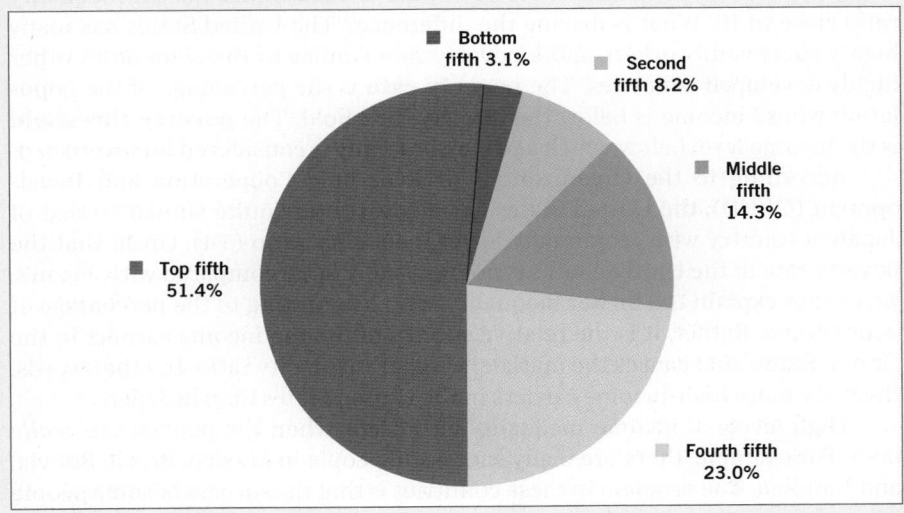

Bottom fifth 3.1%

Second fifth 8.2%

Middle fifth 14.3%

Top fifth 51.4%

Fourth fifth 23.0%

FIGURE 15.3

The Distribution of Income in the United States by Quintile

The top fifth of income earners makes 51.4% of all income, an amount greater than the combined incomes of the four remaining quintiles. Income declines across the quintiles, falling to 3.1% in the lowest fifth.

Source: U.S. Census Bureau, 2017.

TABLE 15.4

Income Inequality Ratios (after controlling for taxes and subsidies) in Selected Countries

Country	Inequality ratio (richest 20% ÷ poorest 20%)
Germany	4.7
Japan	5.4
Canada	5.8
United Kingdom	7.6
United States	9.9
Mexico	11.1
Brazil	16.9
Bolivia	15.2
Namibia	19.6

Source: Adapted from United Nations Development Programme, *Human Development Report*.

Why? More-developed countries have less poverty, so those individuals who are at the bottom of the income ladder in the developed countries earn more than those at the bottom in less developed countries.

UNDERSTANDING OBSERVED INEQUALITY Translating income inequality into a number, as we've done with the income quintiles, can mask the true nature of income inequality. In this section, we step back and consider what the income inequality ratio can tell us and what it cannot tell us.

Because the income inequality ratio measures the success of top earners against that of bottom earners, if the bottom group is doing relatively well, then the inequality ratio will be smaller, which explains why many highly developed countries have ratios under 6. However, the United States has an inequality ratio close to 10. What is driving the difference? The United States has many highly successful workers and a poverty rate similar to those found in other highly developed countries. The **poverty rate** is the percentage of the population whose income is below the poverty threshold. The **poverty threshold** is the income level below which a person or family is considered impoverished.

According to the Organization for Economic Cooperation and Development (OECD), the United States has a poverty rate quite similar to that of Japan, a country with a markedly lower inequality ratio (5.4). Given that the poverty rate in the United States is not unusually large compared with Japan's, we cannot explain the higher inequality ratio by pointing to the percentage of poor people. Rather, it is the relative success of the top income earners in the United States that causes the markedly higher inequality ratio. In other words, there are more high-income earners in the United States than in Japan.

High levels of income inequality also occur when the poorest are *really* poor. For example, there are many successful people in Mexico, Brazil, Bolivia, and Namibia. The problem in these countries is that the success of some people is benchmarked against the extreme poverty of many others. Therefore, high inequality ratios can be a telltale sign of a serious poverty problem. Suppose that the poorest quintile of the population in Bolivia has an average disposable

The **poverty rate** is the percentage of the population whose income is below the poverty threshold.

The **poverty threshold** is the income level below which a person or family is considered impoverished.

income of $4,000, while those in the top quintile have a disposable income of $60,800. The income inequality ratio is $60,800/$4,000 = 15.2. By comparison, consider Canada. If the poorest quintile of the population in Canada has an average disposable income of $10,500, while those in the top quintile have an average of $60,800, the income inequality ratio there is $60,800/$10,500 = 5.8. In both countries, the top quintile is doing equally well, but the widespread poverty in Bolivia produces an alarming income inequality ratio. In this example, the inequality ratio signals a significant poverty problem.

In sum: A high income inequality ratio can occur if people at the bottom earn very little or if the income of high-income earners is much greater than the income of others. The key point to remember is that even though income inequality ratios give us some idea about the degree of inequality in a society, a single number cannot fully reflect the sources of the underlying differences in income.

THE GINI INDEX An alternative way of representing income inequality across countries is to use the **Gini index**, which represents the income distribution of a nation's residents. Its value fluctuates between 0 (no income inequality) and 100 (extreme income inequality). If every individual's income is equal in a society, the Gini index (or Gini coefficient) is 0. A nation where one individual gets all the income, while everyone else gets nothing, would have a Gini index of 100. The average Gini index is approximately 40 (Figure 15.4).

The **Gini index** is a measurement of the income distribution of a country's residents.

FIGURE 15.4

The Gini Index Across the World, 2014

Countries color-coded in green have the lowest Gini index, while those in shades of red have the highest Gini index.

SOURCE: CIA World Factbook.

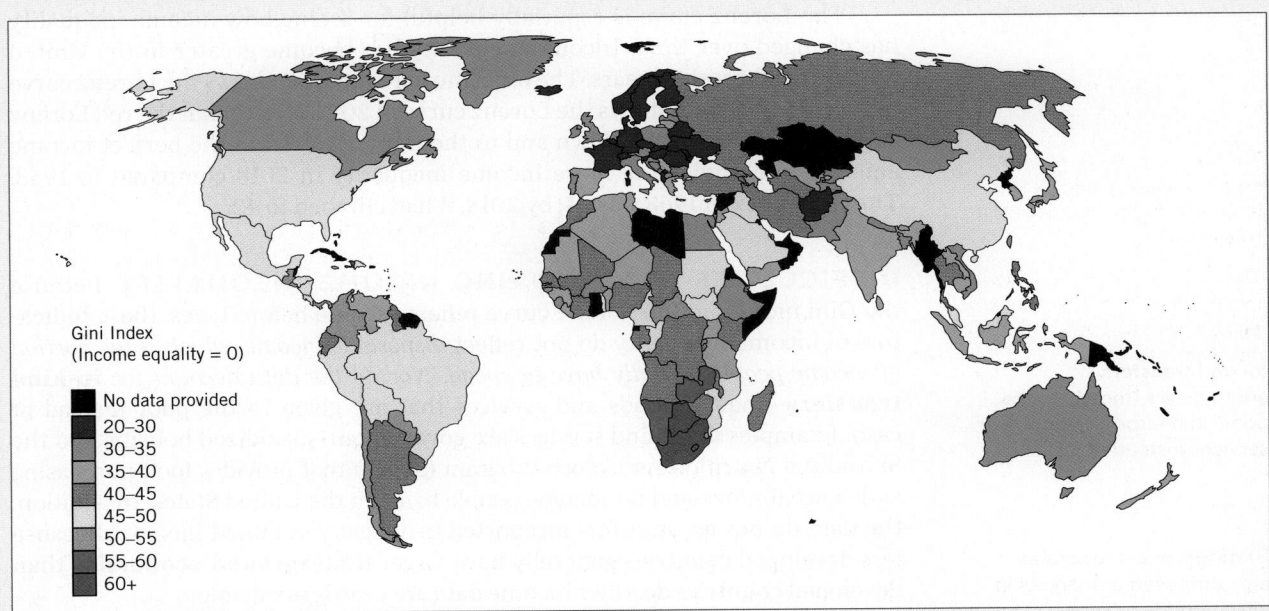

FIGURE 15.5

The Gini Index and the Lorenz Curve

The green curve indicates complete income equality. As income inequality increases, the orange curve shifts down and to the right.

Source: M. Tracy Hunter, https://commons.wikimedia.org/wiki/File:2014_Gini_Index_World_Map,_income_inequality_distribution_by_country_per_World_Bank.svg.

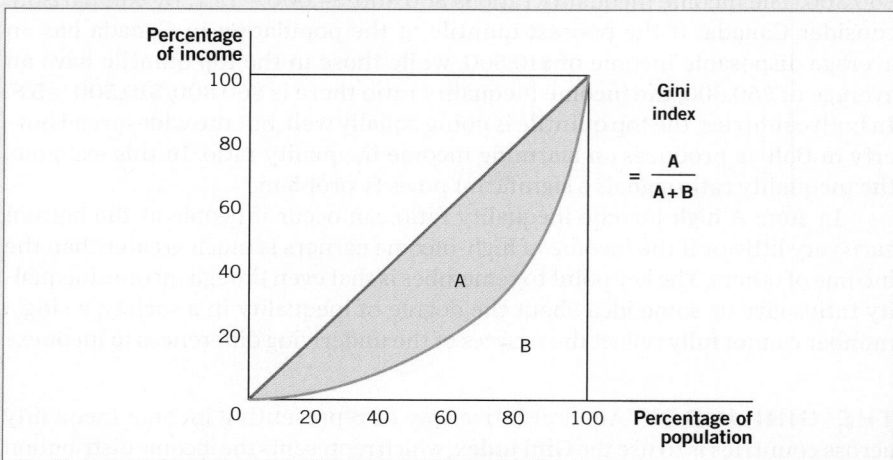

The **Lorenz curve** is a visual representation of the Gini index.

The **Lorenz curve** is a visual way of representing the Gini index. A perfectly equal distribution of income is represented by the green 45-degree line in Figure 15.5. As the income distribution becomes more unequal, the Lorenz curve, represented by the orange line in Figure 15.5, shifts downward and to the right. The Gini index is calculated by taking the area between the two curves, shaded and labeled A, and dividing that amount by the total of area A plus area B. Area A represents the amount of income *inequality* in society, while area B represents the amount of income *equality* in society. Calculating the Gini index gives us a number between 0 and 1. Economists multiply this number by 100 to represent the score as a whole number between 0 and 100.

The Lorenz curve is especially helpful for seeing how income inequality has changed over time. Income inequality has become greater in the United States over the last 50 years. The blue line in Figure 15.6 shows the Lorenz curve in 1968. The red line shows the Lorenz curve in 2018. Notice that the red Lorenz curve from 2018 shifted down and to the right, away from the perfect income equality line, indicating more income inequality in 2018 compared to 1968. The Gini index in 1968 was 34; by 2018, it had climbed to 42.

DIFFICULTIES IN MEASURING INCOME INEQUALITY Because the Gini index and the Lorenz curve reflect income before taxes, these indicators of income inequality do not reflect *disposable income, which is the portion of income people actually have to spend. Nor do the data account for* **in-kind transfers**—that is, goods and services that are given to the poor instead of cash. Examples of in-kind services are government-subsidized housing and the Subsidized Nutrition Assistance Program (SNAP) that provides food-purchasing assistance for low- and no-income people living in the United States. In addition, the data do not account for unreported or illegally obtained income. Because less developed countries generally have larger **underground economies** than developed countries do, their income data are even less reliable.

Many economists also note that income data alone do not capture the value created from goods and services produced in the household. For example, if you

In-kind transfers are transfers (mostly to the poor) in the form of goods or services instead of cash.

Underground economies are composed of markets in which goods or services are traded illegally.

FIGURE 15.6

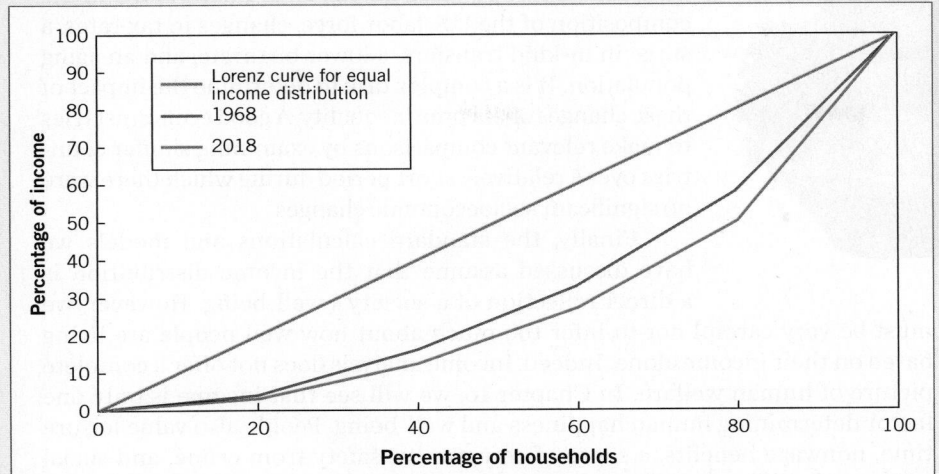

The Gini index in the United States was 34 in 1968. By 2018, it had climbed to 42, indicating an increase in income inequality.

mow your own lawn or grow your own vegetables, those activities have a positive value not expressed in your income data. In less developed countries, many households engage in very few market transactions and produce a large portion of their own goods and services. If we do not count these, our comparison of data with other countries will overstate the amount of inequality present in the less developed countries. Finally, the number of workers per household and the median age of each worker differ from country to country. When households contain more workers or those workers are, on average, older and therefore more experienced, comparing inequality across countries is more likely to be misleading.

Individually, none of these shortcomings poses a serious measurement issue from year to year. However, if we try to measure differences in income across generations, the changes can be significant enough to invalidate the *ceteris paribus* ("all other things being equal") condition that allows us to assume that outside factors are held constant. In short, comparing inequality data from this year with data from last year is generally fine, but comparing inequality data from this year with data from 50 years ago is more difficult. For instance, we might note that income inequality in the United States increased very slightly from 2017 to 2018. However, because we are looking at just two data points, we must be cautious about assuming a trend. To eliminate that problem, we can extend the time frame back to 1968. Comparing the data over that range shows an unmistakable upward

Growing your own vegetables is an activity not counted in official income data.

Income mobility
is the ability of workers to move up or down the economic ladder over time.

trend in income inequality but also violates *ceteris paribus*; after all, the last 50 years have seen dramatic shifts in the composition of the U.S. labor force, changes in tax rates, a surge in in-kind transfers, a lower birthrate, and an aging population. It is a complex task to determine the impact of these changes on income inequality. A good economist tries to make relevant comparisons by examining similar countries over a relatively short period during which there were no significant socioeconomic changes.

Finally, the standard calculations and models we have discussed assume that the income distribution is a direct reflection of a society's well-being. However, we must be very careful not to infer too much about how well people are living based on their income alone. Indeed, income analysis does not offer a complete picture of human welfare. In Chapter 16, we will see that income is only one factor determining human happiness and well-being. People also value leisure time, nonwage benefits, a sense of community, safety from crime, and social networks, among other things.

Income Mobility

When workers have a realistic chance of moving up the economic ladder, each person has an incentive to work harder and invest in human capital. **Income mobility** is the ability of workers to move up or down the economic ladder over time. Think of it this way: if today's poor must remain poor 10 years from now, income inequality remains high. However, if someone in the lowest income category can expect to experience enough economic success to move to a higher income quintile, being poor is a temporary condition. In other words, economic mobility reduces inequality over long periods of time.

The dynamic nature of the U.S. economy is captured by income mobility data. Table 15.5 reports the income mobility in the United States over a series of

TABLE 15.5				
Income Mobility in the United States, 1970–2010				
(1) Ten-year period	(2) % Poorest quintile that move up at least one quintile	(3) % Highest quintile that move down at least one quintile	(4) % Poorest quintile that move up at least two quintiles	(5) % Highest quintile that move down at least two quintiles
1970–1980	43.2%	48.8%	19.1%	22.8%
1975–1985	45.3	50.9	20.6	24.8
1980–1990	45.2	47.6	21.3	25.7
1985–1995	41.8	45.8	17.8	21.5
1990–2000	41.7	46.7	15.2	20.7
1995–2005	41.9	45.0	15.4	20.2
2000–2010	41.8	44.8	14.9	19.9

Source: Katharine Bradbury, *Trends in U.S. Family Income Mobility, 1969–2006*, Working Paper, Federal Reserve Bank of Boston, No. 11-10. Data for 1990–2005 was interpolated. Author's adjustments.

Income Inequality around the world

"The rich get richer, and the poor get poorer" is a simple yet profound way to think about income inequality. As top earners make more and bottom earners make less, the inequality rate increases. It's a combination of these factors, not just extreme wealth or extreme poverty, that leads to huge gaps between those at the very top and those at the very bottom.

$$\text{Inequality Ratio} = \frac{\text{Income Earned by Top 20\%}}{\text{Income Earned by Bottom 20\%}}$$

● Income Earned by Top 20%   ■ Inequality Ratio
● Income Earned by Bottom 20%   ■ Poverty Rate

SOUTH AFRICA 28.4

Less developed countries, like South Africa, have high rates of inequality. Why? Because the poor are extremely poor and earn just a fraction of the income of the affluent.

BRAZIL 15.6

UNITED STATES 9.4

Poverty is not the only factor of inequality, however. When the top earners are highly successful, the gap between rich and poor grows. The United States has a poverty rate similar to Japan's but a top 20% who earn more than Japan's top class.

15.1%

JAPAN 5.4

16.1%

REVIEW QUESTIONS

- Suppose the top 20% of Brazilian earners make, on average, the equivalent of $100,000 a year. What does the average earner in the bottom 20% make?

- A friend tells you he wants to live in a world without income inequality. Discuss the pros and cons using at least one of the five foundations of economics from Chapter 1.

Sources: United Nations Development Programme, Human Development Reports 2018; CIA World Factbook

· ECONOMICS *in the* MEDIA ·

Income Mobility

THE SIMPSONS: EXAMINING ALL OF HOMER'S JOBS

The long-running cartoon series *The Simpsons* features Homer Simpson as a lazy doofus who has somehow managed to work an amazing variety of jobs over the years. In 2017, the website *Vox* did an economic analysis of all the jobs Homer ever held over the course of 600 episodes, from 1989 to 2016. The 100-plus jobs ranged from convenience store clerk, bodyguard, and ordained minister to more exotic gigs such as a moonshine taste tester and a cannonball performance artist (for both of which Homer's practically bomb-proof stomach was an asset). Sometimes Homer caught a break and temporarily ended up in a high-paying position. Other times, his pay was even lower than what he earned in his regular job as a safety inspector ($37,500 in today's money per Homer's paycheck in Season 7) at the local nuclear power plant.

Having identified a hundred or so of Homer's jobs and assigned each a salary, *Vox*'s team then tracked the fluctuations in Homer's average earnings over time. They found that he stays stuck in the lower-middle-class income quintile; he has stagnated like much of the middle class during the time of the show's run. In many ways that is not surprising, since Homer lacks a college education and is not a very motivated worker. After three decades, he remains right where he started: a reminder of why income mobility (or in this case the lack of it) matters so much. When people are able to move across the income quintiles easily, long-term poverty is less likely.

Source: Zachary Crockett, "What Homer Simpson's 100+ jobs tell us about America's middle class," Vox.com, https://www.vox .com/2016/9/6/12752476/the-simpsons-homer-middle-class. Updated Sept 16, 2016.

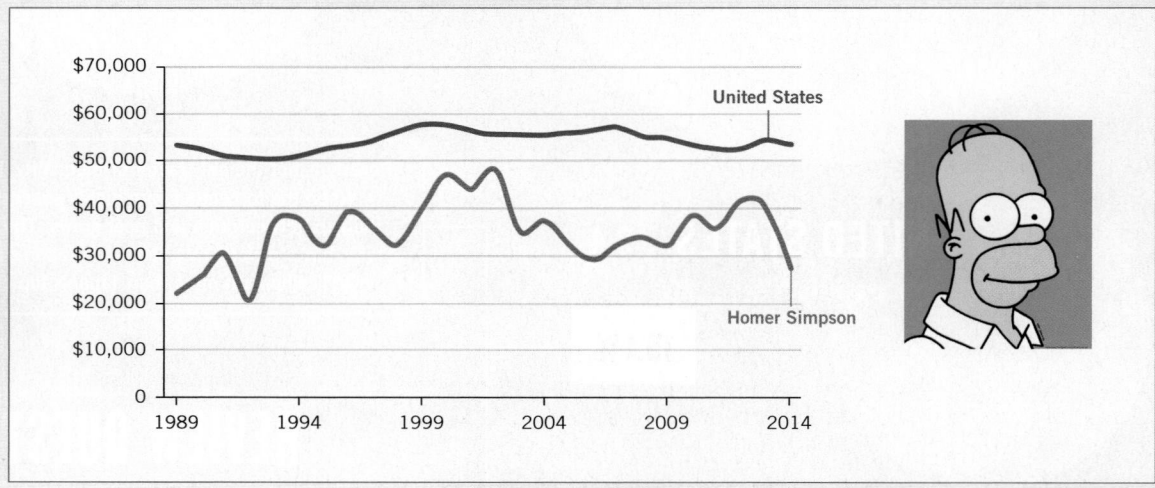

Homer Simpson's fictional pay places him in the lower-middle class.

Income Inequality: The Beginning and End of Inequality

Consider two communities, Alpha and Omega. Alpha has 10 residents, 5 who earn $90,000 and 5 who earn $30,000. Omega also has 10 residents, 5 who earn $250,000 and 5 who earn $50,000.

QUESTION: What is the income inequality ratio in each community?

ANSWER: To answer this question, we must use quintile analysis. Because there are 10 residents in Alpha, the top 2 earners represent the top quintile and the lowest 2 earners represent the bottom quintile. Therefore, the degree of income inequality in Alpha using quintiles analysis is $90,000 ÷ $30,000, or 3. In Omega, the top 2 earners represent the top quintile and the lowest 2 earners represent the bottom quintile. Therefore, the degree of income inequality in Omega is $250,000 ÷ $50,000, or 5.

QUESTION: Which community has the more unequal distribution of income, and why?

ANSWER: Omega has the more unequal distribution of income because the quintile analysis yields an income inequality ratio of 5, versus 3 for Alpha.

QUESTION: Can you think of a reason why someone might prefer to live in Omega?

ANSWER: Each rich citizen of Omega earns more than each rich citizen of Alpha, and each poor citizen of Omega earns more than each poor citizen of Alpha. Admittedly, there is more income inequality in Omega, but there is also more income across the entire income distribution. Thus, one might prefer Omega if the absolute amount of income is what matters more, or one might prefer Alpha if relative equality is what matters more.

The good life: so near, yet so far.

10-year periods from 1970 to 2010. We can see that mobility increased through the late 1980s, but thereafter declined for both the poorest and the highest quintiles. Columns 4 and 5 show the percentage of households that moved up or down at least two quintiles.

Mobility data enable us to separate those at the bottom of the economic ladder into two groups: (1) the *marginal poor*, or people who are poor at a particular point in time but have the skills necessary to advance up the ladder, and (2) the *long-term poor*, or people who lack the skills to advance to the next quintile. The differences in income mobility between these two groups provide a helpful way of understanding how income mobility affects poverty.

For the marginal poor, low earnings are the exception. Because most young workers expect to enjoy higher incomes as they get older, many are willing to borrow in order to make a big purchase—for example, a car or a home. Conversely, middle-aged workers know that a comfortable retirement will be possible only if they save now for the future. As a result, workers in their 50s have much higher savings rates than young workers and retirees. On reaching retirement, earnings fall; but if the worker has saved enough, retirement need

Income Inequality

CAPITAL IN THE TWENTY-FIRST CENTURY

Capital in the Twenty-First Century, by Thomas Piketty, focuses on wealth and income inequality in Europe and the United States since the eighteenth century. The book quickly became a best seller, selling over a million copies in 2014.

Piketty used historical data to examine income inequality beginning with the Industrial Revolution. He found that high levels of income inequality were the norm during the eighteenth and nineteenth centuries. Wealth and income were highly concentrated among rich households. During the twentieth century this pattern changed. Higher tax rates, increased government provision of services, and turbulent economic times caused the concentration of wealth to decline dramatically by the late 1960s. However, Piketty's data show a marked increase in income inequality beginning in the late twentieth century.

Piketty developed a theory that in normal times wealth grows faster than economic output. This means that the world's natural state is a highly unequal distribution of wealth unless economic calamities (such as war or depressions) or government intervention reduce the impact of inherited wealth on the rest of society. For this reason, Piketty recommends that governments increase tax rates on accumulated wealth with the goal of reducing income inequality.

Not all economists are convinced by Piketty's argument. Will the future really look like the past? The answer is not clear. Over time, technological progress

could lead to a more equal income distribution, not a less equal one.

More generally, standard economic theory holds that any asset (wealth included) is subject to diminishing returns. Therefore, the more wealth there is, the harder it is for the wealthy to earn an above-normal return on their investments. In other words, wealth cannot grow faster than economic output indefinitely. Also, inherited wealth accounts for only about 10% of income inequality.

Despite these criticisms, many skeptics have kind words for Piketty because he succeeded in bringing rising income inequality to the forefront of public discussion and debate.

Marginal thinking

not be a period of low consumption. The life-cycle wage pattern argues that changes in borrowing and saving patterns over one's life smooth out the consumption pattern. In other words, for many people, a low income at a point in time does not necessarily reflect a low standard of living.

When we examine how people live in societies with substantial income mobility, we see that the annual income inequality data can create a false impression about the spending patterns of young and old. The young are generally upwardly mobile, so they spend more than one might expect by borrowing. The middle-aged, who have relatively high incomes, spend less than one might expect because they are saving for retirement. And the elderly, who have lower incomes, spend more than one might expect because they are drawing down their retirement savings.

In the next section, we turn our attention to the long-term poor, who do not escape the lowest quintile. Members of this group spend their entire lives near or below the poverty threshold.

How Do Economists Analyze Poverty?

Poverty remains an ongoing challenge in the United States. According to the Census Bureau, close to 15% of all households are below the poverty threshold. To help us understand the issues, we begin with poverty statistics. Then, once we understand the scope of the problem, we examine possible policy solutions.

The Poverty Rate

For the last 50 years, the U.S. Bureau of the Census has been tracking the poverty rate, or the percentage of the population whose income is below the poverty threshold. To keep up with inflation, the poverty threshold is adjusted each year for changes in the overall level of prices in the economy. However, an individual family's threshold is calculated to include only the money that represents income earned by family members in the household. It does not include in-kind transfers, nor are the data adjusted for cost-of-living differences in the family's specific geographical area. For these reasons, poverty thresholds are a crude yardstick. Figure 15.7 shows the poverty rate for households in the United States from 1960 to 2017.

In 1964, Congress passed the Equal Opportunity Act and a number of other measures designed to fight poverty. Despite those initiatives, the rate of poverty today is slightly higher than it was 50 years ago. This result is surprising, because the U.S. economy's output has roughly doubled in that time. One would have hoped that the economy's progress could be enjoyed at the bottom of the economic ladder as well as at the top.

Those below the poverty threshold are unable to make ends meet.

Unfortunately, the stagnant poverty rate suggests that the gains from economic growth over that period have accrued to households in the middle and upper quintiles, rather than to the poor. Poverty has remained persistent, in part, because many low-income workers lack the necessary skills to earn a living wage and, at the same time, investments by firms in automation and technology have reduced the demand for these workers.

Table 15.6 illustrates that children, female heads of household, and certain minorities disproportionately feel the incidence of poverty. When we combine at-risk groups—for example, black or Hispanic women who are heads of household—the poverty rate can exceed 50%.

FIGURE 15.7

Poverty Rate for U.S. Households, 1960–2017

Poverty rates for households fluctuated from 1960 through 2017.

Source: U.S. Bureau of the Census.

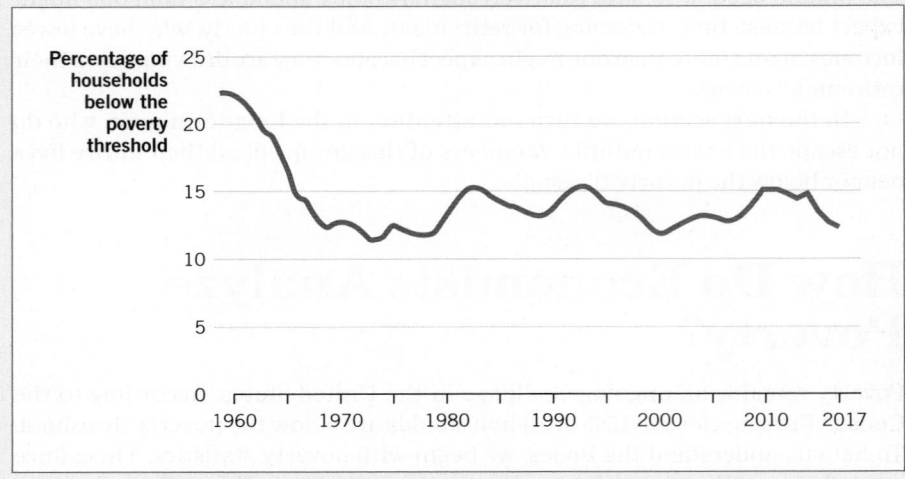

TABLE 15.6

The Poverty Rate for Various Groups, 2017

Group	Poverty rate (percentage)
Age	
Children (under 18)	19
Adults (18–64)	11
Elderly (65 or older)	9
Race/Ethnicity	
White	9
Asian	13
Hispanic	22
Black	20
Type of household	
Married couple	6
Male head only	16
Female head only	31

Source: U.S. Bureau of the Census, 2017.

Poverty Policy

Trade-offs

In this section, we outline a number of policies related to the problem of poverty. These policies are hotly debated because each policy carries both associated costs and assumed benefits, and assumptions about the benefits differ widely.

WELFARE "Welfare" is not the name of a specific government program, but rather an umbrella term for a series of initiatives designed to help the poor by supplementing their income. The term "welfare" in this section should not be confused with our earlier discussions of "social welfare." Here we focus on how government assistance programs ("welfare") operate and the incentives that these programs create.

Welfare can take a variety of forms, such as monetary payments, subsidies and vouchers, health services, or subsidized housing. Welfare is provided by the government and by other public and private organizations. It is intended to help the unemployed, those with illnesses or disabilities that prevent them from working, the elderly, veterans, and households with dependent children. An individual's eligibility for welfare is often limited to a set amount of time and is valid only as long as the recipient's income remains below the eligibility cutoff. Examples of welfare programs include Temporary Assistance for Needy Families (TANF), which provides financial support to families with dependent children; the Supplemental Security Income (SSI) program, which provides financial support to those who are unable to work; and the Subsidized Nutrition Assistance Program (SNAP), which gives financial assistance to those who need help to purchase basic foods.

IN-KIND TRANSFERS In addition to financial assistance, the poor can receive direct assistance in the form of goods and services. The government provides health care to the poor through Medicaid. **Medicaid** is a joint federal and state program that helps low-income individuals and households pay for the costs associated with long-term medical care. Communities or cities often provide organized assistance like shelters, and local community food banks, religious organizations, and private charities like Habitat for Humanity and Toys for Tots all provide in-kind benefits to the poor.

The idea behind in-kind transfers is that they protect recipients from the possibility of making poor decisions if they receive cash instead. For example, some recipients may use cash transfers to support drug or alcohol addictions, to gamble, or to buy unnecessary goods and services. To limit the likelihood of such poor decisions, in-kind transfers can be targeted at essential services. However, not everyone agrees that in-kind transfers are a good idea. Skeptics view them as paternalistic, inefficient, and disrespectful, and they argue that cash payments allow recipients to make the choices that best fit their needs.

THE EARNED INCOME TAX CREDIT (EITC) The Earned Income Tax Credit (EITC) is a tax credit designed to encourage low-income workers to work more. At very low income levels, EITC offers an incentive to work by supplementing earned income with a tax credit of approximately $6,000 a year. The amount is determined, in part, by the number of dependent children in the household and the location. Once a family reaches an income level above its earnings threshold, EITC is phased out, and workers gradually lose the tax credit. Under many welfare and in-kind transfer programs, the qualifying income is a specific cutoff point; an individual or household is either eligible or not. In contrast, EITC is gradually reduced, which means that workers do not face a sizable disincentive to work as the program is phased out.

> **Medicaid**
> is a joint federal and state program that helps low-income individuals and households pay for the costs associated with long-term medical care.

Poverty

THE HUNGER GAMES

The *Hunger Games* series of dystopian-themed books written by Suzanne Collins (and later made into feature films) chronicles the life of Katniss Everdeen, a teenager living in the post-apocalyptic country of Panem, which has been divided into twelve districts. Life in each district is unique, with vast differences in wealth, resources, and production. The wealthy Capitol district governs the economy by heavily regulating all aspects of life in the other poverty-stricken districts. One of the methods of control is the annual Hunger Games, where a boy and a girl are chosen from each district to battle to the death. The survivor earns extra food and a life of luxury.

Katniss Everdeen lives in District 12, an area with striking similarities to the coal mining Appalachian region of the United States. In District 12, inhabitants work in the mines. They struggle to make ends meet, often go hungry, and have a permeating sense of desolation because there is no escape.

The rising income inequality we see in the United States is not as extreme as we find in *The Hunger Games*, but it does remind us that we need to pay attention to income inequality in our society. When an income distribution becomes too unequal, the result

Where would you rather live, the Capitol district or District 12?

is often political and social instability. *The Hunger Games* challenges us to think about economic freedom, the role of institutions in creating growth, the extent to which governments should regulate economic activity, and how policy decisions made today will shape the future world.

Incentives

EITC, which was established in 1975, helps over 25 million families, making it the largest poverty-fighting tool in the United States. The government estimates that EITC payments are sufficient to lift more than 5 million households out of poverty each year. In addition, EITC creates stronger work incentives than those found under traditional antipoverty programs that critics argue discourage recipients from working.

Trade-offs

THE MINIMUM WAGE The minimum wage is often viewed as an antipoverty measure. However, we learned in Chapter 6 that the minimum wage creates trade-offs. Predictably, firms respond to higher minimum wages by hiring fewer workers and utilizing more capital-intensive production processes, such as self-checkout lanes and robotic production. Because the minimum wage does not guarantee employment, the most it offers to a low-skill worker is a slightly larger paycheck. At the same time, a higher minimum wage makes those jobs more difficult to find.

Problems with Traditional Aid

While trying to be well meaning, many welfare programs can create unintended work disincentives, especially when we examine the combined effects of welfare and in-kind transfer programs.

Incentives

As an example, consider a family of five with a combined income of $30,000 a year. Suppose that the family qualifies for public assistance that amounts to another $10,000 in benefits. The family's combined income from employment and benefits thus rises to $40,000. What happens if another family member gets a part-time job and income from wages rises from $30,000 to $40,000? Under the current law, an income of $40,000 disqualifies the family from receiving most of the financial assistance it had been getting. As a result, the family's benefits fall from $10,000 to $2,000 per year. Now the family nets $42,000 total. The person who secured part-time employment may feel that working isn't worth it, because even though the family earned an additional $10,000, they lost $8,000 in welfare benefits. Because the family is able to raise its net income by only $2,000, it has effectively returned $8,000. The loss of those benefits as they are phased out feels like an 80% tax, which creates a large disincentive to work.

This is a basic dilemma that poverty-reducing programs face: those that provide substantial benefits can discourage participation in the workforce because a recipient who starts to work, in many cases, no longer qualifies for the benefits and loses them.

While few people dispute that welfare programs are well intentioned, many economists are concerned about the programs' unintended consequences. A society that establishes a generous welfare package for the poor will find that it faces a Samaritan's dilemma. A **Samaritan's dilemma** occurs when an act of charity creates disincentives for recipients to take care of themselves. President Bill Clinton's 1996 vow "to end welfare as we know it" and for welfare to be "a second chance, not a way of life" attempted to address this dilemma by providing benefits for only a limited period of time. Clinton changed the payout structure for federal assistance and encouraged states to require employment searches as a condition for receiving aid. In addition, the TANF program imposed a five-year maximum for the time during which a recipient can receive benefits. This strategy changed welfare from an entitlement under the law into a temporary safety net, thereby reducing the Samaritan's dilemma.

A **Samaritan's dilemma** occurs when an act of charity creates disincentives for recipients to take care of themselves.

Incentives

ECONOMICS IN THE REAL WORLD

MUHAMMAD YUNUS AND THE GRAMEEN BANK

In 2006, economist Muhammad Yunus received the Nobel Peace Prize for his work helping poor families in Bangladesh. What did Yunus do to win that honor? He founded the Grameen Bank, which was instrumental in creating a new type of loan that has

In 2006, Yunus received the Nobel Peace Prize.

loaned more than $10 billion to poor people in Bangladesh in an effort to eliminate extreme poverty.

The Grameen Bank gives out very small loans, known as *microcredit*, to poor Bangladeshis who are unable to qualify for conventional loans from traditional lenders. The loans are provided without collateral, and repayment is based on an honor system. By conventional standards that sounds preposterous, but it works! The Grameen Bank reports a 97% repayment rate, and according to one survey, over 50% of the families of Grameen borrowers have moved above the poverty line.

It all started with just a few thousand dollars. In 1974, Yunus, who was trained as an economist in the United States, returned to Bangladesh and lent $27 to each of 42 villagers who made bamboo furniture. The loans, which were all paid back, enabled the villagers to cut out middlemen and purchase their own raw materials. A few years later, Yunus won government approval to open the Grameen Bank, named for the Bengali word for "rural."

Yunus had a truly innovative idea. To receive a loan, applicants must belong to a five-member group. Once the first two members begin to pay back their loans, the others can get theirs. While there is no group responsibility for returning the loans, the Grameen Bank believes that it creates a sense of social responsibility, ensuring that all members will pay back their loans. More important, Yunus trusted that people would honor their commitments, and he was proved right.

PRACTICE WHAT YOU KNOW

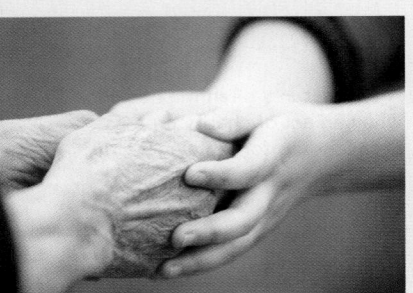

Welfare is an economic means of lending a helping hand.

Incentives

Samaritan's Dilemma: Does Welfare Cause Unemployment?

The state you live in is considering two different welfare programs. The first plan guarantees $8,000 for each person. The second plan does not guarantee any payments, but it doubles any income earned up to $12,000.

QUESTION: Which program creates the lesser amount of unemployment?

ANSWER: Think about incentives. Under the first plan, recipients' benefits are not tied to work. The $8,000 is guaranteed. However, the second plan will pay more if recipients do work. This policy acts as a positive incentive to get a job. For instance, someone who works 20 hours a week and earns $10 per hour would make $200 per week, or about $10,000 a year. Under the second plan, that person would receive an additional $10,000 from the government. Therefore, we can say that the second program reduces the amount of unemployment.

It's Expensive to Be Poor

- The poor pay more for staples than the rich do, since they can't afford to buy in bulk.
- The poor pay more for auto insurance.
- The poor pay more to maintain checking accounts and credit cards.
- The poor are more likely to rent than own their housing, and this is more costly in the long run.

Imagine what it's like to earn $25,000 a year versus $250,000. A person earning $25,000 annually makes about $12.50 an hour—an amount near the minimum wage. A person making $250,000, on the other hand, is in the top five percent of all earners. Suppose these two people with different income levels are trying to do the same things: buy toilet paper and other staples, purchase car insurance, use a checking account and credit cards, and find a place to live.

The person making $25,000 annually is likely to be living paycheck to paycheck. When they buy staples, they rarely have enough extra cash to buy things like toilet paper in bulk, so they end up paying a lot more for those items in smaller units and also spending a lot more time in the process. A study by the Consumer Federation of America (CFA) found that the five major car insurers charge low-income drivers almost $700 a year more for minimum coverage than they do drivers with higher incomes. People living paycheck to paycheck don't have a lot in their checking accounts, so they often pay monthly fees imposed by financial institutions for insufficient deposits. Likewise, people who can't pay off their credit card each month end up paying hefty fees in interest. In addition, most poor people rent a place to live rather than own one. This is costly in two ways: they don't receive the mortgage

"Anyone who has ever struggled with poverty knows how extremely expensive it is to be poor."—James Baldwin

interest deduction on their taxes, and they're not building up equity.

Conversely, our quarter-million per year rich person is able to buy many household items in bulk, receiving a significant discount in the process. Because of the socio-economic group they are in, they get much lower quotes on auto insurance. They have enough in the bank to avoid monthly minimums, and they pay off their credit card bills every month—not only avoiding high interest charges but also profiting from promotions that provide air travel points, cash back, and other goodies. The wealthy also are far more likely to own the home they live in. (For Americans who can afford it, home ownership is often their single biggest financial investment.)

Conclusion

Income and work have long been a subject of discussion and contention. We find that some jobs pay much more than others, and working hard and performing well at one's job do not guarantee good pay. People and jobs differ in many dimensions, and wages usually respond accordingly, though wages are affected by compensating differentials, location, education and human capital, union membership, and efficiency wages, all of which create significant income inequality.

This chapter is ultimately about trade-offs and incentives—two of our five foundations of economics. The debate about how society should handle income, poverty, and inequality is complex, and passions run deep. Depending on your perspective, you can point to data showing that society is improving (the narrowing wage gap between females and males) or worsening (increased levels of income inequality). In economics there are always trade-offs. Policies designed to reduce income inequality may cause highly productive workers to work less. Poverty initiatives may have unintended consequences as well. Unfortunately, good intentions alone won't close the wage gap or decrease income inequality, but the judicious use of incentives just might. ✳

▪ ANSWERING *the* BIG QUESTIONS ▪

What are the determinants of wages?

▪ Supply and demand play a key role in determining wages, along with a number of nonmonetary determinants of earnings, such as compensating differentials, education and human capital, location, lifestyle, union membership, and efficiency wages.

▪ Economic studies estimate that wage discrimination accounts for less than 5% of wage differences.

▪ Despite recent gains, women still earn significantly less than men. Occupational crowding partially explains the wage gap. As long as supply imbalances remain in traditional male and female jobs, significant wage differences will persist.

What causes income inequality?

▪ Five factors can contribute to income inequality: ability, training and education, discrimination, wealth, and corruption. The income inequality ratio is sometimes used to measure a nation's level of inequality. Another measure of income inequality is the Gini index.

▪ Economic mobility reduces income inequality over long periods. Due to the life-cycle wage pattern, distinct borrowing and saving patterns over an individual's life smooth out his or her spending pattern. Therefore, in societies with substantial income mobility, the annual income inequality data overstate the amount of inequality.

How do economists analyze poverty?

- Economists determine the poverty rate by establishing a poverty threshold.
- The poverty rate in the United States is now slightly higher than it was 50 years ago, despite many efforts (welfare, in-kind transfers, and EITC) to reduce it.
- Efforts to reduce poverty are subject to the Samaritan's dilemma because they can create disincentives for recipients to support themselves.

Concepts You Should Know

compensating differential (p. 473)
efficiency wages (p. 476)
Gini index (p. 489)
human capital (p. 473)
income mobility (p. 492)
income inequality ratio (p. 487)
in-kind transfers (p. 490)

life-cycle wage pattern (p. 480)
Lorenz curve (p. 490)
Medicaid (p. 499)
occupational crowding (p. 481)
poverty rate (p. 488)
poverty threshold (p. 488)
productivity (p. 476)

Samaritan's dilemma (p. 501)
strike (p. 475)
underground economies (p. 490)
union (p. 475)
wage discrimination (p. 477)
winner-take-all (p. 484)

Questions for Review

1. Why do garbage collectors sometimes make more than furniture movers?

2. What are efficiency wages? Why are some employers willing to pay them?

3. Why is it difficult to determine the amount of wage discrimination in the workplace?

4. Discuss some of the reasons why full-time working women make, on average, 81% as much as full-time working men.

5. How does the degree of income inequality in the United States compare with that in similarly developed countries? How does U.S. income inequality compare with that in less developed nations?

6. Why do high rates of income mobility mitigate income inequality?

7. Which antipoverty program (welfare, in-kind transfers, or EITC) creates the strongest incentive for recipients to work? Why?

Study Problems (✳ solved at the end of this section)

1. Suppose that society restricted the economic opportunities of right-handed persons to jobs in construction, while left-handed persons can work any job.

    a. Would wages in construction be higher or lower than wages for other jobs?

    b. Would left-handed workers make more or less than right-handed workers?

    c. Now suppose that right-handers are allowed to work any job they like. What effect would this change have on the wages of right-handers and left-handers over time?

2. Internships are considered a vital stepping-stone to full-time employment after college, but not all internship positions are paid. Why do some students take unpaid internships when they could be working summer jobs and earning an income? Include a discussion of human capital in your answer.

3. Consider two communities. In Middletown, two families earn $40,000 each, six families earn $50,000 each, and two earn $60,000 each. In Polarity, four families earn $10,000 each, two earn $50,000 each, and four earn $90,000 each. Which

community has the more unequal distribution of income as measured by the income inequality ratio? Explain your response.

4. The United States has attracted many highly productive immigrants who work in fields such as education, health, and technology. How do these immigrants affect income inequality in the United States? Is this type of immigration good or bad for the United States, and why? What impact is this type of immigration having on the countries that are losing some of their best workers?

✳ 5. Suppose that a wealthy friend asks for your advice on how to reduce income inequality. Your friend wants to know if it would be better to give $100 million to poor people who will never attend college or to offer $100 million in financial aid to students who could not otherwise afford to attend college. What advice would you give, and why?

6. What effect would doubling the minimum wage have on income inequality? Explain your answer.

✳ 7. Suppose that a company has 10 employees. It agrees to pay each worker on the basis of productivity. The individual workers' outputs are 10, 14, 15, 16, 18, 19, 21, 23, 25, and 30 units. However, some of the workers complain that they are earning less than the other workers, so they appeal to management to help reduce the income inequality. As a result, the company decides to pay each worker the same salary. But the next time the company measures each worker's output, they find that 6, 7, 7, 8, 10, 10, 11, 11, 12, and 12 units are produced. Why did this happen? Would you recommend that the company continue the new compensation system? Explain your response.

8. The government is considering three possible welfare programs:

   a. Give each low-income household $10,000.
   b. Give each low-income household $20,000 minus the recipient's income.
   c. Match the income of each low-income household, where the maximum it can receive in benefits is capped at $10,000.

   Which program will do the most to help the poor? Describe the work incentives under each program.

9. A number of very famous people (Ellen DeGeneres, Brad Pitt, Mark Zuckerberg, Bill Gates) all dropped out of college. Why would anyone drop out of college when college graduates typically make significantly more than college dropouts?

✳ 10. Tracy Chapman's song "Fast Car" reminds us how difficult it is to escape poverty. Identify the reasons in the song that keep Tracy trapped in poverty. (To listen to the song, visit www.youtube.com/watch?v=uTIB10eQnA0.)

11. Suppose that next summer you get two job offers, one as a lifeguard and the other as a garbage collector. Each job pays $15 an hour, and you are required to work 30 hours a week.

   a. Which job are you more likely to take?
   b. If no one wants to work as a garbage collector and everyone wants to be a lifeguard, what will happen to the wages in both jobs?

✳ 12. Which of the following explanations (compensating differentials, discrimination, human capital, occupational crowding, winner-take-all) describes each of the following situations?

   a. A person who is perceived as unattractive earns less than a person seen as attractive.
   b. Alexa is more educated and better trained than Felix.
   c. A Nobel-prize winning economist earns significantly more than other economists.
   d. More women work as elementary school teachers than men.

13. In a society where 25% of the people earn $30,000 per year, 50% earn $60,000, and 25% earn $90,000, draw the Lorenz curve and calculate the Gini index.

Solved Problems

5. The return on your wealthy friend's investment will be higher if the money is given to students with the aptitude, but not the income, to go to college. After all, college students earn substantially more than high school graduates do. Therefore, an investment in additional education will raise the marginal revenue product of the poor students' labor. With the higher earning power a college degree provides, more people will be lifted out of poverty, thereby reducing the amount of income inequality in the future.

7. Begin by calculating the average output when each worker's wage is based on the amount he or she produces: $10 + 14 + 15 + 16 + 18 + 19 + 21 + 23 + 25 + 30 = 191$, and $191 (\div 10 = 19.1$. Then compute the average output when the company decides to pay each worker the same wage: $6 + 7 + 7 + 8 + 10 + 10 + 11 + 11 + 12 + 12 + 94$, and $94 (\div 10 = 9.4$. The output has dropped by approximately one-half! Why? The company forgot about incentives. In this case, an attempt to create equal pay caused a disincentive problem (because hard work is not rewarded), and the workers all reduced their work effort. The new compensation system should be scrapped.

10. Tracy's condition is difficult because she lives in the country and the jobs are in the city—which is why she wants a "fast car" to drive away in. She also comes from a broken family; her mother left her father because he had a drinking problem. The lack of nearby job opportunities and the necessity of caring for her father prevents Tracy from taking advantage of economic opportunities elsewhere.

12. **a.** discrimination
    b. human capital
    c. winner-take-all
    d. occupational crowding

PART

V

Special Topics in MICROECONOMICS

Consumer Choice

The More Money You Have, the Happier You'll Be? Not So Fast.

As a college student, you would probably be delighted if someone surprised you with a gift of $100. But to a successful stockbroker, $100 is mere pocket change. The more dollars you have, the less you value each additional one. And there can come a point where more money is actually undesirable. Consider Jack Whittaker, who won a $315 million Powerball jackpot in 2002, which at the time was the biggest single-winner jackpot in American lottery history. He later divorced and went completely broke, was arrested for DUI, and was robbed on two separate occasions while carrying over $100,000. (Who carries *that much* money?) Worst of all, he lost his granddaughter to a drug overdose, which he blamed on the lottery win, as well. Whittaker told an interviewer in 2007: "My wife said she wished that she had torn the ticket up. Well, I wish that we tore the ticket up too." Too much money can make you very unhappy!

Some lottery winners do just fine, of course. But it's so common for winners to deal badly with the sudden wealth, and all the attention from "friends" who suddenly emerge from the woodwork, that there's a name for this phenomenon: the lottery curse. The root problem is that winners suddenly face a whole ton of choices they hadn't faced

"Are we ready to ruin another life? The (un)lucky number is…!" Let's hope winners of these payoffs escape the lottery curse.

before and aren't well-equipped to make. In this chapter, we use our understanding of income constraints, price, and personal satisfaction to determine which economic choices yield the greatest benefits.

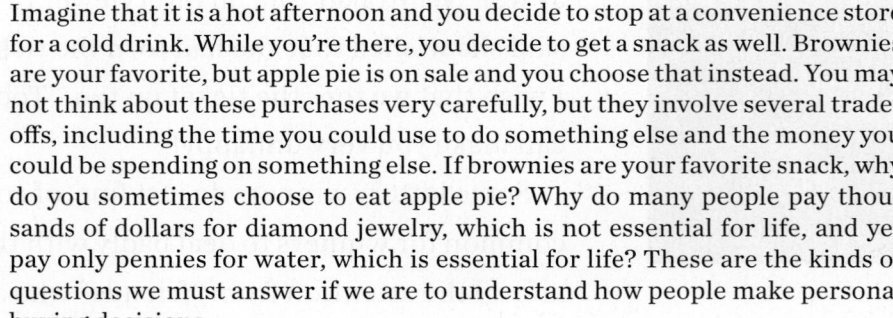

· BIG QUESTIONS ·

- How do economists model consumer satisfaction?
- How do consumers optimize their purchasing decisions?
- What is the diamond-water paradox?

How Do Economists Model Consumer Satisfaction?

Trade-offs

Imagine that it is a hot afternoon and you decide to stop at a convenience store for a cold drink. While you're there, you decide to get a snack as well. Brownies are your favorite, but apple pie is on sale and you choose that instead. You may not think about these purchases very carefully, but they involve several trade-offs, including the time you could use to do something else and the money you could be spending on something else. If brownies are your favorite snack, why do you sometimes choose to eat apple pie? Why do many people pay thousands of dollars for diamond jewelry, which is not essential for life, and yet pay only pennies for water, which is essential for life? These are the kinds of questions we must answer if we are to understand how people make personal buying decisions.

To better understand the decisions that consumers make, economists attempt to measure the satisfaction that consumers get when they make purchases. **Utility** is a measure of the level of satisfaction that a consumer enjoys from the consumption of goods and services. Utility theory seeks to measure contentment, or satisfaction. To understand why people buy the goods and services they do, we need to recognize that some products produce more utility than others and that everyone receives different levels of satisfaction from the same good or service. In other words, utility varies from individual to individual. To quantify this idea of relative satisfaction, economists measure utility with a unit they refer to as a **util**.

There is tremendous value in modeling decisions this way. When we understand utility, we can predict what people are likely to purchase. We model consumer behavior in a manner similar to the way we model how a firm makes

Utility
is a measure of the level of satisfaction that a consumer enjoys from the consumption of goods and services.

A **util** is a personal unit of satisfaction used to measure the enjoyment from consumption of a good or service.

decisions or how the labor market works. We expect the firm to maximize profits, the laborer to accept the best offer, and the consumer to find the combination of goods that gives the most utility. For example, a brownie lover may get 25 utils from her favorite snack, but someone who is less susceptible to the pleasures of chewy, gooey chocolate may rate the same brownie at 10 utils. However, these are not completely accurate measurements of relative utility. Who can say whether one person's 25 utils represents more actual satisfaction than another person's 10? Even if you and a friend agree that you each receive 10 utils from eating brownies, you cannot say that you both experience the same amount of satisfaction; each of you has a unique personal scale. However, the level of enjoyment one receives can be internally consistent. For example, if you rate a brownie at 25 utils and a slice of apple pie at 15 utils, we know that you like brownies more than apple pie.

Utility, or what most of us think of as satisfaction, is a balance between economic and personal factors. Even though there is an inherent problem with equating money and satisfaction, this has not stopped researchers from exploring the connection.

In the next section, we explore the connection between total utility and marginal utility. This connection will help us understand why more money does not necessarily bring more satisfaction.

Do you prefer a slice of apple pie . . .

. . . or a fudge brownie?

ECONOMICS IN THE REAL WORLD

HAPPINESS INDEX

Since 2006, the Organisation for Economic Co-operation and Development (OECD) has published the Better Life Index—popularly called the "happiness index"—which compiles social and economic data for 34 highly developed countries. The OECD measures well-being across these countries, based on 11 topics it has identified as essential in the areas of material living conditions and quality of life.

Which countries are happiest? The OECD doesn't rank them, and the results depend on the relative importance assigned to the different measurements. Australia rates highly in most categories. What makes Australians so happy? It's not their income, which averages only $35,000 per year in U.S. dollars. However, Australians live to an average age of 82 (two years longer than typical in developed countries), experience low amounts of pollution, display a high degree of civic engagement, and enjoy a very high life satisfaction rating.

"Down under" is a satisfying place to live!

In contrast, the OECD identifies the United States as having the highest income, but it scores substantially lower in work-life balance than many of the other top countries do. Just as with individuals, with nations it's hard to make comparisons. Are Australians happier than Americans, or vice versa? Without knowing how much importance people attach to longevity compared to income, it's hard to say. Still, when one country outscores another in virtually every category, we can be pretty sure there's a corresponding difference in happiness levels. Thus it seems clear that Americans and Australians are better off overall than the citizens of Mexico, where safety concerns, poor education, and low levels of income combine to produce a very low rating.

The OECD Better Life Index

The OECD Better Life Index attempts to measure 11 key factors of material well-being in each of its 34 member countries. The goal of the index is to provide member governments with a snapshot of how their citizens are living, thus providing a road map for future policy priorities. Some factors are objectively measured, such as average household income. Others are more subjective, such as "life satisfaction," and are measured from survey responses. Below is a look at the results in three countries.

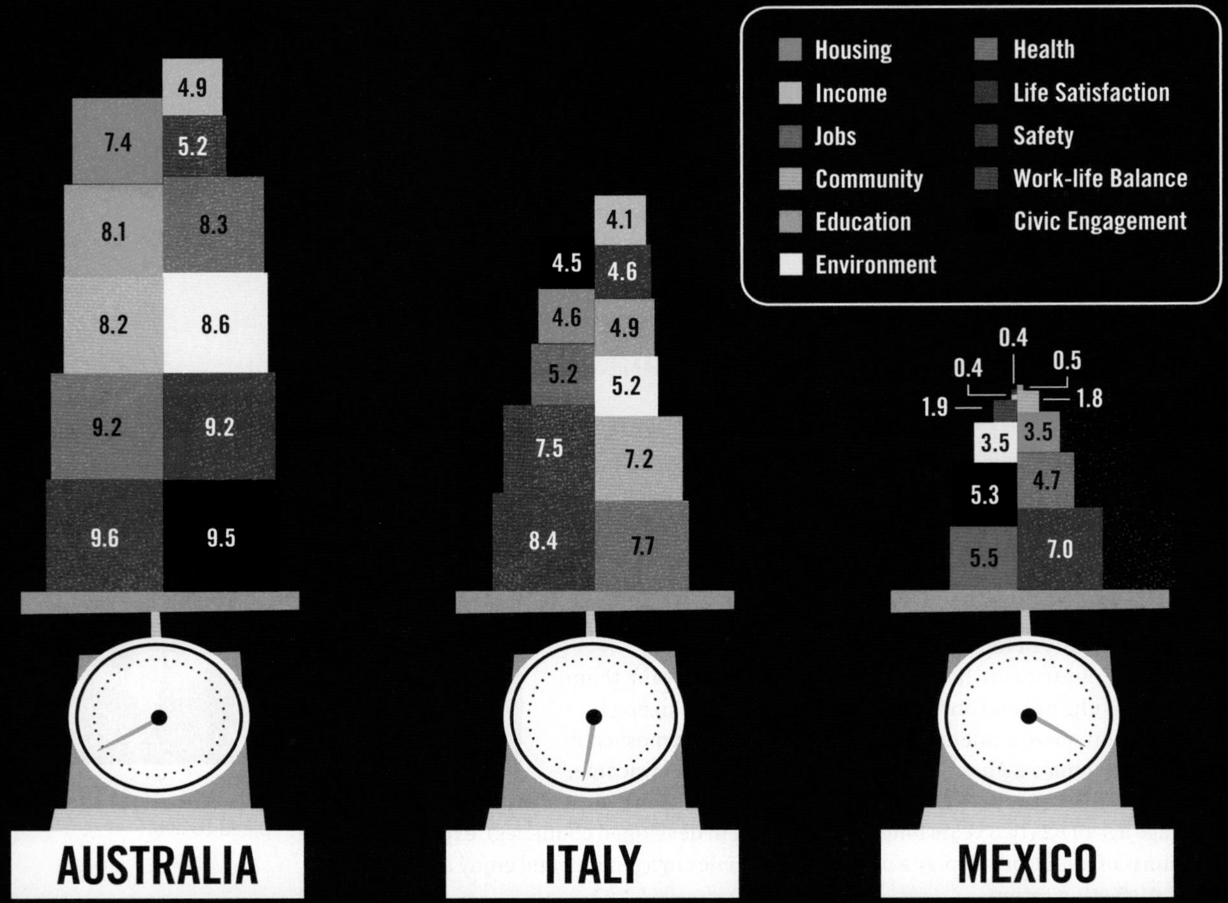

Legend:
- Housing
- Income
- Jobs
- Community
- Education
- Environment
- Health
- Life Satisfaction
- Safety
- Work-life Balance
- Civic Engagement

AUSTRALIA

7.4	4.9
	5.2
8.1	8.3
8.2	8.6
9.2	9.2
9.6	9.5

ITALY

	4.1
4.5	4.6
4.6	4.9
5.2	5.2
7.5	7.2
8.4	7.7

MEXICO

	0.4
0.4	0.5
1.9	1.8
	3.5 3.5
5.3	4.7
5.5	7.0

Each factor is ranked on a scale of zero to 10, with 10 being the highest. One to three indicators go into each measurement. For instance, "Jobs" is measured through the unemployment rate, job security, and personal earnings.

10.0

What do these numbers say about a nation's quality of life? It depends on which factors you think are most important. At www.oecdbetterlifeindex.org you can weight the different categories, create an index, and see how nations compare.

REVIEW QUESTIONS

- Mexico has five glaring challenges to the well-being of its citizens. What are they?

- Visit the OECD website and create your own index. Are any of the 11 factors trade-offs?

Total Utility and Marginal Utility

Thinking about the choices that consumers make can help us understand how to increase total utility. Consider a person who really likes brownies. In this case, the **marginal utility** is the additional satisfaction enjoyed from consuming one more brownie. In the table on the left-hand side of Figure 16.1, we see that the first brownie eaten brings 25 total utils. Eating additional brownies increases total utility until it reaches 75 utils after eating five brownies.

The graph in panel (a) of Figure 16.1 reveals that while the total utility (the green curve) rises until it reaches 75, the rate of increase (that is, the increase

Marginal thinking

Marginal utility
is the additional satisfaction
derived from consuming one
more unit of a good or service.

Total Utility and Marginal Utility

The relationship between total utility and marginal utility can be seen by observing the dashed line that connects panels (a) and (b). Because the marginal utility becomes negative after five brownies are consumed, the total utility eventually falls after a certain number of brownies are eaten. To the left of the dashed line, the marginal utility is positive in panel (b) and the total utility is rising in panel (a). Conversely, to the right of the dashed line, the marginal utility is negative and the total utility is falling.

Number of brownies eaten	Total utility (utils)	Marginal utility (utils per brownie)
0	0	
		25
1	25	
		20
2	45	
		15
3	60	
		10
4	70	
		5
5	75	
		0
6	75	
		−5
7	70	
		−10
8	60	
		−15
9	45	
		−20
10	25	

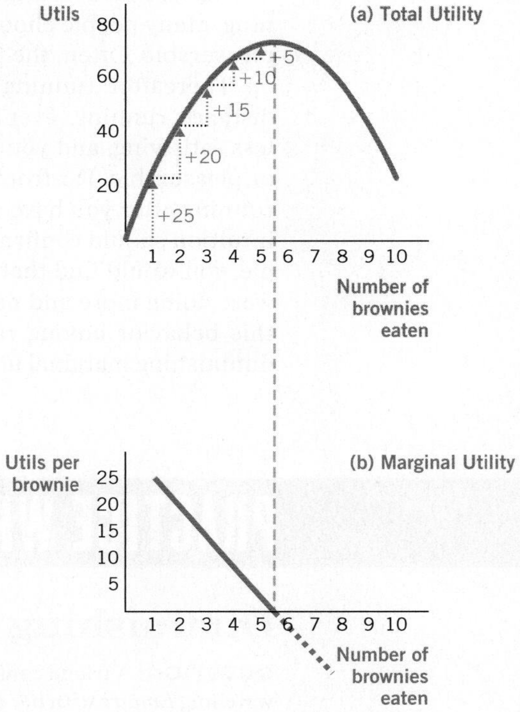

(a) Total Utility

(b) Marginal Utility

Running is fun for only so long.

Diminishing marginal utility occurs when marginal utility declines as consumption increases.

in marginal utility) falls from 25 utils for the first brownie down to 5 additional utils for the fifth. The marginal utility values from the table are plotted in panel (b), which shows that marginal utility declines steadily as consumption rises.

The relationship between total utility and marginal utility is evident when we observe the dashed line that connects panels (a) and (b). Because the marginal utility becomes negative after five brownies are consumed, the total utility eventually falls. To the left of the dashed line, the marginal utility is positive in panel (b) and the total utility is rising in panel (a). Conversely, to the right of the dashed line, the marginal utility is negative and the total utility is falling.

When marginal utility becomes negative, the consumer is tired of eating brownies. At that point, the brownies are no longer adding to the consumer's utility, and he or she will stop eating them.

Diminishing Marginal Utility

As you can see in panel (b) of Figure 16.1, the satisfaction that a consumer derives from consuming a good or service declines with each additional unit consumed. Consider what happens when you participate in a favorite activity for an hour and then decide to do something else. **Diminishing marginal utility** occurs when marginal utility declines as consumption increases. The concept of diminishing marginal utility is so universal that it is one of the most widely held ideas in all of economics.

In rare cases, marginal utility can rise—but only temporarily. Consider running. Many people choose to run for recreation because it is both healthy and pleasurable. Often, the first mile is difficult as the runner's body gets warmed up. Thereafter, running is easier—for a while. No matter how good you are at distance running, eventually the extra miles become more exhausting and less satisfying, and you stop. This does not mean that running is not healthy or pleasurable. Far from it! But it does mean that forcing yourself to do more running after you have already pushed your limit yields less utility. Your own intuition should confirm this theory. If increasing marginal utility were possible, you would find that with every passing second you would enjoy what you were doing more and never want to stop. Because economists do not observe this behavior among rational consumers, we can be highly confident that diminishing marginal utility has tremendous explanatory power.

PRACTICE WHAT YOU KNOW

Diminishing Marginal Utility

QUESTION: A friend confides to you that a third friend has gradually lost interest in watching *Empire* with her and has begun saying she's too busy. How would you advise your friend to handle the situation?

ANSWER: Tell your friend about diminishing marginal utility! Even the best television show runs its course. After a while, the same humor or drama that once made the show interesting no longer seems as interesting. Then suggest to your friend that they mix it up and do something different together. If that doesn't work, it may not be *Empire* that is the problem—it may be that your friend's friend has grown tired of her.

CHALLENGE QUESTION: How could you tell whether the marginal utility someone derived from a TV show had not just gone down to zero but gone negative?

ANSWER: A person whose marginal utility had gone negative would not just show a lack of interest in the show but would be willing to pay a price to avoid watching it. "If you agree to watch something else, I'll do the dishes!"

Cookie Lyon wants you to keep watching.

Table 16.1 highlights how diminishing marginal utility can serve to explain a number of interesting real-world situations. Do not skip this table! It is very useful in helping you understand the concept of diminishing marginal utility.

TABLE 16.1

Examples of Diminishing Marginal Utility

	Example	Explanation using diminishing marginal utility
	Discounts on two-day passes to amusement parks	The excitement on the first day is palpable. You run to rides, don't mind waiting in line, and experience the thrill for the first time. By the second day, the enthusiasm has worn off and the lower price entices you to return.
	Discounts on season tickets	Over the course of any season, people anticipate some games and concerts more highly than other games and concerts. To encourage patrons to buy the entire season package, venues must discount the total price.
	All-you-can-eat buffet	All-you-can-eat buffets offer the promise of unlimited food, but the average diner has a limited capacity. Eating more eventually leads to negative marginal utility. Restaurants assume that diminishing utility will limit how much their customers eat.
	Unlimited minutes with cell phone plans	Cell phone companies rely on the diminishing marginal utility of conversation. Cell phone companies offer "unlimited" plans because they know that consumers will not stay on their phones indefinitely.
	Pokémon GO	Remember the summer of 2016 when Pokémon GO first appeared? Everyone was playing, and capturing digital monsters was so much fun. But you soon tired of the grind . . . and most people quit—that's diminishing marginal utility.
	Nathan's Famous Hot Dog Eating Contest	Many people enjoy eating a hot dog or two or three, but Nathan's Eating Contest is very difficult to watch. The idea of eating so many hot dogs makes a lot of people queasy.

How Do Consumers Optimize Their Purchasing Decisions?

Maximizing utility requires that consumers get the most satisfaction out of every dollar they spend, or what is commonly called "getting the biggest bang for the buck." When a consumer gets the most bang for the buck, we say that the consumer has *optimized* his or her purchasing decisions. However, optimization is easier said than done. Over the course of the year, each of us will make thousands of purchases of different amounts. Our budgets are generally not unlimited, and we try to spend in a way that enables us to meet both our short-run and our long-run needs. The combination of goods and services that maximizes the satisfaction, or utility, we get from our income or budget is the **consumer optimum**. In this section, we examine the decision process that leads to the consumer optimum. We start with two goods and then generalize those findings across a consumer's entire income or budget.

The **consumer optimum** is the combination of goods and services that maximizes the consumer's utility for a given income or budget.

Consumer Purchasing Decisions

Opportunity cost

Let's begin by imagining a world with only two goods: Pepsi and pizza. This example will help us focus on the opportunity cost of purchasing Pepsi instead of pizza, or pizza instead of Pepsi.

Pepsi is available for $1 per can, and each pizza slice costs $2. Suppose you have $10 to spend. How much of each good should you buy in order to maximize your satisfaction? Before we can answer that question, we need a rule for making decisions. To reach your consumer optimum, you must allocate your available money by choosing goods that give you the most utility per dollar spent. By getting the biggest bang for your buck, you will end up optimizing your choices. This relationship, shown below in terms of marginal utility (MU), helps quantify the decision. So if you get more for your money by purchasing Pepsi rather than pizza, then you should buy Pepsi—and vice versa.

$$\frac{MU_{Pepsi}}{Price_{Pepsi}} \quad \textbf{Which is larger?} \quad \frac{MU_{pizza}}{Price_{pizza}}$$

If we divide the marginal utility of a good by its price, we get the utility per dollar spent. Because you wish to optimize your utility, a direct comparison of the marginal utility per dollar spent on Pepsi versus pizza gives you a road map to your consumer satisfaction. Table 16.2 shows the marginal utility for each can of Pepsi (column 2) and the marginal utility for each slice of pizza (column 5).

To decide what to consume first, look at column 3, which lists the marginal utility per dollar spent for Pepsi, and column 6, which lists the marginal utility per dollar spent for pizza. Now it's time to make your first spending decision—whether to drink a Pepsi or eat a slice of pizza. Because the marginal utility per dollar spent for the first slice of pizza (10) is higher than the marginal utility for the first can of Pepsi (9), you order a slice of pizza, which costs $2. You have $8 left.

After eating the first slice of pizza, you can choose between having a second slice of pizza, which brings 8 utils per dollar spent, and having the first can of Pepsi, which brings 9 utils per dollar spent. This time you order a Pepsi, which costs $1. You have $7 left.

TABLE 16.2

The Consumer Optimum with Pepsi and Pizza

(1) Pepsi consumed (cans)	(2) Marginal utility (MU Pepsi)	(3) MU Pepsi / Price Pepsi (Pepsi $1/can)	(4) Pizza consumed (slices)	(5) Marginal utility (MU pizza)	(6) MU pizza / Price pizza (pizza $2/slice)
1	9	9/1 = 9	1	20	20/2 = 10
2	8	8/1 = 8	2	16	16/2 = 8
3	7	7/1 = 7	3	12	12/2 = 6
4	6	6/1 = 6	4	8	8/2 = 4
5	5	5/1 = 5	5	4	4/2 = 2
6	4	4/1 = 4	6	0	0/2 = 0
7	3	3/1 = 3	7	−4	−4/2 = −2
8	2	2/1 = 2	8	−8	−8/2 = −4
9	1	1/1 = 1	9	−12	−12/2 = −6
10	0	0/1 = 0	10	−16	−16/2 = −8

Now you can choose between having a second slice of pizza, representing 8 utils per dollar spent, and having a second can of Pepsi, also 8 utils per dollar spent. Because both choices yield the same amount of utility per dollar spent and you have enough money to afford both, we'll assume you would probably purchase both at the same time. Your purchase costs another $3, which leaves you with $4.

Your next choice is between the third slice of pizza at 6 utils per dollar spent and the third can of Pepsi at 7 utils per dollar spent. Pepsi is the better value, so you buy that. You are left with $3 for your final choice: between the third slice of pizza at 6 utils per dollar spent and the fourth can of Pepsi at 6 utils per dollar spent. Since you have exactly $3 left and the items are of equal utility, you buy both, and you have no money left.

Let's see how well you have done. Looking at column 2 in Table 16.2, we calculate that the four Pepsis you consumed yielded a total utility of 9 + 8 + 7 + 6 = 30 utils. Looking at column 5, we see that three slices of pizza yielded a total utility of 20 + 16 + 12 = 48. Adding the two together (30 + 48) gives 78 total utils of satisfaction. This is the most utility you can afford with $10. To see why, look at Table 16.3, which reports the maximum utility for every affordable combination of Pepsi and pizza.

The optimum combination of Pepsi and pizza is highlighted in red. This is the result we found by comparing the marginal utilities per dollar spent in Table 16.2. Notice that Table 16.3 confirms that this process results in the highest total utility. All other affordable combinations of Pepsi and pizza produce less utility. Table 16.3 also illustrates diminishing marginal utility. If you select either pizza or Pepsi exclusively, you will have a much lower total utility: 60 utils with pizza and 45 utils with Pepsi. In addition, the preferred outcome of four Pepsis and three pizza slices corresponds to a modest amount of each good; this outcome avoids the utility reduction associated with excessive consumption of either good.

By thinking at the margin about which good provides the highest marginal utility, you also maximize your total utility. Of course, most people

TABLE 16.3

The Maximum Utility from Different Combinations of Pepsi and Pizza

Affordable combination of pizza and Pepsi	Total utility
5 pizza slices (20 + 16 + 12 + 8 + 4)	60 utils
2 Pepsis (9 + 8) and 4 pizza slices (20 + 16 + 12 + 8)	73 utils
4 Pepsis (9 + 8 + 7 + 6) and 3 pizza slices (20 + 16 + 12)	78 utils
6 Pepsis (9 + 8 + 7 + 6 + 5 + 4) and 2 pizza slices (20 + 16)	75 utils
8 Pepsis (9 + 8 + 7 + 6 + 5 + 4 + 3 + 2) and 1 pizza slice (20)	64 utils
10 Pepsis (9 + 8 + 7 + 6 + 5 + 4 + 3 + 2 + 1 + 0)	45 utils

rarely think this way. But as consumers we make marginal choices all the time. Instead of adding up utils, we think "that isn't worth it" or "that's a steal." Consumer choice is not so much a conscious calculation as an instinct to seek the most satisfaction. Next we extend our analysis by generalizing the two-good example.

Marginal Thinking with More Than Two Goods

The idea of measuring utility makes our instinctive sense more explicit and enables us to solve simple optimization problems. For instance, when you travel without the aid of GPS, you instinctively make choices about which route to take to save time. The decision to turn left or right when you come to a stop sign is a decision at the margin: one route will be better than the other. If you consistently make the best choices about which way to turn, you will arrive at your destination sooner. This is why economists focus on marginal thinking.

In reality, life is more complex than the simple two-good model implies. When you have $10 to spend, you may choose among many goods. Because you buy many items at all kinds of prices over the course of a year, you must juggle hundreds (or thousands) of purchases so that you enjoy roughly the same utility per dollar spent. Consumer optimum captures this idea by comparing the utility gained with the price paid for every item a consumer buys. In other words, a consumer's income or budget is balanced so that the ratio of the marginal utility (MU) per dollar spent on every item, from good A to good Z, is equal. In mathematical terms:

Marginal thinking

Left or right? One way will get you to your destination sooner.

$$\frac{MU_A}{Price_A} = \frac{MU_B}{Price_B} = \ldots = \frac{MU_Z}{Price_Z}$$

It should be noted that, because goods aren't infinitely divisible (we can't buy a fraction of a soda can), we can't always make the fractions come out exactly equal. Still, we maximize utility by buying the goods with the higher fractions, and in the end the marginal utilities per dollar spent for each good end up approximately equal.

In the next section, we explore the relationship between changes in price and changes in the consumer optimum.

Price Changes and the Consumer Optimum

Recall our example of pizza and Pepsi: you reached an optimum when you purchased four Pepsis and three slices of pizza. At that point, the marginal utility per dollar spent for Pepsi and pizza was equal:

$$\frac{MU_{pizza}\ (12\ utils)}{\$2} = \frac{MU_{Pepsi}\ (6\ utils)}{\$1}$$

In the earlier example, the prices of a slice of pizza ($2) and a can of Pepsi ($1) were held constant. But suppose that the price of a slice of pizza drops to $1.50. This new price causes the ratio of $MU_{pizza} \div Price_{pizza}$ to change from $12 \div 2$, or 6 utils per dollar, to $12 \div 1.5$, or 8 utils per dollar. The lower price for pizza increases the quantity of slices the consumer will buy:

$$\frac{MU_{pizza}\ (12\ utils)}{\$1.50} > \frac{MU_{Pepsi}\ (6\ utils)}{\$1}$$

As a result, we can say that lower prices increase the marginal utility per dollar spent and cause consumers to buy more of a good. Higher prices have the opposite effect by lowering the marginal utility per dollar spent. If that conclusion sounds an awful lot like the law of demand, it is! We have just restated the law of demand in terms of marginal utility.

We know that according to the law of demand (see Chapter 3), the quantity demanded falls when the price rises, and the quantity demanded rises when the price falls—all other things being equal. If we think of consumer desire for a particular product as demand, it makes sense to find a connection between the prices consumers pay, the quantity they buy, and the marginal utility they receive.

A lower price has two effects. First, because the marginal utility per dollar spent is now higher, consumers substitute the product that has become relatively less expensive—this is the **substitution effect**. Second, at the same time, a lower price can also change the purchasing power of income—this is the **real-income effect**. (For a basic discussion of the trends behind these effects, see Chapter 3.)

Let's go back to our Pepsi and pizza example to separate these two effects. A lower price for a slice of pizza makes it more affordable. If slices are $2 each, a consumer with a budget of $10 can afford five slices. If the price drops to $1.50 per slice, the consumer can afford six slices and still have $1 left over.

When the price of a slice of pizza is $2, your optimum is three slices of pizza and four Pepsis. If we drop the price of a slice of pizza to $1.50, you save 50 cents per slice. Because you are purchasing three slices, you save $1.50—which is enough to buy another slice. Looking back at column 5 in Table 16.2, we see that the fourth slice of pizza yields an additional 8 utils. Alternatively, you could use the $1.50 you saved on pizza to buy a fifth can of Pepsi—which has a marginal utility of 5—and still have 50 cents left over.

The lower price of pizza may cause you to substitute pizza for Pepsi because pizza has become relatively less expensive. This is the substitution effect at work. In addition, you have more purchasing power through the money you save from the lower-priced pizza. This is the real-income effect.

The real-income effect matters only when prices change enough to cause a measurable effect on the purchasing power of the consumer's income or

Marginal thinking

The **substitution effect** occurs when consumers substitute a product that has become relatively less expensive as the result of a price change.

The **real-income effect** occurs when there is a change in purchasing power as a result of a change in the price of a good.

budget. For example, suppose that a 10% price reduction in peanut butter cups occurs. Will there be a substitution effect, a real-income effect, or both? The key to answering this question is to consider how much money is saved. Most candy bars cost less than a dollar, so a 10% reduction in price would be less than 10 cents. The lower price will motivate some consumers to switch to peanut butter cups—a substitution effect that can be observed through increased purchases of peanut butter cups. However, the real-income effect is negligible. The consumer has saved less than 10 cents. The money saved could be used to purchase other goods; but very few goods cost so little, and the enhanced purchasing power is effectively zero. Thus, the answer to the question is that there will be a modest substitution effect and essentially no real-income effect.

WOULD YOU PAY $149 FOR A DRINK AT STARBUCKS?

Your favorite Starbucks creation typically costs about $5. Now suppose you do what the guy on the left did, and spend over $100 on extra shots, add-ins, and flavors, all in a punchbowl-sized "cup." Would you enjoy the drink more? Maybe. But 20 times more? Not a chance. How do we know this? The law of diminishing marginal utility tells us that additional units of the same good will eventually bring less marginal utility.

In addition, substantial income and substitution effects are at work when you consider what $149 could buy instead of coffee. For many people, $149 is enough to purchase a month's worth of groceries. It is hard to imagine that a single Starbucks drink could provide more utility than you would experience from the variety of food you would eat over the course of a month. If you are interested in learning more about the curious obsession some people have with purchasing a super-expensive Starbucks creation, check out this link: http://www.caffeineinformer.com/what-is-the-most -expensive-starbucks-drink.

A $149 cup of Starbucks coffee, and yes, that's the actual size. What's the most *you* would pay for your favorite drink?

The **diamond-water paradox** explains why water, which is essential to life, is inexpensive, while diamonds, which do not sustain life, are expensive.

What Is the Diamond-Water Paradox?

Now that you understand the connection between prices and utility, we can tackle one of the most interesting puzzles in economics—the **diamond-water paradox**. First described by Adam Smith in 1776, the diamond-water paradox explains why water, which is essential to life, is inexpensive, while diamonds, which do not sustain life, are expensive. Many people of Smith's era found the paradox perplexing. Today, we can use consumer choice theory to answer the question.

Essentially, the diamond-water paradox unfairly compares the amount of marginal utility a person receives from a small quantity of something rare (the diamond) with the marginal utility received from consuming a small amount of additional water after already consuming a large amount.

We know that marginal utility is captured in the law of demand and therefore by the price of a good. For example, when the price of diamonds increases, the quantity demanded declines. We learned in Chapter 5 that in graphical

Consumer Optimum

QUESTION: Suppose your favorite magazine, *The Economist*, costs $6 per issue and *People* magazine costs $4 per issue. If you receive 20 utils when you read *People*, how many additional utils would you need to get from reading *The Economist* to prompt you to pony up the extra $2 to purchase it instead of *People* magazine?

ANSWER: To answer the question, you first need to equate the marginal utility (MU) per dollar spent for both magazines and solve for the missing variable, the utility from *The Economist*:

$$\frac{MU_{\text{The Economist}} \, (X \text{ utils})}{\$6} = \frac{MU_{\text{People}} \, (20 \text{ utils})}{\$4}$$

$$\frac{X}{\$6} = \frac{20}{\$4}$$

$$X = \frac{\$120}{\$4}$$

$$X = 30$$

When the $MU_{\text{The Economist}}$ is equal to 30 utils, you are indifferent between purchasing either of the two magazines (that is, each magazine would bring you equal satisfaction). Because the question asks how many *additional* utils are needed to justify purchasing *The Economist*, you should subtract the utils from *People*, or 20, to get the difference, which is 30 − 20, or 10 utils.

terms, the consumer surplus is the area under the demand curve and above the price, or the gains from trade that a consumer enjoys. Therefore, if the price of diamonds rises, consumers will enjoy less surplus when buying them.

Figure 16.2 contrasts the demand and supply equilibrium in both the market for water and the market for diamonds. Notice that the consumer surplus is the area highlighted in blue for water and the triangular area highlighted with dots for diamonds. The blue area of total utility for water (TU_w) is much larger than the dotted area of total utility for diamonds (TU_d) because water is essential for life. Therefore, water creates significantly more total utility than diamonds do. However, in most places in the United States, water is very plentiful, so people take additional units of it for granted. In fact, it is so plentiful that if someone were to offer you a gallon of water right now, you would probably hesitate to take it. But what if someone offered you a gallon-size bucket of diamonds? You bet you would take that! Therefore, it should not surprise you that something quite plentiful, water, would yield less marginal utility than something rare, diamonds ($MU_w < MU_d$). However, if water were as rare as diamonds, there is no doubt that the price of water would exceed the price of diamonds.

Let's consider how we use water. We bathe in it, cook with it, and drink it. Each of those uses has high value, so the marginal utility of water is high. But we also use it to water our lawns and fill our fish tanks. Those uses are not nearly as essential, so the marginal utility of water for these uses is much lower. The

FIGURE 16.2

The Diamond-Water Paradox

The diamond-water paradox exists because people fail to recognize that demand and supply are equally important in determining the value a good creates in society. The demand for water is large, while the demand for diamonds is small. If we look at the amount of consumer surplus, we observe that the blue area (TU_w, which represents the consumer surplus for water) is much larger than the dotted area (TU_d, which represents the consumer surplus for diamonds) because water is essential for life. As a result, water creates significantly more total utility (TU) than diamonds. However, because water is abundant in most places, the price, P_{water}, is low. In contrast, diamonds are rare and the price, $P_{diamond}$, is high.

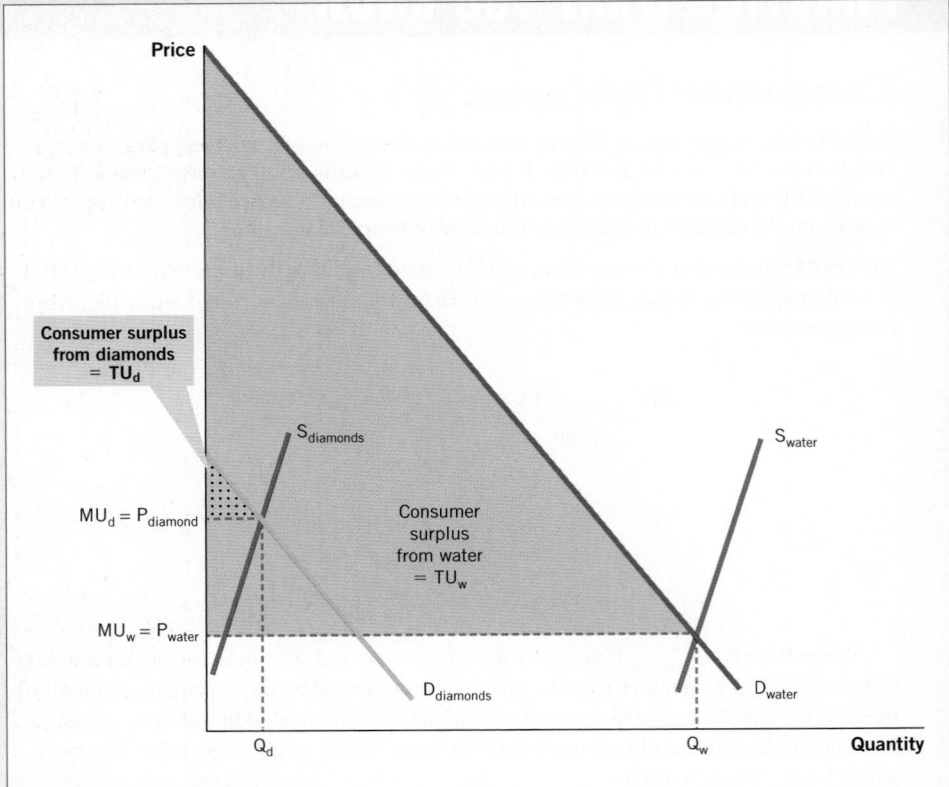

reason we use water in both essential and nonessential ways is that its price is relatively low, so low-value uses, like filling fish tanks, yield enough utility to justify the cost. Because water is abundant in most places, the price (P_{water}) is low. In contrast, diamonds are rare, and their price ($P_{diamond}$) is high. The cost of obtaining a diamond means that a consumer must get a great deal of marginal utility from the purchase of a diamond to justify the expense, which explains why diamonds are given as gifts for extremely special occasions.

Conclusion

Does having more money make people more satisfied? The answer is no. More money enables people to buy more goods, but because of diminishing marginal utility, the increases in satisfaction from being able to buy more goods or higher-quality goods become progressively smaller with rising income. So we could say that having more money makes people somewhat more satisfied. But it seems appropriate to add that the relationship between quality of life and money is not direct. More money sometimes leads to more utility, and at other times more money means more problems.

The Diamond-Water Paradox

SUPER SIZE ME

What would happen if you ate all your meals at McDonald's for an entire month—without ever exercising? *Super Size Me*, a 2004 documentary by Morgan Spurlock, endeavored to find out. It is the absurd nature of Spurlock's adventure that pulls viewers in. No one would *actually* eat every meal at the same restaurant for a month, because diminishing marginal utility would cause the utility from the meals to plunge. (This is especially true with McDonald's, which is not known for high-quality cuisine.)

Why did Spurlock take aim at McDonald's and more generally the fast-food industry? His aim was to reveal how unhealthy fast food really is, but the documentary also happens to unintentionally offer a modern parallel to the diamond-water paradox.

The key is the business model that many fast-food restaurants follow. These restaurants provide filling food at low prices, a combination that encourages consumers to eat more than they would if the price were higher. Eating a lot of food causes diminishing marginal utility; often, the last bite of a sandwich or fries or the last gulp of a 32-ounce drink brings very little additional utility, so it is not uncommon for consumers to discard the excess.

In contrast, consider fine dining. Fancy establishments serve smaller portions by design. A five-course meal is meant to be savored, and the experience trumps price. What makes someone willing to pay

A Big Mac a day for 30 days! What could possibly go wrong?

significantly more when dining out at such places? Upscale restaurants are creating high marginal utility by making every bite mouthwatering. They do not want to diminish the marginal value through overeating.

To summarize, McDonald's is a lot like water in the diamond-water paradox. It is easy to find a McDonald's restaurant almost anywhere, and the chain serves close to 70 million customers a day. Therefore, the total utility the chain creates is high, despite the fact that the marginal utility of the last bite is low. Upscale restaurants are a lot like diamonds: they are uncommon, and the number of customers they serve is small. The total utility that upscale restaurants create is low compared with McDonald's, but the marginal utility of the last individual bite at an upscale restaurant is quite high.

As we have seen in this chapter, price plays a key role in determining utility. Because consumers face a budget and wish to maximize their utility, the prices they pay determine their marginal utility per dollar spent. Comparing the marginal utility per dollar spent across many goods helps us understand individuals' consumption patterns. Diminishing marginal utility also helps to describe consumer choice. Because marginal utility declines with additional consumption, consumers do not exclusively purchase their favorite products. Instead, they diversify their choices in order to gain more utility. In addition,

Worth It

- You really need or want it (inelastic demand).
- No acceptable substitute good is available at a lower price.
- It is a good bang for the buck (MU/P is high).
- You can afford it without spending beyond your means.

Buzzfeed's *Worth It* is the #1 show on YouTube. The show features Steven Lim and Andrew Ilnyckyj. The premise is simple: the hosts try an inexpensive, a moderately-priced, and a very expensive version of the same good. They then debate the merits of each version and explain why it is either "worth it" or not.

Life works the same way! We make thousands of decisions over the course of each year to either make a purchase, not purchase, or find a substitute product instead. *Worth It* is really about the hunt for the consumer optimum, where the extra value we get from buying one more unit of a good is the same across all the items we purchase. Whether something is "worth it" also applies to how we spend our time and energy. In a world of scarcity we must use our limited resources wisely, or else we end up with fewer utils (less enjoyment).

Would you buy a $47 taco and eat it in one bite?

changes in prices have two different effects: one on real income and a separate substitution effect that together determine the composition of the bundle of goods purchased.

In the next chapter, we question how much individuals use consumer choice theory to make their decisions. The approach known as behavioral economics argues that decision-makers are not entirely rational about the choices they make.

Finally, in the appendix that follows, we refine consumer theory by discussing indifference curves. Please read the appendix to get a glimpse into how economists model consumer choice in greater detail. ✳

· ANSWERING *the* BIG QUESTIONS ·

How do economists model consumer satisfaction?

- Economists model consumer satisfaction by examining utility, which is a measure of the level of satisfaction that a consumer enjoys from the consumption of goods and services.

- Utility diminishes with additional consumption. This property limits the amount of any particular good or service that a person will consume.

How do consumers optimize their purchasing decisions?

- Consumers optimize their purchasing decisions by finding the combination of goods and services that maximizes the level of satisfaction from a given income or budget. The consumer optimum occurs when a consumer maximizes the utility from his or her income or budget, so that the marginal utility per dollar spent on every item purchased is equal to that of every other item purchased.

- Changes in price have two distinct effects on consumer behavior. If the price falls, the marginal utility per dollar spent will be higher. As a result, consumers will substitute the product that has become relatively less expensive. This is the substitution effect. If the lower price also results in substantial savings, it causes an increase in purchasing power, known as the real-income effect.

What is the diamond-water paradox?

- The diamond-water paradox explains why water, which is essential to life, is inexpensive, while diamonds, which do not sustain life, are expensive. Many people of Adam Smith's era, in the eighteenth century, found the paradox perplexing. We can solve the diamond-water paradox by recognizing that the price of water is low because its supply is abundant, and the price of diamonds is high because their supply is small. If water were as rare as diamonds, there is no doubt that the price of water would exceed the price of diamonds.

Concepts You Should Know

consumer optimum (p. 518)
diamond-water paradox (p. 522)
diminishing marginal utility (p. 516)

marginal utility (p. 515)
real-income effect (p. 521)
substitution effect (p. 521)

util (p. 512)
utility (p. 512)

Questions for Review

1. After watching a movie, you and your friend both indicate that you liked it. Does this mean that each of you received the same amount of utility? Explain your response.

2. What is the relationship between total utility and marginal utility?

3. How is diminishing marginal utility reflected in the law of demand?

4. What does it mean when we say that the marginal utility per dollar spent is equal for two goods?

Study Problems (✻ solved at the end of the section)

1. A local pizza restaurant charges full price for the first pizza but offers 50% off on a second pizza. Using marginal utility, explain the restaurant's pricing strategy.

2. Suppose that the price of trail mix is $4 per pound and the price of cashews is $6 per pound. If you get 30 utils from the last pound of cashews you consume, how many utils would you have to get from the last pound of trail mix to be in consumer equilibrium?

3. Fill in the missing information in the table below:

Number of cookies	Total utility of cookies	Marginal utility of cookies	Number of pretzels	Total utility of pretzels	Marginal utility of pretzels
0	0	—	0	0	—
1	—	25	1	10	—
2	—	15	2	18	—
3	—	10	3	24	6
4	—	5	4	—	4
5	55	—	5	—	2
6	50	—	6	—	0

4. Use the table in problem 3. Suppose that you have a budget of $8 and that cookies and pretzels cost $1 each. What is the consumer optimum?

5. Use the table in problem 3. What is the consumer optimum if the price of cookies rises from $1 to $1.50 and the price of pretzels remains at $1?

6. You are considering either dining at Cici's, an all-you-can-eat pizza chain, or buying pizza by the slice at a local pizzeria for $2 per slice. At which restaurant are you likely to obtain the most marginal utility from the last slice you eat? Explain your response.

7. In consumer equilibrium, a person buys four cups of coffee at $2 per cup and two muffins at $2 per muffin each day. If the price of a cup of coffee rises to $3, what would you expect to happen to the amount of coffee and muffins this person consumes?

8. How do dollar stores survive when *none* of the items sold brings a high amount of total utility to consumers?

✻ **9.** Imagine that the total utility from consuming five tacos is 10, 16, 19, 20, and 17 utils, respectively. When does marginal utility begin to diminish?

10. You and your friends are considering vacationing in either Cabo San Lucas or Cancun for spring break. When you first researched the cost of your hotel and flights, the total price was $1,000 to each destination. However, a sale has lowered the total cost of going to Cancun to $800. Does this change create a substitution effect, a real-income effect, or both? Explain.

11. Everyone wears underwear, but comparatively few people wear ties. Why are ties so much more expensive than underwear if the demand for underwear is so much greater than the demand for ties?

12. Do you agree with Henry David Thoreau's quote, "Happiness is like a butterfly; the more you chase it, the more it will elude you, but if you turn your attention to other things, it will come and sit softly on your shoulder"? Explain your answer using diminishing marginal utility.

✳ 13. A health study found that patients who experience severe pain may feel better if they curse as a coping mechanism. Based on what you have learned about economics, would you expect to see a difference in pain relief between people who normally use profanity and those who do not normally use profanity?

14. Suppose that Gina's marginal utility from drinking milk is 5 utils per ounce, and her marginal utility from eating cereal is 10 utils per ounce. If the price of milk is 50 cents per ounce and the price of cereal is 80 cents per ounce, is Gina maximizing her utility? If so, explain how you know. If not, explain how she should change her spending to increase her utility.

15. Refer to the following Marginal Utility (MU) table:

$Q_{mangoes}$	$MU_{mangoes}$	$Q_{pineapples}$	$MU_{pineapples}$
1	20	1	24
2	15	2	18
3	10	3	12
4	5	4	6

You have a budget of $10. Pineapples cost $2, and mangoes cost $1. How many of each should you buy to maximize total utility?

Solved Problems

9. The key to answering this question is to realize that the data are expressed in total utils. The first taco brings the consumer 10 utils. Consuming the second taco yields $16 - 10$, or 6 additional utils. Since there are fewer extra utils from the second taco (6) than the utils from the first taco (10), diminishing marginal utility begins after the first taco.

11. Recall that demand is only half of the market. The other half is supply. Far fewer ties are produced than items of underwear. The supply of ties also plays a role in determining the price. In addition, ties are a fashion statement, which makes ties a luxury good. Underwear is a necessity. As a result, ties are a lot like diamonds: there is a small overall market, and prices are high. Underwear is a lot like water: there is a very large overall market, and prices are low. The fact that ties generally cost more does not mean that ties are more valuable to society. Rather, people get more marginal utility from purchasing the "perfect" tie as opposed to finding the "perfect" underwear.

13. The researchers found that patients who infrequently cursed in their daily lives experienced more pain relief when they were in severe pain. Those who regularly cursed in their daily lives experienced almost no pain relief from cursing. This result is not surprising when you recall the law of diminishing marginal utility. For additional information, see http://www .ncbi .nlm.nih.gov/m/pubmed/22078790/.

APPENDIX

16A

Indifference Curve Analysis

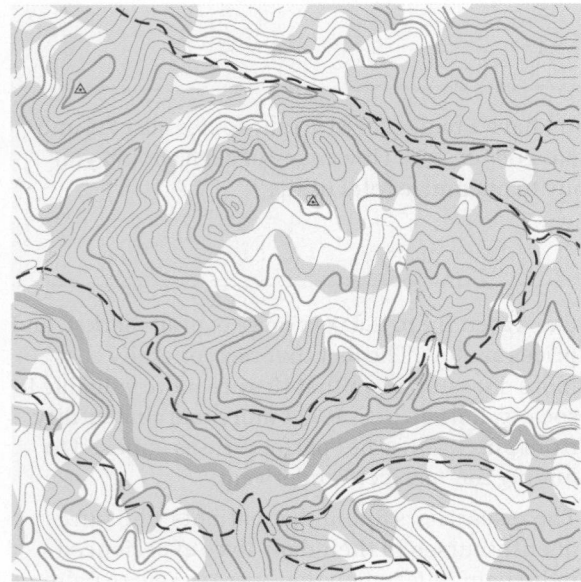

A topographical map and indifference curve analysis share many of the same properties.

An **indifference curve** represents the various combinations of two goods that yield the same level of personal satisfaction, or utility.

A **maximization point** is the point at which a certain combination of two goods yields the greatest possible utility.

There is much more to economic analysis than the simple supply and demand model can capture. Chapter 16 considered how consumers can get the biggest bang for their buck, or the greatest utility out of their purchases. Here we explore the question in more detail, using the tool of indifference curve analysis. The purpose of this appendix is to get you thinking at a deeper level about the connections between price changes and consumption decisions.

Indifference Curves

Indifference curves are a tool that economists use to describe the trade-offs that exist when consumers make decisions.

An **indifference curve** represents the various combinations of two goods that yield the same level of satisfaction, or utility. The simplest way to think about indifference curves is to envision a topographical map on which each line represents a specific elevation. When you look at a topographical map, you see ridges, mountains, valleys, and the subtle flow of the land. An indifference curve conveys the same complex information about personal satisfaction. Indifference curves visually rise to a peak called the **maximization point**, or the point at which utility is maximized. The only limitation of this analysis is that this book is a two-dimensional space used to illustrate a three-dimensional concept. Let's set this concern aside and focus on achieving the maximization point, where total utility is highest.

Returning to our example of pizza and Pepsi, recall that you had $10 to spend and only two items to purchase: Pepsi at $1 per can and pizza at $2 per slice. Like all consumers, you will optimize your utility by maximizing the marginal utility per dollar spent, so you select four Pepsis and three slices of pizza. But what happens if your budget is unlimited? If you're free to spend as much you like, how much pizza and Pepsi would you want?

Economic "Goods" and "Bads"

To answer the question we just posed, we'll start with another question. Are Pepsi and pizza always economic "goods"? This may seem like a strange question, but think about your own consumption habits. Do you keep eating something after you feel full? Do you continue to eat even if your stomach aches? At some point, we all stop eating and drinking. In this sense, economic goods, like Pepsi and pizza, are "good" only up to a point. Once we are full, however, the utility from attaining another unit of the good becomes negative—a "bad."

Each indifference curve represents lines of equal satisfaction. For simplicity, Figure 16A.1 shows the indifference curve as circles around the point of maximum satisfaction. The closer the indifference curve is to the maximization point, the higher the consumer's level of satisfaction.

FIGURE 16A.1

Indifference Curves

The maximization point indicates where a consumer attains the most utility. In quadrant I, both Pepsi and pizza are "goods" (because their consumption involves the reactions of either tasting great or getting full), so attaining more of each will cause utility to rise toward the maximization point. In quadrants II, III, and IV, either pizza or Pepsi is a "bad" or both are (because at those levels of consumption they make the consumer feel either too full or sick). Because the consumer must pay to acquire pizza and Pepsi, and because at least one of the items is reducing the consumer's utility in quadrants II, III, and IV, the most affordable path to the highest utility—that is, the maximization point—is quadrant I. (Notice that the labels are qualitative and reflect decreasing utility with additional consumption.)

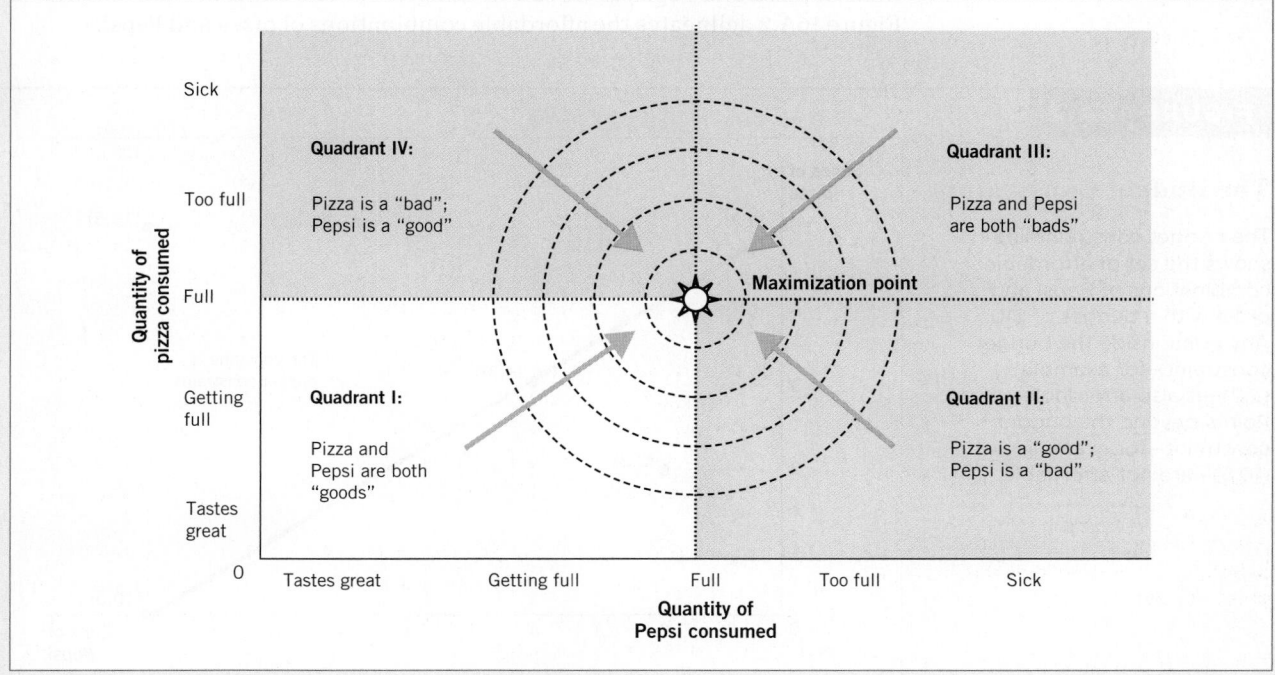

Indifference curves are best seen as approaching the maximization point from all directions (like climbing up a mountain on four different sides). In any hike, some paths are better than others. Figure 16A.1 illustrates four separate ways to reach the maximization point. However, only one of the paths makes any sense. In quadrants II, III, and IV, either pizza or Pepsi is a "bad" or both are "bads" (because at those levels of consumption one or both of them make the consumer feel too full or sick). Because the consumer must pay to acquire pizza and Pepsi, and because at least one of them is reducing the consumer's utility, the consumer's satisfaction will increase by purchasing less of the "bad." In other words, why would anyone willingly pay to feel worse? Quadrants II, III, and IV are highlighted in orange because people are unlikely to choose an option that makes them feel too full or sick. That leaves quadrant I as the preferred path to the highest utility. In quadrant I, increasing amounts of pizza and Pepsi produce more utility. (Notice that the labels in Figure 16A.1 are qualitative and reflect decreasing utility with additional consumption.)

The Budget Constraint

Figure 16A.1 illustrates the choices facing a consumer with an unlimited budget and no opportunity costs. However, in real life we need to account for a person's budget and the cost of acquiring each good. The amount a person has to spend is the **budget constraint**, or the set of consumption bundles that represent the maximum amount the consumer can afford. If you have $10 to spend on pizza ($2 per slice) and Pepsi ($1 per can), you could choose to purchase 10 cans of Pepsi and forgo the pizza. Alternatively, you could purchase 5 slices of pizza and do without the Pepsi. Or you could choose a number of different combinations of pizza and Pepsi, as we saw in Chapter 16. The budget constraint line in Figure 16A.2 delineates the affordable combinations of pizza and Pepsi.

The **budget constraint** is the set of consumption bundles that represent the maximum amount the consumer can afford.

FIGURE 16A.2

The Budget Constraint

The budget constraint line shows the set of affordable combinations of Pepsi and pizza with a budget of $10. Any point inside the budget constraint—for example (2,2)—is also affordable. Points beyond the budget constraint—for example (10,5)—are not affordable.

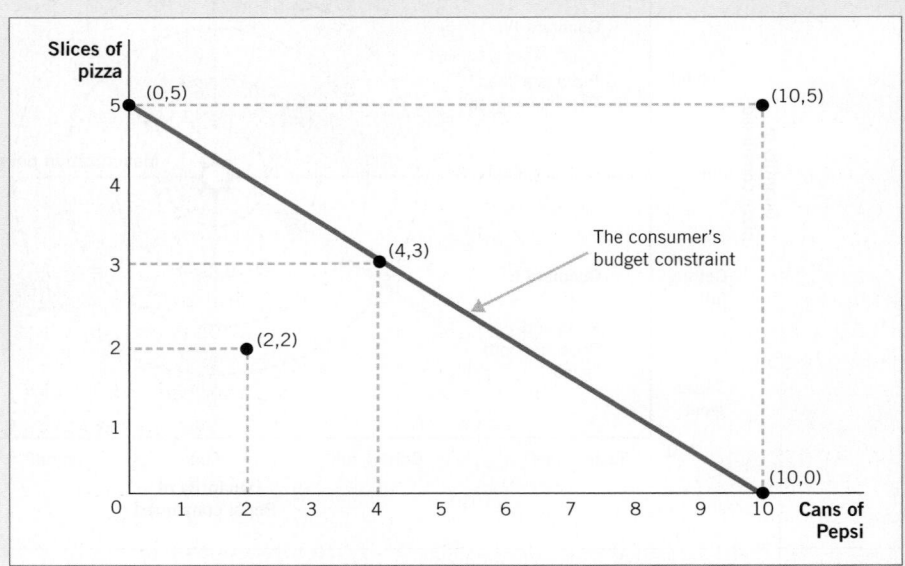

There are many different affordable combinations of the two goods. Let's take the pairs along the budget constraint line first. If you spend your entire $10 on Pepsi, the combination of coordinates would be the point (10,0), which represents 10 cans of Pepsi and 0 slices of pizza. If you spend your entire budget on pizza, the coordinates would be (0,5). These two points are the extreme outcomes. By connecting these two points with a line—the budget constraint—we can see the many combinations that would fully exhaust $10. As a consumer, your goal is to pick the combination that maximizes your satisfaction, subject to your budget constraint. One possibility would be to spend the $10 on four cans of Pepsi and three slices of pizza (4,3), which happens to be the point of utility maximization we discovered in the chapter (see Table 16.3).

What about the points located below and above the budget constraint? For example, looking again at Figure 16A.2, at the point (2,2) you would be spending $6—that is, $2 on Pepsi and $4 on pizza. You would still have $4 to spend on more of either good. Because both goods are desirable, spending the leftover money in your budget will increase your level of satisfaction. So the combination (2,2) represents a failure to maximize utility. On the other side of the budget constraint line, we find the point (10,5). This combination, which would cost you $20 to attain, represents a combination of items you cannot afford. From this example, you can see that the budget constraint is a limiting set of choices, or a constraint imposed by scarcity.

In the next section, we examine indifference curves in greater detail. Once we fully understand the properties that characterize indifference curves, we can join them with the budget constraint to better describe how consumers make choices.

Properties of Indifference Curves

It is useful to keep in mind several assumptions about indifference curves. The properties described in this section help ensure that our model is logically consistent.

Indifference Curves Are Typically Bowed Inward

A rational consumer will operate only in quadrant I in Figure 16A.1. Within that quadrant, the higher indifference curves (those nearer the utility maximization point) are bowed inward (convex) and are preferred to the lower ones (nearer the origin). Our model eliminates any outcome in quadrants II through IV by requiring that goods be "good," not "bad." Because quadrants II through IV result in less utility and greater expenditures, no rational consumer would ever willingly operate in these regions.

Figure 16A.3 shows an indifference curve that reflects the trade-off between two goods. Because the indifference curve bows inward, the **marginal rate of substitution (MRS)**, or the rate at which a consumer is willing to trade one good for another along the indifference curve, varies. The MRS is reflected in the slope of the indifference curve in the figure. Points A and B are both on the same indifference curve, so the consumer finds the combinations (1,5) and (2,3) to be equally attractive. Between points A and B, the consumer must receive two slices of pizza to compensate for the loss of a can of Pepsi. We can see this in the

The **marginal rate of substitution (MRS)** is the rate at which a consumer is willing to trade one good for another along an indifference curve.

Trade-offs

The Marginal Rate of Substitution

The marginal rate of substitution (MRS) along an indifference curve varies, as reflected in the slope of the indifference curve. Because Pepsi and pizza are both subject to diminishing marginal utility, it takes more of the plentiful good to keep the consumer indifferent when giving up another good that is in short supply.

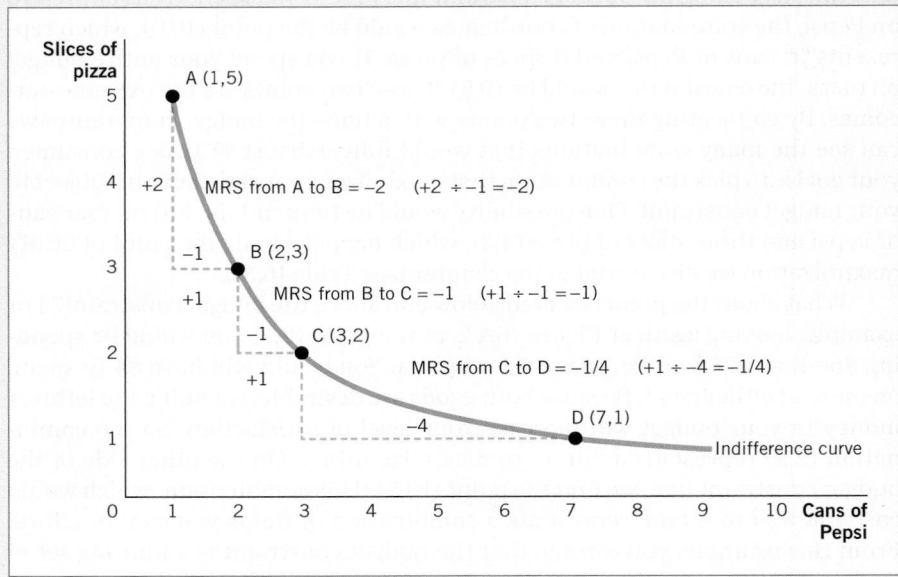

figure by observing that the consumer chooses only two cans of Pepsi and three slices of pizza at (2,3). Because the marginal utility from consuming Pepsi is high when the amount consumed is low, giving up an additional Pepsi requires that the consumer receive back two slices of pizza to reach the point (1,5). Therefore, the marginal rate of substitution (MRS) is −2 (because +2 ÷ −1 = −2).

However, if we examine the same indifference curve between points C and D, we see that the consumer is also indifferent between the combinations (3,2) and (7,1). However, this time the consumer is willing to give up four cans of Pepsi to get one more slice of pizza, so the MRS is −4 (because +1 ÷ −4 = −1/4). Why is there such a big difference between (3,2) and (7,1) compared with (2,3) and (1,5)? At (7,1), the consumer has a lot of Pepsi and very little pizza to enjoy it with. As a result, the marginal utility of the second slice of pizza is so high that it is worth four Pepsis! We can see the change in the marginal rate of substitution visually, because the slope between points A and B is steeper than it is between points C and D.

What explains why Pepsi is more valuable between points A and B? The consumer starts with only two cans. Pizza is more valuable between points C and D because the consumer starts with only two slices of pizza. Because Pepsi and pizza are both subject to diminishing marginal utility, it takes more of the plentiful good to keep the consumer indifferent when giving up another good that is in short supply.

Marginal thinking

Indifference Curves Cannot Be Thick

Another property of indifference curves is that they cannot be thick. If they could be thick, then it would be possible to draw two points inside an indifference curve where one of the two points was preferred to the other. Therefore, a

Slices of pizza (y-axis), Cans of Pepsi (x-axis). Points B (3,3), A (3,2), C (5,2). An impossible indifference curve.

If indifference curves could be thick, it would be possible to draw two points inside the curve in a way that indicates that one of the two points is preferred to the other. Point B has one extra slice of pizza and point C has two extra cans of Pepsi compared with point A. Therefore, the consumer cannot be indifferent between these three points, and the indifference curve cannot be thick.

consumer could be indifferent between those points. In Figure 16A.4, points A, B, and C are all located on the same (impossible) indifference curve. However, points B and C are both strictly preferred to point A. Why? Because point B has one extra slice of pizza compared with point A, and point C has two extra cans of Pepsi compared with point A. Because more pizza and Pepsi adds to the consumer's utility, the consumer cannot be indifferent between these three points.

Indifference Curves Cannot Intersect

Indifference curves, by their very nature, cannot intersect. To understand why, let's look at a hypothetical case. Figure 16A.5 shows two indifference curves crossing at point A. Points A and B are both located along the light orange curve (IC_1), so we know that those two points bring the consumer the same utility. Points A and C are both located along the darker orange curve (IC_2), so those two points also yield the same utility for the consumer. Therefore, the utility at point A equals the utility at point B, and the utility at point A also equals the utility at point C. This means that the utility at point B should also equal the utility at point C, but that cannot be true. Point B is located at (1,3), and point C is located at (2,4). Because (2,4) strictly dominates (1,3), point C is preferred to point B. Therefore, we can say that indifference curves cannot intersect without violating the assumption that consumers are rational utility maximizers.

We have seen that indifference curves have three properties: they are bowed inward toward the origin (convex); they cannot be thick; and they cannot intersect. These properties guarantee that they take the general levels shown in quadrant I of Figure 16A.1.

Indifference Curves Cannot Intersect

The utility at point B should equal the utility at point C, but that cannot be true even though the utility at point B is equal to the utility at point A (along IC₁) and the utility at point C is equal to the utility at point A (along IC₂). Point B is located at (1,3) and point C is located at (2,4). Because (2,4) strictly dominates (1,3), point C is preferred to point B. Indifference curves cannot intersect.

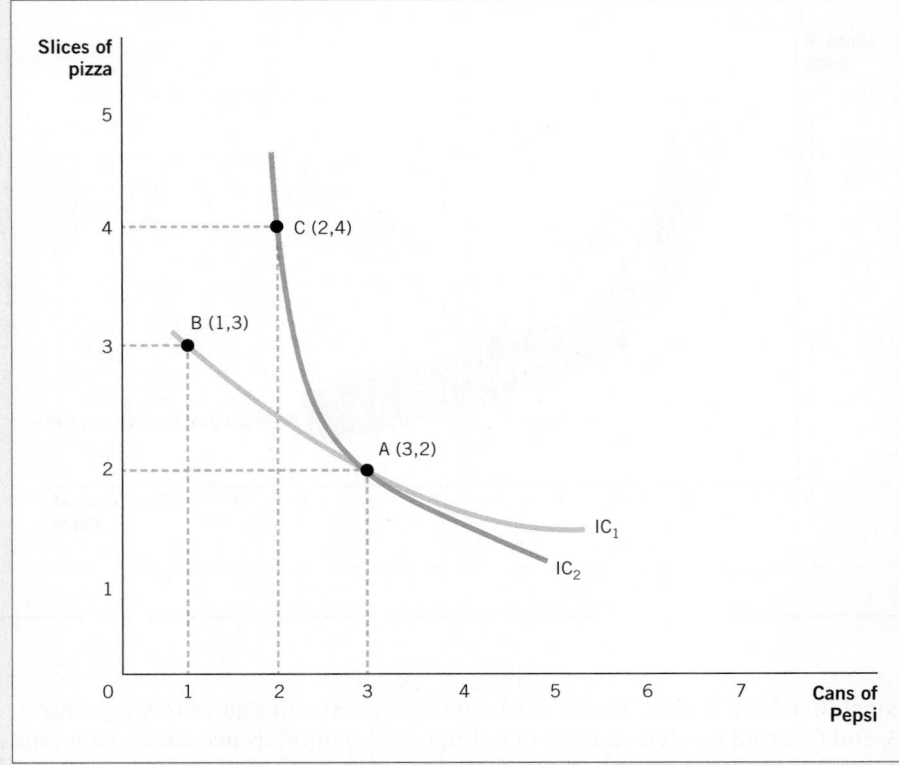

Extreme Preferences: Perfect Substitutes and Perfect Complements

As we have just seen, indifference curves typically are convex and bow inward toward the origin. However, there are two exceptions: *perfect substitutes* and *perfect complements*. These are found on either side of the standard-shaped, convex indifference curve.

Perfect substitutes exist when a consumer is completely indifferent between two goods. Suppose that you cannot taste any difference between Aquafina and Evian bottled water. You would be indifferent between drinking one additional bottle of Aquafina or one additional bottle of Evian. Turning to panel (a) of Figure 16A.6, you can see that the indifference curves (IC₁, IC₂, IC₃, IC₄) for these two goods are straight, parallel lines with a marginal rate of substitution, or slope, of −1 everywhere along the curve. However, it's important to note that the slope of an indifference curve of perfect substitutes need not always be −1; it can be any constant rate. Because perfect substitutes have a marginal rate of substitution with a constant rate, they are drawn as straight lines.

Perfect complements exist when a consumer is interested in consuming two goods in fixed proportions. Shoes are an excellent example. We buy shoes in pairs because the left or right shoe is not valuable by itself; we need both shoes

Perfect substitutes
exist when the consumer is completely indifferent between two goods, resulting in a straight-line indifference curve with a constant marginal rate of substitution.

Perfect complements
exist when the consumer is interested in consuming two goods in fixed proportions, resulting in a right-angle indifference curve.

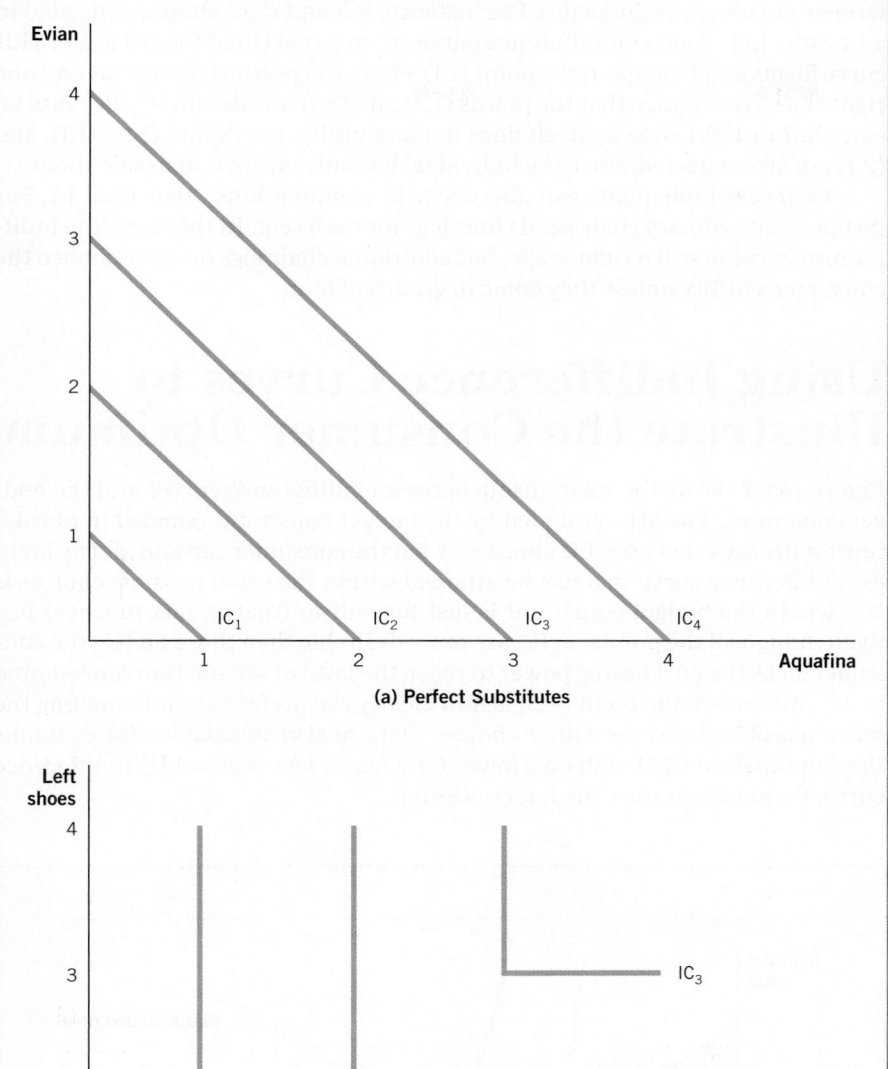

(a) Perfect Substitutes

(b) Perfect Complements

(a) Because perfect substitutes have a marginal rate of substitution that is constant, they are drawn as straight lines. In this case, the MRS, or slope, is –1 everywhere along the lines, or curves. (b) Perfect complements are drawn as right angles. A typical indifference curve that reflects the trade-off between two goods that are not perfect substitutes or perfect complements has a marginal rate of substitution that falls between these two extremes.

to be able to walk comfortably. This explains why shoes are not sold individually. An extra left or right shoe has no marginal value to the consumer, so the indifference curves are right angles. For instance, left and right shoes are needed in a 1:1 ratio. Let's look at indifference curve IC_1 in panel (b) of Figure 16A.6. This curve forms a right angle at the point (1,1) where the person has one left and one right shoe. Now notice that the points (1,2) and (2,1) are also on IC_1. Because an extra left or right shoe by itself does not add utility, the points (1,2), (1,1), and (2,1) are all connected, since the individual has only one pair of usable shoes.

Perfect complements can also occur in combinations other than 1:1. For instance, an ordinary chair needs four legs for each seat. In that case, the indifference curve is still a right angle, but additional chair legs do not enhance the consumer's utility unless they come in groups of four.

Using Indifference Curves to Illustrate the Consumer Optimum

Figure 16A.7 shows the relationship between indifference curves and the budget constraint. The area bounded by the budget constraint (shaded in purple) represents the set of possible choices—what the consumer can afford. The highest indifference curve that can be attained within the set of possible choices is IC_3, where the budget constraint is just tangent to (that is, just touches) IC_3. Even though all the points on IC_4 are more desirable than those on IC_3, the consumer lacks the purchasing power to reach the level of satisfaction represented by IC_4. Moreover, the point (4,3) is now clearly the preferred choice among the set of possible decisions. Other choices that are also affordable—for example, the combination (2,4)—fall on a lower (and hence less preferable) indifference curve. Point (4,3) is the consumer optimum.

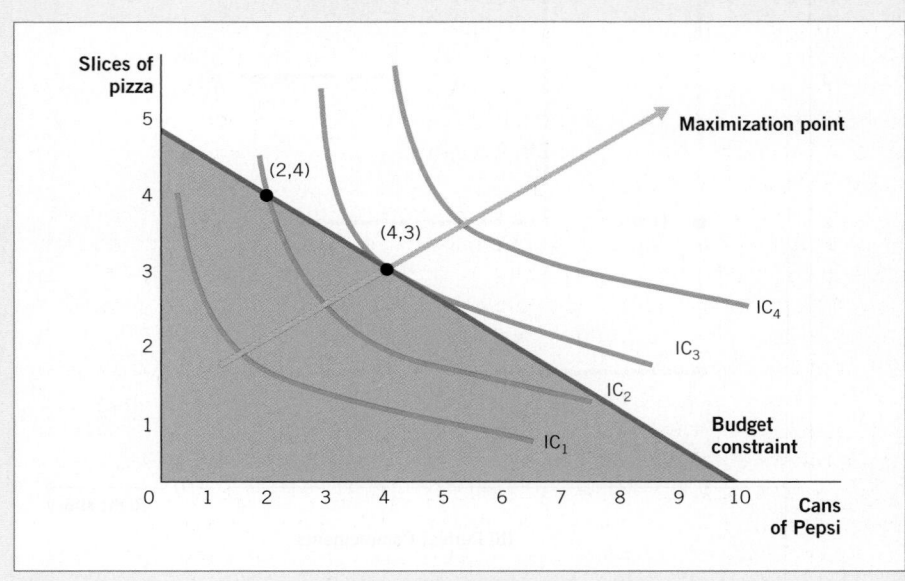

FIGURE 16A.7

Consumer Optimum

Progressively higher indifference curves bring the consumer closer to the maximization point. Because the budget constraint limits what the consumer can afford, the tangency of the budget constraint with the highest indifference curve represents the highest level of affordable satisfaction—that is, the consumer optimum. In this case, the point (4,3) represents the consumer's preferred combination of Pepsi and pizza.

Progressively higher indifference curves bring the consumer closer to the maximization point. Because the budget constraint limits what the consumer can afford, the tangency of the budget constraint with the highest indifference curve represents the highest affordable level of satisfaction—that is, the consumer optimum.

Using Indifference Curves to Illustrate the Real-Income and Substitution Effects

The power of indifference curve analysis is its ability to display how price changes affect consumption choices. Part of the intuition behind the analysis involves understanding when the substitution effect is likely to dominate the real-income effect, and vice versa.

In our example, you have only $10, so a price increase on Pepsi from $1 to $2 per can would represent a financial burden, significantly lowering your real purchasing power. However, we can easily think of cases in which a change in the price of Pepsi wouldn't matter. Suppose yours is a typical American household with a median annual income of $60,000. While out shopping, you observe that a local Toyota car dealer is offering 10% off new cars and a nearby grocery store is selling Pepsi at a 10% discount. Because of the substitution effect, more people will buy Toyotas instead of Hondas, and more people will buy Pepsi instead of Coca-Cola. However, the real-income effects will be quite different. Saving 10% on the price of a new car could easily amount to a savings of $3,000 or more. In contrast, saving 10% on a 2-liter bottle of Pepsi will save only a couple of dimes. In the case of the new car, there is a substantial real-income effect, while the amount you save on the Pepsi is almost immaterial.

As we have just seen, changes in prices can have two distinct effects. The first is a substitution effect, under which changes in price will cause the consumer to substitute toward a good that becomes relatively less expensive. In our Pepsi/pizza example, suppose that the price of Pepsi rises to $2 per can. This price increase reduces your marginal utility per dollar of consuming Pepsi. As a result, you would probably buy fewer Pepsis and use the remaining money to purchase more pizza. In effect, you would substitute the relatively less expensive good (pizza) for the relatively more expensive good (Pepsi).

However, this is not the only effect at work. The change in the product price will also alter the purchasing power of your money, or income. And a change in purchasing power generates a real-income effect. In this case, your $10 will not go as far as it used to. In Figure 16A.8, we can see that the inward rotation of the budget constraint along the x axis from BC_1 to BC_2 is a result of the rise in the price of Pepsi. At $2 per can, you can no longer afford to buy 10 cans; the most you can purchase is 5. Therefore, the budget constraint moves inward along the x axis to 5 units while remaining constant along the y axis (because the price of pizza did not change). As a result, the combination (4,3) is no longer affordable. The higher price of Pepsi produces a new consumer optimum at (2,3) along IC_2. The end result is predictable: a rise in the price of Pepsi causes you to purchase less Pepsi and yields a lower level of satisfaction at IC_2 than your former point on IC_3 did, which is no longer possible.

How a Change in Price Rotates the Budget Constraint

The inward rotation of the budget constraint along the x axis from BC_1 to BC_2 is a result of the rise in the price of Pepsi. At the price of $2 a can, you can no longer afford to buy 10 cans; the most you can purchase is 5. Therefore, the budget constraint moves inward along the x axis to 5 units (causing utility to fall from IC_3 to IC_2) while remaining constant along the y axis (because the price of pizza slices did not change).

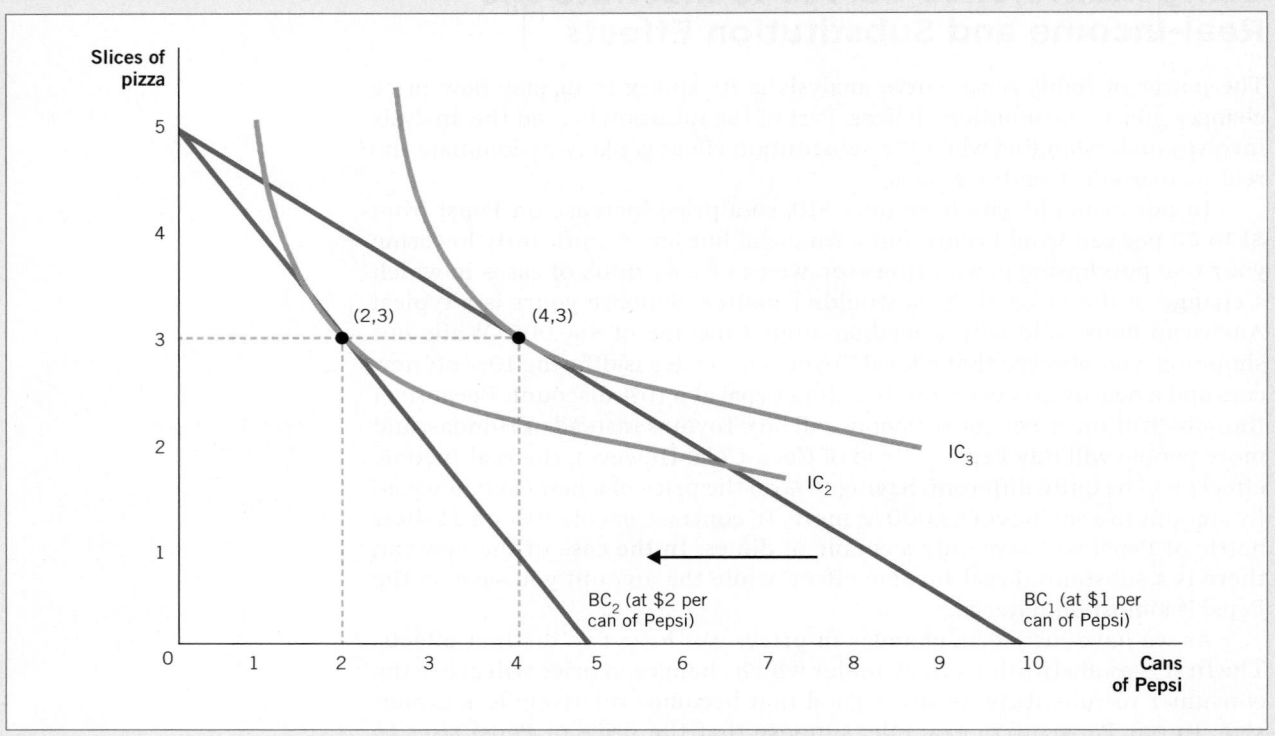

Separating the Substitution Effect from the Real-Income Effect

In this section, we separate the substitution effect from the real-income effect, and we see how the two effects can either reinforce each other or tend to cancel each other out (see Figure 16A.9).

With Pepsi at its new $2-per-can price, you're ready to buy your revised optimum quantities, 2 cans of Pepsi and 3 slices of pizza. Then you learn that Pepsi has briefly gone on sale, at its old price of $1 per can. How will you respond? Since at the old Pepsi price, your optimum was at (4, 3), we know you'll end up back there again. But let's break your move from (2, 3) to (4, 3) into two steps.

Step 1. You were about to content yourself with 2 Pepsis and 3 pizza slices. Since that purchase now comes to $8 instead of $10, you just caught a break. But notice: theoretically you could be equally happy *for even less* than $8. Simply slide along curve IC_2 to the consumption point that is cheapest, given the sale on Pepsi. That would be point A, where you're buying about 2 1/2 cans of Pepsi and 2 1/2 slices of pizza, for a total price of right around $7.50. We can even draw a new budget constraint through this point—call it BC "two point five"—based on the new prices, where we pretend that you have only $7.50 to spend. With that budget, Point A is your consumer optimum. You're just as happy as you would have been at (2, 3), but you've saved money by substituting Pepsi for pizza, because Pepsi is cheaper compared to pizza than it was before. This is the substitution effect. (You would also, by the way, be substituting Pepsi for pizza if instead the price of pizza had gone up. What matters for the substitution effect is how *relative* prices change.)

Step 2. Okay, so you can't actually buy fractional Pepsis and pizza slices. It doesn't matter, though, because you're not actually on a $7.50 budget. You're on a $10 budget, and therefore able to buy both more pizza and more Pepsi. So, we shift the $7.50 line out to make it a $10 constraint, keeping the slope the same to reflect the current pizza-to-Pepsi price ratio. This is the real-income effect,

FIGURE 16A.9

Separating the Substitution Effect from the Real-Income Effect

Breaking down the movement from IC_2 to IC_3 into the substitution effect and the real-income effect allows us to see how each impacts the consumer's choice. The substitution effect increases the amount of Pepsi consumed and decreases the consumption of pizza, as indicated by the blue arrows and the leveling out of the budget constraint, from BC_2 to $BC_{2.5}$. The real-income effect increases the amounts of both Pepsi and pizza, as indicated by the green arrows and the shift of the budget constraint, from $BC_{2.5}$ to BC_3.

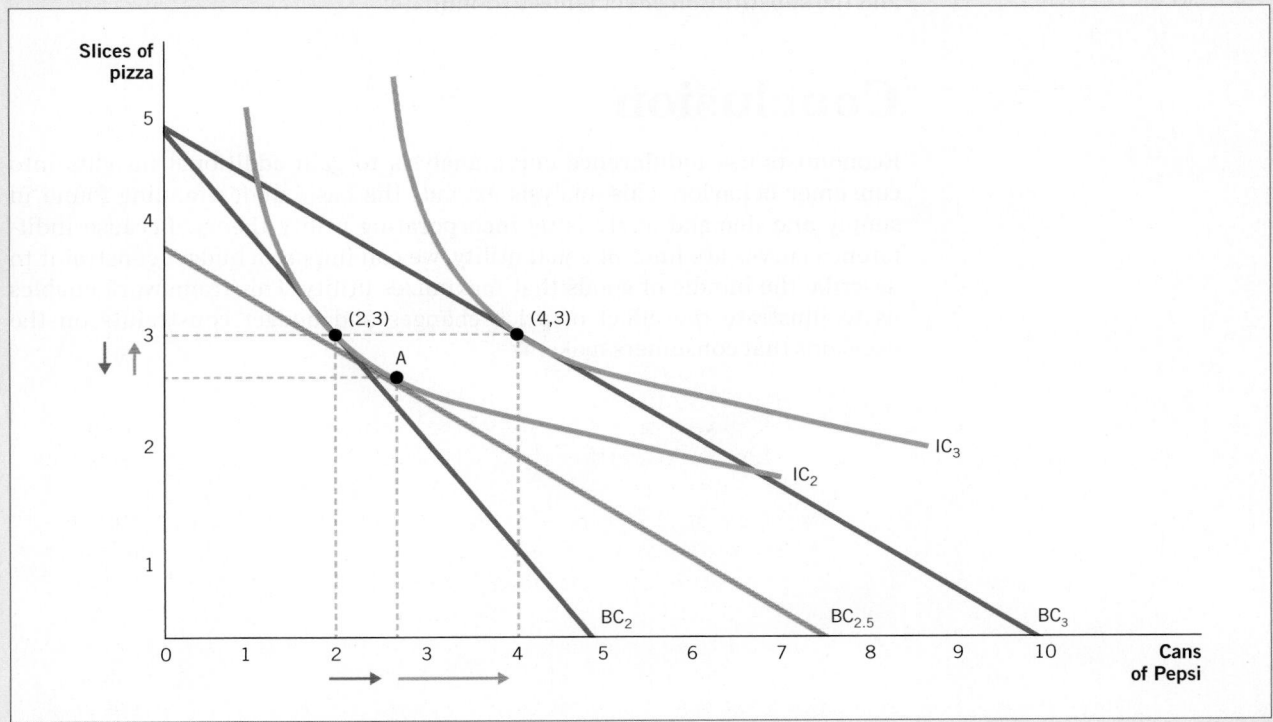

which is based on purchasing power. Again you seek your consumer optimum, where the $10 budget constraint, BC_3 (formerly known as BC_1), grazes curve IC_3, and that's point (4, 3). Enjoy your meal!

The substitution and real-income effects influenced the consumption quantities of pizza and Pepsi in different ways. With pizza the effects canceled out: you bought less pizza because of the substitution effect (the blue arrow pointing down) but more pizza because of the real-income effect (the green arrow pointing up). That's how you started and ended at 3 slices. With Pepsi, on the other hand, the two effects reinforced each other: you bought more Pepsi because of the substitution effect, going from 2 cans to 2 1/2 (the blue arrow pointing right), and yet more because of the real-income effect, going from 2 1/2 cans to 4 (the green arrow pointing right). More generally, whenever the price of a good decreases, the result will be an increase in the amount consumed, because the real-income and substitution effects point in the same direction. By contrast, because the real-income effect and substitution effect move in opposite directions with respect to the good whose price has not changed, the result is ambiguous for that good (pizza), and any change in consumption depends on which effect—the substitution effect or the real-income effect—is greater. Here, they happened to be equal.

In our example, when the price of Pepsi drops back to $1 per can, it produces a large real-income effect. Prior to the price drop, you were spending $4 out of your $10 budget on Pepsi, so Pepsi expenditures represented 40% of your budget. Because Pepsi is a big component of your budget, a halving of its price causes a sizable real-income effect. This is not always the case, however. For example, if the price of a candy bar were to halve, the typical household would barely notice this change. In cases like that, the real-income effect is negligible and the substitution effect tends to dominate.

Conclusion

Economists use indifference curve analysis to gain additional insights into consumer behavior. This analysis extends the basic understanding found in supply and demand analysis by incorporating utility theory. Because indifference curves are lines of equal utility, we can impose a budget constraint to describe the bundle of goods that maximizes utility. This framework enables us to illustrate the effect of price changes and budget constraints on the decisions that consumers make. ✳

Concepts You Should Know

budget constraint (p. 532)
indifference curve (p. 530)
marginal rate of substitution (MRS) (p. 533)

maximization point (p. 530)
perfect complements (p. 536)
perfect substitutes (p. 536)

Questions for Review

1. If your budget increases, what generally happens to the amount of utility you experience?

2. If your budget increases, is it possible for your utility to fall? Explain your response.

3. What is the difference between an economic "good" and an economic "bad"?

4. Describe what happens to your budget constraint if the price of one item in your budget decreases. Show the result on a graph.

5. A friend mentions to you that the campus coffee shop offers a 10% discount each Thursday morning before 10 a.m. Is this discount more likely to cause a significant substitution effect or a significant real-income effect? Explain.

Study Problems *(∗ solved at the end of the section)*

1. Kate has $20. Fish sandwiches cost $5, and a cup of espresso costs $4. Draw Kate's budget constraint. If espresso goes on sale for $2 a cup, what does her new budget constraint look like?

2. When you head home for dinner, your mother always sets the table with one spoon, two forks, and one knife. Draw her indifference curves for forks and knives.

∗ 3. Frank's indifference curves for movies and bowling look like the figure to the right.

Each game of bowling costs $4, and each movie costs $8. If Frank has $24 to spend, how many times will he go bowling? How many times will he go to the movies?

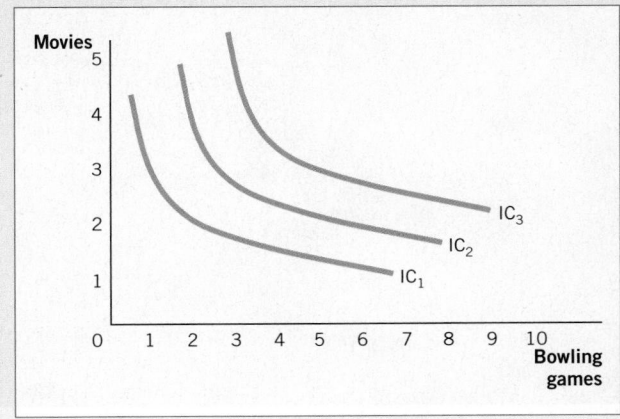

Solved Problem

3. Because Frank has $24 to spend, he can afford $24 ÷ $4, or six games of bowling. If he spends his money instead on movies, he can afford $24 ÷ $8, or three movies. Because Frank's budget constraint (BC) is just tangent to IC_1 at the point (2,2), Frank will go to two movies and bowl two games.

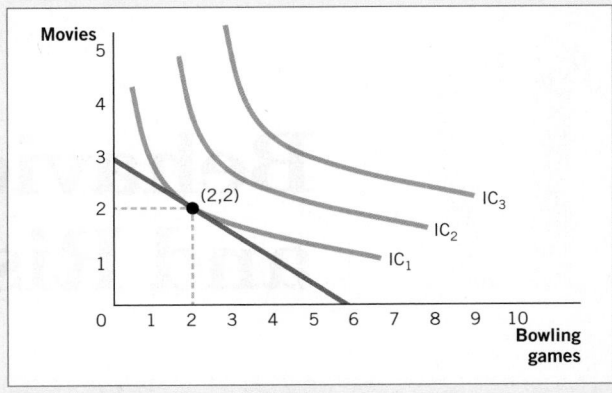

Behavioral Economics and Risk Taking

People Don't Always Make Rational Decisions.

In this textbook, we have proceeded as if every person were *Homo economicus*, a rationally self-interested decision-maker. This idealized individual is acutely aware of opportunities in the environment and strives to maximize the benefits received from each course of action while minimizing the costs. What does *Homo economicus* look like? If you are a fan of *Star Trek,* you'll recall Spock, the Vulcan with perfect logic. He eschewed human emotion and didn't face many of the complications it creates for making decisions. Spock is *Star Trek*'s *Homo economicus*.

Kirk, by contrast, famously goes with his gut when the chips are down. In *Star Trek Into Darkness*, he saves a planet's inhabitants by making a snap decision to ignore the Prime Directive (not for the first time) and letting them see the *Enterprise*. Kirk's seat-of-his-pants style of decision-making often serves him and his shipmates, and various and sundry aliens, well. Remember, though: this is fiction! In the real world, the story is more complicated. Sometimes our instincts do steer us in the right direction. More commonly, however, they lead us astray in various subtle ways. In this chapter, we'll see how that happens. To fold the broadest possible set of human behavior into economic analysis, we must turn to the field of *behavioral*

Yet again, Spock has his mind blown by Kirk trusting his gut and getting away with it. "Why does he *do* that?" he's thinking. Answer: It's a movie, folks. Don't try this at home.

economics, which enables us to capture a wider range of human motivations than the rational-agent model alone affords.

· BIG QUESTIONS ·

- How do economists explain irrational behavior?
- What is the role of risk in decision-making?

How Do Economists Explain Irrational Behavior?

Like economics, psychology endeavors to understand the choices people make. One key difference is that psychologists do not assume that people always behave in a fully rational way. As a result, psychologists have a much broader toolbox at their disposal to describe human behavior. **Behavioral economics** is the field of economics that draws on insights from experimental psychology to explore how people make economic decisions.

Until relatively recently, economists have ignored many human behaviors that do not fit their models. For example, because traditional economic theory assumed that people make optimal decisions, economic theorists did not try to explain why people might make an impulse purchase. Behavioral economists, however, understand that many behaviors contradict standard assumptions about rationality. They employ the idea of **bounded rationality**, which proposes that although decision-makers want a good outcome, either they are not capable of performing the problem-solving that traditional economic theory assumes or they are not inclined to do so.

Bounded rationality, or limited reasoning, can be explained in three ways. First, the information the individual uses to make the decision may be limited or incomplete. Second, the human brain has a limited capacity to process information. Third, there is often a limited amount of time in which to make a decision. These limitations prevent the decision-maker from reaching the results predicted under perfect rationality.

For example, suppose you're about to get married and find yourself at Kleinfeld Bridal with your bridesmaids. You enter the store to begin your search for the perfect wedding dress. You find a dress you like, but its price is higher than you were planning to spend. Do you make the purchase or not? The decision to buy depends on whether you believe that the value is high enough to justify the price. But there is a problem: you have a limited amount of information. In a fully rational world, you would check out alternatives in other stores and on the Internet and then make the decision to purchase the dress only

Behavioral economics is the field of economics that draws on insights from experimental psychology to explore how people make economic decisions.

Bounded rationality (also called limited reasoning) proposes that although decision-makers want a good outcome, either they are not capable of performing the problem solving that traditional economic theory assumes or they are not inclined to do so.

after you were satisfied it was the best possible choice. Full rationality also assumes that your brain is able to recall the features of every dress. However, a dress you tried on at one location often blurs into another dress you tried on elsewhere. Wedding dresses are selected under a binding deadline. This deadline means that you, the bride, must reach a decision quickly. Collectively, these three reasons often prevent a bride from achieving the result that economists' rational models predict. In reality, you walk into a store, see something you love, and make the purchase using partial information. Whenever people end up making decisions without perfect information, the decisions reflect bounded rationality.

We will continue our discussion of behavioral economics by examining various behaviors that do not fit assumptions about fully rational behavior. These include misperceptions of probabilities, inconsistencies in decision-making, and judgments about fairness when making decisions. The goal in this section is to help you recognize and understand many of the behaviors that lead to contradictions between what economic models predict and what people actually do.

Will you say yes to the dress?

Misperceptions of Probabilities

Economic models that assume rationality in decision-making do not account for the way people perceive the probability of events. Low-probability events are often overanticipated, and high-probability events are often underanticipated. To understand why, we consider several familiar examples, including games of chance, difficulties in assessing probabilities, and seeing patterns where none exist.

GAMES OF CHANCE Playing games of chance—for example, a lottery or a slot machine—is generally a losing proposition. Yet even with great odds against winning, millions of people spend money to play games of chance. How can we explain this behavior?

For some people, the remote chance of winning a lottery offers hope that they will be able to purchase something they need but cannot afford or even to escape from poverty. In many cases, people have incomplete information about the probabilities and prize structures. Most lottery players do not calculate the exact odds of winning. Lottery agencies typically highlight winners, as if the game has a positive expected value, which gets people excited about playing. Imagine how sobering it would be if every headline trumpeting the newest lottery millionaire was followed by all the names of people who lost. In fact, almost all games of chance have *negative expected values* for the participants, meaning that players are not likely to succeed at the game.

Players often operate under the irrational belief that they have control over the outcome. They are sure that playing certain numbers or patterns (for example, birthdays, anniversaries, or other lucky numbers) will bring success. Many players also feel they must stick with their favorite numbers to

Many games of chance return only about 50 cents for every dollar played.

Incentives

If you were a contestant, would you make a rational choice?

avoid regret; everyone has heard stories about players who changed from their lucky pattern only to watch it win.

In contrast, some gaming behaviors are rational. For example, the film *21* depicts how skilled blackjack players, working in tandem, can beat the casinos by betting strategically and paying close attention to the cards on the table. In fact, some individuals are able to win at blackjack by counting the cards that have been dealt. Anytime the expected value of a gamble is positive, there is an incentive to play. For instance, if a friend wants to wager $10.00 on the flip of a coin and promises you $25.00 if you guess right, the expected value is half of $25.00, or $12.50. (There are only 2 possible outcomes, heads or tails, so your chances of winning are 1 in 2, or 1/2. So 1/2 × $25.00 = $12.50.) Because $12.50 is greater than the $10.00 you are wagering, we say that the gamble has a *positive expected value*. When the expected value of a gamble is positive, we actually expect that the more you play, the more likely it is that your earnings will be larger than your losses.

Gambles can also make sense when you have very little to lose or no other options. And some people find the thrill of gambling enjoyable as entertainment, whether they win or lose. However, most gambling behaviors do not have rational motivations. Gambling often creates addictions that lead players to make poor financial decisions.

THE DIFFICULTIES IN ASSESSING PROBABILITIES In our discussion of games of chance, we saw that people who gamble do not usually evaluate probabilities in a rational way. But this irrational decision-making also happens with many other behaviors besides gambling. For example, on a per-mile basis, traveling by airplane is approximately 10 times safer than traveling by automobile. However, millions of people who refuse to fly because they are afraid of a crash do not hesitate to get into a car. Driving seems to create a false sense of control over one's surroundings.

The long-running television game show *Let's Make a Deal* provides a well-known example of the difficulties in assessing probabilities accurately. At the end of the show, the host would ask a contestant to choose one of three curtains. Behind each curtain was one of three possible prizes: a car, a nice but less expensive item, or a worthless joke item. Contestants could have maximized their chances of winning the car if they had used probability theory to make a selection. However, contestants rarely chose in a rational way.

Suppose you are a contestant on a game show like *Let's Make a Deal*. You pick curtain number 3. The host, who knows what is behind the curtains, opens a different one—say, curtain number 1, which has a pen filled with chickens (the joke prize). He then offers you the opportunity to switch your choice to curtain number 2. According to probability theory, what is the right thing to do? Most contestants would stay with their original choice because they figure that now they have a 50/50 chance of winning the car. But the probability of winning with your original

Misperceptions of Probabilities

THE BIG BANG THEORY: THE SEPTUM DEVIATION

At the start of the episode, Leonard returns from a visit with his doctor, who explained to Leonard why he snores and gets sinus infections.

SHELDON: Hey, how did it go?

LEONARD: Oh, not fun. The doctor shoved a camera up into my sinuses.

AMY: Did they figure out what's wrong?

LEONARD: Yeah. It's a deviated septum. The surgery to correct it is simple. He's gonna do it next week.

Alarmed, Sheldon tries to convince Leonard that the risk of death from elective surgery is higher than most people realize. However, Sheldon seems fixated on a series of extremely unlikely possibilities.

SHELDON: I've been crunching the numbers, and so far, I've gotten your probability of death all the way to a sphincter-tightening one in 300 . . . What about epilepsy?

LEONARD: I don't have epilepsy.

SHELDON: You don't, but the surgeon might, hmm? And your carotid artery is just one shaky scalpel away from becoming the dancing fountain at Disneyland.

LEONARD: Sheldon, do you realize that driving is riskier than surgery?

Is Sheldon overthinking the risks of Leonard's minor surgery?

SHELDON: I do. I have the drive to the hospital right here. That is if you make it to the car without falling down the stairs.

LEONARD: Buddy, I, I get that you're worried about me and I, I appreciate that, but I'm not going to die.

SHELDON: You don't know that.

LEONARD: Well, I do know that it won't be from an asteroid strike.

SHELDON: You know who else said that? Every cocky *T. Rex* currently swimming around in the gas tank of your car.

choice remains 1/3, because the chance that you guessed correctly the first time is unchanged. Equally, the chance that one of the other curtains contains the car is still 2/3. But with curtain number 1 revealed as the joke prize, that 2/3 probability now belongs entirely to curtain number 2. Therefore, the contestant should take the switch, because it upgrades the chance of winning the car from 1/3 to 2/3. Few contestants make the switch, though. Almost all contestants think that each of the two remaining unopened curtains has an equal probability of holding the car, so they decide not to switch for fear of regretting their decision. Not switching indicates a failure to understand the opportunity costs involved in the decision.

Opportunity cost

The difficulty in recognizing the true underlying probabilities, combined with an irrational fear of regret, leads to many poor decisions. Understanding these tendencies helps economists to evaluate why some decisions are difficult to get right.

SEEING PATTERNS WHERE NONE EXIST Two fallacies, or false ways of thinking, help explain how some people make decisions: the *gambler's fallacy* and the *hot hand fallacy*.

The **gambler's fallacy** is the belief that recent outcomes are unlikely to be repeated and that outcomes that have not occurred recently are due to happen soon. For example, studies examining state lotteries find that bets on recent winning numbers decline. Because the selection of winning numbers is made randomly, just like flipping coins, the probability that a certain number will be a winner in one week is not related to whether the number came up in the previous week. In other words, someone who uses the gambler's fallacy believes that if many "heads" have occurred in a row, then "tails" is more likely to occur next.

The **hot hand fallacy** is the belief that random sequences exhibit a positive correlation (relationship). The classic study in this area examined perceptions about the game of basketball. Most sports enthusiasts believe that a player who has scored several baskets in a row—one with a "hot hand"—is more likely to score a basket with his or her next shot than at another time. However, the study found no positive correlation between success in one shot and success in the next shot.

> The **gambler's fallacy** is the belief that recent outcomes are unlikely to be repeated and that outcomes that have not occurred recently are due to happen soon.

> The **hot hand fallacy** is the belief that random sequences exhibit a positive correlation (relationship).

ECONOMICS IN THE REAL WORLD

HOW BEHAVIORAL ECONOMICS HELPS TO EXPLAIN STOCK PRICE VOLATILITY

Let's examine some of the traps that people fall into when they invest in the stock market. In a fully rational world, the gambler's fallacy and the hot hand fallacy would not exist. In the real world, however, people are prone to seeing patterns in data even when there are none. Investors, for example, often believe that the rise and fall of the stock market is driven by specific events and by underlying metrics such as profitability, market share, and return on investment. But, in fact, investors often react with a herd mentality by rushing into stocks that appear to be doing well—reflecting the hot hand fallacy—and selling off stocks when a downward trend seems to be occurring. Similarly, there are times when investors believe that the stock market has run up or down too rapidly and they expect its direction to change soon—reflecting the gambler's fallacy.

Ulrike Malmendier studies behavioral economics and is a leading expert on how biases affect corporate decisions, stock prices, and markets in general. "Biases don't only affect decision-making by small investors and consumers; they also affect top business leaders," Malmendier says. She likes to quote Warren Buffett, who once remarked, "I'd be a bum on the

Ulrike Malmendier, *Homo economicus* mythbuster.

street with a tin cup if the markets were efficient." In her work on hubris, she found that executives who won prestigious awards, such as "CEO of the Year," tended to underperform their noncelebrity peers in the years just after the prestigious award was bestowed, proving that overconfidence could be detrimental to profits. One likely way this plays out is that award-winning CEOs think they have a hot hand and therefore take risks they shouldn't.[*]

In addition, some segments of the market are driven by investor psychology instead of metrics that measure valuation. Research has also shown that mood matters: believe it or not, there is a small correlation between the weather and how the stock market trades on a particular day. The market is more likely to move higher when it is sunny on Wall Street than when it is cloudy! The very fact that the weather in Lower Manhattan could have anything to do with how the overall stock market performs is strong evidence that some market participants are not rational.

*Source: http://www.haas.berkeley.edu/groups/pubs/berkeleyhaas/summer2014/faculty-rock-stars-toby-stuart-ulrike-malmendier.html.

PRACTICE WHAT YOU KNOW

Gambler's Fallacy or Hot Hand Fallacy? Patterns on Exams

Your instructor is normally conscientious and makes sure that exam answers are randomly distributed. However, you notice that the first five answers on the multiple-choice section are all C. Unsure what this pattern means, you consider the next question. You do not know the answer and are forced to guess. You decide to avoid C because you figure that C cannot happen six times in a row.

QUESTION: Which is at work: the gambler's fallacy or the hot hand fallacy?

ANSWER: According to the gambler's fallacy, recent events are less likely to be repeated again in the near future. So it is the gambler's fallacy at work here in your decision to avoid marking another C. If you had acted on the hot hand fallacy, you would have believed that random sequences exhibit a positive correlation and therefore would have marked the next answer as C.

Do you ever wonder what it means when the same answer comes up many times in a row?

CHALLENGE QUESTION: Suppose that instead of all C's, the first five answers are B, A, C, D, B. Again you are forced to guess. You avoid B because it's the one answer that was already used twice. Is this reasonable?

ANSWER: It's the same gambler's fallacy again, just in subtler form. If the answers are random, it doesn't matter what the first five answers were. They have *nothing to do* with the sixth answer.

Inconsistencies in Decision-Making

Trade-offs

If people were entirely rational, they would always be consistent. So the way a question is asked should not alter our responses, but research has shown that it does. Likewise, rational decision-making requires the ability to take the long-run trade-offs into account: if the returns are large enough, people should be willing to sacrifice current enjoyment for future benefits. Yet many of us make shortsighted decisions. In this section, we examine a variety of decision-making mistakes, including framing effects, priming effects, status quo bias, and inter-temporal decision-making.

FRAMING EFFECTS AND PRIMING EFFECTS We have seen a number of ways in which economic models do not entirely account for the behavior of real people. One common mistake that people make involves the **framing effect,** which occurs when an answer is influenced by the way a question is asked or a decision is influenced by the way alternatives are presented. Consider an employer-sponsored retirement plan. Companies can either (1) ask employees if they want to join or (2) use an automatic enrollment system and ask employees to let them know if they do not wish to participate. Studies have shown that workers who are asked if they want to join tend to participate at a much lower rate than those who are automatically enrolled and must say they want to opt out. Surely, a rational economic decision-maker would determine whether to participate by evaluating the plan itself, not by responding to the way the employer presents the option to participate. However, people are rarely that rational!

> The **framing effect** occurs when people change their answer depending on how the question is asked (or change their decision depending on how alternatives are presented).

Another decision-making pitfall, known as the **priming effect**, occurs when the order of the questions influences the answers. For example, consider two groups of college students. The first group is asked "How happy are you?" followed by "How many dates have you had in the last year?" The second group is asked "How many dates have you had in the last year?" followed by "How happy are you?" The questions are the same, but they are presented in reverse order. In the second group, students who had gone out on more dates reported being much happier than similar students in the first group! In other words, because they were reminded of the number of dates first, those who had more dates believed they were happier.

> The **priming effect** occurs when the order of the questions influences the answers.

STATUS QUO BIAS When people want to keep things the way they are, they may exhibit what is known as the **status quo bias**. This bias leads decision-makers to try to protect what they have, even when an objective evaluation of their circumstances suggests that a change would be beneficial.

> **Status quo bias** exists when decision-makers want to keep things the way they are.

The status quo bias causes people to behave conservatively. The cost of this behavior is missed opportunities that could potentially enhance welfare. For example, an individual with status quo bias would maintain a savings account with a low interest rate instead of actively shopping for better rates elsewhere. This person would lose the potential benefits from higher returns on savings.

Status quo bias also explains why new products and ideas have trouble gaining traction: many potential customers prefer to leave things the way they are, even if something new might make more sense. Consider the $1 coin. It is far more durable than the $1 bill. It is also easier to tell the $1 coin apart from

Framing

INSIDE OUT

Pixar's *Inside Out* (2015) is a hilarious romp that illustrates how five human emotions impact everyday decisions. The film shows that humans do not behave rationally but instead are guided by mental shortcuts and influenced by emotional biases. Moreover, our different emotions provide different ways of framing the same situation. If there's an opportunity to go out in the rain, Joy will ask if we want to go jump around in puddles, while Sadness will ask if we want to stand outside while our boots fill with water. Fear will wonder if it is safe and suggest we stay inside—that's the status quo bias.

Joy, the default emotion in the movie, influences us in ways that are usually good, but not always. Joy helps us face challenges and makes life worth living. Joy also derives utility from small acts of kindness and gives us the pluck to smile when life gets tough. But too much optimism is itself a kind of bias. When we are happy, we don't believe that bad things will happen to us, like traffic accidents—so we may drive too fast. (Joy rides, anyone?) Riley, the teenage girl who is the film's main character,

Our lives are a whirlwind of emotions that make fully rational decisions impossible most of the time.

needed more than simply Joy in her life. Riley also needed Sadness to help her cope with her cross-country move. Our emotions are complex, and each plays a crucial role in helping us navigate life. So it shouldn't be surprising to anyone trying to explain human behavior that our emotional states will influence our choices and how rationally or irrationally we make them.

the other coins and bills in your wallet, and if people used the coin, the government would save about $5 billion in production costs over the next 30 years. That sounds like a slam-dunk policy change, but it is not. Americans like their dollar bills and rarely use the $1 coins in circulation even though they repeatedly use nickels, dimes, and quarters to make change, to feed parking meters, and to buy from vending machines. Introducing more of the $1 coin and eliminating the $1 bill would be rational, but the status quo bias has prevented the change from happening.

ECONOMICS IN THE REAL WORLD

Are you on Team Dollar Bill or Team Dollar Coin?

ARE YOU AN ORGAN DONOR?

More than 25,000 organ transplants take place every year in the United States, with the vast majority coming from deceased donors. Demand greatly exceeds supply. Over 100,000 people are currently on organ donation waiting lists. Most Americans are

In the United States, you must opt in to become an organ donor.

aware of the need, and 90% of all Americans say they support donation. But only 30% know the essential steps to take to become a donor.

There are two main donor systems: the "opt-in" system and the "opt-out" system. In an opt-in system, individuals must give explicit consent to be a donor. In an opt-out system, anyone who has not explicitly refused is considered a donor.

In the United States, donors are required to opt in. Because opting in generally produces fewer donors than opting out, many states have sought to raise donation awareness by allowing consent to be noted on individual driver's licenses.

In Europe, many countries have opt-out systems, where consent is presumed. The difference is crucial. After all, in places with opt-in systems, many people who would be willing to donate organs never actually take the time to complete the necessary steps to opt in. In countries like France and Poland, where people must opt out, over 90% of citizens do not explicitly opt out, which means they give consent. This strategy yields organ donation rates that are significantly higher than those of opt-in programs.

According to traditional economic analysis, opting in or opting out should not matter—the results should be the same. The fact that we find strong evidence to the contrary is a compelling illustration of the framing effect.

INTERTEMPORAL DECISION-MAKING Intertemporal decisions occur across time. **Intertemporal decision-making**—that is, planning to do something over a period of time—requires the ability to value the present and the future consistently. For instance, many people, despite their best intentions, do not end up saving enough for retirement. The temptation to spend money today ends up overwhelming the willpower to save for tomorrow. In a perfectly rational world, a person would not need outside assistance to save enough for retirement. In the real world, however, workers depend on 401(k) plans and other work-sponsored retirement programs to deduct funds from their paycheck so that they don't spend that portion of their income on other things. It may seem odd that people would need an outside agency to help them do something that is in their own long-term interest, but as long as their intertemporal decisions are likely to be inconsistent, the additional commitment helps them to achieve their long-run objectives.

The ability to resist temptation is illustrated by a classic research experiment conducted at a preschool at Stanford University in 1972. One at a time, individual children were led into a room devoid of distractions and were offered a marshmallow. The researchers explained to each child that he or she could eat the marshmallow right away or wait for 15 minutes and be rewarded with a second marshmallow. Very few of the 600 children in the study ate the marshmallow immediately. Most tried to fight the temptation. Of those who tried to wait, approximately one-third held out long enough to earn the second marshmallow. That finding is interesting by itself, but what happened next is truly amazing. Many of the parents of the children in the original study noticed that the children who had delayed gratification seemed to perform better as they progressed through school. Researchers have tracked the participants over the course of 40 years and found that the delayed-gratification group had higher SAT scores, more savings, and larger retirement accounts.

Intertemporal decision-making involves planning to do something over a period of time, which requires valuing the present and the future consistently.

Can you resist eating one marshmallow now in order to get a second one later?

Opt-Out Is Optimal

Some of the most successful applications of behavioral economics are "opt-out" programs, which automatically enroll eligible people unless they explicitly choose not to participate. The incentives and freedom of choice are exactly the same as in "opt-in" programs, where members must choose to participate, but enrollments are significantly higher under opt-out. Here's a look at three remarkable results.

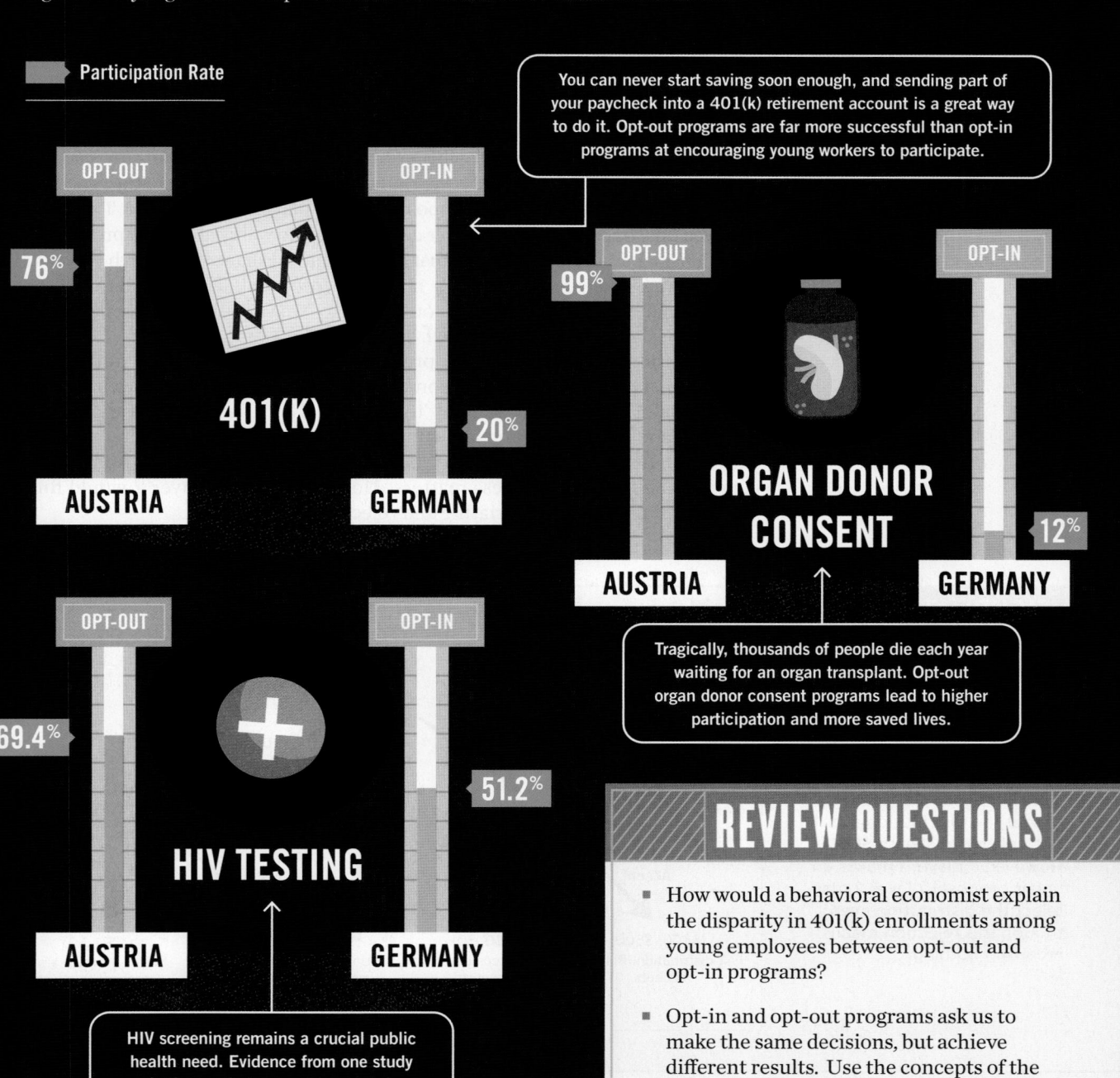

Participation Rate

401(K)

OPT-OUT — **76%** — AUSTRIA

OPT-IN — **20%** — GERMANY

You can never start saving soon enough, and sending part of your paycheck into a 401(k) retirement account is a great way to do it. Opt-out programs are far more successful than opt-in programs at encouraging young workers to participate.

ORGAN DONOR CONSENT

OPT-OUT — **99%** — AUSTRIA

OPT-IN — **12%** — GERMANY

Tragically, thousands of people die each year waiting for an organ transplant. Opt-out organ donor consent programs lead to higher participation and more saved lives.

HIV TESTING

OPT-OUT — **69.4%** — AUSTRIA

OPT-IN — **51.2%** — GERMANY

HIV screening remains a crucial public health need. Evidence from one study indicates that opt-out consent at emergency rooms leads to substantially more individuals agreeing to be tested.

REVIEW QUESTIONS

- How would a behavioral economist explain the disparity in 401(k) enrollments among young employees between opt-out and opt-in programs?

- Opt-in and opt-out programs ask us to make the same decisions, but achieve different results. Use the concepts of the framing effect and non-rational behavior to explain why.

Judgments about Fairness

The pursuit of fairness is another common behavior that is important in economic decisions but that standard economic theory cannot explain. For example, fairness is one of the key drivers in determining tax rate structure for income taxes. Proponents of fairness believe in progressive taxation, whereby the rich pay a higher tax rate on their income than those in lower income brackets do. Likewise, some people object to the high pay of chief executive officers or the high profits of some corporations because they believe there should be an upper limit to what constitutes fair compensation.

While fairness is not normally modeled in economics, behavioral economists have developed experiments to determine the role of fairness in personal decisions. The **ultimatum game** is an economic experiment in which two players decide how to divide a sum of money. The game shows how fairness enters into the rational decision-making process. In the game, player 1 is given a sum of money and is asked to propose a way of splitting it with player 2. Player 2 can either accept or reject the proposal. If player 2 accepts, the sum is split according to the proposal. However, if player 2 rejects the proposal, neither player gets anything. The game is played only once, so the first player does not have to worry about reciprocity.

Consider an ultimatum game that asks player 1 to share $1,000 with player 2. Player 1 must decide how fair to make the proposal. The decision tree in Figure 17.1 highlights four possible outcomes to two very different proposals—a fair proposal and an unfair proposal.

Traditional economic theory presumes that both players are fully rational and wish to maximize their income. Player 1 should therefore maximize his gains by offering the minimum, $1, to player 2. The reasoning is that player 2 values $1 more than nothing and so will accept the proposal, leaving player 1 with $999. But real people are not always economic maximizers because they generally believe that fairness matters. Most of the time, player 2 would find such an unfair division infuriating and reject it.

> The **ultimatum game** is an economic experiment in which two players decide how to divide a sum of money.

FIGURE 17.1

The Decision Tree for the Ultimatum Game

The decision tree for the ultimatum game has four branches. If player 1 makes a fair proposal, player 2 will accept the distribution and both players will earn $500. However, if player 1 makes an unfair proposal, player 2 may reject the distribution even though this rejection means receiving nothing.

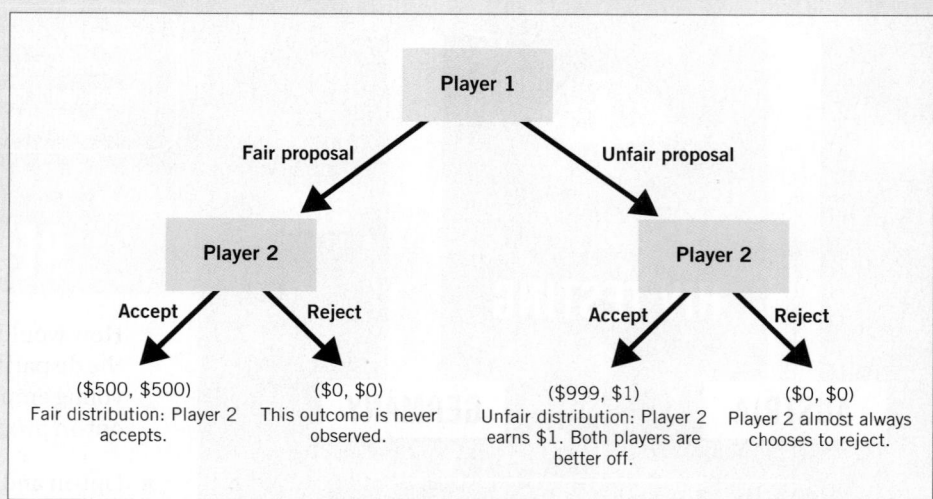

Player 1 knows that player 2 will definitely accept an offer of $500; this division of the money is exactly equal and therefore fair. Thus, the probability of a 50/50 agreement is 100%. In contrast, the probability of player 2 accepting an offer of $1 is close to 0%. Offering increasing amounts from $1 to $500 will continue to raise the probability of an acceptance until it reaches 100% at $500.

Player 2's role is simpler: her only decision is whether to accept or reject the proposal. Player 2 desires a fair distribution but has no direct control over the division. To punish player 1 for being unfair, player 2 must reject the proposal altogether. The trade-off of penalizing player 1 for unfairness is a complete loss of any prize. So while player 2 may not like any given proposal, rejecting it would cause a personal loss. Player 2 might therefore accept a number of unfair proposals because she would rather get something than nothing.

Trade-offs

Each of the ideas that we have presented in this section, including misperceptions of probability, inconsistency in decision-making, and judgments about fairness, represent a departure from the traditional economic model of rational maximization. In the next section, we focus on risk-taking. As you will soon learn, not everyone evaluates risk in the same way. This fact has led economists to reconsider their models of human behavior.

ECONOMICS IN THE REAL WORLD

UNFAIR PAY MATTERS TO CAPUCHIN MONKEYS

Traditional economic theory suggests that when two traders each expect gains from a trade, no matter how unequal those gains may be, the traders will reach an agreement. Researchers on fairness disagree with that conclusion. Frans de Waal, a primatologist, uses capuchin monkeys to argue that fairness matters throughout the animal kingdom. His short TED talk, which is equal parts *America's Funniest Home Videos* and Econ 101, is available on YouTube. It shows how a capuchin monkey given cucumbers as a reward is beside itself when it realizes its companion is receiving grapes. If you're thinking, "Okay, but they're just monkeys," consider how you'd react if you were invited to a party and were served cantaloupe while everyone else got lobster salad. Would you say, "Hey, free cantaloupe"? Or would you find a way to express your displeasure?

Sour grapes? A capuchin monkey throws away cucumber to protest unfairness.

What Is the Role of Risk in Decision-Making?

In this section, we examine the role that risk plays in decision-making. The standard economic model of consumer choice assumes that people are consistent in their risk-taking preferences. However, people's risk tolerances actually vary widely and are subject to change. Thus, risk-taking behavior is not nearly as simple or predictable as economists once believed. We begin with a phenomenon known as *preference reversal*. We then consider how negative surprises can cause people to take more risk, which is explained by *prospect theory*.

Preference Reversals

As you know, trying to predict human behavior is not easy. Maurice Allais, the recipient of the 1988 Nobel Prize in Economics, noticed that people's tolerance for risk appeared to change in different situations. This observation did not agree with the standard economic model, which assumes that an individual's risk tolerance is constant and places the individual into one of three distinct groups: **risk-averse people**, who prefer a sure thing over a gamble with a higher expected value; **risk-neutral people**, who choose the highest expected value regardless of the risk; and **risk-takers**, who prefer gambles with lower expected values, and potentially higher winnings, over a sure thing.

Allais developed a means of assessing risk behavior by presenting the set of choices (known as the Allais paradox) depicted in Table 17.1. Individuals were asked to choose their preferred options between gambles A and B and then again between gambles C and D.

Economic science predicts that people will choose consistently according to their risk preference. As a result, economists understood that risk-averse individuals would choose the pair A and D. Likewise, the pair B and C makes sense if the participants are risk-neutral and wish to maximize the expected value of the gambles. Let's see why.

1. *Risk-Averse People:* People who select gamble A over gamble B take the sure thing. If they are asked to choose between C and D, we would expect them to try to maximize their chances of winning something by selecting D, because it has the higher probability of winning.

2. *Risk-Neutral People:* Gamble B has a higher expected value than gamble A. We know that gamble A always pays $1 million because it occurs 100% of the time. Calculating gamble B's expected value is more complicated. The expected value is computed by multiplying each outcome by its respective probability. For gamble B, this means that the expected value is ($5 million $\times$ 0.10) + ($1 million $\times$ 0.89), which equals $1.39 million. So a risk-neutral player will select gamble B. Likewise, gamble C has a higher expected value than gamble D. Gamble C has an expected value of ($5 million $\times$ 0.10), or $0.5 million. Gamble D's expected value is ($1 million $\times$ 0.11), or $0.11 million. Therefore, a risk-neutral player who thinks at the margin will choose gambles B and C in order to maximize potential winnings from the game.

Risk-averse people prefer a sure thing over a gamble with a higher expected value.

Risk-neutral people choose the highest expected value regardless of the risk.

Risk-takers prefer gambles with lower expected values, and potentially higher winnings, over a sure thing.

Marginal thinking

TABLE 17.1	
The Allais Paradox	

Choose gamble A or B	
Gamble A	**Gamble B**
No gamble—receive $1 million in cash 100% of the time	A lottery ticket that pays $5 million 10% of the time, $1 million 89% of the time, and nothing 1% of the time

Choose gamble C or D	
Gamble C	**Gamble D**
A lottery ticket that pays $5 million 10% of the time and nothing 90% of the time	A lottery ticket that pays $1 million 11% of the time and nothing 89% of the time

Preference Reversals

"MINE"

The music video for Taylor Swift's 2010 hit begins with Swift walking into a coffee shop. When she sits down, she notices a couple arguing at a nearby table. This reminds Swift about her parents arguing when she was very young. Just then, the waiter drops by to take Swift's order. She looks up and dreams of what life would be like with him. We see them running together in the waves at the beach, then unpacking boxes as they move in together. Later, the two argue, resulting in Swift running away from their house and crying, just like she did when she was young and saw her parents arguing. Her boyfriend follows her, and they reconcile. They get married and have two sons. The video ends with Swift reemerging from her dream and ordering her food at the coffee shop.

In the song's refrain, Swift sings, "You made a rebel of a careless man's careful daughter." Think about that line, keeping in mind that a "rebel" is a risk-taker. Does that remind you of a concept from this chapter? It should—this is a preference reversal. The entire song is about someone (Swift) who is normally risk-averse but falls for this guy so hard that she lets her guard down and acts differently. Instead of running

Taylor's dream illustrates one version of a preference reversal.

away when it comes time to fall in love, she stays in the relationship. In other words, the song is about finding someone who makes you believe in love so much that you are willing to take a chance for the first time in your life.

3. *Risk-Takers:* Because risk-takers prefer risk, they would choose gambles B and C even if they were not already the gambles with the highest expected values.

While we would expect people to be consistent in their choices, Allais found that approximately 30% of his research population selected gambles A and C, which are contrasting pairs. Gamble A is the sure thing; however, Gamble C, even though it has the higher expected value, carries more risk. This scenario illustrates a *preference reversal*. A **preference reversal** occurs when risk tolerance is not consistent. Allais argued that a person's risk tolerance depends on his or her financial circumstances. Someone who chooses gamble A over gamble B prefers the certainty of a large financial prize—the guarantee of $1 million over the uncertainty of the larger prize. Choosing gamble A could be seen as similar to purchasing insurance: you pay a fee, known as a *premium*, to protect your winnings. In this case, you forfeit the chance to win $5 million. In contrast,

A **preference reversal** occurs when risk tolerance is not consistent.

Opportunity cost

gambles C and D offer small chances of success, and therefore the choice is more like playing the lottery.

People who play games of chance are more likely to participate in games with large prizes—for example, Powerball—because the winnings will measurably improve their financial status. Allais showed that people care about how much they might win and also how much they stand to lose. This distinction causes people to choose gambles A and C. By establishing that many people behave this way, Allais reshaped the traditional economic view of risk-taking behavior.

It turns out that preference reversals are more common than economists once believed. For example, almost 80% of all income tax filers expect to get a refund because they overpaid in the previous year. This behavior is odd, since there is an opportunity cost of waiting to get money back from the government when it didn't need to be paid in the first place. Employees could have asked their employers to withhold less and enjoyed their money sooner. Individuals who choose to wait to receive their money later are said to have a time preference that is weakly positive. In most circumstances, people have strongly positive time preferences: they prefer to have what they want sooner rather than later. So what do these taxpayers do when they learn the amount of their refund? In many cases, they pay their tax preparers an additional fee to have their refunds sent to their bank accounts electronically so they can receive the money sooner! Traditional economic analysis is unable to explain this behavior; but armed with Allais's insights, we now see this behavior as a preference reversal.

Prospect Theory

The television game show *Deal or No Deal* (2005–2010, 2018–) provides an opportunity for economists to examine the risk choices that contestants make in a high-stakes setting. *Deal or No Deal* creates particular excitement among researchers who study game shows, because it involves no skill whatsoever. Taking skill out of the equation made it easier to analyze the contestants' strategy choices. Other TV game shows, such as *Jeopardy!,* require skill to win prizes. Highly skilled players may have different risk tolerances than their less skilled counterparts. As a result, part of the beauty of studying *Deal or No Deal* is that the outcome is a pure exercise in probability theory.

For those who are unfamiliar with *Deal or No Deal,* here is how the show works. Each of 26 models holds a briefcase containing a sum of money, varying from 1 cent to $1 million. The contestant picks one briefcase as her own and then begins to open the other 25 briefcases one at a time, slowly revealing a little more about what her own case might contain. Suspense builds, and the contestant's chance of a big payoff grows as small sums are eliminated and the $1 million case and other valuable cases remain unopened. As cases are eliminated, a "banker" periodically calls the host to offer the contestant a "deal" in exchange for quitting the game.

At the start of the game, the expected value (EV) of the chosen briefcase is determined as follows:

$$EV_{briefcase} = \$0.01 \times (1/26) + \$1 \times (1/26) + \$5 \times (1/26) + \ldots + \$1M \times (1/26)$$

Deciding when to take the "deal" makes the show compelling.

This value computes to about $131,000. As the game progresses and more and more cases are opened, the "banker's" settlement offers are based on whether the expected value of the briefcase has increased or decreased since the last offer.

Some contestants behave as the traditional model of risk behavior predicts: they maximize the expected value of the briefcase while remaining risk-neutral. Because contestants who are risk neutral don't make for exciting television, the "banker" typically offers a "deal" that is far less than the expected value of the remaining cases throughout the early part of the game. This move encourages contestants to play longer, so that the excitement and tension have a chance to build.

But not all contestants did what the traditional model expected them to do. For example, some contestants took more risks if they suffered setbacks early in the game, such as opening the $1 million briefcase. This behavior is consistent with *prospect theory* from psychology. **Prospect theory**, developed by Daniel Kahneman and Amos Tversky, suggests that people weigh decisions according to subjective utilities of gains and losses. The theory implies that people evaluate the risks that lead to gains separately from the risks that lead to losses. This concept is useful because it explains why some investors try to make up for losses by taking more chances rather than by maximizing the utility they receive from money under a rigid calculation of expected value.

Prospect theory
suggests that individuals weigh the utilities and risks of gains and losses differently.

PRACTICE WHAT YOU KNOW

Risk Aversion: Risk-Taking Behavior

QUESTION: You have a choice between selecting heads or tails. If your guess is correct, you earn $2,000. But you earn nothing if you are incorrect. Alternatively, you can simply take $750 without the gamble. You decide to take the $750. Is your choice evidence of risk aversion or risk-taking?

ANSWER: The expected value of a 50/50 outcome worth $2,000 is $1,000. Therefore, the decision to take the sure thing, which is $250 less, is evidence of risk aversion.

QUESTION: You have a choice between (a) predicting the roll of a six-sided die, with a $3,000 prize for a correct answer, or (b) taking a sure $750. You decide to roll the die. Is your choice evidence of risk aversion or risk-taking?

ANSWER: The expected value of the roll of the die is $1/6 \times \$3,000$, or $500. Therefore, the $750 sure thing has an expected value that is $250 more. By rolling the die, you are taking the option with the lower expected value and also more risk. Therefore, you are a risk-taker.

How do you handle risky decisions?

WHY ARE THERE COLD OPENINGS AT THE BOX OFFICE?

The line for tickets is long. Do you suppose this movie was cold-opened?

Movie studios generally make a film available for review if the screenings are expected to generate a positive buzz. Also, access to movie reviews provides moviegoers with a measure of a film's quality. So a rational moviegoer should infer that if a movie studio releases a film without reviews, it is signaling that the movie is not very good: the studio didn't want to risk negative reviews, so it didn't show the movie to reviewers.

Economists Alexander L. Brown, Colin F. Camerer, and Dan Lovallo studied 856 widely released movies and found that cold openings—movies withheld from critics (that is, not screened) before their release—produced a significant increase (15%) in domestic box office revenue compared with poor films that were reviewed and received predictably negative reviews. Most movie openings are accompanied by a marketing campaign to increase consumer demand. As a consequence, cold openings provide a natural field setting to test how rational moviegoers are. Their results are consistent with the hypothesis that some moviegoers do not infer low quality from a cold opening as they should.

The researchers showed that cold-opened movies earned more than prescreened movies after a number of characteristics were controlled for in the study. An important point is that the researchers also found that cold-opened films did not fare better than expected once they reached foreign film or video rental markets. In both of those cases, movie reviews were widely available, which negated any advantage from cold-opening the films. This finding is consistent with the hypothesis that some moviegoers fail to realize that no advance review is a signal of poor quality. The fact that moviegoer ratings from the Internet Movie Database are lower for movies that were cold-opened also suggests that in the absence of information, moviegoers overestimate the expected quality.

It's not that moviegoers are idiots. But over time, distributors have learned that there's a certain amount of moviegoer naiveté, especially among teenagers. Somebody says "Let's go see *Floundernado,*" and nobody in the group thinks about the fact that they haven't seen any reviews. Or they do think about it, but they don't realize that it's because there *aren't* any reviews out. If they did figure that out, they'd probably know that it's a bad sign. But moviegoers often don't recognize a cold open when they see one, and so distributors have overcome their earlier reluctance and have cold-opened more movies in recent years.

These findings provide evidence that the best movie distribution strategy does not depend entirely on generating positive movie reviews. Cold openings work because some people are unable to process the negative signal implied by incomplete information, despite what traditional economic analysis would lead us to expect.

Bounded Rationality: How to Guard Yourself against Crime

- Raise the probability the criminal will be seen (trim bushes around your property, install motion-sensing lights).
- Raise the costs of entering (deadbolts, security doors, and security bars on windows).
- Raise the probability the criminal will be caught (alarm systems, barking dog).

A rational thief would look for an easier target.

Suppose that a recent crime wave has hit your community and you are concerned about your family's security. Determined to make your house safe, you consider many options: an alarm system, bars on your windows, deadbolts for your doors, better lighting around your house, and a guard dog. Which of these solutions will protect you from a criminal at the lowest cost? All of them provide a measure of protection—but there's another solution that provides deterrence at an extremely low cost.

The level of security you need depends, in part, on how rational you expect the burglar to be. A fully rational burglar would stake out a place, test for an alarm system before breaking in, and choose a home that is an easy target. In other words, the burglar would gather full information. But what if the burglar is not fully rational?

Because criminals look for the easiest target to rob, they will find a house that is easy to break into without detection. If you trim away the shrubs and install floodlights, criminals will realize they can be seen approaching your home. A few hundred dollars spent on better lighting will dramatically lower your chances of being robbed. However, if you believe in bounded rationality, there is an even better answer: a criminal may not know what is inside your house, so a couple of prominently displayed "Beware of

dog!" signs would discourage the burglar for less than $10! In other words, the would-be thief has incomplete information and only a limited amount of time to select a target. A quick scan of your house would identify the "Beware of dog!" signs and cause him to move on.

This is an example of bounded rationality because only limited, and in this case unreliable, information is all that is easily available regarding possible alternatives and their consequences. Knowing that burglars face this constraint can be a key to keeping them away. Of course, you could also buy a "Beware of owner!" sign like the one shown. On the one hand, yes, you'll deter some burglars. On the other hand, you may end up attracting *armed* burglars who are after your (nonexistent) gun collection. Now who's the person with the bounded rationality?

Conclusion

Behavioral economics challenges the traditional economic model and invites a deeper understanding of human behavior. Armed with the insights from behavioral economics, we can answer questions that span a wider range of behaviors. We have seen behavioral economics at work in the examples in this chapter, which include the "opt-in" or "opt-out" debate, the economics of risk-taking, the effects of question design, and the status quo bias. These ideas do not fit squarely into traditional economic analysis. You have learned enough at this point to question the assumptions we have made throughout this book. In the next chapter, we apply all of the tools we have acquired to examine one of the most important sectors of the economy—health care and health insurance. ✳

· ANSWERING *the* BIG QUESTIONS ·

How do economists explain irrational behavior?

* Economists use a number of concepts from behavioral economics to explain how people make choices that display irrational behavior. These concepts include bounded rationality, misperceptions of probabilities, framing effects and priming effects, the status quo bias, intertemporal decision-making, judgments about fairness, preference reversals, and prospect theory.

* Folding the behavioral approach into the standard model makes economists' predictions about human behavior much more robust.

What is the role of risk in decision-making?

* Risk influences decision-making because people can be risk-averse, risk-neutral, or risk-takers.

* In the traditional economic model, risk tolerances are assumed to be constant. If an individual is a risk-taker by nature, he or she will take risks in any circumstance. Likewise, if an individual does not like to take chances, he or she will avoid risk.

* Maurice Allais proved that many people have inconsistent risk preferences, or what are known as preference reversals. Moreover, he showed that simply because some people's preferences are not constant does not necessarily mean that their decisions are irrational.

* Prospect theory suggests that individuals weigh the utilities and risks of gains and losses differently and are therefore willing to take on additional risk to try to recover losses caused by negative shocks.

Concepts You Should Know

Questions for Review

1. What is bounded rationality? How is this concept relevant to economic modeling?

2. What are the hot hand fallacy and the gambler's fallacy? Give an example of each.

3. How does the status quo bias reduce the potential utility that consumers enjoy?

4. Economists use the ultimatum game to test judgments of fairness. What result does economic theory predict?

5. What is prospect theory? Have you ever suffered a setback early in a process (for example, seeking a job or applying for college) that caused you to alter your behavior later on?

Study Problems (✳ solved at the end of the section)

✳ 1. You have a choice between two jobs. The first job pays $50,000 annually. The second job has a base pay of $40,000 with a 30% chance that you will receive an annual bonus of $25,000. You decide to take the $50,000 job. On the basis of this decision, can we tell if you are risk-averse or a risk-taker? Explain your response.

2. Suppose that Danny Ocean decides to play roulette, one of the most popular casino games. Roulette is attractive to gamblers because the house's advantage is small (less than 5%). If Danny Ocean plays roulette and wins big, is this evidence that Danny is risk-averse or a risk-taker? Explain.

3. Many voters go to the polls every four years to cast their ballot for president. The common refrain from those who vote is that their vote "counts" and that voting is important. A skeptical economist points out that with over 100 million ballots cast, the probability that any individual's vote will be decisive is close to 0%. What idea, discussed in this chapter, explains why so many people actually vote?

4. Your instructor is very conscientious and always makes sure that exam answers are randomly distributed. However, you notice that the first five answers on the true/false section are all "true." Unsure what this pattern means, you consider the sixth question. However, you do not know the answer. What answer would you give if you believed in the gambler's fallacy? What answer would you give if you believed in the hot hand fallacy?

✳ 5. Suppose that a university wishes to maximize the response rate for teaching evaluations. The administration develops an easy-to-use online evaluation system that each student can complete at the end of the semester. However, very few students bother to complete the survey. The registrar's office suggests that the online teaching evaluations be linked to course scheduling. When students access the course scheduling system, they are redirected to the teaching evaluations. Under this plan, each student can opt out and go directly to the course scheduling system. Do you think this plan will work to raise the response rate on teaching evaluations? What would traditional economic theory predict? What would a behavioral economist predict?

6. Ray likes his hamburgers with American cheese, lettuce, and ketchup. Whenever he places an order

for a burger, he automatically orders these three toppings. What type of behavior is Ray exhibiting? What does traditional economic theory say about Ray's preferences? What would a behavioral economist say?

7. Many people give to charity and leave tips. What prediction does traditional economic theory make about each of these activities? (*Hint:* Think of the person's narrow self-interest.) What concept from behavioral economics explains this behavior?

8. Given a choice of an extra $1,000 or a gamble with the same expected value, a person prefers the $1,000. But given a choice of a loss of $1,000 or a gamble with the same expected value, the same person prefers the gamble. How would a behavioral economist describe this decision?

✳ 9. A researcher asks you the following question: "Would you rather have a 10% chance of mortality or a 90% chance of survival?" What concept

from behavioral economics is illustrated here? What is the difference between the two choices, if any? Which choice do you think most people make?

✳ 10. How might the concept of diminishing marginal utility, from Chapter 16, be used to compare and contrast the preferences of the risk-averse and the risk-neutral person?

✳ 11. Under what circumstances would it make economic sense to be a risk-taker?

12. Two people are playing an ultimatum game with $100. Player 1 can make an offer to player 2, who can either accept or reject it. If player 2 accepts, then they split the money according to player 1's offer. If player 2 rejects, neither of them get any money. Player 1 offers $2 to player 2. What does *traditional economic theory* say player 2 will do?

Solved Problems

1. The first job pays $50,000 annually, so it has an expected value of $50,000. The second job has a base pay of $40,000 with a 30% chance that you will receive an annual bonus of $25,000. To determine the expected value of the second job, the calculation looks like this: $40,000 + (0.3 × $25,000) = $40,000 + $7,500 = $47,500. Since you decided to take the job with higher expected value, we cannot tell if you are a risk-taker or risk-averse.

5. Because students who access the course scheduling system are redirected to the teaching evaluations, they are forced to opt out if they do not wish to evaluate the instructors. As a result, a behavioral economist would predict that the new system will raise the teaching evaluation response rate. Traditional economic theory would predict that the response rate will not change simply based on whether or not students opt in or opt out.

9. According to traditional economics, how the question is framed should not matter. But behavioral economics correctly predicts that it does: when asked to choose which of the two outcomes they prefer, a significant majority chooses "a 90% chance of survival," even though this statement is equivalent to "a 10% chance of mortality."

10. Let's use Table 17.1 to think about the answer. A person whose marginal utility of money is constant, or decreases only modestly as the amount of money increases, will choose gambles B and C, the gambles with the highest expected monetary value and therefore the highest expected utility. This is the risk-neutral person. The risk-averse person, who chooses gamble A over gamble B, is giving up a 10% chance of getting lots more than $1M in order eliminate a 1% chance of getting nothing. Apparently this person's marginal utility of money diminishes very sharply after $1M.

11. Again let's use Table 17.1 to formulate an answer, and this time imagine a choice between gamble A and gamble C. Someone who prefers a 10% chance of $5M (and otherwise nothing) over a guarantee of $1M would qualify as a risk-taker, because their expected payoff is only $500,000. This kind of preference would make sense for someone in the middle of a very expensive life crisis, where $1M would not be enough to make a difference but $5M would make a big difference.

18

Health Insurance and Health Care

There's No Such Thing as a Free Lunch.

We have come a long way in our exploration of microeconomics. In this chapter, we apply our economic toolkit to one particular industry: health care. The debate over health-care spending is at the core of the healthcare crisis in the United States. The goal of this chapter is not to sway your opinion but to provide a simple set of tools to focus your thinking about how medical care can best serve individuals and society as a whole.

When you are young, health care is often the last thing on your mind—until you need it. Imagine you just turned 26. Out biking the next day, and thinking happy thoughts about the party your friends threw you, you fail to notice a nasty pothole. An instant later, you're sprawled on the pavement, seriously injured. You are no longer covered under your parents' plan. Now what?

Many people believe that the best way to handle all such scenarios would be universal health care: just cover everyone with government-funded national health insurance. As a step in that direction, the Affordable Care Act passed under President Obama (the federal healthcare law often called "Obamacare") mandated expanded coverage. It's the reason you could stay on your parents' plan until your 26th birthday.

But what about the costs? Proponents of universal health care argue that it would make health care less expensive on

A biking accident hurts more when you turn 26 and are no longer able to stay on your parents' insurance plan. Now the damage to your wallet is going to be much greater.

a per-person basis. Conservative policymakers, however, push back and argue that mandatory coverage is inefficient and intrusive, and that universal coverage would be a budget-buster for the government. Even Obamacare is controversial, and neither side of the aisle is satisfied with the political compromises that led to the legislation. So for now, the United States is stuck with a patchwork system of health care and coverage that is neither market based nor government run, and certainly not anywhere near efficient.

Trade-offs

That means we can all benefit from taking a closer look at ways to improve health insurance and health care, and what trade-offs would make sense. In this chapter, we describe how the health-care industry works and how the government and the market can each make the delivery of health care more efficient. We consider how health care is delivered, who pays, and what makes the provision of medical care unlike the delivery of services in any other sector of the economy. Then we use supply and demand analysis to look at how the medical market functions. One important aspect of medical care is the role that information plays in the incentive structure for patients and providers. Finally, we examine a number of case studies to pull all this information together, so you can decide for yourself where you stand on one of the most important issues of the twenty-first century.

· BIG QUESTIONS ·

- What are the important issues in the healthcare industry?
- How does asymmetric information affect healthcare delivery?
- How do demand and supply contribute to high medical costs?
- How do incentives influence the quality of health care?

What Are the Important Issues in the Healthcare Industry?

Health care is big business. If you add the education and automobile sectors together, they represent about 10% of national economic output. But health care alone accounts for more than 17% of the nation's economic output. That's 1 out of every 6 dollars spent annually in the United States—roughly $3.5 trillion, or over $10,000 for every citizen. No matter how you slice it, that is a lot of money.

In this section, we examine the key issues in health care: how much is spent on it, where the money goes, and who the key players in the industry are. The goal is to give you a sense of how the sector functions. Then we turn our attention to supply and demand. First, though, we take a brief look at how health care has changed over the past hundred or so years.

The History of U.S. Health Care

At the start of the twentieth century, life expectancy in the United States was slightly less than 50 years. Now life expectancy is close to 80 years—a longevity gain that would have been unthinkable a few generations ago. Let's go back in time to examine the way medical care was delivered and see some of the advances that have improved the human condition.

Early in the twentieth century, infectious diseases were the most common cause of death in the United States. Typhoid, diphtheria, gangrene, gastritis, smallpox, and tuberculosis were major killers. Today, because of antibiotics, they have either been completely eradicated or are extremely rare. Moreover, the state of medical knowledge was so dismal that a cure was often far worse than the condition it was supposed to treat. For instance, tobacco was recommended for the treatment of bronchitis and asthma, and leeches were used to fight laryngitis. Throughout the first half of the twentieth century, a trip to the doctor was painful, and it rarely produced positive results.

Cutting-edge medical equipment: then . . .

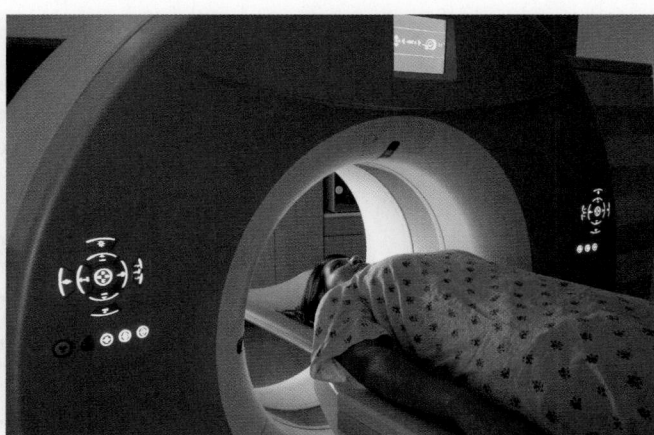

. . . and now.

Since 1950, advances in cellular biology and discoveries in biochemistry have led to a better understanding of diseases and more precise diagnostic tests. In addition, discoveries in biomedical engineering have led to the widespread use of imaging techniques such as ultrasound, computerized axial tomography (CAT scans), and nuclear magnetic resonance imaging (MRI). These and other technological innovations have replaced the medical practices of the past and made medical care safer, gentler, and more effective. In addition, pharmaceutical companies have developed a number of "miracle" drugs for fighting many conditions, including high blood pressure, leukemia, and bad cholesterol, thereby limiting the need for more invasive treatments. Each of these amazing medical advances costs money—sometimes, lots of money. As a society, we have made a trade-off: in exchange for a dramatically longer life expectancy, we now devote much more of our personal and government budgets to health care.

Trade-offs

Healthcare Expenditures

We have noted that healthcare expenditures in the United States are more than 17% of economic output. As you can see in Table 18.1, this total is quite a bit higher than similar expenditures in Canada and Mexico. Canada spends about 10% of its economic output on health care, and Mexico spends slightly more than 5%.

The United States spends significantly more on health care than our neighbors to the north and south, but life expectancy in the United States is lower than in Canada. How does Canada achieve a higher life expectancy while spending less money? And why doesn't Mexico, which spends only about one-tenth of what we do on health care per capita (see Table 18.1), trail farther behind the United States than it does? To answer those questions, consider the usual assumption of *ceteris paribus*, or other things being constant. We all agree that increased healthcare expenditures are making people healthier, probably happier (because they feel better), and more productive—this is true for most countries. However, longevity is also a function of environmental factors, genetics, and lifestyle choices—variables that are not constant across countries. The question we should be asking is not how much money we are spending, but whether we are getting our money's worth. In other words, in this context economists are most concerned with the impediments to the efficient delivery of medical care.

Why does health care take up so much of our budget? There are a number of reasons. Health insurance plays a contributing role. When private insurance covers most treatment costs, many patients agree to tests or medical visits

TABLE 18.1

Selected Healthcare Facts

Country	Total expenditure on health (percentage of economic output)	Per capita expenditure on health (in U.S. dollars)	Life expectancy at birth, total population (in years)
Mexico	5.4	989	75.4
Canada	10.4	4,826	81.9
U.S.	17.2	10,209	78.6

Source: OECD Health Division, *Health Data 2018: Frequently Requested Data.*

they wouldn't be willing to pay for out of pocket. Also, doctors are more willing to order tests that might not be necessary if they know the patient isn't paying directly. Medicare and Medicaid, the two government-sponsored forms of health insurance, add to the overall demand for medical services by providing medical coverage to the elderly and poor. And we know that anytime there is more demand for services, the market price rises in response, as long as supply remains constant.

Another reason for high healthcare costs is the number of uninsured people in the United States—approximately 28 million in 2017. When uninsured people need immediate medical treatment, they often seek care from emergency rooms and clinics, which raises costs in two ways. First, emergency care is extraordinarily expensive—much more so than routine care. Second, waiting until one has an acute condition that requires immediate attention often requires more treatment than would occur with preventive care or an early diagnosis. For example, an insured person who develops a cough with fever is likely to see a physician. If the patient has bronchitis, a few days of medicine and rest will be all it takes to feel better. However, an uninsured person who develops bronchitis is less likely to seek medical help and risks the possibility of a worsening condition, such as pneumonia, which can be difficult and costly to treat.

Medical demand is quite inelastic, so when competition is absent (which is usually the case), hospitals and other providers can charge what they want, and patients will have to pay. In addition, many people are not proactive about their health. Many health problems could be dramatically reduced and costs contained if people curbed habits such as cigarette use, excessive alcohol consumption, and overeating and if they exercised more. Finally, heroic end-of-life efforts are extraordinarily expensive. These efforts may extend life for a few months, days, or hours, and they come at a steep price.

Diminishing Returns

In the United States, it has become the norm to spare no expense in the effort to extend life for even a few days. However, providing more medical care is subject to diminishing returns, as we can see in Figure 18.1. The orange curve shows a society's aggregate health production function, a measure of health reflecting the population's longevity, general health, and quality of life. This function initially rises rapidly when small amounts of health care are provided, but the benefits of additional care are progressively smaller. To understand why, compare points A and B. At point A, only a small amount of medical care is provided (Q_A), but this care has a large impact on health. The slope at point A represents the marginal product of medical care. However, by the time we reach point B at a higher amount of care provided (Q_B), the marginal product of medical care (the slope) is much flatter, indicating that diminishing returns have set in.

Marginal thinking

Higher medical care expenditures, beyond some point, are unlikely to measurably improve longevity and quality of life because many other factors—for example, disease, genetics, and lifestyle—also play a key role in determining health, quality of life, and longevity. As we move out along the medical production function, extending life becomes progressively more difficult, so it is not surprising that medical costs rise appreciably. Given this pattern, society must answer two questions. First, what is the optimal mix of expenditures on medical care? Second, could society get more from each dollar spent by reallocating

FIGURE 18.1

Health Production Function

The marginal product of medical care, indicated by the slope of the health production function, is higher at point A than at point B.

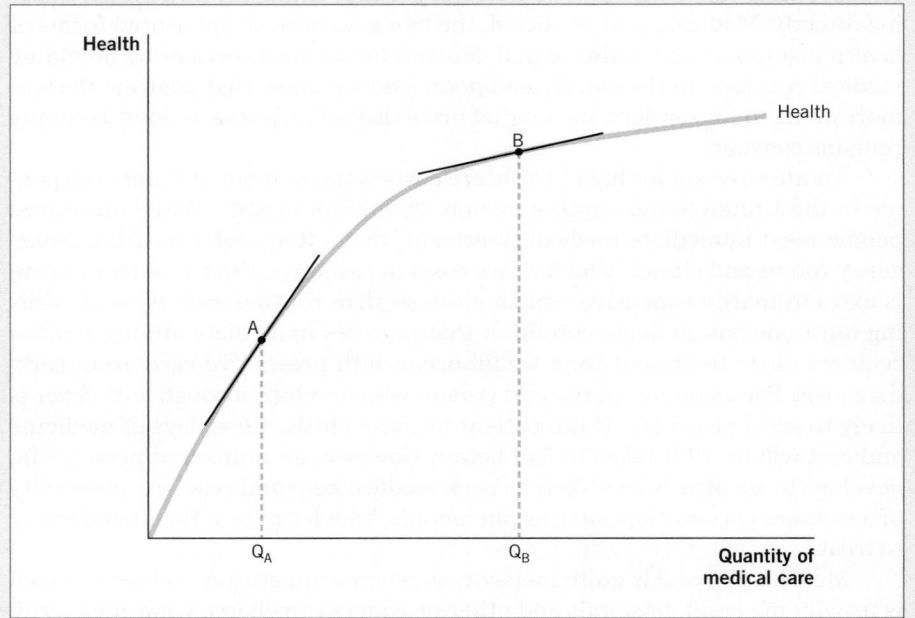

dollars away from heroic efforts to extend life and toward prevention and medical research instead?

Figure 18.2 shows where the typical health dollar goes. Hospital care, physicians, and clinics account for a little more than half of all medical expenses. After that, prescription drugs, dental care, home health care, and nursing homes each represent smaller parts of healthcare expenditures. Here we note a paradox. On the one hand, medical care has become much more efficient as medical records are increasingly computerized and many procedures that required days of hospitalization a generation ago can now take place on an outpatient basis. Thus, reducing medical costs through efficiency gains is ongoing. Yet, on the other hand, costs continue to rise. What is going on? In the next section, we examine the incentives that patients, providers, and insurance companies face when making medical decisions and how the incentive structure contributes to escalating costs.

Who's Who in Health Care, and How Does Insurance Work?

Healthcare consumption is different from that of most other goods and services. Like the others, healthcare services have consumers and producers; but because of intermediaries, such as insurance companies, the two rarely interact directly. This situation generates a unique set of incentives and leads to distortions in the standard supply and demand analysis. It is important to understand how medical care is delivered and paid for, as well as the incentives that patients, medical providers, and insurers face when making decisions.

Incentives

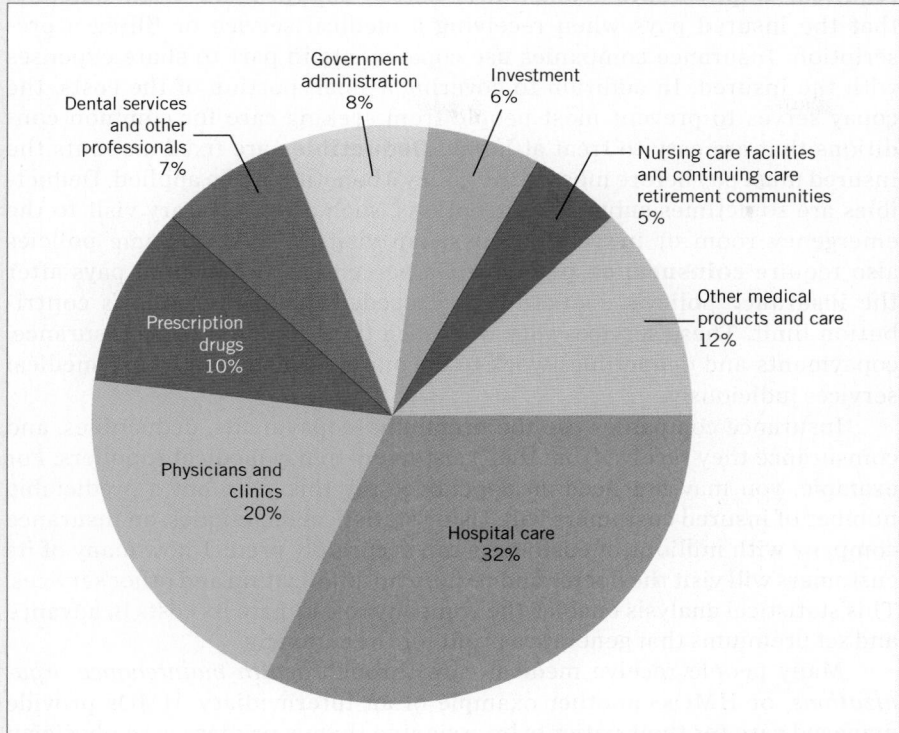

FIGURE 18.2

The Nation's Health Dollar

Hospital care, physicians, and clinics make up over half of all healthcare expenditures, which totaled $3.5 trillion in 2018.

Source: Centers for Medicare and Medicaid Services, Office of the Actuary, National Health Statistics Group. See "National Health Expenditure Data," cms.gov.

Pie chart labels:
- Government administration 8%
- Investment 6%
- Dental services and other professionals 7%
- Nursing care facilities and continuing care retirement communities 5%
- Prescription drugs 10%
- Other medical products and care 12%
- Physicians and clinics 20%
- Hospital care 32%

CONSUMERS The two biggest consumers of medical care are patients and the government. Patients demand medical care to prevent and treat illness. The federal government runs Medicare, a program that provides medical assistance to the elderly, and Medicaid, a program that provides medical assistance to the poor. Medicare and Medicaid are social insurance programs that each serve over 40 million enrollees. The two programs account for approximately one-third of all medical spending in the United States and represent about one-fourth of all U.S. government expenditures.

PRODUCERS The medical care industry employs millions of workers, including doctors, nurses, psychologists, technicians, and many more. There are also over 500,000 medical facilities in this country, including small medical offices, large regional hospitals, nursing homes, pharmacies, and stores that supply medical equipment. In addition, pharmaceutical companies generate over $300 billion in annual sales in the United States.

INTERMEDIARIES Intermediaries—for example, insurance companies—cover certain medical expenses in exchange for a set monthly fee, known as a *premium*. Medical insurance enables consumers to budget their expenses and limit what they will have to pay out of pocket in the event of a serious condition.

Copayments
are fixed amounts the insured must pay when receiving a medical service or filling a prescription.

Deductibles
are fixed amounts the insured must pay before most of the policy's benefits can be applied.

Coinsurance payments
are a percentage of costs the insured must pay after exceeding the insurance policy's deductible up to the policy's contribution limit.

In addition to the premium, a *copayment* or deductible is typically required. **Copayments** (sometimes called "copays") are fixed amounts that the insured pays when receiving a medical service or filling a prescription. Insurance companies use copayments in part to share expenses with the insured. In addition to covering a small portion of the costs, the copay serves to prevent most people from seeking care for common conditions that are easy to treat at home. **Deductibles** are fixed amounts the insured must pay before most of the policy's benefits can be applied. Deductibles are sometimes subject to exceptions, such as a necessary visit to the emergency room or preventive physician visits and tests. Some policies also require **coinsurance payments**, a percentage the insured pays after the insurance policy's deductible is exceeded up to the policy's contribution limit. These services vary with each type of plan. Like coinsurance, copayments and deductibles work to encourage consumers to use medical services judiciously.

Insurance companies use the premiums, copayments, deductibles, and coinsurance they receive from their customers to pay medical suppliers. For example, you may not need an appendectomy this year, but a predictable number of insured customers will. Using statistical techniques, an insurance company with millions of customers can accurately predict how many of its customers will visit the doctor and require hospitalization and other services. This statistical analysis enables the company to estimate its costs in advance and set premiums that generate a profit for the company.

Many people receive medical care through *health maintenance organizations,* or HMOs—another example of an intermediary. HMOs provide managed care for their patients by assigning them a primary care physician (PCP) who oversees their medical care. The HMO then monitors the primary care provider to ensure that unnecessary care is not prescribed. HMOs earn revenue from premiums, copayments, deductibles, and coinsurance. Many insurance plans allow the insured to make choices. *Preferred provider organizations,* or PPOs, are a type of health insurance arrangement that gives plan participants relative freedom to choose the doctors and hospitals they want to visit.

Another kind of insurance company sells insurance against medical malpractice, or negligent treatment on the part of doctors. The doctor pays a set fee to the insurer, which in turn pays for the legal damages that arise if the doctor faces a malpractice claim. By analyzing statistics about the number of malpractice cases for each type of medical procedure performed each year, insurers can estimate the probability that a particular physician will face a malpractice claim; the insurers then incorporate that risk into the premium they charge to doctors.

PHARMACEUTICAL COMPANIES Constituting another major player in the healthcare industry are the many pharmaceutical companies that develop the drugs used to treat a wide variety of conditions. Global pharmaceutical sales are almost $1 trillion. The United States accounts for about 30% of this $1 trillion—that's a lot of prescriptions! Pharmaceutical companies spend billions of dollars developing and testing potential drugs. One drug can take years or decades to develop. Once a drug is developed, it must receive approval by the U. S. Food and Drug Administration (FDA) before it can be sold. The development cost, time required, and risk that a drug may turn out to be problematic or ineffective combine to make the development of new drugs an expensive proposition.

Medical Costs

To understand why medical costs are so high, we must look at the incentives that drive the decisions of the major players. Consumers want every treatment to be covered, providers want a steady stream of business and don't want to be sued for malpractice, and the insurance companies and pharmaceutical companies want to make profits. These market dynamics showcase the inherent conflict that exists between consumers, producers, and intermediaries, and it helps explain the difficulty of providing medical care at a reasonable cost.

Because patient copayments are only a tiny fraction of the total cost of care, the effective marginal cost of seeking medical treatment is quite low. As a result, consumers increase the quantity of medical care they demand. Some physicians prescribe more care than is medically necessary in order to earn more income and to avoid malpractice lawsuits. Meanwhile, insurance companies, which are caught in the middle between patients and medical providers, do their best to contain costs, but they find that controlling the behavior of patients and providers is difficult. Consequently, escalating costs result from a system with poorly designed incentive mechanisms. In the case of Medicare and Medicaid, the government attempts to control costs by setting caps on the reimbursements paid to providers for medical treatments. An unintended consequence of government price setting is that it forces physicians and medical centers to raise prices for other procedures not covered by Medicare and Medicaid.

Incentives

PRACTICE WHAT YOU KNOW

Physical Fitness

QUESTION: You go in for a physical, and your doctor suggests that you get more exercise. So you decide to start working out. The increased physical activity has a big payoff and soon you feel much better, so you decide to double your efforts and get in even better shape. However, you notice that the gains from doubling your workout effort do not make you feel much better. What economic concept explains this effect?

ANSWER: More of a good thing isn't always better. Physical activity extends longevity and increases quality of life up to a point. However, working out is subject to *diminishing returns*. In other words, a small amount of physical activity has a big payoff, but lifting more weights or running more miles, after a certain point, does not increase your overall health—it simply maintains your health.

"I work out . . ."

How Does Asymmetric Information Affect Healthcare Delivery?

We have seen that incentives play an important role in the delivery of medical care. Another important element is the information and lack of information available to participants. Imbalances in information, known as **asymmetric information**, occur whenever one party knows more than the other. Asymmetric information has two forms: *adverse selection* and the *principal-agent problem*.

Asymmetric information is an imbalance in information that occurs when one party knows more than the other.

Adverse Selection

Most of us know very little about medicine. We know when we don't feel well and that we want to feel better, so we seek medical attention. Because we know very little about the service we are buying, we are poor judges of quality. For example, how can you know if your doctor is qualified or better than another doctor? **Adverse selection** exists when one party has information about some aspect of product quality that the other party does not have. As a result, the party with the limited information should be concerned that the other party will misrepresent information to gain an advantage.

When one side knows more than the other, the only way to avoid an adverse outcome is to gather better information. Suppose that you are new in town and need medical care. You haven't had a chance to meet anyone and find out whom to see or where to go for care. Fortunately, there is a way to avoid the worst doctors: websites like ratemds.com provide patient feedback on the quality of care they have received. Armed with knowledge from sources like these, you can request to be treated by doctors whom you know to be competent and have strong reputations. Conducting this research helps new residents avoid below-average care. More generally, it is important for patients to take charge of their own health care and learn all they can about a condition and its treatment so they are prepared to ask questions and make better decisions about treatment options. When patients are better informed, adverse selection is minimized.

Adverse selection also applies when buyers are more likely to seek insurance if they are more likely to need it. Consider a life insurance company. The company wants to avoid selling an inexpensive policy to someone who is likely to die prematurely, so before selling a policy to that applicant, the insurance company has to gather additional information about the person. It can require a medical exam and delay eligibility for full benefits until it can determine that the applicant has no preexisting health conditions. The process of gathering information about the applicant is crucial to minimizing the risk associated with adverse selection. In fact, the process is similar for automobile insurance, in which drivers with poor records pay substantially higher premiums and safe drivers pay substantially lower ones.

Adverse selection exists when one party has information about some aspect of product quality that the other party does not have.

The Principal-Agent Problem

Patients generally trust doctors to make good treatment decisions. A **principal-agent problem** arises when a principal entrusts an agent to complete a task and the agent does not do so in a satisfactory way. Some nonmedical examples will be familiar to you. Parents (the principal) hire a babysitter (the agent) to

A **principal-agent problem** arises when a principal entrusts an agent to complete a task and the agent does not do so in a satisfactory way.

Moral Hazard

"KING-SIZE HOMER"

In this episode of *The Simpsons*, a new corporate fitness policy is intended to help the power plant workers become healthier. Morning exercises are instituted, and the employees are whipped into shape. But Homer hates working out, so he decides to gain a lot of weight in order to claim disability and work at home. To qualify, he must weigh at least 300 pounds. To get to that weight, he must go on an eating binge. Of course, his behavior is not what the designers of the fitness policy had in mind.

This amusing episode is a good example of moral hazard, and it showcases how well-intentioned policies can often be abused.

Moral hazard makes Homer decide to gain weight.

watch their children, but the babysitter might talk on the phone instead. A company manager (the agent) might try to maximize his own salary instead of working to increase value for the shareholders (the principal). Finally, a politician (the agent) might be more likely to grant favors to interest groups than to focus on the needs of his or her constituents (the principal).

In a medical setting, the principal-agent problem occurs whenever patients cannot directly observe how medical providers and insurers are managing their patients' interests. The lack of oversight on the part of patients gives their agents, the physicians and insurance companies, some freedom to pursue other objectives that do not directly benefit patients. In the case of medicine, doctors and hospitals may order more tests, procedures, or visits to specialists than are medically necessary. The physician or the hospital may be more concerned about making profits or avoiding medical malpractice lawsuits than ensuring the patient's health and well-being. At the same time, insurance companies may want to save on treatment costs in order to maximize profit. In both cases, the patient's desire for the best medical care conflicts with the objectives of the agents who deliver their care.

Behavioral Dynamics in Healthcare Delivery

Healthcare is also subject to the problem of **moral hazard**, which is the lack of incentive to guard against risk where one is protected from its consequences. Moral hazard does not necessarily refer to behavior that is "immoral"

Moral hazard is the lack of incentive to guard against risk where one is protected from its consequences.

or "unethical." But it does imply that some people will change their behavior when their risk exposure is reduced and an "it's insured" mentality sets in. This mentality can lead to inefficient outcomes, such as visiting the doctor more often than necessary.

In the example mentioned, there is a moral hazard problem that can be lessened by restructuring the incentives. For the patient, a higher copayment will discourage unnecessary visits to the doctor.

Incentives

To solve a moral hazard problem in medical care, it is necessary to fix the incentive structure. Many health insurance companies address moral hazard by encouraging preventive care, which lowers medical costs. They also impose payment limits on treatments for preventable conditions, such as gum disease and tooth decay.

PRACTICE WHAT YOU KNOW

Asymmetric Information

QUESTION: You decide to use an online dating site, but you are not entirely sure if the posted picture of someone is accurate. Is adverse selection, the principal-agent problem, moral hazard, or some combination of these at work?

ANSWER: Adverse selection is at work. The person you are interested in knows more about herself than you do. She can, and probably would, post a flattering picture of herself. When you finally meet her, you are likely to be disappointed.

QUESTION: You hire a friend to feed your cat and change the litter twice a day while you are on spring break. However, your friend only visits your apartment every other day, and your cat shows its disapproval by using your bedspread as a litter box. Why is this an example of the principal-agent problem?

ANSWER: Because you have arranged for your friend to act on your behalf, but he cares less about your cat than you do and therefore wasn't conscientious about looking after it.

CHALLENGE QUESTION: How are adverse selection and moral hazard also involved in the cat-sitting fiasco?

ANSWER: Adverse selection is involved because you relied on a friend in a one-time arrangement. If you used a professional pet-sitter, you would have more information about his or her performance—first through references and after that through your own experiences. Moral hazard is involved because your friend won't have to sleep in that bed the cat peed on. Because your friend was protected from the consequences of his negligence, he wasn't as worried as you would have been about making sure the cat stuck to the litter box.

How Do Demand and Supply Contribute to High Medical Costs?

Now that we have a basic understanding of how the healthcare industry functions and who the key players are, we can examine the way demand and supply operate in the market for health care. On the demand side, we consider what makes healthcare demand stubbornly inelastic. Health care, when you need it, is not about the price—it is about getting the care you need. When you consider this fact and the presence of third-party payments, or payments made by insurance companies, you can begin to understand why medical expenses have risen so rapidly. On the supply side, medical licensing requirements help explain why the supply of medical services is limited. The combination of strongly inelastic demand and limited supply pushes up prices for medical services.

Healthcare Demand

Health care is usually a necessity, and it doesn't have many good alternatives. These two facts explain why the demand for health care is typically inelastic. For example, going without a heart transplant when you need one isn't an option. In fact, a 2002 RAND Corporation study found that health care has an average price elasticity coefficient of -0.17. This means that a 1% increase in the price of health care will lead to a 0.17% reduction in healthcare expenditures. Recall that as an elasticity coefficient approaches zero, demand becomes more inelastic. So we can say that the demand for medical care is quite inelastic. (For a refresher on elasticity, see Chapter 4.)

But there are some situations in which healthcare expenditures can be reduced. For example, otherwise healthy people with minor colds and other viruses can use home remedies, such as drinking fluids and resting, rather than make an expensive visit to the doctor. So the price elasticity of demand depends on the severity of the medical need and the sense of urgency involved in treatment. Urgent needs have the most inelastic demand. As the time horizon expands from the short run to the long run, the demand for health care becomes progressively more elastic. Nonemergency long-term treatments have the greatest price elasticity. For instance, a significant portion of the adult population postpones routine dental visits, despite the obvious benefits. Later, when a tooth goes bad, some people choose extractions, which are less expensive (though less attractive) than root canals and crowns.

In recent years, demand for health care has grown. As people live longer, demand rises for expensive medical goods and services, including hearing aids, replacement joints, and assisted living and nursing home facilities. In an aging population, the incidence of certain illnesses and conditions—for example, cancer and Alzheimer's disease—rises. In addition, new technologies have made it possible to treat medical conditions for which there previously was no treatment. While these medical advances have improved the quality of life for many consumers, they drive up demand for more advanced medical procedures, equipment, and specialty drugs.

People who are risk averse (see Chapter 17) generally choose to purchase health insurance because it protects them against the possibility of extreme financial hardship in the case of severe illness or other medical problems. But

· ECONOMICS *in the* MEDIA ·

Health Insurance

SUPERSTORE

The sitcom *Superstore* features Amy Dubanowski (America Ferrera) and her fellow employees at Cloud 9, a big-box establishment where you can buy everything from toothpaste to a sofa. In the episode "Health Fund," the employees try to create a fund to pay for medical expenses within their group. While they only mention the word *insurance* with respect to the poor coverage they get through their employer, what they are trying to create is really a group insurance plan. They are attempting to pool their risk by all chipping in up front and then covering actual expenses as they arise.

Within a few hours, however, the plan is overextended by tens of thousands of dollars, due to an immediate flood of participant claims. At this point the simple plan becomes increasingly complex, as Amy and Jonah (Ben Feldman) try to separate people into high- and low-risk groups with differentiated premiums. They also confront traditional insurance problems, like adverse selection, where the high-risk people are the ones most eager to get coverage. There is also evidence of moral hazard, where people change their behavior—or at least their interest in seeing a doctor—due to insurance coverage. Further complex

Do you think America Ferrera and Ben Feldman have better health insurance than the characters they play on Superstore?

adjustments to the plan lead an exasperated employee to declare, "Guys, we're making it too difficult. We just gotta simplify. Cover everything, exclude no one, and make it affordable."

Credit: Thanks to Clair Smith, of St. John Fisher College, for this idea.

insurance may distort their idea of costs and cause them to change their behavior, which creates a moral hazard problem. For example, if an insurance policy does not require the patient to pay anything, or requires very little, to see the doctor, the patient may wind up seeing the doctor more often than necessary.

Consider how this situation affects two patients. Abigail does not have insurance and therefore must pay the full cost of medical care out of pocket. Brett has an insurance policy that requires a small copayment for medical care. Figure 18.3 illustrates the difference between how Abigail (point A) and Brett (point B) might react. Let's suppose they both get sick five times during the year. Because Abigail pays the full cost of seeking treatment ($100 per physician office visit), she will go to the doctor's office only three times. She ends up paying $300. Brett pays $10 per visit, so he will go to the doctor's office five times for a total cost to him of $50. The insurance company picks up the rest of the cost for Brett, or $90 per visit.

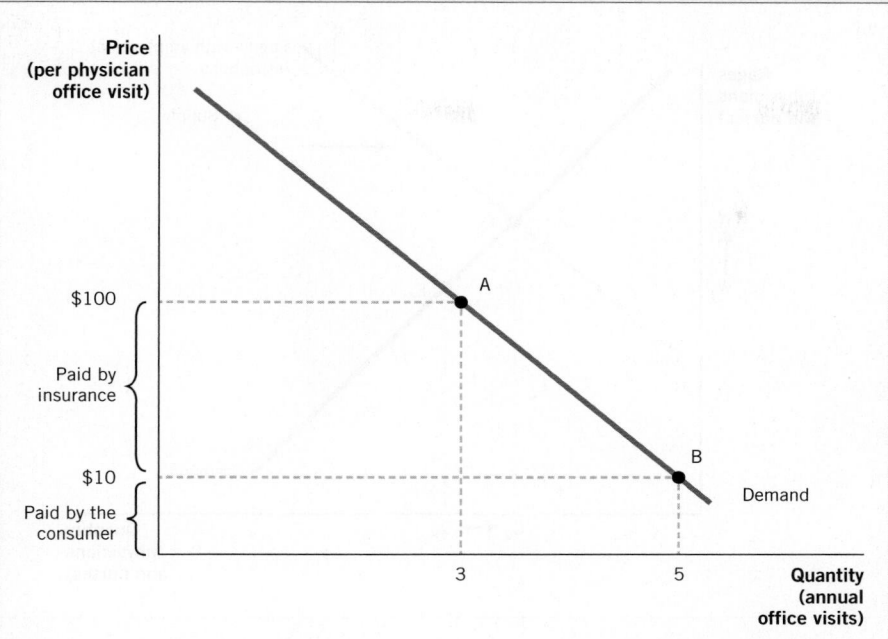

FIGURE 18.3

Price and the Quantity Demanded of Medical Care Services

Without insurance, the consumer bears the entire cost of an office visit, or $100. At this amount, the consumer (Abigail) might think twice about whether the medical care is truly necessary. As a result of these costs, Abigail makes three office visits per year, represented by point A. However, when a consumer has insurance and pays only a $10 copayment per visit, the marginal price drops and the quantity demanded increases. This insured consumer, Brett, makes five office visits per year, represented by point B.

The overall impact of a $10 copayment on healthcare costs is large. In the Abigail/Brett scenario, since each visit costs $100, total healthcare costs for the office visits are only $300 when a patient is uninsured, but $500 with healthcare coverage—a $200 increase in total healthcare costs. Because in our example the insurance companies are paying 90% of the cost, the consumer has little reason not to seek medical attention, even for minor problems that will respond to home treatment. The two extra visits per year illustrate a change in consumer behavior as a result of the lower copayment, helping to explain why insurance costs are so high.

Healthcare Supply

While consumers worry about the price, or premium, they pay for health insurance, producers are concerned about profits. As much as we might like to think that medical providers care only about our health, we must acknowledge that they are providing a service for which they expect to be paid. Therefore, it is more accurate to think of healthcare providers in the same way we think of any other producers: when the price rises, they are willing to supply additional health care. Producers of medical care such as physicians and hospitals also enjoy significant market power. In this section, we consider how licensing requirements limit the supply of certain healthcare providers and thereby impact the market.

Becoming a skilled medical provider is a lengthy process that requires extensive training, education, and certification. Physicians must secure licenses

FIGURE 18.4

Barriers to Entry Limit the Supply of Certain Medical Workers

Restrictions associated with entering the medical profession limit the supply of certain workers. These restrictions cause a decrease in the quantity supplied of physicians and nurses from Q_1 to Q_2 and an increase in wages from W_1 to W_2.

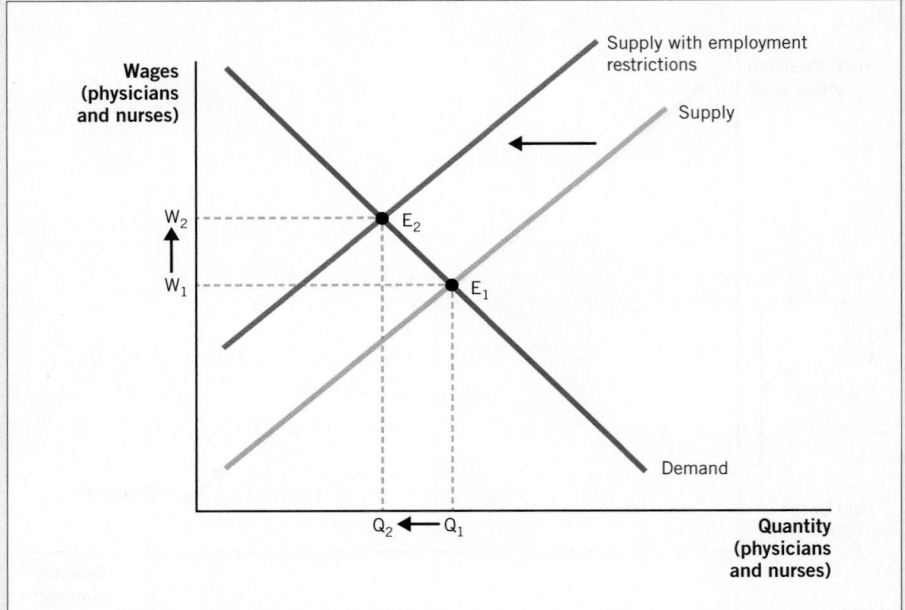

from a medical board before they can practice, and nurses must become registered. Thus, restrictions associated with entering the medical profession limit the supply of workers. This point is captured in Figure 18.4, which illustrates how barriers to entry limit the number of physicians and nurses and the associated effect on their wages.

Barriers to entry in the medical profession restrict the supply of physicians and nurses. The subsequent decrease in the quantity supplied of these medical workers (from Q_1 to Q_2) causes their wages to increase (from W_1 to W_2). In addition, many medical facilities do not face direct competition. For example, many small communities have only one hospital. In these cases, familiarity, the need for immediate care, and convenience make the nearest hospital the default option for most patients. Because economies of scale are important in the provision of medical care, even large metropolitan areas tend to have only a few large hospitals rather than many smaller competitors. As the population base expands, larger hospitals can afford to offer a wider set of services than smaller hospitals do. For instance, the need for pediatric care units, oncology centers, organ transplant centers, and a host of other services require that the hospital develop a particular expertise. The availability of specialized care is, of course, a good thing. However, as hospitals become larger and more highly specialized, competitive pressures subside and they are able to charge higher fees.

The market power of suppliers is held in check to some extent by insurance companies and by the Medicare and Medicaid programs. Also, some services are not reimbursed by insurance. And the insurance companies push back against certain other medical charges by limiting the amount they reimburse, as do Medicare and Medicaid for certain treatments. In addition, elective medical services, such as Lasik eye surgery, are typically not reimbursed by

Demand for Health Care: How Would Universal Health Care Alter the Demand for Medical Care?

QUESTION: Suppose that the United States scraps its current healthcare system, and citizens are 100% covered for all medical care with no copayments or deductibles. How would the new system affect the demand for medical care? Illustrate your answer on a graph.

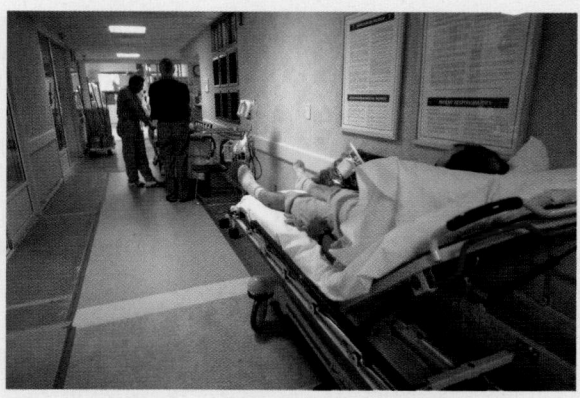

ANSWER: Without any copayment or deductibles, each patient's out-of-pocket expense would be zero. Society would pick up the tab through taxes. As a result, the quantity of medical care demanded by each patient would increase from point A to point B.

An increase in the quantity of medical care demanded for services might mean that "hurry up and wait" becomes a common experience for most patients.

At point B, demand is no longer contingent on price, so this represents the largest potential quantity of care demanded.

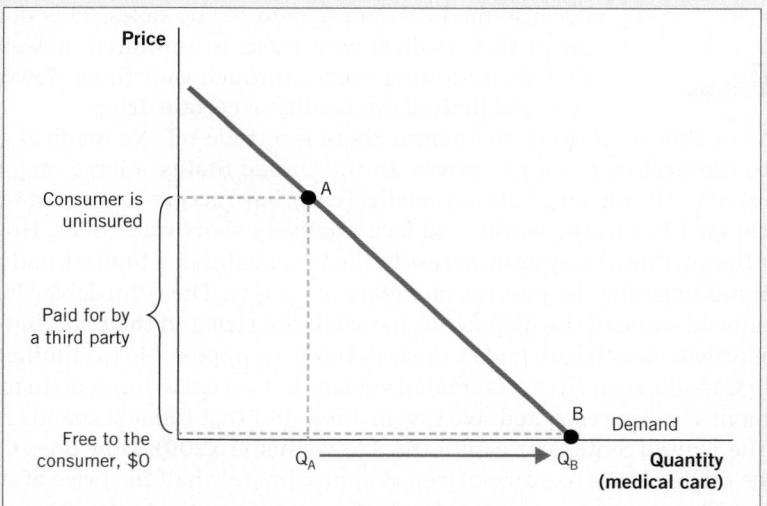

insurance plans. As a result, consumer demand is quite elastic for some services. While high medical care costs continue to be a significant policy concern, one researcher, Melinda Buntin, a professor in the Vanderbilt University School of Health Policy, has found that Medicare spending did not rise as fast as the overall economy and inflation from 2010 to 2016. If this trend holds, healthcare spending as a percentage of GDP will slowly decline over time.[*]

---

[*] Source: https://www.help.senate.gov/imo/media/doc/Buntin.pdf.

How Do Incentives Influence the Quality of Health Care?

Incentives

In this section, we apply what we've learned about health care. First, we look at the universal healthcare debate by comparing the healthcare systems in the United States and Canada. Then we examine the shortage of human organs available for transplant. By considering these two issues, we can see how incentives influence the quality of health care patients receive.

Single-Payer versus Private Health Care

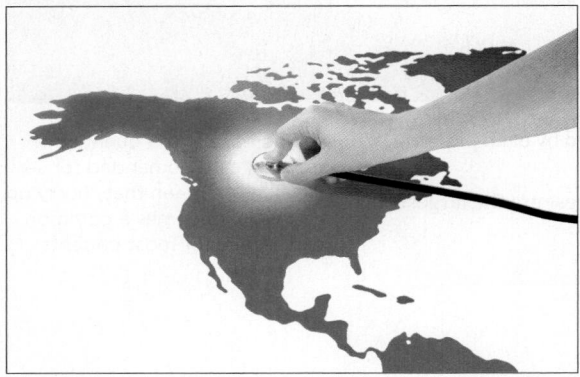

Which country has better health care, the United States or Canada?

Rationing is a fact of life because we live in a world of scarcity. The simplest way of thinking about the healthcare issue is to understand how different rationing mechanisms are used in medical care. In the United States, the primary rationing mechanism is the consumer's ability to pay. One consequence of using prices to ration medical care is that close to 35 million U.S. citizens forgo some medical care because they lack insurance or the means to pay for care on their own. In Canada, no citizen lacks the means to pay because medical care is paid for by taxes. This does not mean that medical care there is unlimited, however. In Canada, rationing occurs through wait times, fewer doctors, and limited availability of certain drugs.

As in almost all things economic, there is a trade-off. No medical system creates the perfect set of incentives. In the United States, a large majority of citizens have the means to pay for medical care, have access to some of the best medical facilities in the world, and face relatively short wait times. However, under the current U.S. system, access to the best facilities is limited, and longer wait times exist for the poorest members of society. The Affordable Care Act has reduced some of the disparities between the rich and the poor, but a system of private health care makes those differences impossible to eliminate.

Trade-offs

In Canada, each citizen is treated equally, but access to immediate medical treatment is more restricted. We saw in Table 18.1 that Canada spends far less than the United States per capita ($4,826 versus $10,209). How does Canada provide medical care to every citizen at approximately half the price of the U.S. system? There are several ways. First, the government sets the rates paid to medical providers. Second, physicians are not permitted to have private practices. Third, hospitals receive grants from the government to cover the costs of providing care. This system, in which there is only a *single payer,* makes the government the single buyer, or monopsonist, of most medical care. (See Chapter 14 for a discussion of monopsony.) In other words, in a **single-payer system**, the government covers the cost of providing most health care, and citizens pay their share through taxes.

In a **single-payer system**, the government covers the cost of providing most health care, and citizens pay their share through taxes.

The Canadian government uses its leverage as a monopsonist to set compensation levels for physicians below the competitive market wage rate. Under Canada's Health Act, government funding is required for medically necessary care, but only if that care is delivered in hospitals or by certified physicians. This means that the Canadian government funds about 70% of all medical expenses,

...ealth: United States vs. Canada

...he healthcare dollar being spent as efficiently as possible to maintain the health of Americans? To answer ...question, it's helpful to compare our situation to other countries, such as Canada. The United States and ...ada have very different healthcare systems. Canada's is primarily a publicly funded, single-payer system ...h the government paying 70% of all health-related expenses. The United States' is primarily a privately ...led, multi-payer system with the government paying approximately 48% of all health-related expenses.

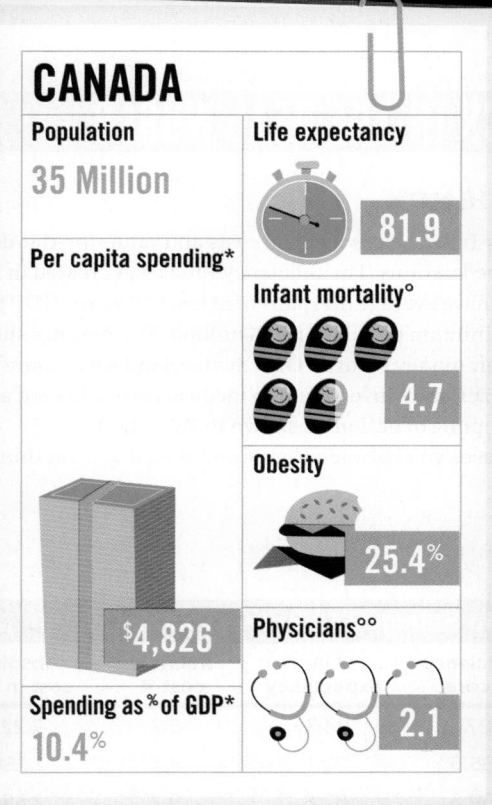

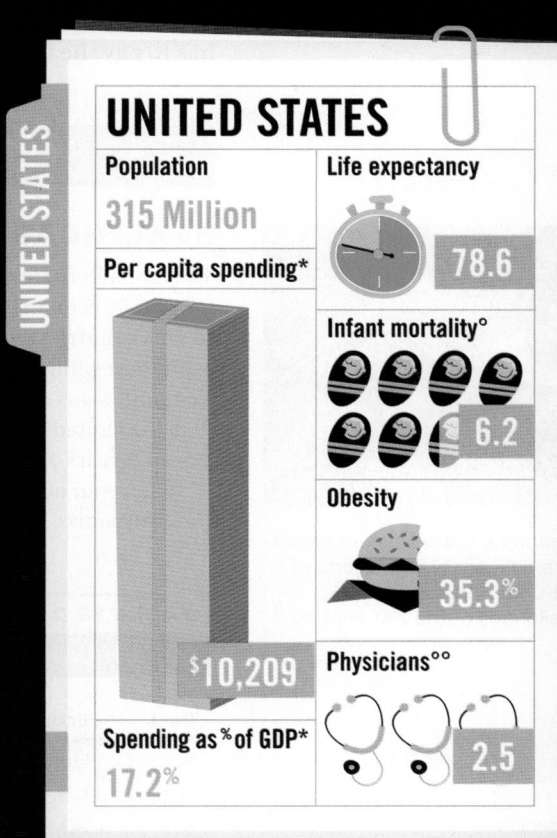

...otal expenditure, public and private   ° Per 1,000 live births   °° Per 1,000 people
...Sources: OECD, World Health Organization, CIA World Factbook.

Both countries achieve similar health outcomes, but health care is a clear example of trade-offs. The Canadian system cuts costs, while patients in the United States benefit from shorter wait times for care and the best medical facilities in the world.

REVIEW QUESTIONS

- How do you think the obesity level in the United States contributes to healthcare costs?

- What are the benefits and costs of a private versu... a public healthcare system?

with the remaining 30% of costs being generated by prescription medications, long-term care, physical therapy, and dental care. In these areas, private insurance operates in much the same way it does in the United States.

Patients seeking medical care in Canada are far more likely to seek additional care in the United States than U.S. patients are to seek care in Canada. This fact might strike you as odd. After all, Canada has national health care, and health services there are covered under the Canadian Health Act. However, there is a difference between access and availability. Because Canada keeps tight control over medical costs, people with conditions that are not life-threatening often face extended waits. Services that are not regulated—for example, veterinarian visits—provide access to medical care without waiting. Dogs in Canada have no trouble getting MRIs and chemotherapy quickly—unlike their human counterparts, who have to wait—but of course the pet owner has to pay the full expense.

ECONOMICS IN THE REAL WORLD

HEALTHCARE EFFICIENCY

The Bloomberg Health Efficiency Index tracks medical costs and value-for-the-dollar for over 50 economically developed nations. The Efficiency Index was created in 2015 to rank countries whose citizens have average lifespans of at least 70 years, GDP per capita exceeding $5,000, and a minimum population of 5 million. The findings show that Americans aren't getting their money's worth. Only Switzerland spent more than the United States—but Switzerland's investment in medical care delivered an extra 4.2 years of extra life. A sampling of nations is shown in Table 18.2.

When your efficiency score places you between Russia and Bulgaria, something is seriously amiss.

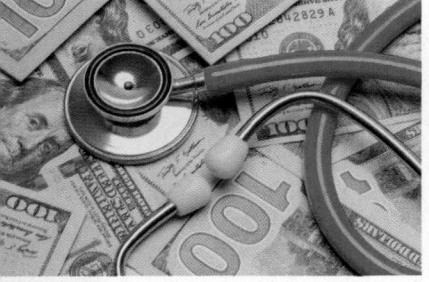

Creating a more efficient health-care delivery system is one of the United States' greatest challenges of the 21st century.

TABLE 18.2

Health Care Efficiency in Selected Countries, 2015

Rank	Economy	Efficiency score	Life expectancy	Relative cost %	Absolute cost in USD
1	Hong King	87.3	84.3	5.7	2,222
2	Singapore	85.6	82.7	4.3	2,280
3	Spain	69.3	82.8	9.2	2,354
7	Japan	64.3	83.8	10.9	3,733
12	Switzerland	58.4	82.9	12.1	9,818
16	Canada	55.5	82.1	10.4	4,508
20	China	54.6	76.1	5.3	426
53	Russia	31.3	71.2	5.6	524
54	United States	29.6	78.7	16.8	9,536
56	Bulgaria	29.4	74.6	8.2	572

Source: https://www.bloomberg.com/news/articles/2018-09-19/u-s-near-bottom-of-health-index-hong-kong-and -singapore-at-top.

The Human Organ Shortage

Many altruistic people donate blood each year to help save the lives of tens of thousands of other people. Their generosity makes transplants and other surgeries possible. Unfortunately, the same level of generosity does not apply to organ donations. The quantity of replacement organs demanded exceeds the quantity of replacement organs supplied each year, resulting in thousands of deaths. Many of these deaths would be preventable if people were allowed to sell organs. However, the National Organ Transplant Act of 1984 makes it illegal to do so in the United States. Restrictions do not cover the entire body: people can sell platelets, sperm, and ova (the female reproductive cell). In those markets, prices determine who donates. With blood, kidneys, livers, and lungs, the donors are not paid. This discrepancy has created two unintended consequences. First, many people die unnecessarily: in the United States, more than 7,000 patients on transplant waiting lists die each year. Second, the demand for human organs has created a billion-dollar-a-year black market.

Let's consider the market for kidneys. Figure 18.5 illustrates how the supply of and demand for human kidneys works. Almost everyone has two kidneys, and a person's life can continue almost normally with only one healthy kidney. Of course, there are risks associated with donation, including complications from the surgery and during recovery, as well as no longer having a backup kidney. However, since there are roughly 300 million "spare" kidneys in the United States (because the population is 300 million), there is

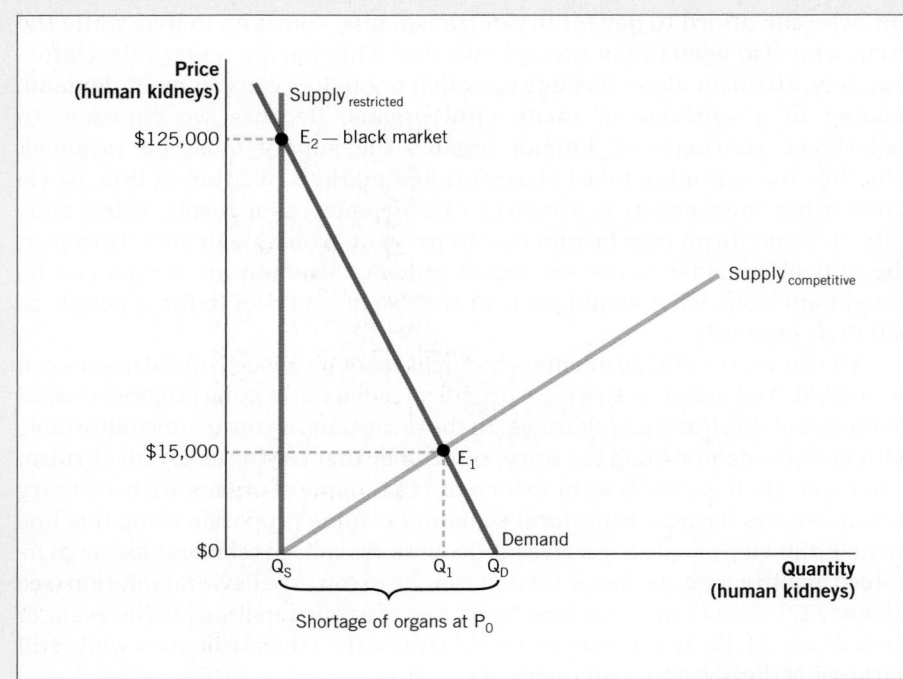

a large pool of potential donors who are good matches for recipients awaiting a transplant.

Because kidneys cannot be legally bought and sold, the supply curve shown in Figure 18.5 does not respond to price. As a result, the curve becomes a vertical line at point Q_S (quantity supplied). Notice that the quantity supplied is not zero because many people donate kidneys to friends and family members in need. Others participate in exchange programs under which they donate a kidney to someone they don't know in exchange for someone else agreeing to donate a kidney to their friend or family member. (Exchange programs help to provide better matches so that the recipient is less likely to reject the kidney transplant.) Moreover, a few altruistic persons donate their kidneys to complete strangers. Nevertheless, the quantity supplied still falls short of the quantity demanded, because $Q_D > Q_S$ at a price of $0.

Trade creates value

Markets would normally reconcile a shortage by increasing prices. In Figure 18.5, an equilibrium market price of $15,000 is shown ($E_1$). Economists have estimated that this would be the market price if the sale of kidneys were legal in the United States. Because such sales are illegal, the nation faces the shortage illustrated in Figure 18.5. Over 4,000 people die each year in this country waiting for a kidney transplant. Many others have a low quality of life while waiting to receive a kidney. Because patients waiting for human organs eventually die without a transplant, a black market for kidney transplants has developed outside the United States. However, the price—typically $125,000 or greater—requires doctors, hospitals, staff, and patients to circumvent the law. As a consequence, the black-market price (at E_2) is much higher than it would be if a competitive market for human kidneys existed.

In its simplest form, the issue is essentially this: why should the affluent, who can afford to pay for organ transplants, continue to live, while the poor, who also need organ transplants, die? That hardly seems fair. Unfortunately, altruism alone has not provided enough organs to meet demand, leading to a shortage of many vital organs. Because we continue to experience shortages of human organs, the supply must be rationed. Whether the rationing takes place through markets, waiting in line, or via some other mechanism is a matter of efficiency. As a result, using markets, in some form, may be one way to prevent avoidable deaths. However, the ethical considerations are significant. For example, if organs can be bought and sold, what would prevent the use of coercion to force people to sell their organs?

Of course, the ethical dilemma becomes moot if viable artificial organs can be created. And in fact, in this regard medical science is making progress toward someday solving the organ shortage. In the meantime, if you are uncomfortable with markets determining the price, remember that relying solely on altruism is not enough. If we really want to increase the supply of organs, we need to try

Incentives

incentives and harness behavioral economics. Some proposals along this line include allowing people to receive tax deductions, college scholarships, or guaranteed health care in exchange for donating an organ. A behavioral solution (see Chapter 17) would require people to opt out of organ donations in the event of their death. All these suggestions would reduce the ethical dilemma while still harnessing the power of economics to save lives.

SELLING OVA TO PAY FOR COLLEGE

Did you know that young, bright, American women with college loans can help pay off their debts by donating their ova? In 2012, *The Atlantic* reported on this phenomenon, exploring the donation process and experience. The donor is paid to travel to a fertility clinic, and several weeks of hormone treatments begin. Afterward, pairs of the donor's ova are removed surgically, then fertilized in a laboratory and implanted inside the womb of a woman who is infertile. With careful lab work and a little luck, the procedure works. The donor receives between $5,000 and $15,000, depending on her track record as a donor. Those whose ova have been successfully implanted and led to the birth of a healthy child are in high demand.

"Baby, baby, baby, oh."

The procedure is not without risks, including rare but potentially serious complications for donors and a high incidence of multiple births among recipients; additionally, long-term risks are not well understood. And, clearly, volunteering for elective surgery isn't a choice everyone would feel comfortable making. But that said, the existence of a market allows a trade that can greatly benefit both the donor and the recipient.

PRACTICE WHAT YOU KNOW

Human Organ Shortage: Liver Transplants

Most liver transplants make use of organs from cadavers. However, liver transplants are also possible with live donors, who give a portion of their liver to a needy recipient. Donating a live liver involves major surgery that lasts between 4 and 12 hours. The complication rate for the donor is low, but the recovery time is typically two to three months. Not surprisingly, there is still a shortage of live livers for transplant.

QUESTION: What solutions can you think of that would motivate more people to donate part of their liver to help save the life of someone else?

ANSWER: One answer would be to repeal the National Organ Transplant Act. This move would create a market for livers and establish a price that would eliminate the shortage. Other ways to increase donations would be to allow donors to claim a tax deduction equal to the value of the portion of the liver donated or to receive scholarships for themselves or members of their family.

The Human Organ Black Market

LAW & ORDER: SPECIAL VICTIMS UNIT

In one episode of *Law & Order: Special Victims Unit*, the officers try to track down a sleazy kidney dealer. What makes the episode compelling is the tension between doing what the law requires—stopping an illegal kidney transplant mid-surgery—and subsequently wrestling with watching the patient suffer as a result. In addition, the officers interview the dealer, the physician, patients on kidney waiting lists, and an administrator of the national kidney wait list. Their opinions, which run a wide gamut, allow the viewer to experience all of the emotions and arguments for and against the purchase of kidneys.

Each character tugs on viewers' emotions in a different way. The sleazy dealer proudly proclaims that he is making his customers happy and that the officers wouldn't be so judgmental if one of their own family members needed a kidney. The physician who does the transplant explains he is not driven by making money but by saving lives. The patients all know where they can get an illegal kidney, but most accept their fate within the current system. The administrator of the wait list argues that "they have enough trouble getting people to volunteer as it is. What would happen if

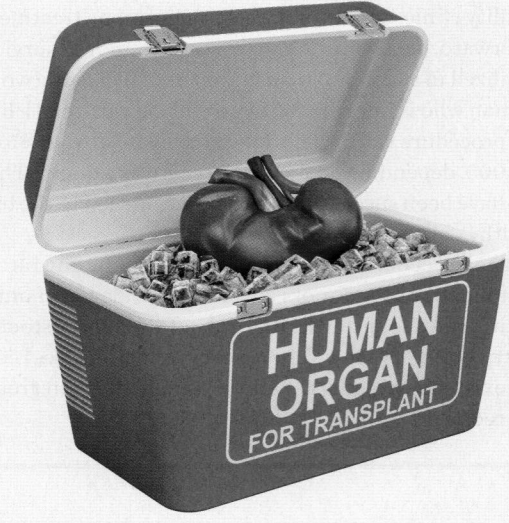

On the track of a black-market kidney dealer.

donors learned that we had made an exception and approved the transplant of an illegally purchased kidney?" By the end of the episode, we see that the economic and ethical dimensions of the issue are not clear-cut.

Conclusion

When people speak about health care, they often debate the merits of universal health care versus private medical care, as if the issue involves just those two factors. This obscures the important economic considerations at work on the micro level. The reality is that the healthcare debate exists on many margins and requires complex trade-offs. The way the various participants deal with different healthcare issues affects how well our nation's overall healthcare system functions. Supply and demand works just fine in explaining the incentives that participants face when considering healthcare options; what complicates the analysis is the impact of third parties on the incentives patients face.

Obamacare: A Primer

Formally called the Affordable Care Act (ACA), Obamacare is a federal law, signed by President Barack Obama in 2010, that provided fundamental reform of the U.S. healthcare and health insurance system, signed by President Barack Obama in 2010. To help you understand the Affordable Care Act, we have created this primer.

Learn about the Affordable Care Act.

1. The ACA does not create health insurance. The legislation regulates the health insurance industry and is designed to increase the quality, affordability, and availability of private insurance.

2. Young adults can stay on their parents' plan until age 26. Before the ACA was passed, it was common for young adults to fall off their parents' plans and, due to low income, forgo health care. Under the ACA, most young adults qualify for federal subsidies or Medicaid through the Health Insurance Marketplace.

3. The ACA created new health insurance exchanges to promote increased enrollment, deliver subsidies, and help spread risk to ensure that the costs associated with expensive medical treatments are shared more broadly across large groups of people, rather than spread across just a few beneficiaries. If you don't have coverage, you can use the Health Insurance Marketplace (healthcare.gov) to buy a private insurance plan. The cost of your marketplace health insurance works on a sliding scale. Those who make less pay less. Poorer Americans are eligible for premium tax credits through the marketplace. These tax credits subsidize the cost of insurance premiums.

4. All new plans sold on or off the marketplace must include a wide range of new benefits. These include wellness visits and preventive tests and treatments at no additional out-of-pocket cost. Preventive care is much cheaper than addressing serious medical issues too late, so this provision of the ACA is intended to lower overall costs.

5. The ACA does away with discrimination based on preexisting conditions and gender, so these factors no longer affect the cost of insurance on or off the marketplace. You can't be denied health coverage based on health status. You can't be dropped from coverage when you are sick. These changes spread risk more evenly and encourage people to get medical care sooner.

Health care straddles the boundary between microeconomic analysis, which focuses on individual behavior, and macroeconomics, in which society's overarching concern is how to best spend so large an amount of money. Moreover, health decisions are an unavoidable part of our individual lives. Medical expenditures account for one out of every six dollars spent in the United States. Therefore, micro forces that lead to fundamental changes to the healthcare system will have a large impact—a macro effect—on our economy. ✳

· ANSWERING *the* BIG QUESTIONS ·

What are the important issues in the healthcare industry?

- The healthcare debate is about efficiency and cost containment. Increases in longevity and quality of life are subject to diminishing returns and require choices with difficult trade-offs.

- The widespread use of insurance alters the incentives consumers and producers face when making healthcare decisions. Consumers pay premiums up front and much smaller deductibles and copayments when seeking medical care. Producers receive the bulk of their revenue from intermediaries such as insurance companies. The result is a system in which consumers demand more medical care because they are insured and many providers have an incentive to order additional tests or procedures that may not be absolutely necessary.

How does asymmetric information affect healthcare delivery?

- Asymmetric information (adverse selection, the principal-agent problem, and moral hazard) affects incentives in healthcare delivery. Insurance companies try to structure their plans to encourage patients to seek care only when it is needed and also to seek preventive care. The companies can achieve these goals by making many preventive care visits free and establishing deductibles and copayments that are high enough to discourage unnecessary trips to the doctor or a demand for additional procedures.

- Inelastic demand for many medical services, combined with third-party payments that significantly lower out-of-pocket expenses to consumers, gives rise to a serious moral hazard problem in which patients demand more medical care than is medically advisable. To solve a moral hazard problem, it is necessary to fix the incentive structure. Moral hazard explains why many insurance companies encourage preventive care: it lowers medical costs. It also explains why insurance companies impose payment limits on preventable conditions.

How do demand and supply contribute to high medical costs?

- Inelastic demand and third-party payments help explain why medical expenses have risen so rapidly. The combination of third-party payments and inelastic demand for medical care increases the quantity of medical care demanded; both factors also result in increased expenditures. As we learned previously, more demand means higher prices, all else equal.

- In addition, licensing requirements limit the supply of key healthcare providers. Licensing requirements provide a supply-side explanation for increased medical expenditures. In addition, hospital charges are rarely subject to competitive pressures. In many small communities, there is only one local hospital, clinic, or specialist nearby. Providers therefore have market power, which they can use in setting prices.

How do incentives influence the quality of health care?

- A single-payer system makes the government the single buyer, or monopsonist, of most medical care. The government uses its leverage as a monopsonist to set compensation levels for providers below the competitive market wage rate.

- Single-payer systems ration medical services through increased wait times, whereas private healthcare systems ration medical care through prices.

- The demand for many replacement organs exceeds the supply made available each year. However, because of the National Organ Transplant Act of 1984, it is illegal to sell most organs in the United States. This restriction results in thousands of deaths annually, many of which would be preventable if people were allowed to sell organs in legal markets.

Concepts You Should Know

adverse selection (p. 578)
asymmetric information (p. 578)
coinsurance payments (p. 576)

copayments (p. 576)
deductibles (p. 576)
moral hazard (p. 579)

principal-agent problem (p. 578)
single-payer system (p. 586)

Questions for Review

1. What is asymmetric information? How is it relevant to medical care?

2. Give one example each of adverse selection, moral hazard, and the principal-agent problem.

3. For each of the examples you gave in question 2, discuss a solution that lessens the asymmetric information problem.

4. Describe why the marginal product of medical care declines as medical expenditures rise.

5. What are two primary reasons healthcare demand has increased dramatically over the last 20 years?

6. What is a supply-related reason for high medical care costs?

7. What are the two primary ways in which health care is rationed?

Study Problems (*solved at the end of the section)

1. Suppose that a medical specialist charges $300 per consultation. If your insurance charges you a $25 copay, what is the marginal cost of your consultation? Suppose that a second patient has a different policy that requires a 25% coinsurance payment, but no copay. What is the second patient's marginal cost of the consultation? Which patient is more likely to see the specialist?

* 2. Newer automobiles have many safety features, including antilock brakes, side air bags, traction control, and rear backup sensors, to help prevent accidents. Do these safety features lead the drivers of newer vehicles to drive more safely? In your answer, consider how an increased number of safety features affects the problem of moral hazard.

3. A customer wants a new life insurance policy. Even though the customer's medical records indicate a good health history, the insurance company requires a physical exam before coverage can be extended. Why would the insurance company insist on a physical exam?

4. Indicate whether the following medical services have elastic or inelastic demand.

   a. an annual physical for someone between the ages of 20 and 35
   b. an MRI used to detect cancer
   c. the removal of a noncancerous mole on your back

   d. seeing a physician when your child has a temperature of 104°F

5. Most people have two working kidneys, but humans need only one working kidney to survive. If the sale of kidneys were legalized, what would happen to the price and the number of kidneys sold in the market? Would a shortage of kidneys continue to exist? Explain your response.

* 6. An isolated community has one hospital. The next closest hospital is 2 hours away. Given what you have learned about monopoly, what prices would you expect the hospital to charge? How much care would you expect it to provide? Compare the prices and amount of care provided to those of a comparably sized hospital in a major metropolitan area where competition is prevalent.

7. One insurance plan costs $100 a month and has a $50 copayment for all services. Another insurance plan costs $50 a month and requires patients to pay a 15% coinsurance. A consumer is trying to decide which plan to purchase. Which plan would the consumer select with an anticipated $200 per month in medical bills? What about $600 per month in medical bills? Set up an equation to determine the monthly amount of medical expenses at which the consumer would be indifferent between the two plans.

8. For each of the following situations, determine whether adverse selection, moral hazard, or the principal-agent problem is at work.

   a. You decide to buy a scalped ticket before a concert, but you are not entirely sure the ticket is legitimate.

   b. A contractor takes a long time to finish the construction work he promised after you gave him his final payment.

   c. You hire a neighborhood teenager to mow your grass once a week over the summer while you are traveling. The teenager mows your grass every three weeks instead.

✳ 9. "To economists, human life is not of infinite value." Explain this statement and its economic implications for end-of-life care.

10. What characteristics make the market for health care different from other markets?

11. Suppose you recently broke your arm, and as part of your recovery process, you are considering how many times to go to physical therapy. The marginal cost (MC) of a visit to the physical therapist is constant and equal to $300. That is what you have to pay per visit, assuming you don't have insurance.

   a. How many times should you visit the physical therapist?

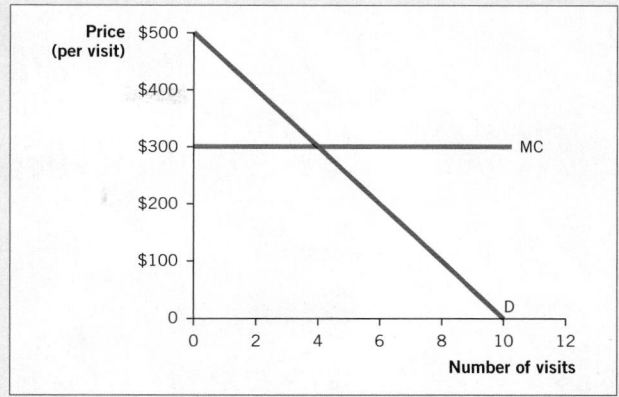

   b. If you have full health coverage (with no copay or deductible) how many times will you visit the physical therapist?

   c. What is the deadweight loss that arises due to full health coverage? (**Hint:** Deadweight loss is the difference between the willingness to pay and the additional cost of production that arises when the consumer has no copay or deductible.)

✳ 12. We learned that when caps are placed on how much a physician can be paid for a service under Medicare, doctors charge more for other services. Can you think of anything else a physician might decide to do if they feel that what Medicare pays is insufficient to cover their costs?

Solved Problems

2. When drivers feel safer, they drive faster—not more safely. The higher speed offsets the safety gain from safety features that help prevent accidents or make them survivable. Drivers of vehicles who feel especially safe are more likely to take on hazardous conditions and become involved in accidents. In other words, they alter their behavior when driving a safer car. The change in behavior is evidence of a moral hazard problem.

6. Because the demand for medical care is quite inelastic, an isolated hospital with significant monopoly power will charge more and offer fewer services. In contrast, a comparably sized hospital in a major metropolitan area where competition is prevalent is forced to charge the market price and offer more services to attract consumers.

9. Human life is not of infinite value because we live in a world of trade-offs. An "infinite value" implies

that the value is so high that all medical paths are worth pursuing. However, one must be mindful of the marginal cost of care versus the amount of additional life that end-of-life care buys. This consideration is especially important at the end of life when extraordinary medical efforts might mean only a few extra days of low-quality life. The law of diminishing returns applies, and the application of this economic principle suggests that resources should be redirected from end-of-life care to preventive care with larger returns.

12. Medicare is a government program, but physicians are not required to participate. Therefore, another option is not to participate, which is exactly what some doctors decide to do. These doctors have decided that as long as they're able to keep their appointment books reasonably full with non-Medicare patients, the opportunity cost of taking Medicare patients is too high.

PART VI

Macroeconomic BASICS

Introduction to Macroeconomics and Gross Domestic Product

Service Industries Play an Increasingly Important Role in the Global Economy.

Amazon is one of the biggest and fastest-growing companies in the world. In 2018, the company was valued at $900 billion. There's no doubt Amazon plays a major role in the global economy, but what does the company actually contribute? It doesn't grow crops, mine minerals, or manufacture goods. What exactly does Amazon do that's economically so significant?

Amazon provides a service: it helps people buy goods produced by others. This service is an important contributor to our U.S. economy, as shown by the fact that most of us have bought something from Amazon at some point.

The service Amazon provides is an intangible but important form of output, and this service provides income to many people throughout the economy. Over the past several decades, the entire U.S. economy has evolved from an economy that primarily manufactured goods to one that provides services like retail, healthcare, financial, and food services. In this chapter, we discuss how economists measure overall production in an economy, production that includes both goods and services. The primary measure is called gross domestic product, or GDP, and this is the focus of this chapter.

Amazon only sold books in the 1990s. Now it's one of the biggest Internet retailers in the world, offering everything from power tools to tropical fruit to movie passes, thanks to high-tech process management. Firms like Amazon are a big reason why the U.S. economy still produces more than one-fifth of all the output in the world, despite the strong growth in China and elsewhere.

- ▪ How is macroeconomics different from microeconomics?
- ▪ What does GDP tell us about the economy?
- ▪ How is GDP computed?
- ▪ What are some shortcomings of GDP data?

How Is Macroeconomics Different from Microeconomics?

Macroeconomics is the study of the economy of an entire nation or society. This is different from microeconomics, which considers the behavior of individual people, firms, and industries. In microeconomics, you study what people buy, what jobs they take, and how they distribute their income between purchases and savings; you also examine the decisions of firms and how they compete with other firms. In macroeconomics, you consider what happens when the *national* output of goods and services rises and falls, when overall *national* employment levels rise and fall, and when the *overall* price level goes up and down.

Here's a more specific example. In microeconomics, you study the markets for particular goods like salmon (an example from Chapter 3). You study the behavior of people who consume salmon and firms that sell salmon—demanders and suppliers. Then you bring them together to see how the equilibrium price depends on the behavior of both demanders and suppliers.

Macroeconomics is the study of the broader economy. It looks at the big picture created by all markets in the economy—the markets for salmon, coffee,

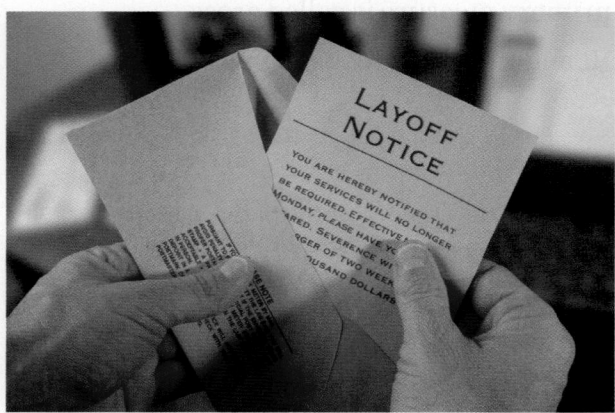

A pink slip for one person is a microeconomic issue . . .   . . . but widespread unemployment is a macroeconomic issue.

TABLE 19.1

Comparing the Perspectives of Microeconomics and Macroeconomics

Topic	Microeconomics	Macroeconomics
Income	The income of a person or the revenue of a firm	The income of an entire nation or a national economy
Output	The production of a single worker, firm, or industry	The production of an entire economy
Employment	The job status and decisions of an individual or firm	The job status of a national population, particularly the number of people who are unemployed
Prices	The price of a single good	The combined prices of all goods in an economy

computers, cars, haircuts, and health care, to name just a few. In macroeconomics, we examine *total* output in an economy rather than just from a single firm or industry. We look at *total* employment across the economy rather than employment at a single firm. We consider *all* prices in the economy rather than the price of just one product, such as salmon. To illustrate these differences, Table 19.1 compares a selection of topics from the different perspectives of microeconomics and macroeconomics.

What Does GDP Tell Us about the Economy?

Economists measure the total output of an economy as a gauge of its overall health. An economy producing more and more valuable output is a healthy economy. If output falls for a certain period, there is something wrong in the economy. The same is true for individuals. If you have a fever for a few days, your output goes down—you don't go to the gym, you study less, and you might call in sick for work. Similarly, we measure national economic output because it gives us a good sense of the overall health of the economy, much as a thermometer that measures your body temperature can give you an indication of your overall health. In this section, we introduce and explain our measure of an economy's output.

Production Equals Income

This chapter is about the measurement of a nation's output, but it's also about the measurement of a nation's income. There's a good reason to cover output and income together: they are essentially the same thing. Nations and individuals that produce large amounts of highly valued output are relatively wealthy. Nations and individuals that don't produce much highly valued output are relatively poor. This is no coincidence.

Adding up dollar sales is a way of measuring both production and income.

Gross domestic product (GDP) is the market value of all final goods and services produced within a country during a specific period.

Let's say you open a coffee shop in your college town. You buy or rent the supplies and equipment you need to produce coffee—everything from coffee beans and espresso machines to electricity. You hire the workers you need to keep the business running. Using these resources, you produce output such as cappuccinos, espressos, and draft coffee. On the first day, you sell 600 coffee drinks at an average price of $4 each, for a total of $2,400. This dollar figure is a measure of your firm's production, or output, on that day, and it is also a measure of the income received. You use the income to pay for your resources and to pay yourself. If you sell even more coffee on the second day, the income generated increases. If you sell less, the income goes down.

The same holds true for nations. **Gross domestic product (GDP)** is the market value of all final goods and services produced within a nation during a specific period of time—typically, a year. GDP is the primary measure of a nation's output and income. Recall our discussion in Chapter 1 about how the circular flow diagram illustrates the relationship between spending and income in a macroeconomy. Households spend to buy goods and services and the spending becomes income to supplier households, in payment for their work and other resources.

GDP is the sum of all the output from coffee shops, doctor's offices, software firms, fast-food restaurants, and all the other firms that produce goods and services within a nation's borders. The sale of this output becomes income to the firms' owners and the resource suppliers. This dual function of GDP is part of the reason we focus on GDP as a barometer of the economy. When GDP goes up, national output and income are both higher. When GDP falls, the economy is producing less than before, and total national income is falling.

Three Uses of GDP Data

Before analyzing the components of GDP, let's see why GDP is such an important indicator. In this section, we briefly explain the three primary uses of GDP data: to measure living standards, to measure economic growth, and to measure business cycles to determine whether an economy is experiencing recession or expansion.

MEASURING LIVING STANDARDS Imagine two very different nations. In the first nation, people work long hours in physically taxing labor, and yet their pay enables them to purchase only life's barest necessities—meager amounts of food, clothing, and shelter. In this nation, very few individuals can afford a high school education or health care from a trained physician. In the second nation, virtually no one starves, people tend to work in climate-controlled environments, almost everyone graduates from high school, and many receive college degrees. The first nation experiences life similar to that in the United States two centuries ago; the second describes life in the United States today. Everyone agrees that living standards are higher in the United States today, because most people can afford more of what they generally desire: goods, services, and leisure.

We can see these differences in living standards in GDP data. Indeed, GDP in the modern United States is much higher than it was in the nineteenth century. Both output and income are higher, which indicates that living standards are also higher. While not perfect, GDP offers us a way of estimating living standards across both time and place.

Let's look at the nations with the highest GDPs in the world. Table 19.2 lists the world's largest economies by GDP in 2016. Column 3 shows GDP for the top 11 economies, giving a picture of each nation's overall output and income. Total world GDP in 2016 was $76 trillion, which means the United States ($18.6 trillion) alone produced 24.5% of all final goods and services in the world. The most significant recent movement on this list has occurred in China, which now stands in second place but was only seventh in 1999.

Although total GDP is important, it is not the best indicator of living standards for a typical person. Table 19.2 reveals that in 2016, China produced more than twice as much GDP as Japan, yet China's population was about 10 times the population of Japan. If we divide each nation's GDP by its population, we find that in Japan there was near $39,000 GDP (or income) for every person, and in China only about $8,000 per person.

When we want to gauge living standards for an average person, we compute **per capita GDP**, which is GDP per person. That is, we divide the country's total GDP by its population. Per capita GDP is listed in the last column of Table 19.2.

Per capita GDP is GDP per person.

MEASURING ECONOMIC GROWTH We also use GDP data to measure economic growth. You can think of *economic growth* as changes in living standards over time. When economies grow, living standards rise, and this outcome is evident in GDP data.

Figure 19.1 shows the change in real per capita GDP in the United States from 1970 to 2018. The overall positive slope of the curve indicates that U.S. living standards rose over the course of 50 years, even though growth was not positive every year. The data show that income for the average person in 2018 was more than double what it was in 1970 (even after adjusting for inflation).

TABLE 19.2

World's Largest Economies by GDP, 2016

Rank	Country	2016 GDP (billions of dollars)	Per capita GDP (U.S. dollars)
1	United States	$18,624	$57,638
2	China	11,199	8,123
3	Japan	4,940	38,901
4	Germany	3,478	42,070
5	United Kingdom	2,648	40,341
6	France	2,465	36,855
7	India	2,264	1,710
8	Italy	1,859	30,675
9	Brazil	1,796	8,650
10	Canada	1,530	42,158
11	Russia	1,283	8,748

Source: World Bank.

FIGURE 19.1

U.S. Real Per Capita GDP, 1970–2018

The positive slope in this graph indicates increased living standards in the United States since 1970. It shows that the average person earns significantly more income today, even after adjusting for inflation. Over this period, real GDP per person increased by an average of 1.8% per year.

Source: U.S. Bureau of Economic Analysis; U.S. Census Bureau.

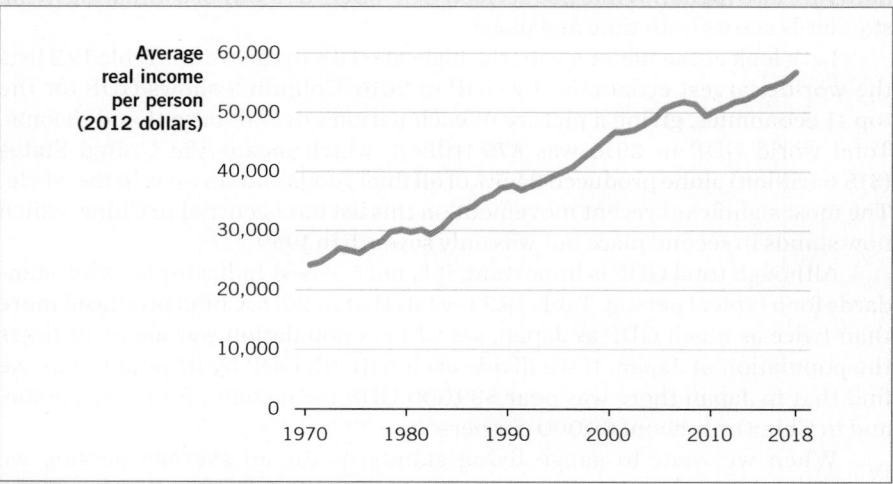

Inflation
is the growth in the overall level of prices in an economy.

Real GDP
is GDP adjusted for changes in prices.

Economic growth
is measured as the percentage change in real per capita GDP.

So the typical person can now afford about twice as much in education, food, vacations, air-conditioning, housing, and cars as the average person in 1970.

You might notice that in this section we have added the word "real" to our discussion of GDP. Figure 19.1 plots *real* per capita GDP. Because we are now looking at data over several years, we have to adjust the GDP data for price changes that occur over time. Prices of goods and services almost always rise through time because of inflation. **Inflation** is the growth in the overall level of prices in an economy. Because GDP is calculated using market values (prices) of goods and services, inflation causes GDP to go up even if there is no change in the quantity of goods and services produced. Therefore, when we look at GDP data over time, we have to adjust it for the effects of inflation. **Real GDP** is GDP adjusted for changes in prices. We discuss how to compute real GDP later in this chapter. For now, just note that any time we evaluate GDP figures across different time periods, we must use real GDP to account for inflation.

Economic growth is measured as the percentage change in real per capita GDP. Notice that this measure starts with GDP data but then adjusts for both population growth and inflation. Given this definition, you should view Figure 19.1 as a picture of economic growth in the United States. But despite what you see in the U.S. GDP data, you should not presume that economic growth is automatic or even typical. Figure 19.2 shows the long-run experience of six other nations with six distinct experiences from 1950 to 2016. In Poland, Turkey, and Mexico, real per capita GDP levels rose significantly, more than doubling between 1950 and 2016. India's remained very low for many years but began growing steadily in the last two decades. Nicaragua is now just slightly wealthier than in 1950 and, sadly, per capita real GDP is now lower in Liberia than it was in 1950.

Economic growth is one of the primary topics that macroeconomists study. In Chapters 24 and 25, we consider the factors that lead to the type of growth that the United States, Poland, Turkey, Mexico, and, more recently, India have enjoyed. We also consider why economies like those of Nicaragua and Liberia struggle to grow. Because real per capita GDP measures living standards, these issues are critical to real people's lives around the globe.

FIGURE 19.2

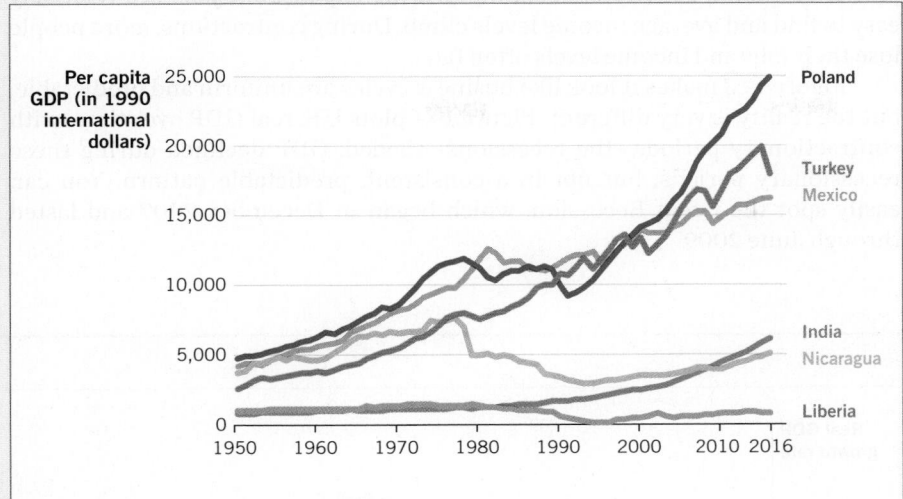

Growth in real per capita
GDP in six nations shows that
growth is not guaranteed. The
levels for Poland, Turkey, and
Mexico more than doubled
since 1950. And while India
and Nicaragua began to
grow more recently, Liberia
has lost ground.

Source: The Maddison-Project, http://
www.ggdc.net/maddison/maddison
-project/home.htm, 2018 version.

MEASURING BUSINESS CYCLES We have seen that GDP data are
used to measure living standards and economic growth. GDP is also used
to determine whether an economy is expanding or contracting in the short
run. In recent years, this use of GDP has received a lot of media attention
because of concerns about recessions. A **recession** is a short-term economic
downturn that typically lasts about six to eighteen months. Even the mere
threat of recession strikes fear in people's hearts because income levels
fall and many individuals lose their jobs or cannot find work during recessions. The U.S. recession that began in December 2007 and lasted until
June 2009 has been dubbed the **Great Recession** because of its length and
depth. The Great Recession was felt across almost all of the globe. In the
United States, it lasted nineteen months, and real GDP fell by more than 8%
in the last three months of 2008. In addition, the recovery from the Great
Recession was very slow.

A **recession** is a short-term
economic downturn.

The **Great Recession** was the
U.S. recession that lasted from
December 2007 to June 2009.

Even if an economy is expanding in the long run, it is normal for it to
experience temporary downturns. A **business cycle** is a short-run fluctuation in economic activity. Figure 19.3 illustrates a theoretical business cycle
in relationship to a long-term trend in real GDP growth. The straight line
represents the long-run trend of real GDP. The slope of the trend line is the
average long-run growth of real GDP. For the United States, this is about 3%
per year. But real GDP doesn't typically grow at exactly 3% per year. Instead
of tracking exactly along the trend line, the economy experiences fluctuations
in output. The wavy line represents the actual path of real GDP over time. It
climbs to peaks when GDP growth is positive and falls to troughs when output
growth is negative.

A **business cycle** is a short-run
fluctuation in economic activity.

The peaks and troughs divide the business cycle into two phases: expansions and contractions. An **economic expansion** occurs from the bottom of a
trough to the next peak, when economic activity is increasing. After a certain
period, the economy enters a recession, or an **economic contraction**—the

An **economic expansion** is a
phase of the business cycle
during which economic activity
is increasing.

An **economic contraction** is
a phase of the business cycle
during which economic activity
is decreasing.

period extending from the peak downward to the next trough. During this phase, economic activity is declining. During expansions, jobs are relatively easy to find and average income levels climb. During contractions, more people lose their jobs and income levels often fall.

Figure 19.3 makes it look like business cycles are uniform and predictable, but the reality is very different. Figure 19.4 plots U.S. real GDP over time, with contractionary periods—the recessions—shaded. GDP declined during these recessionary periods, but not in a consistent, predictable pattern. You can easily spot the Great Recession, which began in December 2007 and lasted through June 2009.

FIGURE 19.3

The Business Cycle

The long-run trend of GDP shows consistent growth. The business cycle reflects the fluctuations an economy typically exhibits. Economic activity increases during the expansion period of the business cycle, but declines during the contraction phase. In real life, the cycle is not nearly as smooth and easy to spot as pictured here.

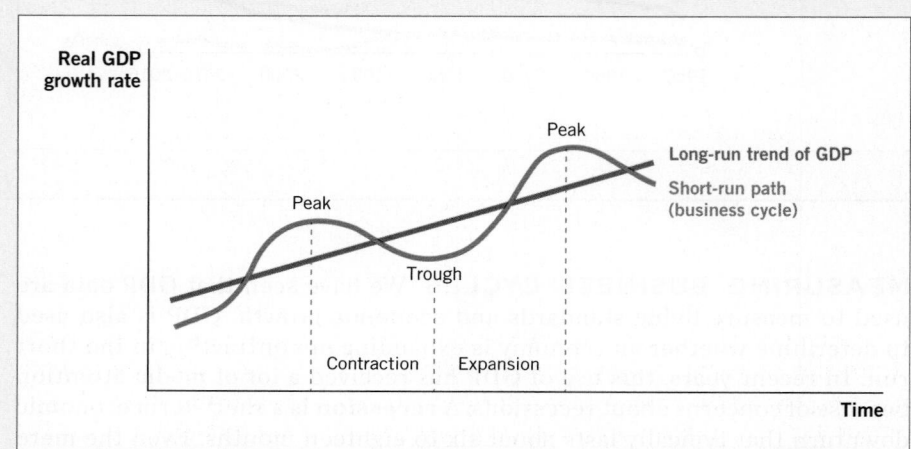

FIGURE 19.4

U.S. Real GDP and Recessions, 1970–2018

Over time, U.S. real GDP fluctuates. The shaded areas indicate periods of recession, when real GDP declines. The Great Recession, which began in December 2007 and lasted through June 2009, was a particularly deep and lengthy modern recession.

Source: U.S. Bureau of Economic Analysis.

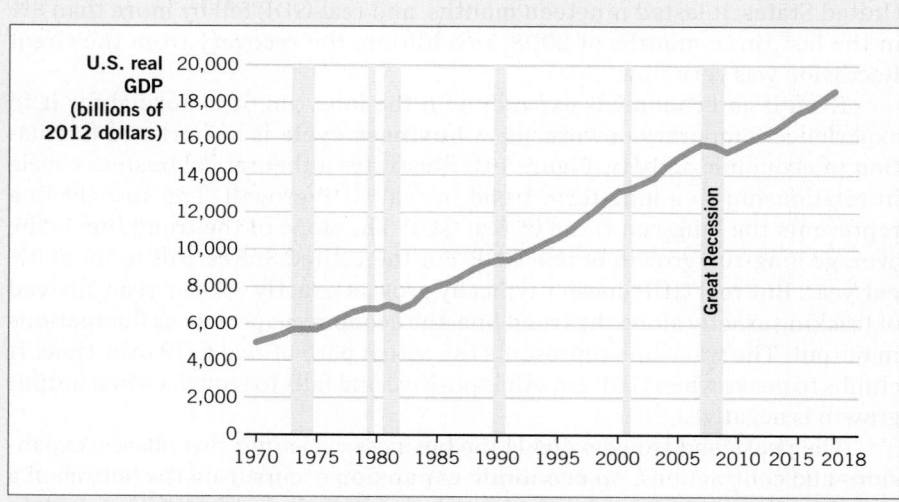

FIGURE 19.5

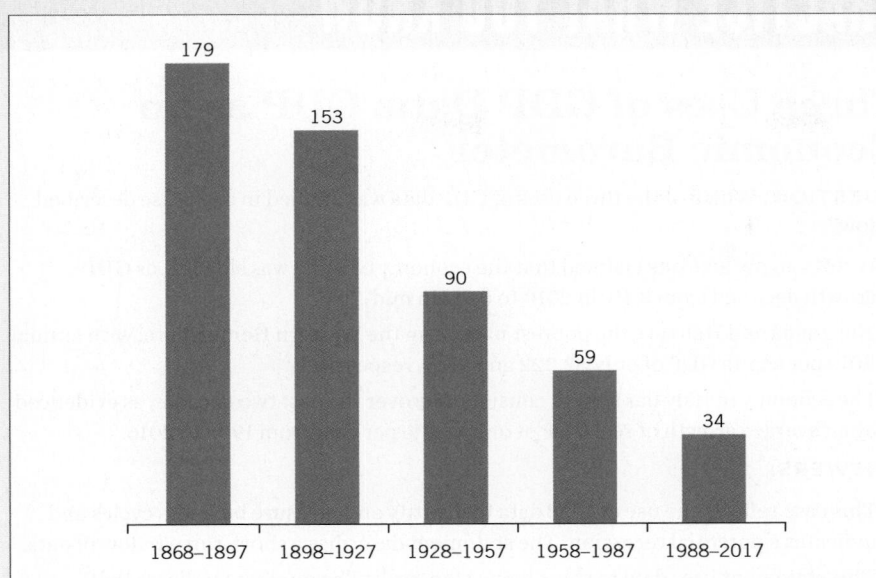

Number of Months U.S. Economy in Recession

Since the Civil War, each successive thirty-year period has brought the U.S. fewer months of recession than the period before it.

Source: National Bureau of Economic Research.

Many people think that recessions are more common today, and/or more severe, than they have been in the past. In fact, the opposite is true. Figure 19.5 shows how U.S. recessions have gotten steadily rarer and shorter in the last 150 years. The graph shows thirty-year intervals, and each bar represents the number of months (out of 360) spent in recession for each interval. The decline is consistent and striking. During the first time window, from 1868 to 1897, about half of the months were spent in recession! But in the most recent thirty-year window, 1988 to 2017, less than 10% of the months experienced recession.

There are at least two reasons why people today overestimate the occurrence of recession. One reason is that our most recent recession, the Great Recession that lasted from 2007 to 2009, was lengthy and deep. Most of us remember that episode vividly: perhaps one of your parents, or a friend's, lost their job during that period. But that recession is clearly an exceptional event, especially in the past thirty years. Another reason is that bad news tends to attract media attention. Whenever something happens that spells potential trouble for the economy, the media take note and people react. The bottom line is that recessions, tough as they may be to go through, are getting rarer all the time, and this good-news trend has been the pattern for over a century now.

How Is GDP Computed?

We have defined GDP as the market value of all final goods and services produced within a country during a specific period. In this section, we examine the definition more carefully, breaking the definition into pieces to give you a deeper understanding of what is counted in GDP and what is not.

Three Uses of GDP Data: GDP as an Economic Barometer

What does GDP data tell us about Haiti?

QUESTION: Which of the three uses of GDP data was applied in each case described below?

a. In 2011, many analysts claimed that the economy of India was slowing, as GDP growth declined from 8.4% in 2010 to 6.9% in mid-2011.

b. Nicaragua and Haiti are the poorest nations in the Western Hemisphere, with annual 2017 per capita GDP of only $2,222 and $740, respectively.

c. The economy of Italy has slowed considerably over the past two decades, as evidenced by an average growth of real GDP of only 0.15% per year from 1996 to 2016.

ANSWERS:

a. This case reflects the use of GDP data to identify and measure business cycles and indicates a potential recession. The statement describes a short-run window of data.

b. This statement uses data to show living standards. The numbers indicate that average Nicaraguans and Haitians have to live on very small amounts of income each year.

c. This observation considers growth rates over 20 years, which means that GDP was applied to look at long-run economic growth.

Counting Market Values

Nations produce a wide variety of goods and services that are measured in various units. Computation of GDP literally requires the addition of apples and oranges, as well as every other final good and service produced in a nation. How can we add everything from cars to corn to haircuts to gasoline to prescription drugs in a way that makes sense? Certainly, we can't just add quantities. For example, in 2014, the United States produced about 8 million motor vehicles and about 12 billion bushels of corn. Looking only at quantities, one might conclude that because the nation produced about 1,500 bushels of corn for every car, corn production is much more important to the U.S. economy. But of course this conclusion is wrong; a bushel of corn is not worth nearly as much as a car.

To add corn and cars and the other goods and services in GDP, economists use market values. That is, we include not only the quantity data but also the price of the good or service. Figure 19.6 offers an example with fairly realistic data. If corn production is 12 billion bushels and these bushels sell for $5 each, the contribution of corn to GDP is $60 billion. If car production is 8 million vehicles and cars sell for $30,000 each, the contribution of cars to GDP is $240 billion. If these were the only goods produced in a given year, GDP would be $60 billion + $240 billion = $300 billion.

As we have said, GDP reflects market values, and these values include both price and quantity information. Remember that one purpose of GDP data is to evaluate the health of an economy. A nation's economic health depends on the

FIGURE 19.6

Using Market Values to Compute GDP

GDP reflects market values added together for many types of goods. In this simple example, the contribution to GDP from corn production is $60 billion, and the contribution from car production is $240 billion.

Good produced	Quantity	×	Unit price	=	Market value
Corn	12 billion bushels	×	$5	=	$60 billion
Cars	8 million vehicles	×	$30,000	=	$240 billion
					$300 billion

total quantities of goods and services produced, as represented in the Quantity column of Figure 19.6. Market values allow us to add together many types of goods. At the same time, market values rely on prices, which can rise when inflation occurs. What if the prices of both cars and corn rise but the quantities produced remain unchanged? In that case, GDP will rise even though the production level stays the same. This is why we compute real GDP by adjusting for inflation (we discuss how to adjust for inflation later in this chapter).

Including Goods and Services

Physical goods are easy to visualize, but less than half of U.S. GDP comes from goods; the majority comes from services. **Services** are outputs that provide benefits without producing a tangible product. Consider a service like a visit to your doctor for a physical. The doctor examines you and offers some medical advice, but you leave with no tangible output.

When considering the proportion of goods and services in U.S. GDP, it is important to note that the composition of U.S. GDP has evolved over time. In the past, the dominant U.S. industries produced manufactured goods, such as autos, steel, and household goods. Today, a majority of U.S. GDP is service output, such as medical, financial, transportation, education, and technology services. Figure 19.7 shows services as a share of U.S. GDP since 1950. As you can see, service output now accounts for about two-thirds of all U.S. output.

Services
are outputs that provide benefits without producing a tangible product.

When you buy a new kitchen appliance, you may pay extra to have it delivered and installed. In that case, you buy both a good (the appliance) and a service (delivery and installation).

FIGURE 19.7

Services as a Share of U.S. GDP, 1950–2016

A century ago, the U.S. economy produced mostly manufactured goods. This trend has shifted in recent decades, and now services account for about two-thirds of U.S. output.

Source: U.S. Bureau of Economic Analysis.

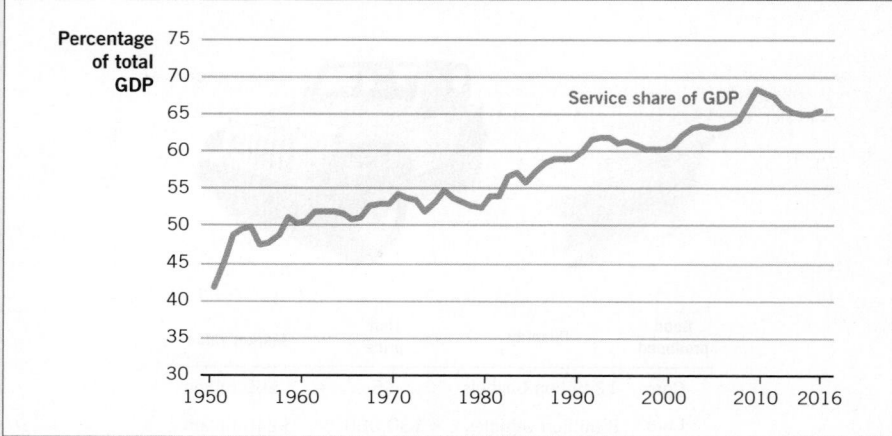

Most economists are not concerned about this move toward a service-dominated economy, but others lament this shift. These others remember that manufacturing industries were a source of prosperity for the U.S. economy and then assume they are still necessary for future growth. This is not a partisan issue; politicians from both major parties take this stand. However, this argument does not allow for the nature of modern economic growth.

A century ago, the significant economic growth in the United States came from manufacturing output. But two centuries ago, U.S. economic growth came from agricultural output. Economies evolve. The fact that innovations in manufacturing spurred past growth does not mean that future growth should not occur through services.

Including Only Final Goods and Services

As we have said, GDP is the summation of spending on goods and services. However, not *all* spending is included. To see why, consider all the spending involved in building a single good—a cell phone. Table 19.3 outlines some intermediate steps required to produce a cell phone that sells for $199. In the process of producing this phone, the manufacturer uses many intermediate goods. **Intermediate goods** are goods that firms repackage or bundle with other goods for sale at a later stage. For example, the cell phone's outer case and keyboard are intermediate goods because the phone manufacturer combines them with other intermediate goods, such as the operating system, to produce the cell phone, which is the final good. **Final goods** are goods that are sold to final users. The sale of the cell phone is included as part of GDP, but the value of the intermediate goods is not.

What happens if we count the value added during each intermediate step in making a cell phone? We start with the outer case and keyboard, which costs $5 to produce. Once the case and keyboard have been purchased, the component

Intermediate goods
are goods that firms repackage or bundle with other goods for sale at a later stage.

Final goods
are goods sold to final users.

TABLE 19.3

Intermediate Steps in Cell Phone Production

Steps	Value added during step	Prices of completed steps
1. Assemble outer case and keyboard	$5	$5
2. Prepare internal hardware	10	15
3. Install operating system	15	30
4. Connect to network	49	79
5. Transact retail sale	120	199
Total	$199	$328

hardware, which costs $10, must be installed, bringing the value of the phone to $15. The operating system software, which costs $15, is then installed, raising the cost to $30. Next, a service provider purchases the phone and connects it to a cellular network; this costs another $49, raising the phone's cost to $79. Finally, the phone is sold to the consumer for $199. The final value in this string of events, the retail price, is the true value that the cell phone creates in the economy. If we counted the value of each intermediate step, we would arrive at a total of $328, which would overstate the phone's value in the economy because it sells for only $199.

This Intel processor is an intermediate good, buried inside your computer.

We cannot get an accurate measure of GDP by summing all the sales made throughout the economy during the year, because many of them reflect intermediate steps in the production process. It is possible to get an accurate measurement of GDP by taking the selling price of the final good or by taking the value added at each step along the way, but not both; that would be double counting. For example, the operating system (OS) is part of the phone, and its value is included as part of the phone in the final sale. If we counted the sale of the OS to the phone manufacturer and then again as a part of the phone, we would be double counting and thus overstating GDP.

Within a Country

The word "domestic" in the phrase "gross domestic product" is important. GDP includes only goods and services produced domestically, or within a nation's physical borders. The output of foreign-owned firms that is produced inside the United States is included in U.S. GDP, but the output of U.S. firms that is produced overseas is included in the GDP of the overseas nation. For example, Nike is a U.S. firm that produces shoes in Thailand. Thus, all the shoes produced in Thailand count as GDP for Thailand.

Gross national product (GNP), an alternative measure of national output, is the output produced by workers and resources owned by residents of the nation. Thus, shoes produced by Nike in Thailand would count as part of U.S. GNP, since the owners of Nike are citizens (and residents) of the

Gross national product (GNP) is the output produced by workers and resources owned by residents of the nation.

United States. Many nations prefer GDP to GNP because much of their domestic output is produced by foreign-owned firms (like Nike shoes produced in Thailand). For these nations, GDP is larger than GNP. These countries prefer GDP because it measures the production that takes place within their borders. Thus, GDP has become the standard measure of international output. As national economies have become more globalized with more production taking place outside the home country, GDP is now used more often than GNP to measure a nation's overall production.

Nike shoes produced in Thailand count as GDP for Thailand.

From a Particular Time Period

GDP only counts goods and services produced during a given time period. Goods or services produced in earlier years do not count in the current year's GDP. For instance, when a new car is produced, it adds to GDP in the year it is sold. However, a used car that is resold does not count in current GDP, because it was already counted in GDP for the year when it was first produced. If we counted the used car when it was resold, we would be counting that car as part of GDP twice (double counting).

In addition, sales of financial assets such as stocks and bonds do not count toward GDP. After all, these kinds of sales, which we will discuss in Chapter 23, do not create anything new; they simply transfer ownership from one person to another. In this way, they are like used goods. However, brokerage fees do count as payment for the brokerage service, and they are included in GDP.

We have now examined the GDP definition in greater detail. In the next section, we consider the way GDP is actually measured by adding together different types of expenditures.

Ice cream cones count as non-durable consumption goods.

Looking at GDP as Different Types of Expenditures

In this section, we look more closely at the different categories of goods and services included in GDP. The Bureau of Economic Analysis (BEA) is the U.S. government agency that tallies GDP data in a process called *national income accounting*. The BEA breaks GDP into four major categories: consumption (C), investment (I), government purchases (G), and net exports (NX). Using this framework, it is possible to express GDP as the following equation:

(EQUATION 19.1)

$$GDP = C + I + G + NX$$

Table 19.4 details the composition of U.S. GDP in 2018. For that year, total GDP was $20,500.6 billion, or about $20 trillion. To get a sense of what that amount represents, imagine laying 20 trillion one-dollar bills from end to end. That would be enough to cover every U.S. highway, street, and county road more than twice!

Looking at Table 19.4, you can see that consumption is by far the largest component of GDP, followed by investment and then by government purchases. Note that the value of net exports is negative. This negative value occurs

TABLE 19.4			
Composition of U.S. GDP, 2018			
Category	Individual expenditures (billions of dollars)	Total expenditures per category (billions of dollars)	Percentage of GDP
Consumption (C)		**$13,951.6**	68.1%
Durable goods	$1,461.5		
Nondurable goods	2,880.7		
Services	9,609.4		
Investment (I)		**3,652.2**	17.8
Fixed Investment	3,595.6		
Change in business inventories	56.5		
Government purchases (G)		**3,522.5**	17.2
Federal	1,319.9		
State and local	2,202.6		
Net Exports (NX)		**−625.6**	−3.1
Exports	2,530.9		
Imports	−3,156.5		
Total GDP		**$20,500.6**	100.0%

Source: Bureau of Economic Analysis

Refrigerators count as durable consumption goods.

because the United States imports more goods than it exports. Let's take a closer look at each of these four components of GDP.

CONSUMPTION **Consumption** (C) is the purchase of final goods and services by households, with the exception of new housing. Most people spend a large majority of their income on consumption goods and services. Consumption goods include everything from groceries to automobiles. You can see in Table 19.4 that services are a very big portion of consumption spending. They include things such as haircuts, doctor's visits, and help from a real estate agent.

> **Consumption**
> is the purchase of final goods and services by households, excluding new housing.

Consumption goods can be divided into two categories: nondurable and durable. *Nondurable* consumption goods are consumed over a short period, and *durable* consumption goods are consumed over a long period. This distinction is important when the economy swings back and forth between good times and bad times. Sales of durable goods—for example, automobiles, appliances, and computers—are subject to significant cyclical fluctuations that correspond to the health of the economy. Because durable goods are generally designed to last for many years, consumers tend to purchase more of these goods when the economy is strong. In contrast, when the economy is weak, they put off purchases of durables and make what they already have last longer—for example, working with an old computer for another year rather than replacing it with a new model right away. However, nondurables don't last very long, so consumers often purchase them regardless of economic conditions.

Investment
is private spending on the tools, plant, and equipment used to produce future output.

When firms buy tools to aid in production, they are making an investment.

Government spending
includes spending by all levels of government on final goods and services.

Net exports
are total exports minus total imports.

INVESTMENT When you hear the word "investment," you likely think of savings or stocks and bonds. But in macroeconomics, **investment** (I) refers to private spending on the tools, plant, and equipment used to produce future output. Investment is something as simple as the purchase of a shovel, a tractor, or a personal computer to help a small business produce goods and services for its customers. But investment also includes more complex endeavors, such as the construction of large factories. For example, when Pfizer builds a new factory to manufacture a new drug, it is making an investment. When Walmart builds a new warehouse, that expense is investment. And when a new house is built, that also counts as investment. This way of accounting for house purchases may seem odd, since most of us think of a home purchase as an act of consumption; but in the national income accounts, such a purchase counts as an investment.

Investment also includes all purchases by businesses that add to their inventories. For example, in preparation for the Christmas buying season, an electronics retailer orders more TVs, cameras, and computers. GDP rises when business inventories increase. GDP is calculated this way because we want to measure output in the period it is produced. Investment in inventory is just one more way that firms spend today to increase output in the future.

Investment spending makes up only about one-sixth of all GDP, but don't underestimate its importance. Most economists agree that investment spending leads to greater future GDP. Tools, including both physical machinery and software, industrial plants to extract raw materials and manufacture goods, and infrastructure such as railways and power grids all help an economy produce more in the future. We will talk more about investment in later chapters.

GOVERNMENT SPENDING National, state, and local governments purchase many goods and services. These purchases are included in GDP as **government spending** (G), which includes spending by all levels of government on final goods and services. For example, every government employee receives a salary, which is considered part of GDP. Similarly, governments spend money purchasing buildings, equipment, and supplies from private-sector firms. Governments also spend on public works projects, including national defense, highway construction, schools, and post offices. *Transfer payments* the government makes to households, such as welfare payments, social security, and unemployment insurance, do not count as GDP, since they are not direct purchases of new goods and services.

NET EXPORTS The United States produces some goods and services that are exported to other countries, and it imports some goods and services produced elsewhere. But only exports add to GDP because they are produced domestically. Imports are tracked, but they do not add to GDP, because our goal is to measure domestic production accurately. As it turns out, imports enter into GDP calculations twice: once positively and once negatively, and the net result is zero. Let's start with net exports. **Net exports** (NX) are total exports minus total imports. We can write the calculation of net exports in equation form as

(EQUATION 19.2)

$$\text{net exports}\,(NX) = \text{exports} - \text{imports}$$

When spending on imports is larger than spending on exports, net exports are negative. Net exports are typically negative for the United States.

Notice that imports enter the GDP calculations as a negative value: GDP = C + I + G + (exports − imports). From this equation you might conclude that imports are harmful to an economy, because they seem to reduce GDP. But imports are then used for one of the other GDP categories (C, I, or G), and so they enter positively there. In this way, imports are accounted for without increasing or decreasing GDP. For example, let's say we import $10 million worth of bananas from Guatemala. These bananas increase consumption by $10 million, but they also increase imports by $10 million, and so net exports falls by $10 million. The net result is that GDP is unaffected, as C rises by the same amount that NX falls.

However, adding the different components together (C, I, G, and NX) in the process of national income accounting really is just that—accounting. The primary goal of the national income accounts is to keep a record of how people are buying the goods and services produced in a nation. More imports coming in means more goods and services for people in that nation. All else equal, imports do not make us worse off.

Real GDP: Adjusting GDP for Price Changes

According to the Bureau of Economic Analysis, in 2010, the U.S. economy produced GDP of $15 trillion. Just eight years later, in 2018, it produced over $20 trillion. That's a 33% increase in just eight years. Is that really possible? Think about this question in long-run historical terms. Is it possible that the nation's economy grew to $15 trillion over more than two centuries, but then just eight years later surpassed $20 trillion? If we look more closely, we'll see that some of this recent increase in GDP data is actually due to inflation.

The raw GDP data, based on market values, is computed on the basis of the prices of goods and services current at the time GDP is calculated. Economists refer to these prices as the *current prices*. The GDP calculated from current prices is called **nominal GDP**. Figure 19.8 compares U.S. nominal and real GDP from 2012 to 2018. Notice that nominal GDP rises much faster than real GDP. While nominal GDP rose by 26%, real GDP increased by 15%. The difference between these percentages reflects price level growth, or inflation.

Nominal GDP is GDP measured in current prices and not adjusted for inflation.

Computing nominal GDP is straightforward: we add the market values (actual prices) of all final goods and services. But to compute real GDP, we also need a measure of overall prices, known as a price level. A **price level** is an index of the average prices of goods and services throughout the economy. It goes up when prices generally rise, and it falls when prices across the economy fall. Chapter 21 explores prices and the calculation of price levels. For now, just take the price data as given, and think of the price level as an indicator of changes in the general level of all prices across the economy.

A **price level** is an index of the average prices of goods and services throughout the economy.

The price level in GDP data, the **GDP deflator**, includes the prices of the final goods and services counted in GDP. The GDP deflator "deflates" all the price inflation out of nominal GDP so that we can see real GDP. Let's look at some actual data. Table 19.5 shows U.S. nominal GDP and price level data from 2009 to 2018. Focus on the years 2012 and 2013 and notice that the price level was set at 100 in 2012 and rose to 102 in 2013. These numbers

The **GDP deflator** is a measure of the price level used to calculate real GDP.

FIGURE 19.8

U.S. Nominal and Real GDP, 2012–2018

Nominal GDP typically rises faster than real GDP because nominal GDP reflects both growth in real production and growth in prices (inflation). From 2012 to 2018, nominal GDP in the United States rose by 26%, but the increase in real GDP (using 2012 as the base year) during the same period was 15%. The difference is price level growth, or inflation.

Source: U.S. Bureau of Economic Analysis.

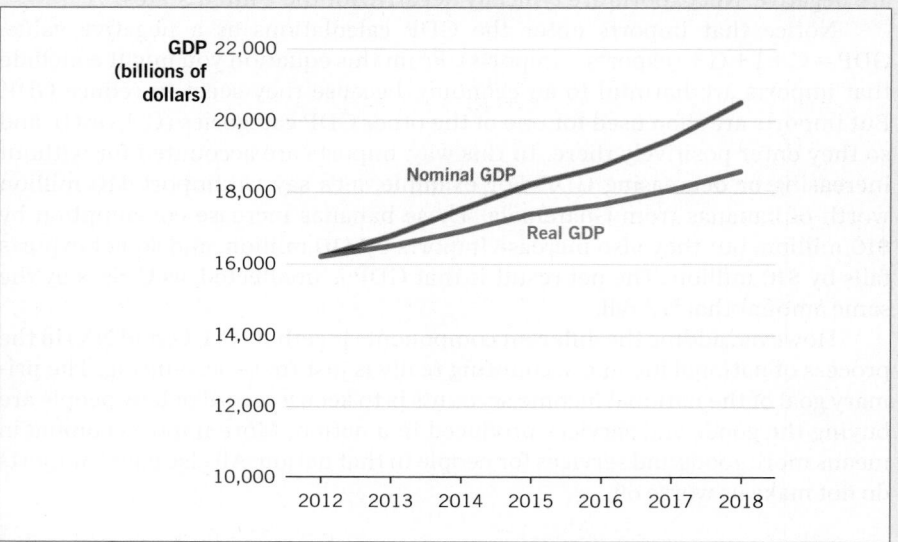

indicate that, on average, prices across the economy rose by 2% between 2012 and 2013.

To compute real GDP, we use the current prices of goods and services and then adjust them to prices from an agreed-upon common time period, or *base period*. We do this in two steps:

1. Divide nominal GDP by the price level.
2. Multiply the result by the price level (100) from the base period.

TABLE 19.5

U.S. Nominal GDP and Price Level, 2009–2018

Year	Nominal GDP (billions of dollars)	Price Level (GDP deflator)
2009	$14,448.9	95
2010	14,992.1	96
2011	15,542.6	98
2012	16,197.0	100
2013	16,784.9	102
2014	17,521.7	104
2015	18,219.3	105
2016	18,707.2	106
2017	19,485.4	108
2018	20,500.6	110

Source: Bureau of Economic Analysis.

TABLE 19.6		
Converting Nominal GDP into Real GDP		
Data for 2018: Nominal GDP = $20,501 billion Price level (GDP deflator) = 110		
General steps	**Our example**	
Step 1: Filter out current prices.	$20,501 ÷ 110 = $186.37	
Step 2: Input base-period prices.	$186.37 × 100 = $18,637	

Putting these two steps together, we compute real GDP for any time period (t) as

$$\text{real GDP}_t = \underbrace{\frac{\text{nominal GDP}_t}{\text{price level}_t}}_{\text{Step 1}} \times \underbrace{100}_{\text{Step 2}}$$

(EQUATION 19.3)

For example, nominal GDP in 2018 was $20,501 billion, and the price level was 110. To convert nominal GDP to real GDP, we divide by 110 and then multiply by 100:

$$= \frac{\$20,501}{110} \times 100 = \$18,637 \text{ billion}$$

Table 19.6 illustrates both steps of this conversion. The figure $18,637 billion is the U.S. real GDP in 2018, adjusted for inflation. Economists and the financial media use other terms for real GDP; sometimes they might say "GDP in 2012 prices" or "GDP in constant 2012 dollars." Whenever you consider changes in GDP over time, you should look for these terms to ensure that the data are not biased by price changes.

Growth Rates

For many macroeconomic applications, it is useful to calculate growth rates. For example, let's say you read that the GDP in Vietnam in 2016 was about $205 billion. This figure may not mean much to you, or you may take it as bad news, since $205 billion is a small fraction of U.S. GDP. But maybe you also read that Vietnam's GDP grew by 6.2% in 2016 (it did!). In that case, you'd have a more positive (and more accurate) impression. In general, growth rates convey additional helpful information.

Growth rates are calculated as percentage changes in a variable. For example, the growth of U.S. nominal GDP in 2018 is computed as

$$\text{nominal GDP growth in 2018} = \frac{\text{GDP}_{2018} - \text{GDP}_{2017}}{\text{GDP}_{2017}} \times 100$$

(EQUATION 19.4)

Unless noted otherwise, the data come from the end of the period. Therefore, the nominal GDP growth computed by Equation 19.4 tells us the percentage change in U.S. GDP from the end of 2017 to the end of 2018, or over the course of 2018. Using actual data, the calculation is

$$\text{nominal GDP growth in 2018} = \text{\% change in nominal GDP}$$

$$= \frac{20{,}501 - 19{,}485}{19{,}485} \times 100 = 5.2\%$$

We can also compute the growth rate of the price level (GDP deflator) for 2018:

$$\text{price level growth rate} = \text{\% change in price level}$$

$$= \frac{110 - 108}{108} \times 100 = 1.9\%$$

This means that throughout the U.S. economy in 2018, inflation was 1.9%.

Armed with these two computations, we can derive one more useful formula for evaluating GDP data. Recall that nominal GDP, which is from raw GDP data, includes information on both the price level and real GDP. When either of these factors changes, nominal GDP is affected. In fact, the growth rate of nominal GDP is approximately equal to the sum of the growth rates of these two factors:

(EQUATION 19.5)   growth of nominal GDP ≈ growth of real GDP + growth of price level

Since growth rates are calculated as percentage changes, we can rewrite Equation 19.5 as

(EQUATION 19.6)   % change in nominal GDP ≈ % change in real GDP

+ % change in price level

Equation 19.6 gives us a simple way of separating GDP growth into its respective parts. For example, since we know that nominal GDP grew by 5.2% in 2018 and the price level grew by 1.9%, the remaining nominal GDP growth of 3.3% (5.2% − 1.9%) is attributable to growth in real GDP.

What Are Some Shortcomings of GDP Data?

We began this chapter with a claim that GDP is the single best measure of economic activity. Along the way, we have learned that nominal GDP fails to account for changes in prices, and so real GDP is a better measure of economic activity. We also talked about how real GDP per capita accounts for population differences. You will be relieved to learn that by now we have finished introducing new variations of GDP! However, there are some problems with relying on GDP data as a measure of a nation's well-being. In this section, we highlight four shortcomings that limit the effectiveness of GDP as a measure of the health of an economy. We also look at the relationship between GDP and happiness. At the end of this section, we consider why economists continue to rely on GDP.

"GDP, OMG!"

THE INDICATOR FROM PLANET MONEY

NPR produces two of the best economics podcast series available; they are called *Planet Money* and *The Indicator* from *Planet Money*. These podcasts are certainly written by knowledgeable economists and are also quite entertaining. They are pitched to popular audiences but are still educational, especially on basic economics. If you are looking for an easy and fun way to learn economics along with your class material this semester, this is the podcast for you.

In July 2018, one *Indicator* episode was on the measurement of GDP. The hosts used the opportunity to consider the very strong growth of the second quarter of 2018. In less than ten minutes, they asked and answered five questions about GDP.

First, they asked "What is GDP?" In answering this question, they gave examples of each type of GDP expenditure. For consumption, they referenced coffee from Starbucks; for investment, they cited purchases of new equipment by Ford, to help produce pickup trucks; for government spending, they pointed to firefighting equipment and tanks for the military; and for exports, they talked about smartphones and financial services.

Their second question was about the 4.1% growth in the second quarter of 2018: "Is that a lot faster than normal?" The answer is "Yes!" In fact, normal growth is less than 3%, so the middle of 2018 was a particularly strong period for GDP growth.

The third question got to the cause of the strong growth: "What made the economy grow so fast in the second quarter?" The answer is that consumption

and exports were particularly high. The tax cuts of the previous year seem to have had an effect on consumer spending in 2018.

Fourth, they asked: "What were the lowlights?" Here they pointed to the cause of the export surge and they postulated that it was due to impending tariffs that threatened to interrupt trade flows in the future. They also noted that business investment didn't grow as much as previously.

Finally, they asked: "Is 4.1% growth sustainable?" Their answer was reasonable and based on a consensus of most economists, which is that 4.1% growth is great but unfortunately not likely to last.

Nonmarket Goods

Many goods and services are produced but not sold in a market. These are then not counted in GDP data even though they create value for society. For instance, work done at home, such as an individual caring for their children, washing their dishes, mowing their lawn, or washing their car, are services produced but

Computing Real and Nominal GDP Growth: GDP Growth in Mexico

How much is Mexico's economy growing?

The following table presents GDP data for Mexico. Use the data from the table to answer the following questions.

QUESTION: What was the rate of growth of real GDP in Mexico in 2016?

ANSWER: Using Equation 19.6,

$$\% \text{ change in real GDP } + \% \text{ change in price level} \approx \% \text{ change in nominal GDP}$$

Rewriting the equation, we can solve for real GDP growth as

$$\% \text{ change in real GDP } \approx \% \text{ change in nominal GDP} - \% \text{ change in price level}$$

For 2016, we have

$$\% \text{ change in real GDP } \approx 6.9 - 4.6 \approx 2.3$$

QUESTION: How would you compute real GDP growth in Mexico in 2013?

ANSWER: Using the 2013 data in the same equation, we get

$$\% \text{ change in real GDP } \approx 3.1 - 1.8 \approx 1.3$$

This means that 2016 was a much better year than 2013 for the Mexican economy.

Year	Nominal GDP growth rate	Price-level growth rate
2013	3.1%	1.8%
2014	7.0	4.7
2015	5.7	3.1
2016	6.9	4.6

Source: World Bank.

CHALLENGE QUESTION: If a citizen of Mexico buys $50,000 worth of stock in Apple Inc. (a U.S. company), and pays a 10% trading fee to a U.S. stock broker, how much is added to U.S. GDP?

ANSWER: $5,000. Only the fee for the broker adds to GDP, since it is a service. The $50,000 stock purchase does not count toward production, since it is just a change of ownership.

not counted in GDP. When the nonmarket segment of an economy is large, the result can be a dramatic undercounting of the annual output being produced. In less-developed societies where many households live off the land and produce goods for their own consumption, GDP—the measure of market activity— is a less reliable measure of economic output.

Underground Economy

The underground, or shadow, economy encompasses transactions that are not reported to the government and therefore are not taxed. These transactions are often settled in cash. Some of these exchanges are for illegal goods and services, such as narcotics and illegal gambling. However, many underground transactions are for legal goods and services, but these activities are not reported in order to avoid taxes. Legal activities that go unreported include tips for waiting tables and tending bar, lawn services, and even home renovations. Because underground transactions are not reported, they are not easily measured and so they are not included in U.S. GDP calculations. However, as we explain in Economics in the Real World (below), many European nations now include illegal underground activities when calculating their GDP.

Not counted in GDP: washing your own car.

How big is the underground economy? No one is exactly sure. Economist Friedrich Schneider has estimated that for wealthy developed economies it is roughly 15% of GDP and that in transitioning economies the percentage rises to between 21% and 30% of GDP. However, in the world's most underdeveloped economies, like those of Nigeria or Armenia, the underground economy can be as much as 40% of GDP.

The United States is widely believed to have one of the smallest shadow economies in the world, with less than 10% of GDP unaccounted for in the official measurement. Why is the underground economy so small in the United States? The simple answer is that in the United States and in many other developed economies, most citizens can earn more by legitimately participating in the economy than by engaging in illegal activities. In short, a strong economy that generates jobs and opportunities for advancement helps to reduce the size of the underground economy. In addition, corruption is much less common. This means that participants in the economy rarely face demands for bribes or kickbacks from authorities or organized crime. This is not the case in many developing nations. For example, Somalia, which ranks last on Transparency International's corruption index, has widespread piracy and virtually no formal economy.

ECONOMICS IN THE REAL WORLD

SEX, DRUGS, AND GDP IN EUROPE

In September 2014, the GDP for the European Union (EU)[*] increased by 3.53% overnight. That is a full year's worth of very solid growth. But it didn't make Europeans any wealthier, because it was actually just the result of a new way of defining and calculating GDP. Eurostat (the economic statistics office of the European Commission) redefined GDP to include many transactions that were previously uncounted and are actually illegal across much of Europe.

The new GDP definition includes illegal drug deals, prostitution, and even sales of stolen goods. Specifically, it includes illegal transactions as long as both parties agree to the transaction.

---

[*]The EU is a group of 28 European nations that have pledged economic cooperation.

FIGURE 19.9

Legality of Cannabis in the European Union

The legality of cannabis varies drastically across the European Union. For example, cannabis is essentially legal in the Netherlands but strictly illegal in France. Previously, only legal transactions were counted as part of GDP in the European Union. However, the new standards adopted in 2014 include illegal transactions in European nations, so long as both parties agree to the transaction. Therefore, illegal trades in France are now counted as part of GDP so that French GDP and Dutch GDP both include transactions for the same goods and services.

Source: Wikimedia Commons.

Ostensibly, Eurostat is trying to capture part of the shadow economy that is typically not measured in GDP. Unfortunately, the process becomes even more complicated when the legality of goods and services varies across nations. For example, Figure 19.9 shows how cannabis laws vary across Europe. Cannabis is essentially legal in some nations (the Netherlands) but strictly illegal in others (France, for example).

Normalizing the accounting standards across nations makes sense. But illegal activities are difficult to measure. In addition, if the illegal activities are a relatively stable portion of GDP, then there is really no bias when they are not included. In fact, the new estimates, in an attempt to provide a more complete measure, may actually introduce more error into GDP measurement due to the difficulty of estimating illegal trade.

So why the change in definition? One possibility is that many European nations are dealing with high deficit- (and debt-) to-GDP ratios, and some of these new measurements (in a backhanded way) help lower these ratios. The European Commission has explicit rules regarding these budget measures: a nation's deficit in a given fiscal year is not to exceed 3% of its GDP, and the national debt is not to exceed 60% of GDP. When nations exceed these bounds, the governing council is directed to use coercive measures called excessive deficit procedures (EDRs). The council has been lax in enforcing EDRs in recent years. However, increasing GDP by simply redefining how it is measured automatically lowers deficit and debt ratios and helps nations that have higher government debt levels.

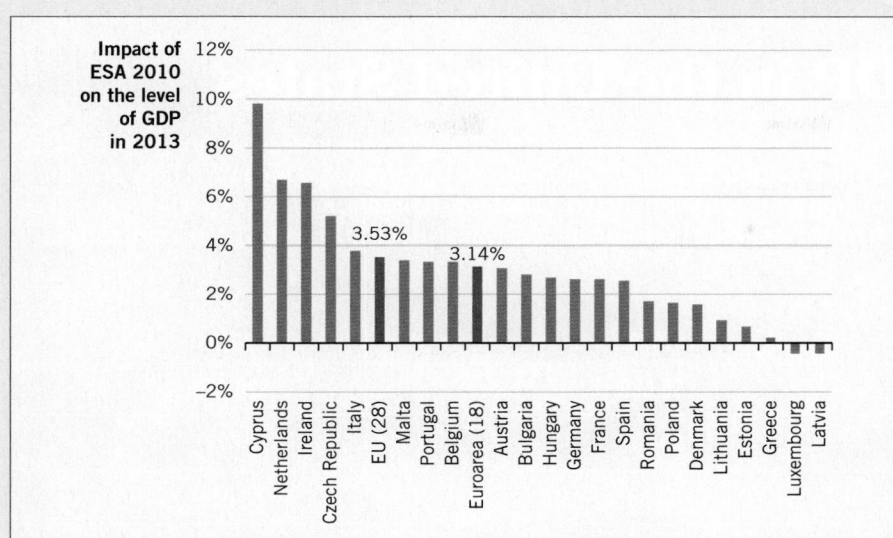

FIGURE 19.10

Impact of ESA 2010 on the level of GDP in 2013

3.53%

3.14%

Cyprus, Netherlands, Ireland, Czech Republic, Italy, EU (28), Malta, Portugal, Belgium, Euroarea (18), Austria, Bulgaria, Hungary, Germany, France, Spain, Romania, Poland, Denmark, Lithuania, Estonia, Greece, Luxembourg, Latvia

Increase in GDP Due to Accounting Change

This data shows how the GDP of each European nation changed as a result of the new GDP accounting rules (ESA). The overall average for the EU was a 3.53% increase in GDP, but the GDP of Cyprus jumped 9.8%. Note that we look at 2013, the year before the law change, to isolate the effects of a definitional change in the accounting of GDP.

Source: Eurostat.

Figure 19.10 shows the effect of the new GDP definition on each nation's GDP level in 2013 (along with the overall EU and Euroarea). Note that we look at 2013, the year before the law change, to isolate the effects of a definitional change in the accounting of GDP. The countries are ordered according to their GDP gains from the new GDP measurements. (ESA 2010 stands for European System Accounts.)

As you can see, GDP for Cyprus jumped 9.8% due to the accounting change, shrinking the country's debt-to-GDP ratio by a full half of a percentage point in 2013—from 5.4% to 4.9%. Clearly, the new accounting rule exaggerates debt reduction in Cyprus as the country tries to move closer to the EU goal of 3%.

In short, while new GDP accounting rules in Europe may normalize national income accounting across the Eurozone, they are particularly helpful to nations that have high government debt levels.

Quality of the Environment

GDP measures the final amount of goods and services produced in a given period, but it does not distinguish how those goods and services are produced. In particular, it does not account for negative environmental side effects that sometimes occur in production. Imagine two economies, both with the same real GDP per capita. One economy relies on clean energy for its production, and the other has weak environmental standards. Citizens in both countries enjoy the same standard of living, but their well-being is not the same. The lax environmental standards in the second economy lead to air and water pollution as well as health problems for its citizens. Since there is more to quality of life than the goods and services we buy, using GDP to infer that both places are equally desirable is unsound.

Not counted in GDP: a clean environment.

ng at GDP in the United States

product (GDP) is the single most important indicator of macroeconomic performance. It gives
the overall health of the economy because it measures both output and income. These graphics
ur pieces of GDP—consumption, investment, government spending, and net exports—and
s changed from 1970 to 2018. On the bottom left, you can also see how real GDP has more than
70.

ollars)	1970	2018
	$5,689	**$20,470**
	$3,408	$14,231
	$633	$3,739
	$1,734	$3,508
	-$87	-$1,009

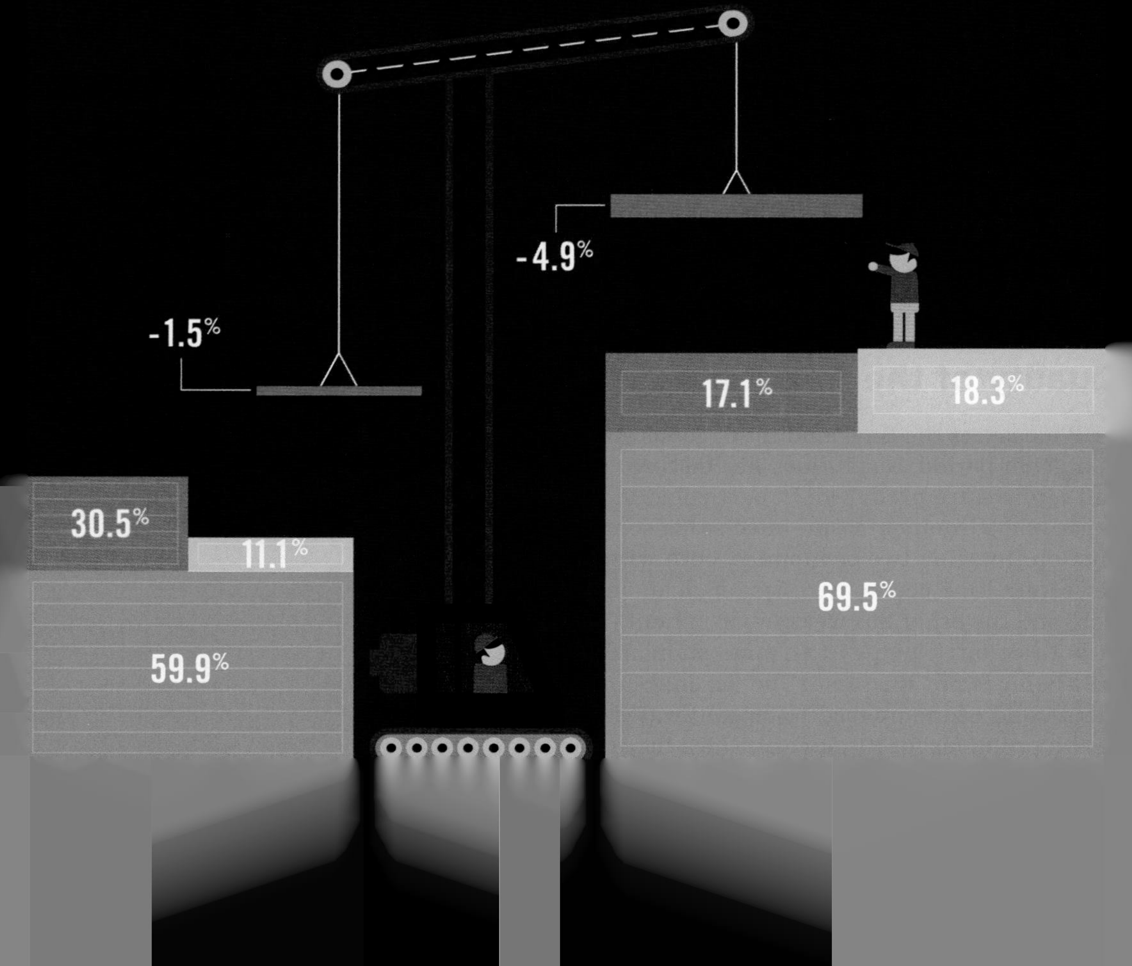

-4.9%

-1.5%

17.1%

18.3%

30.5%

11.1%

59.9%

69.5%

Percentage Breakdowns, 1970 vs. 2018

By measuring the components of each piece of GDP, we can see how the makeup of the U.S. economy has changed over time.

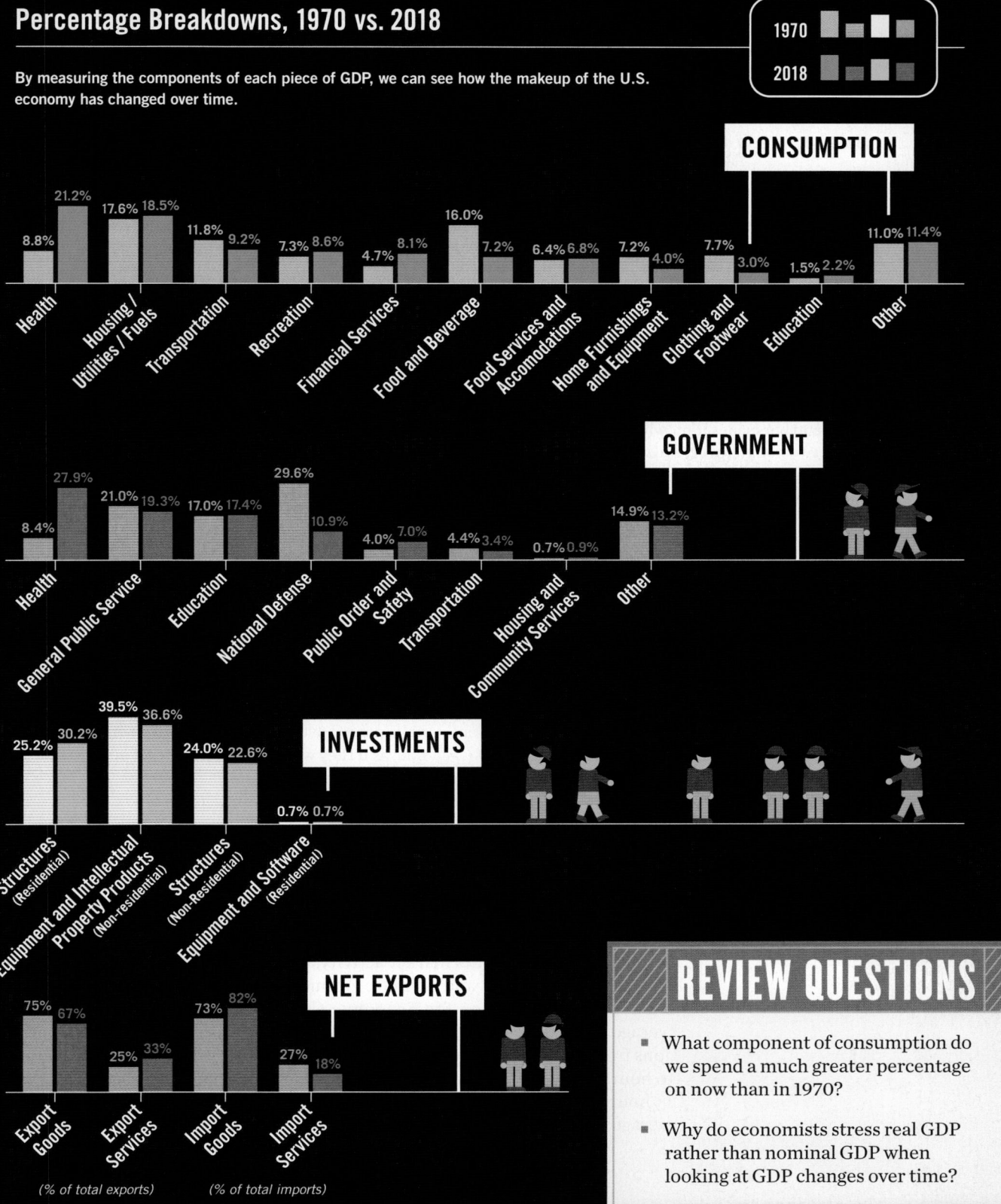

1970
2018

CONSUMPTION

	Health	Housing / Utilities / Fuels	Transportation	Recreation	Financial Services	Food and Beverage	Food Services and Accomodations	Home Furnishings and Equipment	Clothing and Footwear	Education	Other
1970	8.8%	17.6%	11.8%	7.3%	4.7%	16.0%	6.4%	7.2%	7.7%	1.5%	11.0%
2018	21.2%	18.5%	9.2%	8.6%	8.1%	7.2%	6.8%	4.0%	3.0%	2.2%	11.4%

GOVERNMENT

	Health	General Public Service	Education	National Defense	Public Order and Safety	Transportation	Housing and Community Services	Other
1970	8.4%	21.0%	17.0%	29.6%	4.0%	4.4%	0.7%	14.9%
2018	27.9%	19.3%	17.4%	10.9%	7.0%	3.4%	0.9%	13.2%

INVESTMENTS

	Structures (Residential)	Equipment and Intellectual Property Products (Non-residential)	Structures (Non-Residential)	Equipment and Software (Residential)
1970	25.2%	39.5%	24.0%	0.7%
2018	30.2%	36.6%	22.6%	0.7%

NET EXPORTS

	Export Goods	Export Services	Import Goods	Import Services
1970	75%	25%	73%	27%
2018	67%	33%	82%	18%

(% of total exports)   *(% of total imports)*

REVIEW QUESTIONS

- What component of consumption do we spend a much greater percentage on now than in 1970?

- Why do economists stress real GDP rather than nominal GDP when looking at GDP changes over time?

The Underground Economy

BREAKING BAD

Over five tensely plotted seasons, *Breaking Bad* tells the story of Walter White (played by Bryan Cranston), a high school chemistry teacher who becomes a drug kingpin after being diagnosed with terminal lung cancer. By making and selling methamphetamine, he plans to build a fortune that will leave his family financially secure after he dies. As the show progresses, White's priorities shift and we see the outcome of his decisions.

In "Crazy Handful of Nothing" (Season 1, Episode 6), Walter is just getting started. He bluffs his way into a meeting with a feared drug lord named Tuco (Raymond Cruz) and persuades him (with the help of explosives!) to buy two pounds of crystal meth per week, at $35,000 per pound. As Walter's partner Jesse Pinkman (Aaron Paul) later explains, sourcing the chemicals needed for that level of production is going to be a huge challenge. But if the two of them can manage it, they stand to make a lot of money.

Let's think about how this is accounted for in economics. The purchases of those chemicals will be legal and will therefore count toward GDP. So will the purchase of equipment, such as scales to weigh out portions for packaging. But from there on, the market activity goes underground. The sale to Tuco (a sale of goods) is $70,000 per week to a single customer. Then there's Tuco's revenue from selling the drug on the street (a high-markup resale of the same goods), the

"Money up front!" Walter demands.

cut Tuco pays for labor and the associated risk (a sale of services), and the under-the-table money Walter and Jesse later pay their shady lawyer and his gun-toting fixer (more services). All of those transactions are left off the books as far as official GDP is concerned.

One of the ironies of measuring GDP is that even though the many transactions are not part of GDP, the work of the people involved in fighting the war on drugs (police, FBI investigators) is included in GDP. So are the sales of drug paraphernalia passed over the counter, with a wink and a nod, as if they were intended for legal purposes such as tobacco consumption.

Leisure Time

Because GDP only counts market activity, it fails to capture how long workers labor to produce goods and services. For most developed nations, according to the OECD (Organization for Economic Cooperation and Development), the average workweek is slightly over 35 hours. However, there are wide variations from country to country. At the high end, laborers in South Korea average 46 hours per week. In contrast, laborers in the Netherlands average fewer than 28 hours per week. The United States is near the middle of the pack, with an average workweek of 36 hours. This means that comparisons of GDP across countries are problematic because they do not account for the extra time available to workers in countries with substantially fewer hours worked. A comparison between the United States and Japan, which also averages 36 hours per workweek, would be valid; but a comparison of U.S. GDP with that of the Netherlands or South Korea is misleading.

GDP and Happiness

Throughout this chapter, we have presented real per capita GDP as a measure of living standards. But let's be careful; economists do not generally claim that money can buy happiness. However, it is a fact that, *ceteris paribus*, greater wealth does make it easier to afford conveniences, experiences, and even health and well-being that contribute to life satisfaction or happiness. Per capita GDP is positively correlated with many human welfare outcomes that nearly everybody finds desirable: higher life expectancy, higher levels of education, and reduced infant mortality. This probably doesn't surprise you; income allows people to buy better health care, medicines, and education, among other purchases.

Recent research done by economists Betsey Stevenson and Justin Wolfers seems to support these assumptions. Their research has found a consistently positive relationship between self-reported life satisfaction and income. In their research, Stevenson and Wolfers asked questions similar to those found on other surveys used to study happiness and life satisfaction:

"Here is a ladder representing the 'ladder of life.' Let's suppose that the top of the ladder represents the best possible life for you, and the bottom, the worst possible life for you. On which step of the ladder do you feel you personally stand at the present time [0–10 steps]?"

You can imagine how the data will look: people and nations with relatively low life satisfaction will give answers in the 3–4 range, while people and nations with relatively high life satisfaction will give answers in the 6–8 range.

Here are two key results from Stevenson and Wolfers' research:

1. WEALTHIER INDIVIDUALS REPORT GREATER LIFE SATISFACTION THAN POORER PEOPLE IN THE SAME COUNTRY.

Figure 19.11 shows how life satisfaction varies across varying income levels in the 10 most populous countries. The vertical axis measures the life satisfaction variable, and the horizontal axis measures income on a log scale. Clearly, life satisfaction climbs with income: all the lines have a positive and similar slope. Even though Brazilians are especially happy for their given income levels, the general relationship for Brazilians is similar to that for Indians, Russians, and Japanese.

In addition, Stevenson and Wolfers point out the importance of paying attention to percentage changes in that variable, rather than absolute changes. For example, an income change from $400 to $500 is a 25% change, but a change from $40,000 to $50,000 is also a 25% change.

Why do percentage changes matter in this study? Basic economics assumes a diminishing utility of income, which means that increases in life satisfaction (utility) per dollar should decline as income increases. This study demonstrates

FIGURE 19.11

Life Satisfaction and Income by Country

This shows a positive relationship between self-reported life satisfaction (happiness) and household income in ten nations. Wealthier people inside each nation express greater happiness than poorer people in the same nation.

Source: Betsey Stevenson and Justin Wolfers, "Subjective Well-Being and Income: Is There Any Evidence of Satiation?" NBER Working Paper 18992, April 2013.

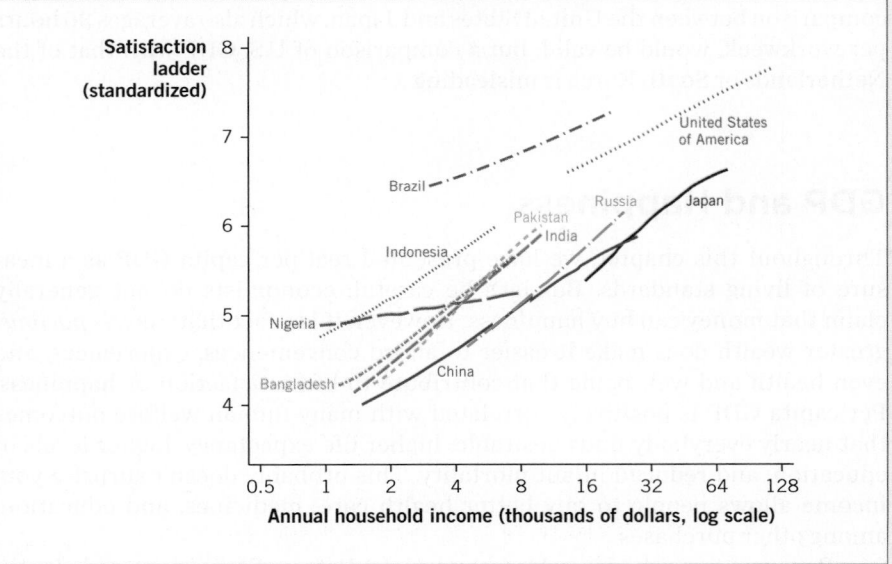

that percentage changes do matter: the data indicate that a doubling of income leads to about a 0.35 unit increase on the life satisfaction ladder.

2. WEALTHIER NATIONS REPORT GREATER LIFE SATISFACTION THAN POORER NATIONS.
Figure 19.12 plots the cross-country data. Each dot represents an individual nation, and the dots together tell a consistent story. First, this shows a clear positive relationship between life satisfaction and income around the globe. Second, there really is a lot of variation in happiness, even at a given income level. For example, compare Mexico and Bulgaria.

In conclusion, survey data from around the globe and across time indicate that increases in income lead to higher life satisfaction, or happiness. Money may not be able to buy happiness, but there is significant evidence that more income presents more opportunities to "pursue happiness."

Not counted in GDP: extra time to relax.

Why Do Economists Continue to Rely on GDP Data?

In addition to the production of goods and services, there are many other measurements that economists might use to determine a country's standard of living: life expectancy, educational levels, access to health care, crime rates, and so on. One problem with including these additional factors in GDP is that they are difficult to measure and rank. Moreover, the combined statistic that we would generate

FIGURE 19.12

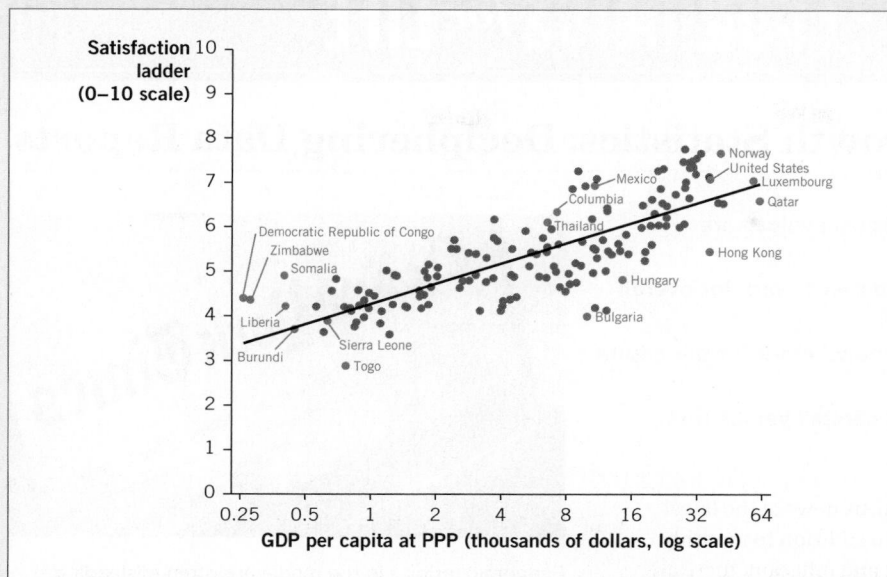

Life Satisfaction and Income around the Globe

Individuals in nations with higher income levels (GDP per capita) report greater happiness on the life satisfaction ladder.

Source: Betsey Stevenson and Justin Wolfers, "Subjective Well-Being and Income: Is There Any Evidence of Satiation?" NBER Working Paper 18992, April 2013.

would be even more challenging to understand. Therefore, we limit GDP to measuring economic production, knowing that it is not a perfect measure of well-being. In addition, GDP is actually correlated with many of the variables we care about, like a cleaner environment, better access to high-quality health care, more education, more leisure time, and lower crime rates.

PRACTICE WHAT YOU KNOW

Shortcomings of GDP Data: Use Caution in Interpreting GDP as an Economic Barometer

In many parts of the world, a significant amount of effort goes into nonmarket production in the household, such as stay-at-home parenting. For example, Zimbabwe has a very high rate of nonmarket household production. In contrast, Canada has a low rate of nonmarket household production.

QUESTION: How does the difference in nonmarket household production affect a comparison of GDP between Zimbabwe and Canada?

ANSWER: The GDP statistics for Zimbabwe are biased downward more than the statistics for Canada, since a larger portion of Zimbabwe's actual production goes unreported. While Zimbabwe is actually a poorer nation than Canada, official statistics exaggerate the difference slightly, making Zimbabwe seem poorer than it is.

Some nations have more stay-at-home parents than others. How does this affect GDP comparisons?

Economic Growth Statistics: Deciphering Data Reports

- Always check that long-run values are adjusted for inflation.
- Three percent is a nice benchmark for overall real GDP growth.
- Two percent is a nice benchmark for per capita GDP growth.
- Context dictates "per capita" versus total income usage.

Economic reports in the media are often misleading.

The media constantly bring us news of the latest economic developments. In addition to monthly reports on unemployment and inflation, there are monthly releases and revisions of GDP data for the United States and other nations. These updates often get a lot of attention. Unfortunately, media reports are not as careful with their economics terminology as we would like. Because they're not worded carefully, the reports can be misleading.

After learning about historical experiences with economic growth, you might find new interest in the economic growth reports that appear almost every month in the mainstream media. However, you must carefully evaluate the data they present. Now that you have perspective on growth statistics, you can determine for yourself whether economic news is positive or negative. For example, an article from the *New York Times* offers the following synopsis of economic growth in China for the previous quarter:

> China's economic output was 6.1 percent higher in the first quarter than a year earlier . . . China's annual growth rate appeared slow in the first quarter after the 6.8 percent rate in the fourth quarter of 2008, partly because it was being compared with the economy's formidable output in the first quarter of last year.[*]

[*]Keith Bradsher, "China's Economic Growth Slows in First Quarter," *New York Times,* April 16, 2009.

China's economy grew at over 6%, and yet this rate is described as "slow." By now, you know that 6% is an incredibly fast rate of growth.

Good economists are very careful with language, and certain terms have very specific meanings. For example, we know that "economic growth" always refers to changes in real *per capita* GDP, not simply GDP or real GDP. But economic reports in mainstream media outlets often blur this distinction. That is exactly the case with the report in the *New York Times* article just cited.

Even though the report's author uses the term "annual growth rate," additional research reveals that he is talking about real GDP growth, but not adjusting the data for population changes. This mistake is fairly common, so you should watch for it when you read economic growth reports. It turns out that the population growth rate in China was about 0.6% in 2009. This means that the growth rate of real per capita GDP in China was actually about 5.5%, which is still very impressive.

Conclusion

We began this chapter describing a changing U.S. economy, one increasing the production of services instead of goods. However, the tool we use to measure both is GDP, and GDP is a measure that works well. In the short run, it helps us recognize business cycles, including the ups of an expansion and the downs of a recession. GDP also serves as a reasonably good indicator of living standards around the globe and over time. Nations with better living conditions are also nations with higher GDP. Thus, even though it has some shortcomings, GDP is a sound indicator of the overall health of an economy.

In the next chapter, we look at another macroeconomic indicator—the unemployment rate. The unemployment rate and other job indicators give us an additional dimension on which to consider the health of an economy. ✳

· ANSWERING *the* BIG QUESTIONS ·

How is macroeconomics different from microeconomics?

- Microeconomics is the study of individuals and firms, but macroeconomics considers the entire economy.
- Many of the topics in both areas of study are the same; these topics include income, employment, and output. But the macro perspective is much broader than the micro perspective.

What does GDP tell us about the economy?

- GDP measures both output and income in a macroeconomy.
- It is a gauge of productivity and the overall level of wealth in an economy.
- We use GDP data to measure living standards, economic growth, and business cycle conditions.

How is GDP computed?

- GDP is the total market value of all final goods and services produced in an economy in a specific time period, usually a year.
- Economists typically compute GDP by adding four types of expenditures in the economy: consumption (C), investment (I), government spending (G), and net exports (NX). Net exports are total exports minus total imports.
- For many applications, it is also necessary to compute real GDP, adjusting GDP for changes in prices (inflation).

What are some shortcomings of GDP data?

- GDP data do not include the production of nonmarket goods, the underground economy, production effects on the environment, or the value placed on leisure time.

Concepts You Should Know

business cycle (p. 607)
consumption (p. 615)
economic contraction (p. 607)
economic expansion (p. 607)
economic growth (p. 606)
final goods (p. 612)
GDP deflator (p. 617)
government spending (p. 616)

Great Recession (p. 607)
gross domestic product (GDP)
(p. 604)
gross national product (GNP)
(p. 613)
inflation (p. 606)
intermediate goods (p. 612)
investment (p. 616)

net exports (p. 616)
nominal GDP (p. 617)
per capita GDP (p. 605)
price level (p. 617)
real GDP (p. 606)
recession (p. 607)
services (p. 611)

Questions for Review

1. Explain the relationship between output and income for both an individual and an entire economy.

2. What is the largest component (C, I, G, or NX) of GDP? Give an example of each component.

3. A farmer sells cotton to a clothing company for $1,000, and the clothing company turns the cotton into T-shirts that it sells to a store for a total of $2,000. How much did GDP increase as a result of these transactions?

4. A friend of yours is reading a financial blog and comes to you for some advice about GDP. She wants to know whether she should pay attention to nominal GDP or real GDP. Which one do you recommend, and why?

5. Is a larger GDP always better than a smaller GDP? Explain your answer with an example.

6. If Max receives an unemployment check, would we include that transfer payment from the government in this year's GDP? Why or why not?

7. Phil owns an old set of golf clubs that he purchased for $1,000 seven years ago. He decides to post them on Craigslist and quickly sells the clubs for $250. How does this sale affect GDP?

8. Real GDP for 2015 is less than nominal GDP for that year. But real GDP for 2000 is more than nominal GDP for that year. Why?

9. What are the four shortcomings with using GDP as a measure of well-being?

10. Economists Betsey Stevenson and Justin Wolfers have researched the relationship between GDP and happiness.

    a. Briefly summarize their two main findings (one or two sentences each).

    b. What two types of evidence (two different empirical tests) did Stevenson and Wolfers use to support their findings?

Study Problems (✳ solved at the end of the section)

1. A friend who knows of your interest in economics comes up to you after reading the latest GDP data and excitedly exclaims, "Did you see that nominal GDP rose from $19 trillion to $19.5 trillion?" What should you tell your friend about this news?

2. In the following situations, explain what is counted (or is not counted) in this year's GDP.

    a. You bought the latest PlayStation model at GameStop last year and resold it on eBay this year.

    b. You purchase a new copy of *Investing for Dummies* at Barnes & Noble.

    c. You purchase a historic home using the services of a real estate agent.

    d. You detail your car so it is spotless inside and out.

    e. You purchase a new hard drive for your old laptop.

    f. Your physical therapist receives $300 for physical therapy but reports only $100.

g. Apple buys 1,000 motherboards for use in making new computers.

h. Toyota produces 10,000 new Camrys that remain unsold at the end of the year.

3. To which component of GDP expenditure (C, I, G, or NX) does each of the following belong?

a. Swiss chocolates imported from Europe

b. a driver's license you receive from the Department of Motor Vehicles

c. a candle you buy at a local store

d. a new house

4. A mechanic builds an engine and then sells it to a customized body shop for $7,000. The body shop installs the engine in a car and sells the car to a dealer for $20,000. The dealer then sells the finished vehicle for $35,000. A consumer drives off with the car. By how much does GDP increase? What is the value added at each step of the production process? How does the total value added compare with the amount by which GDP increased?

5. In this chapter, we used nominal GDP data from Table 19.5 to compute 2018 GDP in 2012 dollars. Using the same steps, use the data from Table 19.5 to compute 2017 GDP in 2012 dollars.

6. Many goods and services are illegally sold or legally sold but not reported to the government. How would increased efforts to count those goods and services affect GDP data?

7. Leisure time is not included in GDP, but what would happen if it was included? Would high-work countries like South Korea fare better in international comparisons of well-being, or worse?

✳ **8.** Fill in the missing data in the following table.

Year	Nominal GDP (thousands of $)	Real GDP (thousands of $)	GDP Deflator
2013	$100	_____	100.0
2014	_____	$110	108.0
2015	130	117	_____
2016	150	_____	120.0
2017	_____	136	125.0

✳ **9.** Consider an economy that only produces two goods: strawberries and cream. Use the following table to compute nominal GDP, real GDP, and the GDP deflator for each year. (Year 2015 is the base year.)

Year	Price of strawberries (per pint)	Quantity of strawberries (pints)	Price of cream (per pint)	Quantity of cream (pints)
2015	$3.00	100	$2.00	200
2016	4.00	125	2.50	400
2017	5.00	150	3.00	500

✳ **10.** The following table presents GDP data for an imaginary economy.

a. Fill in the blanks.

Year	Nominal GDP (in billions)	GDP Deflator (2010 = base year)	Real GDP (billions of 2010 dollars)
1970	$500	20	_____
1980	1,000	25	_____
1990	3,000	_____	$6,000
2000	_____	80	7,500
2010	_____	100	9,000

b. Compute both nominal and real GDP growth from the end of 1970 to the end of 1980. Note that your result is not an annual growth rate; it is the total growth over the entire decade.

11. Determine whether the following are final or intermediate goods:

a. a gallon of milk purchased by you at the supermarket

b. a gallon of milk purchased by Starbucks for their cappuccinos

c. a computer bought by you to surf the internet

d. a computer bought by your college for use in the library

e. a tractor bought by your local county government to mow grass

f. a tractor bought by farmer Glenn to plow his cornfields

g. corn seed used by farmer Glenn to grow corn

12. GDP per capita is a helpful indicator of living standards across nations. But there are short-comings in GDP calculations. In the following examples, determine in which direction, if any, measured GDP will incorrectly estimate the living standards of that country.

a. In India, a greater portion of workers produce nonmarket output. All else equal, this can cause India's measured GDP to _____ its living standards.

b. In China, the air pollution is much greater. All else equal, this can cause China's measured GDP to _____ its living standards.

c. In Greece, many transactions occur in the underground economy—more than in the United States, for example. All else equal, this can cause Greece's measured GDP to _____ its living standards.

d. In France, the average work week is shorter than that in the U.S. All else equal, this can cause France's measured GDP to _____ its living standards.

13. The GDP data in the following table are all end-of-year data for Spain.

a. Fill in the blanks in the table.

	GDP (in millions of current Euros)	GDP (in millions of constant 2010 Euros)	GDP Deflator
2014	$266,227	_____	100.8
2015	275,418	$273,372	_____
2016	_____	281,610	101.6

b. What was the rate of real GDP growth for Spain in 2016?

c. What was the rate of inflation in Spain in 2016?

Solved Problems

8.

Year	Nominal GDP (thousands of $)	Real GDP (thousands of $)	GDP Deflator
2013	$100	$100	100.0
2014	118.8	110	108.0
2015	130	117	111.1
2016	150	125	120.0
2017	170	136	125.0

To solve for the missing data, use the following equation (and 2013 as the base year):

$$\text{real GDP}_{\text{year}} = \frac{\text{nominal GDP}_{\text{year}}}{\text{price level}_{\text{year}}} \times \text{base year price level}$$

For 2013: real GDP$_{2013}$ = ($100 ÷ 100.0)
× 100.0 = $100

For 2014: $110,000 = (nominal GDP$_{2014}$
÷ 108.0) × 100.0

nominal GDP$_{2014}$ = ($110 ÷ 100.0)
× 108.0 = $118.8

For 2015: $117,000 = ($130,000 ÷ GDP
deflator$_{2015}$) × 100.0

GDP deflator$_{2015}$ = ($130 ÷ $117)
× 100.0

GDP deflator$_{2015}$ = 111.1

For 2016: real GDP$_{2016}$ = ($150,000 ÷ 120.0)
× 100.0

real GDP$_{2016}$ = $125

For 2017: $136,000 = (nominal GDP$_{2017}$ ÷ 125.0)
× 100.0

nominal GDP$_{2017}$ = ($136,000 ÷ 100.0)
× 125.0

nominal GDP$_{2017}$ = $170,000

9.

Year	Nominal GDP	Real GDP	GDP Deflator
2015	$700	$700	100.0
2016	1,500	1,175	127.7
2017	2,250	1,450	155.2

First, let's calculate nominal GDP for each of the three years by adding up the market values of the strawberries and cream produced during that year.

For 2015: nominal GDP$_{2015}$ = ($3.00 $\times$ 100) + ($2.00 $\times$ 200) = $700

For 2016: nominal GDP$_{2016}$ = ($4.00 $\times$ 125) + ($2.50 $\times$ 400) = $1,500

For 2017: nominal GDP$_{2017}$ = ($5.00 $\times$ 150) + ($3.00 $\times$ 500) = $2,250

Now, let's calculate real GDP in 2015 dollars by multiplying the quantities produced in each year by the 2015 prices.

For 2015: real GDP$_{2015}$ = ($3.00 $\times$ 100) + ($2.00 $\times$ 200) = $700

For 2016: real GDP$_{2016}$ = ($3.00 $\times$ 125) + ($2.00 $\times$ 400) = $1,175

For 2017: real GDP$_{2017}$ = ($3.00 $\times$ 150) + ($2.00 $\times$ 500) = $1,450

Finally, using the nominal GDP and real GDP numbers we calculated above, let's calculate the GDP deflator by using the following formula:

$$\text{GDP deflator}_{year} = \frac{\text{nominal GDP}_{year}}{\text{real GDP}_{year}} \times 100.0$$

GDP deflator$_{2015}$ = 100.0. Since 2015 is given as the base year, the GDP deflator must be 100.0.

For 2016: GDP deflator$_{2016}$ = ($1,500 $\div$ $1,175) $\times$ 100 = 127.7

For 2017: GDP deflator$_{2017}$ = ($2,250 $\div$ $1,450) $\times$ 100 = 155.2

10.a. Recall Equation 19.3:

$$\text{real GDP}_t = \frac{\text{nominal GDP}_t}{\text{price level}_t} \times 100$$

Year	Nominal GDP (in billions)	GDP Deflator (2010 = base year)	Real GDP (billions of 2010 dollars)
1970	$500	20	$2,500
1980	1,000	25	4,000
1990	3,000	50	6,000
2000	6,000	80	7,500
2010	9,000	100	9,000

Since we know that the GDP deflator is used as the price level, for 1970 we use Equation 19.3 to solve for real GDP:

real GDP$_{1970}$ = ($500/20) $\times$ 100 = $2,500

For 1980, we use Equation 19.3 to solve for real GDP:

real GDP$_{1980}$ = ($1,000/25) $\times$ 100 = $4,000

For 1990, we use Equation 19.3 to solve for the GDP deflator:

$6,000 = ($3,000/price level$_t$) $\times$ 100 = 50

For 2000, we use Equation 19.3 to solve for nominal GDP:

$7,500 = (nominal GDP$_t$/80) $\times$ 100 = $6000

For 2010, we know that nominal GDP is equal to real GDP because this is the base year.

b. nominal GDP growth = (nominal GDP in 1980 – nominal GDP in 1970)/ nominal GDP in 1970 = ($1,000 – $500)/$500 = 1.0 = 100%

real GDP growth = (real GDP in 1980 – real GDP in 1970)/ real GDP in 1970 = ($4,000 – $2,500)/$2,500 = $1,500/$2,500 = 3/5 = 60%

Unemployment

Even Dynamic, Growing Economies Grapple with Unemployment.

The world economy is changing. Some industries are bursting with new job opportunities. Others are shrinking. In the United States, the coal industry continues its century-long decline. In 1923, there were 863,000 coal miners in the United States. By 2018, the number was down by more than 90%, to just 83,000.

The decline in U.S. coal has multiple causes. New exploration and extraction techniques make oil and natural gas cheap alternatives for fueling factories and electric power plants. Wind and solar energy are now major players in the energy market, especially in the Western U.S. Meanwhile, the costs of complying with tightening environmental regulations make it harder for coal plants to operate profitably. Year after year, thousands of laid-off miners have had to look for jobs elsewhere. Miners too old to learn a new trade retire early. Young people who might have gone into mining are turning elsewhere.

But while this is painful for the mining industry, it is normal for specific industries to rise and fall even when the overall economy is progressing. On the whole, the U.S. economy is much better off than it was in 1923: real GDP is now approximately twenty times larger and total

These Colorado coal miners do a very tough job. But they know, as well as anyone, that their industry is on a downward slide. Most economists forecast that the decline of the last 100 years will continue. This is happening even as the overall U.S. economy continues to expand.

employment has grown from about 30 million jobs to more than 150 million. Furthermore, coal is not alone. It is normal for industries to rise and fall over time as economies grow and evolve. The U.S. apparel industry has gone through changes that parallel coal's. These days, automation technology is disrupting even white-collar professions like medicine and law. This textbook, in fact, illustrates the point: books like this were once typeset by hand in the United States, but now they are typeset digitally, and very often overseas. The fact is, industrial churn is normal in a dynamic, growing economy. This churn is one reason why we always have some unemployed workers, even when the economy is growing.

Of course, not all unemployment is caused by economic progress. Much unemployment is caused by economic declines, such as the Great Recession described in Chapter 19. Both normal "churn" unemployment and cyclical, recession-caused unemployment are examined in this chapter.

After GDP, the unemployment rate is the second most important indicator of economic health. In this chapter, we examine the causes of unemployment and explain how it is measured. By looking at some historical data in context, we will begin to understand when unemployment is a matter of concern.

· BIG QUESTIONS ·

- What are the major reasons for unemployment?
- What can we learn from the employment data?

What Are the Major Reasons for Unemployment?

Perhaps you know someone who has lost his or her job. Losing a job is particularly difficult when you are unable to transition easily to another one. After all, many of us depend on our jobs just to survive. Being willing and able to work, but unable to find a job—there are few greater frustrations. **Unemployment** occurs when a worker who is not currently employed is searching for a job without success.

People leave their jobs for many reasons. Some do so voluntarily: they may return to school, take another job, or decide to leave the workforce to care for their children. Others lose a job they wish to keep: an employee might be fired for poor performance or let go because a company is downsizing. When macroeconomists consider unemployment, they explicitly look at workers who seek employment but are unable to secure it. We use the unemployment rate to monitor the level of unemployment in an economy. The **unemployment rate** (u) is the percentage of the labor force that is unemployed. Figure 20.1 plots the U.S. unemployment rate from 1970 to 2018. This graph is one way of quickly measuring national economic frustration. As the unemployment rate climbs, people are more likely to be disappointed in their pursuit of a job. The shaded regions are periods of recession; notice how the unemployment rate spikes during those periods.

Economists distinguish three types of unemployment: structural, frictional, and cyclical. You can think of each type as deriving from a different source. As it turns out, structural and frictional unemployment occur even when the economy is healthy and growing. For this reason, they are often called *natural unemployment*. We consider these first.

Unemployment occurs when a worker who is not currently employed is searching for a job without success.

The **unemployment rate** is the percentage of the labor force that is unemployed.

FIGURE 20.1

U.S. Unemployment Rate, 1970–2018

The unemployment rate is an important indicator of the economy's health. Since 1970, the average unemployment rate in the United States has been about 6%.

Source: U.S. Bureau of Labor Statistics.

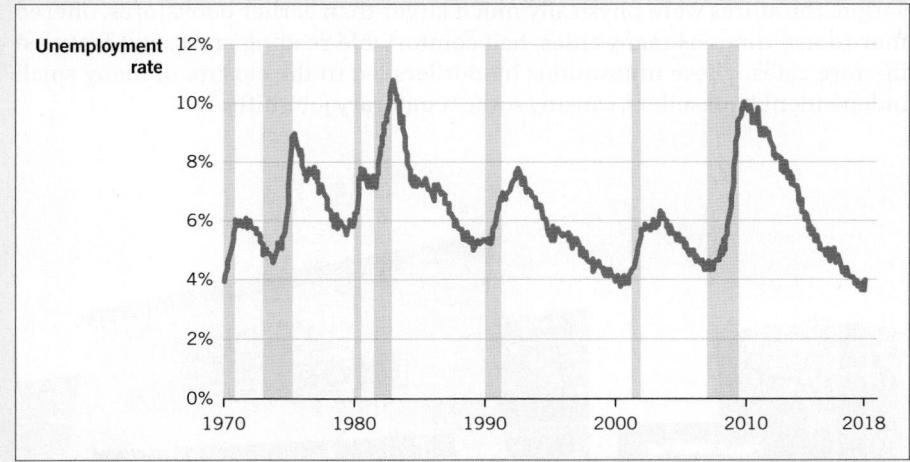

Structural Unemployment

Unemployment is a burden on households and on the whole economy: resources are wasted when idle workers sit on the sidelines. However, a dynamic growing economy is one that adapts and changes. No one would consider it an improvement to return to the economy of early America, where 90% of Americans toiled at manual farmwork and earned subsistence wages that just barely covered the cost of food and shelter. The transformation to our modern economy has brought new jobs but also requires different skills. This makes some jobs obsolete, which inevitably leads to some unemployment, even if just temporarily. And herein lies the dilemma: dynamic growing economies are also evolving economies. If we want an economy that adapts to changes in consumer demands and technology, we must accept some unemployment, at least temporarily, as a by-product of the growth.

Consider that in the past we produced no computers, cell phones, or polio vaccines, and the invention of these products led to great job creation. Improving technologies in these fields enabled us to produce more and better output with fewer resources or fewer employees. Over time, we also produced less of some other things—such as black and white televisions, cassette tapes, and typewriters. These structural changes left some workers unemployed.

CREATIVE DESTRUCTION As new industries are created, some old ones are destroyed. The economist Joseph Schumpeter coined the term *creative destruction* to describe this process of economic evolution. **Creative destruction** occurs when the introduction of new products and technologies leads to the end of other industries and jobs. As some jobs become obsolete, the result is **structural unemployment**, which is caused by changes in the industrial makeup (structure) of the economy. Although structural unemployment can cause transitional problems, it is often a sign of a healthy, growing economy.

The retail book market provides a good example. In the 1980s and 1990s, the Borders book retailer grew from a small Ann Arbor, Michigan, bookseller to a national chain with 1,249 total locations. Borders' success came from innovation: the stores were physically much larger than earlier bookstores, offered four to five times as many titles, had comfortable reading areas, and featured in-store cafés. These innovations by Borders led to the closure of many small independent booksellers, causing some temporary job shifts.

Creative destruction occurs when the introduction of new products and technologies leads to the end of other industries and jobs.

Structural unemployment is unemployment caused by changes in the industrial makeup (structure) of the economy.

Creative destruction in the retail book market means that when new products and jobs are created (like ebook readers), other jobs (like those in physical retail locations) are destroyed.

But innovations in the book market didn't end in the 1990s. The following decade saw greater competition from online booksellers like Amazon.com and the introduction of e-readers like the Kindle, Nook, and iPad. These changes led to the decline of Borders, which had 19,000 employees when it declared bankruptcy in 2011. At that point, Borders's employees found themselves structurally unemployed: they lost their jobs as a result of market innovations.

But this same phenomenon is occurring across the entire macroeconomy. In 2017, real GDP in the United States increased by 2.3%, unemployment rates were low, and 1.8 million new jobs were created overall. Yet even then, there were more than 63 million job separations (workers who quit or were laid off). In a dynamic economy, job turnover is normal.

AN EVOLVING ECONOMY Our evolving economy has led to drastic changes in the type of work Americans do, especially over the long run. Figure 20.2 shows how jobs in the United States have evolved over the past two centuries. In 1800, over 90% of Americans worked in agriculture, either as farmers or as farm laborers. A century later, in 1900, only about half of U.S. workers were employed in farming. The rest were split between manufacturing jobs and service-related jobs. In 1900, manufacturing jobs may have been in railroad or steel production, while service jobs included teaching and accounting. Today, five out of six American workers are employed in service-related jobs. Since 1979, U.S. manufacturing employment has fallen from almost 20 million jobs

FIGURE 20.2

The Evolution of Jobs in the United States

Over the past two centuries, jobs in the United States have evolved from being primarily agricultural to industrial (manufacturing) and then to service.

Source: Federal Reserve Bank of Dallas.

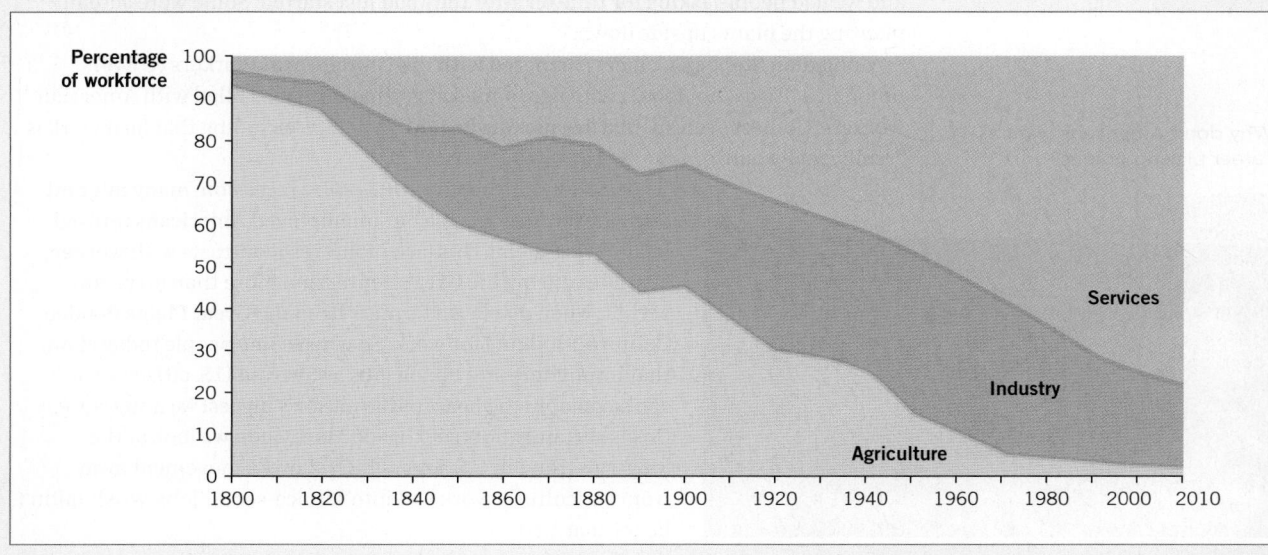

to less than 13 million. Over the same period, employment in service industries has risen from 65 million jobs to nearly 130 million. While we have long had teachers and accountants, there are many new service jobs in fields such as engineering, finance, transportation, health, and government.

The trends presented in Figure 20.2 illustrate creative destruction: the structure of the economy evolves, and this leads to different types of jobs. This long view presents the most positive angle on this process. After all, most of us would prefer working at modern jobs rather than toiling with simple farm tools in a field all day. But along the way, as jobs shift, some temporary structural unemployment inevitably occurs.

While structural unemployment can't be eliminated, it can be reduced in a number of ways. Workers must often retrain, relocate, or change their expectations in some way before they can work elsewhere. Lumberjacks might become computer repair specialists, or autoworkers may need to relocate from Michigan to Kentucky. Government can also enact policies to alleviate the pain of structural unemployment, such as by establishing job training programs and relocation subsidies (paying part of workers' moving costs).

ECONOMICS IN THE REAL WORLD

MOST AMERICANS DON'T WANT FARMWORK

In September 2010, Garance Burke, of the Associated Press (AP), wrote an article about the frustration of U.S. farmers trying to find American workers to harvest fruit and vegetables. Even though the unemployment rate at the time was very high, Americans did not apply for available farm jobs. Burke noted that the few Americans who do take such jobs usually don't stay in the fields for long. The AP analysis showed that from January to June 2010, California farmers advertised 1,160 jobs available to U.S. citizens and legal residents, yet only 36 people were hired. One farmer named Steve Fortin noted problems with American workers: "we saw absentee problems, and we had people asking for time off after they had just started. Some were actually planting the plants upside down."

Comedian Stephen Colbert partnered with the United Farm Workers (UFW) union in a "Take Our Jobs" campaign, aimed at getting farm jobs filled with American workers. Colbert even spent a day picking beans in a field, concluding that farmwork is "really, really hard."

Why don't Americans want a career picking grapes?

Ironically, during the 2007–2009 recession, many migrant farm jobs were available but unemployed Americans refused to apply for them. This lack of interest contrasts with worker attitudes during the Great Depression more than 80 years earlier, when displaced farmers from the Great Plains flooded California looking for work. So when some people today claim that immigrants are taking jobs away from U.S. citizens, we can say that in the heart of the nation's biggest farming state, this is certainly not true. In addition, when we look at the long-run trend in U.S. jobs, which shows a movement away from agricultural work and into service-sector jobs, we shouldn't be too alarmed.

Structural Unemployment

THE OFFICE

In the TV show *The Office*, Angela, Kevin, and Oscar are accountants at the Scranton branch office of Dunder-Mifflin, a paper company. In one episode, a representative from the corporate office (which oversees all branches) unveils a new accounting system. Ryan, from corporate, explains to Angela, Kevin, and Oscar that the new system automates most of the billing process, so that when a customer places an order, it gets emailed to the warehouse and a copy goes directly to the customer's in-box.

Angela then asks, "How do we bill them?" and Ryan responds, "You don't. The invoicing, account reconciliation, and all the follow-up claims just go right to your BlackBerry." At this point, Oscar says, "So what do the accountants do?" Ryan responds, "Well, unless there is a real problem client, nothing."

Angela and Oscar immediately understand that their jobs are becoming obsolete. But Kevin still doesn't understand. So after Ryan has left the room, he crows, "This is the greatest thing that has ever happened to us!" Angela responds, "No, it's not." Kevin still doesn't get it, jumping in with, "Are you kidding me?" Oscar then delivers the bad news: "It was already a stretch that they needed three of us. Now they don't even need one."

In this story, Angela, Oscar, and Kevin are seeing the effects of structural unemployment, as

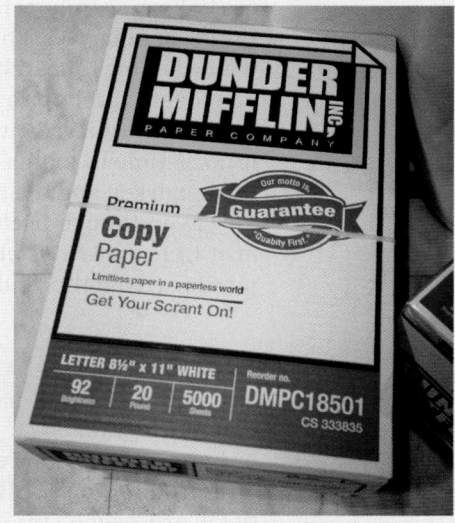

Is technical progress always good news?

technological advances are making their jobs redundant. This is true in the short run because less labor is needed to complete the billing process. However, the structural unemployment that is about to occur is a by-product of a dynamic and growing economy, and most economists would assume that with possibly some additional retraining they will find work elsewhere.

Frictional Unemployment

Even when jobs are available and qualified employees live nearby, it takes time for workers and employers to find one another and agree to terms. **Frictional unemployment** is caused by delays in matching available jobs and workers. Frictional unemployment is another type of natural unemployment: no matter how healthy the economy, there is always some frictional unemployment.

Consider how a successful new product launch at McDonald's affects Burger King. Suppose McDonald's introduces a new product called the "Quadstack," which is really just four Quarter Pounders stacked on top of one another. Now imagine that customers can't get enough of the new sandwich. Because

Frictional unemployment is unemployment caused by delays in matching available jobs and workers.

Searching for a job has never been easier.

of the spike in business, McDonald's needs to hire more employees. At the same time, Burger King loses customers to McDonald's and decides to lay off some workers. Of course, the laid-off Burger King workers will take some time searching for new jobs. And McDonald's will take time deciding how many new workers it needs and which applicants to hire. Because some workers are unemployed during this transition, frictional unemployment results.

Frictional unemployment occurs even in the healthiest economy. Because we live in a world of imperfect information, there are incentives for employees to keep searching for the perfect job and for employers to search longer for the best employees. For example, as you approach graduation from college, you will take time to search for a job and determine which offer to accept. Similarly, employers rarely hire the first applicant they see, even though it is costly to leave a position vacant. Even if there is a perfect job available for every worker, it takes time to match workers and jobs. These time lags create friction in the labor market, and the result is frictional unemployment.

Even though frictional unemployment is natural, its level can rise or fall over time. Let's look at two factors that affect frictional unemployment: information availability and government policies.

INFORMATION AVAILABILITY Any factors that shorten job searches also decrease frictional unemployment. The Internet is a dramatic example: imagine looking for a job without it. You'd read newspaper ads, make dozens or hundreds of phone calls, and make several in-person visits to employers. Yet after all that, you'd still have a great deal of uncertainty about your complete set of job prospects. This was the reality for job searchers as recently as the 1990s.

Today, much of your job search is conducted online. If you are looking for an accounting job, you might search for a job at Indeed.com. In 2018 a nationwide search for accounting job opportunities for CPAs yielded over 38,000 potential matches. Even narrowing this search to, say, the state of Virginia nets 1,300 potential jobs. The point is that the vast pool of information available through the Internet enables workers and companies to find one another more quickly and to make better matches with substantially lower costs. The result is lower frictional unemployment.

GOVERNMENT POLICIES Any factors that lengthen the job search process increase frictional unemployment. These factors include government policies, such as unemployment compensation, and regulations related to the hiring and firing of employees.

Unemployment Insurance and Incentives To reduce the hardship of joblessness, government-provided **unemployment insurance**, also known as *federal jobless benefits*, guarantees that unemployed workers receive a percentage of their former income while unemployed. Governments provide unemployment insurance for many reasons. The benefit cushions the economic consequences of being laid off, and it provides workers time to search for new employment. In addition, unemployment insurance can help contain macroeconomic problems before they spread to other industries. Consider what happens if the auto industry is struggling and workers are laid off: the unemployed autoworkers are no longer able to pay for goods and services they used to buy, and the reduction

Unemployment insurance, also known as federal jobless benefits, is a government program that reduces the hardship of joblessness by guaranteeing that unemployed workers receive a percentage of their former income while unemployed.

in their overall spending hurts other industries. For example, if unemployed workers can't pay their mortgages, lenders will suffer and the downturn will spread to the financial industry. Viewed in this way, unemployment insurance serves to reduce the severity of the overall economic contraction.

However, unemployment insurance creates unintended consequences. For one thing, receiving the cushion of unemployment benefits makes some less inclined to search for and take a job. These workers spend more time unemployed when they have insurance; without unemployment insurance, they have a greater incentive to seek immediate employment. For example, in late 2007, the U.S. economy entered the Great Recession, which ended in mid-2009. But several years after GDP growth resumed and the recession was declared over, the level of unemployment remained high. Why? One reason might be the frictional unemployment that occurred from extensions to unemployment insurance benefits. In particular, the federal government offered extensions of up to 47 weeks after state benefits ran out. These extensions meant that many places offered benefits of up to 99 weeks—nearly two years. While it certainly seems appropriate to help the jobless during recessions, this policy likely created an incentive to search longer for a new job, which in turn contributed to frictional unemployment.

Incentives

Regulations on Hiring and Firing Government regulations on hiring and firing also contribute to frictional unemployment. Regulations on hiring include restrictions on who can and must be interviewed, paperwork that employers must complete for new hires, and additional tax documents that must be filed for new employees. Regulations on firing include mandatory severance pay, written justification, and government fines. While these regulations may be instituted to help workers by giving them greater job security, they have unintended consequences. When it is difficult to hire employees, firms take longer to do so, which increases frictional unemployment. When it is difficult to fire employees, firms take greater care in hiring them. Again, the longer search time increases frictional unemployment.

ECONOMICS IN THE REAL WORLD

EMPLOYMENT, SPANISH STYLE

Relative to most other nations, the United States has relatively few labor market regulations. However, many European nations have especially stringent regulations. Consider Spain, where mandated severance pay is particularly generous. Until 2012, any Spanish firm that wished to fire a worker was required to pay that worker for 45 days for every year the worker had been employed with the company. Thus, if a firm wanted to fire a 10-year employee, it had to pay that person for 450 days after his or her employment ended. (In 2012, the required severance pay was reduced to 20 days of pay for every year of employment.) This regulation makes it very difficult for young workers to break into the labor force. In fact, unemployment rates for workers aged 24 and younger were over 30% in 2018! These regulations also incentivize firms to search longer for the right workers to fill open positions, thereby increasing frictional unemployment. Another regulation seen in Spain is mandated annual increases in wages and benefits. That is, firms are required by law to give pay and benefits raises every year. Think about this regulation as if you were the manager of a Spanish business firm: before you ever hire and retain a worker for more

FIGURE 20.3

Unemployment Rate in the United States and Spain, 2000–2018

From 2000 to 2018, the unemployment rate in Spain was much higher than the unemployment rate in the United States. This difference is largely a result of Spanish labor-market regulations, many of which were put in place to help workers. But the reality is that these regulations increase frictional unemployment.

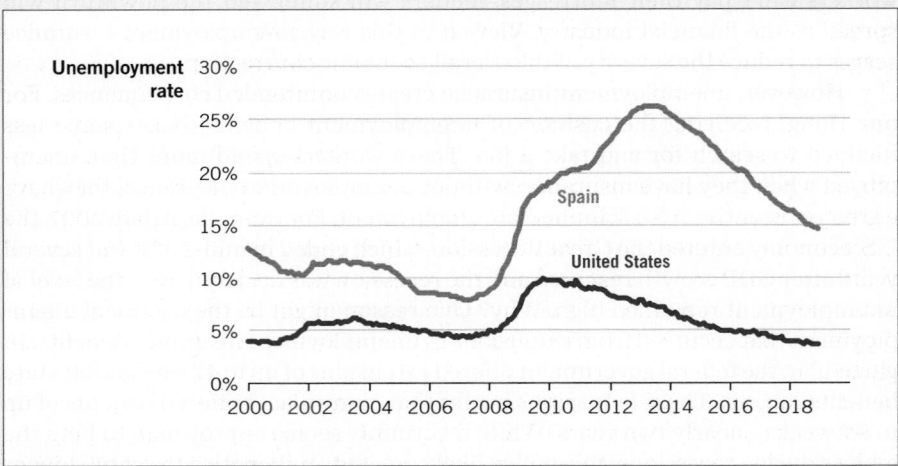

Incentives

than a year, you will want to make sure that this individual is worthy of the current pay plus raises. Like mandatory severance pay, this regulation increases the time firms spend searching for just the right match, again increasing frictional unemployment. Figure 20.3 plots the unemployment rates for Spain and the United States from 2000 to 2018. Notice how much higher the Spanish unemployment rate is. Even in 2017, when the Spanish economy was growing briskly, the unemployment rate remained above 15%. Much of this unemployment is due to frictional unemployment caused by labor market regulations. These regulations were put in place to help workers, but economics tells us that incentives affect behavior, and these regulations change firms' hiring incentives.

Cyclical unemployment is unemployment caused by economic downturns.

During the Great Depression, almost all unemployment was cyclical.

Cyclical Unemployment

The third type of unemployment, **cyclical unemployment**, is caused by recessions, or economic downturns. This type of unemployment generates the greatest concern among economists and policymakers. It is the most serious type of unemployment because it means that jobs are not available for many people who want to work. And while both structural and frictional unemployment are consistent with a growing, evolving economy, the root cause of cyclical unemployment is an unhealthy economy. Referring back to Figure 20.1, notice the spikes in unemployment during recessions. Those spikes are cyclical unemployment. Unlike structural unemployment and frictional unemployment, cyclical unemployment is not considered a natural type of unemployment.

No one knows how long a general macroeconomic downturn might last. Fortunately, many recent recessions in the United States have been fairly short. However, the Great Recession of 2007–2009 lasted for 19 months and led to more cyclical unemployment than at any time in the previous 30 years.

The Natural Rate of Unemployment

We have seen that there are three types of unemployment: structural, frictional, and cyclical. Figure 20.4 illustrates the relationship between these types of unemployment during both recessionary and healthy economic conditions. Notice that structural and frictional unemployment are always present, even when the economy is healthy and growing. During these healthy periods, cyclical unemployment disappears. During recessionary periods, cyclical unemployment emerges. It is also possible for structural and frictional unemployment to increase in economic slowdowns. Structural unemployment might increase if the slowdown leads to changes in the structure of the economy: some jobs or industries may shrink permanently. Frictional unemployment might increase if government policies or other factors increase the job search time for unemployed workers.

Due to natural unemployment from structural and frictional factors, zero unemployment is not attainable. If policymakers consistently strive for zero unemployment, they may take actions that harm the economy. For example, in the 1970s, policymakers tried to push unemployment down past natural levels by putting more and more money into the economy. This strategy led to other complications like inflation, but it failed to reduce unemployment.

Given that some unemployment is natural, it is helpful to identify the normal or expected level. The **natural rate of unemployment** (u^*) is the typical unemployment rate that occurs when the economy is growing normally. Maintaining this natural rate is a more appropriate goal for policymakers. Economists never know the exact numerical value of the natural rate, in part because it changes over time. Currently, most economists feel that the natural rate of unemployment in the United States is between 4 and 5%.

As Table 20.1 summarizes, the actual unemployment rate at any particular time can equal, exceed, or fall below the economy's natural rate of unemployment. Let's think about each of these scenarios in turn. When the economy is healthy, the unemployment rate is equal to its natural rate (no cyclical unemployment exists). When the unemployment rate is equal to the natural rate, the

The **natural rate of unemployment** is the typical unemployment rate that occurs when the economy is growing normally.

FIGURE 20.4

Three Types of Unemployment

Even during healthy economic periods, both structural and frictional unemployment are present. During recessions, cyclical unemployment appears. At the same time, structural and frictional unemployment may grow. As a result, the natural rate of unemployment increases.

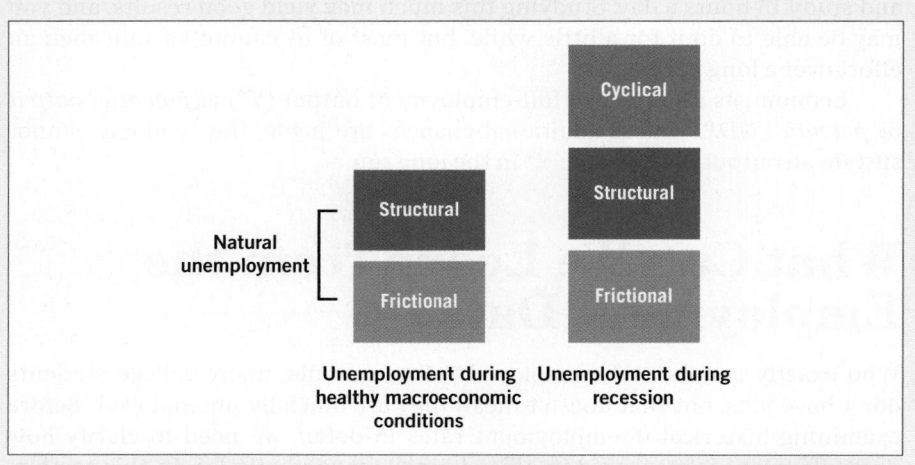

TABLE 20.1

The Natural Rate of Unemployment and Full-Employment Output

	Healthy economy	Recession	Exceptional expansion
Where is the unemployment rate (u) relative to the natural rate of unemployment (u*)?	$u = u^*$	$u > u^*$	$u < u^*$
Where is economic output (Y) relative to full-employment output (Y*)?	$Y = Y^*$	$Y < Y^*$	$Y > Y^*$
What is the level of cyclical unemployment?	Cyclical unemployment is zero.	Cyclical unemployment is positive.	Cyclical unemployment is negative.

Full-employment output, also called potential output or potential GDP, is the economy's output level when the unemployment rate is equal to the natural rate.

output level produced in the economy is called **full-employment output** (Y*). Recall from Chapter 19 that we measure economic output with real GDP (for the rest of the book, our shorthand notation is this: real GDP = Y). When the economy is in recession, cyclical unemployment materializes and the unemployment rate rises above the natural rate (u > u*). At that point, we say the economy is producing at less than full-employment output levels (Y < Y*).

It is possible for the actual unemployment rate to fall below the natural rate (u < u*). This can happen temporarily when the economy is expanding beyond its long-run capabilities. What conditions might bring about a lower-than-natural unemployment rate? Demand for output might be so high that firms keep their factories open for an extra shift and pay their workers overtime. When output is at greater-than-full-employment output (Y > Y*) and the unemployment rate is less than the natural rate (u < u*), resources are being employed at levels that are not sustainable in the long run. To visualize this situation, consider your own productivity as deadlines approach. Perhaps you have several exams in one week, so you decide to set aside most other activities and study 15 hours a day. Studying this much may yield good results, and you may be able to do it for a little while, but most of us cannot sustain such an effort over a long period.

Economists also refer to full-employment output (Y*) as *potential output* or *potential GDP*. Unless additional changes are made, the economy cannot sustain an output greater than Y* in the long run.

What Can We Learn from the Employment Data?

Who exactly counts as "unemployed"? For example, many college students don't have jobs, but that doesn't mean they are officially unemployed. Before examining historical unemployment rates in detail, we need to clarify how unemployment is measured in official employment statistics. In this section, we also look at some challenges of measuring unemployment.

Three Types of Unemployment: Which Type Is It?

QUESTION: In each of the following situations, decide whether the unemployment that occurs is a result of cyclical, frictional, or structural changes. Explain your responses.

a. Workers in a high-end restaurant are laid off when the establishment experiences a decline in demand during a recession.

b. Two hundred automobile workers lose their jobs as a result of a permanent reduction in the demand for automobiles.

c. A new college graduate takes three months to find his first job.

How long will you search for work?

ANSWERS:

a. *Cyclical changes.* Short-run fluctuations in the demand for workers often result from the ebb and flow of the business cycle. When the economy picks up, the laid-off workers may be rehired.

b. *Structural changes.* Since the changes described here are long-run in nature, these workers cannot expect their old jobs to return. Therefore, they must engage in retraining to reenter the labor force. Because they will be unable to find work until the retraining process is complete, the lost jobs represent a fundamental shift in the demand for labor.

c. *Frictional changes.* The recent college graduate has skills that the economy values, but finding an employer still takes time. This short-run job search process is a perfectly natural part of finding a job.

CHALLENGE QUESTION: A recently laid-off paralegal sees on the evening news that the unemployment rate stands at 3.8%. What category of economic change is *unlikely* to be the cause of the paralegal's unemployed status?

ANSWER: The paralegal's job loss is unlikely to be due to cyclical changes, because these occur during economic slowdowns. With the unemployment rate slightly below the natural level of 4% to 5%, the economy is clearly not in a slowdown.

The Unemployment Rate

Earlier in this chapter, we defined the unemployment rate (u) as the percentage of the labor force that is unemployed. We measure the unemployment rate as follows:

$$\text{unemployment rate} = u = \frac{\text{number unemployed}}{\text{labor force}} \times 100$$

(EQUATION 20.1)

Let's look at this definition more closely. To be officially unemployed, a person must be part of the labor force. A member of the **labor force** is defined as someone who is already employed or actively seeking work.

The **labor force** includes people who are already employed or actively seeking work and are part of the work-eligible population.

If a jobless person has not sought a job in four weeks, that person is not counted in the labor force. In addition, only *work-eligible* people are counted. People who are institutionalized, children under the age of 16, and military workers are not considered in the official work-eligible population. Thus, some of the large groups of people not in the labor force are retirees, stay-at-home parents, people in jail, military personnel, children under age 16, and many full-time students. Together, these groups account for just under 25% of the U.S. population. Thus, only three in four Americans are work-eligible.

Figure 20.5 provides a breakdown of the work-eligible population (256,780,000) at the very end of 2018. Approximately two-thirds of this population was in the labor force (161,123,000), and of this number, 6,641,000 were unemployed. Plugging these numbers into Equation 20.1 yields

$$u = \frac{6{,}641{,}000}{161{,}123{,}000} = 4.1\%$$

HISTORICAL UNEMPLOYMENT RATES We now turn to historical data. One of our goals is to give you a good sense of normal conditions. It's also helpful to examine periods when particularly high unemployment rates prevailed. In Chapter 26, we discuss possible reasons for these difficult periods.

Figure 20.6 shows the U.S. unemployment rate from 1970 to 2018, with the blue vertical bars representing periods of recession. Notice how the U.S.

FIGURE 20.5

Unemployment in the United States, December 2018

To compute the unemployment rate, we divide the work-eligible population between those who are in the labor force and those who are not. To be counted in the labor force, a person must either have a job or be actively seeking work. The unemployment rate is the percentage of the labor force that is unemployed.

Source: U.S. Bureau of Labor Statistics.

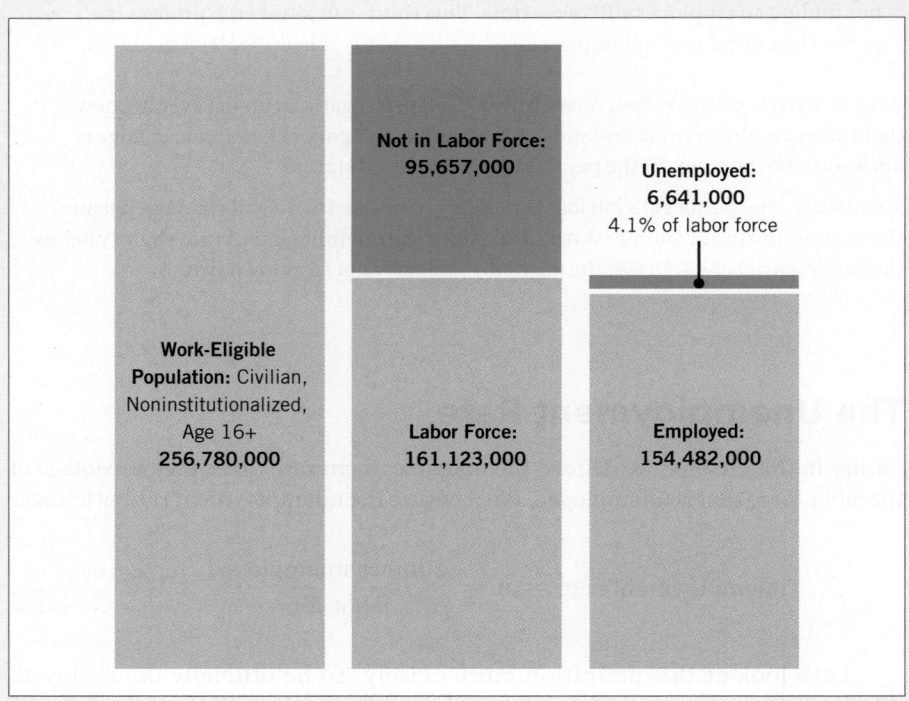

Not in Labor Force: 95,657,000

Unemployed: 6,641,000
4.1% of labor force

Work-Eligible Population: Civilian, Noninstitutionalized, Age 16+
256,780,000

Labor Force: 161,123,000

Employed: 154,482,000

unemployment rate consistently spikes during recessions, and how long it takes for unemployment to return to the natural level of 4% to 5% after each recession. But no matter how lengthy or significant an economic expansion (the nonshaded regions), some unemployment always remains. This unemployment exists because structural and frictional unemployment are always positive. For example, in November 2018, real GDP for the United States was expanding, and the unemployment rate (as Figure 20.6 shows) was 3.7%. That was the lowest U.S. unemployment rate since 1970—but still above zero.

SHORTCOMINGS OF THE UNEMPLOYMENT RATE The unemployment rate, released monthly, is a timely and consistent indicator of the health of the macroeconomy. However, it is not a perfect economic indicator. We now consider two shortcomings in unemployment data.

One shortcoming of the unemployment rate is related to exclusions in the data. People who are unemployed for a long time may just stop looking for work—not because they don't want a job, but because they quit looking. When they stop searching, they fall out of the labor force and no longer count as unemployed; in other words, they are excluded from the statistics. **Marginally attached workers** are defined as those who are not working, have looked for a job in the past 12 months and are willing to work, but have not sought employment in the past four weeks.

Another group not properly accounted for is composed of **underemployed workers**, defined as workers who have part-time jobs but who would like to

Marginally attached workers are not working, have looked for a job in the past 12 months, and are willing to work, but have not sought employment in the past four weeks.

Underemployed workers have part-time jobs but would prefer to work full-time.

FIGURE 20.6

U.S. Unemployment Rate and Recessions, 1970–2018

The U.S. unemployment rate consistently spikes during recessions, which are indicated here by the blue-shaded bars. During recessions, cyclical unemployment rises. During nonrecessionary periods, the unemployment rate drops to (and below) the natural rate of 4 to 5%, with only structural and frictional unemployment remaining.

Source: U.S. Bureau of Labor Statistics.

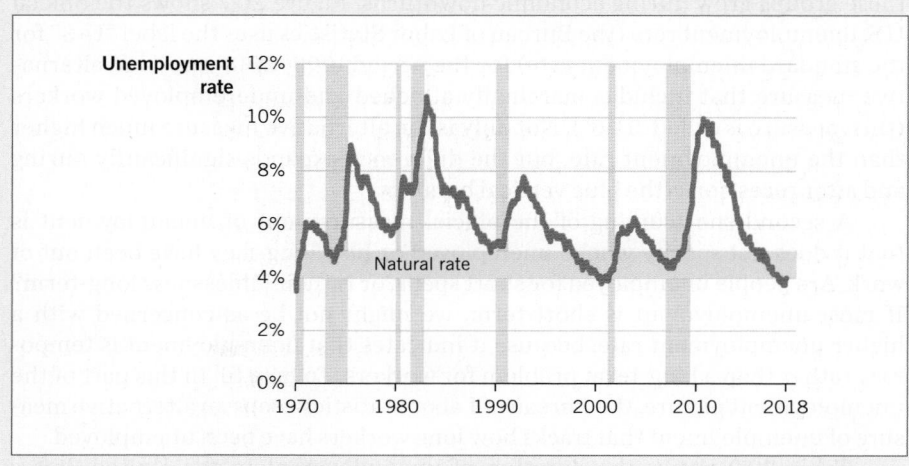

FIGURE 20.7

A Broader Measure of U.S. Labor Market Problems, 1998–2018

The orange line includes workers who are unemployed given the standard definition (U-3). The blue line represents a broader measure of labor market problems (U-6) and includes marginally attached and underemployed workers. The gap between this broader measure and the official unemployment rate grows when the economy enters a recession. Notice how the gap between the two series widens during the Great Recession, which began at the end of 2007.

Source: U.S. Bureau of Labor Statistics.

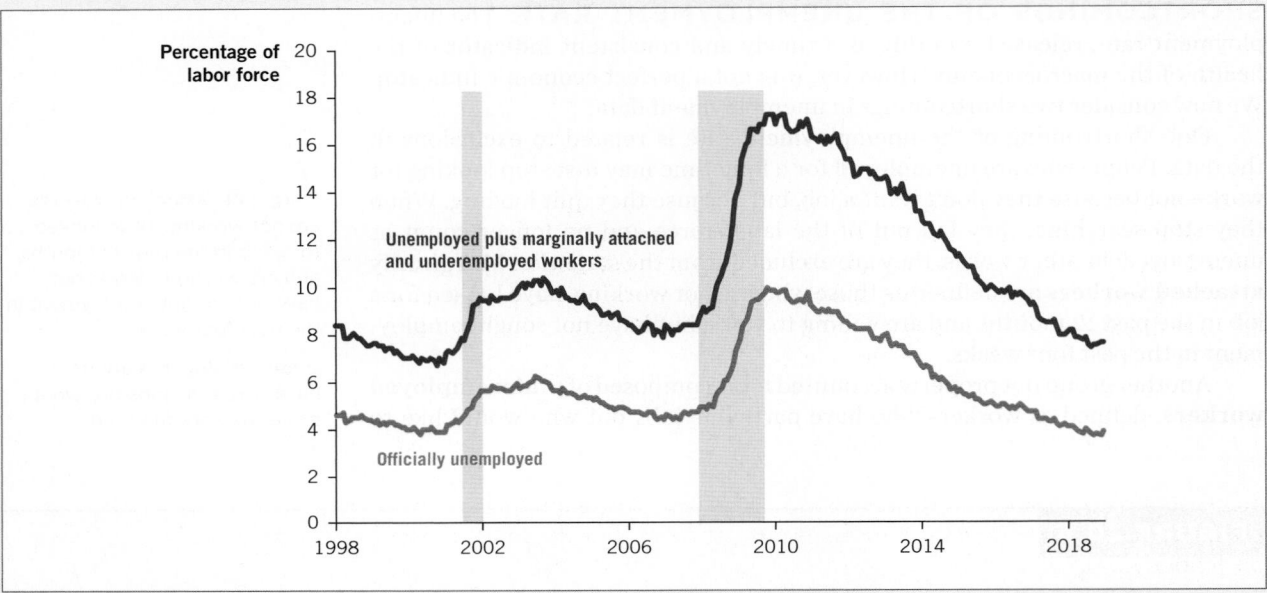

have full-time jobs. These workers are not counted as unemployed. Yet both of these groups grow during economic downturns. Figure 20.7 shows the official U.S. unemployment rate (the Bureau of Labor Statistics uses the label "U-3" for the standard unemployment rate) for the period 1998–2018 versus an alternative measure that includes marginally attached and underemployed workers (this measure is called "U-6"). Not only is the alternative measure much higher than the unemployment rate, but the difference expands significantly during and after recessions (the blue vertical bars).

A second shortcoming of the official measurement of unemployment is that it does not specify who is unemployed or how long they have been out of work. Are people unemployed for short spells, or is their joblessness long-term? If most unemployment is short-term, we might not be as concerned with a higher unemployment rate, because it indicates that unemployment is temporary rather than a long-term problem for workers. To help fill in this part of the unemployment picture, the Bureau of Labor Statistics keeps an alternative measure of unemployment that tracks how long workers have been unemployed.

Table 20.2 shows the duration of unemployment in the United States in January 2010 and January 2019. The year 2010 came just after a long

TABLE 20.2

Duration of Unemployment in the United States, 2010 and 2019

	Percentage of total unemployed	
Duration	2010	2019
Short-term	44.4%	68.9%
Less than 5 weeks	21.5	38.5
5–14 weeks	22.8	30.4
Long-term	56.7	31.1
15–26 weeks	15.9	12.7
27 weeks or longer	39.8	18.4

Source: Bureau of Economic Analysis.

recessionary period in the U.S. economy. At that time, more than 56.7% of total unemployment was long-term (15 weeks or more), with 39.8% of those unemployed out of work 27 weeks or longer. In contrast, consider 2019, nearly a decade after the recession finished. By 2019, 68.9% of unemployment was short-term, and only 31.1% long-term. So when unemployment rates rise, the duration of unemployment often increases too.

Other Labor Market Indicators

Macroeconomists use several other indicators to get a more complete picture of the labor market. These include the labor force participation rate and statistics on gender and race.

LABOR FORCE PARTICIPATION The size of the labor force is itself an important macroeconomic statistic. To see why, consider two hypothetical island economies, each with an overall population of one million people. These two islands, called 2K and 2K18, are identical except in the size of their labor forces. On the first island, 2K, the labor force is 670,000. On the second island, 2K18, the labor force is just 630,000 workers. Island 2K has 40,000 more workers to produce goods and services for a population that is exactly the same size as that of island 2K18. This is why economists watch the **labor force participation rate**, which is the portion of the work-eligible population that is in the labor force:

The **labor force participation rate** is the percentage of the work-eligible population that is in the labor force.

$$\text{labor force participation rate} = \frac{\text{labor force}}{\text{work-eligible population}} \times 100$$

On island 2K, the labor force participation rate is 67%; but on island 2K18, the labor force participation rate is just 63%.

As it turns out, these are the labor force participation rates for the U.S. economy in the years 2000 and 2018. Figure 20.8 shows the evolution of the labor force participation rate in the United States from 1998 to 2018. You can see that it peaks at 67.3% in 2000 but then falls to 62.3% in 2015. All else equal, this means that in 2015 there were fewer people working relative to the overall U.S. population than in any of the previous years shown, including 2000.

FIGURE 20.8

U.S. Labor Force Participation Rate, 1998–2018

The labor force participation rate in the United States peaked at 67.3% in 2000, but it has subsequently fallen to 63%.

Source: U.S. Bureau of Labor Statistics.

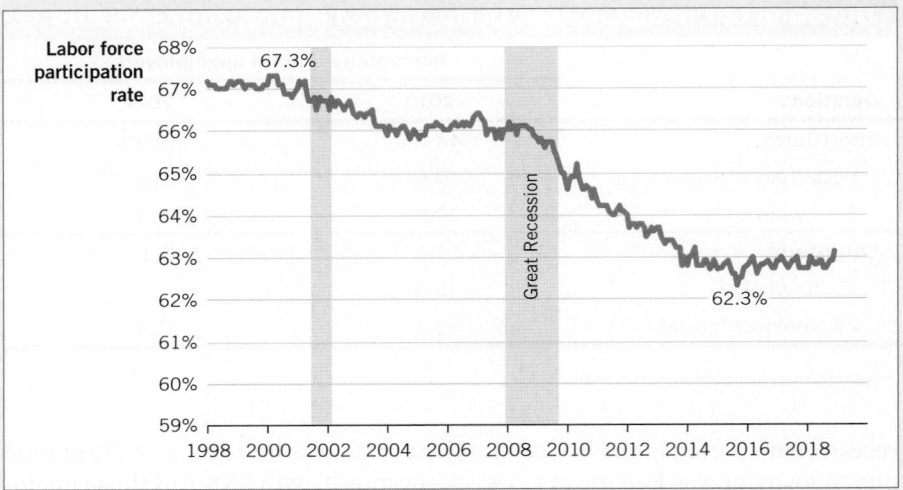

The labor force participation rate in the United States is likely to fall even further over the coming decades, due to the aging of the labor force. The term "baby boom" refers to the period after World War II when U.S. birthrates temporarily rose dramatically. The U.S. Census Bureau pegs this period at 1946–1964. There is now a bubble in the U.S. population known as the "baby boomers." (This might include your parents.) But as the oldest baby boomers are now retiring, the labor force participation rate will naturally fall, all else equal. This means fewer workers contributing to GDP. At the same time, federal expenses allocated toward retirees—for example, Social Security and Medicare—will rise. As you can see in Figure 20.8, these demographic changes are coming at a time when the U.S. labor force participation rate is already declining.

GENDER AND RACE LABOR FORCE STATISTICS Figure 20.9 shows U.S. labor force participation rates for male and female workers, starting in 1950. As you can see, the composition of the labor force today is markedly different from that of two generations ago. Not only are more women working (from 33% in 1950 to 57% in 2018), but male labor force participation has fallen dramatically (from over 86% in 1950 to just 69% in 2018). Men still remain more likely to participate in the labor force than women, but the participation gap has significantly narrowed.

Men are more likely to stay at home today than they were two generations ago.

How do we explain the fact that fewer males are working? A number of reasons account for the decline. Men are living longer, acquiring more education, and spending more time helping to raise families. Because men who are retired, in school, or staying at home to care for children are not counted as part of the labor force, the labor force participation rate for males is lower.

FIGURE 20.9

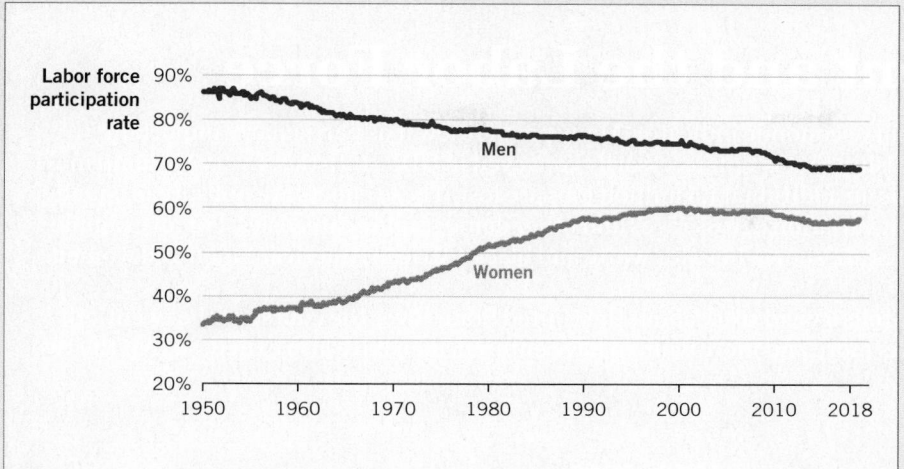

**Trends in U.S. Labor
Force Participation,
1950–2018**

Over the past 70 years, the
composition of the U.S. labor
force has shifted drastically.
While more women have
entered the labor force, the
percentage of men in the
labor force has dropped from
almost 90% to under 70%.

Source: U.S. Bureau of Labor Statistics.

TABLE 20.3

U.S. Unemployment and Labor Force Participation Rates by Gender and Race, January 2019

Group	Unemployment rate	Labor force participation rate
Overall	4.0%	63.2%
Adults (age 20+)		
Black males	7.1	67.9
Black females	5.5	62.8
White males	3.3	72.0
White females	3.2	57.8
Teenagers (age 16–19)		
Black males	24.1	32.2
Black females	17.5	35.8
White males	12.7	37.2
White females	10.5	37.1

Source: U.S. Bureau of Labor Statistics.

Unemployment rates also vary widely across age and race. Table 20.3 breaks down these statistics by age, race, and gender. Looking first at unemployment rates, in January 2019, the overall unemployment rate was 4.0%. But the rate ranges from a low of 3.2% for white females (over 20 years old) to a high of 24.1% for black teenage males. Notice also that labor force participation rates are very low among teenagers, with white teenagers at about 37% but black males at 32.2%.

Unemployment and the Labor Force

The unemployment rate is a primary economic indicator. Many people view it as particularly important because it measures a level of hardship that is not necessarily conveyed in GDP statistics. Every 1% jump in the U.S. unemployment rate means an additional 1.5 million jobs are lost. These effects are not spread equally over society, and there can be great variation across races and other demographic categories. For an example of a demographic comparison, rates are shown here for white and black (African American) men and women.

The labor force participation rate tells a vivid story about the United States over the course of the twentieth and early twenty-first centuries. As more and more women have entered, men have also exited, so that the two rates have converged.

Unemployment Rate by Demographic, 1972–2018

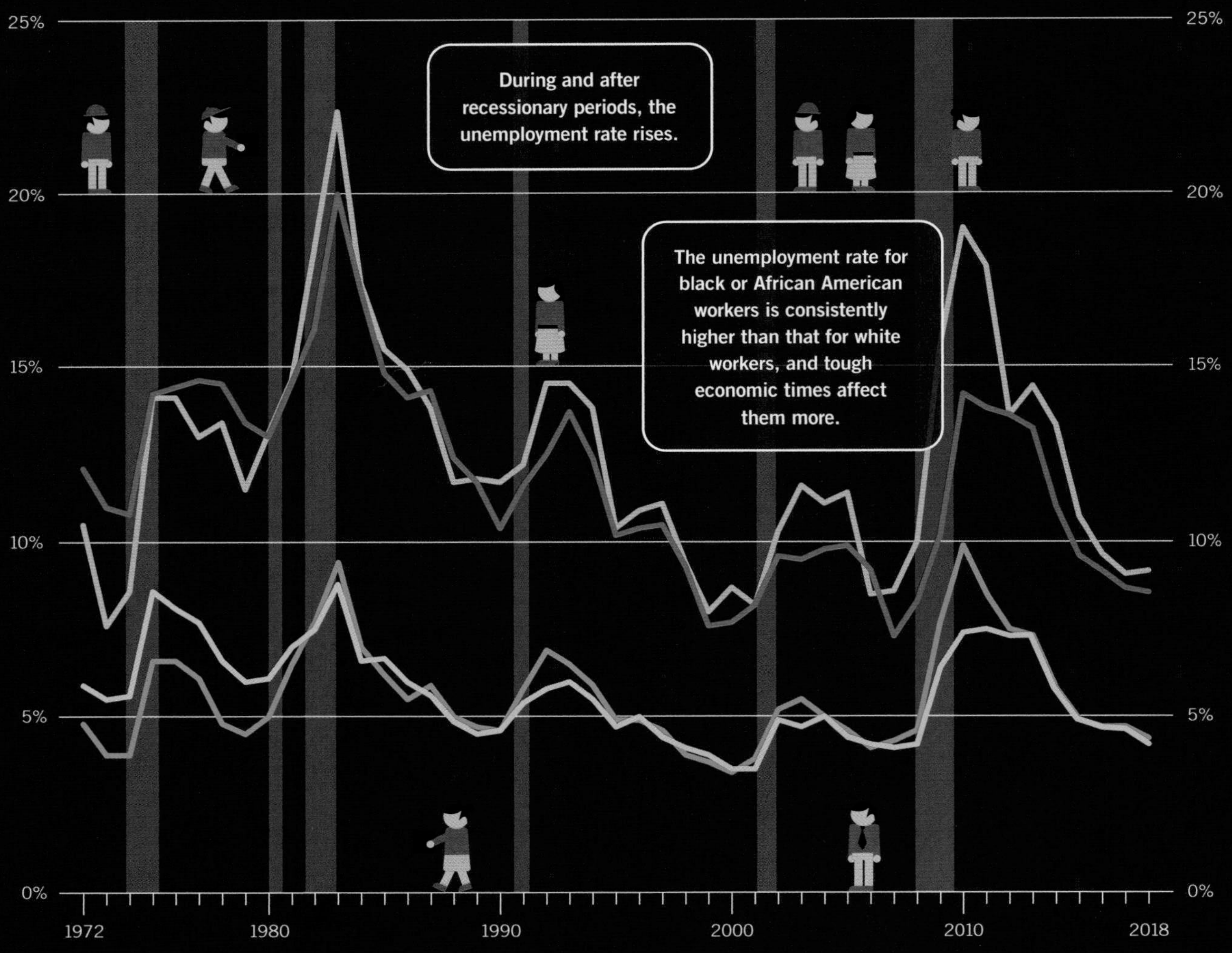

> During and after recessionary periods, the unemployment rate rises.

> The unemployment rate for black or African American workers is consistently higher than that for white workers, and tough economic times affect them more.

25% — 25%

20% — 20%

15% — 15%

10% — 10%

5% — 5%

0% — 0%

1972 1980 1990 2000 2010 2018

REVIEW QUESTIONS

- In the Great Recession of the late 2000s, roughly how many percentage points did the unemployment rate of black or African American men rise?

- How do you explain the labor force participation rate changes between men and women?

Labor Force Participation Rate by Demographic, 1972–2018

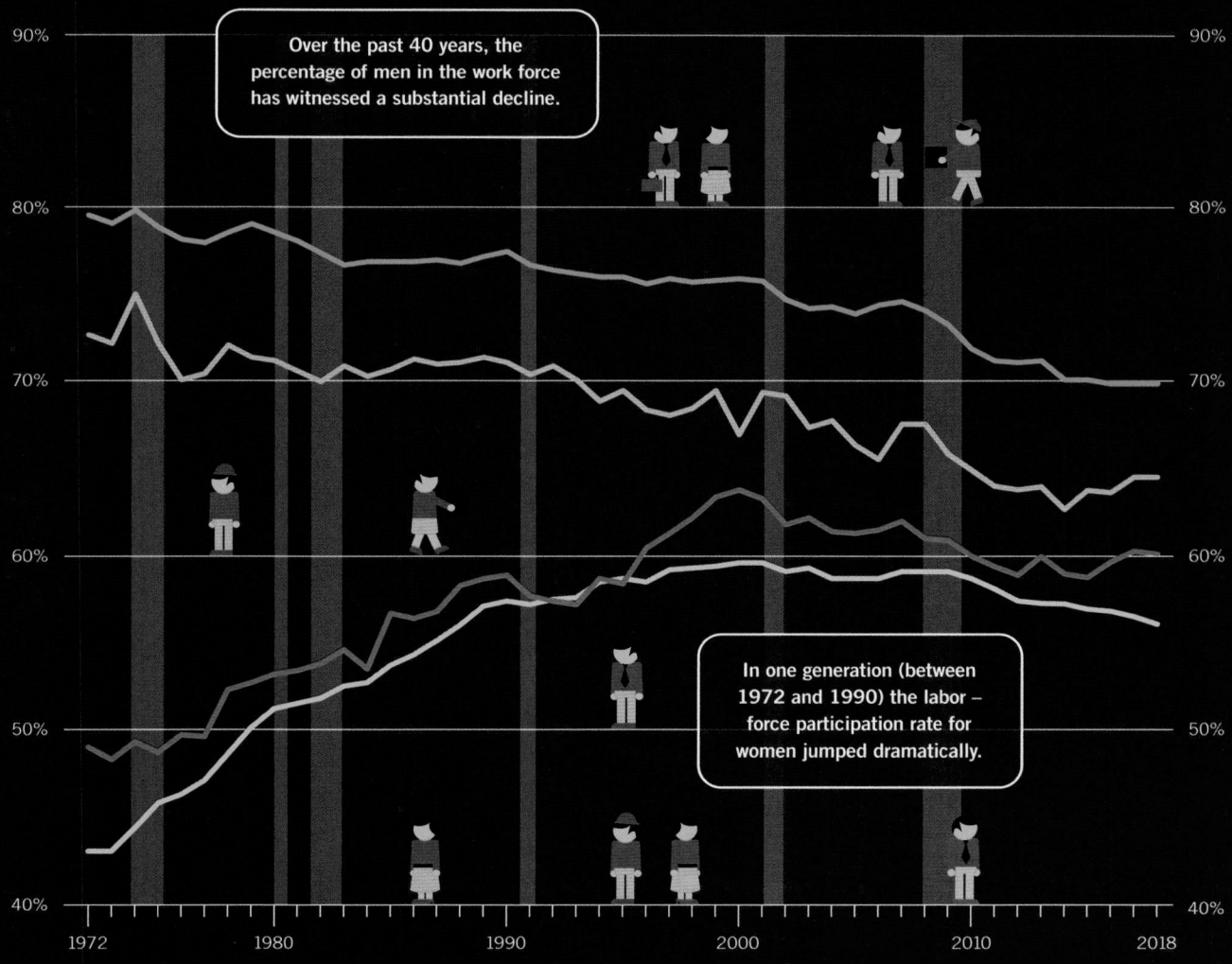

Legend:
- White Men
- White Women
- Black or African American men
- Black or African American women
- Period of Recession

Over the past 40 years, the percentage of men in the work force has witnessed a substantial decline.

In one generation (between 1972 and 1990) the labor force participation rate for women jumped dramatically.

Source: Bureau of Labor Statistics.

This German worker is employed at a textile plant.

Unemployment and Labor Force Participation Rates: Can You Compute the Rates?

The following data are from Germany in 2013:

$$\text{Working-age population} = 71{,}711{,}000$$
$$\text{Labor force} = 44{,}451{,}000$$
$$\text{Employed} = 42{,}269{,}000$$

QUESTION: Using the data, how would you compute the number of unemployed workers, the unemployment rate, and the labor force participation rate for Germany in 2013?

ANSWER: The unemployment rate is the total number of unemployed as a percentage of the labor force. First, determine the number of unemployed as the total labor force minus the number of employed:

$$\text{unemployed} = \text{labor force} - \text{employed} = 2{,}182{,}000$$

Use this information to determine the unemployment rate, which is the number of unemployed divided by the labor force:

$$\text{unemployed} \div \text{labor force} = 4.91\%$$

Finally, the labor force participation rate is the labor force as a percentage of the work-eligible population:

$$\text{labor force participation rate} = \text{labor force} \div \text{working-eligible population}$$
$$= 44{,}451{,}000 \div 71{,}711{,}000$$
$$= 61.99\%$$

Conclusion

This chapter began with the observation that many industries decline as an economy changes and grows, and that these changes inevitably lead to some unemployment. But we have also seen that cyclical unemployment is a reliable indicator of macroeconomic problems. Whenever the unemployment rate is above the natural rate, there is certainly room for improvement. And this also means that policymakers shouldn't aim for zero unemployment— mainly because some unemployment is natural. People pay attention to the unemployment rate because it can affect them personally, but economists monitor the unemployment rate as an important macroeconomic indicator.

Finish Your Degree!

- Getting your Bachelor's degree greatly reduces your chance of unemployment.
- Getting a professional degree typically leads to big jumps in earnings.

College students often fret over which major will increase their chances of getting a good job. Your major certainly matters for getting the job you want, and it may also affect your future income. But the figure below shows just how important it is to finish your degree, no matter what your major may be.

The chart plots unemployment rates by level of educational attainment. The data shown here are from 2017, but you can find current data by visiting the Bureau of Labor Statistics (BLS) at www.bls.gov. Notice how the unemployment rate drops as the level of educational attainment increases. Your choice of major certainly affects your future earnings, but this table shows unemployment rates across all majors. In particular, look at the big drop in the unemployment

rate for those who complete a bachelor's degree or higher. The unemployment rate is about half that of those who earn only a high school diploma. The most important major, it turns out, is the one that holds your interest long enough to guarantee that you graduate!

Want to give yourself the best chance of getting a job?

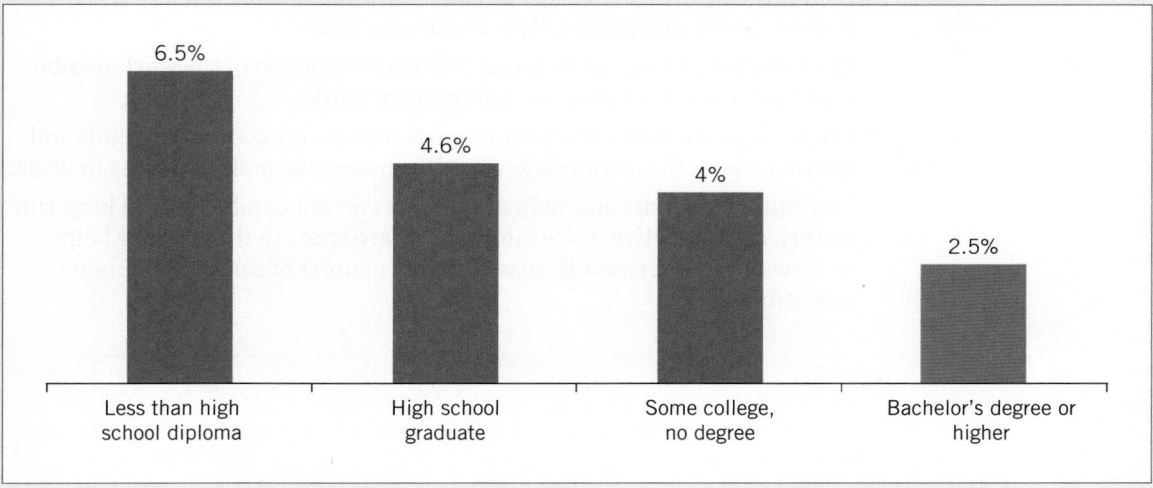

U.S. unemployment rate by educational attainment, 2017.

In addition to real GDP, we use the unemployment rate to assess the position of the economy relative to the business cycle. Because employment data are released more frequently than GDP data, they offer a timely snapshot of current conditions. For this reason, the first Friday of every month, when the employment data are released, tends to be a nervous day, especially during turbulent economic times.

In the next chapter, we will look more closely at a third important macroeconomic indicator—inflation. ✳

· ANSWERING *the* BIG QUESTIONS ·

What are the major reasons for unemployment?

- There are three types of unemployment: structural unemployment, frictional unemployment, and cyclical unemployment.
- Structural unemployment is caused by changes in the structure of the economy that make some jobs obsolete.
- Frictional unemployment is affected by information availability and government policies.
- Cyclical unemployment is caused by recessionary conditions that eliminate jobs during a downturn in the business cycle.

What can we learn from the employment data?

- The unemployment rate, one of the most reliable indicators of an economy's health, reflects the portion of the labor force that is not working and is unsuccessfully searching for a job.
- The labor force participation rate reflects the portion of the work-eligible population that is working or searching for work.
- Unemployment data enable economists to examine economic trends and identify where the labor market conditions are particularly strong or weak.
- Unemployment data also help to evaluate current conditions in a long-run historical perspective. For example, the case study in this chapter helps us view the recent Great Recession in the context of earlier economic downturns.

▪ CHAPTER PROBLEMS

Concepts You Should Know

creative destruction (p. 642)
cyclical unemployment (p. 648)
frictional unemployment
  (p. 645)
full-employment output (p. 650)
labor force (p. 651)

labor force participation rate
  (p. 655)
marginally attached workers
  (p. 653)
natural rate of unemployment
  (p. 649)

structural unemployment (p. 642)
underemployed workers (p. 653)
unemployment (p. 641)
unemployment insurance (p. 646)
unemployment rate (p. 641)

Questions for Review

1. Until the late 1960s, most economists assumed that less unemployment was always preferable to more unemployment. Define and explain the two types of unemployment that are consistent with a dynamic, growing economy.

2. Is there any unemployment when an economy has "full employment"? If so, what type(s)?

3. The news media almost always bemoans the current state of the U.S. economy. How does the most recent unemployment rate relate to the long-run average?

4. What type of unemployment is affected when online job search engines reduce the time necessary for job searches? Does this outcome affect the natural rate of unemployment? If so, how?

5. What groups does the Bureau of Labor Statistics count in the labor force? Explain why the official unemployment rate tends to underestimate the level of labor market problems.

6. Does the duration of unemployment matter? Explain your answer.

7. What does an increase in the natural rate of unemployment imply about each of the three types of unemployment?

8. What can cause an increase in frictional unemployment? Give at least one example. What can cause an increase in structural unemployment? Give at least one example.

Study Problems *(✱solved at the end of the section)*

1. In his song "Allentown," Billy Joel sings about the demise of the steel and coal industries in Pennsylvania. Why do you think the loss of manufacturing jobs was so difficult on the workers in areas like Allentown and parts of the Midwest where manufacturing was once the largest employer? What type of unemployment is the song about?

2. In January 2019, the U.S. economy added 302,000 new jobs. Yet the unemployment rate rose from 3.9% to 4.0%. How is this possible?

3. A country with a civilian (work-eligible) population of 90,000 (all over age 16) has 70,000 employed and 10,000 unemployed persons. Of the unemployed, 5,000 are frictionally unemployed and another 3,000 are structurally unemployed.

On the basis of these data, answer the following questions.
a. What is the size of the labor force?
b. What is the unemployment rate?
c. What is the natural rate of unemployment for this country?
d. Is this economy in recession or expansion? Explain.

4. Visit www.bls.gov and search through the tables on unemployment to answer the following questions.
a. What is the current national unemployment rate for the United States?
b. What is the current unemployment rate among people of your age, sex, and race?

5. Consider a country with 300 million residents, a labor force of 150 million, and 10 million unemployed. Answer the following questions.

   a. What is the labor force participation rate?

   b. What is the unemployment rate?

   c. If 5 million of the unemployed become discouraged and stop looking for work, what is the new unemployment rate?

   d. Suppose instead that 30 million jobs are created, attracting 20 million new people into the labor force. What would be the new rates for labor force participation and unemployment?

✶ **6.** Consider the following hypothetical data from the peaceable nation of Hooland, where there is no military, the entire population is over the age of 16, and no one is institutionalized for any reason. Then answer the questions.

Classification	Number of people
Total population	200 million
Employed	141 million
Full-time students	10 million
Homemakers	25 million
Retired persons	15 million
Seeking work but without a job	9 million

   a. What is the unemployment rate in Hooland?

   b. What is the labor force participation rate in Hooland?

For questions c through f: assume that 15 million Hoolandian homemakers begin seeking jobs, and that 10 million find jobs.

   c. Now what is the rate of unemployment in Hooland?

   d. How does this change affect cyclical unemployment in Hooland?

   e. What will happen to per capita GDP?

   f. Is the economy of Hooland better off after the homemakers enter the labor force? Explain your response.

✶ **7.** In each of the following situations, determine whether or not the person would be considered unemployed.

   a. A 15-year-old offers to pet-sit, but no one hires her.

   b. A college graduate spends the summer after graduation touring Europe before starting a job search.

   c. A part-time teacher works only two days a week, even though he would like a full-time job.

   d. An automobile worker becomes discouraged about the prospects for future employment and decides to stop looking for work.

✶ **8.** The table below presents real data from the U.S. labor market in January 2015. Fill in any numbers that are missing.

Civilian, noninstitutionalized, 16+ population	
Labor force	
Employed	148,201,000
Unemployed	
Labor force participation rate	62.9%
Unemployment rate	5.7%

9. The table below shows employment data for the imaginary country of Karakara in 2018.

Classification	2018
Total population	100
Employed	57
Full-time students	14
Homemakers	16
Retired persons	10
Seeking work, but without a job	3

   a. How many people are in the 2018 labor force for Karakara?

   b. What is the 2018 unemployment rate?

Following a number of very prosperous years, Karakara entered a recession in 2019. As a result, many companies went out of business and 12 people lost their jobs.

c. Assuming everyone who lost their job immediately began to look for a new job, what was the unemployment rate and the labor force participation rate in 2019?

d. Did cyclical unemployment go up, down, or stay the same in 2019?

Classification	2020
Total population	100
Employed	48
Full-time students	18
Homemakers	20
Retired persons	12
Seeking work, but without a job	2

The economy began to recover in 2020. The second table shows the employment data in 2020. As you can see, some of the people who lost their jobs during the recession had trouble finding new jobs, and decided to go back to school, or to become homemakers.

e. What is the economic term used to describe the people who gave up looking for a job?

f. What was the unemployment rate and the labor force participation rate in 2020?

g. Imagine that, as the recovery continues, some of the people who gave up looking for work in 2020 decide to reenter the workforce. In particular, suppose that in 2021, 10 people decide to reenter the labor force, and three of them find jobs. What is the new unemployment rate and the labor force participation rate? Write your answer, in percentage terms, in the table below.

New unemployment rate	_____
Labor force participation rate	_____

Solved Problems

6a. The unemployment rate in Hooland is 6%. To calculate the unemployment rate, use:

unemployment rate = u = (number of unemployed ÷ labor force) × 100

- The number of unemployed: 9 million
- Labor force can be calculated in two ways:
  - Employed plus unemployed:

    141 million + 9 million = 150 million

  - Total population minus those not in labor force (students, homemakers, retirees):

    200 million − (10 million + 25 million + 15 million) = 150 million

Note: Because the total population is only composed of noninstitutionalized civilians over the age of 16, we can use this number (200 million) as the relevant population.

unemployment rate = u = (number of unemployed ÷ labor force) × 100 = (9 ÷ 150) × 100 = 6%

b. The labor force participation rate in Hooland is 75%. To calculate the labor force participation rate, use:

labor force participation rate = (labor force ÷ population) × 100

- Labor force (calculated above): 150 million
- Population: 200 million

labor force participation rate = (labor force ÷ population) × 100 = (150 ÷ 200) × 100 = 75%

c. Now the rate of unemployment in Hooland is 8.5%. To calculate the new unemployment rate, use the same equation as above. However, the figures have changed with new entrants to the labor force:

- The new number of unemployed:

    9 million + 5 million = 14 million

- The new number of employed:

    141 million + 10 million = 151 million

- The new labor force can be calculated in three ways:
  - Previous labor force plus new entrants:

    150 million + 15 million = 165 million

  - Employed plus unemployed:

    151 million + 14 million = 165 million

  - Total population minus those not in labor force (students, homemakers, retirees):

    200 million − (10 million + 10 million + 15 million) = 165 million

    unemployment rate = u = (number of unemployed ÷ labor force) × 100 = (14 ÷ 165) × 100 = 8.5%

Note: Even though the number of employed increased, because the size of the labor force increased by more, the unemployment rate has increased.

d. The change does not affect cyclical unemployment, which is generally associated with economic downturns. Instead, the entrance of new workers into the labor force represents a change in the labor force participation rate. In general, the entry of new workers to the labor force is associated with good economic times. Because most of the homemakers were able to find jobs, we can conclude that the economy of Hooland is growing.

e. With an increase in the number of employed workers, total output in the economy will increase. However, the size of the population has not changed. Thus, per capita GDP will increase as a result of the change.

f. Hooland has a stronger economy with more working homemakers. Even though the unemployment rate has increased as a result of many homemakers entering the labor force, the increase in unemployment is not the result of economic downturn; rather, it is a sign of a growing economy. Hooland has a stronger economy with higher GDP per capita and a greater labor force participation rate as a result of this change.

7a. No. The relevant population used to measure unemployment and the labor force comprises work-eligible individuals 16 years of age or older.

This 15-year-old is not part of the relevant population, so she is not considered unemployed.

b. No. To be counted in the unemployment statistics, an individual must have made efforts to get a job in the past four weeks. This college graduate is not actively seeking work during the summer, so he is not counted as an unemployed individual.

c. No. This part-time teacher is underemployed because he would prefer a full-time position, but under the unemployment rate measurements he is considered to be employed.

d. No. The automobile worker is a marginally attached worker if he has searched for work in the past year but stopped looking for work over four weeks ago. However, since he is not actively looking for work now, he is no longer considered part of the labor force.

8. First, determine the number in the labor force. We know that the labor force is composed of the employed and the unemployed. We also know that the unemployment rate is 5.7% of the labor force, so

$$100\% = 5.7\% + \text{portion of the labor force that is employed}$$

This means that the portion employed is 94.3%.

If 94.3% of the labor force is employed, and the number employed is 148,201,000, then we can determine the size of the labor force as

$$\frac{148,201,000}{\text{labor force}} = 0.943$$

Therefore,

labor force = 157,159,067 (rounding to the nearest whole number)

Next, we find the size of the civilian, noninstitutional, 16+ population (pop). We know that

$$\text{labor force participation rate} = \frac{\text{labor force}}{\text{pop}}$$

and we already know the labor force participation rate and the labor force. Therefore,

$$62.9\% = \frac{157{,}159{,}067}{\text{pop}}$$

$$\text{pop} = \frac{157{,}159{,}067}{0.629}$$

$$\text{population} = \underline{249{,}855{,}432}$$

Finally, we can now solve for the number unemployed because we know the total size of the labor force and the number employed:

$$\text{labor force} = \text{employed} + \text{unemployed}$$

$$157{,}159{,}067 = 148{,}201{,}000 + \text{unemployed}$$

$$\text{unemployed} = \underline{8{,}958{,}067}$$

The Price Level and Inflation

High Inflation Can Be Catastrophic for an Economy.

In 2018, the cost of a dozen eggs in Venezuela climbed to 8 million Bolivars, up from 140 Bolivars just four years earlier. But egg prices weren't the only problem—overall prices rose at a rate of one million percent in 2018. The inflation disaster began in 2014, when the price of oil plunged on the world market. Oil represents about three-fourths of the value of all Venezuelan exports. When oil's price fell, the Venezuelan government desperately needed funds, and so they started printing Bolivars—lots and lots of Bolivars. Over the ensuing years, trying to stay ahead of inflation and expectations, they accelerated the growth of the supply of Bolivars, and this led to more and more inflation. For Venezuelan citizens, it was a disaster. More than half the population earns the minimum wage. But this minimum wage, also set by the government, was just 180 million Bolivars per month in 2018. This meant that an average citizen would have had to work a day and a half just to buy a dozen eggs.

In most of the world inflation is now under control. You may have never experienced significant inflation. Sure, you may notice many prices rising from year to year, but these are slow, steady, often predictable increases. However, as recently as the early 1980s, the annual inflation rate in the

When the price level rises at one million percent per year, paper currency becomes almost worthless. In Venezuela, people have found other creative uses for their Bolivars.

United States was close to 15%—about six times higher than recent experience. And 15% is low by international standards. So it may appear that inflation is not a significant problem. But it certainly has been in the past, and there is no guarantee that we are safe from it in the future.

High inflation can cause the destruction of wealth across an entire economy, and equally important, unpredictable inflation can wreak havoc within an economy—as we will see in the pages ahead.

· BIG QUESTIONS ·

- How is inflation measured?
- What problems does inflation bring?
- What is the cause of inflation?

How Is Inflation Measured?

You might notice price changes on a shopping trip or when you see a reference to prices in an old book or movie. For example, in the 1960 movie *Psycho*, a hotel room for one night was priced at just $10. In Chapter 19, we defined inflation as the growth in the overall level of prices in an economy. When overall prices rise, this affects our budget; it limits how much we can buy with our income. On the other hand, if overall prices fall, our income goes further and we can buy more goods.

Imagine an annual inflation rate of 100%. At this rate, prices double every year. How would this affect your life? Would it change what you buy? Would it change your savings plans? Would it change the salary you negotiate with your employer? Yes, it would change your life on a daily basis. Now imagine that prices double *every day*. This was the situation in Zimbabwe in 2008, when the inflation rate reached almost 80 billion percent per month! This is an example of what economists call *hyperinflation*, an extremely high rate of inflation, and it completely stymies economic activity. In Zimbabwe, for example, average citizens could barely afford necessities like bread and eggs.

Figure 21.1 shows inflation in the United States from 1970 to 2018. Over the past twenty-five years, the long-run average inflation rate in the United States was just 2.25%, which gives us a benchmark for evaluating current inflation rates. In the 1970s and early 1980s, there were periods of very high inflation. At one point in 1980, the inflation rate was almost 15%. But since the early 1980s, inflation seems well controlled in the United States. Looking again at Figure 21.1, you might notice a brief spell of deflation in 2009. **Deflation** occurs when overall prices fall; it is negative inflation. The 2009 deflation was driven largely by falling energy prices at the beginning of a recession.

Zimbabweans show off devalued currency at a 2008 political rally. How is it possible to have 1 billion dollars and not be able to afford dinner?

Measuring inflation is straightforward but requires precision. Prices don't all move together; some prices fall even when most others rise. In addition, some prices affect consumers more than others. A 10% increase in housing prices is significantly more painful than a 10% increase in hot dog prices. So before we can measure inflation, we have to agree on what prices to monitor and how much weight we'll give to each price. In the United States, the Bureau of Labor Statistics (BLS) measures and reports inflation data. In this section, we describe how the BLS estimates the overall price level. (Remember from Chapter 19 that the price level is an index of the average prices of goods and services throughout an economy.) The BLS's goals are to (1) determine the prices of all the goods and services a typical consumer buys and (2) identify how much of a typical consumer's budget is spent on these particular items.

Deflation
occurs when overall prices fall.

The Consumer Price Index (CPI)

We start with the most common price level used to compute inflation. The **consumer price index (CPI)** is the measure of the price level based on the consumption patterns of a typical consumer. When you read or hear about

The **consumer price index (CPI)** is a measure of the price level based on the consumption patterns of a typical consumer.

FIGURE 21.1

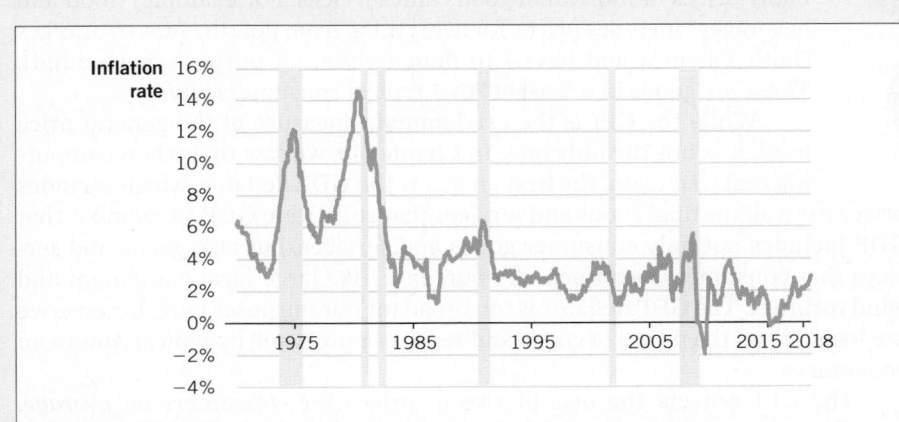

Inflation in the United States, 1970–2018

From 1970 to 2018, inflation rates in the United States averaged 4%. This number is high because of excessive inflation in the 1970s. The inflation rate peaked at over 14% in 1980. In the past twenty-five years, inflation has averaged only about 2.25%.

Source: U.S. Bureau of Labor Statistics.

FIGURE 21.2

The Pieces of the Consumer Price Index, July 2018

The weights assigned to the different categories of expenditures are based on the spending patterns of a typical American. For example, 17% of a typical American's spending is on transportation; this includes car payments and fuel, among other expenses.

Source: U.S. Bureau of Labor Statistics.

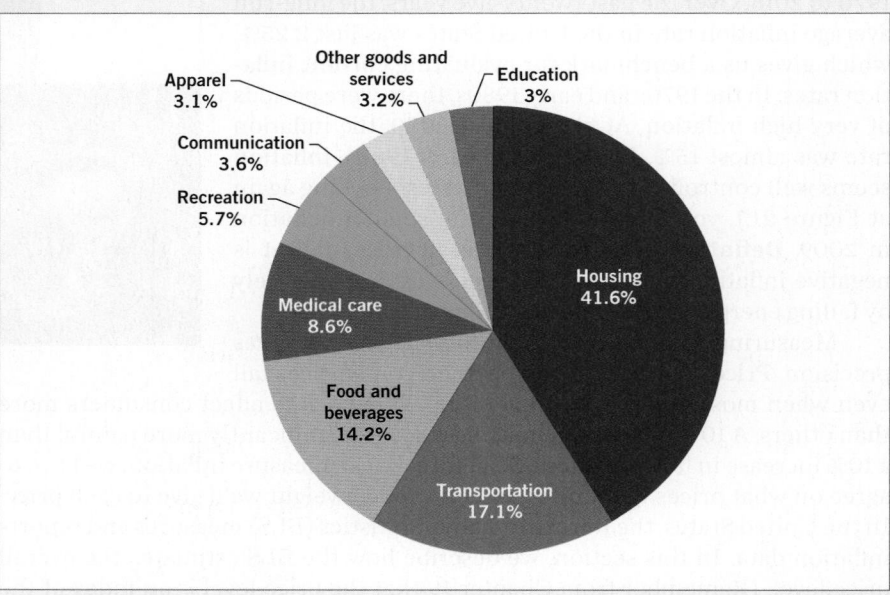

Other goods and services
3.2%

Apparel
3.1%

Education
3%

Communication
3.6%

Recreation
5.7%

Housing
41.6%

Medical care
8.6%

Food and beverages
14.2%

Transportation
17.1%

The CPI is based on prices from a typical "basket" of all consumer goods and services.

inflation in the media, the report almost certainly focuses on this measure. The CPI is essentially the price of a typical "basket" of goods and services purchased by a representative consumer in the United States. What's in that basket? In addition to groceries, there is clothing, transportation, housing, medical care, education, and many other goods and services. The idea is to include everything that a typical consumer buys. Tracking these prices gives us a realistic measure of a typical consumer's cost of living.

Figure 21.2 displays how the CPI was allocated among major spending categories in July 2018. Each of these categories includes many prices of individual goods and services. For example, "food and beverages" includes prices for everything from potato chips to oranges (both Valencia and navel) to flour (white, all purpose, per pound). These are goods in a "basket" that typical consumers buy.

While the CPI is the predominant measure of the general price level, it is not the only one. In Chapter 19, we saw that when computing real GDP data, the best choice is the GDP deflator, which includes prices from all the final goods and services that constitute GDP. Remember that GDP includes not only consumer goods and services, but also goods and services that consumers never actually purchase, like large farm equipment and wind turbines. The GDP deflator is too broad for our purposes here, because we are focusing on the prices of goods and services purchased by typical American consumers.

The CPI reflects the overall rise in prices for consumers *on average*. But of course, none of us is exactly typical in our spending. College students allocate significantly more than average to spending on education; senior citizens spend more than average on medical care; a fashionista spends more than average on clothing; and those with lengthy commutes spend more than average on transportation.

COMPUTING THE CPI Each month, the BLS conducts surveys by sending employees into stores in 38 geographical locations to gather and input price information on over 8,000 goods and services. The BLS collects prices on everything from apples in Chicago, Illinois, to electricity in Scranton, Pennsylvania, to gasoline in San Diego, California. In addition to inputting price information, the BLS surveyors estimate how each good and service affects a typical consumer's budget. Once they do this, they attach a weight to the price of each good or service in the consumer's "basket." For example, Figure 21.2 indicates that the typical consumer spends 17% of his or her budget on transportation. Therefore, transportation prices receive 17% of the total weight in the typical consumer's basket of goods and services. Once the BLS has compiled the prices and budget allocation weights, it can construct the CPI.

To illustrate how this works, let's build a price index using just three goods. Imagine that when you go to the movies you notice you are spending more for that outing than you did last year. You decide to construct a price index to see exactly how the price increases are affecting your budget. You decide to name your index the EPI (entertainment price index). For the sake of this example, assume that a typical night at the movie theater includes two movie tickets, one box of popcorn, and two medium Cokes. This is the basket of goods (the popcorn and Cokes) and service (movie) included in your EPI.

The first four columns in Figure 21.3 show your EPI data for the first year, 2016. The second column shows the respective quantities of goods and service

FIGURE 21.3

Calculating a Simple Price Index

In calculating this entertainment price index (EPI), we use the same steps that the Bureau of Labor Statistics goes through when calculating the CPI. First, we determine the typical basket of goods. Then we calculate the total price of the basket in a base year, 2016 in this example, and set that base year at 100 (creating an index). For subsequent years, we add up the new prices for the same basket of goods, then divide by the basket price in the base year, and then multiply by 100 to determine the new index number.

| | | 2016 | | 2020 | |
Good	Quantity	Unit price	Total cost	Unit price	Total cost
Popcorn	1	$6	$6	$8	$8
Coke	2	$5	$10	$5	$10
Movie ticket	2	$12	$24	$13	$26
Basket price			$40		$44
Index (EPI)		$\frac{$40}{$40} \times 100 = 100$		$\frac{$44}{$40} \times 100 = 110$	

in your basket, and the third column displays the unit prices of these goods and service. The price of popcorn is $6 per box, the Cokes are $5 each, and the movie tickets are $12 each. The fourth column shows how much you pay in total for each good or service; this number is price multiplied by quantity. For example, in 2016, the price of a ticket was $12, so you paid a total of $24 for two tickets. Adding up, we get the total price for your basket of goods and service in 2016, which was $40. This is how much you spent for all goods and service in your EPI in 2016.

Let's now move to 2020. First, note that your consumption pattern hasn't changed; you still buy the same basket of goods and service. But some of the prices did change in 2020. Popcorn is now priced at $8 per box, and the movie ticket costs $13. Note that not all prices have changed; the cost of a Coke remains the same.

To see how the new 2020 prices affect your spending, we compute the total cost required to consume the same goods and service in the same quantities. The last column shows the costs of each component in your basket. The sum of these is now $44.

The final step is to create an index. You need an index because in the real world, adding a lot of prices together yields a huge number that would be difficult to work with. So we create an index that is equal to 100 at a fixed point in time—your base year. In our example, we can use 2016 for the base year. To convert to your index, we divide the basket price in each year by the basket price value from the base year and multiply by 100:

(EQUATION 21.1)
$$\text{price index} = \frac{\text{basket price}}{\text{basket price in base year}} \times 100$$

Using this formula, you can confirm that the EPI for 2016 is 100 and that the EPI for 2020 is 110 (see the last line of Figure 21.3).

When the Bureau of Labor Statistics computes the CPI for the United States, it follows the same basic steps:

1. Define the basket of goods and services and their appropriate weights.
2. Determine the prices of goods across periods.
3. Convert to the index number for each period.

ECONOMICS IN THE REAL WORLD

SLEUTHING FOR PRICES

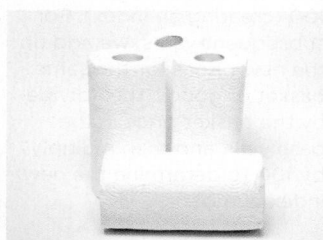

Paper towels are one example of a typical consumer item.

Tracking the prices in the CPI requires a great deal of effort and precision. The Bureau of Labor Statistics (BLS) is the U.S. government agency that is responsible for estimating the consumer price index. As of 2015, the BLS employed 428 "economic assistants." Their job is to fan out around the nation and determine the actual prices of goods and services—every month. This is no easy task because the items in the market basket are constantly changing. In September 2015, Emily Wax-Thibodeaux of the *Washington Post* followed one of these economic assistants on a typical day's work. The BLS employee, Caren Gaffney, drove around the state of Virginia for more than 8 hours tracking prices on gasoline, sugar, and beer.

The priced items were very specific. For the gas price alone, Gaffney needed to determine the octane grade, whether the quoted prices depended on the day of the week, and whether the customer paid with cash or credit. The BLS tracks 200 different price categories, and each category includes the prices of several hundred goods and services. For example, the BLS tracks the prices of four types of margarine (sticks, soft, vegetable blend sticks, and vegetable blend soft). Paper towels may seem like a pretty standard item, but it turns out there are 31 different varieties of some brands.

In macroeconomics, we generally watch a single overall number (the CPI or the GDP deflator) that indicates how much prices have changed. But it's important to remember that thousands of prices are tracked each month by government workers like Caren Gaffney.

Source: https://www.washingtonpost.com/politics/the-governments-human-price-scanners/2013/11/11/a4225dc2-4576-11e3-bf0c-cebf37c6f484_story.html.

Measuring Inflation Rates

Once the CPI is computed, economists use it to measure inflation rates. The inflation rate (i) is a growth rate and is calculated as the percentage change in the price level (P) during a period of time. Using the CPI as the price level, the inflation rate during period 2 is

$$\text{inflation rate (i)} = \frac{P_2 - P_1}{P_1} \times 100$$

(EQUATION 21.2)

In our entertainment price index example, the CPI rose from 100 to 110 in one year. So the inflation rate for that year was 10%, computed as

$$\text{inflation rate (i)} = \frac{110 - 100}{100} \times 100 = 10\%$$

The BLS releases CPI estimates every month. Normally, inflation rates are measured over the course of a year, showing how much the price level grows in 12 months. Figure 21.4 shows the historical relationship between the U.S. inflation rate and the CPI. Panel (a) plots the U.S. CPI from 1970 to 2018. The base period for the CPI is set for 1982–1984, so it goes through 100 in 1983. The CPI was just 38 in 1970 and rose to 251 by 2018. This means that the typical basket of consumer goods and services cost almost seven times as much in 2018 as about 50 years earlier.

Panel (b) of Figure 21.4 plots inflation rates based on the CPI data in panel (a). The inflation graph reveals a number of historical observations that are important to our study of macroeconomics. For example, when you look at the graph, you might wonder what was going on in the 1970s. Since the 1970s, inflation has been relatively low and stable, averaging less than 3%. But from 1970 to 1981, the inflation rate averaged 8%, including the year between April 1979 and March 1980, when it was over 14.5%. We'll explain the reasons for these historically high rates in Chapter 31. For now, in comparing the two graphs in Figure 21.4, notice that the CPI increased more rapidly from 1979 to 1980 than in any other period shown.

FIGURE 21.4

The CPI and Inflation, 1970–2018

Panel (a) shows the CPI from 1970 to 2018. The index of prices for a typical consumer's basket of goods was at 38 in 1970 but rose to 251 by 2018. Panel (b) shows the U.S. inflation rate, computed as the growth rate of the CPI. A rapidly rising CPI, like we see in panel (a) during the 1970s, is reflected in the high inflation rate.

Source: U.S. Bureau of Labor Statistics.

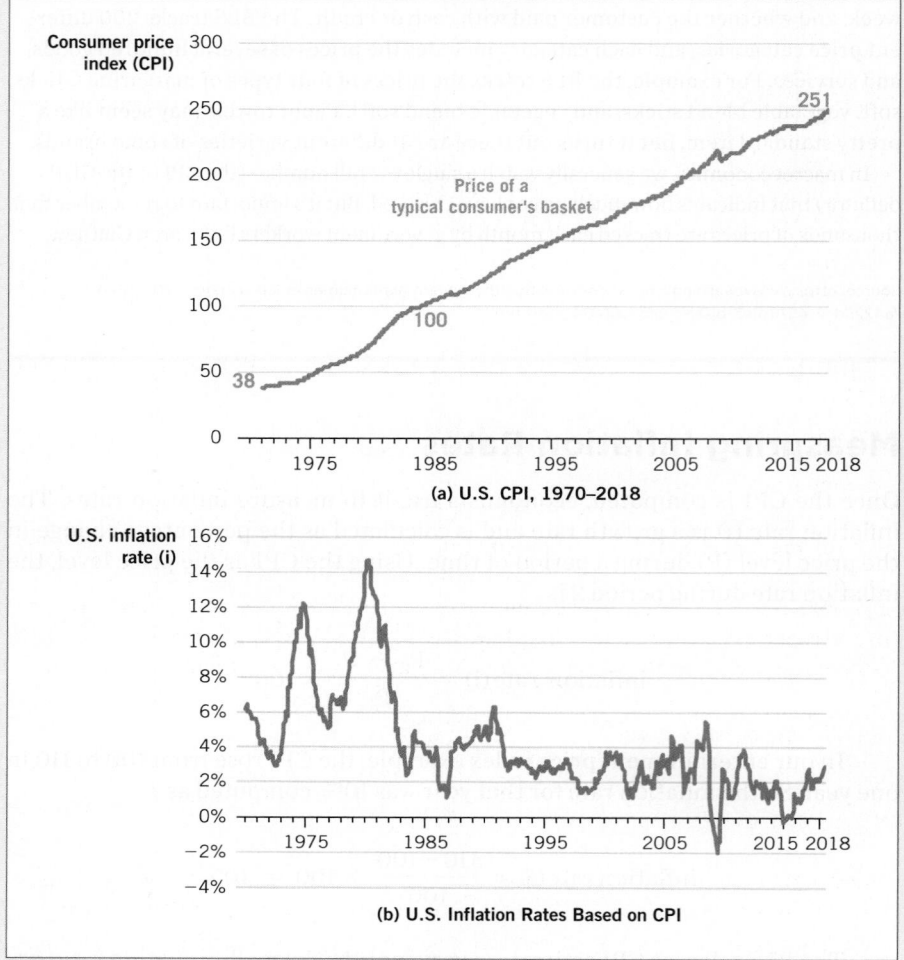

(a) U.S. CPI, 1970–2018

(b) U.S. Inflation Rates Based on CPI

ECONOMICS IN THE REAL WORLD

PRICES DON'T ALL MOVE TOGETHER

While it's clear that prices generally rise, not all prices go up. When the CPI rises, it indicates that the price of the overall consumer basket rises. However, some individual prices stay the same or even fall. For example, consumer electronic prices almost always fall. When flat-panel plasma TVs were introduced in the late 1990s, a 40-inch model cost more than $7,000. Twenty years later, 60-inch flat-panel TVs are available for less than $500. This is the result of technological advancements: as time passes, it often takes fewer resources to produce the same item or something better.

The 1984 Macintosh price was
$2,495 . . .

. . . but this 2018 Apple iMac costs just $1,999.

Computers are another example. In 1984, Apple introduced the Macintosh computer at a price of $2,495. The CPU for the Macintosh ran at 7.83 MHz, and the 9-inch monitor was black and white. Today, you can buy an Apple iMac for less than $2,000. The 2018 iteration has a quad-core processor that runs at 3.5 GHz, and the monitor is 27 inches' worth of ultra high-resolution color. The new computer is better by any measure, yet it costs less than the early model. These kinds of changes in quality make it difficult to measure the CPI, but it is clear that many prices actually fall over time.

Using the CPI to Compare Dollar Values over Time

Prices convey a lot of information, but prices from different periods can be quite confusing. For example, in 1924, a consumer could buy a fully constructed, 1,600-square-foot home through a physical catalog distributed by Sears at a price of just $1,969. But how does that price compare with today's prices? In addition to measuring inflation rates, we can use the CPI to answer these types of questions.

To compare the prices of goods over time, we convert all prices to today's prices, or "prices in today's dollars." Here is the formula:

$$\text{price in today's dollars} = \text{price in earlier time} \times \frac{\text{price level today}}{\text{price level in earlier time}}$$

(EQUATION 21.3)

Following this formula, we can compute the 2018 price of the 1924 Sears home. The CPI in 2018 was 252, and the CPI in 1924 was 17, so the computation is

$$\text{price in 2018} = \$1,969 \times \frac{252}{17} = \$29,188$$

In fact, the 1924 Sears price would be pretty low even today.

The Pieces of the CPI

The price level we often use to measure inflation is the Consumer Price Index (CPI), which is driven by the prices paid by a typical American consumer. The data below shows the various categories in which U.S. citizens spend their income.

PIECES OF THE CPI
FEBRUARY 2019

Category	Percent
SHELTER	33.3%
MISCELLANEOUS GOODS	19.6%
FOOD	13.4%
ENERGY	7.1%
MEDICAL CARE SERVICES	7.0%
TRANSPORTATION SERVICES	6.0%
OTHER	13.6%

SHELTER	33.3%		ENERGY	7.1%
Owner's payments	24.1%		Gasoline	3.5%
Rent	7.9%		Electricity	2.6%
Other	1.3%		Other	1.1%
MISCELLANEOUS GOODS	**19.6%**		**MEDICAL CARE SERVICES**	**7.0%**
New Vehicles	3.7%		Hospital services	2.3%
Apparel	3.0%		Physician's services	1.7%
Used cars and trucks	2.4%		Other	2.9%
Medical care commodities	1.7%		**TRANSPORTATION SERVICES**	**6.0%**
Alcoholic beverages	1.0%		Motor vehicle insurance	2.4%
Tobacco and smoking products	0.7%		Motor vehicle maintenance and repair	1.1%
Other	7.1%		Airline fares	0.7%
FOOD	**13.4%**		Other	1.8%
Food at home	7.3%		**OTHER**	**13.6%**
Food away from home	6.1%			

REVIEW QUESTIONS

- What portion of a monthly budget does a typical U.S. consumer spend on new vehicles?

- Explain how these numbers are used in CPI calculations.

TABLE 21.1

Converting Past Prices into Modern Dollar Values

	Product	Year	Price	Conversion	Today's dollars (2018)	Today's actual price
	Coca-Cola (12 oz.)	1942	$0.05	**$0.05 × (252 ÷ 16)**	$0.79	$0.63
	Hershey's chocolate bar (1 oz.)	1921	0.05	**$0.05 × (252 ÷ 18)**	0.70	0.83
	McDonald's hamburger	1955	0.15	**$0.15 × (252 ÷ 27)**	1.40	1.00
	Nabisco's Oreo cookies (1 lb.)	1922	0.32	**$0.32 × (252 ÷ 17)**	4.74	2.99

Table 21.1 takes past prices from some iconic foods and converts them to today's dollars. For example, the price of a 1-pound bag of Oreo cookies was 32 cents in 1922. Using Equation 21.3, we multiply $0.32 by the modern price level (252) and divide by the 1922 price level (17) to determine the old price in today's dollars. It turns out that, once converted, the old price is $4.74, which is much higher than today's actual price of $2.99. The price in today's dollars corrects for the overall amount of inflation since 1922, helps make sense of historical prices, and dispels the notion that everything was less expensive in the past. This observation is nominally true but not especially interesting. Adjusting for inflation provides a real comparison, which is what good economists always look for.

ECONOMICS IN THE REAL WORLD

WHICH MOVIES ARE MOST POPULAR?

After a successful new movie comes out, the film industry totals up box office receipts and other revenue to see how well the movie has done. But the list is biased toward recent movies, because the data are in nominal terms and not adjusted for inflation.

For example, *Avatar* is ranked as the highest-grossing film of all time, because it earned more dollars (nominal revenue) than any other film, ever. *Titanic* held the top spot from 1998 to 2009, and before that *Star Wars* was number one from 1977 to 1997. Table 21.2 lists the top ten movies of all time, ranked by total nominal receipts. This list may not surprise you—there are several recent movies, like *Black Panther* and *Avengers: Infinity War*. But doesn't it seem odd that *Furious 7* would be the seventh-most-popular movie ever made? Of course, this is only true in nominal terms, the tally of receipts *not* adjusted for inflation.

Is *Avatar* really the most successful movie of all time?

Table 21.3 presents the top ten movies of all time after adjusting for inflation. This list is more meaningful, since the receipts of older movies are now comparable to the newer data, and with that, *Avatar* falls to number 4. The most recent movie still in the

TABLE 21.2

Top Movies of All Time, Ranked by Nominal Receipts

Rank	Movie	Receipts (millions)	Receipts adjusted for inflation, 2018 (millions)
1	*Avatar* (2009)	$2,776	$3,265
2	*Titanic* (1997)	2,208	3,453
3	*Star Wars: Ep. VII- The Force Awakens* (2015)	2,059	2,185
4	*Avengers: Infinity War* (2018)	2,014	2,014
5	*Jurassic World* (2015)	1,672	1,774
6	*The Avengers* (2012)	1,519	1,662
7	*Furious 7* (2015)	1,519	1,612
8	*Avengers: Age of Ultron* (2015)	1,408	1,494
9	*Black Panther* (2018)	1,347	1,347
10	*Harry Potter and the Deathly Hallows- Part 2* (2011)	1,342	1,512

Source: https://www.boxofficemojo.com/alltime/world/.

top ten is *Avengers: Infinity War*, from 2018. But the most impressive result on the list has to come from *Gone with the Wind*. Not only is the 1939 movie ranked number one, but the total revenue is more than twice as much as that from *Titanic*, which holds on to its second-place position. Of course, these rankings are always subject to change. In early 2019, *Avengers: Endgame* raked in over $1 billion worldwide in its first weekend (!) and looked poised to land on both top ten lists in short order.

TABLE 21.3

Top Movies of All Time, Ranked by Real Receipts

	Rank	Movie	Receipts (millions)	Receipts adjusted for inflation, 2018 (millions)
	1	Gone with the Wind (1939)	$391	$6,953
	2	Titanic (1997)	2,208	3,453
	3	Star Wars: Ep. IV- A New Hope (1977)	787	3,340
	4	Avatar (2009)	2,776	3,265
	5	The Exorcist (1973)	403	2,351
	6	The Sound of Music (1965)	286	2,281
	7	Jaws (1975)	471	2,243
	8	Star Wars: Ep. VII- The Force Awakens (2015)	2,059	2,185
	9	ET the Extra- Terrestrial (1982)	793	2,094
	10	Avengers: Infinity War (2018)	2,014	2,014

Source: https://www.boxofficemojo.com/alltime/world/.

The Accuracy of the CPI

We have seen that computing the CPI is not simple. Yet to understand what is happening in the macroeconomy, it is important that the CPI be accurate. For example, sometimes a rapid fall in inflation signals a recession, as it did in 1982 and 2008. Like real GDP and the unemployment rate, inflation is an indicator of national economic conditions.

Wage contracts for over 200,000 UPS employees are adjusted for inflation in reference to the CPI.

But there is another reason the CPI needs to be accurate: when employers adjust wages for inflation, they generally use the CPI. For example, when the United Auto Workers (UAW) union signs a wage agreement with General Motors, the agreement specifies wages for autoworkers several years in advance. Since future inflation is unknown and the UAW wants to protect its workers from excess inflation, the agreement stipulates that wages will be tied to the CPI. Therefore, when the CPI rises, the wages of UAW workers rise; when the CPI falls, the wages of UAW workers fall. So if the CPI overstates inflation, the miscalculation can cost companies millions of dollars. If the CPI understates inflation, this hurts workers, since their wages will not rise as much as they should.

How accurate is the CPI? If consumers always bought the same goods and services from the same suppliers, it would be extremely accurate, and economists could easily track prices over time. But this is not realistic. As time goes by, consumers buy different goods and services from different stores at different locations, and the quality of goods and services changes over time. So the typical basket keeps changing, and this makes it difficult to measure its price. The most common concern is that the CPI overstates true inflation. There are three reasons for this concern: the substitution of different goods and services; changes in quality; and the availability of new goods, services, and locations.

SUBSTITUTION When the price of a good rises, consumers instinctively look to substitute less expensive alternatives. This makes CPI calculations difficult because the typical consumer basket changes. Earlier, when we calculated an entertainment price index, we assumed that you always bought the same quantities of all goods and services, even when the price of popcorn rose and the price of Coke remained the same. However, it is more realistic to assume that if the price of popcorn rises, then some people will choose a less expensive snack. In other words, they find a substitute for popcorn. But when consumers substitute less expensive goods, that change alters the weights of all the goods and services in the typical consumption basket. Without acknowledging the substitution of less expensive items, the CPI would exaggerate the effects of the price increase, leading to upward bias (the reported CPI would be too high). Since 1999, the BLS has used a formula that accounts for both the price increase and the shift in goods and services consumption.

CHANGES IN QUALITY Over time, the quality of goods and services generally improves. For example, the movie theater you frequent may soon begin to offer all movies in 3D. Because this technology is more expensive than the older technology, the price of a ticket might rise from $10 to $12. The increase will seem like inflation, since ticket prices will go up. And yet, consumers get "more" movie for their buck, because the quality will have improved. If the CPI did not account for quality changes, it would have an upward bias in the true cost of living. But the BLS uses an adjustment method to account for quality changes.

NEW GOODS, SERVICES, AND LOCATIONS In a dynamic, growing economy, new goods and services are introduced and new buying options

Equating Dollar Values through Time

AUSTIN POWERS: INTERNATIONAL MAN OF MYSTERY

The Austin Powers series is a hilarious spoof of the James Bond films. In *International Man of Mystery*, we are introduced to British secret agent Austin Powers, who was cryofrozen at the end of the 1960s. Thirty years later, Austin Powers is thawed to help capture his nemesis, Dr. Evil, who was cryofrozen at the same time as Austin and has now stolen a nuclear weapon to hold the world hostage.

Being frozen for 30 years causes Dr. Evil to underestimate how much he should ask for in ransom money: "Gentlemen, it's come to my attention that a breakaway Russian republic called Kreplachistan will be transferring a nuclear warhead to the United Nations in a few days. Here's the plan. We get the warhead, and we hold the world ransom . . . FOR ONE MILLION DOLLARS!"

There is an uncomfortable pause.

Dr. Evil's Number Two speaks up: "Don't you think we should ask for more than a million dollars? A million dollars isn't that much money these days. Virtucon alone makes over nine billion dollars a year."

Dr. Evil responds (pleasantly surprised): "Oh, really? ONE HUNDRED BILLION DOLLARS!"

International Man of Mystery takes place in 1997, and Dr. Evil was frozen in 1967. How much did the price level rise over those 30 years? The CPI was 33.4 in 1967 and 160.5 in 1997. Dividing 160.5 by 33.4 yields

"ONE HUNDRED BILLION DOLLARS!"

a ratio of 4.8. So if Dr. Evil thought that $1 million was a lot of money in 1967, an equivalent amount in 1997 would be $4.8 million. Dr. Evil does not let that stop him from asking for more!

FIGURE 21.5

The Chained CPI versus the Traditional CPI

The chained CPI reduces the upward bias of the traditional CPI by updating the consumer's basket of goods and services every month. This single correction also accounts for price reductions that typically occur during the first few years after a new product has been introduced.

Source: U.S. Bureau of Labor Statistics.

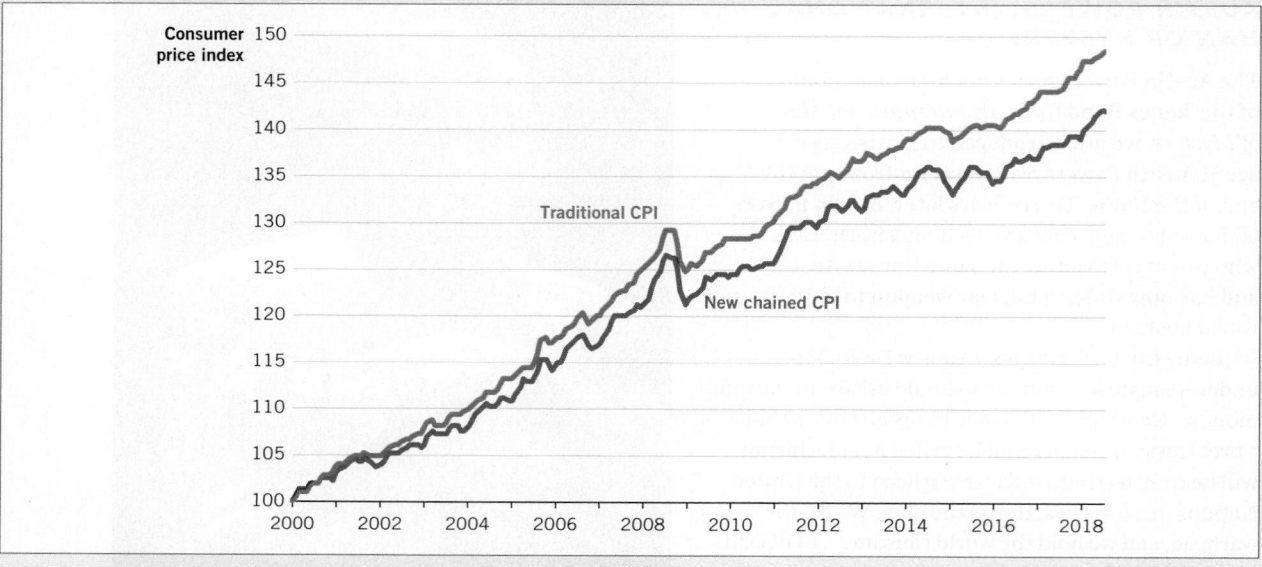

become available. For example, tablet computers, flash drives, and even cell phones weren't in the typical consumer's basket 25 years ago. In addition, Amazon.com and eBay weren't options for consumers to make purchases before the 1990s.

Traditionally, the BLS updated the CPI basket of goods and services only after long time delays. This strategy biased the CPI in an upward direction for two reasons. First, the prices of new products typically drop in the first few years after their introduction. If the CPI basket doesn't include the latest prices, this price drop is lost. Second, new retail outlets such as Internet stores typically offer lower prices than traditional retail stores. If the BLS continued to check prices only at traditional retail stores, it would overstate the price consumers actually pay for goods and services.

In an effort to measure this upward bias, the BLS began computing a chained CPI in 2000. The **chained CPI** is a measure of the CPI in which the typical consumer's basket of goods and services is updated monthly. While it's more difficult to measure and takes longer to estimate, the chained CPI is a better indicator of inflation for the typical consumer. Figure 21.5 shows the two CPI measures together. The vertical distance between the two lines indicates the upward bias of the traditional CPI, which updates the basket of goods and services less often. Notice that the distance grows over time.

The **chained CPI** is a measure of the CPI in which the typical consumer's "basket" of goods and services considered is updated monthly.

THE BILLION PRICES PROJECT

The Billion Prices Project (BPP) is an academic initiative at the Massachusetts Institute of Technology that monitors daily price fluctuations of approximately 5 million items sold by roughly 300 online retailers in more than 70 countries. The BPP is different from the CPI in that it only tracks the prices of goods and services sold online, and it does not weight those prices to reflect their importance in a typical consumer basket. However, even given these differences, the BPP coincides with the CPI rather closely. Figure 21.6 shows the BPP index along with the CPI. The BPP index often overestimates inflation, but the two lines track each other very closely.

Why would researchers create an alternative measure to the CPI? The answer, in part, is because having access to the Internet makes the gathering of real-time price data extremely easy. With time, researchers hope to be able to examine over a billion prices each day across every major sector of the economy. Because the BPP is based only on online sales, there are limitations in generalizing its findings to the entire economy. In relatively stable environments with low inflation, the BPP and CPI are not likely to be very different. When inflation is high (or highly variable), the BPP has the potential to point out meaningful trends in prices long before the CPI data can capture those changes.

FIGURE 21.6

The Billion Prices Project

The Billion Prices Project is an independent index that tracks prices across the Internet as an alternative to the CPI. As the data lines indicate, the BPP index looks very similar to the CPI; however, it is compiled exclusively from online retail prices and requires no input from government workers.

Source: BPP - PriceStats - State Street, http://bpp.mit.edu/usa/.

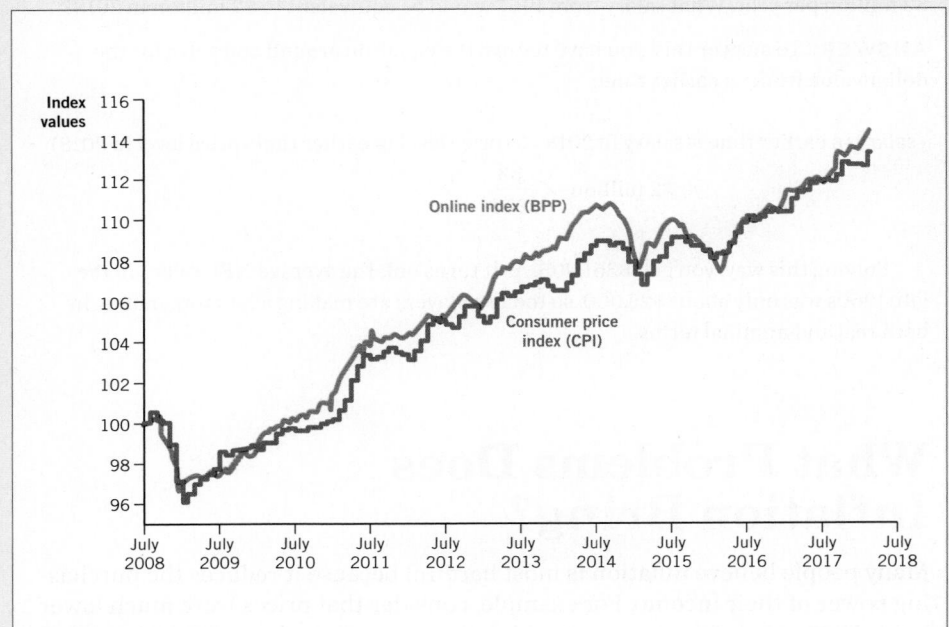

A 1967 Super Bowl ticket.

Using the CPI to Equate Prices over Time: How Cheap Were the First Super Bowl Tickets?

Ticket prices to America's premier sporting event, the Super Bowl, were much lower when it was first played in 1967. In fact, you could have bought a ticket for as little as $6. This seems very low by today's prices. In 2018, many seats sold for more than $5,000 each.

QUESTION: If the CPI from 1967 was 33 and the CPI for 2018 was 252, how would you convert the price of a $6 ticket in 1967 to 2018 dollars?

ANSWER: For this question, we need to use Equation 21.3:

$$\text{price in today's dollars} = \text{price in earlier time} \times \frac{\text{price level today}}{\text{price level in earlier time}}$$

The earlier price was $6, so we substitute this price and the two price levels from above to get

$$\text{price in today's dollars} = \$6 \times \frac{252}{33} = \$45.82$$

It turns out that the old Super Bowl tickets were indeed cheap—you'd be lucky to get a hot dog and a soda at a modern Super Bowl for $45.82.

CHALLENGE QUESTION: NFL players are now paid, on average, more than $2 million per year. What salary from 1967 would be equivalent to $2 million in 2018?

ANSWER: To answer this, you have to turn the equation around and solve for the dollar value from an earlier time:

$$\text{salary in earlier time} = \text{salary in 2018} \times (\text{price level in earlier time/price level in 2018})$$
$$= \$2 \text{ million} \times \frac{33}{252}$$

Solving this way, you get: $261,905. As it turns out, the average NFL salary in the late 1960s was only about $25,000, so today's players are making a lot more money in both real and nominal terms.

What Problems Does Inflation Bring?

Many people believe inflation is most harmful because it reduces the purchasing power of their income. For example, consider that prices were much lower in the 1970s; therefore, it's easy to think that an annual salary of $10,000 at that time could buy a lot more than it can today. Well, this would be true if all else were equal. But salaries are prices, too (prices for labor), and inflation causes them to rise as well. Remember: inflation is an overall rise in prices throughout the economy.

But this does not mean that inflation is harmless. Indeed, inflation does impose many costs on an economy. In this section, we discuss these costs. They include shoe-leather costs, money illusion, menu costs, uncertainty over future price levels, wealth redistribution, price confusion, and tax distortions.

When inflation reaches the levels witnessed in Venezuela in 2018, shoe-leather costs are significant.

Shoe-Leather Costs

Inflation is costly for society when it causes people to do things they wouldn't do in an environment of price stability. The higher the rate of inflation, the more likely people are to change their normal patterns of spending and money-holding. This is because inflation is essentially a tax on holding money. As prices of goods and services rise with inflation, the value of dollars in people's wallets falls. This problem is not currently severe in the United States because inflation rates are very low. But in hyperinflation, the value of dollars falls daily.

To avoid the "tax" on holding money, people hold less money, which means more trips to the bank to make withdrawals. **Shoe-leather costs** are the resources that are wasted when people change their behavior to avoid holding money. In times past, these costs referred to the actual expense of replacing shoes that might get worn out as a result of making many trips to the bank. Today, these include fuel costs and the time used for multiple trips to a bank or ATM.

Shoe-leather costs are the resources that are wasted when people change their behavior to avoid holding money.

Money Illusion

The second problem from inflation is among the least understood. Even when people know inflation has occurred, they do not always react rationally. So although wages and prices might rise because of inflation, people frequently respond as if the prices are higher in real terms. For example, if the price of a movie goes up by 10% but wages and other prices also rise by 10%, nothing changes in real terms. But many people mistakenly conclude that movies have become more expensive. If they treat a price increase from inflation as a change in relative price, they may go see fewer movies or make other decisions based on the new price. Economists call this *money illusion*. **Money illusion** occurs when people interpret nominal changes in wages or prices as real changes.

Money illusion occurs when people interpret nominal changes in wages or prices as real changes.

Money illusion is an easy trap to fall into. Let's see if we can trick you into it. Consider the cost-of-living data presented in Table 21.4. The index scores show relative living costs for an average person living in various U.S. cities. The index is set so that 100 is the cost of living in an average U.S. city.

For this example, let's focus on two particular cities: Philadelphia, Pennsylvania, and Charlotte, North Carolina. The index score for Philadelphia is 126.5; for Charlotte, it is 93.2. These index scores imply that a salary of $93,200 for a person living in Charlotte is equivalent to a salary of $126,500 for a person living in Philadelphia, even though the difference is more than $30,000.

TABLE 21.4

The Cost of Living in Selected U.S. Cities

City	Cost-of-living index number
New York (Manhattan)	216.7
San Francisco, CA	164.0
Washington, DC	140.1
Los Angeles, CA	136.4
Boston, MA	132.5
Philadelphia, PA	126.5
Seattle, WA	121.4
Chicago, IL	116.9
Richmond, VA	104.5
Phoenix, AZ	100.7
Detroit, MI	99.4
Atlanta, GA	95.6
Charlotte, NC	93.2
Dallas, TX	91.9

Source: U.S Census, Annual Average 2010.

Now imagine that you are living in Charlotte and earning $93,200, but your firm offers to relocate you to Philadelphia at a pay rate of $100,000. Doesn't that seem like a pretty large raise? You might be excited to call your parents and tell them you'll be making "six figures." But, in fact, it is actually a real pay cut, since you can buy less with $100,000 in Philadelphia than you can with $93,200 in Charlotte. Money illusion makes it feel like a raise.

The key distinction in this situation is between real wages and nominal wages. The concept of a nominal wage is analogous to nominal GDP. A worker's **nominal wage** is his or her wage expressed in current dollars, like $60 per hour or $120,000 per year. The **real wage** is the nominal wage adjusted for changes in the price level. The real wage is more informative because it describes what the worker earns in terms of purchasing power. So while a salary of $100,000 a year may sound high, if the CPI doubles, that salary does not go far.

Significant macroeconomic problems arise if workers fall victim to money illusion when they interpret the value of their wages, because the illusion causes them to focus on their nominal wage instead of their real wage. For example, when prices fall, any given nominal wage is worth more in real terms. In Chapter 26, we'll see that macroeconomic adjustments can depend on whether workers are willing to let wages fall when other prices fall. Money illusion causes these adjustments to take longer than they should, and this delay tends to lengthen economic downturns.

A worker's **nominal wage** is his or her wage expressed in current dollars.

The **real wage** is the nominal wage adjusted for changes in the price level.

Menu Costs

The act of physically changing prices is also costly. **Menu costs** are the costs of changing prices. While some businesses can change prices easily—for example, gas pumps and signs at gas stations are designed for this

Menu costs are the costs of changing prices.

purpose—businesses such as restaurants can find it expensive to print new menus when their prices change.

Other costs considered in this category are not directly related to menus. For example, changing prices can make regular customers angry enough to take their business elsewhere. Think about your favorite lunch spot. Perhaps you regularly buy a bagel and lemonade for $5 at Bodo's Bagels. What if the price for this combination suddenly increases to $6? You might be annoyed enough to go somewhere else next time.

Menu costs discourage firms from adjusting prices quickly. When some prices are slow to respond, the effects of macroeconomic disturbances are magnified.

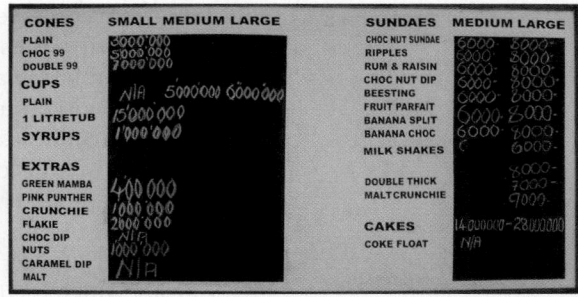

Chalk menus are one way to limit menu costs. This menu is from an ice cream parlor in Zimbabwe during its 2008 hyperinflation. Notice that the price of a small chocolate cone is 5 million Zimbabwean dollars.

Future Price Level Uncertainty

Imagine you decide to open a new coffee shop in your college town. You want to produce espressos, café mochas, and cappuccinos. Of course, you hope to sell these for a profit. But before you can sell a single cup of coffee, you have to spend funds on your resources. You have to buy (that is, invest in) capital goods like an espresso bar, tables, chairs, and a cash register. You also have to hire workers and promise to pay them. All firms, large and small, face this situation. Before any revenue arrives from the sales of output, firms have to spend on resources. This also applies to the overall macroeconomy: to increase GDP in the future, firms must invest today. The funds required to make these investments are typically borrowed from others.

The timeline of production shown in Figure 21.7 illustrates how this process works. At the end, the firm sells its output. **Output** is the product the firm creates. The key point is that in a normal production process, funds are spent today and then repaid in the future—after the output sells. But for this sequence of events to occur, businesses must make promises to deliver payments in the future: these include payments to workers and lenders. Thus, two types of

Output
is the product the firm creates.

FIGURE 21.7

The Timeline of Production

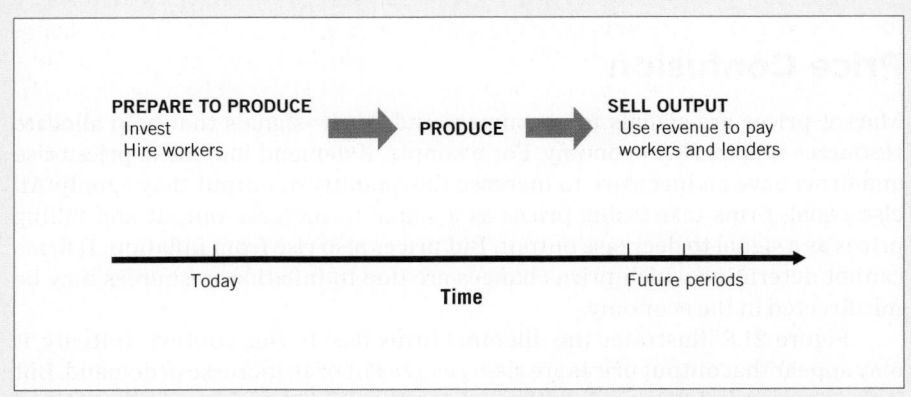

PREPARE TO PRODUCE
Invest
Hire workers

PRODUCE

SELL OUTPUT
Use revenue to pay workers and lenders

Today

Future periods

Time

The way output is typically produced begins with preparation that includes purchases of equipment, labor, and other resources. Actual output and revenue from the sale of output come later. Thus, a firm can only begin production with promises of future payments to resource suppliers.

long-term agreements form the foundation for production: wage and loan contracts. Both of these involve the delivery of dollars in future periods.

But inflation affects the real value of these future dollars. When inflation confuses workers and lenders, these essential long-term agreements seem risky and lenders are less likely to agree to them. Chapter 22 focuses on the market for loans in an economy, and we cover this topic at a deeper level there. For now, we note that inflation can cripple loan markets because people don't know future price levels. When firms cannot borrow money or hire long-term workers, future production is limited. Thus, inflation risk can lead to lower economic output, which is GDP.

Wealth Redistribution

Inflation can also redistribute wealth between borrowers and lenders. Returning to our coffee shop example, imagine that you borrow $50,000 to start your business. You borrow this sum from a bank with the promise of paying back $60,000 in five years. Now if inflation unexpectedly rises during those five years, the inflation devalues your future payment to the bank. As a result, you are better off, but the bank is worse off. Thus, surprise inflation redistributes wealth from lenders to borrowers.

If both you and the bank fully expect the inflation to occur, the bank requires more in return for the loan, so the inflation is less of a problem. In the United States, inflation has been low and steady since the early 1980s. Therefore, surprises are rare. But nations with high inflation rates also have a high variability of inflation, which makes it difficult to predict the future. This is one more reason why high inflation increases the risk of making the loans that are an important source of funding for business ventures.

You might assume that deflation, or falling prices, brings only positive side effects for the economy. After all, wouldn't it be great if the prices of the goods and services you purchase began falling? But unexpected deflation redistributes wealth in the other direction—from borrowers to lenders. Consider again the $50,000 loan with promised repayment of $60,000 in five years. Now, if prices fall unexpectedly over the course of the five years, the real value of the $60,000 loan repayment increases. This helps the lender but harms the borrower. In response, fewer of these loans will be made and this is not helpful to the economy as a whole.

Price Confusion

Market prices are signals to consumers and firms—signals that help allocate resources in a market economy. For example, if demand increases, prices rise and firms have an incentive to increase the quantity of output they supply. All else equal, firms take rising prices as a signal to increase output and falling prices as a signal to decrease output. But prices also rise from inflation. If firms cannot determine which price changes are due to inflation, resources may be misdirected in the economy.

Figure 21.8 illustrates the dilemma firms face in this context. Initially, it may appear that output prices are rising as a result of an increase in demand. But if the cause is inflation, prices throughout the economy rise and the optimal output for the firm should remain at the original output level. If firms always

FIGURE 21.8

"Why Did My Price Change?"

Price changes send information, or signals, to businesses. However, higher prices can be the result of either a real increase in demand or inflation. If upward pressure on prices is the result of greater demand, the profit-maximizing firm should increase its output. But if the price increase is the result of inflation, the firm should not change its level of output.

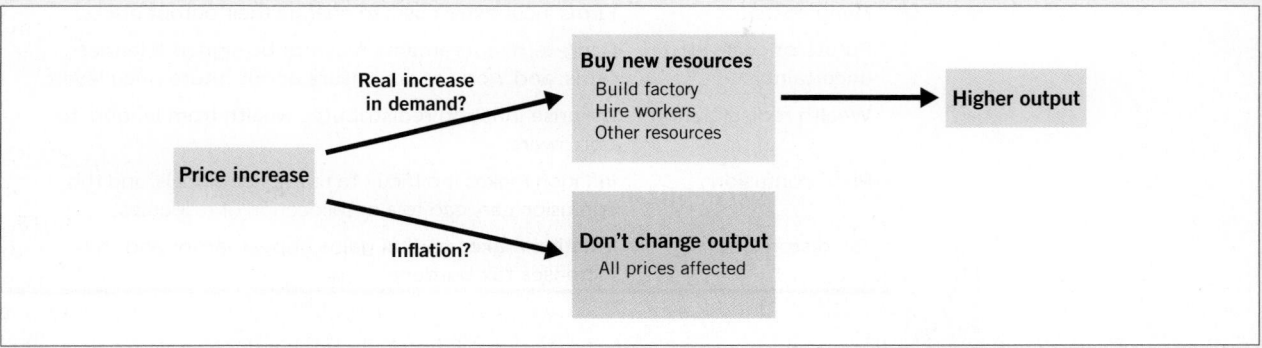

react to price increases by increasing their output, they run the risk of over-building. This can be painful later.

The housing market in the United States provides a good example of price confusion. In 2005, housing prices were high and rising. We can look back now and recognize a price bubble that did not reflect real long-run increases in demand. It appears now that rising housing prices reflected inflation. However, high prices at the time spurred many builders to develop more properties. When housing prices later fell, many of those builders declared bankruptcy. The crash in housing prices was one of the contributing factors to the Great Recession, which began at the end of 2007.

Tax Distortions

Even if inflation causes all prices to rise uniformly, there are still distortionary effects. These will occur because tax laws do not typically account for inflation. One area in which particularly distortionary effects occur is capital gains taxes.

Capital gains taxes are taxes on the gains realized by selling an asset for more than its purchase price. For example, if your parents bought a house in 1980 for $80,000 and then sold it in 2012 for $230,000, they made a $150,000 capital gain on the sale of the house, and this capital gain is taxed. However, it turns out that the CPI rose by exactly the same amount between 1980 and 2012: the CPI was 80 in 1980 and climbed to 230 by 2012. Therefore, the value of your parents' house just kept pace with inflation. In real terms, the value of their house did not climb. But they would still be required to pay a significant tax on the sale of their home. As it turns out, the amount of their tax was determined by inflation and not by the tax laws; if there had been no inflation, your parents would have owed no tax.

Capital gains are realized on more than just home sales. Capital gains also arise with the sales of stocks, bonds, and other financial securities. As we will

Capital gains taxes are taxes on the gains realized by selling an asset for more than its purchase price.

TABLE 21.5

The Costs of Inflation

Cost of inflation	Description
Shoe-leather costs	Time and resources are spent to guard against the effects of inflation.
Money illusion	Consumers misinterpret nominal changes as real changes.
Menu costs	Firms incur extra costs to change their output prices.
Future price level uncertainty	Long-term agreements may not be signed if lenders, firms, and workers are unsure about future price levels.
Wealth redistribution	Surprise inflation redistributes wealth from lenders to borrowers.
Price confusion	Inflation makes it difficult to read price signals, and this confusion can lead to a misallocation of resources.
Tax distortions	Inflation makes capital gains appear larger and thus increases tax burdens.

discuss in Chapter 23, these securities are a crucial ingredient to a growing and expanding economy. But inflation combined with a capital gains tax means that most people will be less likely to make these kinds of purchases. One possible solution is to rewrite the tax laws to take account of inflation's effects.

In this section, we have detailed several economic costs that arise from inflation. Table 21.5 summarizes these costs.

PRACTICE WHAT YOU KNOW

Problems with Inflation: How Big Is Your Raise in Real Terms?

Your boss calls you into his office and tells you he has good news. Because of your stellar performance and hard work, you have earned a 3% raise for next year. But when you think about your future pay, you should also know how much inflation has eroded your current pay. For example, if the inflation rate is 3% per year, then you need a 3% raise just to keep pace with inflation. Note that you can see inflation rates for yourself by visiting the Bureau of Labor Statistics web site (www.bls.gov). Once there, look up inflation rates based on the CPI.

QUESTION: In what situation would a 3% raise signify a lower real wage?

ANSWER: If the inflation rate is greater than 3%, then a 3% raise would actually be a decline in your real wage.

QUESTION: What inflation problem must you overcome to correctly see the value of your raise?

ANSWER: Money illusion. You must evaluate the real, rather than the nominal, value of your pay.

What Is the Cause of Inflation?

Because inflation brings serious macroeconomic costs, you might assume there is significant debate about its cause. But that assumption would be incorrect. Economist Milton Friedman famously said, "Inflation is always and everywhere a monetary phenomenon." What he meant is that inflation is consistently caused by increases in a nation's money supply relative to the quantity of real goods and services in the economy.

Figure 21.9 shows average inflation rates and the money supply growth rates across 138 nations for the years 1996–2016. It is difficult to distinguish all 138 nations, because almost all of the data points are clumped together in the region where average inflation was less than 10 percent. This scatterplot makes it clear that inflation and money growth are certainly tied together. A few nations with very high average inflation rates are easy to pick out. For example, in this sample, the average inflation rate in Angola was 52% per year, and that inflation stemmed from a monetary growth rate of about 66%.

In Chapter 31, we will address this question more formally; we will use a macroeconomic model to show how monetary expansion translates into inflation. But the intuition is straightforward: when the supply of money in an economy grows *relative to the quantity of goods and services*, then it takes more money to buy any particular good or service. Money then becomes less valuable relative to goods and services—and this relationship constitutes inflation. The principle holds true regardless of the type of money used. For example, when Spanish conquistadors brought gold back to Europe from Latin America in the sixteenth century, the supply of money (gold) in Europe increased, and this led to inflation.

The printing press: the cause of inflation.

FIGURE 21.9

Inflation and Money Growth Rates in 138 countries, 1996–2016

The relationship between inflation rates and money growth rates is clear over long periods of time. This relationship applies to nations with low inflation rates and to nations with high inflation rates.

Source: World Bank.

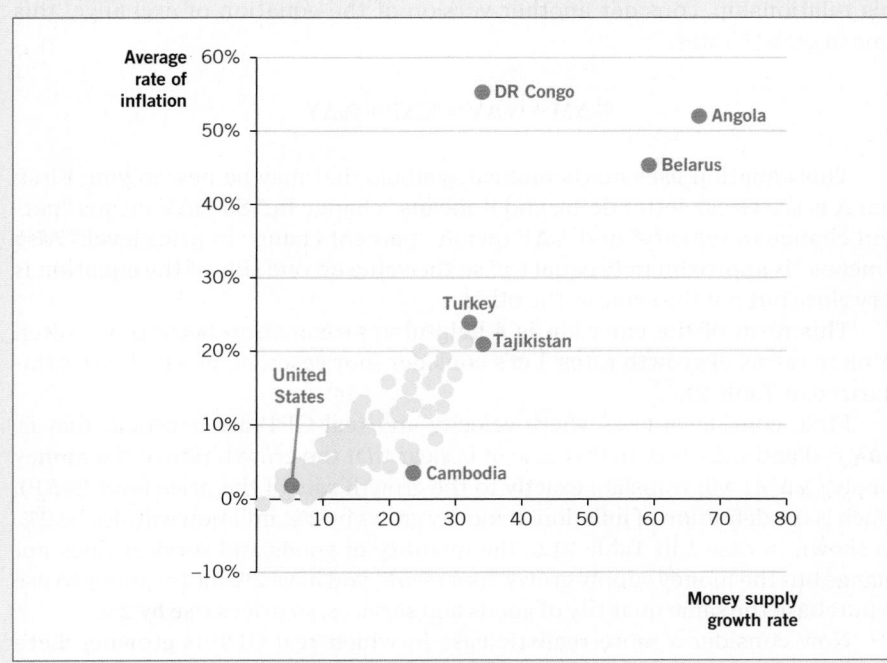

The Equation of Exchange

The data presented in the last section show that more money in an economy generally leads to higher prices. Theoretically, this relationship makes sense. For example, if you have a given level of real GDP in an economy and the money supply doubles, you have twice as many dollars chasing the same quantity of final goods and services. Eventually, it will take about twice as many dollars to buy any particular good or service—which means prices double.

We can summarize that long-run relationship between the price level and the quantity of money with a simple relationship known as the **equation of exchange**. The equation of exchange specifies the long-run relationship between the money supply, the price level, real GDP, and the velocity of money. The actual equation is

$$M \times V = P \times Y$$

The right side of the equation is nominal GDP, or real GDP (Y) times the price level (P). The left side includes the quantity of money in the economy (M) and the velocity of money (V). The **velocity of money** is the number of times a unit of money exchanges hands in a given year. The equation of exchange represents the fact that GDP in a given year is purchased with money, but that money can (and does) turn over more than once in a given year. We'll define money (M) very carefully in Chapter 30, but for now you should know that money includes more than paper currency and coins. Money includes whatever we use in exchange for goods and services. For this reason, the equation of exchange is actually an identity—it is true by definition.

The equation of exchange gives a direct relationship between prices and the size of the money supply, especially if velocity doesn't change much. To see this relationship, consider another version of the equation of exchange, this time in growth rates:

$$\%\Delta M + \%\Delta V \approx \%\Delta P + \%\Delta Y$$

This equation uses mathematical symbols that may be new to you. First, that Δ is the Greek letter delta, and it means "change in." So $\%\Delta V$ means "percent change in velocity" and $\%\Delta P$ means "percent change in price level." Also $\approx$ means "is approximately equal to," so the value on one side of the equation is very close but not the same as the other.

This form of the equation is a helpful approximation because we often think in terms of growth rates. Let's consider four cases, all of which are summarized in Table 21.6.

First, consider a case where velocity and real GDP are constant, that is, $\%\Delta V = 0$ and $\%\Delta Y = 0$. In this case, it is clear that the growth rate of the money supply ($\%\Delta M$) will translate exactly to the growth rate of the price level ($\%\Delta P$), which is the definition of inflation. If money grows by 2%, inflation will also be 2%. As shown in case 1 in Table 21.6, the quantity of goods and services does not change but the money supply grows. As a result, you have 2% more money to use to purchase the same quantity of goods and services, so prices rise by 2%.

Now consider a more realistic case in which real GDP is growing. Let's continue the assumptions that the money supply grows at 2% and velocity does not change. In this case, if real GDP grows at 2% in a given year, then there

The **equation of exchange** specifies the long-run relationship between the money supply, the price level, real GDP, and the velocity of money.

The **velocity of money** is the number of times a unit of money exchanges hands in a given year.

TABLE 21.6

Four Scenarios for the Equation of Exchange

	%ΔM	+	%ΔV	=	%ΔP	+	%ΔY
	Money growth		Velocity growth		Inflation		Real GDP growth
Case 1	2	+	0	=	2	+	0
Case 2	2	+	0	=	0	+	2
Case 3	4	+	0	=	2	+	2
Case 4	9	+	−5	=	2	+	2

is no change in the price level (%ΔP = 0). In this scenario, presented as case 2 in Table 21.6, the money supply grows at exactly the same rate as real GDP, so there is no effect on the price level.

Consider a third, even more realistic case. A typical year brings both real GDP growth and some inflation. In this case, if velocity is constant, the money supply is growing at a greater rate than real GDP growth. Case 3 in Table 21.6 presents such a scenario: real GDP grows at 2% and inflation is also 2%. In this case, with constant velocity, the growth rate of the money supply must be 4%.

Finally, let's consider a case where velocity changes (case 4 in Table 21.6). Changes in velocity occur when those who hold money (for example, individuals and banks) decide to change their spending habits. If people and banks decide to spend their dollars at faster rates, velocity rises. When people and banks decide to hold on to money longer, velocity falls. Let's consider this latter possibility, since it is related to changes in the macroeconomy during the severe recession from 2007 to 2009. What if velocity falls by 5% (%ΔV = −5)? Let's assume that real GDP rises by 2% and that the money supply grows by 9%. Our equation implies that despite the large money supply increase, inflation (%ΔP) is just 2%. Inflation is low because people and banks have decided to hold on to their money longer. The equation of exchange helps us see that changes in all four of these variables—money, velocity, the price level, and real GDP—must be accounted for.

The Reasons Why Governments Inflate the Money Supply

In this chapter, we discussed several problems that stem from inflation: shoe-leather costs, money illusion, menu costs, future price level uncertainty, wealth redistribution, price confusion, and tax distortions. And yet we know what causes inflation. Thus, it is reasonable to wonder why inflation is often still a macroeconomic problem. We point to two reasons: large government debts and short-term gains.

First, large government debts often spur governments to choose to increase the money supply rapidly. When a government owes large sums and also controls the supply of money, there is a natural urge to print more money to pay off debts. After World War I, the German government owed billions of dollars to other nations and to its workers, so it resorted to printing more money—and this action led to inflation rates of almost 30,000% in late 1923.

Second, surprise increases in the money supply can temporarily stimulate an economy toward more rapid growth rates. We'll look at this issue very closely in Chapter 31, but the short-term economic boost is a constant temptation for short-sighted governments. The problems from inflation are often long-term and difficult to overcome. Unfortunately, to realize any benefits from inflation, the government must keep surprising people in the economy. As a result of these attempts to stay ahead of expectations, inflation can spiral out of control.

Conclusion

This chapter began with the story of Venezuela, where hyperinflation has added to the serious woes of that economy. And while inflation rates have been low in the United States for several years now, at times in the past they have been very high—such as during the 1970s. In addition, inflation rates in some other nations remain high.

Inflation, along with the unemployment rate and changes in real GDP, is an important indicator of overall macroeconomic conditions. Now that we have covered these three, we move next to savings and the determination of interest rates. ✳

Inflation Devalues Dollars: Preparing Your Future for Inflation

- Remember that things will likely cost more in the future when you retire due to inflation.
- To keep up, or grow, your savings has to earn an annual return that is at least the same rate or more.
- Money saved in a mattress will always lose value because of inflation! You need to think about investing it somewhere.

In this chapter, we talked about how inflation devalues the money you currently hold and the money you've been promised in the future. One problem you may encounter is how to prepare for retirement in the face of inflation. Perhaps you are not worried about this, since the inflation rate in the United States over the past 50 years has averaged 4%, and more recently the average has been only 2%. But even these low rates mean that dollars will be worth significantly less 40 years from now.

One way to think about the effect of inflation on future dollars is to ask what amount of future dollars it will take to match the real value of $1.00 today. The graph below answers this question based on a retirement date of 40 years in the future. The different inflation rates are specified at the bottom.

How many nest eggs will you need to put aside to keep pace with inflation?

Thus, if the inflation rate averages 4% over the next four decades, you'll need $4.80 just to buy the same goods and services you can buy today for $1.00.

What does this mean for your overall retirement plans? Let's say you decide you could live on $50,000 per year if you retired today. If the inflation rate is 4% between now and your retirement date, you would need enough savings to supply yourself with 50,000 × $4.80, or $240,000 per year, just to keep pace with inflation.

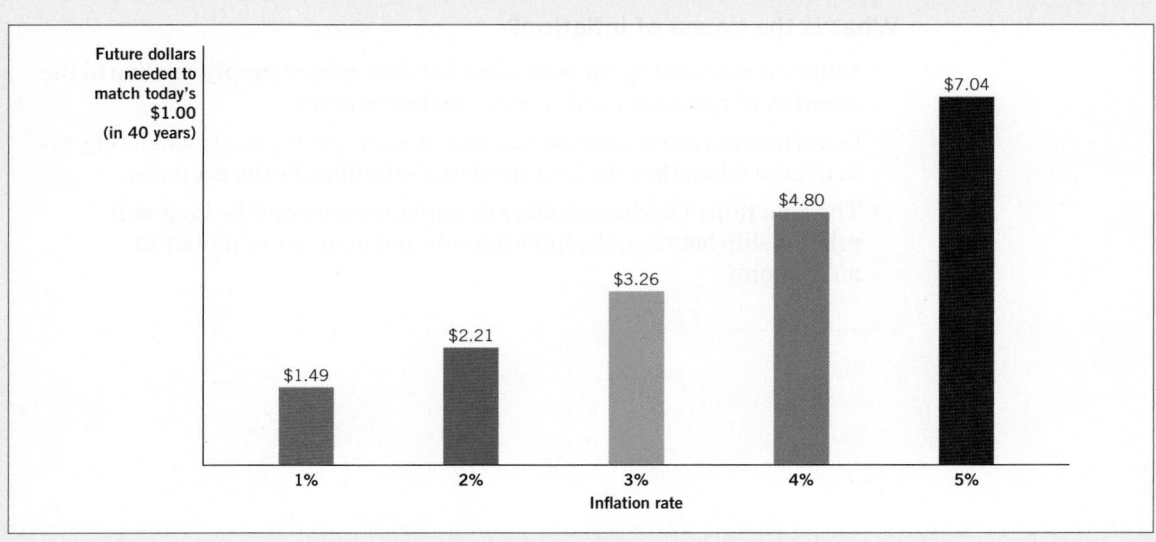

Future dollars needed to match today's $1.00 (in 40 years)

Inflation rate	Value
1%	$1.49
2%	$2.21
3%	$3.26
4%	$4.80
5%	$7.04

· ANSWERING *the* BIG QUESTIONS ·

How is inflation measured?

- The inflation rate is calculated as the percentage change in the overall level of prices.
- Economists use the consumer price index (CPI) to determine the general level of prices in the economy.
- Determining which prices to include in the CPI can be challenging for several reasons: consumers change what they buy over time; the quality of goods and services changes; and new goods, services, and sales locations are introduced.

What problems does inflation bring?

- Inflation imposes shoe-leather costs: it causes people to waste resources as they seek to avoid holding money.
- Inflation can cause people to make decisions based on nominal rather than real monetary values, a problem known as money illusion.
- Inflation adds menu costs, as sellers need to physically change prices.
- Inflation introduces uncertainty about future price levels. Because uncertainty makes it difficult for consumers and producers to plan, it impedes economic progress.
- Unexpected inflation redistributes wealth from lenders to borrowers.
- Inflation creates price confusion: that is, it makes it difficult for producers to read price signals correctly. The result may be a misallocation of resources.
- Inflation distorts people's tax obligations.

What is the cause of inflation?

- Inflation is caused by increases in a nation's money supply relative to the quantity of real goods and services in the economy.
- Governments often increase the money supply too quickly when they are in debt or when they desire a short-run stimulus for the economy.
- The equation of exchange offers a simple summary of the long-run relationship between the inflation rate and quantity of money in an economy.

·CHAPTER PROBLEMS·

Concepts You Should Know

capital gains taxes (p. 691)
chained CPI (p. 684)
consumer price index (CPI) (p. 671)
deflation (p. 671)

equation of exchange (p. 694)
menu costs (p. 688)
money illusion (p. 687)
nominal wage (p. 688)

output (p. 689)
real wage (p. 688)
shoe-leather costs (p. 687)
velocity of money (p. 694)

Questions for Review

1. The price of a typical laptop computer has fallen from $2,000 in 1985 to $800 today. At the same time, the consumer price index has risen from 100 to 252. Adjusting for inflation, how much did the price of laptops change? Does this answer seem right to you, or is it missing something? Explain your response.

2. What three issues are at the center of the debate regarding the accuracy of the CPI? Give an example of each issue.

3. If the prices of homes go up by 5% and the prices of concert tickets rise by 10%, which will have the larger impact on the CPI? Why?

4. If a country is experiencing a relatively high rate of inflation, what impact will this have on the country's long-term rate of economic growth?

5. In a sentence or two, evaluate the accuracy of the following statement, including a clear and precise statement of historical comparison: Inflation in the United States last year was 0%. This is close to the historical level.

6. Wage agreements and loan contracts are two types of multiperiod agreements that are important for economic growth. Suppose you sign a two-year job contract with Wells Fargo stipulating that you will receive an annual salary of $93,500 plus an additional 2% above that in the second year, to account for expected inflation.

   a. If the inflation rate turns out to be 3% rather than 2%, who will be hurt? Why?

   b. If the inflation rate turns out to be 1% rather than 2%, who will be hurt? Why?

Suppose that you also take out a $1,000 loan at the Cavalier Credit Union. The loan agreement stipulates that you must pay it back with 4% interest in one year, and again, the inflation rate is expected to be 2%.

   c. If the inflation rate turns out to be 3% rather than 2%, who will be hurt? Why?

   d. If the inflation rate turns out to be 3% rather than 2%, who will be helped? Why?

7. What are the seven problems caused by inflation? Briefly explain each one.

8. Here is a list of potential problems that inflation might cause. Use the space on the left to name each of these with the terms used in this chapter.

   a. _____ Lenders and workers are reluctant to help firms produce output because the real value of future dollar payoffs is unclear.

   b. _____ Workers make decisions on the basis of nominal rather than real wage changes.

   c. _____ Unexpected inflation reduces the real value of loan repayments.

   d. _____ Firms cannot distinguish whether there is a change in the relative price of their good or a change in the overall price level.

   e. _____ Restaurants need to spend resources to alter the prices on their menus.

   f. _____ Individuals own stock shares for many years and then sell them and are required to pay taxes on the nominal capital gain.

   g. _____ People leave work early to shop before inflation changes prices.

9. Inflation causes a lot of problems for the macroeconomy.

   a. What is the key misconception people have about inflation, and why does this problem generally not accompany inflation?

   b. In this chapter, we discussed the problem of price confusion and the problem of future price uncertainty. Explain the difference between these two problems.

   c. Wealth redistribution is another problem caused by inflation. What is this problem, and how is it related to the future price uncertainty?

10. People often confuse real and nominal variables in macroeconomics.

   a. Give a hypothetical example where nominal wages rise but real wages do not, using specific numbers to illustrate changes in all relevant macroeconomic variables.

   b. Give a hypothetical example of a situation where real wages rise but nominal wages fall, using specific numbers to illustrate changes in all relevant macroeconomic variables.

11. Explain the difference(s) between the CPI and the GDP deflator.

Study Problems (✳ solved at the end of the section)

1. In 1991, the Barenaked Ladies released their hit song "If I Had a Million Dollars." How much money would the group need in 2018 to have the same amount of real purchasing power they had in 1991? Note that the consumer price index in 1991 was 136.2 and in 2018 it was 252.

2. Visit the Bureau of Labor Statistics web site for the CPI (www.bls.gov/cpi), and find the latest news release. Table 1 in that release presents CPI data for all items and also for many individual categories.

   a. How much has the entire index changed (in percentage terms) in the past year?

   b. Now identify and list the five individual categories that have increased the most in the past year.

3. While rooting through the attic, you discover a box of old tax forms. You find that your grand-mother made $75 working part-time during December 1964, when the CPI was 31.3. How much would you need to have earned in January of this year to have at least as much real income as your grandmother did in 1964? To determine the CPI for January of this year, you can visit the Bureau of Labor Statistics web site (www.bls.gov).

✳ 4. Suppose that the residents of Greenland play golf incessantly. In fact, golf is the only thing they spend their money on. They buy golf balls, clubs, and tees. In 2019, they bought 1,000 golf balls for

$2.00 each, 100 clubs for $50.00 each, and 500 tees for $0.10 each. In 2020, they bought 1,000 golf balls for $2.50 each, 100 clubs for $75.00 each, and 500 tees for $0.12 each.

   a. What was the CPI for each year?
   b. What was the inflation rate in 2020?

✳ 5. If healthcare costs make up 10% of total expenditures and they rise by 15% while the other components in the consumer price index remain constant, by how much will the price index rise?

✳ 6. The equation of exchange is helpful for determining the effect of money supply changes on the price level. Use the equation of exchange to answer each of the following questions.

   a. Real GDP grows at 3% and inflation is equal to 2%, but there is no change in velocity. What can you conclude about the change in the money supply?

   b. Real GDP falls by 3% and there is no inflation, but the money supply grew by 5%. What is the implied change in velocity?

   c. Real GDP increases by 3%, velocity does not change, and the money supply grows by 10%. What is the implied rate of inflation?

   d. The money supply grows at 6%, velocity is constant, and inflation is 3%. What can you conclude about the rate of real GDP growth?

7. Let's say you graduate from college and accept a job in 2018. You decide to compare your starting salary with your grandfather's and mother's starting salaries. The salaries you compare are:

- You: $80,000 per year beginning in 2021
- Your mother: $50,000 per year beginning in 1983
- Your grandfather: $20,000 per year beginning in 1965

To compare these salaries, you decide to use the CPI, using 1983 as the base year.

a. Why is the CPI a good price index to use for this comparison?

b. Fill in the missing data point in the following table:

Year	CPI
1965	30
1983	___
2015	238
2018	240

c. Convert both your mother's salary and your grandfather's salary to 2018 dollars. Enter your answers in the table below.

Grandfather's 1965 salary in 2018 dollars	_____
Mother's 1983 salary in 2018 dollars	_____

✳ 8. In the following chart, which of these prices would be included in the CPI? Which would be included in the GDP deflator? Which would be included in both or neither? Mark the correct option for each price.

Price of	CPI	GDP Deflator	Both	Neither
Toothpaste	☐	☐	☐	☐
Industrial coolant	☐	☐	☐	☐
Milk you bought in a grocery store	☐	☐	☐	☐
Milk bought by Starbucks from a food distributor	☐	☐	☐	☐
An Intel computer chip bought by Dell to put into a laptop computer	☐	☐	☐	☐
Bus fare for a trip to a shopping mall	☐	☐	☐	☐
A doctor's appointment, to get a physical	☐	☐	☐	☐

9. In the United States, average income levels vary across racial lines. In particular, Asians tend to earn more than whites, and both groups earn more than Hispanics and blacks. However, economist Jeff Guo looked closely at the data and noted that much of the difference between Asians and other groups can be attributed to the fact that Asians tend to live in more expensive urban areas. In real terms, their wages are not so different from those of other groups.

a. Asian American households earn an average annual income of $82,270, but while the average price level across the United States is 100, the price level where Asian Americans tend to live is 109. Calculate a comparable real income for Asian Americans.

b. Black Americans earn an average of $44,170 per year but live in areas with lower average prices than all races combined. The average price level where Black Americans live is 98.374. Assume that the average price level across the United States is 100, and then compute a real earnings figure that is comparable to average incomes across the United States.

c. Hispanic Americans have an average annual income of $45,320, but when adjusted for the price levels in their area, this number falls to $43,890. Given these two figures, what is the implied price level in the areas where Hispanic Americans live?

Solved Problems

4.a. We'll use the quantities from the first year to designate the weights. To build a price index, we first need to choose which year we will use as the base year. Let 2016 be the base year. Next we define our basket as the goods consumed in 2019: 1,000 golf balls, 100 clubs, and 500 tees. In 2019, this basket cost as follows:

$$(1{,}000 \times \$2) + (100 \times \$50) + (500 \times \$0.10)$$
$$= \$7{,}050$$

In 2020, this basket cost as follows:

$$(1{,}000 \times \$2.50) + (100 \times \$75) + (500 \times \$0.12)$$
$$= \$10{,}060$$

Dividing the cost of the basket in each year by the cost of the basket in the base year and multiplying by 100 gives us the CPI for each year. For 2019, the CPI is calculated as

$$(\$7{,}050 \div \$7{,}050) \times 100 = 100$$

For 2020, the CPI is calculated as

$$(\$10{,}060 \div \$7{,}050) \times 100 = 142.7$$

b. The inflation rate is defined as $[(CPI_2 - CPI_1) \div CPI_1] \times 100$. Plugging the values from part (a) into the formula, we get an inflation rate of 42.7%:

$$[(142.7 - 100) \div 100] \times 100 = 42.7$$

5. The CPI will rise by 1.5%. Suppose the CPI in the first year is 100. If healthcare costs are 10% of total expenditures, then they account for 10 of the 100 points, with the other 90 points falling in other categories. If healthcare costs rise by 15% in the second year, then those 10 points become 11.5 points. Since the prices of the other categories have not changed, the CPI now stands at 101.5, since $11.5 + 90 = 101.5$.

Using our formula for calculating the inflation rate, the rise in healthcare costs has raised the overall price level by 1.5%:

$$[(101.5 - 100) \div 100] \times 100 = 1.5$$

6. Using the equation of exchange in rates of growth, we know that

$$\%\Delta M + \%\Delta V \approx \%\Delta P + \%\Delta Y$$

a. $\%\Delta M + 0 \approx 2\% + 3\%$
Thus, $\%\Delta M \approx 5\%$.

b. $5\% + \%\Delta V \approx 0 + -3\%$
Thus, $\%\Delta V \approx -8\%$.

c. $10\% + 0 \approx \%\Delta P + 3\%$
Thus, $\%\Delta P \approx 7\%$.

d. $6\% + 0 \approx 3\% + \%\Delta Y$
Thus, $\%\Delta Y \approx 3\%$.

8.

Price of	GDP			
	CPI	Deflator	Both	Neither
Toothpaste	☐	☐	■	☐
Industrial coolant	☐	■	☐	☐
Milk you bought in a grocery store	☐	☐	■	☐
Milk bought by Starbucks from a food distributor	☐	☐	☐	■
An Intel computer chip bought by Dell to put into a laptop computer	☐	☐	☐	■
Bus fare for a trip to a shopping mall	☐	☐	■	☐
A doctor's appointment, to get a physical	☐	☐	■	☐

Savings, Interest Rates, and the Market for Loanable Funds

The Market for Loanable Funds Is a Bridge between Savers and Borrowers.

Firms that want to grow have to invest in resources, and these firms generally need someone to lend them funds. Without an efficient and safe market for loans, firms cannot borrow in order to buy what they need to increase their production output. If they don't increase their output, they won't contribute to GDP growth.

Meanwhile, households need to save—for a rainy day, for kids' college tuition, for retirement. Tucking cash under a mattress is one way to go. But a better way is to deposit funds in a bank or other financial institution. After all, why not put one's savings someplace where they're not only safe but will earn more by being loaned out at interest?

Banks take care of the arrangements, allowing savers to become lenders without going to extra trouble. The banks earn a profit by taking a cut. They are the middlemen in the loanable funds market, the bridge between savers and borrowers. When this bridge is safe and functioning well, savers can earn a predictable return on their funds and borrowers can consistently find funds to build, expand, and produce GDP.

In this chapter, we discuss many of the same topics you might study in a course on banking or financial institutions,

The Brooklyn Bridge is one of the most famous bridges in the world. It connects Manhattan, home to many of the United States's biggest financial institutions, and Brooklyn, the largest of New York City's five boroughs and home to many high-tech firms. When those firms need funds for investment, they often look across the river to the financial firms at the other end of the bridge.

but our emphasis is different. We are interested in studying how financial institutions and markets affect the macroeconomy. When we are finished, you will understand why interest rates rise and fall, and you will also appreciate the necessity of the loanable funds market in the larger macroeconomy.

Just about anything you read or hear about interest rates in the popular media leaves you with the impression that the government sets interest rates. This isn't exactly true. For sure, the government can influence many rates. But almost all interest rates in the U.S. economy are determined privately—by the market forces of supply and demand. In fact, you can understand why interest rates rise and fall by applying supply and demand analysis to the market for loans. That's what we do in this chapter. Along the way, we also consider the many factors that influence savers and borrowers.

· BIG QUESTIONS ·

- What is the loanable funds market?
- What factors shift the supply of loanable funds?
- What factors shift the demand for loanable funds?
- How do we apply the loanable funds market model?

What Is the Loanable Funds Market?

Imagine you are an entrepreneur who decides to start a company that will produce and sell college apparel. If you succeed, you'll contribute to national GDP. But you don't really think of it this way; you just hope you've discovered a great business opportunity. Before you sell your first shirt, hat, or sweatpants, however, you have to spend money on the resources you'll use in the production process. For example, if you plan on silk-screening your college logo onto hooded sweatshirts, you have to buy sweatshirts, ink, and a screen-printing press.

Since you have no revenue yet, you need to borrow cash in order to make these investments. For that, you need to go to a financial market. Financial markets are where firms and governments obtain funds, or *financing*, for their operations. These funds come primarily from household savings across the economy.

In economics, we analyze financial markets in the context of a **loanable funds market**. This is the market where savers supply funds for loans to borrowers. This market is not a single physical location but includes places like stock exchanges, investment banks, mutual fund firms, and commercial banks. In this section, we explain the particular characteristics of the loanable funds market and the significant role it plays in the overall economy.

The **loanable funds market** is the market where savers supply funds for loans to borrowers.

Figure 22.1 illustrates the role of the loanable funds market. Savings flow in and become loans for borrowers. We could call it the market for savings or the market for loans. The term "loanable funds" captures the information in both.

On the left side of the figure, the suppliers of funds—those who save—include households and foreign entities. Households are private individuals and families. Foreign entities include foreign governments, firms, and private citizens that choose to save in the United States. For most of the applications we discuss, we focus on households as the primary suppliers of loanable funds. If you have a checking or savings account at a bank, you are a supplier of loanable funds. You deposit funds into your bank account, but these funds don't just sit in a vault; banks loan out the majority of these funds. Household savings in retirement accounts, stocks, bonds, and mutual funds are other big sources of loanable funds.

The demanders, or borrowers, of loanable funds include firms and governments. In this chapter, we focus on firms as the primary borrowers of loanable funds. To reinforce the significance of this market, think about why borrowing takes place: firms borrow to invest, to buy tools and equipment, and to build factories. Firms looking to produce output in the future must borrow to pay their expenses today.

Figure 22.2 shows the production timeline we introduced in Chapter 21. At the end of the timeline is output, or GDP. When output is sold, it produces revenue for the firms, and the revenue serves to pay bills. But future GDP

FIGURE 22.1

The Role of the Loanable Funds Market

The market for loanable funds is where savers bring funds and make them available to borrowers. Households (private individuals and families) are the primary suppliers of loanable funds. Firms are the primary demanders, or borrowers, of loanable funds. When this market is functioning well, firms get the funds necessary for production and savers are paid for lending.

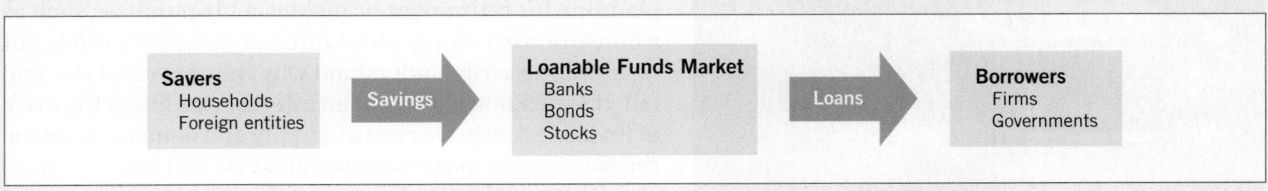

<figure>Savers: Households, Foreign entities → Savings → Loanable Funds Market: Banks, Bonds, Stocks → Loans → Borrowers: Firms, Governments</figure>

FIGURE 22.2

The Timeline of Production

The production timeline illustrates that GDP depends critically on the loanable funds market. At the end of the production timeline we see output, or GDP. But before a firm can produce output, it must purchase resources. Since these purchases occur before the revenue comes in, firms must borrow at the beginning of the timeline.

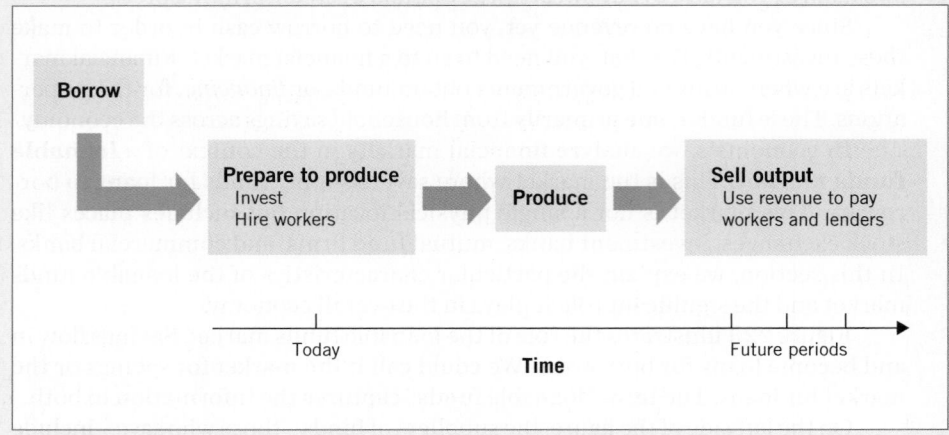

Borrow

Prepare to produce
Invest
Hire workers

Produce

Sell output
Use revenue to pay workers and lenders

Today

Time

Future periods

An **interest rate** is a price of loanable funds, quoted as a percentage of the original loan amount.

Before you can sell college apparel, you have to buy equipment and other supplies.

depends on spending today for necessary resources. This spending comes before any revenue is gained from the sale of output. Therefore, firms must borrow in order to generate future GDP—that's how important the loanable funds market is to the entire economy. Without a well-functioning loanable funds market, future GDP dries up.

Borrowing fuels investment, which creates future output. But notice that *every dollar borrowed requires a dollar saved*. Without savings, we cannot sustain future production. If you want to borrow to buy the resources you need to produce college apparel, someone else has to save. Working backward, the chain of crucial relationships looks like this: output (GDP) requires investment; investment requires borrowing; borrowing requires savings. And all the links in this chain require a loanable funds market that efficiently channels funds from savers to borrowers.

We study this crucial market from the perspective of prices, quantities, supply, and demand—like any other market. The demanders (or consumers) are borrowers who want to invest; the suppliers are savers. Figure 22.3 presents a picture of supply (savings) and demand (investment) for loanable funds, along with a summary of the distinctions of the loanable funds market. The price in this market is the interest rate; the good is loanable funds. These loanable funds are the dollars' worth of savings that are transformed into dollars of investment.

This demand and supply approach helps to clarify the role of interest rates. An **interest rate** is a price of loanable funds. It is like the price of toothpaste or computers or hoodies; it is simply quoted differently—as a percentage of the original loan amount. People who are thinking about planning for retirement or making a big purchase such as a house or a car worry about interest rate fluctuations but do not necessarily understand why interest rates rise and fall. If we acknowledge that an interest rate is just the price of loanable funds, we can use supply and demand to reveal the factors that make interest rates rise and fall.

We now turn to the two different views of interest rates: the saver's view and the borrower's view.

FIGURE 22.3

The Loanable Funds Market

Savings (S) is channeled into investment (D) in the loanable funds market. In this market, loanable funds are the goods bought and sold. The price is an interest rate. This price, like any other market-determined price, is determined by the interaction between supply and demand.

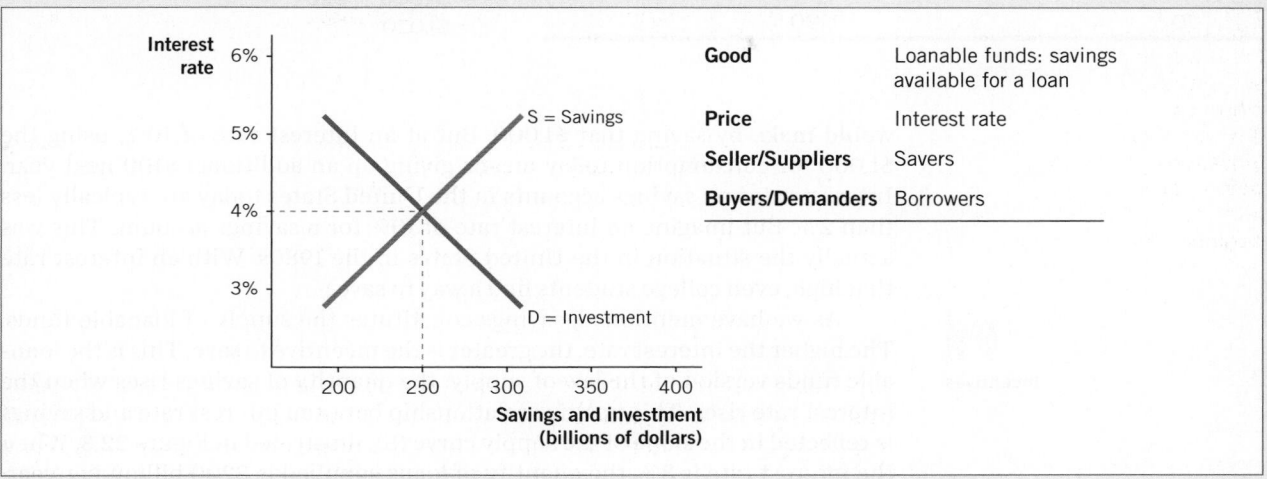

Good	Loanable funds: savings available for a loan
Price	Interest rate
Seller/Suppliers	Savers
Buyers/Demanders	Borrowers

Interest Rates as a Reward for Saving

If you are a saver, the interest rate is the return you get for supplying funds. For example, let's say your parents gave you some cash when you left for college this term. After buying textbooks, groceries, and other supplies, you have $1,000 left, which you consider saving. You go to a bank near campus and inquire about opening a new account. In this transaction, the bank is the buyer, and it offers a certain price for the use of your savings. When it does offer a price, it is not in dollars. The bank quotes a price in an interest rate, or as a percentage of how much you save. But the interest rate communicates the same information. So if you are saving $1,000, the bank might tell you, "We'll pay you 2% if you save that money for a year." Because 2% of $1,000 is $20, this is equivalent to saying, "We'll pay you $20 if you save that money for a year."

If you save $1,000 for one year with an interest rate of 2%, your total amount of savings is $1,020 at the end of the year, which is computed as

$$\$1{,}000 + (2\% \text{ of } \$1{,}000) = \$1{,}000 + \$20 = \$1{,}020$$

For savers, the interest rate is a reward. Every dollar saved today returns more in the saver's account in the future. The higher the interest rate, the greater the return will be in the future. Table 22.1 illustrates how interest rates affect $1,000 worth of savings. An interest rate of 2% yields $1,020 one year later; an interest rate of 10% yields $1,100.

Think of the interest rate as the opportunity cost of consumption. With a 4% interest rate and a $1,000 purchase today, you are giving up the $40 you

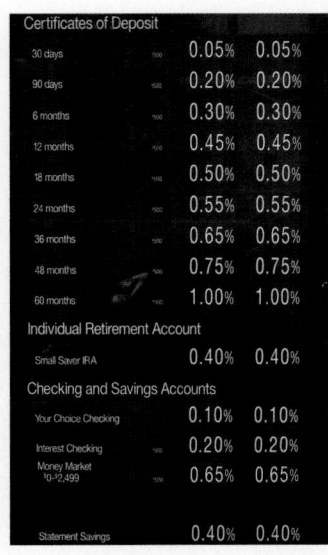

Banks are willing to pay you for your savings. The price they pay is the interest rate.

Opportunity cost

TABLE 22.1

Higher Interest Rates and Greater Future Returns	
Interest rate	Value of $1,000 after one year
2%	$1,020
4	1,040
6	1,060
10	1,100

If you save $1,000 for one year at an interest rate of 2%, this leads to $1,020 next year, computed as

$1,000 + (2% of $1,000)
= $1,000 + (0.02 × $1,000)
= $1,000 + $20
= $1,020

would make by saving that $1,000. But at an interest rate of 10%, using the $1,000 for consumption today means giving up an additional $100 next year. Interest rates on savings accounts in the United States today are typically less than 2%. But imagine an interest rate of 10% for a savings account. This was actually the situation in the United States in the 1980s. With an interest rate that high, even college students find a way to save.

Incentives

As we have mentioned, savings constitutes the supply of loanable funds. The higher the interest rate, the greater is the incentive to save. This is the loanable funds version of the law of supply: the quantity of savings rises when the interest rate rises. This positive relationship between interest rate and savings is reflected in the slope of the supply curve (S), illustrated in Figure 22.3. When the interest rate is 3%, the quantity of loans supplied is $200 billion per year; at 4% the quantity supplied increases to $250 billion; and at 5% it increases to $300 billion.

Interest Rates as a Cost of Borrowing

We now turn to the demand, or borrowing, side of the loanable funds market. For this we shift to the firm's perspective and return to your plan to produce college apparel. Recall that you need to buy the sweatshirts, paint, and a screen-printing press to produce hoodies and other products with a college logo. Assume you need $100,000 to start your business. If you borrow $100,000 for one year at an interest rate of 4%, you'll need to repay $104,000 in one year. It makes sense to do this only if your *expected return* is greater than 4%, or $4,000, on this investment. The **expected return** on a capital investment is the anticipated rate of return based on the probabilities of all possible outcomes. This is a firm's best guess of the future percentage return on an investment.

The **expected return** on a capital investment is the anticipated rate of return based on the probabilities of all possible outcomes.

For borrowers, the interest rate is the cost of borrowing. Firms borrow only if the expected return on their investment is greater than the cost of the loan. For example, at an interest rate of 6%, a firm would borrow only if it expected to make more than a 6% return with its use of the funds. Let's state this as a rule:

Profit-maximizing firms borrow to fund an investment if and only if the expected return on the investment is greater than the interest rate on the loan.

The lower the interest rate, the more likely a business will succeed in earning enough to exceed the interest it will owe at the end of the year. For example, if your firm can borrow at an interest rate of just 3%, you'll need to make a return greater than 3%. There are probably several investments available today that would pay more than a 5% return; but there are even more that would yield returns greater than 3% and more still that would pay greater than 1%. If we apply our rule from above, we'll see a larger quantity of loans demanded as the interest rate drops. This gives us the negative relationship between the interest rate and quantity demanded of loans, reflected in the slope of the demand curve for loanable funds.

The graph of the loanable funds market in Figure 22.3 illustrates the demand curve (D) for loanable funds across the entire U.S. economy. At an interest rate of 5%, the quantity of loans demanded by all business firms in the economy is $200 billion. This indicates that firms believe that only $200 billion worth of investment will pay returns greater than 5%. At an interest rate of 4%, firms estimate that another $50 billion worth of total loans will earn between 4% and 5%, and the quantity of loans demanded rises to $250 billion. Lower interest rates lead to a greater quantity demanded of loanable funds.

How Inflation Affects Interest Rates

If you save $1,000 for a year at an interest rate of 2%, your reward for saving is $20. But inflation affects the real value of this reward. For example, imagine that the inflation rate is exactly 2% during the year you save. This means that next year it will take $1,020 to buy the same quantity of goods and services you are able to buy this year for $1,000. In this case, your interest rate of 2% and the inflation rate of 2% cancel each other out. You break even, and that's not much of a reward.

When making decisions about saving and borrowing, people care more about the real interest rate than the nominal interest rate. The **real interest rate** is the interest rate corrected for inflation; it is the rate of return in terms of real purchasing power. In contrast, the **nominal interest rate** is the interest rate before it is corrected for inflation; it is the *stated* interest rate. In our example, the interest rate of 2% is the nominal interest rate. But with 2% inflation, the real return on your savings disappears, and the real interest rate is zero—or 0%. In general, we can approximate the real interest rate by subtracting the inflation rate from the nominal interest rate in an equation known as the **Fisher equation**:

> The **real interest rate** is the interest rate corrected for inflation. It is the rate of return in terms of real purchasing power.
>
> The **nominal interest rate** is the interest rate before it is corrected for inflation. It is the stated interest rate.
>
> The **Fisher equation** states that the real interest rate equals the nominal interest rate minus the inflation rate.

$$\text{real interest rate} = \text{nominal interest rate} - \text{inflation rate}$$

(EQUATION 22.1)

For example, if the inflation rate this year is 2%, a nominal interest rate of 6% on your savings would yield a 4% real interest rate. The Fisher equation is named after Irving Fisher, the economist who formulated the relationship between inflation and interest rates.

Savers and borrowers care about the real rate of interest on a loan because this is the rate that describes how their funds' real purchasing power changes over the course of the loan. Because the interest rate is a result of supply and demand in the market for loanable funds, higher inflation rates lead to higher nominal interest rates to compensate lenders for the loss of purchasing power. We can rewrite the Fisher equation to see how inflation generally increases nominal interest rates:

$$\text{nominal interest rate} = \text{real interest rate} + \text{inflation rate}$$

(EQUATION 22.2)

For a given real interest rate, the higher the rate of inflation, the higher the nominal interest rate. Table 22.2 shows how the nominal interest rate rises with inflation rates for a given level of the real interest rate. If the real interest rate is

TABLE 22.2

How Inflation Affects Nominal Interest Rates

Inflation rate		Real interest rate		Nominal interest rate
0%	+	4%	=	4%
2	+	4	=	6
4	+	4	=	8

4% and there is no inflation, then the nominal interest rate is also 4%. But if the inflation rate rises to 2%, the nominal interest rate increases to 6%. If the inflation rate rises further to 4%, then the nominal interest rate rises to 8%.

We can picture the Fisher equation by looking at real and nominal interest rates over time. Figure 22.4 plots the real and nominal interest rates in the United States from 1970 to 2018. The difference between them is the inflation rate. Notice that this gap was particularly high during the inflationary 1970s but that it narrowed considerably as inflation rates fell in the 1980s. After 2008, the nominal interest rate in the United States was less than 1%. Because inflation rates were around 2%, the real interest rate was negative.

Unless otherwise stated, in this text we use the nominal interest rate. We do this for two reasons. First, the nominal interest rate is the stated interest rate—the rate you read about and consider in actual financial transactions. Second, low and steady inflation means that the difference between real and nominal interest rates doesn't fluctuate much. That is, while we recognize that savers and borrowers care about the real interest rate, the current inflationary environment throughout much of the developed world leaves us little to gain by focusing on the real interest rate.

In the next two sections, we consider the factors that cause shifts in the supply of and demand for loanable funds.

FIGURE 22.4

Real and Nominal Interest Rates, 1970–2018

The difference between the nominal interest rate and the real interest rate is the rate of inflation. The experience of the 1970s illustrates that the nominal interest rate is historically high when inflation is also high.

Sources: Federal Reserve Bank of St. Louis FRED database; Bureau of Labor Statistics.

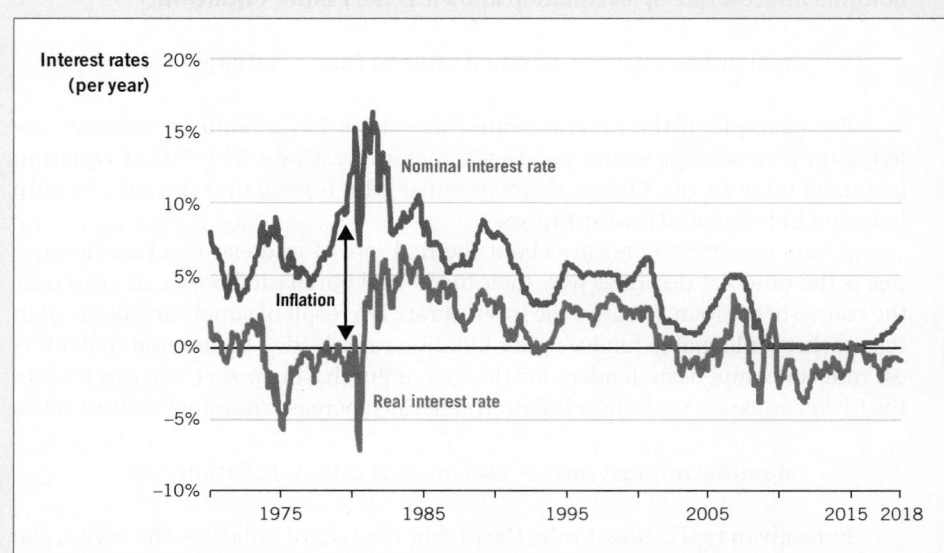

Interest Rates and Quantity Supplied and Demanded: U.S. Interest Rates Have Fallen

In 1981, many interest rates in the United States were 15%, but the inflation rate was 10%. In 2015, many interest rates were less than 1%, and the inflation rate was 2%.

QUESTION: What were the real interest rates in 1981 and 2015?

ANSWER: Using equation 22.1, we compute the real interest rate as

$$\text{real interest rate} = \text{nominal interest rate} - \text{inflation rate}$$

For 1981, the real interest rate was: $15\% - 10\% = 5\%$.
For 2015, the real interest rate was: $1\% - 2\% = -1\%$.

QUESTION: All else equal, how does the drop in interest rates between 1981 and 2015 affect the quantity of loanable funds supplied?

ANSWER: The quantity supplied decreases along the supply curve. Lower interest rates reduce the incentive to save.

CHALLENGE QUESTION: Which would you prefer, a 5% real interest rate, or a −1% real interest rate?

ANSWER: It depends on whether you plan to be a borrower or a lender. If you are borrowing to open a firm, or to buy a house or a car, you like the low rate. But if you are saving for the future by depositing funds at the bank (and thus lending to the bank), you like the high rate.

What Factors Shift the Supply of Loanable Funds?

Recall that the supply of loanable funds comes from savings. If you have either a savings or a checking account, you are a participant in this market. We turn now to three factors that shift the supply curve for loanable funds: income and wealth, time preferences, and consumption smoothing. When these factors change, the supply curve shifts.

Income and Wealth

Imagine that a distant relative dies and you inherit $20,000. What will you do with this unexpected wealth? You might celebrate with a fancy meal and a shopping spree. But most of us would also save some. All else equal, people prefer more savings. Thus, increases in either income or wealth generally produce increases in savings. If income and wealth decline, people save less. These changes shift the loanable funds supply curve.

As India grows from poor to rich, many of the funds its citizens save find their way into the U.S. loanable funds market.

The relationship between income and savings is true across the globe. As nations gain wealth, they save more, and not always in their own nation. Over the past 20 years, the increase in foreign savings has often made its way into the U.S. loanable funds market. For example, a businessman in Mumbai, India, may find himself with extra savings. He likely puts some into an Indian bank and some into Indian stocks and bonds. But there's a good chance he also channels some of his savings into the United States. Historically, U.S. financial markets have offered relatively greater returns than markets in other countries. In addition, the U.S. financial markets are often considered less risky than other global markets because of the size and relative robustness of the U.S. economy. Therefore, as global economies have grown, there has been an increase in foreign savings in the United States.

The increase in foreign savings came at a good time for the United States because domestic savings began falling in the 1980s. Without the influx of foreign funds, U.S. firms would have had difficulty funding investment. Of course, there is no guarantee that foreign savings will continue to flow into the United States at the same rates. But as long as some foreign funds still enter the U.S. financial markets, their presence allows more opportunities for domestic firms to borrow for investment than if firms relied solely on domestic savers.

Time Preferences

The term **time preferences** refers to the fact that people prefer to receive goods and services sooner rather than later.

Do you care when a friend repays your loan?

Imagine that your parents promised you a cash reward for getting a good grade in economics. Does it matter to you if they pay immediately or wait until you graduate? Of course it matters! You want the money as soon as you earn it. This is not unusual. People always prefer to receive funds sooner rather than later, and the same applies to goods and services. The term **time preferences** refers to the fact that people prefer to receive goods and services sooner rather than later. Because people have time preferences, someone must pay them to save. While time preferences are generally stable over time, if the rate of time preference in a society changes, the supply of loanable funds shifts.

While we all prefer sooner to later, some people have greater time preferences than others. Think of those with the strongest time preferences as being the least patient: they *strongly* prefer now to later. Someone with weaker time preferences has more patience. All else equal, people with stronger time preferences save less than people with weaker time preferences.

There are other ways time preferences are observed. For example, people with very strong time preferences may not go to college, since the returns to getting a college education are not typically realized until years later. Time

FIGURE 22.5

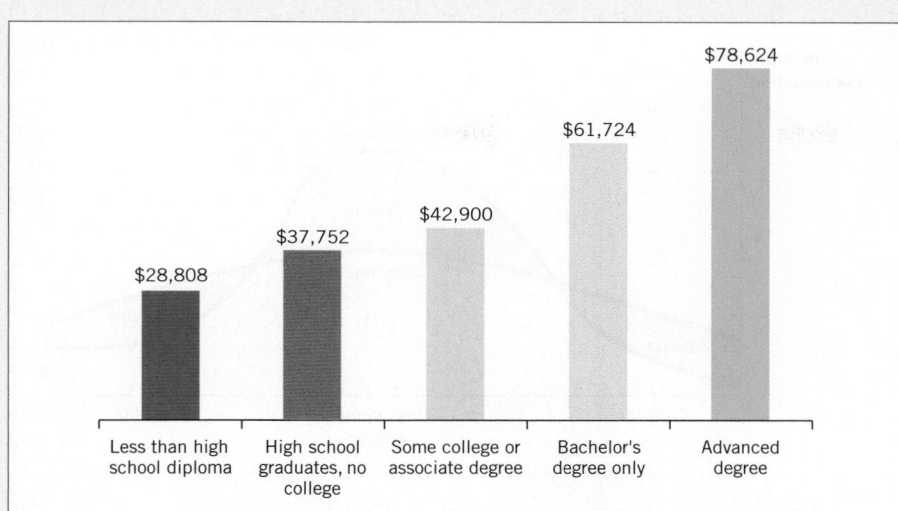

It takes patience, or relatively low time preferences, to stay in school. But annual earnings based on years of schooling shows that education pays off for most graduates.

Source: Bureau of Labor Statistics.

spent in college is time that could have been spent earning income. The fact that you are a college student demonstrates that you are more patient than some others who choose instead to work for more income now.

You'll be happy to know there is a definite payoff to getting a college education. College graduates earn significantly more than high school graduates. Figure 22.5 shows median annual salary in the United States by educational attainment. Some college dropouts—for example, Mark Zuckerberg (creator of Facebook)—earn millions of dollars a year. But Figure 22.5 shows that the median worker with a bachelor's degree earns almost $20,000 more a year than those who don't graduate from college. Patience pays off!

Opportunity cost

Consumption Smoothing

Over the course of a typical lifetime, income varies drastically. Early in life, income levels are relatively low, but income generally rises through midlife. As people near retirement, their income levels fall again. Figure 22.6 illustrates a typical economic life cycle. Income (the green line) is highest in the middle "prime earning years" and lower at both the beginning and end of an individual's work life.

But no one wants to *consume* according to this pattern over the course of a lifetime; most people prefer to consume more evenly over the course of their life. When we are young, we often borrow and spend more than we are earning. We may borrow for a college education or to buy our first home. When we retire, our income levels fall, but we don't want our spending to fall by the same amount. So we generally smooth our consumption over the course of our life. The blue line in Figure 22.6 represents a normal consumption pattern, which is smoother than the income pattern. This **consumption smoothing** is accomplished with the help of the loanable funds market.

Early in life, we borrow so we can spend more than we earn. In Figure 22.6, borrowing is the pink area between income and consumption in early life.

Consumption smoothing occurs when people borrow and save to smooth consumption over their lifetime.

FIGURE 22.6

Savings over a Typical Life Cycle

For most people, income is relatively low in early life, rises in their prime earning years, and falls in later life. But people generally prefer to smooth their consumption over the course of their life. This means they borrow early in life for items like education and their first home; save during midlife when their income is highest; and finally, draw down savings when they retire.

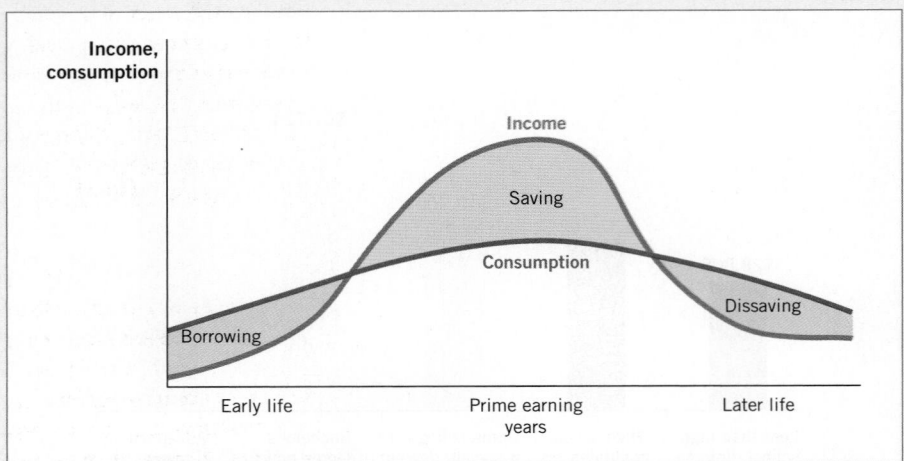

Dissaving
occurs when people withdraw funds from their previously accumulated savings.

Midlife, or the prime earning years, is the time to repay loans and save for retirement. During this period of the life cycle, the income line exceeds the consumption line, and people save—that is the green area. Later in life, when people retire and their income falls, they often live on their savings. Economists call this **dissaving**. Dissaving occurs when people withdraw funds from their previously accumulated savings. Figure 22.6 shows dissavings as the pink area between income and consumption in later life.

We can use the concept of consumption smoothing to clarify a situation currently affecting the U.S. economy. If we have a steady flow of people moving into each life stage, the amount of savings in the economy is stable and there is a steady supply in the market for loanable funds. But if a significant portion of the population leaves the prime earning years at the same time, overall savings will fall. As it turns out, this is the current situation in the United States, because the baby boomers are now retiring from the labor force. The oldest members of this group reached retirement age in 2011. Over the next 10 to 15 years, U.S. workers will enter retirement in record numbers. This means an exit from the prime earning years and, consequently, much less in savings. Furthermore, similar issues are facing other nations, including Japan, Germany, and Italy. We'll come back to this issue later in this chapter.

Figure 22.7 illustrates the effect on the supply of loanable funds when there are changes in income and wealth, time preferences, or consumption smoothing. The initial supply of loanable funds is represented by S_1. The supply of loanable funds increases to S_2 if there is a change that leads to an increase in savings at all levels of the interest rate. For example, an increase in foreign income and wealth increases the supply of savings. Similarly, if people's time preferences fall—if they become more patient—the supply of loanable funds increases. Finally, if a relatively large portion of the population moves into midlife, when savings is highest, this also increases savings from S_1 to S_2.

At other times, however, the supply of loanable funds might decrease. For example, if income and wealth decline, people save less across all interest rates. This is illustrated as a shift from S_1 to S_3 in Figure 22.7. If time preferences

FIGURE 22.7

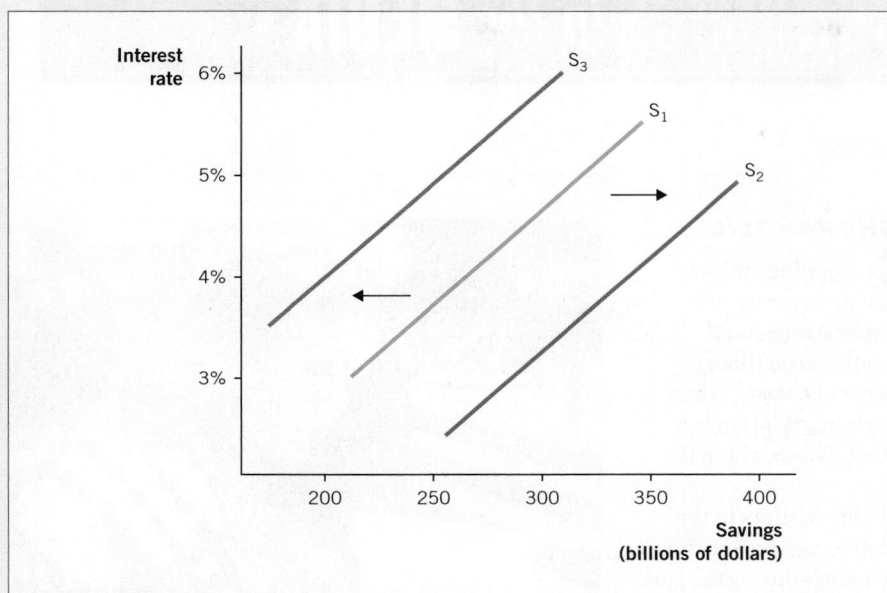

The supply of loanable funds shifts to the right when there are decreases in time preferences, increases in income and wealth, and more people in midlife, when savings is highest. The supply of loanable funds shifts to the left when there are increases in time preferences, decreases in income and wealth, and fewer people in midlife, when savings is highest.

increase, people become more impatient, which reduces the supply of loanable funds. Finally, if a relatively large population group moves out of the prime earning years and into retirement, the supply of loanable funds decreases. This last example describes what is happening in the United States right now.

Table 22.3 summarizes our discussion of the factors that either increase or decrease the supply of loanable funds.

TABLE 22.3

Factors That Shift the Supply of Loanable Funds

Factor	Direction of effect	Explanation
Income and wealth	• *Increases* in income and wealth *increase* the supply of loanable funds. • *Decreases* in income and wealth *decrease* the supply of loanable funds.	Savings is more affordable when people have greater income and wealth.
Time preferences	• *Increases* in time preferences *decrease* the supply of loanable funds. • *Decreases* in time preferences *increase* the supply of loanable funds.	Lower time preferences indicate that people are more patient and more likely to save for the future.
Consumption smoothing	• If *more* people are in midlife and their prime earning years, savings is *higher*. • If *fewer* people are in midlife, savings is *lower*.	Income varies over the life cycle, but people generally like to smooth their consumption.

Time Preferences

CONFESSIONS OF A SHOPAHOLIC

This movie from 2009 follows a shopping junkie, Becky Bloomwood, who must come to terms with her exploding debt. Becky has very strong time preferences: she can't stop spending even though she owes almost $20,000 on her credit cards. When she finally realizes the mess she is in, she attends a Shopaholics Anonymous meeting. This is where the fun really begins.

Becky, like many other first-time visitors to the support group, is reluctant to tell her story. But after listening to others speak of their trials during the past week, the leader turns to Becky, who begins to tell her story. The pure joy she experiences while shopping is immediately obvious to the other members of the support group. As they listen to her describe the fantastic feeling she gets from making new purchases, they long to feel the same way. Her story is not as much about repentance as it is about the need to shop more. This creates a euphoric response from the group. After talking for a short time, Becky has convinced herself— and most of the group—to go on a shopping spree. She bolts from the meeting and races home to her apartment, where she keeps one last credit card in the freezer for emergencies. Gleefully, she takes the card and heads off to find something new to purchase.

This film conveys how easy it is to get into unmanageable debt and how hard it is to break the cycle. Do you know of any friends or relatives—maybe even you yourself—who carry a large amount of credit

Economists would say Becky has very strong time preferences.

card debt? Can you imagine how many people in the entire United States might be in a similar situation? Now think about how those people prefer to borrow rather than save. This perspective helps us to see that in the nation's macroeconomy, the desire to borrow, driven by time preferences, reduces the supply of loanable funds.

ECONOMICS IN THE REAL WORLD

DO AMERICANS SAVE ENOUGH?

Economists recognize the importance of savings for an economy, especially over long time horizons: without savings, firms and governments can't borrow to build the factories and infrastructure we need to produce GDP. But Americans have long had the reputation of being low savers. We should begin by looking at the U.S. personal savings

FIGURE 22.8

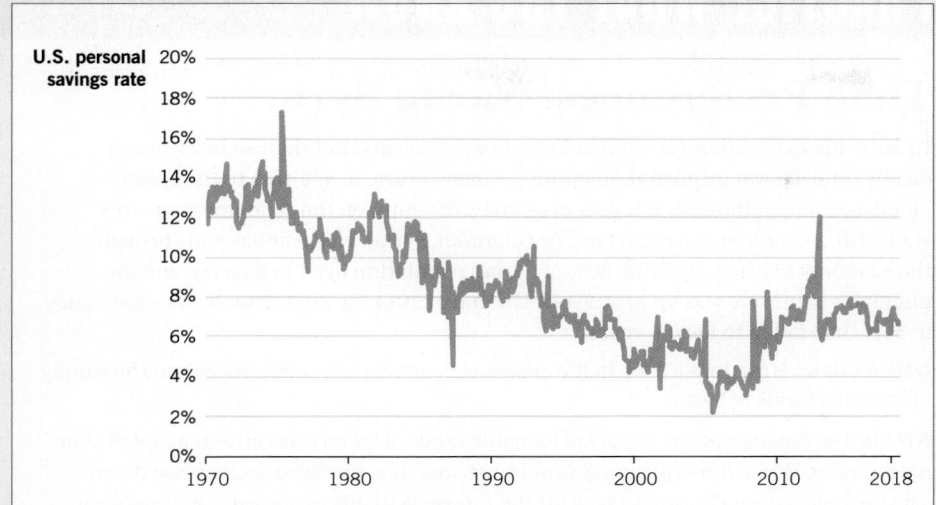

In the United States, the savings rate (savings as a portion of disposable income) fell significantly for about three decades before rising again in 2005. In 1982, the savings rate was over 12%; but it fell to just 2.2% in 2005.

Source: U.S. Bureau of Economic Analysis.

rate, which Figure 22.8 shows for the years 1970 to 2018. The **savings rate** is personal saving as a fraction of disposable (after-tax) income. As you can see, the U.S. savings rate fell consistently for almost 30 years, beginning in the late 1970s. In 1982, the savings rate was over 12%. The decline continued until about 2005, when the savings rate bottomed out at just 2.2%. Since 2005, the savings rate has risen to around 7%, but this is still fairly low in historical terms.

Part of the reason why the U.S. savings rate is so low is the way the rate is defined. In reality, there are several alternative ways to save for the future, not all of which are counted in the official definition of "personal savings." For example, let's say you buy a house for $200,000 and the value of the house rises to $300,000 in just a few years. This means that you now have gained $100,000 in personal wealth. The gain in the value of your house helps you prepare for the future, just as greater savings would. But gains of this nature are not counted as personal savings. In addition to real estate gains, the gains from purchases of stocks and bonds are also not counted in personal savings. In the United States, these capital gains on real estate and financial assets constitute a big part of peoples' savings, which are not accounted for in the official savings rate.

The **savings rate** is personal saving as a fraction of disposable (after-tax) income.

What Factors Shift the Demand for Loanable Funds?

To look at the demand side, we shift perspective to those who borrow in the loanable funds market. As we have seen, the demand for loanable funds derives from the desire to invest or purchase capital goods that aid in future

Time Preferences: War in Syria

One of the difficult side effects of war is a collapse of loanable funds markets.

In 2010, life expectancy for women in Syria was 75 years. But then an intense and deadly internal war gripped that nation for many years. In addition to the massive bloodshed and millions of refugees created by the conflict, the economy came to a standstill. According to a report in *The Guardian*, Syria's civil war basically brought the economy to a halt. By 2015, 80% of Syria's population lived in poverty, and the unemployment rate was up to 57.7% by the end of 2014. By 2014, female life expectancy in Syria had fallen to just 66 years.[*]

QUESTION: How does a drop in life expectancy affect time preferences and the supply of loanable funds in Syria?

ANSWER: Savings, or the supply of loanable funds, depend critically on people's time preferences. When life expectancy is plummeting, time preferences increase drastically: people have no reason to save for the future. With life expectancy plummeting, people are less likely to plan for the future. As time preferences increase, the supply of loanable funds goes down. Thus, when a nation is hit hard by political instability, war, or even a pandemic, one side effect is lower savings, which means a reduced supply of loanable funds—which in turn leads to lower economic output in the future.

Thankfully, by 2017, life expectancy in Syria began to tick up again, rising to 69 years for women. Let's hope this trend continues.

*Source: http://www.theguardian.com/world/2015/mar/12/syrias-war-80-in-poverty-life-expectancy-cut-by-20-years-200bn-lost.

production. We know that the interest rate matters, and this relationship is reflected in the slope of the demand curve. We now turn to factors that cause shifts in the demand for loanable funds. We focus on three: the productivity of capital, investor confidence, and government borrowing.

Productivity of Capital

Consider a firm trying to decide whether to borrow for an investment. Perhaps your own firm is trying to decide whether to borrow to buy a new silk-screening machine, the S-1000, for your college clothing business. This machine is capital, and its purchase counts as an investment. To determine whether you should take a loan, recall our rule: a firm should borrow to fund an investment only if the expected return is greater than the interest rate on the loan. Therefore, if the interest rate on the loan is 4%, you will borrow to buy the S-1000 only if you expect to earn more than a 4% return from it.

Let's say that after crunching the numbers on expected costs and sales from the S-1000, you estimate a return of just 2% from an investment in the S-1000. You decide not to buy the new machine.

But then something changes. That something is the availability of the brand-new S-2000. The S-2000 is an improved machine that prints T-shirts at double the rate of the S-1000. Given this new machine, which is slightly more expensive, you calculate an expected return of 5%, so you decide to take the loan and buy the machine. Thus, your demand for loanable funds increases as a direct result of the availability of the new machine, which is twice as productive as the earlier machine.

What are the implications for the macroeconomy? Remember that firms borrow to finance capital purchases. Therefore, the level of demand for loans depends on the productivity of capital. Changes in capital productivity shift the demand for loanable funds. If capital is more productive, the demand for loans increases; if capital is less productive, the demand for loans decreases.

Productivity can change for a number of reasons. Consider the impact of the Internet. A connection to the Internet provides quick access to data and networking capabilities that people only dreamed about 25 years ago. The Internet also increases the productivity of computers, which are a major capital expense. Over the past 25 years, an increase in expected returns associated with the Internet made investment in computer equipment (capital) more attractive. This means that investment in capital yields greater returns, which in turn increases the demand for loans. When capital is more productive, firms are more likely to borrow to finance purchases of this type of capital.

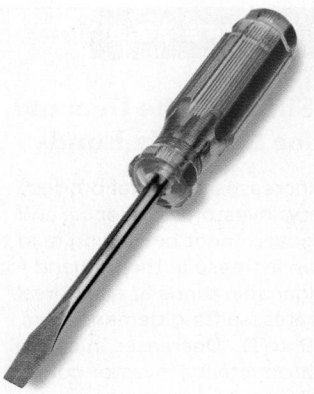

This manual screwdriver depicts capital . . .

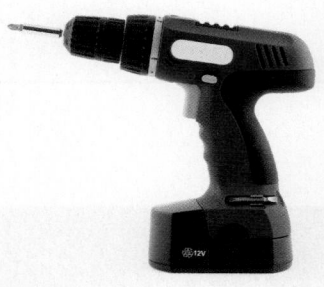

. . . and this electric version of a screwdriver represents an increase in capital productivity.

Investor confidence is a measure of what firms expect for future economic activity.

Investor Confidence

The demand for loanable funds also depends on the beliefs or expectations of the investors at business firms. If a firm believes its sales will increase in the future, it invests more today to build for future sales. If, instead, it believes its future sales will fall, it invests less today. **Investor confidence** is a measure of what firms expect for future economic activity. If confidence is high, they are more likely to borrow for investment at any interest rate. Economist John Maynard Keynes referred to an investor's drive to action as "animal spirits," meaning that investment demand may not even be based on rational decisions or real factors in the economy.

Figure 22.9 illustrates shifts in the demand for loanable funds. If capital productivity increases, demand for investment increases from D_1 to D_2—that is, demand is higher across all interest rates. Similarly, if investor confidence rises, demand for loanable funds increases from D_1 to D_2. In contrast, if capital productivity or investor confidence falls, the demand for loanable funds falls from D_1 to D_3.

Government Borrowing

Governments are big enough borrowers that they can shift the demand for loanable funds all by themselves. We cover this in greater detail in Chapter 28 when we discuss government budgets. For now, just note that increases in government borrowing are reflected as increases in the demand for loanable funds and this shifts the demand curve to the right, while decreases in government borrowing lead to leftward shifts in demand.

FIGURE 22.9

Shifts in the Demand for Loanable Funds

Increases in capital productivity, investor confidence, and government borrowing lead to an increase in the demand for loanable funds at all interest rates, shifting demand from D_1 to D_2. Decreases in capital productivity, investor confidence, and government borrowing decrease the demand for loanable funds from D_1 to D_3.

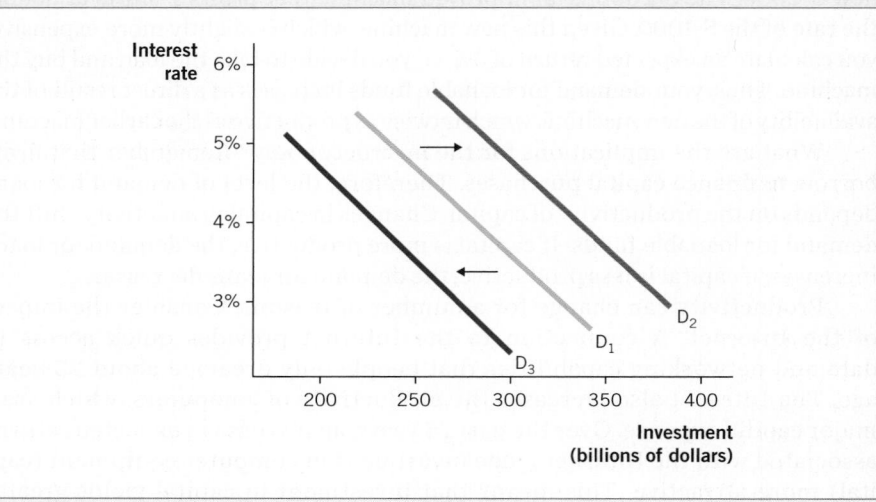

PRACTICE WHAT YOU KNOW

How dangerous is this sponge?

Demand for Loanable Funds: SpongeBob and Loanable Funds

QUESTION: Which one of the following changes would shift the demand for loanable funds, and how?

a. Research shows that watching the cartoon *SpongeBob SquarePants* can shorten a child's attention span. Now assume that an entire generation of children grows up watching this cartoon, resulting in adults who are less patient (their time preferences have increased).

b. A technological advance leads to greater capital productivity.

c. The interest rate falls.

ANSWER:

a. This factor would not affect the demand for loanable funds, but it would affect the supply of loanable funds. Less patience means that time preferences increase and the supply of loanable funds declines.

b. This technological advance would increase the demand for loanable funds.

c. The falling interest rate would lead to a movement along the demand curve, rather than a shift in the demand curve for loanable funds. A decrease in the interest rate could be caused by a decrease in the supply of loanable funds.

How Do We Apply the Loanable Funds Market Model?

We are now ready to use the loanable funds market model to study applications we see in the real world. First, we consider the implications of equilibrium in the loanable funds market. After that, we examine past and future views of the U.S. loanable funds market.

Equilibrium

Equilibrium in the loanable funds market occurs at the interest rate where the plans of savers match the plans of borrowers—that is, where quantity supplied equals quantity demanded. In Figure 22.10, this occurs at an interest rate of 4%, where savers are willing to save $250 billion and borrowers desire $250 billion in loans (in other words, they seek to invest $250 billion). At interest rates above 4%, the quantity of loanable funds supplied exceeds the quantity demanded, and this imbalance leads to downward pressure on the interest rate. At interest rates below 4%, the quantity demanded exceeds the quantity supplied, and this imbalance leads to upward pressure on the interest rate.

The loanable funds market, like other markets, naturally tends to move toward equilibrium, where supply is equal to demand. This equilibrium condition reinforces a key relationship between savings and investment. Equilibrium occurs when

$$savings = investment$$

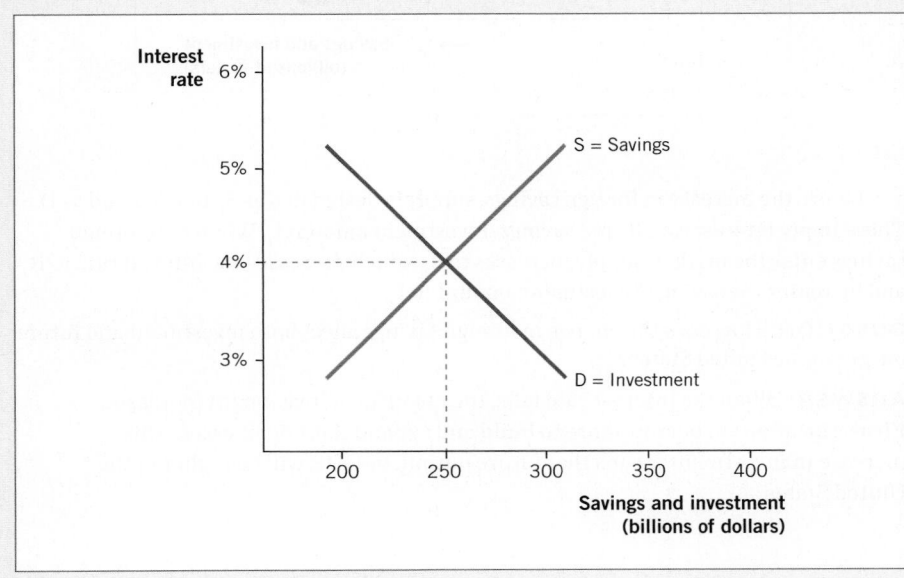

FIGURE 22.10

Equilibrium in the Market for Loanable Funds

Equilibrium in the loanable funds market occurs where supply equals demand, at an interest rate of 4% and a quantity of $250 billion. Because investment is limited by savings, exactly $250 billion is saved and $250 billion is invested.

How does foreign economic growth affect the U.S. loanable funds market?

Working with the Loanable Funds Model: Foreign Savings in the United States

Recently, the economies of China and India have begun to grow very rapidly. This increases their citizens' income and wealth. In turn, these citizens increase their savings in their country and also in the United States.

QUESTION: When foreign savings enter the U.S. loanable funds market, which curve is affected—supply or demand? How is this curve affected?

ANSWER: The supply of loanable funds increases as savings increase.

QUESTION: How would you graph the U.S. loanable funds market both before and after the increase in foreign savings?

ANSWER:

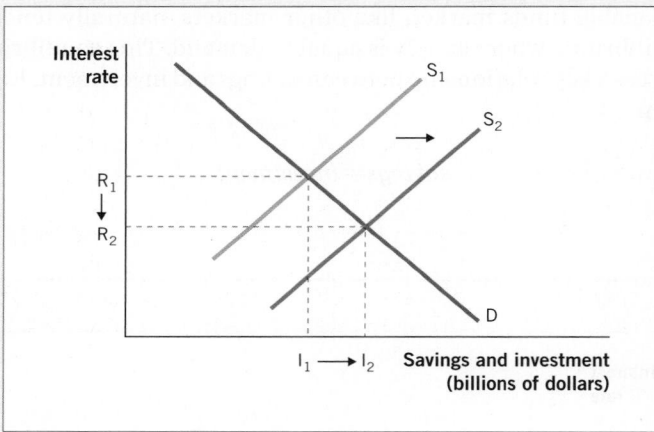

Before the increase in foreign savings, supply is designated as S_1 and demand as D. These imply interest rate R_1 and savings/investment amount I_1. When new foreign savings enter the market, supply increases to S_2, which decreases the interest rate to R_2 and increases the savings/investment amount to I_2.

QUESTION: How does the change in foreign savings affect both investment and future output in the United States?

ANSWER: When the interest rate falls, the quantity of investment increases. Firms can afford to borrow more to build and expand their businesses. This increase in investment means that future output, or GDP, will be higher in the United States.

In Figure 22.10, households and foreign entities have decided to save a combined total of $250 billion at an interest rate of 4%. Subsequently, firms borrow this $250 billion for investment. Thus, dollars that are saved make their way into the loanable funds market and are then channeled to firms for investment purposes.

Equilibrium also helps to clarify an important principle we'll return to often in this text. Investment requires saving because

Every dollar borrowed requires a dollar saved.

If an economy is to grow over time, someone has to invest in capital that helps to produce more in the future. But investment requires savings. Without savings, the economy cannot grow.

Equilibrium is a helpful starting point for understanding how the loanable funds market functions. But in the real world, financial market conditions change frequently. We can account for these changes in our model by using shifts in the supply and demand curves. Let's consider two examples: a shift in demand and a shift in the supply of loanable funds.

A Decrease in the Demand for Loanable Funds

When the overall economy slows, firms often reduce investment, since they expect reduced sales in future periods; this move reflects a decline in investor confidence. This happened recently in the United States during the Great Recession that began at the end of 2007. Panel (a) of Figure 22.11 shows how a decline in investor confidence affects the loanable funds market. When investment demand declines (shown in the figure as a shift from D_{2007} to D_{2008}), the loanable funds model predicts lower interest rates (a drop from R_1 to R_2) and a lower equilibrium level of investment (a drop from I_1 to I_2). Panel (b) of Figure 22.11 shows that investment fell during both recessions (the blue bars) in the years shown. During the Great Recession, real investment fell from $2.2 trillion to just $1.4 trillion—a 36% drop in less than two years.

A Decrease in the Supply of Loanable Funds

Let's now return to the potential effects of the baby boomers' retirement over the next 10 to 15 years. As we saw in the discussion of consumption smoothing, this will likely lead to a decrease in the supply of loanable funds in the United States. Figure 22.12 illustrates this kind of change. The curve labeled S_{2020} represents the supply of loanable funds in 2020. But as the baby boomers retire, supply may shift back to $S_{2030?}$ one decade later.

All else equal, this shift means lower investment (in the figure, a drop from I_1 to I_2) and lower GDP growth going forward. However, many other factors may change over the next few years to increase savings in the United States. For example, as other nations grow, foreigners may continue to increase their savings in the United States. Or perhaps the savings rate in the United States will continue its recent rise. These increases could offset the effects of the baby boomers' retirement and keep interest rates low for U.S. firms.

FIGURE 22.11

A Decline in Investment Demand

(a) When decision-makers at firms lose confidence in the future direction of the economy, investment demand declines and lower investment results. (b) In the United States, real investment declined during both recessions that occurred between 2000 and 2012.

Source: Panel (b): U.S. Bureau of Economic Analysis.

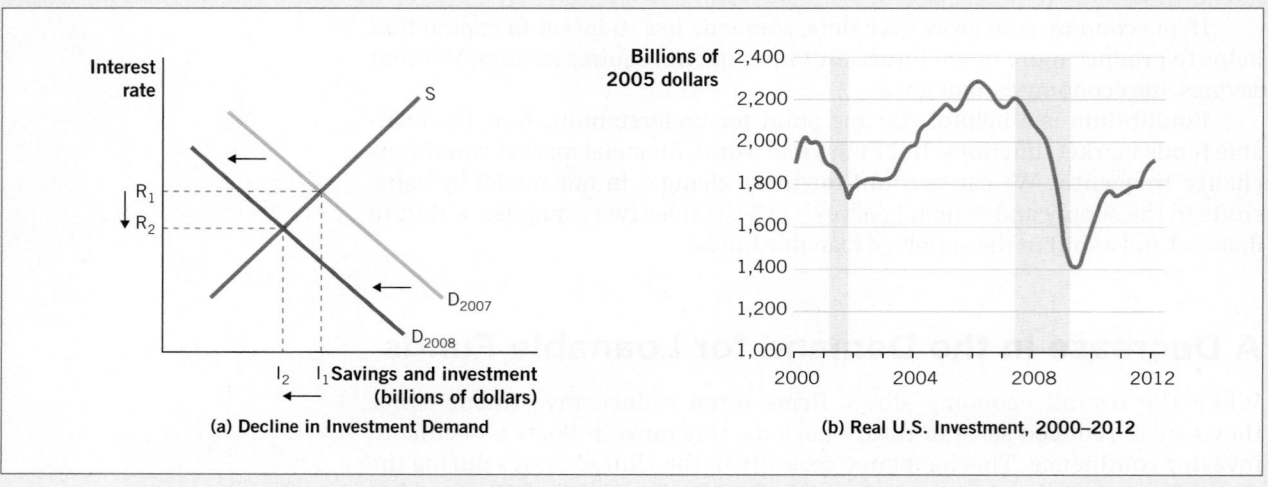

(a) Decline in Investment Demand

(b) Real U.S. Investment, 2000–2012

FIGURE 22.12

The Possible Future of the U.S. Loanable Funds Market

As baby boomers retire and draw down their savings, supply in the loanable funds market will decrease. Then if there are not increases in saving from other sources, interest rates will rise, leading to lower levels of investment.

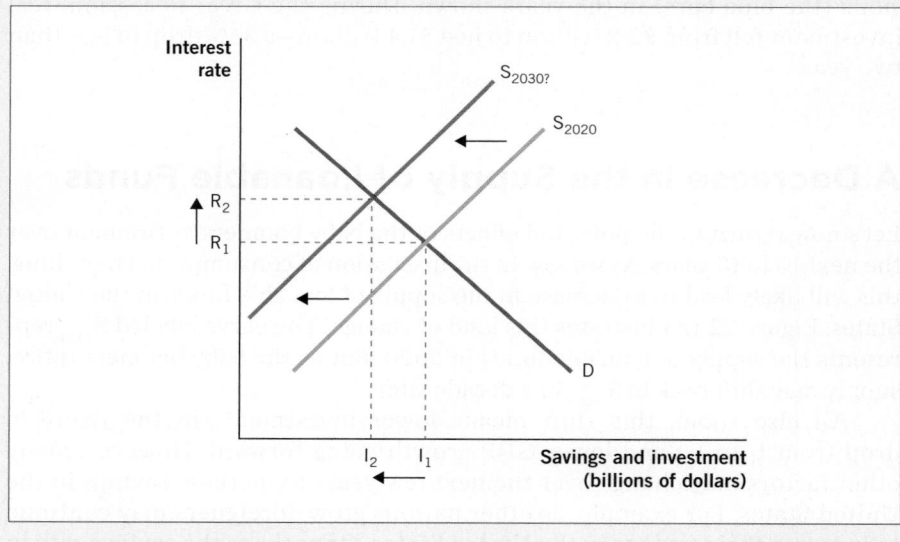

Compound Interest: When Should You Start Saving for Retirement?

- Lower time preferences translate to more savings.
- Small savings early in life lead to big gains later.

When you graduate from college, get a job, and start earning a steady income, you'll have several choices to make. Should you buy or lease a car? Should you buy or rent a home? Should you donate money or time to charity? Regardless of your decisions on issues such as these, you should always make room in your budget for savings.

We know that everyone has positive time preferences, so all else equal, you probably would rather consume now than later. But all else is not equal. That is, a little less consumption now will lead to a lot more consumption later, even under assumptions of very reasonable interest rates. The return to savings is like an exponential function: the longer you save, the greater the return to your savings, even at a constant interest rate. The reason is based on compound interest, which implies that the interest you earn becomes savings—which also bears interest. Let's see how this works.

Consider two people who choose alternate paths. Dirk understands the power of compound interest and chooses to start saving $100 per month when he is 25 years old. Lee has stronger time preferences and decides to wait until age 45 to start saving $100 per month. If both Dirk and Lee work until they are 65 years old, Dirk saves for 40 years and Lee saves for 20.

You might guess that Dirk will end up with twice as much in his retirement account, since he saves twice as long. But you'd be wrong. It turns out that Lee's retirement savings will increase to $53,988. That's not too bad, considering he will have saved just $100 per month over 20 years, or 240 months—the interest payments certainly helped. But what about Dirk? His retirement savings will be worth $281,767! That's more than five times the size of Lee's, and Dirk only made twice as many payments.

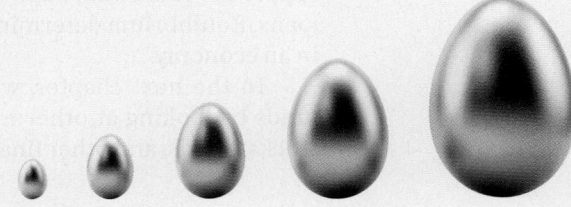

Compound interest produces more interest income.

What did we assume to get these returns? We assumed a 7% interest rate, which is the long-run historical real rate of return on a diversified stock portfolio. But any interest rate would illustrate the key point here: compound interest increases the value of your savings exponentially. So even with very strong time preferences, it makes sense to start saving early.

The graph illustrates the returns to saving $100 per month at an average annual return of 7% until retirement. The only difference is when you start saving. Notice that as you move along the horizontal axis, for each additional five years' worth of savings, the amount by which total savings grows will increase.

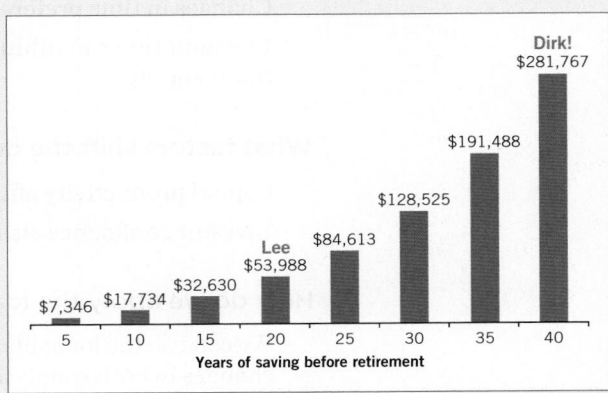

Conclusion

We began this chapter with the misconception that interest rates are set by the government. To be sure, the government influences interest rates, a topic we'll discuss further in Chapter 30. But interest rates are actually set in the market through the interaction of supply and demand. The discussion in this chapter has provided the foundation we need to discuss interest rates and financial markets further.

In macroeconomics, few topics are more important than investment. And investment is the result of equilibrium in the market for loanable funds. Savers supply the funds that support loans; borrowers are investors who demand the loans. Equilibrium determines the quantity of investment and the interest rate in an economy.

In the next chapter, we extend our analysis of the market for loanable funds by looking at other methods for borrowing and lending. These include stocks, bonds, and other financial securities. ✳

▪ ANSWERING *the* BIG QUESTIONS ▪

What is the loanable funds market?

- The loanable funds market connects savers with borrowers.
- Savers are suppliers of loanable funds, and they earn interest as a reward for saving.
- Borrowers are the buyers of loanable funds, and they pay interest as the cost of borrowing.

What factors shift the supply of loanable funds?

- Changes in income and wealth shift the supply of loanable funds.
- Changes in time preferences also affect the supply of loanable funds.
- Consumption smoothing is another factor that shifts the loanable funds supply.

What factors shift the demand for loanable funds?

- Capital productivity affects the demand for loanable funds.
- Investor confidence also affects the demand for loanable funds.

How do we apply the loanable funds market model?

- We can use the loanable funds market model to examine real-world changes in both supply and demand for loanable funds.
- The loanable funds model also clarifies the important conclusion that every dollar borrowed requires a dollar saved.

·CHAPTER PROBLEMS·

Concepts You Should Know

consumption smoothing (p. 715)
dissaving (p. 716)
expected return (p. 710)
Fisher equation (p. 711)

interest rate (p. 708)
investor confidence (p. 721)
loanable funds market (p. 707)
nominal interest rate (p. 711)

real interest rate (p. 711)
savings rate (p. 719)
time preferences (p. 714)

Questions for Review

1. Explain the importance of the loanable funds market to basic GDP in a macroeconomy.

2. All else equal, what does a lower interest rate mean for firms? What does a lower interest rate mean for savers?

3. Consider two alternatives to prepare for retirement: (1) saving in a bank where your funds earn interest and (2) buying fine art that rises in value over time. Each grows your retirement account over time.

   a. If the rates of return on fine art purchases fall, how would you expect the allocation of retirement funds to change across the macroeconomy?

   b. If the national savings rate is based only on the first option (saving in a bank), then what happens to the national savings rate when the allocation of retirement funds shifts as you describe in your response to part (a)?

   c. In addition to art, people often purchase real estate, stocks, and/or bonds as part of their savings, even though these assets are also not counted in the official data on personal savings. Discuss how these purchases affect the official data on a nation's savings rate.

4. List the factors that affect the supply side of the loanable funds market. Which factors shift the curve?

5. List the factors that affect the demand side of the loanable funds market. Which factors shift the curve?

6. Why does inflation have a positive effect on the nominal interest rate?

7. Many people believe that a high interest rate is bad for the economy. Of course, all else equal, a higher interest rate means greater borrowing costs for firms. But a high interest rate is also helpful to some people in the economy.

   a. What group of people benefits from a higher interest rate? Explain how they benefit.

   b. A high interest rate can also indicate that something positive is happening in the economy. Describe how positive factors can lead to an increase in the demand for loanable funds and then an increase in the interest rate.

Study Problems (∗ solved at the end of the section)

1. Assume that the residents of a nation become more patient (experience a reduction in their time preferences).

   a. What will happen to the interest rate in that nation? What will happen to the equilibrium level of investment in that nation? Explain your answers.

   b. In the long run, how will the lower time preferences affect the levels of capital and income growth in that nation?

2. Many interest rates in the United States have fallen over the past couple of decades. Which of the following factors could have been the cause?

   a. increase in the demand for loanable funds
   b. decrease in the demand for loanable funds
   c. increase in the supply of loanable funds
   d. decrease in the supply of loanable funds

3. Use the Fisher equation to fill in the blanks in the following table:

Inflation rate	Real interest rate	Nominal interest rate
_____	2%	7%
_____	0	7
2%	_____	6
9	_____	6
2	2	_____
10	2	_____

✳ **4.** Consider two hypothetical nations: Wahooland and Wildcat Island. Initially, these nations are identical in every way. In particular, they are the same with regard to population size and age, income and wealth, and time preferences. They also have the same interest rate, savings, and investment.

    a. Suddenly, in the year 2015, the interest rate in Wahooland rises. After some investigating, economists determine that nothing has happened to the supply of loanable funds. Therefore, what are the possible reasons for this rise in the interest rate in Wahooland?

    b. Given your answer to part (a), what can you say about the level of investment in Wahooland relative to that in Wildcat Island in 2015? What can you say about future income levels in Wahooland versus Wildcat Island?

    c. Often, we think of a lower interest rate as always being preferable to a higher interest rate. What has this question taught us about that idea?

✳ **5.** Some people have proposed an increase in the retirement age for U.S. citizens. Consider the effects of this proposed new policy.

    a. How would this change affect supply and demand in the market for loanable funds?

    b. How would this change affect the equilibrium interest rate and investment?

    c. In the long run, how would this change affect real GDP in the United States?

6. The Ragged Mountain Running Shop (RMRS) sells running shoes and apparel in Charlottesville, Virginia. The owners of RMRS are considering the possibility of opening new retail locations. After careful market analysis, they estimate the expected returns at five new potential locations. These estimates are listed in the following table, along with the amount RMRS would need to borrow in order to open each location:

Crozet	6%	$100,000
Downtown Charlottesville	4	100,000
Harrisonburg	11	80,000
Waynesboro	2	60,000
West End of Richmond	8	200,000

    a. RMRS approaches the Virginia National Bank (VNB) with hopes of borrowing to expand into other locations. Which locations will RMRS open if VNB offers them a loan at an interest rate of 7%? What if VNB offers loans at a lower interest rate of 5%?

    b. What is the total dollar amount of loans that RMRS takes at an interest rate of 7%? At an interest rate of 5%?

    c. Use the information in the table to graph the demand curve for investment for RMRS.

7. Suppose that several new technological innovations result in greater capital productivity in the U.S. economy. We know that these innovations have several macroeconomic effects. Let's concentrate on the changes in the loanable funds market and assume no other changes occur.

    a. On a sheet of paper, draw the loanable funds market in initial equilibrium. Be sure to label all curves and axes correctly.

    b. On your graph, illustrate how the technological innovations affect the loanable funds market.

    c. Assuming no other changes in the loanable funds market, state how these technological innovations affect the interest rate, the equilibrium level of investment, and future GDP.

8. Assume that the market for loanable funds in the United States is in equilibrium, with a 3% nominal interest rate and $500 billion worth of loans. Now assume that time preferences increase over a generation, due to shorter attention spans and greater impatience.

a. Does this change shift the supply of loanable funds, the demand for loanable funds, or both?
b. How does this change affect the interest rate and the equilibrium quantity of loans?

Solved Problems

4.a. If supply does not change, the rise in the interest rate must be due to a change in demand. If the rate went up, then demand must have increased. An increase in the demand for loanable funds occurs from an increase in the productivity of capital and/or an increase in investor confidence.
  b. Investment will be higher in Wahooland than in Wildcat Island. Future GDP will be higher in Wahooland, and this means that income will be higher.
  c. A higher interest rate can be caused by very productive capital. Thus, an innovative nation that tends to have new productive ideas and then high capital productivity might also have a higher interest rate. A higher interest rate can indicate very high returns to capital investment, which is certainly not bad for an economy.

5.a. The key is to examine how the policy change would affect savings through people's preferences for consumption smoothing. If U.S. workers start working longer, this would delay the dissaving period in their life and increase their savings. So supply would increase (shift outward). Demand would not change.
  b. The equilibrium interest rate would fall, and investment would increase.
  c. Real GDP would be greater, all else equal, due to the increase in investment. Basically, the new savings would become investment in capital. Thus, in the future there would be more tools for production in the United States, and output would be higher.

Financial Markets and Securities

Foreign Loans Lead to Investment in an Economy and Can Pave the Way for Future Growth.

Many people are concerned that foreign nations own significant amounts of U.S. assets. China, in particular, owns many prominent real estate landmarks and more U.S. government debt than any other foreign nation. People worry that since we owe China and other nations money, these nations can control us. And to be sure, owners do have their say. When Chinese investors bought One Chase Manhattan Plaza in New York's financial district, they renamed it 28 Liberty Street—because 8 means good fortune in Chinese culture, and 28 should be twice as lucky.

But think of the situation in terms of loanable funds. From this perspective, the Chinese are lenders who are sending their savings into the United States. These Chinese savings help us build factories and buildings and keep our interest rates lower, helping both our government and private firms in the United States. These exchanges help both Chinese and U.S. citizens.

The financial vehicles we discuss in this chapter are necessary for economic growth and development. These include stocks, bonds, home mortgages, and other financial instruments. Even though we are covering financial topics,

The Waldorf-Astoria in Manhattan is one of the most storied hotel properties in the United States. Built in 1931, it reigned until 1963 as the tallest hotel building in the world. As of 2014, however, it belongs to China's Anbang Insurance Group. The hotel is presently closed for extensive renovations that will provide an even more luxurious experience for guests when it reopens in 2021.

macroeconomics is the common thread that weaves through them; each helps you gain a more detailed understanding of the factors that affect the overall economy. We can both minimize the negative effects of recessions and experience economic growth only when financial markets function efficiently. When there are problems in financial markets, economic growth is impossible.

· BIG QUESTIONS ·

- How do financial markets help the economy?
- What are the key financial tools for the macroeconomy?

How Do Financial Markets Help the Economy?

In financial markets, borrowers and lenders come together. The buyers (or borrowers) in financial markets are firms and governments in search of funds to undertake their daily operations. The sellers (or lenders) are savers looking for opportunities to earn a return on their savings. In Chapter 22, we introduced the loanable funds market as a way of thinking about financial markets through the lens of supply and demand. In this chapter, we present an institutional view of financial markets. That is, we consider what types of firms operate in the middle of financial markets and what types of tools they use to facilitate the exchanges between savers and borrowers.

The major players in the middle of financial markets are called financial intermediaries. **Financial intermediaries** are firms that help to channel funds from savers to borrowers. Banks are one example of a financial intermediary. **Banks** are private firms that accept deposits and extend loans. Banks and other financial intermediaries are important for the macroeconomy because they are at the center of financial markets: they help connect borrowers with savers.

Financial intermediaries are firms that help to channel funds from savers to borrowers.

Banks are private firms that accept deposits and extend loans.

Direct and Indirect Financing

Indirect finance occurs when savers deposit funds into banks, which then loan these funds to borrowers.

When firms seek funding to pay for resources for production, they go to the loanable funds market. There are two different paths through the loanable funds market: indirect finance and direct finance. **Indirect finance** occurs when savers lend funds to financial intermediaries, which then loan these funds to borrowers. In this case, savers are indirectly financing the investments of firms.

Direct finance occurs when borrowers go directly to savers for funds. If you want a loan to start or expand a small business, you might go to a bank. But large established firms can skip financial intermediaries and go directly to these savers when they need funds.

Figure 23.1 shows the two alternate routes through the loanable funds market. The top half illustrates indirect finance, in which banks and other financial intermediaries facilitate the exchanges between lenders (that is, savers) and borrowers. If you have a savings or checking account at a bank, you participate in the loanable funds market as a lender. Banks package together the savings of many depositors like you to extend loans. The bottom half of Figure 23.1 illustrates direct finance, in which borrowers bypass financial intermediaries and go directly to savers for funds.

To undertake direct finance, firms need a contract that specifies the terms and conditions of the loan. These contracts usually take the form of a security. A **security** is a tradable contract that entitles its owner to certain rights. For example, a **bond** is a security that represents a debt to be paid. If you own a bond, it means someone owes you money—it is a formal IOU. Bonds are a tool of direct finance because they enable borrowers to go directly to savers for funds. If a firm sells a bond to an individual, it is borrowing funds that will be repaid at a later date. For example, in 2018 the Target Corporation had $13 billion in bonds outstanding. This means the Target Corporation owed $13 billion to the owners of those bonds.

Direct finance occurs when borrowers go directly to savers for funds.

A **security** is a tradable contract that entitles its owner to certain rights.

A **bond** is a security that represents a debt to be paid.

FIGURE 23.1

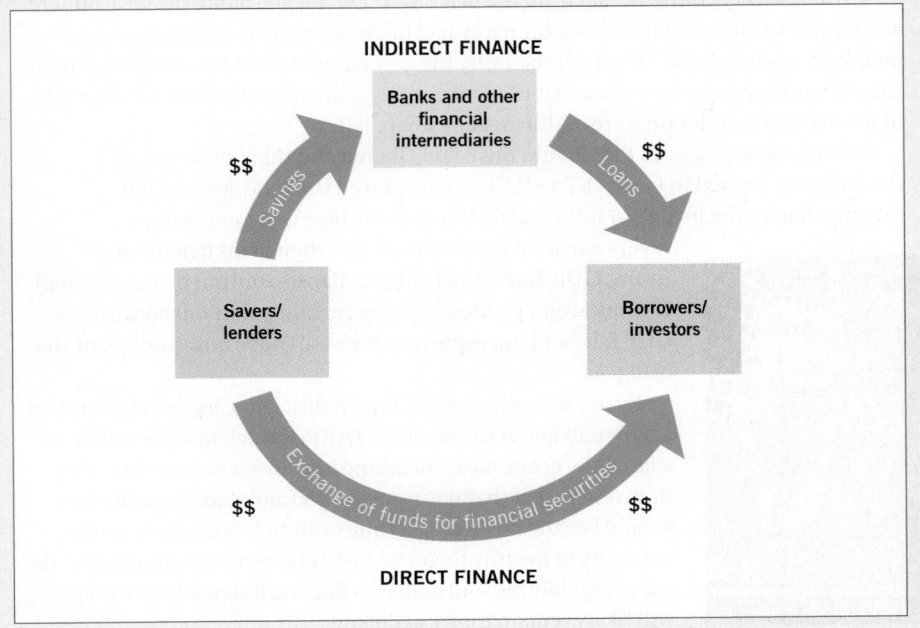

INDIRECT FINANCE

Banks and other financial intermediaries

$$

Loans $$

Savings

$$

Savers/ lenders

Borrowers/ investors

$$

Exchange of funds for financial securities

$$

DIRECT FINANCE

Direct versus Indirect Finance

Funds make their way through the loanable funds market through two distinct paths. Indirect finance occurs when savers and borrowers utilize banks or other financial intermediaries. Alternatively, direct finance occurs when borrowers go directly to savers for their funds.

The Importance of Financial Markets

Financial markets play a vital role in the macroeconomy. Macroeconomic growth is based on the production of GDP across the economy. This production comes from individual firms, such as cupcake shops, department stores, computer producers, and airplane manufacturers. But these firms need funding to build and buy the resources they use to produce their goods and services. These funds come from financial markets.

Consider what happens when financial markets break down. In 2007, several U.S. financial institutions began faltering. In September 2008, Lehman Brothers, a financial intermediary with over $600 billion in assets, went bankrupt. As a result, financial intermediaries all over the world became less inclined to extend loans. Because firms found it more difficult to borrow, economic contraction was inevitable. This contraction was the Great Recession that lasted through mid-2009.

ECONOMICS IN THE REAL WORLD

SHOULD WE BAIL OUT BIG BANKS?

In September 2008, Lehman Brothers, one of the largest financial firms, went bankrupt as many of the real estate loans they were holding went sour. After the Lehman Brothers bankruptcy (which had followed an earlier bankruptcy of Bear Stearns), it appeared there might be a domino effect that would lead to the collapse of many large banks. To avoid this potential disaster, the U.S. government implemented the Troubled Asset Relief Program—which came to be known as TARP—in October 2008. TARP allocated $700 billion to keep banks from failing. The money was used to aid banks that had made bad loans.

TARP was very controversial from the beginning. On the one hand, the government was clearly bailing out big banks after many had made poor business decisions, and people from all walks of life questioned why the government would use taxpayer funds to help banks that seemed to contribute to the recession, especially since most people in the general population were still struggling financially.

Others, including both Presidents Bush and Obama and their secretaries of the treasury, argued in favor of TARP. They considered these large financial intermediaries the bridge to future GDP. When the bridge is strong and safe, savers can lend to borrowers and then firms can invest in future GDP. But if the bridge collapses, output grinds to a halt. If firms aren't producing, they certainly don't need workers. GDP falls and unemployment rises. That's how important the bridge is.

Even today, economists (and politicians) are not in complete agreement about the need for TARP; though many feel this act spared the economy from falling into an even more dire situation, others feel that it was misguided and that no institution should be "too big to fail." While economists do agree on the necessity of healthy financial institutions, bank bailouts and the rules, regulations, and policies affecting financial institutions will likely remain topics of debate.

Do America's wealthiest banks really need taxpayer-funded bailouts?

Direct versus Indirect Finance: Which Is It?

Your friend Krista wants to open a cupcake shop. She needs to buy many resources before she can sell cupcakes and earn revenue. She is uncertain as to whether she should use direct or indirect financing.

QUESTION: For each of the following alternatives, is the financing considered direct or indirect?

a. Krista borrows money from a friend.

b. Krista takes a loan from her small local bank.

c. Krista arranges a loan from a large national bank.

d. Krista issues bonds and sells them to people in her neighborhood.

ANSWERS:

a. This is direct finance: Krista, the borrower, goes directly to a saver without the aid of a financial intermediary.

b. This is indirect finance: the bank makes the loan to Krista from the funds of various savers.

c. This is also indirect finance; the size of the bank does not matter.

d. This is direct finance: Krista goes directly to savers. It doesn't matter if the bonds are sold to people she happens to know.

CHALLENGE QUESTION: Suppose Krista decides to apply for a loan at a local bank. What factors will the bank consider when responding to Krista's application?

ANSWER: The bank will consider how much Krista is asking for, and for how long (the time period before she pays the money back). The bank will also consider the risk that Krista will not be able to repay the loan. Finally, the bank will think about the opportunity cost; that is, the loans the bank could make to others instead, if it turns Krista down. All these factors will go into deciding whether Krista gets the loan and what interest she will pay if she does.

These are some of the resources necessary to produce Lemon Bliss cupcakes.

What Are the Key Financial Tools for the Macroeconomy?

In this section, we explore tools used in financial markets to help fund investment. We focus on tools that matter for the macroeconomy, including bonds, stocks, Treasury securities, home mortgages, and private-sector securities created by the process of securitization. We start with bonds.

Bonds

Firms issue several types of securities to raise funds, but we can view them all as variations of a basic corporate bond.

Let's say your friend Kara wants to open a new website design business. But first she needs a loan to buy computers and software. Initially, Kara goes to a bank for a loan, but it turns her away because her company is new and viewed as very risky. So Kara comes to you and asks for a one-year loan. You know Kara well, so you agree to loan her some money with the understanding that she will repay the funds plus interest exactly one year later.

To formalize your agreement, you decide to draw up an IOU contract like the one presented in Figure 23.2. When you "buy" this contract from Kara, you are lending her funds with the promise that she'll pay you $10,000 in one year. The contract is essentially the same as a corporate or government bond, and it serves the same purpose. This is an example of direct finance, with the borrower going directly to a saver who lends them money.

Like any bond, your contract contains three important pieces of information: the name of the borrower, the repayment date, and the amount due at repayment. In this example, the name of the borrower is Kara Alexis; the repayment date is February 20, 2021. The date on which the loan repayment is due is the **maturity date**. Finally, every bond contract also specifies the face value, or par value, of the bond. The bond's **face value**, or **par value**, is the bond's value at maturity—the amount due at repayment. For notation purposes, we'll call the face value p_m because it is the price, or value, of the bond at maturity.

Perhaps you noticed that Figure 23.2 shows the bond's face value, but not the amount of the initial loan. In fact, you and Kara must come to an agreement about how much you will loan her. But with a bond agreement, the face value is typically set at a round number like $10,000. When you and Kara settle on the initial loan amount, you are agreeing to the dollar price of the bond (p). The price of the bond is the original dollar amount of the loan. For example, if you agree on a price of $8,000 for Kara's bond, that is the amount you loan her. From your perspective, you loan her $8,000 today for the promise that she'll pay you $10,000 in one year. From Kara's perspective, she now has $8,000 she can use to buy computers and software for her website design business, and she can begin producing GDP. But one year from now she has to repay you $10,000.

The **maturity date** of a bond is the date on which the loan repayment is due.

A bond's **face value**, or **par value**, is the bond's value at maturity—the amount due at repayment.

FIGURE 23.2

A Basic Bond Security

A simple IOU contract between two friends is like a bond. It specifies three things: (1) the name of the borrower (here, Kara Alexis); (2) the repayment date (February 20, 2021); (3) the amount due at repayment ($10,000).

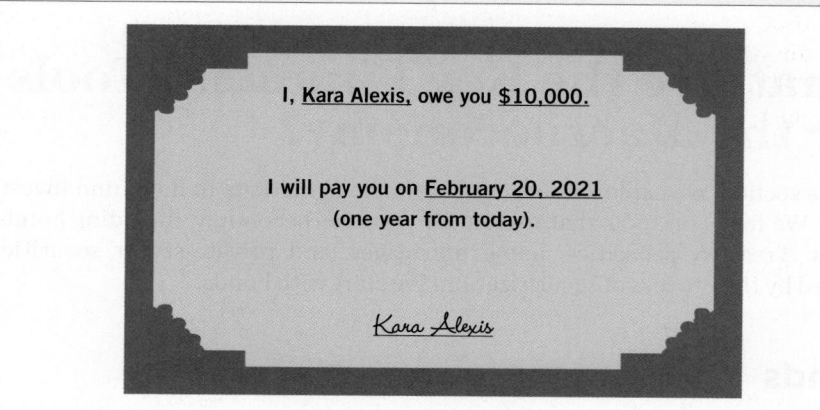

I, <u>Kara Alexis,</u> owe you <u>$10,000.</u>

I will pay you on <u>February 20, 2021</u>
(one year from today).

Kara Alexis

That's how a basic bond security works. Many bonds also include *coupons* that specify periodic interest payments to the bond owner. That distinction is not important for our purposes, so we focus on bonds that entail a single payment when the bond matures.

We now build on this foundation by discussing how interest rates relate to bond prices and how default risk affects the price of a bond.

THE BOND DOLLAR PRICE AND INTEREST RATE In the previous discussion, we described Kara's bond in dollar prices. But loan prices are generally quoted in interest rates. Therefore, we need to consider how the bond's dollar price (p) is related to its interest rate (R). To determine the interest rate on this bond, we have to find the rate of return on the dollars that are loaned. For example, you "buy" Kara's bond for $8,000, and one year later the bond is worth $10,000. In percentage terms, the value of the bond increases by 25%. Thus, the rate of return, or interest rate, is computed as a growth rate, where the price of the bond is growing from its initial value (p_0):

$$\text{interest rate} = R = \frac{\text{face value} - \text{initial price}}{\text{initial price}} = \frac{P_m - P_0}{P_0}$$

(EQUATION 23.1)

If the price of the bond is $8,000, the interest rate is computed as

$$R = \frac{P_m - P_0}{P_0} = \frac{\$10,000 - \$8,000}{\$8,000} = 25\%$$

We used growth rates when we discussed GDP growth and inflation. Here, the interest rate is computed as a growth rate; it is the growth rate of the original funds invested.

With bonds, the face value is fixed—it is printed on the front of the bond. Thus, *the dollar price of a bond determines the bond's interest rate.* If you know the dollar price of a given bond, you can determine the interest rate. Table 23.1 shows several alternative prices for a $10,000 one-year bond. Notice that the lower the price, the higher the interest rate, because it takes fewer dollars for the lender to earn $10,000 one year later.

Each price implies a different interest rate. For example, if Kara sells you the $10,000 bond for only $7,500, the interest rate rises to 33%. This is much better for you, since you buy the bond for $7,500 and are repaid that amount plus $2,500 in interest only one year later. But this is worse for Kara because she is getting just $7,500 this year, with the same promise to repay you $10,000 next year.

TABLE 23.1

Dollar Price and Interest Rate for a $10,000 One-Year Bond

Dollar price (p_0)	Interest rate (R)
$9,000	11%
8,000	25
7,500	33
5,000	100

Notice that as the price of the bond drops, the interest rate on the bond rises. If the bond price drops to $5,000, the interest rate climbs to 100%. This relationship holds by definition: *the dollar price and interest rate of a bond have a negative relationship.*

In Chapter 22, we saw that the interest rate on a loan is the cost of borrowing and the reward for saving. Higher interest rates (lower dollar prices) hurt borrowers and help lenders. As a lender, you want to buy bonds for the lowest price possible because you want the highest possible interest rate on your savings. The borrower wants to sell bonds for the highest price possible so that she can pay the lowest possible interest rate.

A primary factor in determining the interest rate on bonds is the borrower's default risk, a topic to which we now turn.

DEFAULT RISK Some financial transactions are very complex and potentially lead to many different outcomes. But bonds are fairly straightforward. If the bond owner holds the bond until maturity, there are only two possible outcomes: the borrower pays the maturity value of the bond, or the borrower defaults on the loan. These possibilities are illustrated in Figure 23.3. For the bond owner, then, the risk of default is the primary concern. **Default risk** is the risk that the borrower will not pay the face value of a bond on the maturity date.

All else equal, the greater the default risk, the lower the price of a bond. Consider the bond Kara is selling to finance her start-up website design company. If you really trust Kara and believe her business will succeed, you might buy her $10,000 bond for $9,500. At this price, she promises to pay you about 5.25% interest for the use of your funds for a year. However, if you are skeptical about either Kara's integrity or the prospects for her business success, you may be willing to pay only $8,000 for the bond. At this price, she will pay 25%

Default risk
is the risk that the borrower will not pay the face value of a bond on the maturity date.

FIGURE 23.3

Two Possible Outcomes with a Bond

With a bond, both the maturity date and the face value are certain. Thus, there are only two possible outcomes if a bond owner holds the bond until maturity: either the borrower will pay the face value, or she will default. Because these are the only two possible outcomes, default risk is the primary concern of a bond owner.

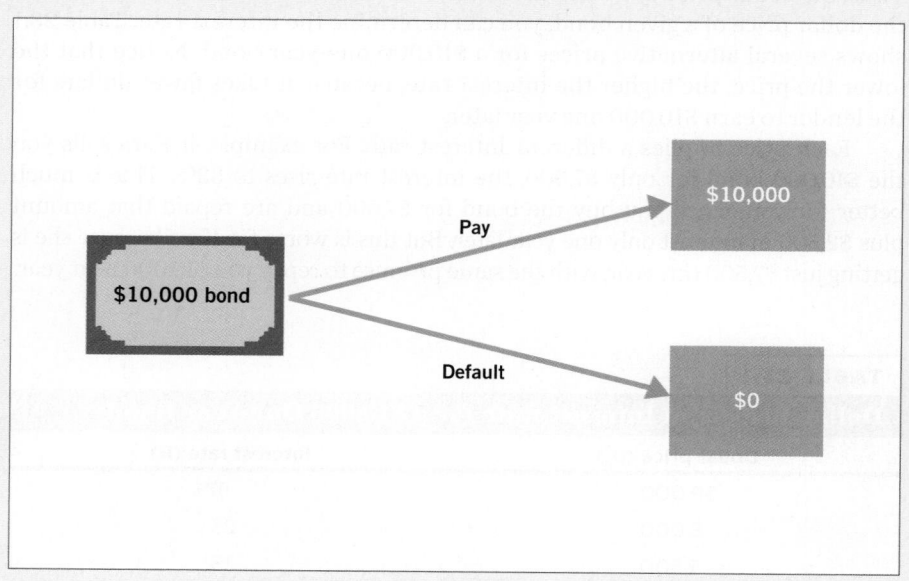

interest for the loan instead. This scenario illustrates an important bond price principle: a *bond's interest rate rises with default risk*.

Consider bonds offered by the Target Corporation. Target is a large company with many capital investments. As mentioned earlier, the Target Corporation had $13 billion in bonds outstanding in 2018. Clearly, there is a significant market for Target bonds. Consider the hypothetical supply and demand for one-year $100,000 Target bonds illustrated in Figure 23.4. Initially, with the demand curve at D_1 and supply at S, the equilibrium price is $98,000.

Now let's assume that something negative happens to the future prospects of Target's business. Perhaps Walmart attracts customers away from Target. This news reduces the probability that Target will pay off its bonds as they mature; in other words, it increases Target's default risk. As such, the demand for Target bonds declines from D_1 to D_2. As demand declines, the market price of Target bonds falls from $98,000 to $97,000, which means the interest rate rises (because the dollar price and interest rate on a bond always move in opposite directions). As a result, we can generalize to say that increases in default risk (1) cause a drop in the price that firms can charge for their bonds and (2) cause an increase in their bonds' interest rate.

BOND RATINGS Default risk is important to bondholders, and it helps to determine the price of the bond. But typical individuals have difficulty judging the default risk of any one company, let alone the thousands of firms that sell bonds in a developed economy. To address this problem, private rating agencies evaluate and then grade the default risk of borrowing entities. They give a grade that reflects the likelihood of default. Three ratings agencies are particularly prominent in the United States: Moody's, Standard and Poor's, and Fitch. The ratings systems are similar for all three firms, so we'll choose Standard and Poor's (S&P) for explanatory purposes.

FIGURE 23.4

How Increased Default Risk Affects the Market for $100,000 Target Bonds

The initial price in the market for Target bonds is $98,000. But an increase in default risk reduces the demand for Target bonds, resulting in a lower price and a higher interest rate. This outcome drives up the borrowing costs for Target.

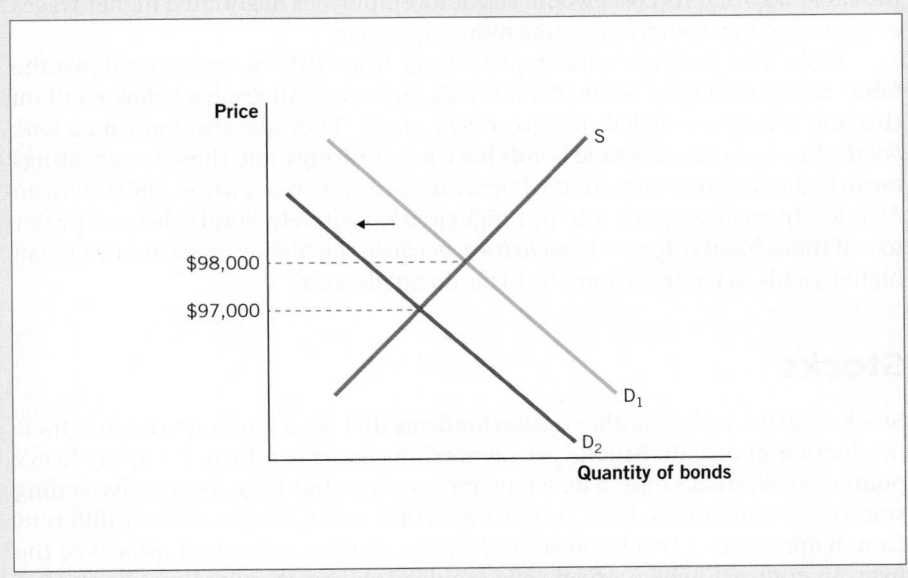

TABLE 23.2

Sample Bond Ratings

S&P*	Grade	Examples
AAA	Prime	Apple, Germany, Harvard University, Johnson & Johnson, Microsoft, University of Virginia
AA	High	Amazon, Berkshire Hathaway, Exxon, Nestle, Nike, Procter & Gamble, Samsung, Toyota, United States, Walmart
A	Upper medium	Anheuser-Busch, Boeing, BP, China, Coca-Cola, Duke University, Ford, GE, IBM, Intel, J.P. Morgan, Louis Vuitton, L'Oreal, Lowe's, Pepsi, Royal Dutch Shell, Siemens, Spain, Target, UnitedHealth Group, Visa, Walt Disney
BBB	Lower medium	American Express, AT&T, Best Buy, eBay, FedEx, General Motors, Goldman Sachs, Heineken, HP, India, Kellogg's, Kraft, McDonald's, McKesson, Mexico, Starbucks, Verizon, Volkswagen
BB	Noninvestment or speculative	American Airlines, Brazil, Marriott, MGM, T-Mobile, Twitter, United Airlines
B	Highly speculative	Argentina, Egypt, Greece, J.C. Penney, Netflix, Office Depot, Staples, Tesla, Turkey, U.S. Steel
CCC	Extremely speculative	Bombardier, P. F. Chang's
CC	In or near default	Neiman Marcus, PetSmart, Sears

*As of 2018.

The most stable firms, those most likely to pay their debts, are given a rating of AAA. In the recent past, firms like Johnson & Johnson and Microsoft have achieved AAA ratings. A high rating is desirable for firms because it directly translates into higher prices and lower interest rates on the firm's bonds. Moreover, the firm's operating costs are directly affected by its bond rating, because the interest rate is the cost of a key resource for its production. If Microsoft's bond rating falls from AAA to AA, this change increases the company's cost in the same way that its costs would rise if its employees negotiated higher wages or if another key resource became more expensive.

Table 23.2 shows selected bond ratings from 2018. As we move down the table, the grade falls and the default risk increases. All grades below medium (BB and lower) are called *noninvestment grade*. They are also known as *junk bonds*. Noninvestment-grade bonds have lower ratings, and these lower ratings mean higher interest rates for the borrowing firms, such as Twitter and American Airlines. In an attempt to spin this higher risk positively, bond salesmen prefer to call these bonds *high-yield securities*, because the higher interest rates mean higher yields to lenders when the firms do not default.

Stocks

Stocks
are ownership shares in a firm.

Stock securities offer another option for firms that need funding to finance their production of output. **Stocks** are ownership shares in a firm. From the firm's point of view, stocks offer a new financing avenue, but they also involve ceding some ownership of the firm. In this important sense, stocks are very different from bank loans or bonds: owners of stock securities are actual owners of the firm. In contrast, when a firm sells bonds, it does not cede direct control of the firm to new owners.

Why would a firm sell stocks instead of bonds? One reason is that bond financing leaves the firm with a lot of bills that must eventually be paid. For example, when IBM sells $10 million worth of 10-year bonds, the company takes on the obligation to pay $10 million in 10 years. If the firm cannot pay this debt, the owners may need to declare bankruptcy and lose the firm altogether. With stocks, however, the owners can sell shares of the firm to others and move forward without the burden of debt.

From the lender's perspective, stock ownership is also different from bond ownership. Because stock owners (shareholders) are owners of the firm, they have some influence on the firm's operations. In fact, a shareholder who owns more than 50% of the shares of the firm is the majority shareholder and controls more than 50% of the ownership votes. A majority shareholder can determine the direction of the company, an influence not available to bondholders.

You can own part of Spotify! To see its current share price, type its ticker symbol (SPOT) into a search engine.

Secondary Markets

Most people who purchase stocks and bonds use brokers, who buy the stocks and bonds in secondary markets. **Secondary markets** are markets in which securities are traded after their first sale. Secondary markets are like used-car markets, but the "used" assets are securities. There's nothing wrong with a used security; it just means the buyer is not purchasing the security directly from the firm whose name is on it. You probably recognize the names of some important secondary stock markets. They include the New York Stock Exchange (NYSE) and NASDAQ (the National Association of Securities Dealers Automated Quotations).

The existence of a secondary market for a given security increases the demand for that security. Consider the difference between a Target Corporation bond and the hypothetical bond you bought from Kara Alexis to help fund her website design company. Whoever buys the Target bond can sell it with a quick call to a broker or with the click of a mouse. The ease of resale is valuable and therefore worth a higher price. But when you buy Kara's bond, you have to hold on to it until you can personally locate another buyer. This sort of complication greatly limits the demand for bonds that cannot be resold in secondary markets, which lowers the price (that is, raises the interest rate).

Figure 23.5 illustrates the impact secondary markets have on security prices. If a secondary market exists for a security, then the demand for the security increases (from D_1 to D_2); in turn, the increased demand causes the price of the security to rise (from p_1 to p_2), all else being equal. For the firm, the existence of a secondary market is helpful because it lowers the interest rate the firm pays on its bonds and therefore its cost of borrowing.

Secondary markets are a valuable institution of market economies because they lower the cost of borrowing. This is true of secondary markets for any asset, not just stocks and bonds. For example, let's say you are considering buying a particular house. Your real estate agent tells you the price is very reasonable, but there is one unusual stipulation: you can never sell the house after you buy it. Of course, this is not a realistic stipulation, but think about how it would affect your willingness to buy the home. The purchase would be more risky,

Secondary markets are markets in which securities are traded after their first sale.

The NYSE is the largest secondary stock market in the world.

FIGURE 23.5

The Effect of Secondary Markets on Security Prices

The existence of secondary markets increases the demand for securities. When demand increases, the price rises (and the interest rate falls). Secondary markets allow firms to borrow at lower interest rates.

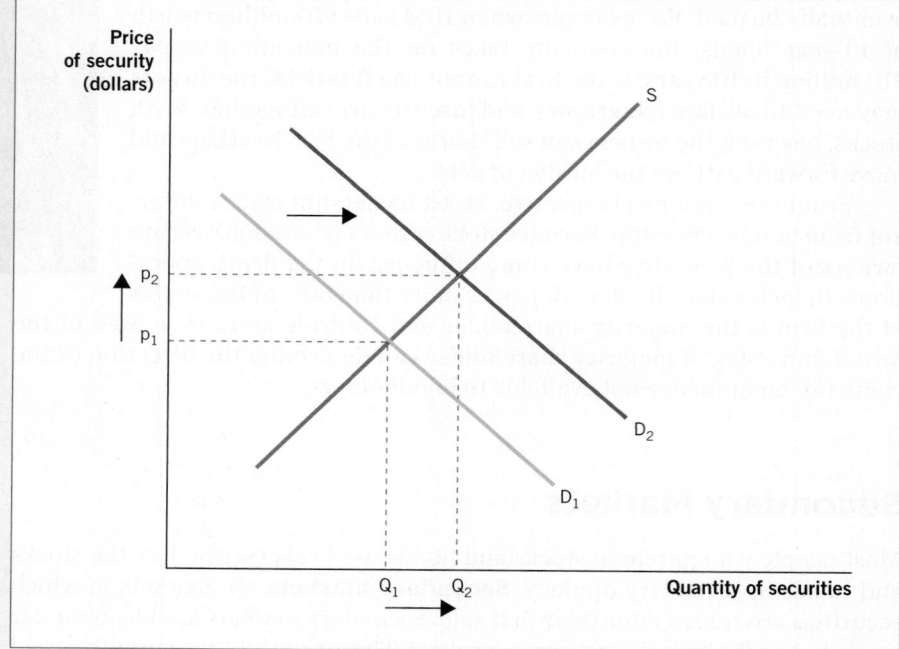

and no buyer would pay as much for that house as for one that could be resold. Secondary markets, by offering future sale opportunities for securities, increase the demand for them.

ECONOMICS IN THE REAL WORLD

STOCK MARKET INDICES: DOW JONES VERSUS S&P

Media reports about the stock market tend to focus on stock price indices like the Dow Jones Industrial Average and the Standard and Poor's 500 (S&P 500). Just as the consumer price index (CPI) tracks general consumer prices, these stock market indices track overall stock prices. The CPI, recall, is a weighted average of all consumer prices, where the weights are determined by the portion of the typical consumer budget spent on any given item. An increase in the CPI indicates a corresponding rise in the general level of consumer prices. Similarly, the rise and fall of stock indices indicate a corresponding rise and fall in the general level of stock prices.

The best-known stock index is the Dow Jones Industrial Average (the Dow). When the Dow was first published in 1896, it tracked 12 companies. Today, it tracks 30 companies selected by the editors of the *Wall Street Journal*. The editors maintain the index so that it represents companies in all the important sectors of the economy. To stay up to date, the Dow must occasionally change the companies in its index. For example, when the technology sector came to the forefront in the late 1990s, Intel and Microsoft were added. In 2015, Apple replaced AT&T. Most recently, General Electric, which had

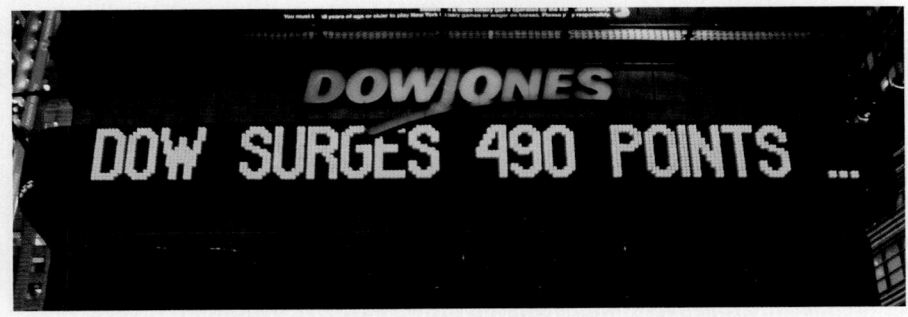

Is it good news when the Dow Jones Industrial Average goes up?

been part of the Dow virtually from the beginning, was replaced in 2018 by the parent company that owns Walgreens drug stores.

One of the advantages of the Dow is that it provides historical data all the way back to May 26, 1896. At that time, the calculation was very simple: an investor added the price of all 12 stocks and divided the sum by 12 to compute a simple average. Today, the Dow incorporates 30 stock prices in the average, but it is essentially computed in the same way. This means the Dow tracks only the price of the stock, not the overall value of a company or the relative values of the companies in the stock market.

The S&P 500 index weights the stock prices by the *market value* of the companies it tracks. The market value is the total number of stock shares multiplied by the price per share. Under a market value–weighted index, the stock prices of large companies have a greater impact than those of smaller companies. For instance, Apple (with a market value of $636 billion in 2015) weighs much more heavily than Facebook (with a market value of $248 billion in 2015). Moreover, there is another difference between the S&P 500 and the Dow Jones index: while the Dow tracks only 30 companies, the S&P 500 tracks 500 companies, thus providing a much broader representation of the stock market.

In many respects, the Dow is an artifact of simpler times, when computing a broadly based index was time intensive. Today, spreadsheets can crunch all the stock price data in milliseconds. Nevertheless, the Dow has been a very reliable measure of market performance, and it also provides a continuous record of historical information that cannot be replaced by more recent indices.

Treasury Securities

So far in our discussion, we have considered firms as the major type of borrowing entity in an economy. But governments are significant borrowers, too. According to the U.S. Treasury Department, the U.S. federal government has about $23 trillion worth of debt—that's more than $68,000 per citizen. All this borrowing takes place through bond sales. **Treasury securities** are the bonds sold by the U.S. government to pay for the national debt.

Treasury securities are sold through auctions to large financial firms. The auction price determines the interest rate. After a Treasury security is sold the first time, anyone can buy it in the large and active secondary market for U.S. Treasury securities.

U.S. Treasury securities are generally considered less risky than any other bond, because borrowers don't expect the U.S. government to default on its debts. Even when politicians threaten actions that could lead to default, the

> **Treasury securities** are the bonds sold by the U.S. government to pay for the national debt.

The Dow Jones Industrial Average

The Dow Jones Industrial Average is perhaps the most closely watched financial market indicator. The Dow tracks average stock prices of 30 firms that represent major industries in the U.S. economy; these include Coca-Cola, Walmart, Disney, Microsoft, Apple, Visa, and Boeing. Since the Dow represents a broad array of industries, movements indicate changes in private investors' expectations about the future direction of the macroeconomy. Increases in the Dow generally reflect confidence in the future of the U.S. economy; decreases mean people are pessimistic. While other economic indicators take months to measure, the Dow is an instantaneous indicator of how private investors view future economic conditions.

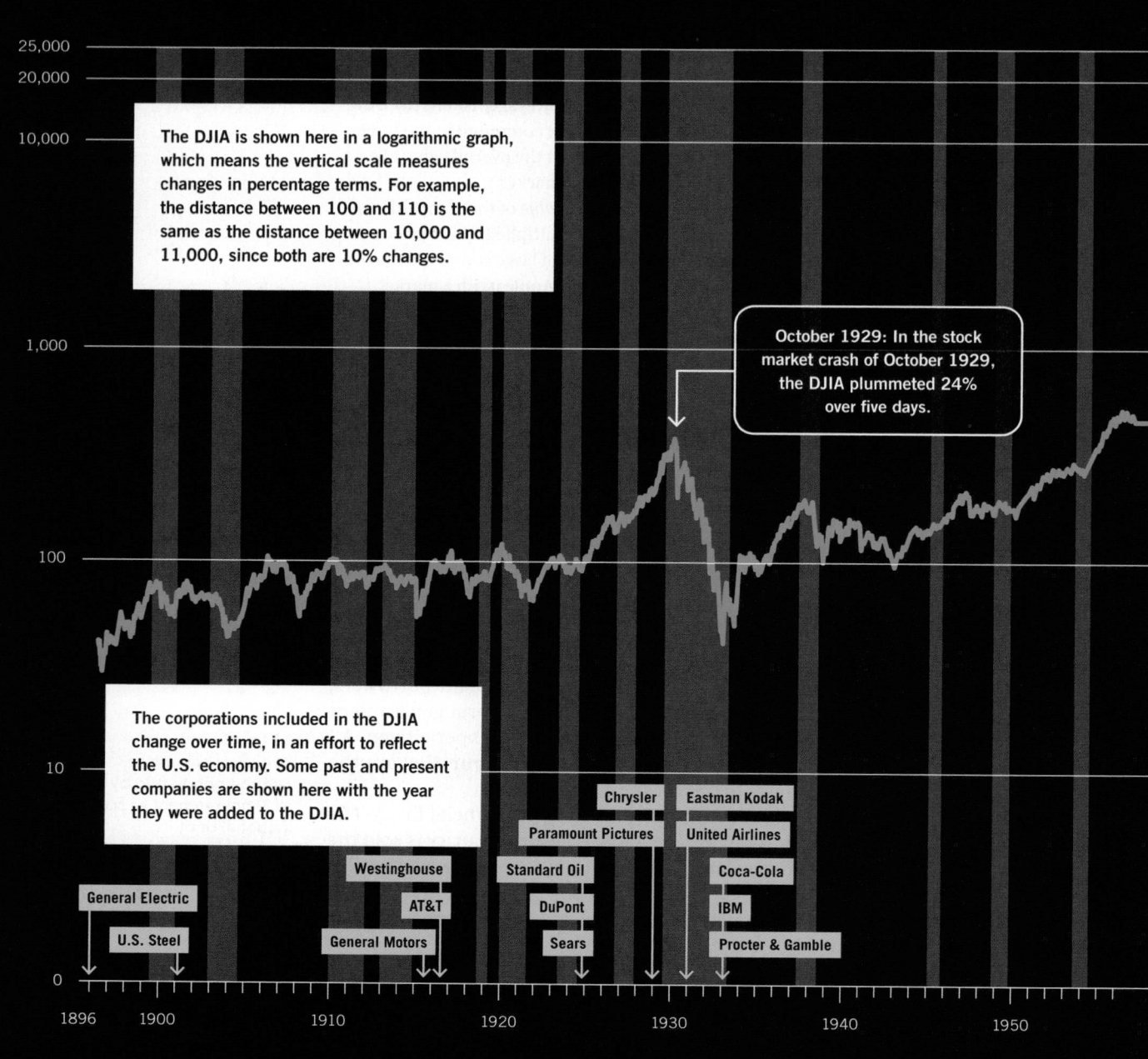

The DJIA is shown here in a logarithmic graph, which means the vertical scale measures changes in percentage terms. For example, the distance between 100 and 110 is the same as the distance between 10,000 and 11,000, since both are 10% changes.

October 1929: In the stock market crash of October 1929, the DJIA plummeted 24% over five days.

The corporations included in the DJIA change over time, in an effort to reflect the U.S. economy. Some past and present companies are shown here with the year they were added to the DJIA.

Chrysler

Paramount Pictures

Eastman Kodak

United Airlines

Westinghouse

Standard Oil

Coca-Cola

General Electric

AT&T

DuPont

IBM

U.S. Steel

General Motors

Sears

Procter & Gamble

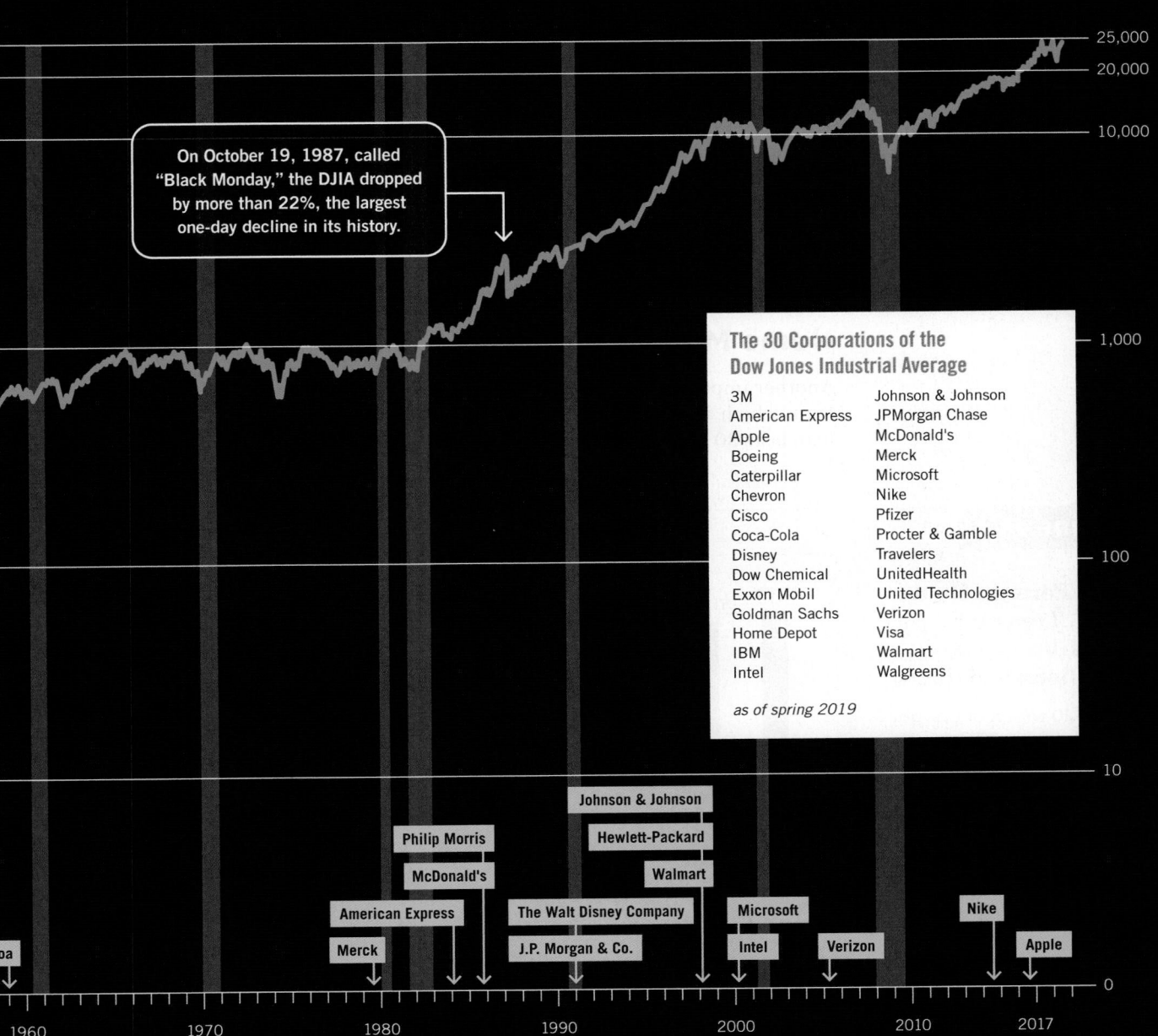

REVIEW QUESTIONS

- Approximately how long did it take the Dow to rise from 1,000 to 10,000? From 10,000 to 25,000?

- Why do movements in overall stock prices indicate something about the entire macroeconomy?

— Dow Jones Industrial Average

■ Period of recession

On October 19, 1987, called "Black Monday," the DJIA dropped by more than 22%, the largest one-day decline in its history.

The 30 Corporations of the Dow Jones Industrial Average

3M	Johnson & Johnson
American Express	JPMorgan Chase
Apple	McDonald's
Boeing	Merck
Caterpillar	Microsoft
Chevron	Nike
Cisco	Pfizer
Coca-Cola	Procter & Gamble
Disney	Travelers
Dow Chemical	UnitedHealth
Exxon Mobil	United Technologies
Goldman Sachs	Verizon
Home Depot	Visa
IBM	Walmart
Intel	Walgreens

as of spring 2019

25,000
20,000
10,000
1,000
100
10
0

Johnson & Johnson

Philip Morris

Hewlett-Packard

McDonald's

Walmart

American Express

The Walt Disney Company

Microsoft

Nike

Merck

J.P. Morgan & Co.

Intel

Verizon

Apple

oa

1960   1970   1980   1990   2000   2010   2017

U.S. Treasury securities are used to pay for government spending when tax revenue falls short.

values of U.S. securities have stayed historically steady because borrowers on the whole have felt that a U.S. loan default is highly unlikely.

Because Treasury bonds are safe, firms and governments from all over the world buy U.S. Treasury securities as a way to limit risk. In 2017, approximately $6.3 trillion (about 30%) of U.S. federal debt was held by foreigners. Figure 23.6 shows the breakdown of foreign ownership of U.S. Treasury securities.

As we noted at the start of the chapter, a common concern is that nations like China will exert undue influence on the U.S. government if we owe them money. But this perspective does not consider a key point: foreign savings keep interest rates lower in the United States than they would otherwise be. This means that U.S. firms and governments can undertake their activities at lower costs. In turn, lower interest rates mean more investment and greater future GDP. That is a clear benefit of foreign investment in the United States.

Treasury securities play many roles in the macroeconomy. For example, they are used when the government alters the supply of money in the economy, which we discuss in Chapter 30. In addition, if the government decides to increase spending without raising taxes, it must pay for the additional spending by borrowing—by selling bonds. We will explore this role of Treasury securities in Chapter 28.

Home Mortgages

Another important borrowing tool in the United States is the home mortgage loan, which individuals use to pay for homes. The most common mortgage loan lasts 30 years from inception and is paid off with 360 monthly payments.

FIGURE 23.6

Major Foreign Holders of U.S. Treasury Securities, 2017 (in billions of dollars)

Of the $20 trillion of U.S. government debt in 2017, foreigners held approximately 30%. China and Japan together owned more than $2 trillion of our national debt, which represents about 10% of the total outstanding.

Source: U.S. Treasury Department.

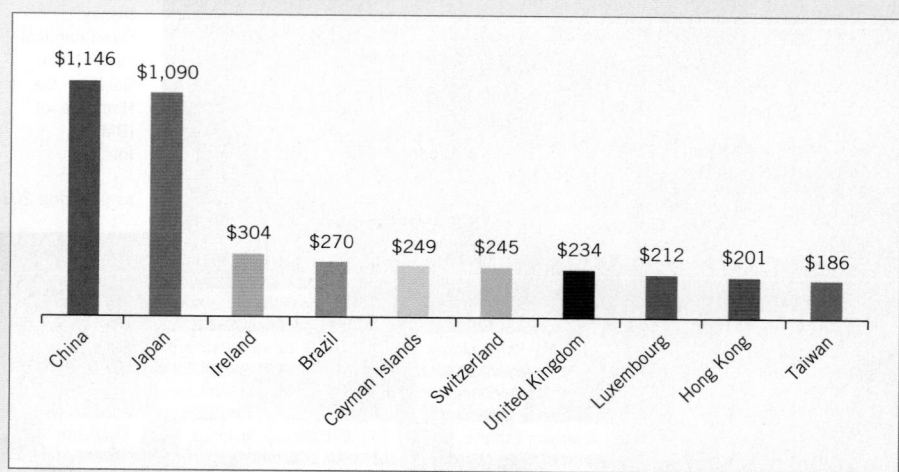

FIGURE 23.7

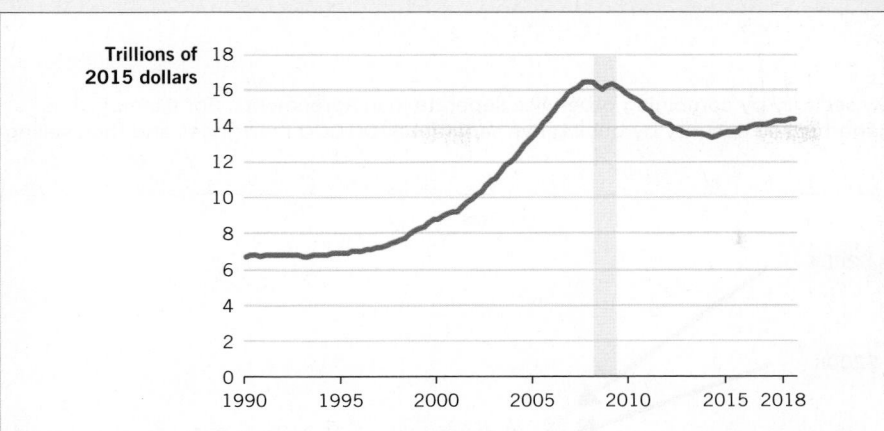

Total Size of U.S. Mortgage Market, 1990–2018

The home mortgage market in the United States expanded greatly, leading up to the recession in 2008. In 1990, there was $6.7 trillion worth of home mortgages in the United States. By 2007, this had expanded to over $16 trillion.

Source: Federal Reserve.

These mortgages are really just variations on the basic bond security we have described in this chapter. When a family wants to buy a home, they take on a mortgage loan, which is a contract that states their willingness to repay the loan over several years—just like a firm signing a bond contract.

The macroeconomic significance of home mortgages has grown over time as more and more people own homes. Figure 23.7 shows the growth in the U.S. mortgage market from 1990 to 2018. The graph plots the total size of the U.S. mortgage market in real (2015) dollars. The period of the Great Recession is shaded (December 2007 to June 2009). The U.S. home mortgage market expanded greatly in the years leading up to the recession. In 1990, there was about $6.7 trillion in home mortgages in the United States. By 2007, the market had expanded to over $16 trillion. However, as you can see in the figure, the U.S. home mortgage market has declined since that high point, and as of the middle of 2018 it was still more than 12% below its highest point.

Securitization

Since the 1980s, bonds, stocks, and other financial securities, including home mortgages, have been bundled together to create new financial assets in a process called securitization. **Securitization** is the creation of a new security by combining otherwise separate loan agreements. These agreements are then bought and sold like any other agreement on secondary markets.

For example, consider two common personal loans: home mortgages and student loans. The United States has secondary markets in which home mortgages and student loans are bought and sold daily. Figure 23.8 illustrates how mortgage-backed securities are created. Each mortgage-backed security (MBS) is a combination, or bundle, of mortgages. The new security is then available for resale in secondary markets.

Most economists believe that these tools are important because opportunities for firms and individuals expand when credit is available. More credit

Securitization is the creation of a new security by combining otherwise separate loan agreements.

FIGURE 23.8

Securitization

Securitization is the creation of a new security by combining otherwise separate loan agreements. For example, it is possible to create a $1 million mortgage-backed security by buying five separate $200,000 mortgages and then selling them together as a bundle.

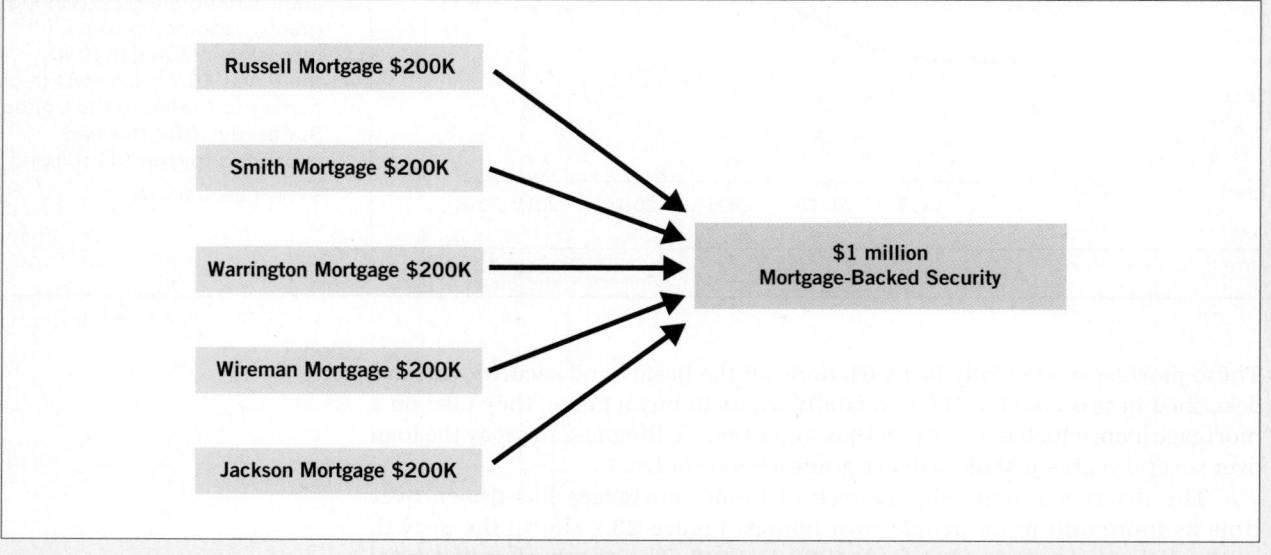

leads to lower borrowing costs, which certainly help borrowers. When interest rates are lower, investment opportunities expand for everything from factories to roads to homes to education. And as we noted earlier, secondary markets reduce borrowing costs. In a few years, you may take out a mortgage to buy a home. There is a chance your mortgage will be bundled together with others into a big security that can be bought and sold. The mere existence of this market means you'll pay a lower interest rate on your mortgage loan. For these reasons, there are incentives to create new markets for all varieties of loan agreements.

Incentives

Indeed, securitization lowers interest rates for borrowers. It also offers new opportunities for lenders. For example, people from all over the globe can now buy securities tied to the U.S. mortgage market. But lenders need to correctly evaluate the risk associated with these newly created securities. When the U.S. home mortgage market began collapsing in 2007, the negative reverberations were felt not only in the United States but worldwide. For example, because Icelandic banks owned a large number of securities tied to the U.S. home mortgage market, both the economy and government of Iceland collapsed during 2008–2009.

The Effects of Foreign Investment: What If We Limit Foreign Ownership of Our National Debt?

Could both of these flags fly over Washington someday?

Imagine that a new law significantly limits foreign ownership of U.S. Treasury bonds.

QUESTION: How would you graph the market for Treasury bonds showing how the new law will affect demand?

ANSWER: Demand will decline because the new law limits foreign demand.

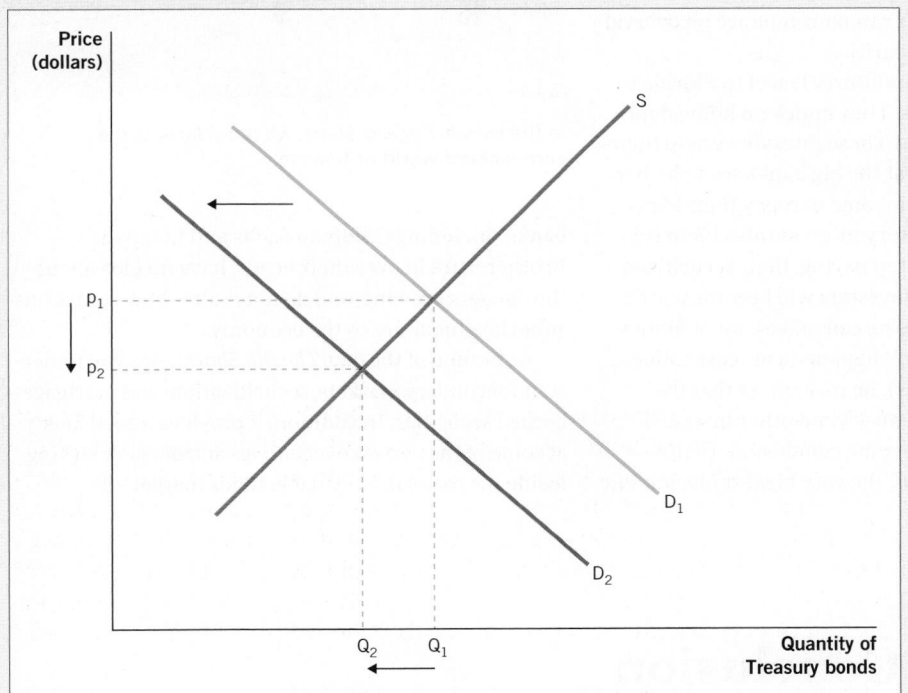

QUESTION: What will happen to the price of Treasury bonds?

ANSWER: The price of Treasury bonds will decline. When demand falls, the new equilibrium price will be lower.

QUESTION: What will happen to the interest rate on Treasury bonds?

ANSWER: The interest rate on Treasury bonds will increase, because dollar price and the interest rate move in opposite directions. A lower price means the government will sell each bond for fewer dollars, so it will be paying higher interest to the bond owner.

   In the end, restrictions on foreign investment will lead to higher domestic interest rates.

Direct Finance

THE BIG SHORT

The Big Short (2015) is based on the book with the same title by Michael Lewis. The movie is essentially a documentary that doesn't feel like a documentary, as the actors carefully explain the details of the financial collapse that led to the Great Recession in 2007.

The movie introduces Mark Baum (played by Steve Carrell) and Michael Burry (played by Christian Bale), who were among the few people who recognized the dangers in the economy's rampant reliance on overvalued mortgage-backed securities.

In the movie, Baum and Burry travel to Florida to interview real borrowers. They knock on home doors and visit local businesses. These interviews help them see what almost nobody at the big banks sees: the borrowers will not have the income to repay their loans when their low introductory interest rates increase. When these borrowers stop paying, their securitized mortgages being sold to investors will become worthless. When Baum realizes he can make a lot of money by betting these losses will happen (a process called "shorting" the mortgages), he recognizes that the economy will take a nosedive when other financial insiders finally reach the same conclusion. In the meantime, he determines, the very biggest investment

In the movie *The Big Short*, we get a look at the complicated world of finance.

banks (including Goldman Sachs and Lehman Brothers) are in over their heads, have no idea about the dangers brewing, and do not realize how dangerous subprime loans are to the economy.

At the end of the day, *The Big Short* helps you understand secondary markets, securitization, and mortgage-backed securities. In addition, it provides a good look at some of the perverse incentives and dangers lurking inside the real-world loanable funds market.

Conclusion

We began this chapter with the idea that borrowing from foreign countries—that is, foreign ownership of a nation's debt—is often helpful to a nation's economy. Funds flowing into the U.S. loanable funds market help lead to economic expansion, no matter where they originate. One of the themes throughout this chapter has been the importance of saving and lending to the macroeconomy. With indirect finance, banks and financial intermediaries help channel funds from savers to borrowers. With direct finance, firms sell securities such as stocks and bonds directly to savers. These securities enable savers to earn returns on their savings while also giving firms access to funds for investment.

In the chapters that follow, we'll see that these financial institutions play a major role in the macroeconomy. ✳

Long-Run Returns for Stocks versus Bonds

- Stocks earn significantly more than bonds over time.
- Stock returns are much riskier than bond returns.

In this chapter, we focused on the importance of stocks and bonds for financing the activities of firms and governments. But you may be wondering which of these instruments would best serve your own personal savings plan.

Let's begin by looking at the historical returns for stocks versus bonds. The bar graph below shows that from 1970 to 2017, the nominal return for long-term Treasury bonds was 7.2%. But over the same period, stocks yielded 10.2%.

Perhaps this doesn't seem like a huge difference. But think of it this way: Imagine that your grandparents decided to set aside $100 for you in 1970. If they bought bonds for you, their savings would have grown to $2,607 in today's dollars. If they instead chose a diversified group of stocks, their savings would have grown to $9,698 in today's dollars. Inflation averaged about 3.6% over this period, but that would affect the real returns on bonds and stocks similarly. These alternatives are plotted in the graph below.

To be sure, stocks are riskier. Just look at how the value of your savings would have fluctuated

Which should you choose: stocks or bonds?

over the years. With stocks, the value of your savings would have sometimes climbed or fallen by more than $1,000 a year. With bonds, the fluctuations would have been much smaller. Therefore, if you are extremely averse to risk, you might choose bonds. But in the long run, taking more risk with stocks has historically been more lucrative. Your grandparents would probably advise you to choose stocks while you are young and then shift toward the safety of bonds as you age and move closer to cashing in.

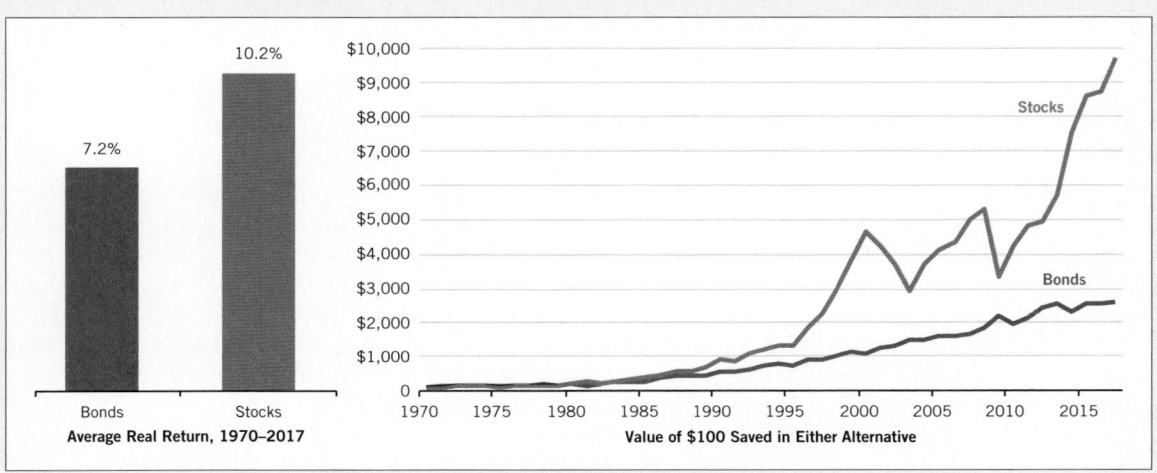

Average Real Return, 1970–2017

Value of $100 Saved in Either Alternative

· ANSWERING *the* BIG QUESTIONS ·

How do financial markets help the economy?

- Financial markets help channel funds to investment opportunities throughout the economy.
- Direct finance occurs when savers lend directly to borrowers; indirect finance occurs when savers and borrowers go through financial intermediaries.

What are the key financial tools for the macroeconomy?

- Bonds serve as a basic instrument of direct finance: they provide a tool with which firms and governments can finance their activities.
- Stocks are an additional source of funds for firms. They give the security holder an ownership share in the firm.
- Secondary markets make securities more valuable and offer more avenues for funds to flow to investors.
- Treasury securities are the bonds sold by the U.S. government to finance the national debt. They play a prominent role in macroeconomic policy.
- Home mortgages are the contracts that people sign to borrow for the purchase of a home. Because the mortgage market is so large, the entire macroeconomy is affected by its condition.

· CHAPTER PROBLEMS ·

Concepts You Should Know

banks (p. 734)
bond (p. 735)
default risk (p. 740)
direct finance (p. 735)
face value (p. 738)

financial intermediaries (p. 734)
indirect finance (p. 734)
maturity date (p. 738)
par value (p. 738)
secondary markets (p. 743)

securitization (p. 749)
security (p. 735)
stocks (p. 742)
Treasury securities (p. 745)

Questions for Review

1. What is the difference between direct and indirect finance? Discuss the reasons why a firm (a borrower) might choose each method. Discuss the reasons why a saver might choose each method.

2. What is securitization? Discuss how securitization benefits borrowers.

3. One principle we learned in this chapter is that the dollar price and the interest rate on a bond move in opposite directions. Why is this always the case?

4. What is the primary use of U.S. Treasury securities? Why are the interest rates on Treasury securities so low? If people worried about the United States defaulting on the national debt, what would you expect to happen to interest rates on U.S. Treasury securities? Why?

5. Why might a firm prefer to finance its investments with bonds rather than stocks? Alternatively, why might a firm prefer stocks to bonds?

6. What is a mortgage-backed security (MBS)? Why is it difficult for ratings agencies to determine the risk of an MBS? Describe how the existence of MBSs helps homebuyers in the United States. Describe how MBS markets spread financial troubles around the world when U.S. home prices dropped in 2008.

7. What is a U.S. Treasury bond? Why are Treasury bonds such a popular asset in world markets?

Study Problems (✶ solved at the end of the section)

1. Toyota bonds are currently rated AA, and Ford bonds are rated BB. Suppose the price of a $1,000 one-year Toyota bond is $970.

   a. What is the rate of return on the one-year Toyota bond?

   b. The price of a $1,000 one-year Ford bond must be:
      i. less than $970
      ii. greater than $970
      iii. $970
      iv. There is insufficient information to answer this question.

   c. The rate of return on a $1,000 one-year Ford bond must be:
      i. less than the return on the Toyota bond
      ii. greater than the return on the Toyota bond
      iii. the same as the return on the Toyota bond
      iv. There is insufficient information to answer this question.

✶ 2. In 2008, when the U.S. automobile industry was struggling, the price of Ford Motor Company bonds rose. In this question, you need to calculate how the price increase also affected the interest rate.

   a. What was the interest rate on a one-year Ford bond with a face value of $5,000 and a price of $4,750?

   b. What was the new interest rate on a one-year Ford bond with a face value of $5,000 and a price of $4,950?

✶ 3. Let's say you own a firm that produces and sells Ping-Pong tables. The name of your company is iPong because your tables have a plug-in jack for all Apple products. To finance a new factory, you decide to sell bonds. Your bonds are rated BBB.

   a. Draw supply and demand curves for your iPong bonds. (The quantity of bonds is measured along the *x* axis and the price along the *y* axis.) Label the supply curve S, the demand curve D, and the equilibrium price p.

b. How will the demand for iPong bonds be affected if a new secondary market agrees to buy and sell iPong bonds? Illustrate the new demand curve in the graph from part (a), and label it D_{SM}. What are the effects on the price and interest rate on iPong bonds?

4. This question involves the hypothetical iPong firm from question 3.

a. How will demand be affected if a ratings agency upgrades your bond rating to AA?

b. How will the ratings upgrade affect the price of your bond?

c. How will the ratings upgrade affect your cost of borrowing?

5. Use supply and demand curves to illustrate how default risk affects both the price and the interest rate of a bond.

6. In this chapter, we discussed Target Corporation bonds to illustrate the effect of default risk on the price of a bond. In particular, when the default risk rises, the demand for a bond falls and then the equilibrium price falls. In our example, the price of a $100,000 Target bond fell from $98,000 to $97,000.

a. What is the interest rate on a one-year $100,000 bond that sells for $98,000?

b. What is the interest rate on a one-year $100,000 bond that sells for $97,000?

✳ **7.** The following table presents partial information for several different bonds that each mature in one year. Use the information given along with Equation 23.1 to fill in the blank cells in the table.

Bond	Face value p_m	Initial price p_o	Interest rate R
A	$10,000	$9,000.00	_____
B	10,000	_____	10%
C	_____	98,039.22	2

8. The data in the following table are for two different bonds that both mature in exactly one year.

Borrower	S&P rating	Face value	Price
Maddie's Pasta	AA	$10,000	$9,500
Tricia's Smoothies	A	10,000	_____

a. What is the annual rate of return (R) for the Maddie bond?

b. Assume that inflation is exactly 2% for the next year. Use the Fisher equation (from Chapter 22) to calculate the real interest rate on the Maddie bond.

c. What is the par value of the Maddie bond?

d. Will the price of the Tricia bond be greater or less than the price of the Maddie bond? Explain your reasoning.

e. Will the interest rate (R) on the Tricia bond be greater or less than the interest rate on the Maddie bond? Explain your reasoning.

9. Recently, a $10,000 one-year AAA University of Virginia (UVA) bond sold for $9,850.

a. What is the implied interest rate on this bond?

b. Since Duke University bonds are rated AA, what can you say about the price of a $10,000 one-year Duke University bond in the context of this question? Explain your reasoning.

c. In 2016, the nominal interest rate on short-term U.S. Treasury securities was 3.0% and the real interest rate was 0.9%. Use this information to determine the rate of inflation in 2016, using the Fisher equation from Chapter 22.

Solved Problems

2.a. Use the formula

$$R = \frac{p_m - p_0}{p_0}$$

Then compute: $R = (\$5{,}000 - \$4{,}750) \div \$4{,}750$
$= \$250 \div \$4{,}750 = 5.26\%$

b. $R = (\$5{,}000 - \$4{,}950) \div \$4{,}950 = \$50$
$\div \$4{,}950 = 1.01\%$

Therefore, when the price of the bond rose by $200, the interest rate decreased from 5.26% to just 1.01%.

3.a.

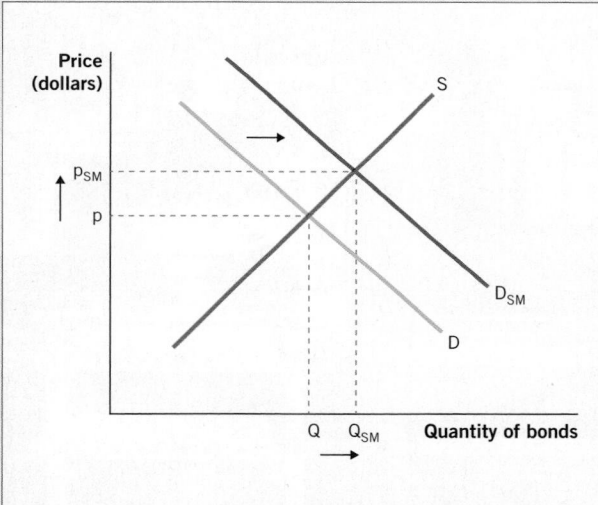

b. If a secondary market is available to sell bonds, the demand for the bonds will increase because the bonds will become more attractive to buyers. When a secondary market exists, you can always resell any bond you own. If there is no secondary market, you are stuck with it once you have it.

In the graph, demand increases and price rises. The result is lower interest rates for your iPong firm.

7. a. For bond A, we are given [...]
(p_0) and the face value (p_m). We [...]
values into Equation 23.1 and then solve for the interest rate:

$$R = \frac{p_m - p_0}{p_0} = \frac{\$10{,}000 - \$9{,}000}{\$9{,}000}$$

$$= \frac{\$1{,}000}{\$9{,}000} = \frac{1}{9} = 11.1\%$$

b. For bond B, we are given the face value (p_m) and the interest rate (R), which we can insert into Equation 23.1 to solve for the initial price (p_0):

$$10\% = 0.10 = \frac{\$10{,}000 - p_0}{p_0}$$

$$0.10p_0 = \$10{,}000 - p_0$$

$$0.10p_0 + p_0 = \$10{,}000$$

$$p_0 = \frac{\$10{,}000}{1.10} = \$9{,}090.91$$

$$p_0 = \frac{\$10{,}000}{1.10} = \$9{,}090.91$$

c. For bond C, we are given the initial price (p_0) and the interest rate R, which we can plug into Equation 23.1 and solve for the price at maturity (p_m):

$$2\% = 0.02 = \frac{p_m - \$98{,}039.22}{\$98{,}039.22}$$

$$0.02 \times \$98{,}039.22 = p_m - \$98{,}039.22$$

$$\$1{,}960.78 = p_m - \$98{,}039.22$$

$$p_m = \$100{,}000$$

PART VII

The Long and Short of MACROECONOMICS

Economic Growth and the Wealth of Nations

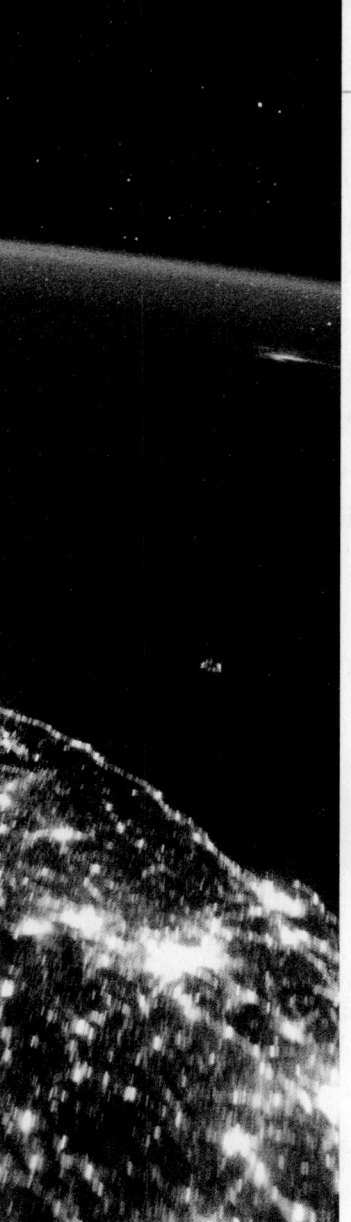

There's More to Prosperity Than Natural Resources.

Many people believe that natural resources, such as trees, oil, and farmland, are the primary sources of economic growth. They believe that nations like the United States and Australia are prosperous because these nations have vast natural resources to use in the production of goods and services. A variation on this idea emphasizes geography: nations with the best shipping locations and the mildest climates have more prosperous economies. But what about the two Koreas? North Korea and South Korea have the same labor force and natural resources—the geography is virtually identical and the people on both sides of the border come from the same families. In 1960, their income levels were very similar and very low, each with less than $1,700 in per capita GDP. Today, however, the two economies are as different as night and day. South Korea is one of the world's leading industrial nations, a major exporter of electronics, automobiles, and other goods to the tune of over $500 billion per year. Meanwhile North Korea, with a population about half the size, manages an output of less than $3 billion, much of that consisting of coal fuel blocks and other minimally processed mineral products. Over the course of this chapter and the next, we explore what economics has to say about

The two Koreas at night, in a satellite image: South Korea, bursting with light, and North Korea, mired in economic darkness. The one sizeable bright spot in North Korea is the capital, Pyongyang. North Korea's self-imposed political and economic isolation has earned it the nickname "The Hermit Kingdom."

differences in economic growth across nations like North and South Korea.

Striving for economic growth is not only about accumulating more wealth. Yes, economic growth brings smartphones and Jet Skis, but it's much more important than that. Economic growth offers the potential for more women and infants to survive childbirth, more people to have access to clean water and better sanitation, and more people to live healthier, longer, and more educated lives.

In this chapter, we begin by looking at the implications of economic growth for human welfare. We then consider the impact of an economy's resources and technology on economic growth. Finally, we discuss the key elements an economy needs in order to grow.

· BIG QUESTIONS ·

- Why does economic growth matter?
- How do resources and technology contribute to economic growth?
- What institutions foster economic growth?
- How are some economists testing new ideas?

Why Does Economic Growth Matter?

In 1900, life expectancy in the United States was 47 years. About 140 of every 1,000 children died before their first birthday. Only about one-third of American homes had running water; and income, in 2018 dollars, was less than $5,000 per person. Most people lived less than a mile from their job and almost nobody owned an automobile. Yes, this is a description of life in the United States in 1900, but it is also a description of life in many poor countries today. What happened in the United States in the meantime? The answer is: economic growth.

In this section, we examine how economic growth affects the lives of people around the world. We also examine the historical data on economic growth and explain some mathematics of growth rates.

Some Ugly Facts

Before looking at data on growth, we need to recall how economists measure economic growth. In Chapter 19, we defined **economic growth** as the percentage change in real per capita GDP. We know that real per capita GDP measures the average level of income in a nation. For most people, life is not all about the pursuit of more income. However, economic growth does alleviate human misery and lengthen lives. Wealthier societies provide better living standards, which include better nutrition, educational opportunities, health care, freedom, and even sources of entertainment.

Economic growth is measured as the percentage change in real per capita GDP.

Let's look around the world and compare life in low-income countries with life in high-income countries. Table 24.1 presents human welfare indicators for some of the world's highest- and lowest-income nations in 2017. Among the poor nations are Bangladesh, Haiti, North Korea, Niger, Liberia, Tanzania, Nepal, Ethiopia, and Zimbabwe. The wealthy nations include Australia, Denmark, Israel, Japan, Germany, South Korea, and the United States.

Consider the first group of indicators, which are related to mortality. In poor countries, 49 out of every 1,000 babies die at birth or in the first year of life, while in rich nations the number is only 5 out of every 1,000. This means that infants are 10 times more likely to die in poor nations. Those that survive one year in poor nations are about 14 times more likely to die before their fifth birthday, as indicated by the under-5 mortality rates. Overall, life expectancy in poor nations is 63 years, while in wealthy nations it is 80 years. Just being born in a wealthy nation adds almost 20 years to an individual's life.

The second group of indicators in Table 24.1 helps to explain the mortality data. Rich nations have about 10 times as many doctors per person: 30 physicians per 10,000 people versus 3 per 10,000. Clean water and sanitation are available to only a fraction of people in poor nations, while these are generally available to all in rich nations. Children in poor nations die every year because

TABLE 24.1

Living Conditions in Poor Nations versus Rich Nations, 2017

Life indicators	Poor	Rich
GDP per capita (PPP)	$2,075	$47,305
Infant mortality rate (per 1,000 live births)	49	5
Under-5 mortality rate (per 1,000)	69	5
Life expectancy at birth (years)	63	80
Physicians (per 10,000)	3	30
Access to improved water (%)	66	100
Access to improved sanitation (%)	28	99
Access to electricity (%)	38.8	100
Mobile cellular subscriptions (per 100 people)	62	125
Secure Internet servers (per million people)	1,053	18,127
Literacy rate, adult male (%)	67	99
Literacy rate, adult female (%)	52	99
Female/male secondary enrollment (ratio)	0.83	0.99

Source: World Bank, World Development Indicators, 2017.

Clean water, even in a bag, saves lives.

they can't get water as clean as the water that comes out of virtually any faucet in the United States. This leads to common ailments like tapeworms and diarrhea that are life-threatening in poor nations. In fact, in 2010, the World Health Organization estimated that 3.6 million people die each year from waterborne diseases.

The last group of indicators in Table 24.1 tells the sobering story about education. First, notice that literacy rates in poor countries are significantly lower than literacy rates in wealthy countries. But there is also a significant difference in literacy rates between men and women in poor nations: 67% of men can read, but only 52% of women are literate. Furthermore, in poor nations women have less access to secondary (high school) education than men; equal access would imply an enrollment ratio of 100%, but in poor nations the ratio is only 83% for secondary school enrollment. So while educational opportunities are rarer for all people in poor nations, women fare worse than men by far.

The data in Table 24.1 support the contention that per capita GDP matters—not for the sake of more income per se, but because it correlates with better human welfare conditions, which matter to everyone.

Learning from the Past

We can learn a lot about the roots of economic growth by considering the past. Historically, any common person's life was focused on subsistence, simply trying to find enough food, shelter, and clothing to survive. As we saw in the previous section, even today many people still live on the margins of subsistence. What can history tell us about how high-income nations achieved economic development? The answer will help clarify possible policy alternatives going forward.

WE WERE ALL POOR ONCE When you look around the globe today, you see rich nations and poor nations. You can probably name many rich nations: the United States, Japan, Taiwan, and the Western European nations, among others. You might also know the very poor nations: almost all of Africa, parts of Latin America, and significant parts of Asia. But the world was not always this way. If we consider the longer history of humankind, only recently did the incomes of common people rise above subsistence level. The Europe of 1750, for instance, was not noticeably richer than Europe at the time of the birth of Jesus of Nazareth.

Consider the very long run. Angus Maddison, a noted economic historian, estimated GDP levels for many nations and for the whole world back to the year AD 1. This remarkable data set is now available at the Maddison Project web site. Figure 24.1 plots Maddison's estimates of real per capita GDP in 2010 U.S. dollars. Clearly, there was a historical break around 1800 that dramatically changed the path of average world living standards.

Maddison estimated the average level of income in the world in 1820 at about $1,100. This would be comparable to you having an annual income of about $1,100. If you had to live on $1,100 for an entire year, it's clear your solitary focus would be on basic necessities like food, clothing, and shelter. Of course, there were certainly rich individuals over the course of history, but until

FIGURE 24.1

Long-Run World Real Per Capita GDP (in 2010 U.S. dollars)

Historical accounts often focus on monarchs and other wealthy people. But for the average person, living standards across the globe didn't change considerably from the time of Jesus to the time of Thomas Jefferson. The data plotted here show per capita GDP in 2010 U.S. dollars, which is adjusted for prices across both time and place.

Source: Angus Maddison, *Statistics on World Population, GDP and Per Capita GDP, 1–2008 AD.* All figures converted to 2010 U.S. dollars.

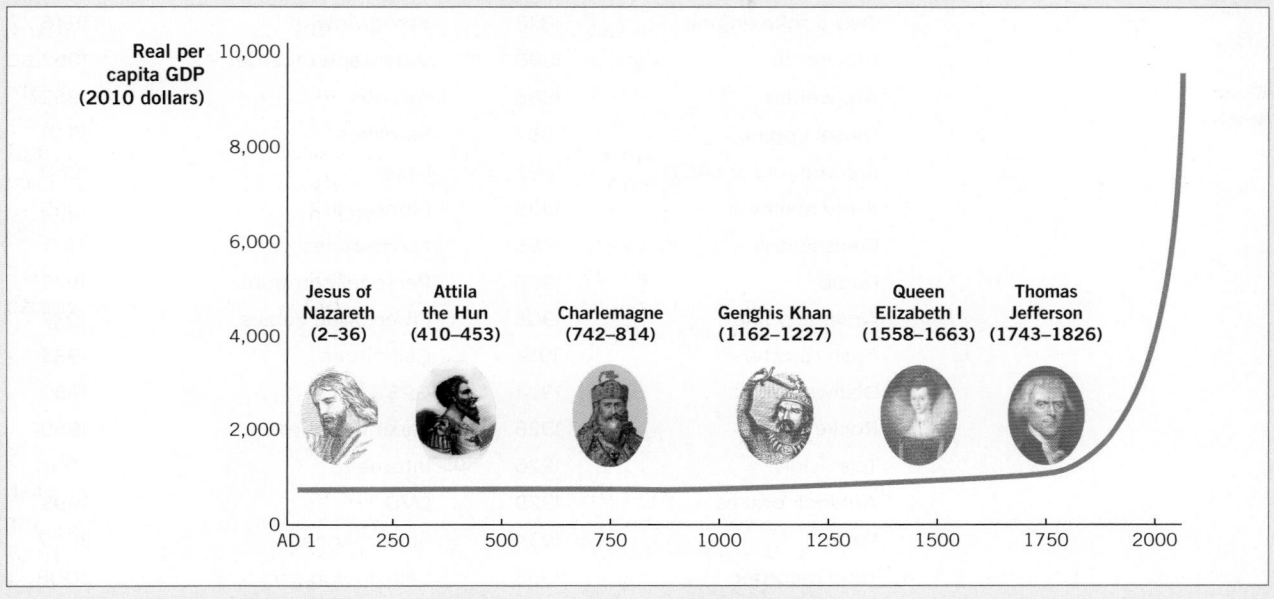

relatively recently, the average person's life was essentially one of subsistence living. Consider Alice Toe, the Liberian girl profiled in the Economics in the Real World feature on page 768. This type of life, where even meals are uncertain, was the basic experience for the average person for nearly all of human history.

Of course, there were global variations in income before 1700. For example, average income in Western Europe in 1600 was about $1,400, while in Latin America it was less than $700. This means Western Europeans were twice as wealthy as Latin Americans in 1600. But average Europeans were still very poor!

The Industrial Revolution, during which many economies moved away from agriculture and toward manufacturing in the 1800s, is at the very center of the big increase in world income growth. Beginning with the Industrial Revolution, the rate of technical progress increased so rapidly, it was able to outpace population growth. The foundation for the Industrial Revolution was laid in the preceding decades, and these foundations included private property protection and several technological innovations. We don't claim that the Industrial Revolution was idyllic for those who lived through it, but the legal and other institutional innovations of that era paved the way for the unprecedented gains in human welfare that people have since experienced.

TABLE 24.2

Important Inventions since the U.S. Civil War

Typewriter	1867	Electron microscope	1939
Sheep shears	1868	Electric clothes dryer	1940
Telephone	1876	Nuclear reactor	1942
Phonograph	1877	Microwave oven	1945
Milking machine	1878	Computer	1946
Two-stroke engine	1878	Xerography	1946
Blowtorch	1880	Videotape recorder	1952
Arc welder	1886	Airbags	1952
Diesel engine	1892	Satellites	1958
Electric motor (AC)	1892	Laser	1960
X-ray machine	1895	Floppy disk	1965
Electric drill	1895	Microprocessor	1971
Radio	1906	Personal computer	1975
Assembly line	1908	Fiber-optic cables	1977
Cash register	1919	Cell phone	1983
Dishwasher	1924	GPS	1989
Rocket	1926	Laser eye surgery	1989
Television	1926	Internet	1991
Antilock brakes	1929	DVD	1995
Radar	1934	Smartphone	2007
Tape recorder	1935	Self-driving cars	2008
Jet engine	1939	Gene-editing technology	2013

Source: Michael Cox and Richard Alm, *Myths of Rich and Poor* (New York: Basic Books, 1999), and miscellaneous other sources.

These data do not imply that life is always easy and predictably comfortable for everyone in the modern world. But opportunities for the average person alive today are very different from those for the average person in past centuries. Table 24.2 lists a sampling of some of the major innovations of the past century and a half. Try to imagine life without any of these, and you'll get a sense of the gains we've made since the Industrial Revolution.

SOME GOT RICH, OTHERS STAYED POOR Although wealth has increased over the past two centuries, it is not evenly distributed around the globe. Figure 24.2 shows real per capita GDP (in 2010 U.S. dollars) for various world regions. In 1800, the income of the average U.S. citizen was about $2,000, or $5.50 per day (in 2010 dollars). Imagine trying to live on $5.50 per day in today's world—that is, $5.50 to buy all the food, clothing, shelter, education, transportation, and anything else you might need to purchase. That was life in the United States in 1800. But it also describes the plight of many people in the world today.

FIGURE 24.2

Real Per Capita GDP over 200 Years (in 2010 U.S. dollars)

Two hundred years ago, all regions and nations were poor. The modern differences in wealth we see around the world today began to emerge before 1900. But the twentieth century saw unprecedented growth take hold in the United States and Western Europe. Unfortunately, some parts of the globe today are no better off than the United States and Western Europe were in 1800.

Source: Angus Maddison, *Statistics on World Population, GDP and Per Capita GDP, 1–2008 AD.* All figures converted to 2010 U.S. dollars.

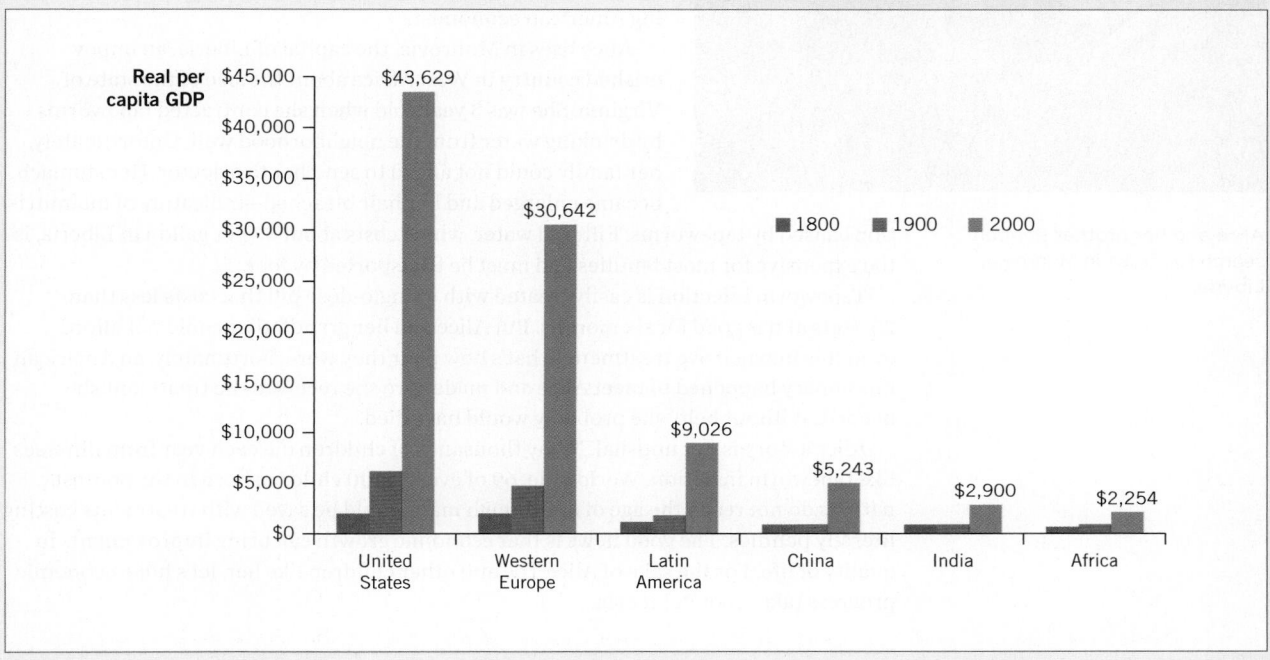

By 1900, some regions had broken the stranglehold of poverty. In 1900, real per capita GDP in Western Europe was $4,701; in the United States, it was $6,153. Prior to 1900, general income levels this high had never been experienced. But in China, India, and Africa, the averages were still less than $1,000 in 1900. The twentieth century proved to be even more prosperous for some, as the income gap widened between the United States and Western Europe and the rest of the world. Unfortunately, real per capita income on the African continent today is still less than that of the United States in 1850, which was $2,768.

While many of the current disparities between nations began about 200 years ago, some nations have moved from poor to rich as recently as the past few decades. In 1950, for example, South Korea, with real per capita GDP of just $1,178, was about as poor as Liberia, at $1,005. Today, South Korea is one of the wealthiest countries in the world, with a per capita income of $36,103, while Liberia is poorer than in 1950, with now just $829 in per capita income.

Alice and her brother Reuben search for crabs in Monrovia, Liberia.

ONE CHILD WHO NEEDS ECONOMIC PROGRESS

This is a true story about a girl named Alice Toe, who is 4 years old. From the look on her face, you can see she is mischievous and has a glowing personality. When this picture was taken, she was digging for crabs for the sole purpose of frightening a visiting American economist.

Alice lives in Monrovia, the capital of Liberia, an impoverished country in West Africa about the size of the state of Virginia. She was 3 years old when she contracted tapeworms by drinking water from the neighborhood well. Unfortunately, her family could not afford to send her to a doctor. Her stomach became enlarged and her hair bleached—indicators of malnutrition caused by tapeworms. Filtered water, which costs about $3 per gallon in Liberia, is too expensive for most families and must be transported by foot.

Tapeworm infection is easily treated with a single-dose pill that costs less than 25 cents and is good for six months. But Alice and her grandfather could not afford even this inexpensive treatment—that's how poor they were. Fortunately, an American missionary happened to meet Alice and made sure she received the treatment she needed. Without help, she probably would have died.

Alice's story is not unusual. Many thousands of children die each year from illnesses like tapeworm infection. Worldwide, 69 of every 1,000 children born in the poorest nations do not reach the age of 5, although many could be saved with treatments costing literally pennies. The good news is that economic growth can bring improvements in quality of life. For the sake of Alice Toe and other children like her, let's hope economic progress takes root in Liberia.

Measuring Economic Growth

Overall, people today are much wealthier than they were 200 years ago. However, this prosperity did not occur overnight. Rather, income grew a little bit each year. There is a striking mathematical truth about growth: small differences in growth rates lead to large differences in wealth levels over time. In this section, we explain how economic growth rates are computed, and we consider the level of growth a nation needs for its population to experience significant improvements in living standards.

THE MATHEMATICS OF GROWTH RATES The big break out of poverty began during the nineteenth century. Table 24.3 shows data on world economic growth in different periods. From 1800 to 1900, average world GDP growth was only 0.64% per year. From 1900 to 1950, world economic growth increased to 1.04%. The difference between 0.64% and 1.04% might seem trivial. But when economic growth increases by 0.4% and is sustained for many years, it makes a big difference. In this section, we show how growth is calculated.

We have seen that economic growth is the annual growth rate of real per capita GDP. It is our measure of how an average person's income changes over

TABLE 24.3

World Economic Growth for Different Historical Eras

Years	Annual Growth rate
AD 1–1800	0.02%
1800–1900	0.64
1900–1950	1.04
1950–2000	2.12

Source: Angus Maddison, *Statistics on World Population, GDP and Per Capita GDP, 1–2008 AD.* All figures converted to 2010 U.S. dollars.

time, including an allowance for price changes. But the government reports overall GDP data in nominal terms. Therefore, to get an accurate growth rate, we need to account for both inflation and population growth. We can use the following equation to approximate economic growth, where %Δ indicates the percentage change in a variable:

economic growth ≈ %Δ in nominal GDP − %Δ price level − %Δ population   **(EQUATION 24.1)**

Let's walk through the equation for economic growth using actual U.S. data as shown in Table 24.4. Starting with nominal GDP data for 2017 and 2018, we compute nominal GDP growth of 5.2%. But part of the increase in nominal GDP is due to inflation. In 2018, the price level, as measured by the GDP deflator, grew by 2.3%. We subtract this inflation rate from nominal GDP growth to get real GDP growth of 2.9%. This number applies to the entire nation, but population also increased by 0.7% in 2018. When we subtract population growth, we are left with 2.2% as the rate of economic growth for the United States in 2018. This growth rate was slightly higher than normal: since 1950, average economic growth in the United States has been about 2%.

A word of caution about terminology is in order. There's a big difference between nominal GDP growth, real GDP growth, and real per capita GDP growth. (In Table 24.4, these terms appear in orange.) But sloppy economic reporting sometimes confuses the terms. You may read something like "the U.S. economy grew by 2.9% in 2018," which refers to real GDP growth and is not calculated on a per capita basis. It would be an even bigger mistake to

TABLE 24.4

Computing an Economic Growth Rate

U.S. GDP in 2017 (in millions)	$19,485,400	
U.S. GDP in 2018 (in millions)	20,500,600	
Nominal GDP growth	5.2%	
− Price growth (inflation)	2.3%	
= Real GDP growth	2.9%	
− Population growth	0.7%	
≈ Real per capita GDP growth	2.2%	≈ Economic growth

Source: GDP data, U.S. Bureau of Economic Analysis; population data, U.S. Census Bureau, www.census.gov/popest/states/NST-ann-est.html.

claim that U.S. economic growth in 2018 was 5.2%, a number not adjusted for either population growth or inflation. Such confusing wording is a common mistake in reports on international economic growth statistics.

GROWTH RATES AND INCOME LEVELS Before we consider policies that might aid economic growth, we need to look more closely at how growth rates affect income levels.

First, consider how significant it is when income doubles, or increases by 100%. If your income doubled today—all else being equal—you could afford twice as much of everything you are currently buying. Now imagine what would happen if income doubled for an entire country or even for all countries. In the United States, real per capita GDP is on track to more than double in the 50 years between 1970 and 2020. This means that the average person living in the United States in 2020 will be able to afford twice as much food, clothing, transportation, education, and even government services as the average U.S. resident in 1970. That's quite a difference.

But increasing real income by 100% in a single year is not realistic. Let's use an annual growth rate closer to reality—say, 2%, which has historically been an average rate of economic growth for the United States. With 2% annual growth, how long does it take to double your income? For example, let's say you graduate and, given your expertise in economics, you get several job offers. One offer is for $50,000 per year with a guaranteed raise of 2% every year. How long would it take for your salary to reach $100,000?

The first answer that pops into your head might be 50 years (based on the idea that 2% growth for 50 years might add to 100% growth). But this answer would be wrong, because it ignores the fact that growth compounds over time. As your salary grows, 2% growth leads to larger and larger dollar increases. Because of this compounding effect, it actually would take only about 35 years to double your income at a 2% growth rate.

Table 24.5 illustrates the process of compounding over time by showing the increase from year to year. Income starts at $50,000 in year 1, and a 2% increase yields $1,000, so one year of growth results in an income of $51,000 in year 2. Subsequent 2% growth in the second year yields $1,020 of new income (2% of $51,000), so after two years your income is $52,020. Looking at year 3, the 2% increase yields $1,040.40. Each year, the dollar increase in income (the green numbers in the third column) gets larger, as 2% of a growing number continues to grow. This scenario corresponds with the experience of the U.S. economy. Since 1970, real per capita

TABLE 24.5

Compound Growth

	Income	2% increase in income	Income in next year
Year 1	$50,000.00	$1,000.00	$51,000.00
Year 2	51,000.00	1,020.00	52,020.00
Year 3	52,020.00	1,040.40	53,060.40
Year 4	53,060.40	1,061.21	54,121.61
Year 5	54,121.61	1,082.43	55,204.04
...			
Year 35	100,000		

TABLE 24.6

A Dollar of Income at Different Growth Rates

Annual growth rate	Years to double	Value after 70 years (approximate)
0%	Never	$1
1	70	2
2	35	4
3	23.3	8
4	17.5	16

GDP in the United States has more than doubled. Yet this jump occurred while U.S. economic growth rates averaged "only" about 2%.

THE RULE OF 70 In the previous example, we saw that when income grows at 2% per year, it doubles in approximately 35 years. A simple rule known as the **rule of 70** determines the length of time necessary for a sum of money to double at a particular growth rate. According to the rule of 70:

> *If the annual growth rate of a variable is x%, the size of that variable doubles approximately every 70 ÷ x years.*

The **rule of 70** states that if the annual growth rate of a variable is *x*%, the size of that variable doubles approximately every 70 ÷ *x* years.

The rule of 70 is an approximation, but it works well with typical economic growth rates.

Table 24.6 illustrates the rule of 70 by showing how long it takes for a single dollar of income to double in value, given different growth rates. At a growth rate of 1%, each dollar of income doubles approximately every 70 ÷ 1 years. If growth increases to 2%, a dollar of income then doubles approximately every 70 ÷ 2 = 35 years. Consider the impact of a 4% growth rate. If this rate can be sustained, income doubles approximately every 70 ÷ 4 = 17.5 years. In 70 years, income doubles 4 times, ending up at approximately 16 times its starting value! China has been recently growing at almost 10% per year, and indeed its per capita income has been doubling about every seven years, which is remarkable and literally world changing.

The rule of 70 shows us that small and consistent growth rates, if sustained for a decade or two, can greatly improve living standards. Over the long course of history, growth rates were essentially zero. But the past two centuries have seen small, consistent growth rates, and the standard of living for many has increased dramatically.

We can look at actual growth rates of various countries over a long period to see the impact on income levels. Table 24.7 presents growth rates of several countries over the 66 years from 1950 to 2016. Let's start with Haiti and Turkey. In 1950, both nations had about $2,500 in annual income per person. But Turkey grew at 3% a year, and Haiti actually experienced negative net growth over these 66 years. As a result, the average income in Turkey is now ten times that of Haiti.

Further down Table 24.7, you see other nations that grew at rates faster even than Turkey. In 1950, Japan's per capita income was just a little higher than Turkey's, at $3,023. Yet 3.9% annual growth for 66 years led to income of $37,465 per person by 2016 in Japan. South Korea, with a staggering 5.3% growth over the entire period, moved from being among the world's very poorest economies to being among the richest.

TABLE 24.7

Economic Growth, 1950–2016

	Average annual growth rate	Real per capita GDP in 1950		Real per capita GDP in 2016
less than 1% growth	−0.5% Haiti	2,485		1,728
	−0.3 Afghanistan	2,392		1,929
	−0.3 Liberia	1,005		829
	0.3 Burundi	536		665
about 1% growth	1.1 Honduras	2,381		4,796
	1.1 Kenya	1,496		3,169
	1.2 Argentina	8,759		18,875
about 2% growth	1.9 United States	15,241		53,015
	2.1 Hungary	6,034		23,279
	2.1 Mexico	4,179		16,133
	2.1 Sweden	11,385		44,659
greater than 2% growth	3.0 Turkey	2,583		17,906
	3.1 Spain	4,098		30,110
	3.1 India	824		6,125
	3.1 Israel	4,192		31,701
	3.9 Japan	3,023		37,465
	4.6 Botswana	779		15,198
	4.6 China	637		12,569
	5.3 South Korea	1,178		36,103

Maddison Project Database, version 2018. Bolt, Jutta, Robert Inklaar, Herman de Jong and Jan Luiten van Zanden (2018), "Rebasing 'Maddison': new income comparisons and the shape of long-run economic development" Maddison Project Working Paper, nr. 10, available for download at www.ggdc.net/maddison.

Note: real GDP per capita figures are rounded to the nearest dollar, population figures are rounded to the nearest 1000.

Perhaps the biggest recent growth story is China's. Only 20 years ago, it was among the world's poorer nations. Over the past 20 years, China has grown at over 8% a year. Even if its astonishing growth slows considerably, China will still likely move into the group of the wealthiest nations in the coming decades.

Clearly, economic growth experiences have varied widely across time and place. But relatively small and consistent growth rates are sufficient to move a nation out of poverty over the period of a few generations. And this movement out of poverty really matters for the people who live in these nations.

ECONOMICS IN THE REAL WORLD

HOW DOES 2% GROWTH AFFECT AVERAGE PEOPLE?

We have seen that annual economic growth in the United States averaged about 2% per year over the past 50 years. What does this economic growth mean for a typical person's everyday life? Another way of thinking about this is to consider what life was like when your grandparents were young. To illustrate, we've assembled some basic data in Table 24.8 to give you an idea of how the average person's life in the United States in 1960 compares to life today.

Average real income in the United States is four times the level of 1960, but what about other factors that affect our everyday lives? For one thing, Americans today live about 13% longer (78.7 years versus 69.7 years). But we also have access to almost twice as many doctors, live in houses more than twice as big, enjoy more education, and own more and better cars and household appliances. On average, we work 6.4 fewer hours per week and hold jobs that are physically less taxing (fewer jobs in agriculture and manufacturing). In 1960, there were no cell phones, and roughly three out of four homes had a single telephone. Today, there are more telephones than there are people in the United States. In addition, many modern amenities were not available in 1960. Can you imagine life without a computer, the Internet, streaming music, microwave ovens, and central air conditioning? Take a look at Table 24.8 to see a striking contrast.

In what ways is life different now from when your grandparents were young?

This entire Shanghai skyline was built in the past 30 years, vividly illustrating the effects of rapid economic growth.

TABLE 24.8

The United States: 1960 versus 2018

General Characteristics	1960	2018
Life expectancy	69.7 years	78.7 years
Physicians per 10,000 people	14.8	26
Years of school completed	10.5 (median)	13 (average)
Portion of income spent on food	27%	11%
Average workweek	40.9 hours	34.5 hours
Workforce in agriculture or manufacturing	37%	16%
Home ownership	61.9%	64.3%
New Home		

Size	1,200 square feet	2,645 square feet
Bedrooms	2	4
Bathrooms	1	3
Central air conditioning?	no	yes
Best-Selling Car		

Model	Chevrolet Impala	Toyota Camry
Price (2018 dollars)	$22,637	$23,645
Miles per gallon	13–16	29–41
Horsepower	135	203
Air conditioning?	optional	standard
Automatic transmission?	optional	standard
Airbags?	no	standard
Power locks and windows?	no	standard
TV		

Size	23 inches	65 inches
Display	black & white	high-definition color
Price (2018 dollars)	$1,594	$699

Source: U.S. Census Bureau, *Statistical Abstract of the United States*, and U.S. Bureau of Labor Statistics.

Computing Economic Growth in Brazil

After several years of solid growth in real per capita GDP, economic growth in Brazil slowed substantially from 2012 to 2016, and then rebounded in 2017. The 2017 Brazilian data below are from the World Bank database called World Development Indicators.

Nominal GDP growth rate	GDP deflator growth rate	Population growth rate
14.58%	3.79%	0.79%

QUESTION: What was the rate of economic growth for Brazil in 2017?

ANSWER: First, recall Equation 24.1:

$$\text{economic growth} \approx \%\Delta \text{ nominal GDP} - \%\Delta \text{price level} - \%\Delta \text{ population}$$

Now, for Brazil, we have

$$\text{economic growth} \approx 14.58 - 3.79 - 0.79 = 10\%$$

QUESTION: If the price level (as measured by the GDP deflator) continues to grow at 3.79% per year, approximately how long will it take for prices to double?

ANSWER: We use the rule of 70:

$$70 \div 3.79 \approx 18.5 \text{ years}$$

CHALLENGE QUESTION: If per capita real GDP was $10,000 in 2017 and the economic growth rate computed above is somehow sustained for 21 years (note that this growth rate, for this long, would be unprecedented), what will be the level of per capita GDP in Brazil in 2038?

ANSWER: By the rule of 70, real per capita GDP will double every $70/x$ years. In this case, $x = 10$, so doubling occurs every 7 years. Over the course of 21 years, real per capita GDP then doubles three times. So the original level of $10,000 turns into $80,000 per person after 21 years.

Data source: International Monetary Fund, World Economic Outlook, April 2017.

How much does inflation affect Brazil's growth data?

Economic Growth, 1950–2016

Economic growth, measured as the growth rate of per capita real GDP, is the key determinant of living standards in nations across time. The map shows the average annual growth rates of nations across the globe from 1950 to 2016. On the right, we give a snapshot of the differences in living conditions between wealthy nations and poor nations.

● LESS THAN 1% GROWTH
With 0% growth, nations are no better off than they were in 1950.

Haiti	-0.55
Liberia	-0.29
Zimbabwe	0.43
Nicaragua	0.46
Venezuelaa	0.71

● 1% – 1.6% GROWTH
With 1% growth, living standards nearly doubled over 58 years.

South Africa	1.07
Argentina	1.17
New Zealand	1.38
El Salvador	1.41
Nigeria	1.54

● 1.7% – 2.5% GROWTH
With 2% growth, living standards almost quadrupled over 58 years.

Morocco	1.86
United States	1.91
Canada	1.94
Mexico	2.07
Brazil	2.40

● GREATER THAN 2.5% GROWTH
With 3% growth, some of the poorest nations are now among the richest.

Israel	3.11
Japan	3.89
Botswana	4.60
China	4.62
South Korea	5.32

Incomplete Data

All dollar figures are 2016 U.S. dollars.

CANADA REAL PER CAPITA GDP
1950	$12,333
2016	$43,745

SOUTH KOREA REAL PER CAPITA GDP
1950	$1,178
2016	$36,103

VENEZUELA REAL PER CAPITA GDP
1950	$9,546
2016	$15,219

SOUTH AFRICA REAL PER CAPITA GDP
1950	$6,015
2016	$12,139

Human Welfare: Highest-Income Versus Lowest-Income Nations

Poor nations include the 34 nations classified as "low income" by the World Bank. Rich nations include the 81 nations classified as "high income."

Poor Nation
Rich Nation

 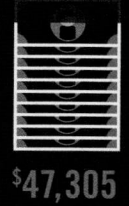
$2,075 $47,305

GDP per Capita

63 80

Life Expectancy at Birth
(Years)

49 5

Infant Mortality Rate
(Per 1,000 Live Births)

69 5

Under-5 Mortality Rate
(Per 1,000)

3 30

Physicians
(Per 10,000 People)

39% 100%

Access to Electricity

66% 100%

Access to Improved Water Source

28% 99%

Access to Improved Sanitation

0.83 0.99

Female to Male Secondary Enrollment
(Ratio)

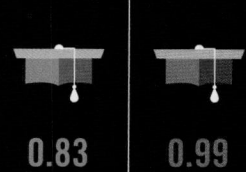
62 125

Mobile Cell Phone Subscriptions
(Per 100 People)

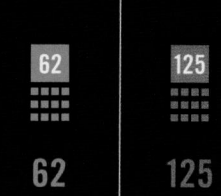
67% 99%

Literacy Rate, Adult Males

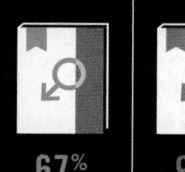 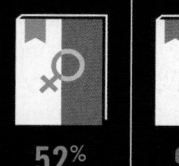
52% 99%

Literacy Rate, Adult Females

REVIEW QUESTIONS

- On average, how much longer do people live in rich versus poor nations?

- If a growth rate of 1.1% persists in South Africa, how long will it take for income to double? Hint: use the Rule of 70.

"The Magic Washing Machine"

Hans Rosling, a Swedish Professor of International Health and the cofounder of the Gapminder Foundation, was particularly good at data visualization, especially as applied to development economics. The web site Gapminder.org shows the uniquely stimulating graphics he helped pioneer.

Rosling was also a gifted public speaker and delivered many TED Talks. One of his best was on how washing machines revolutionize the lives of people around the world. In the video, Rosling recalls the day his mother got her first washing machine, which his parents had saved for years to buy. The grandmother was especially excited to see the new machine. She had spent many years heating water with firewood and then handwashing the laundry for their large family. It was a big day as the Roslings gathered around the new machine to "watch electricity do that work."

As Hans Rosling notes, only a fraction of families in the world can afford washing machines. Well over half the world's population (and in most cultures, this job is almost exclusively done by women) must regularly wash clothes by hand. This time-intensive chore often requires a trip to a lake or river. It can consume most of a day, and it must be repeated over and over again.

But the washing machine is "magic," because it frees people to use their time in other activities. Rosling's mother told him, "Now Hans, we have loaded the laundry. The machine will make the work. And now we can go to the library. Because this is the magic: you load the laundry and what do you get out of the machine? You get books out of the machines, children's books." He added, "And mother got time to read for me. She loved this." There is so much economics in

Hans Rosling showed how the washing machine revolutionized life for women around the globe.

these simple statements. The mother's time was a very scarce resource. And time spent washing clothes had high opportunity costs: it kept her from reading with her son. But the new technology, the washing machine, allowed Hans's mother to both do laundry and read with her children.

Rosling concludes with this flurry of gratitude: "And what we said, my mother and me, 'Thank you industrialization. Thank you steel mill. Thank you power station. And thank you chemical processing industry that gave us time to read books!'" We can all hope for economic growth to spread around the world, so that more people can experience the magic of washing machines.

How Do Resources and Technology Contribute to Economic Growth?

At this point, you may wonder what can be done to provide the best opportunity for economic growth. We see economic growth in many, though certainly not all, nations. But even in those that have grown in the past, future growth is not assured. We now turn to major sources of economic growth.

Economists continue to debate the relative importance of the factors leading to economic growth. However, there is a general consensus on the significance of three factors for economic growth: *resources*, *technology*, and *institutions*. In this section, we examine the first two; later in the chapter, we look at institutions.

Resources

All else equal, the higher the quantity and quality of resources available, the more output a nation can produce. **Resources**, also known as **factors of production**, are the inputs used to produce goods and services. The discovery or cultivation of new resources is a source of economic growth. Economists divide resources into three major categories: natural resources, physical capital, and human capital.

Resources, also known as **factors of production**, are the inputs used to produce goods and services.

NATURAL RESOURCES Natural resources include physical land and the inputs occurring naturally in or on the land. Coal, iron ore, diamonds, and lumber are examples of natural resources. Less obvious examples are mountains, beaches, temperate weather patterns, and scenic views—resources that residents enjoy consuming and that sometimes lead to tourism as a major industry.

Natural resources are an important source of economic wealth for nations. For example, the United States has fertile farmland, forests, coal, iron ore, and oil; the United States supplied more than 12% of the world's oil in 2014.

Geography, or the physical location of a nation, is also a natural resource that can contribute to economic growth. Geographical location facilitates trade and affects other important variables, such as weather and disease control. The world map in Figure 24.3 shows global GDP per square kilometer. As you can see, locations on coasts or along rivers have developed more rapidly than areas inland. These coastal or waterway-based locations were more naturally suited to trade in the days before railroads, trucks, and airplanes.

Natural resources clearly help to increase economic development, but they are not enough to make a nation wealthy. Many poor nations are rich in natural resources. For example, Liberia has mahogany forests, iron ore deposits, rubber tree forests, diamonds, and a beautiful coastline along the Atlantic Ocean. Yet despite all these, Liberia is poor. In contrast, think about Hong Kong, which is now part of China. Hong Kong is very small and densely populated with few natural resources. Yet the citizens of Hong Kong are among the wealthiest in the world.

Diamonds may be a girl's best friend, but are they essential for economic growth?

PHYSICAL CAPITAL The second category of resources is physical capital, or just capital. Recall that capital comprises the tools and equipment used in the production of goods and services. Examples of capital are factories, tractors,

FIGURE 24.3

Global GDP Density

The world's wealthiest areas (shown in darker colors on this map) are often those located near natural shipping lanes along coasts and rivers, where trade naturally flowed. This pattern is evidence that geography matters in economic development.

Source: John Luke Gallup, Jeffrey D. Sachs, and Andrew D. Mellinger, "Geography and Economic Development," Working Paper No. 1, Center for International Development at Harvard University, March 1999.

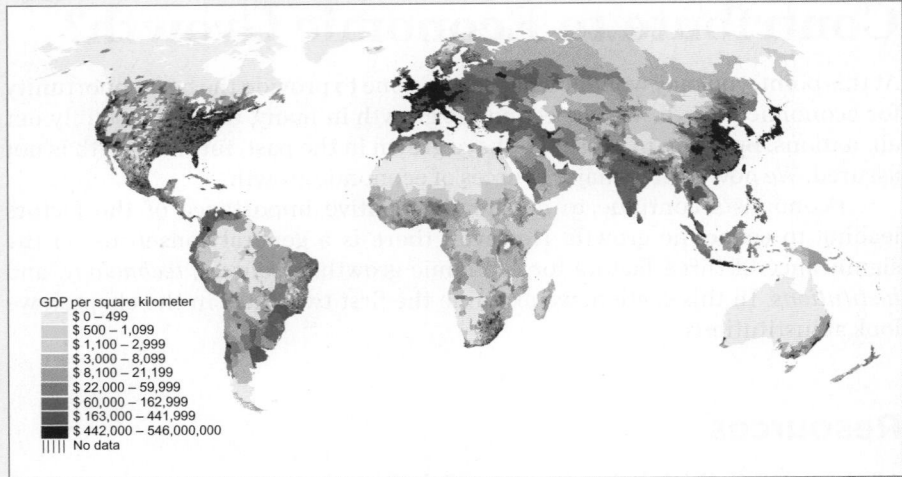

GDP per square kilometer
- $ 0 – 499
- $ 500 – 1,099
- $ 1,100 – 2,999
- $ 3,000 – 8,099
- $ 8,100 – 21,199
- $ 22,000 – 59,999
- $ 60,000 – 162,999
- $ 163,000 – 441,999
- $ 442,000 – 546,000,000
- ||||| No data

roads and bridges, computers, and shovels. The purpose of capital is to aid in the production of future output.

Consider the shipping container, a basic tool that has aided the movement of goods around the globe. A shipping container is a standard-size (20- or 40-foot-long) box used to move goods worldwide. In 1954, a typical cargo ship traveling from New York to Germany might have carried as many as 194,582 individual items. The transportation involved bags, barrels, cartons, and many other different means of packaging and storing goods. Loading and unloading the ship required armies of men working long hours for days on end. Not surprisingly, shipping goods from one country to another was expensive.

The standardized shipping container was first used in 1956. Suddenly, it was possible to move cargo around the globe without repacking every time the mode of transportation changed. Once a cargo ship enters the port, cranes lift the containers 200 feet in the air and unload about 40 large boxes each hour. Dozens of ships are unloaded at a time, and computers run most of the operation. A container full of iPads can be loaded onto the back of a truck in Shenzhen, China, transported to port, and loaded onto a ship that carries 3,000 containers. The ship can bring the iPads to the United States, where the containers are loaded onto a train and, later, a truck. This movement happens without anyone touching the contents. Clearly, the shipping container is a tool that has revolutionized world trade and improved lives.

As the quantity of physical capital per worker rises, so does output per worker: workers are more productive with more and better tools. Look around the world: the productive nations have impressive roads, bridges, buildings, and factories. In poor nations, paved roads are nonexistent or in disrepair, vehicles are of lower quality, and computers are a luxury. Even public electricity and sewage treatment facilities are rare in parts of many developing nations.

This cargo ship, bearing hundreds of individual shipping containers, is arriving at the Port of Oakland, California, with goods from Asia.

Because of the obvious correlation between tools and wealth, many of the early contributions to growth theory focused on the role of physical capital. As a result, much international aid was used to build roads and factories, in the hope that prosperity would follow automatically. But today, most economists understand that capital alone is not sufficient to produce economic growth. Factories, dams, and other large capital projects bring wealth only when they mesh well with the rest of the economy. A steel factory is of little use in a region better suited for growing corn. Without a good rail network or proper roads, a steel factory cannot get the tools it needs and cannot easily sell its products. Dams fall into disrepair within a few years if they are not maintained. Water pipes are a wonderful modern invention, but if they are not kept in good shape, human waste from toilets contaminates the water supply. The point is that simply building new capital in a nation does not ensure future sustained economic growth.

Education enhances human capital, but is it the key ingredient to economic growth?

HUMAN CAPITAL The output of a nation also depends on its workers. **Human capital** is the resource represented by the quantity, knowledge, and skills of the workers in an economy. It is possible to expand human capital by either increasing the number of workers available, educating the existing labor force, or both.

Human capital
is the resource represented by the quantity, knowledge, and skills of the workers in an economy.

We often think in terms of the sheer quantity of workers: all else being equal, a nation with more workers produces more output. But more output does not necessarily mean more economic growth. In fact, economic growth requires more output *per capita*. Adding more workers to an economy may increase total GDP without increasing per capita GDP. However, if more workers from a given population enter the labor force, GDP per capita can increase. For example, as we discussed in Chapter 20, women have entered the U.S. labor force in record numbers over the past 50 years as they have moved from homemaking services not counted in official GDP statistics to the official labor force. As more women join the official labor force, their formally measured output increases both GDP and per capita GDP.

There is another important dimension of human capital: the knowledge and skills of the workers themselves. In this context, it is possible to increase human capital through education and training. Training includes everything from basic literacy to college education and from software competencies to specific job training.

Not many people would doubt that a more educated labor force is more productive. And certainly, to boost per capita output, educating the labor force is more helpful than merely increasing the quantity of workers. But education alone is not enough to ensure economic progress. For many years, for example, India struggled with economic growth, even while its population was significantly more literate than those of other developing nations.

Technology

We know that the world would be much poorer without computers, automobiles, electric light bulbs, and other goods that have resulted from productive ideas. **Technology** is the knowledge available for use in production. Though technology

Technology
is the knowledge available for use in production.

is often embodied in machines and productive techniques, it is really just knowledge. New technology enables us to produce more while using fewer of our limited resources. A **technological advancement** introduces new techniques or methods so that firms can produce more valuable outputs per unit of input. We can either produce more with the same resources or use fewer resources to produce the same quantity.

For example, the assembly line was an important idea. Henry Ford adopted and improved the assembly-line method in 1913 at the Ford Motor Company. In this new approach to the factory, workers focused on well-defined jobs such as screwing on individual parts. A conveyor belt moved the parts around the factory to workers' stations. The workers themselves, by staying put rather than moving around the production floor, experienced a lower rate of accidents and other mishaps.

Agriculture is a sector where technological advances are easy to spot. For example, we know that land resources are necessary to produce corn. But technological advances mean that over time it has become possible to grow and harvest more corn per acre of land. In fact, in the United States, the corn yield per acre is now six times what it was in 1930. In 1930, we produced about 25 bushels of corn per acre, but now the yield is consistently over 150 bushels per acre. Higher yields are a result of technology that has produced hybrid seeds, herbicides, fertilizers, and irrigation techniques.

Figure 24.4 presents another example. There are now significantly fewer milk cows in the United States than at any time since 1920. But total milk

PRACTICE WHAT YOU KNOW

Resources: Growth Policy

The Akosombo Dam in Ghana was built with international aid funds.

Many policies have been advocated to help nations escape poverty, and the policies often focus on the importance of resources.

QUESTION: For each policy listed below, which resource is the primary focus: natural resources, physical capital, or human resources?

a. international loans for infrastructure like roads, bridges, and dams

b. mandated primary education

c. restrictions on the development of forested land

d. population controls

e. international aid for construction of a shoe factory

ANSWERS:

a. Infrastructure is physical capital.

b. Education involves human capital.

c. These restrictions focus on maintaining a certain level of natural resources.

d. Population controls often result from a shortsighted focus on physical capital per capita. The fewer people a nation has, the more tools there are per person.

e. The focus here is physical capital.

FIGURE 24.4

Fewer Cows but More Milk

U.S. dairy cow populations continue to decline, but the average cow now produces five times more milk than in 1924. This means that even with fewer cows, farmers produce 2.3 times more milk than they did in 1924.

Source: USDA.

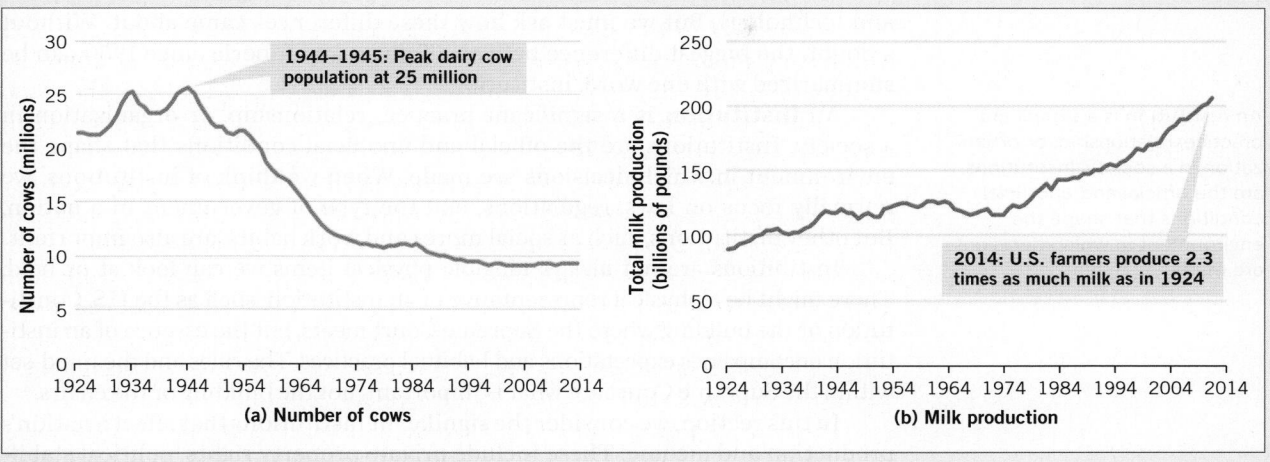

(a) Number of cows

1944–1945: Peak dairy cow population at 25 million

(b) Milk production

2014: U.S. farmers produce 2.3 times as much milk as in 1924

output is at historic highs because dairy farmers can now get about five times as much milk out of each cow. While strategic breeding has played a large role in this increase, even simple technology has factored in this change. For example, farmers now line the cows' stalls with 6 to 8 inches of sand. The sand is comfortable to lie on, it offers uniform support, and it stays cooler in the summer. In the end, the cows produce more milk. This is one simple example of how new ideas or technological advancements enable us to produce more while using fewer resources.

Like capital, technology produces value only when it is combined with other inputs. Simply carrying plans for a shoe factory to Haiti would not generate much economic value. The mere knowledge of how to produce shoes, while important, is only one piece of the growth puzzle. An economy must have the physical capital to produce shoes, must have the human capital to staff the factory and assembly line, and must create favorable conditions and incentives for potential investors. Economic growth occurs when all these conditions come together. That is one reason why it is incorrect to identify technological innovations as the sole cause of differences in wealth across nations.

Moreover, technological innovations do not occur randomly across the globe. Some places produce large clusters of such innovations. Consider that information technology largely comes from MIT and Silicon Valley, movie and television ideas generally come from Hollywood, and new fashion designs regularly come from Paris, Milan, Tokyo, and New York. Technological innovations tend to breed more innovations. This conclusion leads us to reword an earlier question: Why do some regions innovate (and grow) more than others? A large part of the answer lies in our next topic, institutions.

What Institutions Foster Economic Growth?

In 1950, residents in the African nation of Liberia were wealthier than those on the Southeast Asian island of Taiwan. Today, however, per capita GDP in Taiwan is more than 20 times that of Liberia. Yes, much of this wealth gap stems from obvious current differences in physical capital, human capital, and technology. But we must ask how these differences came about. Without a doubt, the biggest difference between Taiwan and Liberia since 1950 can be summarized with one word: institutions.

An **institution** is a significant practice, relationship, or organization in a society. Institutions are the official and unofficial conditions that shape the environment in which decisions are made. When we think of institutions, we normally focus on laws, regulations, and the type of government in a nation. But other institutions, such as social mores and work habits, are also important.

Institutions are not always tangible physical items we can look at or hold. There might be a physical representative of an institution, such as the U.S. Constitution or the building where the Supreme Court meets, but the essence of an institution encompasses expectations and habitual practices. The rules and the mind-set within the Supreme Court are what is important, not the building or the chairs.

In this section, we consider the significant institutions that affect a nation's production and income. These include private property rights, political stability and the rule of law, competitive and open markets, efficient taxes, and stable money and prices. Many of these are examined in detail elsewhere in this book, so we cover them only briefly here.

> An **institution** is a significant practice, relationship, or organization in a society. Institutions are the official and unofficial conditions that shape the environment in which decisions are made.

Private Property Rights

The single greatest incentive for voluntary production is ownership of what you produce. The existence of **private property rights** means individuals can own property—including houses, land, and other resources—and when they use their property in production, they own the resulting output.

> **Private property rights** are the rights of individuals to own property, to use it in production, and to own the resulting output.

Think about the differences in private property rights between Liberia and Taiwan. In Liberia, the system of ownership titles is not dependable. As a result, Liberians who wish to purchase land often must buy the land multiple times from different "owners," because there is no dependable record of true ownership. Taiwan, in contrast, has a well-defined system of law and property rights protection. Without such a system, people have very little incentive to improve the value of their assets.

In the past two decades, the government of China has relaxed its laws against private property ownership, a move that has spurred unprecedented growth. These market reforms began with a risky experiment in the rural community of Xiaogang. In 1978, the heads of 21 families in Xiaogang signed an agreement that became the genesis of private property rights in China. This remarkable document read:

> December 1978, Mr. Yan's Home. We divide the field (land) to every household. Every leader of the household should sign and stamp. If we are able to produce, every household should promise to finish any amount they are required to turn in to the government, no longer asking the government

for food or money. If this fails, even if we go to jail or have our heads shaved, we will not regret. Everyone else (the common people who are not officers and signees of this agreement) also promise to raise our children until they are eighteen years old. First signer: Hong Chang Yan.*

The agreement stipulated each family would continue to produce the government quota for their agricultural output. But they would begin keeping anything they produced above this quota. They also agreed to stop taking food or money from the government. This agreement was dangerous in 1978—so dangerous, they stipulated they would raise one another's children if any of the signees were put in jail.

The Xiaogang agreement led to an agricultural boom that other communities copied. Seeing the success of this property rights experiment, Deng Xiaoping and other Chinese leaders subsequently instituted market reforms in agriculture in the 1980s and then in manufacturing in the 1990s. China's economy is growing rapidly today not because the Chinese found new resources or updated their technology. The Chinese are wealthier because they now recognize private property rights in many different industries.

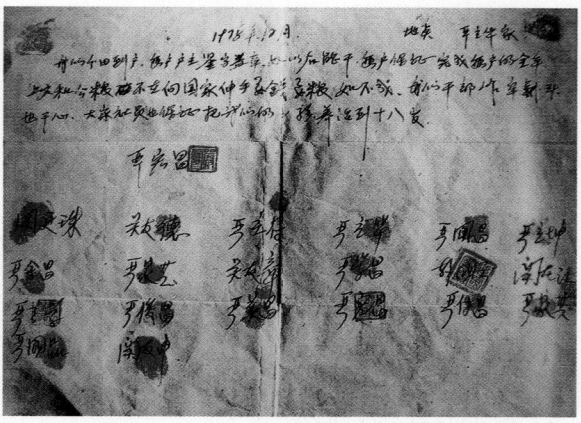

This little Chinese agreement between 21 poor rural families helped to bring private property rights to modern China.

Political Stability and the Rule of Law

To understand the importance of political stability and the rule of law, consider again Liberia and Taiwan. Before 2006, Liberia endured 35 years of political unrest. Government officials assumed office through the use of violence, and national leaders consistently used their power to eradicate their opponents. In contrast, Taiwan's political climate has been relatively stable since 1949. If you were an entrepreneur deciding where to build a factory, would you want to invest millions of dollars in a country with constant violent unrest, or would you choose a peaceful country instead? Which nation would you predict is more likely to see new factories and technological innovation?

Incentives

Political instability is a disincentive for investment. After all, investment makes sense only if there is a fairly certain payoff at the end. In an environment of political instability, there is no incentive to invest in either human or physical capital because there is no predictable future payoff.

Consistent and trustworthy enforcement of a nation's laws is crucial for economic growth. Corruption is one of the most common and dangerous impediments to economic growth. When government officials steal, elicit bribes, or hand out favors to friends, incentives for private investment are reduced. If individuals from all walks of life cannot count on a fair system and the opportunity to earn returns in their investments in human or physical capital, investment declines. And this decline reduces future growth.

The World Justice Project has collected data on the rule of law across the world. Figure 24.5 shows the nations broken down into four groups, based on income, with an average rule-of-law index for each. It is no surprise that nations scoring in the top group on this index are also the nations with the highest levels of per capita GDP. The most corrupt nations are also those with the lowest levels of income.

Bullet casings litter the street in Monrovia, Liberia, in 2003.

---

*Literal translation by Chuhan Wang.

FIGURE 24.5

The Rule of Law and Per Capita Income

Consistent and fair enforcement of a nation's laws pays off with economic growth, and data from the World Justice Project back this up. High-income nations are also nations that adhere most closely to the rule of law, and nations where the law is routinely ignored (where corruption is more rampant) also have lower incomes.

Source: World Justice Project, Annual Report 2011. GDP figures are adjusted using PPP (constant 2005 international $), 2005–2009.

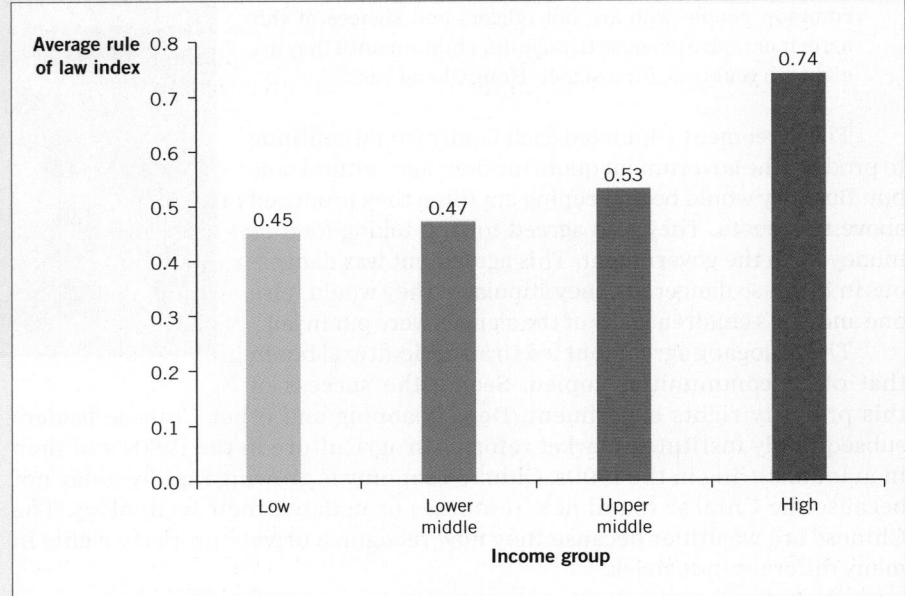

Average rule of law index

Income group	Value
Low	0.45
Lower middle	0.47
Upper middle	0.53
High	0.74

ECONOMICS IN THE REAL WORLD

Would you get more parking tickets if you weren't compelled to pay for them?

WHAT CAN PARKING VIOLATIONS TEACH US ABOUT INTERNATIONAL INSTITUTIONS?

Until 2002, diplomatic immunity protected United Nations diplomats in New York City from fines or arrest stemming from parking violations. This immunity gave economists Raymond Fisman and Edward Miguel the idea for a unique natural experiment: they studied how officials responded to the lack of legal consequences for violating the law. Parking violations under these conditions are an example of corruption because they represent the abuse of power for private gain. Therefore, by comparing the level of parking violations of diplomats from different societies, the economists created a way to compare corruption norms among different cultures.

Fisman and Miguel compared unpaid parking violations with existing survey-based indices on levels of corruption across nations. They found that diplomats from high-corruption nations accumulated significantly more unpaid parking violations than those from low-corruption nations. Among the worst offenders were diplomats from Kuwait, Egypt, Chad, Sudan, and Bulgaria. Among those with zero unpaid parking violations were diplomats from Australia, Canada, Denmark, Japan, and Norway.

This finding suggests that cultural or social norms related to corruption are quite persistent: even when stationed thousands of miles away, diplomats behave as if they are at home. Norms related to corruption are apparently deeply ingrained.

In 2002, enforcement authorities acquired the right to confiscate the diplomatic license plates of violators. And guess what? Unpaid violations dropped by almost 98%. This outcome illustrates the power of incentives in influencing human behavior.

Competitive and Open Markets

In this section, we take a quick look at three institutions essential for economic growth: competitive markets, international trade, and the flow of funds across borders. These market characteristics are covered in detail elsewhere in this book.

COMPETITIVE MARKETS In Chapter 3, we explored how competitive markets ensure consumers can buy goods at the lowest possible prices. When markets aren't competitive, people who want to participate face barriers to entry, which inhibit competition and innovation. Yet many nations monopolize key industries by preventing competition or by establishing government ownership of industries. These policies limit macroeconomic growth.

INTERNATIONAL TRADE Recall from Chapter 2 that trade creates value. In some cases, trade enables nations to consume goods and services they would not produce on their own. Specialization and trade make all nations better off because each can produce goods for which it enjoys a comparative advantage. Output increases when nations (1) produce the goods and services for which they have the lowest opportunity cost and (2) trade for the other goods and services they wish to consume.

Trade creates value

    International trade barriers reduce the benefits available from specialization and trade. Chapter 32 is devoted to the study of international trade.

FLOW OF FUNDS ACROSS BORDERS In Chapter 22, we talked about the importance of savings for economic growth. For example, the inflow of foreign savings has helped to keep interest rates low in the United States even as domestic savings rates have fallen. If firms and individuals are to invest in physical or human capital, someone has to save. Opportunities for investment expand if there is access to savings from around the globe. That is, if foreigners can funnel their savings into your nation's economy, your nation's firms can use these funds to expand. However, many developing nations have restrictions on foreign ownership of land and physical capital within their borders. Restrictions on the flow of capital across borders handcuff domestic firms, which are then forced to seek funds solely from domestic savers.

Efficient Taxes

On the one hand, taxes must be high enough to support effective government. Political stability, the rule of law, and the protection of private property rights all require strong and consistent government. And taxes provide the revenue to pay for government services. On the other hand, if we tax activities fundamental to economic growth, there will be fewer of these activities. In market economies, output and income are strictly intertwined. If we tax income, we are taxing output, and that is GDP. So although taxes are necessary, they can also reduce incentives for production.

Incentives

Before the federal government instituted an income tax, government services were largely funded by taxes on imports. But international trade is also an essential institution for economic growth. So taxes on imports also impede growth.

Efficient taxes are taxes sufficient to fund the activities of government while impeding production and consumption decisions as little as possible. It is not easy to determine the efficient level of taxes or even to determine what activities should be taxed. We will discuss this issue further in Chapter 29, when we discuss fiscal policy.

Stable Money and Prices

High and variable inflation is a sure way to reduce incentives for investment and production. In Chapter 22, we saw that inflation increases uncertainty about future price levels. When people are unsure about future price levels, they are

PRACTICE WHAT YOU KNOW

Hint: The nation's flag is one of those shown here.

Institutions: Can You Guess This Country?

QUESTION: The following is a list of characteristics for a particular country. Can you name it?

1. This country has almost no natural resources.
2. It has no agriculture of its own.
3. It imports water.
4. It is located in the tropics.
5. It has four official languages.
6. It occupies 710 square kilometers.
7. It has one of the world's lowest unemployment rates.
8. It has a literacy rate of 96%.
9. It had a per capita GDP of $56,000 in 2014.
10. It has one of the densest populations per square kilometer on the planet.

ANSWER: Congratulations if you thought of Singapore! At first blush, it seems almost impossible that one of the most successful countries on the planet could have so little going for it in terms of natural resources.

QUESTION: How could a country with so few natural resources survive, let alone flourish? How can an economy grow without any agriculture or enough fresh water?

ANSWER: What Singapore lacks in some areas it more than makes up for in others. Singapore has a lot of human capital from a highly educated and industrious labor force. It has been able to attract plenty of foreign financial funds by creating a stable and secure financial system that protects property rights and encourages free trade. Singapore also has a strategically situated deep-water port in Southeast Asia that benefits from proximity to the emerging economies of China and India.

Learning More and Helping Alleviate Global Poverty

- The best way to learn about global poverty is to travel to low-income nations.
- There are several books you can read to learn more about the economics of global poverty.

The information presented in this chapter reveals a picture of significant and persistent poverty across much of the globe. It is possible that this discussion and your classroom lectures have inspired you to learn more about global poverty or even to try to help those who are less fortunate around the globe. Toward those ends, we can give a little advice.

The surest way to learn about world economic reality is to travel to a developing nation. We suggest taking an alternative spring break or even studying abroad for an entire semester in a developing nation. These are costly ventures, but they will almost certainly change your perspective on life. If you get the chance to travel, be sure to speak directly to people on the streets and ask them to share their personal stories with you. Talk to small business owners, parents, and children. If possible, try to speak to people who have nothing to gain by sharing their story.

You may wish to give financially to help the less fortunate around the globe. There are many international aid charities, but unfortunately, not all are truly helpful or even completely honest. We recommend visiting the website for Givewell (www.givewell.org), which researches charitable organizations from around the world and recommends a few that have proved to be honest and effective.

If you want to study more about growth economics, you should start with two books. The first book is by economist William Easterly, titled *The Elusive Quest for Growth: Economists' Adventures and Misadventures in the Tropics*. In this book, Easterly weaves personal narrative and economic theory together in a unique way to help you understand how economic

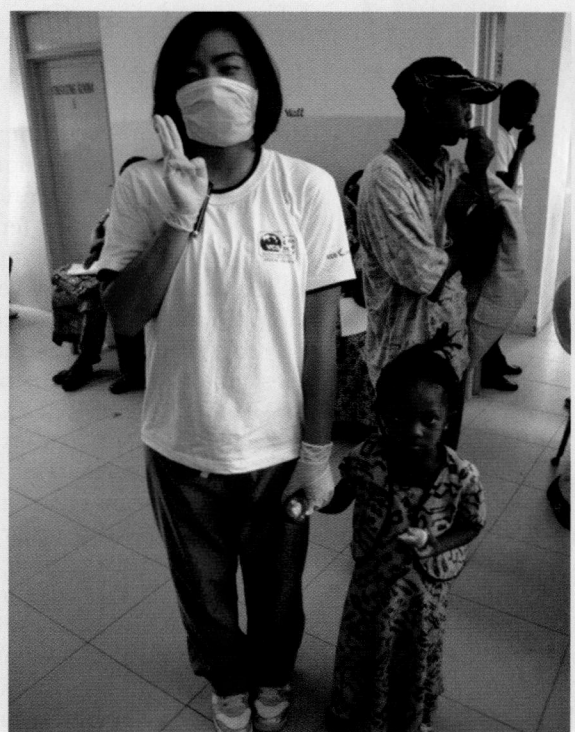

A University of Virginia student helps with eye surgeries in Tema, Ghana.

theories regarding growth have evolved through the years. He both explains past failures and argues compellingly for future policy proposals. The second book, by economists Daron Acemoglu and James Robinson, is called *Why Nations Fail: The Origins of Power, Prosperity, and Poverty*. This book presents the very best arguments for institutions as the primary source of economic growth. Even though this book is written by leading macroeconomists, it is enjoyable reading for mass audiences.

The 2019 Nobel Prize–winning economists Abhijit Banerjee, Esther Duflo, and Michael Kremer transformed the field with their work using randomized controlled trials.

more reluctant to sign contracts that deliver dollar payoffs in the future. Thus, unpredictable inflation diminishes future growth possibilities. In the United States, the Federal Reserve (Fed) is charged with administering monetary policy. The Fed is designed to reduce incentives for politically motivated monetary policy, which typically leads to highly variable inflation rates. We cover the Fed in greater detail in Chapter 30.

How Are Some Economists Testing New Ideas?

Measuring short-term impacts of growth is a challenge in economics. The 2019 Nobel Prize in economics went to the development economists Abhijit Banerjee, Esther Duflo, and Michael Kremer for major contributions in this area. Duflo is the second female winner in economics and the youngest winner ever. The Nobel was given for pioneering fieldwork using randomized controlled trials (RCTs) in developing nations. An RCT randomly groups people to compare and test how policies and incentives affect economic growth.

For example, intestinal hookworms are common in developing countries and often keep students out of school. Using an RCT, Kremer found that deworming programs had a much larger effect than anticipated. Kremer introduced deworming drugs into random school districts and saw improved health and less absenteeism. This included "spillover effects" to nearby communities, where deworming some individuals reduced the chance that others would become infected. The programs have since been expanded.

Using RCTs in India, Banerjee and Duflo found that plans involving "microcredit"—short-term business loans as small as $20, given for no collateral—were not as helpful in reducing poverty as some had thought (though particularly enthusiastic entrepreneurs showed positive results). Duflo and Kremer also studied incentives given to farmers in developing countries to encourage investment in fertilizer for larger crop yields. They found it was most effective to offer discounts to purchase fertilizer at harvest time for future use.

This trio changed the practice of development economics. Economists now fan out around the globe testing new ideas in RCTs.

Conclusion

In this chapter we considered the three sources of economic growth: resources, technology, and institutions. But we also cautioned against an overemphasis on resources and pointed to the necessity of growth-fostering institutions.

In the next chapter, we cover the theory that supports this modern economic analysis. ✳

· ANSWERING *the* BIG QUESTIONS ·

Why does economic growth matter?

- Economic growth affects human welfare in meaningful ways.
- Historical data show that sustained economic growth is a relatively modern phenomenon.
- Relatively small but consistent growth rates are an effective path out of poverty.

How do resources and technology contribute to economic growth?

- Natural resources, physical capital, and human capital all contribute to economic growth.
- Technological advancement, which leads to the production of more output per unit of input, also sustains economic growth.

What institutions foster economic growth?

- Private property rights secure ownership of what an individual produces, creating incentives for increased output.
- Political stability and the rule of law allow people to make production decisions without concern for corrupt government.
- Competitive and open markets allow everyone to benefit from global productivity.
- Efficient taxes are high enough to support effective government, but low enough to provide positive incentives for production.
- Stable money and prices allow people to make long-term production decisions with minimal risk.

How are some economists testing new ideas?

- Fieldwork using randomized controlled trials (RCTs) is changing development economics.
- An RCT randomly groups people to compare and test policies and incentives.

· CHAPTER PROBLEMS ·

Concepts You Should Know

economic growth (p. 763)
factors of production (p. 779)
human capital (p. 781)

institution (p. 784)
private property rights (p. 784)
resources (p. 779)

rule of 70 (p. 771)
technological advancement (p. 782)
technology (p. 781)

Questions for Review

1. What are the three factors influencing economic growth?

2. What is human capital, and how is it different from the quantity of workers available for work? Name three ways to increase a nation's human capital. Is an increase in the size of the labor force also an increase in human capital? Explain your answer.

3. How is economic growth measured?

4. Describe the pattern of world economic growth over the past 2,000 years. Approximately when did economic growth really take off?

5. List five human welfare conditions positively affected by economic growth.

6. Many historical accounts credit the economic success of the United States to its abundance of natural resources.

   a. What is missing from this argument?
   b. Name five poor nations with significant natural resources.

7. The flow of funds across borders is a source of growth for economies. Use what you learned about loanable funds in Chapter 22 to describe how foreign funds might expand output in a nation.

8. In 2011, when the U.S. unemployment rate was over 9%, President Barack Obama said, "There are some structural issues with our economy where a lot of businesses have learned to become much more efficient with a lot fewer workers. You see it when you go to a bank and you use an ATM, you don't go to a bank teller, or you go to the airport and you're using a kiosk instead of checking in at the gate." Discuss the president's quote in terms of both short-run unemployment and long-run growth.

9. The difference between 1% growth and 2% growth seems insignificant. Explain why it really matters.

10. What do economists mean by the term "institutions"? Name five different laws that are institutions affecting production incentives. Name three social practices that affect production in a society.

Study Problems (*solved at the end of the section)

✳ 1. Real per capita GDP in China in 1959 was about $350, but it doubled to about $700 by 1978, when Deng Xiaoping started market reforms.

   a. What was the average annual economic growth rate in China over the 20 years from 1959 to 1978?
   b. Chinese real per capita GDP doubled again in only seven years, reaching $1,400 by 1986. What was the average annual economic growth rate between 1979 and 1986?

✳ 2. The table below presents long-run macroeconomic data for two hypothetical nations, A and B:

	A	B
Nominal GDP growth	12%	5%
Inflation	10	2
Nominal interest	4	4
Unemployment rate	12	5
Population growth	1.5	1

Assume both nations start with real GDP of $1,000 per citizen. Fill in the blanks in the following table, assuming the data on the previous page apply for every year considered.

	A	B
Economic growth rate	_____	_____
Years required for real per capita GDP to double	_____	_____
Real per capita GDP 140 years later	_____	_____

3. Let's revisit the data from Table 24.3, showing the following world economic growth rates for specific historical eras:

Years	Growth rate
AD 1–1800	0.02%
1800–1900	0.64
1900–1950	1.04
1950–2000	2.12

Approximately how many years will it take for average real per capita GDP to double at each of those growth rates?

4. Use the data in the table below to compute economic growth rates for the United States for 2008, 2009, and 2010. Note that all data are from the end of the year specified.

Date	Nominal GDP (billions of current $)	GDP deflator	Population growth rate
2007	$14,061.8	106.30	1.01%
2008	14,369.1	108.62	0.93
2009	14,119.0	109.61	0.87
2010	14,660.4	110.66	0.90

5. The rule of 70 applies in any growth rate application. Let's say you have $1,000 in savings and you have three alternatives:

- a savings account earning 1% interest per year
- a U.S. Treasury bond earning 3% interest per year
- a stock market mutual fund earning 8% interest per year

Approximately how long would it take to double your savings in each of the three accounts?

6. Assume you plan to retire in 40 years and are evaluating the three different accounts listed in question 5. How much would your $1,000 be worth in 40 years under each of the three alternatives?

✳ 7. Economic growth is a very particular concept in economics. The term "economic growth" is not always used correctly in media reports.

a. Define economic growth.
b. Consider the following economy:

Year	Nominal GDP (trillions of dollars)	Price level
2014	$18	240
2015	20	250

Is it possible to calculate the economic growth rate in 2015 given the information above? If so, calculate the economic growth rate. If not, what other information would you need to calculate the economic growth rate?

8. The data below are for the United States in 2009 and 2010.

	Nominal GDP growth rate	GDP deflator growth rate	Money supply growth rate	Nominal interest rate	Real interest rate	Population growth rate	Unemployment rate
2009	−2.0%	0.8%	2.2%	3.0%	2.2%	0.7%	9.5%
2010	3.8	1.2	4.5	2.5	1.3	0.6	9.9

a. Use the approximation formula discussed in the chapter to calculate the approximate rate of economic growth (in percentage terms) for both 2009 and 2010.

b. Determine the approximate number of years it will take for living standards to double in the United States, if the economic growth rate from 2010 is sustained.

9. Understanding economic growth is a significant part of macroeconomics.

a. Define economic growth.

b. The table below shows economic data for the imaginary nation of Lexieland in 2019 and 2020.

Year	Nominal GDP (billions of dollars)	Price level	Population	Nominal interest rate
2019	50	200	50	2%
2020	60	216	55	3

If possible, using the data above, calculate Lexieland's approximate economic growth rate for the year 2020. If you do not have enough information, what other information would you need?

10. The long-run average rate of real GDP growth in the United States is about 3%.

a. The following are other (approximate) long-run annual averages for the United States:

Inflation rate: 4%	Population growth rate: 1%
Immigration rate: 0.5%	Unemployment rate: 6%
Labor force participation rate: 70%	Velocity of money: 2%
Nominal interest rate: 3%	

What is the long run average rate of per capita real GDP growth for the United States?

b. Currently, average annual income in the United States is about $60,000. If the U.S economy grows at the rate you just computed for the next 70 years, what will be the average income level in 70 years?

c. Average annual income in China is now about $9,000. If economic growth in China is 5% for the next 70 years, what will be its average income level in 70 years?

Solved Problems

1a. The rule of 70 tells us we can divide 70 by the rate of growth to approximate the number of years it takes for a variable to double. Therefore, if we know the number of years a variable actually did take to double, we can rearrange the rule of 70 to approximate the average annual growth rate, x:

$$70 \div x = 20$$
$$70 \div 20 = x$$
$$= 3.5$$

Therefore, the Chinese economy grew at an approximate average of 3.5% per year over the 20-year period from 1959 to 1978.

b. Now, with real per capital GDP doubling in approximately seven years, the rule of 70 implies

$$70 \div 7 = 10$$

Therefore, China grew an average of 10% over the seven-year period from 1979 to 1986.

2. To determine economic growth rate, we use the approximations formula:

- Economic growth $\approx$ %Δ in nominal GDP $-$ %Δ price level $-$ %Δ population

- For nation A: 12% − 10% − 1.5% = 0.5%

- For nation B: 5% − 2% − 1% = 2%

To determine the approximate number of years required for real per capita GDP to double, we use the rule of 70:

- For nation A: 70 ÷ 0.5 = 140

- For nation B: 70 ÷ 2 = 35

To determine real per capita GDP 140 years later, we use the rule of 70 results. Nation A's level doubles in exactly 140 years, so it will be two times the original level of $1,000, or $2,000. Nation B's level doubles after 35 years and then doubles again after 35 more. So after 70 years, its level of real per capita GDP is four times the original level. It doubles again in 35 years, so after 105 years, it is eight times the original level. Then it doubles again in 35 more years, so after 140 years, its real per capita GDP is $16,000, which is 16 times the original level.

	A	B
Economic growth rate	0.5%	2%
Years required for real per capita GDP to double	140	35
Real per capita GDP 140 years later	$2,000	$16,000

7a. Economic growth is measured as the percentage change in real per capita GDP.

b. It is not possible to calculate the economic growth rate from the data because we also need the growth rate of the population.

25

Growth Theory

Buildings, Roads, Mosquito Nets, and Other Capital Are Not the Key to Economic Growth.

If we look around the world, it is easy to spot high-income nations and low-income nations. Rich, developed nations have impressive capital, including highways, factories, office buildings, and laboratories. Poor, underdeveloped nations have fewer modern factories and buildings, and their roads and other infrastructure are often in disrepair. Think of North and South Korea, as we saw in the last chapter, where one can literally see the difference from outer space. Clearly, wealth and physical capital go hand in hand, and it is tempting to conclude that physical capital is the *source* of wealth: if poor nations can just acquire more and better tools, they too, can be wealthy.

However, correlation does not prove causation. Modern economic growth theory indicates that physical capital is generally the result of growth, rather than the cause of it, and that institutions, not infrastructure, are the real key to economic vitality. In the last chapter we saw in concrete terms how institutions matter. This chapter now provides the theoretical backbone of growth analysis. We begin with

Remember that satellite image of North and South Korea? Here's a ground-level view of the Ryugyong Hotel in North Korea's capital, Pyongyang. It was supposed to be a showcase piece of infrastructure, but it's been under construction on and off for three decades and is still not done. Behind the sleek façade (a massive LED display recently installed by Egyptian investors) sit unfinished rooms, gathering dust. Why the epic construction fail? Because the institutions of North Korea reward loyalty to the regime over engineering competence.

a brief description of how economic theories develop. After that, we consider the evolution of growth theory, starting with the growth model created by the American economist Robert Solow. The Solow model formed the foundation for growth theory beginning in the 1950s. After discussing the theory and implications of the Solow model, we consider New Growth Theory and its implied policy prescriptions.

· BIG QUESTIONS ·

- How do macroeconomic theories evolve?
- What is the Solow growth model?
- How does technology affect growth?
- Why are institutions the key to economic growth?

How Do Macroeconomic Theories Evolve?

This chapter marks our first major step into macroeconomic theory, or modeling. In Chapter 2, we discussed the characteristics of good economic models: they are simple, flexible, and useful for making accurate predictions. In this chapter, we present a model of economic growth that simplifies from the real world yet also helps us make powerful predictions about economic growth. The stakes are high: growth theory and policy have significant impacts on human lives. Therefore, it's important to consistently reevaluate growth theory in light of real-world results.

Today, economists agree that economic growth is determined by a combination of resources, technology, and institutions. But this consensus is the result of an evolution in growth theory that started almost 60 years ago with the contributions of economist Robert Solow. Although the theory has changed significantly over the past two decades, Solow's growth model still forms the core of New Growth Theory.

In many academic disciplines, new theories are fodder for intellectual debates, with no direct effect on human lives. But in economics, theories are put to the test in the real world, often very soon after they are first articulated. Figure 25.1 illustrates the relationship between economic ideas and real-world events. At the top of the circle, we begin with observations of the real world, which inform a theory as it develops. Once an economic theory is developed, it

FIGURE 25.1

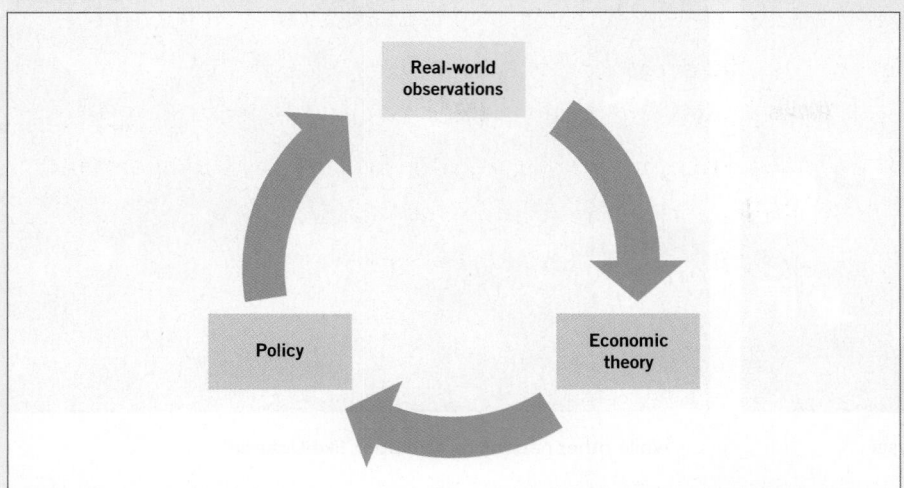

FIGURE 25.1

The Interplay between the Real World and Economic Theory

Observations of the real world shape economic theory. Economic theory then informs policy decisions designed to meet certain economic goals. Once these policies are implemented, they affect the real world. Further real-world observations contribute to additional advances in economic theory, and the cycle continues.

can influence the policies used to pursue certain economic goals. These policies affect the daily lives and well-being of real people. Finally, as economists observe the effects of policy in the real world, they continue to revise economic theory.

Economic growth models affect the welfare of billions of people worldwide. The results can be beneficial. But if growth theory is wrong or incomplete, it can lead to faulty policy prescriptions that result in poverty. We revisit this point toward the end of the chapter.

The Evolution of Growth Theory

In 1776, Adam Smith published his renowned book *An Inquiry into the Nature and Causes of the Wealth of Nations*. This book was the first real economics textbook and, as the title indicates, it focused on what makes a nation wealthy. The central question, paraphrased from the title, is: Why do some nations prosper while others do not? More than two centuries later, we still grapple with the nature and causes of the wealth of nations.

Economists are not alone in their pursuit of answers to this question. Perhaps you or someone you know has visited a developing country. As travel becomes easier and the world economy becomes more integrated, people are more aware of poverty around the globe. Many college students today ask the same questions as economists: Why are so many people poor, and what can be done about it?

This link between economic theory and human welfare is what drives many scholars to study the theory of economic growth. As the Nobel Prize–winning macroeconomist Robert Lucas wrote in 1988:

> Is there some action a government of India could take that would lead the Indian economy to grow like Indonesia's or Egypt's? If so, what exactly? If not, what is it about the "nature of India" that makes it so? The consequences for human welfare involved in questions like these are simply staggering: *Once one starts to think about them it is hard to think of anything else.*

Why are some nations rich, like Malaysia . . .

. . . while other nations remain poor, like Uganda?

Economic growth has not always been the primary focus of macroeconomics. After the Great Depression in the 1930s, macroeconomics focused on the study of business cycles, or short-run expansions and contractions. Growth theory began with the Solow model in the 1950s and still serves as the foundation for growth theory, both in method and in policy. Therefore, while growth theory has evolved, it is helpful to consider the Solow model as both a starting point and the basis of current theory.

What Is the Solow Growth Model?

If you travel around the globe and visit nations with different levels of income, you will notice significant differences in the physical tools available for use in production. Wealthy nations have more factories, better roads, more and better computers—that is, they have more physical capital. Simply viewing the difference in capital, it is easy to conclude that capital automatically yields economic growth.

This was the basic premise of early growth theory: there are rich nations and there are poor nations, and the rich nations are those with capital. Natural resources and human capital are important in the Solow growth model, but the focus is primarily on *physical capital*. So when we speak simply of capital, we mean physical capital; and where human capital is also part of the picture, we will call that labor.

We begin our tour of the Solow model by looking at a nation's production function, which describes how changes in capital affect real output.

A Nation's Production Function

A **production function** for a firm describes the relationship between the inputs the firm uses and the output it creates.

The Solow model starts with a *production function* for the entire economy. In microeconomic theory, a firm's **production function** describes the relationship between the inputs a firm uses and the output it creates. For example, at a single McDonald's restaurant, the daily output depends on both the number of employees and the capital tools employees have to work with. In equation form, the production function for a single firm is

$$q = f(\text{labor, capital})$$

(EQUATION 25.1)

where q is the firm's output. Equation 25.1 says that output *is a function of* the quantities of labor and capital that the firm uses. For McDonald's, the output is the number of meals produced.

In macroeconomics, we extend the production function to an entire nation or macroeconomy. The **aggregate production function** describes the relationship between all the inputs used in the macroeconomy and the economy's total output, where GDP is output. In its simplest form, the aggregate production function tells us that GDP is a function of three broad types of resources, or factors of production, which are the inputs used in producing goods and services. These inputs are capital, labor, and natural resources. We can state the aggregate production function in equation form as

$$\text{GDP} = Y = F(\text{labor, capital, natural resources})$$

The **aggregate production function** describes the relationship between all the inputs used in the macroeconomy and the economy's total output (GDP).

(EQUATION 25.2)

where Y is real output, or GDP.

We can think about the relationship between input and output in a very simple economy. Consider a situation in which there is only one person in the macroeconomy—for example, the character Chuck Noland (played by Tom Hanks) in the 2000 movie *Cast Away*, who finds himself stranded on an island in the South Pacific after his plane crashes. Chuck's individual, or microeconomic, decisions are also macroeconomic decisions, because he is the only person in the economy. The GDP of Chuck's island includes only what he produces with his resources. Let's say Chuck spends his days harvesting fruit on the island. In this case, GDP is equal to whatever fruit Chuck harvests. Table 25.1 shows Chuck's production function and some of the resources he has available.

Chuck's output is the fruit he harvests from around his island. His resources include his labor, the capital of a bamboo ladder, and the island's

In the film *Cast Away*, Chuck Noland's individual, or microeconomic, decisions are also macroeconomic decisions, because he is the only person in the economy.

TABLE 25.1

Chuck Noland's Production Function

	Production function	
	GDP = F(labor, capital, natural resources)	
GDP	**Resources**	**Example**
	Labor	Chuck's time and knowledge
Fruit	Capital	Bamboo ladder
	Natural resources	Fruit trees and bamboo

natural resources, such as bamboo and fruit trees. All else equal, the more Chuck has of any of these resources, the more GDP he can produce. Economic growth occurs when Chuck produces more fruit per week.

In many ways, the production function for a large macroeconomy is the same as for Chuck Noland's one-man economy. Consider the economy of India. In India, output depends on the resources available for production, and India has significant natural resources, such as iron ore, coal, timber, and farmland. In terms of human capital, India has a large labor force with over 520 million workers, and a literacy rate of more than 70%. Finally, India has built up a very large stock of capital—highways, factories, ports, machinery, etc. All of these resources enable the nation to produce an annual GDP of more than $2.6 trillion.

THE FOCUS ON CAPITAL RESOURCES While the Solow model recognizes contributions from both labor and capital, many economists and policymakers focused on capital. As we noted in the chapter opener, early growth theorists saw that capital resources in wealthy nations far exceed those available in developing nations. After all, there are more factories, highways, bridges, and dams in wealthy nations. It seemed logical to conclude that capital is the key to growth.

In addition, periods of investment growth in developed economies are also periods of economic expansion. Figure 25.2 plots U.S. economic growth

FIGURE 25.2

Real GDP and Investment Growth Rates, 1970–2017

Growth in real investment is positively correlated with growth in real GDP. The big question is whether this correlation implies causation.

Source: Bureau of Economic Analysis.

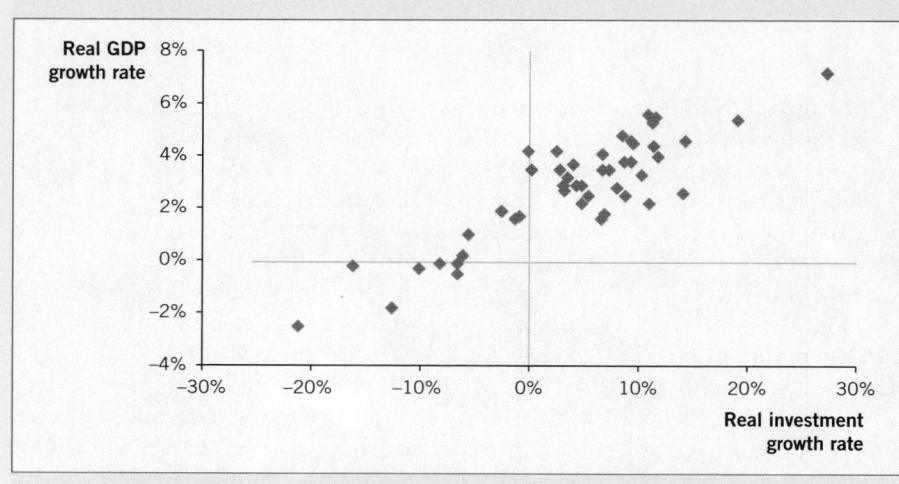

rates with investment growth rates from 1970 to 2017. The data show a clear positive correlation between real GDP growth and the rate of investment growth—another reason to believe that investment and capital are the primary sources of economic growth.

Earlier, we noted the interplay of theory and real-world observations. This is one example. Capital *appears* to cause economic growth, because there is such a strong correlation between capital and output. And, certainly, no one disputes that workers are more productive when they have more tools. For now, however, we continue our focus on capital. Later, we explore alternative growth sources omitted from this early work.

Diminishing Marginal Products

The castaway Chuck Noland would have been happy to find a new grove of mangoes on his island, and his newfound resources would have increased his GDP. Natural resources also help large, developed macroeconomies. For example, discoveries of natural gas in the United States have increased dramatically over the past two decades. This new energy resource enables the United States to produce more with cheaper resources. To quantify how helpful a resource may be, economists employ the concept of *marginal product*. The **marginal product** of an input is the change in output associated with one additional unit of an input. More resources increase output, so we say the marginal product of each resource is positive.

A ladder would help!

The **marginal product** of an input is the change in output divided by the change in input.

DIMINISHING MARGINAL PRODUCT IN A ONE-PERSON ECONOMY

To illustrate some important properties of production functions, let's take a closer look at the production function of Chuck Noland. Initially, Chuck produces GDP by climbing trees and picking fruit. With this method, he is able to gather 1 bushel of fruit in a week. He produces this weekly GDP without the aid of any capital. Now, let's say Chuck decides to take a week to build a bamboo ladder. Building the ladder is a costly investment, because it takes him away from producing fruit for a whole week. But then, after he has the ladder as capital, his weekly output grows to 4 bushels. This means the marginal product (MP) of his ladder is 3 bushels of fruit per week:

$$MP_{capital} = \text{change in output given the change in capital} = 3$$

Marginal thinking

Chuck is so happy with his ladder that he builds a second ladder (perhaps to leave one on each side of the island). Now his weekly output climbs to 6 bushels of fruit. Because he produces 4 bushels with one ladder and 6 bushels with two ladders, the marginal product of the second ladder is 2 bushels. Note that it is less than the marginal product of the first ladder. The marginal product of the second ladder is not as large because while the first ladder completely altered the way Chuck harvests fruit, the second ladder just makes his job a little easier.

Figure 25.3 shows the hypothetical relationship between Chuck's output and the number of ladders he uses. Looking first at the table on the right, note that the second column shows total output (bushels per week), which depends on the number of ladders. The third column shows the marginal product of each ladder. Notice that the marginal product declines as more ladders are added. This outcome reflects the principle of **diminishing marginal product**, which states that the marginal product of an input falls as the quantity of the input

Diminishing marginal product occurs when the marginal product of an input falls as the quantity of the input rises.

FIGURE 25.3

Chuck Noland's Production Function

The table shows how output (bushels per week) increases as the number of ladders increases; it describes the relationship between output and capital inputs. The graph is a picture of the production function. Output increases with capital, but each unit of capital yields less additional output. The shape of the production function, in which the slope is declining, illustrates the diminishing marginal product of capital.

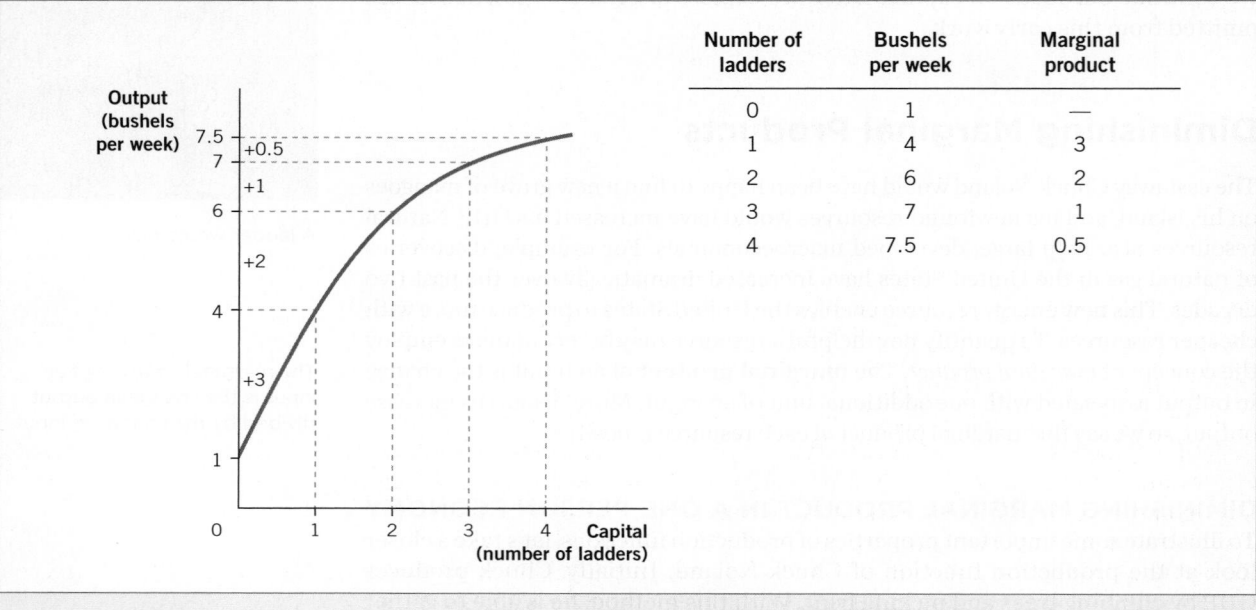

Number of ladders	Bushels per week	Marginal product
0	1	—
1	4	3
2	6	2
3	7	1
4	7.5	0.5

rises. Diminishing marginal product generally applies across all factors of production at both microeconomic and macroeconomic levels.

The left side of Figure 25.3 is a graph of Chuck's production function: it plots the points from the first two columns of the table on the right. With no ladders, the production function indicates 1 bushel of fruit; but then as ladders are added, output climbs along the curve. The slope of the curve flattens out because the marginal product of the added ladders diminishes.

This principle of diminishing marginal productivity is not special to our example of one man alone on an island. It is a phenomenon that holds for resources in a macroeconomy in general, and it is a cornerstone insight of the Solow growth model. Sometimes, the name of this principle is simplified to *diminishing returns*. The following discussion places this concept in the macroeconomic context of the U.S. interstate highway system.

HIGHWAYS AND THE PRODUCTION FUNCTION In the United States, we have a system of interstate highways built by the federal government. This interstate highway system is essentially a 50,000-mile capital good that we use to help produce GDP. The network of highways connects major cities of the United States. These highways increase GDP in the United States, because they help us transport goods and services across the nation. For example, a couch

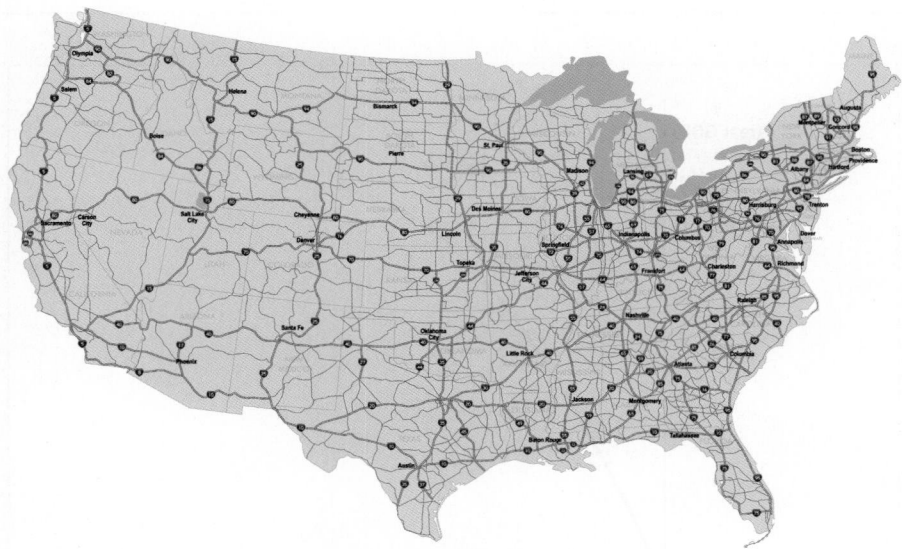

How much would GDP fall without our interstate highways?

manufactured in High Point, North Carolina, can be transported exclusively by interstate highway to Cleveland, Ohio, in less than 8 hours. Before the construction of the interstate system, the same trip between High Point and Cleveland would have taken twice as long, required more gasoline due to inefficient speeds, and caused much more wear and tear on the vehicles used.

If the interstate highway system were somehow to close down completely, GDP would fall immediately. But what would happen to GDP if the government created a second interstate highway system with 50,000 miles of additional roads crisscrossing the United States? That is, what would be the marginal product of an additional interstate highway system? The impact would be positive, but much smaller than that of the original network. This example illustrates diminishing returns: the marginal product of highways declines as more and more become available. The production relationship is just like that of Chuck Noland's ladders.

Figure 25.4 is a graph of the aggregate production function—the production function for the entire economy. On the vertical axis, we have output for the macroeconomy, which is real GDP (Y). To simplify, we assume no population growth and so economic growth is represented as movements up along the vertical axis. On the horizontal axis, capital resources (K) increase from left to right. Notice that the slope of the function is positive, which indicates positive marginal product. But the marginal product of capital also declines as more capital is added. For example, the difference in output from the increase in capital from K_1 to K_2 is larger than the change in output from a change in capital from K_3 to K_4. This outcome illustrates the declining marginal product of capital.

The aggregate production function has formed the basis for most discussions in growth theory since 1956. Economic growth is represented by upward movement along the vertical axis. Indeed, if we focus *only* on this simple formulation, economic growth happens only with investment in capital. Diminishing returns, or declining marginal productivity, is the key assumption of the Solow model. As we shall see, this single assumption leads to striking implications for the macroeconomy.

FIGURE 25.4

The Aggregate Production Function

The aggregate production function graphs the relationship between output (Y, or real GDP) and capital inputs (K). The shape of the production function illustrates two important features of production. First, the marginal production of resources is positive, as indicated by the positive slope. Second, the marginal product of additional resources declines as more resources are added. This result is evident in the declining slope of the function.

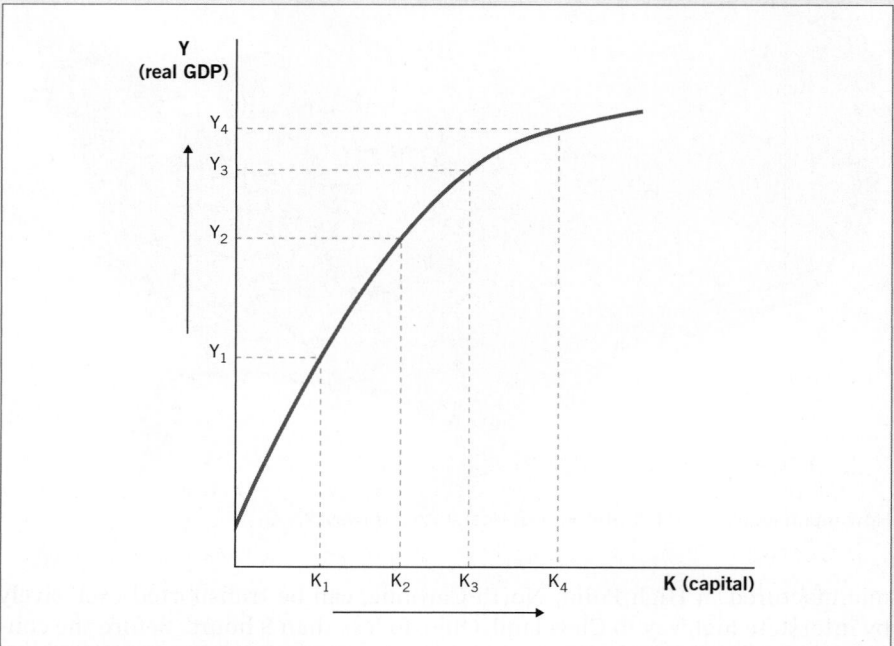

Implications of the Solow Model

We can use the basic framework of the production function with an emphasis on capital and diminishing returns to flesh out the two important implications of the Solow model: the conditions of a *steady state* and *convergence*.

Incentives

THE STEADY STATE How many ladders should Chuck Noland build? It takes a week to build each ladder, and each additional ladder adds less output than the one before. Therefore, at some point Chuck has no incentive to build additional ladders. Perhaps Chuck's incentive declines after he builds two ladders. Looking back at Figure 25.3, you can see that a third ladder yields only 1 more bushel of fruit. Let's assume that Chuck decides it is not worth a week of work (to build a ladder) for 1 more bushel of fruit. Therefore, he builds only two ladders, and his output remains at 6 bushels a week. At this point, economic growth for Chuck stops.

The Solow model implies the same outcome for large macroeconomies. Because the marginal product of capital decreases, at some point there is no reason to build (that is, invest in) more capital. Let's assume this occurs at K_3 in Figure 25.4. This means there is no incentive to build additional capital beyond K_3 because the benefits in terms of additional output no longer exceed the cost of building capital. Since there is no incentive to build capital past K_3, and since we are assuming that capital is the source of growth, the economy stops growing once it reaches K_3. In this example, K_3 is the economy's **steady state**, the condition of a macroeconomy when there is no new net investment.

The **steady state** is the condition of a macroeconomy when there is no new net investment.

An economy at the steady state is like an airplane at its cruising altitude.

Once an economy reaches the steady state, there is no change in either capital or real income. The steady state is a direct implication of diminishing returns: when the marginal return to capital declines, at some point there is no incentive to build more capital. The steady state is not a very encouraging situation. You can think of the steady state as the "stagnant state," because when the economy reaches its steady state, real GDP is no longer increasing and economic growth stops.

It is important to distinguish between *investment* and *net investment*. Over time, capital wears out: roads get potholes, tractors break down, and factories become obsolete. This is known as capital depreciation. **Depreciation** is a decline in the value of a resource over time. Depreciation is natural with capital, and it erodes the capital stock. Without new investment, capital declines over time, so some positive investment is needed to offset depreciation. But if investment is exactly enough to replace depreciated items, the capital stock will not increase—and this means no net investment. **Net investment** is investment minus depreciation. For the capital stock to increase, net investment must be positive.

This distinction between investment and net investment is important when we consider the steady state. In the steady state, net investment equals zero. There may be positive investment, but this is investment to replace worn-out machines and tools. So when an economy reaches its steady state, the capital stock stays constant. For example, if three ladders represent a steady-state condition on Chuck Noland's island, he may repair his ladders periodically. Repairing the ladders to maintain a level of capital counts as investment, but not as positive net investment.

CONVERGENCE If nations with large stocks of capital reach their steady state and stop growing, nations with less capital can catch up by adding to their capital stock. This means that nations all over the globe could potentially converge to the same level of wealth. **Convergence** is the idea that per capita GDPs across nations equalize as nations approach the steady state. Here is the logic of the Solow model: Rich nations are rich because they have more capital. But as these nations approach their steady state, the returns to capital decline and the growth slows. When a nation reaches a steady state, its economic growth stops. But if a nation has not yet reached the steady state, adding capital still leads to growth. Therefore, investment in developing nations should yield

Depreciation
is a fall in the value of a resource over time.

Net investment
is investment minus depreciation.

Convergence
is the idea that per capita GDPs across nations equalize as nations approach the steady state.

Changes in Resources: Natural Disasters

Hurricane Maria caused an estimated $90 billion in damage to Puerto Rico and the U.S. Virgin Islands.

In September 2017, Hurricane Maria slammed into Puerto Rico, killing many people and destroying significant capital, including roads, homes, factories, and bridges.

QUESTION: How would you use an aggregate production function to illustrate the way a major destruction of capital affects a macroeconomy in the short run?

ANSWER:

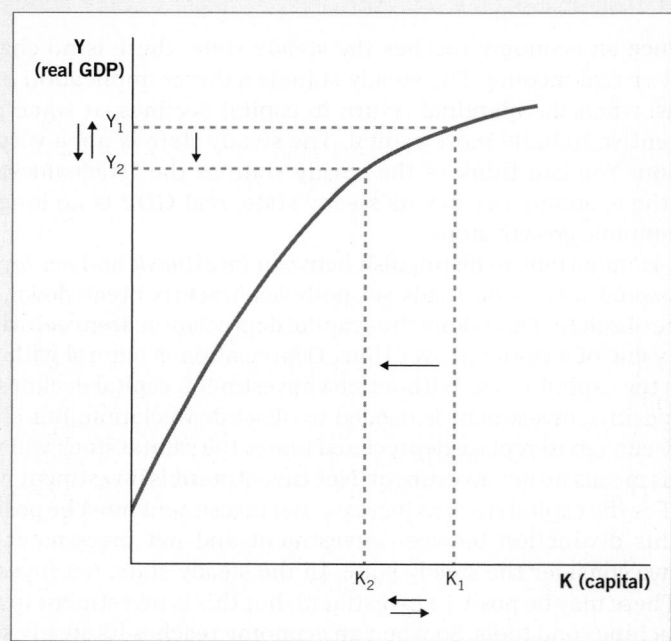

This is an unusual situation, in which the level of capital actually falls. Because capital (K) is on the horizontal axis of the production function, the decline in capital moves Puerto Rico back along its production function. Assuming the original level of capital is indicated as K_1, we can illustrate the effect of Maria as a change to a lower level, say K_2. This means less GDP for Puerto Rico (Y falls from Y_1 to Y_2) until the capital is rebuilt.

QUESTION: With no further changes, what happens to real GDP in the long run?

ANSWER: With no further changes, real GDP returns to the steady-state output level (K_1) in the long run. At the new level of capital after the storm (K_2), the marginal product of additional capital is relatively high, so there is a greater return to building new capital. But in the long run, because there was no shift in the production function, the level of capital returns to the steady-state level (K_1), which means output also returns to its steady-state level (Y_1).

FIGURE 25.5

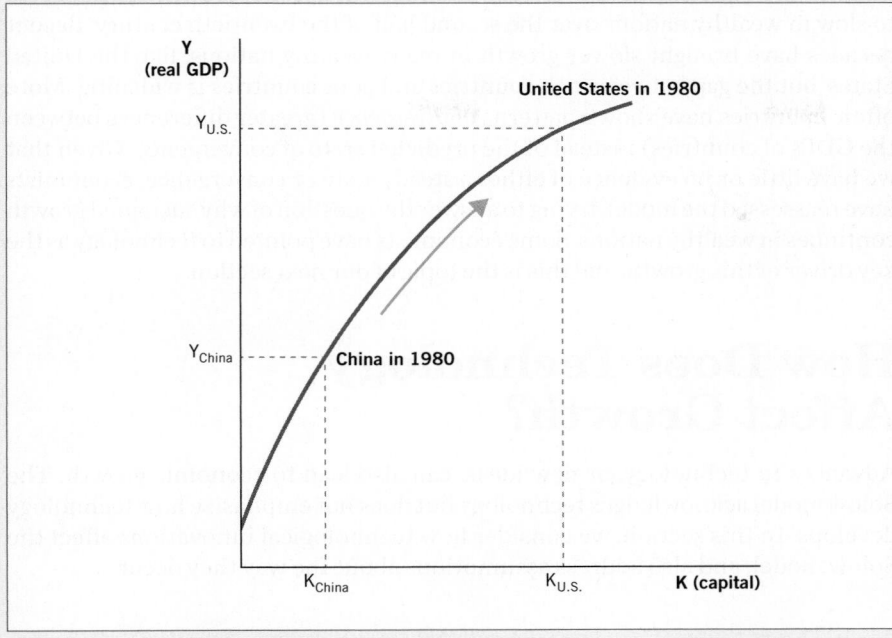

Convergence

In 1980, the United States had much more capital than China did; this was one reason why real GDP for the United States was much higher. But in the years since, China has increased its capital stock substantially and has grown much more rapidly than the United States. The Solow model implies that the United States is closer to its steady state and therefore grows more slowly than China.

relatively greater returns, and this outcome should lead to more capital in developing nations.

Consider the United States and China. In 1980, the United States was wealthy, but China was poor. Figure 25.5 shows both nations as they might have appeared on a production function in 1980. Yet since 1980, growth rates in China have exceeded growth rates in the United States. This blast of growth in China has been accompanied by rapid industrialization—that is, the creation of new capital. According to the Solow model, the new capital in China yields greater returns because the nation started with less capital.

If this basic model were completely realistic, new factories in poor nations would typically yield higher returns than those in rich nations. Investors seeking to build new factories would turn to nations like Haiti, Nicaragua, and North Korea—nations with relatively small capital stocks.

According to the Solow theory, developing nations should catch up because the older, developed economies have already made new discoveries and have documented mistakes to avoid in the development process. Developing nations can jump right into acquiring the best equipment, tools, and practices. For example, if they are building cars, they don't have to start with a Model T and a basic labor-intensive assembly line; they can immediately establish a modern plant resembling those of, say, Ford, Honda, and Volkswagen.

But reality has been much different from what the theory implies. First, although we have seen cases of rapid growth in poor nations, convergence has been rare. In addition to China, the nations of South Korea, Singapore, India, Chile, and others have done well. But they are exceptions. Very recently, it seems some growth is sprouting in African nations, but for the second half of the twentieth century, most poor nations continued to stagnate, rather than converge to the economic levels of wealthier nations. Second, growth did not seem to slow in wealthy nations over the second half of the twentieth century. Recent decades have brought slower growth in many wealthy nations, like the United States, but the gap between rich countries and poor countries is widening. More often, countries have shown patterns of *divergence* (greater differences between the GDPs of countries) instead of the predicted state of convergence. Given that we have little or no evidence of either a steady state or convergence, economists have reassessed the model, trying to answer the question of why sustained growth continues in wealthy nations. Some economists have pointed to technology as the key driver of this growth, and this is the topic of our next section.

How Does Technology Affect Growth?

Advances in technology, or new ideas, can also lead to economic growth. The Solow model acknowledges technology but does not emphasize how technology develops. In this section, we consider how technological innovations affect the Solow model, and also address assumptions about the way they occur.

Technology and the Production Function

In 1994, Intel introduced a revolutionary computer chip for personal computers—the Pentium chip. The original Pentium could perform 166 million operations per second and was more than three times faster than its predecessor chip. But by 2018, just 26 years later, Intel's new chip, the Core i9 9900K, could perform 281 *billion* operations per second. The new chip costs less and uses less energy than the old chip and yet is more than a thousand times faster!

These Intel chips give us a good picture of what technology does. A computer chip is capital—it is a tool that helps us produce. Faster chips mean more output with the same amount of capital.

Now let's see how new technology affects the Solow growth model. First, consider the production function. Figure 25.6 shows two production functions: F_1 is the initial production function, when computers are running on Pentium chips. F_2 is the production function after faster chips arrive. Note the new production function is steeper than the old one. The slope is determined by the marginal product of capital, and the new computer chips make capital more

Older map technology took lots of time . . .   . . . but the new map technology is faster.

FIGURE 25.6

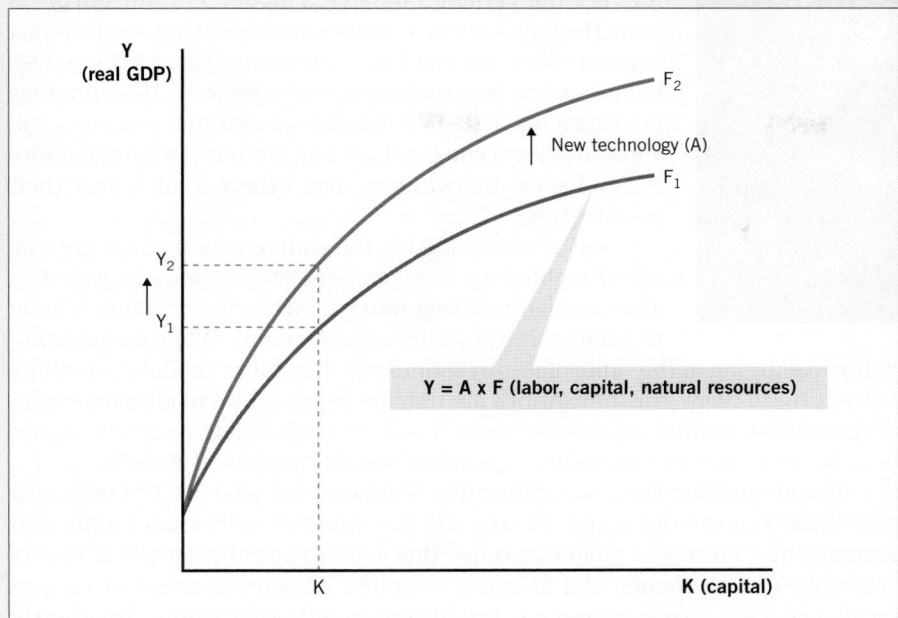

New technology increases the slope of the production function as the marginal product of capital increases. The old production function is shown as F_1 and the new production function as F_2. After the technological innovation (represented by A), capital is more productive, and this outcome leads to new economic growth. If technology continues to advance, economic growth can be sustained.

productive at all levels. For any given level of capital, real GDP is higher. These are the kinds of technological changes that fuel sustained economic growth.

We can also use an equation to see how the production function is altered. The aggregate production function now includes an allowance for technological advancement:

$$Y = A \times F (\text{labor, capital, natural resources})$$

(EQUATION 25.3)

where A accounts for technological change. The addition of A to the basic model helps to explain continued economic growth. Without new technology, the economy eventually reaches a steady state, and growth stops. But new technology means output is higher for any given level of capital, because it makes resources more productive. New technology shifts real output, and therefore income, up to new levels.

Economists and policymakers of course see this shift as very important, and it has driven many political decisions. Before looking at policy implications that derive from the Solow model, let's first look more closely at how technological change occurs in the model.

Exogenous Technological Change

Why do people innovate? What drives them to create better ways of producing? If technology is the source of sustained growth, the answer to this question is critical.

In the Solow model, there is no real answer to the question of what causes technological innovation. The model assumes that technological change occurs

The discovery of the glue used for Post-it Notes was accidental. When the notes are used to paper a friend's car, the act is normally premeditated.

Exogenous growth
is growth that is independent of factors within the economy.

exogenously. Recall from Chapter 2 that exogenous factors are the variables outside a model. For our purposes here, the implication is that technological innovations just happen—they are not based on economics. In this sense, technological innovations occur randomly. If technology is exogenous, it is like rainfall: sometimes you get a lot, and sometimes you don't get any. If some nations get more technological innovations than others, that is just their good fortune.

But if technology is the source of sustained growth, and if technology is exogenous, then economic growth is also exogenous. **Exogenous growth** is growth that is independent of factors within the economy. When we see innovation occurring in the same places over and over, the Solow model chalks it up to luck. In this view, the innovations are not due to any inherent characteristics of the economies that experience them. Similarly, in this view, poor nations are poor because the random technological innovations happened elsewhere.

If you question the assumption that technological advance is a matter of pure luck, you are not alone. So why did the Solow growth model make this assumption? First, the model assumes that technological progress is tied to scientific advancements, and at times scientific discoveries seem to happen by chance. One classic example is the invention of Post-it Notes. Apparently, researchers at 3M accidentally stumbled onto a formula for glue that made Post-it Notes possible. In this sense, the discovery was seemingly random luck.

Second, this model, like most economic models, is developed mathematically. The assumption of exogenous technological change made the theoretical growth models simpler to solve than an alternative model where technological change is dependent upon multiple factors in the economy.

As we will see in the final section of this chapter, economists in the 1980s developed other models (or techniques) to help incorporate technological change into the original model.

Policy Implications of the Solow Model

At the beginning of this chapter, we discussed how macroeconomic theory often translates directly into policy. We are now in a position to consider the policy prescriptions that emerge from the Solow growth model. Proponents of the Solow model emphasize the importance of capital and technology. Thus, for low-income nations to grow, they need the latest technology embedded in capital goods. High-income nations and individuals around the globe can help others grow by providing aid to purchase the latest capital.

As the Solow model grew in popularity in the 1950s, two specific types of aid were developed to implement this approach. First, actual capital goods were built with aid from developed nations. For example, in 1964, with funding from the United States, Great Britain, and the World Bank, the Akosombo Dam was built in the West African nation of Ghana to create hydroelectric power, and to form a lake useful for water transportation and a fishing industry.

Second, international aid was sent directly to developing nations to help them fund investment in infrastructure such as highways, bridges, and modern ports, as well as other types of capital. These aid payments were intended

PRACTICE WHAT YOU KNOW

Technological Innovations: How Is the Production Function Affected?

When new technology is introduced, it makes capital more productive. For example, modern tractors are faster and more powerful than tractors used a century ago.

QUESTION: How does this type of change affect the production function?

ANSWER: The production function gets steeper at each point. For example, when the level of capital is K, the slope of production function F_2 is steeper than the slope of F_1. The reason is that capital is now more productive at every level. The first unit of capital adds more to output than before, and the 500th unit of capital adds more to output than before. The marginal product of capital, which is embedded in the slope of the production function, is now higher at all levels.

This tractor was state-of-the-art technology in 1910.

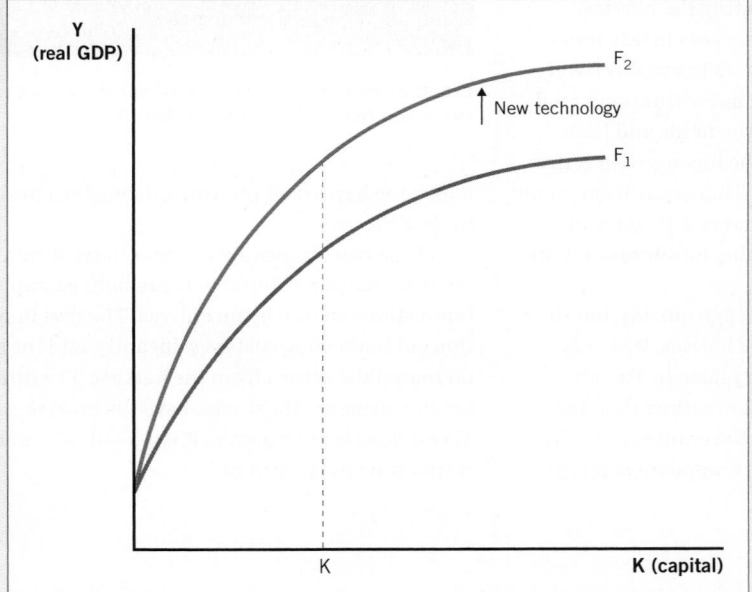

CHALLENGE QUESTION: What happens in the loanable funds market when new technology leads to more productive capital (see Chapter 22 if necessary)?

ANSWER: Productivity of capital shifts the demand for loanable funds. New technology would lead to an increase in demand for loans and, all else equal, interest rates would rise.

to help poor nations build capital infrastructure that would pave the way to economic growth.

While there were of course some successes, economists and policy-makers are largely discouraged by the results of these policy initiatives. For example, fifty-three years after the Akosombo Dam was completed, average

Technological Change

MODERN MARVELS

Modern Marvels is a television series on the History Channel. It often showcases technological innovations that have revolutionized the way goods and services are produced. In Season 13, an episode titled "Harvesters 2" included a look at cranberry harvesting around the globe.

Cranberries are grown on low-lying vines. In the past, cranberry harvesting involved many workers carefully hand-harvesting the berries. But cranberries also have air pockets inside them, and these pockets enable farmers to employ a wet harvest. The big innovation in harvesting occurred when farmers began flooding the fields and then knocking the cranberries off the bushes with water-reel harvesters called beaters. This innovation meant that just a few workers could harvest 10 acres of cranberries in a single day, saving hundreds of hours of labor.

The beaters make the harvest go quickly, but they also tend to damage some of the berries. Recently, Habelman Brothers, a cranberry farm in Tomah, Wisconsin, began using a gentler method than the water-reel so as not to damage the cranberries. Their harvesters use waterwheels with wooden panels to

Cranberries don't grow in water, but they float to the top when farmers flood the fields.

knock the berries off the vines, damaging fewer berries in the process.

These two innovations—water harvesting and the new, gentler waterwheel—are both examples of innovations caused by incentives. The first innovation cut harvesting costs significantly, and the second increased the return from the harvest. The innovators are the farmers—those who have the most to gain. Technology is not random; it is a result of individuals responding to incentives.

Incentives

income levels in Ghana have risen by just $1,200 per person, and this is not an isolated story. After billions of dollars in aid, nations such as Zimbabwe, Liberia, and Haiti are just as poor today as they were in 1960. In contrast, Taiwan, Chile, China, and India received almost no international aid and yet have grown rapidly.

The application of the Solow model to growth policy was often not successful. In fact, most of the twentieth century witnessed very few success stories and a series of failures. Consider the continent of Africa. Thirty-seven African nations achieved independence from 1956 to 1977, offering a unique opportunity to apply the Solow model. Yet by the late twentieth century, it was clear that these policies had failed across the continent, as many African nations were no better off than they were when they gained their independence decades earlier, even while much of the rest of the globe had experienced significant economic gains. Around the end of the twentieth century, these real-world policy results led to a reexamination of growth theory. Economist Dambisa Moyo wrote a book, *Dead Aid: Why Aid Is Not Working and How There Is a Better Way for Africa*, about this failure of international aid across Africa. She argued that foreign aid often led to corruption and nations becoming dependent on this aid. But she also points to policies that can yield growth in low-income nations. We discuss some of these in the next section.

Zambian economist Dambisa Moyo argues that international aid has inhibited growth in Africa.

Why Are Institutions the Key to Economic Growth?

Over the past thirty years, a resurgence in growth theory has been spurred by the belief that some economies grow faster *for reasons particular to those economies*. In some nations, and even in pockets within nations, technology advances more quickly than elsewhere. This resurgent growth theory has been dubbed **New Growth Theory**. It is an approach to long-run growth that focuses on technological change and the incentives fostering innovation inside an economy. The Solow model acknowledges the importance of new ideas and technology, but essentially assumes they spring up exogenously and therefore cannot be predicted. By contrast, New Growth Theory recognizes that economic growth generally appears to be endogenous. **Endogenous growth** is growth driven by factors inside an economy. For example, it is not random coincidence that assembly lines, sewing machines, air conditioning, personal computers, and the Internet were all developed in the United States. These advances spurred economic growth and improved people's lives. Why did they all occur in one nation? This is the focus of New Growth Theory.

New Growth Theory is an approach to long-run growth that focuses on technological change and the incentives fostering innovation inside an economy.

Endogenous growth is growth driven by factors inside an economy.

Economist Paul Romer was awarded the 2018 Nobel Prize in economics in large part based on his work as a founder of New Growth Theory. A famous 1990 paper of his, "Endogenous Technological Change," helped to shift economic theory's focus toward ideas and innovations, and why they occur in some places but not others. Today, many economists stress the importance of institutions as a key factor contributing to endogenous economic growth. We introduced institutions in Chapter 24. In the next section, we examine how institutions can provide a foundation for economic growth.

Endogenous growth originates inside an economy, as it does inside an organism.

The Role of Institutions

Consider the city of Nogales, which straddles the U.S.-Mexico border. The northern half of the city is in Arizona, while the southern half is in the Mexican state of Sonora. But life in these two halves is drastically different: average income in the northern half is three times that in the southern half. The residents of the northern half are much better educated, the roads are much better, and infant mortality is much lower. These are two halves of the same city, so they have the same natural resources, virtually identical geographical

TABLE 25.2
Institutions That Foster Economic Growth

1. Political stability and the rule of law	5. The flow of funds across borders
2. Private property rights	6. Efficient taxes
3. Competitive markets	7. Stable money and prices
4. International trade	

locations, the same ethnicities and weather. Why, then, are they so different? According to economist Daron Acemoglu, who wrote about the city in *Esquire* magazine in 2009:

> The key difference is that those on the north side of the border enjoy law and order and dependable government services—they can go about their daily activities and jobs without fear for their life or safety or property rights. On the other side, the inhabitants have *institutions* that perpetuate crime, graft, and insecurity. [emphasis added]

In other words, Acemoglu and many other economists feel that institutions are a key ingredient in the list of factors driving economic growth. Recall from Chapter 24 that institutions are significant practices, relationships, or organizations in society that frame the incentive structure within which individuals and business firms act. Institutions are the rules of the game, both formal and informal, framing the environment within which production takes place. They help determine the costs and benefits of production. Table 25.2 lists the institutions important for growth.

If we include institutions in the aggregate production function, we have

(EQUATION 25.4)

$$Y = A \times F(\text{labor, capital, natural resources}, \textbf{institutions})$$

Incentives

Institutions can lay the groundwork for natural endogenous growth. With these institutions in place, there are incentives for new technology to emerge and drive growth.

Figure 25.7 shows how institutions can affect the production function, causing it to rise from F_1 to F_2. Notice that the production function shifts up at all points, since institutions affect output across all levels of capital. Consider the shift toward private property rights that has occurred in China since the 1980s. As we discussed in Chapter 24, the shift toward private property rights changed incentives for producers, who now get to keep much of the income from their output. This change created the incentives for the exploding growth we now see in China.

Institutions Determine Incentives

Incentives

We need to consider how institutions affect production decisions. Let's begin with an individual firm's decision to produce. Imagine you are considering whether to open a new website design business. You decide you will start such a business only if you expect to at least break even—that is, your payoff must cover your costs. We can state this common condition as follows:

Voluntary investment and production occur only if *expected payoff* ≥ *costs*.

FIGURE 25.7

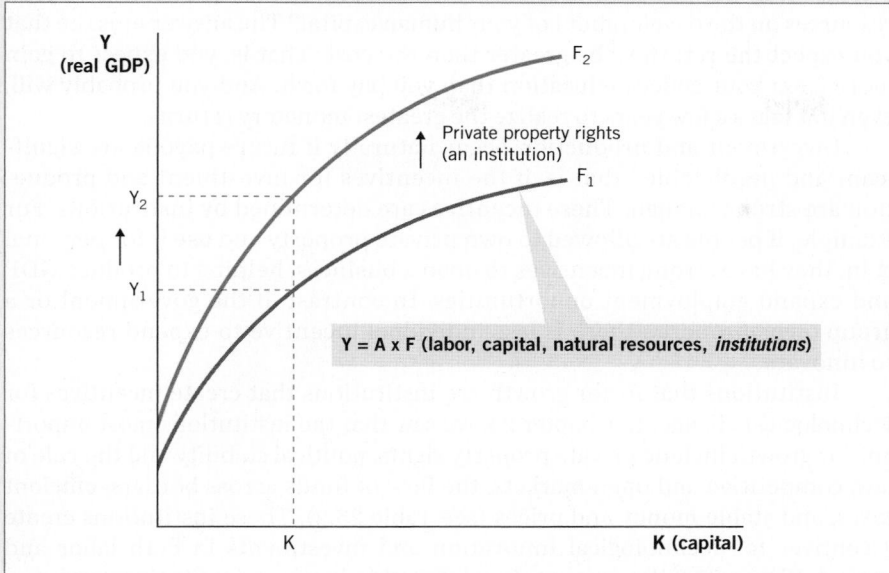

The adoption of efficient institutions shifts a nation's production function upward. The production function shifts up at all points, since institutions affect all levels of capital. Efficient institutions (such as private property rights, shown here) make it possible for nations to produce more with any given level of resources, and they increase incentives for technological innovation.

The payoffs come later than the costs and are uncertain, which is why we call them *expected payoffs*.

No matter what your output—website design, college gear, cupcakes, or tractors—the payoffs come after production and after sales. The exact time lag depends on the type of output, but payoffs from output come sometime after expenditures on resources. Because of the delay and the resources required, firms need to believe that resource expenditures, including time, patience, and effort, will offer a real payoff in the future.

Institutions make a difference: this is how Shanghai, the financial capital of China, looked in 1990 . . .

. . . and this is how Shanghai looked, just 20 years later, in 2010. The difference: institutional changes based on economic incentives for production and growth.

Or consider your decision to invest in your human capital by attending college. Why are you and your family voluntarily spending so much of your resources on the development of your human capital? The answer must be that you expect the return to be greater than the cost. That is, you expect to gain more from your college education than you pay for it. And you probably will, even if it takes a few years to realize the greatest monetary returns.

Investment and production occur naturally if future payoffs are significant and predictable—that is, if the incentives for investment and production are strong enough. These incentives are determined by institutions. For example, if people are allowed to own private property and use it for personal gain, they have strong incentives to open a business, helping to produce GDP and expand employment opportunities. In contrast, if the government or a group owns property, there is less individual incentive to expend resources to innovate.

Institutions that foster growth are institutions that create incentives for technological change. In Chapter 24, we saw that the institutions most important for growth include private property rights, political stability and the rule of law, competitive and open markets, the flow of funds across borders, efficient taxes, and stable money and prices (see Table 25.2). These institutions create incentives for technological innovation and investments in both labor and capital. Figure 25.8 illustrates this relationship between institutions and economic growth. Institutions create incentives for production and investment. If the right incentives are in place, production and investment occur naturally, and the result is more labor, more capital, and technological advancement—all of which lead to economic growth.

Institutions, Incentives, and Endogenous Growth

The goal is economic growth, but it all starts with institutions. Institutions provide the incentives that motivate choices made by people in an economy. The right institutions provide incentives for people to invent new technology and to invest in labor and capital. These actions lead to economic growth.

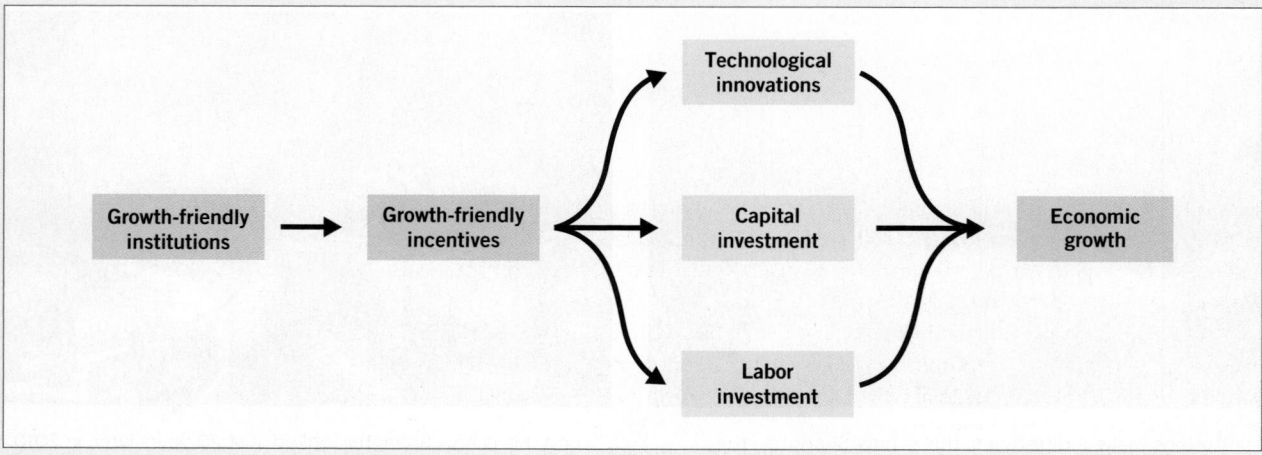

FIGURE 25.9

Institutions That Inhibit Endogenous Growth

People must work and invest today in order to get payoffs from output in the future. Inefficient institutions (such as political instability, corruption, inflation, and high tax rates) reduce the expected future payoffs and thus reduce the incentives for production. Growth-fostering institutions are those that maximize expected future payoffs for producers.

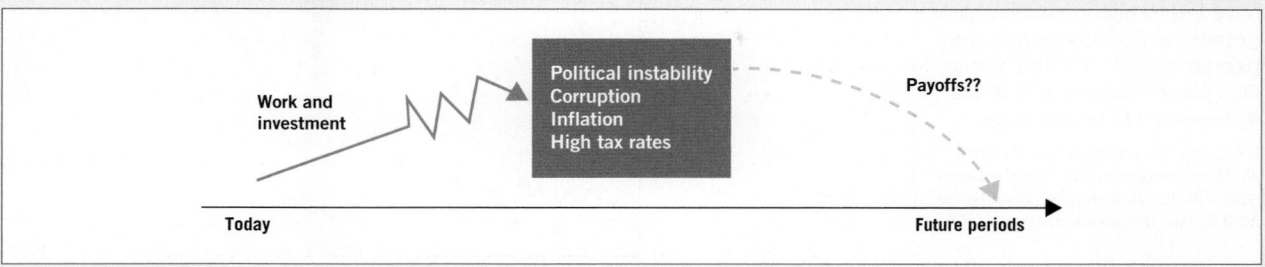

As Acemoglu observed in Nogales, weak or malfunctioning institutions can also act to reduce expected payoffs, through corruption, political instability, high and variable inflation, and high tax rates. A key to sustained growth is to eliminate these barriers. Figure 25.9 illustrates how inefficient institutions impede growth. Because payoffs from productive actions come in the future, anything that reduces the likelihood of these payoffs reduces the incentive for investment today. Resources are not enough. Some nations grow faster due to their institutions. Others grow slowly because of theirs. Unless institutions are the same across nations, we should not expect convergence.

New Growth Theory acknowledges the core truths of the Solow model: resources and technology are sources of economic growth. But it also recognizes the importance of institutions for technological change. This emphasis on institutions matters for policy. For example, international aid, even aid invested in capital goods, cannot lead to growth when corruption and political instability are rampant in the recipient nation. Institutions are the key ingredient to long-run growth.

ECONOMICS IN THE REAL WORLD

CHILE: A MODERN GROWTH MIRACLE

Several nations, after struggling for centuries with little economic growth, have recently begun to grow at impressive rates. The best-known examples are China and India. Not as well known is the recent economic growth in Chile, a country that saw growth even under the rule of a harsh military dictator.

From 1985 to 2016, the growth of real per capita GDP in Chile averaged 3.7%. The rule of 70 (see Chapter 24) tells us that it takes approximately 19 years to double living standards at that rate. In fact, real GDP for Chile rose from just $7,000 per person to over $21,000 per person in the 31 years from 1985 to 2016. You can see this increase in the real per capita GDP shown in panel (a) of Figure 25.10. This is quite a change from Chile's past experience. Chile grew by less than 1% a year from 1900 to 1985.

FIGURE 25.10

Economic Growth and Life Expectancy in Chile

Institutional reforms in Chile have led to historic economic growth, which has helped the people of Chile in many ways. One clear improvement is the increase in life expectancy.

Source: (a) Angus Maddison, *Statistics on World Population, GDP and Per Capita GDP, 1–2008 AD*. All figures converted to 2010 dollars. (b) Gapminder.org.

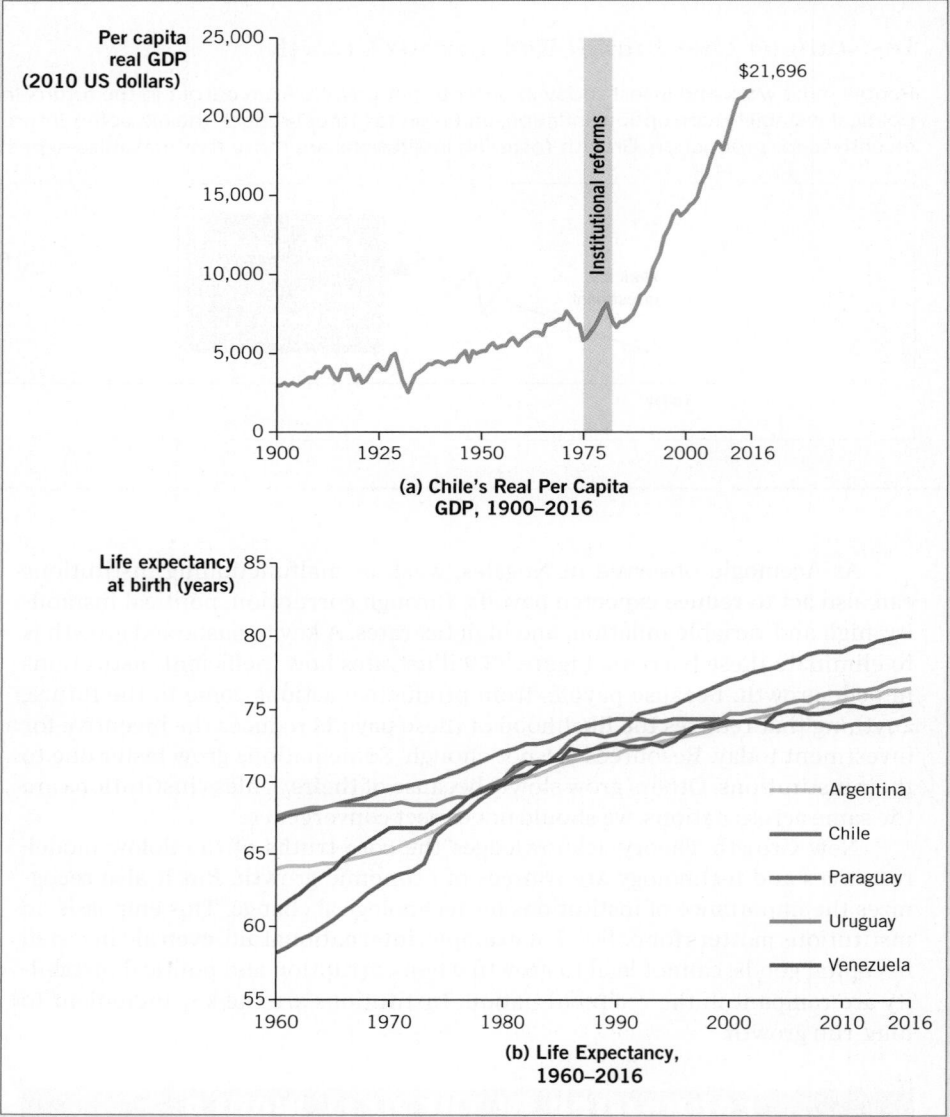

(a) Chile's Real Per Capita GDP, 1900–2016

(b) Life Expectancy, 1960–2016

As we have seen, economic growth means many lives change for the better. One vivid indicator of these changes is life expectancy. Panel (b) of Figure 25.10 shows that life expectancy in Chile increased from 58 years in 1960 to 80 years by 2016. This increase of 22 years in average life span moved Chile ahead of many of its Latin American neighbors.

What is the cause of Chile's growth? In a word—institutions. In 1975, Chile began significant economic reforms. In addition to lowering trade barriers and instituting monetary and price stability (inflation was 665% in 1974), the government privatized many state-owned businesses and removed controls on wages and prices. These reforms were put in place during the regime of a particularly brutal dictator, Augusto Pinochet. While nobody today endorses Pinochet's methods, the results of the institutional changes are still striking.

Chile's recent growth is as breathtaking as the view of Santiago, its capital city.

PRACTICE WHAT YOU KNOW

Solow Growth Theory versus New Growth Theory: What Policy Is Implied?

QUESTION: Below is a list of policy proposals advanced to help the economies of developing nations. Determine whether each proposal is consistent with the Solow model, New Growth Theory, neither, or both.

a. unrestricted international aid to help build a power plant

b. aid for a power plant, dependent on democratic reforms

c. reductions in trade restrictions

ANSWER:

a. This policy proposal is consistent with the Solow model: capital leads to growth.

b. This policy proposal is consistent with both Solow and New Growth Theory. The power plant is capital, but the aid is dependent on institutional reform.

c. This policy proposal is consistent with New Growth Theory. Open trade is an institutional reform that leads to greater competition and more options for citizens in developing nations.

This cargo ship brings goods from Asia to the United States. Which growth model would encourage this kind of international trade?

Institutions of Growth: Applying for a Patent

- Patent laws create incentives for innovation.
- If you have a patentable idea, you can sell it to others.

Patricia Bath is a medical doctor who also invented the laserphaco probe, a device that uses lasers to remove cataracts. Patented by Dr. Bath in 1988, the probe revolutionized cataract surgery. Inventions like this are technological innovations that, as we have seen, are a source of economic growth.

Patent laws are an important institution that has helped to pave the way for many technological advancements. Patents create a 20-year monopoly for the inventor or owner of the patent. This monopoly is an incentive that encourages innovation. Patent laws are thus an institution that encourages new inventions that shift the economy's production function upward.

If you have an idea that you'd like to patent, you need to apply for your patent through the U.S. Patent Office. In addition to a detailed description of your patent, you'll need to create a drawing that specifies exactly how your idea is new and different. Finally, it is a good idea to hire a patent attorney to edit your patent application so you can reduce the chances that someone will copy your idea later.

Even if you don't have the resources to capitalize on your invention, you can always try to sell your patent to someone who can.

You may not be as successful as Patricia Bath, but you can be sure that patents are a legal way to make monopoly profit.

Patricia Bath is a doctor and inventor.

So, you see, patents are a socially beneficial arrangement, both for those who come up with new ideas and for those whose lives will be improved.

Conclusion

We opened this chapter with the misconception that physical capital is the essential ingredient for economic growth. We have seen that while capital is helpful, physical tools are not enough to ensure long-run growth. Without institutions that provide incentives to produce, sustained growth does not take root.

Many people think macroeconomics is all about business cycles and recessions. Our goal in this chapter has been to present the ideas behind long-run growth theory, rather than short-run cycles. In Chapter 26, we present a model that economists use to study short-run business cycles. ✳

· ANSWERING *the* BIG QUESTIONS ·

How do macroeconomic theories evolve?

- Macroeconomic theories evolve in relationship to observations in the real world. Policies often follow from theory. Policies produce results, which in turn influence revisions of economic theory.

What is the Solow growth model?

- The Solow growth model is a model of economic growth based on a production function for the economy.
- The key feature of the production function is diminishing returns.
- The Solow growth model posits that diminishing returns lead economies toward a zero-growth steady state.
- The Solow growth model further posits that given steady states, economies tend to converge over time.

How does technology affect growth?

- Technology is a source of sustained economic growth.
- In the Solow model, technology is exogenous.

Why are institutions the key to economic growth?

- New Growth Theory emphasizes that institutions are the key source of economic growth.
- Institutions determine incentives for production.
- Efficient institutions can lead to endogenous growth.

Concepts You Should Know

aggregate production function
(p. 801)
convergence (p. 807)
depreciation (p. 807)

diminishing marginal product (p. 803)
endogenous growth (p. 815)
exogenous growth (p. 812)
marginal product (p. 803)

net investment (p. 807)
New Growth Theory (p. 815)
production function (p. 800)
steady state (p. 806)

Questions for Review

1. Modern economic theory points to three sources of economic growth. What are these three sources? Give an example of each.

2. About 50 years ago, Robert Solow formulated a simple model of economic growth. What are the two key properties of the aggregate production function at the center of Solow's first contribution?

3. Explain why a nation cannot continue to grow forever by just adding more capital.

4. The Solow model assumes that technological changes are exogenous. What does the term "exogenous" mean? Why does the assumption of exogenous technological change matter for growth policy? What does this assumption imply about growth rates across nations over time?

5. China is a land of vast resources. In addition, technology is easily transportable across international borders. If we rule out these two sources of growth, to what can we attribute the economic growth in China since 1979?

6. The basic Solow growth model implies convergence. What is convergence? What key assumption about the marginal product of capital implies convergence?

7. How can an increase in educational opportunities increase growth? Use a graph to illustrate how educational opportunities affect a nation's production function.

8. Robert Solow formulated a model that still serves as the basis for growth theory.

   a. What is the steady state of an economy, and what key piece of the Solow model implies that the steady state is an inevitable outcome?

   b. Explain the concept of convergence in growth theory. What has been the general experience with regard to convergence across the globe in the years since the Solow papers were published?

9. New Growth Theory uses the basic Solow production function as a starting point, but the emphasis is much different.

   a. What is the key theoretical distinction between New Growth Theory and the Solow growth model?

   b. How does this one difference affect policy recommendations?

10. Explain why the lack of economic growth in North Korea is best understood in the context of New Growth Theory, rather than the Solow model.

11. Diminishing marginal productivity is a key assumption in growth theory, beginning with Solow's model. Name the two important implications of this assumption in the Solow model.

Study Problems (∗ solved at the end of the section)

1. The Solow model focuses on how resources affect output. In this chapter, we focused on capital.

   a. Name the other two major categories of resources.

   b. Draw an aggregate production function with a typical shape; label this function F.

   c. Draw a second production function that indicates a technological advancement; label this new function F_1.

2. Define human capital. Draw a graph that illustrates an increase in effective labor on a production function.

3. Suppose the people in the United States increase their savings rate. How will this change affect the rate of economic growth in the United States?

✳ **4.** The Solow model is still at the core of New Growth Theory.

   a. Draw an aggregate production function for a hypothetical nation. Draw the production function as we do in this chapter, with an emphasis on the capital resource. Label both axes and label your production function F_0.

   b. Suppose several million new workers enter the nation. Show this change on your graph in part (a), carefully distinguishing the new situation from the old. If you have a new production function, label it F_1.

   c. Now suppose the nation invests in new capital, increasing the total capital stock in the nation. Show this change on your graph in part (b), carefully distinguishing the new situation from the old.

✳ **5.** The following list describes policy proposals advanced to help the economies of developing nations. Determine whether each proposal is consistent with the Solow model, New Growth Theory, both, or neither.

   a. microfinance (very small short-term loans for small businesses)
   b. a system of private property rights
   c. international governmental loans to build a shoe factory
   d. international aid for a power plant based on objective corruption controls
   e. unrestricted international aid to build roads
   f. low tax rates

6. Robinson Crusoe is alone on an island. His GDP is the fish he produces using fishing poles (capital). The table below shows how his weekly fish output varies across different numbers of fishing poles.

Fishing poles	Fish per week	MPK
0	0	____
1	30	____
2	40	____
3	48	____

   a. Fill in the blanks in the third column with the marginal product of capital for all units for which this is computable.

   b. Assume Crusoe reaches a steady state at 2 fishing poles. Describe the investment, if any, that Crusoe undertakes once he has 2 fishing poles, assuming no technological changes. Be careful with your terminology here.

   c. Suppose Crusoe, through new ideas, is able to increase his output by 2% per week. How many weeks will it take for Crusoe to increase his output from 40 fish per week to 80 fish per week?

7. The aggregate production function is at the very center of growth theory.

   a. Plot an aggregate production function with its typical shape. Be sure to label both axes. Label this function F_0.

   b. Suppose we discover massive new oil reserves under central Virginia. On the graph you drew in part (a), show how this oil discovery changes the production function. Label the new production function F_1.

Solved Problems

4.a. The key here is to label the graph correctly and have a declining slope.

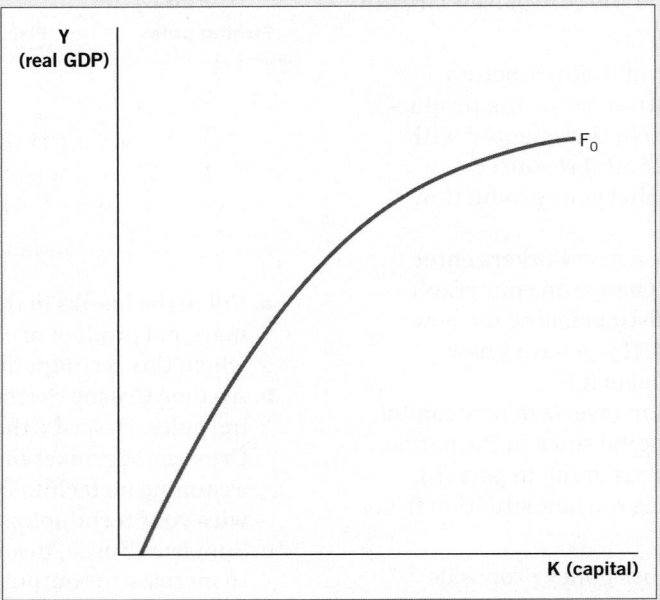

b. The key here is to shift the graph upward. More workers mean more total output because the nation now has more resources.

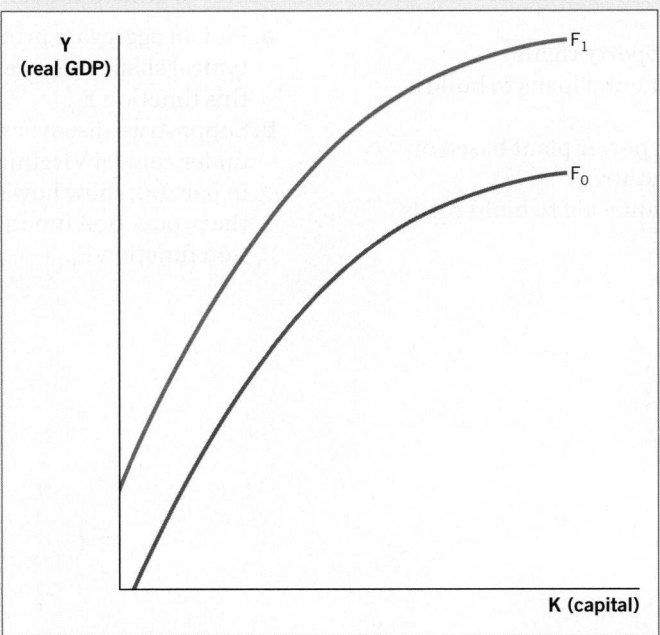

c. The key here is that there is a movement along a given production function, from K_0 to K_1.

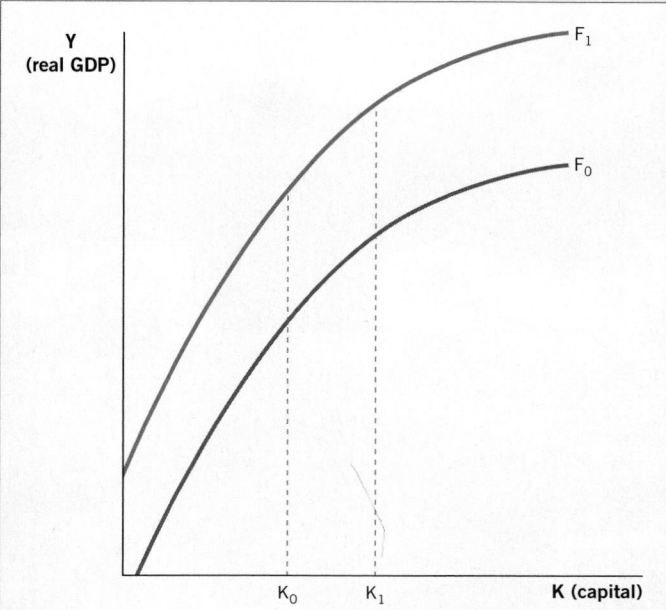

5.a. New Growth Theory or else neither (either answer is defensible): Microfinance loans might help small businesses, and it is possible that the introduction of microfinance could be considered an institutional change. However, if other political and economic institutions are not conducive to growth, microfinance will not be enough.

b. New Growth Theory: Private property rights are an institution shown to foster growth but would not have been relevant before institutions were incorporated into New Growth Theory.

c. Solow: Loans for capital development are a direct policy proposal from the Solow growth model.

d. Both: Here the focus is on capital *along with* institutional changes.

e. Solow: Here the emphasis is solely on capital.

f. New Growth Theory: Low tax rates are an institution focused on growth.

The Aggregate Demand–Aggregate Supply Model

The Economy Does Not Follow a Predictable Cycle of Expansion and Contraction.

Many people believe that the economy goes through a normal and almost predictable cycle, where every few years a recession inevitably arrives, and then the economy moves into an expansionary period for a while before the next recession arrives. Many consider this pattern to be inevitable and even consistent with recessions happening every six to eight years. The term "business cycle" is a popular way to describe the recession-expansion phenomenon, because so many people are convinced that the recession-expansion pattern occurs in a regular cycle.

But in fact, recessions are rarer today than at any other time in our nation's history: while there have been 22 U.S. recessions since 1900, just three have occurred since 1982. In addition, no two recessions are exactly alike in cause or effect. Recessions are certainly painful, as unemployment rises and incomes fall. But thankfully, they are rarer now than ever before.

If your interest in macroeconomics stems from a desire to learn more about recessions and their causes, this is the chapter for you. Chapters 24 and 25 focused on long-run economic growth. In this chapter and the next, we focus

Palm trees and snow—who could resist that combination? In a recession, it turns out, lots of people. Construction of new homes in this Riverside, California, neighborhood sat stalled in February 2009, due to lack of demand. The Great Recession hit this and other communities particularly hard. Housing prices plummeted by 42% over the two years preceding this photo, as the Riverside unemployment rate jumped from under 5% in 2006 to over 14% by 2009.

on short-run fluctuations in the macroeconomy. We begin by building a model of the economy that we can use to consider the causes of business-cycle fluctuations. In the next chapter, we examine historical events in the context of the model and also consider some of the major debates in macroeconomics, which can be framed in terms of our short-run model.

· BIG QUESTIONS ·

- What is the aggregate demand–aggregate supply model?
- What is aggregate demand?
- What is aggregate supply?
- How does the aggregate demand–aggregate supply model help us understand the economy?

What Is the Aggregate Demand–Aggregate Supply Model?

In macroeconomics, there are two major paths of study. One direction explores long-run growth and development. The second direction examines short-run fluctuations, or business cycles. The two paths are complementary: both study GDP growth, employment, and the people, firms, and governments that impact the economy. But they are certainly distinct: growth economics focuses on theories and policies that affect economic progress over several decades, whereas business cycle theory typically focuses on time horizons of five years or less.

In Chapter 19, we presented the idea of a basic business cycle, in which real GDP increases for a while during the expansionary phase and then decreases during the contractionary, or recessionary, phase. The business cycle is most evident in real GDP growth and unemployment rates. During recessions, real GDP growth slows and the unemployment rate rises. During expansions, real GDP growth expands and the unemployment rate falls.

Panel (a) of Figure 26.1 shows real GDP growth rates by quarter for the United States from 1990 to 2019. The blue vertical bars indicate three recessions during this period. During each recession, real GDP growth slowed and even turned negative. The fourth quarter of 2008 registered −8.9% growth, making it the worst quarter since 1958. Panel (b) plots the unemployment rate over the same period. The unemployment rate rose sharply during each of the recessions

FIGURE 26.1

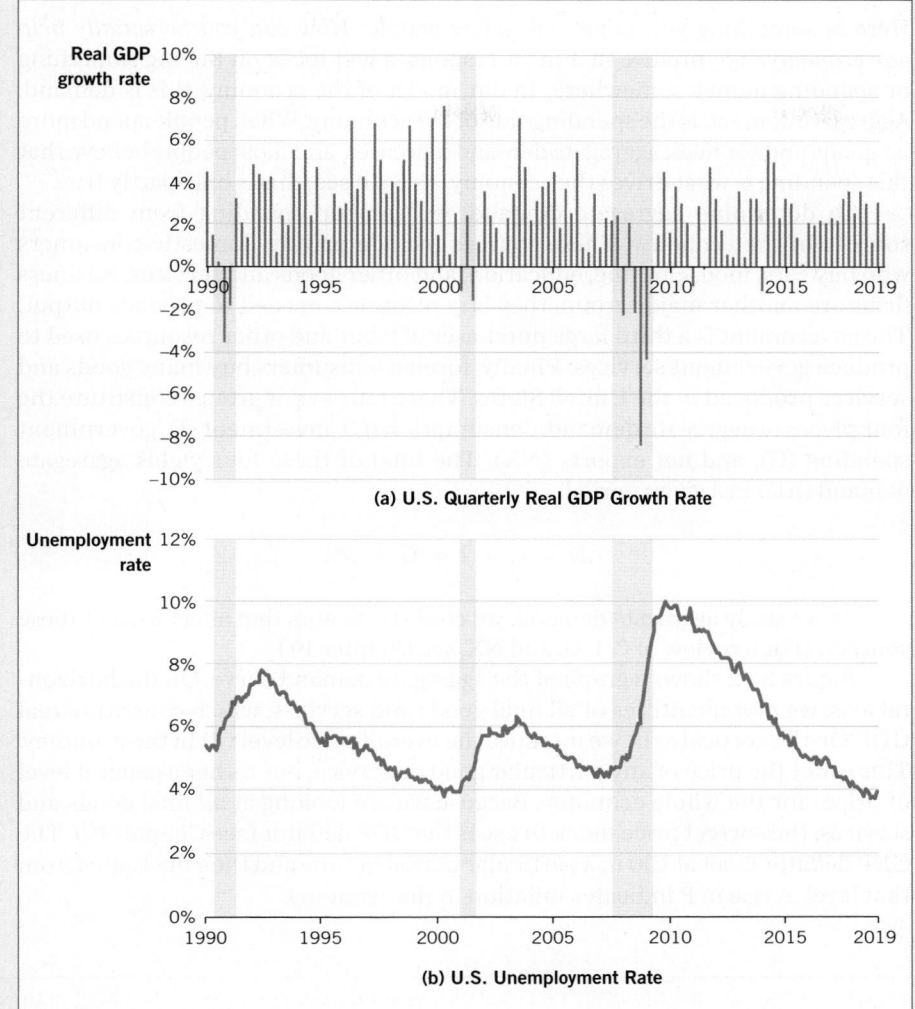

(a) U.S. Quarterly Real GDP Growth Rate

(b) U.S. Unemployment Rate

U.S. Real GDP Growth, Unemployment Rates, and Recessions, 1990–2019

Business cycles are readily observable in real GDP growth and unemployment rates. Panel (a) shows that quarterly real GDP growth often declines during recessionary periods. Panel (b) shows how the unemployment rate spikes during recessions, then gradually falls as the economy expands.

Sources: (a) U.S. Bureau of Economic Analysis; (b) U.S. Bureau of Labor Statistics.

and then slowly fell afterward. The highest unemployment rate during this period was 10% in October 2009.

The model we use to study business cycles is the aggregate demand–aggregate (AD–AS) supply model. At the core of the model are the familiar concepts of demand and supply. In earlier chapters, we looked at the demand and supply of a single good, like pizza or gasoline. Now we consider demand and supply of all final goods and services in an economy—the demand for and supply of GDP. **Aggregate demand** is the total demand for final goods and services in an economy. **Aggregate supply** is the total supply of final goods and services in an economy. The word "aggregate" means total.

We consider each side of the economy separately before bringing them together. The next section explains aggregate demand, and then we turn to aggregate supply.

Aggregate demand
is the total demand for final goods and services in an economy.

Aggregate supply
is the total supply of final goods and services in an economy.

What Is Aggregate Demand?

Here is something you might ask a few people: *How can you personally help our economy?* We predict that most responses will focus on buying something or spending money somewhere. In our model of the economy, this is demand. Aggregate demand is the spending side of the economy. When people spend more on goods and services, aggregate demand increases, and most people believe that this spending is what drives the economy. As we'll see, this is only partly true.

To determine aggregate demand, we sum up spending from different sources in the economy. These sources include private domestic consumers who buy cars, food, clothing, education, and other goods and services. Business firms are another major group; they buy resources needed to produce output. The government is a third large purchaser of labor and other resources used to produce government services. Finally, foreign consumers buy many goods and services produced in the United States. These four major groups constitute the four pieces of aggregate demand: consumption (C), investment (I), government spending (G), and net exports (NX). The total of these four yields aggregate demand (AD) in a given period:

(EQUATION 26.1)

$$AD = C + I + G + NX$$

As we study aggregate demand, we consider factors that affect each of these sources. (For a review of C, I, G, and NX, see Chapter 19.)

Figure 26.2 shows a graph of the aggregate demand curve. On the horizontal axis, we plot quantities of all final goods and services, which constitute real GDP. On the vertical axis, we measure the overall price level (P) in the economy. This is not the price of any particular good or service, but rather a general level of prices for the whole economy. Because we are looking at all final goods and services, the correct price index to use is the GDP deflator (see Chapter 19). The GDP deflator is set at 100 in a particular period of time and then fluctuates from that level. A rise in P indicates inflation in the economy.

FIGURE 26.2

The Aggregate Demand Curve

The aggregate demand curve shows the negative relationship between the quantity demanded of real GDP and the economy's price level (P).

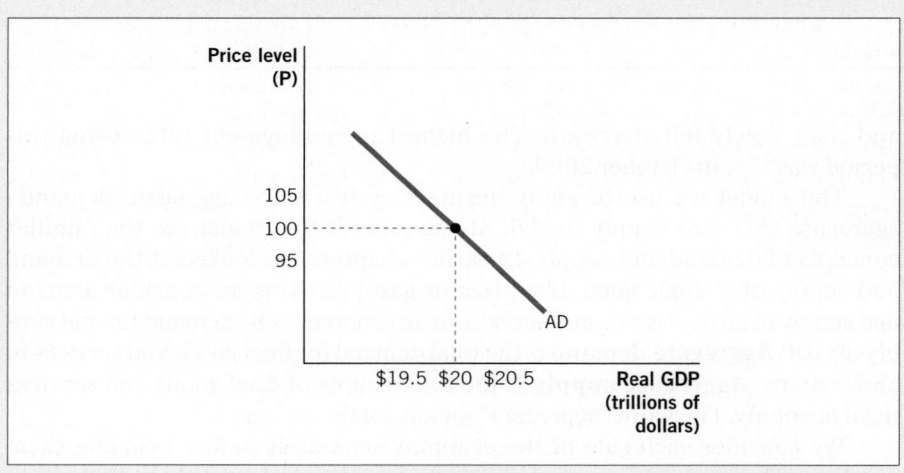

On the graph in Figure 26.2, we have labeled a particular point where the price level is 100 and the quantity of aggregate demand is $20 trillion. The negative slope of the aggregate demand curve means that increases in the price level lead to decreases in the quantity of aggregate demand. When the price level falls, the quantity of aggregate demand rises. But be careful here: aggregate demand does not slope downward for the same reason that individual demand curves slope downward. In the next section, we explain the reasons for the negative slope of the aggregate demand curve.

The Slope of the Aggregate Demand Curve

All else equal, increases in the price level lead to decreases in the quantity of aggregate demand. You might agree with this statement without closely evaluating it, because it sounds like the relationship between the quantity demanded of a single good and its price. But now we are evaluating the whole economy. Remember that the price level is the general price level of all final goods and services. Aggregate demand and aggregate supply don't just measure the quantity of pizzas demanded and supplied; they measure the production of all the firms in all the markets that constitute the economy. Therefore, substitutions from one market to another have no effect on the total amount of output, or real GDP. Substituting out of pizza and into chicken nuggets doesn't change GDP.

There are three reasons for this negative relationship between the quantity of aggregate demand and the price level: the wealth effect, the interest rate effect, and the international trade effect.

THE WEALTH EFFECT If you wake up tomorrow morning and all prices have suddenly doubled, you'll be poorer in real terms than you are today. Because your *wealth* has fallen, you'll likely consume less. **Wealth** is the net value of one's accumulated assets. Your wealth is the total net value of everything you own, including the money in your wallet and in your bank accounts. The **wealth effect** is the change in the quantity of aggregate demand that results from wealth changes due to price-level changes.

For example, if you and your friends have $60 to buy pizza, you can afford to buy four $15 pizzas. But if inflation causes the price of a pizza to rise to $20, you can afford only three pizzas. Similarly, a rise in prices all over the economy reduces real wealth in the economy, and then the quantity of aggregate demand falls. In contrast, if prices fall, real wealth increases, and then the quantity of aggregate demand also increases.

THE INTEREST RATE EFFECT If the price level rises and real wealth falls, people also save less. Therefore, in addition to the wealth effect, an increase in the price level affects people's savings. Let's say you are on a budget that allows you to buy groceries and save a little each month. If the price level rises, you'll probably cut back on both areas. When you spend less on groceries, your actions are reflecting the wealth effect. When you cut back

Wealth
is the net value of one's accumulated assets.

The **wealth effect** is the change in the quantity of aggregate demand that results from wealth changes due to price-level changes.

If you hold money as part of your wealth, the price level affects its real value.

The **interest rate effect** occurs when a change in the price level leads to a change in interest rates and therefore in the quantity of aggregate demand.

The **international trade effect** occurs when a change in the price level leads to a change in the quantity of net exports demanded.

Jeep Grand Cherokee: produced in Toledo, Ohio.

on savings, your action leads to the interest rate effect. The **interest rate effect** occurs when a change in the price level leads to a change in interest rates and therefore in the quantity of aggregate demand. Remember that every dollar borrowed requires a dollar saved. Therefore, when savings decline, the quantity of investment declines, and this is part of aggregate demand.

Figure 26.3 shows the loanable funds market before and after a decrease in savings. Initially, the demand and supply of loanable funds are indicated by curves D and S_1, and the equilibrium interest rate is 3%. If the economy's price level rises, people save less, which shifts supply to S_2. The reduction in supply leads to a higher interest rate of 4%, at which point the quantity of investment falls from I_1 to I_2. Because investment is one piece of aggregate demand, a decrease in investment decreases overall aggregate demand. Thus, a change in the price level initiates a cascade of events with the result that firms invest less at higher interest rates because individuals are saving less.

THE INTERNATIONAL TRADE EFFECT When we draw our aggregate demand curve, the price level and real GDP represent those from the domestic market—in this case the United States. In the context of the world economy, we must also consider U.S. prices *relative to* the prices from other countries. When the U.S. price level rises, all else equal, U.S. goods are relatively more expensive than goods from other countries, and the quantity demanded of U.S. goods falls. The **international trade effect** occurs when a change in the price level leads to a change in the quantity of net exports demanded.

FIGURE 26.3

The Interest Rate Effect in the Loanable Funds Market

If the economy's price level rises, people save less. The decline in savings from S_1 to S_2 leads to an increase in the interest rate from 3% to 4%. At this higher interest rate, the quantity of investment falls from I_1 to I_2 because investment is more costly. Because investment is a component of aggregate demand, a fall in equilibrium investment that occurs with a rise in price level causes the quantity of aggregate demand to fall.

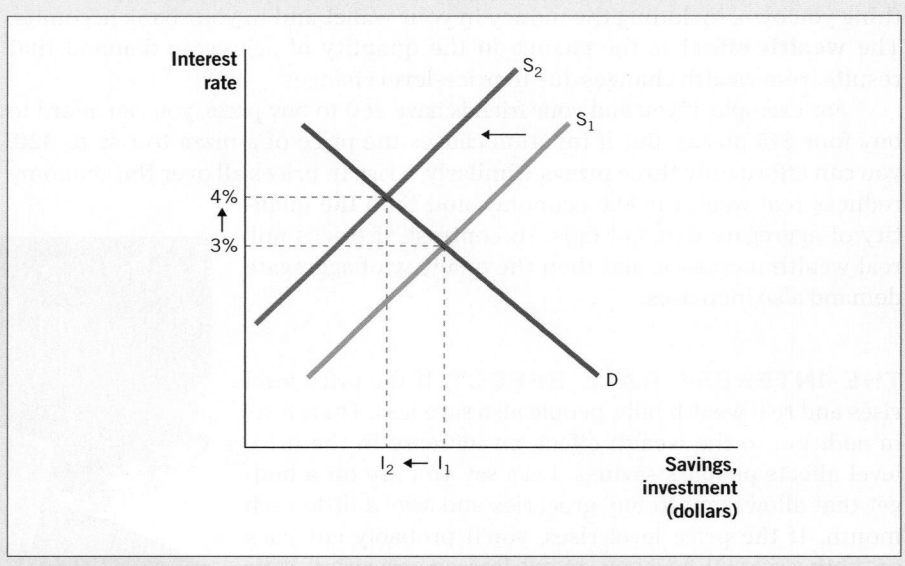

Consider two similar sport utility vehicles: a Jeep Grand Cherokee and a Toyota 4Runner. The Jeep is produced in the United States in Toledo, Ohio. The Toyota is produced in a suburb of Tahara, Aichi, Japan. When the prices of U.S. goods rise relative to the prices of Japanese goods, consumers are more likely to choose the Toyota, so U.S. exports fall and imports rise.

Toyota 4Runner: produced in Tahara, Aichi, Japan.

Figure 26.4 shows all three effects working together to affect the quantity of aggregate demand. Each begins with a change in the economy's price level. When the price level rises from 100 to 110, consumption (C) declines from the wealth effect, investment (I) declines via the interest rate effect, and net exports (NX) fall due to the international trade effect. In reality, the three effects do not influence aggregate demand equally. The international trade effect is relatively small because exports are a relatively small part of GDP. Because consumption is by far the largest component of GDP, the wealth effect is the most significant.

It is important to distinguish between *shifts in* the aggregate demand curve versus *movements along* the aggregate demand curve. In this section, we have identified three effects related to movements along the aggregate demand curve. These all originate with a change in the economy's price level. In contrast, shifts in the demand curve occur when people demand more, or fewer, goods and services at a given price level. These shifts can come from any of the components of aggregate demand: consumption, investment, government spending, or net

FIGURE 26.4

The Slope of the Aggregate Demand Curve

When the price level rises, the quantity of aggregate demand falls. This negative relationship is due to three different effects: (1) the wealth effect implies a lower quantity of consumption (C) demand because real wealth falls at higher price levels; (2) the interest rate effect implies a lower quantity of investment (I) demand due to higher interest rates; (3) the international trade effect implies a lower quantity of net export (NX) demand due to relatively higher domestic prices. Each effect focuses on a different component of aggregate demand.

(Graph: vertical axis "Price level (P)" with values 110 and 100 marked; horizontal axis "Real GDP (trillions of dollars)" with values $19 and $20 marked. A downward-sloping line labeled AD passes through the points (20, 100) and (19, 110). Arrows along the curve labeled −NX, −I, and −C.)

Median U.S. home prices fell from $248,000 to $222,000 between 2007 and 2010. That roughly 10% drop led to a significant decrease in many people's wealth, as well as a decline in aggregate demand.

exports. In the next section, we consider the factors that shift the aggregate demand curve.

Shifts in Aggregate Demand

When people demand more goods and services at all price levels, aggregate demand increases and the AD curve shifts to the right. When people demand fewer goods and services at all price levels, aggregate demand decreases and the AD curve shifts to the left.

In thinking about the many factors that shift aggregate demand, it is helpful to categorize them into the different types of aggregate demand spending: consumption (C), investment (I), government spending (G), and net exports (NX). We begin with factors that cause changes in consumption spending.

SHIFTS IN CONSUMPTION Consumption spending accounts for about 70% of all spending in GDP. In this section, we cover three factors that shift consumption spending. The first is people's current wealth. Imagine for a moment that your wealth increased overnight. If your great-aunt died and left you $1 million, you'd increase your consumption spending: you'd eat out more often, upgrade your wardrobe, and maybe even shop for some bigger-ticket items. This observation also applies to entire nations. When national wealth increases, the consumption component of aggregate demand increases. When wealth falls, consumption declines.

For example, many people own stocks or mutual funds that are tied to the stock market. So when the stock market fluctuates, the wealth of a large portion of the population is affected. When overall stock values rise, wealth increases, which increases aggregate demand. However, if the stock market falls significantly, wealth declines and aggregate demand decreases. Widespread changes in real estate values also affect wealth. Consider that for many people a house represents a large portion of their wealth. When real estate values rise and fall, individual wealth follows, and this outcome affects aggregate demand.

Before moving on, we should clarify that here we are talking about changes in individuals' wealth *not* caused by changes in the price level. When we discussed the slope of the aggregate demand curve, we talked about the wealth effect, which is caused by changes in the economy's price level (P). The wealth effect causes a *movement along* the AD curve, not a shift of the AD curve.

How much income does your future hold?

Expected future income is a second factor that shifts consumption spending. When people expect higher income in the future, they spend more today. For example, graduating college seniors often increase spending immediately after they secure a job offer, even though the job and the corresponding income are typically a few months away. We consume today based on what we anticipate for the future, even though the future is uncertain. Still, the entire economy can be affected by just a change in the general sentiment of consumers.

Perhaps you've heard of the consumer confidence (or consumer sentiment) index. This index, which uses survey data to estimate how consumers feel about the future direction of the economy, is essentially a measure of expected future

Changes in Wealth

DUMB AND DUMBER

In this comedy from 1994, two likable but incredibly simpleminded friends, Harry and Lloyd, try to return a misplaced suitcase to its owner. For most of the movie, they have no idea the suitcase is filled with a million dollars.

When they accidentally open the case while en route to Aspen, Colorado, the friends discover the cash and decide to spend the money freely by writing IOUs and placing them in the suitcase to be repaid later. The newfound money creates a change in Harry and Lloyd's wealth. The two friends immediately enjoy their unexpected wealth by staying at a lavish hotel, giving away $100 bills as tips for the staff, and even using money to wipe their noses when they can't find ordinary tissues to do the job.

In one sense, Harry and Lloyd are much like the rest of us. If our wealth increases, our demand for goods and

What kind of tuxedo would you buy if you had a suitcase full of money?

services increases (via the wealth effect). But Harry and Lloyd are dumb and dumber in that their spending is completely based on someone else's wealth.

income. Confidence, or lack of confidence, in the economy's future changes consumer spending today. Consumer confidence can swing up and down with unpredictable events such as national elections or international turmoil. When these sentiments change, they change consumption spending and shift the aggregate demand curve.

Finally, taxes also affect consumption spending. When consumers pay lower taxes, they can afford to spend more. When taxes rise, consumers have less to spend. In Chapter 29, we cover the effect of taxes on consumption in greater detail. For now, we note that higher taxes lead to lower consumption and lower aggregate demand.

SHIFTS IN INVESTMENT In this section, we consider four factors that shift investment demand. Investment shifts when decision-makers at firms decide to increase or decrease spending on capital goods. One possibility is that business firm confidence changes. Keep in mind that in macroeconomics, business firms are the investors, when they spend on plant and equipment used in future production. When firms decide that the future of their industry or the overall economy is positive, they might decide to purchase tools to increase production and future profits. On the other hand, decreases in business firm confidence lead to decreases in investment and decreases in aggregate demand.

Interest rates also shift investment demand. An increase in interest rates makes investment more expensive for firms, decreasing aggregate demand. In contrast, lower interest rates decrease the cost of borrowing for firms and increase the investment component of aggregate demand. While we typically focus on investment effects from interest rate changes, consumption is also affected by changes in interest rates. At lower interest rates, the return to savings falls and so consumers are more likely to spend their income.

Increases in the quantity of money in an economy also increase aggregate demand through investment. All else equal, more money leads to lower interest rates in the economy. Lower interest rates then mean that firms can borrow

PRACTICE WHAT YOU KNOW

Textile workers in Nicaragua depend on the export economy as a source of jobs.

Aggregate Demand: Shifts in Aggregate Demand versus Movements along the Aggregate Demand Curve

One of the challenges in applying the aggregate demand–aggregate supply model is distinguishing shifts in aggregate demand from movements along the aggregate demand curve. Here we present four scenarios.

QUESTION: Does each scenario below cause a movement along the curve or a shift in the curve? Explain your response each time.

1. Consumers read positive economic news and then expect strong future economic growth.
2. Due to an increase in the price level in the United States, consumers substitute out of clothes made in the United States and into clothes made in Nicaragua.
3. Several European economies go into recession.
4. A decrease in the price level leads to greater real wealth and more savings, which reduces the interest rate and increases investment.

ANSWERS:

1. This scenario involves an increase in expected future income, which increases aggregate demand and causes a positive (rightward) shift in the curve.
2. This scenario begins with a change in the price level, so we know it will involve a movement along the curve. Here the price level rises, so it is a movement back along the curve, signaling a decrease in the quantity of aggregate demand.
3. Foreign recession leads to lower foreign income and wealth, an outcome that decreases the demand for goods and services made in the United States. Less demand for U.S. products causes a decrease in aggregate demand in the United States, leading to a negative (leftward) shift in the aggregate demand curve.
4. Because this scenario involves a change in the price level, it will lead to a movement along the aggregate demand curve. In this case, the lower prices lead to the interest rate effect and an increase in the quantity of aggregate demand.

more cheaply. As a result, investment demand expands. On the other hand, if the money supply decreases, interest rates rise and investment demand falls. This relationship between money and aggregate demand is sometimes more complicated than explained here. For this reason, Chapter 31 is devoted to the effects of money changes on the economy.

SHIFTS IN GOVERNMENT SPENDING Government spending is the third category of aggregate demand, and the piece that policymakers influence most directly. For example, when federal or state governments increase spending to build a new highway, aggregate demand increases. When government spending falls, aggregate demand decreases. Often, these changes are a result of policy decisions made in direct response to economic conditions. For example, if consumption and investment spending fall, the government may increase spending to counteract the decline in aggregate demand. Chapter 29 covers this topic more extensively.

SHIFTS IN NET EXPORTS The fourth and final piece of aggregate demand is net exports. This category of demand shifts in response to changes in foreign income and the value of the U.S. dollar.

When the income of people in foreign nations grows, their demand for U.S. goods increases. The result is an increase in U.S. net exports, which are the final component of aggregate demand. In contrast, if a foreign nation goes into recession, its demand for U.S. goods and services falls. One recent positive example is the growth of large emerging economies and their demand for U.S. goods. As Brazil, China, and India have grown wealthier, their demand for U.S. goods and services has increased.

Exchange rates are another factor that shifts aggregate demand by changing net exports. We cover exchange rates fully in Chapter 33. For now, think in terms of the value of the dollar in world markets. When the value of the dollar rises relative to the currency of other nations, Americans find that imports are less expensive. At the same time, it becomes more expensive for other nations to buy U.S. exports. These two factors combine to reduce net exports, so a stronger dollar leads to a decline in net exports, which reduces aggregate demand.

Figure 26.5 summarizes the effects of the four categories of factors that shift aggregate demand. On the graph, initial aggregate demand is shown as AD_1. Aggregate demand shifts to the right (to AD_2) with *increases* in consumption, investment, government spending, or net exports. In contrast, aggregate demand shifts to the left (to AD_3) with *decreases* in consumption, investment, government spending, or net exports.

What Is Aggregate Supply?

We have seen that aggregate demand embodies the spending desires of an economy. It tells us how many goods and services people want to buy at different price levels. But peoples' wants and desires alone do not determine GDP. We must also consider the supply side of the economy, which tells us about the willingness and ability of producers to supply GDP.

FIGURE 26.5

Factors That Shift the Aggregate Demand Curve

The aggregate demand curve shifts to the right with *increases* in real wealth, expected future income, business firm confidence, the quantity of money, government spending, and foreign income, or with a *decrease* in taxes, interest rates, and the value of the dollar. The aggregate demand curve shifts to the left with *decreases* in real wealth, expected future income, business firm confidence, the quantity of money, government spending, and foreign income, or with an *increase* in taxes, interest rates, and the value of the dollar.

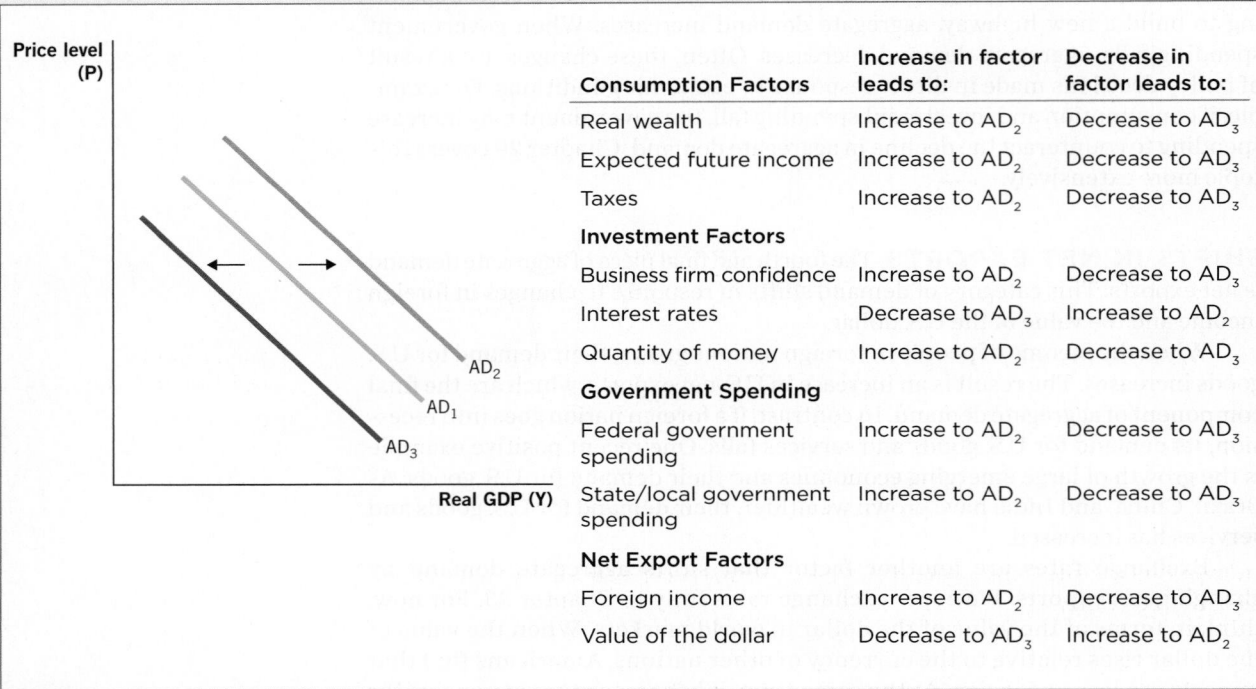

	Increase in factor leads to:	Decrease in factor leads to:
Consumption Factors		
Real wealth	Increase to AD_2	Decrease to AD_3
Expected future income	Increase to AD_2	Decrease to AD_3
Taxes	Increase to AD_2	Decrease to AD_3
Investment Factors		
Business firm confidence	Increase to AD_2	Decrease to AD_3
Interest rates	Decrease to AD_3	Increase to AD_2
Quantity of money	Increase to AD_2	Decrease to AD_3
Government Spending		
Federal government spending	Increase to AD_2	Decrease to AD_3
State/local government spending	Increase to AD_2	Decrease to AD_3
Net Export Factors		
Foreign income	Increase to AD_2	Decrease to AD_3
Value of the dollar	Decrease to AD_3	Increase to AD_2

Most of us relate easily to the demand side because we buy things all the time. To understand the supply side, we need to consider the perspective of those who produce and sell goods and services. For example, imagine you own a coffee shop where you produce drinks such as espressos, lattes, and iced coffee. Your inputs include workers, coffee beans, milk, water, and espresso machines. You buy inputs and combine them in a particular way to produce your output.

Figure 26.6 presents an overview of the basic function of the firm. In the middle is the firm, where inputs are turned into output. The input prices, such as wages and interest rates on loans, help determine the firm's costs. The output prices, such as the cost of an espresso, determine the firm's revenue.

To understand aggregate supply, we need to consider how changes in the overall price level (P) affect the supply decisions of the firm. But the influence of the price level on aggregate supply depends on the time frame. The **long run** in macroeconomics is a period of time sufficient for all prices to adjust. The long run doesn't arrive after a set period of time; it arrives when all prices have adjusted. In the **short run**, some prices change but others take more time.

In macroeconomics, the **long run** is a period of time sufficient for all prices to adjust.

In macroeconomics, the **short run** is the period of time in which some prices have not yet adjusted.

FIGURE 26.6

The Function of the Firm

The firm uses inputs, or factors of production, to produce its output in a particular way. Input prices, such as wages for workers, affect the firm's costs. Output prices affect the firm's revenue.

Inputs
- Labor
- Capital
- Raw materials

Input prices
- Wages
- Interest rates
- Etc.

Firm

Output
- Goods and Services

Output prices
- Set by firm or market

In macroeconomics, the short run is the period of time in which some prices have not yet adjusted.

Long-Run Aggregate Supply

As we've discussed several times in this text, the long-run output of an economy depends on resources, technology, and institutions. The short run may bring fluctuations in real GDP, but in the long run the economy moves toward full-employment output (Y^*). The price level does not affect long-run aggregate supply. Think of it this way: in the long run, the number of paper dollars we exchange for our goods and services does not affect our ability to produce.

Figure 26.7 plots the economy's long-run aggregate supply curve (LRAS). Notice that since we plot LRAS with the economy's price level (P) on the vertical axis and real GDP (Y) on the horizontal axis, long-run aggregate supply is a vertical line at Y^*, which is full-employment output. In Chapter 20, we defined full-employment output as the output produced in the economy when unemployment (u) is at the natural rate (u^*). This is the output level sustainable for the long run in the economy. Because prices don't affect full-employment output, the LRAS curve is a vertical line at Y^*. If the price level is 100, the quantity of aggregate supply is equal to Y^*. If the price level rises to 110 or falls to 90, output in the long run is still Y^*.

SHIFTS IN LONG-RUN AGGREGATE SUPPLY The long-run aggregate supply curve shifts when there is a long-run change in a nation's ability

FIGURE 26.7

The Long-Run Aggregate Supply Curve

The LRAS curve is vertical at Y^* because in the long run the price level does not affect the quantity of aggregate supply. Y^* is full-employment output, where the unemployment rate (u) is equal to the natural rate (u^*).

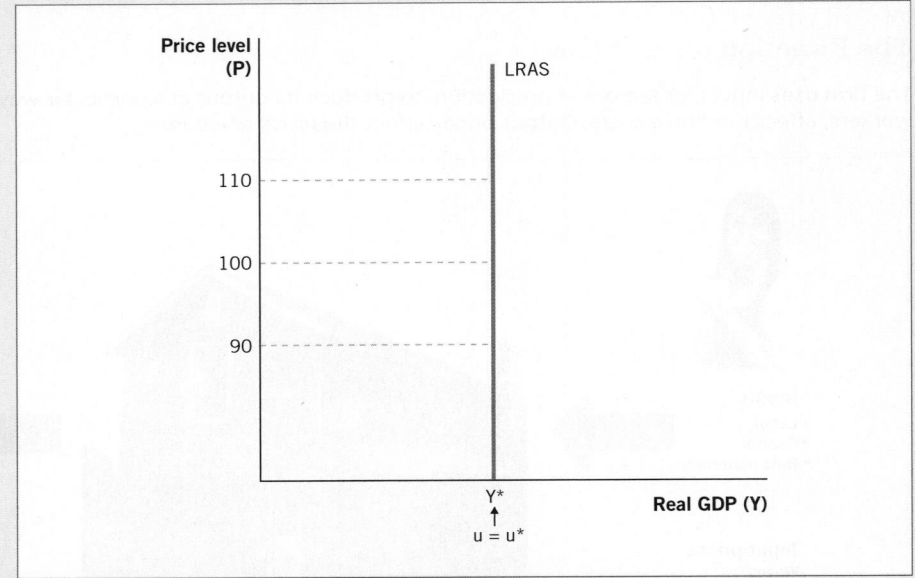

to produce output, or a change in Y^*. The factors that shift long-run aggregate supply are the same factors that determine economic growth: resources, technology, and institutions.

For example, new technology leads to increases in long-run aggregate supply. Consider what happens if driverless cars enable people to travel more quickly and free up congestion on the roads. This new technology will lead to an increase in long-run aggregate supply because it increases productivity in the economy: we can produce more with our limited resources.

Figure 26.8 illustrates a shift in long-run aggregate supply. Initially, the LRAS curve is vertical at Y^*, which depends on resources, technology, and institutions. After the new driverless technology is introduced, $LRAS_1$ shifts to the right (to $LRAS_2$) because now the full-employment output in the economy is greater than before. Notice that both before and after the shift, the unemployment rate is at the natural rate (u^*). The new technology does not reduce the unemployment rate, but workers in the economy are more productive. The new output rate, Y^{**}, is designated with two asterisks because it represents a new full-employment output rate.

In previous chapters, we have used other models to illustrate economic growth by shifting out the economy's production possibilities frontier (PPF) or shifting up the aggregate production function. We illustrate economic growth in the AD–AS model using the long-run aggregate supply curve. As the economy grows over time, full-employment output increases, shifting the LRAS curve to the right. But $LRAS_1$ can also shift to the left (to $LRAS_3$). This shift could occur with a permanent decline in the economy's resources or with the adoption of inefficient

If driverless cars improve traffic conditions and allow people to enjoy work or leisure during their commute, the economy's LRAS curve shifts to the right.

FIGURE 26.8

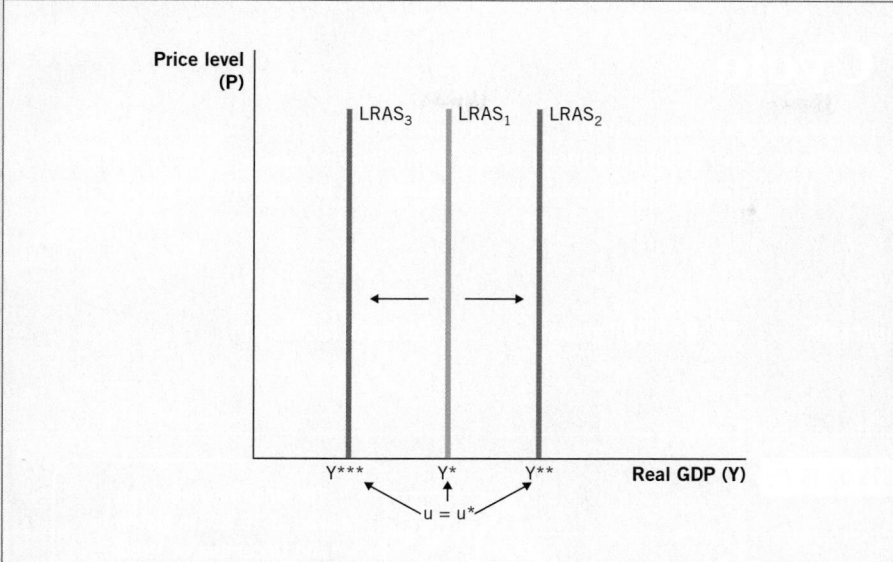

Shifts in the long-run aggregate supply curve occur when there is a change in an economy's resources, technology, or institutions. A technological advance moves an economy from $LRAS_1$ to $LRAS_2$. This is a picture of economic growth. When the LRAS curve shifts to the right, this shift also indicates a change in the economy's full-employment output level from Y^* to Y^{**}. The unemployment rate does not change, but workers are more productive.

institutions. For example, if political instability leads to the overthrow of the government of a nation, LRAS shifts to the left.

Short-Run Aggregate Supply

We just saw that the price level does not affect aggregate supply in the long run. However, in the short run there is a positive relationship between the price level and the quantity of aggregate supply. We consider three reasons for this relationship: inflexible input prices, menu costs, and money illusion.

First, consider input prices. One common input price is worker's wages, and these do not adjust quickly. For example, at your coffee shop, you pay the baristas a particular wage, and this wage is set for a period of time. In addition, interest rates for your business loans are normally fixed. Economists say these input prices are *sticky*, because they "stick" at a certain level and take time to change. In contrast, output prices (like the price of the coffee beverages) are more flexible. Whereas input prices are often set by written contract, output prices are generally easy to change. In a neighborhood coffee shop, prices are often written on a chalkboard, making them very easy to change from day to day.

The distinction between sticky input prices and flexible output prices is at the center of our discussion of aggregate supply, because it affects the way firms react when prices do move. Think about your coffee shop. You might negotiate one-year contracts with your workers. Your coffee bean suppliers fix their prices for a certain period as well. If inflation begins to push up all prices in the macroeconomy, you pull out your chalkboard eraser and raise the price of lattes, espressos, and mochas; these are output prices and they are flexible. But your input prices are sticky (the coffee beans still cost the same, and you have to pay

The Business Cycle

Since 1970, the U.S. economy has experienced seven recessions. These business cycle fluctuations are most visible in observations of real GDP growth and the unemployment rate. During recessions, real GDP typically falls and the unemployment rate climbs. During expansions, real GDP expands and the unemployment rate falls back toward the natural rate.

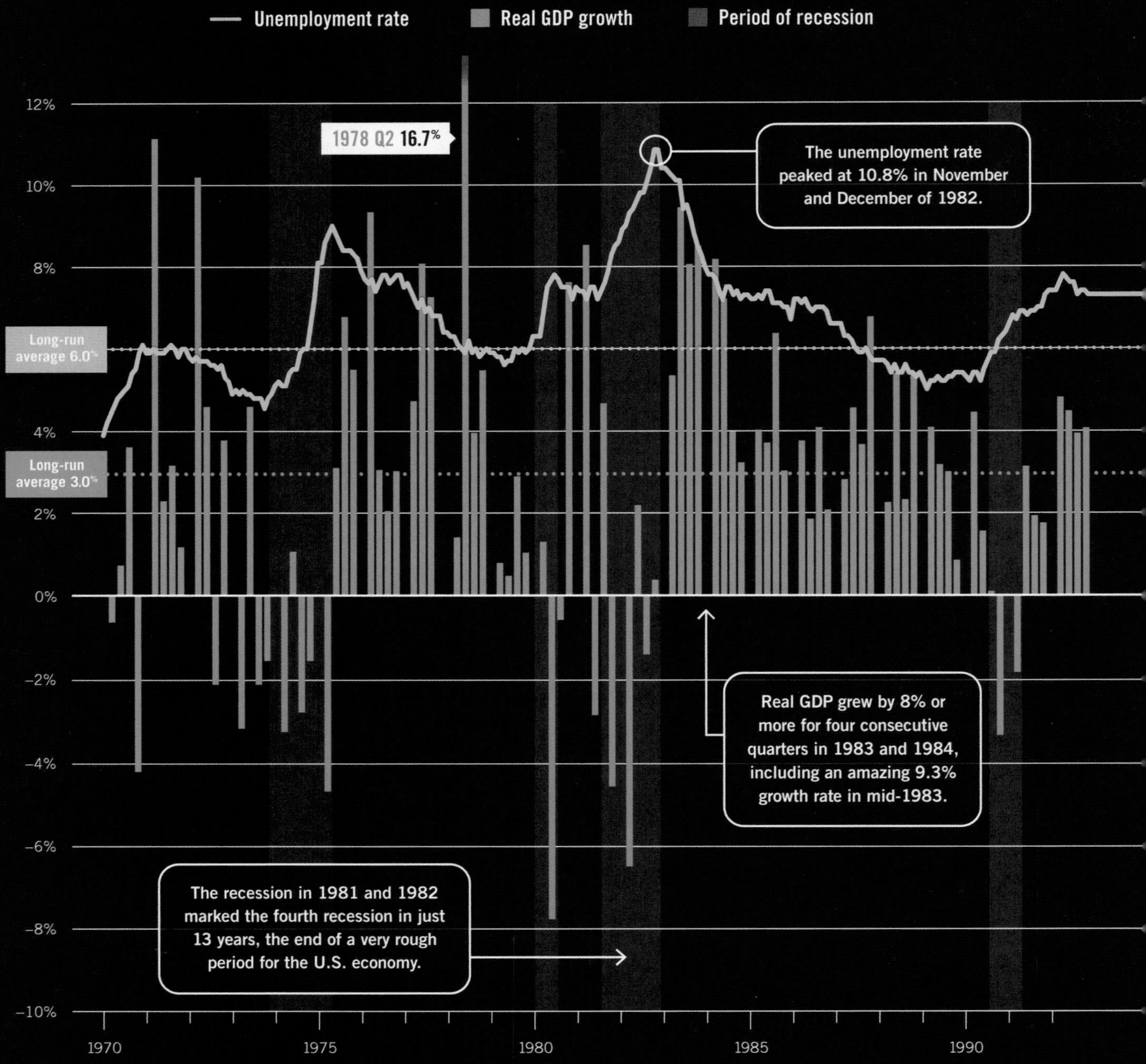

—— Unemployment rate   ▇ Real GDP growth   ▇ Period of recession

1978 Q2 **16.7%**

The unemployment rate peaked at 10.8% in November and December of 1982.

Long-run average 6.0%

Long-run average 3.0%

Real GDP grew by 8% or more for four consecutive quarters in 1983 and 1984, including an amazing 9.3% growth rate in mid-1983.

The recession in 1981 and 1982 marked the fourth recession in just 13 years, the end of a very rough period for the U.S. economy.

12%

10%

8%

6%

4%

2%

0%

-2%

-4%

-6%

-8%

-10%

1970   1975   1980   1985   1990

- Looking at the year immediately following each recession, can you determine which economic recovery was most difficult? On what do you base your answer?

- If the unemployment rate is below the natural rate, what does this imply about aggregate demand?

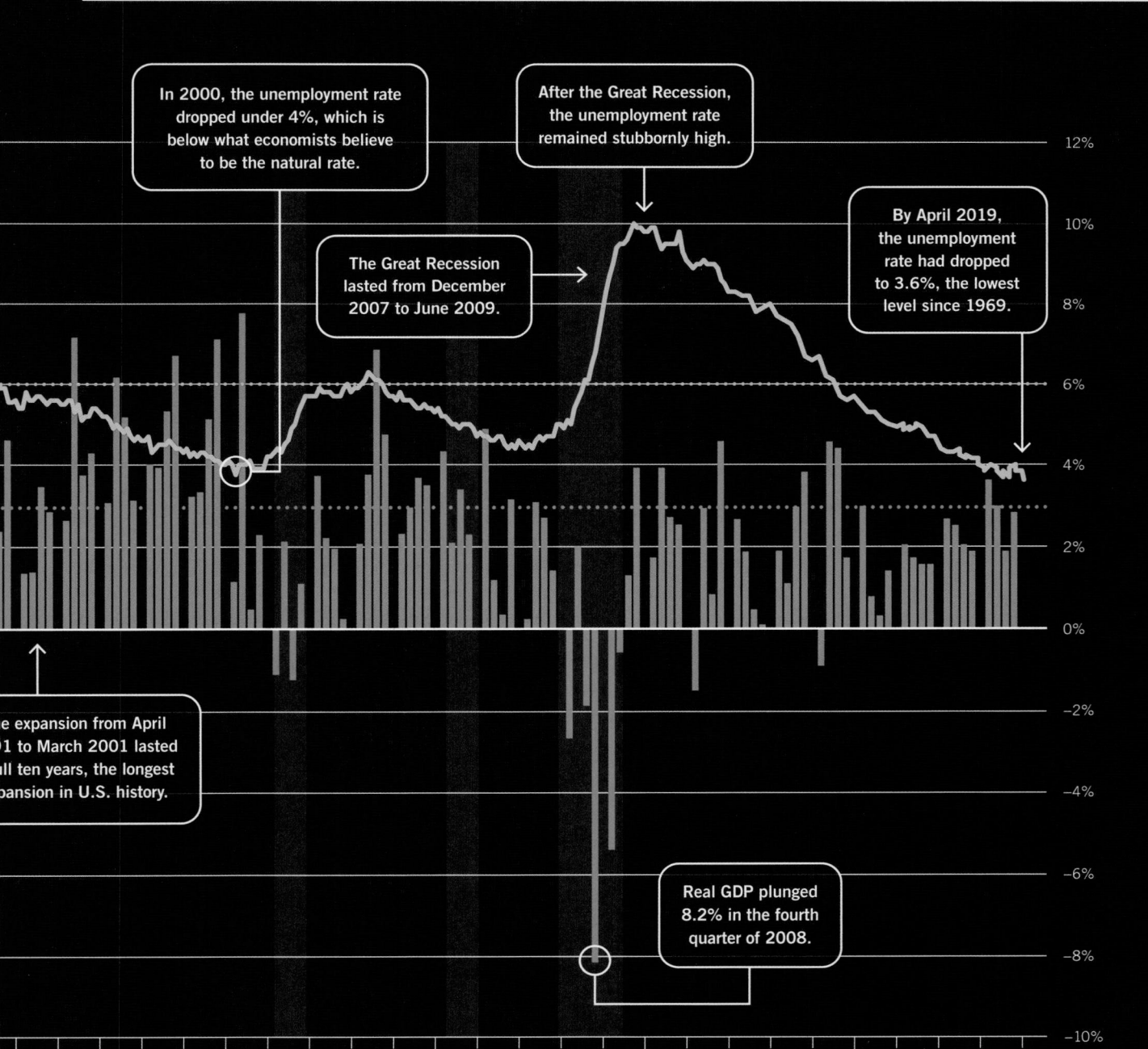

In 2000, the unemployment rate dropped under 4%, which is below what economists believe to be the natural rate.

After the Great Recession, the unemployment rate remained stubbornly high.

The Great Recession lasted from December 2007 to June 2009.

By April 2019, the unemployment rate had dropped to 3.6%, the lowest level since 1969.

e expansion from April
1 to March 2001 lasted
ll ten years, the longest
pansion in U.S. history.

Real GDP plunged 8.2% in the fourth quarter of 2008.

FIGURE 26.9

The Short-Run Aggregate Supply Curve

The positive slope of the short-run aggregate supply curve indicates that increases in the economy's price level lead to an increase in the quantity of aggregate supply in the short run. For example, if the price level rises from 100 to 110, the quantity of aggregate supply rises from $20 trillion to $21 trillion in the short run. The reason is that some prices are sticky in the short run.

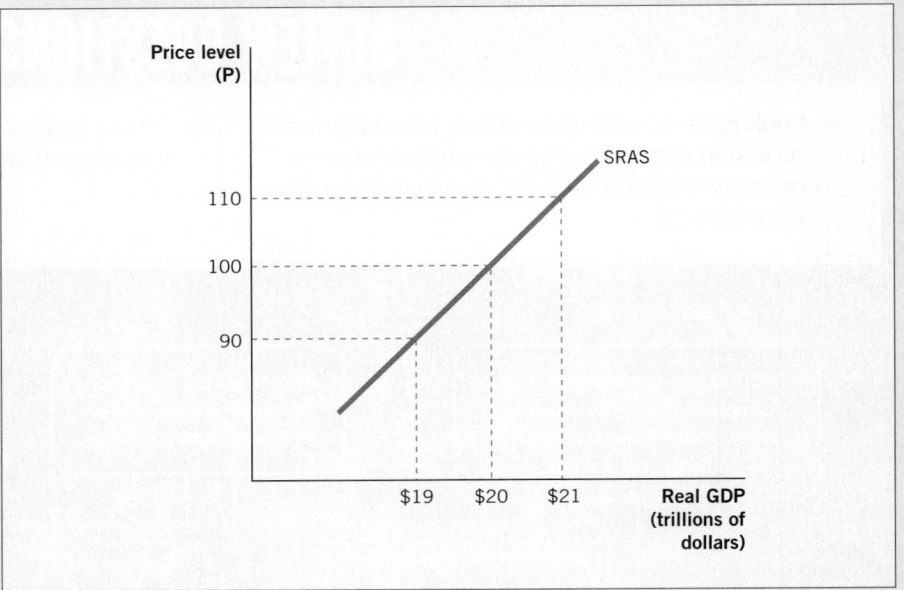

your employees the same amount)—at least for a while. Therefore, your costs remain the same. And here is the link to aggregate supply: because your costs don't rise but your revenues do, it makes sense for you to increase output. When you and other firms raise output, GDP rises.

The dynamic between sticky input prices and flexible output prices explains the positive slope of the short-run aggregate supply curve. Figure 26.9 shows the short-run aggregate supply curve, labeled as SRAS. When the price level rises from 100 to 110, firms produce more in the short run because input prices are sticky, and real GDP rises from $20 trillion to $21 trillion. When the price level falls to 90, firms produce less in the short run because flexible output prices fall but sticky input prices stay relatively high. The result is a decrease in real GDP to $19 trillion.

There are other reasons why aggregate supply might be positively related to the price level in the short run. Menu costs, which we introduced in Chapter 21, are another factor that affects short-run aggregate supply. If the general price level is rising but a firm decides not to adjust its prices because of menu costs, customers will want more of its output. If firms decide to increase output rather than print new menus, the quantity of aggregate supply increases. So again, output is positively related to the price level in the short run.

These output prices are very flexible—they can be changed with the push of a button.

We also talked about the problem of money illusion in Chapter 21. Recall that *money illusion* occurs when people interpret nominal values as real values. In terms of aggregate supply, if output prices are falling but workers are reluctant to accept nominal pay decreases, they reinforce the stickiness of input prices. If input prices don't fall with output prices, firms reduce output in response to general price-level changes.

Any type of price stickiness leads to a positively sloped aggregate supply curve in the short run. But keep in mind that since all prices can change in the long run, the long-run aggregate supply curve is vertical at the full-employment output level.

SHIFTS IN SHORT-RUN AGGREGATE SUPPLY When the long-run aggregate supply curve shifts, it signals a change that affects the economy in both the long run and the short run. Therefore, all long-run aggregate supply curve shifts (caused by changes in resources, technology, and institutions) also cause the short-run aggregate supply curve to shift. But, in addition, the short-run aggregate supply curve sometimes shifts on its own. Typically, these shifts are due to changes that directly affect firms' costs of production and form their incentives for supply.

The primary cause of shifts in short-run aggregate supply is changes in input or resource prices. Aggregate supply is the total quantity of GDP supplied by firms in the economy, as it relates to the overall price level. When input costs fall, production costs fall, and then firms produce more output at any given price level. This means short-run aggregate supply increases, or shifts to the right. The short-run aggregate supply curve exists because input prices and other prices are sticky and do not always adjust immediately when aggregate demand shifts. So when these prices do change, the short-run aggregate supply curve shifts. When input prices rise, short-run aggregate supply declines (the curve shifts to the left).

Although input prices can change for many reasons, we will cover just two main ones. The first is a change in workers' wages. Where workers are unionized, the unions engage in collective bargaining that leads to wage agreements between the workers as a group and their employers. If workers underestimated inflation in the past, this will inform their negotiations for higher wages in the future. For instance, let's say workers sign wage contracts under the assumption that inflation will be about 2% in the next year. If the inflation rate turns out to be 5% instead, the union will push for a more aggressive raise next time. This will cause the short-run aggregate supply curve to shift to the left, as input prices climb.

Along these same lines, if you are going to sign a long-term wage contract by yourself, you'll probably also form some expectation about future prices. After all, the real value of your future income depends on prices in the future. All else equal, when workers and firms expect higher prices in the future, they negotiate higher wages. The result is higher labor costs, which reduce firms' profitability and make them less willing to produce at any price level. Therefore, higher expected future prices lead to a lower aggregate supply. The process works in reverse if workers and firms expect a lower price level. Subsequent negotiations produce a labor agreement with lower wages, which reduces labor costs. When labor costs fall, additional production is more profitable at any price level, and the short-run aggregate supply curve shifts to the right.

A second cause of short-run aggregate supply shifts is *supply shocks*. Sometimes, surprise events occur that

In 2017–2018, Denmark was hit with a drought. This grain farmer in Ejby, Denmark, shows how high his crops would be at that point in a normal growing season. The effects of a nationwide drought can be significant enough to shift the short-run aggregate supply curve.

FIGURE 26.10

Price of Crude Oil

The increase in crude oil prices is an example of a negative supply shock because production costs for firms throughout the economy rise drastically.

Source: U.S. Energy Information Administration.

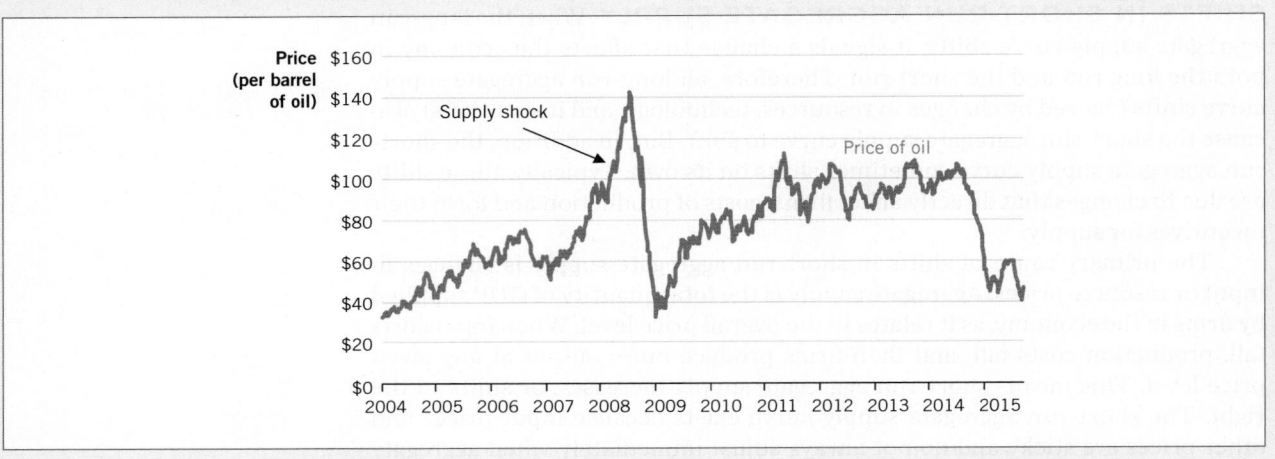

affect input prices. For example, in the summer of 2018, a drought in Denmark led to significantly lower yields of wheat, barley, and rye crops. The drought reduced total output of these crops by 40%. These crops comprise only a small portion of Danish GDP, but when these kinds of events are widespread, the effects can be felt across the macroeconomy. Surprise events that change a firm's production costs are called **supply shocks**. When supply shocks are temporary, they shift only the short-run aggregate supply curve. Supply shocks can be negative or positive. Negative supply shocks lead to higher input prices and higher production costs, shifting the short-run aggregate supply curve to the left; positive supply shocks reduce input prices and production costs, shifting the short-run aggregate supply curve to the right.

> **Supply shocks**
> are surprise events that change a firm's production costs.

A price change in an important factor of production is another supply shock. For example, from July 2007 to July 2008, oil prices in the United States doubled from $70 a barrel to over $140 a barrel. You may recall this period because gas prices rose from about $2 per gallon to more than $4 per gallon in the summer of 2008. Figure 26.10 plots the price of oil from 2004 to 2015. Oil is an important input to many production processes, so when its price doubles, a macroeconomic supply shock occurs. More recently, the drop from over $100 barrel to less than $50 in late 2014 was a positive supply shock for the macroeconomy.

Figure 26.11 shows how changes in input prices shift the short-run aggregate supply curve. Short-run aggregate supply increases (the curve shifts to the right to $SRAS_2$) when resource prices fall. This could occur when negotiation leads to lower worker wages or when there is a positive supply shock. Short-run aggregate supply decreases (the curve shifts to the left to $SRAS_3$) when resource prices rise. This happens when workers negotiate higher wages or when negative supply shocks increase resource prices.

FIGURE 26.11

How Changes in Input Prices Shift the Short-Run Aggregate Supply Curve

The short-run aggregate supply curve shifts to the right (from $SRAS_1$ to $SRAS_2$) when resource prices fall. This could occur when negotiations lead to lower wages or when there is a positive supply shock. The curve shifts to the left (from $SRAS_1$ to $SRAS_3$) when resource prices rise. This happens when workers negotiate higher wages or when negative supply shocks increase resource prices.

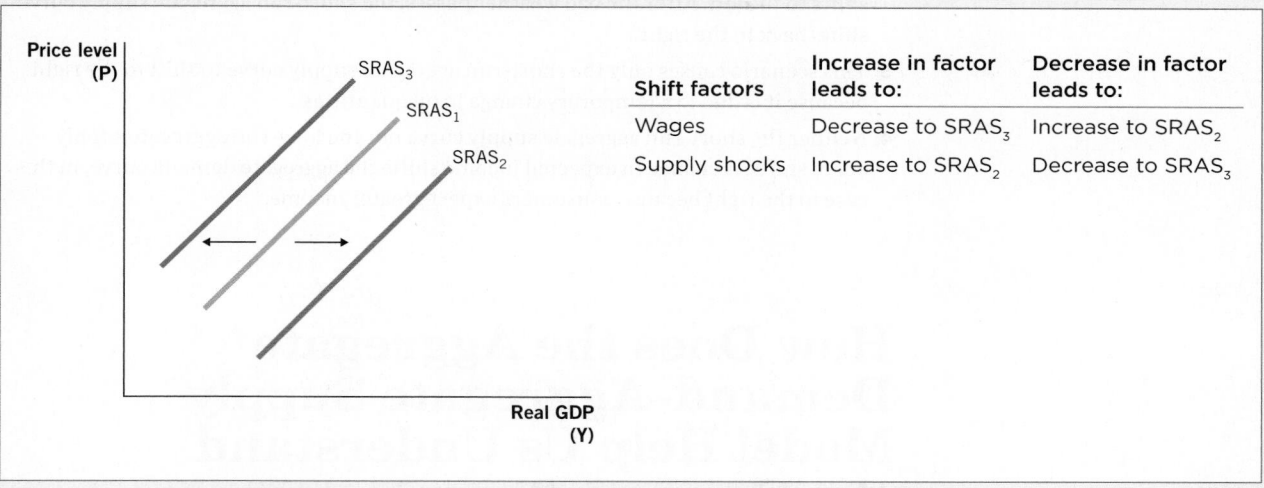

Shift factors	Increase in factor leads to:	Decrease in factor leads to:
Wages	Decrease to $SRAS_3$	Increase to $SRAS_2$
Supply shocks	Increase to $SRAS_2$	Decrease to $SRAS_3$

PRACTICE WHAT YOU KNOW

Long-Run Aggregate Supply and Short-Run Aggregate Supply: Which Curve Shifts?

In the real world, change is typical. In our aggregate demand–aggregate supply model, change means the curves shift. To use the model, you must know which curve shifts, and in which direction, when real-world events occur.

QUESTION: In each of the scenarios listed below, determine whether there is a shift in the long-run aggregate supply curve, the short-run aggregate supply curve, both, or neither. Explain your answer each time.

1. New shale gas deposits are found in North Dakota.
2. Hot weather leads to lower crop yields in the Midwest.
3. The Organization of Petroleum Exporting Countries (OPEC) meets and agrees to increase world oil output, leading to lower oil prices for six months.
4. U.S. consumers expect greater income in 2021.

This oil rig sits atop the Bakken shale formation in North Dakota, where vast new shale gas resources have been discovered.

ANSWERS:

1. This scenario leads to an increase in both long-run aggregate supply and short-run aggregate supply. The shale gas discovery represents new resources, which shifts the long-run aggregate supply curve to the right. In addition, every shift in the long-run aggregate supply curve affects the short-run aggregate supply curve.

2. The lower crop yields are temporary, so only the short-run aggregate supply curve shifts to the left. After the bad weather passes, the short-run aggregate supply curve shifts back to the right.

3. This scenario causes only the short-run aggregate supply curve to shift to the right because it is due to a temporary change in oil quantities.

4. Neither the short-run aggregate supply curve nor the long-run aggregate supply curve shifts. A change in expected income shifts the aggregate demand curve, in this case to the right because consumers expect greater income.

How Does the Aggregate Demand–Aggregate Supply Model Help Us Understand the Economy?

In a market economy, output is determined by exchanges between buyers and sellers, which are represented in our model by aggregate demand and aggregate supply. In this section, we bring aggregate demand and aggregate supply together and also consider how changes in the economy affect real GDP, unemployment, and the price level. As we are about to see, the economy tends to move to the point at which aggregate demand and aggregate supply are equal.

Equilibrium in the Aggregate Demand–Aggregate Supply Model

Figure 26.12 plots the aggregate demand and the aggregate supply curves on the same axes. The point where they intersect, A, is the equilibrium point where the opposing forces of supply and demand are balanced. At point A, the price level is P^* and the output level is Y^*. Prices naturally adjust to move the economy toward this equilibrium point.

To understand why the economy tends toward equilibrium at price level P^*, consider other possible price levels. For example, at price level P_H, which is higher than P^*, aggregate supply is greater than aggregate demand. Here, firms produce more than consumers desire at current prices. Therefore, prices naturally begin to fall to eliminate a potential surplus of goods and services. As prices fall, the quantity of aggregate demand increases and the economy moves toward a new equilibrium at P^*.

In contrast, if the price level is P_L, which is lower than P^*, aggregate demand exceeds aggregate supply. At P_L, buyers desire more than producers are willing to supply. Because aggregate demand exceeds aggregate supply, prices rise and the price level moves toward P^*. The only price level where the plans

FIGURE 26.12

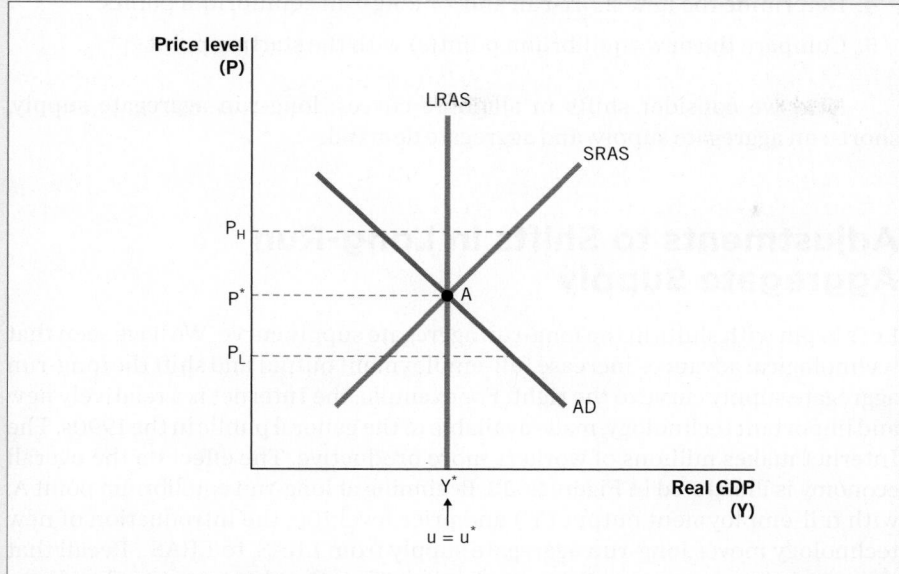

Equilibrium in the Aggregate Demand–Aggregate Supply Model

Forces in the economy naturally move it toward equilibrium at point A, where aggregate supply equals aggregate demand, $P = P^*$, $Y = Y^*$, and $u = u^*$. At P_H, aggregate supply exceeds aggregate demand, which puts downward pressure on prices and moves the economy toward equilibrium at P^*. At P_L, where aggregate demand exceeds aggregate supply, upward pressure on prices moves the economy toward equilibrium at P^*.

of suppliers and demanders match is P^*. Market forces automatically push the economy to the price level where aggregate demand equals aggregate supply.

We can also describe this equilibrium in equation form. In equilibrium, both long-run and short-run aggregate supply are equal to aggregate demand:

$$LRAS = SRAS = AD$$

(EQUATION 26.2)

Aggregate supply is the real GDP produced, which we indicate as Y. Aggregate demand derives from four components: C, I, G, and NX. Therefore, we can rewrite equation 26.2 as:

$$Y = C + I + G + NX$$

(EQUATION 26.3)

Now we know what equilibrium looks like in our model. Equation 26.3 is our reference point for thinking about the economy at a particular point in time.

But the real world brings constant change: everything from technology to weather to wealth and expectations can change. Now that we've built our model of the macroeconomy, we can use it to examine how real-world changes affect the economy.

In what follows, both in this chapter and for the remainder of the book, we consider many real-world factors that lead to changes in the macroeconomy. When we consider a change, we follow a particular sequence of steps to the new equilibrium. Once we determine the new equilibrium, we can assess the effects of the change on real GDP, unemployment, and the price level. The five steps are as follows:

1. Begin with the model in long-run equilibrium.
2. Determine which curve(s) are affected by the change(s), and identify the direction(s) of the change(s).

3. Shift the curve(s) in the appropriate direction(s).

4. Determine the new short-run and/or long-run equilibrium points.

5. Compare the new equilibrium point(s) with the starting point.

Next we consider shifts in all three curves: long-run aggregate supply, short-run aggregate supply, and aggregate demand.

Adjustments to Shifts in Long-Run Aggregate Supply

Let's begin with shifts in the long-run aggregate supply curve. We have seen that technological advances increase full-employment output and shift the long-run aggregate supply curve to the right. For example, the Internet is a relatively new and important technology, made available to the general public in the 1990s. The Internet makes millions of workers more productive. The effect on the overall economy is illustrated in Figure 26.13. Beginning at long-run equilibrium point A, with full-employment output (Y^*) and price level 100, the introduction of new technology moves long-run aggregate supply from $LRAS_1$ to $LRAS_2$. Recall that changes in long-run aggregate supply also affect the short run, so the short-run aggregate supply shifts from $SRAS_1$ to $SRAS_2$. Assuming this technological change is the only change in the economy, we move to long-run equilibrium at point B. Notice that at point B the economy has a new full-employment output level at Y^{**}.

All else equal, technological progress leads to more output and a lower price level, which drops from 100 to 95. Before the Internet, the unemployment

FIGURE 26.13

How Long-Run Aggregate Supply Shifts Affect the Economy

Beginning at long-run equilibrium point A, the price level is 100 and output is at full employment (Y^*). New technology shifts long-run aggregate supply from $LRAS_1$ to $LRAS_2$ (and short-run aggregate supply from $SRAS_1$ to $SRAS_2$) because the economy can now produce more at any price level. The new long-run equilibrium is at point B, and there is now a new, higher full-employment rate of output (Y^{**}). Note that the unemployment rate (u) is equal to the natural rate (u^*) both before and after the shift.

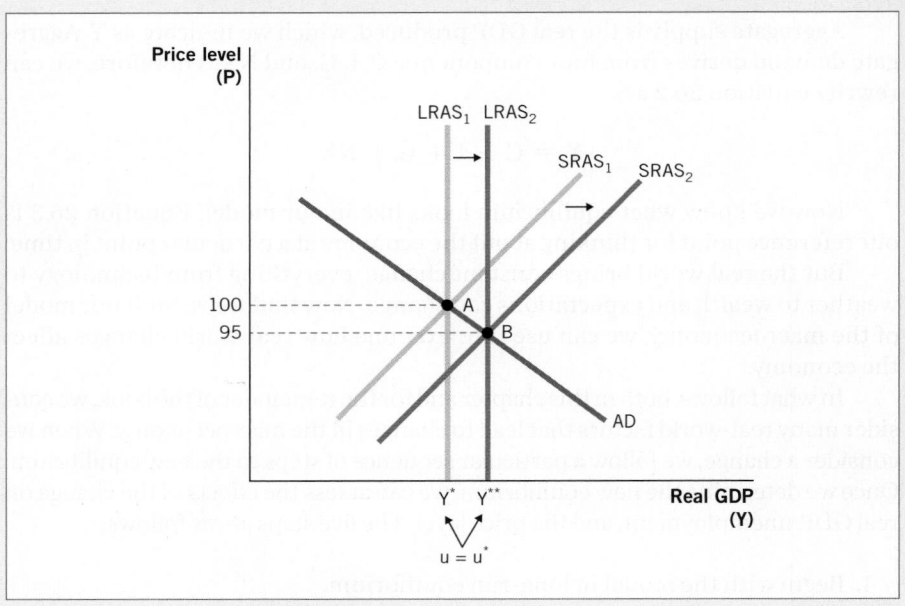

rate was at the natural rate (u*). After the new technology becomes available, employment remains at u*; but better tools mean workers can produce more output (Y** vs. Y*). This also applies to other factors that shift long-run aggregate supply to the right, such as the discovery of new resources or the introduction of new institutions favorable to growth.

Adjustments to Shifts in Short-Run Aggregate Supply

Now let's consider a change in short-run aggregate supply. One possibility is a short-run supply disruption caused by an oil pipeline break, a negative supply shock. Because oil is a widely used input, the disruption temporarily raises production costs. We show this supply shock in Figure 26.14 by shifting short-run aggregate supply to the left, from SRAS$_1$ to SRAS$_2$. The new equilibrium is at point b, with a higher price level (105) and lower level of output (Y$_1$). Because this is a short-run equilibrium, we use the lowercase b. The lower output means increased unemployment in the short run (u > u*). Notice that nothing happens to long-run aggregate supply—in the long run, the pipeline is fixed and oil is produced at full-employment output level Y* again.

Because the disruption is temporary, eventually the short-run aggregate supply curve shifts back to the right until it reaches SRAS$_1$ again. Short-run disruptions in aggregate supply do not alter long-run equilibrium in the economy; eventually, the price level, output, and unemployment rate return to their long-run equilibrium levels at point A. But in the short run, the negative shift brings higher unemployment and lower real GDP.

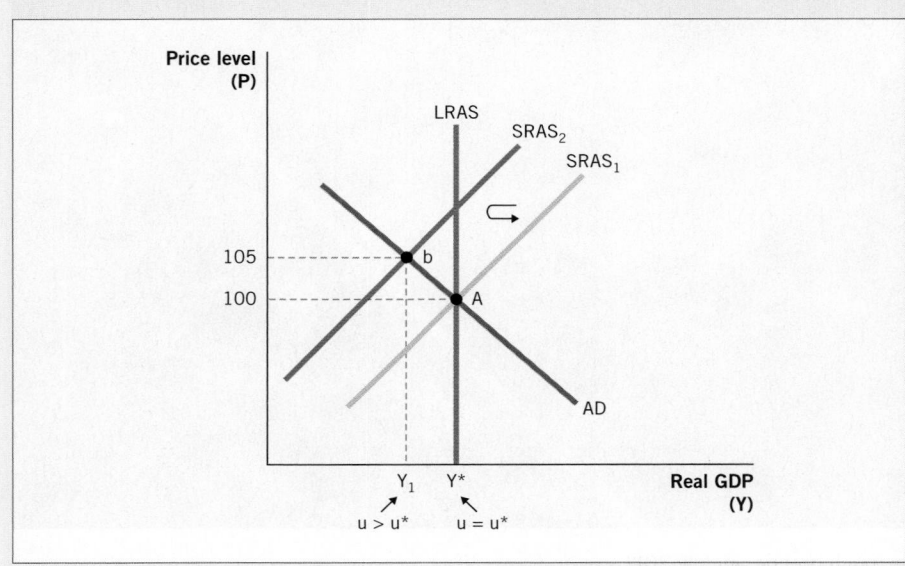

FIGURE 26.14

How Short-Run Aggregate Supply Shifts Affect the Economy

A temporary negative supply shock shifts short-run aggregate supply from SRAS$_1$ to SRAS$_2$. In the short run, the economy moves to equilibrium at point b (denoted with a lowercase letter to distinguish from long-run equilibrium). This equilibrium entails higher prices, lower real GDP, and higher unemployment. In the long run, the economy returns to equilibrium at point A.

THE DROUGHT OF 2012 LED TO MANY HIGHER PRICES

The summer of 2012 was one of the hottest on record for the United States. High temperatures led to extremely low yields in both corn and soybean crops. In fact, in 2012, each acre of corn planted in the United States yielded just 123 bushels, down from 147 bushels the year before and much lower than the 158 bushels in 2013.

Corn is one of those individual goods that also serves as an input to many other types of output, so when the price of corn rises, it takes many other prices with it. For example, corn is an important feed source for cattle. The 2012 jump in corn prices contributed to increases of more than 30% in beef and pork prices over the next few years. Corn is an ingredient in many other consumer products, as well: cereal, soda, cake mixes, candy bars, and even makeup. Thus, when corn prices rise, the prices of all these products also go up, all else equal.

The record temperatures are a classic example of a supply shock, and the result is exactly what the aggregate demand–aggregate supply model predicts: the short-run aggregate supply curve shifts to the left, leading to higher prices throughout the economy.

These Iowa fields were supposed to be much greener in July 2012.

Adjustments to Shifts in Aggregate Demand

Aggregate demand shifts for many reasons. Shifts might even occur from changes in expectations of market participants rather than from real factors in the economy, and yet even these subjective factors affect the macroeconomy. For example, consider an unexpected change in consumer confidence: consumers wake up one morning with expectations of higher future income. This then increases aggregate demand as consumers spend more. Can this kind of change have real effects on the economy? That is, will a change in consumer confidence affect unemployment and real GDP? Let's look at the model.

Figure 26.15 illustrates changes in the economy from an uptick in consumer confidence. We start in long-run equilibrium at point A, where the price level is 100, real GDP is at full-employment output Y^*, and unemployment is equal to the natural rate ($u = u^*$). More spending means aggregate demand shifts from AD_1 to AD_2, and the economy moves to short-run equilibrium at point b. The

FIGURE 26.15

How Aggregate Demand Shifts Affect the Economy

An increase in aggregate demand moves the economy from the initial equilibrium at point A to a new short-run equilibrium at point b. The positive aggregate demand shift increases real GDP and decreases unemployment in the short run ($u < u^*$). In the short run, prices adjust—but only partially, because some prices are sticky. In the long run, when all prices adjust, the short-run aggregate supply curve shifts to $SRAS_2$, and the economy moves to long-run equilibrium at point C, where $Y = Y^*$ and $u = u^*$.

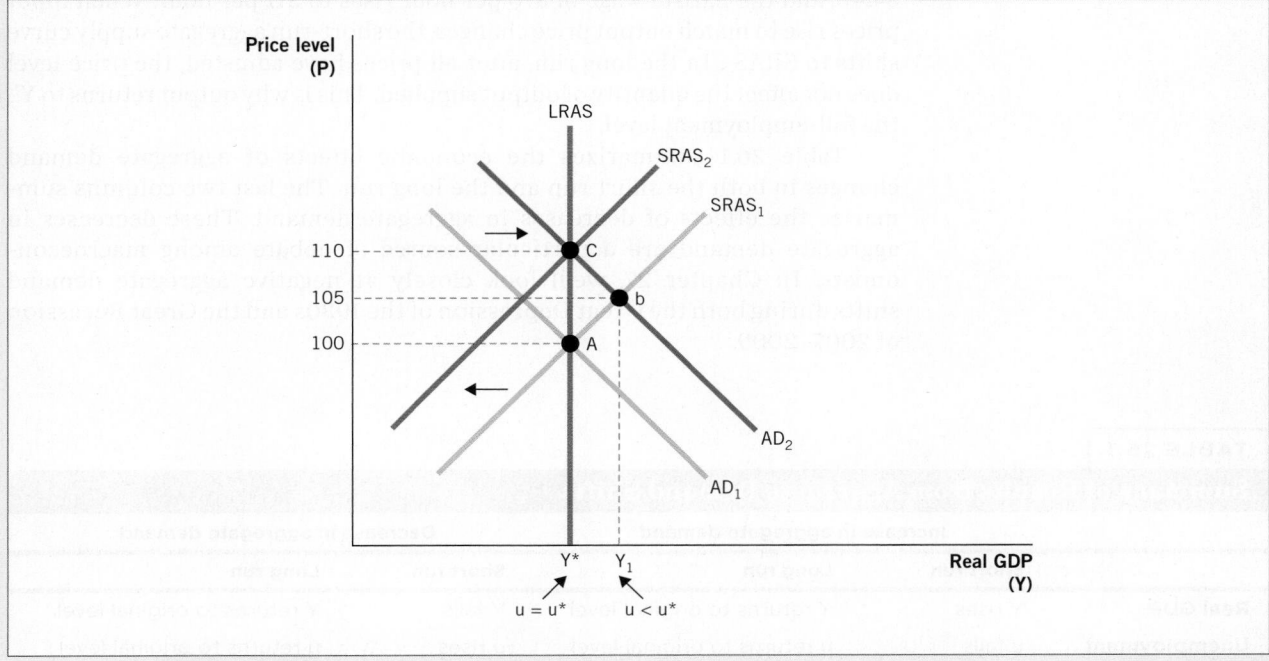

short-run equilibrium is relevant here, because in the short run some prices are sticky, so that even though there is upward pressure on prices, only some prices adjust and the price level rises to 105. But this short-run equilibrium is also associated with higher real GDP (Y_1) and an unemployment rate of u_1, which is less than the natural rate, u^*. Thus, changes in aggregate demand do affect the real economy (Y and u), at least in the short run.

Our initial results seem very positive—after all, unemployment falls and real GDP rises in the short run. But we need to complete the story by following it through to long-run equilibrium. Recall the difference between the long run and the short run: in the long run, all prices adjust. As all prices adjust, short-run aggregate supply shifts back from $SRAS_1$ to $SRAS_2$. The economy then moves to long-run equilibrium at point C. Notice that at C we are back to the original output level (Y^*) and unemployment level (u^*), but prices are higher ($P = 110$). The model is telling us that demand changes have no real effects (on Y and u) in the long run as only the price level (a nominal variable) is affected.

What are the consequences of this move to long-run equilibrium, and how does it compare with the short-run equilibrium? At point b, real GDP is up and unemployment is down. But not everyone is happy. For example, workers with sticky wages must pay more for their final goods and services, but without a wage increase in the short run.

But since all prices can adjust eventually, the economy moves to point C in the long run. Let's consider this whole episode from the view of your small business, the coffee shop. In the short run, output prices (written in chalk) can move up with other macroeconomic prices. But input prices take time to adjust. In the long run, you will renegotiate wages and all other long-term contracts. Thus, if there is a 10% increase in prices throughout the economy, both input and output prices can eventually rise by 10%. The price of a $4 latte rises to $4.40, and the barista wage of $10 per hour rises to $11 per hour. When input prices rise to match output price changes, the short-run aggregate supply curve shifts to $SRAS_2$. In the long run, after all prices have adjusted, the price level does not affect the quantity of output supplied. This is why output returns to Y^*, the full-employment level.

Table 26.1 summarizes the economic effects of aggregate demand changes in both the short run and the long run. The last two columns summarize the effects of decreases in aggregate demand. These decreases in aggregate demand are a particular source of debate among macroeconomists. In Chapter 27, we'll look closely at negative aggregate demand shifts during both the Great Depression of the 1930s and the Great Recession of 2007–2009.

TABLE 26.1

Summary of Results from Aggregate Demand Shifts

	Increase in aggregate demand		Decrease in aggregate demand	
	Short run	Long run	Short run	Long run
Real GDP	Y rises	Y returns to original level	Y falls	Y returns to original level
Unemployment	u falls	u returns to original level	u rises	u returns to original level
Price level	P rises	P rises even further	P falls	P falls even further

Using the Aggregate Demand–Aggregate Supply Model: The Japanese Earthquake and Tsunami of 2011

In 2011, a record-breaking earthquake hit Japan and was followed immediately by a tsunami. This natural disaster destroyed significant capital in Japan, including roads, buildings, and even nuclear power plants.

QUESTION: How would you use the aggregate demand–aggregate supply model to illustrate the effect of this disaster on the Japanese economy?

ANSWER: People often think natural disasters affect only short-run aggregate supply, because the effects are temporary. But if a disaster is so severe that it destroys resources, the long-run aggregate supply will also decline.

These devastating tsunami waves permanently destroyed many capital goods along part of Japan's seacoast.

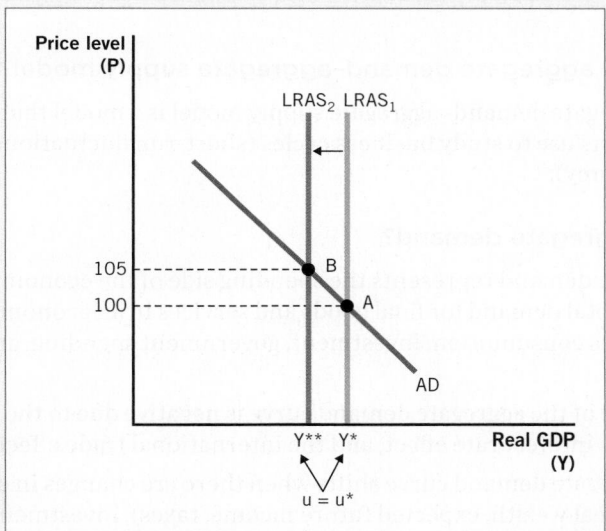

Notice that the unemployment rate (u) is equal to the natural rate (u*) both before and after the shift. Jobs remain because there is plenty of work to do in the aftermath of a natural disaster. However, in the long run Japan has fewer resources after the earthquake than it had before, and this outcome limits the nation's economic growth. Finally, the price level rises since the AD curve doesn't necessarily shift. People may change what they buy (substituting into cleanup and repair-related goods and services), but the AD curve likely stays at approximately the same level.

CHALLENGE QUESTION: What is the effect of the Japanese earthquake and tsunami on the U.S. economy?

ANSWER: Real income falls in Japan, which leads to a decline in aggregate demand for U.S. goods and services.

Conclusion

We began this chapter with the misconception that recessions are normal occurrences that happen every few years. In fact, they are anything but normal. They occur with unpredictable frequency and are caused by many different factors. Recessions in business cycles are often caused by changes in aggregate demand, but the same symptoms can also reflect short-run aggregate supply shifts.

This chapter introduced the aggregate demand–aggregate supply model of the economy, which helps us understand how changes in the real world affect the macroeconomy. In the next chapter, we use the model to evaluate the two biggest macroeconomic disturbances of the past century: the Great Depression of the 1930s and the Great Recession of 2007–2009. ✳

▪ ANSWERING *the* BIG QUESTIONS ▪

What is the aggregate demand–aggregate supply model?

- The aggregate demand–aggregate supply model is a model that economists use to study business cycles (short-run fluctuations in the economy).

What is aggregate demand?

- Aggregate demand represents the spending side of the economy. It is the total demand for final goods and services in an economy. It includes consumption, investment, government spending, and net exports.
- The slope of the aggregate demand curve is negative due to the wealth effect, the interest rate effect, and the international trade effect.
- The aggregate demand curve shifts when there are changes in consumption factors (real wealth, expected future income, taxes), investment factors (firm confidence, interest rates, the quantity of money), government spending (at the federal, state, and local levels), or net export factors (foreign income and the value of the U.S. dollar).

What is aggregate supply?

- Aggregate supply represents the producing side of the economy. It is the total supply of final goods and services in an economy.
- The long-run aggregate supply curve is relevant when all prices are flexible. This curve is vertical at full-employment output and is not influenced by the price level.

- In the short run, when some prices are sticky, the short-run aggregate supply curve is relevant. This curve indicates a positive relationship between the price level and real output supplied.

How does the aggregate demand–aggregate supply model help us understand the economy?

- We can use the aggregate demand–aggregate supply model to see how changes in either aggregate demand or aggregate supply (or both) affect real GDP, unemployment, and the price level.

Concepts You Should Know

aggregate demand (p. 831)
aggregate supply (p. 831)
interest rate effect (p. 834)

international trade effect (p. 834)
long run (p. 840)
short run (p. 840)

supply shocks (p. 848)
wealth (p. 833)
wealth effect (p. 833)

Questions for Review

1. What are three reasons the aggregate demand curve slopes downward? Name at least three factors that shift the aggregate demand curve.

2. What are three reasons the short-run aggregate supply curve slopes upward? Name at least three factors that shift the short-run aggregate supply curve.

3. How are the factors that shift the long-run aggregate supply curve different from those that shift the short-run aggregate supply curve?

4. Why is the long-run aggregate supply curve vertical?

5. How does strong economic growth in China affect aggregate demand in the United States?

6. Suppose the economy is in a recession caused by lower aggregate demand. If no policy action is taken, what will happen to the price level, output, and employment in the long run?

7. Consider two economies, both in recession. In the first economy, all workers have long-term contracts that guarantee high nominal wages for the next five years. In the second economy, all workers have annual contracts indexed to changes in the price level. Which economy will return to the natural rate of output first? Explain your response.

8. The interest rate effect can be viewed as a chain of reactions in the economy.

a. Below is the chain of reactions with some of the steps filled in. Fill in the missing steps in the chain and be sure to indicate the direction of change (using an up or down arrow).

b. What component (or piece) of aggregate demand is primarily affected by the wealth effect?

Study Problems (* solved at the end of the section)

1. Describe whether the following changes cause the short-run aggregate supply to increase, decrease, or neither.

a. The price level increases.
b. Input prices decrease.
c. Firms and workers expect the price level to fall.
d. The price level decreases.
e. New policies increase the cost of meeting government regulations.
f. The number of workers in the labor force increases.

2. Describe whether the following changes cause the long-run aggregate supply to increase, decrease, or neither.

a. The price level increases.
b. The stock of capital in the economy increases.
c. Natural resources increase.
d. The price level decreases.
e. Firms and workers expect the price level to rise.
f. The number of workers in the labor force increases.

3. On the following graph, illustrate the short-run and long-run effects of an increase in aggregate demand. Describe what happens to the price level, output, and employment.

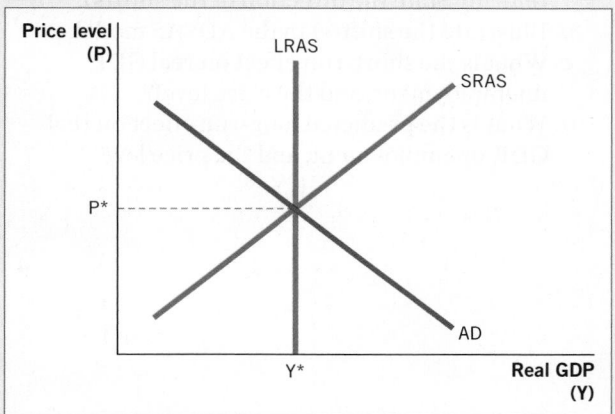

4. How does a lower price level in the United States affect the purchases of imported goods? Explain, using aggregate demand.

✳ **5.** Describe whether the following changes cause aggregate demand to increase, decrease, or neither.

   a. The price level increases.
   b. Investment decreases.
   c. Imports decrease and exports increase.
   d. The price level decreases.
   e. Consumption increases.
   f. Government purchases decrease.

✳ **6.** Suppose a sudden increase in aggregate demand moves the economy from its long-run equilibrium.

   a. Illustrate this change using the aggregate demand–aggregate supply model.
   b. What are the effects of this change in the short run and the long run?

7. In the summer of 2008, global oil prices spiked to extremely high levels before coming down again at the end of that year. This temporary event had global effects because oil is an important resource in the production of many goods and services. Focusing only on the U.S. economy, determine how this kind of event affects the price level,

unemployment rate, and real GDP in both the short run and the long run. Assume the economy was in long-run equilibrium before this change, and consider only this stated change.

✳ **8.** You work for Dr. Zhang, the autocratic dictator of Zhouland. After taking an economics course, you decide that devaluing your currency (Zhoullars) is the way to increase GDP. Following your advice, Dr. Zhang orders massive increases in the supply of Zhoullars, which reduces the value of Zhoullars in world markets. Use the AD–AS model to determine the effects on real GDP, unemployment, and the price level in Zhouland in both the short run and the long run. Assume the economy was in long-run equilibrium before this change, and consider only this stated change.

✳ **9.** Recently, the value of the U.S. dollar has been rising in world markets.

   a. Determine how the rising value of the dollar affects the U.S. price level, real GDP, and the unemployment rate in both the short run and the long run. For this part, assume these changes are unexpected by market participants.
      You can use graphs to derive your answers, but place your answers in the boxes below (using an up arrow, a down arrow, or a dash if the level is consistent). Assume the economy starts in long-run equilibrium, assume no other changes, and make all comparisons to the initial long-run equilibrium.

Short run			Long run		
P	Y	u	P	Y	u

   b. Under certain circumstances, it takes longer for the economy to adjust to long-run equilibrium following unanticipated changes. Do those circumstances apply here? Explain why or why not.
   c. If instead these changes in the value of the dollar are completely anticipated in advance, how will the results differ in the short run?

10. Let's say that in 2022 the United States experiences abnormally good weather. This weather is particularly beneficial for agricultural crop production. Determine how the run of good weather affects the U.S. real GDP, price level, and unemployment rate in both the short run and the long run.

You can use graphs to derive your answers, but place your answers in the boxes below. Assume the economy starts in long-run equilibrium, assume no other changes, and make all comparisons to the initial long-run equilibrium.

Short run			Long run		
P	Y	u	P	Y	u

11. In 2018, the U.S. government passed a tax reform bill that reduced taxes for the prior year (2017) and then also for subsequent years.

a. Which curve(s) is (are) affected by the tax reform? State the direction of the shift(s).
b. Illustrate the shift(s) in the AD–AS model.
c. What is the short-run effect on real GDP, unemployment, and the price level?
d. What is the predicted long-run effect on real GDP, unemployment, and the price level?

Solved Problems

5.a. Neither. A change in the price level (P) leads to a movement along the AD curve. When the price level rises, the quantity of aggregate demand declines along the curve.
b. Investment (I) is one component of aggregate demand, so a decrease in investment decreases aggregate demand.
c. Net exports (NX) is a component of aggregate demand. An increase in exports and a decrease in imports imply that net exports rise, so aggregate demand increases.
d. Aggregate demand neither increases nor decreases with a change in the price level (P). A change in the price level leads to movement along the AD curve. When the price level decreases, the quantity of aggregate demand increases along the curve.
e. Consumption (C) is a component of aggregate demand, so an increase in consumption means an increase in aggregate demand.
f. Government purchases (G) are a component of aggregate demand, so a decrease in government purchases causes a decrease in aggregate demand.

6.a. Aggregate demand increases from AD_1 to AD_2. In the short run, equilibrium will be at point b. In the long run, equilibrium will move to point C.

b. In the short run, real GDP rises, the unemployment rate falls, and the price level rises. In the long run, real GDP goes back to the full-employment level, the unemployment rate returns to the natural rate, and the price level rises further.

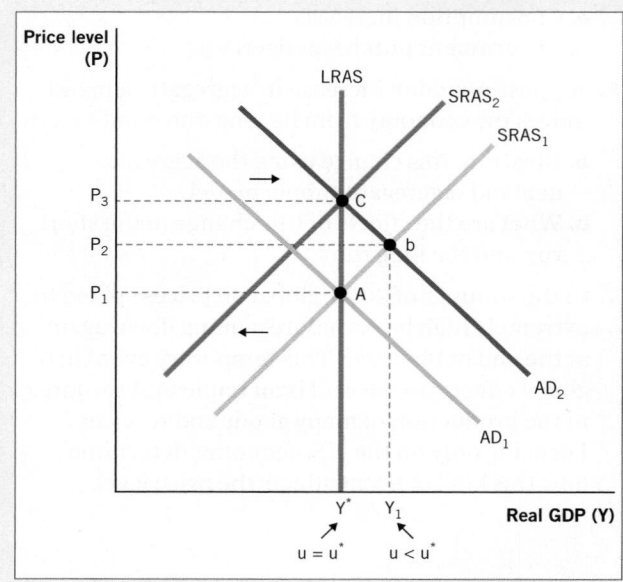

8. The reduction in the value of the Zhoullar means an increase or rightward shift in the aggregate demand curve. This change creates the same scenario pictured in the solution to problem 6; refer again to that figure.

In the short run, there is greater real GDP, lower unemployment, and a higher price level. This short-run equilibrium is pictured as point b in the figure.

In the long run, the only change is an increase in the price level (P), as indicated by the new long-run equilibrium at point C in the figure. Note that this explanation is consistent with the discussion of inflation in Chapter 22. That is, the cause of inflation is monetary expansion. When Dr. Zhang commanded that the number of Zhoullars should increase, he guaranteed that inflation would eventually arrive.

9.a. When the value of the U.S. dollar rises relative to other currencies, it means U.S. exports are relatively more expensive and imports from other nations are relatively less expensive. Therefore,

net export demand falls and AD declines. The fall in AD leads to a new short-run equilibrium with a lower price level, lower real GDP, and higher unemployment. In the long run, the price level falls further, but real GDP and the unemployment rate return to their initial levels.

Short run			Long run		
P	Y	u	P	Y	u
↓	↓	↑	↓	—	—

b. It takes longer for the economy to adjust when prices are falling (rather than rising). That situation does apply here because prices need to fall to restore the economy back to long-run equilibrium.

c. If the results are completely anticipated, then the economy goes immediately to the long-run equilibrium. That is, even in the short run, prices fall, but real GDP and the unemployment rate remain at their long-run equilibrium levels.

Recessions, Expansions, and the Debate over How to Manage Them

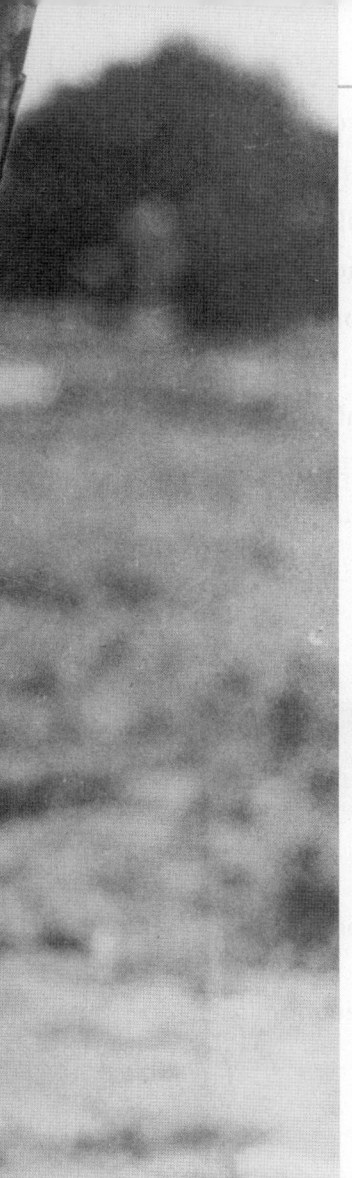

The Great Depression Was Unlike Any Recession We've Experienced Since.

The Great Depression of the 1930s gave birth to macroeconomics as a subdiscipline of economics. Previously, economists were basically microeconomists: they emphasized the interaction of supply and demand in individual markets. But the depth and duration of the Great Depression forced economists to pay more attention to economic aggregates. In 1936, the photographer Dorothea Lange documented the plight of migrant farm workers in California, thousands of whom were living in open-air camps and nearly starving. Driving north on Highway 101, Lange spotted Florence Owens tending to five of her children while her husband and the two oldest boys hiked into town to try to get the family's broken-down car fixed. Published in the *San Francisco News*, Lange's photos of Owens and her children quickly became iconic images of Americans beaten down by the hardships of the time but determined to persevere.

Although according to official statistics, the economy had started to turn the corner, people like Owens and her family still had several lean years ahead of them. The same was true elsewhere in the world, because the Great Depression was a sobering shock to the entire global economy, after the rapid industrial growth of the "Roaring Twenties."

Beside Highway 101, just outside Nipomo, CA, Florence Owens shelters with her children under a roadside lean-to. She and her husband were migrant workers, roaming the southwestern United States in search of work harvesting peas, lettuce, and cotton. When Dorothea Lange took this photo in March of 1936, Owens and her family were stranded due to car trouble.

Fortunately, we've not seen anything so severe since the Great Depression. However, recessions do still occur. In this chapter, we use our aggregate demand–aggregate supply (AD–AS) model to examine some causes of GDP stagnation and high unemployment. We also look closely at two major economic contractions: the Great Depression and the Great Recession of 2007–2009. We then consider some of the major debates about the macroeconomy. All of this sets us up for coverage of government policy responses to business cycles: fiscal policy (Chapters 28 and 29) and monetary policy (Chapters 30 and 31).

· BIG QUESTIONS ·

- Why do recessions occur?
- What happened during the Great Recession and the Great Depression?
- What are the big disagreements in macroeconomics?

Why Do Recessions Occur?

Recessions are short-term economic downturns typically characterized by declines in real GDP growth and increases in the unemployment rate. We can use our AD–AS model to examine some different causes of recessions. In this section, we first consider a decline in aggregate demand and then turn to a decline in aggregate supply.

Declines in Aggregate Demand

Aggregate demand changes in response to many different factors. In Chapter 26 we divided these into four groups: consumption factors, investment factors, government spending, and net export factors. When aggregate demand declines, the economy moves to a new equilibrium, with lower real GDP and higher unemployment. For example, if business firm confidence declines, meaning that firms are less optimistic about future economic conditions, they

FIGURE 27.1

A Demand-Induced Recession

Negative shifts in aggregate demand can move the economy into a recessionary period. In this figure, the economy is initially in long-run equilibrium at point A before a negative shift in aggregate demand, from AD_0 to AD_1. The new equilibrium at point b brings lower real GDP (Y^* falls to Y_1) and higher unemployment ($u > u^*$). This is a classic demand-induced recession.

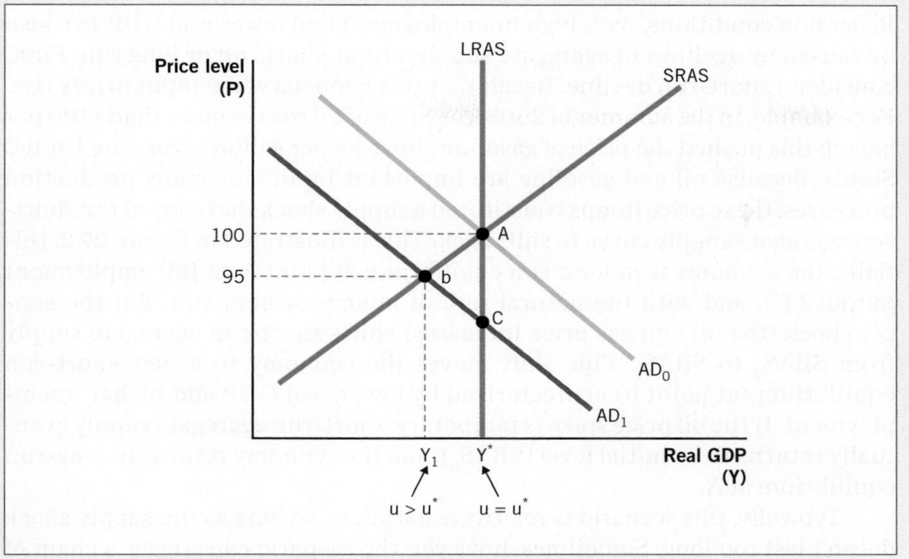

scale back their investment activity, which decreases aggregate demand. We illustrate a decline in AD in Figure 27.1. The economy is initially in long-run equilibrium at point A, with full-employment output (Y^*), unemployment at its natural rate (u^*), and the price level at 100. When aggregate demand declines from AD_0 to AD_1, the economy moves to a new, short-run equilibrium at point b. (Recall that long-run equilibria are denoted with upper-case letters, and short-run with lower case.) The short-run equilibrium is characterized by lower real GDP and a higher unemployment rate—standard recession conditions.

As we discussed in Chapter 26, if prices adjust downward in the long run, eventually the economy moves to a new long-run equilibrium at point C, with full employment output (Y^*) restored and unemployment back to the natural rate (u^*). But the short run is painful. Laid-off workers suffer from lost income, and the retail locations and factories where they worked may be shuttered, no longer generating corporate tax revenue (and instead becoming targets for vandals). To minimize these effects, elected representatives and policymakers often look for ways to help move the economy back to full employment by shifting aggregate demand back to its initial level (AD_0). Economists generally feel that periods of high unemployment are the times when demand-stimulating governmental policies are most effective. Policy options include government spending increases, tax cuts, and expansion of the money supply. (These are each discussed in the next four chapters.)

Many, if not all, recessions can be characterized by a fall in aggregate demand. Even when a decline in aggregate demand is not the initial cause, it often compounds problems, as people spend less due to drops in consumer or business firm confidence. Therefore, when GDP growth slows and unemployment starts rising, economists are quick to dig into the data on aggregate demand. Most economists believe that AD declines contributed to both the Great Depression in the 1930s and the Great Recession from 2007 to 2009, both of which we cover later in this chapter.

Declines in Aggregate Supply

Recession conditions, with high unemployment and lower real GDP, can also be caused by declines in aggregate supply, either short run or long run. First, consider a short-run decline. Recall that this happens when input prices rise. For example, in the summer of 2008, the price of oil rose to more than $100 per barrel; this pushed the price of gasoline above $4 per gallon across the United States. Because oil and gasoline are important inputs for many production processes, these price jumps constituted a supply shock that caused the short-run aggregate supply curve to shift back. This is illustrated in Figure 27.2. Initially, the economy is in long-run equilibrium at point A, at full employment output (Y^*), and with the natural rate of unemployment (u^*). But the supply shock (the oil and gas price increases) shifts short-run aggregate supply from $SRAS_0$ to $SRAS_1$. This shift moves the economy to a new short-run equilibrium (at point b) characterized by lower real GDP and higher unemployment. If the oil price spike is temporary, short-run aggregate supply eventually returns to its initial level ($SRAS_0$), and the economy returns to long-run equilibrium at A.

Typically, this scenario is relatively harmless, so long as the supply shock doesn't last too long. Sometimes, however, the scenario can trigger a chain of events that lead to a longer recession. Many economists believe that in 2008, the oil-and-gas supply shock destabilized an economy already teetering in recession, and that this is what turned a short economic downturn into the Great Recession. The macroeconomic data seem to support this hypothesis. Still, most economists see other factors as bigger contributors to the 2007–2009 recession. We discuss those other factors later in the chapter.

FIGURE 27.2

A Recession Induced by a Shift in Short-Run Aggregate Supply

Shifts in short-run aggregate supply can also bring recessionary conditions. In this figure, the economy is in long-run equilibrium at point A before short-run aggregate supply shifts back (to the left, from $SRAS_0$ to $SRAS_1$), perhaps due to a negative supply shock. The shift then moves the economy to a new short-run equilibrium at point b, where real GDP is lower ($Y_1 < Y^*$) and unemployment is higher ($u > u^*$).

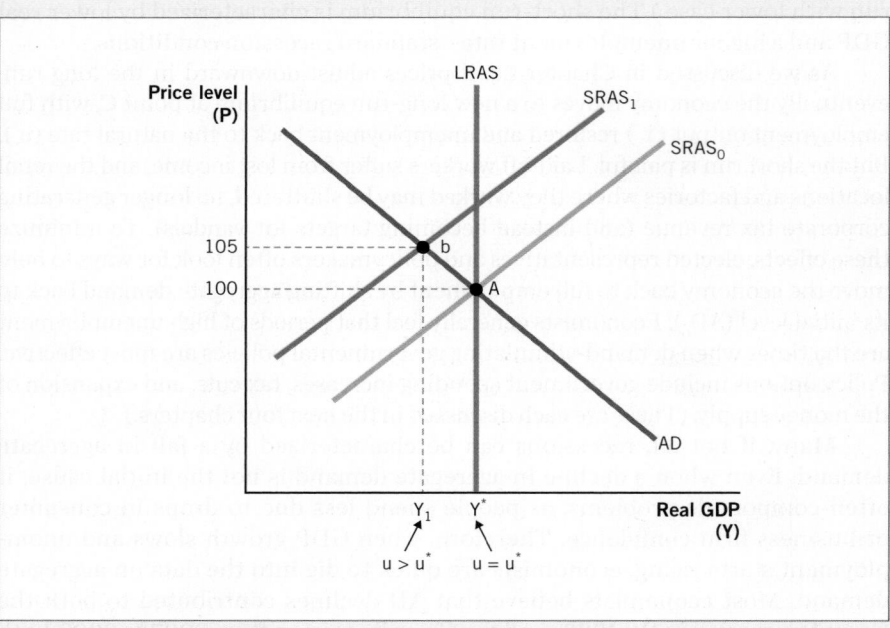

FIGURE 27.3

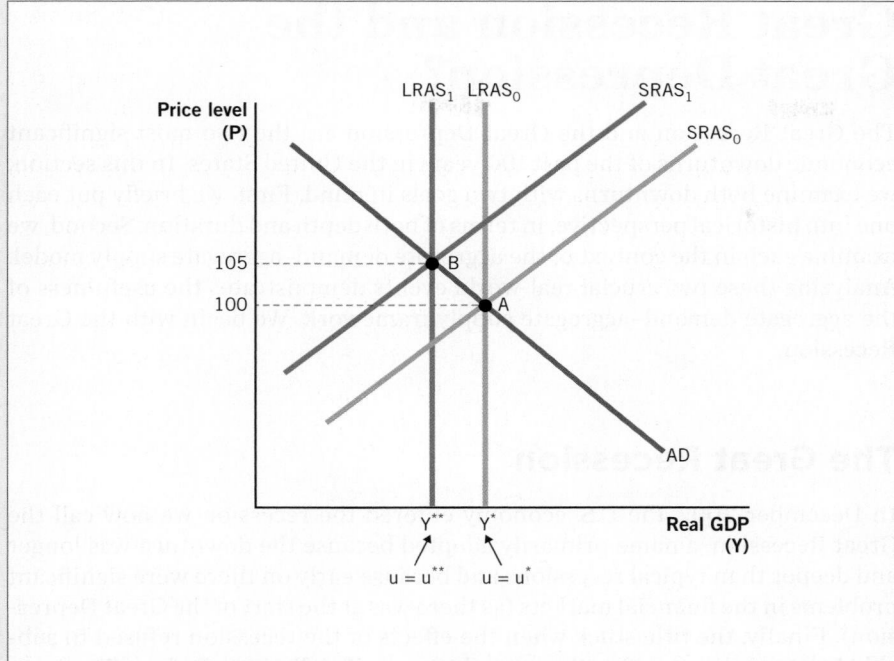

Negative shifts in long-run aggregate supply are less common, but they can also induce recessionary conditions. If long-run aggregate supply declines from $LRAS_0$ to $LRAS_1$ (taking short-run aggregate supply along with it), the economy moves to a new long-run equilibrium at point B, with lower real GDP ($Y^{**} < Y^*$) and higher unemployment ($u^{**} > u^*$). This case is particularly difficult, because the new equilibrium (B) is a long-run equilibrium, and so there is no inherent tendency for the economy to return to the earlier long-run equilibrium. All new growth occurs from Y^{**}.

Now let's consider a decline in long-run aggregate supply. This is caused by negative changes in resources, technology, and institutions. An extreme example is a war fought on home soil; it destroys both labor and capital resources, as soldiers die and buildings or other tools are ruined. But whether the cause is war, natural disaster, or something else, a reduction in resources means full employment output declines and the long-run aggregate supply curve shifts to the left. This is illustrated in Figure 27.3. The reduction of resources moves the economy from long-run equilibrium at point A to a new long-run equilibrium at point B, assuming no other changes take place in the economy. At the new equilibrium, the economy is at a new full employment level of GDP (Y^{**}). While the unemployment rate is technically at the new natural rate of u^{**}, this rate is often higher than the old unemployment rate, since jobs are shifting around in the economy, and this leads to more structural and frictional unemployment. While it's fortunately rare, this type of downturn is particularly painful, because there may not be a policy fix to move the economy back to its initial output level. All new economic growth takes place from the new baseline of Y^{**}, rather than the initial real GDP level of Y^*.

As we move on, remember that no two recessions are exactly alike. We've just considered shifts in aggregate demand, short-run aggregate supply, and long-run aggregate supply. In the textbook and on the chalkboard, it is easy to shift curves and see immediate results. In real life, it is not always clear what is happening, especially during an actual recession. In the next section, we consider the two worst U.S. recessions of the last hundred years.

What Happened during the Great Recession and the Great Depression?

The Great Recession and the Great Depression are the two most significant economic downturns of the past 100 years in the United States. In this section, we examine both downturns with two goals in mind. First, we briefly put each one into historical perspective, in terms of both depth and duration. Second, we examine each in the context of the aggregate demand–aggregate supply model. Analyzing these two crucial real-world events demonstrates the usefulness of the aggregate demand–aggregate supply framework. We begin with the Great Recession.

The Great Recession

In December 2007, the U.S. economy entered the recession we now call the Great Recession, a name primarily adopted because the downturn was longer and deeper than typical recessions and because early on there were significant problems in the financial markets (as there was at the start of the Great Depression). Finally, the title stuck when the effects of the recession refused to subside for several years after the recession was officially over. Before discussing the causes of the Great Recession, let's look more closely at just how serious the contraction was.

THE DEPTH AND DURATION OF THE GREAT RECESSION The official duration of the Great Recession was 18 months (December 2007 to June 2009), making it the longest of all recessions since World War II. But even this length understates how long the U.S. economy was affected by the economic downturn. For several years after the recession was officially over, unemployment remained high and real GDP grew slowly.

One way to grasp the depth and duration of the Great Recession is to compare it with the other recessions since World War II. Figure 27.4 shows comparative data on real GDP and the unemployment rate. Panel (a) compares the pattern of real GDP during the Great Recession and an average pattern of the other recessions since World War II. To illustrate the two paths of GDP, we set them to 100 at the onset of the contraction. Notice that during a typical recession, real GDP falls slightly and then comes back to its original level after about a year and a half. In contrast, during the Great Recession, output fell significantly and then recovered more slowly. In fact, it took nearly four years for real GDP to reach its pre-recession level.

Panel (b) shows the monthly unemployment rate for the Great Recession compared with an average unemployment rate across the other post–World War II recessions. For a typical recession, the unemployment rate climbs to around 7% and then declines after about 12 to 15 months. But for the Great Recession, the unemployment rate climbed to 10% in October 2009 (22 months after the recession began) and remained at or near 8% even five years after the recession began. Taken together, panels (a) and (b) clearly show that the Great Recession was more severe than a typical recession.

FIGURE 27.4

Real GDP and Unemployment Rate, Great Recession versus All Other Post–WWII Recessions

(a) During the Great Recession, real GDP fell further and rebounded more slowly than it otherwise did during a normal postwar recession. (b) Also, the unemployment rate rose to levels far higher than have occurred in typical postwar recessions, and it remained high long after the rate typically falls.

Sources: (a): U.S. Bureau of Economic Analysis; (b): U.S. Bureau of Labor Statistics.

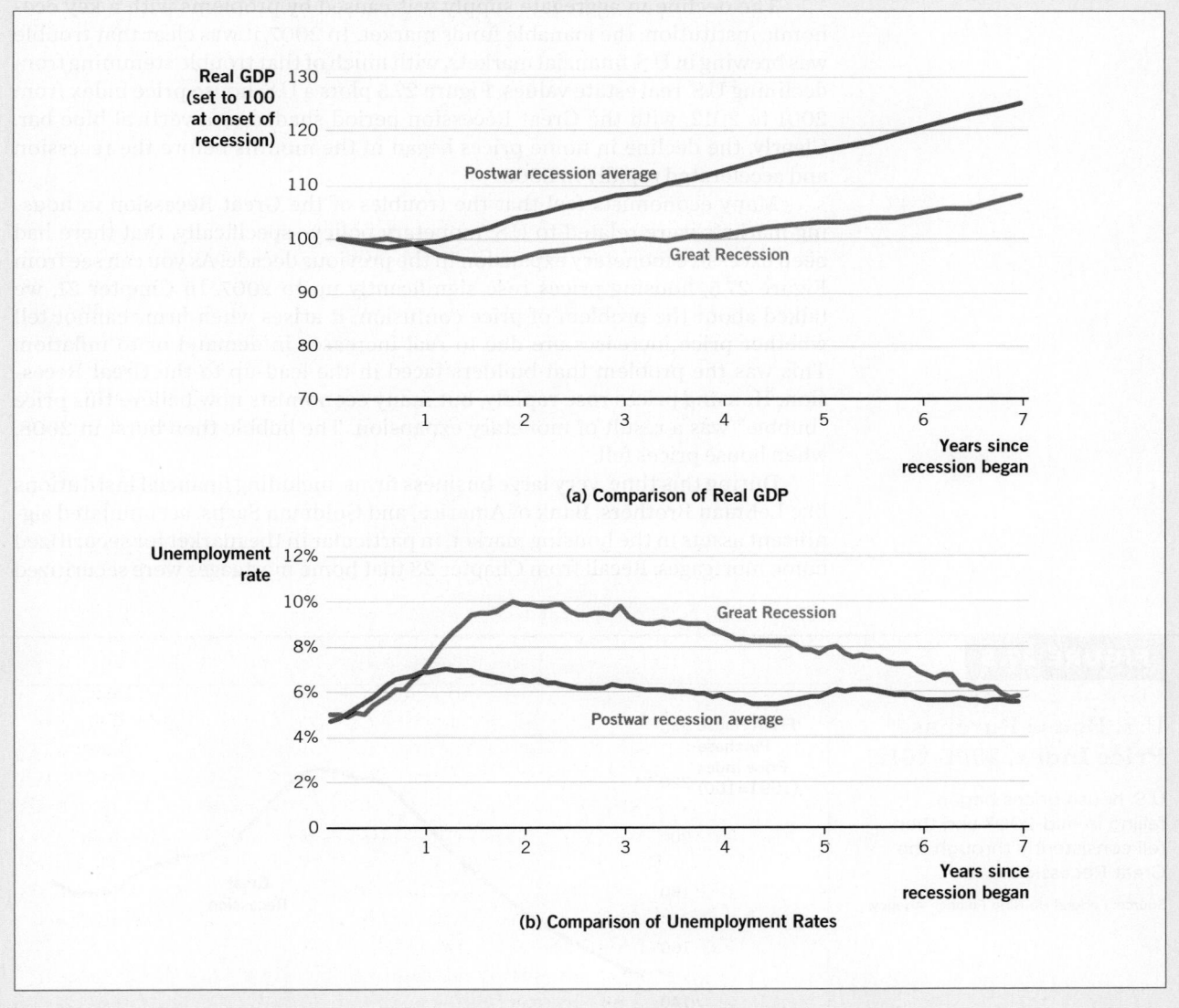

(a) Comparison of Real GDP

(b) Comparison of Unemployment Rates

Why did this happen? First let's briefly review some of the key events of this period. Then we will turn to the aggregate demand–aggregate supply model to examine the factors that contributed to the Great Recession.

USING OUR MODEL TO EXPLAIN THE GREAT RECESSION

Initially, most economists and policymakers assumed that the Great Recession was caused by lower aggregate demand. But while aggregate demand did indeed fall, hindsight reveals that aggregate supply also fell. We begin with the changes in aggregate supply.

The decline in aggregate supply was caused by problems with a key economic institution: the loanable funds market. In 2007, it was clear that trouble was brewing in U.S. financial markets, with much of that trouble stemming from declining U.S. real estate values. Figure 27.5 plots a U.S. house price index from 2001 to 2012, with the Great Recession period shaded as a vertical blue bar. Clearly, the decline in home prices began in the months before the recession and accelerated rapidly in 2008.

Many economists feel that the troubles of the Great Recession in housing markets were related to U.S. monetary policy—specifically, that there had been excessive monetary expansion in the previous decade. As you can see from Figure 27.5, housing prices rose significantly up to 2007. In Chapter 21, we talked about the problem of price confusion: it arises when firms cannot tell whether price increases are due to real increases in demand or to inflation. This was the problem that builders faced in the lead-up to the Great Recession. Housing prices rose rapidly, but many economists now believe this price "bubble" was a result of monetary expansion. The bubble then burst in 2008, when house prices fell.

During this time, very large business firms, including financial institutions like Lehman Brothers, Bank of America, and Goldman Sachs, accumulated significant assets in the housing market, in particular in the market for securitized home mortgages. Recall from Chapter 23 that home mortgages were securitized

---

FIGURE 27.5

U.S. House Purchase Price Index, 2001–2012

U.S. house prices began falling in mid-2007 and then fell consistently through the Great Recession.

Source: Federal Housing Finance Agency.

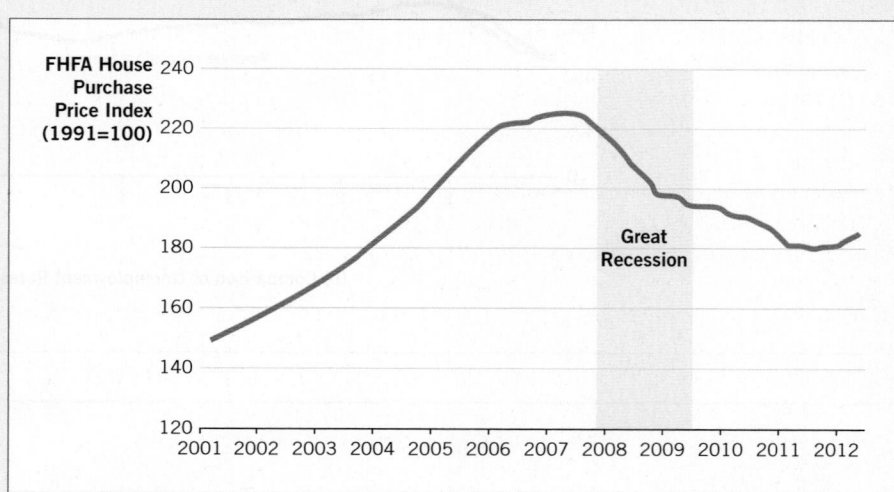

into mortgage-backed securities and that significant quantities of these were held by most of the largest financial institutions. Thus, falling real estate values quickly became a systemic problem for financial markets. Because of the financial firms' interdependence, the problem quickly spread throughout the United States and then to the rest of the world. A financial crisis signals a breakdown in the loanable funds market. When the loanable funds market does not function properly, firms cannot get funding to produce output, and aggregate supply falls.

As we analyze the Great Recession, we have to ask whether the decline in aggregate supply was temporary or permanent. Recall that in the aggregate demand–aggregate supply model, there are different effects from changes in short-run versus long-run aggregate supply. If we model the effect of the financial crisis as temporary, then we view it as a short-run supply shock, illustrated in the AD–AS model with a leftward shift in the short-run aggregate supply curve. After the turmoil ends, the economy returns to its natural rate of output (see Figure 27.2).

In fact, however, the 2008 crisis in the loanable funds market had long-term effects. First off, during the run-up to the Great Recession there was a misallocation of resources. Houses were built that were not needed, using workers and other resources. When the excess of new houses became apparent, the adjustment manifested as a decline in long-run aggregate supply (LRAS). This is like wasting resources, some of which (like materials that went into new homes), we don't get back, and so we can view it as a decline in long-run aggregate supply. Second, new financial regulations changed the financial industry's operating environment. The **Dodd-Frank Act**, signed in July 2010, was the primary regulatory response to the financial turmoil that contributed to the Great Recession. This act established several new oversight bodies and regulations on financial institutions, with the stated aim of reducing risk in financial markets. But while the new regulations may have reduced instability in financial markets, they also affected day-to-day business for banks. These regulations represented a permanent change in how financial institutions operate and shifted the long-run aggregate supply curve to the left.

The **Dodd-Frank Act** is the primary regulatory response to the financial turmoil that contributed to the Great Recession.

Consider an analogy in which financial markets are a bridge between savers and borrowers in an economy. Funds flowing between savers and borrowers are the "traffic" flowing across the bridge. If the economy is to grow, firms must be able to borrow, and so the bridge must be safe and efficient. Financial crises are like accidents on the bridge that disrupt the flow of traffic and temporarily slow the economy. New financial regulations are like speed bumps or stricter speed limits, imposed to reduce the number of accidents and keep the traffic flowing. Thus, we hope the new regulations lead to more stability in financial markets, but we also acknowledge that traffic moves more slowly from now on. In our model, we illustrate the permanent effects of the financial crisis and changes in institutions as a decline in long-run aggregate supply (as in Figure 27.3).

Let's turn now to the decline in aggregate demand during the Great Recession. At least two factors contributed to a large fall in aggregate demand. The first was a fall in wealth: people's homes are often the largest piece of their overall wealth, so when real estate values fall, people's wealth drops. In addition, U.S. stock shares lost one-third of their value during 2008. For millions of people, this meant their retirement savings dropped by a full one-third. Both of these situations contributed to large declines in wealth, so aggregate demand declined significantly.

Aggregate demand also fell because of a decline in expected future income. Beginning in 2007, consumers realized that the economy was slowing. Figure 27.6 shows the Consumer Sentiment Index, which measures consumers' confidence

Consumer Sentiment Index, 2001–2012

The Consumer Sentiment Index is a measure of consumers' confidence about their own financial situation and the future direction of the economy. This index began falling in 2007 and then fell significantly during the Great Recession.

Source: St. Louis Federal Reserve FRED database. The Consumer Sentiment Index was developed at the University of Michigan.

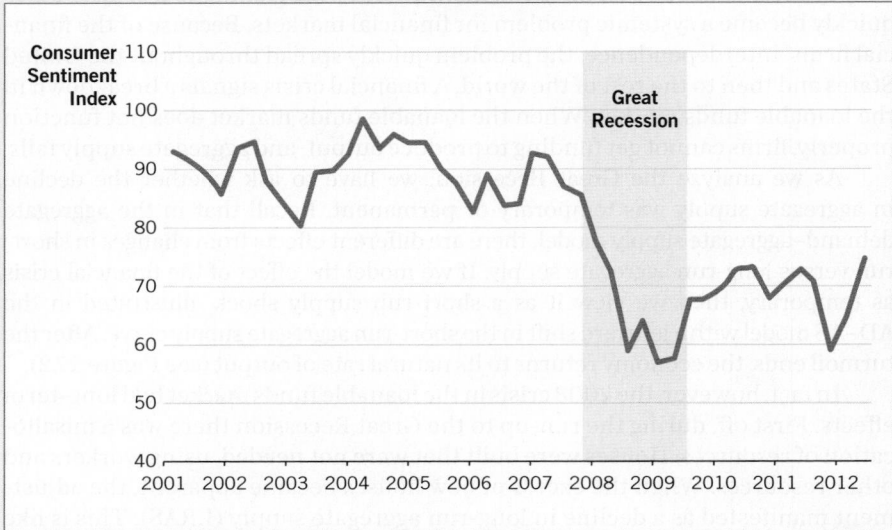

in their own financial situation and in the direction of the overall economy. The Consumer Sentiment Index began falling prior to the recession and then dropped sharply during 2008. Together, these two factors—a decline in wealth and a decline in expected future income—led to a decline in aggregate demand.

Figure 27.7 shows a decline in both aggregate demand and aggregate supply from 2007 to 2008. Aggregate demand shifted from AD_{2007} to AD_{2008}, and long-run aggregate supply shifted from $LRAS_{2007}$ to $LRAS_{2008}$. (Short-run aggregate supply is not pictured here; it shifts with the long-run curve.) In 2007, the economy was in equilibrium at point A; at that time, the unemployment rate (not pictured in Figure 27.7) was below 5%, and real GDP was growing at a 3.6% rate in the second quarter of 2007. Then conditions worsened as housing prices fell and financial market turmoil ensued, leading to lower real wealth and then lower consumer confidence. The declines in aggregate demand and long-run aggregate supply moved the economy to a new equilibrium at point B. During this time, the unemployment rate climbed to 10%, and by the last quarter of 2008, real GDP was declining by 8.9% (on an annual basis).

The unemployment rate rose significantly beginning in 2008 and then continued for several years. This was due in part to an increase in cyclical unemployment, but it was also due to an increase in structural unemployment as the economy adjusted to new types of output in the wake of a decline in long-run aggregate supply.

One reason this recession has been called "Great" is that the decline in real GDP and the increase in the unemployment rate were large by historical standards. But another reason is that symptoms of the recession dragged on for several years after the recession was officially over. In 2012, real GDP was still expanding at less than 2%, and the unemployment rate remained at 8%. In response, the government employed many different tools to try to move the economy back to normal growth and lower levels of unemployment. We will discuss these tools over the next four chapters. But the tools focused primarily on aggregate demand.

FIGURE 27.7

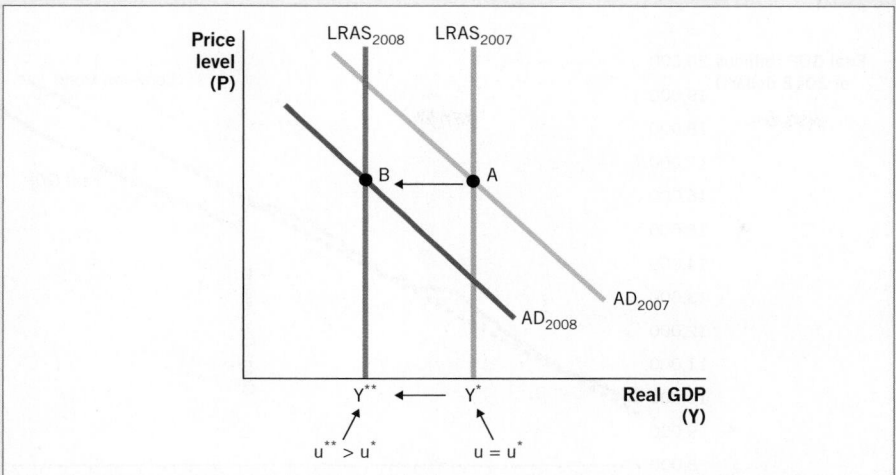

The Decline in Both Long-Run Aggregate Supply and Aggregate Demand, 2007–2008

Financial market turmoil and lower consumer confidence led to decreases in both long-run aggregate supply and aggregate demand. The result was a new, lower level of real GDP and a higher rate of unemployment ($u^{**} > u^*$).

PRACTICE WHAT YOU KNOW

The Great Recession: What Made It "Great"?

QUESTION: What are three reasons why the 2007–2009 recession came to be known as the Great Recession?

ANSWER:

1. Initially, the name appeared because the recession was clearly worse than a typical recession. For example, real GDP fell by an annual rate of 8.9% in the fourth quarter of 2008.

2. There was noticeable stress in financial markets, making the downturn similar to that aspect of the Great Depression.

3. The effects of the Great Recession, in terms of both high unemployment rates and slow real GDP growth, persisted long after the recession was officially over.

CHALLENGE QUESTION: What are two reasons why long-run aggregate supply declined during the Great Recession?

ANSWER:

1. The house price bubble led to overbuilding of housing. This was a misdirection of resources that had long-term consequences.

2. The new financial regulations, implemented to add stability, also meant reduced lending by financial firms.

FIGURE 27.8

Real GDP versus the Previous Trend

There was a significant decline in real GDP during the Great Recession. In addition, there seems to be no tendency for the economy to return to its former trend line, indicating that there has been a permanent decline in long-run aggregate supply. In essence, the Great Recession led to a permanent loss of real GDP that the U.S. economy may never recover.

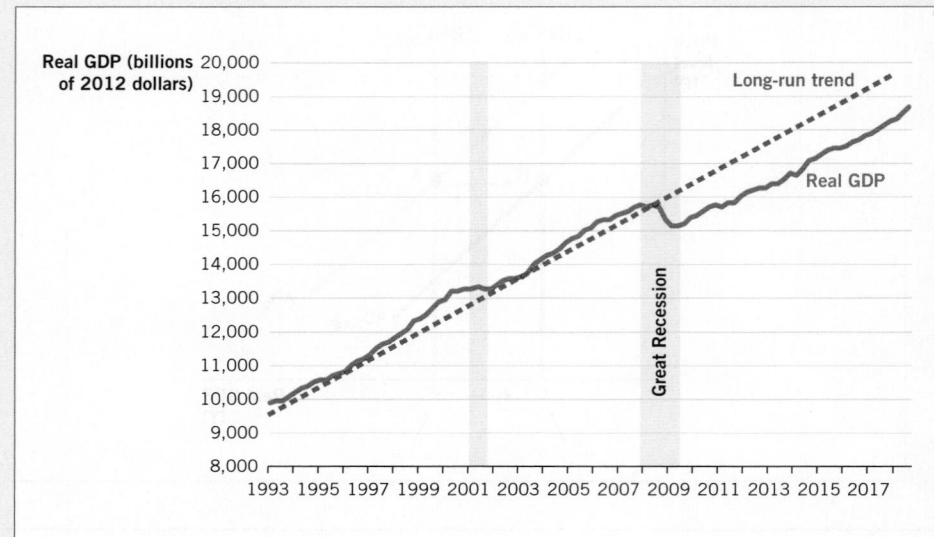

World financial institutions remained in poor health for quite a while after the Great Recession, impacting aggregate supply—and this outcome kept many economies from quickly returning to previous output levels. Figure 27.8 shows U.S. real GDP from 1993 to 2018. In addition, we plot a dashed trend line that indicates the general path of real GDP prior to the Great Recession. These data show that something permanent happened to the U.S. economy during the Great Recession. It is consistent with the theory that long-run aggregate supply declined. The economy began growing again, but from a lower baseline after the Great Recession.

The Great Depression

We have seen that the Great Recession was much worse than typical recessions. However, even though it is named "Great," let's not equate it with the Great Depression. In this section, we look more closely at Depression-era data, and then consider it in terms of our aggregate demand–aggregate supply model.

In this 1937 photo, the "Stalked by Stork" announcement on the man's sandwich board tells passers-by that he is an expectant father.

THE MAGNITUDE OF THE GREAT DEPRESSION To convey the historic magnitude of the Great Depression, we plot extremely long-run U.S. real GDP data in Figure 27.9. The data go all the way back to 1870 and it is easy to identify the Great Depression—it is shown as the massive drop beginning in the 1930s. There have been several contractions in the U.S. economy since 1870, but none even comes close to the Great Depression in severity. Real GDP fell from $1,109 billion in 1929 to $817 billion in 1933 (both in 2012 dollars). Imagine a recession so severe that four years later the economy is producing almost 30% less!

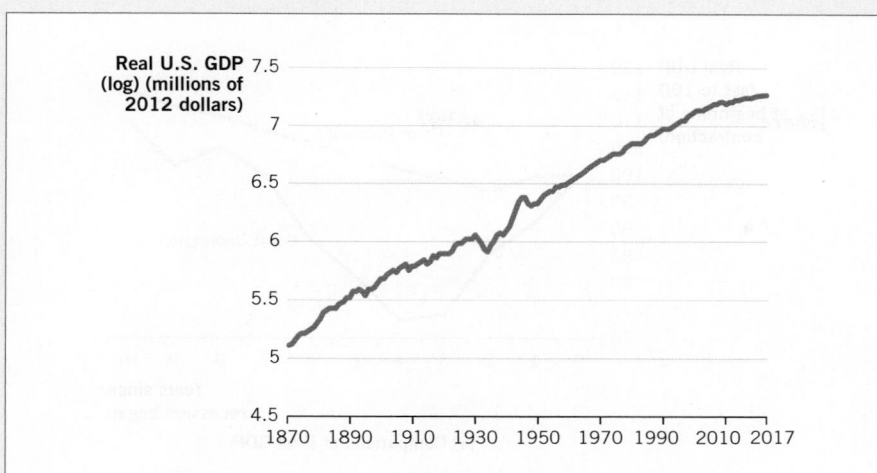

FIGURE 27.9

Real U.S. GDP, 1870–2017

When we look at U.S. real GDP growth over the long run, the Great Depression is easy to spot: it is the severe decline in the 1930s. To normalize across percentage changes, the plotted data appear as the logarithm of real GDP.

Source: U.S. Bureau of Economic Analysis.

Let's compare the Great Depression with the Great Recession that began in 2007. Figure 27.10 shows real GDP growth rates and unemployment rates beginning over the course of each of the two contractions. Panel (a) plots real GDP. Even though we earlier saw that the Great Recession was severe compared with typical U.S. recessions, it looks mild compared to the Great Depression. Real GDP fell by nearly 30% over the four years from 1929 to 1933, and it took seven years for real GDP to return to its pre-recession level.

Panel (b) plots the unemployment rates. In 1929, the unemployment rate was just 2.2%, but just three years later it had climbed to over 25%! In other words, by 1933, one in four workers was without a job. Particularly alarming was the length of the Depression: the unemployment rate remained above 15% for almost the entire decade of the 1930s.

During the Great Depression, shantytowns dubbed "Hoovervilles," after President Hoover, sprang up outside major U.S. cities.

USING OUR MODEL TO EXPLAIN THE GREAT DEPRESSION

The Great Depression was unusual because it was so deep and lasted so long. In fact, it was actually two separate recessions: August 1929 to March 1933 and May 1937 to June 1938. (There is no technical distinction between a recession and a depression—the latter is really just a severe recession.) But the Great Depression was also characterized by another striking condition: prices across the economy declined through the decade. At the end of the 1930s, the price level (measured by the GDP deflator), was still 20% lower than in 1929. The decline in prices indicates that the primary cause of the Great Depression was a decline in aggregate demand.

Figure 27.11 illustrates a significant decline in aggregate demand. In 1929, the economy was in equilibrium at point A, with aggregate demand AD_{1929}. Then

FIGURE 27.10

Unemployment Rate and Real GDP for the Great Recession and the Great Depression

(a) During the Great Depression, real GDP fell by almost a third, and it took seven years to return to its prerecession level. In comparison, the decline in real GDP during the Great Recession seems meager. (b) During the Great Depression, the unemployment rate climbed to over 25% and remained over 15% for most of the entire decade of the 1930s. These levels far exceed the unemployment rates experienced during the Great Recession of 2007–2009.

Source: (a): U.S. Bureau of Economic Analysis; (b): U.S. Bureau of Labor Statistics.

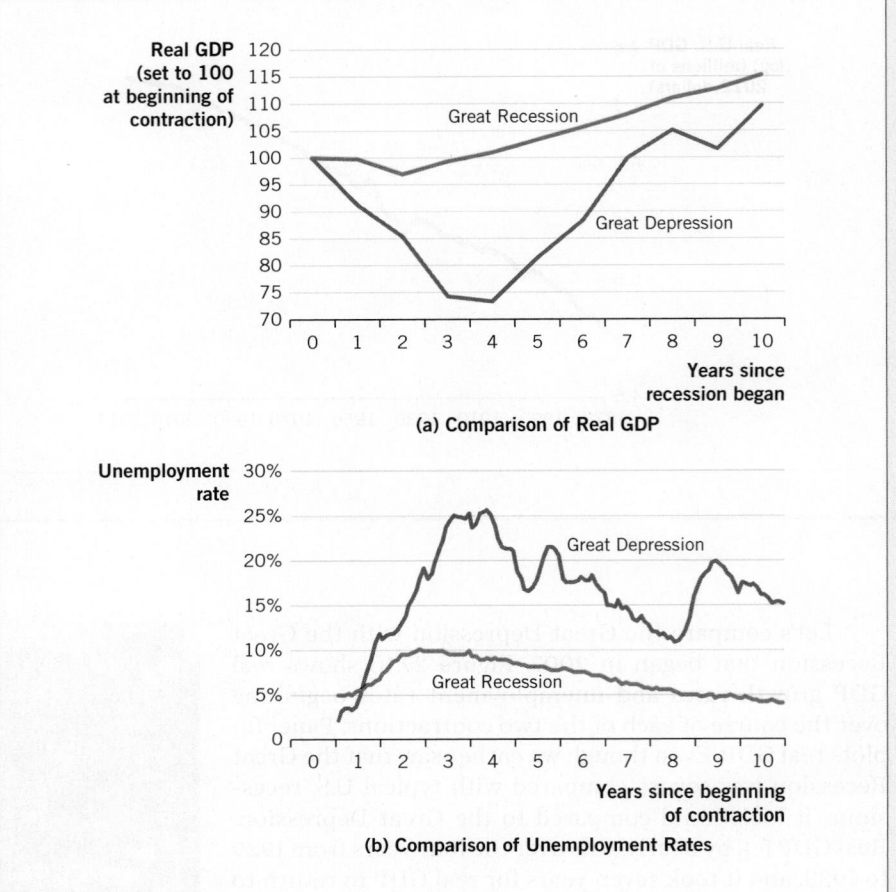

(a) Comparison of Real GDP

(b) Comparison of Unemployment Rates

Macroeconomic policy encompasses governmental acts that influence the macroeconomy.

a significant decline in aggregate demand occurred for several years, as indicated by a shift to AD_{1930+}. As we have seen, lower aggregate demand leads to lower real GDP (shown in the figure as Y_1), higher unemployment rates (25%), and a lower price level (shown here as a decline from 100 to 80). These outcomes match the symptoms of the Great Depression.

There were multiple causes of this aggregate demand decline. First, there was a decline in real wealth. The stock market crashed, beginning on October 24, 1929 (now known as "Black Thursday"). Between 1929 and 1932, stock prices (as measured by the Dow Jones Industrial Average) fell by almost 90%. But the Depression was not caused by the stock market crash alone. A significant reaction to the crash was a change in people's expectations. In particular, expected future income declined—and we know that this factor decreases aggregate demand.

There is, however, a third significant causal factor. Unfortunately, it turns out that much of the decline was due to misguided macroeconomic policy. **Macroeconomic policy** encompasses governmental acts that influence the

FIGURE 27.11

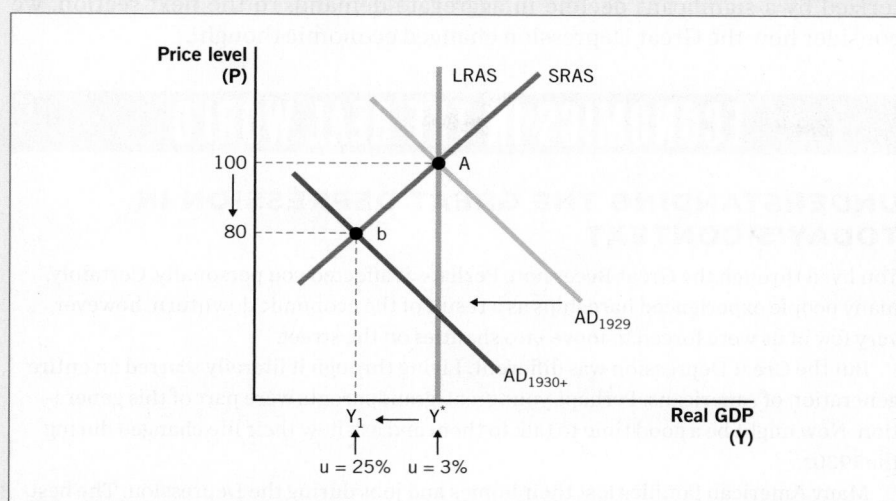

The Decline in Aggregate Demand during the Great Depression

A significant decline in aggregate demand after 1929 can help to explain all three symptoms of the Great Depression: a decline in real GDP (from Y^* to Y_1), an increase in the unemployment rate (from 3% to 25%), and a decrease in the price level (from 100 to 80).

direction of the overall economy. Economists distinguish two different types of macroeconomic policy: fiscal policy and monetary policy. **Fiscal policy** comprises the use of the government's budget tools—government spending and taxes—to influence the macroeconomy. **Monetary policy** involves adjusting the money supply to influence the economy. We are not yet ready to talk in detail about macroeconomic policies (those are the topics of the next section of this book), but we can consider the policy blunders in the context of our aggregate demand and aggregate supply model.

First, consider monetary policy. The government actually reduced the quantity of money in the economy in 1928 and 1929, in hopes of controlling stock prices that policymakers thought were too high. We know that reductions in the money supply lead to lower aggregate demand. Then, when financial panic spread, many people withdrew deposits from banks. As a result, more than 9,000 banks failed in the United States between 1929 and 1933. And while the government had the ability to lend to these ailing banks, it failed to do so. This led to even more shrinking of the money supply. In fact, between 1929 and 1933, the quantity of money circulating through the U.S. economy declined by one-third. Economists today agree that these policy failures led to a significant decline in aggregate demand and were the primary source of economic contraction in the beginning years of the Great Depression.

There were other reasons why the Great Depression dragged on for so long. In the early 1930s, Presidents Hoover and Roosevelt raised taxes to try to balance the federal budget. But higher taxes also reduce aggregate demand. Another policy blunder affected aggregate supply: in 1930, Congress passed the Smoot-Hawley Tariff Act. This legislation imposed tariffs (taxes) on thousands of imported goods and set off a global trade war as other nations reacted by imposing tariffs on U.S. exports.

Fiscal policy
comprises the use of the government's budget tools—government spending and taxes—to influence the macroeconomy.

Monetary policy
involves adjusting the money supply to influence the macroeconomy.

Was the stock market crash the only cause of the Great Depression?

In the end, most analysts agree: the Depression was primarily characterized by a significant decline in aggregate demand. In the next section, we consider how the Great Depression changed economic thought.

ECONOMICS IN THE REAL WORLD

UNDERSTANDING THE GREAT DEPRESSION IN TODAY'S CONTEXT

You lived through the Great Recession. Perhaps it affected you personally. Certainly, many people experienced hardships as a result of the economic downturn, however, very few of us were forced to move into shanties on the street.

But the Great Depression was different. Living through it literally scarred an entire generation of Americans. Perhaps your great-grandparents were part of this generation. Now might be a good time to talk to them and ask how their life changed during the 1930s.

Many American families lost their homes and jobs during the Depression. The best alternative for many in some parts of the country was sharecropping, or living on a farm and harvesting the crops on behalf of the owners. For some other families, the best available living arrangement was in shantytowns outside of major cities. These shanty-towns became known as Hoovervilles, named after President Hoover (who was in office from 1929 to 1933). Although homelessness and unemployment are still issues in the United States, the extent of the problems is far smaller today—and was far smaller during the Great Recession—than it was during the Great Depression.

We can use a familiar consumer item to illustrate the difference between the two contractions. During the Great Recession years of 2007–2009, the number of Starbucks locations in the United States grew from 10,684 to 11,128.* Thus, a chain of coffee shops that sell basic drinks for about $4 each actually expanded during the Great Recession. Yes, the coffee is very good, but that could never have happened during the Great Depression.

Now think again about how the Great Recession affected you or someone you know. How much more extreme might those effects have been during the Great Depression?

Unemployed workers gather together in New York City, December 1937. They have a Christmas tree near their shanty.

Stores like this one would not have survived the Great Depression.

*"Starbucks Company Statistics," *Statistic Brain*, published September 2012. statisticbrain.com.

What Are the Big Disagreements in Macroeconomics?

We now consider the major debates in macroeconomics by building on our discussion of the Great Depression. Most economists agree with the basic implications of the aggregate demand–aggregate supply model. However, economists disagree about the role of government and the economy's ability to self-correct. In this section, we try to clarify some of the issues on which this debate turns.

Perhaps the most contentious issue among macroeconomists involves the economy's adjustment to long-run equilibrium. Consider again the short-run equilibrium, b, in Figure 27.1. Some economists believe that adjustment can and should occur naturally. This group, broadly called **classical economists**, emphasize that all prices eventually adjust and that the economy goes back to long-run equilibrium, at point C. Others, called **Keynesian economists,** see the return to long-run equilibrium as a delayed, unpredictable adjustment. This group stresses the importance of aggregate demand and calls for the government to speed the process back to full employment by shifting aggregate demand using fiscal and monetary policy. While not every economist fits completely in either camp, these distinctions help clarify the debate.

Classical economists stress the importance of aggregate supply and generally believe that the economy can adjust back to full-employment equilibrium on its own.

Keynesian economists stress the importance of aggregate demand and generally believe that the economy needs help returning to full-employment equilibrium.

Classical Economics

At the beginning of the twentieth century, economic theory was basically what we now think of as microeconomics. Economists had a good sense of the merits of supply and demand analysis for individual markets. As you know, when we consider basic supply and demand, the price of the good adjusts to draw the market toward equilibrium. To the extent these economists considered macroeconomic issues, they extended their ideas from microeconomic analysis. In particular, their faith in price flexibility extended to their view of the macroeconomy.

Thus, flexible prices form the foundation of the classical view of the macroeconomy. Consider the implications: if prices are completely flexible, the economy is essentially self-correcting. No matter what factors change in the economy, no matter which curves shift, with fully flexible prices the economy automatically maintains full employment (illustrated by the vertical long-run aggregate supply curve). Figure 27.12 illustrates the strictly classical view. Initially, the economy is in long-run equilibrium at point A. If aggregate demand increases from AD_1 to AD_2, price flexibility means the economy moves to a new equilibrium at point B. At point B, real GDP is at full-employment output (Y^*), and the unemployment rate is at the natural rate ($u = u^*$). In short, increases in aggregate demand are not dangerous when prices quickly adjust.

The results are similar when aggregate demand declines. If aggregate demand falls from AD_1 to AD_3, price flexibility implies that the economy moves to long-run equilibrium at point C. (This outcome is very different from the story we told about the Great Depression, illustrated in Figure 27.8.) If prices are completely flexible, the economy quickly settles back at full-employment output and the natural rate of unemployment. Classical economists probably slept well at night, without worries about long-term economic contractions.

FIGURE 27.12

The Classical View of the Macroeconomy

In the classical view, prices adjust quickly in both directions. Therefore, shifts in aggregate demand do not lead to changes in output or employment because the output level stays at full employment. When prices are completely flexible, aggregate demand becomes less relevant, and changes in long-run aggregate supply are considered the primary source of economic prosperity.

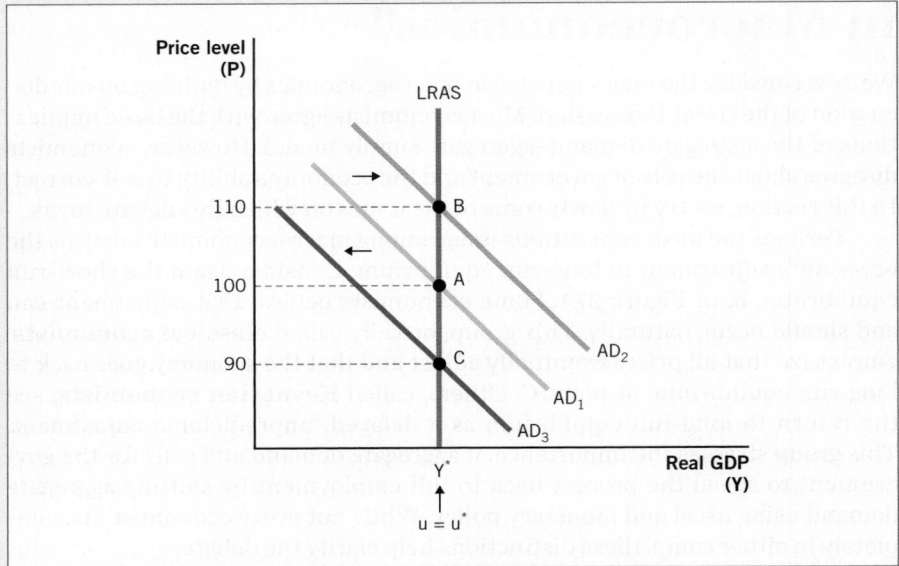

Because they believed that economy self-corrects back to full employment, classical economists were essentially laissez-faire in their policy recommendations. They had faith that market adjustments would take place quickly, so they saw no significant role for a governmental macroeconomic policy focusing on short-run fixes when the economy is underperforming or overperforming.

Today, some economists still lean toward this classical view. They don't worry much about aggregate demand shifts. These economists focus on economic policies designed to promote long-run growth; their main focus is on shifting long-run aggregate supply. Given this perspective, they see savings as a crucial positive factor in the economy: savings translate into investment, which increases capital and shifts the long-run aggregate supply curve to the right.

Keynesian Economics

Although the classical economists dominated economics early in the twentieth century, the experience of the Great Depression presented a challenge to the accepted wisdom. The Great Depression set the stage for a new approach to macroeconomics. John Maynard Keynes, a British economist, formulated this new doctrine. In 1936, Keynes published *The General Theory of Employment, Interest, and Money*. This book vaulted him into the forefront of macroeconomic debates because it offered a theory about why recessions might last a while. Indeed, the title of the book—*The General Theory*—implies that Keynes believed that an economy out of long-run equilibrium is not unusual. Proponents of this view came to be known as Keynesian economists.

Keynesian economists emphasize that after a decline in aggregate demand, some prices, particularly wages, are very slow to adjust downward to move the economy back to full employment. In short, wages and certain other prices are "sticky." As a result, high real wages prevent the labor market from reaching equilibrium and restoring full employment. Here we have an explanation for how prolonged recessions can happen. Keynes advocated governmental intervention to move the economy back to full employment. He argued that the government should try to shift the aggregate demand curve back to its initial level. According to Keynes, it is foolish to wait for long-run adjustments because, as he famously said, "In the long run we are all dead."

To the extent that wages and other prices are indeed sticky, demand declines spell serious trouble for the economy, because there is no natural adjustment back to full employment. So Keynesian economists focus on the demand side of the economy as the source of instability. Look back at Figure 27.11, which shows the decline in aggregate demand between 1929 and 1930+. This large decline was due to a fall in wealth, lower consumer confidence, and bad policy that led to a monetary contraction. If prices don't adjust downward, the short-run equilibrium at b becomes a long-run equilibrium.

Why would wages and other prices be sticky? One explanation is the presence of long-term wage contracts, especially when negotiated through collective bargaining agreements by unions. Certainly, a larger percentage of the labor force was unionized in the 1930s, and this no doubt contributed to wage rigidity. But money illusion may also have played a role (see Chapter 21). Imagine yourself as an employee in the midst of the Great Depression: times are tough, and now your employer is asks you to accept lower wages. This is a tough pill to swallow, even if, with falling consumer prices, you're not looking at a *real* wage decrease. You, or some of your coworkers, might refuse a wage cut. Employees who refuse a pay cut might lose their jobs. This begins a troubling cycle, as workers without jobs drastically cut their spending, and this leads to a reduction in economic activity. Recall the circular flow diagram we discussed in Chapter 1. The welfare of businesses and workers are intertwined.

Keynes recommended that the British and U.S. governments take action to increase aggregate demand. Keynes felt that, with additional government spending, governments could play a role in stopping the global economy's decline. Government spending can increase aggregate demand. Keynes recommended fiscal policy in the form of spending on social programs and additional infrastructure (we discuss this further in Chapter 29). During the Great Depression, a host of programs put into place as part of Franklin Delano Roosevelt's New Deal were designed to create immediate jobs and spending in the economy. If aggregate demand is too low because individuals and firms are reluctant to spend, Keynes argued, the government might fill the void by increasing the government-spending piece of aggregate demand.

The Keynesian view of the economy offered an explanation for the Great Depression (see the appendix to this chapter for more details on this view). In fact, after the nation emerged from the Great Depression, Keynesian theory became dominant in the field of economics.

Table 27.1 summarizes the major differences between classical and Keynesian economists.

TABLE 27.1		
Classical versus Keynesian Economics		
	Classical economics	**Keynesian economics**
Key time period	Long run	Short run
Price flexibility	Prices are flexible	Prices are sticky
Savings	Crucial to growth	A drain on demand
Key side of market	Supply	Demand
Market tendency	Stability, full employment	Instability, cyclical unemployment
Government intervention	Not necessary	Essential

PRACTICE WHAT YOU KNOW

The Big Debates: Guess Which View

QUESTION: Consider the four statements below. Which type of economist, Keynesian or classical, would likely make each statement? Explain your choice each time.

a. "If you want to help the economy, you should increase your spending."

b. "If you want to help the economy, you should increase your savings."

c. "Governmental policy should focus on counteracting short-run fluctuations in the economy."

d. "Governmental policy should not intervene in the business cycle because the economy can correct itself."

Which type of economist would recommend this shopping trip?

ANSWER:

a. *Keynesian.* The Keynesian approach focuses on spending, or aggregate demand, as the fundamental factor in the economy.

b. *Classical.* The classical approach focuses on long-run aggregate supply as the primary source of economic prosperity. In this view, increases in savings are necessary for increased investment, which shifts long-run aggregate supply to the right.

c. *Keynesian.* The Keynesian approach emphasizes inherent instability in the macroeconomy and the resulting need for governmental action to counteract the business cycle.

d. *Classical.* The classical approach emphasizes price flexibility, which means the economy can correct itself and naturally move back to full-employment output levels.

· ECONOMICS *in the* MEDIA ·

The Big Disagreements in Macroeconomics

"FEAR THE BOOM AND THE BUST"

It's Keynes versus Hayek in a YouTube video that has almost 10 million hits. It is a highly original rap video that imagines what two giants of economics, F. A. Hayek and John Maynard Keynes, would have to say to defend their ideas. F. A. Hayek represents the classical economists. Here are some of the best lines:

We've been going back and forth for a century.

[KEYNES] I want to steer markets,

[HAYEK] I want them set free.

There's a boom and bust cycle and good reason to fear it.

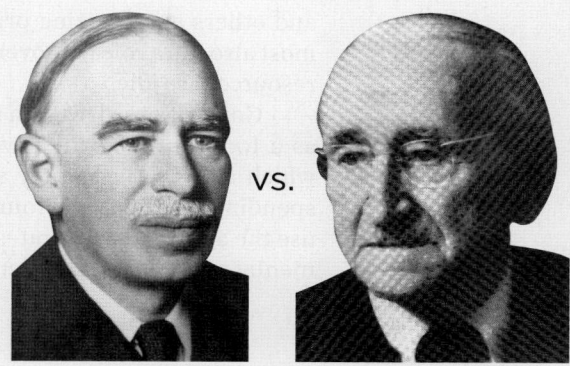

VS.

Keynes (left), sometimes referred to as "the father of macroeconomics," and Hayek, his dogged critic. Check out their "battle" on YouTube!

F. A. Hayek was one of the twentieth century's most significant defenders of free markets. In 1943, he wrote *The Road to Serfdom*, a book that cautions against central planning. Hayek characterizes markets as having the ability to organize spontaneously, to the benefit of an economy. *The Road to Serfdom* appeared in print just a few years after John Maynard Keynes published his *General Theory* in 1936. How could these two giants of economics see the world so differently?

The Austrian-born Hayek, who received the 1974 Nobel Prize in Economics, lived long enough to observe that economics had come full circle. His Nobel acceptance speech was titled "The Pretense of Knowledge." In the talk, he criticized the economics profession for being too quick to adopt Keynesian ideas. Keynes had argued that the economy moves slowly to long-run equilibrium. Hayek countered that efforts to stimulate demand presume that economists know what they are doing; he argued that just because we can build elaborate macroeconomic models does

not mean the models can anticipate every change in the economy. Hayek pointed to the high inflation rates and high unemployment rates of the 1970s as evidence that the Keynesian model was incomplete. Accordingly, he concluded, it would be best to put our faith in the one thing all economists generally agree on: eventually the economy will naturally return to full-employment output levels.

"Fear the Boom and the Bust" presents the views of Hayek and Keynes to make you think. While you might not "get" the many references in the rap just yet, watch it anyway (and tell your friends to watch it). The subject it treats is an important, ongoing debate, and one of the goals of your study of economics is to acquire the information you need to decide for yourself what approach is best for the economy. The video's producers, EconStories, released a sequel a year later. You can view all their work at their YouTube channel: www.youtube.com /user/econstories.

Conclusion

We began this chapter with a look at the severity of the Great Depression. While every recession brings hardship, we have seen that no other modern recession was nearly so severe as the Great Depression. We've now also considered two different views of the macro economy: the classical view and the Keynesian view. The views of most economists probably fall on a continuum between these two views, some emphasizing price adjustments and the importance of supply and others emphasizing price stickiness and the importance of demand. But most also see a role for governmental policy, especially during downturns when resources are idle.

Going forward, we can use the aggregate demand–aggregate supply model as a tool for analyzing governmental policy. This includes monetary policy, which adjusts the money supply, and fiscal policy, which adjusts taxes and spending. Over the next four chapters, we evaluate these policy alternatives and use the aggregate demand–aggregate supply model to understand how governmental policy affects the economy. ✳

⬩ ANSWERING *the* BIG QUESTIONS ⬩

Why do recessions occur?

- Shifts in aggregate demand.
- Shifts in aggregate supply.

What happened during the Great Recession and the Great Depression?

- The Great Recession was characterized by shifts in both long-run aggregate supply and aggregate demand.
- The Great Recession was deeper and longer than typical U.S. recessions.
- The Great Depression was significantly worse than the Great Recession.
- Many factors contributed to the Great Depression, but most significant was a large and persistent decline in aggregate demand.

What are the big disagreements in macroeconomics?

- The big debates in macroeconomics focus on the flexibility of prices and the emphasis on aggregate supply or aggregate demand. The two key schools of thought are classical economics and Keynesian economics.
- If prices are assumed to be flexible, the implication is a generally stable macroeconomy without significant need for government help.
- If prices are assumed to be sticky, the implication is an inherently unstable economy in need of government assistance.

Concepts You Should Know

classical economists (p. 881)   fiscal policy (p. 879)   macroeconomic policy (p. 878)
Dodd-Frank Act (p. 873)   Keynesian economists (p. 881)   monetary policy (p. 879)

Questions for Review

1. What were the cause(s) of the long-run aggregate supply shift during the Great Recession? What were the cause(s) of the aggregate demand shift during the Great Recession?

2. What specific numerical evidence would you give to explain why the Great Depression was so much worse than the Great Recession?

3. What is the key side (supply or demand) of the economy for Keynesian economists? What assumption about prices leads them to this emphasis? What is the key side of the economy (supply or demand) for classical economists? What assumption about prices leads them to this emphasis?

4. In Chapter 26, we covered three factors that shift long-run aggregate supply. What are those factors? Which of those factors changed during the period of the Great Recession, and how did they change?

5. In Chapter 26, we covered a list of factors that shift aggregate demand. Which of those factors changed during the Great Depression, and how did they change?

6. Consider the following statements about the macroeconomy. For each, indicate whether the statement best distinguishes the strict Keynesian view, strict classical view, or neither of these views.

 a. All prices are completely flexible.
 b. The primary focus is on aggregate supply.
 c. Spending is the key determinant of output.
 d. Capital is the key source of economic growth.
 e. Saving can be detrimental to the economy.
 f. The macroeconomy generally takes care of itself.
 g. Every dollar borrowed requires a dollar saved.
 h. The macroeconomy is inherently unstable.
 i. Full employment is at the natural rate of unemployment.
 j. Some prices don't adjust downward.

7. Name two reasons why prices might be sticky in the downward direction.

Study Problems *(✱ solved at the end of the section)*

✱ **1.** Explain whether each of the following statements is more likely to come from a classical economist or a Keynesian economist:

 a. "The recent decline in consumer confidence will likely spell disaster for the economy."
 b. "Business managers making investment decisions play a crucial role in the short-run economy."
 c. "Consumer spending is down, but that is good news because it means savings is up."
 d. "In the long run we are all dead."
 e. "There is no reason to believe that most prices will take more than several months to adjust in either direction."

2. For this problem, we want to practice working with the aggregate demand–aggregate supply model.

 a. Set up an aggregate demand–aggregate supply model in long-run equilibrium, with both short-run and long-run aggregate supply curves and an aggregate demand curve. Label the equilibrium price level as P^* and the equilibrium level of real GDP as Y^*. Draw this model twice.
 b. Using the first set of curves you drew in part (a), now assume that aggregate demand and aggregate supply (both short-run and long-run) decline. If all curves shift by the same amount, what is the resulting change in real GDP and the

price level? What is the implied change in the unemployment rate?

c. Now, using the second set of curves from part (a), let aggregate demand decline by a large amount while the aggregate supply curves decline by a relatively small amount. What are the resulting short-run changes in real GDP and the price level? What is the implied short-run change in the unemployment rate?

d. Parts (b) and (c) describe the two different conditions of the Great Recession and the Great Depression. Which part refers to the Great Recession? Which part refers to the Great Depression?

3. Assume that the economy is in long-run equilibrium, with real GDP at the full employment output level (Y^*) and the unemployment rate equal to the natural rate (u^*).

a. Now assume there is a drop in business firm confidence, that is, decision-makers at firms lose confidence in the future direction of the economy. Illustrate this change using the AD–AS model.

b. What happens to real GDP and unemployment in the short run?

c. What policy or policies would a Keynesian economist recommend to remedy this situation?

d. How would a classical economist respond to this situation?

Solved Problem

1.a. *Keynesian*. The key here is that Keynesian economists emphasize the role of aggregate demand, which depends on consumer confidence.

b. *Keynesian*. The key here is the emphasis on the short run. Investment is a component of aggregate demand and can have an impact on spending in the short run.

c. *Classical*. The key here is the classical emphasis on savings, which can lead to greater levels of

lending in the loanable funds market—an outcome that increases capital in the long run.

d. *Keynesian*. In fact, this is a direct quote from John Maynard Keynes himself. The key here is that the quote de-emphasizes the long run in favor of the short run.

e. *Classical*. The key here is the emphasis on price flexibility.

27A | The Aggregate Expenditures Model

We have used the aggregate demand–aggregate supply (AD–AS) model to explain different reasons why the economy expands and contracts. In addition, we used the AD–AS model to explain the differences between classical economists and Keynesian economists. We observed that Keynesian economists focus on aggregate demand and sticky prices. In this appendix, we develop another model of the economy, the **aggregate expenditures (AE) model**, which extends the Keynesian perspective.

The AE model holds that prices are completely sticky and that aggregate demand therefore determines the economy's level of output and income. In fact, *aggregate expenditures* is another name for aggregate demand.

You may be wondering why some economists are willing to make the assumption that prices do not change. After all, we have seen that all prices adjust in the long run. We can therefore view the AE model strictly as a short-run model of the economy, where prices are inflexible. This model is particularly helpful in understanding economic downturns because, as we have seen, prices can be particularly inflexible in the downward direction.

> The **aggregate expenditures (AE) model** is a short-run model of economic fluctuations. It holds that prices are completely sticky (inflexible) and that aggregate demand (aggregate expenditures) determines the economy's level of output and income.

The Components of Aggregate Expenditures

The four components of aggregate demand are consumption (C), investment (I), government spending (G), and net exports (NX). Aggregate expenditures is another way of describing aggregate demand. Let's consider each component.

Consumption

Recall that consumption expenditures constitute about 71% of all GDP spending. Because this component of aggregate expenditures is so large, it is the key to understanding the AE model. We start with a microeconomic example.

Let's say that your friend Kaitlyn has a job that pays her $3,000 a month after taxes. This $3,000 is Kaitlyn's monthly **disposable income** (Y_d), or income after taxes (Y − T). Kaitlyn is disciplined about saving a part of her income, using 80%, or $2,400 per month, for consumption. She saves the remaining 20%, or $600, of her disposable income. Last year was a productive year for Kaitlyn, and she is

> **Disposable income** is income after taxes (Y − T).

excited because her boss rewarded her with a raise that works out to $200 more disposable income every month. After the raise, Kaitlyn decides to continue saving 20% of her new disposable income, which leaves 80% for consumption.

We are talking about Kaitlyn's propensity to spend her income on consumption as opposed to saving. The **marginal propensity to consume (MPC)** is the portion of additional income spent on consumption. Kaitlyn's MPC is 80%, or 0.8. The **marginal propensity to save (MPS)** is the portion of additional income saved. Kaitlyn's MPS is 20%, or 0.2. MPC and MPS sum to 1 because income is either spent or saved:

$$MPC + MPS = 1$$

This equation applies to individuals like Kaitlyn but also to entire economies. The MPC for a national economy is the average portion of additional income that people in the economy spend on consumption.

We can look at data from the United States over time to see how consumption spending rises with disposable income. Figure 27A.1 shows data on consumption and disposable income for the United States for the years 1965–2014. You can see the positive relationship in the slope: as disposable income rises, so does consumption.

It is helpful to specify the relationship between national consumption spending and disposable income in equation form. This equation is called the **aggregate consumption function**:

$$C = A + MPC \times (Y - T)$$

This equation says that consumption rises with disposable income $(Y - T)$. Whenever disposable income increases by $1, consumption rises by MPC, the marginal propensity to consume. The letter A in the equation represents **autonomous consumption spending**, which is spending on consumption

---

The **marginal propensity to consume (MPC)** is the portion of additional income spent on consumption.

The **marginal propensity to save (MPS)** is the portion of additional income saved.

(EQUATION 27A.1)

The **aggregate consumption function** is an equation that specifies the relationship between national income and national consumption.

(EQUATION 27A.2)

Autonomous consumption spending is spending on consumption independent of the level of income.

U.S. Real Consumption and Disposable Income, 1965–2014

As real disposable income rises, consumption also increases. This is one way of viewing the consumption function for an entire economy.

Source: Bureau of Economic Analysis.

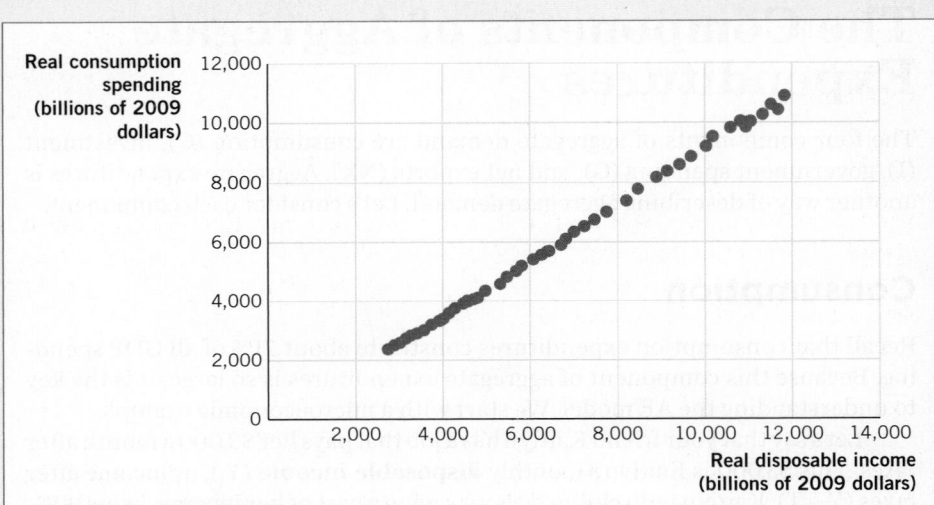

An Aggregate Consumption Function (all dollars in billions; MPC = 0.6)

(1) Y Real GDP	(2) A Autonomous consumption	(3) MPC*Y	(4) C A + MPC*Y
$10,000	$2,800	$6,000	$8,800
11,000	2,800	6,600	9,400
12,000	2,800	7,200	10,000
13,000	2,800	7,800	10,600
14,000	2,800	8,400	11,200

independent of the level of income. (The word "autonomous" means "independent.") Viewed this way, Equation 27A.2 implies that even when income is zero, some consumption must take place (A), and for every dollar rise in disposable income, consumption rises by MPC.

For the remainder of this appendix, we make a simplifying assumption with regard to disposable income. We assume that taxes do not change, so all changes in income (Y) are the same changes in disposable income (Y − T). This assumption does not affect the major implications of the analysis, but it does make the model much simpler. With this assumption, the aggregate consumption function becomes

$$C = A + MPC \times Y$$

(EQUATION 27A.3)

A person's marginal propensity to consume is determined by the portion of disposable income changes they spend (versus save).

Consider the consumption function presented in Table 27A.1 (all dollar values are in billions of dollars). In this example, autonomous consumption is equal to $2,800 billion, and the marginal propensity to consume is 0.6. The first column shows real GDP, or real income levels, ranging from $10,000 billion to $14,000 billion. Column 2 is autonomous consumption spending, which does not change with income level (by definition). Column 3 shows the MPC of 0.6 times the value of Y from column 1. Column 4 is the sum of columns 2 and 3: total consumption (C) = A + MPC*Y.

Figure 27A.2 plots this hypothetical consumption function with real income (Y) on the horizontal axis and consumption spending (C) on the vertical axis (both measured in trillions of dollars). The consumption function starts at $2,800 billion, or $2.8 trillion, which is the level of autonomous consumption spending (A) in the economy. Then, for every dollar of additional income, consumption rises by $0.60, so the slope of the consumption function is 0.6. This slope is the marginal propensity to consume.

Investment

Recall that investment is private spending by firms on tools, plant, equipment, and inventory to produce future output. Inventories play a critical role in the AE model. Inventory investment is not perfectly predictable because firms typically don't know the exact number of goods and services they will sell in a given period.

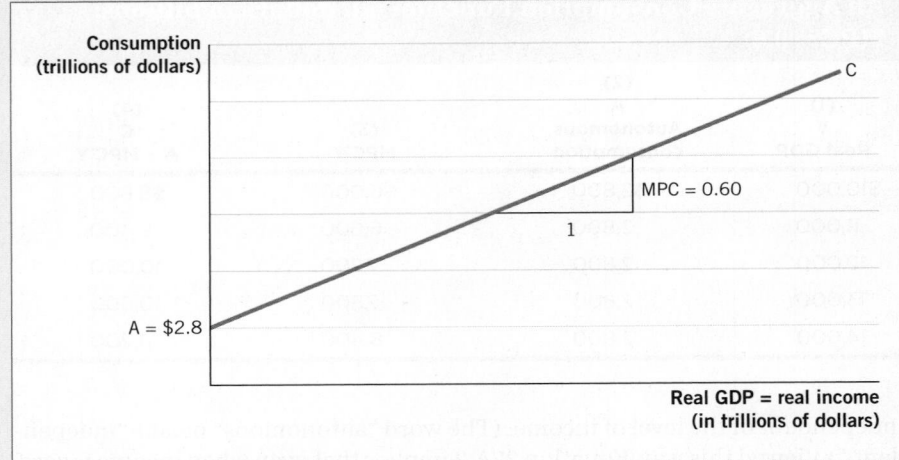

FIGURE 27A.2

Aggregate Consumption Function

The aggregate consumption function shows how consumption is affected by changes in real GDP, which is real income. The equation for this function is C = $2.8 + 0.6˙Y, which implies that autonomous consumption is $2.8 trillion and that the marginal propensity to consume (MPC) is 0.6.

For example, consider a book publisher who is trying to plan for sales of a popular book in 2021. Imagine that the publisher begins the year with an inventory of 1,000 books on hand and anticipates selling 20,000 books in 2021. The publisher would like to have the same level of inventory (1,000 copies) at the end of 2021. Based on these expectations and the current inventory, the publisher prints 20,000 books in 2021.

Now consider the three scenarios displayed in Table 27A.2. In scenario 1, actual sales are 19,000, which is less than the firm anticipated. In scenario 2, actual sales are 21,000, which is more than the firm anticipated. In scenario 3, actual sales are 20,000, exactly equal to anticipated sales.

Consider scenario 1. Here, sales are less than anticipated, and so inventory at the end of 2021 is more than the firm expected. This unplanned inventory is positive **unplanned investment**, which occurs when a firm sells less than expected, causing inventory to rise beyond what was planned. All else being equal, this unplanned investment means the firm enters the next year (2022) with more books on hand than it planned for, and it will react by producing

(Positive) unplanned investment occurs when expected sales exceed actual sales, leading to an increase in inventory.

TABLE 27A.2

Planned and Unplanned Inventory

	Scenario 1 Sales = 19,000 books	Scenario 2 Sales = 21,000 books	Scenario 3 Sales = 20,000 books
Inventory at end of 2020	1,000	1,000	1,000
Production	20,000	20,000	20,000
Actual sales in 2021	19,000	21,000	20,000
Inventory at end of 2021	2,000	0	1,000
Unplanned investment	1,000	-1,000	0
Output adjustment for 2022	Decrease output	Increase output	No change

fewer books in the next year. The last row in the table spells out this important result: positive unplanned investment leads to less output in the future, all else being equal.

Now consider scenario 2, in which actual sales exceed anticipated sales. In this case, inventory at the end of the year is 1,000 books fewer than anticipated. This is an unanticipated decrease in investment, or **negative unplanned investment**. In this case, when people buy more books than the publisher expects, inventories decrease. All else being equal, the publisher will increase production of books in the next year.

The only scenario that does not require future adjustments is scenario 3. In this case, actual sales equal expected sales, and there are no unexpected changes in inventory: actual investment equals planned investment.

This example explains why firms across the economy adjust production each year, even when prices are fixed. When spending on output is greater than anticipated, inventories fall, which leads to output increases in subsequent periods. In contrast, if spending is less than anticipated, inventories pile up and then firms produce less in the future. Equilibrium occurs when spending plans match production plans.

Negative unplanned investment occurs when actual sales exceed anticipated sales, leading to a decrease in inventory.

Increases in inventory count as investment.

An Economy without Government Spending or Net Exports

Before we consider the other components of AE, it is helpful to consider an economy without government spending or net exports. In this case, AE is equal to consumption (C) plus planned investment (PI):

$$AE = C + PI$$

(EQUATION 27A.4)

Let's return to our numerical example. Table 27A.3 is a continuation of the example presented in Table 27A.1 but adds planned investment expenditures. Column 4 indicates $2,000 billion in planned investment expenditures. Note that planned investment expenditures are autonomous with respect to income levels—that is, they don't change with the level of real GDP (Y). In Chapter 26, we identified three factors that do affect the level of investment demand: business firm confidence, interest rates, and the quantity of money in the economy.

TABLE 27A.3

Aggregate Expenditures with No Government Spending or Net Exports (all dollars in billions, MPC = 0.6)

(1) Y Real GDP	(2) A Autonomous consumption	(3) C A + MPC·Y	(4) PI Autonomous planned investment	(5) AE C + PI
$10,000	$2,800	$8,800	$2,000	$10,800
11,000	2,800	9,400	2,000	11,400
12,000	2,800	10,000	2,000	12,000
13,000	2,800	10,600	2,000	12,600
14,000	2,800	11,200	2,000	13,200

Summing Consumption and Planned Investment to Get Aggregate Expenditures

Aggregate expenditures (AE) are the sum of all planned spending: consumption (C) and planned investment (PI). The lower line is consumption expenditures, which depend on the level of income (Y) in the economy. Consumption rises with income at a rate equal to the marginal propensity to consume (MPC). To get AE, we add planned investment (PI), which is assumed to be autonomous (unrelated to income). As a result, the AE line is parallel to the C line. The distance between the two lines is planned investment expenditures.

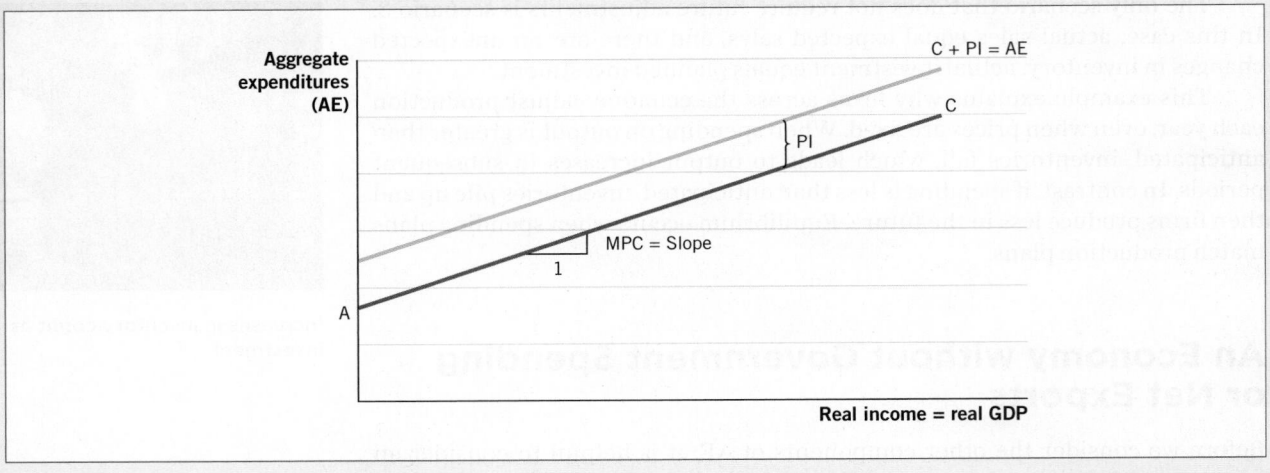

This list does not include real income, and so we assume planned investment expenditures are autonomous with respect to real income (Y). We add consumption (column 3) and autonomous planned investment (column 4) to derive aggregate expenditures in column 5.

Figure 27A.3 graphs the AE line. The lower line, labeled C, is the consumption function, which begins at a level of A. Recall that A is the level of autonomous consumption spending, or the amount consumers spend in a hypothetical case where income (Y) is zero. Consumption increases with Y, and the slope is equal to the marginal propensity to consume (MPC).

To get aggregate expenditures (AE), we add planned investment (PI) and consumption. Because planned investment spending is autonomous, adding PI to C simply shifts up AE by the same amount at all levels.

Equilibrium without Government Spending or Net Exports

Before we examine equilibrium in a general sense, let's consider a numerical example. Table 27A.4 continues our running example but adds column 6 to help us determine equilibrium.

In the AE model, equilibrium occurs when there is no reason for firms to adjust output decisions in the future. As we explained earlier, this point occurs when actual sales equal anticipated sales, so unplanned inventory investment

Equilibrium with No Government Spending or Net Exports
(all dollars in billions; MPC = 0.6)

(1) Y Real GDP	(2) A Autonomous consumption	(3) C A + MPC·Y	(4) PI Autonomous planned investment	(5) AE C + PI	(6) AE − Y
$10,000	$2,800	$8,800	$2,000	$10,800	$800
11,000	2,800	9,400	2,000	11,400	400
12,000	2,800	10,000	2,000	12,000	0
13,000	2,800	10,600	2,000	12,600	−400
14,000	2,800	11,200	2,000	13,200	−800

equals zero. In the language of the AE model, equilibrium occurs when actual spending (Y) is equal to anticipated spending (AE), or when AE = Y.

In our example, equilibrium occurs where real GDP equals $12,000 billion, where there is no difference between AE and Y (indicated in column 6 of Table 27A.4). At real GDP levels below $12,000, aggregate expenditures are greater than actual output (Y). As a result, inventories decrease, and so firms increase output toward $12,000 billion in future periods. On the other hand, at real GDP levels above $12,000 billion, real output exceeds aggregate expenditures. In this case, inventories increase unexpectedly, and firms react in future periods by reducing output toward $12,000 billion. In our example, the only equilibrium point occurs at $12,000 billion.

This is an important result: the equilibrium level of output in the economy is determined by the level of aggregate expenditures. For example, if aggregate expenditures are equal to $11,000 billion, output in the economy will adjust until equilibrium is reached at $11,000 billion. In fact, any point where AE = Y is a possible equilibrium. Panel (a) of Figure 27A.4 plots three possible equilibrium points for a macroeconomy. These always occur where actual real GDP is equal to aggregate expenditures. Panel (b) of Figure 27A.4 presents a line that includes all possible equilibrium points. Notice that this line splits the quadrant into two equal halves and so is at a 45-degree angle. This 45-degree line is a critical piece of the AE model because it shows us all possible equilibrium outcomes.

Let's put the 45-degree line together with aggregate expenditures (AE = C + PI) to determine which equilibrium will result. Figure 27A.5 plots the two lines we need for the AE model. The orange line is the 45-degree line that plots potential equilibrium points for the economy. The blue line is the actual level of AE for the economy, composed of expenditures on consumption and planned investment. Equilibrium occurs where planned AE is equal to actual (real) GDP. In this case, given the total level of AE, equilibrium occurs at $12 trillion. To see why this is the case, let's consider the adjustments that occur when actual (real) GDP is not equal to planned AE.

At a GDP of $11 trillion, planned spending (AE) is above actual output because the AE line (blue) is above the 45-degree equilibrium line (orange). In this case, spending is high relative to actual output, which leads to unplanned decreases in inventories. Thus, in the future, firms increase

Equilibrium Points in the AE Model

Panel (a) shows three points that are possible equilibrium points in the AE model. For example, when AE is $12 trillion and Y is $12 trillion, then actual spending equals planned spending. In this case, there is no unplanned inventory change and the economy is in equilibrium. Panel (b) plots a line through all possible equilibrium points—that is, all points where AE = Y. This line is called the 45-degree line because it emanates from the origin at 45 degrees.

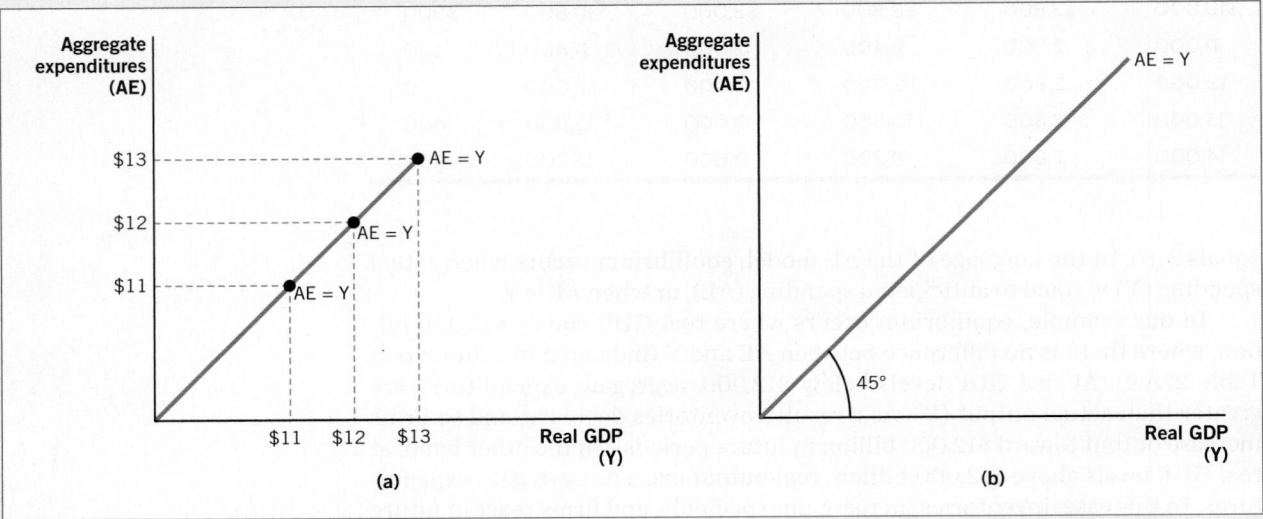

output to adjust to the higher level of planned spending, pushing output toward equilibrium at $12 trillion. This analysis applies to all points where the AE line is above the 45-degree line. That is, at all levels of output less than $12 trillion, firms increase future output and move toward $12 trillion of GDP.

What happens if, instead, firms produce real GDP of $13 trillion? In this case, AE (the blue line) is below actual output (the orange line). This means spending is low relative to output, which leads to unplanned increases in inventories. Firms adjust in the future by reducing real output (Y) down toward equilibrium at $12 trillion.

In this example, output settles to equilibrium at $12 trillion. This is the only output level where firms' plans match the spending patterns of consumers and business firms.

Aggregate Expenditures with Government Spending and Net Exports

More realistically, aggregate expenditures also include government expenditures and net exports:

(EQUATION 27A.5)
$$AE = C + PI + G + NX$$

Equilibrium with No Government Spending or Net Exports

Equilibrium occurs at $12 trillion because that is the only point at which aggregate expenditures (AE) in the economy are exactly equal to what is produced (Y). At output levels below $12 trillion, such as $11 trillion, AE (planned spending, the blue line) is above Y (the orange line), which means spending is above production, which leads to unplanned decreases in inventory. Firms will react by increasing output toward $12 trillion in future periods. At output levels above $12 trillion, such as $13 trillion, AE is below Y, which means spending is above production, and this leads to unplanned increases in inventory. In this case, firms react by decreasing output toward $12 trillion in future periods.

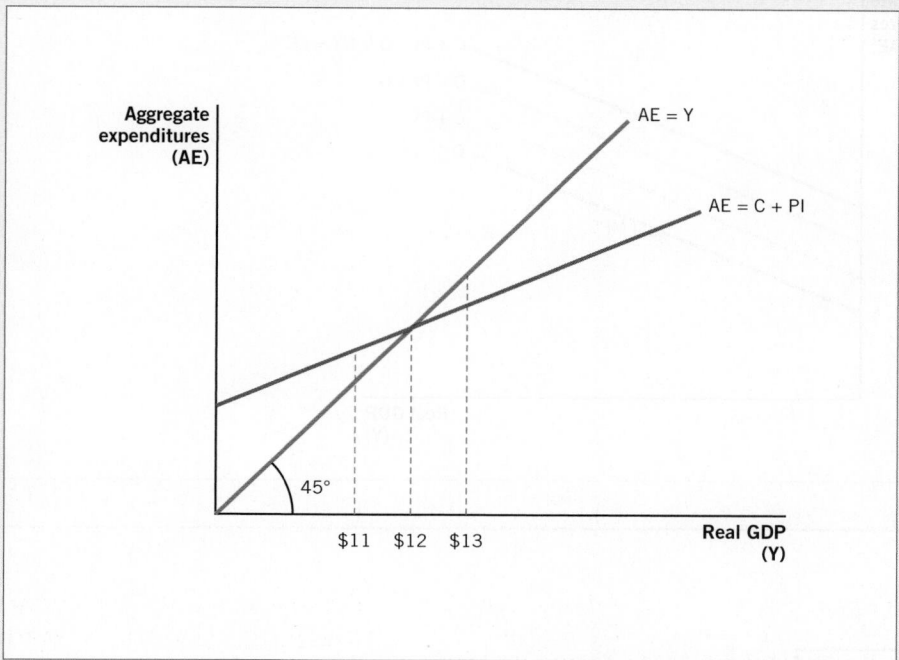

We can now add both government spending (G) and net exports (NX) to see how they affect the macroeconomic equilibrium. Figure 27A.6 shows the aggregate expenditures curve when we include consumption, planned investment, government, and net exports.

Consider the economy presented in Table 27A.5. Looking at the components of aggregate expenditures, we see that autonomous consumption expenditures are $2,800 billion and the MPC is 0.6. Therefore, when income in the economy (Y) is equal to $17,000 billion, total consumption is $2,800 billion + 0.6 ($17,000) billion = $13,000 billion. This number appears in column 3. To get total AE, we also add planned investment ($2,000 billion), government spending ($2,000 billion), and net exports ($400 billion). These four components of aggregate expenditures sum to $17,400 billion. But $17,400 billion is greater than actual GDP, which is $17,000 billion. Inventories decrease by $400 billion, and so in future periods, firms increase output. The only output level that leads to equilibrium is $18,000 billion.

Government purchases, like this military drone, also contribute to aggregate expenditures.

Aggregate Expenditures with All Four Components

Aggregate expenditures (AE) are the total amount of spending in the economy from all four sources: consumption (C), planned investment (PI), government (G), and net exports (NX). Consumption spending depends on the level of income in the economy (Y) and increases at the rate of the marginal propensity to consume (MPC). The other components are assumed to be independent of the level of income, so the AE line shifts up in a parallel fashion when they are added.

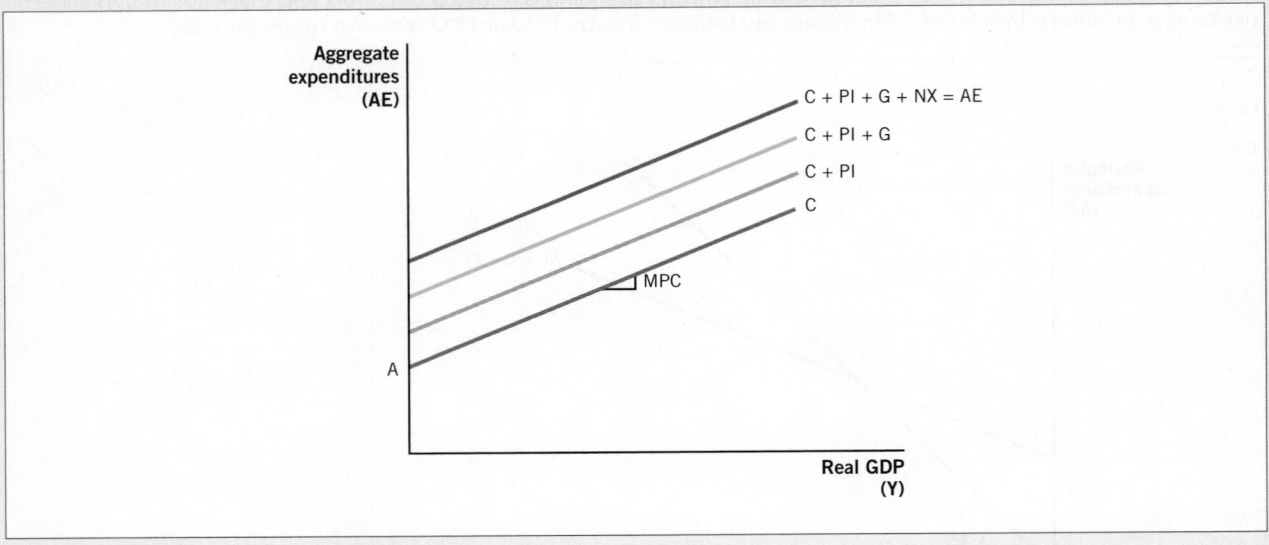

TABLE 27A.5

Equilibrium with All Components of Aggregate Expenditures (all dollars in billions; MPC = 0.6)

(1) Y Real GDP	(2) A Autonomous consumption	(3) C A + MPC·Y	(4) PI Planned investment	(5) G Government spending	(6) NX Net exports	(7) AE C + PI + G + NX	(8) AE − Y
$16,000	$2,800	$12,400	$2,000	$2,000	$400	$16,800	$800
17,000	2,800	13,000	2,000	2,000	400	17,400	400
18,000	2,800	13,600	2,000	2,000	400	18,000	0
19,000	2,800	14,200	2,000	2,000	400	18,600	−400
20,000	2,800	14,800	2,000	2,000	400	19,200	−800

Spending and Equilibrium in a Small Economy

Consider a small economy with autonomous consumption of $700 billion, an MPC of 0.5, planned investment of $150 billion, government spending of $100 billion, and net exports of $50 billion.

QUESTION: Determine AE in this economy when real GDP (Y) is equal to $1,500 billion, $2,000 billion, and $2,500 billion.

ANSWER: We can answer this question by filling in the values in the table below and then summing to get AE in the last column. Note that all dollars are in billions.

(1) Y Real GDP	(2) A Autonomous consumption	(3) C A + MPC·Y	(4) PI Planned investment	(5) G Government spending	(6) NX Net exports	(7) AE C + PI + G + NX
$1,500	$700	$1,450	$150	$100	$50	$1,750
2,000	700	1,700	150	100	50	2,000
2,500	700	1,950	150	100	50	2,250

QUESTION: What is the equilibrium level of real GDP in this economy?

ANSWER: The equilibrium level of real GDP is $2,000 billion because this is the only output level for which AE (the value in the last column) is equal to Y (the value in the first column).

What Are the Implications of the AE Model?

In this section, we examine what the AE model implies about economic outcomes and potential government policy responses to those outcomes.

In the AE model, spending drives the economy. The more people spend, the more income is created for others.

1. Spending Determines Equilibrium Output and Income in the Economy

One key implication of the AE model is that planned aggregate spending dictates the equilibrium level of GDP in an economy. That is, spending determines income completely. Consider the three different levels of aggregate expenditures plotted in Figure 27A.7. When spending is equal to AE_0, the equilibrium level of income in the economy is Y_0. If planned spending increases to AE_1, equilibrium income rises to Y_1. In the AE model, spending increases always lead to increases in real GDP. These increases can result from any of the four

Equilibrium Points in the AE Model

The total level of spending in the economy (AE) determines equilibrium output (Y) in the AE model. When $AE = AE_0$, the level of output is Y_0. If AE shifts up to AE_1, real GDP rises to Y_1. If, instead, AE shifts down to AE_2, real GDP falls to Y_2.

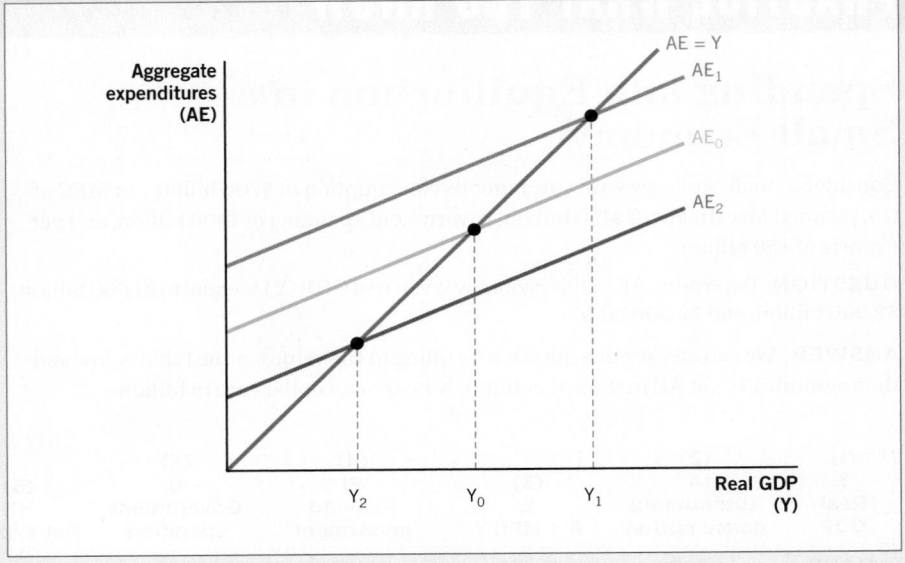

sources: consumption, planned investment, government spending, or net exports. No matter which component increases, the result is the same.

Consider the numerical example we presented earlier in Table 27A.5. In that example, equilibrium output in the economy occurs at real GDP equal to $18 trillion, which comes from consumption spending of $13.6 trillion, planned investment spending of $2 trillion, government spending of $2 trillion, and net exports of $0.4 trillion. Now consider what happens if spending on one of these components increases.

Let's say planned investment rises by $0.4 trillion. Perhaps business firm confidence rises and business decision-makers decide to invest in new factories for future production. Table 27A.6 shows the effect on equilibrium output in the economy. When planned investment rises from $2 trillion to $2.4 trillion, equilibrium real GDP in the economy rises from $18 trillion to $19 trillion. The shift

New Equilibrium with Higher Planned Investment Spending
(all dollars in billions; MPC = 0.6)

(1) Y Real GDP	(2) A Autonomous consumption	(3) C A + MPC·Y	(4) PI Planned investment	(5) G Government spending	(6) NX Net exports	(7) AE C + PI + G + NX	(8) AE − Y
$16,000	$2,800	$12,400	$2,400	$2,000	$400	$17,200	$1,200
17,000	2,800	13,000	2,400	2,000	400	17,800	800
18,000	2,800	13,600	2,400	2,000	400	18,400	400
19,000	2,800	14,200	2,400	2,000	400	19,000	0
20,000	2,800	14,800	2,400	2,000	400	19,600	−400

TABLE 27A.7

New Equilibrium with Lower Planned Investment Spending (all dollars in billions; MPC = 0.6)

(1) Y Real GDP	(2) A Autonomous consumption	(3) C A + MPC·Y	(4) PI Planned investment	(5) G Government spending	(6) NX Net exports	(7) AE C + PI + G + NX	(8) AE − Y
$16,000	$2,800	$12,400	$1,600	$2,000	$400	$16,400	$400
17,000	2,800	13,000	1,600	2,000	400	17,000	0
18,000	2,800	13,600	1,600	2,000	400	17,600	−400
19,000	2,800	14,200	1,600	2,000	400	18,200	−800
20,000	2,800	14,800	1,600	2,000	400	18,800	−1,200

from AE_0 to AE_1 in Figure 27A.7 illustrates how an increase in spending leads to a higher level of real GDP in the economy. Anything that shifts AE upward—whether an increase in C, PI, G, NX, or a combination of these—will lead to an increase in real GDP. In short, spending determines real GDP.

Now consider the opposite scenario. Spending can also decline, and when it does, equilibrium GDP decreases. For example, suppose business firms become pessimistic about the future direction of the economy and decide to decrease investment spending by $0.4 trillion to $1.6 trillion. Table 27A.7 shows the new equilibrium. In this case, the equilibrium level of real GDP falls to $17 trillion.

This result holds no matter what the source of the decreased spending: C, PI, G, NX, or a combination of these components. This is why Keynesians favor government spending in an economic downturn: when G increases, real GDP rises.

2. Equilibrium Can Occur Away from Full Employment

A second important implication of the AE model is that equilibrium output can occur when the economy is not producing full-employment output. In fact, the primary benefit of the AE model is how clearly it can explain the idea of an extended recession when spending is low in an economy. In the AD–AS model we discussed in Chapter 26 and this appendix, there is an inherent tendency for the economy to adjust toward full-employment output, where the unemployment rate is equal to the natural rate of unemployment. But in the AE model, the equilibrium is completely determined by spending, regardless of whether or not the economy is at full employment.

This result implies that the economy can get stuck in a recession, with high unemployment and low real GDP, if spending drops. Notice that the tables and graphs in this appendix have not specified where full-employment output occurs. Equilibrium is determined by the level of spending in the economy, and this equilibrium may occur at less than full-employment output. For example, in Table 27A.5, equilibrium occurs at $18 trillion. But if full-employment output is $19 trillion, the unemployment rate might be 8% when output is at $18 trillion. This means that the economy is in a recession and there is no natural tendency for the economy to move up to $19 trillion.

3. The Spending Multiplier

In the example that accompanies Table 27A.6, we looked at the effects of an increase in planned investment spending from $2 trillion to $2.4 trillion. Let's think about how this spending increase leads to more income in the economy.

First, firms decide to increase planned investment by $0.4 trillion, or $400 billion. This means firms spend $0.4 trillion more on factories, tools, inventory, and other equipment, which they buy from other firms. As a result, the income of these other firms and their employees rises by $400 billion. But that is just the first step, because this new income also generates additional spending in the economy.

If the MPC is 0.6, then $400 billion in new income leads to $240 billion more in consumption spending (0.6 [$400 billion = $240 billion]). So the initial spending increase of $400 billion can generate spending of $640 billion ($400 billion + $240 billion). But the process doesn't stop there. Now there is another $240 billion of income to others in the economy, and they spend 60% of this income, which is $144 billion. And the process continues.

Table 27A.8 follows this spending example out for several rounds. In the end, if we add up all the new spending, we find a total increase in spending of $1,000 billion, or $1 trillion. Thus, any initial change in spending leads to a multiplied effect on real GDP.

To determine the total effect of a spending change on the economy, we use a formula for the **spending multiplier** (m^s), a number that tells us the total impact in spending from an initial change of a given amount. The formula for the spending multiplier is

The **spending multiplier** (m^s) is a number that tells us the total impact on spending from an initial change of a given amount. The total impact on spending is the spending multiplier times the change in spending.

(EQUATION 27A.6)

$$m^s = \frac{1}{1 - MPC}$$

In our example, the MPC is 0.6. We can use this number to solve for the spending multiplier:

$$m^s = \frac{1}{1 - MPC} = \frac{1}{1 - 0.6} = \frac{1}{0.4} = 2.5$$

TABLE 27A.8

Spending Increase Multiplying through the Economy (all dollars in billions; MPC = 0.6)

Round	Spending increase*
1	$400
2	240
3	144
4	86.4
.	.
.	.
.	.
.	.
Total	$1,000

*This table assumes an initial increase in spending of $400 billion.

Thus, an MPC of 0.6 implies that any $1 change in AE eventually leads to a $2.50 change in real GDP. Spending changes are very powerful. But be careful: this statement is true of both increases and decreases. Decreases in AE can lead to large decreases in real GDP. The AE model makes it easier to understand the Keynesian view of the macroeconomy. Spending (aggregate demand or aggregate expenditures) is the key. Therefore, Keynesians often advocate for an increase in government spending. According to the AE model, the new spending in G increases income immediately and then also through the multiplier effect.

Conclusion

The AE model matches the way many people believe the economy works: spending drives the key economic results. Increases in spending lead to more income and lower unemployment. Decreases in spending lead to less income and higher unemployment. It doesn't matter why spending fluctuates—those spending changes have real effects on the macroeconomy.

The AE model implies that the economy is very unstable, driven by consumer and business firm expectations and behavior. The results can be good, but they can also be very bad.

Even though the AE model is helpful in clarifying the Keynesian viewpoint, the same results can be demonstrated with the basic AD–AS model. As such, going forward in this text, we will rely on the AD–AS model to study the macroeconomy. ✳

Concepts You Should Know

aggregate consumption function (p. 890)

aggregate expenditures (AE) model (p. 889)

autonomous consumption spending (p. 890)

disposable income (p. 889)

marginal propensity to consume (MPC) (p. 890)

marginal propensity to save (MPS) (p. 890)

negative unplanned investment (p. 893)

spending multiplier (p. 902)

unplanned investment (p. 892)

Questions for Review

1. The slope of both the consumption function and the aggregate expenditures (AE) line is equal to the marginal propensity to consume (MPC).

   a. Explain why the slope of the consumption function is equal to the MPC.

   b. Explain why the slope of the AE line is equal to the MPC.

2. The AE model implies that a $1 change in government spending eventually leads to more than a $1 change in equilibrium real GDP. Explain how this multiplier process works.

3. Why is it that, in the AE model, all adjustments to equilibrium occur as changes in output? In other words, why does real GDP always change to move the economy to equilibrium?

Study Problem (✳ solved at the end of the section)

✳ **1.** Assume that the following values apply to the Spanish economy:

  • Autonomous consumption (A) is $200 billion.
  • The marginal propensity to consume (MPC) is 0.8.
  • Planned investment expenditure is $50 billion across all income levels.

  • Government spending is $100 billion across all income levels.
  • Net exports are $50 billion across all income levels.

a. Fill in the missing values in the following table. (All dollars are in billions.)

Y Real GDP	A Autonomous consumption	C A + MPC·Y	PI Planned investment	G Government spending	NX Net exports	AE C + PI + G + NX	AE − Y
$1,000	____	____	____	____	____	____	____
1,500	____	____	____	____	____	____	____
2,000	____	____	____	____	____	____	____
2,500	____	____	____	____	____	____	____
3,000	____	____	____	____	____	____	____

b. What is the equilibrium GDP level for Spain as implied by the AE model in this example? How is this equilibrium determined?

c. At the current equilibrium GDP level, the unemployment rate in Spain is relatively high. Therefore, the government of Spain proposes to double the level of government spending (increase G to $200 billion). What is the new equilibrium level of real GDP?

d. What spending multiplier is implied by the MPC of 0.8?

Solved Problem

1.a. All dollars are in billions.

Y Real GDP	A Autonomous consumption	C A + MPC·Y	PI Planned investment	G Government spending	NX Net exports	AE C + PI + G + NX	AE − Y
$1,000	$200	$1,000	$50	$100	$50	$1,200	$200
1,500	200	1,400	50	100	50	1,600	100
2,000	200	1,800	50	100	50	2,000	0
2,500	200	2,200	50	100	50	2,400	−100
3,000	200	2,600	50	100	50	2,800	−200

b. The equilibrium output level will be at $2,000 billion because this is the only level of real GDP where AE = Y.

c. If G doubles to $200 billion, the new equilibrium output level is $2,500 billion because this is where the new AE = Y.

d. The spending multiplier is

$$m^s = \frac{1}{1 - MPC} = \frac{1}{1 - 0.8} = \frac{1}{0.2} = 5$$

PART VIII

Fiscal POLICY

Federal Budgets: The Tools of Fiscal Policy

Federal Governments Typically Spend More Than They Bring In.

You don't have to look far to read about government budget problems. Does *any* government have enough money to pay its bills? Debt problems seem to be mounting all over the globe. The U.S. federal budget has seen record deficits in recent years, with spending vastly surpassing revenue. A big tax cut package passed in 2017 continued this trend and increased deficits, at least in the short term. (More on that later.)

Given the current budget environment, one might assume that governments never balance their budgets. Actually, the United States had a balanced budget as recently as 2001. If deficits are not inevitable, why are they so rampant? That is a question we'll be trying to answer over the course of the next two chapters.

In this chapter, we examine both sides of the government budget (outlays and revenues) and then bring them together to discuss deficits and the national debt. The primary goal of the chapter is to equip you with the knowledge you need to critically examine fiscal policy options. We frame the recent government budget struggles in context to give you a better sense of the magnitude of these problems, both historically and globally.

Budgets for the U.S. government are the result of negotiations between Congress and the president. Any new plans for spending or taxes must be approved by both the Senate and the House of Representatives before the president signs them into law. As a result, passing a budget typically requires a fair amount of arm-twisting and favor-trading.

Of all the chapters in this text, this and the following chapter on fiscal policy are among the most important for your post-college life. Even though you probably won't end up working directly on government budgets, if you vote or otherwise participate in the political process, you'll need to decide what tax and spending plans endorsed by the various candidates make the most sense to you.

In this chapter, we first consider the spending side of the government budget. We then move to the revenue side, where we look closely at taxes. Finally, we bring these two sides together to examine budget deficits and government debt.

· BIG QUESTIONS ·

- How does the government spend?
- How does the government tax?
- What are budget deficits?

How Does the Government Spend?

A government's budget is a plan for both raising and spending funds for governmental activities. It is similar to a budget you may create for your own personal finances. There are two sides to a budget: the sources of funds (income, or revenue) and the uses of funds (spending, or outlays). We start with the spending side. If we were looking at your personal budget, the spending categories might include tuition, books, food, and housing. For a federal (national) government, the budget includes items like national defense, education, highways, health care, and retirement benefits.

Government Outlays

The U.S. government now spends almost $4 trillion each year—more than $12,000 per citizen. Figure 28.1 shows that real U.S. government outlays rose from 1970 to 2017. The trend looks fairly steady until around the year 2000,

FIGURE 28.1

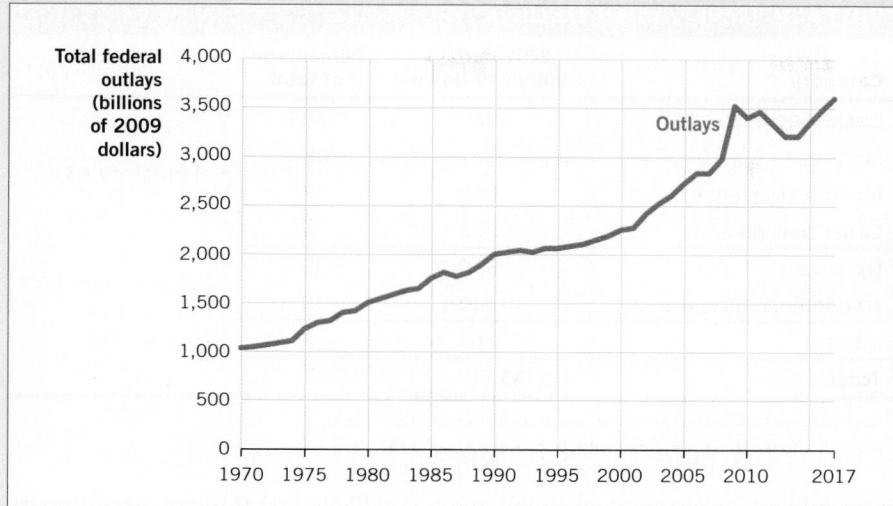

FIGURE 28.1

U.S. Government Outlays, 1970–2017 (in billions of 2009 dollars)

Total outlays represent the spending side of the government budget. This graph shows real outlays (in billions of 2009 dollars) since 1970. In the decade between 2001 and 2010, real outlays grew by 37%. Total (nominal) outlays are now nearly $4 trillion per year, or more than $12,000 per U.S. citizen.

Source: U.S. Office of Management and Budget.

after which the budget's growth becomes more erratic. Perhaps you already know why government outlays varied so much in the past couple of decades; after all, this happened during your lifetime. Over the next two chapters, we will consider the reasons for the wild ride over the past twenty years. Much, but not all, of it is related to the Great Recession, which lasted from 2007 to 2009.

When you think of government spending, your mind probably jumps to goods and services like military hardware, schools, roads, bridges, and wages for government workers. These are part of the government spending component (G) in gross domestic product. But as we examine the total government budget, we also include **transfer payments**, which are payments made to groups or individuals when no good or service is received in return. With transfer payments, the government transfers funds from one group in the country to another. Transfer payments include income assistance (welfare) and Social Security payments to retired or disabled persons. Transfer payments constitute a large and growing share of U.S. federal outlays.

Government budgets combine spending and transfer payments into a broad category called **government outlays**. Table 28.1 shows the breakdown of U.S. government outlays for 2017. We divide outlays into three groups: mandatory outlays, discretionary spending, and interest payments. By far the largest portion of the federal budget is dedicated to **mandatory outlays**, which go to ongoing government programs like Social Security and Medicare. These programs are mandatory because existing laws mandate government funding for them. Mandatory outlays are not generally altered during the budget process; they require changes to existing laws. Sometimes mandatory outlays are called *entitlement programs*, because citizens who meet certain requirements are entitled to the benefits under current laws. We talk more about these in the next section.

Discretionary outlays are subject to adjustment during the annual budget process. Examples of discretionary spending include monies for bridges and roads, payments to government workers, and defense spending. When you think

Transfer payments
are payments made to groups or individuals when no good or service is received in return.

Government outlays
are the part of the government budget that includes both spending and transfer payments.

Mandatory outlays
sometimes called *entitlement programs*, comprise government spending determined by ongoing government programs like Social Security and Medicare.

Discretionary outlays
comprise spending that is adjustable during the annual budget process.

TABLE 28.1

Category	2017 outlays (billions of dollars)	Percentage of total	
2017 U.S. Government Outlays			
Social Security	$939	23%	Mandatory 63%
Medicare	702	18	
Income assistance	668	17	
Other plus receipts	209	5	
Defense	590	15	Discretionary 30%
Nondefense discretionary	610	15	
Interest	263	7	Interest 7%
Total	**$3,981**		

Source: Congressional Budget Office www.cbo.gov/publication/53651.

Note: Due to rounding, these percentages do not add up to 100.

of prominent government spending items, you likely first think of discretionary items. But in fact, discretionary spending accounts for less than one-third of the U.S. government budget, which is now predominantly mandatory spending.

The final category in Table 28.1 is interest payments. These are payments made to current owners of U.S. Treasury bonds. For all practical purposes, these interest payments are also mandatory because they are not easy to alter, given a certain level of debt.

To understand these three broad categories better, imagine applying them to your own budget after you graduate from college. You'll need to plan for groceries, gasoline, car payments, housing payments, utility bills, and perhaps student loan payments. Some of these items are discretionary—you're able to vary them from month to month. These include groceries, gas, and utilities. But others are mandatory, with a predetermined level each month. Mandatory expenses might include your monthly housing and car payments. Finally, student loan payments are like governmental interest payments, in that you're paying off a previously incurred debt.

The distinction between mandatory and discretionary spending helps to explain the recent growth of government spending in many nations: much of the growth is in mandatory spending. Returning to Table 28.1, we see that mandatory spending constituted 63% of the U.S. budget in 2017. In fact, if we include interest payments as obligatory, that leaves just 30% of the U.S. budget where trimming is possible. You might remember this the next time you read or hear about budgetary negotiations: while much of the debate focuses on discretionary spending items like defense, bridges and highways, or educational subsidies, the majority of the budget actually goes to mandatory categories.

It wasn't always this way. Figure 28.2 plots U.S. budget categories as portions of total outlays for 1970–2017. The green-shaded categories represent mandatory spending. Fifty years ago, mandatory spending was about one-third of the federal budget. The cause of the growth in mandatory spending over the last 50 years is both political

Discretionary government spending includes purchases of military equipment.

FIGURE 28.2

Historical Federal Outlay Shares, 1970–2017

The percentage of the budget allocated to mandatory spending programs has almost doubled since 1970. In contrast, discretionary spending is an ever-shrinking percentage of the federal budget.

Source: Congressional Budget Office.

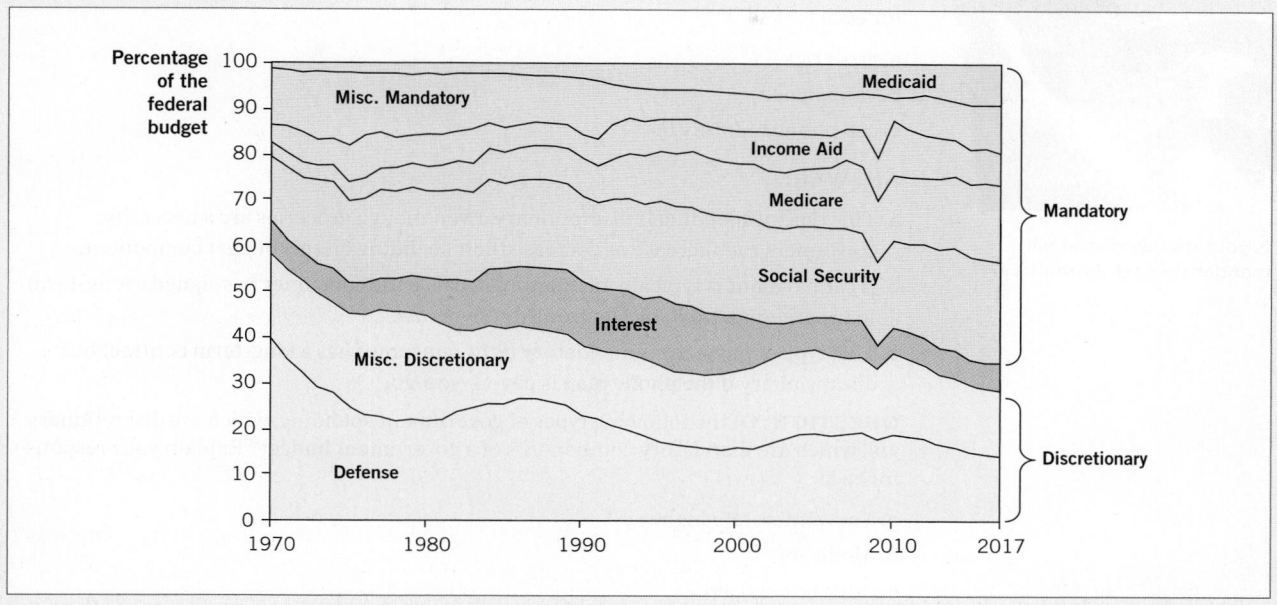

and demographic: new mandatory programs have been added, and an aging population has led to wider eligibility for many programs. Miscellaneous mandatory spending programs include unemployment compensation, income assistance (welfare), and food stamps. Medicare was added in 1966 and then expanded in 2006. By 2017, Social Security and Medicare alone accounted for 42% of the U.S. federal budget, up from just 16% in 1970.

Social Security and Medicare

In this section, we look more closely at Social Security and Medicare so we can try to understand why so many resources are devoted to these programs.

In 1935, as part of the New Deal and in the midst of the Great Depression, the U.S. Congress and President Franklin Roosevelt created the Social Security program. **Social Security** is a government-administered retirement funding program. The program requires workers to contribute a portion of their earnings into the Social Security Trust Fund, with the promise that they'll receive these back (including a modest growth rate) upon retirement.

Congress authorized prescription drug coverage as part of Medicare in 2003.

Social Security
is a U.S. government–administered retirement funding program.

Mandatory versus Discretionary Spending

QUESTION: Of the following types of private spending, which are discretionary and which are mandatory components of a consumer's budget? Explain your response for each.

a. groceries

b. car payment

c. cell phone monthly fee

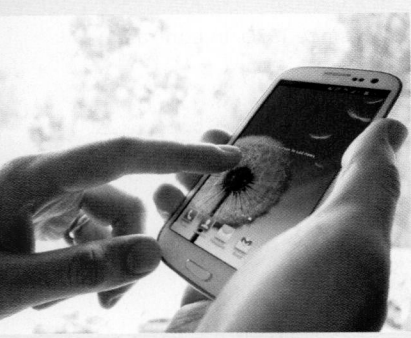

Is your mobile phone bill mandatory or discretionary?

ANSWER:

a. This type of spending is discretionary. Even though groceries are a necessity, consumers can increase or decrease their spending on this budget component.

b. A car payment is typically mandatory because the consumer has signed a long-term loan agreement that entails monthly payments.

c. This type of payment is mandatory if the consumer has a long-term contract but discretionary if the phone plan is pay-as-you-go.

QUESTION: Of the following types of government spending, which are discretionary and which are mandatory components of a government budget? Explain your response for each.

a. a new interstate highway

b. Medicare

c. international aid

ANSWER:

a. This type of spending is discretionary because the government can choose not to fund a new interstate highway.

b. This spending is mandatory because the government is obligated via previously enacted laws to pay Medicare expenses when recipients qualify.

c. This type of spending is discretionary. Each year, the government can choose how much to spend on aid to foreign governments.

The goal of the program is to guarantee that no U.S. worker retires without retirement income.

To understand our current federal budget situation, it helps to consider the financial evolution of the Social Security program over time. At the beginning of the program, there were very few retirees receiving Social Security payouts, and at the same time many workers paying in. As a result, payments into the Trust Fund piled up, even with a low Social Security tax rate of just 2%. However, as time went on, more and more workers naturally retired and became eligible for payouts. At this point, as more workers retire and draw benefits from the program, the Trust Fund balance declines. To keep the Trust Fund from running out of funds, Social Security tax rates have had to increase. The Social Security tax rate is now up to 12.4%.

Medicare is a mandated federal program that funds health care for people aged 65 and older. This program was established in 1965 with the goal of providing medical insurance for all retired workers. Like Social Security, the law requires current workers to pay Medicare taxes with the promise of receiving insurance upon retirement. In 2003, Medicare was extended into reimbursements for prescription drugs for retirees as well.

Both Medicare and Social Security outlays are concentrated on the elderly population and so are greatly affected as population demographics shift. Given that these programs now account for more than 40% of all federal outlays, we should take a closer look at demographic changes before we turn to digging into the dynamics of the federal budget.

DEMOGRAPHICS Entitlement programs have come to dominate the federal budget, with Social Security and Medicare taking up ever-expanding shares. There are three underlying natural demographic reasons. First, people are living longer today than ever before, drawing postretirement benefits for a longer period of time. In 1930, life expectancy after age 60 was less than 14 years, limiting the length of time retirees collected Social Security benefits. Today, Americans live an average of 23 years after age 60. This is a big change from the assumptions on which the system was built.

Second, there are now far more workers retired and drawing benefits than before. To be eligible for Social Security and Medicare payments, workers pay taxes while they work. In the early years, very few were eligible for payouts, but millions were paying in. Both programs naturally generated substantial tax revenue with very few outlays for many years. But with so many workers now retired, the math has changed.

Third, in addition to a normal flow of retirees, the baby boomers (people born between 1946 and 1964) are now retiring. This is a disproportionately large population cohort. Thus, over the next 15 to 20 years, workers will retire in record numbers. This shift will require record outlays for the mandatory programs.

Panel (a) of Figure 28.3 shows the size of the U.S. population aged 65 and over, for every decade since 1900. Each decade brings a larger group of retirement-age workers eligible for mandatory benefits from Social Security and Medicare. This portion will grow even larger over the next two decades. Panel (b) of Figure 28.3 shows the change in the number of U.S. workers per Social Security beneficiary, beginning in 1960. As you can see, in 1960 there were more than five workers per beneficiary in the Social Security system. With that number, it wasn't very difficult to accumulate a large trust fund. But now there are fewer than three workers per beneficiary, and as the baby boomers retire, this number is set to fall to about two, as indicated by the projections for the years 2030 and 2050.

Any substantive discussion about the national debt and deficits must focus on these programs. If we are serious about reducing the national debt, we cannot ignore them.

Medicare is a mandated U.S. federal program that funds health care for people age 65 and older.

Franklin Delano Roosevelt signed the original Social Security Act in 1935.

FIGURE 28.3

The Effects of an Aging Population on Social Security, 1900–2010

Panel (a) shows how the U.S. population is aging, with an increasing percentage being age 65 and older. With the baby boomers now reaching age 65, the percentage will increase even further in coming years. More retirees also means there will be fewer and fewer workers per Social Security beneficiary, as panel (b) illustrates.

Sources: U.S. Census Bureau and Social Security Administration.

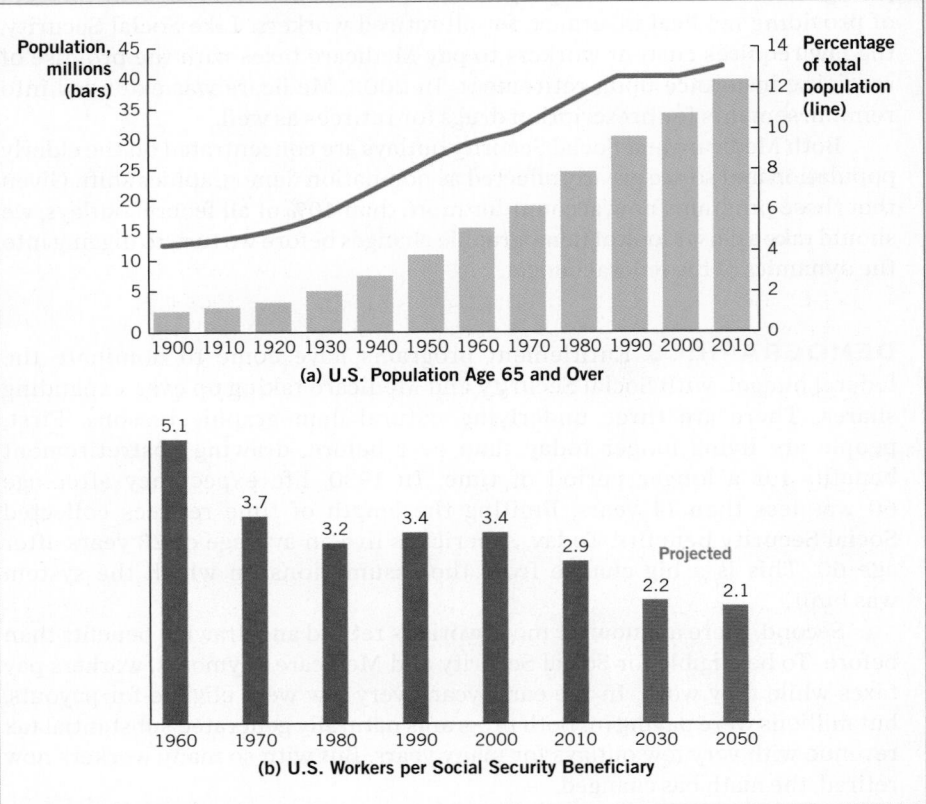

(a) U.S. Population Age 65 and Over

(b) U.S. Workers per Social Security Beneficiary

ECONOMICS IN THE REAL WORLD

ARE THERE SIMPLE FIXES TO THE SOCIAL SECURITY AND MEDICARE FUNDING PROBLEMS?

If current Social Security and Medicare spending trends persist, the U.S. government budget will be severely strained in the not-too-distant future. But it may be possible to alter the spending trajectory, or perhaps even totally resolve the budget issues. Proposed solutions include the following:

1. *Increase the retirement age from 67 to 70.* The logic here begins with the recognition that people are living longer and healthier lives than when these programs were first implemented. If people work three years longer, they will spend three more years contributing to the Trust Fund and three fewer years drawing from it.

2. *Adjust the benefits computation using the consumer price index.* Benefit payments to retirees are adjusted for inflation on the basis of average wage levels when they retire. This policy is in place to ensure that workers' benefits keep up with standard-of-living changes during their working years. Currently, these payments are adjusted on the basis of an average wage index, which has historically increased

faster than the CPI. If, instead, the CPI were used to adjust benefits payments, the payments would grow more slowly and yet still adjust for inflation.

3. *Means-test for benefits.* As it stands now, retirees receive benefits from Medicare and Social Security regardless of their income level. Some analysts have suggested a decrease in benefits paid to wealthier recipients, who can more readily pay for their own retirement and medical care.

These proposed solutions might help to shore up the federal budget. But each would require a change in existing law—and the benefits are not clear-cut across the board. To be sure, raising the retirement age to 70 would definitely mean more revenue for the Trust Fund, and billions of dollars in savings. However, the payoff of indexing benefits to the CPI instead of the average wage index is less certain, since the CPI has actually risen faster than average wages in recent years. As for means-testing benefits, that would change worker incentives going forward, in effect punishing retirees who save on their own and can therefore afford more in retirement. The result? The average person won't save as much for retirement and will be that much more dependent on Uncle Sam. Finally, some people see means-testing as unfair. Medicare and Social Security are mandatory programs all workers must pay into (through taxes) during their time in the labor force. Means-testing implies that some workers won't receive the benefits from a program they were required to pay into.

These changes might reduce the benefits paid out in the short run and, in so doing, reduce pressure on the federal budget. But means-testing might also lead to greater problems in the long run, due to the saving disincentive.

Incentives

Spending and Current Fiscal Issues

Before turning to the revenue side of the budget, we should look at recent history of U.S. government outlays. Figure 28.4 shows real federal government outlays from 1990 to 2017. You can see that federal outlays began growing at a

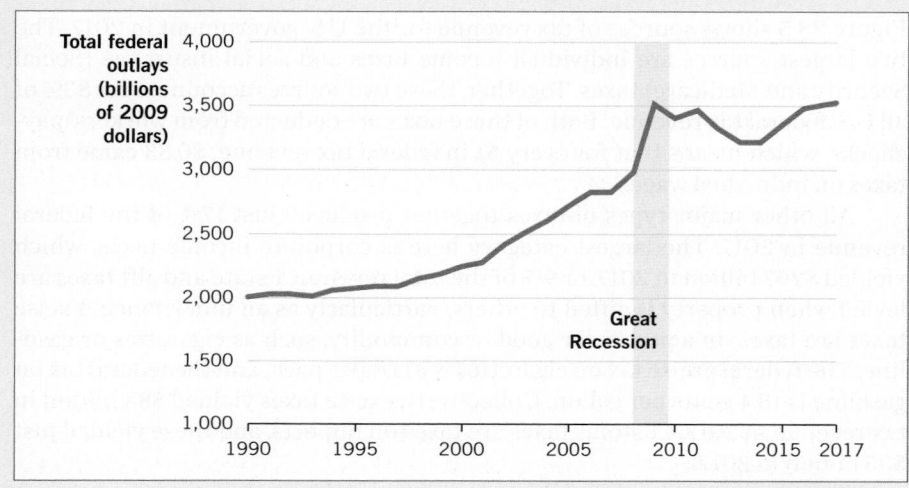

FIGURE 28.4

U.S. Government Outlays, 1990–2017 (in billions of 2009 dollars)

The rate of growth of U.S. government outlays has increased significantly in recent years. It is easy to spot the large spending increases during and after the Great Recession.

Source: U.S. Office of Management and Budget.

faster pace around 2001. While there are many reasons for the increased spending, we can identify three major factors in chronological order:

1. *Defense spending after terrorist attacks on September 11, 2001.*
   Prior to 2001, defense spending consistently declined (as a fraction of the budget) after the fall of the Soviet Union in 1991, to just 16.5% by 2001. But by 2010, defense spending had increased to 19.1% of the federal budget as a result of major conflicts, including the Iraq war.

2. *Increased spending on Social Security and Medicare from program expansions and increased retirement.* As we have seen, spending on these programs has grown significantly in recent years.

3. *Governmental responses to the Great Recession, beginning with fiscal policy in 2008.* We'll cover these policy responses (including their rationale) more fully in Chapter 29, but this is why you see the 25% increase in real outlays from 2007 to 2009.

How Does the Government Tax?

Governments raise revenues in many ways. Fees assessed for government services—for example, admission fees to national parks—contribute small amounts. But almost all government revenue is raised through taxes.

No one enjoys paying taxes, but the government can't provide Social Security, Medicare, national defense, highways, and public education unless it brings in the tax revenue to pay for all those services. Yes, the government can borrow to cover the budget deficits it runs. But the government can't fund its operations entirely through borrowing. In this section, we detail the principal types of tax the U.S. government collects.

Sources of Tax Revenue

Figure 28.5 shows sources of tax revenue for the U.S. government in 2017. The two largest sources are individual income taxes and social insurance (Social Security and Medicare) taxes. Together, these two sources accounted for 83% of all U.S. federal tax revenue. Both of these taxes are deducted from workers' paychecks, which means that for every $1 in federal tax revenue, $0.83 came from taxes on individual wages.

All other major types of taxes together produced just 17% of the federal revenue in 2017. The largest category here is corporate income taxes, which yielded $297 billion in 2017, or 9% of the total revenue. Estate and gift taxes are levied when property is gifted to others, particularly as an inheritance. Excise taxes are taxes on a particular good or commodity, such as cigarettes or gasoline. The federal excise tax on cigarettes is $1.01 per pack, and the federal tax on gasoline is 18.4 cents per gallon. Collectively, excise taxes yielded $84 billion in tax revenue in 2017. Customs taxes are taxes on imports, and these yielded just $35 billion in 2017.

Because income and social insurance taxes play such an outsize role, we will now discuss them in greater detail.

FIGURE 28.5

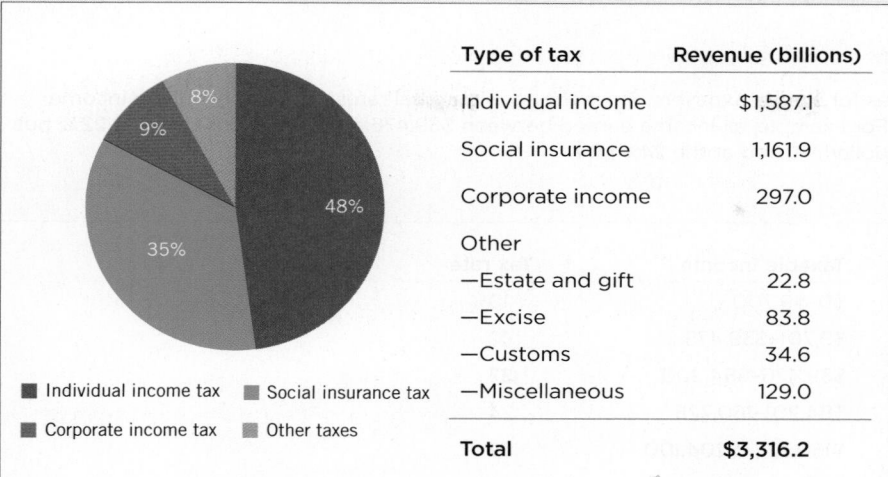

Type of tax	Revenue (billions)
Individual income	$1,587.1
Social insurance	1,161.9
Corporate income	297.0
Other	
—Estate and gift	22.8
—Excise	83.8
—Customs	34.6
—Miscellaneous	129.0
Total	$3,316.2

- ■ Individual income tax
- ■ Social insurance tax
- ■ Corporate income tax
- ■ Other taxes

U.S. Federal Tax Revenue Sources, 2017

The major sources of tax revenue for the U.S. government are the two taxes on income: the individual income tax and the social insurance (Social Security and Medicare) tax. Together, these two categories accounted for 83% of all tax revenue in 2017. Total tax revenue in 2017 was $3.3 trillion.

Source: Congressional Budget Office, Historical Budget Data.

Taxes on Workers' Wages

When you graduate from college and get a full-time job, you'll probably start pulling in bigger paychecks than before. But those paychecks might be smaller than you expect based on your salary alone. Remember, the government pays for activities with tax revenue predominantly raised from taxes on income. Let's look more closely at the major taxes on income: the social insurance tax and the individual income tax.

SOCIAL INSURANCE TAX Earlier, we discussed government outlays for Social Security and Medicare, which together account for more than 40% of total U.S. federal spending. The money spent comes from taxes on workers' paychecks; the benefits received by each retiree depend on taxes paid in during his or her working years. Currently, the tax for these two programs amounts to 15.3% of a worker's pay. This is typically split in half, with 7.65% paid by the employee and 7.65% paid by the employer. People who are self-employed pay the full 15.3% (the Social Security portion of this tax is applicable to the first $118,500 an individual earns). These dollars go into the Social Security and Medicare trust funds that provide income and health care assistance to retirees.

INCOME TAX U.S. federal income taxes are set according to a scale that increases with income levels. In a **progressive income tax system**, people with higher incomes pay a larger percentage of their income in taxes than people with lower incomes do. Figure 28.6 shows 2019 federal income tax rates for single individuals. Notice, the tax rate climbs with income level. That is what is meant when the U.S. income tax system is described as "progressive"; it doesn't mean "a scheme favored by political liberals," even if liberals happen to approve.

The tax rates specified in Figure 28.6 are marginal tax rates. A **marginal tax rate** is the tax rate paid on an individual's "next dollar" of income. Consider a

In a **progressive income tax system**, people with higher incomes pay a larger portion of their income in taxes than people with lower incomes do.

The **marginal tax rate** is the tax rate paid on an individual's next dollar of income.

FIGURE 28.6

2019 U.S. Federal Tax Rates

These tax rates are marginal tax rates for single taxpayers. Since they are marginal rates, they apply only to income dollars within the specified ranges. For example, all income earned between $39,476 and $84,200 is taxed at 22%; but if someone earns $84,201, that last dollar is taxed at the 24% rate.

Source: Internal Revenue Service.

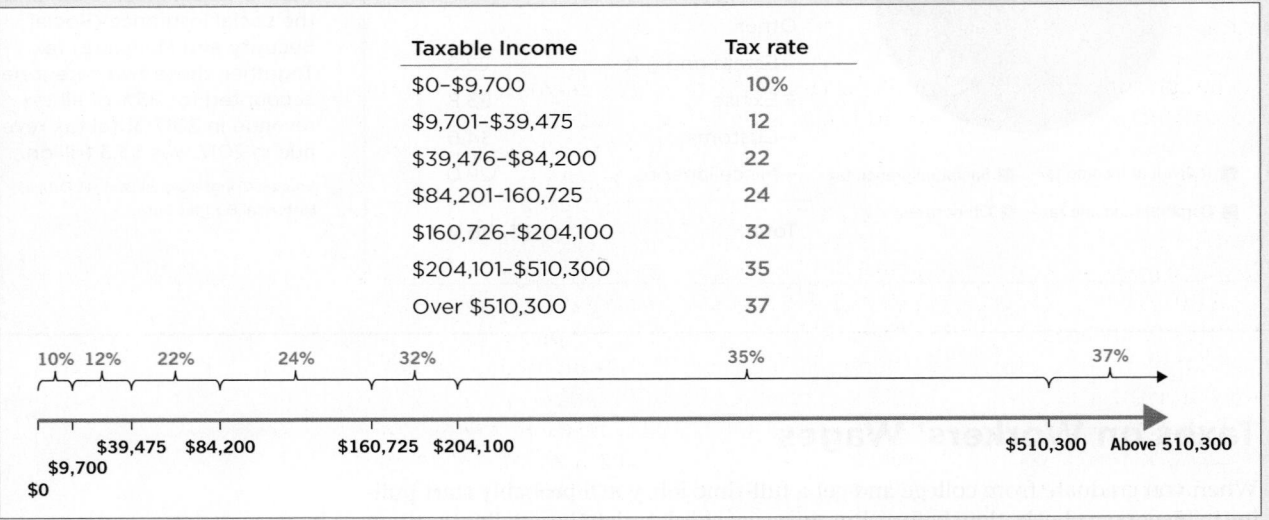

Taxable Income	Tax rate
$0–$9,700	10%
$9,701–$39,475	12
$39,476–$84,200	22
$84,201–160,725	24
$160,726–$204,100	32
$204,101–$510,300	35
Over $510,300	37

Marginal thinking

worker in 2019 with a salary of $72,200. Assume this worker takes the standard tax deduction of $12,200, so taxable income is exactly $60,000. The tax schedule in Figure 28.6 puts someone with $60,000 of taxable income in the 22% tax bracket. This doesn't mean that the worker pays 22% of the entire $60,000 in taxes. What it means is that income *above $39,475* is taxed at 22 cents on the dollar. The same worker will pay 10% on every dollar of income up to $9,700, and 12% on the income between $9,700 and $39,475.

When we consider fiscal policy in Chapter 29, it will be critical to understand how income taxes are computed. For this reason, we now offer a more extended example in which we compute a person's tax bill based on the marginal tax rates from Figure 28.6. Let's use these rates to compute a tax bill based on a taxable income of $60,000.

Before we go through the math, note that three different tax rates apply: 10% on income up to $9,700; 12% on income from $9,701 to $39,475; and 22% on income from $39,476 to $84,200. The total tax bill will be determined as

$$0.10 \times \$9,700 = \$970.00$$
$$+ 0.12 \times (\$39,475 - \$9,700) = \$3,573.00$$
$$+ 0.22 \times (60,000 - \$39,475) = \$4,515.50$$

$$\textbf{Total} = \mathbf{\$9,058.50}$$

Therefore, $60,000 in taxable income will accrue a federal income tax bill of $9,058.50, which is about 15% of the taxable income ($60,000). This 15% is the taxpayer's average tax rate. An **average tax rate** is the total tax paid divided by taxable income. Notice that the average tax rate is below the marginal tax rate (22%). This is generally the case in a progressive tax system, because the marginal tax rate applies to the last few dollars taxed, rather than all income.

Historical Income Tax Rates

Although income taxes seem like a fact of life, the U.S. income tax is only about 100 years old. Prior to 1913, there was no income tax in the United States; most tax revenues were generated by taxes on imports (tariffs). But import taxes were declining, so the government introduced income taxes as another source of revenue. The original income tax in the United States was similar to the current tax system, in that the rates were progressive. But it was very different in terms of the actual tax rates: the highest marginal rate in 1913 was just 6%, and that rate applied only to income greater than $500,000—over $11 million in today's dollars. Very few people were earning that kind of income in 1913. (Not many people earn that kind of income now, for that matter.)

Once income taxes were in place, marginal tax rates rose quickly. By 1918, in fact, the top marginal rate was up to 77%. This rate applied only to income over $2 million, but it meant that every dollar earned beyond $2 million netted only 23 cents to the income earner, after taxes. Figure 28.7 plots the top marginal income tax rates in the United States from 1913 to 2015. Note that while this figure shows only the top rate, it is a good indicator of the general level of rates over time.

We can point to many important dates in the evolution of U.S. income tax rates. During the 1930s, in the midst of the Great Depression, with income

FIGURE 28.7

Historical Top U.S. Marginal Tax Rates, 1913–2015

Marginal rates are a good indicator of overall tax rates since 1913. There are several key historical dates. For example, after 1931, marginal tax rates increased significantly. Major downward revisions occurred in 1963 and in the 1980s.

Source: Internal Revenue Service.

levels plunging, income tax revenues naturally fell. Presidents Hoover and Roosevelt, attempting to balance the federal budget, pressed Congress to increase top marginal rates to 80%. As you might expect, this did not help an already struggling economy. Later, in 1963, with top marginal rates at their historically highest level (over 90%), President Kennedy pushed for tax rate reductions that dropped the top rate to 70%. In the 1980s, President Reagan led the push to lower marginal tax rates even further; by the end of that decade, the top marginal rate was just 28%. In 1993, President Clinton proposed higher rates, and the top rate rose to 39.6%. President George W. Bush pushed through a temporary decrease in this top rate in 2003, and the lower rate of 35% persisted for 10 years, before the top rate returned to 39.6% in 2013. Over the course of a century, there was a great deal of fluctuation in marginal tax rates. Going forward, it is not likely that rates will ever return to the levels witnessed prior to 1980.

PRACTICE WHAT YOU KNOW

Figuring out your income tax bill involves some basic math.

Government Revenue: Federal Taxes

Assume that your taxable income is $100,000. Use the 2019 marginal tax rates from Figure 28.6 to determine your taxes.

QUESTION: How would you compute your federal income tax?

ANSWER: Looking at Figure 28.6, keep in mind that the different rates apply only to the income in the specified bands. For example, the first tax rate of 10% applies only to income up to $9,700. Income between $9,701 and $39,475 is taxed at 12%. Use this pattern to determine the tax paid on all income up to $100,000. Multiply these rates by the income in the respective brackets, and sum these to get the total income tax:

$0.10 \times \$9,700$	=	$970.00
$+ 0.12 \times (\$39,475 - \$9,700)$	=	$3,573.00
$+ 0.22 \times (\$84,200 - \$39,475)$	=	$9,839.50
$+ 0.24 \times (\$100,000 - \$84,200)$	=	$3,792.00

Total = $18,174.50

CHALLENGE QUESTION: Compute the average tax rate and compare it to the marginal tax rate.

ANSWER: The average tax rate is 18.17%, computed as $18,174.50/$100,000. This is less than the marginal tax rate of 24%, the tax rate paid on the last dollar of income. The average rate is below the marginal rate because the higher marginal rate applies only to income above $84,200.

How Are Taxes Distributed across Income Levels in the United States?

In a progressive income tax system, tax rates rise with income. This means that high-income taxpayers pay more than low-income ones, not only in absolute terms (which would be true even with a flat tax) but as a percentage of income, and so they end up paying the lion's share of total taxes. This is certainly true in the United States. Figure 28.8 plots total U.S. federal tax shares paid by different income groups (by household) in the United States from 1980 to 2014. The top line represents the share of taxes paid by the wealthiest 20% of all households. You can see that this has been rising over time and that, by 2014, it had reached 70 percent of all federal taxes paid. In contrast, the twenty percent of U.S. households with the lowest incomes paid just 0.3 percent of all federal taxes in 2014. That year, the top one percent (not pictured) of all households paid more than twice as much in federal taxes (26.6%), as the bottom 60 percent combined (13%).

FIGURE 28.8

Percentage of Total Federal Income and Social Insurance Taxes Paid by Various Income Groups, 1980–2014

In 2014, the middle-income group in the United States (labeled as Middle 20%) paid less than 10% of all income and social insurance taxes paid. The wealthiest 20% (the top line) of income earners paid almost 70% of all income and social insurance taxes in 2014.

Source: Tax Policy Center.

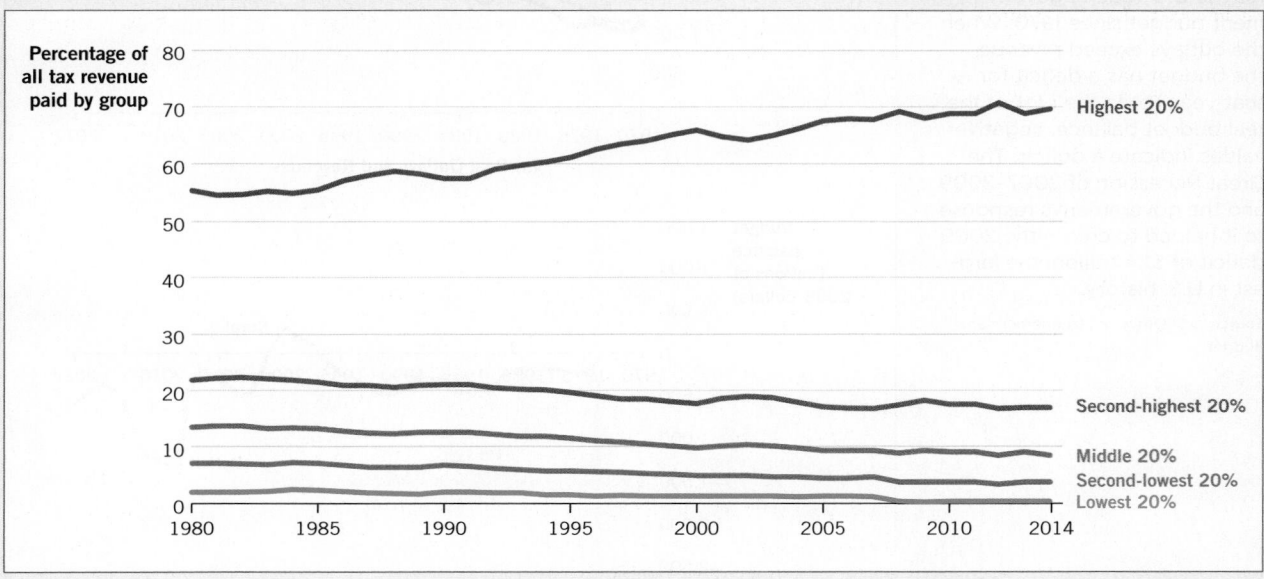

What Are Budget Deficits?

We are now ready to bring both sides of the budget together. Doing so enables us to examine the differences between spending and revenue. In this section, we define budget deficits and debt and also consider these in historical context.

Deficits

A **budget deficit** occurs when government outlays exceed revenue in a given time period, usually a year.

A **budget surplus** occurs when government revenue exceeds outlays in a given time period, usually a year.

A **budget deficit** occurs when government outlays exceed revenue in a given time period, usually a year. Panel (a) of Figure 28.9 plots U.S. budget outlays and revenues from 1970 to 2017, in billions of 2009 dollars. Outlays are displayed in orange and revenues in blue. You can see that outlays generally exceed revenue. The biggest difference came in 2009, when outlays were $3.5 trillion and revenue was just $2.1 trillion. The difference, $1.4 trillion, was the budget deficit for 2009.

It is also possible for the government to have a **budget surplus**, which occurs when revenue exceeds outlays. The most recent U.S. federal surpluses

---

FIGURE 28.9

U.S. Federal Budget Data, 1970–2017 (in billions of 2009 dollars)

(a) Real outlays are shown in orange, and revenue in blue, for the U.S. federal government budget since 1970. When the outlays exceed revenue, the budget has a deficit for that year. (b) In the plot of the real budget balance, negative values indicate a deficit. The Great Recession of 2007–2009 and the government's response to it helped to create the 2009 deficit of $1.4 trillion, the largest in U.S. history.

Source: U.S. Office of Management and Budget.

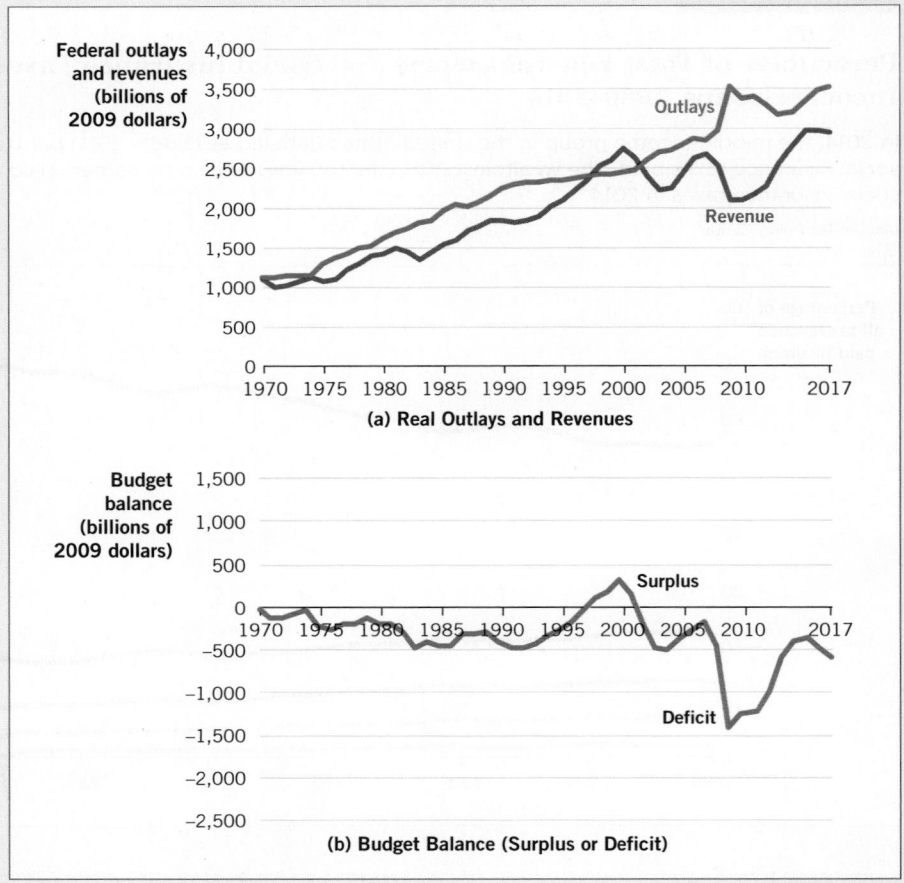

(a) Real Outlays and Revenues

(b) Budget Balance (Surplus or Deficit)

came in the four years from 1998 to 2001. Panel (b) of Figure 28.9 graphs the budget balance from 1970 to 2017. When the budget is in deficit, the balance is negative; when the budget is in surplus, the balance is positive.

The 2009 deficit of $1.4 trillion is the largest in U.S. history—larger in real dollar terms than the deficits generated during World War II in the 1940s. But dollar values for government budget figures, even in real dollars, are misleading over the long run, because the population and the size of the economy change. To control for both population and economic growth, economists look at the deficit as a percentage of GDP. Dividing budget data by GDP scales it to the size of the economy. Figure 28.10 shows the U.S. federal outlays and revenue, both as a fraction of GDP, from 1970 to 2017. Over the entire period, outlays averaged 20.3% of GDP and revenues averaged 17.4% of GDP. These averages are shown as dashed lines in the figure. You can view these long-run averages as a benchmark for future budgets. Both outlays and revenues currently lie outside their long-run averages.

The blue vertical bars in Figure 28.10 indicate economic recessions. When a recession hits, tax revenue, which is largely tied to income, declines. In addition, for reasons we cover in the next chapter, government outlays often increase during recessions. Together these two results cause deficits to increase during recessions.

When the budget is in deficit, the government must borrow funds to pay for the difference between outlays and revenue. In Chapter 23, we introduced U.S. Treasury bonds as important financial assets in the loanable funds market. Now we can understand how those bonds originate: when tax revenues fall short of outlays, the government sells Treasury bonds to cover the difference.

FIGURE 28.10

U.S. Federal Outlays and Revenue as a Percentage of GDP, 1970–2017

The deficit-to-GDP ratio is a helpful gauge of the magnitude of deficits over time because it accounts for changes in population and economic growth. Here we illustrate outlays (orange) and revenue (blue) as a percentage of GDP. The deficit is the vertical distance between the lines. Dashed lines indicate long-run averages. These show us that recent spending has been above the long-run average and recent revenue has been below the long-run average. The blue bars indicate recessionary periods. As you can see, deficits grow during recessions.

Source: U.S. Office of Management and Budget.

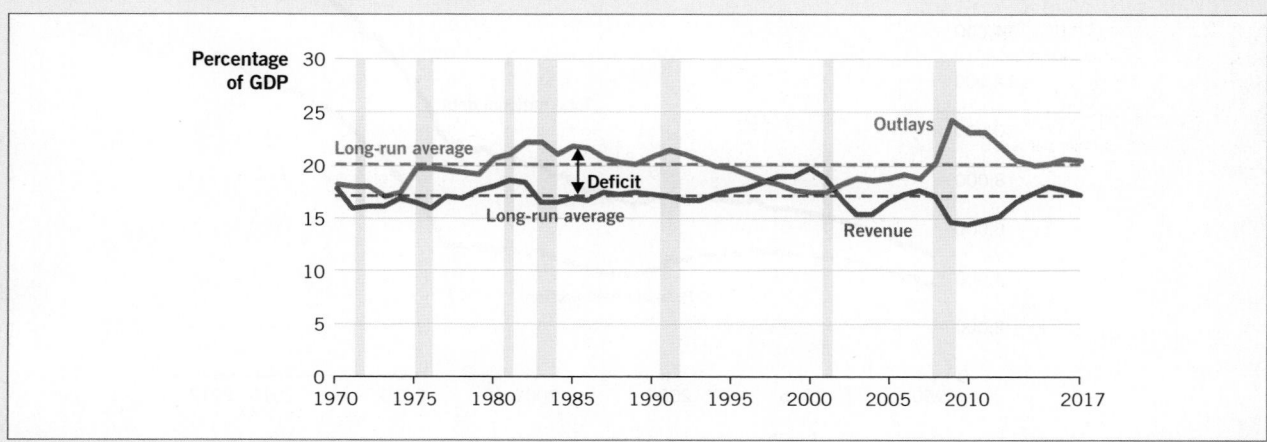

Deficits versus Debt

In your personal budget, it might happen that your spending (outlays) in a given month exceeds your income. In other words, you find you have a deficit. You might rely on funds from parents or grandparents to make up the difference, but this money counts either as income (if it's a gift) or as a loan (if you have to repay it). Often, you will have to borrow, perhaps by using a credit card. A loan, whether it is from a friend, relative, or credit card company, is a debt that must be paid.

A **debt** is the total of all accumulated and unpaid budget deficits.

It's easy to confuse the terms "deficit" and "debt." A deficit is a shortfall in revenue for a particular year's budget. A **debt** is the total of all accumulated and unpaid budget deficits. Consider your tuition bill over the course of your time in college. If you borrow $5,000 to help pay for your first year of college, that is your first-year deficit. If you borrow another $5,000 for your second year, you have a $5,000 deficit for each year, and your debt grows to $10,000. This is the same way that national debt grows. Any year in which there is a budget deficit leads to a larger national debt.

Figure 28.11 shows the U.S. national debt (in real terms) from 1990 to 2017. Notice that we distinguish total national debt and debt held by the public. The

FIGURE 28.11

U.S. National Debt, 1990–2017 (in billions of 2009 dollars)

The total amount of U.S. federal government debt (shown in blue) has grown to almost $20 trillion in recent years, even exceeding annual GDP in the United States. But much of this debt is owned by agencies of the government itself (the government owes money to itself). Therefore, many economists focus instead on the debt held by the general public (anyone besides the U.S. government). This amount (shown in orange) is $13 trillion and constitutes 72% of U.S. GDP. If you are curious about the current size of the U.S. national debt, you can visit the web site www.usdebtclock.org.

Source: U.S. Treasury, *Treasury Bulletin*.

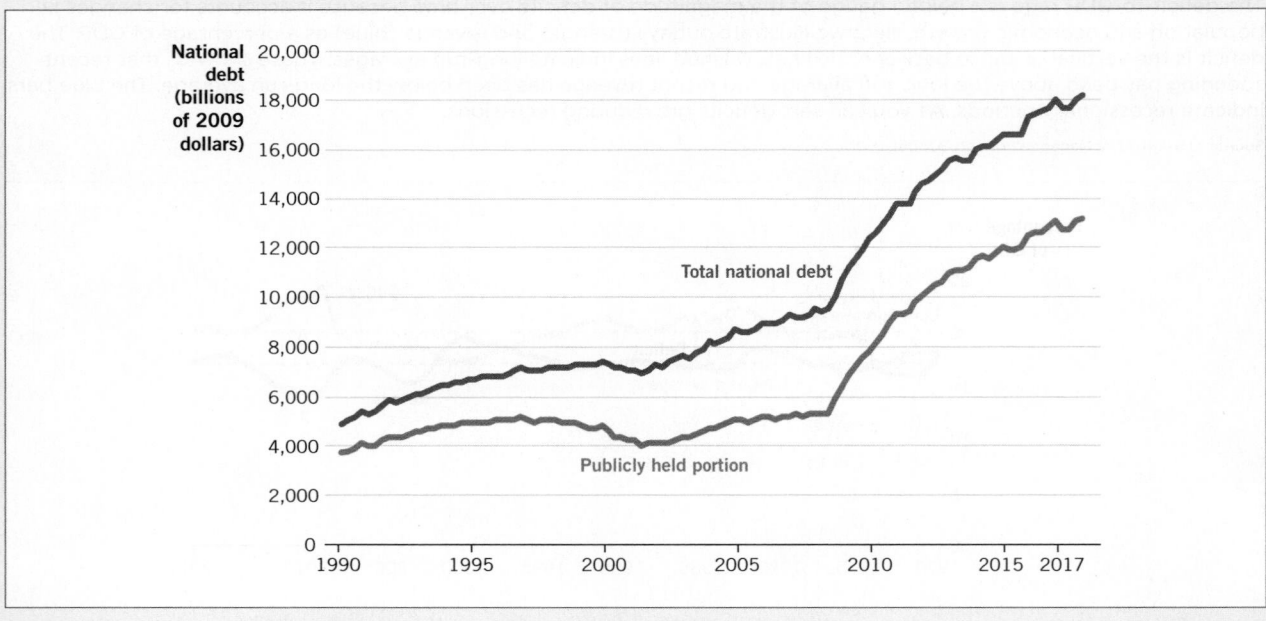

difference between these is debt owned internally by one of the many branches of the U.S. government. Sometimes, a given federal agency purchases Treasury bonds. For example, as part of its mandate to control the money supply, the Federal Reserve typically holds billions of dollars' worth of Treasury securities. Thus, it is helpful to distinguish total government debt that is not also owned by the government itself, and this is the publicly held portion. Figure 28.11 indicates that both measures have risen in recent years, a result of the large budget deficits.

While the U.S. national debt is historically large, relative to the size of the economy it is still smaller than that of many other nations, including many wealthy ones. Figure 28.12 shows publicly held debt-to-GDP ratios for several nations in 2017. The United States comes in at 105%, but Japan's ratio is over 250%.

FIGURE 28.12

International Debt-to-GDP Ratios, 2017

While the U.S. debt-to-GDP ratio has grown to over 100% in recent years, this amount is still smaller than that of some other developed nations.

Source: Eurostat and Trading Economics.

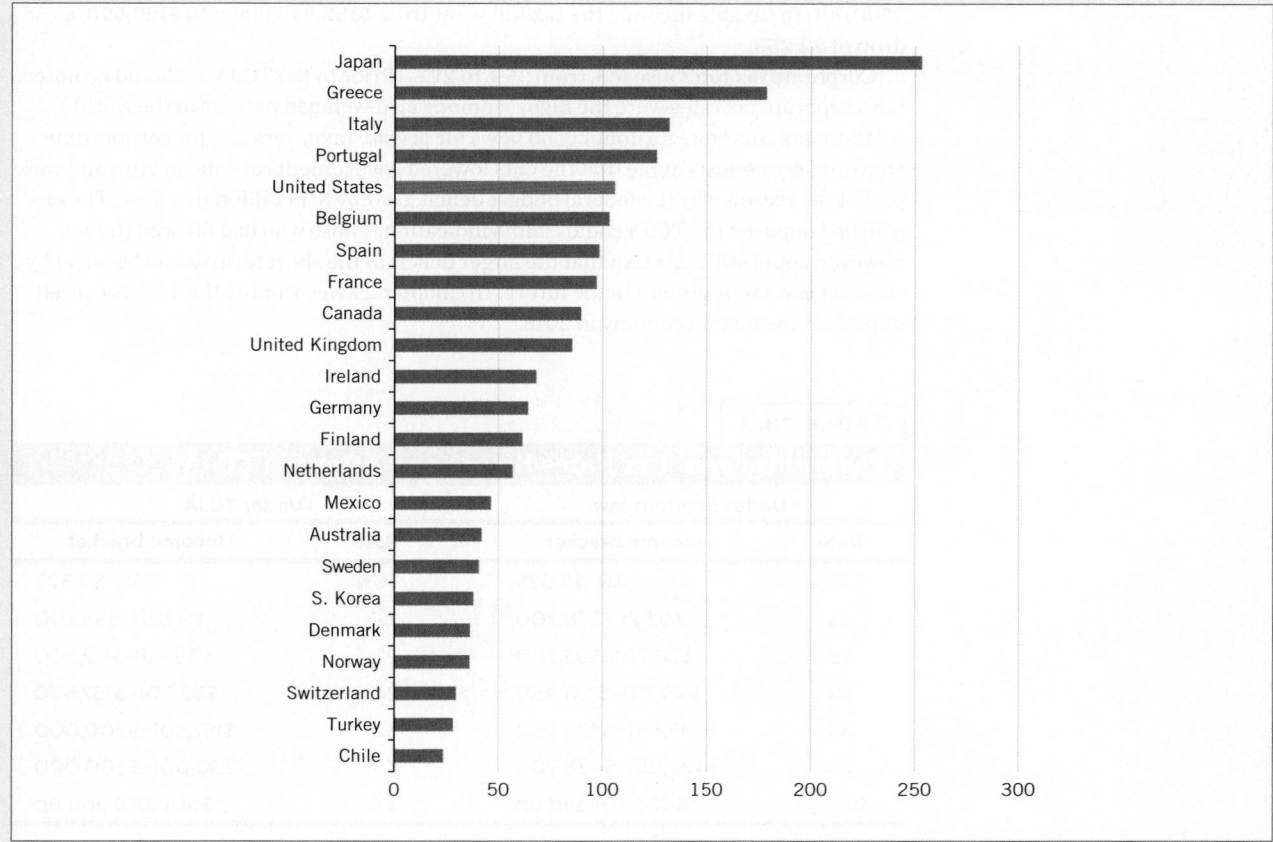

What Are Budget Deficits?

THE TAX CUTS AND JOBS ACT OF 2017

In December of 2017, the U.S. Congress passed, and the President signed into law, the Tax Cuts and Jobs Act of 2017 (TCJA). The two major changes it made to federal tax law were a reduction in personal income tax rates for most taxpayers and a rate reduction for the tax on corporate profits. Many members of Congress voted against the bill, objecting that the federal deficit would rise and that a fiscal policy stimulus should be reserved for a time when the economy is struggling. (At the time the bill passed, the unemployment rate was 4.1%, and real GDP was growing at 2.3% per year.) The act's defenders countered that there was no reason to delay a policy change that would give the economy a long-lasting shot in the arm.

Table 28.2 shows the 2018 tax rate structure for individual taxpayers before and after TCJA. As you can see, rates went down for almost all U.S. taxpayers. The rate for an earner's first $9,525 stayed at 10%, but after that, rates fell from 15%, 25%, and 28% to 12%, 22% and 24%, respectively, all the way up to an annual income of $157,500. Meanwhile, for the highest-income earners, the marginal tax rate fell from 39.6% to 37%. The result was that at the lower end of the income scale, someone earning $30,000 in taxable income paid $3,410 in taxes, rather than $4,024 (without the TCJA), a tax break of $614. At the other end, for someone with $500,000 in taxable income, the tax bill went from $152,943 down to $150,690, a drop of $2,253.

Corporate tax rates also fell, from 35% to 21%. (Prior to the TCJA, it should be noted, U.S. corporate tax rates were the highest among all developed nations in the world.) All these tax cuts were no doubt good news for private taxpayers and for corporations. However, economists agree that the cuts lowered government revenue in 2018 and were part of the reason why the federal budget deficit grew by $114 billion that year. Those who had opposed the TCJA could claim vindication. Those who had favored the act, however, could still maintain that the larger deficit in the short term would be offset by stronger economic growth in the future. In Chapter 29 we examine the TCJA's overall impact on the macroeconomy in 2018.

TABLE 28.2

Federal Income Tax Rates Before and After the TCJA

Under previous law		Under TCJA	
Rate	Income bracket	Rate	Income bracket
10%	$0–$9,525	10%	$0–$9,525
15	$9,526–$38,700	12	$9,526–$38,700
25	$38,701–$93,700	22	$38,701–$82,500
28	$93,701–$195,450	24	$82,501–$157,500
33	$195,451–$424,950	32	$157,501–$200,000
35	$424,951–$426,700	35	$200,001–$500,000
39.6	$426,701 and up	37	$500,001 and up

The TCJA passed both houses of Congress before the President signed it into law in December 2017.

Foreign Ownership of U.S. Federal Debt

As we saw in Chapter 23, many people are concerned about foreign ownership of U.S. debt. The concern stems from a fear that foreigners who own U.S. debt can control the country politically and economically. However, according to the U.S. Treasury, as of 2018, about 70% of U.S. national debt was held domestically, and just 30% internationally. China, Japan, Brazil, and the United Kingdom are the major foreign holders of U.S. debt.

Figure 28.13 shows foreign and domestic ownership of total real U.S. debt from 1990 to 2018. During this period, total national debt grew from less than $5 trillion to over $18 trillion (in 2009 dollars). However, domestic investors and U.S. government agencies were the purchasers of most of the new debt. The portion of U.S. government debt that is foreign owned is only 29 percent.

While this foreign ownership of U.S. government debt is troubling for many Americans, it is important to recognize the benefits of foreign funds to the U.S. loanable funds market. As we discussed in Chapter 23, foreign lending increases the supply of loanable funds in the United States, helping to reduce interest rates. Lower interest rates mean that firms and governments in the United States can borrow at lower cost and thereby increase investment and hire more workers, and ultimately increase future production. Furthermore, the increase in foreign ownership is a natural by-product of emerging foreign economies—as they get wealthier, they buy more U.S. Treasury bonds.

FIGURE 28.13

Foreign and Domestic Ownership of U.S. Government Debt, 1990–2018 (in billions of 2009 dollars)

Most U.S. government debt is owned by Americans or by the U.S. government itself. This graph shows total national debt and internationally owned debt. The percentage owned internationally has grown in recent decades but is still less than one-third of the total.

Source: U.S. Treasury, *Treasury Bulletin*.

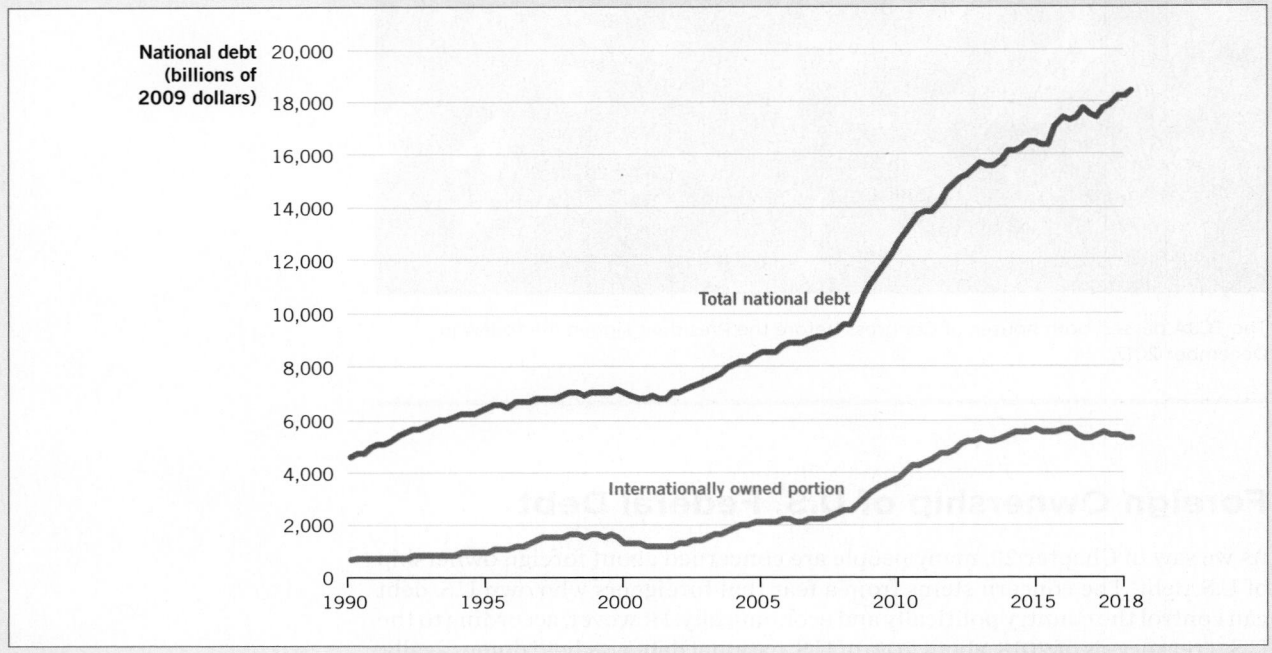

PRACTICE WHAT YOU KNOW

Federal Budgets: The U.S. Debt Crisis

The U.S. national debt grew substantially in the first decade of this century. The table below shows the data on the national debt from both 2001 and 2010.

Year	Total U.S. debt (billions of $)	Nominal GDP (billions of $)
2001	$5,807	$10,286
2010	13,561	14,499

QUESTION: Using the data, compute the U.S. debt-to-GDP ratio in both 2001 and 2010.

ANSWER: For the year 2001, we compute the debt-to-GDP ratio as

$$\$5,807 \div \$10,286 = 0.56$$

For the year 2010, we compute the debt-to-GDP ratio as

$$\$13,561 \div \$14,499 = 0.94$$

QUESTION: What are the major reasons why the national debt increased so much between 2001 and 2010?

ANSWER: First, on the outlay side, U.S. government spending increased due to higher costs for Social Security and Medicare, additional defense spending primarily funding conflicts in Iraq and Afghanistan, and governmental responses to the Great Recession beginning with fiscal policy in 2008.

Second, on the revenue side, tax receipts declined sharply during and after the Great Recession.

This running national debt clock is posted near Times Square in New York City.

Conclusion

We started this chapter with the observation that governments rarely balance their budgets. We then looked more closely at government outlays and revenues. This chapter lays the groundwork for us to examine fiscal policy in Chapter 29. Much of the debt and deficits we observed are a direct result of government budgetary maneuvers to affect the macroeconomy. Going forward, we now understand the institutions of fiscal policy. In Chapter 29, we'll learn about the economic theories that support fiscal policy. ✳

Budgeting for Your Take-Home Pay

- Be sure to budget for your take-home pay rather than your total salary.
- In addition to state and local taxes, you also need to consider the cost of retirement and health benefits.

Many college students have not yet held full-time jobs. So you are probably still planning for that day when you graduate and get your first big paycheck. We certainly don't want to discourage you, but we do offer a few words of caution for when you are budgeting your major expenses.

Let's say you graduate and obtain a good job in the city of your choice. You agree to a salary of $60,000 per year. This is a good starting salary (perhaps due to the economics courses you took!), so you start thinking about your personal budget. Consider a few of the biggest questions: How much can you afford for your monthly housing payment? How large a car payment can you afford? How much can you spend on groceries or dining out? How much should you save each month?

It's smart to think about these questions ahead of time. But when you plan, be sure to recognize that your take-home pay will be far less than $60,000. It is tempting to make a monthly budget based on the $5,000 per month your nominal salary implies. In the table shown here, we estimate the actual size of your paycheck.

First, we subtract federal income tax. Based on 2019 tax rates and assuming a standard deduction of $12,200, we determine that your annual tax bill is $6,375. Next we subtract 7.65% for Social Security and Medicare. After that, we subtract 5% each for state income taxes (this is about average), benefits (like health insurance, dental, and optical), and retirement contributions.

When you put together your budget, be sure to account for all the deductions from your paycheck.

After these deductions, you are left with just $3,186 per month! Your take-home pay is about 35% less than your salary.

Therefore, when you are making major spending decisions about things such as housing and car payments, be sure to budget based on this much smaller figure. If you budget based on your salary alone, you won't be able to save, and you may even become dependent on credit cards.

	Monthly	Yearly
Salary	$5,000	$60,000
Federal income tax	531	6,375
Social Security/Medicare tax	383	4,590
State income tax	250	3,000
Benefits	400	4,800
Retirement	250	3,000
Take-home pay	3,186	38,235

· ANSWERING *the* BIG QUESTIONS ·

How does the government spend?

- Government spending has grown sharply since 2000, and it is now about $4 trillion per year.

- Mandatory spending programs now constitute over 60% of government spending at the U.S. national level. These mandatory programs include Social Security, Medicare, and welfare programs.

- Interest on the national debt is about 7% of federal spending. Defense spending is 15% of federal spending. The remainder of the discretionary budget goes to discretionary government spending like highways, bridges, and the salaries of many government employees.

How does the government tax?

- The U.S. government raises about 83% of its revenues through taxes on paychecks: the income tax and the tax for Social Security and Medicare. The income tax yields about $1.6 trillion in revenue per year. It is a progressive tax, so wealthier Americans pay more in taxes than the poor do.

What are budget deficits?

- If total government outlays exceed revenue in a given year, the budget is in deficit.

- Deficits add to the national debt, which is the accumulated deficit over time.

Concepts You Should Know

average tax rate (p. 921)
budget deficit (p. 924)
budget surplus (p. 924)
debt (p. 926)
discretionary outlays (p. 911)

government outlays (p. 911)
mandatory outlays (p. 911)
marginal tax rate (p. 919)
Medicare (p. 915)

progressive income tax system (p. 919)
Social Security (p. 913)
transfer payments (p. 911)

Questions for Review

1. Since the 1960s, Social Security and Medicare have grown as portions of U.S. government spending.

   a. What major categories of government spending have shrunk during the same period?

   b. Has the U.S. budget become more or less flexible as a result of the growth in the mandatory programs? Explain your response.

2. Explain the difference between a budget deficit and the national debt.

3. Going back to 1965, there have been a few years in which the U.S. government budget was in surplus. What years were these? Why do you think those surpluses disappeared when they did? Figure 28.10 might be helpful in answering this question.

4. This question refers to Figure 28.10, which shows the U.S. outlays and revenue as portions of GDP.

   a. List three periods when the U.S. budget deficit was relatively large.

   b. What historical events were taking place in the United States during these three periods that may have led to these large deficits? Be specific.

5. Explain why mandatory outlays are predicted to grow (as a portion of the total budget) over the next two decades.

6. Explain the difference between average tax rates and marginal tax rates. Is it possible for a person's average tax rate to equal his or her marginal tax rate? If so, how?

7. Determine whether each of the following statements is true or false.

   a. About half of the current U.S. federal budget is allocated to national defense.

   b. About half of the current U.S. federal budget is allocated to mandatory (entitlement) programs.

   c. About ten percent of our current federal budget is allocated to foreign aid.

   d. There was a recent proposal to increase defense spending by $54 billion (true!). If successful, the move will lead to the highest share of the national budget spent on defense since 1970.

   e. More than seventy-five percent of current federal revenue derives from taxes on wages (income and social insurance taxes).

   f. In the 1980s, President Reagan helped to reduce marginal tax rates from the highest level in U.S. history.

   g. Discretionary spending as a total portion of the federal budget is likely to increase as baby boomers retire.

Study Problems (*solved at the end of the section)

1. Use the marginal income tax rates in Figure 28.6 to compute the following:

   a. tax due on taxable income of $100,000, $200,000, and $500,000

   b. average tax rate on taxable income of $100,000, $200,000, and $500,000

2. Greece, Ireland, Portugal, and Spain all went through national budget difficulties a while back. Use the following data to answer questions regarding the sovereign debts of these nations. (All data come from the OECD and are in billions of current U.S. dollars.)

	2000		2010	
	Debt	**GDP**	**Debt**	**GDP**
Greece	$138	$127	$455	$308
Ireland	34	98	124	206
Portugal	62	118	203	231
Spain	292	586	734	1,420

   a. Compute the debt-to-GDP ratio for all four nations in both 2000 and 2010.

   b. Compute the average yearly budget deficit for each of the nations over this period.

   c. In your judgment, which of the four nations was in the worst fiscal shape in 2010? Use your earlier computations to justify your answer.

3. There are three different ways to report budget deficit data: nominal deficits, real deficits, and deficit-to-GDP ratios. Which of the three is most informative? Why?

* 4. Greece experienced significant national budget turmoil after the turn of the present century. In 2010, it was discovered that the government had been concealing the true size of the national debt for several years. The data in the following table reveal just how much the nation's officially reported national debt grew between 2000 and 2010. The data are in billions of U.S. dollars. Use the data to answer the questions that follow.

2000		2010	
Debt	**GDP**	**Debt**	**GDP**
$138	$127	$455	$308

   a. What was the average annual increase in the Greek debt over the 10-year span?

   b. What was the average annual budget deficit for Greece over this period?

* 5. Use the table in problem 4 to compute the debt-to-GDP ratio for Greece in both 2000 and 2010.

Solved Problems

4.a. The debt grew from $138 billion to $455 billion over 10 years, which was an increase of $317 billion, or an average of $31.7 billion per year.

b. Given that the debt increased by $31.7 billion per year, this number was also the figure for the average annual deficit over this period.

5. For 2000: $138 \div 127 = 1.09$

For 2010: $455 \div 308 = 1.48$

Fiscal Policy

Every Few Years, the U.S. Government Uses Fiscal Policy to Try to Boost the Economy.

In February of 2009, newly elected President Barack Obama signed the American Recovery and Reinvestment Act. This act (first passed by both houses of Congress), primarily focused on government spending, is a classic case of fiscal policy used to counteract the business cycle and was passed when the economy was spiraling into a deep recession.

But that was not the last time the U.S. government passed laws to spur on the economy. In December of 2017, President Donald Trump worked with Congress to pass the Tax Cuts and Jobs Act (TCJA), in an effort to move the economy forward. The new law included income tax rate cuts for almost all citizens and corporations. This is fiscal policy: using government spending and taxes to influence the economy. When the TCJA passed, the economy was not in a recession; real GDP was growing at 2.5% per year, and the unemployment rate stood at just 4.1%. Even so, the stated hope of the president and legislators was to increase economic growth in both the short run and the long run.

We won't know for some time how the tax cuts will affect the economy's long-run growth rates. But looking back, we now see that the U.S. economy grew faster in 2018, the first year under the new, lower taxes. Still, the timing of the cuts was hotly debated among economists. Many recommend the use of fiscal

In the United States, fiscal policy must be approved by both the Senate and the House of Representatives, and then requires the president's signature. Sweeping changes are rare. The American Recovery and Reinvestment Act, signed into law in February 2009, is a classic case.

policy to offset the business cycle, implementing tax cuts during recession, not expansion. Economists also generally recommend reducing budget deficits during economic expansion, whereas the TCJA contributed to a larger government budget deficit in 2018.

We won't know the full effects of the TCJA for a few years yet, but this is the chapter where we cover how fiscal policy like the TCJA affects the economy. We begin by framing fiscal policy in the aggregate demand–aggregate supply model. We examine both expansionary and contractionary fiscal policies. We then consider potential shortcomings of fiscal policy and conclude with a view from the supply-side perspective.

· BIG QUESTIONS ·

- What is fiscal policy?
- What are the shortcomings of fiscal policy?
- What is supply-side fiscal policy?

What Is Fiscal Policy?

Fiscal policy
involves the use of government's budget tools, government spending, and taxes to influence the macroeconomy.

When the economy falters, people often look to government to help push the economy forward again. In fact, the government uses many different tools to try to affect the economy. Economists sort these into two types of policy: *monetary policy* and *fiscal policy*. Monetary policy is the use of the money supply to influence the economy. We will study monetary policy in Chapter 31. **Fiscal policy**, the subject of this chapter, involves the use of government budget tools, spending, and taxes to influence the macroeconomy. In the United States, tax and spending changes are legislated and approved by both Congress and the president.

In this section, we first describe how the government can use fiscal policy to try to stimulate the economy; then we discuss how fiscal policy might be used to slow down rapid growth. Along the way, we consider how fiscal policy affects government budget deficits and debt. Finally, we examine the multiplier process, which describes the ways in which the effects of fiscal policy ripple through the economy.

Expansionary Fiscal Policy

In the fall of 2007, the U.S. economy was slipping into recession. When this happens, most citizens expect that the government should do something to keep the recession at bay, and 2007 was no exception. In particular, many expected the government to step in with tax reductions or spending programs to help stimulate the economy. **Expansionary fiscal policy** occurs when the government increases spending or decreases taxes to stimulate the economy toward expansion. In this section, we use the aggregate demand–aggregate supply model to examine the effects of expansionary fiscal policy.

In Chapter 26, we introduced the aggregate demand–aggregate supply model. In that model, we showed that recession can occur as a result of a drop in aggregate demand. In theory, the economy can move itself back to full employment in the long run when all prices adjust. Consider the example presented in Figure 29.1. Initially, the economy is in long-run equilibrium at point A, with $P = 100$, $Y = Y^*$ (full employment), and $u = u^*$ (the natural unemployment rate). If aggregate demand declines from AD_1 to AD_2, the economy moves to short-run equilibrium at point b, with output at Y_1, which is less than full-employment output, and an unemployment rate greater than the natural rate.

At equilibrium point b, government officials can wait for the economy to adjust back to full-employment equilibrium at point C. This adjustment occurs when all prices adjust downward and short-run aggregate supply (SRAS) shifts downward to $SRAS_2$. But prices can take a while to adjust. In addition, recessions are difficult times for many people, and they expect the government to take action to ease their plight. Thus, government officials often choose to use

Expansionary fiscal policy occurs when the government increases spending or decreases taxes to stimulate the economy toward expansion.

FIGURE 29.1

Expansionary Fiscal Policy

A decrease in aggregate demand from AD_1 to AD_2 moves the economy from point A to equilibrium at point b, with less than full-employment output (Y_1) and unemployment (u) greater than the natural rate (u^*). In the long run, all prices adjust (short-run aggregate supply adjusts to $SRAS_2$), moving the economy back to full-employment equilibrium at point C. The goal of expansionary fiscal policy is to shift aggregate demand back to AD_1 so that the economy returns to full employment without waiting for long-run adjustments.

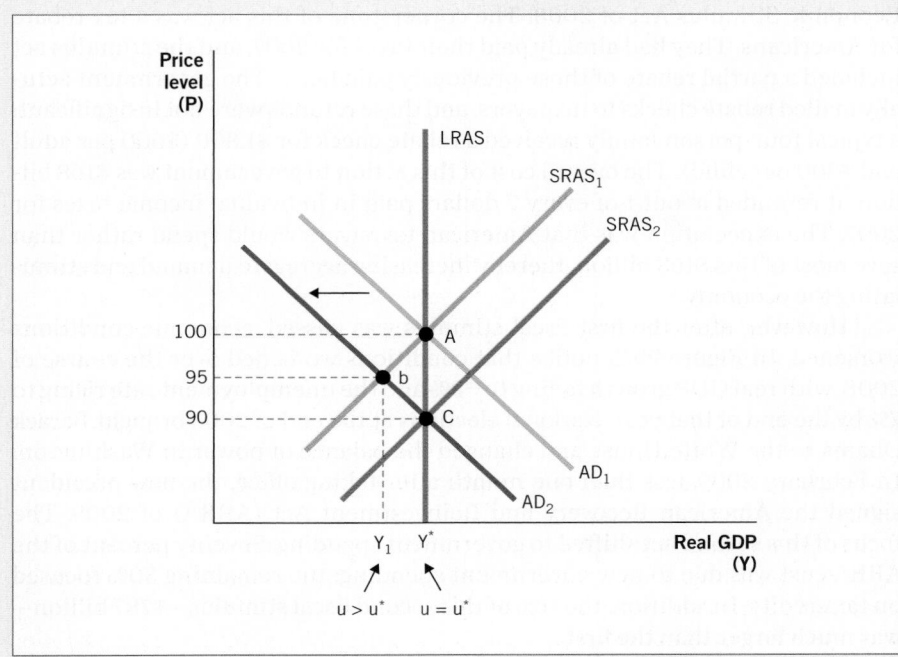

Surrounded by congressional leaders, President Bush signed the Economic Stimulus Act of 2008 . . .

fiscal policy to try to shift aggregate demand back to its original level. If their policy works, the economy returns to full-employment equilibrium at point A.

Fiscal policy can make use of government spending, taxes, or a combination of the two. Recall that aggregate demand has four pieces: consumption (C), Investment (I), government spending (G), and net exports (NX). Therefore, increases in G directly increase aggregate demand. When private spending (consumption, investment, and net exports) is low, the government can increase demand directly by increasing G. Fiscal policy can also focus on consumption (C) by decreasing taxes. Decreases in taxes can increase aggregate demand because people have more of their income left to spend after paying their taxes. When people keep more of their paycheck, they can afford more consumption.

Recent history in the United States offers two prominent examples of expansionary fiscal policy. In the next section, we review these examples to clarify how fiscal policy uses both government spending and taxes.

FISCAL POLICY DURING THE GREAT RECESSION In the fall of 2007, the U.S. unemployment rate climbed from 4.6% to 5%. It was clear that economic conditions were worsening in the United States, and so the government took action. Political leaders decided that fiscal policy could help. Figure 29.2 shows real GDP growth and the unemployment rate in the United States over the period of the Great Recession and beyond. The official period of the recession is shaded blue. The top panel shows quarterly real GDP growth over the period, which was −2.7% at the beginning of 2008. The bottom panel shows the monthly unemployment rate, which began climbing in late 2007 and remained at high levels through 2011, well after the recession officially ended.

In this context, the government enacted two significant fiscal policy initiatives. The first, signed in February 2008 by President George W. Bush, was the Economic Stimulus Act of 2008. The cornerstone of this act was a tax rebate for Americans. They had already paid their taxes for 2007, and the stimulus act included a partial rebate of those previously paid taxes. The government actually mailed rebate checks to taxpayers, and these refunds were not insignificant: a typical four-person family received a rebate check for $1,800 ($600 per adult and $300 per child). The overall cost of this action to government was $168 billion; it refunded about 1 of every 7 dollars paid in individual income taxes for 2007. The expectation was that American taxpayers would spend rather than save most of this $168 billion, thereby increasing aggregate demand and stimulating the economy.

. . . and one year later, President Obama signed the much larger American Recovery and Reinvestment Act of 2009.

However, after the first fiscal stimulus was passed, economic conditions worsened. In Figure 29.2, notice that conditions worsened over the course of 2008, with real GDP growth falling to −8% and the unemployment rate rising to 7% by the end of that year. National elections at the end of 2008 brought Barack Obama to the White House and changed the balance of power in Washington. In February 2009, less than one month after taking office, the new president signed the American Recovery and Reinvestment Act (ARRA) of 2009. The focus of this second act shifted to government spending. Seventy percent of the ARRA cost was due to new government spending; the remaining 30% focused on tax credits. In addition, the size of this second fiscal stimulus—$787 billion— was much larger than the first.

These two major pieces of legislation illustrate the tools of fiscal policy: taxes and spending. The first focused on taxes, the second on government

FIGURE 29.2

Major Fiscal Policy Initiatives during the Great Recession

The Great Recession began in December 2007. In February 2008, President Bush signed the Economic Stimulus Act of 2008, which introduced tax cuts to stimulate the economy and avoid recession. But during 2008, the economy sunk deeper into recession. In February 2009, President Obama signed the American Recovery and Reinvestment Act of 2009, which focused on government spending programs.

Source: GDP data are from the U.S. Bureau of Economic Analysis; unemployment rate data are from the U.S. Bureau of Labor Statistics.

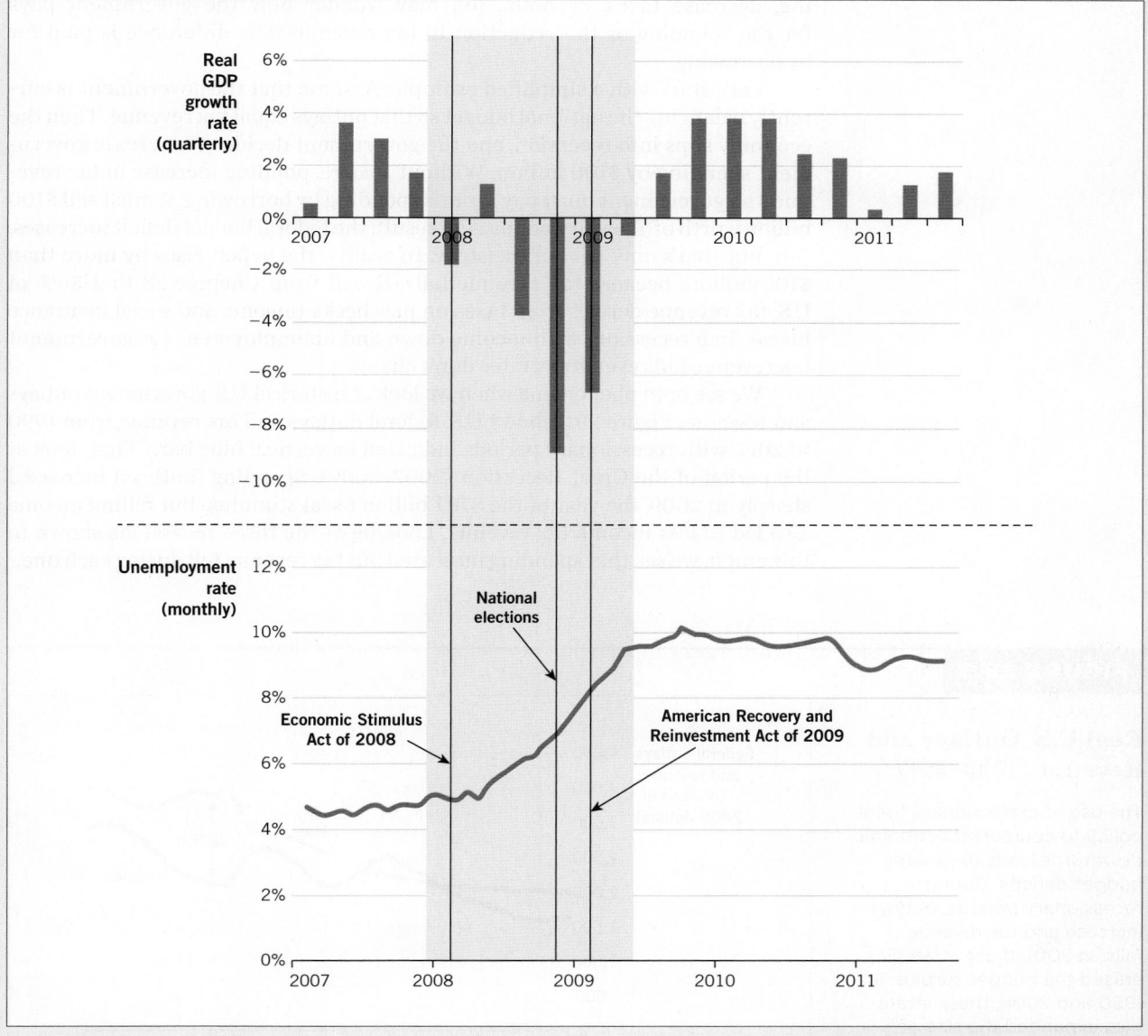

spending. The two acts were very different by most measures, but both sought to increase aggregate demand; they are based on the analysis we presented in Figure 29.1.

Fiscal policy generally focuses on aggregate demand. At the end of this chapter, we consider an alternative approach—one that uses government spending and taxes to affect aggregate supply in the long run.

FISCAL POLICY AND BUDGET DEFICITS We have seen that the typical prescription for an ailing economy is to increase government spending, decrease taxes, or both. You may wonder how the government pays for the spending or the reduction in tax revenue. The difference is paid for by borrowing.

Let's start with a simplified example. Assume that the government is currently balancing the national budget so that outlays equal tax revenue. Then the economy slips into recession, and the government decides to increase government spending by $100 billion. Without a corresponding increase in tax revenue, the government must pay for this spending by borrowing; it must sell $100 billion worth of Treasury bonds. As a result, the federal budget deficit increases.

But that's only part of the story. In reality, the deficit rises by more than $100 billion, because tax revenue falls. Recall from Chapter 28 that 80% of U.S. tax revenue derives from taxes on paychecks (income and social insurance taxes). In a recession, with income down and unemployment up, government tax revenue falls even if tax rates don't change.

We see both phenomena when we look at historical U.S. government outlays and revenue. Figure 29.3 shows U.S. federal outlays and tax revenue from 1990 to 2017, with recessionary periods indicated by vertical blue bars. First, look at the period of the Great Recession (2007–2009). Spending (outlays) increased sharply in 2009, the year of the $787 billion fiscal stimulus. But falling income also led to less income tax revenue. Looking at the three recessions shown in this graph, we see that spending increased but tax revenue fell during each one.

FIGURE 29.3

Real U.S. Outlays and Revenue, 1990–2017

The use of expansionary fiscal policy to counteract economic downturns leads to greater budget deficits. During recessionary periods, outlays increase and tax revenue falls. In 2001, these strategies erased the budget surplus; in 1990 and 2008, these strategies expanded the size of the deficit.

Source: Office of Management and Budget.

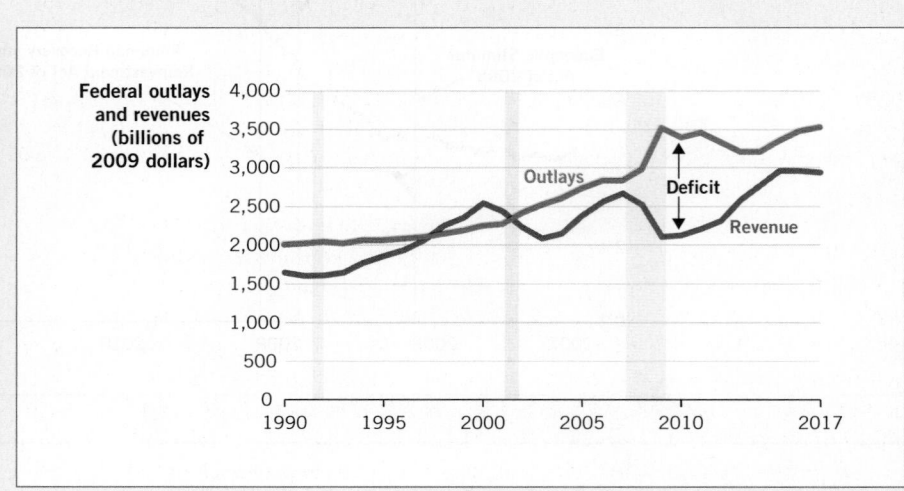

The bottom line is clear: expansionary fiscal policy inevitably leads to increases in budget deficits and the national debt during economic downturns. This policy prescription may seem odd. After all, if you personally fell on rough economic times, you might (reasonably) react differently. For example, if your employer were to cut you back to part-time employment, would it seem like a good idea to go on a spending binge? You might feel better while you were shopping, but it wouldn't help your financial situation much. From a macroeconomic perspective, however, expansionary fiscal policy might work for the overall economy, because spending by one person becomes income to another, which can snowball into income increases throughout the economy. We discuss this "multiplier" aspect of fiscal policy later in this chapter.

Contractionary Fiscal Policy

We have seen that expansionary fiscal policy is often used to try to increase aggregate demand during economic downturns. But there are also times when contractionary fiscal policy is used to reduce aggregate demand. **Contractionary fiscal policy** occurs when the government decreases spending or increases taxes to slow economic expansion.

There are two reasons why a government might want to reduce aggregate demand. First, as we discussed earlier, expansionary fiscal policy creates deficits during recessions. An increase in taxes or a decrease in spending during an economic expansion can work to reduce the budget deficit and pay off some government debt. For example, the U.S. government ran budget surpluses from 1998 to 2001, at the end of an extended period of economic expansion. These surpluses were not large enough to pay off the national debt, but they did shrink it somewhat.

Second, the government might want to reduce aggregate demand if it believes that the economy is expanding beyond its long-run capabilities. Full-employment output (Y^*) is considered the highest level of output sustainable in the long run. But if the unemployment rate falls below the natural rate (u^*), output may be above Y^*. Some economists then worry that the economy may "overheat" from too much spending, which can lead to inflation. Figure 29.4 illustrates this possibility, beginning at short-run equilibrium point a, with aggregate demand equal to AD_1. Notice that this level of aggregate demand leads to short-run equilibrium where real GDP is higher than its full-employment level ($Y_1 > Y^*$). In addition, at point a, the unemployment rate is below the natural rate ($u < u^*$), which is not sustainable in the long run.

When aggregate demand is high enough to drive unemployment below the natural rate, there is upward pressure on the price level, which is at 105 at short-run equilibrium point a. Further, without a reduction in aggregate demand, the economy naturally moves toward equilibrium at point C in the long run as prices fully adjust. But this equilibrium implies even more inflation. Thus, to avoid inflation, the government can use fiscal policy to try to reduce aggregate demand from AD_1 to AD_2. This strategy moves the economy back to long-run equilibrium with price stability at point B.

Together, contractionary and expansionary fiscal policy can serve to counteract the ups and downs of business cycles. We examine this combination more closely in the next section.

FIGURE 29.4

Contractionary Fiscal Policy

When policymakers believe that the economy is producing beyond its long-run capacity ($Y_1 > Y^*$), fiscal policy can be used to reduce aggregate demand. Contractionary fiscal policy moves the economy from short-run equilibrium at point a to equilibrium at point B, thus avoiding the inflationary outcome at point C.

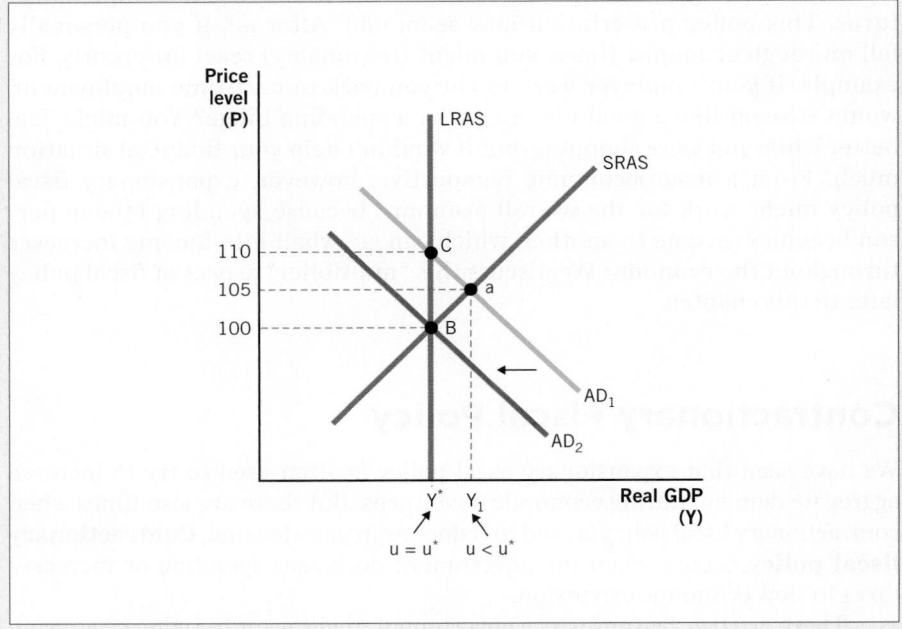

COUNTERCYCLICAL FISCAL POLICY All else being equal, people generally prefer smoothness and predictability in their financial affairs. In Chapter 22, we talked about this characteristic in reference to consumption smoothing; in Chapter 23, we considered how people are risk averse. Along these lines, an economy that grows at a consistent rate is preferable to an economy that grows in an erratic fashion. For these and other reasons, politicians generally employ fiscal policy to counteract the business cycle.

Fiscal policy that seeks to counteract business cycle fluctuations is known as **countercyclical fiscal policy**. It consists of using expansionary policy during economic downturns and contractionary policy during economic expansions. Figure 29.5 illustrates the goals of countercyclical fiscal policy. The natural path of the economy (without countercyclical fiscal policy) includes business cycles during which income and employment fluctuate. The goal for countercyclical fiscal policy is to reduce fluctuations in a business cycle.

You might recall from Chapter 27 that Keynesian economists focus on aggregate demand (total spending) in the economy. Keynesian economics provides the theoretical foundation for countercyclical fiscal policy. In fact, Keynes's ideas provided a theoretical foundation for the New Deal government spending programs implemented in the United States in 1933 and 1935. And these ideas also drove the recent fiscal policy initiatives of 2008 and 2009.

Table 29.1 summarizes the tools of countercyclical fiscal policy, including the timing and effects of the policy on aggregate demand as well as its effects on the government budget deficit.

Countercyclical fiscal policy is fiscal policy that seeks to counteract business cycle fluctuations.

FIGURE 29.5

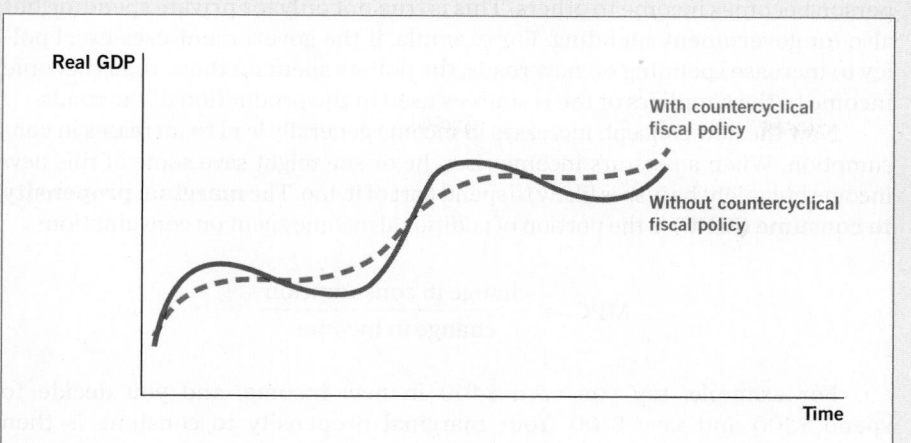

Countercyclical Fiscal Policy and the Business Cycle

The goal of countercyclical fiscal policy is to smooth out the fluctuations in the business cycle.

Multipliers

The tools of fiscal policy are possibly more powerful than our discussion thus far implies, because the initial effect can snowball over time. When fiscal policy shifts aggregate demand, some effects are felt immediately. But a large share of the impact occurs later, as spending effects ripple throughout the economy. To see this process clearly, we need to build on two concepts we learned in previous chapters. One should be familiar; the other is new.

TABLE 29.1

Countercyclical Fiscal Policy Tools

Fiscal policy action	Timing	Objective: How it affects aggregate demand (AD)	By-product: How it affects the budget deficit
Expansionary			
↑ Government spending (G)	When the economy is contracting	G is one component of AD, so increases in G directly increase AD.	Increases budget deficit
↓ Taxes (T)	When the economy is contracting	Decreasing T leaves more funds in the hands of consumers, who then spend more on consumption (C). When C rises, AD rises.	Increases budget deficit
Contractionary			
↓ Government spending (G)	When the economy is expanding	Decreases in G directly decrease AD.	Decreases budget deficit
↑ Taxes (T)	When the economy is expanding	Increasing T leaves fewer funds in the hands of consumers, who then spend less on consumption (C). When C falls, AD falls.	Decreases budget deficit

First, the familiar concept: recall from Chapter 19 that spending by one person becomes income to others. This is true not only for private spending but also for government spending. For example, if the government uses fiscal policy to increase spending on new roads, the dollars spent on those roads become income to the suppliers of the resources used in the production of the roads.

Now the new concept: increases in income generally lead to increases in consumption. When a person's income rises, he or she might save some of this new income but might be just as likely to spend part of it, too. The **marginal propensity to consume (MPC)** is the portion of additional income spent on consumption:

(EQUATION 29.1)

$$MPC = \frac{\text{change in consumption}}{\text{change in income}}$$

For example, say you earn $400 in new income, and you decide to spend $300 and save $100. Your marginal propensity to consume is then $300 ÷ $400 = 0.75. In other words, you spend 75% of your new income. The MPC isn't constant across all people, but it is a fraction between 0 and 1:

$$0 \leq MPC \leq 1$$

Let's consider a simple example of how spending changes affect the economy. For this example, let's say that the government decides to increase spending by $100 billion and spends all of the funds on salaries for government workers. This government spending becomes new income for the government workers. Now let's assume that the MPC of these workers is 0.75, so these workers spend 75 cents of each dollar of their new income. In total, the government workers spend $75 billion and save $25 billion. The new spending becomes $75 billion worth of income to others in the economy. We add this to the initial $100 billion in government spending to get $175 billion in new income. Furthermore, if the recipients of the $75 billion income also turn around and spend 75% of it, they create another $56.25 billion in new income for others in the economy, for a total of $231.25 billion.

It's clear that the initial $100 billion in government spending can create more than $100 billion in income; this effect occurs through the "multiplying" we just described. The effect continues on, round after round, as new income earners spend a portion of their new income.

The multiplier effect is significant when we focus on aggregate demand in the economy. Each time people earn new income, they spend part of it. After all the dust settles, the total effect is a multiple of the original fiscal policy spending.

Figure 29.6 illustrates this multiplier process for our current example. The table in the figure shows how spending becomes income and then how part of the new income is spent. The first round represents the government's initial spending of $100 billion. The following rounds represent the new income generated by consumption spending. Because the MPC is 0.75 in this example, each round generates 75% of the income produced in the preceding round.

In the graph, we show aggregate demand. Each time spending increases, aggregate demand increases (shifts rightward). The initial aggregate demand is labeled AD_1. Each round of spending shifts aggregate demand to the right by less and less, until aggregate demand settles at AD_N, where N represents the completion of the multiplier process.

The **marginal propensity to consume (MPC)** is the portion of additional income spent on consumption.

Your decision to spend or save has macroeconomic consequences.

FIGURE 29.6

The Spending Multiplier Process

Assume that MPC = 0.75 and the government increases spending by $100 billion. In the table, you can see how the spending multiplies throughout the economy; each round is 75% of the prior round. In the end, the total spending increase is four times the initial change in government spending. The graph illustrates the shifting aggregate demand curve as the spending multiplies throughout the economy.

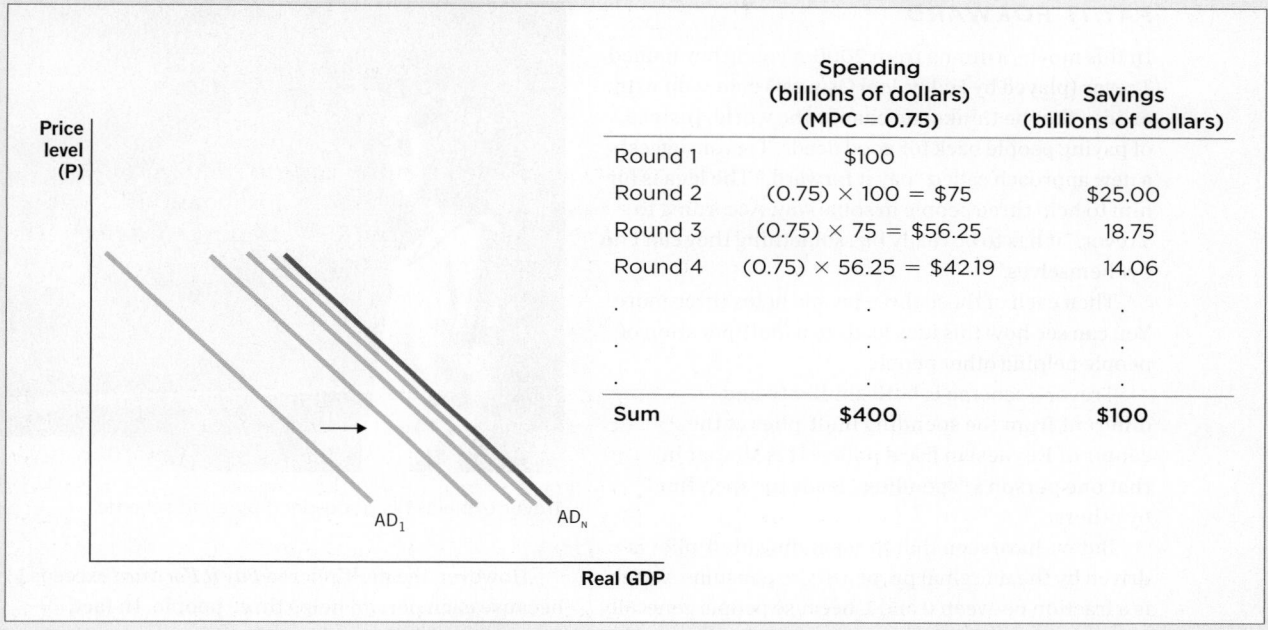

	Spending (billions of dollars) (MPC = 0.75)	Savings (billions of dollars)
Round 1	$100	
Round 2	(0.75) × 100 = $75	$25.00
Round 3	(0.75) × 75 = $56.25	18.75
Round 4	(0.75) × 56.25 = $42.19	14.06
.	.	.
.	.	.
.	.	.
Sum	$400	$100

To determine the total effect on spending from any initial government expenditures, we use the *spending multiplier*. The **spending multiplier** (m^s) tells us the total impact on spending from an initial change of a given amount. The multiplier depends on the marginal propensity to consume: the greater the marginal propensity to consume, the greater the spending multiplier. The formula for the spending multiplier is

The **spending multiplier** is a formula to determine the equation's effect on spending from an initial change of a given amount.

$$m^s = \frac{1}{(1 - \text{MPC})}$$

(EQUATION 29.2)

Because the MPC is a fraction between 0 and 1, in principle the multiplier must come out larger than 1. For example, if the marginal propensity to consume is 0.75, the multiplier is determined as:

$$m^s = \frac{1}{(1 - \text{MPC})} = \frac{1}{1 - 0.75} = \frac{1}{0.25} = 4$$

Sometimes, the spending multiplier is called the *Keynesian multiplier* or *fiscal multiplier*.

Spending Multiplier

PAY IT FORWARD

In this movie, a drama from 2000, a young boy named Trevor (played by Haley Joel Osment) comes up with an idea that he thinks can change the world. Instead of paying people back for good deeds, Trevor suggests a new approach called "pay it forward." The idea is for him to help three people in some way. According to Trevor, "it has to be really big, something they can't do by themselves."

Then each of those three people helps three more. You can see how this idea leads to a multiplication of people helping other people.

Trevor's scheme is both similar to and different from the spending multiplier at the center of Keynesian fiscal policy. It is similar in that one person's "spending" leads to "spending" by others.

But we have seen that the spending multiplier is driven by the marginal propensity to consume, which is a fraction between 0 and 1, because people generally save part of any new income they earn. So the spending multiplication process slows down and eventually dies out.

Trevor explains his good-deed pyramid scheme.

However, the multiplier in *Pay it Forward* exceeds 1 because each person helps three people. In fact, Trevor's multiplier will be infinity because each good deed leads to three more. So the good deeds can continue to expand to more and more good deeds.

The multiplier effects of fiscal policy on an economy are similar to the rippling effects of a stone thrown into the water.

Note that the multiplier concept applies to all spending, no matter whether the spending is public or private. In addition, there is a multiplier associated with tax changes. A reduction in the tax rate leaves more income for consumers to spend. This spending multiplies throughout the economy in much the same way as government spending multiplies.

The multiplier process also works in reverse. If the government reduces spending or increases taxes, people have less income to spend, shifting the aggregate demand curve to the left. In terms of the aggregate demand curve in Figure 29.6, the initial decline in government spending leads to subsequent declines as the effects reverberate through the economy.

In theory, then, the spending multiplier implies that the tools of fiscal policy are very powerful. Not only can the government change its spending and taxing, but multiples of this spending then ripple throughout the economy over several periods. In reality, however, government spending multipliers are not very large. The largest multipliers occur with temporary deficit-financed increases in government spending, but even these rarely go above 1.5. Even

Expansionary Fiscal Policy: Shovel-Ready Projects

In early 2009, with the U.S. economy in deep recession, newly elected President Obama vowed to use fiscal stimulus spending on what was then termed "shovel-ready" projects, because they had already been approved by Congress and were just waiting for funding. Obama expected that his stimulus plan would create new jobs with minimal delays. Let's first examine a simplified version of how economists might try to determine the effect of government spending projects (like the Obama proposal) on the macroeconomy.

QUESTION: Assume that the economy is in short-run equilibrium with less than full-employment output. Also assume that the marginal propensity to consume (MPC) is equal to 0.5. What is the value of the government spending multiplier in this case?

ANSWER: Equation 29.2 gives us the formula for the spending multiplier:

Some government spending projects are more shovel-ready than others.

$$m^s = \frac{1}{(1 - MPC)} = \frac{1}{(1 - 0.5)} = \frac{1}{0.5} = 2$$

QUESTION: Given the size of the multiplier, what would be the implied change in income (GDP) from stimulus spending of $800 billion?

ANSWER: The total implied impact would be: $2 \times \$800$ billion $= \$1.6$ trillion.

more surprisingly, Valerie Ramey, an economist at the University of California, San Diego, estimates that multipliers are typically less than one—not something you'd expect based on how we derived the multiplier from the MPC.[*] This implies that government spending increases don't always translate into more overall spending. In the next section, we cover this more fully, as we discuss shortcomings of fiscal policy.

What Are the Shortcomings of Fiscal Policy?

Valerie Ramey studies the short- and long-term macroeconomic effects of fiscal policy decisions.

At this point, you may wonder why fiscal policy doesn't always work perfectly in the real world. If fiscal policy is as simple as tweaking government spending and taxes and letting the multiplier go to work, why do recessions still happen?

---

[*] Source: Valerie Ramey and Sarah Zubairy, "Government Spending Multipliers in Good Times and in Bad: Evidence from U.S. Historical Data," *Journal of Political Economy*, April 2019. https://econweb.ucsd.edu/~vramey/research/RZUS.pdf.

The first answer is that the real world isn't so simple. Millions of people make individual decisions that collectively affect the entire economy. While economists try to forecast variables and outcomes (how much will people spend versus save?), they can never be certain of the answers to these questions ahead of time. Even the most informed and educated guesses are still guesses and not guarantees.

But there are also more specific shortcomings of fiscal policy. In this section, we consider three issues that arise in the application of fiscal policy: time lags, crowding-out, and savings shifts.

Time Lags

Economic policy is intended to smooth out the economic variations that accompany a business cycle. So timing is important. But there are three time lags that accompany policy decisions: recognition lag, implementation lag, and impact lag.

1. *Recognition lag.* In the real world, it is difficult to determine when the economy is turning up or down. GDP data are released quarterly, and the final estimate for each quarter is not known until three months after the period in question. In addition, it often takes a while for unemployment rates to reflect macroeconomic conditions. Moreover, growth is not constant: one bad quarter does not always signal a recession, and one good quarter is not always the beginning of an expansion. All these factors make it hard to recognize turns in the business cycle.

2. *Implementation lag.* It also takes time to implement fiscal policy. In most nations, one or more governing bodies must approve tax and spending legislation. In the United States, such legislation must pass both houses of Congress and receive presidential approval before becoming law. For this reason, fiscal policy takes much longer to implement than monetary policy. For example, as we discussed earlier in this chapter, the Economic Stimulus Act of 2008 entailed sending tax rebate checks to U.S. taxpayers. The act passed in early February, yet most checks did not go out until about six months later, even though the recipients were known ahead of time.

3. *Impact lag.* Finally, it takes time for the complete effects of fiscal or monetary policy to materialize. The multiplier makes fiscal policy powerful, but it takes time to ripple through the economy.

If lags cause the effects of fiscal policy to be delayed for a year or 18 months, there is a risk that the policy can actually magnify the business cycle. That is, if the effects of expansionary fiscal policy hit when the economy is already expanding, the result may be excessive aggregate demand and inflation. And if contractionary fiscal policy is implemented and followed by time lags, the effects could lead to even deeper recessions.

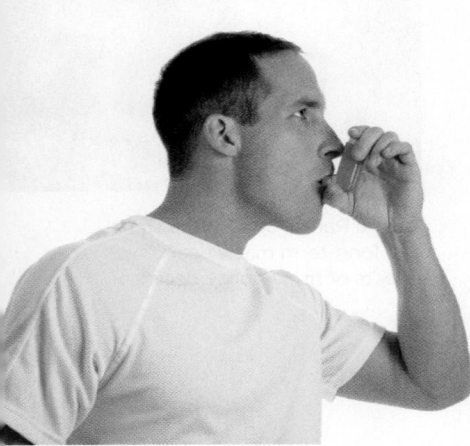

How would you like it if your medications worked with an 18-month lag?

ECONOMICS IN THE REAL WORLD

RECOGNIZING LAGS

Hindsight is 20-20. But in reality, it is very difficult to determine how the economy is performing at any particular point in time. Looking back now, we know the U.S. economy entered a recession in December 2007. But this development was far from clear at the time. In fact, as Edmund Andrews pointed out in a *New York Times* article in February 2008, the Bush administration was not convinced that the economy was in a recession. Reporting on February 12, Andrews wrote:

> The White House predicted on Monday that the economy would escape a recession and that unemployment would remain low this year, though it acknowledged that growth had already slowed. "I don't think we are in a recession right now, and we are not forecasting a recession," said Edward P. Lazear, chairman of the White House Council of Economic Advisers. . . . The administration's forecast calls for the economy to expand 2.7 percent this year and for unemployment to remain at 4.9 percent.

It's not inconceivable that this forecast was biased by political considerations, but according to Andrews, even independent economists were predicting a 1.7% growth rate for 2008. In reality, real GDP fell by 3.5% and the unemployment rate rose to 7.3% by the end of 2008. As this example demonstrates, it is very difficult to accurately recognize current economic conditions.

AUTOMATIC STABILIZERS One possibility for alleviating lag problems are programs that automatically adjust government spending and taxes when economic conditions change. **Automatic stabilizers** are government programs that automatically implement countercyclical fiscal policy in response to economic conditions. Given that the prescription is to increase spending and decrease taxes during downturns and to decrease spending and increase taxes during expansions, there are several government programs that accomplish these goals automatically:

> **Automatic stabilizers** are government programs that automatically implement countercyclical fiscal policy in response to economic conditions.

- *Progressive income tax rates* guarantee that individual tax bills fall when incomes fall (during recessions) and rise when incomes rise (during expansions).

- *Taxes on corporate profits* lower total tax bills when profits are lower (during contractions) and raise tax bills when profits are higher (typically during expansions).

- *Unemployment compensation* increases government spending automatically when the number of unemployed people rises and decreases government spending when fewer people are unemployed.

- *Welfare programs* also increase government spending during downturns and decrease government spending when the economy is doing better.

In short, automatic stabilizers can eliminate recognition lags and implementation lags and thereby alleviate some concerns about the destabilizing effects of fiscal policy.

Crowding-Out

A second challenge in implementing fiscal policy concerns the actual impact of government spending and the multiplier effects. Unfortunately, increases in government spending can lead to decreases in private spending. When government spending substitutes for private spending, the overall change in aggregate demand diminishes. Economists call this effect **crowding-out**. It occurs when private spending falls in response to increases in government spending.

For example, say the government starts a new program in which it buys a new laptop computer for every college student in America. (Don't get too excited; this example is just hypothetical.) If the government buys computers for students, students won't buy as many computers for themselves. Now, students might take all the money they saved on computers and spend it on other items, instead. But if they don't—if they put some of the money in savings—then private spending is "crowded out" by government spending. When crowding-out occurs, aggregate demand does not increase as anticipated, and the fiscal policy is less effective.

Let's look more closely at how crowding-out can work. First, for simplicity, assume that the nation has a balanced government budget and a closed economy (no import or exports). Now suppose the government increases spending by $100 billion but does not raise taxes. This means it must borrow the $100 billion in the loanable funds market. But as we know, every dollar borrowed requires a dollar saved. So when the government borrows $100 billion, the money has to come from $100 billion in savings.

Figure 29.7 illustrates what happens when this government enters the loanable funds market to borrow $100 billion. The graph shows that initially the market is in equilibrium at point A with demand for loans (that is, investment) designated as D_1. The initial interest rate is 5%, and at this rate there is $250 billion worth of savings. This amount of savings funds $250 billion in private borrowing. The table in Figure 29.7 summarizes these initial values in the column labeled "Before stimulus."

Now when the government borrows, the demand for loans increases by $100 billion at all points. This effect is indicated on the graph as a shift from D_1 to D_2. But the new demand for loans changes the equilibrium in the market. The increased demand drives the interest rate up from 5% to 6%, and the new equilibrium quantity of loanable funds increases to $300 billion, shown as point B on the graph. The interest rate rises because of the increase in demand for loans caused by government borrowing.

To demonstrate the overall effects of this new government borrowing, we compare the values of private savings and investment at the two equilibrium points. These are displayed in the table in Figure 29.7. The new equilibrium quantity of loans is $300 billion, but the government has borrowed $100 billion ($G_B$). This means borrowing for private investment spending declines from $250 billion ($I_A$) to $200 billion ($I_B$). Essentially, the higher interest rate discourages some private investment; the government purchases crowd out private investment.

Finally, note that private savings increases from $250 billion ($S_A$) to $300 billion ($S_B$)—that is, by $50 billion—because the higher interest rate (R_B) has caused more individuals to devote more of their income to savings. But if savings rises by $50 billion, consumption must fall by $50 billion. This is a direct relationship. The end result is that an increase of $100 billion in deficit-financed

Crowding-out
occurs when private spending falls in response to increases in government spending.

If the government bought you a new laptop, would you spend your income on another one, too?

FIGURE 29.7

Crowding-Out in the Loanable Funds Market

Initially, at point A, private savings of $250 billion all becomes private investment of $250 billion. But government borrowing shifts the demand for loans from D_1 to D_2. The new demand for loans leads to equilibrium at point B, with a higher interest rate. At the new equilibrium there is $300 billion in private savings (S_B in the table), but $100 billion goes to the government (G_B) and $200 billion is left for private investment (I_B).

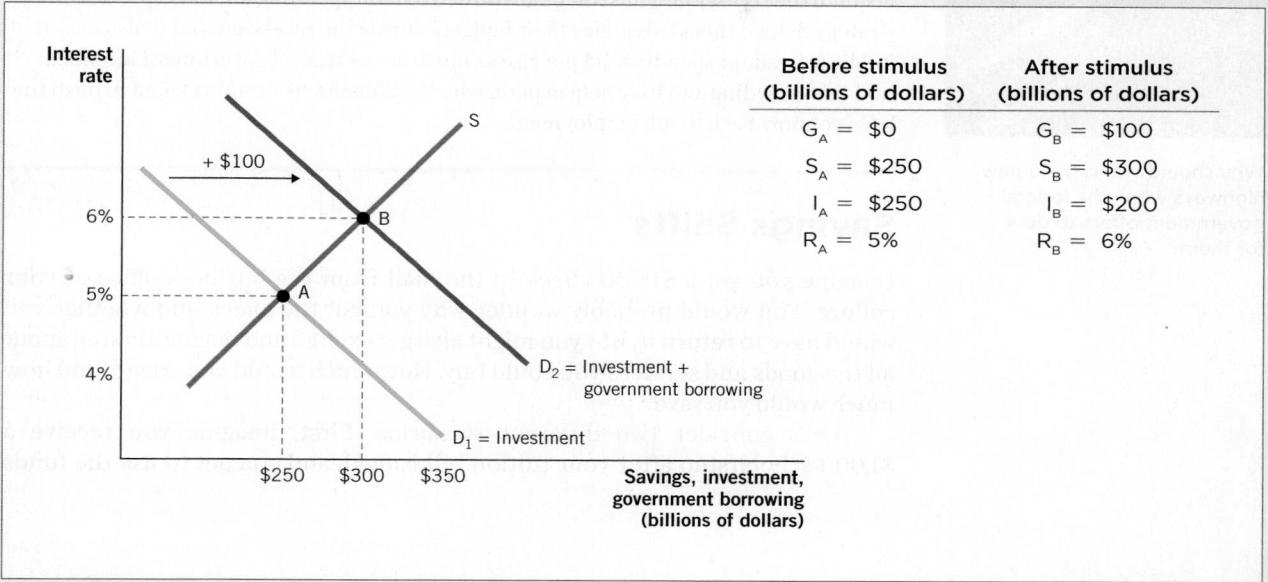

Before stimulus (billions of dollars)	After stimulus (billions of dollars)
$G_A = 0	$G_B = 100
$S_A = 250	$S_B = 300
$I_A = 250	$I_B = 200
$R_A = 5\%$	$R_B = 6\%$

government spending leads to $100 billion less of private spending—$50 billion from lower private investment and $50 billion from higher savings.

In this example, we have complete crowding-out: every dollar of government spending crowds out a dollar of private spending. In reality, crowding-out may be less than complete, if new funds arrive from overseas or if consumers are encouraged to spend more as a result of the government spending. But this example does illustrate an important consideration of economists regarding the effects of fiscal policy.

ECONOMICS IN THE REAL WORLD

DID GOVERNMENT SPENDING REALLY SURGE IN 2009?

In a February 14, 2011, post on his blog, Nobel Prize–winning economist (and prominent Keynesian) Paul Krugman argued that the increases in federal spending in 2009 were offset by reductions in spending at the state government level. He argued that these reductions effectively put a damper on any potential GDP growth and caused the economy to continue to struggle with high unemployment. According to

Why should states build new highways when the federal government offers to do it for them?

Krugman, "Once you take state and local cutbacks into account, there was no surge of government spending."

In a sense, what Krugman was identifying is another challenge of fiscal policy and can be seen as a variation of crowding-out. Technically, crowding-out occurs when private individuals substitute government (federal, state, and local) spending in place of their private spending. But Krugman argued that the crowding-out occurred in the government sector. Federal government spending rose, and then state and local government spending fell. Most states were facing budget crises of their own as a result of the recession. Thus, they substituted federal spending for state spending. This strategy helped them to balance their budgets during the recession. But it also meant total government spending did not rise as much as the federal government intended. And this crowding-out may help explain why the 2009 fiscal stimulus failed to push the U.S. economy back to full employment.

Savings Shifts

Imagine you get a $1,000 check in the mail from the business office at your college. You would probably wonder why you got the check and whether you would have to return it. But you might also get excited and begin thinking about all the goods and services you could buy. How much would you spend, and how much would you save?

Let's consider two different scenarios. First, imagine you receive a $1,000 scholarship after your tuition bill is paid, and you get to use the funds

PRACTICE WHAT YOU KNOW

Without crowding-out, a newly commissioned statue of economist Adam Smith could stimulate the economy.

Crowding-Out: Does Fiscal Policy Lead to More Aggregate Demand?

Imagine that a small country is in recession and the government decides to increase spending. It commissions a very large Adam Smith statue for $50 million. To pay for the statue, the government borrows all of the $50 million. After the government borrows the $50 million, the interest rate rises from 3% to 4% and the equilibrium quantity of loanable funds increases from $500 million to $530 million.

QUESTION: How would you sketch a graph of the loanable funds market representing this scenario? Be sure to indicate on this graph all the changes that take place after the borrowing.

ANSWER: Originally, the market is in equilibrium at point A, with an interest rate of 3% and savings and investment being equal at $500 million. Then the demand for loans increases by $50 million at all points when the government borrows $50 million. This change moves the market to a new equilibrium at point B.

QUESTION: Using the above information and assuming complete crowding-out, what would you predict will happen to C, I, G, and total aggregate demand (AD) in response to the government's action?

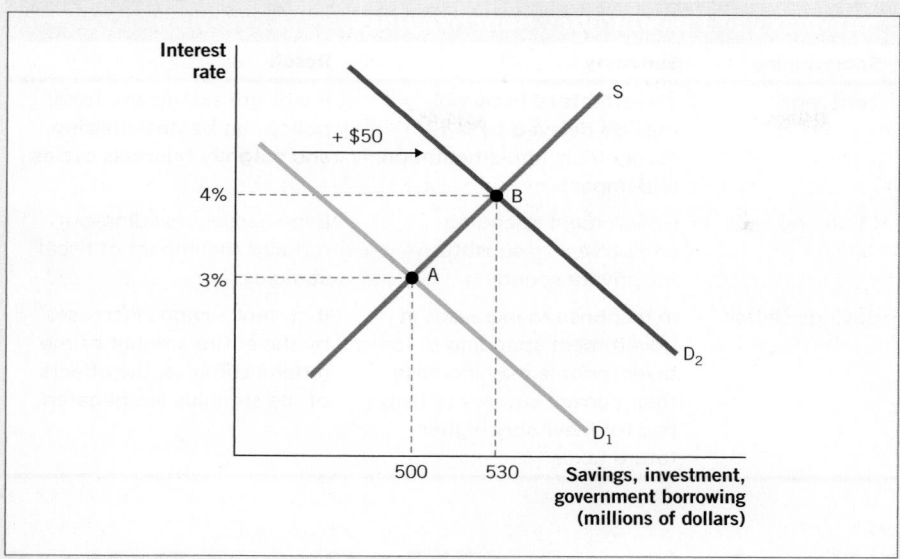

ANSWER: Government spending (G) will increase by $50 million. Total savings will increase from $500 million to $530 million, which means that total savings will increase by $30 million and consumption (C) will fall by $30 million. But because the government is borrowing $50 million of the savings, private investment (I) will fall to $480 million, a decrease of $20 million. All of this means a net change of zero in aggregate demand (AD). These changes are summarized below.

Component	C	I	G	AD
Change (millions of dollars)	−$30	−$20	$50	—

however you like. In that case, you might spend much or all of the $1,000. But now imagine instead that you received the funds in error, and you have to repay them. In this second scenario, you probably wouldn't spend any of the $1,000 you got from the college.

In some ways, government spending in the economy is similar to the second scenario. New spending today has to be paid for someday, which means that taxes must rise sooner or later. The **new classical critique** of fiscal policy, a model developed in the 1970s by a group of economists including Nobel Prize–winners Robert Barro, Robert Lucas, and Thomas Sargent asserts that increases in government spending and decreases in taxes are largely offset by increases in savings, because people know they'll have to pay higher taxes eventually. But if savings increases, consumption falls, and this outcome mitigates the positive effects of the government spending.

Table 29.2 summarizes the three shortcomings that can diminish the effects of fiscal policy.

The **new classical critique** of fiscal policy asserts that increases in government spending and decreases in taxes are largely offset by increases in savings.

TABLE 29.2		
Summary of Fiscal Policy Shortcomings		
Shortcoming	**Summary**	**Result**
Time lags	The effects of fiscal policy may be delayed by lags in recognition, implementation, and impact.	If lags are significant, fiscal policy can be destabilizing and magnify business cycles.
Crowding-out	Government spending can serve as a substitute for private spending.	Even partial crowding-out reduces the impact of fiscal stimulus.
Savings shifts	In response to increases in government spending or lower taxes, people may increase their current savings to help pay for inevitably higher future taxes.	If current savings increases by the entire amount of the federal stimulus, the effects of the stimulus are negated.

What Is Supply-Side Fiscal Policy?

We have considered typical fiscal policy, which focuses squarely on aggregate demand. It is also possible to implement fiscal policy with the intent of affecting the supply side of the economy. In this section, we begin by describing the supply-side perspective and certain popular supply-side policy proposals. We then look more closely at marginal tax rates and consider how changes in tax rates can affect the economy.

The Supply-Side Perspective

Supply-side fiscal policy involves the use of government spending and taxes to affect the production (supply) side of the economy.

Subsidies for college education are a type of supply-side fiscal policy.

We can illustrate the supply-side perspective in the aggregate demand–aggregate supply model. For most of this chapter, we have focused on using fiscal policy to shift the aggregate demand curve. Now we will explore how taxes and government spending can affect long-run aggregate supply. **Supply-side fiscal policy** involves the use of government spending and taxes to affect the supply, or production, side of the economy. Figure 29.8 indicates a shift from $LRAS_1$ to $LRAS_2$. When long-run aggregate supply shifts, the result is a shift to a new level of full-employment output, shown in the figure as a move from Y^* to Y^{**}.

Recall from Chapter 26 that shifts in long-run aggregate supply are caused by changes in resources, technology, and institutions. For example, we know that technological advances increase long-run aggregate supply: a technological advancement allows production of a greater quantity of output using the same or fewer resources. In the long run, much economic growth derives from technological advances. The government can implement fiscal policy and use the tax code to encourage technological advancement. Since 1981, for example, U.S. businesses have received tax credits for expenses related to research and development:

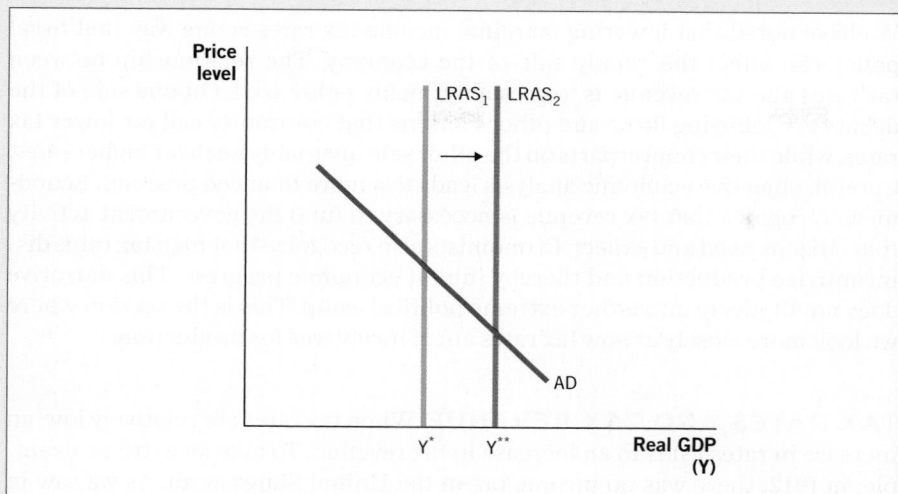

FIGURE 29.8

Supply-Side Fiscal Policy

Typical (demand-side) fiscal policy involves the use of government spending and taxes to shift aggregate demand. In contrast, supply-side fiscal policy involves the use of government spending and taxes to shift long-run aggregate supply (from LRAS$_1$ to LRAS$_2$), which moves the economy from one full-employment output level (Y*) to a new full-employment output level (Y**).

firms that spend on research and development of new technology pay lower taxes than firms that don't. This incentive is designed to encourage innovation and with the goal of ultimately generating a greater supply of output. Thus, the goal of this fiscal policy is to shift long-run aggregate supply.

Many other fiscal policy initiatives are designed to focus on the supply side of the economy. These include:

1. *Research and development (R&D) tax credits.* Tax breaks are given to firms that spend resources to develop new technology. For example, if an alternative energy firm spends resources on a new lab to develop alternative energy sources, this spending reduces its overall tax bill.

2. *Policies that focus on education.* Subsidies or tax breaks for education expenses are given to help create incentives to invest in education. One example is the Pell Grant, which helps to pay for college expenses. Students receive these grants from the federal government to help them pay for college education. Eventually, education and training increase effective labor resources and thus increase aggregate supply.

3. *Lower corporate profit tax rates.* Lower taxes increase the incentives for corporations to undertake activities that generate more profit.

4. *Lower marginal income tax rates.* Lower income tax rates create incentives for individuals to work harder and produce more, because they keep a larger share of their income. We discuss marginal tax rates in the next section.

Incentives

All of these initiatives share two characteristics. First, they increase incentives for productive activities. Second, each initiative takes time to affect aggregate supply. For example, education subsidies may encourage people to go to college and learn skills useful in the workplace. But the full effect of that education isn't felt until after the education is completed. For this reason, supply-side proposals are generally emphasized as long-run solutions to growth problems.

Marginal Income Tax Rates

We have noted that lowering marginal income tax rates is one way that fiscal policy can affect the supply side of the economy. The relationship between tax rates and tax revenue is, regrettably, highly politicized. On one side of the debate are lobbying firms and other factions that constantly call for lower tax rates, while their counterparts on the other side invariably push for higher rates. Careful, objective economic analysis leads to a more nuanced position. Economists recognize that tax revenue is necessary to fund the government activity that citizens need and expect. Economists also recognize that high tax rates disincentivize production and thereby inhibit economic progress. This narrative does not fit nicely into either extreme political camp. This is the section where we look more closely at how tax rates affect incentives for production.

TAX RATES AND TAX REVENUE When tax rates are relatively low, an increase in rates leads to an increase in tax revenue. To take an extreme example: in 1912, there was no income tax in the United States at all. As we saw in Chapter 28, the United States instituted the income tax in 1913 with a top marginal rate of just 6%. Obviously, income tax revenue rose between 1912, when there was no income tax, and 1913, when a modest tax was introduced. At low tax rates, increases in tax rates lead to revenue increases.

But it turns out that if you raise rates too high, tax revenue declines, because the high rates provide negative incentives for production. This means that when tax rates are particularly high, a reduction in tax rates could actually lead to an increase in tax revenue. Tax rate cuts can be creative; that is, they can stimulate work effort, employment, and income and thereby generate *more* income tax revenue for the government.

Consider the following quote:

> The worst deficit comes from a recession. And if we can take the proper action in the proper time, this can be the most important step we can take to prevent another recession. That is the right time to make tax cuts, both for your family budget, and the national budget, resulting from a permanent basic reform and reduction in our rate structure. A creative tax cut, creating more jobs and income and, eventually, more revenue.
>
> —*35th president of the United States*

The president quoted is John F. Kennedy. He made this statement in 1962, when marginal tax rates were as high as 91%. Consider what a 91% marginal tax rate means: these taxpayers keep only 9 cents from an additional dollar's worth of income. Such an astronomical tax rate certainly diminishes incentives for work effort and production! Most economists agree that 91% marginal tax rates stifle economic growth. So although it may seem counterintuitive, it is possible to lower tax rates and increase overall tax revenue.

THE LAFFER CURVE In 1974, University of Chicago professor and economist Arthur Laffer famously tried to illustrate the relationship between tax rates and tax revenue by sketching a drawing on the back of a napkin at dinner. This relationship became known as the Laffer curve. Soon after, it became a centerpiece of Ronald Reagan's presidency in the 1980s and a central component of supply-side economics. Almost since its inception, this curve has been debated.

To understand this curve, let's first clarify the relationship between tax rates and tax revenue. Total income tax revenue depends on the level of income and the tax rate:

$$\text{income tax revenue} = \text{tax rate} \times \text{income}$$

This equation is straightforward. But because human beings react to incentives, it is not always easy to predict how tax revenue will change when tax rates change. The **Laffer curve**, shown in Figure 29.9, illustrates the relationship between tax rates and tax revenue. Notice we have labeled two regions of the Laffer curve. Region I, the blue portion of the curve, illustrates that increasing tax rates leads to increasing tax revenues:

$$\uparrow \text{income tax revenue} = \uparrow \text{tax rate} \times \text{income}$$

But at some point, tax rates become so high that they provide significant disincentives for earning income. This is the case in region II, illustrated by the orange portion of the curve, where increases in the tax rate lead to less tax revenue. Many U.S. taxpayers were in region II in 1962, when some marginal tax rates were above 90% and President Kennedy gave his speech. At this point, an increase in the tax rate reduces income enough (illustrated by the double downward-pointing arrows) that net tax revenue falls:

$$\downarrow \text{income tax revenue} = \uparrow \text{tax rate} \times \downarrow\downarrow \text{income}$$

In region II of the Laffer curve, decreases in the tax rate lead to increases in tax revenue. At the lower rate, people have greater incentives to work and earn more income. Thus, the lower tax rates stimulate the economy and lead to more tax revenue overall.

JFK: Early supply-sider?

The **Laffer curve** is an illustration of the relationship between tax rates and tax revenue.

Incentives

FIGURE 29.9

The Laffer Curve

In region I of the Laffer curve, where tax rates are relatively low, increases in tax rates lead to increases in tax revenue. In region II, where tax rates are relatively high, increases in tax rates decrease tax revenue. Economists disagree over the size of t*, the tax rate that separates the regions.

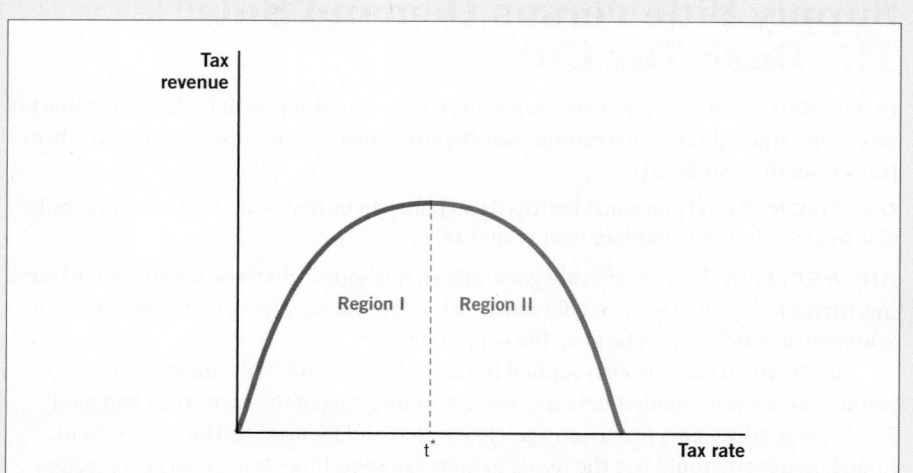

TABLE 29.3			
U.S. Income Tax Revenue for Different Income Levels, 1980 and 1991			
	Income tax revenue per return (2009 dollars)		
	All taxpayers	**Bottom 50%**	**Top 1%**
1980	$6,954	$1,005	$131,307
1991	6,202	692	153,675

At some specific tax rate, tax revenue is maximized. In Figure 29.9, this rate is labeled t*. Economists don't know exactly what this amount is, but it seems to be less than 70% in the United States, based on experience from the 1980s. In 1980, the marginal tax rate on the wealthiest Americans was 70%, but then marginal rates fell across all income brackets over the course of the decade. The result was higher tax revenue from the wealthiest Americans (see Table 29.3) even though tax revenue per taxpayer fell overall. Considering all U.S. taxpayers, average tax revenue (adjusted for both inflation and the number of tax returns filed) went from $6,954 to $6,202 between 1980 and 1991. Many analysts point to these figures and see them as proof that the Laffer curve doesn't exist or even that supply-side economics lacks merit. However, at very high rates, the experience of the 1980s shows that rate reductions can lead to higher revenue.

Table 29.3 shows data from the 1980s regarding tax revenue from taxpayers at different income levels. The rate reductions led to less tax revenue overall, because of drops in tax revenue from the many taxpayers who were paying relatively low taxes to begin with. Overall, revenues declined when we adjust for both inflation and population. But for the wealthiest Americans, a

PRACTICE WHAT YOU KNOW

TAX RELIEF FOR AMERICA

With congressional leaders at his side, President Bush signed a law that reduced top income tax rates from 39.6% to 35%.

Supply Side versus Demand Side: The Bush Tax Cuts

In mid-2001, the Bush administration won congressional approval for lower income tax rates. One stipulation of this rate cut was that the rates also be applied retroactively to taxes from the year 2000.

QUESTION: Would you consider this fiscal policy to be demand-side focused, supply-side focused, or both? Explain your response.

ANSWER: Both! Tax rate cuts are generally supply-side initiatives, because they frame incentives for production going forward. So the rate cuts applying to income taxes for 2001 and beyond were focused on the supply side.

But the Bush tax cuts also applied to taxes already paid. This meant that refund checks were mailed to taxpayers, refunding part of the taxes they had paid for the year 2000. This provision was clearly demand focused, as the government hoped taxpayers would use the funds to increase spending—that is, increase aggregate demand.

Planning for Your Future Taxes

- Recent debt levels will likely lead to higher taxes in the future.
- To reduce your federal tax bill, you can buy municipal bonds.
- You might also want to save more to pay higher future taxes.

The U.S. national debt is currently over $22 trillion, or more than $68,000 per person. And it is growing: in 2007 the national debt per person was only $30,000.

What does this mean for you? It means your taxes are going to be higher in the future. All Americans will need to contribute to pay down this large national debt. So taxes in the future will surely be higher, and you should plan accordingly.

In addition, economic growth will likely be lower until the debt is paid down. We know that higher income taxes reduce incentives for production, so it is safe to say that economic growth will be lower until this debt is paid off and taxes can come down again.

However, you can take actions to lower your future tax bills or make them more manageable. First, you probably ought to budget for higher taxes. This may mean saving more now than you would have saved

Government spending on highway projects was part of fiscal policy legislated during the Great Recession.

otherwise. Second, in terms of personal investments, you might consider buying securities that provide tax-free income. For example, the interest on municipal bonds (bonds issued by state and local governments) is not federally taxed. These simple steps might turn out to have significant benefits when your future tax bills arrive.

rate reduction led to an increase in revenue. The takeaway from Table 29.3 is that data from the 1980s confirm the two distinct regions on the Laffer curve. Generally, conservative public figures tend to stress region II, where tax rate reductions lead to increased revenue. Liberals emphasize region I, where tax rate increases lead to more revenue. Recognizing both regions is important for economic policy.

Conclusion

We began the chapter with a recent example of real life fiscal policy in the United States. Over the next few years, we will be able to see how the 2017 tax cuts actually affected the economy. For sure, the deficit increased. But the growth effects will take some time to work out.

Looking ahead, we turn our attention next to monetary policy. In Chapter 30, we cover money and the Federal Reserve; in Chapter 31, we discuss how monetary policy affects the economy. ✳

· ANSWERING *the* BIG QUESTIONS ·

What is fiscal policy?

- Fiscal policy involves the use of government's budget tools, government spending, and taxes to influence the macroeconomy, often through aggregate demand.
- Countercyclical fiscal policy is designed to counteract business cycle fluctuations by increasing aggregate demand during downturns and decreasing aggregate demand during expansionary periods.

What are the shortcomings of fiscal policy?

- Fiscal policy is subject to three significant lags: a recognition lag, an implementation lag, and an impact lag.
- In addition, crowding-out can diminish the effects of fiscal policy.
- Finally, according to the new classical critique, savings adjustments by private individuals can further diminish the stimulating effects of fiscal policy.

What is supply-side fiscal policy?

- Supply-side fiscal policy involves the use of government spending and taxes to affect the production (supply) side of the economy. This is a long-run view that concentrates on institutional changes.
- A key proposal of supply-side fiscal policy is that lower marginal income tax rates can actually lead to greater tax revenue when tax rates are high.

· CHAPTER PROBLEMS ·

Concepts You Should Know

automatic stabilizers (p. 951)

contractionary fiscal policy
(p. 943)

countercyclical fiscal policy
(p. 944)

crowding-out (p. 952)

expansionary fiscal policy
(p. 939)

fiscal policy (p. 938)

Laffer curve (p. 959)

marginal propensity to consume
(MPC) (p. 946)

new classical critique (p. 955)

spending multiplier (p. 947)

supply-side fiscal policy (p. 956)

Questions for Review

1. How are government budget balances affected by countercyclical fiscal policy? Be sure to describe the effects of both expansionary and contractionary fiscal policy.

2. Using the aggregate demand–aggregate supply model, one might argue that the economy will adjust on its own when aggregate demand drops. How does this adjustment work? Why might this adjustment take some time? (If necessary, review Chapter 26.)

3. Explain why the government budget deficit increases during a recession even without countercyclical fiscal policy.

4. Explain the three types of fiscal policy lags. What are automatic stabilizers? Which lags do automatic stabilizers affect?

5. In what circumstances would contractionary fiscal policy be recommended? How might you

implement this type of policy? Why would you implement this policy—that is, what are the reasons why it might make sense to use fiscal policy to slow the economy?

6. Many people emphasize just one portion of the Laffer curve and forget that there are actually two sides. First, explain the math behind the positively sloped region of the Laffer curve. That is, explain why an increase in the tax rate sometimes leads to an *increase* in tax revenue. Second, explain the math behind the negatively sloped region of the Laffer curve. That is, explain why an increase in the tax rate sometimes leads to a *decrease* in tax revenue.

7. Assuming that complete crowding-out always holds, what happens to consumption, investment, and interest rates if the government *decreases* borrowing, all else being equal?

Study Problems (*solved at the end of the section)

1. Explain the difference between typical demand-side fiscal policy and supply-side fiscal policy. For each of the following fiscal policy proposals, determine whether the primary focus is on aggregate demand or aggregate supply:

   a. a $1,000-per-person tax reduction
   b. a 5% reduction in all tax rates
   c. Pell Grants, which are government subsidies for college education
   d. government-sponsored prizes for new scientific discoveries
   e. an increase in unemployment compensation

2. To explore crowding-out, let's set up a simple loanable funds market in initial equilibrium.

   a. Draw a graph showing initial equilibrium in the loanable funds market at $800 million and an interest rate of 4%. Label your initial supply and demand curves as S_1 and D_1.
   b. Now assume that the government increases spending by $100 million that is entirely deficit financed. Show the new equilibrium in the loanable funds market. (*Note:* There is a range of possible numerical answers for this question. You should choose one number and then be sure

the rest of your answer is consistent with this number.)

c. Write the new equilibrium interest rate and quantity of loanable funds in the blanks below:
New interest rate: _____
New quantity of loanable funds: _____

d. If we assume there was no government debt prior to the fiscal stimulus, determine the following new quantities and write them in the blanks below:
Savings: _____
Investment: _____
Government spending: _____

e. How much did private consumption change as a result of the change in the quantity of savings?

3. The new classical critique of activist fiscal policy is theoretically different from the crowding-out critique. Explain the difference by using a graph of the loanable funds market.

4. Let's consider a small nation, Kaitland, in the context of the aggregate demand–aggregate supply model.

a. Kaitland starts off, in the year 2020, in long-run equilibrium with real GDP of $200 billion, an unemployment rate of 4%, and a price level of 100. On a separate sheet of paper, draw the Kaitland economy in long-run equilibrium and be sure to include AD, SRAS, and LRAS curves.

b. In the year 2021, business firm confidence falls significantly. On your previous graph, show how this affects Kaitland's economy. Be sure to clearly indicate any curve shifts, and state clearly how this affects real GDP, unemployment, and the price level.

c. Which two fiscal policy tools can the government use if they wish to increase aggregate demand? How would they specifically use each tool?

d. If we assume no crowding-out, show how the fiscal policy changes from part (c) affect the Kaitland economy.

＊ **5.** Fill in the blanks in the table below. Assume that the MPC is constant over everyone in the economy.

MPC	Spending multiplier	Change in government spending	Change in income
_____	5	$100	_____
_____	2.5	_____	-$250
0.5	_____	200	_____
0.2	_____	_____	1,000

＊ **6.** Assume that the equilibrium in the loanable funds market is at an interest rate (R) of 3% and the total quantity of loans is $500 billion. In addition, in this initial situation, the government is borrowing $50 billion per year to fund the budget deficit.

a. What is private investment in this initial equilibrium? (It will help to draw a graph of the loanable funds market in this initial equilibrium.)
Now the government increases spending by $200 billion per year and finances this spending completely with additional borrowing.

b. At R = 3%, what would be the quantity demanded of loanable funds?

c. In which direction does the interest rate change to bring the market to equilibrium?
Assume that the new equilibrium is at $575 billion and assume complete crowding-out.

d. Determine the exact amount by which each component of GDP changes, assuming no change in net exports.

e. What is the total change in AD from this action?

Solved Problems

5.

MPC	Spending multiplier	Change in government spending	Change in income
0.8	5	$100	$500
0.6	2.5	−100	−250
0.5	2	200	400
0.2	1.25	800	1,000

6.

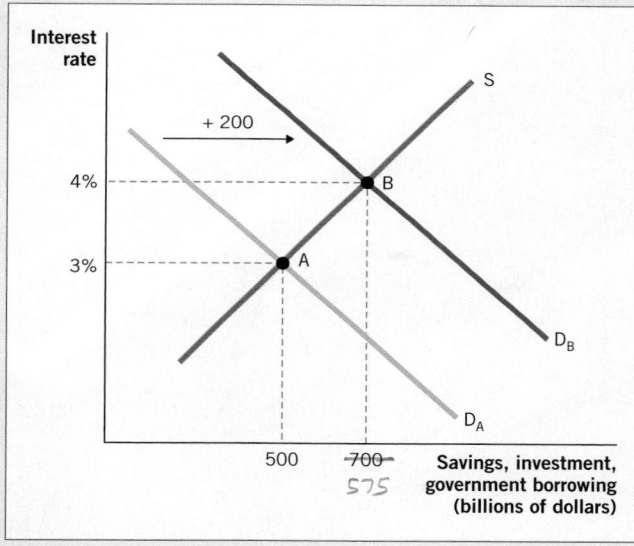

Interest rate / + 200 / 4% / B / 3% / A / S / D_B / D_A / 500 / 700 / 575 / Savings, investment, government borrowing (billions of dollars)

a. The initial equilibrium has an interest rate of 3% and total loans of $500 billion. This equilibrium is pictured as point A in the graph on this page. Because there is a total of $500 billion in loans, but the government is borrowing just $50 billion of this amount, that leaves $450 billion for private investment.

b. The new demand curve is exactly $200 billion to the right of the old demand curve because the government increases the demand for loans by $200 billion at all interest rates. Therefore, at 3%, the new quantity demanded is $700 billion.

c. The interest rate rises to new equilibrium at point B. This increase is normal because at the old interest rate, the quantity demanded exceeds the quantity supplied.

d. Given the new equilibrium at $575 billion, we know that total savings is $575 billion because every dollar borrowed requires a dollar saved. The government is now borrowing $250 billion, which represents an increase in G of +$200 billion. But that leaves just $325 billion for private investment ($575 billion − $250 billion). As a result, I declines by $125 billion from the initial level of $450 billion (see part a). Finally, because total savings was initially $500 billion but is now $575 billion, C (consumption) falls by $75 billion.

e. The change in AD is the sum of the changes in C, I, G, and NX. We assumed no change in NX, but the changes in the others sum to zero (− $75 billion − $125 billion + $200 billion).

PART

IX

Monetary
POLICY

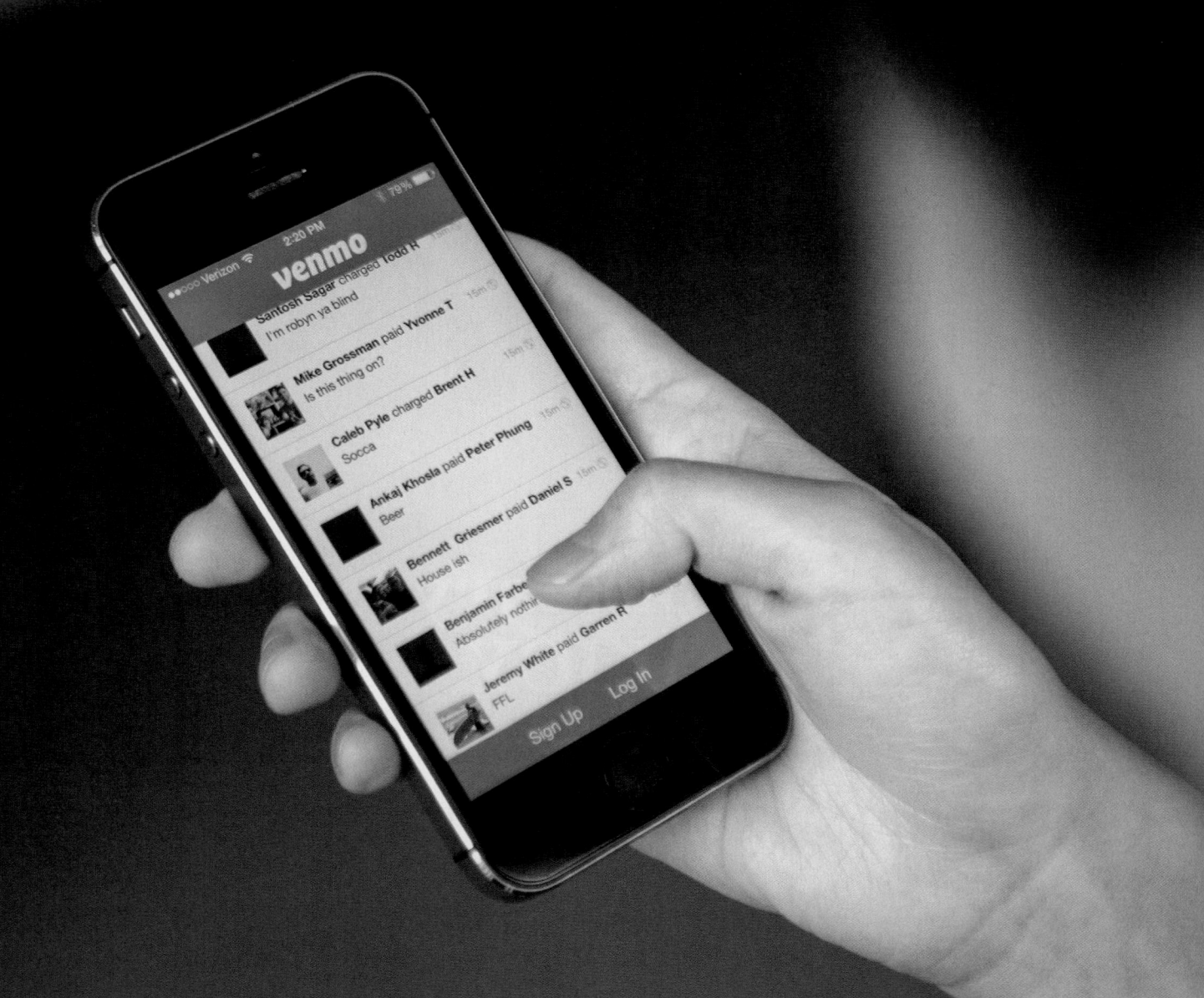

30

Money and the Federal Reserve

Controlling the Money Supply Is Not as Easy as You Think.

Most people believe that controlling the amount of money in the economy is simple. After all, there's a fixed amount of paper currency and coins in circulation, and only the government has the authority to print more. But the size of the overall money supply isn't as securely under the government's control as the printing-press model suggests. In fact, people and firms, not just in the United States but all around the world, have a hand in determining how many American dollars are coursing around the American economy, and the world economy, at any given time.

The main reason for this is that what we use for "money" isn't always paper currency or coins. Just think about your own daily purchases. Many (most?) of them are paid for with something other than actual cash, right? The price of what you pay may be posted in dollars, but depending on the purchase, you might pay with a check, a debit card, or a mobile payment app on your smartphone.

With the range of things that can be used as money, people have a lot more purchasing power than what's represented just by the currency physically in their possession. This makes it hard to get a meaningful exact fix on the size of the money supply. We begin this chapter by looking closely at the definition of money—its functions and its different

Money is more than just green paper! Venmo (owned by PayPal) is a mobile payment app that can be used to make purchases both over the counter and online.

forms. Because banks play an integral role in the money supply process, we will discuss how they operate and how their decisions affect the amount of money in the economy. Finally, we look at the role of the Federal Reserve System and examine how it oversees the amount of money in the economy. This background provides essential preparation for the discussion of monetary policy in Chapter 31.

· BIG QUESTIONS ·

- What is money?
- How do banks create money?
- How does the Federal Reserve control the money supply?

What Is Money?

Currency
is the paper bills and coins used to buy goods and services.

Money
is any generally accepted means of payment.

A **medium of exchange** is what people trade for goods and services.

What is money? The question may seem odd. After all, we use money all the time, right? Even children know that we use coins and paper bills to buy things like food and clothes (goods) and pedicures and car repairs (services). Those coins and bills constitute **currency**. But people also make many purchases without currency. Our definition of *money* is much broader: **money** is any generally accepted means of payment. In this section, we define the functions of money and then explain how the quantity of money is measured.

Money comes in many different colors, shapes, and sizes.

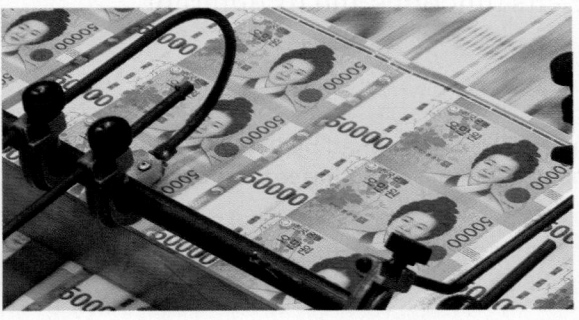

Three Functions of Money

Money has three functions: it is a medium of exchange, a unit of account, and a store of value. Let's look at each function.

A MEDIUM OF EXCHANGE If you want to buy groceries, you offer money in exchange for them; if you work, you accept money as payment for your labor. Money is a common **medium of exchange**—that is, it is what people trade for goods and services.

Modern economies generally have a government-provided medium of exchange. In the United States, the government provides our dollar currency. But even in economies without government provision, a preferred medium of exchange usually emerges. For example, in colonial Virginia, before there was any government mandate regarding money, tobacco became the accepted medium of exchange. Economist Milton Friedman wrote this about tobacco: "It was the money that the colonists used to buy food, clothing, to pay taxes—even to pay for a bride."

Without money, what would you trade for this coffee and bagel?

Invariably, some medium of exchange evolves in any economy; the primary reason is the inefficiency of barter, which is money's alternative. **Barter** occurs when there is no commonly accepted medium of exchange. It involves individuals trading some good or service they already have for something else they want. If you want food in a barter economy, you must find a grocer who also happens to want whatever you have to trade. Maybe you can offer only your labor services, but the grocer wants a new cash register. In that case, you have to try to find someone who has a cash register and also wants to trade it for your labor. This takes more than a coincidence; it takes a double coincidence. Barter requires a **double coincidence of wants**, in which each party in an exchange transaction happens to have what the other party desires. A double coincidence is pretty unusual, which is why a medium of exchange naturally evolves in any exchange environment.

Barter involves the trade of a good or service in the absence of a commonly accepted medium of exchange.

A **double coincidence of wants** occurs when each party in an exchange transaction happens to have what the other party desires.

Historically, the first medium of exchange in an economy has been a commodity that is actually traded for goods and services. **Commodity money** involves the use of an actual good for money. In this situation, the good itself has value apart from its function as money. Examples include gold, silver, and the tobacco of colonial Virginia. But commodities are often difficult to carry around. Due to these transportation costs, money evolved into certificates that represented a fixed quantity of the commodity. These certificates became the medium of exchange but were still tied to the commodity, because they could be traded for the actual commodity if the holder demanded it.

Commodity money involves the use of an actual good for money.

Commodity-backed money is money you can exchange for a commodity at a fixed rate. For example, until 1971, U.S. dollars were fixed in value to specific quantities of silver and gold. A $1 U.S. silver certificate looks much like dollar bills in circulation today, but the print along the bottom of the note reads, "one dollar in silver payable to the bearer on demand." Until 1964, we also had commodity coins in the United States. U.S. quarters from 1964 look like the same quarters we use today, but unlike today's they are made of real silver.

Commodity-backed money is money you can exchange for a commodity at a fixed rate.

While commodity money and commodity-backed money evolve privately in all economies, the type of money used in most modern economies depends on government. In particular, most modern economies make use of fiat money for their medium of exchange. **Fiat money** is money with no value except as the medium of exchange; there is no inherent or intrinsic value to the currency. In the United States, our currency is physically just pieces of green paper, otherwise known as Federal Reserve Notes. This paper has value because the government has mandated that we can use the currency to pay our debts. On U.S. dollar bills, you can read the statement "This note is legal tender for all debts, public and private."

Fiat money is money with no value except as the medium of exchange; there is no inherent or intrinsic value to the currency.

There are advantages and disadvantages to fiat and commodity monies. On the one hand, commodity-backed money ties the value of the holder's money to

The money pictured here looks much like our modern money, but the dollar bill is a commodity-backed silver certificate from 1957. At that time, it could be traded for a dollar's worth of actual silver. The quarter from 1964 is made of real silver.

something real. If the government is obligated to trade silver for every dollar in circulation, a limit is imposed on the number of dollars it can print, which probably limits inflation levels. Fiat money offers no such constraint on the expansion of the money supply. Rapid monetary expansion and then inflation can occur without a commodity standard that ties the value of money to something real. We have and do see this especially in developing and less stable nations; as recently as 2016, Venezuela experienced inflation rates of 1 million percent(!) per year.

On the other hand, tying the value of a nation's currency to a commodity is dangerous when the market value of the commodity fluctuates. Imagine how a new discovery of gold affects prices in a nation with gold-backed currency. An increased supply of gold reduces gold prices, and therefore more gold is required in exchange for all other goods and services. This situation constitutes inflation: the price of everything in terms of the money (gold) rises. This situation occurred in the mid-fifteenth and the mid-seventeenth centuries in Europe as Spanish conquistadors brought back tons of gold from Central and South America. Because a change in the value of a medium of exchange affects the prices of all goods and services in the macroeconomy, it can be risky to tie a currency to a commodity.

A **unit of account** is the measure in which prices are quoted.

A UNIT OF ACCOUNT Money also serves as a unit of account. A **unit of account** is the measure in which prices are quoted. Money enables you and someone you don't know to speak a common language. For example, when the cashier says the mangos you want to buy cost 99 cents each, the cashier is communicating the value of mangos in a way you understand. Consider a world without an accepted unit of account. In that world, goods would be priced in multiple ways. Theoretically, you might go shopping and find goods priced in terms of any possible currency or even other goods. Imagine how difficult it would be to shop! Using money as a unit of account is so helpful that a standard unit of account generally evolves, even in small economies.

Thank goodness each of these fruits is priced in a common unit of account.

Expressing the value of something in terms of dollars and cents also enables people to make accurate comparisons between items. Thus, money also serves as a measuring stick and recording device. Think of your checkbook for a moment. You don't write down in the ledger that you bought a bagel and coffee; instead, you write down that you spent $4. You use dollar amounts to keep track of your account and to record transactions in a consistent manner.

If you keep your money in your sock drawer, you incur an opportunity cost of forgone interest from a bank account.

A **store of value** is a means for holding wealth.

A STORE OF VALUE Money's third function is as a store of value. A **store of value** is a means for holding wealth. Money has long served as an important store of value. Think of bags of gold coins from the Middle Ages. In both fiction and nonfiction stories, pirates' treasures are generally represented by gold; this precious metal was the vehicle for storing great values. But in modern economies, this function is much less important. Today, we have other options for holding our wealth, many of which offer greater returns than keeping dollar bills in a sock drawer or stuffed under a mattress. We can easily put our dollars into bank accounts or investment accounts that earn interest. These options have caused money's role as a store of value to decline.

ECONOMICS IN THE REAL WORLD

THE EVOLUTION OF PRISON MONEY

In the past, cigarettes were often the preferred unit of account and medium of exchange in prisons. This commodity money was useful as currency in addition to its usefulness for smoking. But in 2004 the U.S. government outlawed smoking in federal prisons, and this decision led to the development of a new medium of exchange.

In an October 2008 *Wall Street Journal* article, Justin Scheck reported on one federal facility where cans of mackerel had taken over as the accepted money. According to one prisoner, "It's the coin of the realm." This "bartering" is not legal in federal prisons. Prisoners can lose privileges if they are caught exchanging goods or services for mackerel. Nonetheless, mackerel remains the medium of exchange and the unit of account. For example, haircuts cost about two "macks." The cans of fish also serve as a reliable store of value. Some prisoners even rent lockers from others so they can store their mackerel money.

The evolution of prison money.

But while mackerel is popular, it is not the only commodity used as money in federal prisons. In some prisons, protein bars or cans of tuna serve as money. One reason why mackerel is preferred to other alternatives is that each can costs about one dollar—so it's a simple substitute for U.S. currency, which inmates are not allowed to carry.

Measuring the Quantity of Money

Now that we have defined the three functions of money, we need to consider how the total amount of money in the economy is measured. As we saw in Chapter 21, the quantity of money in an economy affects the overall price level. In particular, a nation's inflation rate is dependent on the rate of growth of its quantity of money. In addition, in Chapter 31 we'll see that the quantity of money can influence real GDP and unemployment rates. Because money has such profound macroeconomic influences, it is important to measure it accurately. But doing so is not quite as simple as just adding up all the currency in an economy.

To get a sense of the difficulties of measuring the money supply, think about all the different ways you make purchases. You might hold some currency for emergencies, to make a vending machine purchase or feed a parking meter, or to do laundry. On top of this, you might write checks to pay your rent, tuition, or utilities bills. Moreover, you probably carry a debit card that enables you to withdraw from your savings or checking account. You may buy your morning coffee or your fast-food lunch with a mobile payment phone app. To measure the quantity of money in an economy, we must somehow find the total value of all these alternative means people use to buy goods and services. Clearly, currency alone is not enough—people buy things all the time without using currency. Currency is money, but it constitutes only a small part of the total money supply.

M1 AND M2 As we broaden our definition of money beyond currency, we first acknowledge bank deposits on which checks can be written. **Checkable deposits** are deposits in bank accounts from which depositors may make withdrawals by writing checks. These deposits represent purchasing power very similar to currency, because personal checks are accepted at many places. Adding checkable deposits to currency gives us a money supply measure known as **M1**, the money supply measure composed of currency and checkable deposits. M1 also includes traveler's checks, but these account for a very small portion of M1.

A broader measure of the money supply, **M2**, includes everything in M1 plus savings deposits. M2 also includes two other types of deposits: money market mutual funds and small-denomination time deposits (certificates of deposit, or CDs). The key point to remember is that the money supply in an economy includes both currency and bank deposits:

$$\text{money supply (M)} = \text{currency} + \text{deposits}$$

Equation 30.1 is an approximation of the general money supply. Actual data for both M1 and M2 are regularly published by the Federal Reserve. Figure 30.1 shows the components of M1 and M2 in the United States as of November 2018. Notice that currency was only $1.6 trillion. Adding checkable deposits of another $2.1 trillion yields M1 of $3.7 trillion. But M2 was more than $14 trillion in 2018, over $9 trillion of which was held in savings accounts. When we discuss monetary policy in the next chapter, it will be important to remember that the money supply includes both currency and bank deposits.

Note that credit cards are not part of the money supply. Purchases made with credit cards involve a loan extended right at the cash register. When the loan is made, a third party is paying for the purchase until the loan is repaid. Because credit card purchases involve the use of borrowed funds, credit cards are not included as part of the money supply.

Until the 1970s, M1 was the most closely monitored money supply measure because it was a reliable estimate of the medium of exchange. But the introduction of automated teller machines (ATMs) rendered M1 obsolete as a reliable money supply measure. Prior to the arrival of the ATM, holding balances in checking accounts was very different from holding funds in savings accounts.

Checkable deposits
are deposits in bank accounts from which depositors may make withdrawals by writing checks.

M1
is the money supply measure composed of currency and checkable deposits.

M2
is the money supply measure that includes everything in M1 plus savings deposits, money market mutual funds, and small-denomination time deposits (CDs).

(EQUATION 30.1)

The invention of the ATM marked the beginning of the end for M1 as a reliable money supply measure.

FIGURE 30.1

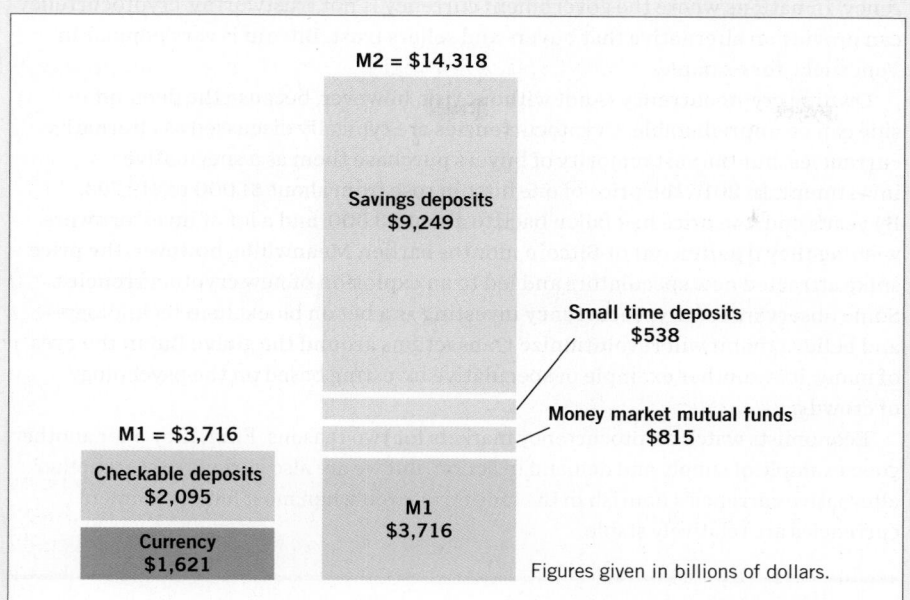

Measures of the U.S. Money Supply, November 2018

M1 and M2 are the most common measures of the money supply. M1 includes currency and checkable deposits. M2 includes everything in M1 plus savings deposits, small-denomination time deposits (CDs), and money market mutual funds.

Source: Federal Reserve, Money Stock Measures.

Funds held in checking accounts are accessed easily by writing checks. However, funds in savings accounts previously required the holder to visit the bank during business hours, wait in line, and fill out a withdrawal slip. Today, because of ATMs, depositors can make withdrawals at any time and at many locations. In addition, debit cards are an even easier way to access your bank deposits. Because both checking and savings accounts are now readily available for purchasing goods and services, M2—which includes both types of deposits—is now a better measure of our economy's medium of exchange.

ECONOMICS IN THE REAL WORLD

CRYPTOCURRENCY IS MONEY, TOO

Bitcoin, Ethereum, and other cryptocurrencies have captured the imagination of many investors around the globe. Although cryptocurrencies are different from traditional money, in that they are not issued by national governments, cryptocurrencies can serve as a medium of exchange and this feature makes them a form of money: they are accepted as payment for goods, services, and debts. You can use bitcoins to buy pizza from Domino's or Pizza Hut, to pay for a download of a Bjork song, or to buy airline tickets via Expedia.com.

A main rationale for cryptocurrencies is that their value can't be deliberately manipulated by the government, or by any other entity, for that matter. Instead, a cryptocurrency's value is determined by supply and demand, where the supply is regulated not by a central bank but by a self-maintaining software technology called blockchain. By allowing the supply of bitcoin to grow only in a very controlled

Dogecoin is a popular cryptocurrency. In 2018, the total market value of all Dogecoins was around $300 million.

fashion, the blockchain code keeps a tight lid on supply-driven inflation of the currency. In nations where the government currency is not trustworthy, cryptocurrency can provide an alternative that buyers and sellers trust. Bitcoin is very popular in Venezuela, for example.

Owning cryptocurrency is not without risk, however, because the demand side can be unpredictable. Cryptocurrencies are typically discussed as alternative currencies, but the vast majority of buyers purchase them as a speculative investment. In 2017, the price of one bitcoin rose from about $1,000 to $19,783. By year's end, the price had fallen back to about $3,000, and a lot of investors were wishing they'd gotten out of Bitcoin months earlier. Meanwhile, however, the price spike attracted new speculators and led to an explosion of new cryptocurrencies. Some observers see cryptocurrency investing as a bet on blockchain technology—and believe that it will revolutionize transactions around the globe. But in the eyes of many, it is another example of speculative investing based on the psychology of crowds.

Economists watch cryptocurrency markets for two reasons. First, they offer another good example of supply and demand in action. But we are also curious to see whether alternative currencies flourish in the long term, even when most fiat government currencies are relatively stable.

PRACTICE WHAT YOU KNOW

Is this M1 or M2? Yes.

The Definition of Money

People sometimes use the word "money" in ways inconsistent with the definition given in this chapter.

QUESTION: Is each of the following statements consistent with our definition of money? Explain your answer each time.

a. "He had a lot of money in his wallet."

b. "She made a lot of money last year."

c. "Do I have money? Yes, I have my credit card."

d. "She has most of her money in the bank."

ANSWERS:

a. This statement is *consistent* with our definition, because currency is part of the medium of exchange.

b. This statement is *inconsistent* with the definition. It refers to income, not to money.

c. This statement is *inconsistent*. Payment with a credit card requires a loan, so using a credit card is technically not counted in the money supply.

d. This statement is *consistent*. Bank deposits count as money because they represent part of our medium of exchange.

How Do Banks Create Money?

We now have a working definition of money: money includes both currency and deposits at banks. And while private individuals and firms aren't permitted to print currency, private actions do influence the total supply of money in the economy, because individuals and banks affect deposits. In this section, we explain how banks create money simply as a by-product of their daily business activity. Note that when we refer to "banks," we are talking about commercial banks, which take in deposits and extend loans. We distinguish commercial banks from investment banks, which serve a different role.

We begin by looking closely at the daily activities at typical banks. After that, we consider how banks influence the money supply.

The Business of Banking

Banks serve two very important roles in the macroeconomy. First, they are critical participants in the market for loanable funds. As we saw in Chapter 23, they provide a way for savers to supply their funds to borrowers without purchasing a financial security. In addition, they play a role in determining the money supply.

To understand how banks create money, let's look at the functions of a bank, illustrated in Figure 30.2. Banks are go-betweens in the market for loans. They are financial intermediaries; that is, they take in deposits and extend loans. Deposits are the primary source of funds, and loans are the primary use of these funds. Banks can be profitable if the interest rate they charge on loans is higher than the interest rate they pay out on deposits.

Figure 30.3 illustrates the gap between interest rates on bank deposits and bank loans for U.S. banks for the period 1990–2018. The two rates go up and down together, but the interest rate on deposits is consistently lower than the interest rate on loans. The difference between the two interest rates pays a bank's operating costs and produces profits.

THE BANK'S BALANCE SHEET Information about a bank's financial operations is available in the bank's balance sheet. A **balance sheet** is an accounting statement that summarizes a firm's key financial information.

A **balance sheet** is an accounting statement that summarizes a firm's key financial information.

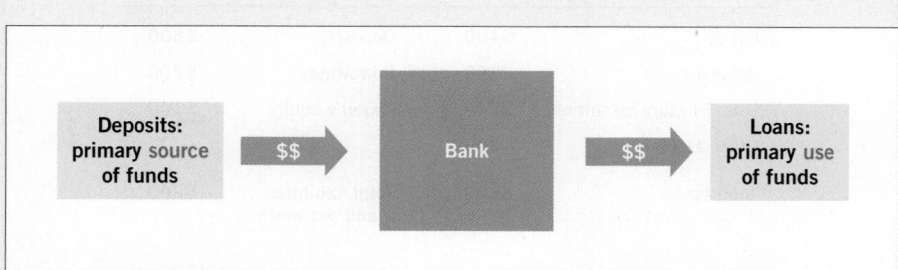

FIGURE 30.2

The Business of Banking: Financial Intermediation

The primary function of commercial banks is financial intermediation: they accept deposits and extend loans.

FIGURE 30.3

Interest Rates on Bank Deposits versus Loans, 1990–2018

Banks charge more interest for loans than they pay for deposits. The difference pays the banks' expenses and produces profits.

Source: FRED data, Federal Reserve Bank of St. Louis. The loan interest rate is the average prime interest rate across the United States; the deposit interest rate is the interest rate on one-month certificates of deposit.

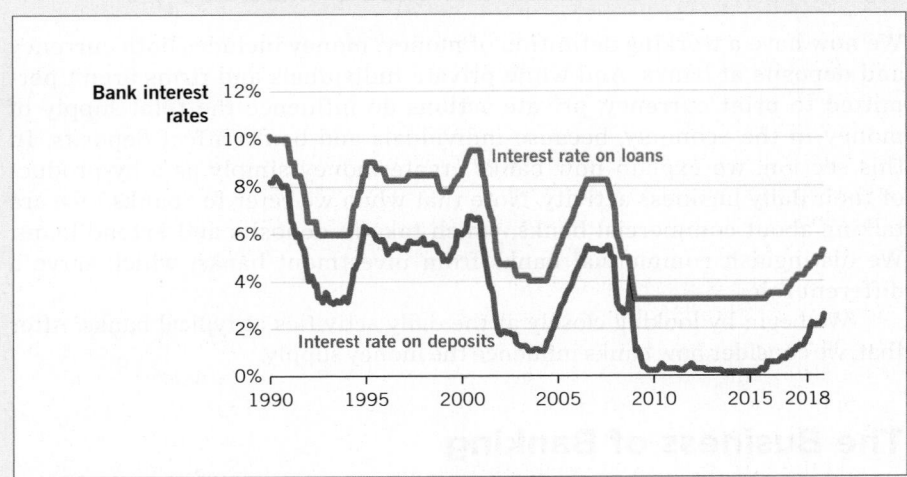

Assets
are the items a firm owns.

Liabilities
are the financial obligations a firm owes to others.

Owner's equity
is the difference between a firm's assets and its liabilities.

Figure 30.4 shows a hypothetical balance sheet for University Bank. The left side of the balance sheet details the bank's **assets**, which are the items the firm owns. Assets indicate how the banking firm uses the funds it has raised from various sources. The right side of the balance sheet details the bank's liabilities and owner's equity. **Liabilities** are the financial obligations the firm owes to others. **Owner's equity** is the difference between the firm's assets and its liabilities. When a firm has more assets than liabilities, it has positive owner's equity. Overall, the right side of the balance sheet identifies the bank's sources of funds.

FIGURE 30.4

Balance Sheet for University Bank

A bank's balance sheet summarizes its key financial information. The bank's assets are recorded on the left side; this side shows how the bank chooses to use its funds. The sources of the firm's funds are recorded on the right side; this side shows liabilities and owner's equity. The two sides of the balance sheet must match for the financial statement to be balanced.

Assets: Uses of funds (in millions)		Liabilities and owner's equity: Sources of funds (in millions)	
Loans	$400	Deposits	$500
Reserves	$60	Borrowings	$200
U.S. Treasury securities	$140	Owner's equity	$100
Other assets	$200		
Total assets	$800	Total liabilities and net worth	$800

As you can see, University Bank has extended $400 million in loans. Many of these loans went to firms to fund investment, but some also went to households to purchase homes, cars, and other consumer items. A second important asset held by banks is reserves. **Reserves** are the portion of bank deposits set aside and not loaned out. Reserves include both currency in the bank's vault and funds that the bank holds in deposit at its own bank, the Federal Reserve. Banks also hold U.S. Treasury securities and other government securities as substantial assets in their portfolio. These securities earn interest and carry very low risk. Finally, banks hold other assets, such as physical buildings and furniture.

Reserves
are the portion of bank deposits that are set aside and not loaned out.

Banks fund their activities primarily by taking in deposits. In fact, the deposits of typical households are the lifeblood of banks. But banks also borrow from other commercial banks and from the Federal Reserve. The third item on the right side of the balance sheet in Figure 30.4 is net worth, or the owner's equity in the bank. Because the University Bank owns $800 million in total assets but owes only $700 million in liabilities ($500 million in deposits plus $200 million in borrowings), the owners of the bank have $100 million in equity.

In the next section, we look more closely at bank reserves, which play an important role in money creation.

BANK RESERVES Our modern system of banking is called fractional reserve banking. **Fractional reserve banking** occurs when banks hold only a fraction of deposits on reserve. The alternative is 100% reserve banking. Banks in a 100% reserve system don't loan out deposits; these banks are essentially just safes, keeping deposits on hand until depositors decide to make a withdrawal.

Fractional reserve banking
occurs when banks hold only a fraction of deposits on reserve.

Figure 30.5 illustrates the process of fractional reserve banking. Deposits come into the banks, and the banks send out a portion of these funds in loans. In recent years, U.S. banks have typically loaned out almost 90% of their deposits, keeping barely over 10% on reserve. Banks loan out most of their deposits because reserves earn very little interest; every dollar kept on reserve costs the bank potential income. In 2015, bank reserves paid just 0.25% interest.

Let's say a local business approaches a bank for a loan to expand its factory. Assume that the bank has reserves available to loan and the current interest rate on these commercial loans is 5%, which the firm is willing to pay. The alternative is to keep the funds on reserve, earning just 0.25% interest. If the bank

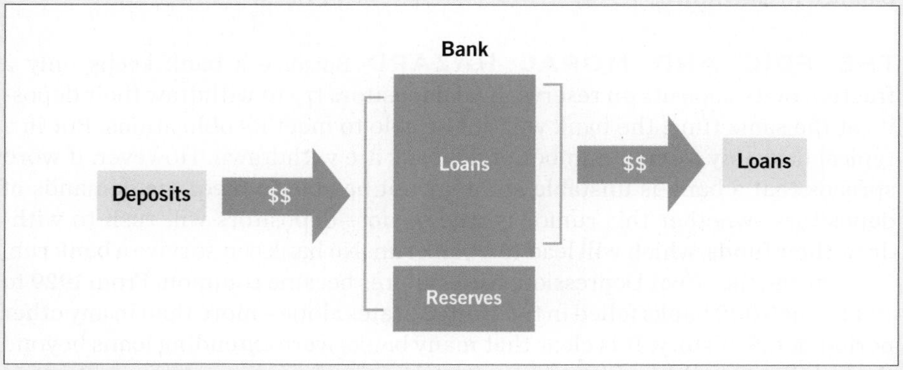

FIGURE 30.5

Fractional Reserve Banking

In a fractional reserve banking system, banks lend out only a fraction of the deposits they take in. The remainder is set aside as reserves.

Opportunity cost

A **bank run** occurs when many depositors attempt to withdraw their funds from a bank at the same time.

The **required reserve ratio** is the portion of deposits that banks are required to keep on reserve.

(EQUATION 30.2)

Excess reserves are any bank reserves held in excess of those required.

(EQUATION 30.3)

rejects the firm's loan application and decides to keep the funds in its vault as reserves, the cost of this decision to the bank is the difference between these two interest rates: $5\% - 0.25\% = 4.75\%$.

Banks hold reserves for two reasons. First, they must accommodate withdrawals by their depositors. You'd be pretty unhappy if you tried to make a withdrawal from your bank and it didn't have enough on reserve to honor your request. If word spread that a bank might have difficulty meeting its depositors' withdrawal requests, that news would probably lead to a bank run. A **bank run** occurs when many depositors attempt to withdraw their funds from a bank at the same time.

Second, banks are legally bound to hold a fraction of their deposits on reserve. The **required reserve ratio** (rr) is the portion of deposits that banks are required to keep on reserve. For a given bank, the dollar amount of reserves it is required to hold is determined by multiplying the required reserve ratio by the bank's total amount of deposits:

$$\text{required reserves} = \text{rr} \times \text{deposits}$$

Currently, the required reserve ratio is 10% for almost all deposits (rr = 0.10). This means your bank can legally lend out up to 90 cents of every dollar you deposit.

Consider University Bank, whose balance sheet was presented in Figure 30.4. The bank currently has $500 million in deposits. University Bank pays some interest on the deposits and offers services, such as checking, to its depositors. University Bank can't afford to keep the $500 million sitting in the vault—the opportunity cost is too high. If the bank is going to stay in business, it will need to loan out at least part of the $500 million. With a reserve requirement of 10% of deposits, required reserves in this case are $50 million, so University Bank can loan out up to $450 million.

Banks rarely keep their level of reserves exactly at the required level. Any reserves above the required level are called **excess reserves**:

$$\text{excess reserves} = \text{total reserves} - \text{required reserves}$$

The balance sheet of University Bank, presented in Figure 30.4, indicates that the bank currently holds total reserves of $60 million. Therefore, it has $10 million in excess reserves. Given the opportunity cost of holding these excess reserves, University Bank will probably seek to loan out most of this balance in the future.

THE FDIC AND MORAL HAZARD Because a bank keeps only a fraction of its deposits on reserve, if all depositors try to withdraw their deposits at the same time, the bank will not be able to meet its obligations. But in a typical day, only a small number of deposits are withdrawn. However, if word spreads that a bank is unstable and may not be able to meet the demands of depositors—whether this rumor is true or not—depositors will rush to withdraw their funds, which will lead to a bank run. No bank can survive a bank run.

During the Great Depression, bank failures became common. From 1929 to 1933, over 9,000 banks failed in the United States alone—more than in any other period in U.S. history. It is clear that many banks were extending loans beyond their ability to collect and pay depositors in a timely manner. As a result, many depositors lost confidence in the banking system. If you became worried about your bank and were not certain you could withdraw your deposits at some later point, wouldn't you run to the bank to get your money out?

This is precisely what happened to many banks during the Great Depression. The Hollywood film classic *It's a Wonderful Life* (1946) captures this situation perfectly. In the movie, the character George Bailey is set to leave on his honeymoon when the financial intermediary he runs is subject to a run. When a depositor asks for his money back, George tells him, "The money's not here. Well, your money's in Joe's house, that's right next to yours. And in the Kennedy house, and Mrs. Macklin's house, and, and a hundred others." This quote summarizes both the beauty and the danger wrapped up in a fractional reserve banking system. Fractional reserve banking allows access to funds by many individuals and firms in an economy, but it can also lead to instability when many depositors demand their funds simultaneously.

To end the bank run, George Bailey offers depositors money from his own wallet.

After the massive rate of bank failures from 1929 to 1933, the U.S. government instituted federal deposit insurance in 1933 through the Federal Deposit Insurance Corporation (FDIC). Deposit insurance now guarantees that depositors will get their deposits back (up to $250,000) even if their bank goes bankrupt. FDIC insurance greatly decreased the frequency of bank runs, but it also created what is referred to as a moral hazard situation. **Moral hazard** is the lack of incentive to guard against risk where one is protected from its consequences. FDIC insurance means that neither banks nor their depositors have an incentive to monitor risk; no matter what happens, they are protected from the consequences of risky behavior.

Moral hazard
is the lack of incentive to guard against risk where one is protected from its consequences.

Consider two types of banks in this environment. Type A banks are conservative, take little risk, and earn relatively low returns on their loans. Type A banks make only very safe loans with very little default risk and, consequently, relatively low rates of return. Type A banks rarely fail, but they make relatively low profit and pay relatively low interest rates to their depositors. In contrast, Type B banks take huge risks, hoping to make extremely large returns on their loans. Type B loans carry greater default risk but also pay higher returns. Type B banks often fail, but the lucky ones—the ones that survive—earn very handsome profits and pay high interest rates on their customers' deposits.

Moral hazard draws individual depositors and bankers to type B banking. There is a tremendous upside and no significant downside, because depositors are protected against losses by FDIC insurance. This is the environment in which our modern banks operate, which is why many analysts argue that reserve requirements and other regulations are necessary to help ensure stability in the financial industry—especially given that recessions often start in the financial industry.

ECONOMICS IN THE REAL WORLD

TWENTY-FIRST-CENTURY BANK RUN

For a modern example of a bank run, consider England's Northern Rock Bank, which experienced a bank run in 2007—the first British bank run in over a century. Northern Rock (which is now owned by Virgin Money) had earned revenue valued over $10 billion

Depositors queue outside a Northern Rock Bank location in September 2007.

per year. But extensive losses stemming from investments in mortgage markets led it to near collapse in 2007.

In September of that year, depositors began queuing outside Northern Rock locations because they feared they would not get their deposits back. Eventually, the British government offered deposit insurance of 100% to Northern Rock depositors—but not before much damage had been done. In February 2008, Northern Rock was taken over by the British government because the bank was unable to repay its debts or find a buyer. To make matters worse, there is some evidence that Northern Rock was solvent at the time of the bank run, meaning that stronger deposit insurance could have saved the bank.

In the United States, over 300 banks failed between 2008 and 2011 without experiencing a bank run. (So these banks failed, but it did not lead to a bank run.) The individual depositors who funded the risky loans got their money back. So why the bank run in England? The difference is a reflection of the level of deposit insurance offered in the two nations. In England, depositors are insured for 100% of their deposits up to a value of $4,000, then for only 90% of their next $70,000. So British depositors get back a fraction of their deposits up to about $74,000. In contrast, FDIC insurance in the United States offers 100% insurance on the first $250,000.

How Banks Create Money

We have seen that banks function as financial intermediaries. But as a by-product of their everyday activity, they also create new money. Modern U.S. banks don't mint currency, but they do create new deposits, and deposits are a part of the money supply.

Money deposited in the banking system leads to more money. To see how, let's start with a hypothetical example that involves the Federal Reserve, which supplies the currency in the United States. Let's say that the Federal Reserve decides to increase the money supply in the United States. It prints a single $1,000 bill and drops it out of a helicopter. Perhaps you are the lucky person who finds this brand-new $1,000 bill. If you keep the $1,000 in your wallet, then the money supply increases by only $1,000. But if you deposit the new money in a bank, then the bank can use it to create even more money.

Let's see how this process works. Consider what happens if you deposit the $1,000 into a savings or checking account at University Bank. When you deposit the $1,000, it is still part of the money supply, because both currency and bank deposits are counted in the money supply. You don't have the currency anymore, but in your wallet you have a debit card that enables you to access the

$1,000 to make purchases. Therefore, the deposit still represents $1,000 worth of the medium of exchange.

But University Bank doesn't keep your $1,000 in reserve; it uses part of your deposit to extend a new loan that earns interest income for the bank. You still have the $1,000 in your account (as a deposit), but someone else receives money from the bank in the form of a loan. Thus, University Bank creates new money by loaning out part of your deposit. You helped the bank in the money creation process because you put your funds into the bank in the first place.

This is just the first step in the money creation process. We'll now explore this process in more detail, utilizing the bank's balance sheet. For this example, we need to make two assumptions to help understand the general picture:

Assumption 1: All currency is deposited in banks.

Assumption 2: Banks hold no excess reserves.

Neither of these assumptions is completely realistic. But let's work through the example under these conditions, and later we can consider the effect of each assumption.

Consider first how your deposit changes the assets and liabilities of University Bank. The following t-account (an abbreviated version of a firm's balance sheet) summarizes all initial changes to the balance sheet of University Bank when you deposit your new $1,000 (assumption 1):

UNIVERSITY BANK

Assets		Liabilities and net worth	
Reserves	+ $1,000	Deposits	+ $1,000

With a required reserve ratio of 10% (rr = 0.10), University Bank loans out $900 of your deposit (assumption 2 implies that only 10% of deposits are held on reserve). Perhaps the bank loans this amount to a student named Kaitlyn so she can pay her tuition bill. When University Bank extends the loan to Kaitlyn, the money supply increases by $900. That is, you still have your $1,000 deposit, and Kaitlyn now has $900.

Including your initial deposit and this $900 loan, the balance sheet changes at University Bank are summarized in this t-account:

UNIVERSITY BANK

Assets		Liabilities and net worth	
Reserves	+$100	Deposits	+$1,000
Loans	+$900		

Kaitlyn gives her college the $900, and the college then deposits this amount into its own bank, named Township Bank. But the money multiplication process does not end here. Township Bank also keeps no excess reserves, so it loans out 90% of the $900, which is $810. This loan creates $810 more in money supply, so total new money is now $1,000 + $900 + $810 = $1,710. Here are the balance sheet changes at Township Bank:

TOWNSHIP BANK

Assets		Liabilities and net worth	
Reserves	+$90	Deposits	+$900
Loans	+$810		

TABLE 30.1

Money Creation

		Round	Deposit	
Assumption 1: All currency is deposited in banks.		1	$1,000	← Initial deposit
Assumption 2: Banks hold no excess reserves.		2	900	
Required reserve ratio (rr) = 10%		3	810	
Initial new money supply = $1,000		4	729	
		•	•	
		•	•	
		•	•	
		Sum	$10,000	← Total money

You can now see that whenever a bank makes a loan, it creates new money. As long as dollars find their way back into the banking system, banks multiply them into more deposits—which means more money. Table 30.1 summarizes this process of money creation. The initial $1,000 deposit ultimately leads to $10,000 worth of money. When monetary funds are deposited into banks, banks can multiply these deposits; and when they do, they create money.

In the end, the impact on the money supply is a large multiple of the initial increase in money. The exact multiple depends on the required reserve ratio (rr). The rate at which banks multiply money when all currency is deposited into banks and they hold no excess reserves is called the **simple money multiplier** (m^m). The formula for the money multiplier is

The **simple money multiplier** is the rate at which banks multiply money when all currency is deposited into banks and they hold no excess reserves.

(EQUATION 30.4)

$$m^m = \frac{1}{rr}$$

In our example, rr = 0.10, so the multiplier is 1/0.10, which is 10. When the money multiplier is 10, a new $1,000 bill produced by the Federal Reserve can eventually lead to $10,000 in new money.

Of course, in the real world our two assumptions don't always hold. There is a more realistic money multiplier that relaxes the two assumptions. Consider how a real-world money multiplier would compare with the simple money multiplier. First, if people hold on to some currency (relaxing assumption 1), banks cannot multiply that currency, so the more realistic multiplier is smaller than the simple money multiplier. Second, if banks hold excess reserves (relaxing assumption 2), these dollars are not multiplied, and again the real multiplier is smaller than the simple version. So, in reality, money doesn't multiply at quite the rate represented by the simple money multiplier. The simple money multiplier represents the *maximum* size of the money multiplier.

Note that the money multiplier process also works in reverse. When funds are withdrawn from the banking system, these are funds that banks cannot multiply. In effect, the money supply contracts. The maximum contraction is the withdrawal times the simple money multiplier.

How Does the Federal Reserve Control the Money Supply?

There's a good chance you've heard of the U.S. Federal Reserve (Fed), even outside economics class. Jerome Powell, the Chair of the Fed's Board of Governors, is one of the most recognized economists in the world. And while we've referred to the Fed periodically throughout this text, now it's time to examine it closely.

In 2018, Jerome Powell replaced Janet Yellen as the chair of the Fed's Board of Governors.

The Many Jobs of the Federal Reserve

The Fed was established in 1913 as the central bank of the United States. The Fed's primary responsibilities are threefold:

1. *Monetary policy*: The Fed controls the U.S. money supply and is charged with regulating it to offset macroeconomic fluctuations.

2. *Central banking*: The Fed serves as a bank for banks, holding their deposits and extending loans to them.

3. *Bank regulation*: The Fed is one of the primary entities charged with ensuring the financial stability of banks, including the determination of reserve requirements.

   In this section, we talk about the Fed's role as central bank and bank regulator. We then look at monetary policy in the remainder of the chapter and into the next chapter.

PRACTICE WHAT YOU KNOW

Fractional Reserve Banking: The B-Money Bank

Use this balance sheet of the B-Money Bank to answer the questions below. Assume that the required reserve ratio is 10%.

B-MONEY BANK

Assets		Liabilities and net worth	
Reserves	$50,000	Deposits	$200,000
Loans	120,000	Net worth	20,000
Treasury securities	50,000		

When banks extend loans, the money supply increases.

QUESTION: What are the required reserves of B-Money Bank?

ANSWER: B-Money is required to hold 10% of deposits, which is $20,000.

QUESTION: What is the maximum new loan B-Money can extend?

ANSWER: B-Money has $30,000 in excess reserves, so it can extend that total amount in new loans.

QUESTION: How would you rewrite B-Money's balance sheet, assuming that this loan is made?

ANSWER: The only items that would change are reserves, which would decline by $30,000, and loans, which would increase by $30,000.

B-MONEY BANK

Assets		Liabilities and net worth	
Reserves	$20,000	Deposits	$200,000
Loans	150,000		
Treasury securities	50,000	Net worth	20,000

QUESTION: If the Federal Reserve now bought all of B-Money's Treasury securities, how large a loan could B-Money now extend?

ANSWER: B-Money would now have $50,000 in excess reserves, so it could make a loan in this amount.

QUESTION: What would be the maximum impact on the money supply from this Fed action?

ANSWER: Using the simple money multiplier, we can see that the money supply could grow by as much as $500,000 from this action alone:

$$\$50,000 \times m^m = \$50,000 \times \frac{1}{rr} = \$50,000 \times 10 = \$500,000$$

CHALLENGE QUESTION: If all banks hold excess reserves of 10%, so that total reserves are 20% of deposits, what is the new money multiplier?

ANSWER: The simple money multiplier would not work in this example any longer because that formula assumes no excess reserves. If total reserves are actually 20%, the multiplier falls to $1/(1/5) = 5$. Banks are not multiplying money as many times, since they are holding more aside on reserve.

The Fed is a "central bank"—that is, it acts as a "bank for banks." In its role as central bank, it offers support and stability to the nation's entire banking system. The first component of this role involves the deposits that banks hold at the Fed. **Federal funds** are deposits that private banks hold on reserve at the Fed. The word "federal" seems to denote that these are government funds, but in fact they are private funds held on deposit at a *federal* agency—the Fed. These deposits are part of the reserves that banks set aside, along with the physical currency in their vaults.

Federal funds
are deposits that private banks hold on reserve at the Federal Reserve.

Banks keep reserves at the Fed in part because the Fed clears loans between banks. When banks loan reserves to other banks, these are *federal funds loans*. The federal funds loans are typically very short term (often overnight), and they enable banks to make quick adjustments to their balance sheets. For example, if our theoretical University Bank somehow dips below its required reserve level, it can approach Township Bank for a short-term loan. If Township Bank happens to have excess reserves, making a short-term loan enables it to earn interest. The interest rate that banks charge each other on interbank loans is known as the **federal funds rate**.

Figure 30.6 illustrates how the relationship between the Federal Reserve and commercial banks is analogous to the relationship between commercial banks and households and firms. First, households and firms hold deposits at banks, and banks hold deposits at the Fed—these are the federal funds. Second, households and firms take out loans from banks, and banks take out loans from the Fed. The loans from the Fed to the private banks are known as **discount loans**.

Discount loans are the vehicle by which the Fed performs its role as "lender of last resort." Given the macroeconomic danger of bank failure, the Fed serves an important role as a backup lender to private banks that find difficulty borrowing elsewhere. The **discount rate** is the interest rate on the discount loans made from the Fed to private banks. The Fed sets this interest rate because it is a loan directly from a branch of the U.S. government to private financial institutions.

Discount loans don't often figure prominently in macroeconomics, but in extremely turbulent times, they reassure financial market participants. For example, when banks were struggling in 2008, financial market participants were assured that troubled banks could rely on the Federal Reserve to fortify failing banks with discount loans. In fact, for the first time in history, other financial firms were allowed to borrow from the Fed. The Fed even extended an $85 billion loan to the insurance company American International Group because it had written insurance policies for financial securities based on failing home mortgages.

The **federal funds rate** is the interest rate on loans between private banks.

Discount loans are loans from the Federal Reserve to private banks.

The **discount rate** is the interest rate on the discount loans made by the Federal Reserve to private banks.

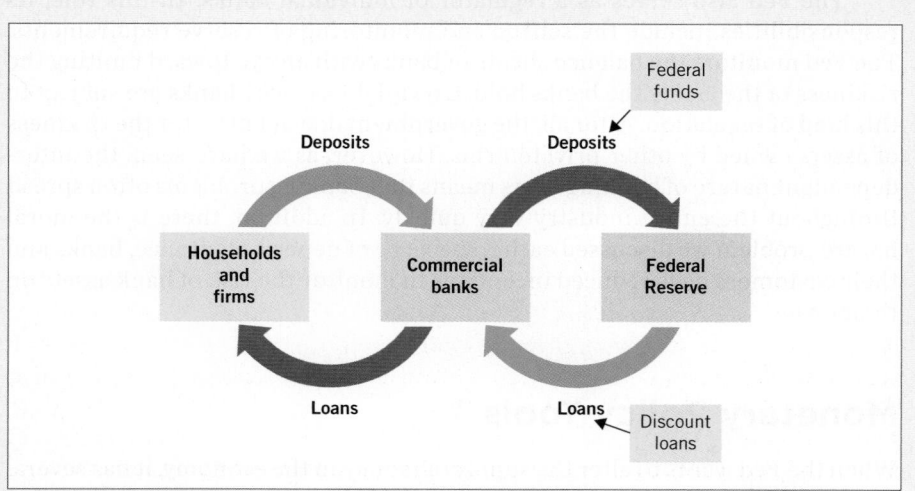

FIGURE 30.6

The Federal Reserve as a Central Bank

The Federal Reserve operates as a central bank for commercial banks. Commercial banks make deposits at the Federal Reserve; these deposits are called federal funds. The Federal Reserve also extends loans to commercial banks; these loans are called discount loans.

Moral Hazard

WALL STREET: MONEY NEVER SLEEPS

This film is a sequel to the 1987 movie *Wall Street*. It focuses on the historical events leading up to and during the financial crisis that began in 2007. One recurring theme in the movie is that some financial firms are "too big to fail." How can a firm be too big to fail?

If one bank fails, it is unable to repay its depositors and other creditors. This situation puts all the bank's creditors into similar financial difficulty. If the failing bank is large enough, its failure can set off a domino effect in which bank after bank fails and the entire financial system collapses. If regulators deem a bank too big to fail, they will use government aid to keep the bank afloat.

However, this situation introduces a particularly strong case of moral hazard. After all, banks have incentives to take on risk so they can earn high profits. If we eliminate the possibility of failure by providing government aid, there is almost no downside risk.

In this movie, Gordon Gecko, played by Michael Douglas, defines moral hazard during a public lecture.

Gordon Gecko understands moral hazard.

His definition is this: "when they take your money and then are not responsible for what they do with it."

Gecko is right: when a financial institution is not required to bear the costs of making poor decisions, it is not legally responsible for mishandling its depositors' funds.

Incentives

The Fed also serves as a regulator of individual banks. In this role, its responsibilities include the setting and monitoring of reserve requirements. The Fed monitors the balance sheets of banks with an eye toward limiting the riskiness of the assets the banks hold. One might ask why banks are subject to this kind of regulation. After all, the government doesn't monitor the riskiness of assets owned by other private firms. However, as we have seen, the interdependent nature of banking firms means that banking problems often spread throughout the entire industry very quickly. In addition, there is the moral hazard problem we discussed earlier: because of deposit insurance, banks and their customers have reduced incentives to monitor the risk of bank assets on their own.

Monetary Policy Tools

AIG: the first (and last?) insurance company to get a discount loan from the Fed.

When the Fed wants to alter the supply of money in the economy, it has several tools at its disposal. In this section we discuss these policy tools, but our emphasis is on the single tool the Fed uses every day: open market operations.

Federal Reserve Terminology

Let's say the reserves at B-Money Bank fall below the required level, so it approaches University Bank for a loan. University Bank agrees to a short-term loan with B-Money Bank.

QUESTION: What is the name of the funds that private banks like University Bank loan to other private banks (like B-Money Bank)? What is the interest rate on these loans called?

ANSWER: The funds are called federal funds. The word "federal" makes it sound as if the funds are a loan from the federal government, but they are not. This wording has been adopted because the loan typically takes place through changes in the two banks' accounts at their bank, the Federal Reserve. The interest rate is the federal funds rate.

Now assume that B-Money Bank has made some particularly troublesome loans (perhaps a lot of high-risk mortgage loans) and that all private parties refuse to lend to B-Money, which then approaches the Fed for a loan to keep its reserves at the required level.

QUESTION: What is the name of this type of loan? What is the name of the interest rate charged for this loan?

ANSWER: This is a discount loan, and the interest rate is the discount rate.

Loans from the Federal Reserve aren't called federal funds. They're called discount loans.

OPEN MARKET OPERATIONS If the Fed decided to increase the money supply, it could do so in a number of direct ways. Here we list three possible means by which the Fed might directly increase the amount of money in the economy. See if you can guess which of the three is actually used:

1. Drop money out of a helicopter.
2. Distribute $50,000 in new $100 bills to every private bank.
3. Use new money to buy something in the economy.

If you chose option 3, you are correct. **Open market operations** involve the purchase or sale of bonds by a central bank. When the Fed wants to increase the money supply, it buys securities; in contrast, when it wishes to decrease the money supply, it sells securities. In Chapter 23, we introduced the U.S. Treasury security as a special bond asset. These are the securities (bonds) that the Fed typically buys and sells when implementing monetary policy.

In principle, the Fed could realize its desired effects through buying any goods and services—real estate, fine art, or, for that matter, tons and tons of coffee and bagels. It would be as if the Fed created a batch of new currency and then went shopping. When it was done shopping, it would leave behind all the new currency in the economy. Whatever it bought during its shopping spree would become an asset on the Fed's balance sheet.

Open market operations involve the purchase or sale of bonds by a central bank.

The Fed buys and sells Treasury securities for two reasons. First, the Fed's goal is to get the funds directly into the market for loanable funds. In this way, financial institutions begin lending the new money, and it quickly moves into the economy. Second, a typical day's worth of open market operations might entail as much as $20 billion in purchases. Imagine being the manager of a bagel shop in Washington, D.C., and having the Fed call in a request for $20 billion worth of bagels. That order would be impossible to fill. But the market for U.S. Treasuries is big enough to accommodate this level of purchases seamlessly. The daily volume in the U.S. Treasury market is over $500 billion, so the Fed can buy and sell without difficulty.

Figure 30.7 summarizes how open market operations work. In panel (a), we see that when the Fed purchases bonds, it creates new money and trades this money with financial institutions for their Treasury bonds. The result is more money in the economy. On the other side, we see in panel (b) that when the Fed sells bonds to financial institutions, it exchanges bonds for existing money, taking the money out of the economy. The result is less money in the economy.

The Fed undertakes open market operations every business day. Typically, it intends to keep market conditions exactly as they were the day before. But open market operations are also the primary tool that the Fed uses to expand or contract the money supply in order to affect the macroeconomy.

QUANTITATIVE EASING The end of 2008 marked the single worst quarter for the U.S. economy in over half a century. Real GDP declined by 8.9%, and the unemployment rate was ratcheting upward. In November 2008, hoping that more money would stimulate the economy, the Federal Reserve determined that it should take additional measures to increase the money supply. The method it chose is a new variety of open market operations known as quantitative easing. **Quantitative easing** is the targeted use of open market

Quantitative easing
is the targeted use of open market operations in which the central bank buys securities specifically targeting certain markets.

FIGURE 30.7

Open Market Operations

In open market purchases, the Fed buys bonds from financial institutions. This action injects new money directly into financial markets. In open market sales, the Fed sells bonds back to financial institutions. This action takes money out of financial markets.

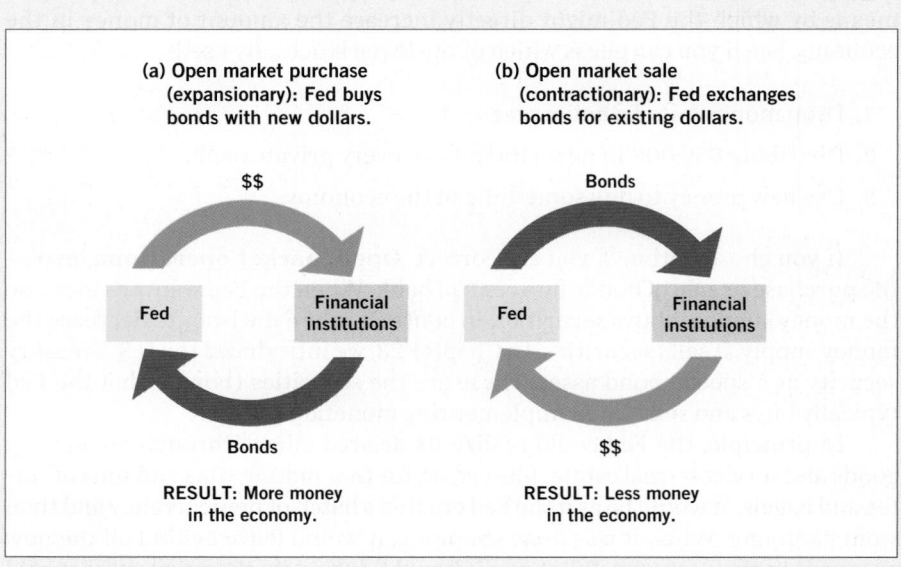

operations in which the central bank buys securities specifically targeting certain markets. Open market operations typically involve buying and selling short-term Treasury securities—that is, bonds that mature in less than one year. But with its quantitative easing in late 2008, the Fed expanded its purchases to include $300 billion in long-term Treasury securities. It also purchased $1.25 trillion in mortgage-backed securities, specifically targeting the housing market. Together with an additional $175 billion in purchases of securities from government-sponsored enterprises, the Fed's purchases amounted to almost $2 trillion in new funds injected into the economy.

This move was bold and unprecedented in both size and scope. It amounted to the Fed creating trillions of new dollars and injecting them into targeted sectors of the economy. The first round of quantitative easing started in November 2008 and continued into the first quarter of 2010. At that point, the Fed was convinced that economic recovery was well under way. But conditions deteriorated over the second half of 2010 as the unemployment rate stayed around 9% and real GDP growth stalled. Because of the lackluster U.S. economic performance in November 2010, the Fed decided to engage in a second round of quantitative easing, dubbed QE 2. This round involved purchasing an additional $600 billion in long-term Treasury securities. The Fed implemented these two rounds of quantitative easing when it was clear that traditional open market operations would not return the economy to stable growth rates.

Then, in September 2011, as the economy continued to struggle toward consistent growth, then-Chairman of the Fed Ben Bernanke announced yet another variation of quantitative easing. In particular, the Fed would buy $400 billion in long-term Treasury securities and simultaneously sell $400 billion in short-term Treasury securities. This action became known as a "twist," because it was not really adding money to the economy but attempting to reduce long-term interest rates and thereby encourage business investment. However, the twist operation did not seem to have a significant effect on the economy, and lackluster growth continued through 2012. Thus, in September 2012, the Fed announced an ongoing program to buy $40 billion worth of securities per month (this amount was later increased to $85 billion). This program, which became known as QE 3, lasted until October 2014. Figure 30.8 illustrates the timeline for these quantitative easing programs along with the quarterly growth rates of real GDP.

In summary, quantitative easing was a new variation of open market operations introduced during the slow recovery from the Great Recession. Because the Fed had already bought so many securities on the open market, the lower interest rates caused by these huge purchases had already pushed short-term interest rates down to zero. Thus, traditional open market operations had reached a boundary and the Fed searched for other actions. Like most moves by the Fed, these actions are hotly debated, as critics of these programs note that quantitative easing did not quickly return the economy to strong growth. In the next chapter, we will look more closely at the Federal Reserve's influence on interest rates.

RESERVE REQUIREMENTS AND DISCOUNT RATES In the past, the Fed made use of two other tools in its administration of monetary policy: reserve requirements and the discount rate. Neither of these has been used recently for monetary policy, but they are available and historically important.

FIGURE 30.8

Quantitative Easing, November 2008–October 2014

Beginning in 2008, the Federal Reserve began the unprecedented practice of quantitative easing (QE) to inject money into the economy. The QE initiatives were each implemented when traditional monetary policy seemed to be failing to push the economy back to consistent growth. QE 3 lasted until October 2014.

Source: GDP data are from the U.S. Bureau of Economic Analysis. QE data are from the Federal Reserve.

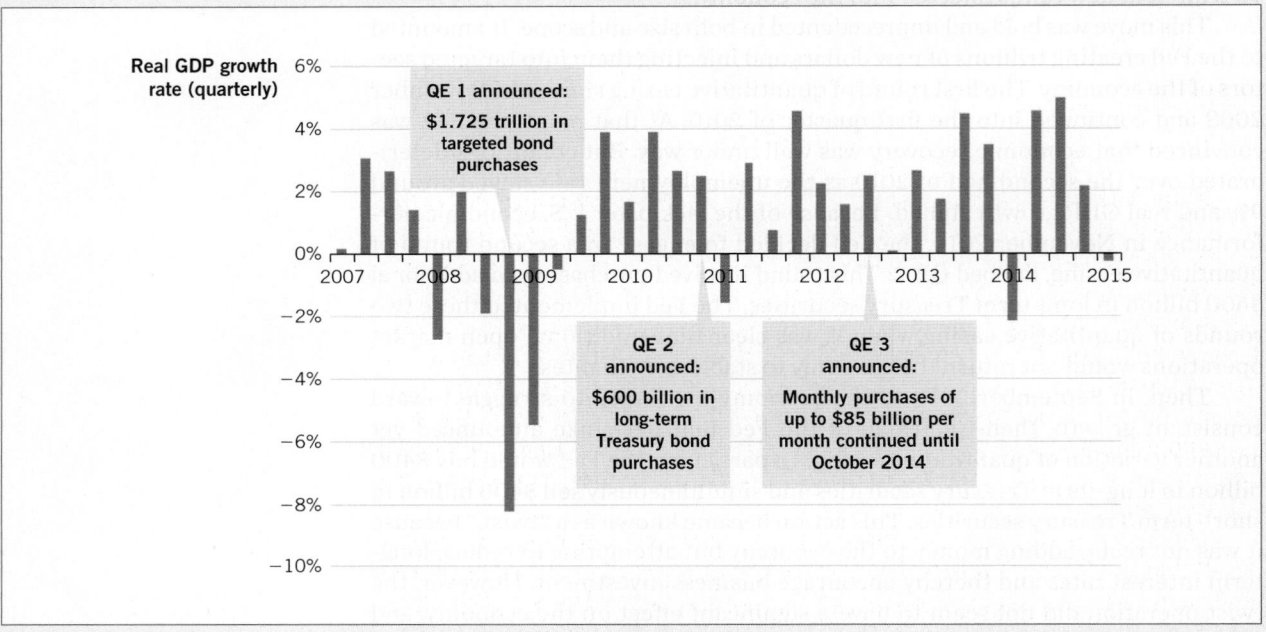

Recall our two earlier observations regarding reserve requirements:

1. The Fed sets the ratio of deposits banks must hold on reserve. This ratio is the required reserve ratio.

2. The simple money multiplier (m^m) depends on the required reserve ratio (rr), because $m^m = \dfrac{1}{rr}$.

Taken together, these observations imply that the Fed can change the money multiplier by changing the required reserve ratio. If the Fed lowers the required reserve ratio, the money multiplier increases. If it raises the required reserve ratio, the money multiplier falls.

For example, consider what would happen if the Fed lowered rr to 5% from its current level of 10%. The new simple money multiplier would be $1 \div 0.05 = 20$. This action alone would double the simple money multiplier. Lowering the required reserve would mean that banks could loan out a larger portion of their deposits, enabling them to create money by multiplying deposits to a greater extent than before.

TABLE 30.2

Required Reserves and the Simple Money Multiplier

$$m^m = \frac{1}{rr}$$

rr	m^m	
0.05	20	Increase in rr → Decrease in m^m
0.10	10	
0.125	8	
0.20	5	Decrease in rr → Increase in m^m
0.25	4	

If, instead, the Fed raised rr to 20%, the simple money multiplier would fall to just $1 \div 0.20 = 5$. Table 30.2 shows different values of the simple money multiplier given different reserve requirements.

This tool is not as precise or predictable as open market operations are. Because small changes in the money multiplier can lead to large swings in the money supply, changing the reserve requirement can cause the money supply to change too much. In addition, changing reserve requirements can have unpredictable outcomes because the overall effects depend on the actions of banks. It is possible that the Fed could lower the reserve requirement to 5% and banks would not change their reserves. For these reasons, the reserve requirement has not been used for monetary policy since 1992.

The Fed has also used the discount rate to administer monetary policy. Recall that the discount rate is the interest rate charged on loans to banks from the Fed in its role as lender of last resort. In the past, the Fed would (1) increase the discount rate to discourage borrowing by banks and to decrease the money supply or (2) decrease the discount rate to encourage borrowing by banks and to increase the money supply. The Fed used this tool actively until the Great Depression era. Currently, the Fed discourages discount borrowing unless banks are struggling. Changing the discount rate to affect bank borrowing is no longer viewed as a helpful tool for changing the money supply.

ECONOMICS IN THE REAL WORLD

EXCESS RESERVES CLIMBED IN THE WAKE OF THE GREAT RECESSION

The simple money multiplier assumes that individuals and banks do not hoard cash: individuals deposit their funds into the banking system, and banks hold no excess reserves. However, these assumptions are not always realistic.

Figure 30.9 shows the excess reserves held by banking institutions in the United States between 1990 and 2018. Until the autumn of 2008, banks held virtually no excess reserves. But then excess reserves climbed to unprecedented levels, reaching over $2,500 billion by 2014.

The cause of this increase was twofold. First, in the wake of the financial turmoil of the Great Recession, banks were probably more risk averse than before. Holding more reserves gave them a buffer against additional failures. But more important, the Federal

Show Me the Money!

In a modern economy, the trade of a good or service involves money as the medium of exchange. Over the centuries, money has evolved from coins made of precious metals to pieces of paper, to numbers on a computer screen. There are two main categories of money in the United States, M1 and M2. M1 is cold, hard cash—that is, actual currency, plus funds in checking deposits at local banks. M2 includes M1 plus savings and money market funds.

M2 ($14,479 billion)

M1 ($3,761 billion)

M1 BREAKDOWN	AMOUNT
Currency	$1,634
Checking Deposits	$2,127

in billions of dollars

Credit cards don't count in the money supply.

M2 BREAKDOWN	AMOUNT
M1	$3,761
Savings Deposits	$9,276
Small Time Deposits	$581
Money Market Mutual Funds	$861

in billions of dollars

A Timeline of Currency

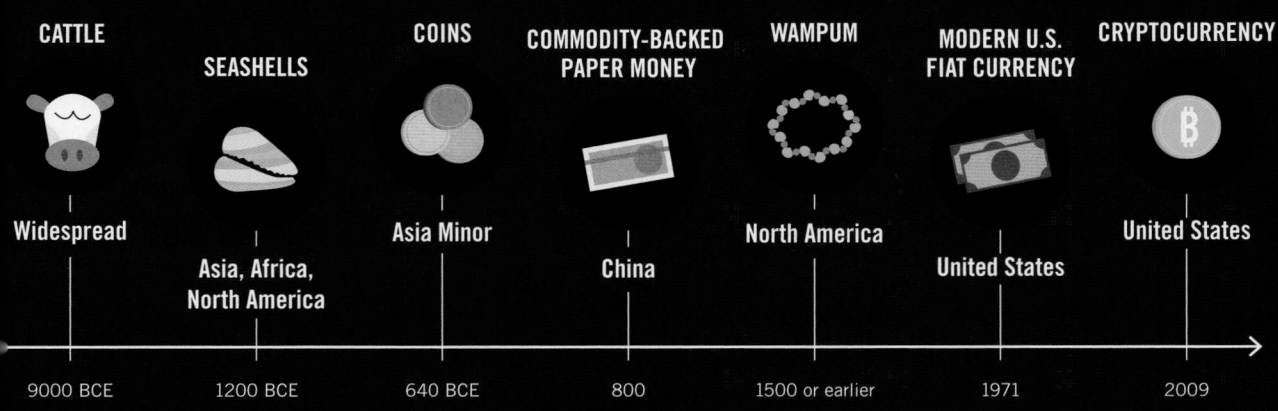

CATTLE	SEASHELLS	COINS	COMMODITY-BACKED PAPER MONEY	WAMPUM	MODERN U.S. FIAT CURRENCY	CRYPTOCURRENCY
Widespread	Asia, Africa, North America	Asia Minor	China	North America	United States	United States
9000 BCE	1200 BCE	640 BCE	800	1500 or earlier	1971	2009

REVIEW QUESTIONS

- What percentage of M1 does currency make up? Of M2?

- Which measure of money, M1 or M2, is the preferred measure of the nation's money supply in the twenty-first century?

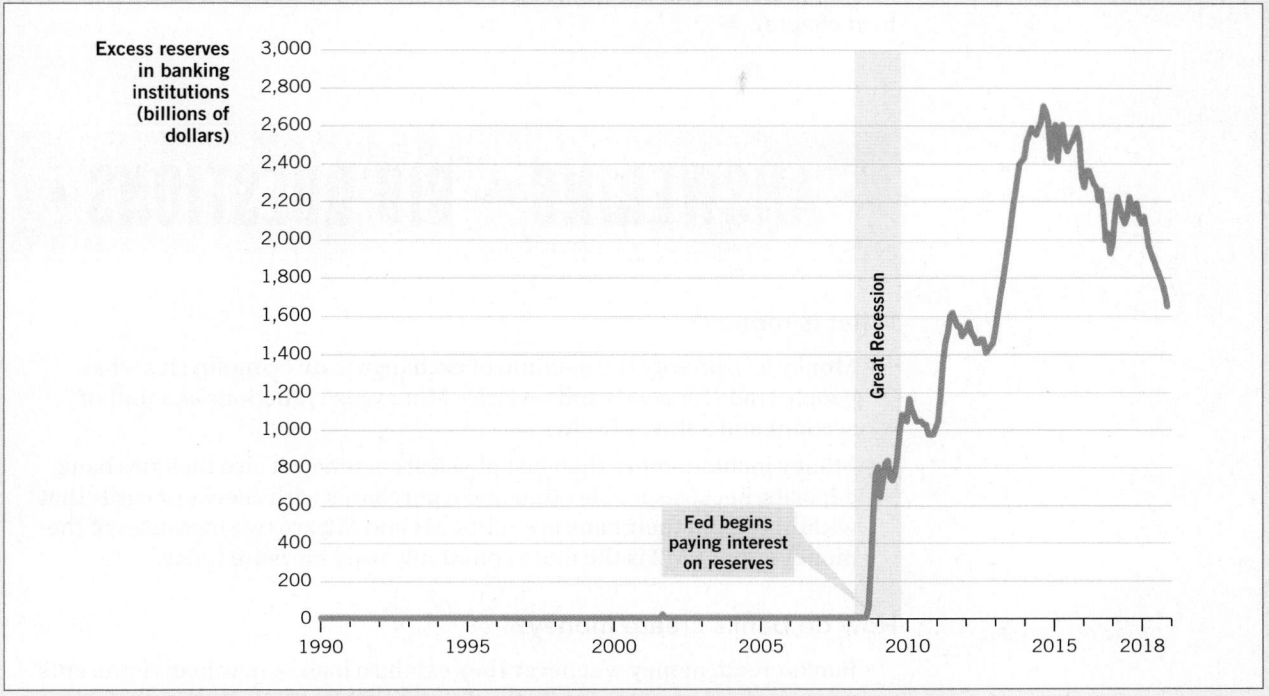

FIGURE 30.9

Excess Reserves, 1990–2018

Banks began holding significant excess reserves in 2008. Part of the explanation lies in the risky nature of loans during the Great Recession, but it is no coincidence that the excess reserves climbed immediately after the Fed began paying interest on reserves.

Source: Federal Reserve Bank of St. Louis, FRED database.

Reserve began paying interest on reserves beginning in October 2008. This historic change in policy means that banks now have less incentive to loan out each dollar above the required reserve threshold. The Fed put this policy in place to reduce the opportunity cost of excess reserves.

The increase in excess reserves means that the money multiplier is much smaller than our earlier analysis implied. When banks hold more dollars on reserve, fewer are loaned out and multiplied throughout the economy.

Incentives

Conclusion

We started this chapter with a common misconception about the supply of money in an economy. Many people believe that it is pretty simple to regulate the quantity of money in an economy. But while currency in modern economies is issued exclusively by government, money also includes bank deposits. Banks expand the money supply when they extend loans, and they contract the money supply when they increase their level of reserves. Even individuals have a significant influence: people like you and me cause the money supply to rise and fall when we change how much currency we hold outside the banking system. Taken together, these facts mean that the Fed's job of monitoring the quantity of money is very difficult. The Fed attempts to expand or contract the money supply, but its efforts may be offset by the actions of banks and individuals.

The material in this chapter sets the stage for a theoretical discussion of monetary policy and the way it affects the economy, which we undertake in the next chapter. ✳

▪ ANSWERING *the* BIG QUESTIONS ▪

What is money?

- Money is primarily the medium of exchange in an economy; it's what people trade for goods and services. Money also functions as a unit of account and a store of value.

- Money includes more than just physical currency; it also includes bank deposits, because people often make purchases with checks or cards that withdraw from their bank accounts. M1 and M2 are two measures of the money supply. M2 is the more commonly used measure today.

How do banks create money?

- Banks create money whenever they extend a loan. A new loan represents new purchasing power, while the deposit that backs the loan is also considered money.

How does the Federal Reserve control the money supply?

- The primary tool of monetary policy is open market operations, which the Fed conducts through the buying and selling of bonds. Quantitative easing is a special form of open market operations introduced in 2008. To increase the money supply, the Fed buys bonds. To decrease the money supply, the Fed sells bonds.

- The Fed has several other tools to control the money supply, including reserve requirements and the discount rate, but these tools have not been used in quite a while.

·CHAPTER PROBLEMS·

Concepts You Should Know

assets (p. 978)
balance sheet (p. 977)
bank run (p. 980)
barter (p. 971)
checkable deposits (p. 974)
commodity-backed money (p. 971)
commodity money (p. 971)
currency (p. 970)
discount loans (p. 987)
discount rate (p. 987)

double coincidence of wants (p. 971)
excess reserves (p. 980)
federal funds (p. 986)
federal funds rate (p. 987)
fiat money (p. 971)
fractional reserve banking (p. 979)
liabilities (p. 978)
M1 (p. 974)
M2 (p. 974)
medium of exchange (p. 970)

money (p. 970)
moral hazard (p. 981)
open market operations (p. 989)
owner's equity (p. 978)
quantitative easing (p. 990)
required reserve ratio (p. 980)
reserves (p. 979)
simple money multiplier (p. 984)
store of value (p. 973)
unit of account (p. 972)

Questions for Review

1. What is the difference between commodity money and fiat money?

2. What are the three functions of money? Which function is the defining characteristic?

3. What are the components of M1 and M2? List them.

4. Suppose you withdraw $100 from your checking account. What impact would this action alone have on the following?

  a. the money supply
  b. your bank's required reserves
  c. your bank's excess reserves

5. Why is the actual money multiplier usually less than the simple money multiplier?

6. Why can't a bank lend out all of its reserves?

7. How does the Fed increase and decrease the money supply through open market operations?

8. How is the discount rate different from the federal funds rate?

9. What is the current required reserve ratio? What would happen to the money supply if the Fed decreased the ratio?

10. Define quantitative easing. How is it different from standard open market operations?

Study Problems (*solved at the end of the section)

1. Suppose that you take $150 in currency out of your pocket and deposit it in your checking account. Assuming a required reserve ratio of 10%, what is the largest amount by which the money supply can increase as a result of your action?

2. Consider the balance sheet for the Wahoo Bank as presented here.

WAHOO BANK BALANCE SHEET

Assets		Liabilities and net worth	
Government securities	$1,600	Liabilities:	
Required reserves	400	Checking deposits	$4,000
Excess reserves	0	Net worth	1,000
Loans	3,000		
Total assests	5,000	Total Liablities and Net worth	5,000

Using a required reserve ratio of 10% and assuming that the bank keeps no excess reserves, write the changes to the balance sheet for each of the following scenarios:

a. Bennett withdraws $200 from his checking account.

b. Roland deposits $500 into his checking account.

c. The Fed buys $1,000 in government securities from the bank.

d. The Fed sells $1,500 in government securities to the bank.

3. Using a required reserve ratio of 10% and assuming that banks keep no excess reserves, which of the following scenarios produces a larger increase in the money supply? Explain why.

a. Someone takes $1,000 from under his or her mattress and deposits it into a checking account.

b. The Fed purchases $1,000 in government securities from a commercial bank.

4. Using a required reserve ratio of 10% and assuming that banks keep no excess reserves, what is the value of government securities the Fed must purchase if it wants to increase the money supply by $2 million?

5. Using a required reserve ratio of 10% and assuming that banks keep no excess reserves, imagine $300 is deposited into a checking account. By how much more does the money supply increase if the Fed lowers the required reserve ratio to 7%?

6. Determine if the following changes affect M1 and/or M2:

a. an increase in savings deposits

b. a decrease in credit card balances

c. a decrease in the amount of currency in circulation

d. the conversion of a savings account to a checking account

7. Determine whether each of the following is considered standard open market operations or quantitative easing:

a. The Fed buys $100 billion in student-loan-backed securities.

b. The Fed sells $400 billion in short-term Treasury securities.

c. The Fed buys $500 billion in 30-year (long-term) Treasury securities.

* **8.** What is the simple money multiplier if the required reserve ratio is 15%? If it is 12.5%?

* **9.** Suppose the Fed buys $1 million in Treasury securities from a commercial bank. What effect will this action have on the bank's reserves and the money supply? Use a required reserve ratio of 10%, and assume that banks hold no excess reserves and all currency is deposited into the banking system.

Solved Problems

8. When the required reserve ratio is 15%:

$$m^m = \frac{1}{rr} = \frac{1}{0.15} = 6.67$$

When the required reserve ratio is 12.5%:

$$m^m = \frac{1}{rr} = \frac{1}{0.125} = 8$$

9. The immediate result is that the commercial bank will have $1 million in excess reserves, because its deposits did not change. The commercial bank will loan out these excess reserves, and the money multiplier process begins. Under the assumptions of this question, the simple money multiplier applies. Therefore, in the end, $10 million in additional deposits will be created.

Monetary Policy

Central Banks' Control of the Economy Is Anything but Certain.

From 1982 to 2007—for 26 years—the U.S. economy hummed along with unprecedented success. There were two recessions during this period, but neither was severe or lengthy. Many economists and other observers believed that the business cycle was essentially tamed once and for all. Some credit for this "great moderation" went to Alan Greenspan, the Chairman of the Board of Governors of the Federal Reserve Board during much of this period. Analysts thought that his savvy handling of interest rates and money supply was the key to the sustained economic growth, and that enlightened supervision of central banks was the path to future economic growth throughout the world.

Unfortunately, the stability did not last. The Great Recession, which started in late 2007, plunged the United States into the worst economic downturn since the Great Depression. Moreover, the slow recovery after 2009 seemed to underscore the limits of monetary policy during significant downturns.

In this chapter, we consider how changes in the money supply and interest rates work their way through the economy. We build on earlier material, drawing heavily

The Federal Reserve plays a powerful role in the world economy, but not as powerful as some people think. Milton Friedman once suggested a thought experiment in which the Fed drops $1,000 bills out of a helicopter all through the economy, to encourage spending. You might enjoy trying to grab some of the money, but it probably won't do much to boost the economy, since prices would quickly rise to match the newly expanded money supply.

on the discussions of monetary policy, the loanable funds market, and the aggregate demand–aggregate supply model. We begin by looking at the short run, when monetary policy is most effective. We then consider why monetary policy can't always turn an economy around. We conclude the chapter by examining the relationship between inflation and unemployment.

· BIG QUESTIONS ·

- What is the effect of monetary policy in the short run?
- Why doesn't monetary policy always work?
- What is the Phillips curve?

What Is the Effect of Monetary Policy in the Short Run?

Across the globe, when economic growth stagnates and unemployment rises, we often look to the central bank to help the economy. Central banks in most countries use monetary policy to reduce interest rates and make it easier for people and businesses to borrow; this action generates new economic activity to get the economy moving again. In the last chapter, we saw that the U.S. Federal Reserve generally uses open market operations to implement monetary policy (increasing or decreasing the money supply). In this chapter, we examine how monetary policy effects ripple through the economy.

We begin by considering the immediate, or short-run, effects. Recall the difference between the short run and the long run in macroeconomics. The *long run* is a period of time long enough for all prices to adjust. But in the *short run*, some prices—often the prices of resources such as wages for workers and interest rates for loans—are inflexible.

An Overview of Monetary Policy in the Short Run

To gain some intuition about the macroeconomic results of money supply changes, let's return to an example we talked about in an earlier chapter: your hypothetical college apparel business. Suppose you already have one retail location where you sell apparel, and you are now considering opening a second.

Before you can open a new store, you need to invest in several resources: a physical location, additional inventory, and some labor. You expect the new store to earn the revenue needed to pay for these resources eventually. But you need a loan to expand the business now, so you go to the bank. The bank is willing to grant you a loan, but the interest rate is higher than your expected return on the investment. So you regretfully decide not to open a new location.

But then the central bank decides to expand the money supply. It buys Treasury securities from banks, which increases the level of reserves in the banking system. As a result, interest rates fall at your local bank. You then take out a loan, open the second apparel shop, and hire a few employees.

In this example, monetary policy affects your actions, and your actions affect the macroeconomy. First, investment increases because you spend on equipment, inventory, and a physical location. Second, aggregate demand increases because your investment demand is part of overall aggregate demand. Finally, as a result of the increase in aggregate demand, real GDP increases and unemployment falls as your output rises and you hire workers. This is what increasing the money supply can do in the short run: it expands the amount of credit (loanable funds) available and paves the way for economic expansion.

Now let's trace the impact of this kind of monetary policy on the entire macroeconomy. In doing so, we draw heavily on what we have presented in preceding chapters. Here, pulled together from previous chapters, is a short list of concepts we will use (the chapters are identified so you can review as necessary):

1. The Fed uses open market operations to implement monetary policy. Open market operations involve the purchase or sale of bonds; normally, these are short-term Treasury securities (Chapter 30).

2. Treasury securities are one important part of the loanable funds market, in which lenders buy securities and borrowers sell securities (Chapter 23).

3. The price in the loanable funds market is the interest rate. Lower interest rates increase the quantity of investment demand, just as lower prices increase the quantity demanded in any product market (Chapter 22).

4. Investment is one component of aggregate demand, so changes in investment indicate corresponding changes in aggregate demand (Chapter 26).

5. In the short run, increases in aggregate demand increase output and lower the unemployment rate (Chapter 26).

We have studied each of these concepts separately. Now it is time to put them together for a complete picture of how monetary policy works.

Expansionary Monetary Policy

There are two types of monetary policy: expansionary and contractionary. **Expansionary monetary policy** occurs when a central bank acts to increase the money supply in an effort to stimulate the economy, and it typically expands the money supply through open market purchases: it buys bonds.

When the Fed buys bonds from financial institutions, new money moves directly into the loanable funds market as an increase in the supply of loanable funds. As we saw in our college apparel store example, this action increases the funds that banks can use for new loans. Figure 31.1 illustrates the short-run

Expansionary monetary policy occurs when a central bank acts to increase the money supply in an effort to stimulate the economy.

FIGURE 31.1

Expansionary Monetary Policy in the Short Run

(a) When the central bank buys bonds, it injects new funds directly into the loanable funds market. This action increases the supply of loanable funds (S_1 shifts to S_2) and decreases the interest rate from 3% to 2%. The lower interest rate leads to an increase in the quantity of investment demand (D) from $200 billion to $210 billion, which increases aggregate demand (AD). (b) The increase in aggregate demand causes real GDP (Y) to rise from $20 trillion to $20.5 trillion and reduces unemployment (u) in the short run. The general price level also rises to 105 but does not fully adjust in the short run.

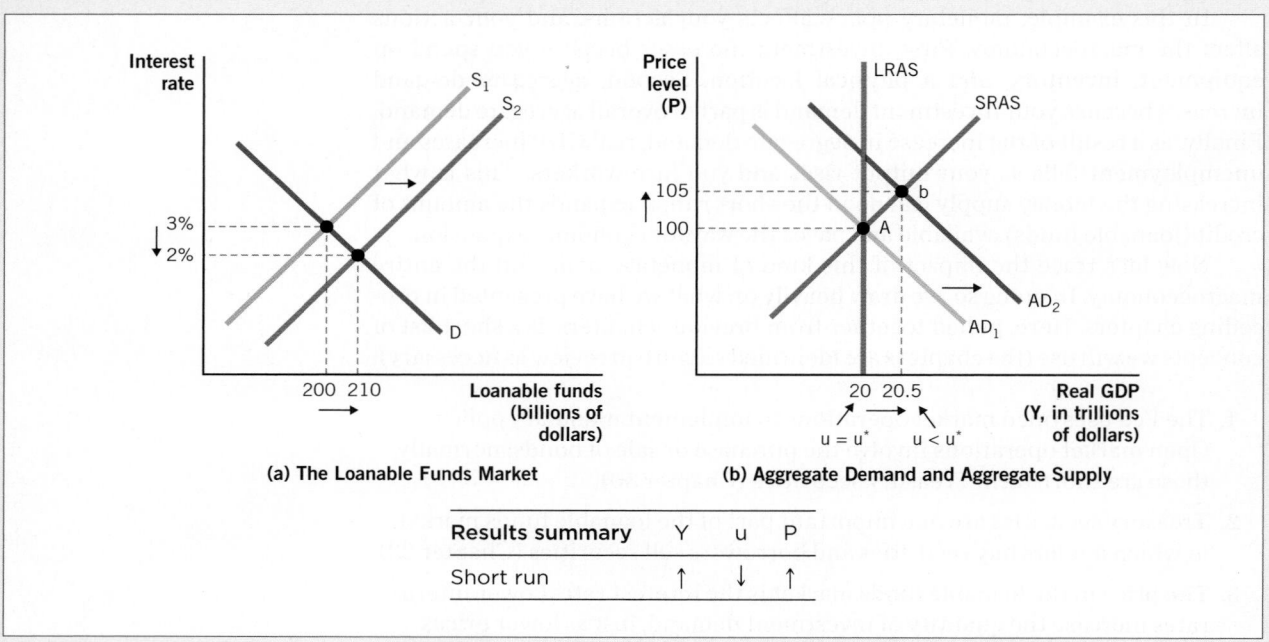

(a) The Loanable Funds Market

(b) Aggregate Demand and Aggregate Supply

Results summary	Y	u	P
Short run	↑	↓	↑

effects of expansionary monetary policy in the loanable funds market and on aggregate demand. First, notice that with open market operations, the new funds directly enter the loanable funds market, as pictured in panel (a). The supply of funds increases from S_1 to S_2. This new supply reduces the interest rate from 3% to 2%. At the lower interest rate, firms take more loans for investment, and the quantity demanded of loanable funds increases from $200 billion to $210 billion.

Because investment is a component of aggregate demand, an increase in the quantity of investment demand also increases aggregate demand, as pictured in panel (b) of Figure 31.1. Remember from Chapter 26 that aggregate demand derives from four sources: C, I, G, and NX. When investment (I) increases, aggregate demand increases from AD_1 to AD_2.

In the short run, increases in aggregate demand lead to increases in real GDP. In panel (b) of Figure 31.1, the economy moves from an initial long-run equilibrium at point A to a short-run equilibrium at point b. Real GDP increases from $20 trillion to $20.5 trillion. The increase in GDP leads to more jobs through the increase in aggregate demand; therefore, it also leads to lower unemployment. Finally, the general price level rises from 100 to 105. This price level increase is only partial; in the short run, output prices are more flexible than input prices, which are sticky and do not adjust.

In summary, in the short run, expansionary monetary policy reduces unemployment (u) and increases real GDP (Y). In addition, the overall price level (P) rises somewhat as flexible prices increase in the short run. These results are summarized in the table at the bottom of Figure 31.1.

Before moving on, let's step back and consider the results of the expansion. They seem positive, right? After all, unemployment goes down, and real GDP goes up. This macroeconomic result is consistent with the way monetary policy affected your hypothetical college apparel firm. Real employment and real output expand from the increase in the money supply. However, later in the chapter, we will see that these benefits do not help everyone in the economy.

ECONOMICS IN THE REAL WORLD

MONETARY POLICY RESPONSES TO THE GREAT RECESSION

In the fall of 2007, it was clear that the U.S. economy was slowing. The unemployment rate rose from 4.4% to 5% between May and June 2007, and real GDP grew by just 1.7% in the fourth quarter. The U.S. economy entered a recession in December 2007. We now know that the nation's economy was entering several years of low growth and high unemployment. Many economists believe that a decline in aggregate demand was one cause of the recession. The Federal Reserve's response was an attempt to increase aggregate demand.

We have seen that open market purchases drive down interest rates. This is exactly how the Federal Reserve responded, beginning in 2007. Figure 31.2 shows the *federal funds rate*, which is the interest rate on short-term loans between banks. Traditional open market operations involve buying short-term Treasury securities, which decreases the short-term interest rate, or selling short-term Treasury securities, which increases the short-term interest rate. As you can see, the Fed actively worked to keep the federal funds rate at nearly 0% for several years. Finally, in 2015, with the unemployment rate down to 5% again, the Fed began inching the federal funds rate back up. It did this by selling off securities it had been holding after three rounds of quantitative easing, a process called "winding down the balance sheet." These decisions reflect the monetary policy prescriptions we discuss in this section—during recessionary periods, expansionary monetary policy aimed at lower interest rates to increase real GDP and reduce unemployment; and between recessions a tightening of the money supply to control inflation.

REAL VERSUS NOMINAL EFFECTS We have seen that changes in the quantity of money lead to real changes in the economy. You may wonder if the process is really that simple. That is, if a central bank can create jobs and real GDP by simply increasing the money supply, why would it ever stop? After all, fiat money is just paper! Well, while there is a short-run incentive to increase the money supply, these effects wear off in the long run as prices adjust and then drive down the value of money.

Think of it this way: Let's say the Fed's preferred method of increasing the money supply is to hand all college students backpacks full of newly printed

FIGURE 31.2

Monetary Policy during the Great Recession

When the Great Recession began, the Fed responded with expansionary monetary policy that led to lower short-term interest rates. The Fed continued to keep the federal funds interest rate near zero through 2015. In 2016, with early signs of inflation beginning to creep into the economic data, the Fed started raising the rate to keep inflation from getting out of hand.

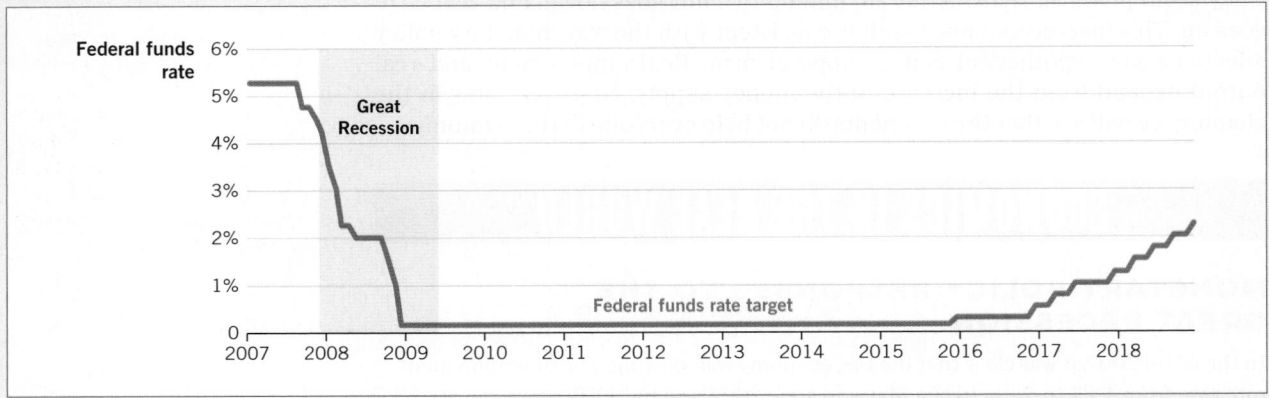

bills. This is a variation on a thought experiment suggested by economist Milton Friedman, involving money dropped from a helicopter. Not a bad idea, right? But let's focus on the macroeconomic effects. Eventually, the new money devalues the entire money supply, because prices rise. But because you get the money first, you get it before any prices adjust. So these new funds represent an increase in real purchasing power for you. This is why monetary policy can have immediate real short-run effects: initially, no prices have adjusted. But as prices adjust in the long run, the effects of the new money wear off.

Injecting new money into the economy eventually causes inflation, but inflation doesn't happen right away and prices do not rise uniformly. During the time that prices are increasing, the value of money is constantly moving downward. Figure 31.3 illustrates the real purchasing power of money as time goes by. Panel (a) shows adjustments to the price level. When new money enters the economy (at time t_0), the price level begins to rise in the short run and then reaches its new level in the long run (at time t_{LR}). Panel (b) shows the value of money relative to these price-level adjustments. When the new money enters the economy, it has its highest value because prices have not yet adjusted. In the short run, as prices rise, the real purchasing power of all money in the economy falls. In the long run, all prices adjust, and the real value of money reaches its lower level. At this point, the real effects of the monetary policy dissipate completely.

How would you like it if new money entered the economy through backpacks full of currency given to all college students?

UNEXPECTED INFLATION HURTS SOME PEOPLE Let's now consider how expansionary monetary policy affects different people across the economy. The basic macroeconomic results, summarized in Figure 31.1, seem very positive: real GDP goes up, the unemployment rate falls, and there

FIGURE 31.3

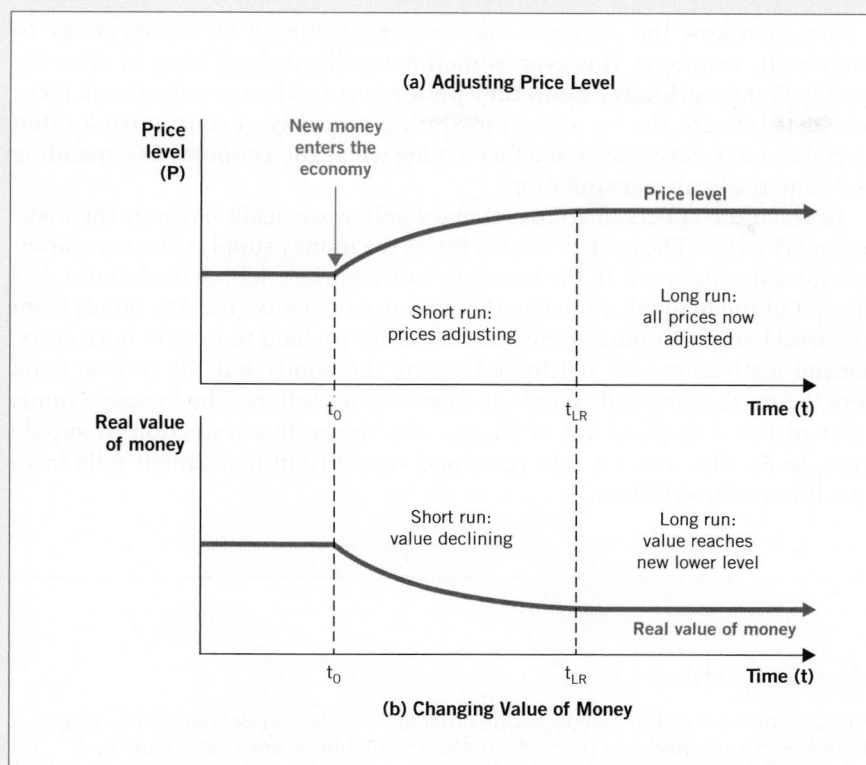

(a) Adjusting Price Level

Price level (P)

New money enters the economy

Price level

Short run: prices adjusting

Long run: all prices now adjusted

t_0 t_{LR} Time (t)

Real value of money

Short run: value declining

Long run: value reaches new lower level

Real value of money

t_0 t_{LR} Time (t)

(b) Changing Value of Money

The Real Value of Money as Prices Adjust

(a) If the central bank increases the money supply at time t_0, the price level begins rising in the short run. In the long run, all prices adjust and the price level reaches its new higher level. (b) As the price level increases, the real value of money declines throughout the short run. In the long run, at t_{LR}, the real value of money reaches a new lower level.

is some inflation. Consider that you are living in an economy where these conditions exist. Everywhere you look, the news seems positive, as the media, politicians, and firms focus on the expanding economy. But this action does not help everybody.

For example, consider workers who signed a two-year contract just before the inflation hit the economy. These workers now pay more for goods and services such as groceries, gasoline, education, and health care—yet their wages were set before the inflation occurred. In real terms, these workers experience a pay cut. Monetary policy derives its potency from sticky prices, but if your price (or wage) is stuck, inflation hurts you.

Inflation harms input suppliers that have sticky prices. In addition to workers, lenders (the suppliers of funds used for expansion) are another prominent group harmed when inflation is greater than anticipated. Imagine that you are a banker who extends a loan with an interest rate of 3%, but then the inflation rate turns out to be 5%. The Fisher equation, discussed in Chapter 22, implies that the loan's real interest rate is actually −2%. A negative interest rate definitely harms your bank!

Later in this chapter, we talk about incentives for these resource suppliers to correctly anticipate inflation. For now, we just note that unexpected inflation, while potentially helpful to the overall economy, is harmful to those who adjust slowly.

Contractionary Monetary Policy

Contractionary monetary policy occurs when a central bank acts to decrease the money supply.

We have seen how the central bank uses expansionary monetary policy to stimulate the economy. However, sometimes policymakers want to slow the economy. **Contractionary monetary policy** occurs when a central bank takes action that reduces the money supply in the economy. A central bank often undertakes contractionary monetary policy when the economy is expanding rapidly and the bank fears inflation.

To trace the effects of contractionary policy, we again begin in the loanable funds market. The central bank reduces the money supply via open market operations: it sells bonds in the loanable funds market. Selling the bonds takes funds out of the loanable funds market because the banks buy the bonds from the central bank with money they might otherwise lend to private borrowers. Financial institutions are not forced to buy the bonds, but the central bank enters the market and sells bonds alongside other sellers. The loanable funds market pictured in panel (a) of Figure 31.4 shows this reduction in supply from S_1 to S_2. The interest rate rises, and equilibrium investment falls from $200 billion to $190 billion.

FIGURE 31.4

Contractionary Monetary Policy in the Short Run

(a) The central bank sells bonds, which pulls funds out of the loanable funds market. This action decreases the supply of loanable funds (S_1 shifts to S_2) and increases the interest rate from 3% to 4%. The higher interest rate leads to a decrease in the quantity of investment demand (D) from $200 billion to $190 billion, and this outcome decreases aggregate demand (AD). (b) The decrease in aggregate demand (from AD_1 to AD_2) causes real GDP to decline from $20 trillion to $19.5 trillion and induces unemployment in the short run. The general price level also falls to 95 but does not fully adjust in the short run.

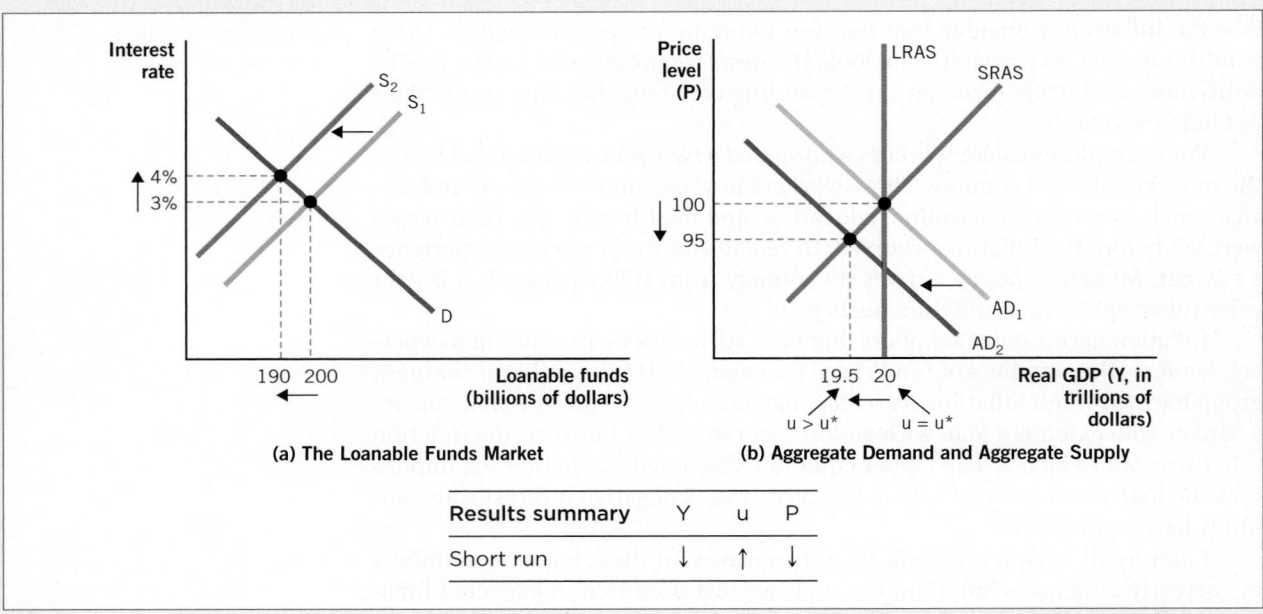

(a) The Loanable Funds Market

(b) Aggregate Demand and Aggregate Supply

Results summary	Y	u	P
Short run	↓	↑	↓

When investment falls, aggregate demand falls. Panel (b) of Figure 31.4 illustrates a fall in aggregate demand from AD_1 to AD_2. In the short run, real GDP decreases from $20 trillion to $19.5 trillion, the unemployment rate increases, and the price level decreases.

These short-run results are again the result of fixed resource prices for the firm. A lower money supply leads to downward pressure on prices (P), but sticky resource prices mean that firms cannot adjust their workers' wages or the terms of their loans in the short run. Therefore, firms reduce output and lay off some workers. This is why we see real GDP (Y) falling and the unemployment rate (u) rising. These results are summarized in the table at the bottom of the figure.

ECONOMICS IN THE REAL WORLD

MONETARY POLICY'S CONTRIBUTION TO THE GREAT DEPRESSION

As if monetary policy is not hard enough, consider that the money supply is not completely controlled by a central bank. In Chapter 30, we explained how the actions of private individuals and banks can increase or decrease the money supply via the money multiplier. Banks increase the money supply when they loan out reserves, and they decrease the money supply when they hold more reserves. In addition, individuals like you and me increase the money supply when we deposit funds into bank accounts, and the banks multiply that money by making loans. When we withdraw our funds and hold on to more currency, we decrease the money supply because banks cannot multiply those funds.

What happens when all these people want to withdraw their funds?

Now imagine a scenario with massive bank failures and very little deposit insurance. As more and more banks fail, people withdraw their funds all over the country. While it makes sense that individuals would want to withdraw their money, as people all over the country continue to remove money from banks, the money supply declines significantly. The reduction in the money supply leads to an economic contraction, similar to the scenario we saw in Figure 31.4.

This type of monetary contraction is exactly what happened at the beginning of the Great Depression. From 1929 to 1933, prior to the establishment of federal deposit insurance, over 9,000 banks failed in the United States. Because of these bank failures, people began holding their money outside the banking system. This action contributed to a significant contraction in the money supply. Figure 31.5 shows the money supply prior to and during the Great Depression. After peaking at $676 billion in 1931, the M2 money supply fell to just $564 billion in 1933. This drastic decline was one of the major causes of the Great Depression. In Chapter 27, we referred to policy errors as one of the causes of the decline in aggregate demand that led to the Great Depression. Economists today agree that the Federal Reserve should have done more to offset the decline in the money supply at the onset of the Great Depression. This was perhaps one of the biggest macroeconomic policy errors in U.S. history.

FIGURE 31.5

U.S. Money Supply before and during the Great Depression

The M2 money supply grew to $676 billion in 1931, but then plummeted to $564 billion by 1933. The huge decline in the money supply was a major contributor to the Great Depression. (Values for real money supply are expressed in 2012 dollars.)

Source: Historical Statistics of the United States, Colonial Times to 1970.

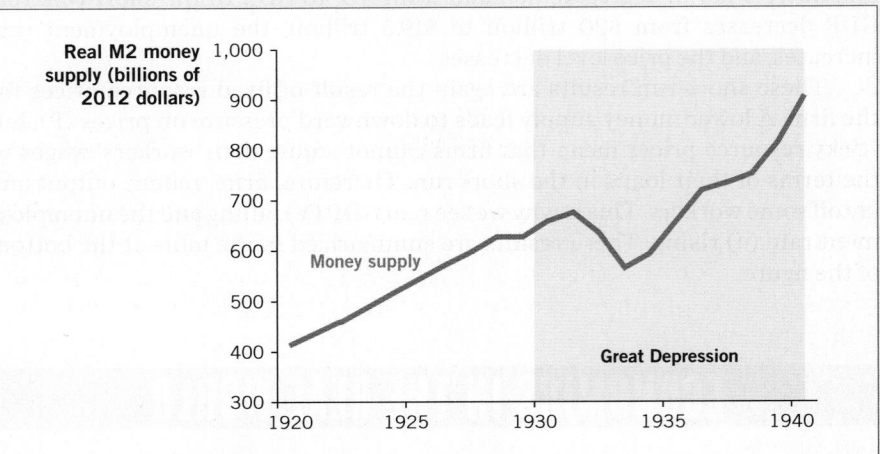

Real M2 money supply (billions of 2012 dollars)

Money supply

Great Depression

PRACTICE WHAT YOU KNOW

The Federal Open Market Committee is the group that determines monetary policy.

Expansionary versus Contractionary Monetary Policy: Monetary Policy in the Short Run

QUESTION: In the short run, how does expansionary monetary policy affect real GDP, unemployment, and the price level in the economy?

ANSWER: Real GDP increases, the unemployment rate falls, and the price level rises as all flexible prices adjust.

QUESTION: In the short run, how does contractionary monetary policy affect real GDP, unemployment, and the price level in the economy?

ANSWER: Real GDP decreases, the unemployment rate rises, and the price level falls as all flexible prices adjust.

QUESTION: What real-world circumstance might lead to contractionary monetary policy?

ANSWER: If members of the Federal Open Market Committee at the Federal Reserve thought that inflation was an imminent danger, they might implement contractionary monetary policy.

CHALLENGE QUESTION: What is the interest rate that the Fed influences most directly, and why is this rate a good gauge of the money supply in the economy?

ANSWER: The Fed targets the federal funds rate, which is the rate that banks charge each other for very short-term loans. This interest rate tells the Fed whether the money supply is too tight or too loose. If the federal funds rate rises, the money supply is deemed too tight. If the federal funds rate falls, the money supply is deemed too loose.

Why Doesn't Monetary Policy Always Work?

So far, we have seen that monetary policy can have real effects on the macroeconomy. By shifting aggregate demand, monetary policy can affect real GDP, unemployment, and the price level. But most economists feel that monetary policy is limited in what it can accomplish. In this section, we consider three of these limitations. First, we look at the diminished effects of monetary policy in the long run. Next, we consider how expectations can dampen the effects of monetary policy. Finally, we examine the limitations of monetary policy when economic downturns are caused by shifts in aggregate supply rather than aggregate demand.

Long-Run Adjustments

We have noted that some prices take longer to adjust than others and that the long run is a period long enough for *all* prices to adjust. Output prices can adjust relatively quickly. Think about the output prices at a coffee shop, which are often displayed in chalk behind the cash register; they are easy to change in the short run. In contrast, input prices, such as workers' wages, are often the slowest prices to adjust. After all, wages are sometimes set by contracts; moreover, money illusion (see Chapter 21) can make input suppliers reluctant to lower their prices. But the long run is a period sufficient for all prices to change, even wage contracts, which eventually expire.

Both types of prices affect the decisions made at firms across the economy, and therefore both affect output and unemployment. For example, consider your hypothetical small business producing and selling college apparel. Earlier in this chapter, you secured a loan to open a new retail location because the Fed increased the money supply, which expanded the supply of loanable funds. When you initially received your loan, costs for resources such as workers, equipment, inventory, and a physical plant were relatively low because prices for these resources are sticky and had not yet adjusted. But in the long run, these resource prices adjust. If everything works out well for you, the monetary expansion leads to new demand for your product and you can keep your new store open. But it is also possible that when the prices of resources rise—in the long run—you may not be able to afford them. At that point, with your costs rising, you may have to reduce your output, lay off some workers, and perhaps even close your new retail location. In the long run, as prices adjust throughout the macroeconomy, the stimulating effects of expansionary monetary policy wear off.

Let's see how this process works for the entire economy. Figure 31.6 illustrates long-run macroeconomic adjustments to expansionary monetary policy. As you can see in the graph, expansionary monetary policy shifts aggregate demand from AD_1 to AD_2. This action moves the economy from long-run equilibrium at point A to short-run equilibrium at point b (with a temporary change in real GDP and unemployment). In the long run, as resource prices rise, short-run aggregate supply shifts to the left from $SRAS_1$ to $SRAS_2$, and the economy moves to a new long-run equilibrium at point C. When we compare the new long-run equilibrium to the situation prior to the application of monetary

FIGURE 31.6

Expansionary Monetary Policy in the Long Run

Beginning in equilibrium at point A, an increase in the money supply shifts aggregate demand from AD₁ to AD₂; this action moves the economy to a new short-run equilibrium at point b. Equilibrium at point b is relevant only in the short run, because all prices have not yet adjusted. In the long run, resource prices adjust. This outcome shifts short-run aggregate supply from SRAS₁ to SRAS₂, and the economy moves to a new long-run equilibrium at point C.

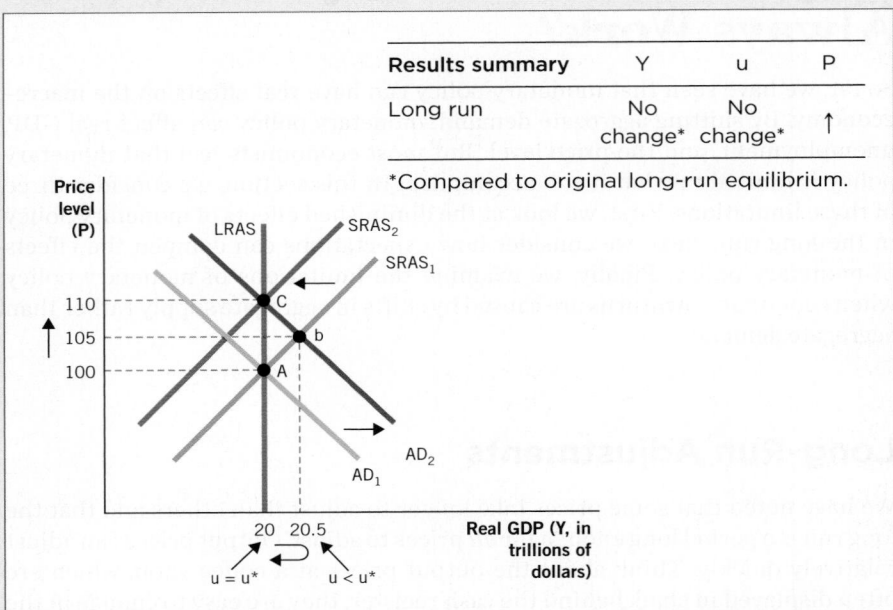

Results summary	Y	u	P
Long run	No change*	No change*	↑

*Compared to original long-run equilibrium.

policy, we see that there is no change in real GDP (Y) or unemployment (u), but there is an increase in the price level from 100 to 110.

One important implication of these long-run results is the lack of real economic effects from monetary policy; in the long run, all prices adjust. Therefore, in the long run, monetary policy does not affect real GDP or unemployment. The only predictable result of more money in the economy over the long run is inflation. As we discussed in Chapter 21, the cause of inflation is monetary growth. You now can understand why, in the context of the aggregate demand–aggregate supply model.

From one perspective, our long-run results may seem strange: central banks can't do much in the long run to affect the real economy. However, this statement might also seem logical, since it's possible to increase the money supply by just printing more paper money. But printing more paper money doesn't affect the economy's long-run productivity or its ability to produce; these outcomes are determined by resources, technology, and institutions. The idea that the money supply does not affect real economic variables is known as **monetary neutrality**.

Given that money is neutral in the long run, why do the Federal Reserve and other central banks employ short-run monetary policy? In fact, many of the substantive debates in macroeconomics focus on the relative importance of the short run versus the long run. Some economists believe it is best to focus on short-run effects, which are very real. After all, during recessions people often lose their jobs, which can be a very painful experience. When the money supply expands, firms can borrow more cheaply and hire more workers. From this perspective, central banks ought to take a very active role in the macroeconomy by increasing the money supply during economic downturns and contracting

Monetary neutrality
is the idea that the money supply does not affect real economic variables.

the money supply during economic expansions. This policy can then potentially smooth out the business cycle.

Other economists discount the short-run expansionary effects of monetary policy and instead focus on the problems of inflation. In Chapter 21, we explored the negative effects of inflation. These include price confusion, wealth redistribution, and uncertainty about future price levels. These by-products of inflation can stifle economic growth.

In the next section, we consider the potency of monetary policy when market participants expect inflation ahead of time.

Adjustments in Expectations

Unexpected inflation harms workers and other resource suppliers who have fixed prices in the short run; therefore, workers normally expect a certain level of inflation and expect to see it reflected by annual pay adjustments or in contractual cost-of-living adjustments that are sometimes tied to inflation rates. The key incentive for anticipating the correct rate of inflation is straightforward: surprise inflation harms people. But when inflation is expected, the real effects on the economy are limited.

Incentives

Let's look at inflation expectations in the context of the aggregate demand–aggregate supply model. Figure 31.7 shows how monetary expansion affects aggregate demand and aggregate supply when it is expected. Expansionary monetary policy shifts aggregate demand from AD_1 to AD_2. But if this effect is expected, short-run aggregate supply shifts to the left from $SRAS_1$ to $SRAS_2$.

In Chapter 26, we discussed how short-run aggregate supply shifts back when workers and resource suppliers expect higher future prices, because they do not want their real prices to fall. If short-run aggregate supply shifts along with the shift in aggregate demand, the economy goes immediately to

FIGURE 31.7

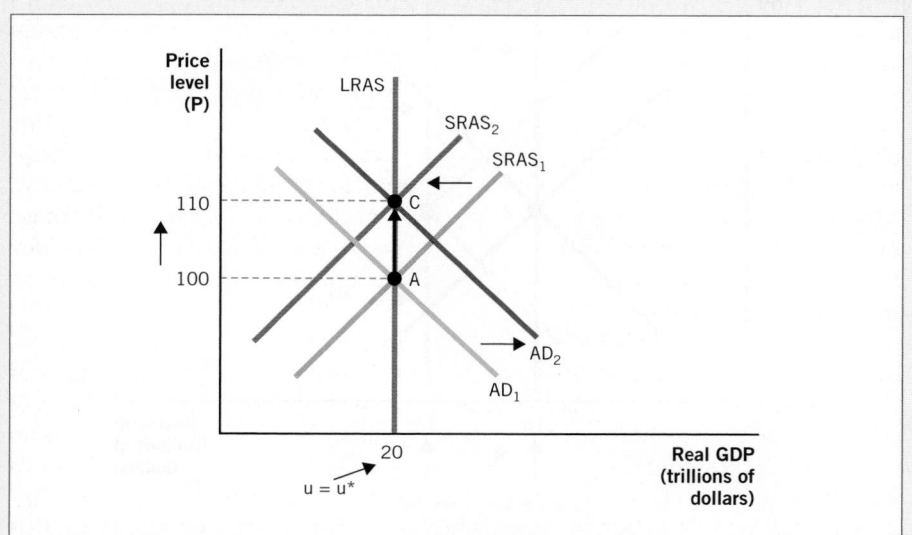

Completely Expected Monetary Policy

If expansionary monetary policy is expected, short-run aggregate supply shifts along with the shift in aggregate demand, and the economy moves directly from equilibrium at point A to point C. In this case, there are no real effects from the monetary policy, even in the short run. The only lasting change is nominal because the price level rises from 100 to 110.

equilibrium at point C. Therefore, monetary policy has no real effect on the economy—real GDP and unemployment do not change. The only lasting change is nominal, because the price level rises from 100 to 110. Monetary policy has real effects only when some prices are sticky. But if inflation is expected, prices are not sticky; they adjust because people plan on the inflation. To the extent that all prices rise, the effect of monetary policy is limited, even in the short run.

Aggregate Supply Shifts and the Great Recession

We have seen that monetary policy affects the economy by shifting aggregate demand. Thus, if a recession results from reduced aggregate demand, monetary policy can stabilize the economy and return it to higher levels of real GDP and lower unemployment. But not all downturns are a result of aggregate demand shifts. Declines in aggregate supply can also lead to recession. And when supply shifts cause the downturn, monetary policy is less likely to restore the economy to its prerecession conditions.

The Great Recession that began in 2007 seems to have included both shifts of aggregate supply and shifts of aggregate demand. In Chapter 27, we argued that the widespread problems in financial markets at that time negatively affected key institutions in the macroeconomy. Further, new financial regulations restricted banks' ability to lend at levels equal to those in effect prior to 2008. The result was a shift backward in long-run aggregate supply. In addition, as people's real wealth and expected future income levels declined, aggregate demand shifted to the left.

Figure 31.8 shows how the decline in both aggregate demand and aggregate supply might affect the economy. Initially, the economy is in equilibrium

FIGURE 31.8

Aggregate Supply–Induced Recession

Initially, in 2007, the economy is in equilibrium at point A. Then the long-run and short-run aggregate supply curves shift to the left, to LRAS$_{2008}$ and SRAS$_{2008}$. In addition, aggregate demand shifts to the left to AD$_{2008}$. This combination of shifts takes the economy to a new equilibrium at point B. At point B, monetary policy is limited in its ability to move the economy back to its original level of real GDP because monetary policy affects the economy through aggregate demand.

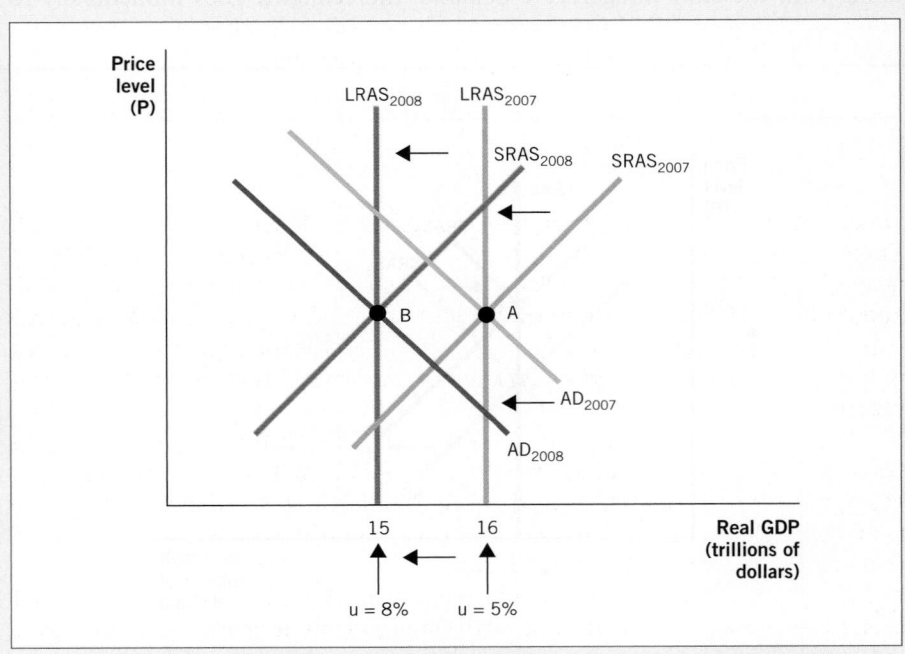

Monetary Policy Isn't Always Effective: Why Couldn't Monetary Policy Pull Us out of the Great Recession?

The Great Recession officially lasted from December 2007 to June 2009. But the effects lingered on for several years thereafter, with slow growth of real GDP and high unemployment rates. These effects all occurred despite several doses of expansionary monetary policy. Not only did the Fed push short-term interest rates to nearly 0%, but it also engaged in several rounds of quantitative easing, purchasing hundreds of billions of dollars' worth of long-term bonds.

QUESTION: What are three possible reasons why monetary policy was not able to restore expansionary growth during and after the Great Recession?

ANSWER:

1. *Monetary policy is ineffective in the long run.* While we don't know the exact length of the short run, all prices certainly had time to adjust by 2010 or 2011, yet the economy was still sluggish. Thus, one possibility is that all prices adjusted, so the effects of monetary policy wore off. This answer alone is probably inadequate, given that the effects of monetary policy were not evident even in the short run.

2. *Monetary policy was expected.* It seems unlikely that monetary policy is much of a surprise nowadays. The Federal Reserve releases official statements after each monetary policy meeting and generally announces the direction it will follow for several months in advance.

3. *The downturn was at least partially due to an aggregate supply shift.* Because monetary policy works through aggregate demand, the effects of monetary policy can be limited if shifts in aggregate supply cause a recession.

at point A, with the aggregate supply and aggregate demand curves from 2007. Then aggregate demand and aggregate supply shift to the left, to the 2008 levels. When this happens, real GDP declines from $16 trillion to $15 trillion, and the unemployment rate rises from 5% to 8%—levels similar to the actual experience during this period. Further, this rise in the unemployment rate was at least partially due to new structural unemployment that raised the natural rate of unemployment.

The dilemma is that at point B, monetary policy is limited in its ability to permanently move output back to its prior level. Even if monetary policy shifts aggregate demand back to AD$_{2007}$, this shift is not enough to eliminate the recession. Furthermore, as we have stressed throughout this chapter, the effects of monetary policy wear off in the long run.

Thus, in the wake of the Great Recession, the U.S. economy continued to struggle with slow growth and high unemployment, even after significant monetary policy interventions. The bottom line is that monetary policy does not enable us to avoid or fix every economic downturn.

What Is the Phillips Curve?

We have seen that monetary policy can stimulate the economy in the short run. Increasing the money supply increases aggregate demand, which can lead to higher real GDP, lower unemployment, and a higher price level (inflation). The relationship between inflation and unemployment is of particular interest to economists and noneconomists alike; it is at the heart of the debate regarding the power of monetary policy to affect the economy. In this section, we examine this relationship by looking at the Phillips curve.

The Traditional Short-Run Phillips Curve

In 1958, British economist A. W. Phillips noted a negative relationship between wage inflation and unemployment rates in the United Kingdom. Soon thereafter, U.S. economists Paul Samuelson and Robert Solow extended the analysis to inflation and unemployment rates in the United States. This short-run negative relationship between inflation and unemployment rates became known as the **Phillips curve**. Before looking at Phillips curve data, let's consider the theory behind the Phillips curve in the context of the aggregate demand–aggregate supply model.

Panel (a) of Figure 31.9 shows how unexpected monetary expansion affects the economy in the short run. Initially, with aggregate demand at AD₁ and the

The **Phillips curve** indicates a short-run negative relationship between inflation and unemployment rates.

FIGURE 31.9

Aggregate Demand, Aggregate Supply, and the Phillips Curve

(a) This graph shows the effect of unexpected monetary expansion in the short run. Initially, the economy is in equilibrium at point A, with a price level of 100, real GDP of $20 trillion, and an unemployment rate of 5%. Aggregate demand shifts from AD₁ to AD₂, which moves the economy to short-run equilibrium at point b. The move to point b is accompanied by an increase in the inflation rate to 5% (the price level rises from 100 to 105) but a lower unemployment rate of just 3%. (b) Here we see the two equilibrium points in a new graph that plots the negative relationship between inflation and unemployment rates. This graph, known as a Phillips curve, clarifies that higher inflation can lead to lower levels of unemployment in the short run.

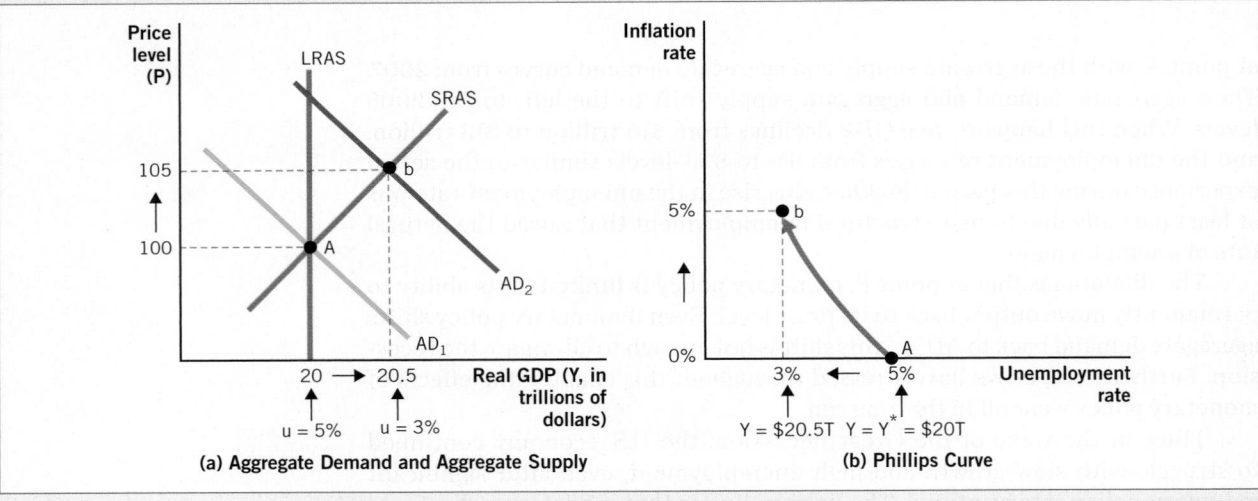

(a) Aggregate Demand and Aggregate Supply

(b) Phillips Curve

price level at 100, the economy is in long-run equilibrium at point A with real GDP (Y) at $20 trillion and the unemployment rate equal to 5%. For this example, we assume the natural rate of unemployment is exactly 5%.

Then expansionary monetary policy shifts aggregate demand to AD_2, which leads to a new short-run equilibrium at point b. Let's focus on the changes to prices and the unemployment rate. The monetary expansion leads to a 5% inflation rate as the price level rises to 105 (indicated in panel b). The unemployment rate drops to 3% as real GDP (Y) expands from $20 trillion to $20.5 trillion. The end result includes both inflation and lower unemployment.

This is the theory behind the Phillips curve relationship: monetary expansion stimulates the economy and brings some inflation, and this outcome reduces the unemployment rate. Similarly, lower inflation is associated with higher unemployment rates. This negative relationship between inflation and unemployment is captured in panel (b) of Figure 31.9, which graphs a Phillips curve. Initially, at point A, the inflation rate is 0% and the unemployment rate is 5%. But when the inflation rate rises to 5%, the unemployment rate drops to 3%.

This negative relationship between inflation and unemployment rates is consistent with Phillips's observations and also with what Samuelson and Solow saw when they plotted historical data. Figure 31.10 plots U.S. inflation and unemployment rates from 1948 to 1969, which includes the period just before and just after the work of Samuelson and Solow. The numerical values plotted represent the years: for example, point 48 represents the year 1948. It is not hard to visualize a Phillips curve relationship in this data: most years with high

FIGURE 31.10

U.S. Inflation and Unemployment Rates, 1948–1969

Data from 1948 to 1969 was very consistent with standard Phillips curve predictions: lower unemployment rates were consistently correlated with higher inflation rates. (Each number in the graph represents a particular year plotted for inflation and unemployment for that year. For example, 51 represents the year 1951, when the inflation rate was about 8% and the unemployment rate was about 3%.)

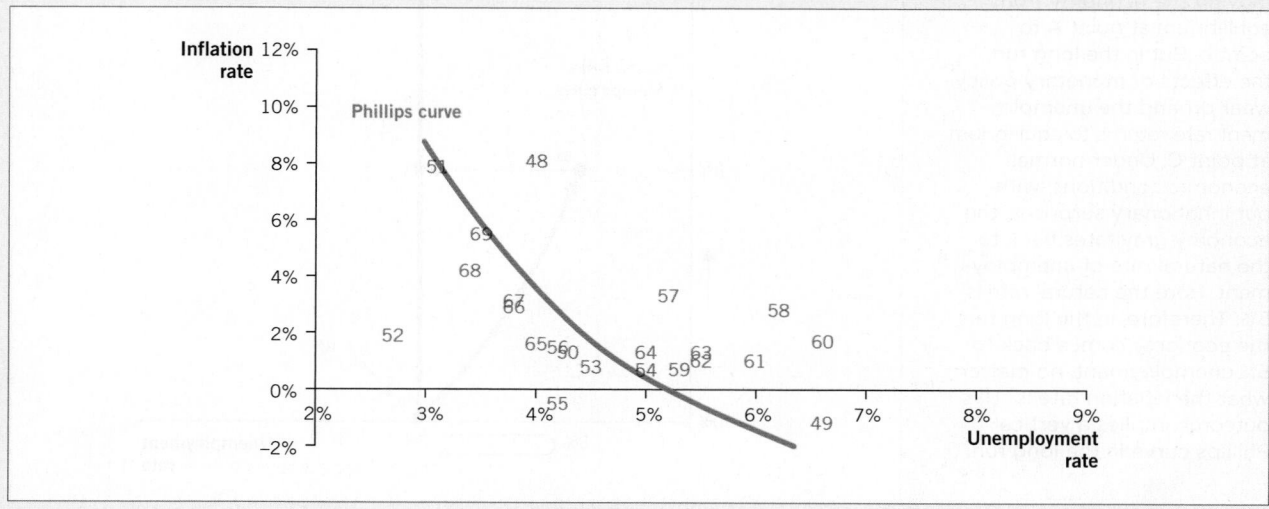

inflation rates had low unemployment rates, while most years with low inflation rates had high unemployment rates.

The Phillips curve implies a powerful role for monetary policy. It implies that a central bank can choose higher or lower unemployment rates simply by adjusting the rate of inflation in an economy. If this is a realistic observation, a central bank can always steer an economy out of recession, simply by creating inflation.

But we have already seen that monetary policy does not always have real effects on the economy. Next we consider the long run, when the real effects of monetary policy wear off. After that, we look at how expectations also mitigate the effects of monetary policy.

The Long-Run Phillips Curve

When all prices adjust, there are no real effects from monetary policy. That is, there are no effects on real GDP or unemployment. Therefore, the long-run Phillips curve looks different from the standard, short-run Phillips curve. Figure 31.11 shows both short-run and long-run Phillips curves. Initially, at point A, there is no inflation in the economy and the unemployment rate is 5%. Then monetary expansion increases the inflation rate to 5%, and the unemployment rate falls to 3% in the short run. This short-run equilibrium is indicated as point b. But when prices adjust in the long run, the unemployment rate returns

FIGURE 31.11

Short-Run and Long-Run Phillips Curves

In the short run, inflation can lead to lower unemployment, moving the economy from equilibrium at point A to point b. But in the long run, the effects of monetary policy wear off and the unemployment rate returns to equilibrium at point C. Under normal economic conditions, without inflationary surprises, the economy gravitates back to the natural rate of unemployment. Here the natural rate is 5%. Therefore, in the long run, the economy comes back to 5% unemployment, no matter what the inflation rate is. This outcome implies a vertical Phillips curve in the long run.

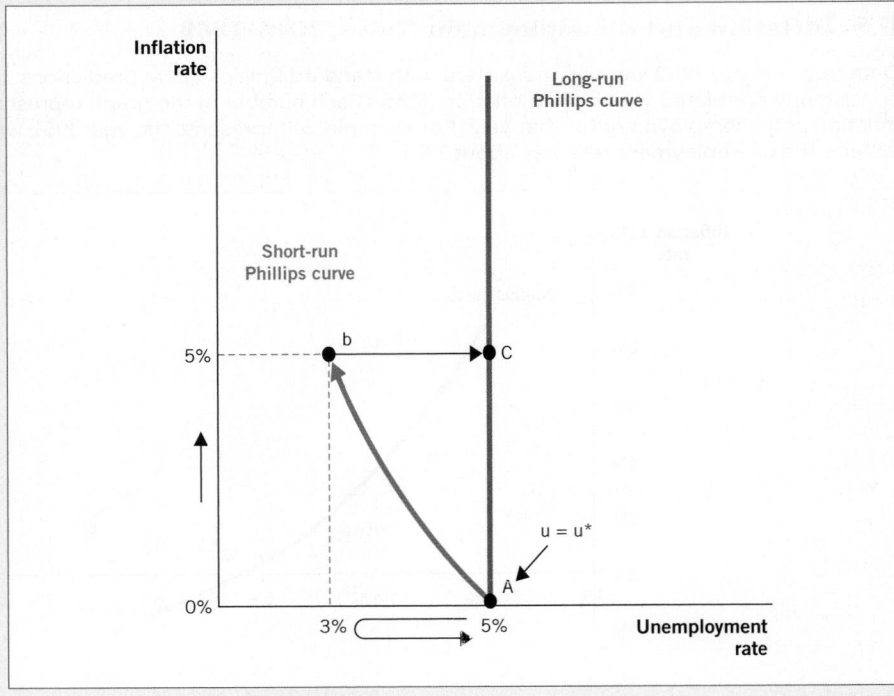

to 5% and the economy moves to a new equilibrium at point C. Inflation is the only result of monetary expansion in the long run.

In Figure 31.11, the unemployment rate is equal to the natural rate (5%) before inflation, and in the long run it returns to the natural rate. Thus, under normal economic conditions, including a scenario with no surprise inflation, we expect the unemployment rate to equal the natural rate ($u = u^*$). Monetary policy can push the unemployment rate down, but only in the short run.

We have also learned that the effects of inflation are dampened or eliminated when inflation is fully expected. We saw this earlier in the context of the aggregate demand–aggregate supply model. Now we look more closely at inflation expectations and how they affect the Phillips curve relationship.

Expectations and the Phillips Curve

We have seen that expected inflation has no real effects on the macroeconomy, even in the short run, because when inflation is expected, all prices adjust. To explore this further, we consider alternative theories of how people form expectations. This topic may seem like one for microeconomics or perhaps even psychology, but it is particularly relevant to monetary policy because the effects of expected inflation are completely different from the effects of unexpected inflation. When inflation is expected, long-term contracts can reflect inflation and mitigate its effects. But when inflation is unexpected, wages and other prices don't adjust immediately, and the result is economic expansion.

ADAPTIVE EXPECTATIONS THEORY In the late 1960s, economists Milton Friedman and Edmund Phelps hypothesized that people adapt their inflation expectations to their prior experience. For example, if the actual inflation rate is consistently 2% year after year, people won't expect 0% inflation; they'll expect 2% inflation. The contributions of Friedman and Phelps came to be known as adaptive expectations. **Adaptive expectations theory** holds that people's expectations of future inflation are based on their most recent experience. If the inflation rate is 5% in 2020, adaptive expectations theory predicts that people will also expect a 5% inflation rate in 2021.

Consider the hypothetical inflation pattern presented in Table 31.1. The second column shows actual inflation over the course of six years. The inflation rate starts at 0% but then goes up to 2% for two years, then increases to 4%

Adaptive expectations theory holds that people's expectations of future inflation are based on their most recent experience.

TABLE 31.1			
Adaptive Expectations			
Year	Actual inflation rate	Expected inflation rate	Error
2016	0%	—	0%
2017	2	0%	−2
2018	2	2	0
2019	4	2	−2
2020	4	4	0
2021	2	4	2

for two years, and then falls to 2% in the last year. If expectations are adaptive, actual inflation in the current period becomes expected inflation for the future. When actual inflation is expected inflation, there is no error, as indicated in the last column. For example, a 2% actual inflation rate in 2017 means people will expect 2% inflation in the future. So when the actual inflation rate is 2% in 2018, people are not surprised. Adaptive expectations theory predicts that people do not always underestimate inflation.

When the inflation rate *accelerates*, however, people do underestimate inflation. For example, if people experience a 2% inflation rate in 2018, they will expect this level for 2019. But in our example, the rate increases to 4% in 2019, which leads to an error of −2%. Note that it is also possible under adaptive expectations theory to overestimate inflation. Overestimation happens when inflation rates fall. For example, in 2021, people might anticipate a 4% inflation rate because they experienced that level in 2020. If the rate is actually 2%, they overestimate inflation by 2%.

The idea behind adaptive expectations theory is not overly complex, but it revolutionized the way economists think about monetary policy. If expectations adapt, then monetary policy may not have real effects, even in the short run. Expansionary monetary policy can stimulate the economy and reduce unemployment—but only if it is unexpected.

Incentives

This was the insight of Friedman and Phelps. Their basic reasoning was that people are not quite as simpleminded as the basic Phillips curve implies. Given that surprise inflation harms people, they have an incentive to anticipate inflation and, at the very least, learn from past experience. And yet, the data from the 1960s, shown in Figure 31.10, were certainly consistent with the traditional Phillips curve interpretation. But Friedman and Phelps challenged the accepted wisdom in 1968 and predicted that the Phillips curve relationship would not last. In particular, they predicted that high inflation would not always deliver low unemployment—a prediction that proved correct.

Figure 31.12 shows U.S. unemployment and inflation rates for the period 1948 to 1979, with data for the 1970s presented in orange. (As in Figure 31.10, the numerical value represents the year.) Clearly, the 1970s were a difficult decade for the macroeconomy. The prior Phillips curve relationship fell apart—compare Figure 31.12 with Figure 31.10. In the 1970s, inflation was high, and so was unemployment. These macroeconomic conditions are now known as **stagflation**, which is the combination of high unemployment rates and high inflation. The stagflation of the 1970s baffled many economists who believed in the validity of the Phillips curve.

Stagflation
is the combination of high unemployment and high inflation.

RATIONAL EXPECTATIONS THEORY Expectations theory evolved yet again in the 1970s and 1980s, in part because of disenchantment with certain implications of adaptive expectations. For example, according to adaptive expectations theory, market participants consistently underestimate inflation when it is accelerating and overestimate inflation when it is decelerating. Expectations are seemingly always a step behind reality. And these errors are predictable.

Rational expectations theory holds that people form expectations on the basis of all available information. If people form expectations rationally, they use more than just today's current level of inflation to predict next year's. Rational expectations are different from adaptive expectations in that they are forward-looking, while adaptive expectations consider only past experience.

Rational expectations theory
holds that people form expectations on the basis of all available information.

FIGURE 31.12

U.S. Inflation and Unemployment Rates, 1948–1979

The 1970s (data points in orange) showed that it is possible to have both high inflation and high unemployment. This decade proved that policymakers could not rely on a permanent, exploitable downward-sloping Phillips curve.

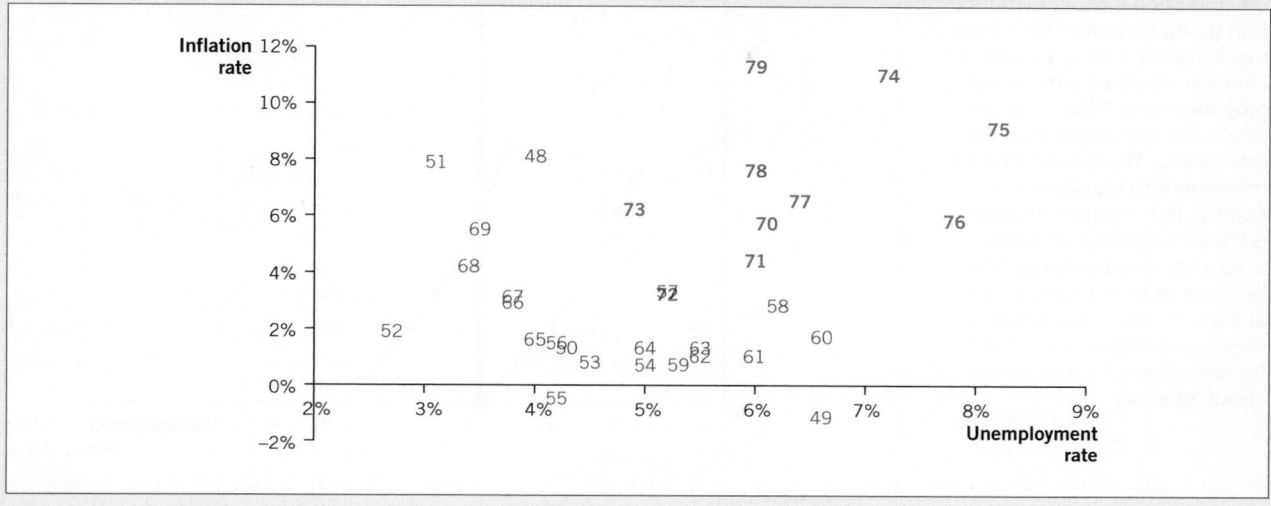

For example, imagine inflation is trending upward. Perhaps the actual inflation rate for three periods is 0%, then 2%, and then 4%. Expectations formed rationally recognize the trend and, looking to the future, predict 6%. This outcome is different from what would occur under adaptive expectations, which would instead imply an expectation of 4% in the fourth period, since that number is consistent with the most recent experience.

Rational expectations theory does not imply that people always predict inflation correctly. No one knows exactly what the level of inflation will be next year. Prediction errors are inevitable. But people are unlikely to underpredict consistently, even when inflation is accelerating. Rational expectations theory identifies prediction errors as random, like the flip of a coin—sometimes positive and sometimes negative.

A Modern View of the Phillips Curve

The short-run Phillips curve is built on the assumption that inflation expectations never adjust. But economists today recognize that the harmful effects of inflation provide an incentive to predict future inflation. Therefore, not all inflation is surprise inflation. And when inflation is not a surprise, it does not affect the unemployment rate. So we need to reconsider how different expectations affect the Phillips curve relationship.

Consider a hypothetical economy in which policymakers have never used inflation to try to stimulate the economy. Let's say that the inflation rate is 0%

. . . tick, tock, tick, tock, tick, _____ . . . What comes next?

Incentives

FIGURE 31.13

The Phillips Curve with Adjusting Expectations

Initially, at point A, inflation is 0% and people expect 0% inflation going forward. This expectation means that any positive inflation will reduce the unemployment rate. If the inflation rate is 5%, the unemployment rate falls to 3%, as indicated by movement to equilibrium at point b. But if actual inflation is 5% and expected inflation is also 5%, the unemployment rate moves to the natural rate at point C. There is a different short-run Phillips curve (SRPC) for each level of expectations about inflation.

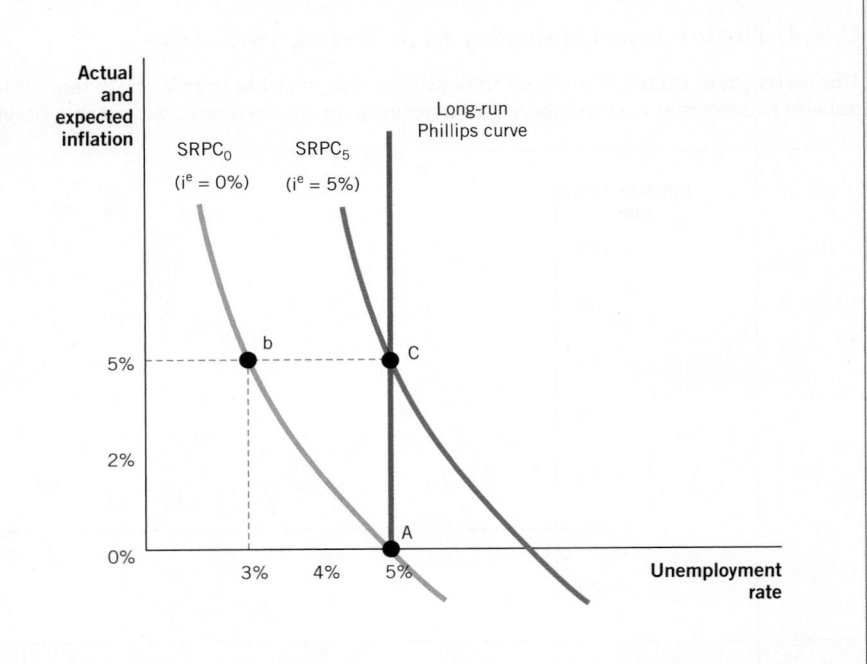

and market participants expect 0% inflation going forward. Figure 31.13 shows this initial situation as point A. Now, if the central bank undertakes policy to raise the inflation rate to 5%, the unemployment rate drops to 3% in the short run. This increase in inflation moves the economy up along the short-run Phillips curve that is labeled SRPC$_0$ (to indicate that expected inflation is 0%: $i^e = 0\%$). The 5% inflation moves the economy to short-run equilibrium at point b on SRPC$_0$.

Now consider what happens if people come to expect a 5% inflation rate. If workers and employers expect 5% inflation, they embed this rate into all long-term contracts. Therefore, when the 5% inflation arrives, it does not stimulate the economy or reduce unemployment. The economy moves to a new equilibrium at point C, which is on SRPC$_5$ (to indicate that expected inflation is now 5%: $i^e = 5\%$). When actual and expected inflation are both 5%, inflation does not reduce the unemployment rate. In summary, the downward-sloping Phillips curve relationship between inflation and unemployment holds only in the short run. In the long run, when expectations adjust, additional inflation does not reduce unemployment.

Figure 31.14 shows unemployment and inflation data from 1948 through 2018. From this complete data set, it seems clear that there is no long-run stable relationship between inflation and unemployment. In fact, the data appear to be randomly distributed. Economists today believe that there are many factors that influence the unemployment rate in the economy, and the inflation rate is just one factor.

FIGURE 31.14

U.S. Inflation and Unemployment Rates, 1948–2018

Data over the long run present a picture of inflation and unemployment rates that looks random. Clearly, the unemployment rate is not always correlated with the inflation rate in the long run.

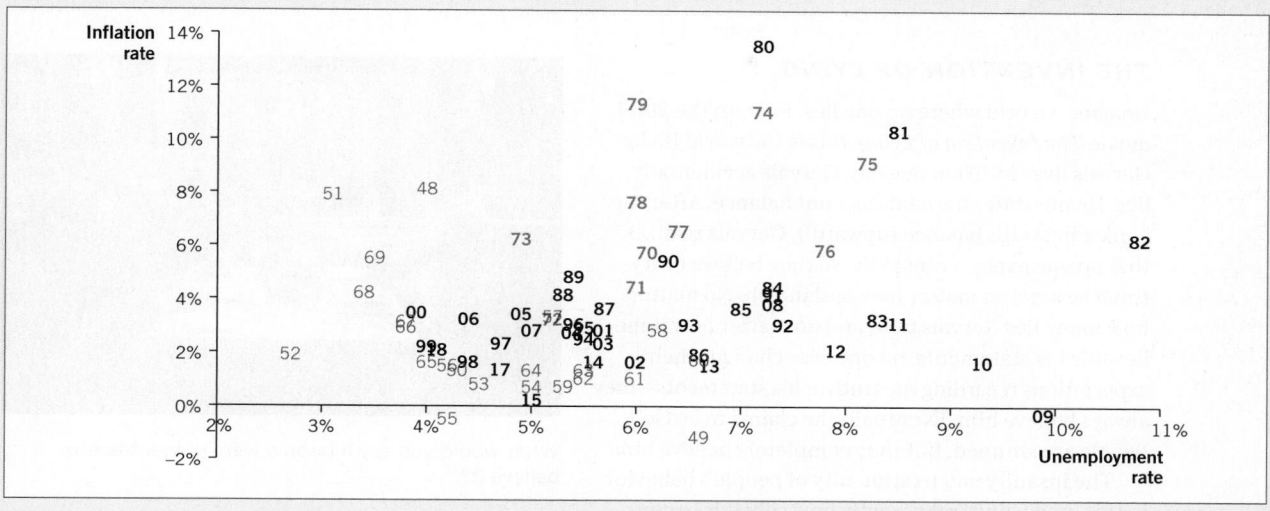

Implications for Monetary Policy

We can now use what we've learned about expectations theory and the Phillips curve to evaluate monetary policy recommendations. **Active monetary policy** involves the strategic use of monetary policy to counteract macroeconomic expansions and contractions. In the 1960s, before the development of expectations theory, monetary policy prescriptions were strictly activist: increase inflation during economic downturns, and reduce inflation when the economy is booming. This policy assumed that the Phillips curve relationship between inflation and unemployment would hold up in the long run.

Modern expectations theory prescribes greater caution. If people anticipate the strategies of the central bank, the power of the monetary policy erodes. If expectations adjust, the optimal monetary policy is to maintain transparency and stability. This conclusion holds if expectations are formed either adaptively or rationally. Let's consider each of these scenarios in turn.

Consider a scenario in which policymakers expand the money supply to decrease the unemployment rate. Say the unemployment rate is clearly above the natural rate, and real GDP is not growing. If expectations are adaptive, inflation reduces the unemployment rate in the short run. Eventually, expectations adjust, and then the central bank needs to increase inflation again just to stay ahead of the adjusting expectations. For monetary policy to succeed in keeping the unemployment rate low, inflation has to accelerate and stay a step ahead of expectations. Essentially, the result is more and more inflation. Worse yet, if the central bank tries to reduce inflation levels, expected inflation then exceeds actual inflation, leading to increased unemployment in the short run. Thus, if

Active monetary policy involves the strategic use of monetary policy to counteract macroeconomic expansions and contractions.

Expectations

THE INVENTION OF LYING

Imagine a world where no one lies. Ever. In the 2009 movie *The Invention of Lying*, this is the world Ricky Gervais lives in. Then one day, Gervais accidentally lies. He misstates his bank account balance. After the bank adjusts his balance (upward!), Gervais realizes that no one expects him to lie, so they believe everything he says, no matter how outlandish. No matter how many lies Gervais tells, and no matter how unbelievable his statements, no one ever changes their expectations regarding the truth of his statements—they always believe him. Eventually, he claims to be God. People are stunned. But they completely believe him.

   The insanity and irrationality of people's behavior in this movie illustrate exactly how silly it is to continually believe lies that come from the same source. The movie succeeds at being funny because no one in the real world would ever be as gullible or stupid as the people in this movie. In the real world, people would come to expect lies from Gervais. In economics lingo: expectations adjust.

What would you say if people were guaranteed to believe it?

   Similarly, in the real world, people come to anticipate inflation when they experience it period after period. It makes no sense to expect 0% inflation if actual inflation has not been 0% for quite some time. In the real world, expectations adjust.

expectations are adaptive, activist monetary policy provides only temporary short-run gains in employment. In the long run, it produces high inflation or unemployment—or both, as it did in the 1970s.

   If, instead, expectations are formed rationally, then activist monetary policy may yield no gains whatsoever. Because market participants use all available information when forming inflation expectations, the central bank is unlikely to achieve positive results from activist monetary policy, even in the short run.

   Many economists feel that monetary policy surprise actions should be minimized. **Passive monetary policy** occurs when central banks purposefully choose only to stabilize the money supply and price levels through monetary policy. In particular, passive policy does not seek to use inflation to affect real variables, including unemployment and real GDP. In the United States, the Federal Reserve has moved markedly in this direction since the early 1980s. Ben Bernanke, Janet Yellen, Jerome Powell, and other chairs of the Federal Reserve Board have consistently taken actions that lead to fewer surprises in monetary policy.

Passive monetary policy occurs when central banks purposefully choose only to stabilize money and price levels through monetary policy.

FEDERAL RESERVE PRESS CONFERENCES

On April 27, 2011, Ben Bernanke held the first press conference by a Fed chairman specifically to talk about the actions of the Fed's policymaking committee. This was an unprecedented leap toward transparency. In the past, the Fed always released carefully worded official statements that often used cryptic language to describe the Fed's outlook for the future.

In the spring of 2011, the economy was struggling to truly emerge from the 2008 recession; unemployment was still over 9%. Yet, in the midst of these economic troubles, the Fed still decided to lay all of its cards on the table. Many observers saw this move as risky. Jacob Goldstein, writing for NPR's *Planet Money* the day before the press conference, explained why it mattered:

> Because everything the head of the Federal Reserve says is a big deal. One off-hand comment can send global markets soaring or plunging. And because Fed chairmen, as a general rule, don't give press conferences. They release official statements that are very, very carefully worded. And they appear before Congress. Since the financial crisis, though, the Fed has come under increased scrutiny. The carefully worded statements and congressional appearances weren't carrying the day. So the leaders of the Fed have decided to send the chairman out for press conferences every few months ("to further enhance the clarity and timeliness of the Federal Reserve's monetary policy communication," in Fedspeak).

Bernanke's moves toward greater Fed openness reflected his belief that central bankers ought to be transparent. Both Janet Yellen and Jerome Powell, Bernanke's successors, have continued the press conferences. The move toward transparency reflects the modern view that expectations matter in macroeconomics—whether they are adaptive or rational.

Modern Fed chairs regularly hold press conferences, reflecting the view that transparency is good monetary policy.

Inflation and Unemployment: Is There a Phillips Curve?

If inflation is unexpected, it can reduce unemployment in the short run. But when inflation is expected, it does not reduce unemployment. In the long run, it is difficult to discern any relationship between inflation and unemployment rates. This suggests that the benefits of activist monetary policy may be severely constrained.

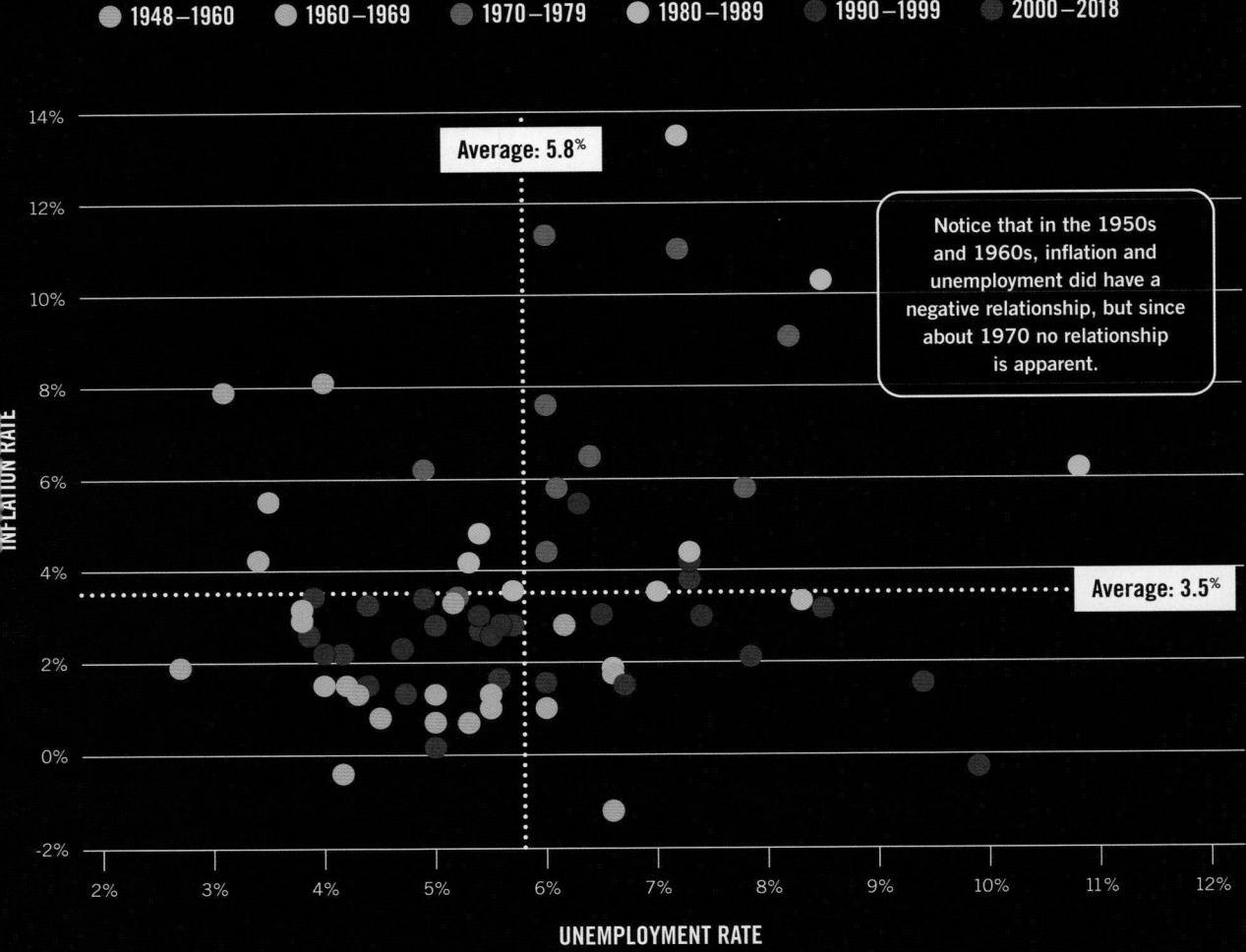

Legend: ● 1948–1960 ● 1960–1969 ● 1970–1979 ● 1980–1989 ● 1990–1999 ● 2000–2018

Average: 5.8%

Average: 3.5%

Notice that in the 1950s and 1960s, inflation and unemployment did have a negative relationship, but since about 1970 no relationship is apparent.

INFLATION RATE

UNEMPLOYMENT RATE

REVIEW QUESTIONS

- Knowing that in the long run inflation is the only result of expansionary monetary policy, why would the government act to increase inflation?

- Can you spot a traditional Phillips Curve in any of the subperiods? If so, which?

Monetary Policy: Expectations

Average unemployment rates in the European Union are about two percentage points higher than those in the United States. Let's consider what might ensue if the European Central Bank (ECB) attempts to use monetary policy to reduce unemployment in Europe. Suppose that in the European economy, all market participants expect a 2% inflation rate but then the European Central Bank (ECB) begins increasing the money supply enough to lead to a 4% inflation rate for a few years.

QUESTION: If expectations are for 2% inflation, what happens to the unemployment rate in the short run?

ANSWER: The unemployment rate falls, because the new inflation is a surprise and it can therefore stimulate the economy.

QUESTION: If expectations are formed adaptively, what happens to the unemployment rate in both the short run and the long run?

ANSWER: The unemployment rate falls in the short run, because the new inflation is different from past experience. In the long run, expectations adapt to the 4% inflation, and all else being equal, the unemployment rises back to its original level (assuming no other changes in the economies).

QUESTION: If expectations are formed rationally, what happens to the unemployment rate in the short run?

ANSWER: If expectations are formed rationally, people understand the incentives of the central bank and therefore may anticipate the expansionary monetary policy. In this case, the unemployment rate does not fall even in the short run.

QUESTION: If the ECB held regular press conferences to describe their thinking and their plans for the money supply, how would this affect the influence of inflation on the unemployment rate?

ANSWER: If the ECB were honest and transparent about their deliberations, it would be that much easier for people to form correct expectations about future inflation, which would tend to erase any remaining influence from inflation on unemployment.

The European Central Bank (ECB) undertakes monetary policy on behalf of the 19 nations that use the euro as their currency.

Conclusion

We began this chapter with the observation that central banks can't always control the macroeconomy. If they could, the U.S. economy certainly would not have experienced the sustained downturn that began at the end of 2007. So what can a central bank do? In the short run, if monetary policy is a surprise, a central bank can stimulate the economy and perhaps lessen the effects of a recession. But these results are mitigated when people come to anticipate monetary policy actions.

In the next two chapters, we turn to the international facets of macroeconomics. International trade, exchange rates, and international finance are becoming more important as the world economy becomes ever more integrated. ✳

How to Protect Yourself from Inflation

- Buying stocks or other assets that rise in value with inflation.
- Buying TIPS, which are Treasury securities that automatically adjust for inflation rates.

In this chapter, we talked about how inflation harms some people. We also talked about how inflation doesn't harm people if they know it is coming—if it is expected.

If you are worried about inflation harming you, you can protect yourself from its effects. In recent history, U.S. inflation has been low and steady. In this case, inflation doesn't really harm anyone because it is easy to predict. But if you live in a country such as Argentina, where inflation has often been a problem because it has been high and unpredictable, or if you are worried about future inflation in the United States, these tips are for you.

The two types of people most often harmed by inflation are workers with fixed wages and lenders with fixed interest rates. Let's look at how to avoid inflation trouble in both instances.

Let's say you are a worker who is worried about inflation. One way to protect yourself is to avoid committing to long-term wage deals. If you must sign a contract, keep it short in duration. Better yet, include a clause in your contract that stipulates cost-of-living adjustments (COLAs) that are tied to a price index like the CPI. This way, your wages are hedged against future inflation.

But perhaps you are more worried about inflation's effect on your savings or retirement funds. In this case, you are a lender and thus susceptible to fixed interest

Gold is not a great long-term investment unless you really fear inflation.

rates. One way to avoid negative returns is to purchase securities or assets that tend to rise in value along with inflation. Stock prices generally go up with inflation, so you may want to invest more of your retirement funds in stocks rather than bonds. Gold is another asset that tends to appreciate in inflationary times because its value is tied to something real.

However, stocks can be risky, and the long-term returns on gold are historically very low. Thus, you might consider buying Treasury Inflation Protected Securities (TIPS). These are low-risk U.S. Treasury bonds that are indexed to inflation rates, so if inflation goes up, you get a higher rate of return. These bonds guarantee a particular real rate of return, no matter what the rate of inflation.

· ANSWERING *the* BIG QUESTIONS ·

What is the effect of monetary policy in the short run?

- In the short run, monetary policy can both speed up and slow down the economy.

- Some prices are sticky in the short run. When some prices fail to adjust, changes in the money supply are essentially a change in real financial resources.

- In the short run, expansionary monetary policy can stimulate the economy, increasing real GDP and reducing the unemployment rate.

- In the short run, contractionary monetary policy can slow the economy, which may help to reduce inflation.

Why doesn't monetary policy always work?

- Monetary policy fails to produce real effects under three different circumstances. First, monetary policy has no real effect in the long run because all prices can adjust. Second, if monetary policy is fully anticipated, prices adjust. Finally, if the economy is experiencing shifts in aggregate supply, monetary policy may be unable to restore normal growth, because monetary policy works primarily through aggregate demand.

What is the Phillips curve?

- The Phillips curve is a theoretical negative relationship between inflation and unemployment rates. The modern consensus is that the Phillips curve is a short-run phenomenon that does not hold in the long run.

- The power of inflation to reduce unemployment is directly related to how people's inflation expectations adjust throughout the economy. Modern expectations theory allows for adjusting expectations, which is why most economists now believe that the Phillips curve relationship does not hold in the long run.

· CHAPTER PROBLEMS ·

Concepts You Should Know

active monetary policy (p. 1023)
adaptive expectations theory (p. 1019)
contractionary monetary policy
   (p. 1008)

expansionary monetary policy
   (p. 1003)
monetary neutrality (p. 1012)
passive monetary policy (p. 1024)

Phillips curve (p. 1016)
rational expectations theory
   (p. 1020)
stagflation (p. 1020)

Questions for Review

1. Why is it possible to change real economic factors in the short run simply by increasing the money supply?

2. Many people focus on the effect of monetary policy on interest rates in the economy.

   a. Use the loanable funds market to explain how unexpected contractionary monetary policy affects interest rates in the short run.

   b. Now explain how these changes affect aggregate demand and aggregate supply in both the short run and the long run. Also explain the changes in real GDP, the unemployment rate, and the price level.

3. During the economic slowdown that began at the end of 2007, the Federal Reserve used monetary

policy to reduce interest rates in the economy. Use what you have learned in this chapter to give a possible explanation as to why the monetary policy failed to restore the economy to long-run equilibrium.

4. Explain why a stable 5% inflation rate can be preferable to one that averages 4% but varies between 1% and 7% regularly.

5. Who is harmed when inflation is less than anticipated? In what ways are they harmed? Who is harmed when inflation is greater than anticipated? In what ways are they harmed?

6. Explain the difference between active and passive monetary policy.

Study Problems *(✳solved at the end of the section)*

1. Use the aggregate demand–aggregate supply model to illustrate the downward-sloping relationship between inflation and unemployment rates in the short-run Phillips curve.

2. Suppose the economy is in long-run equilibrium, with real GDP at $19 trillion and the unemployment rate at 5%. Now assume that the central bank unexpectedly *decreases* the money supply by 6%.

   a. Illustrate the short-run effects on the macroeconomy by using the aggregate demand–aggregate supply model. Be sure to indicate the direction of change in real

GDP, the price level, and the unemployment rate.

   b. Illustrate the long-run effects on the macroeconomy by using the aggregate demand–aggregate supply model. Again, be sure to indicate the direction of change in real GDP, the price level, and the unemployment rate.

   c. Now assume that this monetary contraction was completely expected. Illustrate both short-run and long-run effects on the macroeconomy by using the aggregate demand–aggregate supply model. Be sure to indicate the direction of change in real GDP, the price level, and the unemployment rate.

3. Suppose the economy is in long-run equilibrium, with real GDP at $19 trillion and the unemployment rate at 5%. Now assume that the central bank *increases* the money supply by 6%.

    a. Illustrate the short-run effects on the macroeconomy by using the aggregate demand–aggregate supply model. Be sure to indicate the direction of change in real GDP, the price level, and the unemployment rate.

    b. Illustrate the long-run effects on the macroeconomy by using the aggregate demand–aggregate supply model. Again, be sure to indicate the direction of change in real GDP, the price level, and the unemployment rate.

    c. Now assume that this monetary expansion was completely expected. Illustrate both short-run and long-run effects on the macroeconomy by using the aggregate demand–aggregate supply model. Be sure to indicate the direction of change in real GDP, the price level, and the unemployment rate.

✳ 4. In the past, some people believed that the Federal Reserve routinely expanded the money supply during presidential election years to stimulate the economy and help the incumbent president. For this question, assume that the Fed increases inflation by 3% in every election year.

    a. Describe the effect on the economy during election years if market participants expect 0% inflation.

    b. Describe the effect on the economy during election years if expectations are formed adaptively.

    c. Describe the effect on the economy during election years if expectations are formed rationally.

✳ 5. In each of the following scenarios, estimate the unemployment rate in comparison with the natural rate (u^*).

    a. Inflation is steady at 2% for two years but then increases to 5% for a year.

    b. Inflation is steady at 10% for two years but then decreases to 5% for a year.

    c. Inflation is steady at 8% for several years.

    d. Inflation is steady at 2% for three years, and then the Fed announces that inflation will be 3% one year later.

6. The following table presents actual inflation rates for a hypothetical nation for 10 years.

Column 1	Column 2
Year	Actual inflation rate (i)
Year 1	4%
Year 2	4
Year 3	4
Year 4	6
Year 5	6
Year 6	7
Year 7	6
Year 8	4
Year 9	2
Year 10	1

a. Replicate the table on a separate sheet of paper and leave space for five more columns. Label column 3 "Expected inflation if expectations are adaptive." Fill in this column beginning with year 2.

b. Label column 4 "Unemployment rate if expectations are adaptive." In this column, compare the resulting unemployment rate with the natural rate of unemployment (u^*) using the rule that $u < u^*$ when expected inflation is less than actual inflation, $u > u^*$ when expected inflation is more than actual inflation, and $u = u^*$ when expected inflation is equal to actual inflation.

c. Label column 5 "Random error." To fill in this column, you will need to flip a coin once for each year, beginning in year 2 (nine total coin flips). If the result of your first coin flip is heads, enter a "+1" for year 2, and if the result is tails,

enter "−1." Repeat this process for years 3 through 10.

d. Label column 6 "Expected inflation if expectations are rational." For this column, sum together columns 2 and 5. The result is consistent with rational expectations in a world where errors in expectations are common but random.

e. Finally, label column 7 "Unemployment rate if expectations are rational." In this column, compare the resulting unemployment rate with the natural rate of unemployment (u^*) using the rule that $u < u^*$ when expected inflation is less than actual inflation, $u > u^*$ when expected inflation is more than actual inflation, and $u = u^*$ when expected inflation is equal to actual inflation.

Solved Problems

4.a. If people expect 0% inflation, any positive inflation will stimulate the economy and lower the unemployment rate.

  b. If people form their inflation expectations adaptively, they will not anticipate inflation in an election year because it would be a break from their recent experience. Therefore, inflation in election years will consistently lower the rate of unemployment.

  c. If expectations are formed rationally, then people will consider the incentives of policy-makers during election years. Therefore, they will anticipate higher inflation in those years, and the inflation rate will have no effect on the unemployment rate.

5.a. The increase in inflation is likely a surprise, which means that it stimulates the economy and reduces the unemployment rate to a level below the natural rate.

  b. The decrease in inflation is likely a surprise, which means that it slows the economy and increases the unemployment rate to a level above the natural rate.

  c. Here there are no inflationary surprises, so the inflation rate does not influence the unemployment rate. Therefore, all else being equal, we should expect the unemployment rate to be near the natural rate.

  d. Even though the inflation rate increases, it is not a surprise, so all prices have time to adjust. Therefore, all else being equal, we should expect the unemployment rate to be near the natural rate.

PART

X

International
ECONOMICS

International Trade

Nations Gain through International Trade, Even If They Can Produce Their Goods and Services Domestically.

It's often assumed that nations should try to produce their own goods and services. In particular, it seems intuitive that if the United States *can* produce a particular good more efficiently than any other nation can, then the United States *should* produce that good. But way back in Chapter 2, we learned how individuals gain by specializing in the production of certain goods and obtaining other goods through trade, even when the individuals could produce those other goods more efficiently themselves. Here we will see how the same principles apply to trade between nations. This second look at trade will give us a chance to go deeper into the theory.

International trade is greatly facilitated by an invention that gets little fanfare: the stackable shipping container, conceived and developed in the mid-1950s by trucking magnate Malcolm McLean and engineer Keith Tantlinger. Prior to that time, ships had cargo holds. Wooden crates of cargo were loaded individually and meticulously fitted together like a jigsaw puzzle, to maximize the use of interior space. All of this took time, and more time on the unloading end. McLean and Tantlinger's inspired insight was that on- and off-loading time could be reduced dramatically by using metal containers of uniform shape and size, and using large

Without the invention of the container ship, getting imports from overseas would be a lot more expensive. Imports come into the United States from all over the globe. But does importing goods from other countries harm our economy?

cranes to stack the containers, securely locked together, on the decks of specially configured ships, instead of down in the holds.

Today every container is geo-tagged, so manufacturing plants know exactly when the components they need are offloaded. This arrangement makes just-in-time manufacturing possible. Overall, the "containerization" of shipping has reduced costs by approximately 35% compared to the use of cargo holds. With transoceanic transport dramatically more cost effective, the past few decades have seen the volume of trade among the world's nations rise dramatically.

To help illustrate the extent of international trade, we begin this chapter with a look at global trade data. We then consider how international trade affects an economy. Finally, we have to reckon with the fact that, despite the theoretical arguments for free trade and the practical advances that make it easy and cheap, not everyone is convinced that free trade is a good idea. So we conclude the chapter by examining trade barriers and the reasons for their existence.

· BIG QUESTIONS ·

- Is globalization for real?
- How does international trade help the economy?
- What are the effects of tariffs and quotas?

Is Globalization for Real?

Over the past 75 years, trade among nations all over the world is way up. What this means for you and me is that we can buy fresh Peruvian strawberries (in February!), roses from Kenya, cars from Mexico, and electronics from South Korea. But the United States also exports more now than in any earlier era. Imports and exports are both up for other countries, as well, and that means

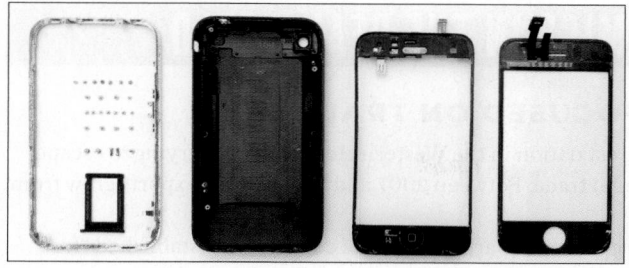
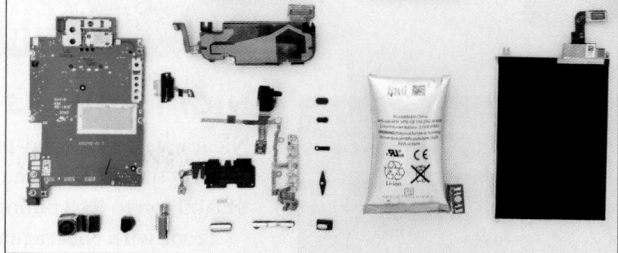

How many borders does an iPhone cross before it is sold?

economies around the globe are more and more interdependent. This interdependence is the essence of *globalization,* and it is changing not only what you purchase but also your future job prospects.

Consider a single popular item: the iPhone. Inside the iPhone are parts made in Germany, Japan, Korea, and the United States. The phone is famously "designed by Apple in California," but it is assembled in China. This single item requires thousands of miles of global shipping before anyone ever touches its screen.

The modern trade explosion has occurred for many reasons. Among these are lower shipping and communication costs, reduced trade barriers, and increased specialization in world economies. Total world exports of goods and services are now about one-fourth the size of world GDP. In this section, we look first at the growth in total world trade and then at trends in U.S. trade.

Trade creates value

Growth in World Trade

World trade has grown, but not just in market value. It has also grown as a percentage of total world output. That is, not only are nations trading more, but they are also trading a greater portion of their GDP. Figure 32.1 shows merchandise trade as a percentage of world GDP. This has expanded dramatically, doubling over 50 years, from 11% in 1970 to 22% in 2017.

FIGURE 32.1

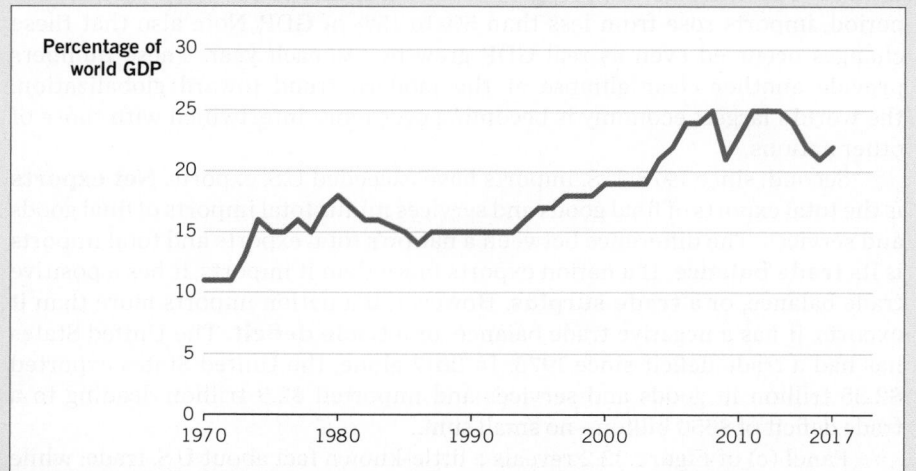

World Trade as a Percentage of World GDP, 1970–2017

Even as a percentage of world GDP, trade has grown significantly. It doubled from 11% in 1970 to 22% in 2017.

Sources: World Trade Organization; World Bank.

NICARAGUA IS FOCUSED ON TRADE

Nicaragua, the second-poorest nation in the Western Hemisphere, is trying to escape poverty through international trade. Between 2007 and 2017, its real exports grew from $1.8 billion to $5.3 billion.

Trade with Nicaragua is growing in part because the country has established "free zones," where companies can produce goods for export and avoid standard corporate tax rates. Typical Nicaraguan companies pay a myriad of sales taxes, value-added taxes, corporate profit taxes, and dividend taxes. But these do not apply to output that a company exports to other nations. U.S. companies that have taken advantage of production in these free zones include Levi's, Under Armour, and Nike.

All else equal, market-driven international trade certainly helps nations to prosper. Yet while the free zones are increasing exports, the effect on domestic consumers in Nicaragua may not be entirely positive. Because the goods have to be exported for the manufacturers to take advantage of the tax breaks, there is very little incentive to produce goods for domestic purchase and consumption.

The Levi-Strauss company produces many of its blue jeans in Nicaragua.

Trends in U.S. Trade

Trends in U.S. international trade are similar to overall global trends. The United States is the world's biggest economy. A huge amount of trade takes place between the individual states *inside* the country. For example, residents of Michigan buy oranges from Florida, and Floridians buy cars from Michigan. Still, even with the ability to produce and trade so much within U.S. borders, the nation's participation in international trade has risen dramatically in recent years. Figure 32.2 shows U.S. exports and imports as a percentage of GDP from 1970 to 2017.

As you look at the data in Figure 32.2, note three features. First, in panel (a), notice that both imports and exports increased significantly over the 50 years from 1970 to 2017. U.S. exports grew from 5% to 12% of GDP. During the same period, imports rose from less than 5% to 15% of GDP. Note also that these changes occurred even as real GDP grew by 3% each year. These numbers provide another clear glimpse at the modern trend toward globalization: the world's largest economy is becoming ever more intertwined with those of other nations.

Second, since 1975, U.S. imports have exceeded U.S. exports. **Net exports** is the total exports of final goods and services minus total imports of final goods and services. The difference between a nation's total exports and total imports is its **trade balance**. If a nation exports more than it imports, it has a positive trade balance, or a **trade surplus**. However, if a nation imports more than it exports, it has a negative trade balance, or a **trade deficit**. The United States has had a trade deficit since 1975. In 2017 alone, the United States exported $2.35 trillion in goods and services and imported $2.9 trillion, leading to a trade deficit of $550 billion—no small sum.

Panel (c) of Figure 32.2 reveals a little-known fact about U.S. trade: while the merchandise (goods) trade deficit is large and growing, the United States actually has a service trade surplus. Popular U.S. service exports include financial,

Net exports is the total exports of final goods and services minus total imports of final goods and services.

A nation's **trade balance** is the difference between its total exports and total imports.

A **trade surplus** occurs when exports exceed imports, indicating a positive trade balance.

A **trade deficit** occurs when imports exceed exports, indicating a negative trade balance.

FIGURE 32.2

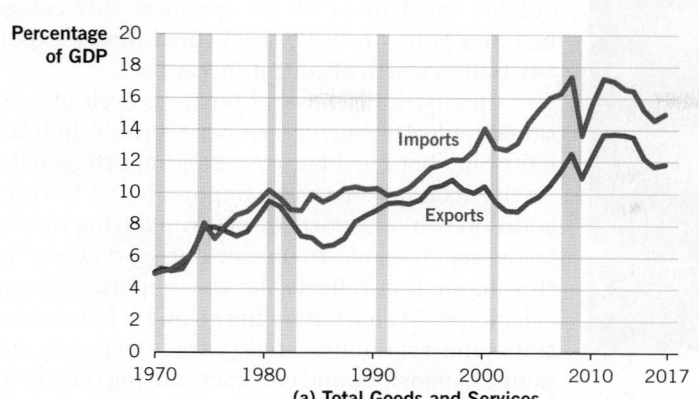

(a) Total Goods and Services

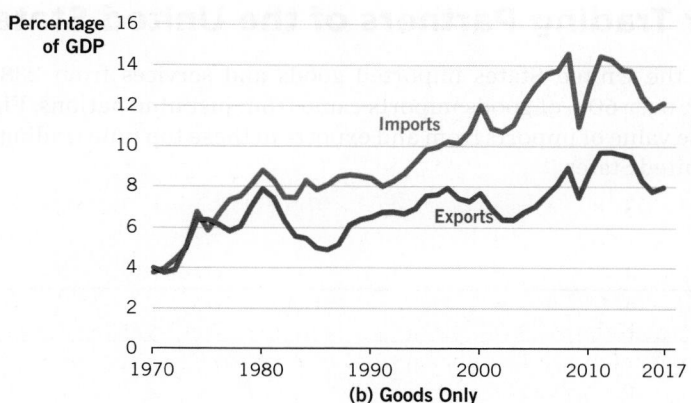

(b) Goods Only

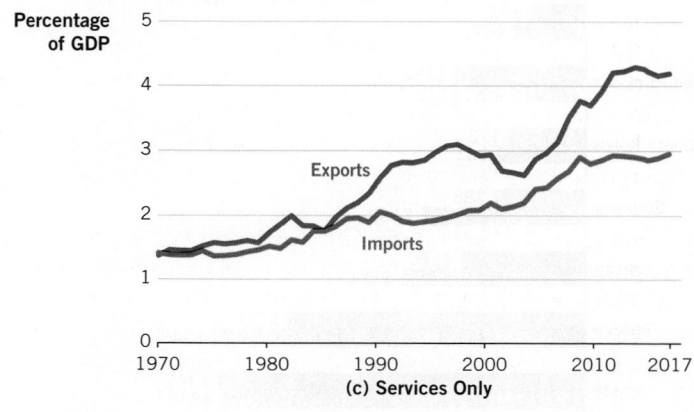

(c) Services Only

U.S. Exports and Imports, 1970–2017 (as a percentage of GDP)

(a) Both imports and exports are rising in the United States. In addition, the trade balance is becoming more negative over time, as imports are exceeding exports by an increasingly wider margin. This trade deficit grows during economic expansions and shrinks during recessions (shaded regions). (b) The trade deficit is driven by a merchandise (goods) deficit, and yet, (c) the United States enjoys a trade surplus in services.

Source: U.S. Bureau of Economic Analysis: *U.S. International Transactions*.

Foreign students who purchase their education in the United States are one type of U.S. service export.

travel, and education services. To put a face on service exports, think about students in your classes who are from outside the United States (perhaps this category even includes you). In 2017, the United States exported over $43 billion worth of education services.

Finally, notice how the business cycle affects international trade. During recessionary periods (indicated by the light blue bars in Figure 32.2a), imports generally drop. As the economy recovers, imports begin to rise again. In addition, while exports often drop during recessions, the trade deficit tends to shrink during downturns. Part of this fluctuation reflects the way imports and exports are calculated. In short, note the strong relationship between trade and economic activity: trade expands during economic expansions and contracts during recessions.

Major Trading Partners of the United States

In 2017, the United States imported goods and services from 238 nations. However, over 60% of goods imports came from just nine nations. Figure 32.3 shows the value of imports from and exports to these top nine trading partners of the United States.

FIGURE 32.3

Major Goods Trading Partners of the United States, 2017 (in billions of dollars)

Fully 64% of all U.S. goods imports come from the nine nations shown here. We export more to Canada and Mexico than to other nations, but we import more from China. The U.S. trade deficit with China is almost $350 billion.

Source: U.S. Bureau of Economic Analysis.

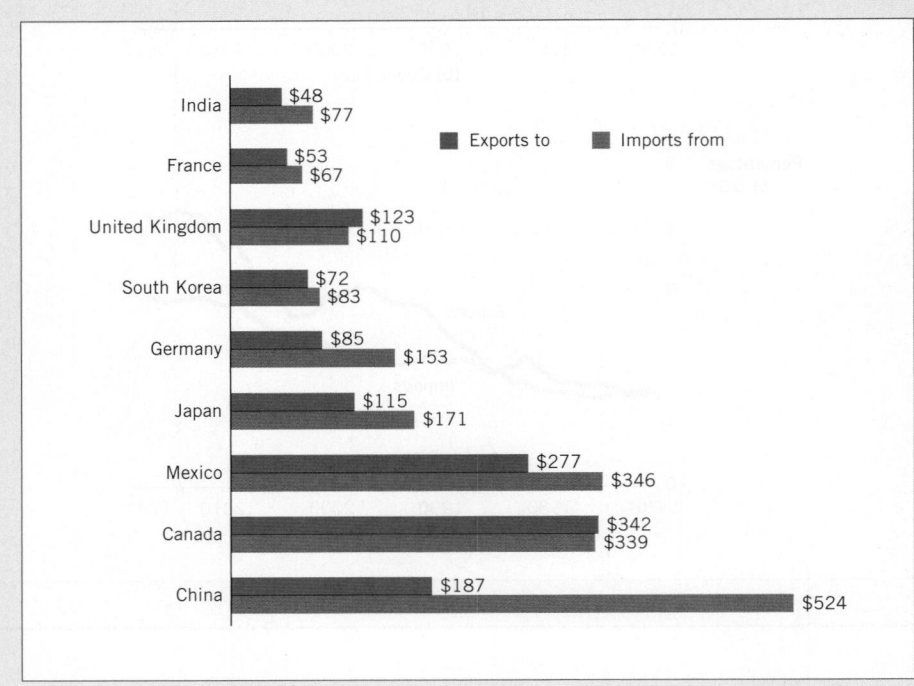

Trade in Goods and Services: Deficit or Surplus?

The United States imports many goods from Japan, including automobiles, electronics, and medical instruments. But we also export many services to Japan, such as financial and travel services. The table below reflects trade between the United States and Japan in 2014. (All figures are in billions of U.S. dollars.)

	Exports to Japan	Imports from Japan
Goods	$20	$103
Services	47	31

Sony PlayStations are a popular U.S. import from Japan.

QUESTION: Using the data shown above, how would you compute the U.S. goods trade balance with Japan? Is the balance a surplus or a deficit?

ANSWER: The U.S. goods trade balance equals

$$\text{goods exports} - \text{goods imports}$$
$$= \$20 \text{ billion} - \$103 \text{ billion} = -\$83 \text{ billion}$$

This is a trade deficit. Imports exceed exports, and the trade balance is negative.

QUESTION: Now how would you compute the U.S. services trade balance with Japan? Is the balance a surplus or a deficit?

ANSWER: The U.S. services trade balance equals

$$\text{service exports} - \text{service imports}$$
$$= \$47 \text{ billion} - \$31 \text{ billion} = \$16 \text{ billion}$$

This is a trade surplus. Exports exceed imports, and the trade balance is positive.

QUESTION: Finally, how would you compute the overall U.S. trade balance with Japan, which includes both goods and services? Is this overall trade balance a surplus or a deficit?

ANSWER: The overall U.S. trade balance equals

$$\text{Goods and service exports} - \text{goods and service imports}$$
$$= \$67 \text{ billion} - \$134 \text{ billion} = -\$67 \text{ billion}$$

This is a trade deficit. Imports exceed exports, and the trade balance is negative.

Data source: Office of the United States Trade Representative.

In this picture from a dollar store, is there anything that is *not* produced in China?

In the past, our closest neighbors—Canada and Mexico—were our chief trading partners. From Canada we get motor vehicles, oil, natural gas, and many other goods and services. From Mexico we get motor vehicles, coffee, computers, household appliances, and gold. More recently, falling transportation costs have led to increased trade with other countries, as well. For example, total imports from China alone are now roughly $524 billion, up from $350 billion (adjusted for inflation) a little more than a decade ago. Popular Chinese imports include electronics, toys, and clothing.

Canada and Mexico buy the most U.S. exports. To Canada we export cars, car parts, computers, and agricultural products. To Mexico we export cars, car parts, computers, and meat, among many other items. Financial and travel services are major U.S. exports to all our major trading partners.

How Does International Trade Help the Economy?

Trade creates value

In this section, we explain how comparative advantage and specialization make it possible to achieve gains from trade between nations. To keep the analysis simple, we assume that two trading partners—the United States and Mexico—produce only two items, clothes and food. This example will enable us to demonstrate that trade creates value in the absence of any restrictions.

Comparative Advantage

Comparative advantage refers to the situation where an individual, business, or country can produce at a lower opportunity cost than a competitor can.

In Chapter 2, we saw that trade creates value and that **comparative advantage** makes the creation of value possible. Gains arise when a nation specializes in production and exchanges its output with a trading partner. In other words, each nation should produce the good it is best at making and trade with other nations for the goods they are best at making. Trade leads to lower costs of production and maximizes the combined output of all nations involved. (Comparative advantage is very important to the discussion that follows. If you don't remember the details of comparative advantage, be sure to review Chapter 2 before proceeding.)

Suppose the United States and Mexico both produce clothing and food. Also assume that the production of one unit of food requires a greater quantity of capital per unit of labor than the production of one unit of clothing (in economics, we say that food is *capital intensive* and clothing is *labor intensive*). Because the United States is generally viewed as abundant in skilled labor but not so much in unskilled labor, while at the same time abundant in capital, it makes sense that it will specialize and produce food. Mexico, which is generally viewed as abundant in unskilled labor, will specialize in clothing.

In Figure 32.4, we see the production possibilities frontier (PPF) for each country when it does *not* specialize and trade. In panel (a), Mexico can produce at any point along its PPF. It can produce 900 million units, or articles, of clothing if it does not make any food, and it can produce 300 million tons of food if it

FIGURE 32.4

The Production Possibilities Frontier for Mexico and the United States without Specialization and Trade

(a) Mexico chooses to operate along its production possibilities curve at 450 million articles of clothing and 150 million tons of food. Each ton of food incurs an opportunity cost of three articles of clothing—a food–clothing ratio of 1:3. (b) The United States chooses to operate along its production possibilities curve at 300 million articles of clothing and 200 million tons of food. Each ton of food incurs an opportunity cost of one-half an article of clothing—a food–clothing ratio of 2:1.

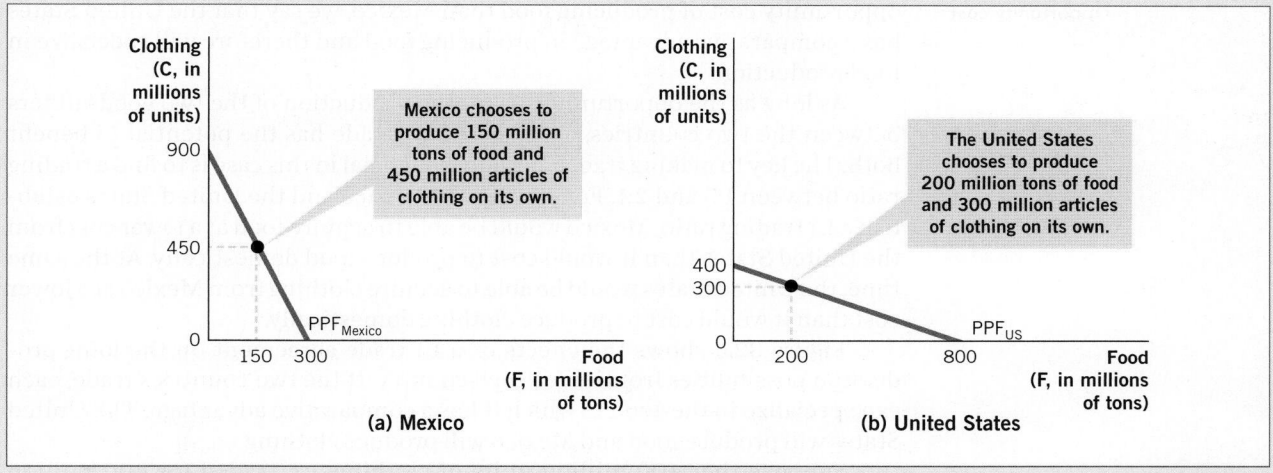

(a) Mexico

(b) United States

does not make any clothing. Neither extreme is especially desirable because it would mean that Mexico would have to do without either clothing or food. As a result, Mexico will prefer to operate somewhere in between the two extremes. We show Mexico operating along its production possibilities frontier at 450 million articles of clothing and 150 million tons of food. Panel (b) shows that the United States can produce 400 million articles of clothing if it does not make any food, and it can produce 800 million tons of food if it does not make any clothing. Like Mexico, the United States will prefer to operate somewhere in between—for example, at 300 million articles of clothing and 200 million tons of food.

To see whether gains from trade are able to make both countries better off, we must first examine the opportunity cost that each country faces when making these two goods. In Mexico, producing 150 million tons of food means giving up the production of 450 million articles of clothing (900 − 450 = 450). Thus, each ton of food incurs an opportunity cost of three articles of clothing, yielding a ratio of 150:450, or 1:3, or one ton of food per three articles of clothing. In the United States, producing 200 million tons of food means giving up production of 100 million articles of clothing (400 − 300 = 100). The ratio here is therefore 200:100, or 2:1. (Notice that both ratios are in the format food:clothing.) In the United States, then, a ton of food incurs an opportunity cost of one-half an article of clothing. Table 32.1 shows the initial production choices and the opportunity costs for both nations. Because the United States has a lower

Opportunity cost

TABLE 32.1

Output and Opportunity Costs for Mexico and the United States

	Chosen output level		Opportunity cost	
	Food (millions of tons)	Clothing (millions of units)	Food (F)	Clothing (C)
Mexico	150	450	3 C	⅓ F
United States	200	300	½ C	2 F

Opportunity cost

opportunity cost of producing food than Mexico, we say that the United States has a comparative advantage in producing food and therefore will specialize in food production.

As long as the opportunity cost of the production of the two goods differs between the two countries, as it does here, trade has the potential to benefit both. The key to making trade mutually beneficial in this case is to find a trading ratio between 1:3 and 2:1. For instance, if Mexico and the United States establish a 1:1 trading ratio, Mexico would be able to acquire food at a lower cost from the United States than it would cost to produce food domestically. At the same time, the United States would be able to acquire clothing from Mexico at a lower cost than it would cost to produce clothing domestically.

Figure 32.5 shows the effects of a 1:1 trade agreement on the joint production possibilities frontier for each country. If the two countries trade, each can specialize in the good in which it has a comparative advantage. The United States will produce food and Mexico will produce clothing.

Suppose that 400 million units of clothing are traded for 400 million tons of food. Let's begin with Mexico, as shown in panel (a). Mexico specializes in the production of clothing, producing 900 million units. It then exports 400 million units of clothing to the United States and imports 400 million tons of food from the United States in return—this is the 1:1 trade ratio we identified previously. Therefore, Mexico ends up at point M_2 with 500 million units of clothing and 400 million tons of food. Notice that Mexico's production without trade (at point M_1) was 450 million units of clothing and 150 tons of food. Therefore, specialization and trade have made Mexico better off by enabling it to consume 50 million more units of clothing and 250 more million tons of food.

Now let's look at the United States in panel (b). The United States specializes in the production of food, producing 800 million tons. It exports 400 million tons of food to Mexico and imports 400 million units of clothing from Mexico in return. Therefore, the United States ends up at point US_2 with 400 million units of clothing and 400 million tons of food. Notice that U.S. production without trade (at point US_1) was 300 million units of clothing and 200 tons of food. Therefore, specialization and trade have made the United States better off by allowing it to consume 100 million more units of clothing and 200 million more tons of food.

The combined benefits that Mexico and the United States enjoy are even more significant. As we saw in Figure 32.4, when Mexico did not specialize and trade, it chose to make 450 million units of clothing and 150 million tons of food. Without specialization and trade, the United States chose to produce 300 million units of clothing and 200 million tons of food. The combined output without specialization was 750 million units of clothing and 350 million tons

FIGURE 32.5

The Production Possibilities Frontier for Mexico and the United States with Specialization and Trade

(a) After Mexico specializes in clothing and trades with the United States, it is better off by 50 million units of clothing and 250 million tons of food (compare points M_1 and M_2). (b) After the United States specializes in food and trades with Mexico, it is better off by 100 million units of clothing and 200 million tons of food (compare points US_1 and US_2).

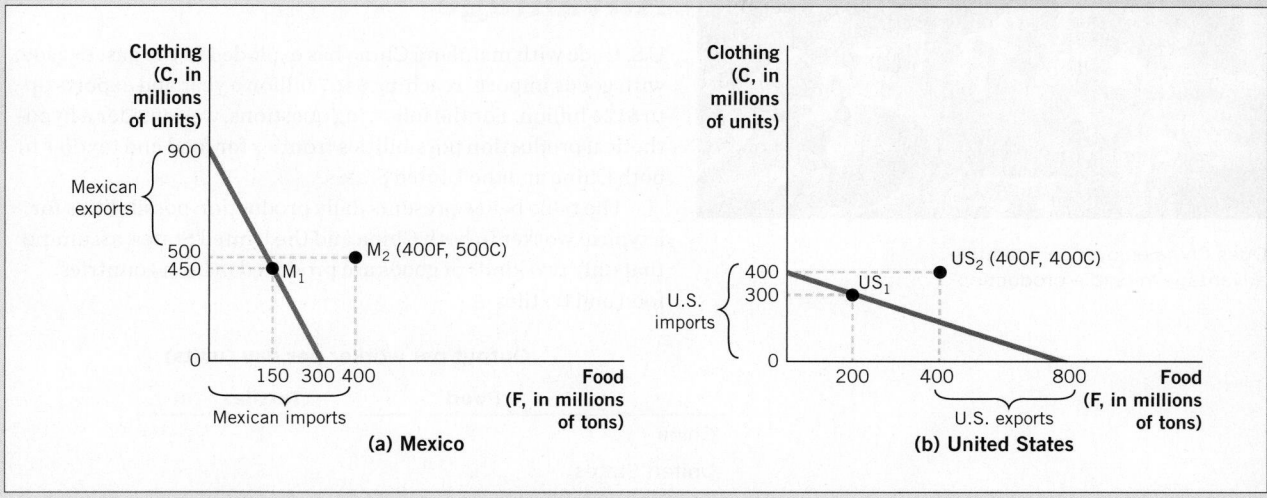

(a) Mexico

(b) United States

of food. However, as we see in Figure 32.5, the joint output with specialization is 900 million units of clothing and 800 million tons of food. In economics, we call this a *positive-sum game* because both players, in this case both countries, win by trading with each other.

Other Advantages of Trade

Although comparative advantage is the biggest reason that many nations trade with other nations, there are other good reasons for nations to engage in trade. In this section, we consider how international trade encourages both economies of scale and increased competition and how these factors can help an economy to grow.

ECONOMIES OF SCALE When a nation specializes its production, it can take advantage of the lower production costs that can accompany large-scale production processes. Economies of scale are especially important for smaller nations that do not have a population big enough to support the domestic production of large-scale items such as automobiles, television sets, steel, and aluminum. However, once a smaller nation has free access to larger markets, it can effectively specialize in what it does best and generate low per-unit costs through exports.

Does China enjoy a comparative advantage in textile production?

Opportunity Cost and Comparative Advantage: Determining Comparative Advantage

U.S. trade with mainland China has exploded in the past decade, with goods imports reaching $467 billion a year and exports up to $124 billion. For the following questions, we consider a hypothetical production possibilities frontier for food and textiles in both China and the United States.

The table below presents daily production possibilities for a typical worker in both China and the United States, assuming that only two kinds of goods are produced in both countries: food and textiles.

	Output per worker per day (units)	
	Food	Textiles
China	1	2
United States	9	3

QUESTION: What are the opportunity costs of food production for both China and the United States?

ANSWER: The opportunity cost of food production in China is the amount of textile production forgone for a single unit of food output. Because a Chinese worker can produce 2 textile units in a day or 1 unit of food, the opportunity cost of 1 unit of food is 2 textile units.

In the United States, a worker can produce 3 textile units in one day or 9 units of food. Thus, the opportunity cost of 1 unit of food is just $\frac{1}{3}$ textile unit.

QUESTION: What are the opportunity costs of textile production for both China and the United States?

ANSWER: The opportunity cost of textile production in China is the amount of food production forgone for a single textile produced. Because a Chinese worker can produce 1 unit of food in a day or 2 textile units, the opportunity cost of 1 textile unit is $\frac{1}{2}$ unit of food.

In the United States, a worker can produce 9 units of food in one day or 3 textile units. Thus, the opportunity cost of 1 textile unit is 3 units of food.

QUESTION: Which nation has a comparative advantage in food production? Which nation has a comparative advantage in textile production?

ANSWER: The United States has a lower opportunity cost of food production ($\frac{1}{3}$ versus 2 textile units), so it has a comparative advantage in food production. China has a lower opportunity cost of textile production ($\frac{1}{2}$ versus 3 units of food), so it has a comparative advantage in textile production.

In Figures 32.4 and 32.5, the production possibilities frontier is shown as a straight line, which makes the computation of the ratios fairly simple and holds the opportunity cost constant. However, in the real world, access to new markets allows countries to take advantage of economies of scale and therefore lower per-unit costs as production expands. Increased production gives companies the opportunity to economize on distribution costs and marketing and to utilize assembly lines and other forms of automation.

Consider how a small textile company based in Mexico fares under this arrangement. With international trade, the company can expand its sales into the United States—a much larger market. This move creates additional demand, which translates into added sales. A larger volume of sales enables the textile firm's production, marketing, and sales to become more efficient. The firm can purchase fabrics in bulk, expand its distribution network, and use volume advertising.

INCREASED COMPETITION Another largely unseen benefit from trade is increased competition. In fact, increased competition from foreign suppliers forces domestic firms to become more innovative and to compete in terms of both price and quality. Competition also gives consumers more options to choose from, which enables consumers to purchase a broader array of products that better match their needs. For example, many cars are produced in the United States, but foreign automobiles offer U.S. consumers greater variety and help to keep the prices of domestically made cars lower than they would be otherwise.

TRADE AGREEMENTS Gains from trade often spur nations to sign trade agreements, to reduce tariffs and clear the way for mutually beneficial exchange. One prominent example is the North American Free Trade Agreement (NAFTA), which was signed in 1992 by the United States, Canada and Mexico. NAFTA eliminated many of the barriers to trade that had been erected between the three nations.

When Donald Trump campaigned for president in 2016, he pledged to make trade more fair for the United States. After he became president, his administration renegotiated the terms of NAFTA and signed a new agreement in 2018. The new agreement, called the United States-Mexico-Canada Agreement (USMCA) altered the provisions of NAFTA slightly but also insured a continuation of trade among the three nations.

Even though trade agreements often stipulate protections for particular industries (most notably, agriculture), they still increase trade between nations. For example, as a result of NAFTA, real U.S. imports and exports of goods with Canada and Mexico have doubled. Between 1993 and 2017, inflation-adjusted exports to Canada rose from $120 billion to $282 billion. Over the same period, inflation-adjusted exports to Mexico grew from $50 billion to $240 billion. The reduction in trade barriers has enabled all three nations to move toward the production of goods and services in which they enjoy a comparative advantage.

The World Trade Organization (WTO) is an international organization that facilitates trade agreements between nations. Created in 1995 by the 123 countries that were then signatories of the General Agreement on Tariffs and Trade, the WTO regulates the trade of various goods and services, including textiles, investment, intellectual property, even agriculture. Moreover, the WTO works to resolve trade disputes. For example, in 2012 the WTO helped to end a 20-year disagreement between Latin American banana exporters and the European Union over a tax on imported bananas.

What Are the Effects of Tariffs and Quotas?

Despite the benefits of free trade, significant trade barriers, such as import taxes, often exist. For example, almost every shoe purchased in the United States is made overseas; but with few exceptions, the U.S. government taxes each pair of shoes that comes across its borders to be sold. For example, a new pair of Nike tennis shoes imported from Vietnam is subject to a 20% import tax. If these shoes are valued at $100, the foreign producer has to pay a $20 tax on them.

Import taxes like those on footwear are not unusual. In this section, we explore two of the most common types of trade barriers: *tariffs* and *quotas*. We then look more closely at common economic and political justifications for **protectionism**, which is a blanket term for governmental actions and policies that restrict or restrain international trade, often with the intent of protecting local businesses and jobs from foreign competition. We close by examining whether or not protectionism is effective.

Protectionism
is a blanket term for governmental actions and policies that restrict or restrain international trade, often with the intent of protecting local businesses and jobs from foreign competition.

Tariffs
are taxes levied on imported goods and services.

Tariffs

Tariffs are taxes levied on imported goods and services. A tariff is paid by the producer of the good when the good arrives in a foreign country. A tariff can be a percentage of the value of the good (called an *ad valorem tax*), a per-unit tax (called a *specific tax*), or a mix of the two. Figure 32.6 illustrates the impact of a per-unit tariff on foreign shoes. To assess how a tariff affects the market price of shoes in the United States, we observe the relationship between domestic demand and domestic supply.

We begin by noting that domestic supply ($S_{domestic only}$) and domestic demand ($D_{domestic}$) would be in equilibrium at $140 per pair of shoes. However, this is not the market price if free trade prevails. If trade is unrestricted, imports are free to enter the domestic market, so that supply increases to $S_{free trade}$. Now, because trade is unrestricted, domestic producers who might wish to charge a price higher than that charged by foreign producers would find that they could not sell their shoes at that price. As a result, the domestic price (P_D) decreases to the world price (P_W), which is $100. At $100, the total quantity demanded is Q_W. Part of this quantity is produced domestically (Q_{DI}), and part is imported from foreign sources ($Q_W - Q_{DI}$).

Now let's see what happens when a tariff of $20 per pair of shoes is levied. When the country imposes the tariff per pair of shoes, the cost that foreign producers must bear when they export shoes rises by $20 per pair, the amount of the tariff. Supply decreases to $S_{with tariff}$. The tariff pushes the domestic price up from $100 to $120 (represented as P_T, reflecting the price with tariff). Foreign producers must pay the tariff, but domestic producers do not have to pay it. One

FIGURE 32.6

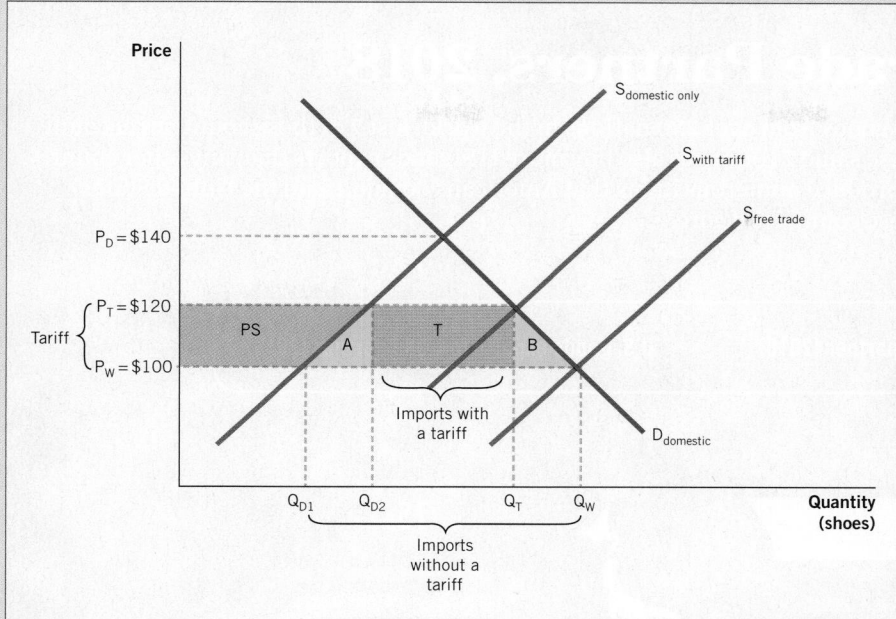

Without a tariff, the domestic market is dominated by imports. However, when a tariff is imposed, the price rises and domestic production expands from Q_{D1} to Q_{D2}. At the same time, imports fall to $Q_T - Q_{D2}$. Tariffs also create deadweight loss (shaded areas A and B), revenue for the government (area T), and increased producer surplus for domestic firms (area PS).

consequence of this situation is that the amount imported drops to $Q_T - Q_{D2}$. At the same time, the amount supplied by domestic producers rises along the domestic-only supply curve from Q_{D1} to Q_{D2}. Because domestic suppliers are now able to charge $120 and also sell more, they are better off.

We can see this outcome visually by noting that domestic suppliers gain producer surplus equal to the shaded area marked PS. The government also benefits from the tariff revenue, shown as shaded area T. The tariff is a pure transfer from foreign suppliers to the government. In this case, the tariff is $20 per pair of shoes, so total tax revenue is $20 times the number of imported pairs of shoes. In addition, there are two areas of deadweight loss, A and B. Consumers are harmed because the price is higher and some people are forced to switch from foreign brands to domestic shoes. In addition, inefficient domestic producers now get to enter the market. Areas A and B represent the efficiency loss associated with the tariff—or the unrealized gains from trade. The economy as a whole loses from the tariff because the loss in consumer surplus is greater than the gains obtained by producers and the government.

Consider for a moment just how damaging a tariff is. Foreign producers are the lowest-cost producer of shoes, but they are limited in how much they can sell. This situation makes little sense from an import/export standpoint. If foreign shoe manufacturers cannot sell as many shoes in the United States, they will acquire fewer dollars to use in purchasing U.S. exports. So not only does the tariff mean higher shoe prices for U.S. consumers, but it also means fewer sales for U.S. exporters.

Major U.S. Trade Partners, 2018

Though the United States imports goods from over 230 nations in the world, just 7 of those countries account for over 60% of these imports. These same 7 countries also buy more U.S. goods exports than any other country. Clearly, our major trade partners produce numerous items that Americans demand, and the United States produces numerous items that these countries desire.

— U.S. goods imports from trade partner (2018)   — U.S. goods exports to trade partner (2018)

JAPAN

TOP IMPORTS FROM
- Passenger cars
- Auto parts
- Industrial machines

TOP EXPORTS TO
- Civilian aircraft
- Pharmaceuticals
- Medical equipment

$75B

$143B

SOUTH KOREA

TOP IMPORTS FROM
- Passenger cars
- Auto parts
- Household goods

TOP EXPORTS TO
- Semiconductors
- Industrial machines
- Civilian aircraft

$56B

$74B

THE UNITED STATES

CHINA

TOP IMPORTS FROM
- Computers
- Household goods
- Apparel

TOP EXPORTS TO
- Soybeans
- Civilian aircraft
- Passenger cars

$120B

$540B

Source: U.S. Bureau of Economic Analysis

- What U.S. industry generates the most universal demand from our trading partners?

- Based on the list of U.S. imports, how would you finish this sentence? "Americans sure love their _____!"

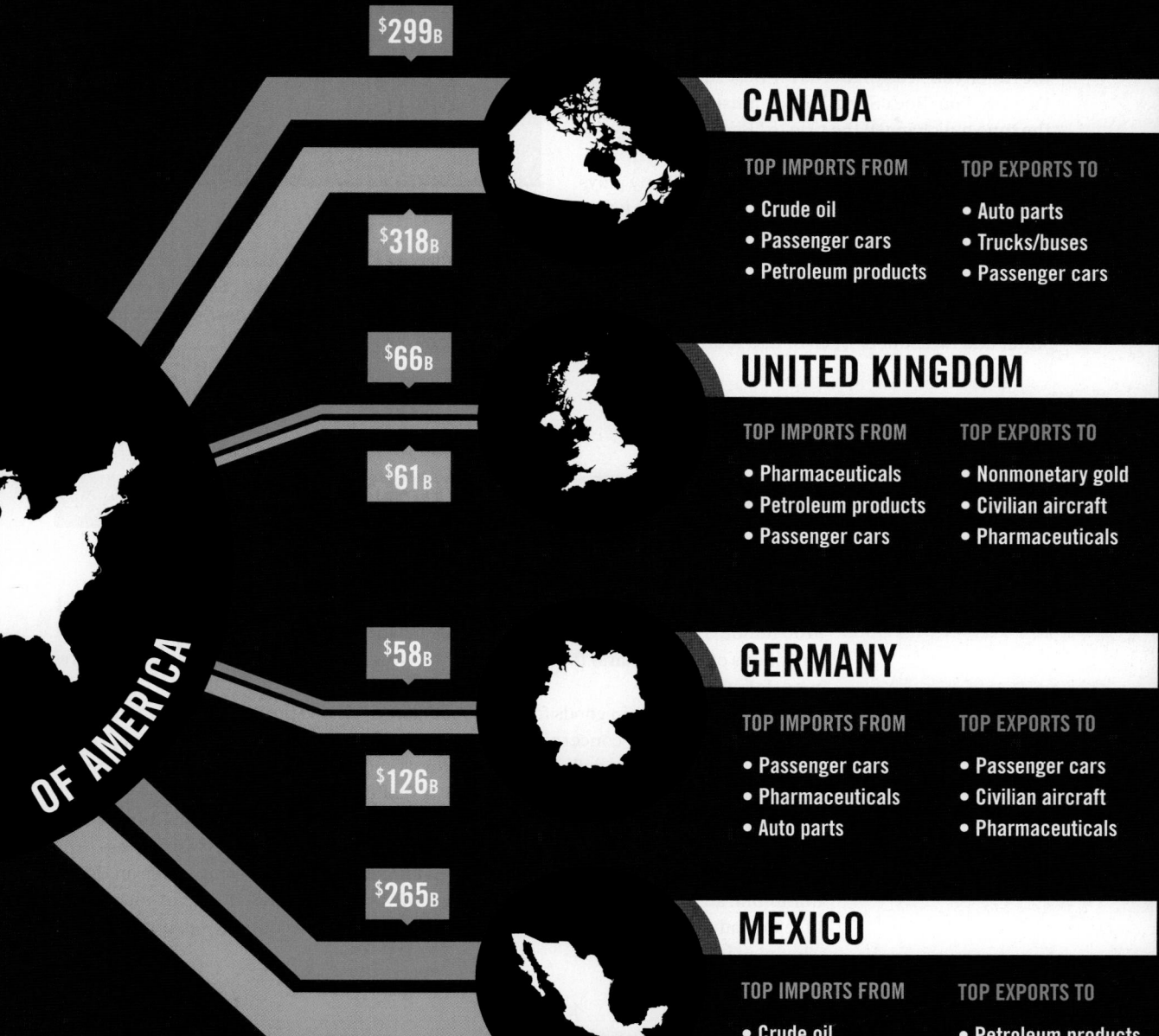

OF AMERICA

$299B

$318B

CANADA

TOP IMPORTS FROM
- Crude oil
- Passenger cars
- Petroleum products

TOP EXPORTS TO
- Auto parts
- Trucks/buses
- Passenger cars

$66B

$61B

UNITED KINGDOM

TOP IMPORTS FROM
- Pharmaceuticals
- Petroleum products
- Passenger cars

TOP EXPORTS TO
- Nonmonetary gold
- Civilian aircraft
- Pharmaceuticals

$58B

$126B

GERMANY

TOP IMPORTS FROM
- Passenger cars
- Pharmaceuticals
- Auto parts

TOP EXPORTS TO
- Passenger cars
- Civilian aircraft
- Pharmaceuticals

$265B

$347B

MEXICO

TOP IMPORTS FROM
- Crude oil
- Passenger cars
- Auto parts

TOP EXPORTS TO
- Petroleum products
- Auto parts
- Computer accessories

Tariffs: A Parody

REMY: "BANANA" (FREE-TRADE "HAVANA" PARODY)

"Havana," recorded by Camila Cabello (with guest vocals by Young Thug) is a very catchy tune that reflects Cabello's Latin roots. In 2018, the song won the American Music Awards for Best Video and Favorite Pop/Rock Song. Parody musician Remy kept the tune but changed the title to "Banana," with lyrics that explain how tariffs would bring back jobs from Havana to East Atlanta. Quite hilariously, Remy plays the president and also all his advisors at a trade policy planning meeting. Each of the advisors weighs in as the song progresses: "Take jobs back from Havana," "Why can't we grow bananas ourselves? They'd taste worse and cost more," and "You'd have to pump in water and heat, dude." If all of this sounds like a bad

THEY SHOULD BE GROWN IN EAST ATLANTA

idea, it is. Placing a tariff on bananas and trying to grow them in the southeast United States is evidence that "We've gone absolutely bananas." Check out the video on YouTube!

ECONOMICS IN THE REAL WORLD

U.S.–CHINA TRADE WAR

Since the 1980s, the U.S. trade deficit with China has increased from $4 billion to almost $400 billion. Figure 32.7 shows the U.S. trade balance with China adjusted for inflation (in billions of 2018 dollars) from 2000 to 2018. Nearly every year brings more and more imports from China.

While this increase in goods for U.S. consumers is viewed positively by economists, the trade deficit is very concerning to some in the United States. President Trump, for example, views the trade deficit as China taking funds from the United States. In March 2018, Trump said the U.S. "lost $500 billion" a year to China.*

To try to reduce this deficit, President Trump began imposing tariffs on Chinese imports in January of 2018. The first items affected were solar panels, washing machines, steel, and aluminum. China retaliated immediately by imposing tariffs on U.S. aluminum, airplanes, cars, pork, and soy beans. By August of 2018, the list of goods affected had grown into the hundreds. Many tariff levels were initially set at 10%, with scheduled increases to 25%.

*Source: Jim Tankersley, "Trump Hates the Trade Deficit. Most Economists Don't," *New York Times*, March 5, 2018, https://www.nytimes.com/2018/03/05/us/politics/trade-deficit-tariffs-economists-trump.html.

FIGURE 32.7

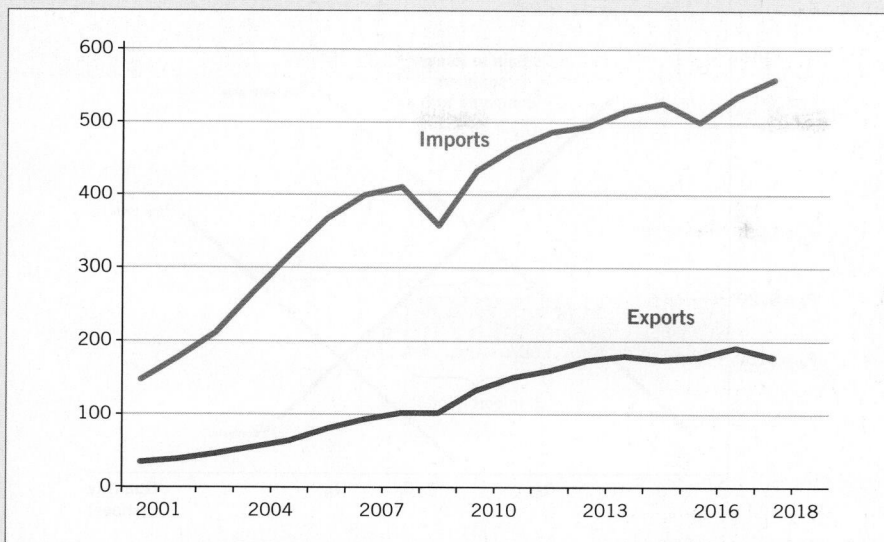

Nearly every year, the United States imports more goods and services from China. Exports typically grow too, but the gap between them (the trade deficit) widens almost every year.

Source: Bureau of Economic Analysis.

If the trade war continues to escalate, trade between the two nations will fall drastically over the next few years, and this is not good news for U.S. consumers. Economists are generally against tariffs, because they limit the value-creating benefits of trade. Put simply: consumers benefit from additional options.

Trade creates value

Quotas

Sometimes, instead of taxing imports, governments use *import quotas* to restrict trade. **Import quotas** are limits on the quantity of products that can be imported into a country. Quotas function like tariffs with one crucial exception: the government does not receive any tax revenue. In the United States today, there are quotas on many products, including milk, tuna, olives, peanuts, cotton, and sugar.

Import quotas are limits on the quantity of products that can be imported into a country.

One famous example of quotas comes from the automobile industry in the 1980s and 1990s. During that period, Japan agreed to a "voluntary" quota on the number of vehicles it would export to the United States. Why would any group of firms agree to supply less than it could? The answer involves politics and economics. By voluntarily limiting the quantity they supply, foreign producers avoid having a tariff applied to their goods. Also, because the quantity supplied is somewhat smaller than it would otherwise be, foreign suppliers can charge higher prices. The net result is that a "voluntary" quota makes financial sense if it helps a producing nation to avoid a tariff.

Figure 32.8 shows how a quota placed on foreign-made shoes would work. The figure looks quite similar to Figure 32.6, which is not an accident. If we set the quota amount on foreign shoes equal to the imports after the tariff illustrated in Figure 32.6, the result is exactly the same with one notable exception: the green tariff rectangle, T, in Figure 32.6 has been replaced with a green rectangle, F, which is called the tariff-equivalent quota.

FIGURE 32.8

The Impact of a Quota

Without a quota, the domestic market is dominated by imports. However, when a quota is imposed, the price rises and domestic production expands from Q_{D1} to Q_{D2}. At the same time, imports fall to $Q_Q - Q_{D2}$. Quotas create deadweight loss (shaded areas A and B), a gain for foreign suppliers (area F), and increased producer surplus for domestic firms (area PS).

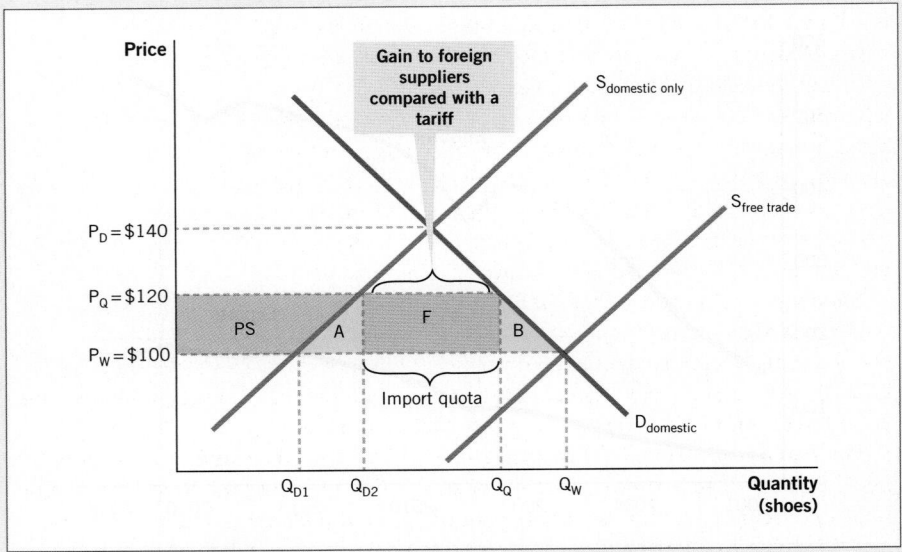

The quota is a strict limit on the number of shoes that may be imported into the United States. This limit pushes up the domestic price of shoes from $100 to $120 (represented as P_Q, reflecting the price under a quota). Because foreign producers must abide by the quota, one consequence is that the amount imported drops to $Q_Q - Q_{D2}$ (where Q_Q represents the total quantity supplied after the imposition of the quota). The smaller amount of imports causes the quantity supplied by domestic producers to rise along the domestic-only supply curve from Q_{D1} to Q_{D2}. Because domestic suppliers are now able to charge $20 more and also sell more, they are better off. We can see this result visually by noting that domestic suppliers gain producer surplus equal to shaded area PS (as we observed in Figure 32.6). As a result, domestic suppliers are indifferent between a tariff and a quota that has the same results. So, like before, there are two areas of deadweight loss, A and B, in which consumers lose because the price is higher and some people are forced to switch from foreign brands to domestic ones.

As you can see by the deadweight loss in shaded areas A and B, a quota results in the same efficiency loss as a tariff. Even though domestic suppliers are indifferent between a tariff and a quota system, foreign producers are not. Under a quota, they are able to keep the revenue generated in the green rectangle, F. Under a tariff, the equivalent rectangle, T, shown in Figure 32.6, is the tax revenue generated by the tariff.

ECONOMICS IN THE REAL WORLD

INEXPENSIVE SHOES FACE THE HIGHEST TARIFFS

Overall, U.S. tariffs average less than 2%, but inexpensive shoes face tariffs that are often at least 10 times more than that amount. What makes inexpensive imported shoes so "dangerous"? To help answer this question, a history lesson is in order.

Just 40 years ago, shoe manufacturers in the United States employed 250,000 workers. Today, the number of shoe workers is less than 3,000—and none of those workers assemble cheap shoes. Most of the shoe jobs have moved to low-labor-cost countries. But the shoe tariff, which was enacted to save domestic jobs, remains the same. Not a single sneaker costing less than $3 a pair is made in the United States, so the protection isn't saving any jobs. In contrast, goods such as cashmere sweaters, snakeskin purses, and silk shirts face low or no import tariffs. Other examples range from the 2.5% tariff on cars, tariffs of 4% and 5% for TV sets, and duty (tax)-free treatment for cell phones.

Shoppers who buy their shoes at Walmart and Zappos face the impact of shoe tariffs approaching 50% for the cheapest shoes, about 20% for a pair of name-brand running shoes, and about 9% for designer shoes from Gucci or Prada. This situation has the unintended consequence of passing along the tax burden to those who are least able to afford it.

One could reasonably argue that the shoe tariff is one of the United States' worst taxes. First, it failed to protect the U.S. shoe industry—the shoe jobs disappeared a long time ago. Second, consumers who are poor pay a disproportionate amount of the tax. And third, families with children pay even more because the more feet in a family, the more shoes are needed.

Why do cheap imported shoes face such a high tariff?

Incentives

Reasons Given for Trade Barriers

Considering all that we have discussed about the gains from trade and the inefficiencies associated with tariffs and quotas, you might be surprised to learn that trade restrictions are quite common. In this section, we consider some of the reasons for the persistence of trade barriers. These include national security, protection of infant industries, retaliation for *dumping*, and favors to special interests.

NATIONAL SECURITY Many people believe that certain industries, such as weapons, energy, and transportation, are vital to our nation's defense. They argue that without the ability to produce its own missiles, firearms, aircraft, and other strategically significant assets, a nation could find itself relying on its enemies. Thus, people often argue that certain industries should be protected in the interest of national security.

Although it is certainly important for any trade arrangement to consider national security, this argument has been used to justify trade restrictions on goods and services from friendly nations with whom we have active, open trade relations. For example, in 2002, the United States imposed tariffs on steel imports. Some policymakers argued that the steel tariffs were necessary because steel is an essential resource for national security. But, in fact, most imported steel comes from Canada and Brazil, which are traditional allies of the United States.

INFANT INDUSTRIES Another argument in support of steel tariffs in the United States was that the U.S. steel industry needed some time to implement new technologies that would enable it to compete with steel producers in other

Free Trade

STAR WARS EPISODE I: THE PHANTOM MENACE

The Phantom Menace (1999) is an allegory about peace, prosperity, taxation, and protectionism. As the movie opens, we see the Republic slowly falling apart. Planetary trade has been at the heart of the galactic economy. The central conflict in the movie is the Trade Federation's attempt to enforce its franchise by trying to intimidate a small planet, Naboo, which believes in free trade and peace.

The leader of the Naboo, Queen Amidala, refuses to pursue any path that might start a war. Her country is subjected to an excessive tariff and blockade, so she decides to appeal to the central government for help in ending the trade restrictions. However, she discovers that the Republic's Galactic Senate is ineffectual, so she returns home and prepares to defend her country.

Meanwhile, two Jedi who work for the Republic are sent to broker a deal between Naboo and the Trade Federation, but they get stranded on Tatooine, a desert planet located in the Outer Rim. In the Outer Rim, three necessary ingredients for widespread trade—the rule of law, sound money, and honesty—are missing. As a consequence, when the Jedi try to purchase some new parts for their ship, they find out that no one accepts the credit-based money of

Disruptive, barriers to trade are!

the Republic. The Jedi are forced to barter, a process that requires each trader to have exactly what the other wants. This situation results in a complicated negotiation between one of the Jedi and a local parts dealer. The scenes on Tatooine show why institutions, economies of scale, and competition matter so much for trade to succeed.

We encourage you to watch *The Phantom Menace* again with a fresh pair of eyes trained on the economics behind the special effects!

The **infant industry argument** states that domestic industries need trade protection until they are established and able to compete internationally.

nations. This **infant industry argument** states that domestic industries need trade protection until they are established and able to compete internationally. According to this point of view, once the fledgling industry gains traction and can support itself, the trade restrictions can be removed.

However, reality doesn't work this way. Firms that lobby for protection are often operating in an established industry. For example, the steel industry in the United States is over 100 years old. Establishing trade barriers is often politically popular, but finding ways to remove them is politically difficult. There was a time when helping to establish the steel, sugar, cotton, or peanut industries might have made sense based on the argument for helping new industries. But the tariffs that protect those industries have remained, in one form or another, for over 100 years.

Tariffs and Quotas: The Winners and Losers from Trade Barriers

We have seen that tariffs definitely affect trade balances. One clear example is the U.S. tariff on Chinese tires that was imposed in 2009. The result of this tariff was a drop in imports of these tires from 13 million tires to just 5.6 million tires in one quarter. In addition, within a year, average radial car tire prices rose by about $8 per tire in the United States: the average price of Chinese tires rose from $30.79 to $37.98, while the average price of tires from all other nations rose from $53.94 to $62.05.

Why would we penalize Chinese tire imports?

QUESTION: Who were the winners and losers domestically from this tire tariff?

ANSWER: The primary winners are domestic tire makers and the government since it collects the tariffs. The primary losers were U.S. tire consumers, who saw prices rise by about $8 per tire, or $32 for a set of four tires.

CHALLENGE QUESTION: Who would be the winners and losers overseas?

ANSWER: The primary winners were the producers of tires from everywhere except China. Because this tariff was targeted at a single nation, it did not affect tire producers in other nations. Non-Chinese tire producers realized an average of $8 more per tire. The losers were Chinese tire manufacturers.

Data Source: Gary Clyde Hufbauer and Sean Lowry, "U.S. Tire Tariffs: Saving Few Jobs at High Cost," Policy Brief (Washington, D.C.: Peterson Institute for International Economics, April 9, 2012).

RETALIATION FOR DUMPING In 2009, the U.S. government imposed tariffs on radial car tires imported from China. These tariffs began at 35% and then gradually decreased to 25% before being phased out after three years. The argument in support of this tariff was that Chinese tire makers were *dumping* their tires in U.S. markets. **Dumping** occurs when a foreign supplier sells a good below the price it charges in its home country. As the name implies, dumping is often a deliberate effort to gain a foothold in a foreign market. It can also be the result of subsidies within foreign countries.

Dumping
occurs when a foreign supplier sells a good below the price it charges in its home country.

In cases of dumping, the WTO allows for special *countervailing duties* to offset the subsidies. Thus, the United States placed a tariff on the imported tires to restore a level playing field. In essence, anytime a foreign entity decides to charge a lower price to penetrate a market, the country that is dumped on is likely to respond by imposing a tariff or quota to protect its domestic industries from foreign takeover. However, retaliation is also problematic. British economist Joan Robinson understood the risks well. She argued that the threat of trade barriers might conceivably work as a negotiation ploy, but when it came to actually enacting a retaliatory tariff, it "would be just as sensible to drop rocks into our harbours because other nations have rocky coasts."*

*Source: Joan Robinson, *Essays in the Theory of Employment* (New York: MacMillan, 1937).

The Impact of Tariffs on Domestic Prices

To help you out, we've identified a few of the products with the highest tariffs, to give you a sense of how much the prices of those imports are affected:

New Balance gets a "kick" out of tariffs on Nike.

- French chocolates—100% tariff
- European truffles—100%
- Sneakers—48%
- Chinese tires—35%

The U.S. International Trade Commission (Office of Tariff Affairs and Trade Agreements) is responsible for publishing the applicable tariff rates for all merchandise imported into the United States. If you are interested in digging deeper, the full schedule can be found here: https://hts.usitc.gov/current. But be warned, the entire tariff schedule runs to almost four thousand pages!

From that list, sneakers are the item that most of us own. U.S. tariffs on sneakers benefit New Balance, the last large shoemaker to keep its entire production process stateside. If you have ever wondered why popular brands of shoes such as Nike and Adidas have higher prices, this is part of the reason. Since Nike and most other retailers produce many of their final products outside the United States, they must pay the tariff that protects domestic suppliers such as New Balance, and they pass those costs through to the customer.

FAVORS TO SPECIAL INTERESTS The imposition of trade barriers is often referred to as "protection." This term raises the questions *Who is being protected?* and *What are they being protected from?* We have seen that trade barriers drive up domestic prices and lead to a lower quantity of goods or services in the market where the barriers are imposed. This situation does not protect consumers. In fact, tariffs and quotas protect domestic producers from international competition. Steel tariffs were put in place to help domestic steel producers, and tire tariffs were put in place to help domestic tire producers.

When we see trade barriers, the publicly stated reason is generally one of the three reasons we have already discussed: national security, infant industry protection, or retaliation for dumping. But we must also recognize that these barriers may be put in place as a favor to special interest groups that have much to gain at the expense of domestic consumers. For example, as a result of sugar import regulations, U.S. consumers pay twice as much for sugar as the rest of the world does. Thus, while sugar tariffs and quotas protect U.S. sugar producers from international competition, they cost U.S. consumers more than $3 billion in 2014 alone. This outcome represents a special interest gain at the expense of U.S. consumers. If it were a tax transferred from consumers to producers, it would likely not persist. However, this kind of favor doesn't appear in the federal budget.

Conclusion

We began this chapter by rejecting the misconception that nations should not trade for goods and services they can produce for themselves. An analysis of the concept of comparative advantage shows that nations can gain by (1) specializing in the production of goods and services for which they have the lowest opportunity cost and then (2) trading for the other goods and services they wish to consume.

International trade is expanding all over the world. The United States now imports and exports more than at any time in its history. Increased trade is generally positive for all nations involved. However, trade barriers still exist around the globe for various reasons, including national security, the protection of infant industries, retaliation for dumping and subsidies, and favors to special interests. ✳

· ANSWERING *the* BIG QUESTIONS ·

Is globalization for real?

- Since 1970, world exports have grown from 11% to about 25% of world GDP. In the United States, imports and exports have both grown rapidly over the past five decades. Between 1965 and 2014, U.S. exports grew from less than 5% of GDP to 13% of GDP. Over the same period, U.S. imports grew from 4% of GDP to over 16% of GDP. There's no doubt that the world economy is becoming more integrated.

How does international trade help the economy?

- Gains from trade occur when a nation specializes in production and exchanges its output with a trading partner. For this arrangement to work, each nation must produce goods for which it is a low-opportunity-cost producer and then trade them for goods for which it is a high-opportunity-cost producer.

- In addition, trade benefits nations' economies through economies of scale and increased international competition.

What are the effects of tariffs and quotas?

- Protectionism in the form of trade restrictions, such as tariffs and quotas, is common. A tariff is a tax on imports; a quota is a quantity restriction on imports.

- Proponents of trade restrictions often cite the need to protect defense-related industries and fledgling firms and to fend off dumping. But protectionist policies can also serve as political favors to special interest groups.

Concepts You Should Know

comparative advantage (p. 1044)
dumping (p. 1059)
import quotas (p. 1055)
infant industry argument (p. 1058)

net exports (p. 1040)
protectionism (p. 1050)
tariffs (p. 1050)

trade balance (p. 1040)
trade deficit (p. 1040)
trade surplus (p. 1040)

Questions for Review

1. What are three problems with trade restrictions? What are three reasons often given in support of trade restrictions?

2. What would happen to the standard of living in the United States if all foreign trade were eliminated?

3. How might a nation's endowment of natural resources, labor, and climate shape the nature of its comparative advantage?

4. Why might foreign producers voluntarily agree to a quota rather than face an imposed tariff?

5. Tariffs reduce the volume of imports. Do tariffs also reduce the volume of exports? Explain your response.

Study Problems *(*solved at the end of the section)*

1. Consider the following table for the neighboring nations of Quahog and Pawnee. Assume that the opportunity cost of producing each good is constant.

Product	Quahog	Pawnee
Meatballs (per hour)	4,000	2,000
Clams (per hour)	8,000	1,000

   a. What is the opportunity cost of producing meatballs in Quahog? What is the opportunity cost of harvesting clams in Quahog?
   b. What is the opportunity cost of producing meatballs in Pawnee? What is the opportunity cost of producing clams in Pawnee?
   c. Based on your answers in parts (a) and (b), which nation has a comparative advantage in producing meatballs? Which nation has a comparative advantage in producing clams?

2. Suppose that the comparative-cost ratios of two products—mangoes and sardines—are as follows in the hypothetical nations of Mangolia and Sardinia:

   Mangolia: 1 mango = 2 cans of sardines
   Sardinia: 1 mango = 4 cans of sardines

In what product should each nation specialize? Explain why the terms of trade of 1 mango = 3 cans of sardines would be acceptable to both nations.

3. What are the two trade restriction policies we discussed in this chapter? Who benefits and who loses from each of these policies? What is the new outcome for society?

*4. Germany and Japan both produce cars and beer. The table below shows production possibilities per worker in each country. For example, one worker in Germany produces 8 cars or 10 cases of beer per week. (For a review of absolute versus comparative advantage, see Chapter 2.)

	Labor force	Cars (C)	Beer (B)
Germany	200	8	10
Japan	100	20	14

   a. Which nation has an absolute advantage in car production? Which one has an absolute advantage in beer production? Explain your answers.
   b. Which nation has a comparative advantage in car production? Which one has a comparative advantage in beer production? Explain your answers.

* 5. Continuing with the example given in the previous problem, assume that Germany and Japan produce their own cars and beer and allocate half their labor force to the production of each.

  a. What quantities of cars and beer does Germany produce? What quantities does Japan produce?

  Now suppose that Germany and Japan produce only the good for which they enjoy a comparative advantage in production. They also agree to trade half of their output for half of what the other country produces.

  b. What quantities of cars and beer does Germany produce now? What quantities does Japan produce?

  c. What quantities of cars and beer does Germany consume now? What quantities does Japan consume?

  d. People often act as if international trade is a zero-sum game, meaning that when one party wins, the other party must lose an equal amount. State this book's foundational principle that contradicts this idea.

* 6. Determine whether each statement is true or false.

  Developing countries stand to gain from international trade because

  a. trade enables them to specialize in producing where they have a comparative advantage.

  b. trade gives them access to the greater variety of goods produced abroad.

  c. trade subjects their local producers to greater competition.

  d. trade allows them to produce larger amounts than they could consume themselves, allowing them to take advantage of increasing returns to scale.

7. Is it possible for a producer to have both an absolute advantage and a comparative advantage?

Solved Problems

4.a. Japan has an absolute advantage in both because $20 > 8$ and $14 > 10$.

  b. Japan has a comparative advantage in car production because its opportunity cost is less than Germany's ($0.7 < 1.25$). Germany has a comparative advantage in beer production because its opportunity cost is less than Japan's ($0.8 < 1.43$).

5.a. Germany: $(C, B) = (800, 1,000)$;
  Japan: $(C, B) = (1,000, 700)$

  b. Germany: $(C, B) = (0, 2,000)$;
  Japan: $(C, B) = (2,000, 0)$

  c. Germany: $(C, B) = (1,000, 1,000)$;
  Japan: $(C, B) = (1,000, 1,000)$

  d. Trade creates value for all involved because each party must benefit from the terms of trade or they would not agree to trade.

6. All four statements are true: (a) Trade is built on the concept of specialization and the application of comparative advantage in that process. (b) Trade allows countries to obtain a greater variety of goods and services from abroad than they could produce on their own. (c) Because trade effectively increases the number of potential competitors in the market, local producers are subject to more competition than would exist without trade. (d) When countries export goods, they benefit from being able to access a larger marketplace, which gives them the opportunity to produce at a larger scale than they would without trade.

International Finance

Trade Deficits Do Not Indicate Economic Problems.

Since 1975, the United States has had a trade deficit with the rest of the world—we import more than we export. Many people believe that trade deficits are bad for an economy. After all, it seems unfair that we buy goods from other nations but they do not buy nearly as many from us. The news media often perpetuate these beliefs by reporting trade deficit data in alarmist tones. The word "deficit" never sounds good. However, economists are not generally bothered by trade deficits. A trade deficit does not indicate economic problems. In fact, a trade deficit usually accompanies a strong and growing economy. A relatively wealthy economy can afford to buy goods and services from all over the world.

In this chapter, we explore the two most important topics in international finance: exchange rates and trade balances. We begin by explaining the determinants of exchange rates in both the short run and the long run, and then we come back to the topic of international trade balances.

Los Angeles, California, is one of the busiest ports in the world. In 2018, the equivalent of 4.9 million twenty-foot shipping containers arrived here, bringing imports from overseas (primarily Asia). The same year, 1.9 million container-equivalents of exports left the same port, which means that 3 million more containers came in than went out. We see the same imbalance at other U.S. ports: far more goods enter the United States than leave it. Is this a bad thing? To whom is it actually unfair?

- Why do exchange rates rise and fall?
- What is purchasing power parity?
- What causes trade deficits?

Why Do Exchange Rates Rise and Fall?

An **exchange rate** is the price of foreign currency, indicating how much a unit of foreign currency costs in terms of another currency.

Have you ever tried to buy a foreign currency? Perhaps you've seen exchange rates displayed on a sign at a bank or airport. If so, you've seen national flags and many potentially confusing numbers. An **exchange rate** is the price of foreign currency. This price tells how much a unit of foreign currency costs in terms of another currency. For example, the price of a single Mexican peso in terms of U.S. dollars is about $0.05, or 5 cents. This is the exchange rate between the peso and the dollar.

A key message from Chapter 32 is that the world economy is becoming ever more integrated: globalization is real and increasing. As more goods and services flow across borders, exchange rates become more important. Exchange rates affect the relative prices of goods and services. Any good that crosses a border requires a foreign currency exchange. For example, the price you pay in the United States for a Samsung television built in South Korea depends on the exchange rate between the U.S. dollar and the won (the currency of South Korea).

Zooming out to the macro view, exchange rates affect the prices of all imports and exports—and therefore GDP. The more integrated the world economy becomes, the more closely economists watch exchange rates because they affect both what nations produce and what they consume.

Are you planning a trip abroad? If so, you'd better figure out how to use signs like this to exchange currency.

CANADA	CAD	0.9512	0.8883
CHINA	CNY	7.3169	6.0910
EURO	EUR	0.6644	0.6100
JAPAN	JPY	109.00	102.00
SINGAPORE	SGD	1.3712	1.2630
HONG KONG	HKD	7.0043	6.4072
NEW ZEALAND	NZD	1.1646	1.0675
MALAYSIA	MYR	3.2536	2.7818

Our approach to exchange rates is straightforward: *exchange rates are prices*. For example, the exchange rate between the U.S. dollar and the won is the dollar price of one won, or the number of dollars required to buy a single won. It is just like the price of other goods we buy. Exchange rates are prices determined in world currency markets. Just as there are global markets where people buy and sell commodities such as sugar, wheat, and roses, there are also world markets, often called *foreign exchange markets*, where people buy and sell currencies.

Exchange rates are determined by the demand for and supply of currency in foreign exchange markets. Thus, if we want to explore the factors that make exchange rates rise and fall, we must consider the factors that affect the demand for and the supply of foreign currency. In this section, we look at some characteristics of foreign exchange markets and then consider the demand for and supply of foreign currency. We will finish up by considering why exchange rates rise and fall.

Characteristics of Foreign Exchange Markets

In a foreign exchange market, the good in question is a foreign currency. Very likely, you've held foreign currency at some point in your life—perhaps because a friend or relative saved some as a souvenir from a trip abroad or perhaps because you were fortunate to vacation or study in a foreign country. The primary reason why people purchase a foreign currency is to buy goods and services produced in the country that uses that currency. Don't lose sight of this simple truth; it is at the core of our entire conversation about exchange rate determination.

The demand for foreign currency is a derived demand. **Derived demand** is demand for a good or service that derives from the demand for another good or service. For example, if you travel to Belgium, you will probably want to buy some chocolate. But first you must buy euros, because the euro is the currency of Belgium. The euro is an unusual currency because it is used by 19 separate European nations, including Belgium, Germany, France, Spain, and Portugal. The demand for euros in world markets is derived from the demand for Belgian chocolate and many other goods, services, and financial assets produced in those 19 nations.

Nowadays it is easier to buy goods in foreign countries by using a credit or debit card; you don't have to physically buy foreign currency. This approach works because your bank or card company is willing to buy the foreign currency for you. To you, it feels like you are paying in U.S. dollars, since you use the same card all over the world and you see deductions from your bank account in dollars. But your bank literally takes dollars from your account and exchanges them for foreign currency so it can pay foreign companies in their own currency. Your bank charges a fee for this service that makes the transaction simpler for you.

> **Derived demand** is demand for a good or service that derives from the demand for another good or service.

EXCHANGE RATES ARE THE PRICE OF FOREIGN CURRENCY

In this section, we look more closely at exchange rates. First, we clarify how exchange rates are quoted; then we consider how appreciation and depreciation—two new terms—affect exchange rates.

Table 33.1 shows a few selected exchange rates from March 2019. Exchange rates can be viewed from either side of the exchange. For example, the exchange rate between the U.S. dollar and the Chinese yuan can be viewed as either of the following:

1. the number of yuan required to buy one U.S. dollar (¥ per $)
2. the number of U.S. dollars required to buy one yuan ($ per ¥)

While these two rates communicate the same information, they are not usually the same number. Instead, they are reciprocals of each other. For consistency, we exclusively use the second option—the number of U.S. dollars required to buy one unit of foreign currency. This number is represented in

TABLE 33.1

Exchange Rates between the U.S. Dollar and Other Currencies, March 2019

	Units of foreign currency you can buy with one U.S. dollar	Number of U.S. dollars required to buy one unit of foreign currency
British pound	0.758	1.320
Chinese yuan	6.667	0.150
Euro	0.877	1.140
Indian rupee	66.667	0.015
Japanese yen	111.111	0.009
Mexican peso	18.868	0.053
South Korean won	1123.596	0.001

Source: Google Public Data.

the last column in Table 33.1. We choose this option for consistency; it is the way we quote all other prices. For example, if you walk into Starbucks and look at the prices posted on the wall, they indicate the number of dollars it takes to buy a single coffee drink. Thus, when we quote exchange rates in this textbook, we always specify the number of dollars required to buy a single unit of foreign currency.

If a currency becomes more valuable in world markets, its price rises, and this increase is called an appreciation. **Currency appreciation** occurs when a currency increases in value relative to other currencies. In contrast, **currency depreciation** occurs when a currency decreases in value relative to other currencies. If the dollar depreciates, it is less valuable in world markets.

Figure 33.1 illustrates appreciation and depreciation with the exchange rate between the U.S. dollar and the Chinese yuan. The exchange rate starts at $0.15. If the exchange rate rises above $0.15, it takes more dollars

Currency appreciation
occurs when a currency becomes more valuable relative to other currencies.

Currency depreciation
occurs when a currency becomes less valuable relative to other currencies.

FIGURE 33.1

Exchange Rates and Currency Appreciation and Depreciation

An exchange rate is the price of a unit of foreign currency. When the exchange rate rises, foreign currency is more expensive, so this is an appreciation of the foreign currency but a depreciation of the domestic currency. When the exchange rate falls, foreign currency is less expensive, so this is a depreciation of the foreign currency but an appreciation of the domestic currency.

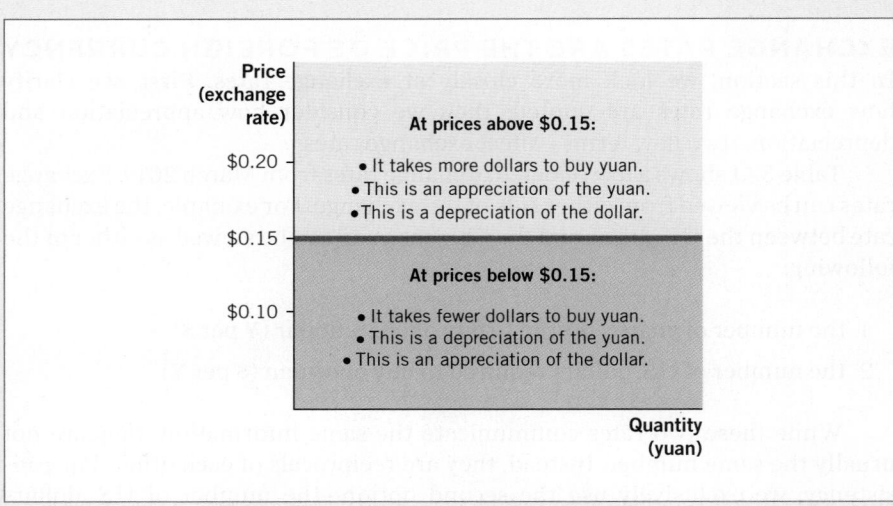

to buy yuan, which signals an appreciation of the yuan and a depreciation of the dollar. If, instead, the price falls below $0.15, it takes fewer dollars to buy yuan, which signals a depreciation of the yuan and an appreciation of the dollar.

SOME HISTORICAL PERSPECTIVE When exchange rates rise, foreign currencies become more expensive relative to the dollar. This means that imports become more expensive. But then U.S. exports become less expensive, so foreigners around the globe can afford to buy more U.S. goods and services. These are the reasons why exchange rates are important macroeconomic indicators to watch.

The recent past offers a mixed picture of the world value of the dollar. Figure 33.2 plots exchange rates for the currencies of two different trading partners of the United States: Europe (the euro) and China (the yuan). The vertical axis in each panel measures the dollar price of one unit of the relevant foreign currency. Panel (a) shows the exchange rate with the euro. The euro exchange rate fluctuated wildly over the 15 years pictured, rising from $1.20 to almost $1.60 during the recession year of 2008 but then falling to under $1.10 by 2015. Between 2013 and 2015, the value of the dollar grew significantly.

Panel (b) shows a similar story for the yuan over the 15-year period. As the price of yuan climbed, dollars were depreciating. But by 2016, the price of the yuan dropped to less than fifteen cuts, indicating a stronger U.S. dollar.

FIGURE 33.2

Two Foreign Exchange Rates, 2004–2018

These exchange rates are reported as the number of U.S. dollars required to purchase a unit of foreign currency. (a) In looking at the euro exchange rate from 2004 to 2018, we see that the price of the euro rose from $1.20 to almost $1.60 but then fell below $1.10 in 2015. (b) The fluctuations in the Chinese yuan exchange rate are much more muted because the Chinese government actively manages (pegs) this exchange rate. Notice the flat regions prior to 2011. These are not produced naturally in world markets.

Source: FRED Economic Data, Federal Reserve Bank of St. Louis.

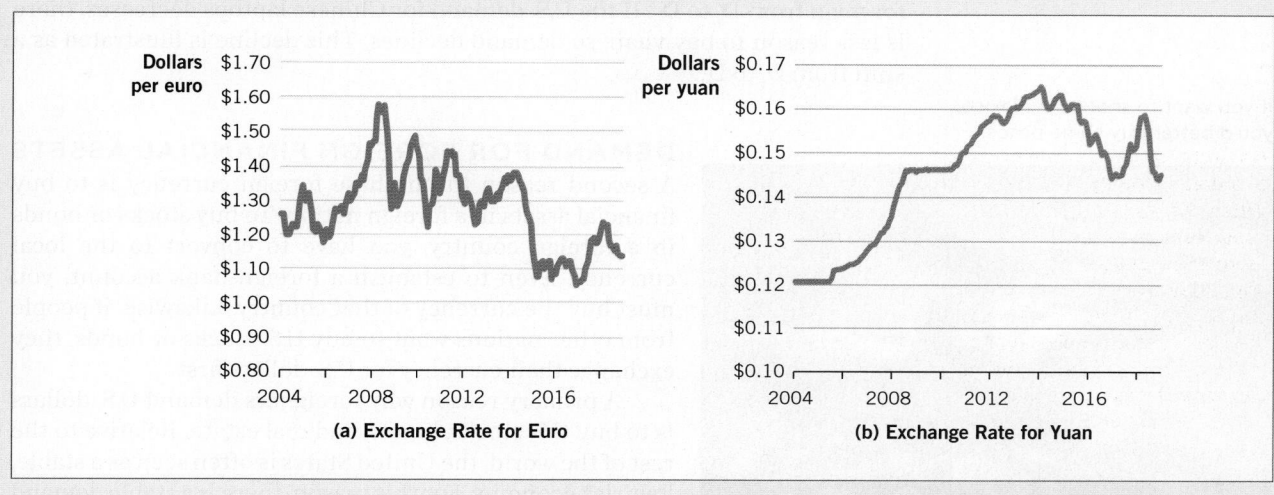

(a) Exchange Rate for Euro

(b) Exchange Rate for Yuan

The Demand for Foreign Currency

In this section, we discuss the factors that affect the demand side of the market for foreign currency. We distinguish three primary factors: the price of the currency (the exchange rate), the demand for foreign goods and services, and the demand for foreign financial assets.

PRICE OF FOREIGN CURRENCY (THE EXCHANGE RATE)

The law of demand holds in foreign currency markets. When the price of the yuan falls, goods and services produced in China (like Lenovo laptops) are less expensive relative to goods and services produced in the United States. Therefore, when the price of yuan falls, the quantity of Chinese goods demanded increases. Conversely, when the price of yuan rises, it becomes more expensive to purchase Chinese goods, and quantity demanded falls.

DEMAND FOR FOREIGN GOODS AND SERVICES

As we emphasized earlier, people generally purchase foreign currency to buy goods or services produced in foreign countries. Perhaps you are thinking, "I buy goods from other countries without purchasing foreign currency." This is true: you can buy imported TVs, cars, fruits, and clothing without ever touching a coin or bill of foreign currency. But those goods were originally purchased with the foreign currency of the nation where they were produced.

For example, a Lenovo laptop computer is produced in China, but you can buy it on the Internet or in a store in the United States. The workers and factory owners in China are paid in yuan. This means that the business firm that imports the Lenovo laptop from China buys yuan to pay for the product. In short, someone has to buy the foreign currency, even if it is not you. For this reason, the demand for a nation's currency derives from (depends on) the demand for its exports.

When the demand for a nation's exports rises, the demand for its currency rises, too. For example, if the U.S. demand for Chinese laptops increases, the demand for yuan increases at all prices. Figure 33.3 illustrates changes in demand for yuan. An increase in demand for Chinese laptops shifts the demand for yuan from D_1 to D_2. If the U.S. demand for Chinese laptops decreases, there is less reason to buy yuan, so demand declines. This decline is illustrated as a shift from D_1 to D_3.

If you want to snorkel in Mexico, you'd better buy some pesos.

DEMAND FOR FOREIGN FINANCIAL ASSETS

A second reason to purchase foreign currency is to buy financial assets in a foreign nation. To buy stocks or bonds in a foreign country, you have to convert to the local currency. Even to establish a foreign bank account, you must buy the currency of that country. Likewise, if people from other nations want to buy U.S. stocks or bonds, they exchange their currency for U.S. dollars first.

A primary reason why foreigners demand U.S. dollars is to buy U.S. stocks, bonds, and real estate. Relative to the rest of the world, the United States is often seen as a stable, low-risk economy. For this reason, there is a stable demand for U.S. dollars.

FIGURE 33.3

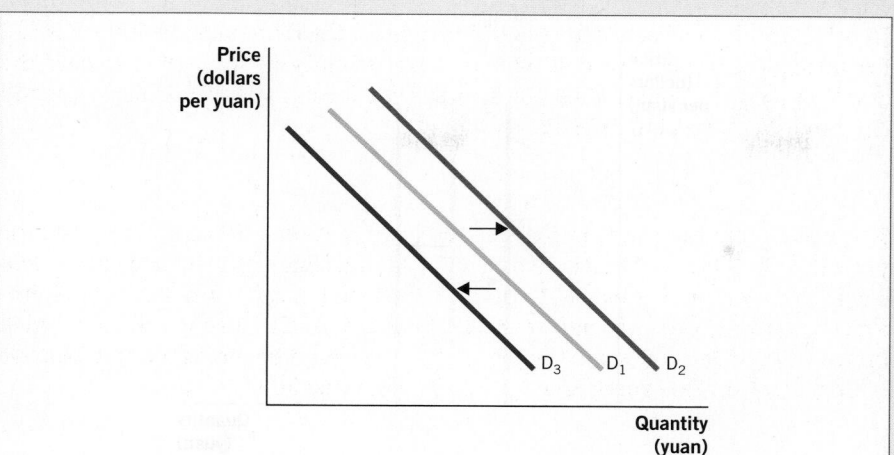

Shifts in the Demand for Foreign Currency

Increases in the demand for foreign currency (D_2) derive from an increased demand for foreign goods and services and/or foreign financial assets. Decreases in the demand for foreign currency (D_3) derive from a decreased demand for foreign goods and services and/or foreign financial assets. Here we illustrate these relationships with the U.S. dollar and the Chinese yuan.

Along these lines, one key factor in foreign exchange markets is interest rates across nations. If interest rates rise in one country (relative to rates in the rest of the world), the demand for its currency increases, since there is a greater demand for the assets with higher returns, all else equal. For example, if interest rates in China rise relative to those in the rest of the world, it means Chinese bonds provide a higher return than previously, and demand rises along with the interest rate. In Figure 33.3, this move is indicated as a shift from D_1 to D_2. When interest rates fall, there is reduced demand for the nation's currency. We see this outcome in Figure 33.3 as a shift from D_1 to D_3.

The Supply of Foreign Currency

In Chapter 30, we discussed fiat currency. This type of currency is printed and supplied by governments. From a market standpoint, it is fixed in quantity at any one time. Governments increase and decrease the supply of fiat currency very often, and when they do, the supply curve shifts, as Figure 33.4 shows. For example, consider the possible actions of the People's Bank of China (PBC), which is the central bank of China, the agency that determines monetary policy for the country. Initially, the supply of yuan is vertical at S_1. If the PBC increases the supply of yuan relative to the supply of dollars, the supply curve shifts outward to S_2. If, instead, the PBC reduces the supply of yuan relative to the supply of dollars, the supply curve shifts in the opposite direction, to S_3.

Applying Our Model of Exchange Rates

In this section, we consider applications of our model of exchange rates. In reality, exchange rates fluctuate daily, and these prices affect the prices of all imports and exports. These fluctuations are the result of shifts in demand, supply, or both. We start with changes in demand.

FIGURE 33.4

Shifts in the Supply of Foreign Currency

The supply of any nation's currency is determined by that nation's government. If the People's Bank of China increases the supply of yuan relative to the supply of dollars, the supply curve shifts from S_1 to S_2. If the supply of yuan decreases relative to the supply of dollars, the curve shifts in the opposite direction, to S_3.

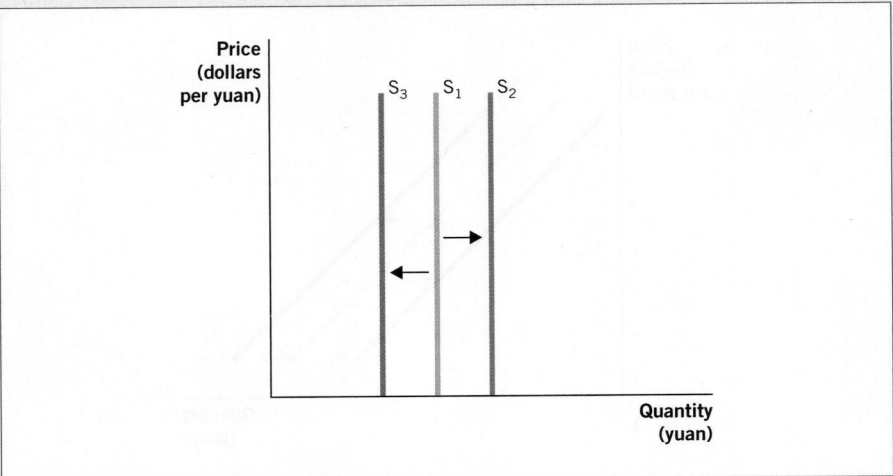

CHANGES IN DEMAND In most of the world, computer shoppers can choose from many varieties; these include Dell (largely produced in the U.S.) and Lenovo (produced in China). In microeconomics, you might study the impact on computer manufacturers from a shift in consumer preferences away from Dells and toward Lenovos. But these kinds of demand changes, which occur quite frequently, also affect the market for foreign currency. For example, if consumer preferences in the United States shift away from Dells and toward Lenovos, the demand for the yuan rises.

Figure 33.5 shows the results of a shift toward Lenovos. Initially, the market (for yuan) is in equilibrium with supply S and demand D_1. The initial equilibrium exchange rate is $0.15. Then, after U.S. consumers demand more Lenovos, the demand for yuan shifts out to D_2. This shift causes the exchange rate to rise to $0.20.

If the cause of the shift is an increase in the demand for Chinese financial assets (like Alibaba bonds), the result is the same. Thus, if interest rates in China rise, this signals investors around the globe to buy financial assets in China. The increase in the yuan demand leads to an increase in the exchange rate. The higher exchange rate implies a yuan appreciation and, by comparison, a dollar depreciation. People want more yuan, so its value rises in relation to the dollar.

If, instead, global demand for goods, services, and financial assets moves away from China and toward the United States, yuan demand falls (shifting to D_3) as people move toward dollars. In this case, the exchange rate falls and the yuan depreciates, while the dollar appreciates.

These shifts in demand occur naturally in a global economy where consumers across different nations choose among products produced in a wide variety of countries. Even just focusing on a single type of good, like cars, we can choose to buy from the United States, Germany,

How are exchange rates affected when consumers choose Lenovo over Dell computers?

FIGURE 33.5

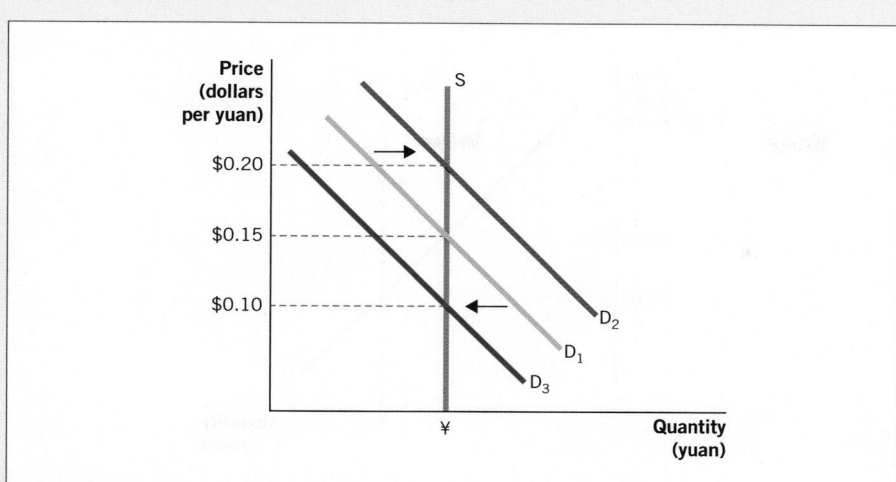

An increase in the demand for foreign currency leads to an increase in the exchange rate from $0.15 to $0.20. This signals a depreciation of the U.S. dollar relative to the yuan. A decrease in the demand for foreign currency leads to a decrease in the exchange rate from $0.15 to $0.10. This signals an appreciation of the U.S. dollar relative to the yuan.

Japan, South Korea, the United Kingdom, Canada, and Italy, to name just a few car-producing countries. But as international demanders' product preferences change, exchange rates are affected. Table 33.2 summarizes how shifts in demand affect foreign exchange rates.

However, there are also "unnatural" changes in exchange rates, caused by intentional actions of government monetary authorities all over the globe. To understand these, we look at shifts in currency supply.

CHANGES IN SUPPLY The supply side of currency markets is determined by government. Figure 33.6 illustrates a scenario in which the People's Bank of China (PBC) increases the supply of yuan. This move shifts supply from S_1 to S_2 and causes the exchange rate to fall from $0.15 to $0.10. The drop in the exchange rate means that the yuan depreciates relative to the dollar—a direct result of the increase in yuan supply. The PBC action means there are now more yuan per dollar, so yuan are worth less in relative terms.

The scenario pictured in Figure 33.6 is actually quite common. Government monetary authorities often intervene in markets to drive down their exchange rates. **Exchange rate manipulation** occurs when a national

Exchange rate manipulation occurs when a national government intentionally adjusts its money supply to affect the exchange rate of its currency.

TABLE 33.2		
Shifts in Demand for Foreign Currency		
Cause	**Demand for foreign currency**	**Exchange rate change**
Increase in demand for foreign goods and services or financial assets	Demand increases.	Exchange rate rises.
Decrease in demand for foreign goods and services or financial assets	Demand decreases.	Exchange rate falls.

FIGURE 33.6

How Supply Shifts Affect the Exchange Rate

All else being equal, an increase in the quantity of yuan shifts the supply of yuan to the right, to ¥₂. This shift causes the exchange rate to decrease from $0.15 to $0.10. Thus, the yuan depreciates and the dollar appreciates.

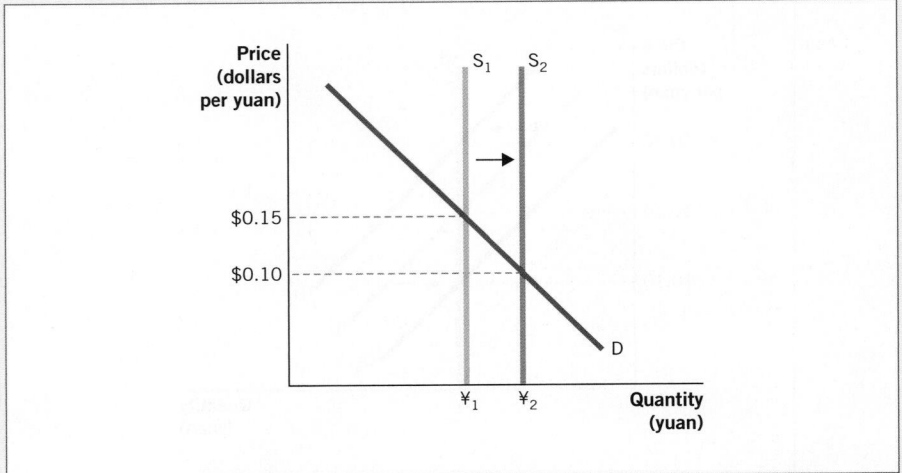

government intentionally adjusts its money supply to affect the exchange rate of its currency.

It may seem odd that a government would take action to purposefully depreciate the value of its own currency. After all, don't we typically want our assets to *appreciate*? If you learned that the value of your car depreciated drastically in the last year, you would not take it as good news. What if the value of your parents' home depreciates; is that good news? No, these are both bad news. However, nations depreciate their own currencies in order to make their exports more affordable to buyers worldwide. When the yuan falls in value, each dollar buys more yuan. And a devalued yuan makes Chinese products more affordable. All else equal, the demand for Chinese products then rises in the United States.

Currency devaluation, by increasing the quantity of currency, can certainly have a short-run impact on aggregate demand. But to see how the currency devaluation affects the Chinese economy, we need to consider it in the context of the aggregate demand–aggregate supply model. In Chapter 26, we included the value of domestic currency among the factors that shift aggregate demand. We noted that a decrease in the value of domestic currency (depreciation) causes an increase in aggregate demand.

Let's now consider this observation in the context of our present discussion. If the PBC acts to depreciate the yuan, aggregate demand for Chinese goods and services increases, as shown in Figure 33.7 as a shift from AD_1 to AD_2. In the short run, this shift leads to greater real GDP (Y_1) and lower unemployment in China. This happens because some prices are inflexible in the short run. But when all prices adjust (shifting SRAS from $SRAS_1$ to $SRAS_2$), output returns to its earlier level, leaving only inflation as the result of the increased quantity of yuan—the price level rises from 100 to 110. In the end, yuan are less expensive; but because of inflation, it takes more yuan to buy Chinese goods. In the long run, there are no real effects from the action: the LRAS curve remains at Y^*.

FIGURE 33.7

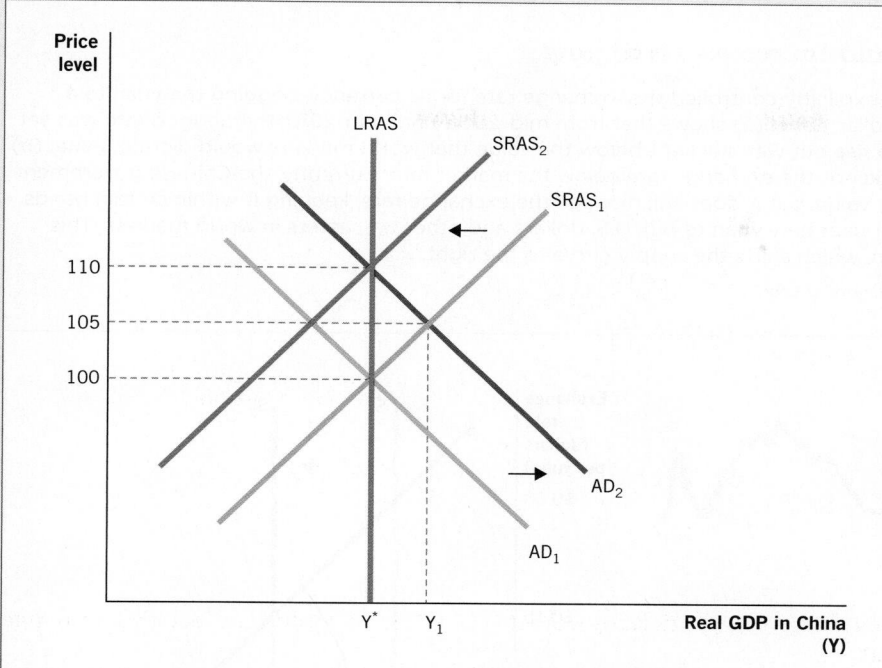

Increase in Aggregate Demand in China Arising from Yuan Depreciation

A depreciation of the yuan increases aggregate demand for Chinese goods and services. In the short run, real GDP increases and unemployment (not pictured here) decreases due to some sticky prices. In the long run, when prices adjust fully, there are no real effects, just inflation, because the price level rises from 100 to 110.

PEGGING EXCHANGE RATES Panel (a) of Figure 33.8 plots the U.S. dollar exchange rate with the Chinese yuan. Notice the flat period between 2008 and 2010, then the gradual, mostly evenly paced increases after that. This pattern is not due to natural market forces; it is because the Chinese government maintained a pegged exchange rate with the dollar. **Pegged (fixed) exchange rates** are exchange rates fixed at a certain level through the actions of a government. The alternative to pegged exchange rates is flexible exchange rates. **Flexible (floating) exchange rates** are exchange rates determined by the market forces of supply of and demand for currency. Previously in this chapter, our discussions have assumed flexible exchange rates.

Many exchange rates today, such as those we have already considered, are flexible. Previously, China explicitly pegged its currency, the yuan, to the U.S. dollar. The yuan was pegged at a value below that which would have prevailed if the exchange rate were flexible; the market-determined rate would have been above $0.160. For instance, the yuan was pegged at $0.147 from 2008 to 2010, as you can see in the flat part of the graph in Figure 33.8, panel (a). Nations cannot just pass laws to peg an exchange rate, because world markets are not subject to the laws of individual nations. Instead, the Chinese government maintained its peg by adjusting the supply of yuan made available to world markets. Currently, the Chinese government does not peg the exchange rate at a specific level, but it does still manage the level by keeping it within a range of values.

To decrease the price of the yuan, the Chinese government increased the supply of yuan relative to the supply of dollars. Panel (b) in Figure 33.8

Pegged (fixed) exchange rates are exchange rates fixed at a certain level through the actions of a government.

Flexible (floating) exchange rates are exchange rates determined by the supply of and demand for currency.

FIGURE 33.8

How China Pegs the Yuan and Increases Its Supply

In the past, the Chinese government explicitly controlled the exchange rate for its currency, pegging the yuan to a particular value relative to the U.S. dollar. Panel (a) shows that from mid-2008 until mid-2010, the pegged rate was set at $0.147; after this, it was allowed to rise but was still kept below the value that world markets would dictate. Panel (b) shows how the Chinese government keeps the exchange rate below the market rate. Currently, the Chinese government doesn't peg the currency to an exact value, but it does still manage the exchange rate, keeping it within certain bands. When it wants to devalue the yuan, it uses new yuan to buy U.S. dollars and other U.S. assets in world markets. This strategy increases the supply of yuan, which shifts the supply curve to the right.

Source: FRED Economic Data, Federal Reserve Bank of St. Louis.

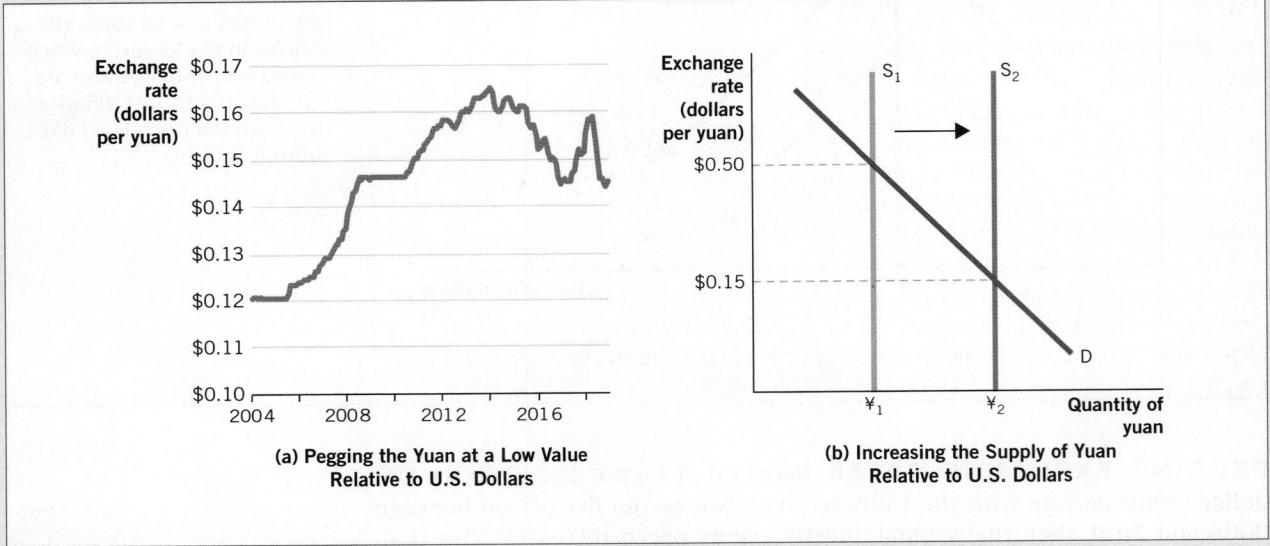

**(a) Pegging the Yuan at a Low Value
Relative to U.S. Dollars**

**(b) Increasing the Supply of Yuan
Relative to U.S. Dollars**

illustrates how an increase in supply drives down the price of the yuan. In practice, when the Chinese government desires a yuan devaluation, it buys U.S. dollars and U.S. Treasury securities in world markets. Notice the word "buy" in the last sentence. That's right: the Chinese government has to buy these, and when it buys them with newly minted yuan, the supply of yuan shifts to the right, to S_2. This action causes the Chinese currency to depreciate. Essentially, the Chinese government is conducting open market operations by purchasing U.S. Treasury securities. Ironically, this is exactly how the U.S. Federal Reserve enacts expansionary monetary policy for the United States.

The Chinese government devalues the yuan so that Chinese goods and services become less expensive on world markets. The government wants Chinese exports to be very affordable because it is trying to build the nation's economy through exports. The Chinese view this as a long-term strategy that will help their economy develop into an industrial economy. Since 2010, the Chinese government has been letting the yuan rise in value, but as the Economics in the Real World feature explains, the Chinese government seems to be having second thoughts.

CHINESE EXPORT GROWTH SLOWS

In August 2015, the Chinese government took action to devalue the yuan, letting the exchange value fall 3% in just two days. The goal of the Chinese government was to cheapen the yuan to make Chinese exports cheaper for Americans and others to buy. The devaluation of the yuan took place while the Chinese economy was struggling to maintain the phenomenal growth of the prior two decades. But many economists question whether continued currency devaluations can lead to sustainable economic growth.

In one sense, it is clear that the Chinese economy has been growing at historically high rates over the past two decades. This fact seems to indicate that the devaluation strategy is helping the Chinese economy overall, not just the export sector. Perhaps this is true, but let's be careful. After all, many other changes have taken place in China over the past two decades. Recall from Chapters 24 and 25 that institutional changes (especially the introduction of private property rights) have significantly altered production incentives in China. Therefore, it is inaccurate to pin China's success on currency devaluation alone.

Will the Chinese government continue to keep the value of the yuan down so that Americans can buy these toys at reduced prices?

In addition, the devaluation of the Chinese currency has other side effects. In particular, devaluation harms Chinese workers, who are paid in yuan. When the government devalues the currency, this move effectively gives the workers a real pay cut. Part of the reason why Chinese exports are so inexpensive is that the nation's labor costs are very low. But this is not a positive outcome for the wage earners.

PRACTICE WHAT YOU KNOW

The Bahamian Dollar Is Pegged to the U.S. Dollar

While the Chinese government keeps the dollar–yuan exchange rate artificially low to encourage exports, other nations peg their currency to the dollar to guarantee stability. In fact, as of 2015, there were still dozens of nations that pegged their currency to the U.S. dollar. Not all the exchange rates are held artificially low with their dollar peg.

This might not look like three U.S. dollars, but that's basically what it is.

QUESTION: Assume that the Bahamian government wants to peg its currency to the U.S. dollar at a 1:1 ratio (one U.S. dollar = one Bahamian dollar). But the current exchange rate is at 90 cents (10 cents below the official peg). What must the Bahamian central bank do to return to the $1 exchange rate?

ANSWER: In this case, as illustrated in the graph on the next page, the initial supply and demand curves intersect at $0.90 before the government intervenes to enforce the peg. Thus, the Bahamian central bank should reduce the supply of Bahamian dollars from S_1 to S_2 to increase the exchange rate to $1.00.

(CONTINUED)

CHALLENGE QUESTION: Assume instead that the Bahamian government wants to alter its exchange rate to exactly $0.45, and the current exchange rate is $0.90. What must the Bahamian central bank do to reach a pegged exchange rate of $0.45?

ANSWER: In this case, the Bahamian central bank will need to double the supply of Bahamian dollars in world markets. This will eventually cause the value of the Bahamian dollar to fall by half.

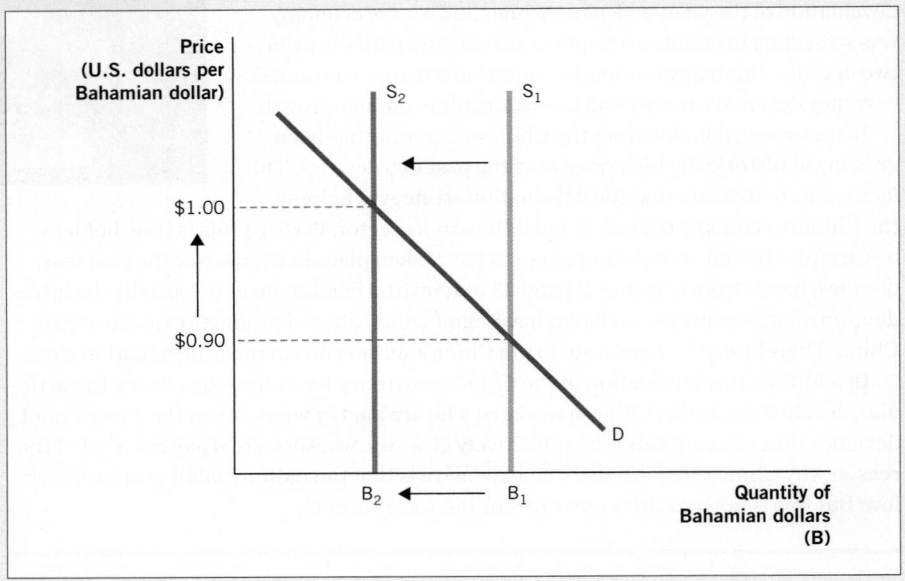

What Is Purchasing Power Parity?

As we have noted, the world economy is becoming ever more integrated. This integration affects both suppliers and demanders of goods and services. Suppliers can often choose where they wish to sell their output, and demanders can often choose where they want to buy their goods and services—even if doing so requires a little extra shipping.

In this section, we discuss the theory of how exchange rates are determined in the long run. We begin by examining how market exchanges determine the price of a particular good at different locations inside a nation. Then we extend this discussion to prices of goods and services in different nations. Finally, we come back and consider limitations to the theory. We begin with the *law of one price*.

The Law of One Price

Let's consider a simplified example of trade within the borders of one country: Florida oranges are consumed in Michigan and many other states. What happens if the price of Florida oranges is different in Michigan and Florida? Figure 33.9 illustrates two different markets for Florida oranges—one in

FIGURE 33.9

The Law of One Price

(a) Initially, the price of a pound of oranges in Florida is $1.80, while (b) the same oranges sell for $2.20 per pound in Michigan. Thus, orange suppliers reduce supply in Florida and increase supply in Michigan. If transportation costs are zero, these supply changes will take place until the price is the same in both locations.

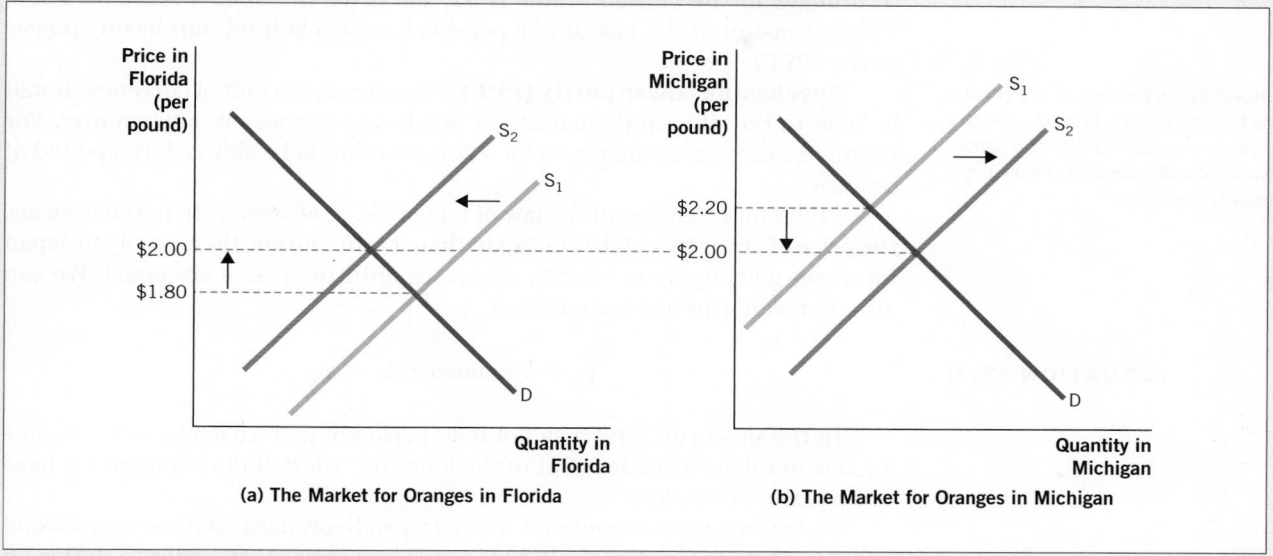

(a) The Market for Oranges in Florida

(b) The Market for Oranges in Michigan

Florida and one in Michigan. Initially, as we see in panel (a), the price of a pound of oranges in Florida is $1.80; as we see in panel (b), the price of a pound of the same oranges in Michigan is $2.20. Assume for now that there are no transportation costs and no trade barriers. In this case, sellers in Florida have an incentive to sell their oranges in Michigan, where the price is 40 cents higher. Thus, the supply in Florida will decline and the supply in Michigan will increase. These supply shifts will lead to an increased price in Florida and a decreased price in Michigan. The adjustment continues until the prices are the same in both locations, at $2.00.

This adjustment process is the logic behind the **law of one price**, which says that after accounting for transportation costs and trade barriers, identical goods sold in different locations must sell for the same price. We can state the law of one price in equation form, where p_A is the price of a good in location A and p_B is the price of the same good in location B:

$$p_A = p_B$$

The law of one price also holds across international borders. For example, if Florida oranges are sold in Japan, the price should be the same once we account for the costs of shipping and trade barriers. But when oranges ship across international borders, a new issue arises because different nations generally use different currencies. We take up this issue in the next section.

Incentives

The **law of one price** says that after accounting for transportation costs and trade barriers, identical goods sold in different locations must sell for the same price.

(EQUATION 33.1)

Purchasing Power Parity and Exchange Rates

In Japan, the medium of exchange is the yen. The exchange rate between the U.S. dollar and the yen is about $0.01. Therefore, since each yen is worth about a penny, the law of one price implies that it should take about 100 times as many yen to buy oranges in Japan as it does dollars to buy the same oranges in the United States. Thus, if the price of a pound of oranges in the United States is $2, the price in Japan should be ¥200. This extension of the law of one price is the idea behind purchasing power parity (PPP).

Purchasing power parity (PPP) is the idea that a unit of currency should be able to buy the same quantity of goods and services in any country. For example, once you exchange $2 for ¥200, you should be able to buy a pound of oranges.

PPP is an extension of the law of one price. If, after converting currencies, the price of oranges is higher in Japan than it is in Florida, then supply to Japan increases and supply in Florida decreases until the prices are equal. We can also represent this in equation form:

(EQUATION 33.2)

$$p_A = \text{exchange rate} \times p_B$$

In the short run, PPP may not hold perfectly, and we explain the reasons for this in the next section. But in the long run, after all the adjustments have taken place, PPP holds.

So far, we have considered a single good—oranges. But we can extend purchasing power parity to all final goods and services in order to derive an important implication regarding exchange rates. If Equation 33.2 holds for all final goods and services, then the price levels (P) in different nations should be related as follows:

(EQUATION 33.3)

$$P_A = \text{exchange rate} \times P_B$$

In Equation 33.3, P_A is the price level in nation A and P_B is the price level in nation B. We can rewrite Equation 33.3 to derive a key implication of PPP:

(EQUATION 33.4)

$$\text{exchange rate} = P_A \div P_B$$

This equation is a direct extension of the law of one price to international trade in all goods and services. We can use Equation 33.4 to learn what causes big swings in exchange rates over time. For example, the exchange rate between the U.S. dollar and the Mexican peso has fallen in recent years, which means that the dollar has appreciated relative to the peso. In 2008, each peso cost approximately $0.10, but over the next decade, the rate fell by half, to $0.05. This long-run change reflects shifts in relative price levels of the United States and Mexico. While inflation in the United States averaged just 1.7% from 2008 to 2018, inflation in Mexico for the same period was 4.2% per year. These changing price levels led to an increase in the exchange rate, because $P_{US} \div P_{Mexico}$ increased between 2008 and 2018. Thus, in the long run, exchange rate fluctuations are driven by relative changes in price levels.

Purchasing power parity (PPP) is the idea that a unit of currency should be able to buy the same quantity of goods and services in any country.

· ECONOMICS *in the* MEDIA ·

Impossible Exchange Rates

EUROTRIP

In this movie from 2004, four American high school graduates travel to Europe and end up in Bratislava, the capital of Slovakia. They are particularly concerned when they pool their remaining money and find they have just $1.83. But it turns out that the U.S. dollar is extremely valuable in Slovakia. Using this small amount of money, the four friends are able to have an amazing night on the town. At one point, they tip a busboy just 5 cents, but this tip is so valuable that the man promptly retires from his job to enjoy his wealth.

An appreciating and strong U.S. dollar is good news to people who are paid in U.S. dollars. The stronger your home currency, the more you can buy around the globe.

But purchasing power parity means that the kind of wild overvaluation of the dollar we see in *Eurotrip* is not possible in the real world. If the dollar were really this strong in some nation, tourists would flood in with

These friends don't have to look far to find a bargain when their dollars are strong relative to the local currency.

dollars and then drive the prices up to a more reasonable level. The movie's story makes for entertaining theater, but the law of one price and purchasing power parity mean these kinds of bargains can't last long in the real world.

ECONOMICS IN THE REAL WORLD

THE BIG MAC INDEX

We have said that purchasing power parity is a condition that should hold in the long run. The British magazine *The Economist* has devised a creative way to test PPP at any given point in time. It compares the price of a McDonald's Big Mac sandwich across many nations. The Big Mac is a good choice because it is roughly the same good all over the world. For example, in July 2018, the price of a Big Mac in the United States was $5.51. Given that the exchange rate between the U.S. dollar and the euro was about $1.16 in July 2018, we can use Equation 33.2 to find the implied price of the Big Mac in the Euro area:

Is the price of this McDonald's sandwich the same all over the world?

$$5.51 = 1.16 \times P_{Europe}$$

Solving for the price in Europe, we find that $5.51 \div 1.16 = 4.75$ euros. In fact, the actual price was 4.56 euros, so the PPP formula worked fairly well in this case.

But PPP doesn't always hold perfectly in the short run. Table 33.3 shows the Big Mac price across seven different nations, along with the price implied by PPP. The first column of numbers gives the actual price of the Big Mac in terms of the domestic currency for each nation. The last column shows the actual price of the Big Mac converted to U.S. dollars using the exchange rate. If PPP held perfectly, the prices in the last column would all be $5.58, the price of a Big Mac in the United States.

In the next section, we examine why PPP might not hold exactly in the short run. One of the key reasons is that the food must be identical across nations.

Why PPP Does Not Hold Perfectly

When we look at the Big Mac index, we see that PPP does not always hold perfectly. There are five reasons why PPP may not hold in the short run.

First, for the law of one price and PPP to hold, the goods or services sold in different locations must be identical. As Table 33.3 notes, the Indian version of the Big Mac is not even a hamburger; it is a chicken sandwich. Thus, we should not expect the prices to be the same.

Second, some goods and services are not tradable. One example is a haircut. Haircuts in China typically cost less than $5 (and often include a massage), whereas haircuts in the United States almost always cost more than $20. But we cannot import a "haircut produced in China"; you'd have to travel to China to buy that service. Therefore, the supply of foreign haircuts cannot adjust to force PPP to hold. This is the case for all nontradable goods and services.

Third, trade barriers inhibit the trade of goods across some international borders. If goods cannot be traded or if tariffs and quotas add to the costs of trade, then prices will not equalize and PPP will not hold. The higher the trade barriers, the higher the price of the good in the foreign country. For example, tariffs and quotas on Florida oranges imported to Japan would lead to higher prices in Japan than in Florida.

Fourth, shipping costs keep prices from completely equalizing. In fact, higher shipping costs will lead to higher prices of the same good in a foreign nation. The greater the shipping costs, the bigger the difference in prices that can persist.

TABLE 33.3

The Big Mac Index, January 2019

	Actual price in domestic currency	Exchange rate	Price in U.S. dollars
U.S. dollar	5.58	1.000	$5.58
Chinese yuan	20.90	6.850	3.05
Euro	4.05	0.872	4.64
Indian rupee*	178.00	69.685	2.55
Japanese yen	390.00	108.440	3.60
Mexican peso	49.00	19.309	2.54
U.K. pound	3.19	0.783	4.07

Source: https://github.com/theeconomist/big-mac-data/releases/tag/2019-01.

*In India, the Big Mac is not sold; the closest comparison is with the Maharaja Mac, which substitutes chicken for beef.

The Law of One Price: What Should the Price Be?

The Ikea furniture company sells Swedish bookshelves all over the world. One popular model is called the BILLY bookcase. The 2015 catalog's base price for the BILLY bookcase in the United States was $59.99, while the price in the United Kingdom was £35.

QUESTION: In 2015, the exchange rate between the U.S. dollar and the British pound sterling was about $1.50. Using this figure, how would you determine the 2015 price implied by PPP for the BILLY bookcase in the United Kingdom? To be clear, we are asking for the price in British pounds sterling that is equal to the $59.99 price in the United States.

BILLY bookcases from Ikea can be shipped all over the world.

ANSWER: From Equation 33.2,

$$\text{price in the United States} = \text{exchange rate} \times \text{price in the United Kingdom}$$

Therefore, substituting in the price in the United States and the exchange rate, we have

$$\$59.99 = \$1.50 \times \text{price in the United Kingdom}$$

Solving this equation, we get

$$\frac{59.99}{1.50} = £39.99$$

QUESTION: The 2015 price implied by PPP was £39.99, but the actual price in the United Kingdom at that time was £35. What are possible reasons why the price in the United Kingdom was slightly lower than PPP would lead us to expect?

ANSWER: Two reasons seem particularly likely. First, shipping costs to the United Kingdom may have been lower than shipping costs to the United States. In addition, there were likely lower trade barriers across Europe than between Europe and the United States.

Data source: Kristian Siedenburg, "Ikea Billy Bookshelf Index," Bloomberg.com, Sept. 15, 2010.

Finally, we have emphasized consistently throughout this book that some prices take longer to adjust than others. PPP is a theory about long-run price adjustments across nations, with prices reacting to changes in demand and supply. The theory is by definition a long-run theory, which only holds after all prices have completely adjusted. Therefore, it will not typically hold perfectly in the short run.

In sum, PPP is a theory that teaches us a lot about the level of exchange rates in the long run—why exchange rates rise and fall over long periods of time. But in the real world, given these limitations, PPP typically does not hold perfectly at any point in time.

What Causes Trade Deficits?

At the beginning of this chapter, we noted that many people think trade deficits are harmful. In this section, we consider why this is a misconception. We also look at the specific causes of trade deficits.

A trade deficit means that more goods and services are coming in than are going out. On a micro level, individuals can have trade deficits with other individuals or business firms. Think about your favorite place to eat lunch. Perhaps you go there once a week. You have a trade deficit with that restaurant; unless you also happen to work there, you buy more from the restaurant than the restaurant buys from you. Does this deficit make you worse off, or indicate weakness on your part? No. In fact, the wealthier you are, the more you may eat at your favorite restaurant and thus further increase your trade deficit. If voluntary trade creates a trade deficit for you, it doesn't mean that you are worse off. Remember: trade creates value.

Your trade deficit with a local lunch spot does not make you worse off.

Trade creates value

When we extend this concept to the entire economy, the result is the same: we are not worse off when more goods and services flow in. In fact, historical data reveal that the U.S. trade deficit often increases during periods of economic growth. Figure 33.10 shows the U.S. trade balance (imports/exports) with recessionary periods shaded as vertical blue bars. The solid blue horizontal line is drawn where exports exactly equal imports. As the orange graph line becomes increasingly negative, it indicates a bigger trade deficit. Notice that the trade deficit widens during periods of expansion and shrinks during recessions. The data show us that trade deficits are often a by-product of positive economic periods.

Before we can explore the various causes of trade deficits, we need to discuss more about the accounting of international trade and financial flows. For this we turn to the balance of payments.

Balance of Payments

In this section, we introduce the terminology of international transactions accounts—the accounts used to track transactions that take place across borders. For a while, it may seem like we have left economics to study accounting. But we need to clarify how international transactions are recorded before we can fully explain the causes of trade deficits and surpluses.

A nation's **balance of payments (BOP)** is a record of payments between that country and the rest of the world. Anytime a payment is made across borders, it is tracked in the BOP. If you buy a car made in Japan, the dollar amount of that transaction is recorded in the balance of payments. If someone from Canada buys shares of stock in a U.S. corporation, that payment is also tracked in the U.S. balance of payments (as well as in Canada's).

The balance of payments is divided into two major accounts: the current account and the capital account. Different types of transactions are entered into each account. The **current account** tracks payments for goods and

The **balance of payments (BOP)** is a record of all payments between one nation and the rest of the world.

The **current account** is the BOP (balance of payments) account that tracks all payments for goods and services, current income from investments, and gifts.

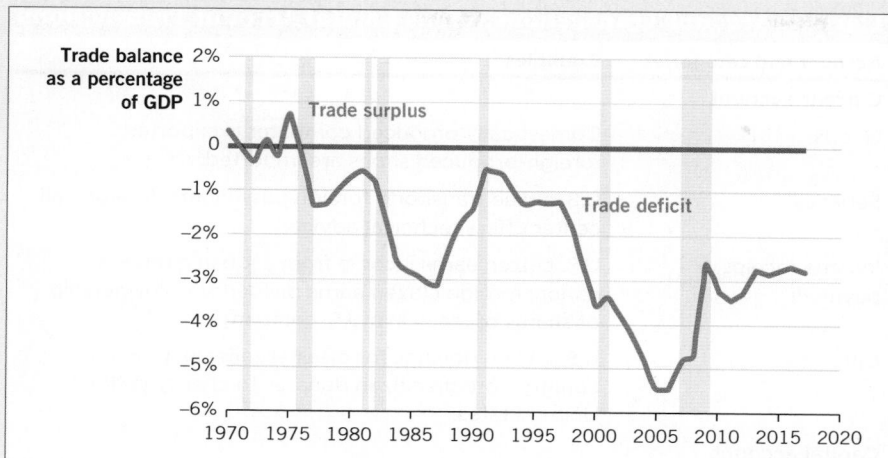

FIGURE 33.10

Trade balance as a percentage of GDP

Trade surplus

Trade deficit

U.S. Trade Balance and Recessions, 1970–2017

Since 1975, the U.S. trade balance has been a deficit, with the deficit reaching its peak in 2006. The trade deficit typically grows during economic expansions and shrinks during recessions, which are indicated here with vertical blue bars.

Source: U.S. Bureau of Economic Analysis, *U.S. International Transactions.*

services, gifts, and current income from investments. When we import TVs from Japan or strawberries from Peru (goods), when we utilize technical advice from a call center in Mumbai, India (a service), and when we supply international aid to refugees in the Middle East (a gift), these transactions are recorded in the current account.

The **capital account** tracks payments for real and financial assets between nations. When residents of one nation buy financial securities such as stocks and bonds from another nation, these payments are recorded in the capital account. When the Chinese government buys U.S. Treasury securities, this transaction is recorded in the capital account. If someone from the United States deposits funds into a Swiss bank account, this transaction is recorded in the capital account. Even if you trade for the currency of another nation, your transaction is recorded in the capital account.

Purchases of real assets also enter in the capital account. If you buy a vacation home in Cozumel, Mexico, it counts as an outgoing payment in the capital account. When Signa Holding (an Austrian real estate company) purchased the Chrysler Building in New York City, the transaction was recorded in the capital account as an incoming payment.

Because much of the activity in the capital account is in financial securities, it is sometimes called the *financial account*. Table 33.4 shows the major categories of the current account and the capital account, along with some examples of the types of transactions entered in each.

Table 33.5 shows actual values for the U.S. current and capital accounts in 2017. Goods and services are by far the largest entry in the current account. For this reason, we focus primarily on goods and services when we discuss the current account.

The dollar amounts in this table represent changes in the various accounts during 2017. For example, on the current account side, the figures indicate that the United States exported about $2.4 trillion worth of goods and services but imported about $2.9 trillion worth. This trade deficit accounts for most of

The **capital account** tracks payments for real and financial assets between nations and extensions of international loans.

Did it hurt the U.S. economy when Signa Holding (an Austrian firm) bought the Chrysler Building in New York City?

TABLE 33.4

Current Account Transactions versus Capital Account Transactions

Account and categories	Examples
Current account	
Goods	Domestically produced computer is exported; foreign-produced shoes are imported.
Services	U.S. airline transports foreign passengers; foreign call center offers technical advice.
Income receipt or payment	U.S. citizen earns income from a job in a foreign nation; foreign citizen earns dividends on ownership of shares of stock in a U.S. company.
Gifts	U.S. citizen donates for disaster relief in a foreign country; foreign citizen donates to charity in the United States.
Capital account	
Financial assets	U.S. citizen buys shares of stock in a foreign company; foreign government buys U.S. Treasury securities.
Real assets	U.S. citizen buys a vacation home in another country; foreign citizen buys an office building in the United States.

TABLE 33.5

U.S. Balance of Payments, 2017

Current account (millions of dollars)		Capital account (millions of dollars)	
Goods and services		Real and financial assets	
Exports	$2,351,072	U.S.-owned assets abroad	−$1,182,749
Imports	−$2,903,349	Foreign-owned assets in United States	$1,537,683
Income			
Receipts	$1,082,167	Net financial derivatives	$23,074
Payments	−$979,031		
Gifts	−$24,746	Statistical discrepancy	$46,387
Balance	−$424,395		$424,395

Source: United States Bureau of Economic Analysis.

the current account deficit. On the capital account side, U.S. individuals (and government) purchased almost $1.2 trillion worth of assets from abroad, but foreigners bought about $1.5 trillion in U.S. assets in 2017. In the short run, statistical discrepancies are common.

When we evaluate the trade balance, we are really focusing on the current account. In fact, when you read about a "trade deficit," you are likely reading about a current account deficit. An **account deficit** exists when more payments are flowing out of an account than into the account. Generally, this means we are importing more goods and services than we are exporting. Table 33.5 shows

An **account deficit** exists when more payments are flowing out of an account than into the account.

that the U.S. current account deficit in 2017 was $552,277 ($2,903,349 − $2,351,072) million.

An **account surplus** exists when more payments are flowing into an account than out of the account. Because goods and services constitute most of the current account, a surplus of the current account is driven by a trade surplus. Table 33.5 shows a capital account surplus of $424,395 for the United States in 2017. You will notice that this surplus is the same size as the current account deficit. This is no coincidence, and we explain the relationship in the next section.

THE KEY IDENTITY OF BALANCE OF PAYMENTS To talk about the major causes of trade deficits, we need to clarify the link between the current and capital accounts. Basically, when one of the accounts increases, the other decreases. We begin with an example before we state an important identity.

Banana imports are recorded with other goods and services in the current account.

An **account surplus** exists when more payments are flowing into an account than out of the account.

Let's say you are shopping for a new car, and you decide on a Toyota manufactured in Japan. Let's assume the following:

- Before you buy a Japanese car, the U.S. trade is completely balanced: imports = exports.

- Before you buy the car, the U.S. capital account is also balanced: U.S. ownership of foreign assets = foreign ownership of U.S. assets.

- The car costs $40,000.

Now when you buy the car, there are two sides to the exchange: from your perspective, you are trading dollars for an imported good; from the perspective of Toyota, the company is trading its car for a U.S. financial asset (dollars). Thus, the exchange is recorded twice in the U.S. balance of payments. First, it is recorded as an import in the current account, and it leads to a current account deficit of $40,000. Second, it is recorded as the purchase of U.S. currency, a U.S. financial asset, in the capital account, and this transaction implies a surplus in the capital account of $40,000. These are entries of equal but offsetting magnitude, which is the principle behind the *balance* of payments.

Now we arrive at an important principle with regard to the balance of payments, which we call the *key identity of the balance of payments*: while either account can be in deficit or surplus, together they sum to zero. A positive balance in the current account means there must be a negative balance in the capital account, and vice versa. We can also write this principle in equation form:

$$\text{current account balance} + \text{capital account balance} = 0$$

(EQUATION 33.5)

Thus, if the current account is in deficit, the capital account is in surplus by the same amount. If the current account is in surplus, the capital account is in deficit by the same amount.

Before moving on, let's consider two other scenarios stemming from our Japanese car example. First, what happens if the new foreign owners of the $40,000 in U.S. currency decide to use it to buy Microsoft software manufactured in the United States? This transaction involves $40,000 worth of U.S. exports, so the current account deficit disappears, as does the capital account surplus.

TABLE 33.6

An Example of Balance of Payments

Example: A U.S. citizen buys a Japanese car for $40,000.

Scenario I: The Japanese company holds on to the $40,000.

$$\begin{array}{ll} \text{U.S. current account:} & -\$40,000 \\ \text{U.S. capital account:} & +\$40,000 \\ \hline \text{Total} & 0 \end{array}$$

Scenario II: The Japanese company buys $40,000 worth of U.S.-produced Microsoft software.

$$\begin{array}{ll} \text{U.S. current account:} & -\$40,000 + \$40,000 = 0 \\ \text{U.S. capital account:} & +\$40,000 - \$40,000 = 0 \\ \hline \text{Total} & 0 \end{array}$$

Scenario III: The Japanese company buys $40,000 worth of Microsoft Corporation stock.

$$\begin{array}{ll} \text{U.S. current account:} & -\$40,000 \\ \text{U.S. capital account:} & +\$40,000 \\ \hline \text{Total} & 0 \end{array}$$

Finally, what happens if, instead, the Japanese owners of $40,000 in U.S. currency use it to purchase shares of Microsoft stock? In this case, the U.S. current account deficit stays at $40,000 and the capital account surplus stays at $40,000, because the Japanese have simply shifted to a different U.S. financial asset. These three scenarios are summarized in Table 33.6. In all cases, the current account changes are offset by opposite capital account changes.

We can see this identity when we examine actual balance of payments data for a nation. Figure 33.11 illustrates the identity with real historical data from

FIGURE 33.11

U.S. Current and Capital Account Balances since 1980

The current account and the capital account are essentially mirror images of each other. If we say that the United States has a current account deficit, we are also saying that it has a capital account surplus.

Source: United States Bureau of Economic Analysis.

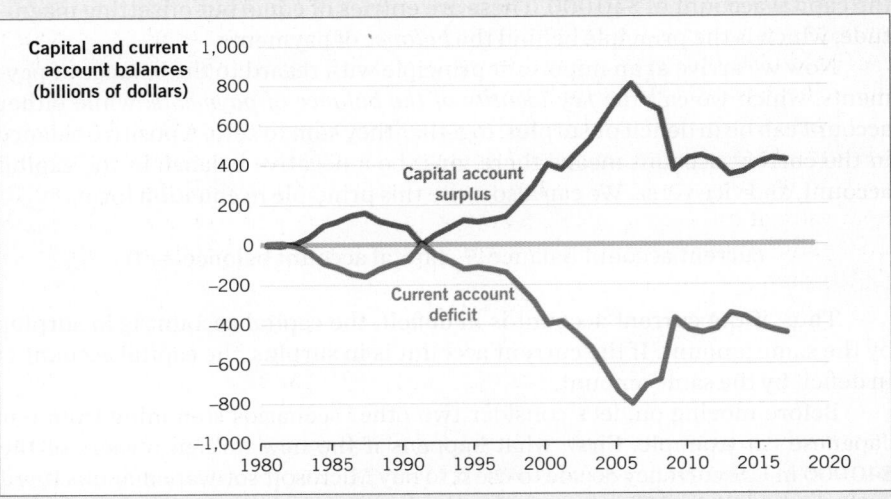

Current Account versus Capital Account Entries

QUESTION: Would the following international transactions be recorded in the U.S. current account or the capital account?

a. the purchase of a Canadian government bond by a resident of Pennsylvania

b. the sale of a U.S. Treasury bond to a resident of Ontario, Canada

c. the purchase of a condominium in Cancun, Mexico, by a U.S. resident

d. the purchase of a Samsung television by Best Buy (a U.S. company)

e. the purchase of an airplane ticket from United Airlines (a U.S. company) by a resident of Chengdu, China, to come to the United States to attend college

If a foreign student buys a ticket on a U.S. airline, how does this transaction affect the balance of payments?

ANSWERS:

a. This would be recorded in the capital account because it is the purchase of a financial asset.

b. This would be recorded in the capital account because it is the sale of a financial asset.

c. This would be recorded in the capital account because it is the purchase of a real asset.

d. This would be recorded in the current account because it is the purchase of a good.

e. This would be recorded in the current account because it is the purchase of a service.

the United States. The orange line is the U.S. current account balance—clearly in deficit since 1991. Figure 33.11 also plots the balance of the capital account, which is clearly in surplus since 1991. Notice that when the capital account surplus grows, it accompanies a larger current account deficit. As the current account deficit exceeded $800 billion in 2006, the capital account surplus also exceeded $800 billion. The two lines are very close to mirror images, which they should be, based on Equation 33.5.

This identity is important for practical purposes because it shows us that anything that affects the capital account also affects the current account. Thus, if we are interested in the major causes of trade deficits, we need to examine not only what causes a current account deficit to increase but also what causes a capital account surplus to increase, because the two are essentially mirror images.

The Causes of Trade Deficits

People who are concerned about trade deficits often think about trade in terms of fairness. After all, if our economy is buying goods from nations around the globe, shouldn't these nations be buying goods from us? The way we calculate GDP seems to reinforce this point of view. Recall that GDP is the sum of four components—consumption (C), investment (I), government expenditures (G), and net exports (NX):

$$GDP = Y = C + I + G + NX$$

The fourth piece is net exports. All else being equal, the net exports component falls when a nation imports more goods. In this sense, the greater current account deficit implies lower GDP. While that implication might make you think that nations are better off with fewer imports or more exports, you shouldn't jump to this conclusion.

There are several causes of deficits in the current account. Although the United States has consistently had a current account deficit since 1975, the cause has varied over time. We consider three primary causes of current account deficits: strong economic growth, lower personal savings rates, and fiscal policy.

STRONG ECONOMIC GROWTH One cause of current account deficits is strong domestic growth. A nation growing and increasing in wealth relative to the rest of the world is also a nation that can afford to import significant quantities of goods and services.

Think of this first in terms of individuals. Imagine that you open a coffee shop and your business does very well. You earn significant profits, and your personal wealth grows. This new wealth enables you to purchase many goods and services that you would not be able to afford if you were less well off. With your new wealth, you'll likely develop trade deficits with many stores and restaurants in your town. You might even establish trade deficits with ski resorts, golf courses, and car dealerships. Bill Gates has personal trade deficits all over the world simply because he buys large quantities of goods and services.

This scenario also applies to nations. During periods of rapid economic expansion in the United States, our current account deficit has grown. The prime example of this is the late 1990s. Look again at Figure 33.11. In the long growth period during the late 1990s, the economy was growing and the current account deficit was growing as well. U.S. wealth was increasing, which enabled us to afford more imports from around the globe. The reverse occurs during economic downturns. When U.S. wealth falls, we are less able to afford imports, and the current account deficit shrinks.

Certain distinct effects cause the trade deficit to grow during economic expansion. The first is in the current account: wealthy domestic consumers can afford to import more goods and services. The second is in the capital account: growing economies offer higher investment returns, so funds from around the globe flow in to take advantage of high rates of return. Table 33.7 summarizes these two complementary effects.

When an economy is growing rapidly relative to the rest of the world, the firms in that economy are willing to pay more for investment funds. This demand for loanable funds shifts to the right and interest rates increase. Subsequently, international funds flow in to take advantage of these higher interest rates.

To clarify, let's return to the example where your coffee shop business is doing very well. One way to expand your business is to offer shares of stock in the business. People buy this stock, hoping to get in on the financial success of your great new business. The stock purchases represent a capital inflow for your business. It works in exactly the same way for nations that are growing

Bill Gates seems to enjoy his trade deficits.

TABLE 33.7

Why Strong Growth Leads to a Current Account Deficit

Primary account	Explanation	Result
Current account	The growing economy leads to wealthier consumers who import more goods and services from around the world.	Net exports fall, which leads to a greater current account deficit.
Capital account	The growing economy offers greater returns, which attracts international funds for investment.	The capital account surplus increases, which reinforces the greater current account deficit.

relatively quickly: funds from around the globe flow in to take advantage of the high returns.

For a macro example, consider the case of China. In recent years, China has periodically experienced a current account deficit, largely owing to its rapid economic growth. This result seems almost counterintuitive, as the rapid Chinese growth has largely been in the area of manufacturing exports. Yet the income surge has also enabled Chinese citizens to import goods and services from all over the globe. In addition, greater returns have brought an influx of global investment funds. These effects were so strong that by late 2010, China was recording current account deficits.

LOWER PERSONAL SAVINGS RATES A second major cause of current account deficits is low domestic savings rates. When households are not saving much, funds must flow in from overseas to supplement domestic investment.

Let's return to the example of your coffee shop. Your business is doing well, and you are considering expansion. You decide you want to open another location for your coffee shop. If you have been frugal and saved a portion of your income, you can use your own savings to expand the business. However, if you have spent your income, you'll need to rely on the savings of others to pay for your expansion. You'll have to borrow from a bank or issue some bonds or perhaps sell shares of stock in your coffee shop business. The purchase of financial assets in your firm is analogous to capital account purchases in the balance of payments.

We can extend the analysis to a macroeconomy. If individuals and governments save a significant portion of their income, the savings can be used to fund investment. In contrast, if savings falls, investment must be funded with outside sources. In the United States, personal savings rates have dropped significantly since the early 1990s (see Figure 22.8). So while the U.S. economy was growing throughout the 1990s and into the first decade of this century, the necessary financing was coming from savers around the globe. This activity increased the capital account surplus. Of course, any increase in the capital account surplus implies an increase in the current account deficit.

As we discussed in Chapter 22, the influx of funds from around the globe was instrumental in keeping interest rates low in the United States and enabling firms to fund expansion. These funds were critical as U.S. savings rates fell, but they did contribute to the widening current account deficit.

TABLE 33.8

Causes of Current Account Deficits

Cause	Explanation
Rapid domestic growth	Domestic buyers are able to afford imports given the increase in wealth, which widens the current account deficit. At the same time, foreign funds are attracted to higher rates of return in the growing economy, which increases the capital account surplus.
Declining domestic savings	Falling domestic savings leaves a finance gap for investment. The gap is filled with foreign funds, which increases the capital account surplus.
Government budget deficits	Increased government borrowing means greater competition for investment funds. All else being equal, more foreign funds are needed to lend to government, and this activity widens the capital account surplus.

FISCAL POLICY Large budget deficits also contribute to current account deficits. This is part of the reason for large U.S. current account deficits in the 1980s and then again after 2000. Large government budget deficits devour both domestic and foreign funds. Recall this important principle from Chapter 22: *Every dollar borrowed requires a dollar saved.* So when the U.S. government borrows trillions each year, this is similar to a further reduction in personal savings: the government is using funds that could have been used for private investment.

Domestic savings are not enough to fund the budget deficit. International funds also flow in to fund the budget deficit. The influx of international funds increases the capital account surplus and thus increases the trade deficit.

Table 33.8 summarizes these different causes of trade deficits. The bottom line is that many factors cause trade deficits, some that don't even seem related to goods and services. The past few decades of U.S. experience offer examples of all three. The 1980s was a time of large budget deficits, and the trade deficit widened. Beginning around 1990, personal savings rates fell and the economy grew rapidly; the trade deficit widened, even as the federal government balanced its budget. Finally, in recent years historically large budget deficits have added to the pressure for capital inflows, reducing any prospects for elimination of the trade deficit in the near future.

Conclusion

We began this chapter with the misconception that trade deficits are harmful to an economy. But we have seen that many factors affect a trade balance, and typically a trade deficit means that the domestic economy is actually doing well. Goods and service flows are interrelated with real and financial asset flows. Given this relationship, changes in personal savings rates and government budget deficits can affect trade balances.

We also studied exchange rates in this chapter and considered them as market prices that depend on the supply of and demand for foreign currency. But exchange rates are also subject to manipulation by governments. Depreciating a nation's currency makes its exports less expensive but doesn't always help all the residents of a nation. ✳

· ANSWERING *the* BIG QUESTIONS ·

Why do exchange rates rise and fall?

- An increase in the exchange rate indicates a depreciation of the domestic currency. The exchange rate increases when there is an increase in demand for foreign goods, services, and financial assets relative to the demand for domestic goods, services, and financial assets.

- The exchange rate also increases when there is a decline in the supply of foreign currency relative to the domestic currency.

- A decrease in the exchange rate indicates an appreciation of the domestic currency. The exchange rate decreases when there is a decrease in demand for foreign goods, services, and financial assets relative to domestic goods, services, and financial assets.

- The exchange rate also falls when there is an increase in the supply of foreign currency relative to the supply of domestic currency.

What is purchasing power parity?

- Purchasing power parity (PPP) is a theory about the determinants of long-run exchange rates. PPP implies that the exchange rate between two nations is determined by a ratio of relative price levels in the two nations. If a nation experiences more inflation than its trading partners do, its exchange rate will rise, indicating a depreciation of its currency.

- PPP is based on the law of one price.

What causes trade deficits?

- Trade deficits are essentially synonymous with current account deficits. As such, they increase when the current account deficit or the capital account surplus increases.

- Economic growth increases the current account deficit as wealthier residents demand more imports. It also works through the capital account as higher rates of return attract foreign funds.

- A second cause of trade deficits is lower personal savings rates.

- A third cause of trade deficits is larger government budget deficits.

Concepts You Should Know

account deficit (p. 1086)
account surplus (p. 1087)
balance of payments (BOP) (p. 1084)
capital account (p. 1085)
currency appreciation (p. 1068)
currency depreciation (p. 1068)

current account (p. 1084)
derived demand (p. 1067)
exchange rate (p. 1066)
exchange rate manipulation (p. 1073)
flexible (floating) exchange rates
   (p. 1075)

law of one price (p. 1079)
pegged (fixed) exchange
   rates (p. 1075)
purchasing power parity (PPP)
   (p. 1080)

Questions for Review

1. The United States imports Molson beer from Canada. Assume that Canada and the United States share the same currency and that a bottle of Molson beer costs $2 in Toronto, Canada, but just $1 in Chicago.

   a. What market adjustments will ensue in this case, assuming no shipping costs or trade barriers?

   b. If Canadians like Molson beer more than the residents of the United States do, can a price differential persist? Why or why not?

2. The United States currently has a current account deficit. How would each of the following events affect this deficit, assuming no other changes?

   a. U.S. economic growth slows relative to the rest of the world.

   b. U.S. personal savings rates increase.

   c. U.S. federal budget deficits decline.

   d. Foreign rates of return (in financial assets) rise relative to rates of return in the United States.

3. Why are current account balances generally mirror images of capital account balances?

4. Sometimes, official government reserves are singled out in the balance of payments accounts. For example, when China buys U.S. financial assets (currency and Treasury securities), this purchase is classified as "Official Government Reserves." On which side of the balance of payments should such purchases be reflected—the current account or the capital account? Explain your logic.

5. What are three factors that might make a capital account surplus grow?

6. Is a trade deficit a sign of economic weakness? Why or why not?

7. The rate of inflation in India from 2007 to 2011 was 8%. Over the same period, the inflation rate in the United States was 2.7%.

   a. What is the implication of these inflation rates for the exchange rate between the dollar and the rupee? In particular, does the PPP condition imply a rise or a fall in the exchange rate? Explain your answer.

   b. Is the change in the exchange rate an appreciation or a depreciation of the dollar? Is it an appreciation or a depreciation of the rupee?

Study Problems (*solved at the end of the section)

1. If interest rates in India rise relative to interest rates around the world, how is the world value of the rupee affected? Illustrate these effects in the market for rupees.

2. From Chapter 21, we know that the primary cause of inflation is expansion of the money supply. In this chapter, we find an additional side effect of monetary expansion. What is this effect? Use

demand and supply of foreign currency to illustrate your answer.

3. Explain the numerical effect on both the U.S. current account and the U.S. capital account from each of these examples.

   a. In the United States, the company Best Buy purchases $1 million worth of TVs from the Samsung corporation, a Korean firm, using U.S.

dollars. In addition, Samsung keeps the U.S. dollars.

b. Best Buy purchases $1 million worth of TVs from the Samsung corporation, using U.S. dollars. Samsung then trades its dollars to a third party for won, the Korean currency.

c. Best Buy trades $1 million for Korean won and then uses the won to buy TVs from Samsung.

4. The price of a dozen roses in the United States is about $30. Use this information, along with the exchange rates given in Table 33.1, to answer the following questions.

a. Assuming that PPP holds perfectly, what is the price of a dozen roses in Turkey? Express your answer in units of Turkish lira.

b. If the actual price in Turkey costs more lira than the answer you found in part (a), how might you account for the discrepancy?

✳ **5.** Explain why the supply curve for foreign currency is vertical. Let's say you return from a trip to Mexico with 1,000 pesos. If you decide to exchange these pesos for dollars, does your action shift the supply of pesos?

✳ **6.** For each of the following transactions, determine whether it will be recorded in the U.S. current account or capital account and whether the entry will be positive or negative.

a. A resident of the United States buys an airplane ticket to England on Virgin Atlantic Airways, a British company.

b. The government of England buys U.S. Treasury securities.

c. A U.S. citizen buys shares of stock in a Chinese corporation.

7. Use our simple model of exchange rates (the market for foreign currency) to determine the effect on the U.S.–Japanese exchange rate from each of the following (assuming no other changes):

a. an increase in Japanese demand for oil produced in the United States

b. an increase in U.S. demand for Japanese real estate

c. an increase in Japanese demand for U.S. Treasury securities

d. a decrease in the supply of Japanese Yen relative to U.S. dollars

8. The Canadian dollar is sometimes called a "loonie," because of the figure of a loon (a duck-like bird) engraved on the dollar coin. The exchange rate between the U.S. dollar and the loonie has recently hovered around $0.75, so each loonie costs about seventy-five U.S. cents. Let's start with this exchange rate but then let it fluctuate. Use what you know about the law of one price to fill in the missing information in the table below. (For this question, assume the law of one price holds perfectly.)

Exchange rate	Price level in U.S.	Price level in Canada
$0.75	100	_____
0.80	100	_____
0.50	100	
0.75	_____	100
0.80	_____	100
0.50	_____	150
_____	100	150
_____	150	100
_____	100	100

Solved Problems

5. The supply curve is vertical because the supply is completely controlled by the government and does not vary with changes in price. Your exchange does not shift the supply of pesos; only the government can do that. Instead, it signals a reduction in demand for pesos.

6.a. This is a purchase of a service, so it enters the current account. It enters negatively because it is an import; thus, funds are flowing out of the U.S. current account.

b. This is a purchase of financial assets in the United States, so it is entered in the U.S. capital account. The entry is positive because funds are flowing into the capital account.

c. This is a purchase of financial assets abroad, so it enters the U.S. capital account. It enters negatively because funds are flowing out.

GLOSSARY

absolute advantage one producer's ability to make more than another producer with the same quantity of resources

account deficit condition existing when more payments are flowing out of an account than into the account

accounting profit profit calculated by subtracting a firm's explicit costs from total revenue

account surplus condition existing when more payments are flowing into an account than out of the account

active monetary policy the strategic use of monetary policy to counteract macroeconomic expansions and contractions

adaptive expectations theory the theory that people's expectations of future inflation are based on their most recent experience

adverse selection phenomenon existing when one party has information about some aspect of product quality that the other party does not have

aggregate consumption function an equation that specifies the relationship between national income and national consumption

aggregate demand the total demand for final goods and services in an economy

aggregate expenditures (AE) model a short-run model of economic fluctuations that holds that prices are completely sticky (inflexible) and that aggregate demand (aggregate expenditures) determines the economy's level of output and income

aggregate production function the relationship between all the inputs used in the macroeconomy and the economy's total output

aggregate supply the total supply of final goods and services in an economy

antitrust laws laws that attempt to prevent collusion (that is, prevent oligopolies from behaving like monopolies)

assets the items a firm owns

asymmetric information an imbalance in information that occurs when one party knows more than the other

austerity policy involving strict budget regulations aimed at debt reduction

automatic stabilizers government programs that automatically implement countercyclical fiscal policy in response to economic conditions

autonomous consumption spending spending on consumption independent of the level of income

average fixed cost (AFC) an amount determined by dividing a firm's total fixed costs by the output

average tax rate the total tax paid divided by the amount of taxable income

average total cost (ATC) the sum of average variable cost and average fixed cost

average variable cost (AVC) an amount determined by dividing a firm's total variable costs by the output

backward-bending labor supply curve supply curve occurring when workers value additional leisure more than additional income

backward induction in game theory, the process of deducing backward from the end of a scenario to infer a sequence of optimal actions

balance of payments (BOP) a record of all payments between one nation and the rest of the world

balance sheet an accounting statement that summarizes a firm's key financial information

bank run event occurring when many depositors attempt to withdraw their funds from a bank at the same time

banks private firms that accept deposits and extend loans

barriers to entry restrictions that make it difficult for new firms to enter a market

barter the trade of a good or service in the absence of a commonly accepted medium of exchange

behavioral economics the field of economics that draws on insights from experimental psychology to explore how people make economic decisions

black markets illegal markets that arise when price controls are in place

bond (1) a security that represents a debt to be paid; (2) an IOU that joins two parties in a contract that specifies the conditions for repayment of a loan, where typically a firm or government the borrower and typically an individual is the lender

bounded rationality the concept that although decision-makers want a good outcome, either they are not capable of performing the problem solving that traditional economic theory assumes or they are not inclined to do so; also called *limited reasoning*

budget constraint the set of consumption bundles that represent the maximum amount the consumer can afford

budget deficit condition occurring when government outlays exceed revenue in a given time period, usually a year

budget surplus condition occurring when government revenue exceeds outlays in a given time period, usually a year

business cycle a short-run fluctuation in economic activity

cap and trade an approach used to curb pollution by creating a system of emissions permits that are traded in an open market

capital account the balance of payments account that tracks payments for real and financial assets between nations and extensions of international loans

capital gains taxes taxes on the gains realized by selling an asset for more than its purchase price

capital goods goods that help produce other valuable goods and services in the future

cartel a group of two or more firms that act in unison

causality condition existing when one variable influences another

ceteris paribus meaning "other things being equal," the concept under which economists examine a change in one variable while holding everything else constant

chained CPI a measure of the consumer price index in which the typical consumer's "basket" of goods and services considered is updated monthly

checkable deposits deposits in bank accounts from which depositors may make withdrawals by writing checks

circular flow diagram a diagram that shows how goods, services, and resources flow through the economy

classical economists economists who stress the importance of aggregate supply and generally believe that the economy can adjust back to full-employment equilibrium on its own

Clayton Act law of 1914 targeting corporate behaviors that reduce competition

club good a good with two characteristics: it is nonrival in consumption and excludable

Coase theorem theorem stating that if there are no barriers to negotiations, and if property rights are fully specified, interested parties will bargain to correct externalities

coinsurance payments a percentage of costs the insured must pay after exceeding the insurance policy's deductible up to the policy's contribution limit

collusion an agreement among rival firms that specifies the price each firm charges and the quantity it produces

commodity-backed money money that can be exchanged for a commodity at a fixed rate

commodity money the use of an actual good for money

common cause a single cause responsible for two phenomena observed to correlate with each other

common-resource good a good with two characteristics: it is rival in consumption and nonexcludable

comparative advantage the situation where an individual, business, or country can produce at a lower opportunity cost than a competitor can

compensating differential the difference in wages offered to offset the desirability or undesirability of a job

competitive market a market in which there are so many buyers and sellers that each has only a small (negligible) impact on the market price and output

complements two goods that are used together; when the price of a complementary good rises, the quantity demanded of that good falls and the demand for the related good goes down

compounding (1) in the context of borrowing money, the situation in which interest is added to an account balance so that the borrower ends up paying interest on an increasingly higher balance; (2) in the context of saving, the situation in which interest is added to the total savings so that you get paid interest on your savings plus any prior interest earned

constant returns to scale condition occurring when long-run average total costs remain constant as output expands

consumer goods goods produced for present consumption

consumer optimum the combination of goods and services that maximizes the consumer's utility for a given income or budget

consumer price index (CPI) a measure of the price level based on the consumption patterns of a typical consumer

consumer surplus the difference between the willingness to pay for a good (or service) and the price paid to get it

consumption the purchase of final goods and services by households, excluding new housing

consumption smoothing behavior occurring when people borrow and save to smooth consumption over their lifetime

contractionary fiscal policy a decrease in government spending or increase in taxes to slow economic expansion

convergence the idea that per capita GDPs across nations equalize as nations approach the steady state

copayments fixed amounts the insured must pay when receiving a medical service or filling a prescription

cost-benefit analysis a process that economists use to determine whether the benefits of providing a public good outweigh the costs

countercyclical fiscal policy fiscal policy that seeks to counteract business cycle fluctuations

CPI see *consumer price index*

creative destruction the introduction of new products and technologies that leads to the end of other industries and jobs

cross-price elasticity of demand measurement of the percentage change of the quantity demanded of one good to the percentage change in the price of a related good

crowding-out phenomenon occurring when private spending falls in response to increases in government spending

currency the paper bills and coins used to buy goods and services

currency appreciation a currency's increase in value relative to other currencies

currency depreciation a currency's decrease in value relative to other currencies

current account the balance of payments account that tracks all payments for goods and services, current income from investments, and gifts

cyclical unemployment unemployment caused by economic downturns

deadweight loss the decrease in economic activity caused by market distortions

debt the total of all accumulated and unpaid budget deficits

decision tree diagram that illustrates all of the possible outcomes in a sequential game

deductibles fixed amounts the insured must pay before most of the policy's benefits can be applied

default risk the risk that a borrower will not pay the face value of a bond on the maturity date

deflation condition occurring when overall prices fall

demand curve a graph of the relationship between the prices in the demand schedule and the quantity demanded at those prices

demand schedule a table that shows the relationship between the price of a good and the quantity demanded

depreciation a fall in the value of a resource over time

derived demand demand for a good or service that derives from the demand for another good or service; the demand for an input used in the production process

diamond-water paradox concept explaining why water, which is essential to life, is inexpensive, while diamonds, which do not sustain life, are expensive

diminishing marginal product condition occurring when successive increases in inputs are associated with a slower rise in output; phenomenon occurring when the marginal product of an input falls as the quantity of the input rises

diminishing marginal utility condition occurring when marginal utility declines as consumption increases

direct finance activity in the loanable funds market when borrowers go directly to savers for funds

discount loans loans from the Federal Reserve to private banks

discount rate the interest rate on the discount loans made by the Federal Reserve to private banks

discouraged workers see *marginally attached workers*

discretionary outlays government spending that is adjustable during the annual budget process

diseconomies of scale condition occurring when long-run average total costs rise as output expands

disposable income income after taxes (Y – T)

dissaving withdrawing funds from previously accumulated savings

dividend a cash payment to stockholders for each share of stock owned

Dodd-Frank Act the primary regulatory response to the financial turmoil that contributed to the Great Recession, enacted in 2010

dominant strategy in game theory, a strategy that a player will always prefer, regardless of what his opponent chooses

double coincidence of wants condition occurring when each party in an exchange transaction happens to have what the other party desires

dumping behavior occurring when a foreign supplier sells a good below the price it charges in its home country

economic contraction a phase of the business cycle during which economic activity is decreasing

economic expansion a phase of the business cycle during which economic activity is increasing

economic growth the percentage change in real per capita GDP

economic profit profit calculated by subtracting both the explicit costs and the implicit costs from a firm's total revenue

economic rent the difference between what a factor of production earns and what it could earn in the next-best alternative

economics the study of how individuals and societies allocate their limited resources to satisfy their unlimited wants

economic thinking a purposeful evaluation of the available opportunities to make the best decision possible

economies of scale condition occurring when long-run average total costs decline as output expands

efficiency wages wages higher than equilibrium wages, offered to increase worker productivity

efficient describing an outcome when allocation of resources maximizes total surplus

efficient scale the output level that minimizes average total cost in the long run

elasticity a measure of the responsiveness of buyers and sellers to changes in price or income

endogenous factors the variables that are inside a model

endogenous growth growth driven by factors inside an economy

equation of exchange an equation that specifies the long-run relationship between the money supply, the price level, real GDP, and the velocity of money

equilibrium condition occurring at the point where the demand curve and the supply curve intersect

equilibrium price the price at which the quantity supplied is equal to the quantity demanded; also known as the *market-clearing price*

equilibrium quantity the amount at which the quantity supplied is equal to the quantity demanded

equity (1) the fairness of the distribution of benefits among the members of a society; (2) the part of an asset that you own; in the case of a house, the part of the selling price you get to keep after paying off the balance on your mortgage

excess capacity phenomenon occurring when a firm produces at an output level smaller than the output level needed to minimize average total costs

excess reserves any bank reserves held in excess of those required

exchange rate the price of foreign currency, indicating how much a unit of foreign currency costs in terms of another currency

exchange rate manipulation a national government's intentional adjustment of its money supply to affect the exchange rate of its currency

excise taxes taxes levied on a particular good or service

excludable good a good for which access can be limited to paying customers

exogenous factors the variables that are outside a model

exogenous growth growth that is independent of factors within the economy

expansionary fiscal policy an increase in government spending or decrease in taxes to stimulate the economy toward expansion

expansionary monetary policy a central bank's action to increase the money supply in an effort to stimulate the economy

expected return the anticipated rate of return on a capital investment based on the probabilities of all possible outcomes

explicit costs tangible out-of-pocket expenses

external costs the costs of a market activity imposed on people who are not participants in that market

externalities the costs or benefits of a market activity that affect a third party

face value the bond's value at maturity—the amount due at repayment; also called *par value*

factors of production the inputs (labor, land, and capital) used in producing goods and services; also called *resources*

federal funds deposits that private banks hold on reserve at the Federal Reserve

federal funds rate the interest rate on loans between private banks

fiat money money with no value except as the medium of exchange; there is no inherent or intrinsic value

final goods goods sold to final users

financial intermediaries firms that help to channel funds from savers to borrowers

fiscal policy the use of government's budget tools, government spending, and taxes to influence the macroeconomy

Fisher equation equation stating that the real interest rate equals the nominal interest rate minus the inflation rate

fixed costs costs that do not vary with a firm's output in the short run; also known as *overhead*

fixed exchange rates see *pegged (fixed) exchange rates*

fixed interest rate an interest rate that remains in effect for the full term of a loan

flexible (floating) exchange rates exchange rates determined by the supply of and demand for currency; also called *floating exchange rates*

floating exchange rates see *flexible (floating) exchange rates*

fractional reserve banking a system in which banks hold only a fraction of deposits on reserve

framing effect a phenomenon seen when people change their answer depending on how the question is asked (or change their decision depending on how alternatives are presented)

free-rider problem phenomenon occurring when someone receives a benefit without having to pay for it

frictional unemployment unemployment caused by delays in matching available jobs and workers

full-employment output the economy's output level when the unemployment rate is equal to the natural rate; also called *potential output* or *potential GDP*

gambler's fallacy the belief that recent outcomes are unlikely to be repeated and that outcomes that have not occurred recently are due to happen soon

game theory a branch of mathematics that economists use to analyze the strategic behavior of decision-makers

GDP see *gross domestic product (GDP)*

GDP deflator a measure of the price level used to calculate real GDP

Gini index a measurement of the income distribution of a country's residents

GNP see *gross national product (GNP)*

government outlays the part of the government budget that includes both spending and transfer payments

government spending spending by all levels of government on final goods and services

Great Recession the U.S. recession that lasted from December 2007 to June 2009

gross domestic product (GDP) the market value of all final goods and services produced within a country during a specific period

gross national product (GNP) the output produced by workers and resources owned by residents of the nation

hot hand fallacy the belief that random sequences exhibit a positive correlation

human capital the resource represented by the quantity, knowledge, and skills of the workers in an economy; the set of skills workers acquire on the job and through education

immediate run a period of time when there is no time for consumers to adjust their behavior

imperfect market a market in which either the buyer or the seller can influence the market price

implicit costs the costs of resources already owned, for which no out-of-pocket payment is made

import quotas limits on the quantity of products that can be imported into a country

incentives factors that motivate a person to act or exert effort

incidence the burden of taxation on the party who pays the tax through higher prices, regardless of whom the tax is actually levied on

income effect phenomenon occurring when laborers work fewer hours at higher wages, using their additional income to demand more leisure

income elasticity of demand measurement of how a change in income affects spending

income inequality ratio ratio calculated by dividing the top quintile's income percentage by the bottom quintile's income percentage

income mobility the ability of workers to move up or down the economic ladder over time

indifference curve a graph representing the various combinations of two goods that yield the same level of personal satisfaction, or utility

indirect finance activity in the loanable funds market when savers deposit funds into banks, which then loan these funds to borrowers

infant industry argument the idea that domestic industries need trade protection until they are established and able to compete internationally

inferior good a good for which demand declines as income rises

inflation the growth in the overall level of prices in an economy

in-kind transfers transfers (mostly to the poor) in the form of goods or services instead of cash

inputs the resources (labor, land, and capital) used in the production process

institution a significant practice, relationship, or organization in a society; the official and unofficial conditions that shape the environment in which decisions are made

interest rate (1) a price of loanable funds, quoted as a percentage of the original loan amount; (2) the price a borrower pays to a lender to use the lender's money

interest rate effect effect occurring when a change in the price level leads to a change in interest rates and therefore in the quantity of aggregate demand

intermediate goods goods that firms repackage or bundle with other goods for sale at a later stage

internal costs the costs of a market activity paid only by an individual participant

internalize relating to a firm's handling of externalities, to take into account the external costs (or benefits) to society that occur as a result of the firm's actions

international trade effect effect occurring when a change in the price level leads to a change in the quantity of net exports demanded

intertemporal decision-making planning to do something over a period of time, which requires valuing the present and the future consistently

investment (1) the process of using resources to create or buy new capital; (2) private spending on the tools, plant, and equipment used to produce future output

investment-grade bonds bonds that pay lower interest rates but are issued by companies that are very likely to repay their creditors

investor confidence a measure of what firms expect for future economic activity

invisible hand a phrase coined by Adam Smith to refer to the unobservable market forces that guide resources to their highest-valued use

junk bonds bonds that pay higher interest rates but are considered speculative

Keynesian economists economists who stress the importance of aggregate demand and generally believe that the economy needs help returning to full-employment equilibrium

labor force those who are already employed or actively seeking work and are part of the work-eligible population

labor force participation rate the percentage of the work-eligible population that is in the labor force

Laffer curve an illustration of the relationship between tax rates and tax revenue

law of demand the law that, all other things being equal, quantity demanded falls when the price rises, and rises when the price falls

law of increasing opportunity cost law stating that the opportunity cost of producing a good rises as a society produces more of it

law of one price law stating that after accounting for transportation costs and trade barriers, identical goods sold in different locations must sell for the same price

law of supply the law that, all other things being equal, the quantity supplied of a good rises when the price of the good rises, and falls when the price of the good falls

law of supply and demand law stating that the market price of any good will adjust to bring the quantity supplied and the quantity demanded into balance

liabilities the financial obligations a firm owes to others

life-cycle wage pattern the predictable effect age has on earnings over the course of a person's working life

loanable funds market the market where savers supply funds for loans to borrowers

long run (1) in microeconomics, the period of time when consumers make decisions that reflect their long-term wants, needs, or limitations and have time to fully adjust to market conditions; (2) in macroeconomics, a period of time sufficient for all prices to adjust

Lorenz curve a visual representation of the Gini index

loss the result when total revenue is less than total cost

M1 the money supply measure composed of currency, checkable deposits, and traveler's checks

M2 the money supply measure that includes everything in M1 plus savings deposits, money market mutual funds, and small-denomination time deposits (CDs)

macroeconomic policy governmental acts to influence the macroeconomy

macroeconomics the study of the overall aspects and workings of an economy

mandatory outlays government spending determined by ongoing programs like Social Security and Medicare; sometimes called *entitlement programs*

marginal cost (MC) the increase in cost that occurs from producing one additional unit of output

marginally attached workers those who are not working, have looked for a job in the past 12 months, and are willing to work, but have not sought employment in the past four weeks

marginal product the change in output divided by the change in input

marginal product of labor the change in output associated with adding one additional worker

marginal propensity to consume (MPC) the portion of additional income spent on consumption

marginal propensity to save (MPS) the portion of additional income saved

marginal rate of substitution (MRS) the rate at which a consumer is willing to trade one good for another along an indifference curve

marginal revenue the change in total revenue a firm receives when it produces one additional unit of output

marginal tax rate the tax rate paid on an individual's next dollar of income

marginal thinking the evaluation of whether the benefit of one more unit of something is greater than its cost

marginal utility the additional satisfaction derived from consuming one more unit of a good or service

market-clearing price see *equilibrium price*

market demand the sum of all the individual quantities demanded by each buyer in the market at each price

market economy an economy in which resources are allocated among households and firms with little or no government interference

market failure condition occurring when there is an inefficient allocation of resources in a market

market power a firm's ability to influence the price of a good or service by exercising control over its demand, supply, or both

markets systems that bring buyers and sellers together to exchange goods and services

market supply the sum of the quantities supplied by each seller in the market at each price

markup the difference between the price the firm charges and the marginal cost of production

maturity date on a bond, the date on which the loan repayment is due

maximization point the point at which a certain combination of two goods yields the greatest possible utility

Medicaid a joint federal and state program that helps low-income individuals and households pay for the costs associated with long-term medical care

Medicare a mandated U.S. federal program that funds health care for people age 65 and older

medium of exchange what people trade for goods and services

menu costs the costs of changing prices

microeconomics the study of the individual units that make up the economy

minimum wage the lowest hourly wage rate that firms may legally pay their workers

monetary neutrality the idea that the money supply does not affect real economic variables

monetary policy the government's adjustment of the money supply to influence the macroeconomy

money any generally accepted means of payment

money illusion the interpretation of nominal changes in wages or prices as real changes

monopolistic competition a type of market structure characterized by low barriers to entry, many different firms, and product differentiation

monopoly condition existing when a single company supplies the entire market for a particular good or service

monopoly power measure of a monopolist's ability to set the price of a good or service

monopsony a situation in which there is only one buyer

moral hazard the lack of incentive to guard against risk where one is protected from its consequences

mutual fund an investment program that trades in diversified holdings and is professionally managed

mutual interdependence a market situation where the actions of one firm have an impact on the price and output of its competitors

Nash equilibrium a phenomenon occurring when all economic decision-makers opt to keep the status quo

natural monopoly the situation that occurs when a single large firm has lower costs than any potential smaller competitor

natural rate of unemployment the typical unemployment rate that occurs when the economy is growing normally

negative correlation condition occurring when two variables move in opposite directions

negative unplanned investment the situation when actual sales exceed anticipated sales, leading to a decrease in inventory

net exports total exports of final goods and services minus total imports of final goods and services

net investment investment minus depreciation

network externality condition occurring when the number of customers who purchase or use a product influences the quantity demanded

new classical critique the assertion that increases in government spending and decreases in taxes are largely offset by increases in savings

New Growth Theory an approach to long-run growth that focuses on technological change and the incentives fostering innovation inside an economy

nominal GDP GDP measured in current prices and not adjusted for inflation

nominal interest rate the interest rate before it is corrected for inflation; the stated interest rate

nominal wage a worker's wage expressed in current dollars

normal good a good consumers buy more of as income rises, holding all other factors constant

normative statement an opinion that cannot be tested or validated; it describes "what ought to be"

occupational crowding the phenomenon of relegating a group of workers to a narrow range of jobs in the economy

oligopoly a form of market structure that exists when a small number of firms sell a differentiated product in a market with high barriers to entry

open market operations operations involving the purchase or sale of bonds by a central bank

opportunity cost the highest-valued alternative that must be sacrificed to get something else

output the product the firm creates

output effect how a change in price affects the number of customers in a market

outsourcing of labor a firm's shifting of jobs to an outside company, usually overseas, where the cost of labor is lower

owner's equity the difference between a firm's assets and its liabilities

par value the bond's value at maturity—the amount due at repayment; also called *face value*

passive monetary policy a central bank's use of monetary policy only to stabilize money and price levels

pegged (fixed) exchange rates exchange rates fixed at a certain level through the actions of a government

per capita GDP GDP per person

perfect complements two goods the consumer is interested in consuming in fixed proportions, resulting in a right-angle indifference curve

perfect price discrimination the practice of selling the same good or service at a unique price to every customer

perfect substitutes two goods the consumer is completely indifferent between, resulting in a straight-line indifference curve with a constant marginal rate of substitution

Phillips curve curve indicating a short-run negative relationship between inflation and unemployment rates

positive correlation condition occurring when two variables move in the same direction

positive statement an assertion that can be tested and validated; it describes "what is"

poverty rate the percentage of the population whose income is below the poverty threshold

poverty threshold the income level below which a person or family is considered impoverished

PPP see *purchasing power parity*

predatory pricing the practice of a firm deliberately setting its prices below average variable costs with the intent of driving rivals out of the market

preference reversal phenomenon arising when risk tolerance is not consistent

price ceiling a legally established maximum price for a good or service

price controls an attempt to set prices through government regulations in the market

price discrimination the practice of selling the same good or service at different prices to different groups of customers

price effect how a change in price affects the firm's revenue

price elasticity of demand a measure of the responsiveness of quantity demanded to a change in price

price elasticity of supply a measure of the responsiveness of the quantity supplied to a change in price; sometimes called *elasticity of supply* or *supply elasticity*

price floor a legally established minimum price for a good or service

price gouging laws temporary ceilings on the prices that sellers can charge during times of emergency

price leadership phenomenon occurring when a dominant firm in an industry sets the price that maximizes its profits and the smaller firms in the industry follow by setting their prices to match the price leader

price level an index of the average prices of goods and services throughout the economy

price maker a firm with some control over the price it charges

price taker a firm with no control over the price set by the market

priming effect phenomenon seen when the order of the questions influences the answers

principal-agent problem a situation in which a principal entrusts an agent to complete a task and the agent does not do so in a satisfactory way

prisoner's dilemma a situation in which decision-makers face incentives that make it difficult to achieve mutually beneficial outcomes

private good a good with two characteristics: it is excludable and rival in consumption

private property provision of an exclusive right of ownership that allows for the use, and especially the exchange, of property

private property rights the rights of individuals to own property, to use it in production, and to own the resulting output

producer surplus the difference between willingness to sell a good (or service) and the price the seller receives

product differentiation the process firms use to make a product more attractive to potential customers

production function the relationship between the inputs a firm uses and the output it creates

production possibilities frontier (PPF) a model that illustrates the combinations of outputs a society can produce if all of its resources are being used efficiently

productivity the effectiveness of effort as measured in terms of the rate of output per unit of input

profit the result when total revenue is higher than total cost

profit-maximizing rule the rule stating that profit maximization occurs when a firm chooses the quantity of output that equates marginal revenue and marginal cost, or MR = MC

progressive income tax system income tax system in which people with higher incomes pay a larger portion of their income in taxes than people with lower incomes do

property rights an owner's ability to exercise control over a resource

prospect theory a theory suggesting that individuals weigh the utilities and risks of gains and losses differently

protectionism a blanket term for governmental actions and policies that restrict or restrain international trade, often with the intent of protecting local businesses and jobs from foreign competition

public good a good that can be consumed by more than one person, and from which nonpayers are difficult to exclude

purchasing power the value of your income expressed in terms of how much you can afford

purchasing power parity (PPP) the idea that a unit of currency should be able to buy the same quantity of goods and services in any country

quantitative easing the targeted use of open market operations in which the central bank buys securities specifically targeting certain markets

quantity demanded the amount of a good or service that buyers are willing and able to purchase at the current price

quantity supplied the amount of a good or service producers are willing and able to sell at the current price

rational expectations theory the theory that people form expectations on the basis of all available information

real GDP GDP adjusted for changes in prices

real-income effect a change in purchasing power as a result of a change in the price of a good

real interest rate the interest rate corrected for inflation; the rate of return in terms of real purchasing power

real wage the nominal wage adjusted for changes in the price level

recession a short-term economic downturn

rent control a price ceiling that applies to the market for apartment rentals

rent seeking occurs when resources are used to secure monopoly rights through the political process

required reserve ratio the portion of deposits that banks are required to keep on reserve

reserves the portion of bank deposits that are set aside and not loaned out

resources the inputs used to produce goods and services; also called *factors of production*

reverse causation condition occurring when causation is incorrectly assigned among associated events

risk-averse people those who prefer a sure thing over a gamble with a higher expected value

risk-neutral people those who choose the highest expected value regardless of the risk

risk-takers those who prefer gambles with lower expected values, and potentially higher winnings, over a sure thing

rival good a good that cannot be enjoyed by more than one person at a time

rule of 70 rule stating that if the annual growth rate of a variable is x%, the size of that variable doubles approximately every $70 \div x$ years

Samaritan's dilemma a situation in which an act of charity creates disincentives for recipients to take care of themselves

savings rate personal saving as a fraction of disposable (after-tax) income

scale the size of the production process

scarcity refers to the inherently limited nature of society's resources, given society's unlimited wants and needs

scatterplot a graph that shows individual (x,y) points

secondary markets markets in which securities are traded after their first sale

securitization the creation of a new security by combining otherwise separate loan agreements

securitized loan a loan in which a borrower's asset serves as collateral

security a tradable contract that entitles its owner to certain rights

services outputs that provide benefits without producing a tangible product

Sherman Antitrust Act the first federal law (1890) limiting cartels and monopolies

shoe-leather costs the resources that are wasted when people change their behavior to avoid holding money

shortage market condition when the quantity supplied of a good is less than the *quantity* demanded; also called *excess demand*

short run (1) in microeconomics, the period of time when consumers make decisions that reflect their short-term wants, needs, or limitations and can partially adjust their behavior; (2) in macroeconomics, the period of time in which some prices have not yet adjusted

signals information conveyed by profits and losses about the profitability of various markets

simple money multiplier the rate at which banks multiply money when all currency is deposited into banks and they hold no excess reserves

single-payer system government coverage of most healthcare costs, with citizens paying their share through taxes

slope the change in the rise along the y axis (vertical) divided by the change in the run along the x axis (horizontal)

social costs the sum of the internal costs and external costs of a market activity

social optimum the price and quantity combination that would exist if there were no externalities

Social Security a U.S. government–administered retirement funding program

social welfare see *total surplus*

specialization the limiting of one's work to a particular area

spending multiplier a number that tells us the total impact on spending from an initial change of a given amount

stagflation the combination of high unemployment and high inflation

status quo bias condition existing when decision-makers want to keep things the way they are

steady state the condition of a macroeconomy when there is no new net investment

stocks ownership shares in a firm

store of value a means for holding wealth

strike a work stoppage designed to aid a union's bargaining position

structural unemployment unemployment caused by changes in the industrial makeup (structure) of the economy

subsidy a payment made by the government to encourage the consumption or production of a good or service

substitutes goods that are used in place of each other; when the price of a substitute good rises, the quantity demanded of that good falls and the demand for the related good goes up

substitution effect (1) the decision by laborers to work more hours at higher wages, substituting labor for leisure; (2) a consumer's substitution of a product that has become relatively less expensive as the result of a price change

sunk costs unrecoverable costs that have been incurred as a result of past decisions

supply curve a graph of the relationship between the prices in the supply schedule and the quantity supplied at those prices

supply schedule a table that shows the relationship between the price of a good and the quantity supplied

supply shocks surprise events that change a firm's production costs

supply-side fiscal policy policy that involves the use of government spending and taxes to affect the production (supply) side of the economy

surplus market condition when the quantity supplied of a good is greater than the quantity demanded; also called *excess supply*

switching costs the costs incurred when a consumer changes from one supplier to another

tariffs taxes levied on imported goods and services

technological advancement the introduction of new techniques or methods so that firms can produce more valuable outputs per unit of input

technology the knowledge available for use in production

third-party problem a situation in which those not directly involved in a market activity experience negative or positive externalities

time preferences the fact that people prefer to receive goods and services sooner rather than later

tit-for-tat a long-run strategy that promotes cooperation among participants by mimicking the opponent's most recent decision with repayment in kind

total cost the amount a firm spends to produce and/or sell goods and services

total revenue the amount a firm receives from the sale of goods and services

total surplus the sum of consumer surplus and producer surplus; a measure of the well-being of all participants in a market, absent any government intervention; also known as *social welfare*

trade the voluntary exchange of goods and services between two or more parties

trade balance the difference between a nation's total exports and total imports

trade deficit condition occurring when imports exceed exports, indicating a negative trade balance

trade surplus condition occurring when exports exceed imports, indicating a positive trade balance

tragedy of the commons the depletion of a common-resource good

transfer payments payments made to groups or individuals when no good or service is received in return

Treasury securities the bonds sold by the U.S. government to pay for the national debt

ultimatum game an economic experiment in which two players decide how to divide a sum of money

underemployed workers those who have part-time jobs but would prefer to work full-time

underground economies markets in which goods or services are traded illegally

unemployment condition occurring when a worker who is not currently employed is searching for a job without success

unemployment insurance a government program that reduces the hardship of joblessness by guaranteeing that unemployed workers receive a percentage of their former income while unemployed; also known as *federal jobless benefits*

unemployment rate the percentage of the labor force that is unemployed

union a group of workers who bargain collectively for better wages and benefits

unit of account the measure in which prices are quoted

unplanned investment also called *positive unplanned investment*; the situation when expected sales exceed actual sales, leading to an increase in inventory

util a personal unit of satisfaction used to measure the enjoyment from consumption of a good or service

utility a measure of the level of satisfaction that a consumer enjoys from the consumption of goods and services

value of the marginal product (VMP) the marginal product of an input multiplied by the price of the output it produces

variable a quantity that can take on more than one value

variable costs costs that change with the rate of output

velocity of money the number of times a unit of money exchanges hands in a given year

wage discrimination unequal payment of workers because of their race, ethnic origin, sex, age, religion, or some other group characteristic

wealth the net value of one's accumulated assets

wealth effect the change in the quantity of aggregate demand that results from wealth changes due to price-level changes

welfare economics the branch of economics that studies how the allocation of resources affects economic well-being

willingness to pay the maximum price a consumer will pay for a good or service; also called the *reservation price*

willingness to sell the minimum price a seller will accept to sell a good or service

winner-take-all phenomenon occurring when extremely small differences in ability lead to sizable differences in compensation

CREDITS

bostanci/iStockphoto; **p. 494** (left): from Vox.com video, "Homer Simpson: An economic analysis", September 9th, 2016. Zachary Crockett/Vox Media, Inc. Data source: The Simpsons (seasons 1-27), BLS, Glassdoor; US Census Bureau. https://www.vox.com/2016/9/6/12752476/the-simpsons-homer-middle-class, (right): ©20th Century Fox Film Corp. All rights reserved/Everett Collection; **p. 495**: Design Pics/Carson Ganci/Getty Images; **p. 496**: Magali Delporte/eyevine/Redux; **p. 497**: Ken Backer/Dreamstime; **p. 500**: Murray Close/©Lionsgate/Courtesy Everett Collection; **p. 502** (top): Roberto Serra/Iguana Press/Getty Images, (bottom): zhang bo/iStockphoto; **p. 503**: Album/Alamy Stock Photo.

PART V

P. 508: Stockbroker/MBI/Alamy Stock Photo.

CHAPTER 16

P. 510: Erik Pendzich/Shutterstock; **p. 513** (top): Stephen Walls/iStockphoto, (center): john shepherd/iStockphoto; (bottom): Rawpixel.com/Shutterstock; **p. 516**: Mathias Wilson/iStockphoto; **p. 517** (top): Chuck Hodes/©Fox/courtesy Everett Collection; **p. 517** (Table 16.1, top to bottom): Christian Degroote/Dreamstime, Robert Billstone/iStockphoto, Juanmonino/iStockphoto, iStockphoto, Stoyan Yotov/Shutterstock, Cal Vornberger/Alamy; **p. 520**: Vividpixels/Dreamstime; **p. 522**: South Florida Reporter; **p. 525**: SUPER SIZE ME, Morgan Spurlock, 2004, ©Samuel Goldwyn/courtesy Everett Collection; **p. 526**: Rimma Bondarenko/Alamy Stock Photo; **p. 530**: AiVectors/Shutterstock.

CHAPTER 17

P. 544: Photo by CBS via Getty Images; **p. 547**: iofoto/iStockphoto; **p. 548** (top): Jennifer Pitiquen/Dreamstime, (bottom): Monty Brinton/CBS Photo Archive/Getty Images; **p. 549**: Monty Brinton/CBS via Getty Images; **p. 550**: Photo courtesy of Ulrike Malmendier. ©Edward Caldwell; **p. 551**: Ryan Balderas/iStockphoto; **p. 553** (top): ©Walt Disney Studios Motion Pictures/Courtesy Everett Collection, (bottom): Filmfoto/Dreamstime; **p. 554** (top): Marc De Simone/Alamy Stock Photo, (bottom): Courtesy of University of Rochester; **p. 557**: National Science Foundation; **p. 559**: Everett Collection Inc/Alamy; **p. 560**: Mark Stahl/iStockphoto; **p. 561** (top): Jason Merritt/FilmMagic/Getty Images, (bottom): Alex Slobodkin/iStockphoto; **p. 562**: Kyodo News via Getty Images; **p. 563**: iunewind/Alamy Stock Vector.

CHAPTER 18

P. 568: Rostyslav Zabolotnyi/Alamy Stock Photo; **p. 571** (left): Brown-Brooks/Photo Researchers/Getty Images, (right): Mark Kostich/iStockphoto; **p. 577**: D Dipasupil/FilmMagic/Getty Images; **p. 579**: Matt Groening/20th Century Fox/Kobal/Shutterstock; **p. 580**: Hero Images Inc./Alamy Stock Photo; **p. 582**: Kathy Hutchins/Shutterstock; **p. 585**: ZUMA Wire Service/Alamy; **p. 586**: Jovan Jaric/iStockphoto; **p. 588**: Michael Burrell/Alamy Stock Photo; **p. 591**: Vesna Andjic/iStockphoto; **p. 592**: Olekcii Mach/Alamy Stock Photo; **p. 593**: sjscreens/Alamy Stock Photo.

PART VI

P. 598: Imaginechina Limited/Alamy Stock Photo.

CHAPTER 19

P. 600: Robert Melen/Alamy Stock Photo; **p. 602** (left): Sailorman/Dreamstime, (right): Emile Wamsteker/Bloomberg via Getty Images; **p. 604**: Eliza Snow/iStockphoto; **p. 610**: Aurora Photos/Alamy Stock Photo; **p. 611** (left): Joe Biafore/iStockphoto, (right): Michael Shake/Dreamstime, (bottom): Hill Street Studios/Getty Images; **p. 613**: AP Photo/Lee Jin-man; **p. 614** (top): Sipa via AP Images, (bottom): Kelpfish/Dreamstime; **p. 615**: Alexander Kharchenko/Dreamstime; **p. 616**: Lezh/iStockphoto; **p. 621**: NPR; **p. 622**: Keith Dannemiller/Alamy Stock Photo; **p. 623**: Katja Bone/iStockphoto; **p. 625**: Jackstraw22/Dreamstime; **p. 628**: Ursula Coyote/©AMC/Courtesy Everett Collection; **p. 630**: kristian sekulic/iStockphoto; **p. 631**: michaeljung/Shutterstock; **p. 632**: Bernardo Ramonfaur/Alamy Stock Photo.

CHAPTER 20

P. 638: Tyler Stableford/Getty Images; **p. 642** (left): Courtesy of Amazon, (right): Kristoffer Tripplaar/Alamy; **p. 644**: Rivertracks/Dreamstime; **p. 645**: Donald Bowers/Getty Images for Quill.com; **p. 646**: Nabeel Zytoon/Dreamstime; **p. 648**: Fotosearch/Getty Images; **p. 651**: Igor Mojzes/Alamy Stock Photo; **p. 656**: iStockPhoto; **p. 660**: dpa picture alliance archive/Alamy Stock Photo; **p. 661**: Mykola Sosiukin/Alamy Stock Photo.

CHAPTER 21

P. 668: Juan Torres/NurPhoto/Getty Images; **p. 671**: Howard Burditt/Reuters/Newscom; **p. 672**: Ljupco/iStockphoto; **p. 673** (top): Ljupco/iStockphoto, (center): AdShooter/iStockphoto, (bottom): hakusan/iStockphoto; **p. 674**: S1001/Shutterstock; **p. 677** (left): alexander kirch/iStockphoto, (right): Krisda/Shutterstock; **p. 679** (top to bottom): Stephen Krow/iStockphoto, Joe Potato Photo/iStockphoto, Michael Neelon(misc)/Alamy, Daniel Bendjy/iStockphoto, (right): AVATAR, Zoe Saldana, Sam Worthington (back), 2009. TM Copyright ©20th Century Fox. All rights reserved/Courtesy Everett Collection; **p. 680** (top to bottom): ©20th Century-Fox Film Corporation, TM Copyright/courtesy Everett Collection, ©20th Century Fox Film Corp. All rights reserved./Courtesy Everett Collection, Lucasfilm/Bad Robot/Walt Disney Studios/Kobal/Shutterstock, ©Marvel/©Walt Disney Studios Motion Pictures/Courtesy Everett Collection, Amblin/Legendary/Universal/Kobal/

Shutterstock, Marvel Enterprises/Kobal/Shutterstock, ©Universal Pictures/Courtesy Everett Collection, Marvel/Walt Disney Pictures/Kobal/Shutterstock, ©Marvel/©Walt Disney Studios Motion Pictures/Courtesy Everett Collection, ©Warner Bros. Ent. All rights reserved./Courtesy Everett Collection; **p. 681** (top to bottom): Selznick/MGM/Kobal/Shutterstock, ©20th Century Fox Film Corp. All rights reserved./Courtesy Everett Collection, Lucasfilm/Fox/Kobal/Shutterstock, ©20th Century-Fox Film Corporation, TM Copyright/courtesy Everett Collection, Universal History Archive/Shutterstock, 20th Century Fox/Kobal/Shutterstock, Universal/Kobal/Shutterstock, ©Walt Disney Studios Motion Pictures/Lucasfilm Ltd./Courtesy Everett Collection, Snap/Shutterstock, ©Marvel/©Walt Disney Studios Motion Pictures/Courtesy Everett Collection; **p. 682**: Jim West/Alamy; **p. 683**: AUSTIN POWERS: THE SPY WHO SHAGGED ME, Mike Myers, 1999, ©New Line/courtesy Everett Collection; **p. 685**: "US Online Price Index" reprinted with permission from State Street PriceStats®; **p. 686**: AP; **p. 687**: Kimberly White/Reuters/Newscom; **p. 689**: Courtesy of Lee Coppock; **p. 692**: Hocus Focus Studio/iStockphoto; **p. 693**: George Peters/iStockphoto; **p. 697**: Cherry b l o s s o m/Shutterstock.

CHAPTER 22

P. 704: Sergey Borisov/Alamy Stock Photo; **p. 708**: Courtesy of Lee Coppock; **p. 709**: Robert Clay/Alamy Stock Photo; **p. 714** (top): Tony Burns/Lonely Planet Images/Getty Images, (bottom): Wesley Thornberry/iStockphoto; **p. 718**: Touchtone/Kobal/Shutterstock; **p. 720**: Ameer Alhalbi/NurPhoto via Getty Images; **p. 721** (top and bottom): DeadDuck/iStockphoto; **p. 722**: SpongeBob Squarepants, 2004, ©Paramount/courtesy Everett Collection; **p. 724**: Feng Li/Getty Images; **p. 727**: creativestockexchange/Shutterstock.

CHAPTER 23

P. 732: Alex Segre/Alamy Stock Photo; **p. 736**: Henk Badenhorst/iStockphoto; **p. 737**: James Baigrie/The Image Bank/Getty Images; **p. 743** (top): Richard Levine/Alamy Stock Photo, (bottom): S. Greg Panosian/iStockPhoto; **p. 745**: Peter Foley/Bloomberg via Getty Images; **p. 748**: Myron Davis/Time Life Pictures/Getty Images; **p. 751**: narvikk/iStockphoto; **p. 752**: Jaap Buitendijk/©Paramount/Courtesy Everett Collection; **p. 753**: Christopher Futcher/iStockphoto.

PART VII

P. 758: Malcolm Fairman/Alamy Stock Photo.

CHAPTER 24

P. 760: NASA/ISS Crew Earth Observations Facility and the Earth Science and Remote Sensing Unit, Johnson Space Center; **p. 764**: Irene Abdou/Alamy Stock Photo; **p. 765** (left

to right): Steven Wynn/iStockphoto, INTERFOTO/Alamy Stock Photo, FALKENSTEINFOTO/Alamy Stock Photo, traveler1116/iStockphoto, Georgios Kollidas/Shutterstock, HultonArchive/iStockphoto; **p. 768**: Courtesy of Lee Coppock; **p. 773** (top): Monkey Business Images/Shutterstock, (bottom): Nicholas Han/Alamy Stock Photo; **p. 774** (clockwise from top left): Onepony/Dreamstime, Sonya Etchison/Dreamstime, Mark Phelan/Detroit Free Press/TNS/Alamy Live News, Cobalt88/Dreamstime, ClassicStock/Alamy, Martyn Goddard/Getty Images; **p. 775**: studio157/iStockphoto; **p. 778**: Moritz Hager/Photoshot/Newscom; **p. 779**: Chris Ratcliffe/Bloomberg via Getty Images; **p. 780**: David Paul Morris/Bloomberg/Getty Images; **p. 781**: Britta Kasholm-Tengve/iStockphoto; **p. 782**: Max Milligan/Getty Images; **p. 785** (top): STR/AFP/Getty Images, (bottom): Carolyn Cole/Los Angeles Times; **p. 786**: Jacom Stephens/iStockphoto; **p. 788**: Alhovik/Dreamstime; **p. 789**: Courtesy of Daniel D. Lee; **p. 790** (top): Bryce Vickmark/MIT/UPI/Alamy Live News, (bottom): Luke MacGregor/Bloomberg via Getty Images.

CHAPTER 25

P. 796: Alexander Demianchuk/ITAR-TASS News Agency/Alamy Stock Photo; **p. 800** (left): Bartosz Hadyniak/iStockphoto, (right): Klaas Lingbeek-van Kranen /iStockphoto; **p. 801**: TM and Copyright ©20th Century Fox Film Corp. All rights reserved. Courtesy: Everett Collection; **p. 803**: Danilo Mongiello/Dreamstime; **p. 805**: Stacey Lynn Payne/iStockphoto; **p. 807**: Ugurhan Betin/Getty Images; **p. 808**: Carl Juste/Miami Herald/TNS/Alamy Live News; **p. 810** (left): tirc83/iStockphoto, (right): Aleksey Boldin/Alamy Stock Photo; **p. 812**: CB2/ZOB/WENN/Newscom; **p. 813**: Dennis Macdonald/Getty Images; **p. 814**: Chris Boswell/iStockphoto; **p. 815** (top) Geraint Lewis/Alamy Stock Photo, (bottom): PaeguS/Shutterstock; **p. 817** (left): China Stringer Network/Reuters/Newscom, (right): Carlos Barria/Reuters/Newscom; **p. 821** (top): Luis Sandoval Mandujano/iStockphoto, (bottom): Alptraum/Dreamstime; **p. 822**: Jemal Countess/Getty Images.

CHAPTER 26

P. 828: David McNew/Getty Images; **p. 833**: Jason Stitt/Dreamstime; **p. 834**: Mike Mareen/Shutterstock; **p. 835**: Marek Uliasz/Alamy Stock Photo; **p. 836** (top): EricVega/iStockphoto, (bottom): Steven Pepple/Dreamstime; **p. 837**: DUMB AND DUMBER, Jim Carrey, Jeff Daniels, 1994. ©New Line Cinema/courtesy Everett Collection; **p. 838**: Christopher Pillitz/Photonica World/Getty Images; **p. 841** (left): EricVega/iStockphoto, (center): Courtesy of Lee Coppock, (right): Vassiliy Mikhailin/iStockphoto; **p. 842**: Justin Sullivan/Getty Images; **p. 846**: Courtesy of Lee Coppock; **p. 847**: Ole Jensen/Getty Images; **p. 849**: Danita Delimont/Gallo Images/Getty Images; **p. 854**: Saul Loeb/AFP/GettyImages; **p. 857**: Jiji Press/AFP/Getty Images.

CHAPTER 27

P. 864: Lange, D., photographer. (1936) Migrant agricultural worker's family. Library of Congress, https://www.loc.gov/item/2017762903/; **p. 876**: Sueddeutsche Zeitung Photo/Alamy Stock Photo; **p. 877**: Universal History Archive/Getty Images; **p. 879**: Underwood Archives/Getty Images; **p. 880** (left): Library of Congress, Prints & Photographs Division, FSA/OWI Collection, LC-DIG-fsa-8a22559, (right): Britta Kasholm-Tengve/iStockphoto; **p. 884**: Monkey Business Images/Shutterstock; **p. 885** (left): Sueddeutsche Zeitung Photo/Alamy Stock Photo, (right): Album/Alamy Stock Photo; **p. 891**: JGI/Jamie Grill/Tetra Images, LLC/Alamy Stock Photo; **p. 893**: Wavebreak Media ltd/Alamy Stock Photo; **p. 897**: U.S. Air Force photo/Staff Sgt. James L. Harper Jr. (The appearance of U.S. Department of Defense visual information does not imply or constitute DOD endorsement); **p. 899**: Ariel Skelley/Digital Vision/Getty Images.

PART VIII

P. 906: AOC Photo/Alamy Stock Photo.

CHAPTER 28

P. 908: Songquan Deng/Alamy Stock Photo; **p. 912**: U.S. Navy photo by Andy Wolfe courtesy of Lockheed Martin; **p. 913**: wavebreakmedia/Shutterstock; **p. 914**: svariophoto/iStockphoto; **p. 915**: AP Photo; **p. 922**: lucky336/iStockphoto; **p. 929**: Shutterstock; **p. 931**: Richard Levine/Alamy Stock Photo; **p. 932**: Hero Images Inc./Alamy Stock Photo.

CHAPTER 29

P. 936: AP Photo/Charles Dharapak; **p. 940** (top): Gerald Martineau/The Washington Post/Getty Images, (bottom): AP Photo/Darin McGregor, Pool; **p. 946**: eurobanks/Shutterstock; **p. 948** (top): PAY IT FORWARD, Haley Joel Osment, 2000/Everett Collection, (bottom): Raja Rc/Dreamstime; **p. 949** (top): Brian Kersey/UPI/Newscom, (bottom): Photo by Erik Jepsen; **p. 950**: Louis-Paul St-Onge/iStockphoto; **p. 952**: Stephen Krow/iStockphoto; **p. 954** (top): Bohuslav Mayer/Dreamstime, (bottom): Ronnie McMillan/Alamy; **p. 956**: Monkey Business Images/Shutterstock; **p. 959**: NASA; **p. 960**: Kevin Lamarque/Reuters/Newscom; **p. 961**: AP Photo/Ed Reinke.

PART IX

P. 966: Konstantin Chagin/Shutterstock.

CHAPTER 30

P. 986: Andrew Harrer/Bloomberg via Getty Images; **p. 970**: Yonhap/EPA/Shutterstock; **p. 971**: Charles Islander/iStockphoto; **p. 972** (left): National Numismatic Collection at the Smithsonian Institution, (right): Scottnodine/Dreamstime, (bottom): DeborahMaxemow/iStockphoto; **p. 973** (top): Ken Tannenbaum/iStockphoto, (left): Versluis Photography/iStockphoto, (right): Maurice Crooks/Alamy; **p. 974**: Baris Simsek/iStockphoto; **p. 975**: Jiri Hera/Alamy Stock Photo; **p. 976**: tomas del amo/Alamy; **p. 981**: RKO/Album/Newscom; **p. 982**: Andy Rain/EPA/Newscom; **p. 985** (top): Federal Reserve/Flickr, (bottom): Ted Foxx/Alamy; **p. 988** (top): TM Copyright ©20th Century Fox Film Corp. All rights reserved. Everett Collection, (bottom): Evan El-Amin/Shutterstock; **p. 989**: Uschools University Images/iStockhoto.

CHAPTER 31

P. 1000: Backyard Productions/Alamy Stock Photo; **p. 1006**: Dani Simmonds/Alamy; **p. 1009**: Bettmann/Getty; **p. 1010**: Britt Leckman/Federal Reserve/Flickr; **p. 1021**: Almir1968/Dreamstime; **p. 1024**: Warner Bros./Courtesy Everett Collection; **p. 1025**: Federal Reserve/Flickr; **p. 1027**: Jackryan89/Dreamstime; **p. 1028**: Oleksiy Mark/Dreamstime.

PART X

P. 1034: stefano baldini/Alamy Stock Photo.

CHAPTER 32

P. 1036: Kiln Enterprises Limited/www.shipmap.org; **p. 1039** (left and right): Phil Crean A/Alamy Stock Photo; **p. 1040**: Aleksandra Yakovleva/iStockphoto; **p. 1042**: Craig Hastings/Getty Images; **p. 1043**: Chris Ratcliffe/Bloomberg via Getty Images; **p. 1044**: UrbanZone/Alamy Stock Photo; **p. 1048**: Andrew Rowat/Getty Images; **p. 1054**: Reason.com; **p. 1057**: AP Photo/Damian Dovarganes; **p. 1058**: Mary Evans/LUCASFILMS/Ronald Grant/Everett Collection; **p. 1059**: Larry Leung/FeatureChina/Newscom; **p. 1060** (left): 2p2play/Shutterstock, (right): Sergio Azenha/Alamy Stock Photo.

CHAPTER 33

P. 1064: Michael Nelson/EPA/Shutterstock; **p. 1066**: david franklin/iStockphoto; **p. 1070**: Patryk Kosmider/iStockphoto; **p. 1072**: Will Ireland/Future/Shutterstock; **p. 1077** (top): Feng Li/Getty Images, (bottom): B.A.E. Inc./Alamy; **p. 1081** (top): 2004, ©DreamWorks/courtesy Everett Collection, (bottom): Niknikopol/Dreamstime; **p. 1083**: Alex Segre/Alamy; **p. 1084**: Courtesy of Lee Coppock; **p. 1085**: btrenkel/iStockphoto; **p. 1087**: AP Photo/Peter Dejong; **p. 1089**: Chmiel/iStockphoto; **p. 1090**: Sean Gallup/Getty Images.

INDEX

Page numbers where key terms are defined are in **boldface.**